4.98

DATE DUE

2/7/80			
11/27/84			
MAY 3 '90			
		JOSTEN'S NO. 30-505	

Works of Charles Dickens

CHARLES DICKENS.

Works of Charles Dickens

Posthumous Papers of the Pickwick Club

The Adventures of Oliver Twist

A Christmas Carol

The Personal History of David Copperfield

Great Expectations

Tale of Two Cities

❧❦❧

With Illustrations by
George Cruikshank, "Phiz" (H.K. Browne), Barnard,
E.G. Dalziel, H. French, and Others

And an Introduction by
Harriet Weitzner

Avenel Books • New York

The original editions of these works were published as
follows:
Posthumous Papers of the Pickwick Club, 1837
The Adventures of Oliver Twist, 1838
A Christmas Carol, 1843
The Personal History of David Copperfield, 1850
Tale of Two Cities, 1859
Great Expectations, 1861

This edition is published by Avenel Books,
distributed by Crown Publishers, Inc.

a   b   c   d   e   f   g   h

Avenel 1978 printing

Library of Congress Cataloging in Publication Data
Dickens, Charles, 1812-1870.
    Works of Charles Dickens.
    CONTENTS: Posthumous papers of the Pickwick club.—
The adventures of Oliver Twist.—A Christmas carol. [etc.]
    I. Cruikshank, George, 1792-1878.
PZ3.D55Wo   1978   [PR4550]   823'.8   78-55407
ISBN 0-517-2631-14

INTRODUCTION.

If any one person can be said to embody the true Victorian spirit, then that person would be Charles Dickens. Dickens, both in his life and in his art, has come to represent all that was joyous in that age of rapid expansion and seemingly unlimited possibilties and all that was tragic in a time when industrialization and urban misery seemed to replace a former pastoral serenity.

Even a sketchy examination of his life reveals the ways in which Dickens reflected his time. When he was a young boy his parents were forced to move from the country to London, like many others in dire financial straits, and, once in London, their situation deteriorated even further, to the point where Dickens' father was put into debtor's prison and Dickens was forced to work in a bootblacking factory. Surely, if he had not seen his parents degraded in his eyes, if he had not experienced child labor first hand, if he had not suffered the besotted ravings of imbecilic grade school teachers, then he could never have portrayed with such feeling the plight of the poor and oppressed.

On the other hand, if his family had not received a reprieve in the form of a small legacy, if his industriousness had not been rewarded with a good job in the field of journalism, and if eventually his writing had not catapulted him to incredible fame, then he could not have brought to his work that sense of optimism and a belief in the possibility of the ultimate triumph of human goodness that makes him such a joy to read.

But Dickens, true Victorian that he was, is still widely read today. His lustre has never diminished, where countless other period novelists have lost their popularity, primarily because the universal verities in which he believed appeal as much to a modern reader as to a Victorian. Even as we reject some of the more sentimental aspects of the novels, we rush to embrace their humanity, their wit, and their concern with poverty and injustice. We appreciate the multidimensionality of the characters, as well as the strength of Dickens' overall conception of the themes and execution of the various plots. We mentally cheer his heroes and boo his villains, but we appreciate even more those characters who combine within themselves the qualities of good and evil, whose moral struggles remind us of our own.

The works chosen for this anthology represent the progression of Dickens' art through various important stages; each is a milestone both in the history of literature and in Dickens' own personal development as a novelist. It is difficult to speak in terms of "best" when discussing Dickens, since each reader has his own particular favorites, but these works certainly reveal Dickens at his most accessible, his most lively, and his most personally involved. And these are also his most enduringly popular stories, every one of which has been dramatized in some form or another, so that literally millions of people are familiar with the characters and plots without ever having read the originals. It is hoped that this edition will change that, since the subtleties of expression and the delightful turns of phrase can only be appreciated through reading the author's own distinctive narrative.

Nowhere is this narrative more readable than in the *Pickwick Papers,* which was supposed to be a simple chronicle of the adventures of a group of sportsmen, the idea having been suggested by an illustrator who wanted to depict such scenes. But Dickens took this conception of a sporting club and turned it into an inventive picaresque novel (minus the sporting motif) with that most lovable of men, Mr. Pickwick, as its driving force. He, together with Mr. Tupman, Mr. Winkle, and Mr. Snodgrass, roam through parts of England, meeting benevolent old gentlemen, giggly young ladies, rogues, imposing matrons, local politicians, and a host of others, all somehow entwined in the charming vagaries of the plot. In addition to the kindly, almost noble Pickwick, the book boasts two of the most verbally brilliant characters in all of Dickens, the reprobate Alfred Jingle and the faithful servant Sam Weller. Sam Weller is to Pickwick what Sancho Panza is to Don Quixote, yet Sancho did not have Weller's sanguine approach to life's problems nor his unquestioning loyalty. As for Jingle, perhaps nowhere in literature has a villain expressed himself with such hilarious succinctness:

> "Conquests! Thousands. Don Bolaro Fizzgig—Grandee—only daughter—Donna Christina—splendid creature—loved me to distraction—jealous father—high-souled daughter—handsome Englishman—Donna Christina in despair—prussic acid—stomach pump in my portmanteau—operation performed—old Bolaro in ecstasies—consent to our union—join hands and floods of tears—romantic story—very."

But later in the novel the tone shifts, as the club's good-natured ramblings and sojourns at a host of cozy and inviting inns ceases and a more serious focus emerges. This occurs when Pickwick is sued for breach of promise (when he tries to explain to his landlady he is hiring a man-servant, she somehow imagines that he is proposing to her). The trial scenes and Pickwick's subsequent removal to debtor's prison deal with issues that Dickens would handle again and again, developing them more fully in later novels, that of the injustice of the courts, the corruption of lawyers, and the horrors of poverty.

The scenes in debtor's prison (where Dickens' family actually lived for a time) are particularly affecting, as we see people who are in large part victims of circumstances they really cannot control, recreating inside those formidable walls a twisted mirror image of the society they left behind. Here are the influential people who have some money at the top of the hierarchy, who manage to live reasonably well, and then, at the lowest end are the most miserable wretches, hopeless and totally abandoned by the outside world. It is this serious reflection on poverty and the law that gives *Pickwick Papers* its depth and takes it out of the realm of the purely comic novel, although the comedy still abounds and a sense of merriment still manages to penetrate even the somberest proceedings.

Once having touched on serious issues, Dickens went on to expand his thoughts on society in *Oliver Twist,* where the plight of an infant abandoned to the questionable mercies of charity is portrayed with a fascinating blend of realism and fantasy. The harsh realities are drawn in Dickens' vivid descriptions of the treatment of an orphan of the workhouse; the mass starvation of the children (embodied in Oliver's pathetic request, "Please, sir, I want some more"), the cruel punishments, and the practice of virtually selling these orphans to the highest bidder to perform various jobs, as Oliver is parceled off to an undertaker's office. Also vividly portrayed is the criminal syndicate of Fagin and Bill Sikes, the back-alley London underworld that takes friendless Oliver to its bosom when the respectable world casts him off. Oliver finds his first friend, the Artful Dodger, who teaches him how to pick pockets and introduces him to the wily Fagin. It is then that the fantasy elements emerge.

Paralleling the sordid depiction of the world of Fagin and Bill Sikes is the sentimental treatment of Oliver's relationship with Mr. Brownlow and Rose. It is during Oliver's first foray with the Artful Dodger that Mr. Brownlow is chosen as the target by the young felons, and it is during a housebreaking attempt that Oliver meets and stays with Rose. It is certainly a case of vice leading to virtue, for Mr. Brownlow turns out to be the best friend of Oliver's father and Rose turns out to be his mother's younger sister, an unlikely set of coincidences, even for Dickens. These contrasts of vice and virtue tend to permeate the novel, as the cleanliness and order of Mr. Brownlow's house, the concern of his housekeeper, and the abundance of food and warmth counter-balance the dismal, barren surroundings of Bill Sikes; and the serene country setting of the Maylie's house with the lovely flower, Rose, at its center makes the creaky, dark lair of Fagin that much more eerie and decrepit. The only person in the book who seems to escape this good-bad dichotomy is Nancy, Bill Sikes mistress. For even though she lives with Bill knowing how venal he is, yet she has some human feeling and a conscience, as indicated by her attempt to save Oliver from Fagin and Sikes and to restore him to the ministrations of Mr. Brownlow.

Oliver Twist, then, has characters who are by and large static—the good remain good, and the bad die unrepentant. The action really follows little Oliver as he bounces back and forth between these two elements, never wavering in his steadfast devotion to goodness and truth. In *A Christmas Carol*, the situation is different, although in its way, it is as much of a fantasy as *Oliver Twist*. Here, the miser Ebeneezer Scrooge goes through a major metamorphosis, with a little help from the supernatural. At the beginning of the tale London seems divided into two opposing camps—the world of Christmas cheer and the shriveled world of Scrooge. Nowhere is Dickens' power of contrast greater than in his depiction of Scrooge's "Bah, humbug!" attitude next to the joy and good will exhibited by the Cratchit family, Scrooge's nephew Fred, and almost all the rest of the city. Scrooge's mean little evening meal, his cold abode appear the more dismal because of Dicken's descriptions of the warmth inside other homes, the happy bustle of last-minute shoppers rushing through the streets, the shop windows replete with holiday goodies, toys, and finery, and the sounds of good fellowship emanating from the neighborhood pubs.

But, unlike the contrasts in *Oliver Twist,* these do not continue to the end of the story. For, on Christmas eve, Scrooge is visited by those now-legendary figures, the ghosts of Christmas Past, Present, and Future. Suddenly Scrooge is outside himself, looking at himself through the reader's eyes, first as a rejected young boy, then as a suitor more interested in the welfare of his money than that of his lovely fiancée. Then he is looking at Christmas as it is being celebrated around London at present, especially at the home of the Cratchits, where the selflessness and love, the high spirits in spite of the failing health of the crippled Tiny Tim, make Scrooge further examine his own baseness. And then, finally, he is looking at his own death, at the lack of mourners, at the people who owe him money feeling relieved at their sudden good fortune. Then the supernatural elements fade, and Scrooge's transformation begins. On Christmas day he dispenses wealth and happiness as if born to be a kindly and humane benefactor, and the reader is entranced and delighted right along with the astonished onlookers in the story.

It is no accident that *A Christmas Carol* is one of Dickens' most beloved works, since it appeals to everyone's fantasy life, everyone's hope that someone who appears unregenerate carries within himself the seeds of reform. But no less beloved is the story of *David Copperfield,* and in that novel the villains are as unregenerate as possible, primarily because the book is so closely related to Dickens' own life story that he could not allow himself to see good where he knew no good existed. For his entire life Dickens resented one aspect of his parents and other close relatives: they, in his eyes, abandoned him at an early age to the horrors and indignities of child labor. Consequently, the figure of Murdstone, the evil stepfather who marries David's mother, is the artist's conception of the bad aspects of Dickens' own father. The more lovable aspects are recognizable in a character in the very same novel, namely Mr. Micawber, that most lovable of all Dickens' childlike grown-ups, for whom something is always promising to turn up. Micawber, like Dickens Senior, could not manage to keep his family solvent, and his famous maxim came straight from the author's own experience: "Annual income twenty pounds, annual expenditure nineteen nineteen six, result happiness. Annual income twenty pounds, annual expenditure twenty pounds ought and six, result misery."

David Copperfield, like the young Dickens, goes to work in a factory, but he frees himself and goes in search of a surrogate father figure, who is, paradoxically, a woman, his aunt Betsy. It is really aunt Betsy who is the driving, masculine force in David's life, always able to come through for him. It is interesting that the only man in her life besides David (and the spectre of a former husband who occasionally flits across the novel) is Mr. Dick, who is so childlike and submissive he is almost a female counterpart to aunt Betsy.

Biographers have often found similarities between Dora, David's first wife, and Dickens' first love Maria Beadnell, as well as between Agnes, David's second wife and Mary Hogarth, Dickens' sister-in-law. In a sense, both are idealized visions of womanhood, probably because Maria rejected Dickens before he could weary of her faults and Mary died quite young. In the book, Dora is portrayed as a childishly lovable creature who is totally helpless, devoted equally to David and to her little dog. A character like this almost has to be "killed off" as a young girl, because it is obvious she could not survive as a woman. Agnes, on the other hand, takes care of her father when he is undercut by that most unctious and slimy miscreant, Uriah Heep, and so the reader is secure in the knowledge that she will not be an inept housekeeper, like Dora, since both David and Dickens seem to have a need for a well-ordered household. Other parallels between the real and fictional characters include their choice of profession, for David Copperfield also becomes a novelist.

When dealing with the theme of adult betrayal, however, Dickens seems to abandon his own life and concentrates on characters for whom there seem to be no model. There is the dashing, spoiled Steerforth who runs off with the innocent Little Em'ly and the dark, seething, scarred Rosa Dartle, who gloats in her bitterness over the poor girl's seduction. The whole setting by the sea of the landed boat where Em'ly lives with her uncle Peggotty and her would-be suitor Ham is a kind of oasis for David during certain pivotal times in his life, and we get the feeling that Steerforth not only violates Em'ly but David as well by shattering the warmth and serenity of that secure environment.

David Copperfield seems to sum up, then, all that the author felt about children growing up, adults who have never grown up, and those who successfully manage to integrate into their personalities the eddying joy of childhood with the responsibilities of adulthood. Mr. and Mrs. Micawber have never grown up, much as Dickens' parents never really managed to look after their own interests with any regularity. Similarly, Dora, Mr. Dick, Agnes' father, and David's mother, all have a kind of ingenuousness that is judged in terms of the novel almost as weakness. The two people who obviously do manage to grow up, in addition to growing together, are David and Agnes, who presumably will enter their future life together fully equipped to avoid those mistakes made by their parents and who will consequently become what Dickens most admired—a stable, middle-class couple able to provide warmth, love, and financial ease for the children we can fairly assume will be the product of so blissful a union.

Having, with *David Copperfield*, exorcised the traumas and agonies of his childhood, Dickens was ready to turn to subjects that did not directly draw upon his own personal experience. In *Tale of Two Cities*, he turned to an examination of the abuses of the French Revolution.

In *Tale of Two Cities*, Dickens, always against the upheavals implicit in revolution, tells a tragic tale of slaughter and false imprisonment, against a backdrop of political intrigue. Dr. Manette, father of the young heroine Lucie, has been imprisoned for many years in the Bastille because he possessed information damaging to a French nobleman. Lucie's husband, Charles Darnay, is really the nephew of this aristocrat but has renounced all association with him. When Darnay is arrested on a trip to France to help a former servant, Dr. Manette, now freed, follows and helps him to freedom because his background as a prisoner is hailed by the revolutionary forces. When Manette's reason for imprisonment is revealed, Darnay is once again arrested, but this time he is saved by the lawyer Sidney Carton, who is in love with Lucie. It is perhaps one of the most melodramatic moments in all of fiction when Carton, about to die on the guillotine in Darnay's stead, utters his famous, "It is a far, far better thing that I do than I have ever done; it is a far, far better rest that I go to than I have ever known." So, as in all of Dickens, the moral order is restored, and the "two cities" are harmoniously linked in the persons of Darnay and Carton, doubles for one another, now spiritually joined by Carton's self-sacrifice and love for Lucie.

Now, in conclusion, we come to what many consider to be Dickens' masterpiece—thematically perfect, brilliantly executed, morally sound, and superbly funny. In *Great Expectations,* Dickens created some of the most memorable characters ever, people both well-rounded and yet sometimes exaggerated. Central to the novel is Pip, who lives with his elder sister and her husband, the blacksmith Joe Gargery, whom Pip describes as "a mild, good-natured, sweet-tempered, easy-going, foolish, dear fellow." Instead of using Joe as a role model, Pip aspires to higher things. When summoned to the mansion of Miss Havisham to play with her ward Estella, he is immediately overcome with his own low station in life and from this point on he cannot escape his fate, the fate of all snobs.

Miss Havisham is no ordinary wealthy spinster: jilted many years ago on her wedding day, she sits in her disintegrating bridal gown while rats gambol through the decaying wedding cake and cobwebs overhang the room. And Estella is no ordinary young girl: brought up by her benefactress as an instrument of revenge against the male sex, she thwarts and torments Pip, looks down on his lowly birth, and throughout the book fulfills what, through upbringing if not native inclination, can only be *her* destiny.

Pip sees all this quite clearly, but he is still seduced by the lure of becoming a gentleman and he quite readily abandons Joe and his manly strength and goodness when an anonymous offer is made to him that will take him to London and make him the very gentleman he dreams of being. The fact that he assumes the offer is being made by Miss Havisham only underscores his self-delusion and shows his value system is already on shaky ground.

Once in London, Pip meets his roommate, the true gentleman of the novel, Herbert Pocket. Herbert immediately understands that Pip's beloved Estella is "hard and haughty and capricious to the last degree" while Pip continues to adore her. And it is Pip, not Herbert, who is ashamed of Joe, with his country blacksmith manners and his shyness. And it is Pip who is totally abashed, chastened, and ashamed when he learns that the person who gave him every advantage in life was not the already-embalmed Miss Havisham but a desperate convict he helped as a child, who has risked his life to return to London and see Pip again. And Pip cannot cope with the knowledge that a convict is behind his every success: "All the truth of my position came flashing on me; and its disappointments, dangers, disgraces, consequences of all kinds, rushed in in such a multitude that I was borne down by them and had to struggle for every breath I drew.''

It is only when Pip accepts Magwitch, the convict, as a human being who has made mistakes but who is nonetheless a part of him that he can begin to return to the reality of life and give up the illusions. Miss Havisham is an illusionary bride who literally goes up in smoke; Estella is an illusionary woman, who can have no feelings in common with other women, though she can outwardly play the part. Only Joe is real, with his inbred kindness and nobility; and Biddy, the young girl who lives with Joe and continually tells Pip the truth about himself though he is too blind to see it; and Herbert, the modest, easy-going friend is also a real person.

But Pip's return to reality is not enough to restore him to his rightful place in society, because he is robbed of that place by virtue of not belonging to either world—his old one or the new. It is only after eleven years of banishment that Pip can return to Joe and Biddy, who are now married, and see the future will be carried on not by him, but by another:

> There, smoking his pipe in the old place by the kitchen firelight, as hale and as strong as ever, though a little grey, sat Joe; and there, fenced into the corner with Joe's leg, and sitting on my own little stool looking at the fire, was—I again!
>
> ''We giv' him the name of Pip for your sake, dear old chap, and we hoped he might grow a little bit like you, and we think he do.''

Harriet Weitzner
April, 1978

CONTENTS.

MR. PICKWICK.

Posthumous Papers
of
The Pickwick Club

by

Charles Dickens

With Illustrations by
"Phiz" (H. K. Browne),
Barnard, and Others

CONTENTS.

*Original edition repeats chapter number XXVIII.

7

ILLUSTRATIONS

TO

PICKWICK PAPERS.

DEDICATION TO THE ORIGINAL EDITION.

TO

MR. SERJEANT TALFOURD, M.P.,

ETC. ETC.

My Dear Sir,

If I had not enjoyed the happiness of your private friendship, I should still have dedicated this work to you, as a slight and most inadequate acknowledgment of the inestimable services you are rendering to the literature of your country, and of the lasting benefits you will confer upon the authors of this and succeeding generations, by securing to them and their descendants a permanent interest in the copyright of their works.

Many a fevered head and palsied hand will gather new vigour in the hour of sickness and distress from your excellent exertions; many a widowed mother and orphan child, who would otherwise reap nothing from the fame of departed genius but its too frequent legacy of poverty and suffering, will bear, in their altered condition, higher testimony to the value of your labours than the most lavish encomiums from lip or pen could ever afford.

Beside such tributes, any avowal of feeling from me, on the question to which you have devoted the combined advantages of your eloquence, character, and genius, would be powerless indeed. Nevertheless, in thus publicly expressing my deep and grateful sense of your efforts in behalf of English literature, and of those who devote themselves to the most precarious of all pursuits, I do but imperfect justice to my own strong feelings on the subject, if I do no service to you.

These few sentences would have comprised all I should have had to say, if I had only known you in your public character. On the score of private feeling, let me add one word more.

Accept the dedication of this book, my dear Sir, as a mark of my warmest regard and esteem—as a memorial of the most gratifying friendship I have ever contracted, and of some of the pleasantest hours I have ever spent—as a token of my fervent admiration of every fine quality of your head and heart—as an assurance of the truth and sincerity with which I shall ever be,

My dear Sir,

Most faithfully and sincerely yours,

CHARLES DICKENS.

48 DOUGHTY STREET,
September 27, 1837.

12

PREFACE TO THE ORIGINAL EDITION.

THE author's object in this work, was to place before the reader a constant succession of characters and incidents; to paint them in as vivid colours as he could command; and to render them, at the same time, life-like and amusing.

Deferring to the judgment of others in the outset of the undertaking, he adopted the machinery of the club, which was suggested as that best adapted to his purpose: but, finding that it tended rather to his embarrassment than otherwise, he gradually abandoned it, considering it a matter of very little importance to the work whether strictly epic justice were awarded to the club, or not.

The publication of the book in monthly numbers, containing only thirty-two pages in each, rendered it an object of paramount importance that, while the different incidents were linked together by a chain of interest strong enough to prevent their appearing unconnected or impossible, the general design should be so simple as to sustain no injury from this detached and desultory form of publication, extending over no fewer than twenty months. In short, it was necessary—or it appeared so to the author—that every number should be, to a certain extent, complete in itself, and yet that the whole twenty numbers, when collected, should form one tolerably harmonious whole, each leading to the other by a gentle and not unnatural progress of adventure.

It is obvious that in a work published with a view to such considerations, no artfully interwoven or ingeniously complicated plot can with reason be expected. The author ventures to express a hope that he has successfully surmounted the difficulties of his undertaking. And if it be objected to the Pickwick Papers, that they are a mere series of adventures, in which the scenes are ever changing, and the characters come and go like the men and women we encounter in the real world, he can only content himself with the reflection, that they claim to be nothing else, and that the same objection has been made to the works of some of the greatest novelists in the English language.

The following pages have been written from time to time, almost as the periodical occasion arose. Having been written for the most part in the society of a very dear young friend who is now no more, they are connected in the author's mind at once with the happiest period of his life, and with its saddest and most severe affliction.

It is due to the gentleman, whose designs accompany the letter-press, to state that the interval has been so short between the production of each number in manuscript and its appearance in print, that the greater portion of the Illustrations have been executed by the artist from the author's mere verbal description of what he intended to write.

The almost unexampled kindness and favour with which these papers have been received by the public will be a never-failing source of gratifying and pleasant recollection while their author lives. He trusts that, throughout this book, no incident or expression occurs which could call a blush into the most delicate cheek, or wound the feelings of the most sensitive person. If any of his imperfect descriptions, while they afford amusement in the perusal, should induce only one reader to think better of his fellow-men, and to look upon the brighter and more kindly side of human nature, he would indeed be proud and happy to have led to such a result.

POSTHUMOUS PAPERS

OF

THE PICKWICK CLUB.

CHAPTER I.

THE PICKWICKIANS.

THE first ray of light which illumines the gloom, and converts into a dazzling brilliancy that obscurity in which the earlier history of the public career of the immortal Pickwick would appear to be involved, is derived from the perusal of the following entry in the Transactions of the Pickwick Club, which the editor of these papers feels the highest pleasure in laying before his readers, as a proof of the careful attention, indefatigable assiduity, and nice discrimination, with which his search among the multifarious documents confided to him has been conducted.

"May 12, 1827. Joseph Smiggers, Esq., P.V.P. M.P.C.* presiding. The following resolutions unanimously agreed to.

"That this Association has heard read, with feelings of unmingled satisfaction, and unqualified approval, the paper communicated by Samuel Pickwick, Esq., G.C. M.P.C.† entitled "Speculations on the Source of the Hampstead Ponds, with Some Observations on the Theory of Tittlebats;" and that this Association does hereby return its warmest thanks to the said Samuel Pickwick, Esq., G.C. M.P.C. for the same.

"That while this Association is deeply sensible of the advantages which must accrue to the cause of science, from the production to which they have just adverted, no less than from the unwearied researches of Samuel Pickwick, Esq., G.C. M.P.C. in Hornsey, Highgate, Brixton, and Camberwell; they cannot but entertain a lively sense of the inestimable benefits which must inevitably result from carrying the speculations of that learned man into a wider field, from extending his travels, and consequently enlarging his sphere of observation; to the advancement of knowledge, and the diffusion of learning.

"That with the view just mentioned, this Association has taken into its serious consideration a proposal, emanating from the aforesaid Samuel Pickwick, Esq., G.C. M.P.C., and three other Pickwickians hereinafter named, for forming a new branch of United Pickwickians, under the title of The Corresponding Society of the Pickwick Club.

"That the said proposal has received the sanction and approval of this Association.

"That the Corresponding Society of the Pickwick Club is therefore hereby constituted; and that Samuel Pickwick, Esq. G.C. M.P.C., Tracy Tupman, Esq., M.P.C., Augustus Snodgrass, Esq., M.P.C., and Nathaniel Winkle, Esq., M.P.C., are hereby nominated and appointed members of the same: and that they be requested to forward, from time to time, authenticated accounts of their journeys and investigations; of their observations of character and manners; and of the whole of their adventures, together with all tales and papers, to which local scenery or associations may give rise, to the Pickwick Club, stationed in London.

* Perpetual Vice President—Member Pickwick Club.—ED.
† General Chairman—Member Pickwick Club.—ED.

"That this Association cordially recognises the principle of every member of the Corresponding Society defraying his own travelling expenses; and that it sees no objection whatever to the members of the said society pursuing their inquiries for any length of time they please, upon the same terms.

"That the members of the aforesaid Corresponding Society, be, and are, hereby informed, that their proposal to pay the postage of their letters, and the carriage of their parcels, has been deliberated upon, by this Association. That this Association considers such proposal worthy of the great minds from which it emanated; and that it hereby signifies its perfect acquiescence therein."

A casual observer, adds the secretary, to whose notes we are indebted for the following account—a casual observer might possibly have remarked nothing extraordinary in the bald head, and circular spectacles, which were intently turned towards his (the secretary's) face, during the reading of the above resolutions. To those who knew that the gigantic brain of Pickwick was working beneath that forehead, and that the beaming eyes of Pickwick were twinkling behind those glasses, the sight was indeed an interesting one. There sat the man who had traced to their source the mighty ponds of Hampstead, and agitated the scientific world with his Theory of Tittlebats, as calm and unmoved as the deep waters of the one on a frosty day, or as a solitary specimen of the other in the inmost recesses of an earthen jar. And how much more interesting did the spectacle become, when, starting into full life and animation, as a simultaneous call for "Pickwick" burst from his followers, that illustrious man slowly mounted into the Windsor chair, on which he had been previously seated, and addressed the club himself had founded. What a study for an artist did that exciting scene present! The eloquent Pickwick, with one hand gracefully concealed behind his coat tails, and the other waving in air to assist his glowing declamation: his elevated position revealing those tights and gaiters, which had they clothed an ordinary man, might have passed without observation, but which, when Pickwick clothed them—if we may use the expression—inspired involuntary awe and respect; surrounded by the men who had volunteered to share the perils of his travels, and who were destined to participate in the glories of his discoveries. On his right hand, sat Mr. Tracy Tupman; the too susceptible Tupman, who to the wisdom and experience of maturer years superadded the enthusiasm and ardour of a boy, in the most interesting and pardonable of human weaknesses—love. Time and feeding had expanded that once romantic form; the black silk waistcoat had become more and more developed; inch by inch had the gold watch-chain beneath it disappeared from within the range of Tupman's vision; and gradually had the capacious chin encroached upon the borders of the white cravat, but the soul of Tupman had known no change—admiration of the

15

MR. PICKWICK ADDRESSES THE CLUB.

fair sex was still its ruling passion. On the left of his great leader sat the poetic Snodgrass, and near him again the sporting Winkle, the former poetically enveloped in a mysterious blue cloak with a canine-skin collar, and the latter communicating additional lustre to a new green shooting coat, plaid neckerchief, and closely-fitted drabs.

Mr. Pickwick's oration upon this occasion, together with the debate thereon, is entered on the Transactions of the Club. Both bear a strong affinity to the discussions of other celebrated bodies; and, as it is always interesting to trace a resemblance between the proceedings of great men, we transfer the entry to these pages.

"Mr. Pickwick observed (says the Secretary) that fame was dear to the heart of every man. Poetic fame was dear to the heart of his friend Snodgrass, the fame of conquest was equally dear to his friend Tupman; and the desire of earning fame, in the sports of the field, the air, and the water, was uppermost in the breast of his friend Winkle. He (Mr. Pickwick) would not deny, that he was influenced by human passions, and human feelings, (cheers)—possibly by human weaknesses—(loud cries of "No"); but this he would say, that if ever the fire of self-importance broke out in his bosom the desire to benefit the human race in preference effectually quenched it. The praise of mankind was his Swing; philanthropy was his insurance office. (Vehement cheering.) He had felt some pride—he acknowledged it freely; and let his enemies make the most of it—he had felt some pride when he presented his Tittlebatian Theory to the world; it might be celebrated or it might not. (A cry of "It is," and great cheering.) He would take the assertion of that honourable Pickwickian whose voice he had just heard—it was celebrated; but if the fame of that treatise were to extend to the farthest confines of the known world, the pride with which he should reflect on the authorship of that production, would be as nothing compared with the pride with which he looked around him, on this, the proudest moment of his existence. (Cheers.) He was a humble individual. (No, no.) Still he could not but feel that they had selected him for a service of great honour, and of some danger. Travelling was in a troubled state, and the minds of coachmen were unsettled. Let them look abroad, and contemplate the scenes which were enacting around them. Stage coaches were upsetting in all directions, horses were bolting, boats were overturning, and boilers were bursting. (Cheers—a voice "No.") No! (Cheers.) Let that honourable Pickwickian who cried "No" so loudly come forward and deny it, if he could. (Cheers.) Who was it that cried "No?" (Enthusiastic cheering.) Was it some vain and disappointed man—he would not say haberdasher—(loud cheers)—who, jealous of the praise which had been—perhaps undeservedly—bestowed on his (Mr. Pickwick's) researches, and smarting under the censure which had been heaped upon his own feeble attempts at rivalry, now took this vile and calumnious mode of—

"Mr. BLOTTON, (of Aldgate,) rose to order. Did the honourable Pickwickian allude to him? (Cries of "Order," "Chair," "Yes," "No," "Go on," "Leave off," &c.)

"Mr. PICKWICK would not put up to be put down by clamour. He had alluded to the honourable gentleman. (Great excitement.)

"Mr. BLOTTON would only say then, that he repelled the hon. gent's false and scurrilous accusation, with profound contempt. (Great cheering.) The hon. gent. was a hum-

bug. (Immense confusion, and loud cries of "chair" and "order.")

"Mr. A. SNODGRASS rose to order. He threw himself upon the chair. (Hear.) He wished to know, whether this disgraceful contest between two members of that club, should be allowed to continue. (Hear, hear.)

"The CHAIRMAN was quite sure the hon. Pickwickian would withdraw the expression he had just made use of.

"Mr. BLOTTON, with all possible respect for the chair, was quite sure he would not.

"The CHAIRMAN felt it his imperative duty to demand of the honourable gentleman, whether he had used the expression which had just escaped him, in a common sense.

"Mr. BLOTTON had no hesitation in saying, that he had not—he had used the word in its Pickwickian sense. (Hear, hear.) He was bound to acknowledge, that, personally, he entertained the highest regard and esteem for the honourable gentleman; he had merely considered him a humbug in a Pickwickian point of view. (Hear, hear.)

"Mr. PICKWICK felt much gratified by the fair, candid, and full explanation of his honourable friend. He begged it to be at once understood, that his own observations had been merely intended to bear a Pickwickian construction. (Cheers.)"

Here the entry terminates, as we have no doubt the debate did also, after arriving at such a highly satisfactory, and intelligible point. We have no official statement of the facts, which the reader will find recorded in the next chapter, but they have been carefully collated from letters and other MS. authorities, so unquestionably genuine, as to justify their narration in a connected form.

CHAPTER II.

THE FIRST DAY'S JOURNEY, AND THE FIRST EVENING'S ADVENTURES; WITH THEIR CONSEQUENCES.

THAT punctual servant of all work, the sun, had just risen, and begun to strike a light on the thirteenth of May, one thousand eight hundred and twenty-seven, when Mr. Samuel Pickwick burst like another sun from his slumbers; threw open his chamber window, and looked out upon the world beneath. Goswell-street was at his feet, Goswell-street was on his right hand—as far as the eye could reach, Goswell-street extended on his left; and the opposite side of Goswell-street was over the way. "Such," thought Mr. Pickwick, "are the narrow views of those philosophers who, content with examining the things that lie before them, look not to the truths which are hidden beyond. As well might I be content to gaze on Goswell-street for ever, without one effort to penetrate to the hidden countries which on every side surround it." And having given vent to this beautiful reflection, Mr. Pickwick proceeded to put himself into his clothes; and his clothes into his portmanteau. Great men are seldom over scrupulous in the arrangement of their attire; the operation of shaving, dressing, and coffee-imbibing was soon performed: and, in another hour, Mr. Pickwick, with his portmanteau in his hand, his telescope in his great-coat pocket, and his note-book in his waistcoat, ready for the reception of any discoveries worthy of being noted down, had arrived at the coach stand in Saint Martin's-le-Grand.

"Cab!" said Mr. Pickwick.

"Here you are, Sir," shouted a strange specimen of the human race, in a sackcloth coat. and apron of the same, who with a brass label and number round his neck, looked as if he were catalogued in some collection of rarities. This was the waterman. "Here you are, Sir. Now, then, fust cab!" And the first cab having been fetched from the public-house, where he had been smoking his first pipe, Mr. Pickwick and his portmanteau were thrown into the vehicle.

"Golden Cross," said Mr. Pickwick.

"Only a bob's vorth, Tommy,"—cried the driver, sulkily, for the information of his friend the waterman, as the cab drove off.

"How old is that horse, my friend?" inquired Mr. Pickwick, rubbing his nose with the shilling he had reserved for the fare.

"Forty-two," replied the driver, eyeing him askant.

"What!" ejaculated Mr. Pickwick, laying his hand upon his note-book. The driver reiterated his former statement. Mr. Pickwick looked very hard at the man's face, but his features were immoveable, so he noted down the fact forthwith.

"And how long do you keep him out at a time?" inquired Mr. Pickwick, searching for further information.

"Two or three veeks," replied the man.

"Weeks!" said Mr. Pickwick in astonishment—and out came the note-book again.

"He lives at Pentonwil when he's at home," observed the driver, coolly, "but we seldom takes him home, on account of his veakness."

"On account of his weakness;" reiterated the perplexed Mr. Pickwick.

"He always falls down, when he's took out o' the cab," continued the driver, "but when he's in it, we bears him up werry tight, and takes him in werry short, so as he can't werry well fall down, and we've got a pair o' precious large wheels on; so ven he does move, they run after him, and he must go on—he can't help it."

Mr. Pickwick entered every word of this statement in his note-book, with the view of communicating it to the club, as a singular instance of the tenacity of life in horses, under trying circumstances. The entry was scarcely completed when they reached the Golden Cross. Down jumped the driver, and out got Mr. Pickwick. Mr. Tupman, Mr. Snodgrass, and Mr. Winkle, who had been anxiously waiting the arrival of their illustrious leader, crowded to welcome him.

"Here's your fare," said Mr. Pickwick, holding out the shilling to the driver.

What was the learned man's astonishment, when that unaccountable person flung the money on the pavement, and requested in figurative terms to be allowed the pleasure of fighting him (Mr. Pickwick) for the amount!

"You are mad," said Mr. Snodgrass.

"Or drunk," said Mr. Winkle.

"Or both," said Mr. Tupman.

"Come on," said the cab-driver, sparring away like clock-work. "Come on—all four on you."

"Here's a lark!" shouted half a dozen hackney coachmen. "Go to vork, Sam,"—and they crowded with great glee round the party.

"What's the row, Sam?" inquired one gentleman in black calico sleeves.

"Row!" replied the cabman, "What did he want my number for?"

"I didn't want your number," said the astonished Mr. Pickwick.

"What did you take it for, then?" inquired the cabman.

"I didn't take it," said Mr. Pickwick, indignantly.

"Would any body believe," continued the cab-driver, appealing to the crowd,—"Would any body believe as an informer 'ud go about in a man's cab, not only takin' down his number, but ev'ry word he says into the bargain, (a light flashed upon Mr. Pickwick—it was the note-book.)"

"Did he though?" inquired another cabman.

"Yes, did he," replied the first—"and then arter aggeráwatin' me to assault him, gets three witnesses here to prove it. But I'll give it him, if I've six months for it. Come on," and the cabman dashed his hat upon the ground, with a reckless disregard of his own private property, and knocked Mr. Pickwick's spectacles off, and followed up the attack with a blow on Mr. Pickwick's nose, and another on Mr. Pickwick's chest, and a third in Mr. Snodgrass's eye, and a fourth, by way of variety, in Mr. Tupman's waistcoat, and then danced into the road, and back again to the pavement, and finally dashed the whole temporary supply of breath out of Mr. Winkle's body; and all in half a dozen seconds.

"Where's an officer?" said Mr. Snodgrass.

"Put 'em under the pump," suggested a hot-pieman.

"You shall smart for this," gasped Mr. Pickwick.

"Informers," shouted the crowd.

"Come on," cried the cabman, who had been sparring without cessation the whole time.

The mob had hitherto been passive spectators of the scene, but as the intelligence of the Pickwickians being informers was spread among them, they began to canvass with considerable vivacity the propriety of enforcing the heated pastry-vendor's proposition: and there is no saying what acts of personal aggression they might have committed, had not the affray been unexpectedly terminated by the interposition of a new comer.

"What's the fun?" said a rather tall thin young man, in a green coat, emerging suddenly from the coach-yard.

"Informers!" shouted the crowd again.

"We are not," roared Mr. Pickwick, in a tone which, to any dispassionate listener, carried conviction with it.

"Ain't you, though,—ain't you?" said the young man, appealing to Mr. Pickwick, and making his way through the crowd, by the infallible process of elbowing the countenances of its component members.

That learned man in a few hurried words explained the real state of the case.

"Come along, then," said he of the green coat, lugging Mr. Pickwick after him by main force, and talking the whole way. "Here, No. 924, take your fare, and take yourself off—respectable gentleman,—know him well—none of your nonsense—this way, Sir—where's your friends?—all a mistake, I see—never mind—accidents will happen—best regulated families—never say die—down upon your luck—pull him up—put that in his pipe—like the flavour—damned rascals." And with a lengthened string of similar broken sentences, delivered with extraordinary volubility, the stranger led the way to the travellers' waiting room, whither he was closely followed by Mr. Pickwick and his disciples.

"Here, waiter," shouted the stranger, ringing the bell

with tremendous violence, "glasses round,—brandy and water, hot and strong, and sweet, and plenty,—eye damaged, sir? Waiter; raw beef-steak for the gentleman's eye,—nothing like raw beef-steak for a bruise, Sir; cold lamp-post very good, but lamp-post inconvenient—damned odd standing in the open street half an hour, with your eye against a lamp-post—eh,—very good—ha! ha!" And the stranger, without stopping to take breath, swallowed at a draught full half a pint of the reeking brandy and water, and flung himself into a chair with as much ease as if nothing uncommon had occurred.

While his three companions were busily engaged in proffering their thanks to their new acquaintance, Mr. Pickwick had leisure to examine his costume and appearance.

He was about the middle height, but the thinness of his body, and the length of his legs, gave him the appearance of being much taller. The green coat had been a smart dress garment in the days of swallow-tails, but had evidently in those times adorned a much shorter man than the stranger, for the soiled and faded sleeves scarcely reached to his wrists. It was buttoned closely up to his chin, at the imminent hazard of splitting the back; and an old stock, without a vestige of shirt collar, ornamented his neck. His scanty black trousers displayed here and there those shiny patches which bespeak long service, and were strapped very tightly over a pair of patched and mended shoes, as if to conceal the dirty white stockings, which were nevertheless distinctly visible. His long black hair escaped in negligent waves from beneath each side of his old pinched up hat; and glimpses of his bare wrist might be observed, between the tops of his gloves, and the cuffs of his coat sleeves. His face was thin and haggard; but an indescribable air of jaunty impudence and perfect self-possession pervaded the whole man.

Such was the individual, on whom Mr. Pickwick gazed through his spectacles (which he had fortunately recovered), and to whom he proceeded, when his friends had exhausted themselves, to return, in chosen terms, his warmest thanks for his recent assistance.

"Never mind," said the stranger, cutting the address very short, "said enough,—no more; smart chap that cabman—handled his fives well; but if I'd been your friend in the green jemmy—damn me—punch his head,—'cod I would,—pig's whisper—pieman too,—no gammon."

This coherent speech was interrupted by the entrance of the Rochester coachman, to announce that "The Commodore" was on the point of starting.

"Commodore!" said the stranger, starting up, "my coach,—place booked,—one outside—leave you to pay for the brandy and water,—want change for a five,—bad silver—Brummagem buttons—won't do—no go—eh?" and he shook his head most knowingly.

Now it so happened that Mr. Pickwick and his three companions had resolved to make Rochester their first halting place too; and having intimated to their new-found acquaintance that they were journeying to the same city, they agreed to occupy the seat at the back of the coach, where they could all sit together.

"Up with you," said the stranger, assisting Mr. Pickwick on to the roof with so much precipitation, as to impair the gravity of that gentleman's deportment very materially.

"Any luggage, Sir?" inquired the coachman.

"Who—I? Brown paper parcel here, that's all, other luggage gone by water,—packing-cases, nailed up—big as houses—heavy, heavy, damned heavy," replied the stranger, as he forced into his pocket as much as he could of the brown paper parcel, which presented most suspicious indications of containing one shirt and a handkerchief.

"Heads, heads, take care of your heads," cried the loquacious stranger, as they came out under the low archway, which in those days formed the entrance to the coachyard. "Terrible place—dangerous work—other day—five children—mother—tall lady, eating sandwiches—forgot the arch—crash—knock—children look round—mother's head off—sandwich in her hand—no mouth to put it in—head of a family off—shocking, shocking. Looking at Whitehall, Sir,—fine place—little window—somebody else's head off there, eh, Sir?—he didn't keep a sharp look-out enough either—eh, sir, eh?"

"I was ruminating," said Mr. Pickwick, "on the strange mutability of human affairs."

"Ah! I see—in at the palace door one day, out at the window the next. Philosopher, Sir?"

"An observer of human nature, Sir," said Mr. Pickwick.

"Ah, so am I. Most people are when they've little to do and less to get. Poet, Sir?"

"My friend Mr. Snodgrass has a strong poetic turn," said Mr. Pickwick.

"So have I," said the stranger. "Epic poem,—ten thousand lines—revolution of July—composed it on the spot—Mars by day, Apollo by night,—bang the field-piece, twang the lyre."

"You were present at that glorious scene, Sir?" said Mr. Snodgrass.

"Present! think I was; fired a musket,—fired with an idea,—rushed into wine shop—wrote it down—back again—whiz, bang—another idea—wine shop again—pen and ink—back again—cut and slash—noble time, Sir. Sportsman, Sir?" abruptly turning to Mr. Winkle.

"A little, Sir," replied that gentleman.

"Fine pursuit, Sir,—fine pursuit.—Dogs, sir?"

"Not just now," said Mr. Winkle.

"Ah! you should keep dogs—fine animals—sagacious creatures—dog of my own once—Pointer—surprising instinct—out shooting one day—entering inclosure—whistled—dog stopped—whistled again—Ponto—no go: stock still—called him—Ponto, Ponto—wouldn't move—dog transfixed—staring at a board—looked up, saw an inscription—'Gamekeeper has orders to shoot all dogs found in this inclosure'—wouldn't pass it—wonderful dog—valuable dog that—very."

"Singular circumstance that," said Mr. Pickwick. "Will you allow me to make a note of it?" *

"Certainly, Sir, certainly—hundred more anecdotes of the same animal.—Fine girl, Sir" (to Mr. Tracy Tupman, who had been bestowing sundry anti-Pickwickian glances on a young lady by the road side.)

"Very!" said Mr. Tupman.

"English girls not so fine as Spanish—noble creatures—

---

* Although we find this circumstance recorded as a "singular" one, in Mr. Pickwick's note-book, we cannot refrain from humbly expressing our dissent from that learned authority. The stranger's anecdote is not one quarter so wonderful as some of Mr. Jesse's "Gleanings." Ponto sinks into utter insignificance before the dogs whose actions he records.—ED.

jet hair—black eyes—lovely forms—sweet creatures—beautiful."

"You have been in Spain, Sir?" said Mr. Tracy Tupman.

"Lived there—ages."

"Many conquests, Sir?" inquired Mr. Tupman.

"Conquests! Thousands. Don Bolaro Fizzgig—Grandee—only daughter—Donna Christina—splendid creature—loved me to distraction—jealous father—high-souled daughter—handsome Englishman—Donna Christina in despair—prussic acid—stomach pump in my portmanteau—operation performed—old Bolaro in ecstacies—consent to our union—join hands and floods of tears—romantic story—very."

"Is the lady in England now, Sir?" inquired Mr. Tupman, on whom the description of her charms had produced a powerful impression.

"Dead, Sir—dead," said the stranger, applying to his right eye the brief remnant of a very old cambric handkerchief. "Never recovered the stomach pump—undermined constitution—fell a victim."

"And her father?" inquired the poetic Snodgrass.

"Remorse and misery," replied the stranger. "Sudden disappearance—talk of the whole city—search made everywhere—without success—public fountain in the great square suddenly ceased playing—weeks elapsed—still a stoppage—workmen employed to clean it—water drawn off—father-in-law discovered sticking head first in the main pipe, with a full confession in his right boot—took him out, and the fountain played away again, as well as ever."

"Will you allow me to note that little romance down, Sir?" said Mr. Snodgrass, deeply affected.

"Certainly, sir, certainly,—fifty more if you like to hear 'em—strange life mine—rather curious history—not extraordinary, but singular."

In this strain, with an occasional glass of ale, by way of parenthesis, when the coach changed horses, did the stranger proceed, until they reached Rochester bridge, by which time the note-books, both of Mr. Pickwick and Mr. Snodgrass, were completely filled with selections from his adventures.

"Magnificent ruin!" said Mr. Augustus Snodgrass, with all the poetic fervour that distinguished him, when they came in sight of the fine old castle.

"What a study for an antiquarian," were the very words which fell from Mr. Pickwick's mouth, as he applied his telescope to his eye.

"Ah! fine place," said the stranger, "glorious pile—frowning walls—tottering arches—dark nooks—crumbling staircases—Old cathedral too—earthy smell—pilgrims' feet worn away the old steps—little Saxon doors—confessionals like money-takers' boxes at theatres—queer customers those monks—Popes, and Lord Treasurers, and all sorts of old fellows, with great red faces, and broken noses, turning up every day—buff jerkins too—match-locks—Sarcophagus—fine place—old legends too—strange stories: capital;" and the stranger continued to soliloquize until they reached the Bull Inn, in the High street, where the coach stopped.

"Do you remain here, Sir?" inquired Mr. Nathaniel Winkle.

"Here—not I—but you'd better—good house—nice beds—Wright's next house, dear—very dear—half-a-crown in the bill, if you look at the waiter—charge you more if you dine at a friend's than they would if you dined in the coffee-room—rum fellows—very."

Mr. Winkle turned to Mr. Pickwick, and murmured a few words; a whisper passed from Mr. Pickwick to Mr. Snodgrass, from Mr. Snodgrass to Mr. Tupman, and nods of assent were exchanged. Mr. Pickwick addressed the stranger.

"You rendered us a very important service, this morning, Sir," said he; "will you allow us to offer a slight mark of our gratitude by begging the favour of your company at dinner?"

"Great pleasure—not presume to dictate, but broiled fowl and mushrooms—capital thing! What time?"

"Let me see," replied Mr. Pickwick, referring to his watch, "it is now nearly three. Shall we say five?"

"Suit me excellently," said the stranger, "five precisely—till then—care of yourselves;" and lifting the pinched up hat a few inches from his head, and carelessly replacing it very much on one side, the stranger, with half the brown paper parcel sticking out of his pocket, walked briskly up the yard, and turned into the high street.

"Evidently a traveller in many countries, and a close observer of men and things," said Mr. Pickwick.

"I should like to see his poem," said Mr. Snodgrass.

"I should like to have seen that dog," said Mr. Winkle.

Mr. Tupman said nothing; but he thought of Donna Christina, the stomach pump, and the fountain; and his eyes filled with tears.

A private sitting-room having been engaged, bed-rooms inspected, and dinner ordered, the party walked out to view the city, and adjoining neighbourhood.

We do not find, from a careful perusal of Mr. Pickwick's notes on the four towns, Stroud, Rochester, Chatham, and Brompton, that his impressions of their appearance differ in any material point, from those of other travellers who have gone over the same ground. His general description is easily abridged.

"The principal productions of these towns," says Mr. Pickwick, "appear to be soldiers, sailors, Jews, chalk, shrimps, officers, and dockyard men. The commodities chiefly exposed for sale in the public streets, are marine stores, hard-bake, apples, flat-fish, and oysters. The streets present a lively and animated appearance, occasioned chiefly by the conviviality of the military. It is truly delightful to a philanthropic mind, to see these gallant men, staggering along under the influence of an overflow, both of animal, and ardent spirits; more especially when we remember that the following them about, and jesting with them, affords a cheap and innocent amusement for the boy population. Nothing (adds Mr. Pickwick) can exceed their good humour. It was but the day before my arrival, that one of them had been most grossly insulted in the house of a publican. The bar-maid had positively refused to draw him any more liquor; in return for which, he had (merely in playfulness) drawn his bayonet, and wounded the girl in the shoulder. And yet this fine fellow was the very first to go down to the house next morning, and express his readiness to overlook the matter, and forget what had occurred!

"The consumption of tobacco in these towns (continues Mr. Pickwick) must be very great: and the smell which pervades the streets must be exceedingly delicious to those who are extremely fond of smoking. A superficial traveller might object to the dirt which is their leading characteristic; but to those who view it as an indication of traffic, and commercial prosperity, it is truly gratifying."

Punctual to five o'clock, came the stranger, and shortly afterwards the dinner. He had divested himself of his brown paper parcel, but had made no alteration in his attire; and was, if possible, more loquacious than ever.

"What's that?" he inquired, as the waiter removed one of the covers.

"Soles, Sir."

"Soles—ah!—capital fish—all come from London—stage-coach proprietors get up political dinners—carriage of soles—dozens of baskets—cunning fellows. Glass of wine, Sir?"

"With pleasure," said Mr. Pickwick—and the stranger took wine; first with him, and then with Mr. Snodgrass, and then with Mr. Tupman, and then with Mr. Winkle, and then with the whole party together, almost as rapidly as he talked.

"Devil of a mess on the staircase, waiter," said the stranger, "Forms going up—carpenters coming down—lamps, glasses, harps. What's going forward?"

"Ball, Sir," said the waiter.

"Assembly—eh?"

"No, Sir, not Assembly, Sir. Ball for the benefit of a charity, Sir."

"Many fine women in this town, do you know, Sir?" inquired Mr. Tupman, with great interest.

"Splendid—capital. Kent, Sir—Every body knows Kent—apples, cherries, hops, and women. Glass of wine, Sir?"

"With great pleasure," replied Mr. Tupman. The stranger filled, and emptied.

"I should very much like to go," said Mr. Tupman, resuming the subject of the ball, "very much."

"Tickets at the bar, Sir," interposed the waiter, "half-a-guinea each, Sir."

Mr. Tupman again expressed an earnest wish to be present at the festivity; but meeting with no response in the darkened eye of Mr. Snodgrass, or the abstracted gaze of Mr. Pickwick, he applied himself with great interest to the port wine and dessert which had just been placed on the table. The waiter withdrew, and the party were left to enjoy the cosy couple of hours succeeding dinner.

"Beg your pardon, Sir," said the stranger, "Bottle stands—pass it round—way of the sun—through the button-hole—no heel-taps," and he emptied his glass, which he had filled about two minutes before; and poured out another, with the air of a man who was used to it.

The wine was passed, and a fresh supply ordered. The visitor talked, the Pickwickians listened. Mr. Tupman felt every moment more disposed for the ball. Mr. Pickwick's countenance glowed with an expression of universal philanthropy; and Mr. Winkle, and Mr. Snodgrass, fell fast asleep.

"They're beginning up stairs," said the stranger—"hear the company—fiddles tuning—now the harp—there they go." The various sounds which found their way down stairs, announced the commencement of the first quadrille.

"How I should like to go," said Mr. Tupman, again.

"So should I," said the stranger,—"confounded luggage—heavy smacks—nothing to go in—odd, an't it?"

Now general benevolence was one of the leading features of the Pickwickian theory, and no one was more remarkable for the zealous manner in which he observed so noble a principle, than Mr. Tracy Tupman. The number of instances, recorded on the transactions of the Society, in which that excellent man referred objects of charity to the houses of other members for left-off garments, or pecuniary relief, is almost incredible.

"I should be very happy to lend you a change of apparel for the purpose," said Mr. Tracy Tupman, "but you are rather slim, and I am—"

"Rather fat—grown up Bacchus—cut the leaves—dismounted from the tub, and adopted kersey, eh?—not double distilled, but doubled milled—ha! ha!—pass the wine."

Whether Mr. Tupman was somewhat indignant at the peremptory tone in which he was desired to pass the wine which the stranger passed so quickly away; or whether he felt very properly scandalized, at an influential member of the Pickwick club being ignominiously compared to a dismounted Bacchus, is a fact not yet completely ascertained. He passed the wine, coughed twice, and looked at the stranger for several seconds with a stern intensity; as that individual, however, appeared perfectly collected, and quite calm under his searching glance, he gradually relaxed, and reverted to the subject of the ball.

"I was about to observe, Sir," he said, "that though my apparel would be too large, a suit of my friend Mr. Winkle's would, perhaps, fit you better."

The stranger took Mr. Winkle's measure with his eye; and that feature glistened with satisfaction as he said—"Just the thing!"

Mr. Tupman looked round him. The wine which had exerted its somniferous influence over Mr. Snodgrass, and Mr. Winkle, had stolen upon the senses of Mr. Pickwick. That gentleman had gradually passed through the various stages which precede the lethargy produced by dinner, and its consequences. He had undergone the ordinary transitions from the height of conviviality, to the depth of misery, and from the depth of misery, to the height of conviviality. Like a gas lamp in the street, with the wind in the pipe, he had exhibited for a moment an unnatural brilliancy: then sunk so low as to be scarcely discernible: after a short interval, he had burst out again, to enlighten for a moment, then flickered with an uncertain, staggering sort of light, and then gone out altogether. His head was sunk upon his bosom; and perpetual snoring, with a partial choke, occasionally, were the only audible indications of the great man's presence.

The temptation to be present at the ball, and to form his first impressions of the beauty of the Kentish ladies, was strong upon Mr. Tupman. The temptation to take the stranger with him, was equally great. He was wholly unacquainted with the place, and its inhabitants; and the stranger seemed to possess as great a knowledge of both, as if he had lived there from his infancy. Mr. Winkle was asleep, and Mr. Tupman had had sufficient experience in such matters to know, that the moment he awoke, he would, in the ordinary course of nature, roll heavily to bed. He was undecided. "Fill your glass, and pass the wine," said the indefatigable visitor.

Mr. Tupman did as he was requested; and the additional stimulus of the last glass settled his determination.

"Winkle's bed-room is inside mine," said Mr. Tupman; "I couldn't make him understand what I wanted, if I woke him now, but I know he has a dress suit, in a carpet bag; and supposing you wore it to the ball, and took it off when we returned, I could replace it without troubling him at all about the matter."

"Capital," said the stranger, "famous plan—damned odd situation—fourteen coats in the packing cases, and obliged to wear another man's—very good notion, that—very."

"We must purchase our tickets," said Mr. Tupman.

"Not worth while splitting a guinea," said the stranger, "toss who shall pay for both—I call; you spin—first time—woman—woman—bewitching woman," and down came the sovereign, with the Dragon (called by courtesy a woman) uppermost.

Mr. Tupman rang the bell, purchased the tickets, and ordered chamber-candlesticks. In another quarter of an hour, the stranger was completely arrayed in a full suit of Mr. Nathaniel Winkle's.

"It's a new coat," said Mr. Tupman, as the stranger surveyed himself with great complacency in a cheval glass. "The first that's been made with our club button,"—and he called his companion's attention to the large gilt button which displayed a bust of Mr. Pickwick in the centre, and the letters "P. C." on either side.

"P. C.," said the stranger,—"Queer set out—old fellow's likeness, and 'P. C.'—What does P. C. stand for—Peculiar Coat, eh?" Mr. Tupman, with rising indignation, and great importance, explained the mystic device.

"Rather short in the waist, a'nt it?" said the stranger, screwing himself round, to catch a glimpse in the glass of the waist buttons which were half way up his back. "Like a general postman's coat—queer coats those—made by contract—no measuring—mysterious dispensations of Providence—all the short men get long coats—all the long men short ones." Running on in this way, Mr. Tupman's new companion adjusted his dress, or rather the dress of Mr. Winkle; and, accompanied by Mr. Tupman, ascended the staircase leading to the ball room.

"What names, Sir?" said the man at the door. Mr. Tracy Tupman was stepping forward to announce his own titles, when the stranger prevented him.

"No names at all,"—and then he whispered Mr. Tupman, "Names wo'nt do—not known—very good names in their way, but not great ones—capital names for a small party, but won't make an impression in public assemblies—*incog*. the thing—Gentlemen from London—distinguished foreigners—anything." The door was thrown open; and Mr. Tracy Tupman, and the stranger, entered the ball room.

It was a long room, with crimson-covered benches, and wax candles in glass chandeliers. The musicians were securely confined in an elevated den, and quadrilles were being systematically got through by two or three sets of dancers. Two card-tables were made up in the adjoining card-room, and two pair of old ladies, and a corresponding number of stout gentlemen, were executing whist therein.

The finale concluded, the dancers promenaded the room, and Mr. Tupman and his companion stationed themselves in a corner, to observe the company.

"Charming women," said Mr. Tupman.

"Wait a minute," said the stranger, "fun presently—nobs not come yet—queer place—Dock-yard people of upper rank don't know Dock-yard people of lower rank—Dock-yard people of lower rank don't know small gentry—small gentry don't know tradespeople—Commissioner don't know anybody."

"Who's that little boy with the light hair and pink eyes, in a fancy dress?" inquired Mr. Tupman.

"Hush, pray—pink eyes—fancy dress—little boy—nonsense—Ensign 97th.—Honourable Wilmot Snipe—great family—Snipes—very."

"Sir Thomas Clubber, Lady Clubber, and the Miss Clubbers!" shouted the man at the door in a stentorian voice. A great sensation was created throughout the room, by the entrance of a tall gentleman in a blue coat and bright buttons, a large lady in blue satin, and two young ladies on a similar scale, in fashionably-made dresses of the same hue.

"Commissioner—head of the yard—great man—remarkably great man," whispered the stranger in Mr. Tupman's ear, as the charitable committee ushered Sir Thomas Clubber and family to the top of the room. The Honourable Wilmot Snipe, and other distinguished gentlemen crowded to render homage to the Miss Clubbers; and Sir Thomas Clubber stood bolt upright, and looked majestically over his black neckerchief at the assembled company.

"Mr. Smithie, Mrs. Smithie, and the Misses Smithie," was the next announcement.

"What's Mr. Smithie?" inquired Mr. Tracy Tupman.

"Something in the yard," replied the stranger. Mr. Smithie bowed deferentially to Sir Thomas Clubber; and Sir Thomas Clubber acknowledged the salute with conscious condescension. Lady Clubber took a telescope view of Mrs. Smithie and family, through her eye-glass, and Mrs. Smithie, stared in her turn, at Mrs. Somebody else, whose husband was not in the dockyard at all.

"Colonel Bulder, Mrs. Colonel Bulder, and Miss Bulder," were the next arrivals.

"Head of the garrison," said the stranger, in reply to Mr. Tupman's inquiring look.

Miss Bulder was warmly welcomed by the Miss Clubbers; the greeting between Mrs. Colonel Bulder, and Lady Clubber, was of the most affectionate description; Colonel Bulder and Sir Thomas Clubber exchanged snuff-boxes, and looked very much like a pair of Alexander Selkirks;—"Monarchs of all they surveyed."

While the aristocracy of the place—the Bulders, and Clubbers, and Snipes—were thus preserving their dignity at the upper end of the room, the other classes of society were imitating their example in other parts of it. The less aristocratic officers of the 97th devoted themselves to the families of the less important functionaries from the dock-yard. The solicitors' wives, and the wine merchant's wife, headed another grade, (the brewer's wife visited the Bulders;) and Mrs. Tomlinson, the post-office keeper, seemed by mutual consent to have been chosen the leader of the trade party.

One of the most popular personages, in his own circle, present, was a little fat man, with a ring of upright black hair round his head, and an extensive bald plain on the top of it—Doctor Slammer, surgeon to the 97th. The Doctor took snuff with every body, chatted with every body, laughed, danced, made jokes, played whist, did everything, and was everywhere. To these pursuits, multifarious as they were, the little Doctor added a more important one than any—he was indefatigable in paying the most unremitting and devoted attention to a little old widow, whose rich dress and profusion of ornament bespoke her a most desirable addition to a limited income.

Upon the doctor, and the widow, the eyes both of Mr. Tupman and his companion had been fixed for some time, when the stranger broke silence.

"Lots of money—old girl—pompous doctor—not a bad idea—good fun," were the intelligible sentences which issued from his lips. Mr. Tupman looked inquisitively in his face.

"I'll dance with the widow," said the stranger.

"Who is she?" inquired Mr. Tupman.

"Don't know—never saw her in all my life—cut out the doctor—here goes." And the stranger forthwith crossed the room; and, leaning against a mantel-piece, commenced gazing with an air of respectful and melancholy admiration on the fat countenance of the little old lady. Mr. Tupman looked on, in mute astonishment. The stranger progressed rapidly; the little doctor danced with another lady—the widow dropped her fan; the stranger picked it up, and presented it,—a smile—a bow—a curtsey—a few words of conversation. The stranger walked boldly up to, and returned with, the master of the ceremonies; a little introductory pantomime; and the stranger and Mrs. Budger took their places in a quadrille.

The surprise of Mr. Tupman at this summary proceeding, great as it was, was immeasurably exceeded by the astonishment of the doctor. The stranger was young and the widow was flattered. The doctor's attentions were unheeded by the widow; and the doctor's indignation was wholly lost on his imperturbable rival. Doctor Slammer was paralyzed. He, Doctor Slammer of the 97th, to be extinguished in a moment, by a man whom nobody had ever seen before, and whom nobody knew even now! Doctor Slammer—Doctor Slammer of the 97th rejected! Impossible! It could not be! Yes, it was; there they were. What! introducing his friend! Could he believe his eyes! He looked again, and was under the painful necessity of admitting the veracity of his optics; Mrs. Budger was dancing with Mr. Tracy Tupman; there was no mistaking the fact. There was the widow before him, bouncing bodily, here and there, with unwonted vigour; and Mr. Tracy Tupman hopping about, with a face expressive of the most intense solemnity, dancing (as a good many people do) as if a quadrille were not a thing to be laughed at, but a severe trial to the feelings, which it requires inflexible resolution to encounter.

Silently and patiently did the doctor bear all this, and all the handings of negus, and watching for glasses, and darting for biscuits, and coquetting, that ensued; but, a few seconds after the stranger had disappeared to lead Mrs. Budger to her carriage, he darted swiftly from the room with every particle of his hitherto-bottled-up indignation effervescing, from all parts of his countenance, in a perspiration of passion.

The stranger was returning, and Mr. Tupman was beside him. He spoke in a low tone, and laughed. The little doctor thirsted for his life. He was exulting. He had triumphed.

"Sir!" said the doctor, in an awful voice, producing a card, and retiring into an angle of the passage, "my name is Slammer, Doctor Slammer, Sir—97th regiment—Chatham Barracks—my card, Sir, my card." He would have added more, but his indignation choked him.

"Ah!" replied the stranger, coolly, "Slammer—much obliged—polite attention—not ill now, Slammer—but when I am—knock you up."

"You—you're a shuffler, Sir," gasped the furious doctor, "a poltroon—a coward—a liar—a—a—a—will nothing induce you to give me your card, Sir."

"Oh! I see," said the stranger, half aside, "negus too strong here—liberal landlord—very foolish—very—lemonade much better—hot rooms—elderly gentlemen—suffer

for it in the morning—cruel—cruel;" and he moved on a step or two.

"You are stopping in this house, Sir," said the indignant little man; "you are intoxicated now, Sir; you shall hear from me in the morning, Sir. I shall find you out, Sir; I shall find you out."

"Rather you found me out, than found me at home," replied the unmoved stranger.

Doctor Slammer looked unutterable ferocity, as he fixed his hat on his head with an indignant knock: and the stranger and Mr. Tupman ascended to the bed-room of the latter to restore the borrowed plumage to the unconscious Winkle.

That gentleman was fast asleep; the restoration was soon made. The stranger was extremely jocose; and Mr. Tracy Tupman, being quite bewildered with wine, negus, lights, and ladies, thought the whole affair an exquisite joke. His new friend departed; and, after experiencing some slight difficulty in finding the orifice in his night-cap, originally intended for the reception of his head, and finally overturning his candlestick in his struggles to put it on, Mr. Tracy Tupman managed to get into bed, by a series of complicated evolutions, and shortly afterwards sank into repose.

Seven o'clock had hardly ceased striking on the following morning, when Mr. Pickwick's comprehensive mind was aroused from the state of unconsciousness, in which slumber had plunged it, by a loud knocking at his chamber door.

"Who's there?" said Mr. Pickwick, starting up in bed.

"Boots, sir."

"What do you want?"

"Please, sir, can you tell me, which gentleman of your party wears a bright blue dress coat, with a gilt button with P. C. on it?"

"It's been given out to brush," thought Mr. Pickwick; and the man has forgotten whom it belongs to—"Mr. Winkle," he called out, "next room but two, on the right hand."

"Thank'ee, sir," said the Boots, and away he went.

"What's the matter?" cried Mr. Tupman, as a loud knocking at *his* door roused *him* from his oblivious repose.

"Can I speak to Mr. Winkle, sir?" replied the Boots from the outside.

"Winkle—Winkle," shouted Mr. Tupman, calling into the inner room.

"Hallo!" replied a faint voice from within the bed-clothes.

"You're wanted—some one at the door—" and having exerted himself to articulate thus much, Mr. Tracy Tupman turned round and fell fast asleep again.

"Wanted!" said Mr. Winkle, hastily jumping out of bed, and putting on a few articles of clothing: "wanted! at this distance from town—who on earth can want me!"

"Gentleman in the coffee room, sir," replied the Boots, as Mr. Winkle opened the door, and confronted him; "gentleman says he'll not detain you a moment, sir, but he can take no denial."

"Very odd!" said Mr. Winkle; "I'll be down directly."

He hurriedly wrapped himself in a travelling-shawl, and dressing-gown, and proceeded down stairs. An old woman and a couple of waiters were cleaning the coffee room, and an officer in undress uniform was looking out of the window. He turned round as Mr. Winkle entered, and made a stiff inclination of the head. Having ordered the attend-

"WHAT! INTRODUCING HIS FRIEND!"

ants to retire, and closed the door very carefully, he said, "Mr. Winkle, I presume?"

"My name *is* Winkle, sir."

"You will not be surprised, sir, when I inform you, that I have called here this morning on behalf of my friend, Dr. Slammer, of the Ninety-seventh."

"Doctor Slammer!" said Mr. Winkle.

"Doctor Slammer. He begged me to express his opinion that your conduct of last evening was of a description which no gentleman could endure: and (he added) which no one gentleman would pursue towards another."

Mr. Winkle's astonishment was too real, and too evident, to escape the observation of Doctor Slammer's friend; he therefore proceeded.—"My friend, Doctor Slammer, requested me to add, that he is firmly persuaded you were intoxicated during a portion of the evening, and possibly unconscious of the extent of the insult you were guilty of. He commissioned me to say, that should this be pleaded as an excuse for your behaviour, he will consent to accept a written apology, to be penned by you, from my dictation."

"A written apology!" repeated Mr. Winkle, in the most emphatic tone of amazement possible.

"Of course you know the alternative," replied the visitor, coolly.

"Were you entrusted with this message to me, by name?" inquired Mr. Winkle, whose intellects were hopelessly confused by this extraordinary conversation.

"I was not present myself," replied the visitor, "and in consequence of your firm refusal to give your card to Doctor Slammer, I was desired by that gentleman to identify the wearer of a very uncommon coat—a bright blue dress coat, with a gilt button, displaying a bust, and the letters 'P. C.'"

Mr. Winkle actually staggered with astonishment, as he heard his own costume thus minutely described. Doctor Slammer's friend proceeded:—

"From the inquiries I made at the bar, just now, I was convinced that the owner of the coat in question arrived here, with three gentlemen, yesterday afternoon. I immediately sent up to the gentleman who was described as appearing the head of the party; and he, at once, referred me to you."

If the principal tower of Rochester Castle had suddenly walked from its foundation, and stationed itself opposite the coffee-room window, Mr. Winkle's surprise would have been as nothing, compared with the profound astonishment with which he had heard this address. His first impression was, that his coat had been stolen. "Will you allow me to detain you one moment?" said he.

"Certainly," replied the unwelcome visitor.

Mr. Winkle ran hastily up-stairs, and with a trembling hand opened the bag. There was the coat in its usual place, but exhibiting, on a close inspection, evident tokens of having been worn on the preceding night.

"It must be so," said Mr. Winkle, letting the coat fall from his hands. "I took too much wine after dinner, and have a very vague recollection of walking about the streets, and smoking a cigar afterwards. The fact is, I was very drunk;—I must have changed my coat—gone somewhere—and insulted somebody—I have no doubt of it; and this message is the terrible consequence." Saying which, Mr. Winkle retraced his steps in the direction of the coffee-room, with the gloomy and dreadful resolve of accepting the challenge of the warlike Doctor

Slammer, and abiding by the worst consequences that might ensue.

To this determination Mr. Winkle was urged by a variety of considerations; the first of which was, his reputation with the club. He had always been looked up to as a high authority on all matters of amusement and dexterity, whether offensive, defensive, or inoffensive; and if, on this very first occasion of being put to the test, he shrunk back from the trial, beneath his leader's eye, his name and standing were lost for ever. Besides, he remembered to have heard it frequently surmised by the uninitiated in such matters, that by an understood arrangement between the seconds, the pistols were seldom loaded with ball; and, furthermore, he reflected that if he applied to Mr. Snodgrass to act as his second, and depicted the danger in glowing terms, that gentleman might possibly communicate the intelligence to Mr. Pickwick, who would certainly lose no time in transmitting it to the local authorities, and thus prevent the killing or maiming of his follower.

Such were his thoughts when he returned to the coffee-room, and intimated his intention of accepting the Doctor's challenge.

"Will you refer me to a friend, to arrange the time and place of meeting?" said the officer.

"Quite unnecessary," replied Mr. Winkle; "name them to me, and I can procure the attendance of a friend, afterwards."

"Shall we say—sunset this evening?" inquired the officer, in a careless tone.

"Very good," replied Mr. Winkle; thinking in his heart it was very bad.

"You know Fort Pitt?"

"Yes; I saw it yesterday."

"If you will take the trouble to turn into the field which borders the trench, take the foot-path to the left, when you arrive at an angle of the fortification; and keep straight on 'till you see me; I will precede you to a secluded place, where the affair can be conducted without fear of interruption."

"*Fear* of interruption!" thought Mr. Winkle.

"Nothing more to arrange, I think," said the officer.

"I am not aware of anything more," replied Mr. Winkle.

"Good morning."

"Good morning:" and the officer whistled a lively air, as he strode away.

That morning's breakfast passed heavily off. Mr. Tupman was not in a condition to rise, after the unwonted dissipation of the previous night; Mr. Snodgrass appeared to labour under a poetical depression of spirits; and even Mr. Pickwick evinced an unusual attachment to silence and soda water. Mr. Winkle eagerly watched his opportunity. It was not long wanting. Mr. Snodgrass proposed a visit to the castle, and as Mr. Winkle was the only other member of the party disposed to walk, they went out together.

"Snodgrass," said Mr. Winkle, when they had turned out of the public street; "Snodgrass, my dear fellow, can I rely upon your secresy?" As he said this, he most devoutly and earnestly hoped he could not.

"You can," replied Mr. Snodgrass. "Hear me swear—"

"No, no;" interrupted Winkle, terrified at the idea of his companion's unconsciously pledging himself not to give information; "don't swear; it's quite unnecessary."

Mr. Snodgrass dropped the hand which he had, in the spirit of poesy, raised towards the clouds, as he made the above appeal, and assumed an attitude of attention.

"I want your assistance, my dear fellow, in an affair of honour," said Mr. Winkle.

"You shall have it," replied Mr. Snodgrass, clasping his friend's hand.

"With a Doctor—Doctor Slammer, of the Ninety-seventh," said Mr. Winkle, wishing to make the matter appear as solemn as possible; "an affair with an officer, seconded by another officer, at sunset this evening, in a lonely field beyond Fort Pitt."

"I will attend you," said Mr. Snodgrass.

He was astonished, but by no means dismayed. It is extraordinary how cool any party but the principal can be in such cases. Mr. Winkle had forgotten this. He had judged of his friend's feelings by his own.

"The consequences may be dreadful," said Mr. Winkle.

"I hope not," said Mr. Snodgrass.

"The Doctor, I believe, is a very good shot," said Mr. Winkle.

"Most of these military men are," observed Mr. Snodgrass, calmly; "but so are you, a'n't you?"

Mr. Winkle replied in the affirmative; and perceiving that he had not alarmed his companion sufficiently, changed his ground.

"Snodgrass," he said, in a voice tremulous with emotion, "if I fall, you will find in a packet which I shall place in your hands a note for my—for my father."

This attack was a failure also. Mr. Snodgrass was affected, but he undertook the delivery of the note, as readily as if he had been a Twopenny Postman.

"If I fall," said Mr. Winkle, "or if the Doctor falls, you, my dear friend, will be tried as an accessory before the fact. Shall I involve my friend in transportation—possibly for life!"

Mr. Snodgrass winced a little at this, but his heroism was invincible. "In the cause of friendship," he fervently exclaimed, "I would brave all dangers."

How Mr. Winkle cursed his companion's devoted friendship internally, as they walked silently along, side by side, for some minutes, each immersed in his own meditations! The morning was wearing away; he grew desperate.

"Snodgrass," he said, stopping suddenly, "do not let me be baulked in this matter—do not give information to the local authorities—do not obtain the assistance of several peace officers, to take either me or Doctor Slammer, of the Ninety-seventh Regiment, at present quartered in Chatham Barracks, into custody, and thus prevent this duel;—I say, do not."

Mr. Snodgrass seized his friend's hand warmly, as he enthusiastically replied, "Not for worlds!"

A thrill passed over Mr. Winkle's frame, as the conviction, that he had nothing to hope from his friend's fears, and that he was destined to become an animated target, rushed forcibly upon him.

The state of the case having been formally explained to Mr. Snodgrass, and a case of satisfaction pistols, with the satisfactory accompaniments of powder, ball, and caps, having been hired from a manufacturer in Rochester, the two friends returned to their inn: Mr. Winkle, to ruminate on the approaching struggle; and Mr. Snodgrass, to arrange the weapons of war, and put them into proper order for immediate use.

It was a dull and heavy evening, when they again sallied forth on their awkward errand. Mr. Winkle was muffled up in a huge cloak to escape observation; and Mr. Snodgrass bore under his the instruments of destruction.

"Have you got ev'rything?" said Mr. Winkle, in an agitated tone.

"Ev'rything," replied Mr. Snodgrass; "plenty of ammunition, in case the shots don't take effect. There's a quarter of a pound of powder in the case, and I have got two newspapers in my pocket, for the loadings."

These were instances of friendship, for which any man might reasonably feel most grateful. The presumption is, that the gratitude of Mr. Winkle was too powerful for utterance, as he said nothing, but continued to walk on—rather slowly.

"We are in excellent time," said Mr. Snodgrass, as they climbed the fence of the first field; "the sun is just going down." Mr. Winkle looked up at the declining orb, and painfully thought of the probability of his "going down" himself, before long.

"There's the officer," exclaimed Mr. Winkle, after a few minutes' walking.

"Where?" said Mr. Snodgrass.

"There;—the gentleman in the blue cloak." Mr. Snodgrass looked in the direction indicated by the forefinger of his friend, and observed a figure, muffled up, as he had described. The officer evinced his consciousness of their presence by slightly beckoning with his hand; and the two friends followed him, at a little distance, as he walked away.

The evening grew more dull every moment, and a melancholy wind sounded through the deserted fields, like a distant giant whistling for his house-dog. The sadness of the scene imparted a sombre tinge to the feelings of Mr. Winkle. He started as they passed the angle of the trench—it looked like a colossal grave.

The officer turned suddenly from the path; and after climbing a paling, and scaling a hedge, entered a secluded field. Two gentlemen were waiting in it; one was a little fat man, with black hair; and the other—a portly personage in a braided surtout—was sitting with perfect equanimity on a camp-stool.

"The other party, and a surgeon, I suppose," said Mr. Snodgrass; "take a drop of brandy." Mr. Winkle seized the wicker bottle, which his friend proffered, and took a lengthened pull at the exhilarating liquid.

"My friend, sir, Mr. Snodgrass," said Mr. Winkle, as the officer approached. Doctor Slammer's friend bowed, and produced a case similar to that which Mr. Snodgrass carried.

"We have nothing further to say, sir, I think," he coldly remarked, as he opened the case; "an apology has been resolutely declined."

"Nothing, sir," said Mr. Snodgrass, who began to feel rather uncomfortable himself.

"Will you step forward?" said the officer.

"Certainly," replied Mr. Snodgrass. The ground was measured, and preliminaries arranged.

"You will find these better than your own," said the opposite second, producing his pistols. "You saw me load them. Do you object to use them?"

"Certainly not," replied Mr. Snodgrass. The offer relieved him from considerable embarrassment; for his previous notions of loading a pistol were rather vague and undefined.

"We may place our men, then, I think," observed the officer, with as much indifference as if the principals were chess-men, and the seconds players.

"I think we may," replied Mr. Snodgrass; who would have assented to any proposition, because he knew nothing about the matter. The officer crossed to Doctor Slammer, and Mr. Snodgrass went up to Mr. Winkle.

"It's all ready," he said, offering the pistol. "Give me your cloak."

"You have got the packet, my dear fellow," said poor Winkle.

"All right," said Mr. Snodgrass. "Be steady, and wing him."

It occurred to Mr. Winkle that this advice was very like that which by-standers invariably give to the smallest boy in a street fight; namely, "Go in, and win:"—an admirable thing to recommend, if you only know how to do it. He took off his cloak, however, in silence—it always took a long time to undo that cloak—and accepted the pistol. The seconds retired, the gentleman on the camp-stool did the same, and the belligerents approached each other.

Mr Winkle was always remarkable for extreme humanity. It is conjectured that his unwillingness to hurt a fellow-creature intentionally, was the cause of his shutting his eyes when he arrived at the fatal spot; and that the circumstance of his eyes being closed, prevented his observing the very extraordinary and unaccountable demeanour of Doctor Slammer. That gentleman started, stared, retreated, rubbed his eyes, stared again; and, finally, shouted "Stop, stop!"

"What's all this?" said Doctor Slammer, as his friend and Mr. Snodgrass came running up—"That's not the man."

"Not the man!" said Doctor Slammer's second.

"Not the man!" said Mr. Snodgrass.

"Not the man!" said the gentleman with the camp-stool in his hand.

"Certainly not," replied the little doctor. "That's not the person who insulted me last night."

"Very extraordinary!" exclaimed the officer.

"Very," said the gentleman with the camp-stool. "The only question is, whether the gentleman, being on the ground, must not be considered, as a matter of form, to be the individual who insulted our friend, Dr. Slammer, yesterday evening, whether he is really that individual or not:" and having delivered this suggestion, with a very sage and mysterious air, the man with the camp-stool took a large pinch of snuff, and looked profoundly round, with the air of an authority in such matters.

Now Mr. Winkle had opened his eyes, and his ears too, when he heard his adversary call out for a cessation of hostilities; and perceiving by what he had afterwards said, that there was, beyond all question, some mistake in the matter, he at once foresaw the increase of reputation he should inevitably acquire, by concealing the real motive of his coming out: he therefore stepped boldly forward, and said—

"I am not the person. I know it."

"Then, that," said the man with the camp-stool, "is an affront to Doctor Slammer, and a sufficient reason for proceeding immediately."

"Pray be quiet, Payne," said the Doctor's second. "Why did you not communicate this fact to me, this morning, sir?"

"To be sure—to be sure," said the man with the camp-stool, indignantly.

"I entreat you to be quiet, Payne," said the other. "May I repeat my question, sir?"

"Because, sir," replied Mr. Winkle, who had had time to deliberate upon his answer—"because, sir, you described an intoxicated and ungentlemanly person as wearing a coat, which I have the honour, not only to wear, but to have invented—the proposed uniform, sir, of the Pickwick Club in London. The honour of that uniform I feel bound to maintain, and I therefore, without inquiry, accepted the challenge which you offered me."

"My dear sir," said the good-humoured little doctor, advancing with extended hand, "I honour your gallantry. Permit me to say, sir, that I highly admire your conduct, and extremely regret having caused you the inconvenience of this meeting, to no purpose."

"I beg you won't mention it, sir," said Mr. Winkle.

"I shall feel proud of your acquaintance, sir," said the little doctor.

"It will afford me the greatest pleasure to know you, sir," replied Mr. Winkle. Thereupon the Doctor and Mr. Winkle shook hands, and then Mr. Winkle and Lieutenant Tappleton (the doctor's second), and then Mr. Winkle and the man with the camp-stool, and, finally, Mr. Winkle and Mr. Snodgrass: the last named gentleman in an excess of admiration at the noble conduct of his heroic friend.

"I think we may adjourn," said Lieutenant Tappleton.

"Certainly," added the Doctor.

"Unless," interposed the man with the camp-stool, "unless Mr. Winkle feels himself aggrieved by the challenge; in which case, I submit, he has a right to satisfaction."

Mr. Winkle, with great self-denial, expressed himself quite satisfied already.

"Or possibly," said the man with the camp-stool, "the gentleman's second may feel himself affronted with some observations which fell from me at an early period of this meeting: if so, I shall be happy to give *him* satisfaction immediately."

Mr. Snodgrass hastily professed himself very much obliged with the handsome offer of the gentleman who had spoken last, which he was only induced to decline, by his entire contentment with the whole proceedings. The two seconds adjusted the cases, and the whole party left the ground in a much more lively manner than they had proceeded to it.

"Do you remain long here?" inquired Doctor Slammer of Mr. Winkle, as they walked on most amicably together.

"I think we shall leave here the day after to-morrow," was the reply.

"I trust I shall have the pleasure of seeing you and your friend at my rooms, and of spending a pleasant evening with you, after this awkward mistake," said the little doctor; "are you disengaged this evening?"

"We have some friends here," replied Mr. Winkle, "and I should not like to leave them to-night. Perhaps you and your friend will join us at the Bull."

"With great pleasure," said the little doctor; "will ten o'clock be too late to look in for half an hour?"

"Oh dear, no," said Mr. Winkle. "I shall be most happy to introduce you to my friends, Mr. Pickwick and Mr. Tupman."

"It will give me great pleasure, I am sure," replied Doctor Slammer, little suspecting who Mr. Tupman was.

"You will be sure to come?" said Mr. Snodgrass.

"Oh certainly."

By this time they had reached the road. Cordial farewells were exchanged, and the party separated. Doctor Slammer and his friends repaired to the barracks, and Mr. Winkle, accompanied by his friend, Mr. Snodgrass, returned to their inn.

CHAPTER III

A NEW ACQUAINTANCE. THE STROLLER'S TALE—A DISAGREEABLE INTERRUPTION; AND AN UN-PLEASANT RENCONTRE.

MR. PICKWICK had felt some apprehensions in consequence of the unusual absence of his two friends, which their mysterious behaviour during the whole morning had by no means tended to diminish. It was, therefore, with more than ordinary pleasure that he rose to greet them when they again entered; and with more than ordinary interest that he inquired what had occurred to detain them from his society. In reply to his questions on this point, Mr. Snodgrass was about to offer an historical account of the circumstances just now detailed, when he was suddenly checked, by observing that there were present, not only Mr. Tupman and their stage-coach companion of the preceding day, but another stranger of equally singular appearance. It was a care-worn looking man, whose sallow face, and deeply sunken eyes, were rendered still more striking than nature had made them, by the straight black hair which hung in matted disorder half way down his face. His eyes were almost unnaturally bright and piercing; his cheek-bones were high and prominent; and his jaws were so long and lank, that an observer would have supposed he was drawing the flesh of his face in, for a moment, by some contraction of the muscles, if his half-opened mouth and immoveable expression had not announced that it was his ordinary appearance. Round his neck he wore a green shawl, with the large ends straggling over his chest, and making their appearance occasionally, beneath the worn button-holes of his old waistcoat. His upper garment was a long black surtout; and below it, he wore wide drab trousers, and large boots, running rapidly to seed.

It was on this uncouth-looking person, that Mr. Winkle's eye rested, and it was towards him that Mr. Pickwick extended his hand when he said, "A friend of our friend's here. We discovered this morning that our friend is connected with the theatre in this place, though he is not desirous to have it generally known, and this gentleman is a member of the same profession. He was about to favour us with a little anecdote connected with it, when you entered."

"Lots of anecdote," said the green-coated stranger of the day before, advancing to Mr. Winkle and speaking in a low confidential tone. "Rum fellow—does the heavy business—no actor—strange man—all sorts of miseries—dismal Jemmy, we call him on the circuit." Mr. Winkle and Mr. Snodgrass politely welcomed the gentleman, elegantly designated as "Dismal Jemmy;" and calling for brandy and water, in imitation of the remainder of the company, seated themselves at the table.

"Now, Sir," said Mr. Pickwick, "will you oblige us with proceeding with what you were going to relate?"

The dismal individual took a dirty roll of paper from his pocket, and turning to Mr. Snodgrass, who had just taken out his note-book, said in a hollow voice, perfectly in keeping with his outward man—"Are you the poet?"

"I—I do a little in that way," replied Mr. Snodgrass, rather taken aback by the abruptness of the question.

"Ah! poetry makes life, what lights and music do the stage. Strip the one of its false embellishments, and the other of its illusions, and what is there real in either, to live or care for?"

"Very true, Sir," replied Mr. Snodgrass.

"To be before the footlights," continued the dismal man, "is like sitting at a grand, court show, and admiring the silken dresses of the gaudy throng—to be behind them, is to be the people who make that finery, uncared for and unknown, and left to sink or swim, to starve or live, as fortune wills it."

"Certainly," said Mr. Snodgrass: for the sunken eye of the dismal man rested on him, and he felt it necessary to say something.

"Go on, Jemmy," said the Spanish traveller, "like black-eyed Susan—all in the Downs—no croaking—speak out—look lively."

"Will you make another glass before you begin, Sir?" said Mr. Pickwick.

The dismal man took the hint, and having mixed a glass of brandy and water, and slowly swallowed half of it, opened the roll of paper and proceeded, partly to read and partly to relate, the following incident, which we find recorded on the Transactions of the club, as "The Stroller's Tale."

THE STROLLER'S TALE.

"THERE is nothing of the marvellous in what I am going to relate," said the dismal man; "there is nothing even uncommon in it. Want and sickness are too common in many stations of life, to deserve more notice than is usually bestowed on the most ordinary vicissitudes of human nature. I have thrown these few notes together, because the subject of them was well known to me for many years. I traced his progress downwards, step by step, until at last he reached that excess of destitution from which he never rose again.

"The man of whom I speak was a low pantomime actor; and, like many people of his class, an habitual drunkard. In his better days, before he had become enfeebled by dissipation and emaciated by disease, he had been in the receipt of a good salary, which, if he had been careful and prudent, he might have continued to receive for some years —not many; because these men either die early, or, by unnaturally taxing their bodily energies, lose, prematurely, those physical powers on which alone they can depend for subsistence. His besetting sin gained so fast upon him, however, that it was found impossible to employ him in the situations in which he really was useful to the theatre. The public-house had a fascination for him which he could not resist. Neglected disease and hopeless poverty were as certain to be his portion as death itself, if he persevered in the same course; yet he *did* persevere, and the result may be guessed. He could obtain no engagement, and he wanted bread.

"Everybody who is at all acquainted with theatrical matters, knows what a host of shabby, poverty-stricken men, hang about the stage of a large establishment—not regularly engaged actors, but ballet people, procession men, tumblers, and so forth, who are taken on during the run of a pantomime, or an Easter piece, and are then discharged, until the production of some heavy spectacle occasions a new demand for their services. To this mode of life the man was compelled to resort: and taking the chair every night, at some low theatrical house, at once put him in possession of a few more shillings weekly, and enabled him to gratify his old propensity. Even this resource shortly failed him; his irregularities were too great to admit of his earning the wretched pittance he might thus have procured, and he was actually reduced to a state bordering on starvation, only procuring a trifle occasionally by borrowing it of some old companion, or by obtaining an appearance at one or other of the commonest of the minor theatres; and when he did earn anything, it was spent in the old way.

"About this time, and when he had been existing for upwards of a year no one knew how, I had a short engagement at one of the theatres on the Surrey side of the water, and here I saw this man, whom I had lost sight of for some time; for I had been travelling in the provinces, and he had been skulking in the lanes and alleys of London. I was dressed to leave the house, and was crossing the stage on my way out, when he tapped me on the shoulder. Never shall I forget the repulsive sight that met my eye when I turned round. He was dressed for the pantomime, in all the absurdity of a clown's costume. The spectral figures in the Dance of Death, the most frightful shapes that the ablest painter ever portrayed on canvas, never presented an appearance half so ghastly. His bloated body and shrunken legs—their deformity enhanced a hundred fold by the fantastic dress—the glassy eyes, contrasting fearfully with the thick white paint with which the face was besmeared: the grotesquely-ornamented head, trembling with paralysis, and the long skinny hands, rubbed with white chalk—all gave him a hideous and unnatural appearance, of which no description could convey an adequate idea, and which, to this day, I shudder to think of. His voice was hollow and tremulous, as he took me aside, and in broken words recounted a long catalogue of sickness and privations, terminating, as usual, with an urgent request for the loan of a trifling sum of money. I put a few shillings in his hand, and, as I turned away, I heard the roar of laughter which followed his first tumble on to the stage.

"A few nights afterwards, a boy put a dirty scrap of paper in my hand, on which were scrawled a few words in pencil, intimating that the man was dangerously ill, and begging me, after the performance, to see him at his lodgings in some street—I forget the name of it now—at no great distance from the theatre. I promised to comply, as soon as I could get away; and, after the curtain fell, sallied forth on my melancholy errand.

"It was late, for I had been playing in the last piece; and, as it was a benefit night, the performances had been protracted to an unusual length. It was a dark cold night, with a chill damp wind, which blew the rain heavily against the windows and house-fronts. Pools of water had collected in the narrow and little-frequented streets, and as many of the thinly-scattered oil-lamps had been blown out by the violence of the wind, the walk was not only a comfortless, but most uncertain one. I had fortunately taken the right course, however, and succeeded, after a little difficulty, in finding the house to which I had been directed—a coal shed, with one story above it, in the back room of which lay the object of my search.

"A wretched-looking woman, the man's wife, met me on the stairs, and, telling me that he had just fallen into a kind of a doze, led me softly in, and placed a chair for me at the bed-side. The sick man was lying with his face turned towards the wall; and as he took no heed of my presence, I had leisure to observe the place in which I found myself.

"He was lying on an old bedstead, which turned up during the day. The tattered remains of a checked curtain were drawn round the bed's head, to exclude the wind, which however made its way into the comfortless room through the numerous chinks in the door, and blew it to and fro every instant. There was a low cinder fire in a rusty unfixed grate; and an old three-cornered stained table, with some medicine-bottles, a broken glass, and a few other domestic articles, was drawn out before it. A little child was sleeping on a temporary bed which had been made for it on the floor, and the woman sat on a chair by its side. There were a couple of shelves, with a few plates and cups and saucers: and a pair of stage shoes and a couple of foils hung beneath them. With the exception of little heaps of rags and bundles which had been carelessly thrown into the corners of the room, these were the only things in the apartment.

"I had had time to note these little particulars, and to mark the heavy breathing and feverish startings of the sick man, before he was aware of my presence. In his restless attempts to procure some easy resting-place for his head, he tossed his hand out of the bed, and it fell on mine. He started up, and stared eagerly in my face.

"'Mr. Hutley, John,' said his wife; 'Mr. Hutley, that you sent for to-night, you know.'

"'Ah!' said the invalid, passing his hand across his forehead; 'Hutley—Hutley—let me see.' He seemed endeavouring to collect his thoughts for a few seconds, and then grasping me tightly by the wrist, said, 'Don't leave me—don't leave me, old fellow. She'll murder me; I know she will.'

"'Has he been long so?' said I, addressing his weeping wife.

"'Since yesterday night,' she replied. 'John, John, don't you know me?'

"'Don't let her come near me,' said the man, with a shudder, as she stooped over him. 'Drive her away; I can't bear her near me.' He stared wildly at her, with a look of deadly apprehension, and then whispered in my ear, 'I beat her, Jem; I beat her yesterday, and many times before. I have starved her, and the boy too; and now I am weak and helpless, Jem, she'll murder me for it; I know she will. If you'd seen her cry, as I have, you'd know it too. Keep her off.' He relaxed his grasp, and sank back exhausted on the pillow.

"I knew but too well what all this meant. If I could have entertained any doubt of it, for an instant, one glance at the woman's pale face and wasted form would have sufficiently explained the real state of the case. 'You had better stand aside,' said I to the poor creature. 'You can do him no good. Perhaps he will be calmer, if he does not see you.' She retired out of the man's sight. He opened his eyes, after a few seconds, and looked anxiously round.

"'Is she gone?' he eagerly inquired.

"'Yes—yes,' said I; 'she shall not hurt you.'

"'I'll tell you what, Jem,' said the man, in a low voice, 'she does hurt me. There's something in her eyes wakes such a dreadful fear in my heart, that it drives me mad. All last night, her large staring eyes and pale face were close to mine; wherever I turned, they turned; and whenever I started up from my sleep, she was at the bed-side looking at me.' He drew me closer to him, as he said in a deep, alarmed whisper—'Jem, she must be an evil spirit—a devil! Hush! I know she is. If she had been a woman, she would have died long ago. No woman could have borne what she has.'

"I sickened at the thought of the long course of cruelty and neglect which must have occurred to produce such an impression on such a man. I could say nothing in reply;

for who could offer hope, or consolation, to the abject being before me?

"I sat there for upwards of two hours, during which time he tossed about, murmuring exclamations of pain or impatience, restlessly throwing his arms here and there, and turning constantly from side to side. At length he fell into that state of partial unconsciousness, in which the mind wanders uneasily from scene to scene, and from place to place, without the control of reason, but still without being able to divest itself of an indescribable sense of present suffering. Finding from his incoherent wanderings that this was the case, and knowing that in all probability the fever would not grow immediately worse, I left him, promising his miserable wife that I would repeat my visit next evening, and, if necessary, sit up with the patient during the night.

"I kept my promise. The last four and twenty hours had produced a frightful alteration. The eyes, though deeply sunk and heavy, shone with a lustre, frightful to behold. The lips were parched, and cracked in many places: the dry hard skin glowed with a burning heat, and there was an almost unearthly air of wild anxiety in the man's face, indicating even more strongly the ravages of the disease. The fever was at its height.

"I took the seat I had occupied the night before, and there I sat for hours, listening to sounds which must strike deep to the heart of the most callous among human beings—the awful ravings of a dying man. From what I had heard of the medical attendant's opinion, I knew there was no hope for him: I was sitting by his death-bed. I saw the wasted limbs, which a few hours before, had been distorted for the amusement of a boisterous gallery, writhing under the tortures of a burning fever—I heard the clown's shrill laugh, blending with the low murmurings of the dying man.

"It is a touching thing to hear the mind reverting to the ordinary occupations and pursuits of health, when the body lies before you weak and helpless; but when those occupations are of a character the most strongly opposed to anything we associate with grave or solemn ideas the impression produced is infinitely more powerful. The theatre, and the public-house, were the chief themes of the wretched man's wanderings. It was evening, he fancied; he had a part to play that night; it was late, and he must leave home instantly. Why did they hold him, and prevent his going—he should lose the money—he must go! No! they would not let him. He hid his face in his burning hands, and feebly bemoaned his own weakness, and the cruelty of his persecutors. A short pause, and he shouted out a few doggerel rhymes—the last he had ever learnt. He rose in bed, drew up his withered limbs, and rolled about in uncouth positions; he was acting—he was at the theatre. A minute's silence, and he murmured the burden of some roaring song. He had reached the old house at last; how hot the room was. He had been ill, very ill, but he was well now, and happy. Fill up his glass. Who was that, that dashed it from his lips? It was the same persecutor that had followed him before. He fell back upon his pillow, and moaned aloud. A short period of oblivion, and he was wandering through a tedious maze of low arched rooms—so low, sometimes, that he must creep upon his hands and knees to make his way along; it was close and dark, and every way he turned, some obstacle impeded his progress. There were insects too, hideous crawling things, with eyes that stared upon him, and filled the very air around: glistening horribly amidst the thick darkness of the place. The walls and ceiling were alive with reptiles—the vault expanded to an enormous size—frightful figures flitted to and fro—and the faces of men he knew, rendered hideous by gibing and mouthing, peered out from among them; they were searing him with heated irons, and binding his head with cords till the blood started; and he struggled madly for life.

"At the close of one of these paroxysms, when I had with great difficulty held him down in his bed, he sank into what appeared to be a slumber. Overpowered with watching and exertion, I had closed my eyes for a few minutes, when I felt a violent clutch on my shoulder. I awoke instantly. He had raised himself up, so as to seat himself in bed—a dreadful change had come over his face, but consciousness had returned, for he evidently knew me. The child who had been long since disturbed by his ravings, rose from its little bed, and ran towards its father, screaming with fright—the mother hastily caught it in her arms, lest he should injure it in the violence of his insanity: but, terrified by the alteration of his features, stood transfixed by the bed-side. He grasped my shoulder convulsively, and, striking his breast with the other hand, made a desperate attempt to articulate. It was unavailing. He extended his arm towards them, and made another violent effort. There was a rattling noise in the throat—a glare of the eye—a short stifled groan—and he fell back—dead!"

It would afford us the highest gratification to be enabled to record Mr. Pickwick's opinion of the foregoing anecdote. We have little doubt that we should have been enabled to present it to our readers, but for a most unfortunate occurrence.

Mr. Pickwick had replaced on the table the glass which, during the last few sentences of the tale, he had retained in his hand; and had just made up his mind to speak—indeed, we have the authority of Mr. Snodgrass's note-book for stating, that he had actually opened his mouth—when the waiter entered the room, and said—

"Some gentlemen, Sir."

It has been conjectured that Mr. Pickwick was on the point of delivering some remarks which would have enlightened the world, if not the Thames, when he was thus interrupted: for he gazed sternly on the waiter's countenance, and then looked round on the company generally, as if seeking for information relative to the new comers.

"Oh!" said Mr. Winkle, rising, "some friends of mine—show them in. Very pleasant fellows," added Mr. Winkle, after the waiter had retired—"Officers of the 97th, whose acquaintance I made rather oddly this morning. You will like them very much."

Mr. Pickwick's equanimity was at once restored. The waiter returned, and ushered three gentlemen into the room.

"Lieutenant Tappleton," said Mr. Winkle, "Lieutenant Tappleton, Mr. Pickwick—Doctor Payne, Mr. Pickwick—Mr. Snodgrass, you have seen before: my friend Mr. Tupman, Doctor Payne—Doctor Slammer, Mr. Pickwick—Mr. Tupman, Doctor Slam—."

Here Mr. Winkle suddenly paused; for strong emotion was visible on the countenance both of Mr. Tupman and the Doctor.

"I have met *this* gentleman before," said the Doctor, with marked emphasis.

"Indeed!" said Mr. Winkle.

"And—and that person, too, if I am not mistaken," said the Doctor, bestowing a scrutinizing glance on the green-coated stranger. "I think I gave that person a very pressing invitation last night, which he thought proper to decline." Saying which, the Doctor scowled magnanimously on the stranger, and whispered his friend Lieutenant Tappleton.

"You don't say so," said that gentleman, at the conclusion of the whisper.

"I do, indeed," replied Doctor Slammer.

"You are bound to kick him on the spot," murmured the owner of the camp-stool, with great importance.

"*Do* be quiet, Payne," interposed the Lieutenant. "Will you allow me to ask you, Sir," he said, addressing Mr. Pickwick, who was considerably mystified by this very unpolite by-play—"Will you allow me to ask you, Sir, whether that person belongs to your party?"

"No, Sir," replied Mr. Pickwick, "he is a guest of ours."

"He is a member of your club, or I am mistaken?" said the Lieutenant, inquiringly.

"Certainly not," responded Mr. Pickwick.

"And never wears your club-button?" said the Lieutenant.

"No—never!" replied the astonished Mr. Pickwick.

Lieutenant Tappleton turned round to his friend Doctor Slammer, with a scarcely perceptible shrug of the shoulder, as if implying some doubt of the accuracy of his recollection. The little Doctor looked wrathful, but confounded; and Mr. Payne gazed with a ferocious aspect on the beaming countenance of the unconscious Pickwick.

"Sir," said the Doctor, suddenly addressing Mr. Tupman, in a tone which made that gentleman start as perceptibly as if a pin had been cunningly inserted in the calf of his leg—"you were at the ball here, last night?"

Mr. Tupman gasped a faint affirmative; looking very hard at Mr. Pickwick all the while.

"That person was your companion," said the Doctor, pointing to the still unmoved stranger.

Mr. Tupman admitted the fact.

"Now, Sir," said the Doctor to the stranger, "I ask you once again, in the presence of these gentlemen, whether you choose to give me your card, and to receive the treatment of a gentleman; or whether you impose upon me the necessity of personally chastising you on the spot?"

"Stay, Sir," said Mr. Pickwick, "I really cannot allow this matter to go any further without some explanation. Tupman, recount the circumstances."

Mr. Tupman, thus solemnly adjured, stated the case in a few words; touched slightly on the borrowing of the coat; expatiated largely on its having been done "after dinner;" wound up with a little penitence on his own account; and left the stranger to clear himself as he best could.

He was apparently about to proceed to do so, when Lieutenant Tappleton, who had been eyeing him with great curiosity, said with considerable scorn—"Haven't I seen you at the theatre, Sir?"

"Certainly," replied the unabashed stranger.

"He is a strolling actor," said the Lieutenant, contemptuously: turning to Dr. Slammer—"He acts in the piece that the Officers of the 52nd get up at the Rochester Theatre to-morrow night. You cannot proceed in this affair, Slammer—impossible!"

"Quite!" said the dignified Payne.

"Sorry to have placed you in this disagreeable situation," said Lieutenant Tappleton, addressing Mr. Pickwick; "allow me to suggest, that the best way of avoiding a recurrence of such scenes in future, will be to be more select in the choice of your companions. Good evening, Sir!" and the Lieutenant bounced out of the room.

"And allow *me* to say, Sir," said the irascible Doctor Payne, "that if I had been Tappleton, or if I had been Slammer, I would have pulled your nose, Sir, and the nose of every man in this company. I would, Sir,—every man. Payne is my name, Sir—Doctor Payne of the 43rd. Good evening, Sir." Having concluded this speech, and uttered the three last words in a loud key, he stalked majestically after his friend, closely followed by Doctor Slammer, who said nothing, but contented himself by withering the company with a look.

Rising rage and extreme bewilderment had swelled the noble breast of Mr. Pickwick, almost to the bursting of his waistcoat, during the delivery of the above defiance. He stood transfixed to the spot, gazing on vacancy. The closing of the door recalled him to himself. He rushed forward with fury in his looks, and fire in his eye. His hand was upon the lock of the door; in another instant it would have been on the throat of Doctor Payne of the 43rd, had not Mr. Snodgrass seized his revered leader by the coat tail, and dragged him backwards.

"Restrain him," cried Mr. Snodgrass, "Winkle, Tupman—he must not peril his distinguished life in such a cause as this."

"Let me go," said Mr. Pickwick.

"Hold him tight," shouted Mr. Snodgrass; and by the united efforts of the whole company, Mr. Pickwick was forced into an arm chair.

"Leave him alone," said the green-coated stranger—"brandy and water—jolly old gentleman—lots of pluck—swallow this—ah!—capital stuff." Having previously tested the virtues of a bumper, which had been mixed by the dismal man, the stranger applied the glass to Mr. Pickwick's mouth; and the remainder of its contents rapidly disappeared.

There was a short pause; the brandy and water had done its work; the amiable countenance of Mr. Pickwick was fast recovering its customary expression.

"They are not worth your notice," said the dismal man.

"You are right, Sir," replied Mr. Pickwick, "they are not. I am ashamed to have been betrayed into this warmth of feeling. Draw your chair up to the table, Sir."

The dismal man readily complied: a circle was again formed round the table, and harmony once more prevailed. Some lingering irritability appeared to find a resting place in Mr. Winkle's bosom, occasioned possibly by the temporary abstraction of his coat—though it is scarcely reasonable to suppose, that so slight a circumstance can have excited even a passing feeling of anger in a Pickwickian breast. With this exception, their good humour was completely restored; and the evening concluded with the conviviality with which it had begun.

CHAPTER IV.

A FIELD-DAY AND BIVOUAC—MORE NEW FRIENDS; AND AN INVITATION TO THE COUNTRY.

MANY authors entertain, not only a foolish, but a really dishonest objection, to acknowledge the sources from whence they derive much valuable information. We have no such feeling. We are merely endeavouring to discharge in an upright manner, the responsible duties of our editorial functions; and whatever ambition we might have felt under other circumstances, to lay claim to the authorship of these adventures, a regard for truth forbids us to do more, than claim the merit of their judicious arrangement, and impartial narration. The Pickwick papers are our New River Head; and we may be compared to the New River Company. The labours of others have raised for us an immense reservoir of important facts. We merely lay them on, and communicate them, in a clear and gentle stream, through the medium of these numbers, to a world thirsting for Pickwickian knowledge.

Acting in this spirit, and resolutely proceeding on our determination to avow our obligations to the authorities we have consulted, we frankly say, that to the note-book of Mr. Snodgrass are we indebted for the particulars recorded in this, and the succeeding chapter—particulars, which, now that we have disburdened our conscience, we shall proceed to detail without further comment.

The whole population of Rochester and the adjoining towns, rose from their beds at an early hour of the following morning, in a state of the utmost bustle and excitement. A grand review was to take place upon the lines. The manœuvres of half a dozen regiments were to be inspected by the eagle eye of the commander-in-chief; temporary fortifications had been erected, the citadel was to be attacked and taken, and a mine was to be sprung.

Mr. Pickwick was, as our readers may have gathered from the slight extract we gave from his description of Chatham, an enthusiastic admirer of the army. Nothing could have been more delightful to him—nothing could have harmonized so well with the peculiar feeling of each of his companions—as this sight. Accordingly they were soon a-foot, and walking in the direction of the scene of action, towards which crowds of people were already pouring, from a variety of quarters.

The appearance of everything on the lines, denoted that the approaching ceremony was one of the utmost grandeur and importance. There were sentries posted to keep the ground for the troops, and servants on the batteries keeping places for the ladies, and sergeants running to and fro, with vellum covered books under their arms, and Colonel Bulder, in full military uniform, on horseback, galloping first to one place and then to another, and backing his horse among the people, and prancing, and curvetting, and shouting in a most alarming manner, and making himself very hoarse in the voice, and very red in the face, without any assignable cause or reason whatever. Officers were running backwards and forwards, first communicating with Colonel Bulder, and then ordering the sergeants, and then running away altogether: and even the very privates themselves looked from behind their glazed stocks with an air of mysterious solemnity, which sufficiently bespoke the special nature of the occasion.

Mr. Pickwick and his three companions stationed themselves in the front rank of the crowd, and patiently awaited the commencement of the proceedings. The throng was increasing every moment; and the efforts they were compelled to make, to retain the position they had gained, sufficiently occupied their attention during the two hours that ensued. At one time there was a sudden pressure from behind; and then Mr. Pickwick was jerked forward for several yards, with a degree of speed and elasticity highly inconsistent with the general gravity of his demeanour; at another moment there was a request to "keep back" from the front, and then the butt end of a musket was either dropped upon Mr. Pickwick's toe, to remind him of the demand, or thrust into his chest to ensure its being complied with. Then some facetious gentlemen on the left, after pressing sideways in a body, and squeezing Mr. Snodgrass into the very last extreme of human torture, would request to know "vere he vos a shovin' to," and when Mr. Winkle had done expressing his excessive indignation at witnessing this unprovoked assault, some person behind would knock his hat over his eyes, and beg the favour of his putting his head in his pocket. These, and other practical witticisms, coupled with the unaccountable absence of Mr. Tupman (who had suddenly disappeared, and was nowhere to be found), rendered their situation upon the whole rather more uncomfortable, than pleasing or desirable.

At length that low roar of many voices ran through the crowd, which usually announces the arrival of whatever they have been waiting for. All eyes were turned in the direction of the sally-port. A few moments of eager expectation, and colours were seen fluttering gaily in the air, arms glistened brightly in the sun: column after column poured on to the plain. The troops halted and formed; the word of command rung through the line, there was a general clash of muskets, as arms were presented; and the commander-in-chief, attended by Colonel Bulder and numerous officers, cantered to the front. The military bands struck up altogether: the horses stood upon two legs each, cantered backwards, and whisked their tails about in all directions: the dogs barked, the mob screamed, the troops recovered, and nothing was to be seen on either side, as far as the eye could reach, but a long perspective of red coats and white trousers, fixed and motionless.

Mr. Pickwick had been so fully occupied in falling about, and disentangling himself, miraculously, from between the legs of horses, that he had not enjoyed sufficient leisure to observe the scene before him, until it assumed the appearance we have just described. When he was at last enabled to stand firmly on his legs, his gratification and delight were unbounded.

"Can anything be finer, or more delightful?" he inquired of Mr. Winkle.

"Nothing," replied that gentleman, who had had a short man standing on each of his feet, for the quarter of an hour immediately preceding.

"It is indeed a noble and a brilliant sight," said Mr. Snodgrass, in whose bosom a blaze of poetry was rapidly bursting forth, "to see the gallant defenders of their country, drawn up in brilliant array before its peaceful citizens: their faces beaming—not with warlike ferocity, but with civilized gentleness: their eyes flashing—not with the rude fire of rapine or revenge, but with the soft light of humanity and intelligence."

Mr. Pickwick fully entered into the spirit of this eulogium, but he could not exactly re-echo its terms; for the soft light of intelligence burnt rather feebly in the eyes of the warriors, inasmuch as the command "eyes front" had been given; and all the spectator saw before him was several thousand pair of optics, staring straight forward, wholly divested of any expression whatever.

"We are in a capital situation, now," said Mr. Pickwick, looking round him. The crowd had gradually dispersed from their immediate vicinity, and they were nearly alone.

"Capital!" echoed both Mr. Snodgrass and Mr. Winkle.

"What are they doing now?" inquired Mr. Pickwick, adjusting his spectacles.

"I—I—rather think," said Mr. Winkle, changing colour—"I rather think they're going to fire."

"Nonsense," said Mr. Pickwick, hastily.

"I—I—really think they are," urged Mr. Snodgrass, somewhat alarmed.

"Impossible," replied Mr. Pickwick. He had hardly uttered the word, when the whole half dozen regiments levelled their muskets as if they had but one common object, and that object the Pickwickians; and burst forth with the most awful and tremendous discharge that ever shook the earth to its centre, or an elderly gentleman off his.

It was in this trying situation, exposed to a galling fire of blank cartridges, and harassed by the operations of the military, a fresh body of whom had begun to fall in, on the opposite side, that Mr. Pickwick displayed that perfect coolness and self-possession, which are the indispensable accompaniments of a great mind. He seized Mr. Winkle by the arm, and placing himself between that gentleman and Mr. Snodgrass, earnestly besought them to remember that beyond the possibility of being rendered deaf by the noise, there was no immediate danger to be apprehended from the firing.

"But—but—suppose some of the men should happen to have ball cartridges by mistake," remonstrated Mr. Winkle, pallid at the supposition he was himself conjuring up. "I heard something whistle through the air just now—so sharp: close to my ear."

"We had better throw ourselves on our faces, hadn't we?" said Mr. Snodgrass.

"No, no—it's over now," said Mr. Pickwick. His lip might quiver, and his cheek might blanch, but no expression of fear or concern escaped the lips of that immortal man.

Mr. Pickwick was right: the firing ceased; but he had scarcely time to congratulate himself on the accuracy of his opinion, when a quick movement was visible in the line: the hoarse shout of the word of command ran along it, and before either of the party could form a guess at the meaning of this new manœuvre, the whole of the half dozen regiments, with fixed bayonets, charged at double quick time down upon the very spot on which Mr. Pickwick and his friends were stationed.

Man is but mortal; and there is a point beyond which human courage cannot extend. Mr. Pickwick gazed through his spectacles for an instant on the advancing mass; and then fairly turned his back and—we will not say fled; first, because it is an ignoble term, and, secondly, because Mr. Pickwick's figure was by no means adapted for that mode of retreat—he trotted away, at as quick a rate as his legs would convey him; so quickly, indeed, that he did not perceive the awkwardness of his situation, to the full extent, until too late.

The opposite troops, whose falling-in had perplexed Mr. Pickwick a few seconds before, were drawn up to repel the mimic attack of the sham besiegers of the citadel; and the consequence was, that Mr. Pickwick and his two companions found themselves suddenly inclosed between two lines of great length; the one advancing at a rapid pace, and the other firmly waiting the collision in hostile array.

"Hoi!" shouted the officers of the advancing line—

"Get out of the way," cried the officers of the stationary one.

"Where are we to go to?" screamed the agitated Pickwickians.

"Hoi—hoi—hoi," was the only reply. There was a moment of intense bewilderment, a heavy tramp of footsteps, a violent concussion; a smothered laugh—the half dozen

regiments were half a thousand yards off, and the soles of Mr. Pickwick's boots were elevated in air.

Mr. Snodgrass and Mr. Winkle had each performed a compulsory summerset with remarkable agility, when the first object that met the eyes of the latter as he sat on the ground, staunching with a yellow silk handkerchief the stream of life which issued from his nose, was his venerated leader at some distance off, running after his own hat, which was gambolling playfully away in perspective.

There are very few moments in a man's existence, when he experiences so much ludicrous distress, or meets with so little charitable commiseration, as when he is in pursuit of his own hat. A vast deal of coolness, and a peculiar degree of judgment, are requisite in catching a hat. A man must not be precipitate, or he runs over it: he must not rush into the opposite extreme, or he loses it altogether. The best way is, to keep gently up with the object of pursuit, to be wary and cautious, to watch your opportunity well, get gradually before it, then make a rapid dive, seize it by the crown, and stick it firmly on your head: smiling pleasantly all the time, as if you thought it as good a joke as anybody else.

There was a fine gentle wind, and Mr. Pickwick's hat rolled sportively before it. The wind puffed, and Mr. Pickwick puffed, and the hat rolled over and over as merrily as a lively porpoise in a strong tide; and on it might have rolled, far beyond Mr. Pickwick's reach, had not its course been providentially stopped, just as that gentleman was on the point of resigning it to its fate.

Mr. Pickwick, we say, was completely exhausted, and about to give up the chase, when the hat was blown with some violence against the wheel of a carriage, which was drawn up in a line with half-a-dozen other vehicles, on the spot to which his steps had been directed. Mr. Pickwick, perceiving his advantage, darted briskly forward, secured his property, planted it on his head, and paused to take breath. He had not been stationary half a minute, when he heard his own name eagerly pronounced by a voice, which he at once recognised as Mr. Tupman's, and, looking upwards, he beheld a sight which filled him with surprise and pleasure.

In an open barouche, the horses of which had been taken out, the better to accommodate it to the crowded place, stood a stout old gentleman, in a blue coat and bright buttons, corderoy breeches and top boots, two young ladies in scarfs and feathers, a young gentleman apparently enamoured of one of the young ladies in scarfs and feathers, a lady of doubtful age, probably the aunt of the aforesaid, and Mr. Tupman, as easy and unconcerned as if he had belonged to the family from the first moments of his infancy. Fastened up behind the barouche was a hamper of spacious dimensions—one of those hampers which always awakens in a contemplative mind, associations connected with cold fowls, tongue, and bottles of wine—and on the box sat a fat and red-faced boy, in a state of somnolency, whom no speculative observer could have regarded for an instant without setting down as the official dispenser of the contents of the before-mentioned hamper, when the proper time for their consumption should arrive.

Mr. Pickwick had bestowed a hasty glance on these interesting objects, when he was again greeted by his faithful disciple.

"Pickwick—Pickwick," said Mr. Tupman; "come up here. Make haste."

"Come along, Sir. Pray, come up," said the stout gentleman. "Joe!—damn that boy, he's gone to sleep again.

MR. PICKWICK IN CHASE OF HIS HAT.

—Joe, let down the steps." The fat boy rolled slowly off the box, let down the steps, and held the carriage door invitingly open. Mr. Snodgrass and Mr. Winkle came up at the moment.

"Room for you all, gentlemen," said the stout man. "Two inside, and one out. Joe, make room for one of these gentlemen on the box. Now, Sir, come along;" and the stout gentleman extended his arm, and pulled first Mr. Pickwick, and then Mr. Snodgrass, into the barouche by main force. Mr. Winkle mounted to the same perch, and the fat boy waddled to the same perch, and fell fast asleep instantly.

"Well, gentlemen," said the stout man, "very glad to see you. Know you very well, gentlemen, though you mayn't remember me. I spent some ev'nins at your club last winter—picked up my friend Mr. Tupman here this morning, and very glad I was to see him. Well, Sir, and how are you? You do look uncommon well, to be sure."

Mr. Pickwick acknowledged the compliment, and cordially shook hands with the stout gentleman in the top boots.

"Well, and how are you, Sir?" said the stout gentle-man, addressing Mr. Snodgrass with paternal anxiety. "Charming, eh? Well, that's right—that's right. And how are you, Sir (to Mr. Winkle)? Well, I am glad to hear you say you are well; very glad I am, to be sure. My daughters, gentlemen—my gals these are; and that's my sister, Miss Rachael Wardle. She's a Miss, she is; and yet she an't a Miss—eh, Sir—eh?" And the stout gentle-man playfully inserted his elbow between the ribs of Mr. Pickwick, and laughed very heartily.

"Lor, brother?" said Miss Wardle, with a deprecating smile.

"True, true," said the stout gentleman; "no one can deny it. Gentlemen, I beg your pardon; this is my friend Mr. Trundle. And now you all know each other, let's be comfortable and happy, and see what's going forward; that's what I say." So the stout gentleman put on his spectacles, and Mr. Pickwick pulled out his glass, and everybody stood up in the carriage, and looked over some-body else's shoulder at the evolutions of the military.

Astounding evolutions they were, one rank firing over the heads of another rank, and then running away; and then the other rank firing over the heads of another rank, and running away in their turn; and then forming squares, with officers in the centre; and then descending the trench on one side with scaling ladders, and ascending it on the other again by the same means; and knocking down barri-cades of baskets, and behaving in the most gallant manner possible. Then there was such a ramming down of the contents of enormous guns on the battery, with instruments like magnified mops; such a preparation before they were let off, and such an awful noise when they did go, that the air resounded with the screams of ladies. The young Miss Wardles were so frightened, that Mr. Trundle was actually obliged to hold one of them up in the carriage, while Mr. Snodgrass supported the other; and Mr. Wardle's sister suffered under such a dreadful state of nervous alarm, that Mr. Tupman found it indispensably necessary to put his arm round her waist, to keep her up at all. Everybody was excited, except the fat boy, and he slept as soundly as if the roaring of cannon were his ordinary lullaby.

"Joe, Joe!" said the stout gentleman, when the citadel was taken, and the besiegers and besieged sat down to dinner. "Damn that boy, he's gone to sleep again. Be good enough to pinch him, Sir—in the leg, if you please; nothing else wakes him—thank you. Undo the hamper, Joe."

The fat boy, who had been effectually roused by the com-pression of a portion of his leg, between the finger and thumb of Mr. Winkle, rolled off the box once again, and proceeded to unpack the hamper, with more expedition than could have been expected from his previous inac-tivity.

"Now, we must sit close," said the stout gentleman. After a great many jokes about squeezing the ladies' sleeves, and a vast quantity of blushing at sundry jocose proposals, that the ladies should sit in the gentlemen's laps, the whole party were stowed down in the barouche; and the stout gentleman proceeded to hand the things from the fat boy (who had mounted up behind for the purpose) into the carriage.

"Now, Joe, knives and forks." The knives and forks were handed in, and the ladies and gentlemen inside, and Mr. Winkle on the box, were each furnished with those useful implements.

"Plates, Joe, plates." A similar process employed in the distribution of the crockery.

"Now, Joe, the fowls. Damn that boy; he's gone to sleep again. Joe! Joe!" (Sundry taps on the head with a stick, and the fat boy, with some difficulty, roused from his lethargy.) "Come, hand in the eatables."

There was something in the sound of the last word, which roused the unctuous boy. He jumped up: and the leaden eyes, which twinkled behind his mountainous cheeks, leered horribly upon the food as he unpacked it from the bas-ket.

"Now, make haste," said Mr. Wardle; for the fat boy was hanging fondly over a capon, which he seemed wholly unable to part with. The boy sighed deeply, and, bestow-ing an ardent gaze upon its plumpness, unwillingly con-signed it to his master.

"That's right—look sharp. Now the tongue—now the pigeon-pie. Take care of that veal and ham—mind the lobsters—take the salad out of the cloth—give me the dress-ing." Such were the hurried orders which issued from the lips of Mr. Wardle, as he handed in the different articles described, and placed dishes in everybody's hands, and on everybody's knees, in endless number.

"Now, ain't this capital?" inquired that jolly person-age, when the work of destruction had commenced.

"Capital!" said Mr. Winkle, who was carving a fowl on the box.

"Glass of wine?"

"With the greatest pleasure."

"You'd better have a bottle to yourself, up there, hadn't you?"

"You're very good."

"Joe!"

"Yes, Sir." (He wasn't asleep this time, having just succeeded in abstracting a veal patty.)

"Bottle of wine to the gentleman on the box. Glad to see you, Sir."

"Thankee." Mr. Winkle emptied his glass, and placed the bottle on the coach-box, by his side.

"Will you permit me to have the pleasure, Sir?" said Mr. Trundle to Mr. Winkle.

"With great pleasure," replied Mr. Winkle to Mr. Trun-dle; and then the two gentlemen took wine, after which they took a glass of wine round, ladies and all.

"How dear Emily is flirting with the strange gentle-man," whispered the spinster aunt, with true spinster-aunt-like envy, to her brother Mr. Wardle.

"Oh! I don't know," said the jolly old gentleman; "all

very natural, I dare say—nothing unusual. Mr. Pickwick, some wine, Sir?" Mr. Pickwick, who had been deeply investigating the interior of the pigeon-pie, readily assented.

"Emily, my dear," said the spinster aunt, with a patronising air, "don't talk so loud, love."

"Lor, aunt!"

"Aunt and the little old gentleman want to have it all to themselves, I think," whispered Miss Isabella Wardle to her sister Emily. The young ladies laughed very heartily, and the old one tried to look amiable, but couldn't manage it.

"Young girls have *such* spirits," said Miss Wardle to Mr. Tupman, with an air of gentle commiseration, as if animal spirits were contraband, and their possession without a permit, a high crime and misdemeanour.

"Oh, they have," replied Mr. Tupman, not exactly making the sort of reply that was expected from him. "It's quite delightful."

"Hem!" said Miss Wardle, rather dubiously.

"Will you permit me?" said Mr. Tupman, in his blandest manner, touching the enchanting Rachael's wrist with one hand, and gently elevating the bottle with the other. "Will you permit me?"

"Oh, Sir!" Mr. Tupman looked most impressive; and Rachael expressed her fear that more guns were going off, in which case, of course, she would have required support again.

"Do you think my dear nieces pretty?" whispered their affectionate aunt to Mr. Tupman.

"I should, if their aunt wasn't here," replied the ready Pickwickian, with a passionate glance.

"Oh, you naughty man—but really, if their complexions were a *little* better, don't you think they would be nice-looking girls—by candle-light?"

"Yes; I think they would;" said Mr. Tupman, with an air of indifference.

"Oh, you quiz—I know what you were going to say."

"What?" inquired Mr. Tupman, who had not precisely made up his mind to say anything at all.

"You were going to say, that Isabella stoops—I know you were—you men are such observers. Well, so she does; it can't be denied; and, certainly, if there is one thing more than another that makes a girl look ugly, it is stooping. I often tell her, that when she gets a little older, she'll be quite frightful. Well, you *are* a quiz!"

Mr. Tupman had no objection to earning the reputation at so cheap a rate: so he looked very knowing, and smiled mysteriously.

"What a sarcastic smile," said the admiring Rachael; "I declare I'm quite afraid of you."

"Afraid of me!"

"Oh, you can't disguise any thing from me—I know what that smile means, very well."

"What?" said Mr. Tupman, who had not the slightest notion himself.

"You mean," said the amiable aunt, sinking her voice still lower—"You mean, that you don't think Isabella's stooping is as bad as Emily's boldness. Well, she *is* bold! You cannot think how wretched it makes me sometimes—I'm sure I cry about it for hours together—my dear brother is so good, and so unsuspicious, that he never sees it; if he did, I'm quite certain it would break his heart. I wish I could think it was only manner—I hope it may be—" (here the affectionate relative heaved a deep sigh, and shook her head despondingly).

"I'm sure aunt's talking about us," whispered Miss Emily Wardle to her sister—"I'm quite certain of it—she looks so malicious."

"Is she?" replied Isabella—"Hem! aunt, dear!"

"Yes, my dear love!"

"I'm *so* afraid you'll catch cold, aunt—have a silk handkerchief to tie round your dear old head—you really should take care of yourself—consider your age!"

However well deserved this piece of retaliation might have been, it was as vindictive a one as could well have been resorted to. There is no guessing in what form of reply the aunt's indignation would have vented itself, had not Mr. Wardle unconsciously changed the subject, by calling emphatically for Joe.

"Damn that boy," said the old gentleman, "he's gone to sleep again."

"Very extraordinary boy, that," said Mr. Pickwick, "does he always sleep in this way?"

"Sleep!" said the old gentleman, "he's always asleep. Goes on errands fast asleep, and snores as he waits at table."

"How very odd!" said Mr. Pickwick.

"Ah! odd indeed," returned the old gentleman; "I'm proud of that boy—wouldn't part with him on any account—damme, he's a natural curiosity! Here, Joe—Joe—take these things away, and open another bottle—d'ye hear?"

The fat boy rose, opened his eyes, swallowed the huge piece of pie he had been in the act of masticating when he last fell asleep, and slowly obeyed his master's orders—gloating languidly over the remains of the feast, as he removed the plates, and deposited them in the hamper. The fresh bottle was produced, and speedily emptied: the hamper was made fast in its old place—the fat boy once more mounted the box—the spectacles and pocket-glass were again adjusted—and the evolutions of the military recommenced. There was a great fizzing and banging of guns, and starting of ladies—and then a mine was sprung, to the gratification of every body—and when the mine had gone off, the military and the company followed its example, and went off too.

"Now, mind," said the old gentleman, as he shook hands with Mr. Pickwick at the conclusion of a conversation which had been carried on at intervals, during the conclusion of the proceedings—"we shall see you all to-morrow."

"Most certainly," replied Mr. Pickwick.

"You have got the address?"

"Manor Farm, Dingley Dell," said Mr. Pickwick, consulting his pocket-book.

"That's it," said the old gentleman. "I don't let you off, mind, under a week; and undertake that you shall see everything worth seeing. If you've come down for a country life, come to me, and I'll give you plenty of it. Joe—damn that boy, he's gone to sleep again—Joe, help Tom put in the horses."

The horses were put in—the driver mounted—the fat boy clambered up by his side—farewells were exchanged—and the carriage rattled off. As the Pickwickians turned round to take a last glimpse of it, the setting sun cast a rich glow on the faces of their entertainers, and fell upon the form of the fat boy. His head was sunk upon his bosom; and he slumbered again.

CHAPTER V.

A SHORT ONE—SHOWING, AMONG OTHER MATTERS,
HOW MR. PICKWICK UNDERTOOK TO DRIVE, AND
MR. WINKLE TO RIDE; AND HOW THEY ·BOTH
DID IT.

BRIGHT and pleasant was the sky, balmy the air, and
beautiful the appearance of every object around, as Mr.
Pickwick leant over the balustrades of Rochester Bridge,
contemplating nature, and waiting for breakfast. The
scene was indeed one, which might well have charmed a far
less reflective mind, than that to which it was presented.

On the left· of the spectator lay the ruined wall, broken
in many places, and in some, overhanging the narrow beach
below in rude and heavy masses. Huge knots of sea-weed
hung upon the jagged and pointed stones, trembling in
every breath of wind; and the green ivy clung mournfully
round the dark, and ruined battlements. Behind it rose
the ancient castle, its towers roofless, and its massive walls
crumbling away, but telling us proudly of its old might
and strength, as when, seven hundred years ago, it rang
with the clash of arms, or resounded with the noise of feasting and revelry. On either side, the banks of the Medway, covered with corn-fields and pastures, with here and
there a windmill, or a distant church, stretched away as far
as the eye could see, presenting a rich and varied landscape, rendered more beautiful by the changing shadows
which passed swiftly across it, as the thin and half-formed
clouds skimmed away in the light of the morning sun.
The river, reflecting the clear blue of the sky, glistened
and sparkled as it flowed noiselessly on; and the oars of
the fishermen dipped into the water with a clear and liquid
sound, as their heavy but picturesque boats glided slowly
down the stream.

Mr. Pickwick was roused from the agreeable reverie into
which he had been led by the objects before him, by a deep
sigh, and a touch on his shoulder. He turned round: and
the dismal man was at his side.

"Contemplating the scene?" inquired the dismal man.

"I was," said Mr. Pickwick.

"And congratulating yourself on being up so soon?"
Mr. Pickwick nodded assent.

"Ah! people need to rise early, to see the sun in all his
splendour, for his brightness seldom lasts the day through.
The morning of day and the morning of life are but too
much alike."

"You speak truly, Sir," said Mr. Pickwick.

"How common the saying," continued the dismal man,
"'The morning's too fine to last.' How well might it be
applied to our every-day existence. God! what would I
forfeit to have the days of my childhood restored, or to be
able to forget them for ever!"

"You have seen much trouble, Sir," said Mr. Pickwick,
compassionately.

"I have," said the dismal man, hurriedly; "I have.
More than those who see me now would believe possible."

He paused for an instant, and then said, abruptly,

"Did it ever strike you, on such a morning as this, that
drowning would be happiness and peace?"

"God bless me, no!" replied Mr. Pickwick, edging a
little from the balustrade, as the possibility of the dismal
man's tipping him over, by way of experiment, occurred to
him rather forcibly.

"*I* have thought so, often," said the dismal man, without noticing the action. "The calm, cool water seems to
me to murmur an invitation to repose and rest. A bound,
a splash, a brief struggle; there is an eddy for an instant,
it gradually subsides into a gentle ripple; the waters have
closed above your head, and the world has closed upon
your miseries and misfortunes for ever." The sunken eye
of the dismal man flashed brightly as he spoke, but the
momentary excitement quickly subsided; and he turned
calmly away, as he said—

"There—enough of that. I wished to see you on another subject. You invited me to read that paper, the
night before last, and listened attentively while I did
so."

"I did," replied Mr. Pickwick; "and I certainly
thought——"

"I asked for no opinion," said the dismal man, interrupting him, "and I want none. You are travelling for amusement and instruction. Suppose I forwarded you a curious
manuscript—observe, not curious because wild or improbable, but curious as a leaf from the romance of real life.
Would you communicate it to the club, of which you have
spoken so frequently?"

"Certainly," replied Mr. Pickwick, "if you wished it;
and it would be entered on their transactions."

"You shall have it," replied the dismal man. "Your
address;" and, Mr. Pickwick having communicated their
probable route, the dismal man carefully noted it down in
a greasy pocket-book, and, resisting Mr. Pickwick's pressing invitation to breakfast, left that gentleman at his inn,
and walked slowly away.

Mr. Pickwick found that his three companions had risen,
and were waiting his arrival to commence breakfast, which
was ready laid in tempting display. They sat down to the
meal; and broiled ham, eggs, tea, coffee, and sundries,
began to disappear with a rapidity which at once bore testimony to the excellence of the fare, and the appetites of
its consumers.

"Now, about Manor Farm," said Mr. Pickwick. "How
shall we go?"

"We had better consult the waiter, perhaps," said Mr.
Tupman; and the waiter was summoned accordingly.

"Dingley Dell, gentlemen—fifteen miles, gentlemen—
cross road—post-chaise, Sir?"

"Post-chaise won't hold more than two," said Mr. Pickwick.

"True, Sir—beg your pardon, Sir.—Very nice four-
wheel chaise, Sir—seat for two behind—one in front for
the gentleman that drives—oh! beg your pardon, Sir—
that'll only hold three."

"What's to be done?" said Mr. Snodgrass.

"Perhaps one of the gentlemen like to ride, Sir," suggested the waiter, looking towards Mr. Winkle; "very
good saddle horses, Sir—any of Mr. Wardle's men coming
to Rochester, bring 'em back, Sir."

"The very thing," said Mr. Pickwick. "Winkle, will
you go on horseback?"

Now Mr. Winkle did entertain considerable misgivings
in the very lowest recesses of his own heart, relative to his
equestrian skill; but, as he would not have them even suspected on any account, he at once replied with great hardihood, "Certainly. I should enjoy it, of all things."

Mr. Winkle had rushed upon his fate; there was no
resource. "Let them be at the door by eleven," said Mr.
Pickwick.

"Very well, Sir," replied the waiter.

The waiter retired; the breakfast concluded; and the travellers ascended to their respective bedrooms, to prepare a change of clothing, to take with them on their approaching expedition.

Mr. Pickwick had made his preliminary arrangements, and was looking over the coffee-room blinds at the passengers in the street, when the waiter entered, and announced that the chaise was ready—an announcement which the vehicle itself confirmed, by forthwith appearing before the coffee-room blinds aforesaid.

It was a curious little green box on four wheels, with a low place like a wine bin for two behind, and an elevated perch for one in front, drawn by an immense brown horse, displaying great symmetry of bone. An hostler stood near it, holding by the bridle another immense horse—apparently a near relative of the animal in the chaise—ready saddled for Mr. Winkle.

"Bless my soul!" said Mr. Pickwick, as they stood upon the pavement while the coats were being put in. "Bless my soul! who's to drive? I never thought of that."

"Oh! you, of course," said Mr. Tupman.

"Of course," said Mr. Snodgrass.

"I!" exclaimed Mr. Pickwick.

"Not the slightest fear, Sir," interposed the hostler. "Warrant him quiet, Sir; a hinfant in arms might drive him."

"He don't shy, does he?" inquired Mr. Pickwick.

"Shy, Sir?—He wouldn't shy if he was to meet a vaggin-load of monkeys, with their tails burnt off."

The last recommendation was indisputable. Mr. Tupman and Mr. Snodgrass got into the bin; Mr. Pickwick ascended to his perch, and deposited his feet on a floor-clothed shelf, erected beneath it, for that purpose.

"Now, shiny Villiam," said the hostler to the deputy hostler, "give the gen'lm'n the ribbins." "Shiny Villiam"—so called, probably, from his sleek hair and oily countenance—placed the reins in Mr. Pickwick's left hand; and the upper hostler thrust a whip into his right.

"Woo," cried Mr. Pickwick, as the tall quadruped evinced a decided inclination to back into the coffee-room window.

"Wo—o," echoed Mr. Tupman and Mr. Snodgrass, from the bin.

"Only his playfulness, gen'lm'n," said the head hostler, encouragingly; "jist kitch hold on him, Villiam." The deputy restrained the animal's impetuosity, and the principal ran to assist Mr. Winkle in mounting.

"T'other side, Sir, if you please."

"Blowed if the gen'lm'n worn't a gettin' up on the wrong side," whispered a grinning post-boy, to the inexpressibly gratified waiter.

Mr. Winkle, thus instructed, climbed into his saddle, with about as much difficulty as he would have experienced in getting up the side of a first-rate man-of-war.

"All right?" inquired Mr. Pickwick, with an inward presentiment that it was all wrong.

"All right," replied Mr. Winkle faintly.

"Let 'em go," cried the hostler,—"Hold him in, Sir;" and away went the chaise, and the saddle horse, with Mr. Pickwick on the box of the one, and Mr. Winkle on the back of the other, to the delight and gratification of the whole inn yard.

"What makes him go sideways?" said Mr. Snodgrass in the bin, to Mr. Winkle in the saddle.

"I can't imagine," replied Mr. Winkle. His horse was going up the street in the most mysterious manner—side first, with his head towards one side of the way, and his tail to the other.

Mr. Pickwick had no leisure to observe either this, or any other particular, the whole of his faculties being concentrated in the management of the animal attached to the chaise, who displayed various peculiarities, highly interesting to a by-stander, but by no means equally amusing to any one seated behind him. Besides constantly jerking his head up, in a very unpleasant and uncomfortable manner, and tugging at the reins to an extent which rendered it a matter of great difficulty for Mr. Pickwick to hold them, he had a singular propensity for darting suddenly every now and then to the side of the road, then stopping short, and then rushing forward for some minutes, at a speed which it was wholly impossible to control.

"What can he mean by this?" said Mr. Snodgrass, when the horse had executed this manœuvre for the twentieth time.

"I don't know," replied Mr. Tupman; "it looks very like shying, don't it?" Mr. Snodgrass was about to reply, when he was interrupted by a shout from Mr. Pickwick.

"Woo," said that gentleman, "I have dropped my whip."

"Winkle," cried Mr. Snodgrass, as the equestrian came trotting up on the tall horse, with his hat over his ears: and shaking all over, as if he would shake to pieces, with the violence of the exercise. "Pick up the whip, there's a good fellow." Mr. Winkle pulled at the bridle of the tall horse till he was black in the face; and having at length succeeded in stopping him, dismounted, handed the whip to Mr. Pickwick, and grasping the reins, prepared to remount.

Now whether the tall horse, in the natural playfulness of his disposition, was desirous of having a little innocent recreation with Mr. Winkle, or whether it occurred to him that he could perform the journey as much to his own satisfaction without a rider as with one, are points upon which, of course, we can arrive at no definite and distinct conclusion. By whatever motives the animal was actuated, certain it is that Mr. Winkle had no sooner touched the reins, than he slipped them over his head, and darted backwards to their full length.

"Poor fellow," said Mr. Winkle, soothingly,—"poor fellow—good old horse." The "poor fellow" was proof against flattery: the more Mr. Winkle tried to get nearer him, the more he sidled away; and, notwithstanding all kinds of coaxing and wheedling, there were Mr. Winkle and the horse going round and round each other for ten minutes, at the end of which time each was at precisely the same distance from the other as when they first commenced—an unsatisfactory sort of thing under any circumstances, but particularly so in a lonely road, where no assistance can be procured.

"What am I to do?" shouted Mr. Winkle, after the dodging had been prolonged for a considerable time. "What am I to do? I can't get on him?"

"You had better lead him till we come to a turnpike," replied Mr. Pickwick from the chaise.

"But he won't come," roared Mr. Winkle. "Do come, and hold him."

Mr. Pickwick was the very personation of kindness and humanity: he threw the reins on the horse's back, and having descended from his seat, carefully drew the chaise into the hedge, lest anything should come along the road, and stepped back to the assistance of his distressed companion, leaving Mr. Tupman and Mr. Snodgrass in the vehicle.

The horse no sooner beheld Mr. Pickwick advancing towards him, with the chaise whip in his hand, than he exchanged the rotary motion in which he had previously indulged, for a retrograde movement of so very determined a character, that it at once drew Mr. Winkle, who was still at the end of the bridle, at a rather quicker rate than fast walking, in the direction from which they had just come. Mr. Pickwick ran to his assistance, but the faster Mr. Pickwick ran forward, the faster the horse ran backward. There was a great scraping of feet, and kicking up of the dust; and at last Mr. Winkle, his arms being nearly pulled out of their sockets, fairly let go his hold. The horse paused, stared, shook his head, turned round, and quietly trotted home to Rochester, leaving Mr. Winkle and Mr. Pickwick gazing on each other with countenances of blank dismay. A rattling noise at a little distance attracted their attention. They looked up.

"Bless my soul!" exclaimed the agonized Mr. Pickwick, "there's the other horse running away!"

It was but too true. The animal was startled by the noise, and the reins were on his back. The result may be guessed. He tore off with the four-wheeled chaise behind him, and Mr. Tupman and Mr. Snodgrass in the four-wheeled chaise. The heat was a short one. Mr. Tupman threw himself into the hedge, Mr. Snodgrass followed his example, the horse dashed the four-wheeled chase against a wooden bridge, separated the wheels from the body, and the bin from the perch; and finally stood stock still, to gaze upon the ruin he had made.

The first care of the two unspilt friends was to extricate their unfortunate companions from their bed of quickset— a process which gave them the unspeakable satisfaction of discovering that they had sustained no injury, beyond sundry rents in their garments, and various lacerations from the brambles. The next thing to be done was, to unharness the horse. This complicated process having been effected, the party walked slowly forward, leading the horse among them, and abandoning the chaise to its fate.

An hour's walking brought the travellers to a little roadside public house, with two elm-trees, a horse trough, and a sign-post, in front; one or two deformed hay-ricks behind, a kitchen garden at the side, and rotten sheds and mouldering out-houses, jumbled in strange confusion, all about it. A red-headed man was working in the garden; and to him Mr. Pickwick called lustily—"Hallo there!"

The red-headed man raised his body, shaded his eyes with his hand, and stared, long and coolly, at Mr. Pickwick and his companions.

"Hallo there!" repeated Mr. Pickwick.

"Hallo!" was the red-headed man's reply.

"How far is it to Dingley Dell?"

"Better er seven mile."

"Is it a good road?"

"No, t'ant." Having uttered this brief reply, and apparently satisfied himself with another scrutiny, the red-headed man resumed his work.

"We want to put this horse up here," said Mr. Pickwick; "I suppose we can, can't we?"

"Want to put that ere horse up, do ee?" repeated the red-headed man, leaning on his spade.

"Of course," replied Mr. Pickwick, who had by this time advanced, horse in hand, to the garden rails.

"Missus"—roared the man with the red head, emerging from the garden, and looking very hard at the horse— "Missus."

A tall bony woman—straight all the way down—in a coarse blue pelisse, with the waist an inch or two below her arm-pits, responded to the call.

"Can we put this horse up here, my good woman?" said Mr. Tupman, advancing, and speaking in his most seductive tones. The woman looked very hard at the whole party; and the red-headed man whispered something in her ear.

"No," replied the woman, after a little consideration, "I'm afeerd on it."

"Afraid!" exclaimed Mr. Pickwick, "what's the woman afraid of!"

"It got us in trouble last time," said the woman, turning into the house; "I woant have nothin' to say to 'un."

"Most extraordinary thing I ever met with in my life," said the astonished Mr. Pickwick.

"I—I—really believe," whispered Mr. Winkle, as his friends gathered round him, "that they think we have come by this horse in some dishonest manner."

"What!" exclaimed Mr. Pickwick, in a storm of indignation. Mr. Winkle modestly repeated his suggestion.

"Hallo, you fellow!" said the angry Mr. Pickwick, "do you think we stole this horse?"

"I'm sure ye did," replied the red-headed man, with a grin which agitated his countenance from one auricular organ to the other. Saying which, he turned into the house, and banged the door after him.

"It's like a dream,"—ejaculated Mr. Pickwick, "a hideous dream. The idea of a man's walking about, all day, with a dreadful horse that he can't get rid of!" The depressed Pickwickians turned moodily away, with the tall quadruped, for which they all felt the most unmitigated disgust, following slowly at their heels.

It was late in the afternoon, when the four friends and their four-footed companion, turned into the lane leading to Manor Farm: and even when they were so near their place of destination, the pleasure they would otherwise have experienced, was materially damped as they reflected on the singularity of their appearance and the absurdity of their situation. Torn clothes, lacerated faces, dusty shoes, exhausted looks, and, above all, the horse. Oh, how Mr. Pickwick cursed that horse: he had eyed the noble animal from time to time with looks expressive of hatred and revenge; more than once he had calculated the probable amount of the expense he would incur by cutting his throat; and now the temptation to destroy him, or to cast him loose upon the world, rushed upon his mind with tenfold force. He was roused from a meditation on these dire imaginings, by the sudden appearance of two figures, at a turn of the lane. It was Mr. Wardle, and his faithful attendant, the fat boy.

"Why, where *have* you been?" said the hospitable old gentleman. "I've been waiting for you all day. Well, you *do* look tired. What! Scratches! Not hurt, I hope —eh? Well, I *am* glad to hear that—very. So you've been spilt, eh? Never mind. Common accident in these parts. Joe—damn that boy, he's asleep again—Joe take that horse from the gentleman, and lead it into the stable."

The fat boy sauntered heavily behind them with the animal; and the old gentleman condoling with his guests in homely phrase, on so much of the day's adventures as they thought proper to communicate, led the way to the kitchen.

"We'll have you put to rights here," said the old gentleman, "and then I'll introduce you to the people in the parlour. Emma, bring out the cherry brandy; now, Jane, a needle and thread here; towels and water, Mary. Come, girls, bustle about."

Three or four buxom girls speedily dispersed in search of the different articles in requisition, while a couple of large-headed, circular-visaged males rose from their seats in the chimney corner, (for although it was a May evening, their attachment to the wood fire appeared as cordial as if it were Christmas,) and dived into some obscure recesses, from which they speedily produced a bottle of blacking, and some half-dozen brushes.

"Bustle," said the old gentleman again, but the admonition was quite unnecessary, for one of the girls poured out the cherry brandy, and another brought in the towels, and one of the men suddenly seizing Mr. Pickwick by the leg, at the imminent hazard of throwing him off his balance, brushed away at his boot, till his corns were red-hot; while the other shampoo'd Mr. Winkle with a heavy clothes brush, indulging, during the operation, in that hissing sound, which hostlers are wont to produce, when engaged in rubbing down a horse.

Mr. Snodgrass, having concluded his ablutions, took a survey of the room, while standing with his back to the fire, sipping his cherry brandy with heartfelt satisfaction. He describes it, as a large apartment, with a red brick floor, and a capacious chimney; the ceiling garnished with hams, sides of bacon, and ropes of onions. The walls were decorated with several hunting-whips, two or three bridles, a saddle, and an old rusty blunderbuss, with an inscription below it, intimating that it was "Loaded"—as it had been, on the same authority, for half a century at least. An old eight-day clock, of solemn and sedate demeanour, ticked gravely in one corner; and a silver watch, of equal antiquity, dangled from one of the many hooks which ornamented the dresser.

"Ready?" said the old gentleman inquiringly, when his guests had washed, mended, brushed, and brandied.

"Quite," replied Mr. Pickwick.

"Come along then," and the party having traversed several dark passages, and being joined by Mr. Tupman, who had lingered behind to snatch a kiss from Emma, for which he had been duly rewarded with sundry pushings and scratchings, arrived at the parlour door.

"Welcome," said their hospitable host, throwing it open and stepping forward to announce them, "Welcome, gentlemen, to Manor Farm."

CHAPTER VI.

AN OLD-FASHIONED CARD-PARTY—THE CLERGYMAN'S VERSES—THE STORY OF THE CONVICT'S RETURN.

SEVERAL guests who were assembled in the old parlour, rose to greet Mr. Pickwick and his friends upon their entrance; and during the performance of the ceremony of introduction, with all due formalities, Mr. Pickwick had leisure to observe the appearance, and speculate upon the characters and pursuits, of the persons by whom he was surrounded—a habit in which he in common with many other great men delighted to indulge.

A very old lady, in a lofty cap and faded silk gown—no less a personage than Mr. Wardle's mother—occupied the post of honour on the right-hand corner of the chimney-piece; and various certificates of her having been brought up in the way she should go when young, and of her not having departed from it when old, ornamented the walls, in the form of samplers of ancient date, worsted landscapes of equal antiquity, and crimson silk tea-kettle holders of a more modern period. The aunt, the two young ladies, and Mr. Wardle, each vying with the other in paying zealous and unremitting attentions to the old lady, crowded round her easy chair, one holding her ear-trumpet, another an orange, and a third a smelling-bottle, while a fourth was busily engaged in patting and punching the pillows, which were arranged for her support. On the opposite side, sat a bald-headed old gentleman, with a good-humoured benevolent face—the clergyman of Dingley Dell; and next him sat his wife, a stout blooming old lady, who looked as if she were well skilled, not only in the art and mystery of manufacturing home-made cordials greatly to other people's satisfaction, but of tasting them occasionally very much to her own. A little hard-headed, Ripstone pippin-faced man, was conversing with a fat old gentleman in one corner; and two or three more old gentlemen, and two or three more old ladies, sat bolt-upright and motionless on their chairs, staring very hard at Mr. Pickwick and his fellow-voyagers.

"Mr. Pickwick, mother," said Mr. Wardle, at the very top of his voice.

"Ah!" said the old lady, shaking her head; "I can't hear you."

"Mr. Pickwick, grandma!" screamed both the young ladies together.

"Ah!" exclaimed the old lady. "Well; it don't much matter. He don't care for an old 'ooman like me, I dare say."

"I assure you, Ma'am," said Mr. Pickwick, grasping the old lady's hand; and speaking so loud that the exertion imparted a crimson hue to his benevolent countenance; "I assure you, Ma'am, that nothing delights me more, than to see a lady of your time of life heading so fine a family, and looking so young and well."

"Ah!" said the old lady, after a short pause; "It's all very fine, I dare say; but I can't hear him."

"Grandma's rather put out now," said Miss Isabella Wardle, in a low tone; "but she'll talk to you presently."

Mr. Pickwick nodded his readiness to humour the infirmities of age, and entered into a general conversation with the other members of the circle.

"Delightful situation this," said Mr. Pickwick.

"Delightful!" echoed Messrs. Snodgrass, Tupman, and Winkle.

"Well, I think it is," said Mr. Wardle.

"There ain't a better spot o' ground in all Kent, Sir," said the hard-headed man with the pippin-face; "there ain't indeed, Sir—I'm sure there ain't, Sir;" and the hard-headed man looked triumphantly round, as if he had been very much contradicted by somebody, but had got the better of him at last.

"There ain't a better spot o' ground in all Kent," said the hard-headed man again, after a pause.

"'Cept Mullins' Meadows," observed the fat man, solemnly.

"Mullins' Meadows!" ejaculated the other, with profound contempt.

"Ah, Mullins' Meadows," repeated the fat man.

"Reg'lar good land that," interposed another fat man.

"And so it is, sure-ly," said a third fat man.

"Everybody knows that," said the corpulent host.

The hard-headed man looked dubiously round, but finding himself in a minority, assumed a compassionate air, and said no more.

"What are they talking about?" inquired the old lady of one of her grand-daughters, in a very audible voice; for, like many deaf people, she never seemed to calculate on the possibility of other persons hearing what she said herself.

"About the land, grandma."

"What about the land?—Nothing the matter, is there?"

"No, no. Mr. Miller was saying our land was better than Mullins' Meadows."

"How should he know anything about it?" inquired the old lady indignantly. "Miller's a conceited coxcomb, and you may tell him I said so." Saying which, the old lady, quite unconscious that she had spoken above a whisper, drew herself up, and looked carving knives at the hard-headed delinquent.

"Come, come," said the bustling host, with a natural anxiety to change the conversation,—"What say you to a rubber, Mr. Pickwick?"

"I should like it of all things," replied that gentleman; "but pray don't make up one on my account."

"Oh, I assure you, mother's very fond of a rubber," said Mr. Wardle; "ain't you mother?"

The old lady, who was much less deaf on this subject than on any other, replied in the affirmative.

"Joe, Joe," said the old gentleman—"Joe—damn that —oh, here he is; put out the card-tables."

The lethargic youth contrived without any additional rousing, to set out two card-tables; the one for Pope Joan, and the other for whist. The whist-players were, Mr. Pickwick and the old lady; Mr. Miller and the fat gentleman. The round game comprised the rest of the company.

The rubber was conducted with all that gravity of deportment, and sedateness of demeanour, which befit the pursuit entitled "whist"—a solemn observance, to which, as it appears to us, the title of "game" has been very irreverently and ignominiously applied. The round-game table on the other hand, was so boisterously merry, as materially to interrupt the contemplations of Mr. Miller, who not being quite so much absorbed as he ought to have been, contrived to commit various high crimes and misdemeanours, which excited the wrath of the fat gentleman to a very great extent, and called forth the good-humour of the old lady in a proportionate degree.

"There!" said the criminal Miller triumphantly, as he took up the odd trick at the conclusion of a hand; "that could not have been played better, I flatter myself;—impossible to have made another trick!"

"Miller ought to have trumped the diamond, oughtn't he, Sir?" said the old lady.

Mr. Pickwick nodded assent.

"Ought I, though?" said the unfortunate, with a doubtful appeal to his partner.

"You ought Sir," said the fat gentleman in an awful voice.

"Very sorry," said the crest-fallen Miller.

"Much use that," growled the fat gentleman.

"Two by honours—makes us eight," said Mr. Pickwick. Another hand. "Can you one?" inquired the old lady.

"I can," replied Mr. Pickwick. "Double, single, and the rub."

"Never was such luck," said Mr. Miller.

"Never was such cards," said the fat gentleman.

A solemn silence; Mr. Pickwick humbrous, the old lady serious, the fat gentleman captious, and Mr. Miller timorous.

"Another double," said the old lady: triumphantly making a memorandum of the circumstance, by placing one sixpence and a battered halfpenny, under the candlestick.

"A double, Sir," said Mr. Pickwick.

"Quite aware of the fact, Sir," replied the fat gentleman, sharply.

Another game, with a similar result, was followed by a revoke from the unlucky Miller; on which the fat gentleman burst into a state of high personal excitement which lasted until the conclusion of the game, when he retired into a corner, and remained perfectly mute for one hour and twenty-seven minutes; at the end of which time, he emerged from his retirement, and offered Mr. Pickwick a pinch of snuff with the air of a man who had made up his mind to a Christian forgiveness of injuries sustained. The old lady's hearing decidedly improved, and the unlucky Miller felt as much out of his element, as a dolphin in a sentry-box.

Meanwhile the round game proceeded right merrily. Isabella Wardle and Mr. Trundle "went partners," and Emily Wardle and Mr. Snodgrass did the same; and even Mr. Tupman and the spinster aunt, established a joint-stock company of fish and flattery. Old Mr. Wardle was in the very height of his jollity; and he was *so* funny in his management of the board, and the old ladies were *so* sharp after their winnings, that the whole table was in a perpetual roar of merriment and laughter. There was one old lady who always had about half a dozen cards to pay for, at which everybody laughed, regularly every round; and when the old lady looked cross at having to pay, they laughed louder than ever; on which the old lady's face gradually brightened up, till at last she laughed louder than any of them. Then, when the spinster aunt got "matrimony," the young ladies laughed afresh, and the spinster aunt seemed disposed to be pettish; till, feeling Mr. Tupman squeezing her hand under the table, *she* brightened up too, and looked rather knowing as if matrimony in reality were not quite so far off as some people thought for; whereupon everybody laughed again, and especially old Mr. Wardle, who enjoyed a joke as much as the youngest. As to Mr. Snodgrass, he did nothing but whisper poetical sentiments into his partner's ear, which made one old gentleman facetiously sly, about partnerships at cards and partnerships for life, and caused the aforesaid old gentleman to make some remarks thereupon, accompanied with divers winks and chuckles, which made the company very merry and the old gentleman's wife especially so. And Mr. Winkle came out with jokes which are very well known in town, but are not at all known in the country; and as everybody laughed at them very heartily, and said they were very capital, Mr. Winkle was in a state of great honour and glory. And the benevolent clergyman looked pleasantly on; for the happy faces which surrounded the table made the good old man feel happy too; and though the merriment was rather boisterous, still it came from the heart and not from the lips: and this is the right sort of merriment, after all.

The evening glided swiftly away, in these cheerful recreations; and when the substantial, though homely supper had been despatched, and the little party formed a social circle round the fire, Mr. Pickwick thought he had never felt so happy in his life, and at no time so much disposed to enjoy, and make the most of, the passing moments.

"Now this," said the hospitable host, who was sitting in

AN OLD FASHIONED CARD PARTY.

great state next the old lady's arm-chair, with her hand fast clasped in his—"This is just what I like—the happiest moments of my life have been passed at this old fireside: and I am so attached to it, that I keep up a blazing fire here every evening, until it actually grows too hot to bear it. Why, my poor old mother, here, used to sit before this fire-place upon that little stool, when she was a girl—didn't you, mother?"

The tear which starts unbidden to the eye when the recollection of old times and the happiness of many years ago, is suddenly recalled, stole down the old lady's face, as she shook her head with a melancholy-smile.

"You must excuse my talking about this old place, Mr. Pickwick," resumed the host, after a short pause—"for I love it dearly, and know no other—the old houses and fields seem like living friends to me: and so does our little church with the ivy,—about which, by-the-by, our excellent friend there, made a song when he first came amongst us. Mr. Snodgrass, have you anything in your glass?"

"Plenty, thank you," replied that gentleman, whose poetic curiosity had been greatly excited by the last observations of his entertainer. "I beg your pardon, but you were talking about the song of the Ivy."

"You must ask our friend opposite about that," said the host knowingly: indicating the clergyman by a nod of his head.

"May I say that I should like to hear you repeat it, Sir?" said Mr. Snodgrass.

"Why really," replied the clergyman, "it's a very slight affair; and the only excuse I have for having ever perpetrated it, is, that I was a young man at the time. Such as it is, however, you shall hear it if you wish."

A murmur of curiosity was of course the reply; and the old gentleman proceeded to recite, with the aid of sundry promptings from his wife, the lines in question. "I call them," said he,

THE IVY GREEN.

Oh, a dainty plant is the Ivy green,
That creepeth o'er ruins old!
Of right choice food are his meals, I ween,
In his cell so lone and cold.
The wall must be crumbled, the stone decayed,
To pleasure his dainty whim:
And the mouldering dust that years have made,
Is a merry meal for him.
    Creeping where no life is seen,
    A rare old plant is the Ivy green.

Fast he stealeth on, though he wears no wings,
And a staunch old heart has he,
How closely he twineth, how tight he clings,
To his friend the huge Oak Tree!
And slily he traileth along the ground,
And his leaves he gently waves,
As he joyously hugs and crawleth round
The rich mould of dead men's graves.
    Creeping where grim death has been,
    A rare old plant is the Ivy green.

Whole ages have fled and their works decayed,
And nations have scattered been;
But the stout old Ivy shall never fade,
From its hale and hearty green.
The brave old plant in its lonely days,
Shall fatten upon the past:
For the stateliest building man can raise,
Is the Ivy's food at last.
    Creeping on, where time has been,
    A rare old plant is the Ivy green.

While the old gentleman repeated these lines a second time, to enable Mr. Snodgrass to note them down, Mr. Pickwick perused the lineaments of his face with an expression of great interest. The old gentleman having concluded his dictation, and Mr. Snodgrass having returned his note-book to his pocket, Mr. Pickwick said,—

"Excuse me, Sir, for making the remark on so short an acquaintance; but a gentleman like yourself cannot fail, I should think, to have observed many scenes and incidents worth recording, in the course of your experience as a minister of the Gospel."

"I have witnessed some certainly," replied the old gentleman; "but the incidents and characters have been of a homely and ordinary nature, my sphere of action being so very limited."

"You *did* make some notes, I think, about John Edmunds, did you not?" inquired Mr. Wardle who appeared very desirous to draw his friend out, for the edification of his new visitors.

The old gentleman slightly nodded his head in token of assent, and was proceeding to change the subject, when Mr. Pickwick said,—

"I beg your pardon, Sir; but pray, if I may venture to inquire, who was John Edmunds?"

"The very thing I was about to ask," said Mr. Snodgrass, eagerly.

"You are fairly in for it," said the jolly host. "You must satisfy the curiosity of these gentlemen, sooner or later; so you had better take advantage of this favourable opportunity, and do so at once."

The old gentleman smiled good-humouredly as he drew his chair forward;—the remainder of the party drew their chairs closer together, especially Mr. Tupman and the spinster aunt, who were possibly rather hard of hearing; and the old lady's ear-trumpet having been duly adjusted, and Mr. Miller (who had fallen asleep during the recital of the verses) roused from his slumbers by an admonitory pinch, administered beneath the table by his ex-partner the solemn fat man, the old gentleman, without further preface, commenced the following tale, to which we have taken the liberty of prefixing the title of

THE CONVICT'S RETURN.

"When I first settled in this village," said the old gentleman, "which is now just five-and-twenty years ago, the most notorious person among my parishioners was a man of the name of Edmunds, who leased a small farm near this spot. He was a morose, savage-hearted, bad man: idle and dissolute in his habits; cruel and ferocious in his disposition. Beyond the few lazy and reckless vagabonds with whom he sauntered away his time in the fields, or sotted in the ale-house, he had not a single friend or acquaintance; no one cared to speak to the man whom many feared, and every one detested—and Edmunds was shunned by all.

"This man had a wife and one son, who, when I first came here, was about twelve years old. Of the acuteness of that woman's sufferings, of the gentle and enduring manner in which she bore them, of the agony of solicitude with which she reared that boy, no one can form an adequate conception. Heaven forgive me the supposition, if it be an uncharitable one, but I do firmly and in my soul believe, that the man systematically tried for many years to break her heart; but she bore it all for her child's sake, and, however strange it may seem to many, for his father's too; for brute as he was and cruelly as he treated her, she had loved him once; and the recollection of what he had been to her, awakened feelings of forbearance and meekness under suffering in her bosom, to which all God's creatures, but women, are strangers.

"They were poor—they could not be otherwise when the man pursued such courses; but the woman's unceasing and unwearied exertions, early and late, morning, noon, and night, kept them above actual want. Those exertions were but ill repaid. People who passed the spot in the evening —sometimes at a late hour of the night—reported that they had heard the moans and sobs of a woman in distress, and the sound of blows: and more than once, when it was past midnight, the boy knocked softly at the door of a neighbour's house, whither he had been sent, to escape the drunken fury of his unnatural father.

"During the whole of this time, and when the poor creature often bore about her marks of ill-usage and violence which she could not wholly conceal, she was a constant attendant at our little church. Regularly every Sunday, morning and afternoon, she occupied the same seat with the boy at her side; and though they were both poorly dressed—much more so than many of their neighbours who were in a lower station—they were always neat and clean. Every one had a friendly nod and a kind word for 'poor Mrs. Edmunds;' and sometimes, when she stopped to exchange a few words with a neighbour at the conclusion of the service in the little row of elm trees which leads to the church porch, or lingered behind to gaze with a mother's pride and fondness upon her healthy boy, as he sported before her with some little companions, her care-worn face would lighten up with an expression of heartfelt gratitude; and she would look, if not cheerful and happy, at least tranquil and contented.

"Five or six years passed away; the boy had become a robust and well-grown youth. The time that had strengthened the child's slight frame and knit his weak limbs into the strength of manhood, had bowed his mother's form, and enfeebled her steps; but the arm that should have supported her was no longer locked in hers; the face that should have cheered her, no more looked upon her own. She occupied her old seat, but there was a vacant one beside her. The Bible was kept as carefully as ever, the places were found and folded down as they used to be: but there was no one to read it with her; and the tears fell thick and fast upon the book, and blotted the words from her eyes. Neighbours were as kind as they were wont to be of old, but she shunned their greetings with averted head. There was no lingering among the old elm trees now—no cheering anticipations of happiness yet in store. The desolate woman drew her bonnet closer over her face, and walked hurriedly away.

"Shall I tell you, that the young man, who, looking back to the earliest of his childhood's days to which memory and consciousness extended, and carrying his recollection down to that moment, could remember nothing which was not in some way connected with a long series of voluntary privations suffered by his mother for his sake, with ill-usage, and insult, and violence, and all endured for him —shall I tell you, that he, with a reckless disregard of her breaking heart, and a sullen wilful forgetfulness of all she had done and borne for him, had linked himself with depraved and abandoned men, and was madly pursuing a

headlong career, which must bring death to him, and shame to her? Alas for human nature! You have anticipated it long since.

"The measure of the unhappy woman's misery and misfortune was about to be completed. Numerous offences had been committed in the neighbourhood; the perpetrators remained undiscovered, and their boldness increased. A robbery of a daring and aggravated nature occasioned a vigilance of pursuit, and a strictness of search, they had not calculated on. Young Edmunds was suspected with three companions. He was apprehended—committed— tried—condemned—to die.

"The wild and piercing shriek from a woman's voice, which resounded through the court when the solemn sentence was pronounced, rings in my ears at this moment. That cry struck a terror to the culprit's heart, which trial, condemnation—the approach of death itself, had failed to awaken. The lips which had been compressed in dogged sullenness throughout, quivered and parted involuntarily; the face turned ashy pale as the cold perspiration broke forth from every pore; the sturdy limbs of the felon trembled, and he staggered in the dock.

"In the first transports of her mental anguish, the suffering mother threw herself upon her knees at my feet, and fervently besought the Almighty Being who had hitherto supported her in all her troubles, to release her from a world of woe and misery, and to spare the life of her only child. A burst of grief, and a violent struggle, such as I hope I may never have to witness again, succeeded. I knew that her heart was breaking from that hour; but I never once heard complaint or murmur escape her lips.

"It was a piteous spectacle to see that woman in the prison yard from day to day, eagerly and fervently attempting, by affection and entreaty, to soften the hard heart of her obdurate son. It was in vain. He remained moody, obstinate, and unmoved. Not even the unlooked-for commutation of his sentence to transportation for fourteen years, softened for an instant the sullen hardihood of his demeanour.

"But the spirit of resignation and endurance that had so long upheld her, was unable to contend against bodily weakness and infirmity. She fell sick. She dragged her tottering limbs from the bed to visit her son once more, but her strength failed her, and she sunk powerless on the ground.

"And now the boasted coldness and indifference of the young man were tested indeed; and the retribution that fell heavily upon him, nearly drove him mad. A day passed away and his mother was not there; another flew by, and she came not near him; a third evening arrived, and yet he had not seen her; and in four-and-twenty hours, he was to be separated from her—perhaps for ever. Oh! how the long-forgotten thoughts of former days rushed upon his mind, as he almost ran up and down the narrow yard—as if intelligence would arrive the sooner for *his* hurrying—and how bitterly a sense of his helplessness and desolation rushed upon him, when he heard the truth! His mother, the only parent he had ever known, lay ill— it might be, dying—within one mile of the ground he stood on; were he free and unfettered, a few minutes would place him by her side. He rushed to the gate, and, grasping the iron rails with the energy of desperation, shook it till it rang again, and threw himself against the thick wall as if to force a passage through the stone; but the strong building mocked his feeble efforts, and he beat his hands together and wept like a child.

"I bore the mother's forgiveness and blessing to her son in prison; and I carried his solemn assurance of repentance, and his fervent supplication for pardon, to her sick bed. I heard with pity and compassion, the repentant man devise a thousand little plans for her comfort and support, when he returned; but I knew that many months before he could reach his place of destination, his mother would be no longer of this world.

"He was removed by night. A few weeks afterwards the poor woman's soul took its flight I confidently hope, and solemnly believe, to a place of eternal happiness and rest. I performed the burial service over her remains. She lies in our little churchyard. There is no stone at her grave's head. Her sorrows were known to man; her virtues to God.

"It had been arranged previously to the convict's departure, that he should write to his mother so soon as he could obtain permission, and that the letter should be addressed to me. The father had positively refused to see his son from the moment of his apprehension; and it was a matter of indifference to him whether he lived or died. Many years passed over without any intelligence of him; and when more than half his term of transportation had expired and I had received no letter, I concluded him to be dead, as, indeed, I almost hoped he might be.

"Edmunds, however, had been sent a considerable distance up the country on his arrival at the settlement; and to this circumstance, perhaps, may be attributed the fact, that though several letters were despatched none of them ever reached my hands. He remained in the same place during the whole fourteen years. At the expiration of the term steadily adhering to his old resolution, and the pledge he gave his mother, he made his way back to England amidst innumerable difficulties, and returned, on foot, to his native place.

"On a fine Sunday evening, in the month of August, John Edmunds set foot in the village he had left with shame and disgrace seventeen years before. His nearest way lay through the churchyard. The man's heart swelled as he crossed the stile. The tall old elms, through whose branches the declining sun cast here and there a rich ray of light upon the shady path, awakened the associations of his earliest days. He pictured himself as he was then, clinging to his mother's hand, and walking peacefully to church. He remembered how he used to look up into her pale face; and how her eyes would sometimes fill with tears as she gazed upon his features—tears which fell hot upon his forehead as she stooped to kiss him, and made him weep too, although he little knew then what bitter tears hers were. He thought how often he had run merrily down that path with some childish playfellow, looking back ever and again, to catch his mother's smile, or hear her gentle voice; and then a veil seemed lifted from his memory, and words of kindness unrequited, and warnings despised, and promises broken, thronged upon his recollection till his heart failed him, and he could bear it no longer.

"He entered the church. The evening service was concluded and the congregation had dispersed, but it was not yet closed. His steps echoed through the low building with a hollow sound, and he almost feared to be alone, it was so still and quiet. He looked round him. Nothing was changed. The place seemed smaller than it used to be; but there were the old monuments on which he had gazed with childish awe a thousand times; the little pulpit with its faded cushion; the Communion table before which he had so often repeated the Commandments he had reverenced as a child, and forgotten as a man. He approached the old seat; it looked cold and desolate. The cushion had been removed, and the Bible was not there. Perhaps his mother now occupied a poorer seat, or possibly she had grown infirm and could not reach the church alone. He dared not think of what he feared. A cold feeling crept over him, and he trembled violently, as he turned away.

"An old man entered the porch just as he reached it. Edmunds started back for he knew him well; many a time had he watched him digging graves in the churchyard. What would *he* say to the returned convict? The old man raised his eyes to the stranger's face, bid him 'good evening,' and walked slowly on. He had forgotten him.

"He walked down the hill, and through the village. The weather was warm, and the people were sitting at their doors, or strolling in their little gardens as he passed, enjoying the serenity of the evening, and their rest from labour. Many a look was turned towards him, and many a doubtful glance he cast on either side to see whether any knew and shunned him. There were strange faces in almost every house; in some he recognised the burly form of some old schoolfellow—a boy when he last saw him—surrounded by a troop of merry children; in others he saw, seated in an easy-chair at the cottage door, a feeble and infirm old man, whom he only remembered as a hale and hearty labourer; but they had all forgotten him, and he passed on unknown.

"The last soft light of the setting sun had fallen on the earth, casting a rich glow on the yellow corn sheaves, and lengthening the shadows of the orchard trees, as he stood before the old house—the home of his infancy—to which his heart had yearned with an intensity of affection not to be described, through long and weary years of captivity and sorrow. The paling was low—though he well remembered the time, when it had seemed a high wall to him; and he looked over into the old garden. There were more seeds and gayer flowers than there used to be, but there were the old trees still—the very tree, under which he had lain a thousand times when tired with playing in the sun, and felt the soft mild sleep of happy boyhood steal gently upon him. There were voices within the house. He listened, but they fell strangely upon his ear; he knew them not. They were merry too; and he well knew that his poor old mother could not be cheerful, and he away. The door opened, and a group of little children bounded out, shouting and romping. The father with a little boy in his arms, appeared at the door, and they crowded round him, clapping their tiny hands, and dragging him out, to join their joyous sports. The convict thought on the many times he had shrunk from his father's sight in that very place. He remembered how often he had buried his trembling head beneath the bed-clothes, and heard the harsh word, and the hard stripe, and his mother's wailing; and though the man sobbed aloud with agony of mind as he left the spot, his fist was clenched, and his teeth were set, in fierce and deadly passion.

"And such was the return to which he had looked through the weary perspective of many years, and for which he had undergone so much suffering! No face of welcome, no look of forgiveness, no house to receive, no hand to help him—and this too in the old village. What was his loneliness in the wild thick woods where man was never seen, to this!

"He felt that in the distant land of his bondage and infamy, he had thought of his native place as it was when he left it;—not as it would be, when he returned. The sad reality struck coldly at his heart, and his spirit sank within him. He had not courage to make inquiries, or to present himself to the only person who was likely to receive him with kindness and compassion. He walked slowly on; and shunning the road-side like a guilty man, turned into a meadow he well remembered; and covering his face with his hands, threw himself upon the grass.

"He had not observed that a man was lying on the bank beside him; his garments rustled as he turned round to steal a look at the new comer: and Edmunds raised his head.

"The man had moved into a sitting posture. His body was much bent, and his face was wrinkled and yellow. His dress denoted him an inmate of the workhouse: he had the appearance of being very old, but it looked more the effect of dissipation or disease, than length of years. He was staring hard at the stranger, and though his eyes were lustreless and heavy at first, they appeared to glow with an unnatural and alarmed expression after they had been fixed upon him for a short time, until they seemed to be starting from their sockets. Edmunds gradually raised himself to his knees, and looked more and more earnestly upon the old man's face. They gazed upon each other in silence.

"The old man was ghastly pale. He shuddered and tottered to his feet. Edmunds sprang to his. He stepped back a pace or two. Edmunds advanced.

"'Let me hear you speak,' said the convict in a thick broken voice.

"'Stand off,' cried the old man, with a dreadful oath. The convict drew closer to him.

"'Stand off,' shrieked the old man. Furious with terror he raised his stick, and struck Edmunds a heavy blow across the face.

"'Father—devil,' murmured the convict, between his set teeth He rushed wildly forward, and clenched the old man by the throat—but he was his father; and his arm fell powerless by his side.

"The old man uttered a loud yell which rang through the lonely fields like the howl of an evil spirit. His face turned black: the gore rushed from his mouth and nose, and dyed the grass a deep dark red, as he staggered and fell. He had ruptured a blood vessel; and he was a dead man before his son could raise him from that thick, sluggish, pool.

*   *   *   *   *   *

"In that corner of the churchyard," said the old gentleman, after a silence of a few moments, "In that corner of the churchyard of which I have before spoken, there lies buried a man, who was in my employment for three years after this event: and who was truly contrite, penitent, and humbled, if ever man was. No one save myself knew in that man's life-time who he was, or whence he came:—it was John Edmunds the returned convict."

CHAPTER VII.

HOW MR. WINKLE, INSTEAD OF SHOOTING AT THE PIGEON AND KILLING THE CROW, SHOT AT THE CROW AND WOUNDED THE PIGEON; HOW THE DINGLEY DELL CRICKET CLUB PLAYED ALL MUG-GLETON, AND HOW ALL MUGGLETON DINED AT THE DINGLEY DELL EXPENSE: WITH OTHER IN-TERESTING AND INSTRUCTIVE MATTERS.

THE fatiguing adventures of the day or the somniferous influence of the clergyman's tale, operated so strongly on the drowsy tendencies of Mr. Pickwick, that, in less than five minutes after he had been shown to his comfortable bed-room, he fell into a sound and dreamless sleep, from which he was only awakened by the morning sun darting his bright beams reproachfully into the apartment. Mr. Pickwick was no sluggard; and he sprang like an ardent warrior from his tent—bedstead.

"Pleasant, pleasant country," sighed the enthusiastic gentleman, as he opened his lattice window. "Who could live to gaze from day to day on bricks and slates, who had once felt the influence of a scene like this? Who could continue to exist, where there are no cows but the cows on the chimney-pots; nothing redolent of Pan but pan-tiles; no crop but stone crop? Who could bear to drag out a life in such a spot? Who I ask could endure it?" and, having cross-examined solitude after the most approved precedents at considerable length, Mr. Pickwick thrust his head out of the lattice, and looked around him.

The rich, sweet smell of the hay-ricks rose to his chamber window; the hundred perfumes of the little flower-garden beneath scented the air around; the deep-green meadows shone in the morning dew that glistened on every leaf as it trembled in the gentle air; and the birds sang as if every sparkling drop were to them a fountain of inspiration. Mr. Pickwick fell into an enchanting, and delicious reverie.

"Hallo!" was the sound that roused him.

He looked to the right but he saw nobody; his eyes wandered to the left, and pierced the prospect; he stared into the sky, but he wasn't wanted there; and then he did what a common mind would have done at once—looked into the garden, and there saw Mr. Wardle.

"How are you?" said that good-humoured individual, out of breath with his own anticipations of pleasure. "Beautiful morning, ain't it? Glad to see you up so early. Make haste down, and come out. I'll wait for you here."

Mr. Pickwick needed no second invitation. Ten minutes sufficed for the completion of his toilet, and at the expiration of that time he was by the old gentleman's side.

"Hallo!" said Mr. Pickwick in his turn: seeing that his companion was armed with a gun, and that another lay ready on the grass. "What's going forward?"

"Why, your friend and I," replied the host, "are going out rook-shooting before breakfast. He's a very good shot ain't he?"

"I've heard him say he's a capital one," replied Mr. Pickwick; "but I never saw him aim at anything."

"Well," said the host, "I wish he'd come. Joe—Joe."

The fat boy, who under the exciting influence of the morning did not appear to be more than three parts and a fraction asleep, emerged from the house.

"Go up, and call the gentleman, and tell him he'll find me and Mr. Pickwick in the rookery. Show the gentleman the way there; d'ye hear?"

The boy departed to execute his commission; and the host, carrying both guns like a second Robinson Crusoe, led the way from the garden.

"This is the place," said the old gentleman, pausing after a few minutes walking, in an avenue of trees. The information was unnecessary; for the incessant cawing of the unconscious rooks, sufficiently indicated their whereabout.

The old gentleman laid one gun on the ground, and loaded the other.

"Here they are," said Mr. Pickwick; and as he spoke, the forms of Mr. Tupman, Mr. Snodgrass, and Mr. Winkle appeared in the distance. The fat boy, not being quite certain which gentleman he was directed to call, had with peculiar sagacity, and to prevent the possibility of any mistake, called them all.

"Come along," shouted the old gentleman, addressing Mr. Winkle; "a keen hand like you ought to have been up long ago, even to such poor work as this."

Mr. Winkle responded with a forced smile, and took up the spare gun with an expression of countenance which a metaphysical rook, impressed with a foreboding of his approaching death by violence, may be supposed to assume. It might have been keenness, but it looked remarkably like misery.

The old gentleman nodded; and two ragged boys who had been marshalled to the spot under the direction of the infant Lambert, forthwith commenced climbing up two of the trees.

"What are those lads for?" inquired Mr. Pickwick abruptly. He was rather alarmed; for he was not quite certain but that the distress of the agricultural interest, about which he had often heard a great deal, might have compelled the small boys, attached to the soil, to earn a precarious and hazardous subsistence by making marks of themselves for inexperienced sportsmen.

"Only to start the game," replied Mr. Wardle, laughing.

"To what?" inquired Mr. Pickwick.

"Why, in plain English to frighten the rooks."

"Oh! Is that all?"

"You are satisfied?"

"Quite."

"Very well. Shall I begin?"

"If you please," said Mr. Winkle, glad of any respite.

"Stand aside, then. Now for it."

The boy shouted, and shook a branch with a nest on it. Half a dozen young rooks in violent conversation, flew out to ask what the matter was. The old gentleman fired by way of reply. Down fell one bird, and off flew the others.

"Take him up, Joe," said the old gentleman.

There was a smile upon the youth's face as he advanced. Indistinct visions of rook-pie floated through his imagination. He laughed as he retired with the bird—it was a plump one.

"Now, Mr. Winkle," said the host, reloading his own gun. "Fire away."

Mr. Winkle advanced, and levelled his gun. Mr. Pickwick and his friends cowered involuntarily to escape damage from the heavy fall of rooks, which they felt quite

certain would be occasioned by the devastating barrel of their friend. There was a solemn pause—a shout—a flapping of wings—a faint click.

"Hallo!" said the old gentleman.

"Won't it go?" inquired Mr. Pickwick.

"Missed fire," said Mr. Winkle, who was very pale, probably from disappointment.

"Odd," said the old gentleman, taking the gun. "Never knew one of them miss fire before. Why, I don't see anything of the cap."

"Bless my soul," said Mr. Winkle. "I declare I forgot the cap!"

The slight omission was rectified. Mr. Pickwick crouched again. Mr. Winkle stepped forward with an air of determination and resolution; and Mr. Tupman looked out from behind a tree. The boy shouted;—four birds flew out. Mr. Winkle fired. There was a scream as of an individual—not a rook—in corporeal anguish. Mr. Tupman had saved the lives of innumerable unoffending birds, by receiving a portion of the charge in his left arm.

To describe the confusion that ensued would be impossible. To tell how Mr. Pickwick in the first transports of his emotion called Mr. Winkle "Wretch!" how Mr. Tupman lay prostrate on the ground; and how Mr. Winkle knelt horror-stricken beside him; how Mr. Tupman called distractedly upon some feminine Christian name, and then opened first one eye, and then the other, and then fell back and shut them both;—all this would be as difficult to describe in detail, as it would be to depict the gradual recovering of the unfortunate individual, the binding up his arm with pocket-handkerchiefs, and the conveying him back by slow degrees supported by the arms of his anxious friends.

They drew near the house. The ladies were at the garden-gate, waiting for their arrival and their breakfast. The spinster aunt appeared; she smiled, and beckoned them to walk quicker. 'Twas evident she knew not of the disaster. Poor thing! There are times when ignorance is bliss indeed.

They approached nearer.

"Why, what *is* the matter with the little old gentleman?" said Isabella Wardle. The spinster aunt heeded not the remark; she thought it applied to Mr. Pickwick. In her eyes Tracy Tupman was a youth; she viewed his years through a diminishing glass.

"Don't be frightened," called out the old host fearful of alarming his daughters. The little party had crowded so completely round Mr. Tupman, that they could not yet clearly discern the nature of the accident.

"Don't be frightened," said the host.

"What's the matter?" screamed the ladies.

"Mr. Tupman has met with a little accident; that's all."

The spinster aunt uttered a piercing scream, burst into an hysteric laugh, and fell backwards in the arms of her nieces.

"Throw some cold water over her," said the old gentleman.

"No, no," murmured the spinster aunt; "I am better now. Bella, Emily—a surgeon! Is he wounded?—Is he dead?—Is he——ha, ha, ha!" Here the spinster aunt burst into fit number two, of hysteric laughter, interspersed with screams.

"Calm yourself," said Mr. Tupman, affected almost to tears by this expression of sympathy with his sufferings. "Dear, dear Madam, calm yourself."

"It is his voice!" exclaimed the spinster aunt; and

strong symptoms of fit number three developed themselves forthwith.

"Do not agitate yourself I entreat you, dearest Madam," said Mr. Tupman, soothingly. "I am very little hurt, I assure you."

"Then you are not dead!" ejaculated the hysterical lady. "Oh, say you are not dead!"

"Don't be a fool, Rachael," interposed Mr. Wardle, rather more roughly than was quite consistent with the poetic nature of the scene. "What the devil's the use of his *saying* he isn't dead?"

"No, no, I am not," said Mr. Tupman. "I require no assistance but yours. Let me lean on your arm," he added, in a whisper, "Oh Miss Rachael!" The agitated female advanced, and offered her arm. They turned into the breakfast parlour. Mr. Tracy Tupman gently pressed her hand to his lips, and sank upon the sofa.

"Are you faint?" inquired the anxious Rachael.

"No," said Mr. Tupman. "It is nothing. I shall be better presently." He closed his eyes.

"He sleeps," murmured the spinster aunt. (His organs of vision had been closed nearly twenty seconds.) "Dear —dear—Mr. Tupman."

Mr. Tupman jumped up—"Oh, say those words again!" he exclaimed.

The lady started. "Surely you did not hear them!" she said, bashfully.

"Oh yes I did!" replied Mr. Tupman; "repeat them. If you would have me recover, repeat them."

"Hush!" said the Lady. "My brother."

Mr. Tracy Tupman resumed his former position; and Mr. Wardle accompanied by a surgeon, entered the room.

The arm was examined, the wound dressed, and pronounced to be a very slight one; and the minds of the company having been thus satisfied, they proceeded to satisfy their appetites with countenances to which an expression of cheerfulness was again restored. Mr. Pickwick alone was silent and reserved. Doubt and distress were exhibited in his countenance. His confidence in Mr. Winkle had been shaken—greatly shaken—by the proceedings of the morning.

"Are you a cricketer?" inquired Mr. Wardle of the marksman.

At any other time, Mr. Winkle would have replied in the affirmative. He felt the delicacy of his situation, and modestly replied, "No."

"Are you, Sir?" inquired Mr. Snodgrass.

"I was once upon a time," replied the host; "but I have given it up now. I subscribe to the club here, but I don't play."

"The grand match is played to-day, I believe," said Mr. Pickwick.

"It is," replied the host. "Of course you would like to see it."

"I, Sir," replied Mr. Pickwick, "am delighted to view any sports which may be safely indulged in, and in which the impotent effects of unskilful people do not endanger human life." Mr. Pickwick paused, and looked steadily on Mr. Winkle, who quailed beneath his leader's searching glance. The great man withdrew his eyes after a few minutes, and added: "Shall we be justified in leaving our wounded friend to the care of the ladies?"

"You cannot leave me in better hands," said Mr. Tupman.

"Quite impossible," said Mr. Snodgrass.

It was therefore settled that Mr. Tupman should be left at home in charge of the females; and that the remainder of the guests under the guidance of Mr. Wardle should proceed to the spot, where was to be held that trial of skill, which had roused all Muggleton from its torpor, and inoculated Dingley Dell with a fever of excitement.

As their walk which was not above two miles long, lay through shady lanes, and sequestered footpaths; and as their conversation turned upon the delightful scenery by which they were on every side surrounded, Mr. Pickwick was almost inclined to regret the expedition they had used, when he found himself in the main street of the town of Muggleton.

Everybody whose genius has a topographical bent, knows perfectly well, that Muggleton is a corporate town, with a mayor, burgesses, and freemen; and anybody who has consulted the addresses of the mayor to the freemen, or the freemen to the mayor, or both to the corporation, or all three to Parliament, will learn from thence what they ought to have known before, that Muggleton is an ancient and loyal borough, mingling a zealous advocacy of Christian principles with a devoted attachment to commercial rights; in demonstration whereof, the mayor, corporation, and other inhabitants, have presented at divers times, no fewer than one thousand four hundred and twenty petitions, against the continuance of negro slavery abroad, and an equal number against any interference with the factory system at home; sixty-eight for permitting the sale of benefices in the church, and eighty-six for abolishing Sunday trading in the streets.

Mr. Pickwick stood in the principal street of this illustrious town, and gazed with an air of curiosity not unmixed with interest, on the objects around him. There was an open square for the market-place; and in the centre of it, a large inn with a sign-post in front, displaying an object very common in art, but rarely met with in nature—to wit, a blue lion with three bow legs in the air, balancing himself on the extreme point of the centre claw of his fourth foot. There were, within sight, an auctioneer's and fire-agency office, a corn-factor's, a linen draper's, a saddler's, a distiller's, a grocer's, and a shoe shop—the last-mentioned warehouse being also appropriated to the diffusion of hats, bonnets, wearing apparel, cotton umbrellas, and useful knowledge. There was a red-brick house with a small paved court-yard in front, which anybody might have known belonged to the attorney: and there was, moreover, another red-brick house with Venetian blinds, and a large brass door-plate, with a very legible announcement that it belonged to the surgeon. A few boys were making their way to the cricket-field; and two or three shopkeepers who were standing at their doors, looked as if they should like to be making their way to the same spot, as indeed to all appearance they might have done, without losing any great amount of custom thereby. Mr. Pickwick having paused to make these observations, to be noted down at a more convenient period, hastened to rejoin his friends, who had turned out of the main street, and were already within sight of the field of battle.

The wickets were pitched, and so were a couple of marquees for the rest and refreshment of the contending parties. The game had not yet commenced. Two or three Dingley Dellers, and All-Muggletonians, were amusing themselves with a majestic air by throwing the ball carelessly from hand to hand; and several other gentlemen dressed like them, in straw hats, flannel jackets, and white trowsers,—a costume in which they looked very much like amateur stone-masons—were sprinkled about the tents, towards one of which Mr. Wardle conducted the party.

Several dozen of "How-are-you's?" hailed the old gentleman's arrival; and a general raising of the straw hats, and bending forward of the flannel jackets, followed his introduction of his guests as gentlemen from London, who were extremely anxious to witness the proceedings of the day, with which, he had no doubt, they would be greatly delighted.

"You had better step into the marquee I think, Sir," said one very stout gentleman, whose body and legs looked like half a gigantic roll of flannel, elevated on a couple of inflated pillow-cases.

"You'll find it much pleasanter, Sir," urged another stout gentleman, who strongly resembled the other half of the roll of flannel aforesaid.

"You're very good," said Mr. Pickwick.

"This way," said the first speaker; "they notch in here—it's the best place in the whole field;" and the cricketer, panting on before, preceded them to the tent.

"Capital game—smart sport—fine exercise—very," were the words which fell upon Mr. Pickwick's ear as he entered the tent; and the first object that met his eyes, was his green-coated friend of the Rochester coach, holding forth, to the no small delight and edification of a select circle of the chosen of All-Muggleton. His dress was slightly improved, and he wore boots; but there was no mistaking him.

The stranger recognised his friends immediately: and, darting forward and seizing Mr. Pickwick by the hand, dragged him to a seat, with his usual impetuosity, talking all the while as if the whole of the arrangements were under his especial patronage and direction.

"This way—this way—capital fun—lots of beer—hogsheads; rounds of beef—bullocks; mustard—cart loads; glorious day—down with you—make yourself at home—glad to see you—very."

Mr. Pickwick sat down as he was bid, and Mr. Winkle and Mr. Snodgrass also complied with the directions of their mysterious friend. Mr. Wardle looked on, in silent wonder.

"Mr. Wardle—a friend of mine," said Mr. Pickwick.

"Friend of yours!—My dear Sir, how are you?—Friend of *my* friend's—give me your hand, Sir"—and the stranger grasped Mr. Wardle's hand with all the fervour of a close intimacy of many years, and then stepped back a pace or two as if to take a full survey of his face and figure, and then shook hands with him again, if possible, more warmly than before.

"Well; and how came you here?" said Mr. Pickwick, with a smile in which benevolence struggled with surprise.

"Come," replied the stranger—"stopping at Crown—Crown at Muggleton—met a party—flannel jackets—white trowsers—anchovy sandwiches—devilled kidneys—splendid fellows—glorious."

Mr. Pickwick was sufficiently versed in the stranger's system of stenography to infer from this rapid and disjointed communication that he had, somehow or other, contracted an acquaintance with the All-Muggletons, which he had converted, by a process peculiar to himself, into

that extent of good fellowship on which a general invitation may be easily founded. His curiosity was therefore satisfied, and putting on his spectacles he prepared himself to watch the play which was just commencing.

All-Muggleton had the first innings; and the interest became intense when Mr. Dumkins and Mr. Podder, two of the most renowned members of that most distinguished club, walked, bat in hand, to their respective wickets. Mr. Luffey, the highest ornament of Dingley Dell, was pitched to bowl against the redoubtable Dumkins, and Mr. Struggles was selected to do the same kind office for the hitherto unconquered Podder. Several players were stationed, to "look out," in different parts of the field, and each fixed himself into the proper attitude by placing one hand on each knee, and stooping very much as if he were "making a back" for some beginner at leap-frog. All the regular players do this sort of thing;—indeed it's generally supposed that it is quite impossible to look out properly in any other position.

The umpires were stationed behind the wickets; the scorers were prepared to notch the runs; a breathless silence ensued. Mr. Luffey retired a few paces behind the wicket of the passive Podder, and applied the ball to his right eye for several seconds. Dumkins confidently awaited its coming, with his eyes fixed on the motions of Luffey.

"Play," suddenly cried the bowler. The ball flew from his hand straight and swift towards the centre stump of the wicket. The wary Dumkins was on the alert; it fell upon the tip of the bat, and bounded far away over the heads of the scouts, who had just stooped low enough to let it fly over them.

"Run—run—another.—Now, then, throw her up—up with her—stop there—another—no—yes—no—throw her up, throw her up."—Such were the shouts which followed the stroke; and, at the conclusion of which All-Muggleton had scored two. Nor was Podder behindhand in earning laurels wherewith to garnish himself and Muggleton. He blocked the doubtful balls, missed the bad ones, took the good ones, and sent them flying to all parts of the field. The scouts were hot and tired; the bowlers were changed and bowled till their arms ached; but Dumkins and Podder remained unconquered. Did an elderly gentleman essay to stop the progress of the ball, it rolled between his legs, or slipped between his fingers. Did a slim gentleman try to catch it, it struck him on the nose, and bounded pleasantly off with redoubled violence, while the slim gentleman's eyes filled with water, and his form writhed with anguish. Was it thrown straight up to the wicket, Dumkins had reached it before the ball. In short, when Dumkins was caught out, and Podder stumped out, All-Muggleton had notched some fifty-four, while the score of the Dingley Dellers was as blank as their faces. The advantage was too great to be recovered. In vain did the eager Luffey, and the enthusiastic Struggles, do all that skill and experience could suggest, to regain the ground Dingley Dell had lost in the contest;—it was of no avail; and in an early period of the winning game Dingley Dell gave in, and allowed the superior prowess of All-Muggleton.

The stranger, meanwhile, had been eating, drinking, and talking, without cessation. At every good stroke he expressed his satisfaction and approval of the player in a most condescending and patronising manner, which could not fail to have been highly gratifying to the party concerned; while at every bad attempt at a catch, and every failure to stop the ball, he launched his personal displeasure at the head of the devoted individual in such denunciations as—"Ah, ah!—stupid"—"Now butter-fingers"—"Muff"—"Humbug"—and so forth—ejaculations which seemed to establish him in the opinion of all around, as a most excellent and undeniable judge of the whole art and mystery of the noble game of cricket.

"Capital game—well played—some strokes admirable," said the stranger as both sides crowded into the tent, at the conclusion of the game.

"You have played it Sir?" inquired Mr. Wardle, who had been much amused by his loquacity.

"Played it! Think I have—thousands of times—not here—West Indies—exciting thing—hot work—very."

"It must be rather a warm pursuit in such a climate," observed Mr. Pickwick.

"Warm!—red hot—scorching—glowing. Played a match once—single wicket—friend the Colonel—Sir Thomas Blazo—who should get the greatest number of runs.—Won the toss—first innings—seven o'clock, A.M.—six natives to look out—went in; kept in—heat intense—natives all fainted—taken away—fresh half-dozen ordered—fainted also—Blazo bowling—supported by two natives—couldn't bowl me out—fainted too—cleared away the Colonel—wouldn't give in—faithful attendant—Quanko Samba—last man left—sun so hot, bat in blisters, ball scorched brown—five hundred and seventy runs—rather exhausted—Quanko mustered up last remaining strength—bowled me out—had a bath, and went out to dinner."

"And what became of what's-his-name, Sir?" inquired an old gentleman.

"Blazo?"

"No—the other gentleman."

"Quanko Samba?"

"Yes Sir."

"Poor Quanko—never recovered it—bowled on, on my account—bowled off, on his own—died Sir." Here the stranger buried his countenance in a brown jug, but whether to hide his emotion or imbibe its contents, we cannot distinctly affirm. We only know that he paused suddenly, drew a long and deep breath, and looked anxiously on, as two of the principal members of the Dingley Dell club approached Mr. Pickwick, and said—

"We are about to partake of a plain dinner at the Blue Lion, Sir; we hope you and your friends will join us."

"Of course," said Mr. Wardle, "among our friends we include Mr. ———;" and he looked towards the stranger.

"Jingle," said that versatile gentleman, taking the hint at once. "Jingle—Alfred Jingle, Esq., of No Hall, Nowhere."

"I shall be very happy, I am sure," said Mr. Pickwick.

"So shall I," said Mr. Alfred Jingle, drawing one arm through Mr. Pickwick's, and another through Mr. Wardle's, as he whispered confidentially in the ear of the former gentleman:—

"Devilish good dinner—cold, but capital—peeped into the room this morning—fowls and pies, and all that sort of thing—pleasant fellows these—well behaved, too—very."

There being no further preliminaries to arrange, the company straggled into the town in little knots of twos and threes; and within a quarter of an hour were all seated in the great room of the Blue Lion Inn Muggleton—Mr. Dumkins acting as chairman, and Mr. Luffey officiating as vice.

There was a vast deal of talking and rattling of knives and forks, and plates: a great running about of three ponderous headed waiters, and a rapid disappearance of the substantial viands on the table; to each and every of which item of confusion, the facetious Mr. Jingle lent the aid of half-a-dozen ordinary men at least. When everybody had eat as much as they could, the cloth was removed, bottles, glasses, and dessert were placed on the table; and the waiters withdrew to "clear away," or in other words, to appropriate to their own private use and emolument, whatever remnants of the eatables and drinkables they could contrive to lay their hands on.

Amidst the general hum of mirth and conversation that ensued, there was a little man with a puffy Say-nothing-to-me,-or-I'll-contradict-you sort of countenance, who remained very quiet; occasionally looking round him when the conversation slackened, as if he contemplated putting in something very weighty: and now and then bursting into a short cough of inexpressible grandeur. At length, during a moment of comparative silence, the little man called out in a very loud, solemn voice,

"Mr. Luffey."

Everybody was hushed into a profound stillness as the individual addressed, replied,

"Sir."

"I wish to address a few words to you Sir, if you will entreat the gentlemen to fill their glasses."

Mr. Jingle uttered a patronizing "hear, hear," which was responded to, by the remainder of the company: and the glasses having been filled the Vice-President assumed an air of wisdom in a state of profound attention; and said,

"Mr. Staple."

"Sir," said the little man, rising, "I wish to address what I have to say to *you* and not to our worthy chairman, because our worthy chairman is in some measure—I may say in a great degree—the subject of what I have to say, or I may say to—to—

"State," suggested Mr. Jingle.

—"Yes, to state," said the little man, "I thank my honourable friend, if he will allow me to call him so—(four hears, and one certainly from Mr. Jingle)—for the suggestion. Sir, I am a Deller—a Dingley Deller, (cheers). I cannot lay claim to the honour of forming an item in the population of Muggleton; nor Sir, I will frankly admit, do I covet that honour: and I will tell you why Sir, (hear); to Muggleton I will readily concede all those honours and distinctions to which it can fairly lay claim—they are too numerous and too well known to require aid or recapitulation from me. But Sir, while we remember that Muggleton has given birth to a Dumkins and a Podder, let us never forget that Dingley Dell can boast a Luffey and a Struggles. (Vociferous cheering.) Let me not be considered as wishing to detract from the merits of the former gentlemen. Sir, I envy them the luxury of their own feelings, on this occasion. (Cheers). Every gentleman who hears me, is probably acquainted with the reply made by an individual, who—to use an ordinary figure of speech—'hung out' in a tub, to the emperor Alexander:—'If I were not Diogenes,' said he, 'I would be Alexander.' I can well imagine these gentlemen to say, 'If I were not Dumkins I would be Luffey; if I were not Podder I would be Struggles.' (Enthusiasm.) But gentlemen of Muggleton is it in cricket alone that your fellow-townsmen stand pre-eminent? Have you never heard of Dumkins and determination? Have you never been taught to associate Podder with property? (Great applause). Have you never, when struggling for your rights, your liberties, and your privileges, been reduced, if only for an instant, to misgiving and despair? And when you have been thus depressed, has not the name of Dumkins laid afresh within your breast, the fire which had just gone out; and has not a word from that man, lighted it again as brightly as if it had never expired? (Great cheering.) Gentlemen, I beg you to surround with a rich halo of enthusiastic cheering, the united names of 'Dumkins and Podder.'"

Here the little man ceased, and here the company commenced a raising of voices, and thumping of tables, which lasted with little intermission during the remainder of the evening. Other toasts were drunk. Mr. Luffey and Mr. Struggles, Mr. Pickwick and Mr. Jingle, were, each in his turn, the subject of unqualified eulogium; and each in due course returned thanks for the honour.

Enthusiastic as we are in the noble cause to which we have devoted ourselves, we should have felt a sensation of pride which we cannot express, and a consciousness of having done something to merit immortality of which we are now deprived, could we have laid the faintest outline of these addresses before our ardent readers. Mr. Snodgrass, as usual, took a great mass of notes, which would no doubt have afforded most useful and valuable information, had not the burning eloquence of the words or the feverish influence of the wine made that gentleman's hand so extremely unsteady, as to render his writing nearly unintelligible, and his style wholly so. By dint of patient investigation, we have been enabled to trace some characters bearing a faint resemblance to the names of the speakers; and we can also discern an entry of a song (supposed to have been sung by Mr. Jingle,) in which the words "bowl" "sparkling" "ruby" "bright," and "wine" are frequently repeated at short intervals. We fancy too, that we can discern at the very end of the notes, some indistinct reference to "broiled bones;" and then the words "cold" "without" occur: but as any hypothesis we could found upon them must necessarily rest upon mere conjecture, we are not disposed to indulge in any of the speculations to which they may give rise.

We will therefore return to Mr. Tupman; merely adding that within some few minutes before twelve o'clock that night, the convocation of worthies of Dingley Dell and Muggleton, were heard to sing with great feeling and emphasis, the beautiful and pathetic national air of

> We won't go home 'till morning,
> We won't go home 'till morning,
> We won't go home 'till morning,
> 'Till daylight doth appear.

CHAPTER VIII.

STRONGLY ILLUSTRATIVE OF THE POSITION, THAT THE COURSE OF TRUE LOVE IS NOT A RAILWAY.

THE quiet seclusion of Dingley Dell, the presence of so many of the gentler sex, and the solicitude and anxiety they evinced in his behalf, were all favourable to the growth and development of those softer feelings which nature had implanted deep in the bosom of Mr. Tracy Tupman, and which now appeared destined to centre in one lovely object. The young ladies were pretty, their manners winning, their dispositions unexceptionable; but there was a dignity in the air, a touch-me-not-ishness in the walk, a majesty in the eye of the spinster aunt, to which, at their time of life they could lay no claim, which distinguished her from any female on whom Mr. Tupman had ever gazed. That there was something kindred in their nature, something congenial in their souls, something mysteriously sympathetic in their bosoms, was evident. Her name was the first that rose to Mr. Tupman's lips as he lay wounded on the grass; and her hysteric laughter, was the first sound that fell upon his ear, when he was supported to the house. But had her agitation arisen from an amiable and feminine sensibility which would have been equally irrepressible in any case; or had it been called forth by a more ardent and passionate feeling, which he, of all men living, could alone awaken? These were the doubts which racked his brain as he lay extended on the sofa: these were the doubts which he determined should be at once and for ever resolved.

It was evening. Isabella and Emily had strolled out with Mr. Trundle; the deaf old lady had fallen asleep in her chair; the snoring of the fat boy, penetrated in a low and monotonous sound from the distant kitchen; the buxom servants were lounging at the side-door, enjoying the pleasantness of the hour, and the delights of a flirtation, on first principles, with certain unwieldy animals attached to the farm; and there sat the interesting pair, uncared for by all, caring for none, and dreaming only of themselves: there they sat, in short, like a pair of carefully-folded kid-gloves—bound up in each other.

"I have forgotten my flowers," said the spinster aunt.

"Water them now," said Mr. Tupman, in accents of persuasion.

"You will take cold in the evening air," urged the spinster aunt, affectionately.

"No, no," said Mr. Tupman, rising; "it will do me good. Let me accompany you."

The lady paused to adjust the sling in which the left arm of the youth was placed, and taking his right arm led him to the garden.

There was a bower at the further end, with honeysuckle, jessamine, and creeping plants—one of those sweet retreats, which humane men erect for the accommodation of spiders.

The spinster aunt took up a large watering-pot which lay in one corner, and was about to leave the arbour. Mr. Tupman detained her, and drew her to a seat beside him.

"Miss Wardle!" said he.

The spinster aunt trembled, till some pebbles which had accidentally found their way into the large watering-pot, shook like an infant's rattle.

"Miss Wardle," said Mr. Tupman, "you are an angel."

"Mr. Tupman!" exclaimed Rachael, blushing as red as the watering-pot itself.

"Nay," said the eloquent Pickwickian—"I know it but too well."

"All women are angels, they say," murmured the lady, playfully.

"Then what can *you* be; or to what, without presumption, can I compare you?" replied Mr. Tupman. "Where was the woman ever seen, who resembled you? Where else could I hope to find so rare a combination of excellence and beauty? Where else could I seek to——Oh!" Here Mr. Tupman paused, and pressed the hand which clasped the handle of the happy watering-pot.

The lady turned aside her head. "Men are such deceivers," she softly whispered.

"They are, they are," ejaculated Mr. Tupman; "but not all men. There lives at least one being who can never change—one being who would be content to devote his whole existence to your happiness—who lives but in your eyes—who breathes but in your smiles—who bears the heavy burden of life itself only for you."

"Could such an individual be found," said the lady——

"But he *can* be found," said the ardent Mr. Tupman, interposing. "He *is* found. He is here Miss Wardle." And ere the lady was aware of his intention, Mr. Tupman had sunk upon his knees at her feet.

"Mr. Tupman, rise," said Rachael.

"Never!" was the valorous reply. "Oh, Rachael!"— He seized her passive hand, and the watering-pot fell to the ground as he pressed it to his lips.—"Oh, Rachael! say you love me."

"Mr. Tupman," said the spinster aunt, with averted head—"I can hardly speak the words; but—but—you are not wholly indifferent to me."

Mr. Tupman no sooner heard this avowal, than he proceeded to do what his enthusiastic emotions prompted, and what, for aught we know, (for we are but little acquainted with such matters,) people so circumstanced always do. He jumped up, and, throwing his arm round the neck of the spinster aunt, imprinted upon her lips numerous kisses, which after a due show of struggling and resistance, she received so passively, that there is no telling how many more Mr. Tupman might have bestowed, if the lady had not given a very unaffected start and exclaimed in an affrighted tone,—

"Mr. Tupman, we are observed!—we are discovered!"

Mr. Tupman looked round. There was the fat boy, perfectly motionless, with his large circular eyes staring into the arbour, but without the slightest expression on his face that the most expert physiognomist could have referred to astonishment, curiosity, or any other known passion that agitates the human breast. Mr. Tupman gazed on the fat boy, and the fat boy stared at him; and the longer Mr. Tupman observed the utter vacancy of the fat boy's countenance, the more convinced he became that he either did not know, or did not understand, anything that had been going forward. Under this impression, he said with great firmness,—

"What do you want here, Sir?"

"Supper's ready, Sir," was the prompt reply.

"Have you just come here Sir?" inquired Mr. Tupman, with a piercing look.

"Just," replied the fat boy.

Mr. Tupman looked at him very hard again; but there was not a wink in his eye, or a curve in his face.

Mr. Tupman took the arm of the spinster aunt, and walked towards the house; the fat boy followed behind.

"He knows nothing of what has happened," he whispered.

"Nothing," said the spinster aunt.

There was a sound behind them, as of an imperfectly suppressed chuckle. Mr. Tupman turned sharply round. No; it could not have been the fat boy; there was not a gleam of mirth, or anything but feeding in his whole visage.

"He must have been fast asleep," whispered Mr. Tupman.

"I have not the least doubt of it," replied the spinster aunt.

They both laughed heartily.

Mr. Tupman was wrong. The fat boy, for once, had not been fast asleep. He was awake—wide awake—to what had been going forward.

The supper passed off without any attempt at a general conversation. The old lady had gone to bed; Isabella Wardle devoted herself exclusively to Mr. Trundle; the spinster aunt's attentions were reserved for Mr. Tupman; and Emily's thoughts appeared to be engrossed by some distant object—possibly they were with the absent Snodgrass.

Eleven—twelve—one o'clock had struck, and the gentlemen had not arrived. Consternation sat on every face. Could they have been waylaid and robbed? Should they send men and lanterns in every direction by which they could be supposed likely to have travelled home? or should they——Hark! there they were. What could have made them so late? A strange voice, too! To whom could it belong? They rushed into the kitchen whither the truants had repaired, and at once obtained rather more than a glimmering of the real state of the case.

Mr. Pickwick, with his hands in his pockets and his hat cocked completely over his left eye, was leaning against the dresser, shaking his head from side to side, and producing a constant succession of the blandest and most benevolent smiles without being moved thereunto by any discernible cause or pretence whatsoever; old Mr. Wardle, with a highly-inflamed countenance, was grasping the hand of a strange gentleman muttering protestations of eternal friendship; Mr. Winkle, supporting himself by the eight-day clock, was feebly invoking destruction upon the head of any member of the family who should suggest the propriety of his retiring for the night; and Mr. Snodgrass had sunk into a chair, with an expression of the most abject and hopeless misery that the human mind can imagine, portrayed in every lineament of his expressive face.

"Is anything the matter?" inquired the three ladies.

"Nothin' the matter," replied Mr. Pickwick. "We—we're—all right.—I say, Wardle, we're all right, ain't we?"

"I should think so," replied the jolly host.—"My dears, here's my friend Mr. Jingle—Mr. Pickwick's friend, Mr. Jingle, come 'pon—little visit."

"Is anything the matter with Mr. Snodgrass Sir?" inquired Emily, with great anxiety.

"Nothing the matter, Ma'am," replied the stranger. "Cricket dinner—glorious party—capital songs—old port —claret—good—very good—wine, Ma'am—wine."

"It wasn't the wine," murmured Mr. Snodgrass, in a broken voice. "It was the salmon." (Somehow or other, it never *is* the wine, in these cases).

"Hadn't they better go to bed Ma'am?" inquired Emma. "Two of the boys will carry the gentlemen up stairs."

"I won't go to bed," said Mr. Winkle, firmly.

"No living boy shall carry me," said Mr. Pickwick, stoutly;—and he went on smiling as before.

"Hurrah!" gasped Mr. Winkle faintly.

"Hurrah!" echoed Mr. Pickwick, taking off his hat and dashing it on the floor, and insanely casting his spectacles into the middle of the kitchen.—At this humorous feat he laughed outright.

"Let's—have—'nother—bottle," cried Mr. Winkle, commencing in a very loud key, and ending in a very faint one. His head dropped upon his breast; and, muttering his invincible determination not to go to his bed, and a sanguinary regret that he had not "done for old Tupman" in the morning, he fell fast asleep; in which condition he was borne to his apartment by two young giants under the personal superintendence of the fat boy, to whose protecting care Mr. Snodgrass shortly afterwards confided his own person. Mr. Pickwick accepted the proffered arm of Mr. Tupman and quietly disappeared, smiling more than ever; and Mr. Wardle after taking as affectionate a leave of the whole family as if he were ordered for immediate execution, consigned to Mr. Trundle the honour of conveying him up stairs, and retired, with a very futile attempt to look impressively solemn and dignified.

"What a shocking scene!" said the spinster aunt.

"Dis-gusting!" ejaculated both the young ladies.

"Dreadful—dreadful!" said Jingle, looking very grave; he was about a bottle and a half ahead of any of his companions. "Horrid spectacle—very."

"What a nice man!" whispered the spinster aunt to Mr. Tupman.

"Good-looking, too!" whispered Emily Wardle.

"Oh, decidedly," observed the spinster aunt.

Mr. Tupman thought of the widow at Rochester: and his mind was troubled. The succeeding half-hour's conversation was not of a nature to calm his perturbed spirit. The new visitor was very talkative, and the number of his anecdotes was only to be exceeded by the extent of his politeness. Mr. Tupman felt, that as Jingle's popularity increased, he (Tupman) retired further into the shade. His laughter was forced—his merriment feigned; and when at last he laid his aching temples between the sheets, he thought, with horrid delight on the satisfaction it would afford him, to have Jingle's head at that moment between the feather bed and the mattrass.

The indefatigable stranger rose betimes next morning, and, although his companions remained in bed overpowered with the dissipation of the previous night, exerted himself most successfully to promote the hilarity of the breakfast-table. So successful were his efforts, that even the deaf old lady insisted on having one or two of his best jokes retailed through the trumpet; and even she condescended to observe to the spinster aunt, that "he" (meaning Jingle) "was an impudent young fellow"—a sentiment in which all her relations then and there present thoroughly coincided.

It was the old lady's habit on the fine summer mornings to repair to the arbour in which Mr. Tupman had already signalised himself, in form and manner following:—first, the fat boy fetched from a peg behind the old lady's bedroom door, a close black satin bonnet, a warm cotton shawl, and a thick stick with a capacious handle; and the old lady having put on the bonnet and shawl at her leisure, would lean one hand on the stick and the other on the fat boy's shoulder, and walk leisurely to the arbour, where the fat boy would leave her to enjoy the fresh air for the space of half an hour; at the expiration of which time he would return and reconduct her back to the house.

The old lady was very precise and very particular; and as this ceremony had been observed for three successive summers without the slightest deviation from the accustomed form, she was not a little surprised on this particular morning, to see the fat boy, instead of leaving the arbour, walk a few paces out of it, look carefully round him in every direction, and return towards her with great stealth and an air of the most profound mystery.

The old lady was timorous—most old ladies are—and her first impression was that the bloated lad was about to do her some grievous bodily harm with the view of possessing himself of her loose coin. She would have cried for assistance, but age and infirmity had long ago deprived her of the power of screaming; she, therefore, watched his motions with feelings of intense terror, which were in no degree diminished by his coming close up to her, and shouting in her ear in an agitated, and as it seemed to her, a threatening tone,—

"Missus!"

Now it so happened that Mr. Jingle was walking in the garden close to the arbour at this moment. He too heard the shout of "Missus," and stopped to hear more. There were three reasons for his doing so. In the first place, he was idle and curious; secondly, he was by no means scrupulous; thirdly, and lastly, he was concealed from view by some flowering shrubs. So there he stood, and there he listened.

"Missus," shouted the fat boy.

"Well Joe," said the trembling old lady. "I'm sure I have been a good mistress to you Joe. You have invariably been treated very kindly. You have never had too much to do; and you have always had enough to eat."

This last was an appeal to the fat boy's most sensitive feelings. He seemed touched as he replied, emphatically,—

"I knows I has."

"Then what can you want to do now?" said the old lady, gaining courage.

"I wants to make your flesh creep," replied the boy.

This sounded like a very blood-thirsty mode of showing one's gratitude; and as the old lady did not precisely understand the process by which such a result was to be attained, all her former horrors returned.

"What do you think I see in this very arbour last night?" inquired the boy.

"Bless us! What?" exclaimed the old lady, alarmed at the solemn manner of the corpulent youth.

"The strange gentleman—him as had his arm hurt—a kissin' and huggin'——"

"Who, Joe—who? None of the servants, I hope."

"Worser than that," roared the fat boy, in the old lady's ear.

"Not one of my grand-da'aters?"

"Worser than that."

"Worse than *that*, Joe!" said the old lady, who had thought this the extreme limit of human atrocity. "Who was it, Joe? I insist upon knowing."

The fat boy looked cautiously round, and having concluded his survey, shouted in the old lady's ear,—

"Miss Rachael."

"What!" said the old lady, in a shrill tone. "Speak louder."

"Miss Rachael," roared the fat boy.

"My da'ater!"

The train of nods which the fat boy gave by way of assent, communicated a *blanc-mange* like motion to his fat cheeks.

"And she suffered him!" exclaimed the old lady.

A grin stole over the fat boy's features as he said,—

"I see her a kissin' of him agin."

If Mr. Jingle, from his place of concealment, could have beheld the expression which the old lady's face assumed at this communication, the probability is that a sudden burst of laughter would have betrayed his close vicinity to the summer-house. He listened attentively. Fragments of angry sentences such as, "Without my permission!"—"At her time of life"—"Miserable old 'ooman like me"—"Might have waited till I was dead," and so forth, reached his ears; and then he heard the heels of the fat boy's boots crunching the gravel, as he retired and left the old lady alone.

It was a remarkable coincidence perhaps, but it was nevertheless a fact, that Mr. Jingle within five minutes after his arrival at Manor Farm on the preceding night, had inwardly resolved to lay siege to the heart of the spinster aunt, without delay. He had observation enough to see, that his off-hand manner was by no means disagreeable to the fair object of his attack; and he had more than a strong suspicion that she possessed that most desirable of all requisites, a small independence. The imperative necessity of ousting his rival by some means or other, flashed quickly upon him, and he immediately resolved to adopt certain proceedings tending to that end and object, without a moment's delay. Fielding tells us that man is fire, and woman tow, and the Prince of Darkness sets a light to 'em. Mr. Jingle knew that young men, to spinster aunts, are as lighted gas to gunpowder, and he determined to essay the effect of an explosion without loss of time.

Full of reflections upon this important decision, he crept from his place of concealment, and, under cover of the shrubs before mentioned, approached the house. Fortune seemed determined to favour his design. Mr. Tupman and the rest of the gentlemen left the garden by the side gate just as he obtained a view of it; and the young ladies he knew, had walked out alone, soon after breakfast. The coast was clear.

The breakfast-parlour door was partially open. He peeped in. The spinster aunt was knitting. He coughed; she looked up and smiled. Hesitation formed no part of Mr. Alfred Jingle's character. He laid his finger on his lips mysteriously, walked in, and closed the door.

"Miss Wardle," said Mr. Jingle, with affected earnestness, "forgive intrusion—short acquaintance—no time for ceremony—all discovered."

"Sir!" said the spinster aunt, rather astonished by the unexpected apparition and somewhat doubtful of Mr. Jingle's sanity.

"Hush!" said Mr. Jingle, in a stage whisper;—"large boy—dumpling face—round eyes—rascal!" Here he shook his head expressively, and the spinster aunt trembled with agitation.

"I presume you allude to Joseph Sir?" said the lady, making an effort to appear composed.

"Yes, Ma'am—damn that Joe!—treacherous dog, Joe—told the old lady—old lady furious—wild—raving—arbour—Tupman—kissing and hugging—all that sort of thing—eh, Ma'am—eh?"

"Mr. Jingle," said the spinster aunt, "if you come here Sir, to insult me—"

"Not at all—by no means," replied the unabashed Mr. Jingle;—"overheard the tale—came to warn you of your danger—tender my services—prevent the hubbub. Never mind—think it an insult—leave the room"—and he turned, as if to carry the threat into execution.

"What shall I do!" said the poor spinster, bursting into tears. "My brother will be furious!"

"Of course he will," said Mr. Jingle pausing—"outrageous."

"Oh Mr. Jingle, what can I say!" exclaimed the spinster aunt, in another flood of despair.

"Say he dreamt it," replied Mr. Jingle, coolly.

A ray of comfort darted across the mind of the spinster aunt at this suggestion. Mr. Jingle perceived it, and followed up his advantage.

"Pooh, pooh!—nothing more easy—blackguard boy—lovely woman—fat boy horsewhipped—you believed—end of the matter—all comfortable."

Whether the probability of escaping from the consequences of this ill-timed discovery was delightful to the spinster's feelings, or whether the hearing herself described as a "lovely woman" softened the asperity of her grief, we know not. She blushed slightly, and cast a grateful look on Mr. Jingle.

That insinuating gentleman sighed deeply, fixed his eyes on the spinster aunt's face for a couple of minutes, started melo-dramatically, and suddenly withdrew them.

"You seem unhappy, Mr. Jingle," said the lady, in a plaintive voice. "May I show my gratitude for your kind interference, by inquiring into the cause, with a view, if possible, to its removal?"

"Ha!" exclaimed Mr. Jingle, with another start—"removal! remove my unhappiness, and your love bestowed upon a man who is insensible to the blessing—who even now contemplates a design upon the affections of the niece of the creature who—but no; he is my friend; I will not expose his vices. Miss Wardle—farewell!" At the conclusion of this address, the most consecutive he was ever known to utter, Mr. Jingle applied to his eyes the remnant of a handkerchief before noticed, and turned towards the door.

"Stay, Mr. Jingle!" said the spinster aunt emphatically. "You have made an allusion to Mr. Tupman—explain it."

"Never!" exclaimed Jingle, with a professional (i.e. theatrical) air. "Never!" and, by way of showing that he had no desire to be questioned further, he drew a chair close to that of the spinster aunt and sat down.

"Mr. Jingle," said the aunt, "I entreat—I implore you, if there is any dreadful mystery connected with Mr. Tupman, reveal it."

"Can I," said Mr. Jingle, fixing his eyes on the aunt's face—"Can I see—lovely creature—sacrificed at the shrine—heartless avarice!" He appeared to be struggling with various conflicting emotions for a few seconds, and then said in a low deep voice—"Tupman only wants your money."

"The wretch!" exclaimed the spinster, with energetic indignation. (Mr. Jingle's doubts were resolved. She had money).

"More than that," said Jingle—"loves another."

"Another!" ejaculated the spinster. "Who?"

"Short girl—black eyes—niece Emily."

There was a pause.

Now if there were one individual in the whole world, of whom the spinster aunt entertained a mortal and deeply-rooted jealousy, it was this identical niece. The colour rushed over her face and neck, and she tossed her head in silence with an air of ineffable contempt. At last, biting her thin lips, and bridling up, she said,—

"It can't be. I won't believe it."

"Watch 'em," said Jingle.

"I will," said the aunt.

"Watch his looks."

"I will."

"His whispers."

"I will."

"He'll sit next her at table."

"Let him."

"He'll flatter her."

"Let him."

"He'll pay her every possible attention."

"Let him."

"And he'll cut you."

"Cut *me!*" screamed the spinster aunt. "*He* cut me;—*will* he!" and she trembled with rage and disappointment.

"You will convince yourself?" said Jingle.

"I will."

"You'll show your spirit?"

"I will."

"You'll not have him afterwards?"

"Never."

"You'll take somebody else?"

"Yes."

"You shall."

Mr. Jingle fell on his knees, remained thereupon for five minutes thereafter: and rose the accepted lover of the spinster aunt—conditionally upon Tupman's perjury being made clear and manifest.

The burden of proof lay with Mr. Alfred Jingle; and he produced his evidence that very day at dinner. The spinster aunt could hardly believe her eyes. Mr. Tracy Tupman was established at Emily's side, ogling, whispering, and smiling, in opposition to Mr. Snodgrass. Not a word, not a look, not a glance, did he bestow upon his heart's pride of the evening before.

"Damn that boy!" thought old Mr. Wardle to himself. —He had heard the story from his mother. "Damn that boy! He *must* have been asleep. It's all imagination."

"Traitor!" thought the spinster aunt to herself. "Dear Mr. Jingle was not deceiving me. Oh! how I hate the wretch!"

The following conversation may serve to explain to our readers, this apparently unaccountable alteration of deportment, on the part of Mr. Tracy Tupman.

The time was evening; the scene the garden. There were two figures walking in a side path; one was rather short and stout; the other rather tall and slim. They were Mr. Tupman and Mr. Jingle. The stout figure commenced the dialogue.

"How did I do it?" he inquired.

"Splendid—capital—couldn't act better myself—you must repeat the part to-morrow—every evening, till further notice."

"Does Rachael still wish it?"

"Of course—she don't like it—but must be done—avert suspicion—afraid of her brother—says there's no help for it—only few days more—when old folks blinded—crown your happiness."

"Any message?"

"Love—best love—kindest regards—unalterable affection. Can I say anything for you?"

"My dear fellow," replied the unsuspicious Mr. Tupman, fervently grasping his "friend's" hand—"carry my best love—say how hard I find it to dissemble—say anything that's kind: but add how sensible I am of the necessity of the suggestion she made to me, through you, this morning. Say I applaud her wisdom and admire her discretion."

"I will. Anything more?"

"Nothing; only add how ardently I long for the time when I may call her mine, and all dissimulation may be unnecessary."

"Certainly, certainly. Anything more?"

"Oh, my friend!" said poor Mr. Tupman, again grasp-ing the hand of his companion, "receive my warmest thanks for your disinterested kindness; and forgive me if I have ever, even in thought, done you the injustice of supposing that you *could* stand in my way. My dear friend can I ever repay you?"

"Don't talk of it," replied Mr. Jingle. He stopped short, as if suddenly recollecting something, and said,—"By-the-by, you can't spare ten pounds, can you?—very particular purpose—pay you in three days."

"I dare say I can," replied Mr. Tupman, in the fulness of his heart. "Three days, you say?"

"Only three days—all over then—no more difficulties."

Mr. Tupman counted the money into his companion's hand, and he dropped it piece by piece into his pocket, as they walked towards the house.

"Be careful," said Mr. Jingle—"not a look."

"Not a wink," said Mr. Tupman.

"Not a syllable."

"Not a whisper."

"All your attentions to the niece—rather rude, than otherwise, to the aunt—only way of deceiving the old ones."

"I'll take care," said Mr. Tupman, aloud.

"And *I*'ll take care," said Mr. Jingle internally; and they entered the house.

The scene of that afternoon was repeated that evening, and on the three afternoons and evenings next ensuing. On the fourth, the host was in high spirits, for he had satisfied himself that there was no ground for the charge against Mr. Tupman. So was Mr. Tupman, for Mr. Jingle had told him that his affair would soon be brought to a crisis. So was Mr. Pickwick, for he was seldom otherwise. So was not Mr. Snodgrass, for he had grown jealous of Mr. Tupman. So was the old lady, for she had been winning at whist. So were Mr. Jingle and Miss Wardle, for reasons of sufficient importance in this eventful history, to be narrated in another chapter.

CHAPTER IX.

A DISCOVERY AND A CHASE.

THE supper was ready laid, the chairs were drawn round the table, bottles, jugs and glasses were arranged upon the sideboard, and everything betokened the approach of the most convivial period in the whole four and twenty hours.

"Where's Rachael?" said Mr. Wardle.

"Aye, and Jingle?" added Mr. Pickwick.

"Dear me," said the host, "I wonder I haven't missed him before. Why, I don't think I've heard his voice for two hours at least. Emily, my dear, ring the bell."

The bell was rung, and the fat boy appeared.

"Where's Miss Rachael?" He couldn't say.

"Where's Mr. Jingle, then?" He didn't know.

Every body looked surprised. It was late—past eleven o'clock. Mr. Tupman laughed in his sleeve. They were loitering somewhere, talking about *him*. Ha, ha! capital notion that—funny.

"Never mind," said Wardle, after a short pause, "they'll turn up presently, I dare say. I never wait supper for anybody."

"Excellent rule, that," said Mr. Pickwick, "admirable."

"Pray, sit down," said the host.

"Certainly," said Mr. Pickwick: and down they sat.

There was a gigantic round of cold beef on the table, and Mr. Pickwick was supplied with a plentiful portion of it. He had raised his fork to his lips, and was on the very point of opening his mouth for the reception of a piece of beef, when the hum of many voices suddenly arose in the kitchen. He paused, and laid down his fork. Mr. Wardle paused too, and insensibly released his hold of the carving-knife, which remained inserted in the beef. He looked at Mr. Pickwick. Mr. Pickwick looked at him.

Heavy footsteps were heard in the passage; the parlour door was suddenly burst open; and the man who had cleaned Mr. Pickwick's boots on his first arrival, rushed into the room, followed by the fat boy, and all the domestics.

"What the devil's the meaning of this?" exclaimed the host.

"The kitchen chimney ain't a-fire, is it, Emma?" inquired the old lady.

"Lor grandma! No," screamed both the young ladies.

"What's the matter?" roared the master of the house.

The man gasped for breath, and faintly ejaculated—

"They ha' gone, Mas'r!—gone right clean off, Sir!" (At this juncture, Mr. Tupman was observed to lay down his knife and fork, and to turn very pale.)

"Who's gone?" said Mr. Wardle, fiercely.

"Mus'r Jingle and Miss Rachael, in a po'-chay, from Blue Lion, Muggleton. I was there; but I couldn't stop 'em; so I run off to tell'ee."

"I paid his expenses!" said Mr. Tupman, jumping up frantically. "He's got ten pounds of mine!—stop him!—he's swindled me!—I won't bear it!—I'll have justice, Pickwick!—I won't stand it!" and with sundry incoherent exclamations of the like nature, the unhappy gentleman spun round and round the apartment, in a transport of frenzy.

"Lord preserve us!" ejaculated Mr. Pickwick, eyeing the extraordinary gestures of his friend with terrified surprise. "He's gone mad! What shall we do?"

"Do!" said the stout host, who regarded only the last words of the sentence. "Put the horse in the gig! I'll get a chaise at the Lion, and follow 'em instantly. Where"—he exclaimed, as the man ran out to execute the commission—"Where's that villain, Joe?"

"Here I am; but I han't a willin'," replied a voice. It was the fat boy's.

"Let me get at him, Pickwick!" cried Wardle, as he rushed at the ill-starred youth. "He was bribed by that scoundrel, Jingle, to put me on a wrong scent, by telling a cock-and-a-bull story of my sister and your friend Tupman!" (Here Mr. Tupman sunk into a chair.) "Let me get at him!"

"Don't let him!" screamed all the women, above whose exclamations, the blubbering of the fat boy, was distinctly audible.

"I won't be held!" cried the old man. "Mr. Winkle, take your hands off! Mr. Pickwick, let me go, Sir!"

It was a beautiful sight, in that moment of turmoil and confusion, to behold the placid and philosophical expression of Mr. Pickwick's face, albeit somewhat flushed with exertion, as he stood with his arms firmly clasped round the extensive waist of their corpulent host, thus restraining the impetuosity of his passion, while the fat boy was scratched, and pulled, and pushed from the room by all the females congregated therein. He had no sooner released his hold, than the man entered to announce that the gig was ready.

"Don't let him go alone!" screamed the females. "He'll kill somebody!"

"I'll go with him," said Mr. Pickwick.

"You're a good fellow, Pickwick," said the host, grasping his hand. "Emma, give Mr. Pickwick a shawl to tie round his neck—make haste. Look after your grandmother, girls; she's fainted away. Now then, are you ready?"

Mr. Pickwick's mouth and chin, having been hastily enveloped in a large shawl: his hat having been put on his head, and his great coat thrown over his arm, he replied in the affirmative.

They jumped into the gig. "Give her, her head, Tom," cried the host; and away they went, down the narrow lanes: jolting in and out of the cart-ruts, and bumping up against the hedges on either side, as if they would go to pieces every moment.

"How much are they a-head?" shouted Wardle, as they drove up to the door of the Blue Lion, round which a little crowd had collected, late as it was.

"Not above three-quarters of an hour," was everybody's reply.

"Chaise and four directly!—out with 'em! Put up the gig afterwards."

"Now, boys!" cried the landlord—"chaise and four out—make haste—look alive there!"

Away ran the hostlers, and the boys. The lanterns glimmered, as the men ran to and fro; the horses' hoofs clattered on the uneven paving of the yard; the chaise rumbled as it was drawn out of the coach-house; and all was noise and bustle.

"Now then!—is that chaise coming out to-night?" cried Wardle.

"Coming down the yard now, Sir," replied the hostler.

Out came the chaise—in went the horses—on sprung the boys—in got the travellers.

"Mind—the seven-mile stage in less than half an hour!" shouted Wardle.

"Off with you!"

The boys applied whip and spur, the waiters shouted, the hostlers cheered, and away they went, fast and furiously.

"Pretty situation," thought Mr. Pickwick, when he had a moment's time for reflection. "Pretty situation for the General Chairman of the Pickwick Club. Damp chaise—strange horses—fifteen miles an hour—and twelve o'clock at night!"

For the first three or four miles, not a word was spoken by either of the gentlemen, each being too much immersed in his own reflections, to address any observations to his companion. When they had gone over that much ground, however, and the horses getting thoroughly warmed began to do their work in really good style, Mr. Pickwick became too much exhilarated with the rapidity of the motion, to remain any longer perfectly mute.

"We're sure to catch them, I think," said he.

"Hope so," replied his companion.

"Fine night," said Mr. Pickwick, looking up at the moon, which was shining brightly.

"So much the worse," returned Wardle; "for they'll have had all the advantage of the moonlight to get the start of us, and we shall lose it. It will have gone down in another hour."

"It will be rather unpleasant going at this rate in the dark, won't it?" inquired Mr. Pickwick.

"I dare say it will," replied his friend drily.

Mr. Pickwick's temporary excitement began to sober down a little, as he reflected upon the inconveniences and dangers of the expedition in which he had so thoughtlessly embarked. He was roused by a loud shouting of the post-boy on the leader.

"Yo—yo—yo—yo—yoe," went the first boy.

"Yo—yo—yo—yoe!" went the second.

"Yo—yo—yo—yoe!" chimed in old Wardle himself, most lustily, with his head and half his body out of the coach window.

"Yo—yo—yo—yoe!" shouted Mr. Pickwick, taking up the burden of the cry, though he had not the slightest notion of its meaning or object. And amidst the yo—yoing of the whole four, the chaise stopped.

"What's the matter?" inquired Mr. Pickwick.

"There's a gate here," replied old Wardle, "We shall hear something of the fugitives."

After a lapse of five minutes, consumed in incessant knocking and shouting, an old man in his shirt and trousers emerged from the turnpike-house, and opened the gate.

"How long is it since a post-chaise went through here?" inquired Mr. Wardle.

"How long?"

"Ah!"

"Why, I don't rightly know. It worn't a long time ago, nor it worn't a short time ago—just between the two, perhaps."

"Has any chaise been by at all?"

"Oh yes, there's been a chay by."

"How long ago, my friend?" interposed Mr. Pickwick, "an hour?"

"Ah, I dare say it might be," replied the man.

"Or two hours?" inquired the post-boy on the wheeler.

"Well, I shouldn't wonder if it was," returned the old man doubtfully.

"Drive on, boys," cried the testy old gentleman: "don't waste any more time with that old idiot!"

"Idiot!" exclaimed the old man with a grin, as he stood in the middle of the road with the gate half closed, watching the chaise which rapidly diminished in the increasing distance. "No—not much o' that either; you've lost ten minutes here, and gone away as wise as you came arter all. If every man on the line as has a guinea give him earns it half as well, you won't catch t'other chay this side Mich'lmas, old short and fat." And with another prolonged grin, the old man closed the gate, re-entered his house, and bolted the door after him.

Meanwhile the chaise proceeded, without any slackening of pace, towards the conclusion of the stage. The moon, as Wardle had foretold, was rapidly on the wane; large tiers of dark heavy clouds which had been gradually overspreading the sky for some time past, now formed one black mass over head; and large drops of rain which pattered every now and then against the windows of the rapid approach of a stormy night. The wind, too, which was directly against them, swept in furious gusts down the narrow road, and howled dismally through the trees which skirted the pathway. Mr. Pickwick drew his coat closer about him, coiled himself more snugly up into the corner of the chaise, and fell into a sound sleep, from which he was only awakened by the stopping of the vehicle, the sound of the hostler's bell, and a loud cry of "Horses on directly!"

But here another delay occurred. The boys were sleeping with such mysterious soundness, that it took five minutes a-piece to wake them. The hostler had somehow or other mislaid the key of the stable, and even when that was found, two sleepy helpers put the wrong harness on the wrong horses, and the whole process of harnessing had to be gone through afresh. Had Mr. Pickwick been alone, these multiplied obstacles would have completely put an end to the pursuit at once, but old Wardle was not to be so easily daunted; and he laid about him with such hearty good-will, cuffing this man, and pushing that; strapping a buckle here, and taking in a link there, that the chaise was ready in a much shorter time than could reasonably have been expected, under so many difficulties.

They resumed their journey; and certainly the prospect before them was by no means encouraging. The stage was fifteen miles long, the night was dark, the wind high, and the rain pouring in torrents. It was impossible to make any great way against such obstacles united: it was hard upon one o'clock already; and nearly two hours were consumed in getting to the end of the stage. Here, however, an object presented itself, which re-kindled their hopes, and re-animated their drooping spirits.

"When did this chaise come in?" cried old Wardle, leaping out of his own vehicle, and pointing to one covered with wet mud, which was standing in the yard.

"Not a quarter of an hour ago, Sir;" replied the hostler, to whom the question was addressed.

"Lady and gentleman?" inquired Wardle, almost breathless with impatience.

"Yes, Sir."

"Tall gentleman—dress coat—long legs—thin body?"

"Yes, Sir."

"Elderly lady—thin face—rather skinny—eh?"

"Yes, Sir."

"By Heavens, it's them, Pickwick," exclaimed the old gentleman.

"Would have been here before," said the hostler, "but they broke a trace."

"'Tis them," said Wardle, "it is, by Jove! Chaise and four instantly. We shall catch them yet, before they reach the next stage. A guinea a-piece, boys—be alive there—bustle about—there's good fellows."

And with such admonitions as these, the old gentleman ran up and down the yard, and bustled to and fro, in a state of excitement which communicated itself to Mr. Pickwick also; and under the influence of which, that gentleman got himself into complicated entanglements with harness, and mixed up with horses and wheels of chaises, in the most surprising manner, firmly believing that by so doing, he was materially forwarding the preparations for their resuming their journey

"Jump in—jump in!" cried old Wardle, climbing into the chaise, pulling up the steps, and slamming the door after him. "Come along, make haste." And before Mr. Pickwick knew precisely what he was about, he felt himself forced in at the other door, by one pull from the old gentleman, and one push from the hostler; and off they were again.

"Ah! we *are* moving now," said the old gentleman exultingly. They were indeed, as was sufficiently testified to Mr. Pickwick, by his constant collisions either with the hard wood-work of the chaise, or the body of his companion.

"Hold up!" said the stout old Mr. Wardle, as Mr. Pickwick dived head foremost into his capacious waistcoat.

"I never did feel such a jolting in my life," said Mr. Pickwick.

"Never mind," replied his companion, "it'll soon be over. Steady, steady."

Mr. Pickwick planted himself into his own corner, as firmly as he could; and on whirled the chaise faster than ever.

They had travelled in this way about three miles, when Mr. Wardle, who had been looking out of the window for two or three minutes, suddenly drew in his face, covered with splashes, and exclaimed in breathless eagerness—

"Here they are!"

Mr. Pickwick thrust his head out of his window. Yes: there was a chaise and four, a short distance before them, dashing along at full gallop.

"Go on, go on," almost shrieked the old gentleman. "Two guineas a-piece, boys—don't let 'em gain on us—keep it up—keep it up."

The horses in the first chaise started on at their utmost speed; and those in Mr. Wardle's galloped furiously behind them.

"I see his head," exclaimed the choleric old man, "Damme, I see his head,"

"So do I," said Mr. Pickwick, "that's he."

Mr. Pickwick was not mistaken. The countenance of Mr. Jingle, completely coated with the mud thrown up by the wheels, was plainly discernible at the window of his chaise; and the motion of his arm, which he was waving violently towards the postilions, denoted that he was encouraging them to increased exertion.

The interest was intense. Fields, trees, and hedges, seemed to rush past them with the velocity of a whirlwind, so rapid was the pace at which they tore along. They were close by the side of the first chaise. Jingle's voice could be plainly heard, even above the din of the wheels, urging on the boys. Old Mr. Wardle foamed with rage and excitement. He roared out scoundrels and villains by the dozen, clenched his fist and shook it expressively at the object of his indignation; but Mr. Jingle only answered with a contemptuous smile, and replied to his menaces by a shout of triumph, as his horses, answering the increased application of whip and spur, broke into a faster gallop, and left the pursuers behind.

Mr. Pickwick had just drawn in his head, and Mr. Wardle, exhausted with shouting, had done the same, when a tremendous jolt threw them forward against the front of the vehicle. There was a sudden bump—a loud crash—away rolled a wheel, and over went the chaise.

After a very few seconds of bewilderment and confusion, in which nothing but the plunging of horses, and breaking of glass, could be made out, Mr. Pickwick felt himself violently pulled out from among the ruins of the chaise; and as soon as he had gained his feet, and extricated his head from the skirts of his great coat which materially impeded the usefulness of his spectacles, the full disaster of the case met his view.

Old Mr. Wardle without a hat, and his clothes torn in several places, stood by his side, and the fragments of the chaise lay scattered at their feet. The post-boys, who had succeeded in cutting the traces, were standing, disfigured with mud and disordered by hard riding, by the horses' heads. About a hundred yards in advance was the other

chaise, which had pulled up on hearing the crash. The postilions, each with a broad grin convulsing his countenance, were viewing the adverse party from their saddles, and Mr. Jingle was contemplating the wreck from the coach-window, with evident satisfaction. The day was just breaking, and the whole scene was rendered perfectly visible by the grey light of the morning.

"Hallo!" shouted the shameless Jingle, "any body damaged?—elderly gentlemen—no light weights—dangerous work—very."

"You're a rascal!" roared Wardle.

"Ha! ha!" replied Jingle; and then he added, with a knowing wink, and a jerk of the thumb towards the interior of the chaise—"I say—she's very well—desires her compliments—begs you won't trouble yourself—love to *Tuppy*—won't you get up behind?—drive on boys."

The postilions resumed their proper attitudes, and away rattled the chaise, Mr. Jingle fluttering in derision a white handkerchief from the coach window.

Nothing in the whole adventure, not even the upset, had disturbed the calm and equable current of Mr. Pickwick's temper. The villany, however, which could first borrow money of his faithful follower, and then abbreviate his name to "Tuppy," was more than he could patiently bear. He drew his breath hard, and coloured up to the very tips of his spectacles, as he said, slowly and emphatically—

"If ever I meet that man again, I'll—"

"Yes, yes," interrupted Wardle, "that's all very well: but while we stand talking here, they'll get their license, and be married in London."

Mr. Pickwick paused, bottled up his vengeance, and corked it down.

"How far is it to the next stage?" inquired Mr. Wardle, of one of the boys.

"Six mile, a'nt it, Tom?"

"Rayther better."

"Rayther better nor six mile, Sir."

"Can't be helped," said Wardle, "we must walk it, Pickwick."

"No help for it," replied that truly great man.

So sending forward one of the boys on horseback, to procure a fresh chaise and horses, and leaving the other behind to take care of the broken one, Mr. Pickwick and Mr. Wardle set manfully forward on the walk, first tying their shawls round their necks, and slouching down their hats to escape as much as possible from the deluge of rain, which after a slight cessation, had again begun to pour heavily down.

CHAPTER X.

CLEARING UP ALL DOUBTS (IF ANY EXISTED) OF THE DISINTERESTEDNESS OF MR. JINGLE'S CHARACTER.

THERE are in London several old inns, once the head-quarters of celebrated coaches in the days when coaches performed their journeys in a graver and more solemn manner than they do in these times; but which have now degenerated into little more than the abiding and booking places of country wagons. The reader would look in vain for any of these ancient hostelries, among the Golden Crosses and Bull and Mouths, which rear their stately fronts in the improved streets of London. If he would

THE BREAKDOWN.

light upon any of these old places, he must direct his steps to the obscurer quarters of the town; and there in some secluded nooks he will find several, still standing with a kind of gloomy sturdiness, amidst the modern innovations which surround them.

In the Borough especially, there still remain some half dozen old inns, which have preserved their external features unchanged, and which have escaped alike the rage for public improvement, and the encroachments of private speculation. Great, rambling, queer, old places they are, with galleries, and passages, and staircases, wide enough and antiquated enough, to furnish materials for a hundred ghost stories, supposing we should ever be reduced to the lamentable necessity of inventing any, and that the world should exist long enough to exhaust the innumerable veracious legends connected with old London Bridge, and its adjacent neighbourhood on the Surrey side.

It was in the yard of one of these inns—of no less celebrated a one than the White Hart—that a man was busily employed in brushing the dirt off a pair of boots, early on the morning succeeding the events narrated in the last chapter. He was habited in a coarse-striped waistcoat, with black calico sleeves, and blue glass buttons: drab breeches and leggings. A bright red handkerchief was wound in a very loose and unstudied style round his neck, and an old white hat was carelessly thrown on one side of his head. There were two rows of boots before him, one cleaned and the other dirty, and at every addition he made to the clean row, he paused from his work, and contemplated its results with evident satisfaction.

The yard presented none of that bustle and activity which are the usual characteristics of a large coach inn. Three or four lumbering wagons, each with a pile of goods beneath its ample canopy, about the height of the second-floor window of an ordinary house, were stowed away beneath a lofty roof which extended over one end of the yard; and another, which was probably to commence its journey that morning, was drawn out into the open space. A double tier of bed-room galleries, with old clumsy balustrades, ran round two sides of the straggling area, and a double row of bells to correspond, sheltered from the weather by a little sloping roof, hung over the door leading to the bar and coffee-room. Two or three gigs and chaise-carts were wheeled up under different little sheds and pent-houses; and the occasional heavy tread of a cart-horse, or rattling of a chain at the further end of the yard, announced to any body who cared about the matter, that the stable lay in that direction. When we add that a few boys in smock frocks, were lying asleep on heavy packages, wool-packs, and other articles that were scattered about on heaps of straw, we have described as fully as need be, the general appearance of the yard of the White Hart Inn, High Street, Borough, on the particular morning in question.

A loud ringing of one of the bells, was followed by the appearance of a smart chambermaid in the upper sleeping gallery, who, after tapping at one of the doors, and receiving a request from within, called over the balustrades.

"Sam!"

"Hallo," replied the man with the white hat.

"Number twenty-two wants his boots."

"Ask number twenty-two, vether he'll have 'em now, or vait till he gets 'em," was the reply.

"Come, don't be a fool, Sam," said the girl, coaxingly, "the gentleman wants his boots directly."

"Well, you are a nice young 'ooman for a musical party, you are," said the boot-cleaner. "Look at these here boots—eleven pair o' boots; and one shoe as b'longs to number six, with the wooden leg. The eleven boots is to be called at half-past eight and the shoe at nine. Who's number twenty-two, that's to put all the others out? No, no; reg'lar rotation, as Jack Ketch said, ven he tied the men up. Sorry to keep you a watin', Sir, but I'll attend to you directly."

Saying which, the man in the white hat set to work upon a top-boot with increased assiduity.

There was another loud ring; and the bustling old landlady of the White Hart made her appearance in the opposite gallery.

"Sam," cried the landlady, "where's that lazy, idle—why Sam—oh, there you are; why don't you answer?"

"Vouldn't be gen-teel to answer, 'till you'd done talking," replied Sam, gruffly.

"Here, clean them shoes for number seventeen directly, and take 'em to private sitting-room, number five, first floor."

The landlady flung a pair of lady's shoes into the yard, and bustled away.

"Number 5," said Sam, as he picked up the shoes, and taking a piece of chalk from his pocket, made a memorandum of their destination on the soles—"Lady's shoes and private sittin' room! I suppose she didn't come in the vaggin."

"She came in early this morning," cried the girl, who was still leaning over the railing of the gallery, "with a gentleman in a hackney-coach, and it's him as wants his boots, and you'd better do 'em, and that's all about it."

"Vy didn't you say so before?" said Sam, with great indignation, singling out the boots in question from the heap before him. "For all I know'd he vas one o' the regular three-pennies. Private room! and a lady too! If he's anything of a gen'lm'n, he's vurth a shillin' a day, let alone the arrands."

Stimulated by this inspiring reflection, Mr. Samuel brushed away with such hearty good will, that in a few minutes the boots and shoes, with a polish which would have struck envy to the soul of the amiable Mr. Warren, (for they used Day and Martin at the White Hart) had arrived at the door of number five.

"Come in," said a man's voice, in reply to Sam's rap at the door.

Sam made his best bow, and stepped into the presence of a lady and gentleman seated at breakfast. Having officiously deposited the gentleman's boots right and left at his feet, and the lady's shoes right and left at hers, he backed towards the door.

"Boots," said the gentleman.

"Sir," said Sam, closing the door, and keeping his hand on the knob of the lock.

"Do you know—what's a-name—Doctors' Commons?"

"Yes Sir."

"Where is it?"

"Paul's Church-yard, Sir; low archway on the carriage-side, bookseller's at one corner, hot-el on the other, and two porters in the middle as touts for licences."

"Touts for licences!" said the gentleman.

"Touts for licences," replied Sam. "Two coves in vhite aprons—touches their hats ven you walk in—'Licence, Sir, licence?' Queer sort, them, and their mas'rs too, Sir—Old Bailey Proctors—and no mistake."

"What do they do?" inquired the gentleman.

"Do! You, Sir! That an't the worst on it, neither.

They put things into old gen'lm'ns heads as they never dreamed of. My father, Sir, vos a coachman. A vidower he vos, and fat enough for anything—uncommon fat, to be sure. His missus dies, and leaves him four hundred pound. Down he goes to the Commons, to see the lawyer and draw the blunt—wery smart—top boots on—nosegay in his button-hole—broad-brimmed tile—green shawl—quite the gen'lm'n. Goes through the archvay, thinking how he should invest the money—up comes the touter, touches his hat—'Licence, Sir, licence?'—'What's that?' says my father.—'Licence, Sir,' says he.—'What licence?' says my father.—'Marriage licence,' says the touter.—'Dash my veskit,' says my father, 'I never thought o' that.'—'I think you wants one, Sir,' says the touter. My father pulls up, and thinks a bit—'No,' says he, 'damme, I'm too old, b'sides I'm a many sizes too large,' says he.—'Not a bit on it, Sir,' says the touter.—'Think not?' says my father.—'I'm sure not,' says he; 'we married a gen'lm'n twice your size, last Monday.'—'Did you, though,' says my father.—'To be sure, ve did,' says the touter, 'you're a babby to him—this vay, Sir—this vay!'—and sure enough my father walks arter him, like a tame monkey behind a horgan, into a little back office, vere a feller sat among dirty papers and tin boxes, making believe he was busy. 'Pray take a seat, vile I makes out the affidavit, Sir,' says the lawyer.—'Thankee, Sir,' says my father, and down he sat, and stared vith all his eyes, and his mouth vide open, at the names on the boxes.—'What's your name, Sir?' says the lawyer.—'Tony Weller,' says my father.—'Parish?' says the lawyer.—'Belle Savage,' says my father; for he stopped there ven he drove up, and he know'd nothing about parishes, he didn't.—'And what's the lady's name?' says the lawyer. My father was struck all of a heap. 'Blessed if I know,' says he.—'Not know!' says the lawyer.—'No more nor you do,' says my father, 'can't I put that in arterwards?'—'Impossible!' says the lawyer.—'Wery well,' says my father, after he'd thought a moment, 'put down Mrs. Clarke.'—'What Clarke?' says the lawyer, dipping his pen in the ink.—'Susan Clarke, Markis o' Granby, Dorking,' says my father; 'she'll have me, if I ask her, I des-say—I never said nothing to her, but she'll have me, I know.' The licence was made out, and she did have him, and what's more she's got him now; and I never had any of the four hundred pound, worse luck. Beg your pardon, Sir," said Sam, when he had concluded, "but vhen I gets on this here grievance, I runs on like a new barrow vith the vheel greased." Having said which, and having paused for an instant to see whether he was wanted for any thing more, Sam left the room.

"Half-past nine—just the time—off at once;" said the gentleman, whom we need hardly introduce as Mr. Jingle.

"Time—for what?" said the spinster aunt, coquettishly.

"Licence, dearest of angels—give notice at the church—call you mine, to-morrow"—said Mr. Jingle, and he squeezed the spinster aunt's hand.

"The licence!" said Rachael, blushing.

"The licence," repeated Mr. Jingle—

"In hurry, post-haste for a licence,
In hurry, ding dong I come back."

"How you run on," said Rachael.

"Run on—nothing to the hours, days, weeks, months, years, when we're united—run on—they'll fly on—bolt—mizzle—steam-engine—thousand-horse power—nothing to it."

"Can't—can't we be married before to-morrow morning?" inquired Rachael.

"Impossible—can't be—notice at the church—leave the licence to-day—ceremony come off to-morrow."

"I am so terrified, lest my brother should discover us!" said Rachael.

"Discover—nonsense—too much shaken by the break down—besides—extreme caution—gave up the post-chaise—walked on—took a hackney coach—came to the Borough—last place in the world that he'd look in—ha! ha!—capital notion that—very."

"Don't be long," said the spinster, affectionately, as Mr. Jingle stuck the pinched up hat on his head.

"Long away from you?—Cruel charmer," and Mr. Jingle skipped playfully up to the spinster aunt, imprinted a chaste kiss upon her lips, and danced out of the room.

"Dear man!" said the spinster, as the door closed after him.

"Rum old girl," said Mr. Jingle, as he walked down the passage.

It is painful to reflect upon the perfidy of our species; and we will not therefore, pursue the thread of Mr. Jingle's meditations, as he wended his way to Doctors' Commons. It will be sufficient for our purpose to relate, that escaping the snares of the dragons in white aprons, who guard the entrance to that enchanted region, he reached the Vicar General's office in safety, and having procured a highly flattering address on parchment, from the Archbishop of Canterbury, to his "trusty and well-beloved Alfred Jingle and Rachael Wardle, greeting," he carefully deposited the mystic document in his pocket, and retraced his steps in triumph to the Borough.

He was yet on his way to the White Hart, when two plump gentlemen and one thin one, entered the yard, and looked round in search of some authorised person of whom they could make a few inquiries. Mr. Samuel Weller happened to be at that moment engaged in burnishing a pair of painted tops, the personal property of a farmer, who was refreshing himself with a slight lunch of two or three pounds of cold beef and a pot or two of porter, after the fatigues of the Borough market; and to him the thin gentleman straightway advanced—

"My friend," said the thin gentleman.

"You're one o' the adwice gratis order," thought Sam, "or you wouldn't be so werry fond o' me all at once." But he only said—"Well Sir."

"My friend," said the thin gentleman, with a conciliatory hem—"Have you got many people stopping here, now? Pretty busy. Eh?"

Sam stole a look at the inquirer. He was a little high-dried man, with a dark squeezed up face, and small restless black eyes, that kept winking and twinkling on each side of his little inquisitive nose, as if they were playing a perpetual game of peep-bo with that feature. He was dressed all in black, with boots as shiny as his eyes, a low white neckcloth, and a clean shirt with a frill to it. A gold watch-chain, and seals, depended from his fob. He carried his black kid gloves in his hands, not on them; and as he spoke, thrust his wrists beneath his coat-tails, with the air of a man who was in the habit of propounding some regular posers.

"Pretty busy, eh?" said the little man.

"Oh, werry well, Sir," replied Sam, "we shan't be bankrupts, and we shan't make our fort'ns. We eats our biled mutton without capers, and don't care for horse-radish ven ve can get beef."

"Ah," said the little man, "you're a wag, a'nt you?"

"My eldest brother was troubled with that complaint," said Sam; "it may be catching—I used to sleep with him."

"This is a curious old house of yours," said the little man, looking round him.

"If you'd sent word you was a coming, we'd ha' had it repaired;" replied the imperturbable Sam.

The little man seemed rather baffled by these several repulses, and a short consultation took place between him and the two plump gentlemen. At its conclusion, the little man took a pinch of snuff from an oblong silver box, and was apparently on the point of renewing the conversation, when one of the plump gentlemen, who in addition to a benevolent countenance, possessed a pair of spectacles, and a pair of black gaiters, interfered—

"The fact of the matter is," said the benevolent gentleman, "that my friend here (pointing to the other plump gentleman,) will give you half a guinea, if you'll answer one or two—"

"Now, my dear Sir—my dear Sir," said the little man, "pray allow me—my dear Sir, the very first principle to be observed in these cases, is this; if you place a matter in the hands of a professional man, you must in no way interfere in the progress of the business; you must repose implicit confidence in him. Really, Mr. (he turned to the other plump gentleman, and said)—I forget your friend's name."

"Pickwick," said Mr. Wardle, for it was no other than that jolly personage.

"Ah, Pickwick—really Mr. Pickwick, my dear Sir, excuse me—I shall be happy to receive any private suggestions of yours, as *amicus curiæ*, but you must see the impropriety of your interfering with my conduct in this case, with such an *ad captandum* argument, as the offer of half a guinea. Really, my dear Sir, really," and the little man took an argumentative pinch of snuff, and looked very profound.

"My only wish, Sir," said Mr. Pickwick, "was to bring this very unpleasant matter to as speedy a close as possible."

"Quite right—quite right," said the little man.

"With which view," continued Mr. Pickwick, "I made use of the argument which my experience of men has taught me is the most likely to succeed in any case."

"Ay, ay," said the little man, "very good, very good, indeed; but you should have suggested it to *me*. My dear Sir, I'm quite certain you cannot be ignorant of the extent of confidence which must be placed in professional men. If any authority can be necessary on such a point, my dear Sir, let me refer you to the well-known case in Barnwell and—"

"Never mind George Barnwell," interrupted Sam, who had remained a wondering listener during this short colloquy; "every body knows vhat sort of a case his was, tho' it's always been my opinion, mind you, that the young 'ooman deserved scragging a precious sight more than he did. Hows'ever, that's neither here nor there. You vant me to accept of half a guinea. Werry well, I'm agreeable: I can't say no fairer than that, can I, Sir? (Mr. Pickwick smiled.) Then the next question is, what the devil do you want with me, as the man said ven he seed the ghost?"

"We want to know"—said Mr. Wardle.

"Now my dear Sir—my dear Sir," interposed the busy little man.

Mr. Wardle shrugged his shoulders, and was silent.

"We want to know," said the little man, solemnly; "and we ask the question of you, in order that we may not awaken apprehensions inside—we want to know who you've got in this house, at present."

"Who there is in the house!" said Sam, in whose mind the inmates were always represented by that particular article of their costume, which came under his immediate superintendence. "There's a vooden leg in number six, there's a pair of Hessians in thirteen, there's two pair of halves in the commercial, there's these here painted tops in the snuggery inside the bar, and five more tops in the coffee-room."

"Nothing more?" said the little man.

"Stop a bit," replied Sam, suddenly recollecting himself. "Yes; there's a pair of Vellingtons a good deal vorn, and a pair o' lady's shoes, in number five."

"What sort of shoes?" hastily inquired Wardle, who, together with Mr. Pickwick, had been lost in bewilderment at the singular catalogue of visitors.

"Country make," replied Sam.

"Any maker's name?"

"Brown."

"Where of?"

"Muggleton."

"It *is* them," exclaimed Wardle. "By Heavens, we've found them!"

"Hush!" said Sam. "The Vellingtons has gone to Doctors' Commons."

"No," said the little man.

"Yes, for a licence."

"We're in time," exclaimed Wardle. "Show us the room; not a moment is to be lost."

"Pray, my dear Sir—pray," said the little man; "caution, caution." He drew from his pocket a red silk purse, and looked very hard at Sam as he drew out a sovereign.

Sam grinned expressively.

"Show us into the room at once, without announcing us," said the little man, "and it's yours."

Sam threw the painted tops into a corner, and led the way through a dark passage, and up a wide staircase. He paused at the end of a second passage, and held out his hand.

"Here it is," whispered the attorney, as he deposited the money in the hand of their guide.

The man stepped forward for a few paces, followed by the two friends and their legal adviser. He stopped at a door.

"Is this the room?" murmured the little gentleman.

Sam nodded assent.

Old Wardle opened the door; and the whole three walked into the room just as Mr. Jingle, who had that moment returned, had produced the licence to the spinster aunt.

The spinster uttered a loud shriek, and, throwing herself in a chair, covered her face with her hands. Mr. Jingle crumpled up the licence, and thrust it into his coat-pocket. The unwelcome visiters advanced into the middle of the room.

"You—you are a nice rascal, ar'n't you?" exclaimed Wardle, breathless with passion.

"My dear Sir, my dear Sir," said the little man, laying his hat on the table. "Pray, consider—pray. *Scandalum magnatum*, defamation of character, action for damages. Calm yourself, my dear Sir, pray—"

"How dare you drag my sister from my house?" said the old man.

"Ay—ay—very good," said the little gentleman, "you may ask that. How dare you, Sir?—eh, Sir?"

"Who the devil are you?" inquired Mr. Jingle, in so fierce a tone, that the little gentleman involuntarily fell back a step or two.

"Who is he, you scoundrel?" interposed Wardle. "He's my lawyer, Mr. Perker, of Gray's inn. Perker, I'll have this fellow prosecuted—indicted—I'll—I'll—damme, I'll ruin him. And you," continued Wardle turning abruptly round to his sister, "you Rachael, at a time of life when you ought to know better, what do *you* mean by running away with a vagabond, disgracing your family, and making yourself miserable. Get on your bonnet, and come back. Call a hackney-coach there, directly, and bring this lady's bill, d'ye hear—d'ye hear?"

"Cert'nly, Sir," replied Sam, who had answered Wardle's violent ringing of the bell with a degree of celerity, which must have appeared marvellous to any body who didn't know that his eye had been applied to the outside of the key-hole during the whole interview.

"Get on your bonnet," repeated Wardle.

"Do nothing of the kind," said Jingle. "Leave the room, Sir—no business here—lady's free to act as she pleases—more than one-and-twenty."

"More than one-and-twenty!" ejaculated Wardle, contemptuously. "More than one-and-forty!"

"I a'nt," said the spinster aunt, her indignation getting the better of her determination to faint.

"You are," replied Wardle, "you're fifty if you're an hour."

Here the spinster aunt uttered a loud shriek, and became senseless.

"A glass of water," said the humane Mr. Pickwick, summoning the landlady.

"A *glass* of water!" said the passionate Wardle. "Bring a bucket, and throw it all over her; it'll do her good, and she richly deserves it."

"Ugh, you brute!" ejaculated the kind-hearted landlady. "Poor dear." And with sundry ejaculations, of "Come now, there's a dear—drink a little of this—it'll do you good—don't give way so—there's a love," &c. &c. the landlady, assisted by a chamber-maid, proceeded to vinegar the forehead, beat the hands, titillate the nose, and unlace the stays of the spinster aunt, and to administer such other restoratives as are usually applied by compassionate females to ladies who are endeavouring to ferment themselves into hysterics.

"Coach is ready, Sir," said Sam, appearing at the door.

"Come along," cried Wardle. "I'll carry her down stairs."

At this proposition, the hysterics came on with redoubled violence.

The landlady was about to enter a very violent protest against this proceeding, and had already given vent to an indignant inquiry whether Mr. Wardle considered himself a lord of the creation, when Mr. Jingle interposed—

"Boots," said he, "get me an officer."

"Stay, stay," said little Mr. Perker. "Consider, Sir, consider."

"I'll *not* consider," replied Jingle, "she's her own mistress—see who dares to take her away—unless she wishes it."

"I *won't* be taken away," murmured the spinster aunt. "I *don't* wish it." (Here there was a frightful relapse.)

"My dear Sir," said the little man, in a low tone, taking Mr. Wardle and Mr. Pickwick apart: "My dear Sir, we're in a very awkward situation. It's a distressing case—very; I never knew one more so; but really, my dear Sir, really we have no power to control this lady's actions. I warned you before we came, my dear Sir, that there was nothing to look to but a compromise."

There was a short pause.

"What kind of compromise would you recommend?" inquired Mr. Pickwick.

"Why, my dear Sir, our friend's in an unpleasant position—very much so. We must be content to suffer some pecuniary loss."

"I'll suffer any, rather than submit to this disgrace, and let her, fool as she is, be made miserable for life," said Wardle.

"I rather think it can be done," said the bustling little man. "Mr. Jingle, will you step with us into the next room for a moment?"

Mr. Jingle assented, and the quartette walked into an empty apartment.

"Now Sir," said the little man, as he carefully closed the door, "is there no way of accommodating this matter—step this way Sir, for a moment—into this window, Sir, where we can be alone—there, Sir, there, pray sit down, Sir. Now, my dear Sir, between you and I, we know very well, my dear Sir, that you have run off with this lady for the sake of her money. Don't frown, Sir, don't frown; I say, between you and I, *we* know it. We are both men of the world, and *we* know very well that our friends here, are not—eh?"

Mr. Jingle's face gradually relaxed; and something distantly resembling a wink, quivered for an instant in his left eye.

"Very good, very good," said the little man, observing the impression he had made. "Now the fact is, that beyond a few hundreds, the lady has little or nothing till the death of her mother—fine old lady, my dear Sir."

"*Old*," said Mr. Jingle, briefly but emphatically.

"Why, yes," said the attorney, with a slight cough. "You are right, my dear Sir, she is *rather* old. She comes of an old family though, my dear Sir; old in every sense of the word. The founder of that family came into Kent, when Julius Cæsar invaded Britain;—only one member of it, since, who hasn't lived to eighty-five, and *he* was beheaded by one of the Henrys. The old lady is not seventy-three now, my dear Sir." The little man paused, and took a pinch of snuff.

"Well," cried Mr. Jingle.

"Well, my dear Sir—you don't take snuff?—ah! so much the better—expensive habit—well, my dear Sir, you're a fine young man, man of the world—able to push your fortune, if you had capital, eh?"

"Well," said Mr. Jingle again.

"Do you comprehend me?"

"Not quite."

"Don't you think—now, my dear Sir, I put it to you, *don't* you think—that fifty pounds and liberty, would be better than Miss Wardle and expectation?"

"Won't do—not half enough!" said Mr. Jingle, rising.

"Nay, nay, my dear Sir," remonstrated the little attorney, seizing him by the button. "Good round sum—a man like you could treble it in no time—great deal to be done with fifty pounds, my dear Sir."

"More to be done with a hundred and fifty," replied Mr. Jingle, coolly.

"Well, my dear Sir, we won't waste time in splitting straws," resumed the little man, "say—say—seventy."

"Won't do," said Mr. Jingle.

"Don't go away, my dear Sir—pray don't hurry," said the little man. "Eighty; come: I'll write you a cheque at once."

"Won't do," said Mr. Jingle.

"Well, my dear Sir, well," said the little man, still detaining him; "just tell me what *will* do."

"Expensive affair," said Mr. Jingle. "Money out of pocket—posting, nine pounds; licence, three—that's twelve—compensation, a hundred—hundred and twelve—Breach of honour—and loss of the lady—"

"Yes, my dear Sir, yes," said the little man, with a knowing look, "never mind the last two items. That's a hundred and twelve—say a hundred—come."

"And twenty," said Mr. Jingle.

"Come, come, I'll write you a cheque," said the little man; and down he sat at the table for that purpose.

"I'll make it payable the day after to-morrow," said the little man, with a look towards Mr. Wardle; "and we can get the lady away, meanwhile." Mr. Wardle sullenly nodded assent.

"A hundred," said the little man.

"And twenty," said Mr. Jingle.

"My dear Sir," remonstrated the little man.

"Give it him," interposed Mr. Wardle, "and let him go."

The cheque was written by the little gentleman, and pocketed by Mr. Jingle.

"Now, leave this house instantly!" said Wardle, starting up.

"My dear Sir," urged the little man.

"And mind," said Mr. Wardle, "that nothing should have induced me to make this compromise—not even a regard for my family—if I had not known, that the moment you got any money in that pocket of yours, you'd go to the devil faster, if possible, than you would without it—"

"My dear Sir," urged the little man again.

"Be quiet, Perker," resumed Wardle. "Leave the room, Sir."

"Off directly," said the unabashed Jingle. "Bye—bye—Pickwick."

If any dispassionate spectator could have beheld the countenance of the illustrious man, whose name forms the leading feature of the title of this work, during the latter part of this conversation, he would have been almost induced to wonder that the indignant fire which flashed from his eyes, did not melt the glasses of his spectacles—so majestic was his wrath. His nostrils dilated, and his fists clenched involuntarily, as he heard himself addressed by the villain. But he restrained himself again—he did *not* pulverise him.

"Here," continued the hardened traitor, tossing the licence at Mr. Pickwick's feet; "get the name altered—take home the lady—do for Tuppy."

Mr. Pickwick was a philosopher, but philosophers are only men in armour, after all. The shaft had reached him, penetrated through his philosophical harness, to his very heart. In the frenzy of his rage, he hurled the inkstand madly forward, and followed it up himself. But Mr. Jingle had disappeared, and he found himself caught in the arms of Sam.

"Hallo," said that eccentric functionary, "furniter's cheap vere you come from. Self-acting ink, that 'ere; it's wrote your mark upon the wall, old gen'lm'n. Hold still,

Sir: wot's the use o' runnin' arter a man as has made his lucky, and got to t' other end of the Borough by this time."

Mr. Pickwick's mind, like those of all truly great men, was open to conviction. He was a quick, and powerful reasoner; and a moment's reflection sufficed to remind him of the impotency of his rage. It subsided as quickly as it had been roused. He panted for breath, and looked benignantly round upon his friends.

Shall we tell the lamentations that ensued, when Miss Wardle found herself deserted by the faithless Jingle? Shall we extract Mr. Pickwick's masterly description of that heart-rending scene? His note-book, blotted with the tears of sympathising humanity, lies open before us; one word, and it is in the printer's hands. But, no! we will be resolute! We will not wring the public bosom, with the delineation of such suffering!

Slowly and sadly did the two friends and the deserted lady, return next day in the Muggleton heavy coach. Dimly and darkly had the sombre shadows of a summer's night fallen upon all around, when they again reached Dingley Dell, and stood within the entrance to Manor Farm.

CHAPTER XI.

INVOLVING ANOTHER JOURNEY, AND AN ANTIQUARIAN DISCOVERY. RECORDING MR. PICKWICK'S DETERMINATION TO BE PRESENT AT AN ELECTION; AND CONTAINING A MANUSCRIPT OF THE OLD CLERGYMAN'S.

A NIGHT of quiet and repose in the profound silence of Dingley Dell, and an hour's breathing of its fresh and fragrant air on the ensuing morning, completely recovered Mr. Pickwick from the effects of his late fatigue of body and anxiety of mind. That illustrious man had been separated from his friends and followers, for two whole days; and it was with a degree of pleasure and delight, which no common imagination can adequately conceive, that he stepped forward to greet Mr. Winkle and Mr. Snodgrass, as he encountered those gentlemen on his return from his early walk. The pleasure was mutual; for who could ever gaze on Mr. Pickwick's beaming face without experiencing the sensation? But still a cloud seemed to hang over his companions which that great man could not but be sensible of, and was wholly at a loss to account for. There was a mysterious air about them both, as unusual as it was alarming.

"And how," said Mr. Pickwick, when he had grasped his followers by the hand, and exchanged warm salutations of welcome; "how is Tupman?"

Mr. Winkle, to whom the question was more peculiarly addressed, made no reply. He turned away his head, and appeared absorbed in melancholy reflection.

"Snodgrass," said Mr. Pickwick, earnestly, "How is our friend—he is not ill?"

"No," replied Mr. Snodgrass; and a tear trembled on his sentimental eye-lid, like a rain-drop on a window-frame. "No; he is not ill."

Mr. Pickwick stopped, and gazed on each of his friends in turn.

"Winkle—Snodgrass," said Mr. Pickwick: "what does

this mean? Where is our friend? What has happened? Speak—I conjure, I entreat—nay, I command you, speak."

There was a solemnity—a dignity—in Mr. Pickwick's manner, not to be withstood.

"He is gone," said Mr. Snodgrass.

"Gone!" exclaimed Mr. Pickwick, "Gone!"

"Gone," repeated Mr. Snodgrass.

"Where?" ejaculated Mr. Pickwick.

"We can only guess, from that communication," replied Mr. Snodgrass, taking a letter from his pocket, and placing it in his friend's hand. "Yesterday morning, when a letter was received from Mr. Wardle, stating that you would be home with his sister at night, the melancholy which had hung over our friend during the whole of the previous day, was observed to increase. He shortly afterwards disappeared: he was missing during the whole day, and in the evening this letter was brought by the hostler from the Crown, at Muggleton. It had been left in his charge in the morning, with a strict injunction that it should not be delivered until night."

Mr. Pickwick opened the epistle. It was in his friend's handwriting, and these were its contents:

"My dear Pickwick,

"You, my dear friend, are placed far beyond the reach of many mortal frailties and weaknesses which ordinary people cannot overcome. You do not know what it is, at one blow, to be deserted by a lovely and fascinating creature, and to fall a victim to the artifices of a villain, who hid the grin of cunning, beneath the mask of friendship. I hope you never may.

"Any letter, addressed to me at the Leather Bottle, Cobham, Kent, will be forwarded—supposing I still exist. I hasten from the sight of that world, which has become odious to me. Should I hasten from it altogether, pity—forgive me. Life, my dear Pickwick, has become insupportable to me. The spirit which burns within us, is a porter's knot, on which to rest the heavy load of worldly cares and troubles; and when that spirit fails us, the burden is too heavy to be borne. We sink beneath it. You may tell Rachael—Ah, that name!—

"TRACY TUPMAN."

"We must leave this place, directly," said Mr. Pickwick, as he refolded the note. "It would not have been decent for us to remain here, under any circumstances, after what has happened; and now we are bound to follow in search of our friend." And so saying, he led the way to the house.

His intention was rapidly communicated. The entreaties to remain were pressing, but Mr. Pickwick was inflexible. Business, he said, required his immediate attendance.

The old clergyman was present.

"You are not really going?" said he, taking Mr. Pickwick aside.

Mr. Pickwick reiterated his former determination.

"Then here," said the old gentleman, "is a little manuscript, which I had hoped to have the pleasure of reading to you myself. I found it on the death of a friend of mine—a medical man, engaged in our County Lunatic Asylum—among a variety of papers, which I had the option of destroying or preserving, as I thought proper. I can hardly believe that the manuscript is genuine, though it certainly is not in my friend's hand. However, whether it be the genuine production of a maniac, or founded upon the ravings of some unhappy being, which I think more probable, read it, and judge for yourself."

Mr. Pickwick received the manuscript, and parted from the benevolent old gentleman with many expressions of good-will and esteem.

It was a more difficult task to take leave of the inmates of Manor Farm, from whom they had received so much hospitality and kindness. Mr. Pickwick kissed the young ladies—we were going to say, as if they were his own daughters, only as he might possibly have infused a little more warmth into the salutation, the comparison would not be quite appropriate—hugged the old lady with filial cordiality: and patted the rosy cheeks of the female servants in a most patriarchal manner, as he slipped into the hands of each, some more substantial expressions of his approval. The exchange of cordialities with their fine old host and Mr. Trundle, were even more hearty and prolonged; and it was not until Mr. Snodgrass had been several times called for, and at last emerged from a dark passage followed soon after by Emily (whose bright eyes looked unusually dim) that the three friends were enabled to tear themselves from their friendly entertainers. Many a backward look they gave at the Farm, as they walked slowly away: and many a kiss did Mr. Snodgrass waft in the air, in acknowledgment of something very like a lady's handkerchief, which was waved from one of the upper windows, until a turn of the lane hid the old house from their sight.

At Muggleton they procured a conveyance to Rochester. By the time they reached the last-named place, the violence of their grief had sufficiently abated to admit of their making a very excellent early dinner; and having procured the necessary information relative to the road, the three friends set forward again in the afternoon to walk to Cobham.

A delightful walk it was: for it was a pleasant afternoon in June, and their way lay through a deep and shady wood, cooled by the light wind which gently rustled the thick foliage, and enlivened by the songs of the birds that perched upon the boughs. The ivy and the moss crept in thick clusters over the old trees, and the soft green turf overspread the ground like a silken mat. They emerged upon an open park, with an ancient hall, displaying the quaint and picturesque architecture of Elizabeth's time. Long vistas of stately oaks and elm trees appeared on every side: large herds of deer were cropping the fresh grass; and occasionally a startled hare scoured along the ground, with the speed of the shadows thrown by the light clouds which sweep across a sunny landscape like a passing breath of summer.

"If this," said Mr. Pickwick, looking about him; "if this were the place to which all who are troubled with our friend's complaint came, I fancy their old attachment to this world would very soon return."

"I think so too," said Mr. Winkle.

"And really," added Mr. Pickwick, after half an hour's walking had brought them to the village, "really for a misanthrope's choice, this is one of the prettiest and most desirable places of residence, I ever met with."

In this opinion also, both Mr. Winkle and Mr. Snodgrass expressed their concurrence; and having been directed to the Leather Bottle, a clean and commodious village alehouse, the three travellers entered, and at once inquired for a gentleman of the name of Tupman.

"Show the gentlemen into the parlour, Tom," said the landlady.

A stout country lad opened a door at the end of the passage, and the three friends entered a long, low-roofed room, furnished with a large number of high-backed leather-cushioned chairs, of fantastic shapes, and embellished with a great variety of old portraits and roughly-coloured prints of some antiquity. At the upper end of the room was a table, with a white cloth upon it, well covered with a roast fowl, bacon, ale, and et ceteras; and at the table sat Mr. Tupman, looking as unlike a man who had taken his leave of the world, as possible.

On the entrance of his friends, that gentleman laid down his knife and fork, and with a mournful air advanced to meet them.

"I did not expect to see you here," he said, as he grasped Mr. Pickwick's hand. "It's very kind."

"Ah!" said Mr. Pickwick, sitting down, and wiping from his forehead the perspiration which the walk had engendered. "Finish your dinner, and walk out with me. I wish to speak to you alone."

Mr. Tupman did as he was desired; and Mr. Pickwick having refreshed himself with a copious draught of ale, waited his friend's leisure. The dinner was quickly despatched, and they walked out together.

For half an hour, their forms might have been seen pacing the churchyard to and fro, while Mr. Pickwick was engaged in combatting his companion's resolution. Any repetition of his arguments would be useless; for what language could convey to them that energy and force which their great originator's manner communicated? Whether Mr. Tupman was already tired of retirement, or whether he was wholly unable to resist the eloquent appeal which was made to him, matters not; he did *not* resist it at last.

"It mattered little to him," he said, "where he dragged out the miserable remainder of his days: and since his friend laid so much stress upon his humble companionship, he was willing to share his adventures."

Mr. Pickwick smiled; they shook hands; and walked back to re-join their companions.

It was at this moment that Mr. Pickwick made that immortal discovery, which has been the pride and boast of his friends, and the envy of every antiquarian in this or any other country. They had passed the door of their inn, and walked a little way down the village, before they recollected the precise spot in which it stood. As they turned back, Mr. Pickwick's eye fell upon a small broken stone, partially buried in the ground, in front of a cottage-door. He paused.

"This is very strange," said Mr. Pickwick.

"What is strange?" inquired Mr. Tupman, staring eagerly at every object near him, but the right one. "God bless me, what's the matter?"

This last was an ejaculation of irrepressible astonishment, occasioned by seeing Mr. Pickwick, in his enthusiasm for discovery, fall on his knees before the little stone, and commence wiping the dust off it with his pocket-handkerchief.

"There is an inscription here," said Mr. Pickwick.

"Is it possible!" said Mr. Tupman.

"I can discern," continued Mr. Pickwick, rubbing away with all his might, and gazing intently through his spectacles: "I can discern a cross, and a B, and then a T. This is important," continued Mr. Pickwick, starting up. "This is some very old inscription, existing perhaps long before the ancient alms-houses in this place. It must not be lost."

He tapped at the cottage-door. A labouring man opened it.

"Do you know how this stone came here, my friend?" inquired the benevolent Mr. Pickwick.

"No, I doan't, Sir," replied the man, civilly. "It was here long afore I war born, or any on us."

Mr. Pickwick glanced triumphantly at his companion.

"You—you—are not particularly attached to it, I dare say," said Mr. Pickwick, trembling with anxiety. "You wouldn't mind selling it, now?"

"Ah! but who'd buy it?" inquired the man; with an expression of face which he probably meant to be very cunning.

"I'll give you ten shillings for it, at once," said Mr. Pickwick, "if you would take it up for me."

The astonishment of the village may be easily imagined, when (the little stone having been raised with one wrench of a spade), Mr. Pickwick, by dint of great personal exertion, bore it with his own hands to the inn, and after having carefully washed it, deposited it on the table.

The exultation and joy of the Pickwickians knew no bounds, when their patience and assiduity, their washing and scraping, were crowned with success. The stone was uneven and broken, and the letters were straggling and irregular, but the following fragment of an inscription was clearly to be deciphered:

Mr. Pickwick's eyes sparkled with delight, as he sat and gloated over the treasure he had discovered. He had attained one of the greatest objects of his ambition. In a county known to abound in remains of the early ages; in a village in which there still existed some memorials of the olden time, he—he, the Chairman of the Pickwick Club—had discovered a strange and curious inscription of unquestionable antiquity, which had wholly escaped the observation of the many learned men who had preceded him. He could hardly trust the evidence of his senses.

"This—this," said he, "determines me. We return to town, to-morrow."

"To-morrow!" exclaimed his admiring followers.

"To-morrow," said Mr. Pickwick. "This treasure must be at once deposited where it can be thoroughly investigated, and properly understood. I have another reason for this step. In a few days, an election is to take place for the borough of Eatanswill, at which Mr. Perker, a gentleman whom I lately met, is the agent of one of the candidates. We will behold, and minutely examine, a scene so interesting to every Englishman."

"We will," was the animated cry of three voices.

Mr. Pickwick looked round him. The attachment and fervour of his followers, lighted up a glow of enthusiasm within him. He was their leader, and he felt it.

"Let us celebrate this happy meeting, with a convivial glass," said he. This proposition, like the other, was received with unanimous applause. And having himself deposited the important stone in a small deal box, purchased from the landlady for the purpose, he placed himself in an arm-chair at the head of the table; and the evening was devoted to festivity and conversation.

"GOD BLESS ME! WHAT'S THE MATTER?"

It was past eleven o'clock—a late hour for the little village of Cobham—when Mr. Pickwick retired to the bed-room which had been prepared for his reception. He threw open the lattice-window, and setting his light upon the table, fell into a train of meditation on the hurried events of the two preceding days.

The hour and the place were both favourable to contemplation; Mr. Pickwick was roused, by the church-clock striking twelve. The first stroke of the hour sounded solemnly in his ear, but when the bell ceased the stillness seemed insupportable;—he almost felt as if he had lost a companion. He was nervous and excited; and hastily undressing himself, and placing his light in the chimney, got into bed.

Every one has experienced that disagreeable state of mind, in which a sensation of bodily weariness in vain contends against an inability to sleep. It was Mr. Pickwick's condition at this moment: he tossed first on one side and then on the other; and perseveringly closed his eyes as if to coax himself to slumber. It was of no use. Whether it was the unwonted exertion he had undergone, or the heat, or the brandy and water, or the strange bed—whatever it was, his thoughts kept reverting very uncomfortably to the grim pictures down stairs, and the old stories to which they had given rise in the course of the evening. After half an hour's tumbling about, he came to the unsatisfactory conclusion, that it was of no use trying to sleep, so he got up and partially dressed himself. Anything, he thought, was better than lying there fancying all kinds of horrors. He looked out of the window—it was very dark. He walked about the room—it was very lonely.

He had taken a few turns from the door to the window, and from the window to the door, when the clergyman's manuscript for the first time entered his head. It was a good thought. If it failed to interest him, it might send him to sleep. He took it from his coat-pocket, and drawing a small table towards his bedside, trimmed the light, put on his spectacles, and composed himself to read. It was a strange handwriting, and the paper was much soiled and blotted. The title gave him a sudden start, too; and he could not avoid casting a wistful glance round the room. Reflecting on the absurdity of giving way to such feelings, however, he trimmed the light again, and read as follows:

A MADMAN'S MANUSCRIPT.

"Yes!—a madman's! How that word would have struck to my heart, many years ago! How it would have roused the terror that used to come upon me sometimes; sending the blood hissing and tingling through my veins, 'till the cold dew of fear stood in large drops upon my skin, and my knees knocked together with fright! I like it now though. It's a fine name. Shew me the monarch whose angry frown was ever feared like the glare of a madman's eye—whose cord and axe, were ever half so sure as a madman's gripe. Ho! ho! It's a grand thing to be mad! to be peeped at like a wild lion through the iron bars—to gnash one's teeth and howl, through the long still night, to the merry ring of a heavy chain—and to roll and twine among the straw, transported with such brave music. Hurrah for the madhouse! Oh it's a rare place!

"I remember days when I was *afraid* of being mad; when I used to start from my sleep, and fall upon my knees, and pray to be spared from the curse of my race; when I rushed from the sight of merriment or happiness, to hide myself in some lonely place, and spend the weary hours in watching the progress of the fever that was to consume my brain. I knew that madness was mixed up with my very blood, and the marrow of my bones; that one generation had passed away without the pestilence appearing among them, and that I was the first in whom it would revive. I knew it *must* be so: that so it always had been, and so it ever would be; and when I cowered in some obscure corner of a crowded room, and saw men whisper, and point, and turn their eyes towards me, I knew they were telling each other of the doomed madman; and I slunk away again to mope in solitude.

"I did this for years; long, long years they were. The nights here are long sometimes—very long; but they are nothing to the restless nights, and dreadful dreams I had at that time. It makes me cold to remember them. Large dusky forms with sly and jeering faces crouched in the corners of the room, and bent over my bed at night, tempting me to madness. They told me in low whispers, that the floor of the old house in which my father's father died, was stained with his own blood, shed by his own hand in raging madness. I drove my fingers into my ears, but they screamed into my head till the room rang with it, that in one generation before him the madness slumbered, but that his grandfather had lived for years with his hands fettered to the ground, to prevent his tearing himself to pieces. I knew they told me the truth—I knew it well. I had found it out years before, though they had tried to keep it from me. Ha! ha! I was too cunning for them, madman as they thought me.

"At last it came upon me, and I wondered how I could ever have feared it. I could go into the world now, and laugh and shout with the best among them. I knew I was mad, but they did not even suspect it. How I used to hug myself with delight, when I thought of the fine trick I was playing them after their old pointing and leering, when I was not mad, but only dreading that I might one day become so! And how I used to laugh for joy, when I was alone, and thought how well I kept my secret, and how quickly my kind friends would have fallen from me, if they had known the truth. I could have screamed with ecstasy when I dined alone with some fine roaring fellow, to think how pale he would have turned, and how fast he would have run, if he had known that the dear friend who sat close to him, sharpening a bright glittering knife, was a madman with all the power, and half the will, to plunge it in his heart. Oh, it was a merry life!

"Riches became mine, wealth poured in upon me, and I rioted in pleasures enhanced a thousand fold to me by the consciousness of my well-kept secret. I inherited an estate. The law—the eagle-eyed law itself, had been deceived, and had handed over disputed thousands to a madman's hands. Where was the wit of the sharp-sighted men of sound mind? Where the dexterity of the lawyers, eager to discover a flaw? The madman's cunning had over-reached them all.

"I had money. How I was courted! I spent it profusely. How I was praised! How those three proud overbearing brothers humbled themselves before me! The old white-headed father, too—such deference—such respect—such devoted friendship—why he worshipped me. The old man had a daughter, and the young men a sister; and all the five were poor. I was rich; and when I married the girl, I saw a smile of triumph play upon the faces of her needy relatives, as they thought of their well-planned scheme, and their fine prize. It was for me to smile. To smile! To laugh outright, and tear my hair, and roll upon the ground with shrieks of merriment. They little thought they had married her to a madman.

"Stay. If they had known it, would they have saved her? A sister's happiness against her husband's gold. The lightest feather I blow into the air, against the gay chain that ornaments my body!

"In one thing I was deceived with all my cunning. If I had not been mad—for though we madmen are sharp-witted enough, we get bewildered sometimes—I should have known that the girl would rather have been placed, stiff and cold in a dull leaden coffin, than borne an envied bride to my rich, glittering, house. I should have known that her heart was with the dark-eyed boy whose name I once heard her breathe in her troubled sleep; and that she had been sacrificed to me, to relieve the poverty of the old white-headed man, and the haughty brothers.

"I don't remember forms or faces now, but I know the girl was beautiful. I *know* she was; for in the bright moonlight nights, when I start up from my sleep, and all is quiet about me, I see, standing still and motionless in one corner of this cell, a slight and wasted figure with long black hair, which streaming down her back, stirs with no earthly wind, and eyes that fix their gaze on me, and never wink or close. Hush! the blood chills at my heart as I write it down—that form is *hers*; the face is very pale, and the eyes are glassy bright; but I know them well. That figure never moves; it never frowns and mouths as others do, that fill this place sometimes; but it is much more dreadful to me, even than the spirits that tempted me many years ago—it comes fresh from the grave; and is so very death-like.

"For nearly a year I saw that face grow paler; for nearly a year, I saw the tears steal down the mournful cheeks, and never knew the cause. I found it out at last though. They could not keep it from me long. She had never liked me; I had never thought she did: she despised my wealth, and hated the splendour in which she lived;—I had not expected that. She loved another. This I had never thought of. Strange feelings came over me, and thoughts forced upon me by some secret power, whirled round and round my brain. I did not hate her, though I hated the boy she still wept for. I pitied—yes, I pitied—the wretched life to which her cold and selfish relations had doomed her. I knew that she could not live long, but the thought that before her death she might give birth to some ill-fated being, destined to hand down madness to its offspring, determined me. I resolved to kill her.

"For many weeks I thought of poison, and then of drowning, and then of fire. A fine sight the grand house in flames, and the madman's wife smouldering away to cinders. Think of the jest of a large reward, too, and of some sane man swinging in the wind for a deed he never did, and all through a madman's cunning! I thought often of this, but I gave it up at last. Oh! the pleasure of stropping the razor day after day, feeling the sharp edge, and thinking of the gash one stroke of its thin bright point would make!

"At last the old spirits who had been with me so often before, whispered in my ear that the time was come, and thrust the open razor into my hand. I grasped it firmly, rose softly from the bed, and leaned over my sleeping wife. Her face was buried in her hands. I withdrew them softly, and they fell listlessly on her bosom. She had been weeping; for the traces of the tears were still wet upon her cheek. Her face was calm and placid; and even as I looked upon it, a tranquil smile lighted up her pale features. I laid my hand softly on her shoulder. She started—it was only a passing dream. I leant forward again. She screamed, and woke.

"One motion of my hand, and she would never again have uttered cry or sound. But I was startled, and drew back. Her eyes were fixed on mine. I know not how it was, but they cowed and frightened me; and I quailed beneath them. She rose from the bed, still gazing fixedly and steadily on me. I trembled; the razor was in my hand, but I could not move. She made towards the door. As she neared it, she turned, and withdrew her eyes from my face. The spell was broken. I bounded forward, and clutched her by the arm. Uttering shriek upon shriek, she sunk upon the ground.

"Now I could have killed her without a struggle; but the house was alarmed. I heard the tread of footsteps on the stairs. I replaced the razor in its usual drawer, unfastened the door, and called loudly for assistance.

"They came, and raised her, and placed her on the bed. She lay bereft of animation for hours; and when life, look, and speech returned, her senses had deserted her, and she raved wildly and furiously.

"Doctors were called in—great men who rolled up to my door in easy carriages, with fine horses and gaudy servants. They were at her bedside for weeks. They had a great meeting, and consulted together in low and solemn voices in another room. One, the cleverest and most celebrated among them, took me aside, and bidding me prepare for the worst, told me—me, the madman!—that my wife was mad. He stood close beside me at an open window, his eyes looking in my face, and his hand laid upon my arm. With one effort, I could have hurled him into the street beneath. It would have been rare sport to have done it; but my secret was at stake, and I let him go. A few days after, they told me I must place her under some restraint: I must provide a keeper for her. I! I went into the open fields where none could hear me, and laughed till the air resounded with my shouts!

"She died next day. The white-headed old man followed her to the grave, and the proud brothers dropped a tear over the insensible corpse of her, whose sufferings they had regarded in her lifetime with muscles of iron. All this was food for my secret mirth, and I laughed behind the white handkerchief which I held up to my face, as we rode home, 'till the tears came into my eyes.

"But though I had carried my object and killed her, I was restless and disturbed, and I felt that before long, my secret must be known. I could not hide the wild mirth and joy which boiled within me, and made me when I was alone, at home, jump up and beat my hands together, and dance round and round, and roar aloud. When I went out, and saw the busy crowds hurrying about the streets: or to the theatre, and heard the sound of music, and beheld the people dancing, I felt such glee, that I could have rushed among them, and torn them to pieces limb from limb, and howled in transport. But I ground my teeth, and struck my feet upon the floor, and drove my sharp nails into my hands. I kept it down; and no one knew I was a madman yet.

"I remember—though it's one of the last things I *can* remember: for now I mix realities with my dreams, and having so much to do, and being always hurried here, have no time to separate the two, from some strange confusion in which they get involved—I remember how I let it out at last. Ha! ha! I think I see their frightened looks now and feel the ease with which I flung them from me, and dashed my clenched fist into their white faces, and then flew like the wind, and left them screaming and shouting far behind. The strength of a giant comes upon me when I think of it. There—see how this iron bar bends beneath my furious wrench. I could snap it like a twig, only there are long galleries here with many doors—I don't think I could find my way along them: and even if I could, I know there are iron gates below which they keep locked and barred. They know what a clever madman I have been, and they are proud to have me here, to show.

"Let me see—yes, I had been out. It was late at night when I reached home, and found the proudest of the three proud brothers, waiting to see me—urgent business he said: I recollect it well. I hated that man with all a madman's hate. Many and many a time had my fingers longed to tear him. They told me he was there. I ran swiftly up stairs. He had a word to say to me. I dismissed the servants. It was late, and we were alone together—*for the first time.*

"I kept my eyes carefully from him at first, for I knew what he little thought—and I gloried in the knowledge—that the light of madness gleamed from them like fire. We sat in silence for a few minutes. He spoke at last. My recent dissipation, and strange remarks, made so soon after his sister's death, were an insult to her memory. Coupling together many circumstances which had at first escaped his observation, he thought I had not treated her well. He wished to know whether he was right in inferring that I meant to cast a reproach upon her memory, and a disrespect upon her family. It was due to the uniform he wore, to demand this explanation.

"This man had a commission in the army—a commission, purchased with my money, and his sister's misery. This was the man who had been foremost in the plot to ensnare me, and grasp my wealth. This was the man who had been the main instrument in forcing his sister to wed me; well knowing that her heart was given to that puling boy. Due! Due to *his* uniform! The livery of his degradation! I turned my eyes upon him—I could not help it—but I spoke not a word.

"I saw the sudden change that came upon him, beneath my gaze. He was a bold man, but the colour faded from his face, and he drew back his chair. I dragged mine nearer to him; and as I laughed—I was very merry then—I saw him shudder. I felt the madness rising within me. He was afraid of me.

"'You were very fond of your sister when she was alive' —I said—'Very.'

"He looked uneasily round him, and I saw his hand grasp the back of his chair: but he said nothing.

"'You villain,' said I, 'I found you out; I discovered your hellish plots against me; I know her heart was fixed on some one else before you compelled her to marry me. I know it—I know it.'

"He jumped suddenly from his chair, brandished it aloft, and bid me stand back—for I took care to be getting closer to him, all the time I spoke.

"I screamed rather than talked, for I felt tumultuous passions eddying through my veins, and the old spirits whispering and taunting me to tear his heart out.

"'Damn you,' said I, starting up, and rushing upon him; 'I killed her. I am a madman. Down with you. Blood, blood, I will have it.'

"I turned aside with one blow, the chair he hurled at me

in his terror, and closed with him; and with a heavy crash, we rolled upon the floor together.

"It was a fine struggle that, for he was a tall strong man, fighting for his life; and I, a powerful madman, thirsting to destroy him. I knew no strength could equal mine, and I was right. Right, again, though a madman! His struggles grew fainter. I knelt upon his chest, and clasped his brawny throat, firmly with both hands. His face grew purple; his eyes were starting from his head, and with protruded tongue, he seemed to mock me. I squeezed the tighter.

"The door was suddenly burst open with a loud noise, and a crowd of people rushed forward, crying aloud to each other, to secure the madman.

"My secret was out; and my only struggle now, was for liberty and freedom. I gained my feet before a hand was on me, threw myself among my assailants, and cleared my way with my strong arm as if I bore a hatchet in my hand, and hewed them down before me. I gained the door, dropped over the banisters, and in an instant was in the street.

"Straight and swift I ran, and no one dared to stop me. I heard the noise of feet behind, and redoubled my speed. It grew fainter and fainter in the distance, and at length died away altogether: but on I bounded, through marsh and rivulet, over fence and wall, with a wild shout which was taken up by the strange beings that flocked around me on every side, and swelled the sound, till it pierced the air. I was borne upon the arms of demons who swept along upon the wind, and bore down bank and hedge before them, and spun me round and round with a rustle and a speed that made my head swim, until at last they threw me from them with a violent shock, and I fell heavily upon the earth. When I woke I found myself here—here in this gay cell where the sun-light seldom comes, and the moon steals in, in rays which only serve to show the dark shadows about me, and that silent figure in its old corner. When I lie awake, I can sometimes hear strange shrieks and cries from distant parts of this large place. What they are, I know not; but they neither come from that pale form, nor does it regard them. For from the first shades of dusk 'till the earliest light of morning, it still stands motionless in the same place, listening to the music of my iron chain, and watching my gambols on my straw bed."

At the end of the manuscript, was written, in another hand, this note:—

[The unhappy man whose ravings are recorded above, was a melancholy instance of the baneful results of energies misdirected in early life, and excesses prolonged until their consequences could never be repaired. The thoughtless riot, dissipation, and debauchery of his younger days, produced fever and delirium. The first effects of the latter, was the strange delusion, founded upon a well-known medical theory, strongly contended for by some, and as strongly contested by others, that an hereditary madness existed in his family. This produced a settled gloom, which in time developed a morbid insanity, and finally terminated in raving madness. There is every reason to believe that the events he detailed, though distorted in the description by his diseased imagination, really happened. It is only matter of wonder to those who were acquainted with the vices of his early career, that his passions, when no longer controlled by reason, did not lead him to the commission of still more frightful deeds.]

Mr. Pickwick's candle was just expiring in the socket, as he concluded the perusal of the old clergyman's manuscript; and when the light went suddenly out, without any previous flicker by way of warning, it communicated a very considerable start to his excited frame. Hastily throwing off such articles of clothing as he had put on when he rose from his uneasy bed, and casting a fearful glance around, he once more scrambled hastily between the sheets, and soon fell fast asleep.

The sun was shining brilliantly into his chamber when he awoke, and the morning was far advanced. The gloom which had oppressed him on the previous night, had disappeared with the dark shadows which shrouded the landscape, and his thoughts and feelings were as light and gay as the morning itself. After a hearty breakfast, the four gentlemen sallied forth to walk to Gravesend, followed by a man bearing the stone in its deal box. They reached that town about one o'clock, (their luggage they had directed to be forwarded to the City, from Rochester,) and being fortunate enough to secure places on the outside of a coach, arrived in London in sound health and spirits, on that same afternoon.

The next three or four days were occupied with the preparations which were necessary for their journey to the borough of Eatanswill. As any reference to that most important undertaking demands a separate chapter, we may devote the few lines which remain at the close of this, to narrate, with great brevity, the history of the antiquarian discovery.

It appears from the Transactions of the Club, then, that Mr. Pickwick lectured upon the discovery at a General Club Meeting, convened on the night succeeding their return, and entered into a variety of ingenious and erudite speculations on the meaning of the inscription. It also appears that a skilful artist executed a faithful delineation of the curiosity, which was engraven on stone, and presented to the Royal Antiquarian Society, and other learned bodies—that heart-burnings and jealousies without number, were created by rival controversies which were penned upon the subject—and that Mr. Pickwick himself wrote a Pamphlet, containing ninety-six pages of very small print, and twenty-seven different readings of the inscription. That three old gentlemen cut off their eldest sons with a shilling a-piece for presuming to doubt the antiquity of the fragment—and that one enthusiastic individual cut himself off prematurely, in despair at being unable to fathom its meaning. That Mr. Pickwick was elected an honorary member of seventeen native and foreign societies, for making the discovery; that none of the seventeen could make anything of it, but that all the seventeen agreed it was very extraordinary.

Mr. Blotton, indeed—and the name will be doomed to the undying contempt of those who cultivate the mysterious and the sublime—Mr. Blotton, we say, with the doubt and cavilling peculiar to vulgar minds, presumed to state a view of the case, as degrading as ridiculous. Mr. Blotton, with a mean desire to tarnish the lustre of the immortal name of Pickwick, actually undertook a journey to Cobham in person, and on his return, sarcastically observed in an oration at the club, that he had seen the man from whom the stone was purchased; that the man presumed the stone to be ancient, but solemnly denied the antiquity of the inscription—inasmuch as he represented it to have been rudely carved by himself in an idle mood, and to display letters intended to bear neither more nor less than the simple construction of—"Bill Stumps, his mark:" and that Mr.

Stumps, being little in the habit of original composition, and more accustomed to be guided by the sound of words than by the strict rules of orthography, had omitted the concluding "L" of his christian name.

The Pickwick Club, as might have been expected from so enlightened an Institution, received this statement with the contempt it deserved, expelled the presumptuous and ill-conditioned Blotton from the society, and voted Mr. Pickwick a pair of gold spectacles, in token of their confidence and approbation; in return for which, Mr. Pickwick caused a portrait of himself to be painted, and hung up in the club-room—which portrait, by the by, he did *not* wish to have destroyed when he grew a few years older.

Mr. Blotton was ejected but not conquered. He also wrote a pamphlet, addressed to the seventeen learned societies, containing a repetition of the statement he had already made, and rather more than half intimating his opinion that the seventeen learned societies aforesaid, were so many "humbugs." Hereupon the virtuous indignation of the seventeen learned societies being roused, several fresh pamphlets appeared; the foreign learned societies corresponded with the native learned societies, the native learned societies translated the pamphlets of the foreign learned societies into English, the foreign learned societies translated the pamphlets of the native learned societies into all sorts of languages: and thus commenced that celebrated scientific discussion so well known to all men, as the Pickwick controversy.

But this base attempt to injure Mr. Pickwick, recoiled upon the head of its calumnious author. The seventeen learned societies unanimously voted the presumptuous Blotton an ignorant meddler; and forthwith set to work upon more treatises than ever. And to this day the stone remains an illegible monument of Mr. Pickwick's greatness, and a lasting trophy of the littleness of his enemies.

CHAPTER XII.

DESCRIPTIVE OF A VERY IMPORTANT PROCEEDING ON THE PART OF MR. PICKWICK; NO LESS AN EPOCH IN HIS LIFE, THAN IN THIS HISTORY.

Mr. Pickwick's apartments in Goswell Street, although on a limited scale, were not only of a very neat and comfortable description, but peculiarly adapted for the residence of a man of his genius and observation. His sitting-room was the first floor front, his bed-room the second floor front; and thus, whether he were sitting at his desk in the parlour, or standing before the dressing-glass in his dormitory, he had an equal opportunity of contemplating human nature in all the numerous phases it exhibits, in that not more populous than popular thoroughfare. His landlady, Mrs. Bardell—the relict and sole executrix of a deceased custom-house officer—was a comely woman of bustling manners and agreeable appearance, with a natural genius for cooking, improved by study and long practice into an exquisite talent. There were no children, no servants, no fowls. The only other inmates of the house were a large man, and a small boy; the first a lodger, the second a production of Mrs. Bardell's. The large man was always home precisely at ten o'clock at night, at which hour he regularly condensed himself into the limits of a dwarfish French bedstead in the back parlour; and the infantine sports and gymnastic exercises of Master Bardell were exclusively confined to the neighbouring pavements and gutters. Cleanliness and quiet reigned throughout the house; and in it Mr. Pickwick's will was law.

To any one acquainted with these points of the domestic economy of the establishment, and conversant with the admirable regulation of Mr. Pickwick's mind, his appearance and behaviour on the morning previous to that which had been fixed upon for the journey to Eatanswill, would have been most mysterious and unaccountable. He paced the room to and fro with hurried steps, popped his head out of the window at intervals of about three minutes each, constantly referred to his watch, and exhibited many other manifestations of impatience, very unusual with him. It was evident that something of great importance was in contemplation, but what that something was not even Mrs. Bardell herself had been enabled to discover.

"Mrs. Bardell," said Mr. Pickwick at last, as that amiable female approached the termination of a prolonged dusting of the apartment—

"Sir," said Mrs. Bardell.

"Your little boy is a very long time gone."

"Why it's a good long way to the Borough, Sir," remonstrated Mrs. Bardell.

"Ah," said Mr. Pickwick, "very true; so it is."

Mr. Pickwick relapsed into silence, and Mrs. Bardell resumed her dusting.

"Mrs. Bardell," said Mr. Pickwick, at the expiration of a few minutes.

"Sir," said Mrs. Bardell again.

"Do you think it's a much greater expense to keep two people, than to keep one?"

"La, Mr. Pickwick," said Mrs. Bardell, colouring up to the very border of her cap, as she fancied she observed a species of matrimonial twinkle in the eyes of her lodger; "La, Mr. Pickwick, what a question!"

"Well, but *do* you?" inquired Mr. Pickwick.

"That depends—" said Mrs. Bardell, approaching the duster very near to Mr. Pickwick's elbow, which was planted on the table; "that depends a good deal upon the person, you know, Mr. Pickwick; and whether it's a saving and careful person, Sir."

"That's very true," said Mr. Pickwick, "but the person I have in my eye (here he looked very hard at Mrs. Bardell) I think possesses these qualities; and has, moreover, a considerable knowledge of the world, and a great deal of sharpness, Mrs. Bardell; which may be of material use to me."

"La, Mr. Pickwick," said Mrs. Bardell; the crimson rising to her cap-border again.

"I do," said Mr. Pickwick, growing energetic, as was his wont in speaking of a subject which interested him, "I do, indeed; and to tell you the truth, Mrs. Bardell, I have made up my mind."

"Dear me, Sir," exclaimed Mrs. Bardell.

"You'll think it very strange now," said the amiable Mr. Pickwick, with a good-humoured glance at his companion, "that I never consulted you about this matter, and never even mentioned it, till I sent your little boy out this morning—eh?"

Mrs. Bardell could only reply by a look. She had long worshipped Mr. Pickwick at a distance, but here she was, all at once, raised to a pinnacle to which her wildest and most extravagant hopes had never dared to aspire. Mr. Pickwick was going to propose—a deliberate plan, too—

sent her little boy to the Borough, to get him out of the way—how thoughtful—how considerate!

"Well," said Mr. Pickwick, "what do you think?"

"Oh, Mr. Pickwick," said Mrs. Bardell, trembling with agitation, "you're very kind, Sir."

"It'll save you a good deal of trouble, won't it?" said Mr. Pickwick.

"Oh, I never thought anything of the trouble, Sir," replied Mrs. Bardell; "and, of course, I should take more trouble to please you then, than ever; but it is so kind of you, Mr. Pickwick, to have so much consideration for my loneliness."

"Ah, to be sure," said Mr. Pickwick; "I never thought of that. When I am in town, you'll always have somebody to sit with you. To be sure, so you will."

"I'm sure I ought to be a very happy woman," said Mrs. Bardell.

"And your little boy—" said Mr. Pickwick.

"Bless his heart," interposed Mrs. Bardell, with a maternal sob.

"He, too, will have a companion," resumed Mr. Pickwick, "a lively one, who'll teach him, I'll be bound, more tricks in a week, than he would ever learn in a year." And Mr. Pickwick smiled placidly.

"Oh you dear—" said Mrs. Bardell.

Mr. Pickwick started.

"Oh you kind, good, playful dear," said Mrs. Bardell; and without more ado, she rose from her chair, and flung her arms round Mr. Pickwick's neck, with a cataract of tears, and a chorus of sobs.

"Bless my soul," cried the astonished Mr. Pickwick;—"Mrs. Bardell my good woman—dear me, what a situation—pray consider.—Mrs. Bardell, don't—if anybody should come—"

"Oh, let them come," exclaimed Mrs. Bardell, frantically; "I'll never leave you—dear, kind, good soul;" and. with these words, Mrs. Bardell clung the tighter.

"Mercy upon me," said Mr. Pickwick, struggling violently; "I hear somebody coming up the stairs. Don't, don't, there's a good creature, don't." But entreaty and remonstrance were alike unavailing: for Mrs. Bardell had fainted in Mr. Pickwick's arms; and before he could gain time to deposit her on a chair, Master Bardell entered the room, ushering in Mr. Tupman, Mr. Winkle, and Mr. Snodgrass.

Mr. Pickwick was struck motionless and speechless. He stood with his lovely burden in his arms, gazing vacantly on the countenances of his friends, without the slightest attempt at recognition or explanation. They, in their turn, stared at him; and Master Bardell, in his turn, stared at everybody.

The astonishment of the Pickwickians was so absorbing, and the perplexity of Mr. Pickwick was so extreme, that they might have remained in exactly the same relative situations until the suspended animation of the lady was restored, had it not been for a most beautiful and touching expression of filial affection on the part of her youthful son. Clad in a tight suit of corderoy, spangled with brass buttons of a very considerable size, he at first stood at the door astounded and uncertain; but by degrees, the impression that his mother must have suffered some personal damage, pervaded his partially developed mind, and considering Mr. Pickwick as the aggressor, he set up an appalling and semi-earthly kind of howling, and butting forward with his head, commenced assailing that immortal gentleman about the back and legs, with such blows and pinches as the strength of his arm, and the violence of his excitement, allowed.

"Take this little villain away," said the agonised Mr. Pickwick, "he's mad."

"What *is* the matter?" said the three tongue-tied Pickwickians.

"I don't know," replied Mr. Pickwick, pettishly. "Take away the boy—(here Mr. Winkle carried the interesting boy, screaming and struggling, to the further end of the apartment.)—Now help me, lead this woman down stairs."

"Oh, I am better now," said Mrs. Bardell, faintly.

"Let me lead you down stairs," said the ever gallant Mr. Tupman.

"Thank you, Sir—thank you;" exclaimed Mrs. Bardell, hysterically. And down stairs she was led accordingly, accompanied by her affectionate son.

"I cannot conceive—" said Mr. Pickwick, when his friend returned—"I cannot conceive what has been the matter with that woman. I had merely announced to her my intention of keeping a man servant, when she fell into the extraordinary paroxysm in which you found her. Very extraordinary thing."

"Very," said his three friends.

"Placed me in such an extremely awkward situation," continued Mr. Pickwick.

"Very," was the reply of his followers, as they coughed slightly, and looked dubiously at each other.

This behaviour was not lost upon Mr. Pickwick. He remarked their incredulity. They evidently suspected him.

"There is a man in the passage now," said Mr. Tupman.

"It's the man I spoke to you about," said Mr. Pickwick, "I sent for him to the Borough this morning. Have the goodness to call him up, Snodgrass."

Mr. Snodgrass did as he was desired; and Mr. Samuel Weller forthwith presented himself.

"Oh—you remember me, I suppose?" said Mr. Pickwick.

"I should think so," replied Sam, with a patronising wink. "Queer start that 'ere, but he was one too many for you, warn't he? Up to snuff and a pinch or two over—eh?"

"Never mind that matter now," said Mr. Pickwick hastily, "I want to speak to you about something else. Sit down."

"Thank'ee, Sir," said Sam. And down he sat without farther bidding, having previously deposited his old white hat on the landing outside the door. "Ta'nt a werry good 'un to look at," said Sam, "but it's an astonishin' 'un to wear; and afore the brim went, it was a werry handsome tile. Hows'ever it's lighter without it, that's one thing, and every hole lets in some air, that's another—wentilation gossamer I calls it." On the delivery of this sentiment, Mr. Weller smiled agreeably upon the assembled Pickwickians.

"Now with regard to the matter on which I, with the concurrence of these gentlemen, sent for you," said Mr. Pickwick.

"That's the pint, Sir," interposed Sam; "out vith it, as the father said to the child, ven he swallowed a farden."

"We want to know, in the first place," said Mr. Pickwick, "whether you have any reason to be discontented with your present situation."

"Afore I answers that 'ere question, gen'l'm'n," replied Mr. Weller, "I should like to know, in the first place, whether you're a goin' to purwide me vith a better."

A sunbeam of placid benevolence played on Mr. Pickwick's features as he said, "I have half made up my mind to engage you myself."

"Have you, though?" said Sam.

Mr. Pickwick nodded in the affirmative.

"Wages?" inquired Sam.

"Twelve pounds a year," replied Mr. Pickwick.

"Clothes?"

"Two suits."

"Work?"

"To attend upon me; and travel about with me and these gentlemen here."

"Take the bill down," said Sam, emphatically. "I'm let to a single gentleman, and the terms is agreed upon."

"You accept the situation?" inquired Mr. Pickwick.

"Cert'nly," replied Sam. "If the clothes fits me half as well as the place, they'll do."

"You can get a character of course?" said Mr. Pickwick.

"Ask the landlady o' the White Hart about that, Sir," replied Sam.

"Can you come this evening?"

"I'll get into the clothes this minute, if they're here," said Sam with great alacrity.

"Call at eight this evening," said Mr. Pickwick; "and if the inquiries are satisfactory, they shall be provided."

With the single exception of one amiable indiscretion, in which an assistant housemaid had equally participated, the history of Mr. Weller's conduct was so very blameless, that Mr. Pickwick felt fully justified in closing the engagement that very evening. With the promptness and energy which characterised not only the public proceedings, but all the private actions of this extraordinary man, he at once led his new attendant to one of those convenient emporiums where gentlemen's new and second-hand clothes are provided, and the troublesome and inconvenient formality of measurement dispensed with; and before night had closed in, Mr. Weller was furnished with a grey coat with the 'P. C.' button, a black hat with a cockade to it, a pink striped waistcoat, light breeches and gaiters, and a variety of other necessaries, too numerous to recapitulate.

"Well," said that suddenly-transformed individual, as he took his seat on the outside of the Eatanswill coach next morning; "I wonder vether I'm meant to be a footman, or a groom, or a gamekeeper, or a seedsman. I looks like a sort of compo of every one on 'em. Never mind; there's change of air, plenty to see, and little to do; and all this suits my complaint uncommon, so long life to the Pickvicks, says I."

CHAPTER XIII.

SOME ACCOUNT OF EATANSWILL: OF THE STATE OF PARTIES THEREIN; AND OF THE ELECTION OF A MEMBER TO SERVE IN PARLIAMENT FOR THAT ANCIENT, LOYAL, AND PATRIOTIC BOROUGH.

WE will frankly acknowledge, that up to the period of our being first immersed in the voluminous papers of the Pickwick club, we had never heard of Eatanswill; we will with equal candour admit, that we have in vain searched for proof of the actual existence of such a place at the present day. Knowing the deep reliance to be placed on every note and statement of Mr. Pickwick's, and not presuming to set up our recollection against the recorded declarations of that great man, we have consulted every authority, bearing upon the subject, to which we could possibly refer. We have traced every name in schedules A and B, without meeting with that of Eatanswill; we have minutely examined every corner of the Pocket County Maps issued for the benefit of society by our distinguished publishers, and the same result has attended our investigation. We are therefore led to believe, that Mr. Pickwick, with that anxious desire to abstain from giving offence to any, and with those delicate feelings for which all who knew him well know he was so eminently remarkable, purposely substituted a fictitious designation, for the real name of the place in which his observations were made. We are confirmed in this belief by a little circumstance, apparently slight and trivial in itself, but when considered in this point of view, not undeserving of notice. In Mr. Pickwick's note-book, we can just trace an entry of the fact, that the places of himself and followers were booked by the Norwich coach; but this entry was afterwards lined through, as if for the purpose of concealing even the direction in which the borough is situated. We will not, therefore, hazard a guess upon the subject, but will at once proceed with this history; content with the materials which its characters have provided for us.

It appears, then, that the Eatanswill people, like the people of many other small towns, considered themselves of the utmost and most mighty importance, and that every man in Eatanswill, conscious of the weight that attached to his example, felt himself bound to unite, heart and soul, with one of the two great parties that divided the town—the Blues and the Buffs. Now the Blues lost no opportunity of opposing the Buffs, and the Buffs lost no opportunity of opposing the Blues; and the consequence was, that whenever the Buffs and Blues met together at public meeting, Town-Hall, fair, or market, disputes and high words arose between them. With these dissensions it is almost superfluous to say that every thing in Eatanswill was made a party-question. If the Buffs proposed to new skylight the market-place, the Blues got up public meetings, and denounced the proceeding; if the Blues proposed the erection of an additional pump in the High Street, the Buffs rose as one man and stood aghast at the enormity. There were Blue shops and Buff shops, Blue inns and Buff inns;—there was a Blue aisle and a Buff aisle, in the very church itself.

Of course it was essentially and indispensably necessary that each of these powerful parties should have its chosen organ and representative: and, accordingly, there were two newspapers in the town—the Eatanswill Gazette and the Eatanswill Independent; the former advocating Blue principles, and the latter conducted on grounds decidedly Buff. Fine newspapers they were. Such leading articles, and such spirited attacks!—"Our worthless contemporary the Gazette"—"That disgraceful and dastardly journal, the Independent"—"That false and scurrilous print, the Independent"—"That vile and slanderous calumniator, the Gazette;"—these, and other spirit-stirring denunciations were strewn plentifully over the columns of each, in every number, and excited feelings of the most intense delight and indignation in the bosoms of the townspeople.

Mr. Pickwick, with his usual foresight and sagacity, had chosen a peculiarly desirable moment for his visit to the borough. Never was such a contest known. The Honourable Samuel Slumkey, of Slumkey Hall, was the Blue candidate; and Horatio Fizkin, Esq., of Fizkin Lodge, near Eatanswill, had been prevailed upon by his friends to stand forward on the Buff interest. The Gazette warned the electors of Eatanswill that the eyes not only of England, but of the whole civilised world, were upon them; and the Independent imperatively demanded to know, whether the constituency of Eatanswill were the grand fellows they had always taken them for, or base and servile tools, undeserving alike of the name of Englishmen and the blessings of freedom. Never had such a commotion agitated the town before.

It was late in the evening, when Mr. Pickwick and his companions, assisted by Sam, dismounted from the roof of the Eatanswill coach. Large blue silk flags were flying from the windows of the Town Arms Inn, and bills were posted in every sash, intimating, in gigantic letters, that the honourable Samuel Slumkey's Committee sat there daily. A crowd of idlers were assembled in the road, looking at a hoarse man in the balcony, who was apparently talking himself very red in the face in Mr. Slumkey's behalf; but the force and point of whose arguments were somewhat impaired by the perpetual beating of four large drums which Mr. Fizkin's committee had stationed at the street corner. There was a busy little man beside him, though, who took off his hat at intervals and motioned to the people to cheer, which they regularly did, most enthusiastically; and as the red-faced gentleman went on talking till he was redder in the face than ever, it seemed to answer his purpose quite as well as if anybody had heard him.

The Pickwickians had no sooner dismounted, than they were surrounded by a branch mob of the honest and independent, who forthwith set up three deafening cheers, which being responded to by the main body (for it's not at all necessary for a crowd to know what they are cheering about), swelled into a tremendous roar of triumph, which stopped even the red-faced man in the balcony.

"Hurrah!" shouted the mob in conclusion.

"One cheer more," screamed the little fugleman in the balcony; and out shouted the mob again, as if lungs were cast iron, with steel works.

"Slumkey for ever!" roared the honest and independent.

"Slumkey for ever!" echoed Mr. Pickwick, taking off his hat.

"No Fizkin," roared the crowd.

"Certainly not," shouted Mr. Pickwick.

"Hurrah!" And then there was another roaring, like that of a whole menagerie when the elephant has rung the bell for the cold meat.

"Who is Slumkey?" whispered Mr. Tupman.

"I don't know," replied Mr. Pickwick in the same tone. "Hush. Don't ask any questions. It's always best on these occasions to do what the mob do."

"But suppose there are two mobs?" suggested Mr. Snodgrass.

"Shout with the largest," replied Mr. Pickwick.

Volumes could not have said more.

They entered the house, the crowd opening right and left to let them pass, and cheering vociferously. The first object of consideration was to secure quarters for the night.

"Can we have beds here?" inquired Mr. Pickwick, summoning the waiter.

"Don't know, Sir," replied the man; "afraid we're full, Sir—I'll inquire, sir." Away he went for that purpose, and presently returned, to ask whether the gentlemen were "Blue."

As neither Mr. Pickwick nor his companions took any vital interest in the cause of either candidate, the question was rather a difficult one to answer. In this dilemma Mr. Pickwick bethought himself of his new friend, Mr. Perker.

"Do you know a gentleman of the name of Perker?" inquired Mr. Pickwick.

"Certainly, Sir; honourable Mr. Samuel Slumkey's agent."

"He is Blue, I think?"

"Oh yes, Sir."

"Then *we* are Blue," said Mr. Pickwick; but observing that the man looked rather doubtful at this accommodating announcement, he gave him his card, and desired him to present it to Mr. Perker forthwith, if he should happen to be in the house. The waiter retired; and re-appearing almost immediately with a request that Mr. Pickwick would follow him, led the way to a large room on the first floor, where, seated at a long table covered with books and papers, was Mr. Perker.

"Ah—ah my dear Sir," said the little man, advancing to meet him; "very happy to see you, my dear Sir, very. Pray sit down. So you have carried your intention into effect. You have come down here to see an election—eh?"

Mr. Pickwick replied in the affirmative.

"Spirited contest, my dear Sir," said the little man.

"I am delighted to hear it," said Mr. Pickwick, rubbing his hands. "I like to see sturdy patriotism, on whatever side it is called forth;—and so it's a spirited contest?"

"Oh yes," said the little man, "very much so indeed. We have opened all the public houses in the place, and left our adversary nothing but the beer-shops—masterly stroke of policy, my dear Sir, eh?"—and the little man smiled complacently, and took a large pinch of snuff.

"And what are the probabilities as to the result of the contest?" inquired Mr. Pickwick.

"Why doubtful, my dear Sir; rather doubtful as yet," replied the little man. "Fizkin's people have got three-and-thirty voters in the lock-up coach-house at the White Hart."

"In the coach-house!" said Mr. Pickwick, considerably astonished by this second stroke of policy.

"They keep 'em locked up there, till they want 'em," resumed the little man. "The effect of that is, you see, to prevent our getting at them; and even if we could, it would be of no use, for they keep them very drunk on purpose. Smart fellow Fizkin's agent—very smart fellow indeed."

Mr. Pickwick stared, but said nothing.

"We are pretty confident, though," said Mr. Perker, sinking his voice almost to a whisper. "We had a little tea-party here, last night—five-and-forty women, my dear Sir—and gave every one of 'em a green parasol when she went away."

"A parasol!" said Mr. Pickwick.

"Fact, my dear Sir, fact. Five-and-forty green parasols, at seven and six-pence a-piece. All women like finery,—extraordinary the effect of those parasols. Secured all their husbands, and half their brothers—beats stockings, and flannel, and all that sort of thing hollow. My idea, my dear Sir, entirely. Hail, rain, or sunshine, you can't

walk half a dozen yards up the street, without encountering half a dozen green parasols."

Here the little man indulged in a convulsion of mirth, which was only checked by the entrance of a third party.

This was a tall, thin man, with a sandy-coloured head inclined to baldness, and a face in which solemn importance was blended with a look of unfathomable profundity. He was dressed in a long brown surtout, with a black cloth waistcoat, and drab trousers. A double eye-glass dangled at his waistcoat: and on his head he wore a very low-crowned hat with a broad brim. The new comer was introduced to Mr. Pickwick as Mr. Pott, the editor of the Eatanswill Gazette. After a few preliminary remarks, Mr. Pott turned round to Mr. Pickwick, and said with solemnity—

"This contest excites great interest in the metropolis, Sir?"

"I believe it does," said Mr. Pickwick.

"To which I have reason to know," said Pott, looking towards Mr. Perker for corroboration,—"to which I have reason to know my article of last Saturday in some degree contributed."

"Not the least doubt of that," said the little man.

"The press is a mighty engine, Sir," said Pott.

Mr. Pickwick yielded his fullest assent to the proposition.

"But I trust, Sir," said Pott, "that I have never abused the enormous power I wield. I trust, Sir, that I have never pointed the noble instrument which is placed in my hands, against the sacred bosom of private life, or the tender breast of individual reputation;—I trust, Sir, that I have devoted my energies to—to endeavours—humble they may be, humble I know they are—to instil those principles of—which—are—"

Here the editor of the Eatanswill Gazette, appearing to ramble, Mr. Pickwick came to his relief, and said—

"Certainly."

"And what, Sir"—said Pott—"what, Sir, let me ask you as an impartial man, is the state of the public mind in London, with reference to my contest with the Independent?"

"Greatly excited, no doubt," interposed Mr. Perker, with a look of slyness which was very likely accidental.

"That contest," said Pott, "shall be prolonged so long as I have health and strength, and that portion of talent with which I am gifted. From that contest, Sir, although it may unsettle men's minds and excite their feelings, and render them incapable for the discharge of the every-day duties of ordinary life; from that contest, Sir, I will never shrink, till I have set my heel upon the Eatanswill Independent. I wish the people of London, and the people of this country to know, Sir, that they may rely upon me;—that I will not desert them, that I am resolved to stand by them, Sir, to the last."

"Your conduct is most noble, Sir," said Mr. Pickwick; and he grasped the hand of the magnanimous Pott.

"You are, Sir, I perceive, a man of sense and talent," said Mr. Pott, almost breathless with the vehemence of his patriotic declaration. "I am most happy, Sir, to make the acquaintance of such a man."

"And I," said Mr. Pickwick," feel deeply honoured by this expression of your opinion. Allow me, Sir, to introduce you to my fellow-travellers, the other corresponding members of the club I am proud to have founded."

"I shall be delighted," said Mr. Pott.

Mr. Pickwick withdrew, and returning with his three friends, presented them in due form to the editor of the Eatanswill Gazette.

"Now my dear Pott," said little Mr. Perker, "the question is, what are we to do with our friends here?"

"We can stop in this house, I suppose," said Mr. Pickwick.

"Not a spare bed in the house, my dear Sir—not a single bed."

"Extremely awkward," said Mr. Pickwick.

"Very;" said his fellow-voyagers.

"I have an idea upon this subject," said Mr. Pott, "which I think may be very successfully adopted. They have two beds at the Peacock, and I can boldly say, on behalf of Mrs. Pott, that she will be delighted to accommodate Mr. Pickwick and any one of his friends, if the other two gentlemen and their servant do not object to shifting, as they best can, at the Peacock."

After repeated pressings on the part of Mr. Pott, and repeated protestations on that of Mr. Pickwick that he could not think of incommoding or troubling his amiable wife, it was decided that this was the only feasible arrangement that could be made. So it *was* made; and after dining together at the Town Arms, the friends separated, Mr. Tupman and Mr. Snodgrass repairing to the Peacock, and Mr. Pickwick and Mr. Winkle proceeding to the mansion of Mr. Pott; it having been previously arranged that they should all re-assemble at the Town Arms in the morning, and accompany the honourable Samuel Slumkey's procession to the place of nomination.

Mr. Pott's domestic circle was limited to himself and his wife. All men whom mighty genius has raised to a proud eminence in the world, have usually some little weakness which appears the more conspicuous from the contrast it presents to their general character. If Mr. Pott had a weakness, it was, perhaps, that he was *rather* too submissive to the somewhat contemptuous control and sway of his wife. We do not feel justified in laying any particular stress upon the fact, because on the present occasion all Mrs. Pott's most winning ways were brought into requisition to receive the two gentlemen.

"My dear," said Mr. Pott, "Mr. Pickwick—Mr. Pickwick of London."

Mrs. Pott received Mr. Pickwick's paternal grasp of the hand with enchanting sweetness: and Mr. Winkle, who had not been announced at all, slided and bowed, unnoticed in an obscure corner.

"P. my dear—" said Mrs. Pott.

"My life," said Mr. Pott.

"Pray introduce the other gentleman."

"I beg a thousand pardons," said Mr Pott. "Permit me—Mrs. Pott, Mr. —"

"Winkle," said Mr. Pickwick.

"Winkle," echoed Mr. Pott; and the ceremony of introduction was complete.

"We owe you many apologies, Ma'am," said Mr. Pickwick, "for disturbing your domestic arrangements at so short a notice."

"I beg you won't mention it, Sir," replied the feminine Pott, with vivacity. "It is a high treat to me, I assure you, to see any new faces; living as I do, from day to day, and week to week, in this dull place, and seeing nobody."

"Nobody, my dear!" exclaimed Mr. Pott, archly.

"Nobody but *you*," retorted Mrs. Pott, with asperity.

"You see, Mr. Pickwick," said the host in explanation of his wife's lament, "that we are in some measure cut off from many enjoyments and pleasures of which we might otherwise partake. My public station, as editor of the Eatanswill Gazette, the position which that paper holds in the country, my constant immersion in the vortex of politics—"

"P. my dear—" interposed Mrs. Pott.

"My life—" said the editor.

"I wish, my dear, you would endeavour to find some topic of conversation in which these gentlemen might take some rational interest."

"But my love," said Mr. Pott, with great humility, "Mr. Pickwick does take an interest in it."

"It's well for him if he can," said Mrs. Pott, emphatically; "I am wearied out of my life with your politics, and quarrels with the Independent, and nonsense. I am quite astonished P. at your making such an exhibition of your absurdity."

"But my dear—" said Mr. Pott.

"Oh, nonsense, don't talk to me;" said Mrs. Pott. "Do you play *écarte*, Sir?"

"I shall be very happy to learn, under your tuition," replied Mr. Winkle.

"Well, then, draw that little table into this window, and let me get out of hearing of those prosy politics."

"Jane," said Mr. Pott, to the servant who brought in candles, "go down into the office, and bring me up the file of the Gazette for Eighteen Hundred and Twenty Eight. I'll just read you—" added the editor, turning to Mr. **Pickwick**, "I'll just read you a few of the leaders I wrote at that time, upon the Buff job of appointing a new toll-man to the turnpike here; I rather think they'll amuse you."

"I should like to hear them very much, indeed," said Mr. Pickwick.

Up came the file, and down sat the editor, with Mr. Pickwick at his side.

We have in vain pored over the leaves of Mr. Pickwick's note-book, in the hope of meeting with a general summary of these beautiful compositions. We have every reason to believe that he was perfectly enraptured with the vigour and freshness of the style; indeed Mr. Winkle has recorded the fact that his eyes were closed, as if with excess of pleasure, during the whole time of their perusal.

The announcement of supper put a stop both to the game at *écarte*, and the recapitulation of the beauties of the Eatanswill Gazette. Mrs. Pott was in the highest spirits and the most agreeable humour. Mr. Winkle had already made considerable progress in her good opinion, and she did not hesitate to inform him, confidentially, that Mr. Pickwick was "a delightful old dear." These terms convey a familiarity of expression, in which few of those who were intimately acquainted with that colossal-minded man, would have presumed to indulge. We have preserved them, nevertheless, as affording at once a touching and a convincing proof of the estimation in which he was held by every class of society, and the ease with which he made his way to their hearts and feelings.

It was a late hour of the night—long after Mr. Tupman and Mr. Snodgrass had fallen asleep in the inmost recesses of the Peacock—when the two friends retired to rest. Slumber soon fell upon the senses of Mr. Winkle, but his feelings had been excited, and his admiration roused; and for many hours after sleep had rendered him insensible to earthly objects, the face and figure of the agreeable Mrs. Pott presented themselves again and again to his wandering imagination.

The noise and bustle which ushered in the morning, were sufficient to dispel from the mind of the most romantic visionary in existence, any associations but those which were immediately connected with the rapidly-approaching election. The beating of drums, the blowing of horns and trumpets, the shouting of men, and tramping of horses, echoed and re-echoed through the streets from the earliest dawn of day; and an occasional fight between the light skirmishers of either party, at once enlivened the preparations, and agreeably diversified their character.

"Well, Sam," said Mr. Pickwick, as his valet appeared at his bed-room door, just as he was concluding his toilet; "all alive to-day, I suppose?"

"Reg'lar game, Sir," replied Mr. Weller; "our people's a col-lecting down at the Town Arms, and they're a hollering themselves hoarse already."

"Ah," said Mr. Pickwick, "do they seem devoted to their party, Sam?"

"Never see such dewotion in my life, Sir."

"Energetic, eh?" said Mr. Pickwick.

"Uncommon," replied Sam; "I never see men eat and drink so much afore. I wonder they a'nt afeer'd o' bustin'."

"That's the mistaken kindness of the gentry here," said Mr. Pickwick.

"Werry likely," replied Sam, briefly.

"Fine, fresh, hearty fellows they seem," said Mr. Pickwick, glancing from the window.

"Werry fresh," replied Sam; "me and the two waiters at the Peacock, has been a pumpin' over the independent woters as supped there last night."

"Pumping over independent voters!" exclaimed Mr. Pickwick.

"Yes," said his attendant, "every man slept vere he fell down; we dragged 'em out, one by one, this mornin' and put 'em under the pump, and they're in reg'lar fine order, now. Shillin' a head the committee paid for that 'ere job."

"Can such things be!" exclaimed the astonished Mr. Pickwick.

"Lord bless your heart, Sir," said Sam, "why where was you half baptized?—that's nothin', that a'nt."

"Nothing?" said Mr. Pickwick.

"Nothin' at all, Sir," replied his attendant. "The night afore the last day o' the last election here, the opposite party bribed the bar-maid at the Town Arms, to hocus the brandy and water of fourteen unpolled electors as was a stoppin' in the house."

"What do you mean by 'hocussing' brandy and water?" inquired Mr. Pickwick.

"Puttin' laud'num in it," replied Sam. "Blessed if she didn't send 'em all to sleep till twelve hours arter the election was over. They took one man up to the booth, in a truck, fast asleep, by way of experiment, but it was no go—they wouldn't poll him; so they brought him back, and put him to bed again."

"Strange practices, these," said Mr. Pickwick; half speaking to himself, and half addressing Sam.

"Not half so strange as a miraculous circumstance as happened to my own father, at an election-time, in this wery place, Sir," replied Sam.

"What was that?" inquired Mr. Pickwick.

"Why he drove a coach down here once," said Sam; "'lection time came on, and he was engaged by vun party to bring down woters from London. Night afore he was a going to drive up, committee on t'other side sends for him quietly, and away he goes vith the messenger, who shows him in;—large room—lots of gen'l'm'n—heaps of papers, pens and ink, and all that 'ere. 'Ah, Mr. Weller,' says the gen'l'm'n in the chair, 'glad to see you, Sir; how are you?'—'Werry well, thank'ee, Sir,' says my father; 'I hope *you're* pretty middlin,' says he—'Pretty well, thank'ee, Sir,' says the gen'l'm'n; 'sit down, Mr. Weller—pray sit down, Sir.' So my father sits down, and he and the gen'l'm'n looks wery hard at each other. 'You don't remember me?' says the gen'l'm'n.—'Can't say I do,' says my father—'Oh, I know you,' says the gen'l'm'n; 'know'd you ven you was a boy,' says he.—'Well, I don't remember you,' says my father—'That's wery odd,' says the gen'l'm'n—'Wery,' says my father—'You must have a bad mem'ry, Mr. Weller,' says the gen'l'm'n—'Well, it is a wery bad 'un,' says my father—'I thought so,' says the gen'l'm'n. So then they pours him out a glass o' wine, and gammons him about his driving, and gets him into a reg'lar good humour, and at last shoves a twenty pound note in his hand. 'It's a wery bad road between this and London,' says the gen'l'm'n—'Here and there it *is* a wery heavy road,' says my father—''Specially near the canal, I think,' says the gen'l'm'n—'Nasty bit, that 'ere,' says my father—'Well, Mr. Weller,' says the gen'l'm'n, 'you're a wery good whip, and can do what you like with your horses, we know. We're all wery fond o' you, Mr. Weller, so in case you *should* have an accident when you're a bringing these here woters down, and *should* tip 'em over into the canal vithout hurtin' 'em, this is for yourself,' says he—'Gen'l'm'n, you're wery kind,' says my father, 'and I'll drink your health in another glass of wine,' says he; vich he did, and then buttons up the money, and bows himself out. You wouldn't believe, Sir," continued Sam, with a look of inexpressible impudence at his master, "that on the wery day as he came down with them woters, his coach *was* upset on that 'ere wery spot, and ev'ry man on 'em was turned into the canal."

"And got out again?" inquired Mr. Pickwick, hastily.

"Why," replied Sam, very slowly, "I rather think one old gentleman was missin'; I know his hat was found, but I a'nt quite certain whether his head was in it or not. But what I look at, is the hex-traordinary, and wonderful coincidence, that arter what that gen'l'm'n said my father's coach should be upset in that wery place, and on that wery day!"

"It is, no doubt, a very extraordinary circumstance indeed," said Mr. Pickwick. "But brush my hat, Sam, for I hear Mr. Winkle calling me to breakfast."

With these words Mr. Pickwick descended to the parlour, where he found breakfast laid, and the family already assembled. The meal was hastily despatched; each of the gentlemen's hats was decorated with an enormous blue favour, made up by the fair hands of Mrs. Pott herself; and as Mr. Winkle had undertaken to escort that lady to a house top, in the immediate vicinity of the hustings, Mr. Pickwick and Mr. Pott repaired alone to the Town Arms, from the back window of which, one of Mr. Slumkey's committee was addressing six small boys, and one girl, whom he dignified, at every second sentence, with the imposing title of "men of Eatanswill," whereat the six small boys aforesaid cheered prodigiously.

The stable-yard exhibited unequivocal symptoms of the glory and strength of the Eatanswill Blues. There was a regular army of blue flags, some with one handle, and some with two, exhibiting appropriate devices, in golden characters four feet high, and stout in proportion. There was a grand band of trumpets, bassoons and drums, marshalled four abreast, and earning their money, if ever men did, especially the drum beaters, who were very muscular. There were bodies of constables with blue staves, twenty committee-men with blue scarfs, and a mob of voters with blue cockades. There were electors on horseback, and electors a-foot. There was an open carriage and four, for the honourable Samuel Slumkey; and there were four carriages and pair, for his friends and supporters: and the flags were rustling, and the band was playing, and the constables were swearing, and the twenty committee-men were squabbling, and the mob were shouting, and the horses were backing, and the post-boys perspiring; and everybody, and everything, then and there assembled, was for the special use, behoof, honour, and renown, of the honourable Samuel Slumkey of Slumkey Hall, one of the candidates for the representation of the Borough of Eatanswill, in the Commons House of Parliament of the United Kingdom.

Loud and long were the cheers, and mighty was the rustling of one of the blue flags, with "Liberty of the Press" inscribed thereon, when the sandy head of Mr. Pott was discerned in one of the windows, by the mob beneath; and tremendous was the enthusiasm when the honourable Samuel Slumkey himself, in top boots, and a blue neckerchief, advanced and seized the hand of the said Pott, and melo-dramatically testified by gestures to the crowd, his ineffaceable obligations to the Eatanswill Gazette.

"Is everything ready?" said the honourable Samuel Slumkey to Mr. Perker.

"Everything, my dear Sir," was the little man's reply.

"Nothing has been omitted, I hope?" said the honourable Samuel Slumkey.

"Nothing has been left undone, my dear Sir—nothing whatever. There are twenty washed men at the street door for you to shake hands with; and six children in arms that you're to pat on the head, and inquire the age of; be particular about the children, my dear Sir,—it has always a great effect, that sort of thing."

"I'll take care," said the honourable Samuel Slumkey.

"And, perhaps, my dear Sir—" said the cautious little man, "perhaps if you could—I don't mean to say it's indispensable—but if you could manage to kiss one of 'em, it would produce a very great impression on the crowd."

"Wouldn't it have as good an effect if the proposer or seconder did that?" said the honourable Samuel Slumkey.

"Why, I am afraid it wouldn't," replied the agent; "if it were done by yourself, my dear Sir, I think it would make you very popular."

"Very well," said the honourable Samuel Slumkey, with a resigned air, "then it must be done. That's all."

"Arrange the procession," cried the twenty committeemen.

Amidst the cheers of the assembled throng, the band, and the constables, and the committee-men, and the voters, and the horsemen, and the carriages, took their places—

each of the two-horse vehicles being closely packed with as many gentlemen as could manage to stand upright in it; and that assigned to Mr. Perker, containing Mr. Pickwick, Mr. Tupman, Mr. Snodgrass, and about half a dozen of the committee beside.

There was a moment of awful suspense as the procession waited for the honourable Samuel Slumkey to step into his carriage. Suddenly the crowd set up a great cheering.

"He has come out," said little Mr. Perker, greatly excited; the more so as their position did not enable them to see what was going forward.

Another cheer, much louder.

"He has shaken hands with the men," cried the little agent.

Another cheer, far more vehement.

"He has patted the babes on the head," said Mr. Perker, trembling with anxiety.

A roar of applause that rent the air.

"He has kissed one of 'em!" exclaimed the delighted little man.

A second roar.

"He has kissed another," gasped the excited manager.

A third roar.

"He's kissing 'em all!" screamed the enthusiastic little gentleman. And hailed by the deafening shouts of the multitude, the procession moved on.

How or by what means it became mixed up with the other procession, and how it was ever extricated from the confusion consequent thereupon, is more than we can undertake to describe, inasmuch as Mr. Pickwick's hat was knocked over his eyes, nose, and mouth, by one poke of a Buff flag staff, very early in the proceedings. He describes himself as being surrounded on every side, when he could catch a glimpse of the scene, by angry and ferocious countenances, by a vast cloud of dust, and by a dense crowd of combatants. He represents himself as being forced from the carriage by some unseen power, and being personally engaged in a pugilistic encounter; but with whom, or how, or why, he is wholly unable to state. He then felt himself forced up some wooden steps by the persons from behind: and on removing his hat, found himself surrounded by his friends, in the very front of the left hand side of the hustings. The right was reserved for the Buff party, and the centre for the mayor and his officers; one of whom—the fat crier of Eatanswill—was ringing an enormous bell, by way of commanding silence, while Mr. Horatio Fizkin and the Honourable Samuel Slumkey, with their hands upon their hearts, were bowing with the utmost affability to the troubled sea of heads that inundated the open space in front; and from whence arose a storm of groans, and shouts, and yells, and hootings, that would have done honour to an earthquake.

"There's Winkle," said Mr. Tupman, pulling his friend by the sleeve.

"Where?" said Mr. Pickwick, putting on his spectacles, which he had fortunately kept in his pocket hitherto.

"There," said Mr. Tupman, "on the top of that house." And there sure enough, in the leaden gutter of a tiled roof, were Mr. Winkle and Mrs. Pott, comfortably seated in a couple of chairs, waving their handkerchiefs in token of recognition—a compliment which Mr. Pickwick returned by kissing his hand to the lady.

The proceedings had not yet commenced; and as an inactive crowd is generally disposed to be jocose, this very innocent action was sufficient to awaken their facetiousness.

"Oh you wicked old rascal," cried one voice, "looking arter the girls, are you?"

"Oh you wenerable sinner," cried another.

"Putting on his spectacles to look at a married 'ooman!" said a third.

"I see him a winkin at her, vith his wicked old eye," shouted a fourth.

"Look arter your wife, Pott," bellowed a fifth;—and then there was a roar of laughter.

As these taunts were accompanied with invidious comparisons between Mr. Pickwick and an aged ram, and several witticisms of the like nature; and as they moreover rather tended to convey reflections upon the honour of an innocent lady, Mr. Pickwick's indignation was excessive; but as silence was proclaimed at the moment, he contented himself by scorching the mob with a look of pity for their misguided minds, at which they laughed more boisterously than ever.

"Silence," roared the mayor's attendants.

"Whiffin, proclaim silence," said the mayor, with an air of pomp befitting his lofty station. In obedience to this command the crier performed another concerto on the bell, whereupon a gentleman in the crowd called out "muffins;" which occasioned another laugh.

"Gentlemen," said the Mayor, at as loud a pitch as he could possibly force his voice to, "Gentlemen. Brother electors of the Borough of Eatanswill. We are met here to-day, for the purpose of choosing a representative in the room of our late—"

Here the Mayor was interrupted by a voice in the crowd.

"Suc-cess to the Mayor!" cried the voice, "and may he never desert the nail and sarspan business, as he got his money by."

This allusion to the professional pursuits of the orator was received with a storm of delight, which, with a bell-accompaniment, rendered the remainder of his speech inaudible, with the exception of the concluding sentence, in which he thanked the meeting for the patient attention with which they had heard him throughout,—an expression of gratitude which elicited another burst of mirth, of about a quarter of an hour's duration.

Next, a tall thin gentleman, in a very stiff white neckerchief, after being repeatedly desired by the crowd to "send a boy home, to ask whether he hadn't left his woice under the pillow," begged to nominate a fit and proper person to represent them in Parliament. And when he said it was Horatio Fizkin, Esquire, of Fizkin Lodge, near Eatanswill, the Fizkinites applauded, and the Slumkeyites groaned, so long, and so loudly, that both he and the seconder might have sung comic songs in lieu of speaking, without anybody's being a bit the wiser.

The friends of Horatio Fizkin, Esquire, having had their innings, a little choleric, pink-faced man stood forward to propose another fit and proper person to represent the electors of Eatanswill in Parliament; and very swimmingly the pink-faced gentleman would have got on, if he had not been rather too choleric to entertain a sufficient perception of the fun of the crowd. But after a very few sentences of figurative eloquence, the pink-faced gentleman got from denouncing those who interrupted him in the mob, to exchanging defiances with the gentlemen on the hustings;

whereupon arose an uproar which reduced him to the necessity of expressing his feelings by serious pantomime, which he did, and then left the stage to his seconder, who delivered a written speech of half an hour's length, and wouldn't be stopped, because he had sent it all to the Eatanswill Gazette, and the Eatanswill Gazette had printed it, every word.

Then Horatio Fizkin, Esquire, of Fizkin Lodge, near Eatanswill, presented himself for the purpose of addressing the electors; which he no sooner did, than the band employed by the honourable Samuel Slumkey, commenced performing with a power to which their strength in the morning was a trifle; in return for which, the Buff crowd belaboured the heads and shoulders of the Blue crowd; on which the Blue crowd endeavoured to dispossess themselves of their very unpleasant neighbours the Buff crowd; and a scene of struggling, and pushing, and fighting, succeeded, to which we can no more do justice than the Mayor could, although he issued imperative orders to twelve constables to seize the ringleaders, who might amount in number to two hundred and fifty, or thereabouts. At all these encounters, Horatio Fizkin, Esquire, of Fizkin Lodge, and his friends, waxed fierce and furious; until at last Horatio Fizkin, Esquire, of Fizkin Lodge, begged to ask his opponent, the honourable Samuel Slumkey, of Slumkey Hall, whether that band played by his consent; which question the honourable Samuel Slumkey declining to answer, Horatio Fizkin, Esquire, of Fizkin Lodge, shook his fist in the countenance of the honourable Samuel Slumkey, of Slumkey Hall; upon which the honourable Samuel Slumkey, his blood being up, defied Horatio Fizkin, Esquire, to mortal combat. At this violation of all known rules and precedents of order, the Mayor commanded another fantasia on the bell, and declared that he would bring before himself, both Horatio Fizkin, Esquire, of Fizkin Lodge, and the honourable Samuel Slumkey, of Slumkey Hall, and bind them over to keep the peace. Upon this terrific denunciation, the supporters of the two candidates interfered, and after the friends of each party had quarrelled in pairs for three-quarters of an hour, Horatio Fizkin, Esquire, touched his hat to the honourable Samuel Slumkey: the honourable Samuel Slumkey touched his to Horatio Fizkin, Esquire: the band was stopped, the crowd were partially quieted, and Horatio Fizkin, Esquire, was permitted to proceed.

The speeches of the two candidates, though differing in every other respect, afforded a beautiful tribute to the merit and high worth of the electors of Eatanswill. Both expressed their opinion that a more independent, a more enlightened, a more public-spirited, a more noble-minded, a more disinterested set of men than those who had promised to vote for him, never existed on earth; each darkly hinted his suspicions that the electors in the opposite interest had certain swinish and besotted infirmities which rendered them unfit for the exercise of the important duties they were called upon to discharge. Fizkin expressed his readiness to do anything he was wanted; Slumkey, his determination to do nothing that was asked of him. Both said that the trade, the manufactures, the commerce, the prosperity, of Eatanswill, would ever be dearer to their hearts than any earthly object; and each had it in his power to state, with the utmost confidence, that he was the man who would eventually be returned.

There was a show of hands; the Mayor decided in

favour of the honourable Samuel Slumkey, of Slumkey Hall. Horatio Fizkin, Esquire, of Fizkin Lodge, demanded a poll, and a poll was fixed accordingly. Then a vote of thanks was moved to the Mayor for his able conduct in the chair; and the Mayor devoutly wishing that he had had a chair to display his able conduct in (for he had been standing during the whole proceedings) returned thanks. The processions re-formed, the carriages rolled slowly through the crowd, and its members screeched and shouted after them as their feelings or caprice dictated.

During the whole time of the polling, the town was in a perpetual fever of excitement. Everything was conducted on the most liberal and delightful scale. Exciseable articles were remarkably cheap at all the public houses; and spring vans paraded the streets for the accommodation of voters who were seized with any temporary dizziness in the head—an epidemic which prevailed among the electors, during the contest, to a most alarming extent, and under the influence of which they might frequently be seen lying on the pavements in a state of utter insensibility. A small body of electors remained unpolled on the very last day. They were calculating and reflecting persons, who had not yet been convinced by the arguments of either party, although they had had frequent conferences with each. One hour before the close of the poll, Mr. Perker solicited the honour of a private interview with these intelligent, these noble, these patriotic men. It was granted. His arguments were brief, but satisfactory. They went in a body to the poll; and when they returned, the honourable Samuel Slumkey, of Slumkey Hall, was returned also.

CHAPTER XIV.

COMPRISING A BRIEF DESCRIPTION OF THE COMPANY AT THE PEACOCK ASSEMBLED; AND A TALE TOLD BY A BAGMAN.

It is pleasant to turn from contemplating the strife and turmoil of political existence, to the peaceful repose of private life. Although in reality no great partisan of either side, Mr. Pickwick was sufficiently fired with Mr. Pott's enthusiasm, to apply his whole time and attention to the proceedings, of which the last chapter affords a description compiled from his own memoranda. Nor while he was thus occupied was Mr. Winkle idle, his whole time being devoted to pleasant walks and short country excursions with Mrs. Pott, who never failed, when such an opportunity presented itself, to seek some relief from the tedious monotony she so constantly complained of. The two gentlemen being thus completely domesticated in the Editor's house, Mr. Tupman and Mr. Snodgrass were in a great measure cast upon their own resources. Taking but little interest in public affairs, they beguiled their time chiefly with such amusements as the Peacock afforded, which were limited to a bagatelle-board in the first floor, and a sequestered skittle-ground in the back yard. In the science and nicety of both these recreations, which are far more abstruse than ordinary men suppose, they were gradually initiated by Mr. Weller, who possessed a perfect knowledge of such pastimes. Thus, notwithstanding that they were in a great measure deprived of the comfort

and advantage of Mr. Pickwick's society, they were still enabled to beguile the time, and to prevent its hanging heavily on their hands.

It was in the evening, however, that the Peacock presented attractions which enabled the two friends to resist, even the invitations of the talented, though prosily inclined, Mr. Pott. It was in the evening that the "commercial room" was filled with a social circle, whose characters and manners it was the delight of Mr. Tupman to observe; whose sayings and doings it was the habit of Mr. Snodgrass to note down.

Most people know what sort of places commercial rooms usually are. That of the Peacock differed in no material respect from the generality of such apartments; that is to say, it was a large bare-looking room, the furniture of which had no doubt been better when it was newer, with a spacious table in the centre, and a variety of smaller dittos in the corners: an extensive assortment of variously shaped chairs, and an old Turkey carpet, bearing about the same relative proportion to the size of the room, as a lady's pocket-handkerchief might to the floor of a watch-box. The walls were garnished with one or two large maps; and several weather-beaten rough great coats, with complicated capes, dangled from a long row of pegs in one corner. The mantel-shelf was ornamented with a wooden inkstand, containing one stump of a pen and half a wafer, a road-book and directory, a county history minus the cover, and the mortal remains of a trout in a glass coffin. The atmosphere was redolent of tobacco-smoke, the fumes of which had communicated a rather dingy hue to the whole room, and more especially to the dusty red curtains which shaded the windows. On the sideboard, a variety of miscellaneous articles were huddled together, the most conspicuous of which were some very cloudy fish-sauce cruets, a couple of driving-boxes, two or three whips, and as many travelling shawls, a tray of knives and forks, and the mustard.

Here it was that Mr. Tupman and Mr. Snodgrass were seated on the evening after the conclusion of the election, with several other temporary inmates of the house, smoking and drinking.

"Well gents," said a stout, hale personage of about forty, with only one eye—a very bright black eye, which twinkled with a roguish expression of fun and good humour, "Our noble selves, gents. I always propose that toast to the company, and drink Mary to myself. Eh, Mary?"

"Get along with you, you wretch," said the handmaiden, obviously not ill pleased with the compliment, however.

"Don't go away, Mary," said the black-eyed man.

"Let me alone, imperence," said the young lady.

"Never mind," said the one-eyed man, calling after the girl as she left the room. "I'll step out by and by, Mary. Keep your spirits up, dear." Here he went through the not very difficult process of winking upon the company with his solitary eye, to the enthusiastic delight of an elderly personage with a dirty face and a clay pipe.

"Rum creeters is women," said the dirty-faced man, after a pause.

"Ah! no mistake about that," said a very red-faced man, behind a cigar.

After this little bit of philosophy there was another pause.

"There's rummer things than women in this world though, mind you," said the man with the black eye, slowly filling a large Dutch pipe, with a most capacious bowl

"Are you married?" inquired the dirty-faced man.

"Can't say I am."

"I thought not." Here the dirty-faced man fell into extasies of mirth at his own retort, in which he was joined by a man of bland voice and placid countenance, who always made it a point to agree with everybody.

"Women after all, gentlemen," said the enthusiastic Mr. Snodgrass, "are the great props and comforts of our existence."

"So they are," said the placid gentleman.

"When they're in a good humour," interposed the dirty-faced man.

"And that's very true," said the placid one.

"I repudiate that qualification," said Mr. Snodgrass, whose thoughts were fast reverting to Emily Wardle, "I repudiate it with disdain—with indignation. Show me the man who says anything against women, as women, and I boldly declare he is not a man." And Mr. Snodgrass took his cigar from his mouth, and struck the table violently with his clenched fist.

"That's good sound argument," said the placid man.

"Containing a position which I deny," interrupted he of the dirty countenance.

"And there's certainly a very great deal of truth in what you observe too, Sir," said the placid gentleman.

"Your health, Sir," said the bagman with the lonely eye, bestowing an approving nod on Mr. Snodgrass.

Mr. Snodgrass acknowledged the compliment.

"I always like to hear a good argument," continued the bagman, "a sharp one, like this; it's very improving; but this little argument about women brought to my mind a story I have heard an old uncle of mine tell, the recollection of which, just now, made me say there were rummer things than women to be met with, sometimes."

"I should like to hear that same story," said the red-faced man with the cigar.

"Should you?" was the only reply of the bagman, who continued to smoke with great vehemence.

"So should I," said Mr. Tupman, speaking for the first time. He was always anxious to increase his stock of experience.

"Should *you*? Well then, I'll tell it. No I won't. I know you won't believe it," said the man with the roguish eye, making that organ look more roguish than ever.

"If you say it's true, of course I shall," said Mr. Tupman.

"Well, upon that understanding I'll tell it," replied the traveller. "Did you ever hear of the great commercial house of Bilson and Slum? But it doesn't matter though, whether you did or not, because they retired from business long since. It's eighty years ago, since the circumstance happened to a traveller for that house, but he was a particular friend of my uncle's: and my uncle told the story to me. It's a queer name; but he used to call it

THE BAGMAN'S STORY,

and he used to tell it, something in this way.

"One winter's evening, about five o'clock, just as it began to grow dusk, a man in a gig might have been seen urging his tired horse along the road which leads across Marlborough Downs, in the direction of Bristol. I say he might have been seen, and I have no doubt he would have been, if anybody but a blind man had happened to pass that way; but the weather was so bad, and the night so cold and wet, that nothing was out but the water, and so the traveller jogged along in the middle of the road, lonesome and dreary enough. If any bagman of that day could have caught sight of the little neck-or-nothing sort of gig, with a clay-coloured body and red wheels, and the vixenish ill-tempered, fast-going bay mare, that looked like a cross between a butcher's horse and a twopenny post-office pony, he would have known at once, that this traveller could have been no other than Tom Smart, of the great house of Bilson and Slum, Cateaton Street, City. However, as there was no bagman to look on, nobody knew anything at all about the matter; and so Tom Smart and his clay-coloured gig with the red wheels, and the vixenish mare with the fast pace, went on together, keeping the secret among them, and nobody was a bit the wiser.

"There are many pleasanter places even in this dreary world, than Marlborough Downs when it blows hard; and if you throw in beside, a gloomy winter's evening, a miry and sloppy road, and a pelting fall of heavy rain, and try the effect, by way of experiment, in your own proper person, you will experience the full force of this observation.

"The wind blew—not up the road or down it, though that's bad enough, but sheer across it, sending the rain slanting down like the lines they used to rule in the copybooks at school, to make the boys slope well. For a moment it would die away, and the traveller would begin to delude himself into the belief that, exhausted with its previous fury, it had quietly lain itself down to rest, when, whoo! he would hear it growling and whistling in the distance, and on it would come rushing over the hill-tops, and sweeping along the plain, gathering sound and strength as it drew nearer, until it dashed with a heavy gust against horse and man, driving the sharp rain into their ears, and its cold damp breath into their very bones; and past them it would scour, far, far away, with a stunning roar, as if in ridicule of their weakness, and triumphant in the consciousness of its own strength and power.

"The bay mare splashed away, through the mud and water, with drooping ears, now and then tossing her head as if to express her disgust at this very ungentlemanly behaviour of the elements, but keeping a good pace notwithstanding, until a gust of wind, more furious than any that had yet assailed them, caused her to stop suddenly, and plant her four feet firmly against the ground, to prevent her being blown over. It's a special mercy that she did this, for if she *had* been blown over, the vixenish mare was so light, and the gig was so light, and Tom Smart such a light weight into the bargain, that they must infallibly have all gone rolling over and over together, until they reached the confines of earth, or until the wind fell; and in either case the probability is, that neither the vixenish mare, nor the clay-coloured gig with the red wheels, nor Tom Smart, would ever have been fit for service again.

"'Well, damn my straps and whiskers,' says Tom Smart, (Tom sometimes had an unpleasant knack of swearing), 'Damn my straps and whiskers,' says Tom, 'if this ain't pleasant, blow me.'

"You'll very likely ask me, why, as Tom Smart had been pretty well blown already, he expressed this wish to be submitted to the same process again. I can't say—all I know is, that Tom Smart said so—or at least he always told my uncle he said so, and it's just the same thing.

"'Blow me,' says Tom Smart; and the mare neighed as if she were precisely of the same opinion.

"'Cheer up old girl,' said Tom, patting the bay mare on the neck with the end of his whip. 'It won't do pushing on, such a night as this; the first house we come to we'll put up at, so the faster you go the sooner it's over. Soho, old girl—gently—gently.'

"Whether the vixenish mare was sufficiently well acquainted with the tones of Tom's voice to comprehend his meaning, or whether she found it colder standing still than moving on, of course I can't say. But I can say that Tom had no sooner finished speaking, than she pricked up her ears, and started forward at a speed which made the clay-coloured gig rattle till you would have supposed every one of the red spokes was going to fly out on the turf of Marlborough Downs; and even Tom, whip as he was, couldn't stop or check her pace, until she drew up, of her own accord, before a road-side inn on the right-hand side of the way, about half a quarter of a mile from the end of the Downs.

"Tom cast a hasty glance at the upper part of the house as he threw the reins to the hostler, and stuck the whip in the box. It was a strange old place, built of a kind of shingle, inlaid, as it were, with cross-beams, with gable-topped windows projecting completely over the pathway, and a low door with a dark porch, and a couple of steep steps leading down into the house, instead of the modern fashion of half a dozen shallow ones, leading up to it. It was a comfortable-looking place though, for there was a strong cheerful light in the bar-window, which shed a bright ray across the road, and even lighted up the hedge on the other side; and there was a red flickering light in the opposite window, one moment but faintly discernible, and the next gleaming strongly through the drawn curtains, which intimated that a rousing fire was blazing within. Marking these little evidences with the eye of an experienced traveller, Tom dismounted with as much agility as his half-frozen limbs would permit, and entered the house.

"In less than five minutes' time, Tom was ensconced in the room opposite the bar—the very room where he had imagined the fire blazing—before a substantial matter-of-fact roaring fire, composed of something short of a bushel of coals, and wood enough to make half a dozen decent gooseberry-bushes, piled half way up the chimney, and roaring and crackling with a sound that of itself would have warmed the heart of any reasonable man. This was comfortable, but this was not all, for a smartly dressed girl, with a bright eye and a neat ankle, was laying a very clean white cloth on the table; and as Tom sat with his slippered feet on the fender, and his back to the open door, he saw a charming prospect of the bar reflected in the glass over the chimney-piece, with delightful rows of green bottles and gold labels, together with jars of pickles and preserves, and cheeses and boiled hams, and rounds of beef, arranged on shelves in the most tempting and delicious array. Well, this was comfortable too; but even this was not all—for in the bar, seated at tea at the nicest possible little table, drawn close up before the brightest possible little fire, was a buxom widow of somewhere about eight and forty or thereabouts, with a face as comfortable as the bar, who was evidently the landlady of the house, and the supreme ruler over all these agreeable possessions. There was only one drawback to the beauty of the whole picture, and that was a tall man—a very tall man—in a brown coat and bright basket buttons, and black whiskers,

and wavy black hair, who was seated at tea with the widow, and who it required no great penetration to discover was in a fair way of persuading her to be a widow no longer, but to confer upon him the privilege of sitting down in that bar, for and during the whole remainder of the term of his natural life.

"Tom Smart was by no means of an irritable or envious disposition, but somehow or other the tall man with the brown coat and the bright basket buttons did rouse what little gall he had in his composition, and did make him feel extremely indignant, the more especially as he could now and then observe, from his seat before the glass, certain little affectionate familiarities passing between the tall man and the widow, which sufficiently denoted that the tall man was as high in favour as he was in size. Tom was fond of hot punch—I may venture to say he was very fond of hot punch—and after he had seen the vixenish mare well fed and well littered down, and eaten every bit of the nice little hot dinner which the widow tossed up for him with her own hands, he just ordered a tumbler of it, by way of experiment. Now if there was one thing in the whole range of domestic art, which the widow could manufacture better than another, it was this identical article; and the first tumbler was adapted to Tom Smart's taste with such peculiar nicety, that he ordered a second with the least possible delay. Hot punch is a pleasant thing, gentlemen—an extremely pleasant thing under any circumstances—but in that snug little parlour, before the roaring fire, with the wind blowing outside till every timber in the old house creaked again, Tom Smart found it perfectly delightful. He ordered another tumbler, and then another—I am not quite certain whether he didn't order another after that—but the more he drank of the hot punch the more he thought of the tall man.

"'Confound his impudence,' said Tom Smart to himself, 'what business has he in that snug bar? Such an ugly villain too!' said Tom. 'If the widow had any taste, she might surely pick up some better fellow than that.' Here Tom's eye wandered from the glass on the chimney-piece, to the glass on the table, and as he felt himself becoming gradually sentimental, he emptied the fourth tumbler of punch and ordered a fifth.

"Tom Smart, gentlemen, had always been very much attached to the public line. It had long been his ambition to stand in a bar of his own, in a green coat, knee-cords, and tops. He had a great notion of taking the chair at convivial dinners, and he had often thought how well he could preside in a room of his own in the talking way, and what a capital example he could set to his customers in the drinking department. All these things passed rapidly through Tom's mind as he sat drinking the hot punch by the roaring fire, and he felt very justly and properly indignant that the tall man should be in a fair way of keeping such an excellent house, while he, Tom Smart, was as far off from it as ever. So, after deliberating over the two last tumblers, whether he hadn't a perfect right to pick a quarrel with the tall man for having contrived to get into the good graces of the buxom widow, Tom Smart at last arrived at the satisfactory conclusion that he was a very ill-used and persecuted individual, and had better go to bed.

"Up a wide and ancient staircase the smart girl preceded Tom, shading the chamber candle with her hand, to protect it from the currents of air which in such a rambling old place might have found plenty of room to disport themselves in, without blowing the candle out, but which did blow it out nevertheless; thus affording Tom's enemies an opportunity of asserting that it was he, and not the wind, who extinguished the candle, and that while he pretended to be blowing it a-light again, he was in fact kissing the girl. Be this as it may, another light was obtained, and Tom was conducted through a maze of rooms, and a labyrinth of passages, to the apartment which had been prepared for his reception, where the girl bid him good-night, and left him alone.

"It was a good large room with big closets, and a bed which might have served for a whole boarding-school, to say nothing of a couple of oaken presses that would have held the baggage of a small army; but what struck Tom's fancy most, was a strange, grim-looking, high-backed chair, carved in the most fantastic manner, with a flowered damask cushion, and the round knobs at the bottom of the legs carefully tied up in red cloth, as if it had got the gout in its toes. Of any other queer chair, Tom would only have thought it *was* a queer chair, and there would have been an end of the matter; but there was something about this particular chair, and yet he couldn't tell what it was, so odd and so unlike any other piece of furniture he had ever seen, that it seemed to fascinate him. He sat down before the fire, and stared at the old chair for half an hour;—Damn the chair, it was such a strange old thing, he couldn't take his eyes off it.

"'Well,' said Tom, slowly undressing himself, and staring at the old chair all the while, which stood with a mysterious aspect by the bedside, 'I never saw such a rum concern as that in my days. Very odd,' said Tom, who had got rather sage with the hot punch, 'Very odd.' Tom shook his head with an air of profound wisdom, and looked at the chair again. He couldn't make anything of it though, so he got into bed, covered himself up warm, and fell asleep.

"In about half an hour, Tom woke up with a start, from a confused dream of tall men and tumblers of punch: and the first object that presented itself to his waking imagination was the queer chair.

"'I won't look at it any more,' said Tom to himself, and he squeezed his eyelids together, and tried to persuade himself he was going to sleep again. No use; nothing but queer chairs danced before his eyes, kicking up their legs, jumping over each other's backs, and playing all kinds of antics.

"'I may as well see one real chair, as two or three complete sets of false ones,' said Tom, bringing out his head from under the bed-clothes. There it was, plainly discernible by the light of the fire, looking as provoking as ever.

"Tom gazed at the chair; and, suddenly as he looked at it, a most extraordinary change seemed to come over it. The carving of the back gradually assumed the lineaments and expression of an old, shrivelled human face; the damask cushion became an antique, flapped waistcoat; the round knobs grew into a couple of feet, encased in red cloth slippers, and the whole chair looked like a very ugly old man, of the previous century, with his arms a-kimbo. Tom sat up in bed, and rubbed his eyes to dispel the illusion. No. The chair was an ugly old gentleman; and what was more, he was winking at Tom Smart.

"Tom was naturally a headlong, careless sort of dog,

and he had had five tumblers of hot punch into the bargain; so, although he was a little startled at first, he began to grow rather indignant when he saw the old gentleman winking and leering at him with such an impudent air. At length he resolved that he wouldn't stand it; and as the old chair still kept winking away as fast as ever, Tom said, in a very angry tone—

"'What the devil are you winking at me for?'

"'Because I like it, Tom Smart,' said the chair; or the old gentleman, whichever you like to call him. He stopped winking though, when Tom spoke, and began grinning like a superannuated monkey.

"'How do you know my name, old nut-cracker face?' inquired Tom Smart, rather staggered;—though he pretended to carry it off so well.

"'Come, come Tom,' said the old gentleman, 'that's not the way to address solid Spanish Mahogany. Dam'me, you couldn't treat me with less respect if I was veneered.' When the old gentleman said this, he looked so fierce that Tom began to grow frightened.

"'I didn't mean to treat you with any disrespect, Sir,' said Tom; in a much humbler tone than he had spoken in at first.

"'Well, well,' said the old fellow, 'perhaps not—perhaps not. Tom—'

"'Sir—'

"'I know everything about you, Tom; everything. You're very poor Tom.'

"'I certainly am,' said Tom Smart. 'But how came you to know that?'

"'Never mind that,' said the old gentleman; 'you're much too fond of punch, Tom.'

"Tom Smart was just on the point of protesting that he hadn't tasted a drop since his last birth-day, but when his eye encountered that of the old gentleman, he looked so knowing that Tom blushed, and was silent.

"'Tom,' said the old gentleman, 'the widow's a fine woman—remarkably fine woman—eh, Tom?' Here the old fellow screwed up his eyes, cocked up one of his wasted little legs, and looked altogether so unpleasantly amorous, that Tom was quite disgusted with the levity of his behaviour;—at his time of life, too!

"'I am her guardian, Tom,' said the old gentleman.

"'Are you?' inquired Tom Smart.

"'I knew her mother, Tom,' said the old fellow; 'and her grandmother. She was very fond of me—made me this waistcoat, Tom.'

"'Did she?' said Tom Smart.

"'And these shoes,' said the old fellow, lifting up one of the red-cloth mufflers; 'but don't mention it, Tom. I shouldn't like to have it known that she was so much attached to me. It might occasion some unpleasantness in the family.' When the old rascal said this, he looked so extremely impertinent, that, as Tom Smart afterwards declared, he could have sat upon him without remorse.

"'I have been a great favourite among the women in my time, Tom,' said the profligate old debauchee; 'hundreds of fine women have sat in my lap for hours together. What do you think of that you dog, eh?' The old gentleman was proceeding to recount some other exploits of his youth, when he was seized with such a violent fit of creaking that he was unable to proceed.

"'Just serves you right, old boy,' thought Tom Smart; but he didn't say anything.

"'Ah!' said the old fellow, 'I am a good deal troubled with this now. I am getting old, Tom, and have lost nearly all my rails. I have had an operation performed, too—a small piece let into my back—and I found it a severe trial, Tom.'

"'I dare say you did, Sir,' said Tom Smart.

"'However,' said the old gentleman, 'that's not the point. Tom, I want you to marry the widow.'

"'Me, Sir!' said Tom.

"'You;' said the old gentleman.

"'Bless your reverend locks,' said Tom—(he had a few scattered horse-hairs left)—'bless your reverend locks, she wouldn't have me.' And Tom sighed involuntarily, as he thought of the bar.

"'Wouldn't she?' said the old gentleman, firmly.

"'No, no,' said Tom; 'there's somebody else in the wind. A tall man—a confoundedly tall man—with black whiskers.'

"'Tom,' said the old gentleman; 'she will never have him.'

"'Won't she?' said Tom. 'If you stood in the bar, old gentleman, you'd tell another story.'

"'Pooh, pooh,' said the old gentleman. 'I know all about that.'

"'About what?' said Tom.

"'The kissing behind the door, and all that sort of thing, Tom,' said the old gentleman, and here he gave another impudent look, which made Tom very wroth, because as you all know, gentlemen, to hear an old fellow, who ought to know better, talking about these things, is very unpleasant—nothing more so.

"'I know all about that, Tom,' said the old gentleman. 'I have seen it done very often in my time, Tom, between more people than I should like to mention to you; but it never came to anything after all.'

"'You must have seen some queer things,' said Tom, with an inquisitive look.

"'You may say that, Tom,' replied the old fellow, with a very complicated wink. 'I am the last of my family, Tom,' said the old gentleman, with a melancholy sigh.

"'Was it a large one?' inquired Tom Smart.

"'There were twelve of us, Tom,' said the old gentleman; 'fine straight-backed, handsome fellows as you'd wish to see. None of your modern abortions—all with arms, and with a degree of polish, though I say it that should not, which it would have done your heart good to behold.'

"'And what's become of the others, Sir?' asked Tom Smart.

"The old gentleman applied his elbow to his eyes as he replied, 'Gone, Tom, gone. We had hard service, Tom, and they hadn't all my constitution. They got rheumatic about the legs and arms, and went into kitchens and other hospitals; and one of 'em, with long service and hard usage, positively lost his senses:—he got so crazy that he was obliged to be burnt. Shocking thing that, Tom.'

"'Dreadful!' said Tom Smart.

"The old fellow paused for a few minutes, apparently struggling with his feelings of emotion, and then said

"'However, Tom, I am wandering from the point. This tall man, Tom, is a rascally adventurer. The moment he married the widow, he would sell off all the furniture, and run away. What would be the consequence? She would be deserted and reduced to ruin, and I should catch my death of cold in some broker's shop.'

"'Yes, but—'

"'Don't interrupt me,' said the old gentleman. 'Of you, Tom, I entertain a very different opinion; for I well know that if you once settled yourself in a public-house, you would never leave it, as long as there was anything to drink within its walls.'

"'I am very much obliged to you for your good opinion, Sir,' said Tom Smart.

"'Therefore,' resumed the old gentleman, in a dictatorial tone; 'you shall have her, and he shall not.'

"'What is to prevent it?' said Tom Smart, eagerly.

"'This disclosure,' replied the old gentleman; 'he is already married.'

"'How can I prove it?' said Tom, starting half out of bed.

"The old gentleman untucked his arm from his side, and having pointed to one of the oaken presses, immediately replaced it, in its old position.

"'He little thinks,' said the old gentleman, 'that in the right hand pocket of a pair of trousers in that press, he has left a letter, entreating him to return to his disconsolate wife, with six—mark me, Tom—six babes, and all of them small ones.'

"As the old gentleman solemnly uttered these words, his features grew less and less distinct, and his figure more shadowy. A film came over Tom Smart's eyes. The old man seemed gradually blending into the chair, the damask waistcoat to resolve into a cushion, the red slippers to shrink into little red cloth bags. The light faded gently away, and Tom Smart fell back on his pillow, and dropped asleep.

"Morning roused Tom from the lethargic slumber, into which he had fallen on the disappearance of the old man. He sat up in bed, and for some minutes vainly endeavoured to recall the events of the preceding night. Suddenly they rushed upon him. He looked at the chair, it was a fantastic and grim-looking piece of furniture, certainly, but it must have been a remarkably ingenious and lively imagination, that could have discovered any resemblance between it and an old man.

"'How are you, old boy?' said Tom. He was bolder in the daylight—most men are.

"The chair remained motionless, and spoke not a word.

"'Miserable morning,' said Tom. No. The chair would not be drawn into conversation.

"'Which press did you point to?—you can tell me that,' said Tom. Devil a word, gentlemen, the chair would say.

"'It's not much trouble to open it, any how,' said Tom, getting out of bed very deliberately. He walked up to one of the presses. The key was in the lock; he turned it, and opened the door. There *was* a pair of trousers there. He put his hand into the pocket, and drew forth the identical letter the old gentleman had described!

"'Queer sort of thing, this,' said Tom Smart; looking first at the chair and then at the press, and then at the letter, and then at the chair again. 'Very queer,' said Tom. But as there was nothing in either to lessen the queerness, he thought he might as well dress himself, and settle the tall man's business at once—just to put him out of his misery.

"Tom surveyed the rooms he passed through, on his way down stairs, with the scrutinising eye of a landlord; thinking it not impossible, that before long, they and their contents would be his property. The tall man was standing in the snug little bar, with his hands behind him, quite at home. He grinned vacantly at Tom. A casual observer might have supposed he did it, only to show his white teeth; but Tom Smart thought that a consciousness of triumph was passing through the place where the tall man's mind would have been, if he had had any. Tom laughed in his face; and summoned the landlady.

"'Good morning, Ma'am,' said Tom Smart, closing the door of the little parlour as the widow entered.

"'Good morning, Sir,' said the widow. 'What will you take for breakfast, Sir?'

"Tom was thinking how he should open the case, so he made no answer.

"'There's a very nice ham,' said the widow, 'and a beautiful cold larded fowl. Shall I send 'em in, Sir?'

"These words roused Tom from his reflections. His admiration of the widow increased as she spoke. Thoughtful creature! Comfortable provider!

"'Who is that gentleman in the bar, Ma'am?' inquired Tom.

"'His name is Jinkins, Sir,' said the widow, slightly blushing.

"'He's a tall man,' said Tom.

"'He is a very fine man, Sir,' replied the widow, 'and a very nice gentleman.'

"'Ah!' said Tom.

"'Is there anything more you want, Sir?' inquired the widow, rather puzzled by Tom's manner.

"'Why, yes,' said Tom. 'My dear Ma'am, will you have the kindness to sit down for one moment?'

"The widow looked much amazed, but she sat down, and Tom sat down too, close beside her. I don't know how it happened—indeed my uncle used to tell me that Tom Smart said *he* didn't know how it happened either—but somehow or other the palm of Tom's hand fell upon the back of the widow's hand, and remained there while he spoke.

"'My dear Ma'am,' said Tom Smart—he had always a great notion of committing the amiable—'My dear Ma'am, you deserve a very excellent husband;—you do indeed.'

"'Lor, Sir!' said the widow—as well she might; Tom's mode of commencing the conversation being rather unusual, not to say startling, the fact of his never having set eyes upon her before the previous night, being taken into consideration. 'Lor, Sir!'

"'I scorn to flatter, my dear Ma'am,' said Tom Smart. 'You deserve a very admirable husband, and whoever he is, he'll be a very lucky man.' As Tom said this, his eye involuntarily wandered from the widow's face to the comforts around him.

"The widow looked more puzzled than ever, and made an effort to rise. Tom gently pressed her hand, as if to detain her, and she kept her seat. Widows, gentlemen, are not usually timorous, as my uncle used to say.

"'I am sure I am very much obliged to you, Sir, for your good opinion,' said the buxom landlady, half-laughing; 'and if ever I marry again'—

"'*If*,' said Tom Smart, looking very shrewdly out at the right-hand corner of his left eye. '*If*'—

"'Well,' said the widow, laughing outright this time '*When* I do, I hope I shall have as good a husband as you describe.'

"'Jinkins to wit,' said Tom.

"'Lor, Sir!' exclaimed the widow.

"'Oh, don't tell me,' said Tom, 'I know him.'

"'I am sure nobody who knows him, knows anything bad of him,' said the widow, bridling up at the mysterious air with which Tom had spoken.

"'Hem,' said Tom Smart.

"The widow began to think it was high time to cry, so she took out her handkerchief, and inquired whether Tom wished to insult her, whether he thought it like a gentleman to take away the character of another gentleman behind his back, why, if he had got anything to say, he didn't say it to the man, like a man, instead of terrifying a poor weak woman in that way; and so forth.

"'I'll say it to him fast enough,' said Tom, 'only I want you to hear it first.'

"'What is it?' inquired the widow, looking intently in Tom's countenance.

"'I'll astonish you,' said Tom, putting his hand in his pocket.

"'If it is, that he wants money,' said the widow, 'I know that already, and you needn't trouble yourself.'

"'Pooh, nonsense, that's nothing,' said Tom Smart; '*I* want money. 'Tan't that.'

"'Oh dear, what can it be?' exclaimed the poor widow.

"'Don't be frightened,' said Tom Smart. He slowly drew forth the letter, and unfolded it. 'You won't scream?' said Tom, doubtfully.

"'No, no,' replied the widow; 'let me see it.'

"'You won't go fainting away, or any of that nonsense?' said Tom.

"'No, no,' returned the widow, hastily.

"'And don't run out, and blow him up,' said Tom, 'because I'll do all that for you; you had better not exert yourself.'

"'Well, well,' said the widow, 'let me see it.'

"'I will,' replied Tom Smart; and, with these words, he placed the letter in the widow's hand.

"Gentlemen, I have heard my uncle say, that Tom Smart said, the widow's lamentations when she heard the disclosure would have pierced a heart of stone. Tom was certainly very tender-hearted, but they pierced his, to the very core. The widow rocked herself to and fro, and wrung her hands.

"'Oh, the deception and villainy of the man!' said the widow.

"'Frightful, my dear Ma'am; but compose yourself,' said Tom Smart.

"'Oh, I can't compose myself,' shrieked the widow. 'I shall never find any one else I can love so much!'

"'Oh yes you will, my dear soul,' said Tom Smart, letting fall a shower of the largest-sized tears, in pity for the widow's misfortunes. Tom Smart, in the energy of his compassion, had put his arm round the widow's waist; and the widow, in a passion of grief, had clasped Tom's hand. She looked up in Tom's face, and smiled through her tears. Tom looked down in hers, and smiled through his.

"I never could find out, gentlemen, whether Tom did or did not kiss the widow at that particular moment. He used to tell my uncle he didn't, but I have my doubts about it. Between ourselves, gentlemen, I rather think he did.

"At all events, Tom kicked the very tall man out at the front door half an hour after, and married the widow a month after. And he used to drive about the country, with the clay-coloured gig with the red wheels, and the vixenish mare with the fast pace, till he gave up business many years afterwards, and went to France with his wife; and then the old house was pulled down."

"Will you allow me to ask you," said the inquisitive old gentleman, "what became of the chair?"

"Why," replied the one-eyed bagman, "it was observed to creak very much on the day of the wedding; but Tom Smart couldn't say for certain, whether it was with pleasure or bodily infirmity. He rather thought it was the latter, though, for it never spoke afterwards."

"Everybody believed the story, didn't they?" said the dirty-faced man.

"Except Tom's enemies," replied the bagman. "Some of 'em said Tom invented it altogether; and others said he was drunk, and fancied it, and got hold of the wrong trousers by mistake before he went to bed. But nobody ever minded what *they* said."

"Tom Smart said it was all true?"

"Every word."

"And your uncle?"

"Every letter."

"They must have been nice men, both of 'em;" said the dirty-faced man.

"Yes, they were," replied the bagman; "very nice men indeed!"

CHAPTER XV.

IN WHICH IS GIVEN A FAITHFUL PORTRAITURE OF TWO DISTINGUISHED PERSONS; AND AN ACCURATE DESCRIPTION OF A PUBLIC BREAKFAST IN THEIR HOUSE AND GROUNDS: WHICH PUBLIC BREAKFAST LEADS TO THE RECOGNITION OF AN OLD ACQUAINTANCE, AND THE COMMENCEMENT OF ANOTHER CHAPTER.

MR. PICKWICK'S conscience had been somewhat reproaching him, for his recent neglect of his friends at the Peacock; and he was just on the point of walking forth in quest of them, on the third morning after the election had terminated, when his faithful valet put into his hand a card, on which was engraved the following inscription,

Mrs. Leo Hunter.

The Den. Eatanswill.

"Person's a waitin'," said Sam, epigrammatically.

"Does the person want me, Sam?" inquired Mr. Pickwick.

"He wants you partickler; and no one else'll do, as the Devil's private secretary said, ven he fetched avay Doctor Faustus," replied Mr. Weller.

"*He.* Is it a gentleman?" said Mr. Pickwick.

"A wery good imitation o' one, if it an't," replied Mr. Weller.

"But this is a lady's card," said Mr. Pickwick.

"Given me by a gen'lm'n, hows'ever," replied Sam, "and he's a waitin' in the drawing-room—said he'd rather wait all day, than not see you."

Mr. Pickwick on hearing this determination, descended to the drawing-room, where sat a grave man, who started up on his entrance, and said, with an air of profound respect—

"Mr. Pickwick, I presume?"

"The same."

"Allow me, Sir, the honour of grasping your hand—permit me Sir, to shake it," said the grave man.

"Certainly," said Mr. Pickwick.

The stranger shook the extended hand, and then continued.

"We have heard of your fame, Sir. The noise of your antiquarian discussion has reached the ears of Mrs. Leo Hunter—my wife, Sir: *I* am *Mr.* Leo Hunter"—the stranger paused, as if he expected that Mr. Pickwick would be overcome by the disclosure; but seeing that he remained perfectly calm, proceeded.

"My wife, Sir—Mrs. Leo Hunter—is proud to number among her acquaintance, all those who have rendered themselves celebrated by their works and talents. Permit me, Sir, to place in a conspicuous part of the list the name of Mr. Pickwick, and his brother members of the club that derives its name from him."

"I shall be extremely happy to make the acquaintance of such a lady, Sir," replied Mr. Pickwick.

"You *shall* make it, Sir," said the grave man. "Tomorrow morning, Sir, we give a public breakfast—a *fête champetre*—to a great number of those who have rendered themselves celebrated by their works and talents. Permit Mrs. Leo Hunter, Sir, to have the gratification of seeing you at the Den."

"With great pleasure," replied Mr. Pickwick.

"Mrs. Leo Hunter has many of these breakfasts, Sir," resumed the new acquaintance—"'Feasts of reason, Sir, and flows of soul,' as somebody who wrote a sonnet to Mrs. Leo Hunter on her breakfasts, feelingly and originally observed."

"Was *he* celebrated for his works, and talents?" inquired Mr. Pickwick.

"He was, Sir," replied the grave man, "all Mrs. Leo Hunter's acquaintance are; it is her ambition, Sir, to have no other acquaintance."

"It is a very noble ambition," said Mr. Pickwick.

"When I inform Mrs. Leo Hunter, that that remark fell from *your* lips, Sir, she will indeed be proud," said the grave man. "You have a gentleman in your train, who has produced some beautiful little poems, I think, Sir."

"My friend Mr. Snodgrass has a great taste for poetry," replied Mr. Pickwick.

"So has Mrs. Leo Hunter, Sir. She dotes on poetry, Sir. She adores it; I may say that her whole soul and mind are wound up, and entwined with it. She has produced some delightful pieces, herself, Sir. You may have met with her 'Ode to an expiring Frog,' Sir."

"I don't think I have," said Mr. Pickwick.

"You astonish me, Sir," said Mr. Leo Hunter. "It created an immense sensation. It was signed with an 'L' and eight stars, and appeared originally in a Lady's Magazine. It commenced

> "Can I view thee panting, lying
> On thy stomach, without sighing;
> Can I unmoved see thee dying
> On a log,
> Expiring frog!"

"Beautiful!" said Mr. Pickwick.

"Fine," said Mr. Leo Hunter, "so simple."

"Very," said Mr. Pickwick.

"The next verse is still more touching. Shall I repeat it?"

"If you please," said Mr. Pickwick.

"It runs thus," said the grave man, still more gravely.

> "Say, have fiends in shape of boys,
> With wild halloo, and brutal noise,
> Hunted thee from marshy joys,
>   With a dog,
>   Expiring frog!"

"Finely expressed," said Mr. Pickwick.

"All point, Sir, all point," said Mr. Leo Hunter, "but you shall hear Mrs. Leo Hunter repeat it. *She* can do justice to it, Sir. She will repeat it, in character, Sir, to-morrow morning."

"In character!"

"As Minerva. But I forgot—it's a fancy dress dejeune."

"Dear me," said Mr. Pickwick, glancing at his own figure—"I can't possibly"—

"Can't Sir; can't!" exclaimed Mr. Leo Hunter. "Solomon Lucas the Jew in the High Street, has thousands of fancy dresses. Consider, Sir, how many appropriate characters are open for your selection. Plato, Zeno, Epicurus, Pythagoras—all founders of clubs."

"I know that," said Mr. Pickwick, "but as I cannot put myself in competition with those great men, I cannot presume to wear their dresses."

The grave man considered deeply, for a few seconds, and then said,

"On reflection, Sir, I don't know whether it would not afford Mrs. Leo Hunter greater pleasure if her guests saw a gentleman of your celebrity in his own costume, rather than in an assumed one. I may venture to promise an exception in your case, Sir—yes, I am quite certain that on behalf of Mrs. Leo Hunter, I may venture to do so."

"In that case," said Mr. Pickwick, "I shall have great pleasure in coming."

"But I waste your time, Sir," said the grave man, as if suddenly recollecting himself. "I know its value, Sir. I will not detain you. I may tell Mrs. Leo Hunter, then, that she may confidently expect you and your distinguished friends? Good morning, Sir, I am proud to have beheld so eminent a personage—not a step, Sir; not a word." And without giving Mr. Pickwick time to offer remonstrance or denial, Mr. Leo Hunter stalked gravely away.

Mr. Pickwick took up his hat, and repaired to the Peacock, but Mr. Winkle had conveyed the intelligence of the fancy ball there, before him.

"Mrs. Pott's going," were the first words with which he saluted his leader.

"Is she?" said Mr. Pickwick.

"As Apollo," replied Mr. Winkle. "Only Pott objects to the tunic."

"He is right. He is quite right," said Mr. Pickwick emphatically.

"Yes;—so she's going to wear a white satin gown with gold spangles."

"They'll hardly know what she's meant for; will they?" inquired Mr. Snodgrass.

"Of course they will," replied Mr. Winkle indignantly. "They'll see her lyre, won't they?"

"True; I forgot that," said Mr. Snodgrass.

"I shall go as a Bandit," interposed Mr. Tupman.

"What!" said Mr. Pickwick, with a sudden start.

"As a bandit," repeated Mr. Tupman, mildly.

"You don't mean to say," said Mr. Pickwick, gazing with solemn sternness at his friend, "You don't mean to say, Mr. Tupman, that it is your intention to put yourself into a green velvet jacket, with a two-inch tail?"

"Such *is* my intention, Sir," replied Mr. Tupman warmly. "And why not, Sir?"

"Because Sir," said Mr. Pickwick, considerably excited —"Because you are too old, Sir."

"Too old!" exclaimed Mr. Tupman.

"And if any further ground of objection be wanting," continued Mr. Pickwick, "you are too fat, Sir."

"Sir," said Mr. Tupman, his face suffused with a crimson glow, "This is an insult."

"Sir," replied Mr. Pickwick in the same tone, "It is not half the insult to you, that your appearance in my presence in a green velvet jacket, with a two-inch tail, would be to me."

"Sir," said Mr. Tupman, "you're a fellow."

"Sir," said Mr. Pickwick, "you're another!"

Mr. Tupman advanced a step or two, and glared at Mr. Pickwick. Mr. Pickwick returned the glare, concentrated into a focus by means of his spectacles, and breathed a bold defiance. Mr. Snodgrass and Mr. Winkle looked on, petrified at beholding such a scene between two such men.

"Sir," said Mr. Tupman, after a short pause, speaking in a low deep voice, "you have called me old."

"I have," said Mr. Pickwick.

"And fat."

"I reiterate the charge."

"And a fellow."

"So you are!"

There was a fearful pause.

"My attachment to your person, Sir," said Mr. Tupman, speaking in a voice tremulous with emotion, and tucking up his wristbands meanwhile, "is great—very great—but upon that person, I must take summary vengeance."

"Come on, Sir," replied Mr. Pickwick. Stimulated by the exciting nature of the dialogue, the heroic man actually threw himself into a paralytic attitude, confidently supposed by the two by-standers to have been intended as a posture of defence.

"What!" exclaimed Mr. Snodgrass, suddenly recovering the power of speech, of which intense astonishment had previously bereft him, and rushing between the two, at the imminent hazard of receiving an application on the temple from each. "What! Mr. Pickwick, with the eyes of the world upon you! Mr. Tupman! who, in common with us all, derives a lustre from his undying name! For shame, gentlemen; for shame."

The unwonted lines which momentary passion had ruled in Mr. Pickwick's clear and open brow, gradually melted away, as his young friend spoke, like the marks of a black-lead pencil beneath the softening influence of India rubber. His countenance had resumed its usual benign expression ere he concluded.

"I have been hasty," said Mr. Pickwick, "very hasty. Tupman; your hand."

The dark shadow passed from Mr. Tupman's face, as he warmly grasped the hand of his friend.

"I have been hasty, too," said he.

"No, no," interrupted Mr. Pickwick, "the fault was mine. You will wear the green velvet jacket?"

"No, no," replied Mr. Tupman.

"To oblige me, you will," resumed Mr. Pickwick.

"Well, well, I will," said Mr. Tupman.

It was accordingly settled that Mr. Tupman, Mr. Winkle, and Mr. Snodgrass, should all wear fancy dresses. Thus Mr. Pickwick was led by the very warmth of his own good feelings to give his consent to a proceeding from which his better judgment would have recoiled—a more striking illustration of his amiable character could hardly have been conceived, even if the events recorded in these pages had been wholly imaginary.

Mr. Leo Hunter had not exaggerated the resources of Mr. Solomon Lucas. His wardrobe was extensive—very extensive—not strictly classical perhaps, nor quite new, nor did it contain any one garment made precisely after the fashion of any age or time, but everything was more or less spangled; and what *can* be prettier than spangles? It may be objected that they are not adapted to the daylight, but everybody knows that they would glitter if there were lamps; and nothing can be clearer than that if people give fancy balls in the day-time, and the dresses do not show quite as well as they would by night, the fault lies solely with the people who give the fancy balls, and is in no wise chargeable on the spangles. Such was the convincing reasoning of Mr. Solomon Lucas; and influenced by such arguments did Mr. Tupman, Mr. Winkle, and Mr. Snodgrass, engage to array themselves in costumes which his taste and experience induced him to recommend as admirably suited to the occasion.

A carriage was hired from the Town Arms, for the accommodation of the Pickwickians, and a chariot was ordered from the same repository, for the purpose of conveying Mr. and Mrs. Pott to Mrs. Leo Hunter's grounds, which Mr. Pott, as a delicate acknowledgment of having received an invitation, had already confidently predicted in the Eatanswill Gazette "would present a scene of varied and delicious enchantment—a bewildering coruscation of beauty and talent—a lavish and prodigal display of hospitality—above all, a degree of splendour softened by the most exquisite taste; and adornment refined with perfect harmony and the chastest good-keeping—compared with which, the fabled gorgeousness of Eastern Fairy Land itself, would appear to be clothed in as many dark and murky colours, as must be the mind of the splenetic and unmanly being who could presume to taint with the venom of his envy, the preparations making by the virtuous and highly distinguished lady, at whose shrine this humble tribute of admiration was offered." This last was a piece of biting sarcasm against the Independent, who in consequence of not having been invited at all, had been through four numbers affecting to sneer at the whole affair, in his very largest type, with all the adjectives in capital letters.

The morning came; it was a pleasant sight to behold Mr. Tupman in full Brigand's costume, with a very tight jacket, sitting like a pincushion over his back and shoulders: the upper portion of his legs encased in the velvet shorts, and the lower part thereof swathed in the complicated bandages to which all Brigands are peculiarly attached. It was pleasing to see his open and ingenuous countenance, well mustachioed and corked, looking out from an open shirt collar; and to contemplate the sugarloaf hat, decorated with ribbons of all colours, which he was compelled to carry on his knee, inasmuch as no known conveyance with a top to it, would admit of any man's carrying it between his head and the roof. Equally humourous and agreeable, was the appearance of Mr. Snodgrass in blue satin trunks and cloak, white silk tights and shoes, and Grecian helmet, which everybody knows (and if they do not, Mr. Solomon Lucas did) to have been the regular, authentic, every-day costume of a Troubadour, from the earliest ages down to the time of their final disappearance from the face of the earth. All this was pleasant, but this was as nothing compared with the shouting of the populace when the carriage drew up, behind Mr. Pott's chariot, which chariot itself drew up at Mr. Pott's door, which door itself opened, and displayed the great Pott accoutred as a Russian officer of justice, with a tremendous knout in his hand—tastefully typical of the stern and mighty power of the Eatanswill Gazette, and the fearful lashings it bestowed on public offenders.

"Bravo!" shouted Mr. Tupman and Mr. Snodgrass from the passage, when they beheld the walking allegory.

"Bravo!" Mr. Pickwick was heard to exclaim, from the passage.

"Hoo—roar Pott," shouted the populace. Amid these salutations, Mr. Pott, smiling with that kind of bland dignity which sufficiently testified that he felt his power, and knew how to exert it, got into the chariot.

Then there emerged from the house, Mrs. Pott, who would have looked very like Apollo if she hadn't had a gown on: conducted by Mr. Winkle, who in his light redcoat, could not possibly have been mistaken for anything but a sportsman, if he had not borne an equal resemblance to a general postman. Last of all, came Mr. Pickwick, whom the boys applauded as loudly as anybody, probably under the impression that his tights and gaiters were some remnants of the dark ages; and then the two vehicles proceeded towards Mrs. Leo Hunter's, Mr. Weller (who was to assist in waiting) being stationed on the box of that in which his master was seated.

Every one of the men, women, boys, girls, and babies, who were assembled to see the visitors in their fancy dresses, screamed with delight and extasy, when Mr. Pickwick, with the Brigand on one arm, and the Troubadour on the other, walked solemnly up the entrance. Never were such shouts heard, as those which greeted Mr. Tupman's efforts to fix the sugar-loaf hat on his head, by way of entering the garden in style.

The preparations were on the most delightful scale; fully realising the prophetic Pott's anticipations about the gorgeousness of Eastern Fairy-land, and at once affording a sufficient contradiction to the malignant statements of the reptile Independent. The grounds were more than an acre and a quarter in extent, and they were filled with people! Never was such a blaze of beauty, and fashion, and literature. There was the young lady who "did" the poetry in the Eatanswill Gazette, in the garb of a sultana, leaning upon the arm of the young gentleman who "did" the review department, and who was appropriately habited in a field marshal's uniform—the boots excepted. There were hosts of these geniuses, and any reasonable person would have thought it honour enough to meet them. But more than these, there were half a dozen lions from London—authors, real authors, who had written whole books, and printed them afterwards—and here you might see 'em, walking about, like ordinary men, smiling and talking—aye, and talking pretty considerable nonsense too, no doubt with the benign intention of rendering themselves intelligible to the common people about them. Moreover, there was a band of music in pasteboard caps; four something-ean singers in the costume of their country, and a dozen hired waiters in the costume of *their* country—and very dirty costume too. And above all, there was Mrs. Leo Hunter in the character of Minerva, receiving the company, and overflowing with pride and gratification at the notion of having called such distinguished individuals together.

"Mr. Pickwick, Ma'am," said a servant, as that gentleman approached the presiding goddess, with his hat in his hand, and the Brigand and Troubadour on either arm.

"What—where!" exclaimed Mrs. Leo Hunter, starting up, in an affected rapture of surprise.

"Here," said Mr. Pickwick.

"Is it possible that I have really the gratification of beholding Mr. Pickwick himself!" ejaculated Mrs. Leo Hunter.

"No other, Ma'am," replied Mr. Pickwick, bowing very low. "Permit me to introduce my friends—Mr. Tupman —Mr. Winkle—Mr. Snodgrass—to the authoress of 'The Expiring Frog.'"

Very few people but those who have tried it, know what a difficult process it is, to bow in green velvet smalls, and a tight jacket and high-crowned-hat, or in blue satin trunks and white silks, or knee-cords and top-boots that were never made for the wearer, and have been fixed upon him without the remotest reference to the comparative dimensions of himself and the suit. Never were such distortions as Mr. Tupman's frame underwent in his efforts to appear easy and graceful—never was such ingenious posturing, as his fancy-dressed friends exhibited.

"Mr. Pickwick," said Mrs. Leo Hunter, "I must make you promise not to stir from my side the whole day. There are hundreds of people here, that I must positively introduce you to."

"You are very kind, Ma'am," said Mr. Pickwick.

"In the first place, here are my little girls; I had almost forgotten them," said Minerva, carelessly pointing towards a couple of full-grown young ladies, of whom one might be about twenty, and the other a year or two older, and who were dressed in very juvenile costumes—whether to make them look young, or their mamma younger, Mr. Pickwick does not distinctly inform us.

"They are very beautiful," said Mr. Pickwick, as the juveniles turned away, after being presented.

"They are very like their mamma, Sir," said Mr. Pott, majestically.

"Oh you naughty man," exclaimed Mrs. Leo Hunter, playfully tapping the Editor's arm with her fan (Minerva with a fan!)

"Why now, my dear Mrs. Hunter," said Mr. Pott, who was trumpeter in ordinary at the Den, "you *know* that when your picture was in the Exhibition of the Royal Academy, last year, everybody inquired whether it was intended for you, or your youngest daughter; for you were so much alike that there was no telling the difference between you."

"Well, and if they did, why need you repeat it, before strangers?" said Mrs. Leo Hunter, bestowing another tap on the slumbering lion of the Eatanswill Gazette.

"Count, Count," screamed Mrs. Leo Hunter to a well-whiskered individual in a foreign uniform, who was passing by.

"Ah! you want me?" said the Count, turning back.

"I want to introduce two very clever people to each other," said Mrs. Leo Hunter. "Mr. Pickwick, I have great pleasure in introducing you to Count Smorltork." She added in a hurried whisper to Mr. Pickwick—"the famous foreigner—gathering materials for his great work on England—hem!—Count Smorltork, Mr. Pickwick."

Mr. Pickwick saluted the Count with all the reverence due to so great a man, and the Count drew forth a set of tablets.

"What you say, Mrs. Hunt?" inquired the Count, smiling graciously on the gratified Mrs. Leo Hunter, "Pig Vig or Big Vig—what you call—Lawyer—eh? I see—that is it. Big Vig"—and the Count was proceeding to enter Mr. Pickwick in his tablets, as a gentleman of the long-robe, who derived his name from the profession to which he belonged, when Mrs. Leo Hunter interposed.

"No, no, Count," said the lady, "Pick-wick."

"Ah, ah, I see," replied the Count. "Peek—christian name; Weeks—surname; good, ver good. Peek Weeks. How you do Weeks?"

"Quite well, I thank you," replied Mr. Pickwick, with all his usual affability. "Have you been long in England?"

"Long—ver long time—fortnight—more."

"Do you stay here long?"

"One week."

"You will have enough to do," said Mr. Pickwick, smiling, "to gather all the materials you want, in that time."

"Eh, they are gathered," said the Count.

"Indeed!" said Mr. Pickwick.

"They are here," added the Count, tapping his forehead significantly. "Large book at home—full of notes—music, picture, science, potry, poltic; all tings."

"The word politics, Sir," said Mr. Pickwick, "comprises, in itself, a difficult study of no inconsiderable magnitude."

"Ah!" said the Count, drawing out the tablets again, "ver good—fine words to begin a chapter. Chapter forty-seven. Poltics. The word poltic surprises by himself—" And down went Mr. Pickwick's remark, in Count Smorltork's tablets, with such variations and additions as the Count's exuberant fancy suggested, or his imperfect knowledge of the language occasioned.

"Count," said Mrs. Leo Hunter.

"Mrs. Hunt," replied the Count.

"This is Mr. Snodgrass, a friend of Mr. Pickwick's, and a poet."

"Stop," exclaimed the Count, bringing out the tablets once more. "Head, potry—chapter, literary friends—name, Snowgrass; ver good. Introduced to Snowgrass—great poet, friend of Peek Weeks—by Mrs. Hunt, which wrote other sweet poem—what is that name?—Frog—Perspiring Frog—ver good—ver good indeed." And the Count put up his tablets, and with sundry bows and acknowledgments walked away, thoroughly satisfied that he had made the most important and valuable additions to his stock of information.

"Wonderful man, Count Smorltork," said Mrs. Leo Hunter.

"Sound philosopher," said Pott.

"Clear-headed, strong-minded person," added Mr. Snodgrass.

A chorus of by-standers took up the shout of Count Smorltork's praise, shook their heads sagely, and unanimously cried "Very!"

As the enthusiasm in Count Smorltork's favour ran very high, his praises might have been sung until the end of the

MRS. LEO HUNTER'S FANCY DRESS DÉJEUNÉ.

festivities, if the four something-ean singers had not ranged themselves in front of a small apple-tree, to look picturesque, and commenced singing their national songs, which appeared by no means difficult of execution, inasmuch as the grand secret seemed to be, that three of the something-ean singers should grunt, while the fourth howled. This interesting performance having concluded amidst the loud plaudits of the whole company, a boy forthwith proceeded to entangle himself with the rails of a chair, and to jump over it, and crawl under it, and fall down with it, and do everything but sit upon it, and then to make a cravat of his legs, and tie them round his neck, and then to illustrate the ease with which a human being can be made to look like a magnified toad—all which feats yielded high delight and satisfaction to the assembled spectators. After which, the voice of Mrs. Pott was heard to chirp faintly forth, something which courtesy interpreted into a song, which was all very classical, and strictly in character, because Apollo was himself a composer, and composers can very seldom sing their own music or anybody else's, either. This was succeeded by Mrs. Leo Hunter's recitation of her far-famed ode to an Expiring Frog, which was encored once, and would have been encored twice, if the major part of the guests, who thought it was high time to get something to eat, had not said that it was perfectly shameful to take advantage of Mrs. Hunter's good nature. So although Mrs. Leo Hunter professed her perfect willingness to recite the ode again, her kind and considerate friends wouldn't hear of it on any account; and the refreshment room being thrown open, all the people who had ever been there before, scrambled in with all possible despatch: Mrs. Leo Hunter's usual course of proceeding, being, to issue cards for a hundred, and breakfast for fifty, or in other words to feed only the very particular lions, and let the smaller animals take care of themselves.

"Where is Mr. Pott?" said Mrs. Leo Hunter, as she placed the aforesaid lions around her.

"Here I am," said the editor, from the very furthest end of the room; far beyond all hope of food, unless something was done for him by the hostess.

"Won't you come up here?"

"Oh pray don't mind him," said Mrs. Pott, in the most obliging voice—"you give yourself a great deal of unnecessary trouble, Mrs. Hunter. You'll do very well there, won't you—dear."

"Certainly—love," replied the unhappy Pott, with a grim smile. Alas for the knout! The nervous arm that wielded it, with such gigantic force upon public characters, was paralysed beneath the glance of the imperious Mrs. Pott.

Mrs. Leo Hunter looked round her in triumph. Count Smorltork was busily engaged in taking notes of the contents of the dishes; Mr. Tupman was doing the honours of the lobster salad to several lionesses, with a degree of grace which no Brigand ever exhibited before; Mr. Snodgrass having cut out the young gentleman who cut up the books for the Eatanswill Gazette, was engaged in an impassioned argument with the young lady who did the poetry: and Mr. Pickwick was making himself universally agreeable. Nothing seemed wanting to render the select circle complete, when Mr. Leo Hunter—whose department on these occasions, was to stand about in door-ways, and talk to the less important people—suddenly called out—

"My dear; here's Mr. Charles Fitz-Marshall."

"Oh dear," said Mrs. Leo Hunter, "how anxiously I have been expecting him. Pray make room, to let Mr.

Fitz-Marshall pass. Tell Mr. Fitz-Marshall, my dear, to come up to me directly, to be scolded for coming so late."

"Coming, my dear Ma'am," cried a voice, "as quick as I can—crowds of people—full room—hard work—very."

Mr. Pickwick's knife and fork fell from his hand. He stared across the table at Mr. Tupman, who had dropped *his* knife and fork, and was looking as if he were about to sink into the ground without further notice.

"Ah!" cried the voice, as its owner pushed his way among the last five and twenty Turks, officers, cavaliers, and Charles the Seconds, that remained between him and the table, "regular mangle—Baker's patent—not a crease in my coat, after all this squeezing—might have 'got up my linen,' as I came along—ha! ha! not a bad idea, that—queer thing to have it mangled when it's upon one, though—trying process—very."

With these broken words, a young man dressed as a naval officer made his way up to the table, and presented to the astonished Pickwickians, the identical form and features of Mr. Alfred Jingle.

The offender had barely time to take Mrs. Leo Hunter's proffered hand, when his eyes encountered the indignant orbs of Mr. Pickwick.

"Hallo!" said Jingle. "Quite forgot—no directions to postilion—give 'em at once—back in a minute."

"The servant, or Mr. Hunter will do it in a moment, Mr. Fitz-Marshall," said Mrs. Leo Hunter.

"No, no—I'll do it—shan't be long—back in no time," replied Jingle. With these words he disappeared among the crowd.

"Will you allow me to ask you, Ma'am," said the excited Mr. Pickwick, rising from his seat, "who that young man is, and where he resides?"

"He is a gentleman of fortune, Mr. Pickwick," said Mrs. Leo Hunter, "to whom I very much want to introduce you. The Count will be delighted with him."

"Yes, yes," said Mr. Pickwick, hastily. **"His resi-**dence—"

"Is at present at the Angel at Bury."

"At Bury?"

"At Bury St. Edmunds, not many miles from here. But dear me, Mr. Pickwick, you are not going to leave us: surely Mr. Pickwick you cannot think of going so soon."

But long before Mrs. Leo Hunter had finished speaking, Mr. Pickwick had plunged through the throng, and reached the garden, whither he was shortly afterwards joined by Mr. Tupman, who had followed his friend closely.

"It's of no use," said Mr. Tupman. "He has gone."

"I know it," said Mr. Pickwick, "and I will follow him."

"Follow him. Where?" inquired Mr. Tupman.

"To the Angel at Bury," replied Mr. Pickwick, speaking very quickly. "How do we know whom he is deceiving there? He deceived a worthy man once, and we were the innocent cause. He shall not do it again, if I can help it; I'll expose him. Sam! Where's my servant?"

"Here you are, Sir," said Mr. Weller, emerging from a sequestered spot, where he had been engaged in discussing a bottle of Madeira, which he had abstracted from the breakfast-table, an hour or two before. "Here's your servant, Sir. Proud o' the title, as the Living Skellinton said, ven they show'd him."

"Follow me instantly," said Mr. Pickwick. "Tupman, if I stay at Bury, you can join me there, when I write. Till then, good-bye."

Remonstrances were useless. Mr. Pickwick was roused,

and his mind was made up. Mr. Tupman returned to his companions; and in another hour had drowned all present recollection of Mr. Alfred Jingle, or Mr. Charles Fitz-Marshall, in an exhilarating quadrille and a bottle of champagne. By that time, Mr. Pickwick and Sam Weller, perched on the outside of a stage coach, were every succeeding minute placing a less and less distance between themselves and the good old town of Bury Saint Edmunds.

CHAPTER XVI.

TOO FULL OF ADVENTURE TO BE BRIEFLY DESCRIBED.

THERE is no month in the whole year, in which nature wears a more beautiful appearance than in the month of August. Spring has many beauties, and May is a fresh and blooming month, but the charms of this time of year, are enhanced by their contrast with the winter season. August has no such advantage. It comes when we remember nothing but clear skies, green fields, and sweet-smelling flowers—when the recollection of snow, and ice, and bleak winds, has faded from our minds as completely as they have disappeared from the earth,—and yet what a pleasant time it is. Orchards and cornfields ring with the hum of labour; trees bend beneath the thick clusters of rich fruit which bow their branches to the ground; and the corn, piled in graceful sheaves, or waving in every light breath that sweeps above it, as if it wooed the sickle, tinges the landscape with a golden hue. A mellow softness appears to hang over the whole earth; the influence of the season seems to extend itself to the very wagon, whose slow motion across the well-reaped field, is perceptible only to the eye, but strikes with no harsh sound upon the ear.

As the coach rolls swiftly past the fields and orchards which skirt the road, groups of women and children, piling the fruit in sieves, or gathering the scattered ears of corn, pause for an instant from their labour, and shading the sun-burnt face with a still browner hand, gaze upon the passengers with curious eyes, while some stout urchin, too small to work, but too mischievous to be left at home, scrambles over the side of the basket in which he has been deposited for security, and kicks and screams with delight. The reaper stops in his work, and stands with folded arms, looking at the vehicle as it whirls past; and the rough cart-horses bestow a sleepy glance upon the smart coach team, which says, as plainly as a horse's glance can, "It's all very fine to look at, but slow going, over a heavy field, is better than warm work like that, upon a dusty road, after all." You cast a look behind you, as you turn a corner of the road. The women and children have resumed their labour, the reaper once more stoops to his work, the cart-horses have moved on, and all are again in motion.

The influence of a scene like this, was not lost upon the well-regulated mind of Mr. Pickwick. Intent upon the resolution he had formed, of exposing the real character of the nefarious Jingle, in any quarter in which he might be pursuing his fraudulent designs, he sat at first taciturn and contemplative, brooding over the means by which his purpose could be best attained. By degrees his attention grew more and more attracted by the objects around him; and at last he derived as much enjoyment from the ride, as if it had been undertaken for the pleasantest reason in the world.

"Delightful prospect, Sam," said Mr. Pickwick.

"Beats the chimbley pots, Sir," replied Mr. Weller, touching his hat.

"I suppose you have hardly seen anything but chimney-pots and bricks and mortar, all your life, Sam," said Mr. Pickwick, smiling.

"I worn't always a boots, Sir," said Mr. Weller, with a shake of the head. "I was a vagginer's boy, once."

"When was that?" inquired Mr. Pickwick.

"When I vas first pitched neck and crop into the world, to play at leap-frog with its troubles," replied Sam. "I vas a carrier's boy at startin': then a vagginer's, then a helper, then a boots. Now I'm a gen'lm'n's servant. I shall be a gen'lm'n myself one of these days, perhaps, with a pipe in my mouth, and a summer-house in the back garden. Who knows? *I* shouldn't be surprised, for once."

"You are quite a philosopher, Sam," said Mr. Pickwick.

"It runs in the family, I b'lieve Sir," replied Mr. Weller. "My father's wery much in that line, now. If my mother-in-law blows him up, he whistles. She flies in a passion, and breaks his pipe; he steps out, and gets another. Then she screams wery loud, and falls into 'sterics; and he smokes wery comfortably 'till she comes to agin. That's philosophy Sir, an't it?"

"A very good substitute for it, at all events," replied **Mr. Pickwick**, laughing. "It must have been of great service to you, in the course of your rambling life, Sam."

"Service Sir," exclaimed Sam. "You may say that. Arter I run away from the carrier, and afore I took up with the vagginer, I had unfurnished lodgin's for a fortnight."

"Unfurnished lodgings?" said Mr. Pickwick.

"Yes—the dry arches of Waterloo Bridge. Fine sleeping-place—vithin ten minutes' walk of all the public offices—only if there is any objection to it, it is that the sitivation's *rayther* too airy. I see some queer sights there."

"Ah, I suppose you did," said Mr. Pickwick, with an air of considerable interest.

"Sights, Sir," resumed Mr. Weller, "as 'ud penetrate your benevolent heart, and come out on the other side. You don't see the reg'lar wagrants there; trust 'em, they knows better than that. Young beggars, male and female, as hasn't made a rise in their profession, takes up their quarters there sometimes; but it's generally the worn-out, starving, houseless creeturs as rolls themselves up in the dark corners o' them lonesome places—poor creeturs as an't up to the twopenny rope."

"And pray Sam, what *is* the twopenny rope?" inquired Mr. Pickwick.

"The twopenny rope, Sir," replied Mr. Weller, "is just a cheap lodgin' house, vere the beds is twopence a night."

"What do they call a bed a rope for?" said Mr. Pickwick.

"Bless your innocence, Sir, that a'nt it," replied Sam. "Ven the lady and gen'lm'n as keeps the Hot-el, first begun business, they used to make the beds on the floor; but this wouldn't do at no price, 'cos instead o' taking a moderate twopenn'orth o' sleep, the lodgers used to lie there half the day. So now they has two ropes, 'bout six foot apart, and three from the floor, which goes right down the room; and the beds are made of slips of coarse sacking, stretched across 'em."

"Well," said Mr. Pickwick.

"Well," said Mr. Weller, "the adwantage o' the plan's hobvious. At six o'clock every mornin', they lets go the ropes at one end, and down falls all the lodgers. 'Consequence is, that being thoroughly waked, they get up wery quietly, and walk away!"

"Beg your pardon, Sir," said Sam, suddenly breaking off in his loquacious discourse. "Is this Bury Saint Edmunds?"

"It is," replied Mr. Pickwick.

The coach rattled through the well paved streets of a handsome little town, of thriving and cleanly appearance, and stopped before a large inn situated in a wide open street, nearly facing the old abbey.

"And this," said Mr. Pickwick, looking up, "is the Angel. We alight here, Sam. But some caution is necessary. Order a private room, and do not mention my name. You understand."

"Right as a trivet, Sir," replied Mr. Weller, with a wink of intelligence; and having dragged Mr. Pickwick's portmanteau from the hind boot, into which it had been hastily thrown when they joined the coach at Eatanswill, Mr. Weller disappeared on his errand. A private room was speedily engaged; and into it, Mr. Pickwick was ushered without delay.

"Now Sam," said Mr. Pickwick, "the first thing to be done is to—"

"Order dinner, Sir," interposed Mr. Weller. "It's wery late, Sir."

"Ah, so it is," said Mr. Pickwick, looking at his watch. "You are right, Sam."

"And if I might adwise, Sir," added Mr. Weller, "I'd just have a good night's rest arterwards, and not begin inquiring arter this here deep 'un 'till the mornin'. There's nothin' so refreshin' as sleep, Sir, as the servant-girl said afore she drank the egg-cup-full o' laudanum."

"I think you are right, Sam," said Mr. Pickwick. "But I must first ascertain that he is in the house, and not likely to go away."

"Leave that to me, Sir," said Sam. "Let me order you a snug little dinner, and make my inquiries below while it's a getting ready; I could worm ev'ry secret out o' the boots's heart, in five minutes."

"Do so," said Mr. Pickwick: and Mr. Weller at once retired.

In half an hour, Mr. Pickwick was seated at a very satisfactory dinner; and in three-quarters Mr. Weller returned with the intelligence that Mr. Charles Fitz-Marshall had ordered his private room to be retained for him, until further notice. He was going to spend the evening at some private house in the neighbourhood, had ordered the boots to sit up until his return, and had taken his servant with him.

"Now Sir," argued Mr. Weller, when he had concluded his report, "if I can get a talk with this here servant in the mornin', he'll tell me all his master's concerns."

"How do you know that?" interposed Mr. Pickwick.

"Bless your heart, Sir, servants always do," replied Mr. Weller.

"Oh, ah, I forgot that," said Mr. Pickwick. "Well."

"Then you can arrange what's best to be done, Sir, and we can act accordingly."

As it appeared that this was the best arrangement that could be made, it was finally agreed upon. Mr. Weller, by his master's permission, retired to spend the evening in his own way; and was shortly afterwards, elected, by the unanimous voice of the assembled company, into the taproom chair, in which honourable post he acquitted himself so much to the satisfaction of the gentlemen-frequenters, that their roars of laughter and approbation penetrated to Mr. Pickwick's bed-room, and shortened the term of his natural rest, by at least three hours.

Early on the ensuing morning, Mr. Weller was dispelling all the feverish remains of the previous evening's conviviality, through the instrumentality of a halfpenny shower-bath (having induced a young gentleman attached to the stable-department, by the offer of that coin, to pump over his head and face, until he was perfectly restored), when he was attracted by the appearance of a young fellow in mulberry-coloured livery, who was sitting on a bench in the yard, reading what appeared to be a hymn-book, with an air of deep abstraction, but who occasionally stole a glance at the individual under the pump, as if he took some interest in his proceedings, nevertheless.

"You're a rum 'un to look at, you are," thought Mr. Weller, the first time his eyes encountered the glance of the stranger in the mulberry-coloured suit, who had a large, sallow, ugly face: very sunken eyes, and a gigantic head, from which depended a quantity of lank black hair. "You're a rum 'un," thought Mr. Weller; and thinking this, he went on washing himself, and thought no more about him.

Still the man kept glancing from his hymn-book to Sam, and from Sam to his hymn-book, as if he wanted to open a conversation. So at last, Sam, by way of giving him an opportunity, said, with a familiar nod—

"How are you, governor?"

"I am happy to say, I am pretty well, Sir," said the man, speaking with great deliberation, and closing the book. "I hope you are the same, Sir?"

"Why, if I felt less like a walking brandy-bottle, I shouldn't be quite so staggery this mornin'," replied Sam "Are you stoppin' in this house, old 'un?"

The mulberry man replied in the affirmative.

"How was it, you worn't one of us, last night?" inquired Sam, scrubbing his face with the towel. "You seem one of the jolly sort—looks as conwivial as a live trout in a lime-basket," added Mr. Weller, in an under tone.

"I was out last night, with my master," replied the stranger.

"What's his name?" inquired Mr. Weller, colouring up very red with sudden excitement, and the friction of the towel combined.

"Fitz-Marshall," said the mulberry man.

"Give us your hand," said Mr. Weller, advancing; "I should like to know you. I like your appearance, old fellow."

"Well, that is very strange," said the mulberry man, with great simplicity of manner. "I like yours so much, that I wanted to speak to you, from the very first moment I saw you under the pump."

"Did you though?"

"Upon my word. Now, isn't that curious?"

"Wery sing'ler," said Sam, inwardly congratulating himself upon the softness of the stranger. "What's your name, my patriarch?"

"Job."

"And a wery good name it is; only one, I know, that ain't got a nickname to it. What's the other name?"

"Trotter," said the stranger. "What is yours?"

Sam bore in mind his master's caution, and replied, "My name's Walker; my master's name's Wilkins. Will you take a drop o' somethin' this mornin', Mr. Trotter?"

Mr. Trotter acquiesced in this agreeable proposal: and having deposited his book in his coat-pocket, accompanied Mr. Weller to the tap, where they were soon occupied in discussing an exhilarating compound, formed by mixing together, in a pewter vessel, certain quantities of British Hollands, and the fragrant essence of the clove.

"And what sort of a place have you got?" inquired Sam, as he filled his companion's glass, for the second time.

"Bad," said Job, smacking his lips, "very bad."

"You don't mean that," said Sam.

"I do, indeed. Worse than that, my master's going to be married."

"No."

"Yes; and worse than that, too, he's going to run away with an immense rich heiress, from boarding-school."

"What a dragon," said Sam, refilling his companion's glass. "It's some boarding-school in this town, I suppose, a'nt it?"

Now, although this question was put in the most careless tone imaginable, Mr. Job Trotter plainly showed, by gestures, that he perceived his new friend's anxiety to draw forth an answer to it. He emptied his glass, looked mysteriously at his companion, winked both of his small eyes, one after the other, and finally made a motion with his arm, as if he were working an imaginary pump-handle: thereby intimating that he (Mr. Trotter) considered himself as undergoing the process of being pumped, by Mr. Samuel Weller.

"No, no," said Mr. Trotter, in conclusion, "that's not to be told to everybody. That is a secret—a great secret, Mr. Walker."

As the mulberry man said this, he turned his glass upside down, by way of reminding his companion that he had nothing left wherewith to slake his thirst. Sam observed the hint; and feeling the delicate manner in which it was conveyed, ordered the pewter vessel to be refilled, whereat the small eyes of the mulberry man glistened.

"And so it's a secret," said Sam.

"I should rather suspect it was," said the mulberry man, sipping his liquor, with a complacent face.

"I suppose your mas'r's very rich?" said Sam.

Mr. Trotter smiled, and holding his glass in his left hand, gave four distinct slaps on the pocket of his mulberry indescribables with his right, as if to intimate that his master might have done the same without alarming anybody much by the chinking of coin.

"Ah," said Sam, "that's the game, is it?"

The mulberry man nodded significantly.

"Well, and don't you think, old feller," remonstrated Mr. Weller, "that if you let your master take in this here young lady, you're a precious rascal?"

"I know that," said Job Trotter, turning upon his companion a countenance of deep contrition, and groaning slightly. "I know that and that's what it is that preys upon my mind. But what am I to do?"

"Do!" said Sam; "di-vulge to the missis, and give up your master."

"Who'd believe me?" replied Job Trotter. "The young lady's considered the very picture of innocence and discretion. She'd deny it, and so would my master. Who'd believe me? I should lose my place, and get indicted for a conspiracy, or some such thing; that's all I should take by my motion."

"There's somethin' in that," said Sam, ruminating; "there's somethin' in that."

"If I knew any respectable gentleman who would take the matter up," continued Mr. Trotter, "I might have some hope of preventing the elopement; but there's the same difficulty, Mr. Walker, just the same. I know no gentleman in this strange place; and ten to one if I did, whether he would believe my story."

"Come this way," said Sam, suddenly jumping up, and grasping the mulberry man by the arm. "My mas'r's the man you want, I see." And after a slight resistance on the part of Job Trotter, Sam led his newly-found friend to the apartment of Mr. Pickwick, to whom he presented him, together with a brief summary of the dialogue we have just repeated.

"I am very sorry to betray my master, Sir," said Job Trotter, applying to his eyes a pink check pocket handkerchief of about three inches square.

"The feeling does you a great deal of honour," replied Mr. Pickwick; "but it is your duty, nevertheless."

"I know it is my duty, Sir," replied Job, with great emotion. "We should all try to discharge our duty, Sir, and I humbly endeavour to discharge mine, Sir; but it is a hard trial to betray a master, Sir, whose clothes you wear, and whose bread you eat, even though he is a scoundrel, Sir."

"You are a very good fellow," said Mr. Pickwick, much affected, "an honest fellow."

"Come, come," interposed Sam, who had witnessed Mr. Trotter's tears with considerable impatience, "blow this here water-cart bis'ness. It won't do no good, this won't."

"Sam," said Mr. Pickwick, reproachfully, "I am sorry to find that you have so little respect for this young man's feelings."

"His feelins is all wery well, Sir," replied Mr. Weller; "and as they're so wery fine, and it's a pity he should lose 'em, I think he'd better keep 'em in his own bussum, than let 'em evaporate in hot water, 'specially as they do no good. Tears never yet wound up a clock, or worked a steam ingin'. The next time you go out to a smoking party, young feller, fill your pipe with that 'ere reflection; and for the present, just put that bit of pink gingham into your pocket. 'T'a'n't so handsome that you need keep waving it about, as if you was a tight-rope dancer."

"My man is in the right," said Mr. Pickwick, accosting Job, "although his mode of expressing his opinion is somewhat homely, and occasionally incomprehensible."

"He is, Sir, very right," said Mr. Trotter, "and I will give way no longer."

"Very well," said Mr. Pickwick. "Now, where is this boarding-school?"

"It is a large, old, red-brick house, just outside the town, Sir," replied Job Trotter.

"And when," said Mr. Pickwick, "when is this villainous design to be carried into execution—when is this elopement to take place?"

"To-night, Sir," replied Job.

"To-night!" exclaimed Mr. Pickwick.

"This very night, Sir," replied Job Trotter. "That is what alarms me so much."

"Instant measures must be taken," said Mr. Pickwick. "I will see the lady who keeps the establishment, immediately."

"I beg your pardon, Sir," said Job, "but that course of proceeding will never do."

"Why not?" inquired Mr. Pickwick.

"My master, Sir, is a very artful man."

"I know he is," said Mr. Pickwick.

"And he has so wound himself round the old lady's heart, Sir," resumed Job, "that she would believe nothing to his prejudice, if you went down on your bare knees, and swore it; especially as you have no proof but the word of a servant, who, for anything she knows (and my master would be sure to say so), was discharged for some fault, and does this, in revenge."

"What had better be done, then?" said Mr. Pickwick.

"Nothing but taking him in the very fact of eloping, will convince the old lady, Sir," replied Job.

"All them old cats *will* run their heads agin mile-stones," observed Mr. Weller in a parenthesis.

"But this taking him in the very act of elopement, would be a very difficult thing to accomplish, I fear," said Mr. Pickwick.

"I don't know, Sir," said Mr. Trotter, after a few moments' reflection. "I think it might be very easily done."

"How?" was Mr. Pickwick's inquiry.

"Why," replied Mr. Trotter, "my master and I, being in the confidence of the two servants, will be secreted in the kitchen at ten o'clock. When the family have retired to rest, we shall come out of the kitchen, and the young lady out of her bed-room. A post-chaise will be waiting, and away we go."

"Well," said Mr. Pickwick.

"Well, Sir, I have been thinking that if you were waiting in the garden behind, alone—"

"Alone," said Mr. Pickwick. "Why alone?"

"I thought it very natural," replied Job, "that the old lady wouldn't like such an unpleasant discovery to be made before more persons than can possibly be helped. The young lady too, Sir—consider her feelings."

"You are very right," said Mr. Pickwick. "The consideration evinces great delicacy of feeling. Go on; you are very right."

"Well Sir, I was thinking that if you were waiting in the back garden alone, and I was to let you in, at the door which opens into it, from the end of the passage, at exactly half-past eleven o'clock, you would be just in the very moment of time, to assist me in frustrating the designs of this bad man, by whom I have been unfortunately ensnared." Here Mr. Trotter sighed deeply.

"Don't distress yourself on that account," said Mr. Pickwick," if he had one grain of the delicacy of feeling which distinguishes you, humble as your station is, I should have some hopes of him."

Job Trotter bowed low; and in spite of Mr. Weller's previous remonstrance, the tears again rose to his eyes.

"I never see such a feller," said Sam. "Blessed if I don't think he's got a main in his head as is always turned on."

"Sam," said Mr. Pickwick, with great severity. "Hold your tongue."

"Wery well, Sir," replied Mr. Weller.

"I don't like this plan," said Mr. Pickwick, after deep meditation. "Why cannot I communicate with the young lady's friends?"

"Because they live one hundred miles from here, Sir," responded Job Trotter.

"That's a clincher," said Mr. Weller, aside.

"Then this garden," resumed Mr. Pickwick. "How am I to get into it?"

"The wall is very low, Sir, and your servant will give you a leg up."

"My servant will give me a leg up," repeated Mr. Pickwick, mechanically. "You will be sure to be near this door, that you speak of?"

"You cannot mistake it, Sir; it's the only one that opens into the garden. Tap at it, when you hear the clock strike, and I will open it instantly."

"I don't like the plan," said Mr. Pickwick; "but as I see no other, and as the happiness of this young lady's whole life is at stake, I adopt it. I shall be sure to be there."

Thus, for the second time, did Mr. Pickwick's innate good-feeling involve him in an enterprise, from which he would most willingly have stood aloof.

"What is the name of the house?" inquired Mr. Pickwick.

"Westgate House, Sir. You turn a little to the right when you get to the end of the town; it stands by itself, some little distance off the high road, with the name on a brass plate on the gate."

"I know it," said Mr. Pickwick. "I observed it once before, when I was in this town. You may depend upon me."

Mr. Trotter made another bow, and turned to depart, when Mr. Pickwick thrust a guinea into his hand.

"You're a fine fellow," said Mr. Pickwick, "and I admire your goodness of heart. No thanks. Remember—eleven o'clock."

"There is no fear of my forgetting it, Sir," replied Job Trotter. With these words he left the room, followed by Sam.

"I say," said the latter, "not a bad notion that 'ere crying. I'd cry like a rain-water spout in a shower, on such good terms. How do you do it?"

"It comes from the heart, Mr. Walker," replied Job solemnly. "Good morning, Sir."

"You're a soft customer, you are;—we've got it all out o' you, any how," thought Mr. Weller, as Job walked away.

We cannot state the precise nature of the thoughts which passed through Mr. Trotter's mind, because we don't know what they were.

The day wore on, evening came, and at a little before ten o'clock Sam Weller reported that Mr. Jingle and Job had gone out together, that their luggage was packed up, and that they had ordered a chaise. The plot was evidently in execution, as Mr. Trotter had foretold.

Half-past ten o'clock arrived, and it was time for Mr. Pickwick to issue forth on his delicate errand. Resisting Sam's tender of his great coat, in order that he might have no incumbrance in scaling the wall, he set forth, followed by his attendant.

There was a bright moon, but it was behind the clouds. It was a fine dry night, but it was most uncommonly dark. Paths, hedges, fields, houses, and trees, were enveloped in one deep shade. The atmosphere was hot and sultry, the summer lightning quivered faintly on the verge of the horizon, and was the only sight that varied the dull gloom in which everything was wrapped—sound there was none, except the distant barking of some restless house-dog.

They found the house, read the brass-plate, walked round the wall, and stopped at that portion of it which divided them from the bottom of the garden.

"You will return to the inn, Sam, when you have assisted me over," said Mr. Pickwick.

"Wery well, Sir."

"And you will sit up, 'till I return."

"Cert'nly, Sir."

"Take hold of my leg; and, when I say 'Over,' raise me gently."

"All right, Sir."

Having settled these preliminaries, Mr. Pickwick grasped the top of the wall, and gave the word "Over," which was very literally obeyed. Whether his body partook in some degree of the elasticity of his mind, or whether Mr. Weller's notions of a gentle push were of a somewhat rougher description than Mr. Pickwick's, the immediate effect of his assistance was to jerk that immortal gentleman completely over the wall on to the bed beneath, where, after crushing three gooseberry-bushes and a rose-tree, he finally alighted at full length.

"You ha'n't hurt yourself, I hope, Sir?" said Sam, in a loud whisper, as soon as he recovered from the surprise consequent upon the mysterious disappearance of his master.

"I have not hurt *myself*, Sam, certainly," replied Mr. Pickwick, from the other side of the wall, "but I rather think that *you* have hurt *me*."

"I hope not, Sir," said Sam.

"Never mind," said Mr. Pickwick, rising, "it's nothing but a few scratches. Go away, or we shall be overheard."

"Good-bye, Sir."

"Good-bye."

With stealthy steps Sam Weller departed, leaving Mr. Pickwick alone in the garden.

Lights occasionally appeared in the different windows of the house, or glanced from the staircases, as if the inmates were retiring to rest. Not caring to go too near the door, until the appointed time, Mr. Pickwick crouched into an angle of the wall, and awaited its arrival.

It was a situation which might well have depressed the spirits of many a man. Mr. Pickwick, however, felt neither depression nor misgiving. He knew that his purpose was in the main a good one, and he placed implicit reliance on the high-minded Job. It was dull, certainly; not to say, dreary; but a contemplative man can always employ himself in meditation. Mr. Pickwick had meditated himself into a doze, when he was roused by the chimes of the neighbouring church ringing out the hour—half-past eleven.

"That's the time," thought Mr. Pickwick, getting cautiously on his feet. He looked up at the house. The lights had disappeared, and the shutters were closed—all in bed, no doubt. He walked on tip-toe to the door, and gave a gentle tap. Two or three minutes passing without any reply, he gave another tap rather louder, and then another rather louder than that.

At length the sound of feet was audible upon the stairs, and then the light of a candle shone through the key-hole of the door. There was a good deal of unchaining and unbolting, and the door was slowly opened.

Now the door opened outwards: and as the door opened wider and wider, Mr. Pickwick receded behind it, more and more. What was his astonishment when he just peeped out, by way of caution, to see that the person who had opened it was—not Job Trotter, but a servant-girl with a candle in her hand! Mr. Pickwick drew in his head again, with the swiftness displayed by that admirable melo-dramatic performer, Punch, when he lies in wait for the flat-headed comedian with the tin box of music.

"It must have been the cat, Sarah," said the girl, addressing herself to some one in the house. "Puss, puss, puss—tit, tit, tit."

But no animal being decoyed by these blandishments, the girl slowly closed the door, and re-fastened it; leaving Mr. Pickwick drawn up straight against the wall.

"This is very curious," thought Mr. Pickwick. "They are sitting up, beyond their usual hour, I suppose. Extremely unfortunate, that they should have chosen this night, of all others, for such a purpose—exceedingly." And with these thoughts, Mr. Pickwick cautiously retired to the angle of the wall in which he had been before ensconced; waiting until such time as he might deem it safe to repeat the signal.

He had not been here five minutes, when a vivid flash of lightning was followed by a loud peal of thunder that crashed and rolled away in the distance with terrific noise—then came another flash of lightning, brighter than the other, and a second peal of thunder louder than the first; and then down came the rain, with a force and fury that swept everything before it.

Mr. Pickwick was perfectly aware that a tree is a very dangerous neighbour in a thunder-storm. He had a tree on his right, a tree on his left, a third before him, and a fourth behind. If he remained where he was, he might fall the victim of an accident; if he showed himself in the centre of the garden, he might be consigned to a constable; —once or twice he tried to scale the wall, but having no other legs this time, than those with which Nature had furnished him, the only effect of his struggles was to inflict a variety of very unpleasant gratings on his knees and shins, and to throw him into a state of the most profuse perspiration.

"What a dreadful situation," said Mr. Pickwick, pausing to wipe his brow after this exercise. He looked up at the house—all was dark. They must be gone to bed now. He would try the signal again.

He walked on tip-toe across the moist gravel, and tapped at the door. He held his breath, and listened at the key-hole. No reply: very odd. Another knock. He listened again. There was a low whispering inside, and then a voice cried—

"Who's there?"

"That's not Job," thought Mr. Pickwick, hastily drawing himself straight up against the wall again. "It's a woman."

He had scarcely had time to form this conclusion, when a window above stairs, was thrown up, and three or four female voices repeated the query—"Who's there?"

Mr. Pickwick dared not move hand or foot. It was clear that the whole establishment was roused. He made up his mind to remain where he was, until the alarm had subsided: and then to make a supernatural effort, and get over the wall, or perish in the attempt.

Like all Mr. Pickwick's determinations, this was the best that could be made under the circumstances; but, unfortunately, it was founded upon the assumption that they would not venture to open the door again. What was his discomfiture, when he heard the chain and bolts withdrawn, and saw the door slowly opening, wider and wider! He retreated into the corner, step by step; but do what he would, the interposition of his own person prevented its being opened to its utmost width.

"Who's there?" screamed a numerous chorus of treble voices from the stair-case inside, consisting of the spinster lady of the establishment, three teachers, five female servants, and thirty boarders, all half-dressed, and in a forest of curl-papers.

Of course Mr. Pickwick didn't say who *was* there: and then the burden of the chorus changed into—"Lor'! I am so frightened."

"Cook," said the lady abbess, who took care to be on the top stair, the very last of the group—"Cook, why don't you go a little way into the garden?"

"Please ma'am, I don't like," responded the cook.

"Lor', what a stupid thing that cook is!" said the thirty boarders.

"Cook," said the lady abbess, with great dignity; "don't answer me, if you please. I insist upon your looking into the garden, immediately."

Here the cook began to cry, and the housemaid said it was "a shame!" for which partisanship she received a month's warning on the spot.

"Do you hear, cook?" said the lady abbess, stamping her foot, impatiently.

"Don't you hear your missis, cook?" said the three teachers.

"What an impudent thing, that cook is!" said the thirty boarders.

The unfortunate cook, thus strongly urged, advanced a step or two, and holding her candle just where it prevented her seeing any thing at all, declared there was nothing there, and it must have been the wind; and the door was just going to be closed in consequence, when an inquisitive boarder, who had been peeping between the hinges, set up a fearful screaming, which called back the cook and the housemaid, and all the more adventurous, in no time.

"What *is* the matter with Miss Smithers?" said the lady abbess, as the aforesaid Miss Smithers proceeded to go into hysterics of four young lady power.

"Lor, Miss Smithers dear," said the other nine-and-twenty boarders.

"Oh, the man—the man—behind the door!" screamed Miss Smithers.

The lady abbess no sooner heard this appalling cry, than she retreated to her own bed-room, double-locked the door, and fainted away all comfortably. The boarders, and the teachers, and the servants, fell back upon the stairs, and upon each other; and never was such a screaming, and fainting, and struggling, beheld. In the midst of the tumult, Mr. Pickwick emerged from his concealment, and presented himself amongst them.

"Ladies—dear ladies," said Mr. Pickwick.

"Oh, he says we're dear," cried the oldest and ugliest teacher. "Oh the wretch."

"Ladies," roared Mr. Pickwick, rendered desperate by the danger of his situation. "Hear me. I am no robber. I want the lady of the house."

"Oh, what a ferocious monster!" screamed another teacher. "He wants Miss Tomkins."

Here there was a general scream.

"Ring the alarm bell, somebody," cried a dozen voices.

"Don't—don't," shouted Mr. Pickwick. "Look at me. Do I look like a robber? My dear ladies—you may bind me hand and leg, or lock me up in a closet, if you like. Only hear what I have got to say—only hear me."

"How did you come in our garden?" faultered the housemaid.

"Call the lady of the house, and I'll tell her everything—everything:" said Mr. Pickwick, exerting his lungs to the utmost pitch. "Call her—only be quiet, and call her, and you shall hear everything."

It might have been Mr. Pickwick's appearance, or it might have been his manner, or it might have been the temptation—so irresistible to a female mind—of hearing something at present enveloped in mystery, that reduced the more reasonable portion of the establishment (some four individuals) to a state of comparative quiet. By them it was proposed, as a test of Mr. Pickwick's sincerity, that he should immediately submit to personal restraint; and that gentleman having consented to hold a conference with Miss Tomkins, from the interior of a closet in which the day boarders hung their bonnets and sandwich-bags, he at once stepped into it, of his own accord, and was securely locked in. This revived the others; and Miss Tomkins having been brought to, and brought down, the conference began.

"What did you do in my garden, man?" said Miss Tomkins, in a faint voice.

"I came to warn you, that one of your young ladies was going to elope to-night," replied Mr. Pickwick, from the interior of the closet.

"Elope!" exclaimed Miss Tomkins, the three teachers, the thirty boarders, and the five servants. "Who with?"

"Your friend, Mr. Charles Fitz-Marshall."

"*My* friend! I don't know any such person."

"Well; Mr. Jingle, then."

"I never heard the name in my life."

"Then, I have been deceived, and deluded," said Mr. Pickwick. "I have been the victim of a conspiracy—a foul and base conspiracy. Send to the Angel, my dear ma'am, if you don't believe me. Send to the Angel for Mr. Pickwick's man-servant, I implore you, ma'am."

"He must be respectable—he keeps a man-servant," said Miss Tomkins to the writing and ciphering governess.

"It's my opinion, Miss Tomkins," said the writing and ciphering governess, "that his man-servant keeps him. *I* think he's a madman, Miss Tomkins, and the other's his keeper."

"I think you are very right, Miss Gwynn," responded Miss Tomkins. "Let two of the servants repair to the Angel, and let the others remain here, to protect us."

So two of the servants were despatched to the Angel in search of Mr. Samuel Weller: and the remaining three stopped behind to protect Miss Tomkins, and the three teachers, and the thirty boarders. And Mr. Pickwick sat down in the closet, beneath a grove of sandwich bags, and awaited the return of the messengers, with all the philosophy and fortitude he could summon to his aid.

An hour and a half elapsed before they came back, and when they did come, Mr. Pickwick recognised, in addition to the voice of Mr. Samuel Weller, two other voices, the tones of which struck familiarly on his ear; but whose they were, he could not for the life of him call to mind.

A very brief conversation ensued. The door was unlocked. Mr. Pickwick stepped out of the closet, and found himself in the presence of the whole establishment of Westgate House, Mr. Samuel Weller, and—old Wardle, and his destined son-in-law, Mr. Trundle!

"My dear friend," said Mr. Pickwick, running forward and grasping Wardle's hand, "my dear friend, pray, for Heaven's sake, explain to this lady the unfortunate and dreadful situation in which I am placed. You must have heard it from my servant; say, at all events, my dear fellow, that I am neither a robber nor a madman."

"I have said so, my dear friend. I have said so already," replied Mr. Wardle, shaking the right hand of his friend, while Mr. Trundle shook the left.

"And whoever says, or has said, he is," interposed Mr. Weller, stepping forward, "says that which is not the truth, but so far from it, on the contrary, quite the rewerse. And if there's any number o' men on these here premises as has said so, I shall be wery happy to give 'em a wery convincing proof o' their being mistaken, in this here wery room, if these wery respectable ladies 'll have the goodness to retire, and order 'em up, one at a time." Having delivered this defiance with great volubility, Mr. Weller struck his open palm emphatically with his clenched fist, and winked pleasantly on Miss Tomkins, the intensity of whose horror at his supposing it within the bounds of possibility that there could be any men on the premises of Westgate House Establishment for Young Ladies, it is impossible to describe.

Mr. Pickwick's explanation having been already partially made, was soon concluded. But neither in the course of his walk home with his friends, nor afterwards when seated before a blazing fire at the supper he so much needed, could a single observation be drawn from him. He seemed bewildered and amazed. Once, and only once, he turned round to Mr. Wardle, and said

"How did you come here?"

"Trundle and I came down here, for some good shooting on the first," replied Wardle. "We arrived to-night and were astonished to hear from your servant that you were here too. But I am glad you are," said the jolly old fellow, slapping him on the back. "I am glad you are. We shall have a jolly party on the first, and we'll give Winkle another chance—eh, old boy?"

Mr. Pickwick made no reply; he did not even ask after his friends at Dingley Dell, and shortly afterwards retired for the night, desiring Sam to fetch his candle when he rung.

The bell did ring in due course, and Mr. Weller presented himself.

"Sam," said Mr. Pickwick, looking out from under the bed-clothes.

"Sir," said Mr. Weller.

Mr. Pickwick paused, and Mr. Weller snuffed the candle.

"Sam," said Mr. Pickwick again, as if with a desperate effort.

"Sir," said Mr. Weller, once more.

"Where is that Trotter?"

"Job, Sir?"

"Yes."

"Gone, Sir."

"With his master, I suppose?"

"Friend or master, or whatever he is, he's gone with him," replied Mr. Weller. "There's a pair on 'em, Sir."

"Jingle suspected my design, and set that fellow on you, with this story, I suppose?" said Mr. Pickwick, half choking.

"Just that, Sir," replied Mr. Weller.

"It was all false, of course?"

"All, Sir," replied Mr. Weller. "Reg'lar do, Sir; artful dodge."

"I don't think he'll escape us quite so easily the next time, Sam?" said Mr. Pickwick.

"I don't think he will, Sir."

"Whenever I meet that Jingle again, wherever it is," said Mr. Pickwick, raising himself in bed, and indenting his pillow with a tremendous blow, "I'll inflict personal chastisement on him, in addition to the exposure he so richly merits. I will, or my name is not Pickwick."

"And venever I catches hold o' that there melan-cholly chap with the black hair," said Sam, "if I don't bring some real water into his eyes, for once in a way, my name a'nt Weller. Good night, Sir."

CHAPTER XVII.

SHOWING THAT AN ATTACK OF RHEUMATISM, IN SOME CASES, ACTS AS A QUICKENER TO INVENTIVE GENIUS.

THE constitution of Mr. Pickwick, though able to sustain a very considerable amount of exertion and fatigue, was not proof against such a combination of attacks as he had undergone on the memorable night, recorded in the last chapter. The process of being washed in the night air, and rough-dried in a close closet, is as dangerous as it is peculiar. Mr. Pickwick was laid up with an attack of rheumatism.

But although the bodily powers of the great man were thus impaired, his mental energies retained their pristine vigour. His spirits were elastic; his good humour was restored. Even the vexation consequent upon his recent adventure had vanished from his mind; and he could join in the hearty laughter which any allusion to it excited in Mr. Wardle, without anger and without embarrassment. Nay, more. During the two days Mr. Pickwick was confined to his bed, Sam was his constant attendant. On the first, he endeavoured to amuse his master by anecdote and conversation; on the second Mr. Pickwick demanded his writing-desk, and pen and ink, and was deeply engaged during the whole day. On the third, being able to sit up in his bed-chamber, he despatched his valet with a message to Mr. Wardle and Mr. Trundle, intimating that if they would take their wine there, that evening, they would greatly oblige him. The invitation was most willingly accepted; and when they were seated over their wine, Mr. Pickwick with sundry blushes, produced the following little tale, as having been "edited" by himself, during his recent indisposition, from his notes of Mr. Weller's unsophisticated recital.

"THE PARISH CLERK—A TALE OF TRUE LOVE.

"Once upon a time, in a very small country town, at a considerable distance from London, there lived a little man named Nathaniel Pipkin, who was the parish clerk of the little town, and lived in a little house in the little high street, within ten minutes' walk of the little church; and who was to be found every day from nine till four, teaching a little learning to the little boys. Nathaniel Pipkin was a harmless, inoffensive, good-natured being, with a turned-up nose, and rather turned-in legs, a cast in his eye, and a halt in his gait; and he divided his time between the church and his school, verily believing that there existed not, on the face of the earth, so clever a man as the curate, so imposing an apartment as the vestry-room, or so well-ordered a seminary as his own. Once, and only once, in his life, Nathaniel Pipkin had seen a bishop—a real bishop, with his arms in lawn sleeves, and his head in a wig. He had seen him walk, and heard him talk at a confirmation, on which momentous occasion Nathaniel Pipkin was so overcome with reverence and awe, when the aforesaid bishop laid his hand on his head, that he fainted right clean away, and was borne out of church in the arms of the beadle.

"This was a great event, a tremendous era, in Nathaniel Pipkin's life, and it was about the only one that had ever occurred to ruffle the smooth current of his quiet existence, when happening one fine afternoon, in a fit of mental abstraction, to raise his eyes from the slate on which he was devising some tremendous problem in compound addition for an offending urchin to solve, they suddenly rested on the blooming countenance of Maria Lobbs, the only daughter of old Lobbs the great saddler over the way. Now, the eyes of Mr. Pipkins had rested on the pretty face of Maria Lobbs many a time and oft before, at church and elsewhere: but the eyes of Maria Lobbs had never looked so bright, the cheeks of Maria Lobbs had never looked so ruddy, as upon this particular occasion. No wonder then, that Nathaniel Pipkin was unable to take his eyes from the countenance of Miss Lobbs; no wonder that Miss Lobbs, finding herself stared at by a young man, withdrew her head from the window out of which she had been peeping, and shut the casement and pulled down the blind; no wonder that Nathaniel Pipkin, immediately thereafter, fell upon the young urchin who had previously offended, and cuffed and knocked him to his heart's content. All this was very natural, and there's nothing at all to wonder at about it.

"It *is* matter of wonder, though, that any one of Mr. Nathaniel Pipkin's retiring disposition, nervous temperament, and most particularly diminutive income, should from this day forth, have dared to aspire to the hand and heart of the only daughter of the fiery old Lobbs—of old Lobbs the great saddler, who could have bought up the whole village at one stroke of his pen, and never felt the outlay—old Lobbs, who was well known to have heaps of money, invested in the bank at the nearest market town—who was reported to have countless and inexhaustible treasures, hoarded up in the little iron safe with the big keyhole, over the chimney-piece in the back parlour—and who, it was well known, on festive occasions garnished his board with a real silver tea-pot, cream ewer, and sugar-basin, which he was wont, in the pride of his heart, to boast should be his daughter's property when he found a man to her mind. I repeat it, to be matter of profound astonishment and intense wonder, that Nathaniel Pipkin should have had the temerity to cast his eyes in this direction. But love is blind, and Nathaniel had a cast in his eye: and perhaps these two circumstances, taken together, prevented his seeing the matter, in its proper light.

"Now, if old Lobbs had entertained the most remote or distant idea of the state of the affections of Nathaniel Pipkin, he would just have razed the school-room to the ground, or exterminated its master from the surface of the earth, or committed some other outrage and atrocity of an equally ferocious and violent description; for he was a terrible old fellow, that Lobbs, when his pride was injured, or his blood was up. Swear! Such trains of oaths would come rolling and pealing over the way, sometimes, when he

was denouncing the idleness of the bony apprentice with the thin legs, that Nathaniel Pipkin would shake in his shoes with horror, and the hair of the pupils' heads would stand on end with fright.

"Well, day after day, when school was over and the pupils gone, did Nathaniel Pipkin sit himself down at the front window, and while he feigned to be reading a book, throw sidelong glances over the way in search of the bright eyes of Maria Lobbs; and he hadn't sat there many days, before the bright eyes appeared at an upper window, apparently deeply engaged in reading too. This was delightful, and gladdening to the heart of Nathaniel Pipkin. It was something to sit there for hours together, and look upon that pretty face when the eyes were cast down; but when Maria Lobbs began to raise her eyes from her book, and dart their rays in the direction of Nathaniel Pipkin, his delight and admiration were perfectly boundless. At last, one day when he knew old Lobbs was out, Nathaniel Pipkin had the temerity to kiss his hand to Maria Lobbs; and Maria Lobbs, instead of shutting the window, and pulling down the blind, kissed *hers* to him, and smiled. Upon which, Nathaniel Pipkin determined, that, come what might, he would develope the state of his feelings, without further delay.

"A prettier foot, a gayer heart, a more dimpled face, or a smarter form, never bounded so lightly over the earth they graced, as did those of Maria Lobbs, the old saddler's daughter. There was a roguish twinkle in her sparkling eyes, that would have made its way to far less susceptible bosoms than that of Nathaniel Pipkin; and there was such a joyous sound in her merry laugh, that the sternest misanthrope must have smiled to hear it. Even old Lobbs himself, in the very height of his ferocity, couldn't resist the coaxing of his pretty daughter; and when she, and her cousin Kate—an arch, impudent-looking, bewitching little person—made a dead set upon the old man together, as, to say the truth, they very often did, he could have refused them nothing, even had they asked for a portion of the countless and inexhaustible treasures, which were hidden from the light, in the iron safe.

"Nathaniel Pipkin's heart beat high within him, when he saw this enticing little couple some hundred yards before him, one summer's evening, in the very field in which he had many a time strolled about till night-time, and pondered on the beauty of Maria Lobbs. But though he had often thought then, how briskly he would walk up to Maria Lobbs and tell her of his passion if he could only meet her, he felt, now that she was unexpectedly before him, all the blood in his body mounting to his face, manifestly to the great detriment of his legs, which, deprived of their usual portion, trembled beneath him. When they stopped to gather a hedge-flower, or listen to a bird, Nathaniel Pipkin stopped too, and pretended to be absorbed in meditation, as indeed he really was; for he was thinking what on earth he should ever do, when they turned back, as they inevitably must in time, and meet him face to face. But though he was afraid to make up to them, he couldn't bear to lose sight of them; so when they walked faster he walked faster, when they lingered he lingered, and when they stopped he stopped; and so they might have gone on, till the darkness prevented them, if Kate had not looked slily back, and encouragingly beckoned Nathaniel to advance. There was something in Kate's manner that was not to be resisted, and so Nathaniel Pipkin complied with the invitation; and after a great deal of blushing on his part, and immoderate laughter on that of the wicked little cousin, Nathaniel Pipkin went down on his knees on the dewy grass, and declared his resolution to remain there for ever, unless he was permitted to rise the accepted lover of Maria Lobbs. Upon this, the merry laughter of Maria Lobbs rang through the calm evening air—without seeming to disturb it, though; it had such a pleasant sound—and the wicked little cousin laughed more immoderately than before, and Nathaniel Pipkin blushed deeper than ever. At length, Maria Lobbs being more strenuously urged by the love-worn little man, turned away her head, and whispered her cousin to say, or at all events Kate *did* say, that she felt much honoured by Mr. Pipkin's addresses, that her hand and heart were at her father's disposal, but that nobody could be insensible to Mr. Pipkin's merits. As all this was said with much gravity, and as Nathaniel Pipkin walked home with Maria Lobbs, and struggled for a kiss at parting, he went to bed a happy man, and dreamed all night long, of softening old Lobbs, opening the strong box, and marrying Maria.

"The next day, Nathaniel Pipkin saw old Lobbs go out upon his old grey poney, and after a great many signs at the window from the wicked little cousin, the object and meaning of which he could by no means understand, the bony apprentice with the thin legs came over to say that his master wasn't coming home all night, and that the ladies expected Mr. Pipkin to tea, at six o'clock precisely. How the lessons were got through that day, neither Nathaniel Pipkin nor his pupils knew any more than you do; but they were got through somehow, and, after the boys had gone, Nathaniel Pipkin took till full six o'clock to dress himself to his satisfaction; not that it took long to select the garments he should wear, inasmuch as he had no choice about the matter, but the putting them on to the best advantage, and touching them up previously, was a task of no inconsiderable difficulty or importance.

"There was a very snug little party, consisting of Maria Lobbs and her cousin Kate, and three or four romping, good-humoured, rosy-cheeked girls. Nathaniel Pipkin had ocular demonstration of the fact, that even the rumours of old Lobbs's treasures were not exaggerated. There were the real solid silver tea-pot, cream-ewer, and sugar-basin, on the table, and real silver spoons to stir the tea with, and real china cups to drink it out of, and plates of the same, to hold the cakes and toast in. The only eye-sore in the whole place, was another cousin of Maria Lobbs's, and brother of Kate, whom Maria Lobbs called 'Henry,' and who seemed to keep Maria Lobbs all to himself, up in one corner of the table. It's a delightful thing to see affection in families, but it may be carried rather too far, and Nathaniel Pipkin could not help thinking that Maria Lobbs must be very particularly fond of her relations, if she paid as much attention to all of them as to this individual cousin. After tea, too, when the wicked little cousin proposed a game at blind man's buff, it somehow or other happened that Nathaniel Pipkin was nearly always blind, and whenever he laid his hand upon the male cousin, he was sure to find that Maria Lobbs was not far off. And though the wicked little cousin and the other girls pinched him, and pulled his hair, and pushed chairs in his way, and all sorts of things, Maria Lobbs never seemed to come near him at all; and once—once—Nathaniel Pipkin could have sworn he heard the sound of a kiss, followed by a faint remonstrance from Maria Lobbs, and a half-suppressed laugh from her female friends. All this was odd—very odd—and

there is no saying what Nathaniel Pipkin might or might not have done, in consequence, if his thoughts had not been suddenly directed into a new channel.

"The circumstance which directed his thoughts into a new channel was a loud knocking at the street-door, and the person who made this loud knocking at the street-door, was no other than old Lobbs himself, who had unexpectedly returned, and was hammering away, like a coffin-maker: for he wanted his supper. The alarming intelligence was no sooner communicated by the bony apprentice with the thin legs, than the girls tripped up stairs to Maria Lobbs's bed-room, and the male cousin and Nathaniel Pipkin were thrust into a couple of closets in the sitting-room, for want of any better places of concealment; and when Maria Lobbs and the wicked little cousin had stowed them away, and put the room to rights, they opened the street door to old Lobbs, who had never left off knocking since he first began.

"Now it did unfortunately happen that old Lobbs being very hungry was monstrous cross. Nathaniel Pipkin could hear him growling away like an old mastiff with a sore throat; and whenever the unfortunate apprentice with the thin legs came into the room, so surely did old Lobbs commence swearing at him in a most Saracenic and ferocious manner, though apparently with no other end or object than that of easing his bosom by the discharge of a few superfluous oaths. At length some supper, which had been warming up, was placed on the table, and then old Lobbs fell to, in regular style; and, having made clear work of it in no time, kissed his daughter, and demanded his pipe.

"Nature had placed Nathaniel Pipkin's knees in very close juxtaposition, but when he heard old Lobbs demand his pipe, they knocked together, as if they were going to reduce each other to powder: for, depending from a couple of hooks, in the very closet in which he stood, was a large brown-stemmed, silver-bowled pipe, which pipe he himself had seen in the mouth of old Lobbs, regularly every afternoon and evening, for the last five years. The two girls went down stairs for the pipe, and up stairs for the pipe, and everywhere but where they knew the pipe was, and old Lobbs stormed away meanwhile, in the most wonderful manner. At last he thought of the closet, and walked up to it. It was of no use a little man like Nathaniel Pipkin pulling the door inwards, when a great strong fellow like old Lobbs was pulling it outwards. Old Lobbs just gave it one tug, and open it flew, disclosing Nathaniel Pipkin standing bolt upright inside, and shaking with apprehension from head to foot. Bless us! what an appalling look old Lobbs gave him, as he dragged him out by the collar, and held him at arm's length.

"'Why, what the devil do you want here?' said old Lobbs, in a fearful voice.

"Nathaniel Pipkin could make no reply, so old Lobbs shook him backwards and forwards, for two or three minutes, by way of arranging his ideas for him.

"'What do you want here?' roared Lobbs, 'I suppose *you* have come after my daughter, now.'

"Old Lobbs merely said this as a sneer: for he did not believe that mortal presumption could have carried Nathaniel Pipkin so far. What was his indignation, when that poor man replied—

"'Yes, I did, Mr. Lobbs—I did come after your daughter. I love her, Mr. Lobbs.'

"'Why, you snivelling, wry-faced little villain,' gasped

old Lobbs, paralysed at the atrocious confession: ' what do you mean by that? Say this to my face! Damme, I'll throttle you.'

"It is by no means improbable that old Lobbs would have carried this threat into execution, in the excess of his rage, if his arm had not been stayed by a very unexpected apparition, to wit, the male cousin, who, stepping out of his closet, and walking up to old Lobbs, said—

" ' I cannot allow this harmless person, Sir, who has been asked here, in some girlish frolic, to take upon himself, in a very noble manner, the fault (if fault it is) which I am guilty of, and am ready to avow. *I* love your daughter, Sir; and *I* came here for the purpose of meeting her.'

"Old Lobbs opened his eyes very wide at this, but not wider than Nathaniel Pipkin.

" ' You did?' said Lobbs: at last finding breath to speak.

" ' I did.'

" ' And I forbade you this house, long ago.'

" ' You did, or I should not have been here, clandestinely, to-night.'

"I am sorry to record it, of old Lobbs, but I think he would have struck the cousin, if his pretty daughter, with her bright eyes swimming in tears, had not clung to his arm.

" ' Don't stop him, Maria,' said the young man: ' if he has the will to strike me, let him. I would not hurt a hair of his grey head, for the riches of the world.'

"The old man cast down his eyes at this reproof, and they met those of his daughter. I have hinted once or twice before, that they were very bright eyes, and, though they were tearful now, their influence was by no means lessened. Old Lobbs turned his head away, as if to avoid being persuaded by them, when, as fortune would have it, he encountered the face of the wicked little cousin, who, half afraid for her brother, and half laughing at Nathaniel Pipkin, presented as bewitching an expression of countenance, with a touch of slyness in it too, as any man, old or young, need look upon. She drew her arm coaxingly through the old man's, and whispered something in his ear; and do what he would, old Lobbs couldn't help breaking out into a smile, while a tear stole down his cheek, at the same time.

"Five minutes after this, the girls were brought down from the bed-room with a great deal of giggling and modesty; and while the young people were making themselves perfectly happy, old Lobbs got down the pipe, and smoked it: and it was a remarkable circumstance about that particular pipe of tobacco, that it was the most soothing and lightful one he ever smoked.

"Nathaniel Pipkin thought it best to keep his own counsel, and by so doing gradually rose into high favour with old Lobbs, who taught him to smoke in time; and they used to sit out in the garden on the fine evenings, for many years afterwards, smoking and drinking in great state. He soon recovered the effects of his attachment, for we find his name in the parish register, as a witness to the marriage of Maria Lobbs to her cousin; and it also appears, by reference to other documents, that on the night of the wedding, he was incarcerated in the village cage, for having, in a state of extreme intoxication, committed sundry excesses in the streets, in all of which he was aided and abetted by the bony apprentice with the thin legs."

CHAPTER XVIII

BRIEFLY ILLUSTRATIVE OF TWO POINTS—FIRST, THE POWER OF HYSTERICS, AND, SECONDLY, THE FORCE OF CIRCUMSTANCES.

FOR two days after the *dejeune* at Mrs. Hunter's, the Pickwickians remained at Eatanswill, anxiously awaiting the arrival of some intelligence from their revered leader. Mr. Tupman and Mr. Snodgrass, were once again left to their own means of amusement; for Mr. Winkle, in compliance with a most pressing invitation, continued to reside at Mr. Pott's house, and to devote his time to the companionship of his amiable lady. Nor was the occasional society of Mr. Pott himself, wanting to complete their felicity. Deeply immersed in the intensity of his speculations for the public weal, and the destruction of the Independent, it was not the habit of that great man to descend from his mental pinnacle to the humble level of ordinary minds. On this occasion, however, and as if expressly in compliment to any follower of Mr. Pickwick's, he unbent, relaxed, stepped down from his pedestal, and walked upon the ground: benignly adapting his remarks to the comprehension of the herd, and seeming in outward form, if not in spirit, to be one of them.

Such having been the demeanour of this celebrated public character towards Mr. Winkle, it will be readily imagined that considerable surprise was depicted on the countenance of the latter gentleman when, as he was sitting alone in the breakfast-room, the door was hastily thrown open, and as hastily closed, on the entrance of Mr. Pott, who, stalking majestically towards him, and thrusting aside his proffered hand, ground his teeth, as if to put a sharper edge on what he was about to utter, and exclaimed, in a saw-like voice,—

"Serpent!"

"Sir!" exclaimed Mr. Winkle, starting from his chair.

"Serpent, Sir," repeated Mr. Pott, raising his voice, and then suddenly depressing it; "I said, Serpent, Sir—make the most of it."

Now when you have parted with a man, at two o'clock in the morning, on terms of the utmost good fellowship, and he meets you again, at half-past nine, and greets you as a serpent, it is not unreasonable to conclude that something of an unpleasant nature has occurred meanwhile. So Mr. Winkle thought. He returned Mr. Pott's gaze of stone, and in compliance with that gentleman's request, proceeded to make the most he could of the "serpent." The most, however, was just nothing at all; so, after a profound silence of some minutes' duration, he said,—

"Serpent, Sir! Serpent, Mr. Pott! What can you mean, Sir?—this is pleasantry."

"Pleasantry, Sir!" exclaimed Pott, with a motion of the hand, indicative of a strong desire to hurl the Britannia metal tea-pot at the head of his visiter. "Pleasantry, Sir! ——but no, I will be calm; I will be calm, Sir;" and in proof of his calmness, Mr. Pott flung himself into a chair, and foamed at the mouth.

"My dear Sir," interposed Mr. Winkle.

"*Dear* Sir!" replied Pott. "How dare you address me, as dear Sir, Sir? How dare you look me in the face and do it?"

"Well, Sir, if you come to that," responded Mr. Winkle,

"how dare you look *me* in the face, and call me a serpent, Sir?"

"Because you are one," replied Mr. Pott.

"Prove it, Sir," said Mr. Winkle, warmly. "Prove it."

A malignant scowl passed over the profound face of the editor, as he drew from his pocket, the Independent of that morning; and laying his finger on a particular paragraph, threw the journal across the table to Mr. Winkle.

That gentleman took it up, and read as follows:—

"Our obscure and filthy contemporary, in some disgusting observations on the recent election for this borough, has presumed to violate the hallowed sanctity of private life, and to refer, in a manner not to be misunderstood, to the personal affairs of our late candidate—aye, and notwithstanding his base defeat, we will add, our future member, Mr. Fizkin. What does our dastardly contemporary mean? What would the ruffian say, if we, setting at naught, like him, the decencies of social intercourse, were to raise the curtain which happily conceals *his* private life from general ridicule, not to say from general execration? What, if we were even to point out, and comment on, facts and circumstances which are publicly notorious, and beheld by every one, but our mole-eyed contemporary—what if we were to print the following effusion, which we received while we were writing the commencement of this article, from a talented fellow-townsman and correspondent:—

"'LINES TO A BRASS POT.

"'Oh Pott! if you'd known
How false she'd have grown,
When you heard the marriage bells tinkle;
You'd have done then, I vow,
What you cannot help now,
And handed her over to W******.'"

"What," said Mr. Pott, solemnly—"what rhymes to 'tinkle,' villain?"

"What rhymes to tinkle?" said Mrs. Pott, whose entrance at the moment forestalled the reply. "What rhymes to tinkle? Why, Winkle, I should conceive:" and saying this, Mrs. Pott smiled sweetly on the disturbed Pickwickian, and extended her hand towards him. The agitated young man would have accepted it, in his confusion, had not Pott indignantly interposed.

"Back, Ma'am—back," said the editor. "Take his hand before my very face!"

"Mr. P.!" said his astonished lady.

"Wretched woman, look here," exclaimed the husband. "Look here, Ma'am—'Lines to a brass Pot,' Ma'am. 'Brass pot;'—that's me, Ma'am. 'False *she*'d have grown;'—that's you, Ma'am—you." With this ebullition of rage, which was not unaccompanied with something like a tremble, at the expression of his wife's face, Mr. Pott dashed the current number of the Eatanswill Independent at her feet.

"Upon my word, Sir," said the astonished Mrs. Pott, stooping to pick up the paper. "Upon my word, Sir."

Mr. Pott winced beneath the contemptuous gaze of his wife. He had made a desperate struggle to screw up his courage, but it was fast coming unscrewed again.

There appears nothing very tremendous in this little sentence, "Upon my word, Sir," when it comes to be read; but the tone of voice in which it was delivered, and the look that accompanied it, both seeming to bear reference to some revenge to be thereafter wreaked upon the head of Pott, produced their full effect upon him. The most un-

skilful observer could have detected in his troubled countenance, a readiness to resign his Wellington boots to any efficient substitute who would have consented to stand in them at that moment.

Mrs. Pott read the paragraph, uttered a loud shriek, and threw herself at full length on the hearth-rug, screaming, and tapping it with the heels of her shoes, in a manner which could leave no doubt of the propriety of her feelings on the occasion.

"My dear," said the terrified Pott,—"I didn't say I believed it;—I——" but the unfortunate man's voice was drowned in the screaming of his partner.

"Mrs. Pott, let me entreat you, my dear Ma'am, to compose yourself," said Mr. Winkle; but the shrieks and tappings were louder, and more frequent, than ever.

"My dear," said Mr. Pott, "I am very sorry. If you won't consider your own health, consider me, my dear. We shall have a crowd round the house." But the more strenuously Mr. Pott entreated, the more vehemently the screams poured forth.

Very fortunately, however, attached to Mrs. Pott's person was a body-guard of one, a young lady whose ostensible employment was to preside over her toilet, but who rendered herself useful in a variety of ways, and in none more so than in the particular department of constantly aiding and abetting her mistress in every wish and inclination opposed to the desires of the unhappy Pott. The screams reached this young lady's ears in due course, and brought her to the room with a speed which threatened to derange materially, the very exquisite arrangement of her cap and ringlets.

"Oh, my dear, dear mistress!" exclaimed the body-guard, kneeling frantically by the side of the prostrate Mrs. Pott. "Oh, my dear mistress, what is the matter?"

"Your master—your brutal master," murmured the patient.

Pott was evidently giving way.

"It's a shame," said the body-guard, reproachfully. "I know he'll be the death on you, Ma'am. Poor dear thing."

He gave way more. The opposite party followed up the attack.

"Oh don't leave me—don't leave, Goodwin," murmured Mrs. Pott, clutching at the wrists of the said Goodwin with an hysteric jerk. "You're the only person that's kind to me, Goodwin."

At this affecting appeal, Goodwin got up a little domestic tragedy of her own, and shed tears copiously. "Never, Ma'am—never," said Goodwin. "Oh, Sir, you should be careful—you should indeed; you don't know what harm you may do Missis; you'll be sorry for it one day, I know —I've always said so."

The unlucky Pott looked timidly on, but said nothing.

"Goodwin," said Mrs. Pott, in a soft voice.

"Ma'am," said Goodwin.

"If you only knew how I have loved that man——"

"Don't distress yourself by recollecting it, Ma'am," said the body-guard.

Pott looked very frightened. It was time for a clencher.

"And now," sobbed Mrs. Pott—"now, after all, to be treated in this way; to be reproached and insulted in the presence of a third party, and that party almost a stranger. But I will not submit to it, Goodwin," continued Mrs. Pott, raising herself, in the arms of her attendant. "My brother, the Lieutenant, shall interfere. I'll be separated, Goodwin."

"It would certainly serve him right, Ma'am," said Goodwin.

Whatever thoughts the threat of a separation might have awakened in Mr. Pott's mind, he forbore to give utterance to them, and contented himself by saying, with great humility,—

"My dear, will you hear me?"

A fresh train of sobs was the only reply, as Mrs. Pott grew more hysterical, requested to be informed why she was ever born, and required sundry other pieces of information of a similar description.

"My dear," remonstrated Mr. Pott, "do not give way to these sensitive feelings. I never believed that the paragraph had any foundation, my dear—impossible. I was only angry, my dear—I may say outrageous—with the Independent people for daring to insert it; that's all:" and Mr. Pott cast an imploring look at the innocent cause of the mischief, as if to entreat him to say nothing about the serpent.

"And what steps, Sir, do you mean to take to obtain redress?" inquired Mr. Winkle, gaining courage as he saw Pott losing it.

"Oh, Goodwin," observed Mrs. Pott, "does he mean to horsewhip the editor of the Independent—does he, Goodwin?"

"Hush, hush, Ma'am; pray keep yourself quiet," replied the body-guard. "I dare say he will, if you wish it, Ma'am."

"Certainly," said Pott, as his wife evinced decided symptoms of going off again—"of course I shall."

"When, Goodwin—when?" said Mrs. Pott, still undecided about the going off.

"Immediately, of course," said Mr. Pott; "before the day is out."

"Oh, Goodwin," resumed Mrs. Pott, "it's the only way of meeting the slander, and setting me right with the world."

"Certainly, Ma'am," replied Goodwin. "No man as is a man, Ma'am, could refuse to do it."

So as the hysterics were still hovering about, Mr. Pott said once more, that he would do it; but Mrs. Pott was so overcome at the bare idea of having ever been suspected, that she was half-a-dozen times on the very verge of a relapse, and most unquestionably would have gone off, had it not been for the indefatigable efforts of the assiduous Goodwin, and repeated entreaties for pardon from the conquered Pott; and finally, when that unhappy individual had been frightened and snubbed down to his proper level, Mrs. Pott recovered, and they went to breakfast.

"You will not allow this base newspaper slander to shorten your stay here, Mr. Pott?" said Mrs. Pott, smiling through the traces of her tears.

"I hope not," said Mr. Pott, actuated, as he spoke, by an internal wish that his visiter would choke himself with the morsel of dry toast which he was raising to his lips at the moment: and so terminate his stay effectually.

"I hope not."

"You are very good," said Mr. Winkle; "but a letter has been received from Mr. Pickwick—so I learn by a note from Mr. Tupman, which was brought up to my bed-room door, this morning—in which he requests us to join him at Bury to-day; and we are to leave by the coach at noon."

"But you will come back?" said Mrs. Pott.

"Oh, certainly," replied Mr. Winkle.

"You are quite sure?" said Mrs. Pott, stealing a tender look at her visitor.

"Quite," responded Mr. Winkle.

The breakfast passed off in silence, for each member of the party was brooding over his, or her, own personal grievances. Mrs. Pott was regretting the loss of a beau; Mr. Pott his rash pledge to horsewhip the Independent; and Mr. Winkle his having placed himself in so awkward a situation. Noon approached, and after many adieux and promises to return, he tore himself away.

"If he ever comes back, I'll poison him," thought Mr. Pott, as he turned into the little back office where he prepared his thunderbolts.

"If I ever do come back, and mix myself up with these people again," thought Mr. Winkle, as he wended his way to the Peacock, "I shall deserve to be horsewhipped myself—that's all."

His friends were ready, the coach was nearly so, and in half an hour they were proceeding on their journey, along the road over which Mr. Pickwick and Sam had so recently travelled, and of which, as we have already said something, we do not feel called upon to extract Mr. Snodgrass's poetical and beautiful description.

Mr. Weller was standing at the door of the Angel, ready to receive them, and by that gentleman they were ushered to the apartment of Mr. Pickwick, where, to the no small surprise of Mr. Winkle and Mr. Snodgrass, and the no small embarrassment of Mr. Tupman, they found old Wardle and Trundle.

"How are you?" said the old man, grasping Mr. Tupman's hand. "Don't hang back, or look sentimental about it; it can't be helped, old fellow. For her sake, I wish you'd had her; for your own, I'm very glad you have not. A young fellow like you, will do better one of these days—eh?" With this consolation, old Wardle slapped Mr. Tupman on the back, and laughed heartily.

"Well, and how are you, my fine fellows?" said the old gentleman, shaking hands with Mr. Winkle and Mr. Snodgrass at the same time. "I have just been telling Pickwick that we must have you all down at Christmas. We're going to have a wedding—a real wedding this time."

"A wedding!" exclaimed Mr. Snodgrass, turning very pale.

"Yes, a wedding. But don't be frightened," said the good-humoured old man; "it's only Trundle there, and Bella."

"Oh, is that all?" said Mr. Snodgrass, relieved from a painful doubt which had fallen heavily on his breast. "Give you joy, Sir. How is Joe?"

"Oh, he;—very well," replied the old gentleman. "Sleepy as ever."

"And your mother, and the clergyman, and all of 'em?"

"Quite well."

"Where," said Mr. Tupman, with an effort—"where is —she, Sir?" and he turned away his head, and covered his eyes with his hand.

"She!" said the old gentleman, with a knowing shake of the head. "Do you mean my single relative—eh?"

Mr. Tupman, by a nod, intimated that his question applied to the disappointed Rachael.

"Oh, she's gone away," said the old gentleman. "She's living at a relation's, far enough off. She couldn't bear to see the girls, so I let her go. But come, here's the dinner. You must be hungry after your ride. I am, without any ride at all; so let us fall to."

Ample justice was done to the meal; and when they were seated round the table, after it had been disposed of, Mr. Pickwick, to the intense horror and indignation of his followers, related the adventure he had undergone, and the success which had attended the base artifices of the diabolical Jingle.

"And the attack of rheumatism which I caught in that garden," said Mr. Pickwick, in conclusion, "renders me lame at this moment."

"I, too, have had something of an adventure," said Mr. Winkle, with a smile; and at the request of Mr. Pickwick, he detailed the malicious libel of the Eatanswill Independent, and the consequent excitement of their friend, the editor.

Mr. Pickwick's brow darkened, during the recital. His friends observed it, and, when Mr. Winkle had concluded, maintained a profound silence. Mr. Pickwick struck the table emphatically with his clenched fist, and spoke as follows:—

"Is it not a wonderful circumstance," said Mr. Pickwick, "that we seem destined to enter no man's house, without involving him in some degree of trouble? Does it not, I ask, bespeak the indiscretion, or, worse than that, the blackness of heart—that I should say so!—of my followers, that, beneath whatever roof they locate, they disturb the peace of mind and happiness of some confiding female? Is it not, I say——"

Mr. Pickwick would in all probability have gone on for some time, had not the entrance of Sam, with a letter, caused him to break off in his eloquent discourse. He passed his handkerchief across his forehead, took off his spectacles, wiped them, and put them on again; and his voice had recovered its wonted softness of tone, when he said,—

"What have you there, Sam?"

"Called at the Post-office just now, and found this here letter, as has laid there for two days," replied Mr. Weller. "It's sealed vith a vafer, and directed in round hand."

"I don't know this hand," said Mr. Pickwick, opening the letter. "Mercy on us! what's this? It must be a jest; it—it—can't be true."

"What's the matter?" was the general inquiry.

"Nobody dead, is there?" said Wardle, alarmed at the horror in Mr. Pickwick's countenance.

Mr. Pickwick made no reply, but, pushing the letter across the table, and desiring Mr. Tupman to read it aloud, fell back in his chair with a look of vacant astonishment quite alarming to behold.

Mr. Tupman, with a trembling voice, read the letter, of which the following is a copy:—

Freeman's Court, Cornhill, August 28th, 1827.

Bardell against Pickwick

Sir,

Having been instructed by Mrs. Martha Bardell, to commence an action against you, for a breach of promise of marriage, for which the plaintiff lays her damages at fifteen hundred pounds, we beg to inform you that a writ has

been issued against you in this suit, in the Court of Common Pleas; and request to know, by return of post, the name of your attorney in London, who will accept service thereof.

We are, Sir,

Your obedient servants,

Dodson and Fogg.

Mr. Samuel Pickwick.

There was something so impressive in the mute astonishment with which each man regarded his neighbour, and every man regarded Mr. Pickwick, that all seemed afraid to speak. The silence was at length broken by Mr. Tupman.

"Dodson and Fogg," he repeated mechanically.

"Bardell and Pickwick," said Mr. Snodgrass, musing.

"Peace of mind and happiness of confiding females," murmured Mr. Winkle, with an air of abstraction.

"It's a conspiracy," said Mr. Pickwick, at length recovering the power of speech;—"a base conspiracy between these two grasping attorneys, Dodson and Fogg. Mrs. Bardell would never do it;—she hasn't the heart to do it;—she hasn't the case to do it. Ridiculous—ridiculous."

"Of her heart," said Wardle, with a smile, "you should certainly be the best judge. I don't wish to discourage you, but I should certainly say that, of her case, Dodson and Fogg are far better judges than any of us, can be."

"It's a vile attempt to extort money," said Mr. Pickwick.

"I hope it is," said Wardle, with a short, dry cough.

"Who ever heard me address her in any way but that in which a lodger would address his landlady?" continued Mr. Pickwick, with great vehemence. "Who ever saw me with her? Not even my friends here——"

"Except on one occasion," said Mr. Tupman.

Mr. Pickwick changed colour.

"Ah," said Wardle. "Well, that's important. There was nothing suspicious then, I suppose?"

Mr. Tupman glanced timidly at his leader. "Why," he said, "there was nothing suspicious; but—I don't know how it happened, mind—she certainly was reclining in his arms."

"Gracious powers!" ejaculated Mr. Pickwick, as the recollection of the scene in question, struck forcibly upon him;—"what a dreadful instance of the force of circumstances! So she was—so she was."

"And our friend was soothing her anguish," said Mr. Winkle, rather maliciously.

"So I was," said Mr. Pickwick. "I won't deny it. So I was."

"Hallo!" said Wardle; "for a case in which there's nothing suspicious, this looks rather queer—eh, Pickwick—eh? Ah, sly dog—sly dog!" and he laughed till the glasses on the side-board, rang again.

"What a dreadful conjunction of appearances!" exclaimed Mr. Pickwick, resting his chin upon his hands. "Winkle—Tupman—I beg your pardon for the observations I made just now. We are all the victims of circumstances, and I the greatest." With this apology, Mr. Pickwick buried his head in his hands, and ruminated; while Wardle measured out a regular circle of nods and winks, addressed to the other members of the company.

"I'll have it explained, though," said Mr. Pickwick, raising his head, and hammering the table. "I'll see this Dodson and Fogg. I'll go to London to-morrow."

"Not to-morrow," said Wardle; "you're too lame."

"Well then, next day."

"Next day is the first of September, and you're pledged to ride out with us, as far as Sir Geoffrey Manning's grounds, at all events, and to meet us at lunch, if you don't take the field."

"Well then, the day after," said Mr. Pickwick; "Thursday.—Sam."

"Sir," replied Mr. Weller.

"Take two places outside to London, on Thursday morning, for yourself and me."

"Wery well, Sir."

Mr. Weller left the room, and departed slowly on his errand, with his hands in his pocket, and his eyes fixed on the ground.

"Rum feller, the hemperor," said Mr. Weller, as he walked slowly up the street. "Think o' his makin' up to that ere Mrs. Bardell—vith a little boy, too! Always the vay vith these here old 'uns hows'ever, as is such steady goers to look at. I didn't think he'd ha' done it, though—I didn't think he'd ha' done it." And moralising in this strain, Mr. Samuel Weller bent his steps towards the booking-office.

CHAPTER XIX.

A PLEASANT DAY, WITH AN UNPLEASANT TERMINATION.

The birds, who, happily for their own peace of mind, and personal comfort, were in blissful ignorance of the preparations which had been making to astonish them, on the first of September, hailed it no doubt, as one of the pleasantest mornings they had seen that season. Many a young partridge who strutted complacently among the stubble, with all the finicking coxcombry of youth, and many an older one who watched his levity out of his little round eye, with the contemptuous air of a bird of wisdom and experience, alike unconscious of their approaching doom, basked in the fresh morning air with lively and blithesome feelings, and a few hours afterwards were laid low upon the earth. But we grow affecting: let us proceed.

In plain common-place matter-of-fact, then, it was a fine morning—so fine that you would scarcely have believed that the few months of an English summer had yet flown by. Hedges, fields, and trees, hill and moorland, presented to the eye their ever-varying shades of deep rich green; scarce a leaf had fallen, scarce a sprinkle of yellow mingled with the hues of summer, warned you that autumn had begun. The sky was cloudless; the sun shone out bright and warm; the songs of birds, and hum of myriads of summer insects, filled the air; and the cottage gardens, crowded with flowers of every rich and beautiful tint, sparkled in the heavy dew, like beds of glittering jewels. Everything bore the stamp of summer, and none of its beautiful colours had yet faded from the die.

Such was the morning, when an open carriage, in which were three Pickwickians, (Mr. Snodgrass having preferred to remain at home,) Mr. Wardle, and Mr. Trundle, with Sam Weller on the box beside the driver, pulled up by a gate at the road-side, before which stood a tall, raw-boned gamekeeper, and a half-booted, leather-legginged boy: each bearing a bag of capacious dimensions, and accompanied by a brace of pointers.

"I say," whispered Mr. Winkle to Wardle, as the man let down the steps, "they don't suppose we're going to kill game enough to fill those bags, do they?"

"Fill them!" exclaimed old Wardle. "Bless you, yes! You shall fill one, and I the other; and when we've done with them, the pockets of our shooting-jackets will hold as much more."

Mr. Winkle dismounted without saying anything in reply to this observation; but he thought within himself, that if the party remained in the open air, till he had filled one of the bags, they stood a considerable chance of catching tolerable colds in the head.

"Hi, Juno, lass—hi, old girl; down, Daph, down," said Wardle, caressing the dogs. "Sir Geoffrey still in Scotland, of course, Martin?"

The tall gamekeeper replied in the affirmative, and looked with some surprise from Mr. Winkle, who was holding his gun as if he wished his coat pocket to save him the trouble of pulling the trigger, to Mr. Tupman, who was holding his, as if he were afraid of it—as there is no earthly reason to doubt that he really was.

"My friends are not much in the way of this sort of thing yet, Martin," said Wardle, noticing the look. "Live and learn, you know. They'll be good shots one of these days. I beg my friend Winkle's pardon, though; he has had some practice."

Mr. Winkle smiled feebly over his blue neckerchief in acknowledgment of the compliment, and got himself so mysteriously entangled with his gun, in his modest confusion, that if the piece had been loaded, he must inevitably have shot himself dead upon the spot.

"You mustn't handle your piece in that ere way, when you come to have the charge in it, Sir," said the tall gamekeeper gruffly, "or I'm damned if you won't make cold meat of some on us."

Mr. Winkle, thus admonished, abruptly altered its position, and in so doing, contrived to bring the barrel into pretty smart contact with Mr. Weller's head.

"Hallo!" said Sam, picking up his hat, which had been knocked off, and rubbing his temple. "Hallo, Sir! if you comes it this vay, you'll fill one o' them bags, and something to spare, at one fire."

Here the leather-legginged boy laughed very heartily, and then tried to look as if it was somebody else, whereat Mr. Winkle frowned majestically.

"Where did you tell the boy to meet us with the snack, Martin?" inquired Wardle.

"Side of One-tree Hill, at twelve o'clock, Sir."

"That's not Sir Geoffrey's land, is it?"

"No, Sir; but it's close by it. It's Captain Boldwig's land; but there'll be nobody to interrupt us, and there's a fine bit of turf there."

"Very well," said old Wardle. "Now the sooner we're off the better. Will you join us at twelve, then, Pickwick?"

Mr. Pickwick was particularly desirous to view the sport, the more especially as he was rather anxious in respect of

Mr. Winkle's life and limbs. On so inviting a morning, too, it was very tantalising to turn back, and leave his friends to enjoy themselves. It was, therefore, with a very rueful air that he replied,—

"Why, I suppose I must."

"An't the gentleman a shot, Sir?" inquired the long gamekeeper.

"No," replied Wardle; "and he's lame besides."

"I should very much like to go," said Mr. Pickwick—"very much."

There was a short pause of commiseration.

"There's a barrow t'other side the hedge," said the boy. "If the gentleman's servant would wheel along the paths, he could keep nigh us, and we could lift it over the stiles and that."

"The wery thing," said Mr. Weller, who was a party interested, inasmuch as he ardently longed to see the sport. "The wery thing. Well said, Small-check; I'll have it out, in a minute."

But here a difficulty arose. The long gamekeeper resolutely protested against the introduction into a shooting-party, of a gentleman in a barrow, as a gross violation of all established rules and precedents.

It was a great objection, but not an insurmountable one. The gamekeeper having been coaxed and feed, and having, moreover, eased his mind by "punching" the head of the inventive youth who had first suggested the use of the machine, Mr. Pickwick was placed in it, and off the party set; Wardle and the long gamekeeper leading the way, and Mr. Pickwick in the barrow, propelled by Sam, bringing up the rear.

"Stop, Sam," said Mr. Pickwick, when they had got half across the first field.

"What's the matter now?" said Wardle.

"I won't suffer this barrow to be moved another step," said Mr. Pickwick, resolutely, "unless Winkle carries that gun of his, in a different manner."

"How *am* I to carry it?" said the wretched Winkle.

"Carry it with the muzzle to the ground," replied Mr. Pickwick.

"It's so unsportsman-like," reasoned Winkle.

"I don't care whether it's unsportsman-like or not," replied Mr. Pickwick; "I am not going to be shot in a wheel-barrow, for the sake of appearances, to please anybody."

"I know the gentleman 'll put that ere charge into somebody afore he's done," growled the long man.

"Well, well—I don't mind," said poor Mr. Winkle, turning his gun stock uppermost;—"there."

"Anythin' for a quiet life," said Mr. Weller; and on they went again.

"Stop," said Mr. Pickwick, after they had gone a few yards further.

"What now?" said Wardle.

"That gun of Tupman's is not safe: I know it isn't," said Mr. Pickwick.

"Eh? What! not safe?" said Mr. Tupman, in a tone of great alarm.

"Not as you are carrying it," said Mr. Pickwick. "I am very sorry to make any further objection, but I cannot consent to go on, unless you carry it, as Winkle does his."

"I think you had better, Sir," said the long gamekeeper, "or you're quite as likely to lodge the charge in your own vestcoat as in anybody else's."

Mr. Tupman, with the most obliging haste, placed his piece in the position required, and the party moved on again; the two amateurs marching with reversed arms, like a couple of privates at a royal funeral.

The dogs suddenly came to a dead stop, and the party advancing stealthily a single pace, stopped too.

"What's the matter with the dogs' legs?" whispered Mr. Winkle. "How queer they're standing."

"Hush, can't you?" replied Wardle, softly. "Don't you see, they're making a point?"

"Making a point!" said Mr. Winkle, staring about him, as if he expected to discover some particular beauty in the landscape, which the sagacious animals were calling special attention to. "Making a point! What are they pointing at?"

"Keep your eyes open," said Wardle, not heeding the question in the excitement of the moment. "Now then."

There was a sharp whirring noise, that made Mr. Winkle start back as if he had been shot himself. Bang, bang, went a couple of guns;—the smoke swept quickly away over the field, and curled into the air.

"Where are they?" said Mr. Winkle, in a state of the highest excitement, turning round and round in all directions. "Where are they? Tell me when to fire. Where are they—where are they?"

"Where are they!" said Wardle, taking up a brace of birds which the dogs had deposited at his feet. "Where are they! why, here they are."

"No, no; I mean the others," said the bewildered Winkle.

"Far enough off, by this time," replied Wardle, coolly reloading his gun.

"We shall very likely be up with another covey in five minutes," said the long gamekeeper. "If the gentleman begins to fire now, perhaps he'll just get the shot out of the barrel by the time they rise."

"Ha! ha! ha!" roared Mr. Weller.

"Sam," said Mr. Pickwick, compassionating his follower's confusion and embarrassment.

"Sir."

"Don't laugh."

"Certainly not, Sir." So, by way of indemnification, Mr. Weller contorted his features from behind the wheel-barrow, for the exclusive amusement of the boy with the leggings, who thereupon burst into a boisterous laugh, and was summarily cuffed by the long gamekeeper, who wanted a pretext for turning round, to hide his own merriment.

"Bravo, old fellow!" said Wardle to Mr. Tupman; "you fired that time, at all events."

"Oh yes," replied Mr. Tupman, with conscious pride. "I let it off."

"Well done. You'll hit something next time, if you look sharp. Very easy, ain't it?"

"Yes, it's very easy," said Mr. Tupman. "How it hurts one's shoulder, though. It nearly knocked me backwards. I had no idea these small fire-arms kicked so."

"Ah," said the old gentleman, smiling; "you'll get used to it, in time. Now then—all ready—all right with the barrow there?"

"All right, Sir," replied Mr. Weller.

"Come along then."

"Hold hard, Sir," said Sam, raising the barrow.

"Aye, aye," replied Mr. Pickwick; and on they went, as briskly as need be.

"Keep that barrow back now," cried Wardle, when it had been hoisted over a stile into another field, and Mr. Pickwick had been deposited in it once more.

"All right, Sir," replied Mr. Weller, pausing.

"Now Winkle," said the old gentleman, "follow me softly, and don't be too late this time."

"Never fear," said Mr. Winkle. "Are they pointing?"

"No, no; not now. Quietly now, quietly." On they crept, and very quietly they would have advanced, if Mr. Winkle, in the performance of some very intricate evolutions with his gun, had not accidentally fired, at the most critical moment, over the boy's head, exactly in the very spot where the tall man's brain would have been, had he been there instead.

"Why, what on earth did you do that for?" said old Wardle, as the birds flew unharmed away.

"I never saw such a gun in my life," replied poor Winkle, looking at the lock, as if that would do any good. "It goes off, of its own accord. It *will* do it."

"Will do it!" echoed Wardle, with something of irritation in his manner. "I wish it would kill something of its own accord."

"It'll do that afore long, Sir," observed the tall man, in a low, prophetic voice.

"What do you mean by that observation, Sir?" inquired Mr. Winkle, angrily.

"Never mind, Sir—never mind," replied the long gamekeeper;—"I've no family myself, Sir; and this here boy's mother will get something handsome from Sir Geoffrey, if he's killed on his land. Load again, Sir—load again."

"Take away his gun," cried Mr. Pickwick from the barrow, horror-stricken at the long man's dark insinuations. "Take away his gun, do you hear, somebody?"

Nobody, however, volunteered to obey the command; and Mr. Winkle, after darting a rebellious glance at Mr. Pickwick, reloaded his gun, and proceeded onwards with the rest.

We are bound, on the authority of Mr. Pickwick, to state, that Mr. Tupman's mode of proceeding evinced far more of prudence and deliberation, than that adopted by Mr. Winkle. Still, this by no means detracts from the great authority of the latter gentleman, on all matters connected with the field; because, as Mr. Pickwick beautifully observes, it has somehow or other happened, from time immemorial, that many of the best and ablest philosophers, who have been perfect lights of science in matters of theory, have been wholly unable to reduce them to practice.

Mr. Tupman's process, like many of our most sublime discoveries, was extremely simple. With the quickness and penetration of a man of genius, he had at once observed that the two great points to be attained were—first, to discharge his piece without injury to himself, and, secondly, to do so, without danger to the by-standers;—obviously, the best thing to do, after surmounting the difficulty of firing at all, was to shut his eyes firmly, and fire into the air.

On one occasion, after performing this feat, Mr. Tupman, on opening his eyes, beheld a plump partridge in the very act of falling wounded to the ground. He was just on the point of congratulating Wardle on his invariable success, when that gentleman advanced towards him, and grasped him warmly by the hand.

"Tupman," said the old gentleman, "you singled out that particular bird?"

"No," said Mr. Tupman—"no."

"You did," said Wardle. "I saw you do it—I observed you pick him out—I noticed you, as you raised your piece to take aim; and I will say this, that the best shot in existence could not have done it more beautifully. You are

an older hand at this, than I thought you, Tupman;—you have been out before."

It was in vain for Mr. Tupman to protest, with a smile of self-denial, that he never had. The very smile was taken as evidence to the contrary; and from that time forth, his reputation was established. It is not the only reputation that has been acquired as easily, nor are such fortunate circumstances confined to partridge-shooting.

Meanwhile, Mr. Winkle flashed, and blazed, and smoked away, without producing any material results worthy of being noted down; sometimes expending his charge in mid-air, and at others sending it skimming along so near the surface of the ground, as to place the lives of the two dogs on a rather uncertain and precarious tenure. As a display of fancy-shooting, it was extremely varied and curious; as an exhibition of firing with any precise object, it was, upon the whole, perhaps a failure. It is an established axiom, that "every bullet has its billet." If it apply in an equal degree to shots, those of Mr. Winkle were unfortunate foundlings, deprived of their natural rights, cast loose upon the world, and billeted nowhere.

"Well," said Wardle, walking up to the side of the barrow, and wiping the streams of perspiration from his jolly red face; "smoking day, isn't it?"

"It is indeed," replied Mr. Pickwick. "The sun is tremendously hot, even to me. I don't know how you must feel it."

"Why," said the old gentleman, "pretty hot. It's past twelve, though. You see that green hill there?"

"Certainly."

"That's the place where we are to lunch; and, by Jove, there's the boy with the basket, punctual as clock-work."

"So he is," said Mr. Pickwick, brightening up. "Good boy, that. I'll give him a shilling, presently. Now, then, Sam, wheel away."

"Hold on, Sir," said Mr. Weller, invigorated with the prospect of refreshments. "Out of the vay, young leathers. If you walley my precious life don't upset me, as the gen-'l'man said to the driver, when they vas a carryin' him to Tyburn." And quickening his pace to a sharp run, Mr. Weller wheeled his master nimbly to the green hill, shot him dexterously out by the very side of the basket, and proceeded to unpack it with the utmost dispatch.

"Weal pie," said Mr. Weller, soliloquising, as he arranged the eatables on the grass. "Very good thing is a weal pie, when you know the lady as made it, and is quite sure it an't kittens; and arter all though, where's the odds, when they're so like weal that the wery piemen themselves don't know the difference?"

"Don't they, Sam?" said Mr. Pickwick.

"Not they, Sir," replied Mr. Weller, touching his hat. "I lodged in the same house vith a pieman once, Sir, and a wery nice man he was—reg'lar clever chap, too—make pies out o' anything, he could. 'What a number o' cats you keep, Mr. Brooks,' says I, when I'd got intimate with him. 'Ah,' says he, 'I do—a good many,' says he. 'You must be wery fond o' cats,' says I. 'Other people is,' says he, a winkin' at me; 'they an't in season till the winter though,' says he. 'Not in season!' says I. 'No,' says he, 'fruits is in, cats is out.' 'Why, what do you mean?' says I. 'Mean?' says he. 'That I'll never be a party to the combination o' the butchers, to keep up the prices o' meat,' says he. 'Mr. Weller,' says he, squeezing my hand wery hard, and vispering in my ear—'don't mention this here agin, but it's the seasonin' as does it. They're all made o' them noble animals,' says he, a pointin' to a wery nice little tabby kitten, 'and I seasons 'em for beef-steak, weal, or kidney, 'cordin' to the demand; and more than that,' says he, 'I can make a weal a beef-steak, or a beef-steak a kidney, or any one on 'em a mutton, at a minute's notice, just as the market changes, and appetites wary!"

"He must have been a very ingenious young man, that, Sam," said Mr. Pickwick, with a slight shudder.

"Just was, Sir," replied Mr. Weller, continuing his occupation of emptying the basket, "and the pies was beautiful. Tongue; well that's a wery good thing, when it an't a woman's. Bread—knuckle o' ham, reg'lar picter—cold beef in slices, wery good. What's in them stone jars, young touch-and-go?"

"Beer in this one," replied the boy, taking from his shoulder a couple of large stone bottles, fastened together by a leathern strap—"cold punch in t'other."

"And a wery good notion of a lunch it is, take it altogether," said Mr. Weller, surveying his arrangement of the repast with great satisfaction. "Now, gen'l'men, 'fall on,' as the English said to the French when they fixed bagginets."

It needed no second invitation to induce the party to yield full justice to the meal; and as little pressing did it require, to induce Mr. Weller, the long gamekeeper, and the two boys, to station themselves on the grass at a little distance, and do good execution upon a decent proportion of the viands. An old oak tree afforded a pleasant shelter to the group, and a rich prospect of arable and meadow land, intersected with luxuriant hedges, and richly ornamented with wood, lay spread out below them.

"This is delightful—thoroughly delightful!" said Mr. Pickwick, the skin of whose expressive countenance, was rapidly peeling off, with exposure to the sun.

"So it is—so it is, old fellow," replied Wardle. "Come; a glass of punch."

"With great pleasure," said Mr Pickwick; and the satisfaction of his countenance after drinking it, bore testimony to the sincerity of the reply.

"Good," said Mr. Pickwick, smacking his lips. "Very good. I'll take another. Cool; very cool. Come, gentlemen," continued Mr. Pickwick, still retaining his hold upon the jar, "a toast. Our friends at Dingley Dell."

The toast was drunk with loud acclamations.

"I'll tell you what I shall do, to get up my shooting again," said Mr. Winkle, who was eating bread and ham with a pocket-knife. "I'll put a stuffed partridge on the top of a post, and practise at it, beginning at a short distance, and lengthening it by degrees. I understand it's capital practice."

"I know a gen'l'man, Sir," said Mr. Weller, "as did that, and begun at two yards; but he never tried it on agin; for he blowed the bird right clean away at the first fire, and nobody ever seed a feather on him arterwards."

"Sam," said Mr. Pickwick.

"Sir," replied Mr. Weller.

"Have the goodness to reserve your anecdotes, 'till they are called for."

"Cert'nly, Sir."

Here Mr. Weller winked the eye which was not concealed by the beer-can he was raising to his lips, with such exquisite facetiousness, that the two boys went into spontaneous convulsions, and even the long man condescended to smile.

"Well, that certainly is most capital cold punch," said Mr. Pickwick, looking earnestly at the stone bottle; "and the day is extremely warm, and—Tupman, my dear friend, a glass of punch?"

"With the greatest delight," replied Mr. Tupman; and having drank that glass, Mr. Pickwick took another, just to see whether there was any orange peel in the punch, because orange peel always disagreed with him; and finding that there was not, Mr. Pickwick took another glass to the health of their absent friend, and then felt himself imperatively called upon to propose another in honour of the punch-compounder, unknown.

This constant succession of glasses, produced considerable effect upon Mr. Pickwick; his countenance beamed with the most sunny smiles, laughter played around his lips, and good-humoured merriment twinkled in his eye. Yielding by degrees to the influence of the exciting liquid, rendered more so by the heat, Mr. Pickwick expressed a strong desire to recollect a song which he had heard in his infancy, and the attempt proving abortive, sought to stimulate his memory with more glasses of punch, which appeared to have quite a contrary effect; for, from forgetting the words of the song, he began to forget how to articulate any words at all; and finally, after rising to his legs to address the company in an eloquent speech, he fell into the barrow, and fast asleep, simultaneously.

The basket having been repacked, and it being found perfectly impossible to awaken Mr. Pickwick from his torpor, some discussion took place whether it would be better for Mr. Weller to wheel his master back again, or to leave him where he was, until they should all be ready to return. The latter course was at length decided on; and as their further expedition was not to exceed an hour's duration, and as Mr. Weller begged very hard to be one of the party, it was determined to leave Mr. Pickwick asleep in the barrow, and to call for him on their return. So away they went, leaving Mr. Pickwick snoring most comfortably in the shade.

That Mr. Pickwick would have continued to snore in the shade until his friends came back, or, in default thereof, until the shades of evening had fallen on the landscape, there appears no reasonable cause to doubt; always supposing that he had been suffered to remain there, in peace. But he was *not* suffered to remain there in peace. And this is what prevented him.

Captain Boldwig was a little fierce man in a stiff black neckerchief and blue surtout, who, when he did condescend to walk about his property, did it in company with a thick rattan stick with a brass ferrule, and a gardener and subgardener with meek faces, to whom (the gardeners, not the stick) Captain Boldwig gave his orders with all due grandeur and ferocity: for Captain Boldwig's wife's sister had married a Marquis, and the Captain's house was a villa, and his land "grounds," and it was all very high, and mighty, and great.

Mr. Pickwick had not been asleep half an hour, when little Captain Boldwig, followed by the two gardeners, came striding along as fast as his size and importance would let him; and when he came near the oak tree, Captain Boldwig paused, and drew a long breath, and looked at the prospect, as if he thought the prospect ought to be highly gratified at having him to take notice of it; and then he struck the ground emphatically with his stick, and summoned the head-gardener.

"Hunt," said Captain Boldwig.

"Yes, Sir," said the gardener.

"Roll this place to-morrow morning—do you hear, Hunt?"

"Yes, Sir."

"And take care that you keep me this place in good order—do you hear, Hunt?"

"Yes, Sir."

"And remind me to have a board done about trespassers, and spring guns, and all that sort of thing, to keep the common people out. Do you hear, Hunt; do you hear?"

"I'll not forget it, Sir."

"I beg your pardon, Sir," said the other man, advancing, with his hand to his hat.

"Well, Wilkins, what's the matter with *you?*" said Captain Boldwig.

"I beg your pardon, Sir—but I think there have been trespassers here to-day."

"Ha!" said the Captain, scowling around him.

"Yes, Sir—they have been dining here, I think, Sir."

"Why, damn their audacity, so they have," said Captain Boldwig, as the crumbs and fragments that were strewn upon the grass, met his eye. "They have actually been devouring their food here. I wish I had the vagabonds here!" said the Captain, clenching the thick stick.

"I wish I had the vagabonds here," said the Captain wrathfully.

"Beg your pardon, Sir," said Wilkins, "but—"

"But what? Eh?" roared the Captain; and following the timid glance of Wilkins, his eyes encountered the wheelbarrow and Mr. Pickwick.

"Who are you, you rascal?" said the Captain, administering several pokes to Mr. Pickwick's body with the thick stick. "What's your name?"

"Cold punch," murmured Mr. Pickwick, as he sunk to sleep again.

"What?" demanded Captain Boldwig

No reply.

"What did he say his name was?" asked the Captain.

"Punch, I think, Sir," replied Wilkins.

"That's his impudence—that's his confounded impudence," said Captain Boldwig. "He's only feigning to be asleep now," said the Captain, in a high passion. "He's drunk; he's a drunken plebeian. Wheel him away, Wilkins, wheel him away directly."

"Where shall I wheel him to, Sir?" inquired Wilkins, with great timidity.

"Wheel him to the Devil," replied Captain Boldwig.

"Very well, Sir," said Wilkins.

"Stay," said the Captain.

Wilkins stopped accordingly.

"Wheel him," said the Captain, "wheel him to the pound; and let us see whether he calls himself Punch, when he comes to himself. He shall not bully me—he shall not bully me. Wheel him away."

Away Mr. Pickwick was wheeled in compliance with this imperious mandate; and the great Captain Boldwig, swelling with indignation, proceeded on his walk.

Inexpressible was the astonishment of the little party when they returned, to find that Mr. Pickwick had disappeared, and taken the wheelbarrow with him. It was the most mysterious and unaccountable thing that was ever heard of. For a lame man to have got upon his legs without any previous notice, and walked off, would have been most extraordinary; but when it came to his wheeling a heavy barrow before him, by way of amusement, it grew positively miraculous. They searched every nook and corner round, together and separately: they shouted, whistled, laughed, called—and all with the same result. Mr. Pickwick was not to be found; and after some hours of fruitless search, they arrived at the unwelcome conclusion, that they must go home without him.

Meanwhile Mr. Pickwick had been wheeled to the Pound, and safely deposited therein, fast asleep in the wheelbarrow, to the immeasurable delight and satisfaction, not only of all the boys in the village, but three fourths of the whole population, who had gathered round in expectation of his waking. If their most intense gratification had been awakened by seeing him wheeled in, how many hundred-fold was their joy increased when, after a few indistinct cries of "Sam!" he sat up in the barrow, and gazed with indescribable astonishment on the faces before him.

A general shout was of course the signal of his having woke up; and his involuntary inquiry of "What's the matter?" occasioned another, louder than the first, if possible.

"Here's a game," roared the populace.

"Where am I?" exclaimed Mr. Pickwick.

"In the Pound," replied the mob.

"How came I here? What was I doing? Where was I brought from?"

"Boldwig—Captain Boldwig," was the only reply.

"Let me out," cried Mr. Pickwick. "Where's my servant? Where are my friends?"

"You an't got no friends. Hurrah!" And then there came a turnip, and then a potato, and then an egg, with a few other little tokens of the playful disposition of the many-headed.

How long this scene might have lasted, or how much Mr. Pickwick might have suffered, no one can tell, had not a carriage which was driving swiftly by, suddenly pulled up, from whence there descended old Wardle and Sam Weller, the former of whom, in far less time than it takes to write it, if not to read it, had made his way to Mr. Pickwick's side, and placed him in the vehicle, just as the latter had concluded the third and last round of a single combat with the town-beadle.

"Run to the Justice's," cried a dozen voices.

"Ah, run avay," said Mr. Weller, jumping up on the box. "Give my compliments—Mr. Veller's compliments—to the Justice, and tell him I've spoilt his beadle, and that, if he'll svear in a new 'un, I'll come back agin to-morrow and spoil him. Drive on, old feller."

"I'll give directions for the commencement of an action for false imprisonment against this Captain Boldwig, directly I get to London," said Mr. Pickwick, as soon as the carriage turned out of the town.

"We were trespassing, it seems," said Wardle.

"I don't care," said Mr. Pickwick, "I'll bring the action."

"No, you won't," said Wardle.

"I will, by—" but as there was a humorous expression in Wardle's face, Mr. Pickwick checked himself, and said—"Why not?"

"Because," said old Wardle, half-bursting with laughter, "because they might turn round on some of us, and say we had taken too much cold punch."

MR. PICKWICK IN THE POUND.

Do what he would, a smile would come into Mr. Pickwick's face; the smile extended into a laugh, the laugh into a roar, and the roar became general. So, to keep up their good humour, they stopped at the first road-side tavern they came to, and ordered a glass of brandy and water all round, with a magnum of extra strength, for Mr. Samuel Weller.

CHAPTER XX.

SHOWING HOW DODSON AND FOGG WERE MEN OF BUSINESS, AND THEIR CLERKS MEN OF PLEASURE; AND HOW AN AFFECTING INTERVIEW TOOK PLACE BETWEEN MR. WELLER AND HIS LONG-LOST PARENT; SHOWING ALSO, WHAT CHOICE SPIRITS ASSEMBLED AT THE MAGPIE AND STUMP, AND WHAT A CAPITAL CHAPTER THE NEXT ONE WILL BE.

In the ground-floor front of a dingy house, at the very furthest end of Freeman's Court, Cornhill, sat the four clerks of Messrs. Dodson and Fogg, two of His Majesty's Attorneys of the Courts of King's Bench and Common Pleas at Westminster, and solicitors of the High Court of Chancery: the aforesaid clerks catching about as favourable glimpses of Heaven's light and Heaven's sun, in the course of their daily labours, as a man might hope to do, were he placed at the bottom of a reasonably deep well; and without the opportunity of perceiving the stars in the day-time, which the latter secluded situation affords.

The clerks' office of Messrs. Dodson and Fogg was a dark, mouldy, earthy-smelling room, with a high wainscotted partition to screen the clerks from the vulgar gaze: a couple of old wooden chairs, a very loud-ticking clock, an almanack, an umbrella-stand, a row of hat pegs, and a few shelves, on which were deposited several ticketed bundles of dirty papers, some old deal boxes with paper labels, and sundry decayed stone ink bottles of various shapes and sizes. There was a glass door leading into the passage which formed the entrance to the court, and on the outer side of this glass door, Mr. Pickwick, closely followed by Sam Weller, presented himself on the Friday morning succeeding the occurrence, of which a faithful narration is given in the last chapter.

"Come in, can't you," cried a voice from behind the partition, in reply to Mr. Pickwick's gentle tap at the door. And Mr. Pickwick and Sam entered accordingly.

"Mr. Dodson or Mr. Fogg at home, Sir?" inquired Mr. Pickwick, gently, advancing, hat in hand, towards the partition.

"Mr. Dodson ain't at home, and Mr. Fogg's particularly engaged," replied the voice; and at the same time the head to which the voice belonged, with a pen behind its ear, looked over the partition, and at Mr. Pickwick.

It was a ragged head, the sandy hair of which, scrupulously parted on one side, and flattened down with pomatum, was twisted into little semi-circular tails round a flat face ornamented with a pair of small eyes, and garnished with a very dirty shirt-collar, and a rusty black stock.

"Mr. Dodson ain't at home, and Mr. Fogg's particularly engaged," said the man to whom the head belonged.

"When will Mr. Dodson be back, Sir?" inquired Mr. Pickwick.

"Can't say."

"Will it be long before Mr. Fogg is disengaged, Sir?"

"Don't know."

Here the man proceeded to mend his pen with great deliberation, while another clerk, who was mixing a Seidlitz powder, under cover of the lid of his desk, laughed approvingly.

"I think I'll wait," said Mr. Pickwick. There was no reply; so Mr. Pickwick sat down unbidden, and listened to the loud ticking of the clock and the murmured conversation of the clerks.

"That was a game, wasn't it?" said one of the gentlemen, in a brown coat and brass buttons, inky drabs, and bluchers, at the conclusion of some inaudible relation of his previous evening's adventures.

"Devilish good—devilish good," said the Seidlitz-powder man.

"Tom Cummins was in the chair," said the man with the brown coat; "It was half-past four when I got to Somers Town, and then I was so precious drunk, that I couldn't find the place where the latch-key went in, and was obliged to knock up the old 'ooman. I say, I wonder what old Fogg 'ud say, if he knew it. I should get the sack, I s'pose—eh?"

At this humorous notion, all the clerks laughed in concert.

"There was such a game with Fogg here, this mornin'," said the man in a brown coat, "while Jack was up stairs sorting the papers, and you two were gone to the stamp-office. Fogg was down here opening the letters, when that chap as we issued the writ against at Camberwell, you know, came in—what's his name again?"

"Ramsey," said the clerk who had spoken to Mr. Pickwick.

"Ah, Ramsey—a precious seedy-looking customer. 'Well, Sir,' says old Fogg, looking at him very fierce—you know his way—'well, Sir, have you come to settle?' 'Yes, I have, Sir,' said Ramsey, putting his hand in his pocket, and bringing out the money, 'the debt's two pound ten, and the costs three pound five, and here it is, Sir;' and he sighed like bricks, as he lugged out the money, done up in a bit of blotting-paper. Old Fogg looked first at the money, and then at him, and then he coughed in his rum way, so that I knew something was coming. 'You don't know there's a declaration filed, which increases the costs materially, I suppose?' said Fogg. 'You don't say that, Sir,' said Ramsey, starting back; 'the time was only out, last night, Sir.' 'I do say it, though,' said Fogg, 'my clerk's just gone to file it. Hasn't Mr. Jackson gone to file that declaration in Bullman and Ramsey, Mr. Wicks?' Of course I said yes, and then Fogg coughed again, and looked at Ramsey. 'My God!' said Ramsey; 'and here have I nearly driven myself mad, scraping this money together, and all to no purpose.' 'None at all,' said Fogg, coolly; 'so you had better go back and scrape some more together, and bring it here in time.' 'I can't get it, by God,' said Ramsey, striking the desk with his fist. 'Don't bully me, Sir,' said Fogg, getting into a passion on purpose. 'I am not bullying you, Sir,' said Ramsey. 'You are,' said Fogg; 'get out, Sir; get out of this office, Sir, and come back, Sir, when you know how to behave yourself.' Well, Ramsey tried to speak, but Fogg wouldn't let him, so he put the money in his pocket, and sneaked out. The door was scarcely shut, when old Fogg turned round to me, with a sweet smile on his face, and drew the declaration out of his coat pocket. 'Here, Wicks,' says Fogg, 'take a cab, and go down to the Temple as quick as you can, and file that. The costs are quite safe, for he's a steady man with a large family, at a salary of five-and twenty-shillings a week, and if he gives us a warrant of attorney, as he must in the end, I know his employers will see it paid; so we may as well get all we can out of him, Mr. Wicks; it's a Christian act to do it, Mr. Wicks, for with his large family and small income, he'll be all the better for a good lesson against getting into debt,—won't he, Mr. Wicks, won't he?'—and he smiled so good-naturedly as he went away, that it was delightful to see him. He is a capital man of business," said Wicks, in a tone of the deepest admiration, "capital, isn't he?"

The other three cordially subscribed to this opinion, and the anecdote afforded the most unlimited satisfaction.

"Nice men these here, Sir," whispered Mr. Weller to his master; "wery nice notion of fun they has, Sir."

Mr. Pickwick nodded assent, and coughed to attract the attention of the young-gentlemen behind the partition, who, having now relaxed their minds by a little conversation among themselves, condescended to take some notice of the stranger.

"I wonder whether Fogg's disengaged now?" said Jackson.

"I'll see," said Wicks, dismounting leisurely from his stool. "What name shall I tell Mr. Fogg?"

"Pickwick," replied the illustrious subject of these memoirs.

Mr. Jackson departed up stairs on his errand, and immediately returned with a message that Mr. Fogg would see Mr. Pickwick in five minutes; and having delivered it, returned again to his desk.

"What did he say his name was?" whispered Wicks.

"Pickwick," replied Jackson; "it's the defendant in Bardell and Pickwick."

A sudden scraping of feet, mingled with the sound of suppressed laughter, was heard from behind the partition

"They're a twiggin' you, Sir," whispered Mr. Weller.

"Twigging me, Sam!" replied Mr. Pickwick; "what do you mean by twigging me?"

Mr. Weller replied by pointing with his thumb over his shoulder: and Mr. Pickwick, on looking up, became sensible of the pleasing fact, that all the four clerks, with countenances expressive of the utmost amusement, and their heads thrust over the wooden partition, were minutely inspecting the figure and general appearance of the supposed trifler with female hearts, and disturber of female happiness. On his looking up, the row of heads suddenly disappeared, and the sound of pens travelling at a furious rate over paper, immediately succeeded.

A sudden ring at the bell which hung in the office, summoned Mr. Jackson to the apartment of Fogg, from whence he came back to say that he (Fogg) was ready to see Mr. Pickwick if he would step up stairs.

Up stairs Mr. Pickwick did step accordingly, leaving Sam Weller below. The room door of the one-pair back, bore inscribed in legible characters the imposing words "Mr. Fogg;" and, having tapped thereat, and been desired to come in, Jackson ushered Mr. Pickwick into the presence.

"Is Mr. Dodson in?" inquired Mr. Fogg.

"Just come in, Sir," replied Jackson.

"Ask him to step here."

"Yes, Sir." Exit Jackson.

"Take a seat, Sir," said Fogg; "there is the paper, Sir: my partner will be here directly, and we can converse about this matter, Sir."

Mr. Pickwick took a seat and the paper, but, instead of reading the latter, peeped over the top of it, and took a survey of the man of business, who was an elderly pimply-faced, vegetable-diet sort of man, in a black coat, dark mixture trousers, and small black gaiters; a kind of being who seemed to be an essential part of the desk at which he was writing, and to have about as much thought or feeling.

After a few minutes' silence, Mr. Dodson, a plump, portly, stern-looking man, with a loud voice, appeared: and the conversation commenced.

"This is Mr. Pickwick," said Fogg.

"Ah! You are the defendant, Sir, in Bardell and Pickwick?" said Dodson.

"I am, Sir," replied Mr. Pickwick.

"Well, Sir," said Dodson, "and what do you propose?"

"Ah!" said Fogg, thrusting his hands into his trousers' pockets, and throwing himself back in his chair, "what do you propose, Mr. Pickwick?"

"Hush, Fogg," said Dodson, "let me hear what Mr. Pickwick has to say."

"I came, gentlemen," replied Mr. Pickwick,—gazing placidly on the two partners,—"I came here, gentlemen, to express the surprise with which I received your letter of the other day, and to inquire what grounds of action you can have against me."

"Grounds of"—Fogg had ejaculated thus much, when he was stopped by Dodson.

"Mr. Fogg," said Dodson, "I am going to speak."

"I beg your pardon, Mr. Dodson," said Fogg.

"For the grounds of action, Sir," continued Dodson, with moral elevation in his air, "you will consult your own conscience and your own feelings. We, Sir, we, are guided entirely by the statement of our client. That statement, Sir, may be true, or it may be false; it may be credible, or it may be incredible; but, if it be true, and if it be credible, I do not hesitate to say, Sir, that our grounds of action, Sir, are strong, and not to be shaken. You may be an unfortunate man, Sir, or you may be a designing one; but if I were called upon as a juryman upon my oath, Sir, to express an opinion of your conduct, Sir, I do not hesitate to assert that I should have but one opinion about it." Here Dodson drew himself up, with an air of offended virtue, and looked at Fogg, who thrust his hands further in his pockets, and, nodding his head sagely, said, in a tone of the fullest concurrence, "Most certainly."

"Well, Sir," said Mr. Pickwick, with considerable pain depicted in his countenance, "you will permit me to assure you, that I am a most unfortunate man, so far as this case is concerned."

"I hope you are, Sir," replied Dodson; "I trust you may be, Sir. If you are really innocent of what is laid to your charge, you are more unfortunate than I had believed any man could possibly be. What do you say, Mr. Fogg?"

"I say precisely what you say," replied Fogg, with a smile of incredulity.

"The writ, Sir, which commences the action," continued Dodson, "was issued regularly. Mr. Fogg, where is the *præcipe* book?"

"Here it is," said Fogg, handing over a square book, with a parchment cover.

"Here is the entry," resumed Dodson. "'Middlesex,

Capias *Martha Bardell, widow*, v. *Samuel Pickwick*. Damages, £1500. Dodson and Fogg for the plaintiff, Aug. 28, 1827.' All regular, Sir; perfectly." And Dodson coughed and looked at Fogg, who said "Perfectly," also. And then they both looked at Mr. Pickwick.

"I am to understand, then," said Mr. Pickwick, "that it really is your intention to proceed with this action?"

"Understand, Sir!—that you certainly may," replied Dodson, with something as near a smile as his importance would allow.

"And that the damages are actually laid at fifteen hundred pounds?" said Mr. Pickwick.

"To which understanding you may add my assurance, that if we could have prevailed upon our client, they would have been laid at treble the amount, Sir:" replied Dodson.

"I believe Mrs. Bardell specially said, however," observed Fogg, glancing at Dodson, "that she would not compromise for a farthing less."

"Unquestionably," replied Dodson, sternly. For the action was only just begun; and it wouldn't have done to let Mr. Pickwick compromise it then, even if he had been so disposed.

"As you offer no terms, Sir," said Dodson, displaying a slip of parchment in his right hand, and affectionately pressing a paper copy of it, on Mr. Pickwick with his left, "I had better serve you with a copy of this writ, Sir. Here is the original, Sir."

"Very well, gentlemen, very well," said Mr. Pickwick, rising in person and wrath at the same time; "you shall hear from my solicitor, gentlemen."

"We shall be very happy to do so," said Fogg, rubbing his hands.

"Very," said Dodson, opening the door.

"And before I go, gentlemen," said the excited Mr. Pickwick, turning round on the landing, "permit me to say, that of all the disgraceful and rascally proceedings—"

"Stay, Sir, stay," interposed Dodson, with great politeness. "Mr. Jackson—Mr. Wicks."

"Sir," said the two clerks, appearing at the bottom of the stairs.

"I just want you to hear what this gentleman says," replied Dodson. "Pray, go on, Sir—disgraceful and rascally proceedings, I think you said."

"I did," said Mr. Pickwick, thoroughly roused. "I said, Sir, that of all the disgraceful and rascally proceedings that ever were attempted, this is the most so. I repeat it, Sir."

"You hear that, Mr. Wicks?" said Dodson.

"You won't forget these expressions, Mr. Jackson?" said Fogg.

"Perhaps you would like to call us swindlers, Sir," said Dodson. "Pray do, Sir, if you feel disposed—now pray do, Sir."

"I do," said Mr. Pickwick. "You *are* swindlers."

"Very good," said Dodson. "You can hear down there, I hope, Mr. Wicks."

"Oh yes, Sir," said Wicks.

"You had better come up a step or two higher, if you can't," added Mr. Fogg.

"Go on, Sir; do go on. You had better call us thieves, Sir; or perhaps you would like to assault one of us. Pray do it, Sir, if you would; we will not make the smallest resistance. Pray do it, Sir."

As Fogg put himself very temptingly within the reach of Mr. Pickwick's clenched fist, there is little doubt that that

gentleman would have complied with his earnest entreaty, but for the interposition of Sam, who, hearing the dispute, emerged from the office, mounted the stairs, and seized his master by the arm.

"You just come avay," said Mr. Weller. "Battledore and shuttlecock's a wery good game, vhen you ain't the shuttlecock and two lawyers the battledores, in vich case it gets too excitin' to be pleasant. Come avay, Sir. If you want to ease your mind by blowing up somebody, come out into the court and blow up me; but it's rayther too expensive work to be carried on here."

And without the slightest ceremony, Mr. Weller hauled his master down the stairs, and down the court, and having safely deposited him in Cornhill, fell behind, prepared to follow whithersoever he should lead.

Mr. Pickwick walked on abstractedly, crossed opposite the Mansion House, and bent his steps up Cheapside. Sam began to wonder where they were going, when his master turned round, and said—

"Sam, I will go immediately to Mr. Perker's."

"That's just exactly the wery place vere you ought to have gone last night," replied Mr. Weller.

"I think it is, Sam," said Mr. Pickwick.

"I *know* it is," said Mr. Weller.

"Well, well, Sam," replied Mr. Pickwick, "we will go there at once, but first, as I have been rather ruffled, I should like a glass of brandy and water warm, Sam. Where can I have it, Sam?"

Mr. Weller's knowledge of London was extensive and peculiar. He replied, without the slightest consideration—

"Second court on the right hand side—last house but vun on the same side the vay—take the box as stands in the first fireplace, 'cos there an't no leg in the middle o' the table, vhich all the others has, and it's wery inconwenient."

Mr. Pickwick observed his valet's directions implicitly, and bidding Sam follow him, entered the tavern he had pointed out, where the hot brandy and water was speedily placed before him; while Mr. Weller, seated at a respectful distance, though at the same table with his master, was accommodated with a pint of porter.

The room was one of a very homely description, and was apparently under the especial patronage of stage coachmen: for several gentlemen, who had all the appearance of belonging to that learned profession, were drinking and smoking in the different boxes. Among the number was one stout, red-faced, elderly man in particular, seated in an opposite box, who attracted Mr. Pickwick's attention. The stout man was smoking with great vehemence, but between every half-dozen puffs, he took his pipe from his mouth, and looked first at Mr. Weller and then at Mr. Pickwick. Then he would bury in a quart-pot, as much of his countenance as the dimensions of the quart-pot admitted of its receiving, and take another look at Sam and Mr. Pickwick. Then he would take another half-dozen puffs with an air of profound meditation, and look at them again. And at last the stout man, putting up his legs on the seat, and leaning his back against the wall, began to puff at his pipe without leaving off at all, and to stare through the smoke at the new comers, as if he had made up his mind to see the most he could of them.

At first the evolutions of the stout man had escaped Mr. Weller's observation, but by degrees as he saw Mr. Pick-

"YOU JUST COME AVAY," SAID MR. WELLER. "BATTLEDORE AND SHUTTLECOCK'S A WERY GOOD GAME, WHEN YOU AIN'T THE SHUTTLECOCK AND TWO LAWYERS THE BATTLEDORES."

wick's eyes every now and then turning towards him, he began to gaze in the same direction, at the same time shading his eyes with his hand, as if he partially recognised the object before him, and wished to make quite sure of its identity. His doubts were speedily dispelled, however; for the stout man having blown a thick cloud from his pipe, a hoarse voice, like some strange effort of ventriloquism, emerged from beneath the capacious shawls which muffled his throat and chest, and slowly uttered these sounds—"Vy, Sammy."

"Who's that, Sam?" inquired Mr. Pickwick.

"Why, I wouldn't ha' believed it, Sir," replied Mr. Weller, with astonished eyes. "It's the old 'un."

"Old one," said Mr. Pickwick. "What old one?"

"My father, Sir," replied Mr. Weller. "How are you, my ancient?" And with this beautiful ebullition of filial affection, Mr. Weller made room on the seat beside him, for the stout man, who advanced pipe in mouth and pot in hand, to greet him.

"Vy, Sammy," said the father, "I han't seen you, for two years and better."

"Nor more you have, old codger," replied the son. "How's mother in law?"

"Vy, I'll tell you what, Sammy," said Mr. Weller, senior, with much solemnity in his manner; "there never was a nicer woman as a widder, than that 'ere second wentur o' mine—a sweet cretur she was, Sammy, and all I can say on her now, is, that as she was such an uncommon pleasant widder, it's a great pity she ever changed her condition. She don't act as a vife, Sammy."

"Don't she, though?" inquired Mr. Weller junior.

The elder Mr. Weller shook his head, as he replied with a sigh, "I've done it once too often, Sammy; I've done it once too often. Take example by your father, my boy, and be very careful o' widders all your life, specially if they've kept a public house, Sammy;" and having delivered this parental advice with great pathos, Mr. Weller senior re-filled his pipe from a tin box he carried in his pocket: and, lighting his fresh pipe from the ashes of the old one, commenced smoking at a great rate.

"Beg your pardon, Sir," he said, renewing the subject, and addressing Mr. Pickwick, after a considerable pause, "nothin' personal, I hope, Sir; I hope you han't got a widder, Sir."

"Not I," replied Mr. Pickwick, laughing; and while Mr. Pickwick laughed, Sam Weller informed his parent in a whisper, of the relation in which he stood towards that gentleman.

"Beg your pardon, Sir," said Mr. Weller, senior, taking off his hat, "I hope you've no fault to find with Sammy, Sir."

"None whatever," said Mr. Pickwick.

"Wery glad to hear it, Sir," replied the old man; "I took a good deal o' pains with his eddication, Sir; let him run in the streets when he was wery young, and shift for his-self. It's the only way to make a boy sharp, Sir."

"Rather a dangerous process, I should imagine," said Mr. Pickwick, with a smile.

"And not a wery sure one, neither," added Mr. Weller; "I got reglarly done the other day."

"No!" said the father.

"I did," said his son; and he proceeded to relate in as few words as possible, how he had fallen a ready dupe to the stratagems of Job Trotter.

Mr. Weller senior listened to the tale with the most profound attention, and, at its termination, said—

"Worn't one o' these chaps slim and tall, with long hair, and the gift o' the gab wery gallopin'?"

Mr. Pickwick did not quite understand the last item of description, but, comprehending the first, said "Yes," at a venture.

"T'other's a black-haired chap in mulberry livery, with a wery large head?"

"Yes, yes, he is," said Mr. Pickwick and Sam, with great earnestness.

"Then I know where they are, and that's all about it," said Mr. Weller; "they're at Ipswich, safe enough, them two."

"No!" said Mr. Pickwick.

"Fact," said Mr. Weller, "and I'll tell you how I know it. I work an Ipswich coach now and then for a friend o' mine. I worked down the wery day arter the night as you caught the rheumatiz, and at the Black Boy at Chelmsford —the wery place they'd come to—I took 'em up, right through to Ipswich, where the man servant—him in the mulberries—told me they was a goin' to put up for a long time."

"I'll follow him," said Mr. Pickwick; "we may as well see Ipswich as any other place. I'll follow him."

"You're quite certain it was them, governor?" inquired Mr. Weller, junior.

"Quite, Sammy, quite," replied his father, "for their appearance is wery sing'ler; besides that 'ere, I wondered to see the gen'lm'n so familiar with his servant; and, more than that, as they sat in front, right behind the box, I heard 'em laughing, and saying how they'd done old Fireworks."

"Old who?" said Mr. Pickwick.

"Old Fireworks, Sir, by which, I've no doubt, they meant you, Sir."

There is nothing positively vile or atrocious in the appellation of "old Fireworks," but still it is by no means a respectful or flattering designation. The recollection of all the wrongs he had sustained at Jingle's hands, had crowded on Mr. Pickwick's mind, the moment Mr. Weller began to speak: it wanted but a feather to turn the scale, and "old Fireworks" did it.

"I'll follow him," said Mr. Pickwick, with an emphatic blow on the table.

"I shall work down to Ipswich the day arter to-morrow, Sir," said Mr. Weller the elder, "from the Bull in Whitechapel; and if you really mean to go, you'd better go with me."

"So we had," said Mr. Pickwick; "very true; I can write to Bury, and tell them to meet me at Ipswich. We will go with you. But don't hurry away, Mr. Weller; won't you take anything?"

"You're wery good, Sir," replied Mr. W., stopping short —"perhaps a small glass of brandy to drink your health, and success to Sammy, Sir, wouldn't be amiss."

"Certainly not," replied Mr. Pickwick. "A glass of brandy here."

The brandy was brought: and Mr. Weller, after pulling his hair to Mr. Pickwick, and nodding to Sam, jerked it down his capacious throat as if it had been a small thimbleful.

"Well done, father," said Sam, "take care, old fellow, or you'll have a touch of your old complaint, the gout."

"I've found a sov'rin' cure for that, Sammy," replied Mr Weller, setting down the glass.

"A sovereign cure for the gout," said Mr. Pickwick, hastily producing his note-book, "what is it?"

"The gout, Sir," replied Mr. Weller, "the gout is a complaint as arises from too much ease and comfort. If ever you're attacked with the gout, Sir, jist you marry a widder as has got a good loud woice, with a decent notion of usin' it, and you'll never have the gout agin. It's a capital prescription, Sir. I takes it reg'lar, and I can warrant it to drive away any illness as is caused by too much jollity." Having imparted this valuable secret, Mr. Weller drained his glass once more, produced a laboured wink, sighed deeply, and slowly retired.

"Well, what do you think of what your father says, Sam?" inquired Mr. Pickwick, with a smile.

"Think, Sir!" replied Mr. Weller; "why, I think he's the wictim o' connubiality, as Blue Beard's domestic chaplain said, with a tear of pity, ven he buried him."

There was no replying to this very apposite conclusion, and, therefore, Mr. Pickwick, after settling the reckoning, resumed his walk to Gray's Inn. By the time he reached its secluded groves, however, eight o'clock had struck, and the unbroken stream of gentlemen in muddy high-lows, soiled white hats, and rusty apparel, who were pouring towards the different avenues of egress, warned him that the majority of the offices had closed for that day.

After climbing two pairs of steep and dirty stairs, he found his anticipations were realised. Mr. Perker's "outer door" was closed; and the dead silence which followed Mr. Weller's repeated kicks thereat, announced that the officials had retired from business for the night.

"This is pleasant, Sam," said Mr. Pickwick; "I shouldn't lose an hour in seeing him; I shall not be able to get one wink of sleep to-night, I know, unless I have the satisfaction of reflecting that I have confided this matter to a professional man."

"Here's an old 'ooman comin' up stairs, Sir," replied Mr. Weller; "p'raps she knows where we can find somebody. Hallo, old lady, vere's Mr. Perker's people?"

"Mr. Perker's people," said a thin, miserable-looking old woman, stopping to recover breath after the ascent of the staircase, "Mr. Perker's people's gone, and I'm a goin' to do the office out."

"Are you Mr. Perker's servant?" inquired Mr. Pickwick.

"I am Mr. Perker's laundress," replied the old woman.

"Ah," said Mr. Pickwick, half aside to Sam, "it's a curious circumstance, Sam, that they call the old women in these inns, laundresses. I wonder what's that for."

"'Cos they has a mortal awersion to washing anythin', I suppose, Sir," replied Mr. Weller.

"I shouldn't wonder," said Mr. Pickwick, looking at the old woman, whose appearance as well as the condition of the office, which she had by this time opened, indicated a rooted antipathy to the application of soap and water; "do you know where I can find Mr. Perker, my good woman?"

"No I don't," replied the old woman, gruffly; "he's out o' town now."

"That's unfortunate," said Mr. Pickwick; "where's his clerk—do you know?"

"Yes, I know where he is, but he wouldn't thank me for telling you," replied the laundress.

"I have very particular business with him," said Mr. Pickwick.

"Won't it do in the morning?" said the woman.

"Not so well," replied Mr Pickwick.

"Well," said the old woman, "if it was anything very particular, I was to say where he was, so I suppose there's no harm in telling. If you just go to the Magpie and Stump, and ask at the bar for Mr. Lowten, they'll show you in to him, and he's Mr. Perker's clerk."

With this direction, and having been furthermore informed that the hostelry in question was situated in a court, happy in the double advantage of being in the vicinity of Clare Market, and closely approximating to the back of New Inn, Mr. Pickwick and Sam descended the rickety staircase in safety, and issued forth in quest of the Magpie and Stump.

This favoured tavern, sacred to the evening orgies of Mr. Lowten and his companions, was what ordinary people would designate a public-house. That the landlord was a man of a money-making turn, was sufficiently testified by the fact of a small bulk-head beneath the tap-room window, in size and shape not unlike a sédan-chair, being underlet to a mender of shoes: and that he was a being of a philanthropic mind, was evident from the protection afforded to a pie-man, who vended his delicacies without fear of interruption, on the very door-step. In the lower windows, which were decorated with curtains of a saffron hue, dangled two or three printed cards, bearing reference to Devonshire cyder and Dantzic spruce, while a large black board, announcing in white letters to an enlightened public, that there were 500,000 barrels of double stout in the cellars of the establishment, left the mind in a state of not unpleasing doubt and uncertainty, as to the precise direction in the bowels of the earth, in which this mighty cavern might be supposed to extend. When we add, that the weather-beaten sign-board bore the half-obliterated semblance of a magpie intently eyeing a crooked streak of brown paint, which the neighbours had been taught from infancy to consider as the "stump," we have said all that need be said, of the exterior of the edifice.

On Mr. Pickwick's presenting himself at the bar, an elderly female emerged from behind a screen therein, and presented herself before him.

"Is Mr. Lowten here, Ma'am?" inquired Mr. Pickwick.

"Yes he is, Sir," replied the landlady. "Here, Charley, show the gentleman in, to Mr. Lowten."

"The gen'lm'n can't go in, just now," said a shambling pot-boy, with a red head, "'cos Mr. Lowten's a singin' a comic song, and he'll put him out. He'll be done d'rectly, Sir."

The red-headed pot-boy had scarcely finished speaking, when a most unanimous hammering of tables, and jingling of glasses, announced that the song had that instant terminated; and Mr. Pickwick, after desiring Sam to solace himself in the tap, suffered himself to be conducted into the presence of Mr. Lowten.

At the announcement of "a gentleman to speak to you, Sir," a puffy-faced young man who filled the chair at the head of the table, looked with some surprise in the direction from whence the voice proceeded: and the surprise seemed to be by no means diminished, when his eyes rested on an individual whom he had never seen before.

"I beg your pardon, Sir," said Mr. Pickwick, "and I am very sorry to disturb the other gentlemen, too, but I come on very particular business; and if you will suffer me to detain you at this end of the room for five minutes, I shall be very much obliged to you."

The puffy-faced young man rose, and drawing a chair close to Mr. Pickwick in an obscure corner of the room, listened attentively to his tale of woe.

"Ah," he said, when Mr. Pickwick had concluded, "Dodson and Fogg—sharp practice theirs—capital men of business is Dodson and Fogg, Sir."

Mr. Pickwick admitted the sharp practice of Dodson and Fogg, and Lowten resumed.

"Perker ain't in town, and he won't be neither, before the end of next week; but if you want the action defended, and will leave the copy with me, I can do all that's needful 'till he comes back."

"That's exactly what I came here for," said Mr. Pickwick, handing over the document. "If anything particular occurs, you can write to me at the post-office, Ipswich."

"That's all right," replied Mr. Perker's clerk; and then seeing Mr. Pickwick's eye wandering curiously towards the table, he added, "Will you join us, for half-an-hour or so? We are capital company here to-night. There's Samkin and Green's managing-clerk, and Smithers and Price's chancery, and Pimkin and Thomas's out o' door—sings a capital song, he does—and Jack Bamber, and ever so many more. You're come out of the country, I suppose. Would you like to join us?"

Mr. Pickwick could not resist so tempting an opportunity of studying human nature. He suffered himself to be led to the table, where, after having been introduced to the company in due form, he was accommodated with a seat near the chairman, and called for a glass of his favourite beverage.

A profound silence, quite contrary to Mr. Pickwick's expectation, succeeded.

"You don't find this sort of thing disagreeable, I hope, Sir?" said his right hand neighbour, a gentleman in a checked shirt and Mosaic studs, with a cigar in his mouth.

"Not in the least," replied Mr. Pickwick, "I like it very much, although I am no smoker myself."

"I should be very sorry to say I wasn't," interposed another gentleman on the opposite side of the table. "It's board and lodging to me, is smoke."

Mr. Pickwick glanced at the speaker, and thought that if it were washing too, it would be all the better.

Here there was another pause. Mr. Pickwick was a stranger, and his coming had evidently cast a damp upon the party.

"Mr. Grundy's going to oblige the company with a song," said the chairman.

"No he ain't," said Mr. Grundy.

"Why not?" said the chairman.

"Because I can't," said Mr. Grundy.

"You had better say you won't," replied the chairman.

"Well, then, I won't," retorted Mr. Grundy. Mr. Grundy's positive refusal to gratify the company, occasioned another silence.

"Won't anybody enliven us?" said the chairman, despondingly.

"Why don't you enliven us yourself, Mr. Chairman?" said a young man with a whisker, a squint, and an open shirt collar (dirty) from the bottom of the table.

"Hear! hear!" said the smoking gentleman, in the Mosaic jewellery.

"Because I only know one song, and I have sung it already, and it's a fine of 'glasses round' to sing the same song twice in a night," replied the chairman.

This was an unanswerable reply, and silence prevailed again.

"I have been to-night, gentlemen," said Mr. Pickwick, hoping to start a subject which all the company could take part in discussing, "I have been to-night in a place which you all know very well, doubtless, but which I have not been in before, for some years, and know very little of; I mean Gray's Inn, gentlemen. Curious little nooks in a great place, like London, these old inns are."

"By Jove," said the chairman, whispering across the table to Mr. Pickwick, "you have hit upon something that one of us, at least, would talk upon for ever. You'll draw old Jack Bamber out; he was never heard to talk about anything else but the Inns, and he has lived alone in them, till he's half crazy."

The individual to whom Lowten alluded, was a little yellow high-shouldered man, whose countenance, from his habit of stooping forward when silent, Mr. Pickwick had not observed before. He wondered though, when the old man raised his shrivelled face, and bent his bright grey eye upon him, with a keen inquiring look, that such remarkable features could have escaped his attention for a moment. There was a fixed grin smile perpetually on his countenance· he leant his chin on a long skinny hand, with nails of extraordinary length; and as he inclined his head to one side, and looked keenly out from beneath his ragged grey eyebrows, there was a strange, wild slyness in his leer, quite repulsive to behold.

This was the figure that now started forward, and burst into an animated torrent of words. As this chapter has been a long one, however, and as the old man was a remarkable personage, it will be more respectful to him, and more convenient to us, to let him speak for himself in a fresh one.

CHAPTER XXI.

IN WHICH THE OLD MAN LAUNCHES FORTH INTO HIS FAVOURITE THEME, AND RELATES A STORY ABOUT A QUEER CLIENT.

"Aha!" said the old man, a brief description of whose manner and appearance concluded the last chapter, "Aha! who was talking about the Inns?"

"I was, Sir," replied Mr. Pickwick—"I was observing what singular old places they are."

"You!" said the old man, contemptuously—"What do you know of the time when young men shut themselves up in those lonely rooms, and read and read, hour after hour, and night after night, till their reason wandered beneath their midnight studies; till their mental powers were exhausted; till morning's light brought no freshness or health to them; and they sank beneath the unnatural devotion of their youthful energies to their dry old books? Coming down to a later time, and a very different day, what do you know of the gradual sinking beneath consumption, or the quick wasting of fever—the grand results of 'life' and dissipation—which men have undergone in those same rooms? How many vain pleaders for mercy, do you think have turned away heart-sick from the lawyer's office, to find a resting-place in the Thames, or a refuge in the gaol? They are no ordinary houses, those. There is not a pannel in the old wainscotting, but what, if it were endowed with the powers of speech and memory, could start from the wall, and tell its tale of horror—the romance of life, Sir, the romance of life. Common-place as they may seem now, I tell you they are strange old places, and I would rather hear many a legend with a terrific-sounding name, than the true history of one old set of chambers."

There was something so odd in the old man's sudden energy, and the subject which had called it forth, that Mr. Pickwick was prepared with no observation in reply; and the old man checking his impetuosity, and resuming the leer, which had disappeared during his previous excitement, said—

"Look at them in another light: their most commonplace and least romantic: what fine places of slow torture they are. Think of the needy man who has spent his all, beggared himself, and pinched his friends, to enter the profession, which is destined never to yield a morsel of bread to him. The waiting—the hope—the disappointment—the fear—the misery—the poverty—the blight on his hopes, and end to his career—the suicide perhaps, or, better still, the shabby, slip-shod drunkard. Am I not right about them, eh?" And the old man rubbed his hands, and leered as if in delight at having found another point of view in which to place his favourite subject.

Mr. Pickwick eyed the old man with great curiosity, and the remainder of the company smiled, and looked on in silence.

"Talk of your German universities," said the little old man—"Pooh, pooh! there's romance enough at home, without going half a mile for it; only people never think of it."

"I never thought of the romance of this particular subject before, certainly," said Mr. Pickwick, laughing.

"To be sure you didn't," said the little old man, "of course not. As a friend of mine used to say to me, 'What is there in chambers, in particular?' 'Queer old places,' said I. 'Not at all,' said he. 'Lonely,' said I. 'Not a bit of it,' said he. He died one morning of apoplexy, as he was going to open his outer door. Fell with his head in his own letter-box, and there he lay for eighteen months. Every body thought he'd gone out of town."

"And how was he found at last?" inquired Mr. Pickwick.

"The benchers determined to break his door open, as he hadn't paid any rent for two years. So they did. Forced the lock; and a very dusty skeleton in a blue coat, black knee-shorts, and silks, fell forward in the arms of the porter who opened the door. Queer, that. Rather, perhaps; rather, eh?" And the little old man put his head more on one side, and rubbed his hands with unspeakable glee.

"I know another case," said the little old man, when his chuckles had in some degree subsided—"It occurred in Clifford's Inn. Tenant of a top set—bad character—shut himself up in his bed-room closet, and took a dose of arsenic. The steward thought he had run away: opened the door, and put a bill up. Another man came, took the chambers, furnished them, and went to live there. Somehow or other he couldn't sleep—always restless and uncomfortable. 'Odd,' says he. 'I'll make the other room my bed-chamber, and this my sitting-room.' He made the change, and slept very well at night, but suddenly found that somehow he couldn't read in the evening: he got nervous and uncomfortable, and used to be always snuffing his candles and staring about him. 'I can't make this out,' said he, when he came home from the play one night, and was drinking a glass of cold grog, with his back to the wall, in order that he mightn't be able to fancy there was any one behind him—'I can't make it out,' said he; and just then his eyes rested on the little closet that had been always locked up, and a shudder ran through his whole frame from top to toe. 'I have felt this strange feeling before,' said he—'I cannot help thinking there's something wrong about that closet.' He made a strong effort, plucked up his courage, shivered the lock with a blow or two of the poker, opened the door, and there, sure enough, standing bolt upright in the corner, was the last tenant, with a little bottle clasped firmly in his hand, and his face livid with the hue of a painful death." As the little old man concluded, he looked round on the attentive faces of his wondering auditory with a smile of grim delight.

"What strange things these are you tell us of, Sir," said Mr. Pickwick, minutely scanning the old man's countenance, by the aid of his glasses.

"Strange!" said the little old man—"Nonsense; you think them strange, because you know nothing about it. They are funny, but not uncommon."

"Funny!" exclaimed Mr. Pickwick, involuntarily.

"Yes, funny, are they not?" replied the little old man, with a diabolical leer; and then, without pausing for an answer, he continued—

"I knew another man—let me see—it's forty years ago now—who took an old, damp, rotten set of chambers, in one of the most ancient Inns, that had been shut up and empty for years and years before. There were lots of old women's stories about the place, and it certainly was very far from being a cheerful one; but he was poor, and the rooms were cheap, and that would have been quite a sufficient reason for him, if they had been ten times worse than they really were. He was obliged to take some mouldering fixtures that were on the place, and, among the rest, was a great lumbering wooden press for papers, with large glass doors, and a green curtain inside; a pretty useless thing for him, for he had no papers to put in it; and as to his clothes, he carried them about with him, and that wasn't very hard work, either. Well, he had moved in all his furniture—it wasn't quite a truck-full—and sprinkled it about the room, so as to make the four chairs look as much like a dozen as possible, and was sitting down before the fire at night, drinking the first glass of two gallons of whiskey he had ordered on credit, wondering whether it would ever be paid for, and if so, in how many years' time, when his eyes encountered the glass doors of the wooden press. 'Ah!' says he—'If I hadn't been obliged to take that ugly article at the old broker's valuation, I might have got something comfortable for the money. I'll tell you what it is, old fellow,' he said, speaking aloud to the press, just because he had got nothing else to speak to—'If it wouldn't cost more to break up your old carcase, than it would ever be worth afterwards, I'd have a fire out of you, in less than no time.' He had hardly spoken the words, when a sound resembling a faint groan, appeared to issue from the interior of the case. It startled him at first, but thinking, on a moment's reflection, that it must be some young fellow in the next chambers, who had been dining out, he put his feet on the fender, and raised the poker to stir the fire. At that moment, the sound was repeated: and one of the glass doors slowly opening, disclosed a pale and emaciated figure in soiled and worn apparel, standing erect in the press. The figure was tall and thin, and the countenance expressive of care and anxiety; but there was something in the hue of the skin, and gaunt and unearthly appearance of the whole form, which no being of this world was ever seen to wear. 'Who are you?' said the new tenant, turning very pale, poising the poker in his hand, however, and taking a very decent aim at the countenance of the figure—'Who are you?' 'Don't throw that poker at me,' replied the form—'If you hurled it with ever so sure an aim, it would pass through me, without resistance, and expend its force on the wood behind. I am a spirit.' 'And, pray, what do you want here?' faltered the tenant. 'In this room,' replied the apparition, 'my worldly ruin was worked, and I and my children beggared. In this press, the papers in a long, long suit, which accumulated for years, were deposited. In this room, when I had died of grief, and long-deferred hope, two wily harpies divided the wealth for which I had contested during a wretched existence, and of which, at last, not one farthing was left for my unhappy descendants. I terrified them from the spot, and since that day have prowled by night—the only period at which I can re-visit the earth—about the scenes of my long-protracted misery. This apartment is mine: leave it to me.' 'If you insist upon making your appearance here,' said the tenant, who had time to collect his presence of mind during this prosy statement of the ghost's —'I shall give up possession with the greatest pleasure; but I should like to ask you one question, if you will allow me.' 'Say on,' said the apparition, sternly. 'Well,' said the tenant, 'I don't apply the observation personally to you, because it is equally applicable to all the ghosts I ever heard of; but it does appear to me, somewhat inconsistent, that when you have an opportunity of visiting the fairest spots of earth—for I suppose space is nothing to you—you should always return exactly to the very places where you have been most miserable.' 'Egad, that's very true; I never thought of that before,' said the ghost. 'You see, Sir,' pursued the tenant, 'this is a very uncomfortable room. From the appearance of that press, I should be disposed to say that it is not wholly free from bugs; and I really think you might find much more comfortable quarters: to say nothing of the climate of London, which is extremely disagreeable.' 'You are very right, Sir,' said the ghost, politely, 'it never struck me till now; I'll try change of air directly'—and, in fact, he began to vanish as he spoke: his legs, indeed, had quite disappeared. 'And if, Sir,' said the tenant, calling after him, 'if you *would* have the goodness to suggest to the other ladies and gentlemen who are now engaged in haunting old empty houses, that they might be much more comfortable elsewhere, you will confer a very great benefit on society.' 'I will,' replied the ghost; 'we must be dull fellows—very dull fellows, indeed; I can't imagine how we can have been so stupid.' With these words, the spirit disappeared; and what is rather remarkable," added the old man, with a shrewd look round the table, "he never came back again."

"That ain't bad, if it's true," said the man in the Mosaic studs, lighting a fresh cigar.

"*If!*" exclaimed the old man, with a look of excessive contempt. "I suppose," he added, turning to Lowten, "he'll say next, that my story about the queer client we had, when I was in an attorney's office, is not true, either —I shouldn't wonder."

"I shan't venture to say anything at all about it, seeing that I never heard the story," observed the owner of the Mosaic decorations.

"I wish you would repeat it, Sir," said Mr. Pickwick.

"Ah, do," said Lowten, "nobody has heard it but me, and I have nearly forgotten it."

The old man looked round the table, and leered more horribly than ever, as if in triumph, at the attention which was depicted in every face. Then rubbing his chin with his hand, and looking up to the ceiling as if to recall the circumstances to his memory, he began as follows:—

THE OLD MAN'S TALE ABOUT THE QUEER CLIENT.

"It matters little," said the old man, "where, or how, I picked up this brief history. If I were to relate it in the order in which it reached me, I should commence in the middle, and when I had arrived at the conclusion, go back for a beginning. It is enough for me to say that some of its circumstances passed before my own eyes; for the remainder I know them to have happened, and there are some persons yet living, who will remember them but too well.

"In the Borough High Street, near Saint George's Church, and on the same side of the way, stands, as most people know, the smallest of our debtors' prisons—the Marshalsea. Although in later times it has been a very different place from the sink of filth and dirt it once was, even its improved condition holds out but little temptation to the extravagant or consolation to the improvident. The condemned felon has as good a yard for air and exercise in Newgate, as the insolvent debtor in the Marshalsea Prison.

"It may be my fancy, or it may be that I cannot separate the place from the old recollections associated with it, but this part of London I cannot bear. The street is broad, the shops are spacious, the noise of passing vehicles, the footsteps of a perpetual stream of people—all the busy sounds of traffic, resound in it from morn to midnight, but the streets around, are mean and close; poverty and debauchery lie festering in the crowded alleys; want and misfortune are pent up in the narrow prison; an air of gloom and dreariness seems, in my eyes at least, to hang about the scene, and to impart to it, a squalid and sickly hue.

"Many eyes, that have long since been closed in the grave, have looked round upon that scene lightly enough, when entering the gate of the old Marshalsea Prison for the first time: for despair seldom comes with the first severe shock of misfortune. A man has confidence in untried friends, he remembers the many offers of service so freely made by his boon companions when he wanted them not; he has hope—the hope of happy inexperience—and however he may bend beneath the first shock, it springs up in his bosom, and flourishes there for a brief space, until it droops beneath the blight of disappointment and neglect. How soon have those same eyes, deeply sunken in the head, glared from faces wasted with famine, and sallow from confinement, in days when it was no figure of speech to say that debtors rotted in prison, with no hope of release, and no prospect of liberty! The atrocity in its full extent no longer exists, but there is enough of it left, to give rise to occurrences that make the heart bleed.

"Twenty years ago, that pavement was worn with the footsteps of a mother and child, who, day by day, so surely as the morning came, presented themselves at the prison gate; often after a night of restless misery and anxious thoughts, were they there, a full hour too soon, and then the young mother turning meekly away, would lead the child to the old bridge, and raising him in her arms to shew him the glistening water, tinted with the light of the morning's sun, and stirring with all the bustling preparations for business and pleasure that the river presents at that early hour, endeavour to interest his thoughts in the objects before him. But she would quickly set him down, and hiding her face in her shawl, give vent to the tears that blinded her, for no expression of interest or amusement lighted up his thin and sickly face. His recollections were few enough, but they were all of one kind—all connected with the poverty and misery of his parents. Hour after hour, had he sat on his mother's knee, and with childish sympathy watched the tears that stole down her face, and then crept quietly away into some dark corner, and sobbed himself to sleep. The hard realities of the world, with many of its worst privations—hunger and thirst, and cold and want—had all come home to him, from the first dawnings of reason; and though the form of childhood was there, its light heart, its merry laugh, and sparkling eyes were wanting.

"The father and mother looked on upon this, and upon each other, with thoughts of agony they dared not breathe in words. The healthy, strong-made man, who could have borne almost any fatigue of active exertion, was wasting beneath the close confinement and unhealthy atmosphere of a crowded prison. The slight and delicate woman was sinking beneath the combined effects of bodily and mental illness; the child's young heart was breaking.

"Winter came, and with it weeks of cold and heavy rain. The poor girl had removed to a wretched apartment close to the spot of her husband's imprisonment; and though the change had been rendered necessary by their increasing poverty, she was happier now, for she was nearer him. For two months, she and her little companion watched the opening of the gate as usual. One day she failed to come, for the first time. Another morning arrived, and she came alone. The child was dead.

"They little know, who coldly talk of the poor man's bereavements, as a happy release from pain to the departed, and a merciful relief from expense to the survivor—they little know, I say, what the agony of those bereavements is. A silent look of affection and regard when all other eyes are turned coldly away—the consciousness that we possess the sympathy and affection of one being when all others have deserted us—is a hold, a stay, a comfort in the deepest affliction, which no wealth could purchase, or power bestow. The child had sat at his parents' feet for hours together, with his little hands patiently folded in each other, and his thin wan face raised towards them. They had seen him pine away, from day to day; and though his brief existence had been a joyless one, and he was now removed to that peace and rest which, child as he was, he had never known in this world, they were his parents, and his loss sunk deep into their souls.

"It was plain to those who looked upon the mother's altered face that death must soon close the scene of her adversity and trial. Her husband's fellow prisoners shrunk from obtruding on his grief and misery, and left to himself alone, the small room he had previously occupied in common with two companions. She shared it with him: and lingering on without pain, but without hope, her life ebbed slowly away.

"She had fainted one evening in her husband's arms, and he had borne her to the open window, to revive her with the air, when the light of the moon falling full upon her face, shewed him a change upon her features, which made him stagger beneath her weight, like a helpless infant.

"'Set me down George,' she said faintly. He did so, and seating himself beside her, covered his face with his hands, and burst into tears.

"'It is very hard to leave you George,' she said, 'but it's God's will, and you must bear it for my sake. Oh! how I thank him for having taken our boy. He is happy, and in heaven now. What would he have done here, without his mother!'

"'You shall not die, Mary, you shall not die;' said the husband, starting up. He paced hurriedly to and fro, striking his head with his clenched fists; then reseating himself beside her, and supporting her in his arms, added more calmly, 'Rouse yourself, my dear girl—pray, pray do. You will revive yet.'

"'Never again George; never again'—said the dying woman. 'Let them lay me by my poor boy now, but promise me, that if ever you leave this dreadful place, and should grow rich, you will have us removed to some quiet country churchyard, a long, long way off—very far from here, where we can rest in peace. Dear George, promise me you will.'

"'I do, I do'—said the man, throwing himself passionately on his knees before her. 'Speak to me Mary, another word; one look—but one—'

"He ceased to speak: for the arm that clasped his neck, grew stiff and heavy. A deep sigh escaped from the wasted form before him; the lips moved, and a smile played upon the face, but the lips were pallid, and the smile faded into a rigid and ghastly stare. He was alone in the world.

"That night, in the silence and desolation of his miserable room, the wretched man knelt down by the dead body of his wife, and called on God to witness a dreadful oath, that from that hour, he devoted himself to revenge her death and that of his child; that from thenceforth to the last moment of his life, his whole energies should be directed to this one object; that his revenge should be protracted and terrible; that his hatred should be undying and unextinguishable; and should hunt its object through the world.

"The deepest despair, and passion scarcely human, had made such fierce ravages on his face and form, in that one night, that his companions in misfortune shrunk affrighted from him as he passed by. His eyes were bloodshot and heavy, his face a deadly white, and his body bent as if with age. He had bitten his under lip nearly through in the violence of his mental suffering, and the blood which had flowed from the wound had trickled down his chin, and stained his shirt and neckerchief. No tear, or sound of complaint escaped him; but the unsettled look, and disordered haste with which he paced up and down the yard, denoted the fever which was burning within.

"It was necessary that his wife's body should be removed from the prison, without delay. He received the communication with perfect calmness, and acquiesced in its propriety. Nearly all the inmates of the prison had assembled to witness its removal; they fell back on either side when the widower appeared; he walked hurriedly forward, and stationed himself, alone, in a little railed area close to the lodge gate, from whence the crowd, with an instinctive feeling of delicacy, had retired. The rude coffin was borne slowly forward on men's shoulders. A dead silence pervaded the throng, broken only by the audible lamentations of the women, and the shuffling steps of the bearers on the stone pavement. They reached the spot where the bereaved husband stood; and stopped. He laid his hand upon the coffin, and mechanically adjusting the pall with which it was covered, motioned them onwards. The turnkeys in the prison lobby took off their hats as it passed through, and in another moment the heavy gate closed behind it. He looked vacantly upon the crowd, and fell heavily to the ground.

"Although for many weeks after this, he was watched night and day, in the wildest ravings of fever, neither the consciousness of his loss, nor the recollection of the vow he had made, ever left him for a moment. Scenes changed before his eyes, place succeeded place, and event followed event, in all the hurry of delirium; but they were all connected in some way with the great object of his mind. He was sailing over a boundless expanse of sea, with a blood-red sky above, and the angry waters lashed into fury beneath, boiling and eddying up, on every side. There was another vessel before them, toiling and labouring in the howling storm; her canvass fluttering in ribbons from the mast, and her deck thronged with figures who were lashed to the sides, over which huge waves every instant burst, sweeping away some devoted creatures into the foaming sea. Onward they bore, amidst the roaring mass of water, with a speed and force which nothing could resist; and striking the stern of the foremost vessel, crushed her, beneath their keel. From the huge whirlpool which the sinking wreck occasioned, arose a shriek so loud and shrill—the death-cry of a hundred drowning wretches, blended into one fierce yell—that it rung far above the war-cry of the elements, and echoed, and re-echoed till it seemed to pierce air, sky, and ocean. But what was that—that old grey-head that rose above the water's surface, and with looks of agony, and screams for aid, buffeted with the waves! One look, and he had sprung from the vessel's side, and with vigorous strokes was swimming towards it. He reached it; he was close upon it. They were *his* features. The old man saw him coming, and vainly strove to elude his grasp. But he clasped him tight, and dragged him beneath the water. Down, down with him, fifty fathoms deep; his struggles grew fainter and fainter, until they wholly ceased. He was dead; he had killed him, and had kept his oath.

"He was traversing the scorching sands of a mighty desert, barefooted and alone. The sand choked and blinded him; its fine thin grains entered the very pores of his skin, and irritated him almost to madness. Gigantic masses of the same material, carried forward by the wind, and shone through, by the burning sun, stalked in the distance like pillars of living fire. The bones of men, who had perished in the dreary waste, lay scattered at his feet; a fearful light fell on everything around; and so far as the eye could reach, nothing but objects of dread and horror presented themselves. Vainly striving to utter a cry of terror, with his tongue cleaving to his mouth, he rushed madly forward. Armed with supernatural strength, he waded through the sand, until exhausted with fatigue and thirst, he fell senseless on the earth. What fragrant coolness revived him; what gushing sound was that? Water! It was indeed a well; and the clear fresh stream was running at his feet. He drank deeply of it, and throwing his aching limbs upon the bank, sunk into a delicious trance. The sound of approaching footsteps roused him. An old grey-headed man tottered forward to slake his burning thirst. It was *he* again. He wound his arms round the old man's body, and

held him back. He struggled in powerful convulsions, and shrieked for water—for but one drop of water to save his life. But he held the old man firmly, and watched his agonies with greedy eyes; and when his lifeless head fell forward on his bosom, he rolled the corpse from him with his feet.

"When the fever left him, and consciousness returned, he awoke to find himself rich and free: to hear that the parent who would have let him die in gaol—*would!* who *had* let those who were far dearer to him than his own existence, die of want and the sickness of heart that medicine cannot cure—had been found, dead in his bed of down. He had all the heart to leave his son a beggar, but proud even of his health and strength, he had put off the act till it was too late, and now might gnash his teeth in the other world, at the thought of the wealth his remissness had left him. He woke to this, and he woke to more. To recollect the purpose for which he lived, and to remember that his enemy was his wife's own father—the man who had cast him into prison, and who, when his daughter and her child sued at his feet for mercy, had spurned them from his door. Oh, how he cursed the weakness that prevented him from being up, and active, in his scheme of vengeance!

"He caused himself to be carried from the scene of his loss and misery, and conveyed to a quiet residence on the sea coast—not in the hope of recovering his peace of mind or happiness, for both were fled for ever; but to restore his prostrate energies, and meditate on his darling object. And here, some evil spirit cast in his way the opportunity for his first, most horrible revenge.

"It was summer time; and wrapped in his gloomy thoughts, he would issue from his solitary lodgings early in the evening, and wandering along a narrow path beneath the cliffs to a wild and lonely spot that had struck his fancy in his ramblings, seat himself on some fallen fragments of the rock, and burying his face in his hands, remain there for hours—sometimes until night had completely closed in, and the long shadows of the frowning cliffs above his head, cast a thick black darkness on every object near him.

"He was seated here, one calm evening in his old position, now and then raising his head, to watch the flight of a seagull, or carry his eye along the glorious crimson path, which commencing in the middle of the ocean, seemed to lead to its very verge where the sun was setting, when the profound stillness of the spot was broken by a loud cry for help; he listened, doubtful of his having heard aright, when the cry was repeated with even greater vehemence than before, and, starting to his feet, he hastened in the direction from whence it proceeded.

"The tale told itself at once: some scattered garments lay on the beach; a human head was just visible above the waves at a little distance from the shore; and an old man, wringing his hands in agony, was running to and fro, shrieking for assistance. The invalid, whose strength was now sufficiently restored, threw off his coat, and rushed towards the sea, with the intention of plunging in, and dragging the drowning man a-shore.

"'Hasten here, Sir, in God's name; help, help, Sir, for the love of Heaven. He is my son, Sir, my only son,' said the old man, frantically, as he advanced to meet him. 'My only son, Sir, and he is dying before his father's eyes.'

"At the first word the old man uttered, the stranger checked himself in his career, and, folding his arms, stood perfectly motionless.

"'Great God!' exclaimed the old man, recoiling—'Heyling!'

"The stranger smiled, and was silent.

"'Heyling!' said the old man, wildly—'My boy, Heyling, my dear boy, look, look;' and, gasping for breath, the miserable father pointed to the spot where the young man was struggling for life.

"'Hark!' said the old man—'He cries once more. He is alive yet. Heyling, save him, save him.'

"The stranger smiled again, and remained immovable as a statue.

"'I have wronged you,' shrieked the old man, falling on his knees, and clasping his hands together—'Be revenged; take my all, my life; cast me into the water at your feet, and, if human nature can repress a struggle, I will die, without stirring hand or foot. Do it, Heyling, do it, but save my boy, he is so young, Heyling, so young to die.'

"'Listen,' said the stranger, grasping the old man fiercely by the wrist—'I will have life for life, and here is ONE. My child died before his father's eyes, a far more agonising and painful death than that young slanderer of his sister's worth is meeting while I speak. You laughed—laughed in your daughter's face, where death had already set his hand—at our sufferings, then. What think you of them now? See there, see there.'

"As the stranger spoke, he pointed to the sea. A faint cry died away upon its surface: the last powerful struggle of the dying man agitated the rippling waves for a few seconds: and the spot where he had gone down into his early grave was undistinguishable from the surrounding water.

*   *   *   *   *

"Three years had elapsed, when a gentleman alighted from a private carriage at the door of a London attorney, then well known to the public as a man of no great nicety in his professional dealings, and requested a private interview on business of importance. Although evidently not past the prime of life, his face was pale, haggard, and dejected; and it did not require the acute perception of the man of business, to discern at a glance, that disease or suffering had done more to work a change in his appearance, than the mere hand of time could have accomplished in twice the period of his whole life.

"'I wish you to undertake some legal business for me,' said the stranger.

"The attorney bowed obsequiously, and glanced at a large packet which the gentleman carried in his hand. His visiter observed the look, and proceeded.

"'It is no common business,' said he; 'nor have these papers reached my hands without long trouble and great expense.'

"The attorney cast a still more anxious look at the packet: and his visiter, untying the string that bound it, disclosed a quantity of promissory notes, with some copies of deeds, and other documents.

"'Upon these papers,' said the client, 'the man whose name they bear, has raised, as you will see, large sums of money, for some years past. There was a tacit understanding between him and the men into whose hands they originally went—and from whom I have by degrees purchased the whole, for treble and quadruple their nominal value—that these loans should be from time to time renewed, until a given period had elapsed. Such an understanding is nowhere expressed. He has sustained many losses of late; and these obligations accumulating upon him at once, would crush him to the earth.'

"'The whole amount is some thousands of pounds,' said the attorney, looking over the papers.

"'It is,' said the client.

"'What are we to do?' inquired the man of business.

"'Do!' replied the client, with sudden vehemence—'Put every engine of the law in force, every trick that ingenuity can devise and rascality execute; fair means and foul; the open oppression of the law, aided by all the craft of its most ingenious practitioners. I would have him die a harassing and lingering death. Ruin him, seize and sell all his lands and goods, drive him from house and home, and drag him forth a beggar in his old age, to die in a common gaol.'

"'But the costs, my dear Sir, the costs of all this,' reasoned the attorney, when he had recovered from his momentary surprise—'If the defendant be a man of straw, who is to pay the costs, Sir?'

"'Name any sum,' said the stranger, his hand trembling so violently with excitement, that he could scarcely hold the pen he seized as he spoke—'Any sum, and it is yours. Don't be afraid to name it, man. I shall not think it dear, if you gain my object.'

"The attorney named a large sum, at hazard, as the advance he should require to secure himself against the possibility of loss; but more with the view of ascertaining how far his client was really disposed to go, than with any idea that he would comply with the demand. The stranger wrote a cheque upon his banker, for the whole amount, and left him.

"The draft was duly honoured, and the attorney, finding that his strange client might be safely relied upon, commenced his work in earnest. For more than two years afterwards, Mr. Heyling would sit whole days together, in the office, poring over the papers as they accumulated, and reading again and again, his eyes gleaming with joy, the letters of remonstrance, the prayers for a little delay, the representations of the certain ruin in which the opposite party must be involved, which poured in, as suit after suit, and process after process, were commenced. To all applications for a brief indulgence, there was but one reply—the money must be paid. Land, house, furniture, each in its turn, was taken under some one of the numerous executions which were issued; and the old man himself would have been immured in prison had he not escaped the vigilance of the officers, and fled.

"The implacable animosity of Heyling, so far from being satiated by the success of his persecution, increased a hundred-fold with the ruin he inflicted. On being informed of the old man's flight, his fury was unbounded. He gnashed his teeth with rage, tore the hair from his head, and assailed with horrid imprecations the men who had been entrusted with the writ. He was only restored to comparative calmness by repeated assurances of the certainty of discovering the fugitive. Agents were sent in quest of him, in all directions; every stratagem that could be invented was resorted to, for the purpose of discovering his place of retreat; but it was all in vain. Half a year had passed over, and he was still undiscovered.

"At length, late one night, Heyling, of whom nothing had been seen for many weeks before, appeared at his attorney's private residence, and sent up word that a gentleman wished to see him instantly. Before the attorney, who had recognised his voice from above stairs, could order the servant to admit him, he had rushed up the staircase, and entered the drawing-room pale and breathless. Having closed the door, to prevent being overheard, he sunk into a chair, and said, in a low voice—

"'Hush! I have found him at last.'

"'No!' said the attorney—'Well done, my dear Sir; well done.'

"'He lies concealed in a wretched lodging in Camden Town,' said Heyling—'Perhaps it is as well, we did lose sight of him, for he has been living alone there, in the most abject misery, all the time, and he is poor—very poor.'

"'Very good,' said the attorney—'You will have the caption made to-morrow, of course?'

"'Yes,' replied Heyling. 'Stay! No! The next day. You are surprised at my wishing to postpone it,' he added, with a ghastly smile; 'but I had forgotten. The next day is an anniversary in his life: let it be done then.'

"'Very good,' said the attorney—'Will you write down instructions for the officer?'

"'No; let him meet me here, at eight in the evening, and I will accompany him myself.'

"They met on the appointed night, and, hiring a hackney-coach, directed the driver to stop at that corner of the old Pancras road, at which stands the parish workhouse. By the time they alighted there, it was quite dark; and, proceeding by the dead wall in front of the Veterinary Hospital, they entered a small bye street, which is, or was at that time, called Little College Street, and which, whatever it may be now, was in those days a desolate place enough, surrounded by little else than fields and ditches.

"Having drawn the travelling-cap he had on, half over his face, and muffled himself in his cloak, Heyling stopped before the meanest-looking house in the street, and knocked gently at the door. It was at once opened by a woman, who dropped a curtesy of recognition, and Heyling whispering the officer to remain below, crept gently up stairs, and, opening the door of the front room, entered at once.

"The object of his search and his unrelenting animosity, now a decrepid old man, was seated at a bare deal table, on which stood a miserable candle. He started on the entrance of the stranger, and rose feebly to his feet.

"'What now, what now?' said the old man—'What fresh misery is this? What do you want here?'

"'A word with you,' replied Heyling. As he spoke, he seated himself at the other end of the table, and, throwing off his cloak and cap, disclosed his features.

"The old man seemed instantly deprived of the power of speech. He fell backward in his chair, and, clasping his hands together, gazed on the apparition with a mingled look of abhorrence and fear.

"'This day six years,' said Heyling, 'I claimed the life you owed me for my child's. Beside the lifeless form of your daughter, old man, I swore to live a life of revenge. I have never swerved from my purpose for a moment's space; but if I had, one thought of her uncomplaining, suffering look, as she drooped away, or of the starving face of our innocent child, would have nerved me to my task. My first act of requital you well remember: this is my last.'

"The old man shivered, and his hands dropped powerless by his side.

"'I leave England to-morrow,' said Heyling, after a moment's pause—'To-night I consign you, to the living death to which you devoted her—a hopeless prison——'

"He raised his eyes to the old man's countenance, and paused. He lifted the light to his face, set it gently down, and left the apartment.

"'You had better see to the old man,' he said to the woman, as he opened the door, and motioned the officer to follow him into the street—'I think he is ill.' The woman closed the door, ran hastily up stairs, and found him lifeless. He had died in a fit.

*   *   *   *   *

"Beneath a plain grave-stone, in one of the most peaceful and secluded church-yards in Kent, where wild flowers mingle with the grass, and the soft landscape around, forms the fairest spot in the garden of England, lie the bones of the young mother and her gentle child. But the ashes of the father do not mingle with theirs; nor from that night forward, did the attorney ever gain the remotest clue, to the subsequent history of his queer client."

As the old man concluded his tale, he advanced to a peg in one corner, and taking down his hat and coat, put them on with great deliberation; and, without saying another word, walked slowly away. As the gentleman with the Mosaic studs had fallen asleep, and the major part of the company were deeply occupied in the humorous process of dropping melted tallow-grease into his brandy and water, Mr. Pickwick departed unnoticed, and having settled his own score, and that of Mr. Weller, he issued forth, in company with that gentleman, from beneath the portal of the Magpie and Stump.

CHAPTER XXII.

MR. PICKWICK JOURNEYS TO IPSWICH, AND MEETS WITH A ROMANTIC ADVENTURE WITH A MIDDLE-AGED LADY IN YELLOW CURL PAPERS.

"THAT 'ere your governor's luggage, Sammy?" inquired Mr. Weller senior, of his affectionate son, as he entered the yard of the Bull Inn, Whitechapel, with a travelling bag and a small portmanteau.

"You might ha' made a worser guess than that, old feller," replied Mr. Weller the younger, setting down his burden in the yard, and sitting himself down upon it afterwards. "The Governor hisself 'll be down here presently."

"He's a cabbin' it, I suppose?" said the father.

"Yes, he's a havin' two mile o' danger at eight-pence," responded the son. "How's mother-in-law this mornin'?"

"Queer, Sammy, queer," replied the elder Mr. Weller, with impressive gravity. "She's been gettin' rayther in the Methodistical order lately, Sammy; and she is uncommon pious, to be sure. She's too good a creetur for me, Sammy—I feel I don't deserve her."

"Ah," said Mr. Samuel, "that's wery self-denyin' o' you."

"Wery," replied his parent, with a sigh. "She's got hold o' some invention for grown-up people being born again, Sammy—the new birth, I thinks they calls it. I should wery much like to see that system in haction, Sammy. I should wery much like to see your mother-in-law born again. Wouldn't I put her out to nurse!"

"What do you think them women does t'other day," continued Mr. Weller, after a short pause, during which he had significantly struck the side of his nose with his fore-finger, some half-dozen times. "What do you think they does, Sammy?"

"Don't know," replied Sam, "what?"

"Goes and gets up a grand tea drinkin' for a feller they

calls their shepherd," said Mr. Weller. "I was a stand-ing starin' in, at the pictur shop down at our place, when I sees a little bill about it; 'tickets half-a-crown. All applications to be made to the committee. Secretary, Mrs. Weller;' and when I got home, there was the committee a sittin' in our back parlour—fourteen women! I wish you could ha' heard 'em Sammy. There they was, a passin' resolutions, and wotin' supplies, and all sorts o' games. Well, what with your mother-in-law a worrying me to go, and what with my looking for'ard to seein' some queer starts if I did, I put my name down for a ticket; at six o'clock on the Friday evenin' I dresses myself out, wery smart, and off I goes vith the old 'ooman, and up we walks into a fust floor where there was tea things for thirty, and a whole lot o' women as begins whisperin' to one another, and lookin' at me, as if they'd never seen a rayther stout gen'lm'n of eight-and-fifty afore. By and bye, there comes a great bustle down stairs, and a lanky chap with a red nose and white neckcloth rushes up, and sings out, 'Here's the shepherd a coming to wisit his faithful flock;' and in comes a fat chap in black, vith a great white face, a smilin' avay like clock-work. Such goin's on, Sammy. 'The kiss of peace,' says the shepherd; and then he kissed the women all round, and ven he'd done, the man vith the red nose began. I was just a thinkin' whether I hadn't better be-gin too—'specially as there was a wery nice lady a sittin' next me—ven in comes the tea, and your mother-in-law, as had been makin' the kettle boil, down stairs. At it they went, tooth and nail. Such a precious loud hymn Sammy, while the tea was a brewing; such a grace, such eatin' and drinkin'. I wish you could ha' seen the shepherd walkin' into the ham and muffins. I never see such a chap to eat and drink—never. The red-nosed man warn't by no means the sort of person you'd like to grub by contract, but he was nothin' to the shepherd. Well; arter the tea was over, they sang another hymn, and then the shepherd began to preach: and wery well he did it, considerin' how heavy them muffins must have lied on his chest. Presently he pulls up, all of sudden, and says, 'Where is the sinner; where is the mis'rable sinner?' upon which, all the women looked at me, and began to groan as if they was dying. I thought it was rather sing'ler, but hows'ever, I says nothing. Presently he pulls up again, and lookin' wery hard at me, says, 'Where is the sinner; where is the mis'rable sinner!' and all the women groans again, ten times louder than afore. I got rather savage at this, so I takes a step or two for'ard and says, 'My friend,' says I, 'did you apply that 'ere observation to me?'—'Stead of beggin' my pardon as any gen'lm'n would ha' done, he got more abusive than ever: called me a wessel, Sammy—a wessel of wrath—and all sorts o' names. So my blood be-ing reg'larly up, I first gave him two or three for himself, and then two or three more to hand over to the man with the red nose, and walked off. I wish you could ha' heard how the women screamed Sammy, ven they picked up the shepherd from under the table——Hallo! here's the gov-ernor, the size of life."

As Mr. Weller spoke, Mr. Pickwick dismounted from a cab, and entered the yard.

"Fine mornin' Sir"—said Mr. Weller senior.

"Beautiful indeed"—replied Mr. Pickwick.

"Beautiful indeed," echoed a red-haired man with an in-quisitive nose and blue spectacles, who had unpacked him-self from a cab at the same moment as Mr. Pickwick. "Going to Ipswich, Sir?"

"I am," replied Mr. Pickwick.

"Extraordinary coincidence. So am I."

Mr. Pickwick bowed.

"Going outside?" said the red-haired man.

Mr. Pickwick bowed again.

"Bless my soul, how remarkable—I am going outside, too," said the red-haired man: "we are positively going together." And the red-haired man, who was an important-looking, sharp-nosed, mysterious-spoken personage, with a bird-like habit of giving his head a jerk every time he said any thing, smiled as if he had made one of the strangest discoveries that ever fell to the lot of human wisdom.

"I am happy in the prospect of your company, Sir," said Mr. Pickwick.

"Ah," said the new-comer, "it's a good thing for both of us, isn't it? Company, you see—company is—is—it's a very different thing from solitude—a'n't it?"

"There's no denyin' that 'ere," said Mr. Weller, joining in the conversation, with an affable smile. "That's what I call a self-evident proposition, as the dog's-meat man said, when the housemaid told him he warn't a gentleman."

"Ah," said the red-haired man, surveying Mr. Weller from head to foot, with a supercilious look. "Friend of yours, Sir?"

"Not exactly a friend," replied Mr. Pickwick, in a low tone. "The fact is, he is my servant, but I allow him to take a good many liberties; for, between ourselves, I flat-ter myself he is an original, and I am rather proud of him."

"Ah," said the red-haired man, "that, you see, is a mat-ter of taste. I am not fond of anything original; I don't like it; don't see the necessity for it. What's your name, Sir?"

"Here is my card, Sir," replied Mr. Pickwick, much amused by the abruptness of the question, and the singular manner of the stranger.

"Ah," said the red-haired man, placing the card in his pocket-book, "Pickwick; very good. I like to know a man's name, it saves so much trouble. That's my card, Sir. Magnus, you will perceive, Sir—Magnus is my name. It's rather a good name, I think, Sir?"

"A very good name, indeed," said Mr. Pickwick, wholly unable to repress a smile.

"Yes, I think it is," resumed Mr. Magnus. "There's a good name before it, too, you will observe. Permit me, Sir—if you hold the card a little slanting, this way, you catch the light upon the up-stroke. There—Peter Magnus —sounds well, I think, Sir."

"Very," said Mr. Pickwick.

"Curious circumstance about those initials, Sir," said Mr. Magnus. "You will observe—P. M.—post meridian. In hasty notes to intimate acquaintance, I sometimes sign myself 'Afternoon.' It amuses my friends very much, Mr. Pickwick."

"It is calculated to afford them the highest gratification, I should conceive," said Mr. Pickwick, rather envying the ease with which Mr. Magnus's friends were entertained.

"Now, gen'lm'n," said the hostler, "coach is ready, if you please."

"Is all my luggage in?" inquired Mr. Magnus.

"All right, Sir."

"Is the red bag in?"

"All right, Sir."

"And the striped bag?"

"Fore boot, Sir."

"And the brown-paper parcel?"

"Under the seat, Sir."

"And the leather hat-box?"

"They're all in, Sir."

"Now, will you get up?" said Mr. Pickwick.

"Excuse me," replied Magnus, standing on the wheel. "Excuse me, Mr. Pickwick. I cannot consent to get up, in this state of uncertainty. I am quite satisfied from that man's manner, that that leather hat-box is *not* in."

The solemn protestations of the hostler being unavailing, the leather hat-box was obliged to be raked up from the lowest depth of the boot, to satisfy him that it had been safely packed; and after he had been assured on this head, he felt a solemn presentiment, first, that the red bag was mislaid, and next that the striped bag had been stolen, and then that the brown paper parcel had "come untied." At length when he had received ocular demonstration of the groundless nature of each and every of these suspicions, he consented to climb up to the roof of the coach, observing that now he had taken every thing off his mind, he felt quite comfortable and happy.

"You're given to nervousness, an't you, Sir?" inquired Mr. Weller senior, eyeing the stranger askance, as he mounted to his place.

"Yes; I always am rather, about these little matters," said the stranger, "but I am all right now—quite right."

"Well, that's a blessin'," said Mr. Weller. "Sammy, help your master up to the box: t'other leg, Sir, that's it; give us your hand, Sir. Up with you. You was a lighter weight when you was a boy, Sir."

"True enough, that, Mr. Weller," said the breathless Mr. Pickwick, good-humouredly, as he took his seat on the box beside him.

"Jump up in front, Sammy," said Mr. Weller. "Now Villam, run 'em out. Take care o' the archvay, gen'lm'n. 'Heads,' as the pieman says. That'll do, Villam. Let 'em alone." And away went the coach up Whitechapel, to the admiration of the whole population of that pretty densely-populated quarter.

"Not a wery nice neighbourhood this, Sir," said Sam, with the touch of the hat which always preceded his entering into conversation with his master.

"It is not indeed, Sam," replied Mr. Pickwick, surveying the crowded and filthy street through which they were passing.

"It's a wery remarkable circumstance, Sir," said Sam, "that poverty and oysters always seems to go together."

"I don't understand you, Sam," said Mr. Pickwick.

"What I mean, Sir," said Sam, "is, that the poorer a place is, the greater call there seems to be for oysters. Look here, Sir; here's a oyster stall to every half-dozen houses—the street's lined vith 'em. Blessed if I don't think that ven a man's wery poor, he rushes out of his lodgings, and eats oysters in reg'lar desperation."

"To be sure he does," said Mr. Weller senior, "and it's just the same vith pickled salmon!"

"Those are two very remarkable facts, which never occurred to me before," said Mr. Pickwick. "The very first place we stop at, I'll make a note of them."

By this time they had reached the turnpike at Mile End; a profound silence prevailed, until they had got two or three miles further on, when Mr. Weller senior turning suddenly to Mr. Pickwick, said—

"Wery queer life is a pike keeper's, Sir."

"A what?" said Mr. Pickwick.

"A pike-keeper."

"What do you mean by a pike-keeper?" inquired Mr. Peter Magnus.

"The old 'un means a turnpike keeper, gen'lm'n," observed Mr. Weller, in explanation.

"Oh," said Mr. Pickwick, "I see. Yes; very curious life. Very uncomfortable."

"They're all on 'em, men as has met vith some disappointment in life," said Mr. Weller senior.

"Ay, ay?" said Mr. Pickwick.

"Yes. Consequence of vich, they retires from the world, and shuts themselves up in pikes; partly vith the view of being solitary, and partly to revenge themselves on mankind, by takin' tolls."

"Dear me," said Mr. Pickwick, "I never knew that before."

"Fact, Sir," said Mr. Weller, "if they was gen'lm'n you'd call 'em misanthropes, but as it is they only takes to pike-keepin'."

With such conversation, possessing the inestimable charm of blending amusement with instruction, did Mr. Weller beguile the tediousness of the journey, during the greater part of the day. Topics of conversation were never wanting, for even when any pause occurred in Mr. Weller's loquacity, it was abundantly supplied by the desire evinced by Mr. Magnus to make himself acquainted with the whole of the personal history of his fellow-travellers, and his loudly-expressed anxiety at every stage, respecting the safety and well-being of the two bags, the leather hat-box, and the brown paper parcel.

In the main street of Ipswich, on the left-hand side of the way, a short distance after you have passed through the open space fronting the Town Hall, stands an inn known far and wide by the appellation of "The Great White Horse," rendered the more conspicuous by a stone statue of some rampacious animal with flowing mane and tail, distantly resembling an insane cart-horse, which is elevated above the principal door. The Great White Horse is famous in the neighbourhood, in the same degree as a prize ox, or county paper-chronicled turnip, or unwieldy pig—for its enormous size. Never were such labyrinths of uncarpeted passages, such clusters of mouldy, badly-lighted rooms, such huge numbers of small dens for eating or sleeping in, beneath any one roof, as are collected together between the four walls of the Great White Horse at Ipswich.

It was at the door of this overgrown tavern, that the London coach stopped, at the same hour every evening; and it was from this same London coach, that Mr. Pickwick, Sam Weller, and Mr. Peter Magnus dismounted, on the particular evening to which this chapter of our history bears reference.

"Do you stop here, Sir?" inquired Mr. Peter Magnus, when the striped bag, and the red bag, and the brown paper parcel, and the leather hat-box, had all been deposited in the passage. "Do you stop here, Sir?"

"I do," said Mr. Pickwick.

"Dear me," said Mr. Magnus, "I never knew anything like these extraordinary coincidences. Why, I stop here, too. I hope we dine together?"

"With pleasure," replied Mr. Pickwick. "I am not quite certain whether I have any friends here or not, though. Is there any gentleman of the name of Tupman here, waiter?"

A corpulent man, with a fortnight's napkin under his

arm, and coeval stockings on his legs, slowly desisted from his occupation of staring down the street, on this question being put to him by Mr. Pickwick; and, after minutely inspecting that gentleman's appearance, from the crown of his hat to the lowest button of his gaiters, replied emphatically—

"No."

"Nor any gentleman of the name of Snodgrass?" inquired Mr. Pickwick.

"No."

"Nor Winkle?"

"No."

"My friends have not arrived to-day, Sir," said Mr. Pickwick. "We will dine alone, then. Shew us a private room, waiter."

On this request being preferred, the corpulent man condescended to order the boots to bring in the gentlemen's luggage, and preceding them down a long dark passage, ushered them into a large badly-furnished apartment, with a dirty grate, in which a small fire was making a wretched attempt to be cheerful, but was fast sinking beneath the dispiriting influence of the place. After the lapse of an hour, a bit of fish and a steak, were served up to the travellers, and when the dinner was cleared away, Mr. Pickwick and Mr. Peter Magnus drew their chairs up to the fire, and having ordered a bottle of the worst possible port wine, at the highest possible price, for the good of the house, drank brandy and water for their own.

Mr. Peter Magnus was naturally of a very communicative disposition, and the brandy and water operated with wonderful effect in warming into life the deepest hidden secrets of his bosom. After sundry accounts of himself, his family, his connexions, his friends, his jokes, his business, and his brothers (most talkative men have a great deal to say about their brothers), Mr. Peter Magnus took a blue view of Mr. Pickwick through his coloured spectacles for several minutes, and then said, with an air of modesty—

"And what do you think—what *do* you think, Mr. Pickwick—I have come down here for?"

"Upon my word," said Mr. Pickwick, "it is wholly impossible for me to guess; on business, perhaps."

"Partly right, Sir," replied Mr. Peter Magnus, "but partly wrong, at the same time: try again, Mr. Pickwick."

"Really," said Mr. Pickwick, "I must throw myself on your mercy, to tell me or not, as you may think best; for I should never guess, if I were to try all night."

"Why, then, he—he—he!" said Mr. Peter Magnus, with a bashful titter, "What should you think, Mr. Pickwick, if I had come down here, to make a proposal, Sir, eh? He—he—he!"

"Think! that you are very likely to succeed," replied Mr. Pickwick, with one of his most beaming smiles.

"Ah!" said Mr. Magnus, "but do you really think so, Mr. Pickwick? Do you, though?"

"Certainly," said Mr. Pickwick.

"No; but you're joking, though."

"I am not, indeed."

"Why, then," said Mr. Magnus, "to let you into a little secret, *I* think so too. I don't mind telling you, Mr. Pickwick, although I'm dreadful jealous by nature—horrid—that the lady is in this house." Here Mr. Magnus took off his spectacles, on purpose to wink, and then put them on again.

"That's what you were running out of the room for, before dinner, then, so often," said Mr. Pickwick, archly.

"Hush—yes, you're right, that was it; not such a fool as to see her, though."

"No!"

"No; wouldn't do, you know, after having just come off a journey. Wait till to-morrow Sir; double the chance then. Mr. Pickwick, Sir, there is a suit of clothes in that bag, and a hat in that box, which I expect, in the effect they will produce, will be invaluable to me, Sir."

"Indeed!" said Mr. Pickwick.

"Yes; you must have observed my anxiety about them to-day. I do not believe that such another suit of clothes, and such a hat, could be bought for money, Mr. Pickwick."

Mr. Pickwick congratulated the fortunate owner of the irresistible garments, on their acquisition; and Mr. Peter Magnus remained for a few moments, apparently absorbed in contemplation.

"She's a fine creature," said Mr. Magnus.

"Is she?" said Mr. Pickwick.

"Very," said Mr. Magnus, "very. She lives about twenty miles from here, Mr. Pickwick. I heard she would be here to-night and all to-morrow forenoon, and came down to seize the opportunity. I think an inn is a good sort of place to propose to a single woman in, Mr. Pickwick. She is more likely to feel the loneliness of her situation in travelling, perhaps, than she would be at home. What do you think, Mr. Pickwick?"

"I think it very probable," replied that gentleman.

"I beg your pardon, Mr. Pickwick," said Mr. Peter Magnus, "but I am naturally rather curious; what may *you* have come down here for?"

"On a far less pleasant errand, Sir," replied Mr. Pickwick, the colour mounting to his face at the recollection—"I have come down here, Sir, to expose the treachery and falsehood of an individual, upon whose truth and honour I placed implicit reliance."

"Dear me," said Mr. Peter Magnus, "that's very unpleasant. It is a lady, I presume? Eh? ah! Sly, Mr. Pickwick, sly. Well, Mr. Pickwick, Sir, I wouldn't probe your feelings for the world. Painful subjects, these, Sir, very painful. Don't mind me, Mr. Pickwick, if you wish to give vent to your feelings. I know what it is to be jilted, Sir; I have endured that sort of thing three or four times."

"I am much obliged to you, for your condolence on what you presume to be my melancholy case," said Mr. Pickwick, winding up his watch, and laying it on the table, "but—"

"No, no," said Mr. Peter Magnus, "not a word more: it's a painful subject, I see, I see. What's the time, Mr. Pickwick?"

"Past twelve."

"Dear me, it's time to go to bed. It will never do, sitting here. I shall be pale to-morrow, Mr. Pickwick."

At the bare notion of such a calamity, Mr. Peter Magnus rang the bell for the chamber-maid; and the striped bag, the red bag, the leather hat-box, and the brown-paper parcel, having been conveyed to his bed-room, he retired in company with a japanned candlestick, to one side of the house, while Mr. Pickwick, and another japanned candlestick, were conducted through a multitude of tortuous windings, to another.

"This is your room, Sir," said the chamber-maid.

"Very well," replied Mr. Pickwick, looking round him. It was a tolerably large double-bedded room, with a fire; upon the whole, a more comfortable-looking apartment than

Mr. Pickwick's short experience of the accommodations of the Great White Horse had led him to expect.

"Nobody sleeps in the other bed, of course," said Mr. Pickwick.

"Oh no, Sir."

"Very good. Tell my servant to bring me up some hot water at half-past eight in the morning, and that I shall not want him any more to-night."

"Yes, Sir." And bidding Mr. Pickwick good night, the chamber-maid retired, and left him alone.

Mr. Pickwick sat himself down in a chair before the fire, and fell into a train of rambling meditations. First he thought of his friends, and wondered when they would join him; then his mind reverted to Mrs. Martha Bardell; and from that lady it wandered, by a natural process, to the dingy counting-house of Dodson and Fogg. From Dodson and Fogg's it flew off at a tangent, to the very centre of the history of the queer client; and then it came back to the Great White Horse at Ipswich, with sufficient clearness to convince Mr. Pickwick that he was falling asleep: so he roused himself, and began to undress, when he recollected he had left his watch on the table down stairs.

Now this watch was a special favourite with Mr. Pickwick, having been carried about, beneath the shadow of his waistcoat, for a greater number of years than we feel called upon to state, at present. The possibility of going to sleep, unless it were ticking gently beneath his pillow, or in the watch-pocket over his head, had never entered Mr. Pickwick's brain. So as it was pretty late now, and he was unwilling to ring his bell at that hour of the night, he slipped on his coat, of which he had just divested himself, and taking the japanned candlestick in his hand, walked quietly down stairs.

The more stairs Mr. Pickwick went down, the more stairs there seemed to be to descend, and again and again, when Mr. Pickwick got into some narrow passage, and began to congratulate himself on having gained the ground-floor, did another flight of stairs appear before his astonished eyes. At last he reached a stone hall, which he remembered to have seen when he entered the house. Passage after passage did he explore; room after room did he peep into; at length, just as he was on the point of giving up the search in despair, he opened the door of the identical room in which he had spent the evening, and beheld his missing property on the table.

Mr. Pickwick seized the watch in triumph, and proceeded to re-trace his steps to his bed-chamber. If his progress downwards had been attended with difficulties and uncertainty, his journey back, was infinitely more perplexing. Rows of doors, garnished with boots of every shape, make, and size, branched off in every possible direction. A dozen times did he softly turn the handle of some bed-room door, which resembled his own, when a gruff cry from within of "Who the devil's that?" or "What do you want here?" caused him to steal away, on tiptoe, with a perfectly marvellous celerity. He was reduced to the verge of despair, when an open door attracted his attention. He peeped in —right at last. There were the two beds, whose situation he perfectly remembered, and the fire still burning. His candle, not a long one when he first received it, had flickered away in the drafts of air through which he had passed, and sunk into the socket, just as he closed the door after him. "No matter," said Mr. Pickwick, "I can undress myself just as well, by the light of the fire."

The bedsteads stood, one on each side of the door; and on the inner side of each, was a little path, terminating in a rush-bottomed chair, just wide enough to admit of a person's getting into, or out of bed, on that side, if he or she thought proper. Having carefully drawn the curtains of his bed on the outside, Mr. Pickwick sat down on the rush-bottomed chair, and leisurely divested himself of his shoes and gaiters. He then took off and folded up, his coat, waistcoat, and neck-cloth, and slowly drawing on his tasseled night-cap, secured it firmly on his head, by tying beneath his chin, the strings which he always had attached to that article of dress. It was at this moment that the absurdity of his recent bewilderment struck upon his mind; and throwing himself back in the rush-bottomed chair, Mr. Pickwick laughed to himself so heartily, that it would have been quite delightful to any man of well-constituted mind to have watched the smiles which expanded his amiable features as they shone forth, from beneath the night-cap.

"It is the best idea," said Mr. Pickwick to himself, smiling till he almost cracked the night-cap strings—"It is the best idea, my losing myself in this place, and wandering about those staircases, that I ever heard of. Droll, droll, very droll." Here Mr. Pickwick smiled again, a broader smile than before, and was about to continue the process of undressing, in the best possible humour, when he was suddenly stopped by a most unexpected interruption; to wit, the entrance into the room of some person with a candle, who, after locking the door, advanced to the dressing table, and set down the light upon it.

The smile that played on Mr. Pickwick's features, was instantaneously lost in a look of the most unbounded and wonder-stricken surprise. The person, whoever it was, had come in so suddenly and with so little noise, that Mr. Pickwick had no time to call out, or oppose their entrance. Who could it be? A robber? Some evil-minded person who had seen him come up stairs with a handsome watch in his hand, perhaps. What was he to do!

The only way in which Mr. Pickwick could catch a glimpse of his mysterious visiter with the least danger of being seen himself, was by creeping on to the bed, and peeping out from between the curtains on the opposite side. To this manoeuvre he accordingly resorted. Keeping the curtains carefully closed with his hand, so that nothing more of him could be seen than his face and night-cap, and putting on his spectacles, he mustered up courage, and looked out.

Mr. Pickwick almost fainted with horror and dismay. Standing before the dressing glass, was a middle-aged lady in yellow curl-papers, busily engaged in brushing what ladies call their "back hair." However the unconscious middle-aged lady came into that room, it was quite clear that she contemplated remaining there for the night; for she had brought a rushlight and shade with her, which, with praiseworthy precaution against fire, she had stationed in a basin on the floor, where it was glimmering away, like a gigantic lighthouse, in a particularly small piece of water.

"Bless my soul," thought Mr. Pickwick, "what a dreadful thing!"

"Hem!" said the lady; and in went Mr. Pickwick's head with automaton-like rapidity.

"I never met with anything so awful as this,"—thought poor Mr. Pickwick, the cold perspiration starting in drops upon his night-cap. "Never. This is fearful."

It was quite impossible to resist the urgent desire to see

THE MIDDLE-AGED LADY IN THE DOUBLE BEDDED ROOM.

what was going forward. So out went Mr. Pickwick's head again. The prospect was worse than before. The middle-aged lady had finished arranging her hair; had carefully enveloped it, in a muslin night-cap with a small plaited border, and was gazing pensively on the fire.

"This matter is growing alarming"—reasoned Mr. Pickwick with himself. "I can't allow things to go on in this way. By the self-possession of that lady, it's clear to me that I must have come into the wrong room. If I call out, she'll alarm the house, but if I remain here the consequences will be still more frightful."

Mr. Pickwick, it is quite unnecessary to say, was one of the most modest and delicate-minded of mortals. The very idea of exhibiting his night-cap to a lady, overpowered him, but he had tied those confounded strings in a knot, and do what he would, he couldn't get it off. The disclosure must be made. There was only one other way of doing it. He shrunk behind the curtains, and called out very loudly—

"Ha—hum."

That the lady started at this unexpected sound was evident, by her falling up against the rush-light shade; that she persuaded herself it must have been the effect of imagination was equally clear, for when Mr. Pickwick, under the impression that she had fainted away, stone-dead from fright, ventured to peep out again, she was gazing pensively on the fire as before.

"Most extraordinary female this," thought Mr. Pickwick, popping in again. "Ha—hum."

These last sounds, so like those in which, as legends inform us, the ferocious giant Blunderbore was in the habit of expressing his opinion that it was time to lay the cloth, were too distinctly audible, to be again mistaken for the workings of fancy.

"Gracious Heaven!" said the middle-aged lady, "what's that!"

"It's—it's—only a gentleman, Ma'am," said Mr. Pickwick from behind the curtains.

"A gentleman!" said the lady with a terrific scream.

"It's all over," thought Mr. Pickwick.

"A strange man!" shrieked the lady. Another instant, and the house would be alarmed. Her garments rustled as she rushed towards the door.

"Ma'am"—said Mr. Pickwick, thrusting out his head, in the extremity of his desperation, "Ma'am."

Now although Mr. Pickwick was not actuated by any definite object in putting out his head, it was instantaneously productive of a good effect. The lady, as we have already stated, was near the door. She must pass it, to reach the staircase, and she would most undoubtedly have done so, by this time, had not the sudden apparition of Mr. Pickwick's night-cap driven her back, into the remotest corner of the apartment, where she stood, staring wildly at Mr. Pickwick, while Mr. Pickwick in his turn, stared wildly at her.

"Wretch,"—said the lady, covering her eyes with her hands, "what do you want here?"

"Nothing, Ma'am—nothing whatever, Ma'am;" said Mr. Pickwick earnestly.

"Nothing!" said the lady, looking up.

"Nothing, Ma'am, upon my honour," said Mr. Pickwick, nodding his head so energetically, that the tassel of his night-cap danced again. "I am almost ready to sink, Ma'am, beneath the confusion of addressing a lady in my night-cap (here the lady hastily snatched off hers), but I can't get it off, Ma'am (here Mr. Pickwick gave it a tremendous tug, in proof of the statement). It is evident to

me Ma'am now, that I have mistaken this bed-room for my own. I had not been here five minutes Ma'am, when you suddenly entered it."

"If this improbable story be really true Sir"—said the lady, sobbing violently, "you will leave it instantly."

"I will Ma'am with the greatest pleasure"—replied Mr. Pickwick.

"Instantly, Sir," said the lady.

"Certainly, Ma'am," interposed Mr. Pickwick very quickly. "Certainly, Ma'am. I—I—am very sorry, Ma'am," said Mr. Pickwick, making his appearance at the bottom of the bed, "to have been the innocent occasion of this alarm and emotion; deeply sorry, Ma'am."

The lady pointed to the door. One excellent quality of Mr. Pickwick's character was beautifully displayed at this moment, under the most trying circumstances. Although he had hastily put on his hat over his night-cap, after the manner of the old patrol; although he carried his shoes and gaiters in his hand, and his coat and waistcoat over his arm, nothing could subdue his native politeness.

"I am exceedingly sorry, Ma'am," said Mr. Pickwick, bowing very low.

"If you are, Sir, you will at once leave the room," said the lady.

"Immediately, Ma'am; this instant, Ma'am," said Mr. Pickwick opening the door, and dropping both his shoes with a loud crash in so doing.

"I trust, Ma'am," resumed Mr. Pickwick, gathering up his shoes, and turning round to bow again. "I trust, Ma'am, that my unblemished character, and the devoted respect I entertain for your sex, will plead as some slight excuse for this "—But before Mr. Pickwick could conclude the sentence, the lady had thrust him into the passage, and locked and bolted the door behind him.

Whatever grounds of self-congratulation Mr. Pickwick might have, for having escaped so quietly from his late awkward situation, his present position was by no means enviable. He was alone, in an open passage, in a strange house, in the middle of the night, half dressed; it was not to be supposed that he could find his way in perfect darkness to a room which he had been wholly unable to discover with a light, and if he made the slightest noise in his fruitless attempts to do so, he stood every chance of being shot at, and perhaps killed, by some wakeful traveller. He had no resource but to remain where he was, until daylight appeared. So after groping his way a few paces down the passage, and to his infinite alarm, stumbling over several pairs of boots in so doing, Mr. Pickwick crouched into a little recess in the wall, to wait for morning, as philosophically as he might.

He was not destined, however, to undergo this additional trial of patience: for he had not been long ensconced in his present concealment when, to his unspeakable horror, a man, bearing a light, appeared at the end of the passage. His horror was suddenly converted into joy, however, when he recognised the form of his faithful attendant. It was indeed Mr. Samuel Weller, who after sitting up thus late, in conversation with the Boots, who was sitting up for the mail, was now about to retire to rest.

"Sam," said Mr. Pickwick, suddenly appearing before him, "Where's my bed-room?"

Mr. Weller stared at his master with the most emphatic surprise; and it was not until the question had been repeated three several times, that he turned round, and led the way to the long-sought apartment.

"Sam," said Mr. Pickwick as he got into bed. "I have

made one of the most extraordinary mistakes to-night, that ever were heard of."

"Wery likely, Sir," replied Mr. Weller drily.

"But of this I am determined, Sam," said Mr. Pickwick; "that if I were to stop in this house for six months, I would never trust myself about it, alone, again."

"That's the wery prudentest resolution as you could come to, Sir," replied Mr. Weller. "You rayther want somebody to look arter you Sir, ven your judgment goes out a wisitin'."

"What do you mean by that, Sam?" said Mr. Pickwick. He raised himself in bed, and extended his hand, as if he were about to say something more; but suddenly checking himself, turned round, and bade his valet "Good night."

"Good night, Sir," replied Mr. Weller. He paused when he got outside the door—shook his head—walked on—stopped—snuffed the candle—shook his head again—and finally proceeded slowly to his chamber, apparently buried in the profoundest meditation.

CHAPTER XXIII.

IN WHICH MR. SAMUEL WELLER BEGINS TO DEVOTE HIS ENERGIES TO THE RETURN MATCH BETWEEN HIMSELF AND MR. TROTTER.

In a small room in the vicinity of the stable-yard, betimes in the morning, which was ushered in by Mr. Pickwick's adventure with the middle-aged lady in the yellow curl-papers, sat Mr. Weller senior, preparing himself for his journey to London. He was sitting in an excellent attitude for having his portrait taken; and here it is.

It is very possible that at some earlier period of his career, Mr. Weller's profile might have presented a bold, and determined outline. His face, however, had expanded under the influence of good living, and a disposition remarkable for resignation; and its bold fleshy curves had so far extended beyond the limits originally assigned them, that unless you took a full view of his countenance in front, it was difficult to distinguish more than the extreme tip of a very rubicund nose. His chin, from the same cause, had acquired the grave and imposing form which is generally described by prefixing the word "double" to that expressive feature, and his complexion exhibited that peculiarly mottled combination of colours which is only to be seen in gentlemen of his profession, and underdone roast beef. Round his neck he wore a crimson travelling shawl, which merged into his chin by such imperceptible gradations, that it was difficult to distinguish the folds of the one, from the folds of the other. Over this, he mounted a long waistcoat of a broad pink-striped pattern, and over that again, a wide-skirted green coat, ornamented with large brass buttons, whereof the two which garnished the waist, were so far apart, that no man had ever beheld them both, at the same time. His hair, which was short, sleek, and black, was just visible beneath the capacious brim of a low-crowned brown hat. His legs were encased in knee-cord breeches, and painted top-boots: and a copper watch-chain terminating in one seal, and a key of the same material, dangled loosely from his capacious waist-band.

We have said that Mr. Weller was engaged in preparing for his journey to London—he was taking sustenance, in fact. On the table before him, stood a pot of ale, a cold round of beef, and a very respectable-looking loaf, to each of which he distributed his favours in turn, with the most rigid impartiality. He had just cut a mighty slice from the latter, when the footsteps of somebody entering the room, caused him to raise his head: and he beheld his son.

"Mornin' Sammy," said the father.

The son walked up to the pot of ale, and nodding significantly to his parent, took a long draught by way of reply.

"Wery good power o' suction, Sammy," said Mr. Weller the elder, looking into the pot, when his first-born had set it down half empty. "You'd ha' made an uncommon fine oyster, Sammy, if you'd been born in that station o' life."

"Yes, I des-say I should ha' managed to pick up a respectable livin'," replied Sam, applying himself to the cold beef, with considerable vigour.

"I'm wery sorry, Sammy," said the elder Mr. Weller, shaking up the ale, by describing small circles with the pot, preparatory to drinking. "I'm wery sorry, Sammy, to hear from your lips, as you let yourself be gammoned by that 'ere mulberry man. I always thought, up to three days ago, that the names of Veller and gammon could never come into contract, Sammy—never."

"Always exceptin' the case of a widder, of course," said Sam.

"Widders, Sammy," replied Mr. Weller, slightly changing colour. "Widders are 'ceptions to ev'ry rule. I *have* heerd how many ord'nary women, one widder's equal to, in pint o' comin' over you. I think it's five-and-twenty, but I don't rightly know vether it an't more."

"Well; that's pretty well," said Sam.

"Besides," continued Mr. Weller, not noticing the interruption, "that's a wery different thing. You know what the counsel said, Sammy, as defended the gen'lem'n as beat his wife with the poker, venever he got jolly. 'And arter all, my Lord,' says he, 'it's a amiable weakness.' So I says respectin' widders, Sammy, and so you'll say, ven you gets as old as I am."

"I ought to ha' know'd better, I know," said Sam.

"Ought to ha' know'd better!" repeated Mr. Weller, striking the table with his fist. "Ought to ha' know'd better! why, I know a young 'un as hasn't had half nor quarter your eddication—as hasn't slept about the markets, no, not six months—who'd ha' scorned to be let in, in such a vay; scorned it, Sammy." In the excitement of feeling produced by this agonising reflection, Mr. Weller rang the bell, and ordered an additional pint of ale.

"Well, it's no use talking about it now," said Sam. "It's over, and can't be helped, and that's one consolation, as they alvays says in Turkey, ven they cuts the wrong man's head off. It's my innings now, gov'rnor, and as soon as I catches hold o' this here Trotter, I'll have a good 'un."

"I hope you will, Sammy. I hope you will," returned Mr. Weller. "Here's your health, Sammy, and may you speedily vipe off the disgrace as you've inflicted on the family name." In honour of this toast Mr. Weller imbibed at a draught, at least two-thirds of the newly-arrived pint, and handed it over to his son, to dispose of the remainder, which he instantaneously did.

"And now, Sammy," said Mr. Weller, consulting the large double-cased silver watch that hung at the end of the copper chain. "Now it's time I was up at the office to get my vay-bill, and see the coach loaded; for coaches,

Sammy, is like guns—they requires to be loaded with wery great care afore they go off."

At this parental and professional joke, Mr. Weller junior smiled a filial smile. His revered parent continued in a solemn tone—

"I'm a goin' to leave you, Samivel my boy, and there's no telling ven I shall see you again. Your mother-in-law may ha' been too much for me, or a thousand things may have happened by the time you next hears any news o' the celebrated Mr. Veller o' the Bell Savage. The family name depends wery much upon you, Samivel, and I hope you'll do wot's right by it. Upon all little pints o' breedin', I know I may trust you as vell as if it was my own self. So I've only this here one little bit of adwice to give you. If ever you gets to up'ards o' fifty, and feels disposed to go a marryin' anybody—no matter who—jist you shut yourself up in your own room, if you've got one, and pison yourself off hand. Hangin's wulgar, so don't you have nothin' to say to that. Pison yourself, Samivel my boy, pison yourself, and you'll be glad on it arterwards." With these affecting words, Mr. Weller looked stedfastly on his son, and turning slowly upon his heel, disappeared from his sight.

In the contemplative mood which these words had awakened, Mr. Samuel Weller walked forth from the Great White Horse when his father had left him; and bending his steps towards Saint Clement's Church, endeavoured to dissipate his melancholy, by strolling among its ancient precincts. He had loitered about, for some time, when he found himself in a retired spot—a kind of court-yard of venerable appearance—which he discovered had no other outlet than the turning by which he had entered. He was about retracing his steps, when he was suddenly transfixed to the spot by a sudden appearance; and the mode and manner of this appearance, we now proceed to relate.

Mr. Samuel Weller had been staring up, at the old red brick houses now and then, in his deep abstraction, bestowing a wink upon some healthy-looking servant girl as she drew up a blind, or threw open a bed-room window, when the green gate of a garden at the bottom of the yard, opened, and a man having emerged therefrom, closed the green gate very carefully after him, and walked briskly towards the very spot where Mr. Weller was standing.

Now taking this, as an isolated fact, unaccompanied by any attendant circumstances, there was nothing very extraordinary in it, because in many parts of the world, men do come out of gardens, close green gates after them, and even walk briskly away, without attracting any particular share of public observation. It is clear, therefore, that there must have been something in the man, or in his manner, or both, to attract Mr. Weller's particular notice. Whether there was, or not, we must leave the reader to determine, when we have faithfully recounted the behaviour of the individual in question.

When the man had shut the green gate after him, he walked, as we have said twice already, with a brisk pace up the court-yard; but he no sooner caught sight of Mr. Weller, than he faltered, and stopped, as if uncertain for the moment what course to adopt. As the green gate was closed behind him, and there was no other outlet but the one in front, however, he was not long in perceiving that he must pass Mr. Samuel Weller to get away. He therefore resumed his brisk pace, and advanced, staring straight before him. The most extraordinary thing about the man was, that he was contorting his face into the most fearful and astonishing grimaces that ever were beheld. Nature's handywork never was disguised with such extraordinary artificial carving, as the man had overlaid his countenance with, in one moment.

"Well,"—said Mr. Weller to himself, as the man approached. "This is wery odd. I could ha' swore it was him."

Up came the man, and his face became more frightfully distorted than ever, as he drew nearer.

"I could take my oath to that 'ere black hair, and mulberry suit," said Mr. Weller; "only I never see such a face as that, afore."

As Mr. Weller said this, the man's features assumed an unearthly twinge, perfectly hideous. He was obliged to pass very near Sam however, and the scrutinising glance of that gentleman enabled him to detect, under all these appalling twists of feature, something too like the small eyes of Mr. Job Trotter, to be easily mistaken.

"Hallo, you Sir," shouted Sam, fiercely.

The stranger stopped.

"Hallo," repeated Sam, still more gruffly.

The man with the horrible face, looked, with the greatest surprise, up the court, and down the court, and in at the windows of the houses—everywhere but at Sam Weller—and took another step forward, when he was brought to again, by another shout.

"Hallo, you Sir,"—said Sam, for the third time.

There was no pretending to mistake where the voice came from now, so the stranger, having no other resource, at last looked Sam Weller full in the face.

"It won't do, Job Trotter," said Sam. "Come, none o' that 'ere nonsense. You ain't so wery 'ansome that you can afford to throw avay many o' your good looks. Bring them 'ere eyes o' your'n back into their proper places, or I'll knock 'em out of your head. D'ye hear?"

As Mr. Weller appeared fully disposed to act up to the spirit of this address, Mr. Trotter gradually allowed his face to resume its natural expression; and then giving a start of joy, exclaimed, "What do I see? Mr. Walker!"

"Ah," replied Sam—"You're wery glad to see me, ain't you?"

"Glad!" exclaimed Job Trotter—"Oh, Mr. Walker, if you had but known how I have looked forward to this meeting! It is too much, Mr. Walker; I cannot bear it, indeed I cannot." And with these words, Mr. Trotter burst into a regular inundation of tears, and, flinging his arms round those of Mr. Weller, embraced him closely, in an ecstacy of joy.

"Get off," cried Sam, highly indignant at this process, and vainly endeavouring to extricate himself from the grasp of his enthusiastic acquaintance, "get off, I tell you. What are you crying over me for, you portable ingine?"

"Because I am so glad to see you," replied Job Trotter, gradually releasing Mr. Weller, as the first symptoms of his pugnacity disappeared. "Oh, Mr. Walker, this is too much."

"Too much!" echoed Sam, "I think it is too much—rayther. Now what have you got to say to me, eh?"

Mr. Trotter made no reply; for the little pink pocket handkerchief was in full force.

"What have you got to say to me, afore I knock your head off?" repeated Mr. Weller, in a threatening manner.

"Eh!" said Mr. Trotter, with a look of virtuous surprise.

"What have you got to say to me?"

"I, Mr. Walker!"

"Don't call me Valker; my name's Veller; you know that vell enough. What have you got to say to me?"

"Bless you, Mr. Walker—Weller I mean—a great many things, if you will come away somewhere, where we can talk comfortably. If you knew how I have looked for you, Mr. Weller—"

"Wery hard, indeed, I s'pose?" said Sam, drily.

"Very, very, Sir," replied Mr. Trotter, without moving a muscle of his face. "But shake hands, Mr. Weller."

Sam eyed his companion for a few seconds, and then, as if actuated by a sudden impulse, complied with his request.

"How," said Job Trotter, as they walked away—"How is your dear, good master? Oh, he is a worthy gentleman, Mr. Weller. I hope he didn't catch cold, that dreadful night, Sir."

There was a momentary look of deep slyness in Job Trotter's eye, as he said this, which ran a thrill through Mr. Weller's clenched fist as he burnt with a desire to make a demonstration on his ribs. Sam constrained himself, however, and replied that his master was extremely well.

"Oh, I am so glad," replied Mr. Trotter, "is he here?"

"Is your'n?" asked Sam, by way of reply.

"Oh, yes, he is here, and I grieve to say, Mr. Weller, he is going on, worse than ever."

"Ah, ah?" said Sam.

"Oh, shocking—terrible."

"At a boarding-school?" said Sam.

"No, not at a boarding-school," replied Job Trotter, with the same sly look which Sam had noticed before—"Not at a boarding-school."

"At the house with the green gate?" inquired Sam, eyeing his companion closely.

"No, no—oh, not there," replied Job, with a quickness very unusual to him, "not there."

"What was *you* a doin' there?" asked Sam, with a sharp glance—"Got inside the gate by accident, perhaps?"

"Why, Mr. Weller," replied Job, "I don't mind telling you my little secrets, because you know we took such a fancy for each other when we first met. You recollect how pleasant we were that morning?"

"Oh yes," said Sam, impatiently—"I remember. Well."

"Well," replied Job, speaking with great precision, and in the low tone of a man who communicates an important secret—"In that house with the green gate, Mr. Weller, they keep a good many servants."

"So I should think, from the look on it," interposed Sam.

"Yes," continued Mr. Trotter, "and one of them is a cook, who has saved up a little money, Mr. Weller, and is desirous, if she can establish herself in life, to open a little shop in the chandlery way, you see."

"Yes."

"Yes, Mr. Weller. Well, Sir, I met her at a chapel that I go to—a very neat little chapel in this town, Mr. Weller, where they sing the number four collection of hymns, which I generally carry about with me, in a little book, which you may perhaps have seen in my hand—and I got a little intimate with her, Mr. Weller, and from that, an acquaintance sprung up between us, and I may venture to say, Mr. Weller, that I am to be the chandler."

"Ah, and a wery amiable chandler you'll make," replied Sam, eyeing Job with a side look of intense dislike.

"The great advantage of this, Mr. Weller," continued Job, his eyes filling with tears as he spoke, "will be, that I shall be able to leave my present disgraceful service with that bad man, and to devote myself to a better and more virtuous life—more like the way in which I was brought up, Mr. Weller."

"You must ha' been wery nicely brought up," said Sam.

"Oh, very, Mr. Weller, very," replied Job; and at the recollection of the purity of his youthful days, Mr. Trotter pulled forth the pink handkerchief, and wept copiously.

"You must ha' been an uncommon nice boy, to go to school vith," said Sam.

"I was Sir," replied Job, heaving a deep sigh. "I was the idol of the place."

"Ah," said Sam, "I don't wonder at it. What a comfort you must ha' been to your blessed mother."

At these words, Mr. Job Trotter inserted an end of the pink handkerchief into the corner of each eye, one after the other, and began to weep copiously.

"Vhat's the matter vith the man," said Sam indignantly. "Chelsea waterworks is nothin' to you. What are you melting vith now—the consciousness o' willainy?"

"I cannot keep my feelings down, Mr. Weller," said Job, after a short pause. "To think that my master should have suspected the conversation I had with yours, and so dragged me away in a post-chaise, and after persuading the sweet young lady to say she knew nothing of him, and bribing the school-mistress to do the same, deserted her for a better speculation,—oh! Mr. Weller, it makes me shudder."

"Oh, that was the vay, was it?" said Mr. Weller.

"To be sure it was," replied Job.

"Vell," said Sam, as they had now arrived near the Hotel, "I vant to have a little bit o' talk with you, Job; so if you're not partickler engaged, I should like to see you at the Great White Horse to-night, somewheres about eight o'clock."

"I shall be sure to come," said Job.

"Yes, you'd better," replied Sam, with a very meaning look, "or else I shall perhaps be askin' arter you, at the other side of the green gate, and then I might cut you out, you know."

"I shall be sure to be with you," said Mr. Trotter; and wringing Sam's hand with the utmost fervour, he walked away.

"Take care, Job Trotter, take care," said Sam, looking after him, "or I shall be one too many for you this time, I shall, indeed." Having uttered this soliloquy, and looked after Job till he was to be seen no more, Mr. Weller made the best of his way to his master's bed-room.

"It's all in training, Sir," said Sam.

"What's in training, Sam?" inquired Mr. Pickwick.

"I have found 'em out, Sir," said Sam.

"Found out who?"

"That 'ere queer customer, and the melancholly chap with the black hair."

"Impossible, Sam!" said Mr. Pickwick, with the greatest energy—"Where are they, Sam; where are they?"

"Hush, hush!" replied Mr. Weller; and as he assisted Mr. Pickwick to dress, he detailed the plan of action on which he proposed to enter.

"But when is this to be done, Sam?" inquired Mr. Pickwick.

"All in good time, Sir," replied Sam.

Whether it was done in good time, or not, will be seen hereafter.

CHAPTER XXIV.

WHEREIN MR. PETER MAGNUS GROWS JEALOUS, AND THE MIDDLE-AGED LADY APPREHENSIVE, WHICH BRINGS THE PICKWICKIANS WITHIN THE GRASP OF THE LAW.

WHEN Mr. Pickwick descended to the room in which he and Mr. Peter Magnus had spent the preceding evening, he found that gentleman with the major part of the contents of the two bags, the leathern hat-box, and the brown-paper parcel, displayed to all possible advantage on his person, while he himself was pacing up and down the room in a state of the utmost excitement and agitation.

"Good morning, Sir," said Mr. Peter Magnus—"What do you think of this, Sir?"

"Very effective indeed," replied Mr. Pickwick, surveying the garments of Mr. Peter Magnus with a good-natured smile.

"Yes, I think it'll do," said Mr. Magnus. "Mr. Pickwick, Sir, I have sent up my card."

"Have you?" said Mr. Pickwick.

"Yes; and the waiter brought back word, that she would see me at eleven—at eleven, Sir; it only wants a quarter now."

"Very near the time," said Mr. Pickwick.

"Yes, it is rather near," replied Mr. Magnus, "rather too near to be pleasant—eh! Mr. Pickwick, Sir?"

"Confidence is a great thing in these cases," observed Mr. Pickwick.

"I believe it is, Sir," said Mr. Peter Magnus. "I am very confident, Sir. Really, Mr. Pickwick, I do not see why a man should feel any fear in such a case as this, Sir. What is it, Sir? There's nothing to be ashamed of; it's a matter of mutual accommodation, nothing more. Husband on one side, wife on the other. That's my view of the matter, Mr. Pickwick."

"It is a very philosophical one," replied Mr. Pickwick. "But breakfast is waiting, Mr. Magnus. Come."

Down they sat to breakfast, but it was evident, notwithstanding the boasting of Mr. Peter Magnus, that he laboured under a very considerable degree of nervousness, of which loss of appetite, a propensity to upset the tea-things, a spectral attempt at drollery, and an irresistible inclination to look at the clock every other second, were among the principal symptoms.

"He—he—he," tittered Mr. Magnus, affecting cheerfulness, and gasping with agitation. "It only wants two minutes, Mr. Pickwick. Am I pale, Sir?"

"Not very," replied Mr. Pickwick.

There was a brief pause.

"I beg your pardon, Mr. Pickwick; but have you ever done this sort of thing in your time?" said Mr. Magnus.

"You mean proposing?" said Mr. Pickwick.

"Yes."

"Never," said Mr. Pickwick, with great energy, "never."

"You have no idea, then, how it's best to begin?" said Mr. Magnus.

"Why," said Mr. Pickwick, "I may have formed some ideas upon the subject, but, as I have never submitted them to the test of experience, I should be sorry if you were induced to regulate your proceedings by them."

"I should feel very much obliged to you, for any advice, Sir," said Mr. Magnus, taking another look at the clock, the hand of which was verging on the five minutes past.

"Well, Sir," said Mr. Pickwick, with the profound solemnity with which that great man could, when he pleased, render his remarks so deeply impressive—"I should commence, Sir, with a tribute to the lady's beauty and excellent qualities; from them, Sir, I should diverge to my own unworthiness."

"Very good," said Mr. Magnus.

"Unworthiness for *her* only, mind, Sir," resumed Mr. Pickwick; "for to shew that I was not wholly unworthy, Sir, I should take a brief review of my past life, and present condition. I should argue, by analogy, that to anybody else, I must be a very desirable object. I should then expatiate on the warmth of my love, and the depth of my devotion. Perhaps I might then be tempted to seize her hand."

"Yes, I see," said Mr. Magnus; "that would be a very great point."

"I should then, Sir," continued Mr. Pickwick, growing warmer as the subject presented itself in more glowing colours before him—"I should, then, Sir, come to the plain and simple question, 'Will you have me?' I think I am justified in assuming that upon this, she would turn away her head."

"You think that may be taken for granted?" said Mr. Magnus; "because, if she did not do that at the right place, it would be embarrassing."

"I think she would," said Mr. Pickwick. "Upon this, Sir, I should squeeze her hand, and I think—I *think*, Mr. Magnus—that after I had done that, supposing there was no refusal, I should gently draw away the handkerchief, which my slight knowledge of human nature leads me to suppose the lady would be applying to her eyes at the moment, and steal a respectful kiss. I think I should kiss her, Mr. Magnus; and at this particular point, I am decidedly of opinion that if the lady were going to take me at all, she would murmur into my ears a bashful acceptance."

Mr. Magnus started: gazed on Mr. Pickwick's intelligent face, for a short time in silence, and then (the dial pointing to the ten minutes past) shook him warmly by the hand, and rushed desperately from the room.

Mr. Pickwick had taken a few strides to and fro; and the small hand of the clock following the latter part of his example, had arrived at the figure which indicates the half hour, when the door suddenly opened. He turned round to greet Mr. Peter Magnus, and encountered in his stead the joyous face of Mr. Tupman, the serene countenance of Mr. Winkle, and the intellectual lineaments of Mr. Snodgrass.

As Mr. Pickwick greeted them, Mr. Peter Magnus tripped into the room.

"My friends, the gentleman I was speaking of, Mr. Magnus," said Mr. Pickwick.

"Your servant, gentlemen," said Mr. Magnus, evidently in a high state of excitement; "Mr. Pickwick, allow me to speak to you, one moment, Sir."

As he said this, Mr. Magnus harnessed his fore-finger to

Mr. Pickwick's button-hole, and, drawing him into a window recess, said—

"Congratulate me, Mr. Pickwick; I followed your advice to the very letter."

"And it was all correct, was it?" inquired Mr. Pickwick.

"It was, Sir—could not possibly have been better," replied Mr. Magnus; "Mr. Pickwick, she is mine."

"I congratulate you, with all my heart," replied Mr. Pickwick, warmly shaking his new friend by the hand.

"You must see her, Sir," said Mr. Magnus; "this way, if you please. Excuse us for one instant, gentlemen." And hurrying on in this way, Mr. Peter Magnus drew Mr. Pickwick from the room. He paused at the next door in the passage, and tapped gently thereat.

"Come in," said a female voice. And in they went.

"Miss Witherfield," said Mr. Magnus, "Allow me to introduce my very particular friend, Mr. Pickwick. Mr. Pickwick, I beg to make you known to Miss Witherfield."

The lady was at the upper end of the room, and as Mr. Pickwick bowed, he took his spectacles from his waistcoat pocket, and put them on, a process which he had no sooner gone through, than, uttering an exclamation of surprise, Mr. Pickwick retreated several paces, and the lady, with a half-suppressed scream, hid her face in her hands, and dropped into a chair, whereupon Mr. Peter Magnus was struck motionless on the spot, and gazed from one to the other, with a countenance expressive of the extremities of horror and surprise.

This certainly was, to all appearance, very unaccountable behaviour, but the fact was, that Mr. Pickwick no sooner put on his spectacles, than he at once recognised in the future Mrs. Magnus the lady into whose room he had so unwarrantably intruded on the previous night; and the spectacles had no sooner crossed Mr. Pickwick's nose, than the lady at once identified the countenance which she had seen surrounded by all the horrors of a night-cap. So the lady screamed, and Mr. Pickwick started.

"Mr. Pickwick!" exclaimed Mr. Magnus, lost in astonishment, "What is the meaning of this, Sir? What is the meaning of it, Sir?" added Mr. Magnus, in a threatening, and a louder tone.

"Sir," said Mr. Pickwick, somewhat indignant at the very sudden manner in which Mr. Peter Magnus had conjugated himself into the imperative mood, "I decline answering that question."

"You decline it, Sir?" said Mr. Magnus.

"I do, Sir," replied Mr. Pickwick; "I object to saying anything which may compromise that lady, or awaken unpleasant recollections in her breast, without her consent and permission."

"Miss Witherfield," said Mr. Peter Magnus, "do you know this person?"

"Know him!" repeated the middle-aged lady, hesitating.

"Yes, know him, Ma'am, I said know him," replied Mr. Magnus, with ferocity.

"I have seen him," replied the middle-aged lady.

"Where?" inquired Mr. Magnus, "where?"

"That," said the middle-aged lady, rising from her seat, and averting her head, "that I would not reveal for worlds."

"I understand you, Ma'am," said Mr. Pickwick, "and respect your delicacy; it shall never be revealed by me, depend upon it."

"Upon my word, Ma'am," said Mr. Magnus, "considering the situation in which I am placed with regard to yourself, you carry this matter off with tolerable coolness—tolerable coolness, Ma'am."

"Cruel Mr. Magnus," said the middle-aged lady; and here she wept very copiously indeed.

"Address your observations to me, Sir," interposed Mr. Pickwick; "I alone am to blame, if anybody be."

"Oh! you alone are to blame, are you, Sir?" said Mr. Magnus; "I—I—see through this, Sir. You repent of your determination now, do you?"

"My determination!" said Mr. Pickwick.

"Your determination, Sir. Oh! don't stare at me, Sir," said Mr. Magnus; "I recollect your words last night, Sir. You came down here, Sir, to expose the treachery and falsehood of an individual on whose truth and honour you had placed implicit reliance—eh?" Here Mr. Peter Magnus indulged in a prolonged sneer; and taking off his green spectacles—which he probably found superfluous in his fit of jealousy—rolled his little eyes about, in a manner which was frightful to behold.

"Eh?" said Mr. Magnus; and then he repeated the sneer with increased effect. "But you shall answer it, Sir."

"Answer what?" said Mr. Pickwick.

"Never mind, Sir," replied Mr. Magnus, striding up and down the room—"Never mind."

There must be something very comprehensive in this phrase of "Never mind," for we do not recollect to have ever witnessed a quarrel in the street, at a theatre, public room, or elsewhere, in which it has not been the standard reply to all belligerent inquiries. "Do you call yourself a gentleman, Sir?"—"Never mind, Sir." "Did I offer to say anything to the young woman, Sir?"—"Never mind, Sir." "Do you want your head knocked up against that wall, Sir?"—"Never mind, Sir." It is observable, too, that there would appear to be some hidden taunt in this universal "Never mind," which rouses more indignation in the bosom of the individual addressed, than the most lavish abuse could possibly awaken.

We do not mean to assert that the application of this brevity to himself, struck exactly that indignation to Mr. Pickwick's soul, which it would infallibly have roused in a vulgar breast. We merely record the fact that Mr. Pickwick opened the room door, and abruptly called out, "Tupman, come here."

Mr. Tupman immediately presented himself, with a look of very considerable surprise.

"Tupman," said Mr. Pickwick, "a secret of some delicacy, in which that lady is concerned, is the cause of a difference which has just arisen between this gentleman and myself. When I assure him, in your presence, that it has no relation to himself, and is not in any way connected with his affairs, I need hardly beg you to take notice that if he continues to dispute it, he expresses a doubt of my veracity, which I shall consider extremely insulting." As Mr. Pickwick said this, he looked encyclopædias at Mr. Peter Magnus.

Mr. Pickwick's upright and honourable bearing, coupled with that force and energy of speech which so eminently distinguished him, would have carried conviction to any reasonable mind; but unfortunately at that particular moment, the mind of Mr. Peter Magnus was in anything but reasonable order. Consequently, instead of receiving Mr. Pickwick's explanation as he ought to have done, he forthwith proceeded to work himself into a red-hot scorching consuming passion, and to talk about what was due to his own feelings, and all that sort of thing, adding force to his declamation by striding to and fro, and pulling his hair, amusements which he would vary occasionally, by shaking his fist in Mr. Pickwick's philanthropic countenance.

Mr. Pickwick, in his turn, conscious of his own innocence and rectitude, and irritated by having unfortunately involved the middle-aged lady in such an unpleasant affair, was not so quietly disposed as was his wont. The consequence was, that words ran high, and voices higher, and at length Mr. Magnus told Mr. Pickwick he should hear from him, to which Mr. Pickwick replied with laudable politeness, that the sooner he heard from him the better; whereupon the middle-aged lady rushed in terror from the room, out of which Mr. Tupman dragged Mr. Pickwick, leaving Mr. Peter Magnus to himself and meditation.

If the middle-aged lady had mingled much with the busy world, or profited at all, by the manners and customs of those who make the laws and set the fashions, she would have known that this sort of ferocity is just the most harmless thing in nature; but as she had lived for the most part in the country, and never read the parliamentary debates, she was little versed in these particular refinements of civilised life. Accordingly, when she had gained her bedchamber, bolted herself in, and begun to meditate on the scene she had just witnessed, the most terrific pictures of slaughter and destruction presented themselves to her imagination; among which, a full-length portrait of Mr. Peter Magnus borne home by four men, with the embellishment of a whole barrel-full of bullets in his left side, was among the very least. The more the middle-aged lady meditated, the more terrified she became; and at length she determined to repair to the house of the principal magistrate of the town, and request him to secure the persons of Mr. Pickwick and Mr. Tupman, without delay.

To this decision, the middle-aged lady was impelled by a variety of considerations, the chief of which, was the incontestable proof it would afford of her devotion to Mr. Peter Magnus, and her anxiety for his safety. She was too well acquainted with his jealous temperament to venture the slightest allusion to the real cause of her agitation on beholding Mr. Pickwick; and she trusted to her own influence and power of persuasion with the little man, to quell his boisterous jealousy, supposing that Mr. Pickwick were removed, and no fresh quarrel could arise. Filled with these reflections, the middle-aged lady arrayed herself in her bonnet and shawl, and repaired to the Mayor's dwelling straightway.

Now George Nupkins, Esquire, the principal magistrate aforesaid, was about as grand a personage as the fastest walker would find out, between sunrise and sunset, on the twenty-first of June, which being, according to the almanacs, the longest day in the whole year, would naturally afford him the longest period for his search. On this particular morning, Mr. Nupkins was in a state of the utmost excitement and irritation, for there had been a rebellion in the town; all the day-scholars at the largest day-school, had conspired to break the windows of an obnoxious appleseller, and had hooted the beadle, and pelted the constabulary—an elderly gentleman in top-boots, who had been called out to repress the tumult; and had been a peace-officer, man and boy, for half a century at least. And Mr. Nupkins was sitting in his easy chair, frowning with majesty, and boiling with rage, when a lady was announced on pressing, private, and particular business. Mr. Nupkins looked calmly terrible, and commanded that the lady

should be shown in, which command, like all the mandates of emperors, and magistrates, and other great potentates of the earth, was forthwith obeyed; and Miss Witherfield, interestingly agitated, was ushered in accordingly.

"Muzzle," said the Magistrate.

Muzzle was an under-sized footman, with a long body and short legs.

"Muzzle."

"Yes, your worship."

"Place a chair and leave the room."

"Yes, your worship."

"Now, Ma'am, will you state your business?" said the Magistrate.

"It is of a very painful kind, Sir," said Miss Witherfield.

"Very likely, Ma'am," said the Magistrate. "Compose your feelings, Ma'am." Here Mr. Nupkins looked benignant. "And then tell me what legal business brings you here, Ma'am." Here the Magistrate triumphed over the man; and he looked stern again.

"It is very distressing to me, Sir, to give this information," said Miss Witherfield, "but I fear a duel is going to be fought here."

"Here, Ma'am," said the Magistrate. "Where, Ma'am?"

"In Ipswich."

"In Ipswich, Ma'am—a duel in Ipswich," said the Magistrate, perfectly aghast at the notion. "Impossible, Ma'am; nothing of the kind can be contemplated in this town, I am persuaded. Bless my soul, Ma'am, are you aware of the activity of our local magistracy? Do you happen to have heard, Ma'am, that I rushed into a prizering on the fourth of May last, attended by only sixty special constables; and, at the hazard of falling a sacrifice to the angry passions of an infuriated multitude, prohibited a pugilistic contest between the Middlesex Dumpling, and the Suffolk Bantam? A duel in Ipswich, Ma'am! I don't think—I do *not* think," said the Magistrate, reasoning with himself, "that any two men can have had the hardihood to plan such a breach of the peace, in this town."

"My information is unfortunately but too correct," said the middle-aged lady, "I was present at the quarrel."

"It's a most extraordinary thing," said the astounded Magistrate. "Muzzle."

"Yes, your worship."

"Send Mr. Jinks here, directly- instantly."

"Yes, your worship."

Muzzle retired; and a pale, sharp-nosed, half-fed, shabbily-clad clerk, of middle age, entered the room.

"Mr. Jinks," said the Magistrate—"Mr. Jinks."

"Sir," said Mr. Jinks.

"This lady, Mr. Jinks, has come here, to give information of an intended duel in this town."

Mr. Jinks, not exactly knowing what to do, smiled a dependant's smile.

"What are you laughing at, Mr. Jinks?" said the Magistrate.

Mr. Jinks looked serious, instantly.

"Mr. Jinks," said the Magistrate, "you're a fool, Sir."

Mr. Jinks looked humbly at the great man, and bit the top of his pen.

"You may see something very comical in this information, Sir; but I can tell you this, Mr. Jinks, that you have very little to laugh at," said the Magistrate.

The hungry-looking Jinks sighed, as if he were quite aware of the fact of his having very little indeed, to be merry about; and, being ordered to take the lady's information, shambled to a seat, and proceeded to write it down.

"This man Pickwick is the principal, I understand," said the Magistrate, when the statement was finished.

"He is," said the middle-aged lady.

"And the other rioter—what's his name, Mr. Jinks?"

"Tupman, Sir."

"Tupman is the second?"

"Yes."

"The other principal you say, has absconded, Ma'am?"

"Yes," replied Miss Witherfield, with a short cough.

"Very well," said the Magistrate. "These are two cut-throats from London, who have come down here, to destroy His Majesty's population, thinking that at this distance from the capital, the arm of the law is weak and paralysed. They shall be made an example of. Draw up the warrants, Mr. Jinks. Muzzle."

"Yes, your worship."

"Is Grummer down stairs?"

"Yes, your worship."

"Send him up."

The obsequious Muzzle retired, and presently returned, introducing the elderly gentleman in the top-boots, who was chiefly remarkable for a bottle nose, a hoarse voice, a snuff-coloured surtout, and a wandering eye.

"Grummer," said the Magistrate.

"Your wash-up."

"Is the town quiet now?"

"Pretty well, your wash-up," replied Grummer. "Pop-'lar feeling has in a measure subsided, consekens o' the boys having dispersed to cricket."

"Nothing but vigorous measures will do, in these times, Grummer," said the Magistrate, in a determined manner. "If the authority of the king's officers is set at nought, we must have the riot act read. If the civil power cannot protect these windows, Grummer, the military must protect the civil power, and the windows too. I believe that is a maxim of the constitution, Mr. Jinks?"

"Certainly, Sir," said Jinks.

"Very good," said the Magistrate, signing the warrants. "Grummer, you will bring these persons before me, this afternoon. You will find them at the Great White Horse. You recollect the case of the Middlesex Dumpling and the Suffolk Bantam, Grummer?"

Mr. Grummer intimated, by a retrospective shake of the head, that he should never forget—as indeed it was not likely he would, so long as it continued to be cited daily.

"This is even more unconstitutional," said the Magistrate; "this is even a greater breach of the peace, and a grosser infringement of His Majesty's prerogative. I believe duelling is one of His Majesty's most undoubted prerogatives, Mr. Jinks?"

"Expressly stipulated in Magna Charta, Sir," said Mr. Jinks.

"One of the brightest jewels in the British crown, wrung from His Majesty by the Political Union of Barons, I believe, Mr. Jinks?" said the Magistrate.

"Just so, Sir," replied Mr. Jinks.

"Very well," said the Magistrate, drawing himself up proudly, "it shall not be violated in this portion of his dominions. Grummer, procure assistance, and execute these warrants with as little delay as possible. Muzzle."

"Yes, your worship."

"Show the lady out."

Miss Witherfield retired, deeply impressed with the Magistrate's learning and research; Mr. Nupkins retired to lunch; Mr. Jinks retired within himself—that being the only retirement he had, except the sofa-bedstead in the small parlour which was occupied by his landlady's family in the day-time—and Mr. Grummer retired, to wash out, by his mode of discharging his present commission, the insult which had been fastened upon himself, and the other representative of His Majesty—the beadle—in the course of the morning.

While these resolute and determined preparations for the conservation of the King's peace, were pending, Mr. Pickwick and his friends, wholly unconscious of the mighty events in progress, had sat quietly down to dinner; and very talkative and companionable they all were; Mr. Pickwick was in the very act of relating his adventure of the preceding night, to the great amusement of his followers, Mr. Tupman especially, when the door opened, and a somewhat forbidding countenance peeped into the room. The eyes in the forbidding countenance looked very earnestly at Mr. Pickwick, for several seconds, and were to all appearance satisfied with their investigation; for the body to which the forbidding countenance belonged, slowly brought itself into the apartment, and presented the form of an elderly individual in top-boots—not to keep the reader any longer in suspense, in short, the eyes were the wandering eyes of Mr. Grummer, and the body was the body of the same gentleman.

Mr. Grummer's mode of proceeding was professional, but peculiar. His first act was to bolt the door on the inside; his second, to polish his head and countenance very carefully with a cotton handkerchief; his third, to place his hat, with the cotton handkerchief in it, on the nearest chair; and his fourth to produce from the breast-pocket of his coat, a short truncheon surmounted by a brazen crown, with which he beckoned to Mr. Pickwick with a grave and ghost-like air.

Mr. Snodgrass was the first to break the astonished silence. He looked steadily at Mr. Grummer for a brief space, and then said emphatically—"This is a private room, Sir—a private room."

Mr. Grummer shook his head, and replied—"No room's private to His Majesty when the street door's once passed. That's law. Some people maintains that an Englishman's house is his castle. That's gammon."

The Pickwickians gazed on each other, with wondering eyes.

"Which is Mr. Tupman?" inquired Mr. Grummer. He had an intuitive perception of Mr. Pickwick; he knew him at once.

"My name's Tupman," said that gentleman.

"My name's Law," said Mr. Grummer.

"What?" said Mr. Tupman.

"Law," replied Mr. Grummer, "law, civil power, and exekative; them's my titles; here's my authority. Blank Tupman, blank Pickwick—against the peace of our sufferin Lord the King—stattit in that case made and purwided—and all regular. I apprehend you Pickwick, Tupman—the aforesaid."

"What do you mean by this insolence?" said Mr. Tupman, starting up—"Leave the room, leave the room."

"Halloo," said Mr. Grummer, retreating very expeditiously to the door, and opening it an inch or two, "Dubbley."

"Well," said a deep voice from the passage.

"Come for'ard, Dubbley," said Mr. Grummer.

At the word of command, a dirty-faced man, something over six feet high, and stout in proportion, squeezed himself through the half-open door, making his face very red in the process, and entered the room.

"Is the other specials outside, Dubbley?" inquired Mr. Grummer.

Mr. Dubbley, who was a man of few words, nodded assent.

"Order in the diwision under your charge, Dubbley," said Mr. Grummer.

Mr. Dubbley did as he was desired; and half a dozen men, each with a short truncheon and a brass crown, flocked into the room. Mr. Grummer pocketed his staff and looked at Mr. Dubbley, Mr. Dubbley pocketed *his* staff and looked at the division; and the division pocketed *their* staves and looked at Messrs. Tupman and Pickwick.

Mr. Pickwick and his followers, rose as one man.

"What is the meaning of this atrocious intrusion upon my privacy?" said Mr. Pickwick.

"Who dares apprehend me?" said Mr. Tupman.

"What do you want here, scoundrels?" said Mr. Snodgrass.

Mr. Winkle said nothing, but he fixed his eyes on Grummer, and bestowed a look upon him, which, if he had had any feeling, must have pierced his brain, and come out on the other side. As it was, however, it had no visible effect upon him whatever.

When the executive perceived that Mr. Pickwick and his friends were disposed to resist the authority of the law, they very significantly turned up their coat sleeves, as if knocking them down in the first instance, and taking them up afterwards, were a mere professional act which had only to be thought of, to be done, as a matter of course. This demonstration was not lost upon Mr. Pickwick. He conferred a few moments with Mr. Tupman apart, and then signified his readiness to proceed to the Mayor's residence, merely begging the parties then and there assembled, to take notice, that it was his firm intention to resent this monstrous invasion of his privileges as an Englishman, the instant he was at liberty, whereat the parties then and there assembled, laughed very heartily, with the single exception of Mr. Grummer, who seemed to consider that any slight cast upon the divine right of Magistrates, was a species of blasphemy, not to be tolerated.

But when Mr. Pickwick had signified his readiness to bow to the laws of his country, and just when the waiters, and hostlers, and chamber-maids, and post-boys, who had anticipated a delightful commotion from his threatened obstinacy, began to turn away, disappointed and disgusted, a difficulty arose which had not been foreseen. With every sentiment of veneration for the constituted authorities, Mr. Pickwick resolutely protested against making his appearance in the public streets, surrounded and guarded by the officers of justice, like a common criminal. Mr. Grummer, in the then disturbed state of public feeling (for it was half-holiday, and the boys had not yet gone home), as resolutely protested against walking on the opposite side of the way, and taking Mr. Pickwick's parole that he would go straight to the Magistrate's; and both Mr. Pickwick and Mr. Tupman as strenuously objected to the expense of a post-coach, which was the only respectable conveyance that could be obtained. The dispute ran high, and the dilemma lasted long; and just as the executive were on the point of overcoming Mr. Pickwick's objection to walking

to the Magistrate's, by the trite expedient of carrying him thither, it was recollected that there stood in the inn yard, an old sedan-chair, which having been originally built for a gouty gentleman with funded property, would hold Mr. Pickwick and Mr. Tupman, at least as conveniently as a modern post-chaise. The chair was hired, and brought into the hall; Mr. Pickwick and Mr. Tupman squeezed themselves inside, and pulled down the blinds; a couple of chairmen were speedily found, and the procession started in grand order. The specials surrounded the body of the vehicle, Mr. Grummer and Mr. Dubbley marched triumphantly in front, Mr. Snodgrass and Mr. Winkle walked arm in arm behind, and the unsoaped of Ipswich brought up the rear.

The shopkeepers of the town, although they had a very indistinct notion of the nature of the offence, could not but be much edified and gratified by this spectacle. Here was the strong arm of the law, coming down with twenty gold-beater force, upon two offenders from the metropolis itself; the mighty engine was directed by their own Magistrate, and worked by their own officers; and both the criminals by their united efforts, were securely boxed up, in the narrow compass of one sedan-chair. Many were the expressions of approval and admiration which greeted Mr. Grummer, as he headed the cavalcade, staff in hand; loud and long were the shouts which were raised by the unsoaped; and amidst these united testimonials of public approbation, the procession moved slowly and majestically along.

Mr. Weller, habited in his morning jacket with the black calico sleeves, was returning in a rather desponding state from an unsuccessful survey of the mysterious house with the green gate, when, raising his eyes, he beheld a crowd pouring down the street, surrounding an object which bore very much the appearance of a sedan-chair. Willing to divert his thoughts from the failure of his enterprise, he stepped aside to see the crowd pass, and finding that they were cheering away, very much to their own satisfaction, forthwith began (just by way of raising his spirits) to cheer too, with all his might and main.

Mr. Grummer passed, and Mr. Dubbley passed, and the sedan passed, and the body-guard of specials passed, and Sam was still responding to the enthusiastic cheers of the mob, and waving his hat about as if he were in the very last extreme of the wildest joy (though of course he had not the faintest idea of the matter in hand), when he was suddenly stopped by the unexpected appearance of Mr. Winkle and Mr. Snodgrass.

"What's the row, genl'm'n?" cried Sam, "Who have they got in this here watch-box in mournin'?"

Both gentlemen replied together, but their words were lost in the tumult.

"Who is it?" roared Sam again.

Once more was a joint reply returned; and though the words were inaudible, Sam saw by the motion of the two pairs of lips that they had uttered the magic word "Pickwick."

This was enough. In another minute Mr. Weller had made his way through the crowd, stopped the chairmen, and confronted the portly Grummer.

"Hallo, old genl'm'n," said Sam, "Who have you got in this here con-wayance?"

"Stand back," said Mr. Grummer, whose dignity, like the dignity of a great many other men, had been wondrously augmented by a little popularity.

"Knock him down, if he don't," said Mr. Dubbley.

"I'm wery much obliged to you, old genl'm'n," replied Sam, "for consulting my conwenience, and I'm still more obliged to the other genl'm'n who looks as if he'd just escaped from a giant's carrywan, for his wery 'ansome suggestion; but I should perfer your givin' me a answer to my question, if it's all the same to you. How are you, Sir?" This last observation was addressed with a patronising air to Mr. Pickwick, who was peeping through the front window.

Mr. Grummer, perfectly speechless with indignation, dragged the truncheon with the brass crown, from its particular pocket, and flourished it before Sam's eyes.

"Ah," said Sam, "it's wery pretty, 'specially the crown, which is uncommon like the real one."

"Stand back," said the outraged Mr. Grummer. By way of adding force to the command, he thrust the brass emblem of royalty into Sam's neckcloth with one hand, and seized Sam's collar with the other, a compliment which Mr. Weller returned by knocking him down out of hand, having previously, with the utmost consideration, knocked down a chairman for him to lie upon.

Whether Mr. Winkle was seized with a temporary attack of that species of insanity which originates in a sense of injury, or animated by this display of Mr. Weller's valour, is uncertain; but certain it is, that he no sooner saw Mr. Grummer fall, than he made a terrific onslaught on a small boy who stood next him; whereupon Mr. Snodgrass, in a truly christian spirit, and in order that he might take no one unawares, announced in a very loud tone that he was going to begin, and proceeded to take off his coat with the utmost deliberation. He was immediately surrounded and secured; and it is but common justice both to him and Mr. Winkle to say, that they did not make the slightest attempt to rescue either themselves or Mr. Weller, who, after a most vigorous resistance, was overpowered by numbers, and taken prisoner. The procession then re-formed, the chairmen resumed their stations, and the march was re-commenced.

Mr. Pickwick's indignation during the whole of this proceeding was beyond all bounds. He could just see Sam upsetting the specials, and flying about, in every direction, and that was all he could see, for the sedan doors wouldn't open, and the blinds wouldn't pull up. At length, with the assistance of Mr. Tupman, he managed to push open the roof; and mounting on the seat, and steadying himself as well as he could, by placing his hand on that gentleman's shoulder, Mr. Pickwick proceeded to address the multitude; to dwell upon the unjustifiable manner in which he had been treated; and to call upon them to take notice that his servant had been first assaulted. And in this order they reached the Magistrate's house; the chairmen trotting, the prisoners following, Mr. Pickwick oratorising, and the crowd shouting.

CHAPTER XXV.

SHOWING, AMONG A VARIETY OF PLEASANT MATTERS, HOW MAJESTIC AND IMPARTIAL MR. NUPKINS WAS; AND HOW MR. WELLER RETURNED MR. JOB TROTTER'S SHUTTLECOCK, AS HEAVILY AS IT CAME. WITH ANOTHER MATTER, WHICH WILL BE FOUND IN ITS PLACE.

VIOLENT was Mr. Weller's indignation as he was borne along; numerous were the allusions to the personal appearance and demeanour of Mr. Grummer and his companion;

and valorous were the defiances to any six of the gentlemen present, in which he vented his dissatisfaction. Mr. Snodgrass and Mr. Winkle listened with gloomy respect to the torrent of eloquence which their leader poured forth, from the sedan-chair, and the rapid course of which, not all Mr. Tupman's earnest entreaties to have the lid of the vehicle closed, were able to check for an instant. But Mr. Weller's anger quickly gave way to curiosity, when the procession turned down the identical court-yard in which he had met with the runaway Job Trotter: and curiosity was exchanged for a feeling of the most gleeful astonishment, when the all-important Mr. Grummer, commanding the sedan-bearers to halt, advanced with dignified and portentous steps, to the very green gate from which Job Trotter had emerged, and gave a mighty pull at the bell-handle which hung at the side thereof. The ring was answered by a very smart and pretty-faced servant-girl, who, after holding up her hands in astonishment at the rebellious appearance of the prisoners, and the impassioned language of Mr. Pickwick, summoned Mr. Muzzle. Mr. Muzzle opened one-half of the carriage gate, to admit the sedan, the captured ones, and the specials; and immediately slammed it in the faces of the mob, who, indignant at being excluded, and anxious to see what followed, relieved their feelings by kicking at the gate and ringing the bell, for an hour or two afterwards. In this amusement they all took part by turns, except three or four fortunate individuals, who having discovered a grating in the gate which commanded a view of nothing, were staring through it, with the same indefatigable perseverance with which people will flatten their noses against the front windows of a chemist's shop, when a drunken man, who has been run over by a dog-cart in the street, is undergoing a surgical inspection in the back-parlour.

At the foot of a flight of steps, leading to the house door, which were guarded on either side by an American aloe in a green tub, the sedan-chair stopped; and Mr. Pickwick and his friends were conducted into the hall, from whence, having been previously announced by Muzzle, and ordered in by Mr. Nupkins, they were ushered into the worshipful presence of that public-spirited officer.

The scene was an impressive one, well calculated to strike terror to the hearts of culprits, and to impress them with an adequate idea of the stern majesty of the law. In front of a big book-case, in a big chair, behind a big table, and before a big volume, sat Mr. Nupkins, looking a full size larger than any one of them, big as they were. The table was adorned with piles of papers: and above the further end of it, appeared the head and shoulders of Mr. Jinks, who was busily engaged in looking as busy as possible. The party having all entered, Muzzle carefully closed the door, and placed himself behind his master's chair to await his orders; Mr. Nupkins threw himself back, with thrilling solemnity, and scrutinised the faces of his unwilling visiters.

"Now, Grummer, who is that person?" said Mr. Nupkins, pointing to Mr. Pickwick, who, as the spokesman of his friends, stood hat in hand, bowing with the utmost politeness and respect.

"This here's Pickvick, your wash-up," said Grummer.

"Come, none o' that 'ere, old Strike-a-light," interposed Mr. Weller, elbowing himself into the front rank—"Beg your pardon, Sir, but this here officer o' yourn in the gamboge tops, 'ull never earn a decent livin' as a master o' the ceremonies any vere. This here, Sir," continued Mr. Weller, thrusting Grummer aside, and addressing the Mag-

MR. WELLER ATTACKS THE EXECUTIVE OF IPSWICH.

istrate with pleasant familiarity—"This here is S. Pick-vick, Esquire; this here's Mr. Tupman; that 'ere's Mr. Snodgrass; and furder on, next him on the t'other side, Mr. Winkle—all wery nice genl'm'n, Sir, as you'll be wery happy to have the acquaintance on; so the sooner you commits these here officers o' yourn to the tread-mill for a month or two, the sooner we shall begin to be on a pleasant understanding. Business first, pleasure arterwards, as King Richard the Third said ven he stabbed the t'other king in the Tower, afore he smothered the babbies."

At the conclusion of this address, Mr. Weller brushed his hat with his right elbow, and nodded benignly to Jinks, who had heard him throughout, with unspeakable awe.

"Who is this man, Grummer?" said the Magistrate.

"Wery desp'rate ch'racter, your wash-up," replied Grummer. "He attempted to rescue the prisoners, and assaulted the officers—so we took him into custody, and brought him here."

"You did quite right," replied the Magistrate. "He is evidently a desperate ruffian."

"He is my servant, Sir," said Mr. Pickwick, angrily.

"Oh! he is your servant, is he?" said Mr. Nupkins. "A conspiracy to defeat the ends of justice, and murder its officers. Pickwick's servant. Put that down, Mr. Jinks." Mr. Jinks did so.

"What's your name, fellow?" thundered Mr. Nupkins.

"Veller," replied Sam.

"A very good name for the Newgate Calendar," said Mr. Nupkins.

This was a joke; so Jinks, Grummer, Dubbley, all the specials, and Muzzle, went into fits of laughter of five minutes' duration.

"Put down his name, Mr. Jinks," said the Magistrate.

"Two L's, old feller," said Sam.

Here an unfortunate special laughed again, whereupon the Magistrate threatened to commit him, instantly. It's a dangerous thing laughing at the wrong man, in these cases.

"Where do you live?" said the Magistrate.

"Vare-ever I can," replied Sam.

"Put down that, Mr. Jinks," said the Magistrate, who was fast rising into a rage.

"Score it under," said Sam.

"He is a vagabond, Mr. Jinks," said the Magistrate. "He is a vagabond on his own statement, is he not, Mr. Jinks?"

"Certainly, Sir."

"Then I'll commit him—I'll commit him, as such," said Mr. Nupkins.

"This is a wery impartial country for justice," said Sam. "There ain't a magistrate going, as don't commit himself, twice as often as he commits other people."

At this sally another special laughed, and then tried to look so supernaturally solemn, that the Magistrate detected him immediately.

"Grummer," said Mr. Nupkins, reddening with passion, "how dare you select such an inefficient and disreputable person for a special constable, as that man? How dare you do it, Sir?"

"I am very sorry, your wash-up," stammered Grummer.

"Very sorry!" said the furious Magistrate. "You shall repent of this neglect of duty, Mr. Grummer; you shall be made an example of. Take that fellow's staff away. He's drunk. You're drunk, fellow."

"I am not drunk, your worship," said the man.

"You *are* drunk," returned the Magistrate. "How dare you say you are not drunk, Sir, when I say you are? Doesn't he smell of spirits, Grummer?"

"Horrid, your wash-up," replied Grummer, who had a vague impression that there was a smell of rum somewhere.

"I knew he did," said Mr. Nupkins. "I saw he was drunk when he first came into the room, by his excited eye. Did you observe his excited eye, Mr. Jinks?"

"Certainly, Sir."

"I haven't touched a drop of spirits this morning," said the man, who was as sober a fellow as need be.

"How dare you tell me a falsehood?" said Mr. Nupkins. "Isn't he drunk at this moment, Mr. Jinks?"

"Certainly, Sir," replied Jinks.

"Mr. Jinks," said the Magistrate, "I shall commit that man, for contempt. Make out his committal, Mr. Jinks."

And committed the special would have been, only Jinks, who was the Magistrate's adviser, having had a legal education of three years in a country attorney's office, whispered the Magistrate that he thought it wouldn't do; so the Magistrate made a speech, and said, that in consideration of the special's family, he would merely reprimand and discharge him. Accordingly, the special was abused vehemently for a quarter of an hour, and sent about his business: and Grummer, Dubbley, Muzzle, and all the other specials murmured their admiration of the magnanimity of Mr. Nupkins.

"Now, Mr. Jinks," said the Magistrate, "swear Grummer."

Grummer was sworn directly; but as Grummer wandered, and Mr. Nupkins' dinner was nearly ready, Mr. Nupkins cut the matter short, by putting leading questions to Grummer, which Grummer answered as nearly in the affirmative as he could. So the examination went off, all very smooth and comfortable; and two assaults were proved against Mr. Weller, and a threat against Mr. Winkle, and a push against Mr. Snodgrass. And when all this was done to the Magistrate's satisfaction, the Magistrate and Mr. Jinks consulted in whispers.

The consultation having lasted about ten minutes, Mr. Jinks retired to his end of the table; and the Magistrate, with a preparatory cough, drew himself up in his chair, and was proceeding to commence his address, when Mr. Pickwick interposed.

"I beg your pardon, Sir, for interrupting you," said Mr. Pickwick; "but before you proceed to express, and act upon, any opinion you may have formed on the statements which have been made here, I must claim my right to be heard, so far as I am personally concerned."

"Hold your tongue, Sir," said the Magistrate, peremptorily.

"I must submit to you, Sir,"—said Mr. Pickwick.

"Hold your tongue, Sir," interposed the Magistrate, "or I shall order an officer to remove you."

"You may order your officers to do whatever you please, Sir," said Mr. Pickwick; "and I have no doubt, from the specimen I have had of the subordination preserved among them, that whatever you order, they will execute; but I shall take the liberty, Sir, of claiming my right to be heard, until I am removed by force."

"Pickwick and principle," exclaimed Mr. Weller, in a very audible voice.

"Sam, be quiet," said Mr. Pickwick.

"Dumb as a drum vith a hole in it," replied Sam.

Mr. Nupkins looked at Mr. Pickwick with a gaze of intense astonishment, at his displaying such unwonted temerity; and was apparently about to return a very angry reply, when Mr. Jinks pulled him by the sleeve, and whispered something in his ear. To this, the Magistrate returned a half-audible answer, and then the whispering was renewed. Jinks was evidently remonstrating.

At length the Magistrate, gulping down with a very bad grace his disinclination to hear anything more, turned to Mr. Pickwick, and said sharply—"What do you want to say?"

"First," said Mr. Pickwick, sending a look through his spectacles, under which even Nupkins quailed. "First, I wish to know what I and my friend have been brought here for?"

"Must I tell him?" whispered the Magistrate to Jinks.

"I think you had better, Sir," whispered Jinks to the Magistrate.

"An information has been sworn before me," said the Magistrate, "that it is apprehended you are going to fight a duel, and that the other man, Tupman, is your aider and abettor in it. Therefore—eh, Mr. Jinks?"

"Certainly, Sir."

"Therefore, I call upon you both, to—I think that's the course, Mr. Jinks?"

"Certainly, Sir."

"To—to—what Mr. Jinks?" said the Magistrate, pettishly.

"To find bail, Sir."

"Yes. Therefore, I call upon you both—as I was about to say, when I was interrupted by my clerk—to find bail."

"Good bail," whispered Mr. Jinks.

"I shall require good bail," said the Magistrate.

"Town's-people," whispered Jinks.

"They must be town's-people," said the Magistrate.

"Fifty pounds each," whispered Jinks, "and householders, of course."

"I shall require two sureties of fifty pounds each," said the Magistrate aloud, with great dignity, "and they must be householders, of course."

"But, bless my heart, Sir," said Mr. Pickwick, who, together with Mr. Tupman, was all amazement and indignation; "we are perfect strangers in this town. I have as little knowledge of any householders here, as I have intention of fighting a duel with any body."

"I dare say," replied the Magistrate, "I dare say—don't you, Mr. Jinks?"

"Certainly, Sir."

"Have you anything more to say?" inquired the Magistrate.

Mr. Pickwick *had* a great deal more to say, which he would no doubt have said, very little to his own advantage, or the Magistrate's satisfaction, if he had not, the moment he ceased speaking, been pulled by the sleeve by Mr. Weller, with whom he was immediately engaged in so earnest a conversation, that he suffered the Magistrate's inquiry to pass wholly unnoticed. Mr. Nupkins was not the man to ask a question of the kind twice over; and so, with another preparatory cough, he proceeded, amidst the reverential and admiring silence of the constables, to pronounce his decision.

He should fine Weller two pounds for the first assault, and three pounds for the second. He should fine Winkle two pounds, and Snodgrass one pound, besides requiring them to enter into their own recognizances to keep the peace towards all His Majesty's subjects, and especially towards his liege servant, Daniel Grummer. Pickwick and Tupman he had already held to bail.

Immediately on the Magistrate ceasing to speak, Mr. Pickwick, with a smile mantling on his again-good-humoured countenance, stepped forward, and said—

"I beg the Magistrate's pardon, but may I request a few minutes' private conversation with him, on a matter of deep importance to himself?"

"What!" said the Magistrate.

Mr. Pickwick repeated his request.

"This is a most extraordinary request," said the Magistrate—"A private interview!"

"A private interview," replied Mr. Pickwick, firmly; "only as a part of the information which I wish to communicate is derived from my servant, I should wish him to be present."

The Magistrate looked at Mr. Jinks, Mr. Jinks looked at the Magistrate, and the officers looked at each other in amazement. Mr. Nupkins turned suddenly pale. Could the man Weller, in a moment of remorse, have divulged some secret conspiracy for his assassination? It was a dreadful thought. He was a public man; and he turned paler, as he thought of Julius Cæsar and Mr. Perceval.

The Magistrate looked at Mr. Pickwick again, and beckoned Mr. Jinks.

"What do you think of this request, Mr. Jinks?" murmured Mr. Nupkins.

Mr. Jinks, who didn't exactly know what to think of it, and was afraid he might offend, smiled feebly, after a dubious fashion, and, screwing up the corners of his mouth, shook his head slowly from side to side.

"Mr. Jinks," said the Magistrate, gravely, "you are an ass, Sir."

At this little expression of opinion, Mr. Jinks smiled again—rather more feebly than before—and edged himself, by degrees, back into his own corner.

Mr. Nupkins debated the matter within himself for a few seconds, and then, rising from his chair, and requesting Mr. Pickwick and Sam to follow him, led the way into a small room which opened into the justice parlour. Desiring Mr. Pickwick to walk to the further end of the little apartment, and holding his hand upon the half-closed door, that he might be able to effect an immediate escape, in case there was the least tendency to a display of hostilities, Mr. Nupkins expressed his readiness to hear the communication, whatever it might be.

"I will come to the point at once, Sir," said Mr. Pickwick, "it affects yourself, and your credit, materially. I have every reason to believe, Sir, that you are harbouring in your house, a gross impostor!"

"Two," interrupted Sam, "Mulberry agin all natur, for tears and willainny."

"Sam," said Mr. Pickwick, "if I am to render myself intelligible to this gentleman, I must beg you to controul your feelings."

"Wery sorry, Sir," replied Mr. Weller; "but when I think o' that 'ere Job, I can't help opening the walve a inch or two."

"In one word, Sir," said Mr. Pickwick, "is my servant right in suspecting that a certain Captain Fitz-Marshall is in the habit of visiting here? Because," added Mr. Pickwick, as he saw that Mr. Nupkins was about to offer a very indignant interruption—"because, if he be, I know that person to be a—"

"Hush, hush," said Mr. Nupkins, closing the door.

"Know him to be what, Sir?"

"An unprincipled adventurer—a dishonourable character—a man who preys upon society, and makes easily-deceived people his dupes, Sir, his absurd, his foolish, his wretched dupes, Sir," said the excited Mr. Pickwick.

"Dear me," said Mr. Nupkins, colouring up very red, and altering his whole manner directly. "Dear me, Mr.—"

"Pickvick," said Sam.

"Pickwick," said the Magistrate, "dear me, Mr. Pickwick—pray take a seat—you cannot mean this? Captain Fitz-Marshall!"

"Don't call him a cap'en," said Sam, "nor Fitz-Marshall neither; he ain't neither one nor t'other. He's a strolling actor, he is, and his name's Jingle; and if ever there was a wolf in a mulberry suit, that ere Job Trotter's him."

"It is very true, Sir," said Mr. Pickwick, replying to the Magistrate's look of amazement; "my only business in this town, is to expose the person of whom we now speak."

And Mr. Pickwick proceeded to pour into the horror-stricken ear of Mr. Nupkins, an abridged account of all Mr. Jingle's atrocities. He related how he had first met him, how he had eloped with Miss Wardle, how he had cheerfully resigned the lady for a pecuniary consideration, how he had entrapped him into a lady's boarding-school at midnight, and how he (Mr. Pickwick) now felt it his duty to expose his assumption of his present name and rank.

As the narrative proceeded, all the warm blood in the body of Mr. Nupkins tingled up into the very tips of his ears. He had picked up the Captain at a neighbouring race-course. Charmed with his long list of aristocratic acquaintance, his extensive travel, and his fashionable demeanour, Mrs. Nupkins and Miss Nupkins had exhibited Captain Fitz-Marshall, and quoted Captain Fitz-Marshall, and hurled Captain Fitz-Marshall at the devoted heads of their select circle of acquaintance, until their bosom friends, Mrs. Porkenham and the Miss Porkenhams, and Mr. Sidney Porkenham, were ready to burst with jealousy and despair. And now, to hear after all, that he was a needy adventurer, a strolling player, and if not a swindler, something so very like it, that it was hard to tell the difference! Heavens! what would the Porkenhams say! What would be the triumph of Mr. Sidney Porkenham when he found that his addresses had been slighted for such a rival! How should he meet the eye of old Porkenham at the next Quarter Sessions!—and what a handle would it be for the opposition magisterial party, if the story got abroad!

"But after all," said Mr. Nupkins, brightening up for a moment, after a long pause; "after all, this is a mere statement. Captain Fitz-Marshall is a man of very engaging manners,—and, I dare say, has many enemies. What proof have you, of the truth of these representations?"

"Confront me with him," said Mr. Pickwick, "that is all I ask, and all I require. Confront him with me, and my friends here; you will want no further proof."

"Why," said Mr. Nupkins, "that might be very easily done, for he will be here to-night, and then there would be no occasion to make the matter public, just—just—for the young man's own sake, you know. I—I—should like to consult Mrs. Nupkins on the propriety of the step, in the first instance, though. At all events, Mr. Pickwick, we must despatch this legal business before we can do anything else. Pray step back into the next room."

Into the next room they went.

"Grummer," said the Magistrate, in an awful voice.

"Your wash-up," replied Grummer, with the smile of a favourite.

"Come, come, Sir," said the Magistrate, sternly, "don't let me see any of this levity here. It is very unbecoming, and I can assure you that you have very little to smile at. Was the account you gave me just now, strictly true? Now be careful, Sir?"

"Your wash-up," stammered Grummer, "I—"

"Oh, you are confused, are you?" said the Magistrate. "Mr. Jinks, you observe this confusion?"

"Certainly, Sir," replied Jinks.

"Now," said the Magistrate, "just repeat your statement, Grummer, and again I warn you to be careful. Mr. Jinks, take his words down."

The unfortunate Grummer proceeded to re-state his complaint, but, what between Mr. Jinks's taking down his words, and the Magistrate's taking them up; his natural tendency to rambling, and his extreme confusion, he managed to get involved, in something under three minutes, in such a mass of entanglement and contradiction, that Mr. Nupkins at once declared he didn't believe him. So the fines were remitted, and Mr. Jinks found a couple of bail in no time. And all these solemn proceedings having been satisfactorily concluded, Mr. Grummer was ignominiously ordered out—an awful instance of the instability of human greatness, and the uncertain tenure of great men's favour.

Mrs. Nupkins was a majestic female in a blue gauze turban and a light brown wig. Miss Nupkins possessed all her mamma's haughtiness without the turban, and all her ill-nature without the wig; and whenever the exercise of these two amiable qualities involved mother and daughter in some unpleasant dilemma, as they not unfrequently did, they both concurred in laying the blame on the shoulders of Mr. Nupkins. Accordingly, when Mr. Nupkins sought Mrs. Nupkins, and detailed the communication which had been made by Mr. Pickwick, Mrs. Nupkins suddenly recollected that she had always expected something of the kind; that she had always said it would be so; that her advice was never taken; that she really did not know what Mr. Nupkins supposed she was; and so forth.

"The idea!" said Miss Nupkins, forcing a tear of very scanty proportions, into the corner of each eye, "the idea of my being made such a fool of!"

"Ah! you may thank your papa, my dear," said Mrs. Nupkins; "how I have implored and begged that man to inquire into the Captain's family connections; how I have urged and entreated him to take some decisive step! I am quite certain nobody would believe it—quite."

"But, my dear," said Mr. Nupkins.

"Don't talk to me, you aggravating thing, don't," said Mrs. Nupkins.

"My love," said Mr. Nupkins, "you professed yourself very fond of Captain Fitz-Marshall. You have constantly asked him here, my dear, and you have lost no opportunity of introducing him elsewhere."

"Didn't I say so, Henrietta?" said Mrs. Nupkins, appealing to her daughter with the air of a much-injured female—"Didn't I say that your papa would turn round, and lay all this, at my door? Didn't I say so?" Here Mrs. Nupkins sobbed.

"Oh pa!" remonstrated Miss Nupkins. And here she sobbed too.

"Isn't it too much, when he has brought all this disgrace and ridicule upon us, for him to taunt me, with being the cause of it?" exclaimed Mrs. Nupkins.

"How can we ever shew ourselves in society!" said Miss Nupkins.

"How can we face the Porkenhams!" said Mrs. Nupkins. "Or the Griggs's!" said Miss Nupkins.

"Or the Slummintowkens!" said Mrs. Nupkins. "But what does your papa care! What is it to *him!*" At this dreadful reflection, Mrs. Nupkins wept with mental anguish, and Miss Nupkins followed on the same side.

Mrs. Nupkins's tears continued to gush forth, with great velocity, until she had gained a little time to think the matter over, when she decided in her own mind, that the best thing to do, would be to ask Mr. Pickwick and his friends to remain until the Captain's arrival, and then to give Mr. Pickwick the opportunity he sought. If it appeared that he had spoken truly, the Captain could be turned out of the house without noising the matter abroad, and they could easily account for his disappearance, by saying that he had been appointed, through the Court influence of his family, to the Governor-Generalship of Sierra Leone, or Sangur Point, or any other of those salubrious climates which enchant Europeans so much, that, when they once get there, they can hardly ever prevail upon themselves to come back again.

When Mrs. Nupkins dried up her tears, Miss Nupkins dried up *hers*, and Mr. Nupkins was very glad to settle the matter as Mrs. Nupkins had proposed. So Mr. Pickwick and his friends, having washed off all marks of their late encounter, were introduced to the ladies, and soon afterwards to their dinner; and Mr. Weller, whom the Magistrate with his peculiar sagacity, had discovered in half an hour to be one of the finest fellows alive, was consigned to the care and guardianship of Mr. Muzzle, who was specially enjoined to take him below, and make much of him.

"How de do, Sir?" said Mr. Muzzle, as he conducted Mr. Weller down the kitchen stairs.

"Why, no con-siderable change has taken place in the state of my system, since I see you cocked up behind your governor's chair in the parlour, a little vile ago," replied Sam.

"You will excuse my not taking more notice of you then," said Mr. Muzzle. "You see, master hadn't introduced us, then. Lor, how fond he is of you, Mr. Weller, to be sure!"

"Ah," said Sam, "what a pleasant chap he is!"

"Ain't he?" replied Mr. Muzzle.

"So much humour," said Sam.

"And such a man to speak," said Mr. Muzzle. "How his ideas flow, don't they?"

"Wonderful," replied Sam; "they comes a pouring out, knocking each other's heads so fast, that they seems to stun one another; you hardly know what he's arter, do you?"

"That's the great merit of his style of speaking," rejoined Mr. Muzzle. "Take care of the last step, Mr. Weller. Would you like to wash your hands, Sir, before we join the ladies? Here's a sink, with the water laid on, Sir, and a clean jack towel behind the door."

"Ah, perhaps I may as vell have a rinse," replied Mr. Weller, applying plenty of yellow soap to the towel, and rubbing away, till his face shone again. "How many ladies are there?"

"Only two in our kitchen," said Mr. Muzzle, "cook and 'ousemaid. We keep a boy to do the dirty work, and a gal besides, but they dine in the washus."

"Oh, they dines in the washus, do they?" said Mr. Weller.

"Yes," replied Mr. Muzzle, "we tried 'em at our table when they first come, but we couldn't keep 'em. The gal's manners is dreadful vulgar; and the boy breathes so very hard while he's eating, that we found it impossible to sit at table with him."

"What a young grampus!" said Mr. Weller.

"Oh, dreadful," rejoined Mr. Muzzle; "but that is the worst of country service, Mr. Weller; the juniors is always so very savage. This way, Sir, if you please—this way."

And preceding Mr. Weller, with the utmost politeness, Mr. Muzzle conducted him into the kitchen.

"Mary," said Mr. Muzzle to the pretty servant-girl, "this is Mr. Weller, a gentleman as master has sent down, to be made as comfortable as possible."

"And your master's a knowin' hand—and has just sent me to the right place," said Mr. Weller, with a glance of admiration at Mary. "If I was master o' this here house, I should alvays find the materials for comfort vere Mary vas."

"Lor, Mr. Weller!" said Mary, blushing.

"Well, I never!" ejaculated the cook.

"Bless me, cook, I forgot you," said Mr. Muzzle. "Mr. Weller, let me introduce you."

"How are you, Ma'am?" said Mr. Weller. "Wery glad to see you, indeed; and hope our acquaintance may be a long 'un, as the gen'lm'n said to the fi' pun' note."

When this ceremony of introduction had been gone through, the cook and Mary retired into the back kitchen to titter for ten minutes; and then returning, all giggles and blushes, they sat down to dinner.

Mr. Weller's easy manner and conversational powers had such irresistible influence with his new friends, that before the dinner was half over, they were on a footing of perfect intimacy, and in possession of a full account of the delinquency of Job Trotter.

"I never could a-bear that Job," said Mary.

"No more you never ought to, my dear," replied Mr. Weller.

"Why not?" inquired Mary.

"Cos ugliness and svindlin' never ought to be formiliar vith elegance and wirtew," replied Mr. Weller. "Ought they, Mr. Muzzle?"

"Not by no means," replied that gentleman.

Here Mary laughed, and said the cook had made her; and the cook laughed, and said she hadn't.

"I han't got a glass," said Mary.

"Drink vith me, my dear," said Mr. Weller. "Put your lips to this here tumbler, and then I can kiss you by deputy."

"For shame, Mr. Weller," said Mary.

"What's a shame, my dear?"

"Talkin' in that way."

"Nonsense; it ain't no harm. It's natur; ain't it, cook?"

"Don't ask me, imperence," replied the cook, in a high state of delight: and hereupon the cook and Mary laughed again, till what between the beer, and the cold meat, and the laughter combined, the latter young lady was brought to the verge of choaking—an alarming crisis from which she was only recovered by sundry pats on the back, and other necessary attentions, most delicately administered by Mr. Samuel Weller.

In the midst of all this jollity and conviviality, a loud ring was heard at the garden-gate, to which the young gentleman who took his meals in the wash-house, immediately responded. Mr. Weller was in the height of his attentions to the pretty housemaid; Mr. Muzzle was busy doing the honours of the table; and the cook had just paused to laugh, in the very act of raising a huge morsel to her lips, when the kitchen-door opened, and in walked Mr. Job Trotter.

We have said in walked Mr. Job Trotter, but the statement is not distinguished by our usual scrupulous adherence to fact. The door opened, and Mr. Trotter appeared. He *would* have walked in, and was in the very act of doing so indeed, when catching sight of Mr. Weller, he involuntarily shrunk back a pace or two, and stood gazing on the unexpected scene before him, perfectly motionless with amazement and terror.

"Here he is," said Sam, rising with great glee. "Why we were that wery moment a speaking o' you. How are you? Vere *have* you been? Come in."

And laying his hand on the mulberry collar of the unresisting Job, Mr. Weller dragged him into the kitchen; and locking the door, handed the key to Mr. Muzzle, who very coolly buttoned it up, in a side-pocket.

"Well, here's a game," cried Sam. "Only think o' my master havin' the pleasure o' meeting your'n, up stairs, and me havin' the joy o' meetin' you down here. How *are* you gettin' on, and how *is* the chandlery bis'ness likely to do? Vell, I am so glad to see you. How happy you look. It's quite a treat to see you, ain't it, Mr. Muzzle?"

"Quite," said Mr. Muzzle.

"So cheerful he is," said Sam.

"In such good spirits," said Muzzle.

"And so glad to see *us*—that makes it so much more comfortable," said Sam. "Sit down; sit down."

Mr. Trotter suffered himself to be forced into a chair by the fireside. He cast his small eyes first on Mr. Weller, and then on Mr. Muzzle, but said nothing.

"Well, now," said Sam, "afore these here ladies, I should just like to ask you, as a sort of curiosity, vether you don't con-sider yourself as nice and vell-behaved a young gen'lm'n as ever used a pink check pocket-handkerchief, and the number four collection?"

"And as was ever a-going to be married to a cook," said that lady, indignantly, "The willin!"

"And leave off his evil ways, and set up in the chandlery line, arterwards," said the housemaid.

"Now, I'll tell you what it is, young man," said Mr. Muzzle, solemnly, enraged at the last two allusions, "this here lady (pointing to the cook) keeps company with me; and when you presume, Sir, to talk of keeping chandlers' shops with her, you injure me in one of the most delicatest points in which one man can injure another. Do you understand that, Sir?"

Here Mr. Muzzle, who had a great notion of his eloquence, in which he imitated his master, paused for a reply. But Mr. Trotter made no reply. So Mr. Muzzle proceeded in a solemn manner—

"It's very probable, Sir, that you won't be wanted up stairs for several minutes, Sir, because *my* master is at this moment particularly engaged in settling the hash of *your* master, Sir; and therefore you'll have leisure, Sir, for a little private talk with me, Sir. Do you understand *that*, Sir?"

Mr. Muzzle again paused for a reply; and again Mr. Trotter disappointed him.

"Well, then," said Mr. Muzzle. "I'm very sorry to have to explain myself before the ladies, but the urgency of the case will be my excuse. The back kitchen's empty, Sir; if you will step in there, Sir, Mr. Weller will see fair, and we can have mutual satisfaction 'till the bell rings. Follow me, Sir."

As Mr Muzzle uttered these words, he took a step or two towards the door; and by way of saving time, began to pull off his coat as he walked along.

Now the cook no sooner heard the concluding words of this desperate challenge, and saw Mr. Muzzle about to put it into execution, than she uttered a loud and piercing shriek; and rushing on Mr. Job Trotter, who rose from his chair on the instant, tore and buffeted his large flat face, with an energy peculiar to excited females, and twining her hands in his long black hair, tore therefrom about enough to make five or six dozen of the very largest-sized mourning-rings. Having accomplished this feat with all the ardour which her devoted love for Mr. Muzzle inspired, she staggered back; and being a lady of very excitable and delicate feelings, instantly fell under the dresser, and fainted away.

At this moment, the bell rang.

"That's for you, Job Trotter," said Sam; and before Mr. Trotter could offer remonstrance or reply—even before he had time to stanch the wounds inflicted by the insensible lady—Sam seized one arm and Mr. Muzzle the other; and one pulling before, and the other pushing behind, they conveyed him up stairs, and into the parlour.

It was an impressive tableau. Alfred Jingle, Esquire, alias Captain Fitz-Marshall, was standing near the door with his hat in his hand, and a smile on his face, wholly unmoved by his very unpleasant situation. Confronting him, stood Mr. Pickwick, who had evidently been inculcating some high moral lesson, for his left hand was beneath his coat tail, and his right extended in air, as was his wont when delivering himself of an impressive address. At a little distance stood Mr. Tupman with indignant countenance, carefully held back by his two younger friends; and at the further end of the room were Mr. Nupkins, Mrs. Nupkins, and Miss Nupkins, gloomily grand, and savagely vexed.

"What prevents me," said Mr. Nupkins, with magisterial dignity, as Job was brought in—"what prevents me from detaining these men as rogues and impostors? It is a foolish mercy. What prevents me?"

"Pride, old fellow, pride," replied Jingle, quite at his ease. "Wouldn't do—no go—caught a captain, eh?—ha! ha! very good—husband for daughter—biter bit—make it public—not for worlds—look stupid—very!"

"Wretch," said Mrs. Nupkins, "we scorn your base insinuations."

"I always hated him," added Henrietta.

"Oh, of course," said Jingle. "Tall young man—old lover—Sidney Porkenham—rich—fine fellow—not so rich as captain, though, eh?—turn him away—off with him—anything for captain—nothing like captain anywhere—all the girls—raving mad—eh, Job, eh?"

Here Mr. Jingle laughed very heartily; and Job, rubbing his hands with delight, uttered the first sound he had given vent to, since he entered the house—a low noiseless chuckle, which seemed to intimate that he enjoyed his laugh too much, to let any of it escape in sound.

"Mr. Nupkins," said the elder lady, "this is not a fit conversation for the servants to overhear. Let these wretches be removed."

"Certainly, my dear," said Mr. Nupkins. "Muzzle."

"Your worship."

"Open the front door."

"Yes, your worship."

"Leave the house," said Mr. Nupkins, waving his hand emphatically.

Jingle smiled, and moved towards the door.

ALFRED JINGLE.

"Stay," said Mr. Pickwick.

Jingle stopped.

"I might," said Mr. Pickwick, "have taken a much greater revenge for the treatment I have experienced at your hands, and that of your hypocritical friend there."

Here Job Trotter bowed with great politeness, and laid his hand upon his heart.

"I say," said Mr. Pickwick, growing gradually angry, "that I might have taken a greater revenge, but I content myself with exposing you, which I consider a duty I owe to society. This is a leniency, Sir, which I hope you will remember."

When Mr. Pickwick arrived at this point, Job Trotter, with facetious gravity, applied his hand to his ear, as if desirous not to lose a syllable he uttered.

"And I have only to add, Sir," said Mr. Pickwick, now thoroughly angry, "that I consider you a rascal, and a—a ruffian—and—and worse than any man I ever saw, or heard of, except that very pious and sanctified vagabond in the mulberry livery."

"Ha! ha!" said Jingle, "good fellow Pickwick—fine heart—stout old boy—but must *not* be passionate—bad thing, very—bye, bye—see you again some day—keep up your spirits—now Job—trot."

With these words, Mr. Jingle stuck on his hat in his old fashion, and strode out of the room. Job Trotter paused, looked round, smiled, and then with a bow of mock solemnity to Mr. Pickwick, and a wink to Mr. Weller, the audacious slyness of which, baffles all description, followed the footsteps of his hopeful master.

"Sam," said Mr. Pickwick, as Mr. Weller was following.

"Sir."

"Stay here."

Mr. Weller seemed uncertain.

"Stay here," repeated Mr. Pickwick.

"Mayn't I polish that ere Job off, in the front garden?" said Mr. Weller.

"Certainly not," replied Mr. Pickwick.

"Mayn't I kick him out o' the gate, Sir?" said Mr. Weller.

"Not on any account," replied his master.

For the first time since his engagement, Mr. Weller looked, for a moment, discontented and unhappy. But his countenance immediately cleared up, for the wily Mr. Muzzle, by concealing himself behind the street door, and rushing violently out, at the right instant, contrived with great dexterity to overturn both Mr. Jingle and his attendant, down the flight of steps, into the American aloe tubs that stood beneath.

"Having discharged my duty, Sir," said Mr. Pickwick to Mr. Nupkins, "I will, with my friends, bid you farewell. While we thank you for such hospitality as we have received, permit me to assure you in our joint names that we should not have accepted it, or consented to extricate ourselves in this way, from our previous dilemma, had we not been impelled by a strong sense of duty. We return to London to-morrow. Your secret is safe with us."

Having thus entered his protest against their treatment of the morning, Mr. Pickwick bowed low to the ladies; and notwithstanding the solicitations of the family, left the room with his friends.

"Get your hat, Sam," said Mr. Pickwick.

"It's below stairs, Sir," said Sam, and he ran down after it.

Now there was nobody in the kitchen, but the pretty housemaid; and as Sam's hat was mislaid, he had to look for it, and the pretty housemaid lighted him. They had to look all over the place for the hat; and the pretty housemaid, in her anxiety to find it, went down on her knees, and turned over all the things that were heaped together in a little corner by the door. It was an awkward corner. You couldn't get at it without shutting the door first.

"Here it is," said the pretty housemaid. "This is it, ain't it?"

"Let me look," said Sam.

The pretty housemaid had stood the candle on the floor; and as it gave a very dim light, Sam was obliged to go down on *his* knees before he could see whether it really was his own hat or not. It was a remarkably small corner, and so—it was nobody's fault but the man's who built the house—Sam and the pretty housemaid were necessarily very close together.

"Yes, this is it," said Sam. "Good bye."

"Good bye," said the pretty housemaid.

"Good bye," said Sam; and as he said it, he dropped the hat that had cost so much trouble looking for.

"How awkward you are," said the pretty housemaid. "You'll lose it again, if you don't take care."

So just to prevent his losing it again, she put it on for him.

Whether it was that the pretty housemaid's face looked prettier still, when it was raised towards Sam's, or whether it was the accidental consequence of their being so near each other, is matter of uncertainty to this day, but Sam kissed her.

"You don't mean to say you did that on purpose," said the pretty housemaid, blushing.

"No, I didn't then," said Sam; "but I will now."

So he kissed her again.

"Sam," said Mr. Pickwick, calling over the bannisters.

"Coming, Sir," replied Sam, running up stairs.

"How long you have been," said Mr. Pickwick.

"There was something behind the door, Sir, which prevented our getting it open, for ever so long," replied Sam.

And this was the first passage of Mr. Weller's first love.

CHAPTER XXVI.

WHICH CONTAINS A BRIEF ACCOUNT OF THE PROGRESS OF THE ACTION OF BARDELL AGAINST PICKWICK.

HAVING accomplished the main end and object of his journey by the exposure of Jingle, Mr. Pickwick resolved on immediately returning to London, with the view of becoming acquainted with the proceedings which had been taken against him, in the mean time, by Messrs. Dodson and Fogg. Acting upon this resolution with all the energy and decision of his character, he mounted to the back seat of the first coach, which left Ipswich on the morning after the memorable occurrences detailed at length in the two preceding chapters; and accompanied by his three friends and Mr. Samuel Weller, arrived in the metropolis in perfect health and safety, the same evening.

Here the friends for a short time separated. Messrs. Tupman, Winkle, and Snodgrass, repaired to their several homes to make such preparations as might be requisite for their forthcoming visit to Dingley Dell; and Mr. Pickwick and Sam took up their present abode in very good, old-fashioned, and comfortable quarters, to wit, the George and Vulture Tavern and Hotel, George Yard, Lombard Street.

Mr. Pickwick had dined, finished his second pint of particular port, pulled his silk handkerchief over his head, put his feet on the fender, and thrown himself back in an easy chair, when the entrance of Mr. Weller with his carpet bag, aroused him from his tranquil meditations.

"Sam," said Mr. Pickwick.

"Sir," said Mr. Weller.

"I have just been thinking, Sam," said Mr. Pickwick, "that having left a good many things at Mrs. Bardell's, in Goswell Street, I ought to arrange for taking them away, before I leave town again."

"Wery good, Sir," replied Mr. Weller.

"I could send them to Mr. Tupman's for the present, Sam," continued Mr. Pickwick, "but, before we take them away, it is necessary that they should be looked up, and put together. I wish you would step up to Goswell Street, Sam, and arrange about it."

"At once, Sir?" inquired Mr. Weller.

"At once," replied Mr. Pickwick. "And stay, Sam," added Mr. Pickwick, pulling out his purse, "there is some rent to pay. The quarter is not due till Christmas, but you may pay it, and have done with it. A month's notice terminates my tenancy. Here it is, written out. Give it, and tell Mrs. Bardell she may put a bill up, as soon as she likes."

"Wery good, Sir," replied Mr. Weller; "anythin' more, Sir?"

"Nothing more, Sam."

Mr. Weller stepped slowly to the door, as if he expected something further; slowly opened it, slowly stepped out, and had slowly closed it within a couple of inches, when Mr. Pickwick called out—

"Sam."

"Yes, Sir," said Mr. Weller, stepping quickly back, and closing the door behind him.

"I have no objection, Sam, to your endeavouring to ascertain how Mrs. Bardell herself, seems disposed towards me, and whether it is really probable that this vile and groundless action is to be carried to extremity. I say I do not object to your doing this, if you wish it, Sam," said Mr. Pickwick.

Sam gave a short nod of intelligence, and left the room. Mr. Pickwick drew the silk handkerchief once more over his head, and composed himself for a nap; Mr. Weller promptly walked forth, to execute his commission.

It was nearly nine o'clock when he reached Goswell Street. A couple of candles were burning in the little front parlour, and a couple of caps were reflected on the window-blind. Mrs. Bardell had got company.

Mr. Weller knocked at the door, and after a pretty long interval—occupied by the party without, in whistling a tune, and by the party within, in persuading a refractory flat candle to allow itself to be lighted—a pair of small boots pattered over the floor-cloth, and Master Bardell presented himself.

"Vell, young townskip," said Sam, "how's mother?"

"She's pretty well," replied Master Bardell, "so am I."

"Vell, that's a mercy," said Sam; "tell her I want to speak to her, my hinfant fernomenon."

Master Bardell, thus adjured, placed the refractory flat candle on the bottom stair, and vanished into the front parlour with his message.

The two caps reflected on the window-blind, were the respective head-dresses of a couple of Mrs. Bardell's most

particular acquaintance, who had just stepped in, to have a quiet cup of tea, and a little warm supper of a couple of sets of pettitoes and some toasted cheese. The cheese was simmering and browning away, most delightfully, in a little Dutch oven before the fire, and the pettitoes were getting on deliciously in a little tin saucepan on the hob; and Mrs. Bardell and her two friends were getting on very well, also, in a little quiet conversation about and concerning all their particular friends and acquaintance, when Master Bardell came back from answering the door, and delivered the message entrusted to him by Mr. Samuel Weller.

"Mr. Pickwick's servant!" said Mrs. Bardell, turning pale.

"Bless my soul!" said Mrs. Cluppins.

"Well, I raly would *not* ha' believed it, unless I had ha' happened to ha' been here!" said Mrs. Sanders.

Mrs. Cluppins was a little brisk, busy-looking woman, and Mrs. Sanders was a big, fat, heavy-faced personage; and the two were the company.

Mrs. Bardell felt it proper to be agitated; and as none of the three exactly knew whether, under existing circumstances, any communication, otherwise than through Dodson and Fogg, ought to be held with Mr. Pickwick's servant, they were all rather taken by surprise. In this state of indecision, obviously the first thing to be done, was to thump the boy for finding Mr. Weller at the door. So his mother thumped him, and he cried melodiously.

"Hold your noise—do—you naughty creetur," said Mrs. Bardell.

"Yes; don't worrit your poor mother," said Mrs. Sanders.

"She's quite enough to worrit her, as it is, without you, Tommy," said Mrs. Cluppins, with sympathising resignation.

"Ah! worse luck, poor lamb!" said Mrs. Sanders.

At all which moral reflections, Master Bardell howled the louder.

"Now, what *shall* I do?" said Mrs. Bardell to Mrs. Cluppins.

"*I* think you ought to see him," replied Mrs. Cluppins. "But on no account without a witness."

"*I* think two witnesses would be more lawful," said Mrs. Sanders, who, like the other friend, was bursting with curiosity.

"Perhaps, he'd better come in here," said Mrs. Bardell.

"To be sure," replied Mrs. Cluppins, eagerly catching at the idea—"Walk in, young man; and shut the street door first, please."

Mr. Weller immediately took the hint; and presenting himself in the parlour, explained his business to Mrs. Bardell, thus—

"Wery sorry to 'casion any personal inconwenience, Ma'am, as the housebreaker said to the old lady when he put her on the fire; but as me and my governor's only just come to town, and is just going away agin, it can't be helped you see."

"Of course, the young man can't help the faults of his master," said Mrs. Cluppins, much struck by Mr. Weller's appearance and conversation.

"Certainly not," chimed in Mrs. Sanders, who, from certain wistful glances at the little tin saucepan, seemed to be engaged in a mental calculation of the probable extent of the pettitoes, in the event of Sam's being asked to stop supper.

"So all I've come about, is just this here," said Sam, disregarding the interruption—"First, to give my governor's notice—there it is. Secondly, to pay the rent—here it is. Thirdly, to say as all his things is to be put together, and given to any body as we sends for 'em. Fourthly, that you may let the place as soon as you like—and that's all."

"Whatever has happened," said Mrs. Bardell, "I always have said and always will say, that in every respect but one, Mr. Pickwick has always behaved himself like a perfect gentleman. His money always was as good as the bank—always."

As Mrs. Bardell said this, she applied her handkerchief to her eyes, and went out of the room to get the receipt.

Sam well knew that he had only to remain quiet, and the women were sure to talk, so he looked alternately at the tin saucepan, the toasted cheese, the wall, and the ceiling, in profound silence.

"Poor dear!" said Mrs. Cluppins.

"Ah, poor thing!" replied Mrs. Sanders.

Sam said nothing. He saw they were coming to the subject.

"I raly cannot contain myself," said Mrs. Cluppins, "when I think of such perjury. I don't wish to say anything to make you uncomfortable, young man, but your master's an old brute, and I wish I had him here to tell him so."

"I vish you had," said Sam.

"To see how dreadful she takes on, going moping about, and taking no pleasure in nothing, except when her friends comes in, out of charity, to sit with her, and make her comfortable," resumed Mrs. Cluppins, glancing at the tin saucepan and the Dutch oven, "it's shocking."

"Barbareous," said Mrs. Sanders.

"And your master, young man, a gentleman with money, as could never feel the expense of a wife, no more than nothing," continued Mrs. Cluppins, with great volubility; "why there ain't the faintest shade of an excuse for his behaviour. Why don't he marry her?"

"Ah," said Sam, "to be sure; that's the question."

"Question, indeed," retorted Mrs. Cluppins; "she'd question him, if she'd my spirit. Hows'ever, there *is* law for us women, mis'rable creeturs as they'd make us, if they could; and that your master will find out, young man, to his cost, afore he's six months older."

At this consolatory reflection, Mrs. Cluppins bridled up, and smiled at Mrs. Sanders, who smiled back again.

"The action's going on, and no mistake," thought Sam, as Mrs. Bardell re-entered with the receipt.

"Here's the receipt, Mr. Weller," said Mrs. Bardell, "and here's the change, and I hope you'll take a little drop of something to keep the cold out, if it's only for old acquaintance' sake, Mr. Weller."

Sam saw the advantage he should gain, and at once acquiesced, whereupon Mrs. Bardell produced from a small closet a black bottle and a wine glass, and so great was her abstraction in her deep mental affliction, that, after filling Mr. Weller's glass, she brought out three more wine glasses, and filled them too.

"Lauk, Mrs. Bardell," said Mrs. Cluppins, "see what you've been and done."

"Well, that is a good one!" ejaculated Mrs. Sanders.

"Ah, my poor head!" said Mrs. Bardell, with a faint smile.

Sam understood all this, of course, so he said at once, that he never could drink before supper, unless a lady drank with him. A great deal of laughing ensued, and then Mrs. Sanders volunteered to humour him, so she took a slight sip out of her glass. Then Sam said it must go all round, so they all took a slight sip. Then little Mrs.

Cluppins proposed as a toast, "Success to Bardell against Pickwick;" and then the ladies emptied their glasses in honour of the sentiment, and got very talkative directly.

"I suppose you've heard what's going forward, Mr. Weller?" said Mrs. Bardell.

"I've heerd somethin' on it," replied Sam.

"It's a terrible thing to be dragged before the public, in that way, Mr. Weller," said Mrs. Bardell; "but I see now, that it's the only thing I ought to do, and my lawyers, Mr. Dodson and Fogg, tell me that, with the evidence as we shall call, we must succeed. I don't know what I should do, Mr. Weller, if I didn't."

The mere idea of Mrs. Bardell's failing in her action, affected Mrs. Sanders so deeply, that she was under the necessity of re-filling and re-emptying her glass immediately; feeling, as she said afterwards, that if she hadn't had the presence of mind to have done so, she must have dropped.

"Ven is it expected to come on?" inquired Sam.

"Either in February or March," replied Mrs. Bardell.

"What a number of witnesses there'll be, won't there?" said Mrs. Cluppins.

"Ah, won't there!" replied Mrs. Sanders.

"And won't Mr. Dodson and Fogg be wild if the plaintiff shouldn't get it?" added Mrs. Cluppins, "when they do it all on speculation!"

"Ah! won't they!" said Mrs. Sanders.

"But the plaintiff must get it," resumed Mrs. Cluppins.

"I hope so," said Mrs. Bardell.

"Oh, there can't be any doubt about it," rejoined Mrs. Sanders.

"Vell," said Sam, rising and setting down his glass. "All I can say is, that I vish you *may* get it."

"Thanke'e, Mr. Weller," said Mrs. Bardell, fervently.

"And of them Dodson and Fogg, as does these sort o' things on spec," continued Mr Weller, "as vell as for the other kind and gen'rous people o' the same purfession, as sets people by the ears free gratis for nothin', and sets their clerks to work to find out little disputes among their neighbours and acquaintance as vants settlin' by means o' law suits—all I can say o' them is, that I vish they had the revard I'd give 'em."

"Ah, I wish they had the reward that every kind and generous heart would be inclined to bestow upon them," said the gratified Mrs. Bardell.

"Amen to that," replied Sam, "and a fat and happy livin' they'd get out of it. Vish you good night, ladies."

To the great relief of Mrs. Sanders, Sam was allowed to depart, without any reference on the part of the hostess to the pettitoes and toasted cheese, to which the ladies, with such juvenile assistance as Master Bardell could afford, soon afterwards rendered the amplest justice—indeed they wholly vanished, before their strenuous exertions.

Mr. Weller wended his way back to the George and Vulture, and faithfully recounted to his master, such indications of the sharp practice of Dodson and Fogg, as he had contrived to pick up in his visit to Mrs. Bardell's. An interview with Mr. Perker next day, more than confirmed Mr. Weller's statement; and Mr. Pickwick was fain to prepare for his Christmas visit to Dingley Bell, with the pleasant anticipation that some two or three months afterwards, an action brought against him for damages sustained by reason of a breach of promise of marriage, would be publicly tried in the Court of Common Pleas; the plaintiff having all the advantages derivable not only from the force of circumstances, but from the sharp practice of Dodson and Fogg to boot.

CHAPTER XXVII.

SAMUEL WELLER MAKES A PILGRIMAGE TO DORKING, AND BEHOLDS HIS MOTHER-IN-LAW.

THERE still remaining an interval of two days, before the time agreed upon, for the departure of the Pickwickians to Dingley Dell, Mr. Weller sat himself down in a back room at the George and Vulture, after eating an early dinner, to muse on the best way of disposing of his time. It was a remarkably fine day; and he had not turned the matter over in his mind ten minutes, when he was suddenly struck filial and affectionate; and it occurred to him so strongly that he ought to go down to see his father, and pay his duty to his mother-in-law, that he was lost in astonishment at his own remissness in never thinking of this moral obligation before. Anxious to atone for his past neglect without another hour's delay, he straightway walked up stairs to Mr. Pickwick, and requested leave of absence for this laudable purpose.

"Certainly, Sam, certainly," said Mr. Pickwick, his eyes glistening with delight at this manifestation of good feeling, on the part of his attendant; "certainly, Sam."

Mr. Weller made a grateful bow.

"I am very glad to see that you have so high a sense of your duties as a son, Sam," said Mr. Pickwick.

"I always had, Sir," replied Mr. Weller.

"That's a very gratifying reflection, Sam," said Mr. Pickwick, approvingly.

"Wery, Sir," replied Mr. Weller; "if ever I vanted anythin' o' my father, I always asked for it in a wery 'spectful and obligin' manner. If he didn't give it me, I took it, for fear I should be led to do anythin' wrong, through not havin' it. I saved him a world o' trouble this vay, Sir."

"That's not precisely what I meant, Sam," said Mr. Pickwick, shaking his head, with a slight smile.

"All good feelin', Sir—the wery best intentions, as the gen'lm'n said ven he run away from his wife, 'cos she seemed unhappy with him," replied Mr. Weller.

"You may go, Sam," said Mr. Pickwick.

"Thank'ee, Sir," replied Mr. Weller; and having made his best bow, and put on his best clothes, Sam planted himself on the top of the Arundel coach, and journeyed on to Dorking.

The Marquis of Granby, in Mrs. Weller's time, was quite a model of a road-side public-house of the better class—just large enough to be convenient, and small enough to be snug. On the opposite side of the road was a large signboard on a high post, representing the head and shoulders of a gentleman with an apoplectic countenance, in a red coat, with deep blue facings, and a touch of the same over his three-cornered hat, for a sky. Over that again, were a pair of flags, and beneath the last button of his coat were a couple of cannon; and the whole formed an expressive and undoubted likeness of the Marquis of Granby of glorious memory. The bar window displayed a choice collection of geranium plants, and a well-dusted row of spirit phials. The open shutters bore a variety of golden inscriptions, eulogistic of good beds and neat wines; and the choice group of countrymen and hostlers lounging about the stable-door and horse-trough, afforded presumptive proof of the excellent quality of the ale and spirits which were sold within. Sam Weller paused, when he dismounted from the coach, to note all these little indications of a thriving business, with the eye of an experienced traveller; and having done so, stepped in at once, highly satisfied with everything he had observed.

"Now, then," said a shrill female voice, the instant Sam thrust in his head at the door, "what do you want, young man?"

Sam looked round in the direction whence the voice proceeded. It came from a rather stout lady of comfortable appearance, who was seated beside the fire-place in the bar, blowing the fire to make the kettle boil for tea. She was not alone, for on the other side of the fire-place, sitting bolt upright in a high-backed chair, was a man in threadbare black clothes, with a back almost as long and stiff as that of the chair itself, who caught Sam's most particular and especial attention at once.

He was a prim-faced, red-nosed man, with a long thin countenance, and a semi-rattlesnake sort of eye—rather sharp, but decidedly bad. He wore very short trousers, and black-cotton stockings, which, like the rest of his apparel, were particularly rusty. His looks were starched, but his white neckerchief was not; and its long limp ends straggled over his closely-buttoned waistcoat in a very uncouth and unpicturesque fashion. A pair of old, worn, beaver gloves, a broad-brimmed hat, and a faded green umbrella, with plenty of whalebone sticking through the bottom, as if to counterbalance the want of a handle at the top, lay on a chair beside him; and being disposed in a very tidy and careful manner, seemed to imply that the red-nosed man, whoever he was, had no intention of going away in a hurry.

To do the red-nosed man justice, he would have been very far from wise if he had entertained any such intention, for, to judge from all appearances, he must have been possessed of a most desirable circle of acquaintance, if he could have reasonably expected to be more comfortable anywhere else. The fire was blazing brightly, under the influence of the bellows, and the kettle was singing gaily, under the influence of both. A small tray of tea-things was arranged on the table; a plate of hot buttered toast was gently simmering before the fire; and the red-nosed man himself was busily engaged in converting a large slice of bread, into the same agreeable edible, through the instrumentality of a long brass toasting-fork. Beside him, stood a glass of reeking hot pine-apple rum and water, with a slice of lemon in it: and every time the red-nosed man stopped to bring the round of bread to his eye, with the view of ascertaining how it got on, he imbibed a drop or two of the hot pine-apple rum and water, and smiled upon the rather stout lady, as she blew the fire.

Sam was so lost in the contemplation of this comfortable scene, that he suffered the first inquiry of the rather stout lady to pass wholly unheeded. It was not until it had been twice repeated, each time in a shriller tone, that he became conscious of the impropriety of his behaviour.

"Governor in?" inquired Sam, in reply to the question.

"No, he isn't," replied Mrs. Weller, for the rather stout lady was no other than the quondam relict and sole executrix of the dead-and-gone Mr. Clarke;—"No, he isn't, and I don't expect him, either."

"I suppose he's a drivin' up to-day?" said Sam.

"He may be, or he may not," replied Mrs. Weller, buttering the round of toast which the red-nosed man had just finished; "I don't know, and, what's more, I don't care. Ask a blessin', Mr. Stiggins."

The red-nosed man did as he was desired, and instantly commenced on the toast with fierce voracity.

The appearance of the red-nosed man had induced Sam, at first sight, to more than half suspect that he was the deputy shepherd, of whom his estimable parent had spoken. The moment he saw him eat, all doubt on the subject was removed, and he perceived at once that if he proposed to take up his temporary quarters where he was, he must make his footing good without delay. He therefore commenced proceedings by putting his arm over the half-door of the bar, coolly unbolting it, and leisurely walking in.

"Mother-in-law," said Sam, "how are you?"

"Why, I do believe he is a Weller," said Mrs. W., raising her eyes to Sam's face, with no very gratified expression of countenance.

"I rayther think he is," said the imperturbable Sam; "and I hope this here reverend gen'lm'n 'll excuse me saying that I wish I was *the* Weller as owns you, mother-in-law."

This was a double-barrelled compliment: it implied that Mrs. Weller was a most agreeable female, and also that Mr. Stiggins had a clerical appearance. It made a visible impression at once; and Sam followed up his advantage by kissing his mother-in-law.

"Get along with you," said Mrs. Weller, pushing him away.

"For shame, young man," said the gentleman with the red nose.

"No offence, Sir, no offence," replied Sam; "you're wery right, though; it ain't the right sort o' thing, ven mothers-in-law is young and good looking, is it, Sir?"

"It's all vanity," said Mr. Stiggins.

"Ah, so it is," said Mrs. Weller, setting her cap to rights.

Sam thought it was, too, but he held his peace.

The deputy shepherd seemed by no means best pleased with Sam's arrival; and when the first effervescence of the compliment had subsided, even Mrs. Weller looked as if she could have spared him without the smallest inconvenience. However, there he was; and as he couldn't be decently turned out, they all three sat down to tea.

"And how's father?" said Sam.

At this inquiry, Mrs. Weller raised her hands and turned up her eyes, as if the subject were too painful to be alluded to. Mr. Stiggins groaned.

"What's the matter with that 'ere gen'lm'n?" inquired Sam.

"He's shocked at the way your father goes on, in—" replied Mrs. Weller.

"Oh, he is, is he?" said Sam.

"And with too good reason," added Mrs. Weller, gravely. Mr. Stiggins took up a fresh piece of toast, and groaned heavily.

"He is a dreadful reprobate," said Mrs. Weller.

"A man of wrath!" exclaimed Mr. Stiggins. And he took a large semi-circular bite out of the toast, and groaned again.

Sam felt very strongly disposed to give the reverend Mr. Stiggins something to groan for, but he repressed his inclination, and merely asked, "What's the old 'un up to, now?"

"Up to, indeed!" said Mrs. Weller, "oh, he has a hard heart. Night after night does this excellent man—don't frown, Mr. Stiggins, I will say you *are* an excellent man —come and sit here, for hours together, and it has not the least effect upon him."

"Well, that is odd," said Sam; "it 'ud have a wery considerable effect upon me, if I wos in his place, I know that."

"The fact is, my young friend," said Mr. Stiggins, solemnly, "he has an obderrate bosom. Oh, my young friend, who else could have resisted the pleading of sixteen of our fairest sisters, and withstood their exhortations to subscribe to our noble society for providing the infant negroes in the West Indies with flannel waistcoats and moral pocket handkerchiefs?"

"What's a moral pocket ankercher?" said Sam; "I never see one o' them articles o' furniter."

"Those which combine amusement with instruction, my young friend," replied Mr. Stiggins, "blending select tales with wood-cuts."

"Oh, I know," said Sam, "them as hangs up in the linen drapers' shops, with beggars' petitions and all that 'ere upon 'em?"

Mr. Stiggins began a third round of toast, and nodded assent.

"And he wouldn't be persuaded by the ladies, wouldn't he?" said Sam.

"Sat and smoked his pipe, and said the infant negroes were—what did he say the infant negroes were?" said Mrs. Weller.

"Little humbugs," replied Mr. Stiggins, deeply affected.

"Said the infant negroes were little humbugs," repeated Mrs. Weller. And they both groaned at the atrocious conduct of the elder Mr. Weller.

A great many more iniquities of a similar nature might have been disclosed, only the toast being all eat, the tea having got very weak, and Sam holding out no indications of meaning to go, Mr. Stiggins suddenly recollected that he had a most pressing appointment with the shepherd, and took himself off accordingly.

The tea-things had been scarcely put away, and the hearth swept up, when the London coach deposited Mr. Weller senior at the door, his legs deposited him in the bar, and his eyes shewed him his son.

"What, Sammy!" exclaimed the father.

"What, old Nobs!" ejaculated the son. And they shook hands heartily.

"Wery glad to see you, Sammy," said the elder Mr. Weller, "though how you've managed to get over your mother-in-law, is a mystery to me. I only vish you'd write me out the receipt, that's all."

"Hush!" said Sam, "she's at home, old feller."

"She ain't vithin hearin'," replied Mr. Weller; "she always goes and blows up, down stairs, for a couple of hours arter tea; so we'll just give ourselves a damp, Sammy."

Saying this, Mr. Weller mixed two glasses of spirits and water, and produced a couple of pipes; and the father and son sitting down opposite each other, Sam on one side the fire, in the high-backed chair, and Mr. Weller senior on the other, in an easy ditto, they proceeded to enjoy themselves with all due gravity.

"Anybody been here, Sammy?" asked Mr. Weller senior, drily, after a long silence.

Sam nodded an expressive assent.

"Red-nosed chap?" inquired Mr. Weller. Sam nodded again.

"Amiable man that 'ere, Sammy," said Mr. Weller, smoking violently.

"Seems so," observed Sam.

"Good hand at accounts," said Mr. Weller.

"Is he?" said Sam.

"Borrows eighteenpence on Monday, and comes on Tuesday for a shillin' to make it up half a crown; calls again on Vensday for another half crown to make it five shillin's, and goes on, doubling, till he gets it up to a five pund note in no time, like them sums in the 'rithmetic book 'bout the nails in the horse's shoes, Sammy."

Sam intimated by a nod that he recollected the problem alluded to by his parent.

"So you vouldn't subscribe to the flannel veskits?" said Sam, after another interval of smoking.

"Cert'nly not," replied Mr. Weller; "what's the good o' flannel veskits to the young niggers abroad? But I'll tell you what it is, Sammy," said Mr. Weller, lowering his voice, and bending across the fire-place, "I'd come down wery handsome towards straight veskits for some people at home."

As Mr. Weller said this, he slowly recovered his former position, and winked at his first-born, in a profound manner.

"It cert'nly seems a queer start to send out pocket ankechers to people as don't know the use on 'em," observed Sam.

"They're alvays a doin' some gammon of that sort, Sammy," replied his father. "T'other Sunday I vas walkin' up the road ven who should I see a standin' at a chapel-door, with a blue soup-plate in her hand, but your mother-in-law. I werily believe there was change for a couple o' suv'rins in it, then, Sammy, all in ha'pence; and as the people come out, they rattled the pennies in, till you'd ha' thought that no mortal plate as ever was baked, could ha' stood the wear and tear. What d'ye think it was all for?"

"For another tea-drinkin', perhaps," said Sam.

"Not a bit on it," replied the father; "for the shepherd's water-rate, Sammy."

"The shepherd's water-rate!" said Sam.

"Ay," replied Mr. Weller, "there was three quarters owin', and the shepherd hadn't paid a farden, not he—perhaps it might be on account that the water warn't o' much use to him, for it's wery little o' that tap he drinks, Sammy, wery; he knows a trick worth a good half dozen of that, he does. Hows'ever, it warn't paid, and so they cuts the water off. Down goes the shepherd to chapel, gives out as he's a persecuted saint, and says he hopes the heart of the turncock as cut the water off, 'll be softened, and turned in the right vay, but he rayther thinks he's booked for somethin' uncomfortable. Upon this, the women calls a meetin', sings a hymn, wotes your mother-in-law into the chair, wolunteers a col-lection next Sunday, and hands it all over to the shepherd. And if he ain't got enough out on 'em, Sammy, to make him free of the water company for life," said Mr. Weller, in conclusion, "I'm one Dutchman, and you're another, and that's all about it."

Mr. Weller smoked for some minutes in silence, and then resumed—

"The worst o' these here shepherds is, my boy, that they reg'larly turns the heads of all the young ladies, about

here. Lord bless their little hearts, they thinks it's all right, and don't know no better; but they're the wictims o' gammon, Samivel, they're the wictims o' gammon."

"I s'pose they are," said Sam.

"Nothin' else," said Mr. Weller, shaking his head gravely; "and wot aggrawates me, Samivel, is to see 'em a wastin' all their time and labour in making clothes for copper-coloured people as don't want 'em, and taking no notice of the flesh-coloured Christians as do. If I'd my vay, Samivel, I'd just stick some o' these here lazy shepherds behind a heavy wheelbarrow, and run 'em up and down a fourteen-inch-wide plank all day. That 'ud shake the nonsense out of 'em, if anythin' vould."

Mr. Weller having delivered this gentle recipe with strong emphasis, eked out by a variety of nods and contortions of the eye, emptied his glass at a draught, and knocked the ashes out of his pipe, with native dignity.

He was engaged in this operation, when a shrill voice was heard in the passage.

"Here's your dear relation, Sammy," said Mr. Weller; and Mrs. W. hurried into the room.

"Oh, you've come back, have you!" said Mrs. Weller.

"Yes, my dear," replied Mr. Weller, filling a fresh pipe.

"Has Mr. Stiggins been back?" said Mrs. Weller.

"No, my dear, he hasn't," replied Mr. Weller, lighting the pipe by the ingenious process of holding to the bowl thereof, between the tongs, a red-hot coal from the adjacent fire; "and what's more, my dear, I shall manage to surwive it, if he don't come back at all."

"Ugh, you wretch," said Mrs. Weller.

"Thank'ee, my love," said Mr Weller.

"Come, come, father," said Sam; "none o' these little lovin's afore strangers. Here's the reverend gen'lm'n a comin' in now."

At this announcement, Mrs. Weller hastily wiped off the tears which she had just begun to force on; and Mr. W. drew his chair sullenly into the chimney corner.

Mr. Stiggins was easily prevailed on, to take another glass of the hot pine-apple rum and water, and a second, and a third, and then to refresh himself with a slight supper, previous to beginning again. He sat on the same side as Mr. Weller senior; and every time he could contrive to do so, unseen by his wife, that gentleman indicated to his son the hidden emotions of his bosom, by shaking his fist over the deputy shepherd's head, a process which afforded his son the most unmingled delight and satisfaction, the more especially as Mr. Stiggins went on, quietly drinking the hot pine-apple rum and water, wholly unconscious of what was going forward.

The major part of the conversation was confined to Mrs. Weller and the reverend Mr. Stiggins; and the topics principally descanted on, were the virtues of the shepherd, the worthiness of his flock, and the high crimes and misdemeanours of everybody beside—dissertations which the elder Mr. Weller occasionally interrupted by half-suppressed references to a gentleman of the name of Walker, and other running commentaries of the same kind.

At length Mr. Stiggins, with several most indubitable symptoms of having quite as much pine-apple rum and water about him, as he could comfortably accommodate, took his hat and his leave; and Sam was, immediately afterwards, shown to bed by his father. The respectable old gentleman wrung his hand fervently, and seemed disposed to address some observations to his son, but on Mrs.

Weller advancing towards him, he appeared to relinquish his intention, and abruptly bade him good night.

Sam was up betimes next day, and having partaken of a hasty breakfast, prepared to return to London. He had scarcely set foot without the house, when his father stood before him.

"Goin', Sammy?" inquired Mr. Weller.

"Off at once," replied Sam.

"I vish you could muffle that 'ere Stiggins, and take him with you," said Mr. Weller.

"I am ashamed o' you, old two-for-his-heels," said Sam, reproachfully, "what do you let him shew his red nose in the Markis o' Granby at all, for?"

Mr. Weller the elder fixed on his son an earnest look, and replied—"'Cause I'm a married man, Samivel, 'cause I'm a married man. Ven you're a married man, Samivel, you'll understand a good many things as you don't understand now; but vether it's worth while goin' through so much, to learn so little; as the charity-boy said ven he got to the end of the alphabet, is a matter o' taste. *I* rayther think it isn't."

"Well," said Sam, "good bye."

"Tar, tar, Sammy," replied his father.

"I've only got to say this here," said Sam, stopping short, "that if *I* was the proprietator o' the Markis o' Granby, and that 'ere Stiggins came and made toast in *my* bar, I'd—"

"What?" interposed Mr. Weller, with great anxiety. "What?"

"—Pison his rum and water," said Sam.

"No!" said Mr. Weller, shaking his son eagerly by the hand, "would you raly, Sammy—would you, though?"

"I would," said Sam. "I wouldn't be too hard upon him, at first: I'd just drop him in the water-butt, and put the lid on; and then if I found he was insensible to kindness, I'd try the other persvasion."

The elder Mr. Weller bestowed a look of deep, unspeakable admiration on his son, and, having once more grasped his hand, walked slowly away, revolving in his mind the numerous reflections to which his advice had given rise.

Sam looked after him, till he turned a corner of the road, and then set forward on his walk to London. He meditated at first on the probable consequences of his own advice, and the likelihood and unlikelihood of his father's adopting it. He dismissed the subject from his mind, however, with the consolatory reflection that time alone would shew; and this is just the reflection we would impress upon the reader.

CHAPTER XXVIII.

A GOOD-HUMOURED CHRISTMAS CHAPTER, CONTAINING AN ACCOUNT OF A WEDDING, AND SOME OTHER SPORTS BESIDE, WHICH ALTHOUGH IN THEIR WAY, EVEN AS GOOD CUSTOMS AS MARRIAGE ITSELF, ARE NOT QUITE SO RELIGIOUSLY KEPT UP, IN THESE DEGENERATE TIMES.

As brisk as bees, if not altogether as light as fairies, did the four Pickwickians assemble on the morning of the twenty-second day of December, in the year of grace in which these, their faithfully-recorded adventures, were undertaken and accomplished. Christmas was close at hand, in all its bluff and hearty honesty; it was the season of hospitality, merriment, and open-heartedness; the old year was preparing, like an ancient philosopher, to call his friends around him, and amidst the sound of feasting and revelry to pass gently and calmly away. Gay and merry was the time; and right gay and merry were at least four of the numerous hearts that were gladdened by its coming.

And numerous indeed are the hearts to which Christmas brings a brief season of happiness and enjoyment. How many families whose members have been dispersed and scattered far and wide, in the restless struggles of life, are then re-united, and meet once again in that happy state of companionship and mutual good-will, which is a source of such pure and unalloyed delight, and one so incompatible with the cares and sorrows of the world, that the religious belief of the most civilised nations, and the rude traditions of the roughest savages, alike number it among the first joys of a future state of existence, provided for the blest and happy! How many old recollections, and how many dormant sympathies, does Christmas time awaken!

We write these words now, many miles distant from the spot at which, year after year, we met on that day, a merry and joyous circle. Many of the hearts that throbbed so gaily then, have ceased to beat; many of the looks that shone so brightly then, have ceased to glow; the hands we grasped, have grown cold; the eyes we sought, have hid their lustre in the grave; and yet the old house, the room, the merry voices and smiling faces, the jest, the laugh, the most minute and trivial circumstance connected with those happy meetings, crowd upon our mind at each recurrence of the season, as if the last assemblage had been but yesterday. Happy, happy Christmas, that can win us back to the delusions of our childish days, that can recall to the old man the pleasures of his youth, and transport the sailor and the traveller, thousands of miles away, back to his own fire-side and his quiet home!

But we are so taken up, and occupied, with the good qualities of Christmas, who, by the way, is quite a country gentleman of the old school, that we are keeping Mr. Pickwick and his friends waiting in the cold, on the outside of the Muggleton coach, which they have just attained, well wrapped up, in great coats, shawls, and comforters. The portmanteaus and carpet-bags have been stowed away, and Mr. Weller and the guard are endeavouring to insinuate into the fore-boot a huge cod-fish several sizes too large for it, which is snugly packed up, in a long brown basket, with a layer of straw over the top, and which has been left to the last, in order that he may repose in safety on the half-dozen barrels of real native oysters, all the property of Mr. Pickwick, which have been arranged in regular order, at the bottom of the receptacle. The interest displayed in Mr Pickwick's countenance is most intense, as Mr. Weller and the guard try to squeeze the cod-fish into the boot, first head first, and then tail first, and then top upwards, and then bottom upwards, and then side-ways, and then long-ways, all of which artifices the implacable cod-fish sturdily resists, until the guard accidentally hits him in the very middle of the basket, whereupon he suddenly disappears into the boot, and with him, the head and shoulders of the guard himself, who, not calculating upon so sudden a cessation of the passive resistance of the cod-fish, experiences a very unexpected shock, to the unsmotherable delight of all the porters and by-standers. Upon this, Mr. Pickwick smiles with great good humour, and drawing a shilling from his waistcoat pocket, begs the guard, as he picks himself out of the boot, to drink his health in a glass of hot brandy and water, at which, the guard smiles too, and Messrs. Snodgrass, Winkle, and Tupman, all smile in company. The guard and Mr. Weller disappear for five minutes, most probably to get the hot brandy and water, for they smell very strongly of it, when they return, the coachman mounts to the box, Mr. Weller jumps up behind, the Pickwickians pull their coats round their legs, and their shawls over their noses; the helpers pull the horse-cloths off, the coachman shouts out a cheery "All right," and away they go.

They have rumbled through the streets, and jolted over the stones, and at length reach the wide and open country. The wheels skim over the hard and frosty ground; and the horses, bursting into a canter at a smart crack of the whip, step along the road as if the load behind them, coach, passengers, cod-fish, oyster barrels, and all, were but a feather at their heels. They have descended a gentle slope, and enter upon a level, as compact and dry as a solid block of marble, two miles long. Another crack of the whip, and on they speed, at a smart gallop, the horses tossing their heads and rattling the harness as if in exhilaration at the rapidity of the motion, while the coachman holding whip and reins in one hand, takes off his hat with the other, and resting it on his knees, pulls out his handkerchief, and wipes his forehead, partly because he has a habit of doing it, and partly because it's as well to shew the passengers how cool he is, and what an easy thing it is to drive four-in-hand, when you have had as much practice as he has. Having done this very leisurely (otherwise the effect would be materially impaired), he replaces his handkerchief, pulls on his hat, adjusts his gloves, squares his elbows, cracks the whip again, and on they speed, more merrily than before.

A few small houses scattered on either side of the road, betoken the entrance to some town or village. The lively notes of the guard's key-bugle vibrate in the clear cold air, and wake up the old gentleman inside, who carefully letting down the window-sash half way, and standing sentry over the air, takes a short peep out, and then carefully pulling it up again, informs the other inside that they're going to change directly; on which the other inside wakes himself up, and determines to postpone his next nap until after the stoppage. Again the bugle sounds lustily forth, and rouses the cottager's wife and children, who peep out at the house-door, and watch the coach till it turns the corner, when they once more crouch round the blazing fire, and throw on another log of wood against father comes home, while father himself, a full mile off, has just exchanged a friendly nod with the coachman, and turned round, to take a good long stare at the vehicle as it whirls away.

And now the bugle plays a lively air as the coach rattles through the ill-paved streets of a country town; and the coachman, undoing the buckle which keeps his ribands together, prepares to throw them off the moment he stops. Mr. Pickwick emerges from his coat collar, and looks about him with great curiosity; perceiving which, the coachman informs Mr. Pickwick of the name of the town, and tells him it was market-day yesterday, both which pieces of information Mr. Pickwick retails to his fellow-passengers, whereupon they emerge from their coat collars too, and look about them also. Mr. Winkle, who sits at the extreme edge, with one leg dangling in the air, is nearly precipitated into the street, as the coach twists round the sharp corner by the cheesemonger's shop, and turns into the market-place; and before Mr. Snodgrass, who sits next to him,

has recovered from his alarm, they pull up at the inn yard, where the fresh horses, with cloths on, are already waiting. The coachman throws down the reins and gets down himself, and the other outside passengers drop down also, except those who have no great confidence in their ability to get up again, and they remain where they are, and stamp their feet against the coach to warm them; looking with longing eyes and red noses at the bright fire in the inn bar, and the sprigs of holly with red berries which ornament the window.

But the guard has delivered at the corn-dealer's shop, the brown paper packet he took out of the little pouch which hangs over his shoulder by a leathern strap, and has seen the horses carefully put to, and has thrown on the pavement the saddle which was brought from London on the coach-roof, and has assisted in the conference between the coachman and the hostler about the grey mare that hurt her off-fore-leg last Tuesday, and he and Mr. Weller are all right behind, and the coachman is all right in front, and the old gentleman inside, who has kept the window down full two inches all this time, has pulled it up again, and the cloths are off, and they are all ready for starting, except the "two stout gentlemen," whom the coachman enquires after with some impatience. Hereupon the coachman, and the guard, and Sam Weller, and Mr. Winkle, and Mr. Snodgrass, and all the hostlers, and every one of the idlers, who are more in number than all the others put together, shout for the missing gentlemen as loud as they can bawl. A distant response is heard from the yard, and Mr. Pickwick and Mr. Tupman come running down it, quite out of breath, for they have been having a glass of ale a-piece, and Mr. Pickwick's fingers are so cold that he has been full five minutes before he could find the sixpence to pay for it. The coachman shouts an admonitory "Now, then, gen'lm'n," the guard re-echoes it—the old gentleman inside, thinks it a very extraordinary thing that people *will* get down when they know there isn't time for it—Mr. Pickwick struggles up on one side, Mr. Tupman on the other, Mr. Winkle cries "All right," and off they start. Shawls are pulled up, coat collars are re-adjusted, the pavement ceases, the houses disappear; and they are once again dashing along the open road, with the fresh clear air blowing in their faces, and gladdening their very hearts within them.

Such was the progress of Mr. Pickwick and his friends by the Muggleton Telegraph, on their way to Dingley Dell; and at three o'clock that afternoon, they all stood, high and dry, safe and sound, hale and hearty, upon the steps of the Blue Lion, having taken on the road quite enough of ale and brandy, to enable them to bid defiance to the frost that was binding up the earth in its iron fetters, and weaving its beautiful net-work upon the trees and hedges. Mr. Pickwick was busily engaged in counting the barrels of oysters, and superintending the disinterment of the cod-fish, when he felt himself gently pulled by the skirts of the coat; and looking round, he discovered that the individual who resorted to this mode of catching his attention, was no other than Mr. Wardle's favourite page, better known to the readers of this unvarnished history by the distinguishing appellation of the fat boy.

"Aha!" said Mr. Pickwick.

"Aha!" said the fat boy.

And as he said it, he glanced from the cod-fish to the oyster barrels, and chuckled joyously. He was fatter than ever.

"Well, you look rosy enough, my young friend," said Mr. Pickwick.

"I've been asleep, right in front of the tap-room fire," replied the fat boy, who had heated himself to the colour of a new chimney-pot, in the course of an hour's nap. "Master sent me over with the chay-cart, to carry your luggage up to the house. He'd ha' sent some saddle horses, but he thought you'd rather walk, being a cold day."

"Yes, yes," said Mr. Pickwick, hastily, for he remembered how they had travelled over nearly the same ground on a previous occasion. "Yes, we would rather walk. Here, Sam."

"Sir," said Mr. Weller.

"Help Mr. Wardle's servant to put the packages into the cart, and then ride on with him. We will walk forward at once."

Having given this direction, and settled with the coachman, Mr. Pickwick and his three friends struck into the footpath across the fields, and walked briskly away, leaving Mr. Weller and the fat boy confronted together for the first time. Sam looked at the fat boy with great astonishment, but without saying a word; and began to stow the things rapidly away in the cart, while the fat boy stood quietly by, and seemed to think it a very interesting sort of thing to see Mr. Weller working by himself.

"There," said Sam, throwing in the last carpet bag. "There they are."

"Yes," said the fat boy, in a very satisfied tone, "there they are."

"Vell, young twenty stun," said Sam, "you're a nice specimen of a prize boy, you are."

"Thankee," said the fat boy.

"You ain't got nothin' on your mind, as makes you fret yourself, have you?" inquired Sam.

"Not as I knows on," replied the boy.

"I should rayther ha' thought, to look at you, that you was a labourin' under an unrequited attachment to some young 'ooman," said Sam.

The fat boy shook his head.

"Vell," said Sam, "I'm glad to hear it. Do you ever drink anythin'?"

"I likes eating, better," replied the boy.

"Ah," said Sam, "I should ha' s'posed that; but what I mean is, should you like a drop of anythin' as'd warm you? but I s'pose you never was cold, with all them elastic fixtures, was you?"

"Sometimes," replied the boy; "and I likes a drop of something, when it's good."

"Oh, you do, do you?" said Sam, "come this vay, then."

The Blue Lion tap was soon gained, and the fat boy swallowed a glass of liquor without so much as winking,—a feat which considerably advanced him in Mr. Weller's good opinion. Mr. Weller having transacted a similar piece of business on his own account, they got into the cart.

"Can you drive?" said the fat boy.

"I should rayther think so," replied Sam.

"There, then," said the fat boy, putting the reins in his hand, and pointing up a lane, "It's as straight as you can go; you can't miss it."

With these words, the fat boy laid himself affectionately down by the side of the cod-fish, and placing an oyster-barrel under his head for a pillow, fell asleep instantaneously.

"Vell," said Sam, "of all the cool boys ever I set my eyes on, this here young gen'lm'n is about the coolest. Come, vake up, young dropsy."

But as young dropsy evinced no symptoms of returning animation, Sam Weller sat himself down in front of the cart, and starting the old horse with a jerk of the rein, jogged steadily on, towards Manor Farm.

Meanwhile, Mr. Pickwick and his friends having walked their blood into active circulation, proceeded cheerfully on; the paths were hard, the grass was crisp and frosty, the air had a fine, dry, bracing coldness, and the rapid approach of the grey twilight (slate-coloured is a better term in frosty weather) made them look forward with pleasant anticipation to the comforts which awaited them at their hospitable entertainer's. It was the sort of afternoon that might induce a couple of elderly gentlemen, in a lonely field, to take off their great coats and play at leap-frog in pure lightness of heart and gaiety; and we firmly believe that had Mr. Tupman at that moment proffered "a back," Mr. Pickwick would have accepted his offer with the utmost avidity.

However, Mr. Tupman did not volunteer any such personal accommodation, and the friends walked on, conversing merrily. As they turned into a lane which they had to cross, the sound of many voices burst upon their ears; and before they had even had time to form a guess as to whom they belonged, they walked into the very centre of the party who were expecting their arrival—a fact which was first notified to the Pickwickians, by the loud "Hurrah," which burst from old Wardle's lips, when they appeared in sight.

First, there was Wardle himself, looking, if that were possible, more jolly than ever; then there were Bella and her faithful Trundle; and, lastly, there were Emily and some eight or ten young ladies, who had all come down to the wedding which was to take place next day, and were in as happy and important a state as young ladies usually are, on such momentous occasions; and they were, one and all, startling the fields and lanes far and wide with their frolic and laughter.

The ceremony of introduction, under such circumstances, was very soon performed, or we should rather say that the introduction was soon over, without any ceremony at all; and in two minutes thereafter, Mr. Pickwick was joking with the young ladies who wouldn't come over the stile while he looked, or who, having pretty feet and unexceptionable ankles, preferred standing on the top-rail for five minutes or so, and declaring that they were too frightened to move, with as much ease and absence of reserve or constraint, as if he had known them for life. It is worthy of remark too, that Mr. Snodgrass offered Emily far more assistance than the absolute terrors of the stile (although it was full three feet high, and had only a couple of stepping-stones) would seem to require; while one black-eyed young lady in a very nice little pair of boots with fur round the top, was observed to scream very loudly, when Mr. Winkle offered to help her over.

All this was very snug and pleasant: and when the difficulties of the stile were at last surmounted, and they once more entered on the open field, old Wardle informed Mr. Pickwick how they had all been down in a body to inspect the furniture and fittings-up of the house, which the young couple were to tenant, after the Christmas holidays; at which communication Bella and Trundle both coloured up, as red as the fat boy after the tap-room fire; and the young lady with the black eyes and the fur round the boots, whispered something in Emily's ear, and then glanced archly at Mr. Snodgrass, to which Emily responded that she was a foolish girl, but turned very red, notwithstanding; and Mr. Snodgrass, who was as modest as all great geniuses usually are, felt the crimson rising to the crown of his head, and devoutly wished, in the inmost recesses of his own heart, that the young lady aforesaid, with her black eyes, and her archness, and her boots with the fur round the top, were all comfortably deposited in the adjacent county.

But if they were social and happy, outside the house what was the warmth and cordiality of their reception when they reached the farm! The very servants grinned with pleasure at sight of Mr. Pickwick; and Emma bestowed a half-demure, half-impudent, and all pretty look of recognition on Mr. Tupman, which was enough to make the statue of Bonaparte in the passage, unfold his arms, and clasp her within them.

The old lady was seated in customary state in the front parlour, but she was rather cross, and by consequence, most particularly deaf. She never went out herself, and like a great many other old ladies of the same stamp, she was apt to consider it an act of domestic treason, if any body else took the liberty of doing what she couldn't. So, bless her old soul, she sat as upright as she could, in her great chair, and looked as fierce as might be—and that was benevolent after all.

"Mother," said Wardle, "Mr. Pickwick. You recollect him."

"Never mind," replied the old lady with great dignity "Don't trouble Mr. Pickwick about an old creetur like me. Nobody cares about me now, and it's very nat'ral they shouldn't." Here the old lady tossed her head, and smoothed down her lavender-coloured silk dress, with trembling hands.

"Come, come, Ma'am," said Mr. Pickwick, "I can't let you cut an old friend in this way. I have come down expressly to have a long talk, and another rubber with you; and we'll show these boys and girls how to dance a minuet, before they're eight-and-forty hours older."

The old lady was rapidly giving way, but she did not like to do it all at once; so she only said, "Ah! I can't hear him."

"Nonsense, mother," said Wardle. "Come, come, don't be cross, there's a good soul. Recollect Bella; come, you must keep her spirits up, poor girl."

The good old lady heard this, for her lip quivered as her son said it. But age has its little infirmities of temper, and she was not quite brought round yet. So, she smoothed down the lavender-coloured dress again, and turning to Mr. Pickwick said, "Ah, Mr. Pickwick, young people was very different, when I was a girl."

"No doubt of that, Ma'am," said Mr. Pickwick, "and that's the reason why I would make much of the few that have any traces of the old stock,"—and saying this, Mr. Pickwick gently pulled Bella towards him, and bestowing a kiss upon her forehead, bade her sit down on the little stool at her grandmother's feet. Whether the expression of her countenance, as it was raised towards the old lady's face, called up a thought of old times, or whether the old lady was touched by Mr. Pickwick's affectionate good nature, or whatever was the cause, she was fairly melted; so, she threw herself on her grand-daughter's neck, and all the little ill-humour evaporated in a gush of silent tears.

A happy party they were, that night. Sedate and solemn were the score of rubbers in which Mr. Pickwick and the old lady played together; and uproarious was the mirth of the round table. Long after the ladies had retired, did the hot elder wine, well qualified with brandy and spice, go round, and round, and round again; and sound was the sleep, and pleasant were the dreams that followed. It is a remarkable fact, that those of Mr. Snodgrass bore constant reference to Emily Wardle; and that the principal figure in Mr. Winkle's visions, was a young lady with black eyes, an arch smile, and a pair of remarkably nice boots, with fur round the tops.

Mr. Pickwick was awakened early in the morning, by a hum of voices and pattering of feet, sufficient to rouse even the fat boy from his heavy slumbers. He sat up in bed, and listened. The female servants and female visitors were running constantly to and fro; and there were such multitudinous demands for warm water, such repeated outcries for needles and thread, and so many half-suppressed entreaties of "Oh, do come and tie me, there's a dear," that Mr. Pickwick in his innocence began to imagine that something dreadful must have occurred, when he grew more awake, and remembered the wedding. The occasion being an important one, he dressed himself with peculiar care, and descended to the breakfast room.

There were all the female servants in a bran new uniform of pink muslin gowns with white bows in their caps, running about the house in a state of excitement and agitation, which it would be impossible to describe. The old lady was dressed out, in a brocaded gown, which had not seen the light for twenty years, saving and excepting such truant rays as had stolen through the chinks in the box in which it had been laid by, during the whole time. Mr. Trundle was in high feather and spirits, but a little nervous withal. The hearty old landlord was trying to look very cheerful and unconcerned, but failing signally in the attempt. All the girls were in tears and white muslin, except a select two or three, who were being honoured with a private view of the bride and bridesmaids, up stairs. All the Pickwickians were in most blooming array; and there was a terrific roaring on the grass in front of the house, occasioned by all the men, boys, and hobbledehoys attached to the farm, each of whom had got a white bow in his button hole, and all of whom were cheering with might and main: being incited thereto, and stimulated therein, by the precept and example of Mr. Samuel Weller, who had managed to become mighty popular already, and was as much at home as if he had been born on the land.

A wedding is a licensed subject to joke upon, but there really is no great joke in the matter after all; we speak merely of the ceremony, and beg it to be distinctly understood that we indulge in no hidden sarcasm upon a married life. Mixed up with the pleasure and joy of the occasion, are the many regrets at quitting home, the tears of parting between parent and child, the consciousness of leaving the dearest and kindest friends of the happiest portion of human life, to encounter its cares and troubles with others still untried, and little known—natural feelings which we would not render this chapter mournful by describing, and which we should be still more unwilling to be supposed to ridicule.

Let us briefly say, then, that the ceremony was performed by the old clergyman, in the parish church of Dingley Dell, and that Mr. Pickwick's name is attached to the register, still preserved in the vestry thereof; that the young lady with the black eyes signed her name in a very unsteady and tremulous manner; and that Emily's signature, as the other bridesmaid, is nearly illegible; that it all went off in very admirable style; that the young ladies generally, thought it far less shocking than they expected; and that although the owner of the black eyes and the arch smile informed Mr. Winkle that she was sure she could never submit to anything so dreadful, we have the very best reasons for thinking she was mistaken. To all this, we may add, that Mr. Pickwick was the first who saluted the bride: and that in so doing, he threw over her neck, a rich gold watch and chain, which no mortal eyes but the jeweller's had ever beheld before. Then the old church bell rang as gaily as it could, and they all returned to breakfast.

"Vere does the mince-pies go, young opium eater?" said Mr. Weller to the fat boy, as he assisted in laying out such articles of consumption as had not been duly arranged on the previous night.

The fat boy pointed to the destination of the pies.

"Wery good," said Sam, "stick a bit o' Christmas in 'em. T'other dish opposite. There; now ve look compact and comfortable, as the father said ven he cut his little boy's head off, to cure him o' squintin'."

As Mr. Weller made the comparison, he fell back a step or two, to give full effect to it, and surveyed the preparations with the utmost satisfaction.

"Wardle," said Mr. Pickwick, almost as soon as they were all seated, "a glass of wine, in honour of this happy occasion!"

"I shall be delighted, my boy," said Wardle. "Joe—damn that boy, he's gone to sleep."

"No, I ain't, Sir," replied the fat boy, starting up from a remote corner, where, like the patron saint of fat boys—the immortal Horner—he had been devouring a Christmas pie, though not with the coolness and deliberation which characterised that young gentleman's proceedings.

"Fill Mr. Pickwick's glass."

"Yes, Sir."

The fat boy filled Mr. Pickwick's glass, and then retired behind his master's chair, from whence he watched the play of the knives and forks, and the progress of the choice morsels, from the dishes, to the mouths of the company, with a kind of dark and gloomy joy that was most impressive.

"God bless you, old fellow," said Mr. Pickwick.

"Same to you, my boy," replied Wardle; and they pledged each other, heartily.

"Mrs. Wardle," said Mr. Pickwick, "we old folks must have a glass of wine together, in honour of this joyful event."

The old lady was in a state of great grandeur just then, for she was sitting at the top of the table in her brocaded gown, with her newly-married grand-daughter on one side, and Mr. Pickwick on the other, to do the carving. Mr. Pickwick had not spoken in a very loud tone, but she understood him at once, and drank off a full glass of wine to his long life and happiness; after which the worthy old soul launched forth into a minute and particular account of her own wedding, with a dissertation on the fashion of wearing high-heeled shoes, and some particulars concerning the life and adventures of the beautiful Lady Tollimglower, deceased, at all of which the old lady herself laughed very heartily indeed, and so did the young ladies too, for they were wondering among themselves what on earth grandma was talking about. When they laughed, the old lady laughed ten times more heartily: and said that they always had been considered capital stories, which caused them all

to laugh again, and put the old lady into the very best of humours. Then the cake was cut, and passed through the ring; and the young ladies saved pieces to put under their pillows to dream of their future husbands on; and a great deal of blushing and merriment was thereby occasioned.

"Mr. Miller," said Mr. Pickwick to his old acquaintance, the hard-headed gentleman, "a glass of wine?"

"With great satisfaction Mr. Pickwick," replied the hard-headed gentleman, solemnly.

"You'll take me in?" said the benevolent old clergyman.

"And me," interposed his wife.

"And me, and me," said a couple of poor relations at the bottom of the table, who had eaten and drank very heartily, and laughed at every thing.

Mr. Pickwick expressed his heartfelt delight at every additional suggestion ; and his eyes beamed with hilarity and cheerfulness.

"Ladies and gentlemen," said Mr. Pickwick, suddenly rising—

"Hear, hear! Hear, hear! Hear, hear!" said Mr. Weller, in the excitement of his feelings.

"Call in all the servants," cried old Wardle, interposing to prevent the public rebuke which Mr. Weller would otherwise most indubitably have received from his master. "Give them a glass of wine each, to drink the toast in. Now, Pickwick."

Amidst the silence of the company, the whispering of the women servants, and the awkward embarrassment of the men, Mr. Pickwick proceeded.

"Ladies and gentlemen—no, I won't say ladies and gentlemen, I'll call you my friends, my dear friends, if the ladies will allow me to take so great a liberty"—

Here Mr. Pickwick was interrupted by immense applause from the ladies, echoed by the gentlemen, during which the owner of the eyes was distinctly heard to state that she could kiss that dear Mr. Pickwick, whereupon Mr. Winkle gallantly inquired if it couldn't be done by deputy, to which the young lady with the black eyes replied, "Go away"—and accompanied the request with a look which said as plainly as a look could do——"if you can."

"My dear friends," resumed Mr. Pickwick, "I am going to propose the health of the bride and bridegroom—God bless 'em (cheers and tears). My young friend Trundle, I believe to be a very excellent and manly fellow; and his wife I know to be a very amiable and lovely girl, well qualified to transfer to another sphere of action the happiness which for twenty years she has diffused around her, in her father's house. (Here, the fat boy burst forth into stentorian blubberings, and was led forth by the coat collar, by Mr. Weller). I wish," added Mr. Pickwick, "I wish I was young enough to be her sister's husband, (cheers); but, failing that, I am happy to be old enough to be her father; for, being so, I shall not be suspected of any latent designs when I say, that I admire, esteem, and love them both (cheers and sobs). The bride's father, our good friend there, is a noble person, and I am proud to know him (great uproar). He is a kind, excellent, independent-spirited, fine-hearted, hospitable, liberal man (enthusiastic shouts from the poor relations, at all the adjectives; and especially at the two last). That his daughter may enjoy all the happiness, even he can desire; and that he may derive from the contemplation of her felicity all the gratification of heart and peace of mind which he so well deserves, is, I am persuaded, our united wish. So, let us drink their healths, and wish them prolonged life, and every blessing."

Mr. Pickwick concluded amidst a whirlwind of applause; and once more were the lungs of the supernumeraries, under Mr. Weller's command, brought into active and efficient operation. Mr. Wardle proposed Mr. Pickwick; and Mr. Pickwick proposed the old lady. Mr. Snodgrass proposed Mr. Wardle, and Mr. Wardle proposed Mr. Snodgrass. One of the poor relations proposed Mr. Tupman, and the other poor relation proposed Mr. Winkle; and all was happiness and festivity, until the mysterious disappearance of both the poor relations beneath the table, warned the party that it was time to adjourn.

At dinner they met again, after a five and twenty mile walk, undertaken by the males at Wardle's recommendation, to get rid of the effects of the wine at breakfast; the poor relations had lain in bed all day, with the view of attaining the same happy consummation, but, as they had been unsuccessful, they stopped there. Mr. Weller kept the domestics in a state of perpetual hilarity; and the fat boy divided his time into small alternate allotments of eating and sleeping.

The dinner was as hearty an affair as the breakfast, and was quite as noisy, without the tears. Then came the dessert and some more toasts. Then came the tea and coffee; and then, the ball.

The best sitting room at Manor Farm was a good, long, dark pannelled room with a high chimney piece, and a capacious chimney, up which you could have driven one of the new patent cabs, wheels and all. At the upper end of the room, seated in a shady bower of holly and evergreens, were the two best fiddlers, and the only harp, in all Muggleton. In all sorts of recesses, and on all kinds of brackets, stood massive and silver candlesticks with four branches each. The carpet was up, the candles burnt bright, the fire blazed and crackled on the hearth; and merry voices and light-hearted laughter rang through the room. If any of the old English yeomen had turned into fairies when they died, it was just the place in which they would have held their revels.

If any thing could have added to the interest of this agreeable scene, it would have been the remarkable fact of Mr. Pickwick's appearing without his gaiters, for the first time within the memory of his oldest friends.

"You mean to dance?" said Wardle.

"Of course I do," replied Mr. Pickwick, "Don't you see I am dressed for the purpose?" and Mr. Pickwick called attention to his speckled silk stockings, and smartly tied pumps.

"*You* in silk stockings!" exclaimed Mr. Tupman jocosely.

"And why not Sir—why not?" said Mr. Pickwick, turning warmly upon him.

"Oh, of course there is no reason why you shouldn't wear them," responded Mr. Tupman.

"I imagine not Sir—I imagine not," said Mr. Pickwick in a very peremptory tone.

Mr. Tupman had contemplated a laugh, but he found it was a serious matter; so he looked grave, and said they were a very pretty pattern.

"I hope they are," said Mr. Pickwick fixing his eyes upon his friend. "You see nothing extraordinary in these stockings, *as* stockings, I trust Sir?"

"Certainly not—oh certainly not," replied Mr. Tupman. He walked away; and Mr. Pickwick's countenance resumed its customary benign expression.

"We are all ready, I believe," said Mr. Pickwick, who was stationed with the old lady at the top of the dance,

and had already made four false starts, in his excessive anxiety to commence.

"Then begin at once," said Wardle. "Now."

Up struck the two fiddles and the one harp, and off went Mr. Pickwick into hands across, when there was a general clapping of hands, and a cry of "Stop, stop."

"What's the matter?" said Mr. Pickwick, who was only brought to, by the fiddles and harp desisting, and could have been stopped by no other earthly power, if the house had been on fire.

"Where's Arabella Allen?" said a dozen voices.

"And Winkle?" added Mr. Tupman.

"Here we are!" exclaimed that gentleman, emerging with his pretty companion from the corner; and, as he did so, it would have been hard to tell which was the redder in the face, he or the young lady with the black eyes.

"What an extraordinary thing it is, Winkle," said Mr. Pickwick, rather pettishly, "that you couldn't have taken your place before."

"Not at all extraordinary," said Mr. Winkle.

"Well," said Mr. Pickwick, with a very expressive smile, as his eyes rested on Arabella, "well, I don't know that it *was* extraordinary, either, after all."

However, there was no time to think more about the matter, for the fiddles and harp began in real earnest. Away went Mr. Pickwick—hands across, down the middle to the very end of the room, and half way up the chimney, back again to the door—poussette everywhere—loud stamp on the ground—ready for the next couple—off again—all the figure over once more—another stamp to beat out the time—next couple, and the next, and the next again—never was such going; and at last, after they had reached the bottom of the dance, and full fourteen couple after the old lady had retired in an exhausted state, and the clergyman's wife had been substituted in her stead, did that gentleman, when there was no demand whatever on his exertions, keep perpetually dancing in his place, to keep time to the music, smiling on his partner all the while with a blandness of demeanour which baffles all description.

Long before Mr. Pickwick was weary of dancing, the newly-married couple had retired from the scene. There was a glorious supper down stairs, notwithstanding, and a good long sitting after it; and when Mr. Pickwick awoke, late the next morning, he had a confused recollection of having, severally and confidentially, invited somewhere about five-and-forty people to dine with him at the George and Vulture, the very first time they came to London; which Mr. Pickwick rightly considered a pretty certain indication of his having taken something besides exercise, on the previous night.

"And so your family has games in the kitchen to-night, my dear, has they?" inquired Sam of Emma.

"Yes, Mr. Weller," replied Emma; "we always have on Christmas eve. Master wouldn't neglect to keep it up on any account."

"Your master's a wery pretty notion of keepin' anythin' up, my dear," said Mr. Weller; "I never see such a sensible sort of man as he is, or such a reg'lar gen'l'm'n."

"Oh, that he is!" said the fat boy, joining in the conversation; "don't he breed nice pork!" and the fat youth gave a semi-cannibalic leer at Mr. Weller, as he thought of the roast legs and gravy.

"Oh, you've woke up, at last, have you?" said Sam.

The fat boy nodded.

"I'll tell you what it is, young boa constructer," said

Mr. Weller, impressively, "if you don't sleep a little less, and exercise a little more, ven you comes to be a man you'll lay yourself open to the same sort o' personal inconvenience as was inflicted on the old gen'lm'n as wore the pig-tail."

"What did they do to him?" inquired the fat boy, in a faltering voice.

"I'm a goin' to tell you," replied Mr. Weller; "he was one o' the largest patterns as was ever turned out—reg'lar fat man, as hadn't caught a glimpse of his own shoes for five-and-forty years."

"Lor!" exclaimed Emma.

"No, that he hadn't, my dear," said Mr. Weller, "and if you'd put an exact model of his own legs on the dinin' table afore him, he wouldn't ha' known 'em. Well, he always walks to his office with a wery handsome gold watch-chain hanging out, about a foot and a half; and a gold watch in his fob pocket as was worth—I'm afraid to say how much, but as much as a watch can be—a large, heavy, round manafacter, as stout for a watch, as he was for a man, and with a big face in proportion. 'You'd better not carry that 'ere watch,' says the old gen'l'm'n's friends, 'you'll be robbed on it,' says they. 'Shall I?' says he. 'Yes, will you,' says they. 'Vell,' says he, 'I should like to see the thief as could get this here watch out, for I'm blessed if I ever can; it's such a tight fit,' says he, 'and venever I vants to know what's o'clock, I'm obliged to stare into the bakers' shops,' he says. Well, then he laughs as hearty as if he was a goin' to pieces, and out he walks agin' with his powdered head and pig-tail, and rolls down the Strand vith the chain hangin' out furder than ever, and the great round watch almost bustin' through his grey kersey smalls. There warn't a pickpocket in all London as didn't take a pull at that chain, but the chain 'ud never break, and the watch 'ud never come out, so they soon got tired o' dragging such a heavy old gen-'l'm'n along the pavement, and he'd go home and laugh till the pig-tail vibrated like the penderlum of a Dutch clock. At last, one day the old gen'l'm'n was a rollin' along, and he sees a pickpocket as he know'd by sight, a-comin' up, arm in arm vith a little boy vith a wery large head. 'Here's a game,' says the old gen'l'm'n to himself, 'they're a-goin' to have another try, but it won't do.' So he begins a chucklin' wery hearty, ven, all of a sudden, the little boy leaves hold of the pickpocket's arm, and rushes headforemost straight into the old gen'l'm'n's stomach, and for a moment doubled him right up vith the pain. 'Murder!' says the old gen'l'm'n. 'All right, Sir,' says the pickpocket, a whisperin' in his ear. And ven he come straight agin', the watch and chain was gone, and what's worse than that, the old gen'l'm'n's digestion was all wrong ever artervards, to the wery last day of his life; so just you look about you, young feller, and take care you don't get too fat."

As Mr. Weller concluded this moral tale, with which the fat boy appeared much affected, they all three wended their way to the large kitchen, in which the family were by this time assembled, according to annual custom on Christmas eve, observed by old Wardle's forefathers from time immemorial.

From the centre of the ceiling of this kitchen, old Wardle had just suspended with his own hands a huge branch of mistletoe, and this same branch of mistletoe instantaneously gave rise to a scene of general and most delightful struggling and confusion; in the midst of which Mr. Pickwick with a gallantry which would have done honour to a descendant of Lady Tollimglower herself, took the old lady by the hand, led her beneath the mystic branch, and saluted her in all courtesy and decorum. The old lady submitted to this piece of practical politeness with all the dignity which befitted so important and serious a solemnity, but the younger ladies not being so thoroughly imbued with a superstitious veneration of the custom, or imagining that the value of a salute is very much enhanced if it cost a little trouble to obtain it, screamed and struggled, and ran into corners, and threatened and remonstrated, and did every thing but leave the room, until some of the less adventurous gentlemen were on the point of desisting, when they all at once found it useless to resist any longer, and submitted to be kissed with a good grace. Mr. Winkle kissed the young lady with the black eyes, and Mr. Snodgrass kissed Emily; and Mr. Weller, not being particular about the form of being under the mistletoe, kissed Emma and the other female servants, just as he caught them. As to the poor relations, they kissed everybody, not even excepting the plainer portion of the young-lady visiters, who, in their excessive confusion, ran right under the mistletoe, directly it was hung up, without knowing it! Wardle stood with his back to the fire, surveying the whole scene, with the utmost satisfaction; and the fat boy took the opportunity of appropriating to his own use, and summarily devouring, a particularly fine mince-pie, that had been carefully put by, for somebody else.

Now the screaming had subsided, and faces were in a glow and curls in a tangle, and Mr. Pickwick, after kissing the old lady as before-mentioned, was standing under the mistletoe, looking with a very pleased countenance on all that was passing around him, when the young lady with the black eyes, after a little whispering with the other young ladies, made a sudden dart forward, and, putting her arm round Mr. Pickwick's neck, saluted him affectionately on the left cheek; and before Mr. Pickwick distinctly knew what was the matter, he was surrounded by the whole body, and kissed by every one of them.

It was a pleasant thing to see Mr. Pickwick in the centre of the group, now pulled this way, and then that, and first kissed on the chin and then on the nose, and then on the spectacles, and to hear the peals of laughter which were raised on every side; but it was a still more pleasant thing to see Mr. Pickwick, blinded shortly afterwards, with a silk-handkerchief, falling up against the wall, and scrambling into corners, and going through all the mysteries of blind-man's buff, with the utmost relish for the game, until at last he caught one of the poor relations; and then had to evade the blind-man himself, which he did with a nimbleness and agility that elicited the admiration and applause of all beholders. The poor relations caught just the people whom they thought would like it; and when the game flagged, got caught themselves. When they were all tired of blind-man's buff, there was a great game at snap-dragon, and when fingers enough were burned with that, and all the raisins gone, they sat down by the huge fire of blazing logs to a substantial supper, and a mighty bowl of wassail, something smaller than an ordinary washhouse copper, in which the hot apples were hissing and bubbling with a rich look, and a jolly sound, that were perfectly irresistible.

"This," said Mr. Pickwick, looking round him, "this is, indeed, comfort."

"Our invariable custom," replied Mr. Wardle. "Everybody sits down with us on Christmas eve, as you see them now—servants and all; and here we wait till the clock strikes twelve, to usher Christmas in, and wile away the time with forfeits and old stories. Trundle, my boy, rake up the fire."

Up flew the bright sparks in myriads as the logs were stirred, and the deep red blaze sent forth a rich glow, that penetrated into the furthest corner of the room, and cast its cheerful tint on every face.

"Come," said Wardle, "a song—a Christmas song. I'll give you one, in default of a better."

"Bravo," said Mr. Pickwick.

"Fill up," cried Wardle. "It will be two hours good, before you see the bottom of the bowl through the deep rich colour of the wassail; fill up all round, and now for the song."

Thus saying, the merry old gentleman, in a good, round, sturdy voice, commenced without more ado—

A CHRISTMAS CAROL.

I CARE not for Spring; on his fickle wing
Let the blossoms and buds be borne:
He woos them amain with his treacherous rain,
And he scatters them ere the morn.
An inconstant elf, he knows not himself,
Or his own changing mind an hour,
He'll smile in your face, and, with wry grimace,
He'll wither your youngest flower.

Let the Summer sun to his bright home run,
He shall never be sought by me;
When he's dimmed by a cloud I can laugh aloud,
And care not how sulky he be;
For his darling child is the madness wild
That sports in fierce fever's train;
And when love is too strong, it don't last long,
As many have found to their pain.

A mild harvest night, by the tranquil light
Of the modest and gentle moon,
Has a far sweeter sheen for me, I ween,
Than the broad and unblushing noon.
But every leaf awakens my grief,
As it lieth beneath the tree;
So let Autumn air be never so fair,
It by no means agrees with me.

But my song I troll out, for CHRISTMAS stout,
The hearty, the true, and the bold;
A bumper I drain, and with might and main
Give three cheers for this Christmas old.
We'll usher him in with a merry din
That shall gladden his joyous heart,
And we'll keep him up while there's bite or sup,
And in fellowship good, we'll part.

In his fine honest pride, he scorns to hide
One jot of his hard-weather scars;
They're no disgrace, for there's much the same trace
On the cheeks of our bravest tars.
Then again I sing 'till the roof doth ring,
And it echoes from wall to wall—
To the stout old wight, fair welcome to-night,
As the King of the Seasons all!

This song was tumultuously applauded, for friends and dependents make a capital audience; and the poor relations especially were in perfect extasies of rapture. Again was the fire replenished, and again went the wassail round.

"How it snows!" said one of the men, in a low tone.

"Snows, does it?" said Wardle.

"Rough, cold night, Sir," replied the man; "and there's a wind got up that drifts it across the fields, in a thick white cloud."

"What does Jem say?" inquired the old lady. "There ain't any thing the matter, is there?"

"No, no, mother," replied Wardle; "he says there's a

snow-drift, and a wind that's piercing cold. I should know that, by the way it rumbles in the chimney."

"Ah!" said the old lady, "there was just such a wind, and just such a fall of snow, a good many years back, I recollect—just five years before your poor father died. It was a Christmas eve, too; and I remember that on that very night he told us the story about the goblins that carried away old Gabriel Grub."

"The story about what?" said Mr. Pickwick.

"Oh, nothing—nothing," replied Wardle. "About an old sexton, that the good people down here suppose to have been carried away by goblins."

"Suppose!" ejaculated the old lady. "Is there any body hardy enough to disbelieve it? Suppose! Haven't you heard ever since you were a child, that he *was* carried away by the goblins, and don't you know he was?"

"Very well, mother, he was, if you like," said Wardle, laughing. "He *was* carried away by goblins, Pickwick; and there's an end of the matter."

"No, no," said Mr. Pickwick, "not an end of it, I assure you; for I must hear how, and why, and all about it."

Wardle smiled, as every head was bent forward to hear; and filling out the wassail with no stinted hand, nodded a health to Mr. Pickwick, and began as follows—

But bless our editorial heart, what a long chapter we have been betrayed into! We had quite forgotten all such petty restrictions as chapters, we solemnly declare. So here goes, to give the goblin a fair start in a new one. A clear stage and no favour for the goblins, ladies and gentlemen, if you please.

CHAPTER XXVIII.*

THE STORY OF THE GOBLINS WHO STOLE A SEXTON.

"IN an old abbey town, down in this part of the country, a long, long while ago—so long, that the story must be a true one, because our great grandfathers implicitly believed it—there officiated as sexton and grave-digger in the church-yard, one Gabriel Grub. It by no means follows that because a man is a sexton, and constantly surrounded by emblems of mortality, therefore he should be a morose and melancholy man; your undertakers are the merriest fellows in the world, and I once had the honour of being on intimate terms with a mute, who in private life, and off duty, was as comical and jocose a little fellow as ever chirped out a devil-may-care song, without a hitch in his memory, or drained off a good stiff glass of grog without stopping for breath. But notwithstanding these precedents to the contrary, Gabriel Grub was an ill-conditioned, cross-grained, surly fellow—a morose and lonely man, who consorted with nobody but himself, and an old wicker bottle which fitted into his large deep waistcoat pocket; and who eyed each merry face as it passed him by, with such a deep scowl of malice and ill-humour, as it was difficult to meet without feeling something the worse for.

"A little before twilight one Christmas Eve, Gabriel shouldered his spade, lighted his lantern, and betook himself towards the old church-yard, for he had got a grave to finish by next morning, and feeling very low he thought it might raise his spirits perhaps, if he went on with his work at once. As he wended his way, up the ancient street, he

*Original edition repeats chapter number XXVIII.

159

saw the cheerful light of the blazing fires gleam through the old casements, and heard the loud laugh and the cheerful shouts of those who were assembled around them; he marked the bustling preparations for next day's good cheer, and smelt the numerous savoury odours consequent thereupon, as they steamed up from the kitchen windows in clouds. All this was gall and wormwood to the heart of Gabriel Grub; and as groups of children, bounded out of the houses, tripped across the road, and were met, before they could knock at the opposite door, by half a dozen curly-headed little rascals who crowded round them as they flocked up stairs to spend the evening in their Christmas games, Gabriel smiled grimly, and clutched the handle of his spade with a firmer grasp, as he thought of measles, scarlet-fever, thrush, hooping-cough, and a good many other sources of consolation beside.

"In this happy frame of mind, Gabriel strode along, returning a short, sullen growl to the good-humoured greetings of such of his neighbours as now and then passed him, until he turned into the dark lane which led to the churchyard. Now Gabriel had been looking forward to reaching the dark lane, because it was, generally speaking, a nice gloomy mournful place, into which the towns-people did not much care to go, except in broad daylight, and when the sun was shining; consequently he was not a little indignant to hear a young urchin roaring out some jolly song about a merry Christmas, in this very sanctuary, which had been called Coffin Lane ever since the days of the old abbey, and the time of the shaven-headed monks. As Gabriel walked on, and the voice drew nearer, he found it proceeded from a small boy, who was hurrying along, to join one of the little parties in the old street, and who, partly to keep himself company, and partly to prepare himself for the occasion, was shouting out the song at the highest pitch of his lungs. So Gabriel waited till the boy came up, and then dodged him into a corner, and rapped him over the head with his lantern five or six times, just to teach him to modulate his voice. And as the boy hurried away with his hand to his head, singing quite a different sort of tune, Gabriel Grub chuckled very heartily to himself, and entered the church-yard, locking the gate behind him.

"He took off his coat, set down his lantern, and getting into the unfinished grave, worked at it for an hour or so, with right good will. But the earth was hardened with the frost, and it was no very easy matter to break it up, and shovel it out; and although there was a moon, it was a very young one, and shed little light upon the grave, which was in the shadow of the church. At any other time, these obstacles would have made Gabriel Grub very moody and miserable, but he was so well pleased with having stopped the small boy's singing, that he took little heed of the scanty progress he had made, and looked down into the grave when he had finished work for the night, with grim satisfaction, murmuring as he gathered up his things—

> Brave lodgings for one, brave lodgings for one,
> A few feet of cold earth, when life is done;
> A stone at the head, a stone at the feet,
> A rich, juicy meal for the worms to eat;
> Rank grass over head, and damp clay around,
> Brave lodgings for one, these, in holy ground!

"'Ho! ho!' laughed Gabriel Grub, as he sat himself down on a flat tombstone which was a favourite resting place of his; and drew forth his wicker bottle. 'A coffin at Christmas—a Christmas Box. Ho! ho! ho!'

"'Ho! ho! ho!' repeated a voice which sounded close behind him.

"Gabriel paused in some alarm, in the act of raising the wicker bottle to his lips, and looked round. The bottom of the oldest grave about him, was not more still and quiet, than the church-yard in the pale moonlight. The cold hoar frost glistened on the tombstones, and sparkled like rows of gems among the stone carvings of the old church. The snow lay hard and crisp upon the ground, and spread over the thickly-strewn mounds of earth, so white and smooth a cover, that it seemed as if corpses lay there, hidden only by their winding sheets. Not the faintest rustle broke the profound tranquillity of the solemn scene. Sound itself appeared to be frozen up, all was so cold and still.

"'It was the echoes,' said Gabriel Grub, raising the bottle to his lips again.

"'It was *not*,' said a deep voice.

"Gabriel started up, and stood rooted to the spot with astonishment and terror; for his eyes rested on a form which made his blood run cold.

"Seated on an upright tombstone, close to him, was a strange unearthly figure, whom Gabriel felt at once, was no being of this world. His long fantastic legs which might have reached the ground, were cocked up, and crossed after a quaint, fantastic fashion; his sinewy arms were bare, and his hands rested on his knees. On his short round body he wore a close covering, ornamented with small slashes; and a short cloak dangled at his back; the collar was cut into curious peaks, which served the goblin in lieu of ruff or neckerchief; and his shoes curled up at the toes into long points. On his head he wore a broad-brimmed sugar loaf hat, garnished with a single feather. The hat was covered with the white frost, and the goblin looked as if he had sat on the same tombstone very comfortably, for two or three hundred years. He was sitting perfectly still; his tongue was put out, as if in derision; and he was grinning at Gabriel Grub with such a grin as only a goblin could call up.

"'It was *not* the echoes,' said the goblin.

"Gabriel Grub was paralysed, and could make no reply.

"'What do you do here on Christmas eve?' said the goblin sternly.

"'I came to dig a grave, Sir,' stammered Gabriel Grub.

"'What man wanders among graves and church-yards on such a night as this?' said the goblin.

"'Gabriel Grub! Gabriel Grub!' screamed a wild chorus of voices that seemed to fill the church-yard. Gabriel looked fearfully round—nothing was to be seen.

"'What have you got in that bottle?' said the goblin.

"'Hollands, Sir,' replied the sexton, trembling more than ever; for he had bought it of the smugglers, and he thought that perhaps his questioner might be in the excise department of the goblins.

"'Who drinks Hollands alone, and in a church-yard, on such a night as this?' said the goblin.

"'Gabriel Grub! Gabriel Grub!' exclaimed the wild voices again.

"The goblin leered maliciously at the terrified sexton, and then raising his voice, exclaimed—

"'And who, then, is our fair and lawful prize?'

"To this inquiry the invisible chorus replied, in a strain that sounded like the voices of many choristers singing to the mighty swell of the old church organ—a strain that seemed borne to the sexton's ears upon a gentle wind, and to die away as its soft breath passed onward—but the burden of the reply was still the same, 'Gabriel Grub! Gabriel Grub!'

"The goblin grinned a broader grin than before, as he said, 'Well, Gabriel, what do you say to this?'

"The sexton gasped for breath.

"'What do you think of this, Gabriel?' said the goblin, kicking up his feet in the air on either side the tombstone, and looking at the turned-up points with as much complacency as if he had been contemplating the most fashionable pair of Wellingtons in all Bond Street.

"'It's—it's—very curious, Sir,' replied the sexton, half dead with fright, 'very curious, and very pretty, but I think I'll go back and finish my work, Sir, if you please.'

"'Work!' said the goblin, 'what work?'

"'The grave, Sir, making the grave,' stammered the sexton.

"'Oh, the grave, eh?' said the goblin, 'who makes graves at à time when all other men are merry, and takes a pleasure in it?'

"Again the mysterious voices replied, 'Gabriel Grub! Gabriel Grub!'

"'I'm afraid my friends want you, Gabriel,' said the goblin, thrusting his tongue further into his cheek than ever—and a most astonishing tongue it was—'I'm afraid my friends want you, Gabriel,' said the goblin.

"'Under favour, Sir,' replied the horror-struck sexton, 'I don't think they can, Sir; they don't know me, Sir; I don't think the gentlemen have ever seen me, Sir.'

"'Oh yes they have,' replied the goblin; 'we know the man with the sulky face and the grim scowl, that came down the street to-night, throwing his evil looks at the children, and grasping his burying spade the tighter. We know the man that struck the boy in the envious malice of his heart, because the boy could be merry, and he could not. We know him, we know him.'

"Here the goblin gave a loud shrill laugh, that the echoes returned twenty-fold, and throwing his legs up in the air, stood upon his head, or rather upon the very point of his sugar-loaf hat, on the narrow edge of the tombstone, from whence he threw a summerset with extraordinary agility, right to the sexton's feet, at which he planted himself in the attitude in which tailors generally sit upon the shop-board.

"'I—I—am afraid I must leave you, Sir,' said the sexton, making an effort to move.

"'Leave us!' said the goblin, 'Gabriel Grub going to leave us. Ho! ho! ho!'

"As the goblin laughed, the sexton observed for one instant a brilliant illumination within the windows of the church, as if the whole building were lighted up; it disappeared, the organ pealed forth a lively air, and whole troops of goblins, the very counterpart of the first one, poured into the church-yard, and began playing at leap-frog with the tombstones, never stopping for an instant to take breath, but overing the highest among them, one after the other, with the most marvellous dexterity. The first goblin was a most astonishing leaper, and none of the others could come near him; even in the extremity of his terror the sexton could not help observing, that while his friends were content to leap over the common-sized grave-stones, the first one took the family vaults, iron railings and all, with as much ease as if they had been so many street posts.

"At last the game reached to a most exciting pitch; the organ played quicker and quicker, and the goblins leaped faster and faster, coiling themselves up, rolling head over heels upon the ground, and bounding over the tombstones like foot-balls. The sexton's brain whirled round with the rapidity of the motion he beheld, and his legs reeled beneath him, as the spirits flew before his eyes, when the goblin king suddenly darting towards him, laid his hand upon his collar, and sank with him through the earth.

"When Gabriel Grub had had time to fetch his breath, which the rapidity of his descent had for the moment taken away, he found himself in what appeared to be a large cavern, surrounded on all sides by crowds of goblins, ugly and grim; in the centre of the room, on an elevated seat, was stationed his friend of the church-yard; and close beside him stood Gabriel Grub himself, without the power of motion.

"'Cold to-night,' said the king of the goblins, 'very cold. A glass of something warm, here.'

"At this command, half a dozen officious goblins, with a perpetual smile upon their faces, whom Gabriel Grub imagined to be courtiers, on that account, hastily disappeared, and presently returned with a goblet of liquid fire, which they presented to the king.

"'Ah!' said the goblin, whose cheeks and throat were quite transparent, as he tossed down the flame, 'This warms one, indeed: bring a bumper of the same, for Mr. Grub.'

"It was in vain for the unfortunate sexton to protest that he was not in the habit of taking anything warm at night; for one of the goblins held him while another poured the blazing liquid down his throat, and the whole assembly screeched with laughter as he coughed and choked, and wiped away the tears which gushed plentifully from his eyes, after swallowing the burning draught.

"'And now,' said the king, fantastically poking the taper corner of his sugar-loaf hat into the sexton's eye, and thereby occasioning him the most exquisite pain—'And now, show the man of misery and gloom a few of the pictures from our own great storehouse.'

"As the goblin said this, a thick cloud which obscured the further end of the cavern, rolled gradually away, and disclosed, apparently at a great distance, a small and scantily furnished, but neat and clean apartment. A crowd of little children were gathered round a bright fire, clinging to their mother's gown, and gambolling round her chair. The mother occasionally rose, and drew aside the window-curtain as if to look for some expected object; a frugal meal was ready spread upon the table, and an elbow chair was placed near the fire. A knock was heard at the door: the mother opened it, and the children crowded round her, and clapped their hands for joy, as their father entered. He was wet and weary, and shook the snow from his garments, as the children crowded round him, and seizing his cloak, hat, stick, and gloves, with busy zeal, ran with them from the room. Then as he sat down to his meal before the fire, the children climbed about his knee, and the mother sat by his side, and all seemed happiness and comfort.

"But a change came upon the view, almost imperceptibly. The scene was altered to a small bed-room, where the fairest and youngest child lay dying; the roses had fled from his cheek, and the light from his eye; and even as the sexton looked upon him with an interest he had never felt or known before, he died. His young brothers and sisters crowded round his little bed, and seized his tiny hand, so cold and heavy; but they shrunk back from its touch, and looked with awe on his infant face; for calm and tranquil as it was, and sleeping in rest and peace as the beautiful child seemed to be, they saw that he was dead, and they knew that he was an angel looking down upon, and blessing them, from a bright and happy Heaven.

"Again the light cloud passed across the picture, and again the subject changed. The father and mother were old and helpless now, and the number of those about them was diminished more than half; but content and cheerfulness sat on every face, and beamed in every eye, as they crowded round the fireside, and told and listened to old stories of earlier and bygone days. Slowly and peacefully the father sank into the grave, and, soon after, the sharer of all his cares and troubles followed him to a place of rest and peace. The few, who yet survived them, knelt by their tomb, and watered the green turf which covered it with their tears; then rose and turned away, sadly and mournfully, but not with bitter cries, or despairing lamentations, for they knew that they should one day meet again; and once more they mixed with the busy world, and their content and cheerfulness were restored. The cloud settled upon the picture, and concealed it from the sexton's view.

"'What do you think of *that?*' said the goblin, turning his large face towards Gabriel Grub.

"Gabriel murmured out something about its being very pretty, and looked somewhat ashamed, as the goblin bent his fiery eyes upon him.

"'*You* a miserable man!' said the goblin, in a tone of excessive contempt. 'You!' He appeared disposed to add more, but indignation choked his utterance, so he lifted up one of his very pliable legs, and flourishing it above his head a little, to insure his aim, administered a good sound kick to Gabriel Grub; immediately after which, all the goblins in waiting crowded round the wretched sexton, and kicked him without mercy, according to the established and invariable custom of courtiers upon earth, who kick whom royalty kicks, and hug whom royalty hugs.

"'Show him some more,' said the king of the goblins.

"At these words the cloud was again dispelled, and a rich and beautiful landscape was disclosed to view—there is just such another to this day, within half a mile of the old abbey town. The sun shone from out the clear blue sky, the water sparkled beneath his rays, and the trees looked greener, and the flowers more gay, beneath his cheering influence. The water rippled on, with a pleasant sound, the trees rustled in the light wind that murmured among their leaves, the birds sang upon the boughs, and the lark carolled on high, her welcome to the morning. Yes, it was morning, the bright, balmy morning of summer; the minutest leaf, the smallest blade of grass, was instinct with life. The ant crept forth to her daily toil, the butterfly fluttered and basked in the warm rays of the sun; myriads of insects spread their transparent wings, and revelled in their brief but happy existence. Man walked forth, elated with the scene; and all was brightness and splendour.

"'*You* a miserable man!' said the king of the goblins, in a more contemptuous tone than before. And again the king of the goblins gave his leg a flourish; again it descended on the shoulders of the sexton; and again the attendant goblins imitated the example of their chief.

"Many a time the cloud went and came, and many a lesson it taught to Gabriel Grub, who although his shoulders smarted with pain from the frequent applications of

the goblin's feet thereunto, looked on with an interest which nothing could diminish. He saw that men who worked hard, and earned their scanty bread with lives of labour, were cheerful and happy; and that to the most ignorant, the sweet face of nature was a never-failing source of cheerfulness and joy. He saw those who had been delicately nurtured, and tenderly brought up, cheerful under privations, and superior to suffering, that would have crushed many of a rougher grain, because they bore within their own bosoms the materials of happiness, contentment, and peace. He saw that women, the tenderest and most fragile of all God's creatures, were the oftenest superior to sorrow, adversity, and distress; and he saw that it was because they bore in their own hearts an inexhaustible wellspring of affection and devotedness. Above all, he saw that men like himself, who snarled at the mirth and cheerfulness of others, were the foulest weeds on the fair surface of the earth; and setting all the good of the world against the evil, he came to the conclusion that it was a very decent and respectable sort of world after all. No sooner had he formed it, than the cloud which had closed over the last picture, seemed to settle on his senses, and lull him to repose. One by one, the goblins faded from his sight, and as the last one disappeared, he sunk to sleep.

"The day had broken when Gabriel Grub awoke, and found himself lying at full length on the flat gravestone in the church-yard, with the wicker bottle lying empty by his side, and his coat, spade, and lantern, all well whitened by the last night's frost, scattered on the ground. The stone on which he had first seen the goblin seated, stood bolt upright before him, and the grave at which he had worked, the night before, was not far off. At first he began to doubt the reality of his adventures, but the acute pain in his shoulders when he attempted to rise, assured him that the kicking of the goblins was certainly not ideal. He was staggered again, by observing no traces of footsteps in the snow on which the goblins had played at leap-frog with the gravestones, but he speedily accounted for this circumstance when he remembered that being spirits, they would leave no visible impression behind them. So Gabriel Grub got on his feet as well as he could, for the pain in his back; and brushing the frost off his coat, put it on, and turned his face towards the town.

"But he was an altered man, and he could not bear the thought of returning to a place where his repentance would be scoffed at, and his reformation disbelieved. He hesitated for a few moments; and then turned away to wander where he might, and seek his bread elsewhere.

"The lantern, the spade, and the wicker bottle, were found that day in the church-yard. There were a great many speculations about the sexton's fate at first, but it was speedily determined that he had been carried away by the goblins; and there were not wanting some very credible witnesses who had distinctly seen him whisked through the air on the back of a chestnut horse blind of one eye, with the hind quarters of a lion, and the tail of a bear. At length all this was devoutly believed; and the new sexton used to exhibit to the curious for a trifling emolument, a good-sized piece of the church weathercock which had been accidentally kicked off by the aforesaid horse in his aërial flight, and picked up by himself in the church-yard, a year or two afterwards.

"Unfortunately these stories were somewhat disturbed by the unlooked-for reappearance of Gabriel Grub himself, some ten years afterwards, a ragged, contented, rheumatic old man. He told his story to the clergyman, and also to the mayor; and in course of time it began to be received as a matter of history, in which form it has continued down to this very day. The believers in the weathercock tale, having misplaced their confidence once, were not easily prevailed upon to part with it again, so they looked as wise as they could, shrugged their shoulders, touched their foreheads, and murmured something about Gabriel Grub's having drunk all the Hollands, and then fallen asleep on the flat tombstone; and they affected to explain what he supposed he had witnessed in the goblin's cavern, by saying that he had seen the world, and grown wiser. But this opinion, which was by no means a popular one at any time, gradually died off; and be the matter how it may, as Gabriel Grub was afflicted with rheumatism to the end of his days, this story has at least one moral, if it teach no better one—and that is, that if a man turns sulky and drinks by himself at Christmas time, he may make up his mind to be not a bit the better for it, let the spirits be ever so good, or let them be even as many degrees beyond proof, as those which Gabriel Grub saw, in the goblin's cavern."

CHAPTER XXIX.

HOW THE PICKWICKIANS MADE AND CULTIVATED THE ACQUAINTANCE OF A COUPLE OF NICE YOUNG MEN BELONGING TO ONE OF THE LIBERAL PROFESSIONS; HOW THEY DISPORTED THEMSELVES ON THE ICE; AND HOW THEIR VISIT CAME TO A CONCLUSION.

"WELL Sam," said Mr. Pickwick as that favoured servitor entered his bed-chamber with his warm water, on the morning of Christmas Day, "Still frosty?"

"Water in the wash-hand basin 's a mask o' ice, Sir," responded Sam.

"Severe weather, Sam," observed Mr. Pickwick.

"Fine time for them as is well wropped up, as the Polar Bear said to himself, ven he was practising his skaiting," replied Mr. Weller.

"I shall be down in a quarter of an hour, Sam," said Mr. Pickwick, untying his night-cap.

"Wery good, Sir," replied Sam. "There's a couple o' Sawbones down stairs."

"A couple of what!" exclaimed Mr. Pickwick, sitting up in bed.

"A couple o' Sawbones," said Sam.

"What's a Sawbones?" inquired Mr. Pickwick, not quite certain whether it was a live animal, or something to eat.

"What! don't you know what a Sawbones is, Sir?" inquired Mr. Weller; "I thought every body know'd as a Sawbones was a Surgeon."

"Oh, a Surgeon, eh?" said Mr. Pickwick with a smile.

"Just that Sir," replied Sam. "These here ones as is below, though, aint reg'lar thorough-bred Sawbones; they're only in trainin'."

"In other words they're Medical Students, I suppose?" said Mr. Pickwick.

Sam Weller nodded assent.

"I am glad of it," said Mr. Pickwick, casting his night-cap energetically on the counterpane, "They are fine fellows; very fine fellows, with judgments matured by observation and reflection; and tastes refined by reading and study. I am very glad of it."

"They're a smokin' cigars by the kitchen fire," said Sam.

"Ah!" observed Mr. Pickwick, rubbing his hands, "overflowing with kindly feelings and animal spirits. Just what I like to see!"

"And one on 'em," said Sam, not noticing his master's interruption, "one on 'em 's got his legs on the table, and is a drinkin' brandy neat, vile the tother one—him in the barnacles—has got a barrel o' oysters atween his knees, vich he's a openin' like steam, and as fast as he eats 'em, he takes a aim vith the shells at young dropsy, who's a settin' down fast asleep, in the chimbley corner."

"Eccentricities of genius, Sam," said Mr. Pickwick. "You may retire."

Sam did retire accordingly; and Mr. Pickwick, at the expiration of the quarter of an hour, went down to breakfast.

"Here he is at last," said old Wardle. "Pickwick, this is Miss Allen's brother, Mr. Benjamin Allen—Ben we call him, and so may you if you like. This gentleman is his very particular friend, Mr.—"

"Mr. Bob Sawyer," interposed Mr. Benjamin Allen, whereupon Mr. Bob Sawyer and Mr. Benjamin Allen laughed in concert.

Mr. Pickwick bowed to Bob Sawyer, and Bob Sawyer bowed to Mr. Pickwick; Bob and his very particular friend then applied themselves most assiduously to the eatables before them; and Mr. Pickwick had an opportunity of glancing at them both.

Mr. Benjamin Allen was a coarse, stout, thick-set young man, with black hair cut rather short, and a white face cut rather long. He was embellished with spectacles, and wore a white neckerchief. Below his single-breasted black surtout, which was buttoned up to his chin, appeared the usual number of pepper-and-salt coloured legs, terminating in a pair of imperfectly polished boots. Although his coat was short in the sleeves, it disclosed no vestige of a linen wristband; and although there was quite enough of his face to admit of the encroachment of a shirt collar, it was not graced by the smallest approach to that appendage. He presented altogether rather a mildewy appearance, and emitted a fragrant odour of full-flavoured Cubas.

Mr. Bob Sawyer, who was habited in a coarse blue coat, which, without being either greatcoat or surtout, partook of the nature and qualities of both, had about him that sort of slovenly smartness, and swaggering gait, which is peculiar to young gentlemen who smoke in the streets by day, shout and scream in the same by night, call waiters by their christian names, and do various other acts and deeds of an equally facetious description. He wore a pair of plaid trousers, and a large rough double-breasted waistcoat; and out of doors, carried a thick stick with a big top. He eschewed gloves, and looked, upon the whole, something like a dissipated Robinson Crusoe.

Such were the two worthies to whom Mr. Pickwick was introduced, as he took his seat at the breakfast table on Christmas morning.

"Splendid morning, gentlemen," said Mr. Pickwick.

Mr. Bob Sawyer slightly nodded his assent to the proposition, and asked Mr. Benjamin Allen for the mustard.

"Have you come far this morning, gentlemen?" inquired Mr. Pickwick.

"Blue Lion at Muggleton," briefly responded Mr. Allen.

"You should have joined us last night," said Mr. Pickwick.

"So we should," replied Bob Sawyer, "but the brandy was too good to leave in a hurry: wasn't it, Ben?"

"Certainly," said Mr. Benjamin Allen; "and the cigars were not bad, or the pork chops either: were they, Bob?"

"Decidedly not," said Bob. And the particular friends resumed their attack upon the breakfast, more freely than before, as if the recollection of last night's supper had imparted a new relish to the meal.

"Peg away, Bob," said Mr. Allen to his companion, encouragingly.

"So I do," replied Bob Sawyer. And so, to do him justice, he did.

"Nothing like dissecting, to give one an appetite," said Mr. Bob Sawyer, looking round the table.

Mr. Pickwick slightly shuddered.

"By the bye, Bob," said Mr. Allen, "have you finished that leg yet?"

"Nearly," replied Sawyer, helping himself to half a fowl as he spoke. "It's a very muscular one for a child's."

"Is it?" inquired Mr. Allen, carelessly.

"Very," said Bob Sawyer, with his mouth full.

"I've put my name down for an arm, at our place," said Mr. Allen. "We're clubbing for a subject, and the list is nearly full, only we can't get hold of any fellow that wants a head. I wish you'd take it."

"No," replied Bob Sawyer; "can't afford expensive luxuries."

"Nonsense!" said Allen.

"Can't indeed," rejoined Bob Sawyer. "I wouldn't mind a brain, but I couldn't stand a whole head."

"Hush, hush, gentlemen, pray," said Mr. Pickwick, "I hear the ladies."

As Mr. Pickwick spoke, the ladies, gallantly escorted by Messrs. Snodgrass, Winkle, and Tupman, returned from an early walk.

"Lor, Ben!" said Arabella, in a tone which expressed more surprise than pleasure at the sight of her brother.

"Come to take you home to-morrow," replied Benjamin. Mr. Winkle turned pale.

"Don't you see Bob Sawyer, Arabella?" enquired Mr. Benjamin Allen, somewhat reproachfully. Arabella gracefully held out her hand, in acknowledgment of Bob Sawyer's presence. A thrill of hatred struck to Mr. Winkle's heart, as Bob Sawyer inflicted on the proffered hand a perceptible squeeze.

"Ben dear!" said Arabella, blushing; "have—have—you been introduced to Mr. Winkle?"

"I have not been, but I shall be very happy to be, Arabella," replied her brother gravely. Here Mr. Allen bowed grimly to Mr. Winkle, while Mr. Winkle and Mr. Bob Sawyer glanced mutual distrust out of the corners of their eyes.

The arrival of the two new visitors, and the consequent check upon Mr. Winkle and the young lady with the fur round her boots, would in all probability have proved a very unpleasant interruption to the hilarity of the party, had not the cheerfulness of Mr. Pickwick, and the good humour of the host, been exerted to the very utmost for the common weal. Mr. Winkle gradually insinuated himself into the good graces of Mr. Benjamin Allen, and even joined in a friendly conversation with Mr. Bob Sawyer; who, enlivened with the brandy, and the breakfast, and the talking, gradually ripened into a state of extreme facetiousness, and related with much glee an agreeable anecdote, about the removal of a tumour on some gentleman's head, which he illustrated by means of an oyster-knife and a half-quartern loaf, to the great edification of the assembled company. Then the whole train went to church, where Mr. Benjamin Allen fell fast asleep; while Mr. Bob Sawyer abstracted his thoughts from worldly matters, by the ingenious process of carving his name on the seat of the pew, in corpulent letters of about four inches long.

"Now," said Wardle, after a substantial lunch, with the agreeable items of strong-beer and cherry-brandy, had been done ample justice to; "what say you to an hour on the ice? We shall have plenty of time."

"Capital!" said Mr. Benjamin Allen.

"Prime!" ejaculated Mr. Bob Sawyer.

"You skait, of course, Winkle?" said Wardle.

"Ye—yes; oh, yes;" replied Mr. Winkle. "I—I—am *rather* out of practice."

"Oh, *do* skait, Mr. Winkle," said Arabella. "I like to see it *so* much."

"Oh, it is *so* graceful," said another young lady.

A third young lady said it was elegant, and a fourth expressed her opinion that it was "swan-like."

"I should be very happy, I'm sure," said Mr. Winkle, reddening; "but I have no skaits."

This objection was at once overruled. Trundle had got a couple of pair, and the fat boy announced that there were half-a-dozen more, down stairs, whereat Mr. Winkle expressed exquisite delight, and looked exquisitely uncomfortable.

Old Wardle led the way to a pretty large sheet of ice; and the fat boy and Mr. Weller, having shovelled and swept away the snow which had fallen on it during the night, Mr. Bob Sawyer adjusted his skaits with a dexterity which to Mr. Winkle was perfectly marvellous, and described circles with his left leg, and cut figures of eight; and inscribed upon the ice, without once stopping for breath, a great many other pleasant and astonishing devices, to the excessive satisfaction of Mr. Pickwick, Mr. Tupman, and the ladies; which reached a pitch of positive enthusiasm, when old Wardle and Benjamin Allen, assisted by the aforesaid Bob Sawyer, performed some mystic evolutions, which they called a reel.

All this time, Mr. Winkle, with his face and hands blue with the cold, had been forcing a gimlet into the soles of his feet, and putting his skaits on, with the points behind, and getting the straps into a very complicated and entangled state, with the assistance of Mr. Snodgrass, who knew rather less about skaits than a Hindoo. At length, however, with the assistance of Mr. Weller, the unfortunate skaits were firmly screwed and buckled on, and Mr. Winkle was raised to his feet.

"Now, then, Sir," said Sam, in an encouraging tone; "off with you, and show 'em how to do it."

"Stop, Sam, stop," said Mr. Winkle, trembling violently, and clutching hold of Sam's arms with the grasp of a drowning man. "How slippery it is, Sam!"

"Not an uncommon thing upon ice, Sir," replied Mr. Weller. "Hold up, Sir."

This last observation of Mr. Weller's bore reference to a demonstration Mr. Winkle made at the instant, of a frantic desire to throw his feet in the air, and dash the back of his head on the ice.

"These—these—are very awkward skaits; ain't they, Sam?" inquired Mr. Winkle, staggering.

"I'm afeerd there's a orkard gen'lm'n in 'em, Sir," replied Sam.

"Now, Winkle," cried Mr. Pickwick, quite unconscious that there was anything the matter. "Come; the ladies are all anxiety."

"Yes, yes," replied Mr. Winkle, with a ghastly smile. "I'm coming."

"Just a goin' to begin," said Sam, endeavouring to disengage himself. "Now, Sir, start off."

"Stop an instant, Sam," gasped Mr. Winkle, clinging most affectionately to Mr. Weller. "I find I've got a couple of coats at home, that I don't want, Sam. You may have them, Sam."

"Thank'ee, Sir," replied Mr. Weller.

"Never mind touching your hat, Sam," said Mr. Winkle, hastily. "You needn't take your hand away, to do that. I meant to have given you five shillings this morning for a Christmas-box, Sam. I'll give it you this afternoon, Sam."

"You're wery good, Sir," replied Mr. Weller.

"Just hold me at first, Sam; will you?" said Mr. Winkle. "There—that's right. I shall soon get in the way of it, Sam. Not too fast, Sam; not too fast."

Mr. Winkle, stooping forward, with his body half doubled up, was being assisted over the ice by Mr. Weller, in a very singular and un-swan-like manner, when Mr. Pickwick most innocently shouted from the opposite bank—

"Sam!"

"Sir?" said Mr. Weller.

"Here. I want you."

"Let go, Sir," said Sam. "Don't you hear the governor a callin'? Let go, Sir."

With a violent effort, Mr. Weller disengaged himself from the grasp of the agonized Pickwickian; and, in so doing, administered a considerable impetus to the unhappy Mr. Winkle. With an accuracy which no degree of dexterity or practice could have insured, that unfortunate gentleman bore swiftly down into the centre of the reel, at the very moment when Mr. Bob Sawyer was performing a flourish of unparalleled beauty. Mr. Winkle struck wildly against him, and with a loud crash they both fell heavily down. Mr. Pickwick ran to the spot. Bob Sawyer had risen to his feet, but Mr. Winkle was far too wise to do anything of the kind in skaits. He was seated on the ice, making spasmodic efforts to smile; but anguish was depicted on every lineament of his countenance.

"Are you hurt?" inquired Mr. Benjamin Allen, with great anxiety.

"Not much," said Mr. Winkle, rubbing his back very hard.

"I wish you'd let me bleed you," said Mr. Benjamin with great eagerness.

"No, thank you," replied Mr. Winkle hurriedly.

"I really think you had better," said Allen.

"Thank you," replied Mr. Winkle; "I'd rather not."

"What do you think, Mr. Pickwick?" inquired Bob Sawyer.

Mr. Pickwick was excited and indignant. He beckoned to Mr. Weller, and said in a stern voice, "Take his skaits off."

"No; but really I had scarcely begun," remonstrated Mr. Winkle.

"Take his skaits off," repeated Mr. Pickwick firmly.

The command was not to be resisted. Mr. Winkle allowed Sam to obey it, in silence.

"Lift him up," said Mr. Pickwick. Sam assisted him to rise.

Mr. Pickwick retired a few paces apart from the bystanders; and, beckoning his friend to approach, fixed a searching look upon him, and uttered in a low, but distinct and emphatic tone, these remarkable words:

"You're a humbug, Sir."

"A what!" said Mr. Winkle, starting.

"A humbug, Sir. I will speak plainer, if you wish it. An impostor, Sir."

With these words, Mr. Pickwick turned slowly on his heel, and rejoined his friends.

While Mr. Pickwick was delivering himself of the sentiment just recorded, Mr. Weller and the fat boy, having by their joint endeavours cut out a slide, were exercising themselves thereupon, in a very masterly and brilliant manner. Sam Weller, in particular, was displaying that beautiful feat of fancy sliding which is currently denominated "knocking at the cobbler's door," and which is achieved by skimming over the ice on one foot, and occasionally giving a two-penny postman's knock upon it with the other. It was a good long slide, and there was something in the motion which Mr. Pickwick, who was very cold with standing still, could not help envying.

"It looks a nice warm exercise that, doesn't it?" he enquired of Wardle, when that gentleman was thoroughly out of breath, by reason of the indefatigable manner in which he had converted his legs into a pair of compasses, and drawn complicated problems on the ice.

"Ah, it does, indeed," replied Wardle. "Do you slide?"

"I used to do so, on the gutters, when I was a boy," replied Mr. Pickwick.

"Try it now," said Wardle.

"Oh, do, please Mr. Pickwick," cried all the ladies.

"I should be very happy to afford you any amusement," replied Mr. Pickwick, "but I haven't done such a thing these thirty years."

"Pooh! pooh! nonsense!" said Wardle, dragging off his skaits with the impetuosity which characterised all his proceedings. "Here; I'll keep you company; come along." And away went the good-tempered old fellow down the slide, with a rapidity which came very close upon Mr. Weller, and beat the fat boy all to nothing.

Mr. Pickwick paused, considered, pulled off his gloves and put them in his hat, took two or three short runs, baulked himself as often, and at last took another run and went slowly and gravely down the slide, with his feet about a yard and a quarter apart, amidst the gratified shouts of all the spectators.

"Keep the pot a bilin', Sir," said Sam; and down went Wardle again, and then Mr. Pickwick, and then Sam, and then Mr. Winkle, and then Mr. Bob Sawyer, and then the fat boy, and then Mr. Snodgrass, following closely upon each other's heels, and running after each other with as much eagerness as if all their future prospects in life depended on their expedition.

It was the most intensely interesting thing, to observe the manner in which Mr. Pickwick performed his share in the ceremony: to watch the torture of anxiety with which he viewed the person behind, gaining upon him at the imminent hazard of tripping him up: to see him gradually expend the painful force which he had put on at first, and turn slowly round on the slide, with his face towards the point from which he had started: to contemplate the playful smile which mantled on his face when he had accomplished the distance, and the eagerness with which he turned round when he had done so, and ran after his predecessor, his black gaiters tripping pleasantly through the snow, and his eyes beaming cheerfulness and gladness through his spectacles. And when he was knocked down, (which happened upon the average every third round), it was the most invigorating sight that can possibly be imagined, to behold him gather up his hat, gloves, and handkerchief, with a glowing countenance, and resume his station in the rank, with an ardour and enthusiasm which nothing could abate.

The sport was at its height, the sliding was at the quickest, the laughter was at the loudest, when a sharp smart crack was heard. There was a quick rush towards the bank, a wild scream from the ladies, and a shout from Mr. Tupman. A large mass of ice disappeared, the water bubbled up over it, and Mr. Pickwick's hat, gloves, and handkerchief were floating on the surface; and this was all of Mr. Pickwick that anybody could see.

Dismay and anguish were depicted on every countenance; the males turned pale, and the females fainted; Mr. Snodgrass and Mr. Winkle grasped each other by the hand, and gazed at the spot where their leader had gone down, with frenzied eagerness; while Mr. Tupman, by way of rendering the promptest assistance, and at the same time conveying to any persons who might be within hearing, the clearest possible notion of the catastrophe, ran off across the country at his utmost speed, screaming "Fire!" with all his might and main.

It was at this very moment, when old Wardle and Sam Weller were approaching the hole with cautious steps, and Mr. Benjamin Allen was holding a hurried consultation with Mr. Bob Sawyer, on the advisability of bleeding the company generally, as an improving little bit of professional practice—it was at this very moment that a face, head, and shoulders emerged from beneath the water, and disclosed the features and spectacles of Mr. Pickwick.

"Keep yourself up for an instant—for only one instant," bawled Mr. Snodgrass.

"Yes, do; let me implore you—for my sake," roared Mr. Winkle, deeply affected. The adjuration was rather unnecessary; the probability being, that if Mr. Pickwick had declined to keep himself up for anybody else's sake, it would have occurred to him that he might as well do so, for his own.

"Do you feel the bottom there, old fellow?" said Wardle.

"Yes, certainly," replied Mr. Pickwick, wringing the water from his head and face, and gasping for breath. "I fell upon my back. I couldn't get on my feet at first."

The clay upon so much of Mr. Pickwick's coat as was yet visible, bore testimony to the accuracy of this statement; and as the fears of the spectators were still further relieved by the fat boy's suddenly recollecting that the water was nowhere more than five feet 'deep, prodigies of valour were performed to get him out. After a vast quantity of splashing, and cracking, and struggling, Mr. Pickwick was at length fairly extricated from his unpleasant position, and once more stood on dry land.

"Oh, he'll catch his death of cold," said Emily.

"Dear old thing!" said Arabella. "Let me wrap this shawl round you, Mr. Pickwick."

"Ah, that's the best thing you can do," said Wardle;

"and when you've got it on, run home as fast as your legs can carry you, and jump into bed directly."

A dozen shawls were offered on the instant; and three or four of the thickest having been selected, Mr. Pickwick was wrapped up, and started off, under the guidance of Mr. Weller; presenting the singular phenomenon of an elderly gentleman dripping wet, and without a hat, with his arms bound down to his sides, skimming over the ground without any clearly defined purpose, at the rate of six good English miles an hour.

But Mr. Pickwick cared not for appearances in such an extreme case, and urged on by Sam Weller, he kept at the very top of his speed until he reached the door of Manor Farm, where Mr. Tupman had arrived some five minutes before, and had frightened the old lady into palpitations of the heart, by impressing her with the unalterable conviction that the kitchen chimney was on fire—a calamity which always presented itself in the most glowing colours to the old lady's mind, when anybody about her evinced the smallest agitation.

Mr. Pickwick paused not an instant until he was snug in bed. Sam Weller lighted a blazing fire in the room, and took up his dinner; a bowl of punch was carried up afterwards, and a grand carouse held in honour of his safety. Old Wardle would not hear of his rising, so they made the bed the chair, and Mr. Pickwick presided. A second and a third bowl were ordered in; and when Mr. Pickwick awoke next morning, there was not a symptom of rheumatism about him, which proves, as Mr. Bob Sawyer very justly observed, that there is nothing like hot punch in such cases, and that if ever hot punch did fail to act as a preventive, it was merely because the patient fell into the vulgar error of not taking enough of it.

The jovial party broke up next morning. Breakings up are capital things in our school days, but in after life they are painful enough. Death, self-interest, and fortune's changes, are every day breaking up many a happy group and scattering them far and wide; and the boys and girls never come back again. We do not mean to say that it was exactly the case in this particular instance; all we wish to inform the reader is, that the different members of the party dispersed to their several homes; that Mr. Pickwick and his friends once more took their seats on the top of the Muggleton coach; and that Arabella Allen repaired to her place of destination, wherever it might have been—we dare say Mr. Winkle knew, but we confess we don't—under the care and guardianship of her brother Benjamin, and his most intimate and particular friend, Mr. Bob Sawyer.

Before they separated, however, that gentleman and Mr. Benjamin Allen drew Mr. Pickwick aside with an air of some mystery; and Mr. Bob Sawyer thrusting his forefinger between two of Mr. Pickwick's ribs, and thereby displaying his native drollery, and his knowledge of the anatomy of the human frame, at one and the same time, enquired—

"I say, old boy, where do you hang out?"

Mr. Pickwick replied that he was at present suspended at the George and Vulture.

"I wish you'd come and see me," said Bob Sawyer.

"Nothing would give me greater pleasure," replied Mr. Pickwick.

"There's my lodgings," said Mr. Bob Sawyer, producing a card, "Lant Street, Borough; it's near Guy's, and handy for me you know. Little distance after you've passed Saint George's Church—turns out of the High Street on the right hand side the way."

"I shall find it," said Mr. Pickwick.

"Come on Thursday week, and bring the other chaps with you," said Mr. Bob Sawyer, "I'm going to have a few medical fellows that night."

Mr. Pickwick expressed the pleasure it would afford him to meet the medical fellows; and after Mr. Bob Sawyer had informed him that he meant to be very cosey, and that his friend Ben was to be one of the party, they shook hands and separated.

We feel that in this place we lay ourself open to the enquiry whether Mr. Winkle was whispering, during this brief conversation, to Arabella Allen, and if so, what he said; and furthermore, whether Mr. Snodgrass was conversing apart with Emily Wardle, and if so, what *he* said. To this, we reply, that whatever they might have said to the ladies, they said nothing at all to Mr. Pickwick or Mr. Tupman for eight-and-twenty miles, and that they sighed very often, refused ale and brandy, and looked gloomy. If our observant lady readers can deduce any satisfactory inferences from these facts, we beg them by all means to do so.

CHAPTER XXX.

WHICH IS ALL ABOUT THE LAW, AND SUNDRY GREAT AUTHORITIES LEARNED THEREIN.

SCATTERED about, in various holes and corners of the Temple, are certain dark and dirty chambers, in and out of which, all the morning in Vacation, and half the evening too in Term time, there may be seen constantly hurrying with bundles of papers under their arms, and protruding from their pockets, an almost uninterrupted succession of Lawyers' Clerks. There are several grades of Lawyers' Clerks. There is the Articled Clerk, who has paid a premium, and is an attorney in perspective, who runs a tailor's bill, receives invitations to parties, knows a family in Gower Street and another in Tavistock Square, goes out of town every Long Vacation to see his father, who keeps live horses innumerable; and who is, in short, the very aristocrat of clerks. There is the salaried clerk—out of door, or in door, as the case may be—who devotes the major part of his thirty shillings a week to his personal pleasure and adornment, repairs half-price to the Adelphi at least three times a week, dissipates majestically at the cider cellars afterwards, and is a dirty caricature of the fashion, which expired six months ago. There is the middle-aged copying clerk, with a large family, who is always shabby, and often drunk. And there are the office lads in their first surtouts, who feel a befitting contempt for boys at day schools, club as they go home at night, for saveloys and porter, and think there's nothing like "life." There are varieties of the genus too numerous to recapitulate, but however numerous they may be, they are all to be seen, at certain regulated business hours, hurrying to and from the places we have just mentioned.

These sequestered nooks are the public offices of the legal profession, where writs are issued, judgments signed, declarations filed, and numerous other ingenious little machines put in motion for the torture and torment of His Majesty's liege subjects, and the comfort and emolument of the practitioners of the law. They are, for the most part, low-roofed, mouldy rooms, where innumerable rolls of parch-

ment, which have been perspiring in secret for the last century, send forth an agreeable odour, which is mingled by day with the scent of the dry rot, and by night with the various exhalations which arise from damp cloaks, festering umbrellas, and the coarsest tallow candles.

About half-past seven o'clock in the evening, some ten days or a fortnight after Mr. Pickwick and his friends returned to London, there hurried into one of these offices, an individual in a brown coat and brass buttons, whose long hair was scrupulously twisted round the rim of his napless hat, and whose soiled drab trousers were so tightly strapped over his Blucher boots, that his knees threatened every moment to start from their concealment. He produced from his coat pockets a long and narrow strip of parchment, on which the presiding functionary impressed an illegible black stamp. He then drew forth four scraps of paper, of similar dimensions, each containing a printed copy of the strip of parchment with blanks for a name; and having filled up the blanks, put all the five documents in his pocket, and hurried away.

The man in the brown coat with the cabalistic documents in his pocket, was no other than our old acquaintance Mr. Jackson, of the house of Dodson and Fogg, Freeman's Court, Cornhill. Instead of returning to the office from whence he came, however, he bent his steps direct to Sun Court, and walking straight into the George and Vulture, demanded to know whether one Mr. Pickwick was within.

"Call Mr. Pickwick's servant, Tom," said the barmaid of the George and Vulture.

"Don't trouble yourself," said Mr. Jackson, "I've come on business. If you'll show me Mr. Pickwick's room, I'll step up myself."

"What name, Sir?" said the waiter.

"Jackson," replied the clerk.

The waiter stepped up stairs to announce Mr. Jackson, but Mr. Jackson saved him the trouble by following close at his heels, and walking into the apartment before he could articulate a syllable.

Mr. Pickwick had that day invited his three friends to dinner; and they were all seated round the fire, drinking their wine, when Mr. Jackson presented himself, as above described.

"How de do, Sir?" said Mr. Jackson, nodding to Mr. Pickwick.

That gentleman bowed, and looked somewhat surprised, for the physiognomy of Mr. Jackson dwelt not in his recollection.

"I have called from Dodson and Fogg's," said Mr. Jackson, in an explanatory tone.

Mr. Pickwick roused at the name. "I refer you to my attorney Sir: Mr. Perker, of Gray's Inn," said he. "Waiter, show this gentleman out."

"Beg your pardon, Mr. Pickwick," said Jackson, deliberately depositing his hat on the floor, and drawing from his pocket the strip of parchment. "But personal service, by clerk or agent, in these cases, you know, Mr. Pickwick—eh, Sir? nothing like caution, Sir, in all legal forms—eh?"

Here Mr. Jackson cast his eye on the parchment; and, resting his hands on the table, and looking round with a winning and persuasive smile, said, "Now come; don't let's have no words about such a little matter as this. Which of you gentlemen's name's Snodgrass?"

At this inquiry, Mr. Snodgrass gave such a very undisguised and palpable start, that no further reply was needed.

"Ah! I thought so," said Mr. Jackson, more affably than

before. "I've got a little something to trouble you with, Sir."

"Me!" exclaimed Mr. Snodgrass.

"It's only a *subpœna* in Bardell and Pickwick on behalf of the plaintiff," replied Jackson, singling out one of the slips of paper, and producing a shilling from his waistcoat pocket. "It'll come on, in the settens after Term; fourteenth of Febooary, we expect; we've marked it a special jury cause, and it's only ten down the paper. That's yours, Mr. Snodgrass." As Jackson said this he presented the parchment before the eyes of Mr. Snodgrass, and slipped the paper and the shilling into his hand.

Mr. Tupman had witnessed this process in silent astonishment, when Jackson, turning sharply upon him, said:

"I think I ain't mistaken when I say your name's Tupman, am I?"

Mr. Tupman looked at Mr. Pickwick; but, perceiving no encouragement in that gentleman's widely-opened eyes to deny his name, said:

"Yes, my name *is* Tupman, Sir."

"And that other gentleman's Mr. Winkle, I think," said Jackson.

Mr. Winkle faltered out a reply in the affirmative; and both gentlemen were forthwith invested with a slip of paper, and a shilling each, by the dexterous Mr. Jackson.

"Now," said Jackson, "I'm afraid you'll think me rather troublesome, but I want somebody else, if it ain't inconvenient. I *have* Samuel Weller's name here, Mr. Pickwick."

"Send my servant here, waiter," said Mr. Pickwick. The waiter retired, considerably astonished, and Mr. Pickwick motioned Jackson to a seat.

There was a painful pause, which was at length broken by the innocent defendant.

"I suppose, Sir," said Mr. Pickwick, his indignation rising while he spoke; "I suppose, Sir, that it is the intention of your employers to seek to criminate me, upon the testimony of my own friends."

Mr. Jackson struck his fore-finger several times against the left side of his nose, to intimate that he was not there to disclose the secrets of the prison-house, and playfully rejoined,

"Not knowin', can't say."

"For what other reason, Sir," pursued Mr. Pickwick, "are these subpœnas served upon them, if not for this?"

"Very good plant, Mr. Pickwick," replied Jackson, slowly shaking his head. "But it won't do. No harm in trying, but there's little to be got out of me."

Here Mr. Jackson smiled once more upon the company; and, applying his left thumb to the tip of his nose, worked a visionary coffee-mill with his right hand, thereby performing a very graceful piece of pantomime (then much in vogue, but now, unhappily, almost obsolete) which was familiarly denominated "taking a grinder."

"No, no, Mr. Pickwick," said Jackson, in conclusion; "Perker's people must guess what we've served these subpœnas for. If they can't, they must wait till the action comes on, and then they'll find out."

Mr. Pickwick bestowed a look of excessive disgust on his unwelcome visitor, and would probably have hurled some tremendous anathema at the heads of Messrs. Dodson and Fogg, had not Sam's entrance at the instant interrupted him.

"Samuel Weller?" said Mr. Jackson, enquiringly.

"Vun o' the truest things as you've said for many a long year," replied Sam, in a most composed manner.

"Here's a subpœna for you, Mr. Weller," said Jackson.

"What's that in English?" enquired Sam.

"Here's the original," said Jackson, declining the required explanation.

"Which?" said Sam.

"This," replied Jackson, shaking the parchment.

"Oh, that's the 'rig'nal, is it?" said Sam. "Well, I'm wery glad I've seen the 'rig'nal, 'cos it's a gratifyin' sort o' thing, and eases vun's mind so much."

"And here's the shilling," said Jackson. "It's from Dodson and Fogg's."

"And it's uncommon handsome o' Dodson and Fogg, as knows so little of me, to come down vith a present," said Sam. "I feel it as a wery high compliment, Sir; and it's a wery hon'rable thing to them, as they knows how to reward merit verever they meets it. Besides vich, it's wery affectin' to one's feelin's."

As Mr. Weller said this, he inflicted a little friction on his right eyelid, with the sleeve of his coat, after the most approved manner of actors when they are in domestic pathetics.

Mr. Jackson seemed rather puzzled by Sam's proceedings; but, as he had served the subpœnas, and had nothing more to say, he made a feint of putting on the one glove which he usually carried in his hand, for the sake of appearances; and returned to the office to report progress.

Mr. Pickwick slept little that night; his memory had received a very disagreeable refresher on the subject of Mrs. Bardell's action. He breakfasted betimes next morning; and, desiring Sam to accompany him, set forth towards Gray's Inn square.

"Sam!" said Mr. Pickwick, looking round, when they got to the end of Cheapside.

"Sir?" said Sam, stepping up to his master.

"Which way?"

"Up Newgate-street."

Mr. Pickwick did not turn round immediately, but looked vacantly in Sam's face for a few seconds, and heaved a deep sigh.

"What's the matter, Sir?" enquired Sam.

"This action, Sam," said Mr. Pickwick, "is expected to come on, on the fourteenth of next month."

"Remarkable coincidence that 'ere, Sir," replied Sam.

"Why remarkable, Sam?" enquired Mr. Pickwick.

"Walentine's day, Sir," responded Sam; "reg'lar good day for a breach o' promise trial."

Mr. Weller's smile awakened no gleam of mirth in his master's countenance. Mr. Pickwick turned abruptly round, and led the way in silence.

They had walked some distance, Mr. Pickwick trotting on before, plunged in profound meditation, and Sam following behind, with a countenance expressive of the most enviable and easy defiance of everything and everybody, when the latter, who was always especially anxious to impart to his master any exclusive information he possessed, quickened his pace until he was close at Mr. Pickwick's heels; and, pointing up at a house they were passing, said,

"Wery nice pork-shop that 'ere, Sir."

"Yes, it seems so," said Mr. Pickwick.

"Celebrated Sassage factory," said Sam.

"Is it?" said Mr. Pickwick.

"Is it!" reiterated Sam, with some indignation; "I should rayther think it was. Why Sir, bless your innocent eyebrows, that's vere the mysterious disappearance of a respectable tradesman took place, four year ago."

"You don't mean to say he was burked, Sam?" said Mr. Pickwick, looking hastily round.

"No I don't indeed, Sir," replied Mr. Weller, "I vish I did; far worse than that. He was the master o' that 'ere shop, Sir, and the inwenter o' the patent-never-leavin'-off sassage steam 'ingine, as ud swaller up a pavin' stone if you put it too near, and grind it into sassages as easy as if it was a tender young babby. Wery proud o' that machine he was, as it was nat'ral he should be; and he'd stand down in the celler a lookin' at it, ven it was in full play, till he got quite melancholy with joy. A wery happy man he'd ha' been, Sir, in the procession o' that 'ere ingine and two more lovely hinfants besides, if it hadn't been for his wife, who was a most ow-dacious wixin. She was always a follerin' him about, and dinnin' in his ears 'till at last he couldn't stand it no longer. 'I'll tell you what it is, my dear,' he says one day; 'if you persewere in this here sort of amusement,' he says, 'I'm blessed if I don't go away to 'Merriker; and that's all about it.' 'You're a idle willin,' says she, 'and I vish the 'Merrikins joy of their bargin.' Arter vich she keeps on abusin' him for half an hour, and then runs into the little parlour behind the shop, sets to a screamin', says he'll be the death on her, and falls in a fit, which lasts for three good hours—one o' them fits which is all screamin' and kickin'. Well, next mornin' the husband was missin'. He hadn't taken nothin' from the till,—hadn't even put on his great coat, so it was quite clear he warn't gone to 'Merriker. Didn't come back next day, didn't come back next week; the Missis had bills printed sayin' that, if he'd come back, he should be forgiven everythin', (which was very liberal, seein' that he hadn't done nothin' at all,) all the canals was dragged, and for two months arterwards venever a body turned up, it was carried, as a reg'lar thing, straight off to the sassage shop. Hows'ever, none on 'em answered, so they gave out that he'd run avay, and she kept on the bis'ness. One Saturday night, a little thin old gen'lm'n comes into the shop in a great passion and says, 'Are you the missis o' this here shop?' 'Yes I am,' says she. 'Well Ma'am,' says he, 'then I've just looked in to say, that me and my family ain't a goin' to be choaked for nothin'; and more than that Ma'am,' he says, 'you'll allow me to observe, that as you don't use the primest parts of the meat in the manafacter o' sassages, I think you'd find beef come nearly as cheap as buttons.' 'Buttons, Sir!' says she, 'Buttons, Ma'am,' says the little old gentleman, unfolding a bit of paper, and shewin' twenty or thirty halves o' buttons. 'Nice seasonin' for sassages, is trousers' buttons, Ma'am.' 'They're my husband's buttons,' says the widder, beginnin' to faint. 'What!' screams the little old gen'lm'n, turnin' wery pale. 'I see it all,' says the widder; 'in a fit of temporary insanity he rashly converted his-self into sassages!' And so he had, Sir," said Mr. Weller, looking steadily into Mr. Pickwick's horror-stricken countenance, "or else he'd been draw'd into the ingine; but however that might ha' been, the little old gen'lm'n, who had been remarkably partial to sassages all his life, rushed out o' the shop in a wild state, and was never heerd on artervards!"

The relation of this affecting incident of private life, brought master and man to Mr. Perker's chambers. Lowten, holding the door half open, was in conversation with a rustily-clad, miserable looking man, in boots without toes, and gloves without fingers. There were traces of privation and suffering—almost of despair—in his lank and careworn countenance; he felt his poverty, for he shrunk to the dark side of the staircase as Mr. Pickwick approached.

"It's very unfortunate," said the stranger with a sigh.

"Very," said Lowten, scribbling his name on the door post with his pen and rubbing it out again with the feather. "Will you leave a message for him?"

"When do you think he'll be back?" enquired the stranger.

"Quite uncertain," replied Lowten, winking at Mr. Pickwick, as the stranger cast his eyes towards the ground.

"You don't think it would be of any use my waiting for him?" said the stranger, looking wistfully into the office.

"Oh, no, I'm sure it wouldn't," replied the clerk, moving a little more into the centre of the door-way. "He's certain not to be back this week, and it's a chance whether he will, next, for when Perker once gets out of town, he's never in a hurry to come back again."

"Out of town!" said Mr. Pickwick; "dear me, how unfortunate!"

"Don't go away, Mr. Pickwick," said Lowten, "I've got a letter for you." The stranger seeming to hesitate, once more looked towards the ground, and the clerk winked slily at Mr. Pickwick as if to intimate that some exquisite piece of humour was going forward; though what it was, Mr. Pickwick could not, for the life of him, divine.

"Step in, Mr. Pickwick," said Lowten. "Well, will you leave a message, Mr. Watty, or will you call again?"

"Ask him to be so kind as to leave out word what has been done in my business," said the man; "for God's sake don't neglect it, Mr. Lowten."

"No, no; I won't forget it," replied the clerk. "Walk in, Mr. Pickwick. Good morning, Mr. Watty; it's a fine day for walking, isn't it?" And, seeing that the stranger still lingered, he beckoned Sam Weller to follow his master in, and shut the door in his face.

"There never was such a pestering bankrupt as that, since the world began, I do believe!" said Lowten, throwing down his pen with the air of an injured man. "His affairs haven't been in Chancery quite four years yet, and I'm d——d if he don't come worrying me twice a-week. Step this way, Mr. Pickwick. Perker is in, and he'll see you, I know. Devilish cold," he added pettishly, "standing at that door, wasting one's time with such seedy vagabonds." And, having very vehemently stirred a particularly large fire, with a particularly small poker, the clerk led the way to his principal's private room, and announced Mr. Pickwick.

"Ah, my dear Sir," said little Mr. Perker, bustling up from his chair; "Well, my dear Sir, and what's the news about your matter—eh? Anything more about our friends in Freeman's-court? They've not been sleeping, I know that. Ah, they're very smart fellows—very smart, indeed."

As the little man concluded, he took an emphatic pinch of snuff, as a tribute to the smartness of Messrs. Dodson and Fogg.

"They are great scoundrels," said Mr. Pickwick.

"Aye, aye," said the little man; "that's a mere matter of opinion, you know, and we won't dispute about terms; because of course you can't be expected to view these subjects with a professional eye. Well, we've done everything that's necessary. I have retained Serjeant Snubbin."

"Is he a good man?" enquired Mr. Pickwick.

"Good man!" replied Perker; "bless your heart and soul, my dear Sir, Serjeant Snubbin is at the very top of his profession. Gets treble the business of any man in court—engaged in every case. You needn't mention it abroad; but we say—we of the profession—that Serjeant Snubbin leads the court by the nose."

The little man took another pinch of snuff as he made this communication, and nodded mysteriously to Mr. Pickwick.

"They have subpœna'd my three friends," said Mr. Pickwick.

"Ah! of course they would," replied Perker. "Important witnesses, saw you in a delicate situation."

"But she fainted of her own accord," said Mr. Pickwick. "She threw herself into my arms."

"Very likely, my dear Sir," replied Perker; "very likely and very natural. Nothing more so, my dear Sir—nothing. But who's to prove it?"

"They have subpœna'd my servant too," said Mr. Pickwick, quitting the other point; for there Mr. Perker's question had somewhat staggered him.

"Sam?" said Perker.

Mr. Pickwick replied in the affirmative.

"Of course, my dear Sir; of course. I knew they would; I could have told *you* that, a month ago. You know, my dear Sir, if you *will* take the management of your affairs into your own hands after entrusting them to your Solicitor, you must also take the consequences." Here Mr. Perker drew himself up with conscious dignity, and brushed some stray grains of snuff from his shirt frill.

"And what do they want him to prove?" asked Mr. Pickwick, after two or three minutes' silence.

"That you sent him up to the Plaintiff's to make some offer of a compromise, I suppose," replied Perker. "It don't matter much, though I don't think many counsel could get a great deal out of *him*."

"I don't think they could," said Mr. Pickwick; smiling, despite his vexation, at the idea of Sam's appearance as a witness. "What course do we pursue?"

"We have only one to adopt, my dear Sir," replied Perker; "cross-examine the witnesses, trust to Snubbin's eloquence, throw dust in the eyes of the judge; and ourselves on the jury."

"And suppose the verdict is against me?" said Mr. Pickwick.

Mr. Perker smiled, took a very long pinch of snuff, stirred the fire, shrugged his shoulders, and remained expressively silent.

"You mean that in that case I must pay the damages?" said Mr. Pickwick, who had watched this telegraphic answer with considerable sternness.

Perker gave the fire another very unnecessary poke, and said "I am afraid so."

"Then I beg to announce to you, my unalterable determination to pay no damages whatever," said Mr. Pickwick, most emphatically. "None, Perker. Not a pound, not a penny, of my money shall find its way into the pockets of Dodson and Fogg. That is my deliberate and irrevocable determination." And Mr. Pickwick gave a heavy blow on the table beside him, in confirmation of the irrevocability of his intention.

"Very well, my dear Sir, very well," said Perker. "You know best, of course."

"Of course," replied Mr. Pickwick hastily. "Where does Serjeant Snubbin live?"

"In Lincoln's Inn Old Square," replied Perker.

"I should like to see him," said Mr. Pickwick.

"See Serjeant Snubbin, my dear Sir!" rejoined Perker, in utter amazement. "Pooh, pooh, my dear Sir, impossible. See Serjeant Snubbin! Bless you, my dear Sir, such a thing was never heard of, without a consultation fee being previously paid, and a consultation fixed. It couldn't be done, my dear Sir; it couldn't be done."

Mr. Pickwick, however, had made up his mind not only that it could be done, but that it should be done; and the consequence was, that within ten minutes after he had received the assurance that the thing was impossible, he was conducted by his solicitor into the outer office of the great Serjeant Snubbin himself.

It was an uncarpeted room of tolerable dimensions, with a large writing-table drawn up near the fire, the baize top of which had long since lost all claim to its original hue of green, and had gradually grown grey with dust and age, except where all traces of its natural colour were obliterated by ink-stains. Upon the table were numerous little bundles of papers tied with red tape; and behind it, sat an elderly clerk, whose sleek appearance and heavy gold watch-chain presented imposing indications of the extensive and lucrative practice of Mr. Serjeant Snubbin.

"Is the Serjeant in his room, Mr. Mallard?" inquired Perker, offering his box with all imaginable courtesy.

"Yes he is," was the reply, "but he's very busy. Look here; not an opinion given yet, on any one of these cases; and an expedition fee paid with all of 'em." The clerk smiled as he said this, and inhaled the pinch of snuff with a zest which seemed to be compounded of a fondness for snuff and a relish for fees.

"Something like practice that," said Perker.

"Yes," said the barrister's clerk, producing his own box, and offering it with the greatest cordiality; "and the best of it, is, that as nobody alive except myself can read the Serjeant's writing, they are obliged to wait for the opinions, when he has given them, till I have copied 'em, ha—ha—ha!"

"Which makes good for we know who, besides the Serjeant, and draws a little more out of the clients, eh?" said Perker; "Ha, ha, ha!" At this the Serjeant's clerk laughed again—not a noisy boisterous laugh, but a silent, internal chuckle, which Mr. Pickwick disliked to hear. When a man bleeds inwardly, it is a dangerous thing for himself; but when he laughs inwardly, it bodes no good to other people.

"You haven't made me out that little list of the fees that I'm in your debt, have you?" said Perker.

"No, I have not," replied the clerk.

"I wish you would," said Perker. "Let me have them, and I'll send you a cheque. But I suppose you're too busy pocketing the ready money, to think of the debtors, eh? ha, ha, ha!" This sally seemed to tickle the clerk amazingly, and he once more enjoyed a little quiet laugh to himself.

"But, Mr. Mallard, my dear friend," said Perker, suddenly recovering his gravity, and drawing the great man's great man into a corner, by the lappel of his coat, "you must persuade the Serjeant to see me, and my client here."

"Come, come," said the clerk, "that's not bad either. See the Serjeant! come, that's too absurd." Notwithstanding the absurdity of the proposal, however, the clerk allowed himself to be gently drawn beyond the hearing of Mr. Pickwick; and after a short conversation conducted in whispers, walked softly down a little dark passage and disappeared into the legal luminary's sanctum, from whence he shortly returned on tiptoe, and informed Mr. Perker and Mr. Pickwick that the Serjeant had been prevailed upon, in violation of all established rules and customs, to admit them at once.

Mr. Serjeant Snubbin was a lantern-faced sallow-complexioned man, of about five-and-forty, or—as the novels say—he might be fifty. He had that dull-looking boiled eye which is so often to be seen in the heads of people who have applied themselves during many years to a weary and laborious course of study; and which would have been sufficient, without the additional eyeglass which dangled from a broad black riband round his neck, to warn a stranger that he was very near-sighted. His hair was thin and weak, which was partly attributable to his having never devoted much time to its arrangement, and partly to his having worn for five-and-twenty years the forensic wig which hung on a block beside him. The marks of hair-powder on his coat-collar, and the ill-washed and worse tied white neckerchief round his throat, showed that he had not found leisure since he left the court to make any alteration in his dress; while the slovenly style of the remainder of his costume warranted the inference that his personal appearance would not have been very much improved if he had. Books of practice, heaps of papers, and opened letters, were scattered over the table without any attempt at order or arrangement; the furniture of the room was old and ricketty; the doors of the book-case were rotting in their hinges; the dust flew out from the carpet in little clouds at every step; the blinds were yellow with age and dirt; and the state of everything in the room showed, with a clearness not to be mistaken, that Mr. Serjeant Snubbin was far too much occupied with his professional pursuits to take any great heed or regard of his personal comforts.

The Serjeant was writing when his clients entered; he bowed abstractedly when Mr. Pickwick was introduced by his solicitor; and then, motioning them to a seat, put his pen carefully in the inkstand, nursed his left leg, and waited to be spoken to.

"Mr. Pickwick is the defendant in Bardell and Pickwick, Serjeant Snubbin," said Perker.

"I am retained in that, am I?" said the Serjeant.

"You are, Sir," replied Perker.

The Serjeant nodded his head, and waited for something else.

"Mr. Pickwick was anxious to call upon you, Serjeant Snubbin," said Perker, "to state to you, before you entered upon the case, that he denies there being any ground or pretence whatever for the action against him; and that unless he came into court with clean hands, and without the most conscientious conviction that he was right in resisting the plaintiff's demand, he would not be there at all. I believe I state your views correctly; do I not, my dear Sir?" said the little man, turning to Mr. Pickwick.

"Quite so," replied that gentleman.

Mr. Serjeant Snubbin unfolded his glasses, raised them to his eyes; and, after looking at Mr. Pickwick for a few seconds with great curiosity, turned to Mr. Perker, and said, smiling slightly as he spoke—

"Has Mr. Pickwick a strong case?"

The attorney shrugged his shoulders.

"Do you purpose calling witnesses?"

"No."

The smile on the Serjeant's countenance became more defined; he rocked his leg with increased violence; and, throwing himself back in his easy-chair, coughed dubiously.

These tokens of the Serjeant's presentiments on the subject, slight as they were, were not lost on Mr. Pickwick. He settled the spectacles, through which he had attentively regarded such demonstrations of the barrister's feeling as he had permitted himself to exhibit, more firmly on his nose; and said with great energy, and in utter disregard of all Mr. Perker's admonitory winkings and frownings—

"My wishing to wait upon you for such a purpose as this, Sir, appears, I have no doubt, to a gentleman who sees so much of these matters as you must necessarily do, a very extraordinary circumstance."

The Serjeant tried to look gravely at the fire, but the smile came back again.

"Gentlemen of your profession, Sir," continued Mr. Pickwick, "see the worst side of human nature—all its disputes, all its ill-will and bad blood, rise up before you. You know from your experience of juries (I mean no disparagement to you, or them) how much depends upon *effect*: and you are apt to attribute to others, a desire to use, for purposes of deception and self-interest, the very instruments which you, in pure honesty and honour of purpose, and with a laudable desire to do your utmost for your client, know the temper and worth of so well, from constantly employing them yourselves. I really believe that to this circumstance may be attributed the vulgar but very general notion of your being, as a body, suspicious, distrustful, and over-cautious. Conscious as I am, Sir, of the disadvantage of making such a declaration to you, under such circumstances, I have come here, because I wish you distinctly to understand, as my friend Mr. Perker has said, that I am innocent of the falsehood laid to my charge; and although I am very well aware of the inestimable value of your assistance, Sir, I must beg to add, that unless you sincerely believe this, I would rather be deprived of the aid of your talents than have the advantage of them."

Long before the close of this address, which we are bound to say was of a very prosy character for Mr. Pickwick, the Serjeant had relapsed into a state of abstraction. After some minutes, however, during which he had reassumed his pen, he appeared to be again aware of the presence of his clients; and, raising his head from the paper, said, rather snappishly—

"Who's with me in this case?"

"Mr. Phunky, Serjeant Snubbin," replied the attorney.

"Phunky, Phunky," said the Serjeant; "I never heard the name before. He must be a very young man."

"Yes, he is a very young man," replied the attorney. "He was only called the other day. Let me see—oh, he hasn't been at the Bar eight years yet."

"Ah, I thought not," said the Serjeant, in that sort of pitying tone in which ordinary folks would speak of a very helpless little child. "Mr. Mallard, send round to Mr.—Mr.—"

"Phunky's—Holborn Court, Gray's Inn," interposed Perker—(Holborn Court, by the bye, is South Square now)—"Mr. Phunky; and say I should be glad if he'd step here, a moment."

Mr. Mallard departed to execute his commission; and Serjeant Snubbin relapsed into abstraction until Mr. Phunky himself was introduced.

Although an infant barrister, he was a full-grown man. He had a very nervous manner, and a painful hesitation in his speech; it did not appear to be a natural defect, but seemed rather the result of timidity, arising from the consciousness of being "kept down" by want of means, or interest, or connexion, or impudence, as the case might be. He was overawed by the Serjeant, and profoundly courteous to the attorney.

"I have not had the pleasure of seeing you before, Mr. Phunky," said Serjeant Snubbin, with haughty condescension.

Mr. Phunky bowed. He *had* had the pleasure of seeing the Serjeant, and of envying him too, with all a poor man's envy, for eight years and a quarter.

"You are with me in this case, I understand?" said the Serjeant.

If Mr. Phunky had been a rich man, he would have instantly sent for his clerk to remind him; if he had been a wise one, he would have applied his fore-finger to his forehead, and endeavoured to recollect whether in the multiplicity of his engagements he had undertaken this one, or not: but as he was neither rich nor wise (in this sense at all events) he turned red, and bowed.

"Have you read the papers, Mr. Phunky?" inquired the Serjeant.

Here again Mr. Phunky should have professed to have forgotten all about the merits of the case; but as he had read such papers as had been laid before him, in the course of the action, and had thought of nothing else, waking or sleeping, throughout the two months during which he had been retained as Mr. Serjeant Snubbin's junior, he turned a deeper red, and bowed again.

"This is Mr. Pickwick," said the Serjeant, waving his pen in the direction in which that gentleman was standing.

Mr. Phunky bowed to Mr. Pickwick with a reverence which a first client must ever awaken; and again inclined his head towards his leader.

"Perhaps you will take Mr. Pickwick away," said the Serjeant, "and—and—and—hear anything Mr. Pickwick may wish to communicate. We shall have a consultation of course." With this hint that he had been interrupted quite long enough, Mr. Serjeant Snubbin, who had been gradually growing more and more abstracted, applied his glass to his eyes for an instant, bowed slightly round, and was once more deeply immersed in the case before him, which arose out of an interminable lawsuit, originating in the act of an individual, deceased a century or so ago, who had stopped up a pathway leading from some place which nobody ever came from, to some other place which nobody ever went to.

Mr. Phunky would not hear of passing through any door until Mr. Pickwick and his solicitor had passed through before him, so it was some time before they got into the Square; and when they did reach it, they walked up and down, and held a long conference, the result of which, was, that it was a very difficult matter to say how the verdict would go; that nobody could presume to calculate on the issue of an action; that it was very lucky they had prevented the other party from getting Serjeant Snubbin; and other topics of doubt and consolation, common in such a position of affairs.

Mr. Weller was then roused by his master from a sweet sleep of an hour's duration; and, bidding adieu to Lowten, they returned to the City.

CHAPTER XXXI.

DESCRIBES, FAR MORE FULLY THAN THE COURT NEWSMAN EVER DID, A BACHELOR'S PARTY, GIVEN BY MR. BOB SAWYER AT HIS LODGINGS IN THE BOROUGH.

THERE is a repose about Lant Street, in the Borough, which sheds a gentle melancholy upon the soul. There are always a good many houses to let in the street: it is a bye-street too, and its dulness is soothing. A house in Lant Street would not come within the denomination of a first-rate residence, in the strict acceptation of the term; but it is a most desirable spot nevertheless. If a man wished to abstract himself from the world; to remove himself from within the reach of temptation; to place himself beyond the possibility of any inducement to look out of the window, we should recommend him by all means to go to Lant Street.

In this happy retreat are colonised a few clear-starchers, a sprinkling of journeymen bookbinders, one or two prison agents for the Insolvent Court, several small housekeepers who are employed in the Docks, a handful of mantua-makers, and a seasoning of jobbing tailors. The majority of the inhabitants either direct their energies to the letting of furnished apartments, or devote themselves to the healthful and invigorating pursuit of mangling. The chief features in the still life of the street, are green shutters, lodging-bills, brass door-plates, and bell-handles; the principal specimens of animated nature, the pot-boy, the muffin youth, and the baked-potato man. The population is migratory, usually disappearing on the verge of quarter-day, and generally by night. His Majesty's revenues are seldom collected in this happy valley, the rents are dubious, and the water communication is very frequently cut off.

Mr. Bob Sawyer embellished one side of the fire, in his first-floor front, early on the evening for which he had invited Mr. Pickwick, and Mr. Ben Allen the other. The preparations for the reception of visitors appeared to be completed. The umbrellas in the passage had been heaped into the little corner outside the back-parlour door; the bonnet and shawl of the landlady's servant had been removed from the bannisters; there were not more than two pair of pattens on the street-door mat; and a kitchen candle, with a very long snuff, burnt cheerfully on the ledge of the staircase window. Mr. Bob Sawyer had himself purchased the spirits at a wine vaults in High Street, and had returned home preceding the bearer thereof, to preclude the possibility of their delivery at the wrong house. The punch was ready-made in a red pan in the bed-room; a little table, covered with a green baize cloth, had been borrowed from the parlour, to play at cards on; and the glasses of the establishment, together with those which had been borrowed for the occasion from the public-house, were all drawn up in a tray, which was deposited on the landing outside the door.

Notwithstanding the highly satisfactory nature of all these arrangements, there was a cloud on the countenance of Mr. Bob Sawyer, as he sat by the fire-side. There was a sympathising expression, too, in the features of Mr. Ben Allen, as he gazed intently on the coals; and a tone of melancholy in his voice, as he said, after a long silence—

"Well, it *is* unlucky that she should have taken it in her head to turn sour, just on this occasion. She might at least have waited till to-morrow."

"That's her malevolence; that's her malevolence," returned Mr. Bob Sawyer vehemently. "She says that if I can afford to give a party I ought to be able to afford to pay her confounded ' little bill.'"

"How long has it been running?" inquired Mr. Ben Allen. A bill, by the bye, is the most extraordinary locomotive engine that the genius of man ever produced. It would keep on running during the longest life-time, without ever once stopping of its own accord.

"Only a quarter, and a month or so," replied Mr. Bob Sawyer.

Ben Allen coughed hopelessly, and directed a searching look between the two top bars of the stove.

"It'll be a deuced unpleasant thing if she takes it into her head to let out, when those fellows are here, won't it?" said Mr. Ben Allen at length.

"Horrible," replied Bob Sawyer, "horrible."

A low tap was heard at the room door. Mr. Bob Sawyer looked expressively at his friend, and bade the tapper come in; whereupon a dirty slipshod girl in black cotton stockings, who might have passed for the neglected daughter of a superannuated dustman in very reduced circumstances, thrust in her head, and said,

"Please, Mister Sawyer, Missis Raddle wants to speak to *you*."

Before Mr. Bob Sawyer could return any answer, the girl suddenly disappeared with a jerk, as if somebody had given her a violent pull behind; this mysterious exit was no sooner accomplished, than there was another tap at the door—a smart pointed tap, which seemed to say, "Here I am, and in I'm coming."

Mr. Bob Sawyer glanced at his friend with a look of abject apprehension, and once more cried "Come in."

The permission was not at all necessary, for, before Mr. Bob Sawyer had uttered the words, a little fierce woman bounced into the room, all in a tremble with passion, and pale with rage.

"Now Mr. Sawyer," said the little fierce woman, trying to appear very calm, "if you'll have the kindness to settle that little bill of mine I'll thank you, because I've got my rent to pay this afternoon, and my landlord's a waiting below now." Here the little woman rubbed her hands, and looked steadily over Mr. Bob Sawyer's head, at the wall behind him.

"I am very sorry to put you to any inconvenience, Mrs. Raddle," said Bob Sawyer deferentially, "but—"

"Oh, it isn't any inconvenience," replied the little woman, with a shrill titter. "I didn't want it particular before to-day; leastways, as it has to go to my landlord directly, it was as well for you to keep it as me. You promised me this afternoon, Mr. Sawyer, and every gentleman as has ever lived here has kept his word, Sir, as of course anybody as calls himself a gentleman, does." And Mrs. Raddle tossed her head, bit her lips, rubbed her hands harder, and looked at the wall more steadily than ever. It was plain to see, as Mr. Bob Sawyer remarked in a style of eastern allegory on a subsequent occasion, that she was "getting the steam up."

"I am very sorry, Mrs. Raddle," said Bob Sawyer with all imaginable humility, "but the fact is, that I have been disappointed in the City to-day."—Extraordinary place that city. We know a most astonishing number of men who always *are* getting disappointed there.

"Well, Mr. Sawyer," said Mrs. Raddle, planting herself firmly on a purple cauliflower in the Kidderminster carpet, "and what's that to me, Sir?"

"I—I—have no doubt, Mrs. Raddle," said Bob Sawyer, blinking this last question, "that before the middle of next week we shall be able to set ourselves quite square, and go on on a better system, afterwards."

This was all Mrs. Raddle wanted. She had bustled up to the apartment of the unlucky Bob Sawyer so bent upon going into a passion, that in all probability payment would have rather disappointed her than otherwise. She was in excellent order for a little relaxation of the kind, having just exchanged a few introductory compliments with Mr. R. in the front kitchen.

"Do you suppose, Mr. Sawyer," said Mrs. Raddle, elevating her voice for the information of the neighbours, "do you suppose that I'm a-going day after day to let a fellar occupy my lodgings as never thinks of paying his rent, nor even the very money laid out for the fresh butter and lump sugar that's bought for his breakfast, and the very milk that's took in, at the street door? Do you suppose a hard-working and industrious woman as has lived in this street for twenty years (ten years over the way, and nine years and three quarters in this very house) has nothing else to do, but to work herself to death after a parcel of lazy idle fellars, that are always smoking and drinking, and lounging, when they ought to be glad to turn their hands to anything that would help 'em to pay their bills? Do you—"

"My good soul," interposed Mr. Benjamin Allen, soothingly.

"Have the goodness to keep your observashuns to yourself, I beg," said Mrs. Raddle, suddenly arresting the rapid torrent of her speech, and addressing the third party with impressive slowness and solemnity. "I am not aweer Sir, that you have any right to address your conversation to me. I don't think I let these apartments to you, Sir."

"No, you certainly did not," said Mr. Benjamin Allen.

"Very good, Sir," responded Mrs. Raddle, with lofty politeness. "Then p'raps, Sir, you'll confine yourself to breaking the arms and legs of the poor people in the hospitals, and keep yourself *to* yourself Sir, or there may be some persons here as will make you, Sir."

"But you are such an unreasonable woman," remonstrated Mr. Benjamin Allen.

"I beg your parding, young man," said Mrs. Raddle, in a cold perspiration of anger. "But will you have the goodness just to call me that, again, Sir?"

"I didn't make use of the word in any invidious manner, ma'am," replied Mr. Benjamin Allen, growing somewhat uneasy on his own account.

"I beg your parding, young man," demanded Mrs. Raddle in a louder and more imperative tone. "But who do you call a woman? Did you make that remark to me, Sir?"

"Why, bless my heart!" said Mr. Benjamin Allen.

"Did you apply that name to me, I ask of you, Sir?" interrupted Mrs. Raddle with intense fierceness, throwing the door wide open.

"Why, of course I did," replied Mr. Benjamin Allen.

"Yes, of course you did," said Mrs. Raddle, backing

gradually to the door, and raising her voice to its loudest pitch, for the special behoof of Mr. Raddle in the kitchen. "Yes, of course you did, and everybody knows that they may safely insult me in my own ouse while my husband sits sleeping down stairs, and taking no more notice than if I was a dog in the streets. He ought to be ashamed of himself (here Mrs. Raddle sobbed) to allow his wife to be treated in this way by a parcel of young cutters and carvers of live people's bodies, that disgraces the lodgings (another sob), and leaving her exposed to all manner of abuse, a base, faint-hearted, timorous wretch, that's afraid to come up stairs, and face the ruffinly creatures—that's afraid—that's afraid to come." Mrs. Raddle paused to listen whether the repetition of the taunt had roused her better half; and, finding that it had not been successful, proceeded to descend the stairs with sobs innumerable, when there came a loud double knock at the street door: whereupon she burst into an hysterical fit of weeping, accompanied with dismal moans, which was prolonged until the knock had been repeated six times, when, in an uncontrollable burst of mental agony, she threw down all the umbrellas, and disappeared into the back parlour, closing the door after her with an awful crash.

"Does Mr. Sawyer live here?" said Mr. Pickwick, when the door was opened.

"Yes," said the girl, "first floor. It's the door straight afore you, when you gets to the top of the stairs."—Having given this instruction, the handmaid, who had been brought up among the aboriginal inhabitants of Southwark, disappeared with the candle in her hand down the kitchen stairs, perfectly satisfied that she had done every thing that could possibly be required of her under the circum stances.

Mr. Snodgrass, who entered last, secured the street door, after several ineffectual efforts, by putting up the chain; and the friends stumbled up stairs, where they were received by Mr. Bob Sawyer, who had been afraid to go down lest he should be waylaid by Mrs. Raddle.

"How are you?" said the discomfited student—"Glad to see you,—take care of the glasses." This caution was addressed to Mr. Pickwick, who had put his hat in the tray.

"Dear me," said Mr. Pickwick, "I beg your pardon."

"Don't mention it, don't mention it," said Bob Sawyer. "I'm rather confined for room here, but you must put up with all that, when you come to see a young bachelor. Walk in. You've seen this gentleman before, I think?" Mr. Pickwick shook hands with Mr. Benjamin Allen, and his friends followed his example. They had scarcely taken their seats when there was another double knock.

"I hope that's Jack Hopkins!" said Mr. Bob Sawyer. "Hush. Yes, it is. Come up, Jack; come up."

A heavy footstep was heard upon the stairs, and Jack Hopkins presented himself. He wore a black velvet waistcoat, with thunder-and-lightning buttons; and a blue striped shirt, with a white false collar.

"You're late, Jack?" said Mr. Benjamin Allen.

"Been detained at Bartholomew's,"—replied Hopkins.

"Anything new?"

"No, nothing particular. Rather a good accident brought into the casualty ward."

"What was that, Sir?" inquired Mr. Pickwick.

"Only a man fallen out of a four pair of stairs' window; —but it's a very fair case—very fair case indeed."

"Do you mean that the patient is in a fair way to recover?" inquired Mr. Pickwick.

"No," replied Hopkins, carelessly. "No, I should

rather say he wouldn't. There must be a splendid operation though, to-morrow—magnificent sight if Slasher does it."

"You consider Mr. Slasher a good operator?" said Mr. Pickwick.

"Best alive," replied Hopkins. "Took a boy's leg out of the socket last week—boy ate five apples and a gingerbread cake—exactly two minutes after it was all over, boy said he wouldn't lie there to be made game of; and he'd tell his mother if they didn't begin."

"Dear me!" said Mr. Pickwick, astonished.

"Pooh! That's nothing, that ain't," said Jack Hopkins. "Is it, Bob?"

"Nothing at all," replied Mr. Bob Sawyer.

"By the bye, Bob," said Hopkins, with a scarcely perceptible glance at Mr. Pickwick's attentive face, "we had a curious accident last night. A child was brought in, who had swallowed a necklace."

"Swallowed what, Sir?" interrupted Mr. Pickwick.

"A necklace," replied Jack Hopkins. "Not all at once, you know, that would be too much—*you* couldn't swallow that, if the child did—eh, Mr. Pickwick, ha! ha!"—Mr. Hopkins appeared highly gratified with his own pleasantry; and continued—"No, the way was this;—child's parents were poor people who lived in a court. Child's eldest sister bought a necklace,—common necklace, made of large black wooden beads. Child, being fond of toys, cribbed the necklace, hid it, played with it, cut the string, and swallowed a bead. Child thought it capital fun, went back next day, and swallowed another bead."

"Bless my heart," said Mr. Pickwick, "what a dreadful thing! I beg your pardon, Sir. Go on."

"Next day, child swallowed two beads; the day after that, he treated himself to three, and so on, till in a week's time he had got through the necklace, five-and-twenty beads in all. The sister, who was an industrious girl, and seldom treated herself to a bit of finery, cried her eyes out, at the loss of the necklace; looked high and low for it; but I needn't say didn't find it. A few days afterwards, the family were at dinner—baked shoulder of mutton, and potatoes under it—the child, who wasn't hungry, was playing about the room, when suddenly there was heard a devil of a noise, like a small hail storm. 'Don't do that, my boy,' said the father. 'I ain't a doin' nothing,' said the child. 'Well, don't do it again,' said the father. There was a short silence, and then the noise began again, worse than ever. 'If you don't mind what I say, my boy,' said the father, 'you'll find yourself in bed, in something less than a pig's whisper.' He gave the child a shake to make him obedient, and such a rattling ensued as nobody ever heard before. 'Why, damme, it's *in* the child!' said the father, 'he's got the croup in the wrong place!' 'No I haven't, father,' said the child, beginning to cry, 'it's the necklace; I swallowed it, father.'—The father caught the child up, and ran with him to the hospital: the beads in the boy's stomach rattling all the way with the jolting; and the people looking up in the air, and down in the cellars to see where the unusual sound came from. He's in the hospital now," said Jack Hopkins, "and he makes such a devil of a noise when he walks about, that they're obliged to muffle him in a watchman's coat, for fear he should wake the patients!"

"That's the most extraordinary case I ever heard of," said Mr. Pickwick, with an emphatic blow on the table.

"Oh, that's nothing," said Jack Hopkins; "is it, Bob?"

"Certainly not," replied Mr. Bob Sawyer.

"Very singular things occur in our profession, I can assure you, Sir," said Hopkins.

"So I should be disposed to imagine," replied Mr. Pickwick.

Another knock at the door, announced a large-headed young man in a black wig, who brought with him a scorbutic youth in a long stock. The next comer was a gentleman in a shirt emblazoned with pink anchors, who was closely followed by a pale youth with a plated watchguard. The arrival of a prim personage in clean linen and cloth boots rendered the party complete. The little table with the green baize cover was wheeled out; the first instalment of punch was brought in, in a white jug; and the succeeding three hours were devoted to *vingt-un* at sixpence a dozen, which was only once interrupted by a slight dispute between the scorbutic youth and the gentleman with the pink anchors, in the course of which, the scorbutic youth intimated a burning desire to pull the nose of the gentleman with the emblems of hope, in reply to which, that individual expressed his decided unwillingness to accept of any "sauce" on gratuitous terms, either from the irascible young gentleman with the scorbutic countenance, or any other person who was ornamented with a head.

When the last "natural" had been declared, and the profit and loss account of fish and sixpences adjusted, to the satisfaction of all parties, Mr. Bob Sawyer rang for supper, and the visitors squeezed themselves into corners while it was getting ready.

It was not so easily got ready as some people may imagine. First of all, it was necessary to awaken the girl, who had fallen asleep with her face on the kitchen table; this took a little time, and, even when she did answer the bell, another quarter of an hour was consumed in fruitless endeavours to impart to her a faint and distant glimmering of reason. The man to whom the order for the oysters had been sent, had not been told to open them; it is a very difficult thing to open an oyster with a limp knife or a two-pronged fork, and very little was done in this way. Very little of the beef was done either; and the ham (which was also from the German sausage-shop round the corner) was in a similar predicament. However, there was plenty of porter in a tin can; and the cheese went a great way, for it was very strong. So upon the whole, perhaps, the supper was quite as good as such matters usually are.

After supper another jug of punch was put upon the table, together with a paper of cigars, and a couple of bottles of spirits. Then there was an awful pause; and this awful pause was occasioned by a very common occurrence in this sort of places, but a very embarrassing one notwithstanding.

The fact is, that the girl was washing the glasses. The establishment boasted four; we do not record the circumstance as at all derogatory to Mrs. Raddle, for there never was a lodging-house yet, that was not short of glasses. The landlady's glasses were little thin blown glass tumblers, and those which had been borrowed from the public house were great, dropsical, bloated articles, each supported on a huge gouty leg. This would have been in itself sufficient to have possessed the company with the real state of affairs; but the young woman of all work had prevented the possibility of any misconception arising in the mind of any gentleman upon the subject, by forcibly dragging every man's glass away, long before he had finished his beer, and audibly stating, despite the winks and interruptions of Mr. Bob Sawyer, that it was to be conveyed down stairs, and washed forthwith.

It is a very ill wind that blows nobody any good. The prim man in the cloth boots, who had been unsuccessfully attempting to make a joke during the whole time the round game lasted, saw his opportunity, and availed himself of it. The instant the glasses disappeared he commenced a long story about a great public character, whose name he had forgotten, making a particularly happy reply to another eminent and illustrious individual whom he had never been able to identify. He enlarged at some length and with great minuteness upon divers collateral circumstances, distantly connected with the anecdote in hand, but for the life of him he couldn't recollect at that precise moment what the anecdote was, although he had been in the habit of telling the story with great applause for the last ten years.

"Dear me," said the prim man in the cloth boots, "it is a very extraordinary circumstance."

"I am sorry you have forgotten it," said Mr. Bob Sawyer, glancing eagerly at the door, as he thought he heard the noise of glasses jingling—"very sorry."

"So am I," responded the prim man, "because I know it would have afforded so much amusement. Never mind; I dare say I shall manage to recollect it, in the course of half an hour or so."

The prim man arrived at this point, just as the glasses came back, when Mr. Bob Sawyer, who had been absorbed in attention during the whole time, said he should very much like to hear the end of it, for, so far as it went, it was, without exception, the very best story he had ever heard.

The sight of the tumblers restored Bob Sawyer to a degree of equanimity which he had not possessed since his interview with his landlady. His face brightened up and he began to feel quite convivial.

"Now, Betsy," said Mr. Bob Sawyer, with great suavity, and dispersing, at the same time, the tumultuous little mob of glasses that the girl had collected in the centre of the table; "now, Betsy, the warm water: be brisk, there's a good girl."

"You can't have no warm water," replied Betsy.

"No warm water!" exclaimed Mr. Bob Sawyer.

"No," said the girl, with a shake of the head which expressed a more decided negative than the most copious language could have conveyed. "Missis Raddle said you warn't to have none."

The surprise depicted on the countenances of his guests imparted new courage to the host.

"Bring up the warm water instantly—instantly!" said Mr. Bob Sawyer, with desperate sternness.

"No; I can't," replied the girl; "Missis Raddle raked out the kitchen fire afore she went to bed, and locked up the kittle."

"Oh, never mind; never mind. Pray don't disturb yourself about such a trifle," said Mr. Pickwick, observing the conflict of Bob Sawyer's passions, as depicted in his countenance, "cold water will do very well."

"Oh, admirably," said Mr. Benjamin Allen.

"My landlady is subject to some slight attacks of mental derangement," remarked Bob Sawyer with a ghastly smile; "I fear I must give her warning."

"No, don't," said Ben Allen.

"I fear I must," said Bob with heroic firmness. "I'll pay her what I owe her, and give her warning to-morrow morning." Poor fellow! how devoutly he wished he could!

Mr. Bob Sawyer's heart-sickening attempts to rally under this last blow communicated a dispiriting influence to the company, the greater part of whom, with the view of rais-

ing their spirits, attached themselves with extra cordiality
to the cold brandy and water, the first perceptible effects of
which were displayed in a renewal of hostilities between
the scorbutic youth and the gentleman in the sanguine
shirt. The belligerents vented their feelings of mutual
contempt, for some time, in a variety of frownings and
snortings, until at last the scorbutic youth felt it necessary
to come to a more explicit understanding on the matter,
when the following clear understanding took place.

"Sawyer," said the scorbutic youth, in a loud voice.

"Well, Noddy," replied Mr. Bob Sawyer.

"I should be very sorry, Sawyer," said Mr. Noddy, "to
create any unpleasantness at any friend's table, and much
less at yours, Sawyer,—very; but I must take this opportunity of informing Mr. Gunter that he is no gentleman."

"And _I_ should be very sorry, Sawyer, to create any disturbance in the street in which you reside," said Mr. Gunter, "but I'm afraid I shall be under the necessity of
alarming the neighbours by throwing the person who has
just spoken, out o' window."

"What do you mean by that, Sir?" inquired Mr. Noddy.

"What I say, Sir," replied Mr. Gunter.

"I should like to see you do it, Sir," said Mr. Noddy.

"You shall _feel_ me do it in half a minute, Sir," replied
Mr. Gunter.

"I request that you'll favour me with your card, Sir,"
said Mr. Noddy.

"I'll do nothing of the kind, Sir," replied Mr. Gunter.

"Why not, Sir?" inquired Mr. Noddy.

"Because you'll stick it up over your chimney-piece, and
delude your visiters into the false belief that a gentleman
has been to see you, Sir," replied Mr. Gunter.

"Sir, a friend of mine shall wait on you in the morning,"
said Mr. Noddy.

"Sir, I'm very much obliged to you for the caution, and
I'll leave particular directions with the servant to lock up
the spoons," replied Mr. Gunter.

At this point the remainder of the guests interposed,
and remonstrated with both parties on the impropriety of
their conduct, on which Mr. Noddy begged to state that
his father was as respectable as Mr. Gunter's father;
to which Mr. Gunter replied that his father was to the full
as respectable as Mr. Noddy's father, and that his father's
son was as good a man as Mr. Noddy, any day in the week.
As this announcement seemed the prelude to a recom-
mencement of the dispute, there was another interference
on the part of the company; and a vast quantity of talking
and clamouring ensued, in the course of which Mr. Noddy
gradually allowed his feelings to overpower him, and professed that he had ever entertained a devoted personal attachment towards Mr. Gunter. To this Mr. Gunter replied
that, upon the whole, he rather preferred Mr. Noddy to
his own brother; on hearing which admission, Mr. Noddy
magnanimously rose from his seat, and proffered his hand
to Mr. Gunter. Mr. Gunter grasped it with affecting fervour; and everybody said that the whole dispute had been
conducted in a manner which was highly honourable to
both parties concerned.

"Now," said Jack Hopkins, "just to set us going again,
Bob, I don't mind singing a song." And Hopkins, incited
thereto, by tumultuous applause, plunged himself at once
into "The King, God bless him," which he sang as loud
as he could, to a novel air, compounded of the "Bay of
Biscay," and "A Frog he would."—The chorus was the

essence of the song, and, as each gentleman sang it to the
tune he knew best, the effect was very striking indeed.

It was at the end of the chorus to the first verse, that
Mr. Pickwick held up his hand in a listening attitude, and
said, as soon as silence was restored—

"Hush! I beg your pardon. I thought I heard somebody
calling from up stairs."

A profound silence immediately ensued; and Mr. Bob
Sawyer was observed to turn pale.

"I think I hear it now," said Mr. Pickwick. "Have the
goodness to open the door."

The door was no sooner opened than all doubt on the
subject was removed.

"Mr. Sawyer—Mr. Sawyer"—screamed a voice from the
two-pair landing.

"It's my landlady," said Bob Sawyer, looking round
him with great dismay. "Yes, Mrs. Raddle."

"What do you mean by this, Mr. Sawyer?" replied the
voice, with great shrillness and rapidity of utterance.
"Ain't it enough to be swindled out of one's rent, and
money lent out of pocket besides, and abused and insulted
by your friends that dares to call themselves men, without
having the house turned out of window, and noise enough
made to bring the fire-engines here, at two o'clock in the
morning?—Turn them wretches away."

"You ought to be ashamed of yourselves," said the voice
of Mr. Raddle, which appeared to proceed from beneath
some distant bed-clothes.

"Ashamed of themselves!" said Mrs. Raddle, "Why
don't you go down and knock 'em every one down stairs?
You would if you was a man."

"I should if I was a dozen men, my dear," replied Mr.
Raddle, pacifically, "but they've rather the advantage of
me in numbers, my dear."

"Ugh, you coward!" replied Mrs. Raddle, with supreme
contempt. "_Do_ you mean to turn them wretches out, or
not, Mr. Sawyer?"

"They're going, Mrs. Raddle, they're going," said the
miserable Bob. "I am afraid you'd better go," said Mr.
Bob Sawyer to his friends. "I _thought_ you were making
too much noise."

"It's a very unfortunate thing," said the prim man.
"Just as we were getting so comfortable too!" The fact
was, the prim man was just beginning to have a dawning
recollection of the story he had forgotten.

"It's hardly to be borne," said the prim man, looking
round. "Hardly to be borne, is it?"

"Not to be endured," replied Jack Hopkins; "let's have
the other verse, Bob. Come, here goes."

"No, no, Jack, don't," interposed Bob Sawyer; "it's a
capital song, but I am afraid we had better not have the
other verse. They are very violent people, the people of
the house."

"Shall I step up stairs, and pitch into the landlord?"
inquired Hopkins, "or keep on ringing the bell, or go and
groan on the staircase? You may command me, Bob."

"I am very much indebted to you for your friendship
and good nature, Hopkins," said the wretched Mr. Bob
Sawyer, "but I think the best plan to avoid any further
dispute is for us to break up at once."

"Now, Mr. Sawyer," screamed the shrill voice of Mrs.
Raddle, "_are_ them brutes going?"

"They're only looking for their hats, Mrs. Raddle,"
said Bob; "they are going directly."

"Going!" said Mrs. Raddle, thrusting her night-cap over the banisters just as Mr. Pickwick, followed by Mr. Tupman, emerged from the sitting-room. "Going! what did they ever come for?"

"My dear ma'am," remonstrated Mr. Pickwick, looking up.

"Get along with you, you old wretch!" replied Mrs. Raddle, hastily withdrawing the night-cap. "Old enough to be his grandfather, you villin! You're worse than any of 'em."

Mr. Pickwick found it in vain to protest his innocence, so hurried down stairs into the street, whither he was closely followed by Mr. Tupman, Mr. Winkle, and Mr. Snodgrass. Mr. Ben Allen, who was dismally depressed with spirits and agitation, accompanied them as far as London Bridge, and in the course of the walk confided to Mr. Winkle, as an especially sensible person to intrust the secret, that he was resolved to cut the throat of any gentleman except Mr. Bob Sawyer who should aspire to the affections of his sister Arabella. Having expressed his determination to perform this painful duty of a brother with proper firmness, he burst into tears, knocked his hat over his eyes, and, making the best of his way back, knocked double knocks at the door of the Borough Market, and took short naps on the steps alternately, until daybreak, under the firm impression that he lived there, and had forgotten the key.

The visiters having all departed, in compliance with the rather pressing request of Mrs. Raddle, the luckless Mr. Bob Sawyer was left alone, to meditate on the probable events of the morrow, and the pleasures of the evening.

CHAPTER XXXII.

MR. WELLER THE ELDER DELIVERS SOME CRITICAL SENTIMENTS RESPECTING LITERARY COMPOSITION; AND, ASSISTED BY HIS SON SAMUEL, PAYS A SMALL INSTALMENT OF RETALIATION TO THE ACCOUNT OF THE REVEREND GENTLEMAN WITH THE RED NOSE.

THE morning of the thirteenth of February, which the readers of this authentic narrative know, as well as we do, to have been the day immediately preceding that which was appointed for the trial of Mrs. Bardell's action, was a busy time for Mr. Samuel Weller, who was perpetually engaged in travelling from the George and Vulture to Mr. Perker's chambers and back again, from and between the hours of nine o'clock in the morning and two in the afternoon, both inclusive. Not that there was anything whatever to be done, for the consultation had taken place, and the course of proceeding to be adopted, had been finally determined on, but Mr. Pickwick being in a most extreme state of excitement, persevered in constantly sending small notes to his attorney, merely containing the enquiry, "Dear Perker —Is all going on well?" to which Mr. Perker invariably forwarded the reply, "Dear Pickwick—As well as possible;" the fact being as we have already hinted that there was nothing whatever to go on, either well or ill, until the sitting of the court on the following morning.

But people who go voluntarily to law, or are taken forci-

bly there, for the first time, may be allowed to labour under some temporary irritation and anxiety: and Sam, with a due allowance for the frailties of human nature, obeyed all his master's behests with that imperturbable good humour and unruffable composure which formed one of his most striking and amiable characteristics.

Sam had solaced himself with a most agreeable little dinner, and was waiting at the bar for the glass of warm mixture in which Mr. Pickwick had requested him to drown the fatigues of his morning's walks, when a young boy of about three feet high, or thereabouts, in a hairy cap and fustian overalls, whose garb bespoke a laudable ambition to attain in time the elevation of an hostler, entered the passage of the George and Vulture, and looked first up the stairs, and then along the passage, and then into the bar, as if in search of somebody to whom he bore a commission; whereupon the barmaid, conceiving it not improbable that the said commission might be directed to the tea or table spoons of the establishment, accosted the boy with

"Now, young man, what do *you* want?"

"Is there anybody here, named Sam?" inquired the youth, in a loud voice of treble quality.

"What's the t'other name?" said Sam Weller, looking round.

"How should I know?" briskly replied the young gentleman below the hairy cap.

"You're a sharp boy, you are," said Mr. Weller; "only I wouldn't show that wery fine edge too much, if I was you, in case anybody took it off. What do you mean by comin' to a hot-el, and asking arter Sam, vith as much politeness as a vild Indian?"

"'Cos an old gen'lm'n told me to," replied the boy.

"What old gen'lm'n?" inquired Sam, with deep disdain.

"Him as drives a Ipswich coach, and uses our parlour" —rejoined the boy. "He told me yesterday mornin' to come to the George in Wultur this afternoon, and ask for Sam."

"It's my father, my dear"—said Mr. Weller, turning with an explanatory air to the young lady in the bar; "blessed if I think he hardly knows wot my other name is. Vell, young brockiley sprout, wot then?"

"Why then," said the boy, "you wos to come to him at six o'clock to our 'ouse 'cos he wants to see you—Blue Boar, Leaden'all Markit. Shall I say you're comin'?"

"You *may* wenture on that 'ere statement, Sir," replied Sam. And thus empowered, the young gentleman walked away, awakening all the echoes in George Yard as he did so, with several chaste and extremely correct imitations of a drover's whistle, delivered in a tone of peculiar richness and volume.

Mr. Weller having obtained leave of absence from Mr. Pickwick, who, in his then state of excitement and worry was by no means displeased at being left alone, set forth long before the appointed hour; and having plenty of time at his disposal, sauntered down as far as the Mansion House, where he paused and contemplated, with a face of great calmness and philosophy, the numerous cads and drivers of short stages who assemble near that famous place of resort, to the great terror and confusion of the old-lady population of these realms. Having loitered here, for half an hour or so, Mr. Weller turned, and began wending his way towards Leadenhall Market, through a variety of bye streets and courts. As he was sauntering away his spare time, and stopped to look at almost every object that met his gaze, it is by no means surprising that Mr. Weller should have paused before a small stationer's and print-seller's window; but without further explanation it does appear surprising that his eyes should have no sooner rested on certain pictures which were exposed for sale therein, than he gave a sudden start, smote his right leg with great vehemence, and exclaimed with energy, "If it hadn't been for this, I should ha' forgot all about it, till it was too late!"

The particular picture on which Sam Weller's eyes were fixed, as he said this, was a highly coloured representation of a couple of human hearts skewered together with an arrow, cooking before a cheerful fire, while a male and female cannibal in modern attire, the gentleman being clad in a blue coat and white trousers, and the lady in a deep red pelisse with a parasol of the same, were approaching the meal with hungry eyes, up a serpentine gravel path leading thereunto. A decidedly indelicate young gentleman, in a pair of wings and nothing else, was depicted as superintending the cooking; a representation of the spire of the church in Langham Place appeared in the distance; and the whole formed a "valentine," of which, as a written inscription in the window testified, there was a large assortment within, which the shopkeeper pledged himself to dispose of to his countrymen generally, at the reduced rate of one and sixpence each.

"I should ha' forgot it; I should certainly ha' forgot it!" said Sam; and so saying, he at once stepped into the stationer's shop, and requested to be served with a sheet of the best gilt-edged letter-paper, and a hard-nibbed pen which could be warranted not to splutter. These articles having been promptly supplied, he walked on direct towards Leadenhall Market at a good round pace, very different from his recent lingering one. Looking round him, he there beheld a sign-board on which the painter's art had delineated something remotely resembling a cerulean elephant with an aquiline nose in lieu of trunk. Rightly conjecturing that this was the Blue Boar himself, he stepped into the house, and inquired concerning his parent.

"He won't be here this three quarters of an hour or more," said the young lady who superintended the domestic arrangements of the Blue Boar.

"Wery good, my dear," replied Sam. "Let me have nine penn'orth o' brandy and water luke, and the inkstand, will you, miss?"

The brandy and water luke and the inkstand having been carried into the little parlour, and the young lady having carefully flattened down the coals to prevent their blazing, and carried away the poker to preclude the possibility of the fire being stirred, without the full privity and concurrence of the Blue Boar being first had and obtained, Sam Weller sat himself down in a box near the stove, and pulled out the sheet of gilt-edged letter paper, and the hard-nibbed pen. Then looking carefully at the pen to see that there were no hairs in it, and dusting down the table, so that there might be no crumbs of bread under the paper, Sam tucked up the cuffs of his coat, squared his elbows, and composed himself to write.

To ladies and gentlemen who are not in the habit of devoting themselves practically to the science of penmanship, writing a letter is no very easy task, it being always considered necessary in such cases for the writer to recline his head on his left arm so as to place his eyes as nearly as possible on a level with the paper, and while glancing sideways at the letters he is constructing, to form with his tongue imaginary characters to correspond. These motions, although unquestionably of the greatest assistance to original composition, retard in some degree the progress of the writer, and Sam had unconsciously been a full hour and a half writing words in small text, smearing out wrong letters with his little finger, and putting in new ones which required going over very often to render them visible through the old blots, when he was roused by the opening of the door and the entrance of his parent.

"Vell, Sammy," said the father.

"Vell, my Prooshan Blue," responded the son, laying down his pen. "What's the last bulletin about mother-in-law?"

"Mrs. Veller passed a wery good night, but is uncommon perwerse, and unpleasant this mornin'—signed upon oath —Tony Veller, Esq. That's the last vun as was issued, Sammy," replied Mr. Weller, untying his shawl.

"No better yet?" inquired Sam.

"All the symptoms aggerawated," replied Mr. Weller, shaking his head. "But wot's that, you're a doin' of—pursuit of knowledge under difficulties—eh Sammy?"

"I've done now," said Sam with slight embarrassment; "I've been a writin'."

"So I see," replied Mr. Weller. "Not to any young 'ooman, I hope, Sammy."

"Why it's no use a sayin' it ain't," replied Sam, "It's a walentine."

"A what!" exclaimed Mr. Weller, apparently horror-stricken by the word.

"A walentine," replied Sam.

"Samivel, Samivel," said Mr. Weller, in reproachful accents, "I didn't think you'd ha' done it. Arter the warnin' you've had o' your father's wicious perpensities; arter all I've said to you upon this here wery subject; arter actiwally seein' and bein' in the company o' your own mother-in-law, vich I should ha' thought wos a moral lesson as no man could ever ha' forgotten to his dyin' day. I didn't think you'd ha' done it, Sammy, I didn't think you'd ha' done it." These reflections were too much for the good old man. He raised Sam's tumbler to his lips and drank off its contents.

"Wot's the matter now!" said Sam.

"Nev'r mind, Sammy," replied Mr. Weller, "it'll be a wery agonizin' trial to me at my time of life, but I'm pretty tough, that's vun consolation, as the wery old turkey remarked ven the farmer said he wos afeerd he should be obliged to kill him, for the London market."

"Wot'll be a trial?" inquired Sam.

"To see you married, Sammy—to see you a dilluded wictim, and thinkin' in your innocence that it's all wery capital," replied Mr. Weller. "It's a dreadful trial to a father's feelin's, that 'ere, Sammy."

"Nonsense," said Sam. "I ain't a goin' to get married, don't you fret yourself about that; I know you're a judge o' these things. Order in your pipe, and I'll read you the letter—there."

We cannot distinctly say whether it was the prospect of the pipe, or the consolatory reflection that a fatal disposition to get married ran in the family and couldn't be helped, which calmed Mr. Weller's feelings, and caused his grief to subside. We should be rather disposed to say that the result was attained by combining the two sources of consolation, for he repeated the second in a low tone, very frequently; ringing the bell meanwhile, to order in the first. He then divested himself of his upper coat; and lighting the pipe and placing himself in front of the fire with his back towards it, so that he could feel its full heat, and recline against the mantel-piece at the same time, turned towards Sam, and, with a countenance greatly mollified by the softening influence of tobacco, requested him to "fire away."

Sam dipped his pen into the ink to be ready for any corrections, and began with a very theatrical air—

"'Lovely——.'"

"Stop," said Mr. Weller, ringing the bell. "A double glass o' the inwariable, my dear."

"Very well, Sir," replied the girl; who with great quickness appeared, vanished, returned, and disappeared.

"They seem to know your ways here," observed Sam.

"Yes," replied his father, "I've been here before, in my time. Go on, Sammy."

"'Lovely creetur,'" repeated Sam.

"'Tain't in poetry, is it?" interposed the father.

"No no," replied Sam.

"Werry glad to hear it," said Mr. Weller. "Poetry's unnat'ral; no man ever talked in poetry 'cept a beadle on boxin' day, or Warren's blackin' or Rowland's oil, or some o' them low fellows; never you let yourself down to talk poetry, my boy. Begin again, Sammy."

Mr. Weller resumed his pipe with critical solemnity, and Sam once more commenced, and read as follows:

"'Lovely creetur i feel myself a dammed'—."

"That ain't proper," said Mr. Weller, taking his pipe from his mouth.

"No; it ain't dammed," observed Sam, holding the letter up to the light, "it's 'shamed,' there's a blot there—'I feel myself ashamed.'"

"Wery good," said Mr. Weller. "Go on."

"'Feel myself ashamed, and completely cir—' I forget wot this here word is," said Sam, scratching his head with the pen, in vain attempts to remember.

"Why don't you look at it, then?" inquired Mr. Weller.

"So I *am* a lookin' at it," replied Sam, "but there's another blot: here's a 'c,' and a 'i,' and a 'd.'"

"Circumwented, p'raps," suggested Mr. Weller.

"No it ain't that," said Sam, "circumscribed, that's it."

"That ain't as good a word as circumwented, Sammy," said Mr. Weller gravely.

"Think not?" said Sam.

"Nothin' like it," replied his father.

"But don't you think it means more?" inquired Sam.

"Vell p'raps it is a more tenderer word," said Mr Weller, after a few moments' reflection. "Go on, Sammy."

"'Feel myself ashamed and completely circumscribed in a dressin' of you, for you *are* a nice gal and nothin' but it.'"

"That's a wery pretty sentiment," said the elder Mr. Weller, removing his pipe to make way for the remark.

"Yes, I think it is rayther good," observed Sam, highly flattered.

"Wot I like in that 'ere style of writin'," said the elder Mr. Weller, "is, that there ain't no callin' names in it,—no Wenuses, nor nothin' o' that kind; wot's the good o' callin' a young 'ooman a Wenus or a angel, Sammy?"

"Ah! what, indeed?" replied Sam.

"You might jist as vell call her a griffin, or a unicorn, or a king's arms at once, which is wery vell known to be a col-lection o' fabulous animals," added Mr. Weller.

"Just as well," replied Sam.

"Drive on, Sammy," said Mr. Weller.

Sam complied with the request, and proceeded as follows; his father continuing to smoke, with a mixed expression of wisdom and complacency, which was particularly edifying.

"'Afore I see you I thought all women was alike.'"

"So they are," observed the elder Mr. Weller, parenthetically.

"'But now,' continued Sam, 'now I find what a reg'lar soft-headed, ink-red-lous turnip I must ha' been for there ain't nobody like you though *I* like you better than nothin' at all.' I thought it best to make that rayther strong," said Sam, looking up.

Mr. Weller nodded approvingly, and Sam resumed.

"'So I take the privilidge of the day, Mary, my dear—as the gen'lem'n in difficulties did, ven he valked out of a Sunday,—to tell you that the first and only time I see you your likeness was took on my hart in much quicker time and brighter colours than ever a likeness was took by the profeel macheen (wich p'r'aps you may have heerd on Mary my dear) altho it *does* finish a portrait and put the frame and glass on complete with a hook at the end to hang it up by and all in two minutes and a quarter.'"

"I am afeerd that werges on the poetical, Sammy," said Mr. Weller, dubiously.

"No it don't," replied Sam, reading on very quickly, to avoid contesting the point.

"'Except of me Mary my dear as your walentine and think over what I've said.—My dear Mary I will now conclude.' That's all," said Sam.

"That's rayther a sudden pull up, ain't it, Sammy?" inquired Mr. Weller.

"Not a bit on it," said Sam; "she'll vish there *wos* more, and that's the great art o' letter writin'."

"Well," said Mr. Weller, "there's somethin' in that; and I wish your mother-in-law 'ud only conduct her conversation on the same gen-teel principle. Ain't you a goin' to sign it?"

"That's the difficulty," said Sam; "I don't know what *to* sign it."

"Sign it—Veller," said the oldest surviving proprietor of that name.

"Won't do," said Sam. "Never sign a walentine with your own name."

"Sign it 'Pickvick,' then," said Mr. Weller; "it's a wery good name, and a easy one to spell."

"The wery thing," said Sam. "I *could* end with a werse; what do you think?"

"I don't like it, Sam," rejoined Mr. Weller. "I never know'd a respectable coachman as wrote poetry, 'cept one, as made an affectin' copy o' werses the night afore he wos hung for a highway robbery; and *he* wos only a Cambervell man, so even that's no rule."

But Sam was not to be dissuaded from the poetical idea that had occurred to him, so he signed the letter—

> "Your love-sick
> Pickwick."

And having folded it, in a very intricate manner, squeezed a down-hill direction in one corner: "To Mary, Housemaid, at Mr. Nupkins's Mayor's, Ipswich, Suffolk"; and put it into his pocket, wafered, and ready for the General Post. This important business having been transacted, Mr. Weller the elder proceeded to open that, on which he had summoned his son.

"The first matter relates to your governor, Sammy,"

said Mr. Weller. "He's a goin' to be tried to-morrow, ain't he?"

"The trial's a comin' on," replied Sam.

"Vell," said Mr. Weller, "Now I s'pose he'll want to call some witnesses to speak to his character, or p'raps to prove a alleybi. I've been a turnin the bus'ness over in my mind, and he may make his-self easy, Sammy. I've got some friends as'll do either for him, but my adwice 'ud be this here—never mind the character, and stick to the alleybi. Nothing like a alleybi, Sammy, nothing." Mr. Weller looked very profound as he delivered this legal opinion; 2 d burying his nose in his tumbler, winked over the top thereof, at his astonished son.

"Why, what do you mean?" said Sam; "you don't think he's a goin' to be tried at the Old Bailey, do you?"

"That ain't no part of the present con-sideration, Sammy," replied Mr. Weller. "Verever he's a goin' to be tried, my boy, a alleybi's the thing to get him off. Ve got Tom Vildspark off that 'ere manslaughter, with a alleybi, ven all the big vigs to a man said as nothing couldn't save him. And my 'pinion is, Sammy, that if your governor don't prove a alleybi, he'll be what the Italians call reg'larly flummoxed, and that's all about it."

As the elder Mr. Weller entertained a firm and unalterable conviction that the Old Bailey was the supreme court of judicature in this country, and that its rules and forms of proceeding regulated and controlled the practice of all other courts of justice whatsoever, he totally disregarded the assurances and arguments of his son, tending to show that the alibi was inadmissible; and vehemently protested that Mr. Pickwick was being "wictimised." Finding that it was of no use to discuss the matter further, Sam changed the subject, and inquired what the second topic was, on which his revered parent wished to consult him.

"That's a pint o' domestic policy, Sammy," said Mr. Weller. "This here Stiggins—"

"Red-nosed man?" inquired Sam.

"The wery same," replied Mr. Weller. "This here red-nosed man, Sammy, wisits your mother-in-law vith a kindness and constancy as I never see equalled. He's sitch a friend o' the family, Sammy, that ven he's avay from us, he can't be comfortable unless he has somethin' to remember us by."

"And I'd give him somethin' as 'ud turpentine and bees'-vax his memory for the next ten years or so, if I wos you," interposed Sam.

"Stop a minute," said Mr. Weller; "I wos a goin to say, he always brings now, a flat bottle as holds about a pint and a half, and fills it vith the pine-apple rum afore he goes avay."

"And empties it afore he comes back, I s'pose," said Sam.

"Clean!" replied Mr. Weller; "never leaves nothin' in it but the cork and the smell: trust him for that, Sammy. Now these here fellows, my boy, are a goin', to-night, to get up the monthly meetin' o' the Brick Lane Branch o' the United Grand Junction Ebenezer Temperance Association. Your mother-in-law wos a goin', Sammy, but she's got the rheumatics, and can't; and I, Sammy—I've got the two tickets as wos sent her." Mr. Weller communicated this secret with great glee, and winked so indefatigably after doing so, that Sam began to think he must have got the tic douloureux in his right eye-lid.

"Well?" said that young gentleman.

"Well," continued his progenitor, looking round him very cautiously, "you and I'll go, punctiwal to the time. The deputy shepherd won't, Sammy; the deputy shepherd won't." Here Mr. Weller was seized with a paroxysm of chuckles, which gradually terminated in as near an approach to a choke, as an elderly gentleman can, with safety, sustain.

"Well, I never see sitch an old ghost in all my born days," exclaimed Sam, rubbing the old gentleman's back, hard enough to set him on fire with the friction. "What are you a laughin' at, corpilence?"

"Hush! Sammy," said Mr. Weller, looking round him with increased caution, and speaking in a whisper: "Two friends o' mine, as works on the Oxford Road, and is up to all kinds o' games, has got the deputy shepherd safe in tow, Sammy; and ven he does come to the Ebenezer Junction, (vich he's sure to do: for they'll see him to the door, and shove him in if necessary) he'll be as far gone in rum and water, as ever he wos at the Markis o' Granby, Dorkin', and that's not sayin' a little either." And with this, Mr. Weller once more laughed immoderately, and once more relapsed into a state of partial suffocation, in consequence.

Nothing could have been more in accordance with Sam Weller's feelings, than the projected exposure of the real propensities and qualities of the red-nosed man; and it being very near the appointed hour of meeting, the father and son took the way at once to Brick Lane: Sam not forgetting to drop his letter into a general post-office as they walked along.

The monthly meetings of the Brick Lane Branch of the United Grand Junction Ebenezer Temperance Association, were held in a large room, pleasantly and airily situated at the top of a safe and commodious ladder. The president was the straight-walking Mr. Anthony Humm, a converted fireman, now a schoolmaster, and occasionally an itinerant preacher; and the secretary was Mr. Jonas Mudge, chandler's shop-keeper, an enthusiastic and disinterested vessel, who sold tea to the members. Previous to the commencement of business, the ladies sat upon forms, and drank tea, till such time as they considered it expedient to leave off; and a large wooden money-box was conspicuously placed upon the green baize cloth of the business table, behind which the secretary stood, and acknowledged, with a gracious smile, every addition to the rich vein of copper which lay concealed within.

On this particular occasion the women drank tea to a most alarming extent; greatly to the horror of Mr. Weller senior, who, utterly regardless of all Sam's admonitory nudgings, stared about him in every direction with the most undisguised astonishment.

"Sammy," whispered Mr. Weller, "if some o' these here people don't want tappin' to-morrow mornin', I ain't your father, and that's wot it is. Why, this here old lady next me is a drownin' herself in tea."

"Be quiet, can't you?" murmured Sam.

"Sam," whispered Mr. Weller, a moment afterwards, in a tone of deep agitation, "mark my vords, my boy: if that 'ere secretary feller keeps on for only five minutes more, he'll blow himself up with toast and water."

"Well, let him, if he likes," replied Sam; "it ain't no bis'ness o' yourn."

"If this here lasts much longer, Sammy," said Mr. Weller, in the same low voice, "I shall feel it my duty, as a human bein', to rise and address the cheer. There's a young 'oman on the next form but two, as has drunk nine breakfast cups and a half; and she's a swellin' wisibly before my wery eyes."

There is little doubt that Mr. Weller would have carried his benevolent intention into immediate execution, if a great noise, occasioned by putting up the cups and saucers, had not very fortunately announced that the tea-drinking was over. The crockery having been removed, the table with the green baize cover was carried out into the centre of the room, and the business of the evening was commenced by a little emphatic man, with a bald head, and drab shorts, who suddenly rushed up the ladder, at the imminent peril of snapping the two little legs encased in the drab shorts, and said:

"Ladies and gentlemen, I move our excellent brother, Mr. Anthony Humm, into the chair."

The ladies waved a choice collection of pocket-handkerchiefs at this proposition; and the impetuous little man literally moved Mr. Humm into the chair, by taking him by the shoulders and thrusting him into a mahogany frame which had once represented that article of furniture. The waving of handkerchiefs was renewed; and Mr. Humm, who was a sleek, white-faced man, in a perpetual perspiration, bowed meekly, to the great admiration of the females, and formally took his seat. Silence was then proclaimed by the little man in the drab shorts, and Mr. Humm rose and said—That, with the permission of his Brick Lane Branch brothers and sisters, then and there present, the secretary would read the report of the Brick Lane Branch committee; —a proposition which was again received with a demonstration of pocket-handkerchiefs.

The secretary having sneezed in a very impressive manner, and the cough which always seizes an assembly, when anything particular is going to be done, having been duly performed, the following document was read:

"REPORT OF THE COMMITTEE OF THE BRICK LANE BRANCH OF THE UNITED GRAND JUNCTION EBENEZER TEMPERANCE ASSOCIATION.

"Your committee have pursued their grateful labours during the past month, and have the unspeakable pleasure of reporting the following additional cases of converts to Temperance.

"H. Walker, tailor, wife, and two children. When in better circumstances, owns to having been in the constant habit of drinking ale and beer; says he is not certain whether he did not twice a week, for twenty years, taste 'dog's nose,' which your committee find upon inquiry, to be compounded of warm porter, moist sugar, gin, and nutmeg (a groan, and 'So it is!' from an elderly female). Is now out of work and pennyless; thinks it must be the porter (cheers) or the loss of the use of his right hand; is not certain which, but thinks it very likely that, if he had drank nothing but water all his life, his fellow workman would never have stuck a rusty needle in him, and thereby occasioned his accident (tremendous cheering). Has nothing but cold water to drink, and never feels thirsty (great applause).

"Betsy Martin, widow, one child, and one eye. Goes out charing and washing, by the day; never had more than one eye, but knows her mother drank bottled stout, and shouldn't wonder if that caused it (immense cheering). Thinks it not impossible that if she had always abstained from spirits, she might have had two eyes by this time

(tremendous applause). Used, at every place she went to, to have eighteen pence a day, a pint of porter, and a glass of spirits; but since she became a member of the Brick Lane Branch, has always demanded three and sixpence instead (the announcement of this most interesting fact was received with deafening enthusiasm).

"Henry Beller was for many years toast-master at various corporation dinners, during which time he drank a great deal of foreign wine; may sometimes have carried a bottle or two home with him; is not quite certain of that, but is sure if he did, that he drank the contents. Feels very low and melancholy, is very feverish, and has a constant thirst upon him; thinks it must be the wine he used to drink (cheers). Is out of employ now; and never touches a drop of foreign wine by any chance (tremendous plaudits).

"Thomas Burton is purveyor of cat's-meat to the Lord Mayor and Sheriffs, and several members of the Common Council (the announcement of this gentleman's name was received with breathless interest). Has a wooden leg; finds a wooden leg expensive going over the stones; used to wear second-hand wooden legs, and drink a glass of hot gin and water regularly every night—sometimes two (deep sighs). Found the second-hand wooden legs split and rot very quickly; is firmly persuaded that their constitution was undermined by the gin and water (prolonged cheering). Buys new wooden legs now, and drinks nothing but water and weak tea. The new legs last twice as long as the others used to do, and he attributes this solely to his temperate habits (triumphant cheers)."

Anthony Humm now moved that the assembly do regale itself with a song. With a view to their rational and moral enjoyment, brother Mordlin had adapted the beautiful words of "Who hasn't heard of a Jolly Young Waterman?" to the tune of the Old Hundredth, which he would request them to join him in singing (great applause). He might take that opportunity of expressing his firm persuasion that the late Mr. Dibdin, seeing the errors of his former life, had written that song to show the advantages of abstinence. It was a Temperance song (whirlwinds of cheers). The neatness of the interesting young man's attire, the dexterity of his feathering, the enviable state of mind which enabled him, in the beautiful words of the poet, to

"Row along, thinking of nothing at all,"

all combined to prove that he must have been a water-drinker (cheers). Oh, what a state of virtuous jollity (rapturous cheering). And what was the young man's reward? Let all young men present mark this:

"The maidens all flock'd to his boat so readily."

(Loud cheers, in which the ladies joined.) What a bright example! The sisterhood, the maidens, flocking round the young waterman, and urging him along the path of duty and of temperance. But, was it the maidens of humble life only, who soothed, consoled, and supported him? No!

"He was always first oars with the fine city ladies."

(Immense cheering.) The soft sex to a man—he begged pardon, to a female—rallied round the young waterman, and turned with disgust from the drinker of spirits (cheers). The Brick Lane Branch brothers were watermen (cheers and laughter). That room was their boat; that audience were the maidens; and he (Mr. Anthony Humm), however unworthily, was "first oars" (unbounded applause).

"Wot does he mean by the soft sex, Sammy?" inquired Mr. Weller, in a whisper.

"The womin," said Sam, in the same tone.

"He ain't far out there, Sammy," replied Mr. Weller; "they *must* be a soft sex,—a wery soft sex, indeed, if they let themselves be gammoned by such fellers as him."

Any further observations from the indignant old gentleman were cut short by the commencement of the song, which Mr. Anthony Humm gave out, two lines at a time, for the information of such of his hearers as were unacquainted with the legend. While it was being sung, the little man with the drab shorts disappeared; he returned immediately on its conclusion, and whispered Mr. Anthony Humm, with a face of the deepest importance.

"My friends," said Mr. Humm, holding up his hand in a deprecatory manner, to bespeak the silence of such of the stout old ladies as were yet a line or two behind; "my friends, a delegate from the Dorking branch of our society, Brother Stiggins, attends below."

Out came the pocket-handkerchiefs again, in greater force than ever, for Mr. Stiggins was excessively popular among the female constituency of Brick Lane.

"He may approach, I think," said Mr. Humm, looking round him, with a fat smile. "Brother Tadger, let him come forth and greet us."

The little man in the drab shorts who answered to the name of Brother Tadger, bustled down the ladder with great speed, and was immediately afterwards heard tumbling up with the Reverend Mr. Stiggins.

"He's a comin', Sammy," whispered Mr. Weller, purple in the countenance with suppressed laughter.

"Don't say nothin' to me," replied Sam, "for I can't bear it. He's close to the door. I hear him a-knockin' his head again the lath and plaster now."

As Sam Weller spoke, the little door flew open, and Brother Tadger appeared, closely followed by the Reverend Mr. Stiggins, who no sooner entered, than there was a great clapping of hands, and stamping of feet, and flourishing of handkerchiefs; to all of which manifestations of delight, Brother Stiggins returned no other acknowledgment than staring with a wild eye, and a fixed smile, at the extreme top of the wick of the candle on the table: swaying his body to and fro, meanwhile, in a very unsteady and uncertain manner.

"Are you unwell, Brother Stiggins?" whispered Mr. Anthony Humm.

"I am all right, Sir," replied Mr. Stiggins, in a tone in which ferocity was blended with an extreme thickness of utterance; "I am all right, Sir."

"Oh, very well," rejoined Mr. Anthony Humm, retreating a few paces.

"I believe no man here, has ventured to say that I am *not* all right, Sir," said Mr. Stiggins.

"Oh, certainly not," said Mr. Humm.

"I should advise him not to, Sir; I should advise him not," said Mr. Stiggins.

By this time the audience were perfectly silent, and waited with some anxiety for the resumption of business.

"Will you address the meeting, brother?" said Mr. Humm, with a smile of invitation.

"No, Sir," rejoined Mr. Stiggins; "No Sir. I will not, Sir."

The meeting looked at each other with raised eye-lids, and a murmur of astonishment ran through the room.

"It's my opinion, Sir," said Mr. Stiggins, unbuttoning his coat, and speaking very loudly; "it's my opinion, Sir, that this meeting is drunk, Sir. Brother Tadger, Sir," said Mr. Stiggins, suddenly increasing in ferocity, and turning sharp round on the little man in the drab shorts, "*you* are drunk, Sir." With this, Mr. Stiggins, entertaining a praiseworthy desire to promote the sobriety of the meeting, and to exclude therefrom all improper characters, hit Brother Tadger on the summit of the nose with such unerring aim, that the drab shorts disappeared like a flash of lightning. Brother Tadger had been knocked, head first, down the ladder.

Upon this, the women set up a loud and dismal screaming; and rushing in small parties before their favourite brothers, flung their arms round them to preserve them from danger. An instance of affection, which had nearly proved fatal to Humm, who, being extremely popular, was all but suffocated by the crowd of female devotees that hung about his neck, and heaped caresses upon him; the greater part of the lights were quickly put out, and nothing but noise and confusion resounded on all sides.

"Now Sammy," said Mr. Weller, taking off his great coat with much deliberation, "just you step out, and fetch in a watchman."

"And wot are you a goin' to do, the while?" inquired Sam.

"Never you mind me, Sammy," replied the old gentleman; "I shall ockipy myself in havin' a small settlement with that 'ere Stiggins." And before Sam could interfere to prevent it, his heroic parent had penetrated into a remote corner of the room, and attacked the Reverend Mr. Stiggins with manual dexterity.

"Come off," said Sam.

"Come on," cried Mr. Weller; and without further invitation he gave the Reverend Mr. Stiggins a preliminary tap on the head, and began dancing round him in a buoyant and cork like manner, which in a gentleman at his time of life was a perfect marvel to behold.

Finding all remonstrances unavailing, Sam pulled his hat firmly on, threw his father's coat over his arm, and taking the old man round the waist, forcibly dragged him down the ladder, and into the street; never releasing his hold, or permitting him to stop, until they reached the corner. As they gained it, they could hear the shouts of the populace, who were witnessing the removal of the Reverend Mr. Stiggins to strong lodgings for the night, and hear the noise occasioned by the dispersion in various directions of the members of the Brick Lane Branch of the United Grand Junction Ebenezer Temperance Association.

CHAPTER XXXIII.

IS WHOLLY DEVOTED TO A FULL AND FAITHFUL REPORT OF THE MEMORABLE TRIAL OF BARDELL AGAINST PICKWICK.

"I wonder what the foreman of the jury, whoever he'll be, has got for breakfast," said Mr. Snodgrass, by way of keeping up a conversation on the eventful morning of the fourteenth of February.

"Ah!" said Perker, "I hope he's got a good one."

"Why so?" inquired Mr. Pickwick.

"Highly important—very important, my dear Sir," replied Perker. "A good, contented, well-breakfasted jury-man, is a capital thing to get hold of. Discontented or hungry jurymen, my dear Sir, always find for the plaintiff."

"Bless my heart," said Mr. Pickwick, looking very blank; "what do they do that for?"

"Why, I don't know," replied the little man, coolly; 'saves time, I suppose. If it's near dinner-time, the fore-man takes out his watch when the jury have retired, and says, 'Dear me, gentlemen, ten minutes to five, I declare! I dine at five, gentlemen.' 'So do I,' says every body else, except two men who ought to have dined at three, and seem more than half disposed to stand out in consequence. The foreman smiles, and puts up his watch:—'Well, gen-tlemen, what do we say?—plaintiff or defendant, gentle-men? I rather think, so far as I am concerned, gentlemen, —I say, I rather think,—but don't let that influence you— I *rather* think the plaintiff's the man.' Upon this, two or three other men are sure to say that they think so too—as of course they do; and then they get on very unanimously and comfortably. Ten minutes past nine!" said the little man, looking at his watch. "Time we were off, my dear Sir; breach of promise trial—court is generally full in such cases. You had better ring for a coach, my dear Sir, or we shall be rather late."

Mr. Pickwick immediately rang the bell, and a coach having been procured, the four Pickwickians and Mr. Perker ensconced themselves therein, and drove to Guild-hall; Sam Weller, Mr. Lowten, and the blue bag, follow-ing in a cab.

"Lowten," said Perker, when they reached the outer hall of the court, "put Mr. Pickwick's friends in the stu-dents' box; Mr. Pickwick himself had better sit by me. This way, my dear Sir,—this way;" and taking Mr. Pick-wick by the coat-sleeve, the little man led him to the low seat just beneath the desks of the King's Counsel, which is constructed for the convenience of attorneys, who from that spot can whisper into the ear of the leading counsel in the case, any instructions that may be necessary during the progress of the trial. The occupants of this seat are in-visible to the great body of spectators, inasmuch as they sit on a much lower level than either the barristers or the audience, whose seats are raised above the floor. Of course they have their backs to both, and their faces towards the judge.

"That's the witness-box, I suppose?" said Mr. Pick-wick, pointing to a kind of pulpit, with a brass rail, on his left hand.

"That's the witness-box, my dear Sir," replied Perker, disinterring a quantity of papers from the blue bag, which Lowten had just deposited at his feet.

"And that," said Mr. Pickwick, pointing to a couple of enclosed seats on his right, "that's where the jurymen sit, is it not?"

"The identical place, my dear Sir," replied Perker, tap-ping the lid of his snuff-box.

Mr. Pickwick stood up in a state of great agitation, and took a glance at the court. There were already a pretty large sprinkling of spectators in the gallery, and a numer-ous muster of gentlemen in wigs in the barristers' seats, who presented, as a body, all that pleasing and extensive variety of nose and whisker for which the bar of England is so justly celebrated. Such of the gentlemen as had got a brief to carry, carried it in as conspicuous a manner as possible, and occasionally scratched their noses therewith, to impress the fact more strongly on the observation of the spectators. Other gentlemen, who had no briefs to show,

carried under their arms goodly octavos, with a red label behind, and that underdone-pie-crust-coloured cover, which is technically known as "law calf." Others, who had neither briefs nor books, thrust their hands into their pockets, and looked as wise as they conveniently could; while others, again, moved here and there with great rest-lessness and earnestness of manner, content to awaken thereby, the admiration and astonishment of the uninitiated strangers. The whole, to the great wonderment of Mr. Pickwick, were divided into little groups, who were chat-ting and discussing the news of the day in the most unfeel-ing manner possible,—just as if no trial at all were com-ing on.

A bow from Mr. Phunky, as he entered, and took his seat behind the row appropriated to the King's Counsel, attracted Mr. Pickwick's attention; and he had scarcely returned it, when Mr. Serjeant Snubbin appeared, followed by Mr. Mallard, who half hid the Serjeant behind a large crimson bag, which he placed on his table, and, after shak-ing hands with Perker, withdrew. Then there entered two or three more Serjeants, and among them, one with a fat body and a red face, who nodded in a friendly manner to Mr. Serjeant Snubbin, and said it was a fine morning.

"Who's that red-faced man, who said it was a fine morning, and nodded to our counsel?" whispered Mr. Pickwick.

"Mr. Serjeant Buzfuz," replied Perker. "He's opposed to us; he leads on the other side. That gentleman behind him, is Mr. Skimpin, his junior."

Mr. Pickwick was just on the point of inquiring, with great abhorrence of the man's cold-blooded villany, how Mr. Serjeant Buzfuz, who was counsel for the opposite party, dared to presume to tell Mr. Serjeant Snubbin, who was counsel for him, that it was a fine morning,—when he was interrupted by a general rising of the barristers, and a loud cry of "Silence!" from the officers of the court. Looking round, he found that this was caused by the en-trance of the judge.

Mr. Justice Stareleigh (who sat in the absence of the Chief Justice, occasioned by indisposition,) was a most particularly short man, and so fat, that he seemed all face and waistcoat. He rolled in, upon two little turned legs, and having bobbed gravely to the bar, who bobbed gravely to him, put his little legs underneath his table, and his lit-tle three-cornered hat upon it; and when Mr. Justice Stare-leigh had done this, all you could see of him was two queer little eyes, one broad pink face, and somewhere about half of a big and very comical-looking wig.

The judge had no sooner taken his seat, than the officer on the floor of the court called out "Silence!" in a com-manding tone, upon which another officer in the gallery cried "Silence!" in an angry manner, whereupon three or four ushers shouted "Silence!" in a voice of indig-nant remonstrance. This being done, a gentleman in black, who sat below the judge, proceeded to call over the names of the jury; and after a great deal of bawling, it was dis-covered that only ten special jurymen were present. Upon this, Mr. Serjeant Buzfuz prayed a *tales*; the gentleman in black then proceeded to press into the special jury two of the common jurymen; and a green-grocer and a chemist were caught directly.

"Answer to your names, gentlemen, that you may be sworn," said the gentleman in black. "Richard Upwitch."

"Here," said the green-grocer.

"Thomas Groffin."

"Here," said the chemist.

"Take the book, gentlemen. You shall well and truly try—"

"I beg this court's pardon," said the chemist, who was a tall, thin, yellow-visaged man, "but I hope this court will excuse my attendance."

"On what grounds, Sir?" said Mr. Justice Stareleigh.

"I have no assistant, my Lord," said the chemist.

"I can't help that, Sir," replied Mr. Justice Stareleigh. "You should hire one."

"I can't afford it, my Lord," rejoined the chemist.

"Then you ought to be able to afford it, Sir," said the Judge, reddening; for Mr. Justice Stareleigh's temper bordered on the irritable, and brooked not contradiction.

"I know I *ought* to do, if I got on as well as I deserved, but I don't, my Lord," answered the chemist.

"Swear the gentleman," said the Judge, peremptorily.

The officer had got no further than the "You shall well and truly try," when he was again interrupted by the chemist.

"I am to be sworn, my Lord, am I?" said the chemist.

"Certainly, Sir," replied the testy little Judge.

"Very well, my Lord," replied the chemist in a resigned manner. "Then there'll be murder before this trial's over; that's all. Swear me if you please, Sir;" and sworn the chemist was, before the Judge could find words to utter.

"I merely wanted to observe, my Lord," said the chemist, taking his seat with great deliberation, "that I've left nobody but an errand-boy in my shop. He is a very nice boy, my Lord, but he is not much acquainted with drugs; and I know that the prevailing impression on his mind is, that Epsom salts means oxalic acid; and syrup of senna, laudanum. That's all, my Lord." With this, the tall chemist composed himself into a comfortable attitude, and, assuming a pleasant expression of countenance, appeared to have prepared himself for the worst.

Mr. Pickwick was regarding the chemist with feelings of the deepest horror, when a slight sensation was perceptible in the body of the court; and immediately afterwards Mrs. Bardell, supported by Mrs. Cluppins, was led in, and placed, in a drooping state, at the other end of the seat on which Mr. Pickwick sat. An extra sized umbrella was then handed in by Mr. Dodson, and a pair of pattens by Mr. Fogg, each of whom had prepared a most sympathising and melancholy face for the occasion. Mrs. Sanders then appeared, leading in Master Bardell. At sight of her child, Mrs. Bardell started; suddenly recollecting herself, she kissed him in a frantic manner; and then relapsing into a state of hysterical imbecility, the good lady requested to be informed where she was. In reply to this, Mrs. Cluppins and Mrs. Sanders turned their heads away and wept, while Messrs. Dodson and Fogg entreated the plaintiff to compose herself. Serjeant Buzfuz rubbed his eyes very hard with a large white handkerchief, and gave an appealing look towards the jury, while the Judge was visibly affected, and several of the beholders tried to cough down their emotions.

"Very good notion that, indeed," whispered Perker to Mr. Pickwick. "Capital fellows those Dodson and Fogg; excellent ideas of effect, my dear Sir, excellent."

As Perker spoke, Mrs. Bardell began to recover by slow degrees, while Mrs. Cluppins, after a careful survey of Master Bardell's buttons and the button-holes to which they severally belonged, placed him on the floor of the court in front of his mother,—a commanding position in which he could not fail to awaken the full commiseration and sympathy of both Judge and jury. This was not done without considerable opposition, and many tears on the part of the young gentleman himself, who had certain inward misgivings that the placing him within the full glare of the Judge's eye was only a formal prelude to his being immediately ordered away for instant execution, or for transportation beyond the seas during the whole term of his natural life, at the very least.

"Bardell and Pickwick," cried the gentleman in black, calling on the case, which stood first on the list.

"I am for the plaintiff, my Lord," said Mr. Serjeant Buzfuz.

"Who is with you, brother Buzfuz?" said the Judge. Mr. Skimpin bowed, to intimate that he was.

"I appear for the defendant, my Lord," said Mr. Serjeant Snubbin.

"Anybody with you, brother Snubbin?" inquired the court.

"Mr. Phunky, my Lord," replied Serjeant Snubbin.

"Serjeant Buzfuz and Mr. Skimpin for the plaintiff," said the Judge, writing down the names in his note-book, and reading as he wrote; "for the defendant, Serjeant Snubbin and Mr. Monkey."

"Beg your Lordship's pardon, Phunky."

"Oh, very good," said the Judge; "I never had the pleasure of hearing the gentleman's name before." Here Mr. Phunky bowed and smiled, and the Judge bowed and smiled too, and then Mr. Phunky, blushing into the very whites of his eyes, tried to look as if he didn't know that everybody was gazing at him, a thing which no man ever succeeded in doing yet, and in all reasonable probability, never will.

"Go on," said the judge.

The ushers again called silence, and Mr. Skimpin proceeded to "open the case;" and the case appeared to have very little inside it when he had opened it, for he kept such particulars as he knew, completely to himself, and sat down, after a lapse of three minutes, leaving the jury in precisely the same advanced stage of wisdom as they were in before.

Serjeant Buzfuz then rose with all the majesty and dignity which the grave nature of the proceedings demanded, and having whispered to Dodson, and conferred briefly with Fogg, pulled his gown over his shoulders, settled his wig, and addressed the jury.

Serjeant Buzfuz began by saying, that never, in the whole course of his professional experience—never, from the very first moment of his applying himself to the study and practice of the law—had he approached a case with feelings of such deep emotion, or with such a heavy sense of the responsibility imposed upon him—a responsibility, he would say, which he could never have supported, were he not buoyed up and sustained by a conviction so strong, that it amounted to positive certainty that the cause of truth and justice, or, in other words, the cause of his much-injured and most oppressed client, must prevail with the high-minded and intelligent dozen of men whom he now saw in that box before him.

Counsel always begin in this way, because it puts the jury on the very best terms with themselves, and makes them think what sharp fellows they must be. A visible effect was produced immediately, several jurymen beginning to take voluminous notes with the utmost eagerness.

"You have heard from my learned friend, gentlemen"—continued Serjeant Buzfuz, well knowing that, from the learned friend alluded to, the gentlemen of the jury had heard just nothing at all—"you have heard from my learned friend, gentlemen, that this is an action for a breach of promise of marriage, in which the damages are laid at 1500*l*. But you have not heard from my learned friend, inasmuch as it did not come within my learned friend's province to tell you, what are the facts and circumstances of the case. Those facts and circumstances, gentlemen, you shall hear detailed by me, and proved by the unimpeachable female whom I will place in that box before you."

Here Mr. Serjeant Buzfuz, with a tremendous emphasis on the word "box," smote his table with a mighty sound, and glanced at Dodson and Fogg, who nodded admiration of the serjeant, and indignant defiance of the defendant.

"The plaintiff, gentlemen," continued Serjeant Buzfuz, in a soft and melancholy voice, "the plaintiff is a widow; yes, gentlemen, a widow. The late Mr. Bardell, after enjoying for many years the esteem and confidence of his sovereign, as one of the guardians of his royal revenues, glided almost imperceptibly from the world, to seek elsewhere for that repose and peace which a custom-house can never afford."

At this pathetic description of the decease of Mr. Bardell, who had been knocked on the head with a quart-pot in a public-house cellar, the learned serjeant's voice faltered, and he proceeded with emotion—

"Some time before his death, he had stamped his likeness upon a little boy. With this little boy, the only pledge of her departed exciseman, Mrs. Bardell shrunk from the world, and courted the retirement and tranquillity of Goswell-street; and here she placed in her front parlour-window a written placard, bearing this inscription—'Apartments furnished for a single gentleman. Enquire within.'"

Here Serjeant Buzfuz paused, while several gentlemen of the jury took a note of the document.

"There is no date to that, is there, Sir?" enquired a juror.

"There is no date, gentlemen," replied Serjeant Buzfuz; "but I am instructed to say that it was put in the plaintiff's parlour-window just this time three years. I entreat the attention of the jury to the wording of this document—'Apartments furnished for a single gentleman!' Mrs. Bardell's opinions of the opposite sex, gentlemen, were derived from a long contemplation of the inestimable qualities of her lost husband. She had no fear—she had no distrust—she had no suspicion—all was confidence and reliance. 'Mr. Bardell,' said the widow; 'Mr. Bardell was a man of honour—Mr. Bardell was a man of his word—Mr. Bardell was no deceiver—Mr. Bardell was once a single gentleman himself; to single gentlemen I look for protection, for assistance, for comfort, and for consolation—in single gentlemen I shall perpetually see something to remind me of what Mr. Bardell was, when he first won my young and untried affections; to a single gentleman, then, shall my lodgings be let.' Actuated by this beautiful and touching impulse, (among the best impulses of our imperfect nature, gentlemen,) the lonely and desolate widow dried her tears, furnished her first floor, caught her innocent boy to her maternal bosom, and put the bill up in her parlour-window. Did it remain there long? No. The serpent was on the watch, the train was laid, the mine was preparing, the sapper and miner was at work. Before the bill had been in the parlour-window three days—three days—gentlemen—a being, erect upon two legs, and bearing all the outward

semblance of a man, and not of a monster, knocked at the door of Mrs. Bardell's house. He enquired within; he took the lodgings; and on the very next day he entered into possession of them. This man was Pickwick—Pickwick, the defendant."

Serjeant Buzfuz, who had proceeded with such volubility that his face was perfectly crimson, here paused for breath. The silence awoke Mr. Justice Stareleigh, who immediately wrote down something with a pen without any ink in it, and looked unusually profound, to impress the jury with the belief that he always thought most deeply with his eyes shut. Serjeant Buzfuz proceeded.

"Of this man Pickwick I will say little; the subject presents but few attractions; and I, gentlemen, am not the man, nor are you, gentlemen, the men, to delight in the contemplation of revolting heartlessness, and of systematic villany."

Here Mr. Pickwick, who had been writhing in silence for some time, gave a violent start, as if some vague idea of assaulting Serjeant Buzfuz, in the august presence of justice and law, suggested itself to his mind. An admonitory gesture from Perker restrained him, and he listened to the learned gentleman's continuation with a look of indignation, which contrasted forcibly with the admiring faces of Mrs. Cluppins and Mrs. Sanders.

"I say systematic villany, gentlemen," said Serjeant Buzfuz, looking through Mr. Pickwick, and talking *at* him; "and when I say systematic villany, let me tell the defendant, Pickwick, if he be in court, as I am informed he is, that it would have been more decent in him, more becoming, in better judgment and in better taste, if he had stopped away. Let me tell him, gentlemen, that any gestures of dissent or disapprobation in which he may indulge in this court will not go down with you; that you will know how to value and how to appreciate them; and let me tell him further, as my lord will tell you, gentlemen, that a counsel, in the discharge of his duty to his client, is neither to be intimidated nor bullied, nor put down; and that any attempt to do either the one or the other, or the first, or the last, will recoil on the head of the attempter, be he plaintiff or be he defendant, be his name Pickwick or Noakes, or Stoakes, or Stiles, or Brown, or Thompson."

This little divergence from the subject in hand, had of course the intended effect of turning all eyes to Mr. Pickwick. Serjeant Buzfuz, having partially recovered from the state of moral elevation into which he had lashed himself, resumed—

"I shall show you, gentlemen, that for two years Pickwick continued to reside constantly, and without interruption or intermission, at Mrs. Bardell's house. I shall show you that Mrs. Bardell, during the whole of that time, waited on him, attended to his comforts, cooked his meals, looked out his linen for the washerwoman when it went abroad, darned, aired, and prepared it for wear, when it came home, and, in short, enjoyed his fullest trust and confidence. I shall show you that, on many occasions, he gave halfpence, and on some occasions even sixpences, to her little boy; and I shall prove to you, by a witness whose testimony it will be impossible for my learned friend to weaken or controvert, that on one occasion he patted the boy on the head, and, after enquiring whether he had won any *alley tors or commoneys* lately (both of which I understand to be a particular species of marbles much prized by the youth of this town), made use of this remarkable expression—'How should you like to have another father?'

THE TRIAL.

I shall prove to you farther, gentlemen, that about a year ago, Pickwick suddenly began to absent himself from home, during long intervals, as if with the intention of gradually breaking off from my client; but I shall show you also, that his resolution was not at that time sufficiently strong, or that his better feelings conquered, if better feelings he has —or that the charms and accomplishments of my client prevailed over his unmanly intentions, by proving to you, that on one occasion, when he returned from the country, he distinctly and in terms, offered her marriage: previously however, taking special care that there should be no witnesses to their solemn contract; and I am in a situation to prove to you, on the testimony of three of his own friends, —most unwilling witnesses, gentlemen—most unwilling witnesses—that on that morning he was discovered by them holding the plaintiff in his arms, and soothing her agitation by his caresses and endearments."

A visible impression was produced upon the auditors by this part of the learned serjeant's address. Drawing forth two very small scraps of paper, he proceeded—

"And now, gentlemen, but one word more. Two letters have passed between these parties, letters which are admitted to be in the handwriting of the defendant, and which speak volumes indeed. These letters, too, bespeak the character of the man. They are not open, fervent, eloquent epistles, breathing nothing but the language of affectionate attachment. They are covert, sly, underhanded communications, but, fortunately, far more conclusive than if couched in the most glowing language and the most poetic imagery—letters that must be viewed with a cautious and suspicious eye—letters that were evidently intended at the time, by Pickwick, to mislead and delude any third parties into whose hands they might fall. Let me read the first:—'Garraway's, twelve o'clock. Dear Mrs. B.—Chops and Tomata sauce. Yours, PICKWICK.' Gentlemen, what does this mean? Chops and Tomata sauce. Yours, Pickwick! Chops! Gracious heavens! and Tomata sauce! Gentlemen, is the happiness of a sensitive and confiding female to be trifled away, by such shallow artifices as these? The next has no date whatever, which is in itself suspicious.—'Dear Mrs. B., I shall not be at home till to-morrow. Slow coach.' And then follows this very remarkable expression—'Don't trouble yourself about the warming-pan.' The warming-pan! Why, gentlemen, who *does* trouble himself about a warming-pan? When was the peace of mind of man or woman broken or disturbed by a warming-pan, which is in itself a harmless, a useful, and I will add, gentlemen, a comforting article of domestic furniture? Why is Mrs. Bardell so earnestly entreated not to agitate herself about this warming-pan, unless (as is no doubt the case) it is a mere cover for hidden fire—a mere substitute for some endearing word or promise, agreeably to a preconcerted system of correspondence, artfully contrived by Pickwick with a view to his contemplated desertion, and which I am not in a condition to explain? And what does this allusion to the slow coach mean? For aught I know, it may be a reference to Pickwick himself, who has most unquestionably been a criminally slow coach during the whole of this transaction, but whose speed will now be very unexpectedly accelerated, and whose wheels, gentlemen, as he will find to his cost, will very soon be greased by you!"

Mr. Serjeant Buzfuz paused in this place, to see whether the jury smiled at his joke; but as nobody took it but the green grocer, whose sensitiveness on the subject was very probably occasioned by his having subjected a chaise-cart to the process in question on that identical morning, the learned serjeant considered it advisable to undergo a slight relapse into the dismals before he concluded.

"But enough of this, gentlemen," said Mr. Serjeant Buzfuz, "it is difficult to smile with an aching heart; it is ill jesting when our deepest sympathies are awakened. My client's hopes and prospects are ruined, and it is no figure of speech to say that her occupation is gone indeed. The bill is down—but there is no tenant. Eligible single gentlemen pass and repass—but there is no invitation for them to enquire within, or without. All is gloom and silence in the house; even the voice of the child is hushed; his infant sports are disregarded when his mother weeps; his 'alley tors' and his 'commoneys' are alike neglected; he forgets the long familiar cry of 'knuckle down,' and at tip-cheese, or odd and even, his hand is out. But Pickwick, gentlemen, Pickwick, the ruthless destroyer of this domestic oasis in the desert of Goswell-street—Pickwick, who has choked up the well, and thrown ashes on the sward —Pickwick, who comes before you to-day with his heartless tomata sauce and warming-pans—Pickwick still rears his head with unblushing effrontery, and gazes without a sigh on the ruin he has made. Damages, gentlemen—heavy damages is the only punishment with which you can visit him; the only recompence you can award to my client. And for those damages she now appeals to an enlightened, a high-minded, a right-feeling, a conscientious, a dispassionate, a sympathising, a contemplative jury of her civilized countrymen." With this beautiful peroration, Mr. Serjeant Buzfuz sat down, and Mr. Justice Stareleigh woke up.

"Call Elizabeth Cluppins," said Serjeant Buzfuz, rising a minute afterwards, with renewed vigour.

The nearest usher called for Elizabeth Tuppins; another one, at a little distance off, demanded Elizabeth Jupkins; and a third rushed in a breathless state into King-street, and screamed for Elizabeth Muffins till he was hoarse.

Meanwhile Mrs. Cluppins, with the combined assistance of Mrs. Bardell, Mrs. Sanders, Mr. Dodson, and Mr. Fogg, was hoisted into the witness-box; and when she was safely perched on the top step, Mrs. Bardell stood on the bottom one, with the pocket-handkerchief and pattens in one hand, and a glass bottle that might hold about a quarter of a pint of smelling salts in the other, ready for any emergency. Mrs. Sanders, whose eyes were intently fixed on the judge's face, planted herself close by, with the large umbrella: keeping her right thumb pressed on the spring with an earnest countenance, as if she were fully prepared to put it up at a moment's notice.

"Mrs. Cluppins," said Serjeant Buzfuz, "pray compose yourself, ma'am;" and, of course, directly Mrs. Cluppins was desired to compose herself she sobbed with increased vehemence, and gave divers alarming manifestations of an approaching fainting fit, or, as she afterwards said, of her feelings being too many for her.

"Do you recollect, Mrs. Cluppins?" said Serjeant Buzfuz, after a few unimportant questions—"do you recollect being in Mrs. Bardell's back one pair of stairs, on one particular morning in July last, when she was dusting Mr. Pickwick's apartment?"

"Yes, my Lord and Jury, I do," replied Mrs. Cluppins.

"Mr. Pickwick's sitting-room was the first-floor front, I believe?"

"Yes, it were, Sir," replied Mrs. Cluppins.

"What were you doing in the back room, ma'am?" inquired the little Judge.

"My Lord and Jury," said Mrs. Cluppins, with interesting agitation, "I will not deceive you."

"You had better not, ma'am," said the little Judge.

"I was there," resumed Mrs. Cluppins, "unbeknown to Mrs. Bardell; I had been out with a little basket, gentlemen, to buy three pound of red kidney pertaties, which was three pound tuppence ha'penny, when I see Mrs. Bardell's street door on the jar."

"On the what?" exclaimed the little Judge.

"Partly open, my Lord," said Serjeant Snubbin.

"She *said* on the jar," said the little Judge, with a cunning look.

"It's all the same, my Lord," said Serjeant Snubbin. The little Judge looked doubtful, and said he'd make a note of it. Mrs. Cluppins then resumed—

"I walked in, gentlemen, just to say good mornin', and went in a permiscuous manner up stairs, and into the back room. Gentlemen, there was the sound of voices in the front room, and—"

"And you listened, I believe, Mrs. Cluppins," said Serjeant Buzfuz.

"Beggin' your pardon, Sir," replied Mrs. Cluppins, in a majestic manner, "I would scorn the haction. The voices was very loud, Sir, and forced themselves upon my ear."

"Well, Mrs. Cluppins, you were not listening, but you heard the voices. Was one of those voices Mr. Pickwick's?"

"Yes, it were, Sir."

And Mrs. Cluppins, after distinctly stating that Mr. Pickwick addressed himself to Mrs. Bardell, repeated by slow degrees, and by dint of many questions, the conversation with which our readers are already acquainted.

The Jury looked suspicious, and Mr. Serjeant Buzfuz smiled and sat down. They looked positively awful when Serjeant Snubbin intimated that he should not cross-examine the witness, for Mr. Pickwick wished it to be distinctly stated that it was due to her to say, that her account was in substance correct.

Mrs. Cluppins having once broken the ice, thought it a very favourable opportunity of entering into a short dissertation on her own domestic affairs; so she straightway proceeded to inform the court that she was the mother of eight children at that present speaking, and that she entertained confident expectations of presenting Mr. Cluppins with a ninth, somewhere about that day six months. At this interesting point, the little Judge interposed most irascibly; and the effect of the interposition was, that both the worthy lady and Mrs. Sanders were politely taken out of court, under the escort of Mr. Jackson, without further parley.

"Nathaniel Winkle," said Mr. Skimpin.

"Here!" replied a feeble voice. And Mr. Winkle entered the witness-box, and having been duly sworn, bowed to the Judge with considerable deference.

"Don't look at me, Sir," said the judge, sharply, in acknowledgment of the salute; "look at the jury."

Mr. Winkle obeyed the mandate, and looked at the place where he thought it most probable the jury might be; for seeing anything in his then state of intellectual complication was wholly out of the question.

Mr. Winkle was then examined by Mr. Skimpin, who, being a promising young man of two or three and forty, was of course anxious to confuse a witness who was notoriously predisposed in favour of the other side, as much as he could.

"Now, Sir," said Mr. Skimpin, "have the goodness to let his Lordship and the jury know what your name is, will you?" and Mr. Skimpin inclined his head on one side to listen with great sharpness to the answer, and glanced at the jury meanwhile, as if to imply that he rather expected Mr. Winkle's natural taste for perjury would induce him to give some name which did not belong to him.

"Winkle," replied the witness.

"What's your Christian name, Sir?" angrily inquired the little judge.

"Nathaniel, Sir."

"Daniel,—any other name?"

"Nathaniel, Sir—my Lord, I mean."

"Nathaniel Daniel, or Daniel Nathaniel?"

"No, my Lord, only Nathaniel—not Daniel at all."

"What did you tell me it was Daniel for, then, Sir?" inquired the judge.

"I didn't, my Lord," replied Mr. Winkle.

"You did, Sir," replied the judge, with a severe frown. "How could I have got Daniel on my notes, unless you told me so, Sir?"

This argument was, of course, unanswerable.

"Mr. Winkle has rather a short memory, my Lord," interposed Mr. Skimpin, with another glance at the jury. "We shall find means to refresh it before we have quite done with him, I dare say."

"You had better be careful, Sir," said the little judge, with a sinister look at the witness.

Poor Mr. Winkle bowed, and endeavoured to feign an easiness of manner, which, in his then state of confusion, gave him rather the air of a disconcerted pickpocket.

"Now, Mr. Winkle," said Mr. Skimpin, "attend to me, if you please, Sir; and let me recommend you, for your own sake, to bear in mind his Lordship's injunctions to be careful. I believe you are a particular friend of Mr. Pickwick, the defendant, are you not?"

"I have known Mr. Pickwick now, as well as I recollect at this moment, nearly—"

"Pray, Mr. Winkle, do not evade the question. Are you, or are you not, a particular friend of the defendant's?"

"I was just about to say, that—"

"Will you, or will you not, answer my question, Sir?"

"If you don't answer the question, you'll be committed, Sir," interposed the little Judge, looking over his note-book.

"Come, Sir," said Mr. Skimpin, "yes or no, if you please."

"Yes, I am," replied Mr. Winkle.

"Yes, you are. And why couldn't you say that at once, Sir? Perhaps you know the plaintiff too? Eh, Mr. Winkle?"

"I don't know her; I've seen her."

"Oh, you don't know her, but you've seen her? Now, have the goodness to tell the gentlemen of the jury what you mean by *that*, Mr. Winkle."

"I mean that I am not intimate with her, but I have seen her when I went to call on Mr. Pickwick, in Goswell-street."

"How often have you seen her, Sir?"

"How often?"

"Yes, Mr. Winkle, how often? I'll repeat the question for you a dozen times, if you require it, Sir." And the learned gentleman, with a firm and steady frown, placed his hands on his hips, and smiled suspiciously to the jury.

On this question there arose the edifying brow-beating, customary on such points. First of all, Mr. Winkle said it was quite impossible for him to say how many times he had seen Mrs. Bardell. Then he was asked if he had seen her twenty times, to which he replied, "Certainly,—more than that." Then he was asked whether he hadn't seen her a hundred times—whether he couldn't swear that he had seen her more than fifty times—whether he didn't know that he had seen her at least seventy-five times, and so forth; the satisfactory conclusion which was arrived at, at last, being—that he had better take care of himself, and mind what he was about. The witness having been by these means reduced to the requisite ebb of nervous perplexity, the examination was continued as follows—

"Pray, Mr. Winkle, do you remember calling on the defendant Pickwick at these apartments in the plaintiff's house in Goswell-street, on one particular morning, in the month of July last?"

"Yes, I do."

"Were you accompanied on that occasion by a friend of the name of Tupman, and another by the name of Snodgrass?"

"Yes, I was."

"Are they here?"

"Yes, they are,"—replied Mr. Winkle, looking very earnestly towards the spot where his friends were stationed.

"Pray attend to me, Mr. Winkle, and never mind your friends"—said Mr. Skimpin, with another expressive look at the jury. "They must tell their stories without any previous consultation with you, if none has yet taken place (another look at the jury). Now, Sir, tell the gentlemen of the jury what you saw on entering the defendant's room, on this particular morning. Come; out with it, Sir; we must have it, sooner or later."

"The defendant, Mr. Pickwick, was holding the plaintiff in his arms, with his hands clasping her waist," replied Mr. Winkle with natural hesitation, "and the plaintiff appeared to have fainted away."

"Did you hear the defendant say anything?"

"I heard him call Mrs. Bardell a good creature, and I heard him ask her to compose herself, for what a situation it was, if any body should come, or words to that effect."

"Now, Mr. Winkle, I have only one more question to ask you, and I beg you to bear in mind his lordship's caution. Will you undertake to swear that Pickwick, the defendant, did not say on the occasion in question—'My dear Mrs. Bardell, you're a good creature; compose yourself to this situation, for to this situation you must come,' or words to *that* effect?"

"I—I didn't understand him so, certainly," said Mr. Winkle, astounded at this ingenious dove-tailing of the few words he had heard. "I was on the staircase, and couldn't hear distinctly; the impression on my mind is—"

"The gentlemen of the jury want none of the impressions on your mind, Mr. Winkle, which I fear would be of little service to honest, straight-forward men," interposed Mr. Skimpin. "You were on the staircase, and didn't distinctly hear; but you will not swear that Pickwick did not make use of the expressions I have quoted? Do I understand that?"

"No, I will not," replied Mr. Winkle; and down sat Mr. Skimpin with a triumphant countenance.

Mr. Pickwick's case had not gone off in so particularly happy a manner, up to this point, that it could very well afford to have any additional suspicion cast upon it. But as it could afford to be placed in a rather better light, if possible, Mr. Phunky rose for the purpose of getting something important out of Mr. Winkle in cross-examination. Whether he did get anything important out of him, will immediately appear.

"I believe, Mr. Winkle," said Mr. Phunky, "that Mr. Pickwick is not a young man?"

"Oh no," replied Mr. Winkle; "old enough to be my father."

"You have told my learned friend that you have known Mr. Pickwick a long time. Had you ever any reason to suppose or believe that he was about to be married?"

"Oh no; certainly not;" replied Mr. Winkle with so much eagerness, that Mr. Phunky ought to have got him out of the box with all possible dispatch. Lawyers hold that there are two kinds of particularly bad witnesses: a reluctant witness, and a too-willing witness; it was Mr. Winkle's fate to figure in both characters.

"I will even go further than this, Mr. Winkle," continued Mr. Phunky in a most smooth and complacent manner. "Did you ever see anything in Mr. Pickwick's manner and conduct towards the opposite sex to induce you to believe that he ever contemplated matrimony of late years, in any case?"

"Oh no; certainly not," replied Mr. Winkle.

"Has his behaviour, when females have been in the case, always been that of a man, who, having attained a pretty advanced period of life, content with his own occupations and amusements, treats them only as a father might his daughters?"

"Not the least doubt of it," replied Mr. Winkle, in the fulness of his heart. "That is—yes—oh yes—certainly."

"You have never known anything in his behaviour towards Mrs. Bardell, or any other female, in the least degree suspicious?" said Mr. Phunky, preparing to sit down, for Serjeant Snubbin was winking at him.

"N—n—no," replied Mr. Winkle, "except on one trifling occasion, which, I have no doubt, might be easily explained."

Now, if the unfortunate Mr. Phunky had sat down when Serjeant Snubbin winked at him, or if Serjeant Buzfuz had stopped this irregular cross-examination at the outset (which he knew better than to do; observing Mr. Winkle's anxiety, and well knowing it would, in all probability, lead to something serviceable to him), this unfortunate admission would not have been elicited. The moment the words fell from Mr. Winkle's lips, Mr. Phunky sat down, and Serjeant Snubbin rather hastily told him he might leave the box, which Mr. Winkle prepared to do with great readiness, when Serjeant Buzfuz stopped him.

"Stay, Mr. Winkle—stay," said Serjeant Buzfuz, "will your lordship have the goodness to ask him, what this one instance of suspicious behaviour towards females on the part of this gentleman, who is old enough to be his father, was?"

"You hear what the learned counsel says, Sir," observed the judge, turning to the miserable and agonized Mr. Winkle. "Describe the occasion to which you refer."

"My lord," said Mr. Winkle, trembling with anxiety, "I—I'd rather not."

"Perhaps so," said the little judge; "but you must."

Amid the profound silence of the whole court, Mr.

Winkle faltered out, that the trifling circumstance of suspicion was Mr. Pickwick's being found in a lady's sleeping apartment at midnight, which had terminated, he believed, in the breaking off of the projected marriage of the lady in question, and led, he knew, to the whole party being forcibly carried before George Nupkins, Esq., magistrate and justice of the peace, for the borough of Ipswich!

"You may leave the box, Sir," said Serjeant Snubbin. Mr. Winkle *did* leave the box, and rushed with delirious haste to the George and Vulture, where he was discovered some hours after, by the waiter, groaning in a hollow and dismal manner, with his head buried beneath the sofa cushions.

Tracy Tupman, and Augustus Snodgrass, were severally called into the box; both corroborated the testimony of their unhappy friend; and each was driven to the verge of desperation by excessive badgering.

Susannah Sanders was then called, and examined by Serjeant Buzfuz, and cross-examined by Serjeant Snubbin. Had always said and believed that Mr. Pickwick would marry Mrs. Bardell; knew that Mrs. Bardell's being engaged to Mr. Pickwick was the current topic of conversation in the neighbourhood, after the fainting in July; had been told it herself by Mrs. Mudberry which kept a mangle, and Mrs. Bunkin which clear-starched, but did not see either Mrs. Mudberry or Mrs. Bunkin in court. Had heard Mr. Pickwick ask the little boy how he should like to have another father. Did not know that Mrs. Bardell was at that time keeping company with the baker, but did know that the baker was then a single man and is now married. Couldn't swear that Mrs. Bardell was not very fond of the baker, but should think that the baker was not very fond of Mrs. Bardell, or he wouldn't have married somebody else. Thought Mrs. Bardell fainted away on the morning in July, because Mr. Pickwick asked her to name the day; knew that she (witness) fainted away stone dead when Mr. Sanders asked *her* to name the day, and believed that everybody as called herself a lady would do the same, under similar circumstances. Heard Mr. Pickwick ask the boy the question about the marbles, but upon her oath did not know the difference between an alley tor and a commoney.

By the COURT—During the period of her keeping company with Mr. Sanders had received love letters, like other ladies. In the course of their correspondence Mr. Sanders had often called her a "duck," but never "chops," or "tomata sauce." He was particularly fond of ducks. Perhaps if he had been as fond of chops and tomata sauce, he might have called her that, as a term of affection.

Serjeant Buzfuz now rose with more importance than he had yet exhibited, if that were possible, and vociferated "Call Samuel Weller."

It was quite unnecessary to call Samuel Weller, for Samuel Weller stepped briskly into the box the instant his name was pronounced; and placing his hat on the floor, and his arms on the rail, took a bird's-eye view of the bar, and a comprehensive survey of the bench with a remarkably cheerful and lively aspect.

"What's your name, Sir?" enquired the judge.

"Sam Weller, my Lord," replied that gentleman.

"Do you spell it with a 'V' or a 'W'?" enquired the Judge.

"That depends upon the taste and fancy of the speller, my Lord," replied Sam, "I never had occasion to spell it more than once or twice in my life, but I spells it with a 'V.'"

Here a voice in the gallery exclaimed aloud, "Quite right too, Samivel; quite right. Put it down a we, my Lord, put it down a we."

"Who is that, that dares to address the Court?" said the little Judge, looking up, "Usher."

"Yes, my Lord."

"Bring that person here instantly."

"Yes, my Lord."

But as the usher didn't find the person, he didn't bring him; and, after a great commotion, all the people who had got up to look for the culprit, sat down again. The little Judge turned to the witness as soon as his indignation would allow him to speak, and said—

"Do you know who that was, Sir?"

"I rayther suspect it was my father, my Lord," replied Sam.

"Do you see him here now?" said the Judge.

"No, I don't, my Lord," replied Sam, staring right up into the lantern in the roof of the Court.

"If you could have pointed him out, I would have committed him instantly," said the Judge. [Sam bowed his acknowledgments and turned, with unimpaired cheerfulness of countenance, towards Serjeant Buzfuz.

"Now, Mr. Weller," said Serjeant Buzfuz.

"Now, Sir," replied Sam.

"I believe you are in the service of Mr. Pickwick, the defendant in this case. Speak up, if you please, Mr. Weller."

"I mean to speak up, Sir," replied Sam, "I am in the service o' that 'ere gen'l'man, and a wery good service it is."

"Little to do, and plenty to get, I suppose?" said Serjeant Buzfuz, with jocularity.

"Oh, quite enough to get, Sir, as the soldier said ven they ordered him three hundred and fifty lashes," replied Sam.

"You must not tell us what the soldier, or any other man, said, Sir," interposed the Judge, "it's not evidence."

"Wery good, my Lord," replied Sam.

"Do you recollect anything particular happening on the morning when you were first engaged by the defendant, eh, Mr. Weller?" said Serjeant Buzfuz.

"Yes I do, Sir," replied Sam.

"Have the goodness to tell the jury what it was."

"I had a reg'lar new fit out o' clothes that mornin', gen'l'men of the jury," said Sam, "and that was a wery partickler and uncommon circumstance vith me in those days."

Hereupon there was a general laugh; and the little Judge, looking with an angry countenance over his desk, said, "You had better be careful, Sir."

"So Mr. Pickwick said at the time, my Lord," replied Sam, "and I was wery careful o' that 'ere suit o' clothes; wery careful indeed, my Lord."

The Judge looked sternly at Sam for full two minutes, but Sam's features were so perfectly calm and serene that he said nothing, and motioned Serjeant Buzfuz to proceed.

"Do you mean to tell me, Mr. Weller," said Serjeant Buzfuz, folding his arms emphatically, and turning half round to the jury, as if in mute assurance that he would bother the witness yet—"Do you mean to tell me, Mr. Weller, that you saw nothing of this fainting on the part of the plaintiff in the arms of the defendant, which you have heard described by the witnesses?"

"Certainly not," replied Sam, "I was in the passage 'till they called me up, and then the old lady was not there."

"Now, attend, Mr. Weller," said Serjeant Buzfuz, dipping a large pen into the inkstand before him, for the purpose of frightening Sam with a show of taking down his answer. "You were in the passage and yet saw nothing of what was going forward. Have you a pair of eyes, Mr. Weller?"

"Yes, I have a pair of eyes," replied Sam, "and that's just it. If they wos a pair o' patent double million magnifyin' gas microscopes of hextra power, p'raps I might be able to see through a flight o' stairs and a deal door; but bein' only eyes you see, my wision's limited."

At this answer, which was delivered without the slightest appearance of irritation, and with the most complete simplicity and equanimity of manner, the spectators tittered, the little Judge smiled, and Serjeant Buzfuz looked particularly foolish. After a short consultation with Dodson and Fogg, the learned Serjeant again turned towards Sam, and said, with a painful effort to conceal his vexation, "Now, Mr. Weller, I'll ask you a question on another point, if you please."

"If you please, Sir," rejoined Sam, with the utmost good-humour.

"Do you remember going up to Mrs. Bardell's house, one night in November last?"

"Oh yes, very well."

"Oh, you *do* remember that, Mr. Weller," said Serjeant Buzfuz, recovering his spirits, "I thought we should get at something at last."

"I rayther thought that, too, Sir," replied Sam; and at this the spectators tittered again.

"Well; I suppose you went up to have a little talk about this trial—eh, Mr. Weller?" said Serjeant Buzfuz, looking knowingly at the jury.

"I went up to pay the rent; but we *did* get a talkin' about the trial," replied Sam.

"Oh you did get a talking about the trial," said Serjeant Buzfuz brightening up with the anticipation of some important discovery. "Now what passed about the trial; will you have the goodness to tell us, Mr. Weller?"

"Vith all the pleasure in life, Sir," replied Sam. "Arter a few unimportant obserwations from the two wirtuous females as has been examined here to-day, the ladies gets into a very great state o' admiration at the honorable conduct of Mr. Dodson and Fogg—them two gen'l'men as is settin' near you now." This, of course, drew general attention to Dodson and Fogg, who looked as virtuous as possible.

"The attornies for the plaintiff," said Mr. Serjeant Buzfuz, "well, they spoke in high praise of the honorable conduct of Messrs. Dodson and Fogg, the attornies for the plaintiff, did they?"

"Yes," said Sam, "they said what a wery gen'rous thing it was o' them to have taken up the case on spec, and to charge nothin' at all for costs, unless they got 'em out of Mr. Pickwick."

At this very unexpected reply, the spectators tittered again, and Dodson and Fogg, turning very red, leant over to Serjeant Buzfuz, and in a hurried manner whispered something in his ear.

"You are quite right," said Serjeant Buzfuz aloud, with affected composure. "It's perfectly useless, my Lord, attempting to get at any evidence through the impenetrable stupidity of this witness. I will not trouble the court by asking him any more questions. Stand down, Sir."

"Would any other gen'l'man like to ask me anythin'?" inquired Sam, taking up his hat, and looking round most deliberately.

"Not I, Mr. Weller, thank you," said Serjeant Snubbin, laughing.

"You may go down, Sir," said Serjeant Buzfuz, waving his hand impatiently. Sam went down accordingly, after doing Messrs. Dodson and Fogg's case as much harm as he conveniently could, and saying just as little respecting Mr. Pickwick as might be, which was precisely the object he had had in view all along.

"I have no objection to admit, my Lord," said Serjeant Snubbin, "if it will save the examination of another witness, that Mr. Pickwick has retired from business, and is a gentleman of considerable independent property."

"Very well," said Serjeant Buzfuz, putting in the two letters for the clerk to read, "Then that's my case, my Lord."

Serjeant Snubbin then addressed the jury on behalf of the defendant; and a very long and a very emphatic address he delivered, in which he bestowed the highest possible eulogiums on the conduct and character of Mr. Pickwick, but inasmuch as our readers are far better able to form a correct estimate of that gentleman's merits and deserts, than Serjeant Snubbin could possibly be, we do not feel called upon to enter at any length into the learned gentleman's observations. He attempted to show that the letters which had been exhibited, merely related to Mr. Pickwick's dinner or to the preparations for receiving him in his apartments on his return from some country excursion. It is sufficient to add in general terms, that he did the best he could for Mr. Pickwick; and the best, as every body knows, on the infallible authority of the old adage, could do no more.

Mr. Justice Stareleigh summed up, in the old-established and most approved form. He read as much of his notes to the jury as he could decipher on so short a notice, and made running comments on the evidence as he went along. If Mrs. Bardell was right, it was perfectly clear Mr. Pickwick was wrong, and if they thought the evidence of Mrs. Cluppins worthy of credence they would believe it, and, if they didn't, why they wouldn't. If they were satisfied that a breach of promise of marriage had been committed, they would find for the plaintiff with such damages as they thought proper; and if, on the other hand, it appears to them that no promise of marriage had ever been given, they would find for the defendant with no damages at all. The jury then retired to their private room to talk the matter over, and the Judge retired to *his* private room, to refresh himself with a mutton chop and a glass of sherry.

An anxious quarter of an hour elapsed; the jury came back, and the judge was fetched in. Mr. Pickwick put on his spectacles, and gazed at the foreman with an agitated countenance and a quickly beating heart.

"Gentlemen," said the individual in black, "are you all agreed upon your verdict?"

"We are," replied the foreman.

"Do you find for the plaintiff, gentlemen, or for the defendant?"

"For the plaintiff."

"With what damages, gentlemen?"

"Seven hundred and fifty pounds."

Mr. Pickwick took off his spectacles, carefully wiped the glasses, folded them into the case, and put them in his pocket; then having drawn on his gloves with great nicety, and stared at the foreman all the while, he mechanically followed Mr. Perker and the blue bag out of court.

They stopped in a side room while Perker paid the court fees; and here Mr. Pickwick was joined by his friends.

Here, too, he encountered Messrs. Dodson and Fogg, rubbing their hands with every token of outward satisfaction.

"Well, gentlemen," said Mr. Pickwick.

"Well, Sir," said Dodson, for self and partner.

"You imagine you'll get your costs, don't you, gentlemen?" said Mr. Pickwick.

Fogg said they thought it rather probable; and Dodson smiled, and said they'd try.

"You may try, and try, and try again, Messrs. Dodson and Fogg," said Mr. Pickwick vehemently, "but not one farthing of costs or damages do you ever get from me, if I spend the rest of my existence in a debtor's prison."

"Ha, ha!" said Dodson, "You'll think better of that, before next term, Mr. Pickwick."

"He, he, he! We'll soon see about that, Mr. Pickwick," grinned Fogg.

Speechless with indignation, Mr. Pickwick allowed himself to be led by his solicitor and friends to the door, and there assisted into a hackney-coach, which had been fetched for the purpose, by the ever watchful Sam Weller.

Sam had put up the steps, and was preparing to jump upon the box, when he felt himself gently touched on the shoulder; and, looking round, his father stood before him. The old gentleman's countenance wore a mournful expression, as he shook his head gravely and said, in warning accents—

"I know'd what 'ud come o' this here mode o' doin' bisness. Oh Sammy, Sammy, vy worn't there a alleybi!"

CHAPTER XXXIV.

IN WHICH MR. PICKWICK THINKS HE HAD BETTER GO TO BATH; AND GOES ACCORDINGLY.

"But surely, my dear Sir," said little Perker, as he stood in Mr. Pickwick's apartment on the morning after the trial—"Surely you don't really mean—really and seriously now, and irritation apart—that you won't pay these costs and damages?"

"Not one halfpenny," said Mr. Pickwick, firmly; "not one halfpenny."

"Hooroar for the principle, as the money-lender said ven he vouldn't renew the bill," observed Mr. Weller, who was clearing away the breakfast things.

"Sam," said Mr. Pickwick, "have the goodness to step down stairs."

"Cert'nly, Sir," replied Mr. Weller; and acting on Mr. Pickwick's gentle hint, Sam retired.

"No, Perker," said Mr. Pickwick, with great seriousness of manner, "my friends here, have endeavoured to dissuade me from this determination, but without avail. I shall employ myself as usual, until the opposite party have the power of issuing a legal process of execution against me; and if they are vile enough to avail themselves of it, and to arrest my person, I shall yield myself up with perfect cheerfulness and content of heart. When can they do this?"

"They can issue execution, my dear Sir, for the amount of the damages and taxed costs, next term," replied Perker, "just two months hence, my dear Sir."

"Very good," said Mr. Pickwick. "Until that time, my dear fellow, let me hear no more of the matter. And now," continued Mr. Pickwick, looking round on his friends with a good-humoured smile, and a sparkle in the eye which no spectacles could dim or conceal, "the only question is, Where shall we go to next?"

Mr. Tupman and Mr. Snodgrass were too much affected by their friend's heroism to offer any reply. Mr. Winkle had not yet sufficiently recovered the recollection of his evidence at the trial, to make any observation on any subject, so Mr. Pickwick paused in vain.

"Well," said that gentleman, "if you leave me to suggest our destination, I say Bath. I think none of us have ever been there."

Nobody had; and as the proposition was warmly seconded by Perker, who considered it extremely probable that if Mr. Pickwick saw a little change and gaiety he would be inclined to think better of his determination, and worse of a debtor's prison, it was carried unanimously: and Sam was at once dispatched to the White Horse Cellar, to take five places by the half-past seven o'clock coach, next morning.

There were just two places to be had inside, and just three to be had out; so Sam Weller booked for them all, and having exchanged a few compliments with the booking-office clerk on the subject of a pewter half-crown which was tendered him as a portion of his "change," walked back to the George and Vulture, where he was pretty busily employed till bed-time in reducing clothes and linen into the smallest possible compass, and exerting his mechanical genius in constructing a variety of ingenious devices for keeping the lids on boxes which had neither locks nor hinges.

The next was a very unpropitious morning for a journey—muggy, damp, and drizzly. The horses in the stages that were going out, and had come through the city, were smoking so, that the outside passengers were invisible. The newspaper-sellers looked moist and smelt mouldy; the wet ran off the hats of the orange-venders as they thrust their heads into the coach windows, and diluted the insides in a refreshing manner. The Jews with the fifty-bladed penknives shut them up in despair; and the men with the pocket-books made pocket-books of them. Watch-guards and toasting-forks were alike at a discount, and pencil-cases and sponge were a drug in the market.

Leaving Sam Weller to rescue the luggage from the seven or eight porters who flung themselves savagely upon it, the moment the coach stopped, and finding that they were about twenty minutes too early, Mr. Pickwick and his friends went for shelter into the travellers' room—the last resource of human dejection.

The travellers' room at the White Horse Cellar is of course uncomfortable; it would be no travellers' room if it were not. It is the right-hand parlour, into which an aspiring kitchen fire-place appears to have walked, accompanied by a rebellious poker, tongs, and shovel. It is divided into boxes, for the solitary confinement of travellers, and is furnished with a clock, a looking-glass, and a live waiter, which latter article is kept in a small kennel for washing glasses, in a corner of the apartment.

One of these boxes was occupied on this particular occasion by a stern-eyed man of about five-and-forty, who had a bald and glossy forehead, with a good deal of black hair at the sides and back of his head, and large black whiskers. He was buttoned up to the chin in a brown coat; and had a large seal-skin travelling-cap, and a great-coat and cloak lying on the seat beside him. He looked up from his breakfast as Mr. Pickwick entered, with a fierce and peremptory air, which was very dignified; and having scrutinized that gentleman and his companions to his entire satisfaction, hummed a tune, in a manner which seemed to say that he rather suspected somebody wanted to take advantage of him, but it wouldn't do.

"Waiter," said the gentleman with the whiskers.

"Sir?" replied a man with a dirty complexion, and a towel of the same, emerging from the kennel before mentioned.

"Some more toast."

"Yes, Sir."

"Buttered toast, mind," said the gentleman, fiercely.

"D'rectly, Sir," replied the waiter.

The gentleman with the whiskers hummed a tune in the same manner as before, and pending the arrival of the toast, advanced to the front of the fire, and, taking his coat tails under his arms, looked at his boots and ruminated.

"I wonder whereabouts in Bath this coach puts up," said Mr. Pickwick, mildly addressing Mr. Winkle.

"Hum—eh—what's that?" said the strange man.

"I made an observation to my friend, Sir," replied Mr. Pickwick, always ready to enter into conversation. "I wondered at what house the Bath coach put up. Perhaps you can inform me."

"Are you going to Bath?" said the strange man.

"I am, Sir," replied Mr. Pickwick.

"And those other gentlemen?"

"They are going also," said Mr. Pickwick.

"Not inside—I'll be damned if you're going inside," said the strange man.

"Not all of us," said Mr. Pickwick.

"No, not all of you," said the strange man emphatically. "I've taken two places. If they try to squeeze six people into an infernal box that only holds four, I'll take a post-chaise and bring an action. I've paid my fare. It won't do; I told the clerk when I took my places that it wouldn't do. I know these things have been done. I know they are done every day, but I never was done, and I never will be. Those who know me best, best know it; crush me!" Here the fierce gentleman rang the bell with great violence, and told the waiter he'd better bring the toast in five seconds, or he'd know the reason why.

"My dear Sir," said Mr. Pickwick, "you will allow me to observe that this is a very unnecessary display of excitement. I have only taken places inside, for two."

"I am glad to hear it," said the fierce man. "I withdraw my expressions. I tender an apology. There's my card. Give me your acquaintance."

"With great pleasure, Sir," replied Mr. Pickwick. "We are to be fellow travellers, and I hope we shall find each other's society mutually agreeable."

"I hope we shall," said the fierce gentleman. "I know we shall. I like your looks; they please me. Gentlemen, your hands and names. Know me."

Of course, an interchange of friendly salutations followed this gracious speech; and the fierce gentleman immediately proceeded to inform the friends in the same short abrupt jerking sentences, that his name was Dowler, that he was going to Bath on pleasure, that he was formerly in the army, that he had now set up in business as a gentleman, that he lived upon the profits, and that the individual for whom the second place was taken, was a personage no less illustrious than Mrs. Dowler, his lady wife.

"She's a fine woman," said Mr. Dowler. "I am proud of her. I have reason."

"I hope I shall have the pleasure of judging," said Mr. Pickwick with a smile.

"You shall," replied Dowler. "She shall know you. She shall esteem you. I courted her under singular circumstances. I won her through a rash vow. Thus. I saw her; I loved her; I proposed; she refused me.—'You love another?'—'Spare my blushes.'—'I know him.'—'You do.' 'Very good, if he remains here, I'll skin him.'"

"Lord bless me!" exclaimed Mr. Pickwick involuntarily.

"Did you skin the gentleman, Sir?" inquired Mr. Winkle, with a very pale face.

"I wrote him a note. I said it was a painful thing. And so it was."

"Certainly," interposed Mr. Winkle.

"I said I had pledged my word as a gentleman to skin him. My character was at stake. I had no alternative. As an officer in His Majesty's service, I was bound to do it. I regretted the necessity, but it must be done. He was open to conviction. He saw that the rules of the service were imperative. He fled. I married her. Here's the coach. That's her head."

As Mr. Dowler concluded, he pointed to a stage which had just driven up: from the open window of which, a rather pretty face in a bright blue bonnet was looking among the crowd on the pavement, most probably for the rash man himself. Mr. Dowler paid his bill and hurried out with his travelling-cap, coat, and cloak; and Mr. Pickwick and his friends followed to secure their places.

Mr. Tupman and Mr. Snodgrass had seated themselves at the back part of the coach; Mr. Winkle had got inside, and Mr. Pickwick was preparing to follow him, when Sam Weller came up to his master, and whispering in his ear, begged to speak to him, with an air of the deepest mystery.

"Well, Sam," said Mr. Pickwick, "what's the matter now?"

"Here's rayther a rum go, Sir," replied Sam.

"What?" inquired Mr. Pickwick.

"This here, Sir," rejoined Sam, "I'm wery much afeerd, Sir, that the proprietor o' this here coach is a playin' some imperence vith us."

"How is that, Sam?" said Mr. Pickwick; "aren't the names down on the way-bill?"

"The names is not only down on the vay-bill, Sir," replied Sam, "but they've painted vun on 'em up, on the door o' the coach." As Sam spoke, he pointed to that part of the coach door on which the proprietor's name usually appears; and there sure enough, in gilt letters of a goodly size, was the magic name of PICKWICK!

"Dear me," exclaimed Mr. Pickwick, quite staggered by the coincidence; "what a very extraordinary thing!"

"Yes, but that ain't all," said Sam, again directing his master's attention to the coach door; "not content vith writin' up Pickwick, they puts 'Moses' afore it, vich I call addin' insult to injury, as the parrot said ven they not only took him from his native land, but made him talk the English langvidge artervards."

"It's odd enough certainly, Sam," said Mr. Pickwick; "but if we stand talking here, we shall lose our places."

"Wot, ain't nothin' to be done in consequence, Sir?" exclaimed Sam, perfectly aghast at the coolness with which Mr. Pickwick prepared to ensconce himself inside.

"Done!" said Mr. Pickwick. "What should be done?"

"Ain't nobody to be whopped for takin' this here liberty, Sir?" said Mr. Weller, who had expected that at least he would have been commissioned to challenge the guard and coachman to a pugilistic encounter on the spot.

"Certainly not," replied Mr. Pickwick eagerly; "not on any account. Jump up to your seat directly."

"I'm wery much afeerd," muttered Sam to himself, as

he turned away, "that somethin' queer's come over the governor, or he'd never ha' stood this so quiet. I hope that 'ere trial hasn't broken his spirit, but it looks bad: wery bad." Mr. Weller shook his head gravely; and it is worthy of remark, as an' illustration of the manner in which he took this circumstance to heart, that he did not speak another word until the coach reached the Kensington turnpike, which was so long a time for him to remain taciturn, that the fact may be considered wholly unprecedented.

Nothing worthy of special mention occurred during the journey. Mr. Dowler related a variety of anecdotes, all illustrative of his own personal prowess and desperation, and appealed to Mrs. Dowler in corroboration thereof; when Mrs. Dowler invariably brought in, in the form of an appendix, some remarkable fact or circumstance which Mr. Dowler had forgotten, or had perhaps through modesty omitted, for the addenda in every instance went to show that Mr. Dowler was even a more wonderful fellow than he made himself out to be. Mr. Pickwick and Mr. Winkle listened with great admiration, and at intervals conversed with Mrs. Dowler, who was a very agreeable and fascinating person. So, what between Mr. Dowler's stories, and Mrs. Dowler's charms, and Mr. Pickwick's good humour, and Mr. Winkle's good listening, the insides contrived to be very companionable all the way.

The outsides did as outsides always do. They were very cheerful and talkative at the beginning of every stage, and very dismal and sleepy in the middle, and very bright and wakeful again, towards the end. There was one young gentleman in an India-rubber cloak, who smoked cigars all day; and there was another young gentleman in a parody upon a great coat, who lighted a good many, and feeling obviously unsettled after the second whiff, threw them away when he thought nobody was looking at him. There was a third young man on the box who wished to be learned in cattle, and an old one behind, who was familiar with farming. There was a constant succession of Christian names in smock frocks and white coats, who were invited to have a "lift" by the guard, and who knew every horse and hostler on the road and off it; and there was a dinner which would have been cheap at half-a-crown a mouth, if any moderate number of mouths could have eat it in the time. And at seven o'clock P.M., Mr. Pickwick and his friends, and Mr. Dowler and his wife, respectively retired to their private sitting-rooms at the White Hart hotel, opposite the great pump room, Bath, where the waiters, from their costume, might be mistaken for Westminster boys, only they destroy the illusion by behaving themselves so much better.

Breakfast had scarcely been cleared away on the succeeding morning, when a waiter brought in Mr. Dowler's card, with a request to be allowed permission to introduce a friend. Mr. Dowler at once followed up the delivery of the card, by bringing himself and the friend also. The friend was a charming young man of not much more than fifty, dressed in a very bright blue coat with resplendent buttons, black trousers, and the thinnest possible pair of highly-polished boots. A gold eye-glass was suspended from his neck by a short broad black ribbon; a gold snuffbox was lightly clasped in his left hand, gold rings innumerable glittered on his fingers, and a large diamond pin set in gold glistened in his shirt frill. He had a gold watch, and a gold curb chain with large gold seals; and he carried a pliant ebony cane with a heavy gold top. His linen was of the very whitest, finest, and stiffest; his wig of the glossiest, blackest, and curliest. His snuff was princes' mixture; his scent *bouquet du roi*. His features were contracted into a perpetual smile; and his teeth were in such perfect order that it was difficult at a small distance to tell the real ones from the false.

"Mr. Pickwick," said Dowler; "my friend, Angelo Cyrus Bantam, Esquire, M. C. Bantam; Mr. Pickwick. Know each other."

"Welcome to Ba—ath, Sir. This is indeed an acquisition. Most welcome to Ba—ath, Sir. It is long—very long, Mr. Pickwick, since you drank the waters. It appears an age, Mr. Pickwick. Re—markable!"

Such were the expressions with which Angelo Cyrus Bantam, Esquire, M. C., took Mr. Pickwick's hand; retaining it in his meantime, and shrugging up his shoulders with a constant succession of bows, as if he really could not make up his mind to the trial of letting it go again.

"It is a very long time since I drank the waters, certainly," replied Mr. Pickwick; "for to the best of my knowledge, I was never here before."

"Never in Ba—ath, Mr. Pickwick!" exclaimed the Grand Master, letting the hand fall in astonishment. "Never in Ba—ath! He! he! Mr. Pickwick, you are a wag. Not bad, not bad. Good, good. He! he! he! Re—markable!"

"To my shame, I must say that I am perfectly serious," rejoined Mr. Pickwick. "I really never was here, before."

"Oh, I see," exclaimed the Grand Master, looking extremely pleased; "Yes, yes—good, good—better and better. You are the gentleman of whom we have heard. Yes; we know you, Mr. Pickwick; we know you."

"The reports of the trial in those confounded papers," thought Mr. Pickwick. "They have heard all about me."

"You are the gentleman residing on Clapham Green," resumed Bantam, "who lost the use of his limbs from imprudently taking cold after port wine—who could not be moved in consequence of acute suffering, and who had the water from the King's Bath bottled at one hundred and three degrees, and sent by waggon to his bed-room in town, where he bathed, sneezed, and same day recovered. Very remarkable!"

Mr. Pickwick acknowledged the compliment which the supposition implied, but had the self-denial to repudiate it, notwithstanding; and taking advantage of a moment's silence on the part of the M. C., begged to introduce his friends, Mr. Tupman, Mr. Winkle, and Mr. Snodgrass—an introduction which of course overwhelmed the M. C. with delight and honour.

"Bantam," said Mr. Dowler, "Mr. Pickwick and his friends are strangers. They must put their names down. Where's the book?"

"The register of the distinguished visitors in Ba—ath will be at the Pump Room this morning at two o'clock," replied the M. C. "Will you guide our friends to that splendid building, and enable me to procure their autographs?"

"I will," rejoined Dowler. "This is a long call. It's time to go. I shall be here again in an hour. Come."

"This is a ball night," said the M. C., again taking Mr. Pickwick's hand, as he rose to go. "The ball-nights in Ba—ath are moments snatched from Paradise; rendered bewitching by music, beauty, elegance, fashion, etiquette, and—and—above all, by the absence of tradespeople, who are quite inconsistent with Paradise, and who have an amalgamation of themselves at the Guildhall every fortnight, which is, to say the least, remarkable. Good bye, good bye!" and protesting all the way down stairs that he was most satisfied, and most delighted, and most overpowered, and most flattered, Angelo Cyrus Bantam, Esquire, M. C., stepped into a very elegant chariot that waited at the door, and rattled off.

At the appointed hour, Mr. Pickwick and his friends, escorted by Dowler, repaired to the Assembly Rooms, and wrote their names down in the book—an instance of condescension at which Angelo Bantam was even more overpowered than before. Tickets of admission to that evening's assembly were to have been prepared for the whole party, but as they were not ready, Mr. Pickwick undertook, despite all the protestations to the contrary of Angelo Bantam, to send Sam for them at four o'clock in the afternoon, to the M. C.'s house in Queen Square. Having taken a short walk through the city, and arrived at the unanimous conclusion that Park Street was very much like the perpendicular streets a man sees in a dream, which he cannot get up for the life of him, they returned to the White Hart, and dispatched Sam on the errand to which his master had pledged him.

Sam Weller put on his hat in a very easy and graceful manner, and thrusting his hands in his waistcoat pockets, walked with great deliberation to Queen Square, whistling as he went along, several of the most popular airs of the day, as arranged with entirely new movements for that noble instrument the organ, either mouth or barrel. Arriving at the number in Queen Square to which he had been directed, he left off whistling, and gave a cheerful knock; which was instantaneously answered by a powdered-headed footman in gorgeous livery, and symmetrical stature.

"Is this here Mr. Bantam's, old feller?" inquired Sam Weller, nothing abashed by the blaze of splendour which burst upon his sight, in the person of the powdered-headed footman with the gorgeous livery.

"Why, young man?" was the haughty inquiry of the powdered-headed footman.

"'Cos if it is, jist you step into him with that 'ere card, and say Mr. Veller's a waitin', will you, six-foot?" said Sam. And saying it, he very coolly walked into the hall, and sat down.

The powdered-headed footman slammed the door very hard, and scowled very grandly, but both the slam and the scowl were lost upon Sam, who was regarding a mahogany umbrella stand with every outward token of critical approval.

Apparently his master's reception of the card had impressed the powdered-headed footman in Sam's favour, for when he came back from delivering it, he smiled in a friendly manner, and said that the answer would be ready directly.

"Wery good," said Sam. "Tell the old gen'lm'n not to put himself in a pespiration. No hurry, six-foot. I've had my dinner."

"You dine early, Sir," said the powdered-headed footman.

"I find I gets on better at supper when I does," replied Sam.

"Have you been long in Bath, Sir?" inquired the powdered-headed footman. "I have not had the pleasure of hearing of you before."

"I haven't created any wery surprisin' sensation here yet," rejoined Sam, "for me and the other fash'nables only come, last night."

"Nice place, Sir," said the powdered-headed footman. "Seems so," observed Sam.

"Pleasant society, Sir," remarked the powdered-headed footman. "Very agreeable servants, Sir."

"I should think they wos," replied Sam. "Affable, unaffected, say-nothin'-to-nobody sort o' fellers."

"Oh, very much so, indeed, Sir," said the powdered-headed footman, evidently taking Sam's remark as a high compliment. "Very much so indeed. Do you do any thing in this way, Sir?" inquired the tall footman, producing a small snuff-box with a fox's head on the top of it.

"Not without sneezing," replied Sam.

"Why, it *is* difficult, Sir, I confess," said the tall footman. "It may be done by degrees, Sir. Coffee is the best practice. I carried coffee, Sir, for a long time. It looks very like rappee, Sir."

Here a sharp peal at the bell reduced the powdered-headed footman to the ignominious necessity of putting the fox's head in his pocket, and hastening with a humble countenance to Mr. Bantam's "study." By the by, we scarcely ever knew a man who never read or wrote either, who hadn't got some small back parlour which he *would* call a study.

"There is the answer, Sir," said the powdered-headed footman. "I am afraid you'll find it inconveniently large."

"Don't mention it," said Sam, taking a letter with a small enclosure. "It's just possible as exhausted natur may manage to surwive it."

"I hope we shall meet again, Sir," said the powdered-headed footman, rubbing his hands, and following Sam out to the doorstep.

"You are wery obligin', Sir," replied Sam. "Now, don't allow yourself to be fatigued beyond your powers, there's a amiable bein'. Consider what you owe to society, and don't let yourself be injured by too much work. For the sake o' your feller creeturs, keep yourself as quiet as you can; only think what a loss you would be." With these pathetic words, Sam Weller departed.

"A very singular young man that," said the powdered-headed footman, looking after Mr. Weller with a countenance which clearly showed he could make nothing of him.

Sam said nothing at all. He winked, shook his head, smiled, winked again; and with an expression of countenance which seemed to denote that he was greatly amused with something or other, walked merrily away.

At precisely twenty minutes before eight o'clock that night, Angelo Cyrus Bantam, Esquire, the Master of the Ceremonies, emerged from his chariot at the door of the Assembly Rooms in the same wig, the same teeth, the same eye-glass, the same watch and seals, the same rings, the same shirt-pin, and the same cane. The only observable alterations in his appearance were, that he wore a brighter blue coat, with a white silk lining, black tights, black silk stockings, and pumps, and a white waistcoat, and was, if possible, just a thought more scented.

Thus attired, the Master of the Ceremonies, in strict discharge of the important duties of his all-important office, planted himself in the rooms to receive the company.

Bath being full, the company, and the sixpences for tea, poured in, in shoals. In the ball-room, the long card-room, the octagonal card-room, the staircases, and the passages, the hum of many voices, and the sound of many feet, were perfectly bewildering. Dresses rustled, feathers waved, lights shone, and jewels sparkled. There was the music—not of the quadrille band, for it had not yet commenced; but the music of soft tiny footsteps, with now and then a clear merry laugh—low and gentle, but very pleasant to hear in a female voice, whether in Bath or elsewhere. Brilliant eyes, lighted up with pleasurable expectation, gleamed from every side; and look where you would, some exquisite form glided gracefully through the throng, and was no sooner lost, than it was replaced by another, as dainty and bewitching.

In the tea-room, and hovering round the card-tables, were a vast number of queer old ladies and decrepid old gentlemen, discussing all the small talk and scandal of the day, with an evident relish and gusto which sufficiently bespoke the intensity of the pleasure they derived from the occupation. Mingled with these groups were three or four matchmaking mammas, appearing to be wholly absorbed by the conversation in which they were taking part, but failing not from time to time to cast an anxious sidelong glance upon their daughters, who, remembering the maternal injunction to make the best use of their time, had already commenced incipient flirtations in the mislaying scarfs, putting on gloves, setting down cups, and so forth, slight matters apparently, but which may be turned to surprisingly good account by expert practitioners.

Lounging near the doors, and in remote corners, were various knots of silly young men, displaying every variety of puppyism and stupidity; amusing all sensible people near them, with their folly and conceit, and happily thinking themselves the objects of general admiration—a wise and merciful dispensation which no good man will quarrel with.

And lastly, seated on some of the back benches, where they had already taken up their positions for the evening, were divers unmarried ladies past their grand climacteric, who, not dancing because there were no partners for them, and not playing cards lest they should be set down as irretrievably single, were in the favourable situation of being able to abuse everybody without reflecting on themselves. In short, they could abuse everybody, because everybody was there. It was a scene of gaiety, glitter, and show; of richly-dressed people, handsome mirrors, chalked floors, girandoles, and wax-candles; and in all parts of the scene, gliding from spot to spot in silent softness, bowing obsequiously to this party, nodding familiarly to that, and smiling complacently on all, was the sprucely attired person of Angelo Cyrus Bantam, Esquire, the Master of the Ceremonies.

"Stop in the tea-room. Take your sixpenn'orth. They lay on hot water, and call it tea. Drink it," said Mr. Dowler, in a loud voice, directing Mr. Pickwick, who advanced at the head of the little party, with Mrs. Dowler on his arm. Into the tea-room Mr. Pickwick turned; and catching sight of him, Mr. Bantam corkscrewed his way through the crowd, and welcomed him with ecstacy.

"My dear Sir, I am highly honoured. Ba—ath is favoured. Mrs. Dowler, you embellish the rooms. I congratulate you on your feathers. Re—markable!"

"Any body here?" inquired Dowler, suspiciously.

"Any body! The *élite* of Ba—ath. Mr. Pickwick, do you see the lady in the gauze turban?"

"The fat old lady?" inquired Mr. Pickwick, innocently.

"Hush, my dear Sir—nobody's fat or old in Ba—ath That's the Dowager Lady Snuphanuph."

"Is it indeed?" said Mr. Pickwick.

"No less a person, I assure you," said the Master of the Ceremonies. "Hush. Draw a little nearer, Mr. Pickwick. You see the splendidly dressed young man coming this way?"

"The one with the long hair, and the particularly small forehead?" inquired Mr. Pickwick.

"The same. The richest young man in Ba—ath at this moment. Young Lord Mutanhed."

"You don't say so?" said Mr. Pickwick.

"Yes. You'll hear his voice in a moment, Mr. Pickwick. He'll speak to me. The other gentleman with him, in the red under waistcoat and dark moustache, is the Honourable Mr. Crushton, his bosom friend. How do you do, my Lord?"

"Veway hot, Bantam," said his Lordship.

"It *is* very warm, my Lord," replied the M. C.

"Confounded," assented the Honourable Mr. Crushton.

"Have you seen his Lordship's mail cart, Bantam?" inquired the Honourable Mr. Crushton, after a short pause, during which young Lord Mutanhed had been endeavouring to stare Mr. Pickwick out of countenance, and Mr. Crushton had been reflecting what subject his Lordship could talk about best.

"Dear me, no," replied the M. C. "A mail cart! What an excellent idea. Re—markable!"

"Gwacious Heavens!" said his Lordship, "I thought evewebody had seen the new mail cart; it's the neatest, pwettiest, gwacefullest thing that ever wan upon wheels—painted wed, with a cweam piebald."

"With a real box for the letters, and all complete," said the Honourable Mr. Crushton.

"And a little seat in fwont, with an iwon wail, for the dwiver," added his Lordship. "I dwove it over to Bwistol the other morning in a cwimson coat, with two servants widing a quarter of a mile behind; and cwucify me if the people didn't wush out of their cottages, and awest my pwogwess, to know if I wasn't the post. Glowwious, glowwious!"

At this anecdote his Lordship laughed very heartily, as did the listeners, of course. Then drawing his arm through that of the obsequious Mr. Crushton, Lord Mutanhed walked away.

"Delightful young man, his Lordship," said the Master of the Ceremonies.

"So I should think," rejoined Mr. Pickwick, drily.

The dancing having commenced, the necessary introductions having been made, and all preliminaries arranged, Angelo Bantam rejoined Mr. Pickwick, and led him into the card-room.

Just at the very moment of their entrance, the Dowager Lady Snuphanuph and two other ladies of an ancient and whist-like appearance, were hovering over an unoccupied card-table; and they no sooner set eyes upon Mr. Pickwick under the convoy of Angelo Bantam, than they exchanged glances with each other, seeing that he was precisely the very person they wanted to make up the rubber.

"My dear Bantam," said the Dowager Lady Snuphanuph, coaxingly, "find us some nice creature to make up this table; there's a good soul." Mr. Pickwick happened to be looking another way at the moment, so her ladyship nodded her head towards him, and frowned expressively.

"My friend Mr. Pickwick, my Lady, will be most happy, I am sure, re—markably so," said the M. C., taking the hint. "Mr. Pickwick, Lady Snuphanuph—Mrs. Colonel Wugsby—Miss Bolo."

Mr. Pickwick bowed to each of the ladies, and finding escape impossible, cut. Mr. Pickwick and Miss Bolo against Lady Snuphanuph and Mrs. Colonel Wugsby.

Just as the trump card was turned up, at the commencement of the second deal, two young ladies hurried into the room, and took their stations on either side of Mrs. Colonel Wugsby's chair, where they waited patiently until the hand was over.

"Now, Jane," said Mrs. Colonel Wugsby, turning to one of the girls, "what is it?"

"I came to ask, Ma, whether I might dance with the youngest Mr. Crawley," whispered the prettier and younger of the two.

"Good God, Jane, how can you think of such things!" replied the mamma, indignantly. "Haven't you repeatedly heard that his father has only eight hundred a-year, which dies with him? I am ashamed of you. Not on any account."

"Ma," whispered the other, who was much older than her sister, and very insipid and artificial, "Lord Mutanhed has been introduced to me. I said I *thought* I wasn't engaged, Ma."

"You're a sweet pet, my love," replied Mrs. Colonel Wugsby, tapping her daughter's cheek with her fan, "and are always to be trusted. He's immensely rich, my dear. Bless you." With these words, Mrs. Colonel Wugsby kissed her eldest daughter most affectionately, and frowning in a warning manner upon the other, sorted her cards.

Poor Mr. Pickwick! he had never played with three thorough-paced female card-players before. They were so desperately sharp that they quite frightened him. If he played a wrong card, Miss Bolo looked a small armoury of daggers; if he stopped to consider which was the right one, Lady Snuphanuph would throw herself back in her chair, and smile with a mingled glance of impatience and pity to Mrs. Colonel Wugsby, at which Mrs. Colonel Wugsby would shrug up her shoulders, and cough, as much as to say she wondered whether he ever would begin. Then, at the end of every hand, Miss Bolo would inquire with a dismal countenance and reproachful sigh, why Mr. Pickwick had not returned that diamond, or led the club, or roughed the spade, or finessed the heart, or led through the honour, or brought out the ace, or played up to the king, or some such thing; and in reply to all these grave charges, Mr. Pickwick would be wholly unable to plead any justification whatever; having by this time forgotten all about the game. People came and looked on, too, which made Mr. Pickwick nervous. Besides all this, there was a great deal of distracting conversation near the table, between Angelo Bantam and the two Miss Matinters, who, being single and singular, paid great court to the Master of the Ceremonies, in the hope of getting a stray partner now and then. All these things, combined with the noises and interruptions of constant comings in and goings out, made Mr. Pickwick play rather badly; the cards were against him, also, and when they left off at ten minutes past eleven, Miss Bolo rose from the table considerably agitated, and went straight home in a flood of tears, and a sedan chair.

Being joined by his friends, who one and all protested that they had scarcely ever spent a more pleasant evening, Mr. Pickwick accompanied them to the White Hart, and having soothed his feelings with something hot, went to bed, and to sleep, almost simultaneously.

CHAPTER XXXV.

THE CHIEF FEATURES OF WHICH WILL BE FOUND TO BE AN AUTHENTIC VERSION OF THE LEGEND OF PRINCE BLADUD, AND A MOST EXTRAORDINARY CALAMITY THAT BEFEL MR. WINKLE.

As Mr. Pickwick contemplated a stay of at least two months in Bath, he deemed it advisable to take private lodgings for himself and friends for that period; and as a favourable opportunity offered for their securing, on moderate terms, the upper portion of a house in the Royal Crescent, which was larger than they required, Mr. and Mrs. Dowler offered to relieve them of a bed-room and sitting-room. This proposition was at once accepted, and in three days' time they were all located in their new abode, when Mr. Pickwick began to drink the waters with the utmost assiduity. Mr. Pickwick took them systematically. He drank a quarter of a pint before breakfast, and then walked up a hill; and another quarter of a pint after breakfast, and then walked down a hill; and after every fresh quarter of a pint, Mr. Pickwick declared, in the most solemn and emphatic terms, that he felt a great deal better, whereat his friends were very much delighted, though they had not been previously aware that there was anything the matter with him.

The great pump-room is a spacious saloon, ornamented with Corinthian pillars, and a music gallery and a Tompion clock, and a statue of Nash, and a golden inscription, to which all the water-drinkers should attend, for it appeals to them in the cause of a deserving charity. There is a large bar with a marble vase, out of which the pumper gets the water, and a number of yellow-looking tumblers, out of which the company get it; and it is a most edifying and satisfactory sight to behold the perseverance and gravity with which they swallow it. There are baths near at hand, in which a part of the company wash themselves, and a band plays afterwards, to congratulate the remainder on their having done so. There is another pump-room, into which infirm ladies and gentlemen are wheeled, in such an astonishing variety of chairs and chaises, that any adventurous individual who goes in with the regular number of toes, is in imminent danger of coming out without them; and there is a third, into which the quiet people go, for it is less noisy than either. There is an immensity of promenading, on crutches and off, with sticks and without: and a great deal of conversation, and liveliness, and pleasantry.

Every morning, the regular water-drinkers, Mr. Pickwick among the number, met each other in the pump-room, took their quarter of a pint, and walked constitutionally. At the afternoon's promenade Lord Mutanhed, and the Honourable Mr. Crushton, the Dowager Lady Snuphanuph, Mrs. Colonel Wugsby, and all the great people, and all the morning water-drinkers, met in grand assemblage. After this, they walked out, or drove out, or were pushed out in bath chairs, and met one another again. After this, the gentlemen went to the reading-rooms and met divisions of the mass. After this, they went home. If it were theatre night, perhaps they met at the theatre; if it were assembly night, they met at the rooms; and if it were neither, they met the next day—a very pleasant routine, with perhaps a slight tinge of sameness.

Mr. Pickwick was sitting up by himself, after a day

spent in this manner, making entries in his journal, his friends having retired to bed, when he was roused by a gentle tap at the room door.

"Beg your pardon, Sir," said Mrs. Craddock, the landlady: peeping in; "but *did* you want anything more, Sir?"

"Nothing more, Ma'am," replied Mr. Pickwick.

"My young girl is gone to bed, Sir," said Mrs. Craddock, "and Mr. Dowler is good enough to say that he'll sit up for Mrs. Dowler, as the party isn't expected to be over till late; so I was thinking that if you wanted nothing more, Mr. Pickwick, I would go to bed."

"By all means, Ma'am," replied Mr. Pickwick.

"Wish you good night, Sir," said Mrs. Craddock.

"Good night, Ma'am," rejoined Mr. Pickwick.

Mrs. Craddock closed the door, and Mr. Pickwick resumed his writing.

In half an hour's time, the entries were concluded. Mr. Pickwick carefully rubbed the last page on the blotting paper, shut up the book, wiped his pen on the bottom of the inside of his coat tail, and opened the drawer of the inkstand to put it carefully away. There were a couple of sheets of writing paper, pretty closely written over, in the inkstand drawer, and they were folded so, that the title, which was in a good round hand, was fully disclosed to him. Seeing from this, that it was no private document; and as it seemed to relate to Bath, and was very short, Mr. Pickwick unfolded it, lighted his bed-room candle that it might burn up well by the time he finished; and drawing his chair nearer the fire, read as follows:—

THE TRUE LEGEND OF PRINCE BLADUD.

"Less than two hundred years agone, on one of the public baths in this city, there appeared an inscription in honour of its mighty founder, the renowned Prince Bladud. That inscription is now erased.

"For many hundred years before that time, there had been handed down from age to age, an old legend, that the illustrious Prince being afflicted with leprosy, on his return from reaping a rich harvest of knowledge in ancient Athens, shunned the court of his royal father, and consorted moodily, with husbandmen and pigs. Among the herd (so said the legend) was a pig of grave and solemn countenance, with whom the Prince had a fellow feeling—for he too was wise—a pig of thoughtful and reserved demeanour; an animal superior to his fellows, whose grunt was terrible, and whose bite was sharp; the young Prince sighed deeply as he looked upon the countenance of the majestic swine;—he thought of his royal father, and his eyes were bedewed with tears.

"This sagacious pig was fond of bathing in rich, moist mud. Not in summer as common pigs do now, to cool themselves, and did even in those distant ages (which is a proof that the light of civilisation had already begun to dawn, though feebly)—but in the cold sharp days of winter. His coat was ever so sleek, and his complexion so clear, that the Prince resolved to essay the purifying qualities of the same water that his friend resorted to. He made the trial. Beneath that black mud, bubbled the hot springs of Bath. He washed, and was cured. Hastening to his father's court, he paid his best respects, and returning quickly hither, founded this city, and its famous baths.

"He sought the pig with all the ardour of their early friendship—but, alas! the waters had been his death. He had imprudently taken a bath at too high a temperature,

and the natural philosopher was no more! He was succeeded by Pliny, who also fell a victim to his thirst for knowledge.

"This *was* the legend. Listen to the true one.

"A great many centuries since, there flourished in great state the famous and renowned Lud Hudibras, king of Britain. He was a mighty monarch. The earth shook when he walked, he was so very stout. His people basked in the light of his countenance, it was so red and glowing. He was, indeed, every inch a king. And there were a good many inches of him too, for although he was not very tall, he was a remarkable size round, and the inches that he wanted in height, he made up in circumference. If any degenerate monarch of modern times could be in any way compared with him, I should say the venerable King Cole would be that illustrious potentate.

"This good king had a queen, who eighteen years before, had had a son, who was called Bladud. He was sent to a preparatory seminary in his father's dominions until he was ten years old, and was then dispatched in charge of a trusty messenger, to a finishing school at Athens; and as there was no extra charge for remaining during the holidays, and no notice required previous to the removal of a pupil, there he remained for eight long years, at the expiration of which time, the king his father sent the lord chamberlain over, to settle the bill, and to bring him home, which the lord chamberlain doing, was received with shouts, and pensioned immediately.

"When King Lud saw the Prince his son, and found he had grown up such a fine young man, he perceived at once what a grand thing it would be to have him married without delay, so that his children might be the means of perpetuating the glorious race of Lud down to the very latest ages of the world. With this view, he sent a special embassy, composed of great noblemen who had nothing particular to do, and wanted lucrative employment, to a neighbouring king, and demanded his fair daughter in marriage for his son, stating at the same time that he was anxious to be on the most affectionate terms with his brother and friend, but that if they couldn't agree in arranging this marriage, he should be under the unpleasant necessity of invading his kingdom, and putting his eyes out. To this, the other king, (who was the weaker of the two) replied that he was very much obliged to his friend and brother for all his goodness and magnanimity, and that his daughter was quite ready to be married, whenever Prince Bladud liked to come and fetch her.

"This answer no sooner reached Britain, than the whole nation were transported with joy. Nothing was heard on all sides but the sounds of feasting and revelry,—except the chinking of money as it was paid in by the people to the collector of the Royal Treasures, to defray the expenses of the happy ceremony. It was upon this occasion that King Lud seated on the top of his throne in full council, rose in the exuberance of his feelings, and commanded the lord chief justice to order in the richest wines and the court minstrels: an act of graciousness which has been, through the ignorance of traditionary historians, attributed to King Cole, in those celebrated lines in which his majesty is represented as

Calling for his pipe, and calling for his pot,
And calling for his fiddlers three.

Which is an obvious injustice to the memory of King

Lud, and a dishonest exaltation of the virtues of King Cole.

"But in the midst of all this festivity and rejoicing, there was one individual present, who tasted not when the sparkling wines were poured forth, and who danced not, when the minstrels played. This was no other than Prince Bladud himself, in honour of whose happiness a whole people were at that very moment, straining alike their throats and purse-strings. The truth was, that the Prince, forgetting the undoubted right of the minister for foreign affairs to fall in love on his behalf, had, contrary to every precedent of policy and diplomacy, already fallen in love on his own account, and privately contracted himself unto the fair daughter of a noble Athenian.

"Here we have a striking example of one of the manifold advantages of civilisation and refinement. If the Prince lived in later days, he might at once have married the object of his father's choice, and then set himself seriously to work, to relieve himself of the burden which rested heavily upon him. He might have endeavoured to break her heart by a systematic course of insult and neglect; or, if the spirit of her sex, and a proud consciousness of her many wrongs had upheld her under this ill treatment, he might have sought to take her life, and so get rid of her effectually. But neither mode of relief suggested itself to Prince Bladud—so he solicited a private audience, and told his father.

"It is an old prerogative of kings to govern everything but their passions. King Lud flew into a frightful rage, tossed his crown up to the ceiling, and caught it again—for in those days kings kept their crowns on their heads, and not in the Tower—stamped the ground, rapped his forehead, wondered why his own flesh and blood rebelled against him, and, finally, calling in his guards, ordered the Prince away to instant confinement in a lofty turret—a course of treatment which the kings of old very generally pursued towards their sons when their matrimonial inclinations did not happen to point to the same quarter as their own.

"When Prince Bladud had been shut up in the lofty turret for the greater part of a year, with no better prospect before his bodily eyes than a stone wall, or before his mental vision than prolonged imprisonment, he naturally began to ruminate on a plan of escape, which after months of preparation he managed to accomplish; considerately leaving his dinner knife in the heart of his gaoler, lest the poor fellow (who had a family) should be considered privy to his flight, and punished accordingly by the infuriated king.

"The monarch was frantic at the loss of his son. He knew not on whom to vent his grief and wrath, until fortunately bethinking himself of the Lord Chamberlain who had brought him home, he struck off his pension and his head together.

"Meanwhile, the young Prince effectually disguised, wandered on foot through his father's dominions, cheered and supported in all his hardships by sweet thoughts of the Athenian maid, who was the innocent cause of his weary trials. One day he stopped to rest in a country village; and seeing that there were gay dances going forward on the green, and gay faces passing to and fro, ventured to inquire of a reveller who stood near him, the reason for this rejoicing.

"'Know you not, O stranger,' was the reply, 'of the recent proclamation of our gracious king?'

"'Proclamation! No. What proclamation?' rejoined the Prince—for he had travelled along the bye and little-frequented ways, and knew nothing of what had passed upon the public roads, such as they were.

"'Why,' replied the peasant, 'the foreign lady that our Prince wished to wed, is married to a foreign noble of her own country; and the king proclaims the fact, and a great public festival besides; for now, of course, Prince Bladud will come back and marry the lady his father chose, who they say is as beautiful as the noon-day sun. Your health, Sir. God save the King!'

"The Prince remained to hear no more. He fled from the spot, and plunged into the thickest recesses of a neighbouring wood. On, on he wandered, night and day, beneath the blazing sun, and the cold pale moon; through the dry heat of noon, and the damp cold of night; in the grey light of morn, and the red glare of eve. So heedless was he of time or object, that being bound for Athens, he wandered as far out of his way as Bath.

"There was no city where Bath stands, then. There was no vestige of human habitation, or sign of man's resort, to bear the name; but there was the same noble country, the same broad expanse of hill and dale, the same beautiful channel stealing on, far away; the same lofty mountains which, like the troubles of life, viewed at a distance, and partially obscured by the bright mist of its morning, lose their ruggedness and asperity, and seem all ease and softness. Moved by the gentle beauty of the scene, the Prince sank upon the green turf, and bathed his swollen feet in his tears.

"'Oh!' said the unhappy Bladud, clasping his hands, and mournfully raising his eyes towards the sky, 'would that my wanderings might end here; would that these grateful tears with which I now mourn hope misplaced, and love despised, might flow in peace for ever!'

"The wish was heard. It was in the time of the heathen deities, who used occasionally to take people at their words, with a promptness, in some cases extremely awkward. The ground opened beneath the Prince's feet; he sunk into the chasm, and instantaneously it closed upon his head for ever, save where his hot tears welled up through the earth, and where they have continued to gush forth ever since.

"It is observable that, to this day, large numbers of elderly ladies and gentlemen who have been disappointed in procuring partners, and almost as many young ones who are anxious to obtain them, repair annually to Bath to drink the waters, from which they derive much strength and comfort. This is most complimentary to the virtue of Prince Bladud's tears, and strongly corroborative of the veracity of this legend."

Mr. Pickwick yawned several times when he had arrived at the end of this little manuscript, carefully refolded, and replaced it in the inkstand drawer, and then, with a countenance expressive of the utmost weariness, lighted his chamber candle, and went up stairs to bed.

He stopped at Mr. Dowler's door, according to custom, and knocked to say, good night.

"Ah!" said Dowler, "going to bed?—I wish I was. Dismal night. Windy; isn't it?"

"Very," said Mr. Pickwick. "Good night."

"Good night."

Mr. Pickwick went to his bed-chamber, and Mr. Dowler resumed his seat before the fire, in fulfilment of his rash promise to sit up till his wife came home.

There are few things more worrying than sitting up for somebody, especially if that somebody be at a party. You cannot help thinking how quickly the time passes with them, which drags so heavily with you; and the more you think of this, the more your hopes of their speedy arrival decline. Clocks tick so loud, too, when you are sitting up alone, and you seem—at least we always do—as if you had got an undergarment of cobwebs on. First, something tickles your right knee, and then the same sensation irritates your left. You have no sooner changed your position, than it comes again in the arms; and when you have fidgeted your limbs into all sorts of queer shapes, you have a sudden relapse in the nose, which you rub as if to rub it off—as there is no doubt you would, if you could. Eyes, too, are mere personal inconveniences; and the wick of one candle gets an inch and a half long, while you are snuffing the other. These, and various other little nervous annoyances, render sitting up for a length of time after everybody else has gone to bed, anything but a cheerful amusement.

This was just Mr. Dowler's opinion, as he sat before the fire, and felt honestly indignant with all the inhuman people at the party, who were keeping him up. He was not put into better humour either, by the reflection that he had taken it into his head, early in the evening, to think he had got an ache there, and so stopped at home. At length, after several droppings asleep, and fallings forward towards the bars, and catchings backward soon enough to prevent being branded in the face, Mr. Dowler made up his mind that he would just throw himself on the bed in the back-room and *think*—not sleep, of course.

"I'm a heavy sleeper," said Mr. Dowler, as he flung himself on the bed. "I must keep awake;—I suppose I shall hear a knock here. Yes. I thought so. I can hear the watchman. There he goes. Fainter now though. A little fainter. He's turning the corner. Ah!" When Mr. Dowler arrived at this point, *he* turned the corner at which he had been so long hesitating, and fell fast asleep.

Just as the clock struck three, there were blown into the crescent a sedan-chair, with Mrs. Dowler inside, borne by one short fat chairman, and one long thin one, who had had much ado all the way to keep their bodies perpendicular, to say nothing of the chair; but on that high ground, and in the crescent, which the wind swept round and round as if it were going to tear the paving stones up, its fury was tremendous. They were very glad to set the chair down, and give a good round loud double-knock at the street door.

They waited some time, but nobody came.

"Servants is in the arms o' Porpus, I think," said the short chairman, warming his hands at the attendant link-boy's torch.

"I wish he'd give 'em a squeeze and wake 'em," observed the long one.

"Knock again, will you, if you please?" cried Mrs. Dowler from the chair. "Knock two or three times, if you please."

The short man was quite willing to get the job over, as soon as possible; so he stood on the step, and gave four or five most startling double-knocks, of eight or ten knocks a piece, while the long man went into the road, and looked up at the windows for a light.

Nobody came. It was all as silent and as dark as ever.

"Dear me!" said Mrs. Dowler. "You must knock again, if you please."

"There ain't a bell, is there, Ma'am?" said the short chairman.

"Yes, there is," interposed the link-boy, "I've been a ringing at it ever so long."

"It's only a handle," said Mrs. Dowler, "the wire's broken."

"I wish the servants' heads wos," growled the long man.

"I must trouble you to knock again, if you please," said Mrs. Dowler with the utmost politeness.

The short man did knock again several times, without producing the smallest effect. The tall man, growing very impatient, then relieved him, and kept on perpetually knocking double-knocks of two loud knocks each, like an insane postman.

At length Mr. Winkle began to dream that he was at a club, and that the members being very refractory, the chairman was obliged to hammer the table a good deal to preserve order; then he had a confused notion of an auction room where there were no bidders, and the auctioneer was buying everything in; and ultimately he began to think it just within the bounds of possibility that somebody might be knocking at the street door. To make quite certain, however, he remained quiet in bed for ten minutes or so, and listened; and when he had counted two or three and thirty knocks, he felt quite satisfied, and gave himself a great deal of credit for being so wakeful.

"Rap rap—rap rap—rap rap—ra, ra, ra, ra, ra, rap," went the knocker.

Mr. Winkle jumped out of bed, wondering very much what could possibly be the matter, and hastily putting on his stockings and slippers, folded his dressing gown round him, lighted a flat candle from the rush-light that was burning in the fire-place, and hurried down stairs.

"Here's somebody comin' at last, Ma'am," said the short chairman.

"I wish I wos behind him vith a bradawl," muttered the long one.

"Who's there?" cried Mr. Winkle, undoing the chain.

"Don't stop to ask questions, cast-iron head," replied the long man, with great disgust; taking it for granted that the inquirer was a footman; "open the door."

"Come, look sharp, timber eye-lids," added the other, encouragingly.

Mr. Winkle, being half asleep, obeyed the command mechanically, opened the door a little, and peeped out. The first thing he saw was the red glare of the link-boy's torch. Startled by the sudden fear that the house might be on fire, he hastily threw the door wide open, and holding the candle above his head, stared eagerly before him, not quite certain whether what he saw was a sedan-chair or a fire engine. At this instant there came a violent gust of wind: the light was blown out; Mr. Winkle felt himself irresistibly impelled on to the steps, and the door blew to, with a loud crash.

"Well, young man, now you *have* done it," said the short chairman.

Mr. Winkle, catching sight of a lady's face at the window of the sedan, turned hastily round, plied the knocker with all his might and main, and called frantically upon the chairman to take the chair away again.

"Take it away, take it away," cried Mr. Winkle. "Here's somebody coming out of another house; put me into the chair. Hide me—do something with me."

All this time he was shivering with cold, and every

time he raised his hand to the knocker the wind took the dressing gown in a most unpleasant manner.

"The people are coming down the Crescent now. There are ladies with 'em; cover me up with something. Stand before me," roared Mr. Winkle. But the chairmen were too much exhausted with laughing to afford him the slightest assistance, and the ladies were every moment approaching nearer and nearer.

Mr. Winkle gave a last hopeless knock; the ladies were only a few doors off. He threw away the extinguished candle which all this time he had held above his head, and fairly bolted into the sedan-chair where Mrs. Dowler was.

Now, Mrs. Craddock had heard the knocking and the voices at last; and, just waiting to put something smarter on her head than her night-cap, ran down into the front drawing-room to make sure that it was the right party, and threw up the window-sash just as Mr. Winkle was rushing into the chair; she no sooner caught sight of what was going forward below, than she raised a vehement and dismal shriek, and implored Mr. Dowler to get up directly, for his wife was running away with another gentleman.

Upon this, Mr. Dowler bounced off the bed as abruptly as an India-rubber ball, and rushing into the front room, arrived at one window just as Mr. Pickwick threw up the other, when the first object that met the gaze of both, was Mr. Winkle bolting into the sedan-chair.

"Watchman," shouted Dowler furiously; "stop him—hold him—keep him tight—shut him in, till I come down. I'll cut his throat—give me a knife—from ear to ear, Mrs. Craddock. I will!" And, breaking from the shrieking landlady, and from Mr. Pickwick, the indignant husband seized a small supper-knife, and tore into the street.

But Mr. Winkle didn't wait for him. He no sooner heard the horrible threat of the valorous Dowler, than he bounced out of the sedan quite as quickly as he had bounced in, and throwing off his slippers into the road, took to his heels and tore round the Crescent, hotly pursued by Dowler and the watchman. He kept ahead; the door was open as he came round the second time, he rushed in, slammed it in Dowler's face, mounted to his bed-room, locked the door, piled a wash-hand-stand, chest of drawers and table against it, and packed up a few necessaries ready for flight with the first light of morning.

Dowler came up to the outside of the door, avowed, through the key-hole, his stedfast determination of cutting Mr. Winkle's throat next day; and, after a great confusion of voices in the drawing-room, amidst which that of Mr. Pickwick was distinctly heard endeavouring to make peace, the inmates dispersed to their several bed-chambers, and all was quiet once more.

It is not unlikely that the inquiry may be made, where Mr. Weller was, all this time? We will state where he was, in the next chapter.

CHAPTER XXXVI.

HONOURABLY ACCOUNTS FOR MR. WELLER'S ABSENCE, BY DESCRIBING A SOIREE TO WHICH HE WAS INVITED AND WENT.—ALSO RELATES HOW HE WAS ENTRUSTED BY MR. PICKWICK WITH A PRIVATE MISSION OF DELICACY AND IMPORTANCE.

"Mr. WELLER," said Mrs. Craddock, upon the morning of this very eventful day, "here's a letter for you."

"Wery odd that," said Sam, "I'm afeerd there must be somethin' the matter, for I don't recollect any gen'lm'n in my circle of acquaintance as is capable o' writin' one."

"Perhaps something uncommon has taken place," observed Mrs. Craddock.

"It must be somethin' wery uncommon indeed, as could produce a letter out o' any friend o' mine," replied Sam, shaking his head dubiously; "nothin' less than a nat'ral conwulsion, as the young gen'lm'n observed ven he wos took with fits. It can't be from the gov'ner," said Sam, looking at the direction. "He always prints, I know, 'cos he learnt writin' from the large bills in the bookin' offices. It's a wery strange thing now, where this here letter can ha' come from."

As Sam said this, he did what a great many people do when they are uncertain about the writer of a note,—looked at the seal, and then at the front, and then at the back, and then at the sides, and then at the superscription; and, as a last resource, thought perhaps he might as well look at the inside, and try to find out from that.

"It's wrote on gilt-edged paper," said Sam, as he unfolded it, "and sealed in bronze vax vith the top of a door-key. Now for it." And, with a very grave face, Mr. Weller slowly read as follows:

"A select company of the Bath footmen presents their compliments to Mr. Weller, and requests the pleasure of his company this evening, to a friendly swarry, consisting of a boiled leg of mutton with the usual trimmings. The swarry to be on table at half-past nine o'clock punctually."

This was inclosed in another note, which ran thus—

"Mr. John Smauker, the gentleman who had the pleasure of meeting Mr. Weller at the house of their mutual acquaintance, Mr. Bantam, a few days since, begs to enclose Mr. Weller the herewith invitation. If Mr. Weller will call on Mr. John Smauker at nine o'clock, Mr. John Smauker will have the pleasure of introducing Mr. Weller.

(Signed) "JOHN SMAUKER."

The envelope was directed to blank Weller, Esq., at Mr. Pickwick's; and, in a parenthesis, in the left hand corner, were the words "airy bell," as an instruction to the bearer.

"Vell," said Sam, "this is comin' it rayther powerful, this is. I never heard a biled leg o' mutton called a swarry afore. I wonder wot they'd call a roast one."

However, without waiting to debate the point, Sam at once betook himself into the presence of Mr. Pickwick, and requested leave of absence for that evening, which was readily granted. With this permission, and the street-door key, Sam Weller issued forth a little before the appointed time, and strolled leisurely towards Queen Square, which he no sooner gained than he had the satisfaction of beholding Mr. John Smauker leaning his powdered head against a lamp post at a short distance off, smoking a cigar through an amber tube.

"How do you do, Mr. Weller?" said Mr. John Smauker, raising his hat gracefully with one hand, while he gently waved the other in a condescending manner. "How do you do, Sir?"

"Why, reasonably conwalessent," replied Sam. "How do you find yourself, my dear feller?"

"Only so so," said Mr. John Smauker.

"Ah, you've been a workin' too hard," observed Sam. "I was fearful you would; it won't do, you know; you must not give way to that 'ere uncompromisin' spirit o' your'n."

"It's not so much that, Mr. Weller," replied Mr. John Smauker, "as, bad wine; I'm afraid I've been dissipating."

"Oh, that's it, is it?" said Sam; "that's a wery bad complaint, that."

"And yet the temptation, you see, Mr. Weller," observed Mr. John Smauker.

"Ah, to be sure," said Sam.

"Plunged into the very vortex of society, you know, Mr. Weller," said Mr. John Smauker with a sigh.

"Dreadful indeed!" rejoined Sam.

"But it's always the way," said Mr. John Smauker; "if your destiny leads you into public life, and public station, you must expect to be subjected to temptations which other people is free from, Mr. Weller."

"Precisely what my uncle said, ven *he* vent into the public line," remarked Sam, "and wery right the old gen'lm'n wos, for he drank hisself to death in somethin' less than a quarter."

Mr. John Smauker looked deeply indignant at any parallel being drawn between himself and the deceased gentleman in question; but as Sam's face was in the most immoveable state of calmness, he thought better of it, and looked affable again.

"Perhaps we had better be walking," said Mr. Smauker, consulting a copper time-piece which dwelt at the bottom of a deep watch-pocket, and was raised to the surface by means of a black string, with a copper key at the other end.

"P'raps we had," replied Sam, "or they'll overdo the swarry, and that'll spile it."

"Have you drank the waters, Mr. Weller?" inquired his companion, as they walked towards High Street.

"Once," replied Sam.

"What did you think of 'em, Sir?"

"I thought they wos particklerly unpleasant," replied Sam.

"Ah," said Mr. John Smauker, "you disliked the killibeate taste, perhaps?"

"I don't know much about that 'ere," said Sam. "I thought they'd a wery strong flavour o' warm flat irons."

"That *is* the killibeate, Mr. Weller," observed Mr. John Smauker, contemptuously.

"Well, if it is, it's a wery inexpressive word, that's all," said Sam. "It may be, but I ain't much in the chimical line myself, so I can't say." And here, to the great horror of Mr. John Smauker, Sam Weller began to whistle.

"I beg your pardon, Mr. Weller," said Mr. John Smauker, agonized at the exceedingly ungenteel sound. "Will you take my arm?"

"Thankee, you're wery good, but I won't deprive you of it," replied Sam. "I've rayther a way o' puttin' my hands in my pockets, if it's all the same to you." As Sam said this, he suited the action to the word, and whistled far louder than before.

"This way," said his new friend, apparently much relieved as they turned down a bye street; "we shall soon be there."

"Shall we?" said Sam, quite unmoved by the announcement of his close vicinity to the select footmen of Bath.

"Yes," said Mr. John Smauker. "Don't be alarmed, Mr. Weller."

"Oh no," said Sam.

"You'll see some very handsome uniforms, Mr. Weller," continued Mr. John Smauker; "and perhaps you'll find some of the gentlemen rather high at first, you know, but they'll soon come round."

"That's wery kind on 'em," replied Sam.

"And you know," resumed Mr. John Smauker, with an air of sublime protection; "you know, as you're a stranger perhaps they'll be rather hard upon you at first."

"They won't be wery cruel, though, will they?" inquired Sam.

"No, no," replied Mr. John Smauker, pulling forth the fox's head, and taking a gentlemanly pinch. "There are some funny dogs among us, and they will have their joke, you know; but you mustn't mind 'em, you mustn't mind 'em."

"I'll try and bear up agin such a reg'lar knock down o' talent," replied Sam.

"That's right," said Mr. John Smauker, putting up the fox's head, and elevating his own; "I'll stand by you."

By this time they had reached a small greengrocer's shop, which Mr. John Smauker entered, followed by Sam, who, the moment he got behind him, relapsed into a series of the very broadest and most unmitigated grins, and manifested other demonstrations of being in a highly enviable state of inward merriment.

Crossing the greengrocer's shop, and putting their hats on the stairs in the little passage behind it, they walked into a small parlour; and here the full splendour of the scene burst upon Mr. Weller's view.

A couple of tables were put together in the middle of the parlour, covered with three or four cloths of different ages and dates of washing, arranged to look as much like one as the circumstances of the case would allow. Upon these, were laid knives and forks for six or eight people. Some of the knife handles were green, others red, and a few more yellow; and as all the forks were black, the combination of colours was exceedingly striking. Plates for a corresponding number of guests were warming behind the fender; and the guests themselves were warming before it, the chief and most important of whom appeared to be a stoutish gentleman in a bright crimson coat with long tails, vividly red breeches, and a cocked hat, who was standing with his back to the fire, and had apparently just entered, for besides retaining his cocked hat on his head, he carried in his hand a high stick, such as gentlemen of his profession usually elevate in a sloping position over the roofs of carriages.

"Smauker, my lad—your fin," said the gentleman with the cocked hat.

Mr. Smauker dovetailed the top joint of his right hand little finger into that of the gentleman with the cocked hat, and said he was charmed to see him looking so well.

"Well, they tell me I am looking pretty blooming," said the man with the cocked hat, "and it's a wonder, too. I've been following our old woman about, two hours a-day for the last fortnight, and if a constant contemplation of the manner in which she hooks-and-eyes that infernal lavender-coloured old gown of hers behind, isn't enough to throw anybody into a low state of despondency for life, stop my quarter's salary."

At this, the assembled selections laughed very heartily; and one gentleman in a yellow waistcoat, with a coach trimming border, whispered a neighbour in green-foil smalls, that Tuckle was in spirits to-night.

"By the by," said Mr. Tuckle, "Smauker, my boy,
you"—— The remainder of the sentence was forwarded
into Mr. John Smauker's ear, by whisper.

"Oh, dear me, I quite forgot," said Mr. John Smauker.
"Gentlemen, my friend Mr. Weller."

"Sorry to keep the fire off you, Weller," said Mr.
Tuckle, with a familiar nod. "Hope you're not cold,
Weller."

"Not by no means, Blazes," replied Sam. "It 'ud be a
wery chilly subject as felt cold ven you stood opposit.
You'd save coals if they put you behind the fender in the
vatin' room at a public office, you would."

As this retort appeared to convey rather a personal allusion to Mr. Tuckle's crimson livery, that gentleman looked
majestic for a few seconds, but gradually edging away from
the fire, broke into a forced smile, and said it wasn't bad.

"Wery much obliged for your good opinion, Sir," replied Sam. "We shall get on by degrees, I des-say.
We'll try a better one, by and by."

At this point the conversation was interrupted by the
arrival of a gentleman in orange-coloured plush, accompanied by another selection in purple cloth, with a great extent of stocking. The new comers having been welcomed
by the old ones, Mr. Tuckle put the question that supper
be ordered in, which was carried unanimously.

The greengrocer and his wife then arranged upon the
table a boiled leg of mutton, hot, with caper sauce, turnips,
and potatoes. Mr. Tuckle took the chair, and was supported at the other end of the board by the gentleman in
orange plush. The greengrocer put on a pair of wash-
leather gloves to hand the plates with, and stationed himself behind Mr. Tuckle's chair.

"Harris," said Mr. Tuckle, in a commanding tone.

"Sir," said the greengrocer.

"Have you got your gloves on?"

"Yes, Sir."

"Then take the kiver off."

"Yes, Sir."

The greengrocer did as he was told, with a show of great
humility, and obsequiously handed Mr. Tuckle the carving
knife; in doing which, he accidentally gaped.

"What do you mean by that, Sir?" said Mr. Tuckle,
with great asperity.

"I beg your pardon, Sir," replied the crest-fallen greengrocer, "I didn't mean to do it, Sir; I was up very late
last night, Sir."

"I tell you what my opinion of you is, Harris," said
Mr. Tuckle with a most impressive air, "you're a vulgar
beast."

"I hope, gentlemen," said Harris, "that you won't be
severe with me, gentlemen. I'm very much obliged to
you indeed, gentlemen, for your patronage, and also for
your recommendations, gentlemen, whenever additional
assistance in waiting is required. I hope, gentlemen, I
give satisfaction."

"No, you don't, Sir," said Mr. Tuckle. "Very far
from it, Sir."

"We consider you an inattentive reskel," said the gentleman in the orange plush.

"And a low thief," added the gentleman in the green-
foil smalls.

"And an unreclaimable blaygaird," added the gentleman
in purple.

The poor greengrocer bowed very humbly while these
little epithets were bestowed upon him, in the true spirit of
the very smallest tyranny; and when every body had said
something to show his superiority, Mr. Tuckle proceeded
to carve the leg of mutton, and to help the company.

This important business of the evening had hardly
commenced, when the door was thrown briskly open, and
another gentleman in a light-blue suit, and leaden buttons,
made his appearance.

"Against the rules," said Mr. Tuckle. "Too late, too
late."

"No, no; positively I couldn't help it," said the gentleman in blue. "I appeal to the company—an affair of gallantry now—an appintment at the theayter."

"Oh, that indeed," said the gentleman in the orange
plush.

"Yes; raly now, honour bright," said the man in blue.
"I made a promese to fetch our youngest daughter at half-
past ten, and she is such an uncauminly fine gal, that I
raly hadn't the art to disappint her. No offence to the
present company, Sir, but a petticut, Sir,—a petticut, Sir, is
irrevokeable."

"I begin to suspect there's something in that quarter,"
said Tuckle, as the new comer took his seat next Sam.
"I've remarked once or twice, that she leans very heavy
on your shoulder when she gets in and out of the carriage."

"Oh raly, raly, Tuckle, you shouldn't," said the man in
blue. "It's not fair. I may have said to one or two
friends that she was a very divine creechure, and had refused one or two offers without any hobvus cause, but—no,
no, no, indeed, Tuckle—before strangers, too—it's not
right—you shouldn't. Delicacy, my dear friend, delicacy." And the man in blue, pulling up his neckerchief,
and adjusting his coat cuffs, nodded and frowned as if
there were more behind which he could say if he liked, but
was bound in honour to suppress.

The man in blue being a light-haired, stiff-necked, free
and easy sort of footman, with a swaggering air and pert
face, had attracted Mr. Weller's especial attention at first,
but when he began to come out in this way, Sam felt more
than ever disposed to cultivate his acquaintance; so he
launched himself into the conversation at once, with characteristic independence.

"Your health, Sir," said Sam. "I like your conwersation much. I think it's wery pretty."

At this the man in blue smiled as if it were a compliment he was well used to; but looked approvingly on Sam
at the same time, and said he hoped he should be better
acquainted with him, for without any flattery at all he
seemed to have the makings of a very nice fellow about
him—just the man after his own heart.

"You're wery good, Sir," said Sam. "What a lucky
feller you are."

"How do you mean?" inquired the gentleman in blue.

"That 'ere young lady," replied Sam. "She knows
wot's wot, she does. Ah, I see." Mr. Weller closed one
eye, and shook his head from side to side in a manner
which was highly gratifying to the personal vanity of the
gentleman in blue.

"I'm afraid you're a cunning fellow, Mr. Weller," said
that individual.

"No, no," said Sam. "I leave all that 'ere to you. It's
a great deal more in your way than mine, as the gen'lm'n
on the right side o' the garden vall said to the man on the
wrong 'un, ven the mad bull wos a cumin' up the lane."

"Well, well, Mr. Weller," said the gentleman in blue,

"I think she has remarked my air and manner, Mr. Weller."

"I should think she couldn't wery well be off o' that," said Sam.

"Have you any little thing of that kind in hand, Sir?" inquired the favoured gentleman in blue, drawing a tooth-pick from his waistcoat pocket.

"Not exactly," said Sam. "There's no daughters at my place, else o' course I should ha' made up to vun on 'em. As it is, I don't think I can do vith any thin' under a female markis. I might take up with a young ooman o' large property as hadn't a title, if she made wery fierce love to me—not else."

"Of course not, Mr. Weller," said the gentleman in blue, "one can't be troubled, you know; and *we* know, Mr. Weller—we, who are men of the world—that a good uniform must work its way with the women, sooner or later. In fact, that's the only thing, between you and I, that makes the service worth entering into."

"Just so," said Sam. "That's it, o' couse."

When this confidential dialogue had gone thus far, glasses were placed round, and every gentleman ordered what he liked best, before the public house shut up. The gentleman in blue and the man in orange, who were the chief exquisites of the party, ordered "cold srub and water," but with the others, gin and water sweet, appeared to be the favourite beverage. Sam called the greengrocer a "desp'rate willin'," and ordered a large bowl of punch—two circumstances which seemed to raise him very much, in the opinion of the selections.

"Gentlemen," said the man in blue, with an air of the most consummate dandyism, "I'll give you the ladies; come."

"Hear, hear!" said Sam, "The young missises."

Here there was a loud cry of "Order," and Mr. John Smauker, as the gentleman who had introduced Mr. Weller into that company, begged to inform him that the word he had just made use of, was unparliamentary.

"Which word was that 'ere, Sir?" inquired Sam.

"Missises, Sir," replied Mr. John Smauker, with an alarming frown. "We don't recognise such distinctions here."

"Oh, wery good," said Sam; "then I'll amend the observation, and call 'em the dear creeturs, if Blazes vill allow me."

Some doubt appeared to exist in the mind of the gentleman in the green-foil smalls, whether the chairman could be legally appealed to, as "Blazes," but as the company seemed more disposed to stand upon their own rights than his, the question was not raised. The man with the cocked hat, breathed short, and looked long at Sam, but apparently thought it as well to say nothing in case he should get the worst of it.

After a short silence, a gentleman in an embroidered coat reaching down to his heels, and a waistcoat of the same which kept one half of his legs warm, stirred his gin and water with great energy, and putting himself upon his feet, all at once, by a violent effort, said he was desirous of offering a few remarks to the company, whereupon the person in the cocked hat had no doubt that the company would be very happy to hear any remarks that the man in the long coat might wish to offer.

"I feel a great delicacy, gentlemen, in coming for'ard," said the man in the long coat, "having the misforchune to be a coachman, and being only admitted as a honorary member of these agreeable swarreys, but I do feel myself bound, gentlemen—drove into a corner, if I may use the expression—to make known an afflicting circumstance which has come to my knowledge; which has happened I may say within the soap of my every day contemplation. Gentlemen, our friend Mr. Whiffers (everybody looked at the individual in orange), our friend Mr. Whiffers has resigned."

Universal astonishment fell upon the hearers. Each gentleman looked in his neighbour's face, and then transferred his glance to the upstanding coachman.

"You may well be sapparised, gentlemen," said the coachman. "I will not wenchure to state the reasons of this irrepairabel loss to the service, but I will beg Mr. Whiffers to state them himself, for the improvement and imitation of his admiring friends."

The suggestion being loudly approved of, Mr. Whiffers explained. He said he certainly could have wished to have continued to hold the appointment which he had just resigned. The uniform was extremely rich and expensive, the females of the family was most agreeable, and the duties of the situation was not, he was bound to say, too heavy; the principal service that was required of him, being, that he should look out of the hall window as much as possible, in company with another gentleman, who had also resigned. He could have wished to have spared that company the painful and disgusting detail on which he was about to enter, but as the explanation had been demanded of him, he had no alternative but to state, boldly and distinctly, that he had been required to eat cold meat.

It is impossible to conceive the disgust which this avowal awakened in the bosoms of the hearers. Loud cries of "Shame," mingled with groans and hisses, prevailed for a quarter of an hour at least.

Mr. Whiffers then added that he feared a portion of this outrage might be traced to his own forbearing and accommodating disposition. He had a distinct recollection of having once consented to eat salt butter, and he had, moreover, on an occasion of sudden sickness in the house, so far forgotten himself as to carry a coal scuttle up to the second floor. He trusted he had not lowered himself in the good opinion of his friends by this frank confession of his faults; and he hoped the promptness with which he had resented the last unmanly outrage on his feelings, to which he had referred, would reinstate him in their good opinion, if he had.

Mr. Whiffers' address was responded to, with a shout of admiration, and the health of the interesting martyr was drunk in a most enthusiastic manner; for this, the martyr returned thanks, and proposed their visitor, Mr. Weller—a gentleman whom he had not the pleasure of an intimate acquaintance with, but who was the friend of Mr. John Smauker, which was a sufficient letter of recommendation to any society of gentlemen whatever, or wherever. On this account he should have been disposed to have given Mr. Weller's health with all the honors, if his friends had been drinking wine, but as they were taking spirits just by way of a change; and as it might be inconvenient to empty a tumbler at every toast, he should propose that the honors be understood.

At the conclusion of this speech, everybody took a sip out of their tumblers in honor of Sam; and Sam having ladled out, and drunk two full glasses of punch in honor of himself, returned thanks in a neat speech.

"Wery much obliged to you, old fellers," said Sam, ladling away at the punch in the most unembarrassed manner possible, "for this here compliment; wich, comin' from sich a quarter, is wery overvelmin'. I've heerd a good deal on you as a body, but I vill say, that I never thought you was sich uncommon nice men as I find you air. I only hope you'll take care o' yourselves, and not compromise nothin' o' your dignity, which is a wery charmin' thing to see, when one's out a walkin', and has always made me wery happy to look at, ever since I was a boy about half as high as the brass-headed stick o' my wery respectable friend, Blazes, there. As to the wictim of oppression in the suit o' brimstone, all I can say of him is, that I hope he'll get jist as good a berth as he deserves; in vich case it's wery little cold swarry as ever he'll be troubled with agin."

Here Sam sat down with a pleasant smile, and his speech having been vociferously applauded, the company broke up.

"Wy, you don't mean to say you're a goin', old feller," said Sam Weller to his friend Mr. John Smauker.

"I must indeed," said Mr. Smauker; "I promised Bantam."

"Oh, wery well," said Sam; "that's another thing. P'raps he'd resign if you disappinted him. You ain't a goin', Blazes?"

"Yes, I am," said the man with the cocked hat.

"Wot, and leave three quarters of a bowl of punch behind you!" said Sam; "nonsense, set down agin."

Mr. Tuckle was not proof against this invitation. He laid aside the cocked hat and stick which he had just taken up, and said he would have one glass just for good fellowship's sake.

As the gentleman in blue went home the same way as Mr. Tuckle, he was prevailed upon to stop too. When the punch was about half gone, Sam ordered in some oysters from the greengrocer's shop; and the effect of both was so extremely exhilarating, that Mr. Tuckle, dressed out with the cocked hat and stick, danced the frog hornpipe among the shells on the table, while the gentleman in blue played an accompaniment upon an ingenious musical instrument formed of a hair comb and a curl-paper. At last, when the punch was all gone, and the night nearly so, they sallied forth to see each other home. Mr. Tuckle no sooner got into the open air, than he was seized with a sudden desire to lie on the curbstone; Sam thought it would be a pity to contradict him, and so let him have his own way. As the cocked hat would have been spoilt if left there, Sam very considerately flattened it down on the head of the gentleman in blue, and putting the big stick in his hand, propped him up against his own street-door, rang the bell, and walked quietly home.

At a much earlier hour next morning than his usual time of rising, Mr. Pickwick walked down stairs completely dressed, and rang the bell.

"Sam," said Mr. Pickwick, when Mr. Weller appeared in reply to the summons, "shut the door."

Mr. Weller did so.

"There was an unfortunate occurrence here, last night, Sam," said Mr. Pickwick, "which gave Mr. Winkle some cause to apprehend violence from Mr. Dowler."

"So I've heerd from the old lady down stairs, Sir," replied Sam.

"And I'm sorry to say, Sam," continued Mr. Pickwick, with a most perplexed countenance, "that in dread of this violence, Mr. Winkle has gone away."

"Gone avay!" said Sam.

"Left the house early this morning without the slightest previous communication with me," replied Mr. Pickwick. "And is gone, I know not where."

"He should ha' stopped and fought it out, Sir," replied Sam, contemptuously. "It vouldn't take much to settle that 'ere Dowler, Sir."

"Well Sam," said Mr. Pickwick, "I may have my doubts of his great bravery and determination, also. But however that may be, Mr. Winkle is gone. He must be found, Sam—found and brought back to me."

"And s'pose he von't come back, Sir," said Sam.

"He must be made, Sam," said Mr. Pickwick.

"Who's to do it, Sir?" enquired Sam with a smile.

"You," replied Mr. Pickwick.

"Wery good, Sir."

With these words Mr. Weller left the room, and immediately afterwards was heard to shut the street door. In two hours' time he returned with as much coolness as if he had been despatched on the most ordinary message possible, and brought the information that an individual in every respect answering Mr. Winkle's description, had gone over to Bristol that morning, by the branch coach from the Royal Hotel.

"Sam," said Mr. Pickwick, grasping his hand, "you're a capital fellow; an invaluable fellow. You must follow him, Sam."

"Cert'nly, Sir," replied Mr. Weller.

"The instant you discover him, write to me immediately, Sam," said Mr. Pickwick. "If he attempts to run away from you, knock him down, or lock him up. You have my full authority, Sam."

"I'll be wery careful, Sir," rejoined Sam.

"You'll tell him," said Mr. Pickwick, "that I am highly excited, highly displeased, and naturally indignant at the very extraordinary course he has thought proper to pursue."

"I will, Sir," replied Sam.

"You'll tell him," said Mr. Pickwick, "that if he does not come back to this very house, with you, he will come back with me, for I will come and fetch him."

"I'll mention that 'ere, Sir," rejoined Sam.

"You think you can find him, Sam?" said Mr. Pickwick, looking earnestly in his face.

"Oh, I'll find him if he's any vere," rejoined Sam, with great confidence.

"Very well," said Mr. Pickwick. "Then the sooner you go the better."

With these instructions Mr. Pickwick placed a sum of money in the hands of his faithful servitor, and ordered him to start for Bristol immediately, in pursuit of the fugitive.

Sam put a few necessaries in a carpet bag, and was ready for starting. He stopped when he had got to the end of the passage, and walking quietly back, thrust his head in at the parlour door.

"Sir," whispered Sam.

"Well, Sam," said Mr. Pickwick.

"I fully understands my instructions, do I, Sir?" inquired Sam.

"I hope so," said Mr. Pickwick.

"It's reg'larly understood about the knockin' down, is it, Sir?" enquired Sam.

"Perfectly," replied Mr. Pickwick. "Thoroughly. Do what you think necessary. You have my orders."

Sam gave a nod of intelligence, and withdrawing his head from the door, set forth on his pilgrimage with a light heart.

CHAPTER XXXVII.

HOW MR. WINKLE, WHEN HE STEPPED OUT OF THE FRYING-PAN, WALKED GENTLY AND COMFORTABLY INTO THE FIRE.

THE ill-starred gentleman who had been the unfortunate cause of the unusual noise and disturbance which alarmed the inhabitants of the Royal Crescent in manner and form already described, after passing a night of great confusion and anxiety, left the roof beneath which his friends still slumbered, bound he knew not whither. The excellent and considerate feelings which prompted Mr. Winkle to take this step can never be too highly appreciated or too warmly extolled. "If"—reasoned Mr. Winkle with himself—"if this Dowler attempts (as I have no doubt he will) to carry into execution his threat of personal violence against myself, it will be incumbent on me to call him out. He has a wife; that wife is attached to, and dependent on him. Heavens! If I should kill him in the blindness of my wrath, what would be my feelings ever afterwards!" This painful consideration operated so powerfully on the feelings of the humane young man, as to cause his knees to knock together, and his countenance to exhibit alarming manifestations of inward emotion. Impelled by these reflections, he grasped his carpet-bag, and creeping stealthily down stairs, shut the detestable street-door with as little noise as possible, and walked off. Bending his steps towards the Royal Hotel, he found a coach on the point of starting for Bristol; and thinking Bristol as good a place for his purpose as any other he could go to, mounted on the box, and reached his place of destination in such time as the pair of horses, who went the whole stage and back again twice a day or more, could be reasonably supposed to arrive there.

He took up his quarters at The Bush; and designing to postpone any communication by letter with Mr. Pickwick until it was probable that Mr. Dowler's wrath might have in some degree evaporated, walked forth to view the city, which struck him as being a shade more dirty than any place he had ever seen. Having inspected the docks and shipping, and viewed the cathedral, he inquired his way to Clifton, and being directed thither, took the route which was pointed out to him. But, as the pavements of Bristol are not the widest or cleanest upon earth, so its streets are not altogether the straightest or least intricate; and Mr. Winkle being greatly puzzled by their manifold windings and twistings, looked about him for a decent shop in which he could apply afresh for counsel and instruction.

His eye fell upon a newly-painted tenement which had been recently converted into something between a shop and a private house, and which a red lamp, projecting over the fan-light of the street-door, would have sufficiently announced as the residence of a medical practitioner, even if the word "Surgery" had not been inscribed in golden characters on a wainscot ground, above the window of what, in times bygone, had been the front parlour. Thinking this an eligible place wherein to make his inquiries, Mr. Winkle stepped into the little shop where the gilt-labelled drawers and bottles were; and finding nobody there, knocked with a half-crown on the counter, to attract the attention of anybody who might happen to be in the back parlour, which he judged to be the innermost and peculiar sanctum of the establishment, from the repetition of the word surgery on the door—painted in white letters this time, by way of taking off the sameness.

At the first knock, a sound, as of persons fencing with fire-irons, which had until now been very audible, suddenly ceased; and at the second, a studious-looking young gentleman in green spectacles, with a very large book in his hand, glided quietly into the shop, and stepping behind the counter, requested to know the visitor's pleasure.

"I am sorry to trouble you, Sir," said Mr. Winkle, "but will you have the goodness to direct me to——"

"Ha! ha! ha!" roared the studious young gentleman, throwing the large book up into the air, and catching it with great dexterity at the very moment when it threatened to smash to atoms all the bottles on the counter. "Here's a start!"

There was, without doubt; for Mr. Winkle was so very much astonished at the extraordinary behaviour of the medical gentleman, that he involuntarily retreated towards the door, and looked very much disturbed at his strange reception.

"What, don't you know me?" said the medical gentleman.

Mr. Winkle murmured, in reply, that he had not that pleasure.

"Why then," said the medical gentleman, "there are hopes for me yet; I may attend half the old women in Bristol if I've decent luck. Get out, you mouldy old villain, get out!" With this adjuration, which was addressed to the large book, the medical gentleman kicked the volume with remarkable agility to the further end of the shop, and pulling off his green spectacles, grinned the identical grin of Robert Sawyer, Esquire, formerly of Guy's Hospital in the Borough, with a private residence in Lant-street.

"You don't mean to say you weren't down upon me?" said Mr. Bob Sawyer, shaking Mr. Winkle's hand with friendly warmth.

"Upon my word I was not," replied Mr. Winkle, returning the pressure.

"I wonder you didn't see the name," said Bob Sawyer, calling his friend's attention to the outer door, on which, in the same white paint, were traced the words "Sawyer, late Nockemorf."

"It never caught my eye," returned Mr. Winkle.

"Lord, if I had known who you were, I should have rushed out, and caught you in my arms," said Bob Sawyer; "but upon my life, I thought you were the King's-taxes."

"No!" said Mr. Winkle.

"I did, indeed," responded Bob Sawyer, "and I was just going to say that I wasn't at home, but if you'd leave a message I'd be sure to give it to myself; for he don't know me, no more does the Lighting and Paving. I think the Church-rates guesses who I am, and I know the Waterworks does, because I drew a tooth of his, when I first came down here.—But come in, come in." Chattering in this way, Mr. Bob Sawyer pushed Mr. Winkle into the back room, where, amusing himself by boring little circular caverns in the chimney-piece with a red-hot poker, sat no less a person than Mr. Benjamin Allen.

"Well," said Mr. Winkle, "this is indeed a pleasure that I did not expect. What a very nice place you have here!"

"Pretty well, pretty well," replied Bob Sawyer. "I

passed soon after that precious party, and my friends came down with the needful for this business; so I put on a black suit of clothes and a pair of spectacles, and came here, to look as solemn as I could."

"And a very snug little business you have, no doubt?" said Mr. Winkle, knowingly.

"Very," replied Bob Sawyer. "So snug, that at the end of a few years you might put all the profits in a wine glass, and cover 'em over with a gooseberry leaf."

"You cannot surely mean that?" said Mr. Winkle. "The stock itself——"

"Dummies, my dear boy," said Bob Sawyer; "half the drawers have got nothing in 'em, and the other half don't open."

"Nonsense!" said Mr. Winkle.

"Fact—honour!" returned Bob Sawyer, stepping out into the shop, and demonstrating the veracity of the assertion by divers hard pulls at the little gilt knobs on the counterfeit drawers. "Hardly anything real in the shop but the leeches, and *they* are secondhand."

"I shouldn't have thought it!" exclaimed Mr. Winkle, much surprised.

"I hope not," replied Bob Sawyer, "else where's the use of appearances, eh? But what will you take? Do as we do?—that's right. Ben, my fine fellow, put your hand into the cupboard, and bring out the patent digester."

Mr. Benjamin Allen smiled his readiness, and produced from the closet at his elbow a black bottle half full of brandy.

"You don't take water, of course?" said Bob Sawyer.

"Thank you," replied Mr. Winkle. "It's *rather* early: I should like to qualify it, if you have no objection."

"None in the least, if you can reconcile it to your conscience," replied Bob Sawyer; tossing off, as he spoke, a glass of the liquor with great relish.—"Ben, the pipkin."

Mr. Benjamin Allen drew forth from the same hiding-place a small brass pipkin, which Bob Sawyer observed he prided himself upon, particularly, because it looked so business-like. The water in the professional pipkin having been made to boil, in course of time, by various little shovels-full of coal, which Mr. Bob Sawyer took out of a practicable window-seat, labelled "Soda Water," Mr. Winkle adulterated his brandy; and the conversation was becoming general, when it was interrupted by the entrance into the shop of a boy, in a sober grey livery and a gold-laced hat, with a small covered basket under his arm, whom Mr. Bob Sawyer immediately hailed with, "Tom, you vagabond, come here."

The boy presented himself accordingly.

"You've been stopping to over all the posts in Bristol, you idle young scamp!" said Mr. Bob Sawyer.

"No, Sir, I haven't," replied the boy.

"You had better not!" said Mr. Bob Sawyer, with a threatening aspect. "Who do you suppose will ever employ a professional man, when they see his boy playing at marbles in the gutter, or flying the garter in the horse-road? Have you no feeling for your profession, you groveller? Did you leave all the medicine?"

"Yes, Sir."

"The powders for the child, at the large house with the new family, and the pills to be taken four times a day at the ill-tempered old gentleman's with the gouty leg?"

"Yes, Sir."

"Then shut the door, and mind the shop."

"Come," said Mr. Winkle, as the boy retired, "things are not quite so bad as you would have me believe, either. There is *some* medicine to be sent out."

Mr. Bob Sawyer peeped into the shop to see that no stranger was within hearing, and leaning forward to Mr. Winkle, said, in a low tone—

"He leaves it all at the wrong houses."

Mr. Winkle looked perplexed, and Bob Sawyer and his friend laughed.

"Don't you see?" said Bob; "he goes up to a house, rings the area bell, pokes a packet of medicine without a direction into the servant's hand, and walks off. Servant takes it into the dining-parlour; master opens it, and reads the label, 'Draught to be taken at bedtime—pills as before—lotion as usual—*the* powder. From Sawyer's, late Nockemorf's. Physicians' prescriptions carefully prepared:' and all the rest of it. Shows it to his wife—she reads the label; it goes down to the servants—*they* read the label. Next day the boy calls: 'Very sorry—his mistake—immense business—great many parcels to deliver—Mr. Sawyer's compliments—late Nockemorf.' The name gets known, and that's the thing, my boy, in the medical way; bless your heart, old fellow, it's better than all the advertising in the world. We have got one four-ounce bottle that's been to half the houses in Bristol, and hasn't done yet."

"Dear me, I see," observed Mr. Winkle; "what an excellent plan!"

"Oh, Ben and I have hit upon a dozen such," replied Bob Sawyer, with great glee. "The lamplighter has eighteen-pence a week to pull the night-bell for ten minutes, every time he comes round; and my boy always rushes into church just before the psalms, when the people have got nothing to do but look about 'em, and calls me out, with horror and dismay depicted on his countenance. 'Bless my soul,' everybody says, 'somebody taken suddenly ill? Sawyer, late Nockemorf, sent for. What a business that young man has!'"

At the termination of this disclosure of some of the mysteries of medicine, Mr. Bob Sawyer and his friend, Ben Allen, threw themselves back in their respective chairs, and laughed boisterously. When they had enjoyed the joke to their hearts' content, the discourse changed to topics in which Mr. Winkle was more immediately interested.

We think we have hinted elsewhere, that Mr. Benjamin Allen had a way of becoming sentimental after brandy. The case is not a peculiar one, as we ourself can testify: having, on a few occasions, had to deal with patients who have been afflicted in a similar manner. At this precise period of his existence, Mr. Benjamin Allen had perhaps a greater predisposition to maudlinism than he had ever known before; the cause of which malady was briefly this. He had been staying nearly three weeks with Mr. Bob Sawyer; Mr. Bob Sawyer was not remarkable for temperance, nor was Mr. Benjamin Allen for the ownership of a very strong head; and the consequence was, that, during the whole space of time just mentioned, Mr. Benjamin Allen had been wavering between intoxication partial and intoxication complete.

"My dear friend," said Mr. Ben Allen, taking advantage of Mr. Bob Sawyer's temporary absence behind the counter, whither he had retired to dispense some of the secondhand leeches, previously referred to, "my dear friend, I am very miserable."

Mr. Winkle professed his heartfelt regret to hear it, and

begged to know whether he could do anything to alleviate the sorrows of the suffering student.

"Nothing, my dear boy—nothing," said Ben. "You recollect Arabella, Winkle—my sister Arabella—a little girl, Winkle, with black eyes—when we were down at Wardle's? I don't know whether you happened to notice her—a nice little girl, Winkle. Perhaps my features may recall her countenance to your recollection?"

Mr. Winkle required nothing to recall the charming Arabella to his mind; and it was rather fortunate he did not, for the features of her brother Benjamin would unquestionably have proved but an indifferent refresher to his memory. He answered, with as much calmness as he could assume, that he perfectly remembered the young lady referred to, and sincerely trusted she was in good health.

"Our friend Bob is a delightful fellow, Winkle," was the only reply of Mr. Ben Allen.

"Very," said Mr. Winkle, not much relishing this close connexion of the two names.

"I designed 'em for each other; they were made for each other, sent into the world for each other, born for each other, Winkle," said Mr. Ben Allen, setting down his glass with great emphasis. "There's a special destiny in the matter, my dear Sir; there's only five years' difference between 'em, and both their birthdays are in August."

Mr. Winkle was too anxious to hear what was to follow, to express much wonderment at this extraordinary circumstance, marvellous as it was; so Mr. Ben Allen, after a tear or two, went on to say, that, notwithstanding all his esteem and respect and veneration for his friend, Arabella had unaccountably and undutifully evinced the most determined antipathy to his person.

"And I think," said Mr. Ben Allen, in conclusion, "*I* think there's a prior attachment."

"Have you any idea who the object of it may be?" asked Mr. Winkle, with great trepidation.

Mr. Ben Allen seized the poker, flourished it, in a warlike manner above his head, inflicted a savage blow on an imaginary skull, and wound up by saying, in a very expressive manner, that he only wished he could guess—that was all.

"I'd show him what I thought of him," said Mr. Ben Allen. And round went the poker again, more fiercely than before.

All this, was of course very soothing to the feelings of Mr. Winkle, who remained silent for a few minutes; but at length mustered up resolution to inquire whether Miss Allen was in Kent.

"No, no," said Mr. Ben Allen, laying aside the poker, and looking very cunning; "I didn't think Wardle's exactly the place for a headstrong girl; so, as I am her natural protector and guardian, our parents being dead, I have brought her down into this part of the country to spend a few months at an old aunt's, in a nice, dull, close place. I think that will cure her, my boy; and if it doesn't, I'll take her abroad for a little while, and see what that'll do."

"Oh, the aunt's is in Bristol, is it?" faltered Mr. Winkle.

"No, no—not in Bristol," replied Mr. Ben Allen, jerking his thumb over his right shoulder: "over that way—down there. But, hush, here's Bob. Not a word, my dear friend—not a word."

Short as this conversation was, it roused in Mr. Winkle the highest degree of excitement and anxiety. The suspected prior attachment rankled in his heart. Could he be the object of it? Could it be for him that the fair Arabella had looked scornfully on the sprightly Bob Sawyer, or had he a successful rival? He determined to see her, cost what it might; but here an insurmountable objection presented itself, for whether the explanatory "over that way," and "down there," of Mr. Ben Allen, meant three miles off, or thirty, or three hundred, he could in no wise guess.

But he had no opportunity of pondering over his love just then, for Bob Sawyer's return was the immediate precursor of the arrival of a meat pie from the baker's, of which that gentleman insisted on his staying to partake. The cloth was laid by an occasional charwoman, who officiated in the capacity of Mr. Bob Sawyer's housekeeper; and a third knife and fork having been borrowed from the mother of the boy in the grey livery (for Mr. Sawyer's domestic arrangements were as yet conducted on a limited scale), they sat down to dinner; the beer being served up, as Mr. Sawyer remarked, "in its native pewter."

After dinner, Mr. Bob Sawyer ordered in the largest mortar in the shop, and proceeded to brew a reeking jorum of rum-punch therein, stirring up and amalgamating the materials with a pestle in a very creditable and apothecary-like manner. Mr. Sawyer being a bachelor, had only one tumbler in the house, which was assigned to Mr. Winkle as a compliment to the visitor, Mr. Ben Allen being accommodated with a funnel with a cork in the narrow end, and Bob Sawyer contenting himself with one of those wide-lipped crystal vessels inscribed with a variety of cabalistic characters, in which chemists are wont to measure out their liquid drugs in compounding prescriptions. These preliminaries adjusted, the punch was tasted, and pronounced excellent; and it having been arranged that Bob Sawyer and Ben Allen should be considered at liberty to fill twice to Mr. Winkle's once, they started fair, with great satisfaction and good-fellowship.

There was no singing, because Mr. Bob Sawyer said it wouldn't look professional; but to make amends for this deprivation there was so much talking and laughing that it might have been heard, and very likely was, at the end of the street: which conversation materially lightened the hours and improved the mind of Mr. Bob Sawyer's boy, who, instead of devoting the evening to his ordinary occupation of writing his name on the counter, and rubbing it out again, peeped through the glass door, and thus listened and looked on, at the same time.

The mirth of Mr. Bob Sawyer was rapidly ripening into the furious, Mr. Ben Allen was fast relapsing into the sentimental, and the punch had well nigh disappeared altogether, when the boy hastily running in, announced that a young woman had just come over, to say that Sawyer late Nockemorf was wanted directly, a couple of streets off. This broke up the party. Mr. Bob Sawyer understanding the message after some twenty repetitions, tied a wet cloth round his head to sober himself, and having partially succeeded, put on his green spectacles and issued forth. Resisting all entreaties to stay till he came back, and finding it quite impossible to engage Mr. Ben Allen in any intelligible conversation on the subject nearest his heart, or indeed on any other, Mr. Winkle took his departure, and returned to the Bush.

The anxiety of his mind, and the numerous meditations which Arabella had awakened, prevented his share of the mortar of punch producing that effect upon him which it would have had, under other circumstances. So, after taking a glass of soda-water and brandy at the bar, he turned into the coffee-room, dispirited rather than elevated by the occurrences of the evening.

Sitting in front of the fire, with his back towards him, was a tallish gentleman in a great-coat: the only other occupant of the room. It was rather a cool evening for the season of the year, and the gentleman drew his chair aside to afford the new comer a sight of the fire. What were Mr. Winkle's feelings when, in doing so, he disclosed to view the face and figure of the vindictive and sanguinary Dowler!

Mr. Winkle's first impulse was to give a violent pull at the nearest bell-handle, but that unfortunately happened to be immediately behind Mr. Dowler's head. He had made one step towards it, before he checked himself. As he did so, Mr. Dowler very hastily drew back.

"Mr. Winkle, Sir. Be calm. Don't strike me. I won't bear it. A blow! Never," said Mr. Dowler, looking meeker than Mr. Winkle had expected in a gentleman of his ferocity.

"A blow, Sir?" stammered Mr. Winkle.

"A blow, Sir," replied Dowler. "Compose your feelings. Sit down. Hear me."

"Sir," said Mr. Winkle, trembling from head to foot, "before I consent to sit down beside, or opposite you, without the presence of a waiter, I must be secured by some further understanding. You used a threat against me last night, Sir—a dreadful threat, Sir." Here Mr. Winkle turned very pale indeed, and stopped short.

"I did," said Dowler, with a countenance almost as white as Mr. Winkle's. "Circumstances were suspicious. They have been explained. I respect your bravery. Your feeling is upright. Conscious innocence. There's my hand. Grasp it."

"Really Sir," said Mr. Winkle, hesitating whether to give his hand or not, and almost fearing that it was demanded in order that he might be taken at an advantage, "really Sir, I——"

"I know what you mean," interposed Dowler. "You feel aggrieved. Very natural. So should I. I was wrong. I beg your pardon. Be friendly. Forgive me." With this, Dowler fairly forced his hand upon Mr. Winkle, and shaking it with the utmost vehemence, declared he was a fellow of extreme spirit, and he had a higher opinion of him than ever.

"Now," said Dowler, "sit down. Relate it all. How did you find me? When did you follow? Be frank. Tell me."

"It's quite accidental," replied Mr. Winkle, greatly perplexed by the curious and unexpected nature of the interview, "Quite."

"Glad of it," said Dowler. "I woke this morning. I had forgotten my threat. I laughed at the accident. I felt friendly. I said so."

"To whom?" inquired Mr. Winkle.

"To Mrs. Dowler. 'You made a vow,' said she. 'I did,' said I. 'It was a rash one,' said she. 'It was,' said I. 'I'll apologise. Where is he?'"

"Who?" inquired Mr. Winkle.

"You," replied Dowler. "I went down stairs. You were not to be found. Pickwick looked gloomy. Shook his head. Hoped no violence would be committed. I saw it all. You felt yourself insulted. You had gone, for a friend perhaps. Possibly for pistols. 'High spirit,' said I. 'I admire him.'"

Mr. Winkle coughed, and beginning to see how the land lay, assumed a look of importance.

"I left a note for you," resumed Dowler. "I said I was sorry. So I was. Pressing business called me here. You were not satisfied. You followed. You required a verbal explanation. You were right. It's all over now. My business is finished. I go back to-morrow. Join me."

As Dowler progressed in his explanation, Mr. Winkle's countenance grew more and more dignified. The mysterious nature of the commencement of their conversation was explained; Mr. Dowler had as great an objection to duelling as himself; in short, this blustering and awful personage was one of the most egregious cowards in existence, and interpreting Mr. Winkle's absence through the medium of his own fears, had actually taken the same step as himself, and prudently retired until all excitement of feeling should have subsided.

As the real state of the case dawned upon Mr. Winkle's mind, he looked very terrible, and said he was perfectly satisfied; but at the same time, said so, with an air that left Mr. Dowler no alternative but to infer that if he had not been, something most horrible and destructive must inevitably have occurred. Mr. Dowler appeared to be impressed with a becoming sense of Mr. Winkle's magnanimity and condescension; and the two belligerents parted for the night, with many protestations of eternal friendship.

About half-past twelve o'clock, when Mr. Winkle had been revelling some twenty minutes in the full luxury of his first sleep, he was suddenly awakened by a loud knocking at his chamber-door, which, being repeated with increased vehemence, caused him to start up in bed, and inquire who was there, and what the matter was.

"Please, Sir, here's a young man which says he must see you directly," responded the voice of the chambermaid.

"A young man!" exclaimed Mr. Winkle.

"No mistake about that 'ere, Sir," replied another voice through the keyhole; "and if that wery same interestin' young creetur ain't let in vithout delay, it's wery possible as his legs vill enter afore his countenance."—The young man gave a gentle kick at one of the lower pannels of the door, after he had given utterance to this hint, as if to add force and point to the remark.

"Is that you, Sam?" inquired Mr. Winkle, springing out of bed.

"Quite unpossible to identify any gen'lm'n vith any degree o' mental satisfaction, vithout lookin' at him, Sir," replied the voice, dogmatically.

Mr. Winkle, not much doubting who the young man was, unlocked the door; which he had no sooner done, than Mr. Samuel Weller entered with great precipitation, and carefully re-locking it on the inside, deliberately put the key in his waistcoat pocket; and, after surveying Mr. Winkle from head to foot, said—

"You're a wery humorous young gen'lm'n, you air, Sir."

"What do you mean by this conduct, Sam?" inquired Mr. Winkle, indignantly. "Get out, Sir, this instant. What do you mean, Sir?"

"What do *I* mean," retorted Sam; "come, Sir, this is rayther too rich, as the young lady said ven she remonstrated with the pastry-cook, arter he'd sold her a pork-pie as had got nothin' but fat inside. What do *I* mean! Well, that ain't a bad 'un, that ain't."

"Unlock that door, and leave this room immediately, Sir," said Mr. Winkle.

"I shall leave this here room, Sir, just percisely at the wery same moment as you leaves it," responded Sam, speaking in a forcible manner, and seating himself with perfect gravity. "If I find it necessary to carry you away, pick-a-back, o' course I shall leave it the least bit o' time possible afore you; but allow me to express a hope as you won't reduce me to ex-tremities: in saying vich, I merely quote wot the nobleman said to the fractious pennywinkle, ven he vouldn't come out of his shell by means of a pin, and he conseqvently began to be aeferd that he should be obliged to crack him in the parlour door." At the end of this address, which was unusually lengthy for him, Mr. Weller planted his hands on his knees, and looked full in Mr. Winkle's face, with an expression of countenance which showed that he had not the remotest intention of being trifled with.

"You're a amiably-disposed young man, Sir, I don't think," resumed Mr. Weller, in a tone of moral reproof, "to go inwolving our precious governor in all sorts o' fanteegs, ven he's made up his mind to go through ev'ry think for principle. You're far worse nor Dodson, Sir; and as for Fogg, I consider him a born angel to you!" Mr. Weller having accompanied this last sentiment with an emphatic slap on each knee, folded his arms with a look of great disgust, and threw himself back in his chair, as if awaiting the criminal's defence.

"My good fellow," said Mr. Winkle, extending his hand—his teeth chattering all the time he spoke, for he had been standing during the whole of Mr. Weller's lecture in his night-gear, "My good fellow, I respect your attachment to my excellent friend, and I am very sorry indeed, to have added to his causes for disquiet. There, Sam, there!"

"Well," said Sam, rather sulkily, but giving the proffered hand a respectful shake at the same time—"Well, so you ought to be, and I am very glad to find you air; for, if I can help it, I won't have him put upon by nobody, and that's all about it."

"Certainly not, Sam," said Mr. Winkle. "There, now go to bed, Sam, and we'll talk further about this, in the morning."

"I'm wery sorry," said Sam, "but I can't go to bed."

"Not go to bed!" repeated Mr. Winkle.

"No," said Sam, shaking his head, "Can't be done."

"You don't mean to say you're going back to-night, Sam?" urged Mr. Winkle, greatly surprised.

"Not unless you particklerly vish it," replied Sam; "but I mustn't leave this here room. The governor's orders wos peremptory."

"Nonsense, Sam," said Mr. Winkle, "I must stop here two or three days; and more than that, Sam, you must stop here too, to assist me in gaining an interview with a young lady—Miss Allen, Sam; you remember her—whom I must and will see before I leave Bristol."

But in reply to each of these positions, Sam shook his head with great firmness, and energetically replied, "It can't be done."

After a great deal of argument and representation on the part of Mr. Winkle, however, and a full disclosure of what had passed in the interview with Dowler, Sam began to waver; and at length a compromise was effected, of which the following were the main and principal conditions—

That Sam should retire, and leave Mr. Winkle in the undisturbed possession of his apartment, on condition that he had permission to lock the door on the outside, and carry off the key; provided always, that in the event of an alarm of fire, or other dangerous contingency, the door should be instantly unlocked. That a letter should be written to Mr. Pickwick early next morning, and forwarded per Dowler, requesting his consent to Sam and Mr. Winkle's remaining at Bristol, for the purpose and with the object already assigned, and begging an answer by the next coach; if favourable, the aforesaid parties to remain accordingly, and if not, to return to Bath immediately on the receipt thereof. And, lastly, that Mr. Winkle should be understood as distinctly pledging himself not to resort to the window, fire-place, or other surreptitious mode of escape in the meanwhile. These stipulations having been concluded, Sam locked the door and departed.

He had nearly got down stairs, when he stopped, and drew the key from his pocket.

"I quite forgot about the knockin' down," said Sam, half turning back. "The governor distinctly said it wos to be done; amazin' stupid o' me, that 'ere now. Never mind," said Sam, brightening up, "it's easily done to-morrow, anyvays."

Apparently much consoled by this reflection, Mr. Weller once more deposited the key in his pocket, and, descending the remainder of the stairs without any fresh visitations of conscience, was soon, in common with the other inmates of the house, buried in profound repose.

CHAPTER XXXVIII.

MR. SAMUEL WELLER, BEING ENTRUSTED WITH A MISSION OF LOVE, PROCEEDS TO EXECUTE IT; WITH WHAT SUCCESS WILL HEREINAFTER APPEAR.

DURING the whole of next day, Sam kept Mr. Winkle steadily in sight, fully determined not to take his eyes off him for one instant, until he should receive express instructions from the fountain-head. However disagreeable Sam's very close watch and great vigilance were to Mr. Winkle, he thought it better to bear with them, than, by any act of violent opposition, to hazard being carried away by force, which Mr. Weller more than once strongly hinted was the line of conduct that a strict sense of duty prompted him to pursue. There is little reason to doubt that Sam would very speedily have quieted his scruples, by bearing Mr. Winkle back to Bath, bound hand and foot, had not Mr. Pickwick's prompt attention to the note, which Dowler had undertaken to deliver, forestalled any such proceeding. In short, at eight o'clock in the evening, Mr. Pickwick himself, walked into the coffee-room of the Bush tavern, and told Sam with a smile, to his very great relief, that he had done quite right, and it was unnecessary for him to mount guard any longer.

"I thought it better to come myself," said Mr. Pickwick, addressing Mr. Winkle, as Sam disencumbered him of his great-coat and travelling shawl, "to ascertain, before I gave my consent to Sam's employment in this matter, that you are quite in earnest and serious, with respect to this young lady."

"Serious, from my heart—from my soul!" returned Mr. Winkle, with great energy.

"Remember," said Mr. Pickwick, with beaming eyes, "we met her at our excellent and hospitable friend's, Winkle. It would be an ill return to tamper lightly, and without due consideration, with this young lady's affections. I'll not allow that, Sir—I'll not allow it."

"I have no such intention, indeed," exclaimed Mr. Winkle warmly. "I have considered the matter well, for a long time, and I feel that my happiness is bound up in her."

"That's wot we call tying it up in a small parcel, Sir," interposed Mr. Weller, with an agreeable smile.

Mr. Winkle looked somewhat stern at this interruption, and Mr. Pickwick angrily requested his attendant not to jest with one of the best feelings of our nature; to which Sam replied, "That he wouldn't, if he was aware on it; but there were so many on 'em, that he hardly know'd which was the best ones ven he heerd 'em mentioned."

Mr. Winkle then recounted what had passed between himself and Mr. Ben Allen, relative to Arabella, stated that his object was to gain an interview with the young lady, and make a formal disclosure of his passion; and declared his conviction, founded on certain dark hints and mutterings of the aforesaid Ben, that, wherever she was at present immured, it was somewhere near the Downs: and this was his whole stock of knowledge or suspicion upon the subject.

With this very slight clue to guide him, it was determined that Mr. Weller should start next morning on an expedition of discovery; it was also arranged that Mr. Pickwick and Mr. Winkle, who were less confident of their powers, should parade the town meanwhile, and accidentally drop in upon Mr. Bob Sawyer in the course of the day, in the hope of seeing or hearing something of the young lady's whereabout.

Accordingly, next morning, Sam Weller issued forth upon his quest, in no way daunted by the very discouraging prospect before him; and away he walked, up one street and down another—we were going to say, up one hill and down another, only it's all uphill at Clifton—without meeting with anything or anybody that tended to throw the faintest light upon the matter in hand. Many were the colloquies into which Sam entered with grooms who were airing horses on roads, and nursemaids who were airing children in lanes; but nothing could Sam elicit from either the first-mentioned or the last, which bore the slightest reference to the object of his artfully-prosecuted inquiries. There were a great many young ladies in a great many houses, the greater part whereof were shrewdly suspected by the male and female domestics to be deeply attached to somebody, or perfectly ready to become so, if opportunity offered. But as none among these young ladies was Miss Arabella Allen, the information left Sam at exactly the old point of wisdom at which he had stood before.

Sam struggled across the Downs against a good high wind, wondering whether it was always necessary to hold your hat on with both hands in that part of the country, and came to a shady by-place, about which were sprinkled several little villas of quiet and secluded appearance. Outside a stable-door at the bottom of a long back lane without a thoroughfare, a groom in undress was idling about, apparently persuading himself that he was doing something with a spade and a wheelbarrow. We may remark, in this place, that we have scarcely ever seen a groom near a stable, in his lazy moments, who has not been, to a greater or less extent, the victim of this singular delusion.

Sam thought he might as well talk to this groom as to any one else, especially as he was very tired with walking, and there was a good large stone just opposite the wheelbarrow; so he strolled down the lane, and, seating himself on the stone, opened a conversation with the ease and freedom for which he was remarkable.

"Mornin', old friend," said Sam.

"Arternoon, you mean," replied the groom, casting a surly look at Sam.

"You're wery right, old friend," said Sam; "I do mean arternoon. How are you?"

"Why, I don't find myself much the better for seeing of you," replied the ill-tempered groom.

"That's wery odd—that is," said Sam, "for you look so uncommon cheerful, and seem altogether so lively, that it does vun's heart good to see you."

The surly groom looked surlier still at this, but not sufficiently so to produce any effect upon Sam, who immediately inquired, with a countenance of great anxiety, whether his master's name was not Walker.

"No, it ain't," said the groom.

"Nor Brown, I s'pose?" said Sam.

"No, it ain't."

"Nor Vilson?"

"No; nor that neither," said the groom.

"Vell," replied Sam, "then I'm mistaken, and he hasn't got the honour o' my acquaintance, which I thought he had. Don't vait here out o' compliment to me," said Sam, as the groom wheeled in the barrow, and prepared to shut the gate. "Ease afore ceremony, old boy; I'll excuse you."

"I'd knock your head off for half-a-crown," said the surly groom, bolting one half of the gate.

"Couldn't afford to have it done on those terms," rejoined Sam. "It 'ud be vurth a life's board vages, at least, to you, and 'ud be cheap at that. Make my compliments in-doors. Tell 'em not to vait dinner for me, and say they needn't mind puttin' any by, for it'll be cold afore I come in."

In reply to this, the groom waxing very wroth, muttered a desire to damage somebody's head; but disappeared without carrying it into execution, slamming the door angrily after him, and wholly unheeding Sam's affectionate request, that he would leave him a lock of his hair, before he went.

Sam continued to sit on the large stone, meditating upon what was best to be done, and revolving in his mind a plan for knocking at all the doors within five miles of Bristol, taking them at a hundred and fifty or two hundred a day, and endeavouring to find Miss Arabella by that expedient, when accident all of a sudden threw in his way what he might have sat there for a twelvemonth and yet not found without it.

Into the lane where he sat, there opened three or four garden gates, belonging to as many houses, which though detached from each other, were only separated by their gardens. As these were large and long, and well planted with trees, the houses were not only at some distance off, but the greater part of them were nearly concealed from view. Sam was sitting with his eyes fixed upon the dust-heap outside the next gate to that by which the groom had disappeared, profoundly turning over in his mind the difficulties of his present undertaking, when the gate opened, and a female servant came out into the lane to shake some bed-side carpets.

Sam was so very busy with his own thoughts, that it is probable he would have taken no more notice of the young woman than just raising his head and remarking that she had a very neat and pretty figure, if his feelings of gallantry had not been most strongly roused by observing that she had no one to help her, and that the carpets seemed too heavy for her single strength. Mr. Weller was a gentleman of great gallantry in his own way, and he no sooner remarked this circumstance than he hastily rose from the large stone, and advanced towards her.

"My dear," said Sam, sliding up with an air of great respect, "you'll spile that wery pretty figure out o' all perportion if you shake them carpets by yourself. Let me help you."

The young lady, who had been coyly affecting not to know that a gentleman was so near, turned round as Sam spoke—no doubt (indeed she said so, afterwards) to decline this offer from a perfect stranger—when instead of speaking, she started back, and uttered a half-suppressed scream. Sam was scarcely less staggered, for in the countenance of the well-shaped female servant, he beheld the very features of his Valentine—the pretty housemaid from Mr. Nupkins's.

"Wy, Mary my dear!" said Sam.

"Lauk, Mr. Weller," said Mary, "how you do frighten one!"

Sam made no verbal answer to this complaint, nor can we precisely say what reply he *did* make. We merely know that after a short pause Mary said, "Lor do adun Mr. Weller," and that his hat had fallen off a few moments before—from both of which tokens we should be disposed to infer that one kiss, or more, had passed between the parties.

"Why, how did you come here?" said Mary, when the conversation to which this interruption had been offered, was resumed.

"O' course I came to look arter you, my darlin'," replied Mr. Weller; for once permitting his passion to get the better of his veracity.

"And how did you know I was here?" inquired Mary. "Who could have told you that I took another service at Ipswich, and that they afterwards moved all the way here? Who *could* have told you that, Mr. Weller?"

"Ah to be sure," said Sam with a cunning look, "that's the pint. Who could ha' told me?"

"It wasn't Mr. Muzzle, was it?" inquired Mary.

"Oh no," replied Sam, with a solemn shake of the head, "it warn't him."

"It must have been the cook," said Mary.

"O' course it must," said Sam.

"Well, I never heard the like of that!" exclaimed Mary.

"No more did I," said Sam. "But Mary, my dear—" here Sam's manner grew extremely affectionate—"Mary my dear, I've got another affair in hand as is wery pressin'. There's one o' my governor's friends—Mr. Winkle—you remember him."

"Him in the green coat?" said Mary. "Oh yes, I remember him."

"Well," said Sam, "he's in a horrid state o' love; reg'larly comfoozled, and done over vith it."

"Lor!" interposed Mary.

"Yes," said Sam; "but that's nothin' if we could only find out the young 'ooman"—and here Sam, with many

digressions upon the personal beauty of Mary, and the unspeakable tortures he had experienced since he last saw her, gave a faithful account of Mr. Winkle's present predicament. "Well!" said Mary, "I never did!"

"O' course not," said Sam, "and nobody never did, nor never vill neither; and here am I a walkin' about like the wanderin' Jew—a sportin' character you have perhaps heerd on Mary my dear, as wos always doin' a match agin' time, and never vent to sleep—looking arter this here Miss Arabella Allen."

"Miss who?" said Mary, in great astonishment.

"Miss Arabella Allen," said Sam.

"Goodness gracious!" said Mary, pointing to the garden-door which the sulky groom had locked after him. "Why it's that very house; she's been living there these six weeks. Their upper housemaid, which is lady's maid too, told me all about it over the wash-house palin's before the family was out of bed, one mornin'."

"Wot, the wery next door to you?" said Sam.

"The very next," replied Mary.

Mr. Weller was so deeply overcome at receiving this intelligence that he found it absolutely necessary to cling to his fair informant for support, and divers little love passages had passed between them, before he was sufficiently collected to return to the subject.

"Vell," said Sam at length, "if this don't beat cock-fightin', nothin' never vill, as the Lord Mayor said ven the chief secretary o' state proposed his missis's health arter dinner. That wery next house! Wy, I've got a message to her as I've been a tryin' all day to deliver."

"Ah," said Mary, "but you can't deliver it now, because she only walks in the garden in the evening, and then only for a very little time; she never goes out, without the old lady."

Sam ruminated for a few moments, and finally hit upon the following plan of operations; that he should return just at dusk—the time at which Arabella invariably took her walk—and being admitted by Mary into the garden of the house to which she belonged, contrive to scramble up the wall, beneath the overhanging boughs of a large pear-tree, which would effectually screen him from observation; there deliver his message, and arrange, if possible, an interview on behalf of Mr. Winkle for the ensuing evening at the same hour.

Having made this arrangement with great dispatch, he assisted Mary in the long-deferred occupation of shaking the carpets.

It is not half as innocent a thing as it looks, that shaking little pieces of carpet—at least, there may be no great harm in the shaking, but the folding is a very insidious process. So long as the shaking lasts, and the two parties are kept the carpet's length apart, it is as innocent an amusement as can well be devised, but when the folding begins, and the distance between them gets gradually lessened from one half its former length to a quarter, and then to an eighth, and then to a sixteenth, and then to a thirty-second if the carpet be long enough, it becomes dangerous. We do not know to a nicety how many pieces of carpet were folded in this instance, but we can venture to state that as many pieces as there were, so many times did Sam kiss the pretty housemaid.

Mr. Weller regaled himself with moderation at the nearest tavern until it was nearly dusk, and then returned to the lane without the thoroughfare. Having been admitted into the garden by Mary, and received from that lady sundry admonitions concerning the safety of his limbs and neck, Sam mounted into the pear-tree, to wait until Arabella should come in sight.

He waited so long without this anxiously-expected event occurring, that he began to think it was not going to take place at all, when he heard light footsteps upon the gravel, and immediately afterwards beheld Arabella walking pensively down the garden. As soon as she came nearly below the tree, Sam began, by way of gently indicating his presence, to make sundry diabolical noises similar to those which would probably be natural to a person who had been afflicted with a combination of inflammatory sore throat, croup, and hooping-cough, from his earliest infancy.

Upon this, the young lady cast a hurried glance towards the spot from whence the dreadful sounds proceeded; and her previous alarm being not at all diminished when she saw a man among the branches, she would most certainly have decamped, and alarmed the house, had not fear fortunately deprived her of the power of moving, and caused her to sink down on a garden-seat which happened by good luck to be near at hand.

"She's a goin' off," soliloquised Sam in great perplexity. "Wot a thing it is, as these here young creeturs *will* go a faintin' avay just ven they oughtn't to. Here, young 'ooman, Miss Sawbones, Mrs. Vinkle, don't."

Whether it was the magic of Mr. Winkle's name, or the coolness of the open air, or some recollection of Mr. Weller's voice, that revived Arabella, matters not. She raised her head and languidly inquired "Who's that, and what do you want?"

"Hush," said Sam, swinging himself on to the wall, and crouching there in as small a compass as he could reduce himself to, "only me, miss, only me."

"Mr. Pickwick's servant!" said Arabella, earnestly.

"The wery same, Miss," replied Sam. "Here's Mr. Vinkle reg'larly sewed up vith desperation, Miss."

"Ah!" said Arabella, drawing nearer the wall.

"Ah indeed," said Sam. "Ve thought ve should ha' been obliged to straight-veskit him last night; he's been a ravin' all day, and he says if he can't see you afore to-morrow night's over, he vishes he may be somethin'-unpleasanted if he don't drown hisself."

"Oh no, no, Mr. Weller," said Arabella, clasping her hands.

"That's wot he says, Miss," replied Sam coolly. "He's a man of his word, and it's my opinion he'll do it, Miss. He's heerd all about you from the Sawbones in barnacles."

"From my brother!" said Arabella, having some faint recognition of Sam's description.

"I don't rightly know which is your brother, Miss," replied Sam. "Is it the dirtiest vun o' the two?"

"Yes, yes, Mr. Weller," returned Arabella, "go on. Make haste, pray."

"Vell Miss," said Sam, "he's heerd all about it from him; and it's the gov'nor's opinion that if you don't see him wery quick, the Sawbones as we've been a speakin' on, 'ull get as much extra lead in his head as'll rayther damage the dewelopement o' the orgins if they ever put it in spirits artervards."

"Oh, what can I do to prevent these dreadful quarrels," exclaimed Arabella.

"It's the suspicion of a priory 'tachment as is the cause of it all," replied Sam. "You'd better see him, Miss."

"But how?—where?" cried Arabella. "I dare not leave the house alone. My brother is so unkind, so unreasonable. I know how strange my talking thus to you must appear, Mr. Weller, but I am very, very unhappy—" and here

poor Arabella wept so bitterly, that Sam grew chivalrous.

"It may seem wery strange talkin' to me about these here affairs, Miss," said Sam with great vehemence; "but all I can say is, that I'm not only ready but villin' to do anythin' as'll make matters agreeable; and if chuckin' either o' them Sawbones out o' winder 'ull do it, I'm the man." As Sam Weller said this, he tucked up his wristbands, at the imminent hazard of falling off the wall in so doing, to intimate his readiness to set to work immediately.

Flattering as these professions of good feeling were, Arabella resolutely declined (most unaccountably, as Sam thought) to avail herself of them. For some time she strenuously refused to grant Mr. Winkle the interview Sam had so pathetically requested; but at length, when the conversation threatened to be interrupted by the unwelcome arrival of a third party, she hurriedly gave him to understand, with many professions of gratitude, that it was barely possible she might be in the garden an hour later, next evening. Sam understood this perfectly well, and Arabella, bestowing upon him one of her sweetest smiles, tripped gracefully away, leaving Mr. Weller in a state of very great admiration of her charms, both personal and mental.

Having descended in safety from the wall, and not forgotten to devote a few moments to his own particular business in the same department, Mr. Weller then made the best of his way back to the Bush, where his prolonged absence had occasioned much speculation and some alarm.

"We must be careful," said Mr. Pickwick, after listening attentively to Sam's tale, "not for our own sakes, but for that of the young lady. We must be very cautious."

"*We!*" said Mr. Winkle, with marked emphasis.

Mr. Pickwick's momentary look of indignation at the tone of this remark, subsided into his characteristic expression of benevolence, as he replied—

"*We,* Sir! I shall accompany you."

"You!" said Mr. Winkle.

"I," replied Mr. Pickwick, mildly. "In affordin' you this interview, the young lady has taken a natural, perhaps, but still a very imprudent step. If I am present at the meeting—a mutual friend, who is old enough to be the father of both parties—the voice of calumny can never be raised against her, hereafter."

Mr. Pickwick's eyes lightened with honest exultation at his own foresight, as he spoke thus. Mr. Winkle was touched at this little trait of his delicate respect for the young *protégée* of his friend, and took his hand with a feeling of regard akin to veneration.

"You *shall* go," said Mr. Winkle.

"I will," said Mr. Pickwick. "Sam, have my greatcoat and shawl ready, and order a conveyance to be at the door to-morrow evening, rather earlier than is absolutely necessary, in order that we may be in good time."

Mr. Weller touched his hat, as an earnest of his obedience, and withdrew to make all needful preparations for the expedition.

The coach was punctual to the time appointed; and Mr. Weller, after duly installing Mr. Pickwick and Mr. Winkle inside, took his seat on the box by the driver. They alighted, as had been agreed on, about a quarter of a mile from the place of rendezvous, and desiring the coachman to await their return, proceeded the remaining distance on foot.

It was at this stage of the undertaking that Mr. Pickwick, with many smiles and various other indications of great self-satisfaction, produced from one of his coat pockets a dark lantern, with which he had specially provided himself for the occasion, and the great mechanical beauty of which, he proceeded to explain to Mr. Winkle, as they walked along, to the no small surprise of the few stragglers they met.

"I should have been the better for something of this kind, in my last garden expedition, at night; eh, Sam?" said Mr. Pickwick, looking good-humouredly round at his follower, who was trudging behind.

"Wery nice things, if they're managed properly, Sir," replied Mr. Weller; "but when you don't want to be seen, I think they're rayther more useful arter the candle's gone out, than ven it's alight."

Mr. Pickwick appeared struck by Sam's remarks, for he put the lantern into his pocket again, and they walked on in silence.

"Down here, Sir," said Sam. "Let me lead the vay. This is the lane, Sir."

Down the lane they.went, and dark enough it was. Mr. Pickwick brought out the lantern once or twice as they groped their way along, and threw a very brilliant little tunnel of light before them, about a foot in diameter. It was very pretty to look at, but seemed to have the effect of rendering surrounding objects rather darker than before.

At length they arrived at the large stone, and here Sam recommended his master and Mr. Pickwick to seat themselves, while he reconnoitred, and ascertained whether Mary was yet in waiting.

After an absence of five or ten minutes, Sam returned, to say that the gate was opened, and all quiet. Following him with stealthy tread, Mr. Pickwick and Mr. Winkle soon found themselves in the garden. Here everybody said "Hush!" a good many times; and that being done, no one seemed to have any very distinct apprehension of what was to be done next.

"Is Miss Allen in the garden yet, Mary?" inquired Mr. Winkle, much agitated.

"I don't know, Sir," replied the pretty housemaid. "The best thing to be done, Sir, will be for Mr. Weller to give you a hoist up into the tree, and perhaps Mr. Pickwick will have the goodness to see that nobody comes up the lane, while I watch at the other end of the garden. Goodness gracious, what's that!"

"That 'ere blessed lantern 'ull be the death on us all," exclaimed Sam, peevishly. "Take care wot you're a doin' on, Sir, you're a sendin' a blaze o' light, right into the back parlour vinder."

"Dear me!" said Mr. Pickwick, turning hastily aside, "I didn't mean to do that."

"Now it's in the next house, Sir," remonstrated Sam.

"Bless my heart!" exclaimed Mr. Pickwick, turning round again.

"Now it's in the stable, and they'll think the place is a' fire," said Sam. "Shut it up, Sir, can't you?"

"It's the most extraordinary lantern I ever met with, in all my life!" exclaimed Mr. Pickwick, greatly bewildered by the effects he had so unintentionally produced. "I never saw such a powerful reflector."

"It'll be vun too powerful for us, if you keep blazin' a vay in that manner, Sir," replied Sam, as Mr. Pickwick, after various unsuccessful efforts, managed to close the slide. "There's the young lady's footsteps. Now, Mr. Vinkle, Sir, up vith you."

"Stop, stop!" said Mr. Pickwick, "I must speak to her first. Help me up, Sam."

"Gently, Sir," said Sam, planting his head against the wall, and making a platform of his back. "Step a top o' that 'ere flower-pot, Sir. Now then, up vith you."

"I'm afraid I shall hurt you, Sam," said Mr. Pickwick.

"Never mind me, Sir," replied Sam. "Lend him a hand, Mr. Vinkle, Sir. Steady, Sir, steady; that's the time o' day."

As Sam spoke, Mr. Pickwick, by exertions almost supernatural in a gentleman of his years and weight, contrived to get upon Sam's back; and Sam gently raising himself up, and Mr. Pickwick holding on fast by the top of the wall, while Mr. Winkle clasped him tight by the legs, they contrived by these means to bring his spectacles just above the level of the coping.

"My dear," said Mr. Pickwick, looking over the wall, and catching sight of Arabella, on the other side, "Don't be frightened, my dear, 'tis only me."

"Oh pray go away, Mr. Pickwick," said Arabella. "Tell them all to go away, I am so dreadfully frightened. Dear, dear Mr. Pickwick, don't stop there. You'll fall down and kill yourself, I know you will."

"Now pray don't alarm yourself, my dear," said Mr. Pickwick, soothingly. "There is not the least cause for fear, I assure you. Stand firm, Sam," said Mr. Pickwick, looking down.

"All right, Sir," replied Mr. Weller. "Don't be longer than you can conweniently help, Sir. You're rayther heavy."

"Only another moment, Sam," replied Mr. Pickwick. "I merely wished you to know, my dear, that I should not have allowed my young friend to see you in this clandestine way, if the situation in which you are placed had left him any alternative; and lest the impropriety of this step should cause you any uneasiness, my love, it may be a satisfaction to you, to know that I am present: that's all, my dear."

"Indeed, Mr. Pickwick, I am very much obliged to you for your kindness and consideration," replied Arabella, drying her tears with her handkerchief. She would probably have said much more, had not Mr. Pickwick's head disappeared with great swiftness, in consequence of a false step on Sam's shoulder, which brought him suddenly to the ground. He was up again in an instant, however; and bidding Mr. Winkle make haste and get the interview over, ran out into the lane to keep watch, with all the courage and ardour of a youth. Mr. Winkle himself, inspired by the occasion, was on the wall in a moment, merely pausing to request Sam to be careful of his master.

"I'll take care on him, Sir," replied Sam. "Leave him to me."

"Where is he? What's he doing, Sam?" inquired Mr. Winkle.

"Bless his old gaiters," rejoined Sam, looking out at the garden-door. "He's a keepin' guard in the lane vith that 'ere dark lantern like a amiable Guy Fawkes. I never see such a fine creetur in my days. Blessed if I don't think his heart must ha' been born five-and-twenty year arter his body, at least!"

Mr. Winkle stayed not to hear the encomium upon his friend. He had dropped from the wall; thrown himself at Arabella's feet; and by this time was pleading the sincerity of his passion with an eloquence worthy even of Mr. Pickwick himself.

While these things were going on in the open air, an elderly gentleman of scientific attainments was seated in his library, two or three houses off, writing a philosophical

"MY DEAR," SAID MR. PICKWICK, LOOKING OVER THE WALL AND CATCHING SIGHT OF ARABELLA ON THE OTHER SIDE, "DON'T BE FRIGHTENED MY DEAR; 'TIS ONLY ME."

treatise, and ever and anon moistening his clay and his labours with a glass of claret from a venerable-looking bottle which stood by his side. In the agonies of composition, the elderly gentleman looked sometimes at the carpet, sometimes at the ceiling, and sometimes at the wall; and when neither carpet, ceiling, nor wall, afforded the requisite degree of inspiration, he looked out of the window.

In one of these pauses of invention, the scientific gentleman was gazing abstractedly on the thick darkness outside, when he was very much surprised by observing a most brilliant light glide through the air a short distance above the ground, and almost instantaneously vanish. After a short time the phenomenon was repeated, not once or twice, but several times: at last the scientific gentleman, laying down his pen, began to consider to what natural causes these appearances were to be assigned.

They were not meteors; they were too low. They were not glow-worms; they were too high. They were not will-o'-the wisps; they were not fire-flies; they were not fire-works. What could they be? Some extraordinary and wonderful phenomenon of nature, which no philosopher had ever seen before; something which it had been reserved for him alone to discover, and which he should immortalise his name by chronicling for the benefit of posterity. Full of this idea, the scientific gentleman seized his pen again, and committed to paper sundry notes of these unparalleled appearances, with the date, day, hour, minute, and precise second at which they were visible, all of which were to form the data of a voluminous treatise of great research and deep learning, which should astonish all the atmospherical wiseacres that ever drew breath in any part of the civilised globe.

He threw himself back in his easy chair, wrapped in contemplations of his future greatness. The mysterious light appeared more brilliantly than before; dancing to all appearance up and down the lane, crossing from side to side, and moving in an orbit as eccentric as comets themselves.

The scientific gentleman was a bachelor. He had no wife to call in and astonish, so he rang the bell for his servant.

"Pruffle," said the scientific gentleman, "there is something very extraordinary in the air to-night. Did you see that?" said the scientific gentleman, pointing out of the window, as the light again became visible.

"Yes I did, Sir."

"What do you think of it, Pruffle?"

"Think of it, Sir?"

"Yes. You have been bred up in the country. What should you say was the cause of those lights, now?"

The scientific gentleman smilingly anticipated Pruffle's reply that he could assign no cause for them at all. Pruffle meditated.

"I should say it was thieves, Sir," said Pruffle at length.

"You're a fool, and may go down stairs"—said the scientific gentleman.

"Thank you Sir"—said Pruffle. And down he went.

But the scientific gentleman could not rest under the idea of the ingenious treatise he had projected, being lost to the world, which must inevitably be the case, if the specula-

tion of the ingenious Mr. Pruffle were not stifled in its birth. He put on his hat and walked quickly down the garden, determined to investigate the matter to the very bottom.

Now, shortly before the scientific gentleman walked out into the garden, Mr. Pickwick had run down the lane as fast as he could, to convey a false alarm that somebody was coming that way, occasionally drawing back the slide of the dark lantern to keep himself from the ditch. The alarm was no sooner given, than Mr. Winkle scrambled back over the wall, and Arabella ran into the house;—the garden-gate was shut, and the three adventurers were making the best of their way down the lane, when they were startled by the scientific gentleman unlocking his garden gate.

"Hold hard," whispered Sam, who was of course the first of the party. "Show a light for just vun second, Sir."

Mr. Pickwick did as he was desired, and Sam seeing a man's head peeping out very cautiously, within half a yard of his own, gave it a gentle tap with his clenched fist, which knocked it with a hollow sound against the gate. Having performed this feat with great suddenness and dexterity, Mr. Weller caught Mr. Pickwick up on his back, and followed Mr. Winkle down the lane at a pace which, considering the burden he carried, was perfectly astonishing.

"Have you got your vind back agin, Sir?" enquired Sam when they had reached the end.

"Quite—quite now," replied Mr. Pickwick.

"Then come along, Sir," said Sam, setting his master on his feet again. "Come betveen us, Sir. Not half a mile to run. Think you're vinnin' a cup, Sir. Now for it."

Thus encouraged, Mr. Pickwick made the very best use of his legs, and it may be confidently stated that a pair of black gaiters never got over the ground in better style than did those of Mr. Pickwick on this memorable occasion.

The coach was waiting, the horses were fresh, the roads were good, and the driver was willing. The whole party arrived in safety at the Bush before Mr. Pickwick had recovered his breath.

"In vith you at once Sir," said Sam, as he helped his master out. "Don't stop a second in the street, arter that 'ere exercise. Beg your pardon, Sir," continued Sam, touching his hat as Mr. Winkle descended, "Hope there warn't a priory 'tachment, Sir."

Mr. Winkle grasped his humble friend by the hand, and whispered in his ear, "It's all right, Sam; quite right"—upon which Mr. Weller struck three distinct blows upon his nose in token of intelligence; smiled, winked, and proceeded to put the steps up with a countenance expressive of lively satisfaction.

As to the scientific gentleman, he demonstrated in a masterly treatise that these wonderful lights were the effect of electricity, and clearly proved the same by detailing how a flash of fire danced before his eyes when he put his head out of the gate, and how he received a shock which stunned him for a full quarter of an hour afterwards; which demonstration delighted all the Scientific Associations beyond measure, and caused him to be considered a light of science ever afterwards.

CHAPTER XXXIX.

INTRODUCES MR. PICKWICK TO A NEW, AND IT IS HOPED NOT UNINTERESTING SCENE, IN THE GREAT DRAMA OF LIFE.

THE remainder of the period which Mr. Pickwick had assigned as the duration of the stay at Bath, passed over without the occurrence of anything material. Trinity Term commenced. On the expiration of its first week, Mr. Pickwick and his friends returned to London, and the former gentleman, attended of course by Sam, straightway repaired to his old quarters at the George and Vulture.

On the third morning after their arrival, just as all the clocks in the city were striking nine individually, and somewhere about nine hundred collectively, Sam was taking the air in George Yard, when a queer sort of fresh painted vehicle drove up, out of which there jumped with great agility, throwing the reins to a stout man who sat beside him, a queer sort of gentleman, who seemed made for the vehicle, and the vehicle for him.

The vehicle was not exactly a gig, neither was it a stanhope. It was not what is currently denominated a dog-cart, neither was it a taxed cart, nor a chaise-cart, nor a guillotined cabriolet; and yet it had something of the character of each and every of these machines. It was painted a bright yellow, with the shafts and wheels picked out in black; and the driver sat in the orthodox sporting style, on cushions piled about two feet above the rail. The horse was a bay, a well-looking animal enough; but with something of a flash and dog-fighting air about him. nevertheless, which accorded admirably, both with the vehicle and his master.

The master himself was a man of about forty, with black hair, and carefully combed whiskers; dressed in a particularly gorgeous manner, with plenty of articles of jewellery about him—all about three sizes larger than those which are usually worn by gentlemen—and a rough great-coat to crown the whole. Into one pocket of this great-coat, he thrust his left hand the moment he dismounted, while from the other he drew forth, with his right, a very bright and glaring silk handkerchief, with which he whisked a speck or two of dust from his boots, and then crumpling it in his hand, swaggered up the court.

It had not escaped Sam's attention that, when this person dismounted, a shabby-looking man in a brown great-coat shorn of divers buttons, who had been previously slinking about on the opposite side of the way, crossed over, and remained stationary close by. Having something more than a suspicion of the object of the gentleman's visit, Sam preceded him to the George and Vulture, and, turning sharp round, planted himself in the centre of the doorway.

"Now, my fine fellow," said the man in the rough coat, in an imperious tone, attempting at the same time to push his way past.

"Now, Sir, wot's the matter?" replied Sam, returning the push with compound interest.

"Come, none of this, my man; this won't do with me," said the owner of the rough coat, raising his voice, and turning very white—"Here, Smouch!"

"Well, wot's amiss here?" growled the man in the brown coat, who had been gradually sneaking up the court during this short dialogue.

"Only some insolence of this young man's," said the principal, giving Sam another push.

"Come, none o' this gammon," growled Smouch, giving him another, and a harder one.

This last push had the effect which it was intended by the experienced Mr. Smouch to produce, for while Sam, anxious to return the compliment, was grinding that gentleman's body against the doorpost, the principal crept past, and made his way to the bar, whither Sam, after bandying a few epithetical remarks with Mr. Smouch, followed at once.

"Good morning, my dear," said the principal, addressing the young lady in the bar, with Botany Bay ease, and New South Wales gentility; "which is Mr. Pickwick's room, my dear?"

"Show him up," said the bar-maid to a waiter, without deigning another look at the exquisite, in reply to his inquiry.

The waiter led the way up stairs as he was desired, and the man in the rough coat followed, with Sam behind him, who, in his progress up the staircase, indulged in sundry gestures indicative of supreme contempt and defiance, to the unspeakable gratification of the servants and other lookers on. Mr. Smouch, who was troubled with a hoarse cough, remained below, and expectorated in the passage.

Mr. Pickwick was fast asleep in bed, when his early visitor, followed by Sam, entered the room. The noise they made, in so doing, awoke him.

"Shaving water, Sam," said Mr. Pickwick, from within the curtains.

"Shave you directly, Mr. Pickwick," said the visitor, drawing one of them back from the bed's head. "I've got an execution against you, at the suit of Bardell.—Here's the warrant.—Common Pleas.—Here's my card. I suppose you'll come over to my house." And giving Mr. Pickwick a friendly tap on the shoulder, the sheriff's officer —for such he was—threw his card on the counterpane, and pulled a gold toothpick from his waistcoat pocket.

"Namby's the name," said the sheriff's deputy, as Mr. Pickwick took his spectacles from under the pillow, and put them on, to read the card. "Namby, Bell Alley, Coleman Street."

At this point, Sam Weller, who had had his eyes fixed hitherto on Mr. Namby's shining beaver, interfered—

"Are you a Quaker?" said Sam.

"I'll let you know who I am, before I've done with you," replied the indignant officer. "I'll teach you manners, my fine fellow, one of these fine mornings."

"Thankee," said Sam. "I'll do the same for you. Take your hat off." With this, Mr. Weller, in the most dexterous manner, knocked Mr. Namby's hat to the other side of the room with such violence, that he had very nearly caused him to swallow the gold toothpick into the bargain.

"Observe this, Mr. Pickwick," said the disconcerted officer, gasping for breath. "I've been assaulted in the execution of my dooty by your servant in your chamber. I'm in bodily fear. I call you to witness this."

"Don't witness nothin', Sir," interposed Sam. "Shut your eyes up tight, Sir. I'd pitch him out o' winder, only he couldn't fall far enough, 'cause o' the leads outside."

"Sam," said Mr. Pickwick in an angry voice, as his attendant made various demonstrations of hostilities, "if you say another word, or offer the slightest interference with this person, I discharge you that instant."

"But, Sir!" said Sam.

"Hold your tongue," interposed Mr. Pickwick "Take that hat up again."

But this, Sam flatly and positively refused to do; and, after he had been severely reprimanded by his master, the officer, being in a hurry, condescended to pick it up himself, venting a great variety of threats against Sam meanwhile, which that gentleman received with perfect composure, merely observing that if Mr. Namby would have the goodness to put his hat on again, he would knock it into the latter end of next week. Mr. Namby, perhaps thinking that such a process might be productive of inconvenience to himself, declined to offer the temptation, and soon after called up Smouch. Having informed him that the capture was made, and that he was to wait for the prisoner until he should have finished dressing, Namby then swaggered out, and drove away. Smouch requesting Mr. Pickwick, in a surly manner, "to be as alive as he could, for it was a busy time," drew up a chair by the door, and sat there till he had finished dressing. Sam was then dispatched for a hackney coach, and in it the triumvirate proceeded to Coleman Street. It was fortunate the distance was short, for Mr. Smouch, besides possessing no very enchanting conversational powers, was rendered a decidedly unpleasant companion in a limited space, by the physical weakness to which we have elsewhere adverted.

The coach having turned into a very narrow and dark street, stopped before a house with iron bars to all the windows; the door-posts of which, were graced by the name and title of "Namby, Officer to the Sheriffs of London;" the inner gate having been opened by a gentleman who might have passed for a neglected twin brother of Mr. Smouch, and who was endowed with a large key for the purpose, Mr. Pickwick was shown into the "coffee-room."

This coffee-room was a front parlour, the principal features of which, were fresh sand and stale tobacco smoke. Mr. Pickwick bowed to the three persons who were seated in it when he entered, and having dispatched Sam for Perker, withdrew into an obscure corner, and from thence looked with some curiosity upon his new companions.

One of these was a mere boy of nineteen or twenty, who, though it was yet barely ten o'clock, was drinking gin and water, and smoking a cigar, amusements to which, judging from his inflamed countenance, he had devoted himself pretty constantly for the last year or two of his life. Opposite him, engaged in stirring the fire with the toe of his right boot, was a coarse, vulgar young man of about thirty, with a sallow face and harsh voice; evidently possessed of that knowledge of the world, and captivating freedom of manner, which is to be acquired in public-house parlours, and at low billiard tables. The third tenant of the apartment was a middle aged man in a very old suit of black, who looked pale and haggard, and paced up and down the room incessantly: stopping now and then to look with great anxiety out of the window as if he expected somebody, and then resuming his walk.

"You'd better have the loan of my razor this morning, Mr. Ayresleigh," said the man who was stirring the fire, tipping the wink to his friend the boy.

"Thank you, no, I shan't want it; I expect I shall be out, in the course of an hour or so," replied the other in a hurried manner. Then walking again up to the window, and once more returning disappointed, he sighed deeply, and left the room; upon which the other two burst into a loud laugh.

"Well, I never saw such a game as that," said the gentleman who had offered the razor, whose name appeared to be Price. "Never!" Mr. Price confirmed the assertion with an oath, and then laughed again, when of course the boy (who thought his companion one of the most dashing fellows alive), laughed also.

"You'd hardly think, would you now," said Price, turning towards Mr. Pickwick, "that that chap's been here a week yesterday, and never once shaved himself yet, because he feels so certain he's going out in half an hour's time, that he thinks he may as well put it off till he gets home?"

"Poor man!" said Mr. Pickwick. "Are his chances of getting out of his difficulties really so great?"

"Chances be d—d," replied Price; "he hasn't half the ghost of one. I wouldn't give *that* for his chance of walking about the streets this time ten years." With this, Mr. Price snapped his fingers contemptuously, and rang the bell.

"Give me a sheet of paper, Crookey," said Mr. Price to the attendant, who in dress and general appearance looked something between a bankrupt grazier, and a drover in a state of insolvency; "and a glass of brandy and water, Crookey, d'ye hear? I'm going to write to my father, and I must have a stimulant, or I shan't be able to pitch it strong enough into the old boy." At this facetious speech, the young boy, it is almost needless to say, was fairly convulsed.

"That's right," said Mr Price. "Never say die. All fun, ain't it?"

"Prime!" said the young gentleman.

"You've some spirit about you, you have," said Price. "You've seen something of life."

"I rather think I have!" replied the boy. He had looked at it through the dirty panes of glass in a bar door.

Mr. Pickwick feeling not a little disgusted with this dialogue, as well as with the air and manner of the two beings by whom it had been carried on, was about to inquire whether he could not be accommodated with a private sitting-room, when two or three strangers of genteel appearance entered, at sight of whom the boy threw his cigar into the fire, and whispering to Mr. Price, that they had come to "make it all right" for him, joined them at a table in the further end of the room.

It would appear, however, that matters were not going to be made all right quite so speedily as the young gentleman anticipated, for a very long conversation ensued, of which Mr. Pickwick could not avoid hearing certain angry fragments regarding dissolute conduct, and repeated forgiveness. At last there were very distinct allusions made by the oldest gentleman of the party to one Whitecross-street, at which the young gentleman, notwithstanding his primeness and his spirit, and his knowledge of life into the bargain, reclined his head upon the table and howled dismally.

Very much satisfied with this sudden bringing down of the youth's valour, and effectual lowering of his tone, Mr. Pickwick rang the bell, and was shown at his own request into a private room furnished with a carpet, table, chairs, sideboard and sofa, and ornamented with a looking-glass, and various old prints. Here he had the advantage of hearing Mrs. Namby's performance on a square piano over head, while the breakfast was getting ready; and when it came, Mr. Perker arrived also.

"Aha, my dear Sir," said the little man, "nailed at last, eh? Come, come, I'm not sorry for it either, because now you'll see the absurdity of this conduct. I've noted down the amount of the taxed costs and damages for which the casa was issued, and we had better settle at once and lose no time. Namby is come home by this time, I dare say.

What say you, my dear Sir, shall I draw a cheque, or will you?" The little man rubbed his hands with affected cheerfulness as he said this, but glancing at Mr. Pickwick's countenance, could not forbear at the same time casting a desponding look towards Sam Weller.

"Perker," said Mr. Pickwick, "let me hear no more of this, I beg. I see no advantage in staying here, so I shall go to prison to-night."

"You can't go to Whitecross-street, my dear Sir," said Perker. "Impossible! There are sixty beds in a ward, and the bolt's on, sixteen hours out of the four-and-twenty."

"I would rather go to some other place of confinement if I can," said Mr. Pickwick. "If not I must make the best I can of that."

"You can go to the Fleet, my dear Sir, if you're determined to go somewhere," said Perker.

"That'll do," said Mr. Pickwick. "I'll go there directly I have finished my breakfast."

"Stop, stop, my dear Sir; not the least occasion for being in such a violent hurry to get into a place that most other men are as eager to get out of," said the good-natured little attorney. "We must have a habeas corpus. There'll be no judge at chambers till four o'clock this afternoon. You must wait till then."

"Very good," said Mr. Pickwick, with unmoved patience. "Then we will have a chop here, at two. See about it Sam, and tell them to be punctual"

Mr. Pickwick remaining firm, despite all the remonstrances and arguments of Perker, the chops appeared and disappeared in due course; he was then put into another hackney coach, and carried off to Chancery Lane; after waiting half an hour or so for Mr. Namby, who had a select dinner party, and could on no account be disturbed before.

There were two judges in attendance at Serjeant's Inn—one King's Bench, and one Common Pleas, and a great deal of business appeared to be transacting before them, if the number of lawyer's clerks who were hurrying in and out with bundles of papers, afforded any test. When they reached the low archway which forms the entrance to the Inn, Perker was detained a few moments parleying with the coachman about the fare and the change; and Mr. Pickwick, stepping to one side to be out of the way of the stream of people that were pouring in and out, looked about him with some curiosity.

The people that attracted his attention most, were three or four men of shabby-genteel appearance, who touched their hats to many of the attorneys who passed, and seemed to have some business there, the nature of which Mr. Pickwick could not divine. They were curious looking fellows. One was a slim and rather lame man in rusty black, and a white neckerchief; another was a stout, burly person, dressed in the same apparel, with a great reddish-black cloth round his neck; a third was a little weazen drunken-looking body with a pimply face. They were loitering about, with their hands behind them, and now and then, with an anxious countenance, whispered something in the ear of some of the gentlemen with papers as they hurried by. Mr. Pickwick remembered to have very often observed them lounging under the archway when he had been walking past, and his curiosity was quite excited to know to what branch of the profession these dingy-looking loungers could possibly belong.

He was about to propound the question to Namby, who kept close beside him sucking a large gold ring on his little finger, when Perker bustled up, and observing that there was no time to lose, led the way into the Inn As Mr. Pickwick followed, the lame man stepped up to him, and civilly touching his hat, held out a written card, which Mr. Pickwick not wishing to hurt the man's feelings by refusing, courteously accepted and deposited in his waistcoat pocket.

"Now," said Perker, turning round before he entered one of the offices, to see that his companions were close behind him. "In here, my dear Sir. Hallo, what do *you* want?"

This last question was addressed to the lame man, who unobserved by Mr. Pickwick, made one of the party. In reply to it, the lame man touched his hat again with all imaginable politeness, and motioned towards Mr. Pickwick.

"No, no," said Perker with a smile. "We don't want you, my dear friend, we don't want you."

"I beg your pardon, Sir," said the lame man. "The gentleman took my card. I hope you will employ me, Sir. The gentleman nodded to me. I'll be judged by the gentleman himself. You nodded to me, Sir?"

"Pooh, pooh, nonsense. You didn't nod to any body, Pickwick? A mistake, a mistake," said Perker.

"The gentleman handed me his card," replied Mr. Pickwick, producing it from his waistcoat pocket. "I accepted it as the gentleman seemed to wish it—in fact I had some curiosity to look at it when I should be at leisure. I——"

The little attorney burst into a loud laugh, and returning the card to the lame man, informing him it was all a mistake, whispered to Mr. Pickwick as the man turned away in dudgeon, that he was only a bail.

"A what!" exclaimed Mr. Pickwick.

"A bail," replied Perker.

"A bail!"

"Yes, my dear Sir, half a dozen of 'em here. Bail you to any amount, and only charge half-a-crown. Curious trade isn't it?" said Perker, regaling himself with a pinch of snuff.

"What! Am I to understand that these men earn a livelihood by waiting about here, to perjure themselves before the judges of the land, at the rate of half-a-crown a crime!" exclaimed Mr. Pickwick, quite aghast at the disclosure.

"Why, I don't exactly know about the perjury, my dear Sir," replied the little gentleman. "Harsh word, my dear Sir, very harsh word indeed. It's a legal fiction, my dear Sir, nothing more." Saying which, the attorney shrugged his shoulders, smiled, took a second pinch of snuff, and led the way into the office of the judge's clerk.

This was a room of specially dirty appearance, with a very low ceiling and old panneled walls; and so badly lighted, that although it was broad day outside, great tallow candles were burning on the desks. At one end, was a door leading to the judge's private apartment, round which were congregated a crowd of attorneys and managing clerks, who were called in, in the order in which their respective appointments stood upon the file. Every time this door was opened to let a party out, the next party made a violent rush to get in; and as in addition to the numerous dialogues which passed between the gentlemen who were waiting to see the judge, a variety of rather personal squabbles ensued between the greater part of those who had seen him, there was as much noise as could well be raised in an apartment of such confined dimensions.

Nor were the conversations of these gentlemen the only

sounds that broke upon the ear. Standing on a box behind a wooden bar at another end of the room was a clerk in spectacles, who was "taking the affidavits," large batches of which were from time to time carried into the private room by another clerk for the judge's signature. There were a large number of attorneys' clerks to be sworn, and it being a moral impossibility to swear them all at once, the struggles of these gentlemen to reach the clerk in spectacles, were like those of a crowd to get in at the pit door of a theatre when His Most Gracious Majesty honours it with his presence. Another functionary, from time to time exercised his lungs in calling over the names of those who had been sworn, for the purpose of restoring to them their affidavits after they had been signed by the judge, which gave rise to a few more scuffles; and all these things going on at the same time, occasioned as much bustle as the most active and excitable person could desire to behold. There were yet another class of persons—those who were waiting to attend summonses their employers had taken out, which it was optional to the attorney on the opposite side to attend or not, and whose business it was from time to time to cry out the opposite attorney's name, to make certain that he was not in attendance without their knowledge.

For example. Leaning against the wall, close beside the seat Mr. Pickwick had taken, was an office lad of fourteen, with a tenor voice, and near him a common-law clerk with a bass one. A clerk hurried in with a bundle of papers, and stared about him. "Sniggle and Blink," cried the tenor.

"Porkin and Snob," growled the bass.

"Stumpy and Deacon," said the new comer.

Nobody answered; and the next man who came in, was hailed by the whole three, and in his turn shouted for another firm, and then somebody else roared in a loud voice for another, and so forth.

All this time, the man in the spectacles was hard at work swearing the clerks; the oath being invariably administered without any effort at punctuation, and usually in the following terms:—

"Take the book in your right hand this in your name and handwriting you swear that the contents of this your affidavit are true so help you God a shilling you must get change I haven't got it."

"Well, Sam," said Mr. Pickwick. "I suppose they are getting the *habeas corpus* ready."

"Yes," said Sam, "and I vish they'd bring out the have-his-carcase. It's wery unpleasant keepin' us vaitin' here. I'd ha' got half a dozen have-his-carcases ready, pack'd up and all, by this time."

What sort of cumbrous and unmanageable machine, Sam Weller imagined a writ of habeas corpus to be does not appear, for Perker at that moment walked up, and took Mr. Pickwick away.

The usual forms having been gone through, the body of Samuel Pickwick was soon afterwards confided to the custody of the tipstaff, to be by him taken to the Warden of the Fleet Prison, and there detained until the amount of the damages and costs in the action of Bardell against Pickwick was fully paid and satisfied.

"And that," said Mr. Pickwick laughing, "will be a very long time. Sam, call another hackney coach. Perker, my dear friend, good bye."

"I shall go with you, and see you safe there," said Perker.

"Indeed," replied Mr. Pickwick, "I would rather go without any other attendant than Sam. As soon as I get settled, I will write and let you know, and I shall expect you immediately. Until then, good bye."

As Mr. Pickwick said this, he got into the coach which had by this time arrived, followed by the tipstaff. Sam having stationed himself on the box, it rolled away.

"A most extraordinary man that," said Perker, as he stopped to pull on his gloves.

"What a bankrupt he'd make, Sir," observed Mr. Lowten who was standing near. "How he would bother the commissioners! He'd set 'em at defiance if they talked of committing him, Sir."

The attorney did not appear very much delighted with his clerk's professional estimate of Mr. Pickwick's character, for he walked away without deigning any reply.

The hackney coach jolted along Fleet Street, as hackney coaches usually do. The horses "went better," the driver said, when they had got anything before them, (they must have gone at a most extraordinary pace when there was nothing,) and so the vehicle kept behind a cart; when the cart stopped, it stopped, and when the cart went on again, it did the same. Mr. Pickwick sat opposite the tipstaff, and the tipstaff sat with his hat between his knees, whistling a tune, and looking out of the coach-window.

Time performs wonders, and, by the powerful old gentleman's aid, even a hackney coach gets over half a mile of ground. They stopped at length, and Mr. Pickwick alighted at the gate of the Fleet.

The tipstaff, just looking over his shoulder to see that his charge was following close at his heels, preceded Mr. Pickwick into the prison; turning to the left, after they had entered, they passed through an open door into a lobby, from which a heavy gate opposite to that by which they had entered, and which was guarded by a stout turnkey with the key in his hand, led at once into the interior of the prison.

Here they stopped, while the tipstaff delivered his papers; and here Mr. Pickwick was apprised that he would remain until he had undergone the ceremony, known to the initiated, as "sitting for your portrait."

"Sitting for my portrait!" said Mr. Pickwick.

"Having your likeness taken, Sir," replied the stout turnkey. "We're capital hands at likenesses here. Take 'em in no time, and always exact. Walk in, Sir, and make yourself at home."

Mr. Pickwick complied with the invitation, and sat himself down, when Mr. Weller, who stationed himself at the back of the chair, whispered that the sitting was merely another term for undergoing an inspection by the different turnkeys, in order that they might know prisoners from visitors.

"Well, Sam," said Mr. Pickwick, "then I wish the artists would come. This is rather a public place."

"They vont be long, Sir, I des-say," replied Sam. "There's a Dutch clock, Sir."

"So I see," observed Mr. Pickwick.

"And a bird-cage, Sir," says Sam. "Veels vithin veels, a prison in a prison. Ain't it, Sir."

As Mr. Weller made this philosophical remark, Mr. Pickwick was aware that his sitting had commenced. The stout turnkey having been relieved from the lock, sat down, and looked at him carelessly from time to time, while a long thin man who had relieved him thrust his hands beneath his coat tails, and planting himself opposite, took a good long view of him. A third rather surly-looking gentleman, who had apparently been disturbed at his tea, for he was disposing of the last remnant of a crust and butter when he came in, stationed himself close to Mr. Pickwick; and, resting his hands on his hips, inspected him narrowly, while two others mixed with the group, and studied his features with most intent and thoughtful faces. Mr. Pickwick winced a good deal under the operation, and appeared to sit very uneasily in his chair: but he made no remark to anybody while it was being performed—not even to Sam, who reclined upon the back of the chair, reflecting, partly on the situation of his master, and partly on the great satisfaction it would have afforded him to make a fierce assault upon all the turnkeys there assembled, one after the other, if it were lawful and peaceable so to do.

At length the likeness was completed, and Mr. Pickwick was informed, that he might now proceed into the prison.

"Where am I to sleep to-night?" inquired Mr. Pickwick.

"Why I don't rightly know about to-night," replied the stout turnkey. "You'll be chummed on somebody to-morrow, and then you'll be all snug and comfortable. The first night's generally rather unsettled, but you'll be set all squares to-morrow."

After some discussion, it was discovered that one of the turnkeys had a bed to let, which Mr. Pickwick could have for that night, and he gladly agreed to hire it.

"If you'll come with me, I'll show it you, at once," said the man. "It ain't a large 'un; but it's an out and outer to sleep in. This way, Sir."

They passed through the inner gate, and descended a short flight of steps. The key was turned after them, and Mr. Pickwick found himself, for the first time in his life, within the walls of a debtor's prison.

CHAPTER XL.

WHAT BEFEL MR. PICKWICK WHEN HE GOT INTO THE FLEET; WHAT DEBTORS HE SAW THERE; AND HOW HE PASSED THE NIGHT.

MR. TOM ROKER, the gentleman who had accompanied Mr. Pickwick into the prison, turned sharp round to the right when he got to the bottom of the little flight of steps, and led the way through an iron gate which stood open, and up another short flight of steps, into a long narrow gallery, dirty and low, paved with stone, and very dimly lighted by a window at each remote end.

"This," said the gentleman, thrusting his hands into his pockets, and looking carelessly over his shoulder to Mr. Pickwick, "This here is the hall flight."

"Oh," replied Mr. Pickwick, looking down a dark and filthy staircase, which appeared to lead to a range of damp and gloomy stone vaults beneath the ground, "and those, I suppose, are the little cellars where the prisoners keep their small quantities of coals. Ah! unpleasant places to have to go down to; but very convenient, I dare say."

"Yes, I shouldn't wonder if they was convenient," replied the gentleman, "seeing that a few people live there pretty snug. That's the Fair, that is."

"My friend," said Mr. Pickwick, "you don't really mean to say that human beings live down in those wretched dungeons?"

"Don't I?" replied Mr. Roker, with indignant astonishment; "why shouldn't I?"

"Live!—Live down there!" exclaimed Mr. Pickwick.

"Live down there! Yes, and die down there, too, wery often!" replied Mr. Roker; "and what of that? Who's got to say anything agin it? Live down there!—Yes, and a wery good place it is to live in, ain't it?"

As Roker turned somewhat fiercely upon Mr. Pickwick in saying this, and moreover muttered, in an excited fashion certain unpleasant invocations concerning his own eyes, limbs, and circulating fluids, the latter gentleman deemed it advisable to pursue the discourse no further. Mr. Roker then proceeded to mount another staircase, as dirty as that which led to the place which had just been the subject of discussion, in which ascent he was closely followed by Mr. Pickwick and Sam.

"There," said Mr. Roker, pausing for breath when they reached another gallery of the same dimensions as the one below, "this is the coffee-room flight: the one above's the third, and the one above that's the top; and the room where you're going to sleep to-night is the warden's room, and it's this way—come on." Having said all this in a breath, Mr. Roker mounted another flight of stairs, with Mr. Pickwick and Sam Weller following at his heels.

These staircases received light from sundry windows placed at some little distance above the floor, and looking into a gravelled area bounded by a high brick wall, with iron *chevaux-de-frise* at the top. This area, it appeared from Mr. Roker's statement, was the racket-ground; and it further appeared, on the testimony of the same gentleman, that there was a smaller area in that portion of the prison which was nearest Farringdon-street, denominated and called "the Painted Ground," from the fact of its walls having once displayed the semblances of various men-of-war in full sail, and other artistical effects, achieved in bygone times by some imprisoned draughtsman in his leisure hours.

Having communicated this piece of information, apparently more for the purpose of discharging his bosom of an important fact, than with any specific view of enlightening Mr. Pickwick, the guide, having at length reached another gallery, led the way into a small passage at the extreme end; opened a door, and disclosed an apartment of an appearance by no means inviting, containing eight or nine iron bedsteads.

"There," said Mr. Roker, holding the door open, and looking triumphantly round at Mr. Pickwick, "There's a room!"

Mr. Pickwick's face, however, betokened such a very trifling portion of satisfaction at the appearance of his lodging, that Mr. Roker looked for a reciprocity of feeling into the countenance of Samuel Weller, who, until now, had observed a dignified silence.

"There's a room, young man," observed Mr. Roker.

"I see it," replied Sam, with a placid nod of the head.

"You wouldn't think to find such a room as this, in the Farringdon Hotel, would you?" said Mr. Roker, with a complacent smile.

To this Mr. Weller replied with an easy and unstudied closing of one eye; which might be considered to mean, either that he would have thought it, or that he would not have thought it, or that he had never thought anything at all about it, just as the observer's imagination suggested. Having executed this feat, and re-opened his eye, Mr. Weller proceeded to inquire which was the individual bedstead that Mr. Roker had so flatteringly described as an out-an-outer to sleep in.

"That's it," replied Mr. Roker, pointing to a very rusty one in a corner. "It would make any one go to sleep, that bedstead would, whether they wanted to or not."

"I should think," said Sam, eyeing the piece of furniture in question with a look of excessive disgust, "I should think poppies was nothin' to it."

"Nothing at all," said Mr. Roker.

"And I s'pose," said Sam, with a sidelong glance at his master, as if to see whether there were any symptoms of his determination being shaken by what passed, "I s'pose the other gen'l'men as sleeps here, are gen'l'men."

"Nothing but it," said Mr. Roker. "One of 'em takes his twelve pints of ale a day, and never leaves off smoking, even at his meals."

"He must be a first-rater," said Sam.

"A, 1," replied Mr. Roker.

Nothing daunted, even by this intelligence, Mr. Pickwick smilingly announced his determination to test the powers of the narcotic bedstead for that night; and Mr. Roker, after informing him that he could retire to rest at whatever hour he thought proper without any further notice or formality, walked off, leaving him standing with Sam in the gallery.

It was getting dark; that is to say, a few gas jets were kindled in this place, which was never light, by way of compliment to the evening, which had set in outside. As it was rather warm, some of the tenants of the numerous little rooms which opened into the gallery on either hand, had set their doors ajar. Mr. Pickwick peeped into them as he passed along, with great curiosity and interest. Here, four or five great hulking fellows, just visible through a cloud of tobacco-smoke, were engaged in noisy and riotous conversation over half-emptied pots of beer, or playing at all-fours with a very greasy pack of cards. In the adjoining room, some solitary tenant might be seen, poring, by the light of a feeble tallow candle, over a bundle of soiled and tattered papers, yellow with dust and dropping to pieces from age, writing, for the hundredth time, some lengthened statement of his grievances, for the perusal of some great man whose eyes it would never reach, or whose heart it would never touch. In a third, a man, with his wife and a whole crowd of children, might be seen making up a scanty bed on the ground, or upon a few chairs, for the younger ones to pass the night in. And in a fourth, and a fifth, and a sixth, and a seventh, the noise, and the beer, and the tobacco-smoke, and the cards, all came over again in greater force than before.

In the galleries themselves, and more especially on the staircases, there lingered a great number of people, who came there, some because their rooms were empty and lonesome; others because their rooms were full and hot; and the greater part because they were restless and uncomfortable, and not possessed of the secret of exactly knowing what to do with themselves. There were many classes of people here, from the labouring man in his fustian jacket, to the broken down spendthrift in his shawl dressing-gown, most appropriately out at elbows; but there was the same air about them all—a kind of listless, jail-bird, careless swagger; a vagabondish who's-afraid sort of bearing, which is wholly indescribable in words; but which any man can understand in one moment if he wishes, by just setting foot in the nearest debtor's prison, and looking at the very first group of people he sees there, with the same interest as Mr. Pickwick did.

"It strikes me, Sam," said Mr. Pickwick, leaning over the iron-rail at the stair-head, "It strikes me, Sam, that imprisonment for debt is scarcely any punishment at all."

"Think not, Sir?" inquired Mr. Weller.

"You see how these fellows drink, and smoke, and roar," replied Mr. Pickwick. "It's quite impossible that they can mind it much."

"Ah, that's just the wery thing, Sir," rejoined Sam, "they don't mind it; it's a reg'lar holiday to them—all porter and skettles. It's the t'other vuns as gets done over vith this sort o' thing: them down-hearted fellers as can't svig avay at the beer, nor play skettles neither; them as vould pay if they could, and gets low by being boxed up. I'll tell you wot it is, Sir; them as is always a idlin' in public houses it don't damage at all, and them as is alvays a vorkin' ven they can, it damages too much. 'It's unekal,' as my father used to say ven his grog worn't made half-and-half—'It's unekal, and that's the fault on it.'"

"I think you're right, Sam," said Mr. Pickwick, after a few moments' reflection, "quite right."

"P'raps, now and then, there's some honest people as likes it," observed Mr. Weller, in a ruminative tone, "but I never heerd o' one as I can call to mind, 'cept the little dirty-faced man in the brown coat, and that was force of habit."

"And who was he?" inquired Mr. Pickwick.

"Vy, that's just the wery point as nobody never know'd," replied Sam.

"But what did he do?"

"Vy he did wot many men as has been much better know'd has done in their time, Sir," replied Sam, "he run a match agin the constable, and vun it."

"In other words, I suppose," said Mr. Pickwick, "he got into debt."

"Just that, Sir," replied Sam, "and in course o' time he come here in consekens. It warn't much—execution for nine pound nothin', multiplied by five for costs; but hows'ever here he stopped for seventeen year. If he got any wrinkles in his face, they were stopped up vith the dirt, for both the dirty face and the brown coat wos just the same at the end o' that time as they wos at the beginnin'. He wos a wery peaceful inoffendin' little creetur, and wos alvays a bustlin' about for somebody, or playin' rackets and never vinnin'; till at last the turnkeys they got quite fond on him, and he wos in the lodge ev'ry night, a chattering vith 'em, and tellin' stories, and all that 'ere. Vun night he wos in there as usual, alone vith a wery old friend of his, as wos on the lock, ven he says all of a sudden, 'I ain't seen the market outside, Bill,' he says (Fleet Market wos there at that time)—'I ain't seen the market outside, Bill,' he says, 'for seventeen year.' 'I know you ain't,' says the turnkey, smoking his pipe. 'I should like to see it for a minit, Bill,' he says. 'Wery probable,' says the turnkey, smoking his pipe wery fierce, and making believe he warn't up to wot the little man wanted. 'Bill,' says the little man, more abrupt than afore, 'I've got the fancy in my head. Let me see the public street once more afore I die; and if I ain't struck with apoplexy, I'll be back in five minits by the clock.' 'And wot 'ud become o' me if you wos struck with apoplexy?' said the turnkey. 'Vy,' says the little creetur, 'whoever found me, 'ud bring me home, for I've got my card in my pocket, Bill,' he says,

'No. 20, Coffee-room Flight:' and that wos true, sure enough, for ven he wanted to make the acquaintance of any new comer, he used to pull out a little limp card vith them words on it and nothin' else; in consideration o' vich, he wos always called Number Tventy. The turnkey takes a fixed look at him, and at last he says in a solemn manner, 'Tventy,' he says, 'I'll trust you; you won't get your old friend into trouble.' 'No, my boy; I hope I've somethin' better behind here,' says the little man, and as he said it, he hit his little veskit wery hard, and then a tear started out o' each eye, which wos wery extraordinary; for it wos supposed as water never touched his face. He shook the turnkey by the hand; out he vent——"

"And never came back again," said Mr. Pickwick.

"Wrong for vunce, Sir," replied Mr. Weller, "for back he come two minits afore the time, a bilin' vith rage, sayin' how he'd been nearly run over by a hackney coach; that he warn't used to it, and he wos blowed if he wouldn't write to the Lord Mayor. They got him pacified at last; and for five year arter that, he never even so much as peeped out o' the lodge-gate."

"At the expiration of that time he died, I suppose," said Mr. Pickwick.

"No he didn't, Sir," replied Sam. "He got a curiosity to go and taste the beer at a new public-house over the way, on the premises; and it wos such a wery nice parlour, that he took it into his head to go there every night, which he did for a long time, alvays comin' back reg'lar about a quarter of an hour afore the gate shut, which wos all wery snug and comfortable. At last he began to get so precious jolly, that he used to forget how the time vent, or care nothin' at all about it, and he vent on gettin' later and later, till vun night his old friend wos just a shuttin' the gate—had turned the key in fact—ven he come up. 'Hold hard, Bill,' he says. 'Wot, ain't you come home yet, Tventy?' says the turnkey, 'I thought you was in long ago.' 'No I wasn't,' says the little man, vith a smile. 'Vell then, I'll tell you wot it is, my friend,' says the turnkey, openin' the gate wery slow and sulky, 'it's my 'pinion as you've got into bad company o' late, which I'm wery sorry to see. Now I don't wish to do anything harsh,' he says, 'but if you can't confine yourself to steady circles, and find your vay back at reg'lar hours, as sure as you're a standin' there, I'll shut you out altogether!' The little man was seized vith a wiolent fit o' tremblin', and never vent outside the prison walls arterwards!"

As Sam concluded, Mr. Pickwick slowly retraced his steps down stairs. After a few thoughtful turns in the Painted Ground, which, as it was now dark, was nearly deserted, he intimated to Mr. Weller that he thought it high time for him to withdraw for the night; requesting him to seek a bed in some adjacent public house, and return early in the morning, to make arrangements for the removal of his master's wardrobe from the George and Vulture. This request Mr. Samuel Weller prepared to obey, with as good a grace as he could assume, but with a very considerable show of reluctance nevertheless. He even went so far as to essay sundry ineffectual hints regarding the expediency of stretching himself on the gravel for that night; but finding Mr. Pickwick obstinately deaf to any such suggestions, finally withdrew.

There is no disguising the fact that Mr. Pickwick felt very low spirited and uncomfortable—not for lack of society, for the prison was very full, and a bottle of wine would at once have purchased the utmost good-fellowship of a few choice spirits, without any more formal ceremony of introduction; but he was alone in the coarse vulgar crowd, and felt the depression of spirit and sinking of heart, naturally consequent upon the reflection that he was cooped and caged up without a prospect of liberation. As to the idea of releasing himself by ministering to the sharpness of Dodson & Fogg, it never for an instant entered his thoughts.

In this frame of mind he turned again into the coffee-room gallery, and walked slowly to and fro. The place was intolerably dirty, and the smell of tobacco-smoke perfectly suffocating. There was a perpetual slamming and banging of doors as the people went in and out, and the noise of their voices and footsteps echoed and re-echoed through the passages constantly. A young woman, with a child in her arms, who seemed scarcely able to crawl, from emaciation and misery, was walking up and down the passage in conversation with her husband, who had no other place to see her in. As they passed Mr. Pickwick, he could hear the female sob bitterly; and once she burst into such a passion of grief, that she was compelled to lean against the wall for support, while the man took the child in his arms, and tried to soothe her.

Mr. Pickwick's heart was really too full to bear it, and he went up stairs to bed.

Now, although the warden's room was a very uncomfortable one, being, in every point of decoration and convenience, several hundred degrees inferior to the commonest infirmary of a county gaol, it had at present the merit of being wholly deserted save by Mr. Pickwick himself. So, he sat down at the foot of his little iron bedstead, and began to wonder how much a year the warden made out of the dirty room. Having satisfied himself, by mathematical calculation, that the apartment was about equal in annual value to the freehold of a small street in the suburbs of London, he took to wondering what possible temptation could have induced a dingy-looking fly that was crawling over his pantaloons, to come into a close prison, when he had the choice of so many airy situations—a course of meditation which led him to the irresistible conclusion that the insect was insane. After settling this point, he began to be conscious that he was getting sleepy; whereupon he took his nightcap out of the pocket in which he had had the precaution to stow it in the morning, and, leisurely undressing himself, got into bed, and fell asleep.

"Bravo! Heel over toe—cut and shuffle—pay away at it, Zephyr! I'm smothered if the Opera House isn't your proper hemisphere. Keep it up. Hooray!" These expressions, delivered in a most boisterous tone, and accompanied with loud peals of laughter, roused Mr. Pickwick from one of those sound slumbers which, lasting in reality some half hour, seem to the sleeper to have been protracted for about three weeks or a month.

The voice had no sooner ceased than the room was shaken with such violence that the windows rattled in their frames, and the bedsteads trembled again. Mr. Pickwick started up, and remained for some minutes fixed in mute astonishment at the scene before him.

On the floor of the room, a man in a broad-skirted green coat, with corderoy knee smalls and grey cotton stockings, was performing the most popular steps of a hornpipe, with a slang and burlesque caricature of grace and lightness, which, combined with the very appropriate character of his costume, was inexpressibly absurd. Another man, evidently very drunk, who had probably been tumbled into bed by his companions, was sitting up between the sheets, warbling as much as he could recollect of a comic song, with the most intensely sentimental feeling and expression; while a third, seated on one of the bedsteads, was applauding both performers with the air of a profound connoisseur, and encouraging them by such ebullitions of feeling as had already roused Mr. Pickwick from his sleep.

This last man was an admirable specimen of a class of gentry which never can be seen in full perfection but in such places;—they may be met with, in an imperfect state, occasionally about stable-yards and public houses; but they never attain their full bloom except in these hot-beds, which would almost seem to be considerately provided by the Legislature for the sole purpose of rearing them.

He was a tall fellow, with an olive complexion, long dark hair, and very thick bushy whiskers meeting under his chin. He wore no neckerchief, as he had been playing rackets all day, and his open shirt collar displayed their full luxuriance. On his head he wore one of the common eighteenpenny French skull-caps, with a gawdy tassel dangling therefrom, very happily in keeping with a common fustian coat. His legs, which, being long, were afflicted with weakness, graced a pair of Oxford-mixture trousers, made to show the full symmetry of the limbs. Being somewhat negligently braced, however, and, moreover, but imperfectly buttoned, they fell in a series of not the most graceful folds over a pair of shoes sufficiently down at heel to display a pair of very soiled white stockings. There was a rakish vagabond smartness, and a kind of boastful rascality, about the whole man, that was worth a mine of gold.

This figure was the first to perceive that Mr. Pickwick was looking on; upon which he winked to the Zephyr, and entreated him, with mock gravity, not to wake the gentleman.

"Why, bless the gentleman's honest heart and soul!" said the Zephyr, turning round and affecting the extremity of surprise; "the gentleman *is* awake. Hem; Shakespeare. How do you do, Sir? How is Mary and Sarah, Sir? and the dear old lady at home, Sir—eh, Sir? Will you have the kindness to put my compliments into the first little parcel you're sending that way, Sir, and say that I would have sent 'em before, only I was afraid they might be broken in the waggon, Sir?"

"Don't overwhelm the gentleman with ordinary civilities when you see he's anxious to have something to drink," said the gentleman with the whiskers, with a jocose air. "Why don't you ask the gentleman what he'll take?"

"Dear me—I quite forgot," replied the other. "What *will* you take, Sir? Will you take port wine, Sir, or sherry wine, Sir? I can recommend the ale, Sir; or perhaps you'd like to taste the porter, Sir? Allow me to have the felicity of hanging up your nightcap, Sir."

With this, the speaker snatched that article of dress from Mr. Pickwick's head, and fixed it in a twinkling on that of the drunken man, who, firmly impressed with the belief that he was delighting a numerous assembly, continued to hammer away at the comic song in the most melancholy strains imaginable.

Taking a man's nightcap from his brow by violent means, and adjusting it on the head of an unknown gentleman of dirty exterior, however ingenious a witticism in itself, is unquestionably one of those which come under the denomination of practical jokes. Viewing the matter precisely in this light, Mr. Pickwick, without the slightest intimation of his purpose, sprang vigorously out of bed; struck the Zephyr so smart a blow in the chest, as to deprive him of a considerable portion of the commodity which sometimes bears his name; and then, recapturing his nightcap, boldly placed himself in an attitude of defence.

"Now," said Mr. Pickwick, gasping no less from excitement than from the expenditure of so much energy, "come on—both of you—both of you." And with this liberal invitation the worthy gentleman communicated a revolving motion to his clenched fists, by way of appalling his antagonists with a display of science.

It might have been Mr. Pickwick's very unexpected gallantry, or it might have been the complicated manner in which he had got himself out of bed, and fallen all in a mass upon the hornpipe man, that touched his adversaries. Touched they were; for, instead of then and there making an attempt to commit manslaughter, as Mr. Pickwick implicitly believed they would have done, they paused, stared at each other a short time, and finally laughed outright.

"Well; you're a trump, and I like you all the better for it," said the Zephyr. "Now jump into bed again, or you'll catch the rheumatics. No malice, I hope?" said the man, extending a hand about the size of the yellow clump of fingers which sometimes swings over a glover's door.

"Certainly not," said Mr. Pickwick, with great alacrity; for, now that the excitement was over, he began to feel rather cool about the legs.

"Allow me the *h*onour, Sir?" said the gentleman with the whiskers, presenting his dexter hand, and aspirating the h.

"With much pleasure, Sir," said Mr. Pickwick; and having executed a very long and solemn shake, he got into bed again.

"My name is Smangle, Sir," said the man with the whiskers.

"Oh," said Mr. Pickwick.

"Mine is Mivins," said the man in the stockings.

"I am delighted to hear it, Sir," said Mr. Pickwick.

"Hem," coughed Mr. Smangle.

"Did you speak, Sir?" said Mr. Pickwick.

"No, I did not, Sir," said Mr. Smangle.

"I thought you did, Sir," said Mr. Pickwick.

All this was very genteel and pleasant; and, to make matters still more comfortable, Mr. Smangle assured Mr. Pickwick a great many times that he entertained a very high respect for the feelings of a gentleman; which sentiment, indeed, did him infinite credit, as he could be in no wise supposed to understand them.

"Are you going through the Court, Sir?" inquired Mr. Mangle.

"Through the what?" said Mr. Pickwick.

"Through the Court—Portugal Street—the Court for the Relief of——you know."

"Oh, no," replied Mr. Pickwick. "No, I am not."

"Going out, perhaps?" suggested Mivins.

"I fear not," replied Mr. Pickwick. "I refuse to pay some damages, and am here in consequence."

"Ah," said Mr. Smangle, "paper has been my ruin."

"A stationer, I presume, Sir?" said Mr. Pickwick, innocently.

"Stationer! No, no; confound and curse me!—not so

low as that. No trade. When I say paper, I mean bills."

"Oh, you use the word in that sense. I see," said Mr. Pickwick.

"Damme? A gentleman must expect reverses," said Smangle. "What of that! Here am I in the Fleet Prison. Well; good. What then? I'm none the worse for that, am I?"

"Not a bit," replied Mr. Mivins. And he was quite right; for, so far from Mr. Smangle being any the worse for it, he was something the better, inasmuch as to qualify himself for the place, he had attained gratuitous possession of certain articles of jewellery, which, long before that, had found their way to the pawnbroker's.

"Well; but come," said Mr. Smangle; "this is dry work. Let's rinse our mouths with a drop of burnt sherry; the last comer shall stand it, Mivins shall fetch it, and I'll help to drink it. That's a fair and gentlemanlike division of labour, any how—curse me!"

Unwilling to hazard another quarrel, Mr. Pickwick gladly assented to the proposition, and consigned the money to Mr. Mivins, who, as it was nearly eleven o'clock, lost no time in repairing to the coffee-room on his errand.

"I say," whispered Smangle, the moment his friend had left the room; "what did you give him?"

"Half a sovereign," said Mr. Pickwick.

"He's a devilish pleasant gentlemanly dog," said Mr. Smangle;—"infernal pleasant. I don't know anybody more so; but——" Here Mr. Smangle stopped short, and shook his head dubiously.

"You don't think there is any probability of his appropriating the money to his own use?" said Mr. Pickwick.

"Oh, no—mind, I don't say that; I expressly say that he's a devilish gentlemanly fellow," said Mr. Smangle. "But I think, perhaps, if somebody went down, just to see that he didn't drop his beak into the jug by accident, or make some confounded mistake in losing the money as he came up stairs, it would be as well. Here, you Sir, just run down stairs, and look after that gentleman, will you?"

This request was addressed to a little timid-looking, nervous man, whose appearance bespoke great poverty, and who had been crouching on his bedstead all this while, apparently quite stupified by the novelty of his situation.

"You know where the coffee-room is," said Smangle; "just run down, and tell that gentleman you've come to help him up with the jug. Or—stop—I'll tell you what —I'll tell you how we'll do him," said Smangle, with a cunning look.

"How?" said Mr. Pickwick.

"Send down word that he's to spend the change in cigars. Capital thought. Run and tell him that; d'ye hear? They shan't be wasted," continued Smangle, turning to Mr. Pickwick. "*I'll* smoke 'em."

This manœuvring was so exceedingly ingenious, and, withal, performed with such immoveable composure and coolness, that Mr. Pickwick would have had no wish to disturb it, even if he had had the power. In a short time Mr. Mivins returned, bearing the sherry, which Mr. Smangle dispensed in two little cracked mugs; considerately remarking, with reference to himself, that a gentleman must not be particular upon such circumstances, and, for his part, he was not too proud to drink out of the jug; in which, to show his sincerity, he forthwith pledged the company in a draught which half emptied it.

An excellent understanding having been, by these means, promoted, Mr. Smangle proceeded to entertain his hearers with a relation of divers romantic adventures in which he had been from time to time engaged, involving various interesting anecdotes of a thorough-bred horse, and a magnificent Jewess, both of surpassing beauty, and much coveted by the nobility and gentry of these kingdoms.

Long before these elegant extracts from the biography of a gentleman were concluded, Mr. Mivins had betaken himself to bed, and set in snoring for the night: leaving the timid stranger and Mr. Pickwick to the full benefit of Mr. Smangle's experiences.

Nor were the two last-named gentlemen as much edified as they might have been by the moving passages which were narrated. Mr. Pickwick had been in a state of slumber for some time, when he had a faint perception of the drunken man bursting out afresh with the comic song, and receiving from Mr. Smangle a gentle intimation, through the medium of the water jug, that his audience were not musically disposed. He then once again dropped off to sleep, with a confused consciousness that Mr. Smangle was still engaged in relating a long story, the chief point of which appeared to be, that, on some occasion particularly stated and set forth, he had "done" a bill and a gentleman at the same time.

CHAPTER XLI.

ILLUSTRATIVE, LIKE THE PRECEDING ONE, OF THE OLD PROVERB, THAT ADVERSITY BRINGS A MAN ACQUAINTED WITH STRANGE BED-FELLOWS. LIKEWISE CONTAINING MR. PICKWICK'S EXTRAORDINARY AND STARTLING ANNOUNCEMENT TO MR. SAMUEL WELLER.

WHEN Mr. Pickwick opened his eyes next morning, the first object upon which they rested was Samuel Weller, seated upon a small black portmanteau, intently regarding, apparently in a condition of profound abstraction, the stately figure of the dashing Mr. Smangle, while Mr. Smangle himself, who was already partially dressed, was seated on his bedstead, occupied in the desperately hopeless attempt of staring Mr. Weller out of countenance. We say desperately hopeless, because Sam, with a comprehensive gaze, which took in Mr. Smangle's cap, feet, head, face, legs, and whiskers, all at the same time, continued to look steadily on with every demonstration of lively satisfaction, but with no more regard to Mr. Smangle's personal sentiments on the subject, than he would have displayed had he been inspecting a wooden statue, or a straw-embowelled Guy Faux.

"Well; will you know me again?" said Mr. Smangle, with a frown.

"I'd svear to you any veres, Sir," replied Sam, cheerfully.

"Don't be impertinent to a gentleman, Sir," said Mr. Smangle.

"Not on no account," replied Sam. "If you'll tell me ven he wakes, I'll be upon the very best extra-super behaviour!" This observation, having a remote tendency to imply that Mr. Smangle was no gentleman, rather kindled his ire.

"Mivins!" said Mr. Smangle, with a passionate air.

"What's the office?" replied that gentleman from his couch.

WORKS OF CHARLES DICKENS

"Who the devil is this fellow?"

"'Gad," said Mr. Mivins, looking lazily out from under the bedclothes, "I ought to ask *you* that. Hasn't he any business here?"

"No," replied Mr. Smangle.

"Then knock him down stairs, and tell him not to presume to get up till I come and kick him," rejoined Mr. Mivins; and with this prompt advice that excellent gentleman again betook himself to slumber.

The conversation exhibiting these unequivocal symptoms of rather verging on the personal, Mr. Pickwick deemed it a fit point at which to interpose.

"Sam," said Mr. Pickwick.

"Sir," rejoined that gentleman.

"Has anything new occurred since last night?"

"Nothin' partickler, Sir," replied Sam, glancing at Mr. Smangle's whiskers; "the late prewailance of a close and confined atmosphere has been rayther favourable to the growth of veeds, of an·alarmin' and sangvinary natur; but vith that 'ere exception things is quiet enough."

"I shall get up," said Mr. Pickwick; "give me some clean things."

Whatever hostile intentions Mr. Smangle might have entertained, his thoughts were speedily diverted by the unpacking of the portmanteau; the contents of which appeared to impress him at once with a most favourable opinion, not only of Mr. Pickwick, but of Sam also, who, he took an early opportunity of declaring, in a tone of voice loud enough for that eccentric personage to overhear, was a regular thorough-bred original, and consequently the very man after his own heart. As to Mr. Pickwick, the affection he conceived for him knew no limits.

"Now is there anything I can do for you, my dear Sir?" said Smangle.

"Nothing that I am aware of, I am obliged to you," replied Mr. Pickwick.

"No linen that you want sent to the washerwoman's? I know a delightful washerwoman outside, that comes for my things twice a week, and, by Jove!—how devilish lucky—this is the very day she calls. Shall I put any of those little things up with mine? Don't say anything about the trouble. Confound and curse it! if one gentleman under a cloud is not to put himself a little out of the way to assist another gentleman in the same condition, what's human nature?"

Thus spake Mr. Smangle, edging himself meanwhile as near as possible to the portmanteau, and beaming forth looks of the most fervent and disinterested friendship.

"There's nothing you want to give out for the man to brush, my dear creature, is there?" resumed Smangle.

"Nothin' whatever, my fine feller," rejoined Sam, taking the reply into his own mouth. "P'raps if vun of us wos to brush, without troubling the man, it 'ud be more agreeable for all parties, as the schoolmaster said ven the young gentleman objected to being flogged by the butler."

"And there's nothing that I can send in my little box to the washerwoman's, is there?" said Smangle, turning from Sam to Mr. Pickwick with an air of some discomfiture.

"Nothin' whatever, Sir," retorted Sam; "I'm afeerd the little box must be chock full o' your own as it is."

This speech was accompanied with such a very expressive look at that particular portion of Mr. Smangle's attire, by the appearance of which the skill of laundresses in getting up gentlemen's linen is generally tested, that he was fain to turn upon his heel, and, for the present at any rate,

to give up all design on Mr. Pickwick's purse and wardrobe. He accordingly retired in dudgeon to the racketground, where he made a light and wholesome breakfast upon a couple of the cigars which had been purchased on the previous night.

Mr. Mivins, who was no smoker, and whose account for small articles of chandlery had also reached down to the bottom of the slate, and been "carried over" to the other side, remained in bed, and, in his own words, "took it out in sleep."

After breakfasting in a small closet attached to the coffee-room, which bore the imposing title of the Snuggery, the temporary inmate of which, in consideration of a small additional charge, has the unspeakable advantage of overhearing all the conversation in the coffee-room aforesaid; and after despatching Mr. Weller on some necessary errands, Mr. Pickwick repaired to the lodge, to consult Mr. Roker concerning his future accommodation.

"Accommodation, eh?" said that gentleman, consulting a large book; "plenty of that, Mr. Pickwick. Your chummage ticket will be on twenty-seven, in the third."

"Oh," said Mr. Pickwick. "My what, did you say?"

"Your chummage ticket," replied Mr. Roker; "you're up to that?"

"Not quite," replied Mr. Pickwick, with a smile.

"Why," said Mr. Roker, "it's as plain as Salisbury. You'll have a chummage ticket upon twenty-seven in the third, and them as is in the room will be your chums."

"Are there many of them?" inquired Mr. Pickwick, dubiously.

"Three," replied Mr. Roker.

Mr. Pickwick coughed.

"One of 'em's a parson," said Mr. Roker, filling up a little piece of paper as he spoke, "another's a butcher."

"Eh?" exclaimed Mr. Pickwick.

"A butcher," repeated Mr. Roker, giving the nib of his pen a tap on the desh to cure it of a disinclination to mark. "What a thorough-paced goer he used to be sure-ly! You remember Tom Martin, Neddy?" said Roker, appealing to another man in the lodge, who was paring the mud off his shoes with a five-and-twenty bladed pocket knife.

"I should think so," replied the party addressed, with a strong emphasis on the personal pronoun.

"Bless my dear eyes," said Mr. Roker, shaking his head slowly from side to side, and gazing abstractedly out of the grated window before him, as if he were fondly recalling some peaceful scene of his early youth; "it seems but yesterday that he whopped the coal-heaver down Fox-under-the-Hill by the wharf there. I think I can see him now, a coming up the Strand between the two street-keepers, a little sobered by the bruising, with a patch o' win-egar and brown paper over his right eyelid, and that 'ere lovely bull-dog, as pinned the little boy arterwards, a following at his heels. What a rum thing time is, ain't it, Neddy?"

The gentleman to whom these observations were addressed, who appeared of a taciturn and thoughtful cast, merely echoed the inquiry; and Mr. Roker, shaking off the poetical and gloomy train of thought into which he had been betrayed, descended to the common business of life, and resumed his pen.

"Do you know what the third gentleman is?" inquired Mr. Pickwick, not very much gratified by this description of his future associates.

"What is that Simpson, Neddy?" said Mr. Roker, turning to his companion.

"What Simpson?" said Neddy.

"Why him in twenty-seven in the third, that this gentleman's going to be chummed on."

"Oh, him!" replied Neddy: "he's nothing exactly. He *was* a horse chaunter: he's a leg now."

"Ah, so I thought," rejoined Mr. Roker, closing the book, and placing the small piece of paper in Mr. Pickwick's hands—"That's the ticket, Sir."

Very much perplexed by this summary disposition of his person, Mr. Pickwick walked back into the prison, revolving in his mind what he had better do. Convinced, however, that before he took any other steps it would be advisable to see, and hold personal converse with, the three gentlemen with whom it was proposed to quarter him, he made the best of his way to the third flight.

After groping about in the gallery for some time, attempting in the dim light to decipher the numbers on the different doors, he at length appealed to a potboy, who happened to be pursuing his morning occupation of gleaning for pewter.

"Which is twenty-seven, my good fellow?" said Mr. Pickwick.

"Five doors further on," replied the potboy. "There's the likeness of a man being hung, and smoking a pipe the while, chalked outside the door."

Guided by this direction, Mr. Pickwick proceeded slowly along the gallery until he encountered the "portrait of a gentleman," above described, upon whose countenance he tapped, with the knuckle of his fore-finger—gently at first, and then audibly. After repeating this process several times without effect, he ventured to open the door and peep in.

There was only one man in the room, and he was leaning out of window as far as he could without over-balancing himself, endeavouring with great perseverance to spit upon the crown of the hat of a personal friend on the parade below. As neither speaking, coughing, sneezing, knocking, nor any other ordinary mode of attracting attention, made this person aware of the presence of a visitor, Mr. Pickwick, after some delay, stepped up to the window, and pulled him gently by the coat-tail. The individual brought in his head and shoulders with great swiftness, and surveying Mr. Pickwick from head to foot, demanded in a surly tone what the—something beginning with a capital H—he wanted.

"I believe," said Mr. Pickwick, consulting his ticket, "I believe this is twenty-seven in the third."

"Well?" replied the gentleman.

"I have come here in consequence of receiving this bit of paper," rejoined Mr. Pickwick.

"Hand it over," said the gentleman.

Mr. Pickwick complied.

"I think Roker might have chummed you somewhere else," said Mr. Simpson (for it was the leg), after a very discontented sort of a pause.

Mr. Pickwick thought so also; but, under all the circumstances, he considered it a matter of sound policy to be silent.

Mr. Simpson mused for a few moments after this, and then, thrusting his head out of the window, gave a shrill whistle, and pronounced some word aloud several times. What the word was, Mr. Pickwick could not distinguish; but he rather inferred that it must be some nickname which distinguished Mr. Martin, from the fact that a great number of gentlemen on the ground below, immediately proceeding to cry "Butcher," in imitation of the tone in which that useful class of society are wont diurnally to make their presence known at area railings.

Subsequent occurrences confirmed the accuracy of Mr. Pickwick's impression; for, in a few seconds, a gentleman, prematurely broad for his years, clothed in a professional blue jean frock, and top-boots with circular toes, entered the room nearly out of breath, closely followed by another gentleman in very shabby black, and a seal-skin cap. The latter gentleman, who fastened his coat all the way up to his chin by means of a pin and a button alternately, had a very coarse red face, and looked like a drunken chaplain, which, indeed, he was.

These two gentlemen having by turns perused Mr. Pickwick's billet, the one expressed his opinion that it was "a rig," and the other his conviction that it was "a go."

Having recorded their feelings in these very intelligible terms, they looked at Mr. Pickwick and each other in awkward silence.

"It's an aggravating thing, just as we got the beds so snug," said the chaplain, looking at three dirty mattresses, each rolled up in a blanket, which occupied one corner of the room during the day, and formed a kind of slab, on which were placed an old cracked basin, ewer, and soapdish, of common yellow earthenware, with a blue flower: "Very aggravating."

Mr. Martin expressed the same opinion in rather stronger terms; Mr. Simpson, after having let a variety of expletive adjectives loose upon society without any substantive to accompany them, tucked up his sleeves, and began to wash the greens for dinner.

While this was going on, Mr. Pickwick had been eyeing the room, which was filthily dirty, and smelt intolerably close. There was no vestige of either carpet, curtain, or blind. There was not even a closet in it. Unquestionably there were but few things to put away, if there had been one; but, however few in number, or small in individual amount, still remnants of loaves, and pieces of cheese, and damp towels, and scraps of meat, and articles of wearing apparel, and mutilated crockery, and bellows without nozzles, and toasting-forks without prongs, *do* present something of an uncomfortable appearance when they are scattered about the floor of a small apartment, which is the common sitting and sleeping room of three idle men.

"I suppose this can be managed somehow," said the butcher, after a pretty long silence. "What will you take to go out?"

"I beg your pardon," replied Mr. Pickwick. "What did you say? I hardly understand you."

"What will you take to be paid out?" said the butcher. "The regular chummage is two-and-sixpence. Will you take three bob?"

"—And a bender," suggested the clerical gentleman.

"Well, I don't mind that; it's only twopence a-piece more," said Mr. Martin.

"What do you say now? We'll pay you out for three-and-sixpence a week. Come."

"And stand a gallon of beer down," chimed in Mr. Simpson. "There."

"And drink it on the spot," said the chaplain. "Now."

"I really am so wholly ignorant of the rules of this place," returned Mr. Pickwick, "that I do not yet comprehend you. Can I live anywhere else? I thought I could not."

At this inquiry Mr. Martin looked with a countenance of excessive surprise at his two friends, and then each gentleman pointed with his right thumb over his left shoulder.

This action, imperfectly described in words by the very feeble term of "over the left," when performed by any number of ladies or gentlemen who are accustomed to act in unison, has a very graceful and airy effect; its expression is one of light and playful sarcasm.

"*Can* you!" repeated Mr. Martin, with a smile of pity.

"Well, if I knew as little of life as that, I'd eat my hat and swallow the buckle," said the clerical gentleman.

"So would I," added the sporting one, solemnly.

After this introductory preface, the three chums informed Mr. Pickwick in a breath, that money was, in the Fleet, just what money was out of it; that it would instantly procure him almost anything he desired; and that, supposing he had got it, and had no objection to spend it, if he only signified his wish to have a room to himself, he might take possession of one, furnished and fitted to boot, in half an hour's time.

With this, the parties separated, very much to their mutual satisfaction; Mr. Pickwick once more retracing his steps to the lodge, and the three companions adjourning to the coffee-room, there to spend the five shillings which the clerical gentleman had, with admirable prudence and foresight, borrowed of him for the purpose.

"I knowed it!" said Mr. Roker, with a chuckle, when Mr Pickwick stated the object with which he had returned. "Didn't I say so, Neddy?"

The philosophical owner of the universal penknife growled an affirmative.

"I knowed you'd want a room for yourself, bless you!" said Mr. Roker. "Let me see. You'll want some furniture. You'll hire that of me, I suppose? That's the reg'lar thing."

"With great pleasure," replied Mr Pickwick.

"There's a capital room up in the coffee-room flight, that belongs to a Chancery prisoner," said Roker. "It'll stand you in a pound a-week. I suppose you don't mind that?"

"Not at all," said Mr. Pickwick.

"Just step there with me," said Roker, taking up his hat with great alacrity; "the matter's settled in five minutes. Lord! why didn't you say at first that you was willing to come down handsome?"

The matter was soon arranged, as the turnkey had foretold. The Chancery prisoner had been there long enough to have lost friends, fortune, home, and happiness, and to have acquired the right of having a room to himself. As he laboured, however, under the slight inconvenience of often wanting a morsel of bread, he eagerly listened to Mr. Pickwick's proposal to rent the apartment; and readily covenanted and agreed to yield him up the sole and undisturbed possession thereof, in consideration of the weekly payment of twenty shillings; from which fund he furthermore contracted to pay out any person or persons that might be chummed upon it.

As they struck the bargain, Mr Pickwick surveyed him with a painful interest. He was a tall, gaunt, cadaverous man, in an old great-coat and slippers, with sunken cheeks, and a restless, eager eye. His lips were bloodless, and his bones sharp and thin. God help him! the iron teeth of confinement and privation had been slowly filing them down for twenty years.

"And where will you live meanwhile, Sir?" said Mr. Pickwick, as he laid the amount of the first week's rent in advance on the tottering table. The man gathered up the money with a trembling hand, and replied that he didn't know yet; he must go and see where he could move his bed to.

"I am afraid, Sir," said Mr. Pickwick, laying his hand gently and compassionately on his arm;—"I am afraid you will have to live in some noisy crowded place. Now, pray, consider this room your own when you want quiet, or when any of your friends come to see you."

"Friends!" interposed the man, in a voice which rattled in his throat. "If I lay dead at the bottom of the deepest mine in the world, tight screwed down and soldered in my coffin, rotting in the dark and filthy ditch that drags its slime along beneath the foundations of this prison, I could not be more forgotten or unheeded than I am here. I am a dead man—dead to society, without the pity they bestow on those whose souls have passed to judgment. Friends to see *me!* My God! I have sunk from the prime of life into old age in this place, and there is not one to raise his hand above my bed, when I lie dead upon it, and say, 'It is a blessing he is gone!'"

The excitement, which had cast an unwonted light over the man's face while he spoke, subsided as he concluded; and, pressing his withered hands together in a hasty and disordered manner, he shuffled from the room.

"Rides rather rusty," said Mr. Roker, with a smile. "Ah! they're like the elephants; they feel it now and then, and it makes 'em wild!"

Having made this deeply-sympathising remark, Mr. Roker entered upon his arrangements with such expedition, that in a short time the room was furnished with a carpet, six chairs, a table, a sofa bedstead, a tea-kettle, and various small *et ceteras*, on hire, at the very reasonable rate of seven-and-twenty shillings and sixpence per week.

"Now, is there anything more we can do for you?" inquired Mr. Roker, looking round with great satisfaction, and gaily chinking the first week's hire in his closed fist.

"Why, yes," said Mr Pickwick, who had been musing deeply for some time. "Are there any people here who run on errands, and so forth?"

"Outside, do you mean?" inquired Mr. Roker.

"Yes; I mean who are able to go outside. Not prisoners."

"Yes, there is," said Roker. "There's an unfortunate devil, who has got a friend on the poor side, that's glad to do anything of that sort. He's been running odd jobs, and that, for the last two months. Shall I send him?"

"If you please," rejoined Mr. Pickwick. "Stay;—no. The poor side, you say. I should like to see it;—I'll go to him myself."

The poor side of a debtor's prison is, as its name imports, that in which the most miserable and abject class of debtors are confined. A prisoner having declared upon the poor side, pays neither rent nor chummage. His fees, upon entering and leaving the gaol, are reduced in amount, and he becomes entitled to a share of some small quantities of food; to provide which, a few charitable persons have, from time to time, left trifling legacies in their wills. Most of our readers will remember, that, until within a very few years past, there was a kind of iron cage in the wall of the Fleet Prison, within which was posted some man of hungry looks, who, from time to time, rattled a money-box, and exclaimed, in a mournful voice, "Pray, remember the poor debtors; pray, remember the poor debtors." The receipts of this box, when there were any, were divided among the poor prisoners, and the men on the poor side relieved each other in this degrading office.

Although this custom has been abolished, and the cage is now boarded up, the miserable and destitute condition of these unhappy persons remains the same. We no longer suffer them to appeal at the prison gates to the charity and compassion of the passers by; but we still leave unblotted in the leaves of our statute book, for the reverence and admiration of succeeding ages, the just and wholesome law which declares that the sturdy felon shall be fed and clothed, and that the penniless debtor shall be left to die of starvation and nakedness. This is no fiction. Not a week passes over our heads but, in every one of our prisons for debt, some of these men must inevitably expire in the slow agonies of want, if they were not relieved by their fellow-prisoners.

Turning these things in his mind, as he mounted the narrow staircase at the foot of which Roker had left him, Mr. Pickwick gradually worked himself to the boiling-over point; and so excited was he with his reflections on this subject, that he had burst into the room to which he had been directed, before he had any distinct recollection either of the place in which he was, or of the object of his visit.

The general aspect of the room recalled him to himself at once; but he had no sooner cast his eyes on the figure of a man who was brooding over the dusty fire, than, letting his hat fall on the floor, he stood perfectly fixed and immoveable with astonishment.

Yes, in tattered garments, and without a coat; his common calico shirt yellow and in rags; his hair hanging over his face; his features changed with suffering, and pinched with famine,—there sat Mr. Alfred Jingle; his head resting upon his hand, his eyes fixed upon the fire, and his whole appearance denoting misery and dejection!

Near him, leaning listlessly against the wall, stood a strong-built countryman, flicking with a worn-out hunting-whip the top-boot that adorned his right foot: his left being thrust into an old slipper. Horses, dogs, and drink had brought him there pell-mell. There was a rusty spur on the solitary boot, which he occasionally jerked into the empty air, at the same time giving the boot a smart blow, and muttering some of the sounds by which a sportsman encourages his horse. He was riding, in imagination, some desperate steeplechase at that moment. Poor wretch! He never rode a match on the swiftest animal in his costly stud, with half the speed at which he had torn along the course that ended in the Fleet.

On the opposite side of the room an old man was seated on a small wooden box, with his eyes rivetted on the floor, and his face settled into an expression of the deepest and most hopeless despair. A young girl—his little granddaughter—was hanging about him, endeavouring, with a thousand childish devices, to engage his attention; but the old man neither saw nor heard her. The voice that had been music to him, and the eyes that had been light, fell coldly on his senses. His limbs were shaking with disease, and the palsy had fastened on his mind.

There were two or three other men in the room, congregated in a little knot, and noisily talking among themselves. There was a lean and haggard woman, too—a prisoner's wife—who was watering, with great solicitude, the wretched stump of a dried-up, withered plant, which, it was plain to see, could never send forth a green leaf again; —too true an emblem, perhaps, of the office she had come there to discharge.

Such were the objects which presented themselves to Mr. Pickwick's view, as he looked round him in amazement. The noise of some one stumbling hastily into the room roused him. Turning his eyes towards the door, they encountered the new comer; and in him, through all

his rags, and dirt, and misery, he recognised the familiar features of Mr. Job Trotter.

"Mr. Pickwick!" exclaimed Job aloud.

"Eh?" said Jingle, starting from his seat. "Mr. ——! So it is—queer place—strange thing—serves me right—very." And with this Mr. Jingle thrust his hands into the place where his trousers pocket used to be, and, dropping his chin upon his breast, sank back into his chair.

Mr. Pickwick was affected; the two men looked so very miserable. The sharp involuntary glance Jingle had cast at a small piece of raw loin of mutton, which Job had brought in with him, said more of their reduced state than two hours' explanation could have done. He looked mildly at Jingle, and said:—

"I should like to speak to you in private. Will you step out for an instant?"

"Certainly," said Jingle, rising hastily. "Can't step far—no danger of overwalking yourself here—spike park—grounds pretty—romantic, but not extensive—open for public inspection—family always in town—housekeeper desperately careful—very."

"You have forgotten your coat," said Mr. Pickwick, as they walked out to the staircase, and closed the door after them.

"Eh?" said Jingle. "Spout—dear relation—uncle Tom—couldn't help it—must eat, you know. Wants of nature—and all that."

"What do you mean?"

"Gone, my dear Sir—last coat—can't help it. Lived on a pair of boots—whole fortnight. Silk umbrella—ivory handle—week—fact—honour—ask Job—knows it."

"Lived for three weeks upon a pair of boots and a silk umbrella with an ivory handle!" exclaimed Mr. Pickwick, who had only heard of such things in shipwrecks, or read of them in Constable's Miscellany.

"True," said Jingle, nodding his head. "Pawnbroker's shop—duplicates here—small sums—mere nothing—all rascals."

"Oh," said Mr. Pickwick, much relieved by this explanation; "I understand you. You have pawned your wardrobe."

"Everything—Job's too—all shirts gone—never mind—saves washing. Nothing soon—lie in bed—starve—die—inquest—little bone-house—poor prisoner—common necessaries—hush it up—gentlemen of the jury—warden's tradesmen—keep it snug—natural death—coroner's order—workhouse funeral—serve him right—all over—drop the curtain."

Jingle delivered this singular summary of his prospects in life with his accustomed volubility, and with various twitches of the countenance to counterfeit smiles. Mr. Pickwick easily perceived that his recklessness was assumed, and looking him full, but not unkindly, in the face, saw that his eyes were moist with tears.

"Good fellow," said Jingle, pressing his hand, and turning his head away. "Ungrateful dog—boyish to cry—can't help it—had fever—weak—ill—hungry. Deserved it all; but suffered much—very." Wholly unable to keep up appearances any longer, and perhaps rendered worse by the effort he had made, the dejected stroller sat down on the stairs, and, covering his face with his hands, sobbed like a child.

"Come, come," said Mr. Pickwick, with considerable emotion, "we'll see what can be done when I know all about the matter. Here, Job; where is that fellow?"

"Here, Sir," replied Job, presenting himself on the staircase. We have described him, by-the-bye, as having deeply-sunken eyes in the best of times; in his present state of want and distress, he looked as if those features had gone out of town altogether.

"Here, Sir," said Job.

"Come here, Sir," said Mr. Pickwick, trying to look stern, with four large tears running down his waistcoat. "Take that, Sir."

Take what? In the ordinary acceptation of such language, it should have been a blow. As the world runs, it ought to have been a sound, hearty cuff; for Mr. Pickwick had been duped, deceived, and wronged by the destitute outcast who was now wholly in his power. Must we tell the truth? It was something from Mr. Pickwick's waistcoat-pocket, which chinked as it was given into Job's hand: and the giving which, somehow or other imparted a sparkle to the eye, and a swelling to the heart of our excellent old friend, as he hurried away.

Sam had returned when Mr. Pickwick reached his own room, and was inspecting the arrangements that had been made for his comfort, with a kind of grim satisfaction which was very pleasant to look upon. Having a decided objection to his master's being there at all, Mr. Weller appeared to consider it a high moral duty not to appear too much pleased with anything that was done, said, suggested, or proposed.

"Well, Sam," said Mr. Pickwick.

"Well, Sir," replied Mr. Weller.

"Pretty comfortable now, eh, Sam?"

"Pretty vell, Sir," responded Sam, looking round him in a disparaging manner.

"Have you seen Mr. Tupman and our other friends?"

"Yes, I *have* seen 'em, Sir, and they're a comin' to-morrow, and wos wery much surprised to hear they warn't to come to-day," replied Sam.

"You have brought the things I wanted?"

Mr. Weller in reply pointed to various packages which he had arranged as neatly as he could, in a corner of the room.

"Very well, Sam," said Mr. Pickwick, after a little hesitation; "listen to what I am going to say, Sam."

"Cert'nly, Sir," rejoined Mr. Weller, "fire avay, Sir."

"I have felt from the first, Sam," said Mr. Pickwick, with much solemnity, "that this is not the place to bring a young man to."

"Nor an old 'un neither, Sir," observed Mr. Weller.

"You're quite right, Sam," said Mr. Pickwick; "but old men may come here through their own heedlessness and unsuspicion, and young men may be brought here by the selfishness of those they serve. It is better for those young men, in every point of view, that they should not remain here. Do you understand me, Sam?"

"Vy no, Sir, I do not," replied Mr. Weller, doggedly.

"Try, Sam," said Mr. Pickwick.

"Vell, Sir," rejoined Sam, after a short pause, "I think I see your drift; and if I do see your drift, it's my 'pinion that you're a comin' it a great deal too strong, as the mail-coachman said to the snow storm, ven it overtook him."

"I see you comprehend me, Sam," said Mr. Pickwick. "Independently of my wish that you should not be idling about a place like this for years to come, I feel that for a debtor in the Fleet to be attended by his man-servant is a monstrous absurdity.—Sam," said Mr. Pickwick, "for a time you must leave me."

"Oh, for a time, eh, Sir?" rejoined Mr. Weller, rather sarcastically.

"Yes, for the time that I remain here," said Mr. Pickwick. "Your wages I shall continue to pay. Any one of my three friends will be happy to take you, were it only out of respect to me. And if I ever do leave this place, Sam," added Mr. Pickwick, with assumed cheerfulness—"if I do, I pledge you my word that you shall return to me instantly."

"Now I'll tell you wot it is, Sir," said Mr. Weller, in a grave and solemn voice. "This here sort o' thing von't do at all, so don't let's hear no more about it."

"I am serious, and resolved, Sam," said Mr. Pickwick.

"You air, air you, Sir?" inquired Mr. Weller, firmly. "Wery good, Sir; then so am I."

Thus speaking, Mr. Weller fixed his hat on his head with great precision, and abruptly left the room.

"Sam," said Mr. Pickwick, calling after him, "Sam. Here."

But the long gallery ceased to re-echo the sound of footsteps. Sam Weller was gone.

CHAPTER XLII.

SHOWING HOW MR. SAMUEL WELLER GOT INTO DIFFICULTIES.

In a lofty room, badly lighted and worse ventilated, situated in Portugal-street, Lincoln's Inn-fields, there sit nearly the whole year round, one, two, three, or four gentlemen in wigs, as the case may be, with little writing desks before them, constructed after the fashion of those used by the judges of the land, barring the French polish; a box of barristers on their right hand; an inclosure of insolvent debtors on their left; and an inclined plane of most especially dirty faces in their front. These gentlemen are the Commissioners of the Insolvent Court, and the place in which they sit is the Insolvent Court itself.

It is, and has been, time out of mind, the remarkable fate of this Court to be somehow or other held and understood by the general consent of all the destitute shabby-genteel people in London, as their common resort, and place of daily refuge. It is always full. The steams of beer and spirits perpetually ascend to the ceiling, and, being condensed by the heat, roll down the walls like rain: there are more old suits of clothes in it at one time, than will be offered for sale in all Houndsditch in a twelve-month; and more unwashed skins and grizzly beards than all the pumps and shaving-shops between Tyburn and Whitechapel could render decent between sunrise and sunset.

It must not be supposed that any of these people have the least shadow of business in, or the remotest connexion with, the place they so indefatigably attend. If they had, it would be no matter of surprise, and the singularity of the thing would cease at once. Some of them sleep during the greater part of the sitting; others carry small portable dinners wrapped in pocket handkerchiefs or sticking out of their worn-out pockets, and munch and listen with equal relish; but no one among them was ever known to have the slightest personal interest in any case that was ever brought forward. Whatever they do, there they sit from the first moment to the last. When it is heavy rainy weather, they all come in wet through; and at such times the vapours of the Court are like those of a fungus-pit.

A casual visitor might suppose this place to be a temple dedicated to the Genius of Seediness. There is not a messenger or process-server attached to it, who wears a coat that was made for him; not a tolerably fresh, or wholesome-looking man in the whole establishment, except a little white-headed apple-faced tipstaff, and even he, like an ill-conditioned cherry preserved in brandy, seems to have artificially dried and withered up into a state of preservation, to which he can lay no natural claim. The very barristers' wigs are ill-powdered, and their curls lack crispness.

But the attorneys, who sit at a large bare table below the Commissioners, are, after all, the greatest curiosities. The professional establishment of the more opulent of these gentlemen, consists of a blue bag and a boy: generally a youth of the Jewish persuasion. They have no fixed offices, their legal business being transacted in the parlours of public-houses, or the yards of prisons, whither they repair in crowds, and canvass for customers after the manner of omnibus cads. They are of a greasy and mildewed appearance; and if they can be said to have any vices at all, perhaps drinking and cheating are the most conspicuous among them. Their residences are usually on the outskirts of "the Rules," chiefly lying within a circle of one mile from the obelisk in St. George's Fields. Their looks are not prepossessing, and their manners are peculiar.

Mr. Solomon Pell, one of this learned body, was a fat flabby pale man, in a surtout which looked green one minute, and brown the next, with a velvet collar of the same cameleon tints. His forehead was narrow, his face wide, his head large, and his nose all on one side, as if Nature, indignant with the propensities she observed in him in his birth, had given it an angry tweak which it had never recovered. Being short-necked and asthmatic, however, he respired principally through this feature; so, perhaps, what it wanted in ornament it made up in usefulness.

"I'm sure to bring him through it," said Mr. Pell.

"Are you though?" replied the person to whom the assurance was pledged.

"Certain sure," replied Pell; "but if he'd gone to any irregular practitioner, mind you, I wouldn't have answered for the consequences."

"Ah!" said the other, with open mouth.

"No, that I wouldn't," said Mr. Pell; and he pursed up his lips, frowned, and shook his head mysteriously.

Now the place where this discourse occurred, was the public house just opposite to the Insolvent Court; and the person with whom it was held was no other than the elder Mr. Weller, who had come there to comfort and console a friend, whose petition to be discharged under the act was to be that day heard, and whose attorney he was at that moment consulting.

"And vere is George?" inquired the old gentleman.

Mr. Pell jerked his head in the direction of a back parlour, whither Mr. Weller at once repairing, was immediately greeted in the warmest and most flattering manner by some half-dozen of his professional brethren, in token of their gratification at his arrival. The insolvent gentleman, who had contracted a speculative but imprudent passion for horsing long stages, which had led to his present embarrassments, looked extremely well, and was soothing the excitement of his feelings with shrimps and porter.

The salutation between Mr. Weller and his friends was strictly confined to the freemasonry of the craft; consisting of a jerking round of the right wrist, and a tossing of the little finger into the air at the same time. We once knew two famous coachmen (they are dead now, poor fellows) who were twins, and between whom an unaffected and devoted attachment existed. They passed each other on the Dover road every day, for twenty-four years, never exchanging any other greeting than this; and yet, when one died, the other pined away, and soon afterwards followed him!

"Vell, George," said Mr. Weller, senior, taking off his upper coat, and seating himself with his accustomed gravity. "How is it? All right behind, and full inside?"

"All right, old feller," replied the embarrassed gentlemen.

"Is the grey mare made over to any body?" inquired Mr. Weller, anxiously.

George nodded in the affirmative.

"Vell, that's all right," said Mr. Weller. "Coach taken care on, also?"

"Con-signed in a safe quarter," replied George, wringing the heads off half-a-dozen shrimps, and swallowing them without any more ado.

"Wery good, wery good," said Mr. Weller. "Alvays see to the drag ven you go down hill. Is the vay-bill all clear and straight for'erd."

"The schedule, Sir," said Pell, guessing at Mr. Weller's meaning, "the schedule is as plain and satisfactory as pen and ink can make it."

Mr. Weller nodded in a manner which bespoke his inward approval of these arrangements; and then, turning to Mr. Pell, said, pointing to his friend George,—

"Ven do you take his cloths off?"

"Why," replied Mr. Pell, "he stands third on the opposed list, and I should think it would be his turn in about half an hour. I told my clerk to come over and tell us when there was a chance."

Mr. Weller surveyed the attorney from head to foot with great admiration, and said emphatically,—

"And what'll you take, Sir?"

"Why, really," replied Mr. Pell, "you're very——. Upon my word and honour, I'm not in the habit of——. It's so very early in the morning, that, actually, I am almost——. Well, you may bring me three penn'orth of rum, my dear."

The officiating damsel, who had anticipated the order before it was given, set the glass of spirits before Pell, and retired.

"Gentlemen," said Mr. Pell, looking round upon the company, "Success to your friend. I don't like to boast, gentlemen; it's not my way; but I can't help saying, that, if your friend hadn't been fortunate enough to fall into hands that——but I won't say what I was going to say. Gentlemen, my service to you." Having emptied the glass in a twinkling, Mr. Pell smacked his lips, and looked complacently round on the assembled coachmen, who evidently regarded him as a species of divinity.

"Let me see," said the legal authority—"What was I a-saying, gentlemen?"

"I think you was remarkin' as you wouldn't have no objection to another o' the same, Sir," said Mr. Weller, with grave facetiousness.

"Ha, ha!" laughed Mr. Pell. "Not bad, not bad. A professional man, too! At this time of the morning it would be rather too good a——. Well, I don't know, my dear—you *may* do that again, if you please. Hem!"

This last sound was a solemn and dignified cough, in which Mr. Pell, observing an indecent tendency to mirth in some of his auditors, considered it due to himself to indulge.

"The late Lord Chancellor, gentlemen, was very fond of me," said Mr. Pell.

"And wery creditable in him, too," interposed Mr. Weller.

"Hear, hear," assented Mr. Pell's client. "Why shouldn't he be?"

"Ah—why, indeed!" said a very red-faced man, who had said nothing yet, and who looked extremely unlikely to say anything more. "Why shouldn't he?"

A murmur of assent ran through the company.

"I remember, gentlemen," said Mr. Pell, "dining with him on one occasion;—there was only us two, but every thing as splendid as if twenty people had been expected; the great seal on a dumb-waiter at his right hand, and a man in a bag-wig and suit of armour guarding the mace with a drawn sword and silk stockings, which is perpetually done, gentlemen, night and day; when he said, ' Pell,' he said; ' no false delicacy, Pell. You're a man of talent; you can get any body through the Insolvent Court, Pell; and your country should be proud of you.' Those were his very words.—' My Lord,' I said, ' you flatter me.'—'Pell,' he said, ' if I do, I'm damned.' "

"Did he say that?" inquired Mr. Weller.

"He did," replied Pell.

"Vell, then," said Mr. Weller, "I say Parliament ought to ha' took it up; and if he'd been a poor man, they would ha' done it."

"But, my dear friend," argued Mr. Pell, "it was in confidence."

"In what?" said Mr. Weller.

"In confidence."

"Oh! wery good," replied Mr. Weller, after a little reflection. "If he damned his-self in confidence, o' course that was another thing."

"Of course it was," said Mr. Pell. "The distinction's obvious, you will perceive."

"Alters the case entirely," said Mr. Weller. "Go on, Sir."

"No; I will not go on, Sir," said Mr. Pell, in a low and serious tone. "You have reminded me, Sir, that this conversation was private—private and confidential, gentlemen. Gentlemen, I am a professional man. It may be that I am a good deal looked up to, in my profession—it may be that I am not. Most people know. I say nothing. Observations have already been made, in this room, injurious to the reputation of my noble friend. You will excuse me, gentlemen; I was imprudent. I feel that I have no right to mention this matter without his concurrence. Thank you, Sir; thank you." Thus delivering himself, Mr. Pell thrust his hands into his pockets, and, frowning grimly around, rattled three-halfpence with terrible determination.

This virtuous resolution had scarcely been formed, when the boy and the blue bag, who were inseparable companions, rushed violently into the room, and said (at least the boy did; for the blue bag took no part in the announcement) that the case was coming on directly. The intelligence was no sooner received than the whole party hurried across the street, and began to fight their way into Court—a preparatory ceremony, which has been calculated to occupy, in ordinary cases, from twenty-five minutes to thirty.

Mr. Weller being stout, cast himself at once into the crowd, with the desperate hope of ultimately turning up in some place which would suit him. His success was not quite equal to his expectations, for having neglected to take his hat off, it was knocked over his eyes by some unseen person, upon whose toes he had alighted with considerable force. Apparently this individual regretted his impetuosity immediately aftewards, for, muttering an indistinct exclamation of surprise, he dragged the old man out into the hall, and, after a violent struggle, released his head and face.

"Samivel!" exclaimed Mr. Weller, when he was thus enabled to behold his rescuer.

Sam nodded.

"You're a dutiful and affectionate little boy, you are, ain't you?" said Mr. Weller, "to come a bonnetin' your father in his old age?"

"How should I know who you wos?" responded the son. "Do you s'pose I wos to tell you by the weight o' your foot?"

"Vell, that's wery true, Sammy," replied Mr. Weller, mollified at once; "but wot are you a doin' on here? Your gov'nor can't do no good here, Sammy. They von't pass that werdict; they von't pass it, Sammy." And Mr. Weller shook his head with legal solemnity.

"Wot a perwerse old file it is!" exclaimed Sam, "always a goin' on about werdicts and alleybis, and that. Who said anything about the werdict?"

Mr. Weller made no reply, but once more shook his head most learnedly.

"Leave off rattlin' that 'ere nob o' yourn, if you don't want it to come off the springs altogether," said Sam impatiently, "and behave reasonable. I vent all the vay down to the Markis o' Granby arter you last night."

"Did you see the Marchionness o' Granby, Sammy?" inquired Mr. Weller, with a sigh.

"Yes, I did," replied Sam.

"How wos the dear creetur lookin'?"

"Wery queer," said Sam. "I think she's a injurin' herself gradually vith too much o' that 'ere pine-apple rum, and other strong medicines o' the same natur."

"You don't mean that, Sammy?" said the senior, earnestly.

"I do, indeed," replied the junior.

Mr. Weller seized his son's hand, clasped it, and let it fall. There was an expression on his countenance in doing so—not of dismay or apprehension, but partaking more of the sweet and gentle character of hope. A gleam of resignation, and even of cheerfulness, passed over his face too, as he slowly said—"I ain't quite certain, Sammy; I wouldn't like to say I wos altogether positive, in case of any subsekent disappintment, but I rayther think, my boy —I rayther think that the shepherd's got the liver complaint!"

"Does he look bad?" inquired Sam.

"He's uncommon pale," replied his father, "'cept about the nose, vich is redder than ever. His appetite is wery so-so, but he imbibes wunderful."

Some thoughts of the rum appeared to obtrude themselves on Mr. Weller's mind as he said this, for he looked gloomy and thoughtful; but very shortly recovered, as was testified by a perfect alphabet of winks, in which he was only wont to indulge when particularly pleased.

"Vell, now," said Sam, "about my affair. Just open

them ears o' yourn, and don't say nothin' till I've done." With this brief preface, Sam related, as succinctly as he could, the last memorable conversation he had had with Mr. Pickwick.

"Stop there by himself, poor creetur!" exclaimed the elder Mr. Weller, "without nobody to take his part! It can't be done, Samivel, it can't be done."

"O' course it can't," asserted Sam; "I know'd that afore I came."

"Vy, they'll eat him up alive, Sammy," exclaimed Mr. Weller.

Sam nodded his concurrence in the opinion.

"He goes in rayther raw, Sammy," said Mr. Weller metaphorically, "and he'll come out done so ex-ceedin' brown, that his most formiliar friends won't know him. Roast pigeon's nothin' to it, Sammy."

Again Sam Weller nodded.

"It oughtn't to be, Samivel," said Mr. Weller, gravely.

"I mustn't be," said Sam.

"Cert'nly no," said Mr. Weller.

"Vell now," said Sam, "you've been a prophecyin' avay wery fine, like a red-faced Nixon, as the sixpenny books gives picters on."

"Who wos he, Sammy?" inquired Mr. Weller.

"Never mind who he was," retorted Sam; "he warn't a coachman, that's enough for you."

"I know'd a ostler o' that name," said Mr. Weller, musing.

"It warn't him," said Sam. "This here gen'lm'n was a prophet."

"Wot's a prophet?" inquired Mr. Weller, looking sternly on his son.

"Vy, a man as tells what's a goin' to happen," replied Sam.

"I wish I'd know'd him, Sammy," said Mr. Weller. "P'raps he might ha' throw'd a small light on that 'ere liver complaint as we wos a speakin' on just now. Hows'-ever, if he's dead, and ain't left the bisness to nobody, there's an end on it. Go on, Sammy," said Mr. Weller, with a sigh.

"Vell," said Sam, "you're been a prophecyin' avay about wot'll happen to the gov'nor if he's left alone. Don't you see any vay o' takin' care on him?"

"No, I don't, Sammy," said Mr. Weller, with a reflect-ive visage.

"No vay at all?" inquired Sam.

"No vay," said Mr. Weller, "unless "—and a gleam of intelligence lighted up his countenance as he sunk his voice to a whisper, and applied his mouth to the ear of his off-spring—"unless it is getting him out in a turn-up bed-stead, unbeknown to the turnkeys, Sammy, or dressin' him up like an old 'ooman vith a green wail."

Sam Weller received both of these suggestions with un-expected contempt, and again propounded his question.

"No," said the old gentleman; "if he von't let you stop there, I see no vay at all. It's no thoroughfare, Sammy— no thoroughfare."

"Well, then, I'll tell you wot it is," said Sam, "I'll trouble you for the loan of five-and-tventy pound."

"Wot good 'ull that do?" inquired Mr. Weller.

"Never mind," replied Sam. "P'raps you may ask for it five minits artervards; p'raps I may say I von't pay, and cut up rough. You von't think o' arrestin' your own son for the money, and sendin' him off to the Fleet, will you, you unnat'ral wagabone?"

At this reply of Sam's, the father and son exchanged a complete code of sly telegraphic nods and gestures, after which, the elder Mr. Weller sat himself down on a stone step, and laughed till he was purple.

"Wot a old image it is!" exclaimed Sam, indignant at this loss of time. "What are you a settin' down there for, con-wertin' your face into a street-door knocker, ven there's so much to be done. Vere's the money?"

"In the boot, Sammy, in the boot," replied Mr. Weller, composing his features. "Hold my hat, Sammy."

Having divested himself of this incumbrance, Mr. Wel-ler gave his body a sudden wrench to one side, and, by a dexterous twist, contrived to get his right hand into a most capacious pocket, from whence, after a great deal of pant-ing and exertion, he extricated a pocket-book of the large octavo size, fastened by a huge leather strap. From thence he drew forth a couple of whip-lashes, three or four buckles, a little sample-bag of corn, and finally a small roll of very dirty bank-notes, from which he selected the required amount, which he handed over to Sam.

"And now, Sammy," said the old gentleman, when the whip-lashes, and the buckles, and the sample, had been all put back, and the book once more deposited at the bottom of the same pocket, "Now, Sammy, I know a gen'lm'n here, as 'll do the rest o' the bisness for us, in no time—a limb o' the law, Sammy, as has got brains like the frogs, dispersed all over his body, and reachin' to the wery tips of his fingers; a friend of the Lord Chancellorship's, Sammy, who'd only have to tell him what he wanted, and he'd lock you up for life, if that wos all."

"I say," said Sam, "none o' that."

"None o' wot?" inquired Mr. Weller.

"Vy, none o' them unconstitootional ways o' doin' it," retorted Sam. "The have-his-carcase, next to the per-petual motion, is vun o' the blessedest things as wos ever made. I've read that 'ere in the newspapers wery of'en."

"Well, wot's that got to do vith it?" inquired Mr. Wel-ler.

"Just this here," said Sam, "that I'll patronise the in-wention, and go in, that vay. No visperin's to the Chan-cellorship—I don't like the notion. It mayn't be alto-gether safe, vith reference to the gettin' out agin."

Deferring to his son's feeling upon this point, Mr. Weller at once sought the erudite Solomon Pell, and ac-quainted him with his desire to issue a writ instantly for the sum of twenty-five pounds, and costs of process, to be executed without delay upon the body of one Samuel Wel-ler; the charges thereby incurred to be paid in advance to Solomon Pell.

The attorney was in high glee, for the embarrassed coach-horse was ordered to be discharged forthwith. He highly approved of Sam's attachment to his master; de-clared that it strongly reminded him of his own feelings of devotion to his friend, the Chancellor; and at once led the elder Mr. Weller down to the Temple to swear the affi-davit of debt, which the boy, with the assistance of the blue bag, had drawn up on the spot.

Meanwhile Sam, having been formally introduced to the white-washed gentleman and his friends, as the offspring of Mr. Weller, of the Belle Sauvage, was treated with marked distinction, and invited to regale himself with them in honour of the occasion—an invitation which he was by no means backward in accepting.

The mirth of gentlemen of this class is of a grave and quiet character usually; but the present instance was one of peculiar festivity, and they relaxed in proportion. After some rather tumultuous toasting of the Chief Commissioner and Mr. Solomon Pell, who had that day displayed such transcendent abilities, a mottled-faced gentleman in a blue shawl proposed that somebody should sing a song. The obvious suggestion was, that the mottled-faced gentleman, being anxious for a song, should sing it himself; but this the mottled-faced gentleman, sturdily, and somewhat offensively, declined to do; upon which, as is not unusual in such cases, a rather angry colloquy ensued.

"Gentlemen," said the coach-horser, "rather than disturb the harmony of this delightful occasion, perhaps Mr. Samuel Weller will oblige the company."

"Raly, gentlemen," said Sam, "I'm not wery much in the habit o' singin' vithout the instrument; but anythin' for a quiet life, as the man said ven he took the sitivation at the light-house."

With this prelude, Mr. Samuel Weller burst at once into the following wild and beautiful legend, which, under the impression that it is not generally known, we take the liberty of quoting. We would beg to call particular attention to the monosyllable at the end of the second and fourth lines, which not only enables the singer to take breath at those points, but greatly assists the metre.

Romance.

I.

Bold Turpin vunce, on Hounslow Heath,
His bold mare Bess bestrode—er;
Ven there he see'd the Bishop's coach
A-comin' along the road—er.
So he gallops close to the orse's legs,
And he claps his head vithin;
And the Bishop says, "Sure as eggs is eggs,
This here's the bold Turpin!"

(CHORUS.) *And the Bishop says, "Sure as eggs is eggs,
This here's the bold Turpin!"*

II.

Says Turpin, "You shall eat your words,
With a sarse of leaden bul—let";
So he puts a pistol to his mouth,
And he fires it down his gul—let.
The coachman, he not likin' the job,
Set off at a full gal—lop,
But Dick put a couple of balls in his nob,
And perwailed on him to stop.

(CHORUS *sarcastically.*) *But Dick put a couple of balls in his nob,
And perwailed on him to stop.*

"I maintain that that 'ere song's personal to the cloth," said the mottled-faced gentleman, interrupting it at this point. "I demand the name o' that coachman."

"Nobody know'd," replied Sam. "He hadn't got his card in his pocket."

"I object to the introduction o' politics," said the mottled-faced gentleman. "I submit that, in the present company, that 'ere song's political; and, wot's much the same, that it ain't true. I say that that coachman did *not* run away; but that he died game—game as pheasants; and I won't hear nothin' said to the contrairey."

As the mottled-faced gentleman spoke with great energy and determination, and as the opinions of the company seemed divided on the subject, it threatened to give rise to fresh altercation, when Mr. Weller and Mr. Pell most opportunely arrived.

"All right, Sammy," said Mr. Weller.

"The officer will be here at four o'clock," said Mr. Pell. "I suppose you won't run away meanwhile—eh? Ha! ha!"

"P'raps my cruel pa 'ull relent afore that," replied Sam, with a broad grin.

"Not I," said the elder Mr. Weller.

"Do," said Sam.

"Not on no account," replied the inexorable creditor.

"I'll give bills for the amount at sixpence a month," said Sam.

"I won't take 'em," said Mr. Weller.

"Ha, ha, ha! very good, very good," said Mr. Solomon Pell, who was making out his little bill of costs; "a very amusing incident indeed. Benjamin, copy that," and Mr. Pell smiled again, as he called Mr. Weller's attention to the amount.

"Thank you, thank you," said the professional gentleman, taking up another of the greasy notes as Mr. Weller took it from the pocket-book. "Three ten and one ten is five. Much obliged to you, Mr. Weller. Your son is a most deserving young man, very much so indeed, Sir. It's a very pleasant trait in a young man's character—very much so," added Mr. Pell, smiling smoothly round, as he buttoned up the money.

"Wot a game it is!" said the elder Mr. Weller, with a chuckle. "A reg'lar prodigy son!"

"Prodigal—prodigal son, Sir," suggested Mr. Pell, mildly.

"Never mind, Sir," said Mr. Weller, with dignity. "I know wot's o'clock, Sir. Ven I don't, I'll ask you, Sir."

By the time the officer arrived, Sam had made himself so extremely popular, that the congregated gentlemen determined to see him to prison in a body. So off they set; the plaintiff and defendant walking arm-in-arm, the officer in front, and eight stout coachmen bringing up the rear. At Serjeants' Inn Coffee-house the whole party halted to refresh; and, the legal arrangements being completed, the procession moved on again.

Some little commotion was occasioned in Fleet Street by the pleasantry of the eight gentlemen in the flank, who persevered in walking four abreast; and it was also found necessary to leave the mottled-faced gentleman behind, to fight a ticket-porter, it being arranged that his friends should call for him as they came back. Nothing but these little incidents occurred on the way. When they reached the gate of the Fleet, the cavalcade, taking the time from the plaintiff, gave three tremendous cheers for the defendant; and, after having shaken hands all round, left him.

Sam having been formally delivered into the warden's custody, to the intense astonishment of Roker, and to the evident emotion of even the phlegmatic Neddy, passed at once into the prison, walked straight to his master's room, and knocked at the door.

"Come in," said Mr. Pickwick.

Sam appeared, pulled off his hat, and smiled.

"Ah, Sam, my good lad," said Mr. Pickwick, evidently delighted to see his humble friend again; "I had no intention of hurting your feelings yesterday, my faithful fellow, by what I said. Put down your hat, Sam, and let me explain my meaning a little more at length."

"Won't presently do, Sir?" inquired Sam.

"Certainly," said Mr. Pickwick; "but why not now?"

"I'd rayther not now, Sir," rejoined Sam.

"Why?" inquired Mr. Pickwick.

"'Cause," said Sam, hesitating.

"Because of what?" inquired Mr. Pickwick, alarmed at his follower's manner. "Speak out, Sam."

"'Cause," rejoined Sam; "'cause I've got a little bisness as I want to do."

"What business?" inquired Mr. Pickwick, surprised at Sam's confused manner.

"Nothin' partickler, Sir," replied Sam.

"Oh, if it's nothing particular," said Mr. Pickwick, with a smile, "you can speak with me first."

"I think I'd better see arter it at once," said Sam, still hesitating.

Mr. Pickwick looked amazed, but said nothing.

"The fact is——" said Sam, stopping short.

"Well!" said Mr. Pickwick. "Speak out, Sam."

"Why, the fact is," said Sam, with a desperate effort, "P'raps I'd better see arter my bed afore I do anythin' else."

"*Your bed!*" exclaimed Mr. Pickwick, in astonishment.

"Yes, my bed, Sir," replied Sam. "I'm a prisoner. I was arrested this here wery arternoon for debt."

"You arrested for debt!" exclaimed Mr. Pickwick, sinking into a chair.

"Yes, for debt, Sir," replied Sam; "and the man as put me in 'ull never let me out, till you go yourself."

"Bless my heart and soul!" ejaculated Mr. Pickwick. "What do you mean?"

"Wot I say, Sir," rejoined Sam. "If it's forty year to come, I shall be a pris'ner, and I'm very glad on it; and if it had been Newgate, it 'ould ha' been just the same. Now the murder's out, and, damme, there's an end on it."

With these words, which he repeated with great emphasis and violence, Sam Weller dashed his hat upon the ground, in a most unusual state of excitement; and then, folding his arms, looked firmly and fixedly in his master's face.

CHAPTER XLIII.

TREATS OF DIVERS LITTLE MATTERS WHICH OCCURRED IN THE FLEET, AND OF MR. WINKLE'S MYSTERIOUS BEHAVIOUR; AND SHOWS HOW THE POOR CHANCERY PRISONER OBTAINED HIS RELEASE AT LAST.

MR. PICKWICK felt a great deal too much touched by the warmth of Sam's attachment, to be able to exhibit any manifestation of anger or displeasure at the precipitate course he had adopted, in voluntarily consigning himself to a debtors' prison for an indefinite period. The only point on which he persevered in demanding any explanation, was, the name of Sam's detaining creditor, but this Mr. Weller as perseveringly withheld.

"It ain't o' no use, Sir," said Sam, again and again. "He's a ma-licious, bad-disposed, vorldly-minded, spiteful, windictive creetur, with a hard heart as there ain't no soft'-nin, as the wirtuous clergyman remarked of the old gen'-lm'n with the dropsy, ven he said, that upon the whole he thought he'd rayther leave his property to his vife than build a chapel vith it."

"But consider, Sam," Mr. Pickwick remonstrated, "the sum is so small that it can very easily be paid, and having made up my mind that you shall stop with me, you should recollect how much more useful you would be, if you could go outside the walls."

"Wery much obliged to you, Sir," replied Mr. Weller gravely; "but I'd rayther not."

"Rather not do what, Sam?"

"Vy, Sir, I'd rayther not let myself down to ask a favor o' this here unremorseful enemy."

"But it is no favor asking him to take the money, Sam," reasoned Mr. Pickwick.

"Beg your pardon, Sir," rejoined Sam; "but it 'ud be a wery great favor to pay it, and he don't deserve none; that's vere it is, Sir."

Here Mr. Pickwick, rubbing his nose with an air of some vexation, Mr. Weller thought it prudent to change the theme of the discourse.

"I takes my determination on principle, Sir," remarked Sam, "and you takes yours on the same ground; vich puts me in mind o' the man as killed his-self on principle, vich o' course you've heerd on, Sir." Mr. Weller paused when he arrived at this point, and cast a comical look at his master out of the corners of his eyes.

"There is no of course in the case, Sam," said Mr. Pickwick, gradually breaking into a smile, in spite of the uneasiness which Sam's obstinacy had given him. "The fame of the gentleman in question never reached my ears."

"No, Sir!" exclaimed Mr. Weller. "You astonish me, Sir; he wos a clerk in a gov'ment office, Sir."

"Was he?" said Mr. Pickwick.

"Yes, he wos, Sir," rejoined Mr. Weller; "and a very pleasant gen'lm'n—one o' the precise and tidy sort, as puts their feet in little India-rubber fire buckets ven its vet veather, and never has no other bosom friends but hare-skins; he saved up his money on principle, vore a clean shirt ev'ry day on principle, never spoke to none of his relations on principle, 'fear they shou'd want to borrow money of him; and wos altogether, in fact, an uncommon agreeable character. He had his hair cut on principle vunce a fortnight, and contracted for his clothes on the economic principle—three suits a year, and send back the old vuns. Being a wery reg-lar gen'lm'n, he din'd ev'ry day at the same place, vere it wos one and ninepence to cut off the joint; and a wery good one and ninepence worth he used to cut, as the landlord often said, vith the tears a tricklin' down his face, let alone the vay he used to poke the fire in the vinter time, vich wos a dead loss o' four-pence ha'penny a day, to say nothin' at all o' the aggra-wation o' seein' him do it. So uncommon grand vith it too! 'Post arter the next gen'lm'n,' he sings out ev'ry day ven he comes in. 'See arter the Times, Thomas; let me look at the Mornin' Herald, ven it's out o' hand; don't forget to bespeak the Chronicle; and just bring the 'Tizer vill you:' and then he'd set vith his eyes fixed on the clock, and rush out just a quarter of a minit afore the time to vaylay the boy as was a comin' in vith the evenin' paper, vich he'd read vith sich intense interest and perse-werance, as vorked the other customers up to the wery confines o' desperation and insanity, 'specially one i-rascible old gen'lm'n as the vaiter wos always obliged to keep a sharp eye on at sich times, 'fear he should be tempted to commit some rash act vith the carving knife. Vell, Sir, here he'd stop, occupyin' the best place for three hours, and never takin' nothin' arter his dinner but sleep, and then he'd go avay to a coffeehouse a few streets off, and have a small pot o' coffee and four crumpets, arter vich he'd valk home to Kensington and go to bed. One night he wos took very ill; sends for the doctor; doctor comes in a green fly, vith a kind o' Robinson Crusoe set o' steps as he could let down ven he got out, and pull up arter him ven he got in, to perwent the necessity o' the coachman's gettin' down, and thereby undeceivin' the public by lettin' 'em see that it wos only a livery coat he'd got on, and not the trousers to match. 'Wot's the matter?' says the doctor. 'Wery ill,' says the patient. 'Wot have you been a eatin' of?' says the doctor. 'Roast weal,' says the patient. 'Wot's the last thing you dewoured?' says the doctor. 'Crumpets,' says the patient. 'That's it,' says the doctor. 'I'll send you a box of pills directly, and don't you never take no more o' them,' he says. 'No more o' wot?' says the patient—'Pills!' 'No; crumpets,' says the doctor. 'Wy?' says the patient, starting up in bed; 'I've eat four crumpets ev'ry night for fifteen year on principle.' 'Vell, then, you'd better leave 'em off on principle,' says the doctor. 'Crumpets is wholesome, Sir,' says the patient. 'Crumpets is *not* wholesome, Sir,' says the doctor, wery fiercely. 'But they're so cheap,' says the patient, comin' down a little, 'and so wery fillin' at the price.' 'They'd be dear to you at any price; dear if you wos paid to eat 'em,' says the doctor. 'Four crumpets a night,' he says, 'vill do your business in six months!' The patient looks him full in the face, and turns it over in his mind for a long time, and at last he says, 'Are you sure o' that 'ere, Sir?' 'I'll stake my professional reputation on it,' says the doctor. 'How many crumpets at a sittin' do you think 'ud kill me off at once?' says the patient. 'I don't know,' says the doctor. 'Do you think half a crown's vurth 'ud do it?' says the patient. 'I think it might,' says the doctor. 'Three shillin's vurth 'ud be sure to do it, I s'pose?' says the patient. 'Certainly,' says the doctor. 'Wery good,' says the patient; 'good night.' Next mornin' he gets up, has a fire lit, orders in three shillins' vurth o' crumpets, toasts 'em all, eats 'em all, and blows his brains out."

"What did he do that for?" enquired Mr. Pickwick abruptly; for he was considerably startled by this tragical termination of the narrative.

"Wot did he do it for, Sir?" reiterated Sam. "Wy, in support of his great principle that crumpets wos wholesome, and to show that he vouldn't be put out of his vay for nobody!"

With such like shiftings and changings of the discourse, did Mr. Weller meet his master's questioning upon the night of his taking up his residence in the Fleet: finding all gentle remonstrance useless, Mr. Pickwick at length yielded a reluctant consent to his taking lodgings by the week, of a bald-headed cobbler, who rented a small slip room in one of the upper galleries. To this humble apartment Mr. Weller moved a mattress and bedding, which he hired of Mr. Roker; and by the time he lay down upon it at night was as much at home as if he had been bred in the prison, and his whole family had vegetated therein for three generations.

"Do you alvays smoke arter you goes to bed, old cock?" enquired Mr. Weller of his landlord, when they had both retired for the night.

"Yes, I does, young bantam," replied the cobbler.

"Vill you allow me to en-quire vy you make up your bed under that 'ere deal table?" said Sam.

"'Cause I was alvays used to a four-poster afore I came here, and I find the legs of the table answer just as well," replied the cobbler.

"You're a character, Sir," said Sam.

"I haven't got anything of the kind belonging to me," rejoined the cobbler, shaking his head; "and if you want

to meet with a good one, I'm afraid you'll find some difficulty in suiting yourself at this register office."

The above short dialogue took place as Mr. Weller lay extended on his mattrass at one end of the room, and the cobbler on his at the other; the apartment being illumined by the light of a rush candle and the cobbler's pipe, which was glowing below the table like a red-hot coal. The conversation, brief as it was, predisposed Mr. Weller strongly in his landlord's favour, and raising himself on his elbow he took a more lengthened survey of his appearance than he had yet had either time or inclination to make.

He was a sallow man—all cobblers are; and had a strong bristly beard—all cobblers have; his face was a queer, good-tempered, crooked featured piece of workmanship, ornamented with a couple of eyes that must have worn a very joyous expression at one time, for they sparkled yet. The man was sixty by years, and Heaven knows how old by imprisonment, so that his having any look approaching to mirth or contentment was singular enough. He was a little man, and being half doubled up as he lay in bed, looked about as long as he ought to have been without his legs. He had got a great red pipe in his mouth, and was smoking and staring at the rushlight in a state of enviable placidity.

"Have you been here long?" enquired Sam, breaking the silence which had lasted for some time.

"Twelve year," replied the cobbler, biting the end of his pipe as he spoke.

"Contempt?" enquired Sam.

The cobbler nodded.

"Vell, then," said Sam, with some sternness, "wot do you persevere in bein' obstinit for, vastin' your precious life avay in this here magnified pound? Vy don't you give in, and tell the Chancellorship that you're wery sorry for makin' his court contemptible, and you won't do so no more?"

The cobbler put his pipe in the corner of his mouth while he smiled, and then brought it back to its old place again, but said nothing.

"Vy don't you?" said Sam, urging his question strenuously.

"Ah," said the cobbler, "you don't quite understand these matters. What do you suppose ruined me, now?"

"Vy," said Sam, trimming the rushlight, "I s'pose the beginnin' wos, that you got into debt, eh?"

"Never owed a farden," said the cobbler; "try again."

"Vell, perhaps," said Sam, "you bought houses, vich is delicate English for goin' mad; or took to buildin', vich is a medical term for bein' incurable."

The cobbler shook his head, and said—"Try again."

"You didn't go to law, I hope?" said Sam, suspiciously.

"Never in my life," replied the cobbler. "The fact is, I was ruined by having money left me."

"Come, come," said Sam, "that von't do. I vish some rich enemy 'ud try to vork my destruction in that 'ere vay. I'd let him."

"Oh, I dare say you don't believe it," said the cobbler, quietly smoking his pipe. "I wouldn't if I was you; but it's true for all that."

"How wos it?" enquired Sam, half induced to believe the fact already by the look the cobbler gave him.

"Just this," replied the cobbler; "an old gentleman, that I worked for, down in the country, and a humble relation of whose I married—she's dead, God bless her, and thank Him for it—was seized with a fit and went off."

"Where?" inquired Sam, who was growing sleepy after the numerous events of the day.

"How should I know where he went?" said the cobbler, speaking through his nose in an intense enjoyment of his pipe. "He went off dead."

"Oh, that indeed," said Sam. "Vell?"

"Well," said the cobbler, "he left five thousand pound behind him."

"And wery gen-teel in him so to do," said Sam.

"One of which," continued the cobbler, "he left to me, 'cause I'd married his relation, you see."

"Wery good," murmured Sam.

"And being surrounded by a great number of nieces and nevys, as was always quarrelling and fighting among themselves for the property, he makes me his executor, and leaves the rest to me in trust, to divide it among 'em as the will prowided."

"Wot do you mean by leavin' it on trust?" inquired Sam, waking up a little. "If it ain't ready money, vere's the use on it?"

"It's a law term, that's all," said the cobbler.

"I don't think that," said Sam, shaking his head. "There's wery little trust at that shop. Hows'ever, go on."

"Well," said the cobbler, "when I was going to take out a probate of the will, the nieces and nevys, who was desperately disappointed at not getting all the money, enters a caveat against it."

"What's that?" inquired Sam.

"A legal instrument, which is as much as to say, it's no go," replied the cobbler.

"I see," said Sam, "a sort of brother-in-law o' the have-his-carcase. Vell."

"But," continued the cobbler, "finding that they couldn't agree among themselves, and consequently couldn't get up a case against the will, they withdrew the caveat, and I paid all the legacies. I'd hardly done it, when one nevy brings an action to set the will aside. The case comes on some months afterwards, before a deaf old gentleman, in a back room somewhere down by Paul's Churchyard; and after four counsels had taken a day a-piece to bother him regularly, he takes a veek or two to consider and read the evidence in six vollums, and then gives his judgment that how the testator was not quite right in his head, and I must pay all the money back again, and all the costs. I appealed; the case come on before three or four very sleepy gentlemen, who had heard it all before in the other court, where they're lawyers without work; the only difference being, that there they're called doctors, and in the other place delegates, if you understand that; and they very dutifully confirmed the decision of the old gentleman below. After that we went into Chancery, where we are still, and where I shall always be. My lawyers have had all my thousand pound long ago; and what between the estate, as they call it, and the costs, I'm here for ten thousand, and shall stop here till I die, mending shoes. Some gentlemen have talked of bringing it before parliament, and I dare say would have done it, only they hadn't time to come to me, and I hadn't power to go to them; and they got tired of my long letters, and dropped the business. And this is God's truth, without one word of suppression or exaggeration, as fifty people, both in this place and out of it, very well know."

The cobbler paused to ascertain what effect his story had produced upon Sam; but finding that he had dropped asleep, knocked the ashes out of his pipe, sighed, put it down, drew the bedclothes over his head, and went to sleep too.

Mr. Pickwick was sitting at breakfast alone next morning, Sam being busily engaged in the cobbler's room, polishing his master's shoes and brushing the black gaiters, when there came a knock at the door, which, before Mr. Pickwick could cry "Come in," was followed by the appearance of a head of hair and a cotton-velvet cap, both of which articles of dress he had no difficulty in recognising as the personal property of Mr. Smangle.

"How are you?" said that worthy, accompanying the inquiry with a score or two of nods; "I say, do you expect anybody this morning? Three men—devilish gentlemanly fellows—have been asking after you down stairs, and knocking at every door on the Hall flight; for which they've been most infernally blown up by the collegians that had the trouble of opening 'em."

"Dear me! How very foolish of them," said Mr. Pickwick, rising. "Yes, I have no doubt they are some friends whom I rather expected to see yesterday."

"Friends of yours," exclaimed Smangle, seizing Mr. Pickwick by the hand. "Say no more. Curse me, they're friends of mine from this minute, and friends of Mivins's too. Infernal pleasant gentlemanly dog, Mivins, isn't he?" said Smangle, with great feeling.

"I know so little of the gentleman," said Mr. Pickwick, hesitating, "that I——"

"I know you do," interposed Smangle, clasping Mr. Pickwick by the shoulder. "You shall know him better, You'll be delighted with him. That man, Sir," said Smangle, with a solemn countenance, "has comic powers that would do honour to Drury Lane Theatre."

"Has he indeed?" said Mr. Pickwick.

"Ah, by Jove he has!" replied Smangle. "Hear him come the four cats in the wheelbarrow—four distinct cats, Sir, I pledge you my honour. Now you know that's infernal clever; dam'me, you can't help liking a man, when you see these sort of traits about him. He's only one fault—that little failing I mentioned to you, you know."

As Mr. Smangle shook his head in a confidential and sympathising manner at this juncture, Mr. Pickwick felt that he was expected to say something, so he said "Ah!" and looked restlessly at the door.

"Ah!" echoed Mr. Smangle, with a long-drawn sigh. "He's delightful company, that man is, Sir—I don't know better company anywhere; but he has that one drawback. If the ghost of his grandfather, Sir, was to rise before him this minute, he'd ask him for the loan of his acceptance on an eighteenpenny stamp."

"Dear me!" exclaimed Mr. Pickwick.

"Yes," added Mr. Smangle; "and if he'd the power of raising him again, he would, in two months and three days from this time, to renew the bill!"

"These are very remarkable traits," said Mr. Pickwick; "but I'm afraid that while we are talking here, my friends may be in a state of great perplexity at not finding me."

"I'll show 'em the way," said Smangle, making for the door. "Good day, I won't disturb you while they're here, you know. By-the-bye——"

As Smangle pronounced the last three words, he stopped suddenly, reclosed the door which he had opened, and, walking softly back to Mr. Pickwick, stepped close up to him on tiptoe, and said in a very soft whisper—

"You couldn't make it convenient to lend me half-a-crown till the latter end of next week, could you?"

Mr. Pickwick could scarcely forbear smiling, but managing to preserve his gravity, he drew forth the coin, and placed it in Mr. Smangle's palm; upon which that gentleman, with many nods and winks, implying profound mystery, disappeared in quest of the three strangers, with whom he presently returned; and having coughed thrice, and nodded as many times, as an assurance to Mr. Pickwick that he should not forget to pay, he shook hands all round in an engaging manner, and at length took himself off.

"My dear friends," said Mr. Pickwick, shaking hands alternately with Mr. Tupman, Mr. Winkle, and Mr. Snodgrass, who were the three visitors in question, "I am delighted to see you."

The triumvirate were much affected. Mr. Tupman shook his head deploringly; Mr. Snodgrass drew forth his handkerchief with undisguised emotion; and Mr. Winkle retired to the window, and sniffed aloud.

"Mornin', gen'l'm'n," said Sam, entering at the moment with the shoes and gaiters; "avay vith melincholly, as the little boy said ven his school missis died. Velcome to the college, gen'l'm'n."

"This foolish fellow," said Mr. Pickwick, tapping Sam on the head as he knelt down to button up his master's gaiters—"this foolish fellow has got himself arrested, in order to be near me."

"What!" exclaimed the three friends.

"Yes, gen'l'm'n," said Sam, "I'm a—stand steady, Sir, if you please—I'm a pris'ner, gen'l'm'n; con-fined, as the lady said."

"A prisoner!" exclaimed Mr. Winkle, with unaccountable vehemence.

"Hallo, Sir!" responded Sam, looking up. "Wot's the matter, Sir?"

"I had hoped, Sam, that—nothing, nothing," said Mr. Winkle, precipitately.

There was something so very abrupt and unsettled in Mr. Winkle's manner, that Mr. Pickwick involuntarily looked at his two friends for an explanation.

"We don't know," said Mr. Tupman, answering this mute appeal aloud. "He has been much excited for two days past, and his whole demeanour very unlike what it usually is. We feared there must be something the matter, but he resolutely denies it."

"No, no," said Mr. Winkle, colouring beneath Mr. Pickwick's gaze; "there is really nothing. I assure you there is nothing, my dear Sir. It will be necessary for me to leave town for a short time on private business, and I had hoped to have prevailed upon you to allow Sam to accompany me."

Mr. Pickwick looked more astonished than before.

"I think," faultered Mr. Winkle, "that Sam would have had no objection to do so; but of course his being a prisoner here, renders it impossible. So I must go alone."

As Mr. Winkle said these words, Mr. Pickwick felt, with some astonishment, that Sam's fingers were trembling at the gaiters, as if he were rather surprised or startled. He looked up at Mr. Winkle, too, when he had finished speaking, and though the glance they exchanged was instantaneous, they seemed to understand each other.

"Do you know anything of this, Sam?" said Mr. Pickwick sharply.

"No, I don't, Sir," replied Mr. Weller, beginning to button with extraordinary assiduity.

"Are you sure, Sam?" said Mr. Pickwick.

"Vy, Sir," responded Mr. Weller; "I'm sure so far, that I've never heerd anythin' on the subject afore this moment. If I makes any guess about it," added Sam, looking at Mr. Winkle, "I haven't got any right to say wot it is, 'fear it should be a wrong 'un."

"I have no right to make any further enquiry into the private affairs of a friend, however intimate a one," said Mr. Pickwick, after a short silence; "at present let me merely say, that I do not understand this at all. There—we have had quite enough of the subject."

Thus expressing himself, Mr. Pickwick led the conversation to different topics, and Mr. Winkle gradually appeared more at ease, though still very far from being completely so. They had all so much to converse about, that the morning very quickly passed away; and when at three o'clock, Mr. Weller produced upon the little dining table, a roast leg of mutton and an enormous meat pie, with sundry dishes of vegetables, and pots of porter, which stood upon the chairs or the sofa-bedstead, or where they could, everybody felt disposed to do justice to the meal, notwithstanding that the meat had been purchased and dressed, and the pie made and baked at the prison cookery hard by.

To these succeeded a bottle or two of very good wine, for which a messenger was dispatched by Mr. Pickwick to the Horn Coffee-house, in Doctors' Commons. The bottle or two, indeed, might be more properly described as a bottle or six, for by the time it was drunk and tea over, the bell began to ring for strangers to withdraw.

But if Mr. Winkle's behaviour had been unaccountable in the morning, it became perfectly unearthly and solemn when, under the influence of his feelings and his share of the bottle or six, he prepared to take leave of his friend. He lingered behind, until Mr. Tupman and Mr. Snodgrass had disappeared, and then fervently clenched Mr. Pickwick's hand with an expression of face, in which deep and mighty resolve was fearfully blended with the very concentrated essence of gloom.

"Good night, my dear Sir," said Mr. Winkle between his set teeth.

"Bless you, my dear fellow," replied the warm-hearted Mr. Pickwick, as he returned the pressure of his young friend's hand.

"Now then," cried Mr. Tupman from the gallery.

"Yes, yes, directly," replied Mr. Winkle. "Good night."

"Good night," said Mr. Pickwick.

There was another good night, and another, and half a dozen more after that, and still Mr. Winkle had fast hold of his friend's hand, and was looking into his face with the same strange expression.

"Is anything the matter?" said Mr. Pickwick at last, when his arm was quite sore with shaking.

"Nothing," said Mr. Winkle.

"Well then, good night," said Mr. Pickwick, attempting to disengage his hand.

"My friend, my benefactor, my honoured companion," murmured Mr. Winkle, catching at his wrist. "Do not judge me harshly; do not, when you hear that driven to extremity by hopeless obstacles, I——"

"Now then," said Mr. Tupman, re-appearing at the door. "Are you coming, or are we to be locked in?"

"Yes, yes, I am ready," replied Mr. Winkle. And with a violent effort he tore himself away.

As Mr. Pickwick was gazing down the passage after

them in silent astonishment, Sam Weller appeared at the stair-head, and whispered for one moment in Mr. Winkle's ear.

"Oh certainly, depend upon me," said that gentleman aloud.

"Thankee, Sir. You von't forget, Sir?" said Sam.

"Of course not," replied Mr. Winkle.

"Vish you luck, Sir," said Sam, touching his hat. "I should very much liked to ha' joined you, Sir; but the gov'ner o' course is pairamount."

"It is very much to your credit that you remain here," said Mr. Winkle. With these words they disappeared down the stairs.

"Very extraordinary," said Mr. Pickwick, going back into his room, and seating himself at the table in a musing attitude. "What can that young man be going to do!"

He had sat ruminating about the matter for some time, when the voice of Roker the turnkey, demanded whether he might come in.

"By all means," said Mr. Pickwick.

"I've brought you a softer pillow, Sir," said Roker, "instead of the temporary one you had last night."

"Thank you," said Mr. Pickwick. "Will you take a glass of wine?"

"You're wery good, Sir," replied Mr. Roker, accepting the proffered glass. "Yours, Sir."

"Thank you," said Mr. Pickwick.

"I'm sorry to say that your landlord's wery bad to-night, Sir," said Roker, setting down the glass, and inspecting the lining of his hat preparatory to putting it on again.

"What! The Chancery prisoner!" exclaimed Mr. Pickwick.

"He won't be a Chancery prisoner wery long, Sir," replied Roker, turning his hat round so as to get the maker's name right side upwards as he looked into it.

"You make my blood run cold," said Mr. Pickwick. "What do you mean?"

"He's been consumptive for a long time past," said Mr. Roker, "and he's taken wery bad in the breath to-night. The doctor said six months ago that nothing but change of air could save him."

"Great Heaven?" exclaimed Mr. Pickwick; "has this man been slowly murdered by the law for six months!"

"I don't know about that, Sir," replied Roker, weighing the hat by the brims in both hands. "I suppose he'd have been took the same wherever he was. He went into the infirmary this morning; the doctor says his strength is to be kept up as much as possible, and the warden's sent him wine and broth and that, from his own house. It's not the warden's fault you know, Sir."

"Of course not," replied Mr. Pickwick hastily.

"I'm afraid however," said Roker shaking his head, "that it's all up with him; I offered Neddy two sixpenno'rths to one upon it just now, but he wouldn't take it, and quite right. Thankee, Sir. Good night, Sir."

"Stay," said Mr. Pickwick earnestly. "Where is this infirmary?"

"Just over where you slept, Sir," replied Roker. "I'll show you if you like to come." Mr. Pickwick snatched up his hat without speaking, and followed at once.

The turnkey led the way in silence; and gently raising the latch of the room-door, motioned Mr. Pickwick to enter. It was a large, bare, desolate room, with a number of stump bedsteads made of iron, on one of which lay stretched the shadow of a man: wan, pale and ghastly. His breathing was hard and thick, and he moaned painfully as it came and went. At the bedside sat a short old man in a cobbler's apron, who by the aid of a pair of horn spectacles, was reading from the Bible aloud. It was the fortunate legatee.

The sick man laid his hand upon his attendant's arm, and motioned him to stop. He closed the book, and laid it on the bed.

"Open the window," said the sick man.

He did so. The noise of carriages and carts, the rattle of wheels, the cries of men and boys; all the busy sounds of a mighty multitude instinct with life and occupation, blended into one deep murmur, floated into the room. Above the hoarse loud hum arose from time to time a boisterous laugh; or a scrap of some jingling song, shouted forth by one of the giddy crowd, would strike upon the ear for an instant, and then be lost amidst the roar of voices and the tramp of footsteps—the breaking of the billows of the restless sea of life that rolled heavily on, without. These are melancholy sounds to a quiet listener at any time; but how melancholy to the watcher by the bed of death!

"There is no air here," said the sick man faintly. "The place pollutes it; it was fresh round about, when I walked there, years ago; but it grows hot and heavy in passing these walls. I cannot breathe it."

"We have breathed it together, a long time," said the old man. "Come, come."

There was a short silence, during which the two spectators approached the bed. The sick man drew a hand of his old fellow prisoner towards him, and pressing it affectionately between both his own, retained it in his grasp.

"I hope," he gasped after a while—so faintly that they bent their ears close over the bed to catch the half-formed sounds his cold blue lips gave vent to—"I hope my merciful Judge will bear in mind my heavy punishment on earth. Twenty years, my friend, twenty years in this hideous grave. My heart broke when my child died, and I could not even kiss him in his little coffin. My loneliness since then, in all this noise and riot, has been very dreadful. May God forgive me! He has seen my solitary, lingering death."

He folded his hands, and murmuring something more they could not hear, fell into a sleep—only a sleep at first, for they saw him smile.

They whispered together for a little time, and the turnkey stooping over the pillow, drew hastily back. "He has got his discharge, by G—!" said the man.

He had. But he had grown so like death in life, that they knew not when he died.

CHAPTER XLIV.

DESCRIPTIVE OF AN AFFECTING INTERVIEW BETWEEN MR. SAMUEL WELLER AND A FAMILY PARTY. MR. PICKWICK MAKES A TOUR OF THE DIMINUTIVE WORLD HE INHABITS, AND RESOLVES TO MIX WITH IT IN FUTURE AS LITTLE AS POSSIBLE.

A FEW mornings after his incarceration, Mr. Samuel Weller, having arranged his master's room with all possible care, and seen him comfortably seated over his books and papers, withdrew to employ himself for an hour or two to come, as he best could. It was a fine morning, and it occurred to Sam that a pint of porter in the open air would lighten his next quarter of an hour or so, as well as any little amusement in which he could indulge.

Having arrived at this conclusion, he betook himself to the tap, and having purchased the beer, and obtained moreover, the day-but-one-before-yesterday's paper, he repaired to the skittle ground, and seating himself on a bench, proceeded to enjoy himself in a very sedate and methodical manner.

First of all, he took a refreshing draught of the beer, and then he looked up at a window, and bestowed a Platonic wink on a young lady who was peeling potatoes thereat. Then he opened the paper, and folded it so as to get the police reports outwards; and this being a vexatious and difficult thing to do when there is any wind stirring, he took another draught of the beer when he had accomplished it. Then he read two lines of the paper, and stopped short to look at a couple of men who were finishing a game at rackets, which, being concluded, he cried out "wery good" in an approving manner, and looked round upon the spectators, to ascertain whether their sentiments coincided with his own. This involved the necessity of looking up at the windows also; and as the young lady was still there, it was an act of common politeness to wink again, and to drink to her good health in dumb show, in another draught of the beer, which Sam did; and having frowned hideously upon a small boy who had noted this latter proceeding with open eyes, he threw one leg over the other, and, holding the newspaper in both hands, began to read in real earnest.

He had hardly composed himself into the needful state of abstraction, when he thought he heard his own name proclaimed in some distant passage. Nor was he mistaken, for it quickly passed from mouth to mouth, and in a few seconds the air teemed with shouts of "Weller."

"Here!" roared Sam, in a stentorian voice. "Wot's the matter? Who wants him? Has an express come to say that his country-house is afire?"

"Somebody wants you in the hall," said a man who was standing by.

"Just mind that 'ere paper and the pot, old feller, will you?" said Sam. "I'm a comin'. Blessed, if they wos a callin' me to the bar, they couldn't make more noise about it."

Accompanying these words with a gentle rap on the head of the young gentleman before noticed, who, unconscious of his close vicinity to the person in request, was screaming "Weller" with all his might, Sam hastened across the ground, and ran up the steps into the hall. Here, the first object that met his eyes was his beloved father sitting on a bottom stair, with his hat in his hand, shouting out, "Weller" in his very loudest tone, at half-minute intervals.

"Wot are you a roarin' at?" said Sam impetuously, when the old gentleman had discharged himself of another shout; "makin' yourself so precious hot that you looks like a aggravated glass blower. Wot's the matter?"

"Aha!" replied the old gentlemen, "I begun to be afeerd that you'd gone for a walk round the Regency Park, Sammy."

"Come," said Sam, "none o' them taunts agin the wictim o' avarice, and come off that 'ere step. Wot are you a settin' down there for? I don't live there."

"I've got sich a game for you, Sammy," said the elder Mr. Weller, rising.

"Stop a minit," said Sam, "you're all vite behind."

"That's right, Sammy, rub it off," said Mr. Weller, as his son dusted him. "It might look personal here, if vun valked about vith any vitevash on vun's clothes, eh, Sammy?"

As Mr. Weller exhibited in this place unequivocal symptoms of an approaching fit of chuckling, Sam interposed to stop it.

"Keep quiet, do," said Sam, "there never vas such a old picter-card born. Vot are you bustin' vith, now?"

"Sammy," said Mr. Weller, wiping his forehead, "I'm afeerd that vun o' these days I shall laugh myself into a appleplexy, my boy."

"Vell, then, wot do you do it for?" said Sam. "Now, then, wot have you got to say?"

"Who do you think's come here vith me, Samivel?" said Mr. Weller, drawing back a pace or two, pursing up his mouth, and extending his eye-brows.

"Pell?" said Sam.

Mr. Weller shook his head, and his red cheeks expanded with the laughter that was endeavouring to find a vent.

"Mottled-faced man, p'r'aps?" suggested Sam.

Again Mr. Weller shook his head.

"Who then?" asked Sam.

"Your mother-in-law," said Mr. Weller; and it was lucky he did say it, or his cheeks must inevitably have cracked from their most unnatural distension.

"Your mother-in-law, Sammy," said Mr. Weller, "and the red-nosed man, my boy; and the red-nosed man. Ho! ho! ho!"

With this, Mr. Weller launched into convulsions of laughter, while Sam regarded him with a broad grin gradually overspreading his whole countenance.

"They've come to have a little serous talk vith you, Samivel," said Mr. Weller, wiping his eyes. "Don't let out nothin' about the unnat'ral creditor, Sammy."

"Wot, don't they know who it is?" inquired Sam.

"Not a bit on it," replied his father.

"Vere are they?" said Sam, reciprocating all the old gentleman's grins.

"In the snuggery," rejoined Mr. Weller. "Catch the red-nosed man a goin' any vere but vere the liquor is; not he, Samivel—not he. Ve'd a wery pleasant ride along the road from the Markis this mornin', Sammy," said Mr. Weller, when he felt himself equal to the task of speaking in an articulate manner. "I drove the old piebald in that 'ere little shay-cart as belonged to your mother-in-law's first venter, into vich a harm-cheer vos lifted for the Shepherd; and I'm blest," said Mr. Weller, with a look of deep scorn—"I'm blest if they didn't bring a portable flight o' steps out into the road a front o' our door, for him to get up by."

"You don't mean that?" said Sam.

"I do mean that, Sammy," replied his father, "and I vish you could ha' seen how tight he held on by the sides ven he did get up, as if he wos afeerd o' being precipitayted down full six foot, and dashed into a million hatoms. He tumbled in at last, however, and avay ve vent; and I rayther think—I say I rayther think, Samivel—that he found his-self a little jolted ven ve turned the corners."

"Wot, I s'pose you happened to drive up agin a post or two?" said Sam.

"I'm afeerd," replied Mr. Weller, in a rapture of winks — "I'm afeerd I took vun or two on 'em, Sammy; he wos a flyin' out o' the harm-cheer all the vay."

Here the old gentleman shook his head from side to side, and was seized with a hoarse internal rumbling, accompanied with a violent swelling of the countenance, and a sudden increase in the breadth of all his features—symptoms which alarmed his son not a little.

"Don't be frightened, Sammy—don't be frightened," said the old gentleman, when, by dint of much struggling, and various convulsive stamps upon the ground he had recovered his voice. "It's only a kind o' quiet laugh as I'm a tryin' to come, Sammy."

"Vell, if that's wot it is," said Sam, "you'd better not try to come it agin. You'll find it rayther a dangerous invention."

"Don't you like it, Sammy?" inquired the old gentleman.

"Not at all," replied Sam.

"Vell," said Mr. Weller, with the tears still running down his cheeks, "it 'ud ha' been a wery great accommodation to me if I could ha' done it, and 'ud ha' saved a good many vords atween your mother-in-law and me, sometimes; but I'm afeerd you're right, Sammy: it's too much in the appleplexy line—a deal too much, Samivel."

This conversation brought them to the door of the snuggery, into which Sam—pausing for an instant to look over his shoulder, and cast a sly leer at his respected progenitor, who was still giggling behind—at once led the way.

"Mother-in-law," said Sam, politely saluting the lady, "wery much obliged to you for this here wisit. Shepherd, how air you?"

"Oh, Samuel!" said Mrs. Weller. "This is dreadful."

"Not a bit on it, mum," replied Sam. "Is it, Shepherd?"

Mr. Stiggins raised his hands, and turned up his eyes, till the whites—or rather the yellows—were alone visible, but made no reply in words.

"Is this here gen'l'm'n troubled with any painful complaint?" said Sam, looking to his mother-in-law for explanation.

"The good man is grieved to see you here, Samuel," replied Mrs. Weller.

"Oh, that's it, is it?" said Sam. "I wos afeerd, from his manner, that he might ha' forgotten to take pepper vith that 'ere last cowcumber he eat. Set down, Sir; ve make no extra charge for the settin' down, as the king remarked ven he blow'd up his ministers."

"Young man," said Mr. Stiggins, ostentatiously, "I fear you are not softened by imprisonment."

"Beg your pardon, Sir," replied Sam, "wot wos you graciously pleased to hobserve?"

"I appehend, young man, that your nature is no softer for this chastening," said Mr. Stiggins, in a loud voice.

"Sir," replied Sam, "you're wery kind to say so. I hope my natur is *not* a soft vun, Sir. Wery much obliged to you for your good opinion, Sir."

At this point of the conversation, a sound, indecorously approaching to a laugh, was heard to proceed from the chair in which the elder Mr. Weller was seated, upon which Mrs. Weller, on a hasty consideration of all the circumstances of the case, considered it her bounden duty to become gradually hysterical.

"Weller," said Mrs. W. (the old gentleman was seated in a corner); "Weller! come forth."

"Werry much obleeged to you, my dear," replied Mr. Weller; "but I'm quite comfortable vere I am."

Upon this, Mrs. Weller burst into tears.

"Wot's gone wrong, mum?" said Sam.

"Oh, Samuel!" replied Mrs. Weller; "your father makes me wretched. Will nothing do him good?"

"Do you hear this here?" said Sam. "Lady vants to know vether nothin' 'ull do you good."

"Wery much indebted to Mrs. Weller for her po-lite inquiries, Sammy," replied the old gentleman. "I think a pipe vould benefit me a good deal. Could I be accommodated, Sammy?"

Here Mrs. Weller let fall some more tears, and Mr. Stiggins groaned.

"Hallo! Here's this unfort'nate gen'lm'n took ill agin," said Sam, looking round. "Vere do you feel it now, Sir?"

"In the same place, young man," rejoined Mr. Stiggins: "in the same place."

"Vere may that be, Sir?" inquired Sam, with great outward simplicity.

"In the buzzim, young man," replied Mr. Stiggins, placing his umbrella on his waistcoat.

At this affecting reply, Mrs. Weller being wholly unable to suppress her feelings, sobbed aloud, and stated her conviction that the red-nosed man was a saint; whereupon Mr. Weller, senior, ventured to suggest, in an undertone, that he must be the representative of the united parishes of Saint Simon Without and Saint Walker Within.

"I'm afeerd, mum," said Sam, "that this here gen'lm'n, vith the tvist in his countenance, feels rayther thirsty, vith the melancholy spectacle afore him. Is it the case, mum?"

The worthy lady looked at Mr. Stiggins for a reply, and that gentleman, with many rollings of the eye, clenched his throat with his right hand, and mimicked the act of swallowing, to intimate that he was athirst.

"I am afraid, Samuel, that his feelings have made him so, indeed," said Mrs. Weller, mournfully.

"Wot's your usual tap, Sir?" replied Sam.

"Oh, my dear young friend!" replied Mr. Stiggins, "all taps is vanities."

"Too true; too true, indeed," said Mrs. Weller, murmuring a groan, and shaking her head assentingly.

"Vell," said Sam, "I des-say they may be, Sir; but vich is your partickler vanity? Vich vanity do you like the flavour on best, Sir?"

"Oh, my dear young friend," replied Mr. Stiggins, "I despise them all. If," said Mr. Stiggins, "if there is any one of them less odious than another, it is the liquor called rum—warm, my dear young friend, with three lumps of sugar to the tumbler."

"Wery sorry to say, Sir," said Sam, "that they don't allow that partickler vanity to be sold in this here establishment."

"Oh, the hardness of heart of these inveterate men!" ejaculated Mr. Stiggins. "Oh, the accursed cruelty of these inhuman persecutors!"

With these words, Mr. Stiggins again cast up his eyes, and rapped his breast with his umbrella; and it is but justice to the reverend gentleman to say, that his indignation appeared very real and unfeigned indeed.

After Mrs. Weller and the red-nosed gentleman had commented on this inhuman usage in a very forcible manner, and vented a variety of pious and holy execrations against its authors, the latter recommended a bottle of port wine, warmed with a little water, spice, and sugar, as being grateful to the stomach, and savouring less of vanity than many other compounds. It was accordingly ordered to be prepared, and pending its preparation the red-nosed man and Mrs. Weller looked at the elder W. and groaned.

"Vell, Sammy," said that gentleman, "I hope you'll find your spirits rose by this here lively wisit. Wery cheerful and improvin' conwersation, ain't it, Sammy?"

"You're a reprobate," replied Sam; "and I desire you von't address no more o' them ungraceful remarks to me."

So far from being edified by this very proper reply, the elder Mr. Weller at once relapsed into a broad grin: and this inexorable conduct causing the lady and Mr. Stiggins to close their eyes and rock themselves to and fro on their chairs, in a troubled manner, he furthermore indulged in several acts of pantomime indicative of a desire to pummel and wring the nose of the aforesaid Stiggins, the performance of which appeared to afford him great mental relief. The old gentleman very narrowly escaped detection, in one instance; for Mr. Stiggins happening to give a start on the arrival of the negus, brought his head in smart contact with the clenched fist with which Mr. Weller had been describing imaginary fireworks in the air, within two inches of his ear for some minutes previous.

"Wot are you a reachin' out your hand for the tumbler in that 'ere sawage vay for?" said Sam, with great promptitude. "Don't you see you've hit the gen'lm'n?"

"I didn't go to do it, Sammy," said Mr. Weller, in some degree abashed by the very unexpected occurrence of the incident.

"Try an invard application, Sir," said Sam, as the red-nosed gentleman rubbed his head with a rueful visage. "Wot do you think o' that for a go o' wanity varm, Sir?"

Mr. Stiggins made no verbal answer, but his manner was expressive. He tasted the contents of the glass which Sam had placed in his hand, put his umbrella on the floor, and tasted it again, passing his hand placidly across his stomach twice or thrice; he then drank the whole at a breath, and smacking his lips, held out the tumbler for more.

Nor was Mrs. Weller behind-hand in doing justice to the composition. The good lady began by protesting that she couldn't touch a drop—then took a small drop—then a large drop—and then a great many drops; and her feelings being of the nature of those substances which are powerfully affected by the application of strong waters, she dropped a tear with every drop of negus, and so got on melting the feelings down, until at length she had arrived at a very pathetic and decent pitch of misery.

The elder Mr. Weller observed these signs and tokens with many manifestations of disgust, and when, after a second jug of the same, Mr. Stiggins began to sigh in a dismal manner, he plainly evinced his disapprobation of the whole proceedings by sundry incoherent ramblings of speech, among which frequent angry repetitions of the word "gammon" were alone distinguishable to the ear.

"I'll tell you wot it is, Samivel, my boy," whispered the old gentleman into his son's ear, after a long and steadfast contemplation of his lady and Mr. Stiggins; "I think there must be somethin' wrong in your mother-in-law's inside, as vell as in that o' the red-nosed man."

"Wot do you mean?" said Sam.

"I mean this here, Sammy," replied the old gentleman, "that wot they drink don't seem no nourishment to 'em; it all turns to varm vater at vunce, and comes a' pourin' out o' their eyes. 'Pend upon it, Sammy, it's a constitootional infirmity."

Mr. Weller delivered this scientific opinion with many confirmatory frowns and nods, which Mrs. Weller remarking, and concluding that they bore some disparaging reference either to herself or to Mr. Stiggins, or to both, was on the point of becoming infinitely worse, when Mr.

Stiggins, getting on his legs as well as he could, proceeded to deliver an edifying discourse for the benefit of the company, but more especially of Mr. Samuel, whom he adjured, in moving terms, to be upon his guard in that sink of iniquity into which he was cast; to abstain from all hypocrisy and pride of heart; and to take in all things exact pattern and copy by him (Stiggins), in which case he might calculate on arriving sooner or later at the comfortable conclusion, that, like him, he was a most estimable and blameless character, and that all his acquaintance and friends were hopelessly abandoned and profligate wretches; which consideration, he said, could not but afford him the liveliest satisfaction.

He furthermore conjured him to avoid, above all things, the vice of intoxication, which he likened unto the filthy habits of swine, and to those poisonous and baleful drugs which being chewed in the mouth are said to filch away the memory. At this point of his discourse the reverend and red-nosed gentleman became singularly incoherent, and staggering to and fro in the excitement of his eloquence, was fain to catch at the back of a chair to preserve his perpendicular.

Mr. Stiggins did not desire his hearers to be upon their guard against those false prophets and wretched mockers of religion, who, without sense to expound its first doctrines, or hearts to feel its first principles, are more dangerous members of society than the common criminal; imposing as they necessarily do upon the weakest and worst informed natures, casting scorn and contempt on what should be held most sacred, and bringing into partial disrepute large bodies of virtuous and well-conducted persons of many excellent sects and persuasions; but as he leant over the back of the chair for a considerable time, and closing one eye, winked a good deal with the other, it is presumed that he thought it all, but kept it to himself.

During the delivery of this oration, Mrs. Weller sobbed and wept at the end of the paragraphs, while Sam, sitting cross-legged on a chair and resting his arms on the top-rail, regarded the speaker with great suavity and blandness of demeanour, occasionally bestowing a look of recognition on the old gentleman, who was delighted at the beginning, and went to sleep about half-way.

"Brayvo! wery pretty!" said Sam, when the red-nosed man having finished, pulled his worn gloves on, thereby thrusting his fingers through the broken tops till the knuckles were disclosed to view—"Wery pretty."

"I hope it may do you good, Samuel," said Mrs. Weller solemnly.

"I think it vill, mum," replied Sam.

"I wish I could hope that it would do your father good," said Mrs. Weller.

"Thankee, my dear," said Mr. Weller, senior. "How do *you* find yourself arter it, my love?"

"Scoffer!" exclaimed Mrs. Weller.

"Benighted man!" said the reverend Mr. Stiggins.

"If I don't get no better light than that 'ere moonshine o' your'n, my vorthy creetur," said the elder Mr. Weller, "it's wery likely as I shall continey to be a night coach till I'm took off the road altogether. Now, Mrs. We, if the piebald stands at livery much longer, he'll stand at nothin' as we go back, and p'raps that 'ere harm cheer ull be tipped over into some hedge or another, vith the shepherd in it."

At this supposition the reverend Mr. Stiggins, in evident consternation, gathered up his hat and umbrella, and proposed an immediate departure, to which Mrs. Weller assented. Sam walked with them to the lodge-gate, and took a dutiful leave.

"A-do, Samivel," said the old gentleman.

"Wot's a-do?" inquired Sam.

"Vell, good bye, then," said the old gentleman.

"Oh, that's wot you're a' aimin' at, is it?" said Sam. "Good bye, old double-vicket."

"Sammy," whispered Mr. Weller, looking cautiously round; "my duty to your gov'ner, and tell him if he thinks better o' this here bis'ness, to com-moonicate vith me. Me and a cab'net-maker has dewised a plan for gettin' him out. A pianner, Samivel—a pianner!" said Mr. Weller, striking his son on the chest with the back of his hand, and falling back a step or two.

"Wot do you mean?" said Sam.

"A pianner forty, Samivel," rejoined Mr. Weller, in a still more mysterious manner, "as he can have on hire; vun as von't play, Sammy."

"And wot 'ud be the good o' that?" said Sam.

"Let him send to my friend, the cab'net maker, to fetch it back, Sammy," replied Mr. Weller. "Are you avake, now?"

"No," rejoined Sam.

"There ain't no vurks in it," whispered his father. "It 'ull hold him easy, vith his hat and shoes on; and breathe through the legs, vich his holler. Have a passage ready taken for 'Merriker. The 'Merrikin gov'ment vill never give him up, ven vunce they finds as he's got money to spend, Sammy. Let the gov'ner stop there till Mrs. Bardell's dead, or Mr. Dodson and Fogg's hung, vich last ewent I think is the most likely to happen first, Sammy; and then let him come back and write a book about the 'Merrikins as'll pay all his expenses and more, if he blows 'em up enough."

Mr. Weller delivered this hurried abstract of his plot with great vehemence of whisper, and then, as if fearful of weakening the effect of the tremendous communication by any further dialogue, gave the coachman's salute, and vanished.

Sam had scarcely recovered his usual composure of countenance, which had been greatly disturbed by the secret communication of his respected relative, when Mr. Pickwick accosted him.

"Sam," said that gentleman.

"Sir," replied Mr. Weller.

"I am going for a walk round the prison, and I wish you to attend me. I see a prisoner we know coming this way, Sam," said Mr. Pickwick, smiling.

"Vich, Sir?" inquired Mr. Weller; "the gen'l'm'n vith the head o' hair, or the interestin' captive in the stockin's?"

"Neither," rejoined Mr. Pickwick. "He is an older friend of yours, Sam."

"O' mine, Sir?" exclaimed Mr. Weller.

"You recollect the gentleman very well, I dare say, Sam," replied Mr. Pickwick, "or else you are more unmindful of your old acquaintances than I think you are. Hush! not a word, Sam—not a syllable. Here he is."

As Mr. Pickwick spoke, Jingle walked up. He looked less miserable than before, being clad in a half-worn suit of clothes, which, with Mr. Pickwick's assistance, had been released from the pawnbroker's. He wore clean linen too, and had had his hair cut. He was very pale and thin, however; and as he crept slowly up, leaning on a stick, it was easy to see that he had suffered severely from illness and want, and was still very weak. He took off his hat as

Mr. Pickwick saluted him, and seemed much humbled and abashed at sight of Sam Weller.

Following close at his heels, came Mr. Job Trotter, in the catalogue of whose vices, want of faith and attachment to his companion could, at all events, find no place. He was still ragged and squalid, but his face was not quite so hollow as on his first meeting with Mr. Pickwick a few days before. As he took off his hat to our benevolent old friend, he murmured some broken expressions of gratitude, and muttered something about having been saved from starving.

"Well, well," said Mr. Pickwick, impatiently interrupting him, "you can follow with Sam. I want to speak to you, Mr. Jingle. Can you walk without his arm?"

"Certainly, Sir—all ready—not too fast—legs shaky—head queer—round and round—earthquaky sort of feeling—very."

"Here, give me your arm," said Mr. Pickwick.

"No, no," replied Jingle; "won't indeed—rather not."

"Nonsense," said Mr. Pickwick; "lean upon me, I desire, Sir."

Seeing that he was confused and agitated, and uncertain what to do, Mr. Pickwick cut the matter short by drawing the invalided stroller's arm through his, and leading him away without saying another word about it.

During the whole of this time, the countenance of Mr. Samuel Weller had exhibited an expression of the most overwhelming and absorbing astonishment that the imagination can pourtray. After looking from Job to Jingle, and from Jingle to Job in profound silence, he softly ejaculated the words, "Vell, I *am* damn'd!" which he repeated at least a score of times, after which exertion he appeared wholly bereft of speech, and again cast his eyes, first upon the one and then upon the other, in mute perplexity and bewilderment.

"Now, Sam," said Mr. Pickwick, looking back.

"I'm a comin', Sir," replied Mr. Weller, mechanically following his master; and still he lifted not his eyes from Mr. Job Trotter, who walked at his side in silence.

Job kept his eyes fixed on the ground for some time, and Sam with his, glued to Job's countenance, ran up against the people who were walking about, and fell over little children, and stumbled against steps and railings, without appearing at all sensible of it, until Job, looking stealthily up, said—

"How do you do, Mr. Weller?"

"It is him!" exclaimed Sam; and having established Job's identity beyond all doubt, he smote his leg, and vented his feelings in a long shrill whistle.

"Things has altered with me, Sir," said Job.

"I should think they had," exclaimed Mr. Weller, surveying his companion's rags with undisguised wonder. "This is rather a change for the worse, Mr. Trotter, as the gen'l'm'n said ven he got two doubtful shillin's and sixpenno'rth o' pocket-pieces for a good half-crown."

"It is indeed," replied Job, shaking his head. "There is no deception now, Mr. Weller. Tears," said Job, with a look of momentary slyness—"tears are not the only proofs of distress, nor the best ones."

"No, they ain't," replied Sam, expressively.

"They may be put on, Mr. Weller," said Job.

"I know they may," said Sam; "some people, indeed, has 'em always ready laid on, and can pull out the plug venever they likes."

"Yes," replied Job; "but *these* sort of things are not

so easily counterfeited, Mr. Weller, and it is a more painful process to get them up." As he spoke, he pointed to his sallow sunken cheeks, and, drawing up his coat sleeve, disclosed an arm which looked as if the bone could be broken at a touch, so sharp and brittle did it appear beneath its thin covering of flesh.

"Wot have you been a doin' to yourself?" said Sam, recoiling.

"Nothing," replied Job.

"Nothin'!" echoed Sam.

"I have been doin' nothing for many weeks past," said Job; "and eating and drinking almost as little."

Sam took one comprehensive glance at Mr. Trotter's thin face and wretched apparel, and then seizing him by the arm, commenced dragging him away with great violence.

"Where are you going, Mr. Weller?" said Job, vainly struggling in the powerful grasp of his old enemy.

"Come on," said Sam; "come on." He deigned no further explanation till they reached the tap, and then called for a pot of porter, which was speedily produced.

"Now," said Sam, "drink that up ev'ry drop on it; and then turn the pot upside down, to let me see as you've took the med'cine."

"But my dear Mr. Weller," remonstrated Job.

"Down vith it," said Sam, peremptorily.

Thus admonished, Mr. Trotter raised the pot to his lips, and, by gentle and almost imperceptible degrees, tilted it into the air. He paused once, and only once, to draw a long breath, but without raising his face from the vessel, which, in a few moments thereafter he held out at arm's length, bottom upwards. Nothing fell upon the ground but a few particles of froth, which slowly detached themselves from the rim and trickled lazily down.

"Vell done," said Sam. "How do you find yourself arter it?"

"Better, Sir. I think I am better," responded Job.

"O' course you air," said Sam, argumentatively. "It's like puttin' gas in a balloon; I can see vith the naked eye that you gets stouter under the operation. Wot do you say to another o' the same di-mensions."

"I would rather not, I am much obliged to you, Sir," replied Job—"much rather not."

"Vell, then, wot do you say to some wittles?" inquired Sam.

"Thanks to your worthy governor, Sir," said Mr. Trotter, "we have half a leg of mutton, baked, at a quarter before three, with the potatoes under it, to save boiling."

"Wot! Has *he* been a purwidin' for you?" asked Sam, emphatically.

"He has, Sir," replied Job. "More than that, Mr. Weller; my master being very ill, he got us a room—we were in a kennel before—and paid for it, Sir; and come to look at us at night when nobody should know. Mr. Weller," said Job, with real tears in his eyes for once, "I could serve that gentleman till I fell down dead at his feet."

"I say," said Sam, "I'll trouble you, my friend—none o' that."

Job Trotter looked amazed.

"None o' that, I say, young feller," repeated Sam firmly. "No vun serves him but me. And now ve're upon it, I'll let you into another secret besides that," said Sam, as he paid for the beer. "I never heerd, mind you, nor read of in story-books, nor see in picters, any angel in tights and gaiters—not even in spectacles, as I remember,

though that may ha' been done, for anythin' I know to the contrairey; but mark my vords, Job Trotter, he's a reg'lar thorough-bred angel for all that; and let me see the man as wenturs to tell me he knows a better vun." With this defiance, Mr. Weller buttoned up his change in a side pocket; and, with many confirmatory nods and gestures by the way, proceeded in search of the subject of discourse.

They found Mr. Pickwick in company with Jingle, talking very earnestly, and not bestowing a look on the groups who were congregated on the racket-ground; they were very motley groups too, and well worth the looking at, if it were only in idle curiosity.

"Well," said Mr. Pickwick, as Sam and his companion drew nigh, "you will see how your health becomes, and think about it meanwhile. Make the statement out for me when you feel yourself equal to the task, and I will discuss the subject with you when I have considered it. Now go to your room. You are tired, and not strong enough to be out long."

Mr. Alfred Jingle, without one spark of his old animation—with nothing even of the dismal gaiety which he had assumed when Mr. Pickwick first stumbled on him in his misery, bowed low without speaking, and motioning to Job not to follow him just yet, crept slowly away.

"Curious scene this, is it not, Sam?" said Mr. Pickwick, looking good-humouredly round.

"Wery much so, Sir," replied Sam. "Vonders vill never cease," added Sam, speaking to himself. "I'm wery much mistaken if that 'ere Jingle worn't a doin' somethin' in the vater-cart vay!"

The area formed by the wall in that part of the Fleet in which Mr. Pickwick stood, was just wide enough to make a good racket court, one side being formed, of course, by the wall itself, and the other by that portion of the prison which looked (or rather would have looked, but for the wall) towards St. Paul's Cathedral. Sauntering or sitting about, in every possible attitude of listless idleness, were a great number of debtors, the major part of whom were waiting in prison until their day of "going up" before the Insolvent Court should arrive, while others had been remanded for various terms, which they were idling away as they best could. Some were shabby, some were smart, many dirty, a few clean; but there they all lounged, and loitered, and slunk about, with as little spirit or purpose as the beasts in a menagerie.

Lolling from the windows which commanded a view of this promenade, were a number of persons; some in noisy conversation with their acquaintance below, others playing at ball with some adventurous throwers outside; and others looking on at the racket-players, or watching the boys as they cried the game. Dirty, slipshod women passed and re-passed on their way to the cooking-house in one corner of the yard; children screamed, and fought, and played together, in another; the tumbling of the skittles, and the shouts of the players, mingled perpetually with these and a hundred other sounds; and all was noise and tumult—save in a little miserable shed a few yards off, where there lay, all quiet and ghastly, the body of the Chancery prisoner who had died the night before, awaiting the mockery of an inquest. The body! It is the lawyer's term for the restless whirling mass of cares and anxieties, affections, hopes, and griefs, that make up the living man. The law had his body, and there it lay, clothed in grave clothes, an awful witness to its tender mercy.

"Would you like to see a whistling-shop, Sir?" inquired Job Trotter.

"What do you mean?" was Mr. Pickwick's counter enquiry.

"A vistlin' shop, Sir," interposed Mr. Weller.

"What is that, Sam?—A bird-fancier's?" enquired Mr. Pickwick.

"Bless your heart, no, Sir," replied Job; "a whistling-shop, Sir, is where they sell spirits." Mr. Job Trotter briefly explained here, that all persons, being prohibited under heavy penalties from conveying spirits into debtors' prisons, and such commodities being highly prized by the ladies and gentlemen confined therein, it had occurred to some speculative turnkey to connive, for certain lucrative considerations, at two or three prisoners retailing the favourite article of gin, for their own profit and advantage.

"This plan you see, Sir, has been gradually introduced into all the prisons for debt," said Mr. Trotter.

"And it has this wery great advantage," said Sam, "that the turnkeys takes wery good care to seize hold o' ev'ry body but them as pays 'em, that attempts the willainny, and ven it gets in the papers they're applauded for their wigilance; so it cuts two vays—frightens other people from the trade, and elevates their own characters."

"Exactly so, Mr. Weller," observed Job.

"Well, but are these rooms never searched to ascertain whether any spirits are concealed in them?" said Mr. Pickwick.

"Cert'nly they are, Sir," replied Sam; "but the turnkeys knows before-hand, and gives the vord to the vistlers, and you *may* vistle for it ven you go to look."

By this time, Job had tapped at a door, which was opened by a gentleman with an uncombed head, who bolted it after them when they had walked in, and grinned; upon which Job grinned, and Sam also: whereupon Mr. Pickwick, thinking it might be expected of him, kept on smiling till the end of the interview.

The gentleman with the uncombed head appeared quite satisfied with this mute announcement of their business; and producing a flat stone bottle, which might hold about a couple of quarts, from beneath his bedstead, he filled out three glasses of gin, which Job Trotter and Sam disposed of in a most workmanlike manner.

"Any more?" said the whistling gentleman.

"No more," replied Job Trotter.

Mr. Pickwick paid; the door was unbolted, and out they came; the uncombed gentleman bestowing a friendly nod upon Mr. Roker, who happened to be passing at the moment.

From this spot Mr. Pickwick wandered along all the galleries, up and down all the staircases, and once again around the whole area of the yard. The great body of the prison population appeared to be Mivins and Smangle, and the parson, and the butcher, and the leg, over and over, and over again. There was the same squalor, the same turmoil and noise, the same general characteristics in every corner; in the best and the worst alike. The whole place seemed restless and troubled; and the people were crowding and flitting to and fro, like the shadows in an uneasy dream.

"I have seen enough," said Mr. Pickwick, as he threw himself into a chair in his little apartment. "My head aches with these scenes, and my heart too. Henceforth I will be a prisoner in my own room."

And Mr. Pickwick stedfastly adhered to this determination. For three long months he remained shut up all day, only stealing out at night to breathe the air when the greater part of his fellow prisoners were in bed or carousing in their rooms. His health was evidently beginning to suffer from the closeness of the confinement, but neither the often-repeated entreaties of Perker and his friends, nor the still more frequently repeated warnings and admonitions of Mr. Samuel Weller, could induce him to alter one jot of his inflexible resolution.

CHAPTER XLV.

RECORDS A TOUCHING ACT OF DELICATE FEELING, NOT UNMIXED WITH PLEASANTRY, ACHIEVED AND PERFORMED BY MESSRS. DODSON AND FOGG.

It was within a week of the close of the month of July, that a hackney cabriolet, number unrecorded, was seen to proceed at a rapid pace up Goswell-street; three people were squeezed into it besides the driver, who sat, of course, in his own particular little dickey at the side; over the apron were hung two shawls, belonging to all appearance to two small vixenish-looking ladies under the apron, between whom, compressed into a very small compass, there was stowed away a gentleman of heavy and subdued demeanour, who, whenever he ventured to make an observation, was snapped up short, by one of the vixenish ladies before-mentioned. Lastly, the two vixenish ladies and the heavy gentleman were giving the driver contradictory directions, all tending to the one point, that he should stop at Mrs. Bardell's door, which the heavy gentleman in direct opposition to, and defiance of, the vixenish ladies, contended was a green door and not a yellow one.

"Stop at the house with the green door, driver," said the heavy gentleman.

"Oh! You perwerse creetur!" exclaimed one of the vixenish ladies. "Drive to the ouse with the yellow door, cabmin."

Upon this the cabman, who in a sudden effort to pull up at the house with the green door, had pulled the horse up so high that he nearly pulled him backwards into the cabriolet, let the animal's fore legs down to the ground again, and paused.

"Now vere am I to pull up?" inquired the driver. "Settle it among yourselves. All I ask is, vere."

Here the contest was renewed with increased violence, and the horse being troubled with a fly on his nose, the cabman humanely employed his leisure in lashing him about the head, on the counter-irritation principle.

"Most wotes carries the day," said one of the vixenish ladies at length. "The ouse with the yellow door, cabmin."

But after the cabriolet had dashed up in splendid style to the house with the yellow door, "making," as one of the vixenish ladies triumphantly said, "acterrally more noise than if one had come in one's own carriage"—and after the driver had dismounted to assist the ladies in getting out, the small round head of Master Thomas Bardell was thrust out of the one pair window of a house with a red door a few numbers off.

"Aggrawatin' thing," said the vixenish lady last mentioned, darting a withering glance at the heavy gentleman.

"My dear, it's not my fault," said the gentleman.

"Don't talk to me, you creetur, don't," retorted the lady. "The house with the red door, cabmin. Oh! if ever a woman was troubled with a ruffinly creetur, that takes a pride and pleasure in disgracing his wife on every possible occasion afore strangers, I am that woman!"

"You ought to be ashamed of yourself, Raddle," said the other little woman, who was no other than Mrs. Cluppins.

"What have I been a doing of?" asked Mr. Raddle.

"Don't talk to me, don't, you brute, for fear I should be perwoked to forgit my sect and strike you," said Mrs. Raddle.

While this dialogue was going on, the driver was most ignominiously leading the horse by the bridle up to the house with the red door, which Master Bardell had already opened. Here was a mean and low way of arriving at a friend's house!—no dashing up with all the fire and fury of the animal, no jumping down of the driver and loud knocking at the door, no opening the apron with a crash at the very last moment for fear of the ladies sitting in a draught, and then the man handing the shawls out afterwards as if he were a private coachman. The whole edge of the thing had been taken off—it was flatter than walking.

"Well Tommy," said Mrs. Cluppins, "How's your poor dear mother?"

"Oh, she's wery well," replied Master Bardell. "She's in the front parlor,—all ready. I'm ready too, I am." Here Master Bardell put his hands in his pockets, and jumped off and on the bottom step of the door.

"Is anybody else a goin', Tommy?" said Mrs. Cluppins, arranging her pelerine.

"Mrs. Sanders is going, she is," replied Tommy. "I'm a goin' too, I am."

"Drat the boy," said little Mrs. Cluppins. "He thinks of nobody but himself. Here Tommy, dear."

"Well," said Master Bardell.

"Who else is a goin', lovey?" said Mrs. Cluppins in an insinuating manner.

"Oh! Mrs. Rogers is a goin'," replied Master Bardell, opening his eyes very wide as he delivered the intelligence.

"What? The lady as has taken the lodgings!" ejaculated Mrs. Cluppins.

Master Bardell put his hands further down into his pockets, and nodded exactly thirty-five times, to imply that it was the lady lodger, and no other.

"Bless us!" said Mrs. Cluppins. "It's quite a party."

"Ah, if you knew what was in the cupboard, you'd say so," replied Master Bardell.

"What is there, Tommy?" said Mrs. Cluppins, coaxingly. "You'll tell me, Tommy, I know."

"No, I won't," replied Master Bardell, shaking his head, and applying himself to the bottom step again.

"Drat the child!" muttered Mrs. Cluppins. "What a prowokin' little wretch it is! Come, Tommy, tell your dear Cluppy."

"Mother said I wasn't to," rejoined Master Bardell, "I'm a goin' to have some, I am." Cheered by this prospect, the precocious boy applied himself to his infantine tread-mill with increased vigour.

The above examination of a child of tender years took place while Mr. and Mrs. Raddle and the cab-driver were having an altercation concerning the fare, which terminating at this point in favour of the cabman, Mrs. Raddle came up tottering.

"Lauk, Mary Ann! what's the matter?" said Mrs. Cluppins.

"It's put me all over in such a tremble, Betsy," replied Mrs. Raddle. "Raddle ain't like a man; he leaves everything to me."

This was scarcely fair upon the unfortunate Mr. Raddle, who had been thrust aside by his good lady in the commencement of the dispute, and peremptorily commanded to hold his tongue. He had no opportunity of defending himself, however, for Mrs. Raddle gave unequivocal signs of fainting; which being perceived from the parlour window, Mrs. Bardell, Mrs. Sanders, the lodger, and the lodger's servant, darted precipitately out, and conveyed her into the house, all talking at the same time, and giving utterance to various expressions of pity and condolence, as if she were one of the most suffering mortals on earth. Being conveyed into the front parlour, she was there deposited on a sofa: and the lady from the first floor running up *to* the first floor, returned with a bottle of sal volatile, which, holding Mrs. Raddle tight round the neck, she applied in all womanly kindness and pity to her nose, until that lady with many plunges and struggles was fain to declare herself decidedly better.

"Ah, poor thing!" said Mrs. Rogers, "I know what her feelin's is, too well."

"Ah, poor thing! so do I," said Mrs. Sanders: and then all the ladies moaned in unison, and said *they* knew what it was, and they pitied her from their hearts, they did; even the lodger's little servant, who was thirteen years old and three feet high, murmured her sympathy.

"But what's been the matter?" said Mrs. Bardell.

"Ah, what has decomposed you, ma'am?" inquired Mrs. Rogers.

"I have been a good deal flurried," replied Mrs. Raddle, in a reproachful manner. Thereupon the ladies cast indignant looks at Mr. Raddle.

"Why, the fact is," said that unhappy gentleman, stepping forward, "when we alighted at this door, a dispute arose with the driver of the cabrioly——" A loud scream from his wife at the mention of this word, rendered all further explanation inaudible.

"You'd better leave us to bring her round, Raddle," said Mrs. Cluppins. "She'll never get better as long as you're here."

All the ladies concurred in this opinion; so Mr. Raddle was pushed out of the room, and requested to give himself an airing in the back yard, which he did for about a quarter of an hour, when Mrs. Bardell announced to him, with a solemn face, that he might come in now, but that he must be very careful how he behaved towards his wife. She knew he didn't mean to be unkind; but Mary Ann was very far from strong, and, if he didn't take care, he might lose her when he least expected it, which would be a very dreadful reflection for him afterwards, and so on. All this, Mr. Raddle heard with great submission, and presently returned to the parlour in a most lamb-like manner.

"Why, Mrs. Rogers, ma'am," said Mrs. Bardell, "you've never been introduced, I declare. Mr. Raddle, ma'am; Mrs. Cluppins, ma'am; Mrs. Raddle, ma'am."

——"Which is Mrs. Cluppins's sister," suggested Mrs. Sanders.

"Oh, indeed!" said Mrs. Rogers, graciously;—for she was the lodger, and her servant was in waiting, so she was more gracious than intimate in right of her position. "Oh, indeed!"

Mrs. Raddle smiled sweetly, Mr. Raddle bowed, and

Mrs. Cluppins said "she was sure she was very happy to have a opportunity of being known to a lady which she had heerd so much in favour of as Mrs. Rogers"—a compliment which the last-named lady acknowledged with graceful condescension.

"Well, Mr. Raddle," said Mrs. Bardell; "I'm sure you ought to feel very much honoured at you and Tommy being the only gentlemen to escort so many ladies all the way to the Spaniard, at Hampstead. Don't you think he ought, Mrs. Rogers, ma'am?"

"Oh, certainly, ma'am," replied Mrs. Rogers; after whom all the other ladies responded, "Oh, certainly."

"Of course I feel it, ma'am," said Mr. Raddle, rubbing his hands, and evincing a slight tendency to brighten up a little. "Indeed, to tell you the truth, I said, as we were coming along in the cabrioily——"

At the recapitulation of the word which awakened so many painful recollections, Mrs. Raddle applied her handkerchief to her eyes again, and uttered a half-suppressed scream; so that Mrs. Bardell frowned upon Mr. Raddle, to intimate that he had better not say anything more; and desired Mrs. Rogers's servant, with an air, to "put the wine on."

This was the signal for displaying the hidden treasures of the closet, which were sundry plates of oranges and biscuits, and a bottle of old crusted port—that at one and nine—with another of the celebrated East India sherry at fourteen-pence, which were all produced in honour of the lodger, and afforded unlimited satisfaction to everybody. After great consternation had been excited in the mind of Mrs. Cluppins, by an attempt on the part of Tommy to recount how he had been cross-examined regarding the cupboard then in action, (which was fortunately nipped in the bud by his imbibing half a glass of the old crusted "the wrong way," and thereby endangering his life for some seconds) the party walked forth in quest of a Hampstead stage. This was soon found, and in a couple of hours they all arrived safely in the Spaniard Tea-gardens, where the luckless Mr. Raddle's very first act nearly occasioned his good lady a relapse, it being neither more nor less than to order tea for seven; whereas (as the ladies one and all remarked), what could have been easier than for Tommy to have drank out of anybody's cup, or everybody's, if that was all, when the waiter wasn't looking, which would have saved one head of tea, and the tea just as good!

However, there was no help for it, and the tea-tray came with seven cups and saucers, and bread and butter on the same scale. Mrs. Bardell was unanimously voted into the chair, and Mrs. Rogers being stationed on her right hand and Mrs. Raddle on her left, the meal proceeded with great merriment and success.

"How sweet the country is, to-be-sure!" sighed Mrs. Rogers; "I almost wish I lived in it always."

"Oh, you wouldn't like that, Ma'am," replied Mrs. Bardell, rather hastily; for it was not at all advisable, with reference to the lodgings, to encourage such notions; "You wouldn't like it, Ma'am."

"Oh! I thould think you was a deal too lively and sought-after, to be content with the country, Ma'am," said little Mrs. Cluppins.

"Perhaps I am, Ma'am. Perhaps I am," sighed the first-floor lodger.

"For lone people as have got nobody to care for them, or take care of them, or as have been hurt in their mind, or that kind of thing," observed Mr. Raddle, plucking up a little cheerfulness, and looking round, "the country is all very well. The country for a wounded spirit they say."

Now, of all things in the world that the unfortunate man could have said, any would have been preferable to this. Of course Mrs. Bardell burst into tears, and requested to be led from the table instantly, upon which the affectionate child began to cry too, most dismally.

"Would any body believe, Ma'am," exclaimed Mrs. Raddle, turning fiercely to the first-floor lodger, "that a woman could be married to such a unmanly creetur, which can tamper with a woman's feelings as he does, every hour in the day, Ma'am?"

"My dear," remonstrated Mr. Raddle, "I didn't mean anything, my dear."

"You didn't mean, Sir!" repeated Mrs. Raddle, with great scorn and contempt. "Go away. I can't bear the sight on you, you brute."

"You must *not* flurry yourself, Mary Ann," interposed Mrs. Cluppins. "You really must consider yourself, my dear, which you never do. Now go away, Raddle, there's a good soul, or you'll only aggravate her."

"You had better take your tea by yourself, Sir, indeed," said Mrs. Rogers, again applying the smelling-bottle.

Mrs. Sanders, who, according to custom, was very busy at the bread and butter, expressed the same opinion, and Mr. Raddle quietly retired.

After this there was a great hoisting up of Master Bardell, who was rather a large size for hugging, into his mother's arms, in which operation he got his boots into the tea-board, and occasioned some confusion among the cups and saucers. But that description of fainting fits, which is contagious among ladies, seldom lasts long, so when he had been well kissed and a little cried over, Mrs. Bardell recovered, set him down again, wondered how she could have been so foolish, and poured out some more tea.

It was at this moment that the sound of approaching wheels was heard, and that the ladies, looking up, saw a hackney-coach stop at the garden-gate.

"More company," said Mrs. Sanders.

"It's a gentleman," said Mrs. Raddle.

"Well, if it ain't Mr. Jackson, the young man from Dodson and Fogg's!" cried Mrs. Bardell. "Why, gracious! Surely Mr. Pickwick can't have paid the damages."

"Or hoffered marriage!" said Mrs. Cluppins.

"Dear me, how slow the gentleman is," exclaimed Mrs. Rogers; "Why doesn't he make haste!"

As the lady spoke these words, Mr. Jackson turned from the coach where he had been addressing some observations to a shabby man in black leggings, who had just emerged from the vehicle with a thick ash stick in his hand, and made his way to the place where the ladies were seated; winding his hair round the brim of his hat as he came along.

"Is anything the matter? Has anything taken place, Mr. Jackson?" said Mrs. Bardell eagerly.

"Nothing whatever, Ma'am," replied Mr. Jackson. "How de do, ladies? I have to ask pardon, ladies, for intruding—but the law, ladies—the law." With this apology Mr. Jackson smiled, made a comprehensive bow, and gave his hair another wind. Mrs. Rogers whispered Mrs. Raddle that he was really an elegant young man.

"I called in Goswell-street," resumed Jackson, "and hearing that you were here, from the slavey, took a coach and came on. Our people want you down in the city directly, Mrs. Bardell."

"Lor!" ejaculated that lady, starting at the sudden nature of the communication.

"Yes," said Jackson, biting his lip. "It's very important and pressing business, which can't be postponed on any account. Indeed, Dodson expressly said so to me, and so did Fogg. I've kept the coach on purpose for you to go back in."

"How very strange!" exclaimed Mrs. Bardell.

The ladies agreed that it *was* very strange, but were unanimously of opinion that it must be very important, or Dodson and Fogg would never have sent; and further, that the business being urgent, she ought to repair to Dodson and Fogg's without any delay.

There was a certain degree of pride and importance about being wanted by one's lawyers in such a monstrous hurry, that was by no means displeasing to Mrs. Bardell, especially as it might be reasonably supposed to enhance her consequence in the eyes of the first-floor lodger. She simpered a little, affected extreme vexation and hesitation, and at last arrived at the conclusion that she supposed she must go.

"But won't you refresh yourself after your walk, Mr. Jackson?" said Mrs. Bardell, persuasively.

"Why, really there ain't much time to lose," replied Jackson; "and I've got a friend here," he continued, looking towards the man with the ash stick.

"Oh, ask your friend to come here, Sir," said Mrs. Bardell. "Pray ask your friend here, Sir."

"Why, thankee, I'd rather not," said Mr. Jackson, with some embarrassment of manner. "He's not much used to ladies' society, and it makes him bashful. If you'll order the waiter to deliver him anything short, he won't drink it off at once, won't he?—only try him." Mr. Jackson's fingers wandered playfully round his nose at this portion of his discourse, to warn his hearers that he was speaking ironically.

The waiter was at once despatched to the bashful gentleman, and the bashful gentleman took something; Mr. Jackson also took something, and the ladies took something for hospitality's sake. Mr. Jackson then said that he was afraid it was time to go; upon which Mrs. Sanders, Mrs. Cluppins, and Tommy (who it was arranged should accompany Mrs. Bardell: leaving the others to Mr. Raddle's protection) got into the coach.

"Isaac," said Jackson, as Mrs. Bardell prepared to get in: looking up at the man with the ash stick, who was seated on the box, smoking a cigar.

"Well."

"*This* is Mrs. Bardell."

"Oh, I know'd that, long ago," said the man.

Mrs. Bardell got in, Mr. Jackson got in after her, and away they drove. Mrs. Bardell could not help ruminating on what Mr. Jackson's friend had said. Shrewd creatures, those lawyers: Lord bless us, how they find people out!

"Sad thing about these costs of our people's, ain't it?" said Jackson, when Mrs. Cluppins and Mrs. Sanders had fallen asleep; "your bill of costs I mean."

"I'm very sorry they can't get them," replied Mrs. Bardell. "But if you law gentlemen do these things on speculation, why you must get a loss now and then, you know."

"You gave them a *cognovit* for the amount of your costs after the trial, I'm told," said Jackson.

"Yes. Just as a matter of form," replied Mrs. Bardell.

"Certainly," replied Jackson drily. "Quite a matter of form. Quite."

On they drove, and Mrs. Bardell fell asleep. She was awakened after some time by the stopping of the coach.

"Bless us!" said the lady, "are we at Freeman's Court?"

"We're not going quite so far," replied Jackson. "Have the goodness to step out."

Mrs. Bardell, not yet thoroughly awake, complied. It was a curious place:—a large wall with a gate in the middle, and a gaslight burning inside.

"Now, ladies," cried the man with the ash stick, looking into the coach, and shaking Mrs. Sanders to wake her, "Come." Rousing her friend, Mrs. Sanders alighted. Mrs. Bardell, leaning on Jackson's arm, and leading Tommy by the hand, had already entered the porch. They followed.

The room they turned into, was even more odd-looking than the porch. Such a number of men standing about! And they stared so!

"What place is this?" inquired Mrs. Bardell, pausing.

"Only one of our public offices," replied Jackson, hurrying her through a door, and looking round to see that the other women were following. "Look sharp, Isaac."

"Safe and sound," replied the man with the ash stick. The door swung heavily after them, and they descended a small flight of steps.

"Here we are, at last. All right and tight, Mrs. Bardell!" said Jackson, looking exultingly round.

"What do you mean?" said Mrs. Bardell, with a palpitating heart.

"Just this," replied Jackson, drawing her a little on one side; "don't be frightened, Mrs. Bardell. There never was a more delicate man than Dodson, ma'am, or a more humane one than Fogg. It was their duty in the way of business to take you in execution for them costs; but they were anxious to spare your feelings as much as they could. What a comfort it must be to you to think how it's been done! This is the Fleet, ma'am. Wish you good night, Mrs. Bardell. Good night, Tommy."

As Jackson hurried away in company with the man with the ash stick, another man, with a key in his hand, who had been looking on, led the bewildered female to a second short flight of steps, leading to a doorway. Mrs. Bardell screamed violently; Tommy roared; Mrs. Cluppins shrunk within herself; and Mrs. Sanders made off, without more ado. For there stood the injured Mr. Pickwick, taking his nightly allowance of air; and beside him leant Samuel Weller, who, seeing Mrs. Bardell, took his hat off with mock reverence, while his master turned indignantly on his heel.

"Don't bother the woman," said the turnkey to Weller; "she's just come in."

"A pris'ner!" said Sam, quickly replacing his hat. "Who's the plaintives? What for? Speak up, old feller."

"Dodson and Fogg," replied the man; "execution on cognovit for costs."

"Here Job, Job," shouted Sam, dashing into the passage, "run to Mr. Perker's, Job; I want him directly. I see some good in this. Here's a game. Hooray! Vere's the gov'nor?"

But there was no reply to these inquiries, for Job had started furiously off, the instant he received his commission, and Mrs. Bardell had fainted in real downright earnest.

CHAPTER XLVI.

IS CHIEFLY DEVOTED TO MATTERS OF BUSINESS,
AND THE TEMPORAL ADVANTAGE OF DODSON
AND FOGG.—MR. WINKLE RE-APPEARS UNDER EX-
TRAORDINARY CIRCUMSTANCES; AND MR. PICK-
WICK'S BENEVOLENCE PROVES STRONGER THAN
HIS OBSTINACY.

JOB TROTTER, abating nothing of his speed, ran up Holborn, sometimes in the middle of the road, sometimes on
the pavement, and sometimes in the gutter, as the chances
of getting along varied with the press of men, women,
children, and coaches, in each division of the thoroughfare,
and regardless of all obstacles, stopped not for an instant
until he reached the gate of Gray's Inn. Notwithstanding all the expedition he had used, however, the gate had
been closed a good half hour when he reached it, and by
the time he had discovered Mr. Perker's laundress, who
lived with a married daughter, who had bestowed her hand
upon a non-resident waiter, and occupied the one-pair of
some number, in some street, closely adjoining to some
brewery, somewhere behind Gray's Inn Lane, it was within fifteen minutes of the time of closing the prison for
the night. Mr. Lowten had still to be ferreted out from
the back parlour of the Magpie and Stump; and Job had
scarcely accomplished this object, and communicated Sam
Weller's message, than the clock struck ten.

"There," said Lowten, "it's too late now. You can't
get in to-night; you've got the key of the street, my
friend."

"Never mind me," replied Job, "I can sleep anywhere.
But won't it be better to see Mr. Perker to-night, so that
we may be there, the first thing in the morning?"

"Why," responded Lowten, after a little consideration,
"if it was in any body else's case, Perker wouldn't be best
pleased at my going up to his house, but as it's Mr. Pickwick's, I think I may venture to take a cab and charge it
to the office." Deciding upon this line of conduct, Mr.
Lowten took up his hat, and begging the assembled company to appoint a deputy chairman during his temporary
absence, led the way to the nearest coach stand, and summoning the cab of most promising appearance, directed the
driver to repair to Montague Place, Russell Square.

Mr. Perker had had a dinner party that day, as was testified by the appearance of lights in the drawing-room
windows, the sound of an improved grand piano, and an
improveable cabinet voice issuing therefrom; and a rather
overpowering smell of meat which pervaded the steps and
entry. In fact a couple of very good country agencies
happening to come up to town at the same time, an agreeable little party had been got together to meet them, comprising Mr. Snicks the Life Office Secretary, Mr. Prosee
the eminent counsel, three solicitors, one commissioner of
bankrupts, a special pleader from the Temple, a small-eyed
peremptory young gentleman, his pupil, who had written
a lively book about the law of demises, with a vast quantity of marginal notes and references; and several other
eminent and distinguished personages. From this society
little Mr. Perker detached himself on his clerk being announced in a whisper; and repairing to the dining-room,
there found Mr. Lowten and Job Trotter, looking very dim
and shadowy by the light of a kitchen candle, which the
gentleman who condescended to appear in plush shorts and
cottons for a quarterly stipend, had, with a becoming con-

tempt for the clerk and all things appertaining to "the
office," placed upon the table.

"Now, Lowten," said little Mr. Perker, shutting the
door, "what's the matter? No important letter come in a
parcel, is there?"

"No, Sir," replied Lowten. "This is a messenger from
Mr. Pickwick, Sir."

"From Pickwick, eh?" said the little man, turning
quickly to Job. "Well; what is it?"

"Dodson and Fogg have taken Mrs. Bardell in execution
for her costs, Sir," said Job.

"No!" exclaimed Perker, putting his hands in his pockets, and reclining against the sideboard.

"Yes," said Job. "It seems they got a cognovit out of
her for the amount of 'em, directly after the trial."

"By Jove!" said Perker, taking both hands out of his
pockets and striking the knuckles of his right against the
palm of his left, emphatically, "those are the cleverest
scamps I ever had anything to do with!"

"The sharpest practitioners *I* ever knew, Sir," observed
Lowten.

"Sharp!" echoed Perker. "There's no knowing where
to have them."

"Very true, Sir, there is not," replied Lowten; and then
both master and man pondered for a few seconds with animated countenances, as if they were reflecting upon one of
the most beautiful and ingenious discoveries that the intellect of man had ever made. When they had in some measure
recovered from their trance of admiration, Job Trotter
discharged himself of the rest of his commission. Perker
nodded his head thoughtfully, and pulled out his watch.

"At ten precisely I will be there," said the little man.
"Sam is quite right. Tell him so. Will you take a glass
of wine, Lowten?"

"No, thank you, Sir."

"You mean yes, I think," said the little man, turning to
the sideboard for a decanter and glasses.

As Lowten *did* mean yes, he said no more on the subject,
but inquired of Job, in an audible whisper, whether the
portrait of Perker, which hung opposite the fire-place,
wasn't a wonderful likeness, to which Job of course replied
that it was. The wine being by this time poured out,
Lowten drank to Mrs. Perker and the children, and Job to
Perker. The gentleman in the plush shorts and cottons
considering it no part of his duty to show the people from
the office out, consistently declined to answer the bell, and
they showed themselves out. The attorney betook himself
to his drawing-room, the clerk to the Magpie and Stump,
and Job to Covent Garden Market to spend the night in a
vegetable basket.

Punctually at the appointed hour next morning the good-
humoured little attorney tapped at Mr. Pickwick's door,
which was opened with great alacrity by Sam Weller.

"Mr. Perker, Sir," said Sam, announcing the visitor to
Mr. Pickwick, who was sitting at the window in a thoughtful attitude. "Wery glad you've looked in accidentally,
Sir. I ryather think the gov'ner vants to have a vord and
a half vith you, Sir."

Perker bestowed a look of intelligence upon Sam, intimating that he understood he was not to say he had been
sent for: and beckoning him to approach, whispered briefly
in his ear.

"Vy, you don't mean that 'ere, Sir?" said Sam, starting back in excessive surprise.

Perker nodded and smiled.

Mr. Samuel Weller looked at the little lawyer, then at Mr. Pickwick, then at the ceiling, then at Perker again; grinned, laughed outright, and finally, catching up his hat from the carpet, without further explanation disappeared.

"What does this mean?" inquired Mr. Pickwick, looking at Perker with astonishment. "What has put Sam into this most extraordinary state?"

"Oh, nothing, nothing," replied Perker. "Come my dear Sir, draw up your chair to the table. I have a good deal to say to you."

"What papers are those?" inquired Mr. Pickwick, as the little man deposited on the table a small bundle of documents tied with red tape.

"The papers in Bardell and Pickwick," replied Perker, undoing the knot with his teeth.

Mr. Pickwick grated the legs of his chair against the ground; and throwing himself into it, folded his hands and looked sternly—if Mr. Pickwick ever could look sternly—at his legal friend.

"You don't like to hear the name of the case?" said the little man, still busying himself with the knot.

"No, I do not indeed," replied Mr. Pickwick.

"Sorry for that," resumed Perker, "because it will form the subject of our conversation."

"I would rather that the subject was never mentioned between us, Perker," interposed Mr. Pickwick hastily.

"Pooh pooh, my dear Sir," said the little man, untying the bundle, and glancing eagerly at Mr. Pickwick out of the corners of his eyes. "It must be mentioned. I have come here on purpose. Now, are you ready to hear what I have to say, my dear Sir? No hurry; if you are not, I can wait. I have got this morning's paper here. Your time shall be mine. There." Hereupon the little man threw one leg over the other, and made a show of beginning to read, with great composure and application.

"Well, well," said Mr. Pickwick with a sigh, but softening into a smile at the same time. "Say what you have to say; it's the old story I suppose?"

"With a difference, my dear Sir; with a difference," rejoined Perker, deliberately folding up the paper and putting it into his pocket again. "Mrs. Bardell, the plaintiff in the action, is within these walls, Sir."

"I know it," was Mr. Pickwick's reply.

"Very good," retorted Perker. "And you know how she comes here, I suppose; I mean on what grounds, and at whose suit?"

"Yes; at least I have heard Sam's account of the matter," said Mr. Pickwick, with affected carelessness.

"Sam's account of the matter," replied Perker, "is, I will venture to say, a perfectly correct one. Well now, my dear Sir, the first question I have to ask, is whether this woman is to remain here?"

"To remain here!" echoed Mr. Pickwick.

"To remain here, my dear Sir," rejoined Perker, leaning back in his chair and looking steadily at his client.

"How can you ask me?" said that gentleman. "It rests with Dodson and Fogg; you know that very well."

"I know nothing of the kind," retorted Perker firmly. "It does *not* rest with Dodson and Fogg; you know the men, my dear Sir, as well as I do. It rests solely, wholly, and entirely with you."

"With me!" ejaculated Mr. Pickwick, rising nervously from his chair, and reseating himself directly afterwards.

The little man gave a double knock on the lid of his snuff-box, opened it, took a great pinch, shut it up again, and repeated the words—"With you."

"I say, my dear Sir," pursued the little man, who seemed to gather confidence from the snuff; "I say that her speedy liberation or perpetual imprisonment rests with you, and with you alone. Hear me out, my dear Sir, if you please, and do not be so very energetic, for it will only put you into a perspiration and do no good whatever. I say," continued Perker, checking off each position on a different finger as he laid it down; "I say that nobody but you can rescue her from this den of wretchedness; and that you can only do that, by paying the costs of this suit—both of plaintiff and defendant—into the hands of these Freeman Court sharks. Now pray be quiet, my dear Sir."

Mr. Pickwick, whose face had been undergoing most surprising changes during this speech, and who was evidently on the verge of a strong burst of indignation, calmed his wrath as well as he could; and Perker, strengthening his argumentative powers with another pinch of snuff, proceeded.

"I have seen the woman this morning. By paying the costs, you can obtain a full release and discharge from the damages; and further—this I know is a far greater object of consideration with you, my dear Sir—a voluntary statement under her hand, in the form of a letter to me, that this business was, from the very first, fomented and encouraged and brought about, by these men, Dodson and Fogg; that she deeply regrets ever having been the instrument of annoyance or injury to you; and that she entreats me to intercede with you, and implore your pardon."

"If I pay her costs for her," said Mr. Pickwick, indignantly; "a valuable document, indeed!"

"No '*if*' in the case, my dear Sir," said Perker, triumphantly. "There is the very letter I speak of. Brought to my office by another woman at nine o'clock this morning, before I had set foot in this place, or held any communication with Mrs. Bardell, upon my honour." And selecting the letter from the bundle, the little lawyer laid it at Mr. Pickwick's elbow, and took snuff for two consecutive minutes without winking.

"Is this all you have to say to me?" inquired Mr. Pickwick, mildly.

"Not quite," replied Perker. "I cannot undertake to say at this moment, whether the wording of the cognovit, the nature of the ostensible consideration, and the proof we can get together about the whole conduct of the suit, will be sufficient to justify an indictment for conspiracy. I fear not, my dear Sir; they are too clever for that, I doubt. I do mean to say, however, that the whole facts, taken together, will be sufficient to justify you in the minds of all reasonable men. And now, my dear Sir, I put it to you. This one hundred and fifty pounds, or whatever it may be—take it in round numbers—is nothing to you. A jury has decided against you; well, their verdict is wrong, but still they decided as they thought right, and it *is* against you. You have now an opportunity, on easy terms, of placing yourself in a much higher position than you ever could by remaining here; which would only be imputed by people who didn't know you to sheer, dogged, wrongheaded, brutal obstinacy: nothing else, my dear Sir, believe me. Can you hesitate to avail yourself of it, when it restores you to your friends, your old pursuits, your health and amusements; when it liberates your faithful and attached servant, whom you otherwise doom to imprisonment for the whole of your life? and above all, when it enables you to take the very magnanimous revenge—which I know, my dear Sir, is one after your own heart—of releasing this woman from a scene of misery and debauchery, to which no man should ever be consigned if I had my will, but the infliction of which, on any female, is frightful and barbarous. Now I ask you, my dear Sir, not only as your legal adviser, but as your very true friend, will you let slip the occasion of attaining all these objects and doing all this good, for the paltry consideration of a few pounds finding their way into the pockets of a couple of rascals, to whom it makes no manner of difference, except that the more they gain the more they'll seek, and so the sooner be led into some piece of knavery that must end in a crash? I have put these considerations to you, my dear Sir, very feebly and imperfectly, but I ask you to think of them—turn them over in your mind as long as you please: I wait here most patiently for your answer."

Before Mr. Pickwick could reply, before Mr. Perker had taken one twentieth part of the snuff which so unusually long an address imperatively required to be followed up, there was a low murmuring of voices outside, and then a hesitating knock at the door.

"Dear, dear," exclaimed Mr. Pickwick, who had been evidently roused by his friend's appeal; "what an annoyance that door is! Who is that?"

"Me, Sir," replied Sam Weller, putting in his head.

"I can't speak to you just now, Sam," said Mr. Pickwick. "I am engaged at this moment, Sam."

"Beg your pardon, Sir," rejoined Mr. Weller. "But here's a lady here, Sir, as says she's somethin' wery partickler to disclose."

"I can't see any lady," replied Mr. Pickwick, whose mind was filled with visions of Mrs. Bardell.

"I vouldn't make too sure o' that, Sir," urged Mr. Weller, shaking his head. "If you know'd who was near, Sir, I rayther think you'd change your note; as the hawk remarked to himself vith a cheerful laugh, ven he heerd the robin redbreast a singin' round the corner."

"Who is it?" enquired Mr. Pickwick.

"Vill you see her, Sir?" asked Mr. Weller, holding the door in his hand, as if he had got some curious live animal on the other side.

"I suppose I must," said Mr. Pickwick, looking at Perker.

"Vell then, all in to begin," cried Sam. "Sound the gong, draw up the curtain, and enter the two con-spirators."

As Sam Weller spoke, he threw the door open, and there rushed tumultuously into the room, Mr. Nathaniel Winkle, leading after him by the hand the identical young lady who, at Dingley Dell, had worn the boots with the fur round the tops; and who, now a very pleasing compound of blushes and confusion, and lilac silk, and a smart hat, and a rich lace veil, looked prettier than ever.

"Miss Arabella Allen!" exclaimed Mr. Pickwick, rising from his chair.

"No," replied Mr. Winkle, dropping on his knees. "Mrs. Winkle. Pardon, my dear friend, pardon."

Mr. Pickwick could scarcely believe the evidence of his own senses, and perhaps would not have done so, but for the corroborative testimony afforded by the smiling countenance of Perker, and the bodily presence, in the background, of Sam and the pretty housemaid, who appeared to contemplate the proceedings with the liveliest satisfaction.

"Oh, Mr. Pickwick," said Arabella in a low voice, as if alarmed at the silence, "can you forgive my imprudence?"

Mr. Pickwick returned no verbal response to this appeal, but he took off his spectacles in great haste, and seizing both the young lady's hands in his, kissed her a great

number of times—perhaps a greater number than was absolutely necessary—and then, still retaining one of her hands, told Mr. Winkle he was an audacious young dog, and bade him get up, which Mr. Winkle, who had been for some seconds scratching his nose with the brim of his hat in a penitent manner, did; whereupon Mr. Pickwick slapped him on the back several times, and then shook hands heartily with Perker, who, not to be behindhand in the compliments of the occasion, saluted both the bride and the pretty housemaid with right good will, and having wrung Mr. Winkle's hand most cordially, wound up his demonstrations of joy by taking snuff enough to set any half dozen men with ordinarily constructed noses, a sneezing for life.

"Why, my dear girl," said Mr. Pickwick, "how has all this come about? Come, sit down, and let me hear it all. How well she looks, doesn't she Perker?" added Mr. Pickwick, surveying Arabella's face with a look of as much pride and exultation, as if she had been his own daughter.

"Delightful, my dear Sir," replied the little man. "If I were not a married man myself, I should be disposed to envy you, you dog, I should." Thus expressing himself, the little lawyer gave Mr. Winkle a poke in the chest, which that gentleman reciprocated; after which they both laughed very loudly, but not so loudly as Mr. Samuel Weller, who had just relieved his feelings by kissing the pretty housemaid under cover of the cupboard door.

"I can never be grateful enough to you, Sam, I am sure," said Arabella, with the sweetest smile imaginable. "I shall not forget your exertions in the garden at Clifton."

"Don't say nothin' wotever about it, Ma'am," replied Sam. "I only assisted natur, Ma'am; as the doctor said to the boy's mother, arter he'd bled him to death."

"Mary, my dear, sit down," said Mr. Pickwick, cutting short these compliments. "Now then—how long have you been married, eh?"

Arabella looked bashfully at her lord and master, who replied, "Only three days."

"Only three days, eh?" said Mr. Pickwick. "Why, what have you been doing these three months?"

"Ah, to be sure," interposed Perker; "come, account for this idleness. You see Pickwick's only astonishment is, that it wasn't all over months ago."

"Why the fact is," replied Mr. Winkle, looking at his blushing young wife, "that I could not persuade Bella to run away for a long time; and when I had persuaded her, it was a long time more before we could find an opportunity. Mary had to give a month's warning, too, before she could leave her place next door, and we couldn't possibly have done it without her assistance."

"Upon my word," exclaimed Mr. Pickwick, who by this time had resumed his spectacles, and was looking from Arabella to Winkle, and from Winkle to Arabella, with as much delight depicted in his countenance as warm-heartedness and kindly feeling can communicate to the human face—"upon my word! you seem to have been very systematic in your proceedings. And is your brother acquainted with all this, my dear?"

"Oh, no, no," replied Arabella, changing colour. "Dear Mr. Pickwick, he must only know it from you—from your lips alone. He is so violent, so prejudiced, and has been so—so anxious in behalf of his friend, Mr. Sawyer," added Arabella, looking down, "that I fear the consequences dreadfully."

"Ah, to be sure," said Perker, gravely. "You must take this matter in hand for them, my dear Sir. These young men will respect you when they would listen to nobody else. You must prevent mischief, my dear Sir. Hot blood—hot blood." And the little man took a warning pinch, and shook his head doubtfully.

"You forget, my love," said Mr. Pickwick, gently, "you forget that I am a prisoner."

"No, indeed I do not, my dear Sir," replied Arabella. "I never have forgotten it; never ceased to think how great your sufferings must have been in this shocking place, but I hoped that what no consideration for yourself would induce you to do, a regard to our happiness might. If my brother hears of this first from you, I feel certain we shall be reconciled. He is my only relation in the world, Mr. Pickwick, and unless you plead for me, I fear I have lost even him. I have done wrong—very, very wrong, I know." Here poor Arabella hid her face in her handkerchief, and wept bitterly.

Mr. Pickwick's nature was a good deal worked upon by these same tears, but when Mrs. Winkle, drying her eyes, took to coaxing and entreating in the sweetest tones of a very sweet voice, he became particularly restless, and evidently undecided how to act, as was evinced by sundry nervous rubbings of his spectacle-glasses, nose, tights, head, and gaiters.

Taking advantage of these symptoms of indecision, Mr. Perker (to whom it appeared the young couple had driven straight that morning) urged with legal point and shrewdness that Mr. Winkle, senior, was still unacquainted with the important rise in life's flight of steps which his son had taken; that the future expectations of the said son depended upon the said Winkle senior continuing to regard him with undiminished feelings of affection and attachment, which it was very unlikely he would do if this great event were long kept a secret from him; that Mr. Pickwick repairing to Bristol to seek Mr. Allen, might with equal reason repair to Birmingham to seek Mr. Winkle, senior; lastly, that Mr. Winkle, senior, had good right and title to consider Mr. Pickwick as in some degree the guardian and adviser of his son, and that it consequently behoved that gentleman, and was indeed due to his personal character, to acquaint the aforesaid Winkle, senior, personally, and by word of mouth, with the whole circumstances of the case, and with the share he had taken in the transaction.

Mr. Tupman and Mr. Snodgrass arrived most opportunely in this stage of the pleadings, and as it was necessary to explain to them all that had occurred, together with the various reasons pro and con, the whole of the arguments were gone over again, after which everybody urged every argument in his own way and at his own length. And at last Mr. Pickwick, fairly argued and remonstrated out of all his resolutions, and being in imminent danger of being argued and remonstrated out of his wits, caught Arabella in his arms, and declaring that she was a very amiable creature, and that he didn't know how it was, but he had always been very fond of her from the first, said he could never find it in his heart to stand in the way of young people's happiness, and they might do with him as they pleased.

Mr. Weller's first act, on hearing this concession, was to dispatch Job Trotter to the illustrious Mr. Pell, with an authority to deliver to the bearer the formal discharge which his prudent parent had had the foresight to leave in the hands of that learned gentleman, in case it should be at any time required on an emergency; his next proceeding was to invest his whole stock of ready money in the purchase of five-and-twenty gallons of mild porter, which he himself dispensed on the racket ground to everybody who would partake of it; this done, he hurra'd in divers parts of the building until he had lost his voice, and then quietly relapsed into his usual collected and philosophical condition.

At three o'clock that afternoon, Mr. Pickwick took a last look at his little room, and made his way as well as he could, through the throng of debtors who pressed eagerly forward to shake him by the hand, until he reached the lodge steps. He turned here to look about him, and his eye lightened as he did so. In all the crowd of wan emaciated faces, he saw not one which was not the happier for his sympathy and charity.

"Perker," said Mr. Pickwick, beckoning one young man towards him, "this is Mr. Jingle, whom I spoke to you about."

"Very good, my dear Sir," replied Perker, looking hard at Jingle. "You will see me again, young man, to-morrow. I hope you may live to remember deeply what I shall have to communicate, Sir."

Jingle bowed respectfully, trembled very much as he took Mr. Pickwick's proffered hand, and withdrew.

"Job you know, I think?" said Mr. Pickwick, presenting that gentleman.

"I know the rascal," replied Perker, good-humouredly. "See after your friend, and be in the way to-morrow at one. Do you hear? Now, is there anything more?"

"Nothing," rejoined Mr. Pickwick. "You have delivered the little parcel I gave you for your old landlord, Sam?"

"I have, Sir," replied Sam. "He bust out a cryin', Sir, and said you wos wery gen'rous and thoughtful, and he only wished you could have him innocklated for a gallopin' consumption, for his old friend as had lived here so long wos dead, and he'd noveres to look for another."

"Poor fellow, poor fellow!" said Mr. Pickwick. "God bless you, my friends!"

As Mr. Pickwick uttered this adieu, the crowd raised a loud shout, and many among them were pressing forward to shake him by the hand again, when he drew his arm through Perker's, and hurried from the prison, far more sad and melancholy, for the moment, than when he had first entered it. Alas! how many sad and unhappy beings had he left behind! and how many of them lie caged there, still!

A happy evening was that for at least one party in the George and Vulture, and light and cheerful were two of the hearts that emerged from its hospitable door next morning; the owners thereof were Mr. Pickwick and Sam Weller, the former of whom was speedily deposited inside a comfortable post coach, with a little dickey behind, in which the latter mounted with great agility.

"Sir," called out Mr. Weller, to his master.

"Well, Sam," replied Mr. Pickwick, thrusting his head out of the window.

"I wish them horses had been three months and better in the Fleet, Sir."

"Why Sam?" inquired Mr. Pickwick.

"Vy, Sir," exclaimed Mr. Weller, rubbing his hands, "how they vould go if they had been!"

CHAPTER XLVII.

RELATES HOW MR. PICKWICK, WITH THE ASSISTANCE
OF SAMUEL WELLER, ESSAYED TO SOFTEN THE
HEART OF MR. BENJAMIN ALLEN, AND TO MOL-
LIFY THE WRATH OF MR. ROBERT SAWYER.

Mr. Ben Allen and Mr. Bob Sawyer sat together in the little surgery behind the shop, discussing minced veal and future prospects, when the discourse, not unnaturally, turned upon the practice acquired by Bob the aforesaid, and his present chances of deriving a competent independence from the honourable profession to which he had devoted himself.

"—Which, I think," observed Mr. Bob Sawyer, pursuing the thread of the subject, "which I think, Ben, are rather dubious."

"What's rather dubious?" inquired Mr. Ben Allen, at the same time sharpening his intellects with a draught of beer. "What's dubious?"

"Why, the chances," responded Mr. Bob Sawyer.

"I forgot," said Mr. Ben Allen. "The beer has reminded me that I forgot, Bob—yes: they *are* dubious."

"It's wonderful how the poor people patronise me," said Mr. Bob Sawyer, reflectively. "They knock me up at all hours of the night, take medicine to an extent which I should have conceived impossible, put on blisters and leeches with a perseverance worthy of a better cause, make additions to their families in a manner which is quite awful. Six of those last-named little promissory notes, all due on the same day Ben, and all entrusted to me."

"It's very gratifying, isn't it?" said Mr. Ben Allen, holding his plate for some more minced veal.

"Oh, very," replied Bob; "only not quite so much so as the confidence of patients, with a shilling or two to spare, would be. This business was capitally described in the advertisement, Ben. It is a practice, a very extensive practice—and that's all."

"Bob," said Mr. Ben Allen, laying down his knife and fork, and fixing his eyes on the visage of his friend—"Bob, I'll tell you what it is."

"What is it?" enquired Mr. Bob Sawyer.

"You must make yourself, with as little delay as possible, master of Arabella's one thousand pounds."

"Three per cent. consolidated Bank annuities, now standing in her name in the book or books of the Governor and Company of the Bank of England," added Bob Sawyer, in legal phraseology.

"Exactly so," said Ben. "She has it when she comes of age, or marries. She wants a year of coming of age, and if you plucked up a spirit she needn't want a month of being married."

"She's a very charming and delightful creature," quoth Mr. Robert Sawyer, in reply; "and has only one fault that I know of, Ben. It happens unfortunately, that that single blemish is a want of taste. She don't like me."

"It's my opinion that she don't know what she does like," said Mr. Ben Allen, contemptuously.

"Perhaps not," remarked Mr. Bob Sawyer. "But it's my opinion that she does know what she doesn't like, and that's of even more importance."

"I wish," said Mr. Ben Allen, setting his teeth together, and speaking more like a savage warrior who fed upon raw wolf's flesh which he carved with his fingers, than a peaceable young gentleman who eat minced veal with a knife and fork—"I wish I knew whether any rascal really has been tampering with her, and attempting to engage her affections. I think I should assassinate him, Bob."

"I'd put a bullet in him if I found him out," said Mr. Sawyer, stopping in the course of a long draught of beer, and looking malignantly out of the porter pot. "If that didn't do his business, I'd extract it afterwards, and kill him that way."

Mr. Benjamin Allen gazed abstractedly on his friend for some minutes in silence, and then said—

"You have never proposed to her point-blank, Bob?"

"No. Because I saw it would be of no use," replied Mr. Robert Sawyer.

"You shall do it before you are twenty-four hours older," retorted Ben, with desperate calmness. "She *shall* have you, or I'll know the reason why—I'll exert my authority."

"Well," said Mr. Bob Sawyer, "We shall see."

"We *shall* see, my friend," replied Mr. Ben Allen, fiercely. He paused for a few seconds, and added in a voice broken by emotion. "You have loved her from a child, my friend—you loved her when we were boys at school together, and even then she was wayward, and slighted your young feelings. Do you recollect, with all the eagerness of a child's love, one day pressing upon her acceptance two small carraway-seed biscuits and one sweet apple, neatly folded into a circular parcel with the leaf of a copy-book?"

"I do," replied Bob Sawyer.

"She slighted that, I think?" said Ben Allen.

"She did," rejoined Bob. "She said I had kept the parcel so long in the pockets of my corduroys, that the apple was unpleasantly warm."

"I remember," said Mr. Allen, gloomily. "Upon which we ate it ourselves, in alternate bites."

Bob Sawyer intimated his recollection of the circumstance last alluded to, by a melancholy frown; and the two friends remained for some time absorbed, each in his own meditations.

While these observations were being exchanged between Mr. Bob Sawyer and Mr. Benjamin Allen, and while the boy in the grey livery, marvelling at the unwonted prolongation of the dinner, cast an anxious look from time to time towards the glass door, distracted by inward misgivings regarding the amount of minced veal which would be ultimately reserved for his individual cravings, there rolled soberly on through the streets of Bristol, a private fly, painted of a sad green colour, drawn by a chubby sort of brown horse, and driven by a surly looking man with his legs dressed like the legs of a groom, and his body attired in the coat of a coachman. Such appearances are common to many vehicles belonging to, and maintained by, old ladies of economical habits; and in this vehicle there sat an old lady who was its mistress and proprietor.

"Martin!" said the old lady, calling to the surly man out of the front window.

"Well?" said the surly man, touching his hat to the old lady.

"Mr. Sawyer's," said the old lady.

"I was going there," said the surly man.

The old lady nodded the satisfaction which this proof of

the surly man's foresight imparted to her feelings; and the surly man giving a smart lash to the chubby horse, they all repaired to Mr. Bob Sawyer's together.

"Martin!" said the old lady, when the fly stopped at the door of Mr. Robert Sawyer late Nockemorf.

"Well?" said Martin.

"Ask the lad to step out and mind the horse."

"I'm going to mind the horse myself," said Martin, laying his whip on the roof of the fly.

"I can't permit it on any account," said the old lady; "your testimony will be very important, and I must take you into the house with me. You must not stir from my side during the whole interview. Do you hear?"

"I hear," replied Martin.

"Well; what are you stopping for?"

"Nothing," replied Martin. So saying, the surly man leisurely descended from the wheel upon which he had been poising himself on the tops of the toes of his right foot, and having summoned the boy in the grey livery, opened the coach-door, flung down the steps, and thrusting in a hand enveloped in a dark wash-leather glove, pulled out the old lady with as much unconcern in his manner as if she were a bandbox.

"Dear me," exclaimed the old lady, "I am so flurried now I have got here Martin, that I'm all in a tremble."

Mr. Martin coughed behind the dark wash-leather glove, but expressed no further sympathy; so the old lady, composing herself, trotted up Mr. Bob Sawyer's steps, and Mr. Martin followed. Immediately upon the old lady's entering the shop, Mr. Benjamin Allen and Mr. Bob Sawyer, who had been putting the spirits and water out of sight, and upsetting nauseous drugs to take off the smell of the tobacco-smoke, issued hastily forth in a transport of pleasure and affection.

"My dear aunt," exclaimed Mr. Ben Allen, "how kind of you to look in upon us. Mr. Sawyer, aunt; my friend Mr. Bob Sawyer that I have spoken to you about, regarding—you know, aunt." And here Mr. Ben Allen, who was not at the moment extraordinarily sober, added the word "Arabella," in what was meant to be a whisper, but which was in fact an especially audible and distinct tone of speech, which nobody could avoid hearing, if anybody were so disposed.

"My dear Benjamin," said the old lady, struggling with a great shortness of breath, and trembling from head to foot—"don't be alarmed, my dear, but I think I had better speak to Mr. Sawyer alone for a moment—only for one moment."

"Bob," said Mr. Ben Allen, "will you take my aunt into the surgery?"

"Certainly," responded Bob, in a most professional voice. "Step this way, my dear Ma'am. Don't be frightened, Ma'am. We shall be able to set you to rights in a very short time, I have no doubt, Ma'am. Here, my dear Ma'am. Now then." With this Mr. Bob Sawyer having handed the old lady to a chair, shut the door, drew another chair close to her, and waited to hear detailed the symptoms of some disorder from which he saw in perspective a long train of profits and advantages.

The first thing the old lady did, was to shake her head a great many times, and begin to cry.

"Nervous," said Bob Sawyer complacently. "Camphor-julep and water three times a day, and composing draught at night."

"I don't know how to begin, Mr. Sawyer," said the old lady. "It is so very painful and distressing."

"You need not begin, Ma'am," rejoined Mr. Bob Sawyer. "I can anticipate all you would say. The head is in fault."

"I should be very sorry to think it was the heart," said the old lady, with a slight groan.

"Not the slightest danger of that, Ma'am," replied Bob Sawyer. "The stomach is the primary cause."

"Mr. Sawyer!" exclaimed the old lady, starting.

"Not the least doubt of it, Ma'am," rejoined Bob, looking wondrous wise. "Medicine, in time, my dear Ma'am, would have prevented it all."

"Mr. Sawyer," said the old lady, more flurried than before, "this conduct is either great impertinence to one in my situation, Sir, or it arises from your not understanding the object of my visit. If it had been in the power of medicine or any foresight I could have used to prevent what has occurred, I should certainly have done so. I had better see my nephew at once," said the old lady, twirling her reticule indignantly, and rising as she spoke.

"Stop a moment, Ma'am," said Bob Sawyer; "I am afraid I have not understood you. What *is* the matter, Ma'am?"

"My niece, Mr. Sawyer," said the old lady—"your friend's sister."

"Yes, Ma'am," said Bob, all impatience; for the old lady, although much agitated, spoke with the most tantalising deliberation, as old ladies often do. "Yes, Ma'am."

"Left my home, Mr. Sawyer, three days ago, on a pretended visit to my sister, another aunt of hers, who keeps the large boarding school just beyond the third mile-stone, where there is a very large laburnum tree and an oak gate," said the old lady, stopping in this place to dry her eyes.

"Oh, devil take the laburnum tree! Ma'am," said Bob, quite forgetting his professional dignity in his anxiety. "Get on a little faster; put a little more steam on, Ma'am, pray."

"This morning," said the old lady, slowly, "this morning, she——"

"She came back, Ma'am, I suppose," said Bob, with great animation. "Did she come back?"

"No, she did not—she wrote," replied the old lady.

"What did she say?" enquired Bob, eagerly.

"She said, Mr. Sawyer," replied the old lady—"and it is this I want you to prepare Benjamin's mind for, gently and by degrees; she said that she was—I have got the letter in my pocket, Mr. Sawyer, but my glasses are in the carriage, and I should only waste the time if I attempted to point out the passage to you, without them; she said, in short, Mr. Sawyer, that she was married."

"What!" said, or rather shouted, Mr. Bob Sawyer.

"Married," repeated the old lady.

Mr. Bob Sawyer stopped to hear no more; but darting from the surgery into the outer shop, cried in a stentorian voice, "Ben, my boy, she's bolted!"

Mr. Ben Allen, who had been slumbering behind the counter with his head half a foot or so below his knees, no sooner heard this appalling communication, than he made a precipitate rush at Mr. Martin, and twisting his hand in the neck-cloth of that taciturn servitor, expressed an obliging intention of choking him where he stood, which intention, with a promptitude often the effect of desperation, he at once commenced carrying into execution with much vigour and surgical skill.

Mr. Martin, who was a man of few words and possessed but little power of eloquence or persuasion, submitted to this operation with a very calm and agreeable expression of countenance, for some seconds; finding, however, that it threatened speedily to lead to a result which would place it beyond his power to claim any wages, board or otherwise, in all times to come, he muttered an inarticulate remonstrance, and felled Mr. Benjamin Allen to the ground. As that gentleman had got his hands entangled in his cravat, he had no alternative but to follow him to the floor. There they both lay struggling, when the shop-door opened, and the party was increased by the arrival of two most unexpected visitors, to wit, Mr. Pickwick and Mr. Samuel Weller.

The impression at once produced upon Mr. Weller's mind by what he saw, was, that Mr. Martin was hired by the establishment of Sawyer late Nockemorf, to take strong medicine, or to go into fits and be experimentalised upon, or to swallow poison now and then with the view of testing the efficacy of some new antidotes, or to do something or other to promote the great science of medicine, and gratify the ardent spirit of enquiry burning in the bosoms of its two young professors. So, without presuming to interfere, Sam stood perfectly still, and looked on as if he were mightily interested in the result of the then pending experiment. Not so, Mr. Pickwick. He at once threw himself upon the astonished combatants with his accustomed energy, and loudly called upon the bystanders to interpose.

This roused Mr. Bob Sawyer, who had been hitherto quite paralysed by the frenzy of his companion; and with that gentleman's assistance, Mr. Pickwick raised Ben Allen to his feet. Mr. Martin finding himself alone on the floor, got up and looked about him.

"Mr. Allen," said Mr. Pickwick, "what is the matter, Sir?"

"Never mind, Sir," replied Mr. Allen, with haughty defiance.

"What is it?" enquired Mr. Pickwick, looking at Bob Sawyer. "Is he unwell?"

Before Bob could reply, Mr. Ben Allen seized Mr. Pickwick by the hand, and murmured, in sorrowful accents, "My sister, my dear Sir; my sister."

"Oh, is that all?" said Mr. Pickwick. "We shall easily arrange that matter, I hope. Your sister is safe and well, and I am here, my dear Sir, to——"

"Sorry to do anythin' as may cause an interruption to such wery pleasant proceedin's, as the king said ven he dissolved the parliament," interposed Mr. Weller, who had been peeping through the glass door; "but there's another experiment here, Sir. Here's a wenerable old lady a lyin' on the carpet vaitin' for dissection, or galwinism, or some other revivin' and scientific inwention."

"I forgot," exclaimed Mr. Ben Allen. "It is my aunt."

"Dear me," said Mr. Pickwick. "Poor lady! gently Sam, gently."

"Strange sitivation for one o' the family," observed Sam Weller, hoisting the aunt into a chair. "Now, depitty Sawbones, bring out the wollatilly."

The latter observation was addressed to the boy in grey, who, having handed over the fly to the care of the street-keeper, had come back to see what all the noise was about. Between the boy in grey, and Mr. Bob Sawyer, and Mr. Benjamin Allen (who having frightened his aunt into a fainting fit, was affectionately solicitous for her recovery) the old lady was at length restored to consciousness; and then Mr. Ben Allen, turning with a puzzled countenance to Mr. Pickwick, asked him what he was about to say when he had been so alarmingly interrupted.

"We are all friends here, I presume?" said Mr. Pickwick, clearing his voice, and looking towards the man of few words with the surly countenance, who drove the fly with the chubby horse.

This reminded Mr. Bob Sawyer that the boy in grey was looking on, with eyes wide open and greedy ears. The incipient chemist having been lifted up by his coat collar and dropped outside the door, Bob Sawyer assured Mr. Pickwick that he might speak without reserve.

"Your sister, my dear Sir," said Mr. Pickwick, turning to Benjamin Allen, "is in London; well and happy."

"Her happiness is no object to me, Sir," said Mr. Benjamin Allen, with a flourish of the hand.

"Her husband *is* an object to *me*, Sir," said Bob Sawyer. "He shall be an object to me, Sir, at twelve paces, and a very pretty object I'll make of him, Sir—a mean-spirited scoundrel!" This, as it stood, was a very pretty denunciation, and magnanimous withal; but Mr. Bob Sawyer rather weakened its effect, by winding up with some general observations concerning the punching of heads and knocking out of eyes, which were commonplace by comparison.

"Stay, Sir," said Mr. Pickwick; "before you apply those epithets to the gentleman in question, consider dispassionately the extent of his fault, and above all remember that he is a friend of mine."

"What!" said Mr. Bob Sawyer.

"His name," cried Ben Allen. "His name."

"Mr. Nathaniel Winkle," said Mr. Pickwick, firmly.

Mr. Benjamin Allen deliberately crushed his spectacles beneath the heel of his boot, and having picked up the pieces and put them into three separate pockets, folded his arms, bit his lips, and looked in a threatening manner at the bland features of Mr. Pickwick.

"Then it's you, is it, Sir, who have encouraged and brought about this match?" inquired Mr. Benjamin Allen, at length.

"And it's this gentleman's servant, I suppose," interrupted the old lady, "who has been skulking about my house, and endeavouring to entrap my servants to conspire against their mistress. Martin!"

"Well?" said the surly man, coming forward.

"Is that the young man you saw in the lane, whom you told me about this morning?"

Mr. Martin, who, as it has already appeared, was a man of few words, looked at Sam Weller, nodded his head, and growled forth, "That's the man."

Mr. Weller, who was never proud, gave a smile of friendly recognition as his eyes encountered those of the surly groom, and admitted, in courteous terms, that he had "knowed him afore."

"And this is the faithful creature," exclaimed Mr. Ben Allen, "that I had nearly suffocated! Mr. Pickwick, how dare you allow your fellow to be employed in the abduction of my sister? I demand that you explain this matter, Sir."

"Explain it, Sir!" cried Bob Sawyer, fiercely.

"It's a conspiracy," said Ben Allen.

"A regular plant," added Mr. Bob Sawyer.

"A disgraceful imposition," observed the old lady.

"Nothing but a do," remarked Martin.

"Pray hear me," urged Mr. Pickwick, as Mr. Ben Allen fell into a chair that patients were bled in, and gave way to his pocket-handkerchief. "I have rendered no assistance in this matter, beyond that of being present at one interview between the young people, which I could not prevent, and from which I conceived my presence would remove any slight colouring of impropriety that it might otherwise have had: this is the whole share I have taken in the transaction, and I had no suspicion that an immediate marriage was even contemplated. Though, mind," added Mr. Pickwick, hastily checking himself, "mind, I do not say I should have prevented it, if I *had* known that it was intended."

"You hear that, all of you; you hear that?" said Mr. Benjamin Allen.

"I hope they do," mildly observed Mr. Pickwick, looking round; "and," added that gentleman, his colour mounting as he spoke, "I hope they hear this, Sir, also,— that from what has been stated to me, Sir, I assert that you were by no means justified in attempting to force your sister's inclinations as you did, and that you should rather have endeavoured by your kindness and forbearance to have supplied the place of other nearer relations whom she has never known from a child. As regards my young friend, I must beg to add, that in every point of worldly advantage, he is at least on an equal footing with yourself, if not on a much better one, and that unless I hear this question discussed with becoming temper and moderation, I decline hearing any more said upon the subject."

"I vish to make a wery few remarks in addition to wot has been put forard by the honorable gen'lm'n as has jist given over," said Mr. Weller, stepping forth, "vich is this here: a indiwidual in company has called me a feller."

"That has nothing whatever to do with the matter, Sam," interposed Mr. Pickwick. "Pray hold your tongue."

"I ain't a goin' to say nothin' on that ere pint, Sir," replied Sam, "but merely this here. P'raps that gen'lm'n may think as there vos a priory 'tachment, but there vorn't nothin' o' the sort, for the young lady said in the wery beginnin' o' the keepin' company that she couldn't abide him. Nobody's cut him out, and it 'ud ha' been just the wery same for him if the young lady had never seen Mr. Vinkle. That's wot I vished to say, Sir, and I hope I've now made that 'ere gen'lm'n's mind easy."

A short pause followed these consolatory remarks of Mr. Weller, and then Mr. Ben Allen rising from his chair, protested that he would never see Arabella's face again, while Mr. Bob Sawyer, despite Sam's flattering assurance, vowed dreadful vengeance on the happy bridegroom.

But, just when matters were at their height and threatening to remain so, Mr. Pickwick found a powerful assistant in the old lady, who, evidently much struck by the mode in which he had advocated her niece's cause, ventured to approach Mr. Benjamin Allen with a few comforting reflections, of which the chief were, that after all, perhaps, it was well it was no worse; the least said the soonest mended, and upon her word she did not know that it was so very bad after all; that what was over couldn't be begun, and what couldn't be cured must be endured, with various other assurances of the like novel and strengthening description. To all of which, Mr. Benjamin Allen replied that he meant no disrespect to his aunt or anybody there, but if it were all the same to them, and they would allow him to have his own way, he would rather have the pleasure of hating his sister till death and after it.

At length when this determination had been announced half a hundred times, the old lady suddenly bridling up and looking very majestic, wished to know what she had done that no respect was to be paid to her years or station, and that she should be obliged to beg and pray in that way of her own nephew, whom she remembered about five-and-twenty years before he was born, and whom she had known personally when he hadn't a tooth in his head; to say nothing of her presence on the first occasion of his having his hair cut, and assistance at numerous other times and ceremonies during his babyhood, of sufficient importance to found a claim upon his affection, obedience, and sympathies, for ever.

While the good lady was bestowing this objurgation on Mr. Ben Allen, Bob Sawyer and Mr. Pickwick had retired in close conversation to the inner room, where the former gentleman was observed to apply himself several times to the mouth of a black bottle, under the influence of which his features gradually assumed a cheerful and even jovial expression. And at last he emerged from the room, bottle in hand, and remarking that he was very sorry to say he had been making a fool of himself, begged to propose the health and happiness of Mr. and Mrs. Winkle, whose felicity, so far from envying, he would be the first to congratulate them upon. Hearing this, Mr. Ben Allen suddenly arose from his chair, and seizing the black bottle drank the toast so heartily, that, the liquor being strong, he became nearly as black in the face as the bottle itself. Finally the black bottle went round till it was empty, and there was so much shaking of hands and interchanging of compliments, that even the metal-visaged Mr. Martin condescended to smile.

"And now," said Bob Sawyer, rubbing his hands, "we'll have a jolly night."

"I am sorry," said Mr. Pickwick, "that I must return to my inn. I have not been accustomed to fatigue lately, and my journey has tired me exceedingly."

"You'll take some tea, Mr. Pickwick?" said the old lady, with irresistible sweetness.

"Thank you, I would rather not," replied that gentleman. The truth is, that the old lady's evidently increasing admiration was Mr. Pickwick's principal inducement for going. He thought of Mrs. Bardell: and every glance of the old lady's eyes threw him into a cold perspiration.

As Mr. Pickwick could by no means be prevailed upon to stay, it was arranged at once, on his own proposition, that Mr. Benjamin Allen should accompany him on his journey to the elder Mr. Winkle's, and that the coach should be at the door at nine o'clock next morning. He then took his leave, and, followed by Samuel Weller, repaired to the Bush. It is worthy of remark, that Mr. Martin's face was horribly convulsed as he shook hands with Sam at parting, and that he gave vent to a smile and an oath simultaneously, from which tokens it has been inferred by those who were best acquainted with that gentleman's peculiarities that he expressed himself much pleased with Mr. Weller's society, and requested the honor of his further acquaintance.

"Shall I order a private room, Sir?" inquired Sam, when they reached the Bush.

"Why, no, Sam," replied Mr. Pickwick; "as I dined in the coffee room, and shall go to bed soon, it is hardly worth while. See who there is in the traveller's room, Sam."

Mr. Weller departed on his errand, and presently returned to say that there was only a gentleman with one eye, and the landlord, who were drinking a bowl of bishop together.

"I will join them," said Mr. Pickwick.

"He's a 'queer customer, the vun-eyed vun, Sir," observed Mr. Weller, as he led the way. "He's a gammonin' that 'ere landlord, he is, Sir, till he don't rightly know vether he's a standing on the soles of his boots or the crown of his hat."

The individual to whom this observation referred, was sitting at the upper end of the room when Mr. Pickwick entered, and was smoking a large Dutch pipe, with his eye intently fixed upon the round face of the landlord, a jolly looking old personage, to whom he had recently been relating some tale of wonder, as was testified by sundry disjointed exclamations of, "Well, I wouldn't have believed it! The strangest thing I ever heard! Couldn't have supposed it possible!" and other expressions of astonishment which burst spontaneously from his lips as he returned the fixed gaze of the one-eyed man.

"Servant, Sir," said the one-eyed man to Mr. Pickwick. "Fine night, Sir."

"Very much so indeed," replied Mr. Pickwick, as the waiter placed a small decanter of brandy, and some hot water before him.

While Mr. Pickwick was mixing his brandy and water, the one-eyed man looked round at him earnestly, from time to time, and at length said—

"I think I've seen you before."

"I don't recollect you," rejoined Mr. Pickwick.

"I dare say not," said the one-eyed man. "You didn't know me, but I knew two friends of yours that were stopping at the Peacock at Eatanswill, at the time of the Election."

"Oh, indeed!" exclaimed Mr. Pickwick.

"Yes," rejoined the one-eyed man. "I mentioned a little circumstance to them about a friend of mine of the name of Tom Smart. Perhaps you've heard them speak of it."

"Often," rejoined Mr. Pickwick, smiling. "He was your uncle, I think?"

"No, no—only a friend of my uncle's," replied the one-eyed man.

"He was a wonderful man, that uncle of yours, though," remarked the landlord, shaking his head.

"Well, I think he was; I think I may say he was," answered the one-eyed man. "I could tell you a story about that same uncle, gentlemen, that would rather surprise you."

"Could you?" said Mr. Pickwick. "Let us hear it by all means."

The one-eyed Bagman ladled out a glass of negus from the bowl, and drank it, smoked a long whiff out of the Dutch pipe, and then calling to Sam Weller who was lingering near the door, that he needn't go away unless he wanted to, because the story was no secret, fixed his eyes upon the landlord's, and proceeded in the words of the next chapter.

CHAPTER XLVIII.

CONTAINING THE STORY OF THE BAGMAN'S UNCLE.

"My uncle, gentlemen," said the bagman, "was one of the merriest, pleasantest, cleverest fellows that ever lived. I wish you had known him, gentlemen. On second thoughts, gentlemen, I *don't* wish you had known him, for if you had, you would have been all by this time in the ordinary course of nature, if not dead, at all events so near it, as to have taken to stopping at home and giving up company, which would have deprived me of the inestimable pleasure of addressing you at this moment. Gentlemen, I wish your fathers and mothers had known my uncle. They would have been amazingly fond of him, especially your respectable mothers, I know they would. If any two of his numerous virtues predominated over the many that adorned his character, I should say they were his mixed punch and his after-supper song. Excuse my dwelling upon these melancholy recollections of departed worth; you won't see a man like my uncle every day in the week.

"I have always considered it a great point in my uncle's character, gentlemen, that he was the intimate friend and companion of Tom Smart, of the great house of Bilson and Slum, Cateaton Street, City. My uncle collected for Tiggin and Welps, but for a long time he went pretty near the same journey as Tom; and the very first night they met, my uncle took a fancy for Tom, and Tom took a fancy for my uncle. They made a bet of a new hat before they had known each other half an hour, who should brew the best quart of punch and drink it the quickest. My uncle was judged to have won the making, but Tom Smart beat him in the drinking by about half a salt-spoon-full. They took another quart a-piece to drink each other's health in, and were staunch friends ever afterwards. There's a destiny in these things gentlemen; we can't help it.

"In personal appearance, my uncle was a trifle shorter than the middle size; he was a thought stouter too, than the ordinary run of people, and perhaps his face might be a shade redder. He had the jolliest face you ever saw, gentlemen: something like Punch, with a handsomer nose and chin; his eyes were always twinkling and sparkling with good humour, and a smile—not one of your unmeaning wooden grins, but a real, merry, hearty, good-tempered smile, was perpetually on his countenance. He was pitched out of his gig once, and knocked head first against a mile-stone. There he lay, stunned, and so cut about the face with some gravel which had been heaped up alongside it, that, to use my uncle's own strong expression, if his mother could have revisited the earth, she wouldn't have known him. Indeed, when I come to think of the matter, gentlemen, I feel pretty sure she wouldn't, for she died when my uncle was two years and seven months old, and I think it's very likely that even without the gravel, his topboots would have puzzled the good lady not a little, to say nothing of his jolly red face. However, there he lay, and I have heard my uncle say many a time that the man said who picked him up that he was smiling as merrily as if he had tumbled out for a treat, and that after they had bled him, the first faint glimmerings of returning animation were, his jumping up in bed, bursting out into a loud laugh, kissing the young woman who held the basin, and demanding a mutton chop and a pickled walnut instantly. He was very fond of pickled walnuts, gentlemen. He said he always found that, taken without vinegar, they relished the beer.

"My uncle's great journey was in the fall of the leaf, at which time he collected debts and took orders in the north: going from London to Edinburgh, from Edinburgh to Glasgow, from Glasgow back to Edinburgh, and thence to London by the smack. You are to understand that this second visit to Edinburgh was for his own pleasure. He used to go back for a week, just to look up his old friends; and what with breakfasting with this one, and lunching with that, and dining with a third, and supping with another, a pretty tight week he used to make of it. I don't know whether any of you, gentlemen, ever partook of a real substantial hospitable Scotch breakfast, and then went out to a slight lunch of a bushel of oysters, a dozen or so of bottled ale, and a noggin or two of whiskey to close up with. If you ever did, you will agree with me that it requires a pretty strong head to go out to dinner and supper afterwards.

"But, bless your heart and eyebrows, all this sort of thing was nothing to my uncle. He was so well seasoned that it was mere child's play. I have heard him say that he could see the Dundee people out any day, and walk home afterwards without staggering; and yet the Dundee people have as strong heads and as strong punch, gentlemen, as you are likely to meet with, between the poles. I have heard of a Glasgow man and a Dundee man drinking against each other for fifteen hours at a sitting. They were both suffocated as nearly as could be ascertained at the same moment, but with this trifling exception, gentlemen, they were not a bit the worse for it.

"One night, within four-and-twenty hours of the time when he had settled to take shipping for London, my uncle supped at the house of a very old friend of his, a Baillie Mac something, and four syllables after it, who lived in the old town of Edinburgh. There were the baillie's wife, and the baillie's three daughters, and the baillie's grown-up son, and three or four stout, bushy eye-browed, canty old Scotch fellows that the baillie had got together to do honour to my uncle, and help to make merry. It was a glorious supper. There was kippered salmon, and Finnan haddocks, and a lamb's head, and a haggis; a celebrated Scotch dish, gentlemen, which my uncle used to say always looked to him, when it came to table, very much like a cupid's stomach; and a great many other things besides, that I forget the names of, but very good things notwithstanding. The lassies were pretty and agreeable; the baillie's wife one of the best creatures that ever lived; and my uncle in thoroughly good cue: the consequence of which was, that the young ladies tittered and giggled, and the old lady laughed out loud, and the baillie and the other old fellows roared till they were red in the face, the whole mortal time. I don't quite recollect how many tumblers of whiskey toddy each man drank after supper, but this I know, that about one o'clock in the morning, the baillie's grown-up son became insensible while attempting the first verse of 'Willie brewed a peck o' maut;' and he having been, for half an hour before, the only other man visible above the mahogany, it occurred to my uncle that it was almost time to think about going, especially as drinking had set in at seven o'clock in order that he might get home at a decent hour. But thinking it might not be quite polite to go just then, my uncle voted himself into the chair, mixed another glass, rose to propose his own health, addressed himself in a neat and complimentary speech, and drank the toast with great enthusiasm. Still nobody woke; so my uncle took a little drop more—neat this time, to prevent the toddy disagreeing with him, and laying violent hands on his hat sallied forth into the street.

"It was a wild gusty night when my uncle closed the baillie's door; and settling his hat firmly on his head to prevent the wind from taking it, thrust his hands into his pockets, and looking upwards, took a short survey of the state of the weather. The clouds were drifting over the moon at their giddiest speed, at one time wholly obscuring her, at another, suffering her to burst forth in full splendour and shed her light on all the objects around; anon, driving over her again with increased velocity, and shrouding everything in darkness. 'Really, this won't do,' said my uncle, addressing himself to the weather, as if he felt himself personally offended. 'This is not at all the kind of thing for my voyage. It will not do at any price,' said my uncle, very impressively. And having repeated this, several times, he recovered his balance with some difficulty —for he was rather giddy with looking up into the sky so long—and walked merrily on.

"The baillie's house was in the Canongate, and my uncle was going to the other end of Leith Walk, rather better than a mile's journey. On either side of him, there shot up against the dark sky, tall, gaunt, straggling houses, with time-stained fronts, and windows that seemed to have shared the lot of eyes in mortals, and to have grown dim and sunken with age. Six, seven, eight stories high were the houses; story piled above story, as children build with cards—throwing their dark shadows over the roughly paved road, and making the night darker. A few oil lamps were scattered, at long distances, but they only served to mark the dirty entrance to some narrow close, or to show where a common stair communicated, by steep and intricate windings with the various flats above. Glancing at all these things with the air of a man who had seen them too often before, to think them worthy of much notice now, my uncle walked up the middle of the street with a thumb in each waistcoat pocket, indulging from time to time in various snatches of song, chaunted forth with such good will and spirit, that the quiet honest folk started from their first sleep and lay trembling in bed till the sound died away in the distance; when, satisfying themselves that it was only some drunken ne'er-do-weel finding his way home, they covered themselves up warm and fell asleep again.

"I am particular in describing how my uncle walked up the middle of the street with his thumbs in his waistcoat pockets, gentlemen, because, as he often used to say (and with great reason too) there is nothing at all extraordinary in this story, unless you distinctly understand at the beginning, that he was not by any means of a marvellous or romantic turn.

"Gentlemen, my uncle walked on with his thumbs in his waistcoat pockets, taking the middle of the street to himself, and singing now a verse of a love song, and then a verse of a drinking one; and when he was tired of both, whistling melodiously, until he reached the North Bridge, which at this point connects the old and new towns of Edinburgh. Here he stopped for a minute to look at the strange irregular clusters of lights piled one above the other, and twinkling afar off so high in the air that they looked like stars gleaming from the castle walls on the one side and the Calton Hill on the other, as if they illuminated veritable castles in the air, while the old picturesque town slept heavily on in gloom and darkness below; its palace and chapel of Holyrood, guarded day and night, as a friend of my uncle's used to say, by old Arthur's Seat, towering, surly and dark like some gruff genius, over the ancient city he has watched so long. I say, gentlemen, my uncle stopped here for a minute to look about him; and then, paying a compliment to the weather which had a little cleared up, though the moon was sinking, walked on again as royally as before, keeping the middle of the road with great dignity, and looking as if he should very much like to meet with somebody who would dispute possession of it with him. There was nobody at all disposed to contest the point, as it happened; and so on he went, with his thumbs in his waistcoat pockets, as peaceable as a lamb.

"When my uncle reached the end of Leith Walk, he had to cross a pretty large piece of waste ground which separated him from a short street which he had to turn down to go direct to his lodging. Now in this piece of waste ground there was at that time an enclosure belonging to some wheelwright, who contracted with the Post-office for the purchase of old worn-out mail coaches; and my uncle being very fond of coaches, old, young, or middle-aged, all at once took it into his head to step out of his road for no other purpose than to peep between the palings at these mails, about a dozen of which he remembered to have seen, crowded together in a very forlorn and dismantled state, inside. My uncle was a very enthusiastic, emphatic sort of person, gentlemen; so, finding that he could not obtain a good peep between the palings, he got over them, and setting himself quietly down on an old axle-tree, began to contemplate the mail coaches with a great deal of gravity.

"There might be a dozen of them, or there might be more—my uncle was never quite certain upon this point, and being a man of very scrupulous veracity about numbers, didn't like to say—but there they stood, all huddled together in the most desolate condition imaginable. The doors had been torn from their hinges and removed, the linings had been stripped off, only a shred hanging here and there by a rusty nail; the lamps were gone, the poles had long since vanished, the iron-work was rusty, the paint worn away; the wind whistled through the chinks in the bare wood-work, and the rain, which had collected on the roofs, fell drop by drop into the insides with a hollow and melancholy sound. They were the decaying skeletons of departed mails, and in that lonely place, at that time of night, they looked chill and dismal.

"My uncle rested his head upon his hands, and thought of the busy bustling people who had rattled about years before, in the old coaches, and were now as silent and changed; he thought of the numbers of people to whom one of those crazy, mouldering vehicles had borne, night after night for many years and through all weathers, the anxiously expected intelligence, the eagerly looked-for remittance, the promised assurance of health and safety, the sudden announcement of sickness and death. The merchant, the lover, the wife, the widow, the mother, the schoolboy, the very child who tottered to the door at the postman's knock—how had they all looked forward to the arrival of the old coach. And where were they all now!

"Gentlemen, my uncle used to *say* that he thought all this at the time, but I rather suspect he learnt it out of some book afterwards, for he distinctly stated that he fell into a kind of doze as he sat on the old axletree looking at the decayed mail coaches, and that he was suddenly awakened by some deep church bell striking two. Now, my uncle was never a fast thinker, and if he had thought all these things, I am quite certain it would have taken him till full half-past two o'clock at the very least. I am, therefore, decidedly of opinion, gentlemen, that my uncle fell into the kind of doze without having thought about anything at all.

"Be this as it may, a church bell struck two. My uncle woke, rubbed his eyes, and jumped up in astonishment.

"In one instant, after the clock struck two, the whole of this deserted and quiet spot had become a scene of the most extraordinary life and animation. The mail coach doors were on their hinges, the lining was replaced, the iron-work was as good as new, the paint was restored, the lamps were alight; cushions and great coats were on every coach box, porters were thrusting parcels into every boot, guards were stowing away letter-bags, hostlers were dashing pails of water against the renovated wheels; numbers of men were rushing about, fixing poles into every coach, passengers arrived, portmanteaus were handed up, horses were put to, and in short it was perfectly clear that every mail there was to be off directly. Gentlemen, my uncle opened his eyes so wide at all this, that, to the very last moment of his life, he used to wonder how it fell out that he had ever been able to shut 'em again.

"'Now, then,' said a voice, as my uncle felt a hand on his shoulder, 'You're booked for one inside. You'd better get in.'

"'*I* booked!' said my uncle, turning round.

"'Yes, certainly.'

"My uncle, gentlemen, could say nothing, he was so very much astonished. The queerest thing of all, was, that although there was such a crowd of persons, and although fresh faces were pouring in, every moment, there was no telling where they came from; they seemed to start up in some strange manner from the ground or the air, and to disappear in the same way. When a porter had put his luggage in the coach and received his fare, he turned round and was gone; and before my uncle had well begun to wonder what had become of him, half-a-dozen fresh ones started up, and staggered along under the weight of parcels which seemed big enough to crush them. The passengers were all dressed so oddly too—large, broad-skirted laced coats with great cuffs and no collars; and wigs, gentlemen, —great formal wigs with a tie behind. My uncle could make nothing of it.

"'Now, *are* you going to get in?' said the person who had addressed my uncle before. He was dressed as a mail guard, with a wig on his head and most enormous cuffs to his coat, and had got a lantern in one hand and a huge blunderbuss in the other, which he was going to stow away in his little arm-chest. '*Are* you going to get in, Jack Martin?' said the guard, holding the lantern to my uncle's face.

"'Hallo!' said my uncle, falling back a step or two. 'That's familiar?'

"'It's so on the way-bill,' replied the guard.

"'Isn't there a Mister before it?' said my uncle—for he felt, gentlemen, that for a guard he didn't know to call him Jack Martin, was a liberty which the Post-office wouldn't have sanctioned if they had known it.

"'No; there is not,' rejoined the guard coolly.

"'Is the fare paid?' inquired my uncle.

"'Of course it is,' rejoined the guard.

"'It is, is it?' said my uncle. 'Then here goes—which coach?'

"'This,' said the guard, pointing to an old-fashioned Edinburgh and London Mail, which had got the steps down, and the door open. 'Stop—here are the other passengers. Let them get in first.'

"As the guard spoke, there all at once appeared, right in front of my uncle, a young gentleman in a powdered wig and a sky blue coat trimmed with silver, made very full and broad in the skirts, which were lined with buck-ram. Tiggin and Welps were in the printed calico and waistcoat piece line, gentlemen, so my uncle knew all the materials at once. He wore knee breeches and a kind of leggings rolled up over his silk stockings, and shoes with buckles; he had ruffles at his wrists, a three-cornered hat on his head, and a long taper sword by his side. The flaps of his waistcoat came half way down his thighs, and the ends of his cravat reached to his waist. He stalked gravely to the coach-door, pulled off his hat, and held it out above his head at arm's length, cocking his little finger in the air at the same time, as some affected people do when they take a cup of tea: then drew his feet together, and made a low grave bow, and then put out his left hand. My uncle was just going to step forward, and shake it heartily, when he perceived that these attentions were directed not towards him, but to a young lady, who just then appeared at the foot of the steps, attired in an old-fashioned green velvet dress, with a long waist and stomacher. She had no bonnet on her head, gentlemen, which was muffled in a black silk hood, but she looked round for an instant as she prepared to get into the coach, and such a beautiful face as she discovered my uncle had never seen —not even in a picture. She got into the coach, holding up her dress with one hand, and as my uncle always said with a round oath, when he told the story, he wouldn't have believed it possible that legs and feet could have been brought to such a state of perfection unless he had seen them with his own eyes.

"But in this one glimpse of the beautiful face, my uncle saw that the young lady had cast an imploring look upon him, and that she appeared terrified and distressed. He noticed too, that the young fellow in the powdered wig, notwithstanding his show of gallantry, which was all very fine and grand, clasped her tight by the wrist when she got in, and followed himself immediately afterwards. An uncommonly ill-looking fellow in a close brown wig, and a plum-coloured suit, wearing a very large sword and boots up to his hips, belonged to the party; and when he sat himself down next to the young lady, who shrunk into a corner at his approach, my uncle was confirmed in his original impression that something dark and mysterious was going forward, or, as he always said himself, that 'there was a screw loose somewhere.' It's quite surprising how quickly he made up his mind to help the lady at any peril, if she needed help.

"'Death and lightning!' exclaimed the young gentleman, laying his hand upon his sword, as my uncle entered the coach.

"'Blood and thunder!' roared the other gentleman. With this he whipped his sword out, and made a lunge at my uncle without further ceremony. My uncle had no weapon about him, but with great dexterity he snatched the ill-looking gentleman's three-cornered hat from his head, and receiving the point of his sword right through the crown, squeezed the sides together, and held it tight.

"'Pink him behind,' cried the ill-looking gentleman to his companion, as he struggled to regain his sword.

"'He had better not,' cried my uncle, displaying the heel of one of his shoes in a threatening manner. 'I'll kick his brains out if he has any, or fracture his skull if he hasn't.' Exerting all his strength at this moment, my uncle wrenched the ill-looking man's sword from his grasp, and flung it clean out of the coach-window, upon which the younger gentleman vociferated 'Death and lightning!' again, and laid his hand upon the hilt of his sword in a

very fierce manner, but didn't draw it. Perhaps, gentlemen, as my uncle used to say, with a smile, perhaps he was afraid of alarming the lady.

"'Now, gentlemen,' said my uncle, taking his seat deliberately, 'I don't want to have any death with or without lightning in a lady's presence, and we have had quite blood and thundering enough for one journey; so if you please, we'll sit in our places like quiet insides—here, guard, pick up that gentleman's carving knife.'

"As quickly as my uncle said the words, the guard appeared at the coach-window with the gentleman's sword in his hand. He held up his lantern, and looked earnestly in my uncle's face as he handed it in, when by its light my uncle saw, to his great surprise, that an immense crowd of mail-coach guards swarmed round the window, every one of whom had his eyes earnestly fixed upon him too. He had never seen such a sea of white faces and red bodies, and earnest eyes, in all his born days.

"'This is the strangest sort of thing I ever had any thing to do with,' thought my uncle—'allow me to return you your hat, Sir.'

"The ill-looking gentleman received his three-cornered hat in silence—looked at the hole in the middle with an enquiring air, and finally stuck it on the top of his wig, with a solemnity the effect of which was a trifle impaired by his sneezing violently at the moment, and jerking it off again.

"'All right!' cried the guard with the lantern, mounting into his little seat behind. Away they went. My uncle peeped out of the coach window as they emerged from the yard, and observed that the other mails, with coachmen, guards, horses, and passengers complete, were driving round and round in circles, at a slow trot of about five miles an hour. My uncle burnt with indignation, gentlemen. As a commercial man, he felt that the mail bags were not to be trifled with, and he resolved to memorialise the Post-office on the subject, the very instant he reached London.

"At present, however, his thoughts were occupied with the young lady who sat in the farthest corner of the coach, with her face muffled closely in her hood: the gentleman with the sky blue coat sitting opposite to her, and the other man in the plum-coloured suit, by her side, and both watching her intently. If she so much as rustled the folds of her hood, he could hear the ill-looking man clap his hand upon his sword, and tell by the other's breathing (it was so dark he couldn't see his face) that he was looking as big as if he were going to devour her at a mouthful. This roused my uncle more and more, and he resolved, come what come might, to see the end of it. He had a great admiration for bright eyes, and sweet faces, and pretty legs and feet; in short he was fond of the whole sex. It runs in our family, gentlemen—so am I.

"Many were the devices which my uncle practised to attract the lady's attention, or at all events, to engage the mysterious gentlemen in conversation. They were all in vain; the gentlemen wouldn't talk, and the lady didn't dare. He thrust his head out of the coach-window at intervals, and bawled out to know why they didn't go faster. But he called till he was hoarse—nobody paid the least attention to him. He leant back in the coach, and thought of the beautiful face, and the feet and legs. This answered better; it wiled away the time, and kept him from wondering where he was going to, and how it was he found himself in such an odd situation. Not that this would have worried him much any way—he was a mighty, free and easy, roving, devil-may-care sort of person, was my uncle, gentlemen.

"All of a sudden the coach stopped. 'Hallo?' said my uncle. 'What's in the wind now?'

"'Alight here,' said the guard, letting down the steps.

"'Here!' cried my uncle.

"'Here,' rejoined the guard.

"'I'll do nothing of the sort,' said my uncle.

"'Very well—then stop where you are,' said the guard.

"'I will,' said my uncle.

"'Do,' said the guard.

"The other passengers had regarded this colloquy with great attention; and finding that my uncle was determined not to alight, the younger man squeezed past him, to hand the lady out. At this moment the ill-looking man was inspecting the hole in the crown of his three-cornered hat. As the young lady brushed past, she dropped one of her gloves into my uncle's hand, and softly whispered with her lips, so close to his face that he felt her warm breath on his nose, the single word 'Help!' Gentlemen, my uncle leaped out of the coach at once with such violence that it rocked on the springs again.

"'Oh! you've thought better of it, have you?' said the guard, when he saw my uncle standing on the ground.

"My uncle looked at the guard for a few seconds, in some doubt whether it wouldn't be better to wrench his blunderbuss from him, fire it in the face of the man with the big sword, knock the rest of the company over the head with the stick, snatch up the young lady, and go off in the smoke. On second thoughts, however, he abandoned this plan as being a shade too melo-dramatic in the execution, and followed the two mysterious men, who, keeping the lady between them, were now entering an old house in front of which the coach had stopped. They turned into the passage, and my uncle followed.

"Of all the ruinous and desolate places my uncle had ever beheld, this was the most so. It looked as if it had once been a large house of entertainment, but the roof had fallen in, in many places, and the stairs were steep, rugged, and broken. There was a huge fire-place in the room into which they walked, and the chimney was blackened with smoke, but no warm blaze lighted it up now. The white feathery dust of burnt wood was still strewed over the hearth, but the stove was cold, and all was dark and gloomy.

"'Well,' said my uncle as he looked about him, 'A mail travelling at the rate of six miles and a half an hour, and stopping for an indefinite time at such a hole as this, is rather an irregular sort of proceeding I fancy. This shall be made known; I'll write to the papers.'

"My uncle said this in a pretty loud voice, and in an open unreserved sort of manner, with the view of engaging the two strangers in conversation if he could. But neither of them took any more notice of him than whispering to each other, and scowling at him as they did so. The lady was at the further end of the room, and once she ventured to wave her hand, as if beseeching my uncle's assistance.

"At length the two strangers advanced a little, and the conversation began in earnest.

"'You don't know this is a private room; I suppose, fellow,' said the gentleman in sky-blue.

"'No I do not, fellow,' rejoined my uncle. 'Only if this is a private room specially ordered for the occasion, I should think the public room must be a *very* comfortable one;' with this, my uncle sat himself down in a high-backed chair and took such an accurate measure of the gentleman with his eyes, that Tiggin and Welps could have supplied him with printed calico for a suit, and not an inch too much or too little, from that estimate alone.

"'Quit this room,' said both men together, grasping their swords.

"'Eh?' said my uncle, not at all appearing to comprehend their meaning.

"'Quit the room, or you are a dead man,' said the ill-looking fellow with the large sword, drawing it at the same time and flourishing it in the air.

"'Down with him!' said the gentleman in sky-blue, drawing his sword also, and falling back two or three yards. 'Down with him!' The lady gave a loud scream.

"Now, my uncle was always remarkable for great boldness and great presence of mind. All the time that he had appeared so indifferent to what was going on, he had been looking slyly about for some missile or weapon of defence, and at the very instant when the swords were drawn, he espied standing in the chimney corner, an old basket-hilted rapier in a rusty scabbard. At one bound, my uncle caught it in his hand, drew it, flourished it gallantly above his head, called aloud to the lady to keep out of the way, hurled the chair at the man in sky-blue, and the scabbard at the man in plum-colour, and taking advantage of the confusion, fell upon them both, pell-mell.

"Gentlemen, there is an old story—none the worse for being true—regarding a fine young Irish gentleman, who being asked if he could play the fiddle, replied he had no doubt he could, but he couldn't exactly say for certain, because he had never tried. This is not inapplicable to my uncle and his fencing. He had never had a sword in his hand before, except once when he played Richard the Third at a private theatre, upon which occasion it was arranged with Richmond that he was to be run through from behind without shewing fight at all; but here he was, cutting and slashing with two experienced swordsmen, thrusting, and guarding, and poking, and slicing, and acquitting himself in the most manful and dexterous manner possible, although up to that time he had never been aware that he had the least notion of the science. It only shows how true the old saying is, that a man never knows what he can do, till he tries, gentlemen.

"The noise of the combat was terrific, each of the three combatants swearing like troopers, and their swords clashing with as much noise as if all the knives and steels in Newport market were rattling together at the same time. When it was at its very height, the lady, to encourage my uncle most probably, withdrew her hood entirely from her face, and disclosed a countenance of such dazzling beauty, that he would have fought against fifty men to win one smile from it and die. He had done wonders before, but now he began to powder away like a raving mad giant.

"At this very moment, the gentleman in sky-blue turning round, and seeing the young lady with her face uncovered, vented an exclamation of rage and jealousy; and turning his weapon against her beautiful bosom, pointed a thrust at her heart which caused my uncle to utter a cry of apprehension that made the building ring. The lady stepped lightly aside, and snatching the young man's sword from his hand before he had recovered his balance, drove him to the wall, and running it through him and the pannelling up to the very hilt, pinned him there hard and fast. It was a splendid example. My uncle, with a loud shout of triumph and a strength that was irresistible, made his adversary retreat in the same direction, and plunging the old rapier into the very centre of a large red flower in the pattern of his waistcoat, nailed him beside his friend; there they both stood, gentlemen, jerking their arms and legs about in agony, like the toy-shop figures that are moved by a piece of packthread. My uncle always said afterwards, that this was one of the surest means he knew of, for disposing of an enemy; but it was liable to one objection on the ground of expense, inasmuch as it involved the loss of a sword for every man disabled.

"'The mail, the mail!' cried the lady, running up to my uncle and throwing her beautiful arms round his neck; 'we may yet escape.'

"'*May!*' cried my uncle; 'why, my dear, there's nobody else to kill, is there?' My uncle was rather disappointed, gentlemen, for he thought a little quiet bit of love-making would be agreeable after the slaughtering, if it were only to change the subject.

"'We have not an instant to lose here,' said the young lady. 'He (pointing to the young gentleman in sky blue) is the only son of the powerful Marquess of Filletoville.'

"'Well then, my dear, I'm afraid he'll never come to the title,' said my uncle, looking coolly at the young gentleman as he stood fixed up against the wall, in the cock-chaffer fashion I have described. 'You have cut off the entail, my love.'

"'I have been torn from my home and friends by these villains,' said the young lady, her features glowing with indignation. 'That wretch would have married me by violence in another hour.'

"'Confound his impudence!' said my uncle, bestowing a very contemptuous look on the dying heir of Filletoville.

"'As you may guess from what you have seen,' said the young lady, 'the party are prepared to murder me if I appeal to any one for assistance. If their accomplices find us here, we are lost. Two minutes hence may be too late. The mail!'—and with these words, overpowered by her feelings and the exertion of sticking the young Marquess of Filletoville, she sunk into my uncle's arms. My uncle caught her up, and bore her to the house-door. There stood the mail with four long-tailed flowing-maned black horses, ready harnessed; but no coachman, no guard, no ostler even, at the horses' heads.

"Gentlemen, I hope I do no injustice to my uncle's memory, when I express my opinion, that although he was a bachelor, he *had* held some ladies in his arms before this time; I believe indeed, that he had rather a habit of kissing barmaids, and I know, that in one or two instances, he had been seen by credible witnesses, to hug a landlady in a very perceptible manner. I mention the circumstance, to show what a very uncommon sort of person this beautiful young lady must have been to have affected my uncle in the way she did; he used to say, that as her long dark hair trailed over his arm, and her beautiful dark eyes fixed themselves upon his face when she recovered, he felt so strange and nervous, that his legs trembled beneath him. But who can look in a sweet soft pair of dark eyes, without feeling queer? I can't, gentlemen. I am afraid to look at some eyes I know, and that's the truth of it.

"'You will never leave me,' murmured the young lady.

"'Never,' said my uncle. And he meant it too.

"'My dear preserver!' exclaimed the young lady. 'My dear, kind brave preserver!'

"'Don't,' said my uncle, interrupting her.

"'Why?' enquired the young lady.

"'Because your mouth looks so beautiful when you speak,' rejoined my uncle, 'that I'm afraid I shall be rude enough to kiss it.'

"The young lady put up her hand as if to caution my uncle not to do so, and said—no, she didn't say anything —she smiled. When you are looking at a pair of the most delicious lips in the world, and see them gently break into a roguish smile—if you are very near them, and nobody else by—you cannot better testify your admiration of their beautiful form and colour than by kissing them at once. My uncle did so, and I honour him for it.

"'Hark!' cried the young lady, starting. 'The noise of wheels and horses.'

"'So it is,' said my uncle, listening. He had a good ear for wheels and the trampling of hoofs, but there appeared to be so many horses and carriages rattling towards them at a distance, that it was impossible to form a guess at their number. The sound was like that of fifty breaks, with six blood cattle in each.

"'We are pursued!' cried the young lady, clasping her hands. 'We are pursued. I have no hope but in you.'

"There was such an expression of terror in her beautiful face, that my uncle made up his mind at once. He lifted her into the coach, told her not to be frightened, pressed his lips to hers once more, and then advising her to draw up the window to keep the cold air out, mounted to the box.

"'Stay, love,' cried the young lady.

"'What's the matter?' said my uncle, from the coach-box.

"'I want to speak to you,' said the young lady; 'only a word—only one word, dearest.'

"'Must I get down?' enquired my uncle. The lady made no answer, but she smiled again. Such a smile, gentlemen!—it beat the other one all to nothing. My uncle descended from his perch in a twinkling.

"'What is it, my dear?' said my uncle, looking in at the coach window. The lady happened to bend forward at the same time, and my uncle thought she looked more beautiful than she had done yet. He was very close to her just then, gentlemen, so he really ought to know.

"'What is it, my dear?' said my uncle.

"'Will you never love any one but me—never marry any one beside?' said the young lady.

"My uncle swore a great oath that he never would marry any body else, and the young lady drew in her head, and pulled up the window. He jumped upon the box, squared his elbows, adjusted the ribands, seized the whip which lay on the roof, gave one flick to the off leader, and away went the four long-tailed, flowing-maned black horses, at fifteen good English miles an hour, with the old mail coach behind them—whew! how they tore along!

"But the noise behind grew louder. The faster went the old mail, the faster came the pursuers—men, horses, dogs, were leagued in the pursuit. The noise was frightful, but above all rose the voice of the young lady, urging my uncle on, and shrieking 'faster! faster!'

"They whirled past the dark trees as feathers would be swept before a hurricane. Houses, gates, churches, hay-stacks, objects of every kind they shot by, with a velocity and noise like roaring waters suddenly let loose. But still the noise of pursuit grew louder, and still my uncle could hear the young lady wildly screaming, 'faster! faster!'

"My uncle plied whip and rein, and the horses flew onward till they were white with foam; and yet the noise behind increased, and yet the young lady cried 'faster! faster!' My uncle gave a loud stamp upon the boot in the energy of the moment, and—found that it was grey morning, and he was sitting in the wheel-wright's yard on the box of an old Edinburgh mail, shivering with the cold and wet, and stamping his feet to warm them! He got down, and looked eagerly inside for the beautiful young lady—alas! there was neither door nor seat to the coach—it was a mere shell.

"Of course my uncle knew very well that there was some mystery in the matter, and that everything had passed exactly as he used to relate it. He remained staunch to the great oath he had sworn to the beautiful young lady: refusing several eligible landladies on her account, and died a bachelor at last. He always said what a curious thing it was that he should have found out, by such a mere accident as his clambering over the palings, that the ghosts of mail-coaches and horses, guards, coachmen, and passengers, were in the habit of making journeys regularly every night; he used to add that he believed he was the only living person who had ever been taken as a passenger on one of these excursions; and I think he was right, gentlemen—at least I never heard of any other."

"I wonder what these ghosts of mail-coaches carry in their bags," said the landlord, who had listened to the whole story with profound attention.

"The dead letters of course," said the Bagman.

"Oh, ah—to be sure," rejoined the landlord. "I never thought of that."

CHAPTER XLIX.

HOW MR. PICKWICK SPED UPON HIS MISSION, AND HOW HE WAS REINFORCED IN THE OUTSET BY A MOST UNEXPECTED AUXILIARY.

THE horses were put to, punctually at a quarter before nine next morning, and Mr. Pickwick and Sam Weller having each taken his seat, the one inside and the other out, the postilion was duly directed to repair in the first instance to Mr. Bob Sawyer's house, for the purpose of taking up Mr. Benjamin Allen.

It was with feelings of no small astonishment, when the carriage drew up before the door with the red lamp, and the very legible inscription of "Sawyer, late Nockemorf," that Mr. Pickwick saw, on popping his head out of the coach-window, the boy in the grey livery very busily employed in putting up the shutters: the which being an unusual and rather un-business-like proceeding at that hour of the morning, at once suggested to his mind two inferences—the one, that some good friend and patient of Mr. Bob Sawyer's was dead; the other, that Mr. Bob Sawyer himself was bankrupt.

"What is the matter?" said Mr. Pickwick to the boy.

"Nothing's the matter, Sir," replied the boy, expanding his mouth to the whole breadth of his countenance.

"All right, all right," cried Bob Sawyer, suddenly appearing at the door, with a small leathern knapsack, limp and dirty, in one hand, and a rough coat and shawl thrown over the other arm. "I'm going, old fellow."

"You!" exclaimed Mr. Pickwick.

"Yes," replied Bob Sawyer, "and a regular expedition we'll make of it. Here, Sam—look out." Thus briefly bespeaking Mr. Weller's attention, Mr. Bob Sawyer jerked the leathern knapsack into the dickey, where it was immediately stowed away under the seat, by Sam, who regarded the proceeding with great admiration. This done, Mr. Bob Sawyer, with the assistance of the boy, forcibly worked himself into the rough coat, which was a few sizes too small for him, and then advancing to the coach window, thrust in his head, and laughed boisterously.

"What a start it is—isn't it?" said Bob, wiping the tears out of his eyes, with one of the cuffs of the rough coat.

"My dear Sir," said Mr. Pickwick, with some embarrassment, "I had no idea of your accompanying us."

"No, that's just the very thing," replied Bob, forcibly working Mr. Pickwick by the lappel of his coat. "That's the joke."

"Oh, that's the joke, is it?" said Mr. Pickwick.

"Of course," replied Bob. "It's the whole point of the thing, you know—that, and leaving the business to take care of itself, as it seems to have made up its mind not to take care of me." With this explanation of the phenomenon of the shutters, Mr. Bob Sawyer pointed to the shop, and relapsed into an ecstacy of mirth.

"Bless me, you are surely not mad enough to think of leaving your patients without anybody to attend them!" remonstrated Mr. Pickwick in a very serious tone.

"Why not?" asked Bob, in reply. "I shall save by it, you know. None of them ever pay. Besides," said Bob, lowering his voice to a confidential whisper, "they will be all the better for it, for being nearly out of drugs and not able to increase my account just now, I should have been obliged to give them calomel all round, and it would have been certain to have disagreed with some of them—so it's all for the best."

There was a philosophy and a strength of reasoning about this reply, which Mr. Pickwick was not prepared for. He paused a few moments, and added, less firmly than before—

"But this chaise, my young friend—this chaise will only hold two; and I am pledged to Mr. Allen."

"Don't think of me for a minute," replied Bob. "I've arranged it all; Sam and I will share the dickey between us. Look here. This little bill is to be wafered on the shop-door: 'Sawyer, late Nockemorf. Enquire of Mrs. Cripps over the way.'—Mrs. Cripps is my boy's mother.—'Mr. Sawyer's very sorry,' says Mrs. Cripps, 'couldn't help it—fetched away early this morning to a consultation of the very first surgeons in the country—couldn't do without him—would have him at any price—tremendous operation.' The fact is," said Bob, in conclusion—"It'll do me more good than otherwise, I expect. If it gets into one of the local papers, it will be the making of me. Here's Ben—now then, jump in!"

With these hurried words, Mr. Bob Sawyer pushed the postboy on one side, jerked his friend into the vehicle, slammed the door, put up the steps, wafered the bill on the street-door, locked it, put the key in his pocket, jumped into the dickey, gave the word for starting; and did the whole with such extraordinary precipitation, that before Mr. Pickwick had well begun to consider whether Mr. Bob Sawyer ought to go or not, they were rolling away with Mr. Bob Sawyer, thoroughly established as part and parcel of the equipage.

So long as their progress was confined to the streets of Bristol, the facetious Bob kept his professional green spectacles on, and conducted himself with becoming steadiness and gravity of demeanour, merely giving utterance to divers verbal witticisms for the exclusive behoof and entertainment of Mr. Samuel Weller, but when they emerged upon the open road, he threw off his green spectacles and his gravity together, and performed a great variety of practical jokes, which were rather calculated perhaps to attract the attention of the passers-by, and to render the carriage and those it contained, objects of more than ordinary curiosity; the least conspicuous among these feats being a most vociferous imitation of a key-bugle, and the ostentatious display of a crimson silk pocket-handkerchief attached to a walking-stick, which was occasionally waved in the air with various gestures indicative of supremacy and defiance.

"I wonder," said Mr. Pickwick, stopping in the midst of a most sedate conversation with Ben Allen, bearing reference to the numerous good qualities of Mr. Winkle and his sister—"I wonder what all the people we pass, can see in us to make them stare so."

"It's a neat turn-out," replied Ben Allen, with something of pride in his tone. "They're not used to see this sort of thing every day, I dare say."

"Possibly," replied Mr. Pickwick. "It may be so. Perhaps it is."

Mr. Pickwick might very probably have reasoned himself into the belief that it really was, had he not, just then happening to look out of the coach window, observed that the looks of the passengers betokened anything but respectful astonishment, and that various telegraphic communications appeared to be passing between them and some persons outside the vehicle, whereupon it all at once occurred to him that those demonstrations might be, in some remote degree, referable to the humorous deportment of Mr. Robert Sawyer.

"I hope," said Mr. Pickwick, "that our volatile friend is committing no absurdities in that dickey behind."

"Oh dear, no," replied Ben Allen. "Except when he's elevated, Bob's the quietest creature breathing."

Here a prolonged imitation of a key-bugle broke upon the ear, succeeded by cheers and screams, all of which evidently proceeded from the throat and lungs of the quietest creature breathing, or in plainer designation, of Mr. Bob Sawyer himself.

Mr. Pickwick and Mr. Ben Allen looked expressively at each other, and the former gentleman taking off his hat, and leaning out of the coach window till nearly the whole of his waistcoat was outside it, was at length enabled to catch a glimpse of his facetious friend.

Mr. Bob Sawyer was seated, not in the dickey, but on the roof of the chaise, with his legs as far asunder as they would conveniently go, wearing Mr. Samuel Weller's hat on one side of his head, and bearing in one hand a most enormous sandwich, while in the other he supported a goodly-sized case-bottle, to both of which he applied himself with intense relish, varying the monotony of the occupation by an occasional howl, or the interchange of some lively *badinage* with any passing stranger. The crimson flag was carefully tied in an erect position to the rail of the dickey, and Mr. Samuel Weller, decorated with Bob Sawyer's hat, was seated in the centre thereof, discussing a twin sandwich with an animated countenance, the expression of which betokened his entire and perfect approval of the whole arrangement.

This was enough to irritate a gentleman with Mr. Pickwick's sense of propriety, but it was not the whole extent of the aggravation, for a stage-coach full, inside and out, was meeting them at the moment, and the astonishment of the passengers was very palpably evinced. The congratulations of an Irish family, too, who were keeping up with the chaise, and begging all the time, were of a rather boisterous description; especially those of its male head, who appeared to consider the display as part and parcel of some political, or other procession of triumph.

"Mr. Sawyer," cried Mr. Pickwick, in a state of great excitement. "Mr. Sawyer, Sir!"

"Hallo!" responded that gentleman, looking over the side of the chaise with all the coolness in life.

"Are you mad, Sir?" demanded Mr. Pickwick.

"Not a bit of it," replied Bob, "only cheerful."

"Cheerful, Sir!" ejaculated Mr. Pickwick. "Take down that scandalous red handkerchief. I beg—I insist, Sir. Sam, take it down."

Before Sam could interpose, Mr. Bob Sawyer gracefully struck his colours, and having put them in his pocket, nodded in a courteous manner to Mr. Pickwick, wiped the mouth of the case-bottle, and applied it to his own; thereby informing him, without any unnecessary waste of words, that he devoted that draught to wishing him all manner of happiness and prosperity. Having done this, Bob replaced the cork with great care, and looking benignantly down on Mr. Pickwick, took a large bite out of the sandwich, and smiled.

"Come," said Mr. Pickwick, whose momentary anger was not quite proof against Bob's immoveable self-possession, "pray let us have no more of this absurdity, Sir."

"No, no," replied Bob, once more exchanging hats with Mr. Weller; "I didn't mean to do it, only I got so enlivened with the ride that I couldn't help it."

"Think of the look of the thing," expostulated Mr. Pickwick, "have some regard to appearances."

"Oh, certainly," said Bob, "it's not the sort of thing at all. All over, governor."

Satisfied with this assurance, Mr. Pickwick once more drew his head into the chaise and pulled up the glass; but he had scarcely resumed the conversation which Mr. Bob Sawyer had interrupted, when he was somewhat startled by the apparition of a small dark body, of an oblong form, on the outside of the window, which gave sundry taps against it, as if impatient of admission.

"What's this?" exclaimed Mr. Pickwick.

"It looks like a case-bottle;" remarked Ben Allen, eyeing the object in question through his spectacles with some interest; "I rather think it belongs to Bob."

The impression was perfectly accurate, for Mr. Bob Sawyer having attached the case-bottle to the end of the walking-stick, was battering the window with it, in token of his wish that his friends inside would partake of its contents, in all good-fellowship and harmony.

"What's to be done?" said Mr. Pickwick, looking at the bottle. "This proceeding is more absurd than the other."

"I think it would be best to take it in," replied Mr. Ben Allen; "it would serve him right to take it in and keep it, wouldn't it?"

"It would," said Mr. Pickwick: "shall I?"

"I think it the most proper course we could possibly adopt," replied Ben.

This advice quite coinciding with his own opinion, Mr. Pickwick gently let down the window and disengaged the bottle from the stick; upon which the latter was drawn up, and Mr. Bob Sawyer was heard to laugh heartily.

"What a merry dog it is," said Mr. Pickwick, looking round at his companion with the bottle in his hand.

"He is," said Mr. Allen.

"You cannot possibly be angry with him," remarked Mr. Pickwick.

"Quite out of the question," observed Benjamin Allen.

During this short interchange of sentiments, Mr. Pickwick had, in an abstracted mood, uncorked the bottle.

"What is it?" enquired Ben Allen, carelessly.

"I don't know," replied Mr. Pickwick, with equal carelessness. "It smells, I think, like milk-punch."

"Oh, indeed!" said Ben.

"I *think* so," rejoined Mr. Pickwick, very properly guarding himself against the possibility of stating an untruth: "mind, I could not undertake to say for certain, without tasting it."

"You had better do so," said Ben; "we may as well know what it is."

"Do you think so?" replied Mr. Pickwick. "Well, if you are curious to know, of course I have no objection."

Ever willing to sacrifice his own feelings to the wishes of his friend, Mr. Pickwick at once took a pretty long taste.

"What is it?" enquired Ben Allen, interrupting him with some impatience.

"Curious," said Mr. Pickwick, smacking his lips, "I hardly know, now. Oh, yes," said Mr. Pickwick, after a second taste, "it *is* punch."

Mr. Ben Allen looked at Mr. Pickwick; Mr. Pickwick looked at Mr. Ben Allen. Mr. Ben Allen smiled; Mr. Pickwick did not.

"It would serve him right," said the last-named gentleman with some severity, "it would serve him right to drink it every drop."

"The very thing that occurred to me," said Ben Allen.

"Is it indeed?" rejoined Mr. Pickwick. "Then here's his health." With these words, that excellent person took a most energetic pull at the bottle, and handed it to Ben Allen, who was not slow to imitate his example. The smiles became mutual, and the milk-punch was gradually and cheerfully disposed of.

"After all," said Mr. Pickwick, as he drained the last drop, "his pranks are really very amusing—very entertaining indeed."

"You may say that," rejoined Mr. Ben Allen. And in proof of Bob Sawyer's being one of the funniest fellows alive, he proceeded to entertain Mr. Pickwick with a long and circumstantial account how that gentleman once drank himself into a fever and got his head shaved; the relation of which pleasant and agreeable history was only stopped by the stoppage of the chaise at the Bell at Berkeley Heath, to change horses.

"I say, we're going to dine here, aren't we?" said Bob, looking in at the window.

"Dine!" said Mr. Pickwick. "Why, we have only come nineteen miles, and have got eighty-seven and a half to go."

"Just the reason why we should take something to enable us to bear up against the fatigue," remonstrated Mr. Bob Sawyer.

"Oh, it's quite impossible to dine at half-past eleven o'clock in the day," replied Mr. Pickwick, looking at his watch.

"So it is," rejoined Bob, "lunch is the very thing. Hallo, you Sir! Lunch for three directly; and keep the horses back for a quarter of an hour. Tell them to put

every thing they have got cold, on the table, and some bottled ale,—and let us taste your very best Madeira." Issuing these orders with monstrous importance and bustle, Mr. Bob Sawyer at once hurried into the house to superintend the arrangements; in less than five minutes he returned and declared them to be excellent.

The quality of the lunch fully justified the eulogium which Bob had pronounced, and very great justice was done to it, not only by that gentleman, but Mr. Ben Allen and Mr. Pickwick also. Under the auspices of the three, the bottled ale and the Madeira were promptly disposed of; and when (the horses being once more put to) they resumed their seats, with the case-bottle full of the best substitute for milk-punch that could be procured on so short a notice, the key-bugle sounded and the red flag waved without the slightest opposition on Mr. Pickwick's part.

At the Hop Pole at Tewkesbury they stopped to dine; upon which occasion there was more bottled ale, with some more Madeira, and some Port besides; and here the case-bottle was replenished for the fourth time. Under the influence of these combined stimulants, Mr. Pickwick and Mr. Ben Allen fell fast asleep for thirty miles, while Bob and Mr. Weller sang duets in the dickey.

It was quite dark when Mr. Pickwick roused himself sufficiently to look out of the window. The straggling cottages by the roadside, the dingy hue of every object visible, the murky atmosphere, the paths of cinders and brick dust, the deep red glow of furnace fires in the distance, the volumes of dense smoke issuing heavily forth from high toppling chimneys, blackening and obscuring every thing around; the glare of distant lights, the ponderous waggons which toiled along the road, laden with clashing rods of iron, or piled with heavy goods—all betokened their rapid approach to the great working town of Birmingham.

As they rattled through the narrow thoroughfares leading to the heart of the turmoil, the sights and sounds of earnest occupation struck more forcibly on the senses. The streets were thronged with working people. The hum of labour resounded from every house; lights gleamed from the long casement windows in the attic stories, and the whirl of wheels and noise of machinery shook the trembling walls. The fires, whose lurid sullen light had been visible for miles, blazed fiercely up in the great works and factories of the town. The din of hammers, the rushing of steam, and the dead heavy clanking of the engines, was the harsh music which arose from every quarter.

The postboy was driving briskly through the open streets and past the handsome and well-lighted shops which intervene between the outskirts of the town and the old Royal Hotel, before Mr. Pickwick had begun to consider the very difficult and delicate nature of the commission which had carried him thither.

The delicate nature of this commission, and the difficulty of executing it in a satisfactory manner, were by no means lessened by the voluntary companionship of Mr. Bob Sawyer: truth to tell, Mr. Pickwick felt that his presence on the occasion, however considerate and gratifying, was by no means an honour he would willingly have sought; in fact he would cheerfully have given a reasonable sum of money to have had Mr. Bob Sawyer removed to any place of not less than fifty miles' distance without delay.

Mr. Pickwick had never held any personal communication with Mr. Winkle, Senior, although he had once or twice corresponded with him by letter, and returned satisfactory answers to his enquiries concerning the moral character and behaviour of his son; he felt nervously sensible that to wait upon him for the first time attended by Bob Sawyer and Ben Allen, both slightly fuddled, was not the most ingenious and likely means that could have been hit upon to prepossess him in his favour.

"However," said Mr. Pickwick, endeavouring to re-assure himself, "I must do the best I can: I must see him to-night, for I faithfully promised to do so; and if they persist in accompanying me, I must make the interview as brief as possible, and be content to hope that, for their own sakes, they will not expose themselves."

As he comforted himself with these reflections, the chaise stopped at the door of the Old Royal. Ben Allen having been partially awakened from a stupendous sleep, and dragged out by the collar by Mr. Samuel Weller, Mr. Pickwick was enabled to alight. They were shown to a comfortable apartment, and Mr. Pickwick at once propounded a question to the waiter concerning the whereabouts of Mr. Winkle's residence.

"Close by, Sir," said the waiter, "not above five hundred yards, Sir. Mr. Winkle is a wharfinger, Sir, at the canal, Sir. Private residence is not—oh dear no, Sir, *not* five hundred yards, Sir." Here the waiter blew a candle out and made a feint of lighting it again, in order to afford Mr. Pickwick an opportunity of asking any further questions, if he felt so disposed.

"Take anything now, Sir?" said the waiter, lighting the candle in desperation at Mr. Pickwick's silence. "Tea or coffee, Sir? dinner, Sir?"

"Nothing now."

"Very good, Sir. Like to order supper, Sir?"

"Not just now."

"*Very* good, Sir." Here he walked softly to the door, and then stopping short, turned round and said with great suavity—

"Shall I send the chambermaid, gentlemen?"

"You may if you please," replied Mr. Pickwick.

"If *you* please, Sir."

"And bring some soda water," said Bob Sawyer.

"Soda water, Sir? Yes, Sir." And with his mind apparently relieved from an overwhelming weight, by having at last got an order for something, the waiter imperceptibly melted away. Waiters never walk or run. They have a peculiar and mysterious power of skimming out of rooms, which other mortals possess not.

Some slight symptoms of vitality having been awakened in Mr. Ben Allen by the soda water, he suffered himself to be prevailed upon to wash his face and hands, and to submit to be brushed by Sam. Mr. Pickwick and Bob Sawyer having also repaired the disorder which the journey had made in their apparel, the three started forth, arm in arm, to Mr. Winkle's; Bob Sawyer impregnating the atmosphere with tobacco smoke as he walked along.

About a quarter of a mile off, in a quiet, substantial-looking street, stood an old red-brick house with three steps before the door, and a brass plate upon it, bearing, in fat Roman capitals the words, "Mr. Winkle." The steps were very white, and the bricks were very red, and the house was very clean; and here stood Mr. Pickwick, Mr. Benjamin Allen, and Mr. Bob Sawyer, as the clock struck ten.

A smart servant girl answered the knock, and started on beholding the three strangers.

"Is Mr. Winkle at home, my dear?" enquired Mr. Pickwick.

"He is just going to supper, Sir," replied the girl.

"Give him that card if you please," rejoined Mr. Pickwick. "Say I am sorry to trouble him at so late an hour; but I am anxious to see him to-night, and have only just arrived."

The girl looked timidly at Mr. Bob Sawyer, who was expressing his admiration of her personal charms by a variety of wonderful grimaces, and casting an eye at the hats and great-coats which hung in the passage, called another girl to mind the door while she went up stairs. The sentinel was speedily relieved, for the girl returned immediately, and begging pardon of the gentlemen for leaving them in the street, ushered them into a floor-clothed back parlour, half office and half dressing room, in which the principal useful and ornamental articles of furniture were a desk, a wash-hand stand and shaving glass, a boot-rack and boot-jack, a high stool, four chairs, a table, and an old eight-day clock. Over the mantel-piece were the sunken doors of an iron safe, while a couple of hanging shelves for books, an almanack, and several files of dusty papers, decorated the walls.

"Very sorry to leave you standing at the door, Sir," said the girl, lighting a lamp, and addressing Mr. Pickwick with a winning smile, "but you was quite strangers to me; and we have such a many trampers that only come to see what they can lay their hands on, that really—"

"There is not the least occasion for any apology, my dear," said Mr. Pickwick good humouredly.

"Not the slightest, my love," said Bob Sawyer, playfully stretching forth his arms, and skipping from side to side, as if to prevent the young lady's leaving the room.

The young lady was not at all softened by these allurements, for she at once expressed her opinion that Mr. Bob Sawyer was an "odous creetur;" and, on his becoming rather more pressing in his attentions, imprinted her fair fingers upon his face, and bounced out of the room with many expressions of aversion and contempt.

Deprived of the young lady's society, Mr. Bob Sawyer proceeded to divert himself by peeping into the desk, looking into all the table-drawers, feigning to pick the lock of the iron safe, turning the almanack with its face to the wall, trying Mr. Winkle senior's boots on, over his own, and making several other humourous experiments upon the furniture, all of which afforded Mr. Pickwick unspeakable horror and agony, and yielded Mr. Bob Sawyer proportionate delight.

At length the door opened, and a little old gentleman in a snuff-coloured suit, with a head and face the precise counterpart of those belonging to Mr. Winkle junior, excepting that he was rather bald, trotted into the room with Mr. Pickwick's card in one hand, and a silver candlestick in the other.

"Mr. Pickwick, Sir, how do you do!" said Winkle the elder, putting down the candlestick and proffering his hand. "Hope I see you well, Sir. Glad to see you. Be seated, Mr. Pickwick, I beg Sir. This gentleman is—"

"My friend Mr. Sawyer," interposed Mr. Pickwick, "your son's friend."

"Oh," said Mr. Winkle the elder, looking rather grimly at Bob. "I hope *you* are well, Sir."

"Right as a trivet," replied Bob Sawyer.

"This other gentleman," cried Mr. Pickwick, "is, as you will see when you have read the letter with which I am entrusted, a very near relative, or should rather say a very particular friend of your son's. His name is Allen."

"*That* gentleman?" enquired Mr. Winkle, pointing with

the card towards Ben Allen, who had fallen asleep in an attitude which left nothing of him visible but his spine and his coat collar.

Mr. Pickwick was on the point of replying to the question, and reciting Mr. Benjamin Allen's name and honourable distinctions at full length, when the sprightly Mr. Bob Sawyer, with the view of rousing his friend to a sense of his situation, inflicted a startling pinch upon the fleshy part of his arm, which caused him to jump up with a loud shriek. Suddenly aware that he was in the presence of a stranger, Mr. Ben Allen advanced and, shaking Mr. Winkle most affectionately by both hands for about five minutes, murmured in some half intelligible fragments of sentences the great delight he felt in seeing him, and a hospitable enquiry, whether he felt disposed to take anything after his walk, or would prefer waiting "till dinner-time;" which done, he sat down and gazed about him with a petrified stare as if he had not the remotest idea where he was, which indeed he had not.

All this was most embarrassing to Mr. Pickwick, the more especially as Mr. Winkle, senior, evinced palpable astonishment at the eccentric—not to say extraordinary—behaviour of his two companions. To bring the matter to an issue at once, he drew a letter from his pocket, and presenting it to Mr. Winkle, senior, said—

"This letter, Sir, is from your son. You will see by its contents that on your favourable and fatherly consideration of it, depend his future happiness and welfare. Will you oblige me by giving it the calmest and coolest perusal, and by discussing the subject afterwards, with me, in the tone and spirit in which alone it ought to be discussed? You may judge of the importance your decision is of, to your son, and his intense anxiety upon the subject, by my waiting upon you without any previous warning at so late an hour; and," added Mr. Pickwick, glancing slightly at his two companions, "and under such unfavourable circumstances."

With this prelude, Mr. Pickwick placed four closely written sides of extra superfine wire-wove penitence in the hands of the astounded Mr. Winkle, senior; and reseating himself in his chair, watched his looks and manner, anxiously it is true, but with the open front of a gentleman who feels he has taken no part which he need excuse or palliate.

The old wharfinger turned the letter over; looked at the front, back, and sides; made a microscopic examination of the fat little boy on the seal; raised his eyes to Mr. Pickwick's face; and then, seating himself on the high stool and drawing the lamp closer to him, broke the wax, unfolded the epistle, and lifting it to the light, prepared to read.

Just at this moment, Mr. Bob Sawyer, whose wit had lain dormant for some minutes, placed his hands upon his knees and made a face after the portraits of the late Mr. Grimaldi, as clown. It so happened that Mr. Winkle, senior, instead of being deeply engaged in reading the letter, as Mr. Bob Sawyer thought, chanced to be looking over the top of it at no less a person than Mr. Bob Sawyer himself; and rightly conjecturing that the face aforesaid was made in ridicule and derision of his own person, he fixed his eyes on Bob with such expressive sternness, that the late Mr. Grimaldi's lineaments gradually resolved themselves into a very fine expression of humility and confusion.

"Did you speak, Sir?" enquired Mr. Winkle, senior, after an awful silence.

"No, Sir," replied Bob, with no remains of the clown about him, save and except the extreme redness of his cheeks.

"You are sure you did not, Sir?" said Mr. Winkle, senior.

"Oh dear! yes, Sir, quite," replied Bob.

"I thought you did, Sir," rejoined the old gentleman, with indignant emphasis. "Perhaps you *looked* at me, Sir?"

"Oh, no! Sir, not at all," replied Bob, with extreme civility.

"I am very glad to hear it, Sir," said Mr. Winkle, senior. Having frowned upon the abashed Bob with great magnificence, the old gentleman again brought the letter to the light, and began to read it seriously.

Mr. Pickwick eyed him intently as he turned from the bottom line of the first page to the top line of the second, and from the bottom of the second to the top of the third, and from the bottom of the third to the top of the fourth; but not the slightest alteration of countenance afforded a clue to the feelings with which he received the announcement of his son's marriage, which Mr. Pickwick knew was in the very first half-dozen lines.

He read the letter to the last word, folded it again with all the carefulness and precision of a man of business; and just when Mr. Pickwick expected some great outbreak of feeling, dipped a pen in the inkstand, and said as quietly as if he were speaking on the most ordinary counting-house topic—

"What is Nathaniel's address, Mr. Pickwick?"

"The George and Vulture, at present," replied that gentleman.

"George and Vulture. Where is that?"

"George Yard, Lombard Street."

"In the City."

"Yes."

The old gentleman methodically indorsed the address on the back of the letter; and then placing it in the desk, which he locked, said as he got off the stool and put the bunch of keys in his pocket—

"I suppose there is nothing else which need detain us, Mr. Pickwick?"

"Nothing else, my dear Sir!" observed that warmhearted person in indignant amazement. "Nothing else! Have you no opinion to express on this momentous event in our young friend's life; no assurance to convey to him, through me, of the continuance of your affection and protection; nothing to say which will cheer and sustain him, and the anxious girl who looks to him for comfort and support? My dear Sir, consider."

"I will consider," replied the old gentleman. "I have nothing to say just now. I am a man of business, Mr. Pickwick; I never commit myself hastily in any affair, and from what I see of this, I by no means like the appearance of it. A thousand pounds is not much, Mr. Pickwick."

"You're very right, Sir," interposed Ben Allen, just awake enough to know that he had spent *his* thousand pounds without the smallest difficulty. "You're an intelligent man; Bob, he's a very knowing fellow this."

"I am very happy to find that *you* do me the justice to make the admission, Sir," said Mr. Winkle, senior, looking contemptuously at Ben Allen, who was shaking his head profoundly. "The fact is, Mr. Pickwick, that when I gave my son a roving license for a year or so to see something of men and manners (which he has done under your auspices), so that he might not enter into life a mere boarding-school milk-sop to be gulled by every body, I never bargained for this. He knows that very well, so if I withdraw my countenance from him on this account, he has no call to be surprised. He shall hear from me, Mr. Pickwick. Good night, Sir. Margaret, open the door."

All this time Bob Sawyer had been nudging Mr. Ben Allen to say something on the right side; and Ben accordingly now burst out, without the slightest preliminary notice, into a brief but impassioned piece of eloquence.

"Sir," said Mr. Ben Allen, staring at the old gentleman, through a pair of very dim and languid eyes, and working his right arm vehemently up and down, "you—you ought to be ashamed of yourself."

"As the lady's brother, of course you are an excellent judge of the question," retorted Mr. Winkle, senior. "There; that's enough. Pray say no more, Mr. Pickwick. Good night, gentlemen."

With these words the old gentleman took up the candlestick, and opening the room door, politely motioned towards the passage.

"You will regret this, Sir," said Mr. Pickwick, setting his teeth close together to keep down his choler; for he felt how important the effort might prove to his young friend.

"I am at present of a different opinion," calmly replied Mr. Winkle, senior. "Once again, gentlemen, I wish you a good night."

Mr. Pickwick walked with angry strides into the street. Mr. Bob Sawyer, completely quelled by the decision of the old gentleman's manner, took the same course; Mr. Ben Allen's hat rolled down the steps immediately afterwards, and Mr. Ben Allen's body followed it directly. The whole party went silent and supperless to bed; and Mr. Pickwick thought, just before he fell asleep, that if he had known Mr. Winkle, senior, had been quite so much of a man of business, it was extremely probable he might never have waited upon him, on such an errand.

CHAPTER L.

IN WHICH MR. PICKWICK ENCOUNTERS AN OLD ACQUAINTANCE, TO WHICH FORTUNATE CIRCUMSTANCE THE READER IS MAINLY INDEBTED FOR MATTER OF THRILLING INTEREST HEREIN SET DOWN, CONCERNING TWO GREAT PUBLIC MEN OF MIGHT AND POWER.

THE morning which broke upon Mr. Pickwick's sight at eight o'clock was not at all calculated to elevate his spirits, or to lessen the depression which the unlooked-for result of his embassy inspired. The sky was dark and gloomy, the air damp and raw, the streets wet and sloppy. The smoke hung sluggishly above the chimney-tops as if it lacked the courage to rise, and the rain came slowly and doggedly down as if it had not even the spirit to pour. A game-cock in the stable-yard, deprived of every spark of his accustomed animation, balanced himself dismally on one leg in a corner: and a donkey, moping with drooping head under the narrow roof of an outhouse, appeared from his meditative and miserable countenance to be contemplating suicide. In the street, umbrellas were the only things to be seen, and the clicking of pattens and splashing of rain-drops, the only sounds to be heard.

The breakfast was interrupted by very little conversation; even Mr. Bob Sawyer felt the influence of the weather, and the previous day's excitement. In his own most expressive language, he was "floored." So was Mr. Ben Allen. So was Mr. Pickwick.

In protracted expectation of the weather clearing up, the last evening paper from London was read and re-read with an intensity of interest only known in cases of extreme destitution; every inch of the carpet was walked over with similar perseverance, the windows were looked out of often enough to justify the imposition of an additional duty upon them, all kinds of topics of conversation were started, and failed; and at length Mr. Pickwick when noon had arrived without a change for the better, rang the bell resolutely and ordered out the chaise.

Although the roads were miry, and the drizzling rain came down harder than it had done yet, and although the mud and wet splashed in at the open windows of the carriage to such an extent that the discomfort was almost as great to the pair of insides as to the pair of outsides, still there was something in the very motion, and the sense of being up and doing, which was so infinitely superior to being pent in a dull room, looking at the dull rain dripping into a dull street, that they all agreed, on starting, that the change was a great improvement, and wondered how they could possibly have delayed making it as long as they had done.

When they stopped to change at Coventry, the steam ascended from the horses in such clouds as wholly to obscure the hostler, whose voice was however heard to declare from the mist, that he expected the first Gold Medal from the Humane Society on their next distribution of rewards, for taking the postboy's hat off; the water descending from the brim of which, the invisible gentleman declared must inevitably have drowned him (the postboy), but for his great presence of mind in tearing it promptly from his head, and drying the gasping man's countenance with a wisp of straw.

"This is pleasant," said Bob Sawyer, turning up his coat collar, and pulling the shawl over his mouth to concentrate the fumes of a glass of brandy just swallowed.

"Wery," replied Sam, composedly.

"You don't seem to mind it," observed Bob.

"Vy, I don't exactly see no good my mindin' on it 'ud do, Sir," replied Sam.

"That's an unanswerable reason, anyhow," said Bob.

"Yes, Sir," rejoined Mr. Weller. "Wotever is, is right, as the young nobleman sweetly remarked ven they put him down in the pension list 'cos his mother's uncle's vife's grandfather vunce lit the king's pipe vith a portable tinder box."

"Not a bad notion that, Sam," said Mr. Bob Sawyer approvingly.

"Just wot the young nobleman said ev'ry quarter-day arterwards for the rest of his life," replied Mr. Weller.

"Wos you ever called in," enquired Sam, glancing at the driver, after a short silence, and lowering his voice to a mysterious whisper, "wos you ever called in, ven you wos 'prentice to a sawbones, to wisit a postboy?"

"I don't remember that I ever was," replied Bob Sawyer.

"You never see a postboy in that 'ere hospital as you *walked* (as they says o' the ghosts), did you?" demanded Sam.

"No," replied Bob Sawyer. "I don't think I ever did."

"Never know'd a churchyard vere there wos a postboy's tombstone, or see a dead postboy, did you?" enquired Sam, pursuing his catechism.

"No," rejoined Bob, "I never did."

"No," rejoined Sam, triumphantly. "Nor never vill; and there's another thing that no man never see, and that's a dead donkey—no man never see a dead donkey, 'cept the gen'l'm'n in the black silk smalls as know'd the young 'ooman as kept a goat; and that wos a French donkey, so wery likely he warn't vun o' the reg'lar breed."

"Well, what has that got to do with the postboys?" asked Bob Sawyer.

"This here," replied Sam. "Vithout goin' so far as to as-sert, as some wery sensible people do, that postboys and donkeys is both immortal, wot I say is this; that venever they feels theirselves gettin' stiff and past their work, they just rides off together, vun postboy to a pair, in the usual vay; wot becomes on 'em nobody knows, but it's wery probable as they starts avay to take their pleasure in some other vorld, for there ain't a man alive as ever see either a donkey or a postboy a takin' his pleasure in this!"

Expatiating upon this learned and remarkable theory, and citing many curious statistical and other facts in its support, Sam Weller beguiled the time until they reached Dunchurch, where a dry postboy and fresh horses were procured; the next stage was Daventry, and the next Towcester; and at the end of each stage it rained harder than it had done at the beginning.

"I say," remonstrated Bob Sawyer, looking in at the coach window, as they pulled up before the door of the Saracen's Head, Towcester, "this won't do you know."

"Bless me!" said Mr. Pickwick, just awaking from a nap, "I'm afraid you are wet."

"Oh you are, are you?" returned Bob. "Yes, I am, a little that way. Uncomfortably damp, perhaps."

Bob did look dampish, inasmuch as the rain was streaming from his neck, elbows, cuffs, skirts, and knees; and his whole apparel shone so with the wet, that it might have been mistaken for a full suit of prepared oilskin.

"I *am* rather wet," said Bob, giving himself a shake, and casting a little hydraulic shower around in so doing, like a Newfoundland dog just emerged from the water.

"I think it's quite impossible to go on to-night," interposed Ben.

"Out of the question, Sir," remarked Sam Weller, coming to assist in the conference; "it's cruelty to animals, Sir, to ask 'em to do it. There's beds here, Sir," said Sam, addressing his master, "everything clean and comfortable. Wery good little dinner, Sir, they can get ready in half an hour—pair of fowls, Sir, and a weal cutlet; French beans, 'taturs, tart, and tidiness. You'd better stop vere you are, Sir, if I might recommend. Take advice, Sir, as the doctor said."

The host of the Saracen's Head opportunely appeared at this moment, to confirm Mr. Weller's statement relative to the accommodations of the establishment, and to back his entreaties with a variety of dismal conjectures regarding the state of the roads, the doubt of fresh horses being to be had at the next stage, the dead certainty of its raining all night, the equally mortal certainty of its clearing up in the morning, and other topics of inducement familiar to innkeepers.

"Well," said Mr. Pickwick, "but I must send a letter to London by some conveyance, so that it may be delivered the very first thing in the morning, or I must go forward at all hazards."

The landlord smiled his delight. Nothing could be easier than for the gentleman to inclose a letter in a sheet of brown paper and send it on either by the mail or the night coach from Birmingham. If the gentleman was particularly anxious to have it left as soon as possible, he might write outside, "To be delivered immediately," which was sure to be attended to; or "pay the bearer half-a-crown extra for instant delivery," which was surer still.

"Very well," said Mr. Pickwick, "then we will stop here."

"Lights in the Sun, John; make up the fire—the gentlemen are wet," cried the landlord. "This way, gentlemen; don't trouble yourselves about the postboy now, Sir. I'll send him to you when you ring for him, Sir. Now John, the candles."

The candles were brought, the fire was stirred up, and a fresh log of wood thrown on. In ten minutes' time a waiter was laying the cloth for dinner, the curtains were drawn, the fire was blazing brightly, and everything looked (as everything always does in all decent English inns) as if the travellers had been expected and their comforts prepared, for days beforehand.

Mr. Pickwick sat down at a side table and hastily indited a note to Mr. Winkle, merely informing him that he was detained by stress of weather, but would certainly be in London next day; until when he deferred any further account of his proceedings. This note was hastily made up into a parcel and despatched to the bar per Mr. Samuel Weller.

Sam left it with the landlady, and was returning to pull his master's boots off, after drying himself by the kitchen fire, when, glancing casually through a half-opened door, he was arrested by the sight of a gentleman with a sandy head who had a large bundle of newspapers lying on the table before him, and was perusing the leading article of one with a settled sneer which curled up his nose and all his other features into a majestic expression of haughty contempt.

"Hallo!" said Sam, "I ought to know that 'ere head and them features; the eye-glass, too, and the broad-brimmed tile! Eatansvill to vit, or I'm a Roman."

Sam was taken with a troublesome cough at once, for the purpose of attracting the gentleman's attention: and the gentleman starting at the sound, raised his head and his eye-glass, and disclosed to view the profound and thoughtful features of Mr. Pott, of the Eatanswill Gazette.

"Beggin' your pardon, Sir," said Sam, advancing with a bow, "my master's here, Mr. Pott."

"Hush, hush!" cried Pott, drawing Sam into the room, and closing the door, with a countenance of mysterious dread and apprehension.

"Wot's the matter, Sir?" enquired Sam, looking vacantly about him.

"Not a whisper of my name," replied Pott—"this is a buff neighbourhood. If the excited and irritable populace knew I was here, I should be torn to pieces."

"No; vould you, Sir?" enquired Sam.

"I should be the victim of their fury," replied Pott. "Now, young man, what of your master?"

"He's a stoppin' here to-night on his vay to town, vith a couple of friends," replied Sam.

"Is Mr. Winkle one of them?" enquired Pott, with a slight frown.

"No Sir; Mr. Vinkle stops at home now," rejoined Sam. "He's married."

"Married!" exclaimed Pott, with frightful vehemence. He stopped, smiled darkly, and added, in a low, vindictive tone, "It serves him right."

Having given vent to this cruel ebullition of deadly malice and cold-blooded triumph over a fallen enemy, Mr. Pott enquired whether Mr. Pickwick's friends were "blue;" receiving a most satisfactory answer in the affirmative from Sam, who knew as much about the matter as Pott himself, he consented to accompany him to Mr. Pickwick's room, where a hearty welcome awaited him, and an agreement to club their dinners together was at once made and ratified.

"And how are matters going on in Eatanswill?" enquired Mr. Pickwick, when Pott had taken a seat near the fire, and the whole party had got their wet boots off, and dry slippers on. "Is the Independent still in being?"

"The Independent, Sir," replied Pott, "is still dragging on a wretched and lingering career, abhorred and despised by even the few who are cognizant of its miserable and disgraceful existence; stifled by the very filth it so profusely scatters; rendered deaf and blind by the exhalations of its own slime, the obscene journal, happily unconscious of its degraded state, is rapidly sinking beneath that treacherous mud which, while it seems to give it a firm standing with the low and debased classes of society, is, nevertheless, rising about its detested head, and will speedily engulf it for ever."

Having delivered this manifesto (which formed a portion of his last week's leader) with vehement articulation, the editor paused to take breath, and looked majestically at Bob Sawyer.

"You are a young man, Sir," said Pott.

Mr. Bob Sawyer nodded.

"So are you, Sir," said Pott, addressing Mr. Ben Allen. Ben admitted the soft impeachment.

"And are both deeply imbued with those blue principles, which so long as I live I have pledged myself to the people of these kingdoms to support and to maintain?" suggested Pott.

"Why, I don't exactly know about that," replied Bob Sawyer, "I am—"

"Not buff, Mr. Pickwick," interrupted Pott, drawing back his chair, "you friend is not buff, Sir?"

"No, no," rejoined Bob, "I'm a kind of plaid at present; a compound of all sort of colours."

"A waverer," said Pott solemnly, "a waverer. I should like to show you a series of eight articles, Sir, that have appeared in the Eatanswill Gazette. I think I may venture to say that you would not be long in establishing your opinions on a firm and solid basis, Sir."

"I dare say I should turn very blue before I got to the end of them," responded Bob.

Mr. Pott looked dubiously at Bob Sawyer for some seconds, and, turning to Mr. Pickwick, said—

"You have seen the literary articles which have appeared at intervals in the Eatanswill Gazette in the course of the last three months, and which have excited such general—I may say such universal attention and admiration?"

"Why," replied Mr. Pickwick, slightly embarrassed by the question, "the fact is, I have been so much engaged in other ways, that I really have not had an opportunity of perusing them."

"You should do so, Sir," said Pott, with a severe countenance.

"I will," said Mr. Pickwick.

"They appeared in the form of a copious review of a work on Chinese metaphysics, Sir," said Pott.

"Oh," observed Mr. Pickwick—"from your pen I hope?"

"From the pen of my critic, Sir," rejoined Pott with dignity.

"An abstruse subject I should conceive," said Mr. Pickwick.

"Very, Sir," responded Pott, looking intensely sage. "He *crammed* for it, to use a technical but expressive term; he read up for the subject, at my desire, in the *Encyclopædia Britannica*."

"Indeed!" said Mr. Pickwick; "I was not aware that that valuable work contained any information respecting Chinese metaphysics."

"He read, Sir," rejoined Pott, laying his hand on Mr. Pickwick's knee, and looking round with a smile of intellectual superiority, "he read for metaphysics under the letter M, and for China under the letter C; and combined his information, Sir!"

Mr. Pott's features assumed so much additional grandeur at the recollection of the power and research displayed in the learned effusions in question, that some minutes elapsed before Mr. Pickwick felt emboldened to renew the conversation; at length, as the Editor's countenance gradually relapsed into its customary expression of moral supremacy, he ventured to resume the discourse by asking—

"Is it fair to enquire what great object has brought you so far from home?"

"That object which actuates and animates me in all my gigantic labours, Sir," replied Pott, with a calm smile—"my country's good."

"I supposed it was some public mission," observed Mr. Pickwick.

"Yes, Sir," resumed Pott, "it is." Here, bending towards Mr. Pickwick, he whispered in a deep hollow voice, "A buff ball, Sir, will take place in Birmingham to-morrow evening."

"God bless me!" exclaimed Mr. Pickwick.

"Yes, Sir, and supper," added Pott.

"You don't say so!" ejaculated Mr. Pickwick.

Pott nodded portentously.

Now, although Mr. Pickwick feigned to stand aghast at this disclosure, he was so little versed in local politics that he was unable to form an adequate comprehension of the importance of the dire conspiracy it referred to; observing which, Mr. Pott, drawing forth the last number of the Eatanswill Gazette, and referring to the same, delivered himself of the following paragraph:—

"Hole-and-Corner Buffery."

"A reptile contemporary has recently sweltered forth his black venom in the vain and hopeless attempt of sullying the fair name of our distinguished and excellent representative, the Honourable Mr. Slumkey—that Slumkey whom we, long before he gained his present noble and exalted position, predicted would one day be, as he now is, at once his country's brightest honour, and her proudest boast: alike her bold defender and her honest pride—our reptile contemporary, we say, has made himself merry at the expense of a superbly embossed plated coal-scuttle, which has been presented to that glorious man by his enraptured constituents, and towards the purchase of which, the nameless wretch insinuates, the Honourable Mr. Slumkey himself contributed, through a confidential friend of his butler's, more than three-fourths of the whole sum subscribed. Why, does not the crawling creature see that even if this be the fact, the Honourable Mr. Slumkey only appears in a still more amiable and radiant light than before, if that be possible? Does not even his obtuseness perceive that this amiable and touching desire to carry out the wishes of the constituent body must for ever endear him to the hearts and souls of such of his fellow townsmen as are not worse than swine; or, in other words, which are not as debased as our contemporary himself? But such is the wretched trickery of hole-and-corner Buffery! These are not its only artifices. Treason is abroad. We boldly state, now that we are goaded to the disclosure, and we throw ourselves on the country and its constables for protection:—we boldly state that secret preparations are at this moment in progress for a Buff ball, which is to be held in a Buff town, in the very heart and centre of a Buff population; which is to be conducted by a Buff master of the ceremonies; which is to be attended by four ultra Buff members of parliament, and the admission to which is to be by Buff tickets. Does our fiendish contemporary wince? Let him writhe in impotent malice as we pen the words, WE WILL BE THERE."

"There, Sir," said Pott, folding up the paper quite exhausted, "that is the state of the case."

The landlord and waiter entering at the moment with dinner, caused Mr. Pott to lay his finger on his lips in token that he considered his life in Mr. Pickwick's hands, and depended on his secrecy. Messrs. Bob Sawyer and Benjamin Allen, who had irreverently fallen asleep during the reading of the quotation from the Eatanswill Gazette and the discussion which followed it, were roused by the mere whispering of the talismanic word "Dinner" in their ears; and to dinner they went with good digestion waiting on appetite, and health on both, and a waiter upon all three.

In the course of the dinner and the sitting which succeeded it, Mr. Pott descending for a few moments to domestic topics, informed Mr. Pickwick that the air of Eatanswill not agreeing with his lady, she was then engaged in making a tour of different fashionable watering-places, with a view to the recovery of her wonted health and spirits; this was a delicate veiling of the fact that Mrs. Pott, acting upon her often repeated threat of separation, had, in virtue of an arrangement negociated by her brother, the Lieutenant, and concluded by Mr. Pott, permanently retired with the faithful body-guard upon one moiety or half-part of the annual income and profits arising from the editorship and sale of the Eatanswill Gazette.

While the great Mr. Pott was dwelling upon this and other matters, enlivening the conversation from time to time with various extracts from his own lucubrations, a stern stranger, calling from the window of a stage-coach, outward bound, which halted at the inn to deliver packages, requested to know whether if he stopped short on his journey and remained there for the night he could be furnished with the necessary accommodation of a bed and bedstead.

"Certainly, Sir," replied the landlord.

"I can, can I?" enquired the stranger, who seemed habitually suspicious in look and manner.

"No doubt of it, Sir," replied the landlord.

"Good," said the stranger. "Coachman, I get down here. Guard, my carpet-bag."

Bidding the other passengers good night in a rather snappish manner, the stranger alighted. He was a shortish gentleman, with very stiff black hair, cut in the porcupine or blacking-brush style, and standing stiff and straight all over his head; his aspect was pompous and threatening; his manner was peremptory; his eyes sharp and restless; and his whole bearing bespoke a feeling of great confidence in himself, and a consciousness of immeasurable superiority over all other people.

This gentleman was shown into the room originally assigned to the patriotic Mr. Pott; and the waiter remarked, in dumb astonishment at the singular coincidence, that he had no sooner lighted the candles than the gentleman, diving into his hat, drew forth a newspaper, and began to read it with the very same expression of indignant scorn which upon the majestic features of Pott had paralysed his energies an hour before. The man observed too, that whereas Mr. Pott's scorn had been roused by a newspaper headed The Eatanswill Independent, this gentleman's withering contempt was awakened by a newspaper entitled The Eatanswill Gazette.

"Send the landlord," said the stranger.

"Yes, Sir," rejoined the waiter.

The landlord was sent, and came.

"Are you the landlord?" enquired the gentleman.

"I am, Sir," replied the landlord.

"Do you know me?" demanded the gentleman.

"I have not that pleasure, Sir," rejoined the landlord.

"My name is Slurk," said the gentleman.

The landlord slightly inclined his head.

"Slurk, Sir," repeated the gentleman, haughtily. "Do you know me now, man?"

The landlord scratched his head, looked at the ceiling, and at the stranger, and smiled feebly.

"Do you know me, man?" enquired the stranger, angrily.

The landlord made a strong effort, and at length, replied, "Well, Sir, I do not know you."

"Good God!" said the stranger, dashing his clenched fist upon the table. "And this is popularity!"

The landlord took a step or two towards the door, and the stranger fixing his eyes upon him, resumed. "This," said the stranger, "this is gratitude for years of labour and study in behalf of the masses. I alight wet and weary; no enthusiastic crowds press forward to greet their champion, the church-bells are silent; the very name elicits no responsive feeling in their torpid bosoms. It is enough," said the agitated Mr. Slurk, pacing to and fro, "to curdle the ink in one's pen, and induce one to abandon their cause for ever."

"Did you say brandy and water, Sir?" said the landlord, venturing a hint.

"Rum," said Mr. Slurk, turning fiercely upon him. "Have you got a fire anywhere?"

"We can light one directly, Sir," said the landlord.

"Which will throw out no heat until it is bed time," interrupted Mr. Slurk. "Is there anybody in the kitchen?"

Not a soul. There was a beautiful fire. Everybody had gone, and the door was closed for the night.

"I will drink my rum and water," said Mr. Slurk, "by the kitchen fire." So, gathering up his hat and newspaper, he stalked solemnly behind the landlord to that humble apartment, and throwing himself on a settle by the fireside, resumed his countenance of scorn, and began to read and drink in silent dignity.

Now some demon of discord, flying over the Saracen's

Head at that moment, on casting down his eyes in mere idle curiosity, happened to behold Slurk established comfortably by the kitchen fire, and Pott slightly elevated with wine in another room; upon which the malicious demon darting down into the last-mentioned apartment with inconceivable rapidity, passed at once into the head of Mr. Bob Sawyer, and prompted him for his (the demon's) own evil purposes to speak as follows:

"I say, we've let the fire out. It's uncommonly cold after the rain, isn't it?"

"It really is," replied Mr. Pickwick, shivering.

"It wouldn't be a bad notion to have a cigar by the kitchen fire, would it?" said Bob Sawyer, still prompted by the demon aforesaid.

"It would be particularly comfortable, I think," replied Mr. Pickwick. "Mr. Pott, what do you say?"

Mr. Pott yielded a ready assent; and all four travellers, each with his glass in his hand, at once betook themselves to the kitchen, with Sam Weller heading the procession to shew them the way.

The stranger was still reading; he looked up and started. Mr. Pott started.

"What's the matter?" whispered Mr. Pickwick.

"That reptile!" replied Pott.

"What reptile?" said Mr. Pickwick, looking about him for fear he should tread on some overgrown black beetle, or dropsical spider.

"That reptile," whispered Pott, catching Mr. Pickwick by the arm, and pointing towards the stranger. "That reptile—Slurk, of the Independent!"

"Perhaps we had better retire," whispered Mr. Pickwick.

"Never, Sir," rejoined Pott,—pot-valiant in a double sense—"never." With these words, Mr. Pott took up his position on an opposite settle, and selecting one from a little bundle of newspapers, began to read against his enemy.

Mr. Pott, of course, read the Independent, and Mr. Slurk, of course, read the Gazette; and each gentleman audibly expressed his contempt of the other's compositions by bitter laughs and sarcastic sniffs; whence they proceeded to more open expressions of opinion, such as "absurd,"— "wretched,"—"atrocity," — "humbug," — "knavery,"— "dirt,"—"filth,"—"slime,"—"ditch water," and other critical remarks of the like nature.

Both Mr. Bob Sawyer and Mr. Ben Allen had beheld these symptoms of rivalry and hatred with a degree of delight which imparted great additional relish to the cigars at which they were puffing most vigorously. The moment they began to flag, the mischievous Mr. Bob Sawyer, addressing Slurk with great politeness, said—

"Will you allow me to look at your paper, Sir, when you have quite done with it?"

"You'll find very little to repay you for your trouble in this contemptible thing, Sir," replied Slurk, bestowing a Satanic frown on Pott.

"You shall have this presently," said Pott, looking up, pale with rage, and quivering in his speech from the same cause. "Ha! ha! you will be amused with this fellow's audacity."

Terrific emphasis was laid upon "thing" and "fellow;" and the faces of both editors began to glow with defiance.

"The ribaldry of this miserable man is despicably disgusting," said Pott, pretending to address Bob Sawyer, and scowling upon Slurk.

Here Mr. Slurk laughed very heartily, and folding the paper so as to get at a fresh column conveniently, said, that the blockhead really amused him.

"What an impudent blunderer this fellow is," said Pott, turning from pink to crimson.

"Did you ever read any of this man's foolery, Sir?" enquired Slurk, of Bob Sawyer.

"Never," replied Bob; "is it very bad?"

"Oh, shocking! shocking!" rejoined Slurk.

"Really, dear me, this is too atrocious!" exclaimed Pott, at this juncture; still feigning to be absorbed in his reading.

"If you can wade through a few sentences of malice, meanness, falsehood, perjury, treachery, and cant," said Slurk, handing the paper to Bob, "you will, perhaps, be somewhat repaid by a laugh at the style of this ungrammatical twaddler."

"What's that you said, Sir?" enquired Pott, looking up, trembling all over with passion.

"What's that to you, Sir?" replied Slurk.

"Ungrammatical twaddler, was it, Sir?" said Pott.

"Yes, Sir, it was," replied Slurk; "and blue bore, Sir, if you like that better; ha! ha!"

Mr. Pott retorted not a word to this jocose insult, but deliberately folding up his copy of the Independent, flattened it carefully down, crushed it beneath his boot, spat upon it with great ceremony, and flung it into the fire.

"There, Sir," said Pott, retreating from the stove, "and that's the way I would serve the viper who produces it, if I were not, fortunately for him, restrained by the laws of my country."

"Serve him so, Sir!" cried Slurk, starting up: "those laws shall never be appealed to by him, Sir, in such a case. Serve him so, Sir!"

"Hear! hear!" said Bob Sawyer.

"Nothing can be fairer," observed Mr. Ben Allen.

"Serve him so, Sir!" reiterated Slurk, in a loud voice.

Mr. Pott darted a look of contempt, which might have withered an anchor.

"Serve him so, Sir!" reiterated Slurk, in a louder voice than before.

"I will not, Sir;" rejoined Pott.

"Oh, you won't! won't you, Sir?" said Mr. Slurk, in a taunting manner; "you hear this, gentlemen! He won't; not that he's afraid; oh, no! he won't. Ha! ha!"

"I consider you, Sir," said Mr. Pott, moved by this sarcasm, "I consider you a viper. I look upon, Sir, you as a man who has placed himself beyond the pale of society, by his most audacious, disgraceful, and abominable public conduct. I view you, Sir, personally or politically, in no other light but as a most unparalleled and unmitigated viper."

The indignant Independent did not wait to hear the end of this personal denunciation; for, catching up his carpet bag which was well stuffed with moveables, he swung it in the air as Pott turned away, and letting it fall with a circular sweep on his head just at that particular angle of the bag where a good thick hair-brush happened to be packed, caused a sharp crash to be heard throughout the kitchen, and brought him at once to the ground.

"Gentlemen," cried Mr. Pickwick, as Pott started up and seized the fire-shovel, "gentlemen, consider for Heaven's sake—help—Sam—here—pray, gentlemen—interfere, somebody."

Uttering these incoherent exclamations, Mr. Pickwick

THE RIVAL EDITORS.

rushed between the infuriated combatants just in time to receive the carpet-bag on one side of his body, and the fire-shovel on the other; whether the representatives of the public feeling of Eatanswill were blinded by animosity, or, being both acute reasoners, saw the advantage of having a third party between them to bear all the blows, certain it is that they paid not the slightest attention to Mr. Pick-wick, but defying each other with great spirit, plied the carpet-bag and the fire-shovel most fearlessly. Mr. Pick-wick would unquestionably have suffered severely from his humane interference, if Mr. Weller, attracted by his mas-ter's cries, had not rushed in at the moment, and, snatch-ing up a meal-sack, effectually stopped the conflict by drawing it over the head and shoulders of the mighty Pott, and clasping him tight round the elbows.

"Take avay that 'ere bag from the t'other madman," said Sam to Ben Allen and Bob Sawyer, who had done nothing but dodge round the group, each with a tortoise-shell lancet in his hand, ready to bleed the first man stunned. "Give it up, you wretched little creetur, or I'll smother you in it."

Awed by these threats, and quite out of breath, the In-dependent suffered himself to be disarmed; and Mr. Weller, removing the extinguisher from Pott, set him free with a caution.

"You take yourselves off to bed quietly," said Sam, "or I'll put you both in it, and let you fight it out vith the mouth tied, as I vould a dozen sich, if they played these games. And you have the goodness to come this here vay, Sir, if you please."

Thus addressing his master, Sam took him by the arm and led him off, while the rival editors were severally re-moved to their beds by the landlord, under the inspection of Mr. Bob Sawyer and Mr. Benjamin Allen; breathing, as they went away, many sanguinary threats, and making vague appointments for mortal combat next day. When they came to think it over, however, it occurred to them that they could do it much better in print, so they recom-menced deadly hostilities without delay; and all Eatans-will rung with their boldness—on paper.

They had taken themselves off in separate coaches, early next morning, before the other travellers were stirring; and the weather having now cleared up, the chaise com-panions once more turned their faces to London.

CHAPTER LI.

INVOLVING A SERIOUS CHANGE IN THE WELLER FAMILY, AND THE UNTIMELY DOWNFALL OF THE RED-NOSED MR. STIGGINS.

CONSIDERING it a matter of delicacy to abstain from intro-ducing either Bob Sawyer or Ben Allen to the young couple, until they were fully prepared to expect them; and wish-ing to spare Arabella's feelings as much as possible, Mr. Pickwick proposed that he and Sam should alight in the neighbourhood of the George and Vulture, and that the two young men should for the present take up their quarters elsewhere; to this they very readily agreed, and the propo-sition was accordingly acted upon: Mr. Ben Allen and Mr. Bob Sawyer betaking themselves to a sequestered pot-shop on the remotest confines of the Borough, behind the bar-door of which their names had in other days very often appeared, at the head of long and complex calculations worked in white chalk.

"Dear me, Mr. Weller," said the pretty housemaid, meeting Sam at the door.

"Dear *me* I vish it wos, my dear," replied Sam, drop-ping behind, to let his master get out of hearing. "Wot a sweet lookin' creetur you are, Mary!"

"Lor, Mr. Weller, what nonsense you do talk!" said Mary. "Oh! *don't*, Mr. Weller."

"Don't what, my dear?" said Sam.

"Why, that," replied the pretty housemaid. "Lor, do get along with you." Thus admonishing him, the pretty housemaid smilingly pushed Sam against the wall, declar-ing that he had tumbled her cap, and put her hair quite out of curl.

"And prevented what I was going to say, besides," added Mary. "There's a letter been waiting here for you four days; you hadn't been gone away half an hour when it came; and more than that, it's got, immediate, on the outside."

"Vere is it, my love?" enquired Sam.

"I took care of it for you, or I dare say it would have been lost long before this," replied Mary. "There, take it; it's more than you deserve."

With these words, after many pretty little coquettish doubts and fears, and wishes that she might not have lost it, Mary produced the letter from behind the nicest little muslin tucker possible, and handed it to Sam, who there-upon kissed it with much gallantry and devotion.

"My goodness me!" said Mary, adjusting the tucker, and feigning unconsciousness, "you seem to have grown very fond of it all at once."

To this Mr. Weller only replied by a wink, the intense meaning of which no description could convey the faint-est idea of; and, setting himself down beside Mary on a window-seat, opened the letter and glanced at the contents.

"Hallo!" exclaimed Sam, "wot's all this?"

"Nothing the matter, I hope?" said Mary, peeping over his shoulder.

"Bless them eyes o' yourn," said Sam, looking up.

"Never mind my eyes; you had much better read your letter," said the pretty housemaid, and as she said this, she made the eyes twinkle with such slyness and beauty that they were perfectly irresistible.

Sam refreshed himself with a kiss, and read as follows:

"*Markis Gran.*
"*By dorken*
"*Wens*^dy.

"My dear Sammle,

"I am wery sorry to have the pleasure of bein a Bear of ill news your Mother in law cort cold consekens of im-prudently settin too long on the damp grass in the rain a hearin of a shepherd who warnt able to leave off till late at night owen to his havin vound his-self up vith brandy and vater and not being able to stop his-self till he got a little sober which took a many hours to do the doctor says that if she svallo'd varm brandy and vater arterwards insted of afore she mightn't have been no vus her veels wos immedetly greased and everythink done to set her a goin as could be inwented your farther had hopes as she vould have vorked round as usual but just as she wos a

turnen the corner my boy she took the wrong road and vent down hill vith a welocity you never see and notvith-standin that the drag was put on drectly by the medikel man it wornt of no use at all for she paid the last pike at tventy minutes afore six o'clock yesterday evenin havin done the jouney wery much under the reglar time vich praps was partly owen to her haven taken in wery little luggage by the vay your father says that if you vill come and see me Sammy he vill take it as a wery great favour for I am wery lonely Samivel. N. B he *vill* have it spelt that vay vich I say ant right and as there is sich a many things to settle he is sure your guvner wont object of course he vill not Sammy for I knows him better so he sends his dooty in vhich I join and am Samivel infernally yours
"TONY VELLER."

"Wot a incomprehensible letter," said Sam; "who's to know wot it means, vith all this he-ing and I-ing! It ain't my father's writin' 'cept this here signater in print letters; that's his."

"Perhaps he got somebody to write it for him, and signed it himself afterwards," said the pretty housemaid.

"Stop a minit," replied Sam, running over the letter again, and pausing here and there to reflect as he did so. "You've hit it. The gen'lm'n as wrote it, wos a tellin' all about the misfortun' in a proper vay, and then my father comes a lookin' over him, and complicates the whole concern by puttin' his oar in. That's just the wery sort o' thing he'd do. You're right, Mary, my dear."

Having satisfied himself on this point, Sam read the letter all over, once more, and, appearing to form a clear notion of its contents for the first time, ejaculated thoughtfully, as he folded it up:—

"And so the poor creature's dead! I'm sorry for it. She warn't a bad-disposed 'ooman if them shepherds had let her alone. I'm werry sorry for it."

Mr. Weller uttered these words in so serious a manner, that the pretty housemaid cast down her eyes and looked very grave.

"Hows'ever," said Sam, putting the letter in his pocket, with a gentle sigh, "it wos to be—and wos, as the old lady said arter she'd married the footman, can't be helped now, can it, Mary?"

Mary shook her head, and sighed too.

"I must apply to the hemperor for leave of absence," said Sam.

Mary sighed again,—the letter was so very affecting.

"Good bye!" said Sam.

"Good bye," rejoined the pretty housemaid, turning her head away.

"Well, shake hands, won't you?" said Sam.

The pretty housemaid put out a hand which, although it was a housemaid's, was a very small one, and rose to go.

"I shan't be wery long avay," said Sam.

"You're always away," said Mary, giving her head the slightest possible toss in the air. "You no sooner come, Mr. Weller, than you go again."

Mr. Weller drew the household beauty closer to him, and entered upon a whispering conversation, which had not proceeded far when she turned her face round and condescended to look at him again. When they parted it was somehow or other indispensably necessary for her to go to her room, and arrange the cap and curls before she could think of presenting herself to her mistress; which prepara-tory ceremony she went off to perform, bestowing many nods and smiles on Sam over the bannisters as she tripped up stairs.

"I shan't be avay more than a day,—or two, Sir, at farthest," said Sam, when he had communicated to Mr. Pickwick the intelligence of his father's loss.

"As long as may be necessary, Sam," replied Mr. Pickwick. "You have my full permission to remain."

Sam bowed.

"You will tell your father, Sam, that if I can be of any assistance to him in his present situation, I shall be most willing and ready to lend him any aid in my power," said Mr. Pickwick.

"Thankee, Sir," rejoined Sam. "I'll mention it, Sir."

And with some expressions of mutual good-will and in-terest, master and man separated.

It was just seven o'clock when Samuel Weller, alighting from the box of a stage coach which passed through Dork-ing, stood within a few hundred yards of the Marquis of Granby. It was a cold dull evening; the little street looked dreary and dismal, and the mahogany countenance of the noble and gallant Marquis seemed to wear a more sad and melancholy expression than it was wont to do, as it swung to and fro, creaking mournfully in the wind. The blinds were pulled down, and the shutters partly closed; of the knot of loungers that usually collected about the door, not one was to be seen; the place was silent and desolate.

Seeing nobody of whom he could ask any preliminary questions, Sam walked softly in, and glancing round, he quickly recognised his parent in the distance.

The widower was seated at a small round table in the little room behind the bar, smoking a pipe, with his eyes intently fixed upon the fire. The funeral had evidently taken place that day, for attached to his hat which he still retained on his head, was a hat-band measuring about a yard and a half in length, which hung over the top rail of the chair and streamed negligently down. Mr. Weller was in a very abstracted and contemplative mood, for notwith-standing that Sam called him by name several times he still continued to smoke with the same fixed and quiet countenance, and was only roused ultimately by his son's placing the palm of his hand on his shoulder.

"Sammy," said Mr. Weller, "you're velcome."

"I've been a callin' to you half a dozen times," said Sam, hanging his hat on a peg, "but you didn't hear me."

"No, Sammy," replied Mr. Weller, again looking thoughtfully at the fire. "I wos in a referee, Sammy."

"Wot about?" enquired Sam, drawing his chair up to the fire.

"In a referee, Sammy," replied the elder Mr. Weller, "regardin' *her*, Samivel." Here Mr. Weller jerked his head in the direction of Dorking churchyard, in mute ex-planation that his words referred to the late Mrs. Weller.

"I wos a thinkin', Sammy," said Mr. Weller, eyeing his son with great earnestness, over his pipe, as if to assure him that however extraordinary and incredible the declar-ation might appear, it was nevertheless calmly and deliber-ately uttered, "I wos a thinkin', Sammy, that upon the whole I wos wery sorry she wos gone."

"Vell, and so you ought to be," replied Sam.

Mr. Weller nodded his acquiescence in the sentiment, and again fastening his eyes on the fire, shrouded himself in a cloud, and mused deeply.

"Those wos wery sensible observations as she made, Sammy?" said Mr. Weller, driving the smoke away with his hand, after a long silence.

"Wot observations?" enquired Sam.

"Them as she made arter she was took ill," replied the old gentleman.

"Wot was they?"

"Somethin' to this here effect. 'Veller,' she says, 'I'm afeard I've not done by you quite wot I ought to have done; you're a wery kind-hearted man, and I might ha' made your home more comfortabler. I begin to see now,' she says, 'ven it's too late, that if a married 'ooman vishes to be religious she should begin vith dischargin' her dooties at home, and makin' them as is about her cheerful and happy, and that vile she goes to church, or chapel, or wot not, at all proper times, she should be wery careful not to con-wert this sort o' thing into an excuse for idleness or self-indulgence, or vurse. I *have* done this,' she says, 'and I've vasted time and substance on them as has done it more than me; but I hope ven I'm gone, Veller, that you'll think on me as I wos afore I know'd them people, and as I raly wos by natur.' 'Susan,' says I,—I wos took up wery short by this, Samivel; I von't deny it, my boy— 'Susan,' I says, 'you've been a wery good vife to me, altogether, don't say nothin' at all about it, keep a good heart my dear, and you'll live to see me punch that 'ere Stiggins's head yet.' She smiled at this, Samivel," said the old gentleman, stifling a sigh with his pipe, "but she died arter all!"

"Vell," said Sam, venturing to offer a little homely consolation after the lapse of three or four minutes, consumed by the old gentleman in slowly shaking his head from side to side, and solemnly smoking; "vell, gov'ner, ve must all come to it, one day or another."

"So we must, Sammy," said Mr. Weller the elder.

"There's a Providence in it all," said Sam.

"O' course there is," replied his father with a nod of grave approval. "Wot 'ud become of the undertakers vithout it, Sammy?"

Lost in the immense field of conjecture opened by this reflection, the elder Mr. Weller laid his pipe on the table, and stirred the fire with a meditative visage.

While the old gentleman was thus engaged, a very buxom-looking cook, dressed in mourning, who had been bustling about in the bar, glided into the room, and bestowing many smirks of recognition upon Sam, silently stationed herself at the back of his father's chair, and announced her presence by a slight cough, the which being disregarded, was followed by a louder one.

"Hallo!" said the elder Mr. Weller, dropping the poker as he looked round, and hastily drew his chair away. "Wot's the matter now?"

"Have a cup of tea, there's a good soul," replied the buxom female, coaxingly.

"I von't," replied Mr. Weller, in a somewhat boisterous manner, "I'll see you——" Mr. Weller hastily checked himself, and added in a low tone, "furder fust."

"Oh, dear, dear; how adversity does change people!" said the lady, looking upwards.

"It's the only thing 'twixt this and the doctor as shall change *my* condition," muttered Mr. Weller.

"I really never saw a man so cross," said the buxom female.

"Never mind—it's all for my own good; vich is the re-flection vith wich the penitent schoolboy comforted his feelin's ven they flogged him," rejoined the old gentleman.

The buxom female shook her head with a compassionate and sympathising air; and, appealing to Sam, enquired whether his father really ought not to make an effort to keep up, and not give way to that lowness of spirits.

"You see, Mr. Samuel," said the buxom female, "as I was telling him yesterday, he *will* feel lonely, he can't expect but what he should, Sir, but he should keep up a good heart, because, dear me, I'm sure we all pity his loss, and are ready to do anything for him; and there's no situation in life so bad, Mr. Samuel, that it can't be mended, which is what a very worthy person said to me when my husband died." Here the speaker, putting her hand before her mouth, coughed again, and looked affectionately at the elder Mr. Weller.

"As I don't rekvire any o' your conversation just now, Mum, vill you have the goodness to re-tire?" enquired Mr. Weller in a grave and steady voice.

"Well, Mr. Weller," said the buxom female, "I'm sure I only spoke to you out of kindness."

"Wery likely, Mum," replied Mr. Weller. "Samivel, show the lady out, and shut the door arter her."

This hint was not lost upon the buxom female, for she at once left the room, and slammed the door behind her, upon which Mr. Weller, senior, falling back in his chair in a violent perspiration, said—

"Sammy, if I wos to stop here alone vun veek—only vun veek, my boy—that 'ere 'ooman 'ud marry me by force and wiolence afore it was over."

"Wot, is she so wery fond o' you?" enquired Sam.

"Fond!" replied his father, "I can't keep her avay from me. If I was locked up in a fire-proof chest vith a patent Brahmin, she'd find means to get at me, Sammy."

"Wot a thing it is to be so sought arter!" observed Sam, smiling.

"I don't take no pride out on it, Sammy," replied Mr. Weller, poking the fire vehemently, "it's a horrid sitiwation. I'm activally drove out o' house and home by it. The breath was scarcely out o' your poor mother-in-law's body, ven vun old 'ooman sends me a pot o' jam, and another a pot o' jelly, and another brews a blessed large jug o' camomile-tea, vich she brings in vith her own hands." Mr. Weller paused with an aspect of intense disgust, and, looking round, added in a whisper, "They wos all widders, Sammy, all on 'em, 'cept the camomile-tea vun, as wos a single young lady o' fifty-three."

Sam gave a comical look in reply, and the old gentleman having broken an obstinate lump of coal, with a countenance expressive of as much earnestness and malice as if it had been the head of one of the widows last-mentioned, said—

"In short, Sammy, I feel that I ain't safe anyveres but on the box."

"How are you safer there than anyveres else," interrupted Sam.

"'Cos a coachman's a privileged indiwidual," replied Mr. Weller, looking fixedly at his son. "'Cos a coachman may do vithout suspicion wot other men may not; 'cos a coachman may be on the very amicablest terms with eighty mile o' females, and yet nobody think that he ever means to marry any vun among 'em. And wot other man can say the same, Sammy?"

"Vell, there's somethin' in that," said Sam.

"If your gov'ner had been a coachman," reasoned Mr. Weller, "do you s'pose as that 'ere jury 'ud ever ha' conwicted him, s'posin' it possible as the matter could ha' gone to that ex-tremity? They dustn't ha' done it."

"Wy not?" said Sam, rather disparagingly.

"Vy not!" rejoined Mr. Weller; "'cos it 'ud ha' gone agin their consciences. A reg'lar coachman's a sort o' connectin' link betvixt singleness and matrimony, and every practicable man knows it."

"Wot you mean, they're gen'ral fav'rites, and nobody takes adwantage on 'em, p'raps?" said Sam.

His father nodded.

"How it ever come to that 'ere pass," resumed the parent Weller, "I can't say; vy it is that long-stage coachmen possess such insiniwations, and is alvays looked up to —a-dored I may say—by ev'ry young 'ooman in ev'ry town he vurks through, I don't know; I only know that so it is; it's a reg'lation of natur—a dispensary, as your poor mother-in-law used to say."

"A dispensation," said Sam, correcting the old gentleman.

"Wery good, Samivel, a dispensation if you like it better," returned Mr. Weller; "I call it a dispensary, and it's alvays writ up so, at the places vere they gives you physic for nothing in your own bottles; that's all."

With these words Mr. Weller re-filled and re-lighted his pipe, and once more summoning up a meditative expression of countenance, continued as follows:—

"Therefore, my boy, as I do not see the adwisability o' stoppin' here to be married vether I vant to or not, and as at the same time I do not vish to separate myself from them interestin' members o' society altogether, I have come to the determination o' drivin' the Safety, and puttin' up vunce more at the Bell Savage, vich is my nat'ral born element, Sammy."

"And wot's to become o' the bis'ness?" enquired Sam.

"The bis'ness, Samivel," replied the old gentleman, "good-vill, stock, and fixters, vill be sold by private contact; and out o' the money, two hundred pound, agreeable to a rekvest o' your mother-in-law's to me, a little afore she died, vill be inwested in your name in—wot do you call them things again?"

"Wot things?" enquired Sam.

"Them things as is always a goin' up and down in the City."

"Omnibuses?" suggested Sam.

"Nonsense," replied Mr. Weller. "Them things as is always a fluctooatin', and gettin' theirselves inwolved somehow or another vith the national debt, and the checquers bills, and all that."

"Oh! the funds," said Sam.

"Ah!" rejoined Mr. Weller, "the funs; two hundred pound o' the money is to be inwested for you, Samivel, in the funs; four and a half per cent. reduced counsels, Sammy."

"Wery kind o' the old lady to think o' me," said Sam, "and I'm wery much obliged to her."

"The rest vill be inwested in my name," continued the elder Mr. Weller; "and ven I'm took off the road, it'll come to you, so take care you don't spend it all at vunst, my boy, and mind that no widder gets a inklin' o' your fortun', or you're done."

Having delivered this warning, Mr. Weller resumed his pipe with a more serene countenance; the disclosure of these matters appearing to have eased his mind considerably.

"Somebody's a tappin' at the door," said Sam.

"Let 'em tap," replied his father, with dignity.

Sam acted upon the direction: upon which there was another tap, and another, and then a long row of taps; upon which Sam enquired why the tapper was not admitted.

"Hush," whispered Mr. Weller, with apprehensive looks, "don't take no notice on 'em, Sammy, it's vun o' the widders, p'raps."

No notice being taken of the taps, the unseen visitor, after a short lapse, ventured to open the door and peep in. It was no female head that was thrust in at the partially opened door, but the long black locks and red face of Mr. Stiggins. Mr. Weller's pipe fell from his hands.

The reverend gentleman gradually opened the door by almost imperceptible degrees, until the aperture was just wide enough to admit of the passage of his lank body, when he glided into the room and closed it after him with great care and gentleness. Turning towards Sam, and raising his hands and eyes in token of the unspeakable sorrow with which he regarded the calamity that had befallen the family, he carried the high-backed chair to his old corner by the fire, and sitting himself down on the very edge of the seat, drew forth a brown pocket-handkerchief, and applied the same to his optics.

While this was going forward, the elder Mr. Weller sat back in his chair with his eyes wide open, his hands planted on his knees, and his whole countenance expressive of absorbing and overwhelming astonishment. Sam sat opposite him in perfect silence, waiting with eager curiosity for the termination of the scene.

Mr. Stiggins kept the brown pocket-handkerchief before his eyes for some minutes, moaning decently meanwhile, and then, mastering his feelings by a strong effort, put it in his pocket and buttoned it up. After this he stirred the fire; after that he rubbed his hands and looked at Sam.

"Oh my young friend," said Mr. Stiggins, breaking the silence in a very low voice, "here's a sorrowful affliction."

Sam nodded very slightly.

"For the man of wrath, too!" added Mr. Stiggins; "it makes a vessel's heart bleed!"

Mr. Weller was overheard by his son to murmur something relative to making a vessel's nose bleed; but Mr. Stiggins heard him not.

"Do you know, young man," whispered Mr. Stiggins, drawing his chair closer to Sam, "whether she has left Emanuel anything?"

"Who's he?" enquired Sam.

"The chapel," replied Mr. Stiggins; "our chapel; our fold, Mr. Samuel."

"She hasn't left the fold nothin', nor the shepherd nothin', nor the animals nothin'," said Sam, decisively; "nor the dogs neither."

Mr. Stiggins looked slyly at Sam, glanced at the old gentleman, who was sitting with his eyes closed, as if asleep; and drawing his chair still nearer, said:

"Nothing for me, Mr. Samuel?"

Sam shook his head.

"I think there's something," said Stiggins, turning as pale as he could turn. "Consider, Mr. Samuel; no little token?"

"Not so much as the vurth o' that 'ere old umberella o' yourn," replied Sam.

"Perhaps," said Mr. Stiggins, hesitatingly, after a few moments' deep thought, "perhaps she recommended me to the care of the man of wrath, Mr. Samuel?"

"I think that's wery likely, from what he said," rejoined Sam; "he wos a speakin' about you, jist now."

"Was he, though?" exclaimed Stiggins, brightening up. "Ah! He's changed, I dare say. We might live very comfortably together now, Mr. Samuel, eh? I could take care of his property when you are away—good care, you see."

Heaving a long-drawn sigh, Mr. Stiggins paused for a response. Sam nodded, and Mr. Weller, the elder, gave vent to an extraordinary sound, which, being neither a groan, nor a grunt, nor a gasp, nor a growl, seemed to partake in some degree of the character of all four.

Mr. Stiggins, encouraged by this sound, which he understood to betoken remorse or repentance, looked about him, rubbed his hands, wept, smiled, wept again, and then, walking softly across the room to a well-remembered shelf in one corner, took down a tumbler, and, with great deliberation, put four lumps of sugar in it. Having got thus far, he looked about him again and sighed grievously; with that he walked softly into the bar, and presently returning with the tumbler half full of pine-apple rum, advanced to the kettle which was singing gaily on the hob, mixed his grog, stirred it, sipped it, sat down, and taking a long and hearty pull at the rum and water, stopped for breath.

The elder Mr. Weller, who still continued to make various strange and uncouth attempts to appear asleep, offered not a single word during these proceedings, but when Mr. Stiggins stopped for breath, he darted upon him, and snatching the tumbler from his hand, threw the remainder of the rum and water in his face, and the glass itself into the grate. Then, seizing the reverend gentleman firmly by the collar, he suddenly fell to kicking him most furiously, accompanying every application of his top-boot to Mr. Stiggins's person with sundry violent and incoherent anathemas upon his limbs, eyes and body.

"Sammy," said Mr. Weller, "put my hat on tight for me."

Sam dutifully adjusted the hat with the long hatband more firmly on his father's head, and the old gentleman, resuming his kicking with greater agility than before, tumbled with Mr. Stiggins through the bar, and through the passage, out at the front door, and so into the street;—the kicking continuing the whole way, and increasing in vehemence, rather than diminishing, every time the top-boot was lifted up.

It was a beautiful and exhilarating sight to see the red-nosed man writhing in Mr. Weller's grasp, and his whole frame quivering with anguish as kick followed kick in rapid succession; it was a still more exciting spectacle to behold Mr. Weller, after a powerful struggle, immersing Mr. Stiggins's head in a horse-trough full of water, and holding it there, till he was all but suffocated.

"There," said Mr. Weller, throwing all his energy into one most complicated kick, as he at length permitted Mr. Stiggins to withdraw his head from the trough, "send any vun o' them lazy shepherds here, and I'll pound him to a jelly first, and drownd him artervards. Sammy, help me in, and fill me a small glass of brandy. I'm out o' breath, my boy."

CHAPTER LII.

COMPRISING THE FINAL EXIT OF MR. JINGLE AND JOB TROTTER; WITH A GREAT MORNING OF BUSINESS IN GRAY'S INN SQUARE. CONCLUDING WITH A DOUBLE KNOCK AT MR. PERKER'S DOOR.

WHEN Arabella, after some gentle preparation, and many assurances that there was not the least occasion for being low-spirited, was at length made acquainted by Mr. Pickwick with the unsatisfactory result of his visit to Birmingham, she burst into tears, and sobbing aloud, lamented in moving terms that she should have been the unhappy cause of any estrangement between a father and his son.

"My dear girl," said Mr. Pickwick, kindly, "it is no fault of yours. It was impossible to foresee that the old gentleman would be so strongly prepossessed against his son's marriage, you know. I am sure," added Mr. Pickwick, glancing at her pretty face, "he can have very little idea of the pleasure he denies himself."

"Oh my dear Mr. Pickwick," said Arabella, "what shall we do, if he continues to be angry with us?"

"Why, wait patiently, my dear, until he thinks better of it," replied Mr. Pickwick, cheerfully.

"But dear Mr. Pickwick, what is to become of Nathaniel if his father withdraws his assistance?" urged Arabella.

"In that case, my love," rejoined Mr. Pickwick, "I will venture to prophecy that he will find some other friend who will not be backward in helping him to start in the world."

The significance of this reply was not so well disguised by Mr. Pickwick but that Arabella understood it. So, throwing her arms round his neck, and kissing him affectionately, she sobbed louder than before.

"Come, come," said Mr. Pickwick, taking her hand, "we will wait here a few days longer, and see whether he writes or takes any other notice of your husband's communication. If not, I have thought of half a dozen plans, any one of which would make you happy at once. There, my dear—there."

With these words, Mr. Pickwick gently pressed Arabella's hand, and bade her dry her eyes, and not distress her husband. Upon which, Arabella, who was one of the best little creatures alive, put her handkerchief in her reticule, and by the time Mr. Winkle joined them, exhibited in full lustre the same beaming smiles and sparkling eyes that had originally captivated him.

"This is a distressing predicament for these young people," thought Mr. Pickwick, as he dressed himself next morning. "I'll walk up to Perker's, and consult him about the matter."

As Mr. Pickwick was further prompted to betake himself to Gray's Inn Square by an anxious desire to come to a pecuniary settlement with the kind-hearted little attorney without further delay, he made a hurried breakfast, and executed his intention so speedily that ten o'clock had not struck when he reached Gray's Inn.

It still wanted ten minutes to the hour when he had ascended the staircase on which Perker's chambers were. The clerks had not arrived yet, and he beguiled the time by looking out of the staircase window.

The healthy light of a fine October morning made even the dingy old houses brighten up a little: some of the dusty windows actually looking almost cheerful as the sun's

IT WAS A STILL MORE EXCITING SPECTACLE TO BEHOLD MR. WELLER ... IMMERSING MR. STIGGINS'S HEAD IN A
HORSE-TROUGH FULL OF WATER, AND HOLDING IT THERE UNTIL HE WAS HALF SUFFOCATED.

rays gleamed upon them. Clerk after clerk hastened into the square by one or other of the entrances, and looking up at the Hall clock, accelerated or decreased his rate of walking according to the time at which his office hours nominally commenced; the half-past nine o'clock people suddenly becoming very brisk, and the ten o'clock gentlemen falling into a pace of most aristocratic slowness. The clock struck ten, and clerks poured in faster than ever, each one in a greater perspiration than his predecessor. The noise of unlocking and opening doors echoed and re-echoed on every side, heads appeared as if by magic in every window, and porters took up their stations for the day, the slipshod laundresses hurried off, the postman ran from house to house, and the whole legal hive was in a bustle.

"You're early, Mr. Pickwick," said a voice behind him.

"Ah, Mr. Lowten," replied that gentleman, looking round, and recognising his old acquaintance.

"Precious warm walking, isn't it?" said Lowten, drawing a Bramah key from his pocket, with a small plug therein, to keep the dust out.

"You appear to feel it so," rejoined Mr. Pickwick, smiling at the clerk, who was literally red hot.

"I've come along, rather, I can tell you," replied Lowten. "It went the half hour as I came through the Polygon. I'm here before *him*, though, so I don't mind."

Comforting himself with this reflection, Mr. Lowten extracted the plug from the door-key; having opened the door, replugged and repocketed his Bramah, and picked up the letters which the postman had dropped through the box, he ushered Mr. Pickwick into the office. Here, in the twinkling of an eye, he divested himself of his coat, put on a thread-bare garment, which he took out of a desk, hung up his hat, pulled forth a few sheets of cartridge and blotting-paper in alternate layers, and sticking a pen behind his ear, rubbed his hands with an air of great satisfaction.

"There you see, Mr. Pickwick," he said "now I'm complete. I've got my office coat on, and my pad out, and let him come as soon as he likes. You haven't got a pinch of snuff about you, have you?"

"No, I have not," replied Mr. Pickwick.

"I'm sorry for it," said Lowten. "Never mind—I'll run out presently, and get a bottle of soda. Don't I look rather queer about the eyes, Mr. Pickwick?"

The individual appealed to, surveyed Mr. Lowten's eyes from a distance, and expressed his opinion that no unusual queerness was perceptible in those features.

"I'm glad of it," said Lowten. "We were keeping it up pretty tolerably at the Stump last night, and I'm rather out of sorts this morning.—Perker's been about that business of yours, by the bye."

"What business?" enquired Mr. Pickwick—"Mrs. Bardell's costs?"

"No, I don't mean that," replied Lowten. "About getting that customer that we paid the ten shillings in the pound to the bill discounter for, on your account—to get him out of the Fleet, you know—about getting him to Demerara."

"Oh, Mr. Jingle," said Mr. Pickwick, hastily. "Yes. Well?"

"Well, it's all arranged," said Lowten, mending his pen. "The agent at Liverpool said he had been obliged to you

many times when you were in business, and he would be glad to take him on your recommendation."

"That's well," said Mr. Pickwick. "I am delighted to hear it."

"But I say," resumed Lowten, scraping the back of the pen preparatory to making a fresh split, "*what* a soft chap that other is!"

"Which other?"

"Why, that servant, or friend, or whatever he is—you know; Trotter."

"Ah!" said Mr. Pickwick, with a smile, "I always thought him the very reverse."

"Well, and so did I, from what little I saw of him," replied Lowten, "it only shows how one may be deceived. What do you think of his going to Demerara, too?"

"What!—and giving up what was offered him here!" exclaimed Mr. Pickwick.

"Treating Perker's offer of eighteen bob a-week, and a rise if he behaved himself, like dirt," replied Lowten. "He said he must go along with the other one, and so they persuaded Perker to write again, and they've got him something on the same estate; not near so good, Perker says, as a convict would get in New South Wales, if he appeared at his trial in a new suit of clothes."

"Foolish fellow," said Mr. Pickwick, with glistening eyes. "Foolish fellow."

"Oh, it's worse than foolish; it's downright sneaking, you know," replied Lowten, nibbing the pen with a contemptuous face. "He says that he's the only friend he ever had, and he's attached to him, and all that. Friendship's a very good thing in its way; we are all very friendly and comfortable at the Stump, for instance, over our grog, where every man pays for himself, but damn hurting yourself for anybody else, you know! No man should have more than two attachments—the first, to number one, and the second to the ladies; that's what I say—ha! ha!" Mr. Lowten concluded with a loud laugh, half in jocularity, and half in derision, which was prematurely cut short by the sound of Perker's footsteps on the stairs, at the first approach of which he vaulted on his stool with an agility most remarkable, and wrote intensely.

The greeting between Mr. Pickwick and his professional adviser was warm and cordial; the client was scarcely ensconced in the attorney's arm chair, however, when a knock was heard at the door, and a voice enquired whether Mr. Perker was within.

"Hark!" said Perker, "that's one of our vagabond friends—Jingle himself, my dear Sir. Will you see him?"

"What do you think?" enquired Mr. Pickwick, hesitating.

"Yes, I think you had better. Here, you Sir, what's your name, walk in, will you?"

In compliance with this unceremonious invitation, Jingle and Job walked into the room, but, seeing Mr. Pickwick, stopped short in some confusion.

"Well," said Perker, "don't you know that gentleman?"

"Good reason to," replied Jingle, stepping forward. "Mr. Pickwick—deepest obligations—life preserver—made a man of me—you shall never repent it, Sir."

"I am happy to hear you say so," said Mr. Pickwick. "You look much better."

"Thanks to you, Sir—great change—Majesty's Fleet—unwholesome place—very," said Jingle, shaking his head.

He was decently and cleanly dressed, and so was Job, who stood bolt upright behind him, staring at Mr. Pickwick with a visage of iron.

"When do they go to Liverpool?" enquired Mr. Pickwick, half aside to Perker.

"This evening, Sir, at seven o'clock," said Job, taking one step forward. "By the heavy coach from the city, Sir."

"Are your places taken?"

"They are, Sir," replied Job.

"You have fully made up your mind to go?"

"I have, Sir," answered Job.

"With regard to such an outfit as was indispensable for Jingle," said Perker, addressing Mr. Pickwick aloud, "I have taken upon myself to make an arrangement for the deduction of a small sum from his quarterly salary, which, being made for only one year, and regularly remitted, will provide for that expense. I entirely disapprove of your doing anything for him, my dear Sir."

"Certainly," interposed Jingle, with great firmness. "Clear head—man of the world—quite right—perfectly."

"By compounding with his creditor, releasing his clothes from the pawnbroker's, relieving him in prison, and paying for his passage," continued Perker, without noticing Jingle's observation, "you have already lost upwards of fifty pounds."

"Not lost," said Jingle, hastily. "Pay it all—stick to business—cash up—every farthing. Yellow fever, perhaps—can't help that—if not—" Here Mr. Jingle paused, and striking the crown of his hat with great violence, passed his hand over his eyes, and sat down.

"He means to say," said Job, advancing a few paces, "that if he is not carried off by the fever, he will pay the money back again. If he lives, he will, Mr. Pickwick. I will see it done. I know he will, Sir," said Job, with great energy. "I could undertake to swear it."

"Well, well," said Mr. Pickwick, who had been bestowing a score or two of frowns upon Perker, to stop his summary of benefits conferred, which the little attorney obstinately disregarded, "you must be careful not to play any more desperate cricket matches, Mr. Jingle, or to renew your acquaintance with Sir Thomas Blazo, and I have little doubt of your preserving your health."

Mr. Jingle smiled at this sally, but looked rather foolish notwithstanding, so Mr. Pickwick changed the subject by saying,

"You don't happen to know, do you, what has become of another friend of yours—a more humble one, whom I saw at Rochester?"

"Dismal Jemmy?" enquired Jingle.

"Yes."

Jingle shook his head.

"Clever rascal—queer fellow, hoaxing genius—Job's brother."

"Job's brother!" exclaimed Mr. Pickwick. "Well, now I look at him closely, there *is* a likeness."

"We were always considered like each other, Sir," said Job, with a cunning look just lurking in the corners of his eyes, "only I was really of a serious nature, and he never was. He emigrated to America, Sir, in consequence of being too much sought after here, to be comfortable; and has never been heard of since."

"That accounts for my not having received the 'page from the romance of real life,' which he promised me one morning when he appeared to be contemplating suicide on Rochester Bridge, I suppose," said Mr. Pickwick, smiling. "I need not enquire whether his dismal behaviour was natural or assumed."

"He could assume anything, Sir," said Job. "You may consider yourself very fortunate in having escaped him so easily. On intimate terms he would have been even a more dangerous acquaintance than—" Job looked at Jingle, hesitated, and finally added, "than—than—myself even."

"A hopeful family yours, Mr. Trotter," said Perker, sealing a letter which he had just finished writing.

"Yes, Sir," replied Job. "Very much so."

"Well," said the little man, laughing; "I hope you are going to disgrace it. Deliver this letter to the agent when you reach Liverpool, and let me advise you, gentlemen, not to be too knowing in the West Indies. If you throw away this chance, you will both richly deserve to be hanged, as I sincerely trust you will be. And now you had better leave Mr. Pickwick and me alone, for we have other matters to talk over, and time is precious." As Perker said this, he looked towards the door with an evident desire to render the leave-taking as brief as possible.

It was brief enough on Mr. Jingle's part. He thanked the little attorney in a few hurried words for the kindness and promptitude with which he had rendered his assistance, and, turning to his benefactor, stood for a few seconds as if irresolute what to say or how to act. Job Trotter relieved his perplexity, for with a humble, grateful bow to Mr. Pickwick, he took his friend gently by the arm, and led him away.

"A worthy couple," said Perker, as the door closed behind them.

"I hope they may become so," replied Mr. Pickwick. "What do you think? Is there any chance of their permanent reformation?"

Perker shrugged his shoulders doubtfully, but observing Mr. Pickwick's anxious and disappointed look, rejoined—

"Of course there is a chance. I hope it may prove a good one. They are unquestionably penitent now; but then, you know, they have the recollection of very recent suffering fresh upon them. What they may become when that fades away, is a problem that neither you nor I can solve. However, my dear Sir," added Perker, laying his hand on Mr. Pickwick's shoulder, "your object is equally honourable, whatever the result is. Whether that species of benevolence which is so very cautious and long-sighted that it is seldom exercised at all, lest its owner should be imposed upon, and so wounded in his self-love, be real charity, or a worldly counterfeit, I leave to wiser heads than mine to determine. But if those two fellows were to commit a burglary to-morrow, my opinion of this action would be equally high."

With these remarks, which were delivered in a much more animated and earnest manner than is usual in legal gentlemen, Perker drew his chair to his desk, and listened to Mr. Pickwick's recital of old Mr. Winkle's obstinacy.

"Give him a week," said Perker, nodding his head prophetically.

"Do you think he will come round?" enquired Mr. Pickwick.

"I think he will," rejoined Perker. "If not, we must

try the young lady's persuasion; and that is what anybody but you would have done at first."

Mr. Perker was taking a pinch of snuff with various grotesque contractions of countenance, eulogistic of the persuasive powers appertaining unto young ladies, when the murmur of enquiry and answer was heard in the outer office, and Lowten tapped at the door.

"Come in," cried the little man.

The clerk came in, and shut the door after him with great mystery.

"What's the matter?" enquired Perker.

"You're wanted, Sir."

"Who wants me?"

Lowten looked at Mr. Pickwick and coughed.

"Who wants me? Can't you speak, Mr. Lowten?"

"Why, Sir," replied Lowten, "it's Mr. Dodson; and Mr. Fogg is with him."

"Bless my life!" said the little man, looking at his watch, "I appointed them to be here at half-past eleven to settle that matter of yours, Pickwick. I gave them an undertaking on which they sent down your discharge; it's very awkward, my dear Sir; what will you do? Would you like to step into the next room?"

The next room being the identical room in which Messrs. Dodson and Fogg were, Mr. Pickwick replied that he would remain where he was, the more especially as Messrs. Dodson and Fogg ought to be ashamed to look him in the face, instead of his being ashamed to see them; which latter circumstance he begged Mr. Perker to note, with a glowing countenance and many marks of indignation.

"Very well, my dear Sir, very well," replied Perker, "I can only say, that if you expect either Dodson or Fogg to exhibit any symptom of shame or confusion at having to look you, or anybody else, in the face, you are the most sanguine man in your expectations that I ever met with. Show them in, Mr. Lowten."

Mr. Lowten disappeared with a grin, and immediately returned ushering in the firm, in due form of precedence—Dodson first, and Fogg afterwards.

"You have seen Mr. Pickwick, I believe?" said Perker to Dodson, inclining his pen in the direction where that gentleman was seated.

"How do you do, Mr. Pickwick?" said Dodson in a loud voice.

"Dear me," cried Fogg, "how do you do, Mr. Pickwick? I hope you are well, Sir. I thought I knew the face," said Fogg, drawing up a chair, and looking round him with a smile.

Mr. Pickwick bent his head very slightly in answer to these salutations, and, seeing Fogg pull a bundle of papers from his coat-pocket, rose and walked to the window.

"There is no occasion for Mr. Pickwick to move, Mr. Perker," said Fogg, untying the red tape which encircled the little bundle, and smiling again, more sweetly than before. "Mr. Pickwick is pretty well acquainted with these proceedings, there are no secrets between us I think. He! he! he!"

"Not many, I think," said Dodson. "Ha! ha! ha!"

Then both the partners laughed together—pleasantly and cheerfully, as men who are going to receive money often do.

"We shall make Mr. Pickwick pay for peeping," said Fogg with considerable native humour, as he unfolded his papers. "The amount of the taxed costs is one hundred and thirty-three, six and fourpence, Mr. Perker."

There was a great comparing of papers and turning over of leaves by Fogg and Perker after this statement of profit and loss, during which Dodson said in an affable manner to Mr. Pickwick—

"I don't think you are looking quite so stout as when I had the pleasure of seeing you last, Mr. Pickwick."

"Possibly not, Sir," replied Mr. Pickwick, who had been flashing forth looks of fierce indignation without producing the smallest effect on either of the sharp practitioners; "I believe I am not, Sir. I have been persecuted and annoyed by scoundrels of late, Sir."

Perker coughed violently, and asked Mr. Pickwick whether he wouldn't like to look at the morning paper, to which enquiry Mr. Pickwick returned a most decided negative.

"True," said Dodson, "I dare say you *have* been annoyed in the Fleet; there are some odd gentry there. Whereabouts were your apartments, Mr. Pickwick?"

"My one room," replied that much-injured gentleman, "was on the Coffee Room flight."

"Oh, indeed!" said Dodson. "I believe that is a very pleasant part of the establishment."

"Very," replied Mr. Pickwick drily.

There was a coolness about all this, which to a gentleman of an excitable temperament had, under the circumstances, rather an exasperating tendency. Mr. Pickwick restrained his wrath by gigantic efforts, but when Perker wrote a cheque for the whole amount, and Fogg deposited it in a small pocket-book, with a triumphant smile playing over his pimply features, which communicated itself likewise to the stern countenance of Dodson, he felt the blood in his cheeks tingling with indignation.

"Now Mr. Dodson," said Fogg, putting up the pocket-book and drawing on his gloves, "I am at your service."

"Very good," said Dodson, rising, "I am quite ready."

"I am very happy," said Fogg, softened by the cheque, "to have had the pleasure of making Mr. Pickwick's acquaintance. I hope you don't think quite so badly of us, Mr. Pickwick, as when we first had the pleasure of seeing you."

"I hope not," said Dodson, with the high tone of calumniated virtue. "Mr. Pickwick now knows us better, I trust; whatever your opinion of gentlemen of our profession may be, I beg to assure you, Sir, that I bear no ill-will or vindictive feelings towards you for the sentiments you thought proper to express in our office in Freeman's Court, Cornhill, on the occasion to which my partner has referred."

"Oh no, no; nor I," said Fogg in a most forgiving manner.

"Our conduct, Sir," said Dodson, "will speak for itself, and justify itself I hope, upon every occasion. We have been in the profession some years, Mr. Pickwick, and have been honoured with the confidence of many excellent clients. I wish you good morning, Sir."

"*Good* morning, Mr. Pickwick," said Fogg; and so saying he put his umbrella under his arm, drew off his right glove, and extended the hand of reconciliation to that most indignant gentleman, who thereupon thrust his hands beneath his coat-tails, and eyed the attorney with looks of scornful amazement.

"Lowten!" cried Perker at this moment. "Open the door."

"Wait one instant," said Mr. Pickwick, "Perker, I *will* speak."

"My dear Sir, pray let the matter rest where it is," said

the little attorney, who had been in a state of nervous apprehension during the whole interview; "Mr. Pickwick, I beg—"

"I will not be put down, Sir," replied Mr. Pickwick hastily. "Mr. Dodson, you have addressed some remarks to me."

Dodson turned round, bent his head meekly, and smiled.

"Some remarks to me," repeated Mr. Pickwick, almost breathless, "and your partner has tendered me his hand, and you have both assumed a tone of forgiveness and high-mindedness, which is an extent of impudence that I was not prepared for, even in you."

"What, Sir!" exclaimed Dodson.

"What, Sir!" reiterated Fogg.

"Do you know that I have been the victim of your plots and conspiracies?" continued Mr. Pickwick. "Do you know that I am the man whom you have been imprisoning and robbing? Do you know that you were the attorneys for the plaintiff in Bardell and Pickwick?"

"Yes, Sir, we do know it," replied Dodson.

"Of course we know it, Sir," rejoined Fogg, slapping his pocket—perhaps by accident.

"I see that you recollect it with satisfaction," said Mr. Pickwick, attempting to call up a sneer for the first time in his life, and failing most signally in so doing. "Although I have long been anxious to tell you in plain terms what my opinion of you is, I should have let even this opportunity pass in deference to my friend Perker's wishes, but for the unwarrantable tone you have assumed, and your insolent familiarity—I say insolent familiarity, Sir," said Mr. Pickwick, turning upon Fogg with a fierceness of gesture which caused that person to retreat towards the door with great expedition.

"Take care, Sir," said Dodson; who, although he was the biggest man of the party, had prudently intrenched himself behind Fogg, and was speaking over his head with a very pale face. "Let him assault you, Mr. Fogg; don't return it on any account."

"No, no, I won't return it," said Fogg, falling back a little more as he spoke; to the evident relief of his partner, who by these means was gradually getting into the outer office.

"You are," continued Mr. Pickwick, resuming the thread of his discourse, "you are a well-matched pair of mean, rascally, pettifogging robbers."

"Well," interposed Perker, "is that all?"

"It is all summed up in that," rejoined Mr. Pickwick; "they are mean, rascally, pettifogging robbers."

"There!" said Perker in a most conciliatory tone, "my dear Sirs, he has said all he has to say: now pray go. Lowten, is that door open?"

Mr. Lowten, with a distant giggle, replied in the affirmative.

"There, there—good morning—good morning—now pray, my dear Sirs,—Mr. Lowten the door," cried the little man, pushing Dodson and Fogg, nothing loath, out of the office, "this way, my dear Sirs—now pray don't prolong this—dear me—Mr. Lowten—the door, Sir, why don't you attend?"

"If there's law in England, Sir," said Dodson, looking towards Mr. Pickwick, as he put on his hat, "you shall smart for this."

"You are a couple of mean—"

"Remember, Sir, you pay dearly for this," said Fogg, shaking his fist.

"—Rascally, pettifogging robbers!" continued Mr. Pickwick, taking not the least notice of the threats that were addressed to him.

"Robbers!" cried Mr. Pickwick, running to the stairhead, as the two attorneys descended.

"Robbers!" shouted Mr. Pickwick, breaking from Lowten and Perker, and thrusting his head out of the staircase window.

When Mr. Pickwick drew in his head again, his countenance was smiling and placid; and, walking quietly back into the office, he declared that he had now removed a great weight from his mind, and that he felt perfectly comfortable and happy.

Perker said nothing at all until he had emptied his snuff-box and sent Lowten out to fill it, when he was seized with a fit of laughing, which lasted for five minutes, at the expiration of which time he said that he supposed he ought to be very angry, but he couldn't think of the business seriously yet—when he could, he would be.

"Well, now," said Mr. Pickwick, "let me have a settlement with you."

"Of the same kind as the last?" enquired Perker, with another laugh.

"Not exactly," rejoined Mr. Pickwick, drawing out his pocket-book, and shaking the little man heartily by the hand, "I only mean a pecuniary settlement. You have done me many acts of kindness that I can never repay, and have no wish to, for I prefer continuing the obligation."

With this preface the two friends dived into some very complicated accounts and vouchers, which having been duly displayed and gone through by Perker, were at once discharged by Mr. Pickwick, with many professions of esteem and friendship.

They had no sooner arrived at this point, than a most violent and startling knocking was heard at the door; it was not an ordinary double knock, but a constant and uninterrupted succession of the loudest single raps, as if the knocker were endowed with the perpetual motion, or the person outside had forgotten to leave off.

"Dear me, what's that?" exclaimed Perker, starting.

"I think it is a knock at the door," said Mr. Pickwick, as if there could be the smallest doubt of the fact!

The knocker made a more energetic reply than words could have yielded, for it continued to hammer with surprising force and noise, without a moment's cessation.

"Dear me!" said Perker, ringing his bell, "we shall alarm the Inn.—Mr. Lowten, don't you hear a knock?"

"I'll answer the door in one moment, Sir," replied the clerk.

The knocker appeared to hear the response, and to assert that it was quite impossible he could wait so long. It made a stupendous uproar.

"It's quite dreadful," said Mr. Pickwick, stopping his ears.

"Make haste, Mr. Lowten," Perker called out, "we shall have the pannels beaten in."

Mr. Lowten, who was washing his hands in a dark closet, hurried to the door, and turning the handle, beheld the appearance which is described in the next chapter.

CHAPTER LIII.

CONTAINING SOME PARTICULARS RELATIVE TO THE
DOUBLE KNOCK, AND OTHER MATTERS, AMONG
WHICH CERTAIN INTERESTING DISCLOSURES
RELATIVE TO MR. SNODGRASS AND A YOUNG
LADY ARE BY NO MEANS IRRELEVANT TO THIS
HISTORY.

THE object that presented itself to the eyes of the astonished clerk was a boy—a wonderfully fat boy—habited as
a serving lad, standing upright on the mat, with his eyes
closed as if in sleep. He had never seen such a fat boy in
or out of a travelling caravan; and this, coupled with the
utter calmness and repose of his appearance, so very different from what was reasonably to have been expected of the
inflicter of such knocks, smote him with wonder.

"What's the matter?" enquired the clerk.

The extraordinary boy replied not a word, but he nodded
once, and seemed, to the clerk's imagination, to snore
feebly.

"Where do you come from?" enquired the clerk.

The boy made no sign. He breathed heavily, but in all
other respects was motionless.

The clerk repeated the question thrice, and receiving no
answer, prepared to shut the door, when the boy suddenly
opened his eyes, winked several times, sneezed once, and
raised his hand as if to repeat the knocking. Finding the
door open he stared about him with great astonishment,
and at length fixed his eyes on Mr. Lowten's face.

"What the devil do you knock in that way for?" enquired the clerk, angrily.

"What way?" said the boy in a slow, sleepy voice.

"Why, like forty hackney coachmen," replied the clerk.

"Because master said I wasn't to leave off knocking till
they opened the door, for fear I should go to sleep," said
the boy.

"Well," said the clerk, "what message have you
brought?"

"He's down stairs," rejoined the boy.

"Who?"

"Master. He wants to know whether you're at home."

Mr. Lowten bethought himself at this juncture of looking out of the window. Seeing an open carriage with a
hearty old gentleman in it, looking up very anxiously, he
ventured to beckon him, on which the old gentleman
jumped out directly.

"That's your master in the carriage, I suppose?" said
Lowten.

The boy nodded.

All further enquiries were superseded by the appearance
of old Wardle, who, running up stairs and just recognising
Lowten, passed at once into Mr. Perker's room.

"Pickwick!" said the old gentleman, "your hand, my
boy; why have I never heard till the day before yesterday
of your suffering yourself to be cooped up in jail? And
why did you let him do it, Perker?"

"I couldn't help it, my dear Sir," replied Perker, with a
smile and a pinch of snuff, "you know how obstinate he is."

"Of course I do, of course I do," replied the old gentleman. "I am heartily glad to see him, notwithstanding.
I will not lose sight of him again in a hurry."

With these words, Wardle shook Mr. Pickwick's hand
once more, and, having done the same to Perker, threw

himself into an arm-chair, his jolly red face shining again
with smiles and health.

"Well," said Wardle, "here are pretty goings on—a
pinch of your snuff, Perker, my boy—never were such
times, eh?"

"What do you mean?" enquired Mr. Pickwick.

"Mean!" replied Wardle, "why, I think the girls are
all running mad; that's no news, you'll say? Perhaps it's
not, but it's true for all that."

"You have not come up to London, of all places in the
world, to tell us *that*, my dear Sir, have you?" enquired
Perker.

"No, not altogether," replied Wardle; "though it was
the main cause of my coming. How's Arabella?"

"Very well," replied Mr. Pickwick, "and will be delighted to see you, I am sure."

"Black-eyed little jilt!" replied Wardle. "I had a
great idea of marrying her myself, one of these odd days
But I am glad of it too, very glad."

"How did the intelligence reach you?" asked Mr. Pick
wick.

"Oh, it came to my girls, of course," replied Wardle.
"Arabella wrote the day before yesterday to say she had
made a stolen match without her husband's father's consent, and so you had gone down to get it when his refusing
it couldn't prevent the match, and all the rest of it. I
though it a very good time to say something serious to my
girls, so I said what a dreadful thing it was that children
should marry without their parents' consent, and so forth;
but, bless your hearts, I couldn't make the least impression
upon them. They thought it such a much more dreadful
thing that there should have been a wedding without
bridesmaids, that I might as well have preached to Joe
himself."

Here the old gentleman stopped to laugh; and having
done so, to his heart's content, presently resumed.

"But this is not the best of it, it seems. This is only
half the love-making and plotting that have been going
forward. We have been walking on mines for the last six
months, and they're sprung at last."

"What do you mean!" exclaimed Mr. Pickwick, turning
pale; "no other secret marriage, I hope?"

"No, no," replied old Wardle; "not so bad as that—no."

"What then?" enquired Mr. Pickwick; "am I interested in it?"

"Shall I answer that question, Perker?" said Wardle.

"If you don't commit yourself by doing so, my dear
Sir."

"Well then, you are," said Wardle.

"How?" asked Mr. Pickwick anxiously. "In what
way?"

"Really," replied Wardle, "you're such a fiery sort of
young fellow that I am almost afraid to tell you; but,
however, if Perker will sit between us to prevent mischief,
I'll venture."

Having closed the room-door, and fortified himself with
another application to Perker's snuff-box, the old gentleman proceeded with his great disclosure in these words.

"The fact is, that my daughter Bella—Bella, that married young Trundle, you know."

"Yes, yes, we know," said Mr. Pickwick impatiently.

"Don't alarm me at the very beginning. My daughter
Bella, Emily having gone to bed with a headache after she
had read Arabella's letter to me, set herself down by my

side the other evening, and began to talk over this marriage affair. 'Well pa,' she says, 'what do you think of it?' 'Why, my dear,' I said, 'I suppose it's all very well; I hope it's for the best.' I answered in this way because I was sitting before the fire at the time, drinking my grog rather thoughtfully, and I knew my throwing in an undecided word now and then, would induce her to continue talking. Both my girls are pictures of their dear mother, and as I grow old I like to sit with only them by me; for their voices and looks carry me back to the happiest period of my life, and make me for the moment as young as I used to be then, though not quite so light-hearted. 'It's quite a marriage of affection, pa,' said Bella, after a short silence. 'Yes, my dear,' said I, 'but such marriages do not always turn out the happiest.'"

"I question that, mind," interposed Mr. Pickwick warmly.

"Very good," responded Wardle, "question anything you like when it's your turn to speak, but don't interrupt me."

"I beg your pardon," said Mr. Pickwick.

"Granted," replied Wardle. "'I am sorry to hear you express your opinion against marriages of affection, pa,' said Bella, colouring a little. 'I was wrong; I ought not to have said so, my dear, either,' said I, patting her cheek as kindly as a rough old fellow like me could pat it, 'for your mother's was one, and so was yours.' 'It's not that I meant, pa,' said Bella. 'The fact is, pa, I wanted to speak to you about Emily.'"

Mr. Pickwick started.

"What's the matter now?" enquired Wardle, stopping in his narrative.

"Nothing," replied Mr. Pickwick. "Pray go on."

"I never could spin out a story," said Wardle abruptly. "It must come out sooner or later, and it'll save us all a great deal of time if it comes at once. The long and the short of it is, then, that Bella at last mustered up courage to tell me that Emily was very unhappy; that she and your young friend Snodgrass had been in constant correspondence and communication ever since last Christmas; that she had very dutifully made up her mind to run away with him, in laudable imitation of her old friend and schoolfellow; but that having some compunctions of conscience on the subject, inasmuch as I had always been rather kindly disposed to both of them, they had thought it better in the first instance to pay me the compliment of asking whether I would have any objection to their being married in the usual matter-of-fact manner. There now, Mr. Pickwick, if you can make it convenient to reduce your eyes to their usual size again, and to let me hear what you think we ought to do, I shall feel rather obliged to you."

The testy manner in which the hearty old gentleman uttered this last sentence was not wholly unwarranted; for Mr. Pickwick's face had settled down into an expression of blank amazement and perplexity quite curious to behold.

"Snodgrass!—since last Christmas!" were the first broken words that issued from the lips of the confounded gentleman.

"Since last Christmas," replied Wardle; "that's plain enough, and very bad spectacles we must have worn, not to have discovered it before."

"I don't understand it," said Mr. Pickwick, ruminating; "I really cannot understand it."

"It's easy enough to understand," replied the choleric old gentleman. "If you had been a younger man, you would have been in the secret long ago; and besides," added Wardle after a moment's hesitation, "the truth is, that, knowing nothing of this matter, I have rather pressed Emily for four or five months past to receive favourably (if she could; I would never attempt to force a girl's inclinations) the addresses of a young gentleman down in our neighbourhood. I have no doubt that, girl-like, to enhance her own value and increase the ardour of Mr. Snodgrass, she has represented this matter in very glowing colours, and that they have both arrived at the conclusion that they are a terribly persecuted pair of unfortunates, and have no resource but clandestine matrimony or charcoal. Now the question is, what's to be done?"

"What have *you* done?" enquired Mr. Pickwick.

"I!"

"I mean what did you do when your married daughter told you this?"

"Oh, I made a fool of myself of course," rejoined Wardle.

"Just so," interposed Perker, who had accompanied this dialogue with sundry twitchings of his watch-chain, vindictive rubbings of his nose, and other symptoms of impatience. "That's very natural; but how?"

"I went into a great passion and frightened my mother into a fit," said Wardle.

"That was judicious," remarked Perker; "and what else, my dear Sir?"

"I fretted and fumed all next day, and raised a great disturbance," rejoined the old gentleman. "At last I got tired of rendering myself unpleasant and making everybody miserable; so I hired a carriage at Muggleton, and, putting my own horses in it, came up to town, under pretence of bringing Emily to see Arabella."

"Miss Wardle is with you, then?" said Mr. Pickwick.

"To be sure she is," replied Wardle. "She is at Osborne's hotel in the Adelphi at this moment, unless your enterprising friend has run away with her since I came out this morning."

"You are reconciled, then?" said Perker.

"Not a bit of it," answered Wardle; "she has been crying and moping ever since, except last night, between tea and supper, when she made a great parade of writing a letter, that I pretended to take no notice of."

"You want my advice in this matter, I suppose?" said Perker, looking from the musing face of Mr. Pickwick to the eager countenance of Wardle, and taking several consecutive pinches of his favourite stimulant.

"I suppose so," said Wardle, looking at Mr. Pickwick.

"Certainly," replied that gentleman.

"Well then," said Perker, rising and pushing his chair back, "my advice is, that you both walk away together, or ride away, or get away by some means or other, for I'm tired of you, and just talk this matter over between you. If you have not settled it by the next time I see you, I'll tell you what to do."

"This is satisfactory," said Wardle, hardly knowing whether to smile or be offended.

"Pooh, pooh, my dear Sir," returned Perker, "I know you both a great deal better than you know yourselves. You have settled it already, to all intents and purposes."

Thus expressing himself, the little gentleman poked his snuff-box, first into the chest of Mr. Pickwick, and then into the waistcoat of Mr. Wardle, upon which they all three laughed, but especially the two last-named gentlemen, who at once shook hands again, without any obvious or particular reason.

"You dine with me to-day," said Wardle to Perker, as he showed them out.

"Can't promise, my dear Sir, can't promise," replied Perker. "I'll look in, in the evening, at all events."

"I shall expect you at five," said Wardle. "Now, Joe;" and Joe having been at length awakened, the two friends departed in Mr. Wardle's carriage, which in common humanity had a dickey behind for the fat boy, who, if there had been a foot-board instead, would have rolled off and killed himself in his very first nap.

Driving to the George and Vulture, they found that Arabella and her maid had sent for a hackney-coach immediately on the receipt of a short note from Emily announcing her arrival in town, and had proceeded straight to the Adelphi. As Wardle had business to transact in the city, they sent the carriage and the fat boy to his hotel, with the information that he and Mr. Pickwick would return together to dinner at five o'clock.

Charged with this message, the fat boy returned, slumbering as peaceably in his dickey over the stones as if it had been a down bed on watch-springs. By some extraordinary miracle he awoke of his own accord, when the coach stopped, and giving himself a good shake to stir up his faculties, went up stairs to execute his commission.

Now, whether the shake had jumbled the fat boy's faculties together instead of arranging them in proper order, or had roused such a quantity of new ideas within him as to render him oblivious of ordinary forms and ceremonies, or (which is also possible) had proved unsuccessful in preventing his falling asleep as he ascended the stairs, it is an undoubted fact that he walked into the sitting room without previously knocking at the door, and so beheld a gentleman, with his arm clasping his young mistress's waist, sitting very lovingly by her side on a sofa, while Arabella and her pretty handmaid feigned to be absorbed in looking out of a window at the other end of the room. At sight of which phenomenon, the fat boy uttered an interjection, the ladies a scream, and the gentleman an oath, almost simultaneously.

"Wretched creature, what do you want here?" said the gentleman, who it is needless to say was Mr. Snodgrass.

To this the fat boy, considerably terrified, briefly responded, "Missis."

"What do you want me for?" enquired Emily, turning her head aside, "you stupid creature."

"Master and Mr. Pickwick is a going to dine here at five," replied the fat boy.

"Leave the room," said Mr. Snodgrass, glaring upon the bewildered youth.

"No, no, no," added Emily hastily. "Bella, dear, advise me."

Upon this, Emily and Mr. Snodgrass, and Arabella and Mary, crowded into a corner and conversed earnestly in whispers for some minutes, during which the fat boy dozed.

"Joe," said Arabella, at length, looking round with a most bewitching smile, "how do you do, Joe?"

"Joe," said Emily, "you're a very good boy; I won't forget you, Joe."

"Joe," said Mr. Snodgrass, advancing to the astonished youth, and seizing his hand, "I didn't know you before. There's five shillings for you, Joe."

"I'll owe you five, Joe," said Arabella, "for old acquaintance sake, you know," and another most captivating smile was bestowed upon the corpulent intruder.

The fat boy's perception being slow, he looked rather puzzled at first to account for this sudden prepossession in his favour, and stared about him in a very alarming manner. At length his broad face began to show symptoms of a grin of proportionately broad dimensions, and then thrusting half a crown into each of his pockets, and a hand and wrist after it, he burst into a horse laugh: being for the first and only time in his existence.

"He understands us, I see," said Arabella.

"He had better have something to eat immediately," remarked Emily.

The fat boy almost laughed again when he heard this suggestion. Mary, after a little more whispering, tripped forth from the group, and said,—

"I am going to dine with you to-day, Sir, if you have no objection."

"This way," said the fat boy, eagerly. "There is such a jolly meat pie."

With these words the fat boy led the way down stairs, his pretty companion captivating all the waiters and angering all the chambermaids as she followed him to the eating room.

There was the meat pie of which the youth had spoken so feelingly: and there were, moreover, a steak and a dish of potatoes, and a pot of porter.

"Sit down," said the fat boy. "Oh, my eye, how prime! I am so hungry."

Having apostrophised his eye in a species of rapture five or six times, the youth took the head of the little table, and Mary set herself at the bottom.

"Will you have some of this?" said the fat boy, plunging into the pie up to the very ferules of the knife and fork.

"A little, if you please," replied Mary.

The fat boy assisted Mary to a little, and himself to a great deal, and was just going to begin eating when he suddenly laid down his knife and fork, leant forward in his chair, and letting his hands, with the knife and fork in them, fall on his knees, said, very slowly,

"I say, how nice you do look!"

This was said in an admiring manner, and was, so far, gratifying; but still there was enough of the cannibal in the young gentleman's eyes to render the compliment a doubtful one.

"Dear me, Joseph," said Mary, affecting to blush, "what do you mean?"

The fat boy, gradually recovering his former position, replied with a heavy sigh, and remaining thoughtful for a few moments, drank a long draught of the porter. Having achieved this feat he sighed again, and applied himself assiduously to the pie.

"What a nice young lady Miss Emily is!" said Mary, after a long silence.

The fat boy had by this time finished the pie. He fixed his eyes on Mary, and replied—

"I knows a nicerer."

"Indeed!" said Mary.

"Yes, indeed!" replied the fat boy, with unwonted vivacity.

"What's her name?" enquired Mary.

"What's yours?"

"Mary."

"So's her's," said the fat boy. "You're her." The boy grinned to add point to the compliment, and put his eyes into something between a squint and a cast, which there is reason to believe he intended for an ogle.

"You mustn't talk to me in that way," said Mary; "you don't mean it."

"Don't I though?" replied the fat boy; "I say—"

"Well."

"Are you going to come here regular?"

"No," rejoined Mary, shaking her head, "I'm going away again to-night. Why?"

"Oh!" said the fat boy, in a tone of strong feeling, "how we should have enjoyed ourselves at meals if you had been!"

"I might come here sometimes, to see you," said Mary, plaiting the table cloth in assumed coyness, "if you would do me a favour."

The fat boy looked from the pie dish to the steak, as if he thought a favour must be in a manner connected with something to eat; and then took out one of the half-crowns and glanced at it nervously.

"Don't you understand me?" said Mary, looking slyly in his fat face.

Again he looked at the half-crown, and said faintly, "No."

"The ladies want you not to say anything to the old gentleman about the young gentleman having been up stairs; and I want you too."

"Is that all?" said the fat boy, evidently very much relieved as he pocketed the half-crown again. "Of course I ain't a going to."

"You see," said Mary, "Mr. Snodgrass is very fond of Miss Emily, and Miss Emily's very fond of him, and if you were to tell about it, the old gentleman would carry you all away miles into the country, where you'd see nobody."

"No, no, I won't tell," said the fat boy, stoutly.

"That's a dear," said Mary. "Now it's time I went up stairs, and got my lady ready for dinner."

"Don't go yet," urged the fat boy.

"I must," replied Mary. "Good bye, for the present."

The fat boy, with elephantine playfulness, stretched out his arms to ravish a kiss; but as it required no great agility to elude him, his fair enslaver had vanished before he closed them again; upon which the apathetic youth ate a pound or so of steak with a sentimental countenance, and fell fast asleep.

There was so much to say up stairs, and there were so many plans to concert for elopement and matrimony in the event of old Wardle continuing to be cruel, that it wanted only half an hour to dinner when Mr. Snodgrass took his final adieu. The ladies ran to Emily's bedroom to dress, and the lover, taking up his hat, walked out of the room. He had scarcely got outside the door, when he heard Wardle's voice talking loudly; and looking over the bannisters, beheld him, followed by some other gentlemen, coming straight upstairs. Knowing nothing of the house, Mr. Snodgrass in his confusion stepped hastily back into the room he had just quitted, and passing from thence into an inner apartment (Mr. Wardle's bedchamber), closed the door softly, just as the persons he had caught a glimpse of entered the sitting room. These were Mr. Wardle, and Mr. Pickwick; Mr. Nathaniel Winkle and Mr. Benjamin Allen, whom he had no difficulty in recognising by their voices.

"Very lucky I had the presence of mind to avoid them," thought Mr. Snodgrass with a smile, and walking on tiptoe

to another door near the bedside, "this opens into the same passage, and I can walk quietly and comfortably away."

There was only one obstacle to his walking quietly and comfortably away, which was, that the door was locked and the key gone.

"Let us have some of your best wine to-day, waiter," said old Wardle, rubbing his hands.

"You shall have some of the very best, Sir," replied the waiter.

"Let the ladies know we have come in."

"Yes, Sir."

Devoutly and ardently did Mr. Snodgrass wish that the ladies could know *he* had come in. He ventured once to whisper "Waiter!" through the keyhole, but the probability of the wrong waiter coming to his relief flashing upon his mind, together with a sense of the strong resemblance between his own situation and that in which another gentleman had been recently found in a neighbouring hotel (an account of whose misfortunes had appeared under the head of "Police" in that morning's paper), he sat himself down upon a portmanteau, and trembled violently.

"We won't wait a minute for Perker," said Wardle, looking at his watch; "he is always exact. He will be here in time if he means to come; and if he does not, it's of no use waiting. Ha! Arabella."

"My sister!" exclaimed Mr. Benjamin Allen, folding her in a most romantic embrace.

"Oh, Ben, dear, how you do smell of tobacco," said Arabella, rather overcome by this mark of affection.

"Do I?" said Mr. Benjamin Allen, "Do I, Bella? Well, perhaps I do."

Perhaps he did, having just left a pleasant little smoking party of twelve medical students in a small back parlour with a large fire.

"But I am delighted to see you," said Mr. Ben Allen. "Bless you, Bella."

"There," said Arabella, bending forward to kiss her brother; "don't take hold of me again, Ben dear, because you tumble me so."

At this point of the reconciliation, Mr. Ben Allen allowed his feelings and the cigars and porter to overcome him; and looked round upon the beholders with damp spectacles.

"Is nothing to be said to me?" cried Wardle, with open arms.

"A great deal," whispered Arabella, as she received the old gentleman's hearty caress and congratulation. "You are a hard-hearted, unfeeling, cruel monster!"

"You are a little rebel," replied Wardle, in the same tone; "and I am afraid I shall be obliged to forbid you the house. People like you, who get married in spite of everybody, ought not to be let loose on society. But come," added the old gentleman aloud, "Here's the dinner; you shall sit by me. Joe; why, damn the boy, he's awake!"

To the great distress of his master, the fat boy was indeed in a state of remarkable vigilance, his eyes being wide open, and looking as if they intended to remain so. There was an alacrity in his manner too which was equally unaccountable; every time his eyes met those of Emily or Arabella, he smirked and grinned; and once Wardle could have sworn he saw him wink.

This alteration in the fat boy's demeanour originated in his increased sense of his own importance, and the dignity he acquired from having been taken into the confidence of the young ladies; and the smirks and grins, and winks, were so many condescending assurances that they might depend upon his fidelity. As these tokens were rather calculated to awaken suspicion than allay it, and were somewhat embarrassing besides, they were occasionally answered by a frown or shake of the head from Arabella, which the fat boy considering as hints to be on his guard, expressed his perfect understanding of, by smirking, grinning, and winking, with redoubled assiduity.

"Joe," said Mr. Wardle after an unsuccessful search in all his pockets, "is my snuff-box on the sofa?"

"No, Sir," replied the fat boy.

"Oh, I recollect; I left it on my dressing table this morning," said Wardle. "Run into the next room and fetch it."

The fat boy went into the next room, and having been absent about a minute, returned with the snuff-box and the palest face that ever a fat boy wore.

"What's the matter with the boy!" exclaimed Wardle.

"Nothen's the matter with me," replied Joe, nervously.

"Have you been seeing any spirits?" enquired the old gentleman.

"Or taking any?" added Ben Allen.

"I think you're right," whispered Wardle across the table. "He is intoxicated, I'm sure."

Ben Allen replied that he thought he was; and as that gentleman had seen a vast deal of the disease in question, Wardle was confirmed in an impression which had been hovering about his mind for half an hour, and at once arrived at the conclusion that the fat boy was very drunk.

"Just keep your eye upon him for a few minutes," murmured Wardle. "We shall soon find out whether he is or not."

The unfortunate youth had only interchanged a dozen words with Mr. Snodgrass, that gentleman having implored him to make a private appeal to some friend to release him, and then pushed him out with the snuff-box, lest his prolonged absence should lead to a discovery. He ruminated a little with a most disturbed expression of face, and left the room in search of Mary.

But Mary had gone home after dressing her mistress, and the fat boy came back again, more disturbed than before.

Wardle and Mr. Ben Allen exchanged glances.

"Joe," said Wardle.

"Yes, Sir."

"What did you go away for?"

The fat boy looked hopelessly in the face of everybody at table, and stammered out that he didn't know.

"Oh," said Wardle, "you don't know, eh? Take this cheese to Mr. Pickwick."

Now, Mr. Pickwick being in the very best health and spirits, had been making himself perfectly delightful all dinner-time, and was at this moment engaged in an energetic conversation with Emily and Mr. Winkle; bowing his head courteously in the emphasis of his discourse, gently waving his left hand to lend force to his observations, and all glowing with placid smiles. He took a piece of cheese from the plate, and was upon the point of turning round to renew the conversation, when the fat boy, stooping so as to bring his head on a level with that of Mr. Pickwick, pointed with his thumb over his shoulder and made the most horrible and hideous face that ever was seen out of a pantomime.

"Dear me!" said Mr. Pickwick, starting, "what a very

—eh?" He stopped, for the fat boy had drawn himself up, and was, or pretended to be, fast asleep.

"What's the matter?" enquired Wardle.

"This is such an extremely singular lad of yours," replied Mr. Pickwick, looking uneasily at the boy. "It seems an odd thing to say, but, upon my word, I am afraid that at times he is a little deranged."

"Oh! Mr. Pickwick, pray don't say so," cried Emily and Arabella, both at once.

"I am not certain, of course," said Mr. Pickwick, amidst profound silence,-and looks of general dismay; "but his manner to me this moment was really very alarming. Oh!" ejaculated Mr. Pickwick, suddenly jumping up with a short scream. "I beg your pardon, ladies, but at that moment he ran some sharp instrument into my leg. Really he is not safe."

"He's drunk," roared old Wardle, passionately. "**Ring the bell, call the waiters! he's drunk.**"

"I ain't," said the fat boy, falling on his knees as his master seized him by the collar. "I ain't drunk."

"Then you're mad—that's worse. Call the waiters," said the old gentleman.

"I ain't mad; I'm sensible," rejoined the fat boy, beginning to cry.

"Then, what the devil did you run sharp instruments into Mr. Pickwick's legs for?" enquired Wardle, angrily.

"He wouldn't look at me," replied the boy. "I wanted to speak to him."

"What did you want to say?" asked half a dozen voices at once.

The fat boy gasped, looked at the bedroom door, gasped again, and wiped two tears away with the knuckle of each of his forefingers.

"What did you want to say?" demanded Wardle, shaking him.

"Stop," said Mr. Pickwick; "allow me. What did you wish to communicate to me, my poor boy?"

"I want to whisper to you," replied the fat boy.

"You want to bite his ear off, I suppose," said Wardle. "Don't come near him, he's vicious; ring the bell, and let him be taken down stairs."

Just as Mr. Winkle caught the bell-rope in his hand, it was arrested by a general expression of astonishment; the captive lover, his face burning with confusion, suddenly walked in from the bedroom, and made a comprehensive bow to the company.

"Hallo!" cried Wardle, releasing the fat boy's collar, and staggering back, "What's this!"

"I have been concealed in the next room, Sir, since you returned," explained Mr. Snodgrass.

"Emily, my girl," said Wardle, reproachfully, "I detest meanness and deceit; this is unjustifiable and indelicate in the highest degree. I don't deserve this, at your hands Emily, indeed."

"Dear papa," said Emily, "Arabella knows—everybody here knows; Joe knows—that I was no party to this concealment. Augustus, for Heaven's sake, explain it."

Mr. Snodgrass, who had only waited for a hearing, at once recounted how he had been placed in his then distressing predicament; how the fear of giving rise to domestic dissensions had alone prompted him to avoid Mr. Wardle on his entrance; and how he merely meant to depart by another door, but, finding it locked, had been compelled to stay against his will. It was a painful situation to be placed in; but he now regretted it the less, inasmuch as it afforded him an opportunity of acknowledging before their mutual friends that he loved Mr. Wardle's daughter deeply and sincerely, that he was proud to avow that the feeling was mutual, and that if thousands of miles were placed between them, or oceans rolled their waters, he could never for an instant forget those happy days when first—et cetera, et cetera.

Having delivered himself to this effect, Mr. Snodgrass bowed again, looked into the crown of his hat, and stepped towards the door.

"Stop!" shouted Wardle. "Why, in the name of all that's——"

"Inflammable," mildly suggested Mr. Pickwick, who thought something worse was coming.

"Well—that's inflammable," said Wardle, adopting the substitute; "couldn't you say all this to me in the first instance?"

"Or confide in me?" added Mr. Pickwick.

"Dear, dear," said Arabella, taking up the defence, "what is the use of asking all that now, especially when you know you had set your covetous old heart on a richer son-in-law, and are so wild and fierce besides, that everybody is afraid of you, except me. Shake hands with him, and order him some dinner, for goodness gracious sake, for he looks half-starved; and pray have your wine up at once, for you'll not be tolerable until you have taken two bottles at least."

The worthy old gentleman pulled Arabella's ear, kissed her without the smallest scruple, kissed his daughter also with great affection, and shook Mr. Snodgrass warmly by the hand.

"She is right upon one point at all events," said the old gentleman, cheerfully. "Ring for the wine."

The wine came, and Perker came up stairs at the same moment. Mr. Snodgrass had dinner at a side table, and when he had dispatched it drew his chair next Emily, without the smallest opposition on the old gentleman's part.

The evening was excellent. Little Mr. Perker came out wonderfully, told various comic stories, and sang a serious song, which was almost as funny as the anecdotes. Arabella was very charming, Mr. Wardle very jovial, Mr. Pickwick very harmonious, Mr. Ben Allen very uproarious, the lovers very silent, Mr. Winkle very talkative, and all of them very happy.

CHAPTER LIV.

MR. SOLOMON PELL, ASSISTED BY A SELECT COMMIT-
TEE OF COACHMEN, ARRANGES THE AFFAIRS OF
THE ELDER MR. WELLER.

"Samivel," said Mr. Weller, accosting his son on the morning after the funeral, "I've found it, Sammy. I thought it vos there."

"Thought wot wos vere?" enquired Sam.

"Your mother-in-law's vill, Sammy," replied Mr. Weller. "In wirtue o' vich, them arrangements is to be made as I told you on last night respectin' the funs."

"Wot, didn't she tell you vere it wos?" enquired Sam.

"Not a bit on it, Sammy," replied Mr. Weller. "Ve vos a adjestin' our little differences, and I vos a cheerin'

her spirits and bearin' her up, so that I forgot to ask anythin' about it. I don't know as I should ha' done it indeed, if I had remembered it," added Mr. Weller, "for it's a rum sort o' thing, Sammy, to go a hankerin' arter anybody's property, ven you're assistin' 'em in illness. It's like helping an outside passenger up ven he's been pitched off a coach, and puttin' your hand in his pocket, vile you ask him vith a sigh how he finds his-self, Sammy."

With this figurative illustration of his meaning, Mr. Weller unclasped his pocket-book, and drew forth a dirty sheet of letter paper, on which were inscribed various characters crowded together in remarkable confusion.

"This here is the dockyment, Sammy," said Mr. Weller. "I found it in the little black teapot on the top shelf o' the bar closet. She used to keep bank notes there 'afore she vos married, Samivel. I've seen her take the lid off to pay a bill, many and many a time. Poor creetur, she might ha' filled all the teapots in the house vith vills, and not have inconwenienced herself neither, for she took wery little of anythin' in that vay lately, 'cept on the Temperance nights, ven they just laid a foundation o' tea to put the spirits a-top on."

"What does it say?" enquired Sam.

"Jist vot I told you, my boy," rejoined his parent. "Two hundred pounds vurth o' reduced counsels to my son-in-law, Samivel, and all the rest o' my property of ev'ry kind and description votsoever to my husband, Mr. Tony Veller, who I appint as my sole eggzekiter."

"That's all, is it?" said Sam.

"That's all," replied Mr. Weller. "And I s'pose as it's all right and satisfactory to you and me, as is the only parties interested, ve may as vell put this bit o' paper into the fire."

"Wot are you a-doin' on, you lunatic?" said Sam, snatching the paper away, as his parent, in all innocence, stirred the fire preparatory to suiting the action to the word. "You're a nice eggzekiter, you are."

"Vy not?" enquired Mr. Weller, looking sternly round with the poker in his hand.

"Vy not!" exclaimed Sam,—"'cos it must be proved, and probated, and sworn to, and all manner o' formalities."

"You don't mean that?" said Mr. Weller, laying down the poker.

Sam buttoned the will carefully in a side pocket, intimating by a look meanwhile, that he did mean it, and very seriously too.

"Then I'll tell you wot it is," said Mr. Weller, after a short meditation, "this is a case for that 'ere confidential pal o' the Chancellorship's. Pell must look into this, Sammy. He's the man for a difficult question at law. Ve'll have this here brought afore the Solvent court directly, Samivel."

"I never did see such a addle-headed old creetur!" exclaimed Sam, irritably, "Old Baileys, and Solvent Courts, and alleybis, and ev'ry species o' gammon alvays a-runnin' through his brain. You'd better get your out o' door clothes on, and come to town about this bisness, than stand a preachin' there about wot you don't understand nothin' of."

"Wery good, Sammy," replied Mr. Weller. "I'm quite agreeable to anythin' as vill hexpedite business, Sammy. But mind this here, my boy, nobody but Pell—nobody but Pell as a legal adviser."

"I don't want anybody else," replied Sam.—"Now, are you a-comin'?"

"Vait a minit, Sammy," replied Mr. Weller, who, having tied his shawl with the aid of a small glass that hung in the window, was now, by dint of the most wonderful exertions, struggling into his upper garments. "Vait a minit, Sammy; ven you grow as old as your father, you won't get into your veskit quite as easy as you do now, my boy."

"If I couldn't get into it easier than that, I'm blessed if I'd vear vun at all," rejoined his son.

"You think so now," said Mr. Weller, with the gravity of age, "but you'll find that as you get vider you'll get viser. Vidth and visdom, Sammy, alvays grows together."

As Mr. Weller delivered this infallible maxim—the result of many years' personal experience and observation—he contrived, by a dexterous twist of his body, to get the bottom button of his coat to perform its office. Having paused a few seconds to recover breath, he brushed his hat with his elbow, and declared himself ready.

"As four heads is better than two, Sammy," said Mr. Weller, as they drove along the London road in the chaise cart, "and as all this here property is a wery great temptation to a legal gen'lm'n, ve'll take a couple o' friends o' mine vith us, as 'll be wery soon down upon him if he comes anythin' irreg'lar; two o' them as saw you to the Fleet that day. They're the wery best judges," added Mr. Weller in a half whisper, "the wery best judges of a horse you ever know'd."

"And of a lawyer too?" enquired Sam.

"The man as can form a ackerate judgment of a animal, can form a ackerate judgment of anythin'," replied his father; so dogmatically, that Sam did not attempt to controvert the position.

In pursuance of this notable resolution, the services of the mottled-faced gentleman and of two other very fat coachmen—selected by Mr. Weller, probably, with a view to their widtth and consequent wisdom—were put into requisition; and this assistance having been secured, the party proceeded to the public-house in Portugal-street, whence a messenger was dispatched to the Insolvent Court over the way, requiring Mr. Solomon Pell's immediate attendance.

The messenger fortunately found Mr. Solomon Pell in court, regaling himself, business being rather slack, with a cold collation of an Abernethy biscuit and a saveloy. The message was no sooner whispered in his ear than he thrust them in his pocket among various professional documents, and hurried over the way with such alacrity that he reached the parlour before the messenger had even emancipated himself from the court.

"Gentlemen," said Mr. Pell, touching his hat, "my service to you all. I don't say it to flatter you, gentlemen, but there are not five other men in the world that I'd have come out of that court for to-day."

"So busy, eh?" said Sam.

"Busy!" replied Pell; "I'm completely sewn up, as my friend the late Lord Chancellor many a time used to say to me, gentlemen, when he came out from hearing appeals in the House of Lords. Poor fellow! he was very susceptible to fatigue; he used to feel those appeals uncommonly. I actually thought more than once that he'd have sunk under them, I did indeed."

Here Mr. Pell shook his head, and paused; upon which the elder Mr. Weller, nudging his neighbour, as begging him to mark the attorney's high connections, asked whether the duties in question produced any permanent ill effects on the constitution of his noble friend.

"I don't think he ever quite recovered them," replied Pell; "in fact I'm sure he never did. 'Pell,' he used to say to me many a time, 'how the blazes you can stand the head-work you do, is a mystery to me.'—'Well,' I used to answer, '*I* hardly know how I do it, upon my life.'—'Pell,' he'd add, sighing, and looking at me with a little envy—friendly envy, you know, gentlemen, mere friendly envy; I never minded it—'Pell, you're a wonder; a wonder.' Ah! you'd have liked him very much if you had known him, gentlemen. Bring me three penn'orth of rum, my dear."

Addressing this latter remark to the waitress in a tone of subdued grief, Mr. Pell sighed, looked at his shoes, and the ceiling; and, the rum having by that time arrived, drank it up.

"However," said Pell, drawing a chair up to the table, "a professional man has no right to think of his private friendships when his legal assistance is wanted. By the bye, gentlemen, since I saw you here before, we have had to weep over a very melancholy occurrence."

Mr. Pell drew out a pocket-handkerchief when he came to the word weep, but he made no further use of it than to wipe away a slight tinge of rum which hung upon his upper lip.

"I saw it in the Advertiser, Mr. Weller," continued Pell. "Bless my soul, not more than fifty-two! dear me —only think."

These indications of a musing spirit were addressed to the mottled-faced man, whose eyes Mr. Pell had accidentally caught; upon which the mottled-faced man, whose apprehension of matters in general was of a foggy nature, moved uneasily in his seat, and opined that indeed, so far as that went, there was no saying how things *was* brought about; which observation involving one of those subtle propositions which it is difficult to encounter in argument, was controverted by nobody.

"I have heard it remarked that she was a very fine woman, Mr. Weller," said Pell in a sympathising manner.

"Yes, Sir, she wos," replied the elder Mr. Weller, not much relishing this mode of discussing the subject, and yet thinking that the attorney, from his long intimacy with the late Lord Chancellor, must know best on all matters of polite breeding. "She wos a wery fine 'ooman, Sir, ven I first know'd her. She wos a widder, Sir, at that time."

"Now, it's curious," said Pell, looking round with a sorrowful smile; "Mrs. Pell was a widow."

"That's very extraordinary," said the mottled-faced man.

"Well, it is a curious coincidence," said Pell.

"Not at all," gruffly remarked the elder Mr. Weller. "More widders is married than single vimin."

"Very good, very good," said Pell, "you're quite right, Mr. Weller. Mrs. Pell was a very elegant and accomplished woman; her manners were the theme of universal admiration in our neighbourhood. I was proud to see that woman dance; there was something so firm and dignified and yet natural, in her motion. Her cutting, gentlemen, was simplicity itself.—Ah! well, well! Excuse my asking the question, Mr. Samuel," continued the attorney in a lower voice, "was your mother-in-law tall?"

"Not wery," replied Sam.

"Mrs. Pell was a tall figure," said Pell, "a splendid woman, with a noble shape, and a nose, gentlemen, formed to command and be majestic. She was very much attached to me—very much—highly connected, too; her mother's brother, gentlemen, failed for eight hundred pound as a Law Stationer."

"Vell," said Mr. Weller, who had grown rather restless during this discussion, "vith regard to bis'ness."

The word was music to Pell's ears. He had been revolving in his mind whether any business was to be transacted, or whether he had been merely invited to partake of a glass of brandy and water, or a bowl of punch, or any similar professional compliment, and now the doubt was set at rest without his appearing at all eager for its solution. His eyes glistened as he laid his hat on the table, and said—

"What is the business upon which—um? Either of these gentlemen wish to go through the court? We require an arrest, a friendly arrest will do, you know; we are all friends here, I suppose?"

"Give me the dockyment, Sammy," said Mr. Weller, taking the will from his son, who appeared to enjoy the interview amazingly. "Wot we rek-vire, Sir, is a probe o' this here."

"Probate, my dear Sir, probate," said Pell.

"Vell, Sir," replied Mr. Weller sharply, "probe and probe it, is wery much the same; if you don't understand wot I mean, Sir, I dessay I can find them as does."

"No offence I hope, Mr. Weller," said Pell, meekly. "You are the executor I see," he added, casting his eyes over the paper.

"I am, Sir," replied Mr. Weller.

"These other gentlemen, I presume, are legatees, are they," enquired Pell with a congratulatory smile.

"Sammy is a leg-at-ease," replied Mr. Weller; "these other gen'l'men is friends o' mine, just come to see fair;—a kind of umpires."

"Oh!" said Pell, "very good. I have no objections, I'm sure. I shall want a matter of five pound of you before I begin, ha! ha! ha!"

It being decided by the committee that the five pounds might be advanced, Mr. Weller produced that sum, after which a long consultation, about nothing particular, took place, in the course whereof Mr. Pell demonstrated, to the perfect satisfaction of the gentlemen who saw fair, that unless the management of the business had been entrusted to him, it must all have gone wrong, for reasons not clearly made out, but no doubt sufficient. This important point being dispatched, Mr. Pell refreshed himself with three chops, and liquids both malt and spirituous, at the expense of the estate, and then they all went away to Doctors' Commons.

The next day there was another visit to Doctors' Commons, and a great to-do with an attesting ostler, who, being inebriated, declined swearing anything but profane oaths, to the great scandal of a proctor and surrogate. Next week there were more visits to Doctors' Commons, and a visit to the Legacy Duty Office besides, and treaties entered into for the disposal of the lease and business, and ratifications of the same, and inventories to be made out, and lunches to be taken, and dinners to be eaten, and so many profitable things to be done, and such a mass of papers accumulated, that Mr. Solomon Pell and the boy, and the blue bag to boot, all got so stout that scarcely anybody would have known them for the same man, boy, and bag, that had loitered about Portugal Street a few days before.

At length all these weighty matters being arranged, a day was fixed for selling out and transferring the stock, and of waiting with that view upon Wilkins Flasher, Esq., stock-broker, of somewhere near the Bank, who had been recommended by Mr. Solomon Pell for the purpose.

It was a kind of festive occasion, and the parties were attired accordingly. Mr. Weller's tops were newly cleaned, and his dress was arranged with peculiar care: the mottled-faced gentleman wore at his button hole a full sized dahlia with several leaves, and the coats of his two friends were adorned with nosegays of laurel and other evergreens. All three were habited in strict holiday costume; that is to say, they were wrapped up to the chins, and wore as many clothes as possible, which is, and has been, a stage-coachman's idea of full dress ever since stage-coaches were invented.

Mr. Pell was waiting at the usual place of meeting at the appointed time; and even he wore a pair of gloves and a clean shirt, the latter much frayed at the collar and wristbands by frequent washings.

"A quarter to two," said Pell, looking at the parlour clock. "If we are with Mr. Flasher at a quarter past, we shall just hit the best time."

"What should you say to a drop o' beer, gen'l'men?" suggested the mottled-faced man.

"And a little bit o' cold beef," said the second coachman.

"Or a oyster," added the third, who was a hoarse gentleman, supported by very round legs.

"Hear, hear!" said Pell; "to congratulate Mr. Weller, on his coming into possession of his property: eh? ha! ha!"

"I'm quite agreeable, gen'l'men," answered Mr. Weller. "Sammy, pull the bell."

Sam complied; and the porter, cold beef, and oysters bieng promptly produced, the lunch was done ample justice to. Where everybody took so active a part, it is almost invidious to make a distinction; but if one individual evinced greater powers than another, it was the coachman with the hoarse voice, who took an imperial pint of vinegar with his oysters, without betraying the least emotion.

"Mr. Pell, Sir," said the elder Mr. Weller, stirring a glass of brandy and water, of which one was placed before every gentleman when the oyster shells were removed; "Mr. Pell, Sir, it wos my intention to have proposed the funs on this occasion, but Samivel has vispered to me—"

Here Mr. Samuel Weller, who had silently ate his oysters with tranquil smiles, cried "Hear!" in a very loud voice.

"—Has vispered to me," resumed his father, "that it vould be better to de-wote the liquor to vishin' you success and prosperity; and thankin' you for the manner in which you've brought this here business through. Here's your health, Sir."

"Hold hard there," interposed the mottled-faced gentleman, with sudden energy, "your eyes on me, gen'l'men."

Saying this, the mottled-faced gentleman rose, as did the other gentlemen. The mottled-faced gentleman reviewed the company, and slowly raised his hand, upon which every man (including he of the mottled countenance) drew a long breath, and lifted his tumbler to his lips. In one instant the mottled-faced gentleman depressed his hand again, and every glass was set down empty. It is impossible to describe the thrilling effect produced by this striking ceremony; at once dignified, solemn, and impressive, it combined every element of grandeur.

"Well, gentlemen," said Mr. Pell, "all I can say is, that such marks of confidence must be very gratifying to a professional man. I don't wish to say anything that might appear egotistical, gentlemen, but I'm very glad, for your own sakes, that you came to me: that's all. If you had gone to any low member of the profession, it's my firm conviction, and I assure you of it as a fact, that you would have found yourselves in Queer Street before this. I could have wished my noble friend had been alive to have seen my management of this case; I don't say it out of pride, but I think—however, gentlemen, I won't trouble you with that. I'm generally to be found here, gentlemen, but if I'm not here, or over the way, that's my address. You'll find my terms very cheap and reasonable, and no man attends more to his clients than I do, and I hope I know a little of my profession besides. If you have any opportunity of recommending me to any of your friends, gentlemen, I shall be very much obliged to you, and so will they too, when they come to know me. *Your* healths, gentlemen."

With this expression of his feelings, Mr. Solomon Pell laid three small written cards before Mr. Weller's friends, and, looking at the clock again, feared it was time to be walking. Upon this hint Mr. Weller settled the bill, and, issuing forth, the executor, legatee, attorney, and umpires, directed their steps towards the city.

The office of Wilkins Flasher, Esquire, of the Stock Exchange, was in a first floor up a court behind the Bank of England; the house of Wilkins Flasher, Esquire, was at Brixton, Surrey; the horse and stanhope of Wilkins Flasher, Esquire, were at an adjacent livery stable; the groom of Wilkins Flasher, Esquire, was on his way to the West End to deliver some game; the clerk of Wilkins Flasher, Esquire, had gone to his dinner; and so Wilkins Flasher, Esquire, himself, cried, "Come in," when Mr. Pell and his companions knocked at the counting-house door.

"Good morning, Sir," said Pell, bowing obsequiously. "We want to make a little transfer, if you please."

"Oh, just come in, will you?" said Mr. Flasher. "Sit down a minute; I'll attend to you directly."

"Thank you, Sir," said Pell, "there's no hurry. Take a chair, Mr. Weller."

Mr. Weller took a chair, and Sam took a box, and the umpires took what they could get, and looked at the almanack and one or two papers which were wafered against the wall, with as much open-eyed reverence as if they had been the finest efforts of the old masters.

"Well, I'll bet you half a dozen of claret on it; come," said Wilkins Flasher, Esquire, resuming the conversation to which Mr. Pell's entrance had caused a momentary interruption.

This was addressed to a very smart young gentleman who wore his hat on his right whisker, and was lounging over the desk killing flies with a ruler. Wilkins Flasher, Esquire, was balancing himself on two legs of an office stool, spearing a wafer-box with a penknife, which he dropped every now and then with great dexterity into the very centre of a small red wafer that was stuck outside. Both gentlemen had very open waistcoats and very rolling collars, and very small boots and very big rings, and very little watches and very large guard chains, and symmetrical inexpressibles and scented pocket handkerchiefs.

"I never bet half a dozen," said the other gentleman. "I'll take a dozen."

"Done, Simmery, done!" said Wilkins Flasher, Esquire.

"P. P., mind," observed the other.

"Of course," replied Wilkins Flasher, Esquire; and Wilkins Flasher, Esquire, entered it in a little book with a gold pencil-case, and the other gentleman entered it also, in another little book with another gold pencil-case.

"I see there's a notice up this morning about Boffer," observed Mr. Simmery. "Poor devil, he's expelled the house."

"I'll bet you ten guineas to five he cuts his throat," said Wilkins Flasher, Esquire.

"Done," replied Mr. Simmery.

"Stop! I bar," said Wilkins Flasher, Esquire, thoughtfully. "Perhaps he may hang himself."

"Very good," rejoined Mr. Simmery, pulling out the gold pencil-case again. "I've no objection to take you that way. Say—makes away with himself."

"Kills himself, in fact," said Wilkins Flasher, Esquire.

"Just so," replied Mr. Simmery, putting it down. "'Flasher—ten guineas to five, Boffer kills himself.' Within what time shall we say?"

"A fortnight?" suggested Wilkins Flasher, Esquire.

"Con-found it, no;" rejoined Mr. Simmery, stopping for an instant to smash a fly with the ruler. "Say a week."

"Split the difference," said Wilkins Flasher, Esquire. "Make it ten days."

"Well; ten days," rejoined Mr. Simmery.

So, it was entered down in the little books that Boffer was to kill himself within ten days, or Wilkins Flasher, Esquire, was to hand over to Frank Simmery, Esquire, the sum of ten guineas; and that if Boffer did kill himself within that time, Frank Simmery, Esquire, would pay to Wilkins Flasher, Esquire, five guineas, instead.

"I'm very sorry he has failed," said Wilkins Flasher, Esquire. "Capital dinners he gave."

"Fine port he had too," remarked Mr. Simmery. "We are going to send our butler to the sale to-morrow, to pick up some of that sixty-four."

"The devil you are!" said Wilkins Flasher, Esquire. "My man's going too. Five guineas my man outbids your man."

"Done."

Another entry was made in the little books, with the gold pencil-cases; and Mr. Simmery having by this time killed all the flies and taken all the bets, strolled away to the Stock Exchange to see what was going forward.

Wilkins Flasher, Esquire, now condescended to receive Mr. Solomon Pell's instructions; and having filled up some printed forms, requested the party to follow him to the Bank, which they did: Mr. Weller and his three friends staring at all they beheld in unbounded astonishment, and Sam encountering every thing with a coolness which nothing could disturb.

Crossing a court-yard which was all noise and bustle; and passing a couple of porters who seemed dressed to match the red fire-engine which was wheeled away into a corner, they passed into an office where their business was to be transacted, where Pell and Mr. Flasher left them standing for a few moments, while they went up stairs into the Will Office.

"Wot place is this here?" whispered the mottled-faced gentleman to the elder Mr. Weller.

"Counsel's Office," replied the executor in a whisper.

"Wot are them gen'l'men a settin' behind the counters?" asked the hoarse coachman.

"Reduced counsels, I s'pose," replied Mr. Weller. "Ain't they the reduced counsels, Samivel?"

"Wy, you don't suppose the reduced counsels is alive, do you?" enquired Sam, with some disdain.

"How should I know?" retorted Mr. Weller; "I thought they looked very like it. Wot are they, then?"

"Clerks," replied Sam.

"Wot are they all a eatin' ham sangwidges for?" enquired his father.

"'Cos it's in their dooty, I suppose," replied Sam, "it's

a part o' the system; they're alvays a doin' it here, all day long!"

Mr. Weller and his friends had scarcely had a moment to reflect upon this singular regulation as connected with the monetary system of the country, when they were rejoined by Pell and Wilkins Flasher, Esquire, who led them to a part of the counter above which was a round black board with a large "W" on it.

"Wot's that for, Sir?" enquired Mr. Weller, directing Pell's attention to the target in question.

"The first letter of the name of the deceased," replied Pell.

"I say," said Mr. Weller, turning round to the umpires. "There's somethin' wrong here. We's our letter—this won't do."

The referees at once gave it as their decided opinion that the business could not be legally proceeded with, under the letter W, and in all probability it would have stood over for one day at least, had it not been for the prompt though at first sight undutiful behaviour of Sam, who seizing his father by the skirt of the coat, dragged him to the counter, and pinned him there until he had affixed his signature to a couple of instruments, which from Mr. Weller's habit of printing, was a work of so much labour and time that the officiating clerk peeled and cut three Ripstone pippins while it was performing.

As the elder Mr. Weller insisted on selling out his portion forthwith, they proceeded from the Bank to the gate of the Stock Exchange, to which Wilkins Flasher, Esq., after a short absence, returned with a cheque on Smith, Payne, and Smith, for five hundred and thirty pounds, that being the sum of money to which Mr. Weller at the market price of the day, was entitled, in consideration of the balance of the second Mrs. Weller's funded savings. Sam's two hundred pounds stood transferred to his name, and Wilkins Flasher, Esquire, having been paid his commission, dropped the money carelessly into his coat pocket, and lounged back to his office.

Mr. Weller was at first obstinately determined upon cashing the cheque in nothing but sovereigns; but on its being represented by the umpires that by so doing he must incur the expense of a small sack to carry them home in, he consented to receive the amount in five-pound notes.

"My son," said Mr. Weller as they came out of the banking-house, "my son and me has a wery partickler engagement this arternoon, and I should like to have this here bis'ness settled out of hand, so let's jest go straight avay someveres, vere ve can hordit the accounts."

A quiet room was soon found, and the accounts were produced and audited. Mr. Pell's bill was taxed by Sam, and some charges were disallowed by the umpires; but, notwithstanding Mr. Pell's declaration, accompanied with many solemn asseverations that they were really too hard upon him, it was by very many degrees the best professional job he had ever had, and one on which he boarded, lodged, and washed, for six months afterwards.

The umpires having partaken of a dram, shook hands and departed, as they had to drive out of town that night. Mr. Solomon Pell, finding that nothing more was going forward either in the eating or drinking way, took a most friendly leave; and Sam and his father were left alone.

"There," said Mr. Weller, thrusting his pocket-book in his side pocket, "vith the bills for the lease and that, there's eleven hundred and eighty pound here. Now Samivel, my boy, turn the horses' heads to the George and Wulter."

CHAPTER LV.

AN IMPORTANT CONFERENCE TAKES PLACE BETWEEN MR. PICKWICK AND SAMUEL WELLER, AT WHICH HIS PARENT ASSISTS.—AN OLD GENTLEMAN IN A SNUFF-COLOURED SUIT ARRIVES UNEXPECTEDLY.

MR. PICKWICK was sitting alone, musing over many things, and thinking, among other considerations, how he could best provide for the young couple whose present unsettled condition was matter of constant regret and anxiety to him, when Mary stepped lightly into the room, and, advancing to the table, said rather hastily—

"O, if you please Sir, Samuel is down stairs, and he says may his father see you?"

"Surely," replied Mr. Pickwick.

"Thank you, Sir," said Mary, tripping towards the door again.

"Sam has not been here long, has he?" enquired Mr. Pickwick.

"Oh no, Sir," replied Mary eagerly. "He has only just come home. He is not going to ask you for any more leave, Sir, he says."

Mary might have been conscious that she had communicated this last intelligence with more warmth than seemed actually necessary, or she might have observed the good-humoured smile with which Mr. Pickwick regarded her when she had finished speaking. She certainly held down her head, and examined the corner of a very smart little apron with more closeness than there appeared any absolute occasion for.

"Tell them they can come up at once, by all means," said Mr. Pickwick.

Mary, apparently much relieved, hurried away with her message.

Mr. Pickwick took two or three turns up and down the room; and, rubbing his chin with his left hand as he did so, appeared lost in thought.

"Well, well," said Mr. Pickwick at length, in a kind but somewhat melancholy tone, "it is the best way in which I could reward him for his attachment and fidelity; let it be so, in Heaven's name. It is the fate of a lonely old man, that those about him should form new and different attachments and leave him. I have no right to expect that it should be otherwise with me. No, no," added Mr. Pickwick more cheerfully, "it would be selfish and ungrateful. I ought to be happy to have an opportunity of providing for him so well. I am—of course I am."

Mr. Pickwick had been so absorbed in these reflections, that a knock at the door was three or four times repeated before he heard it. Hastily seating himself, and calling up his accustomed pleasant looks, he gave the required permission, and Sam Weller entered, followed by his father.

"Glad to see you back again, Sam," said Mr. Pickwick. "How do you do, Mr. Weller?"

"Wery hearty, thankee Sir," replied the widower; "hope I see *you* well, Sir."

"Quite, I thank you," replied Mr. Pickwick.

"I wanted to have a little bit o' conwersation with you, Sir," said Mr. Weller, "if you could spare me five minits or so, Sir."

"Certainly," replied Mr. Pickwick. "Sam, give your father a chair."

"Thankee, Samivel, I've got a cheer here," said Mr. Weller, bringing one forward as he spoke; "uncommon fine day it's been, Sir," added the old gentleman, laying his hat on the floor as he set himself down.

"Remarkably so indeed," replied Mr. Pickwick. "Very seasonable."

"Seasonablest veather I ever see, Sir," rejoined Mr. Weller. Here the old gentleman was seized with a violent fit of coughing, which being terminated, he nodded his head, and winked, and made several supplicatory and threatening gestures to his son, all of which Sam Weller steadily abstained from seeing.

Mr. Pickwick, perceiving that there was some embarrassment on the old gentleman's part, affected to be engaged in cutting the leaves of a book that lay beside him; and waited patiently until Mr. Weller should arrive at the object of his visit.

"I never see sich a aggerawatin' boy as you are, Samivel," said Mr. Weller, looking indignantly at his son; "never in all my born days."

"What is he doing, Mr. Weller?" enquired Mr. Pickwick.

"He von't begin, Sir," rejoined Mr. Weller; "he knows I ain't ekal to ex-pressin' myself ven there's anythin' partickler to be done, and yet he'll stand and see me a settin' here takin' up your walable time, and makin' a regl'ar spectacle o' myself, rayther than help me out vith a syllable. It ain't fillal conduct, Samivel," said Mr. Weller, wiping his forehead; "wery far from it."

"You said you'd speak," replied Sam; "how should I know you wos done up at the wery beginnin'?"

"You might ha' seen I warn't able to start," rejoined his father. "I'm on the wrong side of the road, and backin' into the palins and all manner of unpleasantness, and yet you von't put out a hand to help me. I'm ashamed on you, Samivel."

"The fact is, Sir," said Sam, with a slight bow, "the gov'ner's been a drawin' his money."

"Wery good, Samivel, wery good," said Mr. Weller, nodding his head with a satisfied air, "I didn't mean to speak harsh to you, Sammy. Wery good. That's the vay to begin; come to the pint at once. Wery good indeed, Samivel."

Mr. Weller nodded his head an extraordinary number of times in the excess of his gratification, and waited in a listening attitude for Sam to resume his statement.

"You may sit down, Sam," said Mr. Pickwick, apprehending that the interview was likely to prove rather longer than he had expected.

Sam bowed again and sat down; his father looking round, he continued,

"The gov'ner, Sir, has drawn out five hundred and thirty pounds."

"Reduced counsels," interposed Mr. Weller, senior, in an under tone.

"It don't much matter vether it's reduced counsels, or wot not," said Sam; "five hundred and thirty pound is the sum, ain't it?"

"All right, Samivel," replied Mr. Weller.

"To vich sum, he has added for the house and bisness—"

"Lease, good-vill, stock, and fixters," interposed Mr. Weller.

—"As much as makes it," continued Sam, "altogether, eleven hundred and eighty pound."

"Indeed!" said Mr. Pickwick, "I am delighted to hear it. I congratulate you, Mr. Weller, on having done so well."

"Vait a minit, Sir," said Mr. Weller, raising his hand in a deprecatory manner. "Get on, Samivel."

"This here money," said Sam, with a little hesitation, "he's anxious to put someveres, vere he knows it'll be safe, and I'm wery anxious too, for if he keeps it, he'll go a lendin' it to somebody, or investin' property in horses, or droppin' his pocket-book down a airy, or makin' an Egyptian mummy of his-self in some vay or another."

"Wery good, Samivel," observed Mr. Weller, in as complacent a manner as if Sam had been passing the highest eulogiums on his prudence and foresight. "Wery good."

"For vich reasons," continued Sam, plucking nervously at the brim of his hat; "for vich reasons he's drawn it out to-day, and come here vith me to say, leastvays to offer, or in other vords to—"

"To say this here," said the elder Mr. Weller, impatiently, "that it ain't o' no use to me; I'm a goin' to vork a coach reg'lar, and ha'n't got noveres to keep it in, unless I vos to pay the guard for takin' care on it, or to put it in vun o' the coach pockets, vich 'ud be a temptation to the insides. If you'll take care on it for me, Sir, I shall be wery much obliged to you. P'raps," said Mr. Weller, walking up to Mr. Pickwick and whispering in his ear, "p'raps it'll go a little vay towards the expenses o' that 'ere conviction. All I say is, just you keep it till I ask you for it again." With these words, Mr. Weller placed the pocket-book in Mr. Pickwick's hands, caught up his hat, and ran out of the room with a celerity scarcely to be expected from so corpulent a subject.

"Stop him, Sam," exclaimed Mr. Pickwick, earnestly. "Overtake him; bring him back instantly! Mr. Weller—here—come back!"

Sam saw that his master's injunctions were not to be disobeyed; and catching his father by the arm as he was descending the stairs, dragged him back by main force.

"My good friend," said Mr. Pickwick, taking the old man by the hand; "your honest confidence overpowers me."

"I don't see no occasion for nothin' o' the kind, Sir," replied Mr. Weller, obstinately.

"I assure you, my good friend, I have more money than I can ever need; far more than a man at my age can ever live to spend," said Mr. Pickwick.

"No man knows how much he can spend till he tries," observed Mr. Weller.

"Perhaps not," replied Mr. Pickwick; "but as I have no intention of trying any such experiments, I am not likely to come to want. I must beg you to take this back, Mr. Weller."

"Wery well," said Mr. Weller with a very discontented look. "Mark my vords, Sammy, I'll do somethin' desperate vith this here property; somethin' desperate!"

"You'd better not," replied Sam.

Mr. Weller reflected for a short time, and then buttoning up his coat with great determination, said—

"I'll keep a pike."

"Wot!" exclaimed Sam.

"A pike," rejoined Mr. Weller, through his set teeth; "I'll keep a pike. Say good bye to your father, Samivel; I dewote the remainder o' my days to a pike."

This threat was such an awful one, and Mr. Weller besides appearing fully resolved to carry it into execution, seemed so deeply mortified by Mr. Pickwick's refusal, that that gentleman, after a short reflection, said—

"Well, well, Mr. Weller, I will keep the money. I can do more good with it, perhaps, than you can."

"Just the wery thing, to be sure," said Mr. Weller, brightening up; "o' course you can, Sir."

"Say no more about it," said Mr. Pickwick, locking the pocket-book in his desk; "I am heartily obliged to you, my good friend. Now sit down again; I want to ask your advice."

The internal laughter occasioned by the triumphant success of his visit, which had convulsed not only Mr. Weller's face, but his arms, legs, and body also, during the locking up of the pocket-book, suddenly gave place to the most dignified gravity as he heard these words.

"Wait outside a few minutes, Sam, will you?" said Mr. Pickwick.

Sam immediately withdrew.

Mr. Weller looked uncommonly wise and very much amazed, when Mr. Pickwick opened the discourse by saying—

"You are not an advocate for matrimony, I think, Mr. Weller?"

Mr. Weller shook his head. He was wholly unable to speak; for vague thoughts of some wicked widow having been successful in her designs upon Mr. Pickwick, choked his utterance.

"Did you happen to see a young girl down stairs when you came in just now with your son?" enquired Mr. Pickwick.

"Yes—I see a young gal," replied Mr. Weller, shortly.

"What did you think of her, now?—Candidly, Mr. Weller, what did you think of her?"

"I thought she wos wery plump, and vell made," said Mr. Weller, with a critical air.

"So she is," said Mr. Pickwick, "so she is. What did you think of her manners, from what you saw of her?"

"Wery pleasant," rejoined Mr. Weller. "Wery pleasant and conformable."

The precise meaning which Mr. Weller attached to this last mentioned adjective did not appear, but as it was evident from the tone in which he used it that it was a favourable expression, Mr. Pickwick was as well satisfied as if he had been thoroughly enlightened on the subject.

"I take a great interest in her, Mr. Weller," said Mr. Pickwick.

Mr. Weller coughed.

"I mean an interest in her doing well," resumed Mr. Pickwick; "a desire that she may be comfortable and prosperous. You understand?"

"Wery clearly," replied Mr. Weller, who understood nothing yet.

"That young person," said Mr. Pickwick, "is attached to your son."

"To Samivel Veller!" exclaimed the parent.

"Yes," said Mr. Pickwick.

"It's nat'ral," said Mr. Weller, after some consideration, "nat'ral, but rayther alarmin'. Sammy must be careful."

"How do you mean?" enquired Mr. Pickwick.

"Wery careful that he don't say nothin' to her," responded Mr. Weller. "Wery careful that he ain't led avay in a innocent moment to say anythin' as may lead to a conwiction for breach. You're never safe vith 'em, Mr. Pickwick, ven they vunce has designs on you; there's no

knowin' vere to have 'em, and vile you're a-considering of it they have you. I wos married fust, that vay myself, Sir, and Sammy wos the consekens o' the manoover."

"You give me no great encouragement to conclude what I have to say," observed Mr. Pickwick, "but I had better do so at once. This young person is not only attached to your son, Mr. Weller, but your son is attached to her."

"Vell," said Mr. Weller, "this here's a pretty sort o' thing to come to a father's ears, this is!"

"I have observed them on several occasions," said Mr. Pickwick, making no comment on Mr. Weller's last remark; "and entertain no doubt at all about it. Supposing I were desirous of establishing them comfortably as man and wife in some little business or situation, where they might hope to obtain a decent living, what should you think of it, Mr. Weller?"

At first, Mr. Weller received with wry faces a proposition involving the marriage of anybody in whom he took an interest, but as Mr. Pickwick argued the point with him, and laid great stress upon the fact that Mary was not a widow, he gradually became more tractable. Mr. Pickwick had great influence over him; and he had been much struck with Mary's appearance, having, in fact, bestowed several very unfatherly winks upon her, already. At length he said that it was not for him to oppose Mr. Pickwick's inclination, and that he would be very happy to yield to his advice; upon which Mr. Pickwick joyfully took him at his word and called Sam back into the room.

"Sam," said Mr. Pickwick, clearing his throat, "your father and I have been having some conversation about you."

"About you, Samivel," said Mr. Weller, in a patronising and impressive voice.

"I am not so blind, Sam, as not to have seen, a long time since, that you entertain something more than a friendly feeling towards Mrs. Winkle's maid," said Mr. Pickwick.

"You hear this, Samivel?" said Mr. Weller in the same judicial form of speech as before.

"I hope, Sir," said Sam, addressing his master, "I hope there's no harm in a young man takin' notice of a young 'ooman as is undeniably good-looking and vell-conducted."

"Certainly not," said Mr. Pickwick.

"Not by no means," acquiesced Mr. Weller, affably but magisterially.

"So far from thinking that there is anything wrong in conduct so natural," resumed Mr. Pickwick, "it is my wish to assist and promote your wishes in this respect. With this view I have had a little conversation with your father, and finding that he is of my opinion—"

"The lady not bein' a vidder," interposed Mr. Weller in explanation.

"The lady not being a widow," said Mr. Pickwick, smiling. "I wish to free you from the restraint which your present position imposes upon you: and to mark my sense of your fidelity and many excellent qualities, by enabling you to marry this girl at once, and to earn an independent livelihood for yourself and family. I shall be proud, Sam," said Mr. Pickwick, whose voice had faltered a little hitherto, but now resumed its customary tone, "proud and happy to make your future prospects in life my grateful and peculiar care."

There was a profound silence for a short time, and then Sam said in a low husky sort of voice, but firmly withal—

"I'm very much obliged to you for your goodness, Sir, as is only like yourself, but it can't be done."

"Can't be done!" ejaculated Mr. Pickwick in astonishment.

"Samivel!" said Mr. Weller, with dignity.

"I say it can't be done," repeated Sam in a louder key. "Wot's to become of you, Sir?"

"My good fellow," replied Mr. Pickwick, "the recent changes among my friends will alter my mode of life in future, entirely; besides I am growing older, and want repose and quiet. My rambles, Sam, are over."

"How do I know that 'ere, Sir?" argued Sam; "you think so now! S'pose you wos to change your mind, vich is not unlikely, for you've the spirit o' five-and-twenty in you still,—what 'ud become on you vithout me? It can't be done, Sir, it can't be done."

"Wery good, Samivel, there's a good deal in that," said Mr. Weller, encouragingly.

"I speak after long deliberation, Sam, and with the certainty that I shall keep my word," said Mr. Pickwick, shaking his head. "New scenes have closed upon me; my rambles are at an end."

"Wery good," rejoined Sam. "Then that's the wery best reason wy you should alvays have somebody by you as understands you, to keep you up and make you comfortable. If you vant a more polished sort o' feller, vell and good, have him; but vages or no vages, notice or no notice, board or no board, lodgin' or no lodgin', Sam Veller, as you took from the old inn in the Borough, sticks by you, come what come may; and let ev'rythin' and ev'rybody do their wery fiercest, nothin' shall ever perwent it."

At the close of this declaration, which Sam made with great emotion, the elder Mr. Weller rose from his chair, and forgetting all considerations of time, place, or propriety, waved his hat above his head and gave three vehement cheers.

"My good fellow," said Mr. Pickwick, when Mr. Weller had sat down again, rather abashed at his own enthusiasm, "you are bound to consider the young woman also."

"I do consider the young 'ooman, Sir," said Sam. "I have considered the young 'ooman, I've spoke to her, I've told her how I'm sitivated, she's ready to vait till I'm ready, and I believe she vill. If she don't, she's not the young 'ooman I take her for, and I give her up vith readiness. You've know'd me afore, Sir. My mind's made up, and nothin' can ever alter it."

Who could combat this resolution? Not Mr. Pickwick. He derived at that moment more pride and luxury of feeling from the disinterested attachment of his humble friends, than ten thousand protestations from the greatest men living could have awakened in his heart.

While this conversation was passing in Mr. Pickwick's room, a little old gentleman in a suit of snuff-coloured clothes, followed by a porter carrying a small portmanteau, presented himself below; and after securing a bed for the night, enquired of the waiter whether one Mrs. Winkle was staying there, to which question the waiter of course responded in the affirmative.

"Is she alone?" enquired the little old gentleman.

"I believe she is, Sir," replied the waiter; "I can call her own maid, Sir, if you——"

"No, I don't want her," said the old gentleman quickly. "Show me to her room without announcing me."

"Eh, Sir?" said the waiter.

"Are you deaf?" enquired the little old gentleman.

"No, Sir."

"Then listen, if you please. Can you hear me now?"

"Yes, Sir."

"That's well. Show me to Mrs. Winkle's room, without announcing me."

As the little old gentleman uttered this command, he slipped five shillings into the waiter's hand, and looked steadily at him.

"Really, Sir," said the waiter, "I don't know Sir whether——"

"Ah! you'll do it, I see," said the little old gentleman. "You had better do it at once. It will save time."

There was something so very cool and collected in the gentleman's manner, that the waiter put the five shillings in his pocket, and led him up stairs without another word.

"This is the room, is it?" said the gentleman. "You may go."

The waiter complied, wondering much who the gentleman could be, and what he wanted; the little old gentleman waiting till he was out of sight, tapped at the door.

"Come in," said Arabella.

"Um, a pretty voice at any rate," murmured the little old gentleman; "but that's nothing." As he said this, he opened the door and walked in. Arabella, who was sitting at work, rose on beholding a stranger—a little confused, but by no means ungracefully so.

"Pray don't rise, Ma'am," said the unknown, walking in and closing the door after him. "Mrs. Winkle, I believe?"

Arabella inclined her head.

"Mrs. Nathaniel Winkle, who married the son of the old man at Birmingham?" said the stranger, eyeing Arabella with visible curiosity.

Again Arabella inclined her head, and looked uneasily round, as if uncertain whether to call for assistance.

"I surprise you, I see, Ma'am," said the old gentleman.

"Rather, I confess," replied Arabella, wondering more and more.

"I'll take a chair, if you'll allow me, Ma'am," said the stranger.

He took one; and drawing a spectacle-case from his pocket, leisurely pulled out a pair of spectacles, which he adjusted on his nose.

"You don't know me, Ma'am?" he said, looking so intently at Arabella that she began to feel quite alarmed.

"No, Sir," she replied, timidly.

"No," said the gentleman, nursing his left leg; "I don't know how you should. You know my name, though, Ma'am."

"Do I?" said Arabella, trembling, though she scarcely knew why. "May I ask what it is?"

"Presently, Ma'am, presently," said the stranger, not having yet removed his eyes from her countenance. "You have been recently married, Ma'am?"

"I have," replied Arabella, in a scarcely audible tone, laying aside her work, and becoming greatly agitated as a thought, that had occurred to her before, struck more forcibly upon her mind.

"Without having represented to your husband the propriety of first consulting his father, on whom he is dependent, I think?" said the stranger.

Arabella applied her handkerchief to her eyes.

"Without an endeavour even to ascertain, by some indirect appeal, what were the old man's sentiments on a point in which he would naturally feel much interested?" said the stranger.

"I cannot deny it, Sir," said Arabella.

"And without having sufficient property of your own to afford your husband any permanent assistance in exchange for the worldly advantages which you knew he would have gained if he had married agreeably to his father's wishes?" said the old gentleman. "This is what boys and girls call disinterested affection, till they have boys and girls of their own, and then they see it in a rougher and very different light."

Arabella's tears flowed fast, as she pleaded in extenuation that she was young and inexperienced; that her attachment had alone induced her to take the steps to which she had resorted, and that she had been deprived of the counsel and guidance of her parents almost from infancy.

"It was wrong," said the old gentleman in a milder tone, "very wrong. It was romantic, unbusiness-like, foolish."

"It was my fault; all my fault, Sir," replied poor Arabella, weeping.

"Nonsense," said the old gentleman, "it was not your fault that he fell in love with you, I suppose. Yes it was though," said the old gentleman, looking rather slyly at Arabella. "It was your fault. He couldn't help it."

This little compliment, or the little gentleman's odd way of paying it, or his altered manner—so much kinder than it was at first—or all three together, forced a smile from Arabella in the midst of her tears.

"Where's your husband?" enquired the old gentleman, abruptly; stopping a smile which was just coming over his own face.

"I expect him every instant, Sir," said Arabella. "I persuaded him to take a walk this morning. He is very low and wretched at not having heard from his father."

"Low, is he?" said the old gentleman. "Serve him right."

"He feels it on my account, I am afraid," said Arabella; "and indeed, Sir, I feel it deeply on his. I have been the sole means of bringing him to his present condition."

"Don't mind it on his account, my dear," said the old gentleman. "It serves him right. I am glad of it—actually glad of it, as far as he is concerned."

The words were scarcely out of the old gentleman's lips, when footsteps were heard ascending the stairs, which he and Arabella seemed both to recognize at the same moment. The little gentleman turned pale; and making a strong effort to appear composed, stood up as Mr. Winkle entered the room.

"Father!" said Mr. Winkle, recoiling in amazement.

"Yes, Sir," replied the little gentleman. "Well, Sir, what have you got to say to me?"

Mr. Winkle remained silent.

"You are ashamed of yourself, I hope, Sir," said the old gentleman.

Still Mr. Winkle said nothing.

"Are you ashamed of yourself, Sir, or are you not?" enquired the old gentleman.

"No, Sir," replied Mr. Winkle, drawing Arabella's arm through his. "I am not ashamed of myself, or of my wife either."

"Upon my word!" cried the old gentleman, ironically.

"I am very sorry to have done anything which has lessened your affection for me, Sir," said Mr. Winkle; "but I will say at the same time, that I have no reason to be ashamed of having this lady for my wife, or you for having her for a daughter."

"Give me your hand, Nat.," said the old gentleman in an altered voice. "Kiss me, my love; you *are* a very charming daughter-in-law after all!"

In a few minutes' time Mr. Winkle went in search of Mr. Pickwick, and returning with that gentleman, presented him to his father, whereupon they shook hands for five minutes incessantly.

"Mr. Pickwick, I thank you most heartily for all your kindness to my son," said old Mr. Winkle, in a bluff, straightforward way. "I am a hasty fellow, and when I saw you last, I was vexed and taken by surprise. I have judged for myself now, and am more than satisfied. Shall I make any more apologies, Mr. Pickwick?"

"Not one," replied that gentleman. "You have done the only thing wanting to complete my happiness."

Hereupon there was another shaking of hands for five minutes longer, accompanied by a great number of complimentary speeches, which, besides being complimentary, had the additional and very novel recommendation of being sincere.

Sam had dutifully seen his father to the Belle Sauvage, when, on returning he encountered the fat boy in the court, who had been charged with the delivery of a note from Emily Wardle.

"I say," said Joe, who was unusually loquacious, "what a pretty girl Mary is, isn't she? I am *so* fond of her, I am!"

Mr. Weller made no verbal remark in reply, but eyeing the fat boy for a moment, quite transfixed at his presumption, led him by the collar to the corner, and dismissed him with a harmless but ceremonious kick; after which, he walked home, whistling.

CHAPTER LVI.

IN WHICH THE PICKWICK CLUB IS FINALLY DISSOLVED, AND EVERYTHING CONCLUDED TO THE SATISFACTION OF EVERYBODY.

FOR a whole week after the happy arrival of Mr. Winkle from Birmingham, Mr. Pickwick and Sam Weller were from home all day long, only returning just in time for dinner, and then wearing an air of mystery and importance quite foreign to their natures. It was evident that very grave and eventful proceedings were on foot, but various surmises were afloat respecting their precise character. Some (among whom was Mr. Tupman) were disposed to think that Mr. Pickwick contemplated a matrimonial alliance, but this idea the ladies most strenuously repudiated; others rather inclined to the belief that he had projected some distant tour, and was at present occupied in effecting the preliminary arrangements, but this again was stoutly denied by Sam himself, who had unequivocally stated, when cross-examined by Mary, that no new journeys were to be undertaken. At length, when the brains of the whole party had been racked for six long days by unavailing speculation, it was unanimously resolved that Mr. Pickwick should be called upon to explain his conduct, and to state distinctly why he had thus absented himself from the society of his admiring friends.

With this view, Mr. Wardle invited the full circle to dinner at the Adelphi, and the decanters having been twice sent round, opened the business.

"We are all anxious to know," said the old gentleman,

THE WORDS WERE SCARCELY OUT OF THE OLD GENTLEMAN'S LIPS, WHEN FOOTSTEPS WERE HEARD ASCENDING THE STAIRS, ETC.

"what we have done to offend you, and to induce you to desert us and devote yourself to these solitary walks."

"Are you?" said Mr. Pickwick. "It is singular enough that I had intended to volunteer a full explanation this very day, so if you will give me another glass of wine I will satisfy your curiosity."

The decanters passed from hand to hand with unwonted briskness, and Mr. Pickwick looking round on the faces of his friends with a cheerful smile, proceeded—

"All the changes that have taken place among us," said Mr. Pickwick, "I mean the marriage that *has* taken place, and the marriage that will take place, with the changes they involve, rendered it necessary for me to think soberly and at once upon my future plans. I determined on retiring to some quiet, pretty neighbourhood in the vicinity of London; I saw a house which exactly suited my fancy. I have taken it and furnished it. It is fully prepared for my reception, and I intend entering upon it at once, trusting that I may yet live to spend many quiet years in peaceful retirement; cheered through life by the society of my friends, and followed in death by their affectionate remembrance."

Here Mr. Pickwick paused, and a low murmur ran round the table.

"The house I have taken," said Mr. Pickwick, "is at Dulwich; it has a large garden, and is situated in one of the most pleasant spots near London. It has been fitted up with every attention to substantial comfort; perhaps to a little elegance besides; but of that you shall judge for yourselves. Sam accompanies me there. I have engaged, on Perker's representation, a housekeeper—a very old one —and such other servants as she thinks I shall require. I propose to consecrate this little retreat by having a ceremony, in which I take a great interest, performed there. I wish, if my friend Wardle entertains no objection, that his daughter should be married from my new house, on the day I take possession of it. The happiness of young people," said Mr. Pickwick, a little moved, "has ever been the chief pleasure of my life. It will warm my heart to witness the happiness of those friends who are dearest to me, beneath my own roof."

Mr. Pickwick paused again: and Emily and Arabella sobbed audibly.

"I have communicated, both personally and by letter, with the club," resumed Mr. Pickwick, "acquainting them with my intention. During our long absence it has suffered much from internal dissensions; and the withdrawal of my name, coupled with this and other circumstances, has occasioned its dissolution. The Pickwick Club exists no longer.

"I shall never regret," said Mr. Pickwick in a low voice —"I shall never regret having devoted the greater part of two years to mixing with different varieties and shades of human character, frivolous as my pursuit of novelty may have appeared to many. Nearly the whole of my previous life having been devoted to business and the pursuit of wealth, numerous scenes of which I had no previous conception have dawned upon me—I hope to the enlargement of my mind, and the improvement of my understanding. If I have done but little good, I trust I have done less harm, and that none of my adventures will be other than a source of amusing and pleasant recollections to me in the decline of life. God bless you all."

With these words, Mr. Pickwick filled and drained a bumper with a trembling hand; and his eyes moistened as his friends rose with one accord and pledged him from their hearts.

There were very few preparatory arrangements to be made for the marriage of Mr. Snodgrass. As he had neither father nor mother, and had been in his minority a ward of Mr. Pickwick's, that gentleman was perfectly well acquainted with his possessions and prospects. His account of both was quite satisfactory to Wardle—as almost any other account would have been, for the good old gentleman was overflowing with hilarity and kindness—and a handsome portion having been bestowed upon Emily, the marriage was fixed to take place on the fourth day from that time; the suddenness of which preparations reduced three dress-makers and a tailor to the extreme verge of insanity.

Getting post-horses to the carriage, old Wardle started off next day, to bring his mother up to town. Communicating his intelligence to the old lady with characteristic impetuosity, she instantly fainted away, but being promptly revived, ordered the brocaded silk gown to be packed up forthwith, and proceeded to relate some circumstances of a similar nature attending the marriage of the eldest daughter of Lady Tollinglower, deceased, which occupied three hours in the recital, and were not half finished at last.

Mrs. Trundle had to be informed of all the mighty preparations that were making in London; and being in a delicate state of health was informed thereof through Mr. Trundle, lest the news should be too much for her; but it was not too much for her, inasmuch as she at once wrote off to Muggleton to order a new cap and a black satin gown, and moreover avowed her determination of being present at the ceremony. Hereupon Mr. Trundle called in the doctor, and the doctor said Mrs. Trundle ought to know best how she felt herself, to which Mrs. Trundle replied that she felt herself quite equal to it, and that she had made up her mind to go; upon which the doctor, who was a wise and discreet doctor, and knew what was good for himself as well as for other people, said, that perhaps if Mrs. Trundle stopped at home she might hurt herself more by fretting than by going, so perhaps she had better go. And she did go; the doctor with great attention sending in half a dozen of medicine to be drunk upon the road.

In addition to these points of distraction, Wardle was entrusted with two small letters to two small young ladies who were to act as bridesmaids; upon the receipt of which, the two young ladies were driven to despair by having no "things" ready for so important an occasion, and no time to make them in—a circumstance which appeared to afford the two worthy papas of the two small young ladies rather a feeling of satisfaction than otherwise. However, old frocks were trimmed and new bonnets made, and the young ladies looked as well as could possibly have been expected of them; and as they cried at the subsequent ceremony in the proper places and trembled at the right times, they acquitted themselves to the admiration of all beholders.

How the two poor relations ever reached London— whether they walked, or got behind coaches, or procured lifts in wagons, or carried each other—is uncertain, but there they were, before Wardle; and the very first people that knocked at the door of Mr. Pickwick's house on the bridal morning, were the two poor relations, all smiles and shirt-collar.

They were welcomed heartily though, for riches or poverty had no influence on Mr. Pickwick; the new servants were all alacrity and readiness: Sam in a most unrivalled state of high spirits and excitement, and Mary glowing with beauty and smart ribands.

The bridegroom, who had been staying at the house for two or three days previously, sallied forth gallantly to Dulwich church to meet the bride, attended by Mr. Pickwick, Ben Allen, Bob Sawyer, and Mr. Tupman, with Sam Weller outside, having at his button hole a white favour, the gift of his lady love, and clad in a new and gorgeous suit of livery invented expressly for the occasion. They were met by the Wardles, and the Winkles, and the bride and bridesmaid, and the Trundles; and the ceremony having been performed, the coaches rattled back to Mr. Pickwick's to breakfast, where little Mr. Perker already awaited them.

Here, all the light clouds of the more solemn part of the proceedings passed away; every face shone forth joyously, and nothing was to be heard but congratulations and commendations. Everything was so beautiful! The lawn in front, the garden behind, the miniature conservatory, the dining-room, the drawing-room, the bed-rooms, the smoking-room, and above all the study with its pictures and easy chairs, and odd cabinets, and queer tables, and books out of number, with a large cheerful window opening upon a pleasant lawn and commanding a pretty landscape, just dotted here and there with little houses almost hidden by the trees; and then the curtains, and the carpets, and the chairs, and the sofas! Everything was so beautiful, so compact, so neat and in such exquisite taste, said everybody, that there really was no deciding what to admire most.

And in the midst of all this, stood Mr. Pickwick, his countenance lighted up with smiles, which the heart of no man, woman, or child could resist: himself the happiest of the group, shaking hands over and over again with the same people, and when his own were not so employed, rubbing them with pleasure; turning round in a different direction at every fresh expression of gratification or curiosity, and inspiring everybody with his looks of gladness and delight.

Breakfast is announced. Mr. Pickwick leads the old lady (who has been very eloquent on the subject of Lady Tollinglower), to the top of a long table; Wardle takes the bottom, the friends arrange themselves on either side, Sam takes his station behind his master's chair, the laughter and talking cease; Mr. Pickwick having said grace, pauses for an instant and looks round him. As he does so, the tears roll down his cheeks in the fulness of his joy.

Let us leave our old friend in one of those moments of unmixed happiness, of which, if we seek them, there are ever some to cheer our transitory existence here. There are dark shadows on the earth, but its lights are stronger in the contrast. Some men, like bats or owls, have better eyes for the darkness than for the light; we, who have no such optical powers, are better pleased to take our last parting look at the visionary companions of many solitary hours, when the brief sunshine of the world is blazing full upon them.

It is the fate of most men who mingle with the world and attain even the prime of life, to make many real friends, and lose them in the course of nature. It is the fate of all authors or chroniclers to create imaginary friends, and lose them in the course of art. Nor is this the full extent of their misfortunes; for they are required to furnish an account of them besides.

In compliance with this custom—unquestionably a bad one—we subjoin a few biographical words in relation to the party at Mr. Pickwick's assembled.

Mr. and Mrs. Winkle being fully received into favour by the old gentleman, were shortly afterwards installed in a newly built house, not half a mile from Mr. Pickwick's. Mr. Winkle being engaged in the city as agent or town correspondent of his father, exchanged his old costume for the ordinary dress of Englishmen, and presented all the external appearance of a civilised Christian ever afterwards.

Mr. and Mrs. Snodgrass settled at Dingley Dell, where they purchased and cultivated a small farm, more for occupation than profit. Mr. Snodgrass, being occasionally abstracted and melancholy, is to this day reputed a great poet among his friends and acquaintance, although we do not find that he has ever written anything to encourage the belief. We know many celebrated characters, literary, philosophical, and otherwise, who hold a high reputation on a similar tenure.

Mr. Tupman, when his friends married and Mr. Pickwick settled, took lodgings at Richmond, where he has ever since resided. He walks constantly on the Terrace, during the summer months, with a youthful and janty air, which has rendered him the admiration of the numerous elderly ladies of single condition, who reside in the vicinity. He has never proposed again.

Mr. Bob Sawyer, having previously passed through the Gazette, passed over to Bengal, accompanied by Mr. Benjamin Allen, both gentlemen having received surgical appointments from the East India Company. They each had the yellow fever fourteen times, and then resolved to try a little abstinence, since which period they have been doing well.

Mrs. Bardell let lodgings to many conversable single gentlemen with great profit, but never brought any more actions for a breach of promise of marriage. Her attorneys, Messrs. Dodson and Fogg, continue in business, from which they realise a large income, and in which they are universally considered among the sharpest of the sharp.

Sam Weller kept his word, and remained unmarried for two years. The old housekeeper dying at the end of that time, Mr. Pickwick promoted Mary to the situation, on condition of her marrying Mr. Weller at once, which she did without a murmur. From the circumstance of two sturdy little boys having been repeatedly seen at the gate of the back garden, we have reason to suppose that Sam has some family.

The elder Mr. Weller drove a coach for twelve months, but being afflicted with the gout, was compelled to retire. The contents of the pocket-book had been so well invested for him, however, by Mr. Pickwick, that he had a handsome independence to retire on, upon which he still lives at an excellent public-house near Shooter's Hill, where he is quite reverenced as an oracle, boasting very much of his intimacy with Mr. Pickwick, and retaining a most unconquerable aversion to widows.

Mr. Pickwick himself continued to reside in his new house, employing his leisure hours in arranging the memoranda which he afterwards presented to the secretary of the once famous club, or in hearing Sam Weller read aloud, with such remarks as suggested themselves to his mind, which never failed to afford Mr. Pickwick great amusement. He was much troubled at first by the numerous applications which were made to him by Mr. Snodgrass, Mr. Winkle and Mr. Trundle to act as godfather to their offspring, but he has become used to it now, and officiates as a matter of course. He never had occasion to regret his bounty to Mr. Jingle, for both that person and Job Trotter became in time worthy members of society, although they have always steadily objected to return to the scenes of their old haunts and temptations. He is somewhat infirm now, but he retains all his former juvenility of spirit, and may still be frequently seen contemplating the pictures in the Dulwich Gallery, or enjoying a walk about the pleasant neighbourhood on a fine day. He is known by all the poor people about, who never fail to take their hats off as he passes with great respect; the children idolise him, and so indeed does the whole neighbourhood. Every year he repairs to a large family merrymaking at Mr. Wardle's; on this, as on all other occasions, he is invariably attended by the faithful Sam, between whom and his master there exists a steady and reciprocal attachment, which nothing but death will sever.

The Adventures
of
Oliver Twist

BILL SIKES.

The Adventures

of

Oliver Twist

by

Charles Dickens

With Illustrations by

George Cruikshank

CONTENTS.

ILLUSTRATIONS

TO

OLIVER TWIST

———

OLIVER TWIST.

CHAPTER I.

TREATS OF THE PLACE WHERE OLIVER TWIST WAS BORN; AND OF THE CIRCUMSTANCES ATTENDING HIS BIRTH.

AMONG other public buildings in a certain town, which for many reasons it will be prudent to refrain from mentioning, and to which I will assign no fictitious name, there is one anciently common to most towns, great or small: to wit, a workhouse; and in this workhouse was born: on a day and date which I need not trouble myself to repeat, inasmuch as it can be of no possible consequence to the reader, in this stage of the business at all events: the item of mortality whose name is prefixed to the head of this chapter.

For a long time after it was ushered into this world of sorrow and trouble, by the parish surgeon, it remained a matter of considerable doubt whether the child would survive to bear any name at all; in which case it is somewhat more than probable that these memoirs would never have appeared; or, if they had, that being comprised within a couple of pages, they would have possessed the inestimable merit of being the most concise and faithful specimen of biography, extant in the literature of any age or country.

Although I am not disposed to maintain that the being born in a workhouse, is in itself the most fortunate and enviable circumstance that can possibly befall a human being, I do mean to say that in this particular instance, it was the best thing for Oliver Twist that could by possibility have occurred. The fact is, that there was considerable difficulty in inducing Oliver to take upon himself the office of respiration,—a troublesome practice, but one which custom has rendered necessary to our easy existence; and for some time he lay gasping on a little flock mattress, rather unequally poised between this world and the next: the balance being decidedly in favour of the latter. Now, if, during this brief period, Oliver had been surrounded by careful grandmothers, anxious aunts, experienced nurses, and doctors of profound wisdom, he would most inevitably and indubitably have been killed in no time. There being nobody by, however, but a pauper old woman, who was rendered rather misty by an unwonted allowance of beer; and a parish surgeon who did such matters by contract; Oliver and Nature fought out the point between them. The result was, that, after a few struggles, Oliver breathed, sneezed, and proceeded to advertise to the inmates of the workhouse the fact of a new burden having been imposed upon the parish, by setting up as loud a cry as could reasonably have been expected from a male infant who had not been possessed of that very useful appendage, a voice, for a much longer space of time than three minutes and a quarter.

As Oliver gave this first proof of the free and proper action of his lungs, the patchwork coverlet which was carelessly flung over the iron bedstead, rustled; the pale face of a young woman was raised feebly from the pillow; and a faint voice imperfectly articulated the words, "Let me see the child, and die."

The surgeon had been sitting with his face turned towards the fire: giving the palms of his hands a warm and a rub alternately. As the young woman spoke, he rose, and advancing to the bed's head, said, with more kindness than might have been expected of him:

"Oh, you must not talk about dying yet."

"Lor bless her dear heart, no!" interposed the nurse, hastily depositing in her pocket a green glass bottle, the contents of which she had been tasting in a corner with evident satisfaction. "Lor bless her dear heart, when she has lived as long as I have, Sir, and had thirteen children of her own, and all on 'em dead except two, and them in the wurkus with me, she'll know better than to take on in that way, bless her dear heart! Think what it is to be a mother, there's a dear young lamb, do."

Apparently this consolatory perspective of a mother's prospects failed in producing its due effect. The patient shook her head, and stretched out her hand towards the child.

The surgeon deposited it in her arms. She imprinted her cold white lips passionately on its forehead; passed her hands over her face; gazed wildly round; shuddered; fell back—and died. They chafed her breast, hands, and temples; but the blood had stopped for ever. They talked of hope and comfort. They had been strangers too long.

"It's all over, Mrs. Thingummy!" said the surgeon at last.

"Ah, poor dear, so it is!" said the nurse, picking up the cork of the green bottle which had fallen out on the pillow as she stooped to take up the child. "Poor dear!"

"You needn't mind sending up to me, if the child cries, nurse," said the surgeon, putting on his gloves with great deliberation. "It's very likely it *will* be troublesome. Give it a little gruel if it is." He put on his hat, and, pausing by the bed-side on his way to the door, added "She was a good-looking girl, too; where did she come from?"

"She was brought here last night," replied the old woman, "by the overseer's order. She was found lying in the street. She had walked some distance, for her shoes were worn to pieces; but where she came from, or where she was going to, nobody knows."

The surgeon leaned over the body, and raised the left hand. "The old story," he said, shaking his head: "no wedding-ring, I see. Ah! Good night!"

The medical gentleman walked away to dinner; and the nurse, having once more applied herself to the green bottle, sat down on a low chair before the fire, and proceeded to dress the infant.

What an excellent example of the power of dress, young Oliver Twist was! Wrapped in the blanket which had hitherto formed his only covering, he might have been the child of a nobleman or a beggar; it would have been hard for the haughtiest stranger to have assigned him his proper station in society. But now that he was enveloped in the old calico robes which had grown yellow in the same service, he was badged and ticketed, and fell into his place at once—a parish child—the orphan of a workhouse—the humble, half-starved drudge—to be cuffed and buffeted through the world—despised by all, and pitied by none.

Oliver cried lustily. If he could have known that he was an orphan, left to the tender mercies of churchwardens and overseers, perhaps he would have cried the louder.

CHAPTER II.

TREATS OF OLIVER TWIST'S GROWTH, EDUCATION, AND BOARD.

For the next eight or ten months, Oliver was the victim of a systematic course of treachery and deception. He was brought up by hand. The hungry and destitute situation of the infant orphan was duly reported by the workhouse authorities to the parish authorities. The parish authorities inquired with dignity of the workhouse authorities, whether there was no female then domiciled in "the house" who was in a situation to impart to Oliver Twist, the consolation and nourishment of which he stood in need. The workhouse authorities replied with humility, that there was not. Upon this, the parish authorities magnanimously and humanely resolved, that Oliver should be "farmed," or, in other words, that he should be despatched to a branch-workhouse some three miles off, where twenty or thirty other juvenile offenders against the poor-laws, rolled about the floor all day, without the inconvenience of too much food or too much clothing, under the parental superintendence of an elderly female, who received the culprits at and for the consideration of sevenpence-halfpenny per small head per week. Sevenpence-halfpenny's worth per week is a good round diet for a child; a great deal may be got for sevenpence-halfpenny: quite enough to overload its stomach, and make it uncomfortable. The elderly female was a woman of wisdom and experience; she knew what was good for children; and she had a very accurate perception of what was good for herself. So, she appropriated the greater part of the weekly stipend to her own use, and consigned the rising parochial generation to even a shorter allowance than was originally provided for them. Thereby finding in the lowest depth a deeper still; and proving herself a very great experimental philosopher.

Everybody knows the story of another experimental philosopher, who had a great theory about a horse being able to live without eating, and who demonstrated it so well, that he got his own horse down to a straw a day, and would most unquestionably have rendered him a very spirited and rampacious animal on nothing at all, if he had not died, just four-and-twenty hours before he was to have had his first comfortable bait of air. Unfortunately for the experimental philosophy of the female to whose protecting care Oliver Twist was delivered over, a similar result usually attended the operation of *her* system; for at that very moment when a child had contrived to exist upon the smallest possible portion of the weakest possible food, it did perversely happen in eight and a half cases out of ten, either that it sickened from want and cold, or fell into the fire from neglect, or got half-smothered by accident; in any one of which cases, the miserable little being was usually summoned into another world, and there gathered to the fathers whom it had never known in this.

Occasionally, when there was some more than usually interesting inquest upon a parish child who had been overlooked in turning up a bedstead, or inadvertently scalded to death when there happened to be a washing; though the latter accident was very scarce—anything approaching to a washing being of rare occurrence in the farm—the jury would take it into their heads to ask troublesome questions, or the parishioners would rebelliously affix their signatures to a remonstrance. But these impertinences were speedily checked by the evidence of the surgeon, and

the testimony of the beadle; the former of whom had always opened the body and found nothing inside (which was very probable indeed), and the latter of whom invariably swore whatever the parish wanted; which was very self-devotional. Besides, the board made periodical pilgrimages to the farm, and always sent the beadle the day before, to say they were going. The children were neat and clean to behold, when *they* went; and what more would the people have!

It cannot be expected that this system of farming would produce any very extraordinary or luxuriant crop. Oliver Twist's ninth birth-day found him a pale thin child, somewhat diminutive in stature, and decidedly small in circumference. But nature or inheritance had implanted a good sturdy spirit in Oliver's breast. It had had plenty of room to expand, thanks to the spare diet of the establishment; and perhaps to this circumstance may be attributed his having any ninth birth-day at all. Be this as it may, however, it *was* his ninth birth-day; and he was keeping it in the coal-cellar with a select party of two other young gentlemen, who, after participating with him in a sound thrashing, had been locked up therein for atrociously presuming to be hungry, when Mrs. Mann, the good lady of the house, was unexpectedly startled by the apparition of Mr. Bumble, the beadle, striving to undo the wicket of the garden-gate.

"Goodness gracious! Is that you, Mr. Bumble, Sir?" said Mrs. Mann, thrusting her head out of the window in well-affected ecstasies of joy. "(Susan, take Oliver and them two brats up stairs, and wash 'em directly.)—My heart alive! Mr. Bumble, how glad I am to see you, sure-ly!"

Now, Mr. Bumble was a fat man, and a choleric; so, instead of responding to this open-hearted salutation in a kindred spirit, he gave the little wicket a tremendous shake, and then bestowed upon it a kick which could have emanated from no leg but a beadle's.

"Lor, only think," said Mrs. Mann, running out,—for the three boys had been removed by this time,—"only think of that! That I should have forgotten that the gate was bolted on the inside, on account of them dear children! Walk in, Sir; walk in, pray, Mr. Bumble, do, Sir."

Although this invitation was accompanied with a curtsey that might have softened the heart of a churchwarden, it by no means mollified the beadle.

"Do you think this respectful or proper conduct, Mrs. Mann," inquired Mr. Bumble, grasping his cane, "to keep the parish officers a waiting at your garden-gate, when they come here upon porochial business connected with the porochial orphans? Are you aweer, Mrs. Mann, that you are, as I may say, a porochial delegate, and a stipendiary?"

"I'm sure, Mr. Bumble, that I was only a telling one or two of the dear children as is so fond of you, that it was you a coming," replied Mrs. Mann with great humility.

Mr. Bumble had a great idea of his oratorical powers and his importance. He had displayed the one, and vindicated the other. He relaxed.

"Well, well, Mrs. Mann," he replied in a calmer tone; "it may be as you say; it may be. Lead the way in, Mrs. Mann, for I come on business, and have something to say."

Mrs. Mann ushered the beadle into a small parlour with a brick floor; placed a seat for him; and officiously deposited his cocked hat and cane on the table before him. Mr. Bumble wiped from his forehead the perspiration which his walk had engendered, glanced complacently at the cocked hat, and smiled. Yes, he smiled. Beadles are but men: and Mr. Bumble smiled.

"Now don't you be offended at what I'm going to say," observed Mrs. Mann, with captivating sweetness. "You've had a long walk, you know, or I wouldn't mention it. Now, will you take a little drop of somethink, Mr. Bumble?"

"Not a drop. Not a drop," said Mr. Bumble, waving his right hand in a dignified, but placid manner.

"I think you will," said Mrs. Mann, who had noticed the tone of the refusal, and the gesture that had accompanied it. "Just a leetle drop, with a little cold water, and a lump of sugar."

Mr. Bumble coughed.

"Now, just a leetle drop," said Mrs. Mann persuasively.

"What is it?" inquired the beadle.

"Why, it's what I'm obliged to keep a little of in the house, to put into the blessed infants' Daffy, when they ain't well, Mr. Bumble," replied Mrs. Mann as she opened a corner cupboard, and took down a bottle and glass. "It's gin. I'll not deceive you, Mr. B. It's gin."

"Do you give the children Daffy, Mrs. Mann?" inquired Bumble, following with his eyes the interesting process of mixing.

Ah, bless 'em, that I do, dear as it is," replied the nurse. "I couldn't see 'em suffer before my very eyes, you know, Sir."

"No," said Mr. Bumble approvingly; "no, you could not. You are a humane woman, Mrs. Mann." (Here she set down the glass.) "I shall take a early opportunity of mentioning it to the board, Mrs. Mann." (He drew it towards him.) "You feel as a mother, Mrs. Mann." (He stirred the gin-and-water.) "I—I drink your health with cheerfulness, Mrs. Mann;" and he swallowed half of it.

"And now about business," said the beadle, taking out a leathern pocket-book. "The child that was half-baptized Oliver Twist, is nine year old to-day."

"Bless him!" interposed Mrs. Mann, inflaming her left eye with the corner of her apron.

"And notwithstanding a offered reward of ten pound, which was afterwards increased to twenty pound. Notwithstanding the most superlative, and, I may say, supernat'ral exertions on the part of this parish," said Bumble, "we have never been able to discover who is his father, or what was his mother's settlement, name, or con—dition."

Mrs. Mann raised her hands in astonishment; but added, after a moment's reflection, "How comes he to have any name at all, then?"

The beadle drew himself up with great pride, and said, "I invented it."

"You, Mr. Bumble!"

"I, Mrs. Mann. We name our foundlins in alphabetical order. The last was a S,—Swubble, I named him. This was a T,—Twist, I named *him*. The next one as comes will be Unwin, and the next Vilkins. I have got names ready made to the end of the alphabet, and all the way through it again, when we come to Z."

"Why, you're quite a literary character, Sir!" said Mrs. Mann.

"Well, well," said the beadle, evidently gratified with the compliment; "perhaps I may be. Perhaps I may be, Mrs. Mann." He finished the gin-and-water, and added, "Oliver being now too old to remain here, the board have

determined to have him back into the house. I have come out myself to take him there. So let me see him at once."

"I'll fetch him directly," said Mrs. Mann, leaving the room for that purpose. Oliver, having had by this time as much of the outer coat of dirt which encrusted his face and hands, removed, as could be scrubbed off in one washing, was led into the room by his benevolent protectress.

"Make a bow to the gentleman, Oliver," said Mrs. Mann.

Oliver made a bow, which was divided between the beadle on the chair, and the cocked-hat on the table.

"Will you go along with me, Oliver?" said Mr. Bumble in a majestic voice.

Oliver was about to say that he would go along with anybody with great readiness, when, glancing upwards, he caught sight of Mrs. Mann, who had got behind the beadle's chair, and was shaking her fist at him with a furious countenance. He took the hint at once, for the fist had been too often impressed upon his body not to be deeply impressed upon his recollection.

"Will *she* go with me?" inquired poor Oliver.

"No, she can't," replied Mr. Bumble. "But she'll come and see you sometimes."

This was no very great consolation to the child. Young as he was, however, he had sense enough to make a feint of feeling great regret at going away. It was no very difficult matter for the boy to call the tears into his eyes. Hunger and recent ill-usage are great assistants if you want to cry; and Oliver cried very naturally indeed. Mrs. Mann gave him a thousand embraces, and, what Oliver wanted a great deal more, a piece of bread and butter, lest he should seem too hungry when he got to the workhouse. With the slice of bread in his hand, and the little brown-cloth parish cap on his head, Oliver was then led away by Mr. Bumble from the wretched home where not one kind word or look had never lighted the gloom of his infant years. And yet he burst into an agony of childish grief, as the cottage-gate closed after him. Wretched as were the little companions in misery he was leaving behind, they were the only friends he had ever known; and a sense of his loneliness in the great wide world, sank into the child's heart for the first time.

Mr. Bumble walked on with long strides; little Oliver, firmly grasping his gold-laced cuff, trotted beside him, inquiring at the end of every quarter of a mile whether they were "nearly there." To these interrogations, Mr. Bumble returned very brief and snappish replies; for the temporary blandness which gin-and-water awakens in some bosoms had by this time evaporated: and he was once again a beadle.

Oliver had not been within the walls of the workhouse a quarter of an hour; and had scarcely completed the demolition of a second slice of bread, when Mr. Bumble, who had handed him over to the care of an old woman, returned; and, telling him it was a board night, informed him that the board had said he was to appear before it forthwith.

Not having a very clearly defined notion of what a live board was, Oliver was rather astounded by this intelligence, and was not quite certain whether he ought to laugh or cry. He had no time to think about the matter, however; for Mr. Bumble gave him a tap on the head, with his cane, to wake him up: and another on the back to make him lively: and bidding him follow, conducted him into a large whitewashed room, where eight or ten fat gentlemen were sitting round a table. At the top of the table, seated in an arm-chair rather higher than the rest, was a particularly fat gentleman with a very round, red face.

"Bow to the board," said Bumble. Oliver brushed away two or three tears that were lingering in his eyes; and seeing no board but the table, fortunately bowed to that.

"What's your name, boy?" said the gentleman in the high chair.

Oliver was frightened at the sight of so many gentlemen, which made him tremble; and the beadle gave him another tap behind, which made him cry; and these two causes made him answer in a very low and hesitating voice; whereupon a gentleman in a white waistcoat said he was a fool. Which was a capital way of raising his spirits, and putting him quite at his ease.

"Boy," said the gentleman in the high chair, "listen to me. You know you're an orphan, I suppose?"

"What's that, Sir?" inquired poor Oliver.

"The boy *is* a fool—I thought he was," said the gentleman in the white waistcoat.

"Hush!" said the gentleman who had spoken first. "You know you've got no father or mother, and that you were brought up by the parish, don't you?"

"Yes, Sir," replied Oliver, weeping bitterly.

"What are you crying for?" inquired the gentleman in the white waistcoat. And to be sure it was very extraordinary. What *could* the boy be crying for?

"I hope you say your prayers every night," said another gentleman in a gruff voice; "and pray for the people who feed you, and take care of you—like a Christian."

"Yes, Sir," stammered the boy. The gentleman who spoke last was unconsciously right. It would have been *very* like a Christian, and a marvellously good Christian, too, if Oliver had prayed for the people who fed and took care of *him*. But he hadn't, because nobody had taught him.

"Well! You have come here to be educated, and taught a useful trade," said the red-faced gentleman in the high chair.

"So you'll begin to pick oakum to-morrow morning at six o'clock," added the surly one in the white waistcoat.

For the combination of both these blessings in the one simple process of picking oakum, Oliver bowed low by the direction of the beadle, and was then hurried away to a large ward: where, on a rough hard bed, he sobbed himself to sleep. What a noble illustration of the tender laws of England! They let the paupers go to sleep!

Poor Oliver! He little thought, as he lay sleeping in happy unconsciousness of all around him, that the board had that very day arrived at a decision which would exercise the most material influence over all his future fortunes. But they had. And this was it:—

The members of this board were very sage, deep, philosophical men; and when they came to turn their attention to the workhouse, they found out at once, what ordinary folks would never have discovered—the poor people like it! It was a regular place of public entertainment for the poorer classes; a tavern where there was nothing to pay; a public breakfast, dinner, tea, and supper all the year round; a brick and mortar elysium, where it was all play and no work. "Oho!" said the board, looking very knowing; "we are the fellows to set this to rights; we'll stop it all, in no time." So, they established the rule, that all poor people should have the alternative (for they would compel nobody, not they), of being starved by a gradual process in the house, or by a quick one out of it. With this view, they contracted with the waterworks to lay on an unlimited supply of water; and with a corn-factor to supply periodically small quantities of oatmeal; and issued three meals of thin gruel a day, with an onion twice a week, and half a roll on Sundays. They made a great many other wise and humane regulations, having reference to the ladies, which it is not necessary to repeat; kindly undertook to divorce poor married people, in consequence of the great expense of a suit in Doctors' Commons; and, instead of compelling a man to support his family, as they had theretofore done, took his family away from him, and made him a bachelor! There is no saying how many applicants for relief under these last two heads, might have started up in all classes of society, if it had not been coupled with the workhouse; but the board were long-headed men, and had provided for this difficulty. The relief was inseparable from the workhouse and the gruel; and that frightened people.

For the first six months after Oliver Twist was removed, the system was in full operation. It was rather expensive at first, in consequence of the increase in the undertaker's bill, and the necessity of taking in the clothes of all the paupers, which fluttered loosely on their wasted, shrunken forms, after a week or two's gruel. But the number of workhouse inmates got thin as well as the paupers; and the board were in ecstasies.

The room in which the boys were fed, was a large stone hall, with a copper at one end: out of which the master, dressed in an apron for the purpose, and assisted by one or two women, ladled the gruel at meal-times. Of this festive composition each boy had one porringer, and no more—except on occasions of great public rejoicing, when he had two ounces and a quarter of bread besides. The bowls never wanted washing. The boys polished them with their spoons till they shone again; and when they had performed this operation (which never took very long, the spoons being nearly as large as the bowls), they would sit staring at the copper, with such eager eyes, as if they could have devoured the very bricks of which it was composed; employing themselves, meanwhile, in sucking their fingers most assiduously, with the view of catching up any stray splashes of gruel that might have been cast thereon. Boys have generally excellent appetites. Oliver Twist and his companions suffered the tortures of slow starvation for three months; at last they got so voracious and wild with hunger, that one boy, who was tall for his age, and hadn't been used to that sort of thing (for his father had kept a small cook-shop), hinted darkly to his companions, that unless he had another basin of gruel *per diem*, he was afraid he might some night happen to eat the boy who slept next him, who happened to be a weakly youth of tender age. He had a wild, hungry eye; and they implicitly believed him. A council was held; lots were cast who should walk up to the master after supper that evening, and ask for more; and it fell to Oliver Twist.

The evening arrived; the boys took their places. The master, in his cook's uniform, stationed himself at the copper; his pauper assistants ranged themselves behind him; the gruel was served out; and a long grace was said over the short commons. The gruel disappeared; the boys whispered each other, and winked at Oliver; while his next neighbours nudged him. Child as he was, he was desperate with hunger, and reckless with misery. He rose from the table; and advancing to the master, basin and spoon in hand, said: somewhat alarmed at his own temerity:

"Please, Sir, I want some more."

The master was a fat, healthy man; but he turned very pale. He gazed in stupefied astonishment on the small rebel for some seconds, and then clung for support to the copper. The assistants were paralysed with wonder; the boys with fear.

"What!" said the master at length, in a faint voice.

"Please, Sir," replied Oliver, "I want some more."

The master aimed a blow at Oliver's head with the ladle; pinioned him in his arms; and shrieked aloud for the beadle.

The board were sitting in solemn conclave, when Mr. Bumble rushed into the room in great excitement, and addressing the gentleman in the high chair, said,

"Mr. Limbkins, I beg your pardon, Sir! Oliver Twist has asked for more!"

There was a general start. Horror was depicted on every countenance.

"For *more!*" said Mr. Limbkins. "Compose yourself, Bumble, and answer me distinctly. Do I understand that he asked for more, after he had eaten the supper allotted by the dietary?"

"He did, Sir," replied Bumble.

"That boy will be hung," said the gentleman in the white waistcoat. "I know that boy will be hung."

Nobody controverted the prophetic gentleman's opinion. An animated discussion took place. Oliver was ordered into instant confinement; and a bill was next morning pasted on the outside of the gate, offering a reward of five pounds to anybody who would take Oliver Twist off the hands of the parish. In other words, five pounds and Oliver Twist were offered to any man or woman who wanted an apprentice to any trade, business, or calling.

"I never was more convinced of anything in my life," said the gentleman in the white waistcoat, as he knocked at the gate and read the bill next morning: "I never was more convinced of anything in my life, than I am, that that boy will come to be hung."

As I purpose to show in the sequel whether the white-waistcoated gentleman was right or not, I should perhaps mar the interest of this narrative (supposing it to possess any at all), if I ventured to hint, just yet, whether the life of Oliver Twist had this violent termination or no.

CHAPTER III.

RELATES HOW OLIVER TWIST WAS VERY NEAR GETTING A PLACE, WHICH WOULD NOT HAVE BEEN A SINECURE.

FOR a week after the commission of the impious and profane offence of asking for more, Oliver remained a close prisoner in the dark and solitary room to which he had been consigned by the wisdom and mercy of the board. It appears, at first sight, not unreasonable to suppose, that, if he had entertained a becoming feeling of respect for the prediction of the gentleman in the white waistcoat, he would have established that sage individual's prophetic character, once and for ever, by tying one end of his pocket-handkerchief to a hook in the wall, and attaching himself to the other. To the performance of this feat, however, there was one obstacle: namely, that pocket-handkerchiefs being decided articles of luxury, had been, for all future times and ages, removed from the noses of paupers by the express order of the board, in council assembled: solemnly given and pronounced under their hands and seals. There was a still greater obstacle in Oliver's youth and childishness. He only cried bitterly all day; and when the long, dismal night came on, spread his little hands before his eyes to shut out the darkness, and crouching in the corner, tried to sleep: ever and anon waking with a start and tremble, and drawing himself closer and closer to the wall, as if to feel even its cold hard surface were a protection in the gloom and loneliness which surrounded him.

Let it not be supposed by the enemies of "the system," that, during the period of his solitary incarceration, Oliver was denied the benefit of exercise, the pleasure of society, or the advantages of religious consolation. As for exercise: it was nice cold weather, and he was allowed to perform his ablutions every morning under the pump, in a stone yard, in the presence of Mr. Bumble, who prevented his catching cold, and caused a tingling sensation to pervade his frame, by repeated applications of the cane. As for society: he was carried every other day into the hall where the boys dined, and there sociably flogged as a public warning and example. And so far from being denied the advantages of religious consolation, he was kicked into the same apartment every evening at prayer-time, and there permitted to listen to, and console his mind with, a general supplication of the boys: containing a special clause, therein inserted by authority of the board, in which they entreated to be made good, virtuous, contented, and obedient, and to be guarded from the sins and vices of Oliver Twist: whom the supplication distinctly set forth to be under the exclusive patronage and protection of the powers of wickedness, and an article direct from the manufactory of the very Devil himself.

It chanced one morning, while Oliver's affairs were in this auspicious and comfortable state, that Mr. Gamfield, chimney-sweeper, was wending his way a down the High Street, deeply cogitating in his mind his ways and means of paying certain arrears of rent, for which his landlord had become rather pressing. Mr. Gamfield's most sanguine estimate of his finances could not raise them within full five pounds of the desired amount; and, in a species of arithmetical desperation, he was alternately cudgelling his brains and his donkey, when, passing the workhouse, his eyes encountered the bill on the gate.

"Wo—o!" said Mr. Gamfield to the donkey.

The donkey was in a state of profound abstraction: wondering, probably, whether he was destined to be regaled with a cabbage-stalk or two, when he had disposed of the two sacks of soot with which the little cart was laden; so, without noticing the word of command, he jogged onward.

Mr. Gamfield growled a fierce imprecation on the donkey generally, but more particularly on his eyes; and, running after him, bestowed a blow on his head, which would inevitably have beaten in any skull but a donkey's. Then, catching hold of the bridle, he gave his jaw a sharp wrench, by way of gentle reminder that he was not his own master; and by these means turned him round. He then gave him another blow on the head, just to stun him till he came back again. Having completed these arrangements, he walked up to the gate, to read the bill.

The gentleman with the white waistcoat was standing at the gate with his hands behind him, after having delivered himself of some profound sentiments in the board-room. Having witnessed the little dispute between Mr. Gamfield and the donkey, he smiled joyously when that person came up to read the bill, for he saw at once that Mr. Gamfield was exactly the sort of master Oliver Twist wanted. Mr. Gamfield smiled, too, as he perused the document, for five pounds was just the sum he had been wishing for; and, as to the boy with which it was encumbered, Mr. Gamfield, knowing what the dietary of the workhouse was, well knew he would be a nice small pattern, just the very thing for register stoves. So, he spelt the bill through again, from beginning to end; and then, touching his fur cap in token of humility, accosted the gentleman in the white waistcoat.

"This here boy, Sir, wot the parish wants to 'prentis," said Mr. Gamfield.

"Ay, my man," said the gentleman in the white waist-coat, with a condescending smile. "What of him?"

"If the parish vould like him to learn a light pleasant trade, in a good 'spectable chimbley-sweepin' bisness," said Mr. Gamfield, "I wants a 'prentis, and I am ready to take him."

"Walk in," said the gentleman in the white waistcoat. Mr. Gamfield having lingered behind, to give the donkey another blow on the head, and another wrench of the jaw, as a caution not to run away in his absence: followed the gentleman with the white waistcoat into the room where Oliver had first seen him.

"It's a nasty trade," said Mr. Limbkins, when Gamfield had again stated his wish.

"Young boys have been smothered in chimneys before now," said another gentleman.

"That's acause they damped the straw afore they lit it in the chimbley to make 'em come down agin," said Gamfield; "that's all smoke, and no blaze; vereas smoke ain't o' no use at all in making a boy come down, for it only sinds him to sleep, and that's wot he likes. Boys is wery obstinit, and wery lazy, gen'lmen, and there's nothink like a good hot blaze to make 'em come down vith a run. It's humane too, gen'lmen, acause, even if they've stuck in the chimbley, roasting their feet makes 'em struggle to hextricate theirselves."

The gentleman in the white waistcoat appeared very much amused by this explanation; but his mirth was speedily checked by a look from Mr. Limbkins. The board then proceeded to converse among themselves for a few minutes, but in so low a tone, that the words "saving of expenditure," "looked well in the accounts," "have a printed report published," were alone audible. These only chanced to be heard, indeed, on account of their being very frequently repeated with great emphasis.

At length the whispering ceased; and the members of the board, having resumed their seats and their solemnity, Mr. Limbkins said:

"We have considered your proposition, and we don't approve of it."

"Not at all," said the gentleman in the white waistcoat.

"Decidedly not," added the other members.

As Mr. Gamfield did happen to labour under the slight imputation of having bruised three or four boys to death already, it occurred to him that the board had, perhaps, in some unaccountable freak, taken it into their heads that this extraneous circumstance ought to influence their proceedings. It was very unlike their general mode of doing business, if they had; but still, as he had no particular wish to revive the rumour, he twisted his cap in his hands, and walked slowly from the table.

"So you won't let me have him, gen'lmen?" said Mr. Gamfield, pausing near the door.

"No," replied Mr. Limbkins; "at least, as it's a nasty business, we think you ought to take something less than the premium we offered."

Mr. Gamfield's countenance brightened, as, with a quick step he returned to the table, and said,

"What'll you give, gen'lmen? Come! Don't be too hard on a poor man. What'll you give?"

"I should say three pound ten was plenty," said Mr. Limbkins.

"Ten shillings too much," said the gentleman in the white waistcoat.

"Come!" said Gamfield; "say four pound, gen'lmen. Say four pound, and you've got rid on him for good and all. There!"

"Three pound ten," repeated Mr. Limbkins, firmly.

"Come! I'll split the difference, gen'lmen," urged Gamfield. "Three pound fifteen."

"Not a farthing more," was the firm reply of Mr. Limbkins.

"You're desperate hard upon me, genl'men," said Gamfield, wavering.

"Pooh! pooh! nonsense!" said the gentleman in the white waistcoat. "He'd be cheap with nothing at all, as a premium. Take him, you silly fellow! He's just the boy for you. He wants the stick, now and then: it'll do him good; and his board needn't come very expensive, for he hasn't been over-fed since he was born. Ha! ha! ha!"

Mr. Gamfield gave an arch look at the faces round the table, and, observing a smile on all of them, gradually broke into a smile himself. The bargain was made. Mr. Bumble was at once instructed that Oliver Twist and his indentures were to be conveyed before the magistrate, for signature and approval, that very afternoon.

In pursuance of this determination, little Oliver, to his excessive astonishment, was released from bondage, and ordered to put himself into a clean shirt. He had hardly achieved this very unusual gymnastic performance, when Mr. Bumble brought him, with his own hands, a basin of gruel, and the holiday allowance of two ounces and a quarter of bread. At this tremendous sight, Oliver began to cry very piteously: thinking, not unnaturally, that the board must have determined to kill him for some useful purpose, or they never would have begun to fatten him up in that way.

"Don't make your eyes red, Oliver, but eat your food and be thankful," said Mr. Bumble, in a tone of impressive pomposity. "You're a going to be made a 'prentice of, Oliver."

"A 'prentice, Sir!" said the child, trembling.

"Yes, Oliver," said Mr. Bumble. "The kind and blessed gentlemen which is so many parents to you, Oliver, when you have none of your own: are a going to 'prentice you: and to set you up in life, and make a man of you: although the expense to the parish is three pound ten!—three pound ten, Oliver!—seventy shillins—one hundred and forty sixpences!—and all for a naughty orphan which nobody can't love."

As Mr. Bumble paused to take breath, after delivering this address in an awful voice, the tears rolled down the poor child's face, and he sobbed bitterly.

"Come," said Mr. Bumble, somewhat less pompously, for it was gratifying to his feelings to observe the effect his eloquence had produced; "Come, Oliver! Wipe your eyes with the cuffs of your jacket, and don't cry into your gruel; that's a very foolish action, Oliver." It certainly was, for there was quite enough water in it already.

On their way to the magistrate, Mr. Bumble instructed

Oliver that all he would have to do, would be to look very happy, and say, when the gentleman asked him if he wanted to be apprenticed, that he should like it very much indeed; both of which injunctions Oliver promised to obey: the rather as Mr. Bumble threw in a gentle hint, that if he failed in either particular, there was no telling what would be done to him. When they arrived at the office, he was shut up in a little room by himself, and admonished by Mr. Bumble to stay there, until he came back to fetch him.

There the boy remained, with a palpitating heart, for half an hour. At the expiration of which time Mr. Bumble thrust in his head, unadorned with the cocked hat, and said aloud:

"Now, Oliver, my dear, come to the gentleman." As Mr. Bumble said this, he put on a grim and threatening look, and added, in a low voice, "Mind what I told you, you young rascal!"

Oliver stared innocently in Mr. Bumble's face at this somewhat contradictory style of address; but that gentleman prevented his offering any remark thereupon, by leading him at once into an adjoining room: the door of which was open. It was a large room, with a great window. Behind a desk, sat two old gentlemen with powdered heads: one of whom was reading the newspaper: while the other was perusing, with the aid of a pair of tortoise-shell spectacles, a small piece of parchment which lay before him. Mr. Limbkins was standing in front of the desk on one side; and Mr. Gamfield, with a partially washed face, on the other; while two or three bluff-looking men, in top-boots, were lounging about.

The old gentleman with the spectacles gradually dozed off, over the little bit of parchment; and there was a short pause, after Oliver had been stationed by Mr. Bumble in front of the desk.

"This is the boy, your worship," said Mr. Bumble.

The old gentleman who was reading the newspaper raised his head for a moment, and pulled the other old gentleman by the sleeve; whereupon, the last-mentioned old gentleman woke up.

"Oh, is this the boy?" said the old gentleman.

"This is him, Sir," replied Mr. Bumble. "Bow to the magistrate, my dear."

Oliver roused himself, and made his best obeisance. He had been wondering, with his eyes fixed on the magistrate's powder, whether all boards were born with that white stuff on their heads, and were boards from thenceforth on that account.

"Well," said the old gentleman, "I suppose he's fond of chimney-sweeping?"

"He doats on it, your worship," replied Bumble: giving Oliver a sly pinch, to intimate that he had better not say he didn't.

"And he *will* be a sweep, will he?" inquired the old gentleman.

"If we was to bind him to any other trade to-morrow, he'd run away simultaneous, your worship," replied Bumble.

"And this man that's to be his master—you, Sir—you'll treat him well, and feed him, and do all that sort of thing, will you?" said the old gentleman.

"When I says I will, I means I will," replied Mr. Gamfield doggedly.

"You're a rough speaker, my friend, but you look an honest, open-hearted man," said the old gentleman: turning his spectacles in the direction of the candidate for Oliver's premium, whose villanous countenance was a regular stamped receipt for cruelty. But the magistrate was half blind and half childish, so he couldn't reasonably be expected to discern what other people did.

"I hope I am, Sir," said Mr. Gamfield, with an ugly leer.

"I have no doubt you are, my friend," replied the old gentleman: fixing his spectacles more firmly on his nose, and looking about him for the inkstand.

It was the critical moment of Oliver's fate. If the inkstand had been where the old gentleman thought it was, he would have dipped his pen into it, and signed the indentures, and Oliver would have been straightway hurried off. But, as it chanced to be immediately under his nose, it followed, as a matter of course, that he looked all over his desk for it, without finding it; and happening in the course of his search to look straight before him, his gaze encountered the pale and terrified face of Oliver Twist: who, despite all the admonitory looks and pinches of Bumble, was regarding the repulsive countenance of his future master, with a mingled expression of horror and fear, too palpable to be mistaken, even by a half-blind magistrate.

The old gentleman stopped, laid down his pen, and looked from Oliver to Mr. Limbkins; who attempted to take snuff with a cheerful and unconcerned aspect.

"My boy!" said the old gentleman, leaning over the desk. Oliver started at the sound. He might be excused for doing so: for the words were kindly said; and strange sounds frighten one. He trembled violently, and burst into tears.

"My boy!" said the old gentleman, "you look pale and alarmed. What is the matter?"

"Stand a little away from him, Beadle," said the other magistrate: laying aside the paper, and leaning forward with an expression of interest. "Now, boy, tell us what's the matter: don't be afraid."

Oliver fell on his knees, and clasping his hands together, prayed that they would order him back to the dark room—that they would starve him—beat him—kill him if they pleased—rather than send him away with that dreadful man.

"Well!" said Mr. Bumble, raising his hands and eyes with most impressive solemnity, "Well! of all the artful and designing orphans that ever I see, Oliver, you are one of the most bare-facedest."

"Hold your tongue, Beadle," said the second old gentleman, when Mr. Bumble had given vent to this compound adjective.

"I beg your worship's pardon," said Mr. Bumble, incredulous of his having heard aright. "Did your worship speak to me?"

"Yes. Hold your tongue."

Mr. Bumble was stupefied with astonishment. A beadle ordered to hold his tongue! A moral revolution!

The old gentleman in the tortoise-shell spectacles looked at his companion; he nodded significantly.

"We refuse to sanction these indentures," said the old gentleman: tossing aside the piece of parchment as he spoke.

"I hope," stammered Mr. Limbkins: "I hope the magistrates will not form the opinion that the authorities have been guilty of any improper conduct, on the unsupported testimony of a mere child."

"The magistrates are not called upon to pronounce any opinion on the matter," said the second old gentleman sharply. "Take the boy back to the workhouse, and treat him kindly. He seems to want it."

That same evening, the gentleman in the white waistcoat most positively and decidedly affirmed, not only that Oliver would be hung, but that he would be drawn and quartered into the bargain. Mr. Bumble shook his head with gloomy

**OLIVER ESCAPES BEING BOUND APPRENTICE
TO THE SWEEP.**

mystery, and said he wished he might come to good; where-unto Mr. Gamfield replied, that he wished he might come to him; which, although he agreed with the beadle in most matters, would seem to be a wish of a totally opposite description.

The next morning, the public were once more informed that Oliver Twist was again To Let; and that five pounds would be paid to anybody who would take possession of him.

CHAPTER IV.

OLIVER, BEING OFFERED ANOTHER PLACE, MAKES HIS FIRST ENTRY INTO PUBLIC LIFE.

In great families, when an advantageous place cannot be obtained, either in possession, reversion, remainder, or expectancy, for the young man who is growing up, it is a very general custom to send him to sea. The board, in imitation of so wise and salutary an example, took counsel together on the expediency of shipping off Oliver Twist, in some small trading vessel bound to a good unhealthy port; which suggested itself as the very best thing that could possibly be done with him: the probability being, that the skipper would flog him to death, in a playful mood, some day after dinner, or would knock his brains out with an iron bar; both pastimes being, as is pretty generally known, very favourite and common recreations among gentlemen of that class. The more the case presented itself to the board, in this point of view, the more manifold the advantages of the step appeared; so they came to the conclusion that the only way of providing for Oliver effectually, was to send him to sea without delay.

Mr. Bumble had been despatched to make various pre-liminary inquiries, with the view of finding out some captain or other who wanted a cabin-boy without any friends; and was returning to the workhouse to communicate the result of his mission; when he encountered, just at the gate, no less a person than Mr. Sowerberry, the parochial under-taker.

Mr. Sowerberry was a tall, gaunt, large-jointed man, attired in a suit of thread-bare black, with darned cotton stockings of the same colour, and shoes to answer. His features were not naturally intended to wear a smiling aspect, but he was in general rather given to professional jocosity. His step was elastic, and his face betokened in-ward pleasantry, as he advanced to Mr. Bumble, and shook him cordially by the hand.

"I have taken the measure of the two women that died last night, Mr. Bumble," said the undertaker.

"You'll make your fortune, Mr. Sowerberry," said the beadle, as he thrust his thumb and forefinger into the prof-fered snuff-box of the undertaker: which was an ingenious little model of a patent coffin. "I say you'll make your fortune, Mr. Sowerberry," repeated Mr. Bumble, tapping the undertaker on the shoulder, in a friendly manner, with his cane.

"Think so?" said the undertaker in a tone which half admitted and half disputed the probability of the event. "The prices allowed by the board are very small, Mr. Bumble."

"So are the coffins," replied the beadle: with precisely as near an approach to a laugh as a great official ought to indulge in.

Mr. Sowerberry was much tickled at this: as of course he ought to be; and laughed a long time without cessation. "Well, well, Mr. Bumble," he said at length, "there's no denying that, since the new system of feeding has come in, the coffins are something narrower and more shallow than they used to be; but we must have some profit, Mr. Bumble. Well-seasoned timber is an expensive article, Sir; and all the iron handles come, by canal, from Birmingham."

"Well, well," said Mr. Bumble, "every trade has its drawbacks. A fair profit is, of course, allowable."

"Of course, of course," replied the undertaker; "and if I don't get a profit upon this or that particular article, why, I make it up in the long-run, you see—he! he! he!"

"Just so," said Mr. Bumble.

"Though I must say," continued the undertaker, resuming the current of observations which the beadle had inter-rupted: "though I must say, Mr. Bumble, that I have to contend against one very great disadvantage: which is, that all the stout people go off the quickest. The people who have been better off, and have paid rates for many years, are the first to sink when they come into the house; and let me tell you, Mr. Bumble, that three or four inches over one's calculation makes a great hole in one's profits: especially when one has a family to provide for, Sir."

As Mr. Sowerberry said this, with the becoming indigna-tion of an ill-used man; and as Mr. Bumble felt that it rather tended to convey a reflection on the honour of the parish; the latter gentleman thought it advisable to change the subject. Oliver Twist being uppermost in his mind, he made him his theme.

"By the bye," said Mr. Bumble, "you don't know any-body who wants a boy, do you? A porochial 'prentis, who is at present a deadweight; a millstone, as I may say; round the porochial throat? Liberal terms, Mr. Sower-berry, liberal terms!" As Mr. Bumble spoke, he raised his cane to the bill above him, and gave three distinct raps upon the words "five pounds;" which were printed thereon in Roman capitals of gigantic size.

"Gadso!" said the undertaker: taking Mr. Bumble by the gilt-edged lappel of his official coat; "that's just the very thing I wanted to speak to you about. You know— dear me, what a very elegant button this is, Mr. Bumble! I never noticed it before."

"Yes, I think it is rather pretty," said the beadle, glancing proudly downwards at the large brass buttons which embellished his coat. "The die is the same as the porochial seal—the Good Samaritan healing the sick and bruised man. The board presented it to me on New-year's morning, Mr. Sowerberry. I put it on, I remember, for the first time, to attend the inquest on that reduced trades-man, who died in a doorway at midnight."

"I recollect," said the undertaker. "The jury brought it in, 'Died from exposure to the cold, and want of the common necessaries of life,' didn't they?"

Mr. Bumble nodded.

"And they made it a special verdict, I think," said the undertaker, "by adding some words to the effect, that if the relieving officer had——"

"Tush! Foolery!" interposed the beadle. "If the board attended to all the nonsense that ignorant jurymen talk, they'd have enough to do."

"Very true," said the undertaker; "they would indeed."

"Juries," said Mr. Bumble, grasping his cane tightly, as was his wont when working into a passion: "juries is in-eddicated, vulgar, grovelling wretches."

"So they are," said the undertaker.

"They haven't no more philosophy nor political economy about 'em than that," said the beadle, snapping his fingers contemptuously.

"No more they have," acquiesced the undertaker.

"I despise 'em," said the beadle, growing very red in the face.

"So do I," rejoined the undertaker.

"And I only wish we'd a jury of the independent sort, in the house for a week or two," said the beadle; "the rules and regulations of the board would soon bring their spirit down for 'em."

"Let 'em alone for that," replied the undertaker. So saying, he smiled, approvingly: to calm the rising wrath of the indignant parish officer.

Mr. Bumble lifted off his cocked hat; took a handkerchief from the inside of the crown; wiped from his forehead the perspiration which his rage had engendered; fixed the cocked hat on again; and, turning to the undertaker, said in a calmer voice:

"Well; what about the boy?"

"Oh!" replied the undertaker; "why, you know, Mr. Bumble, I pay a good deal toward the poor's rates."

"Hem!" said Mr. Bumble. "Well?"

"Well," replied the undertaker, "I was thinking that if I pay so much towards 'em, I've a right to get as much out of 'em as I can, Mr. Bumble; and so—and so—I think I'll take the boy myself."

Mr. Bumble grasped the undertaker by the arm, and led him into the building. Mr. Sowerberry was closeted with the board for five minutes; and it was arranged that Oliver should go to him that evening "upon liking"—a phrase which means, in the case of a parish apprentice, that if the master find, upon a short trial, that he can get enough work out of a boy without putting too much food into him, he shall have him for a term of years, to do what he likes with.

When little Oliver was taken before "the gentleman" that evening; and informed that he was to go, that night, as general house-lad to a coffin-maker's; and that if he complained of his situation, or ever came back to the parish again, he would be sent to sea, there to be drowned, or knocked on the head, as the case might be, he evinced so little emotion, that they by common consent pronounced him a hardened young rascal, and ordered Mr. Bumble to remove him forthwith.

Now, although it was very natural that the board, of all people in the world, should feel in a great state of virtuous astonishment and horror at the smallest tokens of want of feeling on the part of anybody, they were rather out, in this particular instance. The simple fact was, that Oliver, instead of possessing too little feeling, possessed rather too much; and was in a fair way of being reduced, for life, to a state of brutal stupidity and sullenness by the ill usage he had received. He heard the news of his destination, in perfect silence; and, having had his luggage put into his hand—which was not very difficult to carry, inasmuch as it was all comprised within the limits of a brown paper parcel, about half a foot square by three inches deep—he pulled his cap over his eyes; and once more attaching himself to Mr. Bumble's coat cuff, was led away by that dignitary to a new scene of suffering.

For some time, Mr. Bumble drew Oliver along, without notice or remark; for the beadle carried his head very erect, as a beadle always should: and, it being a windy day, little Oliver was completely enshrouded by the skirts of Mr. Bumble's coat as they blew open, and disclosed to great advantage his flapped waistcoat and drab plush knee-breeches. As they drew near to their destination, however, Mr. Bumble thought it expedient to look down, and see that the boy was in good order for inspection by his new master: which he accordingly did, with a fit and becoming air of gracious patronage.

"Oliver!" said Mr. Bumble.

"Yes, Sir," replied Oliver, in a low, tremulous voice.

"Pull that cap off your eyes, and hold up your head, Sir."

Although Oliver did as he was desired, at once; and passed the back of his unoccupied hand briskly across his eyes, he left a tear in them when he looked up at his conductor. As Mr. Bumble gazed sternly upon him, it rolled down his cheek. It was followed by another, and another. The child made a strong effort, but it was an unsuccessful one. Withdrawing his other hand from Mr. Bumble's, he covered his face with both; and wept until the tears sprang out from between his thin and bony fingers.

"Well!" exclaimed Mr. Bumble, stopping short, and darting at his little charge a look of intense malignity. "Well! Of *all* the ungratefullest, and worst-disposed boys as ever I see, Oliver, you are the——"

"No, no, Sir," sobbed Oliver, clinging to the hand which held the well-known cane; "no, no, Sir; I will be good indeed; indeed, indeed I will, Sir! I am a very little boy, Sir; and it is so—so—"

"So what?" inquired Mr. Bumble in amazement.

"So lonely, Sir! So very lonely!" cried the child. "Everybody hates me. Oh! Sir, don't, don't pray be cross to me!" The child beat his hand upon his heart; and looked in his companion's face, with tears of real agony.

Mr. Bumble regarded Oliver's piteous and helpless look, with some astonishment, for a few seconds; hemmed three or four times in a husky manner, and, after muttering something about "that troublesome cough," bade Oliver dry his eyes and be a good boy. Then, once more taking his hand, he walked on with him in silence.

The undertaker, who had just put up the shutters of his shop, was making some entries in his day-book by the light of a most appropriately dismal candle, when Mr. Bumble entered.

"Aha!" said the undertaker: looking up from the book, and pausing in the middle of a word; "is that you, Bumble?"

"No one else, Mr. Sowerberry," replied the beadle. "Here! I've brought the boy." Oliver made a bow.

"Oh! that's the boy, is it?" said the undertaker: raising the candle above his head, to get a better view of Oliver. "Mrs. Sowerberry! Will you have the goodness to come here a moment, my dear?"

Mrs. Sowerberry emerged from a little room behind the shop, and presented the form of a short, thin, squeezed-up woman, with a vixenish countenance.

"My dear," said Mr. Sowerberry, deferentially, "this is the boy from the workhouse that I told you of." Oliver bowed again.

"Dear me!" said the undertaker's wife, "he's very small."

"Why, he *is* rather small," replied Mr. Bumble: looking at Oliver as if it were his fault that he was no bigger; "he *is* small. There's no denying it. But he'll grow, Mrs. Sowerberry—he'll grow."

"Ah! I dare say he will," replied the lady pettishly, "on our victuals and our drink. I see no saving in parish children, not I; for they always cost more to keep, than they're worth. However, men always think they know best. There! Get down stairs, little bag o' bones." With this, the undertaker's wife opened a side door, and pushed Oliver down a steep flight of stairs into a stone cell, damp and dark: forming the ante-room to the coal-cellar, and denominated "kitchen:" wherein sat a slatternly girl, in shoes down at heel, and blue worsted stockings very much out of repair.

"Here, Charlotte," said Mrs. Sowerberry, who had followed Oliver down, "give this boy some of the cold bits that were put by for Trip. He hasn't come home since the morning, so he may go without 'em. I dare say the boy isn't too dainty to eat 'em,—are you, boy?"

Oliver, whose eyes had glistened at the mention of meat, and who was trembling with eagerness to devour it, replied in the negative; and a plateful of coarse broken victuals was set before him.

I wish some well-fed philosopher, whose meat and drink turn to gall within him; whose blood is ice, whose heart is iron; could have seen Oliver Twist clutching at the dainty viands that the dog had neglected. I wish he could have witnessed the horrible avidity with which Oliver tore the bits asunder with all the ferocity of famine. There is only one thing I should like better; and that would be to see the Philosopher making the same sort of meal himself, with the same relish.

"Well," said the undertaker's wife, when Oliver had finished his supper: which she had regarded in silent horror, and with fearful auguries of his future appetite: "have you done?"

There being nothing eatable within his reach, Oliver replied in the affirmative.

"Then come with me," said Mrs. Sowerberry: taking up a dim and dirty lamp, and leading the way up stairs; "your bed's under the counter. You don't mind sleeping among the coffins, I suppose? But it doesn't much matter whether you do or don't, for you can't sleep anywhere else. Come; don't keep me here all night!"

Oliver lingered no longer, but meekly followed his new mistress.

CHAPTER V.

OLIVER MINGLES WITH NEW ASSOCIATES. GOING TO A FUNERAL FOR THE FIRST TIME, HE FORMS AN UNFAVORABLE NOTION OF HIS MASTER'S BUSINESS.

OLIVER, being left to himself in the undertaker's shop, set the lamp down on a workman's bench, and gazed timidly about him with a feeling of awe and dread, which many people a good deal older than he will be at no loss to understand. An unfinished coffin on black tressels, which stood in the middle of the shop, looked so gloomy and death-like that a cold tremble came over him, every time his eyes wandered in the direction of the dismal object: from which he almost expected to see some frightful form slowly rear its head, to drive him mad with terror. Against the wall were ranged, in regular array, a long row of elm boards cut into the same shape: looking in the dim light, like high-shouldered ghosts with their hands in their breeches-pockets. Coffin-plates, elm-chips, bright-headed nails, and shreds of

black cloth, lay scattered on the floor; and the wall behind the counter was ornamented with a lively representation of two mutes in very stiff neckcloths, on duty at a large private door, with a hearse drawn by four black steeds, approaching in the distance. The shop was close and hot; and the atmosphere seemed tainted with the smell of coffins. The recess beneath the counter in which his flock mattress was thrust, looked like a grave.

Nor were these the only dismal feelings which depressed Oliver. He was alone in a strange place; and we all know how chilled and desolate the best of us will sometimes feel in such a situation. The boy had no friends to care for, or to care for him. The regret of no recent separation was fresh in his mind; the absence of no loved and well-remembered face sank heavily into his heart. But his heart *was* heavy, notwithstanding; and he wished, as he crept into his narrow bed, that that were his coffin, and that he could be lain in a calm and lasting sleep in the church-yard ground, with the tall grass waving gently above his head, and the sound of the old deep bell to soothe him in his sleep.

Oliver was awakened in the morning, by a loud kicking at the outside of the shop-door: which, before he could huddle on his clothes, was repeated, in an angry and impetuous manner, about twenty-five times. When he began to undo the chain, the legs desisted, and a voice began.

"Open the door, will yer?" cried the voice which belonged to the legs which had kicked at the door.

"I will, directly, Sir," replied Oliver: undoing the chain, and turning the key.

"I suppose yer the new boy, ain't yer?" said the voice through the key-hole.

"Yes, Sir," replied Oliver.

"How old are yer?" inquired the voice.

"Ten, Sir," replied Oliver.

"Then I'll whop yer when I get in," said the voice; "you just see if I don't, that's all, my work'us brat!" and having made this obliging promise, the voice began to whistle.

Oliver had been too often subjected to the process to which the very expressive monosyllable just recorded bears reference, to entertain the smallest doubt that the owner of the voice, whoever he might be, would redeem his pledge, most honourably. He drew back the bolts with a trembling hand, and opened the door.

For a second or two, Oliver glanced up the street, and down the street, and over the way: impressed with the belief that the unknown, who had addressed him through the key-hole, had walked a few paces off, to warm himself; for nobody did he see but a big charity-boy, sitting on a post in front of the house, eating a slice of bread and butter: which he cut into wedges, the size of his mouth, with a clasp knife, and then consumed with great dexterity.

"I beg your pardon, Sir," said Oliver, at length: seeing that no other visitor made his appearance; "did you knock?"

"I kicked," replied the charity-boy.

"Did you want a coffin, Sir?" inquired Oliver, innocently.

At this the charity-boy looked monstrous fierce; and said that Oliver would want one before long, if he cut jokes with his superiors in that way.

"Yer don't know who I am, I suppose, Work'us?" said the charity boy, in continuation: descending from the top of the post, meanwhile, with edifying gravity.

"No, Sir," rejoined Oliver.

"I'm Mister Noah Claypole," said the charity-boy, "and you're under me. Take down the shutters, yer idle young ruffian!" With this, Mr. Claypole administered a kick to Oliver, and entered the shop with a dignified air, which did him great credit. It is difficult for a large-headed, small-eyed youth, of lumbering make and heavy countenance, to look dignified under any circumstances; but it is more especially so, when superadded to these personal attractions are a red nose and yellow smalls.

Oliver, having taken down the shutters, and broken a pane of glass in his efforts to stagger away beneath the weight of the first one to a small court at the side of the house in which they were kept during the day, was graciously assisted by Noah: who, having consoled him with the assurance that "he'd catch it," condescended to help him. Mr. Sowerberry came down soon after. Shortly afterwards, Mrs. Sowerberry appeared; and Oliver having "caught it," in fulfilment of Noah's prediction, followed that young gentleman down stairs to breakfast.

"Come near the fire, Noah," said Charlotte. "I saved a nice little bit of bacon for you from master's breakfast. Oliver, shut that door at Mister Noah's back, and take them bits that I've put out on the cover of the bread-pan. There's your tea; take it away to that box, and drink it there, and make haste, for they'll want you to mind the shop. D'ye hear?"

"D'ye hear, Work'us?" said Noah Claypole.

"Lor, Noah!" said Charlotte, "what a rum creature you are! Why don't you let the boy alone?"

"Let him alone!" said Noah. "Why everybody lets him alone enough, for the matter of that. Neither his father nor his mother will ever interfere with him. All his relations let him have his own way pretty well. Eh, Charlotte? He! he! he!"

"Oh, you queer soul!" said Charlotte, bursting into a hearty laugh, in which she was joined by Noah; after which, they both looked scornfully at poor Oliver Twist, as he sat shivering on the box in the coldest corner of the room, and ate the stale pieces which had been specially reserved for him.

Noah was a charity-boy, but not a workhouse orphan. No chance-child was he, for he could trace his genealogy all the way back to his parents, who lived hard by; his mother being a washerwoman, and his father a drunken soldier, discharged with a wooden leg, and a diurnal pension of twopence-halfpenny and an unstateable fraction. The shop-boys in the neighbourhood had long been in the habit of branding Noah, in the public streets, with the ignominious epithets of "leathers," "charity," and the like; and Noah had borne them without reply. But, now that fortune had cast in his way a nameless orphan, at whom even the meanest could point the finger of scorn, he retorted on him with interest. This affords charming food for contemplation. It shows us what a beautiful thing human nature sometimes is; and how impartially the same amiable qualities are developed in the finest lord and the dirtiest charity-boy.

Oliver had been sojourning at the undertaker's some three weeks or a month. Mr. and Mrs. Sowerberry: the shop being shut up—were taking their supper in the little back-parlour, when Mr. Sowerberry, after several deferential glances at his wife, said,

"My dear—" He was going to say more; but, Mrs. Sowerberry looking up, with a peculiarly unpropitious aspect, he stopped short.

"Well," said Mrs. Sowerberry, sharply.

"Nothing, my dear, nothing," said Mr. Sowerberry.

"Ugh, you brute!" said Mrs. Sowerberry.

"Not at all, my dear," said Mr. Sowerberry humbly. "I thought you didn't want to hear, my dear. I was only going to say——"

"Oh, don't tell me what you were going to say," interposed Mrs. Sowerberry. "I am nobody; don't consult me, pray. I don't want to intrude upon your secrets." As Mrs. Sowerberry said this, she gave an hysterical laugh, which threatened violent consequences.

"But, my dear," said Sowerberry, "I want to ask your advice."

"No, no, don't ask mine," replied Mrs. Sowerberry, in an affecting manner: "ask somebody else's." Here, there was another hysterical laugh, which frightened Mr. Sowerberry very much. This is a very common and much-approved matrimonial course of treatment, which is often very effective. It at once reduced Mr. Sowerberry to begging, as a special favour, to be allowed to say what Mrs. Sowerberry was most curious to hear. After a short altercation of less than three quarters of an hour's duration, the permission was most graciously conceded.

"It's only about young Twist, my dear," said Mr. Sowerberry. "A very good-looking boy that, my dear."

"He need be, for he eats enough," observed the lady.

"There's an expression of melancholy in his face, my dear," resumed Mr. Sowerberry, "which is very interesting. He would make a delightful mute, my love."

Mrs. Sowerberry looked up with an expression of considerable wonderment. Mr. Sowerberry remarked it; and, without allowing time for any observation on the good lady's part, proceeded.

"I don't mean a regular mute to attend grown-up people, my dear, but only for children's practice. It would be very new to have a mute in proportion, my dear. You may depend upon it, it would have a most superb effect."

Mrs. Sowerberry, who had a good deal of taste in the undertaking way, was much struck by the novelty of this idea; but, as it would have been compromising her dignity to have said so, under existing circumstances, she merely inquired, with much sharpness, why such an obvious suggestion had not presented itself to her husband's mind before? Mr. Sowerberry rightly construed this, as an acquiescence in his proposition; it was speedily determined, therefore, that Oliver should be at once initiated into the mysteries of the trade; and, with this view, that he should accompany his master on the very next occasion of his services being required.

The occasion was not long in coming. Half an hour after breakfast next morning, Mr. Bumble entered the shop; and supporting his cane against the counter, drew forth his large leathern pocket-book: from which he selected a small scrap of paper, which he handed over to Sowerberry.

"Aha!" said the undertaker, glancing over it with a lively countenance; "an order for a coffin, eh?"

"For a coffin first, and a porochial funeral afterwards," replied Mr. Bumble, fastening the strap of the leathern pocket-book: which, like himself, was very corpulent.

"Bayton," said the undertaker, looking from the scrap of paper to Mr. Bumble. "I never heard the name before."

Bumble shook his head, as he replied, "Obstinate people, Mr. Sowerberry; very obstinate. Proud, too, I'm afraid, Sir."

"Proud, eh?" exclaimed Mr. Sowerberry with a sneer. "Come, that's too much."

"Oh, it's sickening," replied the beadle. "Antimonial, Mr. Sowerberry!"

"So it is," acquiesced the undertaker.

"We only heard of the family the night before last," said the beadle; "and we shouldn't have known anything about them, then, only a woman who lodges in the same house made an application to the porochial committee for them to send the porochial surgeon to see a woman as was very bad. He had gone out to dinner; but his 'prentice (which is a very clever lad) sent 'em some medicine in a blacking-bottle, off-hand."

"Ah, there's promptness," said the undertaker.

"Promptness, indeed!" replied the beadle. "But what's the consequence; what's the ungrateful behaviour of these rebels, Sir? Why, the husband sends back word that the medicine won't suit his wife's complaint, and so she shan't take it—says she shan't take it, Sir! Good, strong, wholesome medicine, as was given with great success to two Irish labourers and a coalheaver, only a week before— sent 'em for nothing, with a blackin-bottle in,—and he sends back word that she shan't take it, Sir."

As the atrocity presented itself to Mr. Bumble's mind in full force, he struck the counter sharply with his cane, and became flushed with indignation.

"Well," said the undertaker, "I ne—ver—did——"

"Never did, Sir!" ejaculated the beadle. "No, nor nobody never did; but, now she's dead, we've got to bury her; and that's the direction; and the sooner it's done, the better."

Thus saying, Mr. Bumble put on his cocked hat wrong side first, in a fever of parochial excitement; and flounced out of the shop.

"Why, he was so angry, Oliver, that he forgot even to ask after you!" said Mr. Sowerberry, looking after the beadle as he strode down the street.

"Yes, Sir," replied Oliver, who had carefully kept himself out of sight, during the interview; and who was shaking from head to foot at the mere recollection of the sound of Mr. Bumble's voice. He needn't have taken the trouble to shrink from Mr. Bumble's glance, however; for that functionary, on whom the prediction of the gentleman in the white waistcoat had made a very strong impression, thought that now the undertaker had got Oliver upon trial, the subject was better avoided, until such time as he should be firmly bound for seven years, and all danger of his being returned upon the hands of the parish should be thus effectually and legally overcome.

"Well," said Mr. Sowerberry, taking up his hat, "the sooner this job is done, the better. Noah, look after the shop. Oliver, put on your cap, and come with me." Oliver obeyed, and followed his master on his professional mission.

They walked on, for some time, through the most crowded and densely inhabited part of the town; and then, striking down a narrow street more dirty and miserable than any they had yet passed through, paused to look for the house which was the object of their search. The houses on either side were high and large, but very old, and tenanted by people of the poorest class: as their neglected appearance would have sufficiently denoted, without the concurrent testimony afforded by the squalid looks of the few men and women who, with folded arms and bodies half doubled, occasionally skulked along. A great many of the tenements had shop-fronts; but these were fast closed, and mouldering away: only the upper rooms being inhabited. Some houses which had become insecure from age and decay, were prevented from falling into the street, by huge beams of wood reared against the walls, and firmly planted in the road; but even these crazy dens seemed to have been selected as the nightly haunts of some houseless wretches, for many of the rough boards, which supplied the place of door and window, were wrenched from their positions, to afford an aperture wide enough for the passage of a human body. The kennel was stagnant and filthy. The very rats, which here and there lay putrefying in its rottenness, were hideous with famine.

There was neither knocker nor bell-handle at the open door where Oliver and his master stopped; so, groping his way cautiously through the dark passage, and bidding Oliver keep close to him and not be afraid, the undertaker mounted to the top of the first flight of stairs; and stumbling against a door on the landing, rapped at it with his knuckles.

It was opened by a young girl of thirteen or fourteen. The undertaker at once saw enough of what the room contained, to know it was the apartment to which he had been directed. He stepped in; and Oliver followed him.

There was no fire in the room; but a man was crouching, mechanically, over the empty stove. An old woman, too, had drawn a low stool to the cold hearth, and was sitting beside him. There were some ragged children in another corner; and in a small recess, opposite the door, there lay upon the ground, something covered with an old blanket. Oliver shuddered as he cast his eyes towards the place, and crept involuntarily closer to his master; for though it was covered up, the boy felt that it was a corpse.

The man's face was thin and very pale; his hair and beard were grizzly; and his eyes were bloodshot. The old woman's face was wrinkled; her two remaining teeth protruded over her under lip; and her eyes were bright and piercing. Oliver was afraid to look at either her or the man. They seemed so like the rats he had seen outside.

"Nobody shall go near her," said the man, starting fiercely up, as the undertaker approached the recess. "Keep back! D—n you, keep back, if you've a life to lose!"

"Nonsense, my good man," said the undertaker, who was pretty well used to misery in all its shapes. "Nonsense!"

"I tell you," said the man: clenching his hands, and stamping furiously on the floor,—"I tell you I won't have her put into the ground. She couldn't rest there. The worms would worry her—not eat her—she is so worn away."

The undertaker offered no reply to this raving; but, producing a tape from his pocket, knelt down for a moment by the side of the body.

"Ah!" said the man: bursting into tears, and sinking on his knees at the feet of the dead woman; "kneel down, kneel down—kneel round her, every one of you, and mark my words! I say she was starved to death. I never knew how bad she was, till the fever came upon her; and then her bones were starting through the skin. There was neither fire nor candle; she died in the dark—in the dark. She couldn't even see her children's faces, though we heard her gasping out their names. I begged for her in the streets: and they sent me to prison. When I came back, she was dying; and all the blood in my heart has dried up, for they starved her to death. I swear it before the God that saw it! They starved her!" He twined his hands in his hair; and, with a loud scream, rolled grovelling upon the floor: his eyes fixed, and the foam gushing from his lips.

The terrified children cried bitterly; but the old woman, who had hitherto remained as quiet as if she had been wholly deaf to all that passed, menaced them into silence; and having unloosed the man's cravat: who still remained extended on the ground: tottered towards the undertaker.

"She was my daughter," said the old woman, nodding her head in the direction of the corpse; and speaking with an idiotic leer, more ghastly than even the presence of death in such a place. "Lord, Lord! Well, it *is* strange that I who gave birth to her, and was a woman then, should be alive and merry now; and she lying there: so cold and stiff! Lord, Lord!—to think of it;—it's as good as a play —as good as a play!"

As the wretched creature mumbled and chuckled in her hideous merriment, the undertaker turned to go away.

"Stop, stop!" said the old woman in a loud whisper. "Will she be buried to-morrow, or next day, or to-night? I laid her out; and I must walk, you know. Send me a large cloak: a good warm one: for it is bitter cold. We should have cake and wine, too, before we go! Never mind; send some bread—only a loaf of bread and a cup of water. Shall we have some bread, dear?" she said eagerly: catching at the undertaker's coat, as he once more moved towards the door.

"Yes, yes," said the undertaker, "of course. Anything, everything!" He disengaged himself from the old woman's grasp; and, drawing Oliver after him, hurried away.

The next day, (the family having been meanwhile relieved with a half-quartern loaf and a piece of cheese, left with them by Mr. Bumble himself,) Oliver and his master returned to the miserable abode; where Mr. Bumble had already arrived, accompanied by four men from the workhouse, who were to act as bearers. An old black cloak had been thrown over the rags of the old woman and the man; and the bare coffin having been screwed down, was hoisted on the shoulders of the bearers, and carried into the street.

"Now, you must put your best leg foremost, old lady!" whispered Sowerberry in the old woman's ear; "we are rather late; and it won't do, to keep the clergyman waiting. Move on, my men,—as quick as you like!"

Thus directed, the bearers trotted on under their light burden; and the two mourners kept as near them, as they could. Mr. Bumble and Sowerberry walked at a good smart pace in front; and Oliver, whose legs were not so long as his master's, ran by the side.

There was not so great a necessity for hurrying as Mr. Sowerberry had anticipated, however; for when they reached the obscure corner of the churchyard in which the nettles grew, and where the parish graves were made, the clergyman had not arrived; and the clerk, who was sitting by the vestry-room fire, seemed to think it by no means improbable that it might be an hour or so, before he came. So, they put the bier on the brink of the grave; and the two mourners waited patiently in the damp clay, with a cold rain drizzling down: while the ragged boys, whom the spectacle had attracted into the churchyard, played a noisy game at hide-and-seek among the tombstones: or varied their amusements by jumping backwards and forwards over the coffin. Mr. Sowerberry and Bumble, being personal friends of the clerk, sat by the fire with him, and read the paper.

At length, after a lapse of something more than an hour,

Mr. Bumble, and Sowerberry, and the clerk, were seen running towards the grave. Immediately afterwards, the clergyman appeared: putting on his surplice as he came along. Mr. Bumble then thrashed a boy or two, to keep up appearances; and the reverend gentleman, having read as much of the burial service as could be compressed into four minutes, gave his surplice to the clerk, and walked away again.

"Now, Bill!" said Sowerberry to the grave-digger, "fill up."

It was no very difficult task; for the grave was so full, that the uppermost coffin was within a few feet of the surface. The grave-digger shovelled in the earth; stamped it loosely down with his feet; shouldered his spade; and walked off, followed by the boys, who murmured very loud complaints at the fun being over so soon.

"Come, my good fellow!" said Bumble, tapping the man on the back. "They want to shut up the yard."

The man who had never once moved, since he had taken his station by the grave side, started, raised his head, stared at the person who had addressed him, walked forward for a few paces; and fell down in a swoon. The crazy old woman was too much occupied in bewailing the loss of her cloak (which the undertaker had taken off), to pay him any attention; so they threw a can of cold water over him; and when he came to, saw him safely out of the churchyard, locked the gate, and departed on their different ways.

"Well, Oliver," said Sowerberry, as they walked home, "how do you like it?"

"Pretty well, thank you, Sir," replied Oliver, with considerable hesitation. "Not very much, Sir."

"Ah, you'll get used to it in time, Oliver," said Sowerberry. "Nothing when you *are* used to it, my boy."

Oliver wondered, in his own mind, whether it had taken a very long time to get Mr. Sowerberry used to it. But he thought it better not to ask the question; and walked back to the shop: thinking over all he had seen and heard.

CHAPTER VI.

OLIVER, BEING GOADED BY THE TAUNTS OF NOAH, ROUSES INTO ACTION, AND RATHER ASTONISHES HIM.

THE month's trial over, Oliver was formally apprenticed. It was a nice sickly season just at this time. In commercial phrase, coffins were looking up; and, in the course of a few weeks, Oliver had acquired a great deal of experience. The success of Mr. Sowerberry's ingenious speculation, exceeded even his most sanguine hopes. The oldest inhabitants recollected no period at which measles had been so prevalent, or so fatal to infant existence; and many were the mournful processions which little Oliver headed, in a hat-band reaching down to his knees: to the indescribable admiration and emotion of all the mothers in the town. As Oliver accompanied his master in most of his adult expeditions, too, in order that he might acquire that equanimity of demeanour and full command of nerve, which are so essential to a finished undertaker, he had many opportunities of observing the beautiful resignation and fortitude with which some strong-minded people bear their trials and losses.

For instance; when Sowerberry had an order for the

burial of some rich old lady or gentleman, who was surrounded by a great number of nephews and nieces, who had been perfectly inconsolable during the previous illness, and whose grief had been wholly irrepressible even on the most public occasions; they would be as happy among themselves as need be—quite cheerful and contented: conversing together, with as much freedom and gaiety, as if nothing whatever had happened to disturb them. Husbands, too, bore the loss of their wives with the most heroic calmness. Wives, again, put on weeds for their husbands, as if, so far from grieving in the garb of sorrow, they had made up their minds to render it as becoming and attractive as possible. It was observable, too, that ladies and gentlemen who were in passions of anguish during the ceremony of interment, recovered almost as soon as they reached home; and became quite composed before the tea-drinking was over. All this was very pleasant and improving to see; and Oliver beheld it with great admiration.

That Oliver Twist was moved to resignation by the example of these good people, I cannot, although I am his biographer, undertake to affirm with any degree of confidence; but I can most distinctly say, that for many months he continued meekly to submit to the domination and ill-treatment of Noah Claypole: who used him far worse than before, now that his jealousy was roused by seeing the new boy promoted to the black stick and hat-band, while he, the old one, remained stationary in the muffin-cap and leathers. Charlotte treated him badly, because Noah did; and Mrs. Sowerberry was his decided enemy, because Mr. Sowerberry was disposed to be his friend; so, between these three on one side, and a glut of funerals on the other, Oliver was not altogether as comfortable as the hungry pig was, when he was shut up, by mistake, in the grain department of a brewery.

And now I come to a very important passage in Oliver's history; for I have to record an act, slight and unimportant perhaps in appearance, but which indirectly produced a most material change in all his future prospects and proceedings.

One day, Oliver and Noah had descended into the kitchen at the usual dinner-hour, to banquet upon a small joint of mutton—a pound and a half of the worst end of the neck —when, Charlotte being called out of the way, there ensued a brief interval of time, which Noah Claypole, being hungry and vicious, considered he could not possibly devote to a worthier purpose than aggravating and tantalizing young Oliver Twist.

Intent upon this innocent amusement, Noah put his feet on the table-cloth; and pulled Oliver's hair; and twitched his ears; and expressed his opinion that he was a "sneak;" and furthermore announced his intention of coming to see him hanged, whenever that desirable event should take place; and entered upon various other topics of petty annoyance, like a malicious and ill-conditioned charity-boy as he was. But, none of these taunts producing the desired effect of making Oliver cry, Noah attempted to be more facetious still; and in this attempt, did what many small wits, with far greater reputations than Noah, sometimes do to this day, when they want to be funny. He got rather personal.

"Work'us," said Noah, "how's your mother?"

"She's dead," replied Oliver; "don't you say anything about her to me!"

Oliver's colour rose as he said this; he breathed quickly; and there was a curious working of the mouth and nostrils, which Mr. Claypole thought must be the immediate pre-

cursor of a violent fit of crying. Under this impression he returned to the charge.

"What did she die of, Work'us?" said Noah.

"Of a broken heart, some of our old nurses told me," replied Oliver: more as if he were talking to himself, than answering Noah. "I think I know what it must be to die of that!"

"Tol de rol lol lol, right fol lairy, Work'us," said Noah, as a tear rolled down Oliver's cheek. "What's set you a snivelling now?"

"Not *you*," replied Oliver, hastily brushing the tear away. "Don't think it."

"Oh, not me, eh?" sneered Noah.

"No, not you," replied Oliver, sharply. "There; that's enough. Don't say anything more to me about her; you'd better not!"

"Better not!" exclaimed Noah. "Well! Better not! Work'us, don't be impudent. *Your* mother, too! She was a nice 'un, she was. Oh, Lor!" And here, Noah nodded his head expressively; and curled up as much of his small red nose as muscular action could collect together, for the occasion.

"Yer know, Work'us," continued Noah, emboldened by Oliver's silence, and speaking in a jeering tone of affected pity: of all tones the most annoying: "Yer know, Work'us, it can't be helped now; and of course yer couldn't help it then; and I'm very sorry for it; and I'm sure we all are, and pity yer very much. But yer must know, Work'us, yer mother was a regular right-down bad 'un."

"What did you say?" inquired Oliver, looking up very quickly.

"A regular right-down bad 'un, Work'us," replied Noah, coolly. "And it's a great deal better, Work'us, that she died when she did, or else she'd have been hard labouring in Bridewell, or transported, or hung: which is more likely than either, isn't it?"

Crimson with fury, Oliver started up; overthrew the chair and table; seized Noah by the throat; shook him, in the violence of his rage, till his teeth chattered in his head; and, collecting his whole force into one heavy blow, felled him to the ground.

A minute ago, the boy had looked the quiet, mild, dejected creature that harsh treatment had made him. But his spirit was roused at last; the cruel insult to his dead mother had set his blood on fire. His breast heaved; his attitude was erect; his eye bright and vivid; his whole person changed, as he stood glaring over the cowardly tormentor who now lay crouching at his feet: and defied him with an energy he had never known before.

"He'll murder me!" blubbered Noah. "Charlotte! missis! Here's the new boy a murdering of me! Help! help! Oliver's gone mad! Char—lotte!"

Noah's shouts were responded to, by a loud scream from Charlotte, and a louder from Mrs. Sowerberry; the former of whom rushed into the kitchen by a side-door: while the latter paused on the staircase till she was quite certain that it was consistent with the preservation of human life, to come further down.

"Oh, you little wretch!" screamed Charlotte; seizing Oliver with her utmost force, which was about equal to that of a moderately strong man in particularly good training, "Oh, you little un-grate-ful, mur-de-rous, hor-rid vil-lain!" And between every syllable, Charlotte gave Oliver a blow with all her might: accompanying it with a scream, for the benefit of society.

Charlotte's fist was by no means a light one; but, lest it should not be effectual in calming Oliver's wrath, Mrs. Sowerberry plunged into the kitchen, and assisted to hold him with one hand, while she scratched his face with the other. In this favourable position of affairs, Noah rose from the ground: and pommelled him behind.

This was rather too violent exercise to last long. When they were all three wearied out, and could tear and beat no longer, they dragged Oliver, struggling and shouting, but nothing daunted, into the dust-cellar, and there locked him up. This being done, Mrs. Sowerberry sank into a chair, and burst into tears.

"Bless her, she's going off!" said Charlotte. "A glass of water, Noah, dear. Make haste."

"Oh! Charlotte," said Mrs. Sowerberry: speaking as well as she could, through a deficiency of breath, and a sufficiency of cold water, which Noah had poured over her head and shoulders. "Oh! Charlotte, what a mercy we have not all been murdered in our beds!"

"Ah! mercy indeed, ma'am," was the reply. "I only hope this 'll teach master not to have any more of these dreadful creaturs, that are born to be murderers and robbers from their very cradle. Poor Noah! He was all but killed, ma'am, when I come in."

"Poor fellow!" said Mrs. Sowerberry: looking piteously on the charity-boy.

Noah, whose top waistcoat-button might have been somewhere on a level with the crown of Oliver's head, rubbed his eyes with the inside of his wrists while this commiseration was bestowed upon him, and performed same affecting tears and sniffs.

"What's to be done!" exclaimed Mrs. Sowerberry. "Your master's not at home; there's not a man in the house; and he'll kick that door down, in ten minutes." Oliver's vigorous plunges against the bit of timber in question, rendered this occurrence highly probable.

"Dear, dear! I don't know, ma'am," said Charlotte, "unless we send for the police-officers." .

"Or the millingtary," suggested Mr. Claypole.

"No, no," said Mrs. Sowerberry: bethinking herself of Oliver's old friend. "Run to Mr. Bumble, Noah, and tell him to come here directly, and not to lose a minute; never mind your cap! Make haste! You can hold a knife to that black eye, as you run along; and it'll keep the swelling down."

Noah stopped to make no reply, but started off at his fullest speed; and very much it astonished the people who were out walking, to see a charity-boy tearing through the streets pell-mell: with no cap on his head, and a clasp-knife at his eye.

CHAPTER VII.

OLIVER CONTINUES REFRACTORY.

NOAH CLAYPOLE ran along the streets at his swiftest pace; and paused not once for breath, until he reached the workhouse-gate. Having rested here, for a minute or so, to collect a good burst of sobs and an imposing show of tears and terror, he knocked loudly at the wicket; and presented such a rueful face to the aged pauper who opened it, that even he, who saw nothing but rueful faces about him at the best of times, started back in astonishment.

"Why, what's the matter with the boy!" said the old pauper.

"Mr. Bumble! Mr. Bumble!" cried Noah, with well-affected dismay: and in tones so loud and agitated, that they not only caught the ear of Mr. Bumble himself, who happened to be hard by, but alarmed him so much that he rushed into the yard without his cocked hat,—which is a very curious and remarkable circumstance: as showing that even a beadle, acted upon by a sudden and powerful impulse, may be afflicted with a momentary visitation of loss of self-possession, and forgetfulness of personal dignity.

"Oh, Mr. Bumble, Sir!" said Noah: "Oliver, Sir,—Oliver has——"

"What? What?" interposed Mr. Bumble: with a gleam of pleasure in his metallic eyes. "Not run away; he hasn't run away, has he, Noah?"

"No, Sir, no. Not run away, Sir, but he's turned wicious," replied Noah. "He tried to murder me, Sir; and then he tried to murder Charlotte; and then missis. Oh! what dreadful pain it is! Such agony, please, Sir!" And here, Noah writhed and twisted his body into an extensive variety of eel-like positions; thereby giving Mr. Bumble to understand that, from the violent and sanguinary onset of Oliver Twist, he had sustained severe internal injury and damage, from which he was at that moment suffering the acutest torture.

When Noah saw that the intelligence he communicated perfectly paralysed Mr. Bumble, he imparted additional effect thereunto, by bewailing his dreadful wounds ten times louder than before; and, when he observed a gentleman in a white waistcoat crossing the yard, he was more tragic in his lamentations than ever: rightly conceiving it highly expedient to attract the notice, and rouse the indignation, of the gentleman aforesaid.

The gentleman's notice was very soon attracted; for he had not walked three paces, when he turned angrily round, and inquired what that young cur was howling for; and why Mr. Bumble did not favour him with something which would render the series of vocular exclamations so designated, an involuntary process.

"It's a poor boy from the free-school, Sir," replied Mr. Bumble, "who has been nearly murdered—all but murdered, Sir—by young Twist."

"By Jove!" exclaimed the gentleman in the white waistcoat, stopping short. "I knew it! I felt a strange presentiment from the very first, that that audacious young savage would come to be hung!"

"He has likewise attempted, Sir, to murder the female servant," said Mr. Bumble, with a face of ashy paleness.

"And his missis," interposed Mr. Claypole.

"And his master, too, I think you said, Noah?" added Mr. Bumble.

"No; he's out, or he would have murdered him," replied Noah. "He said he wanted to."

"Ah! said he wanted to: did he, my boy?" inquired the gentleman in the white waistcoat.

"Yes, Sir," replied Noah. "And please, Sir, missis wants to know whether Mr. Bumble can spare time to step up there, directly, and flog him: 'cause master's out."

"Certainly, my boy; certainly," said the gentleman in the white waistcoat: smiling benignly, and patting Noah's head, which was about three inches higher than his own. You're a good boy—a very good boy. Here's a penny for you. Bumble, just step up to Sowerberry's with your

OLIVER PLUCKS UP A SPIRIT.

cane, and see what's best to be done. Don't spare him, Bumble."

"No, I will not, Sir," replied the beadle: adjusting the wax-end which was twisted round the bottom of his cane, for purposes of parochial flagellation.

"Tell Sowerberry not to spare him either. They'll never do anything with him, without stripes and bruises," said the gentleman in the white waistcoat.

"I'll take care, Sir," replied the beadle. And the cocked hat and cane having been, by this time, adjusted to their owner's satisfaction: Mr. Bumble and Noah Claypole betook themselves with all speed to the undertaker's shop.

Here, the position of affairs had not at all improved: as Sowerberry had not yet returned, and Oliver continued to kick, with undiminished vigour, at the cellar-door. The accounts of his ferocity, as related by Mrs. Sowerberry and Charlotte, were of so startling a nature, that Mr. Bumble judged it prudent to parley, before opening the door. With this view, he gave a kick at the outside, by way of prelude; and then, applying his mouth to the keyhole, said, in a deep and impressive tone:

"Oliver!"

"Come; you let me out!" replied Oliver, from the inside.

"Do you know this here voice, Oliver?" said Mr. Bumble.

"Yes," replied Oliver.

"Ain't you afraid of it, Sir? Ain't you a-trembling while I speak, Sir?" said Mr. Bumble.

"No!" replied Oliver, boldly.

An answer so different from the one he had expected to elicit, and was in the habit of receiving, staggered Mr. Bumble not a little. He stepped back from the keyhole; drew himself up to his full height; and looked from one to another of the three bystanders, in mute astonishment.

"Oh, you know, Mr. Bumble, he must be mad," said Mrs. Sowerberry. "No boy in half his senses could venture to speak so to you."

"It's not Madness, ma'am," replied Mr. Bumble, after a few moments of deep meditation. "It's Meat."

"What!" exclaimed Mrs. Sowerberry.

"Meat, ma'am, meat," replied Bumble, with stern emphasis. "You've overfed him, ma'am. You've raised a artificial soul and spirit in him, ma'am, unbecoming a person of his condition: as the board, Mrs. Sowerberry, who are practical philosophers, will tell you. What have paupers to do with soul or spirit? It's quite enough that we let 'em have live bodies. If you had kept the boy on gruel, ma'am, this would never have happened."

"Dear, dear!" ejaculated Mrs. Sowerberry, piously raising her eyes to the kitchen ceiling: "this comes of being liberal!"

The liberality of Mrs. Sowerberry to Oliver, had consisted in a profuse bestowal upon him of all the dirty odds and ends which nobody else would eat; so, there was a great deal of meekness and self-devotion in her voluntarily remaining under Mr. Bumble's heavy accusation; of which, to do her justice, she was wholly innocent, in thought, word, or deed.

"Ah!" said Mr. Bumble, when the lady brought her eyes down to earth again; "the only thing that can be done now, that I know of, is to leave him in the cellar for a day or so, till he's a little starved down; and then to take him out, and keep him on gruel all through his apprenticeship. He comes of a bad family. Excitable natures, Mrs. Sowerberry! Both the nurse and doctor said, that that mother of his made her way here, against difficulties and pain that would have killed any well-disposed woman, weeks before."

At this point of Mr. Bumble's discourse, Oliver, just hearing enough to know that some further allusion was being made to his mother, recommenced kicking, with a violence that rendered every other sound inaudible. Sowerberry returned at this juncture; Oliver's offence having been explained to him, with such exaggerations as the ladies thought best calculated to rouse his ire: he unlocked the cellar-door in a twinkling, and dragged his rebellious apprentice out, by the collar.

Oliver's clothes had been torn in the beating he had received; his face was bruised and scratched; and his hair scattered over his forehead. The angry flush had not disappeared, however; and when he was pulled out of his prison, he scowled boldly on Noah, and looked quite undismayed.

"Now, you are a nice young fellow, ain't you?" said Sowerberry: giving Oliver a shake, and a box on the ear.

"He called my mother names," replied Oliver.

"Well, and what if he did, you little ungrateful wretch?" said Mrs. Sowerberry. "She deserved what he said, and worse."

"She didn't," said Oliver.

"She did," said Mrs. Sowerberry.

"It's a lie!" said Oliver.

Mrs. Sowerberry burst into a flood of tears.

This flood of tears left Sowerberry no alternative. If he had hesitated for one instant to punish Oliver most severely, it must be quite clear to every experienced reader that he would have been, according to all precedents in disputes of matrimony established, a brute, an unnatural husband, an insulting creature, a base imitation of a man: and various other agreeable characters too numerous for recital within the limits of this chapter. To do him justice, he was, as far as his power went—it was not very extensive —kindly disposed towards the boy; perhaps because it was his interest to be so; perhaps because his wife disliked him. The flood of tears, however, left him no resource; so he at once gave him a drubbing, which satisfied even Mrs. Sowerberry herself; and rendered Mr. Bumble's subsequent application of the parochial cane, rather unnecessary. For the rest of the day, he was shut up in the back kitchen, in company with a pump and a slice of bread; and, at night, Mrs. Sowerberry, after making various remarks outside the door, by no means complimentary to the memory of his mother, looked into the room: and, amidst the jeers and pointings of Noah and Charlotte, ordered him up stairs to his dismal bed.

It was not until he was left alone in the silence and stillness of the gloomy workshop of the undertaker, that Oliver gave way to the feelings which the day's treatment may be supposed likely to have awakened in a mere child. He had listened to their taunts with a look of contempt; he had borne the lash without a cry: for he felt that pride swelling in his heart which would have kept down a shriek to the last, though they had roasted him alive. But now, when there were none to see or hear him, he fell upon his knees on the floor; and, hiding his face in his hands, wept such tears as, God send for the credit of our nature, few so young may ever have cause to pour out before Him!

For a long time, Oliver remained motionless in this attitude. The candle was burning low in the socket when he rose to his feet. Having gazed cautiously round him, and listened intently, he gently undid the fastenings of the door, and looked abroad.

It was a cold, dark night. The stars seemed, to the boy's eyes, farther from the earth than he had ever seen them before; there was no wind; and the sombre shadows thrown by the trees upon the ground, looked sepulchral and death-like, from being so still. He softly reclosed the door; and, having availed himself of the expiring light of the candle to tie up in a handkerchief the few articles of wearing apparel he had; sat himself down upon a bench, to wait for morning.

With the first ray of light that struggled through the crevices in the shutters, Oliver arose, and again unbarred the door. One timid look around—one moment's pause of hesitation—he had closed it behind him, and was in the open street.

He looked to the right and to the left, uncertain whither to fly. He remembered to have seen the waggons, as they went out, toiling up the hill. He took the same route; and arriving at a footpath across the fields: which he knew, after some distance, led out again into the road: struck into it, and walked quickly on.

Along this same footpath, Oliver well remembered he had trotted beside Mr. Bumble, when he first carried him to the workhouse from the farm. His way lay directly in front of the cottage. His heart beat quickly when he bethought himself of this; and he half resolved to turn back. He had come a long way though, and should lose a great deal of time by doing so. Besides, it was so early that there was very little fear of his being seen; so he walked on.

He reached the house. There was no appearance of its inmates stirring at that early hour. Oliver stopped, and peeped into the garden. A child was weeding one of the little beds; and as he stopped, he raised his pale face, and disclosed the features of one of his former companions. Oliver felt glad to see him, before he went; for, though younger than himself, he had been his little friend and playmate. They had been beaten, and starved, and shut up together, many and many a time.

"Hush, Dick!" said Oliver, as the boy ran to the gate, and thrust his thin arm between the rails to greet him. "Is any one up?"

"Nobody but me," replied the child.

"You mustn't say you saw me, Dick," said Oliver. "I am running away. They beat and ill-use me, Dick; and I am going to seek my fortune, some long way off. I don't know where. How pale you are!"

"I heard the doctor tell them I was dying," replied the child with a faint smile. "I am very glad to see you, dear; but don't stop, don't stop!"

"Yes, yes, I will, to say good-bye to you," replied Oliver. "I shall see you again, Dick; I know I shall. You will be well and happy!"

"I hope so," replied the child. "After I am dead, but not before. I know the doctor must be right, Oliver, because I dream so much of Heaven and Angels; and kind faces that I never see when I am awake. Kiss me," said the child, climbing up the low gate, and flinging his little arms round Oliver's neck: "Good-bye, dear! God bless you!"

The blessing was from a young child's lips, but it was the first that Oliver had ever heard invoked upon his head; and through all the struggles and sufferings, and troubles and changes, of his after life, he never once forgot it.

CHAPTER VIII.

OLIVER WALKS TO LONDON. HE ENCOUNTERS ON THE ROAD A STRANGE SORT OF YOUNG GENTLEMAN.

OLIVER reached the stile at which the bypath terminated; and once more gained the high-road. It was eight o'clock now. Though he was nearly five miles away from the town, he ran, and hid behind the hedges, by turns, till noon: fearing that he might be pursued and overtaken. Then he sat down to rest by the side of the milestone; and began to think, for the first time, where he had better go and try to live.

The stone by which he was seated, bore, in large characters, an intimation that it was just seventy miles from that spot to London. The name awakened a new train of ideas in the boy's mind. London!—that great large place! —nobody—not even Mr. Bumble—could ever find him there! He had often heard the old men in the workhouse, too, say that no lad of spirit need want in London; and that there were ways of living in that vast city, which those who had been bred up in country parts had no idea of. It was the very place for a homeless boy, who must die in the streets unless some one helped him. As these things passed through his thoughts, he jumped upon his feet, and again walked forward.

He had diminished the distance between himself and London by full four miles more, before he recollected how much he must undergo ere he could hope to reach his place of destination. As this consideration forced itself upon him, he slackened his pace a little, and meditated upon his means of getting there. He had a crust of bread, a coarse shirt, and two pairs of stockings, in his bundle. He had a penny too—a gift of Sowerberry's after some funeral in which he had acquitted himself more than ordinarily well —in his pocket. "A clean shirt," thought Oliver, "is a very comfortable thing, very; and so are two pairs of darned stockings; and so is a penny; but they are small helps to a sixty-five miles' walk in winter time." But Oliver's thoughts, like those of most other people, although they were extremely ready and active to point out his difficulties, were wholly at a loss to suggest any feasible mode of surmounting them; so, after a good deal of thinking to no particular purpose, he changed his little bundle over to the other shoulder, and trudged on.

Oliver walked twenty miles that day; and all that time tasted nothing but the crust of dry bread, and a few draughts of water, which he begged at the cottage-doors by the roadside. When the night came, he turned into a meadow; and, creeping close under a hay-rick, determined to lie there, till morning. He felt frightened at first, for the wind moaned dismally over the empty fields: and he was cold and hungry, and more alone than he had ever felt before. Being very tired with his walk, however, he soon fell asleep and forgot his troubles.

He felt cold and stiff, when he got up next morning, and so hungry that he was obliged to exchange the penny for a small loaf, in the very first village through which he passed. He had walked no more than twelve miles, when night closed in again; for his feet were sore, and his legs so weak that they trembled beneath him. Another night passed in the bleak damp air, made him worse; and when he set forward on his journey next morning, he could hardly crawl along.

He waited at the bottom of a steep hill till a stage-coach came up, and then begged of the outside passengers; but there were very few who took any notice of him: and even those told him to wait till they got to the top of the hill, and then let them see how far he could run for a halfpenny. Poor Oliver tried to keep up with the coach a little way, but was unable to do it, by reason of his fatigue and sore feet. When the outsides saw this, they put their halfpence back into their pockets again, declaring that he was an idle young dog, and didn't deserve anything; and the coach rattled away and left only a cloud of dust behind.

In some villages, large painted boards were fixed up; warning all persons who begged within the district, that they would be sent to jail. This frightened Oliver very much, and made him glad to get out of them with all possible expedition. In others, he would stand about the inn-yards, and look mournfully at every one who passed: a proceeding which generally terminated in the landlady's ordering one of the post-boys who were lounging about, to drive that strange boy out of the place, for she was sure he had come to steal something. If he begged at a farmer's house, ten to one but they threatened to set the dog on him; and when he showed his nose in a shop, they talked about the beadle: which brought Oliver's heart into his mouth,—very often the only thing he had there, for many hours together.

In fact, if it had not been for a good-hearted turnpike-man, and a benevolent old lady, Oliver's troubles would have been shortened by the very same process which put an end to his mother's; in other words, he would most assuredly have fallen dead upon the king's highway. But the turnpike-man gave him a meal of bread and cheese; and the old lady, who had a shipwrecked grandson wandering barefooted in some distant part of the earth, took pity upon the poor orphan, and gave him what little she could afford—and more—with such kind and gentle words, and such tears of sympathy and compassion, that they sank deeper into Oliver's soul, than all the sufferings he had ever undergone.

Early on the seventh morning after he had left his native place, Oliver limped slowly into the little town of Barnet. The window-shutters were closed; the street was empty; not a soul had awakened to the business of the day. The sun was rising in all his splendid beauty; but the light only served to show the boy his own lonesomeness and desolation, as he sat, with bleeding feet and covered with dust, upon a cold door-step.

By degrees, the shutters were opened; the window-blinds were drawn up; and people began passing to and fro. Some few stopped to gaze at Oliver for a moment or two, or turned round to stare at him as they hurried by; but none relieved him, or troubled themselves to inquire how he came there. He had no heart to beg. And there he sat.

He had been crouching on the step for some time: wondering at the great number of public-houses (every other house in Barnet was a tavern, large or small): gazing listlessly at the coaches as they passed through: and thinking how strange it seemed that they could do, with ease, in a few hours, what it had taken him a whole week of courage and determination beyond his years to accomplish: when he was roused by observing that a boy, who had passed him carelessly some minutes before, had returned, and was now surveying him most earnestly from the opposite side of the way. He took little heed of this at first; but the boy remained in the same attitude of close observation so long, that Oliver raised his head, and returned his steady look. Upon this, the boy crossed over; and, walking close up to Oliver, said,

"Hullo, my covey, what's the row?"

The boy who addressed this inquiry to the young wayfarer, was about his own age: but one of the queerest looking boys that Oliver had ever seen. He was a snub-nosed, flat-browed, common-faced boy enough; and as dirty a juvenile as one would wish to see; but he had about him all the airs and manners of a man. He was short of his age: with rather bow-legs, and little, sharp, ugly eyes. His hat was stuck on the top of his head so lightly, that it threatened to fall off every moment; and would have done so, very often, if the wearer had not had a knack of every now and then giving his head a sudden twitch, which brought it back to its old place again. He wore a man's coat, which reached nearly to his heels. He had turned the cuffs back, half-way up his arm, to get his hands out of the sleeves: apparently with the ultimate view of thrusting them into the pockets of his corduroy trousers: for there he kept them. He was, altogether, as roystering and swaggering a young gentleman as ever stood four feet six, or something less, in his bluchers.

"Hullo, my covey, what's the row?" said this strange young gentleman to Oliver.

"I am very hungry and tired," replied Oliver: the tears standing in his eyes as he spoke. "I have walked a long way. I have been walking these seven days."

"Walking for sivin days!" said the young gentleman. "Oh, I see. Beak's order, eh? But," he added, noticing Oliver's look of surprise, "I suppose you don't know what a beak is, my flash com-pan-i-on?"

Oliver mildly replied, that he had always heard a bird's mouth described by the term in question.

"My eyes, how green!" exclaimed the young gentleman. "Why, a beak's a madgst'rate; and when you walk by a beak's order, it's not straight forerd, but always agoing up, and nivir a coming down agin. Was you never on the mill?"

"What mill?" inquired Oliver.

"What mill! Why, *the* mill—the mill as takes up so little room that it'll work inside a Stone Jug; and always goes better when the wind's low with people, than when it's high: acos then they can't get workmen. But come," said the young gentleman; "you want grub, and you shall have it. I'm at low-water-mark myself—only one bob and a magpie; but, *as far as* it goes, I'll fork out and stump. Up with you on your pins. There! Now then! Morrice!"

Assisting Oliver to rise, the young gentleman took him to an adjacent chandler's shop, where he purchased a sufficiency of ready-dressed ham and a half-quartern loaf, or, as he himself expressed it, "a fourpenny bran;" the ham being kept clean and preserved from dust, by the ingenious expedient of making a hole in the loaf by pulling out a portion of the crumb, and stuffing it therein. Taking the bread under his arm, the young gentleman turned into a small public-house, and led the way to a tap-room in the rear of the premises. Here, a pot of beer was brought in, by direction of the mysterious youth; and Oliver, falling to, at his new friend's bidding, made a long and hearty meal; during the progress of which, the strange boy eyed him from time to time with great attention.

"Going to London?" said the strange boy, when Oliver had at length concluded.

"Yes."

"Got any lodgings?"

"No."

"Money?"

"No."

The strange boy whistled; and put his arms into his pockets, as far as the big coat sleeves would let them go.

"Do you live in London?" inquired Oliver.

"Yes, I do, when I'm at home," replied the boy. "I suppose you want some place to sleep in to-night, don't you?"

"I do indeed," answered Oliver. "I have not slept under a roof since I left the country."

"Don't fret your eyelids on that score," said the young gentleman. "I've got to be in London to-night; and I know a 'spectable old genelman as lives there, wot'll give you lodgings for nothink, and never ask for the change; that is, if any genelman he knows interduces you. And don't he know me? Oh, no! Not in the least! By no means. Certainly not!"

The young gentleman smiled, as if to intimate that the latter fragments of discourse were playfully ironical; and finished the beer as he did so.

This unexpected offer of shelter was too tempting to be resisted; especially as it was immediately followed up, by the assurance that the old gentleman already referred to, would doubtless provide Oliver with a comfortable place, without loss of time. This led to a more friendly and confidential dialogue; from which Oliver discovered that his friend's name was Jack Dawkins, and that he was a peculiar pet and *protégé* of the elderly gentleman before mentioned.

Mr. Dawkins's appearance did not say a vast deal in favour of the comforts which his patron's interest obtained for those whom he took under his protection; but, as he had a rather flighty and dissolute mode of conversing, and furthermore avowed that among his intimate friends he was better known by the *sobriquet* of "The artful Dodger," Oliver concluded that, being of a dissipated and careless turn, the moral precepts of his benefactor had hitherto been thrown away upon him. Under this impression, he secretly resolved to cultivate the good opinion of the old gentleman as quickly as possible; and, if he found the Dodger incorrigible, as he more than half expected he should, to decline the honour of his farther acquaintance.

As John Dawkins objected to their entering London before nightfall, it was nearly eleven o'clock when they reached the turnpike at Islington. They crossed from the Angel into St. John's Road; struck down the small street which terminates at Sadler's Wells Theatre; through Exmouth Street and Coppice Row; down the little court by the side of the workhouse; across the classic ground which once bore the name of Hockley-in-the-Hole; thence into Little Saffron Hill; and so into Saffron Hill the Great: along which the Dodger scudded at a rapid pace, directing Oliver to follow close at his heels.

Although Oliver had enough to occupy his attention in keeping sight of his leader, he could not help bestowing a few hasty glances on either side of the way as he passed along. A dirtier or more wretched place he had never seen. The street was very narrow and muddy, and the air was impregnated with filthy odours. There were a good many small shops; but the only stock in trade appeared to be heaps of children, who, even at that time of night, were crawling in and out at the doors, or screaming from the inside. The sole places that seemed to prosper, amid the general blight of the place, were the public-houses; and in them, the lowest orders of Irish were wrangling with might and main. Covered ways and yards, which here and there diverged from the main street, disclosed little knots of houses, where drunken men and women were positively wallowing in the filth; and from several of the door-ways, great ill-looking fellows were cautiously emerging, bound, to all appearance, on no very well-disposed or harmless errands.

Oliver was just considering whether he hadn't better run away, when they reached the bottom of the hill. His conductor, catching him by the arm, pushed open the door of a house near Field Lane; and, drawing him into the passage, closed it behind them.

"Now, then!" cried a voice from below, in reply to a whistle from the Dodger.

"Plummy and slam!" was the reply.

This seemed to be some watchword or signal that all was right; for the light of a feeble candle gleamed on the wall at the remote end of the passage; and a man's face peeped out, from where a balustrade of the old kitchen staircase had been broken away.

"There's two on you," said the man, thrusting the candle farther out, and shading his eyes with his hand. "Who's the t'other one?"

"A new pal," replied Jack Dawkins, pulling Oliver forward.

"Where did he come from?"

"Greenland. Is Fagin up stairs?"

"Yes, he's a sortin' the wipes. Up with you!" The candle was drawn back, and the face disappeared.

Oliver, groping his way with one hand, and having the other firmly grasped by his companion, ascended with much difficulty the dark and broken stairs: which his conductor mounted with an ease and expedition that showed he was well acquainted with them. He threw open the door of a back-room, and drew Oliver in after him.

The walls and ceiling of the room were perfectly black with age and dirt. There was a deal table before the fire: upon which were a candle, stuck in a ginger-beer bottle, two or three pewter pots, a loaf and butter, and a plate. In a frying-pan which was on the fire, and which was secured to the mantelshelf by a string, some sausages were cooking; and standing over them, with a toasting-fork in his hand, was a very old shrivelled Jew, whose villanous-looking and repulsive face was obscured by a quantity of matted red hair. He was dressed in a greasy flannel gown, with his throat bare; and seemed to be dividing his attention between the frying-pan and a clothes-horse, over which a great number of silk handkerchiefs were hanging. Several rough beds made of old sacks, were huddled side by side on the floor; and seated round the table were four or five boys, none older than the Dodger, smoking long clay pipes, and drinking spirits with the air of middle aged men. These all crowded about their associate as he whispered a few words to the Jew; and then turned round and grinned at Oliver; as did the Jew himself, toasting-fork in hand.

"This is him, Fagin," said Jack Dawkins; "my friend Oliver Twist."

The Jew grinned; and, making a low obeisance to Oliver, took him by the hand, and hoped he should have the honour of his intimate acquaintance. Upon this, the young gentlemen with the pipes came round him, and shook both his hands very hard—especially the one in which he held his little bundle. One young gentleman was very anxious to hang up his cap for him; and another was so obliging as to put his hands in his pockets, in order tha., as he was very tired, he might not have the trouble of emptying them, himself, when he went to bed. These civilities would probably have been extended much farther, but for a liberal exercise of the Jew's toasting-fork on the heads and shoulders of the affectionate youths who offered them.

"We are very glad to see you, Oliver—very," said the Jew. "Dodger, take off the sausages; and draw a tub near the fire for Oliver. Ah, you're a-staring at the pocket-handkerchiefs! eh, my dear? There are a good many of 'em, ain't there? We've just looked 'em out, ready for the wash; that's all, Oliver; that's all. Ha! ha! ha!"

The latter part of this speech was hailed by a boisterous shout from all the hopeful pupils of the merry old gentleman. In the midst of which, they went to supper.

Oliver ate his share, and the Jew then mixed him a glass of hot gin and water: telling him he must drink it off directly, because another gentleman wanted the tumbler. Oliver did as he was desired. Immediately afterwards, he felt himself gently lifted on to one of the sacks; and then he sank into a deep sleep.

CHAPTER IX.

CONTAINING FURTHER PARTICULARS CONCERNING THE PLEASANT OLD GENTLEMAN, AND HIS HOPEFUL PUPILS.

It was late next morning when Oliver awoke, from a sound, long sleep. There was no other person in the room but the old Jew, who was boiling some coffee in a saucepan for breakfast, and whistling softly to himself as he stirred it round and round, with an iron spoon. He would stop every now and then to listen when there was the least noise below: and when he had satisfied himself, he would go on, whistling and stirring again, as before.

Although Oliver had roused himself from sleep, he was not thoroughly awake. There is a drowsy state, between sleeping and waking, when you dream more in five minutes with your eyes half open, and yourself half conscious of everything that is passing around you, than you would in five nights with your eyes fast closed, and your senses wrapt in perfect unconsciousness. At such times, a mortal knows just enough of what his mind is doing, to form some glimmering conception of its mighty powers, its bounding from earth and spurning time and space, when freed from the restraint of its corporeal associate.

Oliver was precisely in this condition. He saw the Jew with his half-closed eyes; heard his low whistling; and recognised the sound of the spoon grating against the saucepan's sides; and yet the self-same senses were mentally engaged, at the same time, in busy action with almost everybody he had ever known.

When the coffee was done, the Jew drew the saucepan to the hob; and, standing in an irresolute attitude for a few minutes, as if he did not well know how to employ himself, turned round and looked at Oliver, and called him by his name. He did not answer, and was to all appearance asleep.

After satisfying himself upon this head, the Jew stepped gently to the door: which he fastened. He then drew forth: as it seemed to Oliver, from some trap in the floor: a small box, which he placed carefully on the table. His eyes glistened as he raised the lid, and looked in. Dragging an old chair to the table, he sat down; and took from it a magnificent gold watch, sparkling with jewels.

"Aha!" said the Jew, shrugging up his shoulders, and distorting every feature with a hideous grin. "Clever dogs! Clever dogs! Staunch to the last! Never told the old parson where they were. Never peached upon old Fagin! And why should they? It wouldn't have loosened the knot, or kept the drop up, a minute longer. No, no, no! Fine fellows! Fine fellows!"

With these, and other muttered reflections of the like nature, the Jew once more deposited the watch in its place of safety. At least half a dozen more were severally drawn forth from the same box, and surveyed with equal pleasure; besides rings, brooches, bracelets, and other articles of jewellery, of such magnificent materials, and costly workmanship, that Oliver had no idea, even of their names.

Having replaced these trinkets, the Jew took out another: so small that it lay in the palm of his hand. There seemed to be some very minute inscription on it; for the Jew laid it flat upon the table, and shading it with his hand, pored over it, long and earnestly. At length he put it down, as if despairing of success; and, leaning back in his chair, muttered:

"What a fine thing capital punishment is! Dead men never repent; dead men never bring awkward stories to light. Ah, it's a fine thing for the trade! Five of 'em strung up in a row; and none left to play booty, or turn white-livered!"

As the Jew uttered these words, his bright dark eyes, which had been staring vacantly before him, fell on Oliver's face; the boy's eyes were fixed on his in mute curiosity; and, although the recognition was only for an instant—for the briefest space of time that can possibly be conceived—it was enough to show the old man that he had been observed. He closed the lid of the box with a loud crash; and, laying his hand on a bread knife which was on the table, started furiously up. He trembled very much though; for, even in his terror, Oliver could see that the knife quivered in the air.

"What's that?" said the Jew. "What do you watch me for? Why are you awake? What have you seen? Speak out, boy! Quick—quick! for your life!"

"I wasn't able to sleep any longer, Sir," replied Oliver, meekly. "I am very sorry if I have disturbed you, Sir."

"You were not awake an hour ago?" said the Jew, scowling fiercely on the boy.

"No—no, indeed," replied Oliver.

"Are you sure?" cried the Jew: with a still fiercer look than before: and a threatening attitude.

"Upon my word I was not, Sir," replied Oliver, earnestly. "I was not, indeed, Sir."

"Tush, tush, my dear!" said the Jew, abruptly resuming his old manner, and playing with the knife a little, before he laid it down; as if to induce the belief that he had caught it up, in mere sport. "Of course I know that, my dear. I only tried to frighten you. You're a brave boy. Ha! ha! you're a brave boy, Oliver!" The Jew rubbed his hands with a chuckle, but glanced uneasily at the box, notwithstanding.

"Did you see any of these pretty things, my dear?" said the Jew, laying his hand upon it after a short pause.

"Yes, Sir," replied Oliver.

"Ah!" said the Jew, turning rather pale. "They—they're mine, Oliver; my little property. All I have to live upon, in my old age. The folks call me a miser, my dear—only a miser; that's all."

Oliver thought the old gentleman must be a decided miser to live in such a dirty place, with so many watches; but, thinking that perhaps his fondness for the Dodger and the other boys, cost him a good deal of money, he only cast a deferential look at the Jew, and asked if he might get up.

"Certainly, my dear—certainly," replied the old gentleman. "Stay. There's a pitcher of water in the corner by the door. Bring it here; and I'll give you a basin to wash in, my dear."

Oliver got up; walked across the room; and stooped for one instant to raise the pitcher. When he turned his head, the box was gone.

He had scarcely washed himself, and made everything tidy, by emptying the basin out of the window, agreeably to the Jew's directions, when the Dodger returned: accompanied by a very sprightly young friend, whom Oliver had seen smoking on the previous night, and who was now formally introduced to him as Charley Bates. The four sat down, to breakfast on the coffee, and some hot rolls and ham, which the Dodger had brought home in the crown of his hat.

"Well," said the Jew, glancing slyly at Oliver, and addressing himself to the Dodger, "I hope you've been at work this morning, my dears?"

"Hard," replied the Dodger.

"As Nails," added Charley Bates.

"Good boys, good boys!" said the Jew. "What have you got, Dodger?"

"A couple of pocket-books," replied that young gentleman.

"Lined?" inquired the Jew, with eagerness.

"Pretty well," replied the Dodger, producing two pocket-books: one green, and the other red.

"Not so heavy as they might be," said the Jew, after looking at the insides carefully; "but very neat and nicely made. Ingenious workman, ain't he, Oliver?"

"Very, indeed, Sir," said Oliver. At which Mr. Charles Bates laughed uproariously; very much to the amazement of Oliver, who saw nothing to laugh at, in anything that had passed.

"And what have you got, my dear?" said Fagin to Charley Bates.

"Wipes," replied Master Bates; at the same time producing four pocket-handkerchiefs.

"Well," said the Jew, inspecting them closely; "they're very good ones—very. You haven t marked them well, though, Charley; so the marks shall be picked out with a needle, and we'll teach Oliver how to do it. Shall us, Oliver, eh? Ha! ha! ha!"

"If you please, Sir," said Oliver

"You'd like to be able to make pocket-handkerchiefs as easy as Charley Bates, wouldn't you, my dear?" said the Jew.

"Very much indeed, if you'll teach me, Sir," replied Oliver.

Master Bates saw something so exquisitely ludicrous in this reply, that he burst into another laugh; which laugh, meeting the coffee he was drinking, and carrying it down some wrong channel, very nearly terminated in his premature suffocation.

"He is so jolly green!" said Charley when he recovered, as an apology to the company for his unpolite behaviour.

The Dodger said nothing, but he smoothed Oliver's hair down over his eyes, and said he'd know better by-and-bye;

upon which the old gentleman, observing Oliver's colour mounting, changed the subject by asking whether there had been much of a crowd at the execution that morning. This made him wonder more and more; for it was plain from the replies of the two boys that they had both been there; and Oliver naturally wondered how they could possibly have found time to be so very industrious.

When the breakfast was cleared away, the merry old gentleman and the two boys played at a very curious and uncommon game, which was performed in this way. The merry old gentleman, placing a snuff-box in one pocket of his trousers, a note-case in the other, and a watch in his waistcoat pocket, with a guard-chain round his neck, and sticking a mock diamond pin in his shirt: buttoned his coat tight round him, and putting his spectacle-case and handkerchief in his pockets, trotted up and down the room with a stick, in imitation of the manner in which old gentlemen wa'k about the streets any hour in the day. Sometimes he stopped at the fire-place, and sometimes at the door, making believe that he was staring with all his might into shop-windows. At such times, he would look constantly round him, for fear of thieves, and keep slapping all his pockets in turn, to see that he hadn't lost anything, in such a very funny and natural manner, that Oliver laughed till the tears ran down his face. All this time, the two boys followed him closely about: getting out of his sight, so nimbly, every time he turned round, that it was impossible to follow their motions. At last, the Dodger trod upon his toes, or ran upon his boot accidentally, while Charley Bates stumbled up against him behind; and in that one moment they took from him, with the most extraordinary rapidity, snuff-box, note-case, watch-guard, chain, shirt-pin, pocket-handkerchief, even the spectacle-case. If the old gentleman felt a hand in any one of his pockets, he cried out where it was; and then the game began all over again.

When this game had been played a great many times, a couple of young ladies called to see the young gentlemen; one of whom was named Bet, and the other Nancy. They wore a good deal of hair, not very neatly turned up behind, and were rather untidy about the shoes and stockings. They were not exactly pretty, perhaps; but they had a great deal of colour in their faces, and looked quite stout and hearty. Being remarkably free and agreeable in their manners, Oliver thought them very nice girls indeed. As there is no doubt they were.

These visitors stopped a long time. Spirits were produced, in consequence of one of the young ladies complaining of a coldness in her inside; and the conversation took a very convivial and improving turn. At length, Charley Bates expressed his opinion that it was time to pad the hoof. This, it occurred to Oliver, must be French for going out; for, directly afterwards, the Dodger, and Charley, and the two young ladies, went away together, having been kindly furnished by the amiable old Jew with money to spend.

"There, my dear," said Fagin. "That's a pleasant life, isn't it? They have gone out for the day."

"Have they done work, Sir?" inquired Oliver.

"Yes," said the Jew; "that is, unless they should unexpectedly come across any, when they are out; and they won't neglect it, if they do, my dear, depend upon it. Make 'em your models, my dear. Make 'em your models," said the Jew, tapping the fire-shovel on the hearth to add force to his words; "do everything they bid you, and take their advice in all matters—especially the Dodger's, my dear. He'll be a great man himself, and will make you one too, if you take pattern by him. Is my handkerchief hanging out of my pocket, my dear?" said the Jew, stopping short.

"Yes, Sir," said Oliver.

"See if you can take it out, without my feeling it: as you saw them do, when we were at play this morning."

Oliver held up the bottom of the pocket with one hand, as he had seen the Dodger hold it, and drew the handkerchief lightly out of it with the other.

"Is it gone?" cried the Jew.

"Here it is, Sir," said Oliver, showing it in his hand.

"You're a clever boy, my dear," said the playful old gentleman, patting Oliver on the head approvingly. "I never saw a sharper lad. Here's a shilling for you. If you go on, in this way, you'll be the greatest man of the time. And now come here, and I'll show you how to take the marks out of the handkerchiefs."

Oliver wondered what picking the old gentleman's pocket in play, had to do with his chances of being a great man. But, thinking that the Jew, being so much his senior, must know best, he followed him quietly to the table, and was soon deeply involved in his new study.

CHAPTER X.

OLIVER BECOMES BETTER ACQUAINTED WITH THE CHARACTERS OF HIS NEW ASSOCIATES; AND PURCHASES EXPERIENCE AT A HIGH PRICE. BEING A SHORT, BUT VERY IMPORTANT CHAPTER, IN THIS HISTORY.

FOR many days, Oliver remained in the Jew's room, picking the marks out of the pocket-handkerchiefs, (of which a great number were brought home,) and sometimes taking part in the game already described: which the two boys and the Jew played, regularly, every morning. At length, he began to languish for the fresh air, and took many occasions of earnestly entreating the old gentleman to allow him to go out to work, with his two companions.

Oliver was rendered the more anxious to be actively employed, by what he had seen of the stern morality of the old gentleman's character. Whenever the Dodger or Charley Bates came home at night, empty-handed, he would expatiate with great vehemence on the misery of idle and lazy habits; and would enforce upon them the necessity of an active life, by sending them supperless to bed. On one occasion, indeed, he even went so far as to knock them both down a flight of stairs; but this was carrying out his virtuous precepts to an unusual extent.

At length, one morning, Oliver obtained the permission he had so eagerly sought. There had been no handkerchiefs to work upon, for two or three days; and the dinners had been rather meagre. Perhaps these were reasons for the old gentleman's giving his assent; but, whether they were or no, he told Oliver he might go; and placed him under the joint guardianship of Charley Bates, and his friend the Dodger.

The three boys sallied out; the Dodger with his coat-sleeves tucked up, and his hat cocked, as usual; Master Bates sauntering along with his hands in his pockets; and

Oliver between them: wondering where they were going: and what branch of manufacture he would be instructed in, first.

The pace at which they went, was such a very lazy, ill-looking saunter, that Oliver soon began to think his companions were going to deceive the old gentleman, by not going to work at all. The Dodger had a vicious propensity, too, of pulling the caps from the heads of small boys and tossing them down areas; while Charley Bates exhibited some very loose notions concerning the rights of property, by pilfering divers apples and onions from the stalls at the kennel sides, and thrusting them into pockets which were so surprisingly capacious, that they seemed to undermine his whole suit of clothes in every direction. These things looked so bad, that Oliver was on the point of declaring his intention of seeking his way back, in the best way he could; when his thoughts were suddenly directed into another channel, by a very mysterious change of behaviour on the part of the Dodger.

They were just emerging from a narrow court not far from the open square in Clerkenwell, which is yet called, by some strange perversion of terms, "The Green;" when the Dodger made a sudden stop; and, laying his finger on his lip, drew his companions back again, with the greatest caution and circumspection.

"What's the matter?" demanded Oliver.

"Hush!" replied the Dodger. "Do you see that old cove at the book-stall?"

"The old gentleman over the way?" said Oliver. "Yes, I see him."

"He'll do," said the Dodger.

"A prime plant," observed Master Charley Bates.

Oliver looked from one to the other, with the greatest surprise; but he was not permitted to make any inquiries; for the two boys walked stealthily across the road, and slunk close behind the old gentleman towards whom his attention had been directed. Oliver walked a few paces after them; and, not knowing whether to advance or retire, stood looking on in silent amazement.

The old gentleman was a very respectable-looking personage, with a powdered head and gold spectacles. He was dressed in a bottle-green coat with a black velvet collar; wore white trousers; and carried a smart bamboo cane under his arm. He had taken up a book from the stall, and there he stood, reading away, as hard as if he were in his elbow-chair, in his own study. It is very possible that he fancied himself there, indeed; for it was plain, from his utter abstraction, that he saw not the book-stall, nor the street, nor the boys, nor, in short, anything but the book itself; which he was reading straight through; turning over the leaf when he got to the bottom of a page, beginning at the top line of the next one, and going regularly on, with the greatest interest and eagerness.

What was Oliver's horror and alarm as he stood a few paces off, looking on with his eyelids as wide open as they would possibly go, to see the Dodger plunge his hand into the old gentleman's pocket; and draw from thence a handkerchief! To see him hand the same to Charley Bates; and finally to behold them, both, running away round the corner at full speed!

In an instant the whole mystery of the handkerchiefs, and the watches, and the jewels, and the Jew, rushed upon the boy's mind. He stood, for a moment, with the blood so tingling through all his veins from terror, that he felt as if he were in a burning fire; then, confused and frightened, he took to his heels; and, not knowing what he did, made off as fast as he could lay his feet to the ground.

This was all done in a minute's space. In the very instant when Oliver began to run, the old gentleman, putting his hand to his pocket, and missing his handkerchief, turned sharp round. Seeing the boy scudding away at such a rapid pace, he very naturally concluded him to be the depredator; and, shouting "Stop thief!" with all his might made off after him, book in hand.

But the old gentleman was not the only person who raised the hue-and-cry. The Dodger and Master Bates, unwilling to attract public attention by running down the open street, had merely retired into the very first doorway round the corner. They no sooner heard the cry, and saw Oliver running, than, guessing exactly how the matter stood, they issued forth with great promptitude; and, shouting "Stop thief!" too, joined in the pursuit like good citizens.

Although Oliver had been brought up by philosophers, he was not theoretically acquainted with the beautiful axiom that self-preservation is the first law of nature. If he had been, perhaps he would have been prepared for this. Not being prepared, however, it alarmed him the more; so away he went like the wind, with the old gentleman and the two boys roaring and shouting behind him.

"Stop thief! Stop thief!" There is a magic in the sound. The tradesman leaves his counter, and the carman his waggon; the butcher throws down his tray; the baker his basket; the milkman his pail; the errand-boy his parcels; the school-boy his marbles; the paviour his pickaxe; the child his battledore. Away they run, pell-mell, helter-skelter, slap-dash: tearing, yelling, and screaming: knocking down the passengers as they turn the corners, rousing up the dogs, and astonishing the fowls: and streets, squares, and courts, re-echo with the sound.

"Stop thief! Stop thief!" The cry is taken up by a hundred voices, and the crowd accumulate at every turning. Away they fly, splashing through the mud, and rattling along the pavements: up go the windows, out run the people, onward bear the mob, a whole audience desert Punch in the very thickest of the plot, and, joining the rushing throng, swell the shout, and lend fresh vigour to the cry, "Stop thief! Stop thief!"

"Stop thief! Stop thief!" There is a passion *for hunting something* deeply implanted in the human breast. One wretched breathless child, panting with exhaustion; terror in his looks; agony in his eyes; large drops of perspiration streaming down his face; strains every nerve to make head upon his pursuers; and as they follow on his track, and gain upon him every instant, they hail his decreasing strength with still louder shouts, and whoop and scream with joy. "Stop thief!" Ay, stop him for God's sake, were it only in mercy!

Stopped at last. A clever blow. He is down upon the pavement; and the crowd eagerly gather round him: each new comer, jostling and struggling with the others to catch a glimpse. "Stand aside!" "Give him a little air!" "Nonsense! he don't deserve it." "Where's the gentleman?" "Here he is, coming down the street." "Make room there for the gentleman!" "Is this the boy, Sir!" "Yes."

Oliver lay, covered with mud and dust, and bleeding from the mouth, looking wildly round upon the heap of faces that surrounded him, when the old gentleman was officiously dragged and pushed into the circle by the foremost of the pursuers.

"Yes," said the gentleman, "I am afraid it is."

"Afraid!" murmured the crowd. "That's a good 'un."

"Poor fellow!" said the gentleman, "he has hurt himself."

"*I* did that, Sir," said a great lubberly fellow, stepping forward; "and preciously I cut my knuckle agin' his mouth. *I* stopped him, Sir."

The fellow touched his hat with a grin, expecting something for his pains; but the old gentleman, eyeing him with an expression of dislike, looked anxiously round, as if he contemplated running away himself: which it is very possible he might have attempted to do, and thus afforded another chase, had not a police officer (who is generally the last person to arrive in such cases) at that moment made his way through the crowd, and seized Oliver by the collar,

"Come, get up," said the man, roughly.

"It wasn't me indeed, Sir. Indeed, indeed, it was two other boys," said Oliver, clasping his hands passionately, and looking round. "They are here somewhere."

"Oh no, they ain't," said the officer. He meant this to be ironical, but it was true besides; for the Dodger and Charley Bates had filed off down the first convenient court they came to. "Come, get up!"

"Don't hurt him," said the old gentleman, compassionately.

"Oh no, I won't hurt him," replied the officer, tearing his jacket half off his back, in proof thereof. "Come, I know you; it won't do. Will you stand upon your legs, you young devil?"

Oliver, who could hardly stand, made a shift to raise himself on his feet, and was at once lugged along the streets by the jacket-collar, at a rapid pace. The gentleman walked on with them by the officer's side; and as many of the crowd as could achieve the feat, got a little ahead, and stared back at Oliver from time to time. The boys shouted in triumph; and on they went.

CHAPTER XI.

TREATS OF MR. FANG THE POLICE MAGISTRATE; AND FURNISHES A SLIGHT SPECIMEN OF HIS MODE OF ADMINISTERING JUSTICE.

THE offence had been committed within the district, and indeed in the immediate neighbourhood of, a very notorious metropolitan police office. The crowd had only the satisfaction of accompanying Oliver through two or three streets, and down a place called Mutton Hill, when he was led beneath a low archway, and up a dirty court, into this dispensary of summary justice, by the back way. It was a small paved yard into which they turned; and here they encountered a stout man with a bunch of whiskers on his face, and a bunch of keys in his hand.

"What's the matter now?" said the man carelessly.

"A young fogle-hunter," replied the man who had Oliver in charge.

"Are you the party that's been robbed, Sir?" inquired the man with the keys.

"Yes, I am," replied the old gentleman; "but I am not sure that this boy actually took the handkerchief. I—I would rather not press the case."

"Must go before the magistrate now, Sir," replied the

man. "His worship will be disengaged in half a minute. Now, young gallows."

This was an invitation for Oliver to enter through a door which he unlocked as he spoke, and which led into a stone cell. Here he was searched; and, nothing being found upon him, locked up.

This cell was in shape and size something like an area cellar, only not so light. It was most intolerably dirty; for it was Monday morning; and it had been tenanted by six drunken people, who had been locked up elsewhere since Saturday night. But this is little. In our station-houses, men and women are every night confined on the most trivial *charges*—the word is worth noting—in dungeons, compared with which, those in Newgate, occupied by the most atrocious felons, tried, found guilty, and under sentence of death, are palaces. Let any man who doubts this, compare the two.

The old gentleman looked almost as rueful as Oliver when the key grated in the lock. He turned with a sigh to the book, which had been the innocent cause of all this disturbance.

"There is something in that boy's face," said the old gentleman to himself as he walked slowly away, tapping his chin with the cover of the book, in a thoughtful manner; "something that touches and interests me. *Can* he be innocent? He looked like—By the bye," exclaimed the old gentleman, halting very abruptly, and staring up into the sky, "bless my soul!—Where have I seen something like that look before?"

After musing for some minutes, the old gentleman walked, with the same meditative face, into a back ante-room opening from the yard; and there, retiring into a corner, called up before his mind's eye a vast amphitheatre of faces over which a dusky curtain had hung for many years. "No," said the old gentleman, shaking his head; "it must be imagination."

He wandered over them again. He had called them into view, and it was not easy to replace the shroud that had so long concealed them. There were the faces of friends, and foes, and of many that had been almost strangers peering intrusively from the crowd; there were the faces of young and blooming girls that were now old women; there were faces that the grave had changed and closed upon, but which the mind, superior to its power, still dressed in their old freshness and beauty, calling back the lustre of the eyes, the brightness of the smile, the beaming of the soul through its mask of clay, and whispering of beauty beyond the tomb, changed but to be heightened, and taken from earth only to be set up as a light, to shed a soft and gentle glow upon the path to Heaven.

But the old gentleman could recall no one countenance of which Oliver's features bore a trace. So he heaved a sigh over the recollections he had awakened; and being, happily for himself, an absent old gentleman, buried them again in the pages of the musty book.

He was roused by a touch on the shoulder, and a request from the man with the keys to follow him into the office. He closed his book hastily; and was at once ushered into the imposing presence of the renowned Mr. Fang.

The office was a front parlour, with a panelled wall. Mr. Fang sat behind a bar at the upper end; and on one side the door was a sort of wooden pen in which poor little Oliver was already deposited: trembling very much at the awfulness of the scene.

Mr. Fang was a lean, long-backed, stiff-necked, middle-sized man, with no great quantity of hair, and what he had, growing on the back and sides of his head. His face was stern, and much flushed. If he were really not in the habit of drinking rather more than was exactly good for him, he might have brought an action against his countenance for libel, and have recovered heavy damages.

The old gentleman bowed respectfully; and, advancing to the magistrate's desk, said, suiting the action to the word, "That is my name and address, Sir." He then withdrew a pace or two; and, with another polite and gentlemanly inclination of the head, waited to be questioned.

Now, it so happened that Mr. Fang was at that moment perusing a leading article in a newspaper of the morning, adverting to some recent decision of his, and commending him, for the three hundred and fiftieth time, to the special and particular notice of the Secretary of State for the Home Department. He was out of temper; and he looked up with an angry scowl.

"Who are you?" said Mr. Fang.

The old gentleman pointed, with some surprise, to his card.

"Officer!" said Mr. Fang, tossing the card contemptuously away with the newspaper, "who is this fellow?"

"My name, Sir," said the old gentleman, speaking *like* a gentleman, "my name, Sir, is Brownlow. Permit me to inquire the name of the magistrate who offers a gratuitous and unprovoked insult to a respectable person, under the protection of the bench." Saying this, Mr. Brownlow looked round the office as if in search of some person who would afford him the required information.

"Officer!" said Mr. Fang, throwing the paper on one side, "what's this fellow charged with?"

"He's not charged at all, your worship," replied the officer. "He appears against the boy, your worship."

His worship knew this perfectly well; but it was a good annoyance, and a safe one.

"Appears against the boy, does he?" said Fang, surveying Mr. Brownlow contemptuously from head to foot. "Swear him!"

"Before I am sworn, I must beg to say one word," said Mr. Brownlow: "and that is, that I really never, without actual experience, could have believed—"

"Hold your tongue, Sir!" said Mr. Fang, peremptorily.

"I will not, Sir!" replied the old gentleman.

"Hold your tongue this instant, or I'll have you turned out of the office!" said Mr. Fang. "You're an insolent, impertinent fellow. How dare you bully a magistrate!"

"What!" exclaimed the old gentleman, reddening.

"Swear this person!" said Fang to the clerk. "I'll not hear another word. Swear him."

Mr. Brownlow's indignation was greatly roused; but, reflecting perhaps, that he might only injure the boy by giving vent to it, he suppressed his feelings, and submitted to be sworn at once.

"Now," said Fang, "what's the charge against this boy? What have you got to say, Sir?"

"I was standing at a book-stall—" Mr. Brownlow began.

"Hold your tongue, Sir!" said Mr. Fang. "Policeman! Where's the policeman? Here, swear this policeman. Now, policeman, what is this?"

The policeman with becoming humility related how he had taken the charge; how he had searched Oliver, and found nothing on his person; and how that was all he knew about it.

"Are there any witnesses?" inquired Mr. Fang.

"None, your worship," replied the policeman.

Mr. Fang sat silent for some minutes, and then, turning round to the prosecutor, said in a towering passion,

"Do you mean to state what your complaint against this boy is, fellow, or do you not? You have been sworn. Now, if you stand there, refusing to give evidence, I'll punish you for disrespect to the bench; I will, by—"

By whom, nobody knows, for the clerk and jailer coughed very loud, just at the right moment; and the former dropped a heavy book upon the floor, thus preventing the word from being heard—accidentally, of course.

With many interruptions, and repeated insults, Mr. Brownlow contrived to state his case; observing that, in the surprise of the moment, he had run after the boy because he saw him running away; and expressing his hope that, if the magistrate should believe him, although not actually the thief, to be connected with thieves, he would deal as leniently with him as justice would allow.

"He has been hurt already," said the old gentleman in conclusion. "And I fear," he added, with great energy, looking towards the bar, "I really fear that he is very ill."

"Oh! yes, I dare say!" said Mr. Fang, with a sneer. "Come, none of your tricks here, you young vagabond; they won't do. What's your name?"

Oliver tried to reply, but his tongue failed him. He was deadly pale; and the whole place seemed turning round and round.

"What's your name, you hardened scoundrel?" demanded Mr. Fang. "Officer, what's his name?"

This was addressed to a bluff old fellow, in a striped waistcoat, who was standing by the bar. He bent over Oliver, and repeated the inquiry; but finding him really incapable of understanding the question; and knowing that his not replying would only infuriate the magistrate the more, and add to the severity of his sentence; he hazarded a guess.

"He says his name's Tom White, your worship," said this kind-hearted thief-taker.

"Oh, he won't speak out, won't he?" said Fang. "Very well, very well. Where does he live?"

"Where he can, your worship," replied the officer: again pretending to receive Oliver's answer.

"Has he any parents?" inquired Mr. Fang.

"He says they died in his infancy, your worship," replied the officer: hazarding the usual reply.

At this point of the inquiry, Oliver raised his head; and, looking round with imploring eyes, murmured a feeble prayer for a draught of water.

"Stuff and nonsense!" said Mr. Fang: "don't try to make a fool of me."

"I think he really is ill, your worship," remonstrated the officer.

"I know better," said Mr. Fang.

"Take care of him, officer," said the old gentleman, raising his hands instinctively; "he'll fall down."

"Stand away, officer," cried Fang; "let him, if he likes."

Oliver availed himself of the kind permission, and fell heavily to the floor in a fainting fit. The men in the office looked at each other, but no one dared to stir.

"I knew he was shamming," said Fang, as if this were incontestable proof of the fact. "Let him lie there; he'll soon be tired of that."

"How do you propose to deal with the case, Sir?" inquired the clerk in a low voice.

"Summarily," replied Mr. Fang. "He stands committed for three months—hard labour of course. Clear the office."

The door was opened for this purpose, and a couple of men were preparing to carry the insensible boy to his cell; when an elderly man of decent but poor appearance, clad in an old suit of black, rushed hastily into the office, and advanced towards the bench.

"Stop, stop! Don't take him away! For Heaven's sake stop a moment!" cried the new-comer, breathless with haste.

Although the presiding Genii in such an office as this, exercise a summary and arbitrary power over the liberties, the good name, the character, almost the lives, of Her Majesty's subjects, especially of the poorer class; and although, within such walls, enough fantastic tricks are daily played to make the angels blind with weeping; they are closed to the public, save through the medium of the daily press. Mr. Fang was consequently not a little indignant to see an unbidden guest enter in such irreverent disorder.

"What is this? Who is this? Turn this man out. Clear the office!" cried Mr. Fang.

"I will speak," cried the man; "I will not be turned out. I saw it all. I keep the book-stall. I demand to be sworn. I will not be put down. Mr. Fang, you must hear me. You must not refuse, Sir."

The man was right. His manner was bold and determined; and the matter was growing rather too serious to be hushed up.

"Swear the fellow," growled Fang, with a very ill grace. "Now, man, what have you got to say?"

"This," said the man: "I saw three boys: two others and the prisoner here: loitering on the opposite side of the way, when this gentleman was reading. The robbery was committed by another boy. I saw it done; and I saw that this boy was perfectly amazed and stupefied by it." Having by this time recovered a little breath, the worthy book-stall keeper proceeded to relate, in a more coherent manner, the exact circumstances of the robbery.

"Why didn't you come here before?" said Fang, after a pause.

"I hadn't a soul to mind the shop," replied the man. "Everybody who could have helped me, had joined in the pursuit. I could get nobody till five minutes ago; and I've run here all the way."

"The prosecutor was reading, was he?" inquired Fang, after another pause.

"Yes," replied the man. "The very book he has in his hand."

"Oh, that book, eh?" said Fang. "Is it paid for?"

"No, it is not," replied the man, with a smile.

"Dear me, I forgot all about it!" exclaimed the absent old gentleman, innocently.

"A nice person to prefer a charge against a poor boy!" said Fang, with a comical effort to look humane. "I consider, Sir, that you have obtained possession of that book, under very suspicious and disreputable circumstances; and you may think yourself very fortunate that the owner of the property declines to prosecute. Let this be a lesson to you, my man, or the law will overtake you yet. The boy is discharged. Clear the office."

"D—n me!" cried the old gentleman, bursting out with the rage he had kept down so long, "d—n me! I'll—."

"Clear the office!" said the magistrate. "Officers, do you hear? Clear the office!"

The mandate was obeyed; and the indignant Mr. Brownlow was conveyed out, with the book in one hand, and the bamboo cane in the other : in a perfect phrenzy of rage and defiance. He reached the yard; and it vanished in a moment. Little Oliver Twist lay on his back on the pavement, with his shirt unbuttoned, and his temples bathed with water; his face a deadly white; and a cold tremble convulsing his whole frame.

"Poor boy, poor boy!" said Mr. Brownlow, bending over him. "Call a coach, somebody, pray. Directly!"

A coach was obtained, and Oliver, having been carefully laid on one seat, the old gentleman got in and sat himself on the other.

"May I accompany you?" said the book-stall keeper, looking in.

"Bless me, yes, my dear friend," said Mr. Brownlow quickly. "I forgot you. Dear, dear! I have this unhappy book still. Jump in. Poor fellow! There's no time to lose."

The book-stall keeper got into the coach; and away they drove.

CHAPTER XII.

IN WHICH OLIVER IS TAKEN BETTER CARE OF THAN HE EVER WAS BEFORE. AND IN WHICH THE NARRATIVE REVERTS TO THE MERRY OLD GENTLEMAN AND HIS YOUTHFUL FRIENDS.

THE coach rattled away, down Mount Pleasant and up Exmouth Street: over nearly the same ground as that which Oliver had traversed when he first entered London in company with the Dodger; and, turning a different way when it reached the Angel at Islington, stopped at length before a neat house, in a quiet shady street near Pentonville. Here, a bed was prepared, without loss of time, in which Mr. Brownlow saw his young charge carefully and comfortably deposited; and here, he was tended with a kindness and solicitude that knew no bounds.

But, for many days, Oliver remained insensible to all the goodness of his new friends. The sun rose and sank, and rose and sank again, and many times after that; and still the boy lay stretched on his uneasy bed, dwindling away beneath the dry and wasting heat of fever. The worm does not his work more surely on the dead body, than does this slow creeping fire upon the living frame.

Weak, and thin, and pallid, he awoke at last from what seemed to have been a long and troubled dream. Feebly raising himself in the bed, with his head resting on his trembling arm, he looked anxiously round.

"What room is this? Where have I been brought to?" said Oliver. "This is not the place I went to sleep in."

He uttered these words in a feeble voice, being very faint and weak; but they were overheard at once; for the curtain at the bed's head was hastily drawn back; and a motherly old lady, very neatly and precisely dressed, rose as she undrew it, from an armchair close by, in which she had been sitting at needle-work.

"Hush, my dear," said the old lady softly. "You must be very quiet, or you will be ill again; and you have been very bad,—as bad as bad could be, pretty nigh. Lie down again; there's a dear!" With these words, the old lady very gently placed Oliver's head upon the pillow; and,

smoothing back his hair from his forehead, looked so kindly and lovingly in his face, that he could not help placing his little withered hand on hers, and drawing it round his neck.

"Save us!" said the old lady, with tears in her eyes. "What a grateful little dear it is. Pretty creetur! What would his mother feel if she had sat by him as I have, and could see him now!"

"Perhaps she does see me," whispered Oliver, folding his hands together; "perhaps she has sat by me. I almost feel as if she had."

"That was the fever, my dear," said the old lady mildly.

"I suppose it was," replied Oliver, "because Heaven is a long way of; and they are too happy there, to come down to the bed-side of a poor boy. But if she knew I was ill, she must have pitied me, even there; for she was very ill herself before she died. She can't know anything about me though," added Oliver after a moment's silence. "If she had seen me hurt, it would have made her sorrowful; and her face has always looked sweet and happy, when I have dreamed of her."

The old lady made no reply to this; but wiping her eyes first, and her spectacles, which lay on the counterpane, afterwards, as if they were part and parcel of those features, brought some cool stuff for Oliver to drink; and then, patting him on the cheek, told him he must lie very quiet, or he would be ill again.

So, Oliver kept very still; partly because he was anxious to obey the kind old lady in all things; and partly, to tell the truth, because he was completely exhausted with what he had already said. He soon fell into a gentle doze, from which he was awakened by the light of a candle: which, being brought near the bed, showed him a gentleman with a very large and loud-ticking gold watch in his hand, who felt his pulse, and said he was a great deal better.

"You *are* a great deal better, are you not, my dear?" said the gentleman.

"Yes, thank you, Sir," replied Oliver.

"Yes, I know you are," said the gentleman: "You're hungry too, an't you?"

"No, Sir," answered Oliver.

"Hem!" said the gentleman. "No, I know you're not. He is not hungry, Mrs. Bedwin," said the gentleman: looking very wise.

The old lady made a respectful inclination of the head, which seemed to say that she thought the doctor was a very clever man. The doctor appeared very much of the same opinion himself.

"You feel sleepy, don't you, my dear?" said the doctor.

"No, Sir," replied Oliver.

"No," said the doctor, with a very shrewd and satisfied look. "You're not sleepy. Nor thirsty. Are you?"

"Yes, Sir, rather thirsty," answered Oliver.

"Just as I expected, Mrs. Bedwin," said the doctor. "It's very natural that he should be thirsty. You may give him a little tea, ma'am, and some dry toast without any butter. Don't keep him too warm, ma'am; but be careful that you don't let him be too cold—will you have the goodness?"

The old lady dropped a curtsey. The doctor, after tasting the cool stuff, and expressing a qualified approval thereof, hurried away: his boots creaking in a very important and wealthy manner as he went down stairs.

Oliver dozed off again, soon after this; and when he awoke, it was nearly twelve o'clock. The old lady tenderly bade him good-night shortly afterwards; and left him in charge of a fat old woman who had just come: bringing with her, in a little bundle, a small Prayer Book and a large nightcap. Putting the latter on her head and the former on the table, the old woman, after telling Oliver that she had come to sit up with him, drew her chair close to the fire and went off into a series of short naps, chequered at frequent intervals with sundry tumblings forward, and divers moans and chokings, which, however, had no worse effect than causing her to rub her nose very hard, and then fall asleep again. And thus the night crept slowly on. Oliver lay awake for some time, counting the little circles of light which the reflection of the rushlight shade threw upon the ceiling; or tracing with his languid eyes the intricate pattern of the paper on the wall. The darkness and deep stillness of the room were very solemn; and as they brought into the boy's mind the thought that Death had been hovering there, for many days and nights, and might yet fill it with the gloom and dread of his awful presence, he turned his face upon the pillow, and fervently prayed to Heaven.

Gradually, he fell into that deep tranquil sleep which ease from recent suffering alone imparts; that calm and peaceful rest which it is pain to wake from. Who, if this were death, would be roused again to all the struggles and turmoils of life; to all its cares for the present; its anxieties for the future; more than all, its weary recollections of the past!

It had been bright day, for hours, when Oliver opened his eyes; when he did so, he felt cheerful and happy. The crisis of the disease was safely past. He belonged to the world again.

In three days' time, he was able to sit in an easy-chair, well propped up with pillows; and, as he was still too weak to walk, Mrs. Bedwin had him carried down stairs into the little housekeeper's room, which belonged to her: where, having sat him up by the fireside, the good old lady sat herself down too; and, being in a state of considerable delight at seeing him so much better, forthwith began to cry most violently.

"Never mind me, my dear," said the old lady. "I'm only having a regular good cry. There; it's all over now; and I'm quite comfortable."

"You're very, very kind to me, ma'am," said Oliver.

"Well, never you mind that, my dear," said the old lady; "that's got nothing to do with your broth; and it's full time you had it; for the doctor says Mr. Brownlow may come in to see you this morning: and we must get up our best looks, because the better we look, the more he'll be pleased." And with this, the old lady applied herself to warming up in a little saucepan a basin full of broth: strong enough to furnish an ample dinner, when reduced to the regulation strength: for three hundred and fifty paupers, at the very lowest computation.

"Are you fond of pictures, dear?" inquired the old lady, seeing that Oliver had fixed his eyes, most intently, on a portrait which hung against the wall: just opposite his chair.

"I don't quite know, ma'am," said Oliver, without taking his eyes from the canvas; "I have seen so few that I hardly know. What a beautiful, mild face that lady's is!"

"Ah!" said the old lady, "painters always make ladies out prettier than they are, or they wouldn't get any custom, child. The man that invented the machine for taking likenesses might have known *that* would never succeed;

it's a deal too honest. A deal!" said the old lady, laughing very heartily at her own acuteness.

"Is—is that a likeness, ma'am?" said Oliver.

"Yes," said the old lady, looking up for a moment from the broth; "that's a portrait."

"Whose, ma'am?" asked Oliver eagerly.

"Why, really, my dear, I don't know," answered the old lady in a good-humoured manner. "It's not a likeness of anybody that you or I know, I expect. It seems to strike your fancy, dear."

"It is so very pretty," replied Oliver.

"Why, sure you're not afraid of it?" said the old lady: observing, in great surprise, the look of awe with which the child regarded the painting.

"Oh no, no," returned Oliver quickly; "but the eyes look so sorrowful; and where I sit, they seem fixed upon me. It makes my heart beat," added Oliver in a low voice, "as if it was alive, and wanted to speak to me, but couldn't."

"Lord save us!" exclaimed the old lady, starting; "don't talk in that way, child. You're weak and nervous after your illness. Let me wheel your chair round to the other side; and then you won't see it. There!" said the old lady, suiting the action to the word; "you don't see it now, at all events."

Oliver *did* see it in his mind's eye as distinctly as if he had not altered his position; but he thought it better not to worry the kind old lady; so he smiled gently when she looked at him; and Mrs. Bedwin, satisfied that he felt more comfortable, salted and broke bits of toasted bread into the broth, with all the bustle befitting so solemn a preparation. Oliver got through it with extraordinary expedition: and had scarcely swallowed the last spoonful, when there came a soft tap at the door. "Come in," said the old lady; and in walked Mr. Brownlow.

Now, the old gentleman came in as brisk as need be; but he had no sooner raised his spectacles on his forehead, and thrust his hands behind the skirts of his dressing-gown to take a good long look at Oliver, than his countenance underwent a very great variety of odd contortions. Oliver looked very worn and shadowy from sickness: and made an ineffectual attempt to stand up, out of respect to his benefactor: which terminated in his sinking back into the chair again; and the fact is, if the truth must be told, that Mr. Brownlow's heart, being large enough for any six ordinary old gentlemen of humane disposition, forced a supply of tears into his eyes, by some hydraulic process which we are not sufficiently philosophical in a condition to explain.

"Poor boy, poor boy!" said Mr. Brownlow, clearing his throat. "I'm rather hoarse this morning, Mrs. Bedwin. I'm afraid I have caught cold."

"I hope not, Sir," said Mrs. Bedwin. "Everything you have had, has been well aired, Sir."

"I don't know, Bedwin. I don't know," said Mr. Brownlow; "I rather think I had a damp napkin at dinner-time yesterday; but never mind that. How do you feel, my dear?"

"Very happy, Sir," replied Oliver. "And very grateful indeed, Sir, for your goodness to me."

"Good boy," said Mr. Brownlow, stoutly. "Have you given him any nourishment, Bedwin? Any slops, eh?"

"He has just had a basin of beautiful strong broth, Sir," replied Mrs. Bedwin: drawing herself up slightly, and laying a strong emphasis on the last word: to intimate that between slops, and broth well compounded, there existed no affinity or connexion whatsover.

"Ugh!" said Mr. Brownlow, with a slight shudder; "a couple of glasses of port wine would have done him a great deal more good. Wouldn't they, Tom White, eh?"

"My name is Oliver, Sir," replied the little invalid: with a look of great astonishment.

"Oliver," said Mr. Brownlow; "Oliver what? Oliver White, eh?"

"No, Sir, Twist, Oliver Twist."

"Queer name!" said the old gentleman. "What made you tell the magistrate your name was White?"

"I never told him so, Sir," returned Oliver in amazement.

This sounded so like a falsehood, that the old gentleman looked somewhat sternly in Oliver's face. It was impossible to doubt him; there was truth in every one of its thin and sharpened lineaments.

"Some mistake," said Mr. Brownlow. But, although his motive for looking steadily at Oliver no longer existed, the old idea of the resemblance between his features and some familiar face came upon him so strongly, that he could not withdraw his gaze.

"I hope you are not angry with me, Sir?" said Oliver, raising his eyes beseechingly.

"No, no," replied the old gentleman. "Why! what's this? Bedwin, look there!"

As he spoke, he pointed hastily to the picture above Oliver's head; and then to the boy's face. There was its living copy. The eyes, the head, the mouth; every feature was the same. The expression was, for the instant, so precisely alike, that the minutest line seemed copied with startling accuracy!

Oliver knew not the cause of this sudden exclamation; for, not being strong enough to bear the start it gave him, he fainted away. A weakness on his part, which affords the narrative an opportunity of relieving the reader from suspense, in behalf of the two young pupils of the Merry Old Gentleman; and of recording—

That when the Dodger, and his accomplished friend Master Bates, joined in the hue-and-cry which was raised at Oliver's heels, in consequence of their executing an illegal conveyance of Mr. Brownlow's personal property, as has been already described, they were actuated by a very laudable and becoming regard for themselves; and forasmuch as the freedom of the subject and the liberty of the individual are among the first and proudest boasts of a true-hearted Englishman; so I need hardly beg the reader to observe, that this action should tend to exalt them in the opinion of all public and patriotic men, in almost as great a degree as this strong proof of their anxiety for their own preservation and safety goes to corroborate and confirm the little code of laws which certain profound and sound-indulging philosophers have laid down as the mainsprings of all Nature's deeds and actions: the said philosophers very wisely reducing the good lady's proceedings to matters of maxim and theory: and, by a very neat and pretty compliment to her exalted wisdom and understanding, putting entirely out of sight any considerations of heart, or generous impulse and feeling. For these are matters totally beneath a female who is acknowledged by universal admission to be far above the numerous little foibles and weaknesses of her sex.

If I wanted any further proof of the strictly philosophical nature of the conduct of these young gentlemen in their very delicate predicament, I should at once find it in the fact (also recorded in a foregoing part of this narrative), of their quitting the pursuit, when the general attention was fixed upon Oliver; and making immediately for their home by the shortest possible cut. For although I do not mean to assert that it is usually the practice of renowned and learned sages, to shorten the road to any great conclusion (their course indeed being rather to lengthen the distance, by various circumlocutions and discursive staggerings, like unto those in which drunken men under the pressure of a too mighty flow of ideas, are prone to indulge); still I do mean to say, and do say distinctly, that it is the invariable practice of many mighty philosophers, in carrying out their theories, to evince great wisdom and foresight in providing against every possible contingency which can be supposed at all likely to affect themselves. Thus, to do a great right, you may do a little wrong; and you may take any means which the end to be attained will justify; the amount of the right, or the amount of the wrong, or indeed the distinction between the two, being left entirely to the philosopher concerned, to be settled and determined by his clear, comprehensive, and impartial view of his own particular case.

It was not until the two boys had scoured, with great rapidity, through a most intricate maze of narrow streets and courts, that they ventured to halt, by one consent, beneath a low and dark archway. Having remained silent here, just long enough to recover breath to speak, Master Bates uttered an exclamation of amusement and delight; and, bursting into an uncontrollable fit of laughter, flung himself upon a door-step, and rolled thereon in a transport of mirth.

"What's the matter?" inquired the Dodger.

"Ha! ha! ha!" roared Charley Bates.

"Hold your noise," remonstrated the Dodger, looking cautiously round. "Do you want to be grabbed, stupid?"

"I can't help it," said Charley, "I can't help it. To see him splitting away at that pace, and cutting round the corners, and knocking against the posts, and starting on again as if he was made of iron as well as them, and me with the wipe in my pocket, singing out arter him—oh, my eye!" The vivid imagination of Master Bates, presented the scene before him in too strong colours. As he arrived at this apostrophe, he again rolled upon the doorstep, and laughed louder than before.

"What'll Fagin say?" inquired the Dodger; taking advantage of the next interval of breathlessness on the part of his friend to propound the question.

"What!" repeated Charley Bates.

"Ah, what?" said the Dodger.

"Why, what should he say?" inquired Charley: stopping rather suddenly in his merriment; for the Dodger's manner was impressive. "What should he say?"

Mr. Dawkins whistled for a couple of minutes; then, taking off his hat, scratched his head, and nodded thrice.

"What do you mean?" said Charley.

"Toor rul lol loo, gammon and spinnage, the frog he wouldn't, and high cockolorum," said the Dodger: with a slight sneer on his intellectual countenance.

This was explanatory, but not satisfactory. Master Bates felt it so; and again said, "What do you mean?"

The Dodger made no reply; but putting his hat on again, and gathering the skirts of his long-tailed coat under his arm, thrust his tongue into his cheek, slapped the bridge of his nose some half-dozen times in a familiar but ex-

George Cruikshank

OLIVER RECOVERING FROM THE FEVER.

pressive manner, and turning on his heel, slunk down the court. Master Bates followed, with a thoughtful countenance.

The noise of footsteps on the creaking stairs, a few minutes after the occurrence of this conversation, roused the merry old gentleman as he sat over the fire with a saveloy and a small loaf in his left hand; a pocket-knife in his right; and a pewter pot on the trivet. There was a rascally smile on his white face as he turned round; and, looking sharply out from under his thick red eyebrows, bent his ear towards the door, and listened intently.

"Why, how's this?" muttered the Jew: changing countenance; "only two of 'em? Where's the third? They can't have got into trouble. Hark!"

The footsteps approached nearer; they reached the landing. The door was slowly opened; and the Dodger and Charley Bates entered, closing it behind them.

CHAPTER XIII.

SOME NEW ACQUAINTANCES ARE INTRODUCED TO THE INTELLIGENT READER; CONNECTED WITH WHOM, VARIOUS PLEASANT MATTERS ARE RELATED, APPERTAINING TO THIS HISTORY.

"WHERE's Oliver?" said the furious Jew, rising with a menacing look. "Where's the boy?"

The young thieves eyed their preceptor as if they were alarmed at his violence; and looked uneasily at each other. But they made no reply.

"What's become of the boy?" said the Jew, seizing the Dodger tightly by the collar, and threatening him with horrid imprecations. "Speak out, or I'll throttle you!"

Mr. Fagin looked so very much in earnest, that Charley Bates, who deemed it prudent in all cases to be on the safe side; and who conceived it by no means improbable that it might be his turn to be throttled second; dropped upon his knees, and raised a loud, well-sustained, and continuous roar—something between a mad bull and a speaking trumpet.

"Will you speak?" thundered the Jew: shaking the Dodger so much that his keeping in the big coat at all, seemed perfectly miraculous.

"Why, the traps have got him, and that's all about it," said the Dodger, sullenly. "Come, let go o' me, will you!" And, swinging himself, at one jerk, clean out of the big coat, which he left in the Jew's hands, the Dodger snatched up the toasting fork, and made a pass at the merry old gentleman's waistcoat; which, if it had taken effect, would have let a little more merriment out, than could have been easily replaced in a month or two.

The Jew stepped back in this emergency, with more agility than could have been anticipated in a man of his apparent decrepitude; and, seizing up the pot, prepared to hurl it at his assailant's head. But Charley Bates, at this moment, calling his attention by a perfectly terrific howl, he suddenly altered its destination, and flung it full at that young gentleman.

"Why, what the blazes is in the wind now!" growled a deep voice. "Who pitched that 'ere at me? It's well it's the beer, and not the pot, as hit me, or I'd have settled somebody. I might have know'd, as nobody but an in-

fernal, rich, plundering, thundering, old Jew could afford to throw away any drink but water; and not that, unless he done the River Company every quarter. Wot's it all about, Fagin? D—me, if my neck-handkercher an't lined with beer! Come in, you sneaking warmint; wot are you stopping outside for, as if you was ashamed of your master! Come in!"

The man who growled out these words, was a stoutly-built fellow of about five-and-thirty, in a black velveteen coat, very soiled drab breeches, laced-up half boots, and grey cotton stockings, which inclosed a very bulky pair of legs, with large swelling calves; the kind of legs, that in such costume, always look in an unfinished and incomplete state without a set of fetters to garnish them. He had a brown hat on his head, and a dirty Belcher handkerchief round his neck: with the long frayed ends of which he smeared the beer from his face as he spoke; disclosing, when he had done so, a broad heavy countenance with a beard of three days' growth, and two scowling eyes; one of which displayed various parti-coloured symptoms of having been recently damaged by a blow.

"Come in, d'ye hear?" growled this engaging ruffian.

A white shaggy dog, with his face scratched and torn in twenty different places, skulked into the room.

"Why didn't you come in afore?" said the man. "You're getting too proud to own me afore company, are you? Lie down!"

This command was accompanied with a kick, which sent the animal to the other end of the room. He appeared well used to it, however; for he coiled himself up in a corner very quietly, without uttering a sound; and winking his very ill-looking eyes about twenty times in a minute, appeared to occupy himself in taking a survey of the apartment.

"What are you up to? Ill-treating the boys, you covetous, avaricious, in-sa-ti-a-ble old fence?" said the man, seating himself deliberately. "I wonder they don't murder you; I would if I was them. If I'd been your 'prentice, I'd have done it long ago, and—no, I couldn't have sold you arterwards, though; for you're fit for nothing but keeping as a curiosity of ugliness in a glass bottle, and I suppose they don't blow glass bottles large enough."

"Hush! hush! Mr. Sikes," said the Jew, trembling; "don't speak so loud."

"None of your mistering," replied the ruffian; "you always mean mischief when you come that. You know my name: out with it! I shan't disgrace it when the time comes."

"Well, well, then—Bill Sikes," said the Jew with abject humility. "You seem out of humour, Bill."

"Perhaps I am," replied Sikes; "I should think you was rather out of sorts too, unless you mean as little harm when you throw pewter pots about, as you do when you blab and——"

"Are you mad?" said the Jew, catching the man by the sleeve, and pointing towards the boys.

Mr. Sikes contented himself with tying an imaginary knot under his left ear, and jerking his head over on the right shoulder, a piece of dumb show which the Jew appeared to understand perfectly. He then in cant terms, with which his whole conversation was plentifully besprinkled, but which would be quite unintelligible if they were recorded here, demanded a glass of liquor.

"And mind you don't poison it," said Mr. Sikes, laying his hat upon the table.

This was said in jest; but if the speaker could have seen the evil leer with which the Jew bit his pale lip as he turned round to the cupboard, he might have thought the caution not wholly unnecessary, or the wish (at all events) to improve upon the distiller's ingenuity not very far from the old gentleman's merry heart.

After swallowing two or three glassfuls of spirits, Mr. Sikes condescended to take some notice of the young gentlemen; which gracious act led to a conversation, in which the cause and manner of Oliver's capture were circumstantially detailed; with such alterations and improvements on the truth, as to the Dodger appeared most advisable under the circumstances.

"I'm afraid," said the Jew, "that he may say something which will get us into trouble."

"That's very likely," returned Sikes with a malicious grin. "You're blowed upon, Fagin."

"And I'm afraid, you see," added the Jew, speaking as if he had not noticed the interruption; and regarding the other closely as he did so,—"I'm afraid that, if the game was up with us, it might be up with a good many more; and that it would come out rather worse for you than it would for me, my dear."

The man started, and turned fiercely round upon the Jew. But the old gentleman's shoulders were shrugged up to his ears; and his eyes were vacantly staring on the opposite wall.

There was a long pause. Every member of the respectable coterie appeared plunged in his own reflections; not excepting the dog, who by a certain malicious licking of his lips seemed to be meditating an attack upon the legs of the first gentleman or lady he might encounter in the streets when he went out.

"Somebody must find out wot's been done at the office," said Mr. Sikes in a much lower tone than he had taken since he came in.

The Jew nodded assent.

"If he hasn't peached, and is committed, there's no fear till he comes out again," said Mr. Sikes, "and then he must be taken care on. You must get hold of him, somehow."

Again the Jew nodded.

The prudence of this line of action, indeed, was obvious; but unfortunately there was one very strong objection to its being adopted; and this was, that the Dodger, and Charley Bates, and Fagin, and Mr. William Sikes, happened, one and all, to entertain a most violent and deeply-rooted antipathy to going near a police-office, on any ground or pretext whatever.

How long they might have sat and looked at each other, in a state of uncertainty not the most pleasant of its kind, it is difficult to say. It is not necessary to make any guesses on the subject, however; for the sudden entrance of the two young ladies whom Oliver had seen on a former occasion, caused the conversation to flow afresh.

"The very thing!" said the Jew. "Bet will go; won't you, my dear?"

"Wheres?" inquired the young lady.

"Only just up to the office, my dear," said the Jew coaxingly.

It is due to the young lady to say that she did not positively affirm that she would not, but that she merely expressed an emphatic and earnest desire to be "blessed" if she would; a polite and delicate evasion of the request, which shows the young lady to have been possessed of that natural good breeding which cannot bear to inflict upon a fellow-creature, the pain of a direct and pointed refusal.

The Jew's countenance fell; and he turned from this young lady: who was gaily, not to say gorgeously attired, in a red gown, green boots, and yellow curl-papers, to the other female.

"Nancy, my dear," said the Jew in a soothing manner, "what do you say?"

"That it won't do; so it's no use a-trying it on, Fagin," replied Nancy.

"What do you mean by that?" said Mr. Sikes, looking up in a surly manner.

"What I say, Bill," replied the lady collectedly.

"Why, you're just the very person for it," reasoned Mr. Sikes: "nobody about here knows anything of you."

"And as I don't want 'em to, neither," replied Nancy in the same composed manner, "it's rather more no than yes with me, Bill."

"She'll go, Fagin," said Sikes.

"No, she won't, Fagin," said Nancy.

"Yes, she will, Fagin," said Sikes.

And Mr. Sikes was right. By dint of alternate threats, promises, and bribes, the lady in question was ultimately prevailed upon to undertake the commission. She was not, indeed, withheld by the same considerations as her agreeable friend; for, having very recently removed into the neighbourhood of Field Lane from the remote but genteel suburb of Ratcliffe, she was not under the same apprehension of being recognised by any of her numerous acquaintance.

Accordingly, with a clean white apron tied over her gown, and her curl-papers tucked up under a straw bonnet, —both articles of dress being provided from the Jew's inexhaustible stock,—Miss Nancy prepared to issue forth on her errand.

"Stop a minute, my dear," said the Jew, producing a little covered basket. "Carry that in one hand. It looks more respectable, my dear."

"Give her a door-key to carry in her t'other one, Fagin," said Sikes; "it looks real and genivine like."

"Yes, yes, my dear, so it does," said the Jew, hanging a large street-door key on the forefinger of the young lady's right hand. "There; very good! Very good indeed, my dear," said the Jew, rubbing his hands.

"Oh, my brother! My poor, dear, sweet, innocent little brother!" exclaimed Nancy, bursting into tears, and wringing the little basket and the street-door key in an agony of distress. "What has become of him! Where have they taken him to! Oh, do have pity, and tell me what's been done with the dear boy, gentlemen; do, gentlemen, if you please, gentlemen!"

Having uttered those words in a most lamentable and heart-broken tone: to the immeasurable delight of her hearers: Miss Nancy paused, winked to the company, nodded smilingly round, and disappeared.

"Ah! she's a clever girl, my dears," said the Jew, turning round to his young friends, and shaking his head gravely, as if in mute admonition to them to follow the bright example they had just beheld.

"She's a honour to her sex," said Mr. Sikes filling his glass, and smiting the table with his enormous fist. "Here's her health, and wishing they was all like her!"

While these, and many other encomiums, were being passed on the accomplished Nancy, that young lady made the best of her way to the police-office; whither, notwithstanding a little natural timidity consequent upon walking through the streets alone and unprotected, she arrived in perfect safety shortly afterwards.

Entering by the back way, she tapped softly with the key at one of the cell-doors; and listened. There was no sound within: so she coughed and listened again. Still there was no reply: so she spoke.

"Nolly, dear?" murmured Nancy in a gentle voice; "Nolly?"

There was nobody inside but a miserable shoeless criminal, who had been taken up for playing the flute, and who, the offence against society having been clearly proved, had been very properly committed by Mr. Fang to the House of Correction for one month; with the appropriate and amusing remark that since he had so much breath to spare, it would be much more wholesomely expended on the treadmill than in a musical instrument. He made no answer: being occupied in mentally bewailing the loss of the flute, which had been confiscated for the use of the county; so Nancy passed on to the next cell, and knocked there.

"Well!" cried a faint and feeble voice.

"Is there a little boy here?" inquired Nancy, with a preliminary sob.

"No," replied the voice; "God forbid!"

This was a vagrant of sixty-five, who was going to prison for *not* playing the flute; or, in other words, for begging in the streets, and doing nothing for his livelihood. In the next cell, was another man, who was going to the same prison for hawking tin saucepans without a license; thereby doing something for his living, in defiance of the Stamp-office.

But, as neither of these criminals answered to the name of Oliver, or knew anything about him, Nancy made straight up to the bluff officer in the striped waistcoat; and with the most piteous wailings and lamentations: rendered more piteous by a prompt and efficient use of the street-door key and the little basket: demanded her own dear brother.

"I haven't got him, my dear," said the old man.

"Where is he?" screamed Nancy, in a distracted manner.

"Why, the gentleman's got him," replied the officer.

"What gentleman? Oh, gracious Heavens! What gentleman?" exclaimed Nancy.

In reply to this incoherent questioning, the old man informed the deeply affected sister that Oliver had been taken ill in the office, and discharged in consequence of a witness having proved the robbery to have been committed by another boy, not in custody; and that the prosecutor had carried him away, in an insensible condition, to his own residence: of and concerning which, all the informant knew was, that it was somewhere at Pentonville: he having heard that word mentioned in the directions to the coachman.

In a dreadful state of doubt and uncertainty, the agonised young woman staggered to the gate, and then, exchanging her faltering walk for a good, swift, steady run, returned by the most devious and complicated route she could think of, to the domicile of the Jew.

Mr. Bill Sikes no sooner heard the account of the expedition delivered, than he very hastily called up the white dog; and, putting on his hat, expeditiously departed: without devoting any time to the formality of wishing the company good-morning.

"We must know where he is, my dears; he must be found," said the Jew, greatly excited. "Charley, do nothing but skulk about, till you bring home some news of him! Nancy, my dear, I must have him found. I trust to you, my dear,—to you and the Artful for everything! Stay, stay," added the Jew, unlocking a drawer with a shaking hand; "there's money, my dears. I shall shut up this shop to-night. You'll know where to find me! Don't stop here a minute. Not an instant, my dears!"

With these words, he pushed them from the room; and carefully double-locking and barring the door behind them, drew from its place of concealment the box which he had unintentionally disclosed to Oliver. Then, he hastily proceeded to dispose the watches and jewellery beneath his clothing.

A rap at the door startled him in this occupation. "Who's there?" he cried in a shrill tone.

"Me!" replied the voice of the Dodger, through the key-hole.

"What now?" cried the Jew impatiently.

"Is he to be kidnapped to the other ken, Nancy says?" inquired the Dodger.

"Yes," replied the Jew, "wherever she lays hands on him. Find him, find him out, that's all! I shall know what to do next; never fear."

The boy murmured a reply of intelligence; and hurried down stairs after his companions.

"He has not peached so far," said the Jew as he pursued his occupation. "If he means to blab us among his new friends, we may stop his mouth yet."

CHAPTER XIV.

COMPRISING FURTHER PARTICULARS OF OLIVER'S STAY AT MR. BROWNLOW'S, WITH THE REMARKABLE PREDICTION WHICH ONE MR. GRIMWIG UTTERED CONCERNING HIM, WHEN HE WENT OUT ON AN ERRAND.

OLIVER soon recovered from the fainting-fit into which Mr. Brownlow's abrupt exclamation had thrown him; and the subject of the picture was carefully avoided, both by the old gentleman and Mrs. Bedwin, in the conversation that ensued: which indeed bore no reference to Oliver's history or prospects, but was confined to such topics as might amuse without exciting him. He was still too weak to get up to breakfast; but, when he came down into the housekeeper's room next day, his first act was to cast an eager glance at the wall, in the hope of again looking on the face of the beautiful lady. His expectations were disappointed, however, for the picture had been removed.

"Ah!" said the housekeeper, watching the direction of Oliver's eyes. "It is gone, you see."

"I see it is, ma'am," replied Oliver, with a sigh. "Why have they taken it away?"

"It has been taken down, child, because Mr. Brownlow said, that, as it seemed to worry you, perhaps it might prevent your getting well, you know," rejoined the old lady.

"Oh, no, indeed. It didn't worry me, ma'am," said Oliver. "I liked to see it; I quite loved it."

"Well, well!" said the old lady, good-humouredly; "you get well as fast as ever you can, dear, and it shall be hung up again. There! I promise you that! Now let us talk about something else."

This was all the information Oliver could obtain about the picture at that time. As the old lady had been so kind to him in his illness, he endeavoured to think no more of the subject just then; so he listened attentively to a great many stories she told him, about an amiable and handsome daughter of hers, who was married to an amiable and handsome man, and lived in the country; and about a son, who was clerk to a merchant in the West Indies; and who was, also, such a good young man, and wrote such dutiful letters home four times a-year, that it brought the tears into her eyes to talk about them. When the old lady had expatiated, a long time, on the excellences of her children, and the merits of her kind good husband besides, who had been dead and gone, poor dear soul! just six-and-twenty years, it was time to have tea; and after tea she began to teach Oliver cribbage: which he learnt as quickly as she could teach: and at which game they played, with great interest and gravity, until it was time for the invalid to have some warm wine and water, with a slice of dry toast; and then to go cosily to bed.

They were happy days, those of Oliver's recovery. Everything was so quiet, and neat, and orderly; everybody so kind and gentle; that after the noise and turbulence in the midst of which he had always lived, it seemed like Heaven itself. He was no sooner strong enough to put his clothes on, properly, than Mr. Brownlow caused a complete new suit, and a new cap, and a new pair of shoes, to be provided for him. As Oliver was told that he might do what he liked with the old clothes, he gave them to a servant who had been very kind to him, and asked her to sell them to a Jew, and keep the money for herself. This she very readily did; and, as Oliver looked out of the parlour window, and saw the Jew roll them up in his bag and walk away, he felt quite delighted to think that they were safely gone, and that there was now no possible danger of his ever being able to wear them again. They were sad rags, to tell the truth; and Oliver had never had a new suit before.

One evening, about a week after the affair of the picture, as he was sitting talking to Mrs. Bedwin, there came a message down from Mr. Brownlow, that if Oliver Twist felt pretty well, he should like to see him in his study, and talk to him a little while.

"Bless us, and save us! Wash your hands, and let me part your hair nicely for you, child," said Mrs. Bedwin. "Dear heart alive! If we had known he would have asked for you, we would have put you a clean collar on, and made you as smart as sixpence!"

Oliver did as the old lady bade him; and, although she lamented grievously, meanwhile, that there was not even time to crimp the little frill that bordered his shirt-collar; he looked so delicate and handsome, despite that important personal advantage, that she went so far as to say: looking at him with great complacency from head to foot, that she really didn't think it would have been possible, on the longest notice, to have made much difference in him for the better.

Thus encouraged, Oliver tapped at the study door. On Mr. Brownlow calling to him to come in, he found himself in a little back room, quite full of books, with a window, looking into some pleasant little gardens. There was a table drawn up before the window, at which Mr. Brownlow was seated reading. When he saw Oliver, he pushed the book away from him, and told him to come near the table, and sit down. Oliver complied; marvelling where the people could be found to read such a great number of books as seemed to be written to make the world wiser. Which is still a marvel to more experienced people than Oliver Twist, every day of their lives.

"There are a good many books, are there not, my boy?" said Mr. Brownlow: observing the curiosity with which Oliver surveyed the shelves that reached from the floor to the ceiling.

"A great number, Sir," replied Oliver. "I never saw so many."

"You shall read them, if you behave well," said the old gentleman kindly; "and you will like that, better than looking at the outsides,—that is, in some cases; because there *are* books of which the backs and covers are by far the best parts."

"I suppose they are those heavy ones, Sir," said Oliver, pointing to some large quartos, with a good deal of gilding about the binding.

"Not always those," said the old gentleman, patting Oliver on the head, and smiling as he did so; "there are other equally heavy ones, though of a much smaller size. How should you like to grow up a clever man, and write books, eh?"

"I think I would rather read them, Sir," replied Oliver.

"What! wouldn't you like to be a book-writer?" said the old gentleman.

Oliver considered a little while; and at last said, he should think it would be a much better thing to be a book-seller; upon which the old gentleman laughed heartily, and declared he had said a very good thing. Which Oliver felt glad to have done, though he by no means knew what it was.

"Well, well," said the old gentleman, composing his features. "Don't be afraid! We won't make an author of you, while there's an honest trade to be learnt, or brick-making to turn to."

"Thank you, Sir," said Oliver. At the earnest manner of his reply, the old gentleman laughed again; and said something about a curious instinct, which Oliver, not understanding, paid no very great attention to.

"Now," said Mr. Brownlow, speaking if possible in a kinder, but at the same time in a much more serious manner, than Oliver had ever known him assume yet, "I want you to pay great attention, my boy, to what I am going to say. I shall talk to you without any reserve; because I am sure you are as well able to understand me, as many older persons would be."

"Oh, don't tell me you are going to send me away, Sir, pray!" exclaimed Oliver, alarmed at the serious tone of the old gentleman's commencement! "Don't turn me out of doors to wander in the streets again. Let me stay here, and be a servant. Don't send me back to the wretched place I came from. Have mercy upon a poor boy, Sir!"

"My dear child," said the old gentleman, moved by the warmth of Oliver's sudden appeal; "you need not be afraid of my deserting you, unless you give me cause."

"I never, never will, Sir," interposed Oliver.

"I hope not," rejoined the old gentleman. "I do not think you ever will. I have been deceived, before, in the objects whom I have endeavoured to benefit; but I feel strongly disposed to trust you, nevertheless; and I am more interested in your behalf than I can well account for, even to myself. The persons on whom I have bestowed my dearest love, lie deep in their graves; but, although the happiness and delight of my life lie buried there too, I have not made a coffin of my heart, and sealed it up, for ever, on my best affections. Deep affliction has but strengthened and refined them."

As the old gentleman said this in a low voice: more to himself than to his companion; and as he remained silent for a short time afterwards; Oliver sat quite still.

"Well, well!" said the old gentleman at length, in a more cheerful tone, "I only say this, because you have a young heart; and knowing that I have suffered great pain and sorrow, you will be more careful, perhaps, not to wound me again. You say you are an orphan, without a friend in the world; all the inquiries I have been able to make, confirm the statement. Let me hear your story; where you come from; who brought you up; and how you got into the company in which I found you. Speak the truth; and you shall not be friendless while I live."

Oliver's sobs checked his utterance for some minutes; when he was on the point of beginning to relate how he had been brought up at the farm, and carried to the work-house by Mr. Bumble, a peculiarly impatient little double-knock was heard at the street door; and the servant, running up stairs, announced Mr. Grimwig.

"Is he coming up?" inquired Mr. Brownlow.

"Yes, Sir," replied the servant. "He asked if there were any muffins in the house; and, when I told him yes, he said he had come to tea."

Mr. Brownlow smiled; and, turning to Oliver, said that Mr. Grimwig was an old friend of his, and he must not mind his being a little rough in his manners; for he was a worthy creature at bottom, as he had reason to know.

"Shall I go down stairs, Sir?" inquired Oliver.

"No," replied Mr. Brownlow; "I would rather you remained here."

At this moment, there walked into the room: supporting himself by a thick stick: a stout old gentleman, rather lame in one leg, who was dressed in a blue coat, striped waistcoat, nankeen breeches and gaiters, and a broad-brimmed white hat, with the sides turned up with green. A very small-plaited shirt frill stuck out from his waist-coat; and a very long steel watch-chain, with nothing but a key at the end, dangled loosely below it. The ends of his white neckerchief were twisted into a ball about the size of an orange; the variety of shapes into which his countenance was twisted, defy description. He had a manner of screwing his head on one side when he spoke: and of looking out of the corners of his eyes at the same time: which irresistibly reminded the beholder of a parrot. In this attitude, he fixed himself, the moment he made his appearance; and, holding out a small piece of orange-peel at arm's length, exclaimed in a growling, discontented voice,

"Look here! do you see this? Isn't it a most wonderful and extraordinary thing that I can't call at a man's house but I find a piece of this poor surgeon's-friend on the staircase? I've been lamed with orange-peel once, and I know orange-peel will be my death at last. It will, Sir; orange-peel will be my death, or I'll be content to eat my own head, Sir!"

This was the handsome offer with which Mr. Grimwig backed and confirmed nearly every assertion he made; and it was the more singular in his case, because, even admitting for the sake of argument, the possibility of scientific improvements being ever brought to that pass which will enable a gentleman to eat his own head in the event of his being so disposed; Mr. Grimwig's head was such a particularly large one, that the most sanguine man alive could hardly entertain a hope of being able to get through it at a sitting—to put entirely out of the question, a very thick coating of powder.

"I'll eat my head, Sir," repeated Mr. Grimwig, striking his stick upon the ground. "Hallo! what's that!" looking at Oliver, and retreating a pace or two.

"This is young Oliver Twist, whom we were speaking about," said Mr. Brownlow.

Oliver bowed.

"You don't mean to say that's the boy who had the fever, I hope?" said Mr. Grimwig, recoiling a little more. "Wait a minute! Don't speak! Stop—" continued Mr. Grimwig, abruptly, losing all dread of the fever in his triumph at the discovery; "that's the boy who had the orange! If that's not the boy, Sir, who had the orange, and threw this bit of peel upon the staircase, I'll eat my head, and his too."

"No, no, he has not had one," said Mr. Brownlow, laughing. "Come! Put down your hat; and speak to my young friend."

"I feel strongly on this subject, Sir," said the irritable old gentleman, drawing off his gloves. "There's always more or less orange-peel on the pavement in our street; and I *know* it's put there by the surgeon's boy at the corner. A young woman stumbled over a bit last night, and fell against my garden-railings; directly she got up I saw her look towards his infernal red lamp with the pantomime-light. 'Don't go to him,' I called out of the window, 'he's an assassin! A man-trap!' So he is. If he is not——" Here the irascible old gentleman gave a great knock on the ground with his stick; which was always understood, by his friends, to imply the customary offer, whenever it was not expressed in words. Then, still keeping his stick in his hand, he sat down; and, opening a double eye-glass, which he wore attached to a broad black riband, took a view of Oliver: who, seeing that he was the object of inspection, coloured, and bowed again.

"That's the boy, is it?" said Mr. Grimwig, at length.

"That is the boy," replied Mr. Brownlow.

"How are you, boy?" said Mr. Grimwig.

"A great deal better, thank you, Sir," replied Oliver.

Mr. Brownlow, seeming to apprehend that his singular friend was about to say something disagreeable, asked Oliver to step down stairs and tell Mrs. Bedwin they were ready for tea; which, as he did not half like the visitor's manner, he was very happy to do.

"He is a nice-looking boy, is he not?" inquired Mr. Brownlow.

"I don't know," replied Mr. Grimwig, pettishly.

"Don't know?"

"No. I don't know. I never see any difference in boys. I only know two sorts of boys. Mealy boys, and beef-faced boys."

"And which is Oliver?"

"Mealy. I know a friend who has a beef-faced boy; a fine boy, they call him; with a round head, and red cheeks, and glaring eyes; a horrid boy; with a body and limbs that appear to be swelling out of the seams of his blue clothes; with the voice of a pilot, and the appetite of a wolf. I know him! The wretch!"

"Come," said Mr. Brownlow, "these are not the characteristics of young Oliver Twist; so you needn't excite your wrath."

"They are not," replied Mr. Grimwig. "He may have worse."

Here, Mr. Brownlow coughed impatiently; which appeared to afford Mr. Grimwig the most exquisite delight.

"He may have worse, I say," repeated Mr. Grimwig. "Where does he come from? Who is he? What is he? He has had a fever. What of that? Fevers are not peculiar to good people; are they? Bad people have fevers sometimes; haven't they, eh? I knew a man who was hung in Jamaica for murdering his master. He had had a fever six times; he wasn't recommended to mercy on that account. Pooh! nonsense!"

Now, the fact was, that, in the inmost recesses of his own heart, Mr. Grimwig was strongly disposed to admit that Oliver's appearance and manner were unusually prepossessing; but he had a strong appetite for contradiction: sharpened on this occasion by the finding of the orange-peel; and inwardly determining that no man should dictate to him whether a boy was well-looking or not, he had resolved, from the first, to oppose his friend. When Mr. Brownlow admitted that on no one point of inquiry could he yet return a satisfactory answer; and that he had postponed any investigation into Oliver's previous history until he thought the boy was strong enough to bear it; Mr. Grimwig chuckled maliciously. And he demanded, with a sneer, whether the housekeeper was in the habit of counting the plate at night; because, if she didn't find a table-spoon or two missing some sunshiny morning, why, he would be content to—and so forth.

All this, Mr. Brownlow, although himself somewhat of an impetuous gentleman: knowing his friend's peculiarities, bore with great good humour; as Mr. Grimwig, at tea, was graciously pleased to express his entire approval of the muffins, matters went on very smoothly; and Oliver, who made one of the party, began to feel more at his ease than he had yet done in the fierce old gentleman's presence.

"And when are you going to hear a full, true, and particular account of the life and adventures of Oliver Twist?" asked Grimwig of Mr. Brownlow, at the conclusion of the meal: looking sideways at Oliver, as he resumed the subject.

"To-morrow morning," replied Mr. Brownlow. "I would rather he was alone with me at the time. Come up to me to-morrow morning at ten o'clock, my dear."

"Yes, Sir," replied Oliver. He answered with some hesitation, because he was confused by Mr. Grimwig's looking so hard at him.

"I'll tell you what," whispered that gentleman to Mr. Brownlow. "he won't come up to you to-morrow morning. I saw him hesitate. He is deceiving you, my good friend."

"I'll swear he is not," replied Mr. Brownlow, warmly.

"If he is not," said Mr. Grimwig, "I'll——" and down went the stick.

"I'll answer for that boy's truth with my life!" said Mr. Brownlow, knocking the table.

"And I for his falsehood with my head!" rejoined Mr. Grimwig, knocking the table also.

"We shall see," said Mr. Brownlow, checking his rising anger.

"We will," replied Mr. Grimwig, with a provoking smile; "we will."

As fate would have it, Mrs. Bedwin chanced to bring in,

at this moment, a small parcel of books, which Mr. Brownlow had that morning purchased of the identical bookstall-keeper, who has already figured in this history; having laid them on the table, she prepared to leave the room.

"Stop the boy, Mrs. Bedwin!" said Mr. Brownlow; "there is something to go back."

"He has gone, sir," replied Mrs. Bedwin.

"Call after him," said Mr. Brownlow; "it's particular. He is a poor man, and they are not paid for. There are some books to be taken back, too."

The street-door was opened. Oliver ran one way; and the girl ran another; and Mrs. Bedwin stood on the step and screamed for the boy; but there was no boy in sight. Oliver and the girl returned, in a breathless state, to report that there were no tidings of him.

"Dear me, I am very sorry for that," exclaimed Mr. Brownlow; "I particularly wished those books to be returned to-night."

"Send Oliver with them," said Mr. Grimwig, with an ironical smile; "he will be sure to deliver them safely, you know."

"Yes; do let me take them, if you please, Sir," said Oliver. "I'll run all the way, Sir."

The old gentleman was just going to say that Oliver should not go out on any account; when a most malicious cough from Mr. Grimwig determined him that he should; and that, by his prompt discharge of the commission, he should prove to him the injustice of his suspicions: on this head at least: at once.

"You *shall* go, my dear," said the old gentleman. "The books are on a chair by my table. Fetch them down."

Oliver, delighted to be of use, brought down the books under his arm in a great bustle; and waited, cap in hand, to hear what message he was to take.

"You are to say," said Mr. Brownlow, glancing steadily at Grimwig; "you are to say that you have brought those books back; and that you have come to pay the four pound ten I owe him. This is a five-pound note, so you will have to bring me back, ten shillings change."

"I won't be ten minutes, Sir," replied Oliver, eagerly. Having buttoned up the bank-note in his jacket pocket, and placed the books carefully under his arm, he made a respectful bow, and left the room. Mrs. Bedwin followed him to the street-door, giving him many directions about the nearest way, and the name of the bookseller, and the name of the street: all of which Oliver said he clearly understood; and having superadded many injunctions to be sure and not take cold, the old lady at length permitted him to depart.

"Bless his sweet face!" said the old lady, looking after him. "I can't bear, somehow, to let him go out of my sight."

At this moment, Oliver looked gaily round, and nodded before he turned the corner. The old lady smilingly returned his salutation, and, closing the door, went back to her own room.

"Let me see; he'll be back in twenty minutes, at the longest," said Mr. Brownlow, pulling out his watch, and placing it on the table. "It will be dark by that time."

"Oh! you really expect him to come back, do you?" inquired Mr. Grimwig.

"Don't you?" asked Mr. Brownlow, smiling.

The spirit of contradiction was strong in Mr. Grimwig's breast, at the moment; and it was rendered stronger by his friend's confident smile.

"No," he said, smiting the table with his fist, "I do not. The boy has a new suit of clothes on his back; a set of valuable books under his arm; and a five-pound note in his pocket. He'll join his old friends the thieves, and laugh at you. If ever that boy returns to this house, Sir, I'll eat my head."

With these words he drew his chair closer to the table; and there the two friends sat, in silent expectation, with the watch between them.

It is worthy of remark, as illustrating the importance we attach to our own judgments, and the pride with which we put forth our most rash and hasty conclusions, that, although Mr. Grimwig was not by any means a bad-hearted man, and though he would have been unfeignedly sorry to see his respected friend duped and deceived, he really did most earnestly and strongly hope, at that moment, that Oliver Twist might not come back.

It grew so dark, that the figures on the dial-plate were scarcely discernible; but there the two old gentlemen continued to sit, in silence: with the watch between them.

CHAPTER XV.

SHOWING HOW VERY FOND OF OLIVER TWIST, THE MERRY OLD JEW AND MISS NANCY WERE.

IN the obscure parlour of a low public-house, situate in the filthiest part of Little Saffron Hill; a dark and gloomy den, where a flaring gas-light burnt all day in the wintertime: and where no ray of sun ever shone in the summer; there sat, brooding over a little pewter measure and a small glass, strongly impregnated with the smell of liquor, a man in a velveteen coat, drab shorts, half boots, and stockings, whom, even by that dim light, no experienced agent of police would have hesitated for one instant to recognise as Mr. William Sikes. At his feet, sat a white-coated, red-eyed dog; who occupied himself, alternately, in winking at his master with both eyes at the same time; and in licking a large, fresh cut on one side of his mouth, which appeared to be the result of some recent conflict.

"Keep quiet, you warmint! Keep quiet!" 'said Mr. Sikes, suddenly breaking silence. Whether his meditations were so intense as to be disturbed by the dog's winking, or whether his feelings were so wrought upon by his reflections that they required all the relief derivable from kicking an unoffending animal to allay them, is matter for argument and consideration. Whatever was the cause, the effect was a kick and a curse bestowed upon the dog simultaneously.

Dogs are not generally apt to revenge injuries inflicted upon them by their masters; but Mr. Sikes's dog, having faults of temper in common with his owner: and labouring, perhaps, at this moment, under a powerful sense of injury: made no more ado but at once fixed his teeth in one of the half-boots. Having given it a hearty shake, he retired, growling, under a form; thereby just escaping the pewter measure which Mr. Sikes levelled at his head.

"You would, would you?" said Sikes, seizing the poker in one hand, and deliberately opening with the other a large clasp-knife, which he drew from his pocket. "Come here, you born devil! Come here! D'ye hear?"

The dog no doubt heard; because Mr. Sikes spoke in the very harshest key of a very harsh voice; but, appearing to entertain some unaccountable objection to having his throat cut, he remained where he was, and growled more fiercely than before: at the same time grasping the end of the poker between his teeth, and biting at it like a wild beast.

This resistance only infuriated Mr. Sikes the more; who, dropping on his knees, began to assail the animal most furiously. The dog jumped from right to left, and from left to right: snapping, growling, and barking; the man thrust and swore, and struck and blasphemed; and the struggle was reaching a most critical point for one or other; when, the door suddenly opening, the dog darted out: leaving Bill Sikes with the poker and the clasp-knife in his hands.

There must always be two parties to a quarrel, says the old adage. Mr. Sikes, being disappointed of the dog's participation, at once transferred his share in the quarrel to the new-comer.

"What the devil do you come in between me and my dog for?" said Sikes, with a fierce gesture.

"I didn't know, my dear, I didn't know," replied Fagin, humbly—for the Jew was the new-comer.

"Didn't know, you white-livered thief!" growled Sikes. "Couldn't you hear the noise?"

"Not a sound of it, as I'm a living man, Bill," replied the Jew.

"Oh no! You hear nothing, you don't," retorted Sikes with a fierce sneer. "Sneaking in and out, so as nobody hears how you come or go! I wish you had been the dog, Fagin, half a minute ago."

"Why?" inquired the Jew with a forced smile.

"'Cause the government, as cares for the lives of such men as you, as haven't half the pluck of curs, lets a man kill a dog how he likes," replied Sikes, shutting up the knife with a very expressive look; "that's why."

The Jew rubbed his hands; and, sitting down at the table, affected to laugh at the pleasantry of his friend. He was obviously very ill at ease, however.

"Grin away," said Sikes, replacing the poker, and surveying him with savage contempt; "grin away. You'll never have the laugh at me, though, unless it's behind a night-cap. I've got the upper hand over you, Fagin; and, d—me, I'll keep it. There! If I go, you go; so take care of me."

"Well, well, my dear," said the Jew, "I know all that; we—we—have a mutual interest, Bill,—a mutual interest."

"Humph," said Sikes, as if he thought the interest lay rather more on the Jew's side than on his. "Well, what have you got to say to me?"

"It's all passed safe through the melting-pot," replied Fagin, "and this is your share. It's rather more than it ought to be, my dear; but as I know you'll do me a good turn another time, and—"

"Stow that gammon," interposed the robber, impatiently. "Where is it? Hand over!"

"Yes, yes, Bill; give me time, give me time," replied the Jew, soothingly. "Here it is! All safe!" As he spoke, he drew forth an old cotton handkerchief from his breast; and untying a large knot in one corner, produced a small brown-paper packet. Sikes, snatching it from him, hastily opened it; and proceeded to count the sovereigns it contained.

"This is all, is it?" inquired Sikes.

"All," replied the Jew.

"You haven't opened the parcel and swallowed one or

OLIVER TWIST

two as you come along, have you?" inquired Sikes, suspiciously. "Don't put on an injured look at the question; you've done it many a time. Jerk the tinkler."

These words, in plain English, conveyed an injunction to ring the bell. It was answered by another Jew: younger than Fagin, but nearly as vile and repulsive in appearance.

Bill Sikes merely pointed to the empty measure. The Jew, perfectly understanding the hint, retired to fill it: previously exchanging a remarkable look with Fagin, who raised his eyes for an instant, as if in expectation of it, and shook his head in reply; so slightly that the action would have been almost imperceptible to an observant third person. It was lost upon Sikes, who was stooping at the moment to tie the boot-lace which the dog had torn. Possibly, if he had observed the brief interchange of signals, he might have thought that it boded no good to him.

"Is anybody here, Barney?" inquired Fagin; speaking, now that Sikes was looking on, without raising his eyes from the ground.

"Dot a shoul," replied Barney; whose words: whether they came from the heart or not: made their way through the nose.

"Nobody?" inquired Fagin, in a tone of surprise: which perhaps might mean that Barney was at liberty to tell the truth.

"Dobody but Biss Dadsy," replied Barney.

"Nancy!" exclaimed Sikes. "Where? Strike me blind, if I don't honour that 'ere girl, for her native talents."

"She's bid havid a plate of boiled beef id the bar," replied Barney.

"Send her here," said Sikes, pouring out a glass of liquor. "Send her here."

Barney looked timidly at Fagin, as if for permission; the Jew remaining silent, and not lifting his eyes from the ground, he retired; and presently returned, ushering in Nancy: who was decorated with the bonnet, apron, basket, and street-door key, complete.

"You are on the scent, are you, Nancy?" inquired Sikes, proffering the glass.

"Yes, I am, Bill," replied the young lady, disposing of its contents; "and tired enough of it I am, too. The young brat's been ill and confined to the crib; and—"

"Ah, Nancy, dear!" said Fagin, looking up.

Now, whether a peculiar contraction of the Jew's red eyebrows, and a half-closing of his deeply-set eyes, warned Miss Nancy that she was disposed to be too communicative, is not a matter of much importance. The fact is all we need care for here; and the fact is, that she suddenly checked herself: and with several gracious smiles upon Mr. Sikes, turned the conversation to other matters. In about ten minutes' time, Mr. Fagin was seized with a fit of coughing; upon which Nancy pulled her shawl over her shoulders, and declared it was time to go. Mr. Sikes, finding that he was walking a short part of her way himself, expressed his intention of accompanying her; and they went away together, followed, at a little distance, by the dog, who slunk out of a back-yard as soon as his master was out of sight.

The Jew thrust his head out of the room door when Sikes had left it; looked after him as he walked up the dark passage; shook his clenched fist; muttered a deep curse; and then, with a horrible grin, re-seated himself at the table: where he was soon deeply absorbed in the interesting pages of the Hue-and-Cry.

Meanwhile, Oliver Twist, little dreaming that he was within so very short a distance of the merry old gentleman, was on his way to the book-stall. When he got into Clerkenwell, he accidentally turned down a bye-street which was not exactly in his way; but not discovering his mistake until he had got half-way down it, and knowing it must lead in the right direction, he did not think it worth while to turn back; and so marched on, as quickly as he could, with the books under his arm.

He was walking along; thinking how happy and contented he ought to feel; and how much he would give for only one look at poor little Dick, who, starved and beaten, might be weeping bitterly at that very moment; when he was startled by a young woman screaming out very loud, "Oh, my dear brother!" And he had hardly looked up, to see what the matter was, when he was stopped by having a pair of arms thrown tight round his neck.

"Don't," cried Oliver, struggling. "Let go of me. Who is it? What are you stopping me for?"

The only reply to this, was a great number of loud lamentations from the young woman who had embraced him; and who had a little basket and a street-door key in her hand.

"Oh my gracious!" said the young woman, "I've found him! Oh! Oliver! Oliver! Oh you naughty boy, to make me suffer sich distress on your account! Come home, dear, come. Oh, I've found him. Thank gracious goodness heavins, I've found him!" With these incoherent exclamations, the young woman burst into another fit of crying, and got so dreadfully hysterical, that a couple of women who came up at the moment asked a butcher's boy with a shiny head of hair anointed with suet, who was also looking on, whether he didn't think he had better run for the doctor. To which, the butcher's boy: who appeared of a lounging, not to say indolent disposition: replied, that he thought not.

"Oh, no, no, never mind," said the young woman, grasping Oliver's hand; "I'm better now. Come home directly, you cruel boy! Come!"

"What's the matter, ma'am?" inquired one of the women.

"Oh, ma'am," replied the young woman, "he ran away, near a month ago, from his parents, who are hard-working and respectable people; and went and joined a set of thieves and bad characters; and almost broke his mother's heart."

"Young wretch!" said one woman.

"Go home, do, you little brute," said the other.

"I am not," replied Oliver, greatly alarmed. "I don't know her. I haven't any sister, or father and mother either. I'm an orphan; I live at Pentonville."

"Oh, only hear him, how he braves it out!" cried the young woman.

"Why, it's Nancy!" exclaimed Oliver; who now saw her face for the first time; and started back, in irrepressible astonishment.

"You see he knows me!" cried Nancy, appealing to the bystanders. "He can't help himself. Make him come home, there's good people, or he'll kill his dear mother and father, and break my heart!"

"What the devil's this?" said a man, bursting out of a beer-shop, with a white dog at his heels; "young Oliver! Come home to your poor mother, you young dog! Come home directly."

"I don't belong to them. I don't know them. Help!

help!" cried Oliver, struggling in the man's powerful grasp.

"Help!" repeated the man. "Yes; I'll help you, you young rascal! What books are these? You've been a stealing 'em, have you? Give 'em here." With these words, the man tore the volumes from his grasp, and struck him on the head.

"That's right!" cried a looker-on, from a garret-window. "That's the only way of bringing him to his senses!"

"To be sure!" cried a sleepy-faced carpenter, casting an approving look at the garret-window.

"It'll do him good!" said the two women.

"And he shall have it, too!" rejoined the man, administering another blow, and seizing Oliver by the collar. "Come on, you young villain! Here, Bull's-eye, mind him, boy! Mind him!"

Weak with recent illness; stupefied by the blows and the suddenness of the attack; terrified by the fierce growling of the dog, and the brutality of the man; and overpowered by the conviction of the bystanders that he really was the hardened little wretch he was described to be; what could one poor child do! Darkness had set in; it was a low neighbourhood; no help was near; resistance was useless. In another moment, he was dragged into a labyrinth of dark narrow courts, and forced along them, at a pace which rendered the few cries he dared to give utterance to, wholly unintelligible. It was of little moment, indeed, whether they were intelligible or no; for there was nobody to care for them, had they been ever so plain.

The gas-lamps were lighted; Mrs. Bedwin was waiting anxiously at the open door; the servant had run up the street twenty times to see if there were any traces of Oliver; and still the two old gentlemen sat, perseveringly, in the dark parlour: with the watch between them.

CHAPTER XVI.

RELATES WHAT BECAME OF OLIVER TWIST, AFTER HE HAD BEEN CLAIMED BY NANCY.

The narrow streets and courts, at length terminated in a large open space; scattered about which, were pens for beasts, and other indications of a cattle-market. Sikes slackened his pace when they reached this spot: the girl being quite unable to support, any longer, the rapid rate at which they had hitherto walked. Turning to Oliver, he roughly commanded him to take hold of Nancy's hand.

"Do you hear?" growled Sikes, as Oliver hesitated, and looked round.

They were in a dark corner, quite out of the track of passengers. Oliver saw, but too plainly, that resistance would be of no avail. He held out his hand, which Nancy clasped tight in hers.

"Give me the other," said Sikes, seizing Oliver's unoccupied hand. "Here, Bull's-eye!"

The dog looked up, and growled.

"See here, boy!" said Sikes, putting his other hand to Oliver's throat; "if he speaks ever so soft a word, hold him! D'ye mind?"

The dog growled again; and, licking his lips, eyed Oliver as if he were anxious to attach himself to his windpipe without delay.

"He's as willing as a Christian, strike me blind if he isn't!" said Sikes, regarding the animal with a kind of grim and ferocious approval. "Now, you know what you've got to expect, master, so call away as quick as you like; the dog will soon stop that game. Get on, young 'un!"

Bull's-eye wagged his tail in acknowledgment of this unusually endearing form of speech; and, giving vent to another admonitory growl for the benefit of Oliver, led the way onward.

It was Smithfield that they were crossing, although it might have been Grosvenor Square, for anything Oliver knew to the contrary. The night was dark and foggy. The lights in the shops could scarcely struggle through the heavy mist, which thickened every moment and shrouded the streets and houses in gloom; rendering the strange place still stranger in Oliver's eyes; and making his uncertainty the more dismal and depressing.

They had hurried on a few paces, when a deep church-bell struck the hour. With its first stroke, his two conductors stopped: and turned their heads in the direction whence the sound proceeded.

"Eight o'clock, Bill," said Nancy, when the bell ceased.

"What's the good of telling me that; I can hear it, can't I?" replied Sikes.

"I wonder whether *they* can hear it," said Nancy.

"Of course they can," replied Sikes. "It was Bartlemy time when I was shopped; and there warn't a penny trumpet in the fair, as I couldn't hear the squeaking on. Arter I was locked up for the night, the row and din outside made the thundering old jail so silent, that I could almost have beat my head out against the iron plates of the door."

"Poor fellows!" said Nancy, who still had her face turned towards the quarter in which the bell had sounded. "Oh, Bill, such fine young chaps as them!"

"Yes; that's all you women think of," answered Sikes. "Fine young chaps! Well, they're as good as dead, so it don't much matter."

With this consolation, Mr. Sikes appeared to repress a rising tendency to jealousy; and, clasping Oliver's wrist more firmly, told him to step out again.

"Wait a minute!" said the girl: "I wouldn't hurry by, if it was you that was coming out to be hung, the next time eight o'clock struck, Bill. I'd walk round and round the place till I dropped, if the snow was on the ground, and I hadn't a shawl to cover me."

"And what good would that do?" inquired the unsentimental Mr. Sikes. "Unless you could pitch over a file and twenty yards of good stout rope, you might as well be walking fifty mile off, or not walking at all, for all the good it would do me. Come on, will you, and don't stand preaching there."

The girl burst into a laugh; drew her shawl more closely round her; and they walked away. But Oliver felt her hand tremble; and, looking up in her face as they passed a gas-lamp, saw that it had turned a deadly white.

They walked on, by little-frequented and dirty ways, for a full half-hour: meeting very few people, and those appearing from their looks to hold much the same position in society as Mr. Sikes himself. At length they turned into a very filthy narrow street, nearly full of old-clothes shops; the dog, running forward, as if conscious that there was no further occasion for his keeping on guard, stopped before the door of a shop that was closed and apparently untenanted. The house was in a ruinous condition; and on the door was nailed a board, intimating that it was to let: which looked as if it had hung there for many years.

"All right," cried Sikes, glancing cautiously about.

Nancy stooped below the shutters; and Oliver heard the sound of a bell. They crossed to the opposite side of the street: and stood for a few moments under a lamp. A noise, as if a sash window were gently raised, was heard; and soon afterwards the door softly opened. Mr. Sikes then seized the terrified boy by the collar with very little ceremony; and all three were quickly inside the house.

The passage was perfectly dark. They waited, while the person who had let them in, chained and barred the door.

"Anybody here?" inquired Sikes.

"No," replied a voice, which Oliver thought he had heard before.

"Is the old 'un here?" asked the robber.

"Yes," replied the voice; "and precious down in the mouth he has been. Won't he be glad to see you? Oh, no!"

The style of this reply, as well as the voice which delivered it, seemed familiar to Oliver's ears; but it was impossible to distinguish even the form of the speaker in the darkness.

"Let's have a glim," said Sikes, "or we shall go breaking our necks, or treading on the dog. Look after your legs if you do! That's all."

"Stand still a moment, and I'll get you one," replied the voice. The receding footsteps of the speaker were heard; and, in another minute, the form of Mr. John Dawkins, otherwise the Artful Dodger, appeared. He bore in his right hand a tallow candle stuck in the end of a cleft stick.

The young gentleman did not stop to bestow any other mark of recognition upon Oliver than a humorous grin; but, turning away, beckoned the visitors to follow him down a flight of stairs. They crossed an empty kitchen; and, opening the door of a low earthy-smelling room, which seemed to have been built in a small back-yard, were received with a shout of laughter.

"Oh, my wig, my wig!" cried Master Charles Bates, from whose lungs the laughter had proceeded; "here he is! oh, cry, here he is! Oh, Fagin, look at him; Fagin, do look at him! I can't bear it; it is such a jolly game, I can't bear it. Hold me, somebody, while I laugh it out."

With this irrepressible ebullition of mirth, Master Bates laid himself flat on the floor: and kicked convulsively, for five minutes, in an ecstasy of facetious joy. Then, jumping to his feet, he snatched the cleft stick from the Dodger: and, advancing to Oliver, viewed him round and round: while the Jew, taking off his nightcap, made a great number of low bows to the bewildered boy. The Artful meantime, who was of a rather saturnine disposition, and seldom gave way to merriment when it interfered with business, rifled Oliver's pockets with steady assiduity.

"Look at his togs, Fagin!" said Charley, putting the light so close to his new jacket as nearly to set him on fire. "Look at his togs!—Superfine cloth, and the heavy swell cut! Oh, my eye, what a game! And his books, too; nothing but a gentleman, Fagin!"

"Delighted to see you looking so well, my dear," said the Jew, bowing with mock humility. "The Artful shall give you another suit, my dear, for fear you should spoil that Sunday one. Why didn't you write, my dear, and say you were coming? We'd have got something warm for supper."

At this, Master Bates roared again; so loud, that Fagin himself relaxed: and even the Dodger smiled; but as the Artful drew forth the five-pound note at that instant, it is doubtful whether the sally or the discovery awakened his merriment.

"Hallo! what's that?" inquired Sikes, stepping forward as the Jew seized the note. "That's mine, Fagin."

"No, no, my dear," said the Jew. "Mine, Bill, mine. You shall have the books."

"If that ain't mine!" said Bill Sikes, putting on his hat with a determined air; "mine and Nancy's, that is: I'll take the boy back again."

The Jew started. Oliver started too, though from a very different cause; for he hoped that the dispute might really end in his being taken back.

"Come! Hand over, will you?" said Sikes.

"This is hardly fair, Bill; hardly fair, is it, Nancy?" inquired the Jew.

"Fair, or not fair," retorted Sikes, "hand over, I tell you! Do you think Nancy and me has got nothing else to do with our precious time but to spend it in scouting arter, and kidnapping, every young boy as gets grabbed through you? Give it here, you avaricious old skeleton; give it here!"

With this gentle remonstrance, Mr. Sikes plucked the note from between the Jew's finger and thumb; and, looking the old man coolly in the face, folded it up small, and tied it in his neckerchief.

"That's for our share of the trouble," said Sikes; "and not half enough, neither. You may keep the books, if you're fond of reading. If you a'n't, sell 'em."

"They're very pretty," said Charley Bates: who, with sundry grimaces, had been affecting to read one of the volumes in question; "beautiful writing, isn't it, Oliver?" At sight of the dismayed look with which Oliver regarded his tormentors, Master Bates, who was blessed with a lively sense of the ludicrous, fell into another ecstasy, more boisterous than the first.

"They belonged to the old gentleman," said Oliver, wringing his hands; "to the good, kind, old gentleman who took me into his house, and had me nursed, when I was near dying of the fever. Oh, pray send them back; send him back the books and money. Keep me here all my life long; but pray, pray send them back. He'll think I stole them; the old lady: all of them who were so kind to me: will think I stole them. Oh, do have mercy upon me, and send them back!"

With these words, which were uttered with all the energy of passionate grief, Oliver fell upon his knees at the Jew's feet; and beat his hands together, in perfect desperation.

"The boy's right," remarked Fagin, looking covertly round, and knitting his shaggy eyebrows into a hard knot. "You're right, Oliver, you're right; they *will* think you have stolen 'em. Ha! ha!" chuckled the Jew, rubbing his hands; "it couldn't have happened better, if we had chosen our time!"

"Of course it couldn't," replied Sikes; "I know'd that, directly I see him coming through Clerkenwell, with the books under his arm. It's all right enough. They're soft-hearted psalm-singers, or they wouldn't have taken him in at all; and they'll ask no questions after him, fear they should be obliged to prosecute, and so get him lagged. He's safe enough."

George Cruikshank

OLIVER'S RECEPTION BY FAGIN AND THE BOYS.

Oliver had looked from one to the other, while these words were being spoken, as if he were bewildered, and could scarcely understand what passed; but when Bill Sikes concluded, he jumped suddenly to his feet, and tore wildly from the room: uttering shrieks for help, which made the bare old house echo to the roof.

"Keep back the dog, Bill!" cried Nancy, springing before the door, and closing it, as the Jew and his two pupils darted out in pursuit; "keep back the dog; he'll tear the boy to pieces."

"Serve him right!" cried Sikes, struggling to disengage himself from the girl's grasp. "Stand off from me, or I'll split your head against the wall."

"I don't care for that, Bill; I don't care for that," screamed the girl, struggling violently with the man: "the child shan't be torn down by the dog, unless you kill me first."

"Shan't he!" said Sikes, setting his teeth fiercely. "I'll soon do that, if you don't keep off."

The housebreaker flung the girl from him to the further end of the room; just as the Jew and the two boys returned, dragging Oliver among them.

"What's the matter here?" said Fagin, looking round.

"The girl's gone mad, I think," replied Sikes, savagely.

"No, she hasn't," said Nancy, pale and breathless from the scuffle; "no, she hasn't, Fagin; don't think it."

"Then keep quiet, will you?" said the Jew, with a threatening look.

"No, I won't do that, neither," replied Nancy, speaking very loud. "Come! What do you think of that?"

Mr. Fagin was sufficientlly well acquainted with the manners and customs of that particular species of humanity to which Nancy belonged, to feel tolerably certain that it would be rather unsafe to prolong any conversation with her, at present. With the view of diverting the attention of the company, he turned to Oliver.

"So you wanted to get away, my dear, did you?" said the Jew, taking up a jagged and knotted club which lay in a corner of the fireplace; "eh?"

Oliver made no reply. But he watched the Jew's motions; and breathed quickly.

"Wanted to get assistance; called for the police; did you?" sneered the Jew, catching the boy by the arm. "We'll cure you of that, my young master."

The Jew inflicted a smart blow on Oliver's shoulders with the club; and was raising it for a second, when the girl, rushing forward, wrested it from his hand. She flung it into the fire, with a force that brought some of the glowing coals whirling out into the room.

"I won't stand by and see it done, Fagin," cried the girl. "You've got the boy, and what more would you have? Let him be—let him be, or I shall put that mark on some of you, that will bring me to the gallows before my time."

The girl stamped her foot violently on the floor as she vented this threat; and with her lips compressed, and her hands clenched, looked alternately at the Jew and the other robber: her face quite colourless from the passion of rage into which she had gradually worked herself.

"Why, Nancy!" said the Jew, in a soothing tone; after a pause, during which he and Mr. Sikes had stared at one another in a disconcerted manner; "you—you're more clever than ever to-night. Ha! ha! my dear, you are acting beautifully."

"Am I!" said the girl. "Take care I don't overdo it. You will be the worse for it, Fagin, if I do; and so I tell you in good time to keep clear of me."

There is something about a roused woman: especially if she add to all her other strong passions, the fierce impulses of recklessness and despair: which few men like to provoke. The Jew saw that it would be hopeless to affect any further mistake regarding the reality of Miss Nancy's rage; and, shrinking involuntarily back a few paces, cast a glance, half imploring and half cowardly, at Sikes: as if to hint that he was the fittest person to pursue the dialogue.

Mr. Sikes, thus mutely appealed to; and possibly feeling his personal pride and influence interested in the immediate reduction of Miss Nancy to reason; gave utterance to about a couple of score of curses and threats, the rapid production of which reflected great credit on the fertility of his invention. As they produced no visible effect on the object against whom they were discharged, however, he resorted to more tangible arguments.

"What do you mean by this?" said Sikes; backing the inquiry with a very common imprecation concerning the most beautiful of human features: which, if it were heard above, only once out of every fifty thousand times that it is uttered below, would render blindness as common a disorder as measles; "what do you mean by it? Burn my body! Do you know who you are, and what you are?"

"Oh, yes, I know all about it," replied the girl, laughing hysterically; and shaking her head from side to side, with a poor assumption of indifference.

"Well, then, keep quiet," rejoined Sikes, with a growl like that he was accustomed to use when addressing his dog, "or I'll quiet you for a good long time to come."

The girl laughed again: even less composedly than before; and, darting a hasty look at Sikes, turned her face aside and bit her lip till the blood came.

"You're a nice one," added Sikes, as he surveyed her with a contemptuous air, "to take up the humane and gen—teel side! A pretty subject for the child, as you call him, to make a friend of!"

"God Almighty help me, I am!" cried the girl passionately; "and I wish I had been struck dead in the street, or had changed places with them we passed so near tonight, before I had lent a hand in bringing him here. He's a thief, a liar, a devil: all that's bad, from this night forth. Isn't that enough for the old wretch, without blows?"

"Come, come, Sikes," said the Jew, appealing to him in a remonstratory tone, and motioning towards the boys, who were eagerly attentive to all that passed; "we must have civil words; civil words, Bill."

"Civil words!" cried the girl, whose passion was frightful to see. "Civil words, you villain! Yes; you deserve 'em from me. I thieved for you when I was a child not half as old as this!" pointing to Oliver. "I have been in the same trade, and in the same service, for twelve years since. Don't you know it? Speak out! Don't you know it?"

"Well, well," replied the Jew, with an attempt at pacification; "and, if you have, it's your living!"

"Aye, it is!" returned the girl; not speaking, but pouring out the words in one continuous and vehement scream. "It is my living; and the cold, wet, dirty streets are my home; and you're the wretch that drove me to them long ago; and that'll keep me there, day and night, day and night, till I die!"

"I shall do you a mischief!" interposed the Jew, goaded by these reproaches; "a mischief worse than that, if you say much more!"

The girl said nothing more; but, tearing her hair and dress in a transport of frenzy, made such a rush at the Jew as would probably have left signal marks of her revenge upon him, had not her wrists been seized by Sikes at the right moment; upon which, she made a few ineffectual struggles: and fainted.

"She's all right now," said Sikes, laying her down in a corner. "She's uncommon strong in the arms, when she's up in this way."

The Jew wiped his forehead: and smiled, as if it were a relief to have the disturbance over; but neither he, nor Sikes, nor the dog, nor the boys, seemed to consider it in any other light than a common occurrence incidental to business.

"It's the worst of having to do with women," said the Jew, replacing his club; "but they're clever, and we can't get on, in our line, without 'em. Charley, show Oliver to bed."

"I suppose he'd better not wear his best clothes to-morrow, Fagin, had he?" inquired Charley Bates.

"Certainly not," replied the Jew, reciprocating the grin with which Charley put the question.

Master Bates, apparently much delighted with his commission, took the cleft stick: and led Oliver into an adjacent kitchen, where there were two or three of the beds on which he had slept before; and here, with many uncontrollable bursts of laughter, he produced the identical old suit of clothes which Oliver had so much congratulated himself upon leaving off at Mr. Brownlow's; and the accidental display of which, to Fagin, by the Jew who purchased them, had been the very first clue received, of his whereabout.

"Pull off the smart ones," said Charley, "and I'll give 'em to Fagin to take care of. What fun it is!"

Poor Oliver unwillingly complied. Master Bates, rolling up the new clothes under his arm, departed from the room; leaving Oliver in the dark, and locking the door behind him.

The noise of Charley's laughter, and the voice of Miss Betsy, who opportunely arrived to throw water over her friend, and perform other feminine offices for the promotion of her recovery, might have kept many people awake under more happy circumstances than those in which Oliver was placed. But he was sick and weary; and he soon fell sound asleep.

CHAPTER XVII.

OLIVER'S DESTINY CONTINUING UNPROPITIOUS, BRINGS A GREAT MAN TO LONDON TO INJURE HIS REPUTATION.

It is the custom on the stage, in all good murderous melodramas, to present the tragic and the comic scenes, in as regular alternation, as the layers of red and white in a side of streaky well-cured bacon. The hero sinks upon his straw bed, weighed down by fetters and misfortunes; and, in the next scene, his faithful but unconscious squire regales the audience with a comic song. We behold, with throbbing bosoms, the heroine in the grasp of a proud and ruthless baron: her virtue and her life alike in danger; drawing forth her dagger to preserve the one at the cost of the other; and just as our expectations are wrought up to the highest pitch, a whistle is heard: and we are straight-way transported to the great hall of the castle: where a grey-headed seneschal sings a funny chorus with a funnier body of vassals, who are free of all sorts of places from church vaults to palaces, and roam about in company, carolling perpetually.

Such changes appear absurd; but they are not so unnatural as they would seem at first sight. The transitions in real life from well-spread boards to death-beds, and from mourning-weeds to holiday garments, are not a whit less startling; only, there, we are busy actors, instead of passive lookers-on; which makes a vast difference. The actors in the mimic life of the theatre, are blind to violent transitions and abrupt impulses of passion or feeling, which, presented before the eyes of mere spectators, are at once condemned as outrageous and preposterous.

As sudden shiftings of the scene, and rapid changes of time and place, are not only sanctioned in books by long usage, but are by many considered as the great art of authorship: an author's skill in his craft being, by such critics, chiefly estimated with relation to the dilemmas in which he leaves his characters at the end of every chapter: this brief introduction to the present one may perhaps be deemed unnecessary. If so, let it be considered a delicate intimation on the part of the historian that he is going back, directly, to the town in which Oliver Twist was born; the reader taking it for granted that there are good and substantial reasons for making the journey, or he would not be invited to proceed upon such an expedition, on any account.

Mr. Bumble emerged at early morning from the workhouse-gate; and walked, with portly carriage and commanding steps, up the High Street. He was in the full bloom and pride of beadlehood; his cocked hat and coat were dazzling in the morning sun; and he clutched his cane with the vigorous tenacity of health and power. Mr. Bumble always carried his head high; but this morning it was higher than usual. There was an abstraction in his eye, an elevation in his air, which might have warned an observant stranger that thoughts were passing in the beadle's mind, too great for utterance.

Mr. Bumble stopped not to converse with the small shopkeepers and others who spoke to him, deferentially, as he passed along. He merely returned their salutations with a wave of his hand; and relaxed not in his dignified pace, until he reached the farm where Mrs. Mann tended the infant paupers with parochial care.

"Drat that beadle!" said Mrs. Mann, hearing the well-known shaking at the garden-gate. "If it isn't him at this time in the morning! Lauk, Mr. Bumble, only think of its being you! Well, dear me, it *is* a pleasure, this is! Come into the parlour, Sir, please."

The first sentence was addressed to Susan; and the exclamations of delight were uttered to Mr. Bumble: as the good lady unlocked the garden-gate: and showed him, with great attention and respect, into the house.

"Mrs. Mann," said Mr. Bumble; not sitting upon, or dropping himself into a seat, as any common jackanapes would: but letting himself gradually and slowly down into a chair; "Mrs. Mann, ma'am, good morning."

"Well, and good morning to *you*, Sir," replied Mrs. Mann, with many smiles; "and hoping you find yourself well, Sir?"

"So-so, Mrs. Mann," replied the beadle. "A parochial life is not a bed of roses, Mrs. Mann."

"Ah, that it isn't indeed, Mr. Bumble," rejoined the lady. And all the infant paupers might have chorused the rejoinder with great propriety, if they had heard it.

"A porochial life, ma'am," continued Mr. Bumble, striking the table with his cane, "is a life of worrit, and vexation, and hardihood; but all public characters, as I may say, must suffer prosecution."

Mrs. Mann, not very well knowing what the beadle meant, raised her hands with a look of sympathy: and sighed.

"Ah! You may well sigh, Mrs. Mann!" said the beadle.

Finding she had done all right, Mrs. Mann sighed again: evidently to the satisfaction of the public character: who, repressing a complacent smile by looking sternly at his cocked hat, said,

"Mrs. Mann, I am a going to London."

"Lauk, Mr. Bumble!" cried Mrs. Mann, starting back.

"To London, ma'am," resumed the inflexible beadle, "by coach. I and two paupers, Mrs. Mann! A legal action is a coming on, about a settlement; and the board has appointed me—me, Mrs. Mann—to depose to the matter before the quarter-sessions at Clerkinwell. And I very much question," added Mr. Bumble, drawing himself up, "whether the Clerkinwell Sessions will not find themselves in the wrong box before they have done with me."

"Oh! you mustn't be too hard upon them, Sir," said Mrs. Mann, coaxingly.

"The Clerkinwell Sessions have brought it upon themselves, ma'am," replied Mr. Bumble; "and if the Clerkinwell Sessions find that they come off rather worse than they expected, the Clerkinwell Sessions have only themselves to thank."

There was so much determination and depth of purpose about the menacing manner in which Mr. Bumble delivered himself of these words, that Mrs. Mann appeared quite awed by them. At length, she said:

"You're going by coach, Sir? I thought it was always usual to send them paupers in carts."

"That's when they're ill, Mrs. Mann," said the beadle. "We put the sick paupers into open carts in the rainy weather, to prevent their taking cold."

"Oh!" said Mrs. Mann.

"The opposition coach contracts for these two; and takes them cheap," said Mr. Bumble. "They are both in a very low state, and we find it would come two pound cheaper to move 'em than to bury 'em—that is, if we can throw 'em upon another parish, which I think we shall be able to do, if they don't die upon the road to spite us. Ha! ha! ha!"

When Mr. Bumble had laughed a little while, his eyes again encountered the cocked hat; and he became grave.

"We are forgetting business, ma'am," said the beadle; "here is your porochial stipend for the month."

Mr. Bumble produced some silver money rolled up in paper, from his pocket-book; and requested a receipt: which Mrs. Mann wrote.

"It's very much blotted, Sir," said the farmer of infants; "but it's formal enough, I dare say. Thank you, Mr. Bumble, Sir. I am very much obliged to you, I'm sure."

Mr. Bumble nodded, blandly, in acknowledgment of Mrs. Mann's curtsey; and inquired how the children were.

"Bless their dear little hearts!" said Mrs. Mann with emotion, "they're as well as can be, the dears! Of course, except the two that died last week. And little Dick."

"Isn't that boy no better?" inquired Mr. Bumble.

Mrs. Mann shook her head.

"He's a ill-conditioned, wicious, bad-disposed porochial child that," said Mr. Bumble angrily. "Where is he?"

"I'll bring him to you in one minute, Sir," replied Mrs. Mann. "Here, you Dick!"

After some calling, Dick was discovered. Having had his face put under the pump, and dried upon Mrs. Mann's gown, he was led into the awful presence of Mr. Bumble, the beadle.

The child was pale and thin; his cheeks were sunken; and his eyes large and bright. The scanty parish dress, the livery of his misery, hung loosely on his feeble body; and his young limbs had wasted away, like those of an old man.

Such was the little being who stood trembling beneath Mr. Bumble's glance; not daring to lift his eyes from the floor; and dreading even to hear the beadle's voice.

"Can't you look at the gentleman, you obstinate boy?" said Mrs. Mann.

The child meekly raised his eyes, and encountered those of Mr. Bumble.

"What's the matter with you, porochial Dick?" inquired Mr. Bumble, with well-timed jocularity.

"Nothing, Sir," replied the child faintly.

"I should think not," said Mrs. Mann, who had of course laughed very much at Mr. Bumble's humour. "You want for nothing, I'm sure."

"I should like—" faltered the child.

"Heyday!" interposed Mrs. Mann, "I suppose you're going to say that you *do* want for something, now? Why, you little wretch——"

"Stop, Mrs. Mann, stop!" said the beadle, raising his hand with a show of authority. "Like what, Sir; eh?"

"I should like," faltered the child, "if somebody that can write, would put a few words down for me on a piece of paper: and fold it up and seal it: and keep it for me, after I am laid in the ground."

"Why, what does the boy mean?" exclaimed Mr. Bumble, on whom the earnest manner and wan aspect of the child had made some impression: accustomed as he was to such things. "What do you mean, Sir?"

"I should like," said the child, "to leave my dear love to poor Oliver Twist; and to let him know how often I have sat by myself and cried to think of his wandering about in the dark nights with nobody to help him. And I should like to tell him," said the child, pressing his small hands together, and speaking with great fervour, "that I was glad to die when I was very young; for, perhaps, if I had lived to be a man, and had grown old, my little sister, who is in Heaven, might forget me, or be unlike me; and it would be so much happier if we were both children there together."

Mr. Bumble surveyed the little speaker, from head to foot, with indescribable astonishment; and, turning to his companion, said, "They're all in one story, Mrs. Mann. That out-dacious Oliver has demogalized them all!"

"I couldn't have believed it, Sir!" said Mrs. Mann, holding up her hands, and looking malignantly at Dick. "I never see such a hardened little wretch!"

"Take him away, ma'am!" said Mr. Bumble imperiously. "This must be stated to the board, Mrs. Mann."

"I hope the gentlemen will understand that it isn't my fault, Sir?" said Mrs. Mann, whimpering pathetically.

"They shall understand that, ma'am; they shall be acquainted with the true state of the case," said Mr. Bumble. "There; take him away, I can't bear the sight on him."

Dick was immediately taken away, and locked up in the

coal-cellar. Mr. Bumble shortly afterwards took himself off, to prepare for his journey.

At six o'clock next morning, Mr. Bumble: having exchanged his cocked hat for a round one, and encased his person in a blue great-coat with a cape to it: took his place on the outside of the coach, accompanied by the criminals whose settlement was disputed; with whom, in due course of time, he arrived in London. He experienced no other crosses on the way, than those which originated in the perverse behaviour of the two paupers, who persisted in shivering, and complaining of the cold in a manner which, Mr. Bumble declared, caused his teeth to chatter in his head, and made him feel quite uncomfortable; although he had a great-coat on.

Having disposed of these evil-minded persons for the night, Mr. Bumble sat himself down in the house at which the coach stopped: and took a temperate dinner of steaks, oyster sauce, and porter. Putting a glass of hot gin-and-water on the chimney-piece, he drew his chair to the fire; and, with sundry moral reflections on the too prevalent sin of discontent and complaining, composed himself to read the paper.

The very first paragraph upon which Mr. Bumble's eyes rested, was the following advertisement.

"FIVE GUINEAS REWARD.

"Whereas a young boy, named Oliver Twist, absconded, or was enticed, on Thursday evening last, from his home, at Pentonville; and has not since been heard of. The above reward will be paid to any person who will give such information as will lead to the discovery of the said Oliver Twist, or tend to throw any light upon his previous history, in which the advertiser is, for many reasons, warmly interested."

And then followed a full description of Oliver's dress, person, appearance, and disappearance: with the name and address of Mr. Brownlow at full length.

Mr. Bumble opened his eyes; read the advertisement, slowly and carefully, three several times; and in something more than five minutes was on his way to Pentonville: having actually, in his excitement, left the glass of hot gin-and-water, untasted.

"Is Mr. Brownlow at home?" inquired Mr. Bumble of the girl who opened the door.

To this inquiry the girl returned the not uncommon, but rather evasive reply of "I don't know; where do you come from?"

Mr. Bumble no sooner uttered Oliver's name, in explanation of his errand, than Mrs. Bedwin, who had been listening at the parlour door, hastened into the passage in a breathless state.

"Come in—come in," said the old lady: "I knew we should hear of him. Poor dear! I knew we should! I was certain of it. Bless his heart! I said so, all along."

Having said this, the worthy old lady hurried back into the parlour again; and seating herself on a sofa, burst into tears. The girl, who was not quite so susceptible, had run up stairs meanwhile; and now returned with a request that Mr. Bumble would follow her immediately: which he did.

He was shown into the little back study, where sat Mr. Brownlow and his friend Mr. Grimwig, with decanters and glasses before them. The latter gentleman at once burst into the exclamation:

"A beadle! A parish beadle, or I'll eat my head!"

"Pray don't interrupt just now," said Mr. Brownlow. "Take a seat, will you?"

Mr. Bumble sat himself down: quite confounded by the oddity of Mr. Grimwig's manner. Mr. Brownlow moved the lamp, so as to obtain an uninterrupted view of the beadle's countenance; and said, with a little impatience,

"Now, Sir, you come in consequence of having seen the advertisement?"

"Yes, Sir," said Mr. Bumble.

"And you are a beadle, are you not?" inquired Mr. Grimwig.

"I am a porochial beadle, gentlemen," rejoined Mr. Bumble, proudly.

"Of course," observed Mr. Grimwig aside to his friend, "I knew he was. A beadle all over!"

Mr. Brownlow gently shook his head to impose silence on his friend, and resumed:

"Do you know where this poor boy is now?"

"No more than nobody," replied Mr. Bumble.

"Well, what do you know of him?" inquired the old gentleman. "Speak out, my friend, if you have anything to say. What do you know of him?"

"You don't happen to know any good of him, do you?" said Mr. Grimwig, caustically; after an attentive perusal of Mr. Bumble's features.

Mr. Bumble, catching at the inquiry very quickly, shook his head with portentous solemnity.

"You see?" said Mr. Grimwig, looking triumphantly at Mr. Brownlow.

Mr. Brownlow looked apprehensively at Mr. Bumble's pursed-up countenance; and requested him to communicate what he knew regarding Oliver, in as few words as possible.

Mr. Bumble put down his hat; unbuttoned his coat; folded his arms; inclined his head in a retrospective manner; and, after a few moments' reflection, commenced his story.

It would be tedious if given in the beadle's words: occupying, as it did, some twenty minutes in the telling; but the sum and substance of it was, That Oliver was a foundling, born of low and vicious parents. That he had, from his birth, displayed no better qualities than treachery, ingratitude, and malice. That he had terminated his brief career in the place of his birth, by making a sanguinary and cowardly attack on an unoffending lad; and running away in the night-time from his master's house. In proof of his really being the person he represented himself, Mr. Bumble laid upon the table the papers he had brought to town: and, folding his arms again, awaited Mr. Brownlow's observations.

"I fear it is all too true," said the old gentleman sorrowfully, after looking over the papers. "This is not much for your intelligence; but I would gladly have given you treble the money, if it had been favourable to the boy."

It is not at all improbable that if Mr. Bumble had been possessed of this information at an earlier period of the interview, he might have imparted a very different colouring to his little history. It was too late to do it now, however; so he shook his head gravely; and, pocketing the five guineas, withdrew.

Mr. Brownlow paced the room to and fro for some minutes; evidently so much disturbed by the beadle's tale, that even Mr. Grimwig forbore to vex him further.

At length he stopped, and rang the bell violently.

"Mrs. Bedwin," said Mr. Brownlow, when the housekeeper appeared; "that boy, Oliver, is an impostor."

"It can't be, Sir. It cannot be," said the old lady energetically.

"I tell you he is," retorted the old gentleman. "What do you mean by can't be? We have just heard a full account of him from his birth; and he has been a thorough-paced little villain, all his life."

"I never will believe it, Sir," replied the old lady, firmly. "Never!"

"You old women never believe anything but quack-doctors, and lying story-books," growled Mr. Grimwig. "I knew it all along. Why didn't you take my advice in the beginning; you would, if he' hadn't had a fever, I suppose, eh? He was interesting, wasn't he? Interesting! Bah!" And Mr. Grimwig poked the fire with a flourish.

"He was a dear, grateful, gentle child, Sir," retorted Mrs. Bedwin, indignantly. "I know what children are, Sir; and have done these forty years; and people who can't say the same, shouldn't say anything about them. That's my opinion!"

This was a hard hit at Mr. Grimwig, who was a bachelor. As it extorted nothing from that gentleman but a smile, the old lady tossed her head, and smoothed down her apron preparatory to another speech, when she was stopped by Mr. Brownlow.

"Silence!" said the old gentleman, feigning an anger he was far from feeling. "Never let me hear the boy's name again. I rang to tell you that. Never. Never, on any pretence, mind! You may leave the room, Mrs. Bedwin. Remember! I am in earnest."

There were sad hearts at Mr. Brownlow's that night.

Oliver's heart sank within him, when he thought of his good kind friends; it was well for him that he could not know what they had heard, or it might have broken out-right.

CHAPTER XVIII.

HOW OLIVER PASSED HIS TIME IN THE IMPROVING SOCIETY OF HIS REPUTABLE FRIENDS.

ABOUT noon next day, when the Dodger and Master Bates had gone out to pursue their customary avocations, Mr. Fagin took the opportunity of reading Oliver a long lecture on the crying sin of ingratitude: of which he clearly demonstrated he had been guilty, to no ordinary extent, in wilfully absenting himself from the society of his anxious friends; and, still more, in endeavouring to escape from them after so much trouble and expense had been incurred in his recovery. Mr. Fagin laid great stress on the fact of his having taken Oliver in, and cherished him, when, without his timely aid, he might have perished with hunger; and he related the dismal and affecting history of a young lad whom, in his philanthropy, he had succoured under parallel circumstances, but who, proving unworthy of his confidence, and evincing a desire to communicate with the police, had unfortunately come to be hanged at the Old Bailey one morning. Mr. Fagin did not seek to conceal his share in the catastrophe, but lamented with tears in his eyes the wrong-headed and treacherous behaviour of the young person in question, had rendered it necessary that he should become the victim of certain evidence for the Crown: which, if it were not precisely true, was indispensably necessary for the safety of him (Mr.

Fagin) and a few select friends. Mr. Fagin concluded by drawing a rather disagreeable picture of the discomforts of hanging; and, with great friendliness and politeness of manner, expressed his anxious hopes that he might never be obliged to submit Oliver Twist to that unpleasant operation.

Little Oliver's blood ran cold, as he listened to the Jew's words, and imperfectly comprehended the dark threats conveyed in them. That it was possible even for justice itself to confound the innocent with the guilty when they were in accidental companionship, he knew already; and that deeply-laid plans for the destruction of inconveniently knowing or over-communicative persons, had been really devised and carried out by the old Jew on more occasions than one, he thought by no means unlikely, when he recollected the general nature of the altercations between that gentleman and Mr. Sikes: which seemed to bear reference to some foregone conspiracy of the kind. As he glanced timidly up, and met the Jew's searching look, he felt that his pale face and trembling limbs were neither unnoticed nor unrelished by that wary old gentleman.

The Jew smiled hideously; and, patting Oliver on the head, said, that if he kept himself quiet, and applied himself to business, he saw they would be very good friends yet. Then, taking his hat; and covering himself with an old patched great-coat; he went out, and locked the room-door behind him.

And so Oliver remained all that day, and for the greater part of many subsequent days; seeing nobody, between early morning and midnight; and left, during the long hours, to commune with his own thoughts: which, never failing to revert to his kind friends, and the opinion they must long ago have formed of him, were sad indeed.

After the lapse of a week or so, the Jew left the room-door unlocked; and he was at liberty to wander about the house.

It was a very dirty place. The rooms up stairs had great high wooden chimney-pieces and large doors, with panelled walls and cornices to the ceilings: which, although they were black with neglect and dust, were ornamented in various ways; from all of which tokens Oliver concluded that a long time ago, before the old Jew was born, it had belonged to better people, and had perhaps been quite gay and handsome: dismal and dreary as it looked now.

Spiders had built their webs in the angles of the walls and ceilings; and, sometimes, when Oliver walked softly into a room, the mice would scamper across the floor, and run back terrified to their holes. With these exceptions, there was neither sight nor sound of any living thing; and often, when it grew dark, and he was tired of wandering from room to room, he would crouch in the corner of the passage by the street-door, to be as near living people as he could; and would remain there, listening and counting the hours, until the Jew or the boys returned.

In all the rooms, the mouldering shutters were fast closed: and the bars which held them were screwed tight into the wood; the only light which was admitted, stealing its way through round holes at the top: which made the rooms more gloomy, and filled them with strange shadows. There was a back-garret window, with rusty bars outside, which had no shutter; and out of this, Oliver often gazed with a melancholy face for hours together; but nothing was to be descried from it but a confused and crowded mass of house-tops, blackened chimneys, and gable-ends. Sometimes, indeed, a ragged grizzly head might be seen, peering over the parapet-wall of a distant house: but it was quickly withdrawn again; and as the window of Oliver's observatory was nailed down, and dimmed with the rain and smoke of years, it was as much as he could do to make out the forms of the different objects beyond,—which he had as much chance of being, as if he had lived inside the ball of St. Paul's Cathedral.

One afternoon: the Dodger and Master Bates being engaged out that evening: the first-named young gentleman took it into his head to evince some anxiety regarding the decoration of his person (which, to do him justice, was by no means an habitual weakness with him); and, with this end and aim, he condescendingly commanded Oliver to assist him in his toilet, straightway.

Oliver was but too glad to make himself useful; too happy to have some faces, however bad, to look upon; and too desirous to conciliate those about him when he could honestly do so; to throw any objection in the way of this proposal. So he at once expressed his readiness; and, kneeling on the floor, while the Dodger sat upon the table so that he could take his foot in his lap, he applied himself to a process which Mr. Dawkins designated as "japanning his trotter-cases." Which phrase, rendered into plain English, signifieth, cleaning his boots.

Whether it was the sense of freedom and independence which a rational animal may be supposed to feel when he sits on a table in an easy attitude smoking a pipe, swinging one leg carelessly to and fro, and having his boots cleaned all the time, without even the past trouble of having taken them off, or the prospective misery of putting them on, to disturb his reflections; or whether it was the goodness of the tobacco that soothed the feelings of the Dodger, or the mildness of the beer that mollified his thoughts; he was evidently tinctured, for the nonce, with a spice of romance and enthusiasm, foreign to his general nature. He looked down on Oliver, with a thoughtful countenance, for a brief space; and then, raising his head, and heaving a gentle sigh, said, half in abstracton, and half to Master Bates:

"What a pity it is he isn't a prig!"

"Ah!" said Master Charles Bates; "he don't know what's good for him."

The Dodger sighed again, and resumed his pipe: as did Charley Bates. They both smoked, for some seconds, in silence.

"I suppose you don't even know what a prig is?" said the Dodger mournfully.

"I think I know that," replied Oliver, looking up. "It's a th—; you're one, are you not?" inquired Oliver, checking himself.

"I am," replied the Dodger. "I'd scorn to be anything else." Mr. Dawkins gave his hat a ferocious cock, after delivering this sentiment; and looked at Master Bates, as if to denote that he would feel obliged by his saying anything to the contrary.

"I am," repeated the Dodger. "So's Charley. So's Fagin. So's Sikes. So's Nancy. So's Bet. So we all are, down to the dog. And he's the downiest one of the lot!"

"And the least given to peaching," added Charley Bates.

"He wouldn't so much as bark in a witness-box, for fear of committing himself; no, not if you tied him up in one, and left him there without wittles for a fortnight," said the Dodger.

"Not a bit of it," observed Charley.

"He's a rum dog. Don't he look fierce at any strange cove that laughs or sings when he's in company!" pursued the Dodger. "Won't he growl at all, when he hears a fiddle playing! And don't he hate other dogs as ain't of his breed!—Oh, no!"

"He's an out-and-out Christian," said Charley.

This was merely intended as a tribute to the animal's abilities, but it was an appropriate remark in another sense, if Master Bates had only known it; for there are a great many ladies and gentlemen, claiming to be out-and-out Christians, between whom, and Mr. Sikes's dog, there exist very strong and singular points of resemblance.

"Well, well," said the Dodger, recurring to the point from which they had strayed: with that mindfulness of his profession which influenced all his proceedings. "This hasn't got anything to do with young Green here."

"No more it has," said Charley. "Why don't you put yourself under Fagin, Oliver?"

"And make your fortun' out of hand?" added the Dodger, with a grin.

"And so be able to retire on your property, and do the gen-teel: as I mean to, in the very next leap-year but four that ever comes, and the forty-second Tuesday in Trinity-week," said Charley Bates.

"I don't like it," rejoined Oliver, timidly; "I wish they would let me go. I—I—would rather go."

"And Fagin would *rather* not!" rejoined Charley.

Oliver knew this too well; but, thinking it might be dangerous to express his feelings more openly, he only sighed, and went on with his boot-cleaning.

"Go!" exclaimed the Dodger. "Why, where's your spirit? Don't you take any pride out of yourself? Would you go and be dependent on your friends?"

"Oh, blow that!" said Master Bates: drawing two or three silk handkerchiefs from his pocket, and tossing them into a cupboard, "that's too mean; that is."

"*I* couldn't do it," said the Dodger, with an air of haughty disgust.

"You can leave your friends, though," said Oliver with a half smile; "and let them be punished for what you did."

"That," rejoined the Dodger, with a wave of his pipe, "that was all out of consideration for Fagin, 'cause the traps know that we work together, and he might have got into trouble if we hadn't made our lucky; that was the move, wasn't it, Charley?"

Master Bates nodded assent, and would have spoken; but the recollection of Oliver's flight came so suddenly upon him, that the smoke he was inhaling got entangled with a laugh; and went up into his head, and down into his throat: and brought on a fit of coughing and stamping, about five minutes long.

"Look here," said the Dodger, drawing forth a handful of shillings and halfpence. "Here's a jolly life! What's the odds where it comes from? Here, catch hold; there's plenty more where they were took from. You won't, won't you? Oh, you precious flat!"

"It's naughty, ain't it, Oliver?" inquired Charley Bates. "He'll come to be scragged, won't he?"

"I don't know what that means," replied Oliver.

"Something in this way, old feller," said Charley. As he said it, Master Bates caught up an end of his neckerchief; and, holding it erect in the air, dropped his head on his shoulder, and jerked a curious sound through his teeth: thereby indicating, by a lively pantomimic representation, that scragging and hanging were one and the same thing.

"That's what it means," said Charley. "Look how he stares, Jack! I never did see such prime company as that 'ere boy; he'll be the death of me, I know he will." Master Charles Bates, having laughed heartily again, resumed his pipe with tears in his eyes.

"You've been brought up bad," said the Dodger, surveying his boots with much satisfaction when Oliver had polished them. "Fagin will make something of you, though, or you'll be the first he ever had that turned out unprofitable. You'd better begin at once; for you'll come to the trade long before you think of it; and you're only losing time, Oliver."

Master Bates backed this advice with sundry moral admonitions of his own: which, being exhausted, he and his friend Mr. Dawkins launched into a glowing description of the numerous pleasures incidental to the life they led, interspersed with a variety of hints to Oliver that the best thing he could do, would be to secure Fagin's favour without more delay, by the means which they themselves had employed to gain it.

"And always put this in your pipe, Nolly," said the Dodger, as the Jew was heard unlocking the door above, "if you don't take fogles and tickers—"

"What's the good of talking in that way?" interposed Master Bates: "he don't know what you mean."

"If you don't take pocket-handkechers and watches," said the Dodger, reducing his conversation to the level of Oliver's capacity, "some other cove will; so that the coves that lose 'em will be all the worse, and you'll be all the worse too, and nobody half a ha'p'orth the better, except the chaps wot gets them—and you've just as good a right to them as they have."

"To be sure, to be sure!" said the Jew, who had entered, unseen by Oliver. "It all lies in a nutshell, my dear; in a nutshell, take the Dodger's word for it. Ha! ha! He understands the catechism of his trade."

The old man rubbed his hands gleefully together, as he corroborated the Dodger's reasoning in these terms; and chuckled with delight at his pupil's proficiency.

The conversation proceeded no farther at this time, for the Jew had returned home accompanied by Miss Betsy, and a gentleman whom Oliver had never seen before, but who was accosted by the Dodger as Tom Chitling; and who, having lingered on the stairs to exchange a few gallantries with the lady, now made his appearance.

Mr. Chitling was older in years than the Dodger: having perhaps numbered eighteen winters; but there was a degree of deference in his deportment towards that young gentleman which seemed to indicate that he felt himself conscious of a slight inferiority in point of genius and professional acquirements. He had small twinkling eyes, and a pockmarked face; wore a fur cap, a dark corduroy jacket, greasy fustian trousers, and an apron. His wardrobe was, in truth, rather out of repair; but he excused himself to the company by stating that his "time" was only out an hour before; and that, in consequence of having worn the regimentals for six weeks past, he had not been able to bestow any attention on his private clothes. Mr. Chitling added, with strong marks of irritation, that the new way of fumigating clothes up yonder was infernal unconstitutional, for it burnt holes in them, and there was no remedy against the County. The same remark he considered to apply to the regulation mode of cutting the hair: which he held to be decidedly unlawful. Mr. Chitling wound up his observations by stating that he had not touched a drop of anything for forty-two mortal long hard-working days;

and that he "wished he might be busted if he warn't as dry as a lime-basket."

"Where do you think the gentleman has come from, Oliver?" inquired the Jew with a grin, as the other boys put a bottle of spirits on the table.

"I—I—don't know, Sir," replied Oliver.

"Who's that?" inquired Tom Chitling, casting a contemptuous look at Oliver.

"A young friend of mine, my dear," replied the Jew.

"He's in luck then," said the young man, with a meaning look at Fagin. "Never mind where I came from, young 'un; you'll find your way there, soon enough, I'll bet a crown!"

At this sally, the boys laughed. After some more jokes on the same subject, they exchanged a few short whispers with Fagin; and withdrew.

After some words apart between the last comer and Fagin, they drew their chairs towards the fire; and the Jew, telling Oliver to come and sit by him, led the conversation to the topics most calculated to interest his hearers. These were, the great advantages of the trade, the proficiency of the Dodger, the amiability of Charley Bates, and the liberality of the Jew himself. At length these subjects displayed signs of being thoroughly exhausted; and Mr. Chitling did the same: for the House of Correction becomes fatiguing after a week or two. Miss Betsy accordingly withdrew; and left the party to their repose.

From this day, Oliver was seldom left alone; but was placed in almost constant communication with the two boys, who played the old game with the Jew every day: whether for their own improvement or Oliver's, Mr. Fagin best knew. At other times, the old man would tell them stories of robberies he had committed in his younger days: mixed up with so much that was droll and curious, that Oliver could not help laughing heartily, and showing that he was amused in spite of all his better feelings.

In short, the wily old Jew had the boy in his toils; and, having prepared his mind, by solitude and gloom, to prefer any society to the companionship of his own sad thoughts in such a dreary place, was now slowly instilling into his soul the poison which he hoped would blacken it, and change its hue for ever.

CHAPTER XIX.

IN WHICH A NOTABLE PLAN IS DISCUSSED AND DETERMINED ON.

It was a chill, damp, windy night, when the Jew: buttoning his great-coat tight round his shrivelled body, and pulling the collar up over his ears so as completely to obscure the lower part of his face: emerged from his den. He paused on the step as the door was locked and chained behind him; and having listened while the boys made all secure, and until their retreating footsteps were no longer audible, slunk down the street as quickly as he could.

The house to which Oliver had been conveyed, was in the neighbourhood of Whitechapel. The Jew stopped for an instant at the corner of the street; and, glancing suspiciously round, crossed the road, and struck off in the direction of Spitalfields.

The mud lay thick upon the stones: and a black mist hung over the streets; the rain fell sluggishly down: and everything felt cold and clammy to the touch. It seemed just the night when it befitted such a being as the Jew to be abroad. As he glided stealthily along, creeping beneath the shelter of the walls and doorways, the hideous old man seemed like some loathsome reptile, engendered in the slime and darkness through which he moved: crawling forth, by night, in search of some rich offal for a meal.

He kept on his course, through many winding and narrow ways, until he reached Bethnal Green; then, turning suddenly off to the left, he soon became involved in a maze of the mean and dirty streets which abound in that close and densely-populated quarter.

The Jew was evidently too familiar with the ground he traversed, however, to be at all bewildered, either by the darkness of the night, or the intricacies of the way. He hurried through several alleys and streets; and at length turned into one, lighted only by a single lamp at the farther end. At the door of a house in this street, he knocked; and, having exchanged a few muttered words with the person who opened it, walked up stairs.

A dog growled as he touched the handle of a room-door; and a man's voice demanded who was there.

"Only me, Bill; only me, my dear," said the Jew, looking in.

"Bring in your body then," said Sikes. "Lie down, you stupid brute! Don't you know the devil when he's got a great-coat on?"

Apparently, the dog had been somewhat deceived by Mr. Fagin's outer garment; for as the Jew unbuttoned it, and threw it over the back of a chair, he retired to the corner from which he had risen: wagging his tail as he went, to show that he was as well satisfied as it was in his nature to be.

"Well!" said Sikes.

"Well, my dear," replied the Jew. "Ah! Nancy."

The latter recognition was uttered with just enough of embarrassment to imply a doubt of its reception; for Mr. Fagin and his young friend had not met, since she had interfered in behalf of Oliver. All doubts upon the subject, if he had any, were speedily removed by the young lady's behaviour. She took her feet off the fender; pushed back her chair; and bade Fagin draw up his, without saying more about it: for it was a cold night, and no mistake.

"It is cold, Nancy dear," said the Jew, as he warmed his skinny hands over the fire. "It seems to go right through one," added the old man, touching his side.

"It must be a piercer, if it finds its way through *your* heart," said Mr. Sikes. "Give him something to drink, Nancy. Burn my body, make haste! It's enough to turn a man ill, to see his lean old carcase shivering in that way, like a ugly ghost just rose from the grave."

Nancy quickly brought a bottle from a cupboard, in which there were many: which, to judge from the diversity of their appearance, were filled with several kinds of liquids. Sikes, pouring out a glass of brandy, bade the Jew drink it off.

"Quite enough, quite, thankye, Bill," replied the Jew, putting down the glass, after just setting his lips to it.

"What! You're afraid of our getting the better of you, are you?" inquired Sikes, fixing his eyes on the Jew. "Ugh!"

With a hoarse grunt of contempt, Mr. Sikes seized the glass, and threw the remainder of its contents into the ashes: as a preparatory ceremony to filling it again for himself: which he did at once.

The Jew glanced round the room, as his companion tossed down the second glassful; not in curiosity, for he had seen it often before; but in a restless and suspicious manner which was habitual to him. It was a meanly furnished apartment, with nothing but the contents of the closet to induce the belief that its occupier was anything but a working man; and with no more suspicious articles displayed to view than two or three heavy bludgeons which stood in a corner, and a "life-preserver" that hung over the chimney-piece.

"There," said Sikes, smacking his lips. "Now I'm ready."

"For business?" inquired the Jew.

"For business," replied Sikes; "so say what you've got to say."

"About the crib at Chertsey, Bill?" said the Jew, drawing his chair forward, and speaking in a very low voice.

"Yes. Wot about it?" inquired Sikes.

"Ah! you know what I mean, my dear," said the Jew. "He knows what I mean, Nancy; don't he?"

"No, he don't," sneered Mr. Sikes. "Or he won't; and that's the same thing. Speak out, and call things by their right names; don't sit there, winking and blinking, and talking to me in hints: as if you warn't the very first that thought about the robbery. Wot d'ye mean?"

"Hush, Bill, hush!" said the Jew, who had in vain attempted to stop this burst of indignation; "somebody will hear us, my dear. Somebody will hear us."

"Let 'em hear!" said Sikes; "I don't care." But as Mr. Sikes *did* care, upon reflection, he dropped his voice as he said the words, and grew calmer.

"There, there," said the Jew coaxingly. "It was only my caution—nothing more. Now, my dear, about that crib at Chertsey; when is it to be done, Bill, eh? When is it to be done? Such plate, my dears, such plate!" said the Jew: rubbing his hands, and elevating his eyebrows in a rapture of anticipation.

"Not at all," replied Sikes coldly.

"Not to be done at all!" echoed the Jew, leaning back in his chair.

"No, not at all," rejoined Sikes. "At least it can't be a put-up job, as we expected."

"Then it hasn't been properly gone about," said the Jew, turning pale with anger. "Don't tell me."

"But I will tell you," retorted Sikes. "Who are you that's not to be told? I tell you that Toby Crackit has been hanging about the place for a fortnight; and he can't get one of the servants into a line."

"Do you mean to tell me, Bill," said the Jew: softening as the other grew heated: "that neither of the two men in the house can be got over?"

"Yes, I do mean to tell you so," replied Sikes. "The old lady has had 'em these twenty year; and, if you were to give 'em five hundred pound, they wouldn't be in it."

"But do you mean to say, my dear," remonstrated the Jew, "that the women can't be got over?"

"Not a bit of it," replied Sikes.

"Not by flash Toby Crackit?" said the Jew incredulously. "Think what women are, Bill."

"No; not even by flash Toby Crackit," replied Sikes. "He says he's worn sham whiskers, and a canary waistcoat, the whole blessed time he's been loitering down there; and it's all of no use."

"He should have tried mustachios and a pair of military trousers, my dear," said the Jew.

"So he did," rejoined Sikes, "and they warn't of no more use than the other plant."

The Jew looked very blank at this information. After ruminating for some minutes with his chin sunk on his breast, he raised his head, and said, with a deep sigh, that if flash Toby Crackit reported aright, he feared the game was up.

"And yet," said the old man, dropping his hands on his knees, "it's a sad thing, my dear, to lose so much when we had set our hearts upon it."

"So it is," said Mr. Sikes. "Worse luck!"

A long silence ensued; during which, the Jew was plunged in deep thought: with his face wrinkled into an expression of villainy perfectly demoniacal. Sikes eyed him furtively from time to time; Nancy, apparently fearful of irritating the housebreaker, sat with her eyes fixed upon the fire, as if she had been deaf to all that passed.

"Fagin," said Sikes, abruptly breaking the stillness that prevailed, "is it worth fifty shiners extra, if it's safely done from the outside?"

"Yes," said the Jew, as suddenly rousing himself.

"Is it a bargain?" inquired Sikes.

"Yes, my dear, yes," rejoined the Jew; his eyes glistening, and every muscle in his face working, with the excitement that the inquiry had awakened.

"Then," said Sikes, thrusting aside the Jew's hand, with some disdain, "let it come off as soon as you like. Toby and I were over the garden-wall the night afore last, sounding the panels of the door and shutters. The crib's barred up at night like a jail; but there's one part we can crack, safe and softly."

"Which is that, Bill?" asked the Jew eagerly.

"Why," whispered Sikes, "as you cross the lawn——"

"Yes, yes," said the Jew, bending his head forward, with his eyes almost starting out of it.

"Umph!" cried Sikes, stopping short, as the girl: scarcely moving her head: looked suddenly round, and pointed for an instant to the Jew's face. "Never mind which part it is. You can't do it without me, I know; but it's best to be on the safe side when one deals with you."

"As you like, my dear, as you like," replied the Jew. "Is there no help wanted, but yours and Toby's?"

"None," said Sikes. "'Cept a centre-bit and a boy. The first we've both got; the second you must find us."

"A boy!" exclaimed the Jew. "Oh! then it's a panel, eh?"

"Never mind wot it is!" replied Sikes. "I want a boy; and he mustn't be a big un. Lord!" said Mr. Sikes, reflectively, "if I'd only got that young boy of Ned, the chimbley-sweeper's! He kept him small on purpose, and let him out by the job. But the father gets lagged; and then the Juvenile Delinquent Society comes, and takes the boy away from a trade where he was arning money; teaches him to read and write, and in time makes a 'prentice of him. And so they go on," said Mr. Sikes, his wrath rising with the recollection of his wrongs, "so they go on; and, if they'd got money enough (which it's a Providence they have not), we shouldn't have half-a-dozen boys left in the whole trade, in a year or two."

"No more we should," acquiesced the Jew, who had been considering during this speech, and had only caught the last sentence. "What now?" inquired Sikes.

The Jew nodded his head towards Nancy, who was still gazing at the fire; and intimated, by a sign, that he would have her told to leave the room. Sikes shrugged his shoulders impatiently, as if he thought the precaution unnecessary; but complied, nevertheless, by requesting Miss Nancy to fetch him a jug of beer.

"You don't want any beer," said Nancy, folding her arms, and retaining her seat very composedly.

"I tell you I do!" replied Sikes.

"Nonsense," rejoined the girl coolly. "Go on, Fagin. I know what he's going to say, Bill; he needn't mind me."

The Jew still hesitated. Sikes looked from one to the other in some surprise.

"Why, you don't mind the old girl, do you, Fagin?" he asked at length. "You've known her long enough to trust her, or the Devil's in it. She ain't one to blab. Are you, Nancy?"

"*I* should think not!" replied the young lady: drawing her chair up to the table, and putting her elbows upon it.

"No, no, my dear, I know you're not," said the Jew; "but——" and again the old man paused.

"But wot?" inquired Sikes.

"I didn't know whether she mightn't p'r'aps be out of sorts, you know, my dear, as she was the other night," replied the Jew.

At this confession, Miss Nancy burst into a loud laugh; and, swallowing a glass of brandy, shook her head with an air of defiance, and burst into sundry exclamations of "Keep the game a-going!" "Never say die!" and the like. These seemed at once to have the effect of re-assuring both gentlemen; for the Jew nodded his head with a satisfied air, and resumed his seat: as did Mr. Sikes likewise.

"Now, Fagin," said Nancy with a laugh. "Tell Bill at once, about Oliver!"

"Ah! you're a clever one, my dear; the sharpest girl I ever saw!" said the Jew, patting her on the neck. "It *was* about Oliver I was going to speak, sure enough. Ha! ha! ha!"

"What about him?" demanded Sikes.

"He's the boy for you, my dear," replied the Jew in a hoarse whisper; laying his finger on the side of his nose, and grinning frightfully.

"He!" exclaimed Sikes.

"Have him, Bill!" said Nancy. "I would, if I was in your place. He mayn't be so much up, as any of the others; but that's not what you want, if he's only to open a door for you. Depend upon it he's a safe one, Bill."

"I know he is," rejoined Fagin. "He's been in good training these last few weeks; and it's time he began to work for his bread. Besides, the others are all too big."

"Well, he is just the size I want," said Mr. Sikes, ruminating.

"And will do everything you want, Bill, my dear," interposed the Jew; "he can't help himself. That is, if you frighten him enough."

"Frighten him!" echoed Sikes. "It'll be no sham frightening, mind you. If there's anything queer about him when we once get into the work, in for a penny, in for a pound. You won't see him alive again, Fagin. Think of that, before you send him. Mark my words!" said the robber, poising a crowbar, which he had drawn from under the bedstead.

"I've thought of it all," said the Jew with energy. "I've—I've had my eye upon him, my dears, close—close. Once let him feel that he is one of us; once fill his mind with the idea that he has been a thief; and he's ours! Ours for his life! Oho! It couldn't have come about better!" The old man crossed his arms upon his breast; and, drawing his head and shoulders into a heap, literally hugged himself for joy.

"Ours!" said Sikes. "Yours, you mean."

"Perhaps I do, my dear," said the Jew, with a shrill chuckle. "Mine, if you like, Bill."

"And wot," said Sikes, scowling fiercely on his agreeable friend, "wot makes you take so much pains about one chalk-faced kid, when you know there are fifty boys snoozing about Common Garden every night, as you might pick and choose from?"

"Because they're of no use to me, my dear," replied the Jew, with some confusion, "not worth the taking. Their looks convict 'em when they get into trouble; and I lose 'em all. With this boy, properly managed, my dears, I could do what I couldn't with twenty of them. Besides," said the Jew, recovering his self-possession, "he has us now if he could only give us leg-bail again; and he *must* be in the same boat with us. Never mind how he came there; it's quite enough for my power over him that he was in a robbery; that's all I want. Now, how much better this is, than being obliged to put the poor leetle boy out of the way: which would be dangerous, and we should lose by it besides."

"When is it to be done?" asked Nancy, stopping some turbulent exclamation on the part of Mr. Sikes, expressive of the disgust with which he received Fagin's affectation of humanity.

"Ah, to be sure," said the Jew; "when is it to be done, Bill?"

"I planned with Toby, the night arter to-morrow," rejoined Sikes in a surly voice, "if he heerd nothing from me to the contrairy."

"Good," said the Jew; "there's no moon."

"No," rejoined Sikes.

"It's all arranged about bringing off the swag,* is it?" asked the Jew.

Sikes nodded.

"And about—"

"Oh, ah, it's all planned," rejoined Sikes, interrupting him. "Never mind particulars. You'd better bring the boy here to-morrow night; I shall get off the stones an hour arter daybreak. Then you hold your tongue, and keep the melting-pot ready; and that's all you'll have to do."

After some discussion, in which all three took an active part, it was decided that Nancy should repair to the Jew's next evening when the night had set in, and bring Oliver away with her; Fagin craftily observing, that, if he evinced any disinclination to the task, he would be more willing to accompany the girl who had so recently interfered in his behalf, than anybody else. It was also solemnly arranged that poor Oliver should, for the purposes of the contemplated expedition, be unreservedly consigned to the care and custody of Mr. William Sikes; and further, that the said Sikes should deal with him as he thought fit; and should not be held responsible by the Jew for any mischance or evil that might befall the boy, or any punishment with which it might be necessary to visit him: it being understood that, to render the compact in this respect binding, any representations made by Mr. Sikes on his return should be required to be confirmed and corroborated, in all important particulars, by the testimony of flash Toby Crackit.

These preliminaries adjusted, Mr. Sikes proceeded to drink

* Booty.

brandy at a furious rate; and to flourish the crowbar in an alarming manner; yelling forth, at the same time, most unmusical snatches of song, mingled with wild execrations. At length, in a fit of professional enthusiasm, he insisted upon producing his box of housebreaking tools: which he had no sooner stumbled in with, and opened for the purpose of explaining the nature and properties of the various implements it contained, and the peculiar beauties of their construction: than he fell over it upon the floor, and went to sleep where he fell.

"Good night, Nancy," said the Jew, muffling himself up as before.

"Good night."

Their eyes met; and the Jew scrutinised her, narrowly. There was no flinching about the girl. She was as true and earnest in the matter as Toby Crackit himself could be.

The Jew again bade her good night; and, bestowing a sly kick upon the prostrate form of Mr. Sikes, while her back was turned, groped down stairs.

"Always the way!" muttered the Jew to himself as he turned homeward. "The worst of these women is, that a very little thing serves to call up some long-forgotten feeling; and the best of them is, that it never lasts. Ha! ha! The man against the child, for a bag of gold!"

Beguiling the time with these pleasant reflections, Mr. Fagin wended his way, through mud and mire, to his gloomy abode: where the Dodger was sitting up, impatiently awaiting his return.

"Is Oliver a-bed? I want to speak to him," was his first remark as they descended the stairs.

"Hours ago," replied the Dodger, throwing open a door. "Here he is!"

The boy was lying, fast asleep, on a rude bed upon the floor; so pale with anxiety, and sadness, and the closeness of his prison, that he looked like death; not death as it shows in shroud and coffin, but in the guise it wears when life has just departed; when a young and gentle spirit has, but an instant, fled to Heaven, and the gross air of the world has not had time to breathe upon the changing dust it hallowed.

"Not now," said the Jew, turning softly away. "To-morrow. To-morrow."

CHAPTER XX.

WHEREIN OLIVER IS DELIVERED OVER TO MR. WILLIAM SIKES.

WHEN Oliver awoke in the morning, he was a good deal surprised to find that a new pair of shoes, with strong thick soles, had been placed at his bedside; and that his old ones had been removed. At first, he was pleased with the discovery: hoping that it might be the forerunner of his release; but such thoughts were quickly dispelled, on his sitting down to breakfast along with the Jew, who told him in a tone and manner which increased his alarm, that he was to be taken to the residence of Bill Sikes that night.

"To—to—stop there, Sir?" asked Oliver, anxiously.

"No, no, my dear. Not to stop there," replied the Jew. "We shouldn't like to lose you. Don't be afraid, Oliver, you shall come back to us again. Ha! ha! ha! We won't be so cruel as to send you away, my dear. Oh no, no!"

The old man, who was stooping over the fire toasting a piece of bread, looked round as he bantered Oliver thus; and chuckled, as if to shew that he knew he would still be very glad to get away if he could.

"I suppose," said the Jew, fixing his eyes on Oliver, "you want to know what you're going to Bill's for—eh, my dear?"

Oliver coloured, involuntarily, to find that the old thief had been reading his thoughts; but boldly said, Yes, he did want to know.

"Why, do you think?" inquired Fagin, parrying the question.

"Indeed I don't know, Sir," replied Oliver.

"Bah!" said the Jew, turning away with a disappointed countenance from a close perusal of the boy's face. "Wait till Bill tells you, then."

The Jew seemed much vexed by Oliver's not expressing any greater curiosity on the subject; but the truth is, that, although he felt very anxious, he was too much confused by the earnest cunning of Fagin's looks, and his own speculations, to make any further inquiries just then. He had no other opportunity; for the Jew remained very surly and silent till night: when he prepared to go abroad.

"You may burn a candle," said the Jew, putting one upon the table. "And here's a book for you to read, till they come to fetch you. Good night!"

"Good night!" replied Oliver, softly.

The Jew walked to the door: looking over his shoulder at the boy as he went. Suddenly stopping, he called him by his name.

Oliver looked up; the Jew, pointing to the candle, motioned him to light it. He did so; and, as he placed the candlestick upon the table, saw that the Jew was gazing fixedly at him, with lowering and contracted brows, from the dark end of the room.

"Take heed, Oliver! take heed!" said the old man, shaking his right hand before him in a warning manner. "He's a rough man, and thinks nothing of blood when his own is up. Whatever falls out, say nothing; and do what he bids you. Mind!" Placing a strong emphasis on the last word, he suffered his features gradually to resolve themselves into a ghastly grin; and, nodding his head, left the room.

Oliver leaned his head upon his hand when the old man disappeared; and pondered, with a trembling heart, on the words he had just heard. The more he thought of the Jew's admonition, the more he was at a loss to divine its real purpose and meaning. He could think of no bad object to be attained by sending him to Sikes: which would not be equally well answered by his remaining with Fagin; and after meditating for a long time, concluded that he had been selected to perform some ordinary menial offices for the housebreaker, until another boy, better suited for his purpose, could be engaged. He was too well accustomed to suffering, and had suffered too much where he was, to bewail the prospect of change very severely. He remained lost in thought for some minutes; and then, with a heavy sigh, snuffed the candle: and, taking up the book which the Jew had left with him, began to read.

He turned over the leaves. Carelessly at first; but, lighting on a passage which attracted his attention, he soon became intent upon the volume. It was a history of the lives and trials of great criminals; and the pages were soiled and thumbed with use. Here, he read of dreadful crimes that made the blood run cold; of secret murders that had been committed by the lonely wayside: and bodies hidden from the eye of man in deep pits and wells; which would not keep them down, deep as they were, but had yielded them up at last, after many years, and so maddened the murderers with the sight, that in their horror they had confessed their guilt, and yelled for the gibbet to end their agony. Here, too, he read of men who, lying in their beds at dead of night, had been tempted (as they said) and led on, by their own bad thoughts, to such dreadful bloodshed as it made the flesh creep, and the limbs quail, to think of. The terrible descriptions were so real and vivid, that the sallow pages seemed to turn red with gore; and the words upon them, to be sounded in his ears, as if they were whispered, in hollow murmurs, by the spirits of the dead.

In a paroxysm of fear, the boy closed the book, and thrust it from him. Then, falling upon his knees, he prayed Heaven to spare him from such deeds; and rather to will that he should die at once, than be reserved for crimes, so fearful and appalling. By degrees, he grew more calm; and besought, in a low and broken voice, that he might be rescued from his present dangers; and that if any aid were to be raised up for a poor outcast boy, who had never known the love of friends or kindred, it might come to him now: when, desolate and deserted, he stood alone in the midst of wickedness and guilt.

He had concluded his prayer, but still remained with his head buried in his hands, when a rustling noise aroused him.

"What's that!" he cried, starting up, and catching sight of a figure standing by the door. "Who's there?"

"Me. Only me," replied a tremulous voice.

Oliver raised the candle above his head: and looked towards the door. It was Nancy.

"Put down the light," said the girl, turning away her head. "It hurts my eyes."

Oliver saw that she was very pale; and gently inquired if she were ill. The girl threw herself into a chair, with her back towards him: and wrung her hands; but made no reply.

"God forgive me!" she cried after a while, "I never thought of this."

"Has anything happened?" asked Oliver. "Can I help you? I will if I can. I will, indeed."

She rocked herself to and fro; caught her throat; and, uttering a gurgling sound, struggled and gasped for breath.

"Nancy!" cried Oliver, "what is it?"

The girl beat her hands upon her knees, and her feet upon the ground; and, suddenly stopping, drew her shawl close round her: and shivered with cold.

Oliver stirred the fire. Drawing her chair close to it, she sat there, for a little time, without speaking; but at length she raised her head, and looked round.

"I don't know what comes over me sometimes," said she, affecting to busy herself in arranging her dress; "it's this damp, dirty room, I think. Now, Nolly, dear, are you ready?"

"Am I to go with you?" asked Oliver.

"Yes; I have come from Bill," replied the girl. "You are to go with me."

"What for?" asked Oliver, recoiling.

"What for!" echoed the girl, raising her eyes, and averting them again, the moment they encountered the boy's face. "Oh! For no harm."

"I don't believe it," said Oliver: who had watched her closely.

"Have it your own way," rejoined the girl, affecting to laugh. "For no good, then."

Oliver could see that he had some power over the girl's better feelings; and, for an instant, thought of appealing to her compassion for his helpless state. But, then, the thought darted across his mind that it was barely eleven o'clock; and that many people were still in the streets: of whom surely some might be found to give credence to his tale. As the reflection occurred to him, he stepped forward: and said, somewhat hastily, that he was ready.

Neither his brief consideration, nor its purport, was lost on his companion. She eyed him narrowly, while he spoke; and cast upon him a look of intelligence which sufficiently showed that she guessed what had been passing in his thoughts.

"Hush!" said the girl, stooping over him, and pointing to the door as she looked cautiously round. "You can't help yourself. I have tried hard for you, but all to no purpose. You are hedged round and round; and if ever you are to get loose from here, this is not the time."

Struck by the energy of her manner, Oliver looked up in her face with great surprise. She seemed to speak the truth; her countenance was white and agitated; and she trembled with very earnestness.

"I have saved you from being ill-used once: and I will again: and I do now," continued the girl aloud; "for those who would have fetched you, if I had not, would have been far more rough than me. I have promised for your being quiet and silent: if you are not, you will only do harm to yourself and me too: and perhaps be my death. See here! I have borne all this for you already, as true as God sees me show it."

She pointed, hastily, to some livid bruises on her neck and arms; and continued, with great rapidity.

"Remember this! And don't let me suffer more for you, just now. If I could help you, I would; but I have not the power. They don't mean to harm you; and whatever they make you do, is no fault of yours. Hush! Every word from you is a blow for me. Give me your hand. Make haste! Your hand!"

She caught the hand which Oliver instinctively placed in hers; and, blowing out the light, drew him after her up the stairs. The door was opened, quickly, by some one shrouded in the darkness; and was as quickly closed, when they had passed out. A hackney-cabriolet was in waiting; with the same vehemence which she had exhibited in addressing Oliver, the girl pulled him in with her; and drew the curtains close. The driver wanted no directions, but lashed his horse into full speed, without the delay of an instant.

The girl still held Oliver fast by the hand; and continued to pour into his ear, the warnings and assurances she had already imparted. All was so quick and hurried, that he had scarcely time to recollect where he was, or how he came there, when the carriage stopped at the house to which the Jew's steps had been directed on the previous evening.

For one brief moment, Oliver cast a hurried glance along the empty street; and a cry for help hung upon his lips. But the girl's voice was in his ear, beseeching him in such tones of agony to remember her: that he had not the heart to utter it. While he hesitated, the opportunity was gone; for he was already in the house; and the door was shut.

"This way," said the girl, releasing her hold for the first time. "Bill!"

"Hallo!" replied Sikes: appearing at the head of the stairs, with a candle. "Oh! That's the time of day. Come on!"

This was a very strong expression of approbation: an uncommonly hearty welcome: from a person of Mr. Sikes' temperament. Nancy, appearing much gratified thereby, saluted him cordially.

"Bull's-eye's gone home with Tom," observed Sikes, as he lighted them up. "He'd have been in the way."

"That's right," rejoined Nancy.

"So you've got the kid," said Sikes, when they had all reached the room: closing the door as he spoke.

"Yes, here he is," replied Nancy.

"Did he come quiet?" inquired Sikes.

"Like a lamb," rejoined Nancy.

"I'm glad to hear it," said Sikes, looking grimly at Oliver; "for the sake of his young carcase: as would otherways have suffered for it. Come here, young un; and let me read you a lectur', which is as well got over at once."

Thus addressing his new pupil, Mr. Sikes pulled off Oliver's cap and threw it into a corner; and then, taking him by the shoulder, sat himself down by the table, and stood the boy in front of him.

"Now, first: do you know wot this is?" inquired Sikes, taking up a pocket-pistol which lay on the table.

Oliver replied in the affirmative.

"Well then, look here," continued Sikes. "This is powder; that 'ere's a bullet; and this is a little bit of a old hat for waddin'."

Oliver murmured his comprehension of the different bodies referred to; and Mr. Sikes proceeded to load the pistol, with great nicety and deliberation.

"Now it's loaded," said Mr. Sikes, when he had finished.

"Yes, I see it is, Sir," replied Oliver.

"Well," said the robber, grasping Oliver's wrist tightly: and putting the barrel so close to his temple that they touched; at which moment the boy could not repress a start; "if you speak a word when you're out o' doors with me, except when I speak to you, that loading will be in your head without notice. So, if you *do* make up your mind to speak without leave; say your prayers first."

Having bestowed a scowl upon the object of this warning, to increase its effect, Mr. Sikes continued.

"As near as I know, there isn't anybody as would be asking very partickler arter you, if you *was* disposed of; so I needn't take this devil-and-all of trouble to explain matters to you, if it warn't for your own good. D'ye hear me?"

"The short and the long of what you mean," said Nancy: speaking very emphatically: and slightly frowning at Oliver as if to bespeak his serious attention to her words, "is, that if you're crossed by him in this job you have on hand, you'll prevent his ever telling tales afterwards by shooting him through the head; and will take your chance of swinging for it, as you do for a great many other things in the way of business, every month of your life."

"That's it!" observed Mr. Sikes, approvingly; "women can always put things in fewest words. Except when it's blowing up; and then they lengthens it out. And now that he's thoroughly up to it, let's have some supper, and get a snooze before starting."

In pursuance of this request, Nancy quickly laid the cloth; and, disappearing for a few minutes, presently returned with a pot of porter and a dish of sheep's heads: which gave occasion to several pleasant witticisms on the part of Mr. Sikes: founded upon the singular coincidence of "jemmies" being a cant name, common to them, and also to an ingenious implement much used in his profession. Indeed, the worthy gentleman, stimulated perhaps by the immediate prospect of being in active service, was in great spirits and good humour; in proof whereof, it may be here remarked, that he humorously drank all the beer at a draught; and did not utter, on a rough calculation, more than fourscore oaths during the whole progress of the meal.

Supper being ended—it may be easily conceived that Oliver had no great appetite for it—Mr. Sikes disposed of a couple of glasses of spirits and water: and threw himself upon the bed; ordering Nancy, with many imprecations in case of failure, to call him at five precisely. Oliver stretched himself in his clothes, by command of the same authority, on a mattress upon the floor; and the girl, mending the fire, sat before it, in readiness to rouse them at the appointed time.

For a long time Oliver lay awake: thinking it not impossible that Nancy might seek that opportunity of whispering some further advice; but the girl sat brooding over the fire, without moving, save now and then to trim the light. Weary with watching and anxiety, he at length fell asleep.

When he awoke, the table was covered with tea-things; and Sikes was thrusting various articles into the pockets of his great-coat, which hung over the back of a chair: while Nancy was busily engaged in preparing breakfast. It was not yet daylight; for the candle was still burning; and it was quite dark outside. A sharp rain, too, was beating against the window-panes; and the sky looked black and cloudy.

"Now, then!" growled Sikes, as Oliver started up; "half-past five! Look sharp, or you'll get no breakfast; for it's late as it is."

Oliver was not long in making his toilet; and, having taken some breakfast, replied to a surly inquiry from Sikes, by saying that he was quite ready.

Nancy, scarcely looking at the boy, threw him a handkerchief to tie round his throat; and Sikes gave him a large rough cape to button over his shoulders. Thus attired, he gave his hand to the robber, who, merely pausing to show him, with a menacing gesture, that he had the pistol in a side-pocket of his great-coat, clasped it firmly in his; and, exchanging a farewell with Nancy, led him away.

Oliver turned, for an instant, when they reached the door, in the hope of meeting a look from the girl. But she had resumed her old seat in front of the fire; and sat, perfectly motionless, before it.

CHAPTER XXI.

THE EXPEDITION.

It was a cheerless morning when they got into the street; blowing and raining hard; and the clouds looking dull and stormy. The night had been very wet: for large pools of water had collected in the road: and the kennels were overflowing. There was a faint glimmering of the coming day in the sky; but it rather aggravated than relieved the gloom of the scene: the sombre light only serving to pale that which the street lamps afforded, without shedding any warmer or brighter tints upon the wet housetops, and dreary streets. There appeared to be nobody stirring in that quarter of the town; for the windows of the houses were all closely shut; and the streets through which they passed, were noiseless and empty.

By the time they had turned into the Bethnal Green Road, the day had fairly begun to break. Many of the lamps were already extinguished; a few country waggons were slowly toiling on, towards London; and now and then, a stage-coach, covered with mud, rattled briskly by: the driver bestowing, as he passed, an admonitory lash upon the heavy waggoner who, by keeping on the wrong side of the road, had endangered his arriving at the office, a quarter of a minute after his time. The public-houses, with gas-lights burning inside, were already open. By degrees, other shops began to be unclosed; and a few scattered people were met with. Then, came straggling groups of labourers going to their work; then, men and women with fish-baskets on their heads: donkey-carts laden with vegetables; chaise-carts filled with live-stock or whole carcasses of meat; milk-women with pails; and an unbroken concourse of people, trudging out with various supplies to the eastern suburbs of the town. As they approached the City, the noise and traffic gradually increased; and when they threaded the streets between Shoreditch and Smithfield, it had swelled into a roar of sound and bustle. It was as light as it was likely to be, till night came on again; and the busy morning of half the London population had begun.

Turning down Sun Street and Crown Street, and crossing Finsbury Square, Mr. Sikes struck, by way of Chiswell Street, into Barbican: thence into Long Lane: and so into Smithfield; from which latter place arose a tumult of discordant sounds that filled Oliver Twist with surprise and amazement.

It was market-morning. The ground was covered, nearly ankle-deep, with filth and mire; and a thick steam, perpetually rising from the reeking bodies of the cattle, and mingling with the fog, which seemed to rest upon the chimney-tops, hung heavily above. All the pens in the centre of the large area: and as many temporary ones as could be crowded into the vacant space: were filled with sheep; tied up to posts by the gutter side were long lines of beasts and oxen, three or four deep. Countrymen, butchers, drovers, hawkers, boys, thieves, idlers, and vagabonds of every low grade, were mingled together in a dense mass; the whistling of drovers, the barking of dogs, the bellowing and plunging of oxen, the bleating of sheep, the grunting and squeaking of pigs; the cries of hawkers, the shouts, oaths, and quarrelling on all sides; the ringing of bells and roar of voices, that issued from every public-house; the crowding, pushing, driving, beating, whooping, and yelling; the hideous and discordant din that resounded from every corner of the market; and the unwashed, unshaven, squalid, and dirty figures constantly running to and fro, and bursting in and out of the throng; rendered it a stunning and bewildering scene, which quite confounded the senses.

Mr. Sikes, dragging Oliver after him, elbowed his way through the thickest of the crowd; and bestowed very little attention on the numerous sights and sounds which so astonished the boy. He nodded, twice or thrice, to a passing friend; and, resisting as many invitations to take a morning dram, pressed steadily onward, until they were clear of the turmoil, and had made their way through Hosier Lane into Holborn.

"Now, young un!" said Sikes, looking up at the clock of St. Andrew's Church, "hard upon seven! you must step out. Come, don't lag behind already, Lazy-legs!"

Mr. Sikes accompanied this speech with a jerk at his little companion's wrist; Oliver, quickening his pace into a kind of trot, between a fast walk and a run, kept up with the rapid strides of the housebreaker as well as he could.

They held their course at this rate, until they had passed Hyde Park Corner, and were on their way to Kensington: when Sikes relaxed his pace, until an empty cart, which was at some little distance behind, came up. Seeing "Hounslow" written on it, he asked the driver, with as much civility as he could assume, if he would give them a lift as far as Isleworth.

"Jump up," said the man. "Is that your boy?"

"Yes; he's my boy," replied Sikes, looking hard at Oliver, and putting his hand abstractedly into the pocket where the pistol was.

"Your father walks rather too quick for you, don't he, my man?" inquired the driver: seeing that Oliver was out of breath.

"Not a bit of it," replied Sikes, interposing. "He's used to it. Here, take hold of my hand, Ned. In with you!"

Thus addressing Oliver, he helped him into the cart; and the driver, pointing to a heap of sacks, told him to lie down there, and rest himself.

As they passed the different mile-stones, Oliver wondered, more and more, where his companion meant to take him. Kensington, Hammersmith, Chiswick, Kew Bridge, Brentford, were all passed; and yet they went on as steadily as if they had only just begun their journey. At length, they came to a public-house called the Coach and Horses: a little way beyond which, another road appeared to turn off. And here, the cart stopped.

Sikes dismounted with great precipitation: holding Oliver by the hand all the while; and, lifting him down directly, bestowed a furious look upon him, and rapped the side-pocket with his fist, in a very significant manner.

"Good-bye, boy," said the man.

"He's sulky," replied Sikes, giving him a shake; "he's sulky. A young dog! Don't mind him."

"Not I!" rejoined the other, getting into his cart. "It's a fine day, after all." And he drove away.

Sikes waited until he had fairly gone; and then, telling Oliver he might look about him if he wanted, once again led him forward on his journey.

They turned round to the left, a short way past the public-house; and then, taking a right-hand road, walked on for a long time: passing many large gardens and gentlemen's houses on both sides of the way, and stopping for nothing but a little beer, until they reached a town. Here against the wall of a house, Oliver saw, written up in pretty large letters, "Hampton." They lingered about, in the fields, for some hours. At length, they came back into the town; and, turning into an old public-house with a defaced sign-board, ordered some dinner by the kitchen fire.

The kitchen was an old, low-roofed room: with a great beam across the middle of the ceiling: and benches, with high backs to them, by the fire; on which were seated several rough men in smock-frocks, drinking and smoking. They took no notice of Oliver; and very little of Sikes; and, as Sikes took very little notice of them, he and his young comrade sat in a corner by themselves, without being much troubled by their company.

They had some cold meat for dinner; and sat here so long after it, while Mr. Sikes indulged himself with three or four pipes, that Oliver began to feel quite certain they were not going any further. Being much tired with the walk, and getting up so early, he dozed a little at first; and then, quite overpowered by fatigue and the fumes of the tobacco, fell asleep.

It was quite dark when he was awakened by a push from Sikes. Rousing himself sufficiently to sit up and look about him, he found that worthy in close fellowship and communication with a labouring man, over a pint of ale.

"So, you're going on to Lower Halliford, are you?" inquired Sikes.

"Yes, I am," replied the man, who seemed a little the worse—or better, as the case might be—for drinking; "and not slow about it neither. My horse hasn't got a load behind him going back, as he had coming up in the mornin'; and he won't be long a-doing of it. Here's luck to him! Ecod! he's a good un!"

"Could you give my boy and me a lift as far as there?" demanded Sikes, pushing the ale towards his new friend.

"If you're going directly, I can," replied the man, looking out of the pot. "Are you going to Halliford?"

"Going on to Shepperton," replied Sikes.

"I'm your man, as far as I go," replied the other. "Is all paid, Becky?"

"Yes, the other gentleman's paid," replied the girl.

"I say!" said the man, with tipsy gravity; "that won't do, you know."

"Why not?" rejoined Sikes. "You're a-going to accommodate us; and wot's to prevent my standing treat for a pint or so, in return?"

The stranger reflected upon this argument, with a very profound face; and having done so, seized Sikes by the hand: and declared he was a real good fellow. To which Mr. Sikes replied, he was joking; as, if he had been sober, there would have been strong reason to suppose he was.

After the exchange of a few more compliments, they bade the company good night, and went out; the girl gathering up the pots and glasses as they did so: and lounging out to the door, with her hands full, to see the party start.

The horse, whose health had been drunk in his absence, was standing outside: ready harnessed to the cart. Oliver and Sikes got in without any further ceremony; and the man to whom he belonged, having lingered for a minute or two to "bear him up," and to defy the hostler and the world to produce his equal, mounted also. Then, the hostler was told to give the horse his head; and, his head being given him, he made a very unpleasant use of it: tossing it into the air with great disdain, and running into the parlour windows over the way; after performing these feats, and supporting himself for a short time on his hind-legs, he started off at great speed, and rattled out of the town right gallantly.

The night was very dark. A damp mist rose from the river, and the marshy ground about; and spread itself over the dreary fields. It was piercing cold, too; all was gloomy and black. Not a word was spoken; for the driver had grown sleepy; and Sikes was in no mood to lead him into conversation. Oliver sat huddled together, in a corner of the cart; bewildered with alarm and apprehension; and figuring strange objects in the gaunt trees, whose branches waved grimly to and fro, as if in some fantastic joy at the desolation of the scene.

As they passed Sunbury Church, the clock struck seven. There was a light in the ferry-house window opposite: which streamed across the road, and threw into more sombre shadow a dark yew-tree with graves beneath it. There was a dull sound of falling water not far off; and the leaves of the old tree stirred gently in the night wind. It seemed like quiet music for the repose of the dead.

Sunbury was passed through; and they came again into the lonely road. Two or three miles more; and the cart stopped. Sikes alighted; and, taking Oliver by the hand, they once again walked on.

They turned into no house at Shepperton, as the weary boy had expected; but still kept walking on, in mud and darkness, through gloomy lanes and over cold open wastes, until they came within sight of the lights of a town at no great distance. On looking intently forward, Oliver saw that the water was just below them: and that they were coming to the foot of a bridge.

Sikes kept straight on, until they were close upon the bridge; and then turned suddenly down a bank upon the left.

"The water!" thought Oliver, turning sick with fear. "He has brought me to this lonely place to murder me!"

He was about to throw himself on the ground, and make one struggle for his young life, when he saw that they stood before a solitary house: all ruinous and decayed. There was a window on each side of the dilapidated entrance; and one story above; but no light was visible. It was dark, dismantled: and, to all appearance, uninhabited.

Sikes, with Oliver's hand still in his, softly approached the low porch, and raised the latch. The door yielded to the pressure; and they passed in, together.

CHAPTER XXII.

THE BURGLARY.

"Hallo!" cried a loud, hoarse voice, directly they had set foot in the passage.

"Don't make such a row," said Sikes, bolting the door. "Show a glim, Toby."

"Aha! my pal," cried the same voice; "a glim, Barney, a glim! Show the gentleman in, Barney; and wake up first, if convenient."

The speaker appeared to throw a boot-jack, or some such article, at the person he addressed, to rouse him from his slumbers: for the noise of a wooden body, falling violently, was heard; and then an indistinct muttering, as of a man between asleep and awake.

"Do you hear?" cried the same voice. "There's Bill Sikes in the passage with nobody to do the civil to him; and you sleeping there, as if you took laudanum with your meals, and nothing stronger. Are you any fresher now, or do you want the iron candlestick to wake you thoroughly?"

A pair of slipshod feet shuffled, hastily, across the bare floor of the room, as this interrogatory was put; and there issued, from a door on the right hand: first, a feeble candle: and next, the form of the same individual who has been heretofore described as labouring under the infirmity of speaking through his nose, and officiating as waiter at the public-house on Saffron Hill.

"Bister Sikes!" exclaimed Barney, with real or counterfeit joy; "cub id, Sir; cub id."

"Here! you get on first," said Sikes, putting Oliver in front of him. "Quicker! or I shall tread upon your heels."

Muttering a curse upon his tardiness, Sikes pushed Oliver before him; and they entered a low dark room with a smoky fire: two or three broken chairs, a table, and a very old couch: on which, with his legs much higher than his head, a man was reposing at full length, smoking a long clay pipe. He was dressed in a smartly-cut snuff-coloured coat, with large brass buttons; and orange neckerchief; a coarse, staring, shawl-pattern waistcoat; and drab breeches. Mr. Crackit (for he it was) had no very great quantity of hair, either upon his head or face; but what he had, was of a reddish dye, and tortured into long corkscrew curls, through which he occasionally thrust some very dirty fingers, ornamented with large common rings. He was a trifle above the middle size, and apparently rather weak in the legs; but this circumstance by no means detracted from his own admiration of his top-boots, which he contemplated, in their elevated situation, with lively satisfaction.

"Bill, my boy!" said this figure, turning his head towards the door, "I'm glad to see you. I was almost afraid you'd given it up: in which case I should have made a personal wentur. Hallo!"

Uttering this exclamation in a tone of great surprise, as his eye rested on Oliver, Mr. Toby Crackit brought himself into a sitting posture, and demanded who that was.

"The boy. Only the boy!" replied Sikes, drawing a chair towards the fire.

"Wud of Bister Fagid's lads," exclaimed Barney, with a grin.

"Fagin's, eh!" exclaimed Toby, looking at Oliver. "Wot an inwalable boy that'll make, for the old ladies' pockets in chapels. His mug is a fortun' to him."

"There—there's enough of that," interposed Sikes, impatiently; and stooping over his recumbent friend, he whispered a few words in his ear: at which Mr. Crackit laughed immensely, and honoured Oliver with a long stare of astonishment.

"Now," said Sikes, as he resumed his seat, "if you'll give us something to eat and drink while we're waiting, you'll put some heart in us; or in me, at all events. Sit down by the fire, younker, and rest yourself; for you'll have to go out with us again to-night, though not very far off."

Oliver looked at Sikes, in mute and timid wonder; and drawing a stool to the fire, sat with his aching head upon his hands: scarcely knowing where he was, or what was passing around him.

"Here," said Toby, as the young Jew placed some fragments of food, and a bottle, upon the table, "Success to the crack!" He rose to honour the toast; and, carefully depositing his empty pipe in a corner, advanced to the table: filled a glass with spirits: and drank off its contents. Mr. Sikes did the same.

"A drain for the boy," said Toby, half-filling a wine glass. "Down with it, innocence."

"Indeed," said Oliver, looking piteously up into the man's face; "indeed, I——"

"Down with it!" echoed Toby. "Do you think I don't know what's good for you? Tell him to drink it, Bill."

"He had better!" said Sikes, clapping his hand upon his pocket. "Burn my body, if he isn't more trouble than a whole family of Dodgers. Drink it, you perwerse imp; drink it!"

Frightened by the menacing gestures of the two men,

Oliver hastily swallowed the contents of the glass, and immediately fell into a violent fit of coughing: which delighted Toby Crackit and Barney, and even drew a smile from the surly Mr. Sikes.

This done, and Sikes having satisfied his appetite (Oliver could eat nothing but a small crust of bread which they made him swallow), the two men laid themselves down on chairs for a short nap. Oliver retained his stool by the fire; and Barney, wrapped in a blanket, stretched himself on the floor: close outside the fender.

They slept, or appeared to sleep, for some time; nobody stirring but Barney, who rose once or twice to throw coals upon the fire. Oliver fell into a heavy doze; imagining himself straying through the gloomy lanes, or wandering about the dark churchyard, or retracing some one or other of the scenes of the past day: when he was roused by Toby Crackit jumping up and declaring it was half-past one.

In an instant, the other two were on their legs; and all were actively engaged in busy preparation. Sikes and his companion enveloped their necks and chins in large dark shawls, and drew on their great-coats; while Barney, opening a cupboard, brought forth several articles, which he hastily crammed into the pockets.

"Barkers for me, Barney," said Toby Crackit.

"Here they are," replied Barney, producing a pair of pistols. "You loaded them yourself."

"All right!" replied Toby, stowing them away. "The persuaders?"

"I've got 'em," replied Sikes.

"Crape, keys, centre-bits, darkies—nothing forgotten?" inquired Toby: fastening a small crowbar to a loop inside the skirt of his coat.

"All right," rejoined his companion. "Bring them bits of timber, Barney. That's the time of day."

With these words, he took a thick stick from Barney's hands, who, having delivered another to Toby, busied himself in fastening on Oliver's cape.

"Now then!" said Sikes, holding out his hand.

Oliver: who was completely stupefied by the unwonted exercise, and the air, and the drink which had been forced upon him: put his hand mechanically into that which Sikes extended for the purpose.

"Take his other hand, Toby," said Sikes. "Look out, Barney."

The man went to the door, and returned to announce that all was quiet. The two robbers issued forth with Oliver between them. Barney, having made all fast, rolled himself up as before, and was soon asleep again.

It was now intensely dark. The fog was much heavier than it had been in the early part of the night; and the atmosphere was so damp, that, although no rain fell, Oliver's hair and eyebrows, within a few minutes after leaving the house, had become stiff with the half-frozen moisture that was floating about. They crossed the bridge; and kept on towards the lights which he had seen before. They were at no great distance off; and, as they walked pretty briskly, they soon arrived at Chertsey.

"Slap through the town," whispered Sikes; "there'll be nobody in the way, to-night, to see us."

Toby acquiesced; and they hurried through the main street of the little town, which at that late hour was wholly deserted. A dim light shone at intervals from some bed-room-window; and the hoarse barking of dogs occasionally broke the silence of the night. But there was nobody abroad; and they had cleared the town, as the church-bell struck two.

Quickening their pace, they turned up a road upon the left hand. After walking about a quarter of a mile, they stopped before a detached house surrounded by a wall: to the top of which, Toby Crackit, scarcely pausing to take breath, climbed in a twinkling.

"The boy next," said Toby. "Hoist him up; I'll catch hold of him."

Before Oliver had time to look round, Sikes had caught him under the arms; and in three or four seconds he and Toby were lying on the grass on the other side. Sikes followed directly. And they stole cautiously towards the house.

And now, for the first time, Oliver, well-nigh mad with grief and terror, saw that housebreaking and robbery, if not murder, were the objects of the expedition. He clasped his hands together, and involuntarily uttered a subdued exclamation of horror. A mist came before his eyes; the cold sweat stood upon his ashy face; his limbs failed him; and he sank upon his knees.

"Get up!" murmured Sikes, trembling with rage, and drawing the pistol from his pocket; "Get up, or I'll strew your brains upon the grass."

"Oh! for God's sake let me go!" cried Oliver; "let me run away and die in the fields. I will never come near London; never, never! Oh! pray have mercy on me, and do not make me steal. For the love of all the bright angels that rest in Heaven, have mercy upon me!"

The man to whom this appeal was made, swore a dreadful oath, and had cocked the pistol, when Toby, striking it from his grasp, placed his hand upon the boy's mouth, and dragged him to the house.

"Hush!" cried the man; "it won't answer here. Say another word, and I'll do your business myself with a crack on the head. That makes no noise; and is quite as certain, and more genteel. Here, Bill, wrench the shutter open. He's game enough now, I'll engage. I've seen older hands of his age took the same way, for a minute or two, on a cold night."

Sikes, invoking terrific imprecations upon Fagin's head for sending Oliver on such an errand, plied the crowbar vigorously, but with little noise. After some delay, and some assistance from Toby, the shutter to which he had referred, swung open on its hinges.

It was a little lattice window, about five feet and a half above the ground: at the back of the house: which belonged to a scullery, or small brewing-place, at the end of the passage. The aperture was so small, that the inmates had probably not thought it worth while to defend it more securely; but it was large enough to admit a boy of Oliver's size, nevertheless. A very brief exercise of Mr. Sikes's art, sufficed to overcome the fastening of the lattice; and it soon stood wide open also.

"Now listen, you young limb," whispered Sikes, drawing a dark lantern from his pocket, and throwing the glare full on Oliver's face; "I'm a going to put you through there. Take this light; go softly up the steps straight afore you; and along the little hall to the street door; unfasten it, and let us in."

"There's a bolt at the top, you won't be able to reach," interposed Toby. "Stand upon one of the hall chairs. There are three there, Bill, with a jolly large blue unicorn and gold.pitchfork on 'em: which is the old lady's arms."

"Keep quiet, can't you?" replied Sikes, with a threatening look. "The room-door is open, is it?"

"Wide," replied Toby, after peeping in to satisfy himself. "The game of that is, that they always leave it open with a catch, so that the dog, who's got a bed in here, may walk up and down the passage when he feels wakeful. Ha! ha! Barney 'ticed him away to-night. So neat!"

Although Mr. Crackit spoke in a scarcely audible whisper, and laughed without noise, Sikes imperiously commanded him to be silent, and to get to work. Toby complied, by first producing his lantern, and placing it on the ground; then by planting himself firmly with his head against the wall beneath the window, and his hands upon his knees, so as to make a step of his back. This was no sooner done, than Sikes, mounting upon him, put Oliver gently through the window with his feet first; and, without leaving hold of his collar, planted him safely on the floor inside.

"Take this lantern," said Sikes, looking into the room. "You see the stairs afore you?"

Oliver, more dead than alive, gasped out, "Yes." Sikes, pointing to the street-door with the pistol-barrel, briefly advised him to take notice that he was within shot all the way; and that if he faltered, he would fall dead that instant.

"It's done in a minute," said Sikes, in the same low whisper. "Directly I leave go of you, do your work. Hark!"

"What's that?" whispered the other man.

They listened intently.

"Nothing," said Sikes, releasing his hold of Oliver. "Now!"

In the short time he had had to collect his senses, the boy had firmly resolved that, whether he died in the attempt or not, he would make one effort to dart up stairs from the hall, and alarm the family. Filled with this idea, he advanced at once, but stealthily.

"Come back!" suddenly cried Sikes aloud. "Back! back!"

Scared by the sudden breaking of the dead stillness of the place, and by a loud cry which followed it, Oliver let his lantern fall, and knew not whether to advance or fly.

The cry was repeated—a light appeared—a vision of two terrified half-dressed men at the top of the stairs swam before his eyes—a flash—a loud noise—a smoke—a crash somewhere, but where he knew not,—and he staggered back.

Sikes had disappeared for an instant; but he was up again, and had him by the collar before the smoke had cleared away. He fired his own pistol after the men, who were already retreating; and dragged the boy up.

"Clasp your arm tighter," said Sikes, as he drew him through the window. "Give me a shawl here. They've hit him. Quick! Damnation, how the boy bleeds!"

Then, came the loud ringing of a bell: mingled with the noise of firearms, and the shouts of men, and the sensation of being carried over uneven ground at a rapid pace. And then, the noises grew confused in the distance; and a cold deadly feeling crept over the boy's heart; and he saw or heard no more

CHAPTER XXIII.

WHICH CONTAINS THE SUBSTANCE OF A PLEASANT CONVERSATION BETWEEN MR. BUMBLE AND A LADY; AND SHOWS THAT EVEN A BEADLE MAY BE SUSCEPTIBLE ON SOME POINTS.

THE night was bitter cold. The snow lay on the ground, frozen into a hard thick crust; so that only the heaps that had drifted into by-ways and corners were affected by the sharp wind that howled abroad: which, as if expending increased fury on such prey as it found, caught it savagely up in clouds, and, whirling it into a thousand misty eddies, scattered it in air. Bleak, dark, and piercing cold, it was a night for the well-housed and fed to draw round the bright fire and thank God they were at home; and for the homeless starving wretch to lay him down and die. Many hunger-worn outcasts close their eyes in our bare streets, at such times, who, let their crimes have been what they may, can hardly open them in a more bitter world.

Such was the aspect of out-of-doors affairs, when Mrs. Corney, the matron of the workhouse to which our readers have been already introduced as the birthplace of Oliver Twist, sat herself down before a cheerful fire in her own little room; and glanced, with no small degree of complacency, at a small round table: on which stood a tray of corresponding size, furnished with all necessary materials for the most grateful meal that matrons enjoy. In fact, Mrs. Corney was about to solace herself with a cup of tea. As she glanced from the table to the fireplace, where the smallest of all possible kettles was singing a small song in a small voice, her inward satisfaction evidently increased, —so much so, indeed, that Mrs. Corney smiled.

"Well!" said the matron, leaning her elbow on the table, and looking reflectively at the fire; "I'm sure we have all on us a great deal to be grateful for! A great deal, if we did but know it. Ah!"

Mrs. Corney shook her head mournfully, as if deploring the mental blindness of those paupers who did not know it; and thrusting a silver spoon (private property) into the inmost recesses of a two-ounce tin tea-caddy, proceeded to make the tea.

How slight a thing will disturb the equanimity of our frail minds! The black teapot, being very small and easily filled, ran over while Mrs. Corney was moralising; and the water slightly scalded Mrs. Corney's hand.

"Drat the pot!" said the worthy matron, setting it down very hastily on the hob; "a little stupid thing, that only holds a couple of cups! What use is it of, to anybody! Except," said Mrs. Corney, pausing, "except to a poor desolate creature like me. Oh dear!"

With these words, the matron dropped into her chair; and, once more resting her elbow on the table, thought of her solitary fate. The small teapot, and the single cup, had awakened in her mind sad recollections of Mr. Corney (who had not been dead more than five-and-twenty years); and she was overpowered.

"I shall never get another!" said Mrs. Corney, pettishly; "I shall never get another—like him."

Whether this remark bore reference to the husband, or the teapot, is uncertain. It might have been the latter; for Mrs. Corney looked at it as she spoke: and took it up afterwards. She had just tasted her first cup, when she was disturbed by a soft tap at the room-door.

George Cruikshank

A. Dick sc

THE BURGLARY.

"Oh, come in with you!" said Mrs. Corney, sharply. "Some of the old women dying, I suppose. They always die when I'm at meals. Don't stand there, letting the cold air in, don't. What's amiss now, eh?"

"Nothing, ma'am, nothing," replied a man's voice.

"Dear me!" exclaimed the matron, in a much sweeter tone, "is that Mr. Bumble?"

"At your service, ma'am," said Mr. Bumble, who had been stopping outside to rub his shoes clean, and to shake the snow off his coat; and who now made his appearance, bearing the cocked hat in one hand and a bundle in the other. "Shall I shut the door, ma'am?"

The lady modestly hesitated to reply, lest there should be any impropriety in holding an interview with Mr. Bumble, with closed doors. Mr. Bumble taking advantage of the hesitation, and being very cold himself, shut it without further permission.

"Hard weather, Mr. Bumble," said the matron.

"Hard, indeed, ma'am," replied the beadle. "Anti-porochial weather this, ma'am. We have given away, Mrs. Corney, we have given away a matter of twenty quartern loaves, and a cheese and a half, this very blessed afternoon; and yet them paupers are not contented."

"Of course not. When would they be, Mr. Bumble?" said the matron, sipping her tea.

"When, indeed, ma'am!" rejoined Mr. Bumble. "Why, here's one man that, in consideration of his wife and large family, has a quartern loaf and a good pound of cheese, full weight. Is he grateful, ma'am, is he grateful? Not a copper farthing's worth of it! What does he do, ma'am, but ask for a few coals; if it's only a pocket handkerchief full, he says! Coals! What would he do with coals? Toast his cheese with 'em, and then come back for more. That's the way with these people, ma'am; give 'em a apron full of coals to-day: and they'll come back for another, the day after to-morrow, as brazen as alabaster."

The matron expressed her entire concurrence in this intelligible simile; and the beadle went on.

"I never," said Mr. Bumble, "see anything like the pitch it's got to. The day afore yesterday, a man—you have been a married woman, ma'am, and I may mention it to you—a man, with hardly a rag upon his back (here Mrs. Corney looked at the floor), goes to our overseer's door when he has got company coming to dinner; and says, he must be relieved, Mrs. Corney. As he wouldn't go away, and shocked the company very much, our overseer sent him out a pound of potatoes and half a pint of oatmeal. 'My heart!' says the ungrateful villain, 'what's the use of *this* to me? You might as well give me a pair of iron spectacles!' 'Very good,' says our overseer, taking 'em away again, 'you won't get anything else here.' 'Then I'll die in the streets!' says the vagrant. 'Oh no, you won't,' says our overseer."

"Ha! ha! That was very good! So like Mr. Grannett, wasn't it?" interposed the matron. "Well, Mr. Bumble?"

"Well, ma'am," rejoined the beadle, "he went away; and he *did* die in the streets. There's a obstinate pauper for you!"

"It beats anything I could have believed," observed the matron emphatically. "But don't you think out-of-door relief a very bad thing, any way, Mr. Bumble? You're a gentleman of experience, and ought to know. Come."

"Mrs. Corney," said the beadle, smiling as men smile who are conscious of superior information, "out-of-door relief, properly managed: properly managed, ma'am: is the porochial safeguard. The great principle of out-of-door relief is to give the paupers exactly what they don't want; and then they get tired of coming."

"Dear me!" exclaimed Mrs. Corney. "Well, that is a good one, too!"

"Yes. Betwixt you and me, ma'am," returned Mr. Bumble, "that's the great principle; and that's the reason why, if you look at any cases that get into them owdacious newspapers, you'll always observe that sick families have been relieved with slices of cheese. That's the rule now, Mrs. Corney, all over the country. But, however," said the beadle, stopping to unpack his bundle, "these are official secrets, ma'am; not to be spoken of: except, as I may say, among the porochial officers, such as ourselves. This is the port wine, ma'am, that the board ordered for the infirmary; real, fresh, genuine port wine; only out of the cask this forenoon; clear as a bell; and no sediment!"

Having held the first bottle up to the light, and shaken it well to test its excellence, Mr. Bumble placed them both on the top of a chest of drawers; folded the handkerchief in which they had been wrapped; put it carefully in his pocket; and took up his hat, as if to go.

"You'll have a very cold walk, Mr. Bumble," said the matron.

"It blows, ma'am," replied Mr. Bumble, turning up his coat-collar, "enough to cut one's ears off."

The matron looked, from the little kettle, to the beadle, who was moving towards the door; and as the beadle coughed, preparatory to bidding her good night, bashfully inquired whether—whether he wouldn't take a cup of tea?

Mr. Bumble instantaneously turned back his collar again; laid his hat and stick upon a chair; and drew another chair up to the table. As he slowly seated himself, he looked at the lady. She fixed her eyes upon the little teapot. Mr. Bumble coughed again, and slightly smiled.

Mrs. Corney rose to get another cup and saucer from the closet. As she sat down, her eyes once again encountered those of the gallant beadle; she coloured, and applied herself to the task of making his tea. Again Mr. Bumble coughed,—louder this time than he had coughed yet.

"Sweet? " Mr. Bumble," inquired the matron, taking up the sugar-basin.

"Very sweet, indeed, ma'am," replied Mr. Bumble. He fixed his eyes on Mrs. Corney as he said this; and if ever a beadle looked tender, Mr. Bumble was that beadle at that moment.

The tea was made, and handed in silence. Mr. Bumble, having spread a handkerchief over his knees to prevent the crumbs from sullying the splendour of his shorts, began to eat and drink; varying these amusements, occasionally, by fetching a deep sigh; which, however, had no injurious effect upon his appetite, but, on the contrary, rather seemed to facilitate his operations in the tea and toast department.

"You have a cat, ma'am, I see," said Mr. Bumble, glancing at one who, in the centre of her family, was basking before the fire; "and kittens too, I declare!"

"I am so fond of them, Mr. Bumble, you can't think," replied the matron. "They're *so* happy, *so* frolicsome, and *so* cheerful, that they are quite companions for me."

"Very nice animals, ma'am," replied Mr. Bumble, approvingly; "so very domestic."

"Oh, yes!" rejoined the matron, with enthusiasm; "so fond of their home too, that it's quite a pleasure, I'm sure."

"Mrs. Corney, ma'am," said Mr. Bumble, slowly, and marking the time with his teaspoon, "I mean to say this, ma'am; that any cat, or kitten, that could live with you, ma'am, and *not* be fond of its home, must be a ass, ma'am."

"Oh, Mr. Bumble!" remonstrated Mrs. Corney.

"It's of no use disguising facts, ma'am," said Mr. Bumble, slowly flourishing the teaspoon with a kind of amorous dignity which made him doubly impressive; "I would drown it myself, with pleasure."

"Then you're a cruel man," said the matron vivaciously, as she held out her hand for the beadle's cup; "and a very hard-hearted man besides."

"Hard-hearted, ma'am," said Mr. Bumble, "hard!" Mr. Bumble resigned his cup without another word; squeezed Mrs. Corney's little finger as she took it; and inflicting two open-handed slaps upon his laced waistcoat, gave a mighty sigh, and hitched his chair a very little morsel farther from the fire.

It was a round table; and as Mrs. Corney and Mr. Bumble had been sitting opposite each other; with no great space between them, and fronting the fire: it will be seen that Mr. Bumble, in receding from the fire, and still keeping at the table, increased the distance between himself and Mrs. Corney; which proceeding, some prudent readers will doubtless be disposed to admire, and to consider an act of great heroism on Mr. Bumble's part: he being in some sort tempted by time, place, and opportunity, to give utterance to certain soft nothings, which, however well they may become the lips of the light and thoughtless, do seem immeasurably beneath the dignity of judges of the land, members of parliament, ministers of state, lord mayors, and other great public functionaries, but more particularly beneath the stateliness and gravity of a beadle: who (as is well known) should be the sternest and most inflexible among them all.

Whatever were Mr. Bumble's intentions, however: and no doubt they were of the best: it unfortunately happened, as has been twice before remarked, that the table was a round one; consequently Mr. Bumble, moving his chair by little and little, soon began to diminish the distance between himself and the matron; and, continuing to travel round the outer edge of the circle, brought his chair, in time, close to that in which the matron was seated. Indeed, the two chairs touched; and when they did so, Mr. Bumble stopped.

Now, if the matron had moved her chair to the right, she would have been scorched by the fire; and if to the left, she must have fallen into Mr. Bumble's arms; so (being a discreet matron, and no doubt foreseeing these consequences at a glance) she remained where she was, and handed Mr. Bumble another cup of tea.

"Hard-hearted, Mrs. Corney?" said Mr. Bumble, stirring his tea, and looking up into the matron's face; "are *you* hard-hearted, Mrs. Corney?"

"Dear me!" exclaimed the matron, "what a very curious question from a single man. What can you want to know for, Mr. Bumble?"

The beadle drank his tea to the last drop; finished a piece of toast; whisked the crumbs off his knees; wiped his lips; and deliberately kissed the matron.

"Mr. Bumble," cried that discreet lady in a whisper; for the fright was so great, that she had quite lost her voice, "Mr. Bumble, I shall scream!" Mr. Bumble made no reply; but, in a slow and dignified manner, put his arm round the matron's waist.

As the lady had stated her intention of screaming, of course she would have screamed at this additional boldness, but that the exertion was rendered unnecessary by a hasty knocking at the door: which was no sooner heard, than Mr. Bumble darted, with much agility, to the wine bottles, and began dusting them with great violence: while the matron sharply demanded who was there. It is worthy of remark, as a curious physical instance of the efficacy of a sudden surprise in counteracting the effects of extreme fear, that her voice had quite recovered all its official asperity.

"If you please, mistress," said a withered old female pauper, hideously ugly: putting her head in at the door, "Old Sally is a-going fast."

"Well, what's that to me?" angrily demanded the matron. "I can't keep her alive, can I?"

"No, no, mistress," replied the old woman, "nobody can; she's far beyond the reach of help. I've seen a many people die; little babes and great strong men; and I know when death's a-coming, well enough. But she's troubled in her mind; and when the fits are not on her,—and that's not often, for she is dying very hard,—she says she has got something to tell, which you must hear. She'll never die quiet till you come, mistress."

At this intelligence, the worthy Mrs. Corney muttered a variety of invectives against old women who couldn't even die without purposely annoying their betters; and, muffling herself in a thick shawl which she hastily caught up, briefly requested Mr. Bumble to stay till she came back, lest anything particular should occur; and, bidding the messenger walk fast, and not be all night hobbling up the stairs, followed her from the room with a very ill grace: scolding all the way.

Mr. Bumble's conduct on being left to himself, was rather inexplicable. He opened the closet, counted the teaspoons, weighed the sugar-tongs, closely inspected a silver milk-pot to ascertain that it was of the genuine metal; and, having satisfied his curiosity on these points, put on his cocked-hat corner-wise, and danced with much gravity four distinct times round the table. Having gone through this very extraordinary performance, he took off the cocked-hat again; and, spreading himself before the fire with his back towards it, seemed to be mentally engaged in taking an exact inventory of the furniture.

CHAPTER XXIV.

TREATS OF A VERY POOR SUBJECT. BUT IS A SHORT ONE; AND MAY BE FOUND OF IMPORTANCE IN THIS HISTORY.

It was no unfit messenger of death, that had disturbed the quiet of the matron's room. Her body was bent by age; her limbs trembled with palsy; and her face, distorted into a mumbling leer, resembled more the grotesque shaping of some wild pencil, than the work of Nature's hand.

Alas! How few of Nature's faces are left to gladden us with their beauty! The cares, and sorrows, and hungerings, of the world, change them as they change hearts; and it is only when those passions sleep, and have lost their hold for ever, that the troubled clouds pass off, and leave Heaven's surface clear. It is a common thing for the countenances of the dead, even in that fixed and rigid state, to subside into the long-forgotten expression of sleeping infancy, and settle into the very look of early life; so calm, so peaceful, do they grow again, that those who knew them in their happy childhood, kneel by the coffin's side in awe, and see the Angel even upon earth.

The old crone tottered along the passages, and up the stairs, muttering some indistinct answers to the chidings of her companion; and, being at length compelled to pause for breath, gave the light into her hand, and remained behind to follow as she might: while the more nimble superior made her way to the room where the sick woman lay.

It was a bare garret-room, with a dim light burning at the farther end. There was another old woman watching by the bed; and the parish apothecary's apprentice was standing by the fire, making a toothpick out of a quill.

"Cold night, Mrs. Corney," said this young gentleman, as the matron entered.

"Very cold indeed, Sir," replied the mistress, in her most civil tones, and dropping a curtsey as she spoke.

"You should get better coals out of your contractors," said the apothecary's deputy, breaking a lump on the top of the fire with the rusty poker; "these are not at all the sort of thing for a cold night."

"They're the board's choosing, Sir," returned the matron. "The least they could do, would be to keep us pretty warm: for our places are hard enough."

The conversation was here interrupted by a moan from the sick woman.

"Oh!" said the young man, turning his face towards the bed, as if he had previously quite forgotten the patient, "It's all U. P. there, Mrs. Corney."

"It is, is it, Sir?" asked the matron.

"If she lasts a couple of hours, I shall be surprised," said the apothecary's apprentice, intent upon the toothpick's point. "It's a break-up of the system altogether. Is she dozing, old lady?"

The attendant stooped over the bed, to ascertain; and nodded in the affirmative.

"Then perhaps she'll go off in that way, if you don't make a row," said the young man. "Put the light on the floor. She won't see it there."

The attendant did as she was told: shaking her head meanwhile, to intimate that the woman would not die so easily; having done so, she resumed her seat by the side of the other nurse, who had by this time returned. The mistress, with an expression of impatience, wrapped herself in her shawl, and sat at the foot of the bed.

The apothecary's apprentice, having completed the manufacture of the toothpick, planted himself in front of the fire and made good use of it for ten minutes or so: when, apparently growing rather dull, he wished Mrs. Corney joy of her job, and took himself off on tiptoe.

When they had sat in silence for some time, the two old women rose from the bed; and crouching over the fire, held out their withered hands to catch the heat. The flame threw a ghastly light on their shrivelled faces; and made their ugliness appear perfectly terrible, as, in this position, they began to converse in a low voice.

"Did she say any more, Anny dear, while I was gone?" inquired the messenger.

"Not a word," replied the other. "She plucked and tore at her arms for a little time; but I held her hands, and she soon dropped off. She hasn't much strength in her, so I easily kept her quiet. I ain't so weak for an old woman, although I am on parish allowance—no, no!"

"Did she drink the hot wine the doctor said she was to have?" demanded the first.

"I tried to get it down," rejoined the other. "But her teeth were tight set; and she clenched the mug so hard that it was as much as I could do to get it back again. So *I* drank it; and it did me good!"

Looking cautiously round, to ascertain that they were not overheard, the two hags cowered nearer the fire, and chuckled heartily.

"I mind the time," said the first speaker, "when she would have done the same, and made rare fun of it afterwards."

"Ay, that she would," rejoined the other; "she had a merry heart. A many, many, beautiful corpses she laid out, as nice and neat as wax-work. My old eyes have seen them—ay, and these old hands touched them too; for I have helped her, scores of times."

Stretching forth her trembling fingers as she spoke, the old creature shook them exultingly before her face; and fumbling in her pocket, brought out an old time-discoloured tin snuff-box, from which she shook a few grains into the outstretched palm of her companion, and a few more into her own. While they were thus employed, the matron, who had been impatiently watching until the dying woman should awaken from her stupor, joined them by the fire, and sharply asked how long she was to wait.

"Not long, mistress," replied the second woman, looking up into her face. "We have none of us long to wait for Death. Patience, patience! He'll be here soon enough for us all."

"Hold your tongue, you doting idiot!" said the matron, sternly. "You, Martha, tell me; has she been in this way before?"

"Often," answered the first woman.

"But will never be again," added the second one; "that is, she'll never wake again but once—and mind, mistress, that won't be for long."

"Long or short," said the matron, snappishly, "she won't find me here when she does wake; and take care, both of you, how you worry me again for nothing. It's no part of my duty to see all the old women in the house die, and I won't—that's more. Mind that, you impudent old harridans. If you make a fool of me again, I'll soon cure you, I warrant you!"

She was bouncing away, when a cry from the two women, who had turned towards the bed, caused her to look round. The patient had raised herself upright, and was stretching her arms towards them.

"Who's that?" she cried, in a hollow voice.

"Hush, hush!" said one of the women, stooping over her. "Lie down, lie down!"

"I'll never lie down again alive!" said the woman, struggling. "I *will* tell her! Come here! Nearer! Let me whisper in your ear."

She clutched the matron by the arm; and forcing her into a chair by the bedside, was about to speak, when looking round, she caught sight of the two old women bending forward in the attitude of eager listeners.

"Turn them away," said the woman, drowsily; "make haste! make haste!"

The two old crones, chiming in together, began pouring out many piteous lamentations that the poor dear was too far gone to know her best friends; and were uttering sundry protestations that they would never leave her, when the superior pushed them from the room, closed the door, and returned to the bedside. On being excluded, the old ladies changed their tone, and cried through the keyhole that old Sally was drunk; which, indeed, was not unlikely; since, in addition to a moderate dose of opium prescribed by the apothecary, she was labouring under the effects of a final taste of gin-and-water which had been privily administered, in the openness of their hearts, by the worthy old ladies themselves.

"Now listen to me," said the dying woman, aloud, as if making a great effort to revive one latent spark of energy. "In this very room—in this very bed—I once nursed a pretty young creetur', that was brought into the house with her feet cut and bruised with walking, and all soiled with dust and blood. She gave birth to a boy, and died. Let me think—what was the year again?"

"Never mind the year," said the impatient auditor; "what about her?"

"Ay," murmured the sick woman, relapsing into her former drowsy state, "what about her?—what about—I know!" she cried, jumping fiercely up: her face flushed, and her eyes starting from her head—"I robbed her, so I did! She wasn't cold—I tell you she wasn't cold, when I stole it!"

"Stole what, for God's sake?" cried the matron, with a gesture as if she would call for help.

"*It!*" replied the woman, laying her hand over the other's mouth. "The only thing she had. She wanted clothes to keep her warm, and food to eat; but she had kept it safe, and had it in her bosom. It was gold, I tell you! Rich gold, that might have saved her life!"

"Gold!" echoed the matron, bending eagerly over the woman as she fell back. "Go on, go on—yes—what of it? Who was the mother? When was it?"

"She charged me to keep it safe," replied the woman, with a groan, "and trusted me as the only woman about her. I stole it in my heart when she first showed it me hanging round her neck; and the child's death, perhaps, is on me besides! They would have treated him better, if they had known it all!"

"Known what?" asked the other. "Speak!"

"The boy grew so like his mother," said the woman, rambling on, and not heeding the question, "that I could never forget it when I saw his face. Poor girl! poor girl! She was so young, too! Such a gentle lamb! Wait; there's more to tell. I have not told you all, have I?"

"No, no," replied the matron, inclining her head to catch the words, as they came more faintly from the dying woman. "Be quick, or it may be too late!"

"The mother," said the woman, making a more violent effort than before; "the mother, when the pains of death first came upon her, whispered in my ear that if her baby was born alive, and thrived, the day might come when it would not feel so much disgraced to hear its poor young mother named. 'And oh, kind Heaven!' she said, folding her thin hands together, 'whether it be boy or girl, raise up some friends for it in this troubled world; and take pity upon a lonely desolate child, abandoned to its mercy!'"

"The boy's name?" demanded the matron.

"They *called* him Oliver," replied the woman, feebly. "The gold I stole was——"

"Yes, yes—what?" cried the other.

She was bending eagerly over the woman to hear her reply; but drew back, instinctively, as she once again rose, slowly and stiffly, into a sitting posture; then, clutching the coverlid with both hands, muttered some indistinct sounds in her throat, and fell lifeless on the bed.

.   .   .   .

"Stone dead!" said one of the old women, hurrying in, as soon as the door was opened.

"And nothing to tell, after all," rejoined the matron, walking carelessly away.

The two crones, to all appearance, too busily occupied in the preparations for their dreadful duties to make any reply, were left alone: hovering about the body.

CHAPTER XXV.

WHEREIN THIS HISTORY REVERTS TO MR. FAGIN AND COMPANY.

WHILE these things were passing in the country workhouse, Mr. Fagin sat in the old den—the same from which Oliver had been removed by the girl—brooding over a dull, smoky fire. He held a pair of bellows upon his knee, with which he had apparently been endeavouring to rouse it into more cheerful action; but he had fallen into deep thought; and with his arms folded on them, and his chin resting on his thumbs, fixed his eyes, abstractedly, on the rusty bars.

At a table behind him sat the Artful Dodger, Master Charles Bates, and Mr. Chitling: all intent upon a game of whist; the Artful taking dummy against Master Bates and Mr. Chitling. The countenance of the first-named gentleman, peculiarly intelligent at all times, acquired great additional interest from his close observance of the game, and his attentive perusal of Mr. Chitling's hand; upon which, from time to time, as occasion served, he bestowed a variety of earnest glances: wisely regulating his own play by the result of his observations upon his neighbour's cards. It being a cold night, the Dodger wore his hat, as, indeed, was often his custom within doors. He also sustained a clay pipe between his teeth, which he only removed for a brief space when he deemed it necessary to apply for refreshment to a quart pot upon the table, which stood ready filled with gin-and-water for the accommodation of the company.

Master Bates was also attentive to the play; but being of a more excitable nature than his accomplished friend, it was observable that he more frequently applied himself to the gin-and-water; and moreover indulged in many jests and irrelevant remarks, all highly unbecoming a scientific rubber. Indeed, the Artful, presuming upon their close attachment, more than once took occasion to reason gravely with his companion upon these improprieties: all of which remonstrances, Master Bates received in extremely good part; merely requesting his friend to be "blowed," or to insert his head in a sack, or replying with some other neatly-turned witticism of a similar kind, the happy application of which, excited considerable admiration in the mind of Mr. Chitling. It was remarkable that the latter gentleman and his partner invariably lost; and that the circumstance, so far from angering Master Bates, appeared to afford him the highest amusement, inasmuch as he laughed most uproariously at the end of every deal, and protested that he had never seen such a jolly game in all his born days.

"That's two doubles and the rub," said Mr. Chitling, with a very long face, as he drew half-a-crown from his waistcoat-pocket. "I never see such a feller as you, Jack; you win everything. Even when we've good cards, Charley and I can't make nothing of 'em."

Either the matter or the manner of this remark, which was made very ruefully, delighted Charley Bates so much, that his consequent shout of laughter roused the Jew from his reverie, and induced him to inquire what was the matter.

"Matter, Fagin!" cried Charley. "I wish you had watched the play. Tommy Chitling hasn't won a point; and I went partners with him against the Artful and dum."

"Ay, ay!" said the Jew, with a grin, which sufficiently demonstrated that he was at no loss to understand the reason. "Try 'em again, Tom; try 'em again."

"No more of it for me, thankee, Fagin," replied Mr. Chitling; "I've had enough. That 'ere Dodger has such a run of luck that there's no standing again' him."

"Ha! ha! my dear," replied the Jew, "you must get up very early in the morning, to win against the Dodger."

"Morning!" said Charley Bates; "you must put your boots on overnight; and have a telescope at each eye, and a opera-glass between your shoulders, if you want to come over him."

Mr. Dawkins received these handsome compliments with much philosophy, and offered to cut any gentleman in company, for the first picture-card, at a shilling a time. Nobody accepting the challenge, and his pipe being by this time smoked out, he proceeded to amuse himself by sketching a ground-plan of Newgate on the table with the piece of chalk which had served him in lieu of counters; whistling, meantime, with peculiar shrillness.

"How precious dull you are, Tommy!" said the Dodger, stopping short when there had been a long silence; and addressing Mr. Chitling. "What do you think he's thinking of, Fagin?"

"How should I know, my dear?" replied the Jew, looking round as he plied the bellows. "About his losses, maybe; or the little retirement in the country that he's just left, eh? Ha! ha! Is that it, my dear?"

"Not a bit of it," replied the Dodger, stopping the subject of discourse as Mr. Chitling was about to reply. "What do you say, Charley?"

"I should say," replied Master Bates, with a grin, "that he was uncommon sweet upon Betsy. See how he's a-blushing! Oh, my eye! here's a merry-go-rounder! Tommy Chitling's in love! Oh, Fagin, Fagin! what a spree!"

Thoroughly overpowered with the notion of Mr. Chitling being the victim of the tender passion, Master Bates threw himself back in his chair with such violence, that he lost his balance, and pitched over upon the floor; where (the accident abating nothing of his merriment) he lay at full length until his laugh was over, when he resumed his former position, and began another.

"Never mind him, my dear," said the Jew, winking at Mr. Dawkins, and giving Master Bates a reproving tap with the nozzle of the bellows. "Betsy's a fine girl. Stick up to her, Tom. Stick up to her."

"What I mean to say, Fagin," replied Mr. Chitling, very red in the face, "is that that isn't anything to anybody here."

"No more it is," replied the Jew; "Charley will talk. Don't mind him, my dear; don't mind him. Betsy's a fine girl. Do as she bids you, Tom, and you will make your fortune."

"So I do do, as she bids me," replied Mr. Chitling; "I shouldn't have been milled, if it hadn't been for her advice. But it turned out a good job for you; didn't it,

Fagin! And what's six weeks of it? It must come, some time or another, and why not in the winter time when you don't want to go out a-walking so much; eh, Fagin?"

"Ah, to be sure, my dear," replied the Jew.

"You wouldn't mind it again, Tom, would you," asked the Dodger, winking upon Charley and the Jew, "if Bet was all right?"

"I mean to say that I shouldn't," replied Tom, angrily. "There, now! Ah! Who'll say as much as that, I should like to know; eh, Fagin?"

"Nobody, my dear," replied the Jew; "not a soul, Tom. I don't know one of 'em that would do it besides you; not one of 'em, my dear."

"I might have got clear off, if I'd split upon her; mightn't I, Fagin?" angrily pursued the poor half-witted dupe. "A word from me would have done it; wouldn't it, Fagin?"

"To be sure it would, my dear," replied the Jew.

"But I didn't blab it; did I, Fagin?" demanded Tom, pouring question upon question with great volubility.

"No, no, to be sure," replied the Jew; "you were too stout-hearted for that. A deal too stout, my dear!"

"Perhaps I was," rejoined Tom, looking round; "and if I was, what's to laugh at, in that; eh, Fagin?"

The Jew, perceiving that Mr. Chitling was considerably roused, hastened to assure him that nobody was laughing; and, to prove the gravity of the company, appealed to Master Bates, the principal offender. But, unfortunately, Charley, in opening his mouth to reply that he was never more serious in his life, was unable to prevent the escape of such a violent roar, that the abused Mr. Chitling, without any preliminary ceremonies, rushed across the room and aimed a blow at the offender, who, being skilful in evading pursuit, ducked to avoid it; and chose his time so well that it lighted on the chest of the merry old gentleman, and caused him to stagger to the wall, where he stood panting for breath, while Mr. Chitling looked on, in intense dismay.

"Hark!" cried the Dodger at this moment, "I heard the tinkler." Catching up the light, he crept softly up stairs.

The bell was rung again, with some impatience, while the party were in darkness. After a short pause, the Dodger reappeared; and whispered Fagin mysteriously.

"What!" cried the Jew, "alone?"

The Dodger nodded in the affirmative; and, shading the flame of the candle with his hand, gave Charley Bates a private intimation, in dumb show, that he had better not be funny just then. Having performed this friendly office, he fixed his eyes on the Jew's face, and awaited his directions.

The old man bit his yellow fingers, and meditated for some seconds; his face working with agitation the while, as if he dreaded something, and feared to know the worst. At length he raised his head.

"Where is he?" he asked.

The Dodger pointed to the floor above; and made a gesture, as if to leave the room.

"Yes," said the Jew, answering the mute inquiry; "bring him down. Hush! Quiet, Charley! Gently, Tom! Scarce, scarce!"

This brief direction to Charley Bates, and his recent antagonist, was softly and immediately obeyed. There was no sound of their whereabout, when the Dodger descended the stairs, bearing the light in his hand, and followed by a man in a coarse smock-frock; who, after casting a hurried glance round the room, pulled off a large wrapper which had concealed the lower portion of his face, and disclosed: all haggard, unwashed, and unshorn: the features of flash Toby Crackit.

"How are you, Faguey?" said this worthy, nodding to the Jew. "Pop that shawl away in my castor, Dodger, so that I may know where to find it when I cut; that's the time of day! You'll be a fine young cracksman afore the old file now."

With these words he pulled up the smock-frock; and, winding it round his middle, drew a chair to the fire, and placed his feet upon the hob.

"See there, Faguey," he said, pointing disconsolately to his top-boots; "not a drop of Day and Martin since you know when; not a bubble of blacking, by——! But don't look at me in that way, man. All in good time; I can't talk about business till I've eat and drank; so produce the sustenance, and let's have a quiet fill-out for the first time these three days!"

The Jew motioned to the Dodger to place what eatables there were, upon the table; and, seating himself opposite the housebreaker, waited his leisure.

To judge from appearances, Toby was by no means in a hurry to open the conversation. At first, the Jew contented himself with patiently watching his countenance, as if to gain from its expression some clue to the intelligence he brought; but in vain. He looked tired and worn, but there was the same complacent repose upon his features that they always wore; and through dirt, and beard, and whisker, there still shone, unimpaired, the self-satisfied smirk of flash Toby Crackit. Then, the Jew, in an agony of impatience, watched every morsel he put into his mouth; pacing up and down the room, meanwhile, in irrepressible excitement. It was all of no use. Toby continued to eat with the utmost outward indifference, until he could eat no more; then, ordering the Dodger out, he closed the door, mixed a glass of spirits and water, and composed himself for talking.

"First and foremost, Faguey," said Toby.

"Yes, yes!" interposed the Jew, drawing up his chair.

Mr. Crackit stopped to take a draught of spirits and water, and to declare that the gin was excellent; and then, placing his feet against the low mantelpiece, so as to bring his boots to about the level of his eyes, quietly resumed.

"First and foremost, Faguey," said the housebreaker, "how's Bill?"

"What!" screamed the Jew, starting from his seat.

"Why, you don't mean to say——" began Toby, turning pale.

"Mean!" cried the Jew, stamping furiously on the ground. "Where are they? Sikes and the boy! Where are they? Where have they been? Where are they hiding? Why have they not been here?"

"The crack failed," said Toby, faintly.

"I know it," replied the Jew, tearing a newspaper from his pocket, and pointing to it. "What more?"

"They fired and hit the boy. We cut over the fields at the back, with him between us—straight as the crow flies—through hedge and ditch. They gave chase. D——me! the whole country was awake, and the dogs upon us."

"The boy!" gasped the Jew.

"Bill had him on his back, and scudded like the wind. We stopped to take him between us; his head hung down, and he was cold. They were close upon our heels; every man for himself, and each from the gallows! We parted company, and left the youngster lying in a ditch. Alive or dead, that's all I know about him."

The Jew stopped to hear no more; but uttering a loud yell, and twining his hands in his hair, rushed from the room, and from the house.

CHAPTER XXVI.

IN WHICH A MYSTERIOUS CHARACTER APPEARS UPON THE SCENE; AND MANY THINGS, INSEPARABLE FROM THIS HISTORY, ARE DONE AND PERFORMED.

THE old man had gained the street corner, before he began to recover the effect of Toby Crackit's intelligence. He had relaxed nothing of his unusual speed; but was still pressing onward, in the same wild and disordered manner, when the sudden dashing past of a carriage: and a boisterous cry from the foot passengers, who saw his danger: drove him back upon the pavement. Avoiding, as much as possible, all the main streets; and skulking only through the byways and alleys; he at length emerged on Snow Hill. Here he walked even faster than before; nor did he linger until he had again turned into a court; when, as if conscious that he was now in his proper element, he fell into his usual shuffling pace, and seemed to breathe more freely.

Near to the spot on which Snow Hill and Holborn Hill meet, there opens: upon the right hand as you come out of the City: a narrow and dismal alley leading to Saffron Hill. In its filthy shops are exposed for sale bunches of second-hand silk handkerchiefs, of all sizes and patterns; for here reside the traders who purchase them from pick-pockets. Hundreds of these handkerchiefs hang dangling from pegs outside the windows or flaunting from the door-posts; and the shelves, within, are piled with them. Confined as the limits of Field Lane are, it had its barber, its coffee-shop, its beer-shop, and its fried-fish warehouse. It is a commercial colony of itself: the emporium of petty larceny: visited at early morning, and setting-in of dusk, by silent merchants, who traffic in dark back-parlours; and who go as strangely as they come. Here, the clothes-man, the shoe-vamper, and the rag-merchant, display their goods, as signboards to the petty thief; here, stores of old iron and bones, and heaps of mildewy fragments of woollen-stuff and linen, rust and rot in the grimy cellars.

It was into this place that the Jew turned. He was well known to the sallow denizens of the lane; for such of them as were on the look-out to buy or sell, nodded, familiarly, as he passed along. He replied to their salutations in the same way; but bestowed no closer recognition until he reached the further end of the alley; when he stopped, to address a salesman of small stature, who had squeezed as much of his person into a child's chair as the chair would hold, and was smoking a pipe at his warehouse door.

"Why, the sight of you, Mr. Fagin, would cure the hoptalmy!" said this respectable trader, in acknowledgment of the Jew's inquiry after his health.

"The neighbourhood was a little too hot, Lively," said Fagin, elevating his eyebrows, and crossing his hands upon his shoulders.

"Well, I've heerd that complaint of it, once or twice before," replied the trader; "but it soon cools down again; don't you find it so?"

Fagin nodded in the affirmative. Pointing in the direction of Saffron Hill, he inquired whether any one was up yonder to-night.

"At the Cripples?" inquired the man.

The Jew nodded.

"Let me see," pursued the merchant, reflecting. "Yes, there's some half-dozen of 'em gone in, that I knows. I don't think your friend's there."

"Sikes is not, I suppose?" inquired the Jew, with a disappointed countenance.

"*Non istwentus*, as the lawyers say," replied the little man, shaking his head, and looking amazingly sly. "Have you got anything in my line to-night?"

"Nothing to-night," said the Jew, turning away.

"Are you going up to the Cripples, Fagin?" cried the little man, calling after him. "Stop! I don't mind if I have a drop there with you."

But as the Jew, looking back, waved his hand to intimate that he preferred being alone; and, moreover, as the little man could not very easily disengage himself from the chair; the sign of the Cripples was, for a time, bereft of the advantage of Mr. Lively's presence. By the time he had got upon his legs, the Jew had disappeared; so Mr. Lively, after ineffectually standing on tiptoe, in the hope of catching sight of him, again forced himself into the little chair, and, exchanging a shake of the head with a lady in the opposite shop, in which doubt and mistrust were plainly mingled, resumed his pipe with a grave demeanour.

The Three Cripples, or rather the Cripples: which was the sign by which the establishment was familiarly known to its patrons: was the same public-house in which Mr. Sikes and his dog have already figured. Merely making a sign to a man at the bar, Fagin walked straight up stairs; and opening the door of a room, and softly insinuating himself into the chamber, looked anxiously about: shading his eyes with his hand, as if in search of some particular person.

The room was illuminated by two gas-lights; the glare of which was prevented by the barred shutters, and closely-drawn curtains of faded red, from being visible outside. The ceiling was blackened, to prevent its colour from being injured by the flaring of the lamps; and the place was so full of dense tobacco smoke, that at first it was scarcely possible to discern anything more. By degrees, however, as some of it cleared away through the open door, an assemblage of heads, as confused as the noises that greeted the ear, might be made out; and as the eye grew more accustomed to the scene, the spectator gradually became aware of the presence of a numerous company, male and female, crowded round a long table: at the upper end of which, sat a chairman with a hammer of office in his hand; while a professional gentleman, with a bluish nose, and his face tied up for the benefit of a toothache, presided at a jingling piano in a remote corner.

As Fagin stepped softly in, the professional gentleman, running over the keys by way of prelude, occasioned a general cry of order for a song; which, having subsided, a young lady proceeded to entertain the company with a ballad in four verses, between each of which the accompanyist played the melody, all through, as loud as he could. When this was over, the chairman gave a sentiment; after which, the professional gentlemen on the chairman's right and left volunteered a duet, and sang it, with great applause.

It was curious to observe some faces which stood out prominently from among the group. There was the chairman himself (the landlord of the house), a coarse, rough, heavy-built fellow, who, while the songs were proceeding, rolled his eyes hither and thither, and, seeming to give himself up to joviality, had an eye for everything that was done, and an ear for everything that was said—and sharp ones, too. Near him were the singers: receiving, with professional indifference, the compliments of the company, and applying themselves, in turn, to a dozen proffered glasses of spirits and water, tendered by their more boisterous admirers; whose countenances, expressive of almost every vice in almost every grade, irresistibly attracted the attention, by their very repulsiveness. Cunning, ferocity, and drunkenness in all its stages, were there, in their strongest aspects; and women: some with the last lingering tinge of their early freshness almost fading as you looked: others with every mark and stamp of their sex utterly beaten out, and presenting but one loathesome blank of profligacy and crime; some mere girls, others but young women, and none past the prime of life; formed the darkest and saddest portion of this dreary picture.

Fagin, troubled by no grave emotions, looked eagerly from face to face while these proceedings were in progress; but apparently without meeting that of which he was in search. Succeeding, at length, in catching the eye of the man who occupied the chair, he beckoned to him slightly, and left the room, as quietly as he had entered it.

"What can I do for you, Mr. Fagin?" inquired the man, as he followed him out to the landing. "Won't you join us? They'll be delighted, every one of 'em."

The Jew shook his head impatiently, and said in a whisper, "Is *he* here?"

"No," replied the man.

"And no news of Barney?" inquired Fagin.

"None," replied the landlord of the Cripples; for it was he. "He won't stir till it's all safe. Depend on it, they're on the scent down there; and that if he moved, he'd blow upon the thing at once. He's all right enough, Barney is, else I should have heard of him. I'll pound it, that Barney's managing properly. Let him alone for that."

"Will *he* be here to-night?" asked the Jew, laying the same emphasis on the pronoun as before.

"Monks, do you mean?" inquired the landlord, hesitating.

"Hush!" said the Jew. "Yes."

"Certain," replied the man, drawing a gold watch from his fob; "I expected him here, before now. If you'll wait ten minutes, he'll be——"

"No, no," said the Jew, hastily; as though, however desirous he might be to see the person in question, he was nevertheless relieved by his absence. "Tell him I came here to see him; and that he must come to me to-night. No, say to-morrow. As he is not here, to-morrow will be time enough."

"Good!" said the man. "Nothing more?"

"Not a word now," said the Jew, descending the stairs.

"I say," said the other, looking over the rails, and speaking in a hoarse whisper; "what a time this would be for a sell! I've got Phil Barker here: so drunk, that a boy might take him."

"Aha! But it's not Phil Barker's time," said the Jew, looking up. "Phil has something more to do, before we can afford to part with him; so go back to the company, my dear, and tell them to lead merry lives—*while they last.* Ha! ha! ha!"

The landlord reciprocated the old man's laugh; and returned to his guests. The Jew was no sooner alone, than his countenance resumed its former expression of anxiety and thought. After a brief reflection, he called a hack cabriolet, and bade the man drive towards Bethnal Green. He dismissed him within some quarter of a mile of Mr. Sikes's residence; and performed the short remainder of the distance, on foot.

"Now," muttered the Jew, as he knocked at the door, "if there is any deep play here, I shall have it out of you, my girl, cunning as you are."

She was in her room, the woman said. Fagin crept softly up stairs, and entered it without any previous ceremony. The girl was alone; lying with her head upon the table, and her hair straggling over it.

"She has been drinking," thought the Jew, coolly, "or perhaps she is only miserable."

The old man turned to close the door, as he made this reflection; and the noise thus occasioned, roused the girl. She eyed his crafty face narrowly, as she inquired whether there was any news, and listened to his recital of Toby Crackit's story. When it was concluded, she sank into her former attitude, but spoke not a word. She pushed the candle impatiently away; and once or twice, as she feverishly changed her position, shuffled her feet upon the ground; but this was all.

During this silence, the Jew looked restlessly about the room, as if to assure himself that there were no appearances of Sikes having covertly returned. Apparently satisfied with his inspection, he coughed twice or thrice, and made as many efforts to open a conversation; but the girl heeded him no more than if he had been made of stone. At length he made another attempt; and, rubbing his hands together, said, in his most conciliatory tone,

"And where should you think Bill was now, my dear?"

The girl moaned out some half intelligible reply, that she could not tell; and seemed, from the smothered noise that escaped her, to be crying.

"And the boy, too," said the Jew, straining his eyes to catch a glimpse of her face. "Poor leetle child! Left in a ditch, Nance; only think!"

"The child," said the girl, suddenly looking up, "is better where he is, than among us; and if no harm comes to Bill from it, I hope he lies dead in the ditch, and that his young bones may rot there."

"What!" cried the Jew, in amazement.

"Ay, I do," returned the girl, meeting his gaze. "I shall be glad to have him away from my eyes, and to know that the worst is over. I can't bear to have him about me. The sight of him turns me against myself, and all of you."

"Pooh!" said the Jew, scornfully. "You're drunk."

"Am I?" cried the girl, bitterly. "It's no fault of yours, if I am not! You'd never have me anything else, if you had your will, except now;—the humour doesn't suit you, doesn't it?"

"No!" rejoined the Jew, furiously. "It does not."

"Change it, then!" responded the girl, with a laugh.

"Change it!" exclaimed the Jew, exasperated beyond all bounds by his companion's unexpected obstinacy, and the vexation of the night, "I WILL change it! Listen to me, you drab! Listen to me, who, with six words, can strangle Sikes as surely as if I had his bull's throat between my fingers now. If he comes back, and leaves that boy behind him,—if he gets off free; and, dead or alive, he

fails to restore him to me; murder him yourself if you would have him escape Jack Ketch: and do it the moment he sets foot in this room, or, mind me, it will be too late!"

"What is all this?" cried the girl, involuntarily.

"What is it?" pursued Fagin, mad with rage. "When the boy's worth hundreds of pounds to me, am I to lose what chance threw me in the way of getting safely, through the whims of a drunken gang that I could whistle away the lives of! And me bound, too, to a born devil that only wants the will, and has the power to, to——"

Panting for breath, the old man stammered for a word; and in that instant checked the torrent of his wrath, and changed his whole demeanour. A moment before, his clenched hands had grasped the air; his eyes had dilated; and his face grown livid with passion; but now, he shrank into a chair, and, cowering together, trembled with the apprehension of having himself disclosed some hidden villainy. After a short silence, he ventured to look round at his companion. He appeared somewhat reassured, on beholding her in the same listless attitude from which he had first roused her.

"Nancy, dear!" croaked the Jew, in his usual voice. "Did you mind me, dear?"

"Don't worry me, now, Fagin!" replied the girl, raising her head languidly. "If Bill has not done it this time, he will another. He has done many a good job for you, and will do many more when he can; and when he can't, he won't; so no more about that."

"Regarding this boy, my dear?" said the Jew, rubbing the palms of his hands nervously together.

"The boy must take his chance with the rest," interrupted Nancy, hastily; "and I say again, I hope he is dead, and out of harm's way, and out of yours,—that is, if Bill comes to no harm. And if Toby got clear off, he's pretty sure to be safe; for he's worth two of him any time."

"And about what I was saying, my dear?" observed the Jew, keeping his glistening eye steadily upon her.

"You must say it all over again, if it's anything you want me to do," rejoined Nancy; "and if it is, you had better wait till to-morrow. You put me up for a minute; but now I'm stupid again."

Fagin put several other questions: all with the same drift of ascertaining whether the girl had profited by his unguarded hints; but, she answered them so readily, and was withal so utterly unmoved by his searching looks, that his original impression of her being more than a trifle in liquor, was fully confirmed. Nancy, indeed, was not exempt from a failing which was very common among the Jew's female pupils; and in which, in their tenderer years, they were rather encouraged than checked. Her disordered appearance, and a wholesome perfume of Geneva which pervaded the apartment, afforded strong confirmatory evidence of the justice of the Jew's supposition; and when, after indulging in the temporary display of violence above described, she subsided, first into dulness, and afterwards into a compound of feelings: under the influence of which, she shed tears one minute: and in the next gave utterance to various exclamations of "Never say die" and divers calculations as to what might be the amount of the odds so long as a lady or gentleman was happy: Mr. Fagin, who had had considerable experience of such matters in his time, saw, with great satisfaction, that she was very far gone indeed.

Having eased his mind by this discovery; and having accomplished his twofold object of imparting to the girl what he had that night heard, and of ascertaining, with his own eyes, that Sikes had not returned; Mr. Fagin again turned his face homeward: leaving his young friend asleep, with her head upon the table.

It was within an hour of midnight; and the weather being dark and piercing cold, he had no great temptation to loiter. The sharp wind that scoured the streets, seemed to have cleared them of passengers, as of dust and mud, for few people were abroad: and they were to all appearance hastening fast home. It blew from the right quarter for the Jew, however, and straight before it he went: trembling and shivering, as every fresh gust drove him rudely on his way.

He had reached the corner of his own street, and was already fumbling in his pocket for the door-key, when a dark figure emerged from a projecting entrance which lay in deep shadow, and, crossing the road, glided up to him unperceived.

"Fagin!" whispered a voice close to his ear.

"Ah!" said the Jew, turning quickly round, "is that——"

"Yes!" interrupted the stranger, harshly. "I have been lingering here these two hours. Where the devil have you been?"

"On your business, my dear," replied the Jew, glancing uneasily at his companion, and slackening his pace as he spoke. "On your business all night."

"Oh, of course!" said the stranger, with a sneer. "Well; and what's come of it?"

"Nothing good," said the Jew.

"Nothing bad, I hope?" said the stranger, stopping short, and turning a startled look on his companion.

The Jew shook his head, and was about to reply, when the stranger, interrupting him, motioned to the house, before which they had by this time arrived: remarking, that he had better say what he had got to say, under cover: for his blood was chilled with standing about so long, and the wind blew through him.

Fagin looked as if he could have willingly excused himself from taking home a visitor at that unseasonable hour; and, indeed, muttered something about having no fire; but his companion repeating his request in a peremptory manner, he unlocked the door, and requested him to close it softly, while he got a light.

"It's as dark as the grave," said the man, groping forward a few steps. "Make haste!"

"Shut the door," whispered Fagin from the end of the passage. As he spoke, it closed with a loud noise.

"That wasn't my doing," said the other man, feeling his way. "The wind blew it to, or it shut of its own accord; one or the other. Look sharp with the light, or I shall knock my brains out against something in this confounded hole."

Fagin stealthily descended the kitchen stairs. After a short absence, he returned with a lighted candle, and the intelligence that Toby Crackit was asleep in the back room below, and the boys in the front one. Beckoning the man to follow him, he led the way up stairs.

"We can say the few words we've got to say in here, my dear," said the Jew, throwing open a door on the first floor; "and as there are holes in the shutters, and we never show lights to our neighbours, we'll set the candle on the stairs. There!"

With these words, the Jew, stooping down, placed the candle on an upper flight of stairs, exactly opposite to the room door. This done, he led the way into the apartment; which was destitute of all moveables save a broken arm-chair, and an old couch or sofa without covering, which

stood behind the door. Upon this piece of furniture, the stranger flung himself with the air of a weary man; and the Jew, drawing up the arm-chair opposite, they sat face to face. It was not quite dark; for the door was partially open; and the candle outside threw a feeble reflection on the opposite wall.

They conversed for some time in whispers. Though nothing of the conversation was distinguishable beyond a few disjointed words here and there, a listener might easily have perceived that Fagin appeared to be defending himself against some remarks of the stranger; and that the latter was in a state of considerable irritation. They might have been talking, thus, for a quarter of an hour or more, when Monks—by which name the Jew had designated the strange man several times in the course of their colloquy—said, raising his voice a little,

"I tell you again, it was badly planned. Why not have kept him here among the rest, and made a sneaking, snivelling pickpocket of him at once?"

"Only hear him!" exclaimed the Jew, shrugging his shoulders.

"Why, do you mean to say you couldn't have done it, if you had chosen?" demanded Monks, sternly. "Haven't you done it, with other boys, scores of times? If you had had patience for a twelvemonth, at most, couldn't you have got him convicted, and sent safely out of the kingdom; perhaps for life?"

"Who's turn would that have served, my dear?" inquired the Jew, humbly.

"Mine," replied Monks.

"But not mine," said the Jew, submissively. "He might have become of use to me. When there are two parties to a bargain, it is only reasonable that the interests of both should be consulted; is it, my good friend?"

"What then?" demanded Monks, sulkily.

"I saw it was not easy to train him to the business," replied the Jew; "he was not like other boys in the same circumstances."

"Curse him, no!" muttered the man, "or he would have been a thief, long ago."

"I had no hold upon him, to make him worse," pursued the Jew, anxiously watching the countenance of his companion. "His hand was not in. I had nothing to frighten him with; which we always must have in the beginning, or we labour in vain. What could I do? Send him out with the Dodger and Charley? We had enough of that, at first, my dear; I trembled for us all."

"*That* was not my doing," observed Monks.

"No, no, my dear!" renewed the Jew. "And I don't quarrel with it now; because, if it had never happened, you might never have clapped eyes upon the boy to notice him, and so led to the discovery that it was him you were looking for. Well; I got him back for you by means of the girl; and then *she* begins to favour him."

"Throttle the girl!" said Monks, impatiently.

"Why, we can't afford to do that just now, my dear," replied the Jew, smiling; "and, besides, that sort of thing is not in our way; or, one of these days, I might be glad to have it done. I know what these girls are, Monks, well. As soon as the boy begins to harden, she'll care no more for him, than for a block of wood. You want him made a thief. If he is alive, I can make him one from this time; and if—if—" said the Jew, drawing nearer to the other,—"it's not likely, mind,—but if the worst comes to the worst, and he is dead——"

"It's no fault of mine if he is!" interposed the other

man, with a look of terror, and clasping the Jew's arm with trembling hands. "Mind that, Fagin! I had no hand in it. Anything but his death, I told you from the first. I won't shed blood; it's always found out, and haunts a man besides. If they shot him dead, I was not the cause; do you hear me? Fire this infernal den! What's that?"

"What!" cried the Jew, grasping the coward round the body, with both arms, as he sprang to his feet. "Where?"

"Yonder!" replied the man, glaring at the opposite wall. "The shadow! I saw the shadow of a woman, in a cloak and bonnet, pass along the wainscot like a breath!"

The Jew released his hold; and they rushed tumultuously from the room. The candle, wasted by the draught, was standing where it had been placed. It showed them only the empty staircase, and their own white faces. They listened intently; but a profound silence reigned throughout the house.

"It's your fancy," said the Jew, taking up the light, and turning to his companion.

"I'll swear I saw it!" replied Monks, trembling. "It was bending forward, when I saw it first; and when I spoke, it darted away."

The Jew glanced contemptuously at the pale face of his associate, and, telling him he could follow, if he pleased, ascended the stairs. They looked into all the rooms; they were cold, bare, and empty. They descended into the passage, and thence into the cellars below. The green damp hung upon the low walls; and the tracks of the snail and slug glistened in the light of the candle; but all was still as death.

"What do you think now?" said the Jew, when they had regained the passage. "Besides ourselves, there's not a creature in the house except Toby and the boys; and they're safe enough. See here!"

As a proof of the fact, the Jew drew forth two keys from his pocket; and explained, that when he first went down stairs, he had locked them in, to prevent any intrusion on the conference.

This accumulated testimony effectually staggered Mr. Monks. His protestations had gradually become less and less vehement as they proceeded in their search without making any discovery; and, now, he gave vent to several very grim laughs, and confessed it could only have been his excited imagination. He declined any renewal of the conversation, however, for that night: suddenly remembering that it was past one o'clock; and so the amiable couple parted.

CHAPTER XXVII.

ATONES FOR THE UNPOLITENESS OF A FORMER CHAPTER; WHICH DESERTED A LADY, MOST UNCEREMONIOUSLY.

As it would be, by no means, seemly in a humble author to keep so mighty a personage as a beadle waiting, with his back to the fire, and the skirts of his coat gathered up under his arms, until such time as it might suit his pleasure to relieve him; and as it would still less become his station, or his gallantry, to involve in the same neglect a lady on whom that beadle had looked with an eye of tenderness and affection, and in whose ear he had whispered sweet words, which, coming from such a quarter, might well thrill the bosom of maid or matron of whatsoever degree; the historian whose pen traces these words—trusting that he knows his place, and that he entertains a becoming reverence for those upon earth to whom high and important authority is delegated—hastens to pay them that respect which their position demands, and to treat them with all that duteous ceremony which their exalted rank, and (by consequence) great virtues, imperatively claim at his hands. Towards this end, indeed, he had purposed to introduce, in this place, a dissertation touching the divine right of beadles, and elucidative of the position, that a beadle can do no wrong; which could not fail to have been both pleasurable and profitable to the right-minded reader, but which he is unfortunately compelled, by want of time and space, to postpone to some more convenient and fitting opportunity; on the arrival of which, he will be prepared to show, that a beadle properly constituted: that is to say, a parochial beadle, attached to a parochial workhouse, and attending in his official capacity the parochial church: is, in right and virtue of his office, possessed of all the excellences and best qualities of humanity; and that to none of those excellences, can mere companies' beadles, or court-of-law beadles, or even chapel-of-ease beadles (save the last, and they in a very lowly and inferior degree), lay the remotest sustainable claim.

Mr. Bumble had re-counted the tea-spoons, re-weighed the sugar-tongs, made a closer inspection of the milk-pot, and ascertained to a nicety the exact condition of the furniture, down to the very horsehair seats of the chairs; and had repeated each process full half-a-dozen times; before he began to think that it was time for Mrs. Corney to return. Thinking begets thinking; and, as there were no sounds of Mrs. Corney's approach, it occurred to Mr. Bumble that it would be an innocent and virtuous way of spending the time, if he were further to allay his curiosity by a cursory glance at the interior of Mrs. Corney's chest of drawers.

Having listened at the keyhole, to assure himself that nobody was approaching the chamber, Mr. Bumble, beginning at the bottom, proceeded to make himself acquainted with the contents of the three long drawers: which, being filled with various garments of good fashion and texture, carefully preserved between two layers of old newspapers, speckled with dried lavender: seemed to yield him exceeding satisfaction. Arriving, in course of time, at the right-hand corner drawer (in which was the key), and beholding therein a small padlocked box, which, being shaken, gave forth a pleasant sound, as of the chinking of coin, Mr. Bumble returned with a stately walk to the fire-place; and, resuming his old attitude, said, with a grave and determined air, "I'll do it!" He followed up this remarkable declaration, by shaking his head in a waggish manner for ten minutes, as though he were remonstrating with himself for being such a pleasant dog; and then, he took a view of his legs in profile, with much seeming pleasure and interest.

He was still placidly engaged in this latter survey, when Mrs. Corney, hurrying into the room, threw herself, in a breathless state, on a chair by the fireside; and covering her eyes with one hand, placed the other over her heart, and gasped for breath.

"Mrs. Corney," said Mr. Bumble, stooping over the matron, "what is this, ma'am? Has anything happened, ma'am? Pray answer me; I'm on—on—" Mr. Bumble, in his alarm, could not immediately think of the word "tenter-hooks," so he said, "broken bottles."

"Oh, Mr. Bumble!" cried the lady, "I have been so dreadfully put out!"

"Put out, ma'am!" exclaimed Mr. Bumble; "who has dared to—? I know!" said Mr. Bumble, checking himself, with native majesty, "this is them wicious paupers!"

"It's dreadful to think of!" said the lady, shuddering.

"Then *don't* think of it, ma'am," rejoined Mr. Bumble.

"I can't help it," whimpered the lady.

"Then take something, ma'am," said Mr. Bumble, soothingly. "A little of the wine?"

"Not for the world!" replied Mrs. Corney. "I couldn't, —oh! The top shelf in the right-hand corner—oh!" Uttering these words, the good lady pointed, distractedly, to the cupboard; and underwent a convulsion from internal spasms. Mr. Bumble rushed to the closet; and, snatching a pint green-glass bottle from the shelf thus incoherently indicated, filled a tea-cup with its contents, and held it to the lady's lips.

"I'm better now," said Mrs. Corney, falling back, after drinking half of it.

Mr. Bumble raised his eyes piously to the ceiling in thankfulness; and, bringing them down again to the brim of the cup, lifted it to his nose.

"Peppermint," exclaimed Mrs. Corney, in a faint voice, smiling gently on the beadle as she spoke. "Try it! There's a little—a little something else in it."

Mr. Bumble tasted the medicine with a doubtful look; smacked his lips; took another taste; and put the cup down empty.

"It's very comforting," said Mrs. Corney.

"Very much so indeed, ma'am," said the beadle. As he spoke, he drew a chair beside the matron, and tenderly inquired what had happened to distress her.

"Nothing," replied Mrs. Corney. "I am a foolish, excitable, weak creetur."

"Not weak, ma'am," retorted Mr. Bumble, drawing his chair a little closer. "Are you a weak creetur, Mrs. Corney?"

"We are all weak creeturs," said Mrs. Corney, laying down a general principle.

"So we are," said the beadle.

Nothing was said, on either side, for a minute or two afterwards; by the expiration of that time, Mr. Bumble had illustrated the position by removing his left arm from the back of Mrs. Corney's chair, where it had previously rested: to Mrs. Corney's apron-string, round which it gradually became entwined.

"We are all weak creeturs," said Mr. Bumble.

Mrs. Corney sighed.

"Don't sigh, Mrs. Corney," said Mr. Bumble.

"I can't help it," said Mrs. Corney. And she sighed again.

"This is a very comfortable room, ma'am," said Mr. Bumble, looking round. "Another room and this, ma'am, would be a complete thing."

"It would be too much for one," murmured the lady.

"But not for two, ma'am," rejoined Mr. Bumble, in soft accents. "Eh, Mrs. Corney?"

Mrs. Corney drooped her head, when the beadle said this; the beadle drooped his, to get a view of Mrs. Corney's face. Mrs. Corney, with great propriety, turned her head away, and released her hand to get at her pocket-handkerchief; but insensibly replaced it in that of Mr. Bumble.

"The board allow you coals, don't they, Mrs. Corney?" inquired the beadle, affectionately pressing her hand.

"And candles," replied Mrs. Corney, slightly returning the pressure.

"Coals, candles, and house-rent free," said Mr. Bumble. "Oh, Mrs. Corney, what a angel you are!"

The lady was not proof against this burst of feeling. She sank into Mr. Bumble's arms; and that gentleman, in his agitation, imprinted a passionate kiss upon her chaste nose.

"Such porochial perfection!" exclaimed Mr. Bumble, rapturously. "You know that Mr. Slout is worse to-night, my fascinator?"

"Yes," replied Mrs. Corney, bashfully.

"He can't live a week, the doctor says," pursued Mr. Bumble. "He is the master of this establishment; his death will cause a wacancy; that wacancy must be filled up. Oh, Mrs. Corney, what a prospect this opens! What a opportunity for a joining of hearts and housekeepings!"

Mrs. Corney sobbed.

"The little word?" said Mr. Bumble, bending over the bashful beauty. "The one little, little, little word, my blessed Corney?"

"Ye—ye—yes!" sighed out the matron.

"One more," pursued the beadle; "compose your darling feelings for only one more. When is it to come off?"

Mrs. Corney twice essayed to speak; and twice failed. At length, summoning up courage, she threw her arms round Mr. Bumble's neck, and said, it might be as soon as ever he pleased, and that he was "a irresistible duck."

Matters being thus amicably and satisfactorily arranged, the contract was solemnly ratified in another teacupful of the peppermint mixture; which was rendered the more necessary, by the flutter and agitation of the lady's spirits. While it was being disposed of, she acquainted Mr. Bumble with the old woman's decease.

"Very good," said that gentleman, sipping his peppermint. "I'll call at Sowerberry's as I go home, and tell him to send to-morrow morning. Was it that as frightened you, love?"

"It wasn't anything particular, dear," said the lady, evasively.

"It must have been something, love," urged Mr. Bumble. "Won't you tell your own B.?"

"Not now," rejoined the lady; "one of these days. After we're married, dear."

"After we're married!" exclaimed Mr. Bumble. "It wasn't any impudence from any of them male paupers as——"

"No, no, love!" interposed the lady, hastily.

"If I thought it was," continued Mr. Bumble; "if I thought as any one of 'em had dared to lift his wulgar eyes to that lovely countenance——"

"They wouldn't have dared to do it, love," responded the lady.

"They had better not!" said Mr. Bumble, clenching his fist. "Let me see any man, porochial or extra-porochial, as would presume to do it; and I can tell him that he wouldn't do it, a second time!"

Unembellished by any violence of gesticulation, this might have seemed no very high compliment to the lady's charms; but, as Mr. Bumble accompanied the threat with many warlike gestures, she was much touched with this proof of his devotion; and protested, with great admiration, that he was indeed a dove.

The dove then turned up his coat-collar, and put on his cocked-hat; and, having exchanged a long and affectionate embrace with his future partner, once again braved the cold wind of the night; merely pausing, for a few minutes, in the male paupers' ward, to abuse them a little; with the view of satisfying himself that he could fill the office of workhouse-master with needful acerbity. Assured of his qualifications, Mr. Bumble left the building with a light heart, and bright visions of his future promotion: which served to occupy his mind until he reached the shop of the undertaker.

Now, Mr. and Mrs. Sowerberry having gone out to tea and supper: and Noah Claypole not being at any time disposed to take upon himself a greater amount of physical exertion than is necessary to a convenient performance of the two functions of eating and drinking: the shop was not closed, although it was past the usual hour of shutting-up. Mr. Bumble tapped with his cane on the counter several times; but, attracting no attention, and beholding a light shining through the glass-window of the little parlour at the back of the shop, he made bold to peep in and see what was going forward; and, when he saw what *was* going forward, he was not a little surprised.

The cloth was laid for supper; and the table was covered with bread and butter, plates and glasses; a porter-pot and a wine-bottle. At the upper end of the table, Mr. Noah Claypole lolled negligently in an easy-chair, with his legs thrown over one of the arms: an open clasp-knife in one hand, and a mass of buttered bread in the other; close beside him stood Charlotte, opening oysters from a barrel: which Mr. Claypole condescended to swallow, with remarkable avidity. A more than ordinary redness in the region of the young gentleman's nose, and a kind of fixed wink in his right eye, denoted that he was in a slight degree intoxicated; and these symptoms were confirmed by the intense relish with which he took his oysters, for which nothing but a strong appreciation of their cooling properties, in cases of internal fever, could have sufficiently accounted.

"Here's a delicious fat one, Noah, dear!" said Charlotte; "try him, do; only this one."

"What a delicious thing is a oyster!" remarked Mr. Claypole, after he had swallowed it. "What a pity it is, a number of 'em should ever make you feel uncomfortable; isn't it, Charlotte?"

"It's quite a cruelty," said Charlotte.

"So it is," acquiesced Mr. Claypole. "A'nt yer fond of oysters?"

"Not overmuch," replied Charlotte. "I like to see you eat 'em, Noah dear, better than eating 'em myself."

"Lor'!" said Noah, reflectively; "how queer!"

"Have another," said Charlotte. "Here's one with such a beautiful, delicate beard!"

"I can't manage any more," said Noah. "I'm very sorry. Come here, Charlotte, and I'll kiss yer."

"What!" said Mr. Bumble, bursting into the room. "Say that again, Sir."

Charlotte uttered a scream, and hid her face in her apron; Mr. Claypole, without making any further change in his position but suffering his legs to reach the ground, gazed at the beadle in drunken terror.

"Say it again, you vile, owdacious fellow!" said Mr. Bumble. "How dare you mention such a thing, Sir? And how dare you encourage him, you insolent minx? Kiss her!" exclaimed Mr. Bumble, in strong indignation. "Faugh!"

"I didn't mean to do it!" said Noah, blubbering. "She's always a-kissing of me, whether I like it, or not."

"Oh, Noah!" cried Charlotte, reproachfully.

"Yer are; yer know yer are!" retorted Noah. "She's always a-doing of it, Mr. Bumble, Sir; she chucks me under the chin, please Sir; and makes all manner of love!"

"Silence!" cried Mr. Bumble, sternly. "Take yourself down stairs, ma'am. Noah, you shut up the shop; say another word till your master comes home, at your peril; and, when he does come home, tell him that Mr. Bumble said he was to send a old woman's shell after breakfast to-morrow morning. Do you hear, Sir? Kissing!" cried Mr. Bumble, holding up his hands. "The sin and wickedness of the lower orders in this porochial district is frightful! If parliament don't take their abominable courses under consideration, this country's ruined, and the character of the peasantry gone for ever!" With these words, the beadle strode, with a lofty and gloomy air, from the undertaker's premises.

And now that we have accompanied him so far on his road home, and have made all necessary preparations for the old woman's funeral, let us set on foot a few inquiries after young Oliver Twist; and ascertain whether he be still lying in the ditch where Toby Crackit left him.

CHAPTER XXVIII.

LOOKS AFTER OLIVER, AND PROCEEDS WITH HIS ADVENTURES.

"WOLVES tear your throats!" muttered Sikes, grinding his teeth. "I wish I was among some of you; you'd howl the hoarser for it."

As Sikes growled forth this imprecation, with the most desperate ferocity that his desperate nature was capable of, he rested the body of the wounded boy across his bended knee; and turned his head, for an instant, to look back at his pursuers.

There was little to be made out, in the mist and darkness; but the loud shouting of men vibrated through the air; and the barking of the neighbouring dogs, roused by the sound of the alarm-bell, resounded in every direction.

"Stop, you white-livered hound!" cried the robber, shouting after Toby Crackit, who, making the best use of his long legs, was already ahead. "Stop!"

The repetition of the word brought Toby to a dead stand-still. For he was not quite satisfied that he was beyond the range of pistol-shot; and Sikes was in no mood to be played with.

"Bear a hand with the boy," roared Sikes, beckoning furiously to his confederate. "Come back!"

Toby made a show of returning; but ventured, in a low voice, broken for want of breath, to intimate considerable reluctance as he came slowly along.

"Quicker!" cried Sikes, laying the boy in a dry ditch at his feet, and drawing a pistol from his pocket. "Don't play booty with me."

At this moment the noise grew louder. Sikes, again looking round, could discern that the men who had given

MR. CLAYPOLE AS HE APPEARED WHEN HIS MASTER WAS OUT.

chase were already climbing the gate of the field in which he stood; and that a couple of dogs were some paces in advance of them.

"It's all up, Bill!" cried Toby; "drop the kid, and show 'em your heels." With this parting advice, Mr. Crackit: preferring the chance of being shot by his friend, to the certainty of being taken by his enemies: fairly turned tail, and darted off at full speed. Sikes clenched his teeth; took one look round; threw over the prostrate form of Oliver, the cape in which he had been hurriedly muffled; ran along the front of the hedge, as if to distract the attention of those behind, from the spot where the boy lay; paused, for a second, before another hedge which met it at right angles; and whirling his pistol high into the air, cleared it at a bound, and was gone.

"Ho, ho, there!" cried a tremulous voice in the rear. "Pincher! Neptune! Come here, come here!"

The dogs, who, in common with their masters, seemed to have no particular relish for the sport in which they were engaged, readily answered to the command; and three men, who had by this time advanced some distance into the field, stopped to take counsel together.

"My advice, or, leastways, I should say, my *orders*, is," said the fattest man of the party, "that we 'mediately go home again."

"I am agreeable to anything which is agreeable to Mr. Giles," said a shorter man; who was by no means of a slim figure, and who was very pale in the face, and very polite: as frightened men frequently are.

"I shouldn't wish to appear ill-mannered, gentlemen," said the third, who had called the dogs back, "Mr. Giles ought to know."

"Certainly," replied the shorter man; "and whatever Mr. Giles says, it isn't our place to contradict him. No, no, I know my sitiwation! Thank my stars, I know my sitiwation." To tell the truth, the little man *did* seem to know his situation, and to know perfectly well that it was by no means a desirable one; for his teeth chattered in his head as he spoke.

"You are afraid, Brittles," said Mr. Giles.

"I a'n't," said Brittles.

"You are," said Giles.

"You're a falsehood, Mr. Giles," said Brittles.

"You're a lie, Brittles," said Mr. Giles.

Now these four retorts arose from Mr. Giles's taunt; and Mr. Giles's taunt had arisen from his indignation at having the responsibility of going home again, imposed upon himself under cover of a compliment. The third man brought the dispute to a close, most philosophically.

"I'll tell you what it is, gentlemen," said he, "we're all afraid."

"Speak for yourself, Sir," said Mr. Giles, who was the palest of the party.

"So I do," replied the man. "It's natural and proper to be afraid, under such circumstances. *I* am."

"So am I," said Brittles; "only there's no call to tell a man he is, so bounceably."

These frank admissions softened Mr. Giles, who at once owned that *he* was afraid; upon which, they all three faced about, and ran back again with the completest unanimity, until Mr. Giles (who had the shortest wind of the party, and was encumbered with a pitchfork) most handsomely insisted on stopping, to make an apology for his hastiness of speech.

"But it's wonderful," said Mr. Giles, when he had ex-

plained, "what a man will do, when his blood is up. I should have committed murder: I know I should: if we'd caught one of the rascals."

As the other two were impressed with a similar presentiment; and as their blood, like his, had all gone down again; some speculation ensued upon the cause of this sudden change in their temperament.

"I know what it was," said Mr. Giles; "it was the gate."

"I shouldn't wonder if it was," exclaimed Brittles, catching at the idea.

"You may depend upon it," said Giles, "that that gate stopped the flow of the excitement. I felt all mine suddenly going away, as I was climbing over it."

By a remarkable coincidence, the other two had been visited with the same unpleasant sensation at that precise moment; it was quite obvious, therefore, that it was the gate; especially as there was no doubt regarding the time at which the change had taken place, because all three remembered that they had come in sight of the robbers at the very instant of its occurrence.

This dialogue was held between the two men who had surprised the burglars; and a travelling tinker, who had been sleeping in an outhouse; and who had been roused, together with his two mongrel curs, to join in the pursuit. Mr. Giles acted in the double capacity of butler and steward to the old lady of the mansion; and Brittles was a lad of all-work; who, having entered her service a mere child, was treated as a promising young boy still, though he was something past thirty.

Encouraging each other with such converse as this; but keeping very close together, notwithstanding; and looking apprehensively round, whenever a fresh gust rattled through the boughs; the three men hurried back to a tree, behind which they had left their lantern, lest its light should inform the thieves in what direction to fire. Catching up the light, they made the best of their way home, at a good round trot; and long after their dusky forms had ceased to be discernible, it might have been seen twinkling and dancing in the distance, like some exhalation of the damp and gloomy atmosphere through which it was swiftly borne.

The air grew colder, as day came slowly on; and the mist rolled along the ground like a dense cloud of smoke. The grass was wet; the pathways, and low places were all mire and water; and the damp breath of an unwholesome wind went languidly by, with a hollow moaning. Still, Oliver lay motionless and insensible on the spot where Sikes had left him.

Morning drew on apace. The air became more sharp and piercing, as its first dull hue: the death of night, rather than the birth of day: glimmered faintly in the sky. The objects which had looked dim and terrible in the darkness, grew more and more defined and gradually resolved into their familiar shapes. The rain came down, thick and fast, and pattered noisily among the leafless bushes. But, Oliver felt it not, as it beat against him; for he still lay stretched, helpless and unconscious, on his bed of clay.

At length, a low cry of pain broke the stillness that prevailed; and uttering it, the boy awoke. His left arm, rudely bandaged in a shawl, hung heavy and useless at his side: and the bandage was saturated with blood. He was so weak, that he could scarely raise himself into a sitting posture; and when he had done so, he looked feebly round for help, and groaned with pain. Trembling in every joint, from cold and exhaustion, he made an effort to stand upright; but, shuddering from head to foot, fell prostrate on the ground.

After a short return of the stupor in which he had been so long plunged, Oliver: urged by a creeping sickness at his heart, which seemed to warn him that if he lay there, he must surely die: got upon his feet, and essayed to walk. His head was dizzy; and he staggered to and fro like a drunken man; but he kept up, nevertheless, and, with his head drooping languidly on his breast, went stumbling onward, he knew not whither.

And now, hosts of bewildering and confused ideas came crowding on his mind. He seemed to be still walking between long Sikes and Crackit, who were angrily disputing: for the very words they said, sounded in his ears; and when he caught his own attention, as it were, by making some violent effort to save himself from falling, he found that he was talking to them. Then, he was alone with Sikes, plodding on as they had done the previous day; and as shadowy people passed them, he felt the robber's grasp upon his wrist. Suddenly, he started back at the report of firearms; and there rose into the air, loud cries and shouts; lights gleamed before his eyes; and all was noise and tumult, as some unseen hand bore him hurriedly away. Through all these rapid visions, there ran an undefined, uneasy consciousness of pain, which wearied and tormented him incessantly.

Thus he staggered on, creeping, almost mechanically, between the bars of gates, or through hedge-gaps as they came in his way, until he reached a road; here the rain began to fall so heavily, that it roused him.

He looked about, and saw that at no great distance there was a house, which perhaps he could reach. Pitying his condition, they might have compassion on him; and if they did not, it would be better, he thought, to die near human beings, than in the lonely open fields. He summoned up all his strength for one last trial, and bent his faltering steps towards it.

As he drew nearer to this house, a feeling came over him that he had seen it before. He remembered nothing of its details; but the shape and aspect of the building seemed familiar to him.

That garden wall! On the grass inside, he had fallen on his knees last night, and prayed the two men's mercy. It was the very same house they had attempted to rob.

Oliver felt such fear come over him when he recognised the place, that, for the instant, he forgot the agony of his wound, and thought only of flight. Flight! He could scarcely stand: and if he were in full possession of all the best powers of his slight and youthful frame, whither could he fly? He pushed against the garden-gate; it was unlocked, and swung open on its hinges. He tottered across the lawn; climbed the steps; knocked faintly at the door; and, his whole strength failing him, sank down against one of the pillars of the little portico.

It happened that about this time, Mr. Giles, Brittles, and the tinker, were recruiting themselves, after the fatigues and terrors of the night, with tea and sundries, in the kitchen. Not that it was Mr. Giles's habit to admit to too great familiarity the humbler servants: towards whom it was rather his wont to deport himself with a lofty affability, which, while it gratified, could not fail to remind them of his superior position in society. But, death, fires, and burglary, make all men equal; so Mr. Giles sat with his legs stretched out before the kitchen fender, leaning his left arm on the table, while, with his right, he illustrated a circumstantial and minute account of the robbery, to which his hearers (but especially the cook and housemaid, who were of the party) listened with breathless interest.

"It was about half-past two," said Mr. Giles, "or I wouldn't swear that it mightn't have been a little nearer three, when I woke up, and, turning round in my bed, as it might be so (here Mr. Giles turned round in his chair, and pulled the corner of the table-cloth over him to imitate bed-clothes), I fancied I heerd a noise."

At this point of the narrative the cook turned pale, and asked the housemaid to shut the door, who asked Brittles, who asked the tinker, who pretended not to hear.

"—Heerd a noise," continued Mr. Giles. "I says, at first, 'This is illusion;' and was composing myself off to sleep, when I heerd the noise again, distinct."

"What sort of a noise?" asked the cook.

"A kind of a busting noise," replied Mr. Giles, looking round him.

"More like the noise of powdering an iron bar on a nutmeg-grater," suggested Brittles.

"It was, when *you* heerd it, Sir," rejoined Mr. Giles; "but, at this time, it had a busting sound. I turned down the clothes;" continued Giles, rolling back the table-cloth, "sat up in bed; and listened."

The cook and housemaid simultaneously ejaculated "Lor!" and drew their chairs closer together.

"I heerd it now, quite apparent," resumed Mr. Giles. "'Somebody,' I says, 'is forcing of a door, or window;' what's to be done? I'll call up that poor lad, Brittles, and save him from being murdered in his bed; or his throat,' I says, 'may be cut from his right ear to his left, without his ever knowing it.'"

Here, all eyes were turned upon Brittles; who fixed his upon the speaker, and stared at him, with his mouth wide open, and his face expressive of the most unmitigated horror.

"I tossed off the clothes," said Giles, throwing away the table-cloth, and looking very hard at the cook and housemaid, "got softly out of bed; drew on a pair of—"

"Ladies present, Mr. Giles," murmured the tinker.

"—Of *shoes*, Sir," turning upon him, and laying great emphasis on the word; "seized the loaded pistol that always goes up stairs with the plate-basket; and walked on tiptoes to his room. 'Brittles,' I says, when I had woke him, 'don't be frightened!'"

"So you did," observed Brittles, in a low voice.

"'We're dead men, I think, Brittles,' I says," continued Giles; "'but don't be frightened.'"

"*Was* he frightened?" asked the cook.

"Not a bit of it," replied Mr. Giles. "He was as firm —ah! pretty near as firm as I was."

"I should have died at once, I'm sure, if it had been me," observed the housemaid.

"You're a woman," retorted Brittles, plucking up a little.

"Brittles is right," said Mr. Giles, nodding his head, approvingly; "from a woman, nothing else was to be expected. We, being men, took a dark lantern that was standing on Brittles's hob, and groped our way down stairs in the pitch dark,—as it might be so."

Mr. Giles had risen from his seat, and taken two steps with his eyes shut, to accompany his description with appropriate action, when he started violently, in common with the rest of the company, and hurried back to his chair. The cook and housemaid screamed.

"It was a knock," said Mr. Giles, assuming perfect serenity. "Open the door, somebody."

Nobody moved.

"It seems a strange sort of thing, a knock coming at such a time in the morning," said Mr. Giles, surveying the pale faces which surrounded him, and looking very blank himself; "but the door must be opened. Do you hear, somebody?"

Mr. Giles, as he spoke, looked at Brittles; but that young man, being naturally modest, probably considered himself nobody, and so held that the inquiry could not have any application to him; at all events, he tendered no reply. Mr. Giles directed an appealing glance at the tinker; but he had suddenly fallen asleep. The women were out of the question.

"If Brittles would rather open the door, in the presence of witnesses," said Mr. Giles, after a short silence, "I am ready to make one."

"So am I," said the tinker, waking up, as suddenly as he had fallen asleep.

Brittles capitulated on these terms; and the party being somewhat reassured by the discovery (made on throwing open the shutters) that it was now broad day, took their way up stairs; with the dogs in front; and the two women, who were afraid to stay below, bringing up the rear. By the advice of Mr. Giles, they all talked very loud to warn any evil-disposed person outside, that they were strong in numbers; and by a master-stroke of policy, originating in the brain of the same ingenious gentleman, the dogs' tails were well pinched, in the hall, to make them bark savagely.

These precautions having been taken, Mr. Giles held on fast by the tinker's arm (to prevent his running away, as he pleasantly said), and gave the word of command to open the door. Brittles obeyed; and the group, peeping timorously over each other's shoulders, beheld no more formidable object than poor little Oliver Twist, speechless and exhausted, who raised his heavy eyes, and mutely solicited their compassion.

"A boy!" exclaimed Mr. Giles, valiantly pushing the tinker into the background. "What's the matter with the —eh?—Why—Brittles—look here—don't you know?"

Brittles, who had got behind the door to open it, no sooner saw Oliver, than he uttered a loud cry. Mr. Giles, seizing the boy by one leg and one arm: fortunately not the broken limb: lugged him straight into the hall, and deposited him at full length on the floor thereof.

"Here he is!" bawled Giles, calling, in a state of great excitement, up the staircase; "here's one of the thieves, ma'am! Here's a thief, miss! Wounded, miss! I shot him, miss; and Brittles held the light."

"—In a lantern, miss," cried Brittles, applying one hand to the side of his mouth, so that his voice might travel the better.

The two women-servants ran up stairs to carry the intelligence that Mr. Giles had captured a robber; and the tinker busied himself in endeavouring to restore Oliver, lest he should die before he could be hanged. In the midst of all this noise and commotion, there was heard a sweet female voice, which quelled it in an instant.

"Giles!" whispered the voice from the stair-head.

"I'm here, miss," replied Mr. Giles. "Don't be frightened, miss; I ain't much injured. He didn't make a very desperate resistance, miss; I was soon too many for him."

"Hush!" replied the young lady; "you frighten my aunt as much as the thieves did. Is the poor creature much hurt?"

"Wounded desperate, miss," replied Giles, with indescribable complacency.

"He looks as if he was a-going, miss," bawled Brittles, in the same manner as before. "Wouldn't you like to come and look at him, miss, in case he should?"

"Hush, pray; there's a good man!" rejoined the young lady. "Wait quietly one instant, while I speak to aunt."

With a footstep as soft and gentle as the voice, the speaker tripped away; and soon returned, with the direction that the wounded person was to be carried, carefully, up stairs to Mr. Giles's room; and that Brittles was to saddle the pony and betake himself instantly to Chertsey: from which place, he was to despatch, with all speed, a constable and doctor.

"But won't you take one look at him, first, miss?" asked Mr. Giles, with as much pride as if Oliver were some bird of rare plumage, that he had skilfully brought down. "Not one little peep, miss?"

"Not now, for the world," replied the young lady. "Poor fellow! Oh! treat him kindly, Giles, for my sake!"

The old servant looked up at the speaker, as she turned away; with a glance as proud and admiring as if she had been his own child. Then, bending over Oliver, he helped to carry him up stairs, with the care and solicitude of a woman.

CHAPTER XXIX.

HAS AN INTRODUCTORY ACCOUNT OF THE INMATES OF THE HOUSE, TO WHICH OLIVER RESORTED.

In a handsome room: though its furniture had rather the air of old-fashioned comfort, than of modern elegance: there sat two ladies at a well-spread breakfast-table. Mr. Giles, dressed with scrupulous care in a full suit of black, was in attendance upon them. He had taken his station some half-way between the side-board and the breakfast-table; and, with his body drawn up to its full height, his head thrown back, and inclined the merest trifle on one side, his left leg advanced, and his right hand thrust into his waistcoat, while his left hung down by his side, grasping a waiter, looked like one who laboured under a very agreeable sense of his own merits and importance.

Of the two ladies, one was well advanced in years; but the high-backed oaken chair in which she sat, was not more upright than she. Dressed with the utmost nicety and precision, in a quaint mixture of by-gone costume, with some slight concessions to the prevailing taste, which rather served to point the old style pleasantly than to impair its effect, she sat, in a stately manner, with her hands folded on the table before her. Her eyes (and age had dimmed but little of their brightness) were attentively fixed upon her young companion.

George Cruikshank

OLIVER AT THE DOOR OF MRS. MAYLIE.

The younger lady was in the lovely bloom and spring-time of womanhood; at that age, when, if ever angels be for God's good purposes enthroned in mortal forms, they may be, without impiety, supposed to abide in such as hers.

She was not past seventeen. Cast in so slight and exquisite a mould; so mild and gentle; so pure and beautiful; that earth seemed not her element, nor its rough creatures her fit companions. The very intelligence that shone in her deep blue eye, and was stamped upon her noble head, seemed scarcely of her age, or of the world; and yet the changing expression of sweetness and good humour; the thousand lights that played about the face, and left no shadow there; above all, the smile, the cheerful, happy smile, were made for Home, and fireside peace and happiness.

She was busily engaged in the little offices of the table. Chancing to raise her eyes as the elder lady was regarding her, she playfully put back her hair, which was simply braided on her forehead; and threw into one beaming look, such a gush of affection and artless loveliness, that blessed spirits might have smiled to look upon her.

"And Brittles has been gone upwards of an hour, has he?" asked the old lady, after a pause.

"An hour and twelve minutes, ma'am," replied Mr. Giles, referring to a silver watch, which he drew forth by a black ribbon.

"He is always slow," remarked the old lady.

"Brittles always was a slow boy, ma'am," replied the attendant. And seeing, by-the-by, that Brittles had been a slow boy for upwards of thirty years, there appeared no great probability of his ever being a fast one.

"He gets worse instead of better, I think," said the elder lady.

"It is very inexcusable in him if he stops to play with any other boys," said the young lady, smiling.

Mr. Giles was apparently considering the propriety of indulging in a respectful smile himself, when a gig drove up to the garden gate: out of which there jumped a fat gentleman, who ran straight up to the door: and who, getting quickly into the house by some mysterious process, burst into the room, and nearly overturned Mr. Giles and the breakfast-table together.

"I never heard of such a thing!" exclaimed the fat gentleman. "My dear Mrs. Maylie—bless my soul—in the silence of night, too—I *never* heard of such a thing!"

With these expressions of condolence, the fat gentleman shook hands with both ladies; and drawing up a chair, inquired how they found themselves.

"You ought to be dead; positively dead with the fright," said the fat gentleman. "Why didn't you send? Bless me, my man should have come in a minute; and so would I; and my assistant would have been delighted; or anybody, I'm sure, under such circumstances. Dear, dear! So unexpected! In the silence of night, too!"

The doctor seemed especially troubled by the fact of the robbery having been unexpected, and attempted in the night-time; as if it were the established custom of gentlemen in the housebreaking way to transact business at noon, and to make an appointment, by the twopenny post, a day or two previous.

"And you, Miss Rose," said the doctor, turning to the young lady, "I——"

"Oh! very much so, indeed," said Rose, interrupting him; "but there is a poor creature up stairs, whom aunt wishes you to see."

"Ah! to be sure," replied the doctor, "so there is. That was your handiwork, Giles, I understand."

Mr. Giles, who had been feverishly putting the tea-cups to rights, blushed very red, and said that he had had that honour.

"Honour, eh?" said the doctor; "well, I don't know; perhaps it's as honourable to hit a thief in a back kitchen, as to hit your man at twelve paces. Fancy that he fired in the air; and you've fought a duel, Giles."

Mr. Giles, who thought this light treatment of the matter an unjust attempt at diminishing his glory, answered respectfully, that it was not for the like of him to judge about that; but he rather thought it was no joke to the opposite party.

"Gad that's true!" said the doctor. "Where is he? Show me the way. I'll look in again, as I come down, Mrs. Maylie. That's the little window that he got in at, eh? Well, I couldn't have believed it!"

Talking all the way, he followed Mr. Giles up stairs; and while he is going up stairs, the reader may be informed, that Mr. Losberne, a surgeon in the neighbourhood, known through a circuit of ten miles round as "the doctor," had grown fat: more from good-humour than from good living: and was as kind and hearty, and withal as eccentric an old bachelor, as will be found in five times that space, by any explorer alive.

The doctor was absent, much longer than either he or the ladies had anticipated. A large flat box was fetched out of the gig; and a bedroom bell was rung very often; and the servants ran up and down stairs perpetually; from which tokens it was justly concluded that something important was going on above. At length he returned; and in reply to an anxious inquiry after his patient, looked very mysterious, and closed the door, carefully.

"This is a very extraordinary thing, Mrs. Maylie," said the doctor, standing with his back to the door, as if to keep it shut.

"He is not in danger, I hope?" said the old lady.

"Why, that would *not* be an extraordinary thing, under the circumstances," replied the doctor; "though I don't think he is. Have you seen this thief?"

"No," rejoined the old lady.

"Nor heard anything about him?"

"No."

"I beg your pardon, ma'am," interposed Mr. Giles; "but I was going to tell you about him when Doctor Losberne came in."

The fact was, that Mr. Giles had not, at first, been able to bring his mind to the avowal, that he had only shot a boy. Such commendations had been bestowed upon his bravery, that he could not, for the life of him, help postponing the explanation for a few delicious minutes; during which he had flourished, in the very zenith of a brief reputation for undaunted courage.

"Rose wished to see the man," said Mrs. Maylie, "but I wouldn't hear of it."

"Humph!" rejoined the doctor. "There is nothing very alarming in his appearance. Have you any objection to see him in my presence?"

"If it be necessary," replied the old lady, "certainly not."

"Then I think it is necessary," said the doctor; "at all

events, I am quite sure that you would deeply regret not having done so, if you postponed it. He is perfectly quiet and comfortable now. Allow me—Miss Rose, will you permit me? Not the slightest fear, I pledge you my honour!"

CHAPTER XXX.

RELATES WHAT OLIVER'S NEW VISITORS THOUGHT OF HIM.

WITH many loquacious assurances that they would be agreeably surprised in the aspect of the criminal, the doctor drew the young lady's arm through one of his; and offering his disengaged hand to Mrs. Maylie, led them, with much ceremony and stateliness, up stairs.

"Now," said the doctor, in a whisper, as he softly turned the handle of a bedroom-door, "let us hear what you think of him. He has not been shaved very recently, but he don't look at all ferocious notwithstanding. Stop, though! Let me first see that he is in visiting order."

Stepping before them, he looked into the room. Motioning them to advance, he closed the door when they had entered; and gently drew back the curtains of the bed. Upon it, in lieu of the dogged, black-visaged ruffian they had expected to behold, there lay a mere child: worn with pain and exhaustion: and sunk into a deep sleep. His wounded arm, bound and splintered up, was crossed upon his breast; his head reclined upon the other arm, which was half hidden by his long hair, as it streamed over the pillow.

The honest gentleman held the curtain in his hand; and looked on, for a minute or so, in silence. Whilst he was watching the patient thus, the younger lady glided softly past; and seating herself in a chair by the bedside, gathered Oliver's hair from his face. As she stooped over him, her tears fell upon his forehead.

The boy stirred, and smiled in his sleep, as though these marks of pity and compassion had awakened some pleasant dream of a love and affection he had never known; as a strain of gentle music, or the rippling of water in a silent place, or the odour of a flower, or even the mention of a familiar word, will sometimes call up sudden dim remembrances of scenes that never were, in this life; which vanish like a breath; which some brief memory of a happier existence, long gone by, would seem to have awakened; for no voluntary exertion of the mind can ever recall them.

"What can this mean?" exclaimed the elder lady. "This poor child can never have been the pupil of robbers!"

"Vice," sighed the surgeon, replacing the curtain, "takes up her abode in many temples; and who can say that a fair outside shall not enshrine her?"

"But at so early an age!" urged Rose.

"My dear young lady," rejoined the surgeon, mournfully shaking his head; "crime, like death, is not confined to the old and withered alone. The youngest and fairest are too often its chosen victims."

"But, can you—oh, Sir! can you really believe that this delicate boy has been the voluntary associate of the worst outcasts of society?" said Rose.

The surgeon shook his head, in a manner which intimated that he feared it was very possible; and observing that they might disturb the patient, led the way into an adjoining apartment.

"But even if he has been wicked," pursued Rose, "think how young he is; think that he may never have known a mother's love, or the comfort of a home; and that ill-usage and blows, or the want of bread, may have driven him to herd with men who have forced him to guilt. Aunt, dear aunt, for mercy's sake, think of this, before you let them drag this sick child to a prison, which in any case must be the grave of all his chances of amendment. Oh! as you love me, and know that I have never felt the want of parents in your goodness and affection, but that I might have done so, and might have been equally helpless and unprotected with this poor child, have pity upon him before it is too late."

"My dear love!" said the elder lady, as she folded the weeping girl to her bosom, "do you think I would harm a hair of his head?"

"Oh, no!" replied Rose, eagerly.

"No," said the old lady with a trembling lip; "my days are drawing to their close; and may mercy be shown to me as I show it to others! What can I do to save him, Sir?"

"Let me think, ma'am," said the doctor; "let me think."

Mr. Losberne thrust his hands into his pockets; and took several turns up and down the room: often stopping, and balancing himself on his toes: and frowning frightfully. After various exclamations of "I've got it now" and "no, I haven't," and as many renewals of the walking and frowning, he at length made a dead halt, and spoke as follows:

"I think if you give me a full and unlimited commission to bully Giles, and that little boy, Brittles, I can manage it. He is a faithful fellow and an old servant, I know; but you can make it up to him in a thousand ways, and reward him for being such a good shot besides. You don't object to that?"

"Unless there is some other way of preserving the child," replied Mrs. Maylie.

"There is no other," said the doctor. "No other, take my word for it."

"Then my aunt invests you with full power," said Rose, smiling through her tears; "but pray don't be harder upon the poor fellows than is indispensably necessary."

"You seem to think," retorted the doctor, "that everybody is disposed to be hard-hearted to-day, except yourself, Miss Rose. I only hope, for the sake of the rising male sex generally, that you may be found in as vulnerable and soft-hearted a mood by the first eligible young fellow who appeals to your compassion; and I wish I were a young fellow, that I might avail myself, on the spot, of such a favourable opportunity for doing so, as the present."

"You are as great a boy as poor Brittles himself," returned Rose, blushing.

"Well," said the doctor, laughing heartily, "that is no very difficult matter. But to return to this boy. The great point of our agreement is yet to come. He will wake in an hour or so, I dare say; and although I have told that thick-headed constable-fellow down stairs that he mustn't be moved or spoken to, on peril of his life, I think we may converse with him without danger. Now, I make this stipulation—that I shall examine him in your presence, and that if from what he says, we judge, and I can show to the satisfaction of your cool reason, that he is a real and

391

thorough bad one (which is more than possible), he shall be left to his fate, without any further interference on my part, at all events."

"Oh no, aunt!" entreated Rose.

"Oh yes, aunt!" said the doctor. "Is it a bargain?"

"He cannot be hardened in vice," said Rose; "it is impossible."

"Very good," retorted the doctor; "then so much the more reason for acceding to my proposition."

Finally the treaty was entered into; and the parties thereunto sat down to wait, with some impatience, until Oliver should awake.

The patience of the two ladies was destined to undergo a longer trial than Mr. Losberne had led them to expect; for hour after hour passed on, and still Oliver slumbered heavily. It was evening, indeed, before the kind-hearted doctor brought them the intelligence, that he was at length sufficiently restored to be spoken to. The boy was very ill, he said, and weak from the loss of blood; but his mind was so troubled with anxiety to disclose something, that he deemed it better to give him the opportunity, than to insist upon his remaining quiet until next morning: which he should otherwise have done.

The conference was a long one; for Oliver told them all his simple history, and was often compelled to stop, by pain and want of strength. It was a solemn thing, to hear, in the darkened room, the feeble voice of the sick child recounting a weary catalogue of evils and calamities which hard men had brought upon him. Oh! if, when we oppress and grind our fellow-creatures, we bestowed but one thought on the dark evidences of human error, which, like dense and heavy clouds, are rising, slowly it is true, but not less surely, to Heaven, to pour their after-vengeance on our hands; if we heard but one instant, in imagination, the deep testimony of dead men's voices, which no power can stifle, and no pride shut out; where would be the injury and injustice, the suffering, misery, cruelty, and wrong, that each day's life brings with it!

Oliver's pillow was smoothed by gentle hands that night; and loveliness and virtue watched him as he slept. He felt calm and happy; and could have died without a murmur.

The momentous interview was no sooner concluded, and Oliver composed to rest again, than the doctor, after wiping his eyes, and condemning them for being weak all at once, betook himself down stairs to open upon Mr. Giles. And finding nobody about the parlours, it occurred to him, that he could perhaps originate the proceedings with better effect in the kitchen; so into the kitchen he went.

There were assembled, in that lower house of the domestic parliament, the women-servants, Mr. Brittles, Mr. Giles, the tinker (who had received a special invitation to regale himself for the remainder of the day, in consideration of his services), and the constable. The latter gentleman had a large staff, a large head, large features, and large half-boots; and looked as if he had been taking a proportionate allowance of ale, as indeed he had.

The adventures of the previous night were still under discussion; for Mr. Giles was expatiating upon his presence of mind, when the doctor entered; and Mr. Brittles, with a mug of ale in his hand, was corroborating everything, before his superior said it.

"Sit still," said the doctor, waving his hand.

"Thank you, Sir," said Mr. Giles. "Misses wished some ale to be given out, Sir; and as I felt no ways inclined for my own little room, Sir, and was disposed for company, I am taking mine among 'em here."

Brittles headed a low murmur, by which the ladies and gentlemen generally were understood to express the gratification they derived from Mr. Giles's condescension. Mr. Giles looked round with a patronising air, as much as to say that so long as they behaved properly, he would never desert them.

"How is the patient to-night, Sir?" asked Giles.

"So-so;" returned the doctor. "I am afraid you have got yourself into a scrape there, Mr. Giles."

"I hope you don't mean to say, Sir," said Mr. Giles, trembling, "that he's going to die. If I thought it, I should never be happy again. I wouldn't cut a boy off: no, not even Brittles here: not for all the plate in the country, Sir."

"That's not the point," said the doctor, mysteriously. "Mr. Giles, are you a Protestant?"

"Yes, Sir, I hope so," faltered Mr. Giles, who had turned very pale.

"And what are you, boy?" said the doctor, turning sharply upon Brittles.

"Lord bless me, Sir!" replied Brittles, starting violently; "I'm the same as Mr. Giles, Sir."

"Then tell me this," said the doctor, "both of you—both of you! Are you going to take upon yourselves to swear, that that boy up stairs is the boy that was put through the little window last night? Out with it! Come! We are prepared for you!"

The doctor, who was universally considered one of the best-tempered creatures on earth, made this demand in such a dreadful tone of anger, that Giles and Brittles, who were considerably muddled by ale and excitement, stared at each other in a state of stupefaction.

"Pay attention to the reply, constable, will you?" said the doctor, shaking his forefinger with great solemnity of manner, and tapping the bridge of his nose with it, to bespeak the exercise of that worthy's utmost acuteness. "Something may come of this before long."

The constable looked as wise as he could, and took up his staff of office: which had been reclining indolently in the chimney-corner.

"It's a simple question of identity, you will observe," said the doctor.

"That's what it is, Sir," replied the constable, coughing with great violence; for he had finished his ale in a hurry, and some of it had gone the wrong way.

"Here's a house broken into," said the doctor, "and a couple of men catch one moment's glimpse of a boy, in the midst of gunpowder-smoke, and in all the distraction of alarm and darkness. Here's a boy comes to that very same house, next morning, and because he happens to have his arm tied up, these men lay violent hands upon him; by doing which, they place his life in great danger, and swear he is the thief. Now, the question is, whether these men are justified by the fact; and if not, in what situation do they place themselves?"

The constable nodded profoundly. He said, if that wasn't law, he would be glad to know what was.

"I ask you again," thundered the doctor, "are you, on your solemn oaths, able to identify that boy?"

Brittles looked doubtfully at Mr. Giles; Mr. Giles looked doubtfully at Brittles; the constable put his hand behind his ear, to catch the reply; the two women and the tinker leaned forward to listen; and the doctor glanced keenly round; when a ring was heard at the gate, and at the same moment, the sound of wheels.

"It's the runners!" cried Brittles, to all appearances much relieved.

"The what!" exclaimed the doctor, aghast in his turn.

"The Bow Street officers, Sir," replied Brittles, taking up a candle; "me and Mr. Giles sent for 'em this morning."

"What!" cried the doctor.

"Yes," replied Brittles; "I sent a message up by the coachman, and I only wonder why they weren't here before, Sir."

"You did, did you? Then confound your—slow coaches down here; that's all," said the doctor, walking away.

CHAPTER XXXI.

INVOLVES A CRITICAL POSITION.

"Who's that?" inquired Brittles, opening the door a little way, with the chain up, and peeping out, shading the candle with his hand.

"Open the door," replied a man outside; "it's the officers from Bow Street, as was sent to, to-day."

Much comforted by this assurance, Brittles opened the door to its full width, and confronted a portly man in a great-coat, who walked in without saying anything more, and wiped his shoes on the mat, as coolly as if he lived there.

"Just send somebody out to relieve my mate, will you, young man?" said the officer; "he's in the gig, a-minding the prad. Have you got a coach'us here, that you could put it up in, for five or ten minutes?"

Brittles replying in the affirmative, and pointing out the building, the portly man stepped back to the garden-gate, and helped his companion to put up the gig: while Brittles lighted them, in a state of great admiration. This done, they returned to the house; and, being shown into a parlour, took off their great-coats and hats, and showed like what they were.

The man who had knocked at the door, was a stout personage of middle height: aged about fifty: with shiny black hair, cropped pretty close; half-whiskers, a round face, and sharp eyes. The other was a red-headed, bony man, in top-boots; with a rather ill-favoured countenance, and a turned-up sinister-looking nose.

"Tell your governor that Blathers and Duff is here, will you?" said the stouter man, smoothing down his hair, and laying a pair of handcuffs on the table. "O! Good evening, master. Can I have a word or two with you in private, if you please?"

This was addressed to Mr. Losberne, who now made his appearance; that gentleman, motioning Brittles to retire, brought in the two ladies, and shut the door.

"This is the lady of the house," said Mr. Losberne, motioning towards Mrs. Maylie.

Mr. Blathers made a bow. Being desired to sit down, he put his hat upon the floor, and, taking a chair, motioned Duff to do the same. The latter gentleman, who did not appear quite so much accustomed to good society, or quite so much at his ease in it—one of the two—seated himself, after undergoing several muscular affections of the limbs; and forced the head of his stick into his mouth, with some embarrassment.

"Now, with regard to this here robbery, master," said Blathers. "What are the circumstances?"

Mr. Losberne, who appeared desirous of gaining time, recounted them at great length, and with much circumlocution. Messrs. Blathers and Duff looked very knowing meanwhile, and occasionally exchanged a nod.

"I can't say, for certain, till I see the place, of course," said Blathers; "but my opinion at once is,—I don't mind committing myself to that extent,—that this wasn't done by a yokel; eh, Duff?"

"Certainly not," replied Duff.

"And, translating the word yokel for the benefit of the ladies, I apprehend your meaning to be, that this attempt was not made by a countryman?" said Mr. Losberne, with a smile.

"That's it, master," replied Blathers. "This is all about the robbery, is it?"

"All," replied the doctor.

"Now, what is this, about this here boy that the servants are talking on?" said Blathers.

"Nothing at all," replied the doctor. "One of the frightened servants chose to take it into his head, that he had something to do with this attempt to break into the house; but it's nonsense: sheer absurdity."

"Wery easy disposed of, if it is," remarked Duff.

"What he says is quite correct," observed Blathers, nodding his head in a confirmatory way, and playing carelessly with the handcuffs, as if they were a pair of castanets. "Who is the boy? What account does he give of himself? Where did he come from? He didn't drop out of the clouds, did he, master?"

"Of course not," replied the doctor, with a nervous glance at the two ladies. "I know his whole history; but we can talk about that presently. You would like, first, to see the place where the thieves made their attempt, I suppose?"

"Certainly," rejoined Mr. Blathers. "We had better inspect the premises first, and examine the servants arterwards. That's the usual way of doing business."

Lights were then procured; and Messrs. Blathers and Duff, attended by the native constable, Brittles, Giles, and everybody else in short, went into the little room at the end of the passage and looked out at the window; and afterwards went round by way of the lawn, and looked in at the window; and after that, had a candle handed out to inspect the shutter with; and after that, a lantern to trace the footsteps with; and after that, a pitchfork to poke the bushes with. This done, amidst the breathless interest of all beholders, they came in again; and Mr. Giles and Brittles were put through a melodramatic representation of their share in the previous night's adventures: which they performed some six times over: contradicting each other, in not more than one important respect, the first time, and in not more than a dozen the last. This consummation being arrived at, Blathers and Duff cleared the room, and held a long council together, compared with which, for secrecy and solemnity, a consultation of great doctors on the knottiest point in medicine, would be mere child's play.

Meanwhile, the doctor walked up and down the next room in a very uneasy state; and Mrs. Maylie and Rose looked on, with anxious faces.

"Upon my word," he said, making a halt, after a great number of very rapid turns, "I hardly know what to do."

"Surely," said Rose, "the poor child's story, faithfully repeated to these men, will be sufficient to exonerate him."

"I doubt it, my dear young lady," said the doctor, shaking his head. "I don't think it would exonerate him, either with them, or with legal functionaries of a higher grade. What is he, after all, they would say? A runaway. Judged by mere worldly considerations and probabilities, his story is a very doubtful one."

"You believe it, surely?" interrupted Rose.

"*I* believe it, strange as it is; and perhaps I may be an old fool for doing so," rejoined the doctor; "but I don't think it is exactly the tale for a practised police-officer, nevertheless."

"Why not?" demanded Rose.

"Because, my pretty cross-examiner," replied the doctor: "because, viewed with their eyes, there are many ugly points about it; he can only prove the parts that look ill, and none of those that look well. Confound the fellows, they *will* have the why and the wherefore, and will take nothing for granted. On his own showing, you see, he has been the companion of thieves for some time past; he has been carried to a police-office, on a charge of picking a gentleman's pocket; he has been taken away, forcibly, from that gentleman's house, to a place which he cannot describe or point out, and of the situation of which he has not the remotest idea. He is brought down to Chertsey, by men who seem to have taken a violent fancy to him, whether he will or no; and is put through a window to rob a house; and then, just at the very moment when he is going to alarm the inmates, and so do the very thing that would set him all to rights, there rushes into the way, a blundering dog of a half-bred butler, and shoots him; as if on purpose to prevent his doing any good for himself. Don't you see all this?"

"I see it, of course," replied Rose, smiling at the doctor's impetuosity; "but still I do not see anything in it, to criminate the poor child."

"No," replied the doctor; "of course not! Bless the bright eyes of your sex! They never see, whether for good or bad, more than one side of any question; and that is, always, the one which first presents itself to them."

Having given vent to this result of experience, the doctor put his hands into his pockets, and walked up and down the room with even greater rapidity than before.

"The more I think of it," said the doctor, "the more I see that it will occasion endless trouble and difficulty if we put these men in possession of the boy's real story. I am certain it will not be believed; and even if they can do nothing to him in the end, still the dragging it forward, and giving publicity to all the doubts that will be cast upon it, must interfere, materially, with your benevolent plan of rescuing him from misery."

"Oh! what is to be done?" cried Rose. "Dear, dear! why did they send for these people?"

"Why, indeed!" exclaimed Mrs. Maylie. "I would not have had them here, for the world."

"All I know is," said Mr. Losberne at last: sitting down with a kind of desperate calmness, "that we must try and carry it off with a bold face; that's all. The object is a good one, and that must be the excuse. The boy has strong symptoms of fever upon him, and is in no condition to be talked to any more; that's one comfort. We must make the best of it; and if bad be the best, it is no fault of ours. Come in!"

"Well, master," said Blathers, entering the room followed by his colleague, and making the door fast, before he said any more. "This warn't a put-up thing."

"And what the devil's a put-up thing?" demanded the doctor, impatiently.

"We call it a put-up robbery, ladies," said Blathers, turning to them, as if he pitied their ignorance, but had a contempt for the doctor's, "when the servants is in it."

"Nobody suspected them, in this case," said Mrs. Maylie.

"Wery likely not, ma'am," replied Blathers; "but they might have been in it, for all that."

"More likely on that wery account," said Duff.

"We find it was a town hand," said Blathers, continuing his report; "for the style of work is first-rate."

"Wery pretty indeed it is," remarked Duff, in an under tone.

"There was two of 'em in it," continued Blathers; "and they had a boy with 'em; that's plain from the size of the window. That's all to be said at present. We'll see this lad that you've got up stairs at once, if you please."

"Perhaps they will take something to drink first, Mrs. Maylie?" said the doctor: his face brightening, as if some new thought had occurred to him.

"Oh! to be sure!" exclaimed Rose, eagerly. "You shall have it immediately, if you will."

"Why, thank you, miss!" said Blathers, drawing his coat-sleeve across his mouth; "it's dry work, this sort of duty. Anythink that's handy, miss; don't put yourself out of the way, on our accounts."

"What shall it be?" asked the doctor, following the young lady to the sideboard.

"A little drop of spirits, master, if it's all the same," replied Blathers. "It's a cold ride from London, ma'am; and I always find that spirits comes home warmer to the feelings."

This interesting communication was addressed to Mrs. Maylie, who received it very graciously. While it was being conveyed to her, the doctor slipped out of the room.

"Ah!" said Mr. Blathers: not holding his wine-glass by the stem, but grasping the bottom between the thumb and forefinger of his left hand: and placing it in front of his chest; "I have seen a good many pieces of business like this, in my time, ladies."

"That crack down in the back lane at Edmonton, Blathers," said Mr. Duff, assisting his colleague's memory.

"That was something in this way, warn't it?" rejoined Mr. Blathers; "that was done by Conkey Chickweed, that was."

"You always gave that to him," replied Duff. "It was the Family Pet, I tell you. Conkey hadn't any more to do with it than I had."

"Get out!" retorted Mr. Blathers; "I know better. Do you mind that time when Conkey was robbed of his money, though? What a start that was! Better than any novel-book *I* ever see!"

"What was that?" inquired Rose: anxious to encourage any symptoms of good-humour in the unwelcome visitors.

"It was a robbery, miss, that hardly anybody would have been down upon," said Blathers. "This here Conkey Chickweed—"

"Conkey means Nosey, ma'am," interposed Duff.

"Of course the lady knows that, don't she?" demanded Mr. Blathers. "Always interrupting, you are, partner!

This here Conkey Chickweed, miss, kept a public-house over Battlebridge way; and had a cellar, where a good many young lords went to see cock-fighting, and badger-drawing, and that; and a wery intellectual manner the sports was conducted in, for I've seen 'em off'en. He warn't one of the family, at that time; and one night he was robbed of three hundred and twenty-seven guineas in a canvas bag: that was stole out of his bedroom in the dead of night, by a tall man with a black patch over his eye, who had concealed himself under the bed, and after committing the robbery, jumped slap out of window: which was only a story high. He was wery quick about it. But Conkey was quick, too; for he was woke by the noise; and darting out of bed, he fired a blunderbuss arter him, and roused the neighbourhood. They set up a hue-and-cry, directly, and when they came to look about 'em, found that Conkey had hit the robber; for there was traces of blood, all the way to some palings a good distance off; and there they lost 'em. However, he had made off with the blunt; and, consequently, the name of Mr. Chickweed, licensed witler, appeared in the Gazette among the other bankrupts; and all manner of benefits and subscriptions, and I don't know what all, was got up for the poor man, who was in a wery low state of mind about his loss, and went up and down the streets, for three or four days, pulling his hair off in such a desperate manner that many people was afraid he might be going to make away with himself. One day he come up to the office, all in a hurry, and had a private interview with the magistrate, who, after a deal of talk, rings the bell, and orders Jem Spyers in (Jem was a active officer), and tells him to go and assist Mr. Chickweed in apprehending the man as robbed his house. 'I see him, Spyers,' said Chickweed, 'pass my house yesterday morning.' 'Why didn't you up, and collar him?' says Spyers. 'I was so struck all of a heap, that you might have fractured my skull with a toothpick,' says the poor man; 'but we're sure to have him; for between ten and eleven o'clock at night he passed again.' Spyers no sooner heard this, than he put some clean linen and a comb, in his pocket, in case he should have to stop a day or two; and away he goes, and sets himself down at one of the public-house windows behind the little red curtain, with his hat on, all ready to bolt out, at a moment's notice. He was smoking his pipe here, late at night, when all of a sudden Chickweed roars out 'Here he is! Stop thief! Murder!' Jem Spyers dashes out; and there he sees Chickweed, a-tearing down the street full cry. Away goes Spyers; on goes Chickweed; round turns the people; everybody roars out, 'Thieves!' and Chickweed himself keeps on shouting, all the time, like mad. Spyers loses sight of him a minute as he turns the corner; shoots round; sees a little crowd; dives in; 'Which is the man?' 'D—me!' says Chickweed, 'I've lost him again!' It was a remarkable occurrence, but he warn't to be seen nowhere, so they went back to the public-house; and next morning, Spyers took his old place, and looked out, from behind the curtain, for a tall man with a black patch over his eye, till his own two eyes ached again. At last, he couldn't help shutting 'em, to ease 'em a minute; and the very moment he did so, he hears Chickweed a-roaring out, 'Here he is!' Off he starts once more, with Chickweed half-way down the street ahead of him; and after twice as long a run as the yesterday's one, the man's lost again! This was done, once or twice more, till one-half the neigh-bours gave out that Mr. Chickweed had been robbed by the devil, who was playing tricks with him arterwards; and the other half, that poor Mr. Chickweed had gone mad with grief."

"What did Jem Spyers say?" inquired the doctor: who had returned to the room shortly after the commencement of the story.

"Jem Spyers," resumed the officer, "for a long time said nothing at all, and listened to everything without seeming to, which showed he understood his business. But, one morning, he walked into the bar, and taking out his snuff-box, said, 'Chickweed, I've found out who's done this here robbery.' 'Have you?' said Chickweed. 'Oh, my dear Spyers, only let me have wengeance, and I shall die contented! Oh, my dear Spyers, where is the villain?' 'Come!' said Spyers, offering him a pinch of snuff, 'none of that gammon! You did it yourself.' So he had; and a good bit of money he had made by it, too; and nobody would ever have found it out, if he hadn't been so precious anxious to keep up appearances, that's more!" said Mr. Blathers, putting down his wine-glass, and clinking the hand-cuffs together.

"Very curious, indeed," observed the doctor. "Now, if you please, you can walk up stairs."

"If *you* please, Sir," returned Mr. Blathers; and, closely following Mr. Losberne, the two officers ascended to Oliver's bed-room; Mr. Giles preceding the party, with a lighted candle.

Oliver had been dozing; but looked worse, and was more feverish than he had appeared yet. Being assisted by the doctor, he managed to sit up in bed for a minute or so; and looked at the strangers without at all understanding what was going forward—in fact, without seeming to recollect where he was, or what had been passing.

"This," said Mr. Losberne, speaking softly, but with great vehemence notwithstanding, "this is the lad, who, being accidentally wounded by a spring-gun in some boyish trespass on Mr. What-d'ye-call-him's grounds, at the back here, comes to the house for assistance this morning, and is immediately laid hold of and maltreated, by that ingenious gentleman with the candle in his hand: who has placed his life in considerable danger, as I can professionally certify."

Messrs. Blathers and Duff looked at Mr. Giles, as he was thus recommended to their notice; the bewildered butler gazed from them towards Oliver, and from Oliver towards Mr. Losberne, with a most ludicrous mixture of fear and perplexity.

"You don't mean to deny that, I suppose?" said the doctor, laying Oliver gently down again.

"It was all done for the—for the best, Sir!" answered Giles. "I am sure I thought it was the boy, or I wouldn't have meddled with him. I am not of an inhuman disposition, Sir."

"Thought it was what boy?" inquired the senior officer.

"The housebreaker's boy, Sir!" replied Giles. "They—they certainly had a boy."

"Well! Do you think so now?" inquired Blathers.

"Think what, now?" replied Giles, looking vacantly at his questioner.

"Think it's the same boy, Stupid-head?" rejoined Mr. Blathers, impatiently.

"I don't know; I really don't know," said Giles, with a rueful countenance. "I couldn't swear to him."

"What do you think?" asked Mr. Blathers.

"I don't know what to think," replied poor Giles. "I don't think it is the boy; indeed, I'm almost certain that it isn't. You know it can't be."

"Has this man been a-drinking, Sir?" inquired Blathers, turning to the doctor.

"What a precious muddle-headed chap you are!" said Duff, addressing Mr. Giles, with supreme contempt.

Mr. Losberne had been feeling the patient's pulse during this short dialogue; but he now rose from the chair by the bedside, and remarked, that if the officers had any doubts upon the subject, they would perhaps like to step into the next room, and have Brittles before them.

Acting upon this suggestion, they adjourned to a neighbouring apartment, where Mr. Brittles, being called in, involved himself and his respected superior in such a wonderful maze of fresh contradictions and impossibilities, as tended to throw no particular light on anything, but the fact of his own strong mystification; except, indeed, his declarations that he shouldn't know the real boy, if he were put before him that instant; that he had only taken Oliver to be he, because Mr. Giles had said he was; and that Mr. Giles had, five minutes previously, admitted in the kitchen, that he began to be very much afraid that he had been a little too hasty.

Among other ingenious surmises, the question was then raised, whether Mr. Giles had really hit anybody; and, upon examination of the fellow pistol to that which he had fired, it turned out to have no more destructive loading than gunpowder and brown paper: a discovery which made a considerable impression on everybody but the doctor, who had drawn the ball about ten minutes before. Upon no one, however, did it make a greater impression than on Mr. Giles himself; who, after labouring, for some hours, under the fear of having mortally wounded a fellow-creature, eagerly caught at this new idea, and favoured it to the utmost. Finally, the officers, without troubling themselves very much about Oliver, left the Chertsey constable in the house, and took up their rest for that night in the town: promising to return next morning.

With the next morning, there came a rumour, that two men and a boy were in the cage at Kingston, who had been apprehended over night under suspicious circumstances; and to Kingston Messrs. Blathers and Duff journeyed accordingly. The suspicious circumstances, however, resolving themselves, on investigation, into the one fact, that they had been discovered sleeping under a haystack: which, although a great crime, is only punishable by imprisonment, and is, in the merciful eye of the English law, and its comprehensive love of all the King's subjects, held to be no satisfactory proof, in the absence of all other evidence, that the sleeper, or sleepers, have committed burglary accompanied with violence, and have therefore rendered themselves liable to the punishment of death: Messrs. Blathers and Duff came back again, as wise as they went.

In short, after some more examination, and a great deal more conversation, a neighbouring magistrate was readily induced to take the joint bail of Mrs. Maylie and Mr. Losberne for Oliver's appearance if he should ever be called upon; and Blathers and Duff, being rewarded with a couple of guineas, returned to town with divided opinions on the subject of their expedition: the latter gentleman on a mature consideration of all the circumstances, inclining to the belief that the burglarious attempt had originated with the Family Pet; and the former being equally disposed to concede the full merit of it to the great Mr. Conkey Chickweed.

Meanwhile, Oliver gradually throve and prospered under the united care of Mrs. Maylie, Rose, and the kind-hearted Mr. Losberne. If fervent prayers, gushing from hearts overcharged with gratitude, be heard in Heaven—and if they be not, what prayers are!—the blessings which the orphan child called down upon them, sank into their souls, diffusing peace and happiness.

CHAPTER XXXII.

OF THE HAPPY LIFE OLIVER BEGAN TO LEAD WITH HIS KIND FRIENDS.

OLIVER's ailings were neither slight nor few. In addition to the pain and delay attendant upon a broken limb, his exposure to the wet and cold had brought on fever and ague: which hung about him for many weeks, and reduced him sadly. But, at length, he began, by slow degrees, to get better, and to be able to say sometimes, in a few tearful words, how deeply he felt the goodness of the two sweet ladies, and how ardently he hoped that when he grew strong and well again, he could do something to show his gratitude; only something which would let them see the love and duty with which his breast was full; something, however slight, which would prove to them that their gentle kindness had not been cast away; but that the poor boy whom their charity had rescued from misery, or death, was eager to serve them with his whole heart and soul.

"Poor fellow!" said Rose, when Oliver had been one day feebly endeavouring to utter the words of thankfulness that rose to his pale lips: "you shall have many opportunities of serving us, if you will. We are going into the country; and my aunt intends that you shall accompany us. The quiet place, the pure air, and all the pleasures and beauties of spring, will restore you in a few days; and we will employ you in a hundred ways, when you can bear the trouble."

"The trouble!" cried Oliver. "Oh! dear lady, if I could but work for you; if I could only give you pleasure by watering your flowers, or watching your birds, or running up and down the whole day long, to make you happy; what would I give to do it!"

"You shall give nothing at all," said Miss Maylie, smiling; "for, as I told you before, we shall employ you in a hundred ways; and if you only take half the trouble to please us, that you promise now, you will make me very happy indeed."

"Happy, ma'am!" cried Oliver; "how kind of you to say so!"

"You will make me happier than I can tell you," replied the young lady. "To think that my dear good aunt should have been the means of rescuing any one from such sad misery as you have described to us, would be an unspeakable pleasure to me; but to know that the object of her goodness and compassion was sincerely grateful and attached, in consequence, would delight me, more than you can well imagine. Do you understand me?" she inquired, watching Oliver's thoughtful face.

"Oh yes, ma'am, yes!" replied Oliver, eagerly; "but I was thinking that I am ungrateful now."

"To whom?" inquired the young lady.

"To the kind gentleman, and the dear old nurse, who took so much care of me before," rejoined Oliver. "If they knew how happy I am, they would be pleased, I am sure."

"I am sure they would," rejoined Oliver's benefactress; "and Mr. Losberne has already been kind enough to promise that when you are well enough to bear the journey, he will carry you to see them."

"Has he, ma'am?" cried Oliver, his face brightening with pleasure. "I don't know what I shall do for joy when I see their kind faces once again!"

In a short time Oliver was sufficiently recovered to undergo the fatigue of this expedition; and one morning he and Mr. Losberne set out, accordingly, in a little carriage which belonged to Mrs. Maylie. When they came to Chertsey Bridge, Oliver turned very pale, and uttered a loud exclamation.

"What's the matter with the boy?" cried the doctor, as usual, all in a bustle. "Do you see anything—hear anything—feel anything—eh?"

"That, Sir," cried Oliver, pointing out of the carriage window. "That house!"

"Yes; well, what of it? Stop, coachman. Pull up here," cried the doctor. "What of the house, my man; eh?"

"The thieves; the house they took me to," whispered Oliver.

"The devil it is!" cried the doctor. "Halloa, there! let me out!"

But before the coachman could dismount from his box, he had tumbled out of the coach, by some means or other; and, running down to the deserted tenement, began kicking at the door like a madman.

"Halloa!" said a little ugly hump-backed man: opening the door so suddenly, that the doctor, from the very impetus of his last kick, nearly fell forward into the passage. "What's the matter here?"

"Matter!" exclaimed the other, collaring him, without a moment's reflection. "A good deal. Robbery is the matter."

"There'll be murder the matter, too," replied the humpbacked man, coolly, "if you don't take your hands off. Do you hear me?"

"I hear you," said the doctor, giving his captive a hearty shake. "Where's—confound the fellow, what's his rascally name—Sikes; that's it. Where's Sikes, you thief?"

The hump-backed man stared, as if in excess of amazement and indignation; and twisting himself, dexterously, from the doctor's grasp, growled forth a volley of horrid oaths, and retired into the house. Before he could shut the door, however, the doctor had passed into the parlour, without a word of parley. He looked anxiously round; not an article of furniture; not a vestige of anything, animate or inanimate; not even the position of the cupboards; answered Oliver's description!

"Now," said the hump-backed man, who had watched him keenly, "what do you mean by coming into my house, in this violent way? Do you want to rob me, or to murder me? Which is it?"

"Did you ever know a man come out to do either, in a chariot and pair, you ridiculous old vampire?" said the irritable doctor.

"What do you want, then?" demanded the hunchback. "Will you take yourself off, before I do you a mischief? Curse you!"

"As soon as I think proper," said Mr. Losberne, looking into the other parlour; which, like the first, bore no resemblance whatever to Oliver's account of it. "I shall find you out, some day, my friend."

"Will you?" sneered the ill-favoured cripple. "If you

ever want me, I'm here. I haven't lived here mad and all alone, for five-and-twenty years, to be scared by you. You shall pay for this; you shall pay for this." And so saying, the mis-shapen little demon set up a hideous yell, and danced upon the ground, as if frantic with rage.

"Stupid enough, this," muttered the doctor to himself; "the boy must have made a mistake. Here! Put that in your pocket, and shut yourself up again." With these words he flung the hunchback a piece of money, and returned to the carriage.

The man followed to the chariot door, uttering the wildest imprecations and curses all the way; but as Mr. Losberne turned to speak to the driver, he looked into the carriage, and eyed Oliver for an instant with a glance so sharp and fierce, and at the same time so furious and vindictive, that, waking or sleeping, he could not forget it for months afterwards. He continued to utter the most fearful imprecations, until the driver had resumed his seat; and when they were once more on their way, they could see him some distance behind: beating his feet upon the ground, and tearing his hair, in transports of frenzied rage.

"I am an ass!" said the doctor, after a long silence. "Did you know that before, Oliver?"

"No, Sir."

"Then don't forget it another time."

"An ass," said the doctor again, after a further silence of some minutes. "Even if it had been the right place, and the right fellows had been there, what could I have done, single-handed? And if I had had assistance, I see no good that I should have done, except leading to my own exposure, and an unavoidable statement of the manner in which I have hushed up this business. That would have served me right, though. I am always involving myself in some scrape or other, by acting on impulse; and it might have done me good."

Now, the fact was that the excellent doctor had never acted upon anything else but impulse all through his life; and it was no bad compliment to the nature of the impulses which governed him, that so far from being involved in any peculiar troubles or misfortunes, he had the warmest respect and esteem of all who knew him. If the truth must be told, he was a little out of temper, for a minute or two, at being disappointed in procuring corroborative evidence of Oliver's story, on the very first occasion on which he had a chance of obtaining any. He soon came round again, however; and finding that Oliver's replies to his questions, were still as straightforward and consistent, and still delivered with as much apparent sincerity and truth, as they had ever been, he made up his mind to attach full credence to them, from that time forth.

As Oliver knew the name of the street in which Mr. Brownlow resided, they were enabled to drive straight thither. When the coach turned into it, his heart beat so violently, that he could scarcely draw his breath.

"Now, my boy, which house is it?" inquired Mr. Losberne.

"That! That!" replied Oliver, pointing eagerly out of the window. "The white house. Oh! make haste! Pray make haste! I feel as if I should die; it makes me tremble so."

"Come, come!" said the good doctor, patting him on the shoulder. "You will see them directly, and they will be overjoyed to find you safe and well."

"Oh! I hope so!" cried Oliver. "They were so good to me; so very, very good to me."

The coach rolled on. It stopped. No; that was the wrong house; the next door. It went on a few paces, and stopped again. Oliver looked up at the windows, with tears of happy expectation coursing down his face.

Alas! the white house was empty, and there was a bill in the window. "To Let."

"Knock at the next door," cried Mr. Losberne, taking Oliver's arm in his. "What has become of Mr. Brownlow, who used to live in the adjoining house, do you know?"

The servant did not know; but would go and inquire. She presently returned; and said, that Mr. Brownlow had sold off his goods, and gone to the West Indies, six weeks before. Oliver clasped his hands, and sank feebly backwards.

"Has his housekeeper gone, too?" inquired Mr. Losberne, after a moment's pause.

"Yes, Sir," replied the servant. "The old gentleman, the housekeeper, and a gentleman who was a friend of Mr. Brownlow's, all went together."

"Then, turn towards home again," said Mr. Losberne to the driver; "and don't stop to bait the horses, till you get out of this confounded London!"

"The book-stall keeper, Sir?" said Oliver. "I know the way there. See him, pray, Sir! Do see him!"

"My poor boy, this is disappointment enough for one day," said the doctor. "Quite enough for both of us. If we go to the book-stall keeper's, we shall certainly find that he is dead, or has set his house on fire, or run away. No; home again straight!" And in obedience to the doctor's impulse, home they went.

The bitter disappointment caused Oliver much sorrow and grief, even in the midst of his happiness; for he had pleased himself, many times during his illness, with thinking of all that Mr. Brownlow and Mrs. Bedwin would say to him: and what delight it would be to tell them how many long days and nights he had passed in reflecting on what they had done for him, and in bewailing his cruel separation from them. The hope of eventually clearing himself with them, too, and explaining how he had been forced away, had buoyed him up, and sustained him, under many of his recent trials; and now, the idea that they should have gone so far, and carried with them the belief that he was an impostor and a robber: a belief which might remain uncontradicted to his dying day: was almost more than he could bear.

The circumstance occasioned no alteration, however, in the behaviour of his benefactors. After another fortnight: when the fine warm weather had fairly begun, and every tree and flower was putting forth its young leaves and rich blossoms: they made preparations for quitting the house at Chertsey, for some months. Sending the plate, which had so excited the Jew's cupidity, to the banker's; and leaving Giles and another servant in care of the house; they departed to a cottage at some distance in the country; and took Oliver with them.

Who can describe the pleasure and delight, the peace of mind and soft tranquillity, the sickly boy felt in the balmy air, and among the green hills and rich woods, of an inland village! Who can tell how scenes of peace and quietude sink into the minds of pain-worn dwellers in close and noisy places, and carry their own freshness, deep into their jaded hearts! Men who have lived in crowded, pent-up streets, through lives of toil, and never wished for change; men, to whom custom has indeed been second nature, and who have come almost to love each brick and stone that formed the narrow boundaries of their daily walks; even they, with the hand of death upon them, have been known to yearn at last for one short glimpse of Nature's face; and, carried far from the scenes of their old pains and pleasures, have seemed to pass at once into a new state of being; and crawling forth, from day to day, to some green sunny spot, have had such memories wakened up within them by the mere sight of sky, and hill and plain, and glistening water, that a foretaste of heaven itself has soothed their quick decline, and they have sunk into their tombs, as peacefully as the sun, whose setting they watched from their lonely chamber window but a few hours before, faded from their dim and feeble sight! The memories which peaceful country scenes call up, are not of this world, nor its thoughts and hopes. Their gentle influence may teach us how to weave fresh garlands for the graves of those we loved: may purify our thoughts, and bear down before it old enmity and hatred; but beneath all this, there lingers, in the least reflective mind, a vague and half-formed consciousness of having held such feelings long before, in some remote and distant time, which calls up solemn thoughts of distant times to come, and bends down pride and worldliness beneath it.

It was a lovely spot to which they repaired. Oliver, whose days had been spent among squalid crowds, and in the midst of noise and brawling, seemed to enter on a new existence there. The rose and honeysuckle clung to the cottage walls; the ivy crept round the trunks of the trees; and the garden-flowers perfumed the air with delicious odours. Hard by, was a little churchyard; not crowded with tall unsightly gravestones, but full of humble mounds, covered with fresh turf and moss: beneath which, the old people of the village lay at rest. Oliver often wandered here; and, thinking of the wretched grave in which his mother lay, would sometimes sit him down and sob unseen; but, when he raised his eyes to the deep sky overhead, he would cease to think of her as lying in the ground, and would weep for her, sadly, but without pain.

It was a happy time. The days were peaceful and serene; the nights brought with them neither fear nor care; no languishing in a wretched prison, or associating with wretched men; nothing but pleasant and happy thoughts. Every morning he went to a white-headed old gentleman, who lived near the little church: who taught him to read better, and to write; and spoke so kindly, and took such pains, that Oliver could never try enough to please him. Then, he would walk with Mrs. Maylie and Rose, and hear them talk of books; or perhaps sit near them, in some shady place, and listen whilst the young lady read: which he could have done, until it grew too dark to see the letters. Then he had his own lesson for the next day to prepare; and at this, he would work hard, in a little room which looked into the garden, till evening came slowly on, when the ladies would walk out again, and he with them: listening with such pleasure to all they said: and so happy if they wanted a flower that he could climb to reach, or had forgotten anything he could run to fetch: that he could never be quick enough about it. When it became quite dark, and they returned home, the young lady would sit down to the piano, and play some pleasant air, or sing, in a low and gentle voice, some old song which it pleased her aunt to hear. There would be no candles lighted at such times as these; and Oliver would sit by one of the windows, listening to the sweet music, in a perfect rapture.

And when Sunday came, how differently the day was

spent, from any way in which he had ever spent it yet! and how happily too; like all the other days in that most happy time! There was the little church, in the morning, with the green leaves fluttering at the windows: the birds singing without: and the sweet-smelling air stealing in at the low porch, and filling the homely building with its fragrance. The poor people were so neat and clean, and knelt so reverently in prayer, that it seemed a pleasure, not a tedious duty, their assembling there together; and though the singing might be rude, it was real, and sounded more musical (to Oliver's ears at least) than any he had ever heard in church before. Then, there were the walks as usual, and many calls at the clean houses of the labouring men; and at night, Oliver read a chapter or two from the Bible, which he had been studying all the week, and in the performance of which duty he felt more proud and pleased, than if he had been the clergyman himself.

In the morning Oliver would be a-foot by six o'clock, roaming the fields, and plundering the hedges, far and wide, for nosegays of wild flowers, with which he would return laden, home; and which it took great care and consideration to arrange, to the best advantage, for the embellishment of the breakfast-table. There was fresh groundsel, too, for Miss Maylie's birds, with which Oliver, who had been studying the subject under the able tuition of the village clerk, would decorate the cages, in the most approved taste. When the birds were made all spruce and smart for the day, there was usually some little commission of charity to execute in the village; or, failing that, there was rare cricket-playing, sometimes on the green; or, failing that, there was always something to do in the garden, or about the plants, to which Oliver: who had studied this science also, under the same master, who was a gardener by trade: applied himself with hearty goodwill, until Miss Rose made her appearance; when there were a thousand commendations to be bestowed on all he had done.

So three months glided away; three months which, in the life of the most blessed and favoured of mortals, might have been unmingled happiness; and which, in Oliver's, were true felicity indeed. With the purest and most amiable generosity on one side; and the truest, warmest, soul-felt gratitude on the other; it is no wonder that, by the end of that short time, Oliver Twist had become completely domesticated with the old lady and her niece: and that the fervent attachment of his young and sensitive heart, was repaid by their pride in, and attachment to, himself.

CHAPTER XXXIII.

WHEREIN THE HAPPINESS OF OLIVER AND HIS FRIENDS, EXPERIENCES A SUDDEN CHECK.

SPRING flew swiftly by, and summer came; and if the village had been beautiful at first, it was now in the full glow and luxuriance of its richness. The great trees, which had looked shrunken and bare in the earlier months, had now burst into strong life and health; and stretching forth their green arms over the thirsty ground, converted open and naked spots into choice nooks, where was a deep and pleasant shade from which to look upon the wide prospect, steeped in sunshine, which lay stretched out beyond. The earth had donned her mantle of brightest green; and shed her richest perfumes abroad. It was the prime and vigour of the year; all things were glad and flourishing.

Still the same quiet life went on at the little cottage, and the same cheerful serenity prevailed among its inmates. Oliver had long since grown stout and healthy; but health or sickness made no difference in his warm feelings to those about him, though they do in the feelings of a great many people. He was still the same gentle, attached, affectionate creature that he had been when pain and suffering had wasted his strength; and when he was dependent for every slight attention and comfort on those who tended him.

One beautiful night, they had taken a longer walk than was customary with them; for the day had been unusually warm, and there was a brilliant moon; and a light wind had sprung up, which was unusually refreshing. Rose had been in high spirits, too, and they had walked on, in merry conversation, until they had far exceeded their ordinary bounds. Mrs. Maylie being fatigued, they returned more slowly home. The young lady, merely throwing off her simple bonnet, sat down to the piano as usual; after running abstractedly over the keys for a few minutes, she fell into a low and very solemn air; and as she played it, they heard her sob as if she were weeping.

"Rose, my dear!" said the elder lady.

Rose made no reply, but played a little quicker, as though the words had roused her from some painful thoughts.

"Rose, my love!" cried Mrs. Maylie, rising hastily, and bending over her. "What is this? In tears! My dear child, what distresses you?"

"Nothing, aunt; nothing," replied the young lady. "I don't know what it is; I can't describe it; but I feel——"

"Not ill, my love?" interposed Mrs. Maylie.

"No, no! Oh, not ill!" replied Rose: shuddering, as though some deadly chillness were passing over her, while she spoke; "I shall be better presently. Close the window, pray."

Oliver hastened to comply with her request. The young lady, making an effort to recover her cheerfulness, strove to play some livelier tune; but her fingers dropped powerless on the keys: and covering her face with her hands, she sank upon a sofa, and gave vent to the tears which she was now unable to repress.

"My child!" said the elderly lady, folding her arms about her, "I never saw you thus before."

"I would not alarm you if I could avoid it," rejoined Rose; "but indeed I have tried very hard, and cannot help this. I fear I *am* ill, aunt."

She was, indeed; for, when candles were brought, they saw that in the very short time which had elapsed since their return home, the hue of her countenance had changed to a marble whiteness. Its expression had lost nothing of its beauty; but it was changed; and there was an anxious, haggard look about the gentle face, which it had never worn before. Another minute, and it was suffused with a crimson flush: and a heavy wildness came over the soft blue eye; again this disappeared, like the shadow thrown by a passing cloud: and she was once more deadly pale.

Oliver, who watched the old lady anxiously, observed that she was alarmed by these appearances; and so, in truth, was he; but seeing that she affected to make light of them, he endeavoured to do the same; and they so far succeeded, that when Rose was persuaded by her aunt to retire for the night, she was in better spirits; and appeared even in better health: assuring them that she felt certain she should rise in the morning, quite well.

"I hope," said Oliver, when Mrs. Maylie returned, "that

nothing is the matter? She don't look well to-night, but——"

The old lady motioned to him not to speak; and sitting herself down in a dark corner of the room, remained silent for some time. At length, she said, in a trembling voice:

"I hope not, Oliver. I have been very happy with her for some years: too happy, perhaps. It may be time that I should meet with some misfortune; but I hope it is not this."

"What?" inquired Oliver.

"The heavy blow," said the old lady, "of losing the dear girl who has so long been my comfort and happiness."

"Oh! God forbid!" exclaimed Oliver, hastily.

"Amen to that, my child!" said the old lady, wringing her hands.

"Surely there is no danger of anything so dreadful?" said Oliver. "Two hours ago, she was quite well."

"She is very ill now," rejoined Mrs. Maylie; "and will be worse, I am sure. My dear, dear Rose! Oh, what should I do without her!"

She gave way to such great grief, that Oliver, suppressing his own emotion, ventured to remonstrate with her; and to beg, earnestly, that, for the sake of the dear young lady herself, she would be more calm.

"And consider, ma'am," said Oliver, as the tears forced themselves into his eyes, despite his efforts to the contrary. "Oh! consider how young and good she is, and what pleasure and comfort she gives to all about her. I am sure—certain—quite certain—that, for your sake, who are so good yourself; and for her own; and for the sake of all she makes so happy; she will not die. Heaven will never let her die so young."

"Hush!" said Mrs. Maylie, laying her hand on Oliver's head. "You think like a child, poor boy. But you teach me my duty, notwithstanding. I had forgotten it for a moment, Oliver, but I hope I may be pardoned, for I am old, and have seen enough of illness and death to know the agony of separation from the objects of our love. I have seen enough, too, to know that it is not always the youngest and best who are spared to those that love them; but this should give us comfort in our sorrow; for Heaven is just; and such things teach us, impressively, that there is a brighter world than this; and that the passage to it is speedy. God's will be done! I love her; and He knows how well!"

Oliver was surprised to see that as Mrs. Maylie said these words, she checked her lamentations as though by one struggle; and drawing herself up as she spoke, became composed and firm. He was still more astonished to find that this firmness lasted; and that, under all the care and watching which ensued, Mrs. Maylie was ever ready and collected: performing all the duties which devolved upon her, steadily, and, to all external appearance, even cheerfully. But he was young, and did not know what strong minds are capable of, under trying circumstances. How should he, when their possessors so seldom know themselves?

An anxious night ensued. When morning came, Mrs. Maylie's predictions were but too well verified. Rose was in the first stage of a high and dangerous fever.

"We must be active, Oliver, and not give way to useless grief," said Mrs. Maylie, laying her finger on her lip, as she looked steadily into his face; "this letter must be sent, with all possible expedition, to Mr. Losberne. It must be carried to the market-town, which is not more than four miles off, by the footpath across the fields; and thence dis-

patched, by an express on horseback, straight to Chertsey. The people at the inn will undertake to do this; and I can trust to you to see it done, I know."

Oliver could make no reply, but looked his anxiety to be gone at once.

"Here is another letter," said Mrs. Maylie, pausing to reflect; "but whether to send it now, or wait until I see how Rose goes on, I scarcely know. I would not forward it, unless I feared the worst."

"Is it for Chertsey, too, ma'am?" inquired Oliver: impatient to execute his commission, and holding out his trembling hand for the letter.

"No," replied the old lady, giving it to him mechanically. Oliver glanced at it, and saw that it was directed to Harry Maylie, Esquire, at some great lord's house in the country; where, he could not make out.

"Shall it go, ma'am?" asked Oliver, looking up, impatiently.

"I think not," replied Mrs. Maylie, taking it back. "I will wait until to-morrow."

With these words, she gave Oliver her purse, and he started off, without more delay, at the greatest speed he could muster.

Swiftly he ran across the fields, and down the little lanes which sometimes divided them: now almost hidden by the high corn on either side, and now emerging in an open field, where the mowers and haymakers were busy at their work; nor did he stop once, save now and then, for a few seconds, to recover breath, until he came, in a great heat, and covered with dust, on the little market-place of the market-town.

Here he paused, and looked about for the inn. There was a white bank, and a red brewery, and a yellow town-hall; and in one corner there was a large house, with all the wood about it painted green: before which was the sign of "The George." To this he hastened, as soon as it caught his eye.

He spoke to a postboy who was dozing under the gateway; and who, after hearing what he wanted, referred him to the hostler; who after hearing all he had to say again, referred him to the landlord; who was a tall gentleman in a blue neckcloth, a white hat, drab breeches, and boots with tops to match, leaning against a pump by the stable-door, picking his teeth with a silver toothpick.

This gentleman walked with much deliberation into the bar to make out the bill: which took a long time making out: and after it was ready, and paid, a horse had to be saddled, and a man to be dressed, which took up ten good minutes more. Meanwhile Oliver was in such a desperate state of impatience and anxiety, that he felt as if he could have jumped upon the horse himself, and galloped away, full tear, to the next stage. At length, all was ready; and the little parcel having been handed up, with many injunctions and entreaties for its speedy delivery, the man set spurs to his horse, and rattling over the uneven paving of the market-place, was out of the town, and galloping along the turnpike-road, in a couple of minutes.

It was something to feel certain that assistance was sent for; and that no time had been lost. Oliver hurried up the inn-yard, with a somewhat lighter heart: and was turning out of the gateway when he accidentally stumbled against a tall man, wrapped in a cloak: who was at that moment coming out of the inn door.

"Hah!" cried the man, fixing his eyes on Oliver, and suddenly recoiling. "What the devil's this?"

"I beg your pardon, Sir," said Oliver; "I was in a great hurry to get home, and didn't see you were coming."

"Death!" muttered the man to himself, glaring at the boy with his large dark eyes. "Who would have thought it? Grind him to ashes! He'd start up from a marble coffin, to come in my way!"

"I am sorry," stammered Oliver, confused by the strange man's wild look. "I hope I have not hurt you!"

"Rot his bones!" murmured the man, in a horrible passion: between his clenched teeth; "if I had only had the courage to say the word, I might have been free of him in a night. Curses on your head, and black death on your heart, you imp! What are you doing here?"

The man shook his fist and gnashed his teeth, as he uttered these words incoherently. He advanced towards Oliver, as if with the intention of aiming a blow at him, but fell violently on the ground: writhing and foaming, in a fit.

Oliver gazed, for a moment, at the struggles of the madman (for such he supposed him to be); and then darted into the house for help. Having seen him safely carried into the hotel, he turned his face homewards: running as fast as he could, to make up for lost time: and recalling, with a great deal of astonishment and some fear, the extraordinary behaviour of the person from whom he had just parted.

The circumstance did not dwell in his recollection long, however; for when he reached the cottage, there was enough to occupy his mind, and to drive all considerations of self completely from his memory.

Rose Maylie had rapidly grown worse; and before midnight was delirious. A medical practitioner, who resided on the spot, was in constant attendance upon her; and after first seeing the patient, he had taken Mrs. Maylie aside, and pronounced her disorder to be one of a most alarming nature. "In fact," he said, "it would be little short of a miracle, if she recovered."

How often did Oliver start from his bed that night, and stealing out, with noiseless footstep, to the staircase, listen for the slightest sound from the sick chamber! How often did a tremble shake his frame, and cold drops of terror start upon his brow, when a sudden trampling of feet caused him to fear that something too dreadful to think of, had even then occurred! And what had been the fervency of all the prayers he had ever uttered, compared with those he poured forth, now, in the agony and passion of his supplication for the life and health of the gentle creature, who was tottering on the deep grave's verge.

The suspense, the fearful, acute suspense, of standing idly by while the life of one we dearly love, is trembling in the balance; the racking thoughts that crowd upon the mind, and make the heart beat violently, and the breath come thick, by the force of the images they conjure up before it; the desperate anxiety *to be doing something* to relieve the pain, or lessen the danger, which we have no power to alleviate; the sinking of soul and spirit, which the sad remembrance of our helplessness produces; what tortures can equal these; what reflections or endeavours can, in the full tide and fever of the time, allay them!

Morning came; and the little cottage was lonely and still. People spoke in whispers; anxious faces appeared at the gate, from time to time; and women and children went away in tears. All the livelong day, and for hours after it had grown dark, Oliver paced softly up and down the garden: raising his eyes every instant to the sick chamber, and shuddering to see the darkened window, looking as if death lay stretched inside. Late at night, Mr. Losberne arrived. "It is hard," said the good doctor, turning away as he spoke; "so young: so much beloved: but there is very little hope."

Another morning. The sun shone brightly: as brightly as if it looked upon no misery or care; and, with every leaf and flower in full bloom about her: with life, and health, and sounds and sights of joy, surrounding her on every side: the fair young creature lay, wasting fast. Oliver crept away to the old churchyard, and sitting down on one of the green mounds, wept for her, in silence.

There was such peace and beauty in the scene; so much of brightness and mirth in the sunny landscape; such blithesome music in the songs of the summer birds; such freedom in the rapid flight of the rook, careering overhead; so much of life and joyousness in all; that, when the boy raised his aching eyes, and looked about, the thought instinctively occurred to him, that this was not a time for death; that Rose could surely never die when humbler things were all so glad and gay; that graves were for cold and cheerless winter: not for sunlight and fragrance. He almost thought that shrouds were for the old and shrunken; and that they never wrapped the young and graceful form within their ghastly folds.

A knell from the church bell broke harshly on these youthful thoughts. Another! Again! It was tolling for the funeral service. A group of humble mourners entered the gate: wearing white favours; for the corpse was young. They stood uncovered by a grave; and there was a mother: a mother once: among the weeping train. But the sun shone brightly, and the birds sang on.

Oliver turned homeward, thinking on the many kindnesses he had received from the young lady, and wishing that the time could come over again, that he might never cease showing her how grateful and attached he was. He had no cause for self-reproach on the score of neglect, or want of thought, for he had been devoted to her service; and yet a hundred little occasions rose up before him, on which he fancied he might have been more zealous, and more earnest, and wished he had been. We need be careful how we deal with those about us; when every death carries to some small circle of survivors, thoughts of so much omitted, and so little done—of so many things forgotten, and so many more which might have been repaired. There is no remorse so deep as that which is unavailing; if we would be spared its tortures, let us remember this, in time.

When he reached home Mrs. Maylie was sitting in the little parlour. Oliver's heart sank at sight of her; for she had never left the bedside of her niece; and he trembled to think what change could have driven her away. He learnt that she had fallen into a deep sleep, from which she would waken, either to recovery and life, or to bid them farewell, and die.

They sat, listening, and afraid to speak, for hours. The untasted meal was removed; and with looks which showed that their thoughts were elsewhere, they watched the sun as he sank lower and lower, and, at length, cast over sky and earth those brilliant hues which herald his departure. Their quick ears caught the sound of an approaching footstep; and they both involuntarily darted to the door, as Mr. Losberne entered.

"What of Rose?" cried the old lady. "Tell me at once! I can bear it; anything but suspense! Oh, tell me! in the name of Heaven!"

"You must compose yourself," said the doctor, supporting her. "Be calm, my dear ma'am, pray."

"Let me go, in God's name! My dear child! She is dead! She is dying!"

"No!" cried the doctor, passionately. "As He is good and merciful, she will live to bless us all, for years to come."

The lady fell upon her knees, and tried to fold her hands together; but the energy which had supported her so long, fled up to Heaven with her first thanksgiving; and she sank into the friendly arms which were extended to receive her.

CHAPTER XXXIV.

CONTAINS SOME INTRODUCTORY PARTICULARS RELATIVE TO A YOUNG GENTLEMAN WHO NOW ARRIVES UPON THE SCENE; AND A NEW ADVENTURE WHICH HAPPENED TO OLIVER.

IT was almost too much happiness to bear. Oliver felt stunned and stupefied by the unexpected intelligence; he could not weep, or speak, or rest. He had scarcely the power of understanding anything that had passed, until, after a long ramble in the quiet evening air, a burst of tears came to his relief; and he seemed to awaken, all at once, to a full sense of the joyful change that had occurred, and the almost insupportable load of anguish which had been taken from his breast.

The night was fast closing in, when he returned homeward: laden with flowers which he had culled, with peculiar care, for the adornment of the sick chamber. As he walked briskly along the road, he heard behind him the noise of some vehicle, approaching at a furious pace. Looking round, he saw that it was a post-chaise, driven at great speed; and as the horses were galloping, and the road was narrow, he stood leaning against a gate until it should have passed him.

As it dashed on, Oliver caught a glimpse of a man in a white nightcap, whose face seemed familiar to him, although his view was so brief that he could not identify the person. In another second or two, the nightcap was thrust out of the chaise-window; and a stentorian voice bellowed to the driver to stop: which he did as soon as he could pull up his horses. Then, the nightcap once again appeared; and the same voice called Oliver by his name.

"Here!" cried the voice. "Master Oliver, what's the news? Miss Rose! Master O-li-ver!"

"Is it you, Giles?" cried Oliver, running up to the chaise-door.

Giles popped out his nightcap again, preparatory to making some reply, when he was suddenly pulled back by a young gentleman who occupied the other corner of the chaise, and who eagerly demanded what was the news.

"In a word," cried the gentleman, "better or worse?"

"Better—much better!" replied Oliver hastily.

"Thank Heaven!" exclaimed the gentleman. "You are sure?"

"Quite, Sir," replied Oliver. "The change took place only a few hours ago; and Mr. Losberne says, that all danger is at an end."

The gentleman said not another word, but, opening the chaise-door, leaped out, and taking Oliver hurriedly by the arm, led him aside.

"You are quite certain? There is no possibility of any mistake on your part, my boy, is there?" demanded the gentleman in a tremulous voice. "Pray do not deceive me, by awakening any hopes that are not to be fulfilled."

"I would not for the world, Sir," replied Oliver. "Indeed you may believe me. Mr. Losberne's words were, that she would live to bless us all for many years to come. I heard him say so."

The tears stood in Oliver's eyes as he recalled the scene which was the beginning of so much happiness; and the gentleman turned his face away, and remained silent, for some minutes. Oliver thought he heard him sob, more than once; but he feared to interrupt him by any further remark—for he could well guess what his feelings were—and so stood apart, feigning to be occupied with his nosegay.

All this time, Mr. Giles, with the white nightcap on, had been sitting upon the steps of the chaise, supporting an elbow on each knee, and wiping his eyes with a blue cotton pocket-handkerchief dotted with white spots. That the honest fellow had not been feigning emotion, was abundantly demonstrated by the very red eyes with which he regarded the young gentleman, when he turned round and addressed him.

"I think you had better go on to my mother's in the chaise, Giles," said he. "I would rather walk slowly on, so as to gain a little time before I see her. You can say I am coming."

"I beg your pardon, Mr. Harry," said Giles: giving a final polish to his ruffled countenance with the handkerchief; "but if you would leave the postboy to say that, I should be very much obliged to you. It wouldn't be proper for the maids to see me in this state, Sir; I should never have any more authority with them if they did."

"Well," rejoined Harry Maylie, smiling, "you can do as you like. Let him go on with the luggage, if you wish it, and do you follow with us. Only first exchange that nightcap for some more appropriate covering, or we shall be taken for madmen."

Mr. Giles, reminded of his unbecoming costume, snatched off and pocketed his nightcap; and substituted a hat, of grave and sober shape, which he took out of the chaise. This done, the postboy drove off; and Giles, Mr. Maylie, and Oliver, followed at their leisure.

As they walked along, Oliver glanced from time to time with much interest and curiosity at the new-comer. He seemed about five-and-twenty years of age, and was of the middle height; his countenance was frank and handsome; and his demeanour singularly easy and prepossessing. Notwithstanding the difference between youth and age, he bore so strong a likeness to the old lady, that Oliver would have had no great difficulty in imagining their relationship, even if he had not already spoken of her as his mother.

Mrs. Maylie was anxiously waiting to receive her son when he reached the cottage; and the meeting did not take place without great emotion on both sides.

"Mother!" whispered the young man; "why did you not write before?"

"I did," replied Mrs. Maylie; "but, on reflection, I determined to keep back the letter until I had heard Mr. Losberne's opinion."

"But why," said the young man, "why run the chance of that occurring which so nearly happened? If Rose had

—I cannot utter that word now—if this illness had terminated differently, how could you ever have forgiven yourself! How could I ever have known happiness again!"

"If that *had* been the case, Harry," said Mrs. Maylie, "I fear your happiness would have been effectually blighted; and that your arrival here a day sooner or a day later, would have been of very, very little import."

"And who can wonder if it be so, mother?" rejoined the young man; "or why should I say, *if?*—It is—it is—you know it, mother—you must know it!"

"I know that she deserves the best and purest love the heart of man can offer," said Mrs. Maylie; "I know that the devotion and affection of her nature require no ordinary return, but one that shall be deep and lasting. If I did not feel this, and know, besides, that a changed behaviour in one she loved would break her heart, I should not feel my task so difficult of performance, or have to encounter so many struggles in my own bosom, when I take what seems to me to be the strict line of duty."

"This is unkind, mother," said Harry. "Do you still suppose that I am a boy ignorant of my own mind, and mistaking the impulses of my own soul?"

"I think, my dear son," returned Mrs. Maylie, laying her hand upon his shoulder, "that youth has many generous impulses which do not last; and that among them are some, which, being gratified, become only the more fleeting. Above all, I think," said the lady, fixing her eyes on her son's face, "that if an enthusiastic, ardent, and ambitious man marry a wife on whose name there is a stain, which, though it originate in no fault of hers, may be visited by cold and sordid people upon her, and upon his children also; and, in exact proportion to his success in the world, be cast in his teeth, and made the subject of sneers against him: he may—no matter how generous and good his nature—one day repent of the connexion he formed in early life; and she may have the pain and torture of knowing that he does so."

"Mother," said the young man, impatiently, "he would be a selfish brute, unworthy alike of the name of man and of the woman you describe, who acted thus."

"You think so now, Harry," replied his mother.

"And ever will!" said the young man. "The mental agony I have suffered, during the last two days, wrings from me the undisguised avowal to you of a passion which, as you well know, is not one of yesterday, nor one I have lightly formed. On Rose, sweet, gentle girl! my heart is set, as firmly as ever heart of man was set on woman. I have no thought, no view, no hope in life, beyond her; and if you oppose me in this great stake, you take my peace and happiness in your hands, and cast them to the wind. Mother, think better of this, and of me, and do not disregard the happiness of which you seem to think so little."

"Harry," said Mrs. Maylie, "it is because I think so much of warm and sensitive hearts, that I would spare them from being wounded. But we have said enough, and more than enough, on this matter just now."

"Let it rest with Rose, then," interposed Harry. "You will not press these overstrained opinions of yours, so far, as to throw any obstacle in my way?"

"I will not," rejoined Mrs. Maylie; "but I would have you consider——"

"I *have* considered!" was the impatient reply; "Mother, I have considered, years and years. I have considered ever since I have been capable of serious reflection. My feelings remain unchanged, as they ever will; and why should

I suffer the pain of a delay in giving them vent, which can be productive of no earthly good? No! Before I leave this place, Rose shall hear me."

"She shall," said Mrs. Maylie.

"There is something in your manner, which would almost imply that she will hear me coldly, mother," said the young man.

"Not coldly," rejoined the old lady; "far from it."

"How then?" urged the young man. "She has formed no other attachment?"

"No, indeed," replied his mother; "you have, or I mistake, too strong a hold on her affections already. What I would say," resumed the old lady, stopping her son as he was about to speak, "is this. Before you stake your all on this chance; before you suffer yourself to be carried to the highest point of hope; reflect for a few moments, my dear child, on Rose's history, and consider what effect the knowledge of her doubtful birth may have on her decision: devoted as she is to us, with all the intensity of her noble mind, and with that perfect sacrifice of self which, in all matters, great or trifling, has always been her characteristic."

"What do you mean?"

"That I leave you to discover," replied Mrs. Maylie. "I must go back to her. God bless you!"

"I shall see you again to-night?" said the young man, eagerly.

"By and by," replied the lady; "when I leave Rose."

"You will tell her I am here?" said Harry.

"Of course," replied Mrs. Maylie.

"And say how anxious I have been, and how much I have suffered, and how I long to see her. You will not refuse to do this, mother?"

"No," said the old lady; "I will tell her all." And pressing her son's hand, affectionately, she hastened from the room.

Mr. Losberne and Oliver had remained at another end of the apartment while this hurried conversation was proceeding. The former now held out his hand to Harry Maylie; and hearty salutations were exchanged between them. The doctor then communicated, in reply to multifarious questions from his young friend, a precise account of his patient's situation; which was quite as consolatory and full of promise, as Oliver's statement had encouraged him to hope; and to the whole of which, Mr. Giles, who affected to be busy about the luggage, listened with greedy ears.

"Have you shot anything particular, lately, Giles?" inquired the doctor, when he had concluded.

"Nothing particular, Sir," replied Mr. Giles, colouring up to the eyes.

"Nor catching any thieves, nor identifying any housebreakers?" said the doctor.

"None at all, Sir," replied Mr. Giles, with much gravity.

"Well," said the doctor, "I am sorry to hear it, because you do that sort of thing so admirably. Pray, how is Brittles?"

"The boy is very well, Sir," said Mr. Giles, recovering his usual tone of patronage; "and sends his respectful duty, Sir."

That's well," said the doctor. "Seeing you here, reminds me, Mr. Giles, that on the day before that on which I was called away so hurriedly, I executed, at the request of your good mistress, a small commission in your favour. Just step into this corner a moment, will you?"

Mr. Giles walked into the corner with much importance, and some wonder: and was honoured with a short whispering conference with the doctor; on the termination of which, he made a great many bows, and retired with steps of unusual stateliness. The subject matter of this conference was not disclosed in the parlour, but the kitchen was speedily enlightened concerning it; for Mr. Giles walked straight thither, and having called for a mug of ale, announced, with an air of majesty, which was highly effective, that it had pleased his mistress, in consideration of his gallant behaviour on the occasion of that attempted robbery, to deposit, in the local savings-bank, the sum of five and twenty pounds, for his sole use and benefit. At this, the two women-servants lifted up their hands and eyes: and supposed that Mr. Giles would begin to be quite proud now; whereunto Mr. Giles, pulling out his shirt-frill, replied, "No, no;" and that if they observed that he was at all haughty to his inferiors, he would thank them to tell him so. And then he made a great many other remarks, no less illustrative of his humility, which were received with equal favour and applause, and were, withal, as original and as much to the purpose, as the remarks of great men commonly are.

Above stairs, the remainder of the evening passed cheerfully away; for the doctor was in high spirits; and however fatigued or thoughtful Harry Maylie might have been at first, he was not proof against the worthy gentleman's good humour, which displayed itself in a great variety of sallies and professional recollections, and an abundance of small jokes, which struck Oliver as being the drollest things he had ever heard, and caused him to laugh proportionately: to the evident satisfaction of the doctor, who laughed immoderately at himself, and made Harry laugh almost as heartily, by the very force of sympathy. So, they were as pleasant a party as, under the circumstances, they could well have been; and it was late before they retired, with light and thankful hearts, to take that rest of which, after the doubt and suspense they had recently undergone, they stood so much in need.

Oliver rose next morning, in better heart, and went about his usual early occupations, with more hope and pleasure than he had known for many days. The birds were once more hung out, to sing, in their old places; and the sweetest wild flowers that could be found, were once more gathered to gladden Rose with their beauty and fragrance. The melancholy which had seemed to the sad eyes of the anxious boy to hang, for days past, over every object, beautiful as all were, was dispelled by magic. The dew seemed to sparkle more brightly on the green leaves; the air to rustle among them with a sweeter music; and the sky itself to look more blue and bright. Such is the influence which the condition of our own thoughts, exercises, even over the appearance of external objects. Men who look on nature, and their fellow-men, and cry that all is dark and gloomy, are in the right; but the sombre colours are reflections from their own jaundiced eyes and hearts. The real hues are delicate, and need a clearer vision.

It is worthy of remark, and Oliver did not fail to note it at the time, that his morning expeditions were no longer made alone. Harry Maylie, after the very first morning when he met Oliver coming laden home, was seized with such a passion for flowers, and displayed such a taste in their arrangement, as left his young companion far behind. If Oliver were behindhand in these respects, however, he knew where the best were to be found; and morning after

morning they scoured the country together, and brought home the fairest that blossomed. The window of the young lady's chamber was opened now; for she loved to feel the rich summer air stream in, and revive her with its freshness; but there always stood in water, just inside the lattice, one particular little bunch, which was made up with great care, every morning. Oliver could not help noticing that the withered flowers were never thrown away, although the little vase was regularly replenished; nor could he help observing, that whenever the doctor came into the garden, he invariably cast his eyes up to that particular corner, and nodded his head most expressively, as he set forth on his morning's walk. Pending these observations, the days were flying by; and Rose was rapidly recovering.

Nor did Oliver's time hang heavy on his hands; although the young lady had not yet left her chamber; and there were no evening walks, save now and then, for a short distance, with Mrs. Maylie. He applied himself, with redoubled assiduity, to the instructions of the white-headed old gentleman, and laboured so hard that his quick progress surprised even himself. It was while he was engaged in this pursuit, that he was greatly startled and distressed by a most unexpected occurrence.

The little room in which he was accustomed to sit, when busy at his books, was on the ground-floor, at the back of the house. It was quite a cottage-room, with a lattice-window: around which were clusters of jessamine and honeysuckle, that crept over the casement, and filled the place with their delicious perfume. It looked into a garden, whence a wicket-gate opened into a small paddock; all beyond was fine meadow-land and wood. There was no other dwelling near, in that direction; and the prospect it commanded was very extensive.

One beautiful evening, when the first shades of twilight were beginning to settle upon the earth, Oliver sat at this window, intent upon his books. He had been poring over them for some time; and, as the day had been uncommonly sultry, and he had exerted himself a great deal; it is no disparagement to the authors, whoever they may have been, to say, that gradually and by slow degrees, he fell asleep.

There is a kind of sleep that steals upon us sometimes, which, while it holds the body prisoner, does not free the mind from a sense of things about it, and enable it to ramble at its pleasure. So far as an overpowering heaviness, a prostration of strength, and an utter inability to control our thoughts or power of motion, can be called sleep, this is it; and yet we have a consciousness of all that is going on about us; and, if we dream at such a time, words which are really spoken, or sounds which really exist at the moment, accommodate themselves with surprising readiness to our visions, until reality and imagination become so strangely blended that it is afterwards almost a matter of impossibility to separate the two. Nor is this the most striking phenomenon incidental to such a state. It is an undoubted fact, that although our senses of touch and sight be for the time dead, yet our sleeping thoughts, and the visionary scenes that pass before us, will be influenced, and materially influenced, by the *mere silent presence* of some external object: which may not have been near us when we closed our eyes: and of whose vicinity we have had no waking consciousness.

Oliver knew, perfectly well, that he was in his own little room; that his books were lying on the table before him; and that the sweet air was stirring among the creeping plants outside. And yet he was asleep. Suddenly, the scene changed; the air became close and confined; and he thought, with a glow of terror, that he was in the Jew's house again. There sat the hideous old man, in his accustomed corner, pointing at him, and whispering to another man, with his face averted, who sat beside him.

"Hush, my dear!" he thought he heard the Jew say; "it is he, sure enough. Come away."

"He!" the other man seemed to answer; "could I mistake him, think you? If a crowd of devils were to put themselves into his exact shape, and he stood amongst them, there is something that would tell me how to point him out. If you buried him fifty feet deep, and took me across his grave, I should know, if there wasn't a mark above it, that he lay buried there, I should!"

The man seemed to say this, with such dreadful hatred, that Oliver awoke with the fear, and started up.

Good Heaven! what was that, which sent his blood tingling to his heart, and deprived him of his voice, and of power to move! There—there—at the window; close before him; so close, that he could almost have touched him before he started back: with his eyes peering into the room, and meeting his: there stood the Jew! And beside him, white with rage or fear, or both, were the scowling features of the very man who had accosted him at the innyard.

It was but an instant, a glance, a flash, before his eyes; and they were gone. But they had recognised him, and he them; and their look was as firmly impressed upon his memory, as if it had been deeply carved in stone, and set before him from his birth. He stood transfixed for a moment; and then, leaping from the window into the garden, called loudly for help.

CHAPTER XXXV.

CONTAINING THE UNSATISFACTORY RESULT OF OLIVER'S ADVENTURE; AND A CONVERSATION OF SOME IMPORTANCE BETWEEN HARRY MAYLIE AND ROSE.

WHEN the inmates of the house, attracted by Oliver's cries, hurried to the spot from which they proceeded, they found him, pale and agitated, pointing in the direction of the meadows behind the house, and scarcely able to articulate the words, "The Jew! the Jew!"

Mr. Giles was at a loss to comprehend what this outcry meant; but Harry Maylie, whose perceptions were something quicker, and who had heard Oliver's history from his mother, understood it at once.

"What direction did he take?" he asked, catching up a heavy stick which was standing in a corner.

"That," replied Oliver, pointing out the course the men had taken; "I missed them in an instant."

"Then, they are in the ditch!" said Harry. "Follow! And keep as near me, as you can." So saying, he sprang over the hedge, and darted off with a speed which rendered it matter of exceeding difficulty for the others to keep near him.

Giles followed as well as he could; and Oliver followed too; and in the course of a minute or two, Mr. Losberne, who had been out walking, and just then returned, tumbled over the hedge after them, and picking himself up with more agility than he could have been supposed to possess, struck into the same course at no contemptible speed,

shouting all the while, most prodigiously, to know what was the matter.

On they all went; nor stopped they once to breathe, until the leader, striking off into an angle of the field indicated by Oliver, began to search, narrowly, the ditch and hedge adjoining; which afforded time for the remainder of the party to come up; and for Oliver to communicate to Mr. Losberne the circumstances that had led to so vigorous a pursuit.

The search was all in vain. There were not even the traces of recent footsteps, to be seen. They stood, now, on the summit of a little hill, commanding the open fields in every direction for three or four miles. There was the village in the hollow on the left; but, in order to gain that, after pursuing the track Oliver had pointed out, the men must have made a circuit of open ground, which it was impossible they could have accomplished in so short a time. A thick wood skirted the meadow-land in another direction; but they could not have gained that covert for the same reason.

"It must have been a dream, Oliver," said Harry Maylie.

"Oh no, indeed, Sir," replied Oliver, shuddering at the very recollection of the old wretch's countenance; "I saw him too plainly for that. I saw them both, as plainly as I see you now."

"Who was the other?" inquired Harry and Mr. Losberne, together.

"The very same man I told you of, who came so suddenly upon me at the inn," said Oliver. "We had our eyes fixed full upon each other; and I could swear to him."

"They took this way?" demanded Harry; "are you sure?"

"As I am that the men were at the window," replied Oliver, pointing down, as he spoke, to the hedge which divided the cottage-garden from the meadow. "The tall man leaped over, just there; and the Jew, running a few paces to the right, crept through that gap."

The two gentlemen watched Oliver's earnest face, as he spoke; and looking from him to each other, seemed to feel satisfied of the accuracy of what he said. Still, in no direction were there any appearances of the trampling of men in hurried flight. The grass was long; but it was trodden down nowhere, save where their own feet had crushed it. The sides and brinks of the ditches were of damp clay; but in no one place could they discern the print of men's shoes, or the slightest mark which would indicate that any feet had pressed the ground for hours before.

"This is strange!" said Harry.

"Strange!" echoed the doctor. "Blathers and Duff, themselves, could make nothing of it."

Notwithstanding the evidently useless nature of their search, they did not desist until the coming on of night rendered its further prosecution hopeless; and, even then, they gave it up with reluctance. Giles was despatched to the different ale-houses in the village, furnished with the best description Oliver could give of the appearance and dress of the strangers. Of these the Jew was, at all events, sufficiently remarkable to be remembered, supposing he had been seen drinking, or loitering about; but he returned without any intelligence, calculated to dispel or lessen the mystery.

On the next day, further search was made, and the inquiries renewed; but with no better success. On the day following, Oliver and Mr. Maylie repaired to the market-town, in the hope of seeing or hearing something of the

MONKS AND THE JEW.

men there; but this effort was equally fruitless; and after a few days, the affair began to be forgotten, as most affairs are, when wonder, having no fresh food to support it, dies away of itself.

Meanwhile, Rose was rapidly recovering. She had left her room; was able to go out; and mixing once more with the family, carried joy into the hearts of all.

But although this happy change had a visible effect on the little circle; and although cheerful voices and merry laughter were once more heard in the cottage; there was, at times, an unwonted restraint upon some there: even upon Rose herself: which Oliver could not fail to remark. Mrs. Maylie and her son were often closeted together for a long time; and more than once Rose appeared with traces of tears upon her face. After Mr. Losberne had fixed a day for his departure to Chertsey, these symptoms increased; and it became evident that something was in progress which affected the peace of the young lady, and of somebody else besides.

At length, one morning, when Rose was alone in the breakfast-parlour, Harry Maylie entered; and, with some hesitation, begged permission to speak with her for a few moments.

"A few—a very few—will suffice, Rose," said the young man, drawing his chair towards her. "What I shall have to say, has already presented itself to your mind; the most cherished hopes of my heart are not unknown to you, though from my lips you have not yet heard them stated."

Rose had been very pale from the moment of his entrance; but that might have been the effect of her recent illness. She merely bowed; and bending over some plants that stood near, waited in silence for him to proceed.

"I—I—ought to have left here, before," said Harry.

"You should, indeed," replied Rose. "Forgive me for saying so, but I wish you had."

"I was brought here, by the most dreadful and agonising of all apprehensions," said the young man; "the fear of losing the one dear being on whom my every wish and hope are fixed. You had been dying: trembling between earth and heaven. We know that when the young, the beautiful, and good, are visited with sickness, their pure spirits insensibly turn towards their bright home of lasting rest; we know, Heaven help us! that the best and fairest of our kind, too often fade in blooming."

There were tears in the eyes of the gentle girl, as these words were spoken; and when one fell upon the flower over which she bent, and glistened brightly in its cup, making it more beautiful, it seemed as though the outpouring of her fresh young heart, claimed kindred with the loveliest things in nature.

"An angel," continued the young man, passionately; "a creature as fair and innocent of guile as one of God's own angels, fluttered between life and death. Oh! who could hope, when the distant world to which she was akin, half opened to her view, that she would return to the sorrow and calamity of this! Rose, Rose, to know that you were passing away like some soft shadow, which a light from above, casts upon the earth; to have no hope that you would be spared to those who linger here; to know no reason why you should be; to feel that you belonged to that bright sphere whither so many of the fairest and the best have winged their early flight; and yet to pray, amid all these consolations, that you might be restored to those who loved you—these were distractions almost too great to bear. They were mine, by day and night; and with them

came such a rushing torrent of fears, and apprehensions, and selfish regrets, lest you should die, and never know how devotedly I loved you, as almost bore down sense and reason in its course. You recovered; day by day, and almost hour by hour, some drop of health came back, and mingling with the spent and feeble stream of life which circulated languidly within you, swelled it again to a high and rushing tide. I have watched you change almost from death to life, with eyes that moistened with their eagerness and deep affection. Do not tell me that you wish I had lost this; for it has softened my heart to all mankind."

"I did not mean that," said Rose, weeping; "I only wish you had left here, that you might have turned to high and noble pursuits again; to pursuits well worthy of you."

"There is no pursuit more worthy of me: more worthy of the highest nature that exists: than the struggle to win such a heart as yours," said the young man, taking her hand. "Rose, my own dear Rose; for years—for years—I have loved you: hoping to win my way to fame, and then come proudly home and tell you it had been pursued only for you to share; thinking, in my day-dreams, how I would remind you, in that happy moment, of the many silent tokens I had given of a boy's attachment, and claim your hand, as in redemption of some old mute contract that had been sealed between us. That time has not arrived; but here, with no fame won, and no young vision realised, I give to you the heart so long your own, and stake my all upon the words with which you greet the offer."

"Your behaviour has ever been kind and noble," said Rose, mastering the emotions by which she was agitated. "As you believe that I am not insensible or ungrateful, so hear my answer."

"It is, that I may endeavour to deserve you; it is, dear Rose?"

"It is," replied Rose, "that you must endeavour to forget me; not as your old and dearly-attached companion, for that would wound me deeply: but, as the object of your love. Look into the world; think how many hearts you would be proud to gain, are there. Confide some other passion to me, if you will; and I will be the truest, warmest, and most faithful friend you have."

There was a pause, during which, Rose, who had covered her face with one hand, gave free vent to her tears. Harry still retained the other.

"And your reasons, Rose," he said, at length, in a low voice; "your reasons for this decision?"

"You have a right to know them," rejoined Rose. "You can say nothing to alter my resolution. It is a duty that I must perform. I owe it, alike to others, and to myself."

"To yourself?"

"Yes, Harry: I owe it to myself, that I, a friendless, portionless girl, with a blight upon my name, should not give your friends reason to suspect that I had sordidly yielded to your first passion, and fastened myself, a clog, on all your hopes and projects. I owe it to you and yours, to prevent you from opposing, in the warmth of your generous nature, this great obstacle to your progress in the world."

"If your inclinations chime with your sense of duty——" Harry began.

"They do not," replied Rose, colouring deeply.

"Then you return my love?" said Harry. "Say but that, dear Rose; say but that; and soften the bitterness of this hard disappointment!"

"If I could have done so, without doing heavy wrong to him I loved," rejoined Rose, "I could have——"

"Have received this declaration very differently?" said Harry. "Do not conceal that from me, at least, Rose."

"I could," said Rose. "Stay," she added, disengaging her hand, "why should we prolong this painful interview? Most painful to me, and yet productive of lasting happiness notwithstanding; for it *will* be happiness to know that I once held the high place in your regard which I now occupy; and every triumph you achieve in life will animate me with new fortitude and firmness. Farewell, Harry! As we have met to-day, we meet no more; but in other relations than those in which this conversation would have placed us, may we be long and happily entwined; and may every blessing that the prayers of a true and earnest heart can call down from the source of all truth and sincerity, cheer and prosper you!"

"Another word, Rose," said Harry. "Your reason in your own words. From your own lips, let me hear it."

"The prospect before you," answered Rose, firmly, "is a brilliant one; all the honours to which great talents and powerful connexions can help men in public life, are in store for you. But those connexions are proud; and I will neither mingle with such as hold in scorn the mother who gave me life; nor bring disgrace or failure on the son of her who has so well supplied that mother's place. In a word," said the young lady, turning away, as her temporary firmness forsook her, "there is a stain upon my name, which the world visits on innocent heads. I will carry it into no blood but my own; and the reproach shall rest alone on me."

"One word more, Rose. Dearest Rose! one more!" cried Harry, throwing himself before her. "If I had been less—less fortunate, the world would call it; if some obscure and peaceful life had been my destiny; if I had been poor, sick, helpless; would you have turned from me then? Or has my probable advancement to riches and honour, given this scruple birth?"

"Do not press me to reply," answered Rose. "The question does not arise, and never will. It is unfair, un-kind, to urge it."

"If your answer be what I almost dare to hope it is," retorted Harry, "it will shed a gleam of happiness upon my lonely way, and light the dreary path before me. It is not an idle thing to do so much, by the utterance of a few brief words, for one who loves you beyond all else. Oh, Rose! in the name of my ardent and enduring attachment; in the name of all I have suffered for you, and all you doom me to undergo; answer me this one question!"

"Then, if your lot had been differently cast," rejoined Rose; "if you had been even a little, but not so far, above me; if I could have been a help and comfort to you in some humble scene of peace and retirement, and not a blot and drawback in ambitious and distinguished crowds; I should have been spared this trial. I have every reason to be happy, very happy, now; but then, Harry, I own I should have been happier."

Busy recollections of old hopes, cherished as a girl, long ago, crowded into the mind of Rose, while making this avowal; but they brought tears with them, as old hopes will when they come back withered; and they relieved her.

"I cannot help this weakness, and it makes my purpose stronger," said Rose, extending her hand. "I must leave you now, indeed."

"I ask one promise," said Harry. "Once, and only once more,—say within a year, but it may be much sooner,—

—let me speak to you again on this subject, for the last time."

"Not to press me to alter my right determination," replied Rose, with a melancholy smile; "it will be useless."

"No," said Harry; "to hear you repeat it, if you will—finally repeat it. I will lay at your feet, whatever of station or fortune I may possess; and if you still adhere to your present resolution, will not seek, by word or act, to change it."

"Then let it be so," rejoined Rose; "it is but one pang the more, and by that time I may be enabled to bear it better."

She extended her hand again. But the young man caught her to his bosom; and imprinting one kiss on her beautiful forehead, hurried from the room.

CHAPTER XXXVI.

IS A VERY SHORT ONE, AND MAY APPEAR OF NO GREAT IMPORTANCE IN ITS PLACE. BUT IT SHOULD BE READ NOTWITHSTANDING, AS A SE-QUEL TO THE LAST, AND A KEY TO ONE THAT WILL FOLLOW WHEN ITS TIME ARRIVES.

"AND so you are resolved to be my travelling companion this morning, eh?" said the doctor, as Harry Maylie joined him and Oliver at the breakfast-table. "Why, you are not in the same mind or intention two half-hours together."

"You will tell me a different tale one of these days," said Harry, colouring without any perceptible reason.

"I hope I may have good cause to do so," replied Mr. Losberne; "though I confess I don't think I shall. But yesterday morning you had made up your mind, in a great hurry, to stay here, and to accompany your mother, like a dutiful son, to the sea-side. Before noon, you announce that you are going to do me the honour of accompanying me as far as I go, on your road to London. And at night, you urge me, with great mystery, to start before the ladies are stirring; the consequence of which is, that young Oliver here is pinned down to his breakfast when he ought to be ranging the meadows after botanical phenomena of all kinds. Too bad, isn't it, Oliver?"

"I should have been very sorry not to have been at home when you and Mr. Maylie went away, Sir," rejoined Oliver.

"That's a fine fellow," said the doctor; "you shall come and see me when you return. But, to speak seriously, Harry; has any communication from the great nobs produced this sudden anxiety on your part to be gone?"

"The great nobs," replied Harry: "under which desig-nation, I presume, you include my most stately uncle: have not communicated with me at all, since I have been here; nor, at this time of the year, is it likely that any-thing would occur to render necessary my immediate at-tendance among them."

"Well," said the doctor, "you are a queer fellow. But of course they will get you into parliament at the election before Christmas, and these sudden shiftings and changes are no bad preparation for political life. There's some-thing in that; good training is always desirable, whether the race be for place, cup, or sweepstakes."

Harry Maylie looked as if he could have followed up this short dialogue by one or two remarks that would have staggered the doctor not a little; but he contented himself with saying, "We shall see," and pursued the subject no farther. The post-chaise drove up to the door shortly afterwards; and Giles coming in for the luggage, the good doctor bustled out, to see it packed.

"Oliver," said Harry Maylie, in a low voice, "let me speak a word with you."

Oliver walked into the window-recess to which Mr. Maylie beckoned him; much surprised at the mixture of sadness and boisterous spirits, which his whole behaviour displayed.

"You can write well now?" said Harry, laying his hand upon his arm.

"I hope so, Sir," replied Oliver.

"I shall not be at home again, perhaps for some time; I wish you would write to me—say once a fortnight: every alternate Monday: to the General Post Office in London. Will you?"

"Oh! certainly, Sir; I shall be proud to do it," exclaimed Oliver, greatly delighted with the commission.

"I should like to know how—how my mother and Miss Maylie are," said the young man; "and you can fill up a sheet by telling me what walks you take, and what you talk about, and whether she—they, I mean—seem happy and quite well. You understand me?"

"Oh quite, Sir, quite," replied Oliver.

"I would rather you did not mention it to them," said Harry, hurrying over his words; "because it might make my mother anxious to write to me oftener, and it is a trouble and worry to her. Let it be a secret between you and me; and mind you tell me everything; I depend upon you."

Oliver, quite elated and honoured by a sense of his importance, faithfully promised to be secret and explicit in his communications; and Mr. Maylie took leave of him, with many warm assurances of his regard and protection.

The doctor was in the chaise; Giles (who, it had been arranged, should be left behind) held the door open in his hand; and the women-servants were in the garden, looking on. Harry cast one slight glance at the lattice window, and jumped into the carriage.

"Drive on!" he cried, "hard, fast, full gallop. Nothing short of flying will keep pace with me, to-day."

"Halloa!" cried the doctor, letting down the front glass in a great hurry, and shouting to the postilion; "something very short of flying will keep pace with me. Do you hear?"

Jingling and clattering, till distance rendered its noise inaudible, and its rapid progress only perceptible to the eye, the vehicle wound its way along the road, almost hidden in a cloud of dust: now wholly disappearing, and now becoming visible again: as intervening objects, or the intricacies of the way, permitted. It was not until even the dusty cloud was no longer to be seen, that the gazers dispersed.

And there was one looker-on, who remained with eyes fixed upon the spot where the carriage had disappeared, long after it was many miles away; for behind the white curtain which had shrouded her from view when Harry raised his eyes towards the window, sat Rose herself.

"He seems in high spirits and happy," she said, at length. "I feared for a time he might be otherwise. I was mistaken. I am very, very glad."

Tears are signs of gladness as well as grief; but those which coursed down Rose's face, as she sat pensively at the window, still gazing in the same direction, seemed to tell more of sorrow than of joy.

CHAPTER XXXVII.

IN WHICH THE READER MAY PERCEIVE A CONTRAST NOT UNCOMMON IN MATRIMONIAL CASES.

MR. BUMBLE sat in the workhouse parlour, with his eyes moodily fixed on the cheerless grate, whence, as it was summer time, no brighter gleam proceeded, than the reflection of certain sickly rays of the sun, which were sent back from its cold and shining surface. A paper fly-cage dangled from the ceiling, to which he occasionally raised his eyes in gloomy thought; and, as the heedless insects hovered round the gaudy network, Mr. Bumble would heave a deep sigh, while a more gloomy shadow overspread his countenance. Mr. Bumble was meditating; it might be that the insects brought to mind, some painful passage in his own past life.

Nor was Mr. Bumble's gloom the only thing calculated to awaken a pleasing melancholy in the bosom of a spectator. There were not wanting other appearances, and those closely connected with his own person, which announced that a great change had taken place in the position of his affairs. The laced coat, and the cocked-hat; where were they? He still wore knee-breeches, and dark cotton stockings on his nether limbs; but they were not *the* breeches. The coat was wide-skirted; and in that respect like *the* coat, but, oh, how different! The mighty cocked-hat was replaced by a modest round one. Mr. Bumble was no longer a beadle.

There are some promotions in life, which, independent of the more substantial rewards they offer, acquire peculiar value and dignity from the coats and waistcoats connected with them. A field-marshal has his uniform; a bishop his silk apron; a counsellor his silk gown; a beadle his cocked-hat. Strip the bishop of his apron, or the beadle of his hat and lace; what are they? Men. Mere men. Dignity, and even holiness too, sometimes, are more questions of coat and waistcoat than some people imagine.

Mr. Bumble had married Mrs. Corney, and was master of the workhouse. Another beadle had come into power; and on him the cocked-hat, gold-laced coat, and staff, had all three descended.

"And to-morrow two months it was done!" said Mr. Bumble, with a sigh. "It seems a age."

Mr. Bumble might have meant that he had concentrated a whole existence of happiness into the short space of eight weeks; but the sigh—there was a vast deal of meaning in the sigh.

"I sold myself," said Mr. Bumble, pursuing the same train of reflection, "for six teaspoons, a pair of sugar-tongs, and a milk-pot; with a small quantity of second-hand furniture, and twenty pound in money. I went very reasonable. Cheap, dirt cheap!"

"Cheap!" cried a shrill voice in Mr. Bumble's ear: "you would have been dear at any price; and dear enough I paid for you, Lord above knows that!"

Mr. Bumble turned, and encountered the face of his interesting consort, who, imperfectly comprehending the few words she had overheard of his complaint, had hazarded the foregoing remark at a venture.

"Mrs. Bumble, ma'am!" said Mr. Bumble, with sentimental sternness.

"Well?" cried the lady.

"Have the goodness to look at me," said Mr. Bumble, fixing his eyes upon her. ("If she stands such a eye as that," said Mr. Bumble to himself, "she can stand anything. It is a eye I never knew to fail with paupers; and if it fails with her, my power is gone.")

Whether an exceedingly small expansion of eye be sufficient to quell paupers, who, being lightly fed, are in no very high condition; or whether the late Mrs. Corney was particularly proof against eagle glances; are matters of opinion. The matter of fact, is, that the matron was in no way overpowered by Mr. Bumble's scowl, but on the contrary, treated it with great disdain, and even raised a laugh thereat, which sounded as though it were genuine.

On hearing this most unexpected sound, Mr. Bumble looked first incredulous, and afterwards amazed. He then relapsed into his former state; nor did he rouse himself until his attention was again awakened by the voice of his partner.

"Are you going to sit snoring there, all day?" inquired Mrs. Bumble

"I am going to sit here, as long as I think proper, ma'am," rejoined Mr. Bumble; "and although I was *not* snoring, I shall snore, gape, sneeze, laugh, or cry, as the humour strikes me; such being my prerogative."

"Your prerogative!" sneered Mrs. Bumble, with ineffable contempt.

"I said the word, ma'am," observed Mr. Bumble. "The prerogative of a man is to command!"

"And what's the prerogative of a woman, in the name of Goodness?" cried the relict of Mr. Corney deceased.

"To obey, ma'am," thundered Mr. Bumble. "Your late unfort'nate husband should have taught it you; and then, perhaps, he might have been alive now. I wish he was, poor man!"

Mrs. Bumble, seeing at a glance, that the decisive moment had now arrived: and that a blow struck for the mastership on one side or other, must necessarily be final and conclusive: no sooner heard this allusion to the dead and gone, than she dropped into a chair; and with a loud scream that Mr. Bumble was a hard-hearted brute, fell into a paroxysm of tears.

But, tears were not the things to find their way to Mr. Bumble's soul; his heart was waterproof. Like washable beaver hats that improve with rain, his nerves were rendered stouter and more vigorous by showers of tears, which, being tokens of weakness, and so far tacit admissions of his own power, pleased and exalted him. He eyed his good lady with looks of great satisfaction, and begged, in an encouraging manner, that she should cry her hardest: the exercise being looked upon, by the faculty, as strongly conducive to health.

"It opens the lungs, washes the countenance, exercises the eyes, and softens down the temper," said Mr. Bumble. "So, cry away."

As he discharged himself of this pleasantry, Mr. Bumble took his hat from a peg; and putting it on, rather rakishly, on one side, as a man might, who felt he had asserted his superiority in a becoming manner, thrust his hands into his pockets, and sauntered towards the door with much ease and waggishness depicted in his whole appearance.

Now, Mrs. Corney that was, had tried the tears, because they were less troublesome than a manual assault; but she was quite prepared to make trial of the latter mode of proceeding, as Mr. Bumble was not long in discovering.

The first proof he experienced of the fact, was conveyed in a hollow sound, immediately succeeded by the sudden flying off of his hat to the opposite end of the room. This preliminary proceeding laying bare his head, the expert lady, clasping him tight round the throat with one hand, inflicted a shower of blows (dealt with singular vigour and dexterity) upon it with the other. This done, she created a little variety by scratching his face, and tearing his hair off; and having, by this time, inflicted as much punishment as she deemed necessary for the offence, she pushed him over a chair, which was luckily well situated for the purpose: and defied him to talk about his prerogative again, if he dared.

"Get up!" said Mrs. Bumble, in a voice of command. "And take yourself away from here, unless you want me to do something desperate."

Mr. Bumble rose with a very rueful countenance: wondering much what something desperate might be; and, picking up his hat, looked towards the door.

"Are you going?" demanded Mrs. Bumble.

"Certainly, my dear, certainly," rejoined Mr. Bumble, making a quicker motion towards the door. "I didn't intend to—I'm going, my dear! You are so very violent, that really I—"

At this instant, Mrs. Bumble stepped hastily forward to replace the carpet, which had been kicked up in the scuffle. Mr. Bumble immediately darted out of the room, without bestowing another thought on his unfinished sentence: leaving the late Mrs. Corney in full possession of the field.

Mr. Bumble was fairly taken by surprise, and fairly beaten. He had a decided propensity for bullying: derived no inconsiderable pleasure from the exercise of petty cruelty; and, consequently, was (it is needless to say) a coward. This is by no means a disparagement to his character; for many official personages, who are held in high respect and admiration, are the victims of similar infirmities. The remark is made, indeed, rather in his favour than otherwise, and with a view of impressing the reader with a just sense of his qualifications for office.

But, the measure of his degradation was not yet full. After making a tour of the house, and thinking, for the first time, that the poor-laws really were too hard **on** people; and that men who ran away from their wives, leaving them chargeable to the parish, ought, in justice, to be visited with no punishment at all, but rather rewarded as meritorious individuals who had suffered much; Mr. Bumble came to a room where some of the female paupers were usually employed in washing the parish linen: and whence the sound of voices in conversation, now proceeded.

"Hem!" said Mr. Bumble, summoning up all his native dignity. "These women at least shall continue to respect the prerogative. Hallo! hallo there! What do you mean by this noise, you hussies?"

With these words, Mr. Bumble opened the door, and walked in with a very fierce and angry manner: which was at once exchanged for a most humiliated and cowering air, as his eyes unexpectedly rested on the form of his lady wife.

"My dear," said Mr. Bumble, "I didn't know you were here."

"Didn't know I was here!" repeated Mrs. Bumble. "What do *you* do here?"

"I thought they were talking rather too much to be doing their work properly, my dear," replied Mr. Bumble: glancing distractedly at a couple of old women at the wash-tub, who were comparing notes of admiration at the work-house-master's humility.

"*You* thought they were talking too much?" said Mrs. Bumble. "What business is it of yours?"

"Why, my dear—" urged Mr. Bumble, submissively.

"What business is it of yours?" demanded Mrs. Bumble, again.

"It's very true, you're matron here, my dear," submitted Mr. Bumble; "but I thought you mightn't be in the way just then."

"I'll tell you what, Mr. Bumble," returned his lady. "We don't want any of your interference. You're a great deal too fond of poking your nose into things that don't concern you: making everybody in the house laugh, the moment your back is turned: and making yourself look like a fool every hour in the day. Be off; come!"

Mr. Bumble, seeing with excruciating feelings, the delight of the two old paupers, who were tittering together most rapturously, hesitated for an instant. Mrs. Bumble, whose patience brooked no delay, caught up a bowl of soap-suds, and motioning him towards the door, ordered him instantly to depart, on pain of receiving the contents upon his portly person.

What could Mr. Bumble do? He looked dejectedly round, and slunk away; and, as he reached the door, the titterings of the paupers broke into a shrill chuckle of irrepressible delight. It wanted but this. He was degraded in their eyes; he had lost caste and station before the very paupers; he had fallen from all the height and pomp of beadleship, to the lowest depth of the most snubbed hen-peckery.

"All in two months!" said Mr. Bumble, filled with dismal thoughts. "Two months! No more than two months ago, I was not only my own master, but everybody else's, so far as the porochial workhouse was concerned, and now!—"

It was too much. Mr. Bumble boxed the ears of the boy who opened the gate for him (for he had reached the portal in his reverie); and walked, distractedly, into the street.

He walked up one street, and down another, until exercise had abated the first passion of his grief; and then the revulsion of feeling made him thirsty. He passed a great many public-houses; and at length paused before one in a by-way, whose parlour, as he gathered from a hasty peep over the blinds, was deserted, save by one solitary customer. It began to rain, heavily, at the moment. This determined him. Mr. Bumble stepped in; and ordering something to drink, as he passed the bar, entered the apartment into which he had looked from the street.

The man who was seated there, was tall and dark, and wore a large cloak. He had the air of a stranger; and seemed, by a certain haggardness in his look, as well as by the dusty soils on his dress, to have travelled some distance. He eyed Bumble askance, as he entered, but scarcely deigned to nod his head in acknowledgment of his salutation.

Mr. Bumble had quite dignity enough for two: supposing even that the stranger had been more familiar: so he drank his gin-and-water in silence, and read the paper with great show of pomp and circumstance.

It so happened, however: as it will happen very often, when men fall into company under such circumstances: that Mr. Bumble felt, every now and then, a powerful inducement, which he could not resist, to steal a look at the stranger; and that whenever he did so, he withdrew his eyes, in some confusion, to find that the stranger was at that moment stealing a look at him. Mr. Bumble's awkwardness was enhanced by the very remarkable expression of the stranger's eye, which was keen and bright, but shadowed by a scowl of distrust and suspicion, unlike any-

thing he had ever observed before, and most repulsive to behold.

When they had encountered each other's glance several times in this way, the stranger, in a harsh, deep voice, broke silence.

"Were you looking for me," he said, "when you peered in at the window?"

"Not that I am aware of, unless you're Mr.——" Here Mr. Bumble stopped short; for he was curious to know the stranger's name, and thought, in his impatience, he might supply the blank.

"I see you were not," said the stranger; an expression of quiet sarcasm playing about his mouth; "or you would have known my name. You don't know it. I would recommend you not to enquire."

"I meant no harm, young man," observed Mr. Bumble, majestically.

"And have done none," said the stranger.

Another silence succeeded this short dialogue: which was again broken by the stranger.

"I have seen you before, I think," said he. "You were differently dressed at that time, and I only passed you in the street, but I should know you again. You were beadle here, once; were you not?"

"I was," said Mr. Bumble, in some surprise; "porochial beadle."

"Just so," rejoined the other, nodding his head. "It was in that character I saw you. What are you now?"

"Master of the workhouse," rejoined Mr. Bumble, slowly and impressively, to check any undue familiarity the stranger might otherwise assume. "Master of the workhouse, young man!"

"You have the same eye to your own interest, that you always had, I doubt not?" resumed the stranger, looking keenly into Mr. Bumble's eyes, as he raised them in astonishment at the question. "Don't scruple to answer freely, man. I know you pretty well, you see."

"I suppose, a married man," replied Mr. Bumble, shading his eyes with his hand, and surveying the stranger, from head to foot, in evident perplexity, "is not more averse to turning an honest penny when he can, than a single one. Porochial officers are not so well paid that they can afford to refuse any little extra fee when it comes to them in a civil and proper manner."

The stranger smiled, and nodded his head again: as much as to say, he had not mistaken his man; then rang the bell.

"Fill this glass again," he said, handing Mr. Bumble's empty tumbler to the landlord. "Let it be strong and hot. You like it so, I suppose?"

"Not too strong," replied Mr. Bumble, with a delicate cough.

"You understand what that means, landlord!" said the stranger, drily.

The host smiled, disappeared, and shortly afterwards returned with a steaming jorum: of which, the first gulp brought the water into Mr. Bumble's eyes.

"Now listen to me," said the stranger, after closing the door and window. "I came down to this place, to-day, to find you out; and, by one of those chances which the Devil throws in the way of his friends sometimes, you walked into the very room I was sitting in, while you were uppermost in my mind. I want some information from you. I don't ask you to give it for nothing, slight as it is. Put up that, to begin with."

As he spoke, he pushed a couple of sovereigns across the

table to his companion; carefully, as though unwilling that the chinking of money should be heard without. When Mr. Bumble had scrupulously examined the coins, to see that they were genuine, and had put them up, with much satisfaction, in his waistcoat-pocket, he went on:

"Carry your memory back—let me see—twelve years, last winter."

"It's a long time," said Mr. Bumble. "Very good. I've done it."

"The scene, the workhouse."

"Good!"

"And the time, night."

"Yes."

"And the place, the crazy hole wherever it was, in which miserable drabs brought forth the life and health so often denied to themselves; gave birth to puling children for the parish to rear; and hid their shame, rot 'em, in the grave!"

"The lying-in room, I suppose?" said Mr. Bumble, not quite following the stranger's excited description.

"Yes," said the stranger. "A boy was born there."

"A many boys," observed Mr. Bumble, shaking his head, despondingly.

"A murrain on the young devils!" cried the stranger; "I speak of one; a meek-looking, pale-faced hound, who was apprenticed down here, to a coffin-maker: I wish he had made his coffin, and screwed his body in it: and who afterwards ran away to London, as it was supposed."

"Why, you mean Oliver! Young Twist!" said Mr. Bumble; "I remember him, of course. There wasn't a obstinater young rascal——"

"It's not of him I want to hear; I've heard enough of him," said the stranger, stopping Mr. Bumble in the very outset of a tirade on the subject of poor Oliver's vices. "It's of a woman; the hag that nursed his mother. Where is she?"

"Where is she?" said Mr. Bumble, whom the gin-and-water had rendered facetious. "It would be hard to tell. There's no midwifery there, whichever place she's gone to; so I suppose she's out of employment any way."

"What do you mean?" demanded the stranger, sternly.

"That she died last winter," rejoined Mr. Bumble.

The man looked fixedly at him when he had given this information, and although he did not withdraw his eyes for some time afterwards, his gaze gradually became vacant and abstracted, and he seemed lost in thought. For some time, he appeared doubtful whether he ought to be relieved or disappointed by the intelligence; but at length he breathed more freely: and withdrawing his eyes, observed that it was no great matter. With that he rose, as if to depart.

Mr. Bumble was cunning enough; and he at once saw that an opportunity was opened, for the lucrative disposal of some secret in the possession of his better half. He well remembered the night of old Sally's death, which the occurrences of that day had given him good reason to recollect, as the occasion on which he had proposed to Mrs. Corney; and although that lady had never confided to him the disclosure of which she had been the solitary witness, he had heard enough to know that it related to something that had occurred in the old woman's attendance, as workhouse nurse, upon the young mother of Oliver Twist. Hastily calling this circumstance to mind, he informed the stranger, with an air of mystery, that one woman had been closeted with the old harridan shortly before she died; and

that she could, as he had reason to believe, throw some light on the subject of his inquiry.

"How can I find her?" said the stranger, thrown off his guard; and plainly showing that all his fears (whatever they were) were aroused afresh by the intelligence.

"Only through me," rejoined Mr. Bumble.

"When?" cried the stranger, hastily.

"To-morrow," rejoined Bumble.

"At nine in the evening," said the stranger, producing a scrap of paper, and writing down upon it, an obscure address by the water-side, in characters that betrayed his agitation; "at nine in the evening, bring her to me there. I needn't tell you to be secret. It's your interest."

With these words, he led the way to the door, after stopping to pay for the liquor that had been drunk; and shortly remarking that their roads were different, departed without more ceremony than an emphatic repetition of the hour of appointment for the following night.

On glancing at the address, the parochial functionary observed that it contained no name. The stranger had not gone far, so he made after him to ask it.

"What's that?" cried the man, turning quickly round, as Bumble touched him on the arm. "Following me!"

"Only to ask a question," said the other, pointing to the scrap of paper. "What name am I to ask for?"

"Monks!" rejoined the man; and strode, hastily, away.

CHAPTER XXXVIII.

CONTAINING AN ACCOUNT OF WHAT PASSED BETWEEN MR. AND MRS. BUMBLE, AND MONKS, AT THEIR NOCTURNAL INTERVIEW.

IT was a dull, close, overcast summer evening: and the clouds, which had been threatening all day, spread out in a dense and sluggish mass of vapour, already yielded large drops of rain, and seemed to presage a violent thunderstorm: when Mr. and Mrs. Bumble, turning out of the main street of the town, directed their course towards a scattered little colony of ruinous houses, distant from it some mile and a-half, or thereabouts, and erected on a low unwholesome swamp, bordering upon the river.

They were both wrapped in old and shabby outer garments, which might, perhaps, serve the double purpose of protecting their persons from the rain, and sheltering them from observation. The husband carried a lantern, from which, however, no light yet shone; and trudged on, a few paces in front, as though—the way being dirty—to give his wife the benefit of treading in his heavy footprints. They went on, in profound silence; every now and then, Mr. Bumble relaxed his pace, and turned his head as if to make sure that his helpmate was following; then, discovering that she was close at his heels, he mended his rate of walking, and proceeded, at a considerable increase of speed, towards their place of destination.

This was far from being a place of doubtful character; for it had long been known as the residence of none but low and desperate ruffians; who, under various pretences of living by their labour, subsisted chiefly on plunder and crime. It was a collection of mere hovels: some hastily built with loose bricks: others of old worm-eaten ship-timber: jumbled together without any attempt at order or arrangement, and planted, for the most part, within a few feet of the river's bank. A few leaky boats drawn up on the mud, and made fast to the dwarf wall which skirted it: and here and there an oar or coil of rope: appeared, at first, to indicate that the inhabitants of these miserable cottages pursued some avocation on the river; but a glance at the shattered and useless condition of the articles thus displayed, would have led a passer-by, without much difficulty, to the conjecture that they were disposed there, rather for the preservation of appearances than with any view to their being actually employed.

In the heart of this cluster of huts; and skirting the river, which its upper stories overhung; stood a large building, formerly used as a manufactory of some kind: and which had, in its day, probably furnished employment to the inhabitants of the surrounding tenements. But it had long since gone to ruin. The rat, the worm, and the action of the damp, had weakened and rotted the piles on which it stood; and a considerable portion of the building had already sunk down into the water beneath; while the remainder, tottering and bending over the dark stream, seemed to wait a favourable opportunity of following its old companion, and involving itself in the same fate.

It was before this ruinous building that the worthy couple paused, as the first peal of distant thunder reverberated in the air, and the rain commenced pouring violently down.

"The place should be somewhere here," said Bumble, consulting a scrap of paper he held in his hand.

"Halloa there!" cried a voice from above.

Following the sound, Mr. Bumble raised his head, and descried a man looking out of a door, breast-high, on the second story.

"Stand still, a minute," cried the voice; "I'll be with you directly." With which the head disappeared, and the door closed.

"Is that the man?" asked Mr. Bumble's good lady.

Mr. Bumble nodded in the affirmative.

"Then, mind what I told you," said the matron; "and be careful to say as little as you can, or you'll betray us at once."

Mr. Bumble, who had eyed the building with very rueful looks, was apparently about to express some doubts relative to the advisability of proceeding any further with the enterprise just then, when he was prevented by the appearance of Monks: who opened a small door, near which they stood, and beckoned them inwards.

"Come!" he cried impatiently, stamping his foot upon the ground. "Don't keep me here!"

The woman, who had hesitated at first, walked boldly in, without any further invitation. Mr. Bumble, who was ashamed or afraid to lag behind, followed: obviously very ill at his ease and with scarcely any of that remarkable dignity which was usually his chief characteristic.

"What the devil made you stand lingering there, in the wet?" said Monks, turning round, and addressing Bumble, after he had bolted the door behind them.

"We—we were only cooling ourselves," stammered Bumble, looking apprehensively about him.

"Cooling yourselves!" retorted Monks. "Not all the rain that ever fell, or ever will fall, will put as much of hell's fire out, as a man can carry about with him. You won't cool yourselves so easily; don't think it!"

With this agreeable speech, Monks turned short upon the matron, and bent his fierce gaze upon her, till even she, who was not easily cowed, was fain to withdraw her eyes, and turn them towards the ground.

"This is the woman, is it?" demanded Monks.

"Hem! That is the woman," replied Mr. Bumble, mindful of his wife's caution.

"You think women never can keep secrets, I suppose?" said the matron, interposing, and returning, as she spoke, the searching look of Monks.

"I know they will always keep *one* till it's found out," said Monks, contemptuously.

"And what may that be?" asked the matron in the same tone.

"The loss of their own good name," replied Monks. "So, by the same rule, if a woman's a party to a secret that might hang or transport her, I'm not afraid of her telling it to anybody; not I. Do you understand me?"

"No," rejoined the matron, slightly colouring as she spoke?

"Of course you don't!" said Monks. "How should you?"

Bestowing something half-way between a smile and a scowl upon his two companions, and again beckoning them to follow him, the man hastened across the apartment, which was of considerable extent, but low in the roof. He was preparing to ascend a steep staircase, or rather ladder, leading to another floor of warehouses above: when a bright flash of lightning streamed down the aperture, and a peal of thunder followed, which shook the crazy building to its centre.

"Hear it!" he cried, shrinking back. "Hear it! Rolling and crashing on as if it echoed through a thousand caverns where the devils were hiding from it. I hate the sound!"

He remained silent for a few moments; and then, removing his hands suddenly from his face, showed, to the unspeakable discomposure of Mr. Bumble, that it was much distorted, and discoloured.

"These fits come over me, now and then," said Monks, observing his alarm; "and thunder sometimes brings them on. Don't mind me now; it's all over for this once."

Thus speaking, he led the way up the ladder; and hastily closing the window-shutter of the room into which it led, lowered a lantern which hung at the end of a rope and pulley passed through one of the heavy beams in the ceiling: and which cast a dim light upon an old table and three chairs that were placed beneath it.

"Now," said Monks, when they had all three seated themselves, "the sooner we come to our business, the better for all. The woman knows what it is; does she?"

The question was addressed to Bumble; but his wife anticipated the reply, by intimating that she was perfectly acquainted with it.

"He is right in saying that you were with this hag the night she died; and that she told you something—"

"About the mother of the boy you named," replied the matron interrupting him. "Yes."

"The first question is, of what nature was her communication?" said Monks.

"That's the second," observed the woman with much deliberation. "The first is, what may the communication be worth?"

"Who the devil can tell that, without knowing of what kind it is?" asked Monks.

"Nobody better than you, I am persuaded," answered Mrs. Bumble: who did not want for spirit, as her yoke-fellow could abundantly testify.

"Humph!" said Monks significantly, and with a look of eager inquiry; "there may be money's worth to get, eh?"

"Perhaps there may," was the composed reply.

"Something that was taken from her," said Monks. "Something that she wore. Something that—"

"You had better bid," interrupted Mrs. Bumble. "I have heard enough, already, to assure me that you are the man I ought to talk to."

Mr. Bumble, who had not yet been admitted by his better half into any greater share of the secret than he had originally possessed, listened to this dialogue with outstretched neck and distended eyes: which he directed towards his wife and Monks, by turns, in undisguised astonishment; increased, if possible, when the latter sternly demanded what sum was required for the disclosure.

"What's it worth to you?" asked the woman, as collectedly as before.

"It may be nothing; it may be twenty pounds," replied Monks. "Speak out, and let me know which."

"Add five pounds to the sum you have named; give me five-and-twenty pounds in gold," said the woman; "and I'll tell you all I know. Not before."

"Five-and-twenty pounds!" exclaimed Monks, drawing back.

"I spoke as plainly as I could," replied Mrs. Bumble. "It's not a large sum, either."

"Not a large sum for a paltry secret, that may be nothing when it's told!" cried Monks impatiently; "and which has been lying dead for twelve years past or more!"

"Such matters keep well, and, like good wine, often double their value in course of time," answered the matron, still preserving the resolute indifference she had assumed. "As to lying dead, there are those who will lie dead for twelve thousand years to come, or twelve million, for anything you or I know, who will tell strange tales at last!"

"What if I pay it for nothing?" asked Monks, hesitating.

"You can easily take it away again," replied the matron. "I am but a woman; alone here; and unprotected."

"Not alone, my dear, nor unprotected neither," submitted Mr. Bumble, in a voice tremulous with fear; "I am here, my dear. And besides," said Mr. Bumble, his teeth chattering as he spoke, "Mr Monks is too much of a gentleman to attempt any violence on porochial persons. Mr. Monks is aware that I am not a young man, my dear, and also that I am a little run to seed, as I may say; but he has heerd: I say I have no doubt Mr. Monks has heerd, my dear: that I am a very determined officer, with very uncommon strength, if I'm once roused. I only want a little rousing; that's all."

As Mr. Bumble spoke, he made a melancholy feint of grasping his lantern with fierce determination; and plainly showed, by the alarmed expression of every feature, that he *did* want a little rousing, and not a little, prior to making any very warlike demonstration: unless, indeed, against paupers, or other person or persons trained down for the purpose.

"You are a fool," said Mrs. Bumble, in reply; "and had better hold your tongue."

"He had better have cut it out, before he came, if he can't speak in a lower tone," said Monks grimly. "So! He's your husband, eh?"

"He my husband!" tittered the matron, parrying the question.

"I thought as much, when you came in," rejoined Monks, marking the angry glance which the lady darted at her spouse as she spoke. "So much the better; I have less hesitation in dealing with two people, when I find that there's only one will between them. I'm in earnest. See here!"

He thrust his hand into a side-pocket; and producing a canvas bag, told out twenty-five sovereigns on the table, and pushed them over to the woman.

"Now," he said, "gather them up; and when this cursed peal of thunder, which I feel is coming up to break over the house-top, is gone, let's hear your story."

The thunder: which seemed in fact much nearer, and to shiver and break almost over their heads: having subsided, Monks, raising his face from the table, bent forward to listen to what the woman should say. The faces of the three nearly touched, as the two men leant over the small table in their eagerness to hear, and the woman also leant forward to render her whisper audible. The sickly rays of the suspended lantern falling directly upon them, aggravated the paleness and anxiety of their countenances: which, encircled by the deepest gloom and darkness, looked ghastly in the extreme.

"When this woman, that we called old Sally, died," the matron began, "she and I were alone."

"Was there no one by?" asked Monks, in the same hollow whisper; "no sick wretch or idiot in some other bed? No one who could hear, and might, by possibility, understand?"

"Not a soul," replied the woman; "we were alone. *I* stood alone beside the body when death came over it."

"Good," said Monks, regarding her attentively. "Go on."

"She spoke of a young creature," resumed the matron, "who had brought a child into the world some years before; not merely in the same room; but in the same bed in which she then lay dying."

"Ay?" said Monks, with quivering lip, and glancing over his shoulder. "Blood! How things come about!"

"The child was the one you named to him last night," said the matron, nodding carelessly towards her husband; "the mother this nurse had robbed."

"In life?" asked Monks.

"In death," replied the woman, with something like a shudder. "She stole from the corpse, when it had hardly turned to one, that which the dead mother had prayed her, with her last breath, to keep for the infant's sake"

"She sold it?" cried Monks, with desperate eagernesss; "did she sell it? Where? When? To whom? How long before?"

"As she told me, with great difficulty, that she had done this," said the matron; "she fell back and died."

"Without saying more?" cried Monks, in a voice which, from its very suppression, seemed only the more furious. "It's a lie! I'll not be played with. She said more. I'll tear the life out of you both, but I'll know what it was."

"She didn't utter another word," said the woman, to all appearance unmoved (as Mr. Bumble was very far from being) by the strange man's violence; "but she clutched my gown, violently, with one hand, which was partly closed; and when I saw that she was dead, and so removed the hand by force, I found it clasped a scrap of dirty paper."

"Which contained—" interposed Monks, stretching forward.

"Nothing," replied the woman. "It was a pawnbroker's duplicate."

"For what?" demanded Monks.

"In good time I'll tell you," said the woman. "I judge that she had kept the trinket, for some time, in the hope of turning it to better account; and then had pawned it; and had saved or scraped together money to pay the pawnbroker's interest year by year, and prevent its running out; so that if anything came of it, it could still be redeemed. Nothing had come of it; and, as I tell you, she died with the scrap of paper, all worn and tattered, in her hand. The time was out in two days; I thought something might one day come of it too; and so redeemed the pledge."

"Where is it now?" asked Monks quickly.

"*There*," replied the woman. And, as if glad to be relieved of it, she hastily threw upon the table a small kid bag scarcely large enough for a French watch, which Monks pouncing upon, tore open with trembling hands. It contained a little gold locket: in which were two locks of hair, and a plain gold wedding-ring.

"It has the word 'Agnes' engraved on the inside," said the woman. "There is a blank left for the surname; and then follows the date; which is within a year before the child was born. I found out that."

"And this is all?" said Monks, after a close and eager scrutiny of the contents of the little packet.

"All," replied the woman.

Mr. Bumble drew a long breath, as if he were glad to find that the story was over, and no mention made of taking the five-and-twenty pounds back again; and now he took courage to wipe off the perspiration, which had been trickling over his nose, unchecked, during the whole of the previous dialogue.

"I know nothing of the story, beyond what I can guess at," said his wife, addressing Monks, after a short silence, "and I want to know nothing; for it's safer not. But I may ask you two questions, may I?"

"You may ask," said Monks, with some show of surprise; "but whether I answer or not is another question."

"—Which makes three," observed Mr. Bumble, essaying a stroke of facetiousness.

"Is that what you expected to get from me?" demanded the matron.

"It is," replied Monks. "The other question?"

"What you propose to do with it? Can it be used against me?"

"Never," rejoined Monks; "nor against me either. See here! But don't move a step forward, or your life's not worth a bulrush!"

With these words, he suddenly wheeled the table aside, and pulling an iron ring in the boarding, threw back a large trap-door, which opened close at Mr. Bumble's feet, and caused that gentleman to retire several paces backward, with great precipitation.

"Look down," said Monks, lowering the lantern into the gulf. "Don't fear me. I could have let you down, quietly enough, when you were seated over it, if that had been my game."

Thus encouraged, the matron drew near to the brink; and even Mr. Bumble himself, impelled by curiosity, ventured to do the same. The turbid water, swollen by the heavy rain, was rushing rapidly on below; and all other sounds were lost in the noise of its plashing and eddying against the green and slimy piles. There had once been a watermill beneath; and the tide, foaming and chafing round the few rotten stakes, and fragments of machinery that yet remained, seemed to dart onward, with a new impulse, when freed from the obstacles which had unavailingly attempted to stem its headlong course.

"If you flung a man's body down there, where would it be to-morrow morning?" said Monks, swinging the lantern to and fro in the dark well.

"Twelve miles down the river and cut to pieces besides," replied Bumble, recoiling at the very thought.

Monks drew the little packet from his breast, where he had hurriedly thrust it; and tying it to a leaden weight, which had formed a part of some pulley, and was lying on the floor, dropped it into the stream. It fell straight, and true as a die; clove the water with a scarcely audible splash; and was gone.

The three looking into each other's faces, seemed to breathe more freely.

"There!" said Monks, closing the trap-door, which fell heavily back into its former position. "If the sea ever gives up its dead, as books say it will, it will keep its gold and silver to itself, and that trash among it. We have nothing more to say, and may break up our pleasant party."

"By all means," observed Mr. Bumble, with great alacrity.

"You'll keep a quiet tongue in your head, will you?" said Monks, with a threatening look. "I am not afraid of your wife."

"You may depend upon me, young man," answered Mr. Bumble, bowing himself gradually towards the ladder, with excessive politeness. "On everybody's account, young man; on my own, you know, Mr. Monks."

"I am glad, for your sake, to hear it," remarked Monks. "Light your lantern! And get away from here as fast as you can."

It was fortunate that the conversation terminated at this point, or Mr. Bumble, who had bowed himself to within six inches of the ladder, would infallibly have pitched head-long into the room below. He lighted his lantern from that which Monks had detached from the rope, and now carried in his hand; and, making no effort to prolong the discourse, descended in silence, followed by his wife. Monks brought up the rear, after pausing on the steps to satisfy himself that there were no other sounds to be heard than the beating of the rain without, and the rushing of the water.

They traversed the lower room, slowly, and with caution; for Monks started at every shadow; and Mr. Bumble, holding his lantern a foot above the ground, walked not only with remarkable care, but with a marvellously light step for a gentleman of his figure: looking nervously about him for hidden trap-doors. The gate at which they had entered, was softly unfastened and opened by Monks; and, merely exchanging a nod with their mysterious acquaintance, the married couple emerged into the wet and darkness outside.

They were no sooner gone, than Monks, who appeared to entertain an invincible repugnance to being left alone, called to a boy who had been hidden somewhere below; and bidding him go first, and bear the light, returned to the chamber he had just quitted.

THE EVIDENCE DESTROYED.

CHAPTER XXXIX.

INTRODUCES SOME RESPECTABLE CHARACTERS WITH
WHOM THE READER IS ALREADY ACQUAINTED,
AND SHOWS HOW MONKS AND THE JEW LAID
THEIR WORTHY HEADS TOGETHER.

On the evening following that upon which the three
worthies mentioned in the last chapter, disposed of their
little matter of business as therein narrated, Mr. William
Sikes, awakening from a nap, drowsily growled forth an
inquiry what time of night it was.

The room in which Mr. Sikes propounded this question,
was not one of those he had tenanted, previous to the
Chertsey expedition, although it was in the same quarter
of the town, and was situated at no great distance from his
former lodgings. It was not, in appearance, so desirable
a habitation as his old quarters: being a mean and badly-
furnished apartment, of very limited size: lighted only by
one small window in the shelving roof, and abutting on a
close and dirty lane. Nor were there wanting other indications of the good gentleman's having gone down in the
world of late; for a great scarcity of furniture, and total
absence of comfort, together with the disappearance of all
such small moveables as spare clothes and linen, bespoke a
state of extreme poverty; while the meagre and attenuated
condition of Mr. Sikes himself would have fully confirmed
these symptoms, if they had stood in any need of corroboration.

The housebreaker was lying on the bed, wrapped in his
white great-coat, by way of dressing-gown, and displaying
a set of features in no degree improved by the cadaverous
hue of illness, and the addition of a soiled nightcap, and a
stiff, black beard of a week's growth. The dog sat at the
bedside: now eyeing his master with a wistful look, and
now pricking his ears, and uttering a low growl as some
noise in the street, or in the lower part of the house, attracted his attention. Seated by the window, busily engaged in patching an old waistcoat which formed a portion
of the robber's ordinary dress, was a female: so pale and
reduced with watching and privation, that there would have
been considerable difficulty in recognising her as the same
Nancy who has already figured in this tale, but for the
voice in which she replied to Mr. Sikes's question.

"Not long gone seven," said the girl. "How do you
feel to-night, Bill?"

"As weak as water," replied Mr. Sikes, with an imprecation on his eyes and limbs. "Here; lend us a hand; and
let me get off this thundering bed, anyhow."

Illness had not improved Mr. Sikes's temper; for, as the
girl raised him up and led him to a chair, he muttered
various curses on her awkwardness: and struck her.

"Whining, are you?" said Sikes. "Come! Don't stand
snivelling there. If you can't do anything better than
that, cut off altogether. D'ye hear me?"

"I hear you," replied the girl, turning her face aside,
and forcing a laugh. "What fancy have you got in your
head now?"

"Oh! you've thought better of it, have you?" growled
Sikes, marking the tear which trembled in her eye. "All
the better for you, you have."

"Why, you don't mean to say, you'd be hard upon me
to-night, Bill," said the girl, laying her hand upon his
shoulder.

"No!" cried Mr. Sikes. "Why not?"

"Such a number of nights," said the girl, with a touch
of woman's tenderness, which communicated something like
sweetness of tone, even to her voice: "such a number of
nights as I've been patient with you, nursing and caring
for you, as if you had been a child: and this the first that
I've seen you like yourself; you wouldn't have served me
as you did just now, if you'd thought of that, would you?
Come, come; say you wouldn't."

"Well, then," rejoined Mr. Sikes, "I wouldn't. Why,
damme, now, the girl's whining again!"

"It's nothing," said the girl, throwing herself into a chair.
"Don't you seem to mind me. It'll soon be over."

"What'll be over?" demanded Mr. Sikes in a savage
voice. "What foolery are you up to, now, again? Get
up and bustle about, and don't come over me with your
woman's nonsense."

At any other time, this remonstrance, and the tone in
which it was delivered, would have had the desired effect;
but the girl being really weak and exhausted, dropped her
head over the back of the chair, and fainted, before Mr.
Sikes could get out a few of the appropriate oaths with
which, on similar occasions, he was accustomed to garnish
his threats. Not knowing, very well, what to do, in this
uncommon emergency; for Miss Nancy's hysterics were
usually of that violent kind which the patient fights and
struggles out of, without much assistance; Mr. Sikes tried
a little blasphemy: and finding that mode of treatment
wholly ineffectual, called for assistance.

"What's the matter here, my dear?" said the Jew,
looking in.

"Lend a hand to the girl, can't you?" replied Sikes
impatiently. "Don't stand chattering and grinning at
me!"

With an exclamation of surprise, Fagin hastened to the
girl's assistance, while Mr. John Dawkins (otherwise the
Artful Dodger), who had followed his venerable friend into
the room, hastily deposited on the floor a bundle with which
he was laden; and snatching a bottle from the grasp of
Master Charles Bates who came close at his heels, uncorked
it in a twinkling with his teeth, and poured a portion of
its contents down the patient's throat: previously taking
a taste, himself, to prevent mistakes.

"Give her a whiff of fresh air with the bellows, Charley,"
said Mr. Dawkins; "and you slap her hands, Fagin, while
Bill undoes the petticuts."

These united restoratives, administered with great energy; especially that department consigned to Master Bates,
who appeared to consider his share in the proceedings a
piece of unexampled pleasantry: were not long in producing the desired effect. The girl gradually recovered her
senses; and, staggering to a chair by the bedside, hid her
face upon the pillow: leaving Mr. Sikes to confront the
new-comers, in some astonishment at their unlooked-for
appearance.

"Why, what evil wind has blowed you here?" he asked
of Fagin.

"No evil wind at all, my dear," replied the Jew; "for
evil winds blow nobody any good; and I've brought something good with me, that you'll be glad to see. Dodger,
my dear, open the bundle; and give Bill the little trifles
that we spent all our money on, this morning."

In compliance with Mr. Fagin's request, the Artful untied his bundle, which was of large size, and formed of an

George Cruikshank

MR. FAGIN AND HIS PUPIL RECOVERING NANCY.

old table-cloth; and handed the articles it contained, one by one, to Charley Bates: who placed them on the table, with various encomiums on their rarity and excellence.

"Sitch a rabbit pie, Bill," exclaimed that young gentleman, disclosing to view a huge pasty; "sitch delicate creeturs, with sitch tender limbs, Bill, that the wery bones melt in your mouth, and there's no occasion to pick 'em; half a pound of seven and sixpenny green, so precious strong that if you mix it with biling water, it'll go nigh to blow the lid of the tea-pot off; a pound and a-half of moist sugar that the niggers didn't work at all at, afore they got it up to sitch a pitch of goodness,—oh no! Two half-quartern brans; pound of best fresh; piece of double Glo'ster; and to wind up all, some of the richest sort you ever lushed!"

Uttering this last panegyric, Master Bates produced, from one of his extensive pockets, a full-sized wine-bottle, carefully corked; while Mr. Dawkins, at the same instant, poured out a wineglassful of raw spirits from the bottle he carried: which the invalid tossed down his throat without a moment's hesitation.

"Ah!" said the Jew, rubbing his hands with great satisfaction. "You'll do, Bill; you'll do now."

"Do!" exclaimed Mr. Sikes. "I might have been done for, twenty times over, afore you'd have done anything to help me. What do you mean by leaving a man in this state, three weeks and more, you false-hearted wagabond?"

"Only hear him, boys!" said the Jew, shrugging his shoulders. "And us come to bring him all these beau-tiful things."

"The things is well enough in their way," observed Mr. Sikes: a little soothed as he glanced over the table; "but what have you got to say for yourself, why you should leave me here, down in the mouth, health, blunt, and everything else; and take no more notice of me, all this mortal time, than if I was that 'ere dog.—Drive him down, Charley!"

"I never see such a jolly dog as that," cried Master Bates, doing as he was desired. "Smelling the grub like a old lady a going to market! He'd make his fortun on the stage that dog would, and rewive the drayma besides."

"Hold your din," cried Sikes, as the dog retreated under the bed: still growling angrily. "What have you got to say for yourself, you withered old fence, eh?"

"I was away from London, a week and more, my dear, on a plant," replied the Jew.

"And what about the other fortnight?" demanded Sikes. "What about the other fortnight that you've left me lying here, like a sick rat in his hole?"

"I couldn't help it, Bill," replied the Jew. "I can't go into a long explanation before company; but I couldn't help it, upon my honour."

"Upon your what?" growled Sikes, with excessive disgust. "Here! Cut me off a piece of that pie, one of you boys, to take the taste of that out of my mouth, or it'll choke me dead."

"Don't be out of temper, my dear," urged the Jew submissively. "I have never forgot you, Bill; never once."

"No! I'll pound it that you han't," replied Sikes, with a bitter grin. "You've been scheming and plotting away, every hour that I have laid shivering and burning here; and Bill was to do this; and Bill was to do that; and Bill was to do it all, dirt cheap, as soon as he got well: and

was quite poor enough for your work! If it hadn't been for the girl, I might have died."

"There now, Bill," remonstrated the Jew, eagerly catching at the word. "If it hadn't been for the girl! Who but poor ould Fagin was the means of your having such a handy girl about you?"

"He says true enough there!" said Nancy, coming hastily forward. "Let him be; let him be."

Nancy's appearance gave a new turn to the conversation; for the boys, receiving a sly wink from the wary old Jew, began to ply her with liquor: of which, however, she partook very sparingly; while Fagin, assuming an unusual flow of spirits, gradually brought Mr. Sikes into a better temper, by affecting to regard his threats as a little pleasant banter; and, moreover, by laughing very heartily at one or two rough jokes, which, after repeated applications to the spirit-bottle, he condescended to make.

"It's all very well," said Mr. Sikes; "but I must have some blunt from you to-night."

"I haven't a piece of coin about me," replied the Jew.

"Then you've got lots at home," retorted Sikes; "and I must have some from there."

"Lots!" cried the Jew, holding up his hands. "I haven't so much as would——"

"I don't know how much you've got, and I dare say you hardly know yourself, as it would take a pretty long time to count it," said Sikes; "but I must have some to-night; and that's flat."

"Well, well!" said the Jew, with a sigh, "I'll send the Artful round presently."

"You won't do nothing of the kind," rejoined Mr. Sikes. "The Artful's a deal too artful, and would forget to come, or lose his way, or get dodged by traps and so be perwented, or anything for an excuse, if you put him up to it. Nancy shall go to the ken and fetch it, to make all sure; and I'll lie down and have a snooze while she's gone."

After a great deal of haggling and squabbling, the Jew beat down the amount of the required advance from five pounds to three pounds four and sixpence: protesting with many solemn asseverations that that would only leave him eighteenpence to keep house with; Mr. Sikes sullenly remarking that if he couldn't get any more he must be content with that, Nancy prepared to accompany him home; while the Dodger and Master Bates put the eatables in the cupboard. The Jew then, taking leave of his affectionate friend, returned homewards, attended by Nancy and the boys: Mr. Sikes, meanwhile, flinging himself on the bed, and composing himself to sleep away the time until the young lady's return.

In due course, they arrived at the Jew's abode, where they found Toby Crackit and Mr. Chitling intent upon their fifteenth game at cribbage, which it is scarcely necessary to say the latter gentleman lost, and with it, his fifteenth and last sixpence: much to the amusement of his young friends. Mr. Crackit, apparently somewhat ashamed at being found relaxing himself with a gentleman so much his inferior in station and mental endowments, yawned, and inquiring after Sikes, took up his hat to go.

"Has nobody been, Toby?" asked the Jew.

"Not a living leg," answered Mr. Crackit, pulling up his collar; "it's been as dull as swipes. You ought to stand something handsome, Fagin, to recompense me for keeping house so long. Damme, I'm as flat as a juryman; and should have gone to sleep, as fast as Newgate, if I hadn't had the good natur' to amuse this youngster. Horrid dull, I'm blessed if I an't!"

With these and other ejaculations of the same kind, Mr. Toby Crackit swept up his winnings, and crammed them into his waistcoat pocket with a haughty air, as though such small pieces of silver were wholly beneath the consideration of a man of his figure; this done, he swaggered out of the room, with so much elegance and gentility, that Mr. Chitling, bestowing numerous admiring glances on his legs and boots till they were out of sight, assured the company that he considered his acquaintance cheap at fifteen sixpences an interview, and that he didn't value his losses the snap of his little finger.

"Wot a rum chap you are, Tom!" said Master Bates, highly amused by this declaration.

"Not a bit of it," replied Mr. Chitling. "Am I, Fagin?"

"A very clever fellow, my dear," said the Jew, patting him on the shoulder, and winking to his other pupils.

"And Mr. Crackit *is* a heavy swell; an't he, Fagin?" asked Tom.

"No doubt at all of that, my dear," replied the Jew.

"And it *is* a creditable thing to have his acquaintance; an't it, Fagin?" pursued Tom.

"Very much so, indeed, my dear," replied the Jew. "They're only jealous, Tom, because he won't give it to them."

"Ah!" cried Tom, triumphantly, "that's where it is! He has cleaned me out. But I can go and earn some more when I like; can't I, Fagin?"

"To be sure you can," replied the Jew; "and the sooner you go the better, Tom; so make up your loss at once, and don't lose any more time. Dodger! Charley! It's time you were on the lay. Come! It's near ten, and nothing done yet."

In obedience to this hint, the boys, nodding to Nancy, took up their hats, and left the room; the Dodger and his vivacious friend indulging, as they went, in many witticisms at the expense of Mr. Chitling; in whose conduct, it is but justice to say, there was nothing very conspicuous or peculiar: inasmuch as there are a great number of spirited young bloods upon town, who pay a much higher price than Mr. Chitling for being seen in good society: and a great number of fine gentlemen (composing the good society aforesaid) who establish their reputation upon very much the same footing as flash Toby Crackit.

"Now," said the Jew, when they had left the room, "I'll go and get you that cash, Nancy. This is only the key of a little cupboard where I keep a few odd things the boys get, my dear. I never lock up my money, for I've got none to lock up, my dear—ha! ha! ha!—none to lock up. It's a poor trade, Nancy, and no thanks; but I'm fond of seeing the young people about me; and I bear it all, I bear it all. Hush!" he said, hastily concealing the key in his breast; "who's that? Listen!"

The girl, who was sitting at the table with her arms folded, appeared in no way interested in the arrival: or to care whether the person, whoever he was, came or went: until the murmur of a man's voice reached her ears. The instant she caught the sound, she tore off her bonnet and shawl, with the rapidity of lightning, and thrust them under the table. The Jew, turning round immediately afterwards, she muttered a complaint of the heat: in a tone of languor that contrasted, very remarkably, with the extreme haste and violence of this action: which, however,

had been unobserved by Fagin, who had his back towards her at the time.

"Bah!" whispered the Jew, as though nettled by the interruption; "it's the man I expected before; he's coming down stairs. Not a word about the money while he's here, Nance. He won't stop long. Not ten minutes, my dear."

Laying his skinny forefinger upon his lip, the Jew carried a candle to the door, as a man's step was heard upon the stairs without. He reached it, at the same moment as the visitor, who, coming hastily into the room, was close upon the girl before he observed her.

It was Monks.

"Only one of my young people," said the Jew, observing that Monks drew back, on beholding a stranger. "Don't move, Nancy."

The girl drew closer to the table, and glancing at Monks with an air of careless levity, withdrew her eyes; but as he turned his towards the Jew, she stole another look: so keen and searching, and full of purpose, that if there had been any bystander to observe the change, he could hardly have believed the two looks to have proceeded from the same person.

"Any news?" inquired the Jew.

"Great."

"And—and—good?" asked the Jew, hesitating as though he feared to vex the other man by being too sanguine.

"Not bad, any way," replied Monks with a smile. "I have been prompt enough this time. Let me have a word with you."

The girl drew closer to the table, and made no offer to leave the room, although she could see that Monks was pointing to her. The Jew: perhaps fearing that she might say something aloud about the money, if he endeavoured to get rid of her: pointed upwards, and took Monks out of the room.

"Not that infernal hole we were in before," she could hear the man say as they went up stairs. The Jew laughed; and making some reply which did not reach her, seemed, by the creaking of the boards, to lead his companion to the second story.

Before the sound of their footsteps had ceased to echo through the house, the girl had slipped off her shoes; and drawing her gown loosely over her head, and muffling her arms in it, stood at the door, listening with breathless interest. The moment the noise ceased, she glided from the room; ascended the stairs with incredible softness and silence; and was lost in the gloom above.

The room remained deserted for a quarter of an hour or more; the girl glided back with the same unearthly tread; and, immediately afterwards, the two men were heard descending. Monks went at once into the street; and the Jew crawled up stairs again for the money. When he returned, the girl was adjusting her shawl and bonnet, as if preparing to be gone.

"Why, Nance," exclaimed the Jew, starting back as he put down the candle, "how pale you are!"

"Pale!" echoed the girl, shading her eyes with her hands, as if to look steadily at him.

"Quite horrible," said the Jew. "What have you been doing to yourself?"

"Nothing that I know of, except sitting in this close place for I don't know how long and all," replied the girl carelessly. "Come! Let me get back; that's a dear."

With a sigh for every piece of money, Fagin told the amount into her hand. They parted without more conversation, merely interchanging a "good night."

When the girl got into the open street, she sat down upon a doorstep; and seemed, for a few moments, wholly bewildered and unable to pursue her way. Suddenly, she arose; and hurrying on, in a direction quite opposite to that in which Sikes was awaiting her return, quickened her pace, until it gradually resolved into a violent run. After completely exhausting herself, she stopped to take breath; and, as if suddenly recollecting herself, and deploring her inability to do something she was bent upon, wrung her hands, and burst into tears.

It might be that her tears relieved her, or that she felt the full hopelessness of her condition; but she turned back; and hurrying with nearly as great a rapidity in the contrary direction: partly to recover lost time, and partly to keep pace with the violent current of her own thoughts: soon reached the dwelling where she had left the housebreaker.

If she betrayed any agitation, when she presented herself to Mr. Sikes, he did not observe it; for merely inquiring if she had brought the money, and receiving a reply in the affirmative, he uttered a growl of satisfaction, and replacing his head upon the pillow, resumed the slumbers which her arrival had interrupted.

It was fortunate for her that the possession of money occasioned him so much employment next day in the way of eating and drinking; and withal had so beneficial an effect in smoothing down the asperities of his temper; that he had neither time nor inclination to be very critical upon her behaviour and deportment. That she had all the abstracted and nervous manner of one who is on the eve of some bold and hazardous step, which it has required no common struggle to resolve upon, would have been obvious to the lynx-eyed Jew, who would most probably have taken the alarm at once; but Mr. Sikes lacking the niceties of discrimination, and being troubled with no more subtle misgivings than those which resolve themselves into a dogged roughness of behaviour towards everybody; and being, furthermore, in an unusually amiable condition, as has been already observed; saw nothing unusual in her demeanour, and indeed, troubled himself so little about her, that, had her agitation been far more perceptible than it was, it would have been very unlikely to have awakened his suspicions.

As that day closed in, the girl's excitement increased; and, when night came on, and she sat by, watching until the housebreaker should drink himself asleep, there was an unusual paleness in her cheek, and a fire in her eye, that even Sikes observed with astonishment.

Mr. Sikes, being weak from the fever, was lying in bed, taking hot water with his gin to render it less inflammatory; and had pushed his glass towards Nancy to be replenished for the third or fourth time, when these symptoms first struck him.

"Why, burn my body!" said the man, raising himself on his hands as he stared the girl in the face. "You look like a corpse come to life again. What's the matter?"

"Matter!" replied the girl. "Nothing. What do you look at me so hard for?"

"What foolery is this?" demanded Sikes, grasping her by the arm, and shaking her roughly. "What is it? What do you mean? What are you thinking of?"

"Of many things, Bill," replied the girl, shivering, and as she did so, pressing her hands upon her eyes. "But, Lord! What odds in that?"

The tone of forced gaiety in which the last words were spoken, seemed to produce a deeper impression on Sikes than the wild and rigid look which had preceded them.

"I tell you wot it is," said Sikes; "if you haven't caught the fever, and got it comin' on, now, there's something more than usual in the wind, and something dangerous too. You're not a-going to——. No, damme! you wouldn't do that!"

"Do what?" asked the girl.

"There ain't," said Sikes, fixing his eyes upon her, and muttering the words to himself; "there ain't a stauncher-hearted gal going, or I'd have cut her throat three months ago. She's got the fever coming on; that's it."

Fortifying himself with this assurance, Sikes drained the glass to the bottom, and then, with many grumbling oaths, called for his physic. The girl jumped up, with great alacrity; poured it quickly out, but with her back towards him; and held the vessel to his lips, while he drank off the contents.

"Now," said the robber, "come and sit aside of me, and put on your own face; or I'll alter it so, that you won't know it again when you *do* want it."

The girl obeyed. Sikes, locking her hand in his, fell back upon the pillow turning his eyes upon her face. They closed; opened again; closed once more; again opened. He shifted his position restlessly; and, after dozing again, and again, for two or three minutes, and as often springing up with a look of terror, and gazing vacantly about him, was suddenly stricken, as it were, while in the very attitude of rising, into a deep and heavy sleep. The grasp of his hand relaxed; the upraised arm fell languidly by his side; and he lay like one in a profound trance.

"The laudanum has taken effect at last," murmured the girl, as she rose from the bedside. "I may be too late, even now."

She hastily dressed herself in her bonnet and shawl: looking fearfully round, from time to time, as if, despite the sleeping draught, she expected every moment to feel the pressure of Sikes's heavy hand upon her shoulder; then, stooping softly over the bed, she kissed the robber's lips; and then, opening and closing the room-door with noiseless touch, hurried from the house.

A watchman was crying half-past nine, down a dark passage through which she had to pass, in gaining the main thoroughfare.

"Has it long gone the half-hour?" asked the girl.

"It'll strike the hour in another quarter," said the man: raising his lantern to her face.

"And I cannot get there in less than an hour or more," muttered Nancy: brushing swiftly past him, and gliding rapidly down the street.

Many of the shops were already closing in the back lanes and avenues through which she tracked her way, in making from Spitalfields towards the West End of London. The clock struck ten, increasing her impatience. She tore along the narrow pavement: elbowing the passengers from side to side; and darting almost under the horses' heads, crossed crowded streets, where clusters of persons were eagerly watching their opportunity to do the like.

"The woman is mad!" said the people, turning to look after her as she rushed away.

When she reached the more wealthy quarter of the town,

the streets were comparatively deserted; and here her headlong progress excited a still greater curiosity in the stragglers whom she hurried past. Some quickened their pace behind, as though to see whither she was hastening at such an unusual rate; and a few made head upon her, and looked back, surprised at her undiminished speed; but they fell off one by one; and when she neared her place of destination, she was alone.

It was a family hotel in a quiet but handsome street near Hyde Park. As the brilliant light of the lamp which burnt before its door, guided her to the spot, the clock struck eleven. She had loitered for a few paces as though irresolute, and making up her mind to advance; but the sound determined her, and she stepped into the hall. The porter's seat was vacant. She looked round with an air of incertitude, and advanced towards the stairs.

"Now, young woman!" said a smartly-dressed female, looking out from a door behind her, "who do you want here?"

"A lady who is stopping in this house," answered the girl.

"A lady!" was the reply, accompanied with a scornful look. "What lady?"

"Miss Maylie," said Nancy.

The young woman, who had, by this time, noted her appearance, replied only by a look of virtuous disdain; and summoned a man to answer her. To him, Nancy repeated her request.

"What name am I to say?" asked the waiter.

"It's of no use saying any," replied Nancy.

"Nor business?" said the man.

"No, nor that neither," rejoined the girl. "I must see the lady."

"Come!" said the man, pushing her towards the door. "None of this! Take yourself off."

"I shall be carried out, if I go!" said the girl violently; "and I can make that a job that two of you won't like to do. Isn't there anybody here," she said, looking round, "that will see a simple message carried for a poor wretch like me?"

This appeal produced an effect on a good-tempered-faced man-cook, who with some other of the servants was looking on, and who stepped forward to interfere.

"Take it up for her, Joe; can't you?" said this person.

"What's the good?" replied the man. "You don't suppose the young lady will see such as her; do you?"

This allusion to Nancy's doubtful character, raised a vast quantity of chaste wrath in the bosoms of four housemaids, who remarked, with great fervour, that the creature was a disgrace to her sex; and strongly advocated her being thrown, ruthlessly, into the kennel.

"Do what you like with me," said the girl, turning to the men again; "but do what I ask you first, and I ask you to give this message for God Almighty's sake."

The soft-hearted cook added his intercession, and the result was that the man who had first appeared undertook its delivery.

"What's it to be?" said the man, with one foot on the stairs.

"That a young woman earnestly asks to speak to Miss Maylie alone," said Nancy; "and that if the lady will only hear the first word she has to say, she will know whether to hear her business, or to have her turned out of doors as an impostor."

"I say," said the man, "you're coming it strong!"

"You give the message," said the girl firmly; "and let me hear the answer."

The man ran up stairs. Nancy remained, pale and almost breathless, listening with quivering lip to the very audible expressions of scorn, of which the chaste housemaids were very prolific; and of which they became still more so, when the man returned, and said the young woman was to walk up stairs.

"It's no good being proper in this world," said the first housemaid.

"Brass can do better than the gold what has stood the fire," said the second.

The third contented herself with wondering "what ladies was made of;" and the fourth took the first in a quartette of "Shameful!" with which the Dianas concluded.

Regardless of all this: for she had weightier matters at heart: Nancy followed the man, with trembling limbs, to a small ante-chamber, lighted by a lamp from the ceiling. Here he left her and retired.

CHAPTER XL.

A STRANGE INTERVIEW, WHICH IS A SEQUEL TO THE LAST CHAPTER.

THE girl's life had been squandered in the streets, and among the most noisome of the stews and dens of London, but there was something of the woman's original nature left in her still; and when she heard a light step approaching the door opposite to that by which she had entered, and thought of the wide contrast which the small room would in another moment contain, she felt burdened with the sense of her own deep shame, and shrunk as though she could scarcely bear the presence of her with whom she had sought this interview.

But struggling with these better feelings was pride,—the vice of the lowest and most debased creatures no less than of the high and self-assured. The miserable companion of thieves and ruffians, the fallen outcast of low haunts, the associate of the scourings of the jails and hulks, living within the shadow of the gallows itself,—even this degraded being felt too proud to betray a feeble gleam of the womanly feeling which she thought a weakness, but which alone connected her with that humanity, of which her wasting life had obliterated so many, many traces when a very child.

She raised her eyes sufficiently to observe that the figure which presented itself was that of a slight and beautiful girl; and then, bending them on the ground, tossed her head with affected carelessness as she said:

"It's a hard matter to get to see you, lady. If I had taken offence, and gone away, as many would have done, you'd have been sorry for it one day, and not without reason, either."

"I am very sorry if any one has behaved harshly to you," replied Rose. "Do not think of that. Tell me why you wished to see me. I am the person you inquired for."

The kind tone of this answer, the sweet voice, the gentle manner, the absence of any accent of haughtiness or displeasure, took the girl completely by surprise, and she burst into tears.

"Oh, lady, lady!" she said, clasping her hands passionately before her face, "if there was more like you, there would be fewer like me,—there would—there would!"

"Sit down," said Rose, earnestly. "You distress me.

If you are in poverty or affliction I shall be truly glad to relieve you if I can,—I shall indeed. Sit down."

"Let me stand, lady," said the girl, still weeping, "and do not speak to me so kindly till you know me better. It is growing late. Is—is—that door shut?"

"Yes," said Rose, recoiling a few steps, as if to be nearer assistance in case she should require it. "Why?"

"Because," said the girl, "I am about to put my life, and the lives of others in your hands. I am the girl that dragged little Oliver back to old Fagin's, the Jew's, on the night he went out from the house in Pentonville."

"You!" said Rose Maylie.

"I, lady!" replied the girl. "I am the infamous creature you have heard of, that lives among the thieves, and that never from the first moment I can recollect my eyes and senses opening on London streets have known any better life, or kinder words than they have given me, so help me God! Do not mind shrinking openly from me, lady. I am younger than you would think, to look at me, but I am well used to it. The poorest women fall back, as I make my way along the crowded pavement."

"What dreadful things are these!" said Rose, involuntarily falling from her strange companion.

"Thank Heaven upon your knees, dear lady," cried the girl, "that you had friends to care for and keep you in your childhood, and that you were never in the midst of cold and hunger, and riot and drunkenness, and—and something worse than all—as I have been from my cradle; I may use the word, for the alley and the gutter were mine, as they will be my death-bed."

"I pity you!" said Rose, in a broken voice. "It wrings my heart to hear you!"

"Heaven bless you for your goodness!" rejoined the girl. "If you knew what I am sometimes, you would pity me, indeed. But I have stolen away from those who would surely murder me, if they knew I had been here, to tell you what I have overheard. Do you know a man named Monks?"

"No," said Rose.

"He knows you," replied the girl; "and knew you were here, for it was by hearing him tell the place that I found you out."

"I never heard the name," said Rose.

"Then he goes by some other amongst us," rejoined the girl, "which I more than thought before. Some time ago, and soon after Oliver was put into your house on the night of the robbery, I—suspecting this man—listened to a conversation held between him and Fagin in the dark. I found out, from what I heard, that Monks—the man I asked you about, you know—"

"Yes," said Rose, "I understand."

"—That Monks," pursued the girl, "had seen him accidentally with two of our boys on the day we first lost him, and had known him directly to be the same child that he was watching for, though I couldn't make out why. A bargain was struck with Fagin, that if Oliver was got back he should have a certain sum; and he was to have more for making him a thief, which this Monks wanted for some purpose of his own."

"For what purpose?" asked Rose.

"He caught sight of my shadow on the wall as I listened, in the hope of finding out," said the girl; "and there are not many people besides me that could have got out of their way in time to escape discovery. But I did; and I saw him no more till last night."

"And what occurred then?"

"I'll tell you, lady. Last night he came again. Again they went up stairs, and I, wrapping myself up so that my shadow should not betray me, again listened at the door. The first words I heard Monks say were these: 'So the only proofs of the boy's identity lie at the bottom of the river, and the old hag that received them from the mother is rotting in her coffin.' They laughed, and talked of his success in doing this; and Monks, talking on about the boy, and getting very wild, said, that though he had got the young devil's money safely now, he'd rather have had it the other way; for, what a game it would have been to have brought down the boast of the father's will, by driving him through every jail in town, and then hauling him up for some capital felony, which Fagin could easily manage, after having made a good profit of him besides."

"What is all this!" said Rose.

"The truth, lady, though it comes from my lips," replied the girl. "Then, he said, with oaths common enough in my ears, but strange to yours, that if he could gratify his hatred by taking the boy's life without bringing his own neck in danger, he would; but, as he couldn't, he'd be upon the watch to meet him at every turn in life; and if he took advantage of his birth and history, he might harm him yet. 'In short, Fagin,' he says, 'Jew as you are, you never laid such snares as I'll contrive for my young brother, Oliver.'"

"His brother!" exclaimed Rose.

"Those were his words," said Nancy, glancing uneasily round, as she had scarcely ceased to do, since she began to speak, for a vision of Sikes haunted her perpetually. "And more. When he spoke of you and the other lady, and said it seemed contrived by Heaven, or the Devil, against him, that Oliver should come into your hands, he laughed, and said there was some comfort in that too, for how many thousands and hundreds of thousands of pounds would you not give, if you had them, to know who your two-legged spaniel was."

"You do not mean," said Rose, turning very pale, "to tell me that this was said in earnest?"

"He spoke in hard and angry earnest, if a man ever did," replied the girl, shaking her head. "He is an earnest man when his hatred is up. I know many who do worse things; but I'd rather listen to them all a dozen times, than to that Monks once. It is growing late, and I have to reach home without suspicion of having been on such an errand as this. I must get back quickly."

"But what can I do?" said Rose. "To what use can I turn this communication without you? Back! Why do you wish to return to companions you paint in such terrible colours? If you repeat this information to a gentleman whom I can summon in an instant from the next room, you can be consigned to some place of safety without half an hour's delay."

"I wish to go back," said the girl. "I must go back, because—how can I tell such things to an innocent lady like you?—because among the men I have told you of, there is one: the most desperate among them all: that I can't leave; no, not even to be saved from the life I am leading now."

"Your having interfered in this dear boy's behalf before," said Rose; "your coming here, at so great a risk, to tell me what you have heard; your manner, which convinces me of the truth of what you say; your evident contrition, and sense of shame; all lead me to believe that you might be yet reclaimed. Oh!" said the earnest girl, folding her hands as the tears coursed down her face, "do not turn a deaf ear to the entreaties of one of your own sex; the first—the first, I do believe, who ever appealed to you in the voice of pity and compassion. Do hear my words, and let me save you yet, for better things."

"Lady," cried the girl, sinking on her knees, "dear, sweet, angel lady, you *are* the first that ever blessed me with such words as these, and if I had heard them years ago, they might have turned me from a life of sin and sorrow; but it is too late—it is too late!"

"It is never too late," said Rose, "for penitence and atonement."

"It is," cried the girl, writhing in the agony of her mind; "I cannot leave him now! I could not be his death."

"Why should you be?" asked Rose.

"Nothing could save him," cried the girl. "If I told others what I have told you, and led to their being taken, he would be sure to die. He is the boldest, and has been so cruel!"

"Is it possible," cried Rose, "that for such a man as this, you can resign every future hope, and the certainty of immediate rescue? It is madness."

"I don't know what it is," answered the girl; "I only know that it is so, and not with me alone, but with hundreds of others as bad and wretched as myself. I must go back. Whether it is God's wrath for the wrong I have done, I do not know; but I am drawn back to him through every suffering and ill usage: and should be, I believe, if I knew that I was to die by his hand at last."

"What am I to do?" said Rose. "I should not let you depart from me thus."

"You should, lady, and I know you will," rejoined the girl, rising. "You will not stop my going because I have trusted in your goodness, and forced no promise from you, as I might have done."

"Of what use, then, is the communication you have made?" said Rose. "This mystery must be investigated, or how will its disclosure to me, benefit Oliver, whom you are anxious to serve?"

"You must have some kind gentleman about you that will hear it as a secret, and advise you what to do," rejoined the girl.

"But where can I find you again when it is necessary?" asked Rose. "I do not seek to know where these dreadful people live, but where will you be walking or passing at any settled period from this time?"

"Will you promise me that you will have my secret strictly kept, and come alone, or with the only other person that knows it; and that I shall not be watched or followed?" asked the girl.

"I promise you solemnly," answered Rose.

"Every Sunday night, from eleven until the clock strikes twelve," said the girl without hesitation, "I will walk on London Bridge if I am alive."

"Stay another moment," interposed Rose, as the girl moved hurriedly towards the door. "Think once again on your own condition, and the opportunity you have of escaping from it. You have a claim on me: not only as the voluntary bearer of this intelligence, but as a woman lost almost beyond redemption. Will you return to this gang of robbers, and to this man, when a word can save you? What fascination is it that can take you back, and make you cling to wickedness and misery? Oh! is there no chord in your heart that I can touch! Is there nothing

left, to which I can appeal against this terrible infatuation!"

"When ladies as young, and good, and beautiful as you are," replied the girl steadily, "give away your hearts, love will carry you all lengths—even such as you, who have home, friends, other admirers, everything to fill them. When such as I, who have no certain roof but the coffin-lid, and no friend in sickness or death but the hospital nurse, set our rotten hearts on any man, and let him fill the place that has been a blank through all our wretched lives, who can hope to cure us? Pity us, lady—pity us for having only one feeling of the woman left, and for having that turned, by a heavy judgment, from a comfort and a pride, into a new means of violence and suffering."

"You will," said Rose, after a pause, "take some money from me, which may enable you to live without dishonesty—at all events until we meet again?"

"Not a penny," replied the girl, waving her hand.

"Do not close your heart against all my efforts to help you," said Rose, stepping gently forward. "I wish to serve you indeed."

"You would serve me best, lady," replied the girl, wringing her hands, "if you could take my life at once; for I have felt more grief to think of what I am, to-night, than I ever did before, and it would be something not to die in the same hell in which I have lived. God bless you, sweet lady, and send as much happiness on your head as I have brought shame on mine!"

Thus speaking, and sobbing aloud, the unhappy creature turned away; while Rose Maylie, overpowered by this extraordinary interview, which had more the semblance of a rapid dream than an actual occurrence, sank into a chair, and endeavoured to collect her wandering thoughts.

CHAPTER XLI.

CONTAINING FRESH DISCOVERIES, AND SHOWING THAT SURPRISES, LIKE MISFORTUNES, SELDOM COME ALONE.

HER situation was, indeed, one of no common trial and difficulty. While she felt the most eager and burning desire to penetrate the mystery in which Oliver's history was enveloped, she could not but hold sacred the confidence which the miserable woman with whom she had just conversed, had reposed in her, as a young and guileless girl. Her words and manner had touched Rose Maylie's heart; and, mingled with her love for her young charge, and scarcely less intense in its truth and fervour, was her fond wish to win the outcast back to repentance and hope.

They only proposed remaining in London three days, prior to departing for some weeks to a distant part of the coast. It was now midnight of the first day. What course of action could she determine upon, which could be adopted in eight-and-forty hours? Or how could she postpone the journey without exciting suspicion?

Mr. Losberne was with them, and would be for the next two days; but Rose was too well acquainted with the excellent gentleman's impetuosity, and foresaw too clearly the wrath with which, in the first explosion of his indignation, he would regard the instrument of Oliver's re-capture, to trust him with the secret, when her representations in the girl's behalf could be seconded by no experienced person. These were all reasons for the greatest caution and most circumspect behaviour in communicating it to Mrs.

Maylie, whose first impulse would infallibly be to hold a conference with the worthy doctor on the subject. As to resorting to any legal adviser, even if she had known how to do so, it was scarcely to be thought of, for the same reasons. Once the thought occurred to her of seeking assistance from Harry; but this awakened the recollection of their last parting, and it seemed unworthy of her to call him back, when—the tears rose to her eyes as she pursued this train of reflection—he might have by this time learnt to forget her, and to be happier away.

Disturbed by these different reflections; inclining now to one course and then to another, and again recoiling from all, as each successive consideration presented itself to her mind; Rose passed a sleepless and anxious night. After more communing with herself next day, she arrived at the desperate conclusion of consulting Harry.

"If it be painful to him," she thought, "to come back here, how painful will it be to me! But perhaps he will not come; he may write, or he may come himself, and studiously abstain from meeting me—he did when he went away. I hardly thought he would; but it was better for us both." And here Rose dropped the pen, and turned away, as though the very paper which was to be her messenger should not see her weep.

She had taken up the same pen, and laid it down again fifty times, and had considered and reconsidered the first line of her letter without writing the first word, when Oliver, who had been walking in the streets, with Mr. Giles for a body-guard, entered the room in such breathless haste and violent agitation, as seemed to betoken some new cause of alarm.

"What makes you look so flurried?" asked Rose, advancing to meet him.

"I hardly know how; I feel as if I should be choked," replied the boy. "Oh dear! To think that I should see him at last, and you should be able to know that I have told you all the truth!"

"I never thought you had told us anything but the truth," said Rose, soothing him. "But what is this?—of whom do you speak?"

"I have seen the gentleman," replied Oliver, scarcely able to articulate, "the gentleman who was so good to me —Mr. Brownlow, that we have so often talked about."

"Where?" asked Rose.

"Getting out of a coach," replied Oliver, shedding tears of delight, "and going into a house. I didn't speak to him —I couldn't speak to him, for he didn't see me, and I trembled so, that I was not able to go up to him. But Giles asked, for me, whether he lived there, and they said he did. Look here," said Oliver, opening a scrap of paper, "here it is; here's where he lives—I'm going there directly! Oh, dear me, dear me! What shall I do when I come to see him and hear him speak again!"

With her attention not a little distracted by these and a great many other incoherent exclamations of joy, Rose read the address, which was Craven Street, in the Strand, and very soon determined upon turning the discovery to account.

"Quick!" she said, "tell them to fetch a hackney-coach, and be ready to go with me. I will take you there directly, without a minute's loss of time. I will only tell my aunt that we are going out for an hour, and be ready as soon as you are."

Oliver needed no prompting to despatch, and in little more than five minutes they were on their way to Craven Street. When they arrived there, Rose left Oliver in the coach, under pretence of preparing the old gentleman to

receive him; and sending up her card by the servant, requested to see Mr. Brownlow on very pressing business. The servant soon returned, to beg that she would walk up stairs; and, following him into an upper room, Miss Maylie was presented to an elderly gentleman of benevolent appearance, in a bottle-green coat. At no great distance from whom, was seated another old gentleman, in nankeen breeches and gaiters; who did not look particularly benevolent, and who was sitting with his hands clasped on the top of a thick stick, and his chin propped thereupon.

"Dear me," said the gentleman, in the bottle-green coat, hastily rising with great politeness, "I beg your pardon, young lady—I imagined it was some importunate person who—I beg you will excuse me. Be seated, pray."

"Mr. Brownlow, I believe, Sir?" said Rose, glancing from the other gentleman to the one who had spoken.

"That is my name," said the old gentleman. "This is my friend, Mr. Grimwig. Grimwig, will you leave us for a few minutes?"

"I believe," interposed Miss Maylie, "that at this period of our interview, I need not give that gentleman the trouble of going away. If I am correctly informed, he is cognizant of the business on which I wish to speak to you."

Mr. Brownlow inclined his head. Mr. Grimwig, who had made one very stiff bow, and risen from his chair, made another very stiff bow, and dropped into it again.

"I shall surpirse you very much, I have no doubt," said Rose, naturally embarrassed; "but you once showed great benevolence and goodness to a very dear young friend of mine, and I am sure you will take an interest in hearing of him again."

"Indeed!" said Mr. Brownlow.

"Oliver Twist you knew him as," replied Rose.

The words no sooner escaped her lips, than Mr. Grimwig, who had been affecting to dip into a large book that lay on the table, upset it with a great crash, and falling back in his chair, discharged from his features every expression but one of the most unmitigated wonder, and indulged in a prolonged and vacant stare; then, as if ashamed of having betrayed so much emotion, he jerked himself, as it were, by a convulsion into his former attitude, and looking out straight before him emitted a long deep whistle, which seemed, at last, not to be discharged on empty air, but to die away in the innermost recesses of his stomach.

Mr. Brownlow was no less surprised, although his astonishment was not expressed in the same eccentric manner. He drew his chair nearer to Miss Maylie's, and said,

"Do me the favour, my dear young lady, to leave entirely out of the question that goodness and benevolence of which you speak, and of which nobody else knows anything; and if you have it in your power to produce any evidence which will alter the unfavourable opinion I was once induced to entertain of that poor child, in Heaven's name put me in possession of it."

"A bad one! I'll eat my head if he is not a bad one," growled Mr. Grimwig, speaking by some ventriloquial power, without moving a muscle of his face.

"He is a child of a noble nature and a warm heart," said Rose, colouring; "and that Power which has thought fit to try him beyond his years, has planted in his breast affections and feelings which would do honour to many who have numbered his days six times over."

"I'm only sixty-one," said Mr. Grimwig, with the same rigid face. "And, as the devil's in it if this Oliver is not twelve years old at least, I don't see the application of that remark."

"Do not heed my friend, Miss Maylie," said Mr. Brownlow; "he does not mean what he says."

"Yes, he does," growled Mr. Grimwig.

"No, he does not," said Mr. Brownlow, obviously rising in wrath as he spoke.

"He'll eat his head, if he doesn't," growled Mr. Grimwig.

"He would deserve to have it knocked off, if he does," said Mr. Brownlow.

"And he'd uncommonly like to see any man offer to do it," responded Mr. Grimwig, knocking his stick upon the floor.

Having gone thus far, the two old gentlemen severally took snuff, and afterwards shook hands, according to their invariable custom.

"Now, Miss Maylie," said Mr. Brownlow, "to return to the subject in which your humanity is so much interested. Will you let me know what intelligence you have of this poor child: allowing me to premise that I exhausted every means in my power of discovering him, and that since I have been absent from this country, my first impression that he had imposed upon me, and had been persuaded by his former associates to rob me, has been considerably shaken."

Rose, who had had time to collect her thoughts, at once related, in a few natural words, all that had befallen Oliver since he left Mr. Brownlow's house; reserving Nancy's information for that gentleman's private ear, and concluding with the assurance that his only sorrow, for some months past, had been the not being able to meet with his former benefactor and friend.

"Thank God!" said the old gentleman. "This is great happiness to me; great happiness. But you have not told me where he is now, Miss Maylie. You must pardon my finding fault with you,—but why not have brought him?"

"He is waiting in a coach at the door," replied Rose.

"At this door!" cried the old gentleman. With which he hurried out of the room, down the stairs, up the coach-steps, and into the coach, without another word.

When the room-door closed behind him, Mr. Grimwig lifted up his head, and converting one of the hind legs of his chair into a pivot, described three distinct circles with the assistance of his stick and the table: sitting in it all the time. After performing this evolution, he rose and limped as fast as he could up and down the room at least a dozen times, and then stopping suddenly before Rose, kissed her without the slightest preface.

"Hush!" he said, as the young lady rose in some alarm at this unusual proceeding. "Don't be afraid. I'm old enough to be your grandfather. You're a sweet girl. I like you. Here they are!"

In fact, as he threw himself at one dexterous dive into his former seat, Mr. Brownlow returned, accompanied by Oliver, who Mr. Grimwig received very graciously; and if the gratification of that moment had been the only reward for all her anxiety and care in Oliver's behalf, Rose Maylie would have been well repaid.

"There is somebody else who should not be forgotten, by the by," said Mr. Brownlow, ringing the bell. "Send Mrs. Bedwin here, if you please."

The old housekeeper answered the summons with all dispatch; and dropping a curtsey at the door, waited for orders.

"Why, you get blinder every day, Bedwin," said Mr. Brownlow, rather testily.

"Well, that I do, Sir," replied the old lady. "People's eyes, at my time of life, don't improve with age, Sir."

"I could have told you that," rejoined Mr. Brownlow; "but put on your glasses, and see if you can't find out what you were wanted for, will you?"

The old lady began to rummage in her pocket for her spectacles. But Oliver's patience was not proof against this new trial; and yielding to his first impulse, he sprang into her arms.

"God be good to me!" cried the old lady, embracing him; "it is my innocent boy!"

"My dear old nurse!" cried Oliver.

"He would come back—I knew he would," said the old lady, holding him in her arms. "How well he looks, and how like a gentleman's son he is dressed again! Where have you been, this long, long while? Ah! the same sweet face, but not so pale; the same soft eye, but not so sad. I have never forgotten them or his quiet smile, but have seen them every day, side by side with those of my own dear children, dead and gone since I was a lightsome young creature." Running on thus, and now holding Oliver from her to mark how he had grown, now clasping him to her and passing her fingers fondly through his hair, the good soul laughed and wept upon his neck by turns.

Leaving her and Oliver to compare notes at leisure, Mr. Brownlow led the way into another room; and there, heard from Rose a full narration of her interview with Nancy, which occasioned him no little surprise and perplexity. Rose also explained her reasons for not making a confidant of her friend Mr. Losberne in the first instance; the old gentleman considered that she had acted prudently, and readily undertook to hold solemn conference with the worthy doctor himself. To afford him an early opportunity for the execution of this design, it was arranged that he should call at the hotel at eight o'clock that evening, and that in the meantime Mrs. Maylie should be cautiously informed of all that had occurred. These preliminaries adjusted, Rose and Oliver returned home.

Rose had by no means overrated the measure of the good doctor's wrath. Nancy's history was no sooner unfolded to him, than he poured forth a shower of mingled threats and execrations; threatened to make her the first victim of the combined ingenuity of Messrs. Blathers and Duff; and actually put on his hat preparatory to sallying forth immediately to obtain the assistance of those worthies. And, doubtless, he would, in his first outbreak, have carried the intention into effect without a moment's consideration of the consequences, if he had not been restrained, in part, by corresponding violence on the side of Mr. Brownlow, who was himself of an irascible temperament, and partly by such arguments and representations as seemed best calculated to dissuade him from his hotbrained purpose.

"Then what the devil is to be done?" said the impetuous doctor, when they had rejoined the two ladies. "Are we to pass a vote of thanks to all these vagabonds, male and female, and beg them to accept a hundred pounds, or so, apiece, as a trifling mark of our esteem, and some slight acknowledgment of their kindness to Oliver?"

"Not exactly that," rejoined Mr. Brownlow, laughing; "but we must proceed gently and with great care."

"Gentleness and care!" exclaimed the doctor. "I'd send them one and all to——"

"Never mind where," interposed Mr. Brownlow. "But reflect whether sending them anywhere is likely to attain the object we have in view."

"What object?" asked the doctor.

"Simply, the discovery of Oliver's parentage, and regaining for him the inheritance of which, if this story be true, he has been fraudulently deprived."

"Ah!" said Mr. Losberne, cooling himself with his pocket-handkerchief; "I almost forgot that."

"You see," pursued Mr. Brownlow; "placing this poor girl entirely out of the question, and supposing it were possible to bring these scoundrels to justice without compromising her safety, what good should we bring about?"

"Hanging a few of them at least, in all probability," suggested the doctor, "and transporting the rest."

"Very good," replied Mr. Brownlow, smiling; "but no doubt they will bring that about for themselves in the fulness of time, and if we step in to forestal them, it seems to me that we shall be performing a very Quixotic act, in direct opposition to our own interest—or at least to Oliver's, which is the same thing."

"How?" inquired the doctor.

"Thus. It is quite clear that we shall have extreme difficulty in getting to the bottom of this mystery, unless we can bring this man, Monks, upon his knees. That can only be done by stratagem, and by catching him when he is not surrounded by these people. For, suppose he were apprehended, we have no proof against him. He is not even (so far as we know, or as the facts appear to us) concerned with the gang in any of their robberies. If he were not discharged, it is very unlikely that he could receive any further punishment than being committed to prison as a rogue and vagabond; and of course ever afterwards his mouth is so obstinately closed that he might as well, for our purposes, be deaf, dumb, blind, and an idiot."

"Then," said the doctor impetuously, "I put it to you again, whether you think it reasonable that this promise to the girl should be considered binding; a promise made with the best and kindest intentions, but really——"

"Do not discuss the point, my dear young lady, pray," said Mr. Brownlow, interrupting Rose as she was about to speak. "The promise shall be kept. I don't think it will, in the slightest degree, interfere with our proceedings. But, before we can resolve upon any precise course of action, it will be necessary to see the girl; to ascertain from her whether she will point out this Monks, on the understanding that he is to be dealt with by us, and not by the law; or, if she will not, or cannot do that, to procure from her such an account of his haunts and description of his person, as will enable us to identify him. She cannot be seen until next Sunday night; this is Tuesday. I would suggest that, in the meantime, we remain perfectly quiet, and keep these matters secret even from Oliver himself."

Although Mr. Losberne received with many wry faces a proposal involving a delay of five whole days, he was fain to admit that no better course occurred to him just then; and as both Rose and Mrs. Maylie sided very strongly with Mr. Brownlow, that gentleman's proposition was carried unanimously.

"I should like," he said, "to call in the aid of my friend Grimwig. He is a strange creature, but a shrewd one, and might prove of material assistance to us; I should say that he was bred a lawyer, and quitted the Bar in disgust because he had only one brief and a motion of course in twenty years, though whether that is a recommendation or not, you must determine for yourselves."

"I have no objection to your calling in your friend if I may call in mine," said the doctor.

"We must put it to the vote," replied Mr. Brownlow, "who may he be?"

"That lady's son, and this young lady's—very old friend," said the doctor, motioning towards Mrs. Maylie. and concluding with an expressive glance at her niece.

Rose blushed deeply, but she did not make any audible objection to this motion (possibly she felt in a hopeless minority); and Harry Maylie and Mr. Grimwig were accordingly added to the committee.

"We stay in town, of course," said Mrs. Maylie, "while there remains the slightest prospect of prosecuting this inquiry with a chance of success. I will spare neither trouble nor expense in behalf of the object in which we are all so deeply interested, and I am content to remain here, if it be for twelve months, so long as you assure me that any hope remains."

"Good!" rejoined Mr. Brownlow. "And as I see on the faces about me, a disposition to inquire how it happened that I was not in the way to corroborate Oliver's tale, and had so suddenly left the kingdom, let me stipulate that I shall be asked no questions until such time as I may deem it expedient to forestal them by telling my own story. Believe me, I make this request with good reason, for I might otherwise excite hopes destined never to be realised, and only increase difficulties and disappointments already quite numerous enough. Come! Supper has been announced, and young Oliver, who is all alone in the next room, will have begun to think, by this time, that we have wearied of his company, and entered into some dark conspiracy to thrust him forth upon the world."

With these words, the old gentleman gave his hand to Mrs. Maylie, and escorted her into the supper-room. Mr. Losberne followed, leading Rose; and the council was, for the present, effectually broken up.

CHAPTER XLII.

AN OLD ACQUAINTANCE OF OLIVER'S, EXHIBITING DECIDED MARKS OF GENIUS, BECOMES A PUBLIC CHARACTER IN THE METROPOLIS.

Upon the very same night when Nancy, having lulled Mr. Sikes to sleep, hurried on her self-imposed mission to Rose Maylie, there advanced towards London, by the Great North Road, two persons, upon whom it is expedient that this history should bestow some attention.

They were a man and woman; or perhaps they would be better described as a male and female; for the former was one of those long-limbed, knock-kneed, shambling, bony people, to whom it is difficult to assign any precise age,—looking as they do, when they are yet boys, like undergrown men, and when they are almost men, like overgrown boys. The woman was young, but of a robust and hardy make, as she need have been to bear the weight of the heavy bundle which was strapped to her back. Her companion was not encumbered with much luggage, as there merely dangled from a stick, which he carried over his shoulder, a small parcel wrapped in a common handkerchief, and apparently light enough. This circumstance, added to the length of his legs, which were of unusual extent, enabled him with much ease to keep some half-dozen paces in advance of his companion, to whom he occasionally turned with an impatient jerk of the head: as if reproaching her tardiness, and urging her to greater exertion.

Thus, they had toiled along the dusty road, taking little heed of any object within sight, save when they stepped aside to allow a wider passage for the mail-coaches which were whirling out of town, until they passed through High-gate Archway; when the foremost traveller stopped and called impatiently to his companion.

"Come on, can't yer? What a lazybones yer are, Char-lotte."

"It's a heavy load, I can tell you," said the female, coming up, almost breathless with fatigue.

"Heavy! What are yer talking about? What are yer made for?" rejoined the male traveller, changing his own little bundle as he spoke, to the other shoulder. "Oh, there yer are, resting again! Well, if yer ain't enough to tire any body's patience out, I don't know what is!"

"Is it much farther?" asked the woman, resting herself against a bank, and looking up with the perspiration streaming from her face.

"Much farther! Yer as good as there," said the long-legged tramper pointing out before him. "Look there! Those are the lights of London."

"They're a good two mile off, at least," said the woman despondingly.

"Never mind whether they're two mile off, or twenty," said Noah Claypole; for he it was; "but get up and come on, or I'll kick yer, and so I give yer notice."

As Noah's red nose grew redder with anger, and as he crossed the road while speaking, as if fully prepared to put his threat into execution, the woman rose without any further remark, and trudged onward by his side.

"Where do you mean to stop for the night, Noah?" she asked, after they had walked a few hundred yards.

"How should I know?" replied Noah, whose temper had been considerably impaired by walking.

"Near, I hope," said Charlotte.

"No, not near," replied Mr. Claypole. "There! Not near; so don't think it."

"Why not?"

"When I tell yer that I don't mean to do a thing, that's enough, without any why or because either," replied Mr. Claypole with dignity.

"Well, you needn't be so cross," said his companion.

"A pretty thing it would be, wouldn't it, to go and stop at the very first public-house outside the town, so that Sowerberry, if he come up after us, might poke in his old nose, and have us taken back in a cart with handcuffs on," said Mr. Claypole in a jeering tone. "No! I shall go and lose myself among the narrowest streets I can find, and not stop till we come to the very out-of-the-wayest house I can set eyes on. 'Cod, yer may thank yer stars I've got a head; for if we hadn't gone, at first, the wrong road a purpose, and come back across country, yer'd have been locked up hard and fast a week ago, my lady. And serve yer right for being a fool."

"I know I ain't as cunning as you are," replied Char-lotte; "but don't put all the blame on me, and say I should have been locked up. You would have been if I had been, any way."

"Yer took the money from the till, yer know yer did," said Mr. Claypole.

"I took it for you, Noah, dear," rejoined Charlotte.

"Did I keep it?" asked Mr. Claypole.

"No; you trusted in me, and let me carry it like a dear, and so you are," said the lady, chucking him under the chin, and drawing her arm through his.

This was indeed the case; but as it was not Mr. Clay-pole's habit to repose a blind and foolish confidence in any-body, it should be observed, in justice to that gentleman, that he had trusted Charlotte to this extent, in order that, if they were pursued, the money might be found on her: which would leave him an opportunity of asserting his utter innocence of any theft, and would greatly facilitate his chances of escape. Of course, he entered at this juncture, into no explanation of his motives, and they walked on very lovingly together.

In pursuance of this cautious plan Mr. Claypole went on, without halting, until he arrived at the Angel at Isling-ton, where he wisely judged, from the crowd of passengers and number of vehicles, that London began in earnest. Just pausing to observe which appeared the most crowded streets, and consequently the most to be avoided, he crossed into Saint John's Road, and was soon deep in the obscurity of the intricate and dirty ways which, lying be-tween Gray's Inn Lane and Smithfield, render that part of the town one of the lowest and worst that improvement has left in the midst of London.

Through these streets, Noah Claypole walked, dragging Charlotte after him; now stepping into the kennel to em-brace at a glance the whole external character of some small public-house; and now jogging on again, as some fancied appearance induced him to believe it too public for his purpose. At length, he stopped in front of one, more humble in appearance and more dirty than any he had yet seen; and, having crossed over and surveyed it from the opposite pavement, graciously announced his intention of putting up there, for the night.

"So give us the bundle," said Noah, unstrapping it from the woman's shoulders, and slinging it over his own; "and don't yer speak, except when yer spoke to. What's the name of the house—t-h-r—three what?"

"Cripples," said Charlotte.

"Three Cripples," repeated Noah, "and a very good sign too. Now, then! Keep close at my heels, and come along." With these injunctions, he pushed the rattling door with his shoulder, and entered the house, followed by his companion.

There was nobody in the bar but a young Jew, who, with his two elbows on the counter, was reading a dirty news-paper. He stared very hard at Noah, and Noah stared very hard at him.

If Noah had been attired in his charity-boy's dress, there might have been some reason for the Jew opening his eyes so wide; but as he had discarded the coat and badge, and wore a short smock-frock over his leathers, there seemed no particular reason for his appearance exciting so much attention in a public-house.

"Is this the Three Cripples?" asked Noah.

"That is the dabe of this ouse," replied the Jew.

"A gentleman we met on the road, coming up from the country, recommended us here," said Noah, nudging Char-lotte, perhaps to call her attention to this most ingenious device for attracting respect, and perhaps to warn her to betray no surprise. "We want to sleep here to-night."

"I'b dot certain you cad," said Barney, who was the at-tendant sprite; "but I'll idquire."

"Show us the tap, and give us a bit of cold meat and a drop of beer while yer inquiring, will yer?" said Noah.

Barney complied by ushering them into a small back-room, and setting the required viands before them; having done which, he informed the travellers that they could be lodged that night, and left the amiable couple to their refreshment.

Now, this back-room was immediately behind the bar,

and some steps lower, so that any person connected with the house, undrawing a small curtain which concealed a single pane of glass fixed in the wall of the last-named apartment, about five feet from its flooring, could not only look down upon any guests in the back-room without any great hazard of being observed (the glass being in a dark angle of the wall, between which and a large upright beam the observer had to thrust himself), but could, by applying his ear to the partition, ascertain with tolerable distinctness, their subject of conversation. The landlord of the house had not withdrawn his eye from this place of espial for five minutes, and Barney had only just returned from making the communication above related, when Fagin, in the course of his evening's business, came into the bar to inquire after some of his young pupils.

"Hush!" said Barney: "stradegers id the next roob."

"Strangers!" repeated the old man in a whisper.

"Ah! Ad rub uds too," added Barney. "Frob the cuttry, but subthig in your way, or I'b bistaked."

Fagin appeared to receive this communication with great interest. Mounting on a stool, he cautiously applied his eye to the pane of glass, from which secret post he could see Mr. Claypole taking cold beef from the dish, and porter from the pot, and administering homœopathic doses of both to Charlotte, who sat patiently by, eating and drinking at his pleasure.

"Aha!" whispered the Jew, looking round to Barney, "I like that fellow's looks. He'd be of use to us; he knows how to train the girl already. Don't make as much noise as a mouse, my dear, and let me hear 'em talk—let me hear 'em."

The Jew again applied his eye to the glass, and turning his ear to the partition, listened attentively: with a subtle and eager look upon his face, that might have appertained to some old goblin.

"So I mean to be a gentleman," said Mr. Claypole, kicking out his legs, and continuing a conversation, the commencement of which Fagin had arrived too late to hear. "No more jolly old coffins, Charlotte, but a gentleman's life for me; and, if yer like yer shall be a lady."

"I should like that well enough, dear," replied Charlotte; "but tills ain't to be emptied every day, and people to get clear off after it."

"Tills be blowed!" said Mr. Claypole; "there's more things besides tills to be emptied."

"What do you mean?" asked his companion.

"Pockets, women's ridicules, houses, mail-coaches, banks!" said Mr. Claypole, rising with the porter.

"But you can't do all that, dear," said Charlotte.

"I shall look out to get into company with them as can," replied Noah. "They'll be able to make us useful some way or another. Why, you yourself are worth fifty women; I never see such a precious sly and deceitful creetur as yer can be when I let yer."

"Lor, how nice it is to hear you say so!" exclaimed Charlotte, imprinting a kiss upon his ugly face.

"There, that'll do: don't yer be too affectionate, in case I'm cross with yer," said Noah, disengaging himself with great gravity. "I should like to be the captain of some band, and have the whopping of 'em, and follering 'em about, unbeknown to themselves. That would suit me, if there was good profit; and if we could only get in with some gentlemen of this sort, I say it would be cheap at that twenty-pound note you've got,—especially as we don't very well know how to get rid of it ourselves."

After expressing this opinion, Mr. Claypole looked into the porter-pot with an aspect of deep wisdom; and having well shaken its contents, nodded condescendingly to Charlotte, and took a draught, wherewith he appeared greatly refreshed. He was meditating another, when the sudden opening of the door, and the appearance of a stranger, interrupted him.

The stranger was Mr. Fagin. And very amiable he looked, and a very low bow he made, as he advanced, and, setting himself down at the nearest table, ordered something to drink of the grinning Barney.

"A pleasant night, Sir, but cool for the time of year," said Fagin, rubbing his hands. "From the country, I see, Sir?"

"How do yer see that?" asked Noah Claypole.

"We have not so much dust as that in London," replied the Jew, pointing from Noah's shoes to those of his companion, and from them to the two bundles.

"Yer a sharp feller," said Noah. "Ha! ha! only hear that, Charlotte!"

"Why, one need be sharp in this town, my dear," replied the Jew, sinking his voice to a confidential whisper; "and that's the truth."

The Jew followed up this remark by striking the side of his nose with his right forefinger,—a gesture which Noah attempted to imitate, though not with complete success, in consequence of his own nose not being large enough for the purpose. However, Mr. Fagin seemed to interpret the endeavour as expressing a perfect coincidence with his opinion, and put about the liquor which Barney re-appeared with, in a very friendly manner.

"Good stuff that," observed Mr. Claypole, smacking his lips.

"Dear!" said Fagin. "A man need be always emptying a till, or a pocket, or a woman's reticule, or a house, or a mail-coach, or a bank, if he drinks it regularly."

Mr. Claypole no sooner heard this extract from his own remarks than he fell back in his chair, and looked from the Jew to Charlotte with a countenance of ashy paleness and excessive terror.

"Don't mind me, my dear," said Fagin, drawing his chair closer. "Ha! ha! it was lucky it was only me that heard you by chance. It was very lucky it was only me."

"I didn't take it," stammered Noah, no longer stretching out his legs like an independent gentleman, but coiling them up as well as he could under his chair; "it was all her doing: yer've got it now, Charlotte, yer know yer have."

"No matter who's got it, or who did it, my dear!" replied Fagin, glancing, nevertheless, with a hawk's eye at the girl and the two bundles. "I'm in that way myself, and I like you for it."

"In what way?" asked Mr. Claypole, a little recovering.

"In that way of business," rejoined Fagin; "and so are the people of the house. You've hit the right nail upon the head, and are as safe here as you could be. There is not a safer place in all this town than is the Cripples; that is, when I like to make it so, and I have taken a fancy to you and the young woman; so I've said the word, and you may make your minds easy."

Noah Claypole's mind might have been at ease after this assurance, but his body certainly was not; for he shuffled and writhed about, into various uncouth positions: eyeing his new friend meanwhile with mingled fear and suspicion.

"I'll tell you more," said the Jew, after he had reassured

the girl, by dint of friendly nods and muttered encouragements. "I have got a friend that I think can gratify your darling wish, and put you in the right way, where you can take whatever department of the business you think will suit you best at first, and be taught all the others."

"Yer speak as if yer were in earnest," replied Noah.

"What advantage would it be to me to be anything else?" inquired the Jew, shrugging his shoulders. "Here! Let me have a word with you outside."

"There's no occasion to trouble ourselves to move," said Noah, getting his legs by gradual degrees abroad again. "She'll take the luggage up stairs the while. Charlotte, see to them bundles!"

This mandate, which had been delivered with great majesty, was obeyed without the slightest demur; and Charlotte made the best of her way off with the packages while Noah held the door open and watched her out.

"She's kept tolerably well under, ain't she?" he asked as he resumed his seat: in a tone of a keeper who has tamed some wild animal.

"Quite perfect," rejoined Fagin, clapping him on the shoulder. "You're a genius, my dear."

"Why, I suppose if I wasn't, I shouldn't be here," replied Noah. "But, I say, she'll be back if yer lose time."

"Now, what do you think?" said the Jew. "If you was to like my friend, could you do better than join him?"

"Is he in a good way of business; that's where it is!" responded Noah, winking one of his little eyes.

"The top of the tree," said the Jew; "employs a power of hands; and has the very best society in the profession."

"Regular town-maders?" asked Mr. Claypole.

"Not a countryman among 'em; and I don't think he'd take you, even on my recommendation, if he didn't run rather short of assistants just now," replied the Jew.

"Should I have to hand over?" said Noah, slapping his breeches-pocket.

"It couldn't possibly be done without," replied Fagin, in a most decided manner.

"Twenty pound, though,—it's a lot of money!"

"Not when it's in a note you can't get rid of," retorted Fagin. "Number and date taken, I suppose? Payment stopped at the Bank? Ah! It's not worth much to him. It'll have to go abroad, and he couldn't sell it for a great deal in the market!"

"When could I see him?" asked Noah doubtfully.

"To-morrow morning," replied the Jew.

"Where?"

"Here."

"Um!" said Noah. "What's the wages?"

"Live like a gentleman—board and lodging, pipes and spirits free—half of all you earn, and half of all the young woman earns," replied Mr. Fagin.

Whether Noah Claypole, whose rapacity was none of the least comprehensive, would have acceded even to these glowing terms, had he been a perfectly free agent, is very doubtful; but as he recollected that, in the event of his refusal it was in the power of his new acquaintance to give him up to justice immediately (and more unlikely things had come to pass), he gradually relented, and said he thought that would suit him.

"But, yer see," observed Noah, "as she will be able to do a good deal, I should like to take something very light."

"A little fancy work?" suggested Fagin.

"Ah! something of that sort," replied Noah. "What do you think would suit me now? Something not too try-

ing for the strength, and not very dangerous, you know. That's the sort of thing!"

"I heard you talk of something in the spy way upon the others, my dear," said the Jew. "My friend wants somebody who would do that well, very much."

"Why, I did mention that, and I shouldn't mind turning my hand to it sometimes," rejoined Mr. Claypole slowly; "but it wouldn't pay by itself, you know."

"That's true!" observed the Jew, ruminating or pretending to ruminate. "No, it might not."

"What do you think, then?" asked Noah, anxiously regarding him. "Something in the sneaking way, where it was pretty sure work, and not much more risk than being at home."

"What do you think of the old ladies?" asked the Jew. "There's a good deal of money made in snatching their bags and parcels, and running round the corner."

"Don't they holler out a good deal, and scratch sometimes?" asked Noah, shaking his head. "I don't think that would answer my purpose. Ain't there any other line open?"

"Stop!" said the Jew, laying his hand on Noah's knee "The kinchin lay."

"What's that?" demanded Mr. Claypole.

"The kinchins, my dear," said the Jew, "is the young children that's sent on errands by their mothers, with sixpences and shillings; and the lay is just to take their money away—they've always got it ready in their hands,—and then knock 'em into the kennel, and walk off very slow, as if there were nothing else the matter but a child fallen down and hurt itself. Ha! ha! ha!"

"Ha! ha!" roared Mr. Claypole, kicking up his legs in an ecstasy. "Lord, that's the very thing!"

"To be sure it is," replied Fagin; "and you can have a few good beats chalked out in Camden Town, and Battle Bridge, and neighbourhoods like that, where they're always going errands; and you can upset as many kinchins as you want, any hour in the day. Ha! ha! ha!"

With this, Fagin poked Mr. Claypole in the side, and they joined in a burst of laughter both long and loud.

"Well, that's all right!" said Noah, when he had recovered himself, and Charlotte had returned. "What time to-morrow shall we say?"

"Will ten do?" asked the Jew, adding, as Mr. Claypole nodded assent, "What name shall I tell my good friend?"

"Mr. Bolter," replied Noah, who had prepared himself for such an emergency. "Mr. Morris Bolter. This is Mrs. Bolter."

"Mrs. Bolter's humble servant," said Fagin, bowing with grotesque politeness. "I hope I shall know her better very shortly."

"Do you hear the gentleman, Char-lotte?" thundered Mr. Claypole.

"Yes, Noah, dear!" replied Mrs. Bolter, extending her hand.

"She calls me Noah, as a sort of fond way of talking," said Mr. Morris Bolter, late Claypole, turning to the Jew. "You understand?"

"Oh yes, I understand—perfectly," replied Fagin, telling the truth for once. "Good night! Good night!"

With many adieus and good wishes, Mr. Fagin went his way. Noah Claypole, bespeaking his good lady's attention, proceeded to enlighten her relative to the arrangement he had made, with all that haughtiness and air of superiority, becoming, not only a member of the sterner sex, but a gentleman who appreciated the dignity of a special appointment on the kinchin lay, in London and its vicinity.

CHAPTER XLIII.

WHEREIN IS SHOWN HOW THE ARTFUL DODGER GOT INTO TROUBLE.

"AND so it was you that was your own friend, was it?" asked Mr. Claypole, otherwise Bolter, when, by virtue of the compact entered into between them, he had removed next day to the Jew's house. "'Cod, I thought as much last night!"

"Every man's his own friend, my dear," replied Fagin, with his most insinuating grin. "He hasn't as good a one as himself anywhere."

"Except sometimes," replied Morris Bolter, assuming the air of a man of the world. "Some people are nobody's enemies but their own, yer know."

"Don't believe that!" said the Jew. "When a man's his own enemy, it's only because he's too much his own friend; not because he's careful for everybody but himself. Pooh! pooh! There ain't such a thing in nature."

"There oughtn't to be, if there is," replied Mr. Bolter.

"That stands to reason," said the Jew. "Some conjurers say that number three is the magic number, and some say number seven. It's neither, my friend, neither. It's number one."

"Ha! ha!" cried Mr. Bolter. "Number one for ever."

"In a little community like ours, my dear," said the Jew, who felt it necessary to qualify this position, "we have a general number one; that is, you can't consider yourself as number one, without considering me too as the same, and all the other young people."

"Oh, the devil!" exclaimed Mr. Bolter.

"You see," pursued the Jew, affecting to disregard this interruption, "we are so mixed up together, and identified in our interests, that it must be so. For instance, it's your object to take care of number one—meaning yourself."

"Certainly," replied Mr. Bolter. "Yer about right there."

"Well! You can't take care of yourself, number one, without taking care of me, number one."

"Number two, you mean," said Mr. Bolter, who was largely endowed with the quality of selfishness.

"No, I don't!" retorted the Jew. "I'm of the same importance to you, as you are yourself."

"I say," interrupted Mr. Bolter; "yer a very nice man, and I'm very fond of yer; but we ain't quite so thick together, as all that comes to."

"Only think," said the Jew, shrugging his shoulders, and stretching out his hands; "only consider. You've done what's a very pretty thing, and what I love you for doing; but what at the same time would put the cravat round your throat, that's so very easily tied and so very difficult to unloose—in plain English, the halter."

Mr. Bolter put his hand to his neckerchief, as if he felt it inconveniently tight; and murmured an assent, qualified in tone but not in substance.

"The gallows," continued Fagin, "the gallows, my dear, is an ugly finger-post, which points out a very short and sharp turning that has stopped many a bold fellow's career on the broad highway. To keep in the easy road, and keep

it at a distance, is object number one with you."

"Of course it is," replied Mr. Bolter. "What do yer talk about such things for?"

"Only to show you my meaning clearly," said the Jew, raising his eyebrows. "To be able to do that, you depend upon me. To keep my little business all snug, I depend upon you. The first is your number one, the second my number one. The more you value your number one, the more careful you must be of mine; so we come at last to what I told you at first—that a regard for number one holds us all together, and must do so, unless we would all go to pieces in company."

"That's true," rejoined Mr. Bolter, thoughtfully. "Oh! yer a cunning old codger!"

Mr. Fagin saw, with delight, that this tribute to his powers was no mere compliment, but that he had really impressed his recruit with a sense of his wily genius, which it was most important that he should entertain in the outset of their acquaintance. To strengthen an impression so desirable and useful, he followed up the blow by acquainting him, in some detail, with the magnitude and extent of his operations; blending truth and fiction together, as best served his purpose; and bringing both to bear, with so much art, that Mr. Bolter's respect visibly increased, and became tempered, at the same time, with a degree of wholesome fear, which it was highly desirable to awaken.

"It's this mutual trust we have in each other that consoles me under heavy losses," said the Jew. "My best hand was taken from me, yesterday morning."

"Yer don't mean to say he died?" cried Mr. Bolter.

"No, no," replied Fagin, "not so bad as that. Not quite so bad."

"What, I suppose he was——"

"Wanted," interposed the Jew. "Yes, he was wanted."

"Very particular?" inquired Mr. Bolter.

"No," replied the Jew, "not very. He was charged with attempting to pick a pocket, and they found a silver snuff-box on him,—his own, my dear, his own, for he took snuff himself, and was very fond of it. They remanded him till to-day, for they thought they knew the owner. Ah! he was worth fifty boxes, and I'd give the price of as many to have him back. You should have known the Dodger, my dear; you should have known the Dodger."

"Well, but I shall know him, I hope; don't yer think so?" said Mr. Bolter.

"I'm doubtful about it," replied the Jew, with a sigh. "If they don't get any fresh evidence, it'll only be a summary conviction, and we shall have him back again after six weeks or so; but, if they do, it's a case of lagging. They know what a clever lad he is; he'll be a lifer. They'll make the Artful nothing less than a lifer."

"What do yer mean by lagging and a lifer?" demanded Mr. Bolter. "What's the good of talking in that way to me; why don't yer speak so as I can understand yer?"

Fagin was about to translate these mysterious expressions into the vulgar tongue; and, being interpreted, Mr. Bolter would have been informed that they represented that combination of words, "transportation for life," when the dialogue was cut short by the entry of Master Bates, with his hands in his breeches-pockets, and his face twisted into a look of semi-comical woe.

"It's all up, Fagin," said Charley, when he and his new companion had been made known to each other.

"What do you mean?" asked the Jew with trembling lips.

"They've found the gentleman as owns the box; two or three more's a coming to 'dentify him; and the Artful's booked for a passage out," replied Master Bates. "I must have a full suit of mourning, Fagin, and a hatband, to wisit him in, afore he sets out upon his travels. To think of Jack Dawkins—lummy Jack—the Dodger—the Artful Dodger—going abroad for a common twopenny halfpenny sneeze box! I never thought he'd a done it under a gold watch, chain, and seals, at the lowest. Oh, why didn't he rob some rich old gentleman of all his walables, and go out *as* a gentleman, and not like a common prig, without no honour nor glory!"

With this expression of feeling for his unfortunate friend, Master Bates sat himself on the nearest chair with an aspect of chagrin and despondency.

"What do you talk about his having neither honour nor glory for!" exclaimed Fagin, darting an angry look at his pupil. "Wasn't he always top-sawyer among you all! Is there one of you that could touch him or come near him on any scent! Eh?"

"Not one," replied Master Bates, in a voice rendered husky by regret; "not one."

"Then what do you talk of?" replied the Jew angrily; "what are you blubbering for?"

"'Cause it isn't on the rec-ord, is it?" said Charley, chafed into perfect defiance of his venerable friend by the current of his regrets; "'cause it can't come out in the 'dictment; 'cause nobody will never know half of what he was. How will he stand in the Newgate Calendar? P'raps not be there at all. Oh, my eye, my eye, wot a blow it is!"

"Ha! ha!" cried the Jew, extending his right hand, and turning to Mr. Bolter in a fit of chuckling which shook him as though he had the palsy; "see what a pride they take in their profession, my dear. Ain't it beautiful?"

Mr. Bolter nodded assent; and the Jew, after contemplating the grief of Charley Bates for some seconds with evident satisfaction, stepped up to that young gentleman and patted him on the shoulder.

"Never mind, Charley," said Fagin soothingly; "it'll come out, it'll be sure to come out. They'll all know what a clever fellow he was; he'll show it himself, and not disgrace his old pals and teachers. Think how young he is too! What a distinction, Charley, to be lagged at his time of life?"

"Well, it is a honour that is!" said Charley, a little consoled.

"He shall have all he wants," continued the Jew. "He shall be kept in the Stone Jug, Charley, like a gentleman. Like a gentleman! With his beer every day, and money in his pocket to pitch and toss with, if he can't spend it."

"No, shall he though?" cried Charley Bates.

"Ay, that he shall," replied the Jew, "and we'll have a big-wig, Charley: one that's got the greatest gift of the gab: to carry on his defence; and he shall make a speech for himself too, if he likes; and we'll read it all in the papers—'Artful Dodger—shrieks of laughter—here the court was convulsed'—eh, Charley, eh?"

"Ha! ha!" laughed Master Bates, "what a lark that would be, wouldn't it, Fagin? I say, how the Artful would bother 'em, wouldn't he?"

"Would!" cried the Jew. "He shall—he will!"

"Ah, to be sure, so he will," repeated Charley, rubbing his hands.

"I think I see him now," cried the Jew, bending his eyes upon his pupil.

"So do I," cried Charley Bates. "Ha! ha! ha! so do I. I see it all afore me, upon my soul I do, Fagin. What a game! What a regular game! All the big-wigs trying to look solemn, and Jack Dawkins addressing of 'em as intimate and comfortable as if he was the judge's own son making a speech arter dinner—ha ha! ha!"

In fact, the Jew had so well humoured his young friend's eccentric disposition, that Master Bates, who had at first been disposed to consider the imprisoned Dodger rather in the light of a victim, now looked upon him as the chief actor in a scene of most uncommon and exquisite humour, and felt quite impatient for the arrival of the time when his old companion should have so favourable an opportunity of displaying his abilities.

"We must know how he gets on to-day, by some handy means or other," said Fagin. "Let me think."

"Shall I go?" asked Charley.

"Not for the world," replied the Jew. "Are you mad, my dear, stark mad, that you'd walk into the very place where—No, Charley, no. One is enough to lose at a time."

"You don't mean to go yourself, I suppose?" said Charley, with a humorous leer.

"That wouldn't quite fit," replied Fagin, shaking his head.

"Then why don't you send this new cove?" asked Master Bates, laying his hand on Noah's arm. "Nobody knows him."

"Why, if he didn't mind—" observed the Jew.

"Mind!" interposed Charley. "What should *he* have to mind?"

"Really nothing, my dear," said Fagin, turning to Mr. Bolter, "really nothing."

"Oh, I dare say about that, yer know," observed Noah, backing towards the door, and shaking his head with a kind of sober alarm. "No, no—none of that. It's not in my department, that ain't."

"Wot department has he got, Fagin?" inquired Master Bates, surveying Noah's lank form with much disgust. "The cutting away when there's anything wrong, and the eating all the wittles when there's everything right; is that his branch?"

"Never mind," retorted Mr. Bolter; "and don't yer take liberties with your superiors, little boy, or yer'll find yerself in the wrong shop."

Master Bates laughed so vehemently at this magnificent threat, that it was some time before Fagin could interpose, and represent to Mr. Bolter that he incurred no possible danger in visiting the police-office; that, inasmuch as no account of the little affair in which he had been engaged, nor any description of his person, had yet been forwarded to the metropolis, it was very probable that he was not even suspected of having resorted to it for shelter; and that, if he were properly disguised, it would be as safe a spot for him to visit as any in London, inasmuch as it would be, of all places, the very last, to which he could be supposed likely to resort of his own free will.

Persuaded, in part, by these representations, but overborne in a much greater degree by his fear of the Jew, Mr. Bolter at length consented, with a very bad grace, to undertake the expedition. By Fagin's directions, he immediately substituted for his own attire, a waggoner's frock, velveteen breeches, and leather leggings: all of which articles the Jew had at hand. He was likewise furnished with a felt hat well garnished with turnpike tickets; and a carter's whip. Thus equipped, he was to saunter into the office, as some country fellow from Covent Garden Market might be supposed to do for the gratification of his curiosity; and as he was as awkward, ungainly, and raw-boned a fellow as need be, Mr. Fagin had no fear but that he would look the part to perfection.

These arrangements completed, he was informed of the necessary signs and tokens by which to recognise the Artful Dodger, and was conveyed by Master Bates through dark and winding ways to within a very short distance of Bow Street. Having described the precise situation of the office, and accompanied it with copious directions how he was to walk straight up the passage, and when he got into the yard take the door up the steps on the right-hand side, and pull off his hat as he went into the room, Charley Bates bade him hurry on alone, and promised to bide his return on the spot of their parting.

Noah Claypole, or Morris Bolter as the reader pleases, punctually followed the directions he had received, which—Master Bates being pretty well acquainted with the locality—were so exact that he was enabled to gain the magisterial presence without asking any question, or meeting with any interruptions by the way. He found himself jostled among a crowd of people, chiefly women, who were huddled together in a dirty frowsy room, at the upper end of which was a raised platform railed off from the rest, with a dock for the prisoners on the left hand against the wall, a box for the witnesses in the middle, and a desk for the magistrates on the right; the awful locality last named, being screened off by a partition which concealed the bench from the common gaze, and left the vulgar to imagine (if they could) the full majesty of justice.

There were only a couple of women in the dock, who were nodding to their admiring friends, while the clerk read some depositions to a couple of policemen and a man in plain clothes who leant over the table. A jailer stood reclining against the dock-rail, tapping his nose listlessly with a large key, except when he repressed an undue tendency to conversation among the idlers, by proclaiming silence; or looked sternly up to bid some woman "Take that baby out," when the gravity of justice was disturbed by feeble cries, half-smothered in the mother's shawl, from some meagre infant. The room smelt close and unwholesome; the walls were dirt-discoloured; and the ceiling blackened. There was an old smoky bust over the mantelshelf, and a dusty clock above the dock—the only thing present, that seemed to go on as it ought; for depravity, or poverty, or an habitual acquaintance with both, had left a taint on all the animate matter, hardly less unpleasant than the thick greasy scum on every inanimate object that frowned upon it.

Noah looked eagerly about him for the Dodger; but although there were several women who would have done very well for that distinguished character's mother or sister, and more than one man who might be supposed to bear a strong resemblance to his father, nobody at all answering the description given him of Mr. Dawkins was to be seen. He waited in a state of much suspense and uncertainty until the women, being committed for trial, went flaunting out; and then was quickly relieved by the appearance of another prisoner whom he felt at once could be no other than the object of his visit.

It was indeed Mr. Dawkins, who, shuffling into the office with the big coat-sleeves tucked up as usual, his left hand in his pocket, and his hat in his right hand, preceded the jailer, with a rolling gait altogether indescribable, and, taking his place in the dock, requested in an audible voice to know what he was placed in that 'ere disgraceful sitivation for.

"Hold your tongue, will you?" said the jailer.

"I'm an Englishman, an't I?" rejoined the Dodger. "Where are my priwileges?"

"You'll get your privileges soon enough," retorted the jailer, "and pepper with 'em."

"We'll see wot the Secretary of State for the Home Affairs has got to say to the beaks, if I don't," replied Mr. Dawkins. "Now then! Wot is this here business? I shall thank the madg'strates to dispose of this here little affair, and not to keep me while they read the paper, for I've got an appointment with a genelman in the City, and as I'm a man of my word and wery punctual in business matters, he'll go away if I ain't there to my time, and then pr'aps there won't be an action for damage against them as kep me away. Oh no, certainly not!"

At this point, the Dodger, with a show of being very particular with a view to proceedings to be had thereafter, desired the jailer to communicate "the names of them two files as was on the bench," which so tickled the spectators, that they laughed almost as heartily as Master Bates could have done if he had heard the request.

"Silence there!" cried the jailer.

"What is this?" inquired one of the magistrates.

"A pick-pocketing case, your worship."

"Has the boy ever been here before?"

"He ought to have been, a many times," replied the jailer. "He has been pretty well everywhere else. *I* know him well, your worship."

"Oh! you know me, do you?" cried the Artful, making a note of the statement. "Wery good. That's a case of defamation of character, any way."

Here there was another laugh, and another cry of silence.

"Now then, where are the witnesses?" said the clerk.

"Ah! that's right," added the Dodger. "Where are they? I should like to see 'em."

This wish was immediately gratified, for a policeman stepped forward who had seen the prisoner attempt the pocket of an unknown gentleman in a crowd, and indeed take a handkerchief therefrom, which, being a very old one, he deliberately put back again, after trying it on his own countenance. For this reason, he took the Dodger into custody as soon as he could get near him, and the said Dodger, being searched, had upon his person a silver snuffbox, with the owner's name engraved upon the lid. This gentleman had been discovered on reference to the Court Guide, and being then and there present, swore that the snuff-box was his, and that he had missed it on the previous day, the moment he had disengaged himself from the crowd before referred to. He had also remarked a young gentleman in the throng, particularly active in making his way about, and that young gentleman was the prisoner before him.

"Have you anything to ask this witness, boy?" said the magistrate.

"I wouldn't abase myself by descending to hold no conversation with him," replied the Dodger.

"Have you anything to say at all?"

"Do you hear his worship ask if you've anything to say?" inquired the jailer, nudging the silent Dodger with his elbow.

"I beg your pardon," said the Dodger, looking up with an air of abstraction. "Did you redress yourself to me, my man?"

"I never see such an out-and-out young wagabond, your worship," observed the officer with a grin. "Do you mean to say anything, you young shaver?"

"No," replied the Dodger, "not here, for this ain't the shop for justice; besides which, my attorney is a-breakfasting this morning with the Wice President of the House of Commons; but I shall have something to say elsewhere, and so will he, and so will a wery numerous and 'spectable circle of acquaintance as'll make them beaks wish they'd never been born, or that they'd got their footmen to hang 'em up to their own hat-pegs, 'afore they let 'em come out this morning to try it on upon me. I'll——"

"There! He's fully committed!" interposed the clerk. "Take him away."

"Come on," said the jailer.

"Oh ah! I'll come on," replied the Dodger, brushing his hat with the palm of his hand. "Ah! (to the Bench) it's no use your looking frightened; I won't show you no mercy, not a ha'porth of it. *You'll* pay for this, my fine fellers. I wouldn't be you for something! I wouldn't go free, now, if you was to fall down on your knees and ask me. Here, carry me off to prison! Take me away!"

With these last words, the Dodger suffered himself to be led off by the collar; threatening, till he got into the yard, to make a parliamentary business of it; and then grinning in the officer's face, with great glee and self-approval.

Having seen him locked up by himself in a little cell, Noah made the best of his way back to where he had left Master Bates. After waiting here some time, he was joined by that young gentleman, who had prudently abstained from showing himself until he had looked carefully abroad from a snug retreat, and ascertained that his new friend had not been followed by any impertinent person.

The two hastened back together, to bear to Mr. Fagin the animating news that the Dodger was doing full justice to his bringing-up, and establishing for himself a glorious reputation.

CHAPTER XLIV.

THE TIME ARRIVES FOR NANCY TO REDEEM HER PLEDGE TO ROSE MAYLIE. SHE FAILS.

ADEPT as she was, in all the arts of cunning and dissimulation, the girl Nancy could not wholly conceal the effect which the knowledge of the step she had taken, worked upon her mind. She remembered that both the crafty Jew and the brutal Sikes had confided to her schemes, which had been hidden from all others: in the full confidence that she was trustworthy and beyond the reach of their suspicion. Vile as those schemes were, desperate as were their originators, and bitter as were her feelings towards the Jew, who had led her, step by step, deeper and deeper down into an abyss of crime and misery, whence was no escape; still, there were times when, even towards him, she felt some relenting, lest her disclosure would bring him within the iron grasp he had so long eluded, and he should fall at last—richly as he merited such a fate—by her hand.

But, these were the mere wanderings of a mind unable wholly to detach itself from old companions and associations, though enabled to fix itself steadily on one object, and resolved not to be turned aside by any consideration. Her fears for Sikes would have been more powerful inducements to recoil while there was yet time; but she had stipulated that her secret should be rigidly kept, she had dropped no clue which could lead to his discovery, she had refused, even for his sake, a refuge from all the guilt and wretchedness that encompassed her—and what more could she do! She was resolved.

Though all her mental struggles terminated in this conclusion, they forced themselves upon her, again and again, and left their traces too. She grew pale and thin, even within a few days. At times, she took no heed of what was passing before her, or no part in conversations where once, she would have been the loudest. At other times, she laughed without merriment, and was noisy without cause or meaning. At others—often within a moment afterwards—she sat silent and dejected, brooding with her head upon her hands, while the very effort by which she roused herself, told, more forcibly than even these indications, that she was ill at ease, and that her thoughts were occupied with matters very different and distant from those in course of discussion by her companions.

It was Sunday night, and the bell of the nearest church struck the hour. Sikes and the Jew were talking, but they paused to listen. The girl looked up from the low seat on which she crouched, and listened too. Eleven.

"An hour this side of midnight," said Sikes, raising the blind to look out and returning to his seat. "Dark and heavy it is too. A good night for business this."

"Ah!" replied the Jew. "What a pity, Bill, my dear, that there's none quite ready to be done."

"You're right for once," replied Sikes gruffly. "It's a pity, for I'm in the humour too."

The Jew sighed, and shook his head despondingly.

"We must make up for lost time when we've got things into a good train. That's all I know," said Sikes.

"That's the way to talk, my dear," replied the Jew, venturing to pat him on the shoulder. "It does me good to hear you."

"Does you good does it!" cried Sikes. "Well, so be it."

"Ha! ha! ha!" laughed the Jew, as if he were relieved by even this concession. "You're like yourself to-night, Bill! Quite like yourself."

"I don't feel like myself when you lay that withered old claw on my shoulder, so take it away," said Sikes, casting off the Jew's hand.

"It makes you nervous, Bill,—reminds you of being nabbed, does it?" said the Jew, determined not to be offended.

"Reminds me of being nabbed by the Devil," returned Sikes. "There never was another man with such a face as yours, unless it was your father, and I suppose *he* is singeing his grizzled red beard by this time, unless you came straight from the old 'un without any father at all betwixt you; which I shouldn't wonder at, a bit."

Fagin offered no reply to this compliment; but, pulling Sikes by the sleeve, pointed his finger towards Nancy, who had taken advantage of the foregoing conversation to put on her bonnet, and was now leaving the room.

"Hallo!" cried Sikes. "Nance. Where's the gal going to at this time of night?"

"Not far."

"What answer's that?" returned Sikes. "Where are you going?"

"I say, not far."

"And I say where?" retorted Sikes. "Do you hear me?"

"I don't know where," replied the girl.

"Then I do," said Sikes, more in the spirit of obstinacy than because he had any real objection to the girl going where she listed. "Nowhere. Sit down."

"I'm not well. I told you that before," rejoined the girl. "I want a breath of air."

"Put your head out of the winder," replied Sikes.

"There's not enough there," said the girl. "I want it in the street."

"Then you won't have it," replied Sikes. With which assurance he rose, locked the door, took the key out, and pulling her bonnet from her head, flung it up to the top of an old press. "There," said the robber. "Now stop quietly where you are, will you."

"It's not such a matter as a bonnet would keep me," said the girl turning very pale. "What do you mean, Bill? Do you know what you're doing?"

"Know what I'm——Oh!" cried Sikes turning to Fagin, "she's out of her senses, you know, or she daren't talk to me in that way."

"You'll drive me on to something desperate," muttered the girl placing both hands upon her breast, as though to keep down by force some violent outbreak. "Let me go, will you,—this minute—this instant."

"No!" said Sikes.

"Tell him to let me go, Fagin. He had better. It'll be better for him. Do you hear me?" cried Nancy, stamping her foot upon the ground.

"Hear you!" repeated Sikes turning round in his chair to confront her. "Aye! And if I hear you for half a minute longer, the dog shall have such a grip on your throat as'll tear some of that screaming voice out. Wot has come over you, you jade! Wot is it?"

"Let me go," said the girl with great earnestness; then sitting herself down on the floor, before the door, she said, "Bill, let me go; you don't know what you are doing. You don't, indeed. For only one hour—do—do."

"Cut my limbs off one by one!" cried Sikes, seizing her roughly by the arm, "if I don't think the gal's stark raving mad. Get up."

"Not till you let me go—not till you let me go—Never—never!" screamed the girl. Sikes looked on, for a minute, watching his opportunity, and suddenly pinioning her hands dragged her, struggling and wrestling with him by the way, into a small room adjoining, where he sat himself on a bench, and thrusting her into a chair, held her down by force. She struggled and implored by turns until twelve o'clock had struck, and then, wearied and exhausted, ceased to contest the point any further. With a caution, backed by many oaths, to make no more efforts to go out that night, Sikes left her to recover at leisure and rejoined the Jew.

"Whew!" said the housebreaker, wiping the perspiration from his face. "Wot a precious strange gal that is!"

"You may say that, Bill," replied the Jew thoughtfully. "You may say that."

"Wot did she take it into her head to go out to-night for, do you think?" asked Sikes. "Come; you should know her better than me. Wot does it mean?"

"Obstinacy; woman's obstinacy, I suppose, my dear," replied the Jew, shrugging his shoulders.

"Well, I suppose it is," growled Sikes. "I thought I had tamed her, but she's as bad as ever."

"Worse," said the Jew thoughtfully. "I never knew her like this, for such a little cause."

"Nor I," said Sikes. "I think she's got a touch of that fever in her blood yet, and it won't come out—eh?"

"Like enough," replied the Jew.

"I'll let her a little blood, without troubling the doctor, if she's took that way again," said Sikes.

The Jew nodded an expressive approval of this mode of treatment.

"She was hanging about me all day, and night too, when I was stretched on my back; and you, like a blackhearted wolf as you are, kept yourself aloof," said Sikes. "We was very poor too, all the time; and I think, one way or other, it's worried and fretted her; and that being shut up here so long has made her restless—eh?"

"That's it, my dear," replied the Jew in a whisper. "Hush!"

As he uttered these words, the girl herself appeared and resumed her former seat. Her eyes were swollen and red; she rocked herself to and fro; tossed her head; and, after a little time, burst out laughing.

"Why, now she's on the other tack!" exclaimed Sikes, turning a look of excessive surprise on his companion.

Fagin nodded to him to take no further notice just then; and, in a few minutes, the girl subsided into her accustomed demeanour. Whispering Sikes that there was no fear of her relapsing, Fagin took up his hat and bade him good night. He paused when he reached the room-door, and looking round, asked if somebody would light him down the dark stairs.

"Light him down," said Sikes, who was filling his pipe. "It's a pity he should break his neck himself, and disappoint the sightseers. Show him a light."

Nancy followed the old man down stairs, with a candle. When they reached the passage, he laid his finger on his lip, and drawing close to the girl, said, in a whisper,

"What is it, Nancy, dear?"

"What do you mean?" replied the girl, in the same tone.

"The reason of all this," replied Fagin. "If *he*"—he pointed with his skinny fore-finger up the stairs—"is so hard with you (he's a brute, Nance, a brute beast), why don't you—"

"Well!" said the girl, as Fagin paused, with his mouth almost touching her ear, and his eyes looking into hers.

"No matter just now," said the Jew. "We'll talk of this again. You have a friend in me, Nance; a staunch friend. I have the means at hand, quiet and close. If you want revenge on those that treat you like a dog—like a dog! worse than his dog, for he humours him sometimes—come to me. I say, come to me. He is the mere hound of a day, but you know me of old, Nance."

"I know you well," replied the girl, without manifesting the least emotion. "Good night."

She shrank back, as Fagin offered to lay his hand on hers, but said good night again, in a steady voice, and, answering his parting look with a nod of intelligence, closed the door between them.

Fagin walked towards his own home, intent upon the thoughts that were working within his brain. He had conceived the idea—not from what had just passed, though that had tended to confirm him, but slowly and by degrees —that Nancy, wearied of the housebreaker's brutality, had conceived an attachment for some new friend. Her altered manner, her repeated absences from home alone, her comparative indifference to the interests of the gang for which she had once been so zealous, and, added to these, her desperate impatience to leave home that night at a particular hour, all favoured the supposition, and rendered it, to him at least, almost matter of certainty. The object of this new liking was not among his myrmidons. He would be a valuable acquisition with such an assistant as Nancy, and must (thus Fagin argued) be secured without delay.

There was another, and a darker object, to be gained. Sikes knew too much, and his ruffian taunts had not galled the Jew the less, because the wounds were hidden. The girl must know, well, that if she shook him off, she could never be safe from his fury, and that it would be surely wreaked—to the maiming of limbs, or perhaps the loss of life—on the object of her more recent fancy. "With a little persuasion," thought Fagin, "what more likely than that she would consent to poison him! Women have done such things, and worse, to secure the same object before now. There would be the dangerous villain: the man I hate: gone; another secured in his place; and my influence over the girl, with a knowledge of this crime to back it, unlimited."

These things passed through the mind of Fagin, during the short time he sat alone, in the housebreaker's room; and with them uppermost in his thoughts, he had taken the opportunity afterwards afforded him, of sounding the girl in the broken hints he threw out at parting. There was no expression of surprise, no assumption of an inability to understand his meaning. The girl clearly comprehended it. Her glance at parting showed *that*.

But perhaps she would recoil from a plot to take the life of Sikes, and that was one of the chief ends to be attained. "How," thought the Jew, as he crept homewards, "can I increase my influence with her? what new power can I acquire?"

Such brains are fertile in expedients. If, without extracting a confession from herself, he laid a watch, discovered the object of her altered regard, and threatened to reveal the whole history to Sikes (of whom she stood in no common fear) unless she entered into his designs, could he not secure her compliance?

"I can," said Fagin, almost aloud. "She durst not refuse me then. Not for her life, not for her life! I have it all. The means are ready, and shall be set to work. I shall have you yet!"

He cast back a dark look, and a threatening motion of the hand, towards the spot where he had left the bolder villain; and went on his way: busying his bony hands in the folds of his tattered garment, which he wrenched tightly in his grasp, as though there were a hated enemy crushed with every motion of his fingers.

CHAPTER XLV.

NOAH CLAYPOLE IS EMPLOYED BY FAGIN ON A SECRET MISSION.

THE old man was up, betimes, next morning, and waited impatiently for the appearance of his new associate, who, after a delay that seemed interminable, at length presented himself, and commenced a voracious assault on the breakfast.

"Bolter," said the Jew, drawing up a chair and seating himself opposite Morris Bolter.

"Well, here I am," returned Noah. "What's the matter? Don't yer ask me to do anything till I have done eating. That's a great fault in this place. Yer never get time enough over yer meals."

"You can talk as you eat, can't you?" said Fagin, cursing his dear young friend's greediness from the very bottom of his heart.

"Oh yes, I can talk. I get on better when I talk," said Noah, cutting a monstrous slice of bread. "Where's Charlotte?"

"Out," said Fagin. "I sent her out this morning with the other young woman, because I wanted us to be alone."

"Oh!" said Noah. "I wish yer'd ordered her to make some buttered toast first. Well. Talk away. Yer won't interrupt me."

There seemed, indeed, no great fear of anything interrupting him, as he had evidently sat down with a determination to do a great deal of business.

"You did well yesterday, my dear," said the Jew. "Beautiful! Six shillings and ninepence halfpenny on the very first day! The kinchin lay will be a fortune to you."

"Don't yer forget to add three pint-pots and a milk-can," said Mr. Bolter.

"No, no, my dear," replied the Jew. "The pint-pots were great strokes of genius: but the milk-can was a perfect masterpiece."

"Pretty well, I think, for a beginner," remarked Mr. Bolter complacently. "The pots I took off airy railings, and the milk-can was standing by itself outside a public-house. I thought it might get rusty with the rain, or catch cold, yer know. Eh? Ha! ha! ha!"

The Jew affected to laugh very heartily; and Mr. Bolter, having had his laugh out, took a series of large bites, which finished his first hunk of bread and butter, and assisted himself to a second.

"I want you, Bolter," said Fagin, leaning over the table, "to do a piece of work for me, my dear, that needs great care and caution."

"I say," rejoined Bolter, "don't yer go shoving me into danger, or sending me to any more o' yer police-offices. That don't suit me, that don't; and so I tell yer."

"There's not the smallest danger in it—not the very smallest," said the Jew; "it's only to dodge a woman."

"An old woman?" demanded Mr. Bolter.

"A young one," replied Fagin.

"I can do that pretty well, I know," said Bolter. "I was a regular cunning sneak when I was at school. What am I to dodge her for? Not to—"

"Not to do anything," interrupted the Jew, "but to tell me where she goes, who she sees, and, if possible, what she says; to remember the street, if it is a street, or the house, if it is a house; and to bring me back all the information you can."

"What'll yer give me?" asked Noah, setting down his cup, and looking his employer, eagerly, in the face.

"If you do it well, a pound, my dear. One pound," said Fagin, wishing to interest him in the scent as much as possible. "And that's what I never gave yet, for any job of work where there wasn't valuable consideration to be gained."

"Who is she?" inquired Noah.

"One of us."

"Oh Lor!" cried Noah, curling up his nose. "Yer doubtful of her, are yer?"

"She has found out some new friends, my dear, and I must know who they are," replied the Jew.

"I see," said Noah. "Just to have the pleasure of knowing them, if they're respectable people, eh? Ha! ha! ha! I'm your man."

"I knew you would be," cried Fagin, elated by the success of his proposal.

"Of course, of course," replied Noah. "Where is she? Where am I to wait for her? Where am I to go?"

"All that, my dear, you shall hear from me. I'll point her out at the proper time," said Fagin. "You keep ready, and leave the rest to me."

That night, and the next, and the next again, the spy sat booted and equipped in his carter's dress: ready to turn out at a word from Fagin. Six nights passed—six long weary nights—and on each, Fagin came home with a disappointed face, and briefly intimated that it was not yet time. On the seventh, he returned earlier, and with an exultation he could not conceal. It was Sunday.

"She goes abroad to-night," said Fagin, "and on the right errand; for she has been alone all day, and the man she is afraid of, will not be back much before daybreak. Come with me. Quick!"

Noah started up without saying a word; for the Jew was in a state of such intense excitement that it infected him. They left the house stealthily, and, hurrying through a labyrinth of streets, arrived at length before a public-house, which Noah recognised as the same in which he had slept, on the night of his arrival in London.

It was past eleven o'clock, and the door was closed. It opened softly on its hinges as the Jew gave a low whistle. They entered, without noise; and the door was closed behind them.

Scarcely venturing to whisper, but substituting dumb show for words, Fagin, and the young Jew who had admitted them, pointed out the pane of glass to Noah, and signed to him to climb up and observe the person in the adjoining room.

"Is that the woman?" he asked, scarcely above his breath.

The Jew nodded yes.

"I can't see her face well," whispered Noah. "She is looking down, and the candle is behind her."

"Stay there," whispered Fagin. He signed to Barney, who withdrew. In an instant, the lad entered the room adjoining, and, under pretence of snuffing the candle, moved it into the required position, and, speaking to the girl, caused her to raise her face.

"I see her now," cried the spy.

"Plainly?" asked the Jew.

"I should know her among a thousand."

He hastily descended, as the room-door opened, and the girl came out. Fagin drew him behind a small partition which was curtained off, and they held their breaths as she passed within a few feet of their place of concealment, and emerged by the door at which they had entered.

"Hist!" cried the lad who held the door. "Dow."

Noah exchanged a look with Fagin, and darted out.

"To the left," whispered the lad; "take the left had, and keep od the other side."

He did so; and, by the light of the lamps, saw the girl's retreating figure, already at some distance before him. He advanced as near as he considered prudent, and kept on the opposite side of the street, the better to observe her motions. She looked nervously round, twice or thrice, and once stopped to let two men who were following close behind her, pass on. She seemed to gather courage as she advanced, and to walk with a steadier and firmer step. The spy preserved the same relative distance between them, and followed: with his eye upon her.

CHAPTER XLVI.

THE APPOINTMENT KEPT.

THE church clocks chimed three quarters past eleven, as two figures emerged on London Bridge. One, which advanced with a swift and rapid step, was that of a woman, who looked eagerly about her as though in quest of some expected object; the other figure was that of a man, who slunk along in the deepest shadow he could find, and, at some distance, accommodated his pace to hers: stopping when she stopped: and, as she moved again, creeping stealthily on: but never allowing himself, in the ardour of his pursuit, to gain upon her footsteps. Thus, they crossed the bridge, from the Middlesex to the Surrey shore: when the woman, apparently disappointed in her anxious scrutiny of the foot-passengers, turned back. The movement was sudden; but he who watched her, was not thrown off his guard by it; for, shrinking into one of the recesses which surmount the piers of the bridge, and leaning over the parapet the better to conceal his figure, he suffered her to pass by, on the opposite pavement. When she was about the same distance in advance as she had been before, he slipped quietly down, and followed her again. At nearly the centre of the bridge, she stopped. The man stopped too.

It was a very dark night. The day had been unfavourable, and at that hour and place there were few people stirring. Such as there were, hurried quickly past: very possibly without seeing, but certainly without noticing, either the woman, or the man who kept her in view. Their appearance was not calculated to attract the importunate regards of such of London's destitute population, as chanced to take their way over the bridge that night in search of some cold arch or doorless hovel wherein to lay their heads; they stood there in silence: neither speaking nor spoken to, by any one who passed.

A mist hung over the river, deepening the red glare of the fires that burnt upon the small craft moored off the different wharfs, and rendering darker and more indistinct the mirky buildings on the banks. The old smoke-stained storehouses on either side, rose heavy and dull from the dense mass of roofs and gables, and frowned sternly upon water too black to reflect even their lumbering shapes. The tower of old Saint Saviour's Church, and the spire of Saint Magnus, so long the giant-warders of the ancient bridge, were visible in the gloom; but the forest of shipping below bridge, and the thickly scattered spires of churches above, were nearly all hidden from the sight.

The girl had taken a few restless turns to and fro—closely watched meanwhile by her hidden observer—when the heavy bell of St. Paul's tolled for the death of another day. Midnight had come upon the crowded city. The palace, the night-cellar, the jail, the madhouse: the chambers of birth and death, of health and sickness: the rigid face of the corpse and the calm sleep of the child: midnight was upon them all.

The hour had not struck two minutes, when a young lady, accompanied by a grey-haired gentleman, alighted from a hackney-carriage within a short distance of the bridge, and, having dismissed the vehicle, walked straight towards it. They had scarcely set foot upon its pavement, when the girl started, and immediately made towards them. They walked onward, looking about them with the air of persons who entertained some very slight expectation which had little chance of being realised, when they were suddenly joined by this new associate. They halted with an exclamation of surprise, but suppressed it immediately; for a man in the garments of a countryman came close up—brushed against them, indeed—at that precise moment.

"Not here," said Nancy hurriedly, "I am afraid to speak to you here. Come away—out of the public road—down the steps yonder!"

As she uttered these words, and indicated, with her hand, the direction in which she wished them to proceed, the countryman looked round, and roughly asking what they took up the whole pavement for, passed on.

The steps to which the girl pointed, were those which, on the Surrey bank, and on the same side of the bridge as Saint Saviour's Church, form a landing-stairs from the river. To this spot, the man bearing the appearance of a countryman, hastened unobserved; and after a moment's survey of the place, he began to descend.

These stairs are a part of the bridge; they consist of three flights. Just below the end of the second, going down, the stone wall on the left terminates in an ornamental pilaster facing towards the Thames. At this point the lower steps widen: so that a person turning that angle of the wall, is necessarily unseen by any others on the stairs who chance to be above him, if only a step. The countryman looked hastily round, when he reached this point; and as there seemed no better place of concealment, and, the tide being out, there was plenty of room, he slipped aside, with his back to the pilaster, and there waited: pretty certain that they would come no lower, and that even if he could not hear what was said, he could follow them again, with safety.

So tardily stole the time in this lonely place, and so eager was the spy to penetrate the motives of an interview so different from what he had been led to expect, that he more than once gave the matter up for lost, and persuaded himself, either that they had stopped far above, or had resorted to some entirely different spot to hold their mysterious conversation. He was on the very point of emerging from his hiding-place, and regaining the road above, when he heard the sound of footsteps, and directly afterwards of voices almost close at his ear.

He drew himself straight upright against the wall, and scarcely breathing, listened attentively.

"This is far enough," said a voice, which was evidently that of the gentleman. "I will not suffer the young lady to go any farther. Many people would have distrusted you too much to have come even so far, but you see I am willing to humour you."

"To humour me!" cried the voice of the girl whom he had followed. "You're considerate, indeed, Sir. To humour me! Well, well, it's no matter."

"Why, for what," said the gentleman in a kinder tone,

"for what purpose can you have brought us to this strange place? Why not have let me speak to you, above there, where it is light, and there is something stirring, instead of bringing us to this dark and dismal hole?"

"I told you before," replied Nancy, "that I was afraid to speak to you there. I don't know why it is," said the girl, shuddering, "but I have such a fear and dread upon me to-night that I can hardly stand "

"A fear of what?" asked the gentleman, who seemed to pity her.

"I scarcely know of what," replied the girl. "I wish I did. Horrible thoughts of death, and shrouds with blood upon them, and a fear that has made me burn as if I was on fire, have been upon me all day. I was reading a book to-night, to wile the time away, and the same things came into the print."

"Imagination," said the gentleman, soothing her.

"No imagination," replied the girl in a hoarse voice. "I'll swear I saw ' coffin' written in every page of the book in large black letters,—aye, and they carried one close to me, in the streets to-night."

"There is nothing unusual in that," said the gentleman. "They have passed me often."

"*Real ones,*" rejoined the girl. "This was not."

There was something so uncommon in her manner, that the flesh of the concealed listener crept as he heard the girl utter these words, and the blood chilled within him. He had never experienced a greater relief than in hearing the sweet voice of the young lady as she begged her to be calm, and not allow herself to become the prey of such fearful fancies.

"Speak to her kindly," said the young lady to her companion. "Poor creature! She seems to need it."

"Your haughty religious people would have held their heads up to see me as I am to-night, and preached of flames and vengeance," cried the girl. "Oh, dear lady, why ar'n't those who claim to be God's own folks as gentle and as kind to us poor wretches as you, who, having youth, and beauty, and all that they have lost, might be a little proud instead of so much humbler?"

"Ah!" said the gentleman. "A Turk turns his face, after washing it well, to the East, when he says his prayers; these good people, after giving their faces such a rub against the World as to take the smiles off, turn, with no less regularity, to the darkest side of Heaven. Between the Mussulman and the Pharisee, commend me to the first!"

These words appeared to be addressed to the young lady, and were perhaps uttered with the view of affording Nancy time to recover herself. The gentleman, shortly afterwards, addressed himself to her.

"You were not here last Sunday night," he said.

"I couldn't come," replied Nancy; "I was kept by force."

"By whom?"

"Him that I told the young lady of before."

"You were not suspected of holding any communication with anybody on the subject which has brought us here to-night, I hope?" asked the old gentleman.

"No," replied the girl, shaking her head. "It's not very easy for me to leave him unless he knows why; I couldn't have seen the lady when I did, but that I gave him a drink of laudanum before I came away."

"Did he awake before you returned?" inquired the gentleman.

"No; and neither he nor any of them suspect me."

"Good," said the gentleman. "Now listen to me."

"I am ready," replied the girl, as he paused for a moment.

"This young lady," the gentleman began, "has communicated to me, and to some other friends who can be safely trusted, what you told her nearly a fortnight since. I confess to you that I had doubts, at first, whether you were to be implicitly relied upon, but now I firmly believe you are."

"I am," said the girl earnestly.

"I repeat that I firmly believe it. To prove to you that I am disposed to trust you, I tell you without reserve, that we propose to extort the secret, whatever it may be, from the fears of this man Monks. But if—if—" said the gentleman, "he cannot be secured, or, if secured, cannot be acted upon as we wish, you must deliver up the Jew."

"Fagin," cried the girl, recoiling.

"That man must be delivered up by you," said the gentleman.

"I will not do it! I will never do it!" replied the girl. "Devil that he is, and worse than devil as he has been to me, I will never do that."

"You will not?" said the gentleman, who seemed fully prepared for this answer.

"Never!" returned the girl.

"Tell me why?"

"For one reason," rejoined the girl firmly, "for one reason, that the lady knows and will stand by me in, I know she will, for I have her promise; and for this other reason, besides, that, bad life as he has led, I have led a bad life too; there are many of us who have kept the same courses together, and I'll not turn upon them, who might —any of them—have turned upon me, but didn't, bad as they are."

"Then," said the gentleman, quickly, as if this had been the point he had been aiming to attain; "put Monks into my hands, and leave him to me to deal with."

"What if he turns against the others?"

"I promise you that in that case, if the truth is forced from him, there the matter will rest; there must be circumstances in Oliver's little history which it would be painful to drag before the public eye, and if the truth is once elicited, they shall go scot free."

"And if it is not?" suggested the girl.

"Then," pursued the gentleman, "this Jew shall not be brought to justice without your consent. In such a case I could show you reasons, I think, which would induce you to yield it."

"Have I the lady's promise for that?" asked the girl.

"You have," replied Rose. "My true and faithful pledge."

"Monks would never learn how you knew what you do?" said the girl, after a short pause.

"Never," replied the gentleman. "The intelligence should be so brought to bear upon him, that he could never even guess."

"I have been a liar, and among liars from a little child," said the girl after another interval of silence, "but I will take your words."

After receiving an assurance from both, that she might safely do so, she proceeded in a voice so low that it was often difficult for the listener to discover even the purport of what she said, to describe, by name and situation, the public-house whence she had been occasionally followed that night. From the manner in which she occasionally paused, it appeared as if the gentleman were making some hasty notes of the information she communicated. When she had thoroughly explained the localities of the place, the best position from which to watch it without exciting observation, and the night and hour on which Monks was most in the habit of frequenting it, she seemed to consider for a few moments, for the purpose of recalling his features and appearance more forcibly to her recollection.

"He is tall," said the girl, "and a strongly made man, but not stout; he has a lurking walk; and as he walks, constantly looks over his shoulder, first on one side, and then on the other. Don't forget that, for his eyes are sunk in his head so much deeper than any other man's, that you might almost tell him by that alone. His face is dark, like his hair and eyes; and, although he can't be more than six or eight and twenty, withered and haggard. His lips are often discoloured and disfigured with the marks of teeth; for he has desperate fits, and sometimes even bites his hands and covers them with wounds—why did you start?" said the girl, stopping suddenly.

The gentleman replied, in a hurried manner, that he was not conscious of having done so, and begged her to proceed.

"Part of this," said the girl, "I've drawn out from other people at the house I tell you of, for I have only seen him twice, and both times he was covered up in a large cloak. I think that's all I can give you to know him by. Stay though," she added. "Upon his throat: so high that you can see a part of it below his neckerchief when he turns his face: there is—"

"A broad red mark, like a burn or scald," cried the gentleman.

"How's this!" said the girl. "You know him!"

The young lady uttered a cry of surprise, and for a few moments they were so still that the listener could distinctly hear them breathe.

"I think I do," said the gentleman, breaking silence. "I should by your description. We shall see. Many people are singularly like each other. It may not be the same."

As he expressed himself to this effect, with assumed carelessness, he took a step or two nearer the concealed spy, as the latter could tell from the distinctness with which he heard him mutter, "It must be he!"

"Now," he said, returning: so it seemed by the sound: to the spot where he had stood before, "you have given us most valuable assistance, young woman, and I wish you to be the better for it. What can I do to serve you?"

"Nothing," replied Nancy.

"You will not persist in saying that," rejoined the gentleman, with a voice and emphasis of kindness that might have touched a much harder and more obdurate heart. "Think now. Tell me."

"Nothing, Sir," rejoined the girl, weeping. "You can do nothing to help me. I am past all hope, indeed."

"You put yourself beyond its pale," said the gentleman. "The past has been a dreary waste with you, of youthful energies mis-spent, and such priceless treasures lavished, as the Creator bestows but once and never grants again, but, for the future, you may hope. I do not say that it is in our power to offer you peace of heart and mind, for that must come as you seek it; but a quiet asylum, either in England, or, if you fear to remain here, in some foreign country, it is not only within the compass of our ability but our most anxious wish to secure you. Before the dawn of morning, before this river wakes to the first glimpse of daylight, you shall be placed as entirely beyond the reach of your former associates, and leave as utter an absence of all trace behind you, as if you were to disappear from the earth this moment. Come! I would not have you go back to exchange one word with any old companion, or take one look at any old haunt, or breathe the very air which is pestilence and death to you. Quit them all, while there is time and opportunity!"

"She will be persuaded now," cried the young lady. "She hesitates, I am sure."

"I fear not, my dear," said the gentleman.

"No, Sir, I do not," replied the girl, after a short struggle. "I am chained to my old life. I loathe and hate it now, but I cannot leave it. I must have gone too far to turn back,—and yet I don't know, for if you had spoken to me so, some time ago, I should have laughed it off. But," she said, looking hastily round, "this fear comes over me again. I must go home."

"Home!" repeated the young lady, with great stress upon the word.

"Home, lady," rejoined the girl. "To such a home as I have raised for myself with the work of my whole life. Let us part. I shall be watched or seen. Go! Go! If I have done you any service, all I ask is, that you leave me, and let me go my way alone."

"It is useless," said the gentleman, with a sigh. "We compromise her safety, perhaps, by staying here. We may have detained her longer than she expected already."

"Yes, yes," urged the girl. "You have."

"What," cried the young lady, "can be the end of this poor creature's life!"

"What!" repeated the girl. "Look before you, lady. Look at that dark water. How many times do you read of such as I who spring into the tide, and leave no living thing to care for, or bewail them. It may be years hence, or it may be only months, but I shall come to that at last."

"Do not speak thus, pray," returned the young lady, sobbing.

"It will never reach your ears, dear lady, and God forbid such horrors should!" replied the girl. "Good night, good night!"

The gentleman turned away.

"This purse," cried the young lady. "Take it for my sake, that you may have some resource in an hour of need and trouble."

"No!" replied the girl. "I have not done this for money. Let me have that to think of. And yet—give me something that you have worn: I should like to have something—no, no, not a ring—your gloves or handkerchief—anything that I can keep, as having belonged to you, sweet lady. There. Bless you! God bless you. Good night, good night!"

The violent agitation of the girl, and the apprehension of some discovery which would subject her to ill-usage and violence, seemed to determine the gentleman to leave her, as she requested. The sound of retreating footsteps were audible, and the voices ceased.

The two figures of the young lady and her companion soon afterwards appeared upon the bridge. They stopped at the summit of the stairs.

"Hark!" cried the young lady, listening. "Did she call! I thought I heard her voice."

"No, my love," replied Mr. Brownlow, looking sadly back. "She has not moved, and will not till we are gone."

Rose Maylie lingered, but the old gentleman drew her arm through his, and led her, with gentle force, away. As they disappeared, the girl sank down nearly at her full length upon one of the stone stairs, and vented the anguish of her heart in bitter tears.

After a time she arose, and with feeble and tottering steps ascended to the street. The astonished listener remained motionless on his post for some minutes afterwards, and having ascertained, with many cautious glances round him, that he was again alone, crept slowly from his hiding-place, and returned, stealthily and in the shade of the wall, in the same manner as he had descended.

Peeping out, more than once, when he reached the top, to make sure that he was unobserved, Noah Claypole darted away at his utmost speed, and made for the Jew's house as fast as his legs would carry him.

CHAPTER XLVII.

FATAL CONSEQUENCES.

It was nearly two hours before day-break; that time, which, in the autumn of the year, may be truly called the dead of night; when the streets are silent and deserted; when even sound appears to slumber, and profligacy and riot have staggered home to dream; it was at this still and silent hour, that the Jew sat watching in his old lair, with face so distorted and pale, and eyes so red and bloodshot, that he looked less like a man, than like some hideous phantom, moist from the grave, and worried by an evil spirit.

He sat crouching over a cold hearth, wrapped in an old torn coverlet, with his face turned towards a wasting candle that stood upon a table by his side. His right hand was raised to his lips, and as, absorbed in thought, he bit his long black nails, he disclosed among his toothless gums a few such fangs as should have been a dog's or rat's.

Stretched upon a mattress on the floor, lay Noah Claypole, fast asleep. Towards him the old man sometimes directed his eyes for an instant, and then brought them back again to the candle: which, with long-burnt wick drooping almost double, and hot grease falling down in clots upon the table, plainly showed that his thoughts were busy elsewhere.

Indeed they were. Mortification at the overthrow of his notable scheme; hatred of the girl who had dared to palter with strangers; an utter distrust of the sincerity of her refusal to yield him up; bitter disappointment at the loss of his revenge on Sikes; the fear of detection, and ruin, and death; and a fierce and deadly rage kindled by all; these were the passionate considerations which, following close upon each other with rapid and ceaseless whirl, shot through the brain of Fagin, as every evil thought and blackest purpose lay working at his heart.

He sat without changing his attitude in the least, or appearing to take the smallest heed of time, until his quick ear seemed to be attracted by a footstep in the street.

"At last," muttered the Jew, wiping his dry and fevered mouth. "At last!"

The bell rang gently as he spoke. He crept up stairs to the door, and presently returned accompanied by a man muffled to the chin, who carried a bundle under one arm. Sitting down, and throwing back his outer coat, the man displayed the burly frame of Sikes.

"There!" he said, laying the bundle on the table.

"Take care of that, and do the most you can with it. It's been trouble enough to get; I thought I should have been here, three hours ago."

Fagin laid his hand upon the bundle, and locking it in the cupboard, sat down again without speaking. But he did not take his eyes off the robber, for an instant, during this action; and now that they sat over against each other, face to face, he looked fixedly at him, with his lips quivering so violently, and his face so altered by the emotions which had mastered him, that the house-breaker involuntarily drew back his chair, and surveyed him with a look of real affright.

"Wot now?" cried Sikes. "Wot do you look at a man so for?"

Fagin raised his right hand, and shook his trembling forefinger in the air; but his passion was so great, that the power of speech was for the moment gone.

"Damme!" said Sikes, feeling in his breast with a look of alarm. "He's gone mad. I must look to myself here."

"No, no," rejoined Fagin, finding his voice. "It's not —you're not the person, Bill. I've no—no fault to find with you."

"Oh, you haven't, haven't you?" said Sikes, looking sternly at him, and ostentatiously passing a pistol into a more convenient pocket. "That's lucky—for one of us. Which one that is, don't matter."

"I've got that to tell you, Bill," said the Jew, drawing his chair nearer, "will make you worse than me."

"Aye?" returned the robber with an incredulous air. "Tell away! Look sharp, or Nance will think I'm lost."

"Lost!" cried Fagin. "She has pretty well settled that, in her own mind, already."

Sikes looked with an aspect of great perplexity into the Jew's face, and reading no satisfactory explanation of the riddle there, clenched his coat collar in his huge hand and shook him soundly.

"Speak, will you!" he said; "or if you don't, it shall be for want of breath. Open your mouth, and say wot you've got to say in plain words. Out with it, you thundering old cur, out with it!"

"Suppose that lad that's lying there——" Fagin began.

Sikes turned round to where Noah was sleeping, as if he had not previously observed him. "Well!" he said, resuming his former position.

"Suppose that lad," pursued the Jew, "was to peach— to blow upon us all—first seeking out the right folks for the purpose, and then having a meeting with 'em in the street to paint our likenesses, describe every mark that they might know us by, and the crib where we might be most easily taken. Suppose he was to do all this, and besides to blow upon a plant we've all been in, more or less —of his own fancy; not grabbed, trapped, tried, earwigged by the parson and brought to it on bread and water,—but of his own fancy; to please his own taste; stealing out at nights to find those most interested against us, and peaching to them. Do you hear me?" cried the Jew, his eyes flashing with rage. "Suppose he did all this, what then?"

"What then!" replied Sikes, with a tremendous oath. "If he was left alive till I came, I'd grind his skull under the iron heel of my boot into as many grains as there are hairs upon his head."

"What if I did it!" cried the Jew almost in a yell. "I, that know so much, and could hang so many besides myself!"

"I don't know," replied Sikes, clenching his teeth and turning white at the mere suggestion. "I'd do something in the jail that 'ud get me put in irons; and if I was tried along with you, I'd fall upon you with them in the open court, and beat your brains out afore the people. I should have such strength," muttered the robber, poising his brawny arm, "that I could smash your head as if a loaded waggon had gone over it."

"You would?"

"Would I!" said the housebreaker. "Try me."

"If it was Charley, or the Dodger, or Bet, or——"

"I don't care who," replied Sikes impatiently. "Whoever it was, I'd serve them the same."

Fagin again looked hard at the robber; and, motioning him to be silent, stooped over the bed upon the floor, and shook the sleeper to rouse him. Sikes leant forward in his chair: looking on with his hands upon his knees, as if wondering much what all this questioning and preparation was to end in.

"Bolter, Bolter! Poor lad!" said Fagin, looking up with an expression of devilish anticipation, and speaking slowly and with marked emphasis. "He's tired—tired with watching for *her* so long,—watching for *her*, Bill."

"Wot d'ye mean?" asked Sikes, drawing back.

The Jew made no answer, but bending over the sleeper again, hauled him into a sitting posture. When his assumed name had been repeated several times, Noah rubbed his eyes, and, giving a heavy yawn, looked sleepily about him.

"Tell me that again—once again, just for him to hear," said the Jew, pointing to Sikes as he spoke.

"Tell yer what?" asked the sleepy Noah, shaking himself pettishly.

"That about—NANCY," said the Jew, clutching Sikes by the wrist, as if to prevent his leaving the house before he had heard enough. "You followed her?"

"Yes."

"To London Bridge?"

"Yes."

"Where she met two people?"

"So she did."

"A gentleman and a lady that she had gone to of her own accord before, who asked her to give up all her pals, and Monks first, which she did—and to describe him, which she did—and to tell her what house it was that we meet at, and go to, which she did—and where it could be best watched from, which she did—and what time the people went there, which she did. She did all this. She told it all every word without a threat, without a murmur— she did—did she not?" cried the Jew, half mad with fury.

"All right," replied Noah, scratching his head. "That's just what it was!"

"What did they say, about last Sunday?" demanded the Jew.

"About last Sunday!" replied Noah, considering. "Why, I told yer that before."

"Again. Tell it again!" cried Fagin, tightening his grasp on Sikes, and brandishing his other hand aloft, as the foam flew from his lips.

"They asked her," said Noah, who, as he grew more wakeful, seemed to have a dawning perception who Sikes was, "they asked her why she didn't come, last Sunday, as she promised. She said she couldn't."

"Why — why?" interrupted the Jew triumphantly. "Tell him that."

"Because she was forcibly kept at home by Bill, the man she had told them of before," replied Noah.

"What more of him?" cried the Jew. "What more of the man she had told them of before? Tell him that, tell him that."

"Why, that she couldn't very easily get out of doors unless he knew where she was going to," said Noah; "and so the first time she went to see the lady, she—ha! ha! ha! it made me laugh when she said it, that it did—she gave him a drink of laudanum."

"Hell's fire!" cried Sikes, breaking fiercely from the Jew. "Let me go!"

Flinging the old man from him, he rushed from the room, and darted, wildly and furiously, up the stairs.

"Bill, Bill!" cried the Jew, following him hastily. "A word. Only a word."

The word would not have been exchanged, but that the housebreaker was unable to open the door: on which he was expending fruitless oaths and violence, when the Jew came panting up.

"Let me out," said Sikes. "Don't speak to me; it's not safe. Let me out, I say."

"Hear me speak a word," rejoined the Jew, laying his hand upon the lock. "You won't be—"

"Well," replied the other.

"You won't be — too — violent, Bill?" whined the Jew.

The day was breaking, and there was light enough for the men to see each other's faces. They exchanged one brief glance; there was a fire in the eyes of both, which could not be mistaken.

"I mean," said Fagin, showing that he felt all disguise was now useless, "not too violent for safety. Be crafty, Bill, and not too bold."

Sikes made no reply; but, pulling open the door, of which the Jew had turned the lock, dashed into the silent streets.

Without one pause, or moment's consideration; without once turning his head to the right or left, or raising his eyes to the sky, or lowering them to the ground, but looking straight before him with savage resolution: his teeth so tightly compressed that the strained jaw seemed starting through his skin; the robber held on his headlong course, nor muttered a word, nor relaxed a muscle, until he reached his own door. He opened it, softly, with a key; strode lightly up the stairs; and entering his own room, double-locked the door, and lifting a heavy table against it, drew back the curtain of the bed.

The girl was lying, half-dressed, upon it. He had roused her from her sleep, for she raised herself with a hurried and startled look.

"Get up!" said the man.

"It is you, Bill!" said the girl, with an expression of pleasure at his return.

"It is," was the reply. "Get up."

There was a candle burning, but the man hastily drew it from the candlestick, and hurled it under the grate. Seeing the faint light of early day without, the girl rose to undraw the curtain.

"Let it be," said Sikes, thrusting his hand before her. "There's light enough for wot I've got to do."

"Bill," said the girl, in a low voice of alarm, "why do you look like that at me!"

The robber sat regarding her, for a few seconds, with dilated nostrils and heaving breast; and then, grasping her by the head and throat, dragged her into the middle of the room, and looking once towards the door, placed his heavy hand upon her mouth.

"Bill, Bill!" gasped the girl, wrestling with the strength of mortal fear,—"I—I won't scream or cry—not once—hear me—speak to me—tell me what I have done!"

"You know, you she devil!" returned the robber, suppressing his breath. "You were watched to-night; every word you said was heard."

"Then spare my life for the love of Heaven, as I spared yours," rejoined the girl, clinging to him. "Bill, dear Bill, you cannot have the heart to kill me. Oh! think of all I have given up, only this one night, for you. You shall have time to think, and save yourself this crime; I will not loose my hold, you cannot throw me off. Bill, Bill, for dear God's sake, for your own, for mine, stop before you spill my blood! I have been true to you, upon my guilty soul I have!"

The man struggled, violently, to release his arms; but those of the girl were clasped round his, and tear her as he would, he could not tear them away.

"Bill," cried the girl, striving to lay her head upon his breast, "the gentleman, and that dear lady, told me to-night of a home in some foreign country where I could end my days in solitude and peace. Let me see them again, and beg them, on my knees, to show the same mercy and goodness to you; and let us both leave this dreadful place, and far apart lead better lives, and forget how we have lived, except in prayers, and never see each other more. It is never too late to repent. They told me so—I feel it now—but we must have time—a little, little time!"

The house-breaker freed one arm, and grasped his pistol. The certainty of immediate detection if he fired, flashed across his mind even in the midst of his fury; and he beat it twice with all the force he could summon, upon the up-turned face that almost touched his own.

She staggered and fell: nearly blinded with the blood that rained down from a deep gash in her forehead; but raising herself, with difficulty, on her knees, drew from her bosom a white handkerchief—Rose Maylie's own—and holding it up, in her folded hands, as high towards Heaven as her feeble strength would allow, breathed one prayer for mercy to her Maker.

It was a ghastly figure to look upon. The murderer staggering backward to the wall, and shutting out the sight with his hand, seized a heavy club and struck her down.

CHAPTER XLVIII.

THE FLIGHT OF SIKES.

OF all bad deeds that, under cover of the darkness, had been committed within wide London's bounds since night hung over it, that was the worst. Of all the horrors that rose with an ill scent upon the morning air, that was the foulest and most cruel.

The sun—the bright sun, that brings back, not light alone, but new life, and hope, and freshness to man—burst upon the crowded city in clear and radiant glory. Through costly-coloured glass and paper-mended window, through cathedral dome and rotten crevice, it shed its equal ray. It lighted up the room where the murdered woman lay. It did. He tried to shut it out, but it would stream in.

If the sight had been a ghastly one in the dull morning, what was it, now, in all that brilliant light!

He had not moved; he had been afraid to stir. There had been a moan and motion of the hand; and, with terror added to hate, he had struck and struck again. Once he threw a rug over it; but it was worse to fancy the eyes, and imagine them moving towards him, than to see them glaring upward, as if watching the reflection of the pool of gore that quivered and danced in the sunlight on the ceiling. He had plucked it off again. And there was the body—mere flesh and blood, no more—but such flesh, and so much blood!

He struck a light, kindled a fire, and thrust the club into it. There was hair upon the end, which blazed and shrunk into a light cinder, and, caught by the air, whirled up the chimney. Even that frightened him, sturdy as he was; but he held the weapon till it broke, and then piled it on the coals to burn away, and smoulder into ashes. He washed himself, and rubbed his clothes; there were spots that would not be removed, but he cut the pieces out, and burnt them. How those stains were dispersed about the room! The very feet of the dog were bloody.

All this time he had, never once, turned his back upon the corpse; no, not for a moment. Such preparations completed, he moved, backward, towards the door: dragging the dog with him, lest he should soil his feet anew and carry out new evidences of the crime into the streets. He shut the door softly, locked it, took the key, and left the house.

He crossed over, and glanced up at the window, to be sure that nothing was visible from the outside. There was the curtain still drawn, which she would have opened to admit the light she never saw again. It lay nearly under there. *He* knew that. God, how the sun poured down upon the very spot!

The glance was instantaneous. It was a relief to have got free of the room. He whistled on the dog, and walked rapidly away.

He went through Islington; strode up the hill at Highgate on which stands the stone in honour of Whittington; turned down to Highgate Hill, unsteady of purpose, and uncertain where to go; struck off to the right again, almost as soon as he began to descend it; and taking the foot-path across the fields, skirted Caen Wood, and so came out on Hampstead Heath. Traversing the hollow by the Vale of Health, he mounted the opposite bank, and crossing the road which joins the villages of Hampstead and Highgate, made along the remaining portion of the heath to the fields at North End, in one of which he laid himself down under a hedge, and slept.

Soon he was up again, and away,—not far into the country, but back towards London by the high-road—then back again—then over another part of the same ground as he had already traversed—then wandering up and down in fields, and lying on ditches' brinks to rest, and starting up to make for some other spot, and do the same, and ramble on again.

Where could he go, that was near and not too public, to get some meat and drink? Hendon. That was a good place, not far off, and out of most people's way. Thither he directed his steps,—running sometimes, and sometimes, with a strange perversity, loitering at a snail's pace, or stopping altogether and idly breaking the hedges with his stick. But when he got there, all the people he met—the very children at the doors—seemed to view him with sus-

picion. Back he turned again, without the courage to purchase bit or drop, though he had tasted no food for many hours; and once more he lingered on the Heath, uncertain where to go.

He wandered over miles and miles of ground, and still came back to the old place. Morning and noon had passed, and the day was on the wane, and still he rambled to and fro, and up and down, and round and round, and still lingered about the same spot. At last he got away, and shaped his course for Hatfield.

It was nine o'clock at night, when the man, quite tired out, and the dog, limping and lame from the unaccustomed exercise, turned down the hill by the church of the quiet village, and plodding along the little street, crept into a small public-house, whose scanty light had guided them to the spot. There was a fire in the tap-room, and some country-labourers were drinking before it. They made room for the stranger, but he sat down in the furthest corner, and ate and drank alone, or rather with his dog: to whom he cast a morsel of food from time to time.

The conversation of the men assembled here, turned upon the neighbouring land, and farmers; and when those topics were exhausted, upon the age of some old man who had been buried on the previous Sunday: the young men present considering him very old, and the old men present declaring him to have been quite young—not older, one white-haired grandfather said, than he was—with ten or fifteen year of life in him at least—if he had taken care; if he had taken care.

There was nothing to attract attention, or excite alarm in this. The robber, after paying his reckoning, sat silent and unnoticed in his corner, and had almost dropped asleep, when he was half wakened by the noisy entrance of a new-comer.

This was an antic fellow, half pedlar and half mountebank, who travelled about the country on foot to vend hones, strops, razors, washballs, harness-paste, medicine for dogs and horses, cheap perfumery, cosmetics and such-like wares, which he carried in a case slung to his back. His entrance was the signal for various homely jokes with the countrymen, which slackened not until he had made his supper, and opened his box of treasures, when he ingeniously contrived to unite business with amusement.

"And what be that stoof? Good to eat, Harry?" asked a grinning countryman, pointing to some composition-cakes in one corner.

"This," said the fellow, producing one, "this is the infallible and invaluable composition for removing all sorts of stain, rust, dirt, mildew, spick, speck, spot, or spatter, from silk, satin, linen, cambric, cloth, crape, stuff, carpet, merino, muslin, bombazeen, or woollen stuff. Wine-stains, fruit-stains, beer-stains, water-stains, paint-stains, pitch-stains, any stains, all come out at one rub with the infallible and invaluable composition. If a lady stains her honour, she has only need to swallow one cake and she's cured at once—for it's poison. If a gentleman wants to prove his, he has only need to bolt one little square, and he has put it beyond question—for it's quite as satisfactory as a pistol-bullet, and a great deal nastier in the flavour, consequently the more cre... in taking it. One penny a square. With all these virtues, one penny a square!"

There were two buyers directly, and more of the listeners plainly hesitated. The vendor observing this, increased in loquacity.

"It's all bought up as fast as it can be made," said the fellow. "There are fourteen water-mills, six steam-engines, and a galvanic battery, always a-working upon it, and they can't make it fast enough, though the men work so hard that they die off, and the widows is pensioned directly, with twenty pound a-year for each of the children, and a premium of fifty for twins. One penny a square! Two halfpence is all the same, and four farthings is received with joy. One penny a square! Wine-stains, fruit-stains, beer-stains, water-stains, paint-stains, pitch-stains, mud-stains, blood-stains! Here is a stain upon the hat of a gentleman in company, that I'll take clean out, before he can order me a pint of ale."

"Hah!" cried Sikes starting up. "Give that back."

"I'll take it clean out, Sir," replied the man, winking to the company, "before you can come across the room to get it. Gentlemen all, observe the dark stain upon this gentleman's hat, no wider than a shilling, but thicker than a half-crown. Whether it is a wine-stain, fruit-stain, beer-stain, water-stain, paint-stain, pitch-stain, mud-stain, or blood-stain—"

The man got no further, for Sikes with a hideous imprecation overthrew the table, and tearing the hat from him, burst out of the house.

With the same perversity of feeling and irresolution that had fastened upon him, despite himself, all day, the murderer, finding that he was not followed, and that they most probably considered him some drunken sullen fellow, turned back up the town, and getting out of the glare of the lamps of a stage-coach that was standing in the street, was walking past, when he recognised the mail from London, and saw that it was standing at the little post-office. He almost knew what was to come; but he crossed over, and listened.

The guard was standing at the door, waiting for the letter-bag. A man, dressed like a gamekeeper, came up at the moment, and he handed him a basket which lay ready on the pavement.

"That's for your people," said the guard. "Now, look alive in there, will you. Damn that 'ere bag, it warn't ready night afore last; this won't do, you know!"

"Anything new up in town, Ben?" asked the gamekeeper, drawing back to the window-shutters, the better to admire the horses.

"No, nothing that I knows on," replied the man, pulling on his gloves. "Corn's up a little. I heerd talk of a murder, too, down Spitalfields way, but I don't reckon much upon it."

"Oh, that's quite true," said a gentleman inside, who was looking out of the window. "And a dreadful murder it was."

"Was it, Sir?" rejoined the guard, touching his hat. "Man or woman, pray, Sir?"

"A woman," replied the gentleman. "It is supposed—"

"Now, Ben," cried the coachman impatiently.

"Damn that 'ere bag," said the guard; "are you gone to sleep in there?"

"Coming!" cried the office keeper, running out.

"Coming," growled the guard. "Ah, and so's the young 'ooman of property that's going to take a fancy to me, but I don't know when. Here, give hold. All ri—ight!"

The horn sounded a few cheerful notes, and the coach was gone.

Sikes remained standing in the street, apparently unmoved by what he had just heard, and agitated by no stronger feeling than a doubt where to go. At length he went back again, and took the road which leads from Hatfield to St. Albans.

He went on doggedly; but as he left the town behind him, and plunged into the solitude and darkness of the road, he felt a dread and awe creeping upon him which shook him to the core. Every object before him, substance or shadow, still or moving, took the semblance of some fearful thing; but these fears were nothing compared to the sense that haunted him of that morning's ghastly figure following at his heels. He could trace its shadow in the gloom, supply the smallest item of the outline, and note how stiff and solemn it seemed to stalk along. He could hear its garments rustling in the leaves; and every breath of wind came laden with that last low cry. If he stopped it did the same. If he ran, it followed—not running too: that would have been a relief: but like a corpse endowed with the mere machinery of life, and borne on one slow melancholy wind that never rose or fell.

At times, he turned, with desperate determination, resolved to beat this phantom off, though it should look him dead; but the hair rose on his head, and his blood stood still: for it had turned with him and was behind him then. He had kept it before him that morning, but it was behind him now—always. He leaned his back against a bank, and felt that it stood above him, visibly out against the cold night-sky. He threw himself upon the road—on his back upon the road. At his head it stood, silent, erect, and still—a living grave-stone, with its epitaph in blood.

Let no man talk of murderers escaping justice, and hint that Providence must sleep. There were twenty score of violent deaths in one long minute of that agony of fear.

There was a shed in a field he passed, that offered shelter for the night. Before the door, were three tall poplar trees, which made it very dark within; and the wind moaned through them with a dismal wail. He *could not* walk on, till day-light came again; and here he stretched himself close to the wall—to undergo new torture.

For now, a vision came before him, as constant and more terrible than that from which he had escaped. Those widely staring eyes, so lustreless and so glassy, that he had better borne to see them than think upon them, appeared in the midst of the darkness: light in themselves, but giving light to nothing. There were but two, but they were everywhere. If he shut out the sight, there came the room with every well-known object—some, indeed, that he would have forgotten, if he had gone over its contents from memory—each in its accustomed place. The body was in *its* place, and its eyes were as he saw them when he stole away. He got up, and rushed into the field without. The figure was behind him. He re-entered the shed, and shrank down once more. The eyes were there, before he had laid himself along.

And here he remained, in such terror as none but he can know, trembling in every limb, and the cold sweat starting from every pore, when suddenly there arose upon the night-wind the noise of distant shouting, and the roar of voices mingled in alarm and wonder. Any sound of men in that lonely place, even though it conveyed a real cause of alarm, was something to him. He regained his strength and energy at the prospect of personal danger; and, springing to his feet, rushed into the open air.

The broad sky seemed on fire. Rising into the air with

showers of sparks, and rolling one above the other, were sheets of flame, lighting the atmosphere for miles round, and driving clouds of smoke in the direction where he stood. The shouts grew louder as new voices swelled the roar, and he could hear the cry of Fire! mingled with the ringing of an alarm-bell, the fall of heavy bodies, and the crackling of flames as they twined round some new obstacle, and shot aloft as though refreshed by food. The noise increased as he looked. There were people there—men and women—light, bustle. It was like new life to him. He darted onward—straight, lighting, headlong through brier and brake, and leaping gate and fence as madly as the dog, who careered with loud and sounding bark before him.

He came upon the spot. There were half-dressed figures tearing to and fro, some endeavouring to drag the frightened horses from the stables, others driving the cattle from the yard and out-houses, and others laden from the burning pile, amidst a shower of falling sparks, and the tumbling down of redhot beams. The apertures, where doors and windows stood an hour ago, disclosed a mass of raging fire; walls rocked and crumbled into the burning well; the molten lead and iron poured down, white hot, upon the ground. Women and children shrieked, and men encouraged each other with noisy shouts and cheers. The clanking of the engine-pumps, and the spirting and hissing of the water as it fell upon the blazing wood, added to the tremendous roar. He shouted, too, till he was hoarse; and, flying from memory and himself, plunged into the thickest of the throng.

Hither and thither he dived that night: now working at the pumps, and now hurrying through the smoke and flame, but never ceasing to engage himself wherever noise and men were thickest. Up and down the ladders, upon the roofs of buildings, over floors that quaked and trembled with his weight, under the lee of falling bricks and stones, in every part of that great fire was he; but he bore a charmed life, and had neither scratch nor bruise, nor weariness nor thought, till morning dawned again, and only smoke and blackened ruins remained.

This mad excitement over, there returned, with tenfold force, the dreadful consciousness of his crime. He looked suspiciously about him, for the men were conversing in groups, and he feared to be the subject of their talk. The dog obeyed the significant beck of his finger, and they drew off, stealthily, together. He passed near an engine where some men were seated, and they called to him to share in their refreshment. He took some bread and meat; and as he drank a draught of beer, heard the firemen, who were from London, talking about the murder. "He has gone to Birmingham, they say," said one: "but they'll have him yet, for the scouts are out, and by to-morrow night there'll be a cry all through the country."

He hurried off, and walked till he almost dropped upon the ground; then lay down in a lane, and had a long, but broken and uneasy sleep. He wandered on again, irresolute and undecided, and oppressed with the fear of another solitary night.

Suddenly, he took the desperate resolution of going back to London.

"There's somebody to speak to there, at all events," he thought. "A good hiding-place, too. They'll never expect to nab me there, after this country scent. Why can't I lay by for a week or so, and, forcing blunt from Fagin, get abroad to France? Damme, I'll risk it."

He acted upon this impulse without delay, and choosing the least frequented roads began his journey back, resolved to lie concealed within a short distance of the metropolis, and, entering it at dusk by a circuitous route, to proceed straight to that part of it which he had fixed on for his destination.

The dog, though,—if any descriptions of him were out, it would not be forgotten that the dog was missing, and had probably gone with him. This might lead to his apprehension as he passed along the streets. He resolved to drown him, and walked on, looking about for a pond: picking up a heavy stone and tying it to his handkerchief as he went.

The animal looked up into his master's face while these preparations were making; and, whether his instinct apprehended something of their purpose, or the robber's sidelong look at him was sterner than ordinary, skulked a little farther in the rear than usual, and cowered as he came more slowly along. When his master halted at the brink of a pool, and looked round to call him, he stopped outright.

"Do you hear me call? Come here!" cried Sikes.

The animal came up from the very force of habit; but as Sikes stooped to attach the handkerchief to his throat, he uttered a low growl and started back.

"Come back!" said the robber, stamping the ground.

The dog wagged his tail, but moved not. Sikes made a running noose and called him again.

The dog advanced, retreated, paused an instant, turned, and scoured away at his hardest speed.

The man whistled again and again, and sat down and waited in the expectation that he would return. But no dog appeared, and at length he resumed his journey.

CHAPTER XLIX.

MONKS AND MR. BROWNLOW AT LENGTH MEET. THEIR CONVERSATION, AND THE INTELLIGENCE THAT INTERRUPTS IT.

THE twilight was beginning to close in, when Mr. Brownlow alighted from a hackney-coach at his own door, and knocked softly. The door being opened, a sturdy man got out of the coach and stationed himself on one side of the steps, while another man, who had been seated on the box, dismounted too, and stood upon the other side. At a sign from Mr. Brownlow, they helped out a third man, and taking him between them, hurried him into the house. This man was Monks.

They walked in the same manner up the stairs without speaking, and Mr. Brownlow, preceding them, led the way into a back room. At the door of this apartment, Monks, who had ascended with evident reluctance, stopped. The two men looked to the old gentleman as if for instructions.

"He knows the alternative," said Mr. Brownlow. "If he hesitates or moves a finger but as you bid him, drag him into the street, call for the aid of the police, and impeach him as a felon in my name."

"How dare you say this of me?" asked Monks.

"How dare you urge me to it, young man?" replied Mr. Brownlow, confronting him with a steady look. "Are you mad enough to leave this house? Unhand him. There, Sir. You are free to go, and we to follow. But I warn you, by all I hold most solemn and most sacred, that the instant you set foot in the street, that instant will I have you apprehended on a charge of fraud and robbery. I am resolute and immoveable. If you are determined to be the same, your blood be upon your own head!"

"By what authority am I kidnapped in the street and brought here by these dogs?" asked Monks, looking from one to the other of the men who stood by the side of him.

"By mine," replied Mr. Brownlow. "Those persons are indemnified by me. If you complain of being deprived of your liberty—you had power and opportunity to retrieve it as you came along, but you deemed it advisable to remain quiet—I say again, throw yourself for protection on the law. I will appeal to the law too; but when you have gone too far to recede, do not sue to me for leniency, when the power will have passed into other hands; and do not say I plunged you down the gulf into which you rushed yourself."

Monks was plainly disconcerted, and alarmed besides. He hesitated.

"You will decide quickly," said Mr. Brownlow, with perfect firmness and composure. "If you wish me to prefer my charges publicly, and consign you to a punishment the extent of which, although I can, with a shudder, foresee, I cannot control, once more, I say, you know the way. If not, and you appeal to my forbearance, and the mercy of those you have deeply injured, seat yourself, without a word, in that chair. It has waited for you two whole days."

Monks muttered some unintelligible words, but wavered still.

"You will be prompt," said Mr. Brownlow. "A word from me, and the alternative has gone for ever."

Still the man hesitated.

"I have not the inclination to parley," said Mr. Brownlow, "and, as I advocate the dearest interests of others, I have not the right."

"Is there—" demanded Monks with a faltering tongue,—"is there—no middle course?"

"None."

Monks looked at the old gentleman, with an anxious eye; but, reading in his countenance nothing but severity and determination, walked into the room, and, shrugging his shoulders, sat down.

"Lock the door on the outside," said Mr. Brownlow to the attendants, "and come when I ring."

The men obeyed, and the two were left alone together.

"This is pretty treatment, Sir," said Monks, throwing down his hat and cloak, "from my father's oldest friend."

"It is because I was your father's oldest friend, young man," returned Mr. Brownlow; "it is because the hopes and wishes of young and happy years were bound up with him, and that fair creature of his blood and kindred who rejoined her God in youth, and left me here a solitary, lonely man; it is because he knelt with me beside his only sister's death-bed when he was yet a boy, on the morning that would—but Heaven willed otherwise—have made her my young wife; it is because my seared heart clung to him, from that time forth, through all his trials and errors, till he died; it is because old recollections and associations filled my heart, and even the sight of you brings with it old thoughts of him; it is because of all these things that I am moved to treat you gently now—yes, Edward Leeford, even now—and blush for your unworthiness who bear the name."

"What has the name to do with it?" asked the other, after contemplating, half in silence, and half in dogged wonder, the agitation of his companion. "What is the name to me?"

"Nothing," replied Mr. Brownlow, "nothing to you. But it was *hers*, and even at this distance of time brings back to me, an old man, the glow and thrill which I once felt, only to hear it repeated by a stranger. I am very glad you have changed it—very—very."

"This is all mighty fine," said Monks (to retain his assumed designation) after a long silence, during which he had jerked himself in sullen defiance to and fro, and Mr. Brownlow had sat, shading his face with his hand. "But what do you want with me?"

"You have a brother," said Mr. Brownlow, rousing himself: "a brother, the whisper of whose name in your ear when I came behind you in the street, was, in itself, almost enough to make you accompany me hither, in wonder and alarm."

"I have no brother," replied Monks. "You know I was an only child. Why do you talk to me of brothers? You know that, as well as I."

"Attend to what I do know, and you may not," said Mr. Brownlow. "I shall interest you by and by. I know that of the wretched marriage, into which family pride, and the most sordid and narrowest of all ambition, forced your unhappy father when a mere boy, you were the sole and most unnatural issue."

"I don't care for hard names," interrupted Monks with a jeering laugh. "You know the fact, and that's enough for me."

"But I also know," pursued the old gentleman, "the misery, the slow torture, the protracted anguish of that ill-assorted union. I know how listlessly and wearily each of that wretched pair dragged on their heavy chain through a world that was poisoned to them both. I know how cold formalities were succeeded by open taunts; how indifference gave place to dislike, dislike to hate, and hate to loathing, until at last they wrenched the clanking bond asunder, and retiring a wide space apart, carried each a galling fragment, of which nothing but death could break the rivets, to hide it in new society beneath the gayest looks they could assume. Your mother succeeded: she forgot it soon. But it rusted and cankered at your father's heart for years."

"Well, they were separated," said Monks, "and what of that?"

"When they had been separated for some time," returned Mr. Brownlow, "and your mother, wholly given up to Continental frivolities, had utterly forgotten the young husband ten good years her junior, who, with prospects blighted, lingered on at home, he fell among new friends. *This* circumstance, at least, you know already."

"Not I," said Monks, turning away his eyes and beating his foot upon the ground, as a man who is determined to deny everything. "Not I."

"Your manner, no less than your actions, assures me that you have never forgotten it, or ceased to think of it with bitterness," returned Mr. Brownlow. "I speak of fifteen years ago, when you were not more than eleven years old, and your father but one-and-thirty—for he was, I repeat, a boy, when *his* father ordered him to marry. Must I go back to events which cast a shade upon the memory of your parent, or will you spare it, and disclose to me the truth?"

"I have nothing to disclose," rejoined Monks. "You must talk on if you will."

"These new friends, then," said Mr. Brownlow, "were

a naval officer retired from active service, whose wife had died some half-a-year before, and left him with two children—there had been more, but, of all their family, happily but two survived. They were both daughters; one a beautiful creature of nineteen, and the other a mere child of two or three years old."

"What's this to me?" asked Monks.

"They resided," said Mr. Brownlow, without seeming to hear the interruption, "in a part of the country to which your father in his wandering had repaired, and where he had taken up his abode. Acquaintance, intimacy, friendship, fast followed on each other. Your father was gifted as few men are. He had his sister's soul and person. As the old officer knew him more and more, he grew to love him. I would that it had ended there. His daughter did the same."

The old gentleman paused; Monks was biting his lips, with his eyes fixed upon the floor; seeing this, he immediately resumed:

"The end of a year found him contracted, solemnly contracted, to that daughter; the object of the first, true, ardent, only passion of a guileless, untried girl."

"Your tale is of the longest," observed Monks, moving restlessly in his chair.

"It is a true tale of grief and trial, and sorrow, young man," returned Mr. Brownlow, "and such tales usually are; if it were one of unmixed joy and happiness, it would be very brief. At length one of those rich relations to strengthen whose interest and importance your father had been sacrificed, as others are often—it is no uncommon case—died, and to repair the misery he had been instrumental in occasioning, left him *his* panacea for all griefs—Money. It was necessary that he should immediately repair to Rome, whither this man had sped for health, and where he had died, leaving his affairs in great confusion. He went; was seized with mortal illness there; was followed, the moment the intelligence reached Paris, by your mother who carried you with her; he died the day after her arrival, leaving no will—*no will*—so that the whole property fell to her and you."

At this part of the recital Monks held his breath, and listened with a face of intense eagerness, though his eyes were not directed towards the speaker. As Mr. Brownlow paused, he changed his position with the air of one who has experienced a sudden relief, and wiped his hot face and hands.

"Before he went abroad, and as he passed through London on his way," said Mr. Brownlow, slowly, and fixing his eyes upon the other's face, "he came to me."

"I never heard of that," interrupted Monks in a tone intended to appear incredulous, but savouring more of disagreeable surprise.

"He came to me, and left with me, among some other things, a picture—a portrait painted by himself—a likeness of this poor girl—which he did not wish to leave behind, and could not carry forward on his hasty journey. He was worn by anxiety and remorse almost to a shadow; talked in a wild, distracted way, of ruin and dishonour worked by him; confided to me his intention to convert his whole property, at any loss, into money, and, having settled on his wife and you a portion of his recent acquisition, to fly the country—I guessed too well he would not fly alone—and never see it more. Even from me, his old and early friend, whose strong attachment had taken root in the earth that covered one most dear to both—even from me he withheld any more particular confession, promising to write and tell me all, and after that to see me once again, for the last time on earth. Alas! *That* was the last time. I had no letter, and I never saw him more.

"I went," said Mr. Brownlow, after a short pause, "I went, when all was over, to the scene of his—I will use the term the world would freely use, for worldly harshness or favour are now alike to him—of his guilty love: resolved that if my fears were realized that erring child should find one heart and home to shelter and compassionate her. The family had left that part a week before; they had called in such trifling debts as were outstanding, discharged them, and left the place by night. Why, or whither, none can tell."

Monks drew his breath yet more freely, and looked round with a smile of triumph.

"When your brother," said Mr. Brownlow, drawing nearer to the other's chair, "When your brother: a feeble, ragged, neglected child: was cast in my way oy a stronger hand than chance, and rescued by me from a life of vice and infamy—"

"What!" cried Monks.

"By me," said Mr. Brownlow. "I told you I should interest you before long. I say by me—I see that your cunning associate suppressed my name, although, for aught he knew, it would be quite strange to your ears. When he was rescued by me, then, and lay recovering from sickness in my house, his strong resemblance to this picture I have spoken of, struck me with astonishment. Even when I first saw him in all his dirt and misery, there was a lingering expression in his face that came upon me like a glimpse of some old friend flashing on one in a vivid dream. I need not tell you he was snared away before I knew his history—"

"Why not?" asked Monks hastily.

"Because you know it well."

"I!"

"Denial to me is vain," replied Mr. Brownlow. "I shall show you that I know more than that."

"You—you—can't prove anything against me," stammered Monks. "I defy you to do it!"

"We shall see," returned the old gentleman with a searching glance. "I lost the boy, and no efforts of mine could recover him. Your mother being dead, I knew that you alone could solve the mystery if anybody could, and as when I had last heard of you you were on your own estate in the West Indies—whither, as you well know, you retired upon your mother's death to escape the consequences of vicious courses here—I made the voyage. You had left it, months before, and were supposed to be in London, but no one could tell where. I returned. Your agents had no clue to your residence. You came and went, as strangely as you had ever done: sometimes for days together and sometimes not for months: keeping to all appearance the same low haunts and mingling with the same infamous herd who had been your associates when a fierce ungovernable boy. I wearied them with new applications. I paced the streets by night and day, but until two hours ago all my efforts were fruitless, and I never saw you for an instant."

"And now you do see me," said Monks, rising boldly, "what then? Fraud and robbery are high-sounding words—justified, you think, by a fancied resemblance in some young imp to an idle daub of a dead man's. Brother! You don't even know that a child was born of this maudlin pair; you don't even know that."

"I *did not*," replied Mr. Brownlow, rising too; "but within the last fortnight I have learnt it all. You have a brother; you know it, and him. There was a will, which your mother destroyed, leaving the secret and the gain to you at her own death. It contained a reference to some child likely to be the result of this sad connection, which child was born, and accidentally encountered by you, when your suspicions were first awakened by his resemblance to his father. You repaired to the place of his birth. There existed proofs—proofs long suppressed—of his birth and parentage. Those proofs were destroyed by you, and now, in your own words to your accomplice the Jew, '*the only proofs of the boy's identity lie at the bottom of the river, and the old hag that received them from the mother is rotting in her coffin.*' Unworthy son, coward, liar,—you, who hold your councils with thieves and murderers in dark rooms at night,—you, whose plots and wiles have brought a violent death upon the head of one worth millions such as you, —you, who from your cradle were gall and bitterness to your own father's heart, and in whom all evil passions, vice, and profligacy, festered, till they found a vent in a hideous disease which has made your face an index even to your mind—you, Edward Leeford, do you still brave me!"

"No, no, no!" returned the coward, overwhelmed by these accumulated charges.

"Every word!" cried the old gentleman, "every word that has passed between you and this detested villain, is known to me. Shadows on the wall have caught your whispers, and brought them to my ear; the sight of the persecuted child has turned vice itself, and given it the courage and almost the attributes of virtue. Murder has been done, to which you were morally if not really a party."

"No, no," interposed Monks. "I—I—know nothing of that; I was going to inquire the truth of the story when you overtook me. I didn't know the cause. I thought it was a common quarrel."

"It was the partial disclosure of your secrets," replied Mr. Brownlow. "Will you disclose the whole?"

"Yes, I will."

"Set your hand to a statement of truth and facts, and repeat it before witnesses?"

"That I promise too."

"Remain quietly here, until such a document is drawn up, and proceed with me to such a place as I may deem most advisable, for the purpose of attesting it?"

"If you insist upon that, I'll do that also," replied Monks.

"You must do more than that," said Mr. Brownlow. "Make restitution to an innocent and unoffending child, for such he is, although the offspring of a guilty and most miserable love. You have not forgotten the provisions of the will. Carry them into execution so far as your brother is concerned, and then go where you please. In this world you need meet no more."

While Monks was pacing up and down, meditating with dark and evil looks on this proposal and the possibilities of evading it: torn by his fears on the one hand and his hatred on the other: the door was hurriedly unlocked, and a gentleman (Mr. Losberne) entered the room in violent agitation.

"The man will be taken," he cried. "He will be taken to-night!"

"The murderer?" asked Mr. Brownlow.

"Yes, yes," replied the other. "His dog has been seen lurking about some old haunt, and there seems little doubt that his master either is, or will be, there, under cover of the darkness. Spies are hovering about in every direction. I have spoken to the men who are charged with his capture, and they tell me he can never escape. A reward of a hundred pounds is proclaimed by Government to-night."

"I will give fifty more," said Mr. Brownlow, "and proclaim it with my own lips upon the spot, if I can reach it. Where is Mr. Maylie?"

"Harry? As soon as he had seen your friend here, safe in a coach with you, he hurried off to where he heard this," replied the doctor, "and mounting his horse sallied forth to join the first party at some place in the outskirts agreed upon between them."

"The Jew," said Mr. Brownlow; "what of him?"

"When I last heard, he had not been taken, but he will be, or is, by this time. They're sure of him."

"Have you made up your mind?" asked Mr. Brownlow, in a low voice, of Monks.

"Yes," he replied. "You—you—will be secret with me?"

"I will. Remain here till I return. It is your only hope of safety."

They left the room, and the door was again locked.

"What have you done?" asked the doctor in a whisper.

"All that I could hope to do, and even more. Coupling the poor girl's intelligence with my previous knowledge, and the result of our good friend's inquiries on the spot, I left him no loophole of escape, and laid bare the whole villany which by these lights became plain as day. Write and appoint the evening after to-morrow, at seven, for the meeting. We shall be down there, a few hours before, but shall require rest: especially the young lady, who *may* have greater need of firmness than either you or I can quite foresee just now. But my blood boils to avenge this poor murdered creature. Which way have they taken?"

"Drive straight to the office and you will be in time," replied Mr. Losberne. "I will remain here."

The two gentlemen hastily separated; each in a fever of excitement wholly uncontrollable.

CHAPTER L.

THE PURSUIT AND ESCAPE.

NEAR to that part of the Thames on which the church at Rotherhithe abuts, where the buildings on the banks are dirtiest and the vessels on the river blackest with the dust of colliers and the smoke of close-built low-roofed houses, there exists, at the present day, the filthiest, the strangest, the most extraordinary of the many localities that are hidden in London, wholly unknown, even by name, to the great mass of its inhabitants.

To reach this place, the visitor has to penetrate through a maze of close, narrow, and muddy streets, thronged by the roughest and poorest of waterside people, and devoted to the traffic they may be supposed to occasion. The cheapest and least delicate provisions are heaped in the shops; the coarsest and commonest articles of wearing apparel dangle at the salesman's door, and stream from the house-parapet and windows. Jostling with unemployed **labourers of the lowest class, ballast-heavers, coal-whippers, brazen women, ragged children, and the very raff and** refuse of the river, he makes his way with difficulty along, assailed by offensive sights and smells from the narrow alleys which branch off on the right and left, and deafened by the clash of ponderous waggons that bear great piles of merchandise from the stacks of warehouses that rise from every corner. Arriving, at length, in streets remoter and less-frequented than those through which he has passed, he walks beneath tottering house-fronts projecting over the pavement, dismantled walls that seem to totter as he passes, chimneys half crushed half hesitating to fall, windows guarded by rusty iron bars that time and dirt have almost eaten away, and every imaginable sign of desolation and neglect.

In such a neighbourhood, beyond Dockhead in the Borough of Southwark, stands Jacob's Island, surrounded by a muddy ditch, six or eight feet deep and fifteen or twenty wide when the tide is in, once called Mill Pond, but known in these days as Folly Ditch. It is a creek or inlet from the Thames, and can always be filled at high water by opening the sluices at the Lead Mills from which it took its old name. At such times, a stranger, looking from one of the wooden bridges thrown across it at Mill Lane, will see the inhabitants of the houses on either side lowering from their back doors and windows, buckets, pails, domestic utensils of all kinds, in which to haul the water up; and when his eye is turned from these operations to the houses themselves, his utmost astonishment will be excited by the scene before him. Crazy wooden galleries common to the backs of half-a-dozen houses, with holes from which to look upon the slime beneath; windows, broken and patched, with poles thrust out, on which to dry the linen that is never there; rooms so small, so filthy, so confined, that the air would seem too tainted even for the dirt and squalor which they shelter; wooden chambers thrusting themselves out above the mud, and threatening to fall into it—as some have done; dirt-besmeared walls and decaying foundations; every repulsive lineament of poverty, every loathsome indication of filth, rot, and garbage; all these ornament the banks of Folly Ditch.

In Jacob's Island, the warehouses are roofless and empty; the walls are crumbling down; the windows are windows no more; the doors are falling into the streets; the chimneys are blackened, but they yield no smoke. Thirty or forty years ago, before losses and Chancery suits came upon it, it was a thriving place; but now it is a desolate island indeed. The houses have no owners; they are broken open, and entered upon by those who have the courage; and there they live, and there they die. They must have powerful motives for a secret residence, or be reduced to a destitute condition indeed, who seek a refuge in Jacob's Island.

In an upper room of one of these houses—a detached house of fair size, ruinous in other respects, but strongly defended at door and window: of which house the back commanded the ditch in manner already described—there were assembled three men, who, regarding each other every now and then with looks expressive of perplexity and expectation, sat for some time in profound and gloomy silence. One of these was Toby Crackit, another Mr. Chitling, and the third a robber of fifty years, whose nose had been almost beaten in, in some old scuffle, and whose face bore a frightful scar which might probably be traced to the same occasion. This man was a returned transport, and his name was Kags.

"I wish," said Toby turning to Mr. Chitling, "that you had picked out some other crib when the two old ones got too warm, and had not come here, my fine feller."

"Why didn't you, blunder-head?" said Kags.

"Well, I thought you'd have been a little more glad to see me than this," replied Mr. Chitling, with a melancholy air.

"Why look'e, young gentleman," said Toby, "when a man keeps himself so very ex-clusive as I have done, and by that means has a snug house over his head with nobody prying and smelling about it, it's rather a startling thing to have the honour of a wisit from a young gentleman (however respectable and pleasant a person he may be to play cards with at conweniency) circumstanced as you are."

"Especially, when the exclusive young man has got a friend stopping with him, that's arrived sooner than was expected from foreign parts, and is too modest to want to be presented to the Judges on his return," added Mr. Kags.

There was a short silence, after which Toby Crackit, seeming to abandon as hopeless any further effort to maintain his usual devil-may-care swagger, turned to Chitling and said,

"When was Fagin took then?"

"Just at dinner-time—two o'clock this afternoon. Charley and I made our lucky up the wash'us chimney, and Bolter got into the empty water-butt, head downwards; but his legs were so precious long that they stuck out at the top, and so they took him too."

"And Bet?"

"Poor Bet! She went to see the body, to speak to who it was," replied Chitling, his countenance falling more and more, "and went off mad, screaming and raving, and beating her head against the boards; so they put a strait-weskut on her and took her to the hospital—and there she is."

"Wot's come of young Bates?" demanded Kags.

"He hung about, not to come over here afore dark, but he'll be here soon," replied Chitling. "There's nowhere else to go to now, for the people at the Cripples are all in custody, and the bar of the ken—I went up there and see it with my own eyes—is filled with traps."

"This is a smash," observed Toby biting his lips. "There's more than one will go with this."

"The sessions are on," said Kags: "if they get the inquest over, and Bolter turns King's evidence; as of course he will, from what he's said already: they can prove Fagin an accessory before the fact, and get the trial on on Friday, and he'll swing in six days from this, by G—!"

"You should have heard the people groan," said Chitling; "the officers fought like devils, or they'd have torn him away. He was down once, but they made a ring round him, and fought their way along. You should have seen how he looked about him, all muddy and bleeding, and clung to them as if they were his dearest friends. I can see 'em now, not able to stand upright with the pressing of the mob, and dragging him along amongst 'em; I can see the people jumping up, one behind another, and snarling with their teeth and making at him like wild beasts; I can see the blood upon his hair and beard, and hear the cries with which the women worked themselves into the centre of the crowd at the street corner, and swore they'd tear his heart out!"

The horror-stricken witness of this scene pressed his hands upon his ears, and with his eyes closed got up and paced violently to and fro, like one distracted.

Whilst he was thus engaged, and the two men sat by in silence with their eyes fixed upon the floor, a pattering noise was heard upon the stairs, and Sikes's dog bounded into the room. They ran to the window, down stairs, and into the street. The dog had jumped in at an open window; he made no attempt to follow them, nor was his master to be seen.

"What's the meaning of this!" said Toby, when they had returned. "He can't be coming here. I—I—hope not."

"If he was coming here, he'd have come with the dog," said Kags, stooping down to examine the animal, who lay panting on the floor. "Here! Give us some water for him; he has run himself faint."

"He's drunk it all up, every drop," said Chitling, after watching the dog some time in silence. "Covered with mud—lame—half-blind—he must have come a long way."

"Where can he have come from!" exclaimed Toby. "He's been to the other kens of course, and finding them filled with strangers come on here, where he's been many a time and often. But where can he have come from first, and how comes he here alone, without the other!"

"He"—(none of them called the murderer by his old name)—"He can't have made away with himself. What do you think?" said Chitling.

Toby shook his head.

"If he had," said Kags, "the dog 'ud want to lead us away to where he did it. No. I think he's got out of the country, and left the dog behind. He must have given him the slip somehow, or he wouldn't be so easy."

This solution, appearing the most probable one, was adopted as the right; and the dog, creeping under a chair, coiled himself up to sleep, without more notice from anybody.

It being now dark, the shutter was closed, and a candle lighted and placed upon the table. The terrible events of the last two days had made a deep impression on all three, increased by the danger and uncertainty of their own position. They drew their chairs closer together, starting at every sound. They spoke little, and that in whispers, and were as silent and awe-stricken as if the remains of the murdered woman lay in the next room.

They had sat thus, some time, when suddenly was heard a hurried knocking at the door below.

"Young Bates," said Kags, looking angrily round to check the fear he felt himself.

The knocking came again. No, it wasn't he. He never knocked like that.

Crackit went to the window, and, shaking all over, drew in his head. There was no need to tell them who it was; his pale face was enough. The dog too was on the alert in an instant, and ran whining to the door.

"We must let him in," he said, taking up the candle.

"Isn't there any help for it?" asked the other man in a hoarse voice.

"None. He *must* come in."

"Don't leave us in the dark," said Kags, taking down a candle from the chimney-piece, and lighting it, with such a trembling hand that the knocking was twice repeated before he had finished.

Crackit went down to the door, and returned followed by a man with the lower part of his face buried in a handkerchief, and another tied over his head under his hat. He drew them slowly off. Blanched face, sunken eyes, hollow cheeks, beard of three days' growth, wasted flesh, short thick breath; it was the very ghost of Sikes.

He laid his hand upon a chair which stood in the middle of the room, but shuddering as he was about to drop into it, and seeming to glance over his shoulder, dragged it back close to the wall—as close as it would go—ground it against it—and sat down.

Not a word had been exchanged. He looked from one to another in silence. If an eye were furtively raised and met his, it was instantly averted. When his hollow voice broke silence, they all three started. They seemed never to have heard its tones before.

"How came that dog here?" he asked.

"Alone. Three hours ago."

"To-night's paper says that Fagin's taken. Is it true, or a lie?"

"True."

They were silent again.

"Damn you all!" said Sikes, passing his hand across his forehead. "Have you nothing to say to me?"

There was an uneasy movement among them, but nobody spoke.

"You that keep this house," said Sikes, turning his face to Crackit, "do you mean to sell me, or to let me lie here till this hunt is over?"

"You may stop here, if you think it safe," returned the person addressed, after some hesitation.

Sikes carried his eyes slowly up the wall behind him: rather trying to turn his head than actually doing it: and said, "Is—it—the body—is it buried?"

They shook their heads.

"Why isn't it!" he retorted with the same glance behind him. "Wot do they keep such ugly things above the ground for?—Who's that knocking?"

Crackit intimated, by a motion of his hand as he left the room, that there was nothing to fear; and directly came back with Charley Bates behind him. Sikes sat opposite the door, so that the moment the boy entered the room he encountered his figure.

"Toby," said the boy falling back, as Sikes turned his eyes towards him, "why didn't you tell me this, down stairs?"

There had been something so tremendous in the shrinking off of the three, that the wretched man was willing to propitiate even this lad. Accordingly he nodded, and made as though he would shake hands with him.

"Let me go into some other room," said the boy, retreating still farther.

"Charley!" said Sikes, stepping forward, "don't you—don't you know me?"

"Don't come nearer me," answered the boy, still retreating, and looking, with horror in his eyes, upon the murderer's face. "You monster!"

The man stopped half-way, and they looked at each other; but Sikes's eyes sank gradually to the ground.

"Witness you three," cried the boy shaking his clenched fist, and becoming more and more excited as he spoke. "Witness you three—I'm not afraid of him—if they come after him, I'll give him up; I will. I tell you out at once. He may kill me for it if he likes, or if he dares, but if I am here I'll give him up. I'd give him up if he was to be boiled alive. Murder! Help! If there's the pluck of a man among you three, you'll help me. Murder! Help! Down with him!"

Pouring out these cries, and accompanying them with violent gesticulation, the boy actually threw himself, single-handed, upon the strong man, and in the intensity of his energy, and the suddenness of his surprise, brought him heavily to the ground.

The three spectators seemed quite stupefied. They offered no interference, and the boy and man rolled on the ground together; the former, heedless of the blows that showered upon him, wrenching his hands tighter and tighter in the garments about the murderer's breast, and never ceasing to call for help with all his might.

The contest, however, was too unequal to last long. Sikes had him down, and his knee was on his throat, when Crackit pulled him back with a look of alarm, and pointed to the window. There were lights gleaming below, voices in loud and earnest conversation, the tramp of hurried footsteps—endless they seemed in number—crossing the nearest wooden bridge. One man on horseback seemed to be among the crowd; for there was the noise of hoofs rattling on the uneven pavement. The gleam of lights increased; the footsteps came more thickly and noisily on. Then, came a loud knocking at the door, and then a hoarse murmur from such a multitude of angry voices as would have made the boldest quail.

"Help!" shrieked the boy in a voice that rent the air. "He's here! Break down the door!"

"In the King's name," cried the voices without; and the hoarse cry arose again, but louder.

"Break down the door!" screamed the boy. "I tell you they'll never open it. Run straight to the room where the light is. Break down the door!"

Strokes, thick and heavy, rattled upon the door and lower window-shutters as he ceased to speak, and a loud huzzah burst from the crowd; giving the listener, for the first time, some adequate idea of its immense extent.

"Open the door of some place where I can lock this screeching hell-babe," cried Sikes fiercely; running to and fro, and dragging the boy, now, as easily as if he were an empty sack. "That door. Quick!" He flung him in, bolted it, and turned the key. "Is the down-stairs door fast?"

"Double-locked and chained," replied Crackit, who, with the other two men, still remained quite helpless and bewildered.

"The panels—are they strong?"

"Lined with sheet-iron."

"And the windows too?"

"Yes, and the windows."

"Damn you!" cried the desperate ruffian, throwing up the sash and menacing the crowd. "Do your worst! I'll cheat you yet!"

Of all the terrific yells that ever fell on mortal ears, none could exceed the cry of the infuriated throng. Some shouted to those who were nearest to set the house on fire; others roared to the officers to shoot him dead. Among them all, none showed such fury as the man on horseback, who, throwing himself out of the saddle, and bursting through the crowd as if he were parting water, cried, beneath the window, in a voice that rose above all others, "Twenty guineas to the man who brings a ladder!"

The nearest voices took up the cry, and hundreds echoed it. Some called for ladders, some for sledge-hammers; some ran with torches to and fro as if to seek them, and still came back and roared again; some spent their breath in impotent curses and execrations; some pressed forward with the ecstasy of madmen, and thus impeded the progress of those below; some among the boldest attempted to climb up by the water-spout and crevices in the wall; and all waved to and fro, in the darkness beneath, like a field of corn moved by an angry wind: and joined from time to time in one loud furious roar.

"The tide," cried the murderer, as he staggered back into the room, and shut the faces out, "the tide was in as I came up. Give me a rope, a long rope. They're all in front. I may drop into the Folly Ditch, and clear off that way. Give me a rope, or I shall do three more murders and kill myself at last."

The panic-stricken men pointed to where such articles were kept; the murderer, hastily selecting the longest and strongest cord, hurried up to the house-top.

All the windows in the rear of the house had been long ago bricked up, except one small trap in the room where the boy was locked, and that was too small even for the passage of his body. But, from this aperture, he had never ceased to call on those without, to guard the back; and thus, when the murderer emerged at last on the house-top by the door in the roof, a loud shout proclaimed the fact to those in front, who immediately began to pour round, pressing upon each other in one unbroken stream.

He planted a board, which he had carried up with him for the purpose, so firmly against the door that it must be matter of great difficulty to open it from the inside; and creeping over the tiles, looked over the low parapet.

The water was out, and the ditch a bed of mud.

The crowd had been hushed during these few moments, watching his motions and doubtful of his purpose, but the instant they perceived it and knew it was defeated, they raised a cry of triumphant execration to which all their previous shouting had been whispers. Again and again it rose. Those who were at too great a distance to know its meaning, took up the sound; it echoed and re-echoed; it seemed as though the whole city had poured its population out to curse him.

On pressed the people from the front—on, on, on, in a strong struggling current of angry faces, with here and there a glaring torch to light them up, and show them out in all their wrath and passion. The houses on the opposite side of the ditch had been entered by the mob; sashes were thrown up, or torn bodily out; there were tiers and tiers of faces in every window; and cluster upon cluster of people clinging to every house-top. Each little bridge (and there were three in sight) bent beneath the weight of the crowd upon it. Still the current poured on to find some nook or hole from which to vent their shouts, and only for an instant see the wretch.

"They have him now," cried a man on the nearest bridge. "Hurrah!"

The crowd grew light with uncovered heads; and again the shout uprose.

"I promise fifty pounds," cried an old gentleman from the same quarter, "fifty pounds to the man who takes him alive. I will remain here, till he comes to ask me for it."

There was another roar. At this moment the word was passed among the crowd that the door was forced at last, and that he who had first called for the ladder had mounted into the room. The stream abruptly turned, as this intelligence ran from mouth to mouth; and the people at the windows, seeing those upon the bridges pouring back, quitted their stations, and, running into the street, joined the concourse that now thronged pell-mell to the spot they had left: each man crushing and striving with his neighbour, and all panting with impatience to get near the door,

THE LAST CHANCE.

and look upon the criminal as the officers brought him out. The cries and shrieks of those who were pressed almost to suffocation, or trampled down and trodden under foot in the confusion, were dreadful; the narrow ways were completely blocked up; and at this time, between the rush of some to regain the space in front of the house, and the unavailing struggles of others to extricate themselves from the mass, the immediate attention was distracted from the murderer, although the universal eagerness for his capture was, if possible, increased.

The man had shrunk down, thoroughly quelled by the ferocity of the crowd, and the impossibility of escape; but, seeing this sudden change with no less rapidity than it had occurred, he sprang upon his feet, determined to make one last effort for his life by dropping into the ditch, and, at the risk of being stifled, endeavouring to creep away in the darkness and confusion.

Roused into new strength and energy, and stimulated by the noise within the house which announced that an entrance had really been effected, he set his foot against the stack of chimneys, fastened one end of the rope tightly and firmly round it, and with the other made a strong running noose by the aid of his hands and teeth almost in a second. He could let himself down by the cord to within a less distance of the ground than his own height, and had his knife ready in his hand to cut it then and drop.

At the very instant when he brought the loop over his head previous to slipping it beneath his arm-pits, and when the old gentleman before-mentioned (who had clung so tight to the railing of the bridge as to resist the force of the crowd, and retain his position) earnestly warned those about him that the man was about to lower himself down—at that very instant the murderer, looking behind him on the roof, threw his arms above his head, and uttered a yell of terror.

"The eyes again!" he cried, in an unearthly screech.

Staggering as if struck by lightning, he lost his balance and tumbled over the parapet. The noose was at his neck. It ran up with his weight, tight as a bow-string, and swift as the arrow it speeds. He fell for five-and-thirty feet. There was a sudden jerk, a terrific convulsion of the limbs; and there he hung, with the open knife clenched in his stiffening hand.

The old chimney quivered with the shock, but stood it bravely. The murderer swung lifeless against the wall; and the boy, thrusting aside the dangling body which obscured his view, called to the people to come and take him out, for God's sake.

A dog, which had lain concealed till now, ran backwards and forwards on the parapet with a dismal howl, and, collecting himself for a spring, jumped for the dead man's shoulders. Missing his aim, he fell into the ditch, turning completely over as he went; and striking his head against a stone, dashed out his brains.

CHAPTER LI.

AFFORDING AN EXPLANATION OF MORE MYSTERIES THAN ONE, AND COMPREHENDING A PROPOSAL OF MARRIAGE WITH NO WORD OF SETTLEMENT OR PIN-MONEY.

THE events narrated in the last chapter were yet but two days old, when Oliver found himself, at three o'clock in the afternoon, in a travelling-carriage rolling fast towards his native town. Mrs. Maylie, and Rose, and Mrs. Bedwin, and the good doctor, were with him; and Mr. Brownlow followed in a post-chaise, accompanied by one other person whose name had not been mentioned.

They had not talked much upon the way; for Oliver was in a flutter of agitation and uncertainty which deprived him of the power of collecting his thoughts, and almost of speech, and appeared to have scarcely less effect on his companions, who shared it, in at least an equal degree. He and the two ladies had been very carefully made acquainted by Mr. Brownlow with the nature of the admissions which had been forced from Monks; and although they knew that the object of their present journey was to complete the work which had been so well begun, still the whole matter was enveloped in enough of doubt and mystery to leave them in endurance of the most intense suspense.

The same kind friend had, with Mr. Losberne's assistance, cautiously stopped all channels of communication through which they could receive intelligence of the dreadful occurrences that had so recently taken place. "It was quite true," he said, "that they must know them before long, but it might be at a better time than the present, and it could not be at a worse." So, they travelled on in silence: each busied with reflections on the object which had brought them together: and no one disposed to give utterance to the thoughts which crowded upon all.

But if Oliver, under these influences, had remained silent while they journeyed towards his birth-place by a road he had never seen, how the whole current of his recollections ran back to old times, and what a crowd of emotions were wakened up in his breast, when they turned into that which he had traversed on foot: a poor houseless wandering boy, without a friend to help him, or a roof to shelter his head.

"See there, there!" cried Oliver, eagerly clasping the hand of Rose, and pointing out at the carriage window; "that's the stile I came over; there are the hedges I crept behind for fear any one should overtake me and force me back! Yonder is the path across the fields, leading to the old house where I was a little child! Oh Dick, Dick, my dear old friend, if I could only see you now!"

"You will see him soon," replied Rose, gently taking his folded hands between her own. "You shall tell him how happy you are, and how rich you have grown, and that in all your happiness you have none so great as the coming back to make him happy too."

"Yes, yes," said Oliver, "and we'll—we'll take him away from here, and have him clothed and taught, and send him to some quiet country place where he may grow strong and well,—shall we?"

Rose nodded "yes," for the boy was smiling through such happy tears that she could not speak.

"You will be kind and good to him, for you are to every one," said Oliver. "It will make you cry, I know, to hear what he can tell; but never mind, never mind, it will be all over, and you will smile again—I know that too—to think how changed he is; you did the same with me. He said 'God bless you' to me when I ran away," cried the boy with a burst of affectionate emotion; "and I will say 'God bless you' now, and show him how I love him for it!"

As they approached the town, and at length drove through its narrow streets, it became matter of no small difficulty to restrain the boy within reasonable bounds. There was Sowerberry's the undertaker's, just as it used to be, only smaller and less imposing in appearance than he remembered it—there were all the well-known shops and houses, with almost every one of which he had some slight incident connected—there was Gamfield's cart, the very cart he used to have, standing at the old public-house door—there was the workhouse, the dreary prison of his youthful days, with its dismal windows frowning on the street—there was the same lean porter standing at the gate, at sight of whom Oliver involuntarily shrank back, and then laughed at himself for being so foolish, then cried, then laughed again—there were scores of faces at the doors and windows that he knew quite well—there was nearly everything as if he had left it but yesterday, and all his recent life had been but a happy dream.

But it was pure, earnest, joyful reality. They drove straight to the door of the chief hotel (which Oliver used to stare up at, with awe, and think a mighty palace, but which had somehow fallen off in grandeur and size); and here was Mr. Grimwig all ready to receive them, kissing the young lady, and the old one too, when they got out of the coach, as if he were the grandfather of the whole party, all smiles and kindness, and not offering to eat his head—no, not once; not even when he contradicted a very old postboy about the nearest road to London, and maintained he knew it best, though he had only come that way once, and that time fast asleep. There was dinner prepared, and there were bed-rooms ready, and everything was arranged as if by magic.

Notwithstanding all this, when the hurry of the first half-hour was over, the same silence and constraint prevailed that had marked their journey down. Mr. Brownlow did not join them at dinner, but remained in a separate room. The two other gentlemen hurried in and out with anxious faces, and, during the short intervals when they were present, conversed apart. Once, Mrs. Maylie was called away, and after being absent for nearly an hour, returned with eyes swollen with weeping. All these things made Rose and Oliver, who were not in any new secrets, nervous and uncomfortable. They sat wondering, in silence; or, if they exchanged a few words, spoke in whispers, as if they were afraid to hear the sound of their own voices.

At length, when nine o'clock had come, and they began to think they were to hear no more that night, Mr. Losberne and Mr. Grimwig entered the room, followed by Mr. Brownlow and a man whom Oliver almost shrieked with surprise to see; for they told him it was his brother, and it was the same man he had met at the market-town, and seen looking in with Fagin at the window of his little room. Monks cast a look of hate, which, even then, he could not dissemble, at the astonished boy, and sat down near the door. Mr. Brownlow, who had papers in his hand, walked to a table near which Rose and Oliver were seated.

"This is a painful task," said he, "but these declarations, which have been signed in London before many gentlemen, must be in substance repeated here. I would have spared you the degradation, but we must hear them from your own lips before we part, and you know why."

"Go on," said the person addressed, turning away his face. "Quick. I have almost done enough, I think. Don't keep me here."

"This child," said Mr. Brownlow, drawing Oliver to him, and laying his hand upon his head, "is your half-brother; the illegitimate son of your father, my dear friend Edwin Leeford, by poor young Agnes Fleming, who died in giving him birth."

"Yes," said Monks, scowling at the trembling boy: the beating of whose heart he might have heard. "That is their bastard child."

"The term you use," said Mr. Brownlow, sternly, "is a reproach to those who long since passed beyond the feeble censure of the world. It reflects disgrace on no one living, except you who use it. Let that pass. He was born in this town?"

"In the workhouse of this town," was the sullen reply. "You have the story there." He pointed impatiently to the papers as he spoke.

"I must have it here too," said Mr. Brownlow, looking round upon the listeners.

"Listen then! You!" returned Monks. "His father being taken ill at Rome, was joined by his wife, my mother, from whom he had been long separated, who went from Paris and took me with her—to look after his property, for what I know, for she had no great affection for him, nor he for her. He knew nothing of us, for his senses were gone, and he slumbered on till next day, when he died. Among the papers in his desk, were two, dated on the night his illness first came on, directed to yourself;" he addressed himself to Mr. Brownlow; "and enclosed in a few short lines to you, with an intimation on the cover of the package that it was not to be forwarded till after he was dead. One of these papers was a letter to this girl Agnes; the other, a will."

"What of the letter?" asked Mr. Brownlow.

"The letter?—A sheet of paper crossed and crossed again, with a penitent confession, and prayers to God to help her. He had palmed a tale on the girl that some secret mystery—to be explained one day—prevented his marrying her just then; and so she had gone on, trusting patiently to him, until she trusted too far, and lost what none could ever give her back. She was, at that time, within a few months of her confinement. He told her all he had meant to do, to hide her shame, if he had lived, and prayed her, if he died, not to curse his memory, or think the consequences of their sin would be visited on her or their young child; for all the guilt was his. He reminded her of the day he had given her the little locket and the ring with her christian name engraved upon it, and a blank left for that which he hoped one day to have bestowed upon her—prayed her yet to keep it, and wear it next her heart, as she had done before—and then ran on, wildly, in the same words, over and over again, as if he had gone distracted. I believe he had."

"The will," said Mr. Brownlow, as Oliver's tears fell fast. Monks was silent.

"The will," said Mr. Brownlow, speaking for him, "was in the same spirit as the letter. He talked of miseries which his wife had brought upon him; of the rebellious disposition, vice, malice, and premature bad passions of you, his only son, who had been trained to hate him; and left you, and your mother, each an annuity of eight hundred pounds. The bulk of his property he divided into two equal portions—one for Agnes Fleming, and the other for their child, if it should be born alive and ever come of age. If it were a girl, it was to inherit the money unconditionally; but if a boy, only on the stipulation that in his minority he should never have stained his name with any public act of dishonour, meanness, cowardice, or wrong. He did this, he said, to mark his confidence in the mother, and his conviction—only strengthened by approaching death—that the child would share her gentle heart, and noble nature. If he were disappointed in this expectation, then the money was to come to you; for then, and not till then, when both children were equal, would he recognise your prior claim upon his purse, who had none upon his heart, but had, from an infant, repulsed him with coldness and aversion."

"My mother," said Monks, in a louder tone, "did what a woman should have done—she burnt this will. The letter never reached its destination; but that, and other proofs, she kept, in case they ever tried to lie away the blot. The girl's father had the truth from her with every aggravation that her violent hate—I love her for it now—could add. Goaded by shame and dishonour he fled with his children into a remote corner of Wales, changing his very name that his friends might never know of his retreat; and here, no great while afterwards, he was found dead in his bed. The girl had left her home, in secret, some weeks before; he had searched for her, on foot, in every town and village near; and it was on the night when he returned home, assured that she had destroyed herself, to hide her shame and his, that his old heart broke."

There was a short silence here, until Mr. Brownlow took up the thread of the narrative.

"Years after this," he said, "this man's—Edward Leeford's—mother came to me. He had left her, when only eighteen; robbed her of jewels and money; gambled, squandered, forged, and fled to London: where for two years he had associated with the lowest outcasts. She was sinking under a painful and incurable disease, and wished to recover him before she died. Inquiries were set on foot, and strict searches made. They were unavailing for a long time, but ultimately successful; and he went back with her to France."

"There she died," said Monks, "after a lingering illness; and, on her death-bed, she bequeathed these secrets to me, together with her unquenchable and deadly hatred of all whom they involved—though she need not have left me that, for I had inherited it long before. She would not believe that the girl had destroyed herself and the child too, but was filled with the impression that a male child had been born, and was alive. I swore to her, if ever it crossed my path, to hunt it down; never to let it rest; to pursue it with the bitterest and most unrelenting animosity; to vent upon it the hatred that I deeply felt, and to spit upon the empty vaunt of that insulting will by dragging it, if I could, to the very gallows-foot. She was right. He came in my way at last. I began well; and, but for babbling drabs, I would have finished as I began!"

As the villain folded his arms tight together, and muttered curses on himself in the impotence of baffled malice, Mr. Brownlow turned to the terrified group beside him, and explained that the Jew, who had been his old accomplice and confidant, had a large reward for keeping Oliver ensnared: of which some part was to be given up, in the event of his being rescued: and that a dispute on this head had led to their visit to the country house for the purpose of identifying him.

"The locket and ring?" said Mr. Brownlow, turning to Monks.

"I bought them from the man and woman I told you of, who stole them from the nurse, who stole them from the corpse," answered Monks without raising his eyes. "You know what became of them."

Mr. Brownlow merely nodded to Mr. Grimwig, who, disappearing with great alacrity, shortly returned, pushing in

Mrs. Bumble, and dragging her unwilling consort after him.

"Do my hi's deceive me!" cried Mr. Bumble, with ill-feigned enthusiasm, "or is that little Oliver? Oh O-li-ver, if you know'd how I've been a-grieving for you—!"

"Hold your tongue, fool," murmured Mrs. Bumble.

"Isn't natur, natur, Mrs. Bumble!" remonstrated the workhouse master. "Can't I be supposed to feel—*I* as brought him up porochially—when I see him a-setting here, among ladies and gentlemen of the very affablest description! I always loved that boy as if he had been my—my—my own grandfather," said Mr. Bumble, halting for an appropriate comparison. "Master Oliver, my dear, you remember the blessed gentleman in the white waistcoat? Ah! he went to Heaven last week, in a oak coffin with plated handles, Oliver."

"Come, Sir," said Mr. Grimwig, tartly; "suppress your feelings."

"I will do my endeavours, Sir," replied Mr. Bumble. "How do you do, Sir? I hope you are very well."

This salutation was addressed to Mr. Brownlow, who had stepped up to within a short distance of the respectable couple. He inquired, as he pointed to Monks,

"Do you know that person?"

"No," replied Mrs. Bumble flatly.

"Perhaps *you* don't?" said Mr. Brownlow, addressing her spouse.

"I never saw him in all my life," said Mr. Bumble.

"Nor sold him anything, perhaps?"

"No," replied Mrs. Bumble.

"You never had, perhaps, a certain gold locket and ring?" said Mr. Brownlow.

"Certainly not," replied the matron. "Why are we brought here, to answer to such nonsense as this?"

Again Mr. Brownlow nodded to Mr. Grimwig; and again that gentleman limped away, with extraordinary readiness. But not again did he return with a stout man and wife; for this time, he led in two palsied women, who shook and tottered as they walked.

"You shut the door the night old Sally died," said the foremost one, raising her shrivelled hand, "but you couldn't shut out the sound, nor stop the chinks."

"No, no," said the other, looking round her and wagging her toothless jaws. "No, no, no."

"We heard her try to tell you what she'd done, and saw you take a paper from her hand, and watched you too, next day, to the pawnbroker's shop," said the first.

"Yes," added the second, "and it was a 'locket and gold ring.' We found out that, and saw it given you. We were by. Oh! we were by."

"And we know more than that," resumed the first, "for she told us often, long ago, that the young mother had told her that, feeling she should never get over it, she was on her way, at the time that she was taken ill, to die near the grave of the father of the child."

"Would you like to see the pawnbroker himself?" asked Mr. Grimwig with a motion towards the door.

"No," replied the woman; "if he"—she pointed to Monks—"has been coward enough to confess, as I see he has, and you have sounded all these hags till you found the right ones, I have nothing more to say. I *did* sell them, and they're where you'll never get them. What then?"

"Nothing," replied Mr. Brownlow, "except that it remains for us to take care that you are neither of you employed in a situation of trust again. You may leave the room."

"I hope," said Mr. Bumble, looking about him with great ruefulness, as Mr. Grimwig disappeared with the two old women, "I hope that this unfortunate little circumstance will not deprive me of my porochial office?"

"Indeed it will," replied Mr. Brownlow. "You may make up your mind to that, and think yourself well off besides."

"It was all Mrs. Bumble. She *would* do it," urged Mr. Bumble; first looking round to ascertain that his partner had left the room.

"That is no excuse," replied Mr. Brownlow. "You were present on the occasion of the destruction of these trinkets, and, indeed, are the more guilty of the two, in the eye of the law; for the law supposes that your wife acts under your direction."

"If the law supposes that," said Mr. Bumble, squeezing his hat emphatically in both hands, "the law is a ass—a idiot. If that's the eye of the law, the law's a bachelor; and the worst I wish the law is, that his eye may be opened by experience—by experience."

Laying great stress on the repetition of these two words, Mr. Bumble fixed his hat on very tight, and, putting his hands in his pockets, followed his helpmate down stairs.

"Young lady," said Mr. Brownlow, turning to Rose, "give me your hand. Do not tremble. You need not fear to hear the few remaining words we have to say."

"If they have—I do not know how they can, but if they have—any reference to me," said Rose, "pray let me hear them at some other time. I have not strength or spirits now."

"Nay," returned the old gentleman, drawing her arm through his; "you have more fortitude than this, I am sure. Do you know this young lady, Sir?"

"Yes," replied Monks.

"I never saw you before," said Rose faintly.

"I have seen you often," returned Monks.

"The father of the unhappy Agnes had *two* daughters," said Mr. Brownlow. "What was the fate of the other—the child?"

"The child," replied Monks, "when her father died in a strange place, in a strange name, without a letter, book, or scrap of paper that yielded the faintest clue by which his friends or relatives could be traced—the child was taken by some wretched cottagers, who reared it as their own."

"Go on," said Mr. Brownlow, signing to Mrs. Maylie to approach. "Go on!"

"You couldn't find the spot to which these people had repaired," said Monks, "but where friendship fails, hatred will often force a way. My mother found it, after a year of cunning search—ay, and found the child."

"She took it, did she?"

"No. The people were poor, and began to sicken—at least the man did—of their fine humanity; so she left it with them, giving them a small present of money which would not last long, and promising more, which she never meant to send. She didn't quite rely, however, on their discontent and poverty for the child's unhappiness, but told the history of the sister's shame, with such alterations as suited her; bade them take good heed of the child, for she came of bad blood; and told them she was illegitimate, and sure to go wrong at one time or other. The circumstances countenanced all this; the people believed it; and there the child dragged on an existence, miserable enough even to satisfy us, until a widow lady, residing, then, at Chester, saw the girl by chance, pitied her, and took her

home. There was some cursed spell, I think, against us; for in spite of all our efforts she remained there and was happy. I lost sight of her, two or three years ago, and saw her no more until a few months back."

"Do you see her now?"

"Yes. Leaning on your arm."

"But not the less my niece," cried Mrs. Maylie, folding the fainting girl in her arms; "not the less my dearest child. I would not lose her now, for all the treasures of the world. My sweet companion, my own dear girl!"

"The only friend I ever had," cried Rose, clinging to her. "The kindest, best of friends. My heart will burst. I cannot—cannot—bear all this."

"You have borne more, and have been, through all, the best and gentlest creature that ever shed happiness on every one she knew," said Mrs. Maylie, embracing her tenderly. "Come, come, my love; remember who this is who waits to clasp you in his arms, poor child! See here—look, look, my dear!"

"Not aunt," cried Oliver, throwing his arms about her neck: "I'll never call her aunt—sister, my own dear sister, that something taught my heart to love so dearly from the first! Rose, dear, darling Rose!"

Let the tears which fell, and the broken words which were exchanged in the long close embrace between the orphans, be sacred. A father, sister, and mother, were gained, and lost, in that one moment. Joy and grief were mingled in the cup; but there were no bitter tears: for even grief itself arose so softened, and clothed in such sweet and tender recollections, that it became a solemn pleasure, and lost all character of pain.

They were a long, long time alone. A soft tap at the door, at length announced that some one was without. Oliver opened it, glided away, and gave place to Harry Maylie.

"I know it all," he said, taking a seat beside the lovely girl. "Dear Rose, I know it all."

"I am not here by accident," he added after a lengthened silence; "nor have I heard all this to-night, for I knew it yesterday—only yesterday. Do you guess that I have come to remind you of a promise?"

"Stay," said Rose. "You *do* know all?"

"All. You gave me leave, at any time within a year, to renew the subject of our last discourse."

"I did."

"Not to press you to alter your determination," pursued the young man, "but to hear you repeat it, if you would. I was to lay whatever of station or fortune I might possess at your feet, and if you still adhered to your former determination, I pledged myself, by no word or act, to seek to change it."

"The same reasons which influenced me then, will influence me now," said Rose firmly. "If I ever owed a strict and rigid duty to her, whose goodness saved me from a life of indigence and suffering, when should I ever feel it, as I should to-night? It is a struggle," said Rose, "but one I am proud to make; it is a pang, but one my heart shall bear."

"The disclosure of to-night,—" Harry began.

"The disclosure of to-night," replied Rose softly, "leaves me in the same position, with reference to you, as that in which I stood before."

"You harden your heart against me, Rose," urged her lover.

"Oh, Harry, Harry," said the young lady, bursting into tears; "I wish I could, and spare myself this pain."

"Then why inflict it on yourself?" said Harry, taking her hand. "Think, dear Rose, think what you have heard to-night."

"And what have I heard! What have I heard!" cried Rose. "That a sense of his deep disgrace so worked upon my own father that he shunned all—there, we have said enough, Harry, we have said enough."

"Not yet, not yet," said the young man, detaining her as she rose. "My hopes, my wishes, prospects, feeling: every thought in life except my love for you: have undergone a change. I offer you, now, no distinction among a bustling crowd; no mingling with a world of malice and detraction, where the blood is called into honest cheeks by aught but real disgrace and shame; but a home—a heart and home—yes, dearest Rose, and those, and those alone, are all I have to offer."

"What do you mean!" she faltered.

"I mean but this—that when I left you last, I left you with a firm determination to level all fancied barriers between yourself and me; resolved that if my world could not be yours, I would make yours mine; that no pride of birth should curl the lip at you, for I would turn from it. This I have done. Those who have shrunk from me because of this, have shrunk from you, and proved you so far right. Such power and patronage: such relatives of influence and rank: as smiled upon me then, look coldly now; but there are smiling fields and waving trees in England's richest county; and by one village church—mine, Rose, my own —there stands a rustic dwelling which you can make me prouder of, than all the hopes I have renounced, measured a thousandfold. This is *my* rank and station now, and here I lay it down."

. . . . . .

"It's a trying thing waiting supper for lovers," said Mr Grimwig, waking up, and pulling his pocket-handkerchief from over his head.

Truth to tell, the supper had been waiting a most unreasonable time. Neither Mrs. Maylie, nor Harry, nor Rose (who all came in together), could offer a word in extenuation.

"I had serious thoughts of eating my head to-night," said Mr. Grimwig, "for I began to think I should get nothing else. I'll take the liberty, if you'll allow me, of saluting the bride that is to be."

Mr. Grimwig lost no time in carrying this notice into effect upon the blushing girl; and the example, being contagious, was followed both by the doctor and Mr. Brownlow. Some people affirm that Harry Maylie had been observed to set it, originally, in a dark room adjoining; but the best authorities consider this downright scandal: he being young and a clergyman.

"Oliver, my child," said Mrs. Maylie, "where have you been, and why do you look so sad? There are tears stealing down your face at this moment. What is the matter?"

It is a world of disappointment: often to the hopes we most cherish, and hopes that do our nature the greatest honour.

Poor Dick was dead!

CHAPTER LII.

THE JEW'S LAST NIGHT ALIVE.

THE court was paved, from floor to roof, with human faces. Inquisitive and eager eyes peered from every inch of space. From the rail before the dock, away into the sharpest angle of the smallest corner in the galleries, all looks were fixed upon one man—the Jew. Before him and behind: above, below, on the right and on the left: he seemed to stand surrounded by a firmament, all bright with gleaming eyes.

He stood there, in all this glare of living light, with one hand resting on the wooden slab before him, the other held to his ear, and his head thrust forward to enable him to catch with greater distinctness every word that fell from the presiding judge, who was delivering his charge to the jury. At times, he turned his eyes sharply upon them to observe the effect of the slightest featherweight in his favour; and when the points against him were stated with terrible distinctness, looked towards his counsel, in mute appeal that he would, even then, urge something in his behalf. Beyond these manifestations of anxiety, he stirred not hand or foot. He had scarcely moved since the trial began; and now that the judge ceased to speak, he still remained in the same strained attitude of close attention, with his gaze bent on him, as though he listened still.

A slight bustle in the court, recalled him to himself. Looking round, he saw that the jurymen had turned together, to consider of their verdict. As his eyes wandered to the gallery, he could see the people rising above each other to see his face: some hastily applying their glasses to their eyes: and others whispering their neighbours with looks expressive of abhorrence. A few there were, who seemed unmindful of him, and looked only at the jury, in impatient wonder how they could delay. But in no one face—not even among the women, of whom there were many there—could he read the faintest sympathy with himself, or any feeling but one of all-absorbing interest that he should be condemned.

As he saw all this in one bewildered glance, the death-like stillness came again, and looking back, he saw that the jurymen had turned towards the judge. Hush!

They only sought permission to retire.

He looked, wistfully, into their faces, one by one, when they passed out, as though to see which way the greater number leant; but that was fruitless. The jailer touched him on the shoulder. He followed mechanically to the end of the dock, and sat down on a chair. The man pointed it out, or he would not have seen it.

He looked up into the gallery again. Some of the people were eating, and some fanning themselves with handkerchiefs; for the crowded place was very hot. There was one young man sketching his face in a little note-book. He wondered whether it was like, and looked on when the artist broke his pencil-point, and made another with his knife, as any idle spectator might have done.

In the same way, when he turned his eyes towards the judge, his mind began to busy itself with the fashion of his dress, and what it cost, and how he put it on. There was an old fat gentleman on the bench, too, who had gone out, some half an hour before, and now come back. He wondered within himself whether this man had been to get his dinner, what he had had, and where he had had it; and pursued this train of careless thought until some new object caught his eye and roused another.

Not that, all this time, his mind was, for an instant, free from one oppressive overwhelming sense of the grave that opened at his feet; it was ever present to him, but in a vague and general way, and he could not fix his thoughts upon it. Thus, even while he trembled, and turned burning hot at the idea of speedy death, he fell to counting the iron spikes before him, and wondering how the head of one had been broken off, and whether they would mend it or leave it as it was. Then, he thought of all the horrors of the gallows and the scaffold—and stopped to watch a man sprinkling the floor to cool it—and then went on to think again.

At length there was a cry of silence, and a breathless look from all towards the door. The jury returned, and passed him close. He could glean nothing from their faces; they might as well have been of stone. Perfect stillness ensued—not a rustle—not a breath— Guilty.

The building rang with a tremendous shout, and another, and another, and then it echoed deep loud groans, that gathered strength as they swelled out, like angry thunder. It was a peal of joy from the populace outside, greeting the news that he would die on Monday.

The noise subsided, and he was asked if he had anything to say why sentence of death should not be passed upon him. He had resumed his listening attitude, and looked intently at his questioner while the demand was made; but it was twice repeated before he seemed to hear it, and then he only muttered that he was an old man—an old man—an old man—and so, dropping into a whisper, was silent again.

The judge assumed the black cap, and the prisoner still stood with the same air and gesture. A woman in the gallery uttered some exclamation, called forth by this dread solemnity; he looked hastily up as if angry at the interruption, and bent forward yet more attentively. The address was solemn and impressive; the sentence fearful to hear. But he stood, like a marble figure, without the motion of a nerve. His haggard face was still thrust forward, his under-jaw hanging down, and his eyes staring out before him, when the jailer put his hand upon his arm, and beckoned him away. He gazed stupidly about him for an instant, and obeyed.

They led him through a paved room under the court, where some prisoners were waiting till their turns came, and others were talking to their friends, who crowded round a grate which looked into the open yard. There was nobody there, to speak to *him;* but, as he passed, the prisoners fell back to render him more visible to the people who were clinging to the bars: and they assailed him with opprobrious names, and screeched and hissed. He shook his fist, and would have spat upon them; but his conductors hurried him on, through a gloomy passage lighted by a few dim lamps, into the interior of the prison.

Here, he was searched, that he might not have about him the means of anticipating the law; this ceremony performed, they led him to one of the condemned cells, and left him there—alone.

He sat down on a stone bench opposite the door, which served for seat and bedstead; and casting his blood-shot eyes upon the ground, tried to collect his thoughts. After awhile, he began to remember a few disjointed fragments of what the judge had said: though it had seemed to him, at the time, that he could not hear a word. These gradually fell into their proper places, and by degrees suggested more: so that in a little time he had the whole, almost as it was delivered. To be hanged by the neck, till he was dead—that was the end. To be hanged by the neck till he was dead.

As it came on very dark, he began to think of all the men he had known who had died upon the scaffold; some of them through his means. They rose up, in such quick succession, that he could hardly count them. He had seen some of them die,—and had joked too, because they died with prayers upon their lips. With what a rattling noise the drop went down; and how suddenly they changed, from strong and vigorous men to dangling heaps of clothes!

Some of them might have inhabited that very cell—sat upon that very spot. It was very dark; why didn't they bring a light? The cell had been built for many years. Scores of men must have passed their last hours there. It was like sitting in a vault strewn with dead bodies—the cap, the noose, the pinioned arms, the faces that he knew, even beneath that hideous veil.—Light, light!

At length, when his hands were raw with beating against the heavy door and walls, two men appeared: one bearing a candle, which he thrust into an iron candlestick fixed against the wall: the other dragging in a mattress on which to pass the night; for the prisoner was to be left alone no more.

Then came night—dark, dismal, silent night. Other watchers are glad to hear the church-clocks strike, for they tell of life and coming day. To the Jew they brought despair. The boom of every iron bell came laden with the one, deep, hollow sound—Death. What availed the noise and bustle of cheerful morning, which penetrated even there, to him? It was another form of knell, with mockery added to the warning.

The day passed off. Day! There was no day; it was gone as soon as come—and night came on again; night so long, and yet so short; long in its dreadful silence, and short in its fleeting hours. At one time he raved and blasphemed; and at another howled and tore his hair. Venerable men of his own persuasion had come to pray beside him, but he had driven them away with curses. They renewed their charitable efforts, and he beat them off.

Saturday night. He had only one night more to live. And as he thought of this, the day broke—Sunday.

It was not until the night of this last awful day, that a withering sense of his helpless, desperate state came in its full intensity upon his blighted soul; not that he had ever held any defined or positive hope of mercy, but that he had never been able to consider more than the dim probability of dying so soon. He had spoken little to either of the two men, who relieved each other in their attendance upon him; and they, for their parts, made no effort to rouse his attention. He had sat there, awake, but dreaming. Now, he started up, every minute, and with gasping mouth and burning skin, hurried to and fro, in such a paroxysm of fear and wrath that even they—used to such sights—recoiled from him with horror. He grew so terrible, at last, in all the tortures of his evil conscience, that one man could not bear to sit there, eyeing him alone; and so the two kept watch together.

He cowered down upon his stone bed, and thought of the past. He had been wounded with some missiles from the crowd on the day of his capture, and his head was bandaged with a linen cloth. His red hair hung down upon his bloodless face; his beard was torn, and twisted into knots; his eyes shone with a terrible light; his unwashed flesh crackled with the fever that burnt him up. Eight—nine—ten. If it was not a trick to frighten him, and those were the real hours treading on each other's heels, where would he be, when they came round again! Eleven! Another struck, before the voice of the previous hour had ceased to vibrate. At eight, he would be the only mourner in his own funeral train; at eleven——

Those dreadful walls of Newgate, which have hidden so much misery and such unspeakable anguish, not only from the eyes, but, too often and too long, from the thoughts, of men, never held so dread a spectacle as that. The few who lingered as they passed, and wondered what the man was doing who was to be hanged to-morrow, would have slept but ill that night, if they could have seen him.

From early in the evening until nearly midnight, little groups of two and three presented themselves at the lodge-gate, and inquired, with anxious faces, whether any reprieve had been received. These being answered in the negative, communicated the welcome intelligence to clusters in the street, who pointed out to one another the door from which he must come out, and showed where the scaffold would be built, and, walking with unwilling steps away, turned back to conjure up the scene. By degrees they fell off, one by one; and, for an hour, in the dead of night, the street was left to solitude and darkness.

The space before the prison was cleared, and a few strong barriers, painted black, had been already thrown across the road to break the pressure of the expected crowd, when Mr. Brownlow and Oliver appeared at the wicket, and presented an order of admission to the prisoner, signed by one of the sheriffs. They were immediately admitted into the lodge.

"Is the young gentleman to come too, Sir?" said the man whose duty it was to conduct them. "It's not a sight for children, Sir."

"It is not indeed, my friend," rejoined Mr. Brownlow; "but my business with this man is intimately connected with him; and as this child has seen him in the full career of his success and villany, I think it well—even at the cost of some pain and fear—that he should see him now."

These few words had been said apart, so as to be inaudible to Oliver. The man touched his hat; and glancing at Oliver with some curiosity, opened another gate, opposite to that by which they had entered, and led them on, through dark and winding ways, towards the cells.

"This," said the man, stopping in a gloomy passage where a couple of workmen were making some preparations in profound silence,—"this is the place he passes through. If you step this way, you can see the door he goes out at."

He led them into a stone kitchen, fitted with coppers for dressing the prison food, and pointed to a door. There was an open grating above it, through which came the sound of men's voices, mingled with the noise of hammering, and the throwing down of boards. They were putting up the scaffold.

From this place, they passed through several strong gates, opened by other turnkeys from the inner side; and, having entered an open yard, ascended a flight of narrow steps, and came into a passage with a row of strong doors on the left hand. Motioning them to remain where they were, the turnkey knocked at one of these with his bunch of keys. The two attendants, after a little whispering, came out into the passage, stretching themselves as if glad of the temporary relief, and motioned the visitors to follow the jailer into the cell. They did so.

The condemned criminal was seated on his bed, rocking himself from side to side, with a countenance more like that of a snared beast than the face of a man. His mind was evidently wandering to his old life, for he continued to mutter, without appearing conscious of their presence otherwise than as a part of his vision.

"Good boy, Charley — well done —" he mumbled. "Oliver too, ha! ha! ha! Oliver too—quite the gentleman now—quite the—take that boy away to bed!"

The jailer took the disengaged hand of Oliver; and, whispering him not to be alarmed, looked on without speaking.

"Take him away to bed!" cried the Jew. "Do you hear me, some of you? He has been the—the—somehow the cause of all this. It's worth the money to bring him up to it—Bolter's throat, Bill; never mind the girl—Bolter's throat as deep as you can cut. Saw his head off!"

"Fagin," said the jailer.

"That's me!" cried the Jew, falling, instantly, into the attitude of listening he had assumed upon his trial. "An old man, my Lord; a very old, old man!"

"Here," said the turnkey, laying his hand upon his breast to keep him down. "Here's somebody wants to see you, to ask you some questions, I suppose. Fagin, Fagin! Are you a man?"

"I shan't be one long," replied the Jew, looking up with a face retaining no human expression but rage and terror. "Strike them all dead! What right have they to butcher me?"

As he spoke, he caught sight of Oliver and Mr. Brownlow. Shrinking to the furthest corner of the seat, he demanded to know what they wanted there.

"Steady," said the turnkey, still holding him down. "Now, Sir, tell him what you want—quick, if you please, for he grows worse as the time gets on."

"You have some papers," said Mr. Brownlow advancing, "which were placed in your hands, for better security, by a man called Monks."

"It's all a lie together," replied the Jew. "I haven't one—not one."

"For the love of God," said Mr. Brownlow solemnly, "do not say that now, upon the very verge of death; but tell me where they are. You know that Sikes is dead; that Monks has confessed; that there is no hope of any further gain. Where are those papers?"

"Oliver," cried the Jew, beckoning to him. "Here, here! Let me whisper to you."

"I am not afraid," said Oliver in a low voice, as he relinquished Mr. Brownlow's hand.

"The papers," said the Jew, drawing him towards him, "are in a canvas bag, in a hole a little way up the chimney in the top front-room. I want to talk to you, my dear. I want to talk to you."

"Yes, yes," returned Oliver. "Let me say a prayer.

Do! Let me say one prayer. Say only one, upon your knees, with me, and we will talk till morning."

"Outside, outside," replied the Jew, pushing the boy before him towards the door, and looking vacantly over his head. "Say I've gone to sleep—they'll believe *you*. You can get me out, if you take me so. Now then, now then!"

"Oh! God forgive this wretched man!" cried the boy with a burst of tears.

"That's right, that's right," said the Jew. "That'll help us on. This door first. If I shake and tremble, as we pass the gallows, don't you mind, but hurry on. Now, now, now!"

"Have you nothing else to ask him, Sir?" inquired the turnkey.

"No other question," replied Mr. Brownlow. "If I hoped we could recall him to a sense of his position—"

"Nothing will do that, Sir," replied the man, shaking his head. "You had better leave him."

The door of the cell opened, and the attendants returned.

"Press on, press on," cried the Jew. "Softly, but not so slow. Faster, faster!"

The men laid hands upon him, and disengaging Oliver from his grasp, held him back. He struggled with the power of desperation, for an instant; and, then sent up cry upon cry that penetrated even those massive walls, and rang in their ears until they reached the open yard.

It was some time before they left the prison. Oliver nearly swooned after this frightful scene, and was so weak that for an hour or more, he had not the strength to walk.

Day was dawning when they again emerged. A great multitude had already assembled; the windows were filled with people, smoking and playing cards to beguile the time; the crowd were pushing, quarrelling, and joking. Everything told of life and animation, but one dark cluster of objects in the very centre of all—the black stage, the cross-beam, the rope, and all the hideous apparatus of death.

CHAPTER LIII.

AND LAST.

THE fortunes of those who have figured in this tale are nearly closed. The little that remains to their historian to relate, is told in few and simple words.

Before three months had passed, Rose Fleming and Harry Maylie were married in the village church which was henceforth to be the scene of the young clergyman's labours; on the same day they entered into possession of their new and happy home.

Mrs. Maylie took up her abode with her son and daughter-in-law, to enjoy, during the tranquil remainder of her days, the greatest felicity that age and worth can know—the contemplation of the happiness of those on whom the warmest affections and tenderest cares of a well-spent life, have been unceasingly bestowed.

It appeared, on full and careful investigation, that if the wreck of property remaining in the custody of Monks (which had never prospered either in his hands or in those of his mother) were equally divided between himself and Oliver, it would yield, to each, little more than three thousand pounds. By the provisions of his father's will, Oliver would have been entitled to the whole; but Mr. Brownlow, unwilling to deprive the elder son of the oppor-

tunity of retrieving his former vices and pursuing an honest career, proposed this mode of distribution, to which his young charge joyfully acceded.

Monks, still bearing that assumed name, retired with his portion to a distant part of the New World: where, having quickly squandered it, he once more fell into his old courses, and, after undergoing a long confinement for some fresh act of fraud and knavery, at length sank under an attack of his old disorder, and died in prison. As far from home, died the chief remaining members of his friend Fagin's gang.

Mr. Brownlow adopted Oliver as his own son. Removing with him and the old housekeeper to within a mile of the parsonage-house, where his dear friends resided, he gratified the only remaining wish of Oliver's warm and earnest heart, and thus linked together a little society, whose condition approached as nearly to one of perfect happiness as can ever be known in this changing world.

Soon after the marriage of the young people, the worthy doctor returned to Chertsey, where, bereft of the presence of his old friends, he would have been discontented if his temperament had admitted of such a feeling; and would have turned quite peevish if he had known how. For two or three months, he contented himself with hinting that he feared the air began to disagree with him; then, finding that the place really was, to him, no longer what it had been before, he settled his business on his assistant, took a bachelor's cottage just outside the village of which his young friend was pastor, and instantaneously recovered. Here, he took to gardening, planting, fishing, carpentering, and various other pursuits of a similar kind: all undertaken with his characteristic impetuosity; and in each and all, he has since become famous throughout the neighbourhood, as a most profound authority.

Before his removal, he had managed to contract a strong friendship for Mr. Grimwig, which that eccentric gentleman cordially reciprocated. He is accordingly visited by him a great many times in the course of the year. On all such occasions, Mr. Grimwig plants, fishes, and carpenters, with great ardour; doing everything in a very singular and unprecedented manner, but always maintaining, with his favourite asseveration, that his mode is the right one. On Sundays, he never fails to criticise the sermon to the young clergyman's face: always informing Mr. Losberne, in strict confidence afterwards, that he considers it an excellent performance, but deems it as well not to say so. It is a standing and very favourite joke for Mr. Brownlow to rally him on his old prophecy concerning Oliver, and to remind him of the night on which they sat, with the watch between them, waiting his return; but Mr. Grimwig contends that he was right in the main, and, in proof thereof, remarks that Oliver *did not come back*, after all: which always calls forth a laugh on his side, and increases his good humour.

Mr. Noah Claypole: receiving a free pardon from the Crown in consequence of being admitted approver against the Jew: and considering his profession not altogether as safe a one as he could wish: was, for some little time, at a loss for the means of a livelihood, not burthened with too much work. After some consideration, he went into business as an Informer, in which calling he realises a genteel subsistence. His plan is, to walk out once a week during church time, attended by Charlotte in respectable attire. The lady faints away at the doors of charitable publicans, and the gentleman being accommodated with threepenny-worth of brandy to restore her, lays an information next day, and pockets half the penalty. Sometimes Mr. Claypole faints himself, but the result is the same.

Mr. and Mrs. Bumble, deprived of their situations, were gradually reduced to great indigence and misery, and finally became paupers in that very same workhouse in which they had once lorded it over others. Mr. Bumble has been heard to say, that in this reverse and degradation, he has not even spirits to be thankful for being separated from his wife.

As to Mr. Giles and Brittles, they still remain in their old posts, although the former is bald, and the last-named boy quite grey. They sleep at the parsonage, but divide their attentions so equally among its inmates, and Oliver, and Mr. Brownlow, and Mr. Losberne, that to this day the villagers have never been able to discover to which establishment they properly belong.

Master Charles Bates, appalled by Sikes's crime, fell into a train of reflection whether an honest life was not, after all, the best. Arriving at the conclusion that it certainly was, he turned his back upon the scenes of the past, resolved to amend it in some new sphere of action. He struggled hard, and suffered much, for some time; but having a contented disposition, and a good purpose, succeeded in the end; and, from being a farmer's drudge, and a carrier's lad, is now the merriest young grazier in all Northamptonshire.

And now, the hand that traces these words, falters, as it approaches the conclusion of its task: and would weave, for a little longer space, the thread of these adventures.

I would fain linger yet with a few of those among whom I have so long moved, and share their happiness by endeavouring to depict it. I would show Rose Maylie in all the bloom and grace of early womanhood, shedding on her secluded path in life such soft and gentle light, as fell on all who trod it with her, and shone into their hearts. I would paint her the life and joy of the fireside circle and the lively summer group; I would follow her through the sultry fields at noon, and hear the low tones of her sweet voice in the moonlit evening walk; I would watch her in all her goodness and charity abroad, and the smiling untiring discharge of domestic duties at home; I would paint her and her dead sister's child happy in their mutual love, and passing whole hours together in picturing the friends whom they had so sadly lost; I would summon before me, once again, those joyous little faces that clustered round her knee, and listen to their merry prattle; I would recall the tones of that clear laugh, and conjure up the sympathising tear that glistened in the soft blue eye. These, and a thousand looks and smiles, and turns of thought and speech—I would fain recall them every one.

How Mr. Brownlow went on, from day to day, filling the mind of his adopted child with stores of knowledge, and becoming attached to him, more and more, as his nature developed itself, and showed the thriving seeds of all he wished him to become—how he traced in him new traits of his early friend, that awakened in his own bosom old remembrances, melancholy and yet sweet and soothing —how the two orphans, tried by adversity, remembered its lessons in mercy to others, and mutual love, and fervent thanks to Him who had protected and preserved them— these are all matters which need not to be told. I have said that they were truly happy; and without strong affection and humanity of heart, and gratitude to that Being whose code is Mercy, and whose great attribute is Benevolence to all things that breathe, true happiness can never be attained.

Within the altar of the old village church there stands a white marble tablet, which bears as yet but one word: "AGNES." There is no coffin in that tomb; and may it be many, many years, before another name is placed above it! But, if the spirits of the Dead ever come back to earth, to visit spots hallowed by the love—the love beyond the grave —of those whom they knew in life, I believe that the shade of Agnes sometimes hovers round that solemn nook. I believe it none the less because that nook is in a church, and she was weak and erring.

A Christmas Carol

HE HAD BEEN TIM'S BLOOD HORSE ALL THE WAY FROM
CHURCH, AND HAD COME HOME RAMPANT.

A Christmas Carol

In Prose

Being A Ghost Story of Christmas

by

Charles Dickens

With Illustrations

ILLUSTRATIONS

TO

A CHRISTMAS CAROL.

A CHRISTMAS CAROL.

STAVE ONE.

MARLEY'S GHOST.

MARLEY was dead: to begin with. There is no doubt whatever about that. The register of his burial was signed by the clergyman, the clerk, the undertaker, and the chief mourner. Scrooge signed it: and Scrooge's name was good upon 'Change, for anything he chose to put his hand to. Old Marley was as dead as a door-nail.

Mind! I don't mean to say that I know, of my own knowledge, what there is particularly dead about a door-nail. I might have been inclined, myself, to regard a coffin-nail as the deadest piece of ironmongery in the trade. But the wisdom of our ancestors is in the simile; and my unhallowed hands shall not disturb it, or the Country's done for. You will therefore permit me to repeat, emphatically, that Marley was as dead as a door-nail.

Scrooge knew he was dead? Of course he did. How could it be otherwise? Scrooge and he were partners for I don't know how many years. Scrooge was his sole executor, his sole administrator, his sole assign, his sole residuary legatee, his sole friend and sole mourner. And even Scrooge was not so dreadfully cut up by the sad event, but that he was an excellent man of business on the very day of the funeral, and solemnised it with an undoubted bargain.

The mention of Marley's funeral brings me back to the point I started from. There is no doubt that Marley was dead. This must be distinctly understood, or nothing wonderful can come of the story I am going to relate. If we were not perfectly convinced that Hamlet's Father died before the play began, there would be nothing more remarkable in his taking a stroll at night, in an easterly wind, upon his own ramparts, than there would be in any other middle-aged gentleman rashly turning out after dark in a breezy spot—say Saint Paul's Churchyard for instance—literally to astonish his son's weak mind.

Scrooge never painted out Old Marley's name. There it stood, years afterwards, above the warehouse door: Scrooge and Marley. The firm was known as Scrooge and Marley. Sometimes people new to the business called Scrooge Scrooge, and sometimes Marley, but he answered to both names: it was all the same to him.

Oh! But he was a tight-fisted hand at the grindstone, Scrooge! a squeezing, wrenching, grasping, scraping, clutching, covetous, old sinner! Hard and sharp as flint, from which no steel had ever struck out generous fire; secret, and self-contained, and solitary as an oyster. The cold within him froze his old features, nipped his pointed nose, shrivelled his cheek, stiffened his gait; made his eyes red, his thin lips blue; and spoke out shrewdly in his grating voice. A frosty rime was on his head, and on his eyebrows, and his wiry chin. He carried his own low temperature always about with him; he iced his office in the dog-days; and didn't thaw it one degree at Christmas.

External heat and cold had little influence on Scrooge. No warmth could warm, nor wintry weather chill him. No wind that blew was bitterer than he, no falling snow was more intent upon its purpose, no pelting rain less open to entreaty. Foul weather didn't know where to have him. The heaviest rain, and snow, and hail, and sleet, could boast of the advantage over him in only one respect. They often "came down" handsomely, and Scrooge never did.

Nobody ever stopped him in the street to say, with gladsome looks, "My dear Scrooge, how are you? When will you come to see me?" No beggars implored him to bestow a trifle, no children asked him what it was o'clock, no man or woman ever once in all his life inquired the way to such and such a place, of Scrooge. Even the blind men's dogs appeared to know him; and when they saw him coming on, would tug their owners into doorways and up courts; and then would wag their tails as though they said, "No eye at all is better than an evil eye, dark master!"

But what did Scrooge care? It was the very thing he liked. To edge his way along the crowded paths of life, warning all human sympathy to keep its distance, was what the knowing ones call "nuts" to Scrooge.

Once upon a time—of all the good days in the year, on Christmas Eve—old Scrooge sat busy in his counting-house. It was cold, bleak, biting weather: foggy withal: and he could hear the people in the court outside go wheezing up and down, beating their hands upon their breasts, and stamping their feet upon the pavement-stones to warm them. The City clocks had only just gone three, but it was quite dark already: it had not been light all day: and candles were flaring in the windows of the neighbouring offices, like ruddy smears upon the palpable brown air. The fog came pouring in at every chink and keyhole, and was so dense without, that although the court was of the narrowest, the houses opposite were mere phantoms. To see the dingy cloud come drooping down, obscuring everything, one might have thought that Nature lived hard by, and was brewing on a large scale.

The door of Scrooge's counting-house was open that he might keep his eye upon his clerk, who in a dismal little cell beyond, a sort of tank, was copying letters. Scrooge had a very small fire, but the clerk's fire was so very much smaller that it looked like one coal. But he couldn't replenish it, for Scrooge kept the coal-box in his own room; and so surely as the clerk came in with the shovel, the master predicted that it would be necessary for them to part. Wherefore the clerk put on his white comforter, and tried to warm himself at the candle; in which effort, not being a man of a strong imagination, he failed.

"A merry Christmas, uncle! God save you!" cried a cheerful voice. It was the voice of Scrooge's nephew, who came upon him so quickly that this was the first intimation he had of his approach.

"Bah!" said Scrooge, "Humbug!"

He had so heated himself with rapid walking in the fog and frost, that this nephew of Scrooge's, that he was all in a glow; his face was ruddy and handsome; his eyes sparkled, and his breath smoked again.

"Christmas a humbug, uncle!" said Scrooge's nephew. "You don't mean that, I am sure."

"I do," said Scrooge. "Merry Christmas! What right have you to be merry? What reason have you to be merry? You're poor enough."

"Come, then," returned the nephew gaily. "What right

have you to be dismal? What reason have you to be morose? You're rich enough."

Scrooge having no better answer ready on the spur of the moment, said, "Bah!" again; and followed it up with "Humbug."

"Don't be cross, uncle," said the nephew.

"What else can I be," returned the uncle, "when I live in such a world of fools as this? Merry Christmas! Out upon merry Christmas! What's Christmas time to you but a time for paying bills without money; a time for finding yourself a year older, but not an hour richer; a time for balancing your books and having every item in 'em through a round dozen of months presented dead against you? If I could work my will," said Scrooge, indignantly, "every idiot who goes about with 'Merry Christmas,' on his lips, should be boiled with his own pudding, and buried with a stake of holly through his heart. He should!"

"Uncle!" pleaded the nephew.

"Nephew!" returned the uncle, sternly, "keep Christmas in your own way, and let me keep it in mine."

"Keep it!" repeated Scrooge's nephew. "But you don't keep it."

"Let me leave it alone, then," said Scrooge. "Much good may it do you! Much good it has ever done you!"

"There are many things from which I might have derived good, by which I have not profited, I dare say," returned the nephew: "Christmas among the rest. But I am sure I have always thought of Christmas time, when it has come round—apart from the veneration due to its sacred name and origin, if anything belonging to it can be apart from that—as a good time: a kind, forgiving, charitable, pleasant time: the only time I know of, in the long calendar of the year, when men and women seem by one consent to open their shut-up hearts freely, and to think of people below them as if they really were fellow-passengers to the grave, and not another race of creatures bound on other journeys. And therefore, uncle, though it has never put a scrap of gold or silver in my pocket, I believe that it *has* done me good, and *will* do me good; and I say, God bless it!"

The clerk in the Tank involuntarily applauded: becoming immediately sensible of the impropriety, he poked the fire, and extinguished the last frail spark for ever.

"Let me hear another sound from *you*," said Scrooge, "and you'll keep your Christmas by losing your situation. You're quite a powerful speaker, Sir," he added, turning to his nephew. "I wonder you don't go into Parliament."

"Don't be angry, uncle. Come! Dine with us to-morrow."

Scrooge said that he would see him——yes, indeed he did. He went the whole length of the expression, and said that he would see him in that extremity first.

"But why?" cried Scrooge's nephew. "Why?"

"Why did you get married?" said Scrooge.

"Because I fell in love."

"Because you fell in love!" growled Scrooge, as if that were the only one thing in the world more ridiculous than a merry Christmas. "Good afternoon!"

"Nay, uncle, but you never came to see me before that happened. Why give it as a reason for not coming now?"

"Good afternoon," said Scrooge.

"I want nothing from you; I ask nothing of you; why cannot we be friends?"

"Good afternoon," said Scrooge.

"I am sorry, with all my heart, to find you so resolute. We have never had any quarrel, to which I have been a

party. But I have made the trial in homage to Christmas, and I'll keep my Christmas humour to the last. So A Merry Christmas, uncle!"

"Good afternoon!" said Scrooge.

"And A Happy New Year!"

"Good afternoon!" said Scrooge.

His nephew left the room without an angry word, notwithstanding. He stopped at the outer door to bestow the greetings of the season on the clerk, who, cold as he was, was warmer than Scrooge; for he returned them cordially.

"There's another fellow," muttered Scrooge; who overheard him: "my clerk, with fifteen shillings a week, and a wife and family, talking about a merry Christmas. I'll retire to Bedlam."

This lunatic, in letting Scrooge's nephew out, had let two other people in. They were portly gentlemen, pleasant to behold, and now stood, with their hats off, in Scrooge's office. They had books and papers in their hands, and bowed to him.

"Scrooge and Marley's, I believe," said one of the gentlemen, referring to his list. "Have I the pleasure of addressing Mr. Scrooge, or Mr. Marley?"

"Mr. Marley has been dead these seven years," Scrooge replied. "He died seven years ago, this very night."

"We have no doubt his liberality is well represented by his surviving partner," said the gentleman, presenting his credentials.

It certainly was; for they had been two kindred spirits. At the ominous word "liberality," Scrooge frowned, and shook his head, and handed the credentials back.

"At this festive season of the year, Mr. Scrooge," said the gentleman, taking up a pen, "it is more than usually desirable that we should make some slight provision for the poor and destitute, who suffer greatly at the present time. Many thousands are in want of common necessaries; hundreds of thousands are in want of common comforts, Sir."

"Are there no prisons?" asked Scrooge.

"Plenty of prisons," said the gentleman, laying down the pen again.

"And the Union workhouses?" demanded Scrooge. "Are they still in operation?"

"They are. Still," returned the gentleman, "I wish I could say they were not."

"The Treadmill and the Poor Law are in full vigour, then?" said Scrooge.

"Both very busy, Sir."

"Oh! I was afraid, from what you said at first, that something had occurred to stop them in their useful course," said Scrooge. "I'm very glad to hear it."

"Under the impression that they scarcely furnish Christian cheer of mind or body to the multitude," returned the gentleman, "a few of us are endeavouring to raise a fund to buy the Poor some meat and drink, and means of warmth. We choose this time, because it is a time, of all others, when Want is keenly felt, and Abundance rejoices. What shall I put you down for?"

"Nothing!" Scrooge replied.

"You wish to be anonymous?"

"I wish to be left alone," said Scrooge. "Since you ask me what I wish, gentlemen, that is my answer. I don't make merry myself at Christmas, and I can't afford to make idle people merry. I help to support the establishments I have mentioned: they cost enough: and those who are badly off must go there."

"Many can't go there; and many would rather die."

"If they would rather die," said Scrooge, "they had better do it, and decrease the surplus population. Besides—excuse me—I don't know that."

"But you might know it," observed the gentleman.

"It's not my business," Scrooge returned. "It's enough for a man to understand his own business, and not to interfere with other people's. Mine occupies me constantly. Good afternoon, gentlemen!"

Seeing clearly that it would be useless to pursue their point, the gentlemen withdrew. Scrooge resumed his labours with an improved opinion of himself, and in more facetious temper than was usual with him.

Meanwhile the fog and darkness thickened so, that the people ran about with flaring links, proffering their services to go before horses in carriages, and conduct them on their way. The ancient tower of a church, whose gruff old bell was always peeping slily down at Scrooge out of a gothic window in the wall, became invisible, and struck the hours and quarters in the clouds, with tremulous vibrations afterwards as if its teeth were chattering in its frozen head up there. The cold became intense. In the main street at the corner of the court, some labourers were repairing the gas-pipes, and had lighted a great fire in a brazier, round which a party of ragged men and boys were gathered: warming their hands and winking their eyes before the blaze in rapture. The water-plug being left in solitude, its overflowings sullenly congealed, and turned to misanthropic ice. The brightness of the shops where holly sprigs and berries crackled in the lamp heat of the windows, made pale faces ruddy as they passed. Poulterers' and grocers' trades became a splendid joke: a glorious pageant, with which it was next to impossible to believe that such dull principles as bargain and sale had anything to do. The Lord Mayor, in the stronghold of the mighty Mansion House, gave orders to his fifty cooks and butlers to keep Christmas as a Lord Mayor's household should; and even the little tailor, whom he had fined five shillings on the previous Monday for being drunk and bloodthirsty in the streets, stirred up to-morrow's pudding in his garret, while his lean wife and the baby sallied out to buy the beef.

Foggier yet, and colder! Piercing, searching, biting cold. If the good Saint Dunstan had but nipped the Evil Spirit's nose with a touch of such weather as that, instead of using his familiar weapons, then indeed he would have roared to lusty purpose. The owner of one scant young nose, gnawed and mumbled by the hungry cold as bones are gnawed by dogs, stooped down at Scrooge's keyhole to regale him with a Christmas carol: but at the first sound of

> "God bless you, merry gentleman!
> May nothing you dismay!"

Scrooge seized the ruler with such energy of action, that the singer fled in terror, leaving the keyhole to the fog and even more congenial frost.

At length the hour of shutting up the counting-house arrived. With an ill-will Scrooge dismounted from his stool, and tacitly admitted the fact to the expectant clerk in the Tank, who instantly snuffed his candle out, and put on his hat.

"You'll want all day to-morrow, I suppose?" said Scrooge.

"If quite convenient, Sir."

"It's not convenient," said Scrooge, "and it's not fair. If I was to stop half-a-crown for it, you'd think yourself ill-used, I'll be bound?"

The clerk smiled faintly.

"And yet," said Scrooge, "you don't think *me* ill-used, when I pay a day's wages for no work."

The clerk observed that it was only once a year.

"A poor excuse for picking a man's pocket every twenty-fifth of December!" said Scrooge, buttoning his great-coat to the chin. "But I suppose you must have the whole day. Be here all the earlier next morning!"

The clerk promised that he would; and Scrooge walked out with a growl. The office was closed in a twinkling, and the clerk, with the long ends of his white comforter dangling below his waist (for he boasted no great-coat), went down a slide on Cornhill, at the end of a lane of boys, twenty times, in honour of its being Christmas Eve, and then ran home to Camden Town as hard as he could pelt, to play at blindman's-buff.

Scrooge took his melancholy dinner in his usual melancholy tavern; and having read all the newspapers, and beguiled the rest of the evening with his banker's-book, went home to bed. He lived in chambers which had once belonged to his deceased partner. They were a gloomy suite of rooms, in a lowering pile of building up a yard, where it had so little business to be, that one could scarcely help fancying it must have run there when it was a young house, playing at hide-and-seek with other houses, and have forgotten the way out again. It was old enough now, and dreary enough, for nobody lived in it but Scrooge, the other rooms being all let out as offices. The yard was so dark that even Scrooge, who knew its every stone, was fain to grope with his hands. The fog and frost so hung about the black old gateway of the house, that it seemed as if the Genius of the Weather sat in mournful meditation on the threshold.

Now, it is a fact, that there was nothing at all particular about the knocker on the door, except that it was very large. It is also a fact, that Scrooge had seen it, night and morning, during his whole residence in that place; also that Scrooge had as little of what is called fancy about him as any man in the City of London, even including—which is a bold word—the corporation, aldermen, and livery. Let it also be borne in mind that Scrooge had not bestowed one thought on Marley, since his last mention of his seven-years' dead partner that afternoon. And then let any man explain to me, if he can, how it happened that Scrooge, having his key in the lock of the door, saw in the knocker, without its undergoing any intermediate process of change: not a knocker, but Marley's face.

Marley's face. It was not in impenetrable shadow as the other objects in the yard were, but had a dismal light about it, like a bad lobster in a dark cellar. It was not angry or ferocious, but looked at Scrooge as Marley used to look: with ghostly spectacles turned up on its ghostly forehead. The hair was curiously stirred, as if by breath or hot air; and, though the eyes were wide open, they were perfectly motionless. That, and its livid colour, made it horrible; but its horror seemed to be in spite of the face and beyond its control, rather than a part of its own expression.

As Scrooge looked fixedly at this phenomenon, it was a knocker again.

To say that he was not startled, or that his blood was not conscious of a terrible sensation to which it had been a stranger from infancy, would be untrue. But he put his hand upon the key he had relinquished, turned it sturdily, walked in, and lighted his candle.

He *did* pause, with a moment's irresolution, before he shut the door; and he *did* look cautiously behind it first, as if he half-expected to be terrified with the sight of Marley's pigtail sticking out into the hall. But there was nothing on the back of the door, except the screws and nuts that held the knocker on; so he said "Pooh, pooh!" and closed it with a bang.

The sound resounded through the house like thunder. Every room above, and every cask in the wine-merchant's cellars below, appeared to have a separate peal of echoes of its own. Scrooge was not a man to be frightened by echoes. He fastened the door, and walked across the hall, and up the stairs: slowly too: trimming his candle as he went.

You may talk vaguely about driving a coach-and-six up a good old flight of stairs, or through a bad young Act of Parliament; but I mean to say you might have got a hearse up that staircase, and taken it broadwise, with the splinter-bar towards the wall, and the door towards the balustrades: and done it easy. There was plenty of width for that, and room to spare; which is perhaps the reason why Scrooge thought he saw a locomotive hearse going on before him in the gloom. Half-a-dozen gas-lamps out of the street wouldn't have lighted the entry too well, so you may suppose that it was pretty dark with Scrooge's dip.

Up Scrooge went, not caring a button for that: darkness is cheap, and Scrooge liked it. But before he shut his heavy door, he walked through his rooms to see that all was right. He had just enough recollection of the face to desire to do that.

Sitting-room, bedroom, lumber-room. All as they should be. Nobody under the table, nobody under the sofa; a small fire in the grate; spoon and basin ready; and the little saucepan of gruel (Scrooge had a cold in his head) upon the hob. Nobody under the bed; nobody in the closet; nobody in his dressing-gown, which was hanging up in a suspicious attitude against the wall. Lumber-room as usual. Old fire-guard, old shoes, two fish-baskets, washing-stand on three legs, and a poker.

Quite satisfied, he closed his door, and locked himself in; double-locked himself in, which was not his custom. Thus secured against surprise, he took off his cravat; put on his dressing-gown and slippers, and his nightcap; and sat down before the fire to take his gruel.

It was a very low fire indeed; nothing on such a bitter night. He was obliged to sit close to it, and brood over it, before he could extract the least sensation of warmth from such a handful of fuel. The fireplace was an old one, built by some Dutch merchant long ago, and paved all round with quaint Dutch tiles, designed to illustrate the Scriptures. There were Cains and Abels, Pharaoh's daughters, Queens of Sheba, Angelic messengers descending through the air on clouds like feather-beds, Abrahams, Belshazzars, Apostles putting off to sea in butter-boats, hundreds of figures, to attract his thoughts; and yet that face of Marley, seven years dead, came like the ancient Prophet's rod, and swallowed up the whole. If each smooth tile had been a blank at first, with power to shape some picture on its surface from the disjointed fragments of his thoughts, there would have been a copy of old Marley's head on every one.

"Humbug!" said Scrooge; and walked across the room.

After several turns, he sat down again. As he threw his head back in the chair, his glance happened to rest upon a bell, a disused bell, that hung in the room, and communicated for some purpose now forgotten with a chamber in the highest story of the building. It was with great

astonishment, and with a strange, inexplicable dread, that as he looked, he saw this bell begin to swing. It swung so softly in the outset that it scarcely made a sound; but soon it rang out loudly, and so did every bell in the house.

This might have lasted half a minute, or a minute, but it seemed an hour. The bells ceased as they had begun, together. They were succeeded by a clanking noise, deep down below; as if some person were dragging a heavy chain over the casks in the wine-merchant's cellar. Scrooge then remembered to have heard that ghosts in haunted houses were described as dragging chains.

The cellar-door flew open with a booming sound, and then he heard the noise much louder, on the floors below; then coming up the stairs; then coming straight towards his door.

"It's humbug still!" said Scrooge. "I won't believe it."

His colour changed though, when, without a pause, it came on through the heavy door, and passed into the room before his eyes. Upon its coming in, the dying flame leaped up, as though it cried "I know him! Marley's Ghost!" and fell again.

The same face: the very same. Marley in his pigtail, usual waistcoat, tights and boots; the tassels on the latter bristling, like his pigtail, and his coat-skirts, and the hair upon his head. The chain he drew was clasped about his middle. It was long, and wound about him like a tail; and it was made (for Scrooge observed it closely) of cash-boxes, keys, padlocks, ledgers, deeds, and heavy purses wrought in steel. His body was transparent; so that Scrooge, observing him, and looking through his waistcoat, could see the two buttons on his coat behind.

Scrooge had often heard it said that Marley had no bowels, but he had never believed it until now.

No, nor did he believe it even now. Though he looked the phantom through and through, and saw it standing before him; though he felt the chilling influence of its death-cold eyes; and marked the very texture of the folded kerchief bound about its head and chin, which wrapper he had not observed before: he was still incredulous, and fought against his senses.

"How now!" said Scrooge, caustic and cold as ever. "What do you want with me?"

"Much!"—Marley's voice, no doubt about it.

"Who are you?"

"Ask me who I was."

"Who were you then?" said Scrooge, raising his voice. "You're particular—for a shade." He was going to say "to a shade," but substituted this, as more appropriate.

"In life I was your partner, Jacob Marley."

"Can you—can you sit down?" asked Scrooge, looking doubtfully at him.

"I can."

"Do it then."

Scrooge asked the question, because he didn't know whether a ghost so transparent might find himself in a condition to take a chair; and felt that in the event of its being impossible, it might involve the necessity of an embarrassing explanation. But the Ghost sat down on the opposite side of the fireplace, as if he were quite used to it.

"You don't believe in me," observed the Ghost.

"I don't," said Scrooge.

"What evidence would you have of my reality beyond that of your senses?"

"I don't know," said Scrooge.

"Why do you doubt your senses?"

"Because," said Scrooge, "a little thing affects them. A slight disorder of the stomach makes them cheats. You may be an undigested bit of beef, a blot of mustard, a crumb of cheese, a fragment of an underdone potato. There's more of gravy than of grave about you, whatever you are!"

Scrooge was not much in the habit of cracking jokes, nor did he feel, in his heart, by any means waggish then. The truth is, that he tried to be smart, as a means of distracting his own attention, and keeping down his terror; for the spectre's voice disturbed the very marrow in his bones.

To sit, staring at those fixed, glazed eyes, in silence for a moment, would play, Scrooge felt, the very deuce with him. There was something very awful, too, in the spectre's being provided with an infernal atmosphere of its own. Scrooge could not feel it himself, but this was clearly the case; for though the Ghost sat perfectly motionless, its hair, and skirts, and tassels, were still agitated as by the hot vapour from an oven.

"You see this toothpick?" said Scrooge, returning quickly to the charge, for the reason just assigned; and wishing, though it were only for a second, to divert the vision's stony gaze from himself.

"I do," replied the Ghost.

"You are not looking at it," said Scrooge.

"But I see it," said the Ghost, "notwithstanding."

"Well!" returned Scrooge. "I have but to swallow this, and be for the rest of my days persecuted by a legion of goblins, all of my own creation. Humbug, I tell you —humbug!"

At this the spirit raised a frightful cry, and shook its chain with such a dismal and appalling noise, that Scrooge held on tight to his chair, to save himself from falling in a swoon. But how much greater was his horror, when the phantom taking off the bandage round its head, as if it were too warm to wear indoors, its lower jaw dropped down upon its breast!

Scrooge fell upon his knees, and clasped his hands before his face.

"Mercy!" he said. "Dreadful apparition, why do you trouble me?"

"Man of the worldly mind!" replied the Ghost, "do you believe in me or not?"

"I do," said Scrooge. "I must. But why do spirits walk the earth, and why do they come to me?"

"It is required of every man," the Ghost returned, "that the spirit within him should walk abroad among his fellowmen, and travel far and wide; and if that spirit goes not forth in life, it is condemned to do so after death. It is doomed to wander through the world—oh, woe is me!—and witness what it cannot share, but might have shared on earth, and turned to happiness!"

Again the spectre raised a cry, and shook its chain, and wrung its shadowy hands.

"You are fettered," said Scrooge, trembling. "Tell me why?"

"I wear the chain I forged in life," replied the Ghost. "I made it link by link, and yard by yard; I girded it on of my own free will, and of my own free will I wore it. Is its pattern strange to *you*?"

Scrooge trembled more and more.

"Or would you know," pursued the Ghost, "the weight and length of the strong coil you bear yourself? It was full as heavy and as long as this, seven Christmas Eves ago. You have laboured on it, since. It is a ponderous chain!"

Scrooge glanced about him on the floor, in the expectation of finding himself surrounded by some fifty or sixty fathoms of iron cable: but he could see nothing.

"Jacob," he said, imploringly. "Old Jacob Marley, tell me more. Speak comfort to me, Jacob."

"I have none to give," the Ghost replied. "It comes from other regions, Ebenezer Scrooge, and is conveyed by other ministers, to other kinds of men. Nor can I tell you what I would. A very little more, is all permitted to me. I cannot rest, I cannot stay, I cannot linger anywhere. My spirit never walked beyond our counting-house —mark me!—in life my spirit never roved beyond the narrow limits of our money-changing hole; and weary journeys lie before me!"

It was a habit with Scrooge, whenever he became thoughtful, to put his hands in his breeches pockets. Pondering on what the Ghost had said, he did so now, but without lifting up his eyes, or getting off his knees.

"You must have been very slow about it, Jacob," Scrooge observed, in a business-like manner, though with humility and deference.

"Slow!" the Ghost repeated.

"Seven years dead," mused Scrooge. "And travelling all the time!"

"The whole time," said the Ghost. "No rest, no peace. Incessant torture of remorse."

"You travel fast?" said Scrooge.

"On the wings of the wind," replied the Ghost.

"You might have got over a great quantity of ground in seven years," said Scrooge.

The Ghost, on hearing this, set up another cry, and clanked its chain so hideously in the dead silence of the night, that the Ward would have been justified in indicting it for a nuisance.

"Oh! captive, bound, and double-ironed," cried the phantom, "not to know, that ages of incessant labour, by immortal creatures, for this earth must pass into eternity before the good of which it is susceptible is all developed. Not to know that any Christian spirit working kindly in its little sphere, whatever it may be, will find its mortal life too short for its vast means of usefulness. Not to know that no space of regret can make amends for one life's opportunity misused! Yet such was I! Oh! such was I!"

"But you were always a good man of business, Jacob," faltered Scrooge, who now began to apply this to himself.

"Business!" cried the Ghost, wringing its hands again. "Mankind was my business. The common welfare was my business; charity, mercy, forbearance, and benevolence, were, all, my business. The dealings of my trade were but a drop of water in the comprehensive ocean of my business!"

It held up its chain at arm's length, as if that were the cause of all its unavailing grief, and flung it heavily upon the ground again.

"At this time of the rolling year," the spectre said, "I suffer most. Why did I walk through crowds of fellow-beings with my eyes turned down, and never raise them to that blessed Star which led the Wise Men to a poor abode! Were there no poor homes to which its light would have conducted *me*!"

473

Scrooge was very much dismayed to hear the spectre going on at this rate, and began to quake exceedingly.

"Hear me!" cried the Ghost. "My time is nearly gone."

"I will," said Scrooge. "But don't be hard upon me! Don't be flowery, Jacob! Pray!"

"How it is that I appear before you in a shape that you can see, I may not tell. I have sat invisible beside you many and many a day."

It was not an agreeable idea. Scrooge shivered, and wiped the perspiration from his brow.

"That is no light part of my penance," pursued the Ghost. "I am here to-night to warn you, that you have yet a chance and hope of escaping my fate. A chance and hope of my procuring, Ebenezer."

"You were always a good friend to me," said Scrooge. "Thank'ee!"

"You will be haunted," resumed the Ghost, "by Three Spirits."

Scrooge's countenance fell almost as low as the Ghost's had done.

"Is that the chance and hope you mentioned, Jacob?" he demanded, in a faltering voice.

"It is."

"I—I think I'd rather not," said Scrooge.

"Without their visits," said the Ghost, "you cannot hope to shun the path I tread. Expect the first to-morrow, when the bell tolls one."

"Couldn't I take 'em all at once, and have it over, Jacob?" hinted Scrooge.

"Expect the second on the next night at the same hour. The third upon the next night when the last stroke of twelve has ceased to vibrate. Look to see me no more; and look that, for your own sake, you remember what has passed between us!"

When it had said these words, the spectre took its wrapper from the table, and bound it round its head, as before. Scrooge knew this, by the smart sound its teeth made, when the jaws were brought together by the bandage. He ventured to raise his eyes again, and found his supernatural visitor confronting him in an erect attitude, with its chain wound over and about its arm.

The apparition walked backward from him; and at every step it took, the window raised itself a little, so that when the spectre reached it, it was wide open. It beckoned Scrooge to approach, which he did. When they were within two paces of each other, Marley's Ghost held up its hand, warning him to come no nearer. Scrooge stopped.

Not so much in obedience, as in surprise and fear: for on the raising of the hand, he became sensible of confused noises in the air; incoherent sounds of lamentation and regret; wailings inexpressibly sorrowful and self-accusatory. The spectre, after listening for a moment, joined in the mournful dirge; and floated out upon the bleak, dark night.

Scrooge followed to the window: desperate in his curiosity. He looked out.

The air was filled with phantoms, wandering hither and thither in restless haste, and moaning as they went. Every one of them wore chains like Marley's Ghost; some few (they might be guilty governments) were linked together; none were free. Many had been personally known to Scrooge in their lives. He had been quite familiar with one old ghost, in a white waistcoat, with a monstrous iron safe attached to its ankle, who cried piteously at being unable to assist a wretched woman with an infant, whom it saw below, upon a door-step. The misery with them all

was, clearly, that they sought to interfere, for good, in human matters, and had lost the power for ever.

Whether these creatures faded into mist, or mist enshrouded them, he could not tell. But they and their spirit voices faded together; and the night became as it had been when he walked home.

Scrooge closed the window, and examined the door by which the Ghost had entered. It was double-locked, as he had locked it with his own hands, and the bolts were undisturbed. He tried to say "Humbug!" but stopped at the first syllable. And being, from the emotion he had undergone, or the fatigues of the day, or his glimpse of the Invisible World, or the dull conversation of the Ghost, or the lateness of the hour, much in need of repose; went straight to bed, without undressing, and fell asleep upon the instant.

STAVE TWO.

THE FIRST OF THE THREE SPIRITS.

WHEN Scrooge awoke, it was so dark, that looking out of bed, he could scarcely distinguish the transparent window from the opaque walls of his chamber. He was endeavouring to pierce the darkness with his ferret eyes, when the chimes of a neighbouring church struck the four quarters. So he listened for the hour.

To his great astonishment the heavy bell went on from six to seven, and from seven to eight, and regularly up to twelve; then stopped. Twelve! It was past two when he went to bed. The clock was wrong. An icicle must have got into the works. Twelve!

He touched the spring of his repeater, to correct this most preposterous clock. Its rapid little pulse beat twelve; and stopped.

"Why, it isn't possible," said Scrooge, "that I can have slept through a whole day and far into another night. It isn't possible that anything has happened to the sun, and this is twelve at noon!"

The idea being an alarming one, he scrambled out of bed, and groped his way to the window. He was obliged to rub the frost off with the sleeve of his dressing-gown before he could see anything; and could see very little then. All he could make out was, that it was still very foggy and extremely cold, and that there was no noise of people running to and fro, and making a great stir, as there unquestionably would have been if night had beaten off bright day, and taken possession of the world. This was a great relief, because "three days after sight of this First of Exchange pay to Mr. Ebenezer Scrooge or his order," and so forth, would have become a mere United States' security if there were no days to count by.

Scrooge went to bed again, and thought, and thought, and thought it over and over and over, and could make nothing of it. The more he thought, the more perplexed he was; and the more he endeavoured not to think, the more he thought. Marley's Ghost bothered him exceedingly. Every time he resolved within himself, after mature inquiry, that it was all a dream, his mind flew back again, like a strong spring released, to its first position, and presented the same problem to be worked all through, "Was it a dream or not?"

Scrooge lay in this state until the chimes had gone three quarters more, when he remembered, on a sudden, that the Ghost had warned him of a visitation when the bell tolled one. He resolved to lie awake until the hour was passed; and, considering that he could no more go to sleep than go to Heaven, this was perhaps the wisest resolution in his power.

The quarter was so long, that he was more than once convinced he must have sunk into a doze unconsciously, and missed the clock. At length it broke upon his listening ear.

"Ding, dong!"

"A quarter past," said Scrooge, counting.

"Ding, dong!"

"Half-past!" said Scrooge.

"Ding, dong!"

"A quarter to it," said Scrooge.

"Ding, dong!"

"The hour itself," said Scrooge, triumphantly, "and nothing else!"

He spoke before the hour bell sounded, which it now did with a deep, dull, hollow, melancholy ONE. Light flashed up in the room upon the instant, and the curtains of his bed were drawn.

The curtains of his bed were drawn aside, I tell you, by a hand. Not the curtains at his feet, nor the curtains at his back, but those to which his face was addressed. The curtains of his bed were drawn aside; and Scrooge, starting up into a half-recumbent attitude, found himself face to face with the unearthly visitor who drew them: as close to it as I am now to you, and I am standing in the spirit at your elbow.

It was a strange figure—like a child: yet not so like a child as like an old man, viewed through some supernatural medium, which gave him the appearance of having receded from the view, and being diminished to a child's proportions. Its hair, which hung about its neck and down its back, was white as if with age; and yet the face had not a wrinkle in it, and the tenderest bloom was on the skin. The arms were very long and muscular; the hands the same, as if its hold were of uncommon strength. Its legs and feet, most delicately formed, were, like those upper members, bare. It wore a tunic of the purest white; and round its waist was bound a lustrous belt, the sheen of which was beautiful. It held a branch of fresh green holly in its hand; and, in singular contradiction of that wintry emblem, had its dress trimmed with summer flowers. But the strangest thing about it was, that from the crown of its head there sprang a bright clear jet of light, by which all this was visible; and which was doubtless the occasion of its using, in its duller moments, a great extinguisher for a cap, which it now held under its arm.

Even this, though, when Scrooge looked at it with increasing steadiness, was *not* its strangest quality. For as its belt sparkled and glittered now in one part and now in another, and what was light one instant, at another time was dark, so the figure itself fluctuated in its distinctness: being now a thing with one arm, now with one leg, now with twenty legs, now a pair of legs without a head, now a head without a body: of which dissolving parts, no outline would be visible in the dense gloom wherein they melted away. And in the very wonder of this, it would be itself again; distinct and clear as ever.

"Are you the Spirit, Sir, whose coming was foretold to me?" asked Scrooge.

"I am!"

The voice was soft and gentle. Singularly low, as if instead of being so close beside him, it were at a distance.

"Who, and what are you?" Scrooge demanded.

"I am the Ghost of Christmas Past."

"Long past?" inquired Scrooge: observant of its dwarfish stature.

"No. Your past."

Perhaps, Scrooge could not have told anybody why, if anybody could have asked him; but he had a special desire to see the Spirit in his cap; and begged him to be covered.

"What!" exclaimed the Ghost, "would you so soon put out, with worldly hands, the light I give? Is it not enough that you are one of those whose passions made this cap, and force me through whole trains of years to wear it low upon my brow!"

Scrooge reverently disclaimed all intention to offend, or any knowledge of having wilfully "bonneted" the Spirit at any period of his life. He then made bold to inquire what business brought him there.

"Your welfare!" said the Ghost.

Scrooge expressed himself much obliged, but could not help thinking that a night of unbroken rest would have been more conducive to that end. The spirit must have heard him thinking, for it said immediately:

"Your reclamation, then. Take heed!"

It put out its strong hand as it spoke, and clasped him gently by the arm.

"Rise! and walk with me!"

It would have been in vain for Scrooge to plead that the weather and the hour were not adapted to pedestrian purposes; that bed was warm, and the thermometer a long way below freezing; that he was clad but lightly in his slippers, dressing-gown, and nightcap; and that he had a cold upon him at that time. The grasp, though gentle as a woman's hand, was not to be resisted. He rose: but finding that the Spirit made towards the window, clasped its robe in supplication.

"I am a mortal," Scrooge remonstrated, "and liable to fall."

"Bear but a touch of my hand *there*," said the Spirit, laying it upon his heart, "and you shall be upheld in more than this!"

As the words were spoken, they passed through the wall, and stood upon an open country road, with fields on either hand. The city had entirely vanished. Not a vestige of it was to be seen. The darkness and the mist had vanished with it, for it was a clear, cold, winter day, with snow upon the ground.

"Good Heaven!" said Scrooge, clasping his hands together, as he looked about him. "I was bred in this place. I was a boy here!"

The Spirit gazed upon him mildly. Its gentle touch, though it had been light and instantaneous, appeared still present to the old man's sense of feeling. He was conscious of a thousand odours floating in the air, each one connected with a thousand thoughts, and hopes, and joys, and cares long, long forgotten!

"Your lip is trembling," said the Ghost. "And what is that upon your cheek?"

Scrooge muttered, with an unusual catching in his voice, that it was a pimple; and begged the Ghost to lead him where he would.

"You recollect the way?" inquired the Spirit.

"Remember it!" cried Scrooge with fervour—"I could walk it blindfold."

"Strange to have forgotten it for so many years!" observed the Ghost. "Let us go on."

They walked along the road; Scrooge recognising every gate, and post, and tree; until a little market-town appeared in the distance, with its bridge, its church, and winding river. Some shaggy ponies now were seen trotting towards them with boys upon their backs, who called to other boys in country gigs and carts, driven by farmers. All these boys were in great spirits, and shouted to each other, until the broad fields were so full of merry music, that the crisp air laughed to hear it.

"These are but shadows of the things that have been," said the Ghost. "They have no consciousness of us."

The jocund travellers came on; and as they came, Scrooge knew and named them every one. Why was he rejoiced beyond all bounds to see them! Why did his cold eye glisten, and his heart leap up as they went past! Why was he filled with gladness when he heard them give each other Merry Christmas, as they parted at cross-roads and bye-ways, for their several homes! What was merry Christmas to Scrooge? Out upon merry Christmas! What good had it ever done to him?

"The school is not quite deserted," said the Ghost. "A solitary child, neglected by his friends, is left there still."

Scrooge said he knew it. And he sobbed.

They left the high-road, by a well-remembered lane, and soon approached a mansion of dull red brick, with a little weathercock-surmounted cupola, on the roof, and a bell hanging in it. It was a large house, but one of broken fortunes; for the spacious offices were little used, their walls were damp and mossy, their windows broken, and their gates decayed. Fowls clucked and strutted in the stables; and the coach-houses and sheds were overrun with grass. Nor was it more retentive of its ancient state, within; for entering the dreary hall, and glancing through the open doors of many rooms, they found them poorly furnished, cold, and vast. There was an earthy savour in the air, a chilly bareness in the place, which associated itself somehow with too much getting up by candle-light, and not too much to eat.

They went, the Ghost and Scrooge, across the hall, to a door at the back of the house. It opened before them, and disclosed a long, bare, melancholy room, made barer still by lines of plain deal forms and desks. At one of these a lonely boy was reading near a feeble fire; and Scrooge sat down upon a form, and wept to see his poor forgotten self as he had used to be.

Not a latent echo in the house, not a squeak and scuffle from the mice behind the panelling, not a drip from the half-thawed water-spout in the dull yard behind, not a sigh among the leafless boughs of one despondent poplar, not the idle swinging of an empty store-house door, no, not a clicking in the fire, but fell upon the heart of Scrooge with softening influence, and gave a freer passage to his tears.

The Spirit touched him on the arm, and pointed to his younger self, intent upon his reading. Suddenly a man, in foreign garments: wonderfully real and distinct to look at: stood outside the window, with an axe stuck in his belt, and leading an ass laden with wood by the bridle.

"Why, it's Ali Baba!" Scrooge exclaimed in ecstasy. "It's dear old honest Ali Baba! Yes, yes, I know! One Christmas time, when yonder solitary child was left here all alone, he *did* come, for the first time, just like that. Poor boy! And Valentine," said Scrooge, "and his wild brother, Orson; there they go! And what's his name, who

was put down in his drawers, asleep, at the Gate of Damascus; don't you see him! And the Sultan's Groom turned upside down by the Genii; there he is upon his head! Serve him right. I'm glad of it. What business had *he* to be married to the Princess!"

To hear Scrooge expending all the earnestness of his nature on such subjects, in a most extraordinary voice between laughing and crying; and to see his heightened and excited face; would have been a surprise to his business friends in the City, indeed.

"There's the Parrot!" cried Scrooge. "Green body and yellow tail, with a thing like a lettuce growing out of the top of his head; there he is! Poor Robin Crusoe, he called him, when he came home again after sailing round the island. 'Poor Robin Crusoe, where have you been, Robin Crusoe?' The man thought he was dreaming, but he wasn't. It was the Parrot, you know. There goes Friday, running for his life to the little creek! Halloa! Hoop! Halloo!"

Then, with a rapidity of transition very foreign to his usual character, he said, in pity for his former self, "Poor boy!" and cried again.

"I wish," Scrooge muttered, putting his hand in his pocket, and looking about him, after drying his eyes with his cuff: "but it's too late now."

"What is the matter?" asked the Spirit.

"Nothing," said Scrooge. "Nothing. There was a boy singing a Christmas Carol at my door last night. I should like to have given him something: that's all."

The Ghost smiled thoughtfully, and waved its hand: saying as it did so, "Let us see another Christmas!"

Scrooge's former self grew larger at the words, and the room became a little darker and more dirty. The panels shrank, the windows cracked; fragments of plaster fell out of the ceiling, and the naked laths were shown instead; but how all this was brought about, Scrooge knew no more than you do. He only knew that it was quite correct; that everything had happened so; that there he was, alone again, when all the other boys had gone home for the jolly holidays.

He was not reading now, but walking up and down despairingly. Scrooge looked at the Ghost, and with a mournful shaking of his head, glanced anxiously towards the door.

It opened; and a little girl, much younger than the boy, came darting in, and putting her arms about his neck, and often kissing him, addressed him as her "Dear, dear brother."

"I have come to bring you home, dear brother!" said the child, clapping her tiny hands, and bending down to laugh. "To bring you home, home, home!"

"Home, little Fan?" returned the boy.

"Yes!" said the child, brimful of glee. "Home, for good and all. Home, for ever and ever. Father is so much kinder than he used to be, that home's like Heaven! He spoke so gently to me one dear night when I was going to bed, that I was not afraid to ask him once more if you might come home; and he said Yes, you should; and sent me in a coach to bring you. And you're to be a man!" said the child, opening her eyes, "and are never to come back here; but first, we're to be together all the Christmas long, and have the merriest time in all the world."

"You are quite a woman, little Fan!" exclaimed the boy.

She clapped her hands and laughed, and tried to touch

his head; but being too little, laughed again, and stood on tiptoe to embrace him. Then she began to drag him, in her childish eagerness, towards the door; and he, nothing loth to go, accompanied her.

A terrible voice in the hall cried, "Bring down Master Scrooge's box, there!" and in the hall appeared the schoolmaster himself, who glared on Master Scrooge with a ferocious condescension, and threw him into a dreadful state of mind by shaking hands with him. He then conveyed him and his sister into the veriest well of a shivering best-parlour that ever was seen, where the maps upon the wall, and the celestial and terrestrial globes in the windows, were waxy with cold. Here he produced a decanter of curiously light wine, and a block of curiously heavy cake, and administered instalments of those dainties to the young people: at the same time, sending out a meagre servant to offer a glass of "something" to the postboy, who answered that he thanked the gentleman, but if it was the same tap as he had tasted before, he had rather not. Master Scrooge's trunk being by this time tied on to the top of the chaise, the children bade the schoolmaster good-bye right willingly; and getting into it, drove gaily down the garden-sweep: the quick wheels dashing the hoar-frost and snow from off the dark leaves of the evergreens like spray.

"Always a delicate creature, whom a breath might have withered," said the Ghost. "But she had a large heart!"

"So she had," cried Scrooge. "You're right. I'll not gainsay it, Spirit. God forbid!"

"She died a woman," said the Ghost, "and had, as I think, children."

"One child," Scrooge returned.

"True," said the Ghost. "Your nephew!"

Scrooge seemed uneasy in his mind; and answered briefly, "Yes."

Although they had but that moment left the school behind them, they were now in the busy thoroughfares of a city, where shadowy passengers passed and repassed; where shadowy carts and coaches battled for the way, and all the strife and tumult of a real city were. It was made plain enough, by the dressing of the shops, that here too it was Christmas time again; but it was evening, and the streets were lighted up.

The Ghost stopped at a certain warehouse door, and asked Scrooge if he knew it.

"Know it!" said Scrooge. "Was I apprenticed here?"

They went in. At sight of an old gentleman in a Welsh wig, sitting behind such a high desk, that if he had been two inches taller he must have knocked his head against the ceiling, Scrooge cried in great excitement:

"Why, it's old Fezziwig! Bless his heart; it's Fezziwig alive again!"

Old Fezziwig laid down his pen, and looked up at the clock, which pointed to the hour of seven. He rubbed his hands; adjusted his capacious waistcoat; laughed all over himself, from his shoes to his organ of benevolence; and called out in a comfortable, oily, rich, fat, jovial voice:

"Yo ho, there! Ebenezer! Dick!"

Scrooge's former self, now grown a young man, came briskly in, accompanied by his fellow-'prentice.

"Dick Wilkins, to be sure!" said Scrooge to the Ghost. "Bless me, yes. There he is. He was very much attached to me, was Dick. Poor Dick! Dear, dear!"

"Yo ho, my boys!" said Fezziwig. "No more work to-night. Christmas Eve, Dick. Christmas, Ebenezer! Let's

have the shutters up," cried old Fezziwig, with a sharp clap of his hands, "before a man can say Jack Robinson!"

You wouldn't believe how those two fellows went at it! They charged into the street with the shutters—one, two, three—had 'em up in their places—four, five, six—barred 'em and pinned 'em—seven, eight, nine—and came back before you could have got to twelve, panting like race horses.

"Hilli-ho!" cried old Fezziwig, skipping down from the high desk, with wonderful agility. "Clear away, my lads, and let's have lots of room here! Hilli-ho, Dick! Chirrup, Ebenezer!"

Clear away! There was nothing they wouldn't have cleared away, or couldn't have cleared away, with old Fezziwig looking on. It was done in a minute. Every movable was packed off, as if it were dismissed from public life for ever more; the floor was swept and watered, the lamps were trimmed, fuel was heaped upon the fire; and the warehouse was as snug, and warm, and dry, and bright a ball-room, as you would desire to see upon a winter's night.

In came a fiddler with a music-book, and went up to the lofty desk, and made an orchestra of it, and tuned like fifty stomach-aches. In came Mrs. Fezziwig, one vast substantial smile. In came the three Miss Fezziwigs, beaming and lovable. In came the six young followers whose hearts they broke. In came all the young men and women employed in the business. In came the housemaid, with her cousin, the baker. In came the cook, with her brother's particular friend, the milkman. In came the boy from over the way, who was suspected of not having board enough from his master; trying to hide himself behind the girl from next door but one, who was proved to have had her ears pulled by her mistress. In they all came, one after another; some shyly, some boldly, some gracefully, some awkwardly, some pushing, some pulling; in they all came, anyhow and everyhow. Away they all went, twenty couple at once, hands half round and back again the other way; down the middle and up again; round and round in various stages of affectionate grouping; old top couple always turning up in the wrong place; new top couple starting off again as soon as they got there; all top couples at last, and not a bottom one to help them. When this result was brought about, old Fezziwig, clapping his hands to stop the dance, cried out, "Well done!" and the fiddler plunged his hot face into a pot of porter, especially provided for that purpose. But scorning rest upon his reappearance, he instantly began again, though there were no dancers yet, as if the other fiddler had been carried home, exhausted, on a shutter; and he were a bran-new man resolved to beat him out of sight, or perish.

There were more dances, and there were forfeits, and more dances, and there was cake, and there was negus, and there was a great piece of Cold Roast, and there was a great piece of Cold Boiled, and there were mince-pies, and plenty of beer. But the great effect of the evening came after the Roast and Boiled, when the fiddler (an artful dog, mind! The sort of man who knew his business better than you or I could have told it him!) struck up "Sir Roger de Coverley." Then old Fezziwig stood out to dance with Mrs. Fezziwig. Top couple, too; with a good stiff piece of work cut out for them; three or four and twenty pair of partners; people who were not to be trifled with; people who *would* dance, and had no notion of walking.

But if they had been twice as many: ah, four times: old Fezziwig would have been a match for them, and so would

MR. FEZZIWIG'S BALL.

Mrs. Fezziwig. As to *her*, she was worthy to be his partner in every sense of the term. If that's not high praise, tell me higher, and I'll use it. A positive light appeared to issue from Fezziwig's calves. They shone in every part of the dance like moons. You couldn't have predicted, at any given time, what would become of 'em next. And when old Fezziwig and Mrs. Fezziwig had gone all through the dance; advance and retire, hold hands with your partner; bow and curtsey; corkscrew; thread-the-needle, and back again to your place; Fezziwig "cut"—cut so deftly, that he appeared to wink with his legs, and came upon his feet again without a stagger.

When the clock struck eleven, this domestic ball broke up. Mr. and Mrs. Fezziwig took their stations, one on either side the door, and shaking hands with every person individually as he or she went out, wished him or her a Merry Christmas. When everybody had retired but the two 'prentices, they did the same to them; and thus the cheerful voices died away, and the lads were left to their beds; which were under a counter in the back-shop.

During the whole of this time, Scrooge had acted like a man out of his wits. His heart and soul were in the scene, and with his former self. He corroborated everything, remembered everything, enjoyed everything, and underwent the strangest agitation. It was not until now, when the bright faces of his former self and Dick were turned from them, that he remembered the Ghost, and became conscious that it was looking full upon him, while the light upon its head burnt very clear.

"A small matter," said the Ghost, "to make these silly folks so full of gratitude."

"Small!" echoed Scrooge.

The Spirit signed to him to listen to the two apprentices, who were pouring out their hearts in praise of Fezziwig: and when he had done so, said,

"Why! Is it not? He has spent but a few pounds of your mortal money: three or four, perhaps. Is that so much that he deserves this praise?"

"It isn't that," said Scrooge, heated by the remark, and speaking unconsciously like his former, not his latter, self. "It isn't that, Spirit. He has the power to render us happy or unhappy; to make our service light or burdensome; a pleasure or a toil. Say that his power lies in words and looks; in things so slight and insignificant that it is impossible to add and count 'em up: what then? The happiness he gives, is quite as great as if it cost a fortune."

He felt the Spirit's glance, and stopped.

"What is the matter?" asked the Ghost.

"Nothing particular," said Scrooge.

"Something, I think?" the Ghost insisted.

"No," said Scrooge, "No. I should like to be able to say a word or two to my clerk just now! That's all."

His former self turned down the lamps as he gave utterance to the wish; and Scrooge and the Ghost again stood side by side in the open air.

"My time grows short," observed the Spirit. "Quick!"

This was not addressed to Scrooge, or to any one whom he could see, but it produced an immediate effect. For again Scrooge saw himself. He was older now; a man in the prime of life. His face had not the harsh and rigid lines of later years; but it had begun to wear the signs of care and avarice. There was an eager, greedy, restless motion in the eye, which showed the passion that had taken root, and where the shadow of the growing tree would fall.

He was not alone, but sat by the side of a fair young girl in a mourning-dress: in whose eyes there were tears, which sparkled in the light that shone out of the Ghost of Christmas Past.

"It matters little," she said, softly. "To you, very little. Another idol has displaced me; and if it can cheer and comfort you in time to come, as I would have tried to do, I have no just cause to grieve."

"What Idol has displaced you?" he rejoined.

"A golden one."

"This is the even-handed dealing of the world!" he said. "There is nothing on which it is so hard as poverty; and there is nothing it professes to condemn with such severity as the pursuit of wealth!"

"You fear the world too much," she answered, gently. "All your other hopes have merged into the hope of being beyond the chance of its sordid reproach. I have seen your nobler aspirations fall off one by one, until the master-passion, Gain, engrosses you. Have I not?"

"What then?" he retorted. "Even if I have grown so much wiser, what then? I am not changed towards you."

She shook her head.

"Am I?"

"Our contract is an old one. It was made when we were both poor and content to be so, until, in good season, we could improve our worldly fortune by our patient industry. You *are* changed. When it was made, you were another man."

"I was a boy," he said impatiently.

"Your own feeling tells you that you were not what you are," she returned. "I am. That which promised happiness when we were one in heart, is fraught with misery now that we are two. How often and how keenly I have thought of this, I will not say. It is enough that I *have* thought of it, and can release you."

"Have I ever sought release?"

"In words. No. Never."

"In what, then?"

"In a changed nature; in an altered spirit; in another atmosphere of life; another Hope as its great end. In everything that made my love of any worth or value in your sight. If this had never been between us," said the girl, looking mildly, but with steadiness, upon him; "tell me, would you seek me out and try to win me now? Ah, no!"

He seemed to yield to the justice of this supposition, in spite of himself. But he said with a struggle, "You think not."

"I would gladly think otherwise if I could," she answered, "Heaven knows! When *I* have learned a Truth like this, I know how strong and irresistible it must be. But if you were free to-day, to-morrow, yesterday, can even I believe that you would choose a dowerless girl—you who, in your very confidence with her, weigh everything by Gain: or, choosing her, if for a moment you were false enough to your one guiding principle to do so, do I not know that your repentance and regret would surely follow? I do; and I release you. With a full heart, for the love of him you once were."

He was about to speak; but with her head turned from him, she resumed.

"You may—the memory of what is past half makes me

hope you will—have pain in this. A very, very brief time, and you will dismiss the recollection of it, gladly, as an unprofitable dream, from which it happened well that you awoke. May you be happy in the life you have chosen!"

She left him, and they parted.

"Spirit!" said Scrooge, "show me no more! Conduct me home. Why do you delight to torture me?"

"One shadow more!" exclaimed the Ghost.

"No more!" cried Scrooge. "No more. I don't wish to see it. Show me no more!"

But the relentless Ghost pinioned him in both his arms, and forced him to observe what happened next.

They were in another scene and place; a room, not very large or handsome, but full of comfort. Near to the winter fire sat a beautiful young girl, so like the last that Scrooge believed it was the same, until he saw *her*, now a comely matron, sitting opposite her daughter. The noise in this room was perfectly tumultuous, for there were more children there, than Scrooge in his agitated state of mind could count; and, unlike the celebrated herd in the poem, they were not forty children conducting themselves like one, but every child was conducting itself like forty. The consequences were uproarious beyond belief; but no one seemed to care; on the contrary, the mother and daughter laughed heartily, and enjoyed it very much; and the latter, soon beginning to mingle in the sports, got pillaged by the young brigands most ruthlessly. What would I not have given to be one of them! Though I never could have been so rude, no, no! I wouldn't for the wealth of all the world have crushed that braided hair, and torn it down; and for the precious little shoe, I wouldn't have plucked it off, God bless my soul! to save my life. As to measuring her waist in sport, as they did, bold young brood, I couldn't have done it; I should have expected my arm to have grown round it for a punishment, and never come straight again. And yet I should have dearly liked, I own, to have touched her lips; to have questioned her, that she might have opened them; to have looked upon the lashes of her downcast eyes, and never raised a blush; to have let loose waves of hair, an inch of which would be a keepsake beyond price: in short, I should have liked, I do confess, to have had the lightest license of a child, and yet been man enough to know its value.

But now a knocking at the door was heard, and such a rush immediately ensued that she with laughing face and plundered dress was borne towards it the centre of a flushed and boisterous group, just in time to greet the father, who came home attended by a man laden with Christmas toys and presents. Then the shouting and the struggling, and the onslaught that was made on the defenceless porter! The scaling him with chairs for ladders to dive into his pockets, despoil him of brown-paper parcels, hold on tight by his cravat, hug him round the neck, pommel his back, and kick his legs in irrepressible affection! The shouts of wonder and delight with which the development of every package was received! The terrible announcement that the baby had been taken in the act of putting a doll's frying-pan into his mouth, and was more than suspected of having swallowed a fictitious turkey, glued on a wooden platter! The immense relief of finding this a false alarm! The joy, and gratitude, and ecstasy! They are all indescribable alike. It is enough that by degrees the children and their emotions got out of the parlour, and by one stair at a time, up to the top of the house; where they went to bed, and so subsided.

And now Scrooge looked on more attentively than ever, when the master of the house, having his daughter leaning fondly on him, sat down with her and her mother at his own fireside; and when he thought that such another creature, quite as graceful and as full of promise, might have called him father, and been a spring-time in the haggard winter of his life, his sight grew very dim indeed.

"Belle," said the husband, turning to his wife with a smile, "I saw an old friend of yours this afternoon."

"Who was it?"

"Guess!"

"How can I? Tut, don't I know?" she added in the same breath, laughing as he laughed. "Mr. Scrooge."

"Mr. Scrooge it was. I passed his office window; and as it was not shut up, and he had a candle inside, I could scarcely help seeing him. His partner lies upon the point of death, I hear; and there he sat alone. Quite alone in the world, I do believe."

"Spirit!" said Scrooge in a broken voice, "remove me from this place."

"I told you these were shadows of the things that have been," said the Ghost. "That they are what they are, do not blame me!"

"Remove me!" Scrooge exclaimed, "I cannot bear it!"

He turned upon the Ghost, and seeing that it looked upon him with a face, in which in some strange way there were fragments of all the faces it had shown him, wrestled with it.

"Leave me! Take me back. Haunt me no longer!"

In the struggle, if that can be called a struggle in which the Ghost with no visible resistance on its own part was undisturbed by any effort of its adversary, Scrooge observed that its light was burning high and bright; and dimly connecting that with its influence over him, he seized the extinguisher-cap, and by a sudden action pressed it down upon its head.

The Spirit dropped beneath it, so that the extinguisher covered its whole form; but though Scrooge pressed it down with all his force, he could not hide the light, which streamed from under it, in an unbroken flood upon the ground.

He was conscious of being exhausted, and overcome by an irresistible drowsiness; and further, of being in his own bedroom. He gave the cap a parting squeeze, in which his hand relaxed; and had barely time to reel to bed, before he sank into a heavy sleep.

STAVE THREE.

THE SECOND OF THE THREE SPIRITS.

AWAKING in the middle of a prodigiously tough snore, and sitting up in bed to get his thoughts together, Scrooge had no occasion to be told that the bell was again upon the stroke of One. He felt that he was restored to consciousness in the right nick of time, for the especial purpose of holding a conference with the second messenger despatched to him through Jacob Marley's intervention. But, finding that he turned uncomfortably cold when he began to wonder which of his curtains this new spectre would draw back, he put them every one aside with his own hands, and lying down again, established a sharp lookout all round the bed. For he wished to challenge the Spirit on the moment of its appearance, and did not wish to be taken by surprise and made nervous.

Gentlemen of the free-and-easy sort, who plume themselves on being acquainted with a move or two, and being usually equal to the time-of-day, express the wide range of their capacity for adventure by observing that they are good for anything from pitch-and-toss to manslaughter; between which opposite extremes, no doubt, there lies a tolerably wide and comprehensive range of subjects. Without venturing for Scrooge quite as hardily as this, I don't mind calling on you to believe that he was ready for a good broad field of strange appearances, and that nothing between a baby and rhinoceros would have astonished him very much.

Now, being prepared for almost anything, he was not by any means prepared for nothing; and, consequently, when the Bell struck One, and no shape appeared, he was taken with a violent fit of trembling. Five minutes, ten minutes, a quarter of an hour went by, yet nothing came. All this time, he lay upon his bed, the very core and centre of a blaze of ruddy light, which streamed upon it when the clock proclaimed the hour; and which, being only light, was more alarming than a dozen ghosts, as he was powerless to make out what it meant, or would be at; and was sometimes apprehensive that he might be at that very moment an interesting case of spontaneous combustion, without having the consolation of knowing it. At last, however, he began to think—as you or I would have thought at first; for it is always the person not in the predicament who knows what ought to have been done in it, and would unquestionably have done it too—at last, I say, he began to think that the source and secret of this ghostly light might be in the adjoining room, from whence, on further tracing it, it seemed to shine. This idea taking full possession of his mind, he got up softly and shuffled in his slippers to the door.

The moment Scrooge's hand was on the lock, a strange voice called him by his name, and bade him enter. He obeyed.

It was his own room. There was no doubt about that. But it had undergone a surprising transformation. The walls and ceiling were so hung with living green, that it looked a perfect grove, from every part of which, bright gleaming berries glistened. The crisp leaves of holly, mistletoe, and ivy reflected back the light, as if so many little mirrors had been scattered there; and such a mighty blaze went roaring up the chimney, as that dull petrifaction of a hearth had never known in Scrooge's time, or Marley's, or for many and many a winter season gone. Heaped up on the floor, to form a kind of throne, were turkeys, geese, game, poultry, brawn, great joints of meat, sucking-pigs, long wreaths of sausages, mince-pies, plum-puddings, barrels of oysters, red-hot chestnuts, cherry-cheeked apples, juicy oranges, luscious pears, immense twelfth-cakes, and seething bowls of punch, that made the chamber dim with their delicious steam. In easy state upon this couch, there sat a jolly Giant, glorious to see; who bore a glowing torch, in shape not unlike Plenty's horn, and held it up, high up, to shed its light on Scrooge, as he came peeping round the door.

"Come in!" exclaimed the Ghost. "Come in! and know me better, man!"

Scrooge entered timidly, and hung his head before this Spirit. He was not the dogged Scrooge he had been; and though the Spirit's eyes were clear and kind, he did not like to meet them.

"I am the Ghost of Christmas Present," said the Spirit. "Look upon me!"

Scrooge reverently did so. It was clothed in one simple deep green robe, or mantle, bordered with white fur. This garment hung so loosely on the figure, that its capacious breast was bare, as if disdaining to be warded or concealed by any artifice. Its feet, observable beneath the ample folds of the garment, were also bare; and on its head it wore no other covering than a holly wreath set here and there with shining icicles. Its dark brown curls were long and free; free as its genial face, its sparkling eye, its open hand, its cheery voice, its unconstrained demeanour, and its joyful air. Girded round its middle was an antique scabbard; but no sword was in it, and the ancient sheath was eaten up with rust.

"You have never seen the like of me before!" exclaimed the Spirit.

"Never," Scrooge made answer to it.

"Have never walked forth with the younger members of my family; meaning (for I am very young) my elder brothers born in these later years?" pursued the Phantom.

"I don't think I have," said Scrooge. "I am afraid I have not. Have you had many brothers, Spirit?"

"More than eighteen hundred," said the Ghost.

"A tremendous family to provide for!" muttered Scrooge.

The Ghost of Christmas Present rose.

"Spirit," said Scrooge submissively, "conduct me where you will. I went forth last night on compulsion, and I learnt a lesson which is working now. To-night, if you have aught to teach me, let me profit by it."

"Touch my robe!"

Scrooge did as he was told, and held it fast.

Holly, mistletoe, red berries, ivy, turkeys, geese, game, poultry, brawn, meat, pigs, sausages, oysters, pies, puddings, fruit, and punch, all vanished instantly. So did the room, the fire, the ruddy glow, the hour of night, and they stood in the city streets on Christmas morning, where (for the weather was severe) the people made a rough, but brisk and not unpleasant kind of music, in scraping the snow from the pavement in front of their dwellings, and from the tops of their houses: whence it was mad delight to the boys to see it come plumping down into the road below, and splitting into artificial little snow-storms.

The house fronts looked black enough, and the windows blacker, contrasting with the smooth white sheet of snow upon the roofs, and with the dirtier snow upon the ground; which last deposit had been ploughed up in deep furrows by the heavy wheels of carts and waggons; furrows that crossed and re-crossed each other hundreds of times where the great streets branched off, and made intricate channels, hard to trace, in the thick yellow mud and icy water. The sky was gloomy, and the shortest streets were choked up with a dingy mist, half thawed, half frozen, whose heavier particles descended in a shower of sooty atoms, as if all the chimneys in Great Britain had, by one consent, caught fire, and were blazing away to their dear hearts' content. There was nothing very cheerful in the climate or the town, and yet was there an air of cheerfulness abroad that the clearest summer air and brightest summer sun might have endeavoured to diffuse in vain.

For, the people who were shovelling away on the house-tops were jovial and full of glee; calling out to one another from the parapets, and now and then exchanging a facetious snowball—better-natured missile far than many a wordy jest—laughing heartily if it went right and not less heartily if it went wrong. The poulterers' shops were still half open, and the fruiterers' were radiant in their glory. There were great, round, pot-bellied baskets of chestnuts, shaped like the waistcoats of jolly old gentlemen, lolling at the doors, and tumbling out into the street in their apoplectic opulence. There were ruddy, brown-faced broad-girthed Spanish Onions, shining in the fatness of their growth like Spanish Friars; and winking from their shelves in wanton slyness at the girls as they went by, and glanced demurely at the hung-up mistletoe. There were pears and apples, clustered high in blooming pyramids; there were bunches of grapes, made, in the shop-keepers' benevolence, to dangle from conspicuous hooks, that people's mouths might water gratis as they passed; there were piles of filberts, mossy and brown, recalling, in their fragrance, ancient walks among the woods, and pleasant shufflings ankle-deep through withered leaves; there were Norfolk Biffins, squab, and swarthy, setting off the yellow of the oranges and lemons, and, in the great compactness of their juicy persons, urgently entreating and beseeching to be carried home in paper bags and eaten after dinner. The very gold and silver fish, set forth among these choice fruits in a bowl, though members of a dull and stagnant-blooded race, appeared to know that there was something going on; and, to a fish, went gasping round and round their little world in slow and passionless excitement.

The Grocers'! oh the Grocers'! nearly closed, with perhaps two shutters down, or one; but through those gaps such glimpses! It was not alone that the scales descending on the counter made a merry sound, or that the twine and roller parted company so briskly, or that the canisters were rattled up and down like juggling tricks, or even that the blended scents of tea and coffee were so grateful to the nose, or even that the raisins were so plentiful and rare, the almonds so extremely white, the sticks of cinnamon so long and straight, the other spices so delicious, the candied fruits so caked and spotted with molten sugar as to make the coldest lookers-on feel faint and subsequently bilious. Nor was it that the figs were moist and pulpy, or that the French plums blushed in modest tartness from their highly-decorated boxes, or that everything was good to eat and in its Christmas dress: but the customers were all so hurried and so eager in the hopeful promise of the day, that they tumbled up against each other at the door, clashing their wicker baskets wildly, and left their purchases upon the counter, and came running back to fetch them, and committed hundreds of the like mistakes in the best humour possible; while the Grocer and his people were so frank and fresh that the polished hearts with which they fastened their aprons behind might have been their own, worn outside for general inspection, and for Christmas daws to peck at if they chose.

But soon the steeples called good people all, to church and chapel, and away they came, flocking through the streets in their best clothes, and with their gayest faces. And at the same time there emerged from scores of bye-streets, lanes, and nameless turnings, innumerable people, carrying their dinners to the bakers' shops. The sight of these poor revellers appeared to interest the Spirit very much, for he stood with Scrooge beside him in a baker's doorway, and taking off the covers as their bearers passed, sprinkled incense on their dinners from his torch. And it was a very uncommon kind of torch, for once or twice when there were angry words between some dinner-carriers who had jostled with each other, he shed a few drops of water on them from it, and their good humour was restored directly. For they said, it was a shame to quarrel upon Christmas Day. And so it was! God love it, so it was!

In time the bells ceased, and the bakers were shut up; and yet there was a genial shadowing forth of all these dinners and the progress of their cooking, in the thawed blotch of wet above each baker's oven; where the pavement smoked as if its stones were cooking too.

"Is there a peculiar flavour in what you sprinkle from your torch?" asked Scrooge.

"There is. My own."

"Would it apply to any kind of dinner on this day?" asked Scrooge.

"To any kindly given. To a poor one most."

"Why to a poor one most?" asked Scrooge.

"Because it needs it most."

"Spirit," said Scrooge, after a moment's thought, "I wonder you, of all the beings in the many worlds about us, should desire to cramp these people's opportunities of innocent enjoyment."

"I!" cried the Spirit.

"You would deprive them of their means of dining every seventh day, often the only day on which they can be said to dine at all," said Scrooge. "Wouldn't you?"

"I!" cried the Spirit.

"You seek to close these places on the Seventh Day?" said Scrooge. "And it comes to the same thing."

"I seek!" exclaimed the Spirit.

"Forgive me if I am wrong. It has been done in your name, or at least in that of your family," said Scrooge.

"There are some upon this earth of yours," returned the Spirit, "who lay claim to know us, and who do their deeds of passion, pride, ill-will, hatred, envy, bigotry, and selfishness in our name, who are as strange to us and all our kith and kin, as if they had never lived. Remember that, and charge their doings on themselves, not us."

Scrooge promised that he would; and they went on, invisible, as they had been before, into the suburbs of the town. It was a remarkable quality of the Ghost (which Scrooge had observed at the baker's), that notwithstanding his gigantic size, he could accommodate himself to any place with ease; and that he stood beneath a low roof quite as gracefully and like a supernatural creature, as it was possible he could have done in any lofty hall.

And perhaps it was the pleasure the good Spirit had in showing off this power of his, or else it was his own kind, generous, hearty nature, and his sympathy with all poor men, that led him straight to Scrooge's clerk's; for there he went, and took Scrooge with him, holding to his robe; and on the threshold of the door the Spirit smiled, and stopped to bless Bob Cratchit's dwelling with the sprinklings of his torch. Think of that! Bob had but fifteen "Bob" a-week himself; he pocketed on Saturdays but fifteen copies of his Christian name; and yet the Ghost of Christmas Present blessed his four-roomed house!

Then up rose Mrs. Cratchit, Cratchit's wife, dressed out but poorly in a twice-turned gown, but brave in ribbons, which are cheap and make a goodly show for sixpence; and she laid the cloth, assisted by Belinda Cratchit, second of her daughters, also brave in ribbons; while Master Peter Cratchit plunged a fork into the saucepan of potatoes, and getting the corners of his monstrous shirt collar (Bob's private property, conferred upon his son and heir in honour of the day) into his mouth, rejoiced to find himself so gallantly attired, and yearned to show his linen in the fashionable Parks. And now two smaller Cratchits, boy and girl, came tearing in, screaming that outside the baker's they had smelt the goose, and known it for their own; and basking in luxurious thoughts of sage-and-onion, these young Cratchits danced about the table, and exalted Master Peter Cratchit to the skies, while he (not proud, although his collars nearly choked him) blew the fire, until the slow potatoes bubbling up, knocked loudly at the saucepan-lid to be let out and peeled.

"What has ever got your precious father then?" said Mrs. Cratchit. "And your brother, Tiny Tim! And Martha warn't as late last Christmas Day by half-an-hour!"

"Here's Martha, mother!" said a girl, appearing as she spoke.

"Here's Martha, mother!" cried the two young Cratchits. "Hurrah! There's *such* a goose, Martha!"

"Why, bless your heart alive, my dear, how late you are!" said Mrs. Cratchit, kissing her a dozen times, and taking off her shawl and bonnet for her with officious zeal.

"We'd a deal of work to finish up last night," replied the girl, "and had to clear away this morning, mother!"

"Well! Never mind so long as you are come," said Mrs. Cratchit. "Sit ye down before the fire, my dear, and have a warm, Lord bless ye!"

"No, no! There's father coming," cried the two young Cratchits, who were everywhere at once. "Hide, Martha, hide!"

So Martha hid herself, and in came little Bob, the father, with at least three feet of comforter exclusive of the fringe, hanging down before him; and his threadbare clothes darned up and brushed, to look seasonable; and Tiny Tim upon his shoulder. Alas for Tiny Tim, he bore a little crutch, and had his limbs supported by an iron frame!

"Why, where's our Martha?" cried Bob Cratchit, looking round.

"Not coming," said Mrs. Cratchit.

"Not coming!" said Bob, with a sudden declension in his high spirits; for he had been Tim's blood horse all the way from church, and had come home rampant. "Not coming upon Christmas Day!"

Martha didn't like to see him disappointed, if it were only in joke; so she came out prematurely from behind the closet door, and ran into his arms, while the two young Cratchits hustled Tiny Tim, and bore him off into the wash-house, that he might hear the pudding singing in the copper.

"And how did little Tim behave?" asked Mrs. Cratchit, when she had rallied Bob on his credulity, and Bob had hugged his daughter to his heart's content.

"As good as gold," said Bob, "and better. Somehow he gets thoughtful, sitting by himself so much, and thinks the strangest things you ever heard. He told me, coming home, that he hoped the people saw him in the church, because he was a cripple, and it might be pleasant to them to remember upon Christmas Day, who made lame beggars walk and blind men see."

Bob's voice was tremulous when he told them this, and trembled more when he said that Tiny Tom was growing strong and hearty.

His active little crutch was heard upon the floor, and back came Tiny Tim before another word was spoken, escorted by his brother and sister to his stool before the fire; and while Bob, turning up his cuffs—as if, poor fellow, they were capable of being made more shabby—compounded some hot mixture in a jug with gin and lemons, and stirred it round and round and put it on the hob to simmer; Master Peter, and the two ubiquitous young Cratchits went to fetch the goose, with which they soon returned in high procession.

Such a bustle ensued that you might have thought a goose the rarest of all birds; a feathered phenomenon, to which a black swan was a matter of course—and in truth it was something very like it in that house. Mrs. Cratchit made the gravy (ready beforehand in a little saucepan) hissing hot; Master Peter mashed the potatoes with incredible vigour; Miss Belinda sweetened up the apple-sauce; Martha dusted the hot plates; Bob took Tiny Tim beside him in a tiny corner at the table; the two young Cratchits set chairs for everybody, not forgetting themselves, and mounting guard upon their posts, crammed spoons into their mouths, lest they should shriek for goose before their turn came to be helped. At last the dishes were set on, and grace was said. It was succeeded by a breathless pause, as Mrs. Cratchit, looking slowly all along the carving-knife, prepared to plunge it in the breast; but when she did, and when the long expected gush of stuffing issued forth, one murmur of delight arose all round the board, and even Tiny Tim, excited by the two young Cratchits, beat on the table with the handle of his knife, and feebly cried Hurrah!

There never was such a goose. Bob said he didn't believe there ever was such a goose cooked. Its tenderness and flavour, size and cheapness, were the themes of universal admiration. Eked out by the apple sauce and mashed potatoes, it was a sufficient dinner for the whole family; indeed, as Mrs. Cratchit said with great delight (surveying one small atom of a bone upon the dish) they hadn't ate it all at last! Yet every one had had enough, and the youngest Cratchits in particular, were steeped in sage and onion to the eyebrows! But now, the plates being changed by Miss Belinda, Mrs. Cratchit left the room alone—too nervous to bear witnesses—to take the pudding up and bring it in.

Suppose it should not be done enough! Suppose it should break in turning out! Suppose somebody should have got over the wall of the back-yard, and stolen it, while they were merry with the goose—a supposition at which the two young Cratchits became livid! All sorts of horrors were supposed.

Hallo! A great deal of steam! The pudding was out of the copper. A smell like a washing-day! That was the cloth. A smell like an eating-house and a pastrycook's next door to each other, with a laundress's next door to that! That was the pudding! In half a minute Mrs. Cratchit entered—flushed, but smiling proudly—with the pudding like a speckled cannon-ball so hard and firm blazing in half of half-a-quartern of ignited brandy, and bedight with Christmas holly stuck into the top.

Oh, a wonderful pudding! Bob Cratchit said, and calmly too, that he regarded it as the greatest success achieved by Mrs. Cratchit since their marriage. Mrs. Cratchit said that now the weight was off her mind, she would confess she had had her doubts about the quantity of flour. Everybody had something to say about it, but nobody said or thought it was at all a small pudding for a large family. It would have been flat heresy to do so. Any Cratchit would have blushed to hint at such a thing.

At last the dinner was all done, the cloth was cleared, the hearth swept, and the fire made up. The compound in the jug being tasted, and considered perfect, apples and oranges were put upon the table, and a shovel-full of chestnuts on the fire. Then all the Cratchit family drew round the hearth, in what Bob Cratchit called a circle, meaning half a one; and at Bob Cratchit's elbow stood the family display of glass. Two tumblers, and a custard-cup without a handle.

These held the hot stuff from the jug, however, as well as golden goblets would have done; and Bob served it out with beaming looks, while the chestnuts on the fire sputtered and cracked noisily. Then Bob proposed:

"A Merry Christmas to us all, my dears. God bless us!" Which all the family re-echoed.

"God bless us every one!" said Tiny Tim, the last of all.

He sat very close to his father's side upon his little stool. Bob held his withered little hand in his, as if he loved the child, and wished to keep him by his side, and dreaded that he might be taken from him.

"Spirit!" said Scrooge, with an interest he had never felt before, "tell me if Tiny Tim will live."

"I see a vacant seat," replied the Ghost, "in the poor chimney-corner, and a crutch without an owner, carefully preserved. If these shadows remain unaltered by the Future, the child will die."

"No, no," said Scrooge. "Oh no, kind Spirit! say he will be spared."

"If these shadows remain unaltered by the Future, none other of my race," returned the Ghost, "will find him here. What then? If he be like to die, he had better do it, and decrease the surplus population."

Scrooge hung his head to hear his own words quoted by the Spirit, and was overcome with penitence and grief.

"Man," said the Ghost, "if man you be in heart, not adamant, forbear that wicked cant until you have discovered What the surplus is, and Where it is. Will you decide what men shall live, what men shall die? It may be, that in the sight of Heaven, you are more worthless and less fit to live than millions like this poor man's child. Oh God! to hear the Insect on the leaf pronouncing on the too much life among his hungry brothers in the dust!"

Scrooge bent before the Ghost's rebuke, and trembling cast his eyes upon the ground. But he raised them speedily, on hearing his own name.

"Mr. Scrooge!" said Bob; "I'll give you Mr. Scrooge, the Founder of the Feast!"

"The Founder of the Feast indeed!" cried Mrs. Cratchit, reddening. "I wish I had him here. I'd give him a piece of my mind to feast upon, and I hope he'd have a good appetite for it."

"My dear," said Bob, "the children! Christmas Day."

"It should be Christmas Day, I am sure," said she, "on which one drinks the health of such an odious, stingy, hard, unfeeling man as Mr. Scrooge. You know he is, Robert! Nobody knows it better than you do, poor fellow!"

"My dear," was Bob's mild answer, "Christmas Day."

"I'll drink his health for your sake and the Day's," said Mrs. Cratchit, "not for his. Long life to him! A Merry Christmas and a Happy New Year! He'll be very merry and very happy, I have no doubt!"

The children drank the toast after her. It was the first of their proceedings which had no heartiness in it. Tiny Tim drank it last of all, but he didn't care twopence for it. Scrooge was the Ogre of the family. The mention of his name cast a dark shadow on the party, which was not dispelled for full five minutes.

After it had passed away, they were ten times merrier than before, from the mere relief of Scrooge the Baleful being done with. Bob Cratchit told them how he had a situation in his eye for Master Peter, which would bring in, if obtained, full five-and-sixpence weekly. The two young Cratchits laughed tremendously at the idea of Peter's being a man of business; and Peter himself looked thoughtfully at the fire from between his collars, as if he were deliberating what particular investments he should favour when he came into the receipt of that bewildering income. Martha, who was a poor apprentice at a milliner's, then told them what kind of work she had to do, and how many hours she worked at a stretch, and how she meant to lie abed to-morrow morning for a good long rest; to-morrow being a holiday she passed at home. Also how she had seen a countess and a lord some days before, and how the lord "was much about as tall as Peter;" at which Peter pulled up his collars so high that you couldn't have seen his head if you had been there. All this time the chestnuts and the jug went round and round; and bye-and-bye they had a song, about a lost child travelling in the snow, from Tiny Tim, who had a plaintive little voice, and sang it very well indeed.

There was nothing of high mark in this. They were not a handsome family; they were not well dressed; their shoes were far from being water-proof; their clothes were scanty; and Peter might have known, and very likely did, the inside of a pawnbroker's. But, they were happy, grateful, pleased with one another, and contented with the time; and when they faded, and looked happier yet in the bright sprinklings of the Spirit's torch at parting, Scrooge had his eye upon them, and especially on Tiny Tim, until the last.

By this time it was getting dark, and snowing pretty heavily; and as Scrooge and the Spirit went along the streets, the brightness of the roaring fires in kitchens, parlours, and all sorts of rooms, was wonderful. Here, the flickering of the blaze showed preparations for a cosy dinner, with hot plates baking through and through before the fire, and deep red curtains, ready to be drawn to shut out cold and darkness. There, all the children of the house were running out into the snow to meet their married sisters, brothers, cousins, uncles, aunts, and be the first to greet them. Here, again, were shadows on the window-blind of guests assembling; and there a group of handsome girls, all hooded and fur-booted, and all chattering at once, tripped lightly off to some near neighbour's house; where, woe upon the single man who saw them enter—artful witches; well they knew it—in a glow!

But if you had judged from the numbers of people on their way to friendly gatherings, you might have thought that no one was at home to give them welcome when they got there, instead of every house expecting company, and piling up its fires half-chimney high. Blessings on it, how the Ghost exulted! How it bared its breadth of breast, and opened its capacious palm, and floated on, outpouring, with a generous hand, its bright and harmless mirth on everything within its reach! The very lamplighter, who ran on before dotting the dusky street with specks of light, and who was dressed to spend the evening somewhere, laughed out loudly as the Spirit passed: though little kenned the lamplighter that he had any company but Christmas!

And now, without a word of warning from the Ghost, they stood upon a bleak and desert moor, where monstrous masses of rude stone were cast about, as though it were the burial-place of giants; and water spread itself wheresoever it listed, or would have done so, but for the frost that held it prisoner; and nothing grew but moss and furze, and coarse, rank grass. Down in the west the setting sun had left a streak of fiery red, which glared upon the desolation for an instant, like a sullen eye, and frowning lower, lower, lower yet, was lost in the thick gloom of darkest night.

"What place is this?" asked Scrooge.

"A place where Miners live, who labour in the bowels of the earth," returned the Spirit. "But they know me. See!"

A light shone from the window of a hut, and swiftly they advanced towards it. Passing through the wall of mud and stone, they found a cheerful company assembled round a glowing fire. An old, old man and woman, with their children and their children's children, and another generation beyond that, all decked out gaily in their holiday attire. The old man, in a voice that seldom rose above the howling of the wind upon the barren waste, was singing them a Christmas song; it had been a very old song when he was a boy; and from time to time they all joined in the chorus. So surely as they raised their voices, the old man got quite blithe and loud; and so surely as they stopped, his vigour sank again.

The Spirit did not tarry here, but bade Scrooge hold his robe, and passing on above the moor, sped whither? Not to sea? To sea. To Scrooge's horror, looking back, he saw the last of the land, a frightful range of rocks, behind them; and his ears were deafened by the thundering of water, as it rolled, and roared, and raged among the dreadful caverns it had worn, and fiercely tried to undermine the earth.

Built upon a dismal reef of sunken rocks, some league or so from shore, on which the waters chafed and dashed, the wild year through, there stood a solitary lighthouse. Great heaps of seaweed clung to its base, and storm-birds —born of the wind one might suppose, as sea-weed of the water—rose and fell about it, like the waves they skimmed.

But even here, two men who watched the light had made a fire, that through the loophole in the thick stone wall shed out a ray of brightness on the awful sea. Joining their horny hands over the rough table at which they sat, they wished each other Merry Christmas in their can of grog; and one of them, the elder, too, with his face all damaged and scarred with hard weather, as the figure-head of an old ship might be: struck up a sturdy song that was like a Gale in itself.

Again the Ghost sped on, above the black and heaving sea—on, on—until, being far away, as he told Scrooge, from any shore, they lighted on a ship. They stood beside the helmsman at the wheel, the lookout in the bow, the officers who had the watch; dark, ghostly figures in their several stations; but every man among them hummed a Christmas tune, or had a Christmas thought, or spoke below his breath to his companion of some bygone Christmas Day, with homeward hopes belonging to it. And every man on board, waking or sleeping, good or bad, had had a kinder word for another on that day than on any day in the year; and had shared to some extent in its festivities; and had remembered those he cared for at a distance, and had known that they delighted to remember him.

It was a great surprise to Scrooge, while listening to the moaning of the wind, and thinking what a solemn thing it was to move on through the lonely darkness over an unknown abyss, whose depths were secrets as profound as Death: it was a great surprise to Scrooge, while thus engaged, to hear a hearty laugh. It was a much greater surprise to Scrooge to recognise it as his own nephew's, and to find himself in a bright, dry, gleaming room, with the Spirit standing smiling by his side, and looking at that same nephew with approving affability.

"Ha, ha!" laughed Scrooge's nephew. "Ha, ha, ha!"

If you should happen, by any unlikely chance, to know a man more blest in a laugh than Scrooge's nephew, all I can say is, I should like to know him too. Introduce him to me, and I'll cultivate his acquaintance.

It is a fair, even-handed, noble adjustment of things, that while there is infection in disease and sorrow, there is nothing in the world so irresistibly contagious as laughter and good-humour. When Scrooge's nephew laughed in this way: holding his sides, rolling his head, and twisting his face into the most extravagant contortions: Scrooge's niece, by marriage, laughed as heartily as he. And their assembled friends being not a bit behindhand, roared out, lustily.

"Ha, ha! Ha, ha, ha, ha!"

"He said that Christmas was a humbug, as I live!" cried Scrooge's nephew. "He believed it too!"

"More shame for him, Fred!" said Scrooge's niece, indignantly. Bless those women; they never do anything by halves. They are always in earnest.

She was very pretty: exceedingly pretty. With a dimpled, surprised-looking, capital face; a ripe little mouth, that seemed made to be kissed—as no doubt it was; all kinds of good little dots about her chin, that melted into one another when she laughed; and the sunniest pair of eyes you ever saw in any little creature's head. Altogether she was what you would have called provoking, you know; but satisfactory, too. Oh, perfectly satisfactory!

"He's a comical old fellow," said Scrooge's nephew, "that's the truth; and not so pleasant as he might be. However, his offences carry their own punishment, and I have nothing to say against him."

"I'm sure he is very rich, Fred," hinted Scrooge's niece. "At least you always tell me so."

"What of that, my dear!" said Scrooge's nephew. "His wealth is of no use to him. He don't do any good with it. He don't make himself comfortable with it. He hasn't the satisfaction of thinking—ha, ha, ha!—that he is ever going to benefit Us with it."

"I have no patience with him," observed Scrooge's niece. Scrooge's niece's sisters, and all the other ladies, expressed the same opinion.

"Oh, I have!" said Scrooge's nephew "I am sorry for him; I couldn't be angry with him if I tried. Who suffers by his ill whims? Himself, always. Here, he takes it into his head to dislike us, and he won't come and dine with us. What's the consequence! He don't lose much of a dinner——"

"Indeed, I think he loses a very good dinner," interrupted Scrooge's niece. Everybody else said the same, and they must be allowed to have been competent judges, because they had just had dinner; and, with the dessert upon the table, were clustered round the fire, by lamplight.

"Well! I'm very glad to hear it," said Scrooge's nephew, "because I haven't any great faith in these young housekeepers. What do you say, Topper?"

Topper had clearly got his eye upon one of Scrooge's niece's sisters, for he answered that a bachelor was a wretched outcast, who had no right to express an opinion on the subject. Whereat Scrooge's niece's sister—the plump one with the lace tucker: not the one with the roses —blushed.

"Do go on, Fred," said Scrooge's niece, clapping her hands. "He never finishes what he begins to say! He is such a ridiculous fellow!"

Scrooge's nephew revelled in another laugh, and as it was impossible to keep the infection off; though the plump sister tried hard to do it with aromatic vinegar; his example was unanimously followed.

"I was only going to say," said Scrooge's nephew, "that the consequence of his taking a dislike to us, and not making merry with us, is, as I think, that he loses some pleasant moments, which could do him no harm. I am sure he loses pleasanter companions than he can find in his own thoughts, either in his mouldy old office, or his dusty chambers. I mean to give him the same chance every year, whether he likes it or not, for I pity him. He may rail at Christmas till he dies, but he can't help thinking better of it—I defy him—if he finds me going there, in good temper, year after year, and saying 'Uncle Scrooge, how are you?' If it only puts him in the vein to leave his poor clerk fifty pounds, *that's* something; and I think I shook him yesterday."

It was their turn to laugh now at the notion of his shaking Scrooge. But being thoroughly good-natured, and not much caring what they laughed at, so that they laughed at any rate, he encouraged them in their merriment, and passed the bottle joyously.

After tea, they had some music. For they were a musical family, and knew what they were about, when they sang a Glee or Catch, I can assure you: especially Topper, who could growl away in the bass like a good one, and never swell the large veins in his forehead, or get red in the face over it. Scrooge's niece played well upon the harp; and played among other tunes a simple little air (a mere nothing: you might learn to whistle it in two minutes), which had been familiar to the child who fetched Scrooge from the boarding-school, as he had been reminded by the Ghost of Christmas Past. When this strain of music sounded, all the things that Ghost had shown him, came upon his mind; he softened more and more; and thought that if he could have listened to it often, years ago, he might have cultivated the kindnesses of life for his own happiness with his own hands, without resorting to the sexton's spade that buried Jacob Marley.

But they didn't devote the whole evening to music. After a while they played at forfeits; for it is good to be children sometimes, and never better than at Christmas, when its mighty Founder was a child himself. Stop! There was first a game at blind-man's buff. Of course there was. And I no more believe Topper was really blind than I believe he had eyes in his boots. My opinion is, that it was a done thing between him and Scrooge's nephew: and that the Ghost of Christmas Present knew it. The way he went after that plump sister in the lace tucker, was an outrage on the credulity of human nature. Knocking down the fire-irons, tumbling over the chairs, bumping up against the piano, smothering himself among the curtains, wherever she went, there went he. He always knew where the plump sister was. He wouldn't catch anybody else. If you had fallen up against him, as some of them did, and stood there; he would have made a feint of endeavouring to seize you, which would have been an affront to your understanding; and would instantly have sidled off in the direction of the plump sister. She often cried out that it wasn't fair; and it really was not. But when at

last, he caught her; when, in spite of all her silken rustlings, and her rapid flutterings past him, he got her into a corner whence there was no escape; then his conduct was the most execrable. For his pretending not to know her; his pretending that it was necessary to touch her headdress, and further to assure himself of her identity by pressing a certain ring upon her finger, and a certain chain about her neck; was vile, monstrous! No doubt she told him her opinion of it, when, another blind man being in office, they were so very confidential together, behind the curtains.

Scrooge's niece was not one of the blind-man's buff party, but was made comfortable with a large chair and a footstool, in a snug corner, where the Ghost and Scrooge were close behind her. But she joined in the forfeits, and loved her love to admiration with all the letters of the alphabet. Likewise at the game of How, When, and Where, she was very great, and to the secret joy of Scrooge's nephew, beat her sisters hollow: though they were sharp girls too, as Topper could have told you. There might have been twenty people there, young and old, but they all played, and so did Scrooge; for, wholly forgetting in the interest he had in what was going on, that his voice made no sound in their ears, he sometimes came out with his guess quite loud, and very often guessed quite right, too; for the sharpest needle, best Whitechapel, warranted not to cut in the eye, was not sharper than Scrooge: blunt as he took it in his head to be.

The Ghost was greatly pleased to find him in this mood, and looked upon him with such favour, that he begged like a boy to be allowed to stay until the guests departed. But this the Spirit said could not be done.

"Here is a new game," said Scrooge. "One half-hour, Spirit, only one!"

It is a Game called Yes and No, where Scrooge's nephew had to think of something, and the rest must find out what; he only answering to their questions yes or no, as the case was. The brisk fire of questioning to which he was exposed, elicited from him that he was thinking of an animal, a live animal, rather a disagreeable animal, a savage animal, an animal that growled and grunted sometimes, and talked sometimes, and lived in London, and walked about the streets, and wasn't made a show of, and wasn't led by anybody, and didn't live in a menagerie, and was never killed in a market, and was not a horse, or an ass, or a cow, or a bull, or a tiger, or a dog, or a pig, or a cat, or a bear. At every fresh question that was put to him, this nephew burst into a fresh roar of laughter; and was so inexpressibly tickled, that he was obliged to get up off the sofa and stamp. At last the plump sister, falling into a similar state, cried out:

"I have found it out. I know what it is, Fred! I know what it is!"

"What is it?" cried Fred.

"It's your Uncle Scro-o-o-oge!"

Which it certainly was. Admiration was the universal sentiment, though some objected that the reply to "Is it a bear?" ought to have been "Yes;" inasmuch as an answer in the negative was sufficient to have diverted their thoughts from Mr. Scrooge, supposing they had ever had any tendency that way.

"He has given us plenty of merriment, I am sure," said Fred, "and it would be ungrateful not to drink his health. Here is a glass of mulled wine ready to our hand at the moment; and I say, 'Uncle Scrooge!'"

"Well! Uncle Scrooge!" they cried.

"A Merry Christmas and a Happy New Year to the old man, whatever he is!" said Scrooge's nephew. "He wouldn't take it from me, but may he have it, nevertheless. Uncle Scrooge!"

Uncle Scrooge had imperceptibly become so gay and light of heart, that he would have pledged the unconscious company in return, and thanked them in an inaudible speech, if the Ghost had given him time. But the whole scene passed off in the breath of the last word spoken by his nephew; and he and the Spirit were again upon their travels.

Much they saw, and far they went, and many homes they visited, but always with a happy end. The Spirit stood beside sick-beds, and they were cheerful; on foreign lands, and they were close at home; by struggling men, and they were patient in their greater hope; by poverty, and it was rich. In almshouse, hospital, and jail, in misery's every refuge, where vain man in his little brief authority had not made fast the door, and barred the Spirit out, he left his blessing, and taught Scrooge his precepts.

It was a long night, if it were only a night; but Scrooge had his doubts of this, because the Christmas Holidays appeared to be condensed into the space of time they passed together. It was strange, too, that while Scrooge remained unaltered in his outward form, the Ghost grew older, clearly older. Scrooge had observed this change, but never spoke of it, until they left a children's Twelfth Night party, when, looking at the Spirit as they stood together in an open place, he noticed that its hair was grey.

"Are spirits' lives so short?" asked Scrooge.

"My life upon this globe, is very brief," replied the Ghost. "It ends to-night."

"To-night!" cried Scrooge.

"To-night at midnight. Hark! The time is drawing near."

The chimes were ringing the three quarters past eleven at that moment.

"Forgive me if I am not justified in what I ask," said Scrooge, looking intently at the Spirit's robe, "but I see something strange, and not belonging to yourself, protruding from your skirts. Is it a foot or a claw?"

"It might be a claw, for the flesh there is upon it, was the Spirit's sorrowful reply. "Look here."

From the foldings of its robe, it brought two children; wretched, abject, frightful, hideous, miserable. They knelt down at its feet, and clung upon the outside of its garment.

"Oh, Man! look here. Look, look, down here!" exclaimed the Ghost.

They were a boy and girl. Yellow, meagre, ragged, scowling, wolfish; but prostrate, too, in their humility. Where graceful youth should have filled their features out, and touched them with its freshest tints, a stale and shrivelled hand, like that of age, had pinched, and twisted them, and pulled them into shreds. Where angels might have sat enthroned, devils lurked, and glared out menacing. No change, no degradation, no perversion of humanity, in any grade, through all the mysteries of wonderful creation, has monsters half so horrible and dread.

Scrooge started back, appalled. Having them shown to him in this way, he tried to say they were fine children, but the words choked themselves, rather than be parties to a lie of such enormous magnitude.

"Spirit! are they yours?" Scrooge could say no more.

"They are Man's," said the Spirit, looking down upon them. "And they cling to me, appealing from their fathers. This boy is Ignorance. This girl is Want. Beware them both, and all of their degree, but most of all beware this boy, for on his brow I see that written which is Doom, unless the writing be erased. Deny it!" cried the Spirit, stretching out its hand towards the city. "Slander those who tell it ye! Admit it for your factious purposes, and make it worse! And bide the end!"

"Have they no refuge or resource?" cried Scrooge.

"Are there no prisons?" said the Spirit, turning on him for the last time with his own words. "Are there no workhouses?"

The bell struck twelve.

Scrooge looked about him for the Ghost, and saw it not. As the last stroke ceased to vibrate, he remembered the prediction of old Jacob Marley, and lifting up his eyes, beheld a solemn Phantom, draped and hooded, coming, like a mist along the ground, towards him.

STAVE FOUR.

THE LAST OF THE SPIRITS.

THE Phantom slowly, gravely, silently approached. When it came near him, Scrooge bent down upon his knee; for in the very air through which this Spirit moved it seemed to scatter gloom and mystery.

It was shrouded in a deep black garment, which concealed its head, its face, its form, and left nothing of it visible save one outstretched hand. But for this it would have been difficult to detach its figure from the night, and separate it from the darkness by which it was surrounded.

He felt that it was tall and stately when it came beside him, and that its mysterious presence filled him with a solemn dread. He knew no more, for the Spirit neither spoke nor moved.

"I am in the presence of the Ghost of Christmas Yet To Come?" said Scrooge.

The Spirit answered not, but pointed downward with its hand.

"You are about to show me shadows of the things that have not happened, but will happen in the time before us," Scrooge pursued. "Is that so, Spirit?"

The upper portion of the garment was contracted for an instant in its folds, as if the Spirit had inclined its head. That was the only answer he received.

Although well used to ghostly company by this time, Scrooge feared the silent shape so much that his legs trembled beneath him, and he found that he could hardly stand when he prepared to follow it. The Spirit paused a moment, as observing his condition, and giving him time to recover.

But Scrooge was all the worse for this. It thrilled him with a vague uncertain horror, to know that behind the dusky shroud there were ghostly eyes intently fixed upon him, while he, though he stretched his own to the utmost, could see nothing but a spectral hand and one great heap of black.

"Ghost of the Future!" he exclaimed, "I fear you more than any Spectre I have seen. But, as I know your purpose is to do me good, and as I hope to live to be another man from what I was, I am prepared to bear you company, and do it with a thankful heart. Will you not speak to me?"

It gave him no reply. The hand was pointed straight before them.

"Lead on!" said Scrooge. "Lead on! The night is waning fast, and it is precious time to me, I know. Lead on, Spirit!"

The Phantom moved away as it had come towards him. Scrooge followed in the shadow of its dress, which bore him up, he thought, and carried him along.

They scarcely seemed to enter the city; for the city rather seemed to spring up about them, and encompass them of its own act. But there they were, in the heart of it; on 'Change, amongst the merchants; who hurried up and down, and chinked the money in their pockets, and conversed in groups, and looked at their watches, and trifled thoughtfully with their great gold seals; and so forth, as Scrooge had seen them often.

The Spirit stopped beside one little knot of business men. Observing that the hand was pointed to them, Scrooge advanced to listen to their talk.

"No," said a great fat man with a monstrous chin, "I don't know much about it, either way. I only know he's dead."

"When did he die?" inquired another.

"Last night, I believe."

"Why, what was the matter with him?" asked a third, taking a vast quantity of snuff out of a very large snuff-box. "I thought he'd never die."

"God knows," said the first, with a yawn.

"What has he done with his money?" asked a red-faced gentleman with a pendulous excrescence on the end of his nose, that shook like the gills of a turkey-cock.

"I haven't heard," said the man with the large chin, yawning again. "Left it to his Company, perhaps. He hasn't left it to *me*. That's all I know."

This pleasantry was received with a general laugh.

"It's likely to be a very cheap funeral," said the same speaker; "for upon my life I don't know of anybody to go to it. Suppose we make up a party and volunteer?"

"I don't mind going if a lunch is provided," observed the gentleman with the excrescence on his nose. "But I must be fed, if I make one."

Another laugh.

"Well, I am the most disinterested among you, after all," said the first speaker, "for I never wear black gloves, and I never eat lunch. But I'll offer to go, if anybody else will. When I come to think of it, I'm not at all sure that I wasn't his most particular friend; for we used to stop and speak whenever we met. Bye, bye!"

Speakers and listeners strolled away, and mixed with other groups. Scrooge knew the men, and looked towards the Spirit for an explanation.

The Phantom glided on into a street. Its finger pointed to two persons meeting. Scrooge listened again, thinking that the explanation might lie here.

He knew these men, also, perfectly. They were men of business: very wealthy, and of great importance. He had made a point always of standing well in their esteem: in a business point of view, that is; strictly in a business point of view.

"How are you?" said one.

"How are you?" returned the other.

"Well!" said the first. "Old Scratch has got his own at last, hey?"

"So I am told," returned the second. "Cold, isn't it?"

"Seasonable for Christmas time. You're not a skater, I suppose?"

"No. No. Something else to think of. Good morning!"

Not another word. That was their meeting, their conversation, and their parting.

Scrooge was at first inclined to be surprised that the Spirit should attach importance to conversations apparently so trivial; but feeling assured that they must have some hidden purpose, he set himself to consider what it was likely to be. They could scarcely be supposed to have any bearing on the death of Jacob, his old partner, for that was Past, and this Ghost's province was the Future. Nor could he think of any one immediately connected with himself, to whom he could apply them. But nothing doubting that to whomsoever they applied they had some latent moral for his own improvement, he resolved to treasure up every word he heard, and everything he saw; and especially to observe the shadow of himself when it appeared. For he had an expectation that the conduct of his future self would give him the clue he missed, and would render the solution of these riddles easy.

He looked about in that very place for his own image; but another man stood in his accustomed corner, and though the clock pointed to his usual time of day for being there, he saw no likeness of himself among the multitudes that poured in through the Porch. It gave him little surprise, however; for he had been revolving in his mind a change of life, and thought and hoped he saw his new-born resolutions carried out in this.

Quiet and dark, beside him stood the Phantom, with its outstretched hand. When he roused himself from his thoughtful quest, he fancied from the turn of the hand, and its situation in reference to himself, that the Unseen Eyes were looking at him keenly. It made him shudder, and feel very cold.

They left the busy scene, and went into an obscure part of the town, where Scrooge had never penetrated before, although he recognised its situation, and its bad repute. The ways were foul and narrow; the shops and houses wretched; the people half-naked, drunken, slipshod, ugly. Alleys and archways, like so many cesspools, disgorged their offences of smell, and dirt, and life, upon the straggling streets; and the whole quarter reeked with crime, with filth, and misery.

Far in this den of infamous resort, there was a low-browed, beetling shop, below a pent-house roof, where iron, old rags, bottles, bones, and greasy offal, were bought. Upon the floor within, were piled up heaps of rusty keys, nails, chains, hinges, files, scales, weights, and refuse iron of all kinds. Secrets that few would like to scrutinise were bred and hidden in mountains of unseemly rags, masses of corrupted fat, and sepulchres of bones. Sitting in among the wares he dealt in, by a charcoal-stove, made of old bricks, was a grey-haired rascal, nearly seventy years of age; who had screened himself from the cold air without, by a frousy curtaining of miscellaneous tatters, hung upon a line; and smoked his pipe in all the luxury of calm retirement.

Scrooge and the Phantom came into the presence of this man, just as a woman with a heavy bundle slunk into the shop. But she had scarcely entered, when another woman, similarly laden, came in too; and she was closely followed by a man in faded black, who was no less startled by the sight of them, than they had been upon the recognition of each other. After a short period of blank astonishment, in which the old man with the pipe had joined them, they all three burst into a laugh.

"Let the charwoman alone to be the first!" cried she who had entered first. "Let the laundress alone to be the second; and let the undertaker's man alone to be the third. Look here, old Joe, here's a chance! If we haven't all three met here without meaning it!"

"You couldn't have met in a better place," said old Joe, removing his pipe from his mouth. "Come into the parlour. You were made free of it long ago, you know; and the other two an't strangers. Stop till I shut the door of the shop. Ah! How it skreeks! There an't such a rusty bit of metal in the place as its own hinges, I believe; and I'm sure there's no such old bones here, as mine. Ha, ha! We're all suitable to our calling, we're well matched. Come into the parlour. Come into the parlour."

The parlour was the space behind the screen of rags. The old man raked the fire together with an old stair-rod, and having trimmed his smoky lamp (for it was night), with the stem of his pipe, put it in his mouth again.

While he did this, the woman who had already spoken threw her bundle on the floor, and sat down in a flaunting manner on a stool; crossing her elbows on her knees, and looking with a bold defiance at the other two.

"What odds then! What odds, Mrs. Dilber?" said the woman. "Every person has a right to take care of themselves. *He* always did!"

"That's true, indeed!" said the laundress. "No man more so."

"Why, then, don't stand staring as if you was afraid, woman; who's the wiser? We're not going to pick holes in each other's coats, I suppose?"

"No, indeed!" said Mrs. Dilber and the man together. "We should hope not."

"Very well, then!" cried the woman. "That's enough. Who's the worse for the loss of a few things like these? Not a dead man, I suppose."

"No, indeed," said Mrs. Dilber, laughing.

"If he wanted to keep 'em after he was dead, a wicked old screw," pursued the woman, "why wasn't he natural in his lifetime? If he had been, he'd have had somebody to look after him when he was struck with Death, instead of lying gasping out his last there, alone by himself."

"It's the truest word that ever was spoke," said Mrs. Dilber. "It's a judgment on him."

"I wish it was a little heavier one," replied the woman; "and it should have been, you may depend upon it, if I could have laid my hands on anything else. Open that bundle, old Joe, and let me know the value of it. Speak out plain. I'm not afraid to be the first, nor afraid for them to see it. We knew pretty well that we were helping ourselves, before we met here, I believe. It's no sin. Open the bundle, Joe."

But the gallantry of her friends would not allow of this; and the man in faded black, mounting the breach first, produced *his* plunder. It was not extensive. A seal or two, a pencil-case, a pair of sleeve-buttons, and a brooch of no great value, were all. They were severally examined and appraised by old Joe, who chalked the sums he was disposed to give for each, upon the wall, and added them up

into a total when he found there was nothing more to come.

"That's your account," said Joe, "and I wouldn't give another sixpence, if I was to be boiled for not doing it. Who's next?"

Mrs. Dilber was next. Sheets and towels, a little wearing apparel, two old-fashioned silver teaspoons, a pair of sugar-tongs, and a few boots. Her account was stated on the wall in the same manner.

"I always give too much to ladies. It's a weakness of mine, and that's the way I ruin myself," said old Joe. "That's your account. If you asked me for another penny, and made it an open question, I'd repent of being so liberal and knock off half-a-crown."

"And now undo *my* bundle, Joe," said the first woman.

Joe went down on his knees for the greater convenience of opening it, and having unfastened a great many knots, dragged out a large and heavy roll of some dark stuff.

"What do you call this?" said Joe. "Bed-curtains!"

"Ah!" returned the woman, laughing and leaning forward on her crossed arms. "Bed-curtains!"

"You don't mean to say you took 'em down, rings and all, with him lying there?" said Joe.

"Yes I do," replied the woman. "Why not?"

"You were born to make your fortune," said Joe, "and you'll certainly do it."

"I certainly shan't hold my hand, when I can get anything in it by reaching it out, for the sake of such a man as He was, I promise you, Joe," returned the woman coolly. "Don't drop that oil upon the blankets, now."

"His blankets?" asked Joe.

"Whose else's do you think?" replied the woman. "He isn't likely to take cold without 'em, I dare say."

"I hope he didn't die of anything catching? Eh?" said old Joe, stopping in his work, and looking up.

"Don't you be afraid of that," returned the woman. "I an't so fond of his company that I'd loiter about him for such things, if he did. Ah! you may look through that shirt till your eyes ache; but you won't find a hole in it, nor a threadbare place. It's the best he had, and a fine one too. They'd have wasted it, if it hadn't been for me."

"What do you call wasting of it?" asked old Joe.

"Putting it on him to be buried in, to be sure," replied the woman with a laugh. "Somebody was fool enough to do it, but I took it off again. If calico an't good enough for such a purpose, it isn't good enough for anything. It's quite as becoming to the body. He can't look uglier than he did in that one."

Scrooge listened to this dialogue in horror. As they sat grouped about their spoil, in the scanty light afforded by the old man's lamp, he viewed them with a detestation and disgust, which could hardly have been greater, though they had been obscene demons, marketing the corpse itself.

"Ha, ha!" laughed the same woman, when old Joe, producing a flannel bag with money in it, told out their several gains upon the ground. "This is the end of it, you see! He frightened every one away from him when he was alive, to profit us when he was dead! Ha, ha, ha!"

"Spirit!" said Scrooge, shuddering from head to foot. "I see, I see. The case of this unhappy man might be my own. My life tends that way, now. Merciful Heaven, what is this!"

He recoiled in terror, for the scene had changed, and now he almost touched a bed: a bare, uncurtained bed: on which, beneath a ragged sheet, there lay a something covered up, which, though it was dumb, announced itself in awful language.

The room was very dark, too dark to be observed with any accuracy, though Scrooge glanced round it in obedience to a secret impulse, anxious to know what kind of room it was. A pale light, rising in the outer air, fell straight upon the bed; and on it, plundered and bereft, unwatched, unwept, uncared for, was the body of this man.

Scrooge glanced towards the Phantom. Its steady hand was pointed to the head. The cover was so carelessly adjusted that the slightest raising of it, the motion of a finger upon Scrooge's part, would have disclosed the face. He thought of it, felt how easy it would be to do, and longed to do it; but had no more power to withdraw the veil than to dismiss the spectre at his side.

Oh cold, cold, rigid, dreadful Death, set up thine altar here, and dress it with such terrors as thou hast at thy command: for this is thy dominion! But of the loved, revered, and honoured head, thou canst not turn one hair to thy dread purposes, or make one feature odious. It is not that the hand is heavy and will fall down when released; it is not that the heart and pulse are still; but that the hand was open, generous, and true; the heart brave, warm, and tender; and the pulse a man's. Strike, Shadow, strike! And see his good deeds springing from the wound, to sow the world with life immortal!

No voice pronounced these words in Scrooge's ears, and yet he heard them when he looked upon the bed. He thought, if this man could be raised up now, what would be his foremost thoughts? Avarice, hard dealing, griping cares? They have brought him to a rich end, truly!

He lay, in the dark empty house, with not a man, a woman, or a child, to say that he was kind to me in this or that, and for the memory of one kind word I will be kind to him. A cat was tearing at the door, and there was a sound of gnawing rats beneath the hearth-stone. What *they* wanted in the room of death, and why they were so restless and disturbed, Scrooge did not dare to think.

"Spirit!" he said, "this is a fearful place. In leaving it, I shall not leave its lesson, trust me. Let us go!"

Still the Ghost pointed with an unmoved finger to the head.

"I understand you," Scrooge returned, "and I would do it, if I could. But I have not the power, Spirit. I have not the power."

Again it seemed to look upon him.

"If there is any person in the town, who feels emotion caused by this man's death," said Scrooge quite agonised, "show that person to me, Spirit, I beseech you!"

The Phantom spread its dark robe before him for a moment, like a wing; and withdrawing it, revealed a room by daylight, where a mother and her children were.

She was expecting some one, and with anxious eagerness; for she walked up and down the room; started at every sound; looked out from the window; glanced at the clock; tried, but in vain, to work with her needle; and could hardly bear the voices of the children in their play.

At length the long-expected knock was heard. She hurried to the door, and met her husband; a man whose face was careworn and depressed, though he was young. There was a remarkable expression in it now; a kind of serious delight of which he felt ashamed, and which he struggled to repress.

He sat down to the dinner that had been hoarding for him by the fire; and when she asked him faintly what news (which was not until after a long silence), he appeared embarrassed how to answer.

"Is it good," she said, "or bad?"—to help him.

"Bad," he answered.

"We are quite ruined?"

"No. There is hope yet, Caroline."

"If *he* relents," she said, amazed, "there is! Nothing is past hope, if such a miracle has happened."

"He is past relenting," said her husband. "He is dead."

She was a mild and patient creature if her face spoke truth; but she was thankful in her soul to hear it, and she said so, with clasped hands. She prayed forgiveness the next moment, and was sorry; but the first was the emotion of her heart.

"What the half-drunken woman whom I told you of last night, said to me, when I tried to see him and obtain a week's delay; and what I thought was a mere excuse to avoid me; turns out to have been quite true. He was not only very ill, but dying, then."

"To whom will our debt be transferred?"

"I don't know. But before that time we shall be ready with the money; and even though we were not, it would be bad fortune indeed to find so merciless a creditor in his successor. We may sleep to-night with light hearts, Caroline!"

Yes. Soften it as they would, their hearts were lighter. The children's faces, hushed and clustered round to hear what they so little understood, were brighter; and it was a happier house for this man's death! The only emotion that the Ghost could show him, caused by the event, was one of pleasure.

"Let me see some tenderness connected with a death," said Scrooge; "or that dark chamber, Spirit, which we left just now, will be for ever present to me."

The Ghost conducted him through several streets familiar to his feet; and as they went along, Scrooge looked here and there to find himself, but nowhere was he to be seen. They entered poor Bob Cratchit's house; the dwelling he had visited before; and found the mother and the children seated round the fire.

Quiet. Very quiet. The noisy little Cratchits were as still as statues in one corner, and sat looking up at Peter, who had a book before him. The mother and her daughters were engaged in sewing. But surely they were very quiet!

" 'And He took a child, and set him in the midst of them.' "

Where had Scrooge heard those words? He had not dreamed them. The boy must have read them out, as he and the Spirit crossed the threshold. Why did he not go on?

The mother laid her work upon the table, and put her hand up to her face.

"The colour hurts my eyes," she said.

The colour? Ah, poor Tiny Tim!

"They're better now again," said Cratchit's wife. "It makes them weak by candlelight; and I wouldn't show weak eyes to your father when he comes home, for the world. It must be near his time."

"Past it rather," Peter answered, shutting up his book. "But I think he's walked a little slower than he used, these few last evenings, mother."

They were very quiet again. At last she said, and in a steady cheerful voice, that only faltered once:

"I have known him walk with—I have known him walk with Tiny Tim upon his shoulder, very fast indeed."

"And so have I," cried Peter. "Often."

"And so have I," exclaimed another. So had all.

"But he was very light to carry," she resumed, intent upon her work, "and his father loved him so, that it was no trouble—no trouble. And there is your father at the door!"

She hurried out to meet him; and little Bob in his comforter—he had need of it, poor fellow—came in. His tea was ready for him on the hob, and they all tried who should help him to it most. Then the two young Cratchits got upon his knees and laid, each child a little cheek, against his face, as if they said, "Don't mind it, father. Don't be grieved!"

Bob was very cheerful with them, and spoke pleasantly to all the family. He looked at the work upon the table, and praised the industry and speed of Mrs. Cratchit and the girls. They would be done long before Sunday he said.

"Sunday! You went to-day then, Robert?" said his wife.

"Yes, my dear," returned Bob. "I wish you could have gone. It would have done you good to see how green a place it is. But you'll see it often. I promised him that I would walk there on a Sunday. My little, little child!" cried Bob. "My little child!"

He broke down all at once. He couldn't help it. If he could have helped it, he and his child would have been farther apart perhaps than they were.

He left the room, and went up stairs into the room above, which was lighted cheerfully, and hung with Christmas. There was a chair set close beside the child, and there were signs of some one having been there, lately. Poor Bob sat down in it, and when he had thought a little and composed himself, he kissed the little face. He was reconciled to what had happened, and went down again quite happy.

They drew about the fire, and talked; the girls and mother working still. Bob told them of the extraordinary kindness of Mr. Scrooge's nephew, whom he had scarcely seen but once, and who, meeting him in the street that day, and seeing that he looked a little—"just a little down you know," said Bob, inquired what had happened to distress him—"On which," said Bob, "for he is the pleasantest-spoken gentleman you ever heard, I told him. 'I am heartily sorry for it, Mr. Cratchit,' he said, 'and heartily sorry for your good wife.' By the bye, how he ever knew *that*, I don't know."

"Knew what, my dear?"

"Why, that you were a good wife," replied Bob.

"Everybody knows that!" said Peter.

"Very well observed, my boy!" cried Bob. "I hope they do. 'Heartily sorry,' he said, 'for your good wife. If I can be of service to you in any way,' he said, giving me his card, 'that's where I live. Pray come to me.' Now, it wasn't," cried Bob, "for the sake of anything he might be able to do for us, so much as for his kind way, that this was quite delightful. It really seemed as if he had known our Tiny Tim, and felt with us."

"I'm sure he's a good soul!" said Mrs. Cratchit.

"You would be surer of it, my dear," returned Bob, "if you saw and spoke to him. I shouldn't be at all surprised, mark what I say, if he got Peter a better situation."

"Only hear that, Peter," said Mrs. Cratchit.

"And then," cried one of the girls, "Peter will be keeping company with some one, and setting up for himself."

"Get along with you!" retorted Peter, grinning.

"It's just as likely as not," said Bob, "one of these days; though there's plenty of time for that, my dear. But however and whenever we part from one another, I am sure we shall none of us forget poor Tiny Tim—shall we—or this first parting that there was among us?"

"Never, father!" cried they all.

"And I know," said Bob, "I know, my dears, that when we recollect how patient and how mild he was; although he was a little, little child; we shall not quarrel easily among ourselves, and forget poor Tiny Tim in doing it."

"No, never, father!" they all cried again.

"I am very happy," said little Bob, "I am very happy!"

Mrs. Cratchit kissed him, his daughters kissed him, the two young Cratchits kissed him, and Peter and himself shook hands. Spirit of Tiny Tim, thy childish essence was from God!

"Spectre," said Scrooge, "something informs me that our parting moment is at hand. I know it, but I know not how. Tell me what man that was whom we saw lying dead?"

The Ghost of Christmas Yet To Come conveyed him, as before—though at a different time, he thought: indeed, there seemed no order in these latter visions, save that they were in the Future—into the resorts of business men, but showed him not himself. Indeed, the Spirit did not stay for anything, but went straight on, as to the end just now desired, until besought by Scrooge to tarry for a moment.

"This court," said Scrooge, "through which we hurry now, is where my place of occupation is, and has been for a length of time. I see the house. Let me behold what I shall be, in days to come!"

The Spirit stopped; the hand was pointed elsewhere.

"The house is yonder," Scrooge exclaimed. "Why do you point away?"

The inexorable finger underwent no change.

Scrooge hastened to the window of his office, and looked in. It was an office still, but not his. The furniture was not the same, and the figure in the chair was not himself. The Phantom pointed as before.

He joined it once again, and wondering why and whither he had gone, accompanied it until they reached an iron gate. He paused to look round before entering.

A churchyard. Here, then, the wretched man whose name he had now to learn, lay underneath the ground. It was a worthy place. Walled in by houses; overrun by grass and weeds, the growth of vegetation's death, not life; choked up with too much burying; fat with repleted appetite. A worthy place!

The Spirit stood among the graves, and pointed down to One. He advanced towards it trembling. The Phantom was exactly as it had been, but he dreaded that he saw new meaning in its solemn shape.

"Before I draw nearer to that stone to which you point," said Scrooge, "answer me one question. Are these the shadows of the things that Will be, or are they shadows of things that May be, only?"

Still the Ghost pointed downward to the grave by which it stood.

"Men's courses will foreshadow certain ends, to which, if persevered in, they must lead," said Scrooge. "But if the courses be departed from, the ends will change. Say it is thus with what you show me!"

The Spirit was immovable as ever.

Scrooge crept towards it, trembling as he went; and following the finger, read upon the stone of the neglected grave his own name, EBENEZER SCROOGE.

"Am *I* that man who lay upon the bed?" he cried, upon his knees.

The finger pointed from the grave to him, and back again.

"No, Spirit! Oh no, no!"

The finger still was there.

"Spirit!" he cried, tight clutching at its robe, "hear me! I am not the man I was. I will not be the man I must have been but for this intercourse. Why show me this, if I am past all hope!"

For the first time the hand appeared to shake.

"Good Spirit," he pursued, as down upon the ground he fell before it: "Your nature intercedes for me, and pities me. Assure me that I yet may change these shadows you have shown me, by an altered life!"

The kind hand trembled.

"I will honour Christmas in my heart, and try to keep it all the year. I will live in the Past, the Present, and the Future. The Spirits of all Three shall strive within me. I will not shut out the lessons that they teach. Oh, tell me I may sponge away the writing on this stone!"

In his agony, he caught the spectral hand. It sought to free itself, but he was strong in his entreaty, and detained it. The Spirit, stronger yet, repulsed him.

Holding up his hands in one last prayer to have his fate reversed, he saw an alteration in the Phantom's hood and dress. It shrank, collapsed, and dwindled down into a bedpost.

STAVE FIVE.

THE END OF IT.

YES! and the bedpost was his own. The bed was his own, the room was his own. Best and happiest of all, the Time before him was his own, to make amends in!

"I will live in the Past, the Present, and the Future!" Scrooge repeated, as he scrambled out of bed. "The Spirits of all Three shall strive within me. Oh Jacob Marley! Heaven, and the Christmas Time be praised for this! I say it on my knees, old Jacob, on my knees!"

He was so fluttered and so glowing with his good intentions, that his broken voice would scarcely answer to his call. He had been sobbing violently in his conflict with the Spirit, and his face was wet with tears.

"They are not torn down," cried Scrooge, folding one of his bed-curtains in his arms, "they are not torn down, rings and all. They are here: I am here: the shadows of the things that would have been, may be dispelled. They will be. I know they will!"

His hands were busy with his garments all this time: turning them inside out, putting them on upside down, tearing them, mislaying them, making them parties to every kind of extravagance.

"I don't know what to do!" cried Scrooge, laughing and crying in the same breath; and making a perfect Laocoön of himself with his stockings. "I am as light as a feather, I am as happy as an angel, I am as merry as a schoolboy. I am as giddy as a drunken man. A Merry Christmas to everybody! A Happy New Year to all the world. Hallo here! Whoop! Hallo!"

He had frisked into the sitting-room, and was now standing there: perfectly winded.

"There's the saucepan that the gruel was in!" cried Scrooge, starting off again, and frisking round the fireplace. "There's the door, by which the Ghost of Jacob Marley entered! There's the corner where the Ghost of Christmas Present sat! There's the window where I saw the wandering Spirits! It's all right, it's all true, it all happened. Ha, ha, ha!"

Really, for a man who had been out of practice for so many years, it was a splendid laugh, a most illustrious laugh. The father of a long, long line of brilliant laughs!

"I don't know what day of the month it is!" said Scrooge. "I don't know how long I've been among the Spirits. I don't know anything. I'm quite a baby. Never mind. I don't care. I'd rather be a baby. Hallo! Whoop! Hallo here!"

He was checked in his transports by the churches ringing out the lustiest peals he had ever heard. Clash, clang, hammer, ding, dong, bell. Bell, dong, ding, hammer, clang, clash! Oh, glorious, glorious!

Running to the window, he opened it, and put out his head. No fog, no mist; clear, bright, jovial, stirring, cold; cold, piping for the blood to dance to; golden sunlight; heavenly sky; sweet fresh air; merry bells. Oh, glorious. Glorious!

"What's to-day?" cried Scrooge, calling downward to a boy in Sunday clothes, who perhaps had loitered in to look about him.

"EH?" returned the boy, with all his might of wonder.

"What's to-day, my fine fellow?" said Scrooge.

"To-day!" replied the boy. "Why, CHRISTMAS DAY."

"It's Christmas Day!" said Scrooge to himself. "I haven't missed it. The Spirits have done it all in one night. They can do anything they like. Of course they can. Of course they can. Hallo, my fine fellow!"

"Hallo!" returned the boy.

"Do you know the Poulterer's, in the next street but one, at the corner?" Scrooge inquired.

"I should hope I did," replied the lad.

"An intelligent boy!" said Scrooge. "A remarkable boy! Do you know whether they've sold the prize Turkey that was hanging up there? Not the little prize Turkey: the big one?"

"What, the one as big as me?" returned the boy.

"What a delightful boy!" said Scrooge. "It's a pleasure to talk to him. Yes, my buck!"

"It's hanging there now," replied the boy.

"Is it?" said Scrooge. "Go and buy it."

"Walk-ER!" exclaimed the boy.

"No, no," said Scrooge, "I am in earnest. Go and buy it, and tell 'em to bring it here, that I may give them the direction where to take it. Come back with the man, and I'll give you a shilling. Come back with him in less than five minutes, and I'll give you half-a-crown!"

The boy was off like a shot. He must have had a steady hand at a trigger who could have got a shot off half so fast.

"I'll send it to Bob Cratchit's!" whispered Scrooge, rubbing his hands, and splitting with a laugh. "He shan't know who sends it. It's twice the size of Tiny Tim. Joe Miller never made such a joke as sending it to Bob's will be!"

The hand in which he wrote the address was not a steady

one but write it he did, somehow, and went down stairs to open the street door, ready for the coming of the poulterer's man. As he stood there, waiting his arrival, the knocker caught his eye.

"I shall love it, as long as I live!" cried Scrooge, patting it with his hand. "I scarcely ever looked at it before. What an honest expression it has in its face! It's a wonderful knocker!—Here's the Turkey. Hallo! Whoop! How are you! Merry Christmas!"

It *was* a Turkey! He could never have stood upon his legs, that bird. He would have snapped 'em short off in a minute, like sticks of sealing-wax.

"Why, it's impossible to carry that to Camden Town," said Scrooge. "You must have a cab."

The chuckle with which he said this, and the chuckle with which he paid for the turkey, and the chuckle with which he paid for the cab, and the chuckle with which he recompensed the boy, were only to be exceeded by the chuckle with which he sat down breathless in his chair again, and chuckled till he cried.

Shaving was not an easy task, for his hand continued to shake very much; and shaving requires attention, even when you don't dance while you are at it. But if he had cut the end of his nose off, he would have put a piece of sticking-plaster over it, and been quite satisfied.

He dressed himself "all in his best," and at last got out into the streets. The people were by this time pouring forth, as he had seen them with the Ghost of Christmas Present; and walking with his hands behind him, Scrooge regarded everyone with a delighted smile. He looked so irresistibly pleasant, in a word, that three or four good-humoured fellows said, "Good morning, Sir! A Merry Christmas to you!" And Scrooge said often afterwards, that of all the blithe sounds he had ever heard, those were the blithest in his ears.

He had not gone far, when coming on towards him he beheld the portly gentleman, who had walked into his counting-house the day before and said, "Scrooge and Marley's, I believe?" It sent a pang across his heart to think how this old gentleman would look upon him when they met; but he knew what path lay straight before him, and he took it.

"My dear Sir," said Scrooge, quickening his pace, and taking the old gentleman by both his hands. "How do you do? I hope you succeeded yesterday. It was very kind of you. A Merry Christmas to you, Sir!"

"Mr. Scrooge?"

"Yes," said Scrooge. "That is my name, and I fear it may not be pleasant to you. Allow me to ask your pardon. And will you have the goodness"—here Scrooge whispered in his ear.

"Lord bless me," cried the gentleman, as if his breath were gone. "My dear Mr. Scrooge, are you serious?"

"If you please," said Scrooge. "Not a farthing less. A great many back-payments are included in it, I assure you. Will you do me that favour?"

"My dear Sir," said the other, shaking hands with him. "I don't know what to say to such munifi——"

"Don't say anything, please," retorted Scrooge. "Come and see me. Will you come and see me?"

"I will!" cried the old gentleman. And it was clear he meant to do it.

"Thank'ee," said Scrooge. "I am much obliged to you. I thank you fifty times. Bless you!"

He went to church, and walked about the streets, and watched the people hurrying to and fro, and patted children on the head, and questioned beggars, and looked down into the kitchens of houses, and up to the windows; and found that everything could yield him pleasure. He had never dreamed that any walk—that anything—could give him so much happiness. In the afternoon, he turned his steps towards his nephew's house.

He passed the door a dozen times, before he had the courage to go up and knock. But he made a dash, and did it:

"Is your master at home, my dear?" said Scrooge to the girl. Nice girl! Very.

"Yes, Sir"

"Where is he, my love?" said Scrooge.

"He's in the dining-room, Sir, along with mistress. I'll show you up stairs, if you please."

"Thank'ee. He knows me," said Scrooge, with his hand already on the dining-room lock. "I'll go in here, my dear."

He turned it gently, and sidled his face in, round the door. They were looking at the table (which was spread out in great array); for these young housekeepers are always nervous on such points, and like to see that everything is right.

"Fred!" said Scrooge.

Dear heart alive, how his niece by marriage started! Scrooge had forgotten, for the moment, about her sitting in the corner with the footstool, or he wouldn't have done it, on any account.

"Why bless my soul!" cried Fred, "who's that?"

"It's I. Your uncle Scrooge. I have come to dinner. Will you let me in, Fred?"

Let him in! It is a mercy he didn't shake his arm off. He was at home in five minutes. Nothing could be heartier. His niece looked just the same. So did Topper when *he* came. So did the plump sister, when *she* came. So did every one when *they* came. Wonderful party, wonderful games, wonderful unanimity, won-der-ful happiness!

But he was early at the office next morning. Oh he was early there. If he could only be there first, and catch Bob Cratchit coming late! That was the thing he had set his heart upon.

And he did it; yes he did! The clock struck nine. No Bob. A quarter past. No Bob. He was full eighteen minutes and a half behind his time. Scrooge sat with his door wide open, that he might see him come into the Tank.

His hat was off, before he opened the door; his comforter too. He was on his stool in a jiffy; driving away with his pen, as if he were trying to overtake nine o'clock.

"Hallo!" growled Scrooge, in his accustomed voice as near as he could feign it. "What do you mean by coming here at this time of day?"

"I am very sorry, Sir," said Bob. "I *am* behind my time."

"You are?" repeated Scrooge. "Yes. I think you are. Step this way, Sir, if you please."

"It's only once a year, Sir," pleaded Bob, appearing from the Tank. "It shall not be repeated. I was making rather merry yesterday, Sir."

"Now, I'll tell you what, my friend," said Scrooge, "I am not going to stand this sort of thing any longer. And therefore," he continued, leaping from his stool, and giving Bob such a dig in the waistcoat that he staggered back into the Tank again: "and therefore I am about to raise your salary!"

Bob trembled, and got a little nearer to the ruler. He had a momentary idea of knocking Scrooge down with it; holding him; and calling to the people in the court for help and a strait-waistcoat.

"A Merry Christmas, Bob!" said Scrooge, with an earnestness that could not be mistaken, as he clapped him on the back. "A merrier Christmas, Bob, my good fellow, than I have give you for many a year! I'll raise your salary, and endeavour to assist your struggling family, and we will discuss your affairs this very afternoon, over a Christmas bowl of smoking bishop, Bob! Make up the fires, and buy another coal-scuttle before you dot another i, Bob Cratchit!"

Scrooge was better than his word. He did it all, and infinitely more; and to Tiny Tim, who did NOT die, he was a second father. He became as good a friend, as good a master, and as a good a man, as the good old city knew, or any other good old city, town, or borough, in the good old world. Some people laughed to see the alteration in him, but he let them laugh, and little heeded them; for he was wise enough to know that nothing ever happened on this globe, for good, at which some people did not have their fill of laughter in the outset; and knowing that such as these would be blind anyway, he thought it quite as well that they should wrinkle up their eyes in grins, as have the malady in less attractive forms. His own heart laughed: and that was quite enough for him.

He had no further intercourse with Spirits, but lived upon the Total Abstinence Principle, ever afterwards; and it was always said of him, that he knew how to keep Christmas well, if any man alive possessed the knowledge. May that be truly said of us, and all of us! And so, as Tiny Tim observed, God Bless Us, Every One!

The Personal History

of

David Copperfield

CHANGES AT HOME.

The Personal History
of
David Copperfield

by

Charles Dickens

With Illustrations by

"Phiz" (H. K. Browne)
and Others

CONTENTS.

ILLUSTRATIONS

TO

DAVID COPPERFIELD.

———

THE

PERSONAL HISTORY AND EXPERIENCE

OF

DAVID COPPERFIELD THE YOUNGER

CHAPTER I.

I AM BORN.

WHETHER I shall turn out to be the hero of my own life, or whether that station will be held by anybody else, these pages must show. To begin my life with the beginning of my life, I record that I was born (as I have been informed and believe) on a Friday, at twelve o'clock at night. It was remarked that the clock began to strike, and I began to cry, simultaneously.

In consideration of the day and hour of my birth, it was declared by the nurse, and by some sage women in the neighbourhood who had taken a lively interest in me several months before there was any possibility of our becoming personally acquainted, first, that I was destined to be unlucky in life; and secondly, that I was privileged to see ghosts and spirits; both these gifts inevitably attaching, as they believed, to all unlucky infants of either gender, born towards the small hours on a Friday night.

I need say nothing here, on the first head, because nothing can show better than my history whether that prediction was verified or falsified by the result. On the second branch of the question, I will only remark, that unless I ran through that part of my inheritance while I was still a baby, I have not come into it yet. But I do not at all complain of having been kept out of this property; and if anybody else should be in the present enjoyment of it, he is heartily welcome to keep it.

I was born with a caul, which was advertised for sale, in the newspapers, at the low price of fifteen guineas. Whether sea-going people were short of money about that time, or were short of faith and preferred cork jackets, I don't know; all I know is, that there was but one solitary bidding, and that was from an attorney connected with the bill-broking business, who offered two pounds in cash, and the balance in sherry, but declined to be guaranteed from drowning on any higher bargain. Consequently the advertisement was withdrawn at a dead loss—for as to sherry, my poor dear mother's own sherry was in the market then —and ten years afterwards the caul was put up in a raffle down in our part of the country, to fifty members at half-a-crown a head, the winner to spend five shillings. I was present myself, and I remember to have felt quite uncomfortable and confused, at a part of myself being disposed of in that way. The caul was won, I recollect, by an old lady with a hand-basket, who, very reluctantly, produced from it the stipulated five shillings, all in halfpence, and twopence halfpenny short—as it took an immense time and a great waste of arithmetic, to endeavour without any effect to prove to her. It is a fact which will be long remembered as remarkable down there, that she was never drowned, but died triumphantly in bed, at ninety-two. I have under-

stood that it was, to the last, her proudest boast that she never had been on the water in her life, except upon a bridge; and that over her tea (to which she was extremely partial) she, to the last, expressed her indignation at the impiety of mariners and others, who had the presumption to go "meandering" about the world. It was in vain to represent to her that some conveniences, tea perhaps included, resulted from this objectionable practice. She always returned, with greater emphasis and with an instinctive knowledge of the strength of her objection, "Let us have no meandering."

Not to meander myself, at present, I will go back to my birth.

I was born at Blunderstone, in Suffolk, or "thereby," as they say in Scotland. I was a posthumous child. My father's eyes had closed upon the light of this world six months, when mine opened on it. There is something strange to me, even now, in the reflection that he never saw me; and something stranger yet in the shadowy remembrance that I have of my first childish associations with his white gravestone in the churchyard, and of the indefinable compassion I used to feel for it lying out alone there in the dark night, when our little parlour was warm and bright with fire and candle, and the doors of our house were—almost cruelly, it seemed to me sometimes—bolted and locked against it.

An aunt of my father's, and consequently a great-aunt of mine, of whom I shall have more to relate by and by, was the principal magnate of our family. Miss Trotwood, or Miss Betsey, as my poor mother always called her, when she sufficiently overcame her dread of this formidable personage to mention her at all (which was seldom), had been married to a husband younger than herself, who was very handsome, except in the sense of the homely adage, "handsome is, that handsome does"—for he was strongly suspected of having beaten Miss Betsey, and even of having once, on a disputed question of supplies, made some hasty but determined arrangements to throw her out of a two pair of stairs' window. These evidences of an incompatibility of temper induced Miss Betsey to pay him off, and effect a separation by mutual consent. He went to India with his capital, and there, according to a wild legend in our family, he was once seen riding on an elephant, in company with a Baboon; but I think it must have been a Baboo—or a Begum. Anyhow, from India tidings of his death reached home, within ten years. How they affected my aunt, nobody knew; for immediately upon the separation she took her maiden name again, bought a cottage in a hamlet on the sea-coast a long way off, established herself there as a single woman with one servant, and was understood to live secluded, ever afterwards, in an inflexible retirement.

My father had once been a favourite of hers, I believe; but she was mortally affronted by his marriage, on the ground that my mother was "a wax doll." She had never seen my mother, but she knew her to be not yet twenty. My father and Miss Betsey never met again. He was double my mother's age when he married, and of but a delicate constitution. He died a year afterwards, and, as I have said, six months before I came into the world.

This was the state of matters, on the afternoon of, what *I* may be excused for calling, that eventful and important Friday. I can make no claim therefore to have known, at that time, how matters stood; or to have any remembrance, founded on the evidence of my own senses, of what follows.

My mother was sitting by the fire, but poorly in health, and very low in spirits, looking at it through her tears, and desponding heavily about herself and the fatherless little stranger, who was already welcomed by some grosses of prophetic pins, in a drawer up-stairs, to a world not at all excited on the subject of his arrival; my mother, I say, was sitting by the fire, that bright, windy March afternoon, very timid and sad, and very doubtful of ever coming alive out of the trial that was before her, when, lifting her eyes, as she dried them, to the window opposite, she saw a strange lady coming up the garden.

My mother had a sure foreboding at the second glance, that it was Miss Betsey. The setting sun was glowing on the strange lady, over the garden-fence, and she came walking up to the door with a fell rigidity of figure and composure of countenance that could have belonged to nobody else.

When she reached the house, she gave another proof of her identity. My father had often hinted that she seldom conducted herself like any ordinary Christian; and now, instead of ringing the bell, she came and looked in at that identical window, pressing the end of her nose against the glass to that extent, that my poor dear mother used to say it became perfectly flat and white in a moment.

She gave my mother such a turn, that I have always been convinced I am indebted to Miss Betsey for having been born on a Friday.

My mother had left her chair in her agitation, and gone behind it in the corner. Miss Betsey, looking round the room, slowly and inquiringly, began on the other side, and carried her eyes on, like a Saracen's head in a Dutch clock, until they reached my mother. Then she made a frown and a gesture to my mother, like one who was accustomed to be obeyed, to come and open the door. My mother went.

"Mrs. David Copperfield, I *think*," said Miss Betsey; the emphasis referring, perhaps, to my mother's mourning weeds, and her condition.

"Yes," said my mother, faintly.

"Miss Trotwood," said the visitor. "You have heard of her, I dare say?"

My mother answered she had had that pleasure. And she had a disagreeable consciousness of not appearing to imply that it had been an overpowering pleasure.

"Now you see her," said Miss Betsey. My mother bent her head, and begged her to walk in.

They went into the parlour my mother had come from, the fire in the best room on the other side of the passage not being lighted—not having been lighted, indeed, since my father's funeral; and when they were both seated, and Miss Betsey said nothing, my mother, after vainly trying to restrain herself, began to cry.

"Oh, tut, tut, tut!" said Miss Betsey, in a hurry. "Don't do that! Come, come!"

My mother couldn't help it notwithstanding, so she cried until she had had her cry out.

"Take off your cap, child," said Miss Betsey, "and let me see you."

My mother was too much afraid of her to refuse compliance with this odd request, if she had any disposition to do so. Therefore she did as she was told, and did it with such nervous hands that her hair (which was luxuriant and beautiful) fell all about her face.

"Why, bless my heart!" exclaimed Miss Betsey. "You are a very baby!"

My mother was, no doubt, unusually youthful in appearance even for her years; she hung her head, as if it were her fault, poor thing, and said, sobbing, that indeed she was afraid she was but a childish widow, and would be but a childish mother if she lived. In a short pause which ensued, she had a fancy that she felt Miss Betsey touch her hair, and that with no ungentle hand; but, looking at her, in her timid hope, she found that lady sitting with the skirt of her dress tucked up, her hands folded on one knee, and her feet upon the fender, frowning at the fire.

"In the name of Heaven," said Miss Betsey, suddenly, "why Rookery?"

"Do you mean the house, ma'am?" asked my mother.

"Why Rookery?" said Miss Betsey. "Cookery would have been more to the purpose, if you had had any practical ideas of life, either of you."

"The name was Mr. Copperfield's choice," returned my mother. "When he bought the house, he liked to think that there were rooks about it."

The evening wind made such a disturbance just now, among some tall old elm-trees at the bottom of the garden, that neither my mother nor Miss Betsey could forbear glancing that way. As the elms bent to one another, like giants who were whispering secrets, and after a few seconds of such repose, fell into a violent flurry, tossing their wild arms about, as if their late confidences were really too wicked for their peace of mind, some weather-beaten ragged old rooks'-nests, burdening their higher branches, swung like wrecks upon a stormy sea.

"Where are the birds?" asked Miss Betsey.

"The ——?" My mother had been thinking of something else.

"The rooks—what has become of them?" asked Miss Betsey.

"There have not been any since we have lived here," said my mother. "We thought—Mr. Copperfield thought—it was quite a large rookery; but the nests were very old ones, and the birds have deserted them a long while."

"David Copperfield all over!" cried Miss Betsey. "David Copperfield from head to foot! Calls a house a rookery when there's not a rook near it, and takes the birds on trust, because he sees the nests!"

"Mr. Copperfield," returned my mother, "is dead, and if you dare to speak unkindly of him to me——"

My poor dear mother, I suppose, had some momentary intention of committing an assault and battery upon my aunt, who could easily have settled her with one hand, even if my mother had been in far better training for such an encounter than she was that evening. But it passed with the action of rising from her chair; and she sat down again very meekly, and fainted.

When she came to herself, or when Miss Betsey had restored her, whichever it was, she found the latter standing at the window. The twilight was by this time shading down into darkness; and dimly as they saw each other, they could not have done that without the aid of the fire.

"Well?" said Miss Betsey, coming back to her chair, as if she had only been taking a casual look at the prospect; "and when do you expect——"

"I am all in a tremble," faltered my mother. "I don't know what's the matter. I shall die, I am sure!"

"No, no, no," said Miss Betsey. "Have some tea."

"Oh dear me, dear me, do you think it will do me any good?" cried my mother in a helpless manner.

"Of course it will," said Miss Betsey. "It's nothing but fancy. What do you call your girl?"

"I don't know that it will be a girl, yet, ma'am," said my mother.

"Bless the baby!" exclaimed Miss Betsey, unconsciously quoting the second sentiment of the pincushion in the drawer upstairs, but applying it to my mother instead of me, "I don't mean that. I mean your servant-girl."

"Peggotty," said my mother.

"Peggotty!" repeated Miss Betsey, with some indignation. "Do you mean to say, child, that any human being has gone into a Christian church, and got herself named Peggotty?"

"It's her surname," said my mother, faintly. "Mr. Copperfield called her by it, because her Christian name was the same as mine."

"Here! Peggotty!" cried Miss Betsey, opening the parlour-door. "Tea. Your mistress is a little unwell. Don't dawdle."

Having issued this mandate with as much potentiality as if she had been a recognised authority in the house ever since it had been a house, and having looked out to confront the amazed Peggotty coming along the passage with a candle at the sound of a strange voice, Miss Betsey shut the door again, and sat down as before: with her feet on the fender, the skirt of her dress tucked up, and her hands folded on one knee.

"You were speaking about its being a girl," said Miss Betsey. "I have no doubt it will be a girl. I have a presentiment that it must be a girl. Now child, from the moment of the birth of this girl——"

"Perhaps boy," my mother took the liberty of putting in.

"I tell you I have a presentiment that it must be a girl," returned Miss Betsey. "Don't contradict. From the moment of this girl's birth, child, I intend to be her friend. I intend to be her godmother, and I beg you'll call her Betsey Trotwood Copperfield. There must be no mistakes in life with *this* Betsey Trotwood. There must be no trifling with *her* affections, poor dear. She must be well brought up, and well guarded from reposing any foolish confidences where they are not deserved. I must make that *my* care."

There was a twitch of Miss Betsey's head, after each of these sentences, as if her own old wrongs were working within her, and she repressed any plainer reference to them by strong constraint. So my mother suspected, at least, as she observed her by the low glimmer of the fire: too much scared by Miss Betsey, too uneasy in herself, and too subdued and bewildered altogether, to observe anything very clearly, or to know what to say.

"And was David good to you, child?" asked Miss Betsey, when she had been silent for a little while, and these motions of her head had gradually ceased. "Were you comfortable together?"

"We were very happy," said my mother. "Mr. Copperfield was only too good to me."

"What, he spoilt you, I suppose?" returned Miss Betsey. "For being quite alone and dependent on myself in this rough world again, yes, I fear he did indeed," sobbed my mother.

"Well! Don't cry!" said Miss Betsey. "You were not equally matched, child—if any two people *can* be equally matched—and so I asked the question. You were an orphan, weren't you?"

"Yes."

"And a governess?"

"I was nursery-governess in a family where Mr. Copperfield came to visit. Mr. Copperfield was very kind to me, and took a great deal of notice of me, and paid me a good deal of attention, and at last proposed to me. And I accepted him. And so we were married," said my mother simply.

"Ha! Poor baby!" mused Miss Betsey, with her frown still bent upon the fire. "Do you know anything?"

"I beg your pardon, ma'am," faltered my mother.

"About keeping house, for instance," said Miss Betsey.

"Not much, I fear," returned my mother. "Not so much as I could wish. But Mr. Copperfield was teaching me——"

("Much he knew about it himself!") said Miss Betsey in a parenthesis.

—"And I hope I should have improved, being very anxious to learn, and he very patient to teach, if the great misfortune of his death"—my mother broke down again here, and could get no farther.

"Well, well!" said Miss Betsey.

—"I kept my housekeeping-book regularly, and balanced it with Mr. Copperfield every night," cried my mother in another burst of distress, and breaking down again.

"Well, well!" said Miss Betsey. "Don't cry any more."

—"And I am sure we never had a word of difference respecting it, except when Mr. Copperfield objected to my threes and fives being too much like each other, or to my putting curly tails to my sevens and nines," resumed my mother in another burst, and breaking down again.

"You'll make yourself ill," said Miss Betsey, "and you know that will not be good either for you or for my god-daughter. Come! You mustn't do it!"

This argument had some share in quieting my mother, though her increasing indisposition perhaps had a larger one. There was an interval of silence, only broken by Miss Betsey's occasionally ejaculating "Ha!" as she sat with her feet upon the fender.

"David had bought an annuity for himself with his money, I know," said she, by and by. "What did he do for you?"

"Mr. Copperfield," said my mother, answering with some difficulty, "was so considerate and good as to secure the reversion of a part of it to me."

"How much?" asked Miss Betsey.

"A hundred and five pounds a year," said my mother.

"He might have done worse," said my aunt.

The word was appropriate to the moment. My mother was so much worse that Peggotty, coming in with the tea-board and candles, and seeing at a glance how ill she was, —as Miss Betsey might have done sooner if there had been light enough,—conveyed her up-stairs to her own room with all speed; and immediately despatched Ham Peggotty, her nephew, who had been for some days past secreted in the house, unknown to my mother, as a special messenger in case of emergency, to fetch the nurse and doctor.

Those allied powers were considerably astonished, when

they arrived within a few minutes of each other, to find an unknown lady of portentous appearance, sitting before the fire, with her bonnet tied over her left arm, stopping her ears with jewellers' cotton. Peggotty knowing nothing about her, and my mother saying nothing about her, she was quite a mystery in the parlour; and the fact of her having a magazine of jewellers' cotton in her pocket, and sticking the article in her ears in that way, did not detract from the solemnity of her presence.

The doctor having been up-stairs and come down again, and having satisfied himself, I suppose, that there was a probability of this unknown lady and himself having to sit there, face to face, for some hours, laid himself out to be polite and social. He was the meekest of his sex, the mildest of little men. He sidled in and out of a room, to take up the less space. He walked as softly as the Ghost in Hamlet, and more slowly. He carried his head on one side, partly in modest depreciation of himself, partly in modest propitiation of everybody else. It is nothing to say that he hadn't a word to throw at a dog. He couldn't have *thrown* a word at a mad dog. He might have offered him one gently, or half a one, or a fragment of one; for he spoke as slowly as he walked; but he wouldn't have been rude to him, and he couldn't have been quick with him, for any earthly consideration.

Mr. Chillip, looking mildly at my aunt with his head on one side, and making her a little bow, said, in allusion to the jewellers' cotton, as he softly touched his left ear—

"Some local irritation, ma'am?"

"What?" replied my aunt, pulling the cotton out of one ear like a cork.

Mr. Chillip was so alarmed by her abruptness—as he told my mother afterwards—that it was a mercy he didn't lose his presence of mind. But he repeated, sweetly:

"Some local irritation, ma'am?"

"Nonsense!" replied my aunt, and corked herself again, at one blow.

Mr. Chillip could do nothing after this, but sit and look at her feebly, as she sat and looked at the fire, until he was called up-stairs again. After some quarter of an hour's absence, he returned.

"Well?" said my aunt, taking the cotton out of the ear nearest to him.

"Well, ma'am," returned Mr. Chillip, "we are—we are progressing slowly, ma'am."

"Ba—a—ah!" said my aunt, with a perfect shake on the contemptuous interjection. And corked herself, as before.

Really—really—as Mr. Chillip told my mother, he was almost shocked; speaking in a professional point of view alone, he was almost shocked. But he sat and looked at her, notwithstanding, for nearly two hours, as she sat looking at the fire, until he was again called out. After another absence, he again returned.

"Well?" said my aunt, taking out the cotton on that side again.

"Well, ma'am," returned Mr. Chillip, "we are—we are progressing slowly, ma'am."

"Ya—a—ah!" said my aunt. With such a snarl at him, that Mr. Chillip absolutely could not bear it. It was really calculated to break his spirit, he said afterwards. He preferred to go and sit upon the stairs, in the dark and a strong draught, until he was again sent for.

Ham Peggotty, who went to the national school, and was a very dragon at his catechism, and who may therefore be regarded as a credible witness, reported next day, that happening to peep in at the parlour-door an hour after this, he was instantly descried by Miss Betsey, then walking to and fro in a state of agitation, and pounced upon before he could make his escape. That there were now occasional sounds of feet and voices overhead which he inferred the cotton did not exclude, from the circumstance of his evidently being clutched by the lady as a victim on whom to expend her superabundant agitation when the sounds were loudest. That, marching him constantly up and down by the collar (as if he had been taking too much laudanum), she, at those times, shook him, rumpled his hair, made light of his linen, stopped *his* ears as if she confounded them with her own, and otherwise touzled and maltreated him. This was in part confirmed by his aunt, who saw him at half-past twelve o'clock, soon after his release, and affirmed that he was then as red as I was.

The mild Mr. Chillip could not possibly bear malice at such a time, if at any time. He sidled into the parlour as soon as he was at liberty, and said to my aunt in his meekest manner—

"Well, ma'am, I am happy to congratulate you."

"What upon?" said my aunt, sharply.

Mr. Chillip was fluttered again, by the extreme severity of my aunt's manner; so he made her a little bow, and gave her a little smile, to mollify her.

"Mercy on the man, what's he doing!" cried my aunt, impatiently. "Can't he speak?"

"Be calm, my dear ma'am," said Mr. Chillip, in his softest accents. "There is no longer any occasion for uneasiness, ma'am. Be calm."

It has since been considered almost a miracle that my aunt didn't shake him, and shake what he had to say out of him. She only shook her own head at him, but in a way that made him quail.

"Well, ma'am," resumed Mr. Chillip, as soon as he had courage, "I am happy to congratulate you. All is now over, ma'am, and well over."

During the five minutes or so that Mr. Chillip devoted to the delivery of this oration, my aunt eyed him narrowly.

"How is she?" said my aunt, folding her arms with her bonnet still tied on one of them.

"Well, ma'am, she will soon be quite comfortable, I hope," returned Mr. Chillip. "Quite as comfortable as we can expect a young mother to be, under these melancholy domestic circumstances. There cannot be any objection to your seeing her presently, ma'am. It may do her good."

"And *she*. How is *she?*" said my aunt, sharply.

Mr. Chillip laid his head a little more on one side, and looked at my aunt like an amiable bird.

"The baby," said my aunt. "How is she?"

"Ma'am," returned Mr. Chillip, "I apprehended you had known. It's a boy."

My aunt said never a word, but took her bonnet by the strings, in the manner of a sling, aimed a blow at Mr. Chillip's head with it, put it on bent, walked out, and never came back. She vanished like a discontented fairy; or like one of those supernatural beings whom it was popularly supposed I was entitled to see; and never came back any more.

No. I lay in my basket, and my mother lay in her bed; but Betsey Trotwood Copperfield was for ever in the land of dreams and shadows, the tremendous region whence I had so lately travelled; and the light from the window of our room shone out upon the earthly bourne of all such travellers, and the mound above the ashes and the dust that once was he, without whom I had never been.

CHAPTER II.

I OBSERVE.

The first objects that assume a distinct presence before me, as I look far back, into the blank of my infancy, are my mother with her pretty hair and youthful shape, and Peggotty, with no shape at all, and eyes so dark that they seemed to darken their whole neighbourhood in her face, and cheeks and arms so hard and red that I wondered the birds didn't peck her in preference to apples.

I believe I can remember these two at a little distance apart, dwarfed to my sight by stooping down or kneeling on the floor, and I going unsteadily from the one to the other. I have an impression on my mind which I cannot distinguish from actual remembrance, of the touch of Peggotty's fore-finger as she used to hold it out to me, and of its being roughened by needlework, like a pocket nutmeg-grater.

This may be fancy, though I think the memory of most of us can go farther back into such times than many of us suppose; just as I believe the power of observation in numbers of very young children to be quite wonderful for its closeness and accuracy. Indeed, I think that most grown men who are remarkable in this respect, may with greater propriety be said not to have lost the faculty, than to have acquired it; the rather, as I generally observe such men to retain a certain freshness, and gentleness, and capacity of being pleased, which are also an inheritance they have preserved from their childhood.

I might have a misgiving that I am "meandering" in stopping to say this, but that it brings me to remark that I build these conclusions, in part upon my own experience of myself; and if it should appear from anything I may set down in this narrative that I was a child of close observation, or that as a man I have a strong memory of my childhood, I undoubtedly lay claim to both of these characteristics.

Looking back, as I was saying, into the blank of my infancy, the first objects I can remember as standing out by themselves from a confusion of things, are my mother and Peggotty. What else do I remember? Let me see.

There comes out of the cloud, our house—not new to me, but quite familiar, in its earliest remembrance. On the ground-floor is Peggotty's kitchen, opening into a back yard; with a pigeon-house on a pole, in the centre, without any pigeons in it; a great dog-kennel in a corner, without any dog; and a quantity of fowls that look terribly tall to me, walking about, in a menacing and ferocious manner. There is one cock who gets upon a post to crow, and seems to take particular notice of me as I look at him through the kitchen-window, who makes me shiver, he is so fierce. Of the geese outside the side-gate who come waddling after me with their long necks stretched out when I go that way, I

dream at night: as a man environed by wild beasts might dream of lions.

Here is a long passage—what an enormous perspective I make of it!—leading from Peggotty's kitchen to the front-door. A dark storeroom opens out of it, and that is a place to be run past at night; for I don't know what may be among those tubs and jars and old tea-chests, when there is nobody in there with a dimly-burning light, letting a mouldy air come out at the door, in which there is the smell of soap, pickles, pepper, candles, and coffee, all at one whiff. Then there are the two parlours: the parlour in which we sit of an evening, my mother and I and Peggotty—for Peggotty is quite our companion, when her work is done and we are alone—and the best parlour where we sit on a Sunday; grandly, but not so comfortably. There is something of a doleful air about that room to me, for Peggotty has told me—I don't know when, but apparently ages ago—about my father's funeral, and the company having their black cloaks put on. One Sunday night my mother reads to Peggotty and me in there, how Lazarus was raised up from the dead. And I am so frightened that they are afterwards obliged to take me out of bed, and show me the quiet churchyard out of the bedroom window, with the dead all lying in their graves at rest, below the solemn moon.

There is nothing half so green that I know anywhere, as the grass of that churchyard; nothing half so shady as its trees; nothing half so quiet as its tombstones. The sheep are feeding there, when I kneel up, early in the morning, in my little bed in a closet within my mother's room, to look out at it; and I see the red light shining on the sun-dial, and think within myself, "Is the sun-dial glad, I wonder, that it can tell the time again?"

Here is our pew in the church. What a high-backed pew! With a window near it, out of which our house can be seen, and *is* seen many times during the morning's service, by Peggotty, who likes to make herself as sure as she can that it's not being robbed, or is not in flames. But though Peggotty's eye wanders, she is much offended if mine does, and frowns to me, as I stand upon the seat, that I am to look at the clergyman. But I can't always look at him—I know him without that white thing on, and I am afraid of his wondering why I stare so, and perhaps stopping the service to inquire—and what am I to do? It's a dreadful thing to gape, but I must do something. I look at my mother, but *she* pretends not to see me. I look at a boy in the aisle, and *he* makes faces at me. I look at the sunlight coming in at the open door through the porch, and there I see a stray sheep—I don't mean a sinner, but mutton—half making up his mind to come into the church. I feel that if I looked at him any longer, I might be tempted to say something out loud; and what would become of me then! I look up at the monumental tablets on the wall, and try to think of Mr. Bodgers late of this parish, and what the feelings of Mrs. Bodgers must have been, when affliction sore, long time Mr. Bodgers bore, and physicians were in vain. I wonder whether they called in Mr. Chillip, and he was in vain; and if so, how he likes to be reminded of it once a week. I look from Mr. Chillip, in his Sunday neckcloth, to the pulpit; and think what a good place it would be to play in, and what a castle it would make, with another boy coming up the stairs to attack it, and having the velvet cushion with the tassels thrown down on his head. In time my eyes gradually shut up;

and, from seeming to hear the clergyman singing a drowsy song in the heat, I hear nothing, until I fall off the seat with a crash, and am taken out, more dead than alive, by Peggotty.

And now I see the outside of our house, with the latticed bedroom-windows, standing open to let in the sweet-smelling air, and the ragged old rooks'-nests still dangling in the elm-trees at the bottom of the front garden. Now I am in the garden at the back, beyond the yard where the empty pigeon-house and dog-kennel are—a very preserve of butterflies, as I remember it, with a high fence, and a gate and padlock; where the fruit clusters on the trees, riper and richer than fruit has ever been since, in any other garden, and where my mother gathers some in a basket, while I stand by, bolting furtive gooseberries, and trying to look unmoved. A great wind rises, and the summer is gone in a moment. We are playing in the winter twilight, dancing about the parlour. When my mother is out of breath and rests herself in an elbow-chair, I watch her winding her bright curls round her fingers, and straightening her waist, and nobody knows better than I do that she likes to look so well, and is proud of being so pretty.

That is among my very earliest impressions. That, and a sense that we were both a little afraid of Peggotty, and submitted ourselves in most things to her direction, were among the first opinions—if they may be so called—that I ever derived from what I saw.

Peggotty and I were sitting one night by the parlour fire, alone. I had been reading to Peggotty about crocodiles. I must have read very perspicuously, or the poor soul must have been deeply interested, for I remember she had a cloudy impression, after I had done, that they were a sort of vegetable. I was tired of reading, and dead sleepy; but having leave, as a high treat, to sit up until my mother came home from spending the evening at a neighbour's, I would rather have died upon my post (of course) than have gone to bed. I had reached that stage of sleepiness when Peggotty seemed to swell and grow immensely large. I propped my eyelids open with my two forefingers, and looked perseveringly at her as she sat at work; at the little bit of wax-candle she kept for her thread—how old it looked, being so wrinkled in all directions!—at the little house with a thatched roof, where the yard-measure lived; at her work-box with a sliding lid, with a view of St. Paul's Cathedral (with a pink dome) painted on the top; at the brass thimble on her finger; at herself, whom I thought lovely. I felt so sleepy, that I knew if I lost sight of anything, for a moment, I was gone.

"Peggotty," says I, suddenly, "were you ever married?" "Lord, Master Davy," replied Peggotty. "What's put marriage in your head!"

She answered with such a start, that it quite awoke me. And then she stopped in her work, and looked at me, with her needle drawn out to its thread's length.

"But were you ever married, Peggotty?" says I. "You are a very handsome woman, an't you?"

I thought her in a different style from my mother, certainly; but of another school of beauty, I considered her a perfect example. There was a red velvet footstool in the best parlour, on which my mother had painted a nosegay. The ground-work of that stool, and Peggotty's complexion, appeared to me to be one and the same thing. The stool was smooth, and Peggotty was rough, but that made no difference.

"Me handsome, Davy!" said Peggotty. "Lawk, no, my dear. But what put marriage in your head?"

"I don't know!—You mustn't marry more than one person at a time, may you, Peggotty?"

"Certainly not," says Peggotty, with the promptest decision.

"But if you marry a person, and the person dies, why then you may marry another person, mayn't you, Peggotty?"

"You MAY," says Peggotty, "if you choose, my dear. That's a matter of opinion."

"But what is your opinion, Peggotty?" said I.

I asked her, and looked curiously at her, because she looked so curiously at me.

"My opinion is," said Peggotty, taking her eyes from me, after a little indecision and going on with her work, "that I never was married myself, Master Davy, and that I don't expect to be. That's all I know about the subject."

"You an't cross, I suppose, Peggotty, are you?" said I, after sitting quiet for a minute.

I really thought she was, she had been so short with me; but I was quite mistaken: for she laid aside her work (which was a stocking of her own), and opening her arms wide, took my curly head within them, and gave it a good squeeze. I know it was a good squeeze, because, being very plump, whenever she made any little exertion after she was dressed, some of the buttons on the back of her gown flew off. And I recollect two bursting to the opposite side of the parlour, while she was hugging me.

"Now let me hear some more about the Crorkindills", said Peggotty, who was not quite right in the name yet, "for I an't heard half enough."

I couldn't quite understand why Peggotty looked so queer, or why she was so ready to go back to the crocodiles. However, we returned to those monsters, with fresh wakefulness on my part, and we left their eggs in the sand for the sun to hatch; and we ran away from them, and baffled them by constantly turning, which they were unable to do quickly, on account of their unwieldy make; and we went into the water after them, as natives, and put sharp pieces of timber down their throats; and in short we ran the whole crocodile gauntlet. I did, at least; but I had my doubts of Peggotty, who was thoughtfully sticking her needle into various parts of her face and arms, all the time.

We had exhausted the crocodiles, and begun with the alligators, when the garden-bell rang. We went out to the door; and there was my mother, looking unusually pretty, I thought, and with her a gentleman with beautiful black hair and whiskers, who had walked home with us from church last Sunday.

As my mother stooped down on the threshold to take me in her arms and kiss me, the gentleman said I was a more highly privileged little fellow than a monarch—or something like that; for my later understanding comes, I am sensible, to my aid here.

"What does that mean?" I asked him, over her shoulder.

He patted me on the head; but somehow, I didn't like him or his deep voice, and I was jealous that his hand should touch my mother's in touching me—which it did. I put it away, as well as I could.

"Oh, Davy!" remonstrated my mother.

"Dear boy!" said the gentleman. "I cannot wonder at his devotion!"

I never saw such a beautiful colour on my mother's face before. She gently chid me for being rude; and, keeping me close to her shawl, turned to thank the gentleman for taking so much trouble as to bring her home. She put out her hand to him as she spoke, and, as he met it with his own, she glanced, I thought, at me.

"Let us say ' good night,' my fine boy," said the gentle-amn, when he had bent his head—*I* saw him!—over my mother's little glove.

"Good night!" said I.

"Come! Let us be the best friends in the world!" said the gentleman, laughing. "Shake hands!"

My right hand was in my mother's left, so I gave him the other.

"Why, that's the wrong hand, Davy!" laughed the gentleman.

My mother drew my right hand forward, but I was resolved, for my former reason, not to give it him, and I did not. I gave him the other, and he shook it heartily, and said I was a brave fellow, and went away.

At this minute I see him turn round in the garden, and give us a last look with his ill-omened black eyes, before the door was shut.

Peggotty, who had not said a word or moved a finger, secured the fastenings instantly, and we all went into the parlour. My mother, contrary to her usual habit, instead of coming to the elbow-chair by the fire, remained at the other end of the room, and sat singing to herself.

—"Hope you have had a pleasant evening, ma'am," said Peggotty, standing as stiff as a barrel in the centre of the room, with a candlestick in her hand.

"Much obliged to you, Peggotty," returned my mother, in a cheerful voice, "I have had a *very* pleasant evening."

"A stranger or so makes an agreeable change," suggested Peggotty.

"A very agreeable change, indeed," returned my mother.

Peggotty continuing to stand motionless in the middle of the room, and my mother resuming her singing, I fell asleep, though I was not so sound asleep but that I could hear voices, without hearing what they said. When I half awoke from this uncomfortable doze, I found Peggotty and my mother both in tears, and both talking.

"Not such a one as this, Mr. Copperfield wouldn't have liked," said Peggotty. "That I say, and that I swear!"

"Good Heavens!" cried my mother. "You'll drive me mad! Was ever any poor girl so ill-used by her servants as I am? Why do I do myself the injustice of calling myself a girl? Have I never been married, Peggotty?"

"God knows you have, ma'am," returned Peggotty.

"Then, how can you dare," said my mother—"you know I don't mean how can you dare, Peggotty, but how can you have the heart—to make me so uncomfortable and say such bitter things to me, when you are well aware that I haven't, out of this place, a single friend to turn to!"

"The more's the reason," returned Peggotty, "for saying that it won't do. No! That it won't do. No! No price could make it do. No!"—I thought Peggotty would have thrown the candlestick away, she was so emphatic with it.

"How can you be so aggravating," said my mother, shedding more tears than before, "as to talk in such an unjust manner! How can you go on as if it was all settled and arranged, Peggotty, when I tell you over and over again, you cruel thing, that beyond the commonest civili-

ties nothing has passed! You talk of admiration. What am I to do? If people are so silly as to indulge the sentiment, is it my fault? What am I to do, I ask you? Would you wish me to shave my head and black my face, or disfigure myself with a burn, or a scald, or something of that sort? I dare say you would, Peggotty. I dare say you'd quite enjoy it."

Peggotty seemed to take this aspersion very much to heart, I thought.

"And my dear boy," cried my mother, coming to the elbow-chair in which I was, and caressing me, "my own little Davy! Is it to be hinted to me that I am wanting in affection for my precious treasure, the dearest little fellow that ever was!"

"Nobody never went and hinted no such a thing," said Peggotty.

"You did, Peggotty!" returned my mother. "You know you did. What else was it possible to infer from what you said, you unkind creature, when you know as well as I do, that on his account only last quarter I wouldn't buy myself a new parasol, though that old green one is frayed the whole way up, and the fringe is perfectly mangy. You know it is, Peggotty. You can't deny it." Then, turning affectionately to me, with her cheek against mine, "Am I a naughty mama to you, Davy? Am I a nasty, cruel, selfish, bad mama? Say I am, my child; say ' yes,' dear boy, and Peggotty will love you; and Peggotty's love is a great deal better than mine, Davy. *I* don't love you at all, do I?"

At this, we all fell a-crying together. I think I was the loudest of the party, but I am sure we were all sincere about it. I was quite heart-broken myself, and am afraid that in the first transports of wounded tenderness I called Peggotty a "beast." That honest creature was in deep affliction, I remember, and must have become quite button-less on the occasion; for a little volley of those explosives went off, when, after having made it up with my mother, she kneeled down by the elbow-chair, and made it up with me.

We went to bed greatly dejected. My sobs kept waking me, for a long time; and when one very strong sob quite hoisted me up in bed, I found my mother sitting on the coverlet, and leaning over me. I fell asleep in her arms, after that, and slept soundly.

Whether it was the following Sunday when I saw the gentleman again, or whether there was any greater lapse of time before he reappeared, I cannot recall. I don't profess to be clear about dates. But there he was, in church, and he walked home with us afterwards. He came in, too, to look at a famous geranium we had, in the parlour-window. It did not appear to me that he took much notice of it, but before he went he asked my mother to give him a bit of the blossom. She begged him to choose it for himself, but he refused to do that—I could not understand why—so she plucked it for him, and gave it into his hand. He said he would never, never, part with it any more; and I thought he must be quite a fool not to know that it would fall to pieces in a day or two.

Peggotty began to be less with us, of an evening, than she had always been. My mother deferred to her very much—more than usual, it occurred to me—and we were all three excellent friends; still we were different from what we used to be, and were not so comfortable among ourselves. Sometimes I fancied that Peggotty perhaps objected to my mother's wearing all the pretty dresses she had in her drawers, or to her going so often to visit at that neighbour's; but I couldn't, to my satisfaction, make out how it was.

Gradually, I became used to seeing the gentleman with the black whiskers. I liked him no better than at first, and had the same uneasy jealousy of him; but if I had any reason for it beyond a child's instinctive dislike, and a general idea that Peggotty and I could make much of my mother without any help, it certainly was not *the* reason that I might have found if I had been older. No such thing came into my mind, or near it. I could observe, in little pieces, as it were; but as to making a net of a number of these pieces, and catching anybody in it, that was, as yet, beyond me.

One autumn morning I was with my mother in the front garden, when Mr. Murdstone—I knew him by that name now—came by, on horseback. He reined up his horse to salute my mother, and said he was going to Lowestoft to see some friends who were there with a yacht, and merrily proposed to take me on the saddle before him if I would like the ride.

The air was so clear and pleasant, and the horse seemed to like the idea of the ride so much himself, as he stood snorting and pawing at the garden-gate, that I had a great desire to go. So I was sent upstairs to Peggotty to be made spruce; and, in the meantime, Mr. Murdstone dismounted, and, with his horse's bridle drawn over his arm, walked slowly up and down on the outer side of the sweet-briar fence, while my mother walked slowly up and down on the inner, to keep him company. I recollect Peggotty and I peeping out at them from my little window; I recollect how closely they appeared to be examining the sweet-briar between them, as they strolled along; and how, from being in a perfectly angelic temper, Peggotty turned cross in a moment, and brushed my hair the wrong way, excessively hard.

Mr. Murdstone and I were soon off, and trotting along on the green turf by the side of the road. He held me quite easily with one arm, and I don't think I was restless usually; but I could not make up my mind to sit in front of him without turning my head sometimes, and looking up in his face. He had that kind of shallow black eye—I want a better word to express an eye that has no depth in it to be looked into—which, when it is abstracted, seems, from some peculiarity of light, to be disfigured, for a moment, at a time, by a cast. Several times when I glanced at him, I observed that appearance with a sort of awe, and wondered what he was thinking about so closely. His hair and whiskers were blacker and thicker, looked at so near, than even I had given them credit for being. A squareness about the lower part of his face, and the dotted indication of the strong black beard he shaved close every day, reminded me of the wax-work that had travelled into our neighbourhood some half-a-year before. This, his regular eyebrows, and the rich white, and black, and brown, of his complexion—confound his complexion, and his memory!—made me think him, in spite of my misgivings, a very handsome man. I have no doubt that my poor dear mother thought him so too.

We went to an hotel by the sea, where two gentlemen were smoking cigars in a room by themselves. Each of them was lying on at least four chairs, and had a large rough jacket on. In a corner was a heap of coats and boat-cloaks, and a flag, all bundled up together.

They both rolled on to their feet, in an untidy sort of manner, when we came in, and said, "Halloa, Murdstone! We thought you were dead!"

"Not yet," said Mr. Murdstone.

"And who's this shaver?" said one of the gentlemen, taking hold of me.

"That's Davy," returned Mr. Murdstone.

"Davy who?" said the gentleman. "Jones?"

"Copperfield," said Mr. Murdstone.

"What! Bewitching Mrs. Copperfield's incumbrance?" cried the gentleman. "The pretty little widow?"

"Quinion," said Mr. Murdstone, "take care, if you please. Somebody's sharp."

"Who is?" asked the gentleman, laughing.

I looked up, quickly; being curious to know.

"Only Brooks of Sheffield," said Mr. Murdstone.

I was quite relieved to find that it was only Brooks of Sheffield; for, at first, I really thought it was I.

There seemed to be something very comical in the reputation of Mr. Brooks of Sheffield, for both the gentlemen laughed heartily when he was mentioned, and Mr. Murdstone was a good deal amused also. After some laughing, the gentleman whom he had called Quinion said—

"And what is the opinion of Brooks of Sheffield, in reference to the projected business?"

"Why, I don't know that Brooks understands much about it at present," replied Mr. Murdstone; "but he is not generally favourable, I believe."

There was more laughter at this, and Mr. Quinion said he would ring the bell for some sherry in which to drink to Brooks. This he did; and when the wine came, he made me have a little, with a biscuit, and, before I drank it, stand up and say, "Confusion to Brooks of Sheffield!" The toast was received with great applause, and such hearty laughter that it made me laugh too; at which they laughed the more. In short, we quite enjoyed ourselves.

We walked about on the cliff after that, and sat on the grass, and looked at things through a telescope—I could make out nothing myself when it was put to my eye, but I pretended I could—and then we came back to the hotel to an early dinner. All the time we were out, the two gentlemen smoked incessantly—which, I thought, if I might judge from the smell of their rough coats, they must have been doing, ever since the coats had first come home from the tailor's. I must not forget that we went on board the yacht, where they all three descended into the cabin, and were busy with some papers. I saw them quite hard at work, when I looked down through the open skylight. They left me, during this time, with a very nice man, with a 'very large head of red hair and a very small shiny hat upon it, who had got a cross-barred shirt or waistcoat on, with "Skylark" in capital letters across the chest. I thought it was his name; and that as he lived on board ship and hadn't a street-door to put his name on, he put it there instead; but when I called him Mr. Skylark, he said it meant the vessel.

I observed all day that Mr. Murdstone was graver and steadier than the two gentlemen. They were very gay and careless. They joked freely with one another, but seldom with him. It appeared to me that he was more clever and cold than they were, and that they regarded him with something of my own feeling. I remarked that once or twice, when Mr. Quinion was talking, he looked at Mr. Murdstone sideways, as if to make sure of his not being displeased; and that once when Mr. Passnidge (the other gentleman) was in high spirits, he trod upon his foot, and gave him a secret caution with his eyes, to observe Mr. Murdstone, who was sitting stern and silent. Nor do I recollect that Mr. Murdstone laughed at all that day, except at the Sheffield joke—and that, by the bye, was his own.

We went home early in the evening. It was a very fine evening, and my mother and he had another stroll by the sweetbriar, while I was sent in to get my tea. When he was gone, my mother asked me all about the day I had had, and what they had said and done. I mentioned what they had said about her, and she laughed, and told me they were impudent fellows who talked nonsense—but I knew it pleased her. I knew it quite as well as I know it now. I took the opportunity of asking if she was at all acquainted with Mr. Brooks of Sheffield, but she answered No, she supposed he must be a manufacturer in the knife and fork way.

Can I say of her face—altered as I have reason to remember it, perished as I know it is—that it is gone, when here it comes before me at this instant, as distinct as any face that I may choose to look on in a crowded street? Can I say of her innocent and girlish beauty, that it faded, and was no more, when its breath falls on my cheek now, as it fell that night? Can I say she ever changed, when my remembrance brings her back to life, thus only; and, truer to its loving youth than I have been, or man ever is, still holds fast what it cherished then?

I write of her just as she was when I had gone to bed after this talk, and she came to bid me good night. She kneeled down playfully by the side of the bed, and laying her chin upon her hands, and laughing, said—

"What was it they said, Davy? Tell me again. I can't believe it."

"'Bewitching——'" I began.

My mother put her hands upon my lips to stop me.

"It was never bewitching," she said, laughing. "It never could have been bewitching, Davy. Now I know it wasn't!"

"Yes it was. 'Bewitching Mrs. Copperfield,'" I repeated stoutly. "And 'pretty.'"

"No, no, it was never pretty. Not pretty," interposed my mother, laying her fingers on my lips again.

"Yes it was. 'Pretty little widow.'"

"What foolish, impudent creatures!" cried my mother, laughing and covering her face. "What ridiculous men! An't they? Davy dear——"

"Well, ma."

"Don't tell Peggotty; she might be angry with them. I am dreadfully angry with them myself; but I would rather Peggotty didn't know."

I promised, of course; and we kissed one another over and over again, and I soon fell fast asleep.

It seems to me, at this distance of time, as if it were the next day when Peggotty broached the striking and adventurous proposition I am about to mention; but it was probably about two months afterwards.

We were sitting as before, one evening (when my mother was out as before) in company with the stocking and the yard measure, and the bit of wax, and the box with Saint Paul's on the lid, and the crocodile book, when Peggotty, after looking at me several times, and opening her mouth as if she were going to speak, without doing it—which I thought was merely gaping, or I should have been rather alarmed—said coaxingly:

"Master Davy, how should you like to go along with me and spend a fortnight at my brother's at Yarmouth? Wouldn't *that* be a treat?"

"Is your brother an agreeable man, Peggotty?" I inquired, provisionally.

"Oh, what an agreeable man he is!" cried Peggotty, holding up her hands. "Then there's the sea; and the boats and ships; and the fishermen; and the beach; and Am to play with——"

Peggotty meant her nephew Ham, mentioned in my first chapter; but she spoke of him as a morsel of English Grammar.

I was flushed by her summary of delights, and replied that it would indeed be a treat, but what would my mother say?

"Why then I'll as good as bet a guinea," said Peggotty, intent upon her face, "that she'll let us go. I'll ask her, if you like, as soon as ever she comes home. There now!"

"But what's she to do while we are away?" said I, putting my small elbows on the table to argue the point. "She can't live by herself."

If Peggotty were looking for a hole, all of a sudden, in the heel of that stocking, it must have been a very little one indeed, and not worth darning.

"I say! Peggotty! She can't live by herself, you know."

"Oh bless you!" said Peggotty, looking at me again at last. "Don't you know? She's going to stay for a fortnight with Mrs. Grayper. Mrs. Grayper's going to have a lot of company."

Oh! If that was it, I was quite ready to go. I waited, in the utmost impatience, until my mother came home from Mrs. Grayper's (for it was that identical neighbour), to ascertain if we could get leave to carry out this great idea. Without being nearly so much surprised as I had expected, my mother entered into it readily; and it was all arranged that night, and my board and lodging during the visit were to be paid for.

The day soon came for our going. It was such an early day that it came soon, even to me, who was in a fever of expectation, and half afraid that an earthquake or a fiery mountain, or some other great convulsion of nature, might interpose to stop the expedition. We were to go in a carrier's cart, which departed in the morning after breakfast. I would have given any money to have been allowed to wrap myself up overnight, and sleep in my hat and boots.

It touches me nearly now, although I tell it lightly, to recollect how eager I was to leave my happy home; to think how little I suspected what I did leave for ever.

I am glad to recollect that when the carrier's cart was at the gate, and my mother stood there kissing me, a grateful fondness for her and for the old place I had never turned my back upon before, made me cry. I am glad to know that my mother cried too, and that I felt her heart beat against mine.

I am glad to recollect that when the carrier began to move, my mother ran out at the gate, and called to him to stop, that she might kiss me once more. I am glad to dwell upon the earnestness and love with which she lifted up her face to mine, and did so.

As we left her standing in the road, Mr. Murdstone came up to where she was, and seemed to expostulate with her for being so moved. I was looking back round the awning of the cart, and wondered what business it was of his. Peggotty, who was also looking back on the other side, seemed anything but satisfied; as the face she brought back in the cart denoted.

I sat looking at Peggotty for some time, in a reverie on

this supposititious case: whether, if she were employed to lose me like the boy in the fairy tale, I should be able to track my way home again by the buttons she would shed.

CHAPTER III.

I HAVE A CHANGE.

THE carrier's horse was the laziest horse in the world, I should hope, and shuffled along, with his head down, as if he liked to keep the people waiting to whom the packages were directed. I fancied, indeed, that he sometimes chuckled audibly over this reflection, but the carrier said he was only troubled with a cough.

The carrier had a way of keeping his head down, like his horse, and of drooping sleepily forward as he drove, with one of his arms on each of his knees. I say "drove," but it struck me that the cart would have gone to Yarmouth quite as well without him, for the horse did all that; and as to conversation, he had no idea of it but whistling.

Peggotty had a basket of refreshments on her knee, which would have lasted us out handsomely, if we had been going to London by the same conveyance. We ate a good deal, and slept a good deal. Peggotty always went to sleep with her chin upon the handle of the basket, her hold of which never relaxed; and I could not have believed unless I had heard her do it, that one defenceless woman could have snored so much.

We made so many deviations up and down lanes, and were such a long time delivering a bedstead at a public-house, and calling at other places, that I was quite tired, and very glad, when we saw Yarmouth. It looked rather spongy and soppy, I thought, as I carried my eye over the great dull waste that lay across the river; and I could not help wondering, if the world were really as round as my geography-book said, how any part of it came to be so flat. But I reflected that Yarmouth might be situated at one of the poles; which would account for it.

As we drew a little nearer, and saw the whole adjacent prospect lying a straight low line under the sky, I hinted to Peggotty that a mound or so might have improved it; and also that if the land had been a little more separated from the sea, and the town and the tide had not been quite so much mixed up, like toast and water, it would have been nicer. But Peggotty said, with greater emphasis than usual, that we must take things as we found them, and that, for her part, she was proud to call herself a Yarmouth Bloater.

When we got into the street (which was strange enough to me), and smelt the fish, and pitch, and oakum, and tar, and saw the sailors walking about, and the carts jingling up and down over the stones, I felt that I had done so busy a place an injustice; and said as much to Peggotty, who heard my expressions of delight with great complacency, and told me it was well known (I suppose to those who had the good fortune to be born Bloaters) that Yarmouth was, upon the whole, the finest place in the universe.

"Here's my Am!" screamed Peggotty, "growed out of knowledge!"

He was waiting for us, in fact, at the public-house; and asked me how I found myself, like an old acquaintance. I did not feel, at first, that I knew him as well as he knew me, because he had never come to our house since the night I was born, and naturally he had the advantage of me. But our intimacy was much advanced by his taking me on his back to carry me home. He was, now, a huge, strong fellow of six feet high, broad in proportion, and round-shouldered; but with a simpering boy's face and curly light hair that gave him quite a sheepish look. He was dressed in a canvas jacket, and a pair of such very stiff trousers that they would have stood quite as well alone, without any legs in them. And you couldn't so properly have said he wore a hat, as that he was covered in atop, like an old building, with something pitchy.

Ham carrying me on his back and a small box of ours under his arm, and Peggotty carrying another small box of ours, we turned down lanes bestrewn with bits of chips and little hillocks of sand, and went past gas-works, rope-walks, boat-builders' yards, shipwrights' yards, ship-breakers' yards, caulkers' yards, riggers' lofts, smiths' forges, and a great litter of such places, until we came out upon the dull waste I had already seen at a distance; when Ham said,

"Yon's our house, Mas'r Davy!"

I looked in all directions, as far as I could stare over the wilderness, and away at the sea, and away at the river, but no house could I make out. There was a black barge, or some other kind of superannuated boat, not far off, high and dry on the ground, with an iron funnel sticking out of it for a chimney and smoking very cosily; but nothing else in the way of a habitation that was visible to me.

"That's not it?" said I. "That ship-looking thing?"

"That's it, Mas'r Davy," returned Ham.

If it had been Aladdin's palace, roc's egg and all, I suppose I could not have been more charmed with the romantic idea of living in it. There was a delightful door cut in the side, and it was roofed in, and there were little windows in it; but the wonderful charm of it was, that it was a real boat which had no doubt been upon the water hundreds of times, and which had never been intended to be lived in, on dry land. That was the captivation of it to me. If it had ever been meant to be lived in, I might have thought it small, or inconvenient, or lonely; but never having been designed for any such use, it became a perfect abode.

It was beautifully clean inside, and as tidy as possible. There was a table, and a Dutch clock, and a chest of drawers, and on the chest of drawers there was a tea-tray with a painting on it of a lady with a parasol, taking a walk with a military-looking child who was trundling a hoop. The tray was kept from tumbling down, by a bible; and the tray, if it had tumbled down, would have smashed a quantity of cups and saucers and a teapot that were grouped around the book. On the walls there were some common coloured pictures, framed and glazed, of Scripture subjects; such as I have never seen since in the hands of pedlars, without seeing the whole interior of Peggotty's brother's house again, at one view. Abraham in red going to sacrifice Isaac in blue, and Daniel in yellow cast into a den of green lions, were the most prominent of these. Over the little mantel-shelf, was a picture of the *Sarah Jane* lugger, built at Sunderland, with a real little wooden stern stuck on to it; a work of art, combining composition with carpentry, which I considered to be one of the most enviable possessions that the world could afford. There were some hooks in the beams of the ceiling, the use of which I did not divine then; and some lockers and boxes and conveniences of that sort, which served for seats and eked out the chairs.

All this, I saw in the first glance after I crossed the threshold—child-like, according to my theory—and then Peggotty opened a little door and showed me my bedroom. It was the completest and most desirable bedroom ever seen —in the stern of the vessel; with a little window, where the rudder used to go through; a little looking-glass, just the right height for me, nailed against the wall, and framed with oyster-shells; a little bed, which there was just room enough to get into; and a nosegay of seaweed in a blue mug on the table. The walls were whitewashed as white as milk, and the patchwork counterpane made my eyes quite ache with its brightness. One thing I particularly noticed in this delightful house, was the smell of fish; which was so searching, that when I took out my pocket-handkerchief to wipe my nose, I found it smelt exactly as if it had wrapped up a lobster. On my imparting this discovery in confidence to Peggotty, she informed me that her brother dealt in lobsters, crabs, and crawfish; and I afterwards found that a heap of these creatures, in a state of wonderful conglomeration with one another, and never leaving off pinching whatever they laid hold of, were usually to be found in a little wooden outhouse where the pots and kettles were kept.

We were welcomed by a very civil woman in a white apron, whom I had seen curtseying at the door when I was on Ham's back, about a quarter of a mile off. Likewise by a most beautiful little girl (or I thought her so), with a necklace of blue beads on, who wouldn't let me kiss her when I offered to, but ran away and hid herself. By and by, when we had dined in a sumptuous manner off boiled dabs, melted butter, and potatoes, with a chop for me, a hairy man with a very good-natured face came home. As he called Peggotty "Lass," and gave her a hearty smack on the cheek, I had no doubt, from the general propriety of her conduct, that he was her brother; and so he turned out —being presently introduced to me as Mr. Peggotty, the master of the house.

"Glad to see you, Sir," said Mr. Peggotty. "You'll find us rough, Sir, but you'll find us ready."

I thanked him, and replied that I was sure I should be happy in such a delightful place.

"How's your Ma, Sir?" said Mr. Peggotty. "Did you leave her pretty jolly?"

I gave Mr. Peggotty to understand that she was as jolly as I could wish, and that she desired her compliments— which was a polite fiction on my part.

"I'm much obleeged to her, I'm sure," said Mr. Peggotty. "Well, Sir, if you can make out here, for a fortnut, 'long wi' her," nodding at his sister, "and Ham, and little Em'ly, we shall be proud of your company."

Having done the honours of his house in this hospitable manner, Mr. Peggotty went out to wash himself in a kettleful of hot water, remarking that "cold would never get his muck off." He soon returned, greatly improved in appearance; but so rubicund, that I couldn't help thinking his face had this in common with the lobsters, crabs, and crawfish—that it went into the hot water very black and came out very red.

After tea, when the door was shut and all was made snug (the nights being cold and misty now), it seemed to me the most delicious retreat that the imagination of man could conceive. To hear the wind getting up out at sea, to know

that the fog was creeping over the desolate flat outside, and to look at the fire, and think that there was no house near but this one, and this one a boat, was like enchantment. Little Em'ly had overcome her shyness, and was sitting by my side upon the lowest and least of the lockers, which was just large enough for us two, and just fitted into the chimney corner. Mrs. Peggotty, with the white apron, was knitting on the opposite side of the fire. Peggotty at her needlework was as much at home with Saint Paul's and the bit of wax-candle, as if they had never known any other roof. Ham, who had been giving me my first lesson in all-fours, was trying to recollect a scheme of telling fortunes with the dirty cards, and was printing off fishy impressions of his thumb on all the cards he turned. Mr. Peggotty was smoking his pipe. I felt it was a time for conversation and confidence.

"Mr. Peggotty!" says I.

"Sir," says he.

"Did you give your son the name of Ham, because you lived in a sort of ark?"

Mr. Peggotty seemed to think it a deep idea, but answered—

"No, Sir. I never giv him no name."

"Who gave him that name, then?" said I, putting question number two of the catechism to Mr. Peggotty.

"Why, Sir, his father giv it him," said Mr. Peggotty.

"I thought you were his father!"

"My brother Joe was *his* father," said Mr. Peggotty.

"Dead, Mr. Peggotty?" I hinted, after a respectful pause.

"Drownded," said Mr. Peggotty.

I was very much surprised that Mr. Peggotty was not Ham's father, and began to wonder whether I was mistaken about his relationship to anybody else there. I was so curious to know, that I made up my mind to have it out with Mr. Peggotty.

"Little Em'ly," I said, glancing at her. "She is your daughter, isn't she, Mr. Peggotty?"

"No, Sir. My brother-in-law, Tom, was *her* father."

I couldn't help it. "—Dead, Mr. Peggotty?" I hinted, after another respectful silence.

"Drownded," said Mr. Peggotty.

I felt the difficulty of resuming the subject, but had not got to the bottom of it yet, and must get to the bottom somehow. So I said:

"Haven't you *any* children, Mr. Peggotty?"

"No, master," he answered, with a short laugh. "I'm a bacheldore."

"A bachelor!" I said, astonished. "Why, who's that, Mr. Peggotty?" Pointing to the person in the apron who was knitting.

"That's Missis Gummidge," said Mr. Peggotty.

"Gummidge, Mr. Peggotty?"

But at this point Peggotty—I mean my own peculiar Peggotty—made such impressive motions to me not to ask any more questions, that I could only sit and look at all the silent company, until it was time to go to bed. Then, in the privacy of my own little cabin, she informed me that Ham and Em'ly were an orphan nephew and niece, whom my host had at different times adopted in their childhood, when they were left destitute; and that Mrs. Gummidge was the widow of his partner in a boat, who had died very poor. He was but a poor man himself, said Peggotty, but as good as gold and as true as steel—those were her similes. The only subject, she informed me, on which he ever showed a violent temper or swore an oath, was this generosity of his; and if it were ever referred to, by any one of them, he struck the table a heavy blow with his right hand (had split it on one such occasion), and swore a dreadful oath that he would be "Gormed" if he didn't cut and run for good, if it was ever mentioned again. It appeared, in answer to my inquiries, that nobody had the least idea of the etymology of this terrible verb passive to be gormed; but that they all regarded it as constituting a most solemn imprecation.

I was very sensible of my entertainer's goodness, and listened to the women's going to bed in another little crib like mine at the opposite end of the boat, and to him and Ham hanging up two hammocks for themselves on the hooks I had noticed in the roof, in a very luxurious state of mind, enhanced by my being sleepy. As slumber gradually stole upon me, I heard the wind howling out at sea and coming on across the flat so fiercely, that I had a lazy apprehension of the great deep rising in the night. But I bethought myself that I was in a boat, after all; and that a man like Mr. Peggotty was not a bad person to have on board if anything did happen.

Nothing happened, however, worse than morning. Almost as soon as it shone upon the oyster-shell frame of my mirror I was out of bed, and out with little Em'ly, picking up stones upon the beach.

"You're quite a sailor, I suppose?" I said to Em'ly. I don't know that I supposed anything of the kind, but I felt it an act of gallantry to say something; and a shining sail close to us made such a pretty little image of itself, at the moment, in her bright eye, that it came into my head to say this.

"No," replied Em'ly, shaking her head, "I'm afraid of the sea."

"Afraid!" I said, with a becoming air of boldness, and looking very big at the mighty ocean. "*I* an't!"

"Ah! but it's cruel," said Em'ly. "I have seen it very cruel to some of our men. I have seen it tear a boat as big as our house all to pieces."

"I hope it wasn't the boat that——"

"That father was drownded in?" said Em'ly. "No. Not that one. I never see that boat."

"Nor him?" I asked her.

Little Em'ly shook her head. "Not to remember!"

Here was a coincidence. I immediately went into an explanation how I had never seen my own father; and how my mother and I had always lived by ourselves in the happiest state imaginable, and lived so then, and always meant to live so; and how my father's grave was in the churchyard near our house, and shaded by a tree, beneath the boughs of which I had walked and heard the birds sing many a pleasant morning. But there were some differences between Em'ly's orphanhood and mine, it appeared. She had lost her mother before her father; and where her father's grave was no one knew, except that it was somewhere in the depths of the sea.

"Besides," said Em'ly, as she looked about for shells and pebbles, "your father was a gentleman and your mother was a lady; and my father was a fisherman and my mother was a fisherman's daughter, and my uncle Dan is a fisherman."

"Dan is Mr. Peggotty, is he?" said I.

"Uncle Dan—yonder," answered Em'ly, nodding at the boat-house.

"Yes. I mean him. He must be very good, I should think?"

"Good?" said Em'ly. "If I was ever to be a lady, I'd give him a sky-blue coat with diamond buttons, nankeen trousers, a red velvet waistcoat, a cocked hat, a large gold watch, a silver pipe, and a box of money."

I said I had no doubt that Mr. Peggotty well deserved these treasures. I must acknowledge that I felt it difficult to picture him quite at his ease in the raiment proposed for him by his grateful little niece, and that I was particularly doubtful of the policy of the cocked hat; but I kept these sentiments to myself.

Little Em'ly had stopped and looked up at the sky in her enumeration of these articles, as if they were a glorious vision. We went on again, picking up shells and pebbles.

"You would like to be a lady?" I said.

Em'ly looked at me, and laughed and nodded "yes."

"I should like it very much. We would all be gentlefolks together, then. Me, and uncle, and Ham, and Mrs. Gummidge. We wouldn't mind, then, when there come stormy weather.—Not for our own sakes, I mean. We would for the poor fishermen's, to be sure, and we'd help 'em with money when they come to any hurt."

This seemed to me to be a very satisfactory, and therefore not at all improbable picture. I expressed my pleasure in the contemplation of it, and little Em'ly was emboldened to say, shyly,

"Don't you think you are afraid of the sea, now?"

It was quiet enough to reassure me, but I have no doubt if I had seen a moderately large wave come tumbling in, I should have taken to my heels, with an awful recollection of her drowned relations. However, I said "No," and I added, "You don't seem to be, either, though you say you are;"—for she was walking much too near the brink of a sort of old jetty or wooden causeway we had strolled upon, and I was afraid of her falling over.

"I'm not afraid in this way," said little Em'ly. "But I wake when it blows, and tremble to think of Uncle Dan and Ham, and believe I hear 'em crying out for help. That's why I should like so much to be a lady. But I'm not afraid in this way. Not a bit. Look here!"

She started from my side, and ran along a jagged timber which protruded from the place we stood upon, and overhung the deep water at some height, without the least defence. The incident is so impressed on my remembrance, that if I were a draughtsman I could draw its form here, I dare say, accurately as it was that day, and little Em'ly springing forward to her destruction (as it appeared to me), with a look that I have never forgotten, directed far out to sea.

The light, bold, fluttering little figure turned and came back safe to me, and I soon laughed at my fears, and at the cry I had uttered; fruitlessly in any case, for there was no one near. But there have been times since, in my manhood, many times there have been, when I have thought, Is it possible, among the possibilities of hidden things, that in the sudden rashness of the child and her wild look so far off, there was any merciful attraction of her into danger, any tempting her towards him permitted on the part of her dead father, that her life might have a chance of ending that day. There has been a time since when I have wondered whether, if the life before her could have been revealed to me at a glance, and so revealed as that a child could fully comprehend it, and if her preservation could have depended on a motion of my hand, I ought to have held it up to save her. There has been a time since—I do not say it lasted long, but it has been—when I have asked myself the question, would it have been better for little Em'ly to have had the waters close above her head that morning in my sight; and when I have answered Yes, it would have been.

This may be premature. I have set it down too soon, perhaps. But let it stand.

We strolled a long way, and loaded ourselves with things that we thought curious, and put some stranded starfish carefully back into the water—I hardly know enough of the race at this moment to be quite certain whether they had reason to feel obliged to us for doing so, or the reverse —and then made our way home to Mr. Peggotty's dwelling. We stopped under the lee of the lobster-outhouse to exchange an innocent kiss, and went in to breakfast glowing with health and pleasure.

"Like two young mavishes," Mr. Peggotty said. I knew this meant, in our local dialect, like two young thrushes, and received it as a compliment.

Of course I was in love with little Em'ly. I am sure I loved that baby quite as truly, quite as tenderly, with greater purity and more disinterestedness, than can enter into the best love of a later time of life, high and ennobling as it is. I am sure my fancy raised up something round that blue-eyed mite of a child, which etherealised, and made a very angel of her. If, any sunny forenoon, she had spread a little pair of wings, and flown away before my eyes, I don't think I should have regarded it as much more than I had had reason to expect.

We used to walk about that dim old flat at Yarmouth in a loving manner, hours and hours. The day sported by us, as if Time had not grown up himself yet, but were a child too, and always at play. I told Em'ly I adored her, and that unless she confessed she adored me I should be reduced to the necessity of killing myself with a sword. She said she did, and I have no doubt she did.

As to any sense of inequality, or youthfulness, or other difficulty in our way, little Em'ly and I had no such trouble, because we had no future. We made no more provision for growing older, than we did for growing younger. We were the admiration of Mrs. Gummidge and Peggotty, who used to whisper of an evening when we sat, lovingly, on our little locker side by side, "Lor! wasn't it beautiful!" Mr. Peggotty smiled at us from behind his pipe, and Ham grinned all the evening and did nothing else. They had something of the sort of pleasure in us, I suppose, that they might have had in a pretty toy, or a pocket model of the Colosseum.

I soon found out that Mrs. Gummidge did not always make herself so agreeable as she might have been expected to do, under the circumstances of her residence with Mr. Peggotty. Mrs. Gummidge's was rather a fretful disposition, and she whimpered more sometimes than was comfortable for other parties in so small an establishment. I was very sorry for her; but there were moments when it would have been more agreeable, I thought, if Mrs. Gummidge had had a convenient apartment of her own to retire to, and had stopped there until her spirits revived.

Mr. Peggotty went occasionally to a public-house called The Willing Mind. I discovered this, by his being out on the second or third evening of our visit, and by Mrs. Gummidge's looking up at the Dutch clock, between eight and nine, and saying he was there, and that, what was more, she had known in the morning he would go there.

Mrs. Gummidge had been in a low state all day, and had burst into tears in the forenoon, when the fire smoked. "I am a lone lorn creetur'," were Mrs. Gummidge's words, when that unpleasant occurrence took place, "and everythink goes contrary with me."

"Oh, it'll soon leave off," said Peggotty—I again mean our Peggotty—"and besides, you know, it's not more disagreeable to you than to us."

"I feel it more," said Mrs. Gummidge.

It was a very cold day, with cutting blasts of wind. Mrs. Gummidge's peculiar corner of the fireside seemed to me to be the warmest and snuggest in the place, as her chair was certainly the easiest, but it didn't suit her that day at all. She was constantly complaining of the cold, and of its occasioning a visitation in her back which she called "the creeps." At last she shed tears on that subject, and said again that she was "a lone lorn creetur' and everythink went contrary with her."

"It is certainly very cold," said Peggotty. "Everybody must feel it so."

"I feel it more than other people," said Mrs. Gummidge.

So at dinner; when Mrs. Gummidge was always helped immediately after me, to whom the preference was given as a visitor of distinction. The fish were small and bony, and the potatoes were a little burnt. We all acknowledged that we felt this something of a disappointment; but Mrs. Gummidge said she felt it more than we did, and shed tears again, and made that former declaration with great bitterness.

Accordingly, when Mr. Peggotty came home about nine o'clock, this unfortunate Mrs. Gummidge was knitting in her corner, in a very wretched and miserable condition. Peggotty had been working cheerfully. Ham had been patching up a great pair of water-boots; and I, with little Em'ly by my side, had been reading to them. Mrs. Gummidge had never made any other remark than a forlorn sigh, and had never raised her eyes since tea.

"Well, mates," said Mr. Peggotty, taking his seat, "and how are you?"

We all said something, or looked something, to welcome him, except Mrs. Gummidge, who only shook her head over her knitting.

"What's amiss?" said Mr. Peggotty, with a clap of his hands. "Cheer up, old mawther!" (Mr. Peggotty meant old girl.)

Mrs. Gummidge did not appear to be able to cheer up. She took out an old black silk handkerchief and wiped her eyes; but instead of putting it in her pocket, kept it out, and wiped them again, and still kept it out, ready for use.

"What's amiss, dame?" said Mr. Peggotty.

"Nothing," returned Mrs. Gummidge. "You've come from The Willing Mind, Dan'l?"

"Why yes, I've took a short spell at The Willing Mind to-night," said Mr. Peggotty.

"I'm sorry I should drive you there," said Mrs. Gummidge.

"Drive! I don't want no driving," returned Mr. Peggotty, with an honest laugh. "I only go too ready."

"Very ready," said Mrs. Gummidge, shaking her head, and wiping her eyes. "Yes, yes, very ready. I am sorry it should be along of me that you're so ready."

"Along o' you! It an't along o' you!" said Mr. Peggotty. "Don't ye believe a bit on it."

"Yes, yes, it is," cried Mrs. Gummidge. "I know what

I am. I know that I am a lone lorn creetur', and not only that everythink goes contrairy with me, but that I go contrairy with everybody. Yes, yes, I feel more than other people do, and I show it more. It's my misfortun'."

I really couldn't help thinking, as I sat taking in all this, that the misfortune extended to some other members of that family besides Mrs. Gummidge. But Mr. Peggotty made no such retort, only answering with another entreaty to Mrs. Gummidge to cheer up.

"I an't what I could wish myself to be," said Mrs. Gummidge. "I am far from it. I know what I am. My troubles has made me contrairy. I feel my troubles, and they make me contrairy. I wish I didn't feel 'em, but I do. I wish I could be hardened to 'em, but I an't. I make the house uncomfortable. I don't wonder at it. I've made your sister so all day, and Master Davy."

Here I was suddenly melted, and roared out, "No, you haven't, Mrs. Gummidge," in great mental distress.

"It's far from right that I should do it," said Mrs. Gummidge. "It an't a fit return. I had better go into the house and die. I am a lone lorn creetur', and had much better not make myself contrairy here. If things must go contrairy with me, and I must go contrairy myself, let me go contrairy in my parish. Dan'l, I'd better go into the house, and die and be a riddance."

Mrs. Gummidge retired with these words, and betook herself to bed. When she was gone, Mr. Peggotty, who had not exhibited a trace of any feeling but the profoundest sympathy, looked round upon us, and nodding his head with a lively expression of that sentiment still animating his face, said in a whisper:

"She's been thinking of the old 'un!"

I did not quite understand what old one Mrs. Gummidge was supposed to have fixed her mind upon, until Peggotty, on seeing me to bed, explained that it was the late Mr. Gummidge; and that her brother always took that for a received truth on such occasions, and that it always had a moving effect upon him. Some time after he was in his hammock that night, I heard him myself repeat to Ham, "Poor thing! She's been thinking of the old 'un!" And whenever Mrs. Gummidge was overcome in a similar manner during the remainder of our stay (which happened some few times), he always said the same thing in extenuation of the circumstance, and always with the tenderest commiseration.

So the fortnight slipped away, varied by nothing but the variation of the tide, which altered Mr. Peggotty's times of going out and coming in, and altered Ham's engagements also. When the latter was unemployed, he sometimes walked with us to show us the boats and ships, and once or twice he took us for a row. I don't know why one slight set of impressions should be more particularly associated with a place than another, though I believe this obtains with most people, in reference especially to the associations of their childhood. I never hear the name, or read the name, of Yarmouth, but I am reminded of a certain Sunday morning on the beach, the bells ringing for church, little Em'ly leaning on my shoulder, Ham lazily dropping stones into the water, and the sun, away at sea, just breaking through the heavy mist, and showing us the ships, like their own shadows.

At last the day came for going home. I bore up against the separation from Mr. Peggotty and Mrs. Gummidge, but my agony of mind at leaving little Em'ly was piercing. We went arm-in-arm to the public-house where the carrier put up, and I promised, on the road, to write to her. (I redeemed that promise afterwards, in characters larger than those in which apartments are usually announced in manuscript, as being to let.) We were greatly overcome at parting; and if ever, in my life, I have had a void made in my heart, I had one made that day.

Now, all the time I had been on my visit, I had been ungrateful to my home again, and had thought little or nothing about it. But I was no sooner turned towards it, than my reproachful young conscience seemed to point that way with a steady finger; and I felt, all the more for the sinking of my spirits, that it was my nest, and that my mother was my comforter and friend.

This gained upon me as we went along; so that the nearer we drew, and the more familiar the objects became that we passed, the more excited I was to get there, and to run into her arms. But Peggotty, instead of sharing in these transports, tried to check them (though very kindly), and looked confused and out of sorts.

Blunderstone Rookery would come, however, in spite of her, when the carrier's horse pleased—and did. How well I recollect it, on a cold grey afternoon, with a dull sky, threatening rain!

The door opened, and I looked, half laughing and half crying in my pleasant agitation, for my mother. It was not she, but a strange servant.

"Why, Peggotty!" I said, ruefully, "isn't she come home?"

"Yes, yes, Master Davy," said Peggotty. "She's come home. Wait a bit, Master Davy, and I'll—I'll tell you something."

Between her agitation, and her natural awkwardness in getting out of the cart, Peggotty was making a most extraordinary festoon of herself, but I felt too blank and strange to tell her so. When she had got down, she took me by the hand; led me, wondering, into the kitchen; and shut the door.

"Peggotty!" said I, quite frightened. "What's the matter?"

"Nothing's the matter, bless you, Master Davy dear!" she answered, assuming an air of sprightliness.

"Something's the matter, I'm sure. Where's mama?"

"Where's mama, Master Davy?" repeated Peggotty.

"Yes. Why hasn't she come out to the gate, and what have we come in here for? Oh, Peggotty!" My eyes were full, and I felt as if I were going to tumble down.

"Bless the precious boy!" cried Peggotty, taking hold of me. "What is it? Speak, my pet!"

"Not dead, too! Oh, she's not dead, Peggotty?"

Peggotty cried out No! with an astonishing volume of voice; and then sat down, and began to pant, and said I had given her a turn.

I gave her a hug to take away the turn, or to give her another turn in the right direction, and then stood before her, looking at her in anxious inquiry.

"You see, dear, I should have told you before now," said Peggotty, "but I hadn't an opportunity. I ought to have made it, perhaps, but I couldn't azackly"—that was always the substitute for exactly, in Peggotty's militia of words—"bring my mind to it."

"Go on, Peggotty," said I, more frightened than before.

"Master Davy," said Peggotty, untying her bonnet with a shaking hand, and speaking in a breathless sort of way. "What do you think? You have got a Pa!"

I trembled, and turned white. Something—I don't know

what, or how—connected with the grave in the churchyard, and the raising of the dead, seemed to strike me like an unwholesome wind.

"A new one," said Peggotty.

"A new one?" I repeated.

Peggotty gave a gasp, as if she were swallowing something that was very hard, and, putting out her hand, said: "Come and see him."

"I don't want to see him."

—"And your mama," said Peggotty.

I ceased to draw back, and we went straight to the best parlour, where she left me. On one side of the fire, sat my mother; on the other, Mr. Murdstone. My mother dropped her work, and arose hurriedly, but timidly I thought.

"Now, Clara my dear," said Mr. Murdstone. "Recollect! control yourself, always control yourself! Davy boy, how do you do?"

I gave him my hand. After a moment of suspense, I went and kissed my mother: she kissed me, patted me gently on the shoulder, and sat down again to her work. I could not look at her, I could not look at him, I knew quite well that he was looking at us both; and I turned to the window and looked out there, at some shrubs that were drooping their heads in the cold.

As soon as I could creep away, I crept up-stairs. My old dear bedroom was changed, and I was to lie a long way off. I rambled down-stairs to find anything that was like itself, so altered it all seemed; and roamed into the yard. I very soon started back from there, for the empty dog-kennel was filled up with a great dog—deep-mouthed and black-haired like Him—and he was very angry at the sight of me, and sprang out to get at me.

CHAPTER IV.

I FALL INTO DISGRACE.

IF the room to which my bed was removed were a sentient thing that could give evidence, I might appeal to it at this day—who sleeps there now, I wonder!—to bear witness for me what a heavy heart I carried to it. I went up there, hearing the dog in the yard bark after me all the way while I climbed the stairs; and, looking as blank and strange upon the room as the room looked upon me, sat down with my small hands crossed, and thought.

I thought of the oddest things. Of the shape of the room, of the cracks in the ceiling, of the paper on the wall, of the flaws in the window-glass making ripples and dimples on the prospect, of the washing-stand being rickety on its three legs, and having a discontented something about it, which reminded me of Mrs. Gummidge under the influence of the old one. I was crying all the time, but, except that I was conscious of being cold and dejected, I am sure I never thought why I cried. At last in my desolation I began to consider that I was dreadfully in love with little Em'ly, and had been torn away from her to come here where no one seemed to want me, or to care about me, half as much as she did. This made such a very miserable piece of business of it, that I rolled myself up in a corner of the counterpane, and cried myself to sleep.

I was awakened by somebody saying, "Here he is!" and uncovering my hot head. My mother and Peggotty had come to look for me, and it was one of them who had done it.

"Davy," said my mother. "What's the matter?"

I thought it very strange that she should ask me, and answered, "Nothing." I turned over on my face, I recollect, to hide my trembling lip, which answered her with greater truth.

"Davy," said my mother. "Davy, my child!"

I dare say no words she could have uttered would have affected me so much, then, as her calling me her child. I hid my tears in the bedclothes, and pressed her from me with my hand, when she would have raised me up.

"This is your doing, Peggotty, you cruel thing!" said my mother. "I have no doubt at all about it. How can you reconcile it to your conscience, I wonder, to prejudice my own boy against me, or against anybody who is dear to me? What do you mean by it, Peggotty?"

Poor Peggotty lifted up her hands and eyes, and only answered, in a sort of paraphrase of the grace I usually repeated after dinner, "Lord forgive you, Mrs. Copperfield, and for what you have said this minute, may you never be truly sorry!"

"It's enough to distract me," cried my mother. "In my honeymoon, too, when my most inveterate enemy might relent, one would think, and not envy me a little peace of mind and happiness. Davy, you naughty boy! Peggotty, you savage creature! Oh, dear me!" cried my mother, turning from one of us to the other, in her pettish, wilful manner. "What a troublesome world this is, when one has the most right to expect it to be as agreeable as possible!"

I felt the touch of a hand that I knew was neither hers nor Peggotty's, and slipped to my feet at the bed-side. It was Mr. Murdstone's hand, and he kept it on my arm as he said:

"What's this? Clara, my love, have you forgotten?—Firmness, my dear!"

"I am very sorry, Edward," said my mother. "I meant to be very good, but I am so uncomfortable."

"Indeed!" he answered. "That's a bad hearing, so soon, Clara."

"I say it's very hard I should be made so now," returned my mother, pouting; "and it is—very hard—isn't it?"

He drew her to him, whispered in her ear, and kissed her. I knew as well, when I saw my mother's head lean down upon his shoulder, and her arm touch his neck—I knew as well that he could mould her pliant nature into any form he chose, as I know, now, that he did it.

"Go you below, my love," said Mr. Murdstone. "David and I will come down together. My friend," turning a darkening face on Peggotty, when he had watched my mother out, and dismissed her with a nod and a smile: "do you know your mistress's name?"

"She has been my mistress a long time, Sir," answered Peggotty. "I ought to know it."

"That's true," he answered. "But I thought I heard you, as I came up-stairs, address her by a name that is not hers. She has taken mine, you know. Will you remember that?"

Peggotty, with some uneasy glances at me, curtseyed herself out of the room without replying; seeing, I suppose, that she was expected to go, and had no excuse for remaining. When we two were left alone, he shut the door, and sitting on a chair, and holding me standing before him, looked steadily into my eyes. I felt my own attracted, no less steadily, to his. As I recall our being opposed thus, face to face, I seem again to hear my heart beat fast and high.

"David," he said, making his lips thin, by pressing them together, "if I have an obstinate horse or dog to deal with, what do you think I do?"

"I don't know."

"I beat him."

I had answered in a kind of breathless whisper, but I felt, in my silence, that my breath was shorter now.

"I make him wince, and smart. I say to myself, 'I'll conquer that fellow;' and if it were to cost him all the blood he had, I should do it. What is that upon your face?"

"Dirt," I said.

He knew it was the mark of tears as well as I. But if he had asked the question twenty times, each time with twenty blows, I believe my baby heart would have burst before I would have told him so.

"You have a good deal of intelligence for a little fellow," he said, with a grave smile that belonged to him, "and you understood me very well, I see. Wash that face, Sir, and come down with me."

He pointed to the washing-stand, which I had made out to be like Mrs. Gummidge, and motioned me with his head to obey him directly. I had little doubt then, and I have less doubt now, that he would have knocked me down without the least compunction, if I had hesitated.

"Clara, my dear," he said, when I had done his bidding, and he walked me into the parlour, with his hand still on my arm; "you will not be made uncomfortable any more, I hope. We shall soon improve our youthful humours."

God help me, I might have been improved for my whole life, I might have been made another creature perhaps, for life, by a kind word at that season. A word of encouragement and explanation, of pity for my childish ignorance, of welcome home, of reassurance to me that it *was* home, might have made me dutiful to him in my heart henceforth, instead of in my hypocritical outside, and might have made me respect instead of hate him. I thought my mother was sorry to see me standing in the room so scared and strange, and that, presently, when I stole to a chair, she followed me with her eyes more sorrowfully still—missing, perhaps, some freedom in my childish tread—but the word was not spoken, and the time for it was gone.

We dined alone, we three together. He seemed to be very fond of my mother—I am afraid I liked him none the better for that—and she was very fond of him. I gathered from what he said, that an elder sister of his was coming to stay with them, and that she was expected that evening. I am not certain whether I found out then, or afterwards, that, without being actively concerned in any business, he had some share in, or some annual charge upon the profits of, a wine-merchant's house in London, with which his family had been connected from his great-grandfather's time, and in which his sister had a similar interest; but I may mention it in this place, whether or no.

After dinner, when we were sitting by the fire, and I was meditating an escape to Peggotty without having the hardihood to slip away, lest it should offend the master of the house, a coach drove up to the garden-gate, and he went out to receive the visitor. My mother followed him. I was timidly following her, when she turned round at the parlour-door, in the dusk, and taking me in her embrace as she had been used to do, whispered me to love my new father and be obedient to him. She did this hurriedly and secretly, as if it were wrong, but tenderly; and, putting out her hand behind her, held mine in it, until we came near to where he was standing in the garden, where she let mine go, and drew hers through his arm.

It was Miss Murdstone who was arrived, and a gloomy-looking lady she was; dark, like her brother, whom she greatly resembled in face and voice; and with very heavy eyebrows, nearly meeting over her large nose, as if, being disabled by the wrongs of her sex from wearing whiskers, she had carried them to that account. She brought with her two uncompromising hard black boxes, with her initials on the lids in hard brass nails. When she paid the coachman she took her money out of a hard steel purse, and she kept the purse in a very jail of a bag which hung upon her arm by a heavy chain, and shut up like a bite. I had never, at that time, seen such a metallic lady altogether as Miss Murdstone was.

She was brought into the parlour with many tokens of welcome, and there formally recognized my mother as a new and near relation. Then she looked at me, and said:

"Is that your boy, sister-in-law?"

My mother acknowledged me.

"Generally speaking," said Miss Murdstone, "I don't like boys. How d'ye do, boy?"

Under these encouraging circumstances, I replied that I was very well, and that I hoped she was the same; with such an indifferent grace, that Miss Murdstone disposed of me in two words:

"Wants manner!"

Having uttered which, with great distinctness, she begged the favour of being shown to her room, which became to me from that time forth a place of awe and dread, wherein the two black boxes were never seen open or known to be left unlocked, and where (for I peeped in once or twice when she was out) numerous little steel fetters and rivets, with which Miss Murdstone embellished herself when she was dressed, generally hung upon the looking-glass in formidable array.

As well as I could make out, she had come for good, and had no intention of ever going again. She began to "help" my mother next morning, and was in and out of the store-closet all day, putting things to rights, and making havoc in the old arrangements. Almost the first remarkable thing I observed in Miss Murdstone was, her being constantly haunted by a suspicion that the servants had a man secreted somewhere on the premises. Under the influence of this delusion, she dived into the coal-cellar at the most untimely hours, and scarcely ever opened the door of a dark cupboard without clapping it to again, in the belief that she had got him.

Though there was nothing very airy about Miss Murdstone, she was a perfect Lark in point of getting up. She was up (and, as I believe to this hour, looking for that man) before anybody in the house was stirring. Peggotty gave it as her opinion that she even slept with one eye open; but I could not concur in this idea; for I tried it myself after hearing the suggestion thrown out, and found it couldn't be done.

On the very first morning after her arrival she was up and ringing her bell at cock-crow. When my mother came down to breakfast and was going to make the tea, Miss Murdstone gave her a kind of peck on the cheek, which was her nearest approach to a kiss, and said:

"Now, Clara, my dear, I am come here, you know, to relieve you of all the trouble I can. You're much too pretty and thoughtless"—my mother blushed but laughed, and seemed not to dislike this character—"to have any duties imposed upon you that can be undertaken by me. If you'll be so good as give me your keys, my dear, I'll attend to all this sort of thing in future."

From that time, Miss Murdstone kept the keys in her own little jail all day, and under her pillow all night, and my mother had no more to do with them than I had.

My mother did not suffer her authority to pass from her without a shadow of protest. One night when Miss Murdstone had been developing certain household plans to her brother, of which he signified his approbation, my mother suddenly began to cry, and said she thought she might have been consulted.

"Clara!" said Mr. Murdstone sternly. "Clara! I wonder at you."

"Oh, it's very well to say you wonder, Edward!" cried my mother, "and it's very well for you to talk about firmness, but you wouldn't like it yourself."

Firmness, I may observe, was the grand quality on which both Mr. and Miss Murdstone took their stand. However I might have expressed my comprehension of it at that time, if I had been called upon, I nevertheless did clearly comprehend in my own way, that it was another name for tyranny; and for a certain gloomy, arrogant, devil's humour, that was in them both. The creed, as I should state it now, was this. Mr. Murdstone was firm; nobody in his world was to be so firm as Mr. Murdstone; nobody else in his world was to be firm at all, for everybody was to be bent to his firmness. Miss Murdstone was an exception. She might be firm, but only by relationship, and in an inferior and tributary degree. My mother was another exception. She might be firm, and must be; but only in bearing their firmness, and firmly believing there was no other firmness upon earth.

"It's very hard," said my mother, "that in my own house——"

"*My* own house?" repeated Mr. Murdstone. "Clara!"

"*Our* own house, I mean," faltered my mother, evidently frightened—"I hope you must know what I mean, Edward —it's very hard that in *your* own house I may not have a word to say about domestic matters. I am sure I managed very well before we were married. There's evidence," said my mother, sobbing; "ask Peggotty if I didn't do very well when I wasn't interfered with!"

"Edward," said Miss Murdstone, "let there be an end of this. I go to-morrow."

"Jane Murdstone," said her brother, "be silent! How dare you to insinuate that you don't know my character better than your words imply?"

"I am sure," my poor mother went on, at a grievous disadvantage and with many tears, "I don't want anybody to go. I should be very miserable and unhappy if anybody was to go. I don't ask much. I am not unreasonable. I only want to be consulted sometimes. I am very much obliged to anybody who assists me, and I only want to be consulted as a mere form, sometimes. I thought you were pleased, once, with my being a little inexperienced and girlish, Edward—I am sure you said so—but you seem to hate me for it now, you are so severe."

"Edward," said Miss Murdstone, again, "let there be an end of this. I go to-morrow."

"Jane Murdstone," thundered Mr. Murdstone. "Will you be silent? How dare you?"

Miss Murdstone made a jail-delivery of her pocket-handkerchief, and held it before her eyes.

"Clara," he continued, looking at my mother, "you surprise me! You astound me! Yes, I had a satisfaction in the thought of marrying an inexperienced and artless person, and forming her character, and infusing into it some amount of that firmness and decision of which it stood in need. But when Jane Murdstone is kind enough to come to my assistance in this endeavour, and to assume, for my sake, a condition something like a housekeeper's, and when she meets with a base return——"

"Oh, pray, pray, Edward," cried my mother, "don't accuse me of being ungrateful. I am sure I am not ungrateful. No one ever said I was, before. I have many faults, but not that. Oh, don't, my dear!"

"When Jane Murdstone meets, I say," he went on, after waiting until my mother was silent, "with a base return, that feeling of mine is chilled and altered."

"Don't, my love, say that!" implored my mother very piteously. "Oh, don't, Edward! I can't bear to hear it. Whatever I am, I am affectionate. I know I am affectionate. I wouldn't say it, if I wasn't certain that I am. Ask Peggotty. I am sure she'll tell you I'm affectionate."

"There is no extent of mere weakness, Clara," said Mr. Murdstone in reply, "that can have the least weight with me. You lose breath."

"Pray let us be friends," said my mother, "I couldn't live under coldness or unkindness. I am so sorry. I have a great many defects, I know, and it's very good of you, Edward, with your strength of mind, to endeavour to correct them for me. Jane, I don't object to anything. I should be quite broken-hearted if you thought of leaving"—— My mother was too much overcome to go on.

"Jane Murdstone," said Mr. Murdstone to his sister, "any harsh words between us are, I hope, uncommon. It is not my fault that so unusual an occurrence has taken place to-night. I was betrayed into it by another. Nor is it your fault. You were betrayed into it by another. Let us both try to forget it. And as this," he added, after these magnanimous words, "is not a fit scene for the boy— David, go to bed!"

I could hardly find the door, through the tears that stood in my eyes. I was so sorry for my mother's distress; but I groped my way out, and groped my way up to my room in the dark, without even having the heart to say good night to Peggotty, or to get a candle from her. When her coming up to look for me, an hour or so afterwards, awoke me, she said that my mother had gone to bed poorly, and that Mr. and Miss Murdstone were sitting alone.

Going down next morning rather earlier than usual, I paused outside the parlour-door, on hearing my mother's voice. She was very earnestly and humbly entreating Miss Murdstone's pardon, which that lady granted, and a perfect reconciliation took place. I never knew my mother afterwards to give an opinion on any matter, without first appealing to Miss Murdstone, or without having first ascertained, by some sure means, what Miss Murdstone's opinion was; and I never saw Miss Murdstone, when out of temper (she was infirm that way), move her hand towards her bag as if she were going to take out the keys and offer to resign them to my mother, without seeing that my mother was in a terrible fright.

The gloomy taint that was in the Murdstone blood, darkened the Murdstone religion, which was austere and wrathful. I have thought, since, that its assuming that character was a necessary consequence of Mr. Murdstone's firmness, which wouldn't allow him to let anybody off from the utmost weight of the severest penalties he could find any excuse for. Be this as it may, I well remember the tremendous visages with which we used to go to church, and the changed air of the place. Again the dreaded Sunday comes round, and I file into the old pew first, like a guarded captive brought to a condemned service. Again, Miss Murdstone, in a black velvet gown, that looks as if it had been made out of a pall, follows close upon me; then my mother; then her husband. There is no Peggotty now, as in the old time. Again, I listen to Miss Murdstone mumbling the responses, and emphasising all the dread words with a cruel relish. Again, I see her dark eyes roll round the church when she says "miserable sinners," as if she were calling all the congregation names. Again, I catch rare glimpses of my mother, moving her lips timidly between the two, with one of them muttering at each ear like low thunder. Again, I wonder with a sudden fear whether it is likely that our good old clergyman can be wrong, and Mr. and Miss Murdstone right, and that all the angels in heaven can be destroying angels. Again, if I move a finger or relax a muscle of my face, Miss Murdstone pokes me with her prayer-book, and makes my side ache.

Yes, and again, as we walk home, I note some neighbours looking at my mother and at me, and whispering. Again, as the three go on arm-in-arm, and I linger behind alone, I follow some of those looks, and wonder if my mother's step be really not so light as I have seen it, and if the gaiety of her beauty be really almost worried away. Again, I wonder whether any of the neighbours call to mind, as I do, how we used to walk home together, she and I; and I wonder stupidly about that, all the dreary, dismal day.

There had been some talk on occasions of my going to boarding-school. Mr. and Miss Murdstone had originated it, and my mother had of course agreed with them. Nothing, however, was concluded on the subject yet. In the meantime, I learnt lessons at home.

Shall I ever forget those lessons! They were presided over nominally by my mother, but really by Mr. Murdstone and his sister, who were always present, and found them a favourable occasion for giving my mother lessons in that miscalled firmness, which was the bane of both our lives. I believe I was kept at home for that purpose. I had been apt enough to learn, and willing enough, when my mother and I had lived alone together. I can faintly remember learning the alphabet at her knee. To this day, when I look upon the fat black letters in the primer, the puzzling novelty of their shapes, and the easy good-nature of O and Q and S, seem to present themselves again before me as they used to do. But they recall no feeling of disgust or reluctance. On the contrary, I seem to have walked along a path of flowers as far as the crocodile-book, and to have been cheered by the gentleness of my mother's voice and manner all the way. But these solemn lessons which succeeded those, I remember as the death-blow at my peace, and a grievous daily drudgery and misery. They were very long, very numerous, very hard—perfectly unintelligible, some of them, to me—and I was generally as much bewildered by them as I believe my poor mother was herself.

Let me remember how it used to be, and bring one morning back again.

I come into the second-best parlour after breakfast, with my books, and an exercise-book, and a slate. My mother is ready for me at her writing-desk, but not half so ready as Mr. Murdstone in his easy-chair by the window (though he pretends to be reading a book), or as Miss Murdstone, sitting near my mother stringing steel beads. The very sight of these two has such an influence over me, that I begin to feel the words I have been at infinite pains to get into my head, all sliding away, and going I don't know where. I wonder where they do go, by the by?

I hand the first book to mother. Perhaps it is a grammar, perhaps a history, or geography. I take a last drowning look at the page as I give it into her hand, and start off aloud at a racing pace while I have got it fresh. I trip over a word. Mr. Murdstone looks up. I trip over another word. Miss Murdstone looks up. I redden, tumble over half-a-dozen words, and stop. I think my mother would show me the book if she dared, but she does not dare, and she says softly:

"Oh, Davy, Davy!"

"Now, Clara," says Mr. Murdstone, "be firm with the boy. Don't say, 'Oh, Davy, Davy!' That's childish. He knows his lesson, or he does not know it."

"He does not know it," Miss Murdstone interposes awfully.

"I am really afraid he does not," says my mother.

"Then you see, Clara," returns Miss Murdstone, "you should just give him the book back, and make him know it."

"Yes, certainly," says my mother; "that is what I intend to do, my dear Jane. Now, Davy, try once more, and don't be stupid."

I obey the first clause of the injunction by trying once more, but am not so successful with the second, for I am very stupid. I tumble down before I get to the old place, at a point where I was all right before, and stop to think. But I can't think about the lesson. I think of the number of yards of net in Miss Murdstone's cap, or of the price of Mr. Murdstone's dressing-gown, or any such ridiculous problem that I have no business with, and don't want to have anything at all to do with. Mr. Murdstone makes a movement of impatience which I have been expecting for a long time. Miss Murdstone does the same. My mother glances submissively at them, shuts the book, and lays it by as an arrear to be worked out when my other tasks are done.

There is a pile of these arrears very soon, and it swells like a rolling snowball. The bigger it gets, the more stupid I get. The case is so hopeless, and I feel that I am wallowing in such a bog of nonsense, that I give up all idea of getting out, and abandon myself to my fate. The despairing way in which my mother and I look at each other, as I blunder on, is truly melancholy. But the greatest effect in these miserable lessons is when my mother (thinking nobody is observing her) tries to give me the cue by the motion of her lips. At that instant, Miss Murdstone, who has been lying in wait for nothing else all along, says in a deep warning voice:

"Clara!"

My mother starts, colours, and smiles faintly. Mr. Murdstone comes out of his chair, takes the book, throws it at me or boxes my ears with it, and turns me out of the room by the shoulders.

Even when the lessons are done, the worst is yet to happen, in the shape of an appalling sum. This is invented for me, and delivered to me orally by Mr. Murdstone, and begins, "If I go into a cheese-monger's shop, and buy five thousand double-Gloucester cheeses at fourpence-halfpenny each, present payment"—at which I see Miss Murdstone secretly overjoyed. I pore over these cheeses without any result or enlightenment until dinner-time, when, having made a mulatto of myself by getting the dirt of the slate into the pores of my skin, I have a slice of bread to help me out with the cheeses, and am considered in disgrace for the rest of the evening.

It seems to me, at this distance of time, as if my unfortunate studies generally took this course. I could have done very well if I had been without the Murdstones; but the influence of the Murdstones upon me was like the fascination of two snakes on a wretched young bird. Even when I did get through the morning with tolerable credit, there was not much gained but dinner; for Miss Murdstone never could endure to see me untasked, and if I rashly made any show of being unemployed, called her brother's attention to me by saying, "Clara, my dear, there's nothing like work—give your boy an exercise;" which caused me to be clapped down to some new labour there and then. As to any recreation with other children of my age, I had very little of that; for the gloomy theology of the Murdstones made all children out to be a swarm of little vipers (though there *was* a child once set in the midst of the Disciples), and held that they contaminated one another.

The natural result of this treatment, continued, I suppose, for some six months or more, was to make me sullen, dull, and dogged. I was not made the less so, by my sense of being daily more and more shut out and alienated from my mother. I believe I should have been almost stupefied but for one circumstance.

It was this. My father had left a small collection of books in a little room up-stairs, to which I had access (for it adjoined my own) and which nobody else in our house ever troubled. From that blessed little room, Roderick Random, Peregrine Pickle, Humphrey Clinker, Tom Jones, the Vicar of Wakefield, Don Quixote, Gil Blas, and Robinson Crusoe, came out, a glorious host, to keep me company. They kept alive my fancy, and my hope of something beyond that place and time,—they, and the Arabian Nights, and the Tales of the Genii,—and did me no harm; for whatever harm was in some of them was not there for me; *I* knew nothing of it. It is astonishing to me now, how I found time, in the midst of my porings and blunderings over heavier themes, to read those books as I did. It is curious to me how I could ever have consoled myself under my small troubles (which were great troubles to me), by impersonating my favourite characters in them—as I did—and by putting Mr. and Miss Murdstone into all the bad ones—which I did too. I have been Tom Jones (a child's Tom Jones, a harmless creature) for a week together. I have sustained my own idea of Roderick Random for a month at a stretch, I verily believe. I had a greedy relish for a few volumes of Voyages and Travels—I forget what, now—that were on those shelves; and for days and days I can remember to have gone about my region of our house, armed with the centre-piece out of an old set of boot-trees—the perfect realization of Captain Somebody, of the Royal British Navy, in danger of being beset by savages, and resolved to sell his life at a great price. The Captain never lost dignity, from having his ears boxed with the Latin Grammar. I did; but the Captain was a Captain and a hero, in despite of all the grammars of all the languages in the world, dead or alive.

This was my only and my constant comfort. When I think of it, the picture always rises in my mind, of a summer evening, the boys at play in the churchyard, and I sitting on my bed, reading as if for life. Every barn in the neighbourhood, every stone in the church, and every foot of the churchyard, had some association of its own, in my mind, connected with these books, and stood for some locality made famous in them. I have seen Tom Pipes go climbing up the church-steeple; I have watched Strap, with the knapsack on his back, stopping to rest himself upon

the wicket-gate; and I *know* that Commodore Trunnion held that club with Mr. Pickle, in the parlour of our little village alehouse.

The reader now understands, as well as I do, what I was when I came to that point of my youthful history to which I am now coming again.

One morning when I went into the parlour with my books, I found my mother looking anxious, Miss Murdstone looking firm, and Mr. Murdstone binding something round the bottom of a cane—a lithe and limber cane, which he left off binding when I came in, and poised and switched in the air.

"I tell you, Clara," said Mr. Murdstone, "I have been often flogged myself."

"To be sure; of course," said Miss Murdstone.

"Certainly, my dear Jane," faltered my mother, meekly. "But—but do you think it did Edward good?"

"Do you think it did Edward harm, Clara?" asked Mr. Murdstone, gravely.

"That's the point!" said his sister.

To this my mother returned, "Certainly, my dear Jane," and said no more.

I felt apprehensive that I was personally interested in this dialogue, and sought Mr. Murdstone's eye as it lighted on mine.

"Now, David," he said—and I saw that cast again as he said it—"you must be far more careful to-day than usual." He gave the cane another poise, and another switch; and having finished his preparation of it, laid it down beside him, with an impressive look, and took up his book.

This was a good freshener to my presence of mind, as a beginning. I felt the words of my lessons slipping off, not one by one, or line by line, but by the entire page; I tried to lay hold of them; but they seemed, if I may so express it, to have put skates on, and to skim away from me with a smoothness there was no checking.

We began badly, and went on worse. I had come in, with an idea of distinguishing myself rather, conceiving that I was very well prepared; but it turned out to be quite a mistake. Book after book was added to the heap of failures, Miss Murdstone being firmly watchful of us all the time. And when we came at last to the five thousand cheeses (canes he made it that day, I remember), my mother burst out crying.

"Clara!" said Miss Murdstone, in her warning voice.

"I am not quite well, my dear Jane, I think," said my mother.

I saw him wink, solemnly, at his sister, as he rose and said, taking up the cane:

"Why, Jane, we can hardly expect Clara to bear, with perfect firmness, the worry and torment that David has occasioned her to-day. That would be stoical. Clara is greatly strengthened and improved, but we can hardly expect so much from her. David, you and I will go up-stairs, boy."

As he took me out at the door, my mother ran towards us. Miss Murdstone said, "Clara! are you a perfect fool?" and interfered. I saw my mother stop her ears then, and I heard her crying.

He walked me up to my room slowly and gravely—I am certain he had a delight in that formal parade of executing justice—and when we got there, suddenly twisted my head under his arm.

"Mr. Murdstone! Sir!" I cried to him. "Don't! Pray don't beat me! I have tried to learn, Sir, but I can't learn while you and Miss Murdstone are by. I can't indeed!"

"Can't you, indeed, David?" he said. "We'll try that."

He had my head as in a vice, but I twined round him somehow, and stopped him for a moment, entreating him not to beat me. It was only for a moment that I stopped him, for he cut me heavily an instant afterwards, and in the same instant I caught the hand with which he held me in my mouth, between my teeth, and bit it through. It sets my teeth on edge to think of it.

He beat me then, as if he would have beaten me to death. Above all the noise we made, I heard them running up the stairs, and crying out—I heard my mother crying out—and Peggotty. Then he was gone; and the door was locked outside; and I was lying, fevered and hot, and torn, and sore, and raging in my puny way, upon the floor.

How well I recollect, when I became quiet, what an unnatural stillness seemed to reign through the whole house! How well I remember, when my smart and passion began to cool, how wicked I began to feel!

I sat listening for a long while, but there was not a sound. I crawled up from the floor, and saw my face in the glass, so swollen, red, and ugly, that it almost frightened me. My stripes were sore and stiff, and made me cry afresh, when I moved; but they were nothing to the guilt I felt. It lay heavier on my breast than if I had been a most atrocious criminal, I dare say.

It had begun to grow dark, and I had shut the window (I had been lying, for the most part, with my head upon the sill, by turns crying, dozing, and looking listlessly out), when the key was turned, and Miss Murdstone came in with some bread and meat, and milk. These she put down upon the table without a word, glaring at me the while with exemplary firmness, and then retired, locking the door after her.

Long after it was dark I sat there, wondering whether anybody else would come. When this appeared improbable for that night, I undressed, and went to bed; and there, I began to wonder fearfully what would be done to me. Whether it was a criminal act that I had committed? Whether I should be taken into custody, and sent to prison? Whether I was at all in danger of being hanged?

I never shall forget the waking next morning; the being cheerful and fresh for the first moment, and then the being weighed down by the stale and dismal oppression of remembrance. Miss Murdstone reappeared before I was out of bed; told me, in so many words, that I was free to walk in the garden for half-an-hour and no longer; and retired, leaving the door open, that I might avail myself of that permission.

I did so, and did so every morning of my imprisonment, which lasted five days. If I could have seen my mother alone, I should have gone down on my knees to her and besought her forgiveness; but I saw no one, Miss Murdstone excepted, during the whole time—except at evening prayers in the parlour; to which I was escorted by Miss Murdstone after everybody else was placed; where I was stationed, a young outlaw, all alone by myself near the door; and whence I was solemnly conducted by my jailer, before any one arose from the devotional posture. I only observed that my mother was as far off from me as she could be, and kept her face another way, so that I never saw it; and that Mr. Murdstone's hand was bound up in a large linen wrapper.

The length of those five days I can convey no idea of to any one. They occupy the place of years in my remembrance. The way in which I listened to all the incidents of the house that made themselves audible to me; the ringing of bells, the opening and shutting of doors, the murmuring of voices, the footsteps on the stairs; to any laughing, whistling, or singing, outside, which seemed more dismal than anything else to me in my solitude and disgrace—the uncertain pace of the hours, especially at night, when I would wake thinking it was morning, and find that the family were not yet gone to bed, and that all the length of night had yet to come—the depressed dreams and nightmares I had—the return of day, noon, afternoon, evening, when the boys played in the churchyard, and I watched them from a distance within the room, being ashamed to show myself at the window lest they should know I was a prisoner—the strange sensation of never hearing myself speak—the fleeting intervals of something like cheerfulness, which came with eating and drinking, and went away with it—the setting in of rain one evening, with a fresh smell, and its coming down faster and faster between me and the church, until it and gathering night seemed to quench me in gloom, and fear, and remorse—all this appears to have gone round and round for years instead of days, it is so vividly and strongly stamped on my remembrance.

On the last night of my restraint, I was awakened by hearing my own name spoken in a whisper. I started up in bed, and putting out my arms in the dark, said:

"Is that you, Peggotty?"

There was no immediate answer, but presently I heard my name again, in a tone so very mysterious and awful, that I think I should have gone into a fit, if it had not occurred to me that it must have come through the keyhole.

I groped my way to the door, and putting my own lips to the keyhole, whispered:

"Is that you, Peggotty, dear?"

"Yes, my own precious Davy," she replied. "Be as soft as a mouse, or the Cat'll hear us."

I understood this to mean Miss Murdstone, and was sensible of the urgency of the case; her room being close by.

"How's mama, dear Peggotty? Is she very angry with me?"

I could hear Peggotty crying softly on her side of the keyhole, as I was doing on mine, before she answered. "No. Not very."

"What is going to be done with me, Peggotty dear? Do you know?"

"School. Near London," was Peggotty's answer. I was obliged to get her to repeat it, for she spoke it the first time quite down my throat, in consequence of my having forgotten to take my mouth away from the keyhole and put my ear there; and though her words tickled me a good deal, I didn't hear them.

"When, Peggotty?"

"To-morrow."

"Is that the reason why Miss Murdstone took the clothes out of my drawers?" which she had done, though I have forgotten to mention it.

"Yes," said Peggotty. "Box."

"Shan't I see mama?"

"Yes," said Peggotty. "Morning."

Then Peggotty fitted her mouth close to the keyhole, and delivered these words through it with as much feeling and earnestness as a keyhole has ever been the medium of communicating, I will venture to assert: shooting in each broken little sentence in a convulsive little burst of its own.

"Davy, dear. If I ain't been azackly as intimate with you. Lately, as I used to be. It ain't because I don't love you. Just as well and more, my pretty poppet. It's because I thought it better for you. And for some one else besides. Davy, my darling, are you listening? Can you hear?"

"Ye—ye—ye—yes, Peggotty!" I sobbed.

"My own!" said Peggotty, with infinite compassion. "What I want to say, is. That you must never forget me. For I'll never forget you. And I'll take as much care of your mama, Davy. As ever I took of you. And I won't leave her. The day may come when she'll be glad to lay her poor head. On her stupid, cross old Peggotty's arm again. And I'll write to you, my dear. Though I ain't no scholar. And I'll—I'll——" Peggotty fell to kissing the keyhole, as she couldn't kiss me.

"Thank you, dear Peggotty," said I. "Oh, thank you! Thank you! Will you promise me one thing, Peggotty? Will you write and tell Mr. Peggotty and little Em'ly, and Mrs. Gummidge and Ham, that I am not so bad as they might suppose, and that I sent 'em all my love—especially to little Em'ly? Will you, if you please, Peggotty?"

The kind soul promised, and we both of us kissed the keyhole with the greatest affection—I patted it with my hand, I recollect, as if it had been her honest face—and parted. From that night there grew up in my breast a feeling for Peggotty which I cannot very well define. She did not replace my mother; no one could do that; but she came into a vacancy in my heart, which closed upon her, and I felt towards her something I have never felt for any other human being. It was a sort of comical affection, too; and yet if she had died, I cannot think what I should have done, or how I should have acted out the tragedy it would have been to me.

In the morning Miss Murdstone appeared as usual, and told me I was going to school; which was not altogether such news to me as she supposed. She also informed me that when I was dressed, I was to come down-stairs into the parlour, and have my breakfast. There, I found my mother, very pale and with red eyes: into whose arms I ran, and begged her pardon from my suffering soul.

"Oh, Davy!" she said. "That you could hurt any one I love! Try to be better, pray to be better! I forgive you; but I am so grieved, Davy, that you should have such bad passions in your heart."

They had persuaded her that I was a wicked fellow, and she was more sorry for that, than for my going away. I felt it sorely. I tried to eat my parting breakfast, but my tears dropped upon my bread-and-butter, and trickled into my tea. I saw my mother look at me sometimes, and then glance at the watchful Miss Murdstone, and then look down, or look away.

"Master Copperfield's box there!" said Miss Murdstone, when wheels were heard at the gate.

I looked for Peggotty, but it was not she; neither she nor Mr. Murdstone appeared. My former acquaintance, the carrier, was at the door; the box was taken out to his cart, and lifted in.

"Clara!" said Miss Murdstone, in her warning note.

"Ready, my dear Jane," returned my mother. "Good bye, Davy. You are going for your own good. Good bye,

my child. You will come home in the holidays, and be a better boy."

"Clara!" Miss Murdstone repeated.

"Certainly, my dear Jane," replied my mother, who was holding me. "I forgive you, my dear boy. God bless you!"

"Clara!" Miss Murdstone repeated.

Miss Murdstone was good enough to take me out to the cart, and to say on the way that she hoped I would repent, before I came to a bad end; and then I got into the cart, and the lazy horse walked off with it.

CHAPTER V.

I AM SENT AWAY FROM HOME.

WE might have gone about half-a-mile, and my pocket-handkerchief was quite wet through, when the carrier stopped short.

Looking out to ascertain what for, I saw, to my amazement, Peggotty burst from a hedge and climb into the cart. She took me in both her arms, and squeezed me to her stays until the pressure on my nose was extremely painful, though I never thought of that till afterwards when I found it very tender. Not a single word did Peggotty speak. Releasing one of her arms, she put it down in her pocket to the elbow, and brought out some paper bags of cakes which she crammed into my pockets, and a purse which she put into my hand, but not one word did she say. After another and a final squeeze with both arms, she got down from the cart and ran away; and, my belief is, and has always been, without a solitary button on her gown. I picked up one, of several that were rolling about, and treasured it as a keepsake for a long time.

The carrier looked at me, as if to inquire if she were coming back. I shook my head, and said I thought not. "Then, come up," said the carrier to the lazy horse; who came up accordingly.

Having by this time cried as much as I possibly could, I began to think it was of no use crying any more, especially as neither Roderick Random, nor that Captain in the Royal British Navy had ever cried, that I could remember, in trying situations. The carrier, seeing me in this resolution, proposed that my pocket-handkerchief should be spread upon the horse's back to dry. I thanked him, and assented; and particularly small it looked, under those circumstances.

I had now leisure to examine the purse. It was a stiff leather purse, with a snap, and had three bright shillings in it, which Peggotty had evidently polished up with whitening for my greater delight. But its most precious contents were two half-crowns folded together in a bit of paper, on which was written, in my mother's hand, "For Davy. With my love." I was so overcome by this, that I asked the carrier to be so good as reach me my pocket-handkerchief again; but he said he thought I had better do without it; and I thought I really had; so I wiped my eyes on my sleeve and stopped myself.

For good, too; though, in consequence of my previous emotions, I was still occasionally seized with a stormy sob. After we had jogged on for some little time, I asked the carrier if he was going all the way.

"All the way where?" inquired the carrier.

"There," I said.

"Where's there?" inquired the carrier.

"Near London?" I said.

"Why that horse," said the carrier, jerking the rein to point him out, "would be deader than pork afore he got over half the ground."

"Are you only going to Yarmouth, then?" I asked.

"That's about it," said the carrier. "And there I shall take you to the stage-cutch, and the stage-cutch that'll take you to—wherever it is."

As this was a great deal for the carrier (whose name was Mr. Barkis) to say—he being, as I observed in a former chapter, of a phlegmatic temperament, and not at all conversational—I offered him a cake as a mark of attention, which he ate at one gulp, exactly like an elephant, and which made no more impression on his big face than it would have done on an elephant's.

"Did *she* make 'em, now?" said Mr. Barkis, always leaning forward, in his slouching way, on the footboard of the cart with an arm on each knee.

"Peggotty, do you mean, Sir?"

"Ah!" said Mr. Barkis. "Her."

"Yes. She makes all our pastry, and does all our cooking."

"Do she though?" said Mr. Barkis.

He made up his mouth as if to whistle, but he didn't whistle. He sat looking at the horse's ears, as if he saw something new there; and sat so, for a considerable time. By-and-by, he said:

"No sweethearts, I b'lieve?"

"Sweetmeats did you say, Mr. Barkis?" For I thought he wanted something else to eat, and had pointedly alluded to that description of refreshment.

"Hearts," said Mr. Barkis. "Sweethearts; no person walks with her!"

"With Peggotty?"

"Ah!" he said. "Her."

"Oh, no. She never had a sweetheart."

"Didn't she though!" said Mr. Barkis.

Again he made up his mouth to whistle, and again he didn't whistle, but sat looking at the horse's ears.

"So she makes," said Mr. Barkis, after a long interval of reflection, "all the apple parsties, and does all the cooking, do she?"

I replied that such was the fact.

"Well. I'll tell you what," said Mr. Barkis. "P'raps you might be writin' to her?"

"I shall certainly write to her," I rejoined.

"Ah!" he said, slowly turning his eyes towards me. "Well! If you was writin' to her, p'raps you'd recollect to say that Barkis was willin'; would you?"

"That Barkis is willing," I repeated, innocently. "Is that all the message?"

"Ye—es," he said, considering. "Ye—es. Barkis is willin'."

"But you will be at Blunderstone again to-morrow, Mr. Barkis," I said, faltering a little at the idea of my being far away from it then, "and could give your own message so much better."

As he repudiated this suggestion, however, with a jerk of his head, and once more confirmed his previous request by saying, with profound gravity, "Barkis is willin'. That's the message," I readily undertook its transmission. While I was waiting for the coach in the hotel at Yarmouth that very afternoon, I procured a sheet of paper and an ink-stand, and wrote a note to Peggotty, which ran thus: "My dear Peggotty. I have come here safe. Barkis is willing. My love to mama. Yours affectionately. P. S. He says he particularly wants you to know—*Barkis is willing.*"

When I had taken this commission on myself prospectively, Mr. Barkis relapsed into perfect silence; and I, feeling quite worn out by all that had happened lately, lay down on a sack in the cart and fell asleep. I slept soundly until we got to Yarmouth; which was so entirely new and strange to me in the inn-yard to which we drove, that I at once abandoned a latent hope I had had of meeting with some of Mr. Peggotty's family there, perhaps even with little Em'ly herself.

The coach was in the yard, shining very much all over, but without any horses to it as yet; and it looked in that state as if nothing was more unlikely than its ever going to London. I was thinking this, and wondering what would ultimately become of my box, which Mr. Barkis had put down on the yard-pavement by the pole (he having driven up the yard to turn his cart), and also what would ultimately become of me, when a lady looked out of a bow-window where some fowls and joints of meat were hanging up, and said:

"Is that the little gentleman from Blunderstone?"

"Yes, ma'am," I said.

"What name?" inquired the lady.

"Copperfield, ma'am," I said.

"That won't do," returned the lady. "Nobody's dinner is paid for here, in that name."

"Is it Murdstone, ma'am?" I said.

"If you're Master Murdstone," said the lady, "why do you go and give another name, first?"

I explained to the lady how it was, who then rang a bell, and called out, "William! show the coffee-room!" upon which a waiter came running out of a kitchen on the opposite side of the yard to show it, and seemed a good deal surprised when he found he was only to show it to me.

It was a large long room with some large maps in it. I doubt if I could have felt much stranger if the maps had been real foreign countries, and I cast away in the middle of them. I felt it was taking a liberty to sit down, with my cap in my hand, on the corner of the chair nearest the door; and when the waiter laid a cloth on purpose for me, and put a set of castors on it, I think I must have turned red all over with modesty.

He brought me some chops, and vegetables, and took the covers off in such a bouncing manner that I was afraid I must have given him some offence. But he greatly relieved my mind by putting a chair for me at the table, and saying, very affably, "Now, six-foot! come on!"

I thanked him, and took my seat at the board; but found it extremely difficult to handle my knife and fork with anything like dexterity, or to avoid splashing myself with the gravy, while he was standing opposite, staring so hard, and making me blush in the most dreadful manner every time I caught his eye. After watching me into the second chop, he said:

"There's half a pint of ale for you. Will you have it now?"

I thanked him and said "Yes." Upon which he poured it out of a jug into a large tumbler, and held it up against the light, and made it look beautiful.

MY FRIENDLY WAITER AND I.

"My eye!" he said. "It seems a good deal, don't it?"

"It does seem a good deal," I answered with a smile. For it was quite delightful to me to find him so pleasant. He was a twinkling-eyed, pimple-faced man, with his hair standing upright all over his head; and as he stood with one arm a-kimbo, holding up the glass to the light with the other hand, he looked quite friendly.

"There was a gentleman here, yesterday," he said—"a stout gentleman, by the name of Topsawyer—perhaps you know him!"

"No," I said, "I don't think——"

"In breeches and gaiters, broad-brimmed hat, grey coat, speckled choker," said the waiter.

"No," I said bashfully, "I haven't the pleasure——"

"He came in here," said the waiter, looking at the light through the tumbler, "ordered a glass of this ale—*would* order it—I told him not—drank it, and fell dead. It was too old for him. It oughtn't to be drawn; that's the fact."

I was very much shocked to hear of this melancholy accident, and said I thought I had better have some water.

"Why you see," said the waiter, still looking at the light through the tumbler, with one of his eyes shut up, "our people don't like things being ordered and left. It offends 'em. But *I*'ll drink it, if you like. I'm used to it, and use is everything. I don't think it'll hurt me, if I throw my head back, and take it off quick. Shall I?"

I replied that he would much oblige me by drinking it, if he thought he could do it safely, but by no means otherwise. When he did throw his head back, and take it off quick, I had a horrible fear, I confess, of seeing him meet the fate of the lamented Mr. Topsawyer, and fall lifeless on the carpet. But it didn't hurt him. On the contrary, I thought he seemed the fresher for it.

"What have we got here?" he said, putting a fork into my dish. "Not chops?"

"Chops," I said.

"Lord bless my soul!" he exclaimed, "I didn't know they were chops. Why, a chop's the very thing to take off the bad effects of that beer! Ain't it lucky?"

So he took a chop by the bone in one hand, and a potato in the other, and ate away with a very good appetite, to my extreme satisfaction. He afterwards took another chop, and another potato; and after that another chop and another potato. When he had done, he brought me a pudding, and having set it before me, seemed to ruminate, and to become absent in his mind for some moments.

"How's the pie?" he said, rousing himself.

"It's a pudding," I made answer.

"Pudding!" he exclaimed. "Why, bless me, so it is! What!" looking at it nearer. "You don't mean to say it's a batter-pudding!"

"Yes, it is indeed."

"Why, a batter-pudding," he said, taking up a table-spoon, "is my favourite pudding! Ain't that lucky? Come on, little 'un, and let's see who'll get most."

The waiter certainly got most. He entreated me more than once to come in and win, but what with his table-spoon to my tea-spoon, his despatch to my despatch, and his appetite to my appetite, I was left far behind at the first mouthful, and had no chance with him. I never saw anyone enjoy a pudding so much, I think; and he laughed, when it was all gone, as if his enjoyment of it lasted still.

Finding him so very friendly and companionable, it was then that I asked for the pen and ink and paper to write to

Peggotty. He not only brought it immediately, but was good enough to look over me while I wrote the letter. When I had finished it, he asked me where I was going to school.

I said, "Near London," which was all I knew.

"Oh, my eye!" he said, looking very low-spirited, "I am sorry for that."

"Why?" I asked him.

"Oh, Lord!" he said, shaking his head, "that's the school where they broke the boy's ribs—two ribs—a little boy he was. I should say he was—let me see—how old are you, about?"

I told him between eight and nine.

"That's just his age," he said. "He was eight years and six months old when they broke his first rib; eight years and eight months old when they broke his second, and did for him."

I could not disguise from myself, or from the waiter, that this was an uncomfortable coincidence, and inquired how it was done. His answer was not cheering to my spirits, for it consisted of two dismal words, "With whopping."

The blowing of the coach-horn in the yard was a seasonable diversion, which made me get up and hesitatingly inquire, in the mingled pride and diffidence of having a purse (which I took out of my pocket), if there were anything to pay.

"There's a sheet of letter-paper," he returned. "Did you ever buy a sheet of letter-paper?"

I could not remember that I ever had.

"It's dear," he said, "on account of the duty. Three-pence. That's the way we're taxed in this country. There's nothing else, except the waiter. Never mind the ink. *I* lose by that."

"What should you—what should I—how much ought I to—what would it be right to pay the waiter, if you please?" I stammered, blushing.

"If I hadn't a family, and that family hadn't the cow-pock," said the waiter, "I wouldn't take a sixpence. If I didn't support a aged pairint, and a lovely sister,"—here the waiter was greatly agitated—"I wouldn't take a farthing. If I had a good place, and was treated well here, I should beg acceptance of a trifle, instead of taking of it. But I live on broken wittles—and I sleep on the coals"—here the waiter burst into tears.

I was very much concerned for his misfortunes, and felt that any recognition short of ninepence would be mere brutality and hardness of heart. Therefore I gave him one of my three bright shillings, which he received with much humility and veneration, and spun up with his thumb, directly afterwards, to try the goodness of.

It was a little disconcerting to me, to find, when I was being helped up behind the coach, that I was supposed to have eaten all the dinner without any assistance. I discovered this, from overhearing the lady in the bow-window say to the guard, "Take care of that child, George, or he'll burst!" and from observing that the women-servants who were about the place came out to look and giggle at me as a young phenomenon. My unfortunate friend the waiter, who had quite recovered his spirits, did not appear to be disturbed by this, but joined in the general admiration without being at all confused. If I had any doubt of him, I suppose this half-awakened it; but I am inclined to believe that with the simple confidence of a child, and the natural reliance of a child upon superior years (qualities I am very sorry any children should prematurely change for worldly wisdom), I had no serious mistrust of him on the whole, even then.

I felt it rather hard, I must own, to be made, without deserving it, the subject of jokes between the coachman and guard as to the coach drawing heavy behind, on account of my sitting there, and as to the greater expediency of my travelling by waggon. The story of my supposed appetite getting wind among the outside passengers, they were merry upon it likewise; and asked me whether I was going to be paid for, at school, as two brothers or three, and whether I was contracted for, or went upon the regular terms; with other pleasant questions. But the worst of it was, that I knew I should be ashamed to eat anything, when an opportunity offered, and that, after a rather light dinner, I should remain hungry all night—for I had left my cakes behind, at the hotel, in my hurry. My apprehensions were realised. When we stopped for supper I couldn't muster courage to take any, though I should have liked it very much, but sat by the fire and said I didn't want anything. This did not save me from more jokes, either; for a husky-voiced gentleman with a rough face, who had been eating out of a sandwich-box nearly all the way, except when he had been drinking out of a bottle, said I was like a boa constrictor who took enough at one meal to last him a long time; after which, he actually brought a rash out upon himself with boiled beef.

We had started from Yarmouth at three o'clock in the afternoon, and we were due in London about eight next morning. It was midsummer weather, and the evening was very pleasant. When we passed through a village, I pictured to myself what the insides of the houses were like, and what the inhabitants were about; and when boys came running after us, and got up behind and swung there for a little way, I wondered whether their fathers were alive, and whether they were happy at home. I had plenty to think of, therefore, besides my mind running continually on the kind of place I was going to—which was an awful speculation. Sometimes, I remember, I resigned myself to thoughts of home and Peggotty; and to endeavouring, in a confused blind way, to recall how I had felt, and what sort of boy I used to be, before I bit Mr. Murdstone: which I couldn't satisfy myself about by any means, I seemed to have bitten him in such a remote antiquity.

The night was not so pleasant as the evening, for it got chilly; and being put between two gentlemen (the rough-faced one and another) to prevent my tumbling off the coach, I was nearly smothered by their falling asleep, and completely blocking me up. They squeezed me so hard sometimes, that I could not help crying out, "Oh, if you please!"—which they didn't like at all, because it woke them, Opposite me was an elderly lady in a great fur cloak, who looked in the dark more like a haystack than a lady, she was wrapped up to such a degree. This lady had a basket with her, and she hadn't known what to do with it, for a long time, until she found that, on account of my legs being short, it could go underneath me. It cramped and hurt me so, that it made me perfectly miserable; but if I moved in the least, and made a glass that was in the basket rattle against something else (as it was sure to do), she gave me the cruellest poke with her foot, and said, "Come, don't *you* fidget. *Your* bones are young enough I'm sure!"

At last the sun rose, and then my companions seemed to sleep easier. The difficulties under which they had la-

boured all night, and which had found utterance in the most terrific gasps and snorts, are not to be conceived. As the sun got higher, their sleep became lighter, and so they gradually one by one awoke. I recollect being very much surprised by the feint everybody made, then, of not having been to sleep at all, and by the uncommon indignation with which every one repelled the charge. I labour under the same kind of astonishment to this day, having invariably observed that of all human weaknesses, the one to which our common nature is the least disposed to confess (I cannot imagine why) is the weakness of having gone to sleep in a coach.

What an amazing place London was to me when I saw it in the distance, and how I believed all the adventures of all my favourite heroes to be constantly enacting and re-enacting there, and how I vaguely made it out in my own mind to be fuller of wonders and wickedness than all the cities of the earth, I need not stop here to relate. We approached it by degrees, and got, in due time, to the inn in the Whitechapel district, for which we were bound. I forget whether it was the Blue Bull, or the Blue Boar; but I know it was the Blue Something, and that its likeness was painted upon the back of the coach.

The guard's eye lighted on me as he was getting down, and he said at the booking-office door:

"Is there anybody here for a yoongster booked in the name of Murdstone, from Bloonderstone, Sooffolk, to be left till called for?"

Nobody answered.

"Try Copperfield, if you please, Sir," said I, looking helplessly down.

"Is there anybody here for a yoongster, booked in the name of Murdstone, from Bloonderstone, Sooffolk, but owning to the name of Copperfield, to be left till called for?" said the guard. Come! *Is* there anybody?"

No. There was nobody. I looked anxiously around; but the inquiry made no impression on any of the bystanders, if I except a man in gaiters, with one eye, who suggested that they had better put a brass collar round my neck, and tie me up in the stable.

A ladder was brought, and I got down after the lady who was like a haystack: not daring to stir, until her basket was removed. The coach was clear of passengers by that time, the luggage was very soon cleared out, the horses had been taken out before the luggage, and now the coach itself was wheeled and backed off by some hostlers, out of the way. Still, nobody appeared, to claim the dusty youngster from Blunderstone, Suffolk.

More solitary than Robinson Crusoe, who had nobody to look at him and see that he was solitary, I went into the booking-office, and, by invitation of the clerk on duty, passed behind the counter, and sat down on the scale at which they weighed the luggage. Here, as I sat looking at the parcels, packages, and books, and inhaling the smell of stables (ever since associated with that morning), a procession of most tremendous considerations began to march through my mind. Supposing nobody should ever fetch me, how long would they consent to keep me there? Would they keep me long enough to spend seven shillings? Should I sleep at night in one of those wooden bins, with the other luggage, and wash myself at the pump in the yard in the morning; or should I be turned out every night, and expected to come again to be left till called for, when the office opened next day? Supposing there was no mistake in the case, and Mr. Murdstone had devised this plan to get rid of me, what should I do? If they allowed me to remain there until my seven shillings were spent, I couldn't hope to remain there when I began to starve. That would obviously be inconvenient and unpleasant to the customers, besides entailing on the Blue Whatever-it-was, the risk of funeral expenses. If I started off at once, and tried to walk back home, how could I ever find my way, how could I ever hope to walk so far, how could I make sure of any one but Peggotty, even if I got back? If I found out the nearest proper authorities, and offered myself to go for a soldier, or a sailor, I was such a little fellow that it was most likely they wouldn't take me in. These thoughts, and a hundred other such thoughts, turned me burning hot, and made me giddy with apprehension and dismay. I was in the height of my fever when a man entered and whispered to the clerk, who presently slanted me off the scale, and pushed me over to him, as if I were weighed, bought, delivered, and paid for.

As I went out of the office hand-in-hand with this new acquaintance, I stole a look at him. He was a gaunt, sallow young man, with hollow cheeks, and a chin almost as black as Mr. Murdstone's; but there the likeness ended, for his whiskers were shaved off, and his hair, instead of being glossy, was rusty and dry. He was dressed in a suit of black clothes which were rather rusty and dry too, and rather short in the sleeves and legs; and he had a white neck-kerchief on, that was not over-clean. I did not, and do not, suppose that this neck-kerchief was all the linen he wore, but it was all he showed or gave any hint of.

"You're the new boy?" he said.

"Yes, Sir," I said.

I supposed I was. I didn't know.

"I'm one of the masters at Salem House," he said.

I made him a bow and felt very much overawed. I was so ashamed to allude to a commonplace thing like my box, to a scholar and a master at Salem House, that we had gone some little distance from the yard before I had the hardihood to mention it. We turned back, on my humbly insinuating that it might be useful to me hereafter; and he told the clerk that the carrier had instructions to call for it at noon.

"If you please, Sir," I said, when we had accomplished about the same distance as before, "is it far?"

"It's down by Blackheath," he said.

"Is that far, Sir?" I diffidently asked.

"It's a good step," he said. "We shall go by the stage-coach. It's about six miles."

I was so faint and tired, that the idea of holding out for six miles more was too much for me. I took heart to tell him that I had had nothing all night, and that if he would allow me to go buy something to eat I should be very much obliged to him. He appeared surprised at this—I see him stop and look at me now—and after considering for a few moments said he wanted to call on an old person who lived not far off, and that the best way would be for me to buy some bread, or whatever I liked best that was wholesome, and make my breakfast at her house, where we could get some milk.

Accordingly we looked in at a baker's window, and after I had made a series of proposals to buy everything that was bilious in the shop, and he had rejected them one by one, we decided in favour of a nice little loaf of brown bread, which cost me threepence. Then, at a grocer's shop,

we bought an egg and a slice of streaky bacon; which still left what I thought a good deal of change, out of the second of the bright shillings, and made me consider London a very cheap place. These provisions laid in, we went on through a great noise and uproar that confused my weary head beyond description, and over a bridge which, no doubt, was London Bridge (indeed I think he told me so, but I was half asleep), until we came to the poor person's house, which was a part of some almshouses, as I knew by their look, and by an inscription on a stone over the gate, which said they were established for twenty-five poor women.

The Master at Salem House lifted the latch of one of a number of little black doors that were all alike, and had each a little diamond-paned window on one side, and another little diamond-paned window above; and we went into the little house of one of these poor old women, who was blowing a fire to make a little saucepan boil. On seeing the Master enter, the old woman stopped with the bellows on her knee, and said something that I thought sounded like "My Charley!" but on seeing me come in too, she got up, and rubbing her hands made a confused sort of half-curtsey.

"Can you cook this young gentleman's breakfast for him, if you please?" said the Master at Salem House.

"Can I?" said the old woman. "Yes can I, sure!"

"How's Mrs. Fibbitson to-day?" said the Master, looking at another old woman in a large chair by the fire, who was such a bundle of clothes that I feel grateful to this hour for not having sat upon her by mistake.

"Ah, she's poorly," said the first old woman. "It's one of her bad days. If the fire was to go out, through any accident, I verily believe she'd go out too, and never come to life again."

As they looked at her, I looked at her also. Although it was a warm day, she seemed to think of nothing but the fire. I fancied she was jealous even of the saucepan on it; and I have reason to know that she took its impressment into the service of boiling my egg and broiling my bacon, in dudgeon; for I saw her, with my own discomfited eyes, shake her fist at me once, when those culinary operations were going on, and no one else was looking. The sun streamed in at the little window, but she sat with her own back and the back of the large chair towards it, screening the fire as if she were sedulously keeping it warm, instead of it keeping her warm, and watching it in a most distrustful manner. The completion of the preparations for my breakfast, by relieving the fire, gave her such extreme joy that she laughed aloud—and a very unmelodious laugh she had, I must say.

I sat down to my brown loaf, my egg, and my rasher of bacon, with a basin of milk besides, and made a most delicious meal. While I was yet in the full enjoyment of it, the old woman of the house said to the Master:

"Have you got your flute with you?"

"Yes," he returned.

"Have a blow at it," said the old woman, coaxingly. "Do!"

The Master, upon this, put his hand underneath the skirts of his coat, and brought out his flute in three pieces, which he screwed together, and began immediately to play. My impression is, after many years of consideration, that there never can have been anybody in the world who played worse. He made the most dismal sounds I have ever heard produced by any means, natural or artificial. I don't know what the tunes were—if there were such things in the performance at all, which I doubt—but the influence of the strain upon me was, first, to make me think of all my sorrows until I could hardly keep my tears back; then to take away my appetite; and lastly, to make me so sleepy that I couldn't keep my eyes open. They begin to close again, and I begin to nod, as the recollection rises fresh upon me. Once more the little room, with its open corner cupboard, and its square-backed chairs, and its angular little staircase leading to the room above, and its three peacock's feathers displayed over the mantelpiece—I remember wondering when I first went in, what that peacock would have thought if he had known what his finery was doomed to come to—fades from before me, and I nod, and sleep. The flute becomes inaudible, the wheels of the coach are heard instead, and I am on my journey. The coach jolts, I wake with a start, and the flute has come back again, and the Master at Salem House is sitting with his legs crossed, playing it dolefully, while the old woman of the house looks on delighted. She fades in her turn, and he fades, and all fades, and there is no flute, no Master, no Salem House, no David Copperfield, no anything but heavy sleep.

I dreamed, I thought, that once while he was blowing into this dismal flute, the old woman of the house, who had gone nearer and nearer to him in her ecstatic admiration, leaned over the back of his chair and gave him an affectionate squeeze round the neck, which stopped his playing for a moment. I was in the middle state between sleeping and waking, either then or immediately afterwards; for, as he resumed—it was a real fact that he had stopped playing—I saw and heard the same old woman ask Mrs. Fibbitson if it wasn't delicious (meaning the flute), to which Mrs. Fibbitson replied, "Ay, ay! yes!" and nodded at the fire: to which, I am persuaded, she gave the credit of the whole performance.

When I seemed to have been dozing a long while, the Master at Salem House unscrewed his flute into the three pieces, put them up as before, and took me away. We found the coach very near at hand, and got upon the roof; but I was so dead sleepy, that when we stopped on the road to take up somebody else, they put me inside where there were no passengers, and where I slept profoundly, until I found the coach going at a footpace up a steep hill among green leaves. Presently, it stopped, and had come to its destination.

A short walk brought us—I mean the Master and me—to Salem House, which was enclosed with a high brick wall, and looked very dull. Over a door in this wall was a board with SALEM HOUSE upon it; and through a grating in this door we were surveyed, when we rang the bell, by a surly face, which I found, on the door being opened, belonged to a stout man with a bull-neck, a wooden leg, overhanging temples, and his hair cut close all round his head.

"The new boy," said the Master.

The man with the wooden leg eyed me all over—it didn't take long, for there was not much of me—and locked the gate behind us, and took out the key. We were going up to the house, among some dark heavy trees, when he called after my conductor.

"Hallo!"

We looked back, and he was standing at the door of a little lodge, where he lived, with a pair of boots in his hand.

"Here! The cobbler's been," he said, "since you've been out, Mr. Mell, and he says he can't mend 'em any more. He says there an't a bit of the original boot left, and he wonders you expect it."

With these words he threw the boots towards Mr. Mell, who went back a few paces to pick them up, and looked at them (very disconsolately, I was afraid) as we went on together. I observed then, for the first time, that the boots he had on were a good deal the worse for wear, and that his stocking was just breaking out in one place, like a bud.

Salem House was a square brick building with wings; of a bare and unfurnished appearance. All about it was so very quiet, that I said to Mr. Mell I supposed the boys were out; but he seemed surprised at my not knowing that it was holiday-time. That all the boys were at their several homes. That Mr. Creakle, the proprietor, was down by the sea-side with Mrs. and Miss Creakle; and that I was sent in holiday-time as a punishment for my misdoing, all of which he explained to me as we went along.

I gazed upon the schoolroom into which he took me, as the most forlorn and desolate place I had ever seen. I see it now. A long room, with three long rows of desks, and six of forms, and bristling all round with pegs for hats and slates. Scraps of old copybooks and exercises litter the dirty floor. Some silkworms' houses, made of the same materials, are scattered over the desks. Two miserable little white mice, left behind by their owner, are running up and down in a fusty castle made of pasteboard and wire, looking in all the corners with their red eyes for anything to eat. A bird, in a cage very little bigger than himself, makes a mournful rattle now and then in hopping on his perch, two inches high, or dropping from it; but neither sings nor chirps. There is a strange unwholesome smell upon the room, like mildewed corduroys, sweet apples wanting air, and rotten books. There could not well be more ink splashed about it, if it had been roofless from its first construction, and the skies had rained, snowed, hailed, and blown ink through the varying seasons of the year.

Mr. Mell having left me while he took his irreparable boots up-stairs, I went softly to the upper end of the room, observing all this as I crept along. Suddenly I came upon a pasteboard placard, beautifully written, which was lying on the desk, and bore these words—"*Take care of him. He bites.*"

I got upon the desk immediately, apprehensive of at least a great dog underneath. But, though I looked all round with anxious eyes, I could see nothing of him. I was still engaged in peering about, when Mr. Mell came back, and asked me what I did up there.

"I beg your pardon, Sir," says I, "if you please, I'm looking for the dog."

"Dog?" says he. "What dog?"

"Isn't it a dog, Sir?"

"Isn't what a dog?"

"That's to be taken care of, Sir; that bites."

"No, Copperfield," says he gravely, "that's not a dog. That's a boy. My instructions are, Copperfield, to put this placard on your back. I am sorry to make such a beginning with you, but I must do it."

With that, he took me down, and tied the placard, which was neatly constructed for the purpose, on my shoulders like a knapsack; and wherever I went, afterwards, I had the consolation of carrying it.

What I suffered from that placard nobody can imagine. Whether it was possible for people to see me or not, I always fancied that somebody was reading it. It was no relief to turn round and find nobody; for wherever my back was, there I imagined somebody always to be. That cruel man with the wooden leg, aggravated my sufferings. He was in authority; and if he ever saw me leaning against a tree, or a wall, or the house, he roared out from his lodge-door in a stupendous voice, "Hallo, you Sir! You Copperfield! Show that badge conspicuous, or I'll report you!" The playground was a bare gravelled yard, open to all the back of the house and the offices; and I knew that the servants read it, and the butcher read it, and the baker read it; that everybody, in a word, who came backwards and forwards to the house, of a morning when I was ordered to walk there, read that I was to be taken care of, for I bit. I recollect that I positively began to have a dread of myself, as a kind of wild boy who did bite.

There was an old door in this playground, on which the boys had a custom of carving their names. It was completely covered with such inscriptions. In my dread of the end of the vacation and their coming back, I could not read a boy's name, without inquiring in what tone and with what emphasis *he* would read, "Take care of him. He bites." There was one boy—a certain J. Steerforth—who cut his name very deep and very often, who, I conceived, would read it in a rather strong voice, and afterwards pull my hair. There was another boy, one Tommy Traddles, who I dreaded would make game of it, and pretend to be dreadfully frightened of me. There was a third, George Demple, who I fancied would sing it. I have looked, a little shrinking creature, at that door, until the owners of all the names—there were five-and-forty of them in the school then, Mr. Mell said—seemed to send me to Coventry by general acclamation, and to cry out, each in his own way, "Take care of him. He bites!"

It was the same with the places at the desks and forms. It was the same with the groves of deserted bedsteads I peeped at, on my way to, and when I was in, my own bed. I remember dreaming night after night, of being with my mother as she used to be, or of going to a party at Mr. Peggotty's, or of travelling outside the stage-coach, or of dining again with my unfortunate friend the waiter, and in all these circumstances making people scream and stare, by the unhappy disclosure that I had nothing on but my little night-shirt, and that placard.

In the monotony of my life, and in my constant apprehension of the reopening of the school, it was such an insupportable affliction! I had long tasks every day to do with Mr. Mell; but I did them, there being no Mr. and Miss Murdstone here, and got through them without disgrace. Before, and after them, I walked about—supervised, as I have mentioned, by the man with the wooden leg. How vividly I call to mind the damp about the house, the green cracked flagstones in the court, an old leaky water-butt, and the discoloured trunks of some of the grim trees, which seemed to have dripped more in the rain than other trees, and to have blown less in the sun! At one we dined, Mr. Mell and I, at the upper end of a long bare dining-room, full of deal tables, and smelling of fat. Then, we had more tasks until tea, which Mr. Mell drank out of a blue teacup, and I out of a tin pot. All day long,

and until seven or eight in the evening, Mr. Mell, at his own detached desk in the schoolroom, worked hard with pen, ink, ruler, books, and writing-paper, making out the bills (as I found) for last half-year. When he had put up his things for the night, he took out his flute, and blew at it, until I almost thought he would gradually blow his whole being into the large hole at the top, and ooze away at the keys.

I picture my small self in the dimly-lighted rooms, sitting with my head upon my hand, listening to the doleful performance of Mr. Mell, and conning to-morrow's lessons. I picture myself with my books shut up, still listening to the doleful performance of Mr. Mell, and listening through it to what used to be at home, and to the blowing of the wind on Yarmouth flats, and feeling very sad and solitary. I picture myself going up to bed, among the unused rooms, and sitting on my bed-side crying for a comfortable word from Peggotty. I picture myself coming down-stairs in the morning, and looking through a long ghastly gash of a staircase-window at the school-bell hanging on the top of an outhouse, with a weathercock above it; and dreading the time when it shall ring J. Steerforth and the rest to work: which is only second, in my foreboding apprehensions, to the time when the man with the wooden leg shall unlock the rusty gate to give admission to the awful Mr. Creakle. I cannot think I was a very dangerous character in any of these aspects, but in all of them I carried the same warning on my back.

Mr. Mell never said much to me, but he was never harsh to me. I suppose we were company to each other, without talking. I forgot to mention that he would talk to himself sometimes, and grin, and clench his fist, and grind his teeth, and pull his hair in an unaccountable manner. But he had these peculiarities: and at first they frightened me, though I soon got used to them.

CHAPTER VI.

I ENLARGE MY CIRCLE OF ACQUAINTANCE.

I HAD led this life about a month, when the man with the wooden leg began to stump about with a mop and a bucket of water, from which I inferred that preparations were making to receive Mr. Creakle and the boys. I was not mistaken; for the mop came into the schoolroom before long, and turned out Mr. Mell and me, who lived where we could, and got on how we could, for some days, during which we were always in the way of two or three young women, who had rarely shown themselves before, and were so continually in the midst of dust that I sneezed almost as much as if Salem House had been a great snuff-box.

One day I was informed by Mr. Mell, that Mr. Creakle would be home that evening. In the evening, after tea, I heard that he was come. Before bed-time, I was fetched by the man with the wooden leg to appear before him.

Mr. Creakle's part of the house was a good deal more comfortable than ours, and he had a snug bit of garden that looked pleasant after the dusty playground, which was such a desert in miniature, that I thought no one but a camel, or a dromedary, could have felt at home in it. It seemed to me a bold thing even to take notice that the passage looked comfortable, as I went on my way, trembling, to Mr. Creakle's presence: which so abashed me, when I was ushered into it, that I hardly saw Mrs. Creakle or Miss Creakle (who were both there, in the parlour), or anything but Mr. Creakle, a stout gentleman with a bunch of watch-chain and seals, in an arm-chair, with a tumbler and bottle beside him.

"So!" said Mr. Creakle. "This is the young gentleman whose teeth are to be filed! Turn him round."

The wooden-legged man turned me about so as to exhibit the placard; and having afforded time for a full survey of it, turned me about again, with my face to Mr. Creakle, and posted himself at Mr. Creakle's side. Mr. Creakle's face was fiery, and his eyes were small, and deep in his head; he had thick veins in his forehead, a little nose, and a large chin. He was bald on the top of his head; and had some thin wet-looking hair that was just turning grey, brushed across each temple, so that the two sides interlaced on his forehead. But the circumstance about him which impressed me most, was, that he had no voice, but spoke in a whisper. The exertion this cost him, or the consciousness of talking in that feeble way, made his angry face so much more angry, and his thick veins so much thicker, when he spoke, that I am not surprised, on looking back, at this peculiarity striking me as his chief one.

"Now," said Mr. Creakle. "What's the report of this boy?"

"There's nothing against him yet," returned the man with the wooden leg. "There has been no opportunity."

I thought Mr. Creakle was disappointed. I thought Mrs. and Miss Creakle (at whom I now glanced for the first time, and who were, both, thin and quiet) were not disappointed.

"Come here, Sir!" said Mr. Creakle, beckoning to me.

"Come here!" said the man with the wooden leg, repeating the gesture.

"I have the happiness of knowing your father-in-law," whispered Mr. Creakle, taking me by the ear; "and a worthy man he is, and a man of a strong character. He knows me, and I know him. Do *you* know me? Hey?" said Mr. Creakle, pinching my ear with ferocious playfulness.

"Not yet, Sir," I said, flinching with the pain.

"Not yet? Hey?" repeated Mr. Creakle. "But you will soon. Hey?"

"You will soon. Hey?" repeated the man with the wooden leg. I afterwards found that he generally acted, with his strong voice, as Mr. Creakle's interpreter to the boys.

I was very much frightened, and said, I hoped so, if he pleased. I felt, all this while, as if my ear were blazing; he pinched it so hard.

"I'll tell you what I am," whispered Mr. Creakle, letting it go at last, with a screw at parting that brought the water into my eyes, "I'm a Tartar."

"A Tartar," said the man with the wooden leg.

"When I say I'll do a thing, I do it," said Mr. Creakle; "and when I say I will have a thing done, I will have it done."

"—Will have a thing done, I will have it done," repeated the man with the wooden leg.

"I am a determined character," said Mr. Creakle. "That's what I am. I do my duty. That's what *I* do.

My flesh and blood—" he looked at Mrs. Creakle as he said this—"when it rises against me, is not my flesh and blood. I discard it. Has that fellow," to the man with the wooden leg, "been here again?"

"No," was the answer.

"No," said Mr. Creakle. "He knows better. He knows me. Let him keep away. I say let him keep away," said Mr. Creakle, striking his hand upon the table, and looking at Mrs. Creakle, "for he knows me. Now you have begun to know me too, my young friend, and you may go. Take him away."

I was very glad to be ordered away, for Mrs. and Miss Creakle were both wiping their eyes, and I felt as uncomfortable for them as I did for myself. But I had a petition on my mind which concerned me so nearly, that I couldn't help saying, though I wondered at my own courage:

"If you please, Sir——"

Mr. Creakle whispered, "Hah? What's this?" and bent his eyes upon me, as if he would have burnt me up with them.

"If you please, Sir," I faltered, "if I might be allowed (I am very sorry indeed, Sir, for what I did) to take this writing off, before the boys come back——"

Whether Mr. Creakle was in earnest, or whether he only did it to frighten me, I don't know, but he made a burst out of his chair, before which I precipitately retreated, without waiting for the escort of the man with the wooden leg, and never once stopped until I reached my own bedroom, where, finding I was not pursued, I went to bed, as it was time, and lay quaking, for a couple of hours.

Next morning Mr. Sharp came back. Mr. Sharp was the first master, and superior to Mr. Mell. Mr. Mell took his meals with the boys, but Mr. Sharp dined and supped at Mr. Creakle's table. He was a limp, delicate-looking gentleman, I thought, with a good deal of nose, and a way of carrying his head on one side, as if it were a little too heavy for him. His hair was very smooth and wavy; but I was informed by the very first boy who came back that it was a wig (a second-hand one *he* said), and that Mr. Sharp went out every Saturday afternoon to get it curled.

It was no other than Tommy Traddles who gave me this piece of intelligence. He was the first boy who returned. He introduced himself by informing me that I should find his name on the right-hand corner of the gate, over the top bolt; upon that I said, "Traddles?" to which he replied, "The same," and then he asked me for a full account of myself and family.

It was a happy circumstance for me that Traddles came back first. He enjoyed my placard so much, that he saved me from the embarrassment of either disclosure or concealment, by presenting me to every other boy who came back, great or small, immediately on his arrival, in this form of introduction, "Look here! Here's a game!" Happily, too, the greater part of the boys came back low-spirited, and were not so boisterous at my expense as I had expected. Some of them certainly did dance about me like wild Indians, and the greater part could not resist the temptation of pretending that I was a dog, and patting and smoothing me lest I should bite, and saying, "Lie down, Sir!" and calling me Towzer. This was naturally confusing, among so many strangers, and cost me some tears, but on the whole it was much better than I had anticipated.

I was not considered as being formally received into the

school, however, until J. Steerforth arrived. Before this boy, who was reputed to be a great scholar, and was very good-looking, and at least half-a-dozen years my senior, I was carried as before a magistrate. He inquired, under a shed in the playground, into the particulars of my punishment, and was pleased to express his opinion that it was "a jolly shame;" for which I became bound to him ever afterwards.

"What money have you got, Copperfield?" he said, walking aside with me when he had disposed of my affair in these terms.

I told him seven shillings.

"You had better give it to me to take care of," he said. "At least, you can if you like. You needn't if you don't like."

I hastened to comply with his friendly suggestion, and opening Peggotty's purse, turned it upside down into his hand.

"Do you want to spend anything now?" he asked me.

"No, thank you," I replied.

"You can if you like, you know," said Steerforth. "Say the word."

"No, thank you, Sir," I repeated.

"Perhaps you'd like to spend a couple of shillings or so, in a bottle of currant wine by and by, up in the bedroom?" said Steerforth. "You belong to my bedroom, I find."

It certainly had not occurred to me before, but I said, Yes, I should like that.

"Very good," said Steerforth. "You'll be glad to spend another shilling or so, in almond cakes, I dare say?"

I said, Yes, I should like that, too.

"And another shilling or so in biscuits, and another in fruit, eh?" said Steerforth. "I say, young Copperfield, you're going it!"

I smiled because he smiled, but I was a little troubled in my mind, too.

"Well!" said Steerforth. "We must make it stretch as far as we can; that's all. I'll do the best in my power for you. I can go out when I like, and I'll smuggle the prog in." With these words he put the money in his pocket, and kindly told me not to make myself uneasy; he would take care it should be all right.

He was as good as his word, if that were all right which I had a secret misgiving was nearly all wrong—for I feared it was a waste of my mother's two half-crowns—though I had preserved the piece of paper they were wrapped in: which was a precious saving. When we went up-stairs to bed, he produced the whole seven shillings' worth, and laid it out on my bed in the moonlight, saying:

"There you are, young Copperfield, and a royal spread you've got!"

I couldn't think of doing the honours of the feast, at my time of life, while he was by; my hand shook at the very thought of it. I begged him to do me the favour of presiding; and my request being seconded by the other boys who were in that room, he acceded to it, and sat upon my pillow, handing round the viands—with perfect fairness, I must say—and dispensing the currant wine in a little glass without a foot, which was his own property. As to me, I sat on his left hand, and the rest were grouped about us, on the nearest beds and on the floor.

How well I recollect our sitting there, talking in whispers; or their talking, and my respectfully listening, I ought rather to say; the moonlight falling a little way into the room, through the window, painting a pale window on the floor, and the greater part of us in shadow, except when Steerforth dipped a match into a phosphorus-box, when he wanted to look for anything on the board, and shed a blue glare over us that was gone directly! A certain mysterious feeling, consequent on the darkness, the secrecy of the revel, and the whisper in which everything was said, steals over me again, and I listen to all they tell me with a vague feeling of solemnity and awe, which makes me glad that they are all so near, and frightens me (though I feign to laugh) when Traddles pretends to see a ghost in the corner.

I heard all kinds of things about the school and all belonging to it. I heard that Mr. Creakle had not preferred his claim to being a Tartar without reason; that he was the sternest and most severe of masters; that he laid about him, right and left, every day of his life, charging in among the boys like a trooper, and slashing away, unmercifully. That he knew nothing himself, but the art of slashing, being more ignorant (J. Steerforth said) than the lowest boy in the school; that he had been, a good many years ago, a small hop-dealer in the Borough, and had taken to the schooling business after being bankrupt in hops, and making away with Mrs. Creakle's money. With a good deal more of that sort, which I wondered how they knew.

I heard that the man with the wooden leg, whose name was Tungay, was an obstinate barbarian who had formerly assisted in the hop business, but had come into the scholastic line with Mr. Creakle, in consequence, as was supposed among the boys, of his having broken his leg in Mr. Creakle's service, and having done a deal of dishonest work for him, and knowing his secrets. I heard that with the single exception of Mr. Creakle, Tungay considered the whole establishment, masters and boys, as his natural enemies, and that the only delight of his life was to be sour and malicious. I heard that Mr. Creakle had a son, who had not been Tungay's friend, and who, assisting in the school, had once held some remonstrance with his father on an occasion when its discipline was very cruelly exercised, and was supposed, besides, to have protested against his father's usage of his mother. I heard that Mr. Creakle had turned him out of doors, in consequence; and that Mrs. and Miss Creakle had been in a sad way, ever since.

But the greatest wonder that I heard of Mr. Creakle was, there being one boy in the school on whom he never ventured to lay a hand, and that boy being J. Steerforth. Steerforth himself confirmed this when it was stated, and said that he should like to begin to see him do it. On being asked by a mild boy (not me) how he would proceed if he did begin to see him do it, he dipped a match into his phosphorus-box on purpose to shed a glare over his reply, and said he would commence by knocking him down with a blow on the forehead from the seven-and-sixpenny ink-bottle that was always on the mantelpiece. We sat in the dark for some time, breathless.

I heard that Mr. Sharp and Mr. Mell were both supposed to be wretchedly paid; and that when there was hot and cold meat for dinner at Mr. Creakle's table, Mr. Sharp was always expected to say he preferred cold; which was again corroborated by J. Steerforth, the only parlour-boarder. I heard that Mr. Sharp's wig didn't fit him; and that he needn't be so "bounceable"—somebody else said "bumptious"—about it, because his own red hair was very plainly to be seen behind.

I heard that one boy, who was a coal-merchant's son, came as a set-off against the coal-bill, and was called, on that account, "Exchange or Barter"—a name selected from the arithmetic-book as expressing this arrangement. I heard that the table-beer was a robbery of parents, and the pudding an imposition. I heard that Miss Creakle was regarded by the school in general as being in love with Steerforth; and I am sure, as I sat in the dark, thinking of his nice voice, and his fine face, and his easy manner, and his curling hair, I thought it very likely. I heard that Mr. Mell was not a bad sort of fellow, but hadn't a sixpence to bless himself with; and that there was no doubt that old Mrs. Mell, his mother, was as poor as Job. I thought of my breakfast then, and what had sounded like "My Charley!" but I was, I am glad to remember, as mute as a mouse about it.

The hearing of all this, and a good deal more, outlasted the banquet some time. The greater part of the guests had gone to bed as soon as the eating and drinking were over; and we, who had remained whispering and listening half undressed, at last betook ourselves to bed, too.

"Good night, young Copperfield," said Steerforth, "I'll take care of you."

"You're very kind," I gratefully returned. "I am very much obliged to you."

"You haven't got a sister, have you?" said Steerforth, yawning.

"No," I answered.

"That's a pity," said Steerforth. "If you had had one, I should think she would have been a pretty, timid, little, bright-eyed sort of girl. I should have liked to know her. Good night, young Copperfield."

"Good night, Sir," I replied.

I thought of him very much after I went to bed, and raised myself, I recollect, to look at him where he lay in the moonlight, with his handsome face turned up, and his head reclining easily on his arm. He was a person of great power in my eyes; that was, of course, the reason of my mind running on him. No veiled future dimly glanced upon him in the moonbeams. There was no shadowy picture of his footsteps, in the garden that I dreamed of walking in all night.

CHAPTER VII.

MY "FIRST HALF" AT SALEM HOUSE.

School began in earnest next day. A profound impression was made upon me, I remember, by the roar of voices in the schoolroom suddenly becoming hushed as death when Mr. Creakle entered after breakfast, and stood in the doorway looking round upon us like a giant in a story-book surveying his captives.

Tungay stood at Mr. Creakle's elbow. He had no occasion, I thought, to cry out "Silence!" so ferociously, for the boys were all struck speechless and motionless.

Mr. Creakle was seen to speak, and Tungay was heard, to this effect.

"Now, boys, this is a new half. Take care what you're about, in this new half. Come fresh up to the lessons, I advise you, for I come fresh up to the punishment. I won't flinch. It will be of no use your rubbing yourselves; you won't rub the marks out that I shall give you. Now get to work, every boy!"

When this dreadful exordium was over, and Tungay had stumped out again, Mr. Creakle came to where I sat, and told me that if I were famous for biting, he was famous for biting, too. He then showed me the cane, and asked me what I thought of *that*, for a tooth? Was it a sharp tooth, hey? Was it a double tooth, hey? Had it a deep prong, hey? Did it bite, hey? Did it bite? At every question he gave me a fleshy cut with it that made me writhe; so I was very soon made free of Salem House (as Steerforth said), and very soon in tears also.

Not that I mean to say these were special marks of distinction, which only I received. On the contrary, a large majority of the boys (especially the smaller ones) were visited with similar instances of notice, as Mr. Creakle made the round of the schoolroom. Half the establishment was writhing and crying, before the day's work began; and how much of it had writhed and cried before the day's work was over, I am really afraid to recollect, lest I should seem to exaggerate.

I should think there never can have been a man who enjoyed his profession more than Mr. Creakle did. He had a delight in cutting at the boys, which was like the satisfaction of a craving appetite. I am confident that he couldn't resist a chubby boy, especially; that there was a fascination in such a subject, which made him restless in his mind, until he had scored and marked him for the day. I was chubby myself, and ought to know. I am sure when I think of the fellow now, my blood rises against him with the disinterested indignation I should feel if I could have known all about him without having ever been in his power; but it rises hotly, because I know him to have been an incapable brute, who had no more right to be possessed of the great trust he held, than to be Lord High Admiral, or Commander-in-Chief: in either of which capacities, it is probable that he would have done infinitely less mischief.

Miserable little propitiators of a remorseless Idol, how abject we were to him! What a launch in life I think it now, on looking back, to be so mean and servile to a man of such parts and pretensions!

Here I sit at the desk again, watching his eye—humbly watching his eye, as he rules a ciphering-book for another victim whose hands have just been flattened by that identical ruler, and who is trying to wipe the sting out with a pocket-handkerchief. I have plenty to do. I don't watch his eye in idleness, but because I am morbidly attracted to it, in a dread desire to know what he will do next, and whether it will be my turn to suffer, or somebody else's. A lane of small boys beyond me, with the same interest in his eye, watch it too. I think he knows it, though he pretends he don't. He makes dreadful mouths as he rules the ciphering-book; and now he throws his eye sideways down our lane, and we all droop over our books and tremble. A moment afterwards we are again eyeing him. An unhappy culprit, found guilty of imperfect exercise, approaches at his command. The culprit falters excuses, and professes a determination to do better to-morrow. Mr. Creakle cuts a joke before he beats him, and we laugh at it,—miserable little dogs, we laugh, with our visages as white as ashes, and our hearts sinking into our boots.

Here I sit at the desk again, on a drowsy summer afternoon. A buzz and hum go up around me, as if the boys were so many blue-bottles. A cloggy sensation of the lukewarm fat of meat is upon me (we dined an hour or two ago), and my head is as heavy as so much lead. I would give the world to go to sleep. I sit with my eye on Mr. Creakle, blinking at him like a young owl; when sleep overpowers me for a minute, he still looms through my slumber, ruling those ciphering-books; until he softly comes behind me and wakes me to plainer perception of him, with a red ridge across my back.

Here I am in the playground, with my eye still fascinated by him, though I can't see him. The window at a little distance from which I know he is having his dinner, stands for him, and I eye that instead. If he shows his face near it, mine assumes an imploring and submissive expression. If he looks out through the glass, the boldest boy (Steerforth excepted) stops in the middle of a shout or yell, and becomes contemplative. One day, Traddles (the most unfortunate boy in the world) breaks that window accidentally, with a ball. I shudder at this moment with the tremendous sensation of seeing it done, and feeling that the ball has bounded on to Mr. Creakle's sacred head.

Poor Traddles! In a tight sky-blue suit that made his arms and legs like German sausages, or roly-poly puddings, he was the merriest and most miserable of all the boys. He was always being caned—I think he was caned every day that half-year, except one holiday Monday when he was only ruler'd on both hands—and was always going to write to his uncle about it, and never did. After laying his head on the desk for a little while, he would cheer up, somehow, begin to laugh again, and draw skeletons all over his slate, before his eyes were dry. I used at first to wonder what comfort Traddles found in drawing skeletons; and for some time looked upon him as a sort of hermit, who reminded himself by those symbols of mortality that caning couldn't last for ever. But I believe he only did it because they were easy, and didn't want any features.

He was very honourable, Traddles was, and held it as a solemn duty in the boys to stand by one another. He suffered for this on several occasions; and particularly once, when Steerforth laughed in church, and the beadle thought it was Traddles, and took him out. I see him now, going away in custody, despised by the congregation. He never said who was the real offender, though he smarted for it next day, and was imprisoned so many hours that he came forth with a whole churchyard-full of skeletons swarming all over his Latin Dictionary. But he had his reward. Steerforth said there was nothing of the sneak in Traddles, and we all felt that to be the highest praise. For my part, I could have gone through a good deal (though I was much less brave than Traddles, and nothing like so old) to have won such a recompense.

To see Steerforth walk to church before us, arm-in-arm with Miss Creakle, was one of the great sights of my life. I didn't think Miss Creakle equal to little Em'ly in point of beauty, and I didn't love her (I didn't dare); but I thought her a young lady of extraordinary attractions, and in point of gentility not to be surpassed. When Steerforth, in white trousers, carried her parasol for her, I felt proud to know him; and believed that she could not choose but adore him with all her heart. Mr. Sharp and Mr. Mell were both notable personages in my eyes; but Steerforth was to them what the sun was to two stars.

Steerforth continued his protection of me, and proved a very useful friend, since nobody dared to annoy one whom he honoured with his countenance. He couldn't—or, at all events, he didn't—defend me from Mr. Creakle, who was

very severe with me; but whenever I had been treated worse than usual, he always told me that I wanted a little of his pluck, and that he wouldn't have stood it himself; which I felt he intended for encouragement, and considered led to be very kind of him. There was one advantage, and only one that I know of, in Mr. Creakle's severity. He found my placard in his way, when he came up or down behind the form on which I sat, and wanted to make a cut at me in passing; for this reason it was soon taken off, and I saw it no more.

An accidental circumstance cemented the intimacy between Steerforth and me, in a manner that inspired me with great pride and satisfaction, though it sometimes led to inconvenience. It happened on one occasion, when he was doing me the honour of talking to me in the playground, that I hazarded the observation that something or somebody—I forget what now—was like something or somebody in Peregrine Pickle. He said nothing at the time; but when I was going to bed at night, asked me if I had got that book.

I told him no, and explained how it was that I had read it, and all those other books of which I have made mention. "And do you recollect them?" Steerforth said.

Oh yes, I replied; I had a good memory, and I believed I recollected them very well.

"Then I tell you what, young Copperfield," said Steerforth, "you shall tell 'em to me. I can't get to sleep very early at night, and I generally wake rather early in the morning. We'll go over 'em one after another. We'll make some regular Arabian Nights of it."

I felt extremely flattered by this arrangement, and we commenced carrying it into execution that very evening. What ravages I committed on my favourite authors in the course of my interpretation of them, I am not in a condition to say, and should be very unwilling to know; but I had a profound faith in them, and I had, to the best of my belief, a simple, earnest manner of narrating what I did narrate; and these qualities went a long way.

The drawback was, that I was often sleepy at night, or out of spirits and indisposed to resume the story; and then it was rather hard work, and it must be done; for to disappoint or to displease Steerforth was of course out of the question. In the morning too, when I felt weary, and should have enjoyed another hour's repose very much, it was a tiresome thing to be roused, like the Sultana Scheherazade, and forced into a long story before the getting-up bell rang; but Steerforth was resolute; and as he explained to me, in return, my sums and exercises, and anything in my tasks that was too hard for me, I was no loser by the transaction. Let me do myself justice, however. I was moved by no interested or selfish motive, nor was I moved by fear of him. I admired and loved him, and his approval was return enough. It was so precious to me, that I look back on these trifles, now, with an aching heart.

Steerforth was considerate too, and showed his consideration, in one particular instance, in an unflinching manner that was a little tantalising, I suspect, to poor Traddles and the rest. Peggotty's promised letter—what a comfortable letter it was—arrived before "the half" was many weeks old; and with it a cake in a perfect nest of oranges, and two bottles of cowslip wine. This treasure, as in duty bound, I laid at the feet of Steerforth, and begged him to dispense.

"Now, I'll tell you what, young Copperfield," said he: "the wine shall be kept to wet your whistle when you are story-telling."

I blushed at the idea, and begged him, in my modesty,

not to think of it. But he said he had observed I was sometimes hoarse—a little roopy was his exact expression—and it should be, every drop, devoted to the purpose he had mentioned. Accordingly, it was locked up in his box, and drawn off by himself in a phial, and administered to me through a piece of quill in the cork, when I was supposed to be in want of a restorative. Sometimes, to make it a more sovereign specific, he was so kind as to squeeze orange juice into it, or to stir it up with ginger, or dissolve a peppermint drop in it; and although I cannot assert that the flavour was improved by these experiments, or that it was exactly the compound one would have chosen for a stomachic, the last thing at night and the first thing in the morning, I drank it gratefully, and was very sensible of his attention.

We seem, to me, to have been months over Peregrine, and months more over the other stories. The institution never flagged for want of a story, I am certain; and the wine lasted out almost as well as the matter. Poor Traddles—I never think of that boy but with a strange disposition to laugh, and with tears in my eyes—was a sort of chorus, in general; and affected to be convulsed with mirth at the comic parts, and to be overcome with fear when there was any passage of an alarming character in the narrative. This rather put me out, very often. It was a great jest of his, I recollect, to pretend that he couldn't keep his teeth from chattering, whenever mention was made of an Alguazil in connexion with the adventures of Gil Blas; and I remember that, when Gil Blas met the captain of the robbers in Madrid, this unlucky joker counterfeited such an ague of terror, that he was overheard by Mr. Creakle, who was prowling about the passage, and handsomely flogged for disorderly conduct in the bedroom.

Whatever I had within me that was romantic and dreamy, was encouraged by so much story-telling in the dark; and in that respect the pursuit may not have been very profitable to me. But the being cherished as a kind of plaything in my room, and the consciousness that this accomplishment of mine was bruited about among the boys, and attracted a good deal of notice to me though I was the youngest there, stimulated me to exertion. In a school carried on by sheer cruelty, whether it is presided over by a dunce or not, there is not likely to be much learnt. I believe our boys were, generally, as ignorant a set as any schoolboys in existence; they were too much troubled and knocked about to learn; they could no more do that to advantage, than any one can do anything to advantage in a life of constant misfortune, torment, and worry. But my little vanity, and Steerforth's help, urged me on somehow; and without saving me from much, if anything, in the way of punishment, made me, for the time I was there, an exception to the general body, insomuch that I did steadily pick up some crumbs of knowledge.

In this I was much assisted by Mr. Mell, who had a liking for me that I am grateful to remember. It always gave me pain to observe that Steerforth treated him with systematic disparagement, and seldom lost an occasion of wounding his feelings, or inducing others to do so. This troubled me the more for a long time, because I had soon told Steerforth, from whom I could no more keep such a secret than I could keep a cake or any other tangible possession, about the two old women Mr. Mell had taken me to see; and I was always afraid that Steerforth would let it out, and twit him with it.

We little thought, any one of us, I dare say, when I ate my breakfast that first morning, and went to sleep under the shadow of the peacock's feathers to the sound of the flute, what consequences would come of the introduction into those almshouses of my insignificant person. But the visit had its unforeseen consequences; and of a serious sort, too, in their way.

One day when Mr. Creakle kept the house from indisposition, which naturally diffused a lively joy through the school, there was a good deal of noise in the course of the morning's work. The great relief and satisfaction experienced by the boys made them difficult to manage; and though the dreaded Tungay brought his wooden leg in twice or thrice, and took notes of the principal offenders' names, no great impression was made by it, as they were pretty sure of getting into trouble to-morrow, do what they would, and thought it wise, no doubt, to enjoy themselves to-day.

It was, properly, a half-holiday; being Saturday. But as the noise in the playground would have disturbed Mr. Creakle, and the weather was not favourable for going out walking, we were ordered into school in the afternoon, and set some lighter tasks than usual, which were made for the occasion. It was the day of the week on which Mr. Sharp went out to get his wig curled; so Mr. Mell, who always did the drudgery, whatever it was, kept school by himself.

If I could associate the idea of a bull or a bear with any one so mild as Mr. Mell, I should think of him, in connexion with that afternoon when the uproar was at its height, as of one of those animals, baited by a thousand dogs. I recall him bending his aching head, supported on his bony hand, over the book on his desk, and wretchedly endeavouring to get on with his tiresome work, amidst an uproar that might have made the Speaker of the House of Commons giddy. Boys started in and out of their places, playing at puss-in-the-corner with other boys; there were laughing boys, singing boys, talking boys, dancing boys, howling boys; boys shuffled with their feet, boys whirled about him, grinning, making faces, mimicking him behind his back and before his eyes: mimicking his poverty, his boots, his coat, his mother, everything belonging to him that they should have had consideration for.

"Silence!" cried Mr. Mell, suddenly rising up, and striking his desk with the book. "What does this mean! It's impossible to bear it. It's maddening. How can you do it to me, boys?"

It was my book that he struck his desk with; and as I stood beside him, following his eye as it glanced round the room, I saw the boys all stop, some suddenly surprised, some half afraid, and some sorry perhaps.

Steerforth's place was at the bottom of the school, at the opposite end of the long room. He was lounging with his back against the wall, and his hands in his pockets, and looked at Mr. Mell with his mouth shut up as if he were whistling, when Mr. Mell looked at him.

"Silence, Mr. Steerforth!" said Mr. Mell.

"Silence yourself," said Steerforth, turning red. "Whom are you talking to?"

"Sit down," said Mr. Mell.

"Sit down yourself," said Steerforth, "and mind your business."

There was a titter, and some applause; but Mr. Mell was so white, that silence immediately succeeded; and one boy, who had darted out behind him to imitate his mother again, changed his mind, and pretended to want a pen mended.

"If you think, Steerforth," said Mr. Mell, "that I am not acquainted with the power you can establish over any mind here"—he laid his hand, without considering what he did (as I supposed), upon my head—"or that I have not observed you, within a few minutes, urging your juniors on to every sort of outrage against me, you are mistaken."

"I don't give myself the trouble of thinking at all about you," said Steerforth, coolly; "so I'm not mistaken, as it happens."

"And when you make use of your position of favouritism here, Sir," pursued Mr. Mell, with his lip trembling very much, "to insult a gentleman——"

"A what?—where is he?" said Steerforth.

Here somebody cried out, "Shame, J. Steerforth! Too bad!" It was Traddles; whom Mr. Mell instantly discomfited by bidding him hold his tongue.

—"To insult one who is not fortunate in life, Sir, and who never gave you the least offence, and the many reasons for not insulting whom you are old enough and wise enough to understand," said Mr. Mell, with his lip trembling more and more, "you commit a mean and base action. You can sit down or stand up as you please, Sir. Copperfield, go on."

"Young Copperfield," said Steerforth, coming forward up the room, "stop a bit. I tell you what, Mr. Mell, once for all. When you take the liberty of calling me mean or base, or anything of that sort, you are an impudent beggar. You are always a beggar, you know; but when you do that, you are an impudent beggar."

I am not clear whether he was going to strike Mr. Mell, or Mr. Mell was going to strike him, or there was any such intention on either side. I saw a rigidity come upon the whole school as if they had been turned into stone, and found Mr. Creakle in the midst of us, with Tungay at his side, and Mrs. and Miss Creakle looking in at the door as if they were frightened. Mr. Mell, with his elbows on his desk and his face in his hands, sat, for some moments, quite still.

"Mr. Mell," said Mr. Creakle, shaking him by the arm; and his whisper was so audible now, that Tungay felt it unnecessary to repeat his words; "you have not forgotten yourself, I hope?"

"No, Sir, no," returned the Master, showing his face, and shaking his head, and rubbing his hands in great agitation. "No, Sir. No. I have remembered myself, I—no, Mr. Creakle, I have not forgotten myself, I—I have remembered myself, Sir. I—I—could wish you had remembered me a little sooner, Mr. Creakle. It—it—would have been more kind, Sir, more just, Sir. It would have saved me something, Sir."

Mr. Creakle, looking hard at Mr. Mell, put his hand on Tungay's shoulder, and got his feet upon the form close by, and sat upon the desk. After still looking hard at Mr. Mell from this throne, as he shook his head, and rubbed his hands, and remained in the same state of agitation, Mr. Creakle turned to Steerforth, and said:

"Now, Sir, as he don't condescend to tell me, what is this?"

Steerforth evaded the question for a little while; looking in scorn and anger on his opponent, and remaining silent. I could not help thinking even in that interval, I remember, what a noble fellow he was in appearance, and how homely and plain Mr. Mell looked opposed to him.

"What did he mean by talking about favourites, then?" said Steerforth, at length.

"Favourites?" repeated Mr. Creakle, with the veins in his forehead swelling quickly. "Who talked about favourites?"

"He did," said Steerforth.

"And pray, what did you mean by that, Sir?" demanded Mr. Creakle, turning angrily on his assistant.

"I meant, Mr. Creakle," he returned in a low voice, "as I said; that no pupil had a right to avail himself of his position of favouritism to degrade me."

"To degrade you?" said Mr. Creakle. "My stars! But give me leave to ask you, Mr. What's-your-name;" and here Mr. Creakle folded his arms, cane and all, upon his chest, and made such a knot of his brows that his little eyes were hardly visible below them; "whether, when you talk about favourites, you showed proper respect to me? To me, Sir," said Mr. Creakle, darting his head at him suddenly, and drawing it back again, "the principal of this establishment, and your employer."

"It was not judicious, Sir, I am willing to admit," said Mr. Mell. "I should not have done so, if I had been cool."

Here Steerforth struck in.

"Then he said I was mean, and then he said I was base, and then I called him a beggar. If I had been cool, perhaps I shouldn't have called him a beggar. But I did, and I am ready to take the consequences of it."

Without considering, perhaps, whether there were any consequences to be taken, I felt quite in a glow at this gallant speech. It made an impression on the boys too, for there was a low stir among them, though no one spoke a word.

"I am surprised, Steerforth—although your candour does you honour," said Mr. Creakle, "does you honour, certainly —I am surprised, Steerforth, I must say, that you should attach such an epithet to any person employed and paid in Salem House, Sir."

Steerforth gave a short laugh.

"That's not an answer, Sir," said Mr. Creakle, "to my remark. I expect more than that from you, Steerforth."

If Mr. Mell looked homely, in my eyes, before the handsome boy, it would be quite impossible to say how homely Mr. Creakle looked.

"Let him deny it," said Steerforth.

"Deny that he is a beggar, Steerforth?" cried Mr. Creakle. "Why, where does he go a begging?"

"If he is not a beggar himself, his near relation's one," said Steerforth. "It's all the same."

He glanced at me, and Mr. Mell's hand gently patted me upon the shoulder. I looked up, with a flush upon my face and remorse in my heart, but Mr. Mell's eyes were fixed on Steerforth. He continued to pat me kindly on the shoulder, but he looked at him.

"Since you expect me, Mr. Creakle, to justify myself," said Steerforth, "and to say what I mean,—what I have to say is, that his mother lives on charity in an almshouse."

Mr. Mell still looked at him, and still patted me kindly on the shoulder, and said to himself in a whisper, if I heard right: "Yes, I thought so."

Mr. Creakle turned to his assistant, with a severe frown and laboured politeness.

"Now you hear what this gentleman says, Mr. Mell. Have the goodness, if you please, to set him right before the assembled school."

"He is right, Sir, without correction," returned Mr. Mell, in the midst of a dead silence; "what he has said, is true."

"Be so good then as declare publicly, will you," said Mr.

Creakle, putting his head on one side, and rolling his eyes round the school, "whether it ever came to my knowledge until this moment?"

"I believe not directly," he returned.

"Why, you know not," said Mr. Creakle. "Don't you, man?"

"I apprehend you never supposed my worldly circumstances to to be very good," replied the assistant. "You know what my position is, and always has been, here."

"I apprehend, if you come to that," said Mr. Creakle, with his veins swelling again bigger than ever, "that you've been in a wrong position altogether, and mistook this for a charity school. Mr. Mell, we'll part, if you please. The sooner the better."

"There is no time," answered Mr. Mell, rising, "like the present."

"Sir, to you!" said Mr. Creakle.

"I take my leave of you, Mr. Creakle, and of all of you," said Mr. Mell, glancing round the room, and again patting me gently on the shoulder. "James Steerforth, the best wish I can leave you is that you may come to be ashamed of what you have done to-day. At present I would prefer to see you anything rather than a friend, to me, or to any one in whom I feel an interest."

Once more he laid his hand upon my shoulder; and then taking his flute and a few books from his desk, and leaving the key in it for his successor, he went out of the school, with his property under his arm. Mr. Creakle then made a speech, through Tungay, in which he thanked Steerforth for asserting (though perhaps too warmly) the independence and respectability of Salem House; and which he wound up by shaking hands with Steerforth, while we gave three cheers—I did not quite know what for, but I supposed for Steerforth, and so joined in them ardently, though I felt miserable. Mr. Creakle then caned Tommy Traddles for being discovered in tears, instead of cheers, on account of Mr. Mell's departure; and went back to his sofa, or his bed, or wherever he had come from.

We were left to ourselves now, and looked very blank, I recollect, on one another. For myself, I felt so much self-reproach and contrition for my part in what had happened, that nothing would have enabled me to keep back my tears but the fear that Steerforth, who often looked at me, I saw, might think it unfriendly—or, I should rather say, considering our relative ages, and the feeling with which I regarded him, undutiful—if I showed the emotion which distressed me. He was very angry with Traddles, and said he was glad he had caught it.

Poor Traddles, who had passed the stage of lying with his head upon the desk, and was relieving himself as usual with a burst of skeletons, said he didn't care. Mr. Mell was ill-used.

"Who has ill-used him, you girl?" said Steerforth.

"Why, you have," returned Traddles.

"What have I done?" said Steerforth.

"What have you done?" retorted Traddles. "Hurt his feelings, and lost him his situation."

"His feelings!" repeated Steerforth disdainfully. "His feelings will soon get the better of it, I'll be bound. His feelings are not like yours, Miss Traddles. As to his situation—which was a precious one, wasn't it?—do you suppose I am not going to write home, and take care that he gets some money? Polly?"

We thought this intention very noble in Steerforth, whose

mother was a widow, and rich, and would do almost anything, it was said, that he asked her. We were all extremely glad to see Traddles so put down, and exalted Steerforth to the skies: especially when he told us, as he condescended to do, that what he had done had been done expressly for us, and for our cause, and that he had conferred a great boon upon us by unselfishly doing it.

But I must say that when I was going on with a story in the dark that night, Mr. Mell's old flute seemed more than once to sound mournfully in my ears; and that when at last Steerforth was tired, and I lay down in my bed, I fancied it playing so sorrowfully somewhere, that I was quite wretched.

I soon forgot him in the contemplation of Steerforth, who, in an easy amateur way, and without any book (he seemed to me to know everything by heart), took some of his classes until a new master was found. The new master came from a grammar-school, and before he entered on his duties, dined in the parlour one day, to be introduced to Steerforth. Steerforth approved of him highly, and told us he was a Brick. Without exactly understanding what learned distinction was meant by this, I respected him greatly for it, and had no doubt whatever of his superior knowledge: though he never took the pains with me—not that *I* was anybody—that Mr. Mell had taken.

There was only one other event in this half-year, out of the daily school-life, that made an impression upon me which still survives. It survives for many reasons.

One afternoon, when we were all harassed into a state of dire confusion, and Mr. Creakle was laying about him dreadfully, Tungay came in, and called out in his usual strong way: "Visitors for Copperfield!"

A few words were interchanged between him and Mr. Creakle, as, who the visitors were, and what room they were to be shown into; and then I, who had, according to custom, stood up on the announcement being made, and felt quite faint with astonishment, was told to go by the back-stairs and get a clean frill on, before I repaired to the dining-room. These orders I obeyed, in such a flutter and hurry of my young spirits as I had never known before; and when I got to the parlour-door, and the thought came into my head that it might be my mother—I had only thought of Mr. or Miss Murdstone until then—I drew back my hand from the lock, and stopped to have a sob before I went in.

At first I saw nobody; but feeling a pressure against the door, I looked round it, and there, to my amazement, were Mr. Peggotty and Ham, ducking at me with their hats, and squeezing one another against the wall. I could not help laughing; but it was much more in the pleasure of seeing them, than at the appearance they made. We shook hands in a very cordial way; and I laughed and laughed, until I pulled out my pocket-handkerchief and wiped my eyes.

Mr. Peggotty (who never shut his mouth once, I remember, during the visit) showed great concern when he saw me do this, and nudged Ham to say something.

"Cheer up, Mas'r Davy bor'!" said Ham, in his simpering way. "Why, how you have growed!"

"Am I grown?" I said, drying my eyes. I was not crying at anything particular that I know of; but somehow it made me cry to see old friends.

"Growed, Mas'r Davy bor'? Ain't he growed!" said Ham.

"Ain't he growed!" said Mr. Peggotty.

They made me laugh again by laughing at each other, and then we all three laughed until I was in danger of crying again.

"Do you know how mama is, Mr. Peggotty?" I said. "And how my dear, dear, old Peggotty is?"

"Oncommon," said Mr. Peggotty.

"And little Em'ly, and Mrs. Gummidge?"

"On—common," said Mr. Peggotty.

There was a silence. Mr. Peggotty, to relieve it, took two prodigious lobsters, and an enormous crab, and a large canvas bag of shrimps, out of his pockets, and piled them up in Ham's arms.

"You see," said Mr. Peggotty, "knowing as you was partial to a little relish with your wittles when you was along with us, we took the liberty. The old Mawther biled 'em, she did. Mrs. Gummidge biled 'em. Yes," said Mr. Peggotty, slowly, who I thought appeared to stick to the subject on account of having no other subject ready, "Mrs. Gummidge, I do assure you, she biled 'em."

I expressed my thanks. Mr. Peggotty, after looking at Ham, who stood smiling sheepishly over the shell-fish, without making any attempt to help him, said:

"We come, you see, the wind and tide making in our favour, in one of our Yarmouth lugs to Gravesen'. My sister she wrote to me the name of this here place, and wrote to me as if ever I chanced to come to Gravesen', I was to come over and enquire for Mas'r Davy, and gave her dooty, humbly wishing him well, and reporting of the fam'ly as they was oncommon toe-be-sure. Little Em'ly, you see, she'll write to my sister when I go back, as I see you and as you was similarly oncommon, and so we make it quite a merry-go-rounder."

I was obliged to consider a little before I understood what Mr. Peggotty meant by this figure, expressive of a complete circle of intelligence. I then thanked him heartily; and said, with a consciousness of reddening, that I supposed little Em'ly was altered too, since we used to pick up shells and pebbles on the beach.

"She's getting to be a woman, that's wot she's getting to be," said Mr. Peggotty. "Ask him."

He meant Ham, who beamed with delight and assent over the bag of shrimps.

"Her pretty face!" said Mr. Peggotty, with his own shining like a light.

"Her learning!" said Ham.

"Her writing!" said Mr. Peggotty. "Why, it's as black as jet! And so large it is, you might see it anywheres."

It was perfectly delightful to behold with what enthusiasm Mr. Peggotty became inspired when he thought of his little favourite. He stands before me again, his bluff hairy face irradiating with a joyful love and pride for which I can find no description. His honest eyes fire up, and sparkle, as if their depths were stirred by something bright. His broad chest heaves with pleasure. His strong loose hands clench themselves, in his earnestness; and he emphasises what he says with a right arm that shows, in my pigmy view, like a sledge-hammer.

Ham was quite as earnest as he. I dare say they would have said much more about her, if they had not been abashed by the unexpected coming in of Steerforth, who, seeing me in a corner speaking with two strangers, stopped in a song he was singing, and said: "I didn't know you were here, young Copperfield!" (for it was not the usual visiting room), and crossed by us on his way out.

I am not sure whether it was in the pride of having such a friend as Steerforth, or in the desire to explain to him how I came to have such a friend as Mr. Peggotty, that I called to him as he was going away. But I said, modestly —Good Heaven, how it all comes back to me this long time afterwards!—

"Don't go, Steerforth, if you please. These are two Yarmouth boatmen—very kind, good people—who are relations of my nurse, and have come from Gravesend to see me."

"Ay, ay?" said Steerforth, returning. "I am glad to see them. How are you both?"

There was an ease in his manner—a gay and light manner it was, but not swaggering—which I still believe to have borne a kind of enchantment with it. I still believe him, in virtue of this carriage, his animal spirits, his delightful voice, his handsome face and figure, and, for aught I know, of some inborn power of attraction besides (which I think a few people possess), to have carried a spell with him to which it was a natural weakness to yield, and which not many persons could withstand. I could not but see how pleased they were with him, and how they seemed to open their hearts to him in a moment.

"You must let them know at home, if you please, Mr. Peggotty," I said, "when that letter is sent, that Mr. Steerforth is very kind to me, and that I don't know what I should ever do here without him."

"Nonsense!" said Steerforth, laughing. "You mustn't tell them anything of the sort."

"And if Mr. Steerforth ever comes into Norfolk or Suffolk, Mr. Peggotty," I said, "while I am there, you may depend upon it I shall bring him to Yarmouth, if he will let me, to see your house. You never saw such a good house, Steerforth. It's made out of a boat!"

"Made out of a boat, is it?" said Steerforth. "It's the right sort of house for such a thorough-built boatman."

"So 'tis, Sir, so 'tis, Sir," said Ham, grinning. "You're right, young gen'l'm'n. Mas'r Davy bor', gen'l'm'n's right. A thorough-built boatman! Hor, hor! That's what he is, too!"

Mr. Peggotty was no less pleased than his nephew, though his modesty forbade him to claim a personal compliment so vociferously.

"Well, Sir," he said, bowing and chuckling, and tucking in the ends of his neckerchief at his breast: "I thankee, Sir, I thankee! I do my endeavours in my line of life, Sir."

"The best of men can do no more, Mr. Peggotty," said Steerforth. He had got his name already.

"I'll pound it it's wot you do yourself, Sir," said Mr. Peggotty, shaking his head, "and wot you do well—right well! I thankee, Sir. I'm obleeged to you, Sir, for your welcoming manner of me. I'm rough, Sir, but I'm ready —least ways, I hope I'm ready, you understand. My house ain't much for to see, Sir, but it's hearty at your service if ever you should come along with Mas'r Davy to see it. I'm a reg'lar Dodman, I am," said Mr. Peggotty; by which he meant snail, and this was in allusion to his being slow to go, for he had attempted to go after every sentence, and had somehow or other come back again; "but I wish you both well, and I wish you happy!"

Ham echoed this sentiment, and we parted with them in the heartiest manner. I was almost tempted that evening to tell Steerforth about pretty little Em'ly, but I was too timid of mentioning her name, and too much afraid of his laughing at me. .I remember that I thought a good deal, and in an uneasy sort of way, about Mr. Peggotty having said that she was getting on to be a woman; but I decided that was nonsense.

We transported the shell-fish, or the "relish" as Mr. Peggotty had modestly called it, up into our room unobserved, and made a great supper that evening. But Traddles couldn't get happily out of it. He was too unfortunate even to come through a supper like anybody else. He was taken ill in the night—quite prostrate he was—in consequence of crab; and after being drugged with black draughts and blue pills, to an extent which Demple (whose father was a doctor) said was enough to undermine a horse's constitution, received a caning and six chapters of Greek Testament for refusing to confess.

The rest of the half-year is a jumble in my recollection of the daily strife and struggle of our lives; of the waning summer and the changing season; of the frosty mornings when we were rung out of bed, and the cold, cold smell of the dark nights when we were rung into bed again; of the evening schoolroom dimly lighted and indifferently warmed, and the morning schoolroom which was nothing but a great shivering-machine; of the alternation of boiled beef with roast beef, and boiled mutton with roast mutton; of clods of bread-and-butter, dog's-eared lesson-books, cracked slates, tear-blotted copy-books, canings, rulerings, hair-cuttings, rainy Sundays, suet puddings, and a dirty atmosphere of ink surrounding all.

I well remember though, how the distant idea of the holidays, after seeming for an immense time to be a stationary speck, began to come towards us, and to grow and grow. How, from counting months, we came to weeks, and then to days; and how I then began to be afraid that I should not be sent for, and, when I learnt from Steerforth that I had been sent for and was certainly to go home, had dim forebodings that I might break my leg first. How the breaking-up day changed its place fast, at last, from the week after next to next week, this week, the day after to-morrow, to-morrow, to-day, to-night—when I was inside the Yarmouth mail, and going home.

I had many a broken sleep inside the Yarmouth mail, and many an incoherent dream of all these things. But when I awoke at intervals, the ground outside the window was not the playground of Salem House, and the sound in my ears was not the sound of Mr. Creakle giving it to Traddles, but the sound of the coachman touching up the horses.

CHAPTER VIII.

MY HOLIDAYS. ESPECIALLY ONE HAPPY AFTERNOON.

WHEN we arrived before day at the inn where the mail stopped, which was not the inn where my friend the waiter lived, I was shown up to a nice little bedroom, with DOLPHIN painted on the door. Very cold I was, I know, notwithstanding the hot tea they had given me before a large fire down-stairs; and very glad I was to turn into the Dolphin's bed, pull the Dolphin's blankets round my head, and go to sleep.

Mr. Barkis the carrier was to call for me in the morning at nine o'clock. I got up at eight, a little giddy from the shortness of my night's rest, and was ready for him before the appointed time. He received me exactly as if not five minutes had elapsed since we were last together, and I had only been into the hotel to get change for sixpence, or something of that sort.

As soon as I and my box were in the cart, and the carrier seated, the lazy horse walked away with us all at his accustomed pace.

"You look very well, Mr. Barkis," I said, thinking he would like to know it.

Mr. Barkis rubbed his cheek with his cuff, and then looked at his cuff as if he expected to find some of the bloom upon it; but made no other acknowledgment of the compliment.

"I gave your message, Mr. Barkis," I said; "I wrote to Peggotty."

"Ah!" said Mr. Barkis.

Mr. Barkis seemed gruff, and answered drily.

"Wasn't it right, Mr. Barkis?" I asked, after a little hesitation.

"Why, no," said Mr. Barkis.

"Not the message?"

"The message was right enough, perhaps," said Mr Barkis; "but it come to an end there."

Not understanding what he meant, I repeated inquisitively: "Came to an end, Mr. Barkis?"

"Nothing come of it," he explained, looking at me sideways. "No answer."

"There was an answer expected, was there, Mr. Barkis?" said I, opening my eyes. For this was a new light to me.

"When a man says he's willin'," said Mr. Barkis, turning his glance slowly on me again, "it's as much as to say, that man's a waitin' for a answer."

"Well, Mr. Barkis?"

"Well," said Mr. Barkis, carrying his eyes back to his horse's ears; "that man's been a waitin' for a answer ever since."

"Have you told her so, Mr. Barkis?"

"N—no," growled Mr. Barkis, reflecting about it. "I ain't got no call to go and tell her so. I never said six words to her myself. I ain't a goin' to tell her so."

"Would you like me to do it, Mr. Barkis?" said I, doubtfully.

"You might tell her, if you would," said Mr. Barkis, with another slow look at me, "that Barkis was a waitin' for a answer. Says you—what name is it?"

"Her name?"

"Ah!" said Mr. Barkis, with a nod of his head.

"Peggotty."

"Chrisen name? Or nat'ral name?" said Mr. Barkis.

"Oh, it's not her Christian name. Her Christian name is Clara."

"Is it though?" said Mr. Barkis.

He seemed to find an immense fund of reflection in this circumstance, and sat pondering and inwardly whistling for some time.

"Well!" he resumed at length. "Says you, 'Peggotty! Barkis is a waitin' for a answer.' Says she, perhaps, 'Answer to what?' Says you, 'To what I told you.' 'What is that?' says she. 'Barkis is willin',' says you."

This extremely artful suggestion, Mr. Barkis accompanied with a nudge of his elbow that gave me quite a stitch in my side. After that, he slouched over his horse in his usual manner; and made no other reference to the subject except, half an hour afterwards, taking a piece of chalk from his pocket, and writing up, inside the tilt of the cart, "Clara Peggotty"—apparently as a private memorandum.

Ah, what a strange feeling it was to be going home when it was not home, and to find that every object I looked at, reminded me of the happy old home, which was like a dream I could never dream again! The days when my mother and I and Peggotty were all in all to one another, and there was no one to come between us, rose up before me so sorrowfully on the road, that I am not sure I was glad to be there—not sure but that I would rather have remained away, and forgotten it in Steerforth's company. But there I was; and soon I was at our house, where the bare old elm-trees wrung their many hands in the bleak wintry air, and shreds of the old rooks'-nests drifted away upon the wind.

The carrier put my box down at the garden-gate, and left me. I walked along the path towards the house, glancing at the windows, and fearing at every step to see Mr. Murdstone or Miss Murdstone lowering out of one of them. No face appeared, however; and being come to the house, and knowing how to open the door, before dark, without knocking, I went in with a quiet, timid step.

God knows how infantine the memory may have been, that was awakened within me by the sound of my mother's voice in the old parlour, when I set foot in the hall. She was singing in a low tone. I think I must have lain in her arms, and heard her singing so to me when I was but a baby. The strain was new to me, and yet it was so old that it filled my heart brim-full; like a friend come back from a long absence.

I believed, from the solitary and thoughtful way in which my mother murmured her song, that she was alone. And I went softly into the room. She was sitting by the fire, suckling an infant, whose tiny hand she held against her neck. Her eyes were looking down upon its face, and she sat singing to it. I was so far right, that she had no other companion.

I spoke to her, and she started, and cried out. But seeing me, she called me her dear Davy, her own boy! and coming half across the room to meet me, kneeled down upon the ground and kissed me, and laid my head down on her bosom near the little creature that was nestling there, and put its hand up to my lips.

I wish I had died. I wish I had died then, with that feeling in my heart! I should have been more fit for Heaven than I ever have been since.

"He is your brother," said my mother, fondling me. "Davy, my pretty boy! My poor child!" Then she kissed me more and more, and clasped me round the neck. This she was doing when Peggotty came running in, and bounced down on the ground beside us, and went mad about us both for a quarter of an hour.

It seemed that I had not been expected so soon, the carrier being much before his usual time. It seemed, too, that Mr. and Miss Murdstone had gone out upon a visit in the neighbourhood, and would not return before night. I had never hoped for this. I had never thought it possible that we three could be together undisturbed, once more; and I felt, for the time, as if the old days were come back. We dined together by the fireside. Peggotty was in attendance to wait upon us, but my mother wouldn't let her do it, and made her dine with us. I had my own old plate, with a brown view of a man-of-war in full sail upon it, which Peggotty had hoarded somewhere all the time I had been away, and would not have had broken, she said, for a hundred pounds. I had my own old mug with David on it, and my own old little knife and fork that wouldn't cut.

While we were at table, I thought it a favourable occasion to tell Peggotty about Mr. Barkis, who, before I had finished what I had to tell her, began to laugh, and throw her apron over her face.

"Peggotty!" said my mother. "What's the matter?"

Peggotty only laughed the more, and held her apron tight over her face when my mother tried to pull it away, and sat as if her head were in a bag.

"What are you doing, you stupid creature?" said my mother, laughing.

"Oh, drat the man!" cried Peggotty. "He wants to marry me."

"It would be a very good match for you; wouldn't it?" said my mother.

"Oh! I don't know," said Peggotty. "Don't ask me. I wouldn't have him if he was made of gold. Nor I wouldn't have anybody."

"Then, why don't you tell him so, you ridiculous thing?" said my mother.

"Tell him so," retorted Peggotty, looking out of her apron. "He has never said a word to me about it. He knows better. If he was to make so bold as say a word to me, I should slap his face."

Her own was as red as ever I saw it, or any other face, I think; but she only covered it again, for a few moments at a time, when she was taken with a violent fit of laughter; and after two or three of those attacks, went on with her dinner.

I remarked that my mother, though she smiled when Peggotty looked at her, became more serious and thoughtful. I had seen at first that she was changed. Her face was very pretty still, but it looked careworn, and too delicate; and her hand was so thin and white that it seemed to me to be almost transparent. But the change to which I now refer was superadded to this: it was in her manner, which became anxious and fluttered. At last she said, putting out her hand, and laying it affectionately on the hand of her old servant,

"Peggotty, dear, you are not going to be married?"

"Me, ma'am?" returned Peggotty, staring. "Lord bless you, no!"

"Not just yet?" said my mother, tenderly.

"Never!" cried Peggotty.

My mother took her hand, and said:

"Don't leave me, Peggotty. Stay with me. It will not be for long, perhaps. What should I ever do without you?"

"Me leave you, my precious!" cried Peggotty. "Not for all the world and his wife. Why, what's put that in your silly little head?"—For Peggotty had been used of old to talk to my mother sometimes, like a child.

But my mother made no answer, except to thank her, and Peggotty went running on in her own fashion.

"Me leave you? I think I see myself. Peggotty go away from you? I should like to catch her at it! No, no, no," said Peggotty, shaking her head, and folding her arms; "not she, my dear. It isn't that there ain't some Cats that would be well enough pleased if she did, but they shan't be pleased. They shall be aggravated. I'll stay with you till I am a cross cranky old woman. And when I'm too deaf, and too lame, and too blind, and too mumbly for want of teeth, to be of any use at all, even to be found fault with, then I shall go to my Davy, and ask him to take me in."

"And, Peggotty," says I, "I shall be glad to see you, and I'll make you as welcome as a queen."

"Bless your dear heart!" cried Peggotty. "I know you will!" And she kissed me beforehand, in grateful acknowledgment of my hospitality. After that, she covered her head up with her apron again, and had another laugh about Mr. Barkis. After that, she took the baby out of its little cradle, and nursed it. After that, she cleared the dinner-table; after that, came in with another cap on, and her work-box, and the yard-measure, and the bit of wax candle, all just the same as ever.

We sat round the fire, and talked delightfully. I told them what a hard master Mr. Creakle was, and they pitied me very much. I told them what a fine fellow Steerforth was, and what a patron of mine, and Peggotty said she would walk a score of miles to see him. I took the little baby in my arms when it was awake, and nursed it lovingly. When it was asleep again, I crept close to my mother's side, according to my old custom, broken now a long time, and sat with my arms embracing her waist, and my little red cheek on her shoulder, and once more felt her beautiful hair drooping over me—like an angel's wing as I used to think, I recollect—and was very happy indeed.

While I sat thus, looking at the fire, and seeing pictures in the red-hot coals, I almost believed that I had never been away; that Mr. and Miss Murdstone were such pictures, and would vanish when the fire got low; and that there was nothing real in all that I remembered, save my mother, Peggotty, and I.

Peggotty darned away at a stocking as long as she could see, and then sat with it drawn on her left hand like a glove, and her needle in her right, ready to take another stitch whenever there was a blaze. I cannot conceive whose stockings they can have been that Peggotty was always darning, or where such an unfailing supply of stockings in want of darning can have come from. From my earliest infancy she seems to have been always employed in that class of needlework, and never by any chance in any other.

"I wonder," said Peggotty, who was sometimes seized with a fit of wondering on some most unexpected topic, "what's become of Davy's great-aunt?"

"Lor, Peggotty!" observed my mother, rousing herself from a reverie, "what nonsense you talk!"

"Well, but I really do wonder, ma'am," said Peggotty.

"What can have put such a person in your head?" inquired my mother. "Is there nobody else in the world to come there?"

"I don't know how it is," said Peggotty, "unless it's on account of being stupid, but my head never can pick and choose its people. They come and they go, and they don't come and they don't go, just as they like. I wonder what's become of her?"

"How absurd you are, Peggotty," returned my mother. "One would suppose you wanted a second visit from her."

"Lord forbid!" cried Peggotty.

"Well then, don't talk about such uncomfortable things, there's a good soul," said my mother. "Miss Betsey is shut up in her cottage by the sea, no doubt, and will remain there. At all events, she is not likely ever to trouble us again."

"No!" mused Peggotty. "No, that ain't likely at all. —I wonder, if she was to die, whether she'd leave Davy anything?"

"Good gracious me, Peggotty," returned my mother, "what a nonsensical woman you are! when you know that she took offence at the poor dear boy's ever being born at all!"

"I suppose she wouldn't be inclined to forgive him now," hinted Peggotty.

"Why should she be inclined to forgive him now?" said my mother, rather sharply.

"Now that he's got a brother, I mean," said Peggotty.

My mother immediately began to cry, and wondered how Peggotty dared to say such a thing.

"As if this poor little innocent in its cradle had ever done any harm to you or anybody else, you jealous thing!" said she. "You had much better go and marry Mr. Barkis, the carrier. Why don't you?"

"I should make Miss Murdstone happy, if I was to," said Peggotty.

"What a bad disposition you have, Peggotty!" returned my mother. "You are as jealous of Miss Murdstone as it is possible for a ridiculous creature to be. You want to keep the keys yourself, and give out all the things, I suppose? I shouldn't be surprised if you did. When you know that she only does it out of kindness and the best intentions! You know she does, Peggotty—you know it well."

Peggotty muttered something to the effect of "Bother the best intentions!" and something else to the effect that there was a little too much of the best intentions going on.

"I know what you mean, you cross thing," said my mother. "I understand you, Peggotty, perfectly. You know I do, and I wonder you don't colour up like fire. But one point at a time. Miss Murdstone is the point now, Peggotty, and you sha'n't escape it. Haven't you heard her say, over and over again, that she thinks I am too thoughtless and too—a—a—"

"Pretty," suggested Peggotty.

"Well," returned my mother, half laughing, "and if she is so silly as to say so, can I be blamed for it?"

"No one says you can," said Peggotty.

"No, I should hope not, indeed!" returned my mother. "Haven't you heard her say, over and over again, that on this account she wishes to spare me a great deal of trouble, which she thinks I am not suited for, and which I really don't know myself that I *am* suited for; and isn't she up early and late, and going to and fro continually—and doesn't she do all sorts of things, and grope into all sorts of places, coal-holes and pantries and I don't know where, that can't be very agreeable—and do you mean to insinuate that there is not a sort of devotion in that?"

"I don't insinuate at all," said Peggotty.

"You do, Peggotty," returned my mother. "You never do anything else, except your work. You are always insinuating. You revel in it. And when you talk of Mr. Murdstone's good intentions——"

"I never talked of 'em," said Peggotty.

"No, Peggotty," returned my mother, "but you insinuated. That's what I told you just now. That's the worst of you. You *will* insinuate. I said, at the moment, that I understood you, and you see I did. When you talk of Mr. Murdstone's good intentions, and pretend to slight them (for I don't believe you really do, in your heart, Peggotty), you must be as well convinced as I am how good they are, and how they actuate him in everything. If he seems to have been at all stern with a certain person, Peggotty—you understand, and so I am sure does Davy, that I am not alluding to anybody present—it is solely because he is satisfied that it is for a certain person's benefit. He naturally loves a certain person, on my account; and acts solely for a certain person's good. He is better able to judge of it than I am; for I very well know that I am a weak, light, girlish creature, and that he is a firm, grave, serious man. And he takes," said my mother, with the tears which were engendered in her affectionate nature, stealing down her face, "he takes great pains with me; and I ought to be very thankful to him, and very submissive to him even in my thoughts; and when I am not, Peggotty, I worry and condemn myself, and feel doubtful of my own heart, and don't know what to do."

Peggotty sat with her chin on the foot of the stocking, looking silently at the fire.

"There, Peggotty," said my mother, changing her tone, "don't let us fall out with one another, for I couldn't bear it. You are my true friend, I know, if I have any in the world. When I call you a ridiculous creature, or a vexatious thing, or anything of that sort, Peggotty, I only mean that you are my true friend, and always have been, ever since the night when Mr. Copperfield first brought me home here, and you came out to the gate to meet me."

Peggotty was not slow to respond, and ratified the treaty of friendship by giving me one of her best hugs. I think I had some glimpses of the real character of this conversation at the time; but I am sure, now, that the good creature originated it, and took her part in it, merely that my mother might comfort herself with the little contradictory summary in which she had indulged. The design was efficacious; for I remember that my mother seemed more at ease during the rest of the evening, and that Peggotty observed her less.

When we had had our tea, and the ashes were thrown up, and the candles snuffed, I read Peggotty a chapter out of the Crocodile Book, in remembrance of old times—she took it out of her pocket: I don't know whether she had kept it there ever since—and then we talked about Salem House, which brought me round again to Steerforth, who was my great subject. We were very happy; and that evening, as the last of its race, and destined evermore to close that volume of my life, will never pass out of my memory.

It was almost ten o'clock before we heard the sound of wheels. We all got up then; and my mother said hurriedly that, as it was so late, and Mr. and Miss Murdstone approved of early hours for young people, perhaps I had better go to bed. I kissed her, and went up-stairs with my candle directly, before they came in. It appeared to my childish fancy, as I ascended to the bedroom where I had been imprisoned, that they brought a cold blast of air into the house which blew away the old familiar feeling like a feather.

I felt uncomfortable about going down to breakfast in the morning, as I had never set eyes on Mr. Murdstone since the day when I committed my memorable offence. However, as it must be done, I went down, after two or three false starts half-way, and as many runs back on tiptoe to my own room, and presented myself in the parlour.

He was standing before the fire with his back to it, while Miss Murdstone made the tea. He looked at me steadily as I entered, but made no sign of recognition whatever.

I went up to him, after a moment of confusion, and said: "I beg your pardon, Sir. I am very sorry for what I did, and I hope you will forgive me."

"I am glad to hear you are sorry, David," he replied.

The hand he gave me was the hand I had bitten. I could not restrain my eye from resting for an instant on a red spot upon it; but it was not so red as I turned, when I met that sinister expression in his face.

"How do you do, ma'am?" I said to Miss Murdstone.

"Ah, dear me!" sighed Miss Murdstone, giving me the tea-caddy scoop instead of her fingers. "How long are the holidays?"

"A month, ma'am."

"Counting from when?"

"From to-day, ma'am."

"Oh!" said Miss Murdstone. "Then here's *one* day off." She kept a calendar of the holidays in this way, and every morning checked a day off in exactly the same manner. She did it gloomily until she came to ten, but when she got into two figures she became more hopeful, and, as the time advanced, even jocular.

It was on this very first day that I had the misfortune to throw her, though she was not subject to such weaknesses in general, into a state of violent consternation. I came into the room where she and my mother were sitting; and the baby (who was only a few weeks old) being on my mother's lap, I took it very carefully in my arms. Suddenly Miss Murdstone gave such a scream that I all but dropped it.

"My dear Jane!" cried my mother.

"Good Heavens, Clara, do you see?" exclaimed Miss Murdstone.

"See what, my dear Jane?" said my mother; "where?"

"He's got it!" cried Miss Murdstone. "The boy has got the baby!"

She was limp with horror; but stiffened herself to make a dart at me, and take it out of my arms. Then, she turned faint; and was so very ill, that they were obliged to give her cherry-brandy. I was solemnly interdicted by her, on her recovery, from touching my brother any more on any pretence whatever; and my poor mother, who, I could see, wished otherwise, meekly confirmed the interdict, by saying: "No doubt you are right, my dear Jane."

On another occasion, when we three were together, this same dear baby—it was truly dear to me, for our mother's sake—was the innocent occasion of Miss Murdstone's going into a passion. My mother, who had been looking at its eyes as it lay upon her lap, said:

"Davy! come here!" and looked at mine.

I saw Miss Murdstone lay her beads down.

"I declare," said my mother, gently, "they are exactly alike. I suppose they are mine. I think they are the colour of mine. But they are wonderfully alike."

"What are you talking about, Clara?" said Miss Murdstone.

"My dear Jane," faltered my mother, a little abashed by the harsh tone of this inquiry, "I find that the baby's eyes and Davy's are exactly alike."

"Clara!" said Miss Murdstone, rising angrily, "you are a positive fool sometimes."

"My dear Jane," remonstrated my mother.

"A positive fool," said Miss Murdstone. "Who else could compare my brother's baby with your boy? They are not at all alike. They are exactly unlike. They are utterly dissimilar in all respects. I hope they will ever remain so. I will not sit here, and hear such comparisons made." With that she stalked out, and made the door bang after her.

In short, I was not a favourite with Miss Murdstone. In short, I was not a favourite there with anybody, not even with myself; for those who did like me could not show it, and those who did not showed it so plainly that I had a sensitive consciousness of always appearing constrained, boorish, and dull.

I felt that I made them as uncomfortable as they made me. If I came into the room where they were, and they were talking together and my mother seemed cheerful, an anxious cloud would steal over her face from the moment of my entrance. If Mr. Murdstone were in his best humour, I checked him. If Miss Murdstone were in her worst, I intensified it. I had perception enough to know that my mother was the victim always; that she was afraid to speak to me, or be kind to me, lest she should give them some offence by her manner of doing so, and receive a lecture afterwards; that she was not only ceaselessly afraid of her own offending, but of my offending, and uneasily watched their looks if I only moved. Therefore I resolved to keep myself as much out of their way as I could; and many a wintry hour did I hear the church-clock strike, when I was sitting in my cheerless bedroom, wrapped in my little great-coat, poring over a book.

In the evening, sometimes, I went and sat with Peggotty in the kitchen. There I was comfortable, and not afraid of being myself. But neither of these resources was approved of in the parlour. The tormenting humour which was dominant there stopped them both. I was still held to be necessary to my poor mother's training, and, as one of her trials, could not be suffered to absent myself.

"David," said Mr. Murdstone, one day after dinner when I was going to leave the room as usual; "I am sorry to observe that you are of a sullen disposition."

"As sulky as a bear!" said Miss Murdstone.

I stood still, and hung my head.

"Now, David," said Mr. Murdstone, "a sullen obdurate disposition is, of all tempers, the worst."

"And the boy's is, of all such dispositions that ever I have seen," remarked his sister, "the most confirmed and stubborn. I think, my dear Clara, even you must observe it?"

"I beg your pardon, my dear Jane," said my mother, "but are you quite sure—I am certain you'll excuse me, my dear Jane—that you understand Davy?"

"I should be somewhat ashamed of myself, Clara," returned Miss Murdstone, "if I could not understand the boy, or any boy. I don't profess to be profound; but I do lay claim to common sense."

"No doubt, my dear Jane," returned my mother, "your understanding is very vigorous—"

"Oh dear, no! Pray don't say that, Clara," interposed Miss Murdstone, angrily.

"But I am sure it is," resumed my mother; "and everybody knows it is. I profit so much by it myself, in many ways—at least I ought to—that no one can be more convinced of it than myself; and therefore I speak with great diffidence, my dear Jane, I assure you."

"We'll say I don't understand the boy, Clara," returned Miss Murdstone, arranging the little fetters on her wrists. "We'll agree, if you please, that I don't understand him at all. He is much too deep for me. But perhaps my brother's penetration may enable him to have some insight into his character. And I believe my brother was speaking on the subject when we—not very decently—interrupted him."

"I think, Clara," said Mr. Murdstone, in a low grave voice, "that there may be better and more dispassionate judges of such a question than you."

"Edward," replied my mother, timidly, "you are a far better judge of all questions than I pretend to be. Both you and Jane are. I only said——"

"You only said something weak and inconsiderate," he replied. "Try not to do it again, my dear Clara, and keep a watch upon yourself."

My mother's lips moved, as if she answered "Yes, my dear Edward," but she said nothing aloud.

"I was sorry, David, I remarked," said Mr. Murdstone, turning his head and his eyes stiffly towards me, "to observe that you are of a sullen disposition. This is not a character that I can suffer to develop itself beneath my eyes without an effort at improvement. You must endeavour, Sir, to change it. We must endeavour to change it for you."

"I beg your pardon, Sir," I faltered. "I have never meant to be sullen since I came back."

"Don't take refuge in a lie, Sir!" he returned so fiercely, that I saw my mother involuntarily put out her trembling hand as if to interpose between us. "You have withdrawn yourself in your sullenness to your own room. You have kept your own room when you ought to have been here. You know now, once for all, that I require you to be here and not there. Further, that I require you to bring obedience here. You know me, David. I will have it done."

Miss Murdstone gave a hoarse chuckle.

"I will have a respectful, prompt, and ready bearing towards myself," he continued, "and towards Jane Murdstone, and towards your mother. I will not have this room shunned as if it were infected, at the pleasure of a child. Sit down."

He ordered me like a dog, and I obeyed like a dog.

"One thing more," he said. "I observe that you have an attachment to low and common company. You are not to associate with servants. The kitchen will not improve you, in the many respects in which you need improvement. Of the woman who abets you, I say nothing—since you, Clara," addressing my mother in a lower voice, "from old associations and long-established fancies, have a weakness respecting her which is not yet overcome."

"A most unaccountable delusion it is!" cried Miss Murdstone.

"I only say," he resumed, addressing me, "that I disapprove of your preferring such company as Mistress Peggotty, and that it is to be abandoned. Now, David, you understand me, and you know what will be the consequence if you fail to obey me to the letter."

I knew well—better perhaps than he thought, as far as my poor mother was concerned—and I obeyed him to the letter. I retreated to my own room no more; I took refuge with Peggotty no more; but sat wearily in the parlour day after day looking forward to night, and bedtime.

What irksome constraint I underwent, sitting in the same attitude hours upon hours, afraid to move an arm or a leg lest Miss Murdstone should complain (as she did on the least pretence) of my restlessness, and afraid to move an eye lest she should light on some look of dislike or scrutiny that would find new cause for complaint in mine! What intolerable dulness to sit listening to the ticking of the clock; and watching Miss Murdstone's little shiny steel beads as she strung them; and wondering whether she would ever be married, and if so, to what sort of unhappy man; and counting the divisions in the moulding on the chimney-piece; and wandering away, with my eyes, to the ceiling, among the curls and corkscrews in the paper on the wall!

What walks I took alone, down muddy lanes, in the bad winter weather, carrying that parlour, and Mr. and Miss Murdstone in it, everywhere: a monstrous load that I was obliged to bear, a daymare that there was no possibility of breaking in, a weight that brooded on my wits, and blunted them!

What meals I had in silence and embarrassment, always feeling that there were a knife and fork too many, and those mine; an appetite too many, and that mine; a plate and chair too many, and those mine; a somebody too many, and that I!

What evenings, when the candles came, and I was expected to employ myself, but, not daring to read an entertaining book, pored over some hard-headed, harder-hearted treatise on arithmetic; when the tables of weights and measures set themselves to tunes, as Rule Britannia, or Away with Melancholy; when they wouldn't stand still to be learnt, but would go threading my grandmother's needle through my unfortunate head, in at one ear and out at the other!

What yawns and dozes I lapsed into, in spite of all my care; what starts I came out of concealed sleeps with; what answers I never got, to little observations that I rarely made; what a blank space I seemed, which everybody overlooked, and yet was in everybody's way; what a heavy relief it was to hear Miss Murdstone hail the first stroke of nine at night, and order me to bed!

Thus the holidays lagged away, until the morning came when Miss Murdstone said: "Here's the last day off!" and gave me the closing cup of tea of the vacation.

I was not sorry to go. I had lapsed into a stupid state; but I was recovering a little and looking forward to Steerforth, albeit Mr. Creakle loomed behind him. Again Mr. Barkis appeared at the gate, and again Miss Murdstone in her warning voice said: "Clara!" when my mother bent over me, to bid her farewell.

I kissed her, and my baby brother, and was very sorry then; but not sorry to go away, for the gulf between us was there, and the parting was there, every day. And it is not so much the embrace she gave me, that lives in my mind, though it was as fervent as could be, as what followed the embrace.

I was in the carrier's cart when I heard her calling to me. I looked out, and she stood at the garden-gate alone, holding her baby up in her arms for me to see. It was cold still weather; and not a hair of her head, or a fold of her dress, was stirred, as she looked intently at me, holding up her child.

So I lost her. So I saw her afterwards, in my sleep at school—a silent presence near my bed—looking at me with the same intent face—holding up her baby in her arms.

CHAPTER IX.

I HAVE A MEMORABLE BIRTHDAY.

I PASS over all that happened at school, until the anniversary of my birthday came round in March. Except that Steerforth was more to be admired than ever, I remember nothing. He was going away at the end of the half-year, if not sooner, and was more spirited and independent than before in my eyes, and therefore more engaging than before; but beyond this I remember nothing. The great remembrance by which that time is marked in my mind, seems to have swallowed up all lesser recollections, and to exist alone.

It is even difficult for me to believe that there was a gap of full two months between my return to Salem House and the arrival of that birthday. I can only understand that the fact was so, because I know it must have been so; otherwise I should feel convinced that there was no interval, and that the one occasion trod upon the other's heels.

How well I recollect the kind of day it was! I smell the fog that hung about the place; I see the hoar frost, ghostly, through it; I feel my rimy hair fall clammy on my cheek; I look along the dim perspective of the schoolroom, with a sputtering candle here and there to light up the foggy morning, and the breath of the boys wreathing and smoking in the raw cold as they blow upon their fingers, and tap their feet upon the floor.

It was after breakfast, and we had been summoned in from the playground, when Mr. Sharp entered and said:

"David Copperfield is to go into the parlour."

I expected a hamper from Peggotty, and brightened at the order. Some of the boys about me put in their claim not to be forgotten in the distribution of the good things, as I got out of my seat with great alacrity.

"Don't hurry, David," said Mr. Sharp. "There's time enough, my boy, don't hurry."

I might have been surprised by the feeling tone in which he spoke, if I had given it a thought; but I gave it none until afterwards. I hurried away to the parlour; and there I found Mr. Creakle, sitting at his breakfast with the cane and a newspaper before him, and Mrs. Creakle with an opened letter in her hand. But no hamper.

"David Copperfield," said Mrs. Creakle, leading me to a sofa, and sitting down beside me. "I want to speak to you very particularly. I have something to tell you, my child."

Mr. Creakle, at whom of course I looked, shook his head without looking at me, and stopped up a sigh with a very large piece of buttered toast.

"You are too young to know how the world changes every day," said Mrs. Creakle, "and how the people in it pass away. But we all have to learn it, David; some of us when we are young, some of us when we are old, some of us at all times of our lives."

I looked at her earnestly.

"When you came away from home at the end of the vacation," said Mrs. Creakle, after a pause, "were they all well?" After another pause, "Was your mama well?"

I trembled without distinctly knowing why, and still looked at her earnestly, making no attempt to answer.

"Because," said she, "I grieve to tell you that I hear this morning your mama is very ill."

A mist rose between Mrs. Creakle and me, and her figure seemed to move in it for an instant. Then I felt the burning tears run down my face, and it was steady again.

"She is very dangerously ill," she added.

I knew all now.

"She is dead."

There was no need to tell me so. I had already broken out into a desolate cry, and felt an orphan in the wide world.

She was very kind to me. She kept me there all day, and left me alone sometimes; and I cried, and wore myself to sleep, and awoke and cried again. When I could cry no more, I began to think; and then the oppression on my breast was heaviest, and my grief a dull pain that there was no ease for.

And yet my thoughts were idle; not intent on the calamity that weighed upon my heart, but idly loitering near it. I thought of our house shut up and hushed. I thought of the little baby, who, Mrs. Creakle said, had been pining away for some time, and who, they believed, would die too. I thought of my father's grave in the churchyard, by our house, and of my mother lying there beneath the tree I knew so well. I stood upon a chair when I was left alone, and looked into the glass to see how red my eyes were, and how sorrowful my face. I considered, after some hours were gone, if my tears were really hard to flow now, as they seemed to be, what, in connexion with my loss, it would affect me most to think of when I drew near home—for I was going home to the funeral. I am sensible of having felt that a dignity attached to me among the rest of the boys, and that I was important in my affliction.

If ever child were stricken with sincere grief, I was. But I remembered that this importance was a kind of satisfaction to me, when I walked in the playground that afternoon while the boys were in school. When I saw them glancing at me out of the windows, as they went up to their classes, I felt distinguished, and looked more melancholy, and walked slower. When school was over, and they came out and spoke to me, I felt it rather good in myself not to be proud to any of them, and to take exactly the same notice of them all, as before.

I was to go home next night; not by the mail, but by the heavy night-coach, which was called the Farmer, and was principally used by country-people travelling short intermediate distances upon the road. We had no story-telling that evening, and Traddles insisted on lending me his pillow. I don't know what good he thought it would do me, for I had one of my own: but it was all he had to lend, poor fellow, except a sheet of letter-paper full of skeletons; and that he gave me at parting, as a soother of my sorrows and a contribution to my peace of mind.

I left Salem House upon the morrow afternoon. I little thought then that I left it, never to return. We travelled very slowly all night, and did not get into Yarmouth before nine or ten o'clock in the morning. I looked out for Mr. Barkis, but he was not there; and instead of him a fat, short-winded, merry-looking, little old man in black, with rusty little bunches of ribbons at the knees of his breeches, black stockings, and a broad-brimmed hat, came puffing up to the coach-window, and said:

"Master Copperfield?"

"Yes, Sir."

"Will you come with me, young Sir, if you please," he said, opening the door, "and I shall have the pleasure of taking you home."

I put my hand in his, wondering who he was, and we walked away to a shop in a narrow street, on which was written OMER, DRAPER, TAILOR, HABERDASHER, FUNERAL FURNISHER, &c. It was a close and stifling little shop; full of all sorts of clothing, made and unmade, including one window full of beaver-hats and bonnets. We went into a little back-parlour behind the shop, where we found three young women at work on a quantity of black materials, which were heaped upon the table, and little bits of cuttings of which were littered all over the floor. There was a good fire in the room, and a breathless smell of warm black crape —I did not know what the smell was then, but I know now. The three young women, who appeared to be very industrious and comfortable, raised their heads to look at me, and then went on with their work. Stitch, stitch, stitch. At the same time there came from a workshop across a little yard outside the window, a regular sound of hammering that kept a kind of tune: RAT—tat-tat, RAT—tat-tat, RAT—tat-tat, without any variation.

"Well," said my conductor to one of the three young women. "How do you get on, Minnie?"

"We shall be ready by the trying-on time," she replied gaily, without looking up. "Don't you be afraid, father."

Mr. Omer took off his broad-brimmed hat, and sat down and panted. He was so fat that he was obliged to pant some time before he could say:

"That's right."

"Father!" said Minnie, playfully. "What a porpoise you do grow!"

"Well, I don't know how it is, my dear," he replied, considering about it. "I *am* rather so."

"You are such a comfortable man, you see," said Minnie. "You take things so easy."

"No use taking 'em otherwise, my dear," said Mr. Omer.

"No, indeed," returned his daughter. "We are all pretty gay here, thank Heaven! Ain't we, father?"

"I hope so, my dear," said Mr. Omer. "As I have got my breath now, I think I'll measure this young scholar. Would you walk into the shop, Master Copperfield?"

I preceded Mr. Omer, in compliance with his request; and after showing me a roll of cloth which he said was extra super, and too good mourning for anything short of parents, he took my various dimensions, and put them down in a book. While he was recording them he called my attention to his stock in trade, and to certain fashions which he said had "just come up," and to certain other fashions which he said had "just gone out."

"And by that sort of thing we very often lose a little mint of money," said Mr. Omer. "But fashions are like human beings. They come in, nobody knows when, why, or how; and they go out, nobody knows when, why, or how. Everything is like life, in my opinion, if you look at it in that point of view."

I was too sorrowful to discuss the question, which would possibly have been beyond me under any circumstances; and Mr. Omer took me back into the parlour, breathing with some difficulty on the way.

He then called down a little break-neck range of steps behind a door: "Bring up that tea and bread-and-butter!" which, after some time, during which I sat looking about me and thinking, and listening to the stitching in the room and the tune that was being hammered across the yard, appeared on a tray, and turned out to be for me.

"I have been acquainted with you," said Mr. Omer, after

watching me for some minutes, during which I had not made much impression on the breakfast, for the black things destroyed my appetite, "I have been acquainted with you a long time, my young friend."

"Have you, Sir?"

"All your life," said Mr. Omer. "I may say before it. I knew your father before you. He was five foot nine and a half, and he lays in five and twen-ty foot of ground."

"RAT—tat-tat, RAT—tat-tat, RAT—tat-tat," across the yard.

"He lays in five and twen-ty foot of ground, if he lays in a fraction," said Mr. Omer, pleasantly. "It was either his request or her direction, I forget which."

"Do you know how my little brother is, Sir?" I inquired. Mr. Omer shook his head.

"RAT—tat-tat, RAT—tat-tat, RAT—tat-tat."

"He is in his mother's arms," said he.

"Oh, poor little fellow! Is he dead?"

"Don't mind it more than you can help," said Mr. Omer. "Yes. The baby's dead."

My wounds broke out afresh at this intelligence. I left the scarcely tasted breakfast, and went and rested my head on another table in a corner of the little room, which Minnie hastily cleared, lest I should spot the mourning that was lying there with my tears. She was a pretty good-natured girl, and put my hair away from my eyes with a soft kind touch; but she was very cheerful at having nearly finished her work and being in good time, and was so different from me!

Presently the tune left off, and a good-looking young fellow came across the yard into the room. He had a hammer in his hand, and his mouth was full of little nails, which he was obliged to take out before he could speak.

"Well, Joram!" said Mr. Omer. "How do *you* get on?"

"All right," said Joram. "Done, Sir."

Minnie coloured a little, and the other two girls smiled at one another.

"What! you were at it by candle-light last night, when I was at the club, then? Were you?" said Mr. Omer, shutting up one eye.

"Yes," said Joram. "As you said we could make a little trip of it, and go over together, if it was done, Minnie and me—and you—"

"Oh! I thought you were going to leave me out altogether," said Mr. Omer, laughing till he coughed.

"—As you was so good as to say that," resumed the young man, "why I turned to with a will, you see. Will you give me your opinion of it?"

"I will," said Mr. Omer, rising. "My dear;" and he stopped and turned to me; "would you like to see your——"

"No, father," Minnie interposed.

"I thought it might be agreeable, my dear," said Mr. Omer. "But perhaps you're right."

I can't say how I knew it was my dear, dear mother's coffin that they went to look at. I had never heard one making; I had never seen one that I know of: but it came into my mind what the noise was, while it was going on; and when the young man entered, I am sure I knew what he had been doing.

The work being now finished, the two girls, whose names I had not heard, brushed the shreds and threads from their dresses, and went into the shop to put that to rights, and wait for customers. Minnie stayed behind to fold up what they had made, and pack it in two baskets. This she did

upon her knees, humming a lively little tune the while. Joram, who I had no doubt was her lover, came in and stole a kiss from her while she was busy (he didn't appear to mind me, at all), and said her father was gone for the chaise, and he must make haste and get himself ready. Then he went out again; and then she put her thimble and scissors in her pocket, and stuck a needle threaded with black thread neatly in the bosom of her gown, and put on her outer clothing smartly, at a little glass behind the door, in which I saw the reflection of her pleased face.

All this I observed, sitting at the table in the corner with my head leaning on my hand, and my thoughts running on very different things. The chaise soon came round to the front of the shop, and the baskets being put in first, I was put in next, and those three followed. I remember it as a kind of half chaise-cart, half pianoforte-van, painted of a sombre colour, and drawn by a black horse with a long tail. There was plenty of room for us all.

I do not think I have ever experienced so strange a feeling in my life (I am wiser now, perhaps) as that of being with them, remembering how they had been employed, and seeing them enjoy the ride. I was not angry with them; I was more afraid of them, as if I were cast away among creatures with whom I had no community of nature. They were very cheerful. The old man sat in front to drive, and the two young people sat behind him, and whenever he spoke to them leaned forward, the one on one side of his chubby face and the other on the other, and made a great deal of him. They would have talked to me too, but I held back, and moped in my corner; scared by their love-making and hilarity, though it was far from boisterous, and almost wondering that no judgment came upon them for their hardness of heart.

So, when they stopped to bait the horse, and ate and drank and enjoyed themselves, I could touch nothing that they touched, but kept my fast unbroken. So, when we reached home, I dropped out of the chaise behind, as quickly as possible, that I might not be in their company before those solemn windows, looking blindly on me like closed eyes once bright. And oh, how little need I had had to think what would move me to tears when I came back—seeing the window of my mother's room, and next it that which, in the better time, was mine!

I was in Peggotty's arms before I got to the door, and she took me into the house. Her grief burst out when she first saw me; but she controlled it soon, and spoke in whispers, and walked softly, as if the dead could be disturbed. She had not been in bed, I found, for a long time. She sat up at night still, and watched. As long as her poor dear pretty was above the ground, she said, she would never desert her.

Mr. Murdstone took no heed of me when I went into the parlour, where he was, but sat by the fireside, weeping silently, and pondering in his elbow-chair. Miss Murdstone, who was busy at her writing-desk, which was covered with letters and papers, gave me her cold finger-nails, and asked me, in an iron whisper, if I had been measured for my mourning.

I said: "Yes."

"And your shirts," said Miss Murdstone; "have you brought 'em home?"

"Yes, ma'am. I have brought home all my clothes."

This was all the consolation that her firmness administered to me. I do not doubt that she had a choice pleasure in exhibiting what she called her self-command, and her firmness, and her strength of mind, and her common sense, and the whole diabolical catalogue of her unamiable qualities, on such an occasion. She was particularly proud of her turn for business; and she showed it now in reducing everything to pen and ink, and being moved by nothing. All the rest of that day, and from morning to night afterwards, she sat at that desk; scratching composedly with a hard pen, speaking in the same imperturbable whisper to everybody; never relaxing a muscle of her face, or softening a tone of her voice, or appearing with an atom of her dress astray.

Her brother took a book sometimes, but never read it that I saw. He would open it and look at it as if he were reading, but would remain for a whole hour without turning the leaf, and then put it down and walk to and fro in the room. I used to sit with folded hands composedly watching him, and counting his footsteps, hour after hour. He very seldom spoke to her, and never to me. He seemed to be the only restless thing, except the clocks, in the whole motionless house.

In these days before the funeral, I saw but little of Peggotty, except that, in passing up or down stairs, I always found her close to the room where my mother and her baby lay, and except that she came to me every night, and sat by my bed's head while I went to sleep. A day or two before the burial—I think it was a day or two before, but I am conscious of confusion in my mind about that heavy time, with nothing to mark its progress—she took me into the room. I only recollect that underneath some white covering on the bed, with a beautiful cleanliness and freshness all around it, there seemed to me to lie embodied the solemn stillness that was in the house; and that when she would have turned the cover gently back, I cried, "Oh no! oh no!" and held her hand.

If the funeral had been yesterday, I could not recollect it better. The very air of the best parlour, when I went in at the door, the bright condition of the fire, the shining of the wine in the decanters, the patterns of the glasses and plates, the faint sweet smell of cake, the odour of Miss Murdstone's dress, and our black clothes. Mr. Chillip is in the room, and comes to speak to me.

"And how is Master David?" he says, kindly.

I cannot tell him very well. I give him my hand, which he holds in his.

"Dear me!" says Mr. Chillip, meekly smiling, with something shining in his eye. "Our little friends grow up around us. They grow out of our knowledge, ma'am?"

This is to Miss Murdstone, who makes no reply.

"There is a great improvement here, ma'am?" says Mr. Chillip.

Miss Murdstone merely answers with a frown and a formal bend; Mr. Chillip, discomfited, goes into a corner, keeping me with him, and opens his mouth no more.

I remark this, because I remark everything that happens, not because I care about myself, or have done since I came home. And now the bell begins to sound, and Mr. Omer and another come to make us ready. As Peggotty was wont to tell me, long ago, the followers of my father to the same grave were made ready in the same room.

There are Mr. Murdstone, our neighbour Mr. Grayper, Mr. Chillip, and I. When we go out to the door, the bearers and their load are in the garden; and they move before us down the path, and past the elms, and through the gate, and

into the churchyard, where I have so often heard the birds sing on a summer morning.

We stand around the grave. The day seems different to me from every other day, and the light not of the same colour—of a sadder colour. Now there is a solemn hush, which we have brought from home with what is resting in the mould; and while we stand bare-headed, I hear the voice of the clergyman, sounding remote in the open air, and yet distinct and plain, saying, "I am the Resurrection and the Life, saith the Lord!" Then I hear sobs; and, standing apart among the lookers-on, I see that good and faithful servant, whom of all the people upon earth I love the best, and unto whom my childish heart is certain that the Lord will one day say, "Well done."

There are many faces that I know, among the little crowd; faces that I knew in church, when mine was always wondering there; faces that first saw my mother, when she came to the village in her youthful bloom. I do not mind them—I mind nothing but my grief—and yet I see and know them all; and even in the background, far away, see Minnie looking on, and her eye glancing on her sweetheart, who is near me.

It is over, and the earth is filled in, and we turn to come away. Before us stands our house, so pretty and unchanged, so linked in my mind with the young idea of what is gone, that all my sorrow has been nothing to the sorrow it calls forth. But they take me on; and Mr. Chillip talks to me; and when we get home, puts some water to my lips; and when I ask his leave to go up to my room, dismisses me with the gentleness of a woman.

All this, I say, is yesterday's event. Events of later date have floated from me to the shore where all forgotten things will reappear, but this stands like a high rock in the ocean.

I knew that Peggotty would come to me in my room. The Sabbath stillness of the time (the day was so like Sunday! I have forgotten that) was suited to us both. She sat down by my side upon my little bed; and holding my hand, and sometimes putting it to her lips, and sometimes smoothing it with hers, as she might have comforted my little brother, told me, in her way, all that she had to tell concerning what had happened.

"She was never well," said Peggotty, "for a long time. She was uncertain in her mind, and not happy. When her baby was born, I thought at first she would get better, but she was more delicate, and sunk a little every day. She used to like to sit alone before her baby came, and then she cried; but afterwards she used to sing to it—so soft, that I once thought when I heard her, it was like a voice up in the air, that was rising away.

"I think she got to be more timid, and more frightened-like, of late; and that a hard word was like a blow to her. But she was always the same to me. She never changed to her foolish Peggotty, didn't my sweet girl."

Here Peggotty stopped, and softly beat upon my hand a little while.

"The last time that I saw her like her own old self, was the night when you came home, my dear. The day you went away, she said to me, 'I never shall see my pretty darling again. Something tells me so, that tells the truth, I know.'

"She tried to hold up after that; and many a time, when they told her she was thoughtless and light-hearted, made believe to be so; but it was all a bygone then. She never told her husband what she had told me—she was afraid of saying it to anybody else—till one night, a little more than a week before it happened, when she said to him, ' My dear, I think I am dying.'

" 'It's off my mind now, Peggotty,' she told me, when I laid her in her bed that night. " ' He will believe it more and more, poor fellow, every day for a few days to come; and then it will be past. I am very tired. If this is sleep, sit by me while I sleep: don't leave me. God bless both my children! God protect and keep my fatherless boy!'

"I never left her afterwards," said Peggotty. "She often talked to them two down-stairs—for she loved them; she couldn't bear not to love anyone who was about her—but when they went away from her bedside, she always turned to me, as if there was rest where Peggotty was, and never fell asleep in any other way.

"On the last night, in the evening, she kissed me, and said: ' If my baby should die too, Peggotty, please let them lay him in my arms, and bury us together.' (It was done; for the poor lamb lived but a day beyond her.) ' Let my dearest boy go with us to our resting-place,' she said, ' and tell him that his mother, when she lay here, blessed him not once, but a thousand times.' "

Another silence followed this, and another gentle beating on my hand.

"It was pretty far in the night," said Peggotty, "when she asked me for some drink; and when she had taken it, gave me such a patient smile, the dear!—so beautiful!—

"Daybreak had come, and the sun was rising, when she said to me, how kind and considerate Mr. Copperfield had always been to her, and how he had borne with her, and told her, when she doubted herself, that a loving heart was better and stronger than wisdom, and that he was a happy man in hers. ' Peggotty, my dear,' she said then, ' put me nearer to you,' for she was very weak. ' Lay your good arm underneath my neck,' she said, ' and turn me to you, for your face is going far off, and I want it to be near.' I put it as she asked; and oh Davy! the time had come when my first parting words to you were true—when she was glad to lay her poor head on her stupid cross old Peggotty's arm—and she died like a child that had gone to sleep!"

Thus ended Peggotty's narration. From the moment of my knowing of the death of my mother, the idea of her as she had been of late had vanished from me. I remembered her, from that instant, only as the young mother of my earliest impressions, who had been used to wind her bright curls round and round her finger, and to dance with me at twilight in the parlour. What Peggotty had told me now, was so far from bringing me back to the later period, that it rooted the earlier image in my mind. It may be curious, but it is true. In her death she winged her way back to her calm untroubled youth, and cancelled all the rest.

The mother who lay in the grave, was the mother of my infancy; the little creature in her arms was myself, as I had once been, hushed for ever on her bosom.

CHAPTER X.

I BECOME NEGLECTED, AND AM PROVIDED FOR.

THE first act of business Miss Murdstone performed when the day of the solemnity was over, and light was freely admitted into the house, was to give Peggotty a month's warning. Much as Peggotty would have disliked such a service, I believe she would have retained it, for my sake, in preference to the best upon earth. She told me we must part, and told me why; and we condoled with one another, in all sincerity.

As to me or my future, not a word was said, or a step taken. Happy they would have been, I dare say, if they could have dismissed me at a month's warning too. I mustered courage once, to ask Miss Murdstone when I was going back to school; and she answered drily, she believed I was not going back at all. I was told nothing more. I was very anxious to know what was going to be done with me, and so was Peggotty; but neither she nor I could pick up any information on the subject.

There was one change in my condition, which, while it relieved me of a great deal of present uneasiness, might have made me, if I had been capable of considering it closely, yet more uncomfortable about the future. It was this. The constraint that had been put upon me, was quite abandoned. I was so far from being required to keep my dull post in the parlour, that on several occasions, when I took my seat there, Miss Murdstone frowned to me to go away. I was so far from being warned off from Peggotty's society, that, provided I was not in Mr. Murdstone's, I was never sought out or inquired for. At first I was in daily dread of his taking my education in hand again, or of Miss Murdstone's devoting herself to it; but I soon began to think that such fears were groundless, and that all I had to anticipate was neglect.

I do not conceive that this discovery gave me much pain then. I was still giddy with the shock of my mother's death, and in a kind of stunned state as to all tributary things. I can recollect, indeed, to have speculated, at odd times, on the possibility of my not being taught any more, or cared for any more; and growing up to be a shabby moody man, lounging an idle life away, about the village; as well as on the feasibility of my getting rid of this picture by going away somewhere, like the hero in a story, to seek my fortune: but these were transient visions, day dreams I sat looking at sometimes, as if they were faintly painted or written on the wall of my room, and which, as they melted away, left the wall blank again.

"Peggotty," I said in a thoughtful whisper, one evening, when I was warming my hands at the kitchen fire, "Mr. Murdstone likes me less than he used to. He never liked me much, Peggotty; but he would rather not even see me now, if he can help it."

"Perhaps it's his sorrow," said Peggotty, stroking my hair.

"I am sure, Peggotty, I am sorry too. If I believed it was his sorrow, I should not think of it at all. But it's not that; oh no, it's not that."

"How do you know it's not that?" said Peggotty, after a silence.

"Oh, his sorrow is another and quite a different thing. He is sorry at this moment, sitting by the fireside with Miss Murdstone; but if I was to go in, Peggotty, he would be something besides."

"What would he be?" said Peggotty.

"Angry," I answered, with an involuntary imitation of his dark frown. "If he was only sorry, he wouldn't look at me as he does. I am only sorry, and it makes me feel kinder."

Peggotty said nothing for a little while; and I warmed my hands, as silent as she.

"Davy," she said at length.

"Yes, Peggotty?"

"I have tried, my dear, all ways I could think of—all the ways there are, and all the ways there ain't, in short—to get a suitable service here, in Blunderstone; but there's no such a thing, my love."

"And what do mean to do, Peggotty?" says I, wistfully. "Do you mean to go and seek your fortune?"

"I expect I shall be forced to go to Yarmouth," replied Peggotty, "and live there."

"You might have gone farther off," I said, brightening a little, "and been as bad as lost. I shall see you sometimes, my dear old Peggotty, there. You won't be quite at the other end of the world, will you?"

"Contrary ways, please God!" said Peggotty, with great animation. "As long as you are here, my pet, I shall come over every week of my life to see you. One day, every week of my life!"

I felt a great weight taken off my mind by this promise; but even this was not all, for Peggotty went on to say:

"I'm a going, Davy, you see, to my brother's, first, for another fortnight's visit—just till I have had time to look about me, and get to be something like myself again. Now, I have been thinking, that perhaps, as they don't want you here at present, you might be let to go along with me."

If anything, short of being in a different relation to every one about me, Peggotty excepted, could have given me a sense of pleasure at that time, it would have been this project of all others. The idea of being again surrounded by those honest faces, shining welcome on me; of renewing the peacefulness of the sweet Sunday morning, when the bells were ringing, the stones dropping in the water, and the shadowy ships breaking through the mist; of roaming up and down with little Em'ly, telling her my troubles, and finding charms against them in the shells and pebbles on the beach; made a calm in my heart. It was ruffled next moment, to be sure, by a doubt of Miss Murdstone's giving her consent; but even that was set at rest soon, for she came out to take an evening grope in the store-closet while we were yet in conversation, and Peggotty, with a boldness that amazed me, broached the topic on the spot.

"The boy will be idle there," said Miss Murdstone, looking into a pickle-jar, "and idleness is the root of all evil. But, to be sure, he would be idle here—or anywhere, in my opinion."

Peggotty had an angry answer ready, I could see; but she swallowed it for my sake, and remained silent.

"Humph!" said Miss Murdstone, still keeping her eye on the pickles; "it is of more importance than anything else—it is of paramount importance—that my brother should not be disturbed or made uncomfortable. I suppose I had better say yes."

I thanked her, without making any demonstration of joy, lest it should induce her to withdraw her assent. Nor could I help thinking this a prudent course, when she looked at me out of the pickle-jar, with as great an access of sourness as if her black eyes had absorbed its contents. However, the permission was given, and was never retracted; for when the month was out, Peggotty and I were ready to depart.

Mr. Barkis came into the house for Peggotty's boxes. I had never known him to pass the garden-gate before, but on this occasion he came into the house. And he gave me a look as he shouldered the largest box and went out, which I thought had meaning in it, if meaning could ever be said to find its way into Mr. Barkis's visage.

Peggotty was naturally in low spirits at leaving what had been her home so many years, and where the two strong attachments of her life—for my mother and myself—had been formed. She had been walking in the churchyard, too, very early; and she got into the cart, and sat in it with her handkerchief at her eyes.

So long as she remained in this condition, Mr. Barkis gave no sign of life whatever. He sat in his usual place and attitude, like a great stuffed figure. But when she began to look about her, and to speak to me, he nodded his head and grinned several times. I have not the least notion at whom, or what he meant by it.

"It's a beautiful day, Mr. Barkis!" I said, as an act of politeness.

"It ain't bad," said Mr. Barkis, who generally qualified his speech, and rarely committed himself.

"Peggotty is quite comfortable now, Mr. Barkis," I remarked, for his satisfaction.

"Is she, though!" said Mr. Barkis.

After reflecting about it, with a sagacious air, Mr. Barkis eyed her, and said:

"*Are* you pretty comfortable?"

Peggotty laughed, and answered in the affirmative.

"But really and truly, you know. Are you?" growled Mr. Barkis, sliding nearer to her on the seat, and nudging her with his elbow. "Are you? Really and truly, pretty comfortable? Are you? Eh?" At each of these inquiries Mr. Barkis shuffled nearer to her, and gave her another nudge; so that at last we were all crowded together in the left-hand corner of the cart, and I was so squeezed that I could hardly bear it.

Peggotty calling his attention to my sufferings, Mr. Barkis gave me a little more room at once, and got away by degrees. But I could not help observing that he seemed to think he had hit upon a wonderful expedient for expressing himself in a neat, agreeable, and pointed manner, without the inconvenience of inventing conversation. He manifestly chuckled over it for some time. By-and-by he turned to Peggotty again, and repeating, "Are you pretty comfortable though?" bore down upon us as before, until the breath was nearly wedged out of my body. By-and-by he made another descent upon us with the same inquiry, and the same result. At length, I got up whenever I saw him coming, and standing on the footboard, pretended to look at the prospect; after which I did very well.

He was so polite as to stop at a public-house, expressly on our account, and entertain us with broiled mutton and beer. Even when Peggotty was in the act of drinking, he was seized with one of those approaches, and almost choked her. But as we drew nearer to the end of our journey, he had more to do and less time for gallantry; and when we got on Yarmouth pavement, we were all too much shaken and jolted, I apprehend, to have any leisure for anything else.

Mr. Peggotty and Ham waited for us at the old place. They received me and Peggotty in an affectionate manner, and shook hands with Mr. Barkis, who, with his hat on the very back of his head, and a shamefaced leer upon his countenance, and pervading his very legs, presented but a vacant appearance, I thought. They each took one of Peggotty's trunks, and we were going away, when Mr. Barkis solemnly made a sign to me with his forefinger to come under an archway.

"I say," growled Mr. Barkis, "it was all right."

I looked up into his face, and answered, with an attempt to be very profound: "Oh!"

"It didn't come to a end there," said Mr. Barkis, nodding confidentially. "It was all right."

Again I answered: "Oh!"

"You know who was willin'," said my friend. "It was Barkis, and Barkis only."

I nodded assent.

"It's all right," said Mr. Barkis, shaking hands; "I'm a friend of your'n. You made it all right first. It's all right."

In his attempts to be particularly lucid, Mr. Barkis was so extremely mysterious that I might have stood looking in his face for an hour, and most assuredly should have got as much information out of it as out of the face of a clock that had stopped, but for Peggotty's calling me away. As we were going along, she asked me what he had said; and I told her he had said it was all right.

"Like his impudence," said Peggotty, "but I don't mind that! Davy dear, what should you think if I was to think of being married?"

"Why—I suppose you would like me as much then, Peggotty, as you do now?" I returned, after a little consideration.

Greatly to the astonishment of the passengers in the street, as well as of her relations going on before, the good soul was obliged to stop and embrace me on the spot, with many protestations of her unalterable love.

"Tell me what should you say, darling?" she asked again, when this was over, and we were walking on.

"If you were thinking of being married—to Mr. Barkis, Peggotty?"

"Yes," said Peggotty.

"I should think it would be a very good thing. For then you know, Peggotty, you would always have the horse and cart to bring you over to see me, and could come for nothing, and be sure of coming."

"The sense of the dear!" cried Peggotty. "What I have been thinking of, this month back! Yes, my precious; and I think I should be more independent altogether, you see; let alone my working with a better heart in my own house, than I could in anybody else's now. I don't know what I might be fit for, now, as a servant to a stranger. And I shall be always near my pretty's resting-place," said Peggotty musing, "and able to see it when I like; and when I lie down to rest, I may be laid not far off from my darling girl!"

We neither of us said anything for a little while.

"But I wouldn't so much as give it another thought," said Peggotty, cheerily, "if my Davy was anyways against it—not if I had been asked in church thirty times three times over, and was wearing out the ring in my pocket."

"Look at me, Peggotty," I replied; "and see if I am not really glad, and don't truly wish it!" As indeed I did, with all my heart.

"Well, my life," said Peggotty, giving me a squeeze, "I have thought of it night and day, every way I can, and I hope the right way; but I'll think of it again, and speak to my brother about it, and in the meantime we'll keep it to ourselves, Davy, you and me. Barkis is a good plain creetur'," said Peggotty, "and if I tried to do my duty by him, I think it would be my fault if I wasn't—if I wasn't pretty comfortable," said Peggotty, laughing heartily.

This quotation from Mr. Barkis was so appropriate, and tickled us both so much, that we laughed again and again,

and were quite in a pleasant humour when we came within view of Mr. Peggotty's cottage.

It looked just the same, except that it may, perhaps, have shrunk a little in my eyes; and Mrs. Gummidge was waiting at the door as if she had stood there ever since. All within was the same, down to the seaweed in the blue mug in my bedroom. I went into the outhouse to look about me; and the very same lobsters, crabs, and crawfish, possessed by the same desire to pinch the world in general, appeared to be in the same state of conglomeration in the same old corner.

But there was no little Em'ly to be seen, so I asked Mr. Peggotty where she was.

"She's at school, Sir," said Mr. Peggotty, wiping the heat consequent on the porterage of Peggotty's box from his forehead; "she'll be home," looking at the Dutch clock, "in from twenty minutes to half-an-hour's time. We all on us feel the loss of her, bless ye."

Mrs. Gummidge moaned.

"Cheer up, Mawther!" cried Mr. Peggotty.

"I feel it more than anybody else," said Mrs. Gummidge; "I'm a lone lorn creetur', and she used to be a'most the only think that didn't go contrairy with me."

Mrs. Gummidge, whimpering and shaking her head, applied herself to blowing the fire. Mr. Peggotty, looking round upon us while she was so engaged, said in a low voice, which he shaded with his hand: "The old 'un!" From this I rightly conjectured that no improvement had taken place since my last visit in the state of Mrs. Gummidge's spirits.

Now, the whole place was, or it should have been, quite as delightful a place as ever; and yet it did not impress me in the same way. I felt rather disappointed with it. Perhaps it was because little Em'ly was not at home. I knew the way by which she would come, and presently found myself strolling along the path to meet her.

A figure appeared in the distance before long, and I soon knew it to be Em'ly, who was a little creature still in stature, though she was grown. But when she drew nearer, and I saw her blue eyes looking bluer, and her dimpled face looking brighter, and her whole self prettier and gayer, a curious feeling came over me that made me pretend not to know her, and pass by as if I were looking at something a long way off. I have done such a thing since in later life, or I am mistaken.

Little Em'ly didn't care a bit. She saw me well enough; but instead of turning round and calling after me, ran away laughing. This obliged me to run after her, and she ran so fast that we were very near the cottage before I caught her.

"Oh, it's you, is it?" said little Em'ly.

"Why, you knew who it was? Em'ly," said I.

"And didn't *you* know who it was?" said Em'ly. I was going to kiss her, but she covered her cherry lips with her hands, and said she wasn't a baby now, and ran away, laughing more than ever, into the house.

She seemed to delight in teasing me, which was a change in her I wondered at very much. The tea-table was ready, and our little locker was put out in its old place, but instead of coming to sit by me, she went and bestowed her company upon that grumbling Mrs. Gummidge: and on Mr. Peggotty's inquiring why, rumpled her hair all over her face to hide it, and would do nothing but laugh.

"A little puss it is!" said Mr. Peggotty, patting her with his great hand.

DAVID COPPERFIELD

"So sh' is! so sh' is!" cried Ham. "Mas'r Davy bor, so sh' is!" and he sat and chuckled at her for some time, in a state of mingled admiration and delight, that made his face a burning red.

Little Em'ly was spoiled by them all, in fact; and by no one more than Mr. Peggotty himself, whom she could have coaxed into anything, by only going and laying her cheek against his rough whisker. That was my opinion, at least, when I saw her do it; and I held Mr. Peggotty to be thoroughly in the right. But she was so affectionate and sweet-natured, and had such a pleasant manner of being both sly and shy at once, that she captivated me more than ever.

She was tender-hearted, too; for when, as we sat round the fire after tea, an allusion was made by Mr. Peggotty over his pipe to the loss I had sustained, the tears stood in her eyes, and she looked at me so kindly across the table, that I felt quite thankful to her.

"Ah!" said Mr. Peggotty, taking up her curls, and running them over his hand like water, "here's another orphan, you see, Sir. And here," said Mr. Peggotty, giving Ham a back-handed knock in the chest, "is another of 'em, though he don't look much like it."

"If I had you for my guardian, Mr. Peggotty," said I, shaking my head, "I don't think I should _feel_ much like it."

"Well said, Mas'r Davy bor'!" cried Ham, in an ecstasy. "Hoorah! Well said! Nor more you wouldn't! Hor! Hor!"—Here he returned Mr. Peggotty's back-hander, and little Em'ly got up and kissed Mr. Peggotty.

"And how's your friend, Sir?" said Mr. Peggotty to me. "Steerforth?" said I

"That's the name!" cried Mr. Peggotty, turning to Ham. "I knowed it was something in our way."

"You said it was Rudderford," observed Ham, laughing.

"Well?" retorted Mr. Peggotty. "And ye steer with a rudder, don't ye? It ain't fur off. How is he, Sir?"

"He was very well indeed when I came away, Mr. Peggotty."

"There's a friend!" said Mr. Peggotty, stretching out his pipe. "There's a friend, if you talk of friends! Why, Lord love my heart alive, if it ain't a treat to look at him!"

"He is very handsome, is he not?" said I, my heart warming with this praise.

"Handsome!" cried Mr. Peggotty. "He stands up to you like—like a—why, I don't know what he _don't_ stand up to you like. He's so bold!"

"Yes! That's just his character," said I "He's as brave as a lion, and you can't think how frank he is, Mr. Peggotty"

"And I do suppose, now," said Mr Peggotty, looking at me through the smoke of his pipe, "that in the way of book-learning he'd take the wind out of a'most anything."

"Yes," said I, delighted; "he knows everything. He is astonishingly clever."

"There's a friend!" murmured Mr. Peggotty, with a grave toss of his head.

"Nothing seems to cost him any trouble," said I. "He knows a task if he only looks at it. He is the best cricketer you ever saw. He will give you almost as many men as you like at draughts, and beat you easily."

Mr. Peggotty gave his head another toss, as much as to say: "Of course he will."

"He is such a speaker," I pursued, "that he can win anybody over; and I don't know what you'd say if you were to hear him sing, Mr. Peggotty."

Mr. Peggotty gave his head another toss, as much as to say: "I have no doubt of it."

"Then, he's such a generous, fine, noble fellow," said I, quite carried away by my favourite theme, "that it's hardly possible to give him as much praise as he deserves. I am sure I can never feel thankful enough for the generosity with which he has protected me, so much younger and lower in the school than himself."

I was running on, very fast indeed, when my eyes rested on little Em'ly's face, which was bent forward over the table, listening with the deepest attention, her breath held, her blue eyes sparkling like jewels, and the colour mantling in her cheeks. She looked so extraordinarily earnest and pretty, that I stopped in a sort of wonder; and they all observed her at the same time, for, as I stopped, they laughed and looked at her.

"Em'ly is like me," said Peggotty, "and would like to see him."

Em'ly was confused by our all observing her, and hung down her head, and her face was covered with blushes. Glancing up presently through her stray curls, and seeing that we were all looking at her still (I am sure I, for one, could have looked at her for hours), she ran away, and kept away till it was nearly bed-time.

I lay down in the old little bed in the stern of the boat, and the wind came moaning on across the flat as it had done before. But I could not help fancying, now, that it moaned of those who were gone; and instead of thinking that the sea might rise in the night and float the boat away, I thought of the sea that had risen, since I last heard those sounds, and drowned my happy home. I recollect, as the wind and water began to sound fainter in my ears, putting a short clause into my prayers, petitioning that I might grow up to marry little Em'ly, and so dropping lovingly asleep.

The days passed pretty much as they had passed before, except—it was a great exception—that little Em'ly and I seldom wandered on the beach now. She had tasks to learn, and needlework to do; and was absent during a great part of each day. But I felt that we should not have had those old wanderings, even if it had been otherwise. Wild and full of childish whims as Em'ly was, she was more of a little woman than I had supposed. She seemed to have got a great distance away from me, in little more than a year. She liked me, but she laughed at me, and tormented me; and when I went to meet her, stole home another way, and was laughing at the door when I came back, disappointed. The best times were when she sat quietly at work in the doorway, and I sat on the wooden step at her feet, reading to her. It seems to me, at this hour, that I have never seen such sunlight as on those bright April afternoons; that I have never seen such a sunny little figure as I used to see, sitting in the doorway of the old boat; that I have never beheld such sky, such water, such glorified ships sailing away into golden air.

On the very first evening after our arrival, Mr. Barkis appeared in an exceedingly vacant and awkward condition, and with a bundle of oranges tied up in a handkerchief. As he made no allusion of any kind to this property, he was supposed to have left it behind him by accident when he went away; until Ham, running after him to restore it, came back with the information that it was intended for

Peggotty. After that occasion he appeared every evening at exactly the same hour, and always with a little bundle, to which he never alluded, and which he regularly put behind the door, and left there. These offerings of affection were of a most various and eccentric description. Among them I remember a double set of pigs' trotters, a huge pincushion, half a bushel or so of apples, a pair of jet ear-rings, some Spanish onions, a box of dominoes, a canary bird and cage, and a leg of pickled pork.

Mr. Barkis's wooing, as I remember it, was altogether of a peculiar kind. He very seldom said anything; but would sit by the fire in much the same attitude as he sat in, in his cart, and stare heavily at Peggotty, who was opposite. One night, being, as I suppose, inspired by love, he made a dart at the bit of wax-candle she kept for her thread, and put it in his waistcoat-pocket and carried it off. After that his great delight was to produce it when it was wanted, sticking to the lining of his pocket, in a partially melted state, and pocket it again when it was done with. He seemed to enjoy himself very much, and not to feel at all called upon to talk. Even when he took Peggotty out for a walk on the flats, he had no uneasiness on that head, I believe; contenting himself with now and then asking her if she was pretty comfortable; and I remember that sometimes, after he was gone, Peggotty would throw her apron over her face, and laugh for half-an-hour. Indeed, we were all more or less amused, except that miserable Mrs. Gummidge, whose courtship would appear to have been of an exactly parallel nature, she was so continually reminded by these transactions of the old one.

At length, when the term of my visit was nearly expired, it was given out that Peggotty and Mr. Barkis were going to make a day's holiday together, and that little Em'ly and I were to accompany them. I had but a broken sleep the night before, in anticipation of the pleasure of a whole day with Em'ly. We were all astir betimes in the morning; and while we were yet at breakfast, Mr. Barkis appeared in the distance, driving a chaise-cart towards the object of his affections.

Peggotty was dressed as usual, in her neat and quiet mourning; but Mr. Barkis bloomed in a new blue coat, of which the tailor had given him such good measure, that the cuffs would have rendered gloves unnecessary in the coldest weather, while the collar was so high that it pushed his hair up on end on the top of his head. His bright buttons, too, were of the largest size. Rendered complete by drab pantaloons and a buff waistcoat, I thought Mr. Barkis a phenomenon of respectability.

When we were all in a bustle outside the door, I found that Mr. Peggotty was prepared with an old shoe, which was to be thrown after us for luck, and which he offered to Mrs. Gummidge for that purpose.

"No. It had better be done by somebody else, Dan'l," said Mrs. Gummidge. "I'm a lone lorn creetur' myself, and everythink that reminds me of creeturs that ain't lone and lorn, goes contrairy with me."

"Come, old gal!" cried Mr. Peggotty. "Take and heave it!"

"No, Dan'l," returned Mrs. Gummidge, whimpering and shaking her head. "If I felt less, I could do more. You don't feel like me, Dan'l; thinks don't go contrairy with you, nor you with them; you had better do it yourself."

But here Peggotty, who had been going about from one to another in a hurried way, kissing everybody, called out from the cart, in which we all were by this time (Em'ly and I on two little chairs, side by side), that Mrs. Gum-

midge must do it. So Mrs. Gummidge did it; and, I am sorry to relate, cast a damp upon the festive character of our departure, by immediately bursting into tears, and sinking subdued into the arms of Ham, with the declaration that she knowed she was a burden, and had better be carried to the House at once. Which I really thought was a sensible idea, that Ham might have acted on.

Away we went, however, on our holiday excursion; and the first thing we did was to stop at a church, where Mr. Barkis tied the horse to some rails, and went in with Peggotty, leaving little Em'ly and me alone in the chaise. I took that occasion to put my arm round Em'ly's waist, and propose that as I was going away so very soon now, we should determine to be very affectionate to one another, and very happy, all day. Little Em'ly consenting, and allowing me to kiss her, I became desperate; informing her, I recollect, that I never could love another, and that I was prepared to shed the blood of anybody who should aspire to her affections.

How merry little Em'ly made herself about it! With what a demure assumption of being immensely older and wiser than I, the fairy little woman said I was "a silly boy;" and then laughed so charmingly that I forgot the pain of being called by that disparaging name, in the pleasure of looking at her.

Mr. Barkis and Peggotty were a good while in the church, but came out at last, and then we drove away into the country. As we were going along, Mr. Barkis turned to me, and said, with a wink,—by-the-by, I should hardly have thought, before, that he *could* wink:

"What name was it as I wrote up in the cart?"

"Clara Peggotty," I answered.

"What name would it be as I should write up now, if there was a tilt here?"

"Clara Peggotty, again?" I suggested.

"Clara Peggotty BARKIS!" he returned, and burst into a roar of laughter that shook the chaise.

In a word, they were married, and had gone into the church for no other purpose. Peggotty was resolved that it should be quietly done; and the clerk had given her away, and there had been no witnesses of the ceremony. She was a little confused when Mr. Barkis made this abrupt announcement of their union, and could not hug me enough in token of her unimpaired affection; but she soon became herself again, and said she was very glad it was over.

We drove to a little inn in a bye-road, where we were expected, and where we had a very comfortable dinner, and passed the day with great satisfaction. If Peggotty had been married every day for the last ten years, she could hardly have been more at her ease about it; it made no sort of difference in her: she was just the same as ever, and went out for a stroll with little Em'ly and me before tea, while Mr. Barkis philosophically smoked his pipe, and enjoyed himself, I suppose, with the contemplation of his happiness. If so, it sharpened his appetite; for I distinctly call to mind that, although he had eaten a good deal of pork and greens at dinner, and had finished off with a fowl or two, he was obliged to have cold boiled bacon for tea, and disposed of a large quantity without any emotion.

I have often thought, since, what an odd, innocent, out-of-the-way kind of wedding it must have been! We got into the chaise again soon after dark, and drove cosily back, looking up at the stars, and talking about them. I was their chief exponent, and opened Mr. Barkis's mind to an amazing extent. I told him all I knew, but he would have believed anything I might have taken it into my head to impart to him; for he had a profound veneration for my abilities, and informed his wife in my hearing, on that very occasion, that I was "a young Roeshus"—by which I think he meant prodigy.

When we had exhausted the subject of the stars, or rather when I had exhausted the mental faculties of Mr. Barkis, little Em'ly and I made a cloak of an old wrapper, and sat under it for the rest of the journey. Ah, how I loved her! What happiness (I thought) if we were married, and were going away anywhere to live among the trees and in the fields, never growing older, never growing wiser, children ever, rambling hand in hand through sunshine and among flowery meadows, laying down our heads on moss at night, in a sweet sleep of purity and peace, and buried by the birds when we were dead! Some such picture, with no real world in it, bright with the light of our innocence, and vague as the stars afar off, was in my mind all the way. I am glad to think there were two such guileless hearts at Peggotty's marriage as little Em'ly's and mine. I am glad to think the Loves and Graces took such airy forms in its homely procession.

Well, we came to the old boat again in good time at night; and there Mr. and Mrs. Barkis bade us good-bye, and drove away snugly to their own home. I felt then, for the first time, that I had lost Peggotty. I should have gone to bed with a sore heart indeed under any other roof but that which sheltered little Em'ly's head.

Mr. Peggotty and Ham knew what was in my thoughts as well as I did, and were ready with some supper and their hospitable faces to drive it away. Little Em'ly came and sat beside me on the locker for the only time in all that visit; and it was altogether a wonderful close to a wonderful day.

It was a night tide; and soon after we went to bed, Mr. Peggotty and Ham went out to fish. I felt very brave at being left alone in the solitary house, the protector of Em'ly and Mrs. Gummidge, and only wished that a lion or a serpent, or any ill-disposed monster, would make an attack upon us, that I might destroy him, and cover myself with glory. But as nothing of the sort happened to be walking about on Yarmouth flats that night, I provided the best substitute I could by dreaming of dragons until morning.

With morning came Peggotty; who called to me, as usual, under my window, as if Mr. Barkis the carrier had been from first to last a dream too. After breakfast she took me to her own home, and a beautiful little home it was. Of all the movables in it, I must have been most impressed by a certain old bureau of some dark wood in the parlour (the tile-floored kitchen was the general sitting-room), with a retreating top which opened, let down, and became a desk, within which was a large quarto edition of Foxe's Book of Martyrs. This precious volume, of which I do not recollect one word, I immediately discovered and immediately applied myself to; and I never visited the house afterwards, but I kneeled on a chair, opened the casket where this gem was enshrined, spread my arms over the desk, and fell to devouring the book afresh. I was chiefly edified, I am afraid, by the pictures, which were numerous, and represented all kinds of dismal horrors; but the Martyrs and Peggotty's house have been inseparable in my mind ever since, and are now.

I took leave of Mr. Peggotty, and Ham, and Mrs. Gummidge, and little Em'ly, that day; and passed the night at Peggotty's in a little room in the roof (with the crocodile-book on a shelf by the bed's head), which was to be always

mine, Peggotty said, and should always be kept for me in exactly the same state.

"Young or old, Davy dear, as long as I am alive and have this house over my head," said Peggotty, "you shall find it as if I expected you here directly minute. I shall keep it every day, as I used to keep your old little room, my darling; and if you was to go to China, you might think of it as being kept just the same, all the time you were away."

I felt the truth and constancy of my dear old nurse, with all my heart, and thanked her as well as I could. That was not very well, for she spoke to me thus, with her arms round my neck, in the morning, and I was going home in the morning, and I went home in the morning, with herself and Mr. Barkis in the cart. They left me at the gate, not easily or lightly; and it was a strange sight to me to see the cart go on, taking Peggotty away, and leaving me under the old elm-trees looking at the house in which there was no face to look on mine with love or liking any more.

And now I fell into a state of neglect, which I cannot look back upon without compassion. I fell at once into a solitary condition,—apart from all friendly notice, apart from the society of all other boys of my own age, apart from all companionship but my own spiritless thoughts,—which seems to cast its gloom upon this paper as I write.

What would I have given, to have been sent to the hardest school that ever was kept!—to have been taught something, anyhow, anywhere! No such hope dawned upon me. They disliked me; and they sullenly, sternly, steadily, overlooked me. I think Mr. Murdstone's means were straitened at about this time; but it is little to the purpose. He could not bear me; and in putting me from him, he tried, as I believe, to put away the notion that I had any claim upon him—and succeeded.

I was not actively ill-used. I was not beaten, or starved; but the wrong that was done to me had no intervals of relenting, and was done in a systematic, passionless manner. Day after day, week after week, month after month, I was coldly neglected. I wonder sometimes, when I think of it, what they would have done if I had been taken with an illness; whether I should have lain down in my lonely room, and languished through it in my usual solitary way, or whether anybody would have helped me out.

When Mr. and Miss Murdstone were at home, I took my meals with them; in their absence, I ate and drank by myself. At all times I lounged about the house and neighbourhood quite disregarded, except that they were jealous of my making any friends: thinking, perhaps, that if I did, I might complain to some one. For this reason, though Mr. Chillip often asked me to go and see him (he was a widower, having, some years before that, lost a little small light-haired wife, whom I can just remember connecting in my own thoughts with a pale tortoiseshell cat), it was but seldom that I enjoyed the happiness of passing an afternoon in his closet of a surgery; reading some book that was new to me, with the smell of the whole pharmacopœia coming up my nose, or pounding something in a mortar under his mild directions.

For the same reason, added no doubt to the old dislike of her, I was seldom allowed to visit Peggotty. Faithful to her promise, she either came to see me, or met me somewhere near, once every week, and never empty-handed; but many and bitter were the disappointments I had, in being refused permission to pay a visit to her at her house. Some few times, however, at long intervals, I was allowed to go there; and then I found out that Mr. Barkis was something of a miser, or as Peggotty dutifully expressed it, was "a little near," and kept a heap of money in a box under his bed, which he pretended was only full of coats and trousers. In this coffer, his riches hid themselves with such a tenacious modesty, that the smallest instalments could only be tempted out by artifice; so that Peggotty had to prepare a long and elaborate scheme, a very Gunpowder Plot, for every Saturday's expenses.

All this time I was so conscious of the waste of any promise I had given, and of my being utterly neglected, that I should have been perfectly miserable, I have no doubt, but for the old books. They were my only comfort; and I was as true to them as they were to me, and read them over and over I don't know how many times more.

I now approach a period of my life, which I can never lose the remembrance of, while I remember anything; and the recollection of which has often, without my invocation, come before me like a ghost, and haunted happier times.

I had been out, one day, loitering somewhere, in the listless, meditative manner that my way of life engendered, when, turning the corner of a lane near our house, I came upon Mr. Murdstone walking with a gentleman. I was confused, and was going by them, when the gentleman cried:

"What? Brooks?"

"No, Sir, David Copperfield," I said.

"Don't tell me. You are Brooks," said the gentleman. "You are Brooks of Sheffield. That's your name."

At these words, I observed the gentleman more attentively. His laugh coming to my remembrance too, I knew him to be Mr. Quinion, whom I had gone over to Lowestoft with Mr. Murdstone to see, before—it is no matter—I need not recall when.

"And how do you get on, and where are you being educated, Brooks?" said Mr. Quinion.

He had put his hand upon my shoulder, and turned me about, to walk with them. I did not know what to reply, and glanced dubiously at Mr. Murdstone.

"He is at home at present," said the latter. "He is not being educated anywhere. I don't know what to do with him. He is a difficult subject."

That old, double look was on me for a moment; and then his eye darkened with a frown, as it turned, in its aversion, elsewhere.

"Humph!" said Mr. Quinion, looking at us both, I thought. "Fine weather!"

Silence ensued, and I was considering how I could best disengage my shoulder from his hand, and go away, when he said:

"I suppose you are a pretty sharp fellow still? Eh, Brooks?"

"Ay! He is sharp enough," said Mr. Murdstone, impatiently. "You had better let him go. He will not thank you for troubling him."

On this hint, Mr. Quinion released me, and I made the best of my way home. Looking back as I turned into the front garden, I saw Mr. Murdstone leaning against the wicket of the churchyard, and Mr. Quinion talking to him. They were both looking after me, and I felt that they were speaking of me.

Mr. Quinion lay at our house that night. After breakfast, the next morning, I had put my chair away, and was going out of the room, when Mr. Murdstone called me back. He then gravely repaired to another table, where his sister sat herself at her desk. Mr. Quinion, with his hands in his pockets, stood looking out of window; and I stood looking at them all.

"David," said Mr. Murdstone, "to the young this is a world for action; not for moping and droning in."

"—As you do," added his sister.

"Jane Murdstone, leave it to me, if you please. I say, David, to the young this is a world for action, and not for moping and droning in. It is especially so for a young boy of your disposition, which requires a great deal of correcting; and to which no greater service can be done than to force it to conform to the ways of the working world, and to bend it and break it."

"For stubbornness won't do here," said his sister. "What it wants is, to be crushed. And crushed it must be. Shall be, too!"

He gave her a look, half in remonstrance, half in approval, and went on:

"I suppose you know, David, that I am not rich. At any rate, you know it now. You have received some considerable education already. Education is costly; and even if it were not, and I could afford it, I am of opinion that it would not be at all advantageous to you to be kept at a school. What is before you, is a fight with the world; and the sooner you begin it, the better."

I think it occurred to me that I had already begun it, in my poor way: but it occurs to me now, whether or no.

"You have heard 'the counting-house' mentioned sometimes," said Mr. Murdstone.

"The counting-house, Sir?" I repeated.

"Of Murdstone and Grinby, in the wine trade," he replied.

I suppose I looked uncertain, for he went on hastily:

"You have heard the 'counting-house' mentioned, or the business, or the cellars, or the wharf, or something about it."

"I think I have heard the business mentioned, Sir," I said, remembering what I vaguely knew of his and his sister's resources. "But I don't know when."

"It does not matter when," he returned. "Mr. Quinion manages that business."

I glanced at the latter deferentially as he stood looking out of window.

"Mr. Quinion suggests that it gives employment to some other boys, and that he sees no reason why it shouldn't, on the same terms, give employment to you."

"He having," Mr. Quinion observed in a low voice, and half turning round, "no other prospect, Murdstone."

Mr. Murdstone, with an impatient, even an angry gesture, resumed, without noticing what he had said:

"Those terms are, that you will earn enough for yourself to provide for your eating and drinking, and pocket-money. Your lodging (which I have arranged for) will be paid by me. So will your washing."

"Which will be kept down to my estimate," said his sister.

"Your clothes will be looked after for you, too," said Mr. Murdstone; "as you will not be able, yet awhile, to get them for yourself. So you are now going to London, David, with Mr. Quinion, to begin the world on your own account."

"In short, you are provided for," observed his sister; "and will please to do your duty."

Though I quite understood that the purpose of this announcement was to get rid of me, I have no distinct remembrance whether it pleased or frightened me. My impression is, that I was in a state of confusion about it; and, oscillating between the two points, touched neither. Nor had I much time for the clearing of my thoughts, as Mr. Quinion was to go upon the morrow.

Behold me, on the morrow, in a much-worn little white hat, with a black crape round it for my mother, a black jacket, and a pair of hard stiff corduroy trousers—which Miss Murdstone considered the best armour for the legs in that fight with the world which was now to come off: behold me so attired, and with my little worldly all before me in a small trunk, sitting, a lone lorn child (as Mrs. Gummidge might have said), in the post-chaise that was carrying Mr. Quinion to the London coach at Yarmouth! See, how our house and church are lessening in the distance; how the grave beneath the tree is blotted out by intervening objects, how the spire points upward from my old playground no more, and the sky is empty!

CHAPTER XI.

I BEGIN LIFE ON MY OWN ACCOUNT, AND DON'T LIKE IT.

I KNOW enough of the world now, to have almost lost the capacity of being much surprised by anything; but it is matter of some surprise to me, even now, that I can have been so easily thrown away at such an age. A child of excellent abilities, and with strong powers of observation, quick, eager, delicate, and soon hurt bodily or mentally, it seems wonderful to me that nobody should have made any sign in my behalf. But none was made; and I became, at ten years old, a little labouring hind in the service of Murdstone and Grinby.

Murdstone and Grinby's warehouse was at the water-side. It was down in Blackfriars. Modern improvements have altered the place; but it was the last house at the bottom of a narrow street, curving down hill to the river, with some stairs at the end, where people took boat. It was a crazy old house with a wharf of its own, abutting on the water when the tide was in, and on the mud when the tide was out, and literally overrun with rats. Its panelled rooms, discoloured with the dirt and smoke of a hundred years, I dare say; its decaying floors and staircase; the squeaking and scuffling of the old grey rats down in the cellars; and the dirt and rottenness of the place; are things, not of many years ago, in my mind, but of the present instant. They are all before me, just as they were in the evil hour when I went among them for the first time, with my trembling hand in Mr. Quinion's.

Murdstone and Grinby's trade was among a good many kinds of people, but an important branch of it was the supply of wines and spirits to certain packet-ships. I forget now where they chiefly went, but I think there were some among them that made voyages both to the East and West Indies. I know that a great many empty bottles were one of the consequences of this traffic, and that certain men and boys were employed to examine them against the light, and reject those that were flawed, and to rinse and wash them. When the empty bottles ran short, there were labels to be pasted on full ones, or corks to be fitted to them, or seals to be put upon the corks, or finished bottles to be packed in casks. All this work was my work, and of the boys employed upon it I was one.

There were three or four of us, counting me. My working place was established in a corner of the warehouse, where Mr. Quinion could see me, when he chose to stand up on the bottom rail of his stool in the counting-house, and look at me through a window above the desk. Hither, on the first morning of my so auspiciously beginning life on my own account, the oldest of the regular boys was summoned to show me my business. His name was Mick Walker, and he wore a ragged apron and a paper cap. He informed me that his father was a bargeman, and walked, in a black velvet head-dress, in the Lord Mayor's Show. He also informed me that our principal associate would be another boy whom he introduced by the—to me—extraordinary name of Mealy Potatoes. I discovered, however, that this youth had not been christened by that name, but that it had been bestowed upon him in the warehouse, on account of his complexion, which was pale or mealy. Mealy's father was a waterman, who had the additional distinction of being a fireman, and was engaged as such at one of the large theatres; where some young relation of Mealy's—I think his little sister—did Imps in the Pantomimes.

No words can express the secret agony of my soul as I sank into this companionship; compared these henceforth every-day associates with those of my happier childhood—not to say with Steerforth, Traddles, and the rest of those boys; and felt my hopes of growing up to be a learned and distinguished man crushed in my bosom. The deep remembrance of the sense I had, of being utterly without hope now; of the shame I felt in my position; of the misery it was to my young heart to believe that day by day what I had learned, and thought, and delighted in, and raised my fancy and my emulation up by, would pass away from me, little by little, never to be brought back any more; cannot be written. As often as Mick Walker went away in the course of that forenoon, I mingled my tears with the water in which I was washing the bottles; and sobbed as if there were a flaw in my own breast, and it were in danger of bursting.

The counting-house clock was at half-past twelve, and there was general preparation for going to dinner, when Mr. Quinion tapped at the counting-house window, and beckoned to me to go in. I went in, and found there a stoutish, middle-aged person, in a brown surtout and black tights and shoes, with no more hair upon his head (which was a large one, and very shining) than there is upon an egg, and with a very extensive face, which he turned full upon me. His clothes were shabby, but he had an imposing shirt-collar on. He carried a jaunty sort of a stick, with a large pair of rusty tassels to it; and a quizzing-glass hung outside his coat,—for ornament, I afterwards found, as he very seldom looked through it, and couldn't see anything when he did.

"This," said Mr. Quinion, in allusion to myself, "is he."

"This," said the stranger, with a certain condescending roll in his voice, and a certain indescribable air of doing something genteel, which impressed me very much, "is Master Copperfield. I hope I see you well, Sir?"

I said I was very well, and hoped he was. I was sufficiently ill at ease, Heaven knows; but it was not in my nature to complain much at that time of my life, so I said I was very well, and hoped he was.

"I am," said the stranger, "thank Heaven, quite well. I have received a letter from Mr. Murdstone, in which he mentions that he would desire me to receive into an apartment in the rear of my house, which is at present unoccupied—and is, in short, to be let as a—in short," said the stranger, with a smile and in a burst of confidence, "as a bedroom—the young beginner whom I have now the pleasure to——" and the stranger waved his hand, and settled his chin in his shirt-collar.

"This is Mr. Micawber," said Mr. Quinion to me.

"Ahem!" said the stranger, "that is my name."

"Mr. Micawber," said Mr. Quinion, "is known to Mr. Murdstone. He takes orders for us on commission, when he can get any. He has been written to by Mr. Murdstone, on the subject of your lodgings, and he will receive you as a lodger."

"My address," said Mr. Micawber, "is Windsor Terrace, City Road. I—in short," said Mr. Micawber, with the same genteel air, and in another burst of confidence—"I live there."

I made him a bow.

"Under the impression," said Mr. Micawber, "that your peregrinations in this metropolis have not as yet been extensive, and that you might have some difficulty in penetrating the arcana of the Modern Babylon in the direction of the City Road—in short," said Mr. Micawber, in another burst of confidence, "that you might lose yourself—I shall be happy to call this evening, and instal you in the knowledge of the nearest way."

I thanked him with all my heart, for it was friendly in him to offer to take that trouble.

"At what hour," said Mr. Micawber, "shall I——"

"At about eight," said Mr. Quinion.

"At about eight," said Mr. Micawber. "I beg to wish you good day, Mr. Quinion. I will intrude no longer."

So he put on his hat, and went out with his cane under his arm: very upright, and humming a tune when he was clear of the counting-house.

Mr. Quinion then formally engaged me to be as useful as I could in the warehouse of Murdstone and Grinby, at a salary, I think, of six shillings a week. I am not clear whether it was six or seven. I am inclined to believe, from my uncertainty on this head, that it was six at first and seven afterwards. He paid me a week down (from his own pocket, I believe), and I gave Mealy sixpence out of it to get my trunk carried to Windsor Terrace at night: it being too heavy for my strength, small as it was. I paid sixpence more for my dinner, which was a meat pie and a turn at a neighbouring pump; and passed the hour which was allowed for that meal, in walking about the streets.

At the appointed time in the evening, Mr. Micawber reappeared. I washed my hands and face, to do the greater honour to his gentility, and we walked to our house, as I suppose I must now call it, together; Mr. Micawber impressing the names of streets, and the shapes of corner houses upon me, as we went along, that I might find my way back, easily, in the morning.

Arrived at his house in Windsor Terrace (which I noticed was shabby like himself, but also, like himself, made all the show it could), he presented me to Mrs. Micawber, a thin and faded lady, not at all young, who was sitting in the parlour (the first floor was altogether unfurnished, and the blinds were kept down to delude the neighbours), with a baby at her breast. This baby was one of twins; and I may remark here that I hardly ever, in all my experience of the family, saw both the twins detached from Mrs. Micawber at the same time. One of them was always taking refreshment.

There were two other children; Master Micawber, aged about four, and Miss Micawber, aged about three. These, and a dark-complexioned young woman, with a habit of snorting, who was servant to the family, and informed me, before half-an-hour had expired, that she was "a Orfling," and came from St. Luke's workhouse, in the neighbourhood, completed the establishment. My room was at the top of the house, at the back: a close chamber; stencilled all over with an ornament which my young imagination represented as a blue muffin; and very scantily furnished.

"I never thought," said Mrs. Micawber, when she came up, twin and all, to show me the apartment, and sat down to take breath, "before I was married, when I lived with papa and mama, that I should ever find it necessary to take a lodger. But Mr. Micawber being in difficulties, all considerations of private feeling must give way."

I said: "Yes, ma'am."

"Mr. Micawber's difficulties are almost overwhelming just at present," said Mrs. Micawber; "and whether it is possible to bring him through them, I don't know. When I lived at home with papa and mama, I really should have hardly understood what the word meant, in the sense in which I now employ it, but experientia does it—as papa used to say."

I cannot satisfy myself whether she told me that Mr. Micawber had been an officer in the Marines, or whether I have imagined it. I only know that I believe to this hour that he was in the Marines once upon a time, without knowing why. He was a sort of town traveller for a number of miscellaneous houses, now; but made little or nothing of it, I am afraid.

"If Mr. Micawber's creditors will not give him time," said Mrs. Micawber, "they must take the consequences; and the sooner they bring it to an issue the better. Blood cannot be obtained from a stone, neither can anything on account be obtained at present (not to mention law expenses) from Mr. Micawber."

I never can quite understand whether my precocious self-dependence confused Mrs. Micawber in reference to my age, or whether she was so full of the subject that she would have talked about it to the very twins if there had been nobody else to communicate with, but this was the strain in which she began, and she went on accordingly all the time I knew her.

Poor Mrs. Micawber! She said she had tried to exert herself; and so, I have no doubt, she had. The centre of the street-door was perfectly covered with a great brass plate, on which was engraved "Mrs. Micawber's Boarding Establishment for Young Ladies:" but I never found that any young lady had ever been to school there; or that any young lady ever came, or proposed to come; or that the least preparation was ever made to receive any young lady. The only visitors I ever saw or heard of, were creditors. They used to come at all hours, and some of them were quite ferocious. One dirty-faced man, I think he was a bootmaker, used to edge himself into the passage as early as seven o'clock in the morning, and call up the stairs to Mr. Micawber—"Come! You ain't out yet, you know. Pay us, will you? Don't hide, you know; that's mean. I wouldn't be mean if I was you. Pay us, will you? You just pay us, d'ye hear? Come!" Receiving no answer to these taunts, he would mount in his wrath to the words "swindlers" and "robbers;" and these being ineffectual too, would sometimes go to the extremity of crossing the street, and roaring up at the windows of the second floor, where he knew Mr. Micawber was. At these times, Mr. Micawber would be transported with grief and mortification, even to the length (as I was once made aware by a scream from his wife) of making motions at himself with a razor; but within half an hour afterwards, he would polish up his shoes with extraordinary pains, and go out, humming a tune with a greater air of gentility than ever. Mrs. Micawber was quite as elastic. I have known her to be thrown into fainting fits by the King's taxes at three o'clock, and to eat lamb-chops, breaded, and drink warm ale (paid for with two teaspoons that had gone to the pawnbroker's) at four. On one occasion, when an execution had just been put in, coming home through some chance as early as six o'clock, I saw her lying (of course with a twin) under the grate in a swoon, with her hair all torn about her face; but I never knew her more cheerful than she was, that very same night, over a veal-cutlet before the kitchen fire, telling me stories about her papa and mama, and the company they used to keep.

In this house, and with this family, I passed my leisure time. My own exclusive breakfast of a penny loaf and a pennyworth of milk, I provided myself. I kept another small loaf, and a modicum of cheese, on a particular shelf of a particular cupboard, to make my supper on when I came back at night. This made a hole in the six or seven shillings, I know well; and I was out at the warehouse all day, and had to support myself on that money all the week. From Monday morning until Saturday night, I had no advice, no counsel, no encouragement, no consolation, no assistance, no support, of any kind, from any one, that I can call to mind, as I hope to go to heaven!

I was so young and childish, and so little qualified—how could I be otherwise?—to undertake the whole charge of my own existence, that often, in going to Murdstone and Grinby's, of a morning, I could not resist the stale pastry put out for sale at half-price at the pastry-cooks' doors, and spent in that, the money I should have kept for my dinner. Then, I went without my dinner, or bought a roll or a slice of pudding. I remember two pudding-shops, between which I was divided, according to my finances. One was in a court close to St. Martin's Church—at the back of the church,—which is now removed altogether. The pudding at that shop was made of currants, and was rather a special pudding, but was dear, twopennyworth not being larger than a pennyworth of more ordinary pudding. A good shop for the latter was in the Strand—somewhere in that part which has been rebuilt since. It was a stout pale pudding, heavy and flabby, and with great flat raisins in it, stuck in whole at wide distances apart. It came up hot about my time every day, and many a day did I dine off it. When I dined regularly and handsomely, I had a saveloy and a penny loaf, or a fourpenny plate of red beef from a cook's shop; or a plate of bread and cheese and a glass of beer, from a miserable old public-house opposite our place of business, called the Lion, or the Lion and something else that I have forgotten. Once, I remember carrying my own bread (which I had brought from home in the morning) under my arm, wrapped in a piece of paper, like a book, and going to a famous alamode beef-house near Drury Lane, and ordering a "small plate" of that delicacy to eat with it. What the waiter thought of such a strange little apparition coming in all alone, I don't know; but I can see him now, staring at me as I ate my dinner, and bringing up the other waiter

to look. I gave him a halfpenny for himself, and I wish he hadn't taken it.

We had half-an-hour, I think, for tea. When I had money enough, I used to get half-a-pint of ready-made coffee and a slice of bread and butter. When I had none, I used to look at a venison-shop in Fleet Street; or I have strolled, at such a time, as far as Covent Garden Market, and stared at the pine-apples. I was fond of wandering about the Adelphi, because it was a mysterious place, with those dark arches. I see myself emerging one evening from some of these arches, on a little public-house close to the river, with an open space before it, where some coal-heavers were dancing; to look at whom, I sat down upon a bench. I wonder what they thought of me!

I was such a child, and so little, that frequently when I went into the bar of a strange public-house for a glass of ale or porter, to moisten what I had had for dinner, they were afraid to give it me. I remember one hot evening I went into the bar of a public-house, and said to the landlord:

"What is your best—your *very best*—ale a glass?" For it was a special occasion. I don't know what. It may have been my birthday.

"Twopence-halfpenny," says the landlord, "is the price of the Genuine Stunning ale."

"Then," says I, producing the money, "just draw me a glass of the Genuine Stunning, if you please, with a good head to it."

The landlord looked at me in return over the bar, from head to foot, with a strange smile on his face; and instead of drawing the beer, looked round the screen and said something to his wife. She came out from behind it, with her work in her hand, and joined him in surveying me. Here we stand, all three, before me now. The landlord in his shirt-sleeves, leaning against the bar window-frame; his wife looking over the little half-door; and I, in some confusion, looking up at them from outside the partition. They asked me a good many questions; as, what my name was, how old I was, where I lived, how I was employed, and how I came there. To all of which, that I might commit nobody, I invented, I am afraid, appropriate answers. They served me with the ale, though I suspect it was not the Genuine Stunning; and the landlord's wife, opening the little half-door of the bar, and bending down, gave me my money back, and gave me a kiss that was half admiring, and half compassionate, but all womanly and good, I am sure.

I know I do not exaggerate, unconsciously and unintentionally, the scantiness of my resources or the difficulties of my life. I know that if a shilling were given me by Mr. Quinion at any time, I spent it in a dinner or a tea. I know that I worked from morning until night, with common men and boys, a shabby child. I know that I lounged about the streets, insufficiently and unsatisfactorily fed. I know that, but for the mercy of God, I might easily have been, for any care that was taken of me, a little robber or a little vagabond.

Yet I held some station at Murdstone and Grinby's too. Besides that Mr. Quinion did what a careless man so occupied, and dealing with a thing so anomalous, could, to treat me as one upon a different footing from the rest, I never said, to man or boy, how it was that I came to be there, or gave the least indication of being sorry that I was there. That I suffered in secret, and that I suffered exquisitely, no one ever knew but I. How much I suffered, it is, as I have said already, utterly beyond my power to tell. But I kept my own counsel, and I did my work. I knew from the first, that, if I could not do my work as well as any of the rest, I could not hold myself above slight and contempt. I soon became at least as expeditious and as skilful as either of the other boys. Though perfectly familiar with them, my conduct and manner were different enough from theirs to place a space between us. They and the men generally spoke of me as "the little gent," or "the young Suffolker." A certain man named Gregory, who was foreman of the packers, and another named Tipp, who was the carman, and wore a red jacket, used to address me sometimes as "David:" but I think it was mostly when we were very confidential, and when I had made some efforts to entertain them, over our work, with some results of the old readings; which were fast perishing out of my remembrance. Mealy Potatoes uprose once, and rebelled against my being so distinguished; but Mick Walker settled him in no time.

My rescue from this kind of existence I considered quite hopeless, and abandoned, as such, altogether. I am solemnly convinced that I never for one hour was reconciled to it, or was otherwise than miserably unhappy; but I bore it; and even to Peggotty, partly for the love of her and partly for shame, never in any letter (though many passed between us) revealed the truth.

Mr. Micawber's difficulties were an addition to the distressed state of my mind. In my forlorn state I became quite attached to the family, and used to walk about, busy with Mrs. Micawber's calculations of ways and means, and heavy with the weight of Mr. Micawber's debts. On a Saturday night, which was my grand treat,—partly because it was a great thing to walk home with six or seven shillings in my pocket, looking into the shops and thinking what such a sum would buy, and partly because I went home early,—Mrs. Micawber would make the most heart-rending confidences to me; also on a Sunday morning, when I mixed the portion of tea or coffee I had bought overnight, in a little shaving-pot, and sat late at my breakfast. It was nothing at all unusual for Mr. Micawber to sob violently at the beginning of one of these Saturday night conversations, and sing about Jack's delight being his lovely Nan, towards the end of it. I have known him come home to supper with a flood of tears, and a declaration that nothing was now left but a jail; and go to bed making a calculation of the expense of putting bow-windows to the house, "in case anything turned up," which was his favourite expression. And Mrs. Micawber was just the same.

A curious equality of friendship, originating, I suppose, in our respective circumstances, sprang up between me and these people, notwithstanding the ludicrous disparity in our years. But I never allowed myself to be prevailed upon to accept any invitation to eat and drink with them out of their stock (knowing that they got on badly with the butcher and baker, and had often not too much for themselves), until Mrs. Micawber took me into her entire confidence. This she did one evening as follows:—

"Master Copperfield," said Mrs. Micawber, "I make no stranger of you, and therefore do not hesitate to say that Mr. Micawber's difficulties are coming to a crisis."

It made me very miserable to hear it, and I looked at Mrs. Micawber's red eyes with the utmost sympathy.

"With the exception of the heel of a Dutch cheese—which is not adapted to the wants of a young family"—said Mrs. Micawber, "there is really not a scrap of anything in the larder. I was accustomed to speak of the larder when I lived with papa and mama, and I use the word almost unconsciously. What I mean to express is, that there is nothing to eat in the house."

"Dear me!" I said, in great concern.

I had two or three shillings of my week's money in my pocket—from which I presume that it must have been on a Wednesday night when we held this conversation—and I hastily produced them, and with heartfelt emotion begged Mrs. Micawber to accept of them as a loan. But that lady, kissing me, and making me put them back in my pocket, replied that she couldn't think of it.

"No, my dear Master Copperfield," said she, "far be it from my thoughts! But you have a discretion beyond your years, and can render me another kind of service, if you will; and a service I will thankfully accept of."

I begged Mrs. Micawber to name it.

"I have parted with the plate myself," said Mrs. Micawber. "Six tea, two salt, and a pair of sugars, I have at different times borrowed money on, in secret, with my own hands. But the twins are a great tie; and to me, with my recollections of papa and mama, these transactions are very painful. There are still a few trifles that we could part with. Mr. Micawber's feelings would never allow *him* to dispose of them; and Clickett"—this was the girl from the workhouse—"being of a vulgar mind, would take painful liberties if so much confidence was reposed in her. Master Copperfield, if I might ask you"—

I understood Mrs. Micawber now, and begged her to make use of me to any extent. I began to dispose of the more portable articles of property that very evening; and went out on a similar expedition almost every morning, before I went to Murdstone and Grinby's.

Mr. Micawber had a few books on a little chiffonier, which he called the library; and those went first. I carried them, one after another, to a bookstall in the City Road—one part of which, near our house, was almost all bookstalls and bird-shops then—and sold them for whatever they would bring. The keeper of this bookstall, who lived in a little house behind it, used to get tipsy every night, and to be violently scolded by his wife every morning. More than once, when I went there early, I had audience of him in a turn-up bedstead, with a cut in his forehead or a black eye, bearing witness to his excesses overnight (I am afraid he was quarrelsome in his drink), and he with a shaking hand, endeavouring to find the needful shillings in one or other of the pockets of his clothes, which lay upon the floor, while his wife, with a baby in her arms and her shoes down at heel, never left off rating him. Sometimes he had lost his money, and then he would ask me to call again; but his wife had always got some—had taken his, I dare say, while he was drunk—and secretly completed the bargain on the stairs, as we went down together.

At the pawnbroker's shop, too, I began to be very well known. The principal gentleman who officiated behind the counter, took a good deal of notice of me; and often got me, I recollect, to decline a Latin noun or adjective, or to conjugate a Latin verb, in his ear, while he transacted my business. After all these occasions Mrs. Micawber made a little treat, which was generally a supper; and there was a peculiar relish in these meals which I well remember.

At last Mr. Micawber's difficulties came to a crisis, and he was arrested early one morning, and carried over to the King's Bench Prison in the Borough. He told me, as he went out of the house, that the God of day had now gone down upon him—and I really thought his heart was broken and mine too. But I heard, afterwards, that he was seen to play a lively game at skittles, before noon.

On the first Sunday after he was taken there, I was to go and see him, and have dinner with him. I was to ask my way to such a place, and just short of that place I should see another place, and just short of that I should see a yard, which I was to cross, and keep straight on until I saw a turnkey. All this I did; and when at last I did see a turnkey (poor little fellow that I was!), and thought how, when Roderick Random was in a debtors' prison, there was a man there with nothing on him but an old rug, the turnkey swam before my dimmed eyes and my beating heart.

Mr. Micawber was waiting for me within the gate, and we went up to his room (top story but one), and cried very much. He solemnly conjured me, I remember, to take warning by his fate; and to observe that if a man had twenty pounds a year for his income, and spent nineteen pounds nineteen shillings and sixpence, he would be happy, but that if he spent twenty pounds one he would be miserable. After which he borrowed a shilling of me for porter, gave me a written order on Mrs. Micawber for the amount, and put away his pocket-handkerchief, and cheered up.

We sat before a little fire, with two bricks put within the rusted grate, one on each side, to prevent its burning too many coals; until another debtor, who shared the room with Mr. Micawber, came in from the bakehouse with the loin of mutton which was our joint-stock repast. Then I was sent up to "Captain Hopkins" in the room overhead, with Mr. Micawber's compliments, and I was his young friend, and would Captain Hopkins lend me a knife and fork.

Captain Hopkins lent me the knife and fork, with his compliments to Mr. Micawber. There was a very dirty lady in his little room, and two wan girls, his daughters, with shock heads of hair. I thought it was better to borrow Captain Hopkins's knife and fork, than Captain Hopkins's comb. The Captain himself was in the last extremity of shabbiness, with large whiskers, and an old, old brown great-coat with no other coat below it. I saw his bed rolled up in a corner; and what plates and dishes and pots he had, on a shelf; and I divined (God knows how) that though the two girls with the shock heads of hair were Captain Hopkins's children, the dirty lady was not married to Captain Hopkins. My timid station on his threshold was not occupied more than a couple of minutes at most; but I came down again with all this in my knowledge, as surely as the knife and fork were in my hand.

There was something gipsy-like and agreeable in the dinner, after all. I took back Captain Hopkins's knife and fork early in the afternoon, and went home to comfort Mrs. Micawber with an account of my visit. She fainted when she saw me return, and made a little jug of egg-hot afterwards to console us while we talked it over.

I don't know how the household furniture came to be sold for the family benefit, or who sold it, except that *I* did not. Sold it was, however, and carried away in a van; except the bed, a few chairs, and the kitchen-table. With these possessions we encamped, as it were, in the two parlours of the emptied house in Windsor Terrace; Mrs. Micawber, the children, the Orfling, and myself; and lived in those rooms night and day. I have no idea for how long, though it seems to me for a long time. At last Mrs. Micawber resolved to move into the prison, where Mr. Micawber had now secured a room to himself. So I took the key

of the house to the landlord, who was very glad to get it; and the beds were sent over to the King's Bench, except mine, for which a little room was hired outside the walls in the neighbourhood of that Institution, very much to my satisfaction, since the Micawbers and I had become too used to one another, in our troubles, to part. The Orfling was likewise accommodated with an inexpensive lodging in the same neighbourhood. Mine was a quiet back-garret with a sloping roof, commanding a pleasant prospect of a timber-yard; and when I took possession of it, with the reflection that Mr. Micawber's troubles had come to a crisis at last, I thought it quite a paradise.

All this time I was working at Murdstone and Grinby's in the same common way, and with the same common companions, and with the same sense of unmerited degradation as at first. But I never, happily for me no doubt, made a single acquaintance, or spoke to any of the many boys whom I saw daily in going to the warehouse, in coming from it, and in prowling about the streets at meal-times. I led the same secretly unhappy life; but I led it in the same lonely, self-reliant manner. The only changes I am conscious of are, firstly, that I had grown more shabby, and secondly, that I was now relieved of much of the weight of Mr. and Mrs. Micawber's cares; for some relatives or friends had engaged to help them at their present pass, and they lived more comfortably in the prison than they had lived for a long while out of it. I used to breakfast with them now, in virtue of some arrangement, of which I have forgotten the details. I forget, too, at what hour the gates were opened in the morning, admitting of my going in; but I know that I was often up at six o'clock, and that my favourite lounging-place in the interval was old London Bridge, where I was wont to sit in one of the stone recesses, watching the people going by, or to look over the balustrades at the sun shining in the water, and lighting up the golden flame on the top of the Monument. The Orfling met me here sometimes, to be told some astonishing fictions respecting the wharves and the Tower; of which I can say no more than that I hope I believed them myself. In the evening I used to go back to the prison, and walk up and down the parade with Mr. Micawber; or play casino with Mrs. Micawber, and hear reminiscences of her papa and mama. Whether Mr. Murdstone knew where I was, I am unable to say. I never told them at Murdstone and Grinby's.

Mr. Micawber's affairs, although past their crisis, were very much involved by reason of a certain "Deed," of which I used to hear a great deal, and which I suppose, now, to have been some former composition with his creditors, though I was so far from being clear about it then, that I am conscious of having confounded it with those demoniacal parchments which are held to have, once upon a time, obtained to a great extent in Germany. At last this document appeared to be got out of the way, somehow; at all events it ceased to be the rock-ahead it had been; and Mrs. Micawber informed me that "her family" had decided that Mr. Micawber should apply for his release under the Insolvent Debtors' Act, which would set him free, she expected, in about six weeks.

"And then," said Mr. Micawber, who was present, "I have no doubt I shall, please Heaven, begin to be beforehand with the world, and to live in a perfectly new manner, if—in short, if anything turns up."

By way of going in for anything that might be on the cards, I call to mind that Mr. Micawber, about this time, composed a petition to the House of Commons, praying for an alteration in the law of imprisonment for debt. I set down this remembrance here, because it is an instance to myself of the manner in which I fitted my old books to my altered life, and made stories for myself, out of the streets, and out of men and women; and how some main points in the character I shall unconsciously develop, I suppose, in writing my life, were gradually forming all this while.

There was a club in the prison, in which Mr. Micawber, as a gentleman, was a great authority. Mr. Micawber had stated his idea of this petition to the club, and the club had strongly approved of the same. Wherefore Mr. Micawber (who was a thoroughly good-natured man, and as active a creature about everything but his own affairs as ever existed, and never so happy as when he was busy about something that could never be of any profit to him) set to work at the petition, invented it, engrossed it on an immense sheet of paper, spread it out on a table, and appointed a time for all the club, and all within the walls if they chose, to come up to his room and sign it.

When I heard of this approaching ceremony, I was so anxious to see them all come in, one after another, though I knew the greater part of them already, and they me, that I got an hour's leave of absence from Murdstone and Grinby's, and established myself in a corner for that purpose. As many of the principal members of the club as could be got into the small room without filling it, supported Mr. Micawber in front of the petition, while my old friend Captain Hopkins (who had washed himself, to do honour to so solemn an occasion) stationed himself close to it, to read it to all who were unacquainted with its contents. The door was then thrown open, and the general population began to come in, in a long file: several waiting outside, while one entered, affixed his signature, and went out. To everybody in succession, Captain Hopkins said: "Have you read it?"—"No."—"Would you like to hear it read?" If he weakly showed the least disposition to hear it, Captain Hopkins, in a loud sonorous voice, gave him every word of it. The Captain would have read it twenty thousand times, if twenty thousand people would have heard him, one by one. I remember a certain luscious roll he gave to such phrases as "The people's representatives in Parliament assembled," "Your petitioners therefore humbly approach your honourable House," "His gracious Majesty's unfortunate subjects," as if the words were something real in his mouth, and delicious to taste; Mr. Micawber, meanwhile, listening with a little of an author's vanity, and contemplating (not severely) the spikes on the opposite wall.

As I walked to and fro daily between Southwark and Blackfriars, and lounged about at meal-times in obscure streets, the stones of which may, for anything I know, be worn at this moment by my childish feet, I wonder how many of these people were wanting in the crowd that used to come filing before me in review again, to the echo of Captain Hopkins's voice! When my thoughts go back now, to that slow agony of my youth, I wonder how much of the histories I invented for such people hangs like a mist of fancy over well-remembered facts! When I tread the old ground, I do not wonder that I seem to see and pity, going on before me, an innocent romantic boy, making his imaginative world out of such strange experiences and sordid things!

CHAPTER XII.

LIKING LIFE ON MY OWN ACCOUNT NO BETTER, I FORM A GREAT RESOLUTION.

In due time, Mr. Micawber's petition was ripe for hearing; and that gentleman was ordered to be discharged under the Act, to my great joy. His creditors were not implacable; and Mrs. Micawber informed me that even the revengeful bootmaker had declared in open court that he bore him no malice, but that when money was owing to him he liked to be paid. He said he thought it was human nature.

Mr. Micawber returned to the King's Bench when his case was over, as some fees were to be settled, and some formalities observed, before he could be actually released. The club received him with transport, and held an harmonic meeting that evening in his honour; while Mrs. Micawber and I had a lamb's fry in private, surrounded by the sleeping family.

"On such an occasion I will give you, Master Copperfield," said Mrs. Micawber, "in a little more flip," for we had been having some already, "the memory of my papa and mama."

"Are they dead, ma'am?" I inquired, after drinking the toast in a wine-glass.

"My mama departed this life," said Mrs. Micawber, "before Mr. Micawber's difficulties commenced, or at least before they became pressing. My papa lived to bail Mr. Micawber several times, and then expired, regretted by a numerous circle."

Mrs. Micawber shook her head, and dropped a pious tear upon the twin who happened to be in hand.

As I could hardly hope for a more favourable opportunity of putting a question in which I had a near interest, I said to Mrs. Micawber:

"May I ask, ma'am, what you and Mr. Micawber intend to do, now that Mr. Micawber is out of his difficulties, and at liberty? Have you settled yet?"

"My family," said Mrs. Micawber, who always said those two words with an air, though I never could discover who came under the denomination, "my family are of opinion that Mr. Micawber should quit London, and exert his talents in the country. Mr. Micawber is a man of great talent, Master Copperfield."

I said I was sure of that.

"Of great talent," repeated Mrs. Micawber. "My family are of opinion, that, with a little interest, something might be done for a man of his ability in the Custom House. The influence of my family being local, it is their wish that Mr. Micawber should go down to Plymouth. They think it indispensable that he should be upon the spot."

"That he may be ready?" I suggested.

"Exactly," returned Mrs. Micawber. "That he may be ready—in case of anything turning up."

"And do you go too, ma'am?"

The events of the day, in combination with the twins, if not with the flip, had made Mrs. Micawber hysterical, and she shed tears as she replied:

"I never will desert Mr. Micawber. Mr. Micawber may have concealed his difficulties from me in the first instance, but his sanguine temper may have led him to expect that he would overcome them. The pearl necklace and bracelets which I inherited from mama, have been disposed of for less than half their value; and the set of coral, which was the wedding gift of my papa, has been actually thrown away for nothing. But I never will desert Mr. Micawber. No!" cried Mrs. Micawber, more affected than before, "I never will do it! It's of no use asking me!"

I felt quite uncomfortable—as if Mrs. Micawber supposed I had asked her to do anything of the sort!—and sat looking at her in alarm.

"Mr. Micawber has his faults. I do not deny that he is improvident. I do not deny that he has kept me in the dark as to his resources and his liabilities, both," she went on, looking at the wall; "but I never will desert Mr. Micawber!"

Mrs. Micawber having now raised her voice into a perfect scream, I was so frightened that I ran off to the club-room, and disturbed Mr. Micawber in the act of presiding at a long table, and leading the chorus of

"Gee up, Dobbin,
Gee ho, Dobbin,
Gee up, Dobbin,
Gee up, and gee ho—o—o!"

—with the tidings that Mrs. Micawber was in an alarming state, upon which he immediately burst into tears, and came away with me with his waistcoat full of the heads and tails of shrimps, of which he had been partaking.

"Emma, my angel!" cried Mr. Micawber, running into the room; "what is the matter?"

"I never will desert you, Micawber!" she exclaimed.

"My life!" said Mr. Micawber, taking her in his arms. "I am perfectly aware of it."

"He is the parent of my children! He is the father of my twins! He is the husband of my affections," cried Mrs. Micawber, struggling; "and I ne—ver—will—desert Mr. Micawber!"

Mr. Micawber was so deeply affected by this proof of her devotion (as to me, I was dissolved in tears), that he hung over her in a passionate manner, imploring her to look up, and to be calm. But the more he asked Mrs. Micawber to look up, the more she fixed her eyes on nothing; and the more he asked her to compose herself, the more she wouldn't. Consequently Mr. Micawber was soon so overcome, that he mingled his tears with hers and mine; until he begged me to do him the favour of taking a chair on the staircase, while he got her into bed. I would have taken my leave for the night, but he would not hear of my doing that until the strangers' bell should ring. So I sat at the staircase window, until he came out with another chair and joined me.

"How is Mrs. Micawber now, Sir?" I said.

"Very low," said Mr. Micawber, shaking his head; "re-action. Ah, this has been a dreadful day! We stand alone now—everything is gone from us!"

Mr. Micawber pressed my hand, and groaned, and afterwards shed tears. I was greatly touched, and disappointed too, for I had expected that we should be quite gay on this happy and long-looked-for occasion. But Mr. and Mrs. Micawber were so used to their old difficulties, I think, that they felt quite shipwrecked when they came to consider that they were released from them. All their elasticity was departed, and I never saw them half so wretched as on this night; insomuch that when the bell rang, and Mr. Micawber walked with me to the lodge, and parted from me there with a blessing, I felt quite afraid to leave him by himself, he was so profoundly miserable.

But through all the confusion and lowness of spirits in which we had been, so unexpectedly to me, involved, I plainly discerned that Mr. and Mrs. Micawber and their family were going away from London, and that a parting between us was near at hand. It was in my walk home that night, and in the sleepless hours which followed when I lay in bed, that the thought first occurred to me—though I don't know how it came into my head—which afterwards shaped itself into a settled resolution.

I had grown to be so accustomed to the Micawbers, and had been so intimate with them in their distresses, and was so utterly friendless without them, that the prospect of being thrown upon some new shift for a lodging, and going once more among unknown people, was like being that moment turned adrift into my present life, with such a knowledge of it ready made, as experience had given me. All the sensitive feelings it wounded so cruelly, all the shame and misery it kept alive within my breast, became more poignant as I thought of this; and I determined that the life was unendurable.

That there was no hope of escape from it, unless the escape was my own act, I knew quite well. I rarely heard from Miss Murdstone, and never from Mr. Murdstone: but two or three parcels of made or mended clothes had come up for me, consigned to Mr. Quinion, and in each there was a scrap of paper to the effect that J. M. trusted D. C. was applying himself to business, and devoting himself wholly to his duties—not the least hint of my ever being anything else than the common drudge into which I was fast settling down.

The very next day showed me, while my mind was in the first agitation of what it had conceived, that Mrs. Micawber had not spoken of their going away without warrant. They took a lodging in the house where I lived, for a week; at the expiration of which time they were to start for Plymouth. Mr. Micawber himself came down to the counting-house, in the afternoon, to tell Mr. Quinion that he must relinquish me on the day of his departure, and to give me a high character, which I am sure I deserved. And Mr. Quinion, calling in Tipp the carman, who was a married man, and had a room to let, quartered me prospectively on him—by our mutual consent, as he had every reason to think; for I said nothing, though my resolution was now taken.

I passed my evenings with Mr. and Mrs. Micawber, during the remaining term of our residence under the same roof; and I think we became fonder of one another as the time went on. On the last Sunday, they invited me to dinner; and we had a loin of pork and apple sauce, and a pudding. I had bought a spotted wooden horse overnight as a parting gift to little Wilkins Micawber—that was the boy—and a doll for little Emma. I had also bestowed a shilling on the Orfling, who was about to be disbanded.

We had a very pleasant day, though we were all in a tender state about our approaching separation.

"I shall never, Master Copperfield," said Mrs. Micawber, "revert to the period when Mr. Micawber was in difficulties without thinking of you. Your conduct has always been of the most delicate and obliging description. You have never been a lodger. You have been a friend."

"My dear," said Mr. Micawber, "Copperfield," for so he had been accustomed to call me, of late, "has a heart to feel for the distresses of his fellow-creatures when they are behind a cloud, and a head to plan, and a hand to—in short, a general ability to dispose of such available property as could be made away with."

I expressed my sense of this commendation, and said I was very sorry we were going to lose one another.

"My dear young friend," said Mr. Micawber, "I am older than you; a man of some experience in life, and—and of some experience, in short, in difficulties, generally speaking. At present, and until something turns up (which I am, I may say, hourly expecting), I have nothing to bestow but advice. Still my advice is so far worth taking, that—in short, that I have never taken it myself, and am the "—here Mr. Micawber, who had been beaming and smiling, all over his head and face, up to the present moment, checked himself and frowned—"the miserable wretch you behold."

"My dear Micawber!" urged his wife.

"I say," returned Mr. Micawber, quite forgetting himself, and smiling again, "the miserable wretch you behold. My advice is, never do to-morrow what you can do to-day. Procrastination is the thief of time. Collar him!"

"My poor papa's maxim," Mrs. Micawber observed.

"My dear," said Mr. Micawber, "your papa was very well in his way, and Heaven forbid that I should disparage him. Take him for all in all, we ne'er shall—in short, make the acquaintance, probably, of anybody else possessing, at his time of life, the same legs for gaiters, and able to read the same description of print, without spectacles. But he applied that maxim to our marriage, my dear; and that was so far prematurely entered into, in consequence, that I never recovered the expense."

Mr. Micawber looked aside at Mrs. Micawber, and added: "Not that I am sorry for it. Quite the contrary, my love." After which he was grave for a minute or so.

"My other piece of advice, Copperfield," said Mr. Micawber, "you know. Annual income twenty pounds, annual expenditure nineteen nineteen six, result happiness. Annual income twenty pounds, annual expenditure twenty pounds ought and six, result misery. The blossom is blighted, the leaf is withered, the God of day goes down upon the dreary scene and—and in short you are for ever floored. As I am!"

To make his example the more impressive, Mr. Micawber drank a glass of punch with an air of great enjoyment and satisfaction, and whistled the College Hornpipe.

I did not fail to assure him that I would store these precepts in my mind, though indeed I had no need to do so, for, at the time, they affected me visibly. Next morning I met the whole family at the coach-office, and saw them, with a desolate heart, take their places outside, at the back.

"Master Copperfield," said Mrs. Micawber, "God bless you! I never can forget all that, you know, and I never would if I could."

"Copperfield," said Mr. Micawber, "farewell! Every happiness and prosperity! If, in the progress of revolving years, I could persuade myself that my blighted destiny had been a warning to you, I should feel that I had not occupied another man's place in existence altogether in vain. In case of anything turning up (of which I am rather confident), I shall be extremely happy if it should be in my power to improve your prospects."

I think, as Mrs. Micawber sat at the back of the coach, with the children, and I stood in the road looking wistfully at them, a mist cleared from her eyes, and she saw what a little creature I really was. I think so, because she beckoned to me to climb up, with quite a new and motherly expression in her face, and put her arm round my neck, and gave me just such a kiss as she might have given to her own boy. I had barely time to get down again before the coach started,

and I could hardly see the family for the handkerchiefs they waved. It was gone in a minute. The Orfling and I stood looking vacantly at each other in the middle of the road, and then shook hands and said good-bye; she going back, I suppose, to St. Luke's workhouse, as I went to begin my weary day at Murdstone and Grinby's.

But with no intention of passing many more weary days there. No. I had resolved to run away.—To go, by some means or other, down into the country, to the only relation I had in the world, and tell my story to my aunt, Miss Betsey.

I have already observed that I don't know how this desperate idea came into my brain. But once there, it remained there; and hardened into a purpose than which I have never entertained a more determined purpose in my life. I am far from sure that I believed there was anything hopeful in it, but my mind was thoroughly made up that it must be carried into execution.

Again, and again, and a hundred times again, since the night when the thought had first occurred to me and banished sleep, I had gone over that old story of my poor mother's about my birth, which it had been one of my great delights in the old time to hear her tell, and which I knew by heart. My aunt walked into that story, and walked out of it, a dread and awful personage; but there was one little trait in her behaviour which I liked to dwell on, and which gave me some faint shadow of encouragement. I could not forget how my mother had thought that she felt her touch her pretty hair with no ungentle hand; and though it might have been altogether my mother's fancy, and might have had no foundation whatever in fact, I made a little picture, out of it, of my terrible aunt relenting towards the girlish beauty that I recollected so well and loved so much, which softened the whole narrative. It is very possible that it had been in my mind a long time, and had gradually engendered my determination.

As I did not even know where Miss Betsey lived, I wrote a long letter to Peggotty, and asked her, incidentally, if she remembered; pretending that I had heard of such a lady living at a certain place I named at random, and had a curiosity to know if it were the same. In the course of that letter, I told Peggotty that I had a particular occasion for half-a-guinea; and that if she could lend me that sum until I could repay it, I should be very much obliged to her, and would tell her afterwards what I had wanted it for.

Peggotty's answer soon arrived, and was, as usual, full of affectionate devotion. She enclosed the half-guinea (I was afraid she must have had a world of trouble to get it out of Mr. Barkis's box), and told me that Miss Betsey lived near Dover, but whether at Dover itself, at Hythe, Sandgate, or Folkestone, she could not say. One of our men, however, informing me on my asking him about these places, that they were all close together, I deemed this enough for my object, and resolved to set out at the end of that week.

Being a very honest little creature, and unwilling to disgrace the memory I was going to leave behind me at Murdstone and Grinby's, I considered myself bound to remain until Saturday night; and, as I had been paid a week's wages in advance when I first came there, not to present myself in the counting-house at the usual hour, to receive my stipend. For this express reason, I had borrowed the half-guinea, that I might not be without a fund for my travelling expenses. Accordingly, when the Saturday night came, and we were all waiting in the warehouse to be paid, and Tipp the carman, who always took precedence, went in first to draw his money, I shook Mick Walker by the hand; asked him, when it came to his turn to be paid, to say to Mr. Quinion that I had gone to move my box to Tipp's; and, bidding a last good night to Mealy Potatoes, ran away.

My box was at my old lodging over the water, and I had written a direction for it on the back of one of our address cards that we nailed on the casks: "Master David, to be left till called for, at the Coach Office, Dover." This I had in my pocket ready to put on the box, after I should have got it out of the house; and as I went towards my lodging I looked about me for some one who would help me to carry it to the booking-office.

There was a long-legged young man with a very little empty donkey-cart, standing near the Obelisk, in the Black-friars Road, whose eye I caught as I was going by, and who, addressing me as "Sixpen'orth of bad ha'pence," hoped "I should know him again to swear to"—in allusion, I have no doubt, to my staring at him. I stopped to assure him that I had not done so in bad manners, but uncertain whether he might or might not like a job.

"Wot job?" said the long-legged young man.

"To move a box," I answered.

"Wot box?" said the long-legged young man.

I told him mine, which was down that street there, and which I wanted him to take to the Dover coach-office for sixpence.

"Done with you for a tanner!" said the long-legged young man, and directly got upon his cart, which was nothing but a large wooden tray on wheels, and rattled away at such a rate, that it was as much as I could do to keep pace with the donkey.

There was a defiant manner about this young man, and particularly about the way in which he chewed straw as he spoke to me, that I did not much like; as the bargain was made, however, I took him upstairs to the room I was leaving, and we brought the box down, and put it on his cart. Now, I was unwilling to put the direction-card on there, lest any of my landlord's family should fathom what I was doing, and detain me; so I said to the young man that I would be glad if he would stop for a minute, when he came to the dead-wall of the King's Bench Prison. The words were no sooner out of my mouth, than he rattled away as if he, my box, the cart, and the donkey, were all equally mad; and I was quite out of breath with running and calling after him, when I caught him at the place appointed.

Being much flushed and excited, I tumbled my half-guinea out of my pocket in pulling the card out. I put it in my mouth for safety, and though my hands trembled a good deal, had just tied the card on very much to my satisfaction, when I felt myself violently chucked under the chin by the long-legged young man, and saw my half-guinea fly out of my mouth into his hand.

"Wot!" said the young man, seizing me by my jacket collar, with a frightful grin. "This is a pollis case, is it? You're a going to bolt, are you? Come to the pollis, you young warmin, come to the pollis!"

"You give me my money back, if you please," said I, very much frightened; "and leave me alone."

"Come to the pollis!" said the young man. "You shall prove it yourn to the pollis."

"Give me my box and money, will you?" I cried, bursting into tears.

The young man still replied: "Come to the pollis!" and was dragging me against the donkey in a violent manner, as if there were any affinity between that animal and a magistrate, when he changed his mind, jumped into the cart, sat upon my box, and, exclaiming that he would drive to the pollis straight, rattled away harder than ever.

I ran after him as fast as I could, but I had no breath to call out with, and should not have dared to call out, now, if I had. I narrowly escaped being run over, twenty times at least, in half a mile. Now I lost him, now I saw him, now I lost him, now I was cut at with a whip, now shouted at, now down in the mud, now up again, now running into somebody's arms, now running headlong at a post. At length, confused by fright and heat, and doubting whether half London might not by this time be turning out for my apprehension, I left the young man to go where he would with my box and money; and, panting and crying, but never stopping, faced about for Greenwich, which I had understood was on the Dover road: taking very little more out of the world, towards the retreat of my aunt, Miss Betsey, than I had brought into it, on the night when my arrival gave her so much umbrage.

CHAPTER XIII.

THE SEQUEL OF MY RESOLUTION.

For anything I know, I may have had some wild idea of running all the way to Dover, when I gave up the pursuit of the young man with the donkey-cart, and started for Greenwich. My scattered senses were soon collected as to that point, if I had; for I came to a stop in the Kent Road, at a terrace with a piece of water in the middle, and a great foolish image in the middle, blowing a dry shell. Here I sat down on a door-step, quite spent and exhausted with the efforts I had already made, and with hardly breath enough to cry for the loss of my box and half-guinea.

It was by this time dark; I heard the clocks strike ten, as I sat resting. But it was a summer night, fortunately, and fine weather. When I had recovered my breath, and had got rid of a stifling sensation in my throat, I rose up and went on. In the midst of my distress, I had no notion of going back. I doubt if I should have had any, though there had been a Swiss snow-drift in the Kent Road.

But my standing possessed of only three-halfpence in the world (and I am sure I wonder how *they* came to be left in my pocket on a Saturday night!) troubled me none the less because I went on. I began to picture to myself, as a scrap of newspaper intelligence, my being found dead in a day or two, under some hedge; and I trudged on miserably, though as fast as I could, until I happened to pass a little shop, where it was written up that ladies' and gentlemen's wardrobes were bought, and that the best price was given for rags, bones, and kitchen-stuff. The master of this shop was sitting at the door in his shirt-sleeves, smoking; and as there were a great many coats and pairs of trousers dangling from the low ceiling, and only two feeble candles burning inside to show what they were, I fancied that he looked like a man of a revengeful disposition, who had hung all his enemies, and was enjoying himself.

My late experiences with Mr. and Mrs. Micawber suggested to me that here might be a means of keeping off the wolf for a little while. I went up the next bye-street, took off my waistcoat, rolled it neatly under my arm, and came back to the shop-door. "If you please, Sir," I said, "I am to sell this for a fair price."

Mr. Dolloby—Dolloby was the name over the shop-door, at least—took the waistcoat, stood his pipe on its head against the door-post, went into the shop, followed by me, snuffed the two candles with his fingers, spread the waistcoat on the counter, and looked at it there, held it up against the light, and looked at it there, and ultimately said:

"What do you call a price, now, for this here little weskit?"

"Oh! you know best, Sir," I returned, modestly.

"I can't be buyer and seller too," said Mr. Dolloby. "Put a price on this here little weskit."

"Would eighteenpence be?"—I hinted, after some hesitation.

Mr. Dolloby rolled it up again, and gave it me back. "I should rob my family," he said, "if I was to offer ninepence for it."

This was a disagreeable way of putting the business; because it imposed upon me, a perfect stranger, the unpleasantness of asking Mr. Dolloby to rob his family on my account. My circumstances being so very pressing, however, I said I would take ninepence for it, if he pleased. Mr. Dolloby, not without some grumbling, gave ninepence. I wished him good night, and walked out of the shop, the richer by that sum, and the poorer by a waistcoat. But when I buttoned my jacket, that was not much.

Indeed, I foresaw pretty clearly that my jacket would go next, and that I should have to make the best of my way to Dover in a shirt and a pair of trousers, and might deem myself lucky if I got there even in that trim. But my mind did not run so much on this as might be supposed. Beyond a general impression of the distance before me, and of the young man with the donkey-cart having used me cruelly, I think I had no very urgent sense of my difficulties when I once again set off with my ninepence in my pocket.

A plan had occurred to me for passing the night, which I was going to carry into execution. This was, to lie behind the wall at the back of my old school, in a corner where there used to be a haystack. I imagined it would be a kind of company to have the boys, and the bedroom where I used to tell the stories, so near me: although the boys would know nothing of my being there, and the bedroom would yield me no shelter.

I had had a hard day's work, and was pretty well jaded when I came climbing out, at last, upon the level of Blackheath. It cost me some trouble to find out Salem House; but I found it, and I found a haystack in the corner, and I lay down by it; having first walked round the wall, and looked up at the windows, and seen that all was dark and silent within. Never shall I forget the lonely sensation of first lying down, without a roof above my head!

Sleep came upon me as it came on many other outcasts, against whom house-doors were locked, and house-dogs barked, that night—and I dreamed of lying on my old school-bed, talking to the boys in my room; and found myself sitting upright, with Steerforth's name upon my lips, looking wildly at the stars that were glistening and glimmering above me. When I remembered where I was at that untimely hour, a feeling stole upon me that made me get up, afraid of I don't know what, and walk about. But the fainter glimmering of the stars, and the pale light in the sky where the day was coming, reassured me: and my eyes being very heavy, I lay down again, and slept—

though with a knowledge in my sleep that it was cold—until the warm beams of the sun, and the ringing of the getting-up bell at Salem House, awoke me. If I could have hoped that Steerforth was there, I would have lurked about until he came out alone; but I knew he must have left long since. Traddles still remained, perhaps, but it was very doubtful; and I had not sufficient confidence in his discretion or good luck, however strong my reliance was on his good-nature, to wish to trust him with my situation. So I crept away from the wall as Mr. Creakle's boys were getting up, and struck into the long dusty track which I had first known to be the Dover road when I was one of them, and when I little expected that any eyes would ever see me the wayfarer I was now, upon it.

What a different Sunday morning from the old Sunday morning at Yarmouth! In due time I heard the church-bells ringing, as I plodded on; and I met people who were going to church; and I passed a church or two where the congregation were inside, and the sound of singing came out into the sunshine, while the beadle sat and cooled himself in the shade of the porch, or stood beneath the yew-tree, with his hand to his forehead, glowering at me going by. But the peace and the rest of the old Sunday morning were on everything, except me. That was the difference. I felt quite wicked in my dirt and dust, with my tangled hair. But for the quiet picture I had conjured up, of my mother in her youth and beauty, weeping by the fire, and my aunt relenting to her, I hardly think I should have had courage to go on until next day. But it always went before me, and I followed.

I got, that Sunday, through three-and-twenty miles on the straight road, though not very easily, for I was new to that kind of toil. I see myself, as evening closes in, coming over the bridge at Rochester, footsore and tired, and eating bread that I had bought for supper. One or two little houses, with the notice, "Lodgings for Travellers," hanging out, had tempted me; but I was afraid of spending the few pence I had, and was even more afraid of the vicious looks of the trampers I had met or overtaken. I sought no shelter, therefore, but the sky; and toiling into Chatham,—which, in that night's aspect, is a mere dream of chalk, and drawbridges, and mastless ships in a muddy river, roofed like Noah's arks—crept, at last, upon a sort of grass-grown battery overhanging a lane, where a sentry was walking to and fro. Here I lay down, near a cannon; and, happy in the society of the sentry's footsteps, though he knew no more of my being above him than the boys at Salem House had known of my lying by the wall, slept soundly until morning.

Very stiff and sore of foot I was in the morning, and quite dazed by the beating of drums and marching of troops, which seemed to hem me in on every side when I went down towards the long narrow street. Feeling that I could go but a very little way that day, if I were to reserve any strength for getting to my journey's end, I resolved to make the sale of my jacket its principal business. Accordingly, I took the jacket off, that I might learn to do without it; and carrying it under my arm, began a tour of inspection of the various slop-shops.

It was a likely place to sell a jacket in; for the dealers in second-hand clothes were numerous, and were, generally speaking, on the look-out for customers at their shop-doors. But as most of them had, hanging up among their stock, an officer's coat or two, epaulettes and all, I was rendered timid by the costly nature of their dealings, and walked about for a long time without offering my merchandise to any one.

This modesty of mine directed my attention to the marine-store shops, and such shops as Mr. Dolloby's, in preference to the regular dealers. At last I found one that I thought looked promising, at the corner of a dirty lane, ending in an inclosure full of stinging nettles, against the palings of which some second-hand sailors' clothes, that seemed to have overflowed the shop, were fluttering among some cots, and rusty guns, and oilskin hats, and certain trays full of so many old rusty keys of so many sizes that they seemed various enough to open all the doors in the world.

Into this shop, which was low and small, and which was darkened rather than lighted by a little window, overhung with clothes, and was descended into by some steps, I went with a palpitating heart; which was not relieved when an ugly old man, with the lower part of his face all covered with a stubbly grey beard, rushed out of a dirty den behind it, and seized me by the hair of my head. He was a dreadful old man to look at, in a filthy flannel waistcoat, and smelling terribly of rum. His bedstead, covered with a tumbled and ragged piece of patchwork, was in the den he had come from, where another little window showed a prospect of more stinging nettles, and a lame donkey.

"Oh, what do you want?" grinned this old man, in a fierce, monotonous whine. "Oh, my eyes and limbs, what do you want? Oh, my lungs and liver, what do you want? Oh, goroo, goroo!"

I was so much dismayed by these words, and particularly by the repetition of the last unknown one, which was a kind of rattle in his throat, that I could make no answer; hereupon the old man, still holding me by the hair, repeated:

"Oh, what do you want? Oh, my eyes and limbs, what do you want? Oh, my lungs and liver, what do you want? Oh, goroo!"—which he screwed out of himself, with an energy that made his eyes start in his head.

"I wanted to know," I said, trembling, "if you would buy a jacket."

"Oh, let's see the jacket!" cried the old man. "Oh, my heart on fire, show the jacket to us! Oh, my eyes and limbs, bring the jacket out!"

With that he took his trembling hands, which were like the claws of a great bird, out of my hair; and put on a pair of spectacles, not at all ornamental to his inflamed eyes.

"Oh, how much for the jacket?" cried the old man, after examining it. "Oh—goroo!—how much for the jacket?"

"Half-a-crown," I answered, recovering myself.

"Oh, my lungs and liver," cried the old man, "no! Oh, my eyes, no! Oh, my limbs, no! Eighteenpence. Goroo!"

Every time he uttered this ejaculation, his eyes seemed to be in danger of starting out; and every sentence he spoke, he delivered in a sort of tune, always exactly the same, and more like a gust of wind, which begins low, mounts up high, and falls again, than any other comparison I can find for it.

"Well," said I, glad to have closed the bargain, "I'll take eighteenpence."

"Oh, my liver!" cried the old man, throwing the jacket on a shelf. "Get out of the shop! Oh, my lungs, get out of the shop! Oh, my eyes and limbs—goroo!—don't ask for money; make it an exchange."

I never was so frightened in my life, before or since; but I told him humbly that I wanted money, and that nothing else was of any use to me, but that I would wait for it, as he desired, outside, and had no wish to hurry him. So I went outside, and sat down in the shade in a corner. And I sat there so many hours, that the shade became sunlight, and the sunlight became shade again, and still I sat there waiting for the money.

There never was such another drunken madman in that line of business, I hope. That he was well known in the neighbourhood, and enjoyed the reputation of having sold himself to the devil, I soon understood from the visits he received from the boys, who continually came skirmishing about the shop, shouting that legend, and calling to him to bring out his gold. "You ain't poor, you know, Charley, as you pretend. Bring out your gold. Bring out some of the gold you sold yourself to the devil for. Come! It's in the lining of the mattress, Charley. Rip it open and let's have some!" This, and many offers to lend him a knife for the purpose, exasperated him to such a degree, that the whole day was a succession of rushes on his part, and flights on the part of the boys. Sometimes in his rage he would take me for one of them, and come at me, mouthing as if he were going to tear me in pieces; then, remembering me, just in time, would dive into the shop, and lie upon his bed, as I thought from the sound of his voice, yelling in a frantic way, to his own windy tune, the Death of Nelson; with an Oh! before every line, and innumerable Goroos interspersed. As if this were not bad enough for me, the boys, connecting me with the establishment, on account of the patience and perseverance with which I sat outside, half dressed, pelted me, and used me very ill all day.

He made many attempts to induce me to consent to an exchange; at one time coming out with a fishing-rod, at another with a fiddle, at another with a cocked hat, at another with a flute. But I resisted all these overtures, and sat there in desperation; each time asking him, with tears in my eyes, for my money or my jacket. At last he began to pay me in halfpence at a time; and was full two hours getting by easy stages to a shilling.

"Oh, my eyes and limbs!" he then cried, peeping hideously out of the shop, after a long pause, "will you go for twopence more?"

"I can't," I said; "I shall be starved."

"Oh, my lungs and liver, will you go for threepence?"

"I would go for nothing, if I could," I said, "but I want the money badly."

"Oh, go—roo!" (it is really impossible to express how he twisted this ejaculation out of himself, as he peeped round the door-post at me, showing nothing but his crafty old head); "will you go for fourpence?"

I was so faint and weary that I closed with this offer; and taking the money out of his claw, not without trembling, went away more hungry and thirsty than I had ever been, a little before sunset. But at an expense of threepence I soon refreshed myself completely; and, being in better spirits then, limped seven miles upon my road.

My bed at night was under another haystack, where I rested comfortably, after having washed my blistered feet in a stream, and dressed them as well as I was able, with some cool leaves. When I took the road again next morning, I found that it lay through a succession of hop-grounds and orchards. It was sufficiently late in the year for the orchards to be ruddy with ripe apples; and in a few places the hop-pickers were already at work. I thought it all extremely beautiful, and made up my mind to sleep among the hops that night: imagining some cheerful companionship in the long perspectives of poles, with the graceful leaves twining round them.

The trampers were worse than ever that day, and inspired me with a dread that is yet quite fresh in my mind. Some of them were most ferocious-looking ruffians, who stared at me as I went by; and stopped, perhaps, and called after me to come back and speak to them; and when I took to my heels, stoned me. I recollect one young fellow—a tinker, I suppose, from his wallet and brazier—who had a woman with him, and who faced about and stared at me thus; and then roared to me in such a tremendous voice to come back, that I halted and looked round.

"Come here, when you're called," said the tinker, "or I'll rip your young body open."

I thought it best to go back. As I drew nearer to them, trying to propitiate the tinker by my looks, I observed that the woman had a black eye.

"Where are you going?" said the tinker, gripping the bosom of my shirt with his blackened hand.

"I am going to Dover," I said.

"Where do you come from?" asked the tinker, giving his hand another turn in my shirt, to hold me more securely.

"I come from London," I said.

"What lay are you upon?" asked the tinker. "Are you a prig?"

"No—no," I said.

"Ain't you, by G——? If you make a brag of your honesty to me," said the tinker, "I'll knock your brains out."

With his disengaged hand he made a menace of striking me, and then looked at me from head to foot.

"Have you got the price of a pint of beer about you?" said the tinker. "If you have, out with it, afore I take it away!"

I should certainly have produced it, but that I met the woman's look, and saw her very slightly shake her head, and form "No!" with her lips.

"I am very poor," I said, attempting to smile, "and have got no money."

"Why, what do you mean?" said the tinker, looking so sternly at me, that I almost feared he saw the money in my pocket.

"Sir!" I stammered.

"What do you mean," said the tinker, "by wearing my brother's silk handkercher? Give it over here!" And he had mine off my neck in a moment, and tossed it to the woman.

The woman burst into a fit of laughter, as if she thought this a joke, and tossed it back to me, nodded once, as slightly as before, and made the word "Go!" with her lips. Before I could obey, however, the tinker seized the handkerchief out of my hand with a roughness that threw me away like a feather, and putting it loosely round his own neck, turned upon the woman with an oath, and knocked her down. I never shall forget seeing her fall backward on the hard road, and lie there with her bonnet tumbled off, and her hair all whitened in the dust; nor, when I looked back from a distance, seeing her sitting on the pathway, which was a bank by the roadside, wiping the blood from her face with the corner of her shawl, while he went on ahead.

This adventure frightened me so, that, afterwards, when I saw any of these people coming, I turned back until I could find a hiding-place, where I remained until they had

gone out of sight; which happened so often, that I was very seriously delayed. But under this difficulty, as under all the other difficulties of my journey, I seemed to be sustained and led on by my fanciful picture of my mother in her youth, before I came into the world. It always kept me company. It was there, among the hops, when I lay down to sleep; it was with me on my waking in the morning; it went before me all day. I have associated it, ever since, with the sunny street of Canterbury, dozing as it were in the hot light; and with the sight of its old houses and gateways, and the stately, grey cathedral, with the rooks sailing round the towers. When I came, at last, upon the bare, wide downs near Dover, it relieved the solitary aspect of the scene with hope; and not until I reached that first great aim of my journey, and actually set foot in the town itself, on the sixth day of my flight, did it desert me. But then, strange to say, when I stood with my ragged shoes, and my dusty, sunburnt, half-clothed figure, in the place so long desired, it seemed to vanish like a dream, and to leave me helpless and dispirited.

I inquired about my aunt among the boatmen first, and received various answers. One said she lived in the South Foreland Light, and had singed her whiskers by doing so; another, that she was made fast to the great buoy outside the harbour, and could only be visited at half-tide; a third, that she was locked up in Maidstone Jail for child-stealing; a fourth, that she was seen to mount a broom, in the last high wind, and make direct for Calais. The fly-drivers, among whom I inquired next, were equally jocose and equally disrespectful; and the shopkeepers, not liking my appearance, generally replied, without hearing what I had to say, that they had got nothing for me. I felt more miserable and destitute than I had done at any period of my running away. My money was all gone, I had nothing left to dispose of; I was hungry, thirsty, and worn out; and seemed as distant from my end as if I had remained in London.

The morning had worn away in these inquiries, and I was sitting on the step of an empty shop at a street-corner, near the market-place, deliberating upon wandering towards those other places which had been mentioned, when a fly-driver, coming by with his carriage, dropped a horsecloth. Something good-natured in the man's face, as I handed it up, encouraged me to ask him if he could tell me where Miss Trotwood lived; though I had asked the question so often, that it almost died upon my lips.

"Trotwood," said he. "Let me see. I know the name, too. Old lady?"

"Yes," I said, "rather."

"Pretty stiff in the back?" said he, making himself upright.

"Yes," I said. "I should think it very likely."

"Carries a bag?" said he—"bag with a good deal of room in it—is gruffish, and comes down upon you, sharp?"

My heart sank within me as I acknowledged the undoubted accuracy of this description.

"Why then, I tell you what," said he. "If you go up there," pointing with his whip towards the heights, "and keep right on till you come to some houses facing the sea, I think you'll hear of her. My opinion is, she won't stand anything, so here's a penny for you."

I accepted the gift thankfully, and bought a loaf with it. Despatching this refreshment by the way, I went in the direction my friend had indicated, and walked on a good distance without coming to the houses he had mentioned. At length I saw some before me; and approaching them, went into a little shop (it was what we used to call a general shop, at home), and inquired if they could have the goodness to tell me where Miss Trotwood lived. I addressed myself to a man behind the counter, who was weighing some rice for a young woman; but the latter, taking the inquiry to herself, turned round quickly.

"My mistress?" she said. "What do you want with her, boy?"

"I want," I replied, "to speak to her, if you please."

"To beg of her, you mean," retorted the damsel.

"No," I said, "indeed." But suddenly remembering that in truth I came for no other purpose, I held my peace in confusion, and felt my face burn.

My aunt's handmaid, as I supposed she was from what she had said, put her rice in a little basket and walked out of the shop; telling me that I could follow her, if I wanted to know where Miss Trotwood lived. I needed no second permission; though I was by this time in such a state of consternation and agitation, that my legs shook under me. I followed the young woman, and we soon came to a very neat little cottage with cheerful bow-windows: in front of it, a small square gravelled court or garden full of flowers, carefully tended, and smelling deliciously.

"This is Miss Trotwood's," said the young woman. "Now you know; and that's all I have got to say." With which words she hurried into the house, as if to shake off the responsibilty of my appearance; and left me standing at the garden-gate, looking disconsolately over the top of it towards the parlour-window, where a muslin curtain partly undrawn in the middle, a large round green screen or fan fastened on to the window-sill, a small table, and a great chair, suggested to me that my aunt might be at that moment seated in awful state.

My shoes were by this time in a woeful condition. The soles had shed themselves bit by bit, and the upper leathers had broken and burst until the very shape and form of shoes had departed from them. My hat (which had served me for a night-cap, too) was so crushed and bent, that no old battered handleless saucepan on a dunghill need have been ashamed to vie with it. My shirt and trousers, stained with heat, dew, grass, and the Kentish soil on which I had slept—and torn besides—might have frightened the birds from my aunt's garden, as I stood at the gate. My hair had known no comb or brush since I left London. My face, neck, and hands, from unaccustomed exposure to the air and sun, were burnt to a berry-brown. From head to foot I was powdered almost as white with chalk and dust, as if I had come out of a lime-kiln. In this plight, and with a strong consciousness of it, I waited to introduce myself to, and make my first impression on, my formidable aunt.

The unbroken stillness of the parlour-window leading me to infer, after a while, that she was not there, I lifted up my eyes to the window above it, where I saw a florid, pleasant-looking gentleman, with a grey head, who shut up one eye in a grotesque manner, nodded his head at me several times, shook it at me as often, laughed, and went away.

I had been discomposed enough before; but I was so much the more discomposed by this unexpected behaviour, that I was on the point of slinking off, to think how I had best proceed, when there came out of the house a lady with a handkerchief tied over her cap, and a pair of gardening gloves on her hands, wearing a gardening-pocket like a tollman's apron, and carrying a great knife. I knew her immediately to be Miss Betsey, for she came stalking out of the house exactly as my poor mother had so often described her stalking up our garden at Blunderstone Rookery.

"Go away!" said Miss Betsey, shaking her head, and making a distant chop in the air with her knife. "Go along! No boys here!"

I watched her, with my heart at my lips, as she marched to a corner of her garden, and stooped to dig up some little root there. Then, without a scrap of courage, but with a great deal of desperation, I went softly in and stood beside her, touching her with my finger.

"If you please, ma'am," I began.

She started, and looked up.

"If you please, aunt."

"EH?" exclaimed Miss Betsey, in a tone of amazement I have never heard approached.

"If you please, aunt, I am your nephew."

"Oh, Lord!" said my aunt. And sat flat down in the garden-path.

"I am David Copperfield, of Blunderstone, in Suffolk—where you came, on the night when I was born, and saw my dear mama. I have been very unhappy since she died. I have been slighted, and taught nothing, and thrown upon myself, and put to work not fit for me. It made me run away to you. I was robbed at first setting out, and have walked all the way, and have never slept in a bed since I began the journey." Here my self-support gave way all at once; and with a movement of my hands, intended to show her my ragged state, and call it to witness that I had suffered something, I broke into a passion of crying, which I suppose had been pent up within me all the week.

My aunt, with every sort of expression but wonder discharged from her countenance, sat on the gravel, staring at me, until I began to cry; when she got up in a great hurry, collared me, and took me into the parlour. Her first proceeding there was to unlock a tall press, bring out several bottles, and pour some of the contents of each into my mouth. I think they must have been taken out at random, for I am sure I tasted aniseed water, anchovy sauce, and salad dressing. When she had administered these restoratives, as I was still quite hysterical, and unable to control my sobs, she put me on the sofa, with a shawl under my head, and the handkerchief from her own head under my feet, lest I should sully the cover; and then, sitting herself down behind the green fan or screen I have already mentioned, so that I could not see her face, ejaculated at intervals, "Mercy on us!" letting those exclamations off like minute-guns.

After a time she rang the bell. "Janet," said my aunt, when her servant came in. "Go up stairs, give my compliments to Mr. Dick, and say I wish to speak to him."

Janet looked a little surprised to see me lying stiffly on the sofa (I was afraid to move lest it should be displeasing to my aunt) but went on her errand. My aunt, with her hands behind her, walked up and down the room, until the gentleman who had squinted at me from the upper window came in laughing.

"Mr. Dick," said my aunt, "don't be a fool, because nobody can be more discreet than you can, when you choose. We all know that. So don't be a fool, whatever you are."

I MAKE MYSELF KNOWN TO MY AUNT.

The gentleman was serious immediately, and looked at me, I thought, as if he would entreat me to say nothing about the window.

"Mr. Dick," said my aunt, "you have heard me mention David Copperfield? Now don't pretend not to have a memory, because you and I know better."

"David Copperfield?" said Mr. Dick, who did not appear to me to remember much about it. "*David* Copperfield? Oh yes, to be sure. David, certainly."

"Well," said my aunt, "this is his boy—his son. He would be as like his father as it's possible to be, if he was not so like his mother, too."

"His son?" said Mr. Dick. "David's son? Indeed!"

"Yes," pursued my aunt, "and he has done a pretty piece of business. He has run away. Ah! His sister, Betsey Trotwood, never would have run away." My aunt shook her head firmly, confident in the character and behaviour of the girl who never was born.

"Oh! you think she wouldn't have run away?" said Mr. Dick.

"Bless and save the man," exclaimed my aunt, sharply, "how he talks! Don't I know she wouldn't? She would have lived with her godmother, and we should have been devoted to one another. Where, in the name of wonder, should his sister, Betsey Trotwood, have run from, or to?"

"Nowhere," said Mr. Dick.

"Well then," returned my aunt, softened by the reply, "how can you pretend to be wool-gathering, Dick, when you are as sharp as a surgeon's lancet? Now, here you see young David Copperfield, and the question I put to you is, what shall I do with him?"

"What shall you do with him?" said Mr. Dick, feebly, scratching his head. "Oh! do with him?"

"Yes," said my aunt, with a grave look, and her forefinger held up. "Come! I want some very sound advice."

"Why, if I was you," said Mr. Dick, considering, and looking vacantly at me, "I should——" The contemplation of me seemed to inspire him with a sudden idea, and he added, briskly, "I should wash him!"

"Janet," said my aunt, turning round with a quiet triumph, which I did not then understand, "Mr. Dick sets us all right. Heat the bath!"

Although I was deeply interested in this dialogue, I could not help observing my aunt, Mr. Dick, and Janet, while it was in progress, and completing a survey I had already been engaged in making of the room.

My aunt was a tall, hard-featured lady, but by no means ill-looking. There was an inflexibility in her face, in her voice, in her gait and carriage, amply sufficient to account for the effect she had made upon a gentle creature like my mother; but her features were rather handsome than otherwise, though unbending and austere. I particularly noticed that she had a very quick, bright eye. Her hair, which was grey, was arranged in two plain divisions, under what I believe would be called a mob-cap: I mean a cap, much more common then than now, with side-pieces fastening under the chin. Her dress was of a lavender colour, and perfectly neat; but scantily made, as if she desired to be as little encumbered as possible. I remember that I thought it, in form, more like a riding-habit with the superfluous skirt cut off, than anything else. She wore at her side a gentleman's gold watch, if I might judge from its size and make, with an appropriate chain and seals; she had some linen at her throat not unlike a shirt-collar, and things at her wrists like little shirt-wristbands.

Mr. Dick, as I have already said, was grey-headed and florid: I should have said all about him, in saying so, had not his head been curiously bowed—not by age; it reminded me of one of Mr. Creakle's boys' heads after a beating—and his grey eyes prominent and large, with a strange kind of watery brightness in them that made me, in combination with his vacant manner, his submission to my aunt, and his childish delight when she praised him, suspect him of being a little mad; though, if he were mad, how he came to be there puzzled me extremely. He was dressed like any other ordinary gentleman, in a loose grey morning coat and waistcoat, and white trousers; and had his watch in his fob, and his money in his pockets: which he rattled as if he were very proud of it.

Janet was a pretty, blooming girl, of about nineteen or twenty, and a perfect picture of neatness. Though I made no further observation of her at the moment, I may mention here what I did not discover until afterwards, namely, that she was one of a series of protégées whom my aunt had taken into her service expressly to educate in a renouncement of mankind, and who had generally completed their abjuration by marrying the baker.

The room was as neat as Janet or my aunt. As I laid down my pen, a moment since, to think of it, the air from the sea came blowing in again, mixed with the perfume of the flowers; and I saw the old-fashioned furniture brightly rubbed and polished, my aunt's inviolable chair and table by the round green fan in the bow-window, the drugget-covered carpet, the cat, the kettle-holder, the two canaries, the old china, the punch-bowl full of dried rose-leaves, the tall press guarding all sorts of bottles and pots, and, wonderfully out of keeping with the rest, my dusty self upon the sofa, taking note of everything.

Janet had gone away to get the bath ready, when my aunt, to my great alarm, became in one moment rigid with indignation, and had hardly voice to cry out, "Janet! Donkeys!"

Upon which, Janet came running up the stairs as if the house were in flames, darted out on a little piece of green in front, and warned off two saddle-donkeys, lady-ridden, that had presumed to set hoof upon it; while my aunt, rushing out of the house, seized the bridle of a third animal laden with a bestriding child, turned him, led him forth from those sacred precincts, and boxed the ears of the unlucky urchin in attendance who had dared to profane that hallowed ground.

To this hour I don't know whether my aunt had any lawful right of way over that patch of green; but she had settled it in her own mind that she had, and it was all the same to her. The one great outrage of her life, demanding to be constantly avenged, was the passage of a donkey over that immaculate spot. In whatever occupation she was engaged, however interesting to her the conversation in which she was taking part, a donkey turned the current of her ideas in a moment, and she was upon him straight. Jugs of water, and watering-pots, were kept in secret places ready to be discharged on the offending boys; sticks were laid in ambush behind the door; sallies were made at all hours; and incessant war prevailed. Perhaps this was an agreeable excitement to the donkey-boys; or perhaps the more sagacious of the donkeys, understanding how the case stood, delighted with constitutional obstinacy in coming that way. I only know that there were three alarms before the bath was ready; and that on the occasion of the last and most desperate of all, I saw my aunt engage, single-handed, with a sandy-headed lad of fifteen, and bump his sandy head against her own gate, before he seemed to comprehend what was the matter. These interruptions were the more ridiculous to me, because she was giving me broth out of a table spoon at the time (having firmly persuaded herself that I was actually starving, and must receive nourishment at first in very small quantities), and, while my mouth was yet open to receive the spoon, she would put it back into the basin, cry "Janet! Donkeys!" and go out to the assault.

The bath was a great comfort. For I began to be sensible of acute pains in my limbs from lying out in the fields and was now so tired and low that I could hardly keep myself awake for five minutes together. When I had bathed, they (I mean my aunt and Janet) enrobed me in a shirt and a pair of trousers belonging to Mr. Dick, and tied me up in two or three great shawls. What sort of bundle I looked like, I don't know, but I felt a very hot one. Feeling also very faint and drowsy, I soon lay down on the sofa again and fell asleep.

It might have been a dream, originating in the fancy which had occupied my mind so long, but I awoke with the impression that my aunt had come and bent over me, and had put my hair away from my face, and laid my head more comfortably, and had then stood looking at me. The words, "Pretty fellow," or "Poor fellow," seemed to be in my ears, too; but certainly there was nothing else, when I awoke, to lead me to believe that they had been uttered by my aunt, who sat in the bow-window gazing at the sea from behind the green fan, which was mounted on a kind of swivel, and turned any way.

We dined soon after I awoke, off a roast fowl and a pudding; I sitting at table, not unlike a trussed bird myself, and moving my arms with considerable difficulty. But as my aunt had swathed me up, I made no complaint of being inconvenienced. All this time, I was deeply anxious to know what she was going to do with me; but she took her dinner in profound silence, except when she occasionally fixed her eyes on me sitting opposite, and said, "Mercy upon us!" which did not by any means relieve my anxiety.

The cloth being drawn, and some sherry put upon the table (of which I had a glass), my aunt sent up for Mr. Dick again, who joined us, and looked as wise as he could when she requested him to attend to my story, which she elicited from me, gradually, by a course of questions. During my recital, she kept her eyes on Mr. Dick, who I thought would have gone to sleep but for that, and who, whensoever he lapsed into a smile, was checked by a frown from my aunt.

"Whatever possessed that poor unfortunate Baby, that she must go and be married again," said my aunt, when I had finished, "I can't conceive."

"Perhaps she fell in love with her second husband," Mr. Dick suggested.

"Fell in love!" repeated my aunt. "What do you mean? What business had she to do it?"

"Perhaps," Mr. Dick simpered, after thinking a little, "she did it for pleasure."

"Pleasure, indeed!" replied my aunt. "A mighty pleasure for the poor Baby to fix her simple faith upon any dog of a fellow, certain to ill-use her in some way or other. What did she propose to herself, I should like to know! She had had one husband. She had seen David Copperfield

out of the world, who was always running after wax dolls from his cradle. She had got a baby—oh, there were a pair of babies when she gave birth to this child sitting here, that Friday night!—and what more did she want?"

Mr. Dick secretly shook his head at me, as if he thought there was no getting over this.

"She couldn't even have a baby like anybody else," said my aunt. "Where was this child's sister, Betsey Trotwood? Not forthcoming. Don't tell me!"

Mr. Dick seemed quite frightened.

"That little man of a doctor, with his head on one side," said my aunt, "Jellips, or whatever his name was, what was he about? All he could do was to say to me, like a robin redbreast—as he is—'It's a boy.' A boy! Yah, the imbecility of the whole set of 'em!"

The heartiness of the ejaculation startled Mr. Dick exceedingly; and me, too, if I am to tell the truth.

"And then, as if this was not enough, and she had not stood sufficiently in the light of this child's sister, Betsey Trotwood," said my aunt, "she marries a second time—goes and marries a Murderer—or a man with a name like it—and stands in this child's light! And the natural consequence is, as anybody but a baby might have foreseen, that he prowls and wanders. He's as like Cain before he was grown up, as he can be."

Mr. Dick looked hard at me, as if to identify me in this character.

"And then there's that woman with the Pagan name," said my aunt, "that Peggotty, she goes and gets married next. Because she has not seen enough of the evil attending such things, she goes and gets married next, as the child relates. I only hope," said my aunt, shaking her head, "that her husband is one of those Poker husbands who abound in the newspapers, and will beat her well with one."

I could not bear to hear my old nurse so decried, and made the subject of such a wish. I told my aunt that indeed she was mistaken. That Peggotty was the best, the truest, the most faithful, most devoted, and most self-denying friend and servant in the world; who had ever loved me dearly, who had ever loved my mother dearly; who had held my mother's dying head upon her arm, on whose face my mother had imprinted her last grateful kiss. And my remembrance of them both, choking me, I broke down as I was trying to say that her home was my home, and that all she had was mine, and that I would have gone to her for shelter, but for her humble station, which made me fear that I might bring some trouble on her—I broke down, I say, as I was trying to say so, and laid my face in my hands upon the table.

"Well, well!" said my aunt, "the child is right to stand by those who have stood by him.—Janet! Donkeys!"

I thoroughly believe that but for those unfortunate donkeys, we should have come to a good understanding; for my aunt had laid her hand on my shoulder, and the impulse was upon me, thus emboldened, to embrace her and beseech her protection. But the interruption, and the disorder she was thrown into by the struggle outside, put an end to all softer ideas for the present; and kept my aunt indignantly declaiming to Mr. Dick about her determination to appeal for redress to the laws of her country, and to bring actions for trespass against the whole donkey proprietorship of Dover, until tea-time.

After tea, we sat at the window—on the look-out, as I imagined, from my aunt's sharp expression of face, for more invaders—until dusk, when Janet set candles, and a backgammon-board, on the table, and pulled down the blinds.

"Now, Mr. Dick," said my aunt, with her grave look, and her forefinger up as before, "I am going to ask you another question. Look at this child."

"David's son?" said Mr. Dick, with an attentive, puzzled face.

"Exactly so," returned my aunt. "What would you do with him, now?"

"Do with David's son?" said Mr. Dick.

"Ay," replied my aunt, "with David's son."

"Oh!" said Mr. Dick. "Yes. Do with—I should put him to bed."

"Janet!" cried my aunt, with the same complacent triumph that I had remarked before. "Mr. Dick sets us all right. If the bed is ready, we'll take him up to it."

Janet reporting it to be quite ready, I was taken up to it; kindly, but in some sort like a prisoner; my aunt going in front, and Janet bringing up the rear. The only circumstance which gave me any new hope, was my aunt's stopping on the stairs to inquire about a smell of fire that was prevalent there; and Janet's replying that she had been making tinder down in the kitchen, of my old shirt. But there were no other clothes in my room than the odd heap of things I wore; and when I was left there, with a little taper which my aunt forewarned me would burn exactly five minutes, I heard them lock my door on the outside. Turning these things over in my mind, I deemed it possible that my aunt, who could know nothing of me, might suspect I had a habit of running away, and took precautions, on that account, to have me in safe keeping.

The room was a pleasant one, at the top of the house, overlooking the sea, on which the moon was shining brilliantly. After I had said my prayers, and the candle had burnt out, I remember how I still sat looking at the moonlight on the water, as if I could hope to read my fortune in it, as in a bright book; or to see my mother with her child, coming from heaven, along that shining path, to look upon me as she had looked when I last saw her sweet face. I remember how the solemn feeling with which at length I turned my eyes away, yielded to the sensation of gratitude and rest which the sight of the white-curtained bed—and how much more the lying softly down upon it, nestling in the snow-white sheets!—inspired. I remember how I thought of all the solitary places under the night sky where I had slept, and how I prayed that I never might be houseless any more, and never might forget the houseless. I remember how I seemed to float, then, down the melancholy glory of that track upon the sea, away into the world of dreams.

CHAPTER XIV.

MY AUNT MAKES UP HER MIND ABOUT ME.

On going down in the morning, I found my aunt musing so profoundly over the breakfast-table, with her elbow on the tray, that the contents of the urn had overflowed the teapot and were laying the whole table-cloth under water, when my entrance put her meditations to flight. I felt sure that I had been the subject of her reflections, and was more than ever anxious to know her intentions towards me.

Yet I dared not express my anxiety, lest it should give her offence.

My eyes, however, not being so much under control as my tongue, were attracted towards my aunt very often during breakfast. I never could look at her for a few moments together but I found her looking at me—in an odd thoughtful manner, as if I were an immense way off, instead of being on the other side of the small round table. When she had finished her breakfast, my aunt very deliberately leaned back in her chair, knitted her brows, folded her arms, and contemplated me at her leisure with such a fixedness of attention that I was quite overpowered by embarrassment. Not having as yet finished my own breakfast, I attempted to hide my confusion by proceeding with it; but my knife tumbled over my fork, my fork tripped up my knife, I chipped bits of bacon a surprising height into the air instead of cutting them for my own eating, and choked myself with my tea, which persisted in going the wrong way instead of the right one, until I gave in altogether, and sat blushing under my aunt's close scrutiny.

"Hallo!" said my aunt, after a long time.

I looked up, and met her sharp bright glance respectfully.

"I have written to him," said my aunt.

"To——?"

"To your father-in-law," said my aunt. "I have sent him a letter that I'll trouble him to attend to, or he and I will fall out, I can tell him!"

"Does he know where I am, aunt?" I inquired, alarmed.

"I have told him," said my aunt, with a nod.

"Shall I—be—given up to him?" I faltered.

"I don't know," said my aunt. "We shall see."

"Oh! I can't think what I shall do," I exclaimed, "if I have to go back to Mr. Murdstone!"

"I don't know anything about it," said my aunt, shaking her head. "I can't say, I am sure. We shall see."

My spirits sank under these words, and I became very downcast and heavy of heart. My aunt, without appearing to take much heed of me, put on a coarse apron with a bib, which she took out of the press; washed up the teacups with her own hands; and, when everything was washed and set in the tray again, and the cloth folded and put on the top of the whole, rang for Janet to remove it. She next swept up the crumbs with a little broom (putting on a pair of gloves first), until there did not appear to be one microscopic speck left on the carpet; next dusted and arranged the room, which was dusted and arranged to a hair's-breadth already. When all these tasks were performed to her satisfaction, she took off the gloves and apron, folded them up, put them in the particular corner of the press from which they had been taken, brought out her work-box on her own table in the open window, and sat down, with the green fan between her and the light, to work.

"I wish you'd go up-stairs," said my aunt, as she threaded her needle, "and give my compliments to Mr. Dick, and I'll be glad to know how he gets on with his Memorial."

I rose with all alacrity, to acquit myself of this commission.

"I suppose," said my aunt, eyeing me as narrowly as she had eyed her needle in threading it, "you think Mr. Dick a short name, eh?"

"I thought it was rather a short name, yesterday," I confessed.

"You are not to suppose that he hasn't got a longer name, if he chose to use it," said my aunt, with a loftier air. "Babley—Mr. Richard Babley—that's the gentleman's true name."

I was going to suggest, with a modest sense of my youth and the familiarity I had been already guilty of, that I had better give him the full benefit of that name, when my aunt went on to say:

"But don't you call him by it, whatever you do. He can't bear his name. That's a peculiarity of his. Though I don't know that it's much of a peculiarity, either; for he has been ill-used enough, by some that bear it, to have a mortal antipathy for it, Heaven knows. Mr. Dick is his name here, and everywhere else, now—if he ever went anywhere else, which he don't. So take care, child, you don't call him anything *but* Mr. Dick."

I promised to obey, and went up-stairs with my message; thinking, as I went, that if Mr. Dick had been working at his Memorial long, at the same rate as I had seen him working at it, through the open door, when I came down, he was probably getting on very well indeed. I found him still driving at it with a long pen, and his head almost laid upon the paper. He was so intent upon it, that I had ample leisure to observe the large paper kite in a corner, the confusion of bundles of manuscript, the number of pens, and, above all, the quantity of ink (which he seemed to have in, in half-gallon jars by the dozen), before he observed my being present.

"Ha! Phœbus!" said Mr. Dick, laying down his pen. "How does the world go? I'll tell you what," he added, in a lower tone, "I shouldn't wish it to be mentioned, but it's a—" here he beckoned to me, and put his lips close to my ear—"it's a mad world. Mad as Bedlam, boy!" said Mr. Dick, taking snuff from a round box on the table, and laughing heartily.

Without presuming to give my opinion on this question, I delivered my message.

"Well," said Mr. Dick, in answer, "my compliments to her, and I—I believe I have made a start. I think I have made a start," said Mr. Dick, passing his hand among his grey hair, and casting anything but a confident look at his manuscript. "You have been to school?"

"Yes, Sir," I answered; "for a short time."

"Do you recollect the date," said Mr. Dick, looking earnestly at me, and taking up his pen to note it down, "when King Charles the First had his head cut off?"

I said I believed it happened in the year sixteen hundred and forty-nine.

"Well," returned Mr. Dick, scratching his ear with his pen, and looking dubiously at me. "So the books say; but I don't see how that can be. Because, if it was so long ago, how could the people about him have made that mistake of putting some of the trouble out of *his* head, after it was taken off, into *mine?*"

I was very much surprised by the inquiry; but could give no information on this point.

"It's very strange," said Mr. Dick, with a despondent look upon his papers, and with his hand among his hair again, "that I never can get that quite right. I never can make that perfectly clear. But no matter, no matter!" he said cheerfully, and rousing himself, "there's time enough! My compliments to Miss Trotwood, I am getting on very well indeed."

I was going away, when he directed my attention to the kite.

"What do you think of that for a kite?" he said.

I answered that it was a beautiful one. I should think it must have been as much as seven feet high.

"I made it. We'll go and fly it, you and I," said Mr. Dick. "Do you see this?"

He showed me that it was covered with manuscript, very closely and laboriously written; but so plainly, that as I looked along the lines, I thought I saw some allusion to King Charles the First's head again, in one or two places.

"There's plenty of string," said Mr. Dick, "and when it flies high, it takes the facts a long way. That's my manner of diffusing 'em. I don't know where they may come down. It's according to circumstances, and the wind, and so forth; but I take my chance of **that**."

His face was so very **mild** and pleasant, and had something so reverend in it, though it was hale and hearty, that I was not sure but that **he** was having a good-humoured jest with me. So I laughed, and he laughed, and we parted the best friends possible.

"Well, child," said my aunt, when I went down stairs. "And what of Mr. Dick, this morning?"

I informed her that he sent his compliments, and was getting on very well indeed.

"What do you think of him?" said my aunt.

I had some shadowy idea of endeavouring to evade the question, by replying that I thought him a very nice gentleman; but my aunt was not to be so put off, for she laid her work down in her lap, and said, folding her hands upon it:

"Come! Your sister Betsey Trotwood would have told me what she thought of anyone, directly. Be as like your sister as you can, and speak out!"

"Is he—is Mr. Dick—I ask because I don't know, aunt—is he at all out of his mind, then?" I stammered; for I felt I was on dangerous ground.

"Not a morsel," said my aunt.

"Oh, indeed!" I observed faintly.

"If there is anything in the world," said my aunt, with great decision and force of manner, "that Mr. Dick is not, it's that."

I had nothing better to offer, than another timid "Oh, indeed!"

"He has been *called* mad," said my aunt. "I have a selfish pleasure in saying he has been called mad, or I should not have had the benefit of his society and advice for these last ten years and upwards—in fact, ever **since** your sister, Betsey Trotwood, disappointed me."

"So long as that?" I said.

"And nice people they were, who had the audacity to call him mad," pursued my aunt. "Mr. Dick is a sort of distant connexion of mine; it doesn't matter how; I needn't enter into that. If it hadn't been for me, his own brother would have shut him up for life. That's all."

I am afraid it was hypocritical in me, but seeing that my aunt felt strongly on the subject, I tried to look as if I felt strongly too.

"A proud fool!" said my aunt. "Because his brother was a little eccentric—though he is not half so eccentric as a good many people—he didn't like to have him visible about his house, and sent him away to some private asylum-place: though he had been left to his particular care by their deceased father, who thought him almost a natural. And a wise man *he* must have been to think so! Mad himself, no doubt."

Again, as my aunt looked quite convinced, I endeavoured to look quite convinced also.

"So I stepped in," said my aunt, "and made him an offer. I said, ' Your brother's sane—a great deal more sane than you are, or ever will be, it is to be hoped. Let him have his little income, and come and live with me. *I* am not afraid of him, *I* am not proud, *I* am ready to take care of him, and shall not ill-treat him as some people (besides the asylum-folks) have done.' After a good deal of squabbling," said my aunt, "I got him; and he has been here ever since. He is the most friendly and amenable creature in existence; and as for advice!—But nobody knows what that man's mind is, except myself."

My aunt smoothed her dress and shook her head, as if she smoothed defiance of the whole world out of the one, and shook it out of the other.

"He had a favourite sister," said my aunt, "a good creature, and very kind to him. But she did what they all do —took a husband. And *he* did what they all do—made her wretched. It had such an effect upon the mind of Mr. Dick (*that's* not madness, I hope!) that, combined with his fear of his brother, and his sense of his unkindness, it threw him into a fever. That was before he came to me, but the recollection of it is oppressive to him even now. Did he say anything to you about King Charles the First, child?"

"Yes, aunt."

"Ah!" said my aunt, rubbing her nose as if she were a little vexed. "That's his allegorical way of expressing it. He connects his illness with great disturbance and agitation, naturally, and that's the figure, or the simile, or whatever it's called, which he chooses to use. And why shouldn't he, if he thinks proper?"

I said: "Certainly, aunt."

"It's not a business-like way of speaking," said my aunt, "nor a worldly way. I am aware of that; and that's the reason why I insist upon it, that there shan't be a word about it in his Memorial."

"Is it a Memorial about his own history that he is writing, aunt?"

"Yes, child," said my aunt, rubbing her nose again. "He is memorialising the Lord Chancellor, or the Lord Somebody or other—one of those people, at all events, who are paid to *be* memorialised—about his affairs. I suppose it will go in, one of these days. He hasn't been able to draw it up yet, without introducing that mode of expressing himself; but it don't signify; it keeps him employed."

In fact, I found out afterwards that Mr. Dick had been for upwards of ten years endeavouring to keep King Charles the First out of the Memorial; but he had been constantly getting into it, and was there now.

"I say again," said my aunt, "nobody knows what that man's mind is except myself; and he's the most amenable and friendly creature in existence. If he likes to fly a kite sometimes, what of that? Franklin used to fly a kite. He was a Quaker, or something of that sort, if I am not mistaken. And a Quaker flying a kite is a much more ridiculous object than anybody else."

If I could have supposed that my aunt had recounted these particulars for my especial behoof, and as a piece of confidence in me, I should have felt very much distinguished, and should have augured favourably from such a mark of her good opinion. But I could hardly help observing that she had launched into them, chiefly because the question was raised in her own mind, and with very little reference to me, though she had addressed herself to me in the absence of anybody else.

At the same time, I must say that the generosity of her championship of poor harmless Mr. Dick, not only inspired

my young breast with some selfish hope for **myself**, but warmed it unselfishly towards her. I believe that I began to know that there was something about my aunt, notwithstanding her many eccentricities and odd humours, to be honoured and trusted in. Though she was just as sharp that day, as on the day before, and was in and out about the donkeys just as often, and was thrown into a tremendous state of indignation, when a young man, going by, ogled Janet at a window (which was one of the gravest misdemeanours that could be committed against my aunt's dignity), she seemed to me to command more of my respect, if not less of my fear.

The anxiety I underwent, in the interval which necessarily elapsed before a reply could be received to her letter to Mr. Murdstone, was extreme; but I made an endeavour to suppress it, and to be as agreeable as I could in a quiet way, both to my aunt and Mr. Dick. The latter and I would have gone out to fly the great kite; but that I had still no other clothes than the anything but ornamental garments with which I had been decorated on the first day, and which confined me to the house, except for an hour after dark, when my aunt, for my health's sake, paraded me up and down on the cliff outside before going to bed. At length the reply from Mr. Murdstone came, and my aunt informed me, to my infinite terror, that he was coming to speak to her himself on the next day. On the next day, still bundled up in my curious habiliments, I sat counting the time, flushed and heated by the conflict of sinking hopes and rising fears within me; and waiting to be startled by the sight of the gloomy face, whose non-arrival startled me every minute.

My aunt was a little more imperious and stern than usual, but I observed no other token of her preparing herself to receive the visitor so much dreaded by me. She sat at work in the window, and I sat by, with my thoughts running astray on all possible and impossible results of Mr. Murdstone's visit, until pretty late in the afternoon. Our dinner had been indefinitely postponed; but it was growing so late, that my aunt had ordered it to be got ready, when she gave a sudden alarm of donkeys, and to my consternation and amazement, I beheld Miss Murdstone, on a side-saddle, ride deliberately over the sacred piece of green, and stop in front of the house, looking about her.

"Go along with you!" cried my aunt, shaking her head and her fist at the window. "You have no business there. How dare you trespass? Go along! Oh! you bold-faced thing!"

My aunt was so exasperated by the coolness with which Miss Murdstone looked about her, that I really believe she was motionless, and unable for the moment to dart out according to custom. I seized the opportunity to inform her who it was; and that the gentleman now coming near the offender (for the way up was very steep, and he had dropped behind) was Mr. Murdstone himself.

"I don't care who it is!" cried my aunt, still shaking her head, and gesticulating anything but welcome from the bow-window. "I won't be trespassed upon. I won't allow it. Go away! Janet, turn him round. Lead him off!" and I saw, from behind my aunt, a sort of hurried battle-piece, in which the donkey stood resisting everybody, with all his four legs planted different ways, while Janet tried to pull him round by the bridle, Mr. Murdstone tried to lead him on, Miss Murdstone struck at Janet with a parasol, and several boys, who had come to see the engagement, shouted vigorously. But my aunt, suddenly descrying among them the young malefactor who was the donkey's guardian, and who was one of the most inveterate offenders' against her, though hardly in his teens, rushed out to the scene of action, pounced upon him, captured him, dragged him, with his jacket over his head, and his heels grinding the ground, into the garden, and, calling upon Janet to fetch the constables and justices, that he might be taken, tried, and executed on the spot, held him at bay there. This part of the business, however, did not last long; for the young rascal, being expert at a variety of feints and dodges, of which my aunt had no conception, soon went whooping away, leaving some deep impressions of his nailed boots in the flower-beds, and taking his donkey in triumph with him.

Miss Murdstone, during the latter portion of the contest, had dismounted, and was now waiting with her brother at the bottom of the steps, until my aunt should be at leisure to receive them. My aunt, a little ruffled by the combat, marched past them into the house, with great dignity, and took no notice of their presence, until they were announced by Janet.

"Shall I go away, aunt?" I asked, trembling.

"No, Sir," said my aunt. "Certainly not!" With which she pushed me into a corner near her, and fenced me in with a chair, as if it were a prison or a bar of justice. This position I continued to occupy during the whole interview, and from it I now saw Mr. and Miss Murdstone enter the room.

"Oh!" said my aunt, "I was not aware at first to whom I had the pleasure of objecting. But I don't allow anybody to ride over that turf. I make no exceptions. I don't allow anybody to do it."

"Your regulation is rather awkward to strangers," said Miss Murdstone.

"Is it!" said my aunt.

Mr. Murdstone seemed afraid of a renewal of hostilities, and interposing began:

"Miss Trotwood!"

"I beg your pardon," observed my aunt with a keen look. "You are the Mr. Murdstone who married the widow of my late nephew, David Copperfield, of Blunderstone Rookery?—Though why Rookery, I don't know!"

"I am," said Mr. Murdstone.

"You'll excuse my saying, Sir," returned my aunt, "that I think it would have been a much better and happier thing if you had left that poor child alone."

"I so far agree with what Miss Trotwood has remarked," observed Miss Murdstone, bridling, "that I consider our lamented Clara to have been, in all essential respects, a mere child."

"It is a comfort to you and me, ma'am," said my aunt, "who are getting on in life, and are not likely to be made unhappy by our personal attractions, that nobody can say the same of us."

"No doubt!" returned Miss Murdstone, though, I thought, not with a very ready or gracious assent. "And it certainly might have been, as you say, a better and happier thing for my brother if he had never entered into such a marriage. I have always been of that opinion."

"I have no doubt you have," said my aunt. "Janet," ringing the bell, "my compliments to Mr. Dick, and beg him to come down."

Until he came, my aunt sat perfectly upright and stiff, frowning at the wall. When he came, my aunt performed the ceremony of introduction.

"Mr. Dick. An old and intimate friend. On whose judgment," said my aunt, with emphasis, as an admonition to Mr. Dick, who was biting his forefinger and looking rather foolish, "I rely."

Mr. Dick took his finger out of his mouth, on this hint, and stood among the group, with a grave and attentive expression of face. My aunt inclined her head to Mr. Murdstone, who went on:

"Miss Trotwood. On the receipt of your letter, I considered it an act of greater justice to myself, and perhaps of more respect to you——"

"Thank you," said my aunt, still eyeing him keenly. "You needn't mind me."

"To answer it in person, however inconvenient the journey," pursued Mr. Murdstone, "rather than by letter. This unhappy boy who has run away from his friends and his occupation——"

"And whose appearance," interposed his sister, directing general attention to me in my indefinable costume, "is perfectly scandalous and disgraceful."

"Jane Murdstone," said her brother, "have the goodness not to interrupt me. This unhappy boy, Miss Trotwood, has been the occasion of much domestic trouble and uneasiness; both during the lifetime of my late dear wife, and since. He has a sullen, rebellious spirit; a violent temper; and an untoward, intractable disposition. Both my sister and myself have endeavoured to correct his vices, but ineffectually. And I have felt—we both have felt, I may say; my sister being fully in my confidence—that it is right you should receive this grave and dispassionate assurance from our lips."

"It can hardly be necessary for me to confirm anything stated by my brother," said Miss Murdstone; "but I beg to observe, that, of all the boys in the world, I believe this is the worst boy."

"Strong!" said my aunt, shortly.

"But not at all too strong for the facts," returned Miss Murdstone.

"Ha!" said my aunt. "Well, Sir?"

"I have my own opinions," resumed Mr. Murdstone, whose face darkened more and more, the more he and my aunt observed each other, which they did very narrowly, "as to the best mode of bringing him up; they are founded, in part, on my knowledge of him, and in part on my knowledge of my own means and resources. I am responsible for them to myself, I act upon them, and I say no more about them. It is enough that I place this boy under the eye of a friend of my own, in a respectable business; that it does not please him; that he runs away from it; makes himself a common vagabond about the country; and comes here, in rags, to appeal to you, Miss Trotwood. I wish to set before you, honourably, the exact consequences—so far as they are within my knowledge—of your abetting him in this appeal."

"But about the respectable business first," said my aunt. "If he had been your own boy, you would have put him to it, just the same, I suppose?"

"If he had been my brother's own boy," returned Miss Murdstone, striking in, "his character, I trust, would have been altogether different."

"Or if the poor child, his mother, had been alive, he would still have gone into the respectable business, would he?" said my aunt.

"I believe," said Mr. Murdstone, with an inclination of his head, "that Clara would have disputed nothing, which myself and my sister Jane Murdstone were agreed was for the best."

Miss Murdstone confirmed this with an audible murmur.

"Humph!" said my aunt. "Unfortunate baby!"

Mr. Dick, who had been rattling his money all this time, was rattling it so loudly now, that my aunt felt it necessary to check him with a look, before saying:

"The poor child's annuity died with her?"

"Died with her," replied Mr. Murdstone.

"And there was no settlement of the little property—the house and garden—the what's-its-name Rookery without any rooks in it—upon her boy?"

"It had been left to her, unconditionally, by her first husband," Mr. Murdstone began, when my aunt caught him up with the greatest irascibility and impatience.

"Good Lord, man, there's no occasion to say that. Left to her unconditionally! I think I see David Copperfield looking forward to any condition of any sort or kind, though it stared him point-blank in the face! Of course it was left to her unconditionally. But when she married again—when she took that most disastrous step of marrying you, in short," said my aunt, "to be plain—did no one put in a word for the boy at that time?"

"My late wife loved her second husband, madam," said Mr. Murdstone, "and trusted implicitly in him."

"Your late wife, Sir, was a most unworldly, most unhappy, most unfortunate baby," returned my aunt, shaking her head at him. "That's what *she* was. And now, what have you got to say next?"

"Merely this, Miss Trotwood," he returned. "I am here to take David back; to take him back unconditionally, to dispose of him as I think proper, and to deal with him as I think right. I am not here to make any promise, or give any pledge to anybody. You may possibly have some idea, Miss Trotwood, of abetting him in his running away, and in his complaints to you. Your manner, which I must say does not seem intended to propitiate, induces me to think it possible. Now I must caution you that if you abet him once, you abet him for good and all; if you step in between him and me, now, you must step in, Miss Trotwood, for ever. I cannot trifle, or be trifled with. I am here, for the first and last time, to take him away. Is he ready to go? If he is not—and you tell me he is not; on any pretence; it is indifferent to me what—my doors are shut against him henceforth, and yours, I take it for granted, are open to him."

To this address, my aunt had listened with the closest attention, sitting perfectly upright, with her hands folded on one knee, and looking grimly on the speaker. When he had finished, she turned her eyes so as to command Miss Murdstone, without otherwise disturbing her attitude, and said:

"Well, ma'am, have *you* got anything to remark?"

"Indeed, Miss Trotwood," said Miss Murdstone, "all that I could say has been so well said by my brother, and all that I know to be the fact has been so plainly stated by him, that I have nothing to add except my thanks for your politeness. For your very great politeness, I am sure," said Miss Murdstone; with an irony which no more affected my aunt than it discomposed the cannon I had slept by at Chatham.

"And what does the boy say?" said my aunt. "Are you ready to go, David?"

I answered no, and entreated her not to let me go. I

said that neither Mr. nor Miss Murdstone had ever liked me, or had ever been kind to me. That they had made my mama, who always loved me dearly, unhappy about me, and that I knew it well, and that Peggotty knew it. I said that I had been more miserable than I thought anybody could believe who only knew how young I was. And I begged and prayed my aunt—I forget in what terms now, but I remember that they affected me very much then—to befriend and protect me, for my father's sake.

"Mr. Dick," said my aunt; "what shall I do with this child?"

Mr. Dick considered, hesitated, brightened, and rejoined, "Have him measured for a suit of clothes directly."

"Mr. Dick," said my aunt triumphantly, "give me your hand, for your common sense is invaluable." Having shaken it with great cordiality, she pulled me towards her and said to Mr. Murdstone:

"You can go when you like; I'll take my chance with the boy. If he's all you say he is, at least I can do as much for him then, as you have done. But I don't believe a word of it."

"Miss Trotwood," rejoined Mr. Murdstone, shrugging his shoulders, as he rose, "if you were a gentleman——"

"Bah! Stuff and nonsense!" said my aunt. "Don't talk to me!"

"How exquisitely polite!" exclaimed Miss Murdstone, rising. "Overpowering, really!"

"Do you think I don't know," said my aunt, turning a deaf ear to the sister, and continuing to address the brother, and to shake her head at him with infinite expression, "what kind of life you must have led that poor, unhappy, misdirected baby? Do you think I don't know what a woeful day it was for the soft little creature when *you* first came in her way—smirking and making great eyes at her, I'll be bound, as if you couldn't say boh! to a goose!"

"I never heard anything so elegant!" said Miss Murdstone.

"Do you think I can't understand you as well as if I had seen you," pursued my aunt, "now that I *do* see and hear you—which I tell you candidly, is anything but a pleasure to me? Oh yes, bless us! who so smooth and silky as Mr. Murdstone at first! The poor, benighted innocent had never seen such a man. He was made of sweetness. He worshipped her. He doted on her boy—tenderly doted on him. He was to be another father to him, and they were all to live together in a garden of roses, weren't they? Ugh! Get along with you, do!" said my aunt.

"I never heard anything like this person in my life!" exclaimed Miss Murdstone.

"And when you had made sure of the poor little fool," said my aunt—"God forgive me that I should call her so, and she gone where *you* won't go in a hurry—because you had not done wrong enough to her and hers, you must begin to train her, must you? begin to break her, like a poor caged bird, and wear her deluded life away, in teaching her to sing *your* notes?"

"This is either insanity or intoxication," said Miss Murdstone, in a perfect agony at not being able to turn the current of my aunt's address towards herself; "and my suspicion is that it's intoxication."

Miss Betsey, without taking the least notice of the interruption, continued to address herself to Mr. Murdstone as if there had been no such thing.

"Mr. Murdstone," she said, shaking her finger at him, "you were a tyrant to the simple baby, and you broke her heart. She was a loving baby—I know that; I knew it, years before *you* ever saw her—and through the best part of her weakness, you gave her the wounds she died of. There is the truth for your comfort, however you like it. And you and your instruments may make the most of it."

"Allow me to inquire, Miss Trotwood," interposed Miss Murdstone, "whom you are pleased to call, in a choice of words in which I am not experienced, my brother's instruments?"

Still stone-deaf to the voice, and utterly unmoved by it, Miss Betsey pursued her discourse.

"It was clear enough, as I have told you, years before *you* ever saw her—and why, in the mysterious dispensations of Providence, you ever did see her, is more than humanity can comprehend—it was clear enough that the poor soft little thing would marry somebody, at some time or other; but I did hope it wouldn't have been as bad as it has turned out. That was the time, Mr. Murdstone, when she gave birth to her boy here," said my aunt; "to the poor child you sometimes tormented her through afterwards, which is a disagreeable remembrance, and makes the sight of him odious now. Ay, ay! you needn't wince!" said my aunt. "I know it's true without that."

He had stood by the door, all this while, observant of her, with a smile upon his face, though his black eyebrows were heavily contracted. I remarked now, that, though the smile was on his face still, his colour had gone in a moment, and he seemed to breathe as if he had been running.

"Good day, Sir," said my aunt, "and good-bye. Good day to you too, ma'am," said my aunt, turning suddenly upon his sister. "Let me see you ride a donkey over *my* green again, and as sure as you have a head upon your shoulders, I'll knock your bonnet off, and tread upon it!"

It would require a painter, and no common painter too, to depict my aunt's face as she delivered herself of this very unexpected sentiment, and Miss Murdstone's face as she heard it. But the manner of the speech, no less than the matter, was so fiery, that Miss Murdstone, without a word in answer, discreetly put her arm through her brother's, and walked haughtily out of the cottage; my aunt remaining in the window looking after them; prepared, I have no doubt, in case of the donkey's reappearance, to carry her threat into instant execution.

No attempt at defiance being made, however, her face gradually relaxed, and became so pleasant, that I was emboldened to kiss and thank her; which I did with great heartiness, and with both my arms clasped round her neck. I then shook hands with Mr. Dick, who shook hands with me a great many times, and hailed this happy close of the proceedings with repeated bursts of laughter.

"You'll consider yourself guardian, jointly with me, of this child, Mr. Dick," said my aunt.

"I shall be delighted," said Mr. Dick, "to be the guardian of David's son."

"Very good," returned my aunt, "*that's* settled. I have been thinking, do you know, Mr. Dick, that I might call him Trotwood?"

"Certainly, certainly. Call him Trotwood, certainly," said Mr. Dick. "David's son's Trotwood."

"Trotwood Copperfield, you mean," returned my aunt.

"Yes, to be sure. Yes. Trotwood Copperfield," said Mr. Dick, a little abashed.

My aunt took so kindly to the notion, that some ready made clothes, which were purchased for me that afternoon, were marked "Trotwood Copperfield," in her own hand-writing, and in indelible marking-ink, before I put them on; and it was settled that all the other clothes which were ordered to be made for me (a complete outfit was bespoke that afternoon) should be marked in the same way.

Thus I began my new life, in a new name, and with everything new about me. Now that the state of doubt was over, I felt, for many days, like one in a dream. I never thought that I had a curious couple of guardians, in my aunt and Mr. Dick. I never thought of anything about myself, distinctly. The two things clearest in my mind were, that a remoteness had come upon the old Blunderstone life—which seemed to lie in the haze of an immeasurable distance; and that a curtain had for ever fallen on my life at Murdstone and Grinby's. No one has ever raised that curtain since. I have lifted it for a moment, even in this narrative, with a reluctant hand, and dropped it gladly. The remembrance of that life is fraught with so much pain to me, with so much mental suffering and want of hope, that I have never had the courage even to examine how long I was doomed to lead it. Whether it lasted for a year, or more, or less, I do not know. I only know that it was, and ceased to be; and that I have written, and there I leave it.

CHAPTER XV.

I MAKE ANOTHER BEGINNING.

Mr. Dick and I soon became the best of friends, and very often, when his day's work was done, went out together to fly the great kite. Every day of his life he had a long sitting at the Memorial, which never made the least progress, however hard he laboured, for King Charles the First always strayed into it, sooner or later, and then it was thrown aside, and another one begun. The patience and hope with which he bore these perpetual disappointments, the mild perception he had that there was something wrong about King Charles the First, the feeble efforts he made to keep him out, and the certainty with which he came in, and tumbled the Memorial out of all shape, made a deep impression upon me. What Mr. Dick supposed would come of the Memorial, if it were completed; where he thought it was to go, or what he thought it was to do; he knew no more than anybody else, I believe. Nor was it at all necessary that he should trouble himself with such questions, for if anything were certain under the sun, it was certain that the Memorial never would be finished.

It was quite an affecting sight, I used to think, to see him with the kite when it was up a great height in the air. What he had told me, in his room, about his belief in its disseminating the statements pasted on it, which were nothing but old leaves of abortive Memorials, might have been a fancy with him sometimes; but not when he was out, looking up at the kite in the sky, and feeling it pull and tug at his hands. He never looked so serene as he did then. I used to fancy, as I sat by him of an evening, on a green slope, and saw him watch the kite high in the quiet air, that it lifted his mind out of its confusion, and bore it (such was my boyish thought) into the skies. As he wound the string in, and it came lower and lower down out of the beautiful light, until it fluttered to the ground, and lay there like a dead thing, he seemed to wake gradually out of a dream; and I remember to have seen him take it up, and look about him in a lost way, as if they had both come down together, so that I pitied him with all my heart.

While I advanced in friendship and intimacy with Mr. Dick, I did not go backward in the favour of his staunch friend, my aunt. She took so kindly to me, that, in the course of a few weeks, she shortened my adopted name of Trotwood into Trot; and even encouraged me to hope that if I went on as I had begun, I might take equal rank in her affections with my sister Betsey Trotwood.

"Trot," said my aunt one evening, when the backgammon-board was placed as usual for herself and Mr. Dick, "we must not forget your education."

This was my only subject of anxiety, and I felt quite delighted by her referring to it.

"Should you like to go to school at Canterbury?" said my aunt.

I replied that I should like it very much, as it was so near her.

"Good," said my aunt. "Should you like to go to-morrow?"

Being already no stranger to the general rapidity of my aunt's evolutions, I was not surprised by the suddenness of the proposal, and said: "Yes."

"Good," said my aunt again. "Janet, hire the grey pony and chaise to-morrow morning at ten o'clock, and pack up Master Trotwood's clothes to-night."

I was greatly elated by these orders; but my heart smote me for my selfishness, when I witnessed their effect on Mr. Dick, who was so low-spirited at the prospect of our separation, and played so ill in consequence, that my aunt, after giving him several admonitory raps on the knuckles with her dice-box, shut up the board, and declined to play with him any more. But, on hearing from my aunt that I should sometimes come over on a Saturday, and that he could sometimes come and see me on a Wednesday, he revived; and vowed to make another kite for those occasions, of proportions greatly surpassing the present one. In the morning he was down-hearted again, and would have sustained himself by giving me all the money he had in his possession, gold and silver too, if my aunt had not interposed, and limited the gift to five shillings, which, at his earnest petition, were afterwards increased to ten. We parted at the garden-gate in a most affectionate manner, and Mr. Dick did not go into the house until my aunt had driven me out of sight of it.

My aunt, who was perfectly indifferent to public opinion, drove the grey pony through Dover in a masterly manner; sitting high and stiff like a state coachman, keeping a steady eye upon him wherever he went, and making a point of not letting him have his own way in any respect. When we came into the country road, she permitted him to relax a little, however; and looking at me down in a valley of cushion by her side, asked me whether I was happy?

"Very happy indeed, thank you, aunt," I said.

She was much gratified; and both her hands being occupied, patted me on the head with her whip.

"Is it a large school, aunt?" I asked.

"Why, I don't know," said my aunt. "We are going to Mr. Wickfield's first."

"Does *he* keep a school?" I asked.

"No, Trot," said my aunt. "He keeps an office."

I asked for no more information about Mr. Wickfield, as she offered none, and we conversed on other subjects until we came to Canterbury, where, as it was market-day, my aunt had a great opportunity of insinuating the grey pony among carts, baskets, vegetables, and hucksters' goods. The hair-breadth turns and twists we made, drew down upon us a variety of speeches from the people standing about, which were not always complimentary; but my aunt drove on with perfect indifference, and I dare say would have taken her own way with as much coolness through an enemy's country.

At length we stopped before a very old house bulging out over the road; a house with long low lattice-windows bulging out still farther, and beams with carved heads on the ends bulging out too, so that I fancied the whole house was leaning forward, trying to see who was passing on the narrow pavement below. It was quite spotless in its cleanliness. The old-fashioned brass knocker on the low arched door, ornamented with carved garlands of fruit and flowers, twinkled like a star; the two stone steps descending to the door were as white as if they had been covered with fair linen; and all the angles and corners, and carvings and mouldings, and quaint little panes of glass, and quainter little windows, though as old as the hills, were as pure as any snow that ever fell upon the hills.

When the pony-chaise stopped at the door, and my eyes were intent upon the house, I saw a cadaverous face appear at a small window on the ground floor (in a little round tower that formed one side of the house), and quickly disappear. The low arched door then opened, and the face came out. It was quite as cadaverous as it had looked in the window, though in the grain of it there was that tinge of red which is sometimes to be observed in the skins of red-haired people. It belonged to a red-haired person—a youth of fifteen, as I take it now, but looking much older—whose hair was cropped as close as the closest stubble; who had hardly any eyebrows, and no eyelashes, and eyes of a red-brown, so unsheltered and unshaded, that I remember wondering how he went to sleep. He was high-shouldered and bony; dressed in decent black, with a white wisp of a neckcloth; buttoned up to the throat; and had a long, lank, skeleton hand, which particularly attracted my attention, as he stood at the pony's head, rubbing his chin with it, and looking up at us in the chaise.

"Is Mr. Wickfield at home, Uriah Heep?" said my aunt.

"Mr. Wickfield's at home, ma'am," said Uriah Heep, "if you'll please to walk in there—" pointing with his long hand to the room he meant.

We got out; and leaving him to hold the pony, went into a long low parlour looking towards the street, from the window of which I caught a glimpse, as I went in, of Uriah Heep breathing into the pony's nostrils, and immediately covering them with his hand, as if he were putting some spell upon him. Opposite to the tall old chimney-piece, were two portraits: one of a gentleman with grey hair (though not by any means an old man) and black eyebrows, who was looking over some papers tied together with red tape; the other, of a lady, with a very placid and sweet expression of face, who was looking at me.

I believe I was turning about in search of Uriah's picture, when, a door at the farther end of the room opening, a gentleman entered, at sight of whom I turned to the first-mentioned portrait again, to make quite sure that it had not come out of its frame. But it was stationary; and as the gentleman advanced into the light, I saw that he was some years older than when he had had his picture painted.

"Miss Betsey Trotwood," said the gentleman, "pray walk in. I was engaged for a moment, but you'll excuse my being busy. You know my motive. I have but one in life."

Miss Betsey thanked him, and we went into his room, which was furnished as an office, with books, papers, tin boxes, and so forth. It looked into a garden, and had an iron safe let into the wall; so immediately over the mantel-shelf, that I wondered, as I sat down, how the sweeps got round it when they swept the chimney.

"Well, Miss Trotwood," said Mr. Wickfield; for I soon found that it was he, and that he was a lawyer, and steward of the estates of a rich gentleman of the county; "what wind blows you here? Not an ill wind, I hope?"

"No," replied my aunt, "I have not come for any law."

"That's right, ma'am," said Mr. Wickfield. "You had better come for anything else."

His hair was quite white now, though his eyebrows were still black. He had a very agreeable face, and, I thought, was handsome. There was a certain richness in his complexion, which I had been long accustomed, under Peggotty's tuition, to connect with port wine; and I fancied it was in his voice too, and referred his growing corpulency to the same cause. He was very cleanly dressed, in a blue coat, striped waistcoat, and nankeen trousers; and his fine frilled shirt and cambric neckcloth looked unusually soft and white, reminding my strolling fancy (I call to mind) of the plumage on the breast of a swan.

"This is my nephew," said my aunt.

"Wasn't aware you had one, Miss Trotwood," said Mr. Wickfield.

"My grand-nephew, that is to say," observed my aunt.

"Wasn't aware you had a grand-nephew, I give you my word," said Mr. Wickfield.

"I have adopted him," said my aunt, with a wave of her hand, importing that his knowledge and his ignorance were all one to her, "and I have brought him here, to put him to a school where he may be thoroughly well taught, and well treated. Now tell me where that school is, and what it is, and all about it."

"Before I can advise you properly," said Mr. Wickfield, —"the old question, you know. What's your motive in this?"

"Deuce take the man!" exclaimed my aunt. "Always fishing for motives, when they're on the surface! Why, to make the child happy and useful."

"It must be a mixed motive, I think," said Mr. Wickfield, shaking his head and smiling incredulously.

"A mixed fiddlestick!" returned my aunt. "You claim to have one plain motive in all you do yourself. You don't suppose, I hope, that you are the only plain dealer in the world?"

"Ay, but I have only one motive in life, Miss Trotwood," he rejoined, smiling. "Other people have dozens, scores, hundreds. I have only one. There's the difference. However, that's beside the question. The best school? Whatever the motive, you want the best?"

My aunt nodded assent.

"At the best we have," said Mr. Wickfield, considering, "your nephew couldn't board just now."

"But he could board somewhere else, I suppose?" suggested my aunt.

Mr. Wickfield thought I could. After a little discussion, he proposed to take my aunt to the school, that she might see it and judge for herself; also, to take her, with the same object, to two or three houses where he thought I could be boarded. My aunt embracing the proposal, we were all three going out together, when he stopped and said:

"Our little friend here might have some motive, perhaps, for objecting to the arrangements. I think we had better leave him behind?"

My aunt seemed disposed to contest the point; but to facilitate matters I said I would gladly remain behind, if they pleased; and returned into Mr. Wickfield's office, where I sat down again, in the chair I had first occupied, to await their return.

It so happened that this chair was opposite a narrow passage, which ended in the little circular room where I had seen Uriah Heep's pale face looking out of window. Uriah, having taken the pony to a neighbouring stable, was at work at a desk in this room, which had a brass frame on the top to hang papers upon, and on which the writing he was making a copy of was then hanging. Though his face was towards me, I thought, for some time, the writing being between us, that he could not see me; but looking that way more attentively, it made me uncomfortable to observe that, every now and then, his sleepless eyes would come below the writing, like two red suns, and stealthily stare at me for I dare say a whole minute at a time, during which his pen went, or pretended to go, as cleverly as ever. I made several attempts to get out of their way—such as standing on a chair to look at a map on the other side of the room, and poring over the columns of a Kentish newspaper—but they always attracted me back again; and whenever I looked towards those two red suns, I was sure to find them, either just rising, or just setting.

At length, much to my relief, my aunt and Mr. Wickfield came back, after a pretty long absence. They were not so successful as I could have wished; for though the advantages of the school were undeniable, my aunt had not approved of any of the boarding-houses proposed for me.

"It's very unfortunate," said my aunt. "I don't know what to do, Trot."

"It *does* happen unfortunately," said Mr. Wickfield. "But I'll tell you what you can do, Miss Trotwood."

"What's that?" inquired my aunt.

"Leave your nephew here, for the present. He's a quiet fellow. He won't disturb me at all. It's a capital house for study. As quiet as a monastery, and almost as roomy. Leave him here."

My aunt evidently liked the offer, though she was delicate of accepting it. So did I.

"Come, Miss Trotwood," said Mr. Wickfield. "This is the way out of the difficulty. It's only a temporary arrangement, you know. If it don't act well, or don't quite accord with our mutual convenience, he can easily go to the right-about. There will be time to find some better place for him in the meanwhile. You had better determine to leave him here for the present!"

"I am very much obliged to you," said my aunt; "and so is he, I see; but——"

"Come! I know what you mean," cried Mr. Wickfield. "You shall not be oppressed by the receipt of favours, Miss

Trotwood. You may pay for him, if you like. We won't be hard about terms, but you shall pay if you will."

"On that understanding," said my aunt, "though it doesn't lessen the real obligation, I shall be very glad to leave him."

"Then come and see my little housekeeper," said Mr. Wickfield.

We accordingly went up a wonderful old staircase; with a balustrade so broad that we might have gone up that, almost as easily; and into a shady old drawing-room, lighted by some three or four of the quaint windows I had looked up at from the street: which had old oak seats in them, that seemed to have come of the same trees as the shining oak floor, and the great beams in the ceiling. It was a prettily furnished room, with a piano and some lively furniture in red and green, and some flowers. It seemed to be all old nooks and corners; and in every nook and corner there was some queer little table, or cupboard, or bookcase, or seat, or something or other, that made me think there was not such another good corner in the room; until I looked at the next one, and found it equal to it, if not better. On everything there was the same air of retirement and cleanliness that marked the house outside.

Mr. Wickfield tapped at a door in a corner of the panelled wall, and a girl of about my own age came quickly out and kissed him. On her face, I saw immediately the placid and sweet expression of the lady whose picture had looked at me down-stairs. It seemed to my imagination as if the portrait had grown womanly, and the original remained a child. Although her face was quite bright and happy, there was a tranquillity about it, and about her—a quiet, good, calm spirit—that I never have forgotten; that I never shall forget.

This was his little housekeeper, his daughter Agnes, Mr. Wickfield said. When I heard how he said it, and saw how he held her hand, I guessed what the one motive of his life was.

She had a little basket-trifle hanging at her side, with keys in it; and looked as staid and as discreet a housekeeper as the old house could have. She listened to her father as he told her about me, with a pleasant face; and when he had concluded, proposed to my aunt that we should go up-stairs and see my room. We all went together, she before us: and a glorious old room it was, with more oak beams, and diamond panes; and the broad balustrade going all the way up to it.

I cannot call to mind where or when, in my childhood, I had seen a stained-glass window in a church. Nor do I recollect its subject. But I know that when I saw her turn round, in the grave light of the old staircase, and wait for us, above, I thought of that window; and that I associated something of its tranquil brightness with Agnes Wickfield ever afterwards.

My aunt was as happy as I was, in the arrangement made for me; and we went down to the drawing-room again, well pleased and gratified. As she would not hear of staying to dinner, lest she should by any chance fail to arrive at home with the grey pony before dark; and as I apprehended Mr. Wickfield knew her too well, to argue any point with her; some lunch was provided for her there, and Agnes went back to her governess, and Mr. Wickfield to his office. So we were left to take leave of one another without any restraint.

She told me that everything would be arranged for me by Mr. Wickfield, and that I should want for nothing, and gave me the kindest words and the best advice.

"Trot," said my aunt in conclusion, "be a credit to yourself, to me, and Mr. Dick, and Heaven be with you!"

I was greatly overcome, and could only thank her, again and again, and send my love to Mr. Dick.

"Never," said my aunt, "be mean in anything; never be false; never be cruel. Avoid those three vices, Trot, and I can always be hopeful of you."

I promised, as well as I could, that I would not abuse her kindness or forget her admonition.

"The pony's at the door," said my aunt, "and I am off! Stay here."

With these words she embraced me hastily, and went out of the room, shutting the door after her. As first I was startled by so abrupt a departure, and almost feared I had displeased her; but when I looked into the street, and saw how dejectedly she got into the chaise, and drove away without looking up, I understood her better, and did not do her that injustice.

By five o'clock, which was Mr. Wickfield's dinner-hour, I had mustered up my spirits again, and was ready for my knife and fork. The cloth was only laid for us two; but Agnes was waiting in the drawing-room before dinner, went down with her father, and sat opposite to him at table. I doubted whether he could have dined without her.

We did not stay there, after dinner, but came up-stairs into the drawing-room again: in one snug corner of which, Agnes set glasses for her father, and a decanter of port wine. I thought he would have missed its usual flavour, if it had been put there for him by any other hands.

There he sat, taking his wine, and taking a good deal of it, for two hours; while Agnes played on the piano, worked, and talked to him and me. He was, for the most part, gay and cheerful with us; but sometimes his eyes rested on her, and he fell into a brooding state, and was silent. She always observed this quickly, as I thought, and always roused him with a question or caress. Then he came out of his meditation, and drank more wine.

Agnes made the tea, and presided over it; and the time passed away after it, as after dinner, until she went to bed; when her father took her in his arms and kissed her, and, she being gone, ordered candles in his office. Then I went to bed too.

But in the course of the evening I had rambled down to the door, and a little way along the street, that I might have another peep at the old houses, and the grey Cathedral; and might think of my coming through that old city on my journey, and of my passing the very house I lived in, without knowing it. As I came back, I saw Uriah Heep shutting up the office; and, feeling friendly towards everybody, went in and spoke to him, and at parting, gave him my hand. But oh, what a clammy hand his was! as ghostly to the touch as to the sight! I rubbed mine afterwards, to warm it, *and to rub his off*.

It was such an uncomfortable hand, that, when I went to my room, it was still cold and wet upon my memory. Leaning out of window, and seeing one of the faces on the beam-ends looking at me sideways, I fancied it was Uriah Heep got up there somehow, and shut him in a hurry.

CHAPTER XVI.

I AM A NEW BOY IN MORE SENSES THAN ONE.

NEXT morning, after breakfast, I entered on school life again. I went, accompanied by Mr. Wickfield, to the scene of my future studies—a grave building in a court-yard, with a learned air about it that seemed very well suited to the stray rooks and jackdaws who came down from the Cathedral towers to walk with a clerkly bearing on the grass-plot—and was introduced to my new master, Doctor Strong.

Doctor Strong looked almost as rusty, to my thinking, as the tall iron rails and gates outside the house; and almost as stiff and heavy as the great stone urns that flanked them, and were set up, on the top of the red-brick wall, at regular distances all round the court, like sublimated skittles, for Time to play at. He was in his library (I mean Doctor Strong was), with his clothes not particularly well brushed, and his hair not particularly well combed; his knee-smalls unbraced; his long black gaiters unbuttoned; and his shoes yawning like two caverns on the hearth-rug. Turning upon me a lustreless eye, that reminded me of a long-forgotten blind old horse who once used to crop the grass, and tumble over the graves, in Blunderstone churchyard, he said he was glad to see me: and then he gave me his hand; which I didn't know what to do with, as it did nothing for itself.

But, sitting at work, not far off from Doctor Strong, was a very pretty young lady—whom he called Annie, and who was his daughter, I supposed—who got me out of my difficulty by kneeling down to put Doctor Strong's shoes on, and button his gaiters, which she did with great cheerfulness and quickness. When she had finished, and we were going out to the schoolroom, I was much surprised to hear Mr. Wickfield, in bidding her good morning, address her as "Mrs. Strong;" and I was wondering could she be Doctor Strong's son's wife, or could she be Mrs. Doctor Strong, when Doctor Strong himself unconsciously enlightened me.

"By the bye, Wickfield," he said, stopping in a passage with his hand on my shoulder; "you have not found any suitable provision for my wife's cousin yet?"

"No," said Mr. Wickfield. "No. Not yet."

"I could wish it done as soon as it *can* be done, Wickfield," said Doctor Strong, "for Jack Maldon is needy, and idle; and of those two bad things, worse things sometimes come. What does Doctor Watts say," he added, looking at me, and moving his head to the time of his quotation, "'Satan finds some mischief still, for idle hands to do.'"

"Egad, Doctor," returned Mr. Wickfield, "if Doctor Watts knew mankind, he might have written, with as much truth, 'Satan finds some mischief still, for busy hands to do.' The busy people achieve their full share of mischief in the world, you may rely upon it. What have the people been about, who have been the busiest in getting money, and in getting power, this century or two? No mischief?"

"Jack Maldon will never be very busy in getting either, I expect," said Doctor Strong, rubbing his chin thoughtfully.

"Perhaps not," said Mr. Wickfield; "and you bring me back to the question, with an apology for digressing. No, I have not been able to dispose of Mr. Jack Maldon yet. I believe," he said this with some hesitation, "I penetrate your motive, and it makes the thing more difficult."

"My motive," returned Doctor Strong, "is to make some suitable provision for a cousin, and an old playfellow, of Annie's."

"Yes, I know," said Mr. Wickfield, "at home or abroad."

"Ay!" replied the Doctor, apparently wondering why he emphasised those words so much. "At home or abroad."

"Your own expression, you know," said Mr. Wickfield. "Or abroad."

"Surely," the Doctor answered. "Surely. One or other."

"One or other? Have you no choice?" asked Mr. Wickfield.

"No," returned the Doctor.

"No?" with astonishment.

"Not the least."

"No motive," said Mr. Wickfield, "for meaning abroad, and not at home?"

"No," returned the Doctor.

"I am bound to believe you, and of course I do believe you," said Mr. Wickfield. "It might have simplified my office very much, if I had known it before. But I confess I entertained another impression."

Doctor Strong regarded him with a puzzled and doubting look, which almost immediately subsided into a smile that gave me great encouragement; for it was full of amiability and sweetness, and there was a simplicity in it, and indeed in his whole manner, when the studious, pondering frost upon it was got through, very attractive and hopeful to a young scholar like me. Repeating "no," and "not the least," and other short assurances to the same purport, Doctor Strong jogged on before us, at a queer, uneven pace; and we followed; Mr. Wickfield looking grave, I observed, and shaking his head to himself, without knowing that I saw him.

The schoolroom was a pretty large hall, on the quietest side of the house, confronted by the stately stare of some half-dozen of the great urns, and commanding a peep of an old secluded garden belonging to the Doctor, where the peaches were ripening on the sunny south wall. There were two great aloes, in tubs, on the turf outside the windows; the broad hard leaves of which plant (looking as if they were made of painted tin) have ever since, by association, been symbolical to me of silence and retirement. About five-and-twenty boys were studiously engaged at their books when we went in, but they rose to give the Doctor good morning, and remained standing when they saw Mr. Wickfield and me.

"A new boy, young gentlemen," said the Doctor; "Trotwood Copperfield."

One Adams, who was the head-boy, then stepped out of his place and welcomed me. He looked like a young clergyman, in his white cravat, but he was very affable and good-humoured; and he showed me my place, and presented me to the masters, in a gentlemanly way that would have put me at my ease, if anything could.

It seemed to me so long, however, since I had been among such boys, or among any companions of my own age, except Mick Walker and Mealy Potatoes, that I felt as strange as ever I have done in all my life. I was so conscious of having passed through scenes of which they could have no knowledge, and of having acquired experiences foreign to my age, appearance, and condition as one of them, that I half believed it was an imposture to come there as an ordinary little schoolboy. I had become, in the Murdstone and Grinby time, however short or long it may have been, so unused to the sports and games of boys, that I knew I was awkward and inexperienced in the commonest things belonging to them. Whatever I had learnt, had so slipped away from me in the sordid cares of my life from day to night, that now, when I was examined about what I knew, I knew nothing, and was put into the lowest form of the school. But, troubled as I was, by my want of boyish skill, and of book-learning too, I was made infinitely more uncomfortable by the consideration, that, in what I did know, I was much farther removed from my companions than in what I did not. My mind ran upon what they would think, if they knew of my familiar acquaintance with the King's Bench Prison? Was there anything about me which would reveal my proceedings in connexion with the Micawber family—all those pawnings, and sellings, and suppers—in spite of myself? Suppose some of the boys had seen me coming through Canterbury, wayworn and ragged, and should find me out? What would they say, who made so light of money, if they could know how I had scraped my halfpence together, for the purchase of my daily saveloy and beer, or my slices of pudding? How would it affect them, who were so innocent of London life and London streets, to discover how knowing I was (and was ashamed to be) in some of the meanest phases of both? All this ran in my head so much, on that first day at Doctor Strong's, that I felt distrustful of my slightest look and gesture; shrank within myself whensoever I was approached by one of my new school-fellows; and hurried off, the minute school was over, afraid of committing myself in my response to any friendly notice or advance.

But there was such an influence in Mr. Wickfield's old house, that when I knocked at it, with my new school-books under my arm, I began to feel my uneasiness softening away. As I went up to my airy old room, the grave shadow of the staircase seemed to fall upon my doubts and fears, and to make the past more indistinct. I sat there, sturdily conning my books, until dinner-time (we were out of school for good at three); and went down, hopeful of becoming a passable sort of boy yet.

Agnes was in the drawing-room, waiting for her father, who was detained by some one in his office. She met me with her pleasant smile, and asked me how I liked the school. I told her I should like it very much, I hoped; but I was a little strange to it at first.

"You have never been to school," I said, "have you?"

"Oh, yes! Every day."

"Ah, but you mean here, at your own home?"

"Papa couldn't spare me to go anywhere else," she answered, smiling and shaking her head. "His house-keeper must be in his house, you know."

"He is very fond of you, I am sure," I said.

She nodded "Yes," and went to the door to listen for his coming up, that she might meet him on the stairs. But, as he was not there, she came back again.

"Mama has been dead ever since I was born," she said, in her quiet way. "I only know her picture, down stairs. I saw you looking at it yesterday. Did you think whose it was?"

I told her yes, because it was so like herself.

"Papa says so, too," said Agnes, pleased. "Hark! That's papa now!"

Her bright calm face lighted up with pleasure as she went to meet him, and as they came in, hand in hand. He

greeted me cordially; and told me I should certainly be happy under Doctor Strong, who was one of the gentlest of men.

"There may be some, perhaps—I don't know that there are—who abuse his kindness," said Mr. Wickfield. "Never be one of those, Trotwood, in anything. He is the least suspicious of mankind; and whether that's a merit, or whether it's a blemish, it deserves consideration in all dealings with the Doctor, great or small."

He spoke, I thought, as if he were weary, or dissatisfied with something; but I did not pursue the question in my mind, for dinner was just then announced, and we went down and took the same seats as before.

We had scarcely done so, when Uriah Heep put in his red head and his lank hand at the door, and said:

"Here's Mr. Maldon begs the favour of a word, Sir."

"I am but this moment quit of Mr. Maldon," said his master.

"Yes, Sir," returned Uriah; "but Mr. Maldon has come back, and he begs the favour of a word."

As he held the door open with his hand, Uriah looked at me, and looked at Agnes, and looked at the dishes, and looked at the plates, and looked at every object in the room, I thought,—yet seemed to look at nothing; he made such an appearance all the while of keeping his red eyes dutifully on his master.

"I beg your pardon. It's only to say, on reflection," observed a voice behind Uriah, as Uriah's head was pushed away, and the speaker's substituted—"pray excuse me for this intrusion—that as it seems I have no choice in the matter, the sooner I go abroad the better. My cousin Annie did say, when we talked of it, that she liked to have her friends within reach rather than to have them banished, and the old Doctor——"

"Doctor Strong, was that?" Mr. Wickfield interposed, gravely.

"Doctor Strong of course," returned the other; "I call him the old Doctor—it's all the same, you know."

"I don't know," returned Mr. Wickfield.

"Well, Doctor Strong," said the other—"Doctor Strong was of the same mind, I believed. But as it appears from the course you take with me that he has changed his mind, why there's no more to be said, except that the sooner I am off, the better. Therefore, I thought I'd come back and say, that the sooner I am off the better. When a plunge is to be made into the water, it's of no use lingering on the bank."

"There shall be as little lingering as possible, in your case, Mr. Maldon, you may depend upon it," said Mr. Wickfield.

"Thank'ee," said the other. "Much obliged. I don't want to look a gift-horse in the mouth, which is not a gracious thing to do; otherwise, I dare say, my cousin Annie could easily arrange it in her own way. I suppose Annie would only have to say to the old Doctor——"

"Meaning that Mrs. Strong would only have to say to her husband—do I follow you?" said Mr. Wickfield.

"Quite so," returned the other, "—would only have to say, that she wanted such and such a thing to be so and so; and it would be so and so, as a matter of course."

"And why as a matter of course, Mr. Maldon?" asked Mr. Wickfield, sedately eating his dinner.

"Why, because Annie's a charming young girl, and the old Doctor—Doctor Strong, I mean—is not quite a charming young boy," said Mr. Jack Maldon, laughing. "No offence to anybody, Mr. Wickfield. I only mean that I suppose some compensation is fair and reasonable, in that sort of marriage."

"Compensation to the lady, Sir?" asked Mr. Wickfield gravely.

"To the lady, Sir," Mr. Jack Maldon answered, laughing. But appearing to remark that Mr. Wickfield went on with his dinner in the same sedate, immovable manner, and that there was no hope of making him relax a muscle of his face, he added:

"However, I have said what I came back to say, and, with another apology for this intrusion, I may take myself off. Of course I shall observe your directions, in considering the matter as one to be arranged between you and me solely, and not to be referred to, up at the Doctor's."

"Have you dined?" asked Mr. Wickfield, with a motion of his hand towards the table.

"Thank'ee. I am going to dine," said Mr. Maldon, "with my cousin Annie. Good-bye!"

Mr. Wickfield, without rising, looked after him thoughtfully as he went out. He was rather a shallow sort of young gentleman, I thought, with a handsome face, a rapid utterance, and a confident, bold air. And this was the first I ever saw of Mr. Jack Maldon; whom I had not expected to see so soon, when I heard the Doctor speak of him that morning.

When we had dined, we went up-stairs again, where everything went on exactly as on the previous day. Agnes set the glasses and decanters in the same corner, and Mr. Wickfield sat down to drink, and drank a good deal. Agnes played the piano to him, sat by him, and worked and talked, and played some games at dominoes with me. In good time she made tea; and afterwards, when I brought down my books, looked into them, and showed me what she knew of them (which was no slight matter, though she said it was), and what was the best way to learn and understand them. I see her, with her modest, orderly, placid manner, and I hear her beautiful calm voice, as I write these words. The influence for all good, which she came to exercise over me at a later time, begins already to descend upon my breast. I love little Em'ly, and I don't love Agnes—no, not at all in that way—but I feel that there are goodness, peace, and truth, wherever Agnes is; and that the soft light of the coloured window in the church, seen long ago, falls on her always, and on me when I am near her, and on everything around.

The time having come for her withdrawal for the night, and she having left us, I gave Mr. Wickfield my hand, preparatory to going away myself. But he checked me and said: "Should you like to stay with us, Trotwood, or to go elsewhere?"

"To stay," I answered, quickly.

"You are sure?"

"If you please. If I may!"

"Why, it's but a dull life that we lead here, boy, I am afraid," he said.

"Not more dull for me than Agnes, Sir. Not dull at all!"

"Than Agnes," he repeated, walking slowly to the great chimney-piece, and leaning against it. "Than Agnes!"

He had drunk wine that evening (or I fancied it), until his eyes were bloodshot. Not that I could see them now, for they were cast down, and shaded by his hand; but I had noticed them a little while before.

"Now I wonder," he muttered, "whether my Agnes tires of me. When should I ever tire of her? But that's different, that's quite different."

He was musing, not speaking to me; so I remained quiet.

"A dull old house," he said, "and a monotonous life; but I must have her near me. I must keep her near me. If the thought that I may die and leave my darling, or that my darling may die and leave me, comes like a spectre, to distress my happiest hours, and is only to be drowned in——"

He did not supply the word; but pacing slowly to the place where he had sat, and mechanically going through the action of pouring wine from the empty decanter, set it down and paced back again.

"If it is miserable to bear when she is here," he said, "what would it be, and she away? No, no, no. I cannot try that."

He leaned against the chimney-piece, brooding so long that I could not decide whether to run the risk of disturbing him by going, or to remain quietly where I was, until he should come out of his reverie. At length he aroused himself, and looked about the room until his eyes encountered mine.

"Stay with us, Trotwood, eh?" he said, in his usual manner, and as if he were answering something I had just said. "I am glad of it. You are company to us both. It is wholesome to have you here. Wholesome for me, wholesome for Agnes, wholesome perhaps for all of us."

"I am sure it is for me, Sir," I said. "I am so glad to be here."

"That's a fine fellow!" said Mr. Wickfield. "As long as you are glad to be here, you shall stay here." He shook hands with me upon it, and clapped me on the back; and told me that when I had anything to do at night after Agnes had left us, or when I wished to read for my own pleasure, I was free to come down to his room, if he were there and if I desired it for company's sake, and to sit with him. I thanked him for his consideration; and, as he went down soon afterwards, and I was not tired, went down too, with a book in my hand, to avail myself, for half-an-hour, of his permission.

But, seeing a light in the little round office, and immediately feeling myself attracted towards Uriah Heep, who had a sort of fascination for me, I went in there instead. I found Uriah reading a great fat book, with such demonstrative attention, that his lank fore-finger followed up every line as he read, and made clammy tracks along the page (or so I fully believed) like a snail.

"You are working late to-night, Uriah," says I.

"Yes, Master Copperfield," says Uriah.

As I was getting on the stool opposite, to talk to him more conveniently, I observed that he had not such a thing as a smile about him, and that he could only widen his mouth and make two hard creases down his cheeks, one on each side, to stand for one.

"I am not doing office-work, Master Copperfield," said Uriah.

"What work, then?" I asked.

"I am improving my legal knowledge, Master Copperfield," said Uriah. "I am going through Tidd's Practice. Oh, what a writer Mr. Tidd is, Master Copperfield!"

My stool was such a tower of observation, that as I watched him reading on again, after this rapturous exclamation, and following up the lines with his fore-finger, I observed that his nostrils, which were thin and pointed, with sharp dints in them, had a singular and most uncomfortable way of expanding and contracting themselves; that they seemed to twinkle instead of his eyes, which hardly ever twinkled at all.

"I suppose you are quite a great lawyer?" I said, after looking at him for some time.

"Me, Master Copperfield?" said Uriah. "Oh, no. I'm a very umble person."

It was no fancy of mine about his hands, I observed; for he frequently ground the palms against each other as if to squeeze them dry and warm, besides often wiping them, in a stealthy way, on his pocket-handkerchief.

"I am well aware that I am the umblest person going," said Uriah Heep, modestly; "let the other be where he may. My mother is likewise a very umble person. We live in a numble abode, Master Copperfield, but have much to be thankful for. My father's former calling was umble. He was a sexton."

"What is he now?" I asked.

"He is a partaker of glory at present, Master Copperfield," said Uriah Heep. "But we have much to be thankful for. How much have I to be thankful for in living with Mr. Wickfield!"

I asked Uriah if he had been with Mr. Wickfield long?

"I have been with him going on four year, Master Copperfield," said Uriah; shutting up his book, after carefully marking the place where he had left off. "Since a year after my father's death. How much have I to be thankful for, in that! How much have I to be thankful for, in Mr. Wickfield's kind intention to give me my articles, which would otherwise not lay within the umble means of mother and self!"

"Then, when your articled time is over, you'll be a regular lawyer, I suppose?" said I.

"With the blessing of Providence, Master Copperfield," returned Uriah.

"Perhaps you'll be a partner in Mr. Wickfield's business, one of these days," I said, to make myself agreeable; "and it will be Wickfield and Heep, or Heep late Wickfield."

"Oh, no, Master Copperfield," returned Uriah, shaking his head, "I am much too umble for that!"

He certainly did look uncommonly like the carved face on the beam outside my window, as he sat, in his humility, eyeing me sideways, with his mouth widened, and the creases in his cheeks.

"Mr. Wickfield is a most excellent man, Master Copperfield," said Uriah. "If you have known him long, you know it, I am sure, much better than I can inform you."

I replied that I was certain he was; but that I had not known him long myself, though he was a friend of my aunt's.

"Oh, indeed, Master Copperfield," said Uriah. "Your aunt is a sweet lady, Master Copperfield!"

He had a way of writhing when he wanted to express enthusiasm, which was very ugly; and which diverted my attention from the compliment he had paid my relation, to the snaky twistings of his throat and body.

"A sweet lady, Master Copperfield!" said Uriah Heep. "She has a great admiration for Miss Agnes, Master Copperfield, I believe?"

I said, "Yes," boldly; not that I knew anything about it, Heaven forgive me!

"I hope you have, too, Master Copperfield," said Uriah. "But I am sure you must have."

"Everybody must have," I returned.

"Oh, thank you, Master Copperfield," said Uriah Heep, "for that remark! It is so true! Umble as I am, I know it is *so* true! Oh, thank you, Master Copperfield!"

He writhed himself quite off his stool in the excitement of his feelings, and, being off, began to make arrangements for going home.

"Mother will be expecting me," he said, referring to a pale, inexpressive-faced watch in his pocket, "and getting uneasy; for though we are very umble, Master Copperfield, we are much attached to one another. If you would come and see us, any afternoon, and take a cup of tea at our lowly dwelling, mother would be as proud of your company as I should be."

I said I should be glad to come.

"Thank you, Master Copperfield," returned Uriah, putting his book away upon the shelf. "I suppose you stop here, some time, Master Copperfield?"

I said I was going to be brought up there, I believed, as long as I remained at school.

"Oh, indeed!" exclaimed Uriah. "I should think *you* would come into the business at last, Master Copperfield!"

I protested that I had no views of that sort, and that no such scheme was entertained in my behalf by anybody; but Uriah insisted on blandly replying to all my assurances, "Oh, yes, Master Copperfield, I should think you would, indeed!" and, "Oh, indeed, Master Copperfield, I should think you would, certainly!" over and over again. Being, at last, ready to leave the office for the night, he asked me if it would suit my convenience to have the light put out; and on my answering "Yes," instantly extinguished it. After shaking hands with me—his hand felt like a fish, in the dark—he opened the door into the street a very little, and crept out, and shut it, leaving me to grope my way back into the house: which cost me some trouble and a fall over his stool. This was the proximate cause, I suppose, of my dreaming about him, for what appeared to me to be half the night; and dreaming, among other things, that he had launched Mr. Peggotty's house on a piratical expedition, with a black flag at the mast-head, bearing the inscription "Tidd's Practice," under which diabolical ensign he was carrying me and little Em'ly to the Spanish Main, to be drowned.

I got a little better of my uneasiness when I went to school next day, and a good deal the better next day, and so shook it off by degrees, that in less than a fortnight I was quite at home, and happy, among my new companions. I was awkward enough in their games, and backward enough in their studies; but custom would improve me in the first respect, I hoped, and hard work in the second. Accordingly, I went to work very hard, both in play and in earnest, and gained great commendation. And, in a very little while, the Murdstone and Grinby life became so strange to me that I hardly believed in it, while my present life grew so familiar, that I seemed to have been leading it a long time.

Doctor Strong's was an excellent school; as different from Mr. Creakle's as good is from evil. It was very gravely and decorously ordered, and on a sound system; with an appeal, in everything, to the honour and good faith of the boys, and an avowed intention to rely on their possession of those qualities unless they proved themselves unworthy of it, which worked wonders. We all felt that we had a part in the management of the place, and in sustaining its character and dignity. Hence, we soon became warmly attached to it—I am sure I did for one, and I never knew, in all my time, of any other boy being otherwise—and learnt with a good will, desiring to do it credit. We had noble games out of hours, and plenty of liberty; but even then, as I remember, we were well spoken of in the town, and rarely did any disgrace, by our appearance or manner, to the reputation of Doctor Strong and Doctor Strong's boys.

Some of the higher scholars boarded in the Doctor's house, and through them I learned, at second hand, some particulars of the Doctor's history—as how he had not yet been married twelve months to the beautiful young lady I had seen in the study, whom he had married for love; for she had not a sixpence, and had a world of poor relations (so our fellows said) ready to swarm the Doctor out of house and home. Also, how the Doctor's cogitating manner was attributable to his being always engaged in looking out for Greek roots; which, in my innocence and ignorance, I supposed to be a botanical furore on the Doctor's part, especially as he always looked at the ground when he walked about, until I understood that they were roots of words, with a view to a new Dictionary which he had in contemplation. Adams, our head-boy, who had a turn for mathematics, had made a calculation, I was informed, of the time this Dictionary would take in completing, on the Doctor's plan, and at the Doctor's rate of going. He considered that it might be done in one thousand six hundred and forty-nine years, counting from the Doctor's last, or sixty-second, birthday.

But the Doctor himself was the idol of the whole school: and it must have been a badly-composed school if he had been anything else, for he was the kindest of men; with a simple faith in him that might have touched the stone hearts of the very urns upon the wall. As he walked up and down that part of the courtyard which was at the side of the house, with the stray rooks and jackdaws looking after him with their heads cocked slyly, as if they knew how much more knowing they were in worldly affairs than he, if any sort of vagabond could only get near enough to his creaking shoes to attract his attention to one sentence of a tale of distress, that vagabond was made for the next two days. It was so notorious in the house, that the masters and head-boys took pains to cut these marauders off at angles, and to get out of windows, and turn them out of the courtyard, before they could make the Doctor aware of their presence; which was sometimes happily effected within a few yards of him, without his knowing anything of the matter, as he jogged to and fro. Outside his own domain, and unprotected, he was a very sheep for the shearers. He would have taken his gaiters off his legs, to give away. In fact, there was a story current among us (I have no idea, and never had, on what authority, but I have believed it for so many years that I feel quite certain it is true), that on a frosty day, one winter-time, he actually did bestow his gaiters on a beggar-woman, who occasioned some scandal in the neighbourhood by exhibiting a fine infant from door to door, wrapped in those garments, which were universally recognised, being as well known in the vicinity as the Cathedral. The legend added that the only person who did not identify them was the Doctor himself, who, when they were shortly afterwards displayed at the door of a little second-hand shop of no very good repute, where such things were taken in exchange for gin, was more than once observed to handle them approvingly, as if admiring some curious novelty in the pattern, and considering them an improvement on his own.

It was very pleasant to see the Doctor with his pretty young wife. He had a fatherly, benignant way of showing his fondness for her, which seemed in itself to express a good man. I often saw them walking in the garden where the peaches were, and I sometimes had a nearer observation of them in the study or the parlour. She appeared to me to take great care of the Doctor, and to like him very much, though I never thought her vitally interested in the Dictionary: some cumbrous fragments of which work the Doctor always carried in his pockets, and in the lining of his hat, and generally seemed to be expounding to her as they walked about.

I saw a good deal of Mrs. Strong, both because she had taken a liking for me on the morning of my introduction to the Doctor, and was always afterwards kind to me, and interested in me; and because she was very fond of Agnes, and was often backwards and forwards at our house. There was a curious constraint between her and Mr. Wickfield, I thought (of whom she seemed to be afraid), that never wore off. When she came there of an evening, she always shrank from accepting his escort home, and ran away with me instead. And sometimes, as we were running gaily across the Cathedral yard together, expecting to meet nobody, we would meet Mr. Jack Maldon, who was always surprised to see us.

Mrs. Strong's mama was a lady I took great delight in. Her name was Mrs. Markleham; but our boys used to call her the Old Soldier, on account of her generalship, and the skill with which she marshalled great forces of relations against the Doctor. She was a little, sharp-eyed woman, who used to wear, when she was dressed, one unchangeable cap, ornamented with some artificial flowers, and two artificial butterflies supposed to be hovering above the flowers. There was a superstition among us that this cap had come from France, and could only originate in the workmanship of that ingenious nation: but all I certainly know about it is, that it always made its appearance of an evening, wheresoever Mrs. Markleham made *her* appearance; that it was carried about to friendly meetings in a Hindoo basket; that the butterflies had the gift of trembling constantly; and that they improved the shining hours at Doctor Strong's expense, like busy bees.

I observed the Old Soldier—not to adopt the name disrespectfully—to pretty good advantage, on a night which is made memorable to me by something else I shall relate. It was the night of a little party at the Doctor's, which was given on the occasion of Mr. Jack Maldon's departure for India, whither he was going as a cadet, or something of that kind: Mr. Wickfield having at length arranged the business. It happened to be the Doctor's birthday, too. We had had a holiday, had made presents to him in the morning, had made a speech to him through the head-boy, and had cheered him until we were hoarse, and until he had shed tears. And now, in the evening, Mr. Wickfield, Agnes, and I, went to have tea with him in his private capacity.

Mr. Jack Maldon was there, before us. Mrs. Strong, dressed in white, with cherry-coloured ribbons, was playing the piano, when we went in; and he was leaning over her to turn the leaves. The clear red and white of her complexion was not so blooming and flower-like as usual, I thought, when she turned round; but she looked very pretty, wonderfully pretty.

"I have forgotten, Doctor," said Mrs. Strong's mama, when we were seated, "to pay you the compliments of the day: though they are, as you may suppose, very far from being mere compliments in my case. Allow me to wish you many happy returns."

"I thank you, ma'am," replied the Doctor.

"Many, many, many happy returns," said the Old Soldier. "Not only for your own sake, but for Annie's and John Maldon's, and many other people's. It seems but yesterday to me, John, when you were a little creature, a head shorter than Master Copperfield, making baby love to Annie behind the gooseberry bushes in the back-garden."

"My dear mama," said Mrs. Strong, "never mind that now."

"Annie, don't be absurd," returned her mother. "If you are to blush to hear of such things, now you are an old married woman, when are you not to blush to hear of them?"

"Old?" exclaimed Mr. Jack Maldon. "Annie? Come!"

"Yes, John," returned the Soldier. "Virtually, an old married woman. Although not old by years—for when did you ever hear me say, or who has ever heard me say, that a girl of twenty was old by years!—your cousin is the wife of the Doctor, and, as such, what I have described her. It is well for you, John, that your cousin *is* the wife of the Doctor. You have found in him an influential and kind friend, who will be kinder yet, I venture to predict, if you deserve it. I have no false pride. I never hesitate to admit, frankly, that there are some members of our family who want a friend. You were one yourself, before your cousin's influence raised up one for you."

The Doctor, in the goodness of his heart, waved his hand as if to make light of it, and save Mr. Jack Maldon from any further reminder. But Mrs. Markleham changed her chair for one next the Doctor's, and putting her fan on his coat-sleeve said:

"No, really, my dear Doctor, you must excuse me if I appear to dwell on this rather, because I feel so very strongly. I call it quite my monomania, it is such a subject of mine. You are a blessing to us. You really are a boon, you know."

"Nonsense, nonsense," said the Doctor.

"No, no, I beg your pardon," retorted the Old Soldier. "With nobody present, but our dear and confidential friend Mr. Wickfield, I cannot consent to be put down. I shall begin to assert the privileges of a mother-in-law, if you go on like that, and scold you. I am perfectly honest and outspoken. What I am saying, is what I said when you first overpowered me with surprise—you remember how surprised I was?—by proposing for Annie. Not that there was anything so very much out of the way, in the mere fact of the proposal—it would be ridiculous to say that!—but because, you having known her poor father, and having known her from a baby six months old, I hadn't thought of you in such a light at all, or indeed as a marrying man in any way—simply that, you know."

"Ay, ay," returned the Doctor, good-humouredly. "Never mind."

"But I *do* mind," said the Old Soldier, laying her fan upon his lips. "I mind very much. I recall these things

that I may be contradicted if I am wrong. Well! Then I spoke to Annie, and I told her what had happened. I said, 'My dear, here's Doctor Strong has positively been and made you the subject of a handsome declaration and an offer.' Did I press it in the least? No. I said, 'Now, Annie, tell me the truth this moment; is your heart free?' 'Mama,' she said, crying, 'I am extremely young'—which was perfectly true—' and I hardly know if I have a heart at all.' 'Then, my dear,' I said, 'you may rely upon it, it's free. At all events, my love,' said I, 'Doctor Strong is in an agitated state of mind, and must be answered. He cannot be kept in his present state of suspense.' 'Mama,' said Annie, still crying, 'would he be unhappy without me? If he would, I honour and respect him so much, that I think I will have him.' So it was settled. And then, and not till then, I said to Annie, 'Annie, Doctor Strong will not only be your husband, but he will represent your late father: he will represent the head of our family, he will represent the wisdom and station, and I may say the means, of our family; and will be, in short, a boon to it.' I used the word at the time, and I have used it again, to-day. If I have any merit, it is consistency."

The daughter had sat quite silent and still during this speech, with her eyes fixed on the ground; her cousin standing near her, and looking on the ground too. She now said very softly, in a trembling voice:

"Mama, I hope you have finished?"

"No, my dear Annie," returned the Soldier, "I have not quite finished. Since you ask me, my love, I reply that I have *not*. I complain that you really are a little unnatural towards your own family; and, as it is of no use complaining to you, I mean to complain to your husband. Now, my dear Doctor, do look at that silly wife of yours."

As the Doctor turned his kind face, with its smile of simplicity and gentleness, towards her, she drooped her head more. I noticed that Mr. Wickfield looked at her steadily.

"When I happened to say to that naughty thing, the other day," pursued her mother, shaking her head and her fan at her, playfully, "that there was a family circumstance she might mention to you—indeed, I think, was bound to mention—she said, that to mention it was to ask a favour; and that, as you were too generous, and as for her to ask was always to have, she wouldn't."

"Annie, my dear," said the Doctor. "That was wrong. It robbed me of a pleasure."

"Almost the very words I said to her!" exclaimed her mother. "Now really, another time, when I know what she would tell you but for this reason, and won't, I have a great mind, my dear Doctor, to tell you myself."

"I shall be glad if you will," returned the Doctor.

"Shall I?"

"Certainly."

"Well, then, I will!" said the Old Soldier. "That's a bargain." And having, I suppose, carried her point, she tapped the Doctor's hand several times with her fan (which she kissed first), and returned triumphantly to her former station.

Some more company coming in, among whom were the two masters and Adams, the talk became general; and it naturally turned on Mr. Jack Maldon, and his voyage, and the country he was going to, and his various plans and prospects. He was to leave that night, after supper, in a post-chaise, for Gravesend; where the ship, in which he was to make the voyage, lay; and was to be gone—unless he came home on leave, or for his health—I don't know how many years. I recollect it was settled by general consent that India was quite a misrepresented country, and had nothing objectionable in it, but a tiger or two, and a little heat in the warm part of the day. For my own part, I looked on Mr. Jack Maldon as a modern Sindbad, and pictured him the bosom friend of all the Rajahs in the East, sitting under canopies, smoking curly golden pipes—a mile long, if they could be straightened out.

Mrs. Strong was a very pretty singer: as I knew, who often heard her singing by herself. But, whether she was afraid of singing before people, or was out of voice that evening, it was certain that she couldn't sing at all. She tried a duet, once, with her cousin Maldon, but could not so much as begin; and afterwards, when she tried to sing by herself, although she began sweetly, her voice died away on a sudden, and left her quite distressed, with her head hanging down over the keys. The good Doctor said she was nervous, and, to relieve her, proposed a round game at cards; of which he knew as much as of the art of playing the trombone. But I remarked that the Old Soldier took him into custody directly, for her partner; and instructed him, as the first preliminary of initiation, to give her all the silver he had in his pocket.

We had a merry game, not made the less merry by the Doctor's mistakes, of which he committed an innumerable quantity, in spite of the watchfulness of the butterflies, and to their great aggravation. Mrs. Strong had declined to play, on the ground of not feeling very well; and her cousin Maldon had excused himself because he had some packing to do. When he had done it, however, he returned, and they sat together, talking, on the sofa. From time to time she came and looked over the Doctor's hand, and told him what to play. She was very pale, as she bent over him, and I thought her finger trembled as she pointed out the cards; but the Doctor was quite happy in her attention, and took no notice of this, if it were so.

At supper, we were hardly so gay. Every one appeared to feel that a parting of that sort was an awkward thing, and that the nearer it approached, the more awkward it was. Mr. Jack Maldon tried to be very talkative, but was not at his ease, and made matters worse. And they were not improved, as it appeared to me, by the Old Soldier: who continually recalled passages of Mr. Jack Maldon's youth.

The Doctor, however, who felt, I am sure, that he was making everybody happy, was well pleased, and had no suspicion but that we were all at the utmost height of enjoyment.

"Annie, my dear," said he, looking at his watch, and filling his glass, "it is past your cousin Jack's time, and we must not detain him, since time and tide—both concerned in this case—wait for no man. Mr. Jack Maldon, you have a long voyage, and a strange country, before you; but many men have had both, and many men will have both, to the end of time. The winds you are going to tempt, have wafted thousands upon thousands to fortune, and brought thousands upon thousands happily back."

"It's an affecting thing," said Mrs. Markleham, "however it's viewed, it's affecting, to see a fine young man one has known from an infant, going away to the other end of the world, leaving all he knows behind, and not knowing what's before him. A young man really well deserves constant support and patronage," looking at the Doctor, "who makes such sacrifices."

"Time will go fast with you, Mr. Jack Maldon," pursued the Doctor, "and fast with all of us. Some of us can hardly expect, perhaps, in the natural course of things, to greet you on your return. The next best thing is to hope to do it, and that's my case. I shall not weary you with good advice. You have long had a good model before you, in your cousin Annie. Imitate her virtues as nearly as you can."

Mrs. Markleham fanned herself, and shook her head.

"Farewell, Mr. Jack," said the Doctor, standing up; on which we all stood up. "A prosperous voyage out, a thriving career abroad, and a happy return home!"

We all drank the toast, and all shook hands with Mr. Jack Maldon; after which he hastily took leave of the ladies who were there, and hurried to the door, where he was received, as he got into the chaise, with a tremendous broadside of cheers discharged by our boys, who had assembled on the lawn for the purpose. Running in among them to swell the ranks, I was very near the chaise when it rolled away; and I had a lively impression made upon me, in the midst of the noise and dust, of having seen Mr. Jack Maldon rattle past with an agitated face, and something cherry-coloured in his hand.

After another broadside for the Doctor, and another for the Doctor's wife, the boys dispersed, and I went back into the house, where I found the guests all standing in a group about the Doctor, discussing how Mr. Jack Maldon had gone away, and how he had borne it, and how he had felt it, and all the rest of it. In the midst of these remarks, Mrs. Markleham cried: "Where's Annie?"

No Annie was there; and when they called to her, no Annie replied. But all pressing out of the room, in a crowd, to see what was the matter, we found her lying on the hall floor. There was great alarm at first, until it was found that she was in a swoon, and that the swoon was yielding to the usual means of recovery; when the Doctor, who had lifted her head upon his knee, put her curls aside with his hand, and said, looking around:

"Poor Annie! She's so faithful and tender-hearted! It's the parting from her old playfellow and friend—her favourite cousin—that has done this. Ah! It's a pity! I am very sorry!"

When she opened her eyes, and saw where she was, and that we were all standing about her, she arose with assistance: turning her head, as she did so, to lay it on the Doctor's shoulder—or to hide it, I don't know which. We went into the drawing-room, to leave her with the Doctor and her mother; but she said, it seemed, that she was better than she had been since morning, and that she would rather be brought among us; so they brought her in, looking very white and weak, I thought, and sat her on a sofa.

"Annie, my dear," said her mother, doing something to her dress. "See here! You have lost a bow. Will anybody be so good as find a ribbon; a cherry-coloured ribbon?"

It was the one she had worn at her bosom. We all looked for it; I myself looked everywhere, I am certain—but nobody could find it.

"Do you recollect where you had it last, Annie?" said her mother.

I wondered how I could have thought she looked white, or anything but burning red, when she answered that she had had it safe, a little while ago, she thought, but it was not worth looking for.

Nevertheless, it was looked for again, and still not found.

She entreated that there might be no more searching; but it was still sought for in a desultory way, until she was quite well, and the company took their departure.

We walked very slowly home, Mr. Wickfield, Agnes, and I—Agnes and I admiring the moonlight, and Mr. Wickfield scarcely raising his eyes from the ground. When we, at last, reached our own door, Agnes discovered that she had left her little reticule behind. Delighted to be of any service to her, I ran back to fetch it.

I went into the supper-room where it had been left, which was deserted and dark. But a door of communication between that and the Doctor's study, where there was a light, being open, I passed on there, to say what I wanted, and to get a candle.

The Doctor was sitting in his easy-chair by the fireside, and his young wife was on a stool at his feet. The Doctor, with a complacent smile, was reading aloud some manuscript explanation or statement of a theory out of that interminable Dictionary, and she was looking up at him. But, with such a face as I never saw. It was so beautiful in its form, it was so ashy pale, it was so fixed in its abstraction, it was so full of a wild, sleep-walking, dreamy horror of I don't know what. The eyes were wide open, and her brown hair fell in two rich clusters on her shoulders, and on her white dress, disordered by the want of the lost ribbon. Distinctly as I recollect her look, I cannot say of what it was expressive. I cannot even say of what it is expressive to me now, rising again before my older judgment. Penitence, humiliation, shame, pride, love, and trustfulness—I see them all; and in them all, I see that horror of I don't know what.

My entrance, and my saying what I wanted, roused her. It disturbed the Doctor too, for when I went back to replace the candle I had taken from the table, he was patting her head, in his fatherly way, and saying he was a merciless drone to let her tempt him into reading on; and he would have her go to bed.

But she asked him, in a rapid, urgent manner, to let her stay—to let her feel assured (I heard her murmur some broken words to this effect) that she was in his confidence that night. And, as she turned again towards him, after glancing at me as I left the room and went out at the door, I saw her cross her hands upon his knee, and look up at him with the same face, something quieted, as he resumed his reading.

It made a great impression on me, and I remembered it a long time afterwards; as I shall have occasion to narrate when the time comes.

CHAPTER XVII.

SOMEBODY TURNS UP.

It has not occurred to me to mention Peggotty since I ran away; but, of course, I wrote her a letter almost as soon as I was housed at Dover, and another and a longer letter, containing all particulars fully related, when my aunt took me formally under her protection. On my being settled at Doctor Strong's I wrote to her again, detailing my happy condition and prospects. I never could have derived anything like the pleasure from spending the money Mr. Dick had given me, that I felt in sending a gold half-guinea to Peggotty, per post, inclosed in this last letter, to discharge the sum I had borrowed of her: in which epistle, not before, I mentioned about the young man with the donkey-cart.

To these communications Peggotty replied as promptly, if not as concisely, as a merchant's clerk. Her utmost powers of expression (which were certainly not great in ink) were exhausted in the attempt to write what she felt on the subject of my journey. Four sides of incoherent and interjectional beginnings of sentences, that had no end, except blots, were inadequate to afford her any relief. But the blots were more expressive to me than the best composition; for they showed me that Peggotty had been crying all over the paper, and what could I have desired more?

I made out, without much difficulty, that she could not take quite kindly to my aunt yet. The notice was too short after so long a prepossession the other way. We never knew a person, she wrote; but to think that Miss Betsey should seem to be so different from what she had been thought to be, was a Moral!—That was her word. She was evidently still afraid of Miss Betsey, for she sent her grateful duty to her but timidly; and she was evidently afraid of me, too, and entertained the probability of my running away again soon: if I might judge from the repeated hints she threw out, that the coach-fare to Yarmouth was always to be had of her for the asking.

She gave me one piece of intelligence which affected me very much, namely, that there had been a sale of the furniture at our old home, and that Mr. and Miss Murdstone were gone away, and the house was shut up, to be let or sold. God knows I had no part in it while they remained there, but it pained me to think of the dear old place as altogether abandoned; of the weeds growing tall in the garden, and the fallen leaves lying thick and wet upon the paths. I imagined how the winds of winter would howl round it, how the cold rain would beat upon the window-glass, how the moon would make ghosts on the walls of the empty rooms, watching their solitude all night. I thought afresh of the grave in the churchyard, underneath the tree; and it seemed as if the house were dead too, now, and all connected with my father and mother were faded away.

There was no other news in Peggotty's letters. Mr. Barkis was an excellent husband, she said, though still a little near; but we all had our faults, and she had plenty (though I am sure I don't know what they were); and he sent his duty, and my little bedroom was always ready for me. Mr. Peggotty was well, and Ham was well, and Mrs. Gummidge was but poorly, and little Em'ly wouldn't send her love, but said that Peggotty might send it, if she liked.

All this intelligence I dutifully imparted to my aunt, only reserving to myself the mention of little Em'ly, to whom I instinctively felt that she would not very tenderly incline.

While I was yet new at Doctor Strong's, she made several excursions over to Canterbury to see me, and always at unseasonable hours: with the view, I suppose, of taking me by surprise. But, finding me well employed, and bearing a good character, and hearing on all hands that I rose fast in the school, she soon discontinued these visits. I saw her on a Saturday, every third or fourth week, when I went over to Dover for a treat; and I saw Mr. Dick every alternate Wednesday, when he arrived by stage-coach at noon, to stay until next morning.

On these occasions Mr. Dick never travelled without a leathern writing-desk, containing a supply of stationery and

I RETURN TO THE DOCTOR'S AFTER THE PARTY.

the Memorial; in relation to which document he had a notion that time was beginning to press now, and that it really must be got out of hand.

Mr. Dick was very partial to gingerbread. To render his visits the more agreeable, my aunt had instructed me to open a credit for him at a cake-shop, which was hampered with the stipulation that he should not be served with more than one shilling's-worth in the course of any one day. This, and the reference of all his little bills at the County Inn where he slept, to my aunt, before they were paid, induced me to suspect that he was only allowed to rattle his money, and not to spend it. I found on further investigation that this was so, or at least there was an agreement between him and my aunt that he should account to her for all his disbursements. As he had no idea of deceiving her, and always desired to please her, he was thus made chary of launching into expense. On this point, as well as on all other possible points, Mr. Dick was convinced that my aunt was the wisest and most wonderful of women; as he repeatedly told me with infinite secrecy, and always in a whisper.

"Trotwood," said Mr. Dick, with an air of mystery, after imparting this confidence to me, one Wednesday; "who's the man that hides near our house and frightens her?"

"Frightens my aunt, Sir?"

Mr. Dick nodded. "I thought nothing would have frightened her," he said, "for she's——" here he whispered softly, "don't mention it—the wisest and most wonderful of women." Having said which, he drew back, to observe the effect which this description of her made upon me.

"The first time he came," said Mr. Dick, "was—let me see—sixteen hundred and forty-nine was the date of King Charles's execution. I think you said sixteen hundred and forty-nine?"

"Yes, Sir."

"I don't know how it can be," said Mr. Dick, sorely puzzled and shaking his head. "I don't think I am as old as that."

"Was it in that year that the man appeared, Sir?" I asked.

"Why, really," said Mr. Dick, "I don't see how it can have been in that year, Trotwood. Did you get that date out of history?"

"Yes, Sir."

"I suppose history never lies, does it?" said Mr. Dick, with a gleam of hope.

"Oh dear, no, Sir!" I replied, most decisively. I was ingenuous and young, and I thought so.

"I can't make it out," said Mr. Dick, shaking his head. "There's something wrong, somewhere. However, it was very soon after the mistake was made of putting some of the trouble out of King Charles's head into my head, that the man first came. I was walking out with Miss Trotwood after tea, just at dark, and there he was, close to our house."

"Walking about?" I inquired.

"Walking about?" repeated Mr. Dick. "Let me see. I must recollect a bit. N—no, no; he was not walking about."

I asked, as the shortest way to get at it, what he was doing.

"Well, he wasn't there at all," said Mr. Dick, "until he came up behind her, and whispered. Then she turned round and fainted, and I stood still and looked at him, and he walked away; but that he should have been hiding ever

since (in the ground or somewhere), is the most extraordinary thing!"

"Has he been hiding ever since?" I asked.

"To be sure he has," retorted Mr. Dick, nodding his head gravely. "Never came out, till last night! We were walking last night, and he came up behind her again, and I knew him again."

"And did he frighten my aunt again?"

"All of a shiver," said Mr. Dick, counterfeiting that affection and making his teeth chatter. "Held by the palings. Cried. But, Trotwood, come here," getting me close to him, that he might whisper very softly; "why did she give him money, boy, in the moonlight?"

"He was a beggar, perhaps."

Mr. Dick shook his head, as utterly renouncing the suggestion; and having replied a great many times, and with great confidence, "No beggar, no beggar, no beggar, Sir!" went on to say, that from his window he had afterwards, and late at night, seen my aunt give this person money outside the garden rails in the moonlight, who then slunk away—into the ground again, as he thought probable—and was seen no more: while my aunt came hurriedly and secretly back into the house, and had, even that morning, been quite different from her usual self; which preyed on Mr. Dick's mind.

I had not the least belief, in the outset of this story, that the unknown was anything but a delusion of Mr. Dick's, and one of the line of that ill-fated Prince who occasioned him so much difficulty; but after some reflection I began to entertain the question whether an attempt, or threat of an attempt, might have been twice made to take poor Mr. Dick himself from under my aunt's protection, and whether my aunt, the strength of whose kind feeling towards him I knew from herself, might have been induced to pay a price for his peace and quiet. As I was already much attached to Mr. Dick, and very solicitous for his welfare, my fears favoured this supposition; and for a long time his Wednesday hardly ever came round, without my entertaining a misgiving that he would not be on the coach-box as usual. There he always appeared, however, grey-headed, laughing, and happy; and he never had anything more to tell of the man who could frighten my aunt.

These Wednesdays were the happiest days of Mr. Dick's life; they were far from being the least happy of mine. He soon became known to every boy in the school; and though he never took an active part in any game but kite-flying, was as deeply interested in all our sports as any one among us. How often have I seen him, intent upon a match at marbles or pegtop, looking on with a face of unutterable interest, and hardly breathing at the critical times. How often, at hare and hounds, have I seen him mounted on a little knoll, cheering the whole field on to action, and waving his hat above his grey head, oblivious of King Charles the Martyr's head, and all belonging to it! How many a summer-hour have I known to be but blissful minutes to him in the cricket-field! How many winter days have I seen him, standing blue-nosed, in the snow and east wind, looking at the boys going down the long slide, and clapping his worsted gloves in rapture!

He was a universal favourite, and his ingenuity in little things was transcendent. He could cut oranges into such devices as none of us had an idea of. He could make a boat out of anything, from a skewer upwards. He could turn crampbones into chessmen; fashion Roman chariots from old court cards; make spoked wheels out of cotton reels, and birdcages of old wire. But he was greatest of all, perhaps, in the articles of string and straw; with which we were all persuaded he could do anything that could be done by hands.

Mr. Dick's renown was not long confined to us. After a few Wednesdays, Doctor Strong himself made some inquiries of me about him, and I told him all my aunt had told me; which interested the Doctor so much that he requested, on the occasion of his next visit, to be presented to him. This ceremony I performed; and the Doctor begging Mr. Dick, whensoever he should not find me at the coach-office, to come on there, and rest himself until our morning's work was over, it soon passed into a custom for Mr. Dick to come on as a matter of course, and, if we were a little late, as often happened on a Wednesday, to walk about the courtyard, waiting for me. Here he made the acquaintance of the Doctor's beautiful young wife (paler than formerly, all this time; more rarely seen by me or any one, I think, and not so gay, but not less beautiful), and so became more and more familiar by degrees, until, at last, he would come into the school and wait. He always sat in a particular corner, on a particular stool, which was called "Dick," after him; here he would sit, with his grey head bent forward, attentively listening to whatever might be going on with a profound veneration for the learning he had never been able to acquire.

This veneration Mr. Dick extended to the Doctor, whom he thought the most subtle and accomplished philosopher of any age. It was long before Mr. Dick ever spoke to him otherwise than bareheaded; and even when he and the Doctor had struck up quite a friendship, and would walk together by the hour, on that side of the courtyard which was known among us as The Doctor's Walk, Mr. Dick would pull off his hat at intervals to show his respect for wisdom and knowledge. How it ever came about, that the Doctor began to read out scraps of the famous Dictionary, in these walks, I never knew; perhaps he felt it all the same, at first, as reading to himself. However, it passed into a custom too; and Mr. Dick, listening with a face shining with pride and pleasure, in his heart of hearts believed the Dictionary to be the most delightful book in the world.

As I think of them going up and down before those schoolroom windows—the Doctor reading with his complacent smile, an occasional flourish of the manuscript, or grave motion of his head; and Mr. Dick listening, enchained by interest, with his poor wits calmly wandering God knows where, upon the wings of hard words—I think of it as one of the pleasantest things, in a quiet way, that I have ever seen. I feel as if they might go walking to and fro for ever, and the world might somehow be the better for it—as if a thousand things it makes a noise about, were not one-half so good for it or me.

Agnes was one of Mr. Dick's friends, very soon; and in often coming to the house, he made acquaintance with Uriah. The friendship between himself and me increased continually, and it was maintained on this odd footing: that, while Mr. Dick came professedly to look after me as my guardian, he always consulted me in any little matter of doubt that arose, and invariably guided himself by my advice; not only having a high respect for my native sagacity, but considering that I inherited a good deal from my aunt.

One Thursday morning, when I was about to walk with Mr. Dick from the hotel to the coach-office before going back to school (for we had an hour's school before breakfast), I met Uriah in the street, who reminded me of the promise I had made to take tea with himself and his mother: adding, with a writhe, "but I didn't expect you to keep it, Master Copperfield, we're so very umble."

I really had not yet been able to make up my mind whether I liked Uriah or detested him; and I was very doubtful about it still, as I stood looking him in the face in the street. But I felt it quite an affront to be supposed proud, and said I only wanted to be asked.

"Oh, if that's all, Master Copperfield," said Uriah, "and it really isn't our umbleness that prevents you, will you come this evening? But if it is our umbleness, I hope you won't mind owning to it, Master Copperfield; for we are well aware of our condition."

I said I would mention it to Mr. Wickfield, and if he approved, as I had no doubt he would, I would come with pleasure. So, at six o'clock that evening, which was one of the early office evenings, I announced myself as ready, to Uriah.

"Mother will be proud, indeed," he said, as we walked away together. "Or she would be proud, if it wasn't sinful, Master Copperfield."

"Yet you didn't mind supposing I was proud this morning," I returned.

"Oh dear, no, Master Copperfield!" returned Uriah. "Oh, believe me, no! Such a thought never came into my head! I shouldn't have deemed it at all proud if you had thought us too umble for you. Because we are so very umble."

"Have you been studying much law lately?" I asked, to change the subject.

"Oh, Master Copperfield," he said, with an air of self-denial, "my reading is hardly to be called study. I have passed an hour or two in the evening, sometimes, with Mr. Tidd."

"Rather hard, I suppose?" said I.

"He is hard to me sometimes," returned Uriah. "But I don't know what he might be, to a gifted person."

After beating a little tune on his chin as we walked on, with the two forefingers of his skeleton right-hand, he added:

"There are expressions, you see, Master Copperfield—Latin words and terms—in Mr. Tidd, that are trying to a reader of my umble attainments."

"Would you like to be taught Latin?" I said, briskly. "I will teach it you with pleasure as I learn it."

"Oh, thank you, Master Copperfield," he answered, shaking his head. "I am sure it's very kind of you to make the offer, but I am much too umble to accept it."

"What nonsense, Uriah!"

"Oh, indeed you must excuse me, Master Copperfield! I am greatly obliged, but I should like it of all things, I assure you; but I am far too umble. There are people enough to tread upon me in my lowly state, without my doing outrage to their feelings by possessing learning. Learning ain't for me. A person like myself had better not aspire. If he is to get on in life, he must get on umbly, Master Copperfield."

I never saw his mouth so wide, or the creases in his cheeks so deep, as when he delivered himself of these sentiments: shaking his head all the time, and writhing modestly.

"I think you are wrong, Uriah," I said. "I dare say

there are several things that I could teach you, if you would like to learn them."

"Oh, I don't doubt that, Master Copperfield," he answered; "not in the least. But not being umble yourself, you don't judge well, perhaps, for them that are. I won't provoke my betters with knowledge, thank you. I'm much too umble. Here is my umble dwelling, Master Copperfield!"

We entered a low, old-fashioned room, walked straight into from the street, and found there Mrs. Heep, who was the dead image of Uriah, only short. She received me with the utmost humility, and apologized to me for giving her son a kiss, observing that, lowly as they were, they had their natural affections, which they hoped would give no offence to any one. It was a perfectly decent room, half parlour and half kitchen, but not at all a snug room. The tea-things were set upon the table, and the kettle was boiling on the hob. There was a chest of drawers with an escritoire top, for Uriah to read or write at of an evening; there was Uriah's blue bag lying down and vomiting papers; there was a company of Uriah's books commanded by Mr. Tidd; there was a corner cupboard; and there were the usual articles of furniture. I don't remember that any individual object had a bare, pinched, spare look; but I do remember that the whole place had.

It was perhaps a part of Mrs. Heep's humility, that she still wore weeds. Notwithstanding the lapse of time that had occurred since Mr. Heep's decease, she still wore weeds. I think there was some compromise in the cap; but otherwise she was as weedy as in the early days of her mourning.

"This is a day to be remembered, my Uriah, I am sure," said Mrs. Heep, making the tea, "when Master Copperfield pays us a visit."

"I said you'd think so, mother," said Uriah.

"If I could have wished father to remain among us for any reason," said Mrs. Heep, "it would have been, that he might have known his company this afternoon."

I felt embarrassed by these compliments; but I was sensible, too, of being entertained as an honoured guest, and I thought Mrs. Heep an agreeable woman.

"My Uriah," said Mrs. Heep, "has looked forward to this, Sir, a long while. He had his fears that our umbleness stood in the way, and I joined in them myself. Umble we are, umble we have been, umble we shall ever be," said Mrs. Heep.

"I am sure you have no occasion to be so, ma'am," I said, "unless you like."

"Thank you, Sir," retorted Mrs. Heep. "We know our station and are thankful in it."

I found that Mrs. Heep gradually got nearer to me, and that Uriah gradually got opposite to me, and that they respectfully plied me with the choicest of the eatables on the table. There was nothing particularly choice there, to be sure; but I took the will for the deed, and felt that they were very attentive. Presently they began to talk about aunts, and then I told them about mine; and about fathers and mothers, and then I told them about mine; and then Mrs. Heep began to talk about fathers-in-law, and then I began to tell her about mine; but stopped, because my aunt had advised me to observe a silence on that subject. A tender young cork, however, would have had no more chance against a pair of corkscrews, or a tender young tooth against a pair of dentists, or a little shuttlecock against two battledores, than I had against Uriah and Mrs. Heep.

They did just what they liked with me; and wormed things out of me that I had no desire to tell, with a certainty I blush to think of the more especially as, in my juvenile frankness, I took some credit to myself for being so confidential, and felt that I was quite the patron of my two respectful entertainers.

They were very fond of one another: that was certain. I take it, that had its effect upon me, as a touch of nature; but the skill with which the one followed up whatever the other said, was a touch of art which I was still less proof against. When there was nothing more to be got out of me about myself (for on the Murdstone and Grinby life, and on my journey, I was dumb), they began about Mr. Wickfield and Agnes. Uriah threw the ball to Mrs. Heep, Mrs. Heep caught it and threw it back to Uriah, Uriah kept it up a little while, then sent it back to Mrs. Heep, and so they went on tossing it about until I had no idea who had got it, and was quite bewildered. The ball itself was always changing too. Now it was Mr. Wickfield, now Agnes, now the excellence of Mr. Wickfield, now my admiration of Agnes; now the extent of Mr. Wickfield's business and resources, now our domestic life after dinner; now, the wine that Mr. Wickfield took, the reason why he took it, and the pity that it was he took so much; now one thing, now another, then everything at once; and all the time, without appearing to speak very often, or to do anything but sometimes encourage them a little, for fear they should be overcome by their humility and the honour of my company, I found myself perpetually letting out something or other that I had no business to let out, and seeing the effect of it in the twinkling of Uriah's dinted nostrils.

I had begun to be a little uncomfortable, and to wish myself well out of the visit, when a figure coming down the street passed the door—it stood open to air the room, which was warm, the weather being close for the time of year—came back again, looked in, and walked in, exclaiming loudly, "Copperfield! Is it possible?"

It was Mr. Micawber! It was Mr. Micawber, with his eye-glass, and his walking-stick, and his shirt-collar, and his genteel air, and the condescending roll in his voice, all complete!

"My dear Copperfield," said Mr. Micawber, putting out his hand, "this is indeed a meeting which is calculated to impress the mind with a sense of the instability and uncertainty of all human—in short, it is a most extraordinary meeting. Walking along the street, reflecting upon the probability of something turning up (of which I am at present rather sanguine), I find a young but valued friend turn up, who is connected with the most eventful period of my life; I may say, with the turning-point of my existence. Copperfield, my dear fellow, how do you do?"

I cannot say—I really cannot say—that I was glad to see Mr. Micawber there; but I was glad to see him too, and shook hands with him heartily, inquiring how Mrs. Micawber was.

"Thank you," said Mr. Micawber, waving his hand as of old, and settling his chin in his shirt-collar. "She is tolerably convalescent. The twins no longer derive their sustenance from Nature's founts—in short," said Mr. Micawber, in one of his bursts of confidence, "they are weaned—and Mrs. Micawber is, at present, my travelling companion. She will be rejoiced, Copperfield, to renew her acquaintance with one who has proved himself in all respects a worthy minister at the sacred altar of friendship."

I said I should be delighted to see her.

"You are very good," said Mr. Micawber.

Mr. Micawber then smiled, settled his chin again, and looked about him.

"I have discovered my friend Copperfield," said Mr. Micawber genteelly, and without addressing himself particularly to any one, "not in solitude, but partaking of a social meal in company with a widow lady, and one who is apparently her offspring—in short," said Mr. Micawber, in another of his bursts of confidence, "her son. I shall esteem it an honour to be presented."

I could do no less, under these circumstances, than make Mr. Micawber known to Uriah Heep and his mother; which I accordingly did. As they abased themselves before him, Mr. Micawber took a seat, and waved his hand in his most courtly manner.

"Any friend of my friend Copperfield's," said Mr. Micawber, "has a personal claim upon myself."

"We are too umble, Sir," said Mrs. Heep, "my son and me, to be the friends of Master Copperfield. He has been so good as take his tea with us, and we are thankful to him for his company; also to you, Sir, for your notice."

"Ma'am," returned Mr. Micawber, with a bow, "you are very obliging: and what are you doing, Copperfield? Still in the wine trade?"

I was excessively anxious to get Mr. Micawber away; and replied, with my hat in my hand, and a very red face, I have no doubt, that I was a pupil at Doctor Strong's.

"A pupil?" said Mr. Micawber, raising his eyebrows. "I am extremely happy to hear it. Although a mind like my friend Copperfield's"—to Uriah and Mrs. Heep,—"does not require that cultivation which, without his knowledge of men and things, it would require, still it is a rich soil teeming with latent vegetation—in short," said Mr. Micawber, smiling, in another burst of confidence, "it is an intellect capable of getting up the classics to any extent."

Uriah, with his long hands slowly twining over one another, made a ghastly writhe from the waist upwards, to express his concurrence in this estimation of me.

"Shall we go and see Mrs. Micawber, Sir?" I said, to get Mr. Micawber away.

"If you will do her that favour, Copperfield," replied Mr. Micawber, rising. "I have no scruple in saying, in the presence of our friends here, that I am a man who has, for some years, contended against the pressure of pecuniary difficulties." I knew he was certain to say something of this kind; he always would be so boastful about his difficulties. "Sometimes I have risen superior to my difficulties. Sometimes my difficulties have—in short, have floored me. There have been times when I have administered a succession of facers to them; there have been times when they have been too many for me, and I have given in, and said to Mrs. Micawber in the words of Cato, 'Plato, thou reasonest well. It's all up now. I can show fight no more.' But at no time of my life," said Mr. Micawber, "have I enjoyed a higher degree of satisfaction than in pouring my griefs (if I may describe difficulties, chiefly arising out of warrants of attorney and promissory notes at two and four months, by that word) into the bosom of my friend Copperfield."

Mr. Micawber closed this handsome tribute by saying, "Mr. Heep! Good evening. Mrs. Heep! Your servant,"

and then walking out with me in his most fashionable manner, making a good deal of noise on the pavement with his shoes, and humming a tune as we went.

It was a little inn where Mr. Micawber put up, and he occupied a little room in it, partitioned off from the commercial room, and strongly flavoured with tobacco-smoke. I think it was over the kitchen, because a warm greasy smell appeared to come up through the chinks in the floor, and there was a flabby perspiration on the walls. I know it was near the bar, on account of the smell of spirits and jingling of glasses. Here, recumbent on a small sofa, underneath a picture of a racehorse, with her head close to the fire, and her feet pushing the mustard off the dumbwaiter at the other end of the room, was Mrs. Micawber, to whom Mr. Micawber entered first, saying, "My dear, allow me to introduce to you a pupil of Doctor Strong's."

I noticed, by-the-by, that although Mr. Micawber was just as much confused as ever about my age and standing, he always remembered, as a genteel thing, that I was a pupil of Doctor Strong's.

Mrs. Micawber was amazed, but very glad to see me. I was very glad to see her too, and, after an affectionate greeting on both sides, sat down on the small sofa near her.

"My dear," said Mr. Micawber, "if you will mention to Copperfield what our present position is, which I have no doubt he will like to know, I will go and look at the paper the while, and see whether anything turns up among the advertisements."

"I thought you were at Plymouth, ma'am," I said to Mrs. Micawber, as he went out.

"My dear Master Copperfield," she replied, "we went to Plymouth."

"To be on the spot," I hinted.

"Just so," said Mrs. Micawber. "To be on the spot. But, the truth is, talent is not wanted in the Custom House. The local influence of my family was quite unavailing to obtain any employment in that department, for a man of Mr. Micawber's abilities. They would rather *not* have a man of Mr. Micawber's abilities. He would only show the deficiency of the others. Apart from which," said Mrs. Micawber, "I will not disguise from you, my dear Master Copperfield, that when that branch of my family which is settled in Plymouth became aware that Mr. Micawber was accompanied by myself, and by little Wilkins and his sister, and by the twins, they did not receive him with that ardour which he might have expected, being so newly released from captivity. In fact," said Mrs. Micawber, lowering her voice,—"this is between ourselves—our reception was cool."

"Dear me!" I said.

"Yes," said Mrs. Micawber. "It is truly painful to contemplate mankind in such an aspect, Master Copperfield, but our reception was, decidedly, cool. There is no doubt about it. In fact, that branch of my family which is settled in Plymouth became quite personal to Mr. Micawber, before we had been there a week."

I said, and thought, that they ought to be ashamed of themselves.

"Still, so it was," continued Mrs. Micawber. "Under such circumstances, what could a man of Mr. Micawber's spirit do. But one obvious course was left. To borrow of that branch of my family the money to return to London, and to return at any sacrifice."

"Then you all came back again, ma'am?" I said.

"We all came back again," replied Mrs. Micawber. "Since then, I have consulted other branches of my family on the course which it is most expedient for Mr. Micawber to take—for I maintain that he must take some course, Master Copperfield," said Mrs. Micawber, argumentatively. "It is clear that a family of six, not including a domestic, cannot live upon air."

"Certainly, ma'am," said I.

"The opinion of those other branches of my family," pursued Mrs. Micawber, "is, that Mr. Micawber should immediately turn his attention to coals."

"To what, ma'am?"

"To coals," said Mrs. Micawber. "To the coal trade. Mr. Micawber was induced to think, on inquiry, that there might be an opening for a man of his talent in the Medway Coal Trade. Then, as Mr. Micawber very properly said, the first step to be taken clearly was, to come and *see* the Medway. Which we came and saw. I say 'we,' Master Copperfield; for I never will," said Mrs. Micawber with emotion, "I never will desert Mr. Micawber."

I murmured my admiration and approbation.

"We came," repeated Mrs. Micawber, "and saw the Medway. My opinion of the coal trade on that river, is, that it may require talent, but that it certainly requires capital. Talent, Mr. Micawber has; capital, Mr. Micawber has not. We saw, I think, the greater part of the Medway; and that is my individual conclusion. Being so near here, Mr. Micawber was of opinion that it would be rash not to come on, and see the Cathedral. Firstly, on account of its being so well worth seeing, and our never having seen it; and secondly, on account of the great probability of something turning up in a cathedral town. We have been here," said Mrs. Micawber, "three days. Nothing has, as yet, turned up; and it may not surprise you, my dear Master Copperfield, so much as it would a stranger, to know that we are at present waiting for a remittance from London, to discharge our pecuniary obligations at this hotel. Until the arrival of that remittance," said Mrs. Micawber with much feeling, "I am cut off from my home (I allude to lodgings in Pentonville), from my boy and girl, and from my twins."

I felt the utmost sympathy for Mr. and Mrs. Micawber in this anxious extremity, and said as much to Mr. Micawber, who now returned: adding that I only wished I had money enough, to lend them the amount they needed. Mr. Micawber's answer expressed the disturbance of his mind. He said, shaking hands with me, "Copperfield, you are a true friend; but when the worst comes to the worst, no man is without a friend who is possessed of shaving materials." At this dreadful hint Mrs. Micawber threw her arms round Mr. Micawber's neck and entreated him to be calm. He wept; but so far recovered, almost immediately, as to ring the bell for the waiter, and bespeak a hot kidney pudding and a plate of shrimps for breakfast in the morning.

When I took my leave of them, they both pressed me so much to come and dine before they went away, that I could not refuse. But, as I knew I could not come next day, when I should have a good deal to prepare in the evening, Mr. Micawber arranged that he would call at Doctor Strong's in the course of the morning (having a presentiment that the remittance would arrive by that post), and propose the day after, if it would suit me better.

Accordingly I was called out of school next forenoon, and found Mr. Micawber in the parlour; who had called to say that the dinner would take place as proposed. When I asked him if the remittance had come, he pressed my hand and departed.

As I was looking out of the window that same evening, it surprised me, and made me rather uneasy, to see Mr. Micawber and Uriah Heep walk past, arm-in-arm: Uriah humbly sensible of the honour that was done him, and Mr. Micawber taking a bland delight in extending his patronage to Uriah. But I was still more surprised, when I went to the little hotel next day at the appointed dinner-hour, which was four o'clock, to find, from what Mr. Micawber said, that he had gone home with Uriah, and had drunk brandy-and-water at Mrs. Heep's.

"And I'll tell you what, my dear Copperfield," said Mr. Micawber, "your friend Heep is a young fellow who might be Attorney-General. If I had known that young man, at the period when my difficulties came to a crisis, all I can say is, that I believe my creditors would have been a great deal better managed than they were."

I hardly understood how this could have been, seeing that Mr. Micawber had paid them nothing at all as it was; but I did not like to ask. Neither did I like to say, that I hoped he had not been too communicative to Uriah; or to inquire if they had talked much about me. I was afraid of hurting Mr. Micawber's feelings, or, at all events, Mrs. Micawber's, she being very sensitive; but I was uncomfortable about it, too, and often thought about it afterwards.

We had a beautiful little dinner. Quite an elegant dish of fish; the kidney-end of a loin of veal, roasted; fried sausage meat; a partridge, and a pudding. There was wine, and there was strong ale; and after dinner Mrs. Micawber made us a bowl of hot punch with her own hands.

Mr. Micawber was uncommonly convivial. I never saw him such good company. He made his face shine with the punch, so that it looked as if it had been varnished all over. He got cheerfully sentimental about the town, and proposed success to it; observing that Mrs. Micawber and himself had been made extremely snug and comfortable there, and that he never should forget the agreeable hours they had passed in Canterbury. He proposed me afterwards; and he, and Mrs. Micawber, and I, took a review of our past acquaintance, in the course of which, we sold the property all over again. Then I proposed Mrs. Micawber; or, at least, said, modestly, "If you'll allow me, Mrs. Micawber, I shall now have the pleasure of drinking *your* health, ma'am." On which Mr. Micawber delivered an eulogium on Mrs. Micawber's character, and said she had ever been his guide, philosopher, and friend, and that he would recommend me, when I came to a marrying-time of life, to marry such another woman, if such another woman could be found.

As the punch disappeared, Mr. Micawber became still more friendly and convivial. Mrs. Micawber's spirits becoming elevated, too, we sang "Auld Lang Syne." When we came to "Here's a hand, my trusty frere," we all joined hands round the table; and when we declared we would "take a right gude willie-waught," and hadn't the least idea what it meant, we were really affected.

In a word, I never saw anybody so thoroughly jovial as Mr. Micawber was, down to the very last moment of the evening, when I took a hearty farewell of himself and his amiable wife. Consequently, I was not prepared, at seven o'clock next morning, to receive the following communication, dated half-past nine in the evening; a quarter of an hour after I had left him.

"MY DEAR YOUNG FRIEND,

"The die is cast—all is over. Hiding the ravages of care with a sickly mask of mirth, I have not informed you, this evening, that there is no hope of the remittance! Under these circumstances, alike humiliating to endure, humiliating to comtemplate, and humiliating to relate, I have discharged the pecuniary liability contracted at this establishment, by giving a note of hand, made payable fourteen days after date, at my residence, Pentonville, London. When it becomes due, it will not be taken up. The result is destruction. The bolt is impending, and the tree must fall.

"Let the wretched man who now addresses you, my dear Copperfield, be a beacon to you through life. He writes with that intention, and in that hope. If he could think himself of so much use, one gleam of day might, by possibility, penetrate into the cheerless dungeon of his remaining existence—though his longevity is, at present (to say the least of it), extremely problematical.

"This is the last communication, my dear Copperfield, you will ever receive

"From
"The
"Beggared Outcast,
"WILKINS MICAWBER."

I was so shocked by the contents of this heartrending letter, that I ran off directly towards the little hotel with the intention of taking it on my way to Doctor Strong's, and trying to soothe Mr. Micawber with a word of comfort. But, half-way there, I met the London coach with Mr. and Mrs. Micawber up behind; Mr. Micawber, the very picture of tranquil enjoyment, smiling at Mrs. Micawber's conversation, eating walnuts out of a paper bag, with a bottle sticking out of his breast-pocket. As they did not see me, I thought it best, all things considered, not to see them. So, with a great weight taken off my mind, I turned into a by-street that was the nearest way to school, and felt, upon the whole, relieved that they were gone; though I still liked them very much, nevertheless.

CHAPTER XVIII.

A RETROSPECT.

MY schooldays! The silent gliding on of my existence—the unseen, unfelt progress of my life—from childhood up to youth! Let me think, as I look back upon that flowing water, now a dry channel overgrown with leaves, whether there are any marks along its course, by which I can remember how it ran.

A moment, and I occupy my place in the Cathedral, where we all went together every Sunday morning, assembling first at school for that purpose. The earthy smell, the sunless air, the sensation of the world being shut out, the resounding of the organ through the black and white arched galleries and aisles, are wings that take me back,

and hold me hovering above those days, in a half-sleeping and half-waking dream.

I am not the last boy in the school. I have risen, in a few months, over several heads. But the first boy seems to me a mighty creature, dwelling afar off, whose giddy height is unattainable. Agnes says "No," but I say "Yes," and tell her that she little thinks what stores of knowledge have been mastered by the wonderful Being, at whose place she thinks I, even I, weak aspirant, may arrive in time. He is not my private friend and public patron, as Steerforth was; but I hold him in a reverential respect. I chiefly wonder what he'll be, when he leaves Doctor Strong's, and what mankind will do to maintain any place against him.

But who is this that breaks upon me? This is Miss Shepherd, whom I love.

Miss Shepherd is a boarder at the Misses Nettingalls' establishment. I adore Miss Shepherd. She is a little girl, in a spencer, with a round face and curly flaxen hair. The Misses Nettingalls' young ladies come to the Cathedral too. I cannot look upon my book, for I must look upon Miss Shepherd. When the choristers chaunt, I hear Miss Shepherd. In the service I mentally insert Miss Shepherd's name—I put her in among the Royal Family. At home, in my own room, I am sometimes moved to cry out, "Oh, Miss Shepherd!" in a transport of love.

For some time, I am doubtful of Miss Shepherd's feelings, but, at length, Fate being propitious, we meet at the dancing-school. I have Miss Shepherd for my partner. I touch Miss Shepherd's glove, and feel a thrill go up the right arm of my jacket, and come out at my hair. I say nothing tender to Miss Shepherd, but we understand each other. Miss Shepherd and myself live but to be united.

Why do I secretly give Miss Shepherd twelve Brazil nuts for a present, I wonder? They are not expressive of affection, they are difficult to pack into a parcel of any regular shape, they are hard to crack, even in room-doors, and they are oily when cracked; yet I feel that they are appropriate to Miss Shepherd. Soft, seedy biscuits, also, I bestow upon Miss Shepherd; and oranges innumerable. Once, I kiss Miss Shepherd in the cloak-room. Ecstasy! What are my agony and indignation next day, when I hear a flying rumour that the Misses Nettingall have stood Miss Shepherd in the stocks for turning in her toes!

Miss Shepherd being the one pervading theme and vision of my life, how do I ever come to break with her? I can't conceive. And yet a coolness grows between Miss Shepherd and myself. Whispers reach me of Miss Shepherd having said she wished I wouldn't stare so, and having I avowed a preference for Master Jones—for Jones! a boy of no merit whatever. The gulf between me and Miss Shepherd widens. At last, one day, I meet the Misses Nettingalls' establishment out walking. Miss Shepherd makes a face as she goes by, and laughs to her companion. All is over. The devotion of a life—it seems a life, it is all the same—is at an end; Miss Shepherd comes out of the morning service, and the Royal Family know her no more.

I am higher in the school, and no one breaks my peace. I am not at all polite, now, to the Misses Nettingalls' young ladies, and shouldn't dote on any of them, if they were twice as many and twenty times as beautiful. I think the dancing-school a tiresome affair, and wonder why the girls can't dance by themselves and leave us alone. I am growing great in Latin verses, and neglect the laces of my boots. Doctor Strong refers to me in public as a promising young scholar. Mr. Dick is wild with joy, and my aunt remits me a guinea by the next post.

The shade of a young butcher rises, like the apparition of an armed head in Macbeth. Who is this young butcher? He is the terror of the youth of Canterbury. There is a vague belief abroad, that the beef suet with which he anoints his hair gives him unnatural strength, and that he is a match for a man. He is a broad-faced, bull-necked young butcher, with rough red cheeks, an ill-conditioned mind, and an injurious tongue. His main use of this tongue, is, to disparage Doctor Strong's young gentlemen. He says, publicly, that if they want anything he'll give it 'em. He names individuals among them (myself included), whom he could undertake to settle with one hand, and the other tied behind him. He waylays the smaller boys to punch their unprotected heads, and calls challenges after me in the open streets. For these sufficient reasons I resolve to fight the butcher.

It is a summer evening, down in a green hollow, at the corner of a wall. I meet the butcher by appointment. I am attended by a select body of our boys; the butcher, by two other butchers, a young publican, and a sweep. The preliminaries are adjusted, and the butcher and myself stand face to face. In a moment the butcher lights ten thousand candles out of my left eyebrow. In another moment, I don't know where the wall is, or where I am, or where anybody is. I hardly know which is myself and which the butcher, we are always in such a tangle and tussle, knocking about upon the trodden grass. Sometimes I see the butcher, bloody but confident; sometimes I see nothing, and sit gasping on my second's knee; sometimes I go in at the butcher madly, and cut my knuckles open against his face, without appearing to discompose him at all. At last I awake, very queer about the head, as from a giddy sleep, and see the butcher walking off, congratulated by the two other butchers and the sweep and publican, and putting on his coat as he goes; from which I augur, justly, that the victory is his.

I am taken home in a sad plight, and I have beef-steaks put to my eyes, and am rubbed with vinegar and brandy, and find a great white puffy place bursting out on my upper lip, which swells immoderately. For three or four days I remain at home, a very ill-looking subject, with a green shade over my eyes; and I should be very dull, but that Agnes is a sister to me, and condoles with me, and reads to me, and makes the time light and happy. Agnes has my confidence completely, always; I tell her all about the butcher, and the wrongs he has heaped upon me; and she thinks I couldn't have done otherwise than fight the butcher, while she shrinks and trembles at my having fought him.

Time has stolen on unobserved, for Adams is not the head-boy in the days that are come now, nor has he been this many and many a day. Adams has left the school so long, that when he comes back, on a visit to Doctor Strong, there are not many there, besides myself, who know him. Adams is going to be called to the bar almost directly, and is to be an advocate, and to wear a wig. I am surprised to find him a meeker man than I had thought, and less imposing in appearance. He has not staggered the world yet, either; for it goes on (as well as I can make out) pretty much the same as if he had never joined it.

A blank, through which the warriors of poetry and history march on in stately hosts that seem to have no end—

and what comes next! *I* am the head-boy, now; and look down on the line of boys below me, with a condescending interest in such of them as bring to my mind the boy I was myself, when I first came there. That little fellow seems to be no part of me; I remember him as something left behind upon the road of life—as something I have passed, rather than have actually been—and almost think of him as of some one else.

And the little girl I saw on that first day at Mr. Wickfield's, where is she? Gone also. In her stead, the perfect likeness of the picture, a child likeness no more, moves about the house; and Agnes—my sweet sister, as I call her in my thoughts, my counsellor and friend, the better angel of the lives of all who come within her calm, good, self-denying influence—is quite a woman.

What other changes have come upon me, besides the changes in my growth and looks, and in the knowledge I have garnered all this while? I wear a gold watch and chain, a ring upon my little finger, and a long-tailed coat; and I use a great deal of bear's grease—which, taken in conjunction with the ring, looks bad. Am I in love again? I am. I worship the eldest Miss Larkins.

The eldest Miss Larkins is not a little girl. She is a tall, dark, black-eyed, fine figure of a woman. The eldest Miss Larkins is not a chicken; for the youngest Miss Larkins is not that, and the eldest must be three or four years older. Perhaps the eldest Miss Larkins may be about thirty. My passion for her is beyond all bounds.

The eldest Miss Larkins knows officers. It is an awful thing to bear. I see them speaking to her in the street. I see them cross the way to meet her, when her bonnet (she has a bright taste in bonnets) is seen coming down the pavement, accompanied by her sister's bonnet. She laughs and talks, and seems to like it. I spend a good deal of my own spare time in walking up and down to meet her. If I can bow to her once in the day (I know her to bow to, knowing Mr. Larkins), I am happier. I deserve a bow now and then. The raging agonies I suffer on the night of the Race Ball, where I know the eldest Miss Larkins will be dancing with the military, ought to have some compensation, if there be even-handed justice in the world.

My passion takes away my appetite, and makes me wear my newest silk neck-kerchief continually. I have no relief but in putting on my best clothes, and having my boots cleaned over and over again. I seem, then, to be worthier of the eldest Miss Larkins. Everything that belongs to her, or is connected with her, is precious to me. Mr. Larkins (a gruff old gentleman with a double chin, and one of his eyes immovable in his head) is fraught with interest to me. When I can't meet his daughter, I go where I am likely to meet him. To say, "How do you do, Mr. Larkins? Are the young ladies and all the family quite well?" seems so pointed, that I blush.

I think continually about my age. Say I am seventeen, and say that seventeen is young for the eldest Miss Larkins, what of that? Besides, I shall be one-and-twenty in no time almost. I regularly take walks outside Mr. Larkins's house in the evening, though it cuts me to the heart to see the officers go in, or to hear them up in the drawing-room, where the eldest Miss Larkins plays the harp. I even walk, on two or three occasions, in a sickly, spoony manner, round and round the house after the family are gone to bed, wondering which is the eldest Miss Larkins's chamber (and pitching, I dare say now, on Mr. Larkins's instead); wishing that a fire would burst out; that the assembled crowd would stand appalled; that I, dashing through them with a ladder, might rear it against her window, save her in my arms, go back for something she had left behind, and perish in the flames. For I am generally disinterested in my love, and think I could be content to make a figure before Miss Larkins, and expire.—Generally, but not always. Sometimes brighter visions rise before me. When I dress (the occupation of two hours), for a great ball given at the Larkins's (the anticipation of three weeks), I indulge my fancy with pleasing images. I picture myself taking courage to make a declaration to Miss Larkins. I picture Miss Larkins sinking her head upon my shoulder, and saying, "Oh, Mr. Copperfield, can I believe my ears!" I picture Mr. Larkins waiting on me next morning, and saying, "My dear Copperfield, my daughter has told me all. Youth is no objection. Here are twenty thousand pounds. Be happy!" I picture my aunt relenting, and blessing us; and Mr. Dick and Doctor Strong being present at the marriage ceremony. I am a sensible fellow, I believe—I believe, on looking back, I mean—and modest I am sure; but all this goes on notwithstanding.

I repair to the enchanted house, where there are lights, chattering, music, flowers, officers (I am sorry to see), and the eldest Miss Larkins, a blaze of beauty. She is dressed in blue, with blue flowers in her hair—forget-me-nots. As if *she* had any need to wear forget-me-nots! It is the first really grown-up party that I have ever been invited to, and I am a little uncomfortable; for I appear not to belong to anybody, and nobody appears to have anything to say to me, except Mr. Larkins, who asks me how my schoolfellows are, which he needn't do, as I have not come there to be insulted. But after I have stood in the doorway for some time, and feasted my eyes upon the goddess of my heart, she approaches me—she, the eldest Miss Larkins!—and asks me pleasantly, if I dance.

I stammer, with a bow, "With you, Miss Larkins."

"With no one else?" inquires Miss Larkins.

"I should have no pleasure in dancing with any one else."

Miss Larkins laughs and blushes (or I think she blushes) and says, "Next time but one, I shall be very glad."

The time arrives. "It is a waltz, I think," Miss Larkins doubtfully observes, when I present myself. "Do you waltz? If not, Captain Bailey——"

But I do waltz (pretty well, too, as it happens), and I take Miss Larkins out. I take her sternly from the side of Captain Bailey. He is wretched, I have no doubt; but he is nothing to me. I have been wretched, too. I waltz with the eldest Miss Larkins! I don't know where, among whom, or how long. I only know that I swim about in space, with a blue angel, in a state of blissful delirium, until I find myself alone with her in a little room, resting on a sofa. She admires a flower (pink camellia japonica, price half-a-crown), in my buttonhole. I give it her, and say:

"I ask an inestimable price for it, Miss Larkins."

"Indeed! What is that?" returns Miss Larkins.

"A flower of yours, that I may treasure it as a miser does gold."

"You're a bold boy," says Miss Larkins. "There."

She gives it me, not displeased; and I put it to my lips, and then into my breast. Miss Larkins, laughing, draws her hand through my arm, and says, "Now take me back to Captain Bailey."

I am lost in the recollection of this delicious interview, and the waltz, when she comes to me again, with a plain elderly gentleman, who has been playing whist all night, upon her arm, and says:

"Oh, here is my bold friend! Mr. Chestle wants to know you, Mr. Copperfield."

I feel at once that he is a friend of the family, and am much gratified.

"I admire your taste, Sir," says Mr. Chestle. "It does you credit. I suppose you don't take much interest in hops; but I am a pretty large grower myself; and if you ever like to come over to our neighbourhood—neighbourhood of Ashford—and take a run about our place, we shall be glad for you to stop as long as you like."

I thank Mr. Chestle warmly, and shake hands. I think I am in a happy dream. I waltz with the eldest Miss Larkins once again—she says I waltz so well! I go home in a state of unspeakable bliss, and waltz in imagination, all night long, with my arm round the blue waist of my dear divinity. For some days afterwards, I am lost in rapturous reflections; but I neither see her in the street, nor when I call. I am imperfectly consoled for this disappointment by the sacred pledge, the perished flower.

"Trotwood," says Agnes, one day after dinner. "Who do you think is going to be married to-morrow? Some one you admire."

"Not you, I suppose, Agnes?"

"Not me!" raising her cheerful face from the music she is copying. "Do you hear him, papa?—The eldest Miss Larkins."

"To—to Captain Bailey?" I have just power enough to ask.

"No; to no Captain. To Mr. Chestle, a hop-grower."

I am terribly dejected for about a week or two. I take off my ring, I wear my worst clothes, I use no bear's grease, and I frequently lament over the late Miss Larkins's faded flower. Being, by that time, rather tired of this kind of life, and having received new provocation from the butcher, I throw the flower away, go out with the butcher, and gloriously defeat him.

This, and the resumption of my ring, as well as of the bear's grease in moderation, are the last marks I can discern, now, in my progress to seventeen.

CHAPTER XIX.

I LOOK ABOUT ME, AND MAKE A DISCOVERY.

I AM doubtful whether I was at heart glad or sorry, when my schooldays drew to an end, and the time came for my leaving Doctor Strong's. I had been very happy there, I had a great attachment for the Doctor, and I was eminent and distinguished in that little world. For these reasons I was sorry to go; but for other reasons, unsubstantial enough, I was glad. Misty ideas of being a young man at my own disposal, of the importance attaching to a young man at his own disposal, of the wonderful things to be seen and done by that magnificent animal, and the wonderful effects he could not fail to make upon society, lured me away. So powerful were these visionary considerations in my boyish mind, that I seem, according to my present way of thinking, to have left school without natural regret. The separation has not made the impression on me, that other separations have. I try in vain to recall how I felt about it, and what its circumstances were; but it is not momentous in my recollection. I suppose the opening prospect confused me. I know that my juvenile experiences went for little or nothing then; and that life was more like a great fairy story, which I was just about to begin to read, than anything else.

My aunt and I had held many grave deliberations on the calling to which I should be devoted. For a year or more I had endeavoured to find a satisfactory answer to her often-repeated question, "What I would like to be?" But I had no particular liking, that I could discover, for anything. If I could have been inspired with a knowledge of the science of navigation, taken the command of a fast-sailing expedition, and gone round the world on a triumphant voyage of discovery, I think I might have considered myself completely suited. But in the absence of any such miraculous provision, my desire was to apply myself to some pursuit that would not lie too heavily upon her purse; and to do my duty in it, whatever it might be.

Mr. Dick had regularly assisted at our councils, with a meditative and sage demeanour. He never made a suggestion but once; and on that occasion (I don't know what put it in his head), he suddenly proposed that I should be "a brazier." My aunt received this proposal so very ungraciously, that he never ventured on a second; but ever afterwards confined himself to looking watchfully at her for her suggestions, and rattling his money.

"Trot, I tell you what, my dear," said my aunt, one morning in the Christmas season when I left school; "as this knotty point is still unsettled, and as we must not make a mistake in our decision if we can help it, I think we had better take a little breathing-time. In the meanwhile, you must try to look at it from a new point of view, and not as a schoolboy."

"I will, aunt."

"It has occurred to me," pursued my aunt, "that a little change, and a glimpse of life out of doors, may be useful, in helping you to know your own mind, and form a cooler judgment. Suppose you were to take a little journey now. Suppose you were to go down into the old part of the country again, for instance, and see that—that out-of-the-way woman with the savagest of names," said my aunt, rubbing her nose, for she could never thoroughly forgive Peggotty for being so called.

"Of all things in the world, aunt, I should like it best!"

"Well," said my aunt, "that's lucky, for I should like it too. But it's natural and rational that you should like it. And I am very well persuaded that whatever you do, Trot, will always be natural and rational."

"I hope so, aunt."

"Your sister, Betsey Trotwood," said my aunt, "would have been as natural and rational a girl as ever breathed. You'll be worthy of her, won't you?"

"I hope I shall be worthy of *you*, aunt. That will be enough for me."

"It's a mercy that poor dear baby of a mother of yours didn't live," said my aunt, looking at me approvingly, "or she'd have been so vain of her boy by this time, that her soft little head would have been completely turned, if there was anything of it left to turn." (My aunt always excused any weakness of her own in my behalf, by transferring it in this way to my poor mother.) "Bless me, Trotwood, how you do remind me of her!"

"Pleasantly, I hope, aunt?" said I.

"He's as like her, Dick," said my aunt, emphatically, "he's as like her, as she was that afternoon, before she began to fret—bless my heart, he's as like her, as he can look at me out of his two eyes!"

"Is he indeed?" said Mr. Dick.

"And he's like David, too," said my aunt, decisively.

"He is very like David!" said Mr. Dick.

"But what I want you to be, Trot," resumed my aunt, "—I don't mean physically, but morally; you are very well physically—is, a firm fellow. A fine firm fellow, with a will of your own. With resolution," said my aunt, shaking her cap at me, and clenching her hand. "With determination. With character, Trot—with strength of character that is not to be influenced, except on good reason, by anybody, or by anything. That's what I want you to be. That's what your father and mother might both have been, Heaven knows, and been the better for it."

I intimated that I hoped I should be what she described.

"That you may begin, in a small way, to have a reliance upon yourself, and to act for yourself," said my aunt, "I shall send you upon your trip, alone. I did think, once, of Mr. Dick's going with you; but, on second thoughts, I shall keep him to take care of me."

Mr. Dick, for a moment, looked a little disappointed; until the honour and dignity of having to take care of the most wonderful woman in the world, restored the sunshine to his face.

"Besides," said my aunt, "there's the Memorial."

"Oh, certainly," said Mr. Dick, in a hurry, "I intend, Trotwood, to get that done immediately—it really must be done immediately! And then it will go in, you know—and then—," said Mr. Dick, after checking himself, and pausing a long time, "there'll be a pretty kettle of fish!"

In pursuance of my aunt's kind scheme, I was shortly afterwards fitted out with a handsome purse of money, and a portmanteau, and tenderly dismissed upon my expedition. At parting, my aunt gave me some good advice, and a good many kisses; and said that as her object was that I should look about me, and should think a little, she would recommend me to stay a few days in London, if I liked it, either on my way down into Suffolk, or in coming back. In a word, I was at liberty to do what I would, for three weeks or a month; and no other conditions were imposed upon my freedom than the before-mentioned thinking and looking about me, and a pledge to write three times a week and faithfully report myself.

I went to Canterbury first, that I might take leave of Agnes and Mr. Wickfield (my old room in whose house I had not yet relinquished), and also of the good Doctor. Agnes was very glad to see me, and told me that the house had not been like itself since I had left it.

"I am sure I am not like myself when I am away," said I. "I seem to want my right hand, when I miss you. Though that's not saying much; for there's no head in my right hand, and no heart. Every one who knows you, consults with you, and is guided by you, Agnes."

"Every one who knows me, spoils me, I believe," she answered, smiling.

"No. It's because you are like no one else. You are so good, and so sweet-tempered. You have such a gentle nature, and you are always right."

"You talk," said Agnes, breaking into a pleasant laugh, as she sat at work, "as if I were the late Miss Larkins."

"Come! It's not fair to abuse my confidence," I answered, reddening at the recollection of my blue enslaver.

"But I shall confide in you, just the same, Agnes. I can never grow out of that. Whenever I fall into trouble, or fall in love, I shall always tell you, if you'll let me—even when I come to fall in love in earnest."

"Why, you have always been in earnest!" said Agnes, laughing again.

"Oh! that was as a child, or a schoolboy," said I, laughing in my turn, not without being a little shamefaced. "Times are altering now, and I suppose I shall be in a terrible state of earnestness one day or other. My wonder is, that you are not in earnest yourself, by this time, Agnes."

Agnes laughed again, and shook her head.

"Oh, I know you are not!" said I, "because if you had been, you would have told me. Or at least—" for I saw a faint blush in her face, "you would have let me find it out for myself. But there is no one that I know of, who deserves to love *you*, Agnes. Some one of a nobler character, and more worthy altogether than anyone I have ever seen here, must rise up, before I give *my* consent. In the time to come, I shall have a wary eye on all admirers; and shall exact a great deal from the successful one, I assure you."

We had gone on, so far, in a mixture of confidential jest and earnest, that had long grown naturally out of our familiar relations, begun as mere children. But Agnes, now suddenly lifting up her eyes to mine, and speaking in a different manner, said:

"Trotwood, there is something that I want to ask you, and that I may not have another opportunity of asking for a long time, perhaps—something I would ask, I think, of no one else. Have you observed any gradual alteration in papa?"

I had observed it, and had often wondered whether she had too. I must have shown as much, now, in my face; for her eyes were in a moment cast down, and I saw tears in them.

"Tell me what it is," she said, in a low voice.

"I think—shall I be quite plain, Agnes, liking him so much?"

"Yes," she said.

"I think he does himself no good by the habit that has increased upon him since I first came here. He is often very nervous—or I fancy so."

"It is not fancy," said Agnes, shaking her head.

"His hand trembles, his speech is not plain, and his eyes look wild. I have remarked that at those times, and when he is least like himself, he is most certain to be wanted on some business."

"By Uriah," said Agnes.

"Yes; and the sense of being unfit for it, or of not having understood it, or of having shown his condition in spite of himself, seems to make him so uneasy, that next day he is worse, and next day worse, and so he becomes jaded and haggard. Do not be alarmed by what I say, Agnes, but in this state I saw him, only the other evening, lay down his head upon his desk, and shed tears like a child."

Her hand passed softly before my lips while I was yet speaking, and in a moment she had met her father at the door of the room, and was hanging on his shoulder. The expression of her face, as they both looked towards me, I felt to be very touching. There was such deep fondness for him, and gratitude to him for all his love and care, in her beautiful look; and there was such a fervent appeal to me to deal tenderly by him, even in my inmost thoughts, and to let no harsh construction find any place against him; she was, at once, so proud of him and devoted to him, yet so compassionate and sorry, and so reliant upon me to be so, too; that nothing she could have said would have expressed more to me, or moved me more.

We were to drink tea at the Doctor's. We went there at the usual hour; and round the study-fireside found the Doctor, and his young wife, and her mother. The Doctor, who made as much of my going away as if I were going to China, received me as an honoured guest; and called for a log of wood to be thrown on the fire, that he might see the face of his old pupil reddening in the blaze.

"I shall not see many more new faces in Trotwood's stead, Wickfield," said the Doctor, warming his hands; "I am getting lazy, and want ease. I shall relinquish all my young people in another six months, and lead a quieter life."

"You have said so, any time these ten years, Doctor," Mr. Wickfield answered.

"But now I mean to do it," returned the Doctor. "My first master will succeed me—I am in earnest at last—so you'll soon have to arrange our contracts, and to bind us firmly to them, like a couple of knaves."

"And to take care," said Mr. Wickfield, "that you're not imposed on, eh? As you certainly would be, in any contract you should make for yourself. Well! I am ready. There are worse tasks than that, in my calling."

"I shall have nothing to think of then," said the Doctor, with a smile, "but my Dictionary; and this other contract-bargain—Annie."

As Mr. Wickfield glanced towards her, sitting at the tea-table by Agnes, she seemed to me to avoid his look with such unwonted hesitation and timidity, that his attention became fixed upon her, as if something were suggested to his thoughts.

"There is a post come in from India, I observe," he said, after a short silence.

"By-the-by! and letters from Mr. Jack Maldon!" said the Doctor.

"Indeed?"

"Poor dear Jack!" said Mrs. Markleham, shaking her head. "That trying climate. Like living, they tell me, on a sand-heap, underneath a burning-glass! He looked strong, but he wasn't. My dear Doctor, it was his spirit, not his constitution, that he ventured on so boldly. Annie, my dear, I am sure you must perfectly recollect that your cousin never was strong—not what can be called *robust*, you know," said Mrs. Markleham, with emphasis, and looking round upon us generally—"from the time when my daughter and himself were children together, and walking about, arm in arm, the livelong day."

Annie, thus addressed, made no reply.

"Do I gather from what you say, ma'am, that Mr. Maldon is ill?" asked Mr. Wickfield.

"Ill!" replied the Old Soldier. "My dear Sir, he's all sorts of things."

"Except well?" said Mr. Wickfield.

"Except well, indeed!" said the Old Soldier. "He has had dreadful strokes of the sun, no doubt, and jungle fevers and agues, and every kind of thing you can mention. As to his liver," said the Old Soldier resignedly, "that, of course, he gave up altogether, when he first went out!"

"Does he say all this?" asked Mr. Wickfield.

"Say? My dear Sir," returned Mrs. Markleham, shaking her head and her fan, "you little know my poor Jack Maldon when you ask that question. Say? Not he. You might drag him at the heels of four wild horses first."

"Mama!" said Mrs. Strong.

"Annie, my dear," returned her mother, "once for all, I must really beg that you will not interfere with me, unless it is to confirm what I say. You know as well as I do, that your cousin Maldon would be dragged at the heels of any number of wild horses—why should I confine myself to four! I *won't* confine myself to four—eight, sixteen, two-and-thirty, rather than say anything calculated to overturn the Doctor's plans."

"Wickfield's plans," said the Doctor, stroking his face, and looking penitently at his adviser. "That is to say, our joint plans for him. I said myself, abroad or at home."

"And I said," added Mr. Wickfield gravely, "abroad. I was the means of sending him abroad. It's my responsibility."

"Oh! Responsiblity!" said the Old Soldier. "Everything was done for the best, my dear Mr. Wickfield; everything was done for the kindest and best, we know. But if the dear fellow can't live there, he can't live there. And if he can't live there, he'll die there, sooner than he'll overturn the Doctor's plans. I know him," said the Old Soldier, fanning herself, in a sort of calm prophetic agony, "and I know he'll die there, sooner than he'll overturn the Doctor's plans."

"Well, well, ma'am," said the Doctor cheerfully, "I am not bigoted to my plans, and I can overturn them myself. I can substitute some other plans. If Mr. Jack Maldon comes home on account of ill health, he must not be allowed to go back, and we must endeavour to make some more suitable and fortunate provision for him in this country."

Mrs. Markleham was so overcome by this generous speech (which, I need not say, she had not at all expected or led up to) that she could only tell the Doctor it was like himself, and go several times through that operation of kissing the sticks of her fan, and then tapping his hand with it. After which she gently chid her daughter Annie, for not being more demonstrative when such kindnesses were showered, for her sake, on her old playfellow: and entertained us with some particulars concerning other deserving members of her family, whom it was desirable to set on their deserving legs.

All this time, her daughter Annie never once spoke, or lifted up her eyes. All this time, Mr. Wickfield had his glance upon her as she sat by his own daughter's side. It appeared to me that he never thought of being observed by any one; but was so intent upon her, and upon his own thoughts in connexion with her, as to be quite absorbed. He now asked what Mr. Jack Maldon had actually written in reference to himself, and to whom he had written it?

"Why, here," said Mrs. Markleham, taking a letter from the chimney-piece above the Doctor's head, "the dear fellow says to the Doctor himself—where is it? Oh!—'I am sorry to inform you that my health is suffering severely, and that I fear I may be reduced to the necessity of returning home for a time, as the only hope of restoration.' That's pretty plain, poor fellow! His only hope of restoration! But Annie's letter is plainer still. Annie, show me that letter again."

"Not now, mama," she pleaded in a low tone.

"My dear, you absolutely are, on some subjects, one of the most ridiculous persons in the world," returned her mother, "and perhaps the most unnatural to the claims of your own family. We never should have heard of the letter at all, I believe, unless I had asked for it myself. Do you call that confidence, my love, towards Doctor Strong? I am surprised. You ought to know better."

The letter was reluctantly produced; and as I handed it to the old lady, I saw how the unwilling hand from which I took it, trembled.

"Now let us see," said Mrs. Markleham, putting her glass to her eye, "where the passage is. 'The remembrance of old times, my dearest Annie'—and so forth—it's not there. 'The amiable old Proctor'—who's he? Dear me, Annie, how illegibly your cousin Maldon writes, and how stupid I am! 'Doctor,' of course. Ah! amiable indeed!'" Here she left off, to kiss her fan again, and shake it at the Doctor, who was looking at us in a state of placid satisfaction. "Now I have found it. '*You* may not be surprised to hear, Annie'—no, to be sure, knowing that he never was really strong; what did I say just now?—'that I have undergone so much in this distant place, as to have decided to leave it at all hazards; on sick leave, if I can; on total resignation, if that is not to be obtained. What I have endured, and do endure here, is insupportable.' And but for the promptitude of that best of creatures," said Mrs. Markleham, telegraphing the Doctor as before, and refolding the letter, "it would be insupportable to me to think of."

Mr. Wickfield said not one word, though the old lady looked to him as if for his commentary on this intelligence; but sat severely silent, with his eyes fixed on the ground. Long after the subject was dismissed, and other topics occupied us, he remained so; seldom raising his eyes, unless to rest them for a moment, with a thoughtful frown, upon the Doctor, or his wife, or both.

The Doctor was very fond of music. Agnes sang with great sweetness and expression, and so did Mrs. Strong. They sang together, and played duets together, and we had quite a little concert. But I remarked two things: first, that though Annie soon recovered her composure, and was quite herself, there was a blank between her and Mr. Wickfield which separated them wholly from each other; secondly, that Mr. Wickfield seemed to dislike the intimacy between her and Agnes, and to watch it with uneasiness. And now, I must confess, the recollection of what I had seen on that night when Mr. Maldon went away, first began to return upon me with a meaning it had never had, and to trouble me. The innocent beauty of her face was not as innocent to me as it had been; I mistrusted the natural grace and charm of her manner; and when I looked at Agnes by her side, and thought how good and true Agnes was, suspicions arose within me that it was an ill-assorted friendship.

She was so happy in it herself, however, and the other was so happy too, that they made the evening fly away as if it were but an hour. It closed in an incident which I well remember. They were taking leave of each other, and Agnes was going to embrace her and kiss her, when Mr. Wickfield stepped between them, as if by accident, and drew Agnes quickly away. Then I saw, as though all the intervening time had been cancelled, and I were still standing in the doorway on the night of the departure, the expression of that night in the face of Mrs. Strong, as it confronted his.

I cannot say what an impression this made upon me, or how impossible I found it, when I thought of her afterwards, to separate her from this look, and remember her face in its innocent loveliness again. It haunted me when I got home. I seemed to have left the Doctor's roof with a dark cloud lowering on it. The reverence that I had for his grey head, was mingled with commiseration for his faith in those who were treacherous to him, and with resentment against those who injured him. The impending shadow of a great affliction, and a great disgrace that had no distinct form in it yet, fell like a stain upon the quiet place where I had worked and played as a boy, and did it a cruel wrong. I had no pleasure in thinking, any more, of the grave old broad-leaved aloe-trees which remained shut up in themselves a hundred years together, and of the trim smooth grass-plot, and the stone urns, and the Doctor's Walk, and the congenial sound of the Cathedral bell hovering above them all. It was as if the tranquil sanctuary of my boyhood had been sacked before my face, and its peace and honour given to the winds.

But morning brought with it my parting from the old house, which Agnes had filled with her influence; and that occupied my mind sufficiently. I should be there again soon, no doubt; I might sleep again—perhaps often—in my old room; but the days of my inhabiting there were gone, and the old time was past. I was heavier at heart when I packed up such of my books and clothes as still remained there to be sent to Dover, than I cared to show to Uriah Heep: who was so officious to help me, that I uncharitably thought him mighty glad that I was going.

I got away from Agnes and her father, somehow, with an indifferent show of being very manly, and took my seat upon the box of the London coach. I was so softened and forgiving, going through the town, that I had half a mind to nod to my old enemy the butcher, and throw him five shillings to drink. But he looked such a very obdurate butcher as he stood scraping the great block in the shop, and moreover, his appearance was so little improved by the loss of a front tooth which I had knocked out, that I thought it best to make no advances.

The main object on my mind, I remember, when we got fairly on the road, was to appear as old as possible to the coachman, and to speak extremely gruff. The latter point I achieved at great personal inconvenience; but I stuck to it, because I felt it was a grown-up sort of thing.

"You are going through, Sir?" said the coachman.

"Yes, Willliam," I said, condescendingly (I knew him); "I am going to London. I shall go down into Suffolk afterwards."

"Shooting, Sir?" said the coachman.

He knew as well as I did that it was just as likely, at that time of year, I was going down there whaling; but I felt complimented, too.

"I don't know," I said, pretending to be undecided, "whether I shall take a shot or not."

"Birds is got wery shy, I'm told," said William.

"So I understand," said I.

"Is Suffolk your county, Sir?" asked William.

"Yes," I said, with some importance. "Suffolk's my county."

"I'm told the dumplings is uncommon fine down there," said William.

I was not aware of it myself, but I felt it necessary to uphold the institutions of my county, and to evince a famil-iarity with them; so I shook my head, as much as to say, "I believe you!"

"And the Punches," said William. "There's cattle! A Suffolk Punch, when he's a good 'un, is worth his weight in gold. Did you ever breed any Suffolk Punches yourself, Sir?"

"N—no," I said, "not exactly."

"Here's a gen'lm'n behind me, I'll pound it," said William, "as has bred 'em by wholesale."

The gentleman spoken of was a gentleman with a very unpromising squint, and a prominent chin, who had a tall white hat on with a narrow flat brim, and whose close-fitting drab trousers seemed to button all the way up outside his legs from his boots to his hips. His chin was cocked over the coachman's shoulder, so near to me, that his breath quite tickled the back of my head; and as I looked round at him, he leered at the leaders with the eye with which he didn't squint, in a very knowing manner.

"Ain't you?" said William.

"Ain't I what?" asked the gentleman behind.

"Bred them Suffolk Punches by wholesale?"

"I should think so," said the gentleman. "There ain't no sort of orse that I ain't bred, and no sort of dorg. Orses and dorgs is some men's fancy. They're wittles and drink to me—lodging, wife, and children—reading, writing, and 'rithmetic—snuff, tobacker, and sleep."

"That ain't a sort of man to see sitting behind a coach-box, is it though?" said William in my ear, as he handled the reins.

I construed this remark into an indication of a wish that he should have my place, so I blushingly offered to resign it.

"Well, if you don't mind, Sir," said William, "I think it *would* be more correct."

I have always considered this as the first fall I had in life. When I booked my place at the coach-office, I had had "Box Seat" written against the entry, and had given the book-keeper half-a-crown. I was got up in a special great-coat and shawl, expressly to do honour to that distinguished eminence; had glorified myself upon it a good deal; and had felt that I was a credit to the coach. And here, in the very first stage, I was supplanted by a shabby man with a squint, who had no other merit than smelling like a livery-stables, and being able to walk across me, more like a fly than a human being, while the horses were at a canter!

A distrust of myself, which has often beset me in life on small occasions, when it would have been better away, was assuredly not stopped in its growth by this little incident outside the Canterbury coach. It was in vain to take refuge in gruffness of speech. I spoke from the pit of my stomach for the rest of the journey, but I felt completely extinguished, and dreadfully young.

It was curious and interesting, nevertheless, to be sitting up there, behind four horses: well educated, well dressed, and with plenty of money in my pocket; and to look out for the places where I had slept on my weary journey. I had abundant occupation for my thoughts, in every conspicuous landmark on the road. When I looked down at the tramps whom we passed, and saw that well-remembered style of face turned up, I felt as if the tinker's blackened hand were in the bosom of my shirt again. When we clattered through the narrow street of Chatham, and I caught a glimpse, in passing, of the lane where the old monster lived who had bought my jacket, I stretched my neck eagerly to look for the place where I had sat, in the sun and in the shade, waiting for my money. When we came, at last, within a stage of London, and passed the veritable Salem House where Mr. Creakle had laid about him with a heavy hand, I would have given all I had, for lawful permission to get down and thrash him, and let all the boys out like so many caged sparrows.

We went to the Golden Cross, at Charing Cross, then a mouldy sort of establishment in a close neighbourhood. A waiter showed me into the coffee-room; and a chambermaid introduced me to my small bed-chamber, which smelt like a hackney-coach, and was shut up like a family vault. I was still painfully conscious of my youth, for nobody stood in any awe of me at all: the chambermaid being utterly indifferent to my opinions on any subject, and the waiter being familiar with me, and offering advice to my inexperience.

"Well now," said the waiter, in a tone of confidence, "what would you like for dinner? Young gentlemen likes poultry in general: have a fowl!"

I told him, as majestically as I could, that I wasn't in the humour for a fowl.

"Ain't you!" said the waiter. "Young gentlemen is generally tired of beef and mutton: have a weal cutlet!"

I assented to this proposal, in default of being able to suggest anything else.

"Do you care for taters?" said the waiter, with an insinuating smile, and his head on one side. "Young gentlemen generally has been overdosed with taters."

I commanded him, in my deepest voice, to order a veal cutlet and potatoes, and all things fitting; and to inquire at the bar if there were any letters for Trotwood Copperfield, Esquire—which I knew there were not, and couldn't be, but thought it manly to appear to expect.

He soon came back to say that there were none (at which I was much surprised) and began to lay the cloth for my dinner in a box by the fire. While he was so engaged, he asked me what I would take with it; and on my replying "Half a pint of sherry," thought it a favourable opportunity, I am afraid, to extract that measure of wine from the stale leavings at the bottoms of several small decanters. I am of this opinion, because, while I was reading the newspaper, I observed him behind a low wooden partition, which was his private apartment, very busy pouring out of a number of those vessels into one, like a chemist and druggist making up a prescription. When the wine came, too, I thought it flat; and it certainly had more English crumbs in it, than were to be expected in a foreign wine in anything like a pure state; but I was bashful enough to drink it, and say nothing.

Being then in a pleasant frame of mind (from which I infer that poisoning is not always disagreeable in some stages of the process), I resolved to go to the play. It was Covent Garden Theatre that I chose; and there, from the back of a centre box, I saw Julius Cæsar and the new Pantomime. To have all those noble Romans alive before me, and walking in and out for my entertainment, instead of being the stern taskmasters they had been at school, was a most novel and delightful effect. But the mingled reality and mystery of the whole show, the influence upon me of the poetry, the lights, the music, the company, the smooth stupendous changes of glittering and brilliant scenery, were so dazzling, and opened up such illimitable regions of delight, that when I came out into the rainy street, at twelve o'clock at night, I felt as if I had come from the clouds, where I had been leading a romantic life for ages, to a bawling, splashing, link-lighted, umbrella-struggling, hackney-coach-jostling, patten-clinking, muddy, miserable world.

I had emerged by another door, and stood in the street for a little while, as if I really were a stranger upon earth: but the unceremonious pushing and hustling that I received, soon recalled me to myself, and put me in the road back to the hotel; whither I went, revolving the glorious vision all the way; and where, after some porter and oysters, I sat revolving it still, at past one o'clock, with my eyes on the coffee-room fire.

I was so filled with the play, and with the past—for it was, in a manner, like a shining transparency, through which I saw my earlier life moving along—that I don't know when the figure of a handsome well-formed young man, dressed with a tasteful easy negligence which I have reason to remember very well, became a real presence to me. But I recollect being conscious of his company without having noticed his coming in—and my still sitting, musing, over the coffee-room fire.

At last I rose to go to bed, much to the relief of the sleepy waiter, who had got the fidgets in his legs, and was twisting them, and hitting them, and putting them through all kinds of contortions in his small pantry. In going towards the door, I passed the person who had come in, and saw him plainly. I turned directly, came back, and looked again. He did not know me, but I knew him in a moment.

At another time I might have wanted the confidence or the decision to speak to him, and might have put it off until next day, and might have lost him. But, in the then condition of my mind, where the play was still running high, his former protection of me appeared so deserving of my gratitude, and my old love for him overflowed my breast so freshly and spontaneously, that I went up to him at once, with a fast-beating heart, and said:

"Steerforth! won't you speak to me?"

He looked at me—just as he used to look, sometimes—but I saw no recognition in his face.

"You don't remember me, I am afraid," said I.

"My God!" he suddenly exclaimed. "It's little Copperfield!"

I grasped him by both hands, and could not let them go. But for very shame, and the fear that it might displease him, I could have held him round the neck and cried.

"I never, never, never was so glad! My dear Steerforth, I am so overjoyed to see you!"

"And I am rejoiced to see you, too!" he said, shaking my hands heartily. "Why, Copperfield, old boy, don't be overpowered!" And yet he was glad, too, I thought, to see how the delight I had in meeting him affected me.

I brushed away the tears that my utmost resolution had not been able to keep back, and I made a clumsy laugh of it, and we sat down together, side by side.

"Why, how do you come to be here?" said Steerforth, clapping me on the shoulder.

"I came here by the Canterbury coach, to-day. I have been adopted by an aunt down in that part of the country, and have just finished my education there. How do you come to be here, Steerforth?"

"Well, I am what they call an Oxford man," he returned; "that is to say, I get bored to death down there, periodically—and I am on my way now to my mother's. You're a devilish amiable-looking fellow, Copperfield. Just what you used to be, now I look at you! Not altered in the least!"

"I knew *you* immediately," I said; "but you are more easily remembered."

He laughed as he ran his hand through the clustering curls of his hair, and said gaily:

"Yes, I am on an expedition of duty. My mother lives a little way out of town; and the roads being in a beastly condition, and our house tedious enough, I remained here to-night instead of going on. I have not been in town half-a-dozen hours, and those I have been dozing and grumbling away at the play."

"I have been at the play, too," said I. "At Covent Garden. What a delightful and magnificent entertainment, Steerforth!"

Steerforth laughed heartily.

"—My dear young Davy," he said, clapping me on the shoulder again, "you are a very Daisy. The daisy of the field, at sunrise, is not fresher than you are! I have been at Covent Garden, too, and there never was a more miserable business.—Holloa, you Sir!"

This was addressed to the waiter, who had been very attentive to our recognition, at a distance, and now came forward deferentially.

"Where have you put my friend, Mr. Copperfield?" said Steerforth.

"Beg your pardon, Sir?"

"Where does he sleep? What's his number? You know what I mean," said Steerforth.

"Well, Sir," said the waiter, with an apologetic air. "Mr. Copperfield is at present in forty-four, Sir."

"And what the devil do you mean," retorted Steerforth, "by putting Mr. Copperfield into a little loft over a stable?"

"Why, you see we wasn't aware, Sir," returned the waiter, still apologetically, "as Mr. Copperfield was anyways particular. We can give Mr. Copperfield seventy-two, Sir, if it would be preferred. Next you, Sir."

"Of course it would be preferred," said Steerforth. "And do it at once."

The waiter immediately withdrew to make the exchange. Steerforth, very much amused at my having been put into forty-four, laughed again, and clapped me on the shoulder again, and invited me to breakfast with him next morning at ten o'clock—an invitation I was only too proud and happy to accept. It being now pretty late, we took our candles and went up-stairs, where we parted with friendly heartiness at his door, and where I found my new room a great improvement on my old one, it not being at all musty, and having an immense four-post bedstead in it, which was quite a little landed estate. Here, among pillows enough for six, I soon fell asleep in a blissful condition, and dreamed of ancient Rome, Steerforth, and friendship, until the early morning coaches, rumbling out of the archway underneath, made me dream of thunder and the gods.

CHAPTER XX.

STEERFORTH'S HOME.

WHEN the chambermaid tapped at my door at eight o'clock, and informed me that my shaving-water was out-

side, I felt severely the having no occasion for it, and blushed in my bed. The suspicion that she laughed too, when she said it, preyed upon my mind all the time I was dressing; and gave me, I was conscious, a sneaking and guilty air when I passed her on the staircase, as I was going down to breakfast. I was so sensitively aware, indeed, of being younger than I could have wished, that for some time I could not make up my mind to pass her at all, under the ignoble circumstances of the case; but, hearing her there with a broom, stood peeping out of the window at King Charles on horseback, surrounded by a maze of hackney-coaches and looking anything but regal in a drizzling rain and a dark-brown fog, until I was admonished by the waiter that the gentleman was waiting for me.

It was not in the coffee-room that I found Steerforth expecting me, but in a snug private apartment, red-curtained and Turkey-carpeted, where the fire burnt bright, and a fine hot breakfast was set forth on a table covered with a clean cloth; and a cheerful miniature of the room, the fire, the breakfast, Steerforth, and all, was shining in the little round mirror over the sideboard. I was rather bashful at first, Steerforth being so self-possessed, and elegant, and superior to me in all respects (age included); but his easy patronage soon put that to rights, and made me quite at home. I could not enough admire the change he had wrought in the Golden Cross; or compare the dull forlorn state I had held yesterday, with this morning's comfort and this morning's entertainment. As to the waiter's familiarity, it was quenched as if it had never been. He attended on us, as I may say, in sackcloth and ashes.

"Now, Copperfield," said Steerforth, when we were alone, "I should like to hear what you are doing, and where you are going, and all about you. I feel as if you were my property."

Glowing with pleasure to find that he had still this interest in me, I told him how my aunt had proposed the little expedition that I had before me, and whither it tended.

"As you are in no hurry, then," said Steerforth, "come home with me to Highgate, and stay a day or two. You will be pleased with my mother—she is a little vain and prosy about me, but that you can forgive her—and she will be pleased with you."

"I should like to be as sure of that, as you are kind enough to say you are," I answered, smiling.

"Oh!" said Steerforth, "every one who likes me, has a claim on her that is sure to be acknowledged."

"Then I think I shall be a favourite," said I.

"Good!" said Steerforth. "Come and prove it. We will go and see the lions for an hour or two—it's something to have a fresh fellow like you to show them to, Copperfield—and then we'll journey out to Highgate by the coach."

I could hardly believe but that I was in a dream, and that I should wake presently in number forty-four, to the solitary box in the coffee-room and the familiar waiter again. After I had written to my aunt and told her of my fortunate meeting with my admired old schoolfellow, and my acceptance of his invitation, we went out in a hackney chariot, and saw a Panorama and some other sights, and took a walk through the Museum, where I could not help observing how much Steerforth knew, on an infinite variety of subjects, and of how little account he seemed to make his knowledge.

"You'll take a high degree at college, Steerforth," said

I, "if you have not done so already; and they will have good reason to be proud of you."

"*I* take a degree!" cried Steerforth. "Not I! my dear Daisy—will you mind my calling you Daisy?"

"Not at all!" said I.

"That's a good fellow! My dear Daisy," said Steerforth, laughing, "I have not the least desire or intention to distinguish myself in that way. I have done quite sufficient for my purpose. I find that I am heavy company enough for myself, as I am."

"But the fame——" I was beginning.

"You romantic Daisy!" said Steerforth, laughing still more heartily; "why should I trouble myself, that a parcel of heavy-headed fellows may gape and hold up their hands? Let them do it at some other man. There's fame for him, and he's welcome to it."

I was abashed at having made so great a mistake, and was glad to change the subject. Fortunately it was not difficult to do, for Steerforth could always pass from one subject to another with a carelessness and lightness that were his own.

Lunch succeeded to our sight-seeing, and the short winter day wore away so fast, that it was dusk when the stage-coach stopped with us at an old brick house at Highgate on the summit of the hill. An elderly lady, though not very far advanced in years, with a proud carriage and a handsome face, was in the doorway as we alighted; and greeting Steerforth as "My dearest James," folded him in her arms. To this lady he presented me as his mother, and she gave me a stately welcome.

It was a genteel old-fashioned house, very quiet and orderly. From the windows of my room I saw all London lying in the distance like a great vapour, with here and there some lights twinkling through it. I had only time, in dressing, to glance at the solid furniture, the framed pieces of work (done, I supposed, by Steerforth's mother when she was a girl), and some pictures in crayons of ladies with powdered hair and bodices, coming and going on the walls, as the newly-kindled fire crackled and sputtered, when I was called to dinner.

There was a second lady in the dining-room, of a slight short figure, dark, and not agreeable to look at, but with some appearance of good looks too, who attracted my attention: perhaps because I had not expected to see her; perhaps because I found myself sitting opposite to her; perhaps because of something really remarkable in her. She had black hair and eager black eyes, and was thin, and had a scar upon her lip. It was an old scar—I should rather call it, seam, for it was not discoloured, and had healed years ago—which had once cut through her mouth, downward towards the chin, but was now barely visible across the table, except above and on her upper lip, the shape of which it had altered. I concluded in my own mind that she was about thirty years of age, and that she wished to be married. She was a little dilapidated—like a house—with having been so long to let; yet had, as I have said, an appearance of good looks. Her thinness seemed to be the effect of some wasting fire within her, which found a vent in her gaunt eyes.

She was introduced as Miss Dartle and both Steerforth and his mother called her Rosa. I found that she lived there, and had been for a long time Mrs. Steerforth's companion. It appeared to me that she never said anything she wanted to say, outright; but hinted it, and made a great deal more of it by this practice. For example, when Mrs. Steerforth observed, more in jest than earnest, that she

feared her son led but a wild life at college, Miss Dartle put in thus:

"Oh, really? You know how ignorant I am, and that I only ask for information, but isn't it always so? I thought that kind of life was on all hands understood to be—eh?"

"It is education for a very grave profession, if you mean that, Rosa," Mrs. Steerforth answered with some coldness.

"Oh! Yes! That's very true," returned Miss Dartle. "But isn't it, though?—I want to be put right, if I am wrong—isn't it really?"

"Really what?" said Mrs. Steerforth.

"Oh! You mean it's *not!*" returned Miss Dartle. "Well, I'm very glad to hear it! Now, I know what to do. That's the advantage of asking. I shall never allow people to talk before me about wastefulness and profligacy, and so forth, in connexion with that life, any more."

"And you will be right," said Mrs. Steerforth. "My son's tutor is a conscientious gentleman; and if I had not implicit reliance on my son, I should have reliance on him."

"Should you?" said Miss Dartle. "Dear me! Conscientious, is he? Really conscientious, now?"

"Yes, I am convinced of it," said Mrs. Steerforth.

"How very nice!" exclaimed Miss Dartle. "What a comfort! Really conscientious? Then he's not—but of course he can't be, if he's really conscientious. Well, I shall be quite happy in my opinion of him, from this time. You can't think how it elevates him in my opinion, to know for certain that he's really conscientious!"

Her own views of every question, and her correction of everything that was said to which she was opposed, Miss Dartle insinuated in the same way: sometimes, I could not conceal from myself, with great power, though in contradiction even of Steerforth. An instance happened before dinner was done. Mrs. Steerforth speaking to me about my intention of going down into Suffolk, I said at hazard how glad I should be, if Steerforth would only go there with me; and explaining to him that I was going to see my old nurse, and Mr. Peggotty's family, I reminded him of the boatman whom he had seen at school.

"Oh! That bluff fellow!" said Steerforth. "He had a son with him, hadn't he?"

"No. That was his nephew," I replied; "whom he adopted, though, as a son. He has a very pretty little niece too, whom he adopted as a daughter. In short, his house (or rather his boat, for he lives in one, on dry land) is full of people who are objects of his generosity and kindness. You would be delighted to see that household."

"Should I?" said Steerforth. "Well, I think I should. I must see what can be done. It would be worth a journey—not to mention the pleasure of a journey with you, Daisy—to see that sort of people together, and to make one of 'em."

My heart leaped with a new hope of pleasure. But it was in reference to the tone in which he had spoken of "that sort of people," that Miss Dartle, whose sparkling eyes had been watchful of us, now broke in again.

"Oh, but, really? Do tell me. Are they, though?" she said.

"Are they what? And are who what?" said Steerforth.

"That sort of people.—Are they really animals and clods, and beings of another order? I want to know *so* much."

"Why, there's a pretty wide separation between them and us," said Steerforth, with indifference. "They are not to be expected to be as sensitive as we are. Their delicacy is not to be shocked, or hurt very easily. They are wonderfully virtuous, I dare say—some people contend for that, at least; and I am sure I don't want to contradict them—but they have not very fine natures, and they may be thankful that, like their coarse rough skins, they are not easily wounded."

"Really!" said Miss Dartle. "Well, I don't know, now, when I have been better pleased to hear that. It's so consoling! It's such a delight to know that when they suffer, they don't feel! Sometimes I have been quite uneasy for that sort of people; but now I shall just dismiss the idea of them, altogether. Live and learn. I had my doubts, I confess, but now they're cleared up. I didn't know, and now I do know; and that shows the advantage of asking—don't it?"

I believed that Steerforth had said what he had, in jest, or to draw Miss Dartle out; and I expected him to say as much when she was gone, and we two were sitting before the fire. But he merely asked me what I thought of her.

"She is very clever, is she not?" I asked.

"Clever! She brings everything to a grindstone," said Steerforth, "and sharpens it, as she has sharpened her own face and figure these years past. She has worn herself away by constant sharpening. She is all edge."

"What a remarkable scar that is upon her lip!" I said.

Steerforth's face fell, and he paused a moment.

"Why, the fact is," he returned, "—I did that."

"By an unfortunate accident!"

"No. I was a young boy, and she exasperated me, and I threw a hammer at her. A promising young angel I must have been!"

I was deeply sorry to have touched on such a painful theme, but that was useless now.

"She has borne the mark ever since, as you see," said Steerforth; "and she'll bear it to her grave, if she ever rests in one; though I can hardly believe she will ever rest anywhere. She was the motherless child of a sort of cousin of my father's. He died one day. My mother, who was then a widow, brought her here to be company to her. She has a couple of thousand pounds of her own, and saves the interest of it every year, to add to the principal. There's the history of Miss Rosa Dartle for you."

"And I have no doubt she loves you like a brother?' said I.

"Humph!" retorted Steerforth, looking at the fire. "Some brothers are not loved over much; and some love—but help yourself, Copperfield! We'll drink the daisies of the field, in compliment to you; and the lilies of the valley that toil not, neither do they spin, in compliment to me—the more shame for me!" A moody smile that had overspread his features cleared off as he said this merrily, and he was his own frank, winning self again.

I could not help glancing at the scar with a painful interest when we went to tea. It was not long before I observed that it was the most susceptible part of her face, and that, when she turned pale, that mark altered first, and became a dull, lead-coloured streak, lengthening out to its full extent, like a mark in invisible ink brought to the fire. There was litlte altercation between her and Steerforth about a cast of the dice at backgammon—when I thought her, for one moment, in a storm of rage; and then I saw it start forth like the old writing on the wall.

It was no matter of wonder to me that Mrs. Steerforth devoted to her son. She seemed to be able to speak or think about nothing else. She showed me his picture as an infant, in a locket, with some of his baby-hair in it; she showed me his picture as he had been when I first knew him; and she wore at her breast his picture as he was now. All the letters he had ever written to her, she kept in a cabinet near her own chair by the fire; and she would have read me some of them, and I should have been very glad to hear them too, if he had not interposed, and coaxed her out of the design.

"It was at Mr. Creakle's, my son tells me, that you first became acquainted," said Mrs. Steerforth, as she and I were talking at one table, while they played backgammon at another. "Indeed, I recollect his speaking, at that time, of a pupil younger than himself who had taken his fancy there; but your name, as you may suppose, has not lived in my memory."

"He was very generous and noble to me in those days, I assure you, ma'am," said I, "and I stood in need of such a friend. I should have been quite crushed without him."

"He is always generous and noble," said Mrs. Steerforth, proudly.

I subscribed to this with all my heart, God knows. She knew I did; for the stateliness of her manner already abated toward me, except when she spoke in praise of him, and then her air was always lofty.

"It was not a fit school generally for my son," said she; "far from it; but there were particular circumstances to be considered at the time, of more importance even than that selection. My son's high spirit made it desirable that he should be placed with some man who felt its superiority, and would be content to bow himself before it; and we found such a man there."

I knew that, knowing the fellow. And yet I did not despise him the more for it, but thought it a redeeming quality in him—if he could be allowed any grace for not resisting one so irresistible as Steerforth.

"My son's great capacity was tempted on, there, by a feeling of voluntary emulation and conscious pride," the fond lady went on to say. "He would have risen against all constraint; but he found himself the monarch of the place, and he haughtily determined to be worthy of his station. It was like himself."

I echoed, with all my heart and soul, that it was like himself.

"So my son took, of his own will, and on no compulsion, to the course in which he can always, when it is his pleasure, outstrip every competitor," she pursued. "My son informs me, Mr. Copperfield, that you were quite devoted to him, and that when you met yesterday you made yourself known to him with tears of joy. I should be an affected woman if I made any pretence of being surprised by my son's inspiring such emotions; but I can not be indifferent to any one who is so sensible of his merit, and I am very glad to see you here, and can assure you that he feels an unusual friendship for you, and that you may rely on his protection."

Miss Dartle played backgammon as eagerly as she did everything else. If I had seen her, first, at the board, I should have fancied that her figure had got thin, and her eyes had got large, over that pursuit, and no other in the world. But I am very much mistaken if she missed a word of this, or lost a look of mine as I received it with the utmost pleasure, and, honoured by Mrs. Steerforth's confidence, felt older than I had done since I left Canterbury.

When the evening was pretty far spent, and a tray of glasses and decanters came in, Steerforth promised, over the fire, that he would seriously think of going down into the country with me. There was no hurry, he said; a week hence would do; and his mother hospitably said the same. While we were talking, he more than once called me Daisy; which brought Miss Dartle out again.

"But really, Mr. Copperfield," she asked, "is it a nickname? And why does he give it you? Is it—eh?—because he thinks you young and innocent? I am so stupid in these things."

I colored in replying that I believed it was.

"Oh!" said Miss Dartle. "Now I am glad to know that! I ask for information, and I am glad to know it. He thinks you young and innocent; and so you are his friend? Well, that's quite delightful!"

She went to bed soon after this, and Mrs. Steerforth retired too. Steerforth and I, after lingering for half an hour over the fire, talking about Traddles and all the rest of them at old Salem House, went up-stairs together. Steerforth's room was next to mine, and I went in to look at it. It was a picture of comfort, full of easy-chairs, cushions, and footstools, worked by his mother's hand, and with no sort of thing omitted that could help to render it complete. Finally, her handsome features looked down on her darling from a portrait on the wall, as if it were even something to her that her likeness should watch him while he slept.

I found the fire burning clear enough in my room by this time, and the curtains drawn before the windows and round the bed, giving it a very snug appearance. I sat down in a great chair upon the hearth to meditate on my happiness; and had enjoyed the contemplation of it for some time, when I found a likeness of Miss Dartle looking eagerly at me from above the chimney-piece.

It was a startling likeness, and necessarily had a startling look. The painter hadn't made the scar, but *I* made it; and there it was, coming and going: now confined to the upper lip as I had seen it at dinner, and now showing the whole extent of the wound inflicted by the hammer, as I had seen it when she was passionate.

I wondered peevishly why they couldn't put her anywhere else instead of quartering her on me. To get rid of her, I undressed quickly, extinguished my light, and went to bed. But, as I fell asleep, I could not forget that she was still there looking, "Is it really, though? I want to know;" and when I awoke in the night, I found that I was uneasily asking all sorts of people in my dreams whether it really was or not—without knowing what I meant.

CHAPTER XXI.

LITTLE EM'LY.

THERE was a servant in that house, a man who, I understood, was usually with Steerforth, and had come into his service at the University, who was in appearance a pattern of respectability. I believe there never existed in his station a more respectable-looking man. He was taciturn, soft-footed, very quiet in his manner, deferential, observant, always at hand when wanted, and never near when not wanted; but his great claim to consideration was his respectability. He had not a pliant face, he had rather a

stiff neck, rather a tight smooth head with short hair clinging to it at the sides, a soft way of speaking, with a peculiar habit of whispering the letter S so distinctly, that he seemed to use it oftener than any other man; but every peculiarity that he had he made respectable. If his nose had been upside-down, he would have made that respectable. He surrounded himself with an atmosphere of respectability, and walked secure in it. It would have been next to impossible to suspect him of anything wrong, he was so thoroughly respectable. Nobody could have thought of putting him in a livery, he was so highly respectable. To have imposed any derogatory work upon him, would have been to inflict a wanton insult on the feelings of a most respectable man. And of this, I noticed the women-servants in the household were so intuitively conscious, that they always did such work themselves, and generally while he read the paper by the pantry fire.

Such a self-contained man I never saw. But in that quality, as in every other he possessed, he only seemed to be the more respectable. Even the fact that no one knew his Christian name, seemed to form a part of his respectability. Nothing could be objected against his surname **Littimer**, by which he was known. Peter might have been hanged, or Tom transported; but Littimer was perfectly respectable.

It was occasioned, I suppose, by the reverend nature of respectability in the abstract, but I felt particularly young in this man's presence. How old he was himself, I could not guess—and that again went to his credit on the same score; for in the calmness of respectability he might have numbered fifty years as well as thirty.

Littimer was in my room in the morning before I was up, to bring me that reproachful shaving-water, and to put out my clothes. When I undrew the curtains and looked out of bed, I saw him, in an equable temperature of respectability, unaffected by the east wind of January, and not even breathing frostily, standing my boots right and left in the first dancing position, and blowing specks of dust off my coat as he laid it down like a baby.

I gave him good morning, and asked him what o'clock it was. He took out of his pocket the most respectable hunting watch I ever saw, and preventing the spring with his thumb from opening far, looked in at the face as if he were consulting an oracular oyster, shut it up again, and said, if I pleased, it was half-past eight.

"Mr. Steerforth will be glad to hear how you have rested, Sir."

"Thank you," said I, "very well indeed. Is Mr. Steerforth quite well?"

"Thank you, Sir, Mr. Steerforth is tolerably well." Another of his characteristics,—no use of superlatives. A cool calm medium always.

"Is there anything more I can have the honour of doing for you, Sir? The warning bell will ring at nine; the family take breakfast at half-past nine."

"Nothing, I thank you."

"I thank *you*, Sir, if you please;" and with that, and with a little inclination of his head when he passed the bedside, as an apology for correcting me, he went out, shutting the door as delicately as if I had just fallen into a sweet sleep on which my life depended.

Every morning we held exactly this conversation: never any more, and never any less; and yet, invariably, however far I might have been lifted out of myself overnight, and advanced towards maturer years, by Steerforth's companionship, or Mrs. Steerforth's confidence, or Miss Dartle's conversation, in the presence of this most respectable man I became, as our smaller poets sing "a boy again."

He got horses for us; and Steerforth, who knew everything, gave me lessons in riding. He provided foils for us, and Steerforth gave me lessons in fencing—gloves, and I began, of the same master, to improve in boxing. It gave me no manner of concern that Steerforth should find me a novice in these sciences, but I never could bear to show my want of skill before the respectable Littimer. I had no reason to believe that Littimer understood such arts himself; he never led me to suppose anything of the kind, by so much as the vibration of one of his respectable eyelashes; yet whenever he was by, while we were practising, I felt myself the greenest and most inexperienced of mortals.

I am particular about this man, because he made a particular effect on me at that time, and because of what took place thereafter.

The week passed away in a most delightful manner. It passed rapidly, as may be supposed, to one entranced as I was; and yet it gave me so many occasions for knowing Steerforth better, and admiring him more in a thousand respects, that at its close I seemed to have been with him for a much longer time. A dashing way he had of treating me like a plaything, was more agreeable to me than any behaviour he could have adopted. It reminded me of our old acquaintance; it seemed the natural sequel of it; it showed me that he was unchanged; it relieved me of any uneasiness I might have felt, in comparing my merits with his, and measuring my claims upon his friendship by any equal standard; above all, it was a familiar, unrestrained, affectionate demeanour that he used towards no one else. As he had treated me at school differently from all the rest, I joyfully believed that he treated me in life unlike any other friend he had. I believed that I was nearer to his heart than any other friend, and my own heart warmed with attachment to him.

He made up his mind to go with me into the country, and the day arrived for our departure. He had been doubtful at first whether to take Littimer or not, but decided to leave him at home. The respectable creature, satisfied with his lot whatever it was, arranged our portmanteaus on the little carriage that was to take us into London, as if they were intended to defy the shocks of ages; and received my modestly proffered donation with perfect tranquillity.

We bade adieu to Mrs. Steerforth and Miss Dartle, with many thanks on my part, and much kindness on the devoted mother's. The last thing I saw was Littimer's unruffled eye; fraught, as I fancied, with the silent conviction that I was very young indeed.

What I felt, in returning so auspiciously to the old familiar places, I shall not endeavour to describe. We went down by the Mail. I was so concerned, I recollect, even for the honour of Yarmouth, that when Steerforth said, as we drove through its dark streets to the inn, that, as well as he could make out, it was a good, queer, out-of-the-way kind of hole, I was highly pleased. We went to bed on our arrival (I observed a pair of dirty shoes and gaiters in connexion with my old friend the Dolphin as we passed that door), and breakfasted late in the morning. Steerforth, who was in great spirits, had been strolling about the beach before I was up, and had made acquaintance, he said, with half the boatmen in the place. Moreover he had seen, in the distance, what he was sure must be the identical house of Mr. Peggotty, with smoke coming out of the chimney; and had had a great mind, he told me, to walk in and swear he was myself grown out of knowledge.

"When do you propose to introduce me there, Daisy?" he said. "I am at your disposal. Make your own arrangements."

"Why, I was thinking that this evening would be a good time, Steerforth, when they are all sitting round the fire. I should like you to see it when it's snug, it's such a curious place."

"So be it!" returned Steerforth. "This evening."

"I shall not give them any notice that we are here, you know," said I, delighted. "We must take them by surprise."

"Oh, of course! It's no fun," said Steerforth, "unless we take them by surprise. Let us see the natives in their aboriginal condition."

"Though they *are* that sort of people that you mentioned," I returned.

"Aha! What! you recollect my skirmishes with Rosa, do you?" he exclaimed with a quick look. "Confound the girl, I am half afraid of her. She's like a goblin to me. But never mind her. Now what are you going to do? You are going to see your nurse, I suppose?"

"Why, yes," I said, "I must see Peggotty first of all."

"Well," replied Steerforth, looking at his watch. "Suppose I deliver you up to be cried over for a couple of hours. Is that long enough?"

I answered, laughing, that I thought we might get through it in that time, but that he must come also; for he would find that his renown had preceded him, and that he was almost as great a personage as I was.

"I'll come anywhere you like," said Steerforth, "or do anything you like. Tell me where to come to; and in two hours I'll produce myself in any state you please, sentimental or comical."

I gave him minute directions for finding the residence of Mr. Barkis, carrier to Blunderstone and elsewhere; and, on this understanding, went out alone. There was a sharp bracing air; the ground was dry; the sea was crisp and clear; the sun was diffusing abundance of light, if not much warmth; and everything was fresh and lively. I was so fresh and lively myself, in the pleasure of being there, that I could have stopped the people in the streets and shaken hands with them.

The streets looked small, of course. The streets that we have only seen as children always do, I believe, when we go back to them. But I had forgotten nothing in them, and found nothing changed, until I came to Mr. Omer's shop. OMER AND JORAM was now written up, where OMER used to be; but the inscription, DRAPER, TAILOR, HABERDASHER, FUNERAL FURNISHER, &c., remained as it was.

My footsteps seemed to tend so naturally to the shop-door, after I had read these words from over the way, that I went across the road and looked in. There was a pretty woman at the back of the shop, dancing a little child in her arms, while another little fellow clung to her apron. I had no difficulty in recognising either Minnie or Minnie's children. The glass door of the parlour was not open; but in the workshop across the yard I could faintly hear the old tune playing, as if it had never left off.

"Is Mr. Omer at home?" said I, entering. "I should like to see him, for a moment, if he is."

"Oh yes, Sir, he is at home," said Minnie; "this weather don't suit his asthma out of doors. Joe, call your grandfather!"

The little fellow, who was holding her apron, gave such a lusty shout, that the sound of it made him bashful, and he buried his face in her skirts, to her great admiration. I heard a heavy puffing and blowing coming towards us, and soon Mr. Omer, shorter-winded than of yore, but not much older-looking, stood before me.

"Servant, Sir," said Mr. Omer. "What can I do for you, Sir?"

"You can shake hands with me, Mr. Omer, if you please," said I, putting out my own. "You were very good-natured to me once, when I am afraid I didn't show that I thought so."

"Was I though?" returned the old man. "I'm glad to hear it, but I don't remember when. Are you sure it was me?"

"Quite."

"I think my memory has got as short as my breath," said Mr. Omer, looking at me and shaking his head; "for I don't remember you."

"Don't you remember your coming to the coach to meet me, and my having breakfast here, and our riding out to Blunderstone together: you, and I, and Mrs. Joram, and Mr. Joram too—who wasn't her husband then?"

"Why, Lord bless my soul!" exclaimed Mr. Omer, after being thrown by his surprise into a fit of coughing, "you don't say so! Minnie, my dear, you recollect? Dear me, yes—the party was a lady, I think?"

"My mother," I rejoined.

"To—be—sure," said Mr. Omer, touching my waistcoat with his forefinger, "and there was a little child too! There was two parties. The little party was laid along with the other party. Over at Blunderstone it was, of course. Dear me! And how have you been since?"

Very well, I thanked him, as I hoped he had been too.

"Oh! nothing to grumble at, you know," said Mr. Omer. "I find my breath gets short, but it seldom gets longer as a man gets older. I take it as it comes, and make the best of it. That's the best way, ain't it?"

Mr. Omer coughed again, in consequence of laughing, and was assisted out of his fit by his daughter, who now stood close beside us, dancing her smallest child on the counter.

"Dear me!" said Mr. Omer. "Yes, to be sure. Two parties! Why, in that very ride, if you'll believe me, the day was named for my Minnie to marry Joram. 'Do name it, Sir,' says Joram. 'Yes, do, father,' says Minnie. And now he's come into the business. And look here! The youngest!"

Minnie laughed, and stroked her banded hair upon her temples, as her father put one of his fat fingers into the hand of the child she was dancing on the counter.

"Two parties, of course!" said Mr. Omer, nodding his head retrospectively. "Ex-actly so! And Joram's at work, at this minute, on a grey one with silver nails, not this measurement"—the measurement of the dancing child—

upon the counter—"by a good two inches. Will you take something?"

I thanked him, but declined.

"Let me see," said Mr. Omer. "Barkis's the carrier's wife—Peggotty's the boatman's sister—she had something to do with your family? She was in service there, sure?"

My answering in the affirmative gave him great satisfaction.

"I believe my breath will get long next, my memory's getting so much so," said Mr. Omer. "Well, Sir, we've got a young relation of hers here, under articles to us, that has as elegant a taste in the dressmaking business—I assure you I don't believe there's a duchess in England can touch her."

"Not little Em'ly?" said I, involuntarily.

"Em'ly's her name," said Mr. Omer, "and she's little too. But if you'll believe me, she has such a face of her own that half the women in this town are mad against her."

"Nonsense, father!" cried Minnie.

"My dear," said Mr. Omer, "I don't say it's the case with you," winking at me, "but I say that half the women in Yarmouth—ah! and in five mile round—are mad against that girl."

"Then she should have kept to her own station in life, father," said Minnie, "and not have given them any hold to talk about her, and then they couldn't have done it."

"Couldn't have done it, my dear!" retorted Mr. Omer. "Couldn't have done it! Is that *your* knowledge of life? What is there that any woman couldn't do, that she shouldn't do—especially on the subject of another woman's good looks?"

I really thought it was all over with Mr. Omer, after he had uttered this libellous pleasantry. He coughed to that extent, and his breath eluded all his attempts to recover it with that obstinacy, that I fully expected to see his head go down behind the counter, and his little black breeches, with the rusty little bunches of ribbons at the knees, come quivering up in a last ineffectual struggle. At length, however, he got better, though he still panted hard, and was so exhausted that he was obliged to sit on the stool of the shop-desk.

"You see," he said, wiping his head, and breathing with difficulty, "she hasn't taken much to any companions here; she hasn't taken kindly to any particular acquaintances and friends, not to mention sweethearts. In consequence, an ill-natured story got about, that Em'ly wanted to be a lady. Now, my opinion is, that it came into circulation principally on account of her sometimes saying, at the school, that if she was a lady she would like to do so and so for her uncle—don't you see?—and buy him such and such fine things."

"I assure you, Mr. Omer, she has said so to me," I returned eagerly, "when we were both children."

Mr. Omer nodded his head and rubbed his chin. "Just so. Then out of a very little, she could dress herself, you see, better than most others could out of a deal, and *that* made things unpleasant. Moreover, she was rather what might be called wayward—I'll go so far as to say what I should call wayward myself," said Mr. Omer—"didn't know her own mind quite—a little spoiled—and couldn't, at first, exactly bind herself down. No more than that was ever said against her, Minnie?"

"No, father," said Mrs. Joram. "That's the worst, I believe."

"So when she got a situation," said Mr. Omer, "to keep a fractious old lady company, they didn't very well agree, and she didn't stop. At last she came here, apprenticed for three years. Nearly two of 'em are over, and she has been as good a girl as ever was. Worth any six! Minnie, is she worth any six, now?"

"Yes, father," replied Minnie. "Never say I detracted from her!"

"Very good," said Mr. Omer. "That's right. And so, young gentleman," he added, after a few moments' further rubbing of his chin, "that you may not consider me long-winded as well as short-breathed, I believe that's all about it."

As they had spoken in a subdued tone, while speaking of Em'ly, I had no doubt that she was near. On my asking now, if that were not so, Mr. Omer nodded yes, and nodded towards the door of the parlour. My hurried inquiry if I might peep in, was answered with a free permission; and, looking through the glass, I saw her sitting at her work. I saw her, a most beautiful little creature, with the cloudless blue eyes, that had looked into my childish heart, turned laughingly upon another child of Minnie's who was playing near her; with enough of wilfulness in her bright face to justify what I had heard; with much of the old capricious coyness lurking in it; but with nothing in her pretty looks, I am sure, but what was meant for goodness and for happiness, and what was on a good and happy course.

The tune across the yard that seemed as if it never had left off—alas! it was the tune that never *does* leave off—was beating, softly, all the while.

"Wouldn't you like to step in," said Mr. Omer, "and speak to her? Walk in and speak to her, Sir! Make yourself at home!"

I was too bashful to do so then—I was afraid of confusing her, and I was no less afraid of confusing myself: but I informed myself of the hour at which she left of an evening, in order that our visit might be timed accordingly; and taking leave of Mr. Omer, and his pretty daughter, and her little children, went away to my dear old Peggotty's.

Here she was, in the tiled kitchen, cooking dinner! The moment I knocked at the door she opened it, and asked me what I pleased to want. I looked at her with a smile, but she gave me no smile in return. I had never ceased to write to her, but it must have been seven years since we had met.

"Is Mr. Barkis at home, ma'am?" I said, feigning to speak roughly to her.

"He's at home, Sir," returned Peggotty, "but he's bad abed with the rheumatics."

"Don't he go over to Blunderstone now?" I asked.

"When he's well, he do," she answered.

"Do *you* ever go over there, Mrs. Barkis?"

She looked at me more attentively, and I noticed a quick movement of her hands towards each other.

"Because I want to ask a question about a house there, that they call the—what is it?—the Rookery," said I.

She took a step backward, and put out her hands in an undecided frightened way, as if to keep me off.

"Peggotty!" I cried to her.

She cried, "My darling boy!" and we both burst into tears, and were locked in one another's arms.

What extravagances she committed; what laughing and crying over me; what pride she showed, what joy, what sorrow that she whose pride and joy I might have been,

could never hold me in a fond embrace; I have not the heart to tell. I was troubled with no misgiving that it was young in me to respond to her emotions. I had never laughed and cried in all my life, I dare say—not even in her—more freely than I did that morning."

"Barkis will be so glad," said Peggotty, wiping her eyes with her apron, "that it'll do him more good than pints of liniment. May I go and tell him you are here? Will you come up and see him, my dear?"

Of course I would. But Peggotty could not get out of the room as easily as she meant to, for as often as she got to the door and looked round at me, she came back again to have another laugh and another cry upon my shoulder. At last, to make the matter easier, I went up-stairs with her; and having waited outside for a minute, while she said a word of preparation to Mr. Barkis, presented myself before that invalid.

He received me with absolute enthusiasm. He was too rheumatic to be shaken hands with, but he begged me to shake the tassel on the top of his nightcap, which I did most cordially. When I sat down by the side of the bed, he said that it did him a world of good to feel as if he was driving me on the Blunderstone road again. As he lay in bed, face upward, and so covered, with that exception, that he seemed to be nothing but a face—like a conventional cherubim—he looked the queerest object I ever beheld.

"What name was it as I wrote up in the cart, Sir?" said Mr. Barkis, with a slow rheumatic smile.

"Ah! Mr. Barkis, we had some grave talks about that matter, hadn't we?"

"I was willin' a long time, Sir?" said Mr. Barkis.

"A long time," said I.

"And I don't regret it," said Mr. Barkis. "Do you remember what you told me once, about her making all the apple parsties and doing all the cooking?"

"Yes, very well," I returned.

"It was as true," said Mr. Barkis, "as turnips is. It was as true," said Mr. Barkis, nodding his nightcap, which was his only means of emphasis, "as taxes is. And nothing's truer than them."

Mr. Barkis turned his eyes upon me, as if for my assent to this result of his reflections in bed; and I gave it.

"Nothing's truer than them," repeated Mr. Barkis; "a man as poor as I am finds that out in his mind when he's laid up. I'm a very poor man, Sir."

"I am sorry to hear it, Mr. Barkis."

"A very poor man, indeed I am," said Mr. Barkis.

Here his right hand came slowly and feebly from under the bed-clothes, and with a purposeless uncertain grasp took hold of a stick which was loosely tied to the side of the bed. After some poking about with this instrument, in the course of which his face assumed a variety of distracted expressions, Mr. Barkis poked it against a box, an end of which had been visible to me all the time. Then his face became composed.

"Old clothes," said Mr. Barkis.

"Oh!" said I.

"I wish it was Money, Sir," said Mr. Barkis.

"I wish it was, indeed," said I.

"But it AIN'T," said Mr. Barkis, opening both his eyes as wide as he possibly could.

I expressed myself quite sure of that, and Mr. Barkis, turning his eyes more gently to his wife, said:

"She's the usefullest and best of women, C. P. Barkis.

All the praise that any one can give to C. P. Barkis, she deserves, and more! My dear, you'll get a dinner to-day, for company; something good to eat and drink, will you?"

I should have protested against this unnecessary demonstration in my honour, but that I saw Peggotty, on the opposite side of the bed, extremely anxious I should not. So I held my peace.

"I have got a trifle of money somewhere about me, my dear," said Mr. Barkis, "but I'm a little tired. If you and Mr. David will leave me for a short nap, I'll try and find it when I wake."

We left the room, in compliance with this request. When we got outside the door, Peggotty informed me that Mr. Barkis, being now "a little nearer" than he used to be, always resorted to this same device before producing a single coin from his store; and that he endured unheard-of agonies in crawling out of bed alone, and taking it from that unlucky box. In effect, we presently heard him uttering suppressed groans of the most dismal nature, as this magpie proceeding racked him in every joint; but while Peggotty's eyes were full of compassion for him, she said his generous impulse would do him good, and it was better not to check it. So he groaned on, until he had got into bed again, suffering, I have no doubt, a martyrdom; and then called us in, pretending to have just woke up from a refreshing sleep, and to produce a guinea from under his pillow. His satisfaction in which happy imposition on us, and in having preserved the impenetrable secret of the box, appeared to be a sufficient compensation to him for all his tortures.

I prepared Peggotty for Steerforth's arrival, and it was not long before he came. I am persuaded she knew no difference between his having been a personal benefactor of hers and a kind friend to me, and that she would have received him with the utmost gratitude and devotion in any case. But his easy, spirited good-humour; his genial manner, his handsome looks, his natural gift of adapting himself to whomsoever he pleased, and making direct, when he cared to do it, to the main point of interest in anybody's heart; bound her to him wholly in five minutes. His manner to me, alone, would have won her. But, through all these causes combined, I sincerely believe she had a kind of adoration for him before he left the house that night.

He stayed there with me to dinner—if I were to say willingly, I should not half express how readily and gaily. He went into Mr. Barkis's room like light and air, brightening and refreshing it as if he were healthy weather. There was no noise, no effort, no consciousness, in anything he did; but in everything an indescribable lightness, a seeming impossibility of doing anything else, or doing anything better, which was so graceful, so natural, and agreeable, that it overcomes me, even now, in the remembrance.

We made merry in the little parlour, where the Book of Martyrs, unthumbed since my time, was laid out upon the desk as of old, and where I now turned over its terrific pictures, remembering the old sensations they had awakened, but not feeling them. When Peggotty spoke of what she called my room, and of its being ready for me at night, and of her hoping I would occupy it, before I could so much as look at Steerforth, hesitating, he was possessed of the whole case.

"Of course," he said. "You'll sleep here, while we stay, and I shall sleep at the hotel."

"But to bring you so far," I returned, "and to separate, seems bad companionship, Steerforth."

"Why, in the name of Heaven, where do you naturally belong!" he said. "What is 'seems,' compared to that!" It was settled at once.

He maintained all his delightful qualities to the last, until we started forth, at eight o'clock, for Mr. Peggotty's boat. Indeed, they were more and more brightly exhibited as the hours went on; for I thought even then, and I have no doubt now, that the consciousness of success in his determination to please, inspired him with a new delicacy of perception, and made it, subtle as it was, more easy to him. If any one had told me, then, that all this was a brilliant game, played for the excitement of the moment, for the employment of high spirits, in the thoughtless love of superiority, in a mere wasteful careless course of winning what was worthless to him, and next minute thrown away—I say, if any one had told me such a lie that night, I wonder in what manner of receiving it my indignation would have found a vent!

Probably only in an increase, had that been possible, of the romantic feelings of fidelity and friendship with which I walked beside him, over the dark wintry sands, towards the old boat; the wind sighing around us even more mournfully than it had sighed and moaned upon the night when I first darkened Mr. Peggotty's door.

"This is a wild kind of place, Steerforth, is it not?"

"Dismal enough in the dark," he said; "and the sea roars as if it were hungry for us. Is that the boat, where I see a light yonder?"

"That's the boat," said I.

"And it's the same I saw this morning," he returned. "I came straight to it, by instinct, I suppose."

We said no more as we approached the light, but made softly for the door. I laid my hand upon the latch; and whispering Steerforth to keep close to me, went in.

A murmur of voices had been audible on the outside, and, at the moment of our entrance, a clapping of hands: which latter noise, I was surprised to see, proceeded from the generally disconsolate Mrs. Gummidge. But Mrs. Gummidge was not the only person there who was unusually excited. Mr. Peggotty, his face lighted up with uncommon satisfaction, and laughing with all his might, held his rough arms wide open, as if for little Em'ly to run into them; Ham, with a mixed expression in his face of admiration, exultation, and a lumbering sort of bashfulness that sat upon him very well, held little Em'ly by the hand, as if he were presenting her to Mr. Peggotty; little Em'ly herself, blushing and shy, but delighted with Mr. Peggotty's delight, as her joyous eyes expressed, was stopped by our entrance (for she saw us first) in the very act of springing from Ham to nestle in Mr. Peggotty's embrace. In the first glimpse we had of them all, and at the moment of our passing from the dark cold night into the warm light room, this was the way in which they were all employed: Mrs. Gummidge in the background, clapping hands like a madwoman.

The little picture was so instantaneously dissolved by our going in, that one might have doubted whether it had ever been. I was in the midst of the astonished family, face to face with Mr. Peggotty, and holding out my hand to him, when Ham shouted:

"Mas'r Davy! It's Mas'r Davy!"

In a moment we were all shaking hands with one another, and asking one another how we did, and telling one another how glad we were to meet, and all talking at once. Mr. Peggotty was so proud and overjoyed to see us, that he did not know what to say or do, but kept over and over again

WE WERE UNEXPECTEDLY AT MR. PEGGOTTY'S FIRESIDE.

shaking hands with me, and then with Steerforth, and then with me, and then ruffling his shaggy hair all over his head, and laughing with such glee and triumph, that it was a treat to see him.

"Why, that you two gent'lmen—gent'lmen growed—should come to this here roof to-night, of all nights in my life," said Mr. Peggotty, "is such a thing as never happened afore, I do rightly believe! Em'ly, my darling, come here! Come here, my little witch! There's Mas'r Davy's friend, my dear! There's the gent'lman as you've heerd on, Em'ly. He comes to see you, along with Mas'r Davy, on the brightest night of your uncle's life as ever was or will be, Gorm the t'other one, and horroar for it!"

After delivering this speech all in a breath, and with extraordinary animation and pleasure, Mr. Peggotty put one of his large hands rapturously on each side of his niece's face, and kissing it a dozen times, laid it with a gentle pride and love upon his broad chest, and patted it as if his hand had been a lady's. Then he let her go; and as she ran into the little chamber where I used to sleep, looked round upon us, quite hot and out of breath with his uncommon satisfaction.

"If you two gent'lmen—gent'lmen growed now, and such gent'lmen——" said Mr. Peggotty.

"So th' are, so th' are!" cried Ham. "Well said! So th' are. Mas'r Davy bor—gent'lmen growed—so th' are!"

"If you two gent'lmen, gent'lmen growed," said Mr. Peggotty, "don't ex-cuse me for being in a state of mind, when you understand matters, I'll arks your pardon. Em'ly, my dear!—She knows I'm a going to tell," here his delight broke out again, "and has made off. Would you be so good as look arter her, Mawther, for a minute?"

Mrs. Gummidge nodded and disappeared.

"If this ain't," said Mr. Peggotty, sitting down among us by the fire, "the brightest night o' my life, I'm a shell-fish—biled too—and more I can't say. This here little Em'ly, Sir," in a low voice to Steerforth,—"her as you see a blushing here just now——"

Steerforth only nodded; but with such a pleased expression of interest, and of participation in Mr. Peggotty's feelings, that the latter answered him as if he had spoken.

"To be sure," said Mr. Peggotty, "that's her, and so she is. Thank'ee, Sir."

Ham nodded to me several times, as if he would have said so too.

"This here little Em'ly of ours," said Mr. Peggotty, "has been, in our house, what I suppose (I'm a ignorant man, but that's my belief) no one but a little bright-eyed creetur *can* be in a house. She ain't my child; I never had one; but I couldn't love her more. You understand! I couldn't do it!"

"I quite understand," said Steerforth.

"I know you do, Sir," returned Mr. Peggotty, "and thank'ee again. Mas'r Davy, he can remember what she was; you may judge for your own self what she is; but neither of you can't fully know what she has been, is, and will be, to my loving 'art. I am rough, Sir," said Mr. Peggotty, "I am as rough as a Sea Porkypine; but no one, unless, mayhap, it is a woman, can know, I think, what our little Em'ly is to me. And betwixt ourselves," sinking his voice lower yet, "*that* woman's name ain't Missis Gummidge neither, though she has a world of merits."

Mr. Peggotty ruffled his hair again with both hands, as a further preparation for what he was going to say, and went on, with a hand upon each of his knees:

"There was a certain person as had know'd our Em'ly, from the time when her father was drownded; as had seen her constant; when a babby, when a young gal, when a woman. Not much of a person to look at, he warn't," said Mr. Peggotty, "something o' my own build—rough—a good deal o' the sou'-wester in him—wery salt—but, on the whole, a honest sort of a chap, with his 'art in the right place."

I thought I had never seen Ham grin to anything like the extent to which he sat grinning at us now.

"What does this here blessed tarpaulin go and do," said Mr. Peggotty, with his face one high moon of enjoyment, "but he loses that there 'art of his to our little Em'ly. He follers her about, he makes hisself a sort o' sarvant to her, he loses in a great measure his relish for his wittles, and in the long run he makes it clear to me wot's amiss. Now I could wish myself, you see, that our little Em'ly was in a fair way of being married. I could wish to see her, at all ewents, under articles to a honest man as had a right to defend her. I don't know how long I may live, or how soon I may die; but I know that if I was capsized, any night, in a gale of wind in Yarmouth Roads here, and was to see the town-lights shining for the last time over the rollers as I couldn't make no head aginst, I could go down quieter for thinking 'There's a man ashore there, iron-true to my little Em'ly, God bless her, and no wrong can touch my Em'ly while so be as that man lives.'"

Mr. Peggotty, in simple earnestness, waved his right arm, as if he were waving it at the town-lights for the last time, and then, exchanging a nod with Ham, whose eye he caught, proceeded as before:

"Well! I counsels him to speak to Em'ly. He's big enough, but he's bashfuller than a little 'un, and he don't like. So *I* speak. 'What! *Him?*' says Em'ly. '*Him* that I've know'd so intimate so many years, and like so much! Oh, uncle! I never can have *him*. He's such a good fellow!' I gives her a kiss, and I says no more to her than 'My dear, you're right to speak out, you're to choose for yourself, you're as free as a little bird.' Then I aways to him, and says, 'I wish it could have been so, but it can't. But you can both be as you was, and wot I say to you is, Be as you was with her, like a man.' He says to me, a shaking of my hand, 'I will!' he says. And he was—honourable and manful—for two year going on, and we was just the same at home here as afore."

Mr. Peggotty's face, which had varied in its expression with the various stages of his narrative, now resumed all its former triumphant delight, as he laid a hand upon my knee and a hand upon Steerforth's (previously wetting them both, for the greater emphasis of the action), and divided the following speech between us:

"All of a sudden, one evening—as it might be to-night—comes little Em'ly from her work, and him with her! There ain't so much in *that*, you'll say. No, because he takes care on her, like a brother, arter dark, and indeed afore dark, and at all times. But this tarpaulin chap, he takes hold of her hand, and he cries out to me, joyful, Look here! This is to be my little wife!' And she says, half bold and half shy, and half a laughing and half a crying, 'Yes, uncle! If you please.'—If I please!" cried Mr. Peggotty, rolling his head in an ecstasy at the idea; "Lord, as if I should do anythink else!—' If you please, I am steadier now, and I have thought better of it, and I'll be as good a little wife as I can to him, for he's a dear, good fellow!' Then Missis Gummidge, she claps her hands like a play, and you come in. Theer! the murder's out!" said Mr. Peggotty—"You come in! It took place this here present hour; and here's the man that'll marry her, the minute she's out of her time."

Ham staggered, as well he might, under the blow Mr. Peggotty dealt him in his unbounded joy, as a mark of confidence and friendship; but feeling called upon to say something to us, he said, with much faltering and great difficulty:

"She warn't no higher than you was, Mas'r Davy—when you first come—when I thought what she'd grow up to be. I see her grow up—gent'lmen—like a flower. I'd lay down my life for her—Mas'r Davy—Oh! most content and cheerful! She's more to me—gent'lmen—than—she's all to me that ever I can want, and more than ever I—than ever I could say. I—I love her true. There ain't a gent'lman in all the land—nor yet sailing upon all the sea—that can love his lady more than I love her, though there's many a common man—would say better—what he meant."

I thought it affecting to see such a sturdy fellow as Ham was now, trembling in the strength of what he felt for the pretty little creature who had won his heart. I thought the simple confidence reposed in us by Mr. Peggotty and by himself, was, in itself, affecting. I was affected by the story altogether. How far my emotions were influenced by the recollections of my childhood, I don't know. Whether I had come there with any lingering fancy that I was still to love little Em'ly, I don't know. I know that I was filled with pleasure by all this; but, at first, with an indescribably sensitive pleasure, that a very little would have changed to pain.

Therefore, if it had depended upon me to touch the prevailing chord among them with any skill, I should have made a poor hand of it. But it depended upon Steerforth; and he did it with such address, that in a few minutes we were all as easy and as happy as it was possible to be.

"Mr. Peggotty," he said, "you are a thoroughly good fellow, and deserve to be as happy as you are to-night. My hand upon it! Ham, I give you joy, my boy. My hand upon that, too! Daisy, stir the fire, and make it a brisk one! and Mr. Peggotty, unless you can induce your gentle niece to come back (for whom I vacate this seat in the corner), I shall go. Any gap at your fireside on such a night—such a gap least of all—I wouldn't make, for the wealth of the Indies!"

So Mr. Peggotty went into my old room to fetch little Em'ly. At first, little Em'ly didn't like to come, and then Ham went. Presently they brought her to the fireside, very much confused, and very shy,—but she soon became more assured when she found how gently and respectfully Steerforth spoke to her; how skilfully he avoided anything that would embarrass her; how he talked to Mr. Peggotty of boats, and ships, and tides, and fish; how he referred to me about the time when he had seen Mr. Peggotty at Salem House; how delighted he was with the boat and all belonging to it; how lightly and easily he carried on, until he brought us, by degrees, into a charmed circle, and we were all talking away without any reserve.

Em'ly, indeed, said little all the evening; but she looked, and listened, and her face got animated, and she was charming. Steerforth told a story of a dismal shipwreck (which arose out of his talk with Mr. Peggotty), as if he saw it all before him—and little Em'ly's eyes were fastened on him all the time, as if she saw it too. He told us a merry adventure of his own, as a relief to that, with as much gaiety as if the narrative were as fresh to him as it was to us—and little Em'ly laughed until the boat rang with the musical sounds, and we all laughed (Steerforth too), in irresistible sympathy with what was so pleasant and light-hearted. He got Mr. Peggotty to sing, or rather to roar, "When the stormy winds do blow, do blow, do blow;" and he sang a sailor's song himself, so pathetically and beautifully, that I could have almost fancied that the real wind creeping sorrowfully round the house, and murmuring low through our unbroken silence, was there to listen.

As to Mrs. Gummidge, he roused that victim of despondency with a success never attained by anyone else (so Mr. Peggotty informed me), since the decease of the old one. He left her so little leisure for being miserable, that she said next day she thought she must have been bewitched.

But he set up no monopoly of the general attention, or the conversation. When little Em'ly grew more courageous, and talked (but still bashfully) across the fire to me, of our old wanderings upon the beach, to pick up shells and pebbles; and when I asked her if she recollected how I used to be devoted to her; and when we both laughed and reddened, casting these looks back on the pleasant old times, so unreal to look at now; he was silent and attentive, and observed us thoughtfully. She sat, at this time, and all the evening, on the old locker in her old little corner by the fire—Ham beside her, where I used to sit. I could not satisfy myself whether it was in her own little tormenting way, or in a maidenly reserve before us, that she kept quite close to the wall, and away from him; but I observed that she did so, all the evening.

As I remember, it was almost midnight when we took our leave. We had had some biscuit and dried fish for supper, and Steerforth had produced from his pocket a full flask of Hollands, which we men (I may say we men, now, without a blush) had emptied. We parted merrily; and as they all stood crowded round the door to light us as far as they could upon our road, I saw the sweet blue eyes of little Em'ly peeping after us, from behind Ham, and heard her soft voice calling to us to be careful how we went.

"A most engaging little beauty!" said Steerforth, taking my arm. "Well! It's a quaint place, and they are quaint company, and it's quite a new sensation to mix with them."

"How fortunate we are, too," I returned, "to have arrived to witness their happiness in that intended marriage! I never saw people so happy. How delightful to see it, and to be made the sharers in their honest joy, as we have been!"

"That's rather a chuckle-headed fellow for the girl; isn't he?" said Steerforth.

He had been so hearty with him, and with them all, that I felt a shock in this unexpected and cold reply. But turning quickly upon him, and seeing a laugh in his eyes, I answered, much relieved:

"Ah, Steerforth! It's well for you to joke about the poor! You may skirmish with Miss Dartle, or try to hide your sympathies in jest from me, but I know better. When I see how perfectly you understand them, how exquisitely you can enter into happiness like this plain fisherman's, or humour a love like my old nurse's, I know that there is not a joy or sorrow, not an emotion, of such people, that can be indifferent to you. And I admire and love you for it, Steerforth, twenty times the more!"

He stopped, and looking in my face, said, "Daisy, I believe you are in earnest, and are good. I wish we all were!" Next moment he was gaily singing Mr. Peggotty's song, as we walked at a round pace back to Yarmouth.

CHAPTER XXII.

SOME OLD SCENES, AND SOME NEW PEOPLE.

STEERFORTH and I stayed for more than a fortnight in that part of the country. We were very much together, I need not say; but occasionally we were asunder for some hours at a time. He was a good sailor, and I was but an indifferent one; and when he went out boating with Mr. Peggotty, which was a favourite amusement of his, I generally remained ashore. My occupation of Peggotty's spare room put a constraint upon me, from which he was free: for, knowing how assiduously she attended on Mr. Barkis all day, I did not like to remain out late at night; whereas Steerforth, lying at the Inn, had nothing to consult but his own humour. Thus it came about, that I heard of his making little treats for the fishermen at Mr. Peggotty's house of call, "The Willing Mind," after I was in bed, and of his being afloat, wrapped in fishermen's clothes, whole moonlight nights, and coming back when the morning tide was at flood. By this time, however, I knew that his restless nature and bold spirits delighted to find a vent in rough toil and hard weather, as in any other means of excitement that presented itself freshly to him; so none of his proceedings surprised me.

Another cause of our being sometimes apart was, that I had naturally an interest in going over to Blunderstone, and revisiting the old familiar scenes of my childhood; while Steerforth, after being there once, had naturally no great interest in going there again. Hence, on three or four days that I can at once recall, we went our several ways after an early breakfast, and met again at a late dinner. I had no idea how he employed his time in the interval, beyond a general knowledge that he was very popular in the place, and had twenty means of actively diverting himself where another man might not have found one.

For my own part, my occupation in my solitary pilgrimages was to recall every yard of the old road as I went along it, and to haunt the old spots, of which I never tired. I haunted them, as my memory had often done, and lingered among them as my younger thoughts had lingered when I was far away. The grave beneath the tree, where both my parents lay—on which I had looked out, when it was my father's only, with such curious feelings of compassion, and by which I had stood, so desolate, when it was opened to receive my pretty mother and her baby—the grave which Peggotty's own faithful care had ever since kept neat, and made a garden of, I walked near, by the hour. It lay a little off the churchyard path, in a quiet corner, not so far removed but I could read the names upon the stone as I walked to and fro, startled by the sound of the church-bell when it struck the hour, for it was like a departed voice to me. My reflections at these times were always associated with the figure I was to make in life, and the distinguished things I was to do. My echoing footsteps went to no other tune, but were as constant to that as if I had come home to build my castles in the air at a living mother's side.

There were great changes in my old home. The ragged nests, so long deserted by the rooks, were gone; and the trees were lopped and topped out of their remembered shapes. The garden had run wild, and half the windows of the house were shut up. It was occupied, but only by a poor lunatic gentleman, and the people who took care of him. He was always sitting at my little window, looking out into the churchyard; and I wondered whether his rambling thoughts ever went upon any of the fancies that used to occupy mine, on the rosy mornings when I peeped out of that same little window in my night-clothes, and saw the sheep quietly feeding in the light of the rising sun.

Our old neighbours, Mr. and Mrs. Grayper, were gone to South America, and the rain had made its way through the roof of their empty house, and stained the outer walls. Mr. Chillip was married again to a tall, raw-boned, high-nosed wife; and they had a weazen little baby, with a heavy head that it couldn't hold up, and two weak staring eyes, with which it seemed to be always wondering why it had ever been born.

It was with a singular jumble of sadness and pleasure that I used to linger about my native place, until the reddening winter sun admonished me that it was time to start on my returning walk. But, when the place was left behind, and especially when Steerforth and I were happily seated over our dinner by a blazing fire, it was delicious to think of having been there. So it was, though in a softened degree, when I went to my neat room at night; and, turning over the leaves of the crocodile-book (which was always there, upon a little table), remembered with a grateful heart how blest I was in having such a friend as Steerforth, such a friend as Peggotty, and such a substitute for what I had lost as my excellent and generous aunt.

My nearest way to Yarmouth, in coming back from these long walks, was by a ferry. It landed me on the flat between the town and the sea, which I could make straight across, and so save myself a considerable circuit by the high road. Mr. Peggotty's house being on that waste-place, and not a hundred yards out of my tract, I always looked in as I went by. Steerforth was pretty sure to be there expecting me, and we went on together through the frosty air and gathering fog towards the twinkling lights of the town.

One dark evening, when I was later than usual—for I had, that day, been making my parting visit to Blunderstone, as we were now about to return home—I found him alone in Mr. Peggotty's house, sitting thoughtfully before the fire. He was so intent upon his own reflections that he was quite unconscious of my approach. This, indeed, he might easily have been if he had been less absorbed, for footsteps fell noiselessly on the sandy ground outside; but even my entrance failed to rouse him. I was standing close to him, looking at him; and still, with a heavy brow, he was lost in his meditations.

He gave such a start when I put my hand upon his shoulder, that he made me start too.

"You come upon me," he said, almost angrily, "like a reproachful ghost!"

"I was obliged to announce myself somehow," I replied. 'Have I called you down from the stars?"

"No," he answered. "No."

"Up from anywhere, then?" said I, taking my seat near him.

"I was looking at the pictures in the fire," he returned.

"But you are spoiling them for me," said I, as he stirred

it quickly with a piece of burning wood, striking out of it a train of red-hot sparks that went careering up the little chimney, and roaring out into the air.

"You would not have seen them," he returned. "I detest this mongrel time, neither day nor night. How late you are! Where have you been?"

"I have been taking leave of my usual walk," said I.

"And I have been sitting here," said Steerforth, glancing round the room, "thinking that all the people we found so glad on the night of our coming down, might—to judge from the present wasted air of the place—be dispersed, or dead, or come to I don't know what harm. David, I wish to God I had had a judicious father these last twenty years!"

"My dear Steerforth, what is the matter?"

"I wish with all my soul I had been better guided!" he exclaimed. "I wish with all my soul I could guide myself better!"

There was a passionate dejection in his manner that quite amazed me. He was more unlike himself than I could have supposed possible.

"It would be better to be this poor Peggotty, or his lout of a nephew," he said, getting up and leaning moodily against the chimney-piece, with his face towards the fire, "than to be myself, twenty times richer and twenty times wiser, and be the torment to myself that I have been, in this Devil's bark of a boat, within the last half-hour!"

I was so confounded by the alteration in him, that at first I could only observe him in silence, as he stood leaning his head upon his hand, and looking gloomily down at the fire. At length I begged him, with all the earnestness I felt, to tell me what had occurred so cross him so unusually, and to let me sympathise with him, if I could not hope to advise him. Before I had well concluded, he began to laugh—fretfully at first, but soon with returning gaiety.

"Tut, it's nothing, Daisy! nothing!" he replied. "I told you, at the inn in London, I am heavy company for myself, sometimes. I have been a nightmare to myself, just now—must have had one, I think. At odd dull times, nursery tales come up into the memory, unrecognised for what they are. I believe I have been confounding myself with the bad boy who 'didn't care,' and became food for lions—a grander kind of going to the dogs, I suppose. What old women call the horrors, have been creeping over me from head to foot. I have been afraid of myself."

"You are afraid of nothing else, I think," said I.

"Perhaps not, and yet may have enough to be afraid of too," he answered. "Well! So it goes by! I am not about to be hipped again, David; but I tell you, my good fellow, once more, that it would have been well for me (and for more than me) if I had had a steadfast and judicious father!"

His face was always full of expression, but I never saw it express such a dark kind of earnestness as when he said these words, with his glance bent on the fire.

"So much for that!" he said, making as if he tossed something light into the air, with his hand.

"'Why, being gone, I am a man again,'

like Macbeth. And now for dinner! If I have not (Macbeth-like) broken up the feast with most admired disorder, Daisy."

"But where are they all, I wonder!" said I.

"God knows," said Steerforth. "After strolling to the ferry looking for you, I strolled in here and found the place deserted. That set me thinking, and you found me thinking."

The advent of Mrs. Gummidge with a basket, explained how the house had happened to be empty. She had hurried out to buy something that was needed, against Mr. Peggotty's return with the tide; and had left the door open in the meanwhile, lest Ham and little Em'ly, with whom it was an early night, should come home while she was gone. Steerforth, after very much improving Mrs. Gummidge's spirits by a cheerful salutation and a jocose embrace, took my arm, and hurried me away.

He had improved his own spirits, no less than Mrs. Gummidge's, for they were again at their usual flow, and he was full of vivacious conversation as we went along.

"And so," he said, gaily, "we abandon this buccaneer life to-morrow, do we?"

"So we agreed," I returned. "And our places by the coach are taken, you know."

"Ay! there's no help for it, I suppose," said Steerforth. "I have almost forgotten that there is anything to do in the world but to go out tossing on the sea here. I wish there was not."

"As long as the novelty should last," said I, laughing.

"Like enough," he returned; "though there's a sarcastic meaning in that observation for an amiable piece of innocence like my young friend. Well! I dare say I am a capricious fellow, David. I know I am; but while the iron is hot, I can strike it vigorously too. I could pass a reasonably good examination already, as a pilot in these waters, I think."

"Mr. Peggotty says you are a wonder," I returned.

"A nautical phenomenon, eh?" laughed Steerforth.

"Indeed he does, and you know how truly; knowing how ardent you are in any pursuit you follow, and how easily you can master it. And that amazes me most in you, Steerforth—that you should be contented with such fitful uses of your powers."

"Contented?" he answered, merrily. "I am never contented, except with your freshness, my gentle Daisy. As to fitfulness, I have never learnt the art of binding myself to any of the wheels on which the Ixions of these days are turning round and round. I missed it somehow in a bad apprenticeship, and now don't care about it.—You know I have bought a boat down here?"

"What an extraordinary fellow you are, Steerforth!" I exclaimed, stopping—for this was the first I had heard of it. "When you may never care to come near the place again!"

"I don't know that," he returned. "I have taken a fancy to the place. At all events," walking me briskly on, "I have bought a boat that was for sale—a clipper, Mr. Peggotty says; and so she is—and Mr. Peggotty will be master of her in my absence."

"Now I understand you, Steerforth!" said I, exultingly. "You pretend to have bought it for yourself, but you have really done so to confer a benefit on him. I might have known as much at first, knowing you. My dear kind Steerforth, how can I tell you what I think of your generosity?"

"Tush!" he answered, turning red. "The less said, the better."

"Didn't I know?" cried I, "didn't I say that there was not a joy, or sorrow, or any emotion of such honest hearts that was indifferent to you?"

"Ay, ay," he answered, "you told me all that. There let it rest. We have said enough!"

Afraid of offending him by pursuing the subject when he made so light of it, I only pursued it in my thoughts as we went on at even a quicker pace than before.

"She must be newly rigged," said Steerforth, "and I shall leave Littimer behind to see it done, that I may know she is quite complete. Did I tell you Littimer had come down?"

"No."

"Oh, yes! came down this morning, with a letter from my mother."

As our looks met, I observed that he was pale even to his lips, though he looked very steadily at me. I feared that some difference between him and his mother might have led to his being in the frame of mind in which I had found him at the solitary fireside. I hinted so.

"Oh no!" he said, shaking his head, and giving a slight laugh. "Nothing of the sort! Yes. He is come down, that man of mine."

"The same as ever?" said I.

"The same as ever," said Steerforth. "Distant and quiet as the North Pole. He shall see to the boat being fresh named. She's the Stormy Petrel now. What does Mr. Peggotty care for Stormy Petrels! I'll have her christened again."

"By what name?" I asked.

"The Little Em'ly."

As he had continued to look steadily at me, I took it as a reminder that he objected to being extolled for his consideration. I could not help showing in my face how much it pleased me, but I said little, and he resumed his usual smile, and seemed relieved.

"But see here," he said, looking before us, "where the original little Em'ly comes! And that fellow with her, eh? Upon my soul, he's a true knight. He never leaves her!"

Ham was a boat-builder in these days, having improved a natural ingenuity in that handicraft, until he had become a skilled workman. He was in his working-dress, and looked rugged enough, but manly withal, and a very fit protector for the blooming little creature at his side. Indeed, there was a frankness in his face, an honesty, and an undisguised show of his pride in her, and his love for her, which were, to me, the best of good looks. I thought, as they came towards us, that they were well matched even in that particular.

She withdrew her hand timidly from his arm as we stopped to speak to them, and blushed as she gave it to Steerforth and to me. When they passed on, after we had exchanged a few words, she did not like to replace that hand, but, still appearing timid and constrained, walked by herself. I thought all this very pretty and engaging, and Steerforth seemed to think so too, as we looked after them fading away in the light of a young moon.

Suddenly there passed us—evidently following them—a young woman whose approach we had not observed, but whose face I saw as she went by, and thought I had a faint remembrance of. She was lightly dressed; looked bold, and haggard, and flaunting, and poor; but seemed, for the time, to have given all that to the wind which was blowing, and to have nothing in her mind but going after them. As the dark distant level, absorbing their figures into itself, left but itself visible between us and the sea and clouds, her figure disappeared in like manner, still no nearer to them than before.

"That is a black shadow to be following the girl," said Steerforth, standing still; "what does it mean?"

He spoke in a low voice that sounded almost strange to me.

"She must have it in her mind to beg of them, I think," said I.

"A beggar would be no novelty," said Steerforth, "but it is a strange thing that the beggar should take that shape to-night."

"Why?" I asked him.

"For no better reason, truly, than because I was thinking," he said, after a pause, "of something like it, when it came by. Where the Devil did it come from, I wonder!"

"From the shadow of this wall, I think," said I, as we emerged upon a road on which a wall abutted.

"It's gone!" he returned, looking over his shoulder. "And all ill go with it. Now for our dinner!"

But he looked again over his shoulder towards the sea-line glimmering afar off; and yet again. And he wondered about it, in some broken expressions, several times, in the short remainder of our walk; and only seemed to forget it when the light of fire and candle shone upon us, seated warm and merry, at table.

Littimer was there, and had his usual effect upon me. When I said to him that I hoped Mrs. Steerforth and Miss Dartle were well, he answered respectfully (and of course respectably), that they were tolerably well, he thanked me, and had sent their compliments. This was all, and yet he seemed to me to say as plainly as a man could say: "You are very young, Sir; you are exceedingly young."

We had almost finished dinner, when taking a step or two towards the table, from the corner where he kept watch upon us, or rather upon me, as I felt, he said to his master:

"I beg your pardon, Sir. Miss Mowcher is down here."

"Who?" cried Steerforth, much astonished.

"Miss Mowcher, Sir."

"Why, what on earth does *she* do here?" said Steerforth.

"It appears to be her native part of the country, Sir. She informs me that she makes one of her professional visits here, every year, Sir. I met her in the street this afternoon, and she wished to know if she might have the honour of waiting on you after dinner, Sir."

"Do you know the giantess in question, Daisy?" inquired Steerforth.

I was obliged to confess—I felt ashamed, even of being at this disadvantage before Littimer—that Miss Mowcher and I were wholly unacquainted.

"Then you shall know her," said Steerforth, "for she is one of the seven wonders of the world. When Miss Mowcher comes, show her in."

I felt some curiosity and excitement about this lady, especially as Steerforth burst into a fit of laughing when I referred to her, and positively refused to answer any question of which I made her the subject. I remained, therefore, in a state of considerable expectation until the cloth had been removed some half-an-hour, and we were sitting over our decanter of wine before the fire, when the door opened, and Littimer, with his habitual serenity quite undisturbed, announced:

"Miss Mowcher!"

I looked at the doorway and saw nothing. I was still looking at the doorway, thinking that Miss Mowcher was a long while making her appearance, when, to my infinite astonishment, there came waddling round a sofa which stood between me and it, a pursy dwarf, of about forty or forty-five, with a very large head and face, a pair of roguish grey eyes, and such extremely little arms, that, to enable herself to lay a finger archly against her snub nose as she ogled Steerforth, she was obliged to meet the finger half-way, and lay her nose against it. Her chin, which was what is called a double chin, was so fat that it entirely swallowed up the strings of her bonnet, bow and all. Throat she had none; waist she had none; legs she had none, worth mentioning; for though she was more than full-sized down to where her waist would have been, if she had had any, and though she terminated, as human beings generally do, in a pair of feet, she was so short that she stood at a common-sized chair as at a table, resting a bag she carried on the seat. This lady; dressed in an off-hand, easy style; bringing her nose and her forefinger together, with the difficulty I have described; standing with her head necessarily on one side, and, with one of her sharp eyes shut up, making an uncommonly knowing face; after ogling Steerforth for a few moments, broke into a torrent of words.

"What! My flower!" she pleasantly began, shaking her large head at him. "You're there, are you! Oh, you naughty boy, fie for shame, what do you do so far away from home? Up to mischief, I'll be bound. Oh, you're a downy fellow, Steerforth, so you are, and I'm another, ain't I? Ha, ha, ha! You'd have betted a hundred pound to five, now, that you wouldn't have seen me here, wouldn't you? Bless you, man alive, I'm everywhere. I'm here, and there, and where not, like the conjuror's half-crown in the lady's hankercher. Talking of hankerchers—and talking of ladies—what a comfort you are to your blessed mother, ain't you, my dear boy, over one of my shoulders, and I don't say which!"

Miss Mowcher untied her bonnet, at this passage of her discourse, threw back the strings, and sat down, panting, on a foot-stool in front of the fire—making a kind of arbour of the dining-table, which spread its mahogany shelter above her head.

"Oh my stars and what's-their-names!" she went on, clapping a hand on each of her little knees, and glancing shrewdly at me. "I'm of too full a habit, that's the fact, Steerforth. After a flight of stairs, it gives me as much trouble to draw every breath I want, as if it was a bucket of water. If you saw me looking out of an upper window, you'd think I was a fine woman, wouldn't you?"

"I should think that, wherever I saw you," replied Steerforth.

"Go along, you dog, do!" cried the little creature, making a whisk at him with the handkerchief with which she was wiping her face, "and don't be impudent! But I give you my word and honour I was at Lady Mithers's last week—there's a woman! How she wears!—and Mithers himself came into the room where I was waiting for her—there's a man! How he wears! and his wig too, for he's had it these ten years—and he went on at that rate in the compliment-ary line, that I began to think I should be obliged to ring the bell. Ha! ha! ha! He's a pleasant wretch, but he wants principle."

"What were you doing for Lady Mithers?" asked Steer-forth.

"That's tellings, my blessed infant," she retorted, tap-ping her nose again, screwing up her face, and twinkling her eyes like an imp of supernatural intelligence. "Never you mind! You'd like to know whether I stop her hair from falling off, or dye it, or touch up her complexion, or improve her eyebrows, wouldn't you? And so you shall,

my darling—when I tell you! Do you know what my great grandfather's name was?"

"No," said Steerforth.

"It was Walker, my sweet pet," replied Miss Mowcher, "and he came of a long line of Walkers, that I inherit all the Hookey estates from."

I never beheld anything approaching to Miss Mowcher's wink, except Miss Mowcher's self-possession. She had a wonderful way too, when listening to what was said to her, or when waiting for an answer to what she had said herself, of pausing with her head cunningly on one side, and one eye turned up like a magpie's. Altogether I was lost in amaze-ment, and sat staring at her, quite oblivious, I am afraid, of the laws of politeness.

She had by this time drawn the chair to her side, and was busily engaged in producing from the bag (plunging in her short arm to the shoulder, at every dive) a number of small bottles, sponges, combs, brushes, bits of flannel, little pairs of curling-irons, and other instruments, which she tumbled in a heap upon the chair. From this employment she suddenly desisted, and said to Steerforth, much to my confusion·

"Who's your friend?"

"Mr. Copperfield," said Steerforth; "he wants to know you."

"Well then, he shall! I thought he looked as if he did!" returned Miss Mowcher, waddling up to me, bag in hand, and laughing on me as she came. "Face like a peach!" standing on tiptoe to pinch my cheek as I sat. "Quite tempting! I'm very fond of peaches Happy to make your acquaintance, Mr. Copperfield, I'm sure."

I said that I congratulated myself on having the honour to make hers, and that the happiness was mutual.

"Oh my goodness, how polite we are!" exclaimed Miss Mowcher, making a preposterous attempt to cover her large face with her morsel of a hand. "What a world of gam-mon and spinnage it is, though, ain't it!"

This was addressed confidentially to both of us, as the morsel of a hand came away from the face, and buried itself, arm and all, in the bag again.

"What do you mean, Miss Mowcher?" said Steerforth.

"Ha! ha! ha! What a refreshing set of humbugs we are, to be sure, ain't we, my sweet child?" replied that morsel of a woman, feeling in the bag with her head on one side, and her eye in the air. "Look here!" taking something out. "Scraps of the Russian Prince's nails! Prince Alphabet turned topsy-turvy, I call him, for his name's got all the letters in it, higgledy-piggledy."

"The Russian Prince is a client of yours, is he?" said Steerforth.

"I believe you, my pet," replied Miss Mowcher. "I keep his nails in order for him. Twice a week! Fingers and toes!"

"He pays well, I hope?" said Steerforth.

"Pays as he speaks, my dear child,—through the nose," replied Miss Mowcher. "None of your close shavers the Prince ain't. You'd say so, if you saw his moustachios. Red by nature, black by art."

"By your art, of course," said Steerforth.

Miss Mowcher winked assent. "Forced to send for me. Couldn't help it. The climate affected his dye; it did very well in Russia, but it was no go here. You never saw such a rusty prince in all your born days as he was. Like old iron!"

"Is that why you called him a humbug, just now?" inquired Steerforth.

"Oh, you're a broth of a boy, ain't you?" returned Miss

Mowcher, shaking her head violently. "I said, what a set of humbugs we were in general, and I showed you the scraps of the Prince's nails to prove it. The Prince's nails do more for me in private families of the genteel sort, than all my talents put together. I always carry 'em about. They're the best introduction. If Miss-Mowcher cuts the Prince's nails, she *must* be all right. I give 'em away to the young ladies. They put 'em in albums, I believe. Ha! ha! ha! Upon my life, 'the whole social system' (as the men call it when they make speeches in Parliament) is a system of Prince's nails!" said this least of women, trying to fold her short arms, and nodding her large head.

Steerforth laughed heartily, and I laughed too. Miss Mowcher continuing all the time to shake her head (which was very much on one side), and to look into the air with one eye, and to wink with the other.

"Well, well!" she said, smiting her small knees, and rising, "this is not business. Come, Steerforth, let's explore the polar regions, and have it over."

She then selected two or three of the little instruments, and a little bottle, and asked (to my surprise) if the table would bear. On Steerforth's replying in the affirmative, she pushed a chair against it, and begging the assistance of my hand, mounted up, pretty nimbly, to the top, as if it were a stage.

"If either of you saw my ankles," she said, when she was safely elevated, "say so, and I'll go home and destroy myself."

"*I* did not," said Steerforth.

"*I* did not," said I.

"Well then," cried Miss Mowcher, "I'll consent to live. Now, ducky, ducky, ducky, come to Mrs. Bond and be killed!"

This was an invocation to Steerforth to place himself under her hands; who, accordingly, sat himself down, with his back to the table, and his laughing face towards me, and submitted his head to her inspection, evidently for no other purpose than our entertainment. To see Miss Mowcher standing over him, looking at his rich profusion of brown hair through a large round magnifying-glass, which she took out of her pocket, was a most amazing spectacle.

"*You're* a pretty fellow!" said Miss Mowcher, after a brief inspection. "You'd be as bald as a friar on the top of your head in twelve months, but for me. Just half-a-minute, my young friend, and we'll give you a polishing that shall keep your curls on for the next ten years!"

With this, she tilted some of the contents of the little bottle on to one of the little bits of flannel, and, again imparting some of the virtues of that preparation to one of the little brushes, began rubbing and scraping away with both on the crown of Steerforth's head in the busiest manner I ever witnessed, talking all the time.

"There's Charley Pyegrave, the Duke's son," she said. "You know Charley?" peeping round into his face.

"A little," said Steerforth.

"What a man *he* is! *There's* a whisker! As to Charley's legs, if they were only a pair (which they ain't), they'd defy competition. Would you believe he tried to do without me—in the Life-Guards, too?"

"Mad!" said Steerforth.

"It looks like it. However, mad or sane, he tried," returned Miss Mowcher. "What does he do, but, lo and behold you, he goes into a perfumer's shop, and wants to buy a bottle of the Madagascar Liquid."

"Charley does?" said Steerforth.

"Charley does. But they haven't got any of the Madagascar Liquid."

"What is it? Something to drink?" asked Steerforth.

"To drink?" returned Miss Mowcher, stopping to slap his cheek. "To doctor his own moustachios with, you *know*. There was a woman in the shop—elderly female —quite a Griffin—who had never even heard of it by name. ' Begging pardon, Sir,' said the Griffin to Charley, ' it's not—not—not ROUGE, is it?' ' Rouge,' said Charley to the Griffin. ' What the unmentionable to ears polite, do you think I want with rouge?' ' No offence, Sir,' said the Griffin; ' we have it asked for by so many names, I thought it might be.' Now that, my child," continued Miss Mowcher, rubbing all the time as busily as ever, "is another instance of the refreshing humbug I was speaking of. *I* do something in that way myself—perhaps a good deal— perhaps a little—sharp's the word, my dear boy—never mind!"

"In what way do you mean? In the rouge way?" said Steerforth.

"Put this and that together, my tender pupil," returned the wary Mowcher, touching her nose, "work it by the rule of Secrets in all trades, and the product will give you the desired result. I say *I* do a little in that way myself. One Dowager, *she* calls it lip-salve. Another, *she* calls it gloves. Another, *she* calls it tucker-edging. Another, *she* calls it a fan. *I* call it whatever *they* call it. I supply it for 'em, but we keep up the trick so, to one another, and make believe with such a face, that they'd as soon think of laying it on, before a whole drawing-room, as before me. And when I wait upon 'em, they'll say to me sometimes— *with it on*—thick, and no mistake—' How am I looking, Mowcher? Am I pale?' Ha! ha! ha! ha! Isn't *that* refreshing, my young friend!"

I never did in my days behold anything like Mowcher as she stood upon the dining-table, intensely enjoying this refreshment, rubbing busily at Steerforth's head, and winking at me over it.

"Ah!" she said. "Such things are not much in demand hereabouts. That sets me off again! I haven't seen a pretty woman since I've been here, Jemmy."

"No?" said Steerforth.

"Not the ghost of one," replied Miss Mowcher.

"We could show her the substance of one, I think?" said Steerforth, addressing his eyes to mine. "Eh, Daisy?"

"Yes, indeed," said I.

"Aha?" cried the little creature, glancing sharply at my face, and then peeping round at Steerforth's. "Umph?"

The first exclamation sounded like a question put to both of us, and the second like a question put to Steerforth only. She seemed to have found no answer to either, but continued to rub, with her head on one side and her eye turned up, as if she were looking for an answer in the air, and were confident of its appearing presently.

"A sister of yours, Mr. Copperfield?" she cried, after a pause, and still keeping the same look-out. "Ay, ay?"

"No," said Steerforth, before I could reply. "Nothing of the sort. On the contrary, Mr. Copperfield used—or I am much mistaken—to have a great admiration for her."

"Why, hasn't he now?" returned Miss Mowcher. "Is he fickle? oh, for shame! Did he sip every flower, and change every hour, until Polly his passion requited? Is her name Polly?"

The elfin suddenness with which she pounced upon me with this question, and a searching look, quite disconcerted me for a moment.

"No, Miss Mowcher," I replied. "Her name is Emily."

"Aha?" she cried exactly as before. "Umph? What a rattle I am! Mr. Copperfield, ain't I volatile?"

Her tone and look implied something that was not agreeable to me in connexion with the subject. So I said, in a graver manner than any of us had yet assumed:

"She is as virtuous as she is pretty. She is engaged to be married to a most worthy and deserving man in her own station of life. I esteem her for her good sense, as much as I admire her for her good looks."

"Well said!" cried Steerforth. "Hear, hear, hear! Now, I'll quench the curiosity of this little Fatima, my dear Daisy, by leaving her nothing to guess at. She is at present apprenticed, Miss Mowcher, or articled, or whatever it may be, to Omer and Joram, Haberdashers, Milliners, and so forth, in this town. Do you observe? Omer and Joram. The promise of which my friend has spoken, is made and entered into with her cousin; Christian name, Ham; surname, Peggotty; occupation, boat-builder; also of this town. She lives with a relative; Christian name, unknown; surname, Peggotty; occupation, seafaring; also of this town. She is the prettiest and most engaging little fairy in the world. I admire her—as my friend does—exceedingly. If it were not that I might appear to disparage her intended, which I know my friend would not like, I would add, that to me she seems to be throwing herself away; that I am sure she might do better; and that I swear she was born to be a lady."

Miss Mowcher listened to these words, which were very slowly and distinctly spoken, with her head on one side, and her eye in the air, as if she were still looking for that answer. When he ceased she became brisk again in an instant, and rattled away with surprising volubility.

"Oh, and that's all about it, is it?" she exclaimed, trimming his whiskers with a little restless pair of scissors, that went glancing round his head in all directions. "Very well: *very* well! Quite a long story. Ought to end 'and they lived happy ever afterwards;' oughtn't it? Ah! What's that game at forfeits? I love my love with an E, because she's enticing: I hate her with an E, because she's engaged. I took her to the sign of the exquisite, and treated her with an elopement; her name's Emily, and she lives in the east? Ha! ha! ha! Mr. Copperfield, ain't I volatile?"

Merely looking at me with extravagant slyness, and not waiting for any reply, she continued, without drawing breath:

"There! If ever any scapegrace was trimmed and touched up to perfection, you are, Steerforth. If I understand any noddle in the world, I understand yours. Do you hear me when I tell you that, my darling? I understand yours," peeping down into his face. "Now you may mizzle, Jemmy (as we say at Court), and if Mr. Copperfield will take the chair I'll operate on him."

"What do you say, Daisy?" inquired Steerforth, laughing, and resigning his seat "Will you be improved?"

"Thank you, Miss Mowcher, not this evening."

"Don't say no," returned the little woman, looking at me with the aspect of a connoisseur; "a little bit more eyebrow?"

"Thank you," I returned, "some other time."

"Have it carried half a quarter of an inch towards the temple," said Miss Mowcher. "We can do it in a fortnight."

"No, I thank you. Not at present."

"Go in for a tip," she urged. "No? Let's get the scaffolding up, then, for a pair of whiskers. Come!"

I could not help blushing as I declined, for I felt we were on my weak point, now. But Miss Mowcher, finding that I was not at present disposed for any decoration within the range of her art, and that I was, for the time being, proof against the blandishments of the small bottle which she held up before one eye to enforce her persuasions, said she would make a beginning on an early day, and requested the aid of my hand to descend from her elevated station. Thus assisted, she skipped down with much agility, and began to tie her double chin into her bonnet.

"The fee," said Steerforth, "is——"

"Five bob," replied Miss Mowcher, "and dirt cheap, my chicken. Ain't I volatile, Mr. Copperfield?"

I replied politely: "Not at all." But I thought she was rather so, when she tossed up his two half-crowns like a goblin pieman, caught them, dropped them in her pocket, and gave it a loud slap.

"That's the Till!" observed Miss Mowcher, standing at the chair again, and replacing in the bag a miscellaneous collection of little objects she had emptied out of it. "Have I got all my traps? It seems so. It won't do to be like long Ned Beadwood, when they took him to church 'to marry him to somebody,' as he says, and left the bride behind. Ha! ha! ha! A wicked rascal, Ned, but droll! Now, I know I'm going to break your hearts, but I am forced to leave you. You must call up all your fortitude, and try to bear it. Good bye, Mr. Copperfield! Take care of yourself, Jockey of Norfolk! How I *have* been rattling on! It's all the fault of you two wretches. *I* forgive you! 'Bob swore!'—as the Englishman said for 'Good night,' when he first learnt French, and thought it so like English. 'Bob swore,' my ducks!"

With the bag slung over her arm, and rattling as she waddled away, she waddled to the door; where she stopped to inquire if she should leave us a lock of her hair. "Ain't I volatile?" she added, as a commentary on this offer, and, with her finger on her nose, departed.

Steerforth laughed to that degree, that it was impossible for me to help laughing too; though I am not sure I should have done so, but for this inducement. When we had had our laugh quite out, which was after some time, he told me that Miss Mowcher had quite an extensive connexion, and made herself useful to a variety of people in a variety of ways. Some people trifled with her as a mere oddity, he said; but she was as shrewdly and sharply observant as anyone he knew, and as long-headed as she was short-armed. He told me that what she had said of being here, and there, and everywhere, was true enough; for she made little darts into the provinces, and seemed to pick up customers everywhere, and to know everybody. I asked him what her disposition was: whether it was at all mischievous, and if her sympathies were generally on the right side of things: but, not succeeding in attracting his attention to these questions after two or three attempts, I forebore or forgot to repeat them. He told me instead, with much rapidity, a good deal about her skill, and her profits; and about her being a scientific cupper, if I should ever have occasion for her service in that capacity.

She was the principal theme of our conversation during the evening: and when we parted for the night Steerforth called after me over the banisters, "Bob swore!" as I went downstairs.

I was surprised, when I came to Mr. Barkis's house, to

find Ham walking up and down in front of it, and still more surprised to learn from him that little Em'ly was inside. I naturally inquired why he was not there too, instead of pacing the street by himself?

"Why, you see, Mas'r Davy," he rejoined, in a hesitating manner, "Em'ly, she's talking to some 'un in here."

"I should have thought," said I, smiling, "that that was a reason for your being in here too, Ham."

"Well, Mas'r Davy, in a general way, so 't would be," he returned; "but look'ee here, Mas'r Davy," lowering his voice, and speaking very gravely. "It's a young woman, Sir—a young woman, that Em'ly knowed once, and doen't ought to know no more."

When I heard these words, a light began to fall upon the figure I had seen following them, some hours ago.

"It's a poor wurem, Mas'r Davy," said Ham, "as is trod under foot by all the town. Up street and down street. The mowld o' the churchyard don't hold any that the folk shrink away from, more."

"Did I see her to-night, Ham, on the sands, after we met you?"

"Keeping us in sight?" said Ham. "It's like you did, Mas'r Davy. Not that I know'd then, she was theer, Sir, but along of her creeping soon arterwards under Em'ly's little winder, when she see a light come, and whisp'ring 'Em'ly, Em'ly, for Christ's sake, have a woman's heart towards me. I was once like you!' Those was solemn words, Mas'r Davy, fur to hear!"

"They were indeed, Ham. What did Em'ly do?"

"Says Em'ly, 'Martha, is it you? Oh, Martha, can it be you?'—for they had sat at work together, many a day, at Mr. Omer's."

"I recollect her now!" cried I, recalling one of the two girls I had seen when I first went there. "I recollect her quite well!"

"Martha Endell," said Ham. "Two or three year older than Em'ly, but was at the school with her."

"I never heard her name," said I. "I didn't mean to interrupt you."

"For the matter o' that, Mas'r Davy," replied Ham, "all's told a'most in them words, 'Em'ly, Em'ly, for Christ's sake, have a woman's heart towards me. I was once like you!' She wanted to speak to Em'ly. Em'ly couldn't speak to theer, for her loving uncle was come home, and he wouldn't—no, Mas'r Davy," said Ham, with great earnestness, "he couldn't, kind-natur'd, tender-hearted as he is, see them two together, side by side, for all the treasures that's wrecked in the sea."

I felt how true this was. I knew it, on the instant, quite as well as Ham.

"So Em'ly writes in pencil on a bit of paper," he pursued, "and gives it to her out o' window to bring here. 'Show that,' she says, 'to my aunt, Mrs. Barkis, and she'll set you down by her fire, for the love of me, till uncle is gone out, and I can come.' By-and-by she tells me what I tell you, Mas'r Davy, and asks me to bring her. What can I do? She doen't ought to know any such, but I can't deny her, when the tears is on her face."

He put his hand into the breast of his shaggy jacket, and took out with great care a pretty little purse.

"And if I could deny her when the tears was on her face, Mas'r Davy," said Ham, tenderly adjusting it on the rough palm of his hand, "how could I deny her when she give me this to carry for her—knowing what she brought it for? Such a toy as it is!" said Ham, thoughtfully looking on it. "With such a little money in it, Em'ly my dear!"

I shook him warmly by the hand when he had put it away again—for that was more satisfactory to me than saying anything—and we walked up and down, for a minute or two, in silence. The door opened then, and Peggotty appeared, beckoning to Ham to come in. I would have kept away, but she came after me, entreating me to come in too. Even then, I would have avoided the room where they all were, but for its being the neat-tiled kitchen I have mentioned more than once. The door opening immediately into it, I found myself among them, before I considered whither I was going.

The girl—the same I had seen upon the sands—was near the fire. She was sitting on the ground, with her head and one arm lying on a chair. I fancied, from the disposition of her figure, that Em'ly had but newly risen from the chair, and that the forlorn head might perhaps have been lying on her lap. I saw but little of the girl's face, over which her hair fell loose and scattered, as if she had been disordering it with her own hands; but I saw that she was young, and of a fair complexion. Peggotty had been crying. So had little Em'ly. Not a word was spoken when we first went in; and the Dutch clock by the dresser seemed, in the silence, to tick twice as loud as usual.

Em'ly spoke first.

"Martha wants," she said to Ham, "to go to London."

"Why to London?" returned Ham.

He stood between them, looking on the prostrate girl with a mixture of compassion for her, and of jealousy of her holding any companionship with her whom he loved so well, which I have always remembered distinctly. They both spoke as if she were ill; in a soft, suppressed tone that was plainly heard, although it hardly rose above a whisper.

"Better there than here," said a third voice aloud—Martha's, though she did not move. "No one knows me there. Everybody knows me here."

"What will she do there?" inquired Ham.

She lifted up her head, and looked darkly round at him for a moment; then laid it down again, and curved her right arm about her neck, as a woman in a fever, or in an agony of pain from a shot, might twist herself.

"She will try to do well," said little Em'ly. "You don't know what she has said to us. Does he—do they—aunt?"

Peggotty shook her head compassionately.

"I'll try," said Martha, "if you'll help me away. I never can do worse than I have done here. I may do better. Oh!" with a dreadful shiver, "take me out of these streets, where the whole town knows me from a child!"

As Em'ly held out her hand to Ham, I saw him put in it a little canvas bag. She took it, as if she thought it were her purse, and made a step or two forward; but finding her mistake, came back to where he had retired near me, and showed it to him.

"It's all yourn, Em'ly," I could hear him say. "I haven't nowt in all the wureld that ain't yourn, my dear. It ain't of no delight to me, except for you!"

The tears rose freshly in her eyes, but she turned away and went to Martha. What she gave her, I don't know. I saw her stooping over her, and putting money in her bosom. She whispered something, and asked was that enough? "More than enough," the other said, and took her hand and kissed it.

Then Martha arose, and gathering her shawl about her,

covering her face with it, and weeping aloud, went slowly to the door. She stopped a moment before going out, as if she would have uttered something or turned back; but no word passed her lips. Making the same low, dreary, wretched moaning in her shawl, she went away.

As the door closed, little Em'ly looked at us three in a hurried manner, and then hid her face in her hands, and fell to sobbing.

"Doen't, Em'ly!" said Ham, tapping her gently on the shoulder. "Doen't, my dear! You doen't ought to cry so, pretty!"

"Oh, Ham!" she exclaimed, still weeping pitifully, "I am not as good a girl as I ought to be! I know I have not the thankful heart, sometimes, I ought to have!"

"Yes, yes, you have, I'm sure," said Ham.

"No! no! no!" cried little Em'ly, sobbing, and shaking her head. "I am not as good a girl as I ought to be. Not near! not near!"

And still she cried, as if her heart would break.

"I try your love too much. I know I do!" she sobbed. "I'm often cross to you, and changeable with you, when I ought to be far different. You are never so to me. Why am I ever so to you, when I should think of nothing but how to be grateful, and to make you happy!"

"You always make me so," said Ham, "my dear! I am happy in the sight of you. I am happy, all day long, in the thoughts of you."

"Ah! that's not enough!" she cried. "That is because you are good; not because I am! Oh, my dear, it might have been a better fortune for you, if you had been fond of some one else—of some one steadier and much worthier than me, who was all bound up in you, and never vain and changeable like me!"

"Poor little tender-heart," said Ham, in a low voice. "Martha has overset her, altogether."

"Please, aunt," sobbed Em'ly, "come here, and let me lay my head upon you. Oh, I am very miserable to-night, aunt! Oh, I am not as good a girl as I ought to be. I am not, I know!"

Peggotty had hastened to the chair before the fire. Em'ly, with her arms around her neck, kneeled by her, looking up most earnestly into her face.

"Oh, pray, aunt, try to help me! Ham, dear, try to help me! Mr. David, for the sake of old times, do, please, try to help me! I want to be a better girl than I am. I want to feel a hundred times more thankful than I do. I want to feel more, what a blessed thing it is to be the wife of a good man, and to lead a peaceful life. Oh me, oh me! Oh my heart, my heart!"

She dropped her face on my old nurse's breast, and, ceasing this supplication, which in its agony and grief was half a woman's, half a child's, as all her manner was (being, in that, more natural, and better suited to her beauty, as I thought, than any other manner could have been), wept silently, while my old nurse hushed her like an infant.

She got calmer by degrees, and then we soothed her; now talking encouragingly, and now jesting a little with her, until she began to raise her head and speak to us. So we got on, until she was able to smile, and then to laugh, and then to sit up, half ashamed; while Peggotty recalled her stray ringlets, dried her eyes, and made her neat again, lest her uncle should wonder, when she got home, why his darling had been crying.

I saw her do, that night, what I had never seen her do before. I saw her innocently kiss her chosen husband on the cheek, and creep close to his bluff form as if it were her best support. When they went away together, in the waning moonlight, and I looked after them, comparing their departure in my mind with Martha's, I saw that she held his arm with both her hands, and still kept close to him.

CHAPTER XXIII.

I CORROBORATE MR. DICK, AND CHOOSE A PROFESSION.

When I awoke in the morning I thought very much of little Em'ly, and her emotion last night, after Martha had left. I felt as if I had come into the knowledge of those domestic weaknesses and tendernesses in a sacred confidence, and that to disclose them, even to Steerforth, would be wrong. I had no gentler feeling towards anyone than towards the pretty creature who had been my playmate, and whom I have always been persuaded, and shall always be persuaded, to my dying day, I then devotedly loved. The repetition to any ears—even to Steerforth's—of what she had been unable to repress when her heart lay open to me by an accident, I felt would be a rough deed, unworthy of myself, unworthy of the light of our poor childhood, which I always saw encircling her head. I made a resolution, therefore, to keep it in my own breast; and there it gave her image a new grace.

While we were at breakfast, a letter was delivered to me from my aunt. As it contained matter on which I thought Steerforth could advise me as well as anyone, and on which I knew I should be delighted to consult him, I resolved to make it a subject of discussion on our journey home. For the present we had enough to do, in taking leave of all our friends. Mr. Barkis was far from being the last among them, in his regret at our departure; and I believe would even have opened the box again, and sacrificed another guinea, if it would have kept us eight-and-forty hours in Yarmouth. Peggotty, and all her family, were full of grief at our going. The whole house of Omer and Joram turned out to bid us good bye; and there were so many seafaring volunteers in attendance on Steerforth, when our portmanteaus went to the coach, that if we had had the baggage of a regiment with us, we should hardly have wanted porters to carry it. In a word, we departed to the regret and admiration of all concerned, and left a great many people very sorry behind us.

"Do you stay long here, Littimer?" said I, as he stood waiting to see the coach start.

"No, Sir," he replied; "probably not very long, Sir."

"He can hardly say just now," observed Steerforth, carelessly. "He knows what he has to do, and he'll do it."

"That I am sure he will," said I.

Littimer touched his hat in acknowledgment of my good opinion, and I felt about eight years old. He touched it once more, wishing us a good journey; and we left him standing on the pavement, as respectable a mystery as any pyramid in Egypt.

For some little time we held no conversation, Steerforth being unusually silent, and I being sufficiently engaged in wondering, within myself, when I should see the old places again, and what new changes might happen to me or them in the meanwhile. At length Steerforth, becoming gay and talkative in a moment, as he could become anything he liked at any moment, pulled me by the arm:

"Find a voice, David. What about the letter you were speaking of at breakfast?"

"Oh!" said I, taking it out of my pocket. "It's from my aunt."

"And what does she say, requiring consideration!"

"Why, she reminds me, Steerforth," said I, "that I came out on this expedition to look about me, and to think a little."

'Which, of course, you have done?"

"Indeed I can't say I have, particularly. To tell you the truth, I am afraid I had forgotten it."

"Well! look about you now, and make up for your negligence," said Steerforth. "Look to the right, and you'll see a flat country, with a good deal of marsh in it; look to the left, and you'll see the same. Look to the front, and you'll find no difference; look to the rear, and there it is still."

I laughed, and replied that I saw no suitable profession in the whole prospect; which was perhaps to be attributed to its flatness.

"What says our aunt on the subject?" inquired Steerforth, glancing at the letter in my hand. "Does she suggest anything?"

"Why, yes," said I. "She asks me, here, if I think I should like to be a proctor? What do you think of it?"

"Well, I don't know," replied Steerforth, coolly. "You may as well do that as anything else, I suppose."

I could not help laughing again, at his balancing all callings and professions so equally; and I told him so.

"What *is* a proctor, Steerforth?" said I.

"Why, he is a sort of monkish attorney," replied Steerforth. "He is, to some faded courts held in Doctors' Commons—a lazy old nook near St. Paul's Churchyard— what solicitors are to the courts of law and equity. He is a functionary whose existence, in the natural course of things, would have terminated about two hundred years ago. I can tell you best what he is, by telling you what Doctors' Commons is. It's a little out-of-the-way place, where they administer what is called ecclesiastical law, and play all kinds of tricks with obsolete old monsters of Acts of Parliament, which three-fourths of the world know nothing about, and the other fourth supposes to have been dug up, in a fossil state, in the days of the Edwards. It's a place that has an ancient monopoly in suits about people's wills and people's marriages, and disputes among ships and boats."

"Nonsense, Steerforth!" I exclaimed. "You don't mean to say that there is any affinity between nautical matters and ecclesiastical matters?"

"I don't, indeed, my dear boy," he returned; "but I mean to say that they are managed and decided by the same set of people, down in that same Doctors' Commons. You shall go there one day, and find them blundering through half the nautical terms in Young's Dictionary, apropos of the 'Nancy' having run down the 'Sarah Jane,' or Mr. Peggotty and the Yarmouth boatmen having put off in a gale of wind with an anchor and cable to the 'Nelson' Indiaman in distress; and you shall go there another day, and find them deep in the evidence, pro and con, respecting a clergyman who has misbehaved himself; and you shall find the judge in the nautical case, the advocate in the clergyman case, or contrariwise. They are like actors: now a man's a judge, and now he is not a judge; now he's one thing, now he's another; now he's something else, change and change about; but it's always a very pleasant profitable little affair of private theatricals, presented to an uncommonly select audience."

"But advocates and proctors are not one and the same?" said I, a little puzzled. "Are they?"

"No," returned Steerforth, "the advocates are civilians —men who have taken a doctor's degree at college—which is the first reason of my knowing anything about it. The proctors employ the advocates. Both get very comfortable fees, and altogether they make a mighty snug little party. On the whole, I would recommend you to take to Doctors' Commons kindly, David. They plume themselves on their gentility there, I can tell you, if that's any satisfaction."

I made allowance for Steerforth's light way of treating the subject, and, considering it with reference to the staid air of gravity and antiquity which I associated with that "lazy old nook near St. Paul's Churchyard," did not feel indisposed towards my aunt's suggestion; which she left to my free decision, making no scruple of telling me that it had occurred to her, on her lately visiting her own proctor in Doctors' Commons for the purpose of settling her will in my favour.

"That's a laudable proceeding on the part of our aunt, at all events," said Steerforth, when I mentioned it; "and one deserving of all encouragement. Daisy, my advice is that you take kindly to Doctors' Commons."

I quite made up my mind to do so. I then told Steerforth that my aunt was in town awaiting me (as I found from her letter), and that she had taken lodgings for a week at a kind of private hotel in Lincoln's Inn Fields, where there was a stone staircase, and a convenient door in the roof; my aunt being firmly persuaded that every house in London was going to be burnt down every night.

We achieved the rest of our journey pleasantly, sometimes recurring to Doctors' Commons, and anticipating the distant days when I should be a proctor there, which Steerforth pictured in a variety of humorous and whimsical lights, that made us both merry. When we came to our journey's end, he went home, engaging to call upon me next day but one; and I drove to Lincoln's Inn Fields, where I found my aunt up, and waiting supper.

If I had been round the world since we parted, we could hardly have been better pleased to meet again. My aunt cried outright as she embraced me; and said, pretending to laugh, that if my poor mother had been alive, that silly little creature would have shed tears, she had no doubt.

"So you have left Mr. Dick behind, aunt?" said I. "I am sorry for that. Ah, Janet, how do you do?"

As Janet curtsied, hoping I was well, I observed my aunt's visage lengthen very much.

"I am sorry for it, too," said my aunt, rubbing her nose. "I have had no peace of mind, Trot, since I have been here."

Before I could ask why, she told me.

"I am convinced," said my aunt; laying her hand with melancholy firmness on the table, "that Dick's character is not a character to keep the donkeys off. I am confident he wants strength of purpose. I ought to have left Janet at home, instead, and then my mind might perhaps have been at ease. If ever there was a donkey trespassing on my green," said my aunt, with emphasis, "there was one this afternoon at four o'clock. A cold feeling came over me from head to foot, and I *know* it was a donkey!"

I tried to comfort her on this point, but she rejected consolation.

"It was a donkey," said my aunt; "and it was the one with the stumpy tail which that Murdering sister of a woman rode, when she came to my house." This had been, ever since, the only name my aunt knew for Miss Murdstone. "If there is any donkey in Dover, whose audacity it is harder to me to bear than another's, that," said my aunt, striking the table, "is the animal."

Janet ventured to suggest that my aunt might be disturbing herself unnecessarily, and that she believed the donkey in question was then engaged in the sand-and-gravel line of business, and was not available for purposes of trespass. But my aunt wouldn't hear of it.

Supper was comfortably served and hot, though my aunt's rooms were very high up—whether that she might have more stone stairs for her money, or might be nearer to the door in the roof, I don't know—and consisted of a roast fowl, a steak, and some vegetables, to all of which I did ample justice, and which were all excellent. But my aunt had her own ideas concerning London provision, and ate but little.

"I suppose this unfortunate fowl was born and brought up in a cellar," said my aunt, "and never took the air except on a hackney coach-stand. I *hope* the steak may be beef, but I don't believe it. Nothing's genuine in the place, in my opinion, but the dirt."

"Don't you think the fowl may have come out of the country, aunt?" I hinted.

"Certainly not," returned my aunt. "It would be no pleasure to a London tradesman to sell anything which was what he pretended it was."

I did not venture to controvert this opinion, but I made a good supper, which it greatly satisfied her to see me do. When the table was cleared, Janet assisted her to arrange her hair, to put on her nightcap, which was of a smarter construction than usual ("in case of fire," my aunt said), and to fold her gown back over her knees, these being her usual preparations for warming herself before going to bed. I then made her, according to certain established regulations from which no deviation, however slight, could ever be permitted, a glass of hot white wine and water, and a slice of toast cut into long thin strips. With these accompaniments we were left alone to finish the evening, my aunt sitting opposite to me drinking her wine and water; soaking her strips of toast in it, one by one, before eating them; and looking benignantly on me, from among the borders of her nightcap.

"Well, Trot," she began, "what do you think of the proctor plan? Or have you not begun to think about it yet?"

"I have thought a good deal about it, my dear aunt, and I have talked a good deal about it with Steerforth. I like it very much indeed. I like it exceedingly."

"Come!" said my aunt. "That's cheering!"

"I have only one difficulty, aunt."

"Say what it is, Trot," she returned.

"Why, I want to ask, aunt, as this seems, from what I understand, to be a limited profession, whether my entrance into it would not be very expensive?"

"It will cost," returned my aunt, "to article you, just a thousand pounds."

"Now, my dear aunt," said I, drawing my chair nearer, "I am uneasy in my mind about that. It's a large sum of money. You have expended a great deal on my education, and have always been as liberal to me in all things, as it was possible to be. You have been the soul of generosity. Surely there are some ways in which I might begin life with hardly any outlay, and yet begin with a good hope of getting on by resolution and exertion. Are you sure that it would not be better to try that course? Are you certain that you can afford to part with so much money, and that it is right that it should be so expended? I only ask you, my second mother, to consider. Are you certain?"

My aunt finished eating the piece of toast on which she was then engaged, looking me full in the face all the while; and then setting her glass on the chimney-piece, and folding her hands upon her folded skirts, replied as follows:

"Trot, my child, if I have any object in life, it is to provide for your being a good, a sensible, and a happy man. I am bent upon it—so is Dick. I should like some people that I know to hear Dick's conversation on the subject. Its sagacity is wonderful. But no one knows the resources of that man's intellect, except myself!"

She stopped for a moment to take my hand between hers, and went on:

"It's in vain, Trot, to recall the past, unless it works some influence upon the present. Perhaps I might have been better friends with your poor father. Perhaps I might have been better friends with that poor child your mother, even after your sister Betsey Trotwood disappointed me. When you came to me, a little runaway boy, all dusty and wayworn, perhaps I thought so. From that time until now, Trot, you have ever been a credit to me and a pride and pleasure. I have no other claim upon my means; at least"—here to my surprise she hesitated, and was confused— "no, I have *no* other claim upon my means—and you are my adopted child. Only be a loving child to me in my age, and bear with my whims and fancies; and you will do more for an old woman whose prime of life was not so happy or conciliating as it might have been, than ever that old woman did for you."

It was the first time I had heard my aunt refer to her past history. There was a magnanimity in her quiet way of doing so, and of dismissing it, which would have exalted her in my respect and affection, if anything could.

"All is agreed and understood between us now, Trot," said my aunt, "and we need talk of this no more. Give me a kiss, and we'll go to the Commons after breakfast to-morrow."

We had a long chat by the fire before we went to bed. I slept in a room on the same floor with my aunt's, and was a little disturbed in the course of the night by her knocking at my door as often as she was agitated by a distant sound of hackney-coaches or market-carts, and inquiring "if I heard the engines?" But towards morning she slept better, and suffered me to do so too.

At about midday, we set out for the office of Messrs. Spenlow and Jorkins, in Doctors' Commons. My aunt, who had this other general opinion in reference to London, that every man she saw was a pickpocket, gave me her purse to carry for her, which had ten guineas in it and some silver.

We made a pause at the toy-shop in Fleet Street, to see the giants of Saint Dunstan's strike upon the bells—we had timed our going, so as to catch them at it, at twelve o'clock —and then went on towards Ludgate Hill and St. Paul's Churchyard. We were crossing to the former place, when I found that my aunt greatly accelerated her speed and looked frightened. I observed, at the same time, that a lowering ill-dressed man who had stopped and stared at us in passing, a little before, was coming so close after us, as to brush against her.

"Trot! My dear Trot!" cried my aunt, in a terrified whisper, and pressing my arm. "I don't know what I am to do."

"Don't be alarmed," said I. "There's nothing to be afraid of. Step into a shop, and I'll soon get rid of this fellow."

"No, no, child!" she returned. "Don't speak to him for the world. I entreat, I order you!"

"Good Heaven, aunt!" said I. "He is nothing but a sturdy beggar."

"You don't know what he is!" replied my aunt. "You don't know who he is! You don't know what you say!"

We had stopped in an empty doorway, while this was passing, and he had stopped too.

"Don't look at him!" said my aunt, as I turned my head indignantly, "but get me a coach, my dear, and wait for me in St. Paul's Churchyard."

"Wait for you?" I repeated.

"Yes," rejoined my aunt. "I must go alone. I must go with him."

"With him, aunt? This man?"

"I am in my senses," she replied, "and I tell you I *must.* Get me a coach!"

However much astonished I might be, I was sensible that I had no right to refuse compliance with such a peremptory command. I hurried away a few paces, and called a hackney-chariot which was passing empty. Almost before I could let down the steps, my aunt sprang in, I don't know how, and the man followed. She waved her hand to me to go away, so earnestly, that, all confounded as I was, I turned from them at once. In doing so, I heard her say to the coachman, "Drive anywhere! Drive straight on!" and presently the chariot passed me, going up the hill.

What Mr. Dick had told me, and what I had supposed to be a delusion of his, now came into my mind. I could not doubt that this person was the person of whom he had made such mysterious mention, though what the nature of his hold upon my aunt could possibly be, I was quite unable to imagine. After half an hour's cooling in the Churchyard, I saw the chariot coming back. The driver stopped beside me, and my aunt was sitting in it alone.

She had not yet sufficiently recovered from her agitation to be quite prepared for the visit we had to make. She desired me to get into the chariot, and to tell the coachman to drive slowly up and down a little while. She said no more, except, "My dear child, never ask me what it was, and don't refer to it," until she had perfectly regained her composure, when she told me she was quite herself now, and we might get out. On her giving me her purse, to pay the driver, I found that all the guineas were gone, and only the loose silver remained.

Doctors' Commons was approached by a little low archway. Before we had taken many paces down the street beyond it, the noise of the city seemed to melt, as if by magic, into a softened distance. A few dull courts, and narrow ways, brought us to the sky-lighted offices of Spenlow and Jorkins; in the vestibule of which temple, accessible to pilgrims without the ceremony of knocking, three or four clerks were at work as copyists. One of these, a little dry man, sitting by himself, who wore a stiff brown wig that looked as if it were made of gingerbread, rose to receive my aunt, and show us into Mr. Spenlow's room.

"Mr. Spenlow's in Court, ma'am," said the dry man; "it's an Arches day; but it's close by, and I'll send for him directly."

As we were left to look about us while Mr. Spenlow was fetched, I availed myself of the opportunity. The furniture of the room was old-fashioned and dusty; and the green baize on the top of the writing-table had lost all its colour, and was as withered and pale as an old pauper. There were a great many bundles of papers on it, some indorsed as Allegations, and some (to my surprise) as Libels, and some as being in the Consistory Court, and some in the Arches Court, and some in the Prerogative Court, and some in the Admiralty Court, and some in the Delegates' Court; giving me occasion to wonder much, how many Courts there might be in the gross, and how long it would take to understand them all. Besides these, there were sundry immense manuscript Books of Evidence taken on affidavit, strongly bound, and tied together in massive sets, a set to each cause, as if every cause were a history in ten or twenty volumes. All this looked tolerably expensive, I thought, and gave me an agreeable notion of a proctor's business. I was casting my eyes with increasing complacency over these and many similar objects, when hasty footsteps were heard in the room outside, and Mr. Spenlow, in a black gown trimmed with white fur, came hurrying in, taking off his hat as he came.

He was a little light-haired gentleman, with undeniable boots, and the stiffest of white cravats and shirt-collars. He was buttoned up mighty trim and tight, and must have taken a great deal of pains with his whiskers, which were accurately curled. His gold watch-chain was so massive, that a fancy came across me, that he ought to have a sinewy golden arm, to draw it out with, like those which are put up over the gold-beaters' shops. He was got up with such care, and was so stiff, that he could hardly bend himself; being obliged, when he glanced at some papers on his desk, after sitting down in his chair, to move his whole body, from the bottom of his spine, like Punch.

I had previously been presented by my aunt, and had been courteously received. He now said:

"And so, Mr. Copperfield, you think of entering into our profession? I casually mentioned to Miss Trotwood, when I had the pleasure of an interview with her the other day," —with another inclination of his body—Punch again— "that there was a vacancy here. Miss Trotwood was good enough to mention that she had a nephew who was her peculiar care, and for whom she was seeking to provide genteelly in life. That nephew, I believe, I have now the pleasure of "—Punch again.

I bowed my acknowledgments, and said, my aunt had mentioned to me that there was that opening, and that I believed I should like it very much. That I was strongly inclined to like it, and had taken immediately to the proposal. That I could not absolutely pledge myself to like

WORKS OF CHARLES DICKENS

it, until I knew something more about it. That although it was little else than a matter of form, I presumed I should have an opportunity of trying how I liked it, before I bound myself to it irrevocably.

"Oh surely! surely!" said Mr. Spenlow. "We always, in this house, propose a month—an initiatory month. I should be happy, myself, to propose two months—three—an indefinite period, in fact—but I have a partner. Mr. Jorkins."

"And the premium, Sir," I returned, "is a thousand pounds."

"And the premium, stamp included, is a thousand pounds," said Mr. Spenlow. "As I have mentioned to Miss Trotwood, I am actuated by no mercenary considerations; few men are less so, I believe; but Mr. Jorkins has his opinions on these subjects, and I am bound to respect Mr. Jorkins's opinions. Mr. Jorkins thinks a thousand pounds too little, in short."

"I suppose, Sir," said I, still desiring to spare my aunt, "that it is not the custom here, if an articled clerk were particularly useful, and made himself a perfect master of his profession"—I could not help blushing, this looked so like praising myself—"I suppose it is not the custom, in the later years of his time, to allow him any——"

Mr. Spenlow, by a great effort, just lifted his head far enough out of his cravat, to shake it, and answered, anticipating the word "salary:"

"No. I will not say what consideration I might give to that point myself, Mr. Copperfield, if I were unfettered. Mr. Jorkins is immovable."

I was quite dismayed by the idea of this terrible Jorkins. But I found out afterwards that he was a mild man of a heavy temperament, whose place in the business was to keep himself in the background, and be constantly exhibited by name as the most obdurate and ruthless of men. If a clerk wanted his salary raised, Mr. Jorkins wouldn't listen to such a proposition. If a client were slow to settle his bill of costs, Mr. Jorkins was resolved to have it paid; and however painful these things might be (and always were) to the feelings of Mr. Spenlow, Mr. Jorkins would have his bond. The heart and hand of the good angel Spenlow would have been always open, but for the restraining demon Jorkins. As I have grown older, I think I have had experience of some other houses doing business on the principle of Spenlow and Jorkins!

It was settled that I should begin my month's probation as soon as I pleased, and that my aunt need neither remain in town nor return at its expiration, as the articles of agreement, of which I was to be the subject, could easily be sent to her at home for her signature. When we had got so far, Mr. Spenlow offered to take me into Court then and there, and show me what sort of place it was. As I was willing enough to know, we went out with this object, leaving my aunt behind; who would trust herself, she said, in no such place, and who, I think, regarded all Courts of Law as a sort of powder-mills that might blow up at any time.

Mr. Spenlow conducted me through a paved courtyard formed of grave brick houses, which I inferred, from the Doctors' names upon the doors, to be the official abiding-places of the learned advocates of whom Steerforth had told me; and into a large dull room, not unlike a chapel to my thinking, on the left hand. The upper part of this room was fenced off from the rest; and there, on the two sides of a raised platform of the horseshoe form, sitting on easy old-fashioned dining-room chairs, were sundry gentlemen in red gowns and grey wigs, whom I found to be the Doctors aforesaid. Blinking over a little desk like a pulpit-desk, in the curve of the horseshoe, was an old gentleman, whom, if I had seen him in an aviary, I should certainly have taken for an owl, but who I learned was the presiding judge. In the space within the horseshoe, lower than these, that is to say, on about the level of the floor, were sundry other gentlemen of Mr. Spenlow's rank, and dressed like him in black gowns with white fur upon them, sitting at a long green table. Their cravats were in general stiff, I thought, and their looks haughty; but in this last respect, I presently conceived I had done them an injustice, for when two or three of them had to rise and answer a question of the presiding dignitary, I never saw anything more sheepish. The public, represented by a boy with a comforter, and a shabby-genteel man secretly eating crumbs out of his coat pockets, was warming itself at a stove in the centre of the Court. The languid stillness of the place was only broken by the chirping of this fire and by the voice of one of the Doctors, who was wandering slowly through a perfect library of evidence, and stopping to put up, from time to time, at little roadside inns of argument on the journey. Altogether, I have never, on any occasion, made one at such a cosey, dozey, old-fashioned, time-forgotten, sleepy-headed little family-party in all my life; and I felt it would be quite a soothing opiate to belong to it in any character—except perhaps as a suitor.

Very well satisfied with the dreamy nature of this retreat, I informed Mr. Spenlow that I had seen enough for that time, and we rejoined my aunt; in company with whom I presently departed from the Commons, feeling very young when I went out of Spenlow and Jorkins's, on account of the clerks poking one another with their pens to point me out.

We arrived at Lincoln's Inn Fields without any new adventures, except encountering an unlucky donkey in a costermonger's cart, who suggested painful associations to my aunt. We had another long talk about my plans, when we were safely housed; and as I knew she was anxious to get home, and between fire, food, and pickpockets, could never be considered at her ease for half-an-hour in London, I urged her not to be uncomfortable on my account, but to leave me to take care of myself.

"I have not been here a week to-morrow, without considering that too, my dear," she returned. "There is a furnished little set of chambers to be let in the Adelphi, Trot, which ought to suit you to a marvel."

With this brief introduction, she produced from her pocket an advertisement, carefully cut out of a newspaper, setting forth that in Buckingham Street in the Adelphi there was to be let furnished, with a view of the river, a singularly desirable and compact set of chambers, forming a genteel residence for a young gentleman, a member of one of the Inns of Court, or otherwise, with immediate possession. Terms moderate, and could be taken for a month only if required.

"Why, this is the very thing, aunt!" said I, flushed with the possible dignity of living in chambers.

"Then come," replied my aunt, immediately resuming the bonnet she had a minute before laid aside. "We'll go and look at 'em."

Away we went. The advertisement directed us to apply

to Mrs. Crupp on the premises, and we rang the area bell, which we supposed to communicate with Mrs. Crupp. It was not until we had rung three or four times that we could prevail on Mrs. Crupp to communicate with us, but at last she appeared, being a stout lady with a flounce of flannel petticoat below a nankeen gown.

"Let us see these chambers of yours, if you please, ma'am," said my aunt.

"For this gentleman?" said Mrs. Crupp, feeling in her pocket for her keys.

"Yes, for my nephew," said my aunt.

"And a sweet set they is for sich!" said Mrs. Crupp.

So we went up-stairs.

They were on the top of the house—a great point with my aunt, being near the fire-escape—and consisted of a little half-blind entry where you could see hardly anything, a little stone-blind pantry where you could see nothing at all, a sitting-room, and a bedroom. The furniture was rather faded, but quite good enough for me; and, sure enough, the river was outside the windows.

As I was delighted with the place, my aunt and Mrs. Crupp withdrew into the pantry to discuss the terms, while I remained on the sitting-room sofa, hardly daring to think it possible that I could be destined to live in such a noble residence. After a single combat of some duration they returned, and I saw, to my joy, both in Mrs. Crupp's countenance and in my aunt's, that the deed was done.

"Is it the last occupant's furniture?" inquired my aunt.

"Yes it is, ma'am," said Mrs. Crupp.

"What's become of him?" asked my aunt.

Mrs. Crupp was taken with a troublesome cough, in the midst of which she articulated with much difficulty. "He was took ill here, ma'am, and—ugh! ugh! ugh! dear me! —and he died!"

"Hey! What did he die of?" asked my aunt.

"Well, ma'am, he died of drink," said Mrs. Crupp, in confidence. "And smoke."

"Smoke? You don't mean chimneys?" said my aunt.

"No, ma'am," returned Mrs. Crupp. "Cigars and pipes."

"*That's* not catching, Trot, at any rate," remarked my aunt, turning to me.

"No, indeed," said I.

In short, my aunt, seeing how enraptured I was with the premises, took them for a month, with leave to remain for twelve months when that time was out. Mrs. Crupp was to find linen, and to cook; every other necessary was already provided; and Mrs. Crupp expressly intimated that she should always yearn towards me as a son. I was to take possession the day after to-morrow, and Mrs. Crupp said, thank Heaven she had now found summun she could care for!

On our way back, my aunt informed me how she confidently trusted that the life I was now to lead would make me firm and self-reliant, which was all I wanted. She repeated this several times next day, in the intervals of our arranging for the transmission of my clothes and books from Mr. Wickfield's; relative to which, and to all my late holiday, I wrote a long letter to Agnes, of which my aunt took charge, as she was to leave on the succeeding day. Not to lengthen these particulars, I need only add, that she made a handsome provision for all my possible wants during my month of trial; that Steerforth, to my great

disappointment and hers too, did not make his appearance before she went away; that I saw her safely seated in the Dover coach, exulting in the coming discomfiture of the vagrant donkeys, with Janet at her side; and that when the coach was gone, I turned my face to the Adelphi, pondering on the old days when I used to roam about its subterranean arches, and on the happy changes which had brought me to the surface.

CHAPTER XXIV.

MY FIRST DISSIPATION.

IT was a wonderfully fine thing to have that lofty castle to myself, and to feel, when I shut my outer door, like Robinson Crusoe, when he had got into his fortification, and pulled his ladder up after him. It was a wonderfully fine thing to walk about town with the key of my house in my pocket, and to know that I could ask any fellow to come home, and make quite sure of its being inconvenient to nobody, if it were not so to me. It was a wonderfully fine thing to let myself in and out, and to come and go without a word to any one, and to ring Mrs. Crupp up, gasping, from the depths of the earth, when I wanted her—and when she was disposed to come. All this, I say, was wonderfully fine; but I must say, too, that there were times when it was very dreary.

It was fine in the morning, particularly in the fine mornings. It looked a very fresh, free life, by daylight: still fresher, and more free, by sunlight. But as the day declined, the life seemed to go down too. I don't know how it was; it seldom looked well by candle-light. I wanted somebody to talk to, then. I missed Agnes. I found a tremendous blank, in the place of that smiling repository of my confidence. Mrs. Crupp appeared to be a long way off. I thought about my predecessor, who had died of drink and smoke; and I could have wished he had been so good as to live, and not bother me with his decease.

After two days and nights, I felt as if I had lived there for a year, and yet I was not an hour older, but was quite as much tormented by my own youthfulness as ever.

Steerforth not yet appearing, which induced me to apprehend that he must be ill, I left the Commons early on the third day, and walked out to Highgate. Mrs. Steerforth was very glad to see me, and said that he had gone away with one of his Oxford friends to see another who lived near St. Albans, but that she expected him to return to-morrow. I was so fond of him, that I felt quite jealous of his Oxford friends.

As she pressed me to stay to dinner, I remained, and I believe we talked about nothing but him all day. I told her how much the people liked him at Yarmouth, and what a delightful companion he had been. Miss Dartle was full of hints and mysterious questions, but took a great interest in all our proceedings there, and said, "Was it really, though?" and so forth, so often, that she got everything out of me she wanted to know. Her appearance was exactly what I have described it, when I first saw her; but the society of the two ladies was so agreeable, and came so natural to me, that I felt myself falling a little in love with her. I could not help thinking, several times in the course of the evening, and particularly when I walked home at night, what delightful company she would be in Buckingham Street.

I was taking my coffee and roll in the morning, before going to the Commons—and I may observe in this place that it is surprising how much coffee Mrs. Crupp used, and how weak it was, considering—when Steerforth himself walked in, to my unbounded joy.

"My dear Steerforth," cried I, "I began to think I should never see you again!"

"I was carried off by force of arms," said Steerforth, "the very next morning after I got home. Why, Daisy, what a rare old bachelor you are here!"

I showed him over the establishment, not omitting the pantry, with no little pride, and he commended it highly. "I tell you what, old boy," he added, "I shall make quite a town-house of this place, unless you give me notice to quit."

This was a delightful hearing. I told him if he waited for that, he would have to wait till doomsday.

"But you shall have some breakfast!" said I, with my hand on the bell-rope, "and Mrs. Crupp shall make you some fresh coffee, and I'll toast you some bacon in a bachelor's Dutch-oven that I have got here."

"No, no!" said Steerforth. "Don't ring! I can't! I am going to breakfast with one of these fellows who is at the Piazza Hotel, in Covent Garden."

"But you'll come back to dinner?" said I.

"I can't, upon my life. There's nothing I should like better, but I *must* remain with these two fellows. We are all three off together to-morrow morning."

"Then bring them here to dinner," I returned. "Do you think they would come?"

"Oh! they would come fast enough," said Steerforth; "but we should inconvenience you. You had better come and dine with us somewhere."

I would not by any means consent to this, for it occurred to me that I really ought to have a little house-warming, and that there never could be a better opportunity. I had a new pride in my rooms after his approval of them, and burned with a desire to develop their utmost resources. I therefore made him promise positively in the names of his two friends, and we appointed six o'clock as the dinner-hour.

When he was gone, I rang for Mrs. Crupp, and acquainted her with my desperate design. Mrs. Crupp said, in the first place, of course it was well known she couldn't be expected to wait, but she knew a handy young man, who she thought could be prevailed upon to do it, and whose terms would be five shillings, and what I pleased. I said, certainly we would have him. Next, Mrs. Crupp said it was clear she couldn't be in two places at once (which I felt to be reasonable), and that "a young gal" stationed in the pantry with a bedroom candle, there never to desist from washing plates, would be indispensable. I said, what would be the expense of this young female, and Mrs. Crupp said she supposed eighteen-pence would neither make me nor break me. I said I supposed not; and *that* was settled. Then Mrs. Crupp said, Now about the dinner.

It was a remarkable instance of want of forethought on the part of the ironmonger who had made Mrs. Crupp's kitchen fireplace, that it was capable of cooking nothing but chops and mashed potatoes. As to a fish-kittle, Mrs. Crupp said, well! would I only come and look at the range? She couldn't say fairer than that. Would I come and look

at it? As I should not have been much the wiser if I *had* looked at it, I declined, and said, "Never mind fish." But Mrs. Crupp said, Don't say that; oysters was in, and why not them? So *that* was settled. Mrs. Crupp then said what she would recommend would be this. A pair of hot roast fowls—from the pastrycook's; a dish of stewed beef, with vegetables—from the pastrycook's; two little corner things, as a raised pie and a dish of kidneys—from the pastrycook's; a tart, and (if I liked) a shape of jelly—from the pastrycook's. This, Mrs. Crupp said, would leave her at full liberty to concentrate her mind on the potatoes, and to serve up the cheese and celery as she could wish to see it done.

I acted on Mrs. Crupp's opinion, and gave the order at the pastrycook's myself. Walking along the Strand, afterwards, and observing a hard mottled substance in the window of a ham and beef shop, which resembled marble, but was labelled "Mock Turtle," I went in and bought a slab of it, which I have since seen reason to believe would have sufficed for fifteen people. This preparation, Mrs. Crupp, after some difficulty, consented to warm up; and it shrank so much in a liquid state, that we found it what Steerforth called "rather a tight fit" for four.

These preparations happily completed, I bought a little dessert in Covent Garden Market, and gave a rather extensive order at a retail wine-merchant's in that vicinity. When I came home in the afternoon, and saw the bottles drawn up in a square on the pantry-floor, they looked so numerous (though there were two missing, which made Mrs. Crupp very uncomfortable), that I was absolutely frightened at them.

One of Steerforth's friends was named Grainger, and the other Markham. They were both very gay and lively fellows; Grainger, something older than Steerforth; Markham, youthful-looking, and I should say not more than twenty. I observed that the latter always spoke of himself indefinitely, as "a man," and seldom or never in the first person singular.

"A man might get on very well here, Mr. Copperfield," said Markham—meaning himself.

"It's not a bad situation," said I, "and the rooms are really commodious."

"I hope you have both brought appetites with you?" said Steerforth.

"Upon my honour," returned Markham, "town seems to sharpen a man's appetite. A man is hungry all day long. A man is perpetually eating."

Being a little embarrassed at first, and feeling much too young to preside, I made Steerforth take the head of the table when dinner was announced, and seated myself opposite to him. Everything was very good; we did not spare the wine; and he exerted himself so brilliantly to make the thing pass off well, that there was no pause in our festivity. I was not quite such good company during dinner as I could have wished to be, for my chair was opposite the door, and my attention was distracted by observing that the handy young man went out of the room very often, and that his shadow always presented itself, immediately afterwards, on the wall of the entry, with a bottle at its mouth. The "young gal" likewise occasioned me some uneasiness: not so much by neglecting to wash the plates, as by breaking them. For being of an inquisitive disposition, and unable to confine herself (as her positive instructions were) to the pantry, she was constantly peering in at us, and constantly imagining herself detected; in which belief, she several times retired upon the plates (with which she had carefully paved the floor), and did a great deal of destruction.

These, however, were small drawbacks, and easily forgotten when the cloth was cleared, and the dessert put on the table; at which period of the entertainment the handy young man was discovered to be speechless. Giving him private directions to seek the society of Mrs. Crupp, and to remove the "young gal" to the basement also, I abandoned myself to enjoyment.

I began, by being singularly cheerful and light-hearted; all sorts of half-forgotten things to talk about, came rushing into my mind, and made me hold forth in a most unwonted manner. I laughed heartily at my own jokes, and everybody else's; called Steerforth to order for not passing the wine; made several engagements to go to Oxford; announced that I meant to have a dinner-party exactly like that, once a week until further notice; and madly took so much snuff out of Grainger's box, that I was obliged to go into the pantry, and have a private fit of sneezing ten minutes long.

I went on, by passing the wine faster and faster yet, and continually starting up with a corkscrew to open more wine, long before any was needed. I proposed Steerforth's health. I said he was my dearest friend, the protector of my boyhood, and the companion of my prime. I said I was delighted to propose his health. I said I owed him more obligations than I could ever repay, and held him in a higher admiration than I could ever express. I finished by saying, "I'll give you Steerforth! God bless him! Hurrah!" We have him three times three, and another, and a good one to finish with. I broke my glass in going round the table to shake hands with him, and I said (in two words) "Steerforth you're the guiding star of my existence."

I went on, by finding suddenly that somebody was in the middle of a song. Markham was the singer, and he sang "When the heart of a man is depressed with care." He said, when he had sung it, he would give us "Woman!" I took objection to that, and I couldn't allow it. I said it was not a respectful way of proposing the toast, and I would never permit that toast to be drunk in my house otherwise than as "The Ladies!" I was very high with him, mainly I think because I saw Steerforth and Grainger laughing at me—or at him—or at both of us. He said a man was not to be dictated to. I said a man was. He said a man was not to be insulted, then. I said he was right there—never under my roof, where the Lares were sacred, and the laws of hospitality paramount. He said it was no derogation from a man's dignity to confess that I was a devilish good fellow. I instantly proposed his health.

Somebody was smoking. We were all smoking. I was smoking, and trying to suppress a rising tendency to shudder. Steerforth had made a speech about me, in the course of which I had been affected almost to tears. I returned thanks, and hoped the present company would dine with me to-morrow, and the day after—each day at five o'clock, that we might enjoy the pleasures of conversation and society through a long evening. I felt called upon to propose an individual. I would give them my aunt. Miss Betsey Trotwood, the best of her sex!

Somebody was leaning out of my bedroom window, refreshing his forehead against the cool stone of the parapet, and feeling the air upon his face. It was myself. I was addressing myself as "Copperfield," and saying, "Why

did you try to smoke? You might have known you couldn't do it." Now, somebody was unsteadily contemplating his features in the looking-glass. That was I too. I was very pale in the looking-glass; my eyes had a vacant appearance; and my hair—only my hair, nothing else—looked drunk.

Somebody said to me, "Let us go to the theatre, Copperfield!" There was no bedroom before me, but again the jingling table covered with glasses; the lamp; Grainger on my right hand, Markham on my left, and Steerforth opposite—all sitting in a mist, and a long way off. The theatre? To be sure. The very thing. Come along! But they must excuse me if I saw everybody out first, and turned the lamp off—in case of fire.

Owing to some confusion in the dark, the door was gone. I was feeling for it in the window-curtains, when Steerforth, laughing, took me by the arm and led me out. We went down-stairs, one behind another. Near the bottom, somebody fell, and rolled down. Somebody else said it was Copperfield. I was angry at that false report, until, finding myself on my back in the passage, I began to think there might be some foundation for it.

A very foggy night, with great rings round the lamps in the streets! There was an indistinct talk of its being wet. I considered it frosty. Steerforth dusted me under a lamp-post, and put my hat into shape, which somebody produced from somewhere in a most extraordinary manner, for I hadn't had it on before. Steerforth then said, "You are all right, Copperfield, are you not?" and I told him, "Neverberrer."

A man, sitting in a pigeon-hole place, looked out of the fog, and took money from somebody, inquiring if I was one of the gentlemen paid for, and appearing rather doubtful (as I remember in the glimpse I had of him) whether to take the money for me or not. Shortly afterwards, we were very high up in a very hot theatre, looking down into a large pit, that seemed to me to smoke; the people with whom it was crammed were so indistinct. There was a great stage, too, looking very clean and smooth after the streets; and there were people upon it, talking about something or other, but not at all intelligibly. There was an abundance of bright lights, and there was music, and there were ladies down in the boxes, and I don't know what more. The whole building looked to me, as if it were learning to swim; it conducted itself in such an unaccountable manner, when I tried to steady it.

On somebody's motion, we resolved to go down-stairs to the dress-boxes, where the ladies were. A gentleman lounging, full dressed, on a sofa, with an opera-glass in his hand, passed before my view, and also my own figure at full length in a glass. Then I was being ushered into one of these boxes, and found myself saying something as I sat down, and people about me crying "Silence!" to somebody, and ladies casting indignant glances at me, and—what! yes!—Agnes, sitting on the seat before me, in the same box, with a lady and gentleman beside her, whom I didn't know. I see her face now, better than I did then, I dare say, with its indelible look of regret and wonder turned upon me.

"Agnes!" I said, thickly, "Lorblessmer! Agnes!"

"Hush! Pray!" she answered, I could not conceive why. "You disturb the company. Look at the stage!"

I tried, on her injunction, to fix it, and to hear something of what was going on there, but quite in vain. I looked at her again by-and-by, and saw her shrink into her corner, and put her gloved hand to her forehead.

"Agnes!" I said. "I'mafraidyou'renorwell."

"Yes, yes. Do not mind me, Trotwood," she returned. "Listen! Are you going away soon?"

"Amigoarawaysoo?" I repeated.

"Yes."

I had a stupid intention of replying that I was going to wait, to hand her down-stairs. I suppose I expressed it, somehow; for, after she had looked at me attentively for a little while, she appeared to understand, and replied in a low tone:

"I know you will do as I ask you, if I tell you I am very earnest in it. Go away now, Trotwood, for my sake, and ask your friends to take you home."

She had so far improved me, for the time, that though I was angry with her, I felt ashamed, and with a short "Goori!" (which I intended for "Good night") got up and went away. They followed, and I stepped at once out of the box-door into my bedroom, where only Steerforth was with me, helping me to undress, and where I was by turns telling him that Agnes was my sister, and adjuring him to bring the corkscrew, that I might open another bottle of wine.

How somebody, lying in my bed, lay saying and doing all this over again, at cross purposes, in a feverish dream all night—the bed a rocking sea that was never still! How, as that somebody slowly settled down into myself, did I begin to parch, and feel as if my outer covering of skin were a hard board; my tongue the bottom of an empty kettle, furred with long service, and burning up over a slow fire; the palms of my hands, hot plates of metal which no ice could cool!

But the agony of mind, the remorse, and shame I felt, when I became conscious next day! My horror of having committed a thousand offences I had forgotten, and which nothing could ever expiate—my recollection of that indelible look which Agnes had given me—the torturing impossibility of communicating with her, not knowing, beast that I was, how she came to be in London, or where she stayed—my disgust of the very sight of the room where the revel had been held—my racking head—the smell of smoke, the sight of glasses, the impossibility of going out, or even getting up! Oh, what a day it was!

Oh, what an evening, when I sat down by my fire to a basin of mutton broth, dimpled all over with fat, and thought I was going the way of my predecessor, and should succeed to his dismal story as well as to his chambers, and had half a mind to rush express to Dover and reveal all! What an evening, when Mrs. Crupp, coming in to take away the broth-basin, produced one kidney on a cheese-plate as the entire remains of yesterday's feast, and I was really inclined to fall upon her nankeen breast, and say, in heart-felt penitence, "Oh, Mrs. Crupp, Mrs. Crupp, never mind the broken meats! I am very miserable!"—only that I doubted, even at that pass, if Mrs. Crupp were quite the sort of woman to confide in!

CHAPTER XXV.

GOOD AND BAD ANGELS.

I was going out at my door on the morning after that deplorable day of headache, sickness, and repentance, with an odd confusion in my mind relative to the date of my dinner-party, as if a body of Titans had taken an enormous lever and pushed the day before yesterday some months back, when I saw a ticket-porter coming up-stairs, with a letter in his hand. He was taking his time about his errand, then; but when he saw me on the top of the staircase, looking at him over the banisters, he swung into a trot, and came up panting as if he had run himself into a state of exhaustion.

"T. Copperfield, Esquire," said the ticket-porter, touching his hat with his little cane.

I could scarcely lay claim to the name: I was so disturbed by the conviction that the letter came from Agnes. However, I told him I was T. Copperfield, Esquire, and he believed it, and gave me the letter, which he said required an answer. I shut him out on the landing to wait for the answer, and went into my chambers again, in such a nervous state that I was fain to lay the letter down on my breakfast-table, and familiarise myself with the outside of it a little, before I could resolve to break the seal.

I found, when I did open it, that it was a very kind note, containing no reference to my condition at the theatre. All it said was, "My dear Trotwood. I am staying at the house of papa's agent, Mr. Waterbrook, in Ely Place, Holborn. Will you come and see me to-day, at any time you like to appoint? Ever yours affectionately, AGNES."

It took me such a long time to write an answer at all to my satisfaction, that I don't know what the ticket-porter can have thought, unless he thought I was learning to write. I must have written half a dozen answers at least. I began one, "How can I ever hope, my dear Agnes, to efface from your remembrance the disgusting impression"—there I didn't like it, and then I tore it up. I began another, "Shakspeare has observed, my dear Agnes, how strange it is that a man should put an enemy into his mouth"—that reminded me of Markham, and it got no farther. I even tried poetry. I began one note, in a six-syllable line, "Oh, do not remember"—but that associated itself with the Fifth of November, and became an absurdity. After many attempts, I wrote, "My dear Agnes. Your letter is like you, and what could I say of it that would be higher praise than that? I will come at four o'clock. Affectionately and sorrowfully, T. C." With this missive (which I was in twenty minds at once about recalling, as soon as it was out of my hands), the ticket-porter at last departed.

If the day were half as tremendous to any other professional gentleman in Doctors' Commons as it was to me, I sincerely believe he made some expiation for his share in that rotten old ecclesiastical cheese. Although I left the office at half-past three, and was prowling about the place of appointment within a few minutes afterwards, the appointed time was exceeded by a full quarter of an hour, according to the clock of St. Andrew's, Holborn, before I could muster up sufficient desperation to pull the private bell-handle let into the left-hand door-post of Mr. Waterbrook's house.

The professional business of Mr. Waterbrook's establishment was done on the ground floor, and the genteel business (of which there was a good deal) in the upper part of the building. I was shown into a pretty but rather close drawing-room, and there sat Agnes, netting a purse.

She looked so quiet and good, and reminded me so strongly of my airy fresh school days at Canterbury, and the sodden, smoky, stupid wretch I had been the other night, that, nobody being by, I yielded to my self-reproach and shame, and—in short, made a fool of myself. I cannot deny that I shed tears. To this hour I am undecided whether it was upon the whole the wisest thing I could have done, or the most ridiculous.

"If it had been any one but you, Agnes," said I, turning away my head, "I should not have minded it half so much. But that it should have been you who saw me! I almost wish I had been dead, first."

She put her hand—its touch was like no other hand—upon my arm for a moment; and I felt so befriended and comforted, that I could not help moving it to my lips, and gratefully kissing it.

"Sit down," said Agnes, cheerfully. "Don't be unhappy, Trotwood. If you cannot confidently trust me, whom will you trust?"

"Ah, Agnes!" I returned. "You are my good Angel!"

She smiled rather sadly, I thought, and shook her head.

"Yes, Agnes, my good Angel! Always my good Angel!"

"If I were, indeed, Trotwood," she returned, "there is one thing that I should set my heart on very much."

I looked at her inquiringly; but already with a fore-knowledge of her meaning.

"On warning you," said Agnes, with a steady glance, "against your bad Angel."

"My dear Agnes," I began, "if you mean Steerforth——"

"I do, Trotwood," she returned.

"Then, Agnes, you wrong him very much. He my bad Angel, or anyone's! He, anything but a guide, a support, and a friend to me! My dear Agnes! Now, is it not unjust, and unlike you, to judge him from what you saw of me the other night?"

"I do not judge him from what I saw of you the other night," she quietly replied.

"From what, then?"

"From many things—trifles in themselves, but they do not seem to me to be so, when they are put together. I judge him, partly from your account of him, Trotwood, and your character, and the influence he has over you."

There was always something in her modest voice that seemed to touch a chord within me, answering to that sound alone. It was always earnest; but when it was very earnest, as it was now, there was a thrill in it that quite subdued me. I sat looking at her as she cast her eyes down on her work; I sat seeming still to listen to her; and Steerforth, in spite of all my attachment to him, darkened in that tone.

"It is very bold in me," said Agnes, looking up again, "who have lived in such seclusion, and can know so little of the world, to give you my advice so confidently, or even to have this strong opinion. But I know in what it is engendered, Trotwood,—in how true a remembrance of our having grown up together, and in how true an interest in all relating to you. It is that which makes me bold. I am certain that what I say is right. I am quite sure it is. I feel as if it were some one else speaking to you, and not I, when I caution you that you have made a dangerous friend."

Again I looked at her, again I listened to her after she was silent, and again his image, though it was still fixed in my heart, darkened.

"I am not so unreasonable as to expect," said Agnes, resuming her usual tone, after a little while, "that you will, or that you can, at once, change any sentiment that has become a conviction to you; least of all a sentiment that is rooted in your trusting disposition. You ought not hastily to do that. I only ask you, Trotwood, if you ever think of me—I mean," with a quiet smile, for I was going to

interrupt her, and she knew why, "as often as you think of me—to think of what I have said. Do you forgive me for all this?"

"I will forgive you, Agnes," I replied, "when you come to do Steerforth justice, and to like him as well as I do."

"Not until then?" said Agnes.

I saw a passing shadow on her face when I made this mention of him, but she returned my smile, and we were again as unreserved in our mutual confidence as of old.

"And when, Agnes," said I, "will you forgive me the other night?"

"When I recall it," said Agnes.

She would have dismissed the subject so, but I was too full of it to allow that, and insisted on telling her how it happened that I had disgraced myself, and what chain of accidental circumstances had had the theatre for its final link. It was a great relief to me to do this, and to enlarge on the obligation that I owed to Steerforth for his care of me when I was unable to take care of myself.

"You must not forget," said Agnes, calmly changing the conversation as soon as I had concluded, "that you are always to tell me, not only when you fall into trouble, but when you fall in love. Who has succeeded to Miss Larkins, Trotwood?"

"No one, Agnes."

"Some one, Trotwood," said Agnes, laughing, and holding up her finger.

"No, Agnes, upon my word! There is a lady, certainly, at Mrs. Steerforth's house, who is very clever, and whom I like to talk to—Miss Dartle—but I don't adore her."

Agnes laughed again at her own penetration, and told me that if I were faithful to her in my confidence she thought she should keep a little register of my violent attachments, with the date, duration, and termination of each, like the table of the reigns of the kings and queens, in the History of England. Then she asked me if I had seen Uriah.

"Uriah Heep?" said I. "No. Is he in London?"

"He comes to the office down-stairs, every day," returned Agnes. "He was in London a week before me. I am afraid on disagreeable business, Trotwood."

"On some business that makes you uneasy, Agnes, I see," said I. "What can that be?"

Agnes laid aside her work, and replied, folding her hands upon one another, and looking pensively at me out of those beautiful soft eyes of hers:

"I believe he is going to enter into partnership with papa."

"What? Uriah? That mean, fawning fellow, worm himself into such promotion!" I cried, indignantly. "Have you made no remonstrance about it, Agnes? Consider what a connexion it is likely to be. You must speak out. You must not allow your father to take such a mad step. You must prevent it, Agnes, while there's time."

Still looking at me, Agnes shook her head while I was speaking, with a faint smile at my warmth: and then replied:

"You remember our last conversation about papa? It was not long after that—not more than two or three days—when he gave me the first intimation of what I tell you. It was sad to see him struggling between his desire to represent it to me as a matter of choice on his part, and his inability to conceal that it was forced upon him. I felt very sorry."

"Forced upon him, Agnes! Who forces it upon him?"

"Uriah," she replied, after a moment's hesitation, "has

made himself indispensable to papa. He is subtle and watchful. He has mastered papa's weaknesses, fostered them, and taken advantage of them, until—to say all that I mean in a word Trotwood—until papa is afraid of him."

There was more that she might have said; more that she knew, or that she suspected; I clearly saw. I could not give her pain by asking what it was, for I, knew that she withheld it from me, to spare her father. It had long been going on to this, I was sensible: yes, I could not but feel, on the least reflection, that it had been going on to this for a long time. I remained silent.

"His ascendancy over papa," said Agnes, "is very great. He professes humility and gratitude—with truth, perhaps: I hope so—but his position is really one of power, and I fear he makes a hard use of his power."

I said he was a hound, which, at the moment, was a great satisfaction to me.

"At the time I speak of, as the time when papa spoke to me," pursued Agnes, "he had told papa that he was going away; that he was very sorry, and unwilling to leave, but that he had better prospects. Papa was very much depressed then, and more bowed down by care than ever you or I have seen him; but he seemed relieved by this expedient of the partnership, though at the same time he seemed hurt by it and ashamed of it."

"And how did you receive it, Agnes?"

"I did, Trotwood," she replied, "what I hope was right. Feeling sure that it was necessary for papa's peace that the sacrifice should be made, I entreated him to make it. I said it would lighten the load of his life—I hope it will!—and that it would give me increased opportunities of being his companion. Oh, Trotwood!" cried Agnes, putting her hands before her face, as her tears started on it, "I almost feel as if I had been papa's enemy, instead of his loving child. For I know how he has altered, in his devotion to me. I know how he has narrowed the circle of his sympathies and duties, in the concentration of his whole mind upon me. I know what a multitude of things he has shut out for my sake, and how his anxious thoughts of me have shadowed his life, and weakened his strength and energy, by turning them always upon one idea. If I could ever set this right! If I could ever work out his restoration, as I have so innocently been the cause of his decline!"

I had never before seen Agnes cry. I had seen tears in her eyes when I had brought new honours home from school, and I had seen them there when we last spoke about her father, and I had seen her turn her gentle head aside when we took leave of one another; but I had never seen her grieve like this. It made me so sorry that I could only say, in a foolish, helpless manner, "Pray, Agnes, don't! Don't, my dear sister!"

But Agnes was too superior to me in character and purpose, as I know well now, whatever I might know or not know then, to be long in need of my entreaties. The beautiful, calm manner, which makes her so different in my remembrance from everybody else, came back again, as if a cloud had passed from a serene sky.

"We are not likely to remain alone much longer," said Agnes, "and while I have an opportunity, let me earnestly entreat you, Trotwood, to be friendly to Uriah. Don't repel him. Don't resent (as I think you have a general disposition to do) what may be uncongenial to you in him. He may not deserve it, for we know no certain ill of him. In any case, think first of papa and me!"

Agnes had no time to say more, for the room-door opened, and Mrs. Waterbrook, who was a large lady—or who wore a large dress: I don't exactly know which, for I don't know which was dress and which was lady—came sailing in. I had a dim recollection of having seen her at the theatre, as if I had seen her in a pale magic-lantern; but she appeared to remember me perfectly, and still to suspect me of being in a state of intoxication.

Finding by degrees, however, that I was sober, and (I hope) that I was a modest young gentleman, Mrs. Waterbrook softened towards me considerably, and inquired, firstly, if I went much into the parks, and secondly, if I went much into society. On my replying to both these questions in the negative, it occurred to me that I fell again in her good opinion; but she concealed the fact gracefully, and invited me to dinner next day. I accepted the invitation, and took my leave, making a call on Uriah in the office as I went out, and leaving a card for him in his absence.

When I went to dinner next day, and, on the street-door being opened, plunged into a vapour-bath of haunch of mutton, I divined that I was not the only guest, for I immediately identified the ticket-porter in disguise, assisting the family servant, and waiting at the foot of the stairs to carry up my name. He looked, to the best of his ability, when he asked me for it confidentially, as if he had never seen me before; but well did I know him, and well did he know me. Conscience made cowards of us both.

I found Mr. Waterbrook to be a middle-aged gentleman, with a short throat, and a good deal of shirt collar, who only wanted a black nose to be the portrait of a pug-dog. He told me he was happy to have the honour of making my acquaintance; and when I had paid my homage to Mrs. Waterbrook, presented me, with much ceremony, to a very awful lady in a black velvet dress, and a great black velvet hat, whom I remember as looking like a near relation of Hamlet's—say his aunt.

Mrs. Henry Spiker was this lady's name; and her husband was there too: so cold a man, that his head, instead of being grey, seemed to be sprinkled with hoar-frost. Immense deference was shown to the Henry Spikers, male and female; which Agnes told me was on account of Mr. Henry Spiker being solicitor to something or to somebody, I forget what or which, remotely connected with the Treasury.

I found Uriah Heep among the company, in a suit of black, and in deep humility. He told me, when I shook hands with him, that he was proud to be noticed by me, and that he really felt obliged to me for my condescension. I could have wished he had been less obliged to me, for he hovered about me in his gratitude all the rest of the evening; and whenever I said a word to Agnes, was sure, with his shadowless eyes and cadaverous face, to be looking gauntly down upon us from behind.

There were other guests—all iced for the occasion, as it struck me, like the wine. But, there was one who attracted my attention before he came in, on account of my hearing him announced as Mr. Traddles! My mind flew back to Salem House; and could it be Tommy, I thought, who used to draw the skeletons!

I looked for Mr. Traddles with unusual interest. He was a sober, steady-looking young man of retiring manners, with a comic head of hair, and eyes that were rather wide open; and he got into an obscure corner so soon, that I had some difficulty in making him out. At length I had a good view of him, and either my vision deceived me, or it was the old unfortunate Tommy.

I made my way to Mr. Waterbrook, and said, that I believed I had the pleasure of seeing an old schoolfellow there.

"Indeed?" said Mr. Waterbrook, surprised. "You are too young to have been at school with Mr. Henry Spiker?"

"Oh, I don't mean him!" I returned. "I mean the gentleman named Traddles."

"Oh! Ay, ay! indeed!" said my host, with much diminished interest. "Possibly."

"If it's really the same person," said I, glancing towards him, "it was at a place called Salem House where we were together, and he was an excellent fellow."

"Oh yes. Traddles is a good fellow," returned my host, nodding his head with an air of toleration. "Traddles is quite a good fellow."

"It's a curious coincidence," said I.

"It is really," returned my host, "quite a coincidence, that Traddles should be here at all: as Traddles was only invited this morning, when the place at table, intended to be occupied by Mrs. Henry Spiker's brother, became vacant, in consequence of his indisposition. A very gentlemanly man, Mrs. Henry Spiker's brother, Mr. Copperfield."

I murmured an assent, which was full of feeling, considering that I knew nothing at all about him; and I inquired what Mr. Traddles was by profession.

"Traddles," returned Mr. Waterbrook, "is a young man reading for the bar. Yes. He is quite a good fellow—nobody's enemy but his own."

"Is he his own enemy?" said I, sorry to hear this.

"Well," returned Mr. Waterbrook, pursing up his mouth, and playing with his watch-chain, in a comfortable, prosperous sort of way. "I should say he was one of those men who stand in their own light. Yes, I should say he would never, for example, be worth five hundred pound. Traddles was recommended to me, by a professional friend. Oh yes. Yes. He has a kind of talent, for drawing briefs, and stating a case in writing, plainly. I am able to throw something in Traddles's way, in the course of the year; something—for him—considerable. Oh yes. Yes."

I was much impressed by the extremely comfortable and satisfied manner in which Mr. Waterbrook delivered himself of this little word "Yes," every now and then. There was wonderful expression in it. It completely conveyed the idea of a man who had been born, not to say with a silver spoon, but with a scaling-ladder, and had gone on mounting all the heights of life one after another, until now he looked, from the top of the fortifications, with the eye of a philosopher and a patron, on the people down in the trenches.

My reflections on this theme were still in progress when dinner was announced. Mr. Waterbrook went down with Hamlet's aunt. Mr. Henry Spiker took Mrs. Waterbrook. Agnes, whom I should have liked to take myself, was given to a simpering fellow with weak legs. Uriah, Traddles, and I, as the junior part of the company, went down last, how we could. I was not so vexed at losing Agnes as I might have been, since it gave me an opportunity of making myself known to Traddles on the stairs, who greeted me with great fervour: while Uriah writhed with such obtrusive satisfaction and self-abasement, that I could gladly have pitched him over the banisters.

Traddles and I were separated at table, being billeted in two remote corners: he in the glare of a red velvet lady; I, in the gloom of Hamlet's aunt. The dinner was very long, and the conversation was about the Aristocracy—and Blood. Mrs. Waterbrook repeatedly told us, that if she had a weakness, it was Blood.

It occurred to me several times that we should have got on better, if we had not been quite so genteel. We were so exceedingly genteel, that our scope was very limited. A Mr. and Mrs. Gulpidge were of the party, who had something to do at second-hand (at least, Mr. Gulpidge had), with the law business of the Bank; and what with the Bank, and what with the Treasury, we were as exclusive as the Court Circular. To mend the matter, Hamlet's aunt had the family failing of indulging in soliloquy, and held forth in a desultory manner, by herself, on every topic that was introduced. These were few enough, to be sure; but as we always fell back upon Blood, she had as wide a field for abstract speculation as her nephew himself.

We might have been a party of ogres, the conversation assumed such a sanguine complexion.

"I confess I am of Mrs. Waterbrook's opinion," said Mr. Waterbrook, with his wine-glass at his eye. "Other things are all very well in their way, but give me Blood!"

"Oh! There is nothing," observed Hamlet's aunt, "so satisfactory to one! There is nothing that is so much one's *beau-idéal* of—of all that sort of thing, speaking generally. There are some low minds (not many, I am happy to believe, but there are *some*) that would prefer to do what *I* should call bow down before idols. Positively idols! Before services, intellect, and so on. But these are intangible points. Blood is not so. We see Blood in a nose, and we know it. We meet with it in a chin, and we say, 'There it is! That's Blood!' It is an actual matter of fact. We point it out. It admits of no doubt."

The simpering fellow with the weak legs, who had taken Agnes down, stated the question more decisively yet, I thought.

"Oh, you know, deuce take it," said this gentleman, looking round the board with an imbecile smile, "we can't forego Blood, you know. We must have Blood, you know. Some young fellows, you know, may be a little behind their station, perhaps, in point of education and behaviour, and may go a little wrong, you know, and get themselves and other people into a variety of fixes—and all that—but deuce take it, it's delightful to reflect that they've got Blood in 'em! Myself, I'd rather at any time be knocked down by a man who had got Blood in him, than I'd be picked up by a man who hadn't!"

This sentiment, as compressing the general question into a nutshell, gave the utmost satisfaction, and brought the gentleman into great notice until the ladies retired. After that, I observed that Mr. Gulpidge and Mr. Henry Spiker, who had hitherto been very distant, entered into a defensive alliance against us, the common enemy, and exchanged a mysterious dialogue across the table for our defeat and overthrow.

"That affair of the first bond for four thousand five hundred pounds has not taken the course that was expected, Gulpidge," said Mr. Henry Spiker.

"Do you mean the D. of A.'s?" said Mr. Spiker.

"The C. of B.'s?" said Mr. Gulpidge.

Mr. Spiker raised his eyebrows, and looked much concerned.

"When the question was referred to Lord—I needn't name him," said Mr. Gulpidge, checking himself—

"I understand," said Mr. Spiker, "N."

Mr. Gulpidge darkly nodded—"was referred to him, his answer was, 'Money, or no release.'"

"Lord bless my soul!" cried Mr. Spiker.

"Money, or no release," repeated Mr. Gulpidge firmly. "The next in reversion—you understand me?"

"K.," said Mr. Spiker, with an ominous look.

"—K. then positively refused to sign. He was attended at Newmarket for that purpose, and he point-blank refused to do it."

Mr. Spiker was so interested, that he became quite stony.

"So the matter rests at this hour," said Mr. Gulpidge, throwing himself back in his chair. "Our friend Waterbrook will excuse me if I forbear to explain myself generally, on account of the magnitude of the interests involved."

Mr. Waterbrook was only too happy, as it appeared to me, to have such interests, and such names, even hinted at, across his table. He assumed an expression of gloomy intelligence (though I am persuaded he knew no more about the discussion than I did), and highly approved of the discretion that had been observed. Mr. Spiker, after the receipt of such a confidence, naturally desired to favour his friend with a confidence of his own; therefore the foregoing dialogue was succeeded by another, in which it was Mr. Gulpidge's turn to be surprised, and that by another in which the surprise came round to Mr. Spiker's turn again, and so on, turn and turn about. All this time we, the outsiders, remained oppressed by the tremendous interests involved in the conversation; and our host regarded us with pride, as the victims of a salutary awe and astonishment.

I was very glad indeed to get up-stairs to Agnes, and to talk with her in a corner, and to introduce Traddles to her, who was shy, but agreeable, and the same good-natured creature still. As he was obliged to leave early, on account of going away next morning for a month, I had not nearly so much conversation with him as I could have wished; but we exchanged addresses, and promised ourselves the pleasure of another meeting when he should come back to town. He was greatly interested to hear that I knew Steerforth, and spoke of him with such warmth that I made him tell Agnes what he thought of him. But Agnes only looked at me the while, and very slightly shook her head when only I observed her.

As she was not among people with whom I believed she could be very much at home, I was almost glad to hear that she was going away within a few days, though I was sorry at the prospect of parting from her again so soon. This caused me to remain until all the company were gone. Conversing with her, and hearing her sing, was such a delightful reminder to me of my happy life in the grave old house she had made so beautiful, that I could have remained there half the night; but, having no excuse for staying any longer, when the lights of Mr. Waterbrook's society were all snuffed out, I took my leave very much against my inclination. I felt then, more than ever, that she was my better Angel; and if I thought of her sweet face and placid smile, as though they had shone on me from some removed being, like an Angel, I hope I thought no harm.

I have said that the company were all gone; but I ought to have excepted Uriah, whom I don't include in that denomination, and who had never ceased to hover near us. He was close behind me when I went down-stairs. He was close beside me, when I walked away from the house, slowly fitting his long skeleton fingers into the still longer fingers of a great Guy Fawkes pair of gloves.

It was in no disposition for Uriah's company, but in remembrance of the entreaty Agnes had made to me, that I asked him if he would come home to my rooms and have some coffee.

"Oh, really, Master Copperfield," he rejoined,—"I beg your pardon, Mister Copperfield, but the other comes so natural,—I don't like that you should put a constraint upon yourself to ask a numble person like me to your ouse."

"There is no constraint in the case," said I. "Will you come?"

"I should like to, very much," replied Uriah, with a writhe.

"Well, then, come along!" said I.

I could not help being rather short with him, but he appeared not to mind it. We went the nearest way, without conversing much upon the road; and he was so humble in respect of those scarecrow gloves, that he was still putting them on, and seemed to have made no advance on that labour, when we got to my place.

I led him up the dark stairs, to prevent his knocking his head against anything, and really his damp cold hand felt so like a frog in mine, that I was tempted to drop it and run away. Agnes and hospitality prevailed, however, and I conducted him to my fireside. When I lighted my candles, he fell into meek transports with the room that was revealed to him; and when I heated the coffee in an unassuming block-tin vessel in which Mrs. Crupp delighted to prepare it (chiefly, I believe, because it was not intended for the purpose, being a shaving-pot, and because there was a patent invention of great price mouldering away in the pantry), he professed so much emotion, that I could joyfully have scalded him.

"Oh, really, Master Copperfield,—I mean Mister Copperfield," said Uriah, "to see you waiting upon me is what I never could have expected! But, one way and another, so many things happen to me which I never could have expected, I am sure, in my umble station, that it seems to rain blessings on my ed. You have heard something, I des-say, of a change in my expectations, Master Copperfield, —I should say, Mister Copperfield?"

As he sat on my sofa, with his long knees drawn up under his coffee-cup, his hat and gloves upon the ground close to him, his spoon going softly round and round, his shadowless red eyes, which looked as if they had scorched their lashes off, turned towards me without looking at me, the disagreeable dints I have formerly described in his nostrils coming and going with his breath, and a snaky undulation pervading his frame from his chin to his boots, I decided in my own mind that I disliked him intensely. It made me very uncomfortable to have him for a guest, for I was young then, and unused to disguise what I so strongly felt.

"You have heard something, I des-say, of a change in my expectations, Master Copperfield—I should say, Mister Copperfield?" observed Uriah.

"Yes," said I, "something."

"Ah! I thought Miss Agnes would know of it!" he quietly returned. "I'm glad to find Miss Agnes knows of it. Oh, thank you, Master—Mister Copperfield!"

I could have thrown my bootjack at him (it lay ready on the rug), for having entrapped me into the disclosure of anything concerning Agnes, however immaterial. But I only drank my coffee.

"What a prophet you have shown yourself, Mister Copperfield!" pursued Uriah. "Dear me, what a prophet you have proved yourself to be! Don't you remember saying to me once, that perhaps I should be a partner in Mr. Wickfield's business, and perhaps it might be Wickfield and Heep? *You* may not recollect it; but when a person is umble, Master Copperfield, a person treasures such things up!"

"I recollect talking about it," said I, ".though I certainly did not think it very likely then."

"Oh! who *would* have thought it likely, Mister Copperfield!" returned Uriah, enthusiastically. "I am sure I didn't myself. I recollect saying with my own lips that I was much too umble. So I considered myself really and truly."

He sat, with that carved grin on his face, looking at the fire as I looked at him.

"But the umblest persons, Master Copperfield," he presently resumed, "may be the instruments of good. I am glad to think I have been the instrument of good to Mr. Wickfield, and that I may be more so. Oh, what a worthy man he is, Mister Copperfield, but how imprudent he has been!"

"I am sorry to hear it," said I. I could not help adding, rather pointedly, "on all accounts."

"Decidedly so, Mister Copperfield," replied Uriah. "On all accounts. Miss Agnes's above all! You don't remember your own eloquent expressions, Master Copperfield; but *I* remember how you said one day that everybody must admire her, and how I thanked you for it! You have forgot that I have no doubt, Master Copperfield?"

"No," said I, drily.

"Oh how glad I am, you have not!" exclaimed Uriah. "To think that you should be the first to kindle the sparks of ambition in my umble breast, and that you've not forgot it! Oh!——Would you excuse me asking for a cup more coffee?"

Something in the emphasis he laid upon the kindling of those sparks, and something in the glance he directed at me as he said it, had made me start as if I had seen him illuminated by a blaze of light. Recalled by his request, preferred in quite another tone of voice, I did the honours of the shaving-pot; but I did them with an unsteadiness of hand, a sudden sense of being no match for him, and a perplexed suspicious anxiety as to what he might be going to say next, which I felt could not escape his observation.

He said nothing at all. He stirred his coffee round and round, he sipped it, he felt his chin softly with his grisly hand, he looked at the fire, he looked about the room, he gasped rather than smiled at me, he writhed and undulated about, in his deferential servility, he stirred and sipped again, but he left the renewal of the conversation to me.

"So, Mr. Wickfield," said I, at last, "who is worth five hundred of you—or me;" for my life, I think, I could not have helped dividing that part of the sentence with an awkward jerk; "has been imprudent, has he, Mr. Heep?"

"Oh very imprudent indeed, Master Copperfield," returned Uriah, sighing modestly. "Oh very much so! But I wish you'd call me Uriah, if you please. It's like old times."

"Well! Uriah," said I, bolting it out with some difficulty.

"Thank you!" he returned, with fervour. "Thank you, Master Copperfield! It's like the blowing of old breezes or the ringing of old bellses to hear *you* say Uriah. I beg your pardon. Was I making any observation?"

"About Mr. Wickfield," I suggested.

"Oh! Yes, truly," said Uriah. "Ah! Great imprudence, Master Copperfield. It's a topic that I wouldn't touch upon, to any soul but you. Even to you I can only touch upon it, and no more. If any one else had been in my place during the last few years, by this time he would have had Mr. Wickfield (oh, what a worthy man he is, Master Copperfield, too!) under his thumb. Un—der—his thumb," said Uriah, very slowly, as he stretched out his cruel-looking hand above my table, and pressed his own thumb down upon it, until it shook, and shook the room.

If I had been obliged to look at him with his splay foot on Mr. Wickfield's head, I think I could scarcely have hated him more.

"Oh dear, yes, Master Copperfield," he proceeded, in a soft voice, most remarkably contrasting with the action of his thumb, which did not diminish its hard pressure in the least degree, "there's no doubt of it. There would have been loss, disgrace, I don't know what all. Mr. Wickfield knows it. I am the umble instrument of umbly serving him, and he puts me on an eminence I hardly could have hoped to reach. How thankful should I be!" With his face turned towards me, as he finished, but without looking at me, he took his crooked thumb off the spot where he had planted it, and slowly and thoughtfully scraped his lank jaw with it, as if he were shaving himself.

I recollect well how indignantly my heart beat, as I saw his crafty face, with the appropriately red light of the fire upon it, preparing for something else.

"Master Copperfield," he began—"but am I keeping you up?"

"You are not keeping me up. I generally go to bed late."

"Thank you, Master Copperfield! I have risen from my umble station since first you used to address me, it is true; but I am umble still. I hope I never shall be otherwise than umble. You will not think the worse of my umbleness, if I make a little confidence to you, Master Copperfield? Will you?"

"Oh no," said I, with an effort.

"Thank you!" He took out his pocket-handkerchief, and began wiping the palms of his hands. "Miss Agnes, Master Copperfield——"

"Well, Uriah?"

"Oh, how pleasant to be called Uriah, spontaneously!" he cried; and gave himself a jerk, like a convulsive fish. "You thought her looking very beautiful to-night, Master Copperfield?"

"I thought her looking as she always does: superior, in all respects, to every one around her," I returned.

"Oh, thank you! It's so true!" he cried. "Oh, thank you very much for that!"

"Not at all," I said, loftily. "There is no reason why you should thank me."

"Why that, Master Copperfield," said Uriah, "is, in fact, the confidence that I am going to take the liberty of reposing. Umble as I am," he wiped his hands harder, and looked at them and at the fire by turns, "umble as my mother is, and lowly as our poor but honest roof has ever been, the image of Miss Agnes (I don't mind trusting you with my secret, Master Copperfield, for I have always overflowed towards you since the first moment I had the pleasure of beholding you in a pony-shay) has been in my breast for years. Oh, Master Copperfield, with what a pure affection do I love the ground my Agnes walks on!"

I believe I had a delirious idea of seizing the red-hot poker out of the fire, and running him through with it. It went from me with a shock, like a ball fired from a rifle: but the image of Agnes, outraged by so much as a thought of this red-headed animal's, remained in my mind when I looked at him, sitting all awry as if his mean soul griped his body, and made me giddy. He seemed to swell and grow before my eyes; the room seemed full of the echoes of his voice; and the strange feeling (to which, perhaps, no one is quite a stranger) that all this had occurred before, at some indefinite time, and that I knew what he was going to say next, took possession of me.

A timely observation of the sense of power that there was in his face, did more to bring back to my remembrance the entreaty of Agnes, in its full force, than any effort I could have made. I asked him, with a better appearance of composure than I could have thought possible a minute before, whether he had made his feelings known to Agnes.

"Oh, no, Master Copperfield!" he returned; "oh dear, no! Not to anyone but you. You see I am only just emerging from my lowly station. I rest a good deal of hope on her observing how useful I am to her father (for I trust to be very useful to him indeed, Master Copperfield), and how I smooth the way for him, and keep him straight. She's so much attached to her father, Master Copperfield (oh what a lovely thing it is in a daughter!), that I think she may come, on his account to be kind to me."

I fathomed the depth of the rascal's whole scheme, and understood why he laid it bare.

"If you'll have the goodness to keep my secret, Master Copperfield," he pursued, "and not, in general, to go against me, I shall take it as a particular favour. You wouldn't wish to make unpleasantness. I know what a friendly heart you've got; but having only known me on my umble footing (on my umblest, I should say, for I am very umble still), you might, unbeknown, go against me rather, with my Agnes. I call her mine, you see, Master Copperfield. There's a song that says, 'I'd crowns resign, to call her mine!' I hope to do it, one of these days."

Dear Agnes! So much too loving and too good for anyone that I could think of, was it possible that she was reserved to be the wife of such a wretch as this!

"There's no hurry at present, you know, Master Copperfield," Uriah proceeded, in his slimy way, as I sat gazing at him, with this thought in my mind. "My Agnes is very young still; and mother and me will have to work our way upwards, and make a good many new arrangements, before it would be quite convenient. So I shall have time gradually to make her familiar with my hopes, as opportunities offer. Oh, I'm so much obliged to you for this confidence! Oh, it's such a relief, you can't think, to know that you understand our situation, and are certain (as you wouldn't wish to make unpleasantness in the family) not to go against me!"

He took the hand which I dared not withhold, and having given it a damp squeeze, referred to his pale-faced watch.

"Dear me!" he said, "it's past one. The moments slip away so, in the confidence of old times, Master Copperfield, that it's almost half-past one!"

I answered that I had thought it was later. Not that I had really thought so, but because my conversational powers were effectually scattered.

"Dear me!" he said, considering. "The ouse that I am stopping at—a sort of a private hotel and boarding ouse, Master Copperfield, near the New River ed—will have gone to bed these two hours."

"I am sorry," I returned, "that there is only one bed here, and that I——"

"Oh, don't think of mentioning beds, Master Copperfield!" he rejoined ecstatically, drawing up one leg. "But *would* you have any objections to my laying down before the fire?"

"If it comes to that," I said, "pray take my bed, and I'll lie down before the fire."

His repudiation of this offer was almost shrill enough, in the excess of its surprise and humility, to have penetrated to the ears of Mrs. Crupp, then sleeping, I suppose, in a distant chamber, situated at about the level of low-water mark, soothed in her slumbers by the ticking of an incorrigible clock, to which she always referred me when we had any little difference on the score of punctuality, and which was never less than three-quarters of an hour too slow, and had always been put right in the morning by the best authorities. As no arguments I could urge, in my bewildered condition, had the least effect upon his modesty in inducing him to accept my bedroom, I was obliged to make the best arrangements I could, for his repose before the fire. The mattress of the sofa (which was a great deal too short for his lank figure), the sofa pillows, a blanket, the table-cover, a clean breakfast-cloth, and a great-coat, made him a bed and covering, for which he was more than thankful. Having lent him a nightcap, which he put on at once, and in which he made such an awful figure that I have never worn one since, I left him to his rest.

I never shall forget that night. I never shall forget how I turned and tumbled; how I wearied myself with thinking about Agnes and this creature; how I considered what could I do, and what ought I to do; how I could come to no other conclusion than that the best course for her peace, was to do nothing, and to keep to myself what I had heard. If I went to sleep for a few moments, the image of Agnes with her tender eyes, and of her father looking fondly on her, as I had so often seen him look, arose before me with appealing faces, and filled me with vague terrors. When I awoke, the recollection that Uriah was lying in the next room sat heavy on me like a waking nightmare; and oppressed me with a leaden dread, as if I had had some meaner quality of devil for a lodger.

The poker got into my dozing thoughts besides, and wouldn't come out. I thought, between sleeping and waking, that it was still red-hot, and I had snatched it out of the fire, and run him through the body. I was so haunted at last by the idea, though I knew there was nothing in it, that I stole into the next room to look at him. There I saw him, lying on his back, with his legs extending to I don't know where, gurglings taking place in his throat, stoppages in his nose, and his mouth open like a post-office. He was so much worse in reality than in my distempered fancy, that afterwards I was attracted to him in very repulsion, and could not help wandering in and out every half-hour or so, and taking another look at him. Still, the long, long night seemed heavy and hopeless as ever, and no promise of day was in the murky sky.

When I saw him going down-stairs early in the morning (for, thank Heaven! he would not stay to breakfast), it appeared to me as if the night was going away in his person. When I went out to the Commons, I charged Mrs. Crupp with particular directions to leave the windows open, that my sitting-room might be aired, and purged of his presence.

CHAPTER XXVI.

I FALL INTO CAPTIVITY.

I saw no more of Uriah Heep, until the day when Agnes left town. I was at the coach-office to take leave of her and see her go; and there was he, returning to Canterbury by the same conveyance. It was some small satisfaction to me to observe his spare, short-waisted, high-shouldered, mulberry-coloured great-coat perched up, in company with an umbrella like a small tent, on the edge of the back seat on the roof, while Agnes was, of course, inside; but what I underwent in my efforts to be friendly with him, while Agnes looked on, perhaps deserved that little recompense. At the coach-window, as at the dinner-party, he hovered about us without a moment's intermission, like a great vulture: gorging himself on every syllable that I said to Agnes, or Agnes said to me.

In the state of trouble into which his disclosure by my fire had thrown me, I had thought very much of the words Agnes had used in reference to the partnership: "I did what I hope was right. Feeling sure that it was necessary for papa's peace that the sacrifice should be made, I entreated him to make it." A miserable foreboding that she would yield to, and sustain herself by, the same feeling in reference to any sacrifice for his sake, had oppressed me ever since. I knew how she loved him. I knew what the devotion of her nature was. I knew from her own lips that she regarded herself as the innocent cause of his errors, and as owing him a great debt she ardently desired to pay. I had no consolation in seeing how different she was from this detestable Rufus with the mulberry-coloured great-coat, for I felt that in the very difference between them, in the self-denial of her pure soul and the sordid baseness of his, the greatest danger lay. All this, doubtless, he knew thoroughly, and had, in his cunning, considered well.

Yet, I was so certain that the prospect of such a sacrifice afar off, must destroy the happiness of Agnes; and I was so sure, from her manner, of its being unseen by her then, and having cast no shadow on her yet; that I could as soon have injured her, as given her any warning of what impended. Thus it was that we parted without explanation: she waving her hand and smiling farewell from the coach-window; her evil genius writhing on the roof, as if he had her in his clutches and triumphed.

I could not get over this farewell glimpse of them for a long time. When Agnes wrote to tell me of her safe arrival, I was as miserable as when I saw her going away. Whenever I fell into a thoughtful state, this subject was sure to present itself, and all my uneasiness was sure to be redoubled. Hardly a night passed without my dreaming of it. It became a part of my life, and as inseparable from my life as my own head.

I had ample leisure to refine upon my uneasiness: for Steerforth was at Oxford, as he wrote to me, and when I was not at the Commons, I was very much alone. I believe I had at this time some lurking distrust of Steerforth. I wrote to him most affectionately in reply to his, but I think I was glad, upon the whole, that he could not come to London just then. I suspect the truth to be, that the influence of Agnes was upon me, undisturbed by the sight of him; and that it was the more powerful with me, because she had so large a share in my thoughts and interest.

In the meantime, days and weeks slipped away. I was articled to Spenlow and Jorkins. I had ninety pounds a year (exclusive of my house-rent and sundry collateral matters) from my aunt. My rooms were engaged for twelve months certain: and though I still found them dreary of an evening, and the evenings long, I could settle down into a state of equable low spirits, and resign myself to coffee; which I seem, on looking back, to have taken by the gallon at about this period of my existence. At about this time, too, I made three discoveries: first, that Mrs. Crupp was a martyr to a curious disorder called "the spazzums," which was generally accompanied with inflammation of the nose, and required to be constantly treated with peppermint; secondly, that something peculiar in the temperature of my pantry, made the brandy-bottles burst; thirdly, that I was alone in the world, and much given to record that circumstance in fragments of English versification.

On the day when I was articled, no festivity took place, beyond my having sandwiches and sherry into the office for the clerks, and going alone to the theatre at night. I went to see "The Stranger" as a Doctors' Commons sort of play, and was so dreadfully cut up, that I hardly knew myself in my own glass when I got home. Mr. Spenlow remarked, on this occasion, when we concluded our business, that he should have been happy to have seen me at his house at Norwood to celebrate our becoming connected, but for his domestic arrangements being in some disorder, on account of the expected return of his daughter from finishing her education at Paris. But, he intimated that when she came home he should hope to have the pleasure of entertaining me. I knew that he was a widower with one daughter, and expressed my acknowledgments.

Mr. Spenlow was as good as his word. In a week or two, he referred to this engagement, and said, that if I would do him the favour to come down next Saturday, and stay till Monday, he would be extremely happy. Of course I said I *would* do him the favour; and he was to drive me down in his phaeton, and to bring me back.

When the day arrived, my very carpet-bag was an object of veneration to the stipendiary clerks, to whom the house at Norwood was a sacred mystery. One of them informed me that he had heard that Mr. Spenlow ate entirely off plate and china; and another hinted at champagne being constantly on draught, after the usual custom of table beer. The old clerk with the wig, whose name was Mr. Tiffey, had been down on business several times in the course of his career, and had on each occasion penetrated to the breakfast-parlour. He described it as an apartment of the most sumptuous nature, and said that he had drank brown East India sherry there, of a quality so precious as to make a man wink.

We had an adjourned cause in the Consistory that day—about excommunicating a baker who had been objecting in a vestry to a paving-rate—and as the evidence was just twice the length of Robinson Crusoe, according to a calculation I made, it was rather late in the day before we finished. However, we got him excommunicated for six weeks, and sentenced in no end of costs; and then the baker's proctor, and the judge, and the advocates on both sides (who were all nearly related), went out of town together, and Mr. Spenlow and I drove away in the phaeton.

The phaeton was a very handsome affair; the horses arched their necks and lifted up their legs as if they knew they belonged to Doctors' Commons. There was a good deal of competition in the Commons on all points of display, and it turned out some very choice equipages then; though I always have considered, and always shall consider, that in my time the great article of competition there was starch: which I think was worn among the proctors to as great an extent as it is in the nature of man to bear.

We were very pleasant, going down, and Mr. Spenlow gave me some hints in reference to my profession. He said it was the genteelest profession in the world, and must on no account be confounded with the profession of a solicitor: being quite another sort of thing, infinitely more exclusive, less mechanical, and more profitable. We took things much more easily in the Commons than they could be taken anywhere else, he observed, and that sets us, as a privileged class, apart. He said it was impossible to conceal the disagreeable fact, that we were chiefly employed by solicitors; but he gave me to understand that they were an inferior race of men, universally looked down upon by all proctors of any pretensions.

I asked Mr. Spenlow what he considered the best sort of professional business? He replied, that a good case of a disputed will, where there was a neat little estate of thirty or forty thousand pounds, was, perhaps, the best of all. In such a case, he said, not only were there very pretty pickings, in the way of arguments at every stage of the proceedings, and mountains upon mountains of evidence on interrogatory and counter-interrogatory (to say nothing of an appeal lying, first to the Delegates, and then to the Lords); but, the costs being pretty sure to come out of the estate at last, both sides went at it in a lively and spirited manner, and expense was no consideration. Then, he launched into a general eulogium on the Commons. What was to be particularly admired (he said) in the Commons, was its compactness. It was the most conveniently organised place in the world. It was the complete idea of snugness. It lay in a nutshell. For example: You brought a divorce case, or a restitution case, into the Consistory. Very good. You tried it in the Consistory. You made a quiet little round game of it, among a family group, and you played it out at leisure. Suppose you were not satisfied with the Consistory, what did you do then? Why, you went into the Arches. What was the Arches? The same court, in the same room, with the same bar, and the same practitioners, but another judge, for there the Consistory judge could plead any court-day as an advocate. Well, you played your round game out again. Still you were not satisfied. Very good. What did you do then? Why, you went to the Delegates. Who were the Delegates? Why, the Ecclesiastical Delegates were the advocates without any business, who had looked on at the round game when it was playing in both courts, and had seen the cards shuffled, and cut, and played, and had talked to all the players about it, and now came fresh, as judges, to settle the matter to the satisfaction of everybody! Discontented people might talk of corruption in the Commons, closeness in the Commons, and the necessity of reforming the Commons, said Mr. Spenlow solemnly in conclusion; but when the price of wheat per bushel had been highest, the Commons had been busiest; and a man might lay his hand upon his heart, and say this to the whole world,— "Touch the Commons, and down comes the country!"

I listened to all this with attention; and though, I must say, I had my doubts whether the country was quite as much obliged to the Commons as Mr. Spenlow made out, I

respectfully deferred to his opinion. That about the price of wheat per bushel, I modestly felt was too much for my strength, and quite settled the question. I have never, to this hour, got the better of that bushel of wheat. It has reappeared to annihilate me, all through my life, in connexion with all kinds of subjects. I don't know now, exactly, what it has to do with me, or what right it has to crush me, on an infinite variety of occasions; but whenever I see my old friend the bushel brought in by the head and shoulders (as he always is, I observe), I give up a subject for lost.

This is a digression. *I* was not the man to touch the Commons, and bring down the country. I submissively expressed, by my silence, my acquiescence in all I had heard from my superior in years and knowledge; and we talked about "The Stranger" and the Drama, and the pair of horses, until we came to Mr. Spenlow's gate.

There was a lovely garden to Mr. Spenlow's house; and though that was not the best time of the year for seeing a garden, it was so beautifully kept, that I was quite enchanted. There was a charming lawn, there were clusters of trees, and there were perspective walks that I could just distinguish in the dark, arched over with trellis-work, on which shrubs and flowers grew in the growing season. "Here Miss Spenlow walks by herself," I thought. "Dear me!"

We went into the house, which was cheerfully lighted up, and into a hall where there were all sorts of hats, caps, great-coats, plaids, gloves, whips, and walking-sticks. "Where is Miss Dora?" said Mr. Spenlow to the servant. "Dora!" I thought. "What a beautiful name!"

We turned into a room near at hand (I think it was the identical breakfast-room, made memorable by the brown East India sherry), and I heard a voice say, "Mr. Copperfield, my daughter Dora, and my daughter Dora's confidential friend!" It was, no doubt, Mr. Spenlow's voice, but I didn't know it, and I didn't care whose it was. All was over in a moment. I had fulfilled my destiny. I was a captive and a slave. I loved Dora Spenlow to distraction!

She was more than human to me. She was a Fairy, a Sylph, I don't know what she was—anything that no one ever saw, and everything that everybody ever wanted. I was swallowed up in an abyss of love in an instant. There was no pausing on the brink; no looking down, or looking back; I was gone, headlong, before I had sense to say a word to her.

"*I*," observed a well-remembered voice, when I had bowed and murmured something, "have seen Mr. Copperfield before."

The speaker was not Dora. No; the confidential friend, Miss Murdstone!

I don't think I was much astonished. To the best of my judgment, no capacity of astonishment was left in me. There was nothing worth mentioning in the material world, but Dora Spenlow, to be astonished about. I said, "How do you do, Miss Murdstone? I hope you are well." She answered, "Very well." I said, "How is Mr. Murdstone?" She replied, "My brother is robust, I am obliged to you."

Mr. Spenlow, who, I suppose, had been surprised to see us recognise each other, then put in his word.

"I am glad to find," he said, "Copperfield, that you and Miss Murdstone are already acquainted."

"Mr. Copperfield and myself," said Miss Murdstone, with severe composure, "are connexions. We were once slightly

I FALL INTO CAPTIVITY.

acquainted. It was in his childish days. Circumstances have separated us since. I should not have known him."

I replied that I should have known her, anywhere. Which was true enough.

"Miss Murdstone has had the goodness," said Mr. Spenlow to me, "to accept the office—if I may so describe it—of my daughter Dora's confidential friend. My daughter Dora having, unhappily, no mother, Miss Murdstone is obliging enough to become her companion and protector."

A passing thought occurred to me that Miss Murdstone, like the pocket-instrument called a life-preserver, was not so much designed for purposes of protection as of assault. But as I had none but passing thoughts for any subject save Dora, I glanced at her, directly afterwards, and was thinking that I saw, in her prettily pettish manner, that she was not very much inclined to be particularly confidential to her companion and protector, when a bell rang, which Mr. Spenlow said was the first dinner-bell, and so carried me off to dress.

The idea of dressing one's self, or doing anything in the way of action, in that state of love, was a little too ridiculous. I could only sit down before my fire, biting the key of my carpet-bag, and think of the captivating, girlish, bright-eyed, lovely Dora. What a form she had, what a face she had, what a graceful, variable, enchanting manner!

The bell rang again so soon that I made a mere scramble of my dressing, instead of the careful operation I could have wished under the circumstances, and went downstairs. There was some company. Dora was talking to an old gentleman with a grey head. Grey as he was—and a great-grandfather into the bargain, for he said so—I was madly jealous of him.

What a state of mind I was in! I was jealous of everybody. I couldn't bear the idea of anybody knowing Mr. Spenlow better than I did. It was torturing to me to hear them talk of occurrences in which I had no share. When a most amiable person, with a highly polished bald head, asked me across the dinner-table, if that were the first occasion of my seeing the grounds, I could have done anything to him that was savage and revengeful.

I don't remember who was there, except Dora. I have not the least idea what we had for dinner, besides Dora. My impression is, that I dined off Dora entirely, and sent away half-a-dozen plates untasted. I sat next to her. I talked to her. She had the most delightful little voice, the gayest little laugh, the pleasantest and most fascinating little ways, that ever led a lost youth into hopeless slavery. She was rather diminutive altogether. So much the more precious, I thought.

When she went out of the room with Miss Murdstone (no other ladies were of the party), I fell into a reverie, only disturbed by the cruel apprehension that Miss Murdstone would disparage me to her. The amiable creature with the polished head told me a long story, which I think was about gardening. I think I heard him say, "my gardener," several times. I seemed to pay the deepest attention to him, but I was wandering in a garden of Eden all the while, with Dora.

My apprehensions of being disparaged to the object of my engrossing affection were revived when we went into the drawing-room, by the grim and distant aspect of Miss Murdstone. But I was relieved of them in an unexpected manner.

"David Copperfield," said Miss Murdstone, beckoning me aside into a window. "A word."

I confronted Miss Murdstone alone.

"David Copperfield," said Miss Murdstone, "I need not enlarge upon family circumstances. They are not a tempting subject."

"Far from it, ma'am," I returned.

"Far from it," assented Miss Murdstone. "I do not wish to revive the memory of past differences, or of past outrages. I have received outrages from a person—a female, I am sorry to say, for the credit of my sex—who is not to be mentioned without scorn and disgust; and therefore I would rather not mention her."

I felt very fiery on my aunt's account; but I said it would certainly be better, if Miss Murdstone pleased, *not* to mention her. I could not hear her disrespectfully mentioned, I added, without expressing my opinion in a decided tone.

Miss Murdstone shut her eyes, and disdainfully inclined her head; then, slowly opening her eyes, resumed:

"David Copperfield, I shall not attempt to disguise the fact, that I formed an unfavourable opinion of you in your childhood. It may have been a mistaken one, or you may have ceased to justify it. That is not in question between us now. I belong to a family remarkable, I believe, for some firmness; and I am not the creature of circumstance or change. I may have my opinion of you. You may have your opinion of me."

I inclined my head, in my turn.

"But it is not necessary," said Miss Murdstone, "that these opinions should come into collision here. Under existing circumstances, it is as well on all accounts that they should not. As the chances of life have brought us together again, and may bring us together on other occasions, I would say let us meet here as distant acquaintances. Family circumstances are a sufficient reason for our only meeting on that footing, and it is quite unnecessary that either of us should make the other the subject of remark. Do you approve of this?"

"Miss Murdstone," I returned, "I think you and Mr. Murdstone used me very cruelly, and treated my mother with great unkindness. I shall always think so, as long as I live. But I quite agree in what you propose."

Miss Murdstone shut her eyes again, and bent her head. Then, just touching the back of my hand with the tips of her cold, stiff fingers, she walked away, arranging the little fetters on her wrists and round her neck: which seemed to be the same set, in exactly the same state, as when I had seen her last. These reminded me, in reference to Miss Murdstone's nature, of the fetters over a jail-door; suggesting on the outside, to all beholders, what was to be expected within.

All I know of the rest of the evening is, that I heard the empress of my heart sing enchanted ballads in the French language, generally to the effect that, whatever was the matter, we ought always to dance, Ta ra la, Ta ra la! accompanying herself on a glorified instrument, resembling a guitar. That I was lost in blissful delirium. That I refused refreshment. That my soul recoiled from punch particularly. That when Miss Murdstone took her into custody and led her away, she smiled and gave me her delicious hand. That I caught a view of myself in a mirror, looking perfectly imbecile and idiotic. That I retired to bed in a most maudlin state of mind, and got up in a crisis of feeble infatuation.

It was a fine morning, and early, and I thought I would go and take a stroll down one of those wire-arched walks, and indulge my passion by dwelling on her image. On my way through the hall, I encountered her little dog, who was called Jip—short for Gipsy. I approached him tenderly, for I loved even him; but he showed his whole set of teeth, got under a chair expressly to snarl, and wouldn't hear of the least familiarity.

The garden was cool and solitary. I walked about, wondering what my feelings of happiness would be, if I could ever become engaged to this dear wonder. As to marriage, and fortune, and all that, I believe I was almost as innocently undesigning then, as when I loved little Em'ly. To be allowed to call her "Dora," to write to her, to dote upon and worship her, to have reason to think that when she was with other people she was yet mindful of me, seemed to me the summit of human ambition—I am sure it was the summit of mine. There is no doubt whatever that I was a lackadaisical young spooney; but there was a purity of heart in all this still, that prevents my having quite a contemptuous recollection of it, let me laugh as I may.

I had not been walking long, when I turned a corner, and met her. I tingle again from head to foot as my recollection turns that corner, and my pen shakes in my hand.

"You—are—out early, Miss Spenlow," said I.

"It's so stupid at home," she replied, "and Miss Murdstone is so absurd! She talks such nonsense about its being necessary for the day to be aired, before I come out. Aired!" (She laughed, here, in the most melodious manner.) "On a Sunday morning, when I don't practise, I must do something. So I told papa last night I *must* come out. Besides, it's the brightest time of the whole day. Don't you think so?"

I hazarded a bold flight, and said (not without stammering) that it was very bright to me then, though it had been very dark to me a minute before.

"Do you mean a compliment?" said Dora, "or that the weather has really changed?"

I stammered worse than before, in replying that I meant no compliment, but the plain truth; though I was not aware of any change having taken place in the weather. It was in the state of my own feelings, I added bashfully; to clench the explanation.

I never saw such curls—how could I, for there never were such curls!—as those she shook out to hide her blushes. As to the straw hat and blue ribbons which was on the top of the curls, if I could only have hung it up in my room in Buckingham Street, what a priceless possession it would have been!

"You have just come home from Paris," said I.

"Yes," said she. "Have you ever been there?"

"No."

"Oh! I hope you'll go soon. You would like it so much!"

Traces of deep-seated anguish appeared in my countenance. That she should hope I would go, that she should think it possible I *could* go, was insupportable. I depreciated Paris; I depreciated France. I said I wouldn't leave England, under existing circumstances, for any earthly consideration. Nothing should induce me. In short, she was shaking the curls again, when the little dog came running along the walk to our relief.

He was mortally jealous of me, and persisted in barking at me. She took him up in her arms—oh my goodness!—and caressed him, but he insisted upon barking still. He wouldn't let me touch him, when I tried; and then she beat him. It increased my sufferings greatly to see the pats she gave him for punishment on the bridge of his blunt nose, while he winked his eyes, and licked her hand, and still growled within himself like a little double-bass. At length he was quiet—well he might be with her dimpled chin upon his head!—and we walked away to look at a greenhouse.

"You are not very intimate with Miss Murdstone, are you?" said Dora.—"My pet!"

(The two last words were to the dog. Oh, if they had only been to me!)

"No," I replied. "Not at all so."

"She is a tiresome creature," said Dora, pouting. "I can't think what papa can have been about, when he chose such a vexatious thing to be my companion. Who wants a protector! I am sure *I* don't want a protector. Jip can protect me a great deal better than Miss Murdstone,—can't you, Jip dear?"

He only winked lazily, when she kissed his ball of a head.

"Papa calls her my confidential friend, but I am sure she is no such thing—is she, Jip? We are not going to confide in any such cross people, Jip and I. We mean to bestow our confidence where we like, and to find out our own friends, instead of having them found out for us—don't we, Jip?"

Jip made a comfortable noise, in answer, a little like a tea-kettle when it sings. As for me, every word was a new heap of fetters, rivetted above the last.

"It is very hard, because we have not a kind Mama, that we are to have, instead, a sulky, gloomy old thing like Miss Murdstone, always following us about—isn't it, Jip? Never mind, Jip. We won't be confidential, and we'll make ourselves as happy as we can in spite of her, and we'll tease her, and not please her,—won't we, Jip?"

If it had lasted any longer, I think I must have gone down on my knees on the gravel, with the probability before me of grazing them, and of being presently ejected from the premises besides. But, by good fortune the greenhouse was not far off, and these words brought us to it.

It contained quite a show of beautiful geraniums. We loitered along in front of them, and Dora often stopped to admire this one or that one, and I stopped to admire the same one, and Dora, laughing, held the dog up childishly, to smell the flowers; and if we were not all three in Fairyland, certainly *I* was. The scent of a geranium leaf, at this day, strikes me with a half comical, half serious wonder as to what change has come over me in a moment; and then I see a straw hat and blue ribbons, and a quantity of curls, and a little black dog being held up, in two slender arms, against a bank of blossoms and bright leaves.

Miss Murdstone had been looking for us. She found us here; and presented her uncongenial cheek, the little wrinkles in it filled with hair powder, to Dora to be kissed. Then she took Dora's arm in hers, and marched us in to breakfast as if it were a soldier's funeral.

How many cups of tea I drank, because Dora made it, I don't know. But, I perfectly remember that I sat swilling tea until my whole nervous ssytem, if I had had any in those days, must have gone by the board. By-and-by we went to church. Miss Murdstone was between Dora and me in the pew; but I heard her sing, and the congregation vanished. A sermon was delivered—about Dora, of course—and I am afraid that is all I know of the service.

We had a quiet day. No company, a walk, a family dinner of four, and an evening of looking over books and pictures; Miss Murdstone with a homily before her, and her eye upon us, keeping guard vigilantly. Ah! little did Mr. Spenlow imagine, when he sat opposite to me after dinner that day, with his pocket-handkerchief over his head, how fervently I was embracing him, in my fancy, as his son-in-law! Little did he think, when I took leave of him at night, that he had just given his full consent to my being engaged to Dora, and that I was invoking blessings on his head!

We departed early in the morning, for we had a Salvage case coming on in the Admiralty Court, requiring a rather accurate knowledge of the whole science of navigation, in which (as we couldn't be expected to know much about those matters in the Commons) the judge had entreated two old Trinity Masters, for charity's sake, to come and help him out. Dora was at the breakfast-table to make the tea again, however; and I had the melancholy pleasure of taking off my hat to her in the phaeton, as she stood on the door-step with Jip in her arms.

What the Admiralty was to me that day; what nonsense I made of our case in my mind, as I listened to it; how I saw "DORA" engraved upon the blade of the silver oar which they lay upon the table, as the emblem of that high jurisdiction; and how I felt, when Mr. Spenlow went home without me (I had had an insane hope that he might take me back again), as if I were a mariner myself, and the ship to which I belonged had sailed away and left me on a desert island; I shall make no fruitless effort to describe. If that sleepy old Court could rouse itself, and present in any visible form the day-dreams I have had in it about Dora, it would reveal my truth.

I don't mean the dreams that I dreamed on that day alone, but day after day, from week to week, and term to term. I went there, not to attend to what was going on, but to think about Dora. If ever I bestowed a thought upon the cases, as they dragged their slow length before me, it was only to wonder, in the matrimonial cases (remembering Dora), how it was that married people could ever be otherwise than happy; and, in the Prerogative cases, to consider, if the money in question had been left to me, what were the foremost steps I should immediately have taken in regard to Dora. Within the first week of my passion, I bought four sumptuous waistcoats—not for myself; I had no pride in them; for Dora—and took to wearing straw-coloured kid gloves in the streets, and laid the foundations of all the corns I have ever had. If the boots I wore at that period could only be produced and compared with the natural size of my feet, they would show what the state of my heart was, in a most affecting manner.

And yet, wretched cripple as I made myself by this act of homage to Dora, I walked miles upon miles daily in the hope of seeing her. Not only was I soon as well known on the Norwood Road as the postmen on that beat, but I pervaded London likewise. I walked about the streets where the best shops for ladies were, I haunted the Bazaar like an unquiet spirit, I fagged through the Park again and again, long after I was quite knocked up. Sometimes, at long intervals, and on rare occasions, I saw her. Perhaps I saw her glove waved in a carriage window; perhaps I met her, walked with her and Miss Murdstone a little way, and spoke to her. In the latter case I was always very

miserable afterwards, to think that I had said nothing to the purpose; or that she had no idea of the extent of my devotion, or that she cared nothing about me. I was always looking out, as may be supposed, for another invitation to Mr. Spenlow's house. I was always being disappointed, for I got none.

Mrs. Crupp must have been a woman of penetration; for when this attachment was but a few weeks old, and I had not had the courage to write more explicitly even to Agnes, than that I had been to Mr. Spenlow's house, "whose family," I added, "consists of one daughter;"—I say Mrs. Crupp must have been a woman of penetration, for, even in that early stage, she found it out. She came up to me one evening, when I was very low, to ask (she being then afflicted with the disorder I have mentioned) if I could oblige her with a little tincture of cardamums mixed with rhubarb, and flavoured with seven drops of the essence of cloves, which was the best remedy for her complaint;—or, if I had not such a thing by me, with a little brandy, which was the next best. It was not, she remarked, so palatable to her, but it was the next best. As I had never even heard of the first remedy, and always had the second in the closet, I gave Mrs. Crupp a glass of the second, which (that I might have no suspicion of its being devoted to any improper use) she began to take in my presence.

"Cheer up, Sir," said Mrs. Crupp. "I can't abear to see you so, Sir: I'm a mother myself."

I did not quite perceive the application of this fact to *my*self, but I smiled on Mrs. Crupp, as benignly as was in my power.

"Come, Sir," said Mrs. Crupp. "Excuse me. I know what it is, Sir. There's a young lady in the case."

"Mrs. Crupp?" I returned, reddening.

"Oh, bless you! Keep a good heart, Sir!" said Mrs. Crupp, nodding encouragement. "Never say die, Sir! If She don't smile upon you, there's a many as will. You're a young gentleman to *be* smiled on, Mr. Copperfull, and you must learn your walue, Sir."

Mrs. Crupp always called me Mr. Copperfull: firstly, no doubt, because it was not my name; and secondly, I am inclined to think, in some indistinct association with a washing-day.

"What makes you suppose there is any young lady in the case, Mrs. Crupp?" said I.

"Mr. Copperfull," said Mrs. Crupp, with a great deal of feeling, "I'm a mother myself."

For some time Mrs. Crupp could only lay her hand upon her nankeen bosom, and fortify herself against returning pain with sips of her medicine. At length she spoke again.

"When the present set were took for you by your dear aunt, Mr. Copperfull," said Mrs. Crupp, "my remark were, I had now found summun I could care for. 'Thank Ev'in!' were the expression, 'I have now found summun I can care for!'—You don't eat enough, Sir, nor yet drink."

"Is that what you found your supposition on, Mrs. Crupp?" said I.

"Sir," said Mrs. Crupp, in a tone approaching to severity, "I've laundressed other young gentlemen besides yourself. A young gentleman may be over-careful of himself, or he may be under-careful of himself. He may brush his hair too regular, or too unregular. He may wear his boots much too large for him, or much too small. That is according as the young gentleman has his original character formed. But let him go to which extreme he may, Sir, there's a young lady in both of 'em."

Mrs. Crupp shook her head in such a determined manner, that I had not an inch of 'vantage ground left.

"It was but the gentleman which died here before yourself," said Mrs. Crupp, "that fell in love—with a barmaid —and had his waistcoats took in directly, though much swelled by drinking."

"Mrs. Crupp," said I, "I must beg you not to connect the young lady in my case with a barmaid, or anything of that sort, if you please."

"Mr. Copperfull," returned Mrs. Crupp, "I'm a mother myself, and not likely. I ask your pardon, Sir, if I intrude. I should never wish to intrude where I were not welcome. But you are a young gentleman, Mr. Copperfull, and my adwice to you is, to cheer up, Sir, to keep a good heart, and to know your own walue. If you was to take to something, Sir," said Mrs. Crupp, "if you was to take to skittles, now, which is healthy, you might find it divert your mind, and do you good."

With these words, Mrs. Crupp, affecting to be very careful of the brandy—which was all gone—thanked me with a majestic curtsey, and retired. As her figure disappeared into the gloom of the entry, this counsel certainly presented itself to my mind in the light of a slight liberty on Mrs. Crupp's part; but, at the same time, I was content to receive it, in another point of view, as a word to the wise, and a warning in future to keep my secret better.

CHAPTER XXVII.

TOMMY TRADDLES.

It may have been in consequence of Mrs. Crupp's advice, and, perhaps, for no better reason than because there was a certain similarity in the sound of the word skittles and Traddles, that it came into my head, next day, to go and look after Traddles. The time he had mentioned was more than out, and he lived in a little street near the Veterinary College at Camden Town, which was principally tenanted, as one of our clerks who lived in that direction informed me, by gentlemen students, who bought live donkeys, and made experiments on those quadrupeds in their private apartments. Having obtained from this clerk a direction to the academic grove in question, I set out, the same afternoon, to visit my old schoolfellow.

I found that the street was not as desirable a one as I could have wished it to be, for the sake of Traddles. The inhabitants appeared to have a propensity to throw any little trifles they were not in want of, into the road: which not only made it rank and sloppy, but untidy too, on account of the cabbage-leaves. The refuse was not wholly vegetable either, for I myself saw a shoe, a doubled-up saucepan, a black bonnet, and an umbrella, in various stages of decomposition, as I was looking out for the number I wanted.

The general air of the place reminded me forcibly of the days when I lived with Mr. and Mrs. Micawber. An indescribable character of faded gentility that attached to the house I sought, and made it unlike all the other houses in the street—though they were all built on one monoto-

nous pattern, and looked like the early copies of a blundering boy who was learning to make houses, and had not yet got out of his cramped brick-and-mortar pothooks—reminded me still more of Mr. and Mrs. Micawber. Happening to arrive at the door as it was opened to the afternoon milkman, I was reminded of Mr. and Mrs. Micawber more forcibly yet.

"Now," said the milkman to a very youthful servant-girl. "Has that there little bill of mine been heerd on?"

"Oh, master says he'll attend to it immediate," was the reply.

"Because," said the milkman, going on as if he had received no answer, and speaking, as I judged from his tone, rather for the edification of somebody within the house, than of the youthful servant—an impression which was strengthened by his manner of glaring down the passage— "Because that there little bill has been running so long, that I begin to believe it's run away altogether, and never won't be heerd of. Now, I'm not a going to stand it, you know!" said the milkman, still throwing his voice into the house, and glaring down the passage.

As to his dealing in the mild article of milk, by-the-by, there never was a greater anomaly. His deportment would have been fierce in a butcher or a brandy-merchant.

The voice of the youthful servant became faint, but she seemed to me, from the action of her lips, again to murmur that it would be attended to immediate.

"I tell you what," said the milkman, looking hard at her for the first time, and taking her by the chin, "are you fond of milk?"

"Yes, I likes it," she replied.

"Good," said the milkman. "Then you won't have none to-morrow. D'ye hear? Not a fragment of milk you won't have to-morrow."

I thought she seemed, upon the whole, relieved, by the prospect of having any to-day. The milkman, after shaking his head at her, darkly, released her chin, and with anything rather than good-will opened his can, and deposited the usual quantity in the family jug. This done, he went away, muttering, and uttered the cry of his trade next door, in a vindictive shriek.

"Does Mr. Traddles live here?" I then inquired.

A mysterious voice from the end of the passage replied "Yes." Upon which the youthful servant replied "Yes."

"Is he at home?" said I.

Again the mysterious voice replied in the affirmative, and again the servant echoed it. Upon this, I walked in, and in pursuance of the servant's directions walked upstairs; conscious, as I passed the back parlour-door, that I was surveyed by a mysterious eye, probably belonging to the mysterious voice.

When I got to the top of the stairs—the house was only a story high above the ground floor—Traddles was on the landing to meet me. He was delighted to see me, and gave me welcome, with great heartiness, to his little room. It was in the front of the house, and extremely neat, though sparely furnished. It was his only room, I saw; for there was a sofa-bedstead in it, and his blacking-brushes and blacking were among his books—on the top shelf, behind a dictionary. His table was covered with papers, and he was hard at work in an old coat. I looked at nothing, that I know of, but I saw everything, even to the prospect of a church upon his china inkstand, as I sat down—and this, too, was a faculty confirmed in me in the old Micawber times. Various ingenious arrangements he had made, for the disguise of his chest of drawers, and the accommodation of his boots, his shaving-glass, and so forth, particularly impressed themselves upon me, as evidences of the same Traddles who used to make models of elephants' dens in writing-paper to put flies in; and to comfort himself, under ill-usage, with the memorable works of art I have so often mentioned.

In a corner of the room was something neatly covered up with a large white cloth. I could not make out what that was.

"Traddles," said I, shaking hands with him again, after I had sat down. "I am delighted to see you."

"I am delighted to see *you*, Copperfield," he returned. "I am very glad indeed to see you. It was because I was thoroughly glad to see you when we met in Ely Place, and was sure you were thoroughly glad to see me, that I gave you this address instead of my address at chambers."

"Oh! You have chambers?" said I.

"Why, I have the fourth of a room and a passage, and the fourth of a clerk," returned Traddles. "Three others and myself unite to have a set of chambers—to look business-like—and we quarter the clerk too. Half-a-crown a week he costs me."

His old simple character and good temper, and something of his old unlucky fortune also, I thought, smiled at me in the smile with which he made this explanation.

"It's not because I have the least pride, Copperfield, you understand," said Traddles, "that I don't usually give my address here. It's only on account of those who come to me, who might not like to come here. For myself, I am fighting my way on in the world against difficulties, and it would be ridiculous if I made a pretence of doing anything else."

"You are reading for the bar, Mr. Waterbrook informed me?" said I.

"Why, yes," said Traddles, rubbing his hands, slowly over one another, "I am reading for the bar. The fact is, I have just begun to keep my terms, after rather a long delay. It's some time since I was articled, but the payment of that hundred pounds was a great pull. A great pull!" said Traddles, with a wince, as if he had had a tooth out.

"Do you know what I can't help thinking of, Traddles, as I sit here looking at you?" I asked him.

"No," said he.

"That sky-blue suit you used to wear."

"Lord, to be sure!" cried Traddles, laughing. "Tight in the arms and legs, you know? Dear me! Well! Those were happy times, weren't they?"

"I think our schoolmaster might have made them happier, without doing any harm to any of us, I acknowledge," I returned.

"Perhaps he might," said Traddles. "But dear me, there was a good deal of fun going on. Do you remember the nights in the bed-room? When we used to have the suppers? And when you used to tell the stories? Ha, ha, ha! And do you remember when I got caned for crying about Mr. Mell? Old Creakle! I should like to see him again, too!"

"He was a brute to you, Traddles," said I, indignantly; for his good humour made me feel as if I had seen him beaten but yesterday.

"Do you think so?" returned Traddles. "Really? Perhaps he was, rather. But it's all over, a long while. Old Creakle!"

"You were brought up by an uncle, then?" said I.

"Of course I was!" said Traddles. "The one I was always going to write to. And always didn't, eh! Ha, ha, ha! Yes, I had an uncle then. He died soon after I left school."

"Indeed!"

"Yes. He was a retired—what do you call it?—draper—cloth-merchant—and had made me his heir. But he didn't like me when I grew up."

"Do you really mean that?" said I. He was so composed, that I fancied he must have some other meaning.

"Oh dear yes, Copperfield! I mean it," replied Traddles. "It was an unfortunate thing, but he didn't like me at all. He said I wasn't at all what he expected, and so he married his housekeeper."

"And what did you do?" I asked.

"I didn't do anything in particular," said Traddles. "I lived with them, waiting to be put out in the world, until his gout unfortunately flew to his stomach—and so he died, and so she married a young man, and so I wasn't provided for."

"Did you get nothing, Traddles, after all?"

"Oh dear yes!" said Traddles. "I got fifty pounds. I had never been brought up to any profession, and at first I was at a loss what to do for myself. However, I began, with the assistance of the son of a professional man, who had been to Salem House—Yawler, with his nose on one side. Do you recollect him?"

No. He had not been there with me; all the noses were straight, in my day.

"It don't matter," said Traddles. "I began, by means of his assistance, to copy law writings. That didn't answer very well; and then I began to state cases for them, and make abstracts, and do that sort of work. For I am a plodding kind of fellow, Copperfield, and had learnt the way of doing such things pithily. Well! That put it in my head to enter myself as a law student; and that ran away with all that was left of the fifty pounds. Yawler recommended me to one or two other offices, however—Mr. Waterbrook's for one—and I got a good many jobs. I was fortunate enough, too, to become acquainted with a person in the publishing way, who was getting up an Encyclopædia, and he set me to work; and, indeed" (glancing at his table), "I am at work for him at this minute. I am not a bad compiler, Copperfield," said Traddles, preserving the same air of cheerful confidence in all he said, "but I have no invention at all; not a particle. I suppose there never was a young man with less originality than I have."

As Traddles seemed to expect that I should assent to this as a matter of course, I nodded; and he went on, with the same sprightly patience—I can find no better expression—as before.

"So, by little and little, and not living high, I managed to scrape up the hundred pounds at last," said Traddles; "and thank Heaven that's paid—though it was—though it certainly was," said Traddles, wincing again as if he had had another tooth out, "a pull. I am living by the sort of work I have mentioned, still, and I hope, one of these days, to get connected with some newspaper: which would almost be the making of my fortune. Now, Copperfield, you are so exactly what you used to be, with that agreeable face, and it's so pleasant to see you, that I sha'n't conceal anything. Therefore you must know that I am engaged."

Engaged! Oh Dora!

"She is a curate's daughter," said Traddles; "one of

ten, down in Devonshire. Yes!" For he saw me glance, involuntarily, at the prospect on the inkstand. "That's the church! You come round here, to the left, out of this gate," tracing his finger along the inkstand, "and exactly where I hold this pen, there stands the house—facing, you understand, towards the church."

The delight with which he entered into these particulars, did not fully present itself to me until afterwards; for my selfish thoughts were making a ground-plan of Mr. Spenlow's house and garden at the same moment.

"She is such a dear girl!" said Traddles; "a little older than me, but the dearest girl! I told you I was going out of town? I have been down there. I walked there, and I walked back, and I had the most delightful time! I dare say ours is likely to be a rather long engagement, but our motto is 'Wait and hope!' We always say that. 'Wait and hope,' we always say. And she would wait, Copperfield, till she was sixty—any age you can mention—for me!"

Traddles rose from his chair, and with a triumphant smile, put his hand upon the white cloth I had observed.

"However," he said; "it's not that we haven't made a beginning towards housekeeping. No, no; we have begun. We must get on by degrees, but we have begun. Here," drawing the cloth off with great pride and care, "are two pieces of furniture to commence with. This flower-pot and stand, she bought herself. You put that in a parlour-window," said Traddles, falling a little back from it to survey it with the greater admiration, "with a plant in it, and—and there you are! This little round table with the marble top (it's two feet ten in circumference), *I* bought. You want to lay a book down, you know, or somebody comes to see you or your wife, and wants a place to stand a cup of tea upon, and—and there you are again!" said Traddles. "It's an admirable piece of workmanship—firm as a rock!"

I praised them both, highly, and Traddles replaced the covering as carefully as he had removed it.

"It's not a great deal towards the furnishing," said Traddles, "but it's something. The table-cloths, and pillow-cases, and articles of that kind, are what discourage me most, Copperfield. So does the ironmongery—candle-boxes, and gridirons, and that sort of necessaries—because those things tell, and mount up. However, 'wait and hope!' And I assure you she's the dearest girl!"

"I am quite certain of it," said I.

"In the meantime," said Traddles, coming back to his chair; "and this is the end of my prosing about myself, I get on as well as I can. I don't make much, but I don't spend much. In general, I board with the people down-stairs, who are very agreeable people indeed. Both Mr. and Mrs. Micawber have seen a good deal of life, and are excellent company."

"My dear Traddles!" I quickly exclaimed. "What are you talking about!"

Traddles looked at me, as if he wondered what *I* was talking about.

"Mr. and Mrs. Micawber!" I repeated. "Why, I am intimately acquainted with them!"

An opportune double-knock at the door, which I knew well from old experience in Windsor Terrace, and which nobody but Mr. Micawber could ever have knocked at that door, resolved any doubt in my mind as to their being my old friends. I begged Traddles to ask his landlord to walk up. Traddles accordingly did so, over the banister; and

Mr. Micawber, not a bit changed—his tights, his stick, his shirt-collar, and his eye-glass, all the same as ever—came into the room with a genteel and youthful air.

"I beg your pardon, Mr. Traddles," said Mr. Micawber, with the old roll in his voice, as he checked himself in humming a soft tune. "I was not aware that there was any individual, alien to this tenement, in your sanctum."

Mr. Micawber slightly bowed to me, and pulled up his shirt-collar.

"How do you do, Mr. Micawber?" said I.

"Sir," said Mr. Micawber, "you are exceedingly obliging. I am *in statu quo.*"

"And Mrs. Micawber?" I pursued.

"Sir," said Mr. Micawber, "she is also, thank God, *in statu quo.*"

"And the children, Mr. Micawber?"

"Sir," said Mr. Micawber, "I rejoice to reply that they are, likewise, in the enjoyment of salubrity."

All this time, Mr. Micawber had not known me in the least, though he had stood face to face with me. But now, seeing me smile, he examined my features with more attention, fell back, cried, "Is it possible! Have I the pleasure of again beholding Copperfield!" and shook me by both hands with the utmost fervour.

"Good Heaven, Mr. Traddles!" said Mr. Micawber, "to think that I should find you acquainted with the friend of my youth, the companion of earlier days! My dear!" calling over the banisters to Mrs. Micawber, while Traddles looked (with reason) not a little amazed at this description of me. "Here is a gentleman in Mr. Traddles's apartment, whom he wishes to have the pleasure of presenting to you, my love!"

Mr. Micawber immediately reappeared, and shook hands with me again.

"And how is our good friend the Doctor, Copperfield?" said Mr. Micawber, "and all the circle at Canterbury?"

"I have none but good accounts of them," said I.

"I am most delighted to hear it," said Mr. Micawber. "It was at Canterbury where we last met. Within the shadow, I may figuratively say, of that religious edifice, immortalized by Chaucer, which was anciently the resort of pilgrims from the remotest corners of—in short," said Mr. Micawber, "in the immediate neighbourhood of the Cathedral."

I replied that it was. Mr. Micawber continued talking as volubly as he could; but not, I thought, without showing, by some marks of concern in his countenance, that he was sensible of sounds in the next room, as of Mrs. Micawber washing her hands, and hurriedly opening and shutting drawers that were uneasy in their action.

"You find us, Copperfield," said Mr. Micawber, with one eye on Traddles, "at present established, on what may be designated as a small and unassuming scale; but, you are aware that I have, in the course of my career, surmounted difficulties, and conquered obstacles. You are no stranger to the fact, that there have been periods of my life, when it has been requisite that I should pause, until certain expected events should turn up; when it has been necessary that I should fall back, before making what I trust I shall not be accused of presumption in terming—a spring. The present is one of those momentous stages in the life of man. You find me, fallen back, *for* a spring; and I have every reason to believe that a vigorous leap will shortly be the result."

I was expressing my satisfaction, when Mrs. Micawber

came in; a little more slatternly than she used to be, or so she seemed now, to my unaccustomed eyes, but still with some preparation of herself for company, and with a pair of brown gloves on.

"My dear," said Mr. Micawber, leading her towards me. "Here is a gentleman of the name of Copperfield, who wishes to renew his acquaintance with you."

It would have been better, as it turned out, to have led gently up to his announcement, for Mrs. Micawber, being in a delicate state of health, was overcome by it, and was taken so unwell, that Mr. Micawber was obliged, in great trepidation, to run down to the water-butt in the back yard, and draw a basinful to lave her brow with. She presently revived, however, and was really pleased to see me. We had half-an-hour's talk, all together; and I asked her about the twins, who, she said, were "grown great creatures;" and after Master and Miss Micawber, whom she described as "absolute giants," but they were not produced on that occasion.

Mr. Micawber was very anxious that I should stay to dinner. I should not have been averse to do so, but that I imagined I detected trouble, and calculation relative to the extent of the cold meat, in Mrs. Micawber's eye. I therefore pleaded another engagement; and observing that Mrs. Micawber's spirits were immediately lightened, I resisted all persuasion to forego it.

But I told Traddles, and Mr. and Mrs. Micawber, that before I could think of leaving, they must appoint a day when they would come and dine with me. The occupations to which Traddles stood pledged, rendered it necessary to fix a somewhat distant one; but an appointment was made for the purpose, that suited us all, and then I took my leave.

Mr. Micawber, under pretence of showing me a nearer way than that by which I had come, accompanied me to the corner of the street; being anxious (he explained to me) to say a few words to an old friend, in confidence.

"My dear Copperfield," said Mr. Micawber, "I need hardly tell you that to have beneath our roof, under existing circumstances, a mind like that which gleams—if I may be allowed the expression—which gleams—in your friend Traddles, is an unspeakable comfort. With a washerwoman, who exposes hard-bake for sale in her parlour-window, dwelling next door, and a Bow Street officer residing over the way, you may imagine that his society is a source of consolation to myself and to Mrs. Micawber. I am at present, my dear Copperfield, engaged in the sale of corn upon commission. It is not an avocation of a remunerative description—in other words, it does *not* pay—and some temporary embarrassments of a pecuniary nature have been the consequence. I am, however, delighted to add that I have now an immediate prospect of something turning up (I am not at liberty to say in what direction), which I trust will enable me to provide, permanently, both for myself and for your friend Traddles, in whom I have an unaffected interest. You may, perhaps, be prepared to hear that Mrs. Micawber is in a state of health which renders it not wholly improbable that an addition may be ultimately made to those pledges of affection which—in short, to the infantine group. Mrs. Micawber's family have been so good as to express their dissatisfaction with this state of things. I have merely to observe, that I am not aware it is any business of theirs, and that I repel that exhibition of feeling with scorn, and with defiance!"

Mr. Micawber then shook hands with me again, and left me.

CHAPTER XXVIII.

MR. MICAWBER'S GAUNTLET.

UNTIL the day arrived on which I was to entertain my newly-found old friends, I lived principally on Dora and coffee. In my love-lorn condition, my appetite languished; and I was glad of it, for I felt as though it would have been an act of perfidy towards Dora to have a natural relish for my dinner. The quantity of walking exercise I took, was not in this respect attended with its usual consequence, as the disappointment counteracted the fresh air. I have my doubts, too, founded on the acute experience acquired at this period of my life, whether a sound enjoyment of animal food can develop itself freely in any human subject who is always in torment from tight boots. I think the extremities require to be at peace before the stomach will conduct itself with vigour.

On the occasion of this domestic little party, I did not repeat my former extensive preparations. I merely provided a pair of soles, a small leg of mutton, and a pigeon-pie. Mrs. Crupp broke out into rebellion on my first bashful hint in reference to the cooking of the fish and joint, and said, with a dignified sense of injury, "No! No, Sir! You will not ask me sich a thing, for you are better acquainted with me than to suppose me capable of doing what I cannot do with ampial satisfaction to my own feelings!" But, in the end, a compromise was effected; and Mrs. Crupp consented to achieve this feat, on condition that I dined from home for a fortnight afterwards.

And here I may remark, that what I underwent from Mrs. Crupp, in consequence of the tyranny she established over me, was dreadful. I never was so much afraid of anyone. We made a compromise of everything. If I hesitated, she was taken with that wonderful disorder which was always lying in ambush in her system, ready, at the shortest notice, to prey upon her vitals. If I rang the bell impatiently, after half-a-dozen unavailing modest pulls, and she appeared at last—which was not by any means to be relied upon—she would appear with a reproachful aspect, sink breathless on a chair near the door, lay her hand upon her nankeen bosom, and become so ill, that I was glad, at any sacrifice of brandy or anything else, to get rid of her. If I objected to having my bed made at five o'clock in the afternoon—which I *do* still think an uncomfortable arrangement—one motion of her hand towards the same nankeen region of wounded sensibility was enough to make me falter an apology. In short, I would have done anything in an honourable way rather than give Mrs. Crupp offence; and she was the terror of my life.

I bought a second-hand dumb-waiter for this dinner-party, in preference to re-engaging the handy young man; against whom I had conceived a prejudice, in consequence of meeting him in the Strand, one Sunday morning, in a waistcoat remarkably like one of mine, which had been missing since the former occasion. The "young gal" was re-engaged; but on the stipulation that she should only bring in the dishes, and then withdraw to the landing-place, beyond the outer door; where a habit of sniffing she had contracted would be lost upon the guests, and where her retiring on the plates would be a physical impossibility.

Having laid in the materials for a bowl of punch, to be compounded by Mr. Micawber; having provided a bottle of lavender-water, two wax candles, a paper of mixed pins, and a pincushion, to assist Mrs. Micawber in her toilette, at my dressing-table; having also caused the fire in my bed-room to be lighted for Mrs. Micawber's convenience; and having laid the cloth with my own hands, I awaited the result with composure.

At the appointed time, my three visitors arrived together. Mr. Micawber with more shirt-collar than usual, and a new ribbon to his eye-glass; Mrs. Micawber with her cap in a whity-brown paper parcel; Traddles carrying the parcel, and supporting Mrs. Micawber on his arm. They were all delighted with my residence. When I conducted Mrs. Micawber to my dressing-table, and she saw the scale on which it was prepared for her, she was in such raptures, that she called Mr. Micawber to come in and look.

"My dear Copperfield," said Mr. Micawber, "this is luxurious. This is a way of life which reminds me of the period when I was myself in a state of celibacy, and Mrs. Micawber had not yet been solicited to plight her faith at the Hymeneal altar."

"He means, solicited by him, Mr. Copperfield," said Mrs. Micawber, archly. "He cannot answer for others."

"My dear," returned Mr. Micawber with sudden seriousness, "I have no desire to answer for others. I am too well aware that when, in the inscrutable decrees of Fate, you were reserved for me, it is possible you may have been reserved for one, destined, after a protracted struggle, at length to fall a victim to pecuniary involvements of a complicated nature. I understand your allusion, my love. I regret it, but I can bear it."

"Micawber!" exclaimed Mrs. Micawber, in tears. "Have I deserved this! I, who never have deserted you; who never *will* desert you, Micawber!"

"My love," said Mr. Micawber, much affected, "you will forgive, and our old and tried friend Copperfield will, I am sure, forgive, the momentary laceration of a wounded spirit, made sensitive by a recent collision with the Minion of Power—in other words, with a ribald Turncock attached to the waterworks—and will pity, not condemn, its excesses."

Mr. Micawber then embraced Mrs. Micawber, and pressed my hand; leaving me to infer from this broken allusion that his domestic supply of water had been cut off that afternoon, in consequence of default in the payment of the company's rates.

To divert his thoughts from this melancholy subject, I informed Mr. Micawber that I relied upon him for a bowl of punch, and led him to the lemons. His recent despondency, not to say despair, was gone in a moment. I never saw a man so thoroughly enjoy himself amid the fragrance of lemon-peel and sugar, the odour of burning rum, and the steam of boiling water, as Mr. Micawber did that afternoon. It was wonderful to see his face shining at us out of a thin cloud of these delicate fumes, as he stirred, and mixed, and tasted, and looked as if he were making, instead of punch, a fortune for his family down to the latest posterity. As to Mrs. Micawber, I don't know whether it was the effect of the cap, or the lavender-water, or the pins, or the fire, or the wax candles, but she came out of my room, comparatively speaking, lovely. And the lark was never gayer than that excellent woman.

I suppose—I never ventured to inquire, but I suppose—that Mrs. Crupp, after frying the soles, was taken ill. Because we broke down at that point. The leg of mutton came up very red within, and very pale without: besides having a foreign substance of a gritty nature sprinkled over it, as if it had had a fall into the ashes of that remarkable kitchen fireplace. But we were not in a condition to judge of this fact from the appearance of the gravy, forasmuch as the "young gal" had dropped it all upon the stairs—where it remained, by-the-by, in a long train, until it was worn out. The pigeon-pie was not bad, but it was a delusive pie: the crust being like a disappointing head, phrenologically speaking: full of lumps and bumps, with nothing particular underneath. In short, the banquet was such a failure that I should have been quite unhappy—about the failure, I mean, for I was always unhappy about Dora—if I had not been relieved by the great good-humour of my company, and by a bright suggestion from Mr. Micawber.

"My dear friend Copperfield," said Mr. Micawber, "accidents will occur in the best-regulated families; and in families not regulated by that pervading influence which sanctifies while it enhances the—a—I would say in short, by the influence of Woman, in the lofty character of Wife, they may be expected with confidence, and must be borne with philosophy. If you will allow me to take the liberty of remarking that there are few comestibles better, in their way, than a Devil, and that I believe, with a little division of labour, we could accomplish a good one if the young person in attendance could produce a gridiron, I would put it to you, that this little misfortune may be easily repaired."

There was a gridiron in the pantry, on which my morning rasher of bacon was cooked. We had it in, in a twinkling, and immediately applied ourselves to carrying Mr. Micawber's idea into effect. The divison of labour to which he had referred was this:—Traddles cut the mutton into slices; Mr. Micawber (who could do anything of this sort to perfection) covered them with pepper, mustard, salt, and cayenne; I put them on the gridiron, turned them with a fork, and took them off, under Mr. Micawber's direction; and Mrs. Micawber heated, and continually stirred, some mushroom ketchup in a little saucepan. When we had slices enough done to begin upon, we fell-to, with our sleeves still tucked up at the wrists, more slices sputtering and blazing on the fire, and our attention divided between the mutton on our plates, and the mutton then preparing.

What with the novelty of this cookery, the excellence of it, the bustle of it, the frequent starting up to look after it, the frequent sitting down to dispose of it as the crisp slices came off the gridiron hot and hot, the being so busy, so flushed with the fire, so amused, and in the midst of such a tempting noise and savour, we reduced the leg of mutton to the bone. My own appetite came back miraculously. I am ashamed to record it, but I really believe I forgot Dora for a little while. I am satisfied that Mr. and Mrs. Micawber could not have enjoyed the feast more, if they had sold a bed to provide it. Traddles laughed as heartily, almost the whole time, as he ate and worked. Indeed we all did, all at once; and I dare say there never was a greater success.

We were at the height of our enjoyment, and were all busily engaged, in our several departments, endeavouring to bring the last batch of slices to a state of perfection that should crown the feast, when I was aware of a strange presence in the room, and my eyes encountered those of the staid Littimer, standing hat in hand before me.

"What's the matter!" I involuntarily asked.

"I beg your pardon, Sir, I was directed to come in. Is my master not here, Sir?"

"No."

"Have you not seen him, Sir?"

"No; don't you come from him?"

"Not immediately so, Sir."

"Did he tell you you would find him here?"

"Not exactly so, Sir. But I should think he might be here to-morrow, as he has not been here to-day."

"Is he coming up from Oxford?"

"I beg, Sir," he returned respectfully, "that you will be seated, and allow me to do this." With which he took the fork from my unresisting hand, and bent over the gridiron, as if his whole attention were concentrated on it.

We should not have been much discomposed, I dare say, by the appearance of Steerforth himself; but we became in a moment the meekest of the meek before his respectable serving-man. Mr. Micawber, humming a tune, to show that he was quite at ease, subsided into his chair, with the handle of a hastily-concealed fork sticking out of the bossom of his coat, as if he had stabbed himself. Mrs. Micawber put on her brown gloves, and assumed a genteel languor. Traddles ran his greasy hands through his hair, and stood it bolt upright, and stared in confusion at the table-cloth. As for me, I was a mere infant at the head of my own table; and hardly ventured to glance at the respectable phenomenon, who had come from Heaven knows where, to put my establishment to rights.

Meanwhile he took the mutton off the gridiron, and gravely handed it round. We all took some, but our appreciation of it was gone, and we merely made a show of eating it. As we severally pushed away our plates, he noiselessly removed them, and set on the cheese. He took that off, too, when it was done with; cleared the table; piled everything on the dumb-waiter; gave us our wine-glasses; and, of his own accord, wheeled the dumb-waiter into the pantry. All this was done in a perfect manner, and he never raised his eyes from what he was about. Yet, his very elbows, when he had his back towards me, seemed to teem with the expression of his fixed opinion that I was extremely young.

"Can I do anything more, Sir?"

I thanked him and said, No; but would he take no dinner himself?

"None, I am obliged to you, Sir."

"Is Mr. Steerforth coming from Oxford?"

"I beg your pardon, Sir?"

"Is Mr. Steerforth coming from Oxford?"

"I should imagine that he might be here to-morrow, Sir. I rather thought he might have been here to-day, Sir. The mistake is mine no doubt, Sir."

"If you should see him first——" said I.

"If you'll excuse me, Sir, I don't think I shall see him first."

"In case you do," said I, "pray say that I am sorry he was not here to-day, as an old schoolfellow of his was here."

"Indeed, Sir!" and he divided a bow between me and Traddles, with a glance at the latter.

He was moving softly to the door, when, in a forlorn hope of saying something naturally—which I never could, to this man—I said:

"Oh! Littimer!"

"Sir!"

"Did you remain long at Yarmouth, that time?"

"Not particularly so, Sir."

"You saw the boat completed?"

"Yes, Sir. I remained behind on purpose to see the boat completed."

"I know!" He raised his eyes to mine respectfully. "Mr. Steerforth has not seen it yet, I suppose?"

"I really can't say, Sir. I think—but I really can't say, Sir. I wish you good night, Sir."

He comprehended everybody present, in the respectful bow with which he followed these words, and disappeared. My visitors seemed to breathe more freely when he was gone; but my own relief was very great, for besides the constraint, arising from that extraordinary sense of being at a disadvantage which I always had in this man's presence, my conscience had embarrassed me with whispers that I had mistrusted his master, and I could not repress a vague uneasy dread that he might find it out. How was it, having so little in reality to conceal, that I always *did* feel as if this man were finding me out?

Mr. Micawber roused me from this reflection, which was blended with a certain remorseful apprehension of seeing Steerforth himself, by bestowing many encomiums on the absent Littimer as a most respectable fellow, and a thoroughly admirable servant. Mr. Micawber, I may remark, had taken his full share of the general bow, and had received it with infinite condescension.

"But punch, my dear Copperfield," said Mr. Micawber, tasting it, "like time and tide, waits for no man. Ah! it is at the present moment in high flavour. My love, will you give me your opinion?"

Mrs. Micawber pronounced it excellent.

"Then I will drink," said Mr. Micawber, "if my friend Copperfield will permit me to take that social liberty, to the days when my friend Copperfield and myself were younger, and fought our way in the world side by side. I may say, of myself and Copperfield, in words we have sung together before now, that

> 'We twa hae run about the braes
> And pu'd the gowans fine'

—in a figurative point of view—on several occasions. I am not exactly aware," said Mr. Micawber, with the old roll in his voice, and the old indescribable air of saying something genteel, "what gowans may be, but I have no doubt that Copperfield and myself would frequently have taken a pull at them, if it had been feasible."

Mr. Micawber, at the then present moment, took a pull at his punch. So we all did: Traddles evidently lost in wondering at what distant time Mr. Micawber and I could possibly have been comrades in the battle of the world.

"Ahem!" said Mr. Micawber, clearing his throat, and warming with the punch and with the fire. "My dear, another glass?"

Mrs. Micawber said it must be very little; but we couldn't allow that, so it was a glassful.

"As we are quite confidential here, Mr. Copperfield," said Mrs. Micawber, sipping her punch, "Mr. Traddles being a part of our domesticity, I should much like to have your opinion on Mr. Micawber's prospects. For corn," said Mrs. Micawber argumentatively, "as I have repeatedly said to Mr. Micawber, may be gentlemanly, but it is not remunerative. Commission to the extent of two and ninepence in a fortnight cannot, however limited our ideas, be considered remunerative."

We were all agreed upon that.

"Then," said Mrs. Micawber, who prided herself on taking a clear view of things, and keeping Mr. Micawber straight by her woman's wisdom, when he might otherwise go a little crooked, "then I ask myself this question. If corn is not to be relied upon, what is? Are coals to be relied upon? Not at all. We have turned our attention to that experiment, on the suggestion of my family, and we find it fallacious."

Mr. Micawber, leaning back in his chair with his hands in his pockets, eyed us aside, and nodded his head, as much as to say that the case was very clearly put.

"The articles of corn and coals," said Mrs. Micawber, still more argumentatively, "being equally out of the question, Mr. Copperfield, I naturally look round the world, and say, ' What is there in which a person of Mr. Micawber's talent is likely to succeed?' And I exclude the doing anything on commission, because commission is not a certainty. What is best suited to a person of Mr. Micawber's peculiar temperament is, I am convinced, a certainty."

Traddles and I both expressed, by a feeling murmur, that this great discovery was no doubt true of Mr. Micawber, and that it did him much credit.

"I will not conceal from you, my dear Mr. Copperfield," said Mrs. Micawber, "that *I* have long felt the brewing business to be particularly adapted to Mr. Micawber. Look at Barclay and Perkins! Look at Truman, Hanbury, and Buxton! It is on that extensive footing that Mr. Micawber, I know from my own knowledge of him, is calculated to shine; and the profits, I am told, are e-nor-mous! But if Mr. Micawber cannot get into those firms —which decline to answer his letters, when he offers his services even in an inferior capacity—what is the use of dwelling upon that idea? None. I may have a conviction that Mr. Micawber's manners——"

"Hem! Really, my dear," interposed Mr. Micawber.

"My love, be silent," said Mrs. Micawber, laying her brown glove on his hand. "I may have a conviction, Mr. Copperfield, that Mr. Micawber's manners peculiarly qualify him for the banking business. I may argue within myself, that if *I* had a deposit at a banking-house, the manners of Mr. Micawber, as representing that banking-house, would inspire confidence, and must extend the connexion. But if the various banking-houses refuse to avail themselves of Mr. Micawber's abilities, or receive the offer of them with contumely, what is the use of dwelling upon *that* idea? None. As to originating a banking business, I may know that there are members of my family who, if they chose to place their money in Mr. Micawber's hands, might found an establishment of that description. But if they do *not* choose to place their money in Mr. Micawber's hands— which they don't—what is the use of that? Again I contend that we are no farther advanced than we were before."

I shook my head, and said, "Not a bit." Traddles also shook his head, and said, "Not a bit."

"What do I deduce from this?" Mrs. Micawber went on to say, still with the same air of putting a case lucidly. "What is the conclusion, my dear Mr. Copperfield, to which I am irresistibly brought? Am I wrong in saying, it is clear that we must live?"

I answered, "Not at all!" and Traddles answered, "Not at all!" and I found myself afterwards sagely adding, alone, that a person must either live or die.

"Just so," returned Mrs. Micawber. "It is precisely that. And the fact is, my dear Mr. Copperfield, that we can *not* live without something widely different from existing circumstances shortly turning up. Now I am convinced, myself, and this I have pointed out to Mr. Micaw-

ber several times of late, that things cannot be expected to turn up of themselves. We must, in a measure, assist to turn them up. I may be wrong, but I have formed that opinion."

Both Traddles and I applauded it highly.

"Very well," said Mrs. Micawber. "Then what do I recommend? Here is Mr. Micawber with a variety of qualifications—with great talent——"

"Really, my love," said Mr. Micawber.

"Pray, my dear, allow me to conclude. Here is Mr. Micawber, with a variety of qualifications, with great talent—*I* should say, with genius, but that may be the partiality of a wife——"

Traddles and I both murmured "No."

"And here is Mr. Micawber without any suitable position or employment. Where does that responsibility rest? Clearly on society. Then I would make a fact so disgraceful known, and boldly challenge society to set it right. It appears to me, my dear Mr. Copperfield," said Mrs. Micawber, forcibly, "that what Mr. Micawber has to do, is to throw down the gauntlet to society, and say, in effect, ' Show me who will take that up. Let the party immediately step forward.'"

I ventured to ask Mrs. Micawber how this was to be done.

"By advertising," said Mrs. Micawber—"in all the papers. It appears to me, that what Mr. Micawber has to do, in justice to himself, in justice to his family, and I will even go so far as to say in justice to society, by which he has been hitherto overlooked, is to advertise in all the papers; to describe himself plainly as so-and-so, with such and such qualifications, and to put it thus: ' *Now* employ me, on remunerative terms, and address, post-paid, to W. M., Post Office, Camden Town.'"

"This idea of Mrs. Micawber's, my dear Copperfield," said Mr. Micawber, making his shirt-collar meet in front of his chin, and glancing at me sideways, "is, in fact, the Leap to which I alluded, when I last had the pleasure of seeing you."

"Advertising is rather expensive," I remarked, dubiously.

"Exactly so!" said Mrs. Micawber, preserving the same logical air. "Quite true, my dear Mr. Copperfield! I have made the identical observation to Mr. Micawber. It is for that reason especially, that I think Mr. Micawber ought (as I have already said, in justice to himself, in justice to his family, and in justice to society) to raise a certain sum of money—on a bill."

Mr. Micawber, leaning back in his chair, trifled with his eyeglass, and cast his eyes up at the ceiling; but I thought him observant of Traddles, too, who was looking at the fire.

"If no member of my family," said Mrs. Micawber, "is possessed of sufficient natural feeling to negotiate that bill —I believe there is a better business term to express what I mean——"

Mr. Micawber, with his eyes still cast up at the ceiling, suggested "Discount."

"To discount that bill," said Mrs. Micawber, "then my opinion is, that Mr. Micawber should go into the City, should take that bill into the Money Market, and should dispose of it for what he can get. If the individuals in the Money Market oblige Mr. Micawber to sustain a great sacrifice, that is between themselves and their consciences. I view it, steadily, as an investment. I recommend Mr. Micawber, my dear Mr. Copperfield, to do the same; to regard it as an investment which is sure of return, and to make up his mind to *any* sacrifice."

I felt, but I am sure I don't know why, that this was self-denying and devoted in Mrs. Micawber, and I uttered a murmur to that effect. Traddles, who took his tone from me, did likewise, still looking at the fire.

"I will not," said Mrs. Micawber, finishing her punch, and gathering her scarf about her shoulders, preparatory to her withdrawal to my bedroom: "I will not protract these remarks on the subject of Mr. Micawber's pecuniary affairs. At your fireside, my dear Mr. Copperfield, and in the presence of Mr. Traddles, who, though not so old a friend, is quite one of ourselves, I could not refrain from making you acquainted with the course *I* advise Mr. Micawber to take. I feel that the time is arrived when Mr. Micawber should exert himself and—I will add—assert himself, and it appears to me that these are the means. I am aware that I am merely a female, and that a masculine judgment is usually considered more competent to the discussion of such questions; still I must not forget that, when I lived at home with my papa and mama, my papa was in the habit of saying, 'Emma's form is fragile, but her grasp of a subject is inferior to none.' That my papa was too partial, I well know; but that he was an observer of character in some degree, my duty and my reason equally forbid me to doubt."

With these words, and resisting our entreaties that she would grace the remaining circulation of the punch with her presence, Mrs. Micawber retired to my bedroom. And really I felt that she was a noble woman—the sort of woman who might have been a Roman matron, and done all manner of heroic things, in times of public trouble.

In the fervour of this impression, I congratulated Mr. Micawber on the treasure he possessed. So did Traddles. Mr. Micawber extended his hand to each of us in succession, and then covered his face with his pocket-handkerchief, which I think had more snuff upon it than he was aware of. He then returned to the punch, in the highest state of exhilaration.

He was full of eloquence. He gave us to understand that in our children we lived again, and that, under the pressure of pecuniary difficulties, any accession to their number was doubly welcome. He said that Mrs. Micawber had latterly had her doubts on this point, but that he had dispelled them, and reassured her. As to her family, they were totally unworthy of her, and their sentiments were utterly indifferent to him, and they might—I quote his own expression—go to the Devil.

Mr. Micawber then delivered a warm eulogy on Traddles. He said Traddles's was a character, to the steady virtues of which he (Mr. Micawber) could lay no claim, but which, he thanked Heaven, he could admire. He feelingly alluded to the young lady, unknown, whom Traddles had honoured with his affection, and who had reciprocated that affection by honouring and blessing Traddles with *her* affection. Mr. Micawber pledged her. So did I. Traddles thanked us both, by saying, with a simplicity and honesty I had sense enough to be quite charmed with, "I am very much obliged to you indeed. And I do assure you, she's the dearest girl!——"

Mr. Micawber took an early opportunity, after that, of hinting, with the utmost delicacy and ceremony, at the state of *my* affections. Nothing but the serious assurance of his friend Copperfield to the contrary, he observed, could deprive him of the impression that his friend Copperfield loved and was beloved. After feeling very hot and uncomfortable for some time, and after a good deal of blushing, stammering, and denying, I said, having my glass in my hand, "Well! I would give them D.!" which so excited and gratified Mr. Micawber, that he ran with a glass of punch into my bedroom, in order that Mrs. Micawber might drink D., who drank it with enthusiasm, crying from within, in a shrill voice, "Hear, hear! My dear Mr. Copperfield, I am delighted. Hear!" and tapping at the wall, by way of applause.

Our conversation, afterwards, took a more worldly turn; Mr. Micawber telling us that he found Camden Town inconvenient, and that the first thing he contemplated doing, when the advertisement should have been the cause of something satisfactory turning up, was to move. He mentioned a terrace at the western end of Oxford Street, fronting Hyde Park, on which he had always had his eye, but which he did not expect to attain immediately, as it would require a large establishment. There would probably be an interval, he explained, in which he should content himself with the upper part of a house, over some respectable place of business—say in Piccadilly,—which would be a cheerful situation for Mrs. Micawber; and where, by throwing out a bow window, or carrying up the roof another story, or making some little alteration of that sort, they might live, comfortably and reputably, for a few years. Whatever was reserved for him, he expressly said, or wherever his abode might be, we might rely on this—there would always be a room for Traddles, and a knife and fork for me. We acknowledged his kindness; and he begged us to forgive his having launched into these practical and business-like details, and to excuse it as natural in one who was making entirely new arrangements in life.

Mrs. Micawber, tapping at the wall again, to know if tea were ready, broke up this particular phase of our friendly conversation. She made tea for us in a most agreeable manner; and, whenever I went near her, in handing about the teacups and bread-and-butter, asked me, in a whisper, whether D. was fair, or dark, or whether she was short, or tall: or something of that kind; which I think I liked. After tea, we discussed a variety of topics before the fire; and Mrs. Micawber was good enough to sing us (in a small, thin, flat voice, which I remembered to have considered, when I first knew her, the very table-beer of acoustics) the favourite ballads of "The Dashing White Serjeant," and "Little Tafflin." For both of these songs Mrs. Micawber had been famous when she lived at home with her papa and mama. Mr. Micawber told us, that when he heard her sing the first one, on the first occasion of his seeing her beneath the parental roof, she had attracted his attention in an extraordinary degree; but that when it came to Little Tafflin, he had resolved to win that woman or perish in the attempt.

It was between ten and eleven o'clock when Mrs. Micawber rose to replace her cap in the whity-brown paper parcel, and to put on her bonnet. Mr. Micawber took the opportunity of Traddles putting on his great-coat, to slip a letter into my hand, with a whispered request that I would read it at my leisure. I also took the opportunity of my holding a candle over the banisters to light them down, when Mr. Micawber was going first, leading Mrs. Micawber, and Traddles was following with the cap, to detain Traddles for a moment on the top of the stairs.

"Traddles," said I, "Mr. Micawber don't mean any

harm, poor fellow; but, if I were you, I wouldn't lend him anything."

"My dear Copperfield," returned Traddles, smiling, "I haven't got anything to lend."

"You have got a name, you know," said I.

"Oh! You call *that* something to lend?" returned Traddles, with a thoughtful look.

"Certainly."

"Oh!" said Traddles. "Yes, to be sure! I am very much obliged to you, Copperfield; but—I am afraid I have lent him that already."

"For the bill that is to be a certain investment?" I inquired.

"No," said Traddles. "Not for that one. This is the first I have heard of that one. I have been thinking that he will most likely propose that one, on the way home. Mine's another."

"I hope there will be nothing wrong about it," said I.

"I hope not," said Traddles. "I should think not, though, because he told me, only the other day, that it was provided for. That was Mr. Micawber's expression. 'Provided for.'"

Mr. Micawber looking up at this juncture to where we were standing, I had only time to repeat my caution. Traddles thanked me, and descended. But I was much afraid, when I observed the good-natured manner in which he went down with the cap in his hand, and gave Mrs. Micawber his arm, that he would be carried into the Money Market neck and heels.

I returned to my fireside, and was musing, half gravely and half laughing, on the character of Mr. Micawber and the old relations between us, when I heard a quick step ascending the stairs. At first, I thought it was Traddles coming back for something Mrs. Micawber had left behind; but as the step approached, I knew it, and felt my heart beat high, and the blood rush to my face, for it was Steerforth's.

I was never unmindful of Agnes, and she never left that sanctuary in my thoughts—if I may call it so—where I had placed her from the first. But when he entered, and stood before me with his hand out, the darkness that had fallen on him changed to light, and I felt confounded and ashamed of having doubted one I loved so heartily. I loved her none the less; I thought of her as the same benignant, gentle angel in my life; I reproached myself, not her, with having done him an injury; and I would have made him any atonement, if I had known what to make, and how to make it.

"Why, Daisy, old boy, dumbfoundered!" laughed Steerforth, shaking my hand heartily, and throwing it gaily away. "Have I detected you in another feast, you Sybarite! These Doctors' Commons fellows are the gayest men in town, I believe, and beat us sober Oxford people all to nothing!" His bright glance went merrily round the room, as he took the seat on the sofa opposite to me, which Mrs. Micawber had recently vacated, and stirred the fire into a blaze.

"I was so surprised at first," said I, giving him welcome with all the cordiality I felt, "that I had hardly breath to greet you with, Steerforth."

"Well, the sight of me *is* good for sore eyes, as the Scotch say," replied Steerforth, "and so is the sight of you, Daisy, in full bloom. How are you, my Bacchanal?"

"I am very well," said I; "and not at all Bacchanalian to-night, though I confess to another party of three."

"All of whom I met in the street, talking loud in your praise," returned Steerforth. "Who's our friend in the tights?"

I gave him the best idea I could, in a few words, of Mr. Micawber. He laughed heartily at my feeble portrait of that gentleman, and said he was a man to know, and he must know him.

"But who do you suppose our other friend is?" said I, in my turn.

"Heaven knows," said Steerforth. "Not a bore, I hope? I thought he looked a little like one."

"Traddles!" I replied, triumphantly.

"Who's he?" asked Steerforth, in his careless way.

"Don't you remember Traddles? Traddles in our room at Salem House?"

"Oh! That fellow!" said Steerforth, beating a lump of coal on the top of the fire, with the poker. "Is he as soft as ever? And where the deuce did you pick *him* up?"

I extolled Traddles in reply, as highly as I could; for I felt that Steerforth rather slighted him. Steerforth, dismissing the subject with a light nod, and a smile, and the remark that he would be glad to see the old fellow too, for he had always been an odd fish, inquired if I could give him anything to eat? During most of this short dialogue, when he had not been speaking in a wild vivacious manner, he had sat idly beating on the lump of coal with the poker. I observed that he did the same thing while I was getting out the remains of the pigeon-pie, and so forth.

"Why, Daisy, here's a supper for a king!" he exclaimed, starting out of his silence with a burst, and taking his seat at the table. "I shall do it justice, for I have come from Yarmouth."

"I thought you came from Oxford?" I returned.

"Not I," said Steerforth. "I have been seafaring—better employed."

"Littimer was here to-day, to inquire for you," I remarked, "and I understood him that you were at Oxford; though, now I think of it, he certainly did not say so."

"Littimer is a greater fool than I thought him, to have been inquiring for me at all," said Steerforth, jovially pouring out a glass of wine, and drinking to me. "As to understanding him, you are a cleverer fellow than most of us, Daisy, if you can do that."

"That's true, indeed," said I, moving my chair to the table. "So you have been at Yarmouth, Steerforth!" interested to know all about it. "Have you been there long?"

"No," he returned. "An *escapade* of a week or so."

"And how are they all? Of course, little Emily is not married yet?"

"Not yet. Going to be, I believe—in so many weeks, or months, or something or other. I have not seen much of 'em. By-the-by;" he laid down his knife and fork, which he had been using with great diligence, and began feeling in his pockets; "I have a letter for you."

"From whom?"

"Why, from your old nurse," he returned, taking some papers out of his breast-pocket. "'J. Steerforth, Esquire, debtor, to the Willing Mind;' that's not it. Patience, and we'll find it presently. Old what's-his-name's in a bad way, and it's about that, I believe."

"Barkis, do you mean?"

"Yes!" still feeling in his pockets, and looking over

their contents: "it's all over with poor Barkis, I am afraid I saw a little apothecary there—surgeon, or whatever he is —who brought your worship into the world. He was mighty learned about the case, to me; but the upshot of his opinion was, that the carrier was making his last journey rather fast.—Put your hand into the breast-pocket of my great-coat on the chair yonder, and I think you'll find the letter. Is it there?"

"Here it is!" said I.

"That's right!"

It was from Peggotty; something less legible than usual, and brief. It informed me of her husband's hopeless state, and hinted at his being "a little nearer" than heretofore, and consequently more difficult to manage for his own comfort. It said nothing of her weariness and watching, and praised him highly. It was written with a plain, unaffected, homely piety that I knew to be genuine, and ended with "my duty to my ever darling"—meaning myself.

While I deciphered it, Steerforth continued to eat and drink.

"It's a bad job," he said, when I had done; "but the sun sets every day, and people die every minute, and we mustn't be scared by the common lot. If we failed to hold our own, because that equal foot at all men's doors was heard knocking somewhere, every object in this world would slip from us. No! Ride on! Rough-shod if need be, smooth-shod if that will do, but ride on! Ride on over all obstacles, and win the race!"

"And win what race?" said I.

"The race that one has started in," said he. "Ride on!"

I noticed, I remember, as he paused, looking at me with his handsome head a little thrown back, and his glass raised in his hand, that, though the freshness of the sea-wind was on his face, and it was ruddy, there were traces in it, made since I last saw it, as if he had applied himself to some habitual strain of the fervent energy which, when roused, was so passionately roused within him. I had it in my thoughts to remonstrate with him upon his desperate way of pursuing any fancy that he took—such as this buffeting of rough seas, and braving of hard weather, for example—when my mind glanced off to the immediate subject of our conversation again, and pursued that instead.

"I tell you what, Steerforth," said I, "if your high spirits will listen to me——"

"They are potent spirits, and will do whatever you like," he answered, moving from the table to the fireside again.

"Then I tell you what, Steerforth. I think I will go down and see my old nurse. It is not that I can do her any good, or render her any real service; but she is so attached to me that my visit will have as much effect on her, as if I could do both. She will take it so kindly, that it will be a comfort and support to her. It is no great effort to make, I am sure, for such a friend as she has been to me. Wouldn't you go a day's journey, if you were in my place?"

His face was thoughtful, and he sat considering a little before he answered, in a low voice, "Well! Go. You can do no harm."

"You have just come back," said I, "and it would be in vain to ask you to go with me?"

"Quite," he returned. "I am for Highgate to-night. I have not seen my mother this long time, and it lies upon my conscience, for it's something to be loved as she loves her prodigal son.—Bah! Nonsense!—You mean to go to-morrow, I suppose?" he said, holding me out at arm's length, with a hand on each of my shoulders.

"Yes, I think so."

"Well, then, don't go till next day. I wanted you to come and stay a few days with us. Here I am, on purpose to bid you, and you fly off to Yarmouth!"

"You are a nice fellow to talk of flying off, Steerforth, who are always running wild on some unknown expedition or other!"

He looked at me for a moment without speaking, and then rejoined, still holding me as before, and giving me a shake:

"Come! Say the next day, and pass as much of to-morrow as you can with us! Who knows when we may meet again, else? Come! Say the next day! I want you to stand between Rosa Dartle and me, and keep us asunder."

"Would you love each other too much, without me?"

"Yes; or hate," laughed Steerforth; "no matter which. Come! Say the next day!"

I said the next day; and he put on his great-coat, and lighted his cigar, and set off to walk home. Finding him in this intention, I put on my own great-coat (but did not light my own cigar, having had enough of that for one while) and walked with him as far as the open road; a dull road, then, at night. He was in great spirits all the way; and when we parted, and I looked after him going so gallantly and airily homeward, I thought of his saying, "Ride on over all obstacles, and win the race!" and wished, for the first time, that he had some worthy race to run.

I was undressing in my own room, when Mr. Micawber's letter tumbled on the floor. Thus reminded of it, I broke the seal and read as follows. It was dated an hour and a half before dinner. I am not sure whether I have mentioned that, when Mr. Micawber was at any particularly desperate crisis, he used a sort of legal phraseology: which he seemed to think equivalent to winding up his affairs.

"Sir—for I dare not say, my dear Copperfield,

"It is expedient that I should inform you that the undersigned is Crushed. Some flickering efforts to spare you the premature knowledge of his calamitous position, you may observe in him this day; but hope has sunk beneath the horizon, and the undersigned is Crushed.

"The present communication is penned within the personal range (I cannot call it the society) of an individual, in a state closely bordering on intoxication, employed by a broker. That individual is in legal possession of the premises, under a distress for rent. His inventory includes, not only the chattels and effects of every description belonging to the undersigned, as yearly tenant of this habitation, but also those appertaining to Mr. Thomas Traddles, lodger, a member of the Honourable Society of the Inner Temple.

"If any drop of gloom were wanting in the overflowing cup, which is now 'commended' (in the language of an immortal Writer) to the lips of the undersigned, it would be found in the fact, that a friendly acceptance granted to the undersigned, by the before-mentioned Mr. Thomas Traddles, for the sum of £23 4s. 9½d. is overdue, and is NOT provided for. Also, in the fact, that the living responsibilities clinging to the undersigned, will, in the course of nature, be increased by the sum of one more helpless victim; whose miserable appearance may be looked for—in round numbers—at the expiration of a period not exceeding six lunar months from the present date.

"After premising thus much, it would be a work of

supererogation to add, that dust and ashes are for ever scattered

"On
"The
"Head
"Of
"WILKINS MICAWBER."

Poor Traddles! I knew enough of Mr. Micawber by this time, to foresee that *he* might be expected to recover the blow; but my night's rest was sorely distressed by thoughts of Traddles, and of the curate's daughter, who was one of ten, down in Devonshire, and who was such a dear girl, and who would wait for Traddles (ominous praise!) until she was sixty, or any age that could be mentioned.

CHAPTER XXIX.

I VISIT STEERFORTH AT HIS HOME, AGAIN.

I MENTIONED to Mr. Spenlow in the morning, that I wanted leave of absence for a short time; and as I was not in the receipt of any salary, and consequently was not obnoxious to the implacable Jorkins, there was no difficulty about it. I took that opportunity, with my voice sticking in my throat, and my sight failing as I uttered the words, to express my hope that Miss Spenlow was quite well; to which Mr. Spenlow replied, with no more emotion than if he had been speaking of an ordinary human being, that he was much obliged to me, and she was very well.

We articled clerks, as germs of the patrician order of proctors, were treated with so much consideration, that I was almost my own master at all times. As I did not care, however, to get to Highgate before one or two o'clock in the day, and as we had another little excommunication case in court that morning, which was called The office of the Judge promoted by Tipkins against Bullock for his soul's correction, I passed an hour or two in attendance on it with Mr. Spenlow very agreeably. It arose out of a scuffle between two churchwardens, one of whom was alleged to have pushed the other against a pump; the handle of which pump projecting into a school-house, which school-house was under a gable of the church-roof, made the push an ecclesiastical offence. It was an amusing case; and sent me up to Highgate, on the box of the stage-coach, thinking about the Commons, and what Mr. Spenlow had said about touching the Commons and bringing down the country.

Mrs. Steerforth was pleased to see me, and so was Rosa Dartle. I was agreeably surprised to find that Littimer was not there, and that we were attended by a modest little parlour-maid, with blue ribbons in her cap, whose eye it was much more pleasant, and much less disconcerting, to catch by accident, than the eye of that respectable man. But what I particularly observed, before I had been half-an-hour in the house, was the close and attentive watch Miss Dartle kept upon me; and the lurking manner in which she seemed to compare my face with Steerforth's, and Steerforth's with mine, and to lie in wait for something to come out between the two. So surely as I looked towards her, did I see that eager visage, with its gaunt black eyes and searching brow, intent on mine; or passing suddenly from mine to Steerforth's; or comprehending both of us at once. In this lynx-like scrutiny she was so far from faltering when she saw I observed it, that at such a time she only fixed her piercing look upon me with a more intent expression still. Blameless as I was, and knew that I was, in reference to any wrong she could possibly suspect me of, I shrank before her strange eyes, quite unable to endure their hungry lustre.

All day, she seemed to pervade the whole house. If I talked to Steerforth in his room, I heard her dress rustle in the little gallery outside. When he and I engaged in some of our old exercises on the lawn behind the house, I saw her face pass from window to window, like a wandering light, until it fixed itself in one, and watched us. When we all four went out walking in the afternoon, she closed her thin hand on my arm like a spring, to keep me back, while Steerforth and his mother went on out of hearing: and then spoke to me.

"You have been a long time," she said, "without coming here. Is your profession really so engaging and interesting as to absorb your whole attention? I ask because I always want to be informed, when I am ignorant. Is it really, though?"

I replied that I liked it well enough, but that I certainly could not claim so much for it.

"Oh! I am glad to know that, because I always like to be put right when I am wrong," said Rosa Dartle. "You mean it is a little dry, perhaps?"

Well, I replied; perhaps it *was* a little dry.

"Oh! and that's a reason why you want relief and change—excitement, and all that?" said she. "Ah! very true! But isn't it a little——Eh?—for him; I don't mean you?"

A quick glance of her eye towards the spot where Steerforth was walking, with his mother leaning on his arm, showed me whom she meant; but beyond that, I was quite lost. And I looked so, I have no doubt.

"Don't it—I don't say that it *does*, mind, I want to know —don't it rather engross him? Don't it make him, perhaps, a little more remiss than usual in his visits to his blindly-doting—eh?" With another quick glance at them, and such a glance at me as seemed to look into my innermost thoughts.

"Miss Dartle," I returned, "pray do not think——"

"I don't!" she said. "Oh dear me, don't suppose that I think anything! I am not suspicious. I only ask a question. I don't state any opinion. I want to found an opinion on what you tell me. Then, it's not so? Well! I am very glad to know it."

"It certainly is not the fact," said I, perplexed, "that I am accountable for Steerforth's having been away from home longer than usual—if he has been: which I really don't know at this moment, unless I understand it from you. I have not seen him this long while, until last night."

"No?"

"Indeed, Miss Dartle, no!"

As she looked full at me, I saw her face grow sharper and paler, and the marks of the old wound lengthen out until it cut through the disfigured lip, and deep into the nether lip, and slanted down the face. There was something positively awful to me in this, and in the brightness of her eyes, as she said, looking fixedly at me:

"What is he doing?"

I repeated the words, more to myself than her, being so amazed.

"What is he doing?" she said, with an eagerness that seemed enough to consume her like a fire. "In what is that man assisting him, who never looks at me without an inscrutable falsehood in his eyes? If you are honourable and faithful, I don't ask you to betray your friend. I ask you only to tell me, is it anger, is it hatred, is it pride, is it restlessness, is it some wild fancy, is it love, *what is it*, that is leading him?"

"Miss Dartle," I returned, "how shall I tell you, so that you will believe me, that I know of nothing in Steerforth different from what there was when I first came here? I can think of nothing. I hardly understand, even, what you mean."

As she still looked fixedly at me, a twitching or throbbing, from which I could not dissociate the idea of pain, came into that cruel mark; and lifted up the corner of her lip as if with scorn, or with a pity that despised its object. She put her hand upon it hurriedly—a hand so thin and delicate, that when I had seen her hold it up before the fire to shade her face, I had compared it in my thoughts to fine porcelain—and saying, in a quick, fierce, passionate way, "I swear you to secrecy about this!" said not a word more.

Mrs. Steerforth was particularly happy in her son's society, and Steerforth was, on this occasion, particularly attentive and respectful to her. It was very interesting to me to see them together, not only on account of their mutual affection, but because of the strong personal resemblance between them, and the manner in which what was haughty or impetuous in him was softened by age and sex, in her, to a gracious dignity. I thought, more than once, that it was well no serious cause of division had ever come between them; or two such natures—I ought rather to express it, two such shades of the same nature—might have been harder to reconcile than the two extremest opposites in creation. The idea did not originate in my own discernment, I am bound to confess, but in a speech of Rosa Dartle's.

She said at dinner:

"Oh, but do tell me, though, somebody, because I have been thinking about it all day, and I want to know."

"You want to know what, Rosa?" returned Mrs. Steerforth. "Pray, pray, Rosa, do not be mysterious."

"Mysterious!" she cried. "Oh! really? Do you consider me so?"

"Do I constantly entreat you," said Mrs. Steerforth, "to speak plainly, in your own natural manner?"

"Oh! then, this is *not* my natural manner?" she rejoined. "Now you must really bear with me, because I ask for information. We never know ourselves."

"It has become a second nature," said Mrs. Steerforth, without any displeasure; "but I remember,—and so must you, I think,—when your manner was different, Rosa; when it was not so guarded, and was more trustful."

"I am sure you are right," she returned; "and so it is that bad habits grow upon one! Really? Less guarded and more trustful? How *can* I, imperceptibly, have changed, I wonder! Well, that's very odd! I must study to regain my former self."

"I wish you would," said Mrs. Steerforth, with a smile.

"Oh! I really will, you know!" she answered. "I will learn frankness from—let me see—from James."

"You cannot learn frankness, Rosa," said Mrs. Steerforth, quickly—for there was always some effect of sarcasm in what Rosa Dartle said, though it was said, as this was, in the most unconscious manner in the world—"in a better school."

"That I am sure of," she answered, with uncommon fervour. "If I am sure of anything, of course, you know, I am sure of that."

Mrs. Steerforth appeared to me to regret having been a little nettled; for she presently said, in a kind tone:

"Well, my dear Rosa, we have not heard what it is that you want to be satisfied about?"

"That I want to be satisfied about?" she replied, with provoking coldness. "Oh! it was only whether people, who are like each other in their moral constitution—is that the phrase?"

"It's as good a phrase as another," said Steerforth.

"Thank you:—whether people, who are like each other in their moral constitution, are in greater danger than people not so circumstanced, supposing any serious cause of variance to arise between them, of being divided angrily and deeply?"

"I should say yes," said Steerforth.

"Should you?" she retorted. "Dear me! Supposing then, for instance—any unlikely thing will do for a supposition—that you and your mother were to have a serious quarrel."

"My dear Rosa," interposed Mrs. Steerforth, laughing good-naturedly, "suggest some other supposition! James and I know our duty to each other better, I pray Heaven!"

"Oh!" said Miss Dartle, nodding her head thoughtfully. "To be sure. *That* would prevent it? Why, of course it would. Ex-actly. Now, I am glad I have been so foolish as to put the case, for it is so very good to know that your duty to each other would prevent it! Thank you very much."

One other little circumstance connected with Miss Dartle I must not omit; for I had reason to remember it thereafter, when all the irremediable past was rendered plain. During the whole of this day, but especially from this period of it, Steerforth exerted himself with his utmost skill, and that was with his utmost ease, to charm this singular creature into a pleasant and pleased companion. That he should succeed, was no matter of surprise to me. That she should struggle against the fascinating influence of his delightful art—delightful nature I thought it then—did not surprise me either; for I knew that she was sometimes jaundiced and perverse. I saw her features and her manner slowly change; I saw her look at him with growing admiration; I saw her try, more and more faintly, but always angrily, as if she condemned a weakness in herself, to resist the captivating power that he possessed; and finally, I saw her sharp glance soften, and her smile become quite gentle, and I ceased to be afraid of her as I had really been all day, and we all sat about the fire, talking and laughing together, with as little reserve as if we had been children.

Whether it was because we had sat there so long, or because Steerforth was resolved not to lose the advantage he had gained, I do not know; but we did not remain in the dining-room more than five minutes after her departure. "She is playing her harp," said Steerforth, softly, at the drawing-room door, "and nobody but my mother has heard her do that, I believe, these three years." He said it with a curious smile, which was gone directly; and we went into the room and found her alone.

"Don't get up!" said Steerforth (which she had already done); "my dear Rosa, don't! Be kind for once, and sing us an Irish song."

"What do you care for an Irish song?" she returned.

"Much!" said Steerforth. "Much more than for any other. Here is Daisy, too, loves music from his soul. Sing us an Irish song, Rosa! and let me sit and listen as I used to do."

He did not touch her, or the chair from which she had risen, but sat himself near the harp. She stood beside it for some little while, in a curious way, going through the motion of playing it with her right hand, but not sounding it. At length she sat down, and drew it to her with one sudden action, and played and sang.

I don't know what it was, in her touch or voice, that made that song the most unearthly I have ever heard in my life, or can imagine. There was something fearful in the reality of it. It was as if it had never been written, or set to music, but sprung out of the passion within her; which found imperfect utterance in the low sounds of her voice, and crouched again when all was still. I was dumb when she leaned beside the harp again, playing it, but not sounding it, with her right hand.

A minute more, and this had roused me from my trance: —Steerforth had left his seat, and gone to her, and had put his arm laughingly about her, and had said, "Come, Rosa, for the future we will love each other very much!" And she had struck him, and had thrown him off with the fury of a wild cat, and had burst out of the room.

"What is the matter with Rosa?" said Mrs. Steerforth, coming in.

"She has been an angel, mother," returned Steerforth, "for a little while; and has run into the opposite extreme, since, by way of compensation."

"You should be careful not to irritate her, James. Her temper has been soured, remember, and ought not to be tried."

Rosa did not come back; and no other mention was made of her, until I went with Steerforth into his room to say Good-night. Then he laughed about her, and asked me if I had ever seen such a fierce little piece of incomprehensibility.

I expressed as much of my astonishment as was then capable of expression, and asked if he could guess what it was that she had taken so much amiss, so suddenly.

"Oh, Heaven knows," said Steerforth. "Anything you like—or nothing! I told you she took everything, herself included, to a grindstone, and sharpened it. She is an edge-tool, and requires great care in dealing with. She is always dangerous. Good night!"

"Good night!" said I, "my dear Steerforth! I shall be gone before you wake in the morning. Good night!"

He was unwilling to let me go; and stood, holding me out, with a hand on each of my shoulders, as he had done in my own room.

"Daisy," he said, with a smile—"for though that's not the name your godfathers and godmothers gave you, it's the name I like best to call you by—and I wish, I wish, I wish, you could give it to me!"

"Why, so I can, if I choose," said I.

"Daisy, if anything should ever separate us, you must think of me at my best, old boy. Come! Let us make that bargain. Think of me at my best, if circumstances should ever part us!"

"You have no best to me, Steerforth," said I, "and no worst. You are always equally loved, and cherished in my heart."

So much compunction for having ever wronged him, even by a shapeless thought, did I feel within me, that the confession of having done so was rising to my lips. But for the reluctance I had, to betray the confidence of Agnes, but for my uncertainty how to approach the subject with no risk of doing so, it would have reached them before he said, "God bless you, Daisy, and good night!" In my doubt, it did *not* reach them; and we shook hands, and we parted.

I was up with the dull dawn, and, having dressed as quietly as I could, looked into his room. He was fast asleep; lying, easily, with his head upon his arm, as I had often seen him lie at school.

The time came in its season, and that was very soon, when I almost wondered that nothing troubled his repose, as I looked at him.

But he slept—let me think of him so again—as I had often seen him sleep at school; and thus, in this silent hour, I left him.

—Never more, oh God forgive you, Steerforth! to touch that passive hand in love and friendship. Never, never more!

CHAPTER XXX.

A LOSS.

I GOT down to Yarmouth in the evening, and went to the inn. I knew that Peggotty's spare room—my room—was likely to have occupation enough in a little while, if that great Visitor, before whose presence all the living must give place, were not already in the house; so I betook myself to the inn, and dined there, and engaged my bed.

It was ten o'clock when I went out. Many of the shops were shut, and the town was dull. When I came to Omer and Joram's, I found the shutters up, but the shop-door standing open. As I could obtain a perspective view of Mr. Omer inside, smoking his pipe by the parlour-door, I entered, and asked him how he was.

"Why, bless my life and soul!" said Mr. Omer, "how do you find yourself? Take a seat.—Smoke not disagreeable, I hope?"

"By no means," said I. "I like it—in somebody else's pipe."

"What, not in your own, eh?" Mr. Omer returned, laughing. "All the better, Sir. Bad habit for a young man. Take a seat. I smoke, myself, for the asthma."

Mr. Omer had made room for me, and placed a chair. He now sat down again, very much out of breath, gasping at his pipe as if it contained a supply of that necessary, without which he must perish.

"I am sorry to have heard bad news of Mr. Barkis," said I.

Mr. Omer looked at me, with a steady countenance, and shook his head.

"Do you know how he is to-night?" I asked.

"The very question I should have put to you, Sir," returned Mr. Omer, "but on account of delicacy. It's one of the drawbacks of our line of business. When a party's ill, we *can't* ask how the party is."

The difficulty had not occurred to me; though I had had my apprehensions too, when I went in, of hearing the old tune. On its being mentioned, I recognised it, however, and said as much.

"Yes, yes, you understand," said Mr. Omer, nodding his head. "We durs'n't do it. Bless you, it would be a shock that the generality of parties mightn't recover, to say ' Omer and Joram's compliments, and how do you find yourself this morning?'—or this afternoon—as it may be."

Mr. Omer and I nodded at each other, and Mr. Omer recruited his wind by the aid of his pipe.

"It's one of the things that cut the trade off from attentions they could often wish to show," said Mr. Omer. "Take myself. If I have known Barkis a year, to move to as he went by, I have known him forty year. But _I_ can't go and say, ' How is he?'"

I felt it was rather hard on Mr. Omer, and I told him so.

"I'm not more self-interested, I hope, than another man," said Mr. Omer. "Look at me! My wind may fail me at any moment, and it ain't likely that, to my own knowledge, I'd be self-interested under such circumstances. I say it ain't likely, in a man who knows his wind will go, when it _does_ go, as if a pair of bellows was cut open; and that man a grandfather," said Mr. Omer.

I said, "Not at all."

"It ain't that I complain of my line of business," said Mr. Omer. "It ain't that. Some good and some bad goes, no doubt, to all callings. What I wish is, that parties was brought up stronger-minded."

Mr. Omer, with a very complacent and amiable face, took several puffs in silence; and then said, resuming his first point:

"Accordingly we're obleeged, in ascertaining how Barkis goes on, to limit ourselves to Em'ly. She knows what our real objects are, and she don't have any more alarms or suspicions about us, than if we was so many lambs. Minnie and Joram have just stepped down to the house, in fact (she's there, after hours, helping her aunt a bit), to ask her how he is to-night; and if you was to please to wait till they come back, they'd give you full particulars. Will you take something? A glass of srub and water, now? I smoke on srub and water, myself," said Mr. Omer, taking up his glass, "because it's considered softening to the passages, by which this troublesome breath of mine gets into action. But, Lord bless you," said Mr. Omer, huskily, "it ain't the passages that's out of order! ' Give me breath enough,' says I to my daughter Minnie, 'and _I'll_ find passages, my dear.'"

He really had no breath to spare, and it was very alarming to see him laugh. When he was again in a condition to be talked to, I thanked him for the proffered refreshment, which I declined, as I had just had dinner; and, observing that I would wait, since he was so good as to invite me, until his daughter and his son-in-law came back, I inquired how little Emily was?

"Well, Sir," said Mr. Omer, removing his pipe, that he might rub his chin; "I tell you truly, I shall be glad when her marriage has taken place."

"Why so?" I inquired.

"Well, she's unsettled at present," said Mr. Omer. "It aint that she's not as pretty as ever, for she's prettier—I do assure you, she is prettier. It ain't that she don't work as well as ever, for she does. She _was_ worth any six, and she _is_ worth any six. But somehow she wants heart. If you understand," said Mr. Omer, after rubbing his chin again, and smoking a little, "what I mean in a general way by the expression, 'A long pull, and a strong pull, and

a pull altogether, my hearties, hurrah!' I should say to you, that _that_ was—in a general way—what I miss in Emily."

Mr. Omer's face and manner went for so much, that I could conscientiously nod my head, as divining his meaning. My quickness of apprehension seemed to please him, and he went on:

"Now, I consider this is principally on account of her being in an unsettled state, you see. We have talked it over a good deal, her uncle and myself, and her sweetheart and myself, after business; and I consider it is principally on account of her being unsettled. You must always recollect of Em'ly," said Mr. Omer, shaking his head gently, "that she's a most extraordinary affectionate little thing. The proverb says, ' You can't make a silk purse out of a sow's ear.' Well, I don't know about that. I rather think you may, if you begin early in life. She has made a home out of that old boat, Sir, that stone and marble couldn't beat."

"I am sure she has!" said I.

"To see the clinging of that pretty little thing to her uncle," said Mr. Omer; "to see the way she holds on to him, tighter and tighter, and closer and closer, every day, is to see a sight. Now, you know, there's a struggle going on when that's the case. Why should it be made a longer one than is needful?"

I listened attentively to the good old fellow, and acquiesced, with all my heart, in what he said.

"Therefore, I mentioned to them," said Mr. Omer, in a comfortable, easy-going tone, "this. I say, ' Now, don't consider Em'ly nailed down in point of time, at all. Make it your own time. Her services have been more valuable than was supposed; her learning has been quicker than was supposed; Omer and Joram can run their pen through what remains; and she's free when you wish. If she likes to make any little arrangement, afterwards, in the way of doing any little thing for us at home, very well. If she don't, very well still. We're no losers, anyhow.' For—don't you see," said Mr. Omer, touching me with his pipe, "it ain't likely that a man so short of breath as myself, and a grandfather too, would go and strain points with a little bit of a blue-eyed blossom, like _her_?"

"Not at all, I am certain," said I.

"Not at all! You're right!" said Mr. Omer. "Well, Sir, her cousin—you know it's a cousin she's going to be married to?"

"Oh yes," I replied. "I know him well."

"Of course you do," said Mr. Omer. "Well, Sir! Her cousin being, as it appears, in good work, and well to do, thanked me in a very manly sort of manner for this (conducting himself altogether, I must say, in a way that gives me a high opinion of him), and went and took as comfortable a little house as you or I could wish to clap eyes on. That little house is now furnished, right through, as neat and complete as a doll's parlour; and but for Barkis's illness having taken this bad turn, poor fellow, they would have been man and wife—I dare say, by this time. As it is, there's a postponement."

"And Emily, Mr. Omer?" I inquired. "Has she become more settled?"

"Why that, you know," he returned, rubbing his double-chin again, "can't naturally be expected. The prospect of the change and separation, and all that, is, as one may say, close to her and far away from her, both at once. Barkis's death needn't put it off much, but his lingering might. Anyway, it's an uncertain state of matters, you see."

"I see," said I.

"Consequently," pursued Mr. Omer, "Em'ly's still a little down and a little fluttered; perhaps, upon the whole, she's more so than she was. Every day she seems to get fonder and fonder of her uncle, and more loth to part from all of us. A kind word from me brings the tears into her eyes; and if you was to see her with my daughter Minnie's little girl, you'd never forget it. Bless my heart alive!" said Mr. Omer, pondering, "how she loves that child!"

Having so favourable an opportunity, it occurred to me to ask Mr. Omer, before our conversation should be interrupted by the return of his daughter and her husband, whether he knew anything of Martha.

"Ah!" he rejoined, shaking his head, and looking very much dejected. "No good. A sad story, Sir, however you come to know it. I never thought there was any harm in the girl. I wouldn't wish to mention it before my daughter Minnie—for she'd take me up directly—but I never did. None of us ever did."

Mr. Omer, hearing his daughter's footstep before I heard it, touched me with his pipe, and shut up one eye, as a caution. She and her husband came in immediately afterwards.

Their report was, that Mr. Barkis was "as bad as bad could be;" that he was quite unconscious; and that Mr. Chillip had mournfully said in the kitchen, on going away just now, that the College of Physicians, the College of Surgeons, and Apothecaries' Hall, if they were all called in together, couldn't help him. He was past both Colleges, Mr. Chillip said, and the Hall could only poison him.

Hearing this, and learning that Mr. Peggotty was there, I determined to go to the house at once. I bade good night to Mr. Omer, and to Mr. and Mrs. Joram; and directed my steps thither, with a solemn feeling, which made Mr. Barkis quite a new and different creature.

My low tap at the door was answered by Mr. Peggotty. He was not so much surprised to see me as I had expected. I remarked this in Peggotty, too, when she came down; and I have seen it since; and I think, in the expectation of that dread surprise, all other changes and surprises dwindle into nothing.

I shook hands with Mr. Peggotty, and passed into the kitchen, while he softly closed the door. Little Emily was sitting by the fire, with her hands before her face. Ham was standing near her.

We spoke in whispers; listening, between whiles, for any sound in the room above. I had not thought of it on the occasion of my last visit, but how strange it was to me now, to miss Mr. Barkis out of the kitchen!

"This is very kind of you, Mas'r Davy," said Mr. Peggotty.

"It is oncommon kind," said Ham.

"Em'ly, my dear," cried Mr. Peggotty. "See here! Here's Mas'r Davy come! What, cheer up, pretty! Not a wured to Mas'r Davy?"

There was a trembling upon her, that I can see now. The coldness of her hand when I touched it, I can feel yet. Its only sign of animation was to shrink from mine; and then she glided from the chair, and, creeping to the other side of her uncle, bowed herself, silently and trembling still, upon his breast.

"It's such a loving art," said Mr. Peggotty, smoothing her rich hair with his great hard hand, "that it can't abear the sorrer of this. It's nat'ral in young folk, Mas'r Davy, when they're new to these here trials, and timid, like my little bird,—it's nat'ral."

She clung closer to him, but neither lifted up her face, nor spoke a word.

"It's getting late, my dear," said Mr. Peggotty, "and here's Ham come fur to take you home. Theer! Go along with t'other loving art! What, Em'ly? Eh, my pretty?"

The sound of her voice had not reached me, but he bent his head as if he listened to her, and then said:

"Let you stay with your uncle? Why, you doen't mean to ask me that! Stay with your uncle, Moppet? When your husband that'll be so soon, is here fur to take you home? Now a person wouldn't think it, fur to see this little thing alongside a rough-weather chap like me," said Mr. Peggotty, looking round at both of us, with infinite pride; "but the sea ain't more salt in it than she has fondness in her for her uncle—a foolish little Em'ly!"

"Em'ly's in the right in that, Mas'r Davy!" said Ham. "Look'ee here! As Em'ly wishes of it, and as she's hurried and frightened, like, besides, I'll leave her till morning. Let me stay too!"

"No, no," said Mr. Peggotty. "You doen't ought—a married man like you—or what's as good—to take and hull away a day's work. And you doen't ought to watch and work both. That won't do. You go home and turn in. You ain't afeerd of Em'ly not being took good care on, *I* know."

Ham yielded to this persuasion, and took his hat to go. Even when he kissed her,—and I never saw him approach her, but I felt that nature had given him the soul of a gentleman,—she seemed to cling closer to her uncle, even to the avoidance of her chosen husband. I shut the door after him, that it might cause no disturbance of the quiet that prevailed; and when I turned back, I found Mr. Peggotty still talking to her.

"Now, I'm a going up-stairs to tell your aunt as Mas'r Davy's here, and that'll cheer her up a bit," he said. "Sit ye down by the fire, the while, my dear, and warm these mortal cold hands. You doen't need to be so fearsome, and take on so much. What? You'll go along with me? —Well! come along with me—come! If her uncle was turned out of house and home, and forced to lay down in a dyke, Mas'r Davy," said Mr. Peggotty, with no less pride than before, "it's my belief she'd go along with him, now! But there'll be some one else, soon,—some one else, soon, Em'ly!"

Afterwards, when I went up-stairs, as I passed the door of my little chamber, which was dark, I had an indistinct impression of her being within it, cast down upon the floor. But, whether it was really she, or whether it was a confusion of the shadows in the room, I don't know now.

I had leisure to think, before the kitchen-fire, of pretty little Em'ly's dread of death—which, added to what Mr. Omer had told me, I took to be the cause of her being so unlike herself—and I had leisure, before Peggotty came down, even to think more leniently of the weakness of it: as I sat counting the ticking of the clock, and deepening my sense of the solemn hush around me. Peggotty took me in her arms, and blessed and thanked me over and over again for being such a comfort to her (that was what she said) in her distress. She then entreated me to come up-stairs, sobbing that Mr. Barkis had always liked me and admired me; that he had often talked of me, before he fell into a stupor; and that she believed, in case of his coming to himself again, he would brighten up at sight of me, if he could brighten up at any earthly thing.

The probability of his ever doing so, appeared to me, when I saw him, to be very small. He was lying with his head and shoulders out of bed, in an uncomfortable attitude, half resting on the box which had cost him so much pain and trouble. I learned that, when he was past creeping out of bed to open it, and past assuring himself of its safety by means of the divining-rod I had seen him use, he had required to have it placed on the chair at the bedside, where he had ever since embraced it, night and day. His arm lay on it now. Time and the world were slipping from beneath him, but the box was there; and the last words he had uttered were (in an explanatory tone) "Old Clothes!"

"Barkis, my dear!" said Peggotty, almost cheerfully: bending over him, while her brother and I stood at the bed's foot. "Here's my dear boy—my dear boy, Master Davy, who brought us together, Barkis! That you sent messages by, you know! Won't you speak to Master Davy?"

He was as mute and senseless as the box, from which his form derived the only expression it had.

"He's a going out with the tide," said Mr. Peggotty to me, behind his hand.

My eyes were dim, and so were Mr. Peggotty's; but I repeated in a whisper, "With the tide?"

"People can't die, along the coast," said Mr. Peggotty, "except when the tide's pretty nigh out. They can't be born, unless it's pretty nigh in—not properly born, till flood. He's a going out with the tide. It's ebb at half-arter three, slack water half-an-hour. If he lives till it turns, he'll hold his own till past the flood, and go out with the next tide."

We remained there, watching him, a long time—hours. What mysterious influence my presence had upon him in that state of his senses, I shall not pretend to say; but when he at last began to wander feebly, it is certain he was muttering about driving me to school.

"He's coming to himself," said Peggotty.

Mr. Peggotty touched me, and whispered with much awe and reverence, "They are both a going out fast."

"Barkis, my dear!" said Peggotty.

"C. P. Barkis," he cried faintly. "No better woman anywhere!"

"Look! Here's Master Davy!" said Peggotty. For he now opened his eyes.

I was on the point of asking him if he knew me, when he tried to stretch out his arm, and said to me, distinctly, with a pleasant smile:

"Barkis is willin'!"

And, it being low water, he went out with the tide.

CHAPTER XXXI.

A GREATER LOSS.

It was not difficult for me, on Peggotty's solicitation, to resolve to stay where I was, until after the remains of the poor carrier should have made their last journey to Blun-

derstone. She had long ago bought, out of her own savings, a little piece of ground in our old churchyard near the grave "of her sweet girl," as she always called my mother; and there they were to rest.

In keeping Peggotty company, and doing all I could for her (little enough at the utmost), I was as grateful, I rejoice to think, as even now I could wish myself to have been. But I am afraid I had a supreme satisfaction, of a personal and professional nature, in taking charge of Mr. Barkis's will, and expounding its contents.

I may claim the merit of having originated the suggestion that the will should be looked for in the box. After some search, it was found in the box, at the bottom of a horse's nose-bag; wherein (besides hay) there was discovered an old gold watch, with chain and seals, which Mr. Barkis had worn on his wedding-day, and which had never been seen before or since; a silver tobacco-stopper in the form of a leg; an imitation lemon, full of minute cups and saucers, which I have some idea Mr. Barkis must have purchased to present to me when I was a child, and afterwards found himself unable to part with; eighty-seven guineas and a half, in guineas and half-guineas; two hundred and ten pounds, in perfectly clean bank-notes; certain receipts for Bank of England stock; an old horseshoe, a bad shilling, a piece of camphor, and an oyster-shell. From the circumstance of the latter article having been much polished, and displaying prismatic colours on the inside, I conclude that Mr. Barkis had some general ideas about pearls, which never resolved themselves into anything definite.

For years and years, Mr. Barkis had carried this box, on all his journeys, every day. That it might the better escape notice, he had invented a fiction that it belonged to "Mr. Blackboy," and was "to be left with Barkis till called for;" a fable he had elaborately written on the lid, in characters now scarcely legible.

He had hoarded, all these years, I found, to good purpose. His property in money amounted to nearly three thousand pounds. Of this he bequeathed the interest of one thousand to Mr. Peggotty for his life; on his decease, the principal to be equally divided between Peggotty, little Emily, and me or the survivor or survivors of us, share and share alike. All the rest he died possessed of, he bequeathed to Peggotty; whom he left residuary legatee, and sole executrix of that his last will and testament.

I felt myself quite a proctor when I read this document aloud with all possible ceremony, and set forth its provisions, any number of times, to those whom they concerned. I began to think there was more in the Commons than I had supposed. I examined the will with the deepest attention, pronounced it perfectly formal in all respects, made a pencil-mark or so in the margin, and thought it rather extraordinary that I knew so much.

In this abstruse pursuit; in making an account for Peggotty, of all the property into which she had come; in arranging all the affairs in an orderly manner; and in being her referee and adviser on every point, to our joint delight; I passed the week before the funeral. I did not see little Emily in that interval, but they told me she was to be quietly married in a fortnight.

I did not attend the funeral in character, if I may venture to say so. I mean I was not dressed up in a black cloak and a streamer, to frighten the birds; but I walked over to Blunderstone early in the morning, and was in the churchyard when it came, attended only by Peggotty and her brother. The mad gentleman looked on, out of my little window; Mr. Chillip's baby wagged its heavy head, and rolled its goggle eyes, at the clergyman, over its nurse's shoulder; Mr. Omer breathed short in the background; no one else was there; and it was very quiet. We walked about the churchyard for an hour, after all was over; and pulled some young leaves from the tree above my mother's grave.

A dread falls on me here. A cloud is lowering on the distant town, towards which I retraced my solitary steps. I fear to approach it. I cannot bear to think of what did come, upon that memorable night; of what must come again, if I go on.

It is no worse, because I write it. It would be no better, if I stopped my most unwilling hand. It is done. Nothing can undo it; nothing can make it otherwise than as it was.

My old nurse was to go to London with me next day, on the business of the will. Little Emily was passing that day at Mr. Omer's. We were all to meet in the old boathouse that night. Ham would bring Emily at the usual hour. I would walk back at my leisure. The brother and sister would return as they had come, and be expecting us, when the day closed in, at the fireside.

I parted from them at the wicket-gate, where visionary Straps had rested with Roderick Random's knapsack in the days of yore; and, instead of going straight back, walked a little distance on the road to Lowestoft. Then I turned, and walked back towards Yarmouth. I stayed to dine at a decent alehouse, some mile or two from the ferry I have mentioned before; and thus the day wore away, and it was evening when I reached it. Rain was falling heavily by that time, and it was a wild night; but there was a moon behind the clouds, and it was not dark.

I was soon within sight of Mr. Peggotty's house, and of the light within it shining through the window. A little floundering across the sand, which was heavy, brought me to the door, and I went in.

It looked very comfortable indeed. Mr. Peggotty had smoked his evening pipe, and there were preparations for some supper by-and-by. The fire was bright, the ashes were thrown up, the locker was ready for little Emily in her old place. In her own old place sat Peggotty, once more, looking (but for her dress) as if she had never left it. She had fallen back, already, on the society of the work-box with Saint Paul's upon the lid, the yard-measure in the cottage, and the bit of wax candle: and there they all were, just as if they had never been disturbed. Mrs. Gummidge appeared to be fretting a little, in her old corner; and consequently looked quite natural, too.

"You're first of the lot, Mas'r Davy!" said Mr. Peggotty, with a happy face. "Doen't keep in that coat, Sir, if it's wet."

"Thank you, Mr. Peggotty," said I, giving him my outer coat to hang up. "It's quite dry."

"So 'tis!" said Mr. Peggotty, feeling my shoulders. "As a chip! Sit ye down, Sir. It ain't o' no use saying welcome to you, but you're welcome, kind and hearty."

"Thank you, Mr. Peggotty, I am sure of that. Well, Peggotty!" said I, giving her a kiss. "And how are you, old woman?"

"Ha, ha!" laughed Mr. Peggotty, sitting down beside us, and rubbing his hands in his sense of relief from recent trouble, and in the genuine heartiness of his nature;

"there's not a woman in the wureld, Sir—as I tell her—that need to feel more easy in her mind than her! She done her dooty by the departed, and the departed know'd it; and the departed done what was right by her, as she done what was right by the departed;—and—and—and it's *all* right!"

Mrs. Gummidge groaned.

"Cheer up, my pretty mawther!" said Mr. Peggotty. (But he shook his head aside at us, evidently sensible of the tendency of the late occurrences to recall the memory of the old one.) "Doen't be down! Cheer up, for your own self, on'y a little bit, and see if a good deal more doen't come nat'ral!"

"Not to me, Dan'l," returned Mrs. Gummidge. "Nothink's nat'ral to me but to be lone and lorn."

"No, no," said Mr. Peggotty, soothing her sorrows.

"Yes, yes, Dan'l!" said Mrs. Gummidge. "I ain't a person to live with them as has had money left. Things go too contrairy with me. I had better be a riddance."

"Why, how should I ever spend it without you?" said Mr. Peggotty, with an air of serious remonstrance. "What are you talking on? Doen't I want you more now, than ever I did?"

"I know'd I was never wanted before!" cried Mrs. Gummidge, with a pitiable whimper, "and now I'm told so! How could I expect to be wanted, being so lone and lorn, and so contrairy!"

Mr. Peggotty seemed very much shocked at himself for having made a speech capable of this unfeeling construction, but was prevented from replying, by Peggotty's pulling his sleeve, and shaking her head. After looking at Mrs. Gummidge for some moments, in sore distress of mind, he glanced at the Dutch clock, rose, snuffed the candle, and put it in the window.

"Theer!" said Mr. Peggotty, cheerily. "Theer we are, Missis Gummidge!" Mrs. Gummidge slightly groaned. "Lighted up, accordin' to custom! You're a wonderin' what that's fur, Sir! Well, it's fur our little Em'ly. You see, the path ain't over light or cheerful arter dark; and when I'm here at the hour as she's a comin' home, I puts the light in the winder. That, you see," said Mr. Peggotty, bending over me with great glee, "meets two objects. She says, says Em'ly, 'Theer's home!' she says. And likewise, says Em'ly, 'My uncle's theer!' Fur if I ain't theer, I never have no light showed."

"You're a baby!" said Peggotty; very fond of him for it, if she thought so.

"Well," returned Mr. Peggotty, standing with his legs pretty wide apart, and rubbing his hands up and down them in his comfortable satisfaction, as he looked alternately at us and at the fire, "I doen't know but I am. Not, you see, to look at."

"Not azackly," observed Peggotty.

"No," laughed Mr. Peggotty, "not to look at, but to—to consider on, you know. *I* doen't care, bless you! Now I tell you. When I go a looking and looking about that theer pritty house of our Em'ly's, I'm—I'm Gormed," said Mr. Peggotty, with sudden emphasis—"theer! I can't say more—if I doen't feel as if the littlest things was her, a'most. I takes 'em up and I puts 'em down, and I touches of em as delicate as if they was our Em'ly. So 'tis with her little bonnets and that. I couldn't see one on em rough used a purpose—not fur the whole wureld. There's a babby for you, in the form of a great Sea Porkypine!"

said Mr. Peggotty, relieving his earnestness with a roar of laughter.

Peggotty and I both laughed, but not so loud.

"It's my opinion, you see," said Mr. Peggotty, with a delighted face, after some further rubbing of his legs, "as this is along of my havin' played with her so much, and made believe as we was Turks, and French, and sharks, and every wariety of forinners—bless you, yes; and lions and whales, and I doen't know what all!—when she warn't no higher than my knee. I've got into the way on it, you know. Why, this here candle now!" said Mr. Peggotty, gleefully holding out his hand towards it, "*I* know wery well that arter she's married and gone, I shall put that candle theer, just that same as now. I know wery well that when I'm here o' nights (and where else should *I* live, bless your arts, whatever fortun I come into?) and she ain't here, or I ain't theer, I shall put the candle in the winder, and sit afore the fire, pretending I'm expecting of her, like I'm a doing now. *There's* a babby for you," said Mr. Peggotty, with another roar, "in the form of a Sea Porky-pine! Why, at the present minute, when I see the candle sparkle up, I says to myself, 'She's a looking at it! Em'ly's a coming!' *There's* a babby for you, in the form of a Sea Porkypine! Right for all that," said Mr. Peggotty, stopping in his roar, and smiting his hands together; "fur here she is!"

It was only Ham. The night should have turned more wet since I came in, for he had a large sou'-wester hat on, slouched over his face.

"Wheer's Em'ly?" said Mr. Peggotty.

Ham made a motion with his head, as if she were outside. Mr. Peggotty took the light from the window, trimmed it, put it on the table, and was busily stirring the fire, when Ham, who had not moved, said:

"Mas'r Davy, will you come out a minute, and see what Em'ly and me has got to show you?"

We went out. As I passed him at the door, I saw, to my astonishment and fright, that he was deadly pale. He pushed me hastily into the open air, and closed the door upon us. Only upon us two.

"Ham! what's the matter?"

"Mas'r Davy!——" Oh, for his broken heart, how dreadfully he wept!

I was paralysed by the sight of such grief. I don't know what I thought, or what I dreaded. I could only look at him.

"Ham! Poor good fellow! For Heaven's sake, tell me what's the matter!"

"My love, Mas'r Davy—the pride and hope of my art—her that I'd have died for, and would die for now—she's gone!"

"Gone?"

"Em'ly's run away! Oh, Mas'r Davy, think *how* she's run away, when I pray my good and gracious God to kill her (her that is so dear above all things) sooner than let her come to ruin and disgrace!"

The face he turned up to the troubled sky, the quivering of his clasped hands, the agony of his figure, remain associated with that lonely waste, in my remembrance, to this hour. It is always night there, and he is the only object in the scene.

"You're a scholar," he said, hurriedly, "and know what's right and best. What am I to say, indoors? How am I ever to break it to him, Mas'r Davy?"

I saw the door move, and instinctively tried to hold the latch on the outside, to gain a moment's time. It was too late. Mr. Peggotty thrust forth his face; and never could I forget the change that came upon it when he saw us, if I were to live five hundred years.

I remember a great wail and cry, and the women hanging about him, and we all standing in the room; I with a paper in my hand, which Ham had given me; Mr. Peggotty, with his vest torn open, his hair wild, his face and lips quite white, and blood trickling down his bosom (it had sprung from his mouth, I think), looking fixedly at me.

"Read it, Sir," he said, in a low shivering voice. "Slow, please. I doen't know as I can understand."

In the midst of this silence of death, I read thus, from a blotted letter:—

"'When you, who love me so much better than I ever have deserved, even when my mind was innocent, see this, I shall be far away.'"

"I shall be fur away," he repeated slowly. "Stop! Em'ly fur away. Well!"

"'When I leave my dear home—my dear home—oh, my dear home!—in the morning,'"

the letter bore date on the previous night:

'—it will be never to come back, unless he brings me back a lady. This will be found at night, many hours after, instead of me. Oh, if you knew how my heart is torn. If even you, that I have wronged so much, that never can forgive me, could only know what I suffer! I am too wicked to write about myself. Oh, take comfort in thinking that I am so bad. Oh, for mercy's sake, tell uncle that I never loved him half so dear as now. Oh, don't remember how affectionate and kind you have all been to me—don't remember we were ever to be married—but try to think as if I died when I was little, and was buried somewhere. Pray Heaven that I am going away from, have compassion on my uncle! Tell him that I never loved him half so dear. Be his comfort. Love some good girl, that will be what I was once to uncle, and be true to you, and worthy of you, and know no shame but me. God bless all! I'll pray for all, often, on my knees. If he doen't bring me back a lady, and I don't pray for my own self, I'll pray for all. My parting love to uncle. My last tears, and my last thanks, for uncle!'"

That was all.

He stood, long after I had ceased to read, still looking at me. At length I ventured to take his hand, and to entreat him, as well as I could, to endeavour to get some command of himself. He replied, "I thank'ee, Sir, I thank'ee!" without moving.

Ham spoke to him. Mr. Peggotty was so far sensible of *his* affliction, that he wrung his hand; but, otherwise, he remained in the same state, and no one dared to disturb him.

Slowly, at last, he moved his eyes from my face, as if he were waking from a vision, and cast them round the room. Then he said, in a low voice:

"Who's the man? I want to know his name."

Ham glanced at me, and suddenly I felt a shock that struck me back.

"There's a man suspected," said Mr. Peggotty. "Who is it?"

"Mas'r Davy!" implored Ham. "Go out a bit, and let me tell him what I must. You doen't ought to hear it, Sir."

I felt the shock again. I sank down in a chair, and tried to utter some reply; but my tongue was fettered, and my sight was weak.

"I want to know his name!" I heard said, once more.

"For some time past," Ham faltered, "there's been a servant about here, at odd times. There's been a gen'lm'n too. Both of 'em belonged to one another."

Mr. Peggotty stood fixed as before, but now looking at him.

"The servant," pursued Ham, "was seen along with—our poor girl—last night. He's been in hiding about here, this week or over. He was thought to have gone, but he was hiding. Doen't stay, Mas'r Davy, doen't!"

I felt Peggotty's arm round my neck, but I could not have moved if the house had been about to fall upon me.

"A strange chay and hosses was outside town, this morning, on the Norwich road, a'most afore the day broke," Ham went on. "The servant went to it, and come from it, and went to it again. When he went to it again, Em'ly was nigh him. The t'other was inside. He's the man."

"For the Lord's love," said Mr. Peggotty, falling back, and putting out his hand, as if to keep off what he dreaded. "Doen't tell me his name's Steerforth."

"Mas'r Davy," exclaimed Ham, in a broken voice, "it ain't no fault of yourn—and I am far from laying of it to you—but his name is Steerforth, and he's a damned villain!"

Mr. Peggotty uttered no cry, and shed no tear, and moved no more, until he seemed to wake again, all at once, and pulled down his rough coat from its peg in a corner.

"Bear a hand with this! I'm struck of a heap, and can't do it," he said, impatiently. "Bear a hand, and help me. Well!" when somebody had done so. "Now give me that theer hat!"

Ham asked him whither he was going.

"I'm a going to seek my niece. I'm a going to seek my Em'ly. I'm a going, first, to stave in that theer boat, and sink it where I would have drownded him, as I'm a livin' soul, if I had had one thought of what was in him! As he sat afore me," he said, wildly, holding out his clenched right hand, "as he sat afore me, face to face, strike me down dead, but I'd have drownded him, and thought it right!—I'm a going to seek my niece."

"Where?" cried Ham, interposing himself before the door.

"Anywhere! I'm a going to seek my niece through the wureld. I'm a going to find my poor niece in her shame, and bring her back. No one stop me! I tell you I'm a going to seek my niece!"

"No, no!" cried Mrs. Gummidge, coming between them, in a fit of crying. "No, no, Dan'l, not as you are now. Seek her in a little while, my lone lorn Dan'l, and that'll be but right; but not as you are now. Sit ye down, and give me your forgiveness for having ever been a worrit to you, Dan'l—what have *my* contrairies ever been to this!—and let us speak a word about them times when she was first an orphan, and when Ham was too, and when I was a poor widder woman, and you took me in. It'll soften your poor heart, Dan'l," laying her head upon his shoulder, "and you'll bear your sorrow better; for you know the promise, Dan'l, 'As you have done it unto one of the least of these, you have done it unto Me'; and that can never fail under this roof, that's been our shelter for so many, many year!"

He was quite passive now; and when I heard him crying, the impulse that had been upon me to go down upon my knees, and ask their pardon for the desolation I had caused, and curse Steerforth, yielded to a better feeling. My overcharged heart found the same relief, and I cried too.

CHAPTER XXXII.

THE BEGINNING OF A LONG JOURNEY.

WHAT is natural in me, is natural in many other men, I infer, and so I am not afraid to write that I never had loved Steerforth better than when the ties that bound me to him were broken. In the keen distress of the discovery of his unworthiness, I thought more of all that was brilliant in him, I softened more towards all that was good in him, I did more justice to the qualities that might have made him a man of a noble nature and a great name, than ever I had done in the height of my devotion to him. Deeply as I felt my own unconscious part in his pollution of an honest home, I believed that if I had been brought face to face with him, I could not have uttered one reproach. I should have loved him so well still—though he fascinated me no longer—I should have held in so much tenderness the memory of my affection for him, that I think I should have been as weak as a spirit-wounded child, in all but the entertainment of a thought that we could ever be re-united. That thought I never had. I felt, as he had felt, that all was at an end between us. What his remembrances of me were, I have never known—they were light enough, perhaps, and easily dismissed—but mine of him were as the remembrances of a cherished friend, who was dead.

Yes, Steerforth, long removed from the scenes of this poor history! My sorrow may bear involuntary witness against you at the Judgment Throne; but my angry thoughts or my reproaches never will, I know!

The news of what had happened soon spread through the town; insomuch that as I passed along the streets next morning, I overheard the people speaking of it at their doors. Many were hard upon her, some few were hard upon him, but towards her second father and her lover there was but one sentiment. Among all kinds of people a respect for them in their distress prevailed, which was full of gentleness and delicacy. The seafaring men kept apart, when those two were seen early, walking with slow steps on the beach; and stood in knots, talking compassionately among themselves.

It was on the beach, close down by the sea, that I found them. It would have been easy to perceive that they had not slept all last night, even if Peggotty had failed to tell me of their still sitting just as I left them, when it was broad day. They looked worn; and I thought Mr. Peggotty's head was bowed in one night more than in all the years I had known him. But they were both as grave and steady as the sea itself: then lying beneath a dark sky, waveless—yet with a heavy roll upon it, as if it breathed in its rest—and touched, on the horizon, with a strip of silvery light from the unseen sun.

"We have had a mort of talk, Sir," said Mr. Peggotty to me, when we had all three walked a little while in silence, "of what we ought and doen't ought to do. But we see our course now."

I happened to glance at Ham, then looking out to sea

upon the distant light, and a frightful thought came into my mind—not that his face was angry, for it was not; I recall nothing but an expression of stern determination in it—that if ever he encountered Steerforth, he would kill him.

"My dooty here, Sir," said Mr. Peggotty, "is done. I'm a going to seek my——" he stopped, and went on in a firmer voice: "I'm a going to seek her. That's my dooty evermore."

He shook his head when I asked him where he would seek her, and inquired if I were going to London to-morrow? I told him I had not gone to-day, fearing to lose the chance of being of any service to him; but that I was ready to go when he would.

"I'll go along with you, Sir," he rejoined, "if you're agreeable, to-morrow."

We walked again, for a while, in silence.

"Ham," he presently resumed, "he'll hold to his present work, and go and live along with my sister. The old boat yonder——"

"Will you desert the old boat, Mr. Peggotty?" I gently interposed.

"My station, Mas'r Davy," he returned, "ain't there no longer; and if ever a boat foundered, since there was darkness on the face of the deep, that one's gone down. But no, Sir, no; I doen't mean as it should be deserted. Fur from that."

We walked again for a while, as before, until he explained:

"My wishes is, Sir, as it shall look, day and night, winter and summer, as it has always looked, since she first know'd it. If ever she should come a wandering back, I wouldn't have the old place seem to cast her off, you understand, but seem to tempt her to draw nigher to't, and to peep in, maybe, like a ghost, out of the wind and rain, through the old winder, at the old seat by the fire. Then, maybe, Mas'r Davy, seein' none but Missis Gummidge there, she might take heart to creep in, trembling; and might come to be laid down in her old bed, and rest her weary head where it was once so gay."

I could not speak to him in reply, though I tried.

"Every night," said Mr. Peggotty, "as reg'lar as the night comes, the candle must be stood in its old pane of glass, that if ever she should see it, it may seem to say 'Come back, my child, come back!' If ever there's a knock, Ham (partic'ler a soft knock), arter dark, at your aunt's door, doen't you go nigh it. Let it be her—not you—that sees my fallen child!"

He walked a little in front of us, and kept before us for some minutes. During this interval, I glanced at Ham again, and observing the same expression on his face, and his eyes still directed to the distant light, I touched his arm.

Twice I called him by his name, in the tone in which I might have tried to rouse a sleeper, before he heeded me. When I at last inquired on what his thoughts were so bent, he replied:

"On what's afore me, Mas'r Davy; and over yon."

"On the life before you, do you mean?" He had pointed confusedly out to sea.

"Ay, Mas'r Davy. I doen't right know how 'tis, but from over yon there seemed to me to come—the end of it like;" looking at me as if he were waking, but with the same determined face.

"What end?" I asked, possessed by my former fear.

"I doen't know," he said, thoughtfully; "I was calling to mind that the beginning of it all did take place here—and then the end come. But it's gone! Mas'r Davy," he added; answering, as I think, my look; "you han't no call to be afeerd of me: but I'm kiender muddled; I don't fare to feel no matters,"—which was as much as to say that he was not himself, and quite confounded.

Mr. Peggotty stopping for us to join him: we did so, and said no more. The remembrance of this, in connexion with my former thought, however, haunted me at intervals, even until the inexorable end came at its appointed time.

We insensibly approached the old boat, and entered. Mrs. Gummidge, no longer moping in her especial corner, was busy preparing breakfast. She took Mr. Peggotty's hat, and placed his seat for him, and spoke so comfortably and softly, that I hardly knew her.

"Dan'l, my good man," said she, "you must eat and drink, and keep up your strength, for without it you'll do nowt. Try, that's a dear soul! And if I disturb you with my clicketten," she meant her chattering, "tell me so, Dan'l, and I won't."

When she had served us all, she withdrew to the window, where she sedulously employed herself in repairing some shirts and other clothes belonging to Mr. Peggotty, and neatly folding and packing them in an old oilskin bag, such as sailors carry. Meanwhile, she continued talking, in the same quiet manner:

"All times and seasons, you know, Dan'l," said Mrs. Gummidge, "I shall be allus here, and everythink will look accordin' to your wishes. I'm a poor scholar, but I shall write to you, odd times, when you're away, and send my letters to Mas'r Davy. Maybe you'll write to me too, Dan'l, odd times, and tell me how you fare to feel upon your lone lorn journeys."

"You'll be a solitary woman here, I'm afeerd!" said Mr. Peggotty.

"No, no, Dan'l," she returned, "I shan't be that. Doen't you mind me. I shall have enough to do to keep a Beein' for you" (Mrs. Gummidge meant a home), "again you come back—to keep a Beein' here for any that may hap to come back, Dan'l. In the fine time, I shall set outside the door as I used to do. If any should come nigh, they shall see the old widder woman true to 'em, a long way off."

What a change in Mrs. Gummidge in a little time! She was another woman. She was so devoted, she had such a quick perception of what it would be well to say, and what it would be well to leave unsaid; she was so forgetful of herself, and so regardful of the sorrow about her, that I held her in a sort of veneration. The work she did that day! There were many things to be brought up from the beach and stored in the outhouse—as oars, nets, sails, cordage, spars, lobster-pots, bags of ballast, and the like; and though there was abundance of assistance rendered, there being not a pair of working hands on all that shore but would have laboured hard for Mr. Peggotty, and been well paid in being asked to do it, yet she persisted all day long in toiling under weights that she was quite unequal to, and fagging to and fro on all sorts of unnecessary errands. As to deploring her misfortunes, she appeared to have entirely lost the recollection of ever having had any. She preserved an equable cheerfulness in the midst of her sympathy, which was not the least astonishing part of the change that had come over her. Querulousness was out of the question. I did not even observe her voice to falter, or a tear to escape from her eyes, the whole day through, until twilight; when she and I and Mr. Peggotty being alone together, and he having fallen asleep in perfect exhaustion, she broke into a half-suppressed fit of sobbing and crying, and taking me to the door, said, "Ever bless you, Mas'r Davy, be a friend to him, poor dear!" Then she immediately ran out of the house to wash her face, in order that she might sit quietly beside him, and be found at work there, when he should awake. In short I left her, when I went away at night, the prop and staff of Mr. Peggotty's affliction; and I could not meditate enough upon the lesson that I read in Mrs. Gummidge, and the new experience she unfolded to me.

It was between nine and ten o'clock when, strolling in a melancholy manner through the town, I stopped at Mr. Omer's door. Mr. Omer had taken it so much to heart, his daughter told me, that he had been very low and poorly all day, and had gone to bed without his pipe.

"A deceitful, bad-hearted girl," said Mrs. Joram. "There was no good in her, ever!"

"Don't say so," I returned. "You don't think so."

"Yes, I do!" cried Mrs. Joram, angrily.

"No, no," said I.

Mrs. Joram tossed her head, endeavouring to be very stern and cross; but she could not command her softer self, and began to cry. I was young, to be sure; but I thought much the better of her for this sympathy, and fancied it became her, as a virtuous wife and mother, very well indeed.

"What will she ever do!" sobbed Minnie. "Where will she go! What will become of her! Oh, how could she be so cruel, to herself and him!"

I remembered the time when Minnie was a young and pretty girl; and I was glad that she remembered it too, so feelingly.

"My little Minnie," said Mrs. Joram, "has only just now been got to sleep. Even in her sleep she is sobbing for Em'ly. All day long, little Minnie has cried for her, and asked me, over and over again, whether Em'ly was wicked? What can I say to her, when Em'ly tied a ribbon off her own neck round little Minnie's the last night she was here, and laid her head down on the pillow beside her till she was fast asleep! The ribbon's round my little Minnie's neck now. It ought not to be, perhaps, but what can I do? Em'ly is very bad, but they were fond of one another. And the child knows nothing!"

Mrs. Joram was so unhappy, that her husband came out to take care of her. Leaving them together, I went home to Peggotty's; more melancholy myself, if possible, than I had been yet.

That good creature—I mean Peggotty—all untired by her late anxieties and sleepless nights, was at her brother's, where she meant to stay till morning. An old woman, who had been employed about the house for some weeks past, while Peggotty had been unable to attend to it, was the house's only other occupant besides myself. As I had no occasion for her services, I sent her to bed, by no means against her will; and sat down before the kitchen fire a little while, to think about all this.

I was blending it with the deathbed of the late Mr. Barkis, and was driving out with the tide towards the distance at which Ham had looked so singularly in the morning, when I was recalled from my wanderings by a knock at the door. There was a knocker upon the door, but it was not that which made the sound. The tap was from a hand, and low down upon the door, as if it were given by a child.

It made me start as much as if it had been the knock of a footman to a person of distinction. I opened the door; and at first looked down, to my amazement, on nothing but a great umbrella that appeared to be walking about of itself. But presently I discovered underneath it, Miss Mowcher.

I might not have been prepared to give the little creature a very kind reception, if, on her removing the umbrella, which her utmost efforts were unable to shut up, she had shown me the "volatile" expression of face which had made so great an impression on me at our first and last meeting. But her face, as she turned it up to mine, was so earnest; and when I relieved her of the umbrella (which would have been an inconvenient one for the Irish Giant) she wrung her little hands in such an afflicted manner; that I rather inclined towards her.

"Miss Mowcher!" said I, after glancing up and down the empty street, without distinctly knowing what I expected to see besides; "how do you come here? What is the matter?"

She motioned to me with her short right arm, to shut the umbrella for her; and passing me hurriedly, went into the kitchen. When I had closed the door, and followed, with the umbrella in my hand, I found her sitting on the corner of the fender—it was a low iron one, with two flat bars at top to stand plates upon—in the shadow of the boiler, swaying herself backwards and forwards, and chafing her hands upon her knees like a person in pain.

Quite alarmed at being the only recipient of this untimely visit, and the only spectator of this portentous behaviour, I exclaimed again: "Pray tell me, Miss Mowcher, what is the matter! are you ill?"

"My dear young soul," returned Miss Mowcher, squeezing her hands upon her heart one over the other. "I am ill here, I am very ill. To think that it should come to this, when I might have known it and perhaps prevented it, if I hadn't been a thoughtless fool!"

Again her large bonnet (very disproportionate to her figure) went backwards and forwards, in her swaying of her little body to and fro; while a most gigantic bonnet rocked, in unison with it, upon the wall.

"I am surprised," I began, "to see you so distressed and serious"—when she interrupted me.

"Yes, it's always so!" she said. "They are all surprised, these inconsiderate young people, fairly and full grown, to see any natural feeling in a little thing like me! They make a plaything of me, use me for their amusement, throw me away when they are tired, and wonder that I feel more than a toy horse or a wooden soldier! Yes, yes, that's the way. The old way!"

"It may be, with others," I returned, "but I do assure you it is not with me. Perhaps I ought not to be at all surprised to see you as you are now: I know so little of you. I said, without consideration, what I thought."

"What can I do?" returned the little woman, standing up and holding out her arms to show herself. "See! What I am, my father was; and my sister is; and my brother is. I have worked for sister and brother these many years—hard, Mr. Copperfield—all day. I must live. I do no harm. If there are people so unreflecting or so cruel, as to make a jest of me, what is left for me to do but to make a jest of myself, them, and everything? If I do so, for the time, whose fault is that? Mine?"

No. Not Miss Mowcher's, I perceived.

"If I had shown myself a sensitive dwarf to your false friend," pursued the little woman, shaking her head at me, with reproachful earnestness, "how much of his help or good will do you think *I* should ever have had? If little Mowcher (who had no hand, young gentleman, in the making of herself) addressed herself to him, or the like of him, because of her misfortunes, when do you suppose her small voice would have been heard? Little Mowcher would have as much need to live, if she was the bitterest and dullest of pigmies; but she couldn't do it. No. She might whistle for her bread and butter till she died of Air!"

Miss Mowcher sat down on the fender again, and took out her handkerchief, and wiped her eyes.

"Be thankful for me, if you have a kind heart, as I think you have," she said, "that while I know well what I am, I can be cheerful and endure it all. I am thankful for myself, at any rate, that I can find my tiny way through the world, without being beholden to anyone; and that in return for all that is thrown at me, in folly or vanity, as I go along, I can throw bubbles back. If I don't brood over all I want, it is the better for me, and not the worse for anyone. If I am a plaything for you giants, be gentle with me."

Miss Mowcher replaced her handkerchief in her pocket, looking at me with very intent expression all the while, and pursued:

"I saw you in the street just now. You may suppose I am not able to walk as fast as you, with my short legs and short breath, and I couldn't overtake you; but I guessed where you came, and came after you. I have been here before, to-day, but the good woman wasn't at home."

"Do you know her?" I demanded.

"I know *of* her, and about her," she replied, "from Omer and Joram. I was there at seven o'clock this morning. Do you remember what Steerforth said to me about this unfortunate girl, that time when I saw you both at the inn?"

The great bonnet on Miss Mowcher's head, and the greater bonnet on the wall, began to go backwards and forwards again when she asked this question.

I remembered very well what she referred to, having had it in my thoughts many times that day. I told her so.

"May the Father of all Evil confound him," said the little woman, holding up her forefinger between me and her sparkling eyes; "and ten times more confound that wicked servant; but I believed it was *you* who had a boyish passion for her!"

"I?" I repeated.

"Child, child! In the name of blind ill-fortune," cried Miss Mowcher, wringing her hands impatiently, as she went to and fro again upon the fender, "why did you praise her so, and blush, and look disturbed?"

I could not conceal from myself that I had done this, though for a reason very different from her supposition.

"What did I know?" said Miss Mowcher, taking out her handkerchief again, and giving one little stamp on the ground whenever, at short intervals, she applied it to her eyes with both hands at once. "He was crossing you and wheedling you, I saw; and you were soft wax in his hands, I saw. Had I left the room a minute, when his man told me that 'Young Innocence' (so he called you, and you

may call him 'Old Guilt' all the days of your life) had set his heart upon her, and she was giddy and liked him, but his master was resolved that no harm should come of it—more for your sake than for hers—and that that was their business here? How could I *but* believe him? I saw Steerforth soothe and please you by his praise of her! You were the first to mention her name. You owned to an old admiration of her. You were hot and cold, and red and white, all at once when I spoke to you of her. What could I think—what *did* I think—but that you were a young libertine in everything but experience, and had fallen into hands that had experience enough, and could manage you (having your fancy) for your own good? Oh! oh! oh! They were afraid of my finding out the truth," exclaimed Miss Mowcher, getting off the fender, and trotting up and down the kitchen with her two short arms distressfully lifted up, "because I am a sharp little thing—I need be, to get through the world at all!—and they deceived me altogether, and I gave the poor unfortunate girl a letter, which I fully believe was the beginning of her ever speaking to Littimer, who was left behind on purpose!"

I stood amazed at the revelation of all this perfidy, looking at Miss Mowcher as she walked up and down the kitchen until she was out of breath: when she sat upon the fender again, and, drying her face with her handkerchief, shook her head for a long time, without otherwise moving, and without breaking silence.

"My country rounds," she added at length, "brought me to Norwich, Mr. Copperfield, the night before last. What I happened to find out there, about their secret way of coming and going, without you—which was strange—led to my suspecting something wrong. I got into the coach from London last night, as it came through Norwich, and was here this morning. Oh, oh, oh! too late!"

Poor little Mowcher turned so chilly after all her crying and fretting, that she turned round on the fender, putting her poor little wet feet in among the ashes to warm them, and sat looking at the fire, like a large doll. I sat in a chair on the other side of the hearth, lost in unhappy reflections, and looking at the fire too, and sometimes at her.

"I must go," she said at last, rising as she spoke. "It's late. You don't mistrust me?"

Meeting her sharp glance, which was as sharp as ever when she asked me, I could not on that short challenge answer no, quite frankly.

"Come!" said she, accepting the offer of my hand to help her over the fender, and looking wistfully up into my face, "you know you wouldn't mistrust me, if I was a full-sized woman!"

I felt that there was much truth in this; and I felt rather ashamed of myself.

"You are a young man," she said, nodding. "Take a word of advice, even from three foot nothing. Try not to associate bodily defects with mental, my good friend, except for a solid reason."

She had got over the fender now, and I had got over my suspicion. I told her that I believed she had given me a faithful account of herself, and that we had both been hapless instruments in designing hands. She thanked me, and said I was a good fellow.

"Now, mind!" she exclaimed, turning back on her way to the door, and looking shrewdly at me, with her forefinger up again. "I have some reason to suspect, from what I have heard—my ears are always open; I can't afford to spare what powers I have—that they are gone abroad. But if ever they return, if ever any one of them returns, while I am alive, I am more likely than another, going about as I do, to find it out soon. Whatever I know, you shall know. If ever I can do anything to serve the poor betrayed girl, I will do it faithfully, please Heaven! And Littimer had better have a bloodhound at his back, than little Mowcher!"

I placed implicit faith in this last statement, when I marked the look with which it was accompanied.

"Trust me no more, but trust me no less, than you would trust a full-sized woman," said the little creature, touching me appealingly on the wrist. "If ever you see me again, unlike what I am now, and like what I was when you first saw me, observe what company I am in. Call to mind that I am a very helpless and defenceless little thing. Think of me at home with my brother like myself and sister like myself, when my day's work is done. Perhaps you won't, then, be very hard upon me, or surprised if I can be distressed and serious. Good night!"

I gave Miss Mowcher my hand, with a very different opinion of her from that which I had hitherto entertained, and opened the door to let her out. It was not a trifling business to get the great umbrella up, and properly balanced in her grasp; but at last I successfully accomplished this, and saw it go bobbing down the street through the rain, without the least appearance of having anybody underneath it, except when a heavier fall than usual from some overcharged waterspout sent it toppling over, on one side, and discovered Miss Mowcher struggling violently to get it right. After making one or two sallies to her relief, which were rendered futile by the umbrella's hopping on again, like an immense bird, before I could reach it, I came in, went to bed, and slept till morning.

In the morning I was joined by Mr. Peggotty and by my old nurse, and we went at an early hour to the coach-office, where Mrs. Gummidge and Ham were waiting to take leave of us.

"Mas'r Davy," Ham whispered, drawing me aside, while Mr. Peggotty was stowing his bag among the luggage, "his life is quite broke up. He doen't know wheer he's going; he doen't know what's afore him; he's bound upon a voyage that'll last, on and off, all the rest of his days, take my wured for't, unless he finds what he's a seeking of. I am sure you'll be a friend to him, Mas'r Davy?"

"Trust me, I will indeed," said I, shaking hands with Ham earnestly.

"Thank'ee. Thank'ee, very kind, Sir. One thing furder. I'm in good employ, you know, Mas'r Davy, and I han't no way now of spending what I gets. Money's of no use to me no more, except to live. If you can lay it out for him, I shall do my work with a better art. Though as to that, Sir," and he spoke very steadily and mildly, "you're not to think but I shall work at all times, like a man, and act the best that lays in my power!"

I told him I was well convinced of it; and I hinted that I hoped the time might even come, when he would cease to lead the lonely life he naturally contemplated now.

"No, Sir," he said, shaking his head, "all that's past and over with me, Sir. No one can never fill the place that's empty. But you'll bear in mind about the money, as theer's at all times some laying by for him?"

Reminding him of the fact, that Mr. Peggotty derived a steady, though certainly a very moderate income from the bequest of his late brother-in-law, I promised to do so. We then took leave of each other. I cannot leave him, even now, without remembering with a pang, at once his modest fortitude and his great sorrow.

As to Mrs. Gummidge, if I were to endeavour to describe how she ran down the street by the side of the coach, seeing nothing but Mr. Peggotty on the roof, through the tears she tried to repress, and dashing herself against the people who were coming in the opposite direction, I should enter on a task of some difficulty. Therefore I had better leave her sitting on a baker's doorstep, out of breath, with no shape at all remaining in her bonnet, and one of her shoes off, lying on the pavement at a considerable distance.

When we got to our journey's end, our first pursuit was to look about for a little lodging for Peggotty, where her brother could have a bed. We were so fortunate as to find one, of a very clean and cheap description, over a chandler's shop, only two streets removed from me. When we had engaged this domicile, I bought some cold meat at an eating-house, and took my fellow-travellers home to tea; a proceeding, I regret to state, which did not meet with Mrs. Crupp's approval, but quite the contrary. I ought to observe, however, in explanation of that lady's state of mind, that she was much offended by Peggotty's tucking up her widow's gown before she had been ten minutes in the place, and setting to work to dust my bedroom. This Mrs. Crupp regarded in the light of a liberty, and a liberty, she said, was a thing she never allowed.

Mr. Peggotty had made a communication to me on the way to London, for which I was not unprepared. It was, that he purposed first seeing Mrs. Steerforth. As I felt bound to assist him in this, and also to mediate between them; with the view of sparing the mother's feelings as much as possible, I wrote to her that night. I told her as mildly as I could what his wrong was, and what my own share in his injury. I said he was a man in very common life, but of a most gentle and upright character; and that I ventured to express a hope that she would not refuse to see him in his heavy trouble. I mentioned two o'clock in the afternoon as the hour of our coming, and I sent the letter myself by the first coach in the morning.

At the appointed time, we stood at the door—the door of that house where I had been, a few days since, so happy: where my youthful confidence and warmth of heart had been yielded up so freely: which was closed against me henceforth: which was now a waste, a ruin.

No Littimer appeared. The pleasanter face which had replaced his, on the occasion of my last visit, answered to our summons, and went before us to the drawing-room. Mrs. Steerforth was sitting there. Rosa Dartle glided, as we went in, from another part of the room, and stood behind her chair.

I saw, directly, in his mother's face, that she knew from himself what he had done. It was very pale, and bore the traces of deeper emotion than my letter alone, weakened by the doubts her fondness would have raised upon it, would have been likely to create. I thought her more like him than ever I had thought her; and I felt, rather than saw, that the resemblance was not lost on my companion.

She sat upright in her arm-chair, with a stately, immovable, passionless air, that it seemed as if nothing could disturb. She looked very steadfastly at Mr. Peggotty when he stood before her; and he looked quite as steadfastly at her. Rosa Dartle's keen glance comprehended all of us. For some moments not a word was spoken. She motioned to Mr. Peggotty to be seated. He said, in a low voice, "I shouldn't feel it nat'ral, ma'am, to sit down in this house. I'd sooner stand." And this was succeeded by another silence, which she broke thus:

"I know, with deep regret, what has brought you here. What do you want of me? What do you ask me to do?"

He put his hat under his arm, and feeling in his breast for Emily's letter, took it out, unfolded it, and gave it to her.

"Please to read that, ma'am. That's my niece's hand!"

She read it, in the same stately and impassive way,—untouched by its contents, as far as I could see,—and returned it to him.

"'Unless he brings me back a lady,'" said Mr. Peggotty, tracing out that part with his finger. "I come to know, ma'am, whether he will keep his wured?"

"No," she returned.

"Why not?" said Mr. Peggotty.

"It is impossible. He would disgrace himself. You cannot fail to know that she is far below him."

"Raise her up!" said Mr. Peggotty.

"She is uneducated and ignorant."

"Maybe she's not; maybe she is," said Mr. Peggotty. "*I* think not, ma'am; but I'm no judge of them things. Teach her better!"

"Since you oblige me to speak more plainly, which I am very unwilling to do, her humble connexions would render such a thing impossible, if nothing else did."

"Hark to this, ma'am," he returned, slowly and quietly. "You know what it is to love your child. So do I. If she was a hundred times my child, I couldn't love her more. You doen't know what it is to lose your child. I do. All the heaps of riches in the wureld would be nowt to me (if they was mine) to buy her back! But, save her from this disgrace, and she shall never be disgraced by us. Not one of us that she's growed up among, not one of us that's lived along with her, and had her for their all in all, these many year, will ever look upon her pritty face again. We'll be content to let her be; we'll be content to think of her, far off, as if she was underneath another sun and sky; we'll be content to trust her to her husband,—to her little children, p'raps,—and bide the time when all of us shall be alike in quality afore our God!"

The rugged eloquence with which he spoke, was not devoid of all effect. She still preserved her proud manner, but there was a touch of softness in her voice, as she answered:

"I justify nothing. I make no counter-accusations. But I am sorry to repeat, it is impossible. Such a marriage would irretrievably blight my son's career, and ruin his prospects. Nothing is more certain than that it never can take place, and never will. If there is any other compensation——"

"I am looking at the likeness of the face," interrupted Mr. Peggotty, with a steady but a kindling eye, "that has looked at me, in my home, at my fireside, in my boat,—wheer not?—smiling and friendly, when it was so treacherous, that I go half wild when I think of it. If the likeness of that face don't turn to burning fire, at the thought

of offering money to me for my child's blight and ruin, it's as bad. I doen't know, being a lady's, but what it's worse."

She changed now, in a moment. An angry flush overspread her features; and she said, in an intolerant manner, grasping the arm-chair tightly with her hands:

"What compensation can you make to *me* for opening such a pit between me and my son? What is your love to mine? What is your separation to ours?"

Miss Dartle softly touched her, and bent down her head to whisper, but she would not hear a word.

"No, Rosa, not a word! Let the man listen to what I say! My son, who has been the object of my life, to whom its every thought has been devoted, whom I have gratified from a child in every wish, from whom I have had no separate existence since his birth,—to take up in a moment with a miserable girl, and avoid me! To repay my confidence with systematic deception, for her sake, and quit me for her! To set this wretched fancy, against his mother's claims upon his duty, love, respect, gratitude—claims that every day and hour of his life should have strengthened into ties that nothing could be proof against! Is this no injury?"

Again Rosa Dartle tried to soothe her; again ineffectually.

"I say, Rosa, not a word! If he can stake his all upon the lightest object, I can stake my all upon a greater purpose. Let him go where he will, with the means that my love has secured to him! Does he think to reduce me by long absence? He knows his mother very little if he does. Let him put away his whim now, and he is welcome back. Let him not put her away now, and he never shall come near me, living or dying, while I can raise my hand to make a sign against it, unless, being rid of her for ever, he comes humbly to me and begs for my forgiveness. This is my right. This is the acknowledgment I *will* have. This is the separation that there is between us! And is this," she added, looking at her visitor with the proud intolerant air with which she had begun, "no injury?"

While I heard and saw the mother as she said these words, I seemed to hear and see the son, defying them. All that I had ever seen in him of an unyielding, wilful spirit, I saw in her. All the understanding that I had now of his misdirected energy, became an understanding of her character too, and a perception that it was, in its strongest springs, the same.

She now observed to me, aloud, resuming her former restraint, that it was useless to hear more, or to say more, and that she begged to put an end to the interview. She rose with an air of dignity to leave the room, when Mr. Peggotty signified that it was needless.

"Doen't fear me being any hindrance to you, I have no more to say, ma'am," he remarked, as he moved towards the door. "I come heer with no hope, and I take away no hope. I have done what I thowt should be done, but I never looked fur any good to come of my stan'ning where I do. This has been too evil a house fur me and mine, fur me to be in my right senses and expect it."

With this, we departed; leaving her standing by her elbow-chair, a picture of a noble presence and a handsome face.

We had, on our way out, to cross a paved hall, with glass sides and roof, over which a vine was trained. Its leaves and shoots were green then, and the day being sunny, a pair of glass doors leading to the garden were thrown open. Rosa Dartle, entering this way with a noiseless step, when we were close to them, addressed herself to me:

"You do well," she said, "indeed, to bring this fellow here!"

Such a concentration of rage and scorn as darkened her face, and flashed in her jet-black eyes, I could not have thought compressible even into that face. The scar made by the hammer was, as usual in this excited state of her features, strongly marked. When the throbbing I had seen before, came into it as I looked at her, she absolutely lifted up her hand and struck it.

"This is a fellow," she said, "to champion and bring here, is he not? You are a true man!"

"Miss Dartle," I returned, "you are surely not so unjust as to condemn *me?*"

"Why do you bring division between these two mad creatures?" she returned. "Don't you know that they are both mad with their own self-will and pride?"

"Is it my doing?" I returned.

"Is it your doing!" she retorted. "Why do you bring this man here?"

"He is a deeply injured man, Miss Dartle," I replied. "You may not know it."

"I know that James Steerforth," she said, with her hand on her bosom, as if to prevent the storm that was raging there, from being loud, "has a false, corrupt heart, and is a traitor. But what need I know or care about this fellow, and his common niece?"

"Miss Dartle," I returned, "you deepen the injury. It is sufficient already. I will only say, at parting, that you do him a great wrong."

"I do him no wrong," she returned. "They are a depraved, worthless set. I would have her whipped!"

Mr. Peggotty passed on, without a word, and went out at the door.

"Oh, shame, Miss Dartle! shame!" I said indignantly. "How can you bear to trample on his undeserved affliction!"

"I would trample on them all," she answered. "I would have his house pulled down. I would have her branded on the face, drest in rags, and cast out in the streets to starve. If I had the power to sit in judgment on her, I would see it done. See it done? I would do it! I detest her. If I ever could reproach her with her infamous condition, I would go anywhere to do so. If I could hunt her to her grave, I would. If there was any word of comfort that would be a solace to her in her dying hour, and only I possessed it, I wouldn't part with it for Life itself."

The mere vehemence of her words can convey, I am sensible, but a weak impression of the passion by which she was possessed, and which made itself articulate in her whole figure, though her voice, instead of being raised, was lower than usual. No description I could give of her would do justice to my recollection of her, or to her entire deliverance of herself to her anger. I have seen passion in many forms, but I have never seen it in such a form as that.

When I joined Mr. Peggotty, he was walking slowly and thoughtfully down the hill. He told me, as soon as I came up with him, that having now discharged his mind of what he had purposed doing in London, he meant "to set out on his travels," that night. I asked him where he meant to go? He only answered, "I'm a going, Sir, to seek my niece."

We went back to the little lodging over the chandler's shop, and there I found an opportunity of repeating to Peggotty what he had said to me. She informed me, in return, that he had said the same to her that morning. She knew no more than I did, where he was going, but she thought he had some project shaped out in his mind.

I did not like to leave him, under such circumstances, and we all three dined together off a beefsteak pie—which was one of the many good things for which Peggotty was famous—and which was curiously flavoured on this occasion, I recollect well, by a miscellaneous taste of tea, coffee, butter, bacon, cheese, new loaves, firewood, candles, and walnut ketchup, continually ascending from the shop. After dinner we sat for an hour or so near the window, without talking much; and then Mr. Peggotty got up, and brought his oilskin bag and his stout stick, and laid them on the table.

He accepted, from his sister's stock of ready money, a small sum on account of his legacy; barely enough, I should have thought, to keep him for a month. He promised to communicate with me, when anything befell him; and he slung his bag about him, took his hat and stick, and bade us both "Good bye!"

"All good attend you, dear old woman," he said, embracing Peggotty, "and you too, Mas'r Davy!" shaking hands with me. "I'm a going to seek her, fur and wide. If she should come home while I'm away—but ah, that ain't like to be!—or if I should bring her back, my meaning is, that she and me shall live and die where no one can't reproach her. If any hurt should come to me, remember that the last words I left for her was, 'My unchanged love is with my darling child, and I forgive her!'"

He said this solemnly, bare-headed; then, putting on his hat, he went down the stairs, and away. We followed to the door. It was a warm, dusty evening, just the time when, in the great main thoroughfare out of which that by-way turned, there was a temporary lull in the eternal tread of feet upon the pavement, and a strong red sunshine. He turned, alone, at the corner of our shady street, into a glow of light, in which we lost him. Rarely did that hour of the evening come, rarely did I wake at night, rarely did I look up at the moon, or stars, or watch the falling rain, or hear the wind, but I thought of his solitary figure toiling on, poor pilgrim, and recalled the words:

"I'm a going to seek her, fur and wide. If any hurt should come to me, remember that the last words I left for her was, 'My unchanged love is with my darling child, and I forgive her!'"

CHAPTER XXXIII.

BLISSFUL.

ALL this time, I had gone on loving Dora, harder than ever. Her idea was my refuge in disappointment and distress, and made some amends to me, even for the loss of my friend. The more I pitied myself, or pitied others, the more I sought for consolation in the image of Dora. The greater the accumulation of deceit and trouble in the world, the brighter and the purer shone the star of Dora high above the world. I don't think I had any definite idea where Dora came from, or in what degree she was related to a higher order of beings; but I am quite sure I should have scouted the notion of her being simply human, like any other young lady, with indignation and contempt.

If I may so express it, I was steeped in Dora. I was not merely over head and ears in love with her, but I was saturated through and through. Enough love might have been wrung out of me, metaphorically speaking, to drown anybody in; and yet there would have remained enough within me, and all over me, to pervade my entire existence.

The first thing I did, on my own account, when I came back, was to take a night-walk to Norwood, and, like the subject of a venerable riddle of my childhood, to go "round and round the house, without ever touching the house," thinking about Dora. I believe the theme of this incomprehensible conundrum was the moon. No matter what it was, I, the moon-struck slave of Dora, perambulated round and round the house and garden for two hours, looking through crevices in the palings, getting my chin by dint of violent exertion above the rusty nails on the top, blowing kisses at the lights in the windows, and romantically calling on the night, at intervals, to shield my Dora—I don't exactly know what from, I suppose from fire. Perhaps from mice, to which she had a great objection.

My love was so much on my mind, and it was so natural to me to confide in Peggotty, when I found her again by my side of an evening with the old set of industrial implements, busily making the tour of my wardrobe, that I imparted to her, in a sufficiently roundabout way, my great secret. Peggotty was strongly interested, but I could not get her into my view of the case at all. She was audaciously prejudiced in my favour, and quite unable to understand why I should have any misgivings, or be low-spirited about it. "The young lady might think herself well off," she observed, "to have such a beau. And as to her Pa," she said, "what *did* the gentleman expect, for gracious sake!"

I observed, however, that Mr. Spenlow's Proctorial gown and stiff cravat took Peggotty down a little, and inspired her with a greater reverence for the man who was gradually becoming more and more etherealized in my eyes every day, and about whom a reflected radiance seemed to me to beam when he sat erect in Court among his papers, like a little lighthouse in a sea of stationery. And by-the-by, it used to be uncommonly strange to me to consider, I remember, as I sat in Court too, how those dim old judges and doctors wouldn't have cared for Dora, if they had known her; how they wouldn't have gone out of their senses with rapture, if marriage with Dora had been proposed to them; how Dora might have sung and played upon that glorified guitar, until she led *me* to the verge of madness, yet not have tempted one of those slow-goers an inch out of his road!

I despised them, to a man. Frozen-out old gardeners in the flower-beds of the heart, I took a personal offence against them all. The Bench was nothing to me but an insensible blunderer. The Bar had no more tenderness or poetry in it, than the bar of a public-house.

Taking the management of Peggotty's affairs into my own hands, with no little pride, I proved the will, and came to a settlement with the Legacy Duty Office, and took her to the Bank, and soon got everything into an orderly train. We varied the legal character of these proceedings by going to see some perspiring Waxwork, in Fleet Street (melted, I should hope, these twenty years); and by visiting Miss Linwood's Exhibition, which I remember as a Mausoleum of needlework, favourable to self-examination and repentance; and by inspecting the Tower of London; and going to the top of St. Paul's. All these wonders afforded Peggotty as much pleasure as she was able to enjoy, under existing circumstances: except, I think, St. Paul's, which from her long attachment to her workbox, became a rival of the picture on the lid, and was, in some particulars, vanquished, she considered, by that work of art.

Peggotty's business, which was what we used to call "common-form business" in the Commons (and very light and lucrative the common-form business was), being settled, I took her down to the office one morning to pay her bill. Mr. Spenlow had stepped out, old Tiffey said, to get a gentleman sworn for a marriage licence; but as I knew he would be back directly, our place lying close to the Surrogate's, and to the Vicar-General's Office too, I told Peggotty to wait.

We were a little like undertakers, in the Commons, as regarded Probate transactions; generally making it a rule to look more or less cut up, when we had to deal with clients in mourning. In a similar feeling of delicacy, we were always blithe and light-hearted with the licence clients. Therefore I hinted to Peggotty that she would find Mr. Spenlow much recovered from the shock of Mr. Barkis's decease; and indeed he came in like a bridegroom.

But neither Peggotty nor I had eyes for him, when we saw, in company with him, Mr. Murdstone. He was very little changed. His hair looked as thick, and was certainly as black as ever; and his glance was as little to be trusted as of old.

"Ah, Copperfield?" said Mr. Spenlow. "You know this gentleman, I believe?"

I made my gentleman a distant bow, and Peggotty barely recognised him. He was, at first, somewhat disconcerted to meet us two together; but quickly decided what to do, and came up to me.

"I hope," he said, "that you are doing well?"

"It can hardly be interesting to you," said I. "Yes, if you wish to know."

We looked at each other, and he addressed himself to Peggotty.

"And you," said he. "I am sorry to observe that you have lost your husband."

"It's not the first loss I have had in my life, Mr. Murdstone," replied Peggotty, trembling from head to foot. "I am glad to hope that there is nobody to blame for this one, —nobody to answer for it."

"Ha!" said he; "that's a comfortable reflection. You have done your duty?"

"I have not worn anybody's life away," said Peggotty, "I am thankful to think! No, Mr. Murdstone, I have not worried and frightened any sweet creetur to an early grave!"

He eyed her gloomily—remorsefully I thought—for an instant; and said, turning his head towards me, but looking at my feet instead of my face:

"We are not likely to encounter soon again;—a source of satisfaction to us both, no doubt, for such meetings as this can never be agreeable. I do not expect that you, who always rebelled against my just authority, exerted for your benefit and reformation, should owe me any good-will now There is an antipathy between us——"

"An old one, I believe?" said I, interrupting him.

He smiled, and shot as evil a glance at me as could come from his dark eyes.

"It rankled in your baby breast," he said. "It embittered the life of your poor mother. You are right. I hope you may do better, yet; I hope you may correct yourself."

Here he ended the dialogue, which had been carried on in a low voice, in a corner of the outer office, by passing into Mr. Spenlow's room, and saying aloud, in his smoothest manner:

"Gentlemen of Mr. Spenlow's profession are accustomed to family differences, and know how complicated and difficult they always are!" With that, he paid the money for his licence; and, receiving it neatly folded from Mr. Spenlow, together with a shake of the hand, and a polite wish for his happiness and the lady's, went out of the office.

I might have had more difficulty in constraining myself to be silent under his words, if I had had less difficulty in impressing upon Peggotty (who was only angry on my account, good creature!) that we were not in a place for recrimination, and that I besought her to hold her peace. She was so unusually roused, that I was glad to compound for an affectionate hug, elicited by this revival in her mind of our old injuries, and to make the best I could of it, before Mr. Spenlow and the clerks.

Mr. Spenlow did not appear to know what the connexion between Mr. Murdstone and myself was; which I was glad of, for I could not bear to acknowledge him, even in my own breast, remembering what I did of the history of my poor mother. Mr. Spenlow seemed to think, if he thought anything about the matter, that my aunt was the leader of the state party in our family, and that there was a rebel party commanded by somebody else—so I gathered at least from what he said, while we were waiting for Mr. Tiffey to make out Peggotty's bill of costs.

"Miss Trotwood," he remarked, "is very firm, no doubt, and not likely to give way to opposition. I have an admiration for her character, and I may congratulate you, Copperfield, on being on the right side. Differences between relations are much to be deplored—but they are extremely general—and the great thing is, to be on the right side:" meaning, I take it, on the side of the moneyed interest.

"Rather a good marriage this, I believe?" said Mr. Spenlow.

I explained that I knew nothing about it.

"Indeed!" he said. "Speaking from the few words Mr. Murdstone dropped—as a man frequently does on these occasions—and from what Miss Murdstone let fall, I should say it was rather a good marriage."

"Do you mean that there is money, Sir?" I asked.

"Yes," said Mr. Spenlow, "I understand there's money. Beauty too, I am told."

"Indeed? Is his new wife young?"

"Just of age," said Mr. Spenlow. "So lately, that I should think they had been waiting for that."

"Lord deliver her!" said Peggotty. So very emphatically and unexpectedly, that we were all three discomposed; until Tiffey came in with the bill.

Old Tiffey soon appeared, however, and handed it to Mr. Spenlow, to look over. Mr. Spenlow, settling his chin in his cravat and rubbing it softly, went over the items with a deprecatory air—as if it were all Jorkins's doing—and handed it back to Tiffey with a bland sigh.

"Yes," he said. "That's right. Quite right. I should have been extremely happy, Copperfield, to have limited these charges to the actual expenditure out of pocket; but it is an irksome incident in my professional life, that I am not at liberty to consult my own wishes. I have a partner —Mr. Jorkins."

As he said this with a gentle melancholy, which was the next thing to making no charge at all, I expressed my acknowledgments on Peggotty's behalf, and paid Tiffey in bank-notes. Peggotty then retired to her lodging, and Mr. Spenlow and I went into Court, where we had a divorce suit coming on, under an ingenious little statute (repealed now, I believe, but in virtue of which I have seen several marriages annulled), of which the merits were these. The husband, whose name was Thomas Benjamin, had taken out his marriage licence as Thomas only; suppressing the Benjamin, in case he should not find himself as comfortable as he expected. *Not* finding himself as comfortable as he expected, or being a little fatigued with his wife, poor fellow, he now came forward, by a friend, after being married a year or two, and declared that his name was Thomas Benjamin, and therefore he was not married at all. Which the Court confirmed, to his great satisfaction.

I must say that I had my doubts about the strict justice of this, and was not even frightened out of them by the bushel of wheat which reconciles all anomalies.

But Mr. Spenlow argued the matter with me. He said, Look at the world, there was good and evil in that; look at the ecclesiastical law, there was good and evil in *that*. It was all part of a system. Very good. There you were!

I had not the hardihood to suggest to Dora's father that possibly we might even improve the world a little, if we got up early in the morning, and took off our coats to the work; but I confessed that I thought we might improve the Commons. Mr. Spenlow replied that he would particularly advise me to dismiss that idea from my mind, as not being worthy of my gentlemanly character; but that he would be glad to hear from me of what improvement I thought the Commons susceptible?

Taking that part of the Commons which happened to be nearest to us—for our man was unmarried by this time, and we were out of Court, and strolling past the Prerogative Office—I submitted that I thought the Prerogative Office rather a queerly managed institution. Mr. Spenlow inquired in what respect? I replied, with all due deference to his experience (but with more deference, I am afraid, to his being Dora's father), that perhaps it was a little nonsensical that the Registry of that Court, containing the original wills of all persons leaving effects within the immense province of Canterbury, for three whole centuries, should be an accidental building, never designed for the purpose, leased by the registrars for their own private emolument, unsafe, not even ascertained to be fireproof, choked with the important documents it held, and positively, from the roof to the basement, a mercenary speculation of the registrars, who took great fees from the public, and crammed the public's wills away anyhow and anywhere, having no other object than to get rid of them cheaply. That, perhaps, it was a little unreasonable that these registrars in the receipt of profits amounting to eight or nine thousand pounds a year (to say nothing of the profits of the deputy-registrars, and clerks of seats), should not be obliged to spend a little of that money, in finding a reasonably safe place for the important documents which all classes of people were compelled to hand over to them, whether they would or no. That, perhaps, it was a little unjust that all the great offices in this great office, should be magnificent sinecures, while the unfortunate working-clerks in the cold dark room up-stairs were the worst rewarded, and the least considered men, doing important services, in London. That perhaps it was a little indecent that the principal registrar of all, whose duty it was to find the public, constantly resorting to this place, all needful accommodation, should be an enormous sinecurist in virtue of that post (and might be, besides, a clergyman, a pluralist, the holder of a stall in a cathedral, and what not), while the public was put to the inconvenience of which we had a specimen every afternoon when the office was busy, and which we knew to be quite monstrous. That, perhaps, in short, this Prerogative Office of the diocese of Canterbury was altogether such a pestilent job, and such a pernicious absurdity, that but for its being squeezed away in a corner of St. Paul's Churchyard, which few people knew, it must have been turned completely inside out, and upside down, long ago.

Mr. Spenlow smiled as I became modestly warm on the subject, and then argued this question with me as he had argued the other. He said, What was it after all? It was a question of feeling. If the public felt that their wills were in safe keeping, and took it for granted that the office was not to be made better, who was the worse for it? Nobody. Who was the better for it? All the sinecurists. Very well. Then the good predominated. It might not be a perfect system; nothing *was* perfect; but what he objected to, was, the insertion of the wedge. Under the Prerogative Office, the country had been glorious. Insert the wedge into the Prerogative Office, and the country would cease to be glorious. He considered it the principle of a gentleman to take things as he found them; and he had no doubt the Prerogative Office would last our time. I deferred to his opinion, though I had great doubts of it myself. I find he was right, however; for it has not only lasted to the present moment, but has done so in the teeth of a great parliamentary report made (not too willingly) eighteen years ago, when all these objections of mine were set forth in detail, and when the existing stowage for wills was described as equal to the accumulation of only two years and a half more. What they have done with them since; whether they have lost many, or whether they sell any, now and then, to the butter-shops; I don't know. I am glad mine is not there, and I hope it may not go there, yet awhile.

I have set all this down, in my present blissful chapter, because here it comes into its natural place. Mr. Spenlow and I falling into this conversation, prolonged it and our saunter to and fro, until we diverged into general topics. And so it came about, in the end, that Mr. Spenlow told me this day week was Dora's birthday, and he would be glad if I would come down and join a little picnic on the occasion. I went out of my senses immediately; became a mere driveller next day, on receipt of a little lace-edged sheet of note-paper, "Favoured by papa. To remind;" and passed the intervening period in a state of dotage.

I think I committed every possible absurdity, in the way of preparation for this blessed event. I turn hot when I remember the cravat I bought. My boots might be placed in any collection of instruments of torture. I provided, and sent down by the Norwood coach the night before, a delicate little hamper, amounting in itself, I thought, almost to a declaration. There were crackers in it with the tenderest mottoes that could be got for money. At six in the morning, I was in Covent Garden Market, buying a bouquet for Dora. At ten I was on horseback (I hired a gallant grey, for the occasion), with the bouquet in my hat, to keep it fresh, trotting down to Norwood.

I suppose that when I saw Dora in the garden and pretended not to see her, and rode past the house pretending to be anxiously looking for it, I committed two small fooleries which other young gentlemen in my circumstances might have committed—because they came so very natural to me. But oh! when I *did* find the house, and *did* dismount at the garden gate, and drag those stony-hearted boots across the lawn to Dora sitting on a garden-seat under a lilac-tree, what a spectacle she was, upon that beautiful morning, among the butterflies, in a white chip bonnet and a dress of celestial blue!

There was a young lady with her—comparatively stricken in years—almost twenty, I should say. Her name was Miss Mills, and Dora called her Julia. She was the bosom friend of Dora. Happy Miss Mills!

Jip was there, and Jip *would* bark at me again. When I presented my bouquet, he gnashed his teeth with jealousy. Well he might. If he had the least idea how I adored his mistress, well he might!

"Oh, thank you, Mr. Copperfield! What dear flowers!" said Dora.

I had had an intention of saying (and had been studying the best form of words for three miles) that I thought them beautiful before I saw them so near *her*. But I couldn't manage it. She was too bewildering. To see her lay the flowers against her little dimpled chin, was to lose all presence of mind and power of language in a feeble ecstasy. I wonder I didn't say, "Kill me, if you have a heart, Miss Mills. Let me die here!"

Then Dora held my flowers to Jip to smell. Then Jip growled, and wouldn't smell them. Then Dora laughed, and held them a little closer to Jip, to make him. Then Jip laid hold of a bit of geranium with his teeth, and worried imaginary cats in it. Then Dora beat him, and pouted, and said, "my poor beautiful flowers!" as compassionately, I thought, as if Jip had laid hold of me. I wished he had!

"You'll be so glad to hear, Mr. Copperfield," said Dora, "that that cross Miss Murdstone is not here. She has gone to her brother's marriage, and will be away at least three weeks. Isn't that delightful?"

I said I was sure it must be delightful to her, and all that was delightful to her was delightful to me. Miss

Mills, with an air of superior wisdom and benevolence, smiled upon us.

"She is the most disagreeable thing I ever saw," said Dora. "You can't believe how ill-tempered and shocking she is, Julia."

"Yes, I can, my dear!" said Julia.

"*You* can, perhaps, love," returned Dora, with her hand on Julia's. "Forgive my not excepting you, my dear, at first."

I learnt, from this, that Miss Mills had had her trials in the course of a chequered existence; and that to these, perhaps, I might refer that wise benignity of manner which I had already noticed. I found, in the course of the day, that this was the case: Miss Mills having been unhappy in a misplaced affection, and being understood to have retired from the world on her awful stock of experience, but still to take a calm interest in the unblighted hopes and loves of youth.

But now Mr. Spenlow came out of the house, and Dora went to him, saying, "Look, papa, what beautiful flowers!" And Miss Mills smiled thoughtfully, as who should say, "Ye May-flies, enjoy your brief existence in the bright morning of life!" And we all walked from the lawn towards the carriage, which was getting ready.

I shall never have such a ride again. I have never had such another. There were only those three, their hamper, my hamper, and the guitar-case, in the phaeton; and, of course, the phaeton was open; and I rode behind it, and Dora sat with her back to the horses, looking towards me. She kept the bouquet close to her on the cushion, and wouldn't allow Jip to sit on that side of her at all, for fear he should crush it. She often carried it in her hand, often refreshed herself with its fragrance. Our eyes at those times often met; and my great astonishment is that I didn't go over the head of my gallant grey into the carriage.

There was dust, I believe. There was a good deal of dust, I believe. I have a faint impression that Mr. Spenlow remonstrated with me for riding in it; but I knew of none. I was sensible of a mist of love and beauty about Dora, but of nothing else. He stood up sometimes, and asked me what I thought of the prospect. I said, it was delightful, and I dare say it was; but it was all Dora to me. The sun shone Dora, and the birds sang Dora. The south wind blew Dora, and the wild flowers in the hedges were all Dora, to a bud. My comfort is, Miss Mills understood me. Miss Mills alone could enter into my feelings thoroughly.

I don't know how long we were going, and to this hour I know as little where we went. Perhaps it was near Guildford. Perhaps some Arabian-night magician opened up the place for the day, and shut it for ever when we came away. It was a green spot, on a hill, carpeted with soft turf. There were shady trees, and heather, and, as far as the eye could see, a rich landscape.

It was a trying thing to find people here, waiting for us; and my jealousy, even of the ladies, knew no bounds. But all of my own sex—especially one impostor, three or four years my elder, with a red whisker, on which he established an amount of presumption not to be endured—were my mortal foes.

We all unpacked our baskets, and employed ourselves in getting dinner ready. Red Whisker pretended he could make a salad (which I don't believe), and obtruded himself on public notice. Some of the young ladies washed the lettuces for him, and sliced them under his directions. Dora was among these. I felt that Fate had pitted me against this man, and one of us must fall.

Red Whisker made his salad (I wondered how they could eat it. Nothing should have induced *me* to touch it!) and voted himself into the charge of the wine-cellar, which he constructed, being an ingenious beast, in the hollow trunk of a tree. By-and-by I saw him, with the majority of a lobster on his plate, eating his dinner at the feet of Dora!

I have but an indistinct idea of what happened for some time after this baleful object presented itself to my view. I was very merry, I know; but it was hollow merriment. I attached myself to a young creature in pink, with little eyes, and flirted with her desperately. She received my attentions with favour; but whether on my account solely, or because she had any designs on Red Whisker, I can't say. Dora's health was drunk. When I drank it, I affected to interrupt my conversation for that purpose, and to resume it immediately afterwards. I caught Dora's eye as I bowed to her, and I thought it looked appealing. But it looked at me over the head of Red Whisker, and I was adamant.

The young creature in pink had a mother in green; and I rather think the latter separated us from motives of policy. Howbeit, there was a general breaking up of the party, while the remnants of the dinner were being put away; and I strolled off by myself among the trees, in a raging and remorseful state. I was debating whether I should pretend that I was not well, and fly—I don't know where—upon my gallant grey, when Dora and Miss Mills met me.

"Mr. Copperfield," said Miss Mills, "you are dull."

I begged her pardon. Not at all.

"And, Dora," said Miss Mills, "*you* are dull."

Oh dear no! Not in the least.

"Mr. Copperfield and Dora," said Miss Mills, with an almost venerable air. "Enough of this. Do not allow a trivial misunderstanding to wither the blossoms of spring, which, once put forth and blighted, can not be renewed. I speak," said Miss Mills, "from experience of the past—the remote irrevocable past. The gushing fountains which sparkle in the sun, must not be stopped in mere caprice; the oasis in the Desert of Sahara, must not be plucked up idly."

I hardly knew what I did, I was burning all over to that extraordinary extent; but I took Dora's little hand and kissed it—and she let me! I kissed Miss Mills's hand; and we all seemed, to my thinking, to go straight up to the seventh heaven.

We did not come down again. We stayed up there all the evening. At first we strayed to and fro among the trees: I with Dora's shy arm drawn through mine: and Heaven knows, folly as it all was, it would have been a happy fate to have been struck immortal with those foolish feelings, and have strayed among the trees for ever!

But, much too soon, we heard the others laughing and talking, and calling "where's Dora!" So we went back, and they wanted Dora to sing. Red Whisker would have got the guitar-case out of the carriage, but Dora told him nobody knew where it was but I. So Red Whisker was done for in a moment; and *I* got it, and *I* unlocked it, and *I* took the guitar out, and *I* sat by her, and *I* held her handkerchief and gloves, and *I* drank in every note of her dear voice, and she sang to *me* who loved her, and all the others might applaud as much as they liked, but they had nothing to do with it!

I was intoxicated with joy. I was afraid it was too happy to be real, and that I should wake in Buckingham Street presently, and hear Mrs. Crupp clinking the teacups in getting breakfast ready. But Dora sang, and others sang, and Miss Mills sang—about the slumbering echoes in the caverns of Memory; as if she were a hundred years old —and the evening came on; and we had tea, with the kettle boiling gipsy-fashion; and I was still as happy as ever.

I was happier than ever when the party broke up, and the other people, defeated Red Whisker and all, went their several ways, and we went ours through the still evening and the dying light, with sweet scents rising up around us. Mr. Spenlow being a little drowsy after the champagne— honour to the soil that grew the grape, to the grape that made the wine, to the sun that ripened it, and to the merchant who adulterated it!—and being fast asleep in a corner of the carriage, I rode by the side, and talked to Dora. She admired my horse and patted him—oh, what a dear little hand it looked upon a horse!—and her shawl would not keep right, and now and then I drew it round her with my arm; and I even fancied that Jip began to see how it was, and to understand that he must make up his mind to be friends with me.

That sagacious Miss Mills, too; that amiable, though quite used-up recluse; that little patriarch of something less than twenty, who had done with the world, and mustn't on any account have the slumbering echoes in the caverns of Memory awakened; what a kind thing she did!

"Mr. Copperfield," said Miss Mills, "come to this side of the carriage a moment—if you can spare a moment. I want to speak to you."

Behold me, on my gallant grey, bending at the side of Miss Mills, with my hand upon the carriage-door!

"Dora is coming to stay with me. She is coming home with me the day after to-morrow. If you would like to call, I am sure papa would be happy to see you."

What could I do but invoke a silent blessing on Miss Mills's head, and store Miss Mills's address in the securest corner of my memory! What could I do but tell Miss Mills, with grateful looks and fervent words, how much I appreciated her good offices, and what an inestimable value I set upon her friendship!

Then Miss Mills benignantly dismissed me, saying, "Go back to Dora!" and I went; and Dora leaned out of the carriage to talk to me, and we talked all the rest of the way; and I rode my gallant grey so close to the wheel that I grazed his near fore-leg against it, and "took the bark off," as his owner told me, "to the tune of three pun' sivin" —which I paid, and thought extremely cheap for so much joy. What time Miss Mills sat looking at the moon, murmuring verses and recalling, I suppose, the ancient days when she and earth had anything in common.

Norwood was many miles too near, and we reached it many hours too soon; but Mr. Spenlow came to himself a little short of it and said, "You must come in, Copperfield, and rest!" and I consenting, we had sandwiches and wine-and-water. In the light room, Dora blushing looked so lovely, that I could not tear myself away, but sat there staring, in a dream, until the snoring of Mr. Spenlow inspired me with sufficient consciousness to take my leave. So we parted; I riding all the way to London with the farewell touch of Dora's hand still light on mine, recalling every incident and word ten thousand times; lying down in my own bed at last, as enraptured a young noodle as ever was carried out of his five wits by love.

When I awoke next morning, I was resolute to declare my passion to Dora, and know my fate. Happiness or misery was now the question. There was no other question that I knew of in the world, and only Dora could give the answer to it. I passed three days in a luxury of wretchedness, torturing myself by putting every conceivable variety of discouraging construction on all that ever had taken place between Dora and me. At last, arrayed for the purpose at a vast expense, I went to Miss Mills's, fraught with a declaration.

How many times I went up and down the street, and round the square—painfully aware of being a much better answer to the old riddle than the original one—before I could persuade myself to go up the steps and knock, is no matter now. Even when, at last, I had knocked, and was waiting at the door, I had some flurried thought of asking if that were Mr. Blackboy's (in imitation of poor Barkis), begging pardon, and retreating. But I kept my ground.

Mr. Mills was not at home. I did not expect he would be. Nobody wanted *him*. Miss Mills was at home. Miss Mills would do.

I was shown into a room up-stairs, where Miss Mills and Dora were. Jip was there. Miss Mills was copying music (I recollect, it was a new song, called Affection's Dirge), and Dora was painting flowers. What were my feelings, when I recognised my own flowers; the identical Covent Garden Market purchase! I cannot say that they were very like, or that they particularly resembled any flowers that have ever come under my observation; but I knew from the paper round them, which was accurately copied, what the composition was.

Miss Mills was very glad to see me, and very sorry her Papa was not at home: though I thought we all bore that with fortitude. Miss Mills was conversational for a few minutes, and then, laying down her pen upon Affection's Dirge, got up, and left the room.

I began to think I would put it off till to-morrow.

"I hope your poor horse was not tired, when he got home at night," said Dora, lifting up her beautiful eyes. "It was a long way for him."

I began to think I would do it to-day.

"It was a long way for *him*," said I, "for he had nothing to uphold him on the journey."

"Wasn't he fed, poor thing?" asked Dora.

I began to think I would put it off till to-morrow.

"Ye—yes," I said, "he was well taken care of. I mean he had not the unutterable happiness that I had in being so near you."

Dora bent her head over her drawing, and said, after a little while—I had sat, in the interval, in a burning fever, and with my legs in a very rigid state—

"You didn't seem to be sensible of that happiness yourself, at one time of the day."

I saw now that I was in for it, and it must be done on the spot.

"You didn't care for that happiness in the least," said Dora, slightly raising her eyebrows, and shaking her head, "when you were sitting by Miss Kitt."

DAVID COPPERFIELD

Kitt, I should observe, was the name of the creature in pink, with the little eyes.

"Though certainly I don't know why you should," said Dora, "or why you should call it a happiness at all. But of course you don't mean what you say. And I am sure no one doubts your being at liberty to do whatever you like. Jip, you naughty boy, come here!"

I don't know how I did it. I did it in a moment. I intercepted Jip. I had Dora in my arms. I was full of eloquence. I never stopped for a word. I told her how I loved her. I told her I should die without her. I told her that I idolised and worshipped her. Jip barked madly all the time.

When Dora hung her head and cried, and trembled, my eloquence increased so much the more. If she would like me to die for her, she had but to say the word, and I was ready. Life without Dora's love was not a thing to have on any terms. I couldn't bear it, and I wouldn't. I had loved her every minute, day and night, since I first saw her. I loved her at that minute to distraction. I should always love her, every minute, to distraction. Lovers had loved before, and lovers would love again; but no lover had ever loved, might, could, would, or should ever love, as I loved Dora. The more I raved, the more Jip barked. Each of us, in his own way, got more mad every moment.

Well, well! Dora and I were sitting on the sofa by-and-by, quiet enough, and Jip was lying in her lap, winking peacefully at me. It was off my mind. I was in a state of perfect rapture. Dora and I were engaged.

I suppose we had some notion that this was to end in marriage. We must have had some, because Dora stipulated that we were never to be married without her papa's consent. But, in our youthful ecstasy, I don't think that we really looked before us or behind us; or had any aspiration beyond the ignorant present. We were to keep our secret from Mr. Spenlow; but I am sure the idea never entered my head, then, that there was anything dishonourable in that.

Miss Mills was more than usually pensive when Dora, going to find her, brought her back;—I apprehend, because there was a tendency in what had passed to awaken the slumbering echoes in the caverns of Memory. But she gave us her blessing, and the assurance of her lasting friendship, and spoke to us, generally, as became a Voice from the Cloister.

What an idle time it was! What an unsubstantial, happy, foolish time it was!

When I measured Dora's finger for a ring that was to be made of forget-me-nots, and when the jeweller, to whom I took the measure, found me out, and laughed over his order-book, and charged me anything he liked for the pretty little toy, with its blue stones—so associated in my remembrance with Dora's hand, that yesterday, when I saw such another, by chance, on the finger of my own daughter, there was a momentary stirring in my heart, like pain!

When I walked about, exalted with my secret, and full of my own interest, and felt the dignity of loving Dora, and of being beloved, so much, that if I had walked the air, I could not have been more above the people not so situated, who were creeping on the earth!

When we had those meetings in the garden of the square, and sat within the dingy summer-house, so happy, that I love the London sparrows to this hour, for nothing else, and see the plumage of the tropics in their smoky feathers!

When we had our first great quarrel (within a week of our betrothal), and when Dora sent me back the ring, enclosed in a despairing cocked-hat note, wherein she used the terrible expression that "our love had begun in folly, and ended in madness!" which dreadful words occasioned me to tear my hair, and cry that all was over!

When, under cover of the night, I flew to Miss Mills, whom I saw by stealth in a back-kitchen where there was a mangle, and implored Miss Mills to interpose between us and avert insanity. When Miss Mills undertook the office and returned with Dora, exhorting us, from the pulpit of her own bitter youth, to mutual concession, and the avoidance of the Desert of Sahara!

When we cried, and made it up, and were so blest again, that the back-kitchen, mangle and all, changed to Love's own temple, where we arranged a plan of correspondence through Miss Mills, always to comprehend at least one letter on each side every day!

What an idle time! What an unsubstantial, happy, foolish time! Of all the times of mine that Time has in his grip, there is none that in one retrospection I can smile at half so much, and think of half so tenderly.

CHAPTER XXXIV.

MY AUNT ASTONISHES ME.

I WROTE to Agnes as soon as Dora and I were engaged. I wrote her a long letter, in which I tried to make her comprehend how blest I was, and what a darling Dora was. I entreated Agnes not to regard this as a thoughtless passion which would ever yield to any other, or had the least resemblance to the boyish fancies that we used to joke about. I assured her that its profundity was quite unfathomable, and expressed my belief that nothing like it had ever been known.

Somehow, as I wrote to Agnes on a fine evening by my open window, and the remembrance of her clear calm eyes and gentle face came stealing over me, it shed such a peaceful influence upon the hurry and agitation in which I had been living lately, and of which my very happiness partook in some degree, that it soothed me into tears. I remember that I sat resting my head upon my hand, when the letter was half done, cherishing a general fancy as if Agnes were one of the elements of my natural home. As if, in the retirement of the house made almost sacred to me by her presence, Dora and I must be happier than anywhere. As if, in love, joy, sorrow, hope, or disappointment; in all emotions; my heart turned naturally there, and found its refuge and best friend.

Of Steerforth, I said nothing. I only told her there had been sad grief at Yarmouth, on account of Emily's flight; and that on me it made a double wound, by reason of the circumstances attending it. I knew how quick she always was to divine the truth, and that she would never be the first to breathe his name.

To this letter, I received an answer by return of post. As I read it, I seemed to hear Agnes speaking to me. It was like her cordial voice in my ears. What can I say more?

While I had been away from home lately, Traddles had called twice or thrice. Finding Peggotty within, and being informed by Peggotty (who always volunteered that information to whomsoever would receive it), that she was my old nurse, he had established a good-humoured acquaintance with her, and had stayed to have a little chat with her about me. So Peggotty said; but I am afraid the chat was all on her own side, and of immoderate length, as she was very difficult indeed to stop, God bless her! when she had me for her theme.

This reminds me, not only that I expected Traddles on a certain afternoon of his own appointing, which was now come, but that Mrs. Crupp had resigned everything appertaining to her office (the salary excepted) until Peggotty should cease to present herself. Mrs. Crupp, after holding divers conversations respecting Peggotty, in a very high-pitched voice, on the staircase—with some invisible Familiar it would appear, for corporeally speaking she was quite alone at those times—addressed a letter to me, developing her views. Beginning it with that statement of universal application, which fitted every occurrence of her life, namely, that she was a mother herself, she went on to inform me that she had once seen very different days, but that at all periods of her existence she had had a constitutional objection to spies, intruders, and informers. She named no names, she said; let them the cap fitted, wear it; but spies, intruders, and informers, especially in widders' weeds (this clause was underlined), she had ever accustomed herself to look down upon. If a gentleman was the victim of spies, intruders, and informers (but still naming no names), that was his own pleasure. He had a right to please himself; so let him do. All that she, Mrs. Crupp, stipulated for, was, that she should not be "brought in contract" with such persons. Therefore she begged to be excused from any further attendance on the top set, until things were as they formerly was, and as they could be wished to be; and further mentioned that her little book would be found upon the breakfast-table every Saturday morning, when she requested an immediate settlement of the same, with the benevolent view of saving trouble, "and an ill-conwenience" to all parties.

After this, Mrs. Crupp confined herself to making pitfalls on the stairs, principally with pitchers, and endeavouring to delude Peggotty into breaking her legs. I found it rather harassing to live in this state of siege, but was too much afraid of Mrs. Crupp to see any way out of it.

"My dear Copperfield," cried Traddles, punctually appearing at my door, in spite of all these obstacles, "how do you do?"

"My dear Traddles," said I, "I am delighted to see you at last, and very sorry I have not been at home before. But I have been so much engaged——"

"Yes, yes, I know," said Traddles, "of course. Yours lives in London, I think."

"What did you say?"

"She—excuse me—Miss D., you know," said Traddles, colouring in his great delicacy, "lives in London, I believe?"

"Oh yes. Near London."

"Mine, perhaps you recollect," said Traddles, with a serious look, "lives down in Devonshire—one of ten. Consequently, I am not so much engaged as you—in that sense."

"I wonder you can bear," I returned, "to see her so seldom."

"Hah!" said Traddles, thoughtfully. "It does seem a wonder. I suppose it is, Copperfield, because there's no help for it?"

"I suppose so," I replied with a smile, and not without a blush. "And because you have so much constancy and patience, Traddles."

"Dear me!" said Traddles, considering about it, "do I strike you in that way, Copperfield? Really I didn't know that I had. But she is such an extraordinarily dear girl herself, that it's possible she may have imparted something of those virtues to me. Now you mention it, Copperfield, I shouldn't wonder at all. I assure you she is always forgetting herself, and taking care of the other nine."

"Is she the eldest?" I inquired.

"Oh dear, no," said Traddles. "The eldest is a Beauty."

He saw, I suppose, that I could not help smiling at the simplicity of this reply; and added, with a smile upon his own ingenuous face:

"Not, of course, but that my Sophy—pretty name, Copperfield, I always think?"

"Very pretty!" said I.

"Not, of course, but that Sophy is beautiful too in my eyes, and would be one of the dearest girls that ever was, in anybody's eyes (I should think). But when I say the eldest is a Beauty, I mean she really is a——" he seemed to be describing clouds about himself, with both hands: "Splendid, you know," said Traddles, energetically.

"Indeed!" said I.

"Oh, I assure you," said Traddles, "something very uncommon, indeed! Then, you know, being formed for society and admiration, and not being able to enjoy much of it, in consequence of their limited means, she naturally gets a little irritable and exacting, sometimes. Sophy puts her in good humour!"

"Is Sophy the youngest?" I hazarded.

"Oh dear, no!" said Traddles, stroking his chin. "The two youngest are only nine and ten. Sophy educates 'em."

"The second daughter, perhaps?" I hazarded.

"No," said Traddles. "Sarah's the second. Sarah has something the matter with her spine, poor girl. The malady will wear out by-and-by, the doctors say, but in the meantime she has to lie down for a twelvemonth. Sophy nurses her. Sophy's the fourth."

"Is the mother living?" I inquired.

"Oh yes," said Traddles, "she is alive. She is a very superior woman, indeed, but the damp country is not adapted to her constitution, and—in fact, she has lost the use of her limbs."

"Dear me!" said I.

"Very sad, is it not?" returned Traddles. "But in a merely domestic view it is not so bad as it might be, because Sophy takes her place. She is quite as much a mother *to* her mother, as she is to the other nine."

I felt the greatest admiration for the virtues of this young lady; and, honestly with the view of doing my best to prevent the good-nature of Traddles from being imposed upon, to the detriment of their joint prospects in life, inquired how Mr. Micawber was?

"He is quite well, Copperfield, thank you," said Traddles. "I am not living with him at present."

"No?"

"No. You see the truth is," said Traddles, in a whisper, "he has changed his name to Mortimer, in consequence of his temporary embarrassments; and he don't come out till after dark—and then in spectacles. There was an execution put into our house, for rent. Mrs. Micawber was in such a dreadful state that I really couldn't resist giving my name to that second bill we spoke of here. You may imagine how delightful it was to my feelings, Copperfield, to see the matter settled with it, and Mrs. Micawber recover her spirits."

"Hum!" said I.

"Not that her happiness was of long duration," pursued Traddles, "for, unfortunately, within a week another execution came in. It broke up the establishment. I have been living in a furnished apartment since then, and the Mortimers have been very private indeed. I hope you won't think it selfish, Copperfield, if I mention that the broker carried off my little round table with the marble top, and Sophy's flower-pot and stand?"

"What a hard thing!" I exclaimed indignantly.

"It was a——it was a pull," said Traddles, with his usual wince at that expression. "I don't mention it reproachfully, however, but with a motive. The fact is, Copperfield, I was unable to repurchase them at the time of their seizure; in the first place, because the broker, having an idea that I wanted them, ran the price up to an extravagant extent; and, in the second place, because I—hadn't any money. Now, I have kept my eye since, upon the broker's shop," said Traddles, with a great enjoyment of his mystery, "which is up at the top of Tottenham Court Road, and, at last, to-day I find them put out for sale. I have only noticed them from over the way, because if the broker saw *me*, bless you, he'd ask any price for them! What has occurred to me, having now the money, is, that perhaps you wouldn't object to ask that good nurse of yours to come with me to the shop—I can show it her from round the corner of the next street—and make the best bargain for them, as if they were for herself, that she can!"

The delight with which Traddles propounded this plan to me, and the sense he had of its uncommon artfulness, are among the freshest things in my remembrance.

I told him that my old nurse would be delighted to assist him, and that we would all three take the field together, but on one condition. That condition was, that he should make a solemn resolution to grant no more loans of his name, or anything else, to Mr. Micawber.

"My dear Copperfield," said Traddles, "I have already done so, because I begin to feel that I have not only been inconsiderate, but that I have been positively unjust to Sophy. My word being passed to myself, there is no longer any apprehension; but I pledge it to you, too, with the greatest readiness. That first unlucky obligation, I have paid. I have no doubt Mr. Micawber would have paid it if he could, but he could not. One thing I ought to mention, which I like very much in Mr. Micawber, Copperfield. It refers to the second obligation, which is not yet due. He don't tell me that it *is* provided for, but he says it *will be*. Now, I think there is something very fair and honest about that!"

I was unwilling to damp my good friend's confidence, and therefore assented. After a little further conversation, we went round to the chandler's shop, to enlist Peggotty; Traddles declining to pass the evening with me, both because he endured the liveliest apprehensions that his property would be bought by somebody else before he could repurchase it, and because it was the evening he always devoted to writing to the dearest girl in the world.

I never shall forget him peeping round the corner of the street in Tottenham Court Road, while Peggotty was bargaining for the precious articles; or his agitation when she came slowly towards us after vainly offering a price, and was hailed by the relenting broker, and went back again. The end of the negotiation was that she bought the property on tolerably easy terms, and Traddles was transported with pleasure.

"I am very much obliged to you, indeed," said Traddles, on hearing it was to be sent to where he lived, that night. "If I might ask one other favour, I hope you would not think it absurd, Copperfield?"

I said beforehand, certainly not.

"Then if you *would* be good enough," said Traddles to Peggotty, "to get the flower-pot now, I think I should like (it being Sophy's, Copperfield) to carry it home myself!"

Peggotty was glad to get it for him, and he overwhelmed her with thanks, and went his way up Tottenham Court Road, carrying the flower-pot affectionately in his arms, with one of the most delighted expressions of countenance I ever saw.

We then turned back towards my chambers. As the shops had charms for Peggotty which I never knew them possess in the same degree for anybody else, I sauntered easily along, amused by her staring in at the windows, and waiting for her as often as she chose. We were thus a good while in getting to the Adelphi.

On our way upstairs, I called her attention to the sudden disappearance of Mrs. Crupp's pitfalls, and also to the prints of recent footsteps. We were both very much surprised, coming higher up, to find my outer door standing open (which I had shut), and to hear voices inside.

We looked at one another, without knowing what to make of this, and went into the sitting-room. What was my amazement to find, of all people upon earth, my aunt there, and Mr. Dick! My aunt sitting on a quantity of luggage, with her two birds before her, and her cat on her knee, like a female Robinson Crusoe, drinking tea. Mr. Dick leaning thoughtfully on a great kite, such as we had often been out together to fly, with more luggage piled about him!

"My dear aunt!" cried I. "Why, what an unexpected pleasure!"

We cordially embraced; and Mr. Dick and I cordially shook hands; and Mrs. Crupp, who was busy making tea, and could not be too attentive, cordially said she had knowed well as Mr. Copperfull would have his heart in his mouth, when he see his dear relations.

"Halloa!" said my aunt to Peggotty, who quailed before her awful presence. "How are *you?*"

"You remember my aunt, Peggotty?" said I.

"For the love of goodness, child," exclaimed my aunt, "don't call the woman by that South Sea Island name! If she married and got rid of it, which was the best thing she could do, why don't you give her the benefit of the change?

What's your name now,—P.?" said my aunt, as a compromise for the obnoxious appellation.

"Barkis, ma'am," said Peggotty, with a curtsey.

"Well! That's human," said my aunt. "It sounds less as if you wanted a Missionary. How d'ye do, Barkis? I hope you're well?"

Encouraged by these gracious words, and by my aunt's extending her hand, Barkis came forward, and took the hand, and curtsied her acknowledgments.

"We are older than we were, I see." said my aunt. "We have only met each other once before, you know. A nice business we made of it then! Trot, my dear, another cup."

I handed it dutifully to my aunt, who was in her usual inflexible state of figure; and ventured a remonstrance with her on the subject of her sitting on a box.

"Let me draw the sofa here, or the easy-chair, aunt," said I. "Why should you be so uncomfortable?"

"Thank you, Trot," replied my aunt, "I prefer to sit upon my property." Here my aunt looked hard at Mrs. Crupp, and observed, "We needn't trouble you to wait, ma'am."

"Shall I put a little more tea in the pot afore I go, ma'am?" said Mrs. Crupp.

"No, I thank you, ma'am," replied my aunt.

"Would you let me fetch another pat of butter, ma'am?" said Mrs. Crupp. "Or would you be persuaded to try a new-laid hegg? or should I brile a rasher? Ain't there nothing I could do for your dear aunt, Mr. Copperfull?"

"Nothing, ma'am," returned my aunt. "I shall do very well, I thank you."

Mrs. Crupp, who had been incessantly smiling to express sweet temper, and incessantly holding her head on one side, to express a general feebleness of constitution, and incessantly rubbing her hands, to express a desire to be of service to all deserving objects, gradually smiled herself, one-sided herself, and rubbed herself, out of the room.

"Dick!" said my aunt. "You know what I told you about time-servers and wealth-worshippers?"

Mr. Dick—with rather a scared look, as if he had forgotten it—returned a hasty answer in the affirmative.

"Mrs. Crupp is one of them," said my aunt. "Barkis, I'll trouble you to look after the tea, and let me have another cup, for I don't fancy that woman's pouring-out!"

I knew my aunt sufficiently well to know that she had something of importance on her mind, and that there was far more matter in this arrival than a stranger might have supposed. I noticed how her eye lighted on me, when she thought my attention otherwise occupied; and what a curious process of hesitation appeared to be going on within her, while she preserved her outward stiffness and composure. I began to reflect whether I had done anything to offend her; and my conscience whispered me that I had not yet told her about Dora. Could it by any means be that, I wondered!

As I knew she would only speak in her own good time, I sat down near her, and spoke to the birds, and played with the cat, and was as easy as I could be. But I was very far from being really easy; and I should still have been so, even if Mr. Dick, leaning over the great kite behind my aunt, had not taken every secret opportunity of shaking his head darkly at me, and pointing at her.

"Trot," said my aunt at last, when she had finished her tea, and carefully smoothed down her dress, and wiped her lips—"you needn't go, Barkis!—Trot, have you got to be firm and self-reliant?"

"I hope so, aunt."

"What do you think?" inquired Miss Betsey.

"I think so, aunt."

"Then why, my love," said my aunt, looking earnestly at me, "why do you think I prefer to sit upon this property of mine to-night?"

I shook my head, unable to guess.

"Because," said my aunt, "it's all I have. Because I'm ruined, my dear!"

If the house, and every one of us, had tumbled out into the river together, I could hardly have received a greater shock.

"Dick knows it," said my aunt, laying her hand calmly on my shoulder. "I am ruined, my dear Trot! All I have in the world is in this room, except the cottage; and that I have left Janet to let. Barkis, I want to get a bed for this gentleman to-night. To save expense, perhaps you can make up something here for myself. Anything will do. It's only for to-night. We'll talk about this, more, to-morrow."

I was roused from my amazement, and concern for her—I am sure, for her—by her falling on my neck, for a moment, and crying that she only grieved for me. In another moment, she suppressed this emotion; and said with an aspect more triumphant than dejected:

"We must meet reverses boldly, and not suffer them to frighten us, my dear. We must learn to act the play out. We must live misfortune down, Trot!"

CHAPTER XXXV.

DEPRESSION.

As soon as I could recover my presence of mind, which quite deserted me in the first overpowering shock of my aunt's intelligence, I proposed to Mr. Dick to come round to the chandler's shop, and take possession of the bed which Mr. Peggotty had lately vacated. The chandler's shop being in Hungerford Market, and Hungerford Market being a very different place in those days, there was a low wooden colonnade before the door (not very unlike that before the house where the little man and woman used to live, in the old weather-glass), which pleased Mr. Dick mightily. The glory of lodging over this structure would have compensated him, I dare say, for many inconveniences; but, as there were really few to bear, beyond the compound of flavours I have already mentioned, and perhaps the want of a little more elbow-room, he was perfectly charmed with his accommodation. Mrs. Crupp had indignantly assured him that there wasn't room to swing a cat there; but, as Mr. Dick justly observed to me, sitting down on the foot of the bed, nursing his leg, "You know, Trotwood, I don't want to swing a cat. I never do swing a cat. Therefore, what does that signify to *me!*"

I tried to ascertain whether Mr. Dick had any understanding of the causes of this sudden and great change in my aunt's affairs. As I might have expected, he had none at all. The only account he could give of it, was, that my

MY AUNT ASTONISHES ME.

aunt had said to him, the day before yesterday, "Now, Dick, are you really and truly the philosopher I take you for?" That then he had said, Yes, he hoped so. That then my aunt had said, "Dick, I am ruined." That then he had said, "Oh, indeed!" That then my aunt had praised him highly, which he was very glad of. And that then they had come to me, and had had bottled porter and sand- wiches on the road.

Mr. Dick was so very complacent, sitting on the foot of the bed, nursing his leg, and telling me this, with his eyes wide open and a surprised smile, that I am sorry to say I was provoked into explaining to him that ruin meant dis- tress, want, and starvation; but I was soon bitterly re- proved for this harshness, by seeing his face turn pale, and tears course down his lengthened cheeks, while he fixed upon me a look of such unutterable woe, that it might have softened a far harder heart than mine. I took infinitely greater pains to cheer him up again than I had taken to depress him; and I soon understood (as I ought to have known at first) that he had been so confident, merely be- cause of his faith in explaining to him that ruin meant dis- women, and his unbounded reliance on my intellectual re- sources. The latter, I believe, he considered a match for any kind of disaster not absolutely mortal.

"What can we do, Trotwood?" said Mr. Dick. "There's the Memorial——"

"To be sure there is," said I. "But all we can do just now, Mr. Dick, is to keep a cheerful countenance, and not let my aunt see that we are thinking about it."

He assented to this in the most earnest manner; and implored me, if I should see him wandering an inch out of the right course, to recall him by some of those superior methods which were always at my command. But I regret to state that the fright I had given him proved too much for his best attempts at concealment. All the evening his eyes wandered to my aunt's face, with an expression of the most dismal apprehension, as if he saw her growing thin on the spot. He was conscious of this, and put a constraint upon his head; but his keeping that immovable, and sitting rolling his eyes like a piece of machinery, did not mend the matter at all. I saw him look at the loaf at supper (which happened to be a small one), as if nothing else stood between us and famine; and when my aunt insisted on his making his customary repast, I detected him in the act of pocketing fragments of his bread and cheese; I have no doubt for the purpose of reviving us with those savings, when we should have reached an advanced stage of attenuation.

My aunt, on the other hand, was in a composed frame of mind, which was a lesson to all of us—to me, I am sure. She was extremely gracious to Peggotty, except when I inadvertently called her by that name; and, strange as I knew she felt in London, appeared quite at home. She was to have my bed, and I was to lie in the sitting-room, to keep guard over her. She made a great point of being so near the river, in case of a conflagration; and I suppose really did find some satisfaction in that circumstance.

"Trot, my dear," said my aunt, when she saw me making preparations for compounding her usual night-draught, "No!"

"Nothing, aunt?"

"Not wine, my dear. Ale."

"But there is wine here, aunt. And you always have it made of wine."

"Keep that, in case of sickness," said my aunt. "We mustn't use it carelessly, Trot. Ale for me. Half a pint."

I thought Mr. Dick would have fallen, insensible. My aunt being resolute, I went out and got the ale myself. As it was growing late, Peggotty and Mr. Dick took that op- portunity of repairing to the chandler's shop together. I parted from him, poor fellow, at the corner of the street, with his great kite at his back, a very monument of human misery.

My aunt was walking up and down the room when I returned, crimping the borders of her nightcap with her fingers. I warmed the ale and made the toast on the usual infallible principles. When it was ready for her, she was ready for it, with her nightcap on, and the skirt of her gown turned back on her knees.

"My dear," said my aunt, after taking a spoonful of it; "it's a great deal better than wine. Not half so bilious."

I suppose I looked doubtful, for she added:

"Tut, tut, child. If nothing worse than Ale happens to us, we are well off."

"I should think so myself, aunt, I am sure," said I.

"Well, then, why *don't* you think so?" said my aunt.

"Because you and I are very different people," I returned.

"Stuff and nonsense, Trot!" replied my aunt.

My aunt went on with a quiet enjoyment, in which there was very little affectation, if any; drinking the warm ale with a teaspoon, and soaking her strips of toast in it.

"Trot," said she, "I don't care for strange faces in gen- eral, but I rather like that Barkis of yours, do you know!"

"It's better than a hundred pounds to hear you say so!" said I.

"It's a most extraordinary world," observed my aunt, rubbing her nose; "how that woman ever got into it with that name, is unaccountable to me. It would be much more easy to be born a Jackson, or something of that sort, one would think."

"Perhaps she thinks so, too; it's not her fault," said I.

"I suppose not," returned my aunt, rather grudging the admission; "but it's very aggravating. However, she's Barkis now. That's some comfort. Barkis is uncommonly fond of you, Trot."

"There is nothing she would leave undone to prove it," said I.

"Nothing, I believe," returned my aunt. "Here, the poor fool has been begging and praying about handing over some of her money—because she has got too much of it! A simpleton!"

My aunt's tears of pleasure were positively trickling down into the warm ale.

"She's the most ridiculous creature that ever was born," said my aunt. "I knew, from the first moment when I saw her with that poor dear blessed baby of a mother of yours, that she was the most ridiculous of mortals. But there are good points in Barkis!"

Affecting to laugh, she got an opportunity of putting her hand to her eyes. Having availed herself of it, she re- sumed her toast and her discourse together.

"Ah! Mercy upon us!" sighed my aunt. "I know all about it, Trot! Barkis and myself had quite a gossip while you were out with Dick. I know all about it. I don't know where these wretched girls expect to go to, for my part. I wonder they don't knock out their brains against —against mantelpieces," said my aunt; an idea which was probably suggested to her by her contemplation of mine.

"Poor Emily!" said I.

"Oh, don't talk to me about poor," returned my aunt. "She should have thought of that, before she caused so much misery! Give me a kiss, Trot. I am sorry for your early experience."

As I bent forward, she put her tumbler on my knee to detain me, and said:

"Oh, Trot, Trot! And so you fancy yourself in love! Do you?"

"Fancy, aunt!" I exclaimed, as red as I could be. "I adore her with my whole soul!"

"Dora, indeed!" returned my aunt. "And you mean to say the little thing is very fascinating, I suppose?"

"My dear aunt," I replied, "no one can form the least idea of what she is!"

"Ah! And not silly?" said my aunt.

"Silly, aunt!"

I seriously believe it had never once entered my head for a single moment, to consider what she was or not. I resented the idea, of course; but I was in a manner struck by it, as a new one altogether.

"Not light-headed?" said my aunt.

"Light-headed, aunt!" I could only repeat this daring speculation with the same kind of feeling with which I had repeated the preceding question.

"Well, well!" said my aunt. "I only ask. I don't depreciate her. Poor little couple! And so you think you were formed for one another, and are to go through a party-supper-table kind of life, like two pretty pieces of confectionery, do you, Trot?"

She asked me this so kindly, and with such a gentle air, half playful and half sorrowful, that I was quite touched.

"We are young and inexperienced, aunt, I know," I replied; "and I dare say we say and think a good deal that is rather foolish. But we love one another truly, I am sure. If I thought Dora could ever love anybody else, or cease to love me; or that I could ever love anybody else, or cease to love her; I don't know what I should do—go out of my mind, I think!"

"Ah, Trot!" said my aunt, shaking her head, and smiling gravely; "blind, blind, blind!"

"Some one that I know, Trot," my aunt pursued, after a pause, "though of a very pliant disposition, has an earnestness of affection in him that reminds me of poor Baby. Earnestness is what that Somebody must look for, to sustain him and improve him, Trot. Deep, downright, faithful earnestness."

"If you only knew the earnestness of Dora, aunt!" I cried.

"Oh, Trot!" she said again; "blind, blind!" and without knowing why, I felt a vague unhappy loss or want of something overshadow me like a cloud.

"However," said my aunt, "I don't want to put two young creatures out of conceit with themselves, or to make them unhappy; so, though it is a girl and boy attachment, and girl and boy attachments very often—mind! I don't say always!—come to nothing, still we'll be serious about it, and hope for a prosperous issue one of these days. There's time enough for it to come to anything!"

This was not upon the whole very comforting to a rapturous lover; but I was glad to have my aunt in my confidence, and I was mindful of her being fatigued. So I thanked her ardently for this mark of her affection, and for all her other kindnesses towards me; and after a tender good night, she took her nightcap into my bedroom.

How miserable I was, when I lay down! How I thought and thought about my being poor, in Mr. Spenlow's eyes; about my not being what I thought I was, when I proposed to Dora; about the chivalrous necessity of telling Dora what my worldly condition was, and releasing her from her engagement if she thought fit; about how I should contrive to live, during the long term of my articles, when I was earning nothing; about doing something to assist my aunt, and seeing no way of doing anything; about coming down to have no money in my pocket, and to wear a shabby coat, and to be able to carry Dora no little presents, and to ride no gallant greys, and to show myself in no agreeable light! Sordid and selfish as I knew it was, and as I tortured myself by knowing that it was, to let my mind run on my own distress so much, I was so devoted to Dora that I could not help it. I knew that it was base in me not to think more of my aunt, and less of myself; but, so far, selfishness was inseparable from Dora, and I could not put Dora on one side for any mortal creature. How exceedingly miserable I was, that night!

As to sleep, I had dreams of poverty in all sorts of shapes, but I seemed to dream without the previous ceremony of going to sleep. Now I was ragged, wanting to sell Dora matches, six bundles for a halfpenny; now I was at the office in a nightgown and boots, remonstrated with by Mr. Spenlow on appearing before the clients in that airy attire; now I was hungrily picking up the crumbs that fell from old Tiffey's daily biscuit, regularly eaten when St. Paul's struck one; now I was hopelessly endeavouring to get a licence to marry Dora, having nothing but one of Uriah Heep's gloves to offer in exchange, which the whole Commons rejected; and still, more or less conscious of my own room, I was always tossing about like a distressed ship in a sea of bedclothes.

My aunt was restless, too, for I frequently heard her walking to and fro. Two or three times in the course of the night, attired in a long flannel wrapper in which she looked seven feet high, she appeared, like a disturbed ghost, in my room, and came to the side of the sofa on which I lay. On the first occasion I started up in alarm, to learn that she inferred from a particular light in the sky, that Westminster Abbey was on fire; and to be consulted in reference to the probability of its igniting Buckingham Street, in case the wind changed. Lying still, after that, I found that she sat down near me, whispering to herself "Poor boy!" And then it made me twenty times more wretched, to know how unselfishly mindful she was of me, and how selfishly mindful I was of myself.

It was difficult to believe that a night so long to me, could be short to anybody else. This consideration set me thinking and thinking of an imaginary party where people were dancing the hours away, until that became a dream too, and I heard the music incessantly playing one tune, and saw Dora incessantly dancing one dance, without taking the least notice of me. The man who had been playing the harp all night, was trying in vain to cover it with an ordinary-sized nightcap, when I awoke; or I should rather say, when I left off trying to go to sleep, and saw the sun shining in through the window at last.

There was an old Roman bath in those days at the bottom of one of the streets out of the Strand—it may be there still —in which I have had many a cold plunge. Dressing myself as quietly as I could, and leaving Peggotty to look after my aunt, I tumbled head foremost into it, and then went for a walk to Hampstead. I had a hope that this brisk treatment might freshen my wits a little; and I think it did them good, for I soon came to the conclusion that the first step I ought to take was to try if my articles could be cancelled and the premium recovered. I got some breakfast on the Heath, and walked back to Doctors' Commons, along the watered roads and through a pleasant smell of summer flowers, growing in gardens and carried into town on hucksters' heads, intent on this first effort to meet our altered circumstances.

I arrived at the office so soon, after all, that I had half an hour's loitering about the Commons, before old Tiffey, who was always first, appeared with his key. Then I sat down in my shady corner, looking up at the sunlight on the opposite chimney-pots, and thinking about Dora; until Mr. Spenlow came in, crisp and curly.

"How are you, Copperfield?" said he. "Fine morning!"

"Beautiful morning, Sir," said I. "Could I say a word to you before you go into Court?"

"By all means," said he. "Come into my room."

I followed him into his room, and he began putting on his gown, and touching himself up before a little glass he had, hanging inside a closet door.

"I am sorry to say," said I, "that I have some rather disheartening intelligence from my aunt."

"No!" said he. "Dear me! Not paralysis, I hope?"

"It has no reference to her health, Sir," I replied. "She has met with some large losses. In fact, she has very little left, indeed."

"You as-tound me, Copperfield!" cried Mr. Spenlow.

I shook my head. "Indeed, Sir," said I, "her affairs are so changed, that I wished to ask you whether it would be possible—at a sacrifice on our part of some portion of the premium, of course," I put in this, on the spur of the moment, warned by the blank expression of his face—"to cancel my articles?"

What it cost me to make this proposal, nobody knows. It was like asking, as a favour, to be sentenced to transportation from Dora.

"To cancel your articles, Copperfield? Cancel?"

I explained with tolerable firmness, that I really did not know where my means of subsistence were to come from, unless I could earn them for myself. I had no fear for the future, I said—and I laid great emphasis on that, as if to imply that I should still be decidedly eligible for a son-in-law one of these days—but, for the present, I was thrown upon my own resources.

"I am extremely sorry to hear this, Copperfield," said Mr. Spenlow. "Extremely sorry. It is not usual to cancel articles for any such reason. It is not a professional course of proceeding. It is not a convenient precedent at all. Far from it. At the same time——"

"You are very good, Sir," I murmured, anticipating a concession.

"Not at all. Don't mention it," said Mr. Spenlow. "At the same time, I was going to say, if it had been my lot to have my hands unfettered—if I had not a partner—Mr. Jorkins——"

My hopes were dashed in a moment, but I made another effort.

"Do you think, Sir," said I, "if I were to mention it to Mr. Jorkins——"

Mr. Spenlow shook his head discouragingly. "Heaven forbid, Copperfield," he replied, "that I should do any

man an injustice; still less, Mr. Jorkins. But I know my partner, Copperfield. Mr. Jorkins is *not* a man to respond to a proposition of this peculiar nature. Mr. Jorkins is very difficult to move from the beaten track. You know what he is!"

I am sure I knew nothing about him, except that he had originally been alone in the business, and now lived by himself in a house near Montagu Square, which was fearfully in want of painting; that he came very late of a day, and went away very early; that he never appeared to be consulted about anything; and that he had a dingy little black-hole of his own up-stairs, where no business was ever done, and where there was a yellow old cartridge-paper pad upon his desk, unsoiled by ink, and reported to be twenty years of age.

"Would you object to my mentioning it to him, Sir?" I asked.

"By no means," said Mr. Spenlow. "But I have some experience of Mr. Jorkins, Copperfield. I wish it were otherwise, for I should be happy to meet your views in any respect. I cannot have the least objection to your mentioning it to Mr. Jorkins, Copperfield, if you think it worth while."

Availing myself of this permission, which was given with a warm shake of the hand, I sat thinking about Dora, and looking at the sunlight stealing from the chimney-pots down the wall of the opposite house until Mr. Jorkins came. I then went up to Mr. Jorkins's room, and evidently astonished Mr. Jorkins very much by making my appearance there.

"Come in, Mr. Copperfield," said Mr. Jorkins. "Come in!"

I went in, and sat down; and stated my case to Mr. Jorkins pretty much as I had stated it to Mr. Spenlow. Mr. Jorkins was not by any means the awful creature one might have expected, but a large, mild, smooth-faced man of sixty, who took so much snuff that there was a tradition in the Commons that he lived principally on that stimulant, having little room in his system for any other article of diet.

"You have mentioned this to Mr. Spenlow, I suppose?" said Mr. Jorkins; when he had heard me, very restlessly, to an end.

I answered Yes, and told him that Mr. Spenlow had introduced his name.

"He said I should object?" asked Mr. Jorkins.

I was obliged to admit that Mr. Spenlow had considered it probable.

"I am sorry to say, Mr. Copperfield, I can't advance your object," said Mr. Jorkins, nervously. "The fact is—but I have an appointment at the Bank, if you'll have the goodness to excuse me."

With that he rose in a great hurry, and was going out of the room, when I made bold to say that I feared, then, there was no way of arranging the matter?

"No!" said Mr. Jorkins, stopping at the door to shake his head. "Oh, no! I object, you know," which he said very rapidly, and went out. "You must be aware, Mr. Copperfield," he added, looking restlessly in at the door again, "if Mr. Spenlow objects——"

"Personally, he does not object, Sir," said I.

"Oh! Personally!" repeated Mr. Jorkins, in an impatient manner. "I assure you there's an objection, Mr. Copperfield. Hopeless! What you wish to be done, can't be done. I—I really have got an appointment at the Bank." With that he fairly ran away; and to the best of my knowledge, it was three days before he showed himself in the Commons again.

Being very anxious to leave no stone unturned, I waited until Mr. Spenlow came in, and then described what had passed; giving him to understand that I was not hopeless of his being able to soften the adamantine Jorkins, if he would undertake that task.

"Copperfield," returned Mr. Spenlow, with a gracious smile, "you have not known my partner, Mr. Jorkins, as long as I have. Nothing is farther from my thoughts than to attribute any degree of artifice to Mr. Jorkins. But Mr. Jorkins has a way of stating his objections which often deceives people. No, Copperfield!" shaking his head. "Mr. Jorkins is not to be moved, believe me!"

I was completely bewildered between Mr. Spenlow and Mr. Jorkins, as to which of them really was the objecting partner; but I saw with sufficient clearness that there was obduracy somewhere in the firm, and that the recovery of my aunt's thousand pounds was out of the question. In a state of despondency, which I remember with anything but satisfaction, for I know it still had too much reference to myself (though always in connexion with Dora), I left the office, and went homeward.

I was trying to familiarise my mind with the worst, and to present to myself the arrangements we should have to make for the future in their sternest aspect, when a hackney-chariot coming after me, and stopping at my very feet, occasioned me to look up. A fair hand was stretched forth to me from the window; and the face I had never seen without a feeling of serenity and happiness, from the moment when it first turned back on the old oak staircase with the great broad balustrade, and when I associated its softened beauty with the stained-glass window in the church, was smiling on me.

"Agnes!" I joyfully exclaimed. "Oh, my dear Agnes, of all people in the world, what a pleasure to see you!"

"Is it, indeed?" she said, in her cordial voice.

"I want to talk to you so much!" said I. "It's such a lightening of my heart, only to look at you! If I had had a conjuror's cap, there is no one I should have wished for but you!"

"What?" returned Agnes.

"Well! perhaps Dora first," I admitted, with a blush.

"Certainly, Dora first, I hope," said Agnes, laughing.

"But you next!" said I. "Where are you going?"

She was going to my rooms to see my aunt. The day being very fine, she was glad to come out of the chariot, which smelt (I had my head in it all this time) like a stable put under a cucumber-frame. I dismissed the coachman, and she took my arm, and we walked on together. She was like Hope embodied, to me. How different I felt in one short minute, having Agnes at my side!

My aunt had written her one of the odd, abrupt notes—very little longer than a bank-note—to which her epistolary efforts were usually limited. She had stated therein that she had fallen into adversity, and was leaving Dover for good, but had quite made up her mind to it, and was so well that nobody need be uncomfortable about her. Agnes had come to London to see my aunt, between whom and herself there had been a mutual liking these many years:

indeed, it dated from the time of my taking up my residence in Mr. Wickfield's house. She was not alone, she said. Her papa was with her—and Uriah Heep.

"And now they are partners," said I. "Confound him!"

"Yes," said Agnes. "They have some business here; and I took advantage of their coming, to come too. You must not think my visit all friendly and disinterested, Trotwood, for—I am afraid I may be cruelly prejudiced—I do not like to let papa go away alone, with him."

"Does he exercise the same influence over Mr. Wickfield still, Agnes?"

Agnes shook her head. "There is such a change at home," said she, "that you would scarcely know the dear old house. They live with us now."

"They?" said I.

"Mr. Heep and his mother. He sleeps in your old room," said Agnes, looking up into my face.

"I wish I had the ordering of his dreams," said I. "He wouldn't sleep there long."

"I keep my own little room," said Agnes, "where I used to learn my lessons. How the time goes! You remember? The little panelled room that opens from the drawing-room?"

"Remember, Agnes? When I saw you, for the first time, coming out at the door, with your quaint little basket of keys hanging at your side?"

"It is just the same," said Agnes, smiling. "I am glad you think of it so pleasantly. We were very happy."

"We were indeed," said I.

"I keep that room to myself still; but I cannot always desert Mrs. Heep, you know. And so," said Agnes quietly, "I feel obliged to bear her company, when I might prefer to be alone. But I have no other reason to complain of her. If she tires me, sometimes, by her praises of her son, it is only natural in a mother. He is a very good son to her."

I looked at Agnes when she said these words, without detecting in her any consciousness of Uriah's design. Her mild but earnest eyes met mine with their own beautiful frankness, and there was no change in her gentle face.

"The chief evil of their presence in the house," said Agnes, "is that I cannot be as near papa as I could wish—Uriah Heep being so much between us—and cannot watch over him, if that is not too bold a thing to say, as closely as I would. But, if any fraud or treachery is practising against him, I hope that simple love and truth will be stronger in the end. I hope that real love and truth are stronger in the end than any evil or misfortune in the world."

A certain bright smile, which I never saw on any other face, died away, even while I thought how good it was, and how familiar it had once been to me; and she asked me, with a quick change of expression (we were drawing very near my street), if I knew how the reverse in my aunt's circumstances had been brought about. On my replying no, she had not told me yet, Agnes became thoughtful, and I fancied I felt her arm tremble in mine.

We found my aunt alone, in a state of some excitement. A difference of opinion had arisen between herself and Mrs. Crupp, on an abstract question (the propriety of chambers being inhabited by the gentler sex); and my aunt, utterly indifferent to spasms on the part of Mrs. Crupp, had cut the dispute short, by informing that lady that she smelt of my brandy, and that she would trouble her to walk out. Both of these expressions Mrs. Crupp considered actionable, and had expressed her intention of bringing before a "British Judy"—meaning, it was supposed, the bulwark of our national liberties.

My aunt, however, having had time to cool, while Peggotty was out showing Mr. Dick the soldiers at the Horse Guards—and being, besides, greatly pleased to see Agnes—rather plumed herself on the affair than otherwise, and received us with unimpaired good-humour. When Agnes laid her bonnet on the table, and sat down beside her, I could not but think, looking on her mild eyes and her radiant forehead, how natural it seemed to have her there, how trustfully, although she was so young and inexperienced, my aunt confided in her; how strong she was, indeed, in simple love and truth.

We began to talk about my aunt's losses, and I told them what I had tried to do that morning.

"Which was injudicious, Trot," said my aunt, "but well meant. You are a generous boy—I suppose I must say, young man, now—and I am proud of you, my dear. So far, so good. Now, Trot and Agnes, let us look the case of Betsey Trotwood in the face, and see how it stands."

I observed Agnes turn pale, as she looked very attentively at my aunt. My aunt, patting her cat, looked very attentively at Agnes.

"Betsey Trotwood," said my aunt, who had always kept her money matters to herself: "—I don't mean your sister, Trot, my dear, but myself—had a certain property. It don't matter how much; enough to live on. More; for she had saved a little, and added to it. Betsey funded her property for some time, and then, by the advice of her man of business, lent it out on landed security. That did very well, and returned very good interest, till Betsey was paid off. I am talking of Betsey as if she was a man-of-war. Well! Then, Betsey had to look about her, for a new investment. She thought she was wiser, now, than her man of business, who was not such a good man of business by this time, as he used to be—I am alluding to your father, Agnes—and she took it into her head to lay it out for herself. So she took her pigs," said my aunt, "to a foreign market; and a very bad market it turned out to be. First, she lost in the mining way, and then she lost in the diving way—fishing up treasure, or some such Tom Tidler nonsense," explained my aunt, rubbing her nose; "and then she lost in the mining way again, and, last of all, to set the thing entirely to rights, she lost in the banking way. I don't know what the bank shares were worth for a little while," said my aunt; "cent per cent was the lowest of it, I believe; but the bank was at the other end of the world, and tumbled into space, for what I know; anyhow, it fell to pieces, and never will and never can pay sixpence; and Betsey's sixpences were all there, and there's an end of them. Least said, soonest mended!"

My aunt concluded this philosophical summary, by fixing her eyes with a kind of triumph on Agnes, whose colour was gradually returning.

"Dear Miss Trotwood, is that all the history?" said Agnes.

"I hope it's enough, child," said my aunt. "If there had been more money to lose, it wouldn't have been all, I dare say. Betsey would have contrived to throw that after the rest, and make another chapter, I have little doubt. But, there was no more money, and there's no more story."

Agnes had listened at first with suspended breath. Her colour still came and went, but she breathed more freely. I thought I knew why. I thought she had had some fear that her unhappy father might be in some way to blame for what had happened. My aunt took her hand in hers, and laughed.

"Is that all?" repeated my aunt. "Why, yes, that's all, except, 'And she lived happy ever afterwards.' Perhaps I may add that of Betsey yet, one of these days. Now, Agnes, you have a wise head. So have you, Trot, in some things, though I can't compliment you always;" and here my aunt shook her own at me, with an energy peculiar to herself. "What's to be done? Here's the cottage, taking one time with another, will produce, say seventy pounds a year. I think we may safely put it down at that. Well! —That's all we've got," said my aunt; with whom it was an idiosyncrasy, as it is with some horses, to stop very short when she appeared to be in a fair way of going on for a long while.

"Then," said my aunt, after a rest, "there's Dick. He's good for a hundred a year, but of course that must be expended on himself. I would sooner send him away, though I know I am the only person who appreciates him, than have him, and not spend his money on himself. How can Trot and I do best, upon our means? What do you say, Agnes?"

"I say, aunt," I interposed, "that I must do something!"

"Go for a soldier, do you mean?" returned my aunt, alarmed; "or go to sea? I won't hear of it. You are to be a proctor. We're not going to have any knockings on the head in this family, if you please, Sir."

I was about to explain that I was not desirous of introducing that mode of provision into the family, when Agnes inquired if my rooms were held for any long term?

"You come to the point, my dear," said my aunt. "They are not to be got rid of, for six months at least, unless they could be underlet, and that I don't believe. The last man died here. Five people out of six would die—of course—of that woman in nankeen with the flannel petticoat. I have a little ready money; and I agree with you, the best thing we can do, is, to live the term out here, and get Dick a bedroom hard by."

I thought it my duty to hint at the discomfort my aunt would sustain, from living in a continual state of guerilla warfare with Mrs. Crupp; but she disposed of that objection summarily by declaring that, on the first demonstration of hostilities, she was prepared to astonish Mrs. Crupp for the whole remainder of her natural life.

"I have been thinking, Trotwood," said Agnes, diffidently, "that if you had time——"

"I have a good deal of time, Agnes. I am always disengaged after four or five o'clock, and I have time early in the morning. In one way and another," said I, conscious of reddening a little as I thought of the hours and days I had devoted to fagging about town, and to and fro upon the Norwood Road, "I have abundance of time."

"I knew you would not mind," said Agnes, coming to me, and speaking in a low voice, so full of sweet and hopeful consideration that I hear it now, "the duties of a secretary."

"Mind, my dear Agnes?"

"Because," continued Agnes, "Doctor Strong has acted on his intention of retiring, and has come to live in London; and he asked papa, I know, if he could recommend him one.

Don't you think he would rather have his favourite old pupil near him, than anybody else?"

"Dear Agnes!" said I. "What should I do without you! You are always my good angel. I told you so. I never think of you in any other light."

Agnes answered with her pleasant laugh, that one good angel (meaning Dora) was enough; and went on to remind me that the Doctor had been used to occupy himself in his study, early in the morning, and in the evening—and that probably my leisure would suit his requirements very well. I was scarcely more delighted with the prospect of earning my own bread, than with the hope of earning it under my old master; in short, acting on the advice of Agnes, I sat down and wrote a letter to the Doctor, stating my object, and appointing to call on him next day at ten in the forenoon. This I addressed to Highgate—for in that place, so memorable to me, he lived—and went out and posted, myself, without losing a minute.

Wherever Agnes was, some agreeable token of her noiseless presence seemed inseparable from the place. When I came back, I found my aunt's birds hanging, just as they had hung so long in the parlour window of the cottage; and my easy-chair imitating my aunt's much easier chair in its position at the open window; and even the round green fan, which my aunt had brought away with her, screwed on to the window-sill. I knew who had done all this, by its seeming to have quietly done itself; and I should have known in a moment who had arranged my neglected books in the old order of my school days, even if I had supposed Agnes to be miles away, instead of seeing her busy with them, and smiling at the disorder into which they had fallen.

My aunt was quite gracious on the subject of the Thames (it really did look very well with the sun upon it, though not like the sea before the cottage), but she could not relent towards the London smoke, which, she said, "peppered everything." A complete revolution, in which Peggotty bore a prominent part, was being effected in every corner of my rooms, in regard to this pepper; and I was looking on, thinking how little even Peggotty seemed to do with a good deal of bustle, and how much Agnes did without any bustle at all, when a knock came at the door.

"I think," said Agnes, turning pale, "it's papa. He promised me that he would come."

I opened the door, and admitted, not only Mr. Wickfield, but Uriah Heep. I had not seen Mr. Wickfield for some time. I was prepared for a great change in him, after what I had heard from Agnes, but his appearance shocked me.

It was not that he looked many years older, though still dressed with the old scrupulous cleanliness; or that there was an unwholesome ruddiness upon his face; or that his eyes were full and bloodshot; or that there was a nervous trembling in his hand, the cause of which I knew, and had for some years seen at work. It was not that he had lost his good looks, or his old bearing of a gentleman—for that he had not—but the thing that struck me most was, that with the evidences of his native superiority still upon him, he should submit himself to that crawling impersonation of meanness, Uriah Heep. The reversal of the two natures, in their relative positions, Uriah's of power, and Mr. Wickfield's of dependence, was a sight more painful to me than I can express. If I had seen an Ape taking command of a Man, I should hardly have thought it a more degrading spectacle.

He appeared to be only too conscious of himself. When he came in, he stood still; and with his head bowed, as if he felt it. This was only for a moment; for Agnes softly said to him, "Papa! Here is Miss Trotwood—and Trotwood, whom you have not seen for a long while!" and then he approached, and constrainedly gave my aunt his hand, and shook hands more cordially with me. In the moment's pause I speak of, I saw Uriah's countenance form itself into a most ill-favoured smile. Agnes saw it too, I think, for she shrank from him.

What my aunt saw, or did not see, I defy the science of physiognomy to have made out, without her own consent. I believe there never was anybody with such an imperturbable countenance when she chose. Her face might have been a dead wall on the occasion in question, for any light it threw upon her thoughts; until she broke silence with her usual abruptness.

"Well, Wickfield!" said my aunt; and he looked up at her for the first time. "I have been telling your daughter how well I have been disposing of my money for myself, because I couldn't trust it to you, as you were growing rusty in business matters. We have been taking counsel together, and getting on very well, all things considered. Agnes is worth the whole firm, in my opinion."

"If I may umbly make the remark," said Uriah Heep, with a writhe, "I fully agree with Miss Betsey Trotwood, and should be only too appy if Miss Agnes was a partner."

"You're a partner yourself, you know," returned my aunt, "and that's about enough for you, I expect. How do you find yourself, Sir?"

In acknowledgment of this question, addressed to him with extraordinary curtness, Mr. Heep, uncomfortably clutching the blue bag he carried, replied that he was pretty well, he thanked my aunt, and hoped she was the same.

"And you, Master—I should say, Mister Copperfield," pursued Uriah. "I hope I see you well! I am rejoiced to see you, Mister Copperfield, even under present circumstances." I believed that; for he seemed to relish them very much. "Present circumstances is not what your friends would wish for you, Mister Copperfield, but it isn't money makes the man: it's—I am really unequal with my umble powers to express what it is," said Uriah, with a fawning jerk, "but it isn't money!"

Here he shook hands with me: not in the common way, but standing at a good distance from me, and lifting my hand up and down like a pump-handle, that he was a little afraid of.

"And how do you think we are looking, Master Copperfield,—I should say, Mister?" fawned Uriah. "Don't you find Mr. Wickfield blooming, Sir? Years don't tell much in our firm, Master Copperfield, except in raising up the umble, namely, mother and self—and in developing," he added, as an afterthought, "the beautiful, namely, Miss Agnes."

He jerked himself about, after this compliment, in such an intolerable manner, that my aunt, who had sat looking straight at him, lost all patience.

"Deuce take the man!" said my aunt, sternly, "what's he about? Don't be galvanic, Sir!"

"I ask your pardon, Miss Trotwood," returned Uriah; "I'm aware you're nervous."

"Go along with you, Sir!" said my aunt, anything but appeased. "Don't presume to say so! I am nothing of the sort. If you're an eel, Sir, conduct yourself like one.

If you're a man, control your limbs, Sir! Good God!" said my aunt, with great indignation, "I am not going to be serpentined and corkscrewed out of my senses!"

Mr. Heep was rather abashed, as most people might have been, by this explosion; which derived great additional force from the indignant manner in which my aunt afterwards moved in her chair, and shook her head as if she were making snaps or bounces at him. But, he said to me aside in a meek voice:

"I am well aware, Master Copperfield, that Miss Trotwood, though an excellent lady, has a quick temper (indeed I think I had the pleasure of knowing her, when I was a numble clerk, before you did, Master Copperfield), and it's only natural, I am sure, that it should be made quicker by present circumstances. The wonder is, that it isn't much worse! I only called to say that if there was anything we could do, in present circumstances, mother or self, or Wickfield and Heep, we should be really glad. I may go so far?" said Uriah, with a sickly smile at his partner.

"Uriah Heep," said Mr. Wickfield, in a monotonous forced way, "is active in the business, Trotwood. What he says, I quite concur in. You know I had an old interest in you. Apart from that, what Uriah says I quite concur in!"

"Oh, what a reward it is," said Uriah, drawing up one leg, at the risk of bringing down upon himself another visitation from my aunt, "to be so trusted in! But I hope I am able to do something to relieve him from the fatigues of business, Master Copperfield!"

"Uriah Heep is a great relief to me," said Mr. Wickfield, in the same dull voice. "It's a load off my mind, Trotwood, to have such a partner."

The red fox made him say all this, I knew, to exhibit him to me in the light he had indicated on the night when he poisoned my rest. I saw the same ill-favoured smile upon his face again, and saw how he watched me.

"You are not going, papa?" said Agnes, anxiously. "Will you not walk back with Trotwood and me?"

He would have looked to Uriah, I believe, before replying, if that worthy had not anticipated him.

"I am bespoke myself," said Uriah, "on business; otherwise I should have been appy to have kept with my friends. But I leave my partner to represent the firm. Miss Agnes, ever yours! I wish you good-day, Master Copperfield, and leave my umble respects for Miss Betsey Trotwood."

With those words, he retired, kissing his great hand, and leering at us like a mask.

We sat there, talking about our pleasant old Canterbury days, an hour or two. Mr. Wickfield, left to Agnes, soon became more like his former self; though there was a settled depression upon him, which he never shook off. For all that, he brightened; and had an evident pleasure in hearing us recall the little incidents of our old life, many of which he remembered very well. He said it was like those times, to be alone with Agnes and me again; and he wished to Heaven they had never changed. I am sure there was an influence in the placid face of Agnes, and in the very touch of her hand upon his arm, that did wonders for him.

My aunt (who was busy nearly all this while with Peggotty, in the inner room) would not accompany us to the place where they were staying, but insisted on my going; and I went. We dined together. After dinner, Agnes sat beside him, as of old, and poured out his wine. He took what she gave him, and no more—like a child—and we all

three sat together at a window as the evening gathered in. When it was almost dark, he lay down on a sofa, Agnes pillowing his head and bending over him a little while; and when she came back to the window, it was not so dark but I could see tears glittering in her eyes.

I pray Heaven that I never may forget the dear girl in her love and truth, at that time of my life; for if I should, I must be drawing near the end, and then I would desire to remember her best! She filled my heart with such good resolutions, strengthened my weakness so, by her example, so directed—I know not how, she was too modest and gentle to advise me in many words—the wandering ardour and unsettled purpose within me, that all the little good I have done, and all the harm I have forborne, I solemnly believe I may refer to her.

And how she spoke to me of Dora, sitting at the window in the dark; listened to my praises of her; praised again; and round the little fairy-figure shed some glimpses of her own pure light, that made it yet more precious and more innocent to me! Oh, Agnes, sister of my boyhood, if I had known then, what I knew long afterwards!—

There was a beggar in the street, when I went down; and as I turned my head towards the window, thinking of her calm seraphic eyes, he made me start by muttering, as if he were an echo of the morning:

"Blind! Blind! Blind!"

CHAPTER XXXVI.

ENTHUSIASM.

I BEGAN the next day with another dive into the Roman bath, and then started for Highgate. I was not dispirited now. I was not afraid of the shabby coat, and had no yearnings after gallant greys. My whole manner of thinking of our late misfortune was changed. What I had to do, was, to show my aunt that her past goodness to me had not been thrown away on an insensible, ungrateful object. What I had to do, was, to turn the painful discipline of my younger days to account, by going to work with a resolute and steady heart. What I had to do, was, to take my woodman's axe in my hand, and clear my own way through the forest of difficulty, by cutting down the trees until I came to Dora. And I went on at a mighty rate, as if it could be done by walking.

When I found myself on the familiar Highgate road, pursuing such a different errand from that old one of pleasure, with which it was associated, it seemed as if a complete change had come on my whole life. But that did not discourage me. With the new life, came new purpose, new intention. Great was the labour; priceless the reward. Dora was the reward, and Dora must be won.

I got into such a transport, that I felt quite sorry my coat was not a little shabby already. I wanted to be cutting at those trees in the forest of difficulty, under circumstances that should prove my strength. I had a good mind to ask an old man, in wire spectacles, who was breaking stones upon the road, to lend me his hammer for a little while, and let me begin to beat a path to Dora out of granite. I stimulated myself into such a heat, and got so out of breath, that I felt as if I had been earning I don't know how much. In this state, I went into a cottage that I saw was to let, and examined it narrowly,—for I felt it necessary to be practical.

It would do for me and Dora admirably: with a little front garden for Jip to run about in, and bark at the trades-people through the railings, and a capital room up-stairs for my aunt. I came out again, hotter and faster than ever, and dashed up to Highgate, at such a rate that I was there an hour too early; and, though I had not been, should have been obliged to stroll about to cool myself, before I was at all presentable.

My first care, after putting myself under this necessary course of preparation, was to find the Doctor's house. It was not in that part of Highgate where Mrs. Steerforth lived, but quite on the opposite side of the little town. When I had made this discovery, I went back, in an attraction I could not resist, to a lane by Mrs. Steerforth's, and looked over the corner of the garden wall. His room was shut up close. The conservatory doors were standing open, and Rosa Dartle was walking, bareheaded, with a quick, impetuous step, up and down a gravel walk on one side of the lawn. She gave me the idea of some fierce thing, that was dragging the length of its chain to and fro upon a beaten track, and wearing its heart out.

I came softly away from my place of observation, and avoiding that part of the neighbourhood, and wishing I had not gone near it, strolled about until it was ten o'clock. The church with the slender spire, that stands on the top of the hill now, was not there then to tell me the time. An old red-brick mansion, used as a school, was in its place; and a fine old house it must have been to go to school at, as I recollect it.

When I approached the Doctor's cottage—a pretty old place, on which he seemed to have expended some money, if I might judge from the embellishments and repairs that had the look of being just completed—I saw him walking in the garden at the side, gaiters and all, as if he had never left off walking since the days of my pupilage. He had his old companions about him, too; for there were plenty of high trees in the neighbourhood, and two or three rooks were on the grass, looking after him, as if they had been written to about him by the Canterbury rooks, and were observing him closely in consequence.

Knowing the utter hopelessness of attracting his attention from that distance, I made bold to open the gate, and walk after him, so as to meet him when he should turn round. When he did, and came towards me, he looked at me thoughtfully for a few moments, evidently without thinking about me at all; and then his benevolent face expressed extraordinary pleasure, and he took me by both hands.

"Why, my dear Copperfield," said the Doctor; "you are a man! How do you do? I am delighted to see you. My dear Copperfield, how very much you have improved! You are quite—yes—dear me!"

I hoped he was well, and Mrs. Strong too.

"Oh dear, yes!" said the Doctor; "Annie's quite well, and she'll be delighted to see you. You were always her favourite. She said so, last night, when I showed her your letter. And—yes, to be sure—you recollect Mr. Jack Maldon, Copperfield?"

"Perfectly, Sir."

"Of course," said the Doctor. "To be sure. *He's* pretty well, too."

"Has he come home, Sir?" I inquired.

"From India?" said the Doctor. "Yes. Mr. Jack Maldon couldn't bear the climate, my dear. Mrs. Markleham—you have not forgotten Mrs. Markleham?"

Forgotten the Old Soldier! And in that short time!

"Mrs. Markleham," said the Doctor, "was quite vexed about him, poor thing; so we have got him at home again; and we have bought him a little Patent place, which agrees with him much better."

I knew enough of Mr. Jack Maldon to suspect from this account that it was a place where there was not much to do, and which was pretty well paid. The Doctor, walking up and down with his hand on my shoulder, and his kind face turned encouragingly to mine, went on:

"Now, my dear Copperfield, in reference to this proposal of yours. It's very gratifying and agreeable to me, I am sure; but don't you think you could do better? You achieved distinction, you know, when you were with us. You are qualified for many good things. You have laid a foundation that any edifice may be raised upon; and is it not a pity that you should devote the spring-time of your life to such a poor pursuit as I can offer?"

I became very glowing again, and, expressing myself in a rhapsodical style, I am afraid, urged my request strongly; reminding the Doctor that I had already a profession.

"Well, well," returned the Doctor, "that's true. Certainly, your having a profession, and being actually engaged in studying it, makes a difference. But, my good young friend, what's seventy pounds a year?"

"It doubles our income, Doctor Strong," said I.

"Dear me!" replied the Doctor. "To think of that! Not that I mean to say it's rigidly limited to seventy pounds a year, because I have always contemplated making any young friend I might thus employ, a present too. Undoubtedly," said the Doctor, still walking me up and down with his hand on my shoulder. "I have always taken an annual present into account."

"My dear tutor," said I (now, really, without any nonsense), "to whom I owe more obligations already than I can ever acknowledge——"

"No, no," interposed the Doctor. "Pardon me!"

"If you will take such time as I have, and that is my mornings and evenings, and can think it worth seventy pounds a year, you will do me such a service as I cannot express."

"Dear me!" said the Doctor, innocently. "To think that so little should go for so much! Dear, dear! And when you can do better, you will? On your word, now?" said the Doctor,—which he had always made a very grave appeal to the honour of us boys.

"On my word, Sir!" I returned, answering in our old school manner.

"Then be it so!" said the Doctor, clapping me on the shoulder, and still keeping his hand there, as we still walked up and down.

"And I shall be twenty times happier, Sir," said I, with a little—I hope innocent—flattery, "if my employment is to be on the Dictionary."

The Doctor stopped, smilingly clapped me on the shoulder again, and exclaimed, with a triumph most delightful to behold, as if I had penetrated to the profoundest depths of mortal sagacity, "My dear young friend, you have hit it. It is the Dictionary!"

How could it be anything else? His pockets were as

full of it as his head. It was sticking out of him in all directions. He told me that since his retirement from scholastic life, he had been advancing with it wonderfully; and that nothing could suit him better than the proposed arrangements for morning and evening work, as it was his custom to walk about in the day-time with his considering cap on. His papers were in a little confusion, in consequence of Mr. Jack Maldon having lately proffered his occasional services as an amanuensis, and not being accustomed to that occupation; but we should soon put right what was amiss, and go on swimmingly. Afterwards, when we were fairly at our work, I found Mr. Jack Maldon's efforts more troublesome to me than I had expected, as he had not confined himself to making numerous mistakes, but had sketched so many soldiers, and ladies' heads, over the Doctor's manuscript, that I often became involved in labyrinths of obscurity.

The Doctor was quite happy in the prospect of our going to work together on that wonderful performance, and we settled to begin next morning at seven o'clock. We were to work two hours every morning, and two or three hours every night, except on Saturdays, when I was to rest. On Sundays, of course, I was to rest also, and I considered these very easy terms.

Our plans being thus arranged to our mutual satisfaction, the Doctor took me into the house to present me to Mrs. Strong, whom we found in the Doctor's new study, dusting his books,—a freedom which he never permitted anybody else to take with those sacred favourites.

They had postponed their breakfast on my account, and we sat down to table together. We had not been seated long, when I saw an approaching arrival in Mrs. Strong's face, before I heard any sound of it. A gentleman on horseback came to the gate, and leading his horse into the little court, with the bridle over his arm, as if he were quite at home, tied him to a ring in the empty coach-house wall, and came into the breakfast parlour, whip in hand. It was Mr. Jack Maldon; and Mr. Jack Maldon was not at all improved by India, I thought. I was in a state of ferocious virtue, however, as to young men who were not cutting down the trees in the forest of difficulty; and my impression must be received with due allowance.

"Mr. Jack!" said the Doctor, "Copperfield!"

Mr. Jack Maldon shook hands with me; but not very warmly, I believed; and with an air of languid patron age, at which I secretly took great umbrage. But his languor altogether was quite a wonderful sight; except when he addressed himself to his cousin Annie.

"Have you breakfasted this morning, Mr. Jack?" said the Doctor.

"I hardly ever take breakfast, Sir," he replied, with his head thrown back in an easy-chair. "I find it bores me."

"Is there any news to-day?" inquired the Doctor.

"Nothing at all, Sir," replied Mr. Maldon. "There's an account about the people being hungry and discontented down in the North, but they are always being hungry and discontented somewhere."

The Doctor looked grave, and said, as though he wished to change the subject, "Then there's no news at all; and no news, they say, is good news."

"There's a long statement in the papers, Sir, about a murder," observed Mr. Maldon. "But somebody's always being murdered, and I didn't read it."

A display of indifference to all the actions and passions of mankind was not supposed to be such a distinguished quality at that time, I think, as I have observed it to be considered since. I have known it very fashionable indeed. I have seen it displayed with such success, that I have encountered some fine ladies and gentlemen who might as well have been born caterpillars. Perhaps it impressed me the more then, because it was new to me, but it certainly did not tend to exalt my opinion of, or to strengthen my confidence in, Mr. Jack Maldon.

"I came out to inquire whether Annie would like to go to the opera to-night," said Mr. Maldon, turning to her. "It's the last good night there will be, this season; and there's a singer there, whom she really ought to hear. She is perfectly exquisite. Besides which, she is so charmingly ugly," relapsing into languor.

The Doctor, ever pleased with what was likely to please his young wife, turned to her and said:

"You must go, Annie. You must go."

"I would rather not," she said to the Doctor. "I prefer to remain at home. I would much rather remain at home."

Without looking at her cousin, she then addressed me, and asked me about Agnes, and whether she should see her, and whether she was not likely to come that day; and was so much disturbed, that I wondered how even the Doctor, buttering his toast, could be blind to what was so obvious.

But he saw nothing. He told her, good-naturedly, that she was young and ought to be amused and entertained, and must not allow herself to be made dull by a dull old fellow. However, he said, he wanted to hear her sing all the new singer's songs to him; and how could she do that well, unless she went? So the Doctor persisted in making the engagement for her, and Mr. Jack Maldon was to come back to dinner. This concluded, he went to his Patent place, I suppose; but at all events went away on his horse, looking very idle.

I was curious to find out next morning, whether she had been. She had not, but had sent into London to put her cousin off; and had gone out in the afternoon to see Agnes, and had prevailed upon the Doctor to go with her; and they had walked home by the fields, the Doctor told me, the evening being delightful. I wondered then, whether she would have gone if Agnes had not been in town, and whether Agnes had some good influence over her too!

She did not look very happy, I thought; but it was a good face, or a very false one. I often glanced at it, for she sat in the window all the time we were at work; and made our breakfast, which we took by snatches as we were employed. When I left, at nine o'clock, she was kneeling on the ground at the Doctor's feet, putting on his shoes and gaiters for him. There was a softened shade upon her face, thrown from some green leaves overhanging the open window of the low room; and I thought all the way to Doctors' Commons, of the night when I had seen it looking at him as he read.

I was pretty busy now; up at five in the morning, and home at nine or ten at night. But I had infinite satisfaction in being so closely engaged, and never walked slowly on any account, and felt enthusiastically that the more I tired myself, the more I was doing to deserve Dora. I had not revealed myself in my altered character to Dora yet, because she was coming to see Miss Mills in a few days, and I deferred all I had to tell her until then; merely informing her in my letters (all our communications were secretly forwarded through Miss Mills), that I had much to tell her. In the meantime, I put myself on a short allowance of bear's grease, wholly abandoned scented soap and lavender water, and sold off three waistcoats at a prodigious sacrifice, as being too luxurious for my stern career.

Not satisfied with all these proceedings, but burning with impatience to do something more, I went to see Traddles, now lodging up behind the parapet of a house in Castle Street, Holborn. Mr. Dick, who had been with me to Highgate twice already, and had resumed his companionship with the Doctor, I took with me.

I took Mr. Dick with me, because, acutely sensitive to my aunt's reverses, and sincerely believing that no galley-slave or convict worked as I did, he had begun to fret and worry himself out of spirits and appetite, as having nothing useful to do. In this condition, he felt more incapable of finishing the Memorial than ever; and the harder he worked at it, the oftener that unlucky head of King Charles the First got into it. Seriously apprehending that his malady would increase, unless we put some innocent deception upon him and caused him to believe that he was useful, or unless we could put him in the way of being really useful (which would be better), I made up my mind to try if Traddles could help us. Before we went I wrote Traddles a full statement of all that had happened, and Traddles wrote me back a capital answer, expressive of his sympathy and friendship.

We found him hard at work with his inkstand and papers, refreshed by the sight of the flowerpot-stand and the little round table in a corner of the small apartment. He received us cordially, and made friends with Mr. Dick in a moment. Mr. Dick professed an absolute certainty of having seen him before, and we both said, "Very likely."

The first subject on which I had to consult Traddles was this.—I had heard that many men distinguished in various pursuits had begun life by reporting the debates in Parliament. Traddles having mentioned newspapers to me, as one of his hopes, I had put the two things together, and told Traddles in my letter that I wished to know how I could qualify myself for this pursuit. Traddles now informed me, as the result of his inquiries, that the mere mechanical acquisition necessary, except in rare cases, for thorough excellence in it, that is to say, a perfect and entire command of the mystery of shorthand writing and reading, was about equal in difficulty to the mastery of six languages; and that it might perhaps be attained, by dint of perseverance, in the course of a few years. Traddles reasonably supposed that this would settle the business; but I, only feeling that here indeed were a few tall trees to be hewn down, immediately resolved to work my way on to Dora through this thicket, axe in hand.

"I am very much obliged to you, my dear Traddles," said I. "I'll begin to-morrow."

Traddles looked astonished, as he well might; but he had no notion as yet of my rapturous condition.

"I'll buy a book," said I, "with a good scheme of this art in it; I'll work at it at the Commons, where I haven't half enough to do; I'll take down the speeches in our court for practice—Traddles, my dear fellow, I'll master it!"

"Dear me," said Traddles, opening his eyes, "I had no idea you were such a determined character, Copperfield!"

I don't know how he should have had, for it was new enough to me. I passed that off, and brought Mr. Dick on the carpet.

"You see," said Mr. Dick wistfully, "if I could exert myself, Mr. Traddles—if I could beat a drum or blow anything!"

Poor fellow! I have little doubt he would have preferred such an employment in his heart to all others. Traddles, who would not have smiled for the world, replied composedly:

"But you are a very good penman, Sir. You told me so, Copperfield?"

"Excellent!" said I. And indeed he was. He wrote with extraordinary neatness.

"Don't you think," said Traddles, "you could copy writings, Sir, if I got them for you?"

Mr. Dick looked doubtfully at me. "Eh, Trotwood?"

I shook my head. Mr. Dick shook his, and sighed. "Tell him about the Memorial," said Mr. Dick.

I explained to Traddles that there was a difficulty in keeping King Charles the First out of Mr. Dick's manuscripts; Mr. Dick in the meanwhile looking very deferentially and seriously at Traddles, and sucking his thumb.

"But these writings, you know, that I speak of, are already drawn up and finished," said Traddles, after a little consideration. "Mr. Dick has nothing to do with them. Wouldn't that make a difference, Copperfield? At all events, wouldn't it be well to try?"

This gave us new hope. Traddles and I laying our heads together apart, while Mr. Dick anxiously watched us from his chair, we concocted a scheme in virtue of which we got him to work next day, with triumphant success.

On a table by the window in Buckingham Street, we set out the work Traddles procured for him—which was to make, I forget how many copies of a legal document about some right of way—and on another table we spread the last unfinished original of the great Memorial. Our instructions to Mr. Dick were that he should copy exactly what he had before him, without the least departure from the original; and that when he felt it necessary to make the slightest allusion to King Charles the First, he should fly to the Memorial. We exhorted him to be resolute in this, and left my aunt to observe him. My aunt reported to us, afterwards, that, at first, he was like a man playing the kettle-drums, and constantly divided his attentions between the two; but that, finding this confuse and fatigue him, and having his copy there, plainly before his eyes, he soon sat at it in an orderly business-like manner, and postponed the Memorial to a more convenient time. In a word, although we took great care that he should have no more to do than was good for him, and although he did not begin with the beginning of the week, he earned by the following Saturday night ten shillings and ninepence; and never, while I live, shall I forget his going about to all the shops in the neighbourhood to change this treasure into sixpences, or his bringing them to my aunt arranged in the form of a heart upon a waiter, with tears of joy and pride in his eyes. He was like one under the propitious influence of a charm, from the moment of his being usefully employed; and if there were a happy man in the world, that Saturday night, it was the grateful creature who thought my aunt the most wonderful woman in existence, and me the most wonderful young man.

"No starving now, Trotwood," said Mr. Dick, shaking hands with me in a corner. "I'll provide for her, Sir!" and he flourished his ten fingers in the air, as if they were ten banks.

I hardly know which was the better pleased, Traddles or I. "It really," said Traddles, suddenly, taking a letter out of his pocket, and giving it to me, "put Mr. Micawber quite out of my head!"

The letter (Mr. Micawber never missed any possible opportunity of writing a letter) was addressed to me, "By the kindness of T. Traddles, Esquire, of the Inner Temple." It ran thus:—

"My dear Copperfield,

"You may possibly not be unprepared to receive the intimation that something has turned up. I may have mentioned to you on a former occasion that I was in expectation of such an event.

"I am about to establish myself in one of the provincial towns of our favoured island (where the society may be described as a happy admixture of the agricultural and the clerical), in immediate connexion with one of the learned professions. Mrs. Micawber and our offspring will accompany me. Our ashes, at a future period, will probably be found commingled in the cemetery attached to a venerable pile, for which the spot to which I refer, has acquired a reputation, shall I say from China to Peru?

"In bidding adieu to the modern Babylon, where we have undergone many vicissitudes, I trust not ignobly, Mrs. Micawber and myself cannot disguise from our minds that we part, it may be for years and it may be for ever, with an individual linked by strong associations to the altar of our domestic life. If, on the eve of such a departure, you will accompany our mutual friend, Mr. Thomas Traddles, to our present abode, and there reciprocate the wishes natural to the occasion, you will confer a Boon

"On
"One
"Who
"Is
"Ever yours,
"Wilkins Micawber."

I was glad to find that Mr. Micawber had got rid of his dust and ashes, and that something really had turned up at last. Learning from Traddles that the invitation referred to the evening then wearing away, I expressed my readiness to do honour to it; and we went off together to the lodging which Mr. Micawber occupied as Mr. Mortimer, and which was situated near the top of the Gray's Inn Road.

The resources of this lodging were so limited, that we found the twins, now some eight or nine years old, reposing in a turn-up bedstead in the family sitting-room, where Mr. Micawber had prepared, in a washhand-stand jug, what he called a "Brew" of the agreeable beverage for which he was famous. I had the pleasure, on this occasion, of renewing the acquaintance of Master Micawber, whom I found a promising boy of about twelve or thirteen, very subject to that restlessness of limb which is not an unfrequent phenomenon in youths of his age. I also became once more known to his sister, Miss Micawber, in whom, as Mr. Micawber told us, "her mother renewed her youth, like the phœnix."

"My dear Copperfield," said Mr. Micawber, "yourself and Mr. Traddles find us on the brink of migration, and will excuse any little discomforts incidental to that position."

Glancing round as I made a suitable reply, I observed that the family effects were already packed, and that the amount of luggage was by no means overwhelming. I congratulated Mrs. Micawber on the approaching change.

"My dear Mr. Copperfield," said Mrs. Micawber, "of your friendly interest in all our affairs, I am well assured. My family may consider it banishment, if they please; but I am a wife and mother, and I never will desert Mr. Micawber."

Traddles, appealed to, by Mrs. Micawber's eye, feelingly acquiesced.

"That," said Mrs. Micawber, "that, at least, is my view, my dear Mr. Copperfield and Mr. Traddles, of the obligation which I took upon myself when I repeated the irrevocable words, 'I, Emma, take thee, Wilkins.' I read the service over with a flat-candle on the previous night, and the conclusion I derived from it was, that I never could desert Mr. Micawber. And," said Mrs. Micawber, "though it is possible I may be mistaken in my view of the ceremony, I never will!"

"My dear," said Mr. Micawber, a little impatiently, "I am not conscious that you are expected to do anything of the sort."

"I am aware, my dear Mr. Copperfield," pursued Mrs. Micawber, "that I am now about to cast my lot among strangers; and I am also aware that the various members of my family, to whom Mr. Micawber has written in the most gentlemanly terms, announcing that fact, have not taken the least notice of Mr. Micawber's communication. Indeed I may be superstitious," said Mrs. Micawber, "but it appears to me that Mr. Micawber is destined never to receive any answers whatever to the great majority of the communications he writes. I may augur from the silence of my family, that they object to the resolution I have taken; but I should not allow myself to be swerved from the path of duty, Mr. Copperfield, even by my papa and mama, were they still living.

I expressed my opinion that this was going in the right direction.

"It may be a sacrifice," said Mrs. Micawber, "to immure one's self in a Cathedral town; but surely, Mr. Copperfield, if it is a sacrifice in me, it is much more a sacrifice in a man of Mr. Micawber's abilities."

"Oh! You are going to a Cathedral town?" said I.

Mr. Micawber, who had been helping us all, out of the washhand-stand jug, replied:

"To Canterbury. In fact, my dear Copperfield, I have entered into arrangements, by virtue of which I stand pledged and contracted to our friend, Heep, to assist and serve him in the capacity of—and to be—his confidential clerk."

I stared at Mr. Micawber, who greatly enjoyed my surprise.

"I am bound to state to you," he said, with an official air, "that the business habits, and the prudent suggestions, of Mrs. Micawber, have in a great measure conduced to this result. The gauntlet, to which Mrs. Micawber referred upon a former occasion, being thrown down in the form of an advertisement, was taken up by my friend Heep, and led to a mutual recognition. Of my friend Heep," said Mr. Micawber, "who is a man of remarkable shrewdness, I desire to speak with all possible respect. My friend Heep has not fixed the positive remuneration at too high a figure, but he has made a great deal, in the way of extrication from the pressure of pecuniary difficulties, contingent on the value of my services; and on the value of those services, I pin my faith. Such address and intelligence as I chance to possess," said Mr. Micawber, boastfully disparaging himself, with the old genteel air, "will be devoted to my friend Heep's service. I have already some acquaintance with the law—as a defendant on civil process—and I shall immediately apply myself to the Commentaries of one of the most eminent and remarkable of our English jurists. I believe it is unnecessary to add that I allude to Mr. Justice Blackstone."

These observations, and indeed the greater part of the observations made that evening, were interrupted by Mrs. Micawber's discovering that Master Micawber was sitting on his boots, or holding his head on with both arms as if he felt it loose, or accidentally kicking Traddles under the table, or shuffling his feet over one another, or producing them at distances from himself apparently outrageous to nature, or lying sideways with his hair among the wine-glasses, or developing his restlessness of limb in some other form incompatible with the general interests of society; and by Master Micawber's receiving those discoveries in a resentful spirit. I sat all the while, amazed by Mr. Micawber's disclosure, and wondering what it meant; until Mrs. Micawber resumed the thread of the discourse, and claimed my attention.

"What I particularly request Mr. Micawber to be careful of, is," said Mrs. Micawber, "that he does not, my dear Mr. Copperfield, in applying himself to this subordinate branch of the law, place it out of his power to rise, ultimately, to the top of the tree. I am convinced that Mr. Micawber, giving his mind to a profession so adapted to his fertile resources, and his flow of language, *must* distinguish himself. Now, for example, Mr. Traddles," said Mrs. Micawber, assuming a profound air, "a judge, or even say a chancellor. Does an individual place himself beyond the pale of those preferments by entering on such an office as Mr. Micawber has accepted?"

"My dear," observed Mr. Micawber—but glancing inquisitively at Traddles, too; "we have time enough before us, for the consideration of those questions."

"Micawber," she returned, "no! Your mistake in life is, that you do not look forward far enough. You are bound, in justice to your family, if not to yourself, to take in at a comprehensive glance the extremest point in the horizon to which your abilities may lead you."

Mr. Micawber coughed, and drank his punch with an air of exceeding satisfaction—still glancing at Traddles, as if he desired to have his opinion.

"Why, the plain state of the case, Mrs. Micawber," said Traddles, mildly breaking the truth to her, "I mean the real prosaic fact, you know——"

"Just so," said Mrs. Micawber, "my dear Mr. Traddles, I wish to be as prosaic and literal as possible on a subject of so much importance."

"—Is," said Traddles, "that this branch of the law, even if Mr. Micawber were a regular solicitor——"

"Exactly so," returned Mrs. Micawber. ("Wilkins, you are squinting, and will not be able to get your eyes back.")

"—Has nothing," pursued Traddles, "to do with that. Only a barrister is eligible for such preferments; and Mr. Micawber could not be a barrister, without being entered at an inn of court as a student, for five years."

"Do I follow you?" said Mrs. Micawber, with her most affable air of business. "Do I understand, my dear Mr. Traddles, that, at the expiration of that period, Mr. Micawber would be eligible as a judge or chancellor?"

"He would be *eligible*," returned Traddles, with a strong emphasis on that word.

"Thank you," said Mrs. Micawber. "That is quite sufficient. If such is the case, and Mr. Micawber forfeits no privilege by entering on these duties, my anxiety is set at rest. I speak," said Mrs. Micawber, "as a female, necessarily; but I have always been of opinion that Mr. Micawber possesses what I have heard my papa call, when I lived at home, the judicial mind; and I hope Mr. Micawber is now entering on a field where that mind will develop itself, and take a commanding station."

I quite believe that Mr. Micawber saw himself, in his judicial mind's eye, on the woolsack. He passed his hand complacently over his bald head, and said with ostentatious resignation:

"My dear, we will not anticipate the decrees of fortune. If I am reserved to wear a wig, I am at least prepared, externally," in allusion to his baldness, "for that distinction. I do not," said Mr. Micawber, "regret my hair, and I may have been deprived of it for a specific purpose. I cannot say. It is my intention, my dear Copperfield, to educate my son for the Church; I will not deny that I should be happy, on his account, to attain to eminence."

"For the Church?" said I, still pondering, between whiles, on Uriah Heep.

"Yes," said Mr. Micawber. "He has a remarkable head-voice, and will commence as a chorister. Our residence at Canterbury, and our local connexion, will, no doubt, enable him to take advantage of any vacancy that may arise in the Cathedral corps."

On looking at Master Micawber again, I saw that he had a certain expression of face, as if his voice were behind his eyebrows; where it presently appeared to be, on his singing us (as an alternative between that and bed), "The Wood-Pecker tapping." After many compliments on this performance, we fell into some general conversation; and as I was too full of my desperate intentions to keep my altered circumstances to myself, I made them known to Mr. and Mrs. Micawber. I cannot express how extremely delighted they both were, by the idea of my aunt's being in difficulties; and how comfortable and friendly it made them.

When we were nearly come to the last round of the punch, I addressed myself to Traddles, and reminded him that we must not separate, without wishing our friends health, happiness, and success in their new career. I begged Mr. Micawber to fill us bumpers, and proposed the toast in due form: shaking hands with him across the table, and kissing Mrs. Micawber, to commemorate that eventful occasion. Traddles imitated me in the first particular, but did not consider himself a sufficiently old friend to venture on the second.

"My dear Copperfield," said Mr. Micawber, rising with one of his thumbs in each of his waistcoat-pockets, "the companion of my youth: if I may be allowed the expression—and my esteemed friend Traddles: if I may be permitted to call him so—will allow me, on the part of Mrs. Micawber, myself, and our offspring, to thank them in the warmest and most uncompromising terms for their good wishes. It may be expected that on the eve of a migration which will consign us to a perfectly new existence," Mr. Micawber spoke as if they were going five hundred thousand miles, "I should offer a few valedictory remarks to two such friends as I see before me. But all that I have to say in this way, I have said. Whatever station in society I may attain, through the medium of the learned profession of which I am about to become an unworthy member, I shall endeavour not to disgrace, and Mrs. Micawber will be safe to adorn. Under the temporary pressure of pecuniary liabilities, contracted with a view to their immediate liquidation, but remaining unliquidated through a combination of circumstances, I have been under the necessity of assuming a garb from which my natural instincts recoil—I allude to spectacles—and possessing myself of a cognomen, to which I can establish no legitimate pretensions. All I have to say on that score is, that the cloud has passed from the dreary scene, and the God of Day is once more high upon the mountain tops. On Monday next, on the arrival of the four o'clock afternoon coach at Canterbury, my foot will be on my native heath—my name, Micawber!"

Mr. Micawber resumed his seat on the close of these remarks, and drank two glasses of punch in grave succession. He then said with much solemnity:

"One thing more I have to do, before this separation is complete, and that is to perform an act of justice. My friend Mr. Thomas Traddles has, on two several occasions, 'put his name,' if I may use a common expression, to bills of exchange for my accommodation. On the first occasion Mr. Thomas Traddles was left—let me say, in short, in the lurch. The fulfilment of the second has not yet arrived. The amount of the first obligation," here Mr. Micawber carefully referred to papers, "was, I believe, twenty-three, four, nine, and a half; of the second, according to my entry of that transaction, eighteen, six, two. These sums, united, make a total, if my calculation is correct, amounting to forty-one, ten, eleven, and a half. My friend Copperfield will perhaps do me the favour to check that total?"

I did so and found it correct.

"To leave this metropolis," said Mr. Micawber, "and my friend Mr. Thomas Traddles, without acquitting myself of the pecuniary part of this obligation, would weigh upon my mind to an insupportable extent. I have, therefore, prepared for my friend Mr. Thomas Traddles, and I now hold in my hand, a document, which accomplishes the desired object. I beg to hand to my friend Mr. Thomas Traddles my I. O. U. for forty-one, ten, eleven and a half, and I am happy to recover my moral dignity, and to know that I can once more walk erect before my fellow-man!"

With this introduction (which greatly affected him), Mr. Micawber placed his I. O. U. in the hands of Traddles, and said he wished him well in every relation of life. I am persuaded, not only that this was quite the same to Mr. Micawber as paying the money, but that Traddles himself hardly knew the difference until he had had time to think about it.

Mr. Micawber walked so erect before his fellow-man, on the strength of this virtuous action, that his chest looked half as broad again when he lighted us down stairs. We parted with great heartiness on both sides; and when I had seen Traddles to his own door, and was going home alone, I thought, among the other odd and contradictory things I mused upon, that, slippery as Mr. Micawber was, I was probably indebted to some compassionate recollection he retained of me as his boy-lodger, for never having been asked by him for money. I certainly should not have had the moral courage to refuse it; and I have no doubt he knew that (to his credit be it written), quite as well as I did.

CHAPTER XXXVII.

A LITTLE COLD WATER.

MY new life had lasted for more than a week, and I was stronger than ever in those tremendous practical resolutions that I felt the crisis required. I continued to walk extremely fast, and to have a general idea that I was getting on. I made it a rule to take as much out of myself as I possibly could, in my way of doing everything to which I applied my energies. I made a perfect victim of myself. I even entertained some idea of putting myself on a vegetable diet, vaguely conceiving that, in becoming a graminivorous animal, I should sacrifice to Dora.

As yet, little Dora was quite unconscious of my desperate firmness, otherwise than as my letters darkly shadowed it forth. But, another Saturday came, and on that Saturday evening she was to be at Miss Mills's; and when Mr. Mills had gone to his whist-club (telegraphed to me in the street, by a birdcage in the drawing-room middle window), I was to go there to tea.

By this time, we were quite settled down in Buckingham Street, where Mr. Dick continued his copying in a state of absolute felicity. My aunt had obtained a signal victory over Mrs. Crupp, by paying her off, throwing the first pitcher she planted on the stairs out of window, and protecting in person, up and down the staircase, a supernumerary whom she engaged from the outer world. These vigorous measures struck such terror to the breast of Mrs. Crupp, that she subsided into her own kitchen, under the impression that my aunt was mad. My aunt being supremely indifferent to Mrs. Crupp's opinion and everybody else's, and rather favouring than discouraging the idea, Mrs. Crupp, of late the bold, became within a few days so faint-hearted, that rather than encounter my aunt upon the staircase, she would endeavour to hide her portly form behind doors—leaving visible, however, a wide margin of flannel petticoat—or would shrink into dark corners. This gave my aunt such unspeakable satisfaction, that I believe she took a delight in prowling up and down, with her bonnet insanely perched on the top of her head, at times when Mrs. Crupp was likely to be in the way.

My aunt, being uncommonly neat and ingenious, made so many little improvements in our domestic arrangements, that I seemed to be richer instead of poorer. Among the rest, she converted the pantry into a dressing-room for me; and purchased and embellished a bedstead for my occupation, which looked as like a bookcase in the daytime, as a bedstead could. I was the object of her constant solicitude; and my poor mother herself could not have loved me better, or studied more how to make me happy.

Peggotty had considered herself highly privileged in being allowed to participate in these labours; and, although she still retained something of her old sentiment of awe in reference to my aunt, had received so many marks of encouragement and confidence, that they were the best friends possible. But the time had now come (I am speaking of the Saturday when I was to take tea at Miss Mills's) when it was necessary for her to return home, and enter on the discharge of the duties she had undertaken in behalf of Ham. "So good bye, Barkis," said my aunt, "and take care of yourself! I am sure I never thought I could be sorry to lose you!"

I took Peggotty to the coach-office, and saw her off. She cried at parting, and confided her brother to my friendship as Ham had done. We had heard nothing of him since he went away, that sunny afternoon.

"And now, my own dear Davy," said Peggotty, "if, while you're a prentice, you should want any money to spend; or if, when you're out of your time, my dear, you should want any to set you up (and you must do one or other, or both, my darling); who has such a good right to ask leave to lend it you, as my sweet girl's own old stupid me!"

I was not so savagely independent as to say anything in reply, but that if ever I borrowed money of anyone, I would borrow it of her. Next to accepting a large sum on the spot, I believe this gave Peggotty more comfort than anything I could have done.

"And, my dear!" whispered Peggotty, "tell the pretty little angel that I should so have liked to see her, only for a minute! And tell her that before she marries my boy, I'll come and make your house so beautiful for you, if you'll let me!"

I declared that nobody else should touch it; and this gave Peggotty such delight, that she went away in good spirits.

I fatigued myself as much as I possibly could in the Commons all day, by a variety of devices, and at the appointed time in the evening repaired to Mr. Mills's street. Mr. Mills, who was a terrible fellow to fall asleep after dinner, had not yet gone out, and there was no birdcage in the middle window.

He kept me waiting so long, that I fervently hoped the Club would fine him for being late. At last he came out; and then I saw my own Dora hang up the birdcage, and peep into the balcony to look for me, and run in again when she saw I was there, while Jip remained behind, to bark injuriously at an immense butcher's dog in the street, who could have taken him like a pill.

Dora came to the drawing-room door to meet me; and Jip came scrambling out, tumbling over his own growls, under the impression that I was a Bandit; and we all three went in, as happy and loving as could be. I soon carried desolation into the bosom of our joys—not that I meant to do it, but that I was so full of the subject—by asking Dora, without the smallest preparation, if she could love a beggar?

My pretty, little, startled Dora! Her only association with the word was a yellow face and a nightcap, or a pair of crutches, or a wooden leg, or a dog with a decanter-stand in his mouth, or something of that kind; and she stared at me with the most delightful wonder.

"How can you ask me anything so foolish!" pouted Dora. "Love a beggar!"

"Dora, my own dearest!" said I. "*I* am a beggar!"

"How can you be such a silly thing," replied Dora, slapping my hand, "as to sit there, telling such stories? I'll make Jip bite you!"

Her childish way was the most delicious way in the world to me, but it was necessary to be explicit, and I solemnly repeated:

"Dora, my own life, I am your ruined David!"

"I declare I'll make Jip bite you!" said Dora, shaking her curls, "if you are so ridiculous."

But I looked so serious, that Dora left off shaking her curls, and laid her trembling little hand upon my shoulder, and first looked scared and anxious, then began to cry. That was dreadful. I fell upon my knees before the sofa, caressing her, and imploring her not to rend my heart; but, for some time, poor little Dora did nothing but exclaim Oh dear! oh dear! And oh, she was so frightened! And where was Julia Mills! And oh, take her to Julia Mills, and go away, please! until I was almost beside myself.

At last, after an agony of supplication and protestation, I got Dora to look at me, with a horrified expression of face, which I gradually soothed until it was only loving, and her soft, pretty cheek was lying against mine. Then I told her, with my arms clasped round her, how I loved her, so dearly, and so dearly; how I felt it right to offer to release her from her engagement, because now I was poor; how I never could bear it, or recover it, if I lost her; how I had no fears of poverty, if she had none, my arm being nerved and my heart inspired by her; how I was already working with a courage such as none but lovers knew; how I had begun to be practical, and to look into the future; how a crust well-earned was sweeter far than a feast inherited; and much more to the same purpose, which I delivered in a burst of passionate eloquence quite surprising to myself, though I had been thinking about it, day and night, ever since my aunt had astonished me.

"Is your heart mine still, dear Dora?" said I, rapturously, for I knew by her clinging to me that it was.

"Oh, yes!" cried Dora. "Oh, yes, it's all yours. Oh, don't be dreadful!"

I dreadful! To Dora!

"Don't talk about being poor, and working hard!" said Dora, nestling closer to me. "Oh, don't, don't!"

"My dearest love," said I, "the crust well-earned——"

"Oh, yes; but I don't want to hear any more about crusts!" said Dora. "And Jip must have a mutton-chop every day at twelve, or he'll die!"

I was charmed with her childish, winning way. I fondly explained to Dora that Jip should have his mutton-chop with his accustomed regularity. I drew a picture of our frugal home, made independent by my labour—sketching in the little house I had seen at Highgate, and my aunt in her room up-stairs.

"I am not dreadful now, Dora?" said I, tenderly.

"Oh, no, no!" cried Dora. "But I hope your aunt will keep in her own room a good deal! And I hope she's not a scolding old thing!"

If it were possible for me to love Dora more than ever, I am sure I did. But I felt she was a little impracticable. It damped my new-born ardour, to find that ardour so difficult of communication to her. I made another trial. When she was quite herself again, and was curling Jip's ears, as he lay upon her lap, I became grave, and said:

"My own! May I mention something?"

"Oh, please don't be practical!" said Dora, coaxingly. "Because it frightens me so!"

"Sweet heart!" I returned; "there is nothing to alarm you in all this. I want you to think of it quite differently. I want to make it nerve you, and inspire you, Dora."

"Oh, but that's so shocking!" cried Dora.

"My love, no. Perseverance and strength of character will enable us to bear much worse things."

"But I haven't got any strength at all," said Dora, shaking her curls. "Have I, Jip? Oh, do kiss Jip, and be agreeable!"

It was impossible to resist kissing Jip, when she held him up to me for that purpose, putting her own bright, rosy little mouth into kissing form, as she directed the operation, which she insisted should be performed symmetrically, on the centre of his nose. I did as she bade me—rewarding myself afterwards for my obedience—and she charmed me out of my graver character for I don't know how long.

"But, Dora, my beloved!" said I, at last resuming it; "I was going to mention something."

The Judge of the Prerogative Court might have fallen in love with her, to see her fold her little hands and hold them up, begging and praying me not to be dreadful any more.

"Indeed I am not going to be, my darling!" I assured her. "But, Dora, my love, if you will sometimes think—not despondingly, you know; far from that!—but if you will sometimes think—just to encourage yourself—that you are engaged to a poor man——"

"Don't, don't! Pray don't!" cried Dora. "It's so very dreadful!"

"My soul, not at all!" said I, cheerfully. "If you will sometimes think of that, and look about now and then at your papa's housekeeping, and endeavour to acquire a little habit of accounts, for instance——"

Poor little Dora received this suggestion with something that was half a sob and half a scream.

"—It will be so useful to us afterwards," I went on. "And if you would promise me to read a little—a little Cookery Book that I would send you, it would be so excellent for both of us. For our path in life, my Dora," said I, warming with the subject, "is stony and rugged now, and it rests with us to smooth it. We must fight our way onward. We must be brave. There are obstacles to be met, and we must meet, and crush them!"

I was going on at a great rate, with a clenched hand, and a most enthusiastic countenance; but it was quite unnecessary to proceed. I had said enough. I had done it again. Oh, she was so frightened! Oh, where was Julia Mills! Oh, take her to Julia Mills, and go away, please! So that, in short, I was quite distracted, and raved about the drawing-room.

I thought I had killed her, this time. I sprinkled water on her face. I went down on my knees. I plucked at my hair. I denounced myself as a remorseless brute and a ruthless beast. I implored her forgiveness. I besought her to look up. I ravaged Miss Mills's work-box for a smelling-bottle, and in my agony of mind applied an ivory needle-case instead, and dropped all the needles over Dora. I shook my fists at Jip, who was as frantic as myself. I did every wild extravagance that could be done, and was a long way beyond the end of my wits when Miss Mills came into the room.

"Who has done this!" exclaimed Miss Mills, succouring her friend.

I replied, "*I*, Miss Mills! *I* have done it! Behold the destroyer!"—or words to that effect—and hid my face from the light, in the sofa cushion.

At first Miss Mills thought it was a quarrel, and that we were verging on the Desert of Sahara; but she soon found out how matters stood, for my dear affectionate little Dora, embracing her, began exclaiming that I was "a poor labourer;" and then cried for me, and embraced me, and asked me would I let her give me all her money to keep, and then fell on Miss Mills's neck, sobbing as if her tender heart were broken.

Miss Mills must have been born to be a blessing to us. She ascertained from me in a few words what it was all about, comforted Dora, and gradually convinced her that I was not a labourer—from my manner of stating the case I believe Dora concluded that I was a navigator, and went balancing myself up and down a plank all day with a wheelbarrow—and so brought us together in peace. When we were quite composed, and Dora had gone up-stairs to put some rose-water to her eyes, Miss Mills rang for tea. In the ensuing interval, I told Miss Mills that she was evermore my friend, and that my heart must cease to vibrate ere I could forget her sympathy.

I then expounded to Miss Mills what I had endeavoured, so very unsuccessfully, to expound to Dora. Miss Mills replied, on general principles, that the Cottage of content was better than the Palace of cold splendour, and that where love was, all was.

I said to Miss Mills that this was very true, and who should know it better than I, who loved Dora with a love that never mortal had experienced yet? But on Miss Mills observing, with despondency, that it were well indeed for some hearts if this were so, I explained that I begged leave to restrict the observation to mortals of the masculine gender.

I then put it to Miss Mills, to say whether she considered that there was or was not any practical merit in the suggestion I had been anxious to make, concerning the accounts, the housekeeping, and the Cookery Book?

Miss Mills, after some consideration, thus replied:

"Mr. Copperfield, I will be plain with you. Mental suffering and trial supply, in some natures, the place of years, and I will be as plain with you as if I were a Lady Abbess. No. The suggestion is not appropriate to our Dora. Our dearest Dora is a favourite child of nature. She is a thing of light, and airiness, and joy. I am free to confess that if it could be done, it might be well, but——" and Miss Mills shook her head.

I was encouraged by this closing admission on the part of Miss Mills to ask her, whether, for Dora's sake, if she had any opportunity of luring her attention to such preparations for an earnest life, she would avail herself of it? Miss Mills replied in the affirmative so readily, that I further asked her if she would take charge of the Cookery Book; and, if she ever could insinuate it upon Dora's acceptance, without frightening her, undertake to do me that crowning service. Miss Mills accepted this trust, too; but was not sanguine.

And Dora returned, looking such a lovely little creature, that I really doubted whether she ought to be troubled with anything so ordinary. And she loved me so much, and was so captivating (particularly when she made Jip stand on his hind-legs for toast, and when she pretended to hold that nose of his against the hot teapot for punishment because he wouldn't), that I felt like a sort of Monster who had got into a Fairy's bower, when I thought of having frightened her, and made her cry.

After tea we had the guitar; and Dora sang those same dear old French songs about the impossibility of ever on any account leaving off dancing, La ra la, La ra la, until I felt a much greater Monster than before.

We had only one check to our pleasure, and that happened a little while before I took my leave, when, Miss Mills chancing to make some allusion to to-morrow morning, I unluckily let out that, being obliged to exert myself now, I got up at five o'clock. Whether Dora had any idea that I was a Private Watchman, I am unable to say; but it made a great impression on her, and she neither played nor sang any more.

It was still on her mind when I bade her adieu; and she said to me, in her pretty coaxing way—as if I were a doll, I used to think:

"Now don't get up at five o'clock, you naughty boy. It's so nonsensical!"

"My love," said I, "I have work to do."

"But don't do it!" returned Dora. "Why should you?"

It was impossible to say to that sweet little surprised face, otherwise than lightly and playfully, that we must work, to live.

"Oh! How ridiculous!" cried Dora.

"How shall we live without, Dora?" said I.

"How? Anyhow!" said Dora.

She seemed to think she had quite settled the question, and gave me such a triumphant little kiss, direct from her innocent heart, that I would hardly have put her out of conceit with her answer, for a fortune.

Well! I loved her, and I went on loving her, most absorbingly, entirely, and completely. But going on, too, working pretty hard, and busily keeping red-hot all the irons I now had in the fire, I would sit sometimes of a night, opposite my aunt, thinking how I had frightened Dora that time, and how I could best make my way with a guitar-case through the forest of difficulty, until I used to fancy that my head was turning quite grey.

CHAPTER XXXVIII.

A DISSOLUTION OF PARTNERSHIP.

I DID not allow my resolution, with respect to the Parliamentary Debates, to cool. It was one of the irons I began to heat immediately, and one of the irons I kept hot, and hammered at, with a perseverance I may honestly admire. I bought an approved scheme of the noble art and mystery of stenography (which cost me ten and sixpence); and plunged into a sea of perplexity that brought me, in a few weeks, to the confines of distraction. The changes that were rung upon dots, which in such a position meant such a thing, and in such another position something else, entirely different; the wonderful vagaries that were played by circles; the unaccountable consequences that resulted from marks like flies' legs; the tremendous effects of a curve in a wrong place; not only troubled my waking hours, but reappeared before me in my sleep. When I had groped my way, blindly, through these difficulties, and had mastered the alphabet, which was an Egyptian Temple in itself, there then appeared a procession of new horrors, called arbitrary characters; the most despotic characters I have ever known; who insisted, for instance, that a thing like the beginning of a cobweb, meant expectation, and that a pen-and-ink sky-rocket stood for disadvantageous. When I had fixed these wretches in my mind, I found that they had driven everything else out of it; then, beginning again, I forgot them; while I was picking them up, I dropped the other fragments of the system; in short, it was almost heartbreaking.

It might have been quite heartbreaking, but for Dora, who was the stay and anchor of my tempest-driven bark.

Every scratch in the scheme was a gnarled oak in the forest of difficulty, and I went on cutting them down, one after another, with such vigour, that in three or four months I was in a condition to make an experiment on one of our crack speakers in the Commons. Shall I ever forget how the crack speaker walked off from me before I began, and left my imbecile pencil staggering about the paper as if it were in a fit!

This would not do, it was quite clear. I was flying too high, and should never get on, so. I resorted to Traddles for advice; who suggested that he should dictate speeches to me, at a pace, and with occasional stoppages, adapted to my weakness. Very grateful for this friendly aid, I accepted the proposal; and night after night, almost every night, for a long time, we had a sort of private Parliament in Buckingham Street, after I came home from the Doctor's.

I should like to see such a Parliament anywhere else! My aunt and Mr. Dick represented the Government or the Opposition (as the case might be), and Traddles, with the assistance of Enfield's Speaker or a volume of Parliamentary orations, thundered astonishing invectives against them. Standing by the table, with his finger in the page to keep the place, and his right arm flourishing above his head, Traddles, as Mr. Pitt, Mr. Fox, Mr. Sheridan, Mr. Burke, Lord Castlereagh, Viscount Sidmouth, or Mr. Canning, would work himself into the most violent heats, and deliver the most withering denunciations of the profligacy and corruption of my aunt and Mr. Dick; while I used to sit, at a little distance, with my note-book on my knee, fagging after him with all my might and main. The inconsistency and recklessness of Traddles were not to be exceeded by any real politician. He was for any description of policy, in the compass of a week; and nailed all sorts of colours to every denomination of mast. My aunt, looking very like an immovable Chancellor of the Exchequer, would occasionally throw in an interruption or two, as "Hear!" or "No!" or "Oh!" when the text seemed to require it: which was always a signal to Mr. Dick (a perfect country gentleman) to follow lustily with the same cry. But Mr. Dick got taxed with such things in the course of his Parliamentary career, and was made responsible for such awful consequences, that he became uncomfortable in his mind sometimes. I believe he actually began to be afraid he really had been doing something, tending to the annihilation of the British constitution, and the ruin of the country.

Often and often we pursued these debates until the clock pointed to midnight, and the candles were burning down. The result of so much good practice was, that by-and-by I began to keep pace with Traddles pretty well, and should have been quite triumphant if I had had the least idea what my notes were about. But, as to reading them after I had got them, I might as well have copied the Chinese inscriptions on an immense collection of tea-chests, or the golden characters on all the great red and green bottles in the chemists' shops!

There was nothing for it, but to turn back and begin all over again. It was very hard, but I turned back, though with a heavy heart, and began laboriously and methodically to plod over the same tedious ground at a snail's pace; stopping to examine minutely every speck in the way, on all sides, and making the most desperate efforts to know these elusive characters by sight wherever I met them. I was always punctual at the office; at the Doctor's too: and I really did work, as the common expression is, like a cart-horse.

One day, when I went to the Commons as usual, I found Mr. Spenlow in the doorway looking extremely grave, and talking to himself. As he was in the habit of complaining of pains in his head—he had naturally a short throat, and I do seriously believe he overstarched himself—I was at first alarmed by the idea that he was not quite right in that direction; but he soon relieved my uneasiness.

Instead of returning my "Good morning" with his usual affability, he looked at me in a distant, ceremonious manner, and coldly requested me to accompany him to a certain coffee-house, which, in those days, had a door opening into the Commons, just within the little archway in St. Paul's Churchyard. I complied, in a very uncomfortable state, and with a warm shooting all over me, as if my apprehensions were breaking out into buds. When I allowed him to go on a little before, on account of the narrowness of the way, I observed that he carried his head with a lofty air that was particularly unpromising; and my mind misgave me that he had found out about my darling Dora.

If I had not guessed this, on the way to the coffee-house, I could hardly have failed to know what was the matter when I followed him into an up-stairs room, and found Miss Murdstone there, supported by a background of sideboard, on which were several inverted tumblers sustaining lemons, and two of those extraordinary boxes, all corners and flutings, for sticking knives and forks in, which, happily for mankind, are now obsolete.

Miss Murdstone gave me her chilly finger-nails, and sat severely rigid. Mr. Spenlow shut the door, motioned me to a chair, and stood on the hearth-rug in front of the fireplace.

"Have the goodness to show Mr. Copperfield," said Mr. Spenlow, "what you have in your reticule, Miss Murdstone."

I believe it was the old identical steel-clasped reticule of my childhood, that shut up like a bite. Compressing her lips, in sympathy with the snap, Miss Murdstone opened it—opening her mouth a little at the same time—and produced my last letter to Dora, teeming with expressions of devoted affection.

"I believe that is your writing, Mr. Copperfield?" said Mr. Spenlow.

I was very hot, and the voice I heard was very unlike mine, when I said, "It is, Sir!"

"If I am not mistaken," said Mr. Spenlow, as Miss Murdstone brought a parcel of letters out of her reticule, tied round with the dearest bit of blue ribbon, "those are also from your pen, Mr. Copperfield?"

I took them from her with a most desolate sensation; and, glancing at such phrases at the top, as "My ever dearest and own Dora," "My best beloved angel," "My blessed one for ever," and the like, blushed deeply, and inclined my head.

"No, thank you!" said Mr. Spenlow coldly, as I mechanically offered them back to him. "I will not deprive you of them. Miss Murdstone, be so good as to proceed!"

That gentle creature, after a moment's thoughtful survey of the carpet, delivered herself with much dry unction as follows:

"I must confess to having entertained my suspicions of Miss Spenlow, in reference to David Copperfield, for some time. I observed Miss Spenlow and David Copperfield, when they first met; and the impression made upon me then was not agreeable. The depravity of the human heart is such——"

"You will oblige me, ma'am," interrupted Mr. Spenlow, "by confining yourself to facts."

Miss Murdstone cast down her eyes, shook her head as if protesting against this unseemly interruption, and with frowning dignity resumed.

"Since I am to confine myself to facts, I will state them as dryly as I can. Perhaps that will be considered an acceptable course of proceeding. I have already said, Sir, that I have had my suspicions of Miss Spenlow, in reference to David Copperfield, for some time. I have frequently endeavoured to find decisive corroboration of those suspicions, but without effect. I have therefore forborne to mention them to Miss Spenlow's father;" looking severely at him; "knowing how little disposition there usually is in such cases, to acknowledge the conscientious discharge of duty."

Mr. Spenlow seemed quite cowed by the gentlemanly sternness of Miss Murdstone's manner, and deprecated her severity with a conciliatory little wave of his hand.

"On my return to Norwood, after the period of absence occasioned by my brother's marriage," pursued Miss Murdstone in a disdainful voice, "and on the return of Miss Spenlow from her visit to her friend Miss Mills, I imagined that the manner of Miss Spenlow gave me greater occasion for suspicion than before. Therefore I watched Miss Spenlow closely."

Dear, tender little Dora, so unconscious of this Dragon's eye!

"Still," resumed Miss Murdstone, "I found no proof until last night. It appeared to me that Miss Spenlow received too many letters from her friend Miss Mills; but Miss Mills being her friend with her father's full concurrence," another telling blow at Mr. Spenlow, "it was not for me to interfere. If I may not be permitted to allude to the natural depravity of the human heart, at least I may—I must—be permitted, so far to refer to misplaced confidence."

Mr. Spenlow apologetically murmured his assent.

"Last evening after tea," pursued Miss Murdstone, "I observed the little dog starting, rolling, and growling about the drawing-room, worrying something. I said to Miss Spenlow, 'Dora, what is that the dog has in his mouth? It's paper.' Miss Spenlow immediately put her hand to her frock, gave a sudden cry, and ran to the dog. I interposed, and said, 'Dora my love, you must permit me.'"

Oh Jip, miserable Spaniel, this wretchedness, then, was your work!

"Miss Spenlow endeavoured," said Miss Murdstone, "to bribe me with kisses, work-boxes, and small articles of jewellery—that, of course, I pass over. The little dog retreated under the sofa on my approaching him, and was with great difficulty dislodged by the fire-irons. Even when dislodged, he still kept the letter in his mouth; and on my endeavouring to take it from him, at the imminent risk of being bitten, he kept it between his teeth so pertinaciously as to suffer himself to be held suspended in the air by means of the document. At length I obtained possession of it. After perusing it, I taxed Miss Spenlow with having many such letters in her possession; and ultimately obtained from her, the packet which is now in David Copperfield's hand."

Here she ceased; and snapping her reticule again, and shutting her mouth, looked as if she might be broken, but could never be bent.

"You have heard Miss Murdstone," said Mr. Spenlow,

turning to me. "I beg to ask, Mr. Copperfield, if you have anything to say in reply?"

The picture I had before me, of the beautiful little treasure of my heart, sobbing and crying all night—of her being alone, frightened, and wretched, then—of her having so piteously begged and prayed that stony-hearted woman to forgive her—of her having vainly offered her those kisses, work-boxes, and trinkets—of her being in such grievous distress, and all for me—very much impaired the little dignity I had been able to muster. I am afraid I was in a tremulous state for a minute or so, though I did my best to disguise it.

"There is nothing I can say, Sir," I returned, "except that all the blame is mine. Dora——"

"Miss Spenlow, if you please," said her father, majestically.

——"was induced and persuaded by me," I went on, swallowing that colder designation, "to consent to this concealment, and I bitterly regret it."

"You are very much to blame, Sir," said Mr. Spenlow, walking to and fro upon the hearth-rug, and emphasizing what he said with his whole body instead of his head, on account of the stiffness of his cravat and spine. "You have done a stealthy and unbecoming action, Mr. Copperfield. When I take a gentleman to my house, no matter whether he is nineteen, twenty-nine, or ninety, I take him there in a spirit of confidence. If he abuses my confidence, he commits a dishonourable action, Mr. Copperfield."

"I feel it, Sir, I assure you," I returned. "But I never thought so, before. Sincerely, honestly, indeed, Mr. Spenlow, I never thought so, before. I love Miss Spenlow to that extent——"

"Pooh! nonsense!" said Mr. Spenlow, reddening. "Pray don't tell me to my face that you love my daughter, Mr. Copperfield!"

"Could I defend my conduct if I did not, Sir?" I returned, with all humility.

"Can you defend your conduct if you do, Sir?" said Mr. Spenlow, stopping short upon the hearth-rug. "Have you considered your years, and my daughter's years, Mr. Copperfield? Have you considered what it is to undermine the confidence that should subsist between my daughter and myself? Have you considered my daughter's station in life, the projects I may contemplate for her advancement, the testamentary intentions I may have with reference to her? Have you considered anything, Mr. Copperfield?"

"Very little, Sir, I am afraid;" I answered, speaking to him as respectfully and sorrowfully as I felt; "but pray believe me, I have considered my own worldly position. When I explained it to you, we were already engaged——"

"I BEG," said Mr. Spenlow, more like Punch than I had ever seen him, as he energetically struck one hand upon the other—I could not help noticing that even in my despair; "that you will NOT talk to me of engagements, Mr. Copperfield!"

The otherwise immovable Miss Murdstone laughed contemptuously in one short syllable.

"When I explained my altered position to you, Sir," I began again, substituting a new form of expression for what was so unpalatable to him, "this concealment, into which I am so unhappy as to have led Miss Spenlow, had begun. Since I have been in that altered position, I have strained every nerve, I have exerted every energy, to improve it. I am sure I shall improve it in time. Will you grant me time —any length of time? We are both so young, Sir——"

"You are right," interrupted Mr. Spenlow, nodding his head a great many times, and frowning very much, "you are both very young. It's all nonsense. Let there be an end of the nonsense. Take away those letters, and throw them in the fire. Give me Miss Spenlow's letters to throw in the fire; and although our future intercourse must, you are aware, be restricted to the Commons here, we will agree to make no further mention of the past. Come, Mr. Copperfield, you don't want sense; and this is the sensible course."

No. I couldn't think of agreeing to it. I was very sorry, but there was a higher consideration than sense. Love was above all earthly considerations, and I loved Dora to idolatry, and Dora loved me. I didn't exactly say so; I softened it down as much as I could; but I implied it, and I was resolute upon it. I don't think I made myself very ridiculous, but I know I was resolute.

"Very well, Mr. Copperfield," said Mr. Spenlow, "I must try my influence with my daughter."

Miss Murdstone, by an expressive sound, a long-drawn respiration, which was neither a sigh nor a moan, but was like both, gave it as her opinion that he should have done this at first.

"I must try," said Mr. Spenlow, confirmed by this support, "my influence with my daughter. Do you decline to take those letters, Mr. Copperfield?" For I had laid them on the table.

Yes. I told him I hoped he would not think it wrong, but I couldn't possibly take them from Miss Murdstone.

"Nor from me?" said Mr. Spenlow.

No, I replied with the profoundest respect; nor from him.

"Very well!" said Mr. Spenlow.

A silence succeeding, I was undecided whether to go or stay. At length I was moving quietly towards the door, with the intention of saying that perhaps I should consult his feelings best by withdrawing: when he said, with his hands in his coat-pockets, into which it was as much as he could do to get them; and with what I should call, upon the whole, a decidedly pious air:

"You are probably aware, Mr. Copperfield, that I am not altogether destitute of worldly possessions, and that my daughter is my nearest and dearest relative?"

I hurriedly made him a reply to the effect, that I hoped the error into which I had been betrayed by the desperate nature of my love, did not induce him to think me mercenary too?

"I don't allude to the matter in that light," said Mr. Spenlow. "It would be better for yourself, and all of us, if you *were* mercenary, Mr. Copperfield—I mean, if you were more discreet, and less influenced by all this youthful nonsense. No. I merely say, with quite another view, you are probably aware I have some property to bequeath to my child!"

I certainly supposed so.

"And you can hardly think," said Mr. Spenlow, "having experience of what we see, in the Commons here, every day, of the various unaccountable and negligent proceedings of men, in respect of their testamentary arrangements—of all subjects, the one on which perhaps the strangest revelations of human inconsistency are to be met with—but that mine are made?"

I inclined my head in acquiescence.

"I should not allow," said Mr. Spenlow, with an evident increase of pious sentiment, and slowly shaking his head as he poised himself upon his toes and heels alternately, "my suitable provision for my child to be influenced by a piece of youthful folly like the present. It is mere folly. Mere nonsense. In a little while, it will weigh lighter than any feather. But I might—I might—if this silly business were not completely relinquished altogether, be induced in some anxious moment to guard her from, and surround her with protections against, the consequences of any foolish step in the way of marriage. Now, Mr. Copperfield, I hope that you will not render it necessary for me to open, even for a quarter of an hour, that closed page in the book of life, and unsettle, even for a quarter of an hour, grave affairs long since composed."

There was a serenity, a tranquillity, a calm-sunset air about him, which quite affected me. He was so peaceful and resigned—clearly had his affairs in such perfect train, and so systematically wound up—that he was a man to feel touched in the contemplation of. I really think I saw tears rise to his eyes, from the depth of his own feeling of all this.

But what could I do? I could not deny Dora and my own heart. When he told me I had better take a week to consider of what he had said, how could I say I wouldn't take a week, yet how could I fail to know that no amount of weeks could influence such love as mine?

"In the meantime, confer with Miss Trotwood, or with any person with any knowledge of life," said Mr. Spenlow, adjusting his cravat with both hands. "Take a week, Mr. Copperfield."

I submitted; and, with a countenance as expressive as I was able to make it of dejected and despairing constancy, came out of the room. Miss Murdstone's heavy eyebrows followed me to the door—I say her eyebrows rather than her eyes, because they were much more important in her face—and she looked so exactly as she used to look, at about that hour of the morning, in our parlour at Blunderstone, that I could have fancied I had been breaking down in my lessons again, and that the dead weight on my mind was that horrible old spelling-book with oval woodcuts, shaped, to my youthful fancy, like the glasses out of spectacles.

When I got to the office, and, shutting out old Tiffey and the rest of them with my hands, sat at my desk, in my own particular nook, thinking of this earthquake that had taken place so unexpectedly, and in the bitterness of my spirit cursing Jip, I fell into such a state of torment about Dora, that I wonder I did not take up my hat and rush insanely to Norwood. The idea of their frightening her, and making her cry, and of my not being there to comfort her, was so excruciating, that it impelled me to write a wild letter to Mr. Spenlow, beseeching him not to visit upon her the consequences of my awful destiny. I implored him to spare her gentle nature—not to crush a fragile flower—and addressed him generally, to the best of my remembrance, as if, instead of being her father, he had been an Ogre, or the Dragon of Wantley. This letter I sealed and laid upon his desk before he returned; and when he came in, I saw him, through the half-opened door of his room, take it up and read it.

He said nothing about it all the morning; but before he went away in the afternoon he called me in, and told me that I need not make myself at all uneasy about his daughter's happiness. He had assured her, he said, that it was all nonsense; and he had nothing more to say to her.

He believed he was an indulgent father (as indeed he was), and I might spare myself any solicitude on her account.

"You may make it necessary, if you are foolish or obstinate, Mr. Copperfield," he observed, "for me to send my daughter abroad again, for a term; but I have a better opinion of you. I hope you will be wiser than that, in a few days. As to Miss Murdstone," for I had alluded to her in the letter, "I respect that lady's vigilance, and feel obliged to her; but she has strict charge to avoid the subject. All I desire, Mr. Copperfield, is, that it should be forgotten. All you have got to do, Mr. Copperfield, is to forget it."

All! In the note I wrote to Miss Mills, I bitterly quoted this sentiment. All I had to do, I said, with gloomy sarcasm, was to forget Dora. That was all, and what was that! I entreated Miss Mills to see me, that evening. If it could not be done with Mr. Mills's sanction and concurrence, I besought a clandestine interview in the back kitchen where the mangle was. I informed her that my reason was tottering on its throne, and only she, Miss Mills, could prevent its being deposed. I signed myself, hers distractedly; and I couldn't help feeling, when I read this composition over, before sending it by a porter, that it was something in the style of Mr. Micawber.

However, I sent it. At night I repaired to Miss Mills's street, and walked up and down, until I was stealthily fetched in by Miss Mills's maid, and taken the area way to the back kitchen. I have since seen reason to believe that there was nothing on earth to prevent my going in at the front door, and being shown up into the drawing-room, except Miss Mills's love of the romantic and mysterious.

In the back kitchen, I raved as became me. I went there, I suppose, to make a fool of myself, and I am quite sure I did it. Miss Mills had received a hasty note from Dora, telling her that all was discovered, and saying, "Oh pray come to me, Julia, do, do!" But Miss Mills, mistrusting the acceptability of her presence to the higher powers, had not yet gone; and we were all benighted in the Desert of Sahara.

Miss Mills had a wonderful flow of words, and liked to pour them out. I could not help feeling, though she mingled her tears with mine, that she had a dreadful luxury in our afflictions. She petted them, as I may say, and made the most of them. A deep gulf, she observed, had opened between Dora and me, and Love could only span it with it rainbow. Love must suffer in this stern world; it ever had been so, it ever would be so. No matter, Miss Mills remarked. Hearts confined by cobwebs would burst at last, and then Love was avenged.

This was small consolation, but Miss Mills wouldn't encourage fallacious hopes. She made me much more wretched than I was before, and I felt (and told her with the deepest gratitude) that she was indeed a friend. We resolved that she should go to Dora the first thing in the morning, and find some means of assuring her, either by looks or words, of my devotion and misery. We parted, overwhelmed with grief; and I think Miss Mills enjoyed herself completely.

I confided all to my aunt when I got home; and in spite of all she could say to me, went to bed despairing. I got up despairing, and went out despairing. It was Saturday morning, and I went straight to the Commons.

I was surprised, when I came within sight of our office-door, to see the ticket-porters standing outside talking together, and some half-dozen stragglers gazing at the windows, which were shut up. I quickened my pace, and, passing among them, wondering at their looks, went hurriedly in.

The clerks were there, but nobody was doing anything. Old Tiffey, for the first time in his life, I should think, was sitting on somebody else's stool, and had not hung up his hat.

"This is a dreadful calamity, Mr. Copperfield," said he, as I entered.

"What is?" I exclaimed. "What's the matter?"

"Don't you know?" cried Tiffey, and all the rest of them, coming round me.

"No!" said I, looking from face to face.

"Mr. Spenlow," said Tiffey.

"What about him!"

"Dead!"

I thought it was the office reeling, and not I, as one of the clerks caught hold of me. They sat me down in a chair, untied my neckcloth, and brought me some water. I have no idea whether this took any time.

"Dead?" said I.

"He dined in town yesterday, and drove down in the phaeton by himself," said Tiffey, "having sent his own groom home by the coach, as he sometimes did, you know——"

"Well?"

"The phaeton went home without him. The horses stopped at the stable gate. The man went out with a lantern. Nobody in the carriage."

"Had they run away?"

"They were not hot," said Tiffey, putting on his glasses; "no hotter, I understand, than they would have been, going down at the usual pace. The reins were broken, but they had been dragging on the ground. The house was roused up directly, and three of them went out along the road. They found him a mile off."

"More than a mile off, Mr. Tiffey," interposed a junior.

"Was it? I believe you are right," said Tiffey,—"*more* than a mile off—not far from the church—lying partly on the road-side, and partly on the path, upon his face. Whether he fell out in a fit, or got out, feeling ill before the fit came on—or even whether he was quite dead then, though there is no doubt he was quite insensible—no one appears to know. If he breathed, certainly he never spoke. Medical assistance was got as soon as possible, but it was quite useless."

I cannot describe the state of mind into which I was thrown by this intelligence. The shock of such an event happening so suddenly, and happening to one with whom I had been in any respect at variance—the appalling vacancy in the room he had occupied so lately, where his chair and table seemed to wait for him, and his handwriting of yesterday was like a ghost—the indefinable impossibility of separating him from the place, and feeling, when the door opened, as if he might come in—the lazy hush and rest there was in the office, and the insatiable relish with which our people talked about it, and other people came in and out all day, and gorged themselves with the subject—this is easily intelligible to any one. What I cannot describe is, how, in the innermost recesses of my own heart, I had a lurking jealousy even of Death. How I felt as if its might

would push me from my ground in Dora's thoughts. How I was, in a grudging way I have no words for, envious of her grief. How it made me restless to think of her weeping to others, or being consoled by others. How I had a grasping, avaricious wish to shut out everybody from her but myself, and to be all in all to her, at that unseasonable time of all times.

In the trouble of this state of mind—not exclusively my own, I hope, but known to others—I went down to Norwood that night; and finding from one of the servants, when I made my inquiries at the door, that Miss Mills was there, got my aunt to direct a letter to her, which I wrote. I deplored the untimely death of Mr. Spenlow most sincerely, and shed tears in doing so. I entreated her to tell Dora, if Dora were in a state to hear it, that he had spoken to me with the utmost kindness and consideration; and had coupled nothing but tenderness, not a single or reproachful word, with her name. I know I did this selfishly, to have my name brought before her; but I tried to believe it was an act of justice to his memory. Perhaps I did believe it.

My aunt received a few lines next day in reply; addressed, outside, to her; within, to me. Dora was overcome by grief; and when her friend had asked her should she send her love to me, had only cried, as she was always crying, "Oh, dear papa! oh, poor papa!" But she had not said No, and that I made the most of.

Mr. Jorkins, who had been at Norwood since the occurrence, came to the office a few days afterwards. He and Tiffey were closeted together for some few moments, and then Tiffey looked out at the door and beckoned me in.

"Oh!" said Mr. Jorkins. "Mr. Tiffey and myself, Mr. Copperfield, are about to examine the desk, the drawers, and other such repositories of the deceased, with the view of sealing up his private papers, and searching for a Will. There is no trace of any, elsewhere. It may be as well for you to assist us, if you please."

I had been in agony to obtain some knowledge of the circumstances in which my Dora would be placed—as, in whose guardianship, and so forth—and this was something towards it. We began the search at once; Mr. Jorkins unlocking the drawers and desks, and we all taking out the papers. The office-papers we placed on one side, and the private papers (which were not numerous) on the other. We were very grave; and when we came to a stray seal, or pencil-case, or ring, or any little article of that kind which we associated personally with him, we spoke very low.

We had sealed up several packets; and were still going on dustily and quietly, when Mr. Jorkins said to us, applying exactly the same words to his late partner as his late partner had applied to him:

"Mr. Spenlow was very difficult to move from the beaten track. You know what he was! I am disposed to think he had made no will."

"Oh, I know he had!" said I.

They both stopped and looked at me.

"On the very day when I last saw him," said I, "he told me that he had, and that his affairs were long since settled."

Mr. Jorkins and old Tiffey shook their heads with one accord.

"That looks unpromising," said Tiffey.

"Very unpromising," said Mr. Jorkins.

"Surely you don't doubt——" I began.

"My good Mr. Copperfield!" said Tiffey, laying his

hand upon my arm, and shutting up both his eyes as he shook his head: "if you had been in the Commons as long as I have, you would know that there is no subject on which men are so inconsistent, and so little to be trusted."

"Why, bless my soul, he made that very remark!" I replied persistently.

"I should call that almost final," observed Tiffey. "My opinion is—no will."

It appeared a wonderful thing to me, but it turned out that there *was* no will. He had never so much as thought of making one, so far as his papers afforded any evidence; for there was no kind of hint, sketch, or memorandum, of any testamentary intention whatever. What was scarcely less astonishing to me was, that his affairs were in a most disordered state. It was extremely difficult, I heard, to make out what he owed, or what he had paid, or of what he died possessed. It was considered likely that for years he could have had no clear opinion on these subjects himself. By little and little it came out, that, in the competition on all points of appearance and gentility that his running high in the Commons, he had spent more than his professional income, which was not a very large one, and had reduced his private means, if they ever had been great (which was exceedingly doubtful), to a very low ebb indeed. There was a sale of the furniture and lease, at Norwood; and Tiffey told me, little thinking how interested I was in the story, that, paying all the just debts of the deceased, and deducting his share of outstanding bad and doubtful debts due to the firm, he wouldn't give a thousand pounds for all the assets remaining.

This was at the expiration of about six weeks. I had suffered tortures all the time, and thought I really must have laid violent hands upon myself, when Miss Mills still reported to me, that my broken-hearted little Dora would say nothing, when I was mentioned, but "Oh, poor papa! Oh, dear papa!" Also, that she had no other relations than two aunts, maiden sisters of Mr. Spenlow, who lived at Putney, and who had not held any other than chance communication with their brother for many years. Not that they had ever quarrelled (Miss Mills informed me); but that having been, on the occasion of Dora's christening, invited to tea, when they considered themselves privileged to be invited to dinner, they had expressed their opinion in writing, that it was "better for the happiness of all parties" that they should stay away. Since which they had gone their road, and their brother had gone his.

These two ladies now emerged from their retirement, and proposed to take Dora to live at Putney. Dora, clinging to them both, and weeping, exclaimed, "Oh yes, aunts! Please take Julia Mills and me and Jip to Putney!" So they went, very soon after the funeral.

How I found time to haunt Putney, I am sure I don't know; but I contrived, by some means or other, to prowl about the neighbourhood pretty often. Miss Mills, for the more exact discharge of the duties of friendship, kept a journal; and she used to meet me sometimes, on the Common, and read it, or (if she had not time to do that) lend it to me. How I treasured up the entries, of which I subjoin a sample!

"Monday. My sweet D. still much depressed. Headache. Called attention to J. as being beautifully sleek. D. fondled J. Associations thus awakened, opened floodgates of sorrow. Rush of grief admitted. (Are tears the dewdrops of the heart? J. M.)

"Tuesday. D. weak and nervous. Beautiful in pallor. (Do we not remark this in moon likewise? J. M.) D., J. M., and J. took airing in carriage. J. looking out of window, and barking violently at dustman, occasioned smile to overspread features of D. (Of such slight links is chain of life composed! J. M.)

"Wednesday. D. comparatively cheerful. Sang to her, as congenial melody, Evening Bells. Effect not soothing, but reverse. D. inexpressibly affected. Found sobbing afterwards, in own room. Quoted verses respecting self and young Gazelle. Ineffectually. Also referred to Patience on Monument. (Qy. Why on monument? J. M.)

"Thursday. D. certainly improved. Better night. Slight tinge of damask revisiting cheek. Resolved to mention name of D. C. Introduced same, cautiously, in course of airing. D. immediately overcome. 'Oh, dear, dear Julia! Oh, I have been a naughty and undutiful child!' Soothed and caressed. Drew ideal picture of D. C. on verge of tomb. D. again overcome. 'Oh, what shall I do, what shall I do? Oh, take me somewhere!' Much alarmed. Fainting of D. and glass of water from public-house. (Poetical affinity. Chequered sign on doorpost: chequered human life. Alas! J. M.)

"Friday. Day of incident. Man appears in kitchen, with blue bag, 'for lady's boots left out to heel.' Cook replies, 'No such orders.' Man argues point. Cook withdraws to inquire, leaving man alone with J. On Cook's return, man still argues point, but ultimately goes. J. missing. D. distracted. Information sent to police. Man to be identified by broad nose, and legs like balustrades of bridge. Search made in every direction. No J. D. weeping bitterly, and inconsolable. Renewed reference to young Gazelle. Appropriate, but unavailing. Towards evening, strange boy calls. Brought into parlour. Broad nose, but no balustrades. Says he wants a pound, and knows a dog. Declines to explain further, though much pressed. Pound being produced by D., takes Cook to little house, where J. alone tied up to leg of table. Joy of D., who dances round J. while he eats his supper. Emboldened by this happy change, mention D. C. upstairs. D. weeps afresh, cries piteously, 'Oh, don't, don't, don't!' It is so wicked to think of anything but poor papa!'—embraces J. and sobs herself to sleep. (Must not D. C. confine himself to the broad pinions of Time? J. M.)"

Miss Mills and her journal were my sole consolation at this period. To see her, who had seen Dora, but a little while before—to trace the initial letter of Dora's name through her sympathetic pages—to be made more and more miserable by her—were my only comforts. I felt as if I had been living in a palace of cards, which had tumbled down, leaving only Miss Mills and me among the ruins; as if some grim enchanter had drawn a magic circle round the innocent goddess of my heart, which nothing indeed but those same strong pinions, capable of carrying so many people over so much, would enable me to enter!

CHAPTER XXXIX.

WICKFIELD AND HEEP.

My aunt, beginning, I imagine, to be made seriously uncomfortable by my prolonged dejection, made a pretence of being anxious that I should go to Dover, to see that all was working well at the cottage, which was let; and to conclude an agreement, with the same tenant, for a longer term of occupation. Janet was drafted into the service of Mrs. Strong, where I saw her every day. She had been undecided, on leaving Dover, whether or no to give the finishing touch to that renunciation of mankind in which she had been educated, by marrying a pilot; but she decided against that venture. Not so much for the sake of principle, I believe, as because she happened not to like him.

Although it required an effort to leave Miss Mills, I fell rather willingly into my aunt's pretence, as a means of enabling me to pass a few tranquil hours with Agnes. I consulted the good Doctor relative to an absence of three days; and the Doctor wishing me to take that relaxation,—he wished me to take more; but my energy could not bear that,—I made up my mind to go.

As to the Commons, I had no great occasion to be particular about my duties in that quarter. To say the truth, we were getting in no very good odour among the tip-top proctors, and were rapidly sliding down to but a doubtful position. The business had been indifferent under Mr. Jorkins, before Mr. Spenlow's time; and although it had been quickened by the infusion of new blood, and by the display which Mr. Spenlow made, still it was not established on a sufficiently strong basis to bear, without being shaken, such a blow as the sudden loss of its active manager. It fell off very much. Mr. Jorkins, notwithstanding his reputation in the firm, was an easy-going, incapable sort of man, whose reputation out of doors was not calculated to back it up. I was turned over to him now, and when I saw him take his snuff and let the business go, I regretted my aunt's thousand pounds more than ever.

But this was not the worst of it. There were a number of hangers-on and outsiders about the Commons, who, without being proctors themselves, dabbled in common-form business, and got it done by real proctors, who lent their names in consideration of a share in the spoil;—and there were a good many of these too. As our house now wanted business on any terms, we joined this noble band; and threw out lures to the hangers-on and outsiders, to bring their business to us. Marriage licences and small probates were what we all looked for, and what paid us best; and the competition for these ran very high indeed. Kidnappers and inveiglers were planted in all the avenues of entrance to the Commons, with instructions to do their utmost to cut off all persons in mourning, and all gentlemen with anything bashful in their appearance, and entice them to the offices in which their respective employers were interested; which instructions were so well observed, that I myself, before I was known by sight, was twice hustled into the premises of our principal opponent. The conflicting interests of these touting gentlemen being of a nature to irritate their feelings, personal collisions took place; and the Commons was even scandalized by our principal inveigler (who had formerly been in the wine trade, and afterwards in the sworn brokery line) walking about for some days with a black eye. Any one of these scouts used to think nothing of politely assisting an old lady in black out of a vehicle, killing any proctor whom she inquired for, representing his employer as the lawful successor and representative of that proctor, and bearing the old lady off (sometimes greatly affected) to his employer's office. Many captives were brought to me in this way. As to marriage licences, the competition rose to such a pitch, that a shy gentleman in want of one, had nothing to do but submit himself to the first inveigler, or be fought for, and become the prey of the strongest. One of our clerks, who was an outsider, used, in the height of this contest, to sit with his hat on, that he might be ready to rush out and swear before a surrogate any victim who was brought in. The system of inveigling continues, I believe, to this day. The last time I was in the Commons, a civil able-bodied person in a white apron pounced out upon me from a doorway, and whispering the word "Marriage-licence" in my ear, was with great difficulty prevented from taking me up in his arms and lifting me into a proctor's.

From this digression, let me proceed to Dover.

I found everything in a satisfactory state at the cottage; and was enabled to gratify my aunt exceedingly by reporting that the tenant inherited her feud, and waged incessant war against donkeys. Having settled the little business I had to transact there, and slept there one night, I walked on to Canterbury early in the morning. It was now winter again; and the fresh, cold windy day, and the sweeping downland, brightened up my hopes a little.

Coming into Canterbury, I loitered through the old streets with a sober pleasure that calmed my spirits, and eased my heart. There were the old signs, the old names over the shops, the old people serving in them. It appeared so long, since I had been a schoolboy there, that I wondered the place was so little changed, until I reflected how little I was changed myself. Strange to say, that quiet influence which was inseparable in my mind from Agnes, seemed to pervade even the city where she dwelt. The venerable Cathedral towers, and the old jackdaws and rooks whose airy voices made them more retired than perfect silence would have done; the battered gateways, once stuck full with statues, long thrown down, and crumbled away, like the reverential pilgrims who had gazed upon them; the still nooks, where the ivied growth of centuries crept over gabled ends and ruined walls; the ancient houses, the pastoral landscape of field, orchard, and garden; everywhere—on everything—I felt the same serener air, the same calm, thoughtful, softening spirit.

Arrived at Mr. Wickfield's house, I found, in the little lower room on the ground-floor, where Uriah Heep had been of old accustomed to sit, Mr. Micawber plying his pen with great assiduity. He was dressed in a legal-looking suit of black, and loomed, burly and large, in that small office.

Mr. Micawber was extremely glad to see me, but a little confused too. He would have conducted me immediately into the presence of Uriah, but I declined.

"I know the house of old, you recollect," said I, "and will find my way up-stairs. How do you like the law, Mr. Micawber?"

"My dear Copperfield," he replied. "To a man possessed of the higher imaginative powers, the objection to legal studies is the amount of detail which they involve. Even in our professional correspondence," said Mr. Micawber, glancing at some letters he was writing, "the mind is not at liberty to soar to any exalted form of expression. Still, it is a great pursuit. A great pursuit!"

He then told me that he had become the tenant of Uriah Heep's old house; and that Mrs. Micawber would be delighted to receive me, once more, under her own roof.

"It is humble," said Mr. Micawber, "to quote a favourite expression of my friend Heep; but it may prove the stepping-stone to more ambitious domiciliary accommodation."

I asked him whether he had reason, so far, to be satisfied with his friend Heep's treatment of him? He got up to ascertain if the door were close shut, before he replied, in a lower voice:

"My dear Copperfield, a man who labours under the pressure of pecuniary embarrassments, is, with the generality of people, at a disadvantage. That disadvantage is not diminished, when that pressure necessitates the drawing of stipendiary emoluments, before those emoluments are strictly due and payable. All I can say is, that my friend Heep has responded to appeals to which I need not more particularly refer, in a manner calculated to redound equally to the honour of his head, and of his heart."

"I should not have supposed him to be very free with his money either," I observed.

"Pardon me!" said Mr. Micawber, with an air of constraint, "I speak of my friend Heep as I have experience."

"I am glad your experience is so favourable," I returned.

"You are very obliging, my dear Copperfield," said Mr. Micawber; and hummed a tune.

"Do you see much of Mr. Wickfield?" I asked, to change the subject.

"Not much," said Mr. Micawber, slightingly. "Mr. Wickfield is, I dare say, a man of very excellent intentions; but he is—in short, he is obsolete."

"I am afraid his partner seeks to make him so," said I.

"My dear Copperfield!" returned Mr. Micawber, after some uneasy evolutions on his stool, "allow me to offer a remark! I am here, in a capacity of confidence. I am here, in a position of trust. The discussion of some topics, even with Mrs. Micawber herself (so long the partner of my various vicissitudes, and a woman of a remarkable lucidity of intellect), is, I am led to consider, incompatible with the functions now devolving on me. I would therefore take the liberty of suggesting that in our friendly intercourse—which I trust will never be disturbed!—we draw a line. On one side of this line," said Mr. Micawber, representing it on the desk with the office ruler, "is the whole range of the human intellect, with a trifling exception; on the other, *is* that exception; that is to say, the affairs of Messrs. Wickfield and Heep, with all belonging and appertaining thereunto. I trust I give no offence to the companion of my youth, in submitting this proposition to his cooler judgment?"

Though I saw an uneasy change in Mr. Micawber, which sat tightly on him, as if his new duties were a misfit, I felt I had no right to be offended. My telling him so, appeared to relieve him; and he shook hands with me.

"I am charmed, Copperfield," said Mr. Micawber, "let me assure you, with Miss Wickfield. She is a very superior young lady, of very remarkable attractions, graces, and virtues. Upon my honour," said Mr. Micawber, indefinitely kissing his hand and bowing with his genteelest air, "I do homage to Miss Wickfield! Hem!"

"I am glad of that, at least," said I.

"If you had not assured us, my dear Copperfield, on the occasion of that agreeable afternoon we had the happiness of passing with you, that D. was your favourite letter," said Mr. Micawber, "I should unquestionably have supposed that A. had been so."

We have all some experience of a feeling, that comes over us occasionally, of what we are saying and doing having been said and done before, in a remote time—of our having been surrounded, dim ages ago, by the same faces, objects, and circumstances—of our knowing perfectly what will be said next, as if we suddenly remembered it! I never had this mysterious impression more strongly in my life, than before he uttered those words.

I took my leave of Mr. Micawber, for the time, charging him with my best remembrances to all at home. As I left him, resuming his stool and his pen, and rolling his head in his stock, to get it into easier writing order, I clearly perceived that there was something interposed between him and me, since he had come into his new functions, which prevented our getting at each other as we used to do, and quite altered the character of our intercourse.

There was no one in the quaint old drawing-room, though it presented tokens of Mrs. Heep's whereabout. I looked into the room still belonging to Agnes, and saw her sitting by the fire, at a pretty old-fashioned desk she had, writing.

My darkening the light made her look up. What a pleasure to be the cause of that bright change in her attentive face, and the object of that sweet regard and welcome!

"Ah, Agnes!" said I, when we were sitting together, side by side; "I have missed you so much, lately!"

"Indeed?" she replied. "Again! And so soon?"

I shook my head.

"I don't know how it is, Agnes; I seem to want some faculty of mind that I ought to have. You were so much in the habit of thinking for me, in the happy old days here, and I came so naturally to you for counsel and support, that I really think I have missed acquiring it!"

"And what is it?" said Agnes, cheerfully.

"I don't know what to call it," I replied. "I think I am earnest and persevering?"

"I am sure of it," said Agnes.

"And patient, Agnes?" I inquired, with a little hesitation.

"Yes," returned Agnes, laughing. "Pretty well."

"And yet," said I, "I get so miserable and worried, and am so unsteady and irresolute in my power of assuring myself, that I know I must want—shall I call it—reliance, of some kind?"

"Call it so, if you will," said Agnes.

"Well," I returned. "See here! You come to London, I rely on you, and I have an object and a course at once. I am driven out of it, I come here, and in a moment I feel an altered person. The circumstances that distressed me are not changed, since I came into this room; but an influence comes over me in that short interval that alters me, oh, how much for the better! What is it? What is your secret, Agnes?"

Her head was bent down, looking at the fire.

"It's the old story," said I. "Don't laugh, when I say it was always the same in little things as it is in greater ones. My old troubles were nonsense, and now they are serious; but whenever I have gone away from my adopted sister——"

Agnes looked up—with such a heavenly face!—and gave me her hand, which I kissed.

"Whenever I have not had you, Agnes, to advise and approve in the beginning, I have seemed to go wild, and to get into all sorts of difficulty. When I have come to you, at last (as I have always done), I have come to peace and happiness. I come home, now, like a tired traveller, and find such a blessed sense of rest!"

I felt so deeply what I said, it affected me so sincerely, that my voice failed, and I covered my face with my hand,

and broke into tears. I write the truth. Whatever contradictions and inconsistencies there were within me, as there are within so many of us; whatever might have been so different, and so much better; whatever I had done, in which I had perversely wandered away from the voice of my own heart; I knew nothing of. I only knew that I was fervently in earnest, when I felt the rest and peace of having Agnes near me.

In her placid sisterly manner; with her beaming eyes; with her tender voice; and with that sweet composure, which had long ago made the house that held her quite a sacred place to me; she soon won me from this weakness, and led me on to tell all that had happened since our last meeting.

"And there is not another word to tell, Agnes," said I, when I had made an end of my confidence. "Now, my reliance is on you."

"But it must not be on me, Trotwood," returned Agnes, with a pleasant smile. "It must be on some one else."

"On Dora?" said I.

"Assuredly."

"Why, I have not mentioned, Agnes," said I, a little embarrassed, "that Dora is rather difficult to—I would not, for the world, say, to rely upon, because she is the soul of purity and truth—but rather difficult to—I hardly know how to express it, really, Agnes. She is a timid little thing, and easily disturbed and frightened. Some time ago, before her father's death, when I thought it right to mention to her—but I'll tell you, if you will bear with me, how it was."

Accordingly, I told Agnes about my declaration of poverty, about the Cookery Book, the housekeeping accounts, and all the rest of it.

"Oh, Trotwood!" she remonstrated, with a smile. "Just your old headlong way! You might have been in earnest in striving to get on in the world, without being so very sudden with a timid, loving, inexperienced girl. Poor Dora!"

I never heard such sweet forbearing kindness expressed in a voice, as she expressed in making this reply. It was as if I had seen her admiringly and tenderly embracing Dora, and tacitly reproving me, by her considerate protection, for my hot haste in fluttering that little heart. It was as if I had seen Dora, in all her fascinating artlessness, caressing Agnes, and thanking her, and coaxingly appealing against me, and loving me with all her childish innocence.

I felt so grateful to Agnes, and admired her so! I saw those two together, in a bright perspective, such well-associated friends, each adorning the other so much!

"What ought I to do then, Agnes?" I inquired, after looking at the fire a little while. "What would it be right to do?"

"I think," said Agnes, "that the honourable course to take, would be to write to those two ladies. Don't you think that any secret course is an unworthy one?"

"Yes. If you think so," said I.

"I am poorly qualified to judge of such matters," replied Agnes, with a modest hesitation, "but I certainly feel—in short, I feel that your being secret and clandestine, is not being like yourself."

"Like myself, in the too high opinion you have of me, Agnes, I am afraid," said I.

"Like yourself, in the candour of your nature," she

returned; "and therefore I would write to those two ladies. I would relate, as plainly and as openly as possible, all that has taken place; and I would ask their permission to visit sometimes, at their house. Considering that you are young, and striving for a place in life, I think it would be well to say that you would readily abide by any conditions they might impose upon you. I would entreat them not to dismiss your request, without a reference to Dora; and to discuss it with her when they should think the time suitable. I would not be too vehement," said Agnes, gently, "or propose too much. I would trust to my fidelity and perseverance—and to Dora."

"But if they were to frighten Dora again, Agnes, by speaking to her," said I. "And if Dora were to cry, and say nothing about me!"

"Is that likely?" inquired Agnes, with the same sweet consideration in her face.

"God bless her, she is as easily scared as a bird," said I. "It might be! Or if the two Miss Spenlows (elderly ladies of that sort are odd characters sometimes) should not be likely persons to address in that way!"

"I don't think, Trotwood," returned Agnes, raising her soft eyes to mine, "I would consider that. Perhaps it would be better only to consider whether it is right to do this; and, if it is, to do it."

I had no longer any doubt on the subject. With a lightened heart, though with a profound sense of the weighty importance of my task, I devoted the whole afternoon to the composition of the draft of this letter; for which great purpose, Agnes relinquished her desk to me. But first I went down stairs to see Mr. Wickfield and Uriah Heep.

I found Uriah in possession of a new, plaster-smelling office, built out in the garden; looking extraordinarily mean, in the midst of a quantity of books and papers. He received me in his usual fawning way, and pretended not to have heard of my arrival from Mr. Micawber; a pretence I took the liberty of disbelieving. He accompanied me into Mr. Wickfield's room, which was the shadow of its former self—having been divested of a variety of conveniences, for the accommodation of the new partner—and stood before the fire, warming his back, and shaving his chin with his bony hand, while Mr. Wickfield and I exchanged greetings.

"You stay with us, Trotwood, while you remain in Canterbury?" said Mr. Wickfield, not without a glance at Uriah for his approval.

"Is there room for me?" said I.

"I am sure, Master Copperfield—I should say Mister, but the other comes so natural," said Uriah,—"I would turn out of your old room with pleasure, if it would be agreeable."

"No, no," said Mr. Wickfield. "Why should you be inconvenienced? There's another room. There's another room."

"Oh, but you know," returned Uriah, with a grin, "I should really be delighted!"

To cut the matter short, I said I would have the other room or none at all; so it was settled that I should have the other room: and, taking my leave of the firm until dinner, I went up stairs again.

I had hoped to have no other companion than Agnes. But Mrs. Heep had asked permission to bring herself and her knitting near the fire, in that room; on pretence of its having an aspect more favourable for her rheumatics, as the wind then was, than the drawing-room or dining-parlour. Though I could almost have consigned her to the mercies of the wind on the topmost pinnacle of the Cathedral, without remorse, I made a virtue of necessity, and gave her a friendly salutation.

"I'm umbly thankful to you, Sir," said Mrs. Heep, in acknowledgment of my inquiries concerning her health, "but I'm only pretty well. I haven't much to boast of. If I could see my Uriah well settled in life, I couldn't expect much more, I think. How do you think my Ury looking, Sir?"

I thought him looking as villainous as ever, and I replied that I saw no change in him.

"Oh, don't you think he's changed?" said Mrs. Heep. "There I must umbly beg leave to differ from you. Don't you see a thinness of him?"

"Not more than usual," I replied.

"*Don't* you though!" said Mrs. Heep. "But you don't take notice of him with a mother's eye!"

His mother's eye was an evil eye to the rest of the world, I thought as it met mine, howsoever affectionate to him; and I believe she and her son were devoted to one another. It passed me, and went on to Agnes.

"Don't *you* see a wasting and a wearing in him, Miss Wickfield?" inquired Mrs. Heep.

"No," said Agnes, quietly pursuing the work on which she was engaged. "You are too solicitous about him. He is very well."

Mrs. Heep, with a prodigious sniff, resumed her knitting. She never left off, or left us for a moment. I had arrived early in the day, and we had still three or four hours before dinner; but she sat there, plying her knitting-needles as monotonously as an hour-glass might have poured out its sands. She sat on one side of the fire; I sat at the desk in front of it; a little beyond me, on the other side, sat Agnes. Whensoever, slowly pondering over my letter, I lifted up my eyes, and meeting the thoughtful face of Agnes, saw it clear, and beam encouragement upon me, with its own angelic expression, I was conscious presently of the evil eye passing me, and going on to her, and coming back to me again, and dropping furtively upon the knitting. What the knitting was, I don't know, not being learned in that art; but it looked like a net; and as she worked away with those Chinese chopsticks of knitting-needles, she showed in the firelight like an ill-looking enchantress, baulked as yet by the radiant goodness opposite, but getting ready for a cast of her net by-and-by.

At dinner she maintained her watch, with the same unwinking eyes. After dinner, her son took his turn; and when Mr. Wickfield, himself, and I were left alone together, leered at me, and writhed until I could hardly bear it. In the drawing-room, there was the mother knitting and watching again. All the time that Agnes sang and played, the mother sat at the piano. Once she asked for a particular ballad, which she said her Ury (who was yawning in a great chair) doted on; and at intervals she looked round at him, and reported to Agnes that he was in raptures with the music. But she hardly ever spoke—I question if she ever did—without making some mention of him. It was evident to me that this was the duty assigned to her.

This lasted until bedtime. To have seen the mother and son, like two great bats hanging over the whole house, and darkening it with their ugly forms, made me so uncomfortable, that I would rather have remained down-stairs, knitting and all, than gone to bed. I hardly got any sleep. Next day the knitting and watching began again, and lasted all day.

I had not an opportunity of speaking to Agnes, for ten minutes. I could barely show her my letter. I proposed to her to walk out with me; but Mrs. Heep repeatedly complaining that she was worse, Agnes charitably remained within, to bear her company. Towards the twilight I went out by myself, musing on what I ought to do, and whether I was justified in withholding from Agnes, any longer, what Uriah Heep had told me in London: for that began to trouble me again, very much.

I had not walked out far enough to be quite clear of the town, upon the Ramsgate road, where there was a good path, when I was hailed, through the dust, by somebody behind me. The shambling figure, and the scanty greatcoat, were not to be mistaken. I stopped, and Uriah Heep came up.

"Well?" said I.

"How fast you walk!" said he. "My legs are pretty long, but you've given 'em quite a job."

"Where are you going?" said I.

"I am coming with you, Master Copperfield, if you'll allow me the pleasure of a walk with an old acquaintance." Saying this, with a jerk of his body, which might have been either propitiatory or derisive, he fell into step beside me.

"Uriah!" said I, as civilly as I could, after a silence.

"Master Copperfield!" said Uriah.

"To tell you the truth (at which you will not be offended), I came out to walk alone, because I have had so much company."

He looked at me sideways, and said with his hardest grin: "You mean mother?"

"Why yes, I do," said I.

"Ah! But you know we're so very umble," he returned. "And having such a knowledge of our own umbleness, we must really take care that we're not pushed to the wall by them as isn't umble. All stratagems are fair in love, Sir."

Raising his great hands until they touched his chin, he rubbed them softly, and softly chuckled; looking as like a malevolent baboon, I thought, as anything human could look.

"You see," he said, still hugging himself in that unpleasant way, and shaking his head at me, "you're quite a dangerous rival, Master Copperfield. You always was, you know."

"Do you set a watch upon Miss Wickfield, and make her home no home, because of me?" said I.

"Oh! Master Copperfield! Those are very arsh words," he replied.

"Put my meaning into any words you like," said I. "You know what it is, Uriah, as well as I do."

"Oh no! You must put it into words," he said. "Oh, really! I couldn't myself."

"Do you suppose," said I, constraining myself to be very temperate and quiet with him, on account of Agnes, "that I regard Miss Wickfield otherwise than as a very dear sister?"

"Well, Master Copperfield," he replied, "you perceive I

am not bound to answer that question. You may not, you know. But then, you see, you may!"

Anything to equal the low cunning of his visage, and of his shadowless eyes, without the ghost of an eyelash, I never saw.

"Come, then!" said I. "For the sake of Miss Wickfield——"

"My Agnes!" he exclaimed, with a sickly, angular contortion of himself. "Would you be so good as call her Agnes, Master Copperfield?"

"For the sake of Agnes Wickfield—Heaven bless her!"

"Thank you for that blessing, Master Copperfield!" he interposed.

"I will tell you what I should, under any other circumstances, as soon have thought of telling to—Jack Ketch."

"To who, Sir?" said Uriah, stretching out his neck, and shading his ear with his hand.

"To the hangman," I returned. "The most unlikely person I could think of,"—though his own face had suggested the allusion quite as a natural sequence. "I am engaged to another young lady. I hope that contents you."

"Upon your soul?" said Uriah.

I was about indignantly to give my assertion the confirmation he required, when he caught hold of my hand, and gave it a squeeze.

"Oh, Master Copperfield," he said. "If you had only had the condescension to return my confidence when I poured out the fulness of my art, the night I put you so much out of the way by sleeping before your sitting-room fire, I never should have doubted you. As it is, I'm sure I'll take off mother directly, and only too appy. I know you'll excuse the precautions of affection, won't you? What a pity, Master Copperfield, that you didn't condescend to return my confidence! I'm sure I gave you every opportunity. But you never have condescended to me, as much as I could have wished. I know you have never liked me, as I have liked you!"

All this time he was squeezing my hand with his damp fishy fingers, while I made every effort I decently could to get it away. But I was quite unsuccessful. He drew it under the sleeve of his mulberry-coloured great-coat, and I walked on, almost upon compulsion, arm in arm with him.

"Shall we turn?" said Uriah, by-and-by wheeling me face about towards the town, on which the early moon was now shining, silvering the distant windows.

"Before we leave the subject, you ought to understand," said I, breaking a pretty long silence, "that I believe Agnes Wickfield to be as far above you, and as far removed from all your aspirations, as that moon herself!"

"Peaceful! Ain't she!" said Uriah. "Very! Now confess, Master Copperfield, that you haven't liked me quite as I have liked you. All along you've thought me too umble now, I shouldn't wonder?"

"I am not fond of professions of humility," I returned, "or professions of anything else."

"There now!" said Uriah, looking flabby and lead-coloured in the moonlight. "Didn't I know it! But how little you think of the rightful umbleness of a person in my station, Master Copperfield! Father and me was both brought up at a foundation school for boys; and mother, she was likewise brought up at a public, sort of charitable, establishment. They taught us all a deal of umbleness—not much else that I know of, from morning to night. We was to be umble to this person, and umble to that; and to pull off our caps here, and to make bows there; and always to know our place, and abase ourselves before our betters. And we had such a lot of betters! Father got the monitor-medal by being umble. So did I. Father got made a sexton by being umble. He had the character, among the gentlefolks, of being such a well-behaved man, that they were determined to bring him in. 'Be umble, Uriah,' says father to me, 'and you'll get on. It was what was always being dinned into you and me at school; it's what goes down best. Be umble,' says father, 'and you'll do!' And really it ain't done bad!"

It was the first time it had ever occurred to me, that this detestable cant of false humility might have originated out of the Heep family. I had seen the harvest, but had never thought of the seed.

"When I was quite a young boy," said Uriah, "I got to know what umbleness did, and I took to it. I ate umble pie with an appetite. I stopped at the umble point of my learning, and says I, 'Hold hard!' When you offered to teach me Latin, I knew better. 'People like to be above you,' says father, 'keep yourself down.' I am very umble to the present moment, Master Copperfield, but I've got a little power!"

And he said all this—I knew, as I saw his face in the moonlight—that I might understand he was resolved to recompense himself by using his power. I had never doubted his meanness, his craft and malice; but I fully comprehended now, for the first time, what a base, unrelenting, and revengeful spirit, must have been engendered by this early, and this long suppression.

His account of himself was so far attended with an agreeable result, that it led to his withdrawing his hand in order that he might have another hug of himself under the chin. Once apart from him, I was determined to keep apart; and we walked back, side by side, saying very little more by the way.

Whether his spirits were elevated by the communication I had made to him, or by his having indulged in this retrospect, I don't know; but they were raised by some influence. He talked more at dinner than was usual with him; asked his mother (off duty, from the moment of our re-entering the house), whether he was not growing too old for a bachelor; and once looked at Agnes so, that I would have given all I had, for leave to knock him down.

When we three males were left alone after dinner, he got into a more adventurous state. He had taken little or no wine; and I presume it was the mere insolence of triumph that was upon him, flushed perhaps by the temptation my presence furnished to its exhibition.

I had observed yesterday, that he tried to entice Mr. Wickfield to drink; and, interpreting the look which Agnes had given me as she went out, had limited myself to one glass, and then proposed that we should follow her. I would have done so again to-day; but Uriah was too quick for me.

"We seldom see our present visitor, Sir," he said, addressing Mr. Wickfield, sitting, such a contrast to him, at the end of the table, "and I should propose to give him welcome in another glass or two of wine, if you have no objections. Mr. Copperfield, your elth and appiness!"

I was obliged to make a show of taking the hand he

stretched across to me; and then, with very different emotions, I took the hand of the broken gentleman, his partner.

"Come, fellow-partner," said Uriah, "if I may take the liberty,—now, suppose you give us something or another appropriate to Copperfield!"

I pass over Mr. Wickfield's proposing my aunt, his proposing Mr. Dick, his proposing Doctors' Commons, his proposing Uriah, his drinking everything twice; his consciousness of his own weakness, the ineffectual effort that he made against it; the struggle between his shame in Uriah's deportment, and his desire to conciliate him; the manifest exultation with which Uriah twisted and turned, and held him up before me. It made me sick at heart to see, and my hand recoils from writing it.

"Come, fellow-partner!" said Uriah, at last, "*I*'ll give you another one, and I umbly ask for bumpers, seeing I intend to make it the divinest of her sex."

Her father had his empty glass in his hand. I saw him set it down, look at the picture she was so like, put his hand to his forehead, and shrink back in his elbow-chair.

"I'm an umble individual to give you her elth," proceeded Uriah, "but I admire—adore her."

No physical pain that her father's grey head could have borne, I think could have been more terrible to me, than the mental endurance I saw compressed now within both his hands.

"Agnes," said Uriah, either not regarding him, or not knowing what the nature of his action was, "Agnes Wickfield is, I am safe to say, the divinest of her sex. May I speak out, among friends? To be her father is a proud distinction, but to be her husband——"

Spare me from ever again hearing such a cry, as that with which her father rose up from the table!

"What's the matter?" said Uriah, turning of a deadly colour. "You are not gone mad, after all, Mr. Wickfield, I hope? If I say, I've an ambition to make your Agnes my Agnes, I have as good a right to it as another man. I have a better right to it than any other man!"

I had my arms round Mr. Wickfield, imploring him by everything I could think of, oftenest of all by his love for Agnes, to calm himself a little. He was mad for the moment; tearing out his hair, beating his head, trying to force me from him, and to force himself from me, not answering a word, not looking at or seeing any one; blindly striving for he knew not what, his face all staring and distorted—a frightful spectacle.

I conjured him, incoherently, but in the most impassioned manner, not to abandon himself to this wildness, but to hear me. I besought him to think of Agnes, to connect me with Agnes, to recollect how Agnes and I had grown up together, how I honoured her and loved her, how she was his pride and joy. I tried to bring her idea before him in any form; I even reproached him with not having firmness to spare her the knowledge of such a scene as this. I may have effected something, or his wildness may have spent itself; but by degrees he struggled less, and began to look at me—strangely at first, then with recognition in his eyes. At length he said, "I know, Trotwood! My darling child and you—I know! But look at him!"

He pointed to Uriah, pale and glowering in a corner, evidently very much out in his calculations, and taken by surprise.

"Look at my torturer," he replied. "Before him I have step by step abandoned name and reputation, peace and quiet, house and home."

"I have kept your name and reputation for you, and your peace and quiet, and your house and home too," said Uriah, with a sulky, hurried, defeated air of compromise. "Don't be foolish, Mr. Wickfield. If I have gone a little beyond what you were prepared for, I can go back, I suppose? There's no harm done."

"I looked for single motives in every one," said Mr. Wickfield, "and I was satisfied I had bound him to me by motives of interest. But see what he is—oh, see what he is!"

"You had better stop him, Copperfield, if you can," cried Uriah, with his long forefinger pointing towards me. "He'll say something presently—mind you!—he'll be sorry to have said afterwards, and you'll be sorry to have heard!"

"I'll say anything!" cried Mr. Wickfield, with a desperate air. "Why should I not be in all the world's power if I am in yours!"

"Mind! I tell you!" said Uriah, continuing to warn me. "If you don't stop his mouth, you're not his friend! Why shouldn't you be in all the world's power, Mr. Wickfield? Because you have got a daughter. You and me know what we know, don't we? Let sleeping dogs lie—who wants to rouse 'em? I don't. Can't you see I am as umble as I can be? I tell you, if I've gone too far, I'm sorry. What would you have, Sir?"

"Oh, Trotwood, Trotwood!" exclaimed Mr. Wickfield, wringing his hands. "What I have come down to be, since I first saw you in this house! I was on my downward way then, but the dreary, dreary road I have traversed since! Weak indulgence has ruined me. Indulgence in remembrance, and indulgence in forgetfulness. My natural grief for my child's mother turned to disease; my natural love for my child turned to disease. I have infected everything I touched. I have brought misery on what I dearly love, I know—*you* know! I thought it possible that I could truly love one creature in the world, and not love the rest; I thought it possible that I could truly mourn for one creature gone out of the world, and not have some part in the grief of all who mourned. Thus the lessons of my life have been perverted! I have preyed on my own morbid coward heart, and it has preyed on me. Sordid in my grief, sordid in my love, sordid in my miserable escape from the darker side of both, oh see the ruin I am, and hate me, shun me!"

He dropped into a chair, and weakly sobbed. The excitement into which he had been roused was leaving him. Uriah came out of his corner.

"I don't know all I have done, in my fatuity," said Mr. Wickfield, putting out his hands, as if to deprecate my condemnation. "*He* knows best," meaning Uriah Heep, "for he has always been at my elbow, whispering me. You see the millstone that he is about my neck. You find him in my house, you find him in my business. You heard him, but a little time ago. What need have I to say more?"

"You haven't need to say so much, nor half so much, nor anything at all," observed Uriah, half defiant, and half fawning. "You wouldn't have took it up so, if it hadn't been for the wine. You'll think better of it to-morrow, Sir. If I have said too much, or more than I meant, what of it? I haven't stood by it!"

The door opened, and Agnes, gliding in, without a vestige of colour in her face, put her arm round his neck, and steadily said, "Papa, you are not well. Come with me!". He laid his head upon her shoulder, as if he were oppressed with heavy shame, and went out with her. Her eyes met mine for but an instant, yet I saw how much she knew of what had passed.

"I didn't expect he'd cut up so rough, Master Copperfield," said Uriah. "But it's nothing. I'll be friends with him to-morrow. It's for his good. I'm umbly anxious for his good."

I gave him no answer, and went upstairs into the quiet room where Agnes had so often sat beside me at my books. Nobody came near me until late at night. I took up a book and tried to read. I heard the clocks strike twelve, and was still reading, without knowing what I read, when Agnes touched me.

"You will be going early in the morning, Trotwood. Let us say good-bye, now!"

She had been weeping, but her face then was so calm and beautiful!

"Heaven bless you!" she said, giving me her hand.

"Dearest Agnes!" I returned, "I see you ask me not to speak of to-night—but is there nothing to be done?"

"There is God to trust in!" she replied.

"Can *I* do nothing—I, who come to you with *my* poor sorrows?"

"And make mine so much lighter," she replied. "Dear Trotwood, no!"

"Dear Agnes," I said, "it is presumptuous for me, who am so poor in all in which you are so rich—goodness, resolution, all noble qualities—to doubt or direct you; but you know how much I love you, and how much I owe you. You will never sacrifice yourself to a mistaken sense of duty, Agnes?"

More agitated for a moment than I had ever seen her, she took her hand from me, and moved a step back.

"Say you have no such thought, dear Agnes! Much more than sister! Think of the priceless gift of such a heart as yours, of such a love as yours!"

Oh! long, long afterwards, I saw that face rise up before me, with its momentary look, not wondering, not accusing, not regretting. Oh, long, long afterwards, I saw that look subside, as it did now, into the lovely smile, with which she told me she had no fear for herself—I need have none for her—and parted from me by the name of Brother, and was gone!

It was dark in the morning, when I got upon the coach at the inn door. The day was just breaking when we were about to start, and then, as I sat thinking of her, came struggling up the coach side, through the mingled day and night, Uriah's head.

"Copperfield!" said he, in a croaking whisper, as he hung by the iron on the roof, "I thought you'd be glad to hear before you went off, that there are no squares broke between us. I've been into his room already, and we've made it all smooth. Why, though I'm umble, I'm useful to him, you know; and he understands his interest when he isn't in liquor! What an agreeable man he is, after all, Master Copperfield!"

I obliged myself to say that I was glad he had made his apology.

"Oh, to be sure!" said Uriah. "When a person's umble, you know, what's an apology? So easy! I say!

I suppose," with a jerk, "you have sometimes plucked a pear before it was ripe, Master Copperfield?"

"I suppose I have," I replied.

"*I* did that last night," said Uriah; "but it'll ripen yet! It only wants attending to. I can wait!"

Profuse in his farewells, he got down again as the coachman got up. For anything I know, he was eating something to keep the raw morning air out; but, he made motions with his mouth as if the pear were ripe already, and he were smacking his lips over it.

CHAPTER XL.

THE WANDERER.

WE had a very serious conversation in Buckingham Street that night, about the domestic occurrences I have detailed in the last chapter. My aunt was deeply interested in them, and walked up and down the room with her arms folded, for more than two hours afterwards. Whenever she was particularly discomposed, she always performed one of these pedestrian feats; and the amount of her discomposure might always be estimated by the duration of her walk. On this occasion she was so much disturbed in mind as to find it necessary to open the bedroom door, and make a course for herself, comprising the full extent of the bedrooms from wall to wall; and while Mr. Dick and I sat quietly by the fire, she kept passing in and out, along this measured track, at an unchanging pace, with the regularity of a clock pendulum.

When my aunt and I were left to ourselves by Mr. Dick's going out to bed, I sat down to write my letter to the two old ladies. By that time she was tired of walking, and sat by the fire with her dress tucked up as usual. But instead of sitting in her usual manner, holding her glass upon her knee, she suffered it to stand neglected on the chimneypiece; and, resting her left elbow on her right arm, and her chin on her left hand, looked thoughtfully at me. As often as I raised my eyes from what I was about, I met hers. "I am in the lovingest of tempers, my dear," she would assure me with a nod, "but I am fidgetted and sorry!"

I had been too busy to observe, until after she was gone to bed, that she had left her night-mixture, as she always called it, untasted on the chimney-piece. She came to her door, with even more than her usual affection of manner, when I knocked to acquaint her with this discovery; but only said, "I have not the heart to take it, Trot, to-night," and shook her head, and went in again.

She read my letter to the two old ladies, in the morning, and approved of it. I posted it, and had nothing to do then, but wait, as patiently as I could, for the reply. I was still in this state of expectation, and had been, for nearly a week; when I left the Doctor's one snowy night, to walk home.

It had been a bitter day, and a cutting north-east wind had blown for some time. The wind had gone down with the light, and so the snow had come on. It was a heavy, settled fall, I recollect, in great flakes; and it lay thick. The noise of wheels and tread of people were as hushed, as if the streets had been strewn that depth with feathers.

My shortest way home,—and I naturally took the shortest way on such a night—was through Saint Martin's Lane.

Now, the church which gives its name to the lane, stood in a less free situation at that time; there being no open space before it, and the lane winding down to the Strand. As I passed the steps of the portico, I encountered, at the corner, a woman's face. It looked in mine, passed across the narrow lane, and disappeared. I knew it. I had seen it somewhere. But I could not remember where. I had some association with it, that struck upon my heart directly; but I was thinking of anything else when it came upon me, and was confused.

On the steps of the church, there was the stooping figure of a man, who had put down some burden on the smooth snow, to adjust it; my seeing the face, and my seeing him, were simultaneous. I don't think I had stopped in my surprise; but, in any case, as I went on, he rose, turned, and came down towards me. I stood face to face with Mr. Peggotty!

Then I remembered the woman. It was Martha, to whom Emily had given the money that night in the kitchen. Martha Endell—side by side with whom, he would not have seen his dear niece, Ham had told me, for all the treasures wrecked in the sea.

We shook hands heartily. At first, neither of us could speak a word.

"Mas'r Davy!" he said, gripping me tight, "it do my art good to see you, Sir. Well met, well met!"

"Well met, my dear old friend!" said I.

"I had my thowts o' coming to make inquiration for you, Sir, to-night," he said, "but knowing as your aunt was living along wi' you—for I've been down yonder—Yarmouth way—I was afeerd it was too late. I should have come early in the morning, Sir, afore going away."

"Again?" said I.

"Yes, Sir," he replied, patiently shaking his head, "I'm away to-morrow."

"Where were you going now?" I asked.

"Well!" he replied, shaking the snow out of his long hair, "I was a going to turn in somewheers."

In those days there was a side-entrance to the stable-yard of the Golden Cross, the inn so memorable to me in connexion with his misfortune, nearly opposite to where we stood. I pointed out the gateway, put my arm through his, and we went across. Two or three public-rooms opened out of the stable-yard; and looking into one of them, and finding it empty, and a good fire burning, I took him in there.

When I saw him in the light, I observed, not only that his hair was long and ragged, but that his face was burnt dark by the sun. He was greyer, the lines in his face and forehead were deeper, and he had every appearance of having toiled and wandered through all varieties of weather; but he looked very strong, and like a man upheld by steadfastness of purpose, whom nothing could tire out. He shook the snow from his hat and clothes, and brushed it away from his face, while I was inwardly making these remarks. As he sat down opposite to me at a table, with his back to the door by which we had entered, he put out his rough hand again, and grasped mine warmly.

"I'll tell you, Mas'r Davy," he said,—"wheer all I've been, and what all we've heerd. I've been fur, and we've heerd little; but I'll tell you!"

I rang the bell for something hot to drink. He would have nothing stronger than ale; and while it was being brought, and being warmed at the fire, he sat thinking. There was a fine massive gravity in his face, I did not venture to disturb.

"When she was a child," he said, lifting up his head soon after we were left alone, "she used to talk to me a deal about the sea, and about them coasts where the sea got to be dark blue, and to lay a shining and a shining in the sun. I thowt, odd times, as her father being drownded made her think on it so much. I doen't know, you see, but maybe she believed—or hoped—he had drifted out to them parts, where the flowers is always a blowing, and the country bright."

"It is likely to have been a childish fancy," I replied.

"When she was—lost," said Mr. Peggotty, "I know'd in my mind, as he would take her to them countries. I know'd in my mind, as he'd have told her wonders of 'em, and how she was to be a lady theer, and how he got her listen to him fust, along o' sech like. When we see his mother, I know'd quite well as I was right. I went across-Channel to France, and landed theer, as if I'd fell down from the sky."

I saw the door move, and the snow drift in. I saw it move a little more, and a hand softly interpose to keep it open.

"I found out a English gentleman as was in authority," said Mr. Peggotty, "and told him I was a going to seek my niece. He got me them papers as I wanted fur to carry me through—I doen't rightly know how they're called—and he would have give me money, but that I was thankful to have no need on. I thank him kind, for all he done, I'm sure! 'I've wrote afore you,' he says to me, 'and I shall speak to many as will come that way, and many will know you, fur distant from here, when you're a travelling alone.' I told him, best as I was able, what my gratitoode was, and went away through France."

"Alone, and on foot?" said I.

"Mostly afoot," he rejoined; "sometimes in carts along with people going to market; sometimes in empty coaches. Many mile a day afoot, and often with some poor soldier or another, travelling to see his friends. I couldn't talk to him," said Mr. Peggotty, "nor he to me; but we was company for one another, too, along the dusty roads."

I should have known that by his friendly tone.

"When I come to any town," he pursued, "I found the inn, and waited about the yard till some one turned up (some one mostly did) as know'd English. Then I told how that I was on my way to seek my niece, and they told me what manner of gentlefolks was in the house, and I waited to see any as seemed like her, going in or out. When it warn't Em'ly, I went on agen. By little and little, when I come to a new village or that, among the poor people, I found they know'd about me. They would set me down at their cottage doors, and give me what-not fur to eat and drink, and show me where to sleep; and many a woman, Mas'r Davy, as has had a daughter of about Em'ly's age, I've found a waiting for me, at Our Saviour's Cross outside the village, fur to do me sim'lar kindnesses. Some has had daughters as was dead. And God only knows how good them mothers was to me!"

It was Martha at the door. I saw her haggard, listening face distinctly. My dread was lest he should turn his head, and see her too.

"They would often put their children—partic'lar their little girls," said Mr. Peggotty, "upon my knee; and many a time you might have seen me sitting at their doors, when night was coming on, a'most as if they'd been my darling's children. Oh, my darling!"

Overpowered by sudden grief, he sobbed aloud. I laid my trembling hand upon the hand he put before his face. "Thank'ee, Sir," he said, "doen't take no notice."

In a very little while he took his hand away and put it on his breast, and went on with his story.

"They often walked with me," he said, "in the morning, maybe a mile or two upon my road; and when we parted, and I said, 'I'm very thankful to you! God bless you!' they always seemed to understand, and answered pleasant. At last I come to the sea. It warn't hard, as you may suppose, for a seafaring man like me to work his way over to Italy. When I got theer, I wandered on as I had done afore. The people was just as good to me, and I should have gone from town to town, maybe the country through, but that I got news of her being seen among them Swiss mountains yonder. One as know'd his servant see 'em there, all three, and told me how they travelled, and where they was. I made for them mountains, Mas'r Davy, day and night. Ever so fur as I went, ever so fur the mountains seemed to shift away from me. But I come up with 'em, and I crossed 'em. When I got nigh the place as I had been told of, I began to think within my own self, 'What shall I do when I see her?'"

The listening face, insensible to the inclement night, still drooped at the door, and the hands begged me—prayed me —not to cast it forth.

"I never doubted her," said Mr. Peggotty. "No! Not a bit! On'y let her see my face—on'y let her heer my voice—on'y let my stanning still afore her bring to her thoughts the home she had fled away from, and the child she had been—and if she had growed to be a royal lady, she'd have fell down at my feet! I know'd it well. Many a time in my sleep had I heerd her cry out, 'Uncle!' and seen her fall like death afore me. Many a time in my sleep had I raised her up, and whispered to her, 'Em'ly, my dear, I am come fur to bring forgiveness, and to take you home!'"

He stopped and shook his head, and went on with a sigh.

"*He* was nowt to me now. Em'ly was all. I bought a country dress to put upon her; and I know'd that, once found, she would walk beside me over them stony roads, go where I would, and never, never, leave me more. To put that dress upon her, and to cast off what she wore—to take her on my arm again, and wander towards home—to stop sometimes upon the road, and heal her bruised feet and her worse-bruised heart—was all that I thowt of now. I doen't believe I should have done so much as look at him. But, Mas'r Davy, it warn't to be—not yet! I was too late, and they was gone. Wheer, I couldn't learn. Some said heer, some said theer. I travelled heer, and I travelled theer, but I found no Em'ly, and I travelled home."

"How long ago?" I asked.

"A matter o' fower days," said Mr. Peggotty. "I sighted the old boat arter dark, and the light a shining in the winder. When I come nigh and looked in through the glass, I see the faithful creetur Missis Gummidge sittin' by the fire, as we had fixed upon, alone. I called out, 'Doen't be afeerd! It's Dan'l!' and I went in. I never could have thowt the old boat would have been so strange!"

From some pocket in his breast he took out, with a very careful hand, a small paper bundle containing two or three letters or little packets, which he laid upon the table.

"This fust one come," he said, selecting it from the rest, "afore I had been gone a week. A fifty pound bank-note, in a sheet of paper, directed to me, and put underneath the door in the night. She tried to hide her writing, but she couldn't hide it from Me!"

He folded up the note again, with great patience and care, in exactly the same form, and laid it on one side.

"This come to Missis Gummidge," he said, opening another, "two or three months ago." After looking at it for some moments, he gave it to me, and added in a low voice, "Be so good as read it, Sir."

I read as follows:

"Oh, what will you feel when you see this writing, and know it comes from my wicked hand! But try, try—not for my sake, but for uncle's goodness, try to let your heart soften to me, only for a little little time! Try, pray do, to relent towards a miserable girl, and write down on a bit of paper whether he is well, and what he said about me before you left off ever naming me among yourselves —and whether, of a night, when it is my old time of coming home, you ever see him look as if he thought of one he used to love so dear. Oh, my heart is breaking when I think about it! I am kneeling down to you, begging and praying you not to be as hard with me as I deserve—as I well, well know I deserve—but to be so gentle and so good, as to write down something of him, and to send it to me. You need not call me Little, you need not call me by the name I have disgraced; but oh, listen to my agony, and have mercy on me so far as to write me some word of uncle, never, never to be seen in this world by my eyes again!

"Dear, if your heart is hard towards me—justly hard, I know— but, Listen, if it is hard, dear, ask him I have wronged the most— him whose wife I was to have been—before you quite decide against my poor poor prayer! If he should be so compassionate as to say that you might write something for me to read—I think he would, oh, I think he would, if you would only ask him, for he always was so brave and so forgiving—tell him then (but not else), that when I hear the wind blowing at night, I feel as if it was passing angrily from seeing him and uncle, and was going up to God against me. Tell him that if I was to die to-morrow (and oh, if I was fit, I would be so glad to die!) I would bless him and uncle with my last words, and pray for his happy home with my last breath!"

Some money was enclosed in this letter also. Five pounds. It was untouched like the previous sum, and he refolded it in the same way. Detailed instructions were added relative to the address of a reply, which, although they betrayed the intervention of several hands, and made it difficult to arrive at any very probable conclusion in reference to her place of concealment, made it at least not unlikely that she had written from that spot where she was stated to have been seen.

"What answer was sent?" I inquired of Mr. Peggotty.

"Missis Gummidge," he returned, "not being a good scholar, Sir, Ham kindly drawed it out, and she made a copy on it. They told her I was gone to seek her, and what my parting words was."

"Is that another letter in your hand?" said I.

"It's money, Sir," said Mr. Peggotty, unfolding it a little way. "Ten pound, you see. And wrote inside, 'From a true friend,' like the fust. But the fust was put underneath the door, and this come by the post, day afore yesterday. I'm a going to seek her at the post-mark."

He showed it to me. It was a town on the Upper Rhine. He had found out, at Yarmouth, some foreign dealers who knew that country, and they had drawn him a rude map on paper, which he could very well understand. He laid it between us on the table; and, with his chin resting on one hand, tracked his course upon it with the other.

I asked him how Ham was? He shook his head.

"He works," he said, "as bold as a man can. His name's as good, in all that part, as any man's is, anywheres in the wureld. Anyone's hand is ready to help him, you understand, and his is ready to help them. He's never been heerd fur to complain. But my sister's belief is ('twixt ourselves) as it has cut him deep."

"Poor fellow, I can believe it!"

"He ain't no care, Mas'r Davy," said Mr. Peggotty in a solemn whisper—"keinder no care no-how for his life. When a man's wanted for rough sarvice in rough weather, he's theer. When there's hard duty to be done with danger in it, he steps for'ard afore all his mates. And yet he's as gentle as any child. There ain't a child in Yarmouth that doen't know him."

He gathered up the letters thoughtfully, smoothing them with his hand; put them into their little bundle; and placed it tenderly in his breast again. The face was gone from the door. I still saw the snow drifting in; but nothing else was there.

"Well!" he said, looking to his bag, "having seen you to-night, Mas'r Davy (and that doos me good!) I shall away betimes to-morrow morning. You have seen what I've got heer;" putting his hand on where the little packet lay; "all that troubles me is, to think that any harm might come to me, afore that money was give back. If I was to die, and it was lost, or stole, or elseways made away with, and it was never know'd by him but what I'd took it, I believe the t'other wureld wouldn't hold me! I believe I must come back!"

He rose, and I rose too; we grasped each other by the hand again, before going out.

"I'd go ten thousand mile," he said, "I'd go till I dropped dead, to lay that money down afore him. If I do that, and find my Em'ly, I'm content. If I doen't find her, maybe she'll come to hear, sometime, as her loving uncle only ended his search for her when he ended his life; and if I know her, even that will turn her home at last!"

As he went out into the rigorous night, I saw the lonely figure flit away before us. I turned him hastily on some pretence, and held him in conversation until it was gone.

He spoke of a travellers' house on the Dover road, where he knew he could find a clean, plain lodging for the night. I went with him over Westminster Bridge, and parted from him on the Surrey shore. Everything seemed, to my imagination, to be hushed in reverence for him, as he resumed his solitary journey through the snow.

I returned to the inn yard, and, impressed by my remembrance of the face, looked awfully around for it. It was not there. The snow had covered our late footprints; my new track was the only one to be seen; and even that began to die away (it snowed so fast) as I looked back over my shoulder.

CHAPTER XLI.

DORA'S AUNTS.

At last, an answer came from the two old ladies. They presented their compliments to Mr. Copperfield, and informed him that they had given his letter their best consideration, "with a view to the happiness of both parties"—which I thought rather an alarming expression, not only because of the use they had made of it in relation to the family difference before-mentioned, but because I had (and have all my life) observed that conventional phrases are a sort of fireworks, easily let off, and liable to take a great variety of shapes and colours not at all suggested by their original form. The Misses Spenlow added that they begged to forbear expressing, "through the medium of correspondence," an opinion on the subject of Mr. Copperfield's communication; but that if Mr. Copperfield would do them the favour to call, upon a certain day (accompanied, if he thought proper, by a confidential friend), they would be happy to hold some conversation on the subject.

To this favour, Mr. Copperfield immediately replied, with his respectful compliments, that he would have the honour of waiting on the Misses Spenlow, at the time appointed; accompanied, in accordance with their kind permission, by his friend Mr. Thomas Traddles of the Inner Temple. Having despatched which missive, Mr. Copperfield fell into a condition of strong nervous agitation; and so remained until the day arrived.

It was a great augmentation of my uneasiness to be bereaved, at this eventful crisis, of the inestimable services of Miss Mills. But Mr. Mills, who was always doing something or other to annoy me—or I felt as if he were, which was the same thing—had brought his conduct to a climax, by taking it into his head that he would go to India. Why should he go to India, except to harass me? To be sure he had nothing to do with any other part of the world, and had a good deal to do with that part; being entirely in the India trade, whatever that was (I had floating dreams myself concerning golden shawls and elephants' teeth); having been at Calcutta in his youth; and designing now to go out there again, in the capacity of resident partner. But this was nothing to me. However, it was so much to him that for India he was bound, and Julia with him; and Julia went into the country to take leave of her relations; and the house was put into a perfect suit of bills, announcing that it was to be let or sold, and that the furniture (Mangle and all) was to be taken at a valuation. So, here was another earthquake of which I became the sport, before I had recovered from the shock of its predecessor!

I was in several minds how to dress myself on the important day; being divided between my desire to appear to advantage, and my apprehensions of putting on anything that might impair my severely practical character in the eyes of the Misses Spenlow. I endeavoured to hit a happy medium between these two extremes; my aunt approved the result; and Mr. Dick threw one of his shoes after Traddles and me, for luck, as we went down-stairs.

Excellent fellow as I knew Traddles to be, and warmly attached to him as I was, I could not help wishing, on that delicate occasion, that he had never contracted the habit of brushing his hair so very upright. It gave him a surprised look—not to say a hearth-broomy kind of expression—which, my apprehensions whispered, might be fatal to us.

I took the liberty of mentioning it to Traddles, as we were walking to Putney; and saying that if he *would* smooth it down a little——

"My dear Copperfield," said Traddles, lifting off his hat and rubbing his hair all kinds of ways, "nothing would give me greater pleasure. But it won't."

"Won't be smoothed down?" said I.

"No," said Traddles. "Nothing will induce it. If I was to carry a half-hundredweight upon it, all the way to Putney, it would be up again the moment the weight was taken off. You have no idea what obstinate hair mine is, Copperfield. I am quite a fretful porcupine."

I was a little disappointed, I must confess, but thoroughly charmed by his good-nature too. I told him how I esteemed his good-nature; and said that his hair must have taken all the obstinacy out of his character, for *he* had none.

"Oh!" returned Traddles, laughing, "I assure you, it's quite an old story, my unfortunate hair. My uncle's wife couldn't bear it. She said it exasperated her. It stood very much in my way, too, when I first fell in love with Sophy. Very much!"

"Did she object to it?"

"*She* didn't," rejoined Traddles; "but her eldest sister—the one that's the Beauty—quite made game of it, I understand. In fact, all the sisters laugh at it."

"Agreeable!" said I.

"Yes," returned Traddles with perfect innocence, "it's a joke for us. They pretend that Sophy has a lock of it in her desk, and is obliged to shut it in a clasped book, to keep it down. We laugh about it."

"By-the-bye, my dear Traddles," said I, "your experience may suggest something to me. When you became engaged to the young lady whom you have just mentioned, did you make a regular proposal to her family? Was there anything like—what we are going through to-day, for instance?" I added, nervously.

"Why," replied Traddles, on whose attentive face a thoughtful shade had stolen, "it was rather a painful transaction, Copperfield, in my case. You see, Sophy being of so much use in the family, none of them could endure the thought of her ever being married. Indeed, they had quite settled among themselves that she never was to be married, and they called her the old maid. Accordingly, when I mentioned it, with the greatest precaution, to Mrs. Crewler——"

"The mama?" said I.

"The mama," said Traddles—"Reverend Horace Crewler—when I mentioned it with every possible precaution to Mrs. Crewler, the effect upon her was such that she gave a scream and became insensible. I couldn't approach the subject again, for months."

"You did at last?" said I.

"Well, the Reverend Horace did," said Traddles. "He is an excellent man, most exemplary in every way; and he pointed out to her that she ought, as a Christian, to reconcile herself to the sacrifice (especially as it was so uncertain), and to bear no uncharitable feeling towards me. As to myself, Copperfield, I give you my word, I felt a perfect bird of prey towards the family."

"The sisters took your part, I hope, Traddles?"

"Why, I can't say they did," he returned. "When we had comparatively reconciled Mrs. Crewler to it, we had to break it to Sarah. You recollect my mentioning Sarah, as the one that has something the matter with her spine?"

"Perfectly!"

"She clenched both her hands," said Traddles, looking at me in dismay; "shut her eyes; turned lead-colour; became perfectly stiff; and took nothing for two days but toast-and-water, administered with a teaspoon."

"What a very unpleasant girl, Traddles!" I remarked.

"Oh, I beg your pardon, Copperfield!" said Traddles.

"She is a very charming girl, but she has a great deal of feeling. In fact, they all have. Sophy told me afterwards, that the self-reproach she underwent while she was in attendance upon Sarah, no words could describe. I know it must have been severe, by my own feelings, Copperfield; which were like a criminal's. After Sarah was restored, we still had to break it to the other eight; and it produced various effects upon them of a most pathetic nature. The two little ones, whom Sophy educates, have only just left off de-testing me."

"At any rate, they are all reconciled to it now, I hope?" said I.

"Ye—yes, I should say they were, on the whole, resigned to it," said Traddles, doubtfully. "The fact is, we avoid mentioning the subject; and my unsettled prospects and indifferent circumstances are a great consolation to them. There will be a deplorable scene, whenever we are married. It will be much more like a funeral, than a wedding. And they'll all hate me for taking her away!"

His honest face, as he looked at me with a serio-comic shake of his head, impresses me more in the remembrance than it did in the reality, for I was by this time in a state of such excessive trepidation and wandering of mind, as to be quite unable to fix my attention on anything. On our approaching the house where the Misses Spenlow lived, I was at such a discount in respect of my personal looks and presence of mind, that Traddles proposed a gentle stimulant in the form of a glass of ale. This having been administered at a neighbouring public-house, he conducted me, with tottering steps, to the Misses Spenlows' door.

I had a vague sensation of being, as it were, on view, when the maid opened it; and of wavering, somehow, across a hall with a weather-glass in it, into a quiet little drawing-room on the ground-floor, commanding a neat garden. Also of sitting down here, on a sofa, and seeing Traddles's hair start up, now his hat was removed, like one of those obtrusive little figures made of springs, that fly out of fictitious snuff-boxes when the lid is taken off. Also of hearing an old-fashioned clock ticking away on the chimney-piece, and trying to make it keep time to the jerking of my heart,—which it wouldn't. Also of looking round the room for any sign of Dora, and seeing none. Also of thinking that Jip once barked in the distance, and was instantly choked by somebody. Ultimately I found myself backing Traddles into the fireplace, and bowing in great confusion to two dry little elderly ladies, dressed in black, and each looking wonderfully like a preparation in chip or tan of the late Mr. Spenlow.

"Pray," said one of the two little ladies, "be seated."

When I had done tumbling over Traddles, and had sat upon something which was not a cat—my first seat was—I so far recovered my sight, as to perceive that Mr. Spenlow had evidently been the youngest of the family; that there was a disparity of six or eight years between the two sisters; and that the younger appeared to be the manager of the conference, inasmuch as she had my letter in her hand—so familiar as it looked to me, and yet so odd!—and was referring to it through an eye-glass. They were dressed alike, but this sister wore her dress with a more youthful air than the other; and perhaps had a trifle more frill, or tucker, or brooch, or bracelet, or some little thing of that kind, which made her look more lively. They were both upright in their carriage, formal, precise, composed, and quiet. The sister who had not my letter, had her arms crossed on her breast, and resting on each other, like an Idol.

"Mr. Copperfield, I believe," said the sister who had got my letter, addressing herself to Traddles.

This was a frightful beginning. Traddles had to indicate that I was Mr. Copperfield, and I had to lay claim to myself, and they had to divest themselves of a preconceived opinion that Traddles was Mr. Copperfield, and altogether we were in a nice condition. To improve it, we all distinctly heard Jip give two short barks, and receive another choke.

"Mr. Copperfield!" said the sister with the letter.

I did something—bowed, I suppose—and was all attention, when the other sister struck in.

"My sister Lavinia," said she, "being conversant with matters of this nature, will state what we consider most calculated to promote the happiness of both parties."

I discovered afterwards that Miss Lavinia was an authority in affairs of the heart, by reason of there having anciently existed a certain Mr. Pidger, who played short whist, and was supposed to have been enamoured of her. My private opinion is, that this was entirely a gratuitous assumption, and that Pidger was altogether innocent of any such sentiments—to which he had never given any sort of expression that I could ever hear of. Both Miss Lavinia and Miss Clarissa had a superstition, however, that he would have declared his passion, if he had not been cut short in his youth (at about sixty) by over-drinking his constitution, and over-doing an attempt to set it right again by swilling Bath water. They had a lurking suspicion even, that he died of secret love; though I must say there was a picture of him in the house with a damask nose, which concealment did not appear to have ever preyed upon.

"We will not," said Miss Lavinia, "enter on the past history of this matter. Our poor brother Francis's death has cancelled that."

"We had not," said Miss Clarissa, "been in the habit of frequent association with our brother Francis; but there was no decided division or disunion between us. Francis took his road; we took ours. We considered it conducive to the happiness of all parties that it should be so. And it was so."

Each of the sisters leaned a little forward to speak, shook her head after speaking, and became upright again when silent. Miss Clarissa never moved her arms. She sometimes played tunes upon them with her fingers—minuets and marches, I should think—but never moved them.

"Our niece's position, or supposed position, is much changed by our brother Francis's death," said Miss Lavinia; "and therefore we consider our brother's opinions as regarded her position as being changed too. We have no reason to doubt, Mr. Copperfield, that you are a young gentleman possessed of good qualities and honourable character; or that you have an affection—or are fully persuaded that you have an affection—for our niece."

I replied, as I usually did whenever I had a chance, that nobody had ever loved anybody else as I loved Dora. Traddles came to my assistance with a confirmatory murmur.

Miss Lavinia was going on to make some rejoinder, when Miss Clarissa, who appeared to be incessantly beset by a desire to refer to her brother Francis, struck in again:

"If Dora's mamma," she said, "when she married our brother Francis, had at once said that there was not room

for the family at the dinner-table, it would have been better for the happiness of all parties."

"Sister Clarissa," said Miss Lavinia. "Perhaps we needn't mind that now."

"Sister Lavinia," said Miss Clarissa, "it belongs to the subject. With your branch of the subject, on which alone you are competent to speak, I should not think of interfering. On this branch of the subject I have a voice and an opinion. It would have been better for the happiness of all parties, if Dora's mamma, when she married our brother Francis, had mentioned plainly what her intentions were. We should then have known what we had to expect. We should have said 'pray do not invite us, at any time;' and all possibility of misunderstanding would have been avoided."

When Miss Clarissa had shaken her head, Miss Lavinia resumed: again referring to my letter through her eyeglass. They both had little bright round twinkling eyes, by the way, which were like birds' eyes. They were not unlike birds, altogether; having a sharp, brisk, sudden manner, and a little short, spruce way of adjusting themselves, like canaries.

Miss Lavinia, as I have said, resumed:

"You ask permission of my sister Clarissa and myself, Mr. Copperfield, to visit here, as the accepted suitor of our niece."

"If our brother Francis," said Miss Clarissa, breaking out again, if I may call anything so calm a breaking out, "wished to surround himself with an atmosphere of Doctors' Commons, and of Doctors' Commons only, what right or desire had we to object? None, I am sure. We have ever been far from wishing to obtrude ourselves on anyone. But why not say so? Let our brother Francis and his wife have their society. Let my sister Lavinia and myself have our society. We can find it for ourselves, I hope!"

As this appeared to be addressed to Traddles and me, both Traddles and I made some sort of reply. Traddles was inaudible. I think I observed, myself, that it was highly creditable to all concerned. I don't in the least know what I meant.

"Sister Lavinia," said Miss Clarissa, having now relieved her mind, "you can go on, my dear."

Miss Lavinia proceeded:

"Mr. Copperfield, my sister Clarissa and I have been very careful indeed in considering this letter; and we have not considered it without finally showing it to our niece, and discussing it with our niece. We have no doubt that you think you like her very much."

"Think, ma'am," I rapturously began, "oh——!"

But Miss Clarissa giving me a look (just like a sharp canary), as requesting that I would not interrupt the oracle, I begged pardon.

"Affection," said Miss Lavinia, glancing at her sister for corroboration, which she gave in the form of a little nod to every clause, "mature affection, homage, devotion, does not easily express itself. Its voice is low. It is modest and retiring, it lies in ambush, waits and waits. Such is the mature fruit. Sometimes a life glides away, and finds it still ripening in the shade."

Of course I did not understand then that this was an allusion to her supposed experience of the stricken Pidger; but I saw, from the gravity with which Miss Clarissa nodded her head, that great weight was attached to these words.

"The light—for I call them, in comparison with such

TRADDLES AND I IN CONFERENCE WITH THE MISSES SPENLOW.

sentiments, the light—inclinations of very young people," pursued Miss Lavinia, "are dust, compared to rocks. It is owing to the difficulty of knowing whether they are likely to endure or have any real foundation, that my sister Clarissa and myself have been very undecided how to act, Mr. Copperfield, and Mr.——"

"Traddles," said my friend, finding himself looked at.

"I beg pardon. Of the Inner Temple, I believe?" said Miss Lavinia, again glancing at my letter.

Traddles said "Exactly so," and became pretty red in the face.

Now, although I had not received any express encouragement as yet, I fancied that I saw in the two little sisters, and particularly in Miss Lavinia, an intensified enjoyment of this new and fruitful subject of domestic interest, a settling down to make the most of it, a disposition to pet it, in which there was a good bright ray of hope. I thought I perceived that Miss Lavinia would have uncommon satisfaction in superintending two young lovers, like Dora and me; and that Miss Clarissa would have hardly less satisfaction in seeing her superintend us, and in chiming in with her own particular department of the subject whenever that impulse was strong upon her. This gave me courage to protest most vehemently that I loved Dora better than I could tell, or anyone believe; that all my friends knew how I loved her; that my aunt, Agnes, Traddles, everyone who knew me, knew how I loved her, and how earnest my love had made me. For the truth of this, I appealed to Traddles. And Traddles, firing up as if he were plunging into a Parliamentary Debate, really did come out nobly: confirming me in good round terms, and in a plain sensible practical manner, that evidently made a favourable impression.

"I speak, if I may presume to say so, as one who has some little experience of such things," said Traddles, "being myself engaged to a young lady—one of ten, down in Devonshire—and seeing no probability, at present, of our engagement coming to a termination."

"You may be able to confirm what I have said, Mr. Traddles," observed Miss Lavinia, evidently taking a new interest in him, "of the affection that is modest and retiring; that waits and waits?"

"Entirely, ma'am," said Traddles.

Miss Clarissa looked at Miss Lavinia, and shook her head gravely. Miss Lavinia looked consciously at Miss Clarissa, and heaved a little sigh.

"Sister Lavinia," said Miss Clarissa, "take my smelling-bottle."

Miss Lavinia revived herself with a few whiffs of aromatic vinegar—Traddles and I looking on with great solicitude the while; and then went on to say, rather faintly:

"My sister and myself have been in great doubt, Mr. Traddles, what course we ought to take in reference to the likings, or imaginary likings, of such very young people as your friend Mr. Copperfield and our niece."

"Our brother Francis's child," remarked Miss Clarissa. "If our brother Francis's wife had found it convenient in her lifetime (though she had an unquestionable right to act as she thought best) to invite the family to her dinner-table, we might have known our brother Francis's child better at the present moment. Sister Lavinia, proceed."

Miss Lavinia turned my letter, so as to bring the superscription towards herself, and referred through her eye-glass to some orderly-looking notes she had made on that part of it.

"It seems to us," said she, "prudent, Mr. Traddles, to bring these feelings to the test of our own observation. At present we know nothing of them, and are not in a situation to judge how much reality there may be in them. Therefore we are inclined so far to accede to Mr. Copperfield's proposal, as to admit his visits here."

"I shall never, dear ladies," I exclaimed, relieved of an immense load of apprehension, "forget your kindness!"

"But," pursued Miss Lavinia,—"but, we would prefer to regard those visits, Mr. Traddles, as made, at present, to us. We must guard ourselves from recognising any positive engagement between Mr. Copperfield and our niece, until we have had an opportunity——"

"Until you have had an opportunity, sister Lavinia," said Miss Clarissa.

"Be it so," assented Miss Lavinia, with a sigh—"until I have had an opportunity of observing them."

"Copperfield," said Traddles, turning to me, "you feel, I am sure, that nothing could be more reasonable or considerate."

"Nothing!" cried I. "I am deeply sensible of it."

"In this position of affairs," said Miss Lavinia, again referring to her notes, "and admitting his visits on this understanding only, we must require from Mr. Copperfield a distinct assurance, on his word of honour, that no communication of any kind shall take place between him and our niece without our knowledge. That no project whatever shall be entertained with regard to our niece, without being first submitted to us——"

"To you, sister Lavinia," Miss Clarissa interposed.

"Be it so, Clarissa!" assented Miss Lavinia resignedly—"to me—and receiving our concurrence. We must make this a most express and serious stipulation, not to be broken on any account. We wished Mr. Copperfield to be accompanied by some confidential friend to-day," with an inclination of her head towards Traddles, who bowed, "in order that there might be no doubt or misconception on this subject. If Mr. Copperfield, or if you, Mr. Traddles, feel the least scruple, in giving this promise, I beg you to take time to consider it."

I exclaimed, in a state of high ecstatic fervour, that not a moment's consideration could be necessary. I bound myself by the required promise, in a most impassioned manner; called upon Traddles to witness it; and denounced myself as the most atrocious of characters if I ever swerved from it in the least degree.

"Stay!" said Miss Lavinia, holding up her hand; "we resolved, before we had the pleasure of receiving you two gentlemen, to leave you alone for a quarter of an hour, to consider this point. You will allow us to retire."

It was in vain for me to say that no consideration was necessary. They persisted in withdrawing for the specified time. Accordingly, these little birds hopped out with great dignity; leaving me to receive the congratulations of Traddles, and to feel as if I were translated to regions of exquisite happiness. Exactly at the expiration of the quarter of an hour, they reappeared with no less dignity than they had disappeared. They had gone rustling away as if their little dresses were made of autumn-leaves: and they came rustling back, in like manner.

I then bound myself once more to the prescribed conditions.

"Sister Clarissa," said Miss Lavinia, "the rest is with you."

Miss Clarissa, unfolding her arms for the first time, took the notes and glanced at them.

"We shall be happy," said Miss Clarissa, "to see Mr. Copperfield to dinner, every Sunday, if it should suit his convenience. Our hour is three."

I bowed.

"In the course of the week," said Miss Clarissa, "we shall be happy to see Mr. Copperfield to tea. Our hour is half-past six."

I bowed again.

"Twice in the week," said Miss Clarissa, "but, as a rule, not oftener."

I bowed again.

"Miss Trotwood," said Miss Clarissa, "mentioned in Mr. Copperfield's letter, will perhaps call upon us. When visiting is better for the happiness of all parties, we are glad to receive visits, and return them. When it is better for the happiness of all parties that no visiting should take place (as in the case of our brother Francis, and his establishment), that is quite different."

I intimated that my aunt would be proud and delighted to make their acquaintance; though I must say I was not quite sure of their getting on very satisfactorily together. The conditions being now closed, I expressed my acknowledgments in the warmest manner; and, taking the hand, first of Miss Clarissa, and then of Miss Lavinia, pressed it, in each case, to my lips.

Miss Lavinia then arose, and begging Mr. Traddles to excuse us for a minute, requested me to follow her. I obeyed, all in a tremble, and was conducted into another room. There, I found my blessed darling stopping her ears behind the door, with her dear little face against the wall; and Jip in the plate-warmer with his head tied up in a towel.

Oh! How beautiful she was in her black frock, and how she sobbed and cried at first, and wouldn't come out from behind the door! How fond we were of one another, when she did come out at last; and what a state of bliss I was in, when we took Jip out of the plate-warmer, and restored him to the light, sneezing very much, and were all three reunited!

"My dearest Dora! Now, indeed, my own for ever!"

"Oh DON'T!" pleaded Dora. "Please!"

"Are you not my own for ever, Dora?"

"Oh yes, of course I am!" cried Dora, "but I am so frightened!"

"Frightened, my own?"

"Oh yes! I don't like him," said Dora. "Why don't he go?"

"Who, my life?"

"Your friend," said Dora. "It isn't any business of his. What a stupid he must be."

"My love!" (There never was anything so coaxing as her childish ways.) "He is the best creature!"

"Oh, but we don't want any best creatures!" pouted Dora.

"My dear," I argued, "you will soon know him well, and like him of all things. And here is my aunt coming soon; and you'll like her of all things too, when you know her."

"No, please don't bring her!" said Dora, giving me a horrified little kiss, and folding her hands. "Don't. I know she's a naughty, mischief-making old thing! Don't

let her come here, Doady!" which was a corruption of David.

Remonstrance was of no use, then; so I laughed, and admired, and was very much in love and very happy; and she showed me Jip's new trick of standing on his hind-legs in a corner—which he did for about the space of a flash of lightning, and then fell down—and I don't know how long I should have stayed there, oblivious of Traddles, if Miss Lavinia had not come in to take me away. Miss Lavinia was very fond of Dora (she told me Dora was exactly like what she had been herself at her age—she must have altered a good deal), and she treated Dora just as if she had been a toy. I wanted to persuade Dora to come and see Traddles, but on my proposing it she ran off to her own room, and locked herself in; so I went to Traddles without her, and walked away with him on air.

"Nothing could be more satisfactory," said Traddles; "and they are very agreeable old ladies, I am sure. I shouldn't be at all surprised if you were to be married years before me, Copperfield."

"Does your Sophy play on any instrument, Traddles?" I inquired, in the pride of my heart.

"She knows enough of the piano to teach it to her little sisters," said Traddles.

"Does she sing at all?" I asked.

"Why, she sings ballads, sometimes, to freshen up the others a little when they're out of spirits," said Traddles "Nothing scientific."

"She doesn't sing to the guitar?" said I

"Oh dear no!" said Traddles.

"Paint at all?"

"Not at all," said Traddles.

I promised Traddles that he should hear Dora sing, and see some of her flower-painting. He said he should like it very much, and we went home arm-in-arm in great good-humour and delight. I encouraged him to talk about Sophy, on the way; which he did with a loving reliance on her that I very much admired. I compared her in my mind with Dora, with considerable inward satisfaction; but I candidly admitted to myself that she seemed to be an excellent kind of girl for Traddles, too.

Of course my aunt was immediately made acquainted with the successful issue of the conference, and with all that had been said and done in the course of it. She was happy to see me so happy, and promised to call on Dora's aunts without loss of time. But she took such a long walk up and down our rooms that night, while I was writing to Agnes, that I began to think she meant to walk till morning.

My letter to Agnes was a fervent and grateful one, narrating all the good effects that had resulted from my following her advice. She wrote, by return of post, to me. Her letter was hopeful, earnest, and cheerful. She was always cheerful from that time.

I had my hands more full than ever, now. My daily journeys to Highgate considered, Putney was a long way off; and I naturally wanted to go there as often as I could. The proposed tea-drinkings being quite impracticable, I compounded with Miss Lavinia for permission to visit every Saturday afternoon, without detriment to my privileged Sundays. So, the close of every week was a delicious time for me; and I got through the rest of the week by looking forward to it.

I was wonderfully relieved to find that my aunt and

Dora's aunts rubbed on, all things considered, much more smoothly than I could have expected. My aunt made her promised visit within a few days of the conference; and within a few more days, Dora's aunts called upon her, in due state and form. Similar but more friendly exchanges took place afterwards, usually at intervals of three or four weeks. I know that my aunt distressed Dora's aunts very much, by utterly setting at naught the dignity of fly-conveyance, and walking out to Putney at extraordinary times, as shortly after breakfast or just before tea; likewise by wearing her bonnet in any manner that happened to be comfortable to her head, without at all deferring to the prejudices of civilisation on that subject. But Dora's aunts soon agreed to regard my aunt as an eccentric and somewhat masculine lady, with a strong understanding; and although my aunt occasionally ruffled the feathers of Dora's aunts, by expressing heretical opinions on various points of ceremony, she loved me too well not to sacrifice some of her little peculiarities to the general harmony.

The only member of our small society, who positively refused to adapt himself to circumstances, was Jip. He never saw my aunt without immediately displaying every tooth in his head, retiring under a chair, and growling incessantly: with now and then a doleful howl, as if she really were too much for his feelings. All kinds of treatment were tried with him—coaxing, scolding, slapping, bringing him to Buckingham Street (where he instantly dashed at the two cats, to the terror of all beholders); but he never could prevail upon himself to bear my aunt's society. He would sometimes think he had got the better of his objection, and be amiable for a few minutes; and then would put up his snub nose, and howl to that extent, that there was nothing for it but to blind him and put him in the plate-warmer. At length, Dora regularly muffled him in a towel and shut him up there, whenever my aunt was reported at the door.

One thing troubled me much, after we had fallen into this quiet train. It was, that Dora seemed by one consent to be regarded like a pretty toy or plaything. My aunt, with whom she gradually became familiar, always called her Little Blossom; and the pleasure of Miss Lavinia's life was to wait upon her, curl her hair, make ornaments for her, and treat her like a pet child. What Miss Lavinia did, her sister did as a matter of course. It was very odd to me; but they all seemed to treat Dora, in her degree, much as Dora treated Jip in his.

I made up my mind to speak to Dora about this; and one day when we were out walking (for we were licensed by Miss Lavinia, after a while, to go out walking by ourselves), I said to her that I wished she could get them to behave towards her differently.

"Because you know, my darling," I remonstrated, "you are not a child."

"There!" said Dora. "Now you're going to be cross!"

"Cross, my love?"

"I am sure they're very kind to me," said Dora, "and I am very happy."

"Well! But, my dearest life!" said I, "you might be very happy, and yet treated rationally."

Dora gave me a reproachful look—the prettiest look!—and then began to sob, saying, if I didn't like her, why had I ever wanted so much to be engaged to her? And why didn't I go away now, if I couldn't bear her?

What could I do, but kiss away her tears, and tell her how I doted on her, after that!

"I am sure I am very affectionate," said Dora; "you oughtn't to be cruel to me, Doady!"

"Cruel, my precious love! As if I would—or could—be cruel to you, for the world!"

"Then don't find fault with me," said Dora, making a rosebud of her mouth; "and I'll be good."

I was charmed by her presently asking me, of her own accord, to give her that Cookery Book I had once spoken of, and to show her how to keep accounts, as I had once promised I would. I brought the volume with me on my next visit (I got it prettily bound, first, to make it look less dry and more inviting); and as we strolled about the Common, I showed her an old housekeeping-book of my aunt's, and gave her a set of tablets, and a pretty little pencil-case, and box of leads, to practise housekeeping with.

But the Cookery Book made Dora's head ache, and the figures made her cry. They wouldn't add up, she said. So she rubbed them out, and drew little nosegays, and likenesses of me and Jip, all over the tablets.

Then I playfully tried verbal instruction in domestic matters, as we walked about on a Saturday afternoon. Sometimes, for example, when we passed a butcher's shop, I would say:

"Now suppose, my pet, that we were married, and you were going to buy a shoulder of mutton for dinner, would you know how to buy it?"

My pretty little Dora's face would fall, and she would make her mouth into a bud again, as if she would very much prefer to shut mine with a kiss.

"Would you know how to buy it, my darling?" I would repeat, perhaps, if I were very inflexible.

Dora would think a little, and then reply, perhaps, with great triumph:

"Why, the butcher would know how to sell it, and what need I know? Oh, you silly boy!"

So, when I once asked Dora, with an eye to the Cookery Book, what she would do, if we were married, and I were to say I should like a nice Irish stew, she replied that she would tell the servant to make it; and then clapped her little hands together across my arm, and laughed in such a charming manner that she was more delightful than ever.

Consequently, the principal use to which the Cookery Book was devoted, was being put down in the corner for Jip to stand upon. But Dora was so pleased, when she had trained him to stand upon it without offering to come off, and at the same time to hold the pencil-case in his mouth, that I was very glad I had bought it.

And we fell back on the guitar-case, and the flower-painting, and the songs about never leaving off dancing, Ta ra la! and were as happy as the week was long. I occasionally wished I could venture to hint to Miss Lavinia, that she treated the darling of my heart a little too much like a plaything; and I sometimes awoke, as it were, wondering to find that I had fallen into the general fault, and treated her like a plaything too—but not often.

CHAPTER XLII.

MISCHIEF.

I FEEL as if it were not for me to record, even though this manuscript is intended for no eyes but mine, how hard I worked at that tremendous shorthand, and all improvement appertaining to it, in my sense of responsibility to

Dora and her aunts. I will only add, to what I have already written of my perseverance at this time of my life, and of a patient and continuous energy which then began to be matured within me, and which I know to be the strong part of my character, if it have any strength at all, that there, on looking back, I find the source of my success. I have been very fortunate in worldly matters; many men have worked much harder, and not succeeded half so well; but I never could have done what I have done, without the habits of punctuality, order, and diligence, without the determination to concentrate myself on one object at a time, no matter how quickly its successor should come upon its heels, which I then formed. Heaven knows I write this, in no spirit of self-laudation. The man who reviews his own life, as I do mine, in going on here, from page to page, had need to have been a good man indeed, if he would be spared the sharp consciousness of many talents neglected, many opportunities wasted, many erratic and perverted feelings constantly at war within his breast, and defeating him. I do not hold one natural gift, I daresay, that I have not abused. My meaning simply is, that whatever I have tried to do in life, I have tried with all my heart to do well; that whatever I have devoted myself to, I have devoted myself to completely; that, in great aims and in small, I have always been thoroughly in earnest. I have never believed it possible that any natural or improved ability can claim immunity from the companionship of the steady, plain, hard-working qualities, and hope to gain its end. There is no such thing as such fulfilment on this earth. Some happy talent, and some fortunate opportunity, may form the two sides of the ladder on which some men mount, but the rounds of that ladder must be made of stuff to stand wear and tear; and there is no substitute for thorough-going, ardent, and sincere earnestness. Never to put one hand to anything, on which I could throw my whole self; and never to affect depreciation of my work, whatever it was; I find, now, to have been my golden rules.

How much of the practice I have just reduced to precept, I owe to Agnes, I will not repeat here. My narrative proceeds to Agnes, with a thankful love.

She came on a visit of a fortnight to the Doctor's. Mr. Wickfield was the Doctor's old friend, and the Doctor wished to talk with him, and do him good. It had been matter of conversation with Agnes when she was last in town, and this visit was the result. She and her father came together. I was not much surprised to hear from her that she had engaged to find a lodging in the neighbourhood for Mrs. Heep, whose rheumatic complaint required change of air, and who would be charmed to have it in such company. Neither was I surprised when, on the very next day, Uriah, like a dutiful son, brought his worthy mother to take possession.

"You see, Master Copperfield," said he, as he forced himself upon my company for a turn in the Doctor's garden, "where a person loves, a person is a little jealous—leastways, anxious to keep an eye on the beloved one."

"Of whom are you jealous, now?" said I.

"Thanks to you, Master Copperfield," he returned, "of no one in particular just at present—no male person, at least."

"Do you mean that you are jealous of a female person?"

He gave me a sidelong glance out of his sinister red eyes, and laughed.

"Really, Master Copperfield," he said, "—I should say

Mister, but I know you'll excuse the abit I've got into—you're so insinuating, that you draw me like a corkscrew! Well, I don't mind telling you," putting his fish-like hand on mine, "I'm not a lady's man in general, Sir, and I never was, with Mrs. Strong."

His eyes looked green now, as they watched mine with a rascally cunning.

"What do you mean?" said I.

"Why, though I am a lawyer, Master Copperfield," he replied, with a dry grin, "I mean, just at present, what I say."

"And what do you mean by your look?" I retorted, quietly.

"By my look? Dear me, Copperfield, that's sharp practice! What do I mean by my look?"

"Yes," said I. "By your look."

He seemed very much amused, and laughed as heartily as it was in his nature to laugh. After some scraping of his chin with his hand, he went on to say, with his eyes cast downward—still scraping, very slowly:

"When I was but a numble clerk, she always looked down upon me. She was for ever having my Agnes backwards and forwards at her ouse, and she was for ever being a friend to you, Master Copperfield; but I was too far beneath her, myself, to be noticed."

"Well?" said I; "suppose you were!"

"—And beneath him too," pursued Uriah, very distinctly, and in a meditative tone of voice, as he continued to scrape his chin.

"Don't you know the Doctor better," said I, "than to suppose him conscious of your existence, when you were not before him?"

He directed his eyes at me in that sidelong glance again, and he made his face very lantern-jawed, for the greater convenience of scraping, as he answered:

"Oh dear, I am not referring to the Doctor! Oh no, poor man! I mean Mr. Maldon!"

My heart quite died within me. All my old doubts, and apprehensions on that subject, all the Doctor's happiness and peace, all the mingled possibilities of innocence and compromise, that I could not unravel, I saw, in a moment, at the mercy of this fellow's twisting.

"He never could come into the office, without ordering and shoving me about," said Uriah. "One of your fine gentlemen he was! I was very meek and umble—and I am. But I didn't like that sort of thing—and I don't!"

He left off scraping his chin, and sucked in his cheeks until they seemed to meet inside; keeping his sidelong glance upon me all the while.

"She is one of your lovely women, she is," he pursued, when he had slowly restored his face to its natural form; "and ready to be no friend to such as me, I know. She's just the person as would put my Agnes up to higher sort of game. Now, I ain't one of your lady's men, Master Copperfield; but I've had eyes in my ed, a pretty long time back. We umble ones have got eyes, mostly speaking—and we look out of 'em."

I endeavoured to appear unconscious and not disquieted, but, I saw in his face, with poor success.

"Now, I'm not a going to let myself be run down, Copperfield," he continued, raising that part of his countenance where his red eyebrows would have been if he had had any, with malignant triumph, "and I shall do what I can to put a stop to this friendship. I don't approve of it. I don't mind acknowledging to you that I've got rather a grudging disposition, and want to keep off all intruders. I ain't a going, if I know it, to run the risk of being plotted against."

"You are always plotting, and delude yourself into the belief that everybody else is doing the like, I think," said I.

"Perhaps so, Master Copperfield," he replied. "But I've got a motive, as my fellow-partner used to say; and I go at it tooth and nail. I mustn't be put upon, as a numble person, too much. I can't allow people in my way. Really they must come out of the cart, Master Copperfield!"

"I don't understand you," said I.

"Don't you, though?" he returned, with one of his jerks. "I'm astonished at that, Master Copperfield, you being usually so quick! I'll try to be plainer, another time.—Is that Mr. Maldon a-norseback, ringing at the gate, Sir?"

"It looks like him," I replied, as carelessly as I could.

Uriah stopped short, put his hands between his great knobs of knees, and doubled himself up with laughter. With perfectly silent laughter. Not a sound escaped from him. I was so repelled by his odious behaviour, particularly by this concluding instance, that I turned away without any ceremony; and left him doubled up in the middle of the garden, like a scarecrow in want of support.

It was not on that evening; but, as I well remember, on the next evening but one, which was a Saturday; that I took Agnes to see Dora. I had arranged the visit, beforehand, with Miss Lavinia; and Agnes was expected to tea.

I was in a flutter of pride and anxiety; pride in my dear little betrothed, and anxiety that Agnes should like her. All the way to Putney, Agnes being inside the stage-coach, and I outside, I pictured Dora to myself in every one of the pretty looks I knew so well; now making up my mind that I should like her to look exactly as she looked at such a time, and then doubting whether I should not prefer her looking as she looked at such another time; and almost worrying myself into a fever about it.

I was troubled by no doubt of her being very pretty, in any case; but it fell out that I had never seen her look so well. She was not in the drawing-room when I presented Agnes to her little aunts, but was shyly keeping out of the way. I knew where to look for her, now; and sure enough I found her stopping her ears again, behind the same dull old door.

At first she wouldn't come at all; and then she pleaded for three minutes by my watch. When at length she put her arm through mine, to be taken to the drawing-room, her charming little face was flushed, and had never been so pretty. But, when we went into the room, and it turned pale, she was ten thousand times prettier yet.

Dora was afraid of Agnes. She had told me that she knew Agnes was "too clever." But when she saw her looking at once so cheerful and so earnest, and so thoughtful, and so good, she gave a faint little cry of pleased surprise, and just put her affectionate arms round Agnes's neck, and laid her innocent cheek against her face.

I never was so happy. I never was so pleased as when I saw those two sit down together, side by side. As when I saw my little darling looking up so naturally to those cordial eyes. As when I saw the tender, beautiful regard which Agnes cast upon her.

Miss Lavinia and Miss Clarissa partook, in their way, of my joy. It was the pleasantest tea-table in the world. Miss Clarissa presided. I cut and handed the sweet seed-cake—the little sisters had a birdlike fondness for picking up seeds and pecking at sugar; Miss Lavinia looked on with benignant patronage, as if our happy love

were all her work; and we were perfectly contented with ourselves and one another.

The gentle cheerfulness of Agnes went to all their hearts. Her quiet interest in everything that interested Dora; her manner of making acquaintance with Jip (who responded instantly); her pleasant way, when Dora was ashamed to come over to her usual seat by me; her modest grace and ease, eliciting a crowd of blushing little marks of confidence from Dora; seemed to make our circle quite complete.

"I am so glad," said Dora, after tea, "that you like me. I didn't think you would; and I want, more than ever, to be liked, now Julia Mills is gone."

I have omitted to mention it, by-the-bye. Miss Mills had sailed, and Dora and I had gone aboard a great East Indiaman at Gravesend to see her; and we had had preserved ginger, and guava, and other delicacies of that sort for lunch; and we had left Miss Mills weeping on a camp-stool on the quarter-deck, with a large new diary under her arm, in which the original reflections awakened by the contemplation of Ocean were to be recorded under lock and key.

Agnes said, she was afraid, I must have given her an unpromising character; but Dora corrected that directly.

"Oh no!" she said, shaking her curls at me; "it was all praise. He thinks so much of your opinion, that I was quite afraid of it."

"My good opinion cannot strengthen his attachment to some people whom he knows," said Agnes, with a smile; "it is not worth their having."

"But please let me have it," said Dora, in her coaxing way, "if you can!"

We made merry about Dora's wanting to be liked, and Dora said I was a goose, and she didn't like me at any rate, and the short evening flew away on gossamer-wings. The time was at hand when the coach was to call for us. I was standing alone before the fire, when Dora came stealing softly in, to give me that usual precious little kiss before I went.

"Don't you think, if I had had her for a friend a long time ago, Doady," said Dora, her bright eyes shining very brightly, and her little right hand idly busying itself with one of the buttons of my coat, "I might have been more clever perhaps?"

"My love!" said I, "what nonsense!"

"Do you think it is nonsense?" returned Dora, without looking at me. "Are you sure it is?"

"Of course I am!"

"I have forgotten," said Dora, still turning the button round and round, "what relation Agnes is to you, you dear bad boy."

"No blood-relation," I replied; "but we were brought up together, like brother and sister."

"I wonder why you ever fell in love with me?" said Dora, beginning on another button of my coat.

"Perhaps because I couldn't see you, and not love you, Dora!"

"Suppose you had never seen me at all," said Dora, going to another button.

"Suppose we had never been born!" said I, gaily.

I wondered what she was thinking about, as I glanced in admiring silence at the little soft hand travelling up the row of buttons on my coat, and at the clustering hair that lay against my breast, and at the lashes of her downcast eyes, slightly rising as they followed her idle fingers. At length her eyes were lifted up to mine, and she stood on tiptoe to give me, more thoughtfully than usual, that precious little kiss—once, twice, three times—and went out of the room.

They all came back together within five minutes afterwards, and Dora's unusual thoughtfulness was quite gone then. She was laughingly resolved to put Jip through the whole of his performances, before the coach came. They took some time (not so much on account of their variety, as Jip's reluctance), and were still unfinished when it was heard at the door. There was a hurried but affectionate parting between Agnes and herself; and Dora was to write to Agnes (who was not to mind her letters being foolish, she said), and Agnes was to write to Dora; and they had a second parting at the coach-door, and a third when Dora, in spite of the remonstrances of Miss Lavinia, would come running out once more to remind Agnes at the coach-window about writing, and to shake her curls at me on the box.

The stage-coach was to put us down near Covent Garden, where we were to take another stage-coach for Highgate. I was impatient for the short walk in the interval, that Agnes might praise Dora to me. Ah! what praise it was! How lovingly and fervently did it commend the pretty creature I had won, with all her artless graces best displayed, to my most gentle care. How thoughtfully remind me, yet with no pretence of doing so, of the trust in which I held the orphan child!

Never, never, had I loved Dora so deeply and truly, as I loved her that night. When we had again alighted, and were walking in the starlight along the quiet road that led to the Doctor's house, I told Agnes it was her doing.

"When you were sitting by her," said I, "you seemed to be no less _her_ guardian angel than mine; and you seem so now, Agnes."

"A poor angel," she returned, "but faithful."

The clear tone of her voice, going straight to my heart, made it natural to me to say:

"The cheerfulness that belongs to you, Agnes (and to no one else that ever I have seen), is so restored, that I have observed to-day, that I have begun to hope you are happier at home?"

"I am happier in myself," she said; "I am quite cheerful and light-hearted."

I glanced at the serene face looking upward, and thought it was the stars that made it seem so noble.

"There has been no change at home," said Agnes, after a few moments.

"No fresh reference," said I, "to—I wouldn't distress you, Agnes, but I cannot help asking—to what we spoke of, when we parted last?"

"No, none," she answered.

"I have thought so much about it."

"You must think less about it. Remember that I confide in simple love and truth at last. Have no apprehensions for me, Trotwood," she added, after a moment; "the step you dread my taking, I shall never take."

Although I think I had never really feared it, in any season of cool reflection, it was an unspeakable relief to me to have this assurance from her own truthful lips. I told her so, earnestly.

"And when this visit is over," said I,—"for we may not be alone another time,—how long is it likely to be, my dear Agnes, before you come to London again?"

"Probably a long time," she replied; "I think it will be best—for papa's sake—to remain at home. We are not likely to meet often, for some time to come; but I shall be a good correspondent of Dora's, and we shall frequently hear of one another that way."

We were now within the little courtyard of the Doctor's cottage. It was growing late. There was a light in the window of Mrs. Strong's chamber, and Agnes, pointing to it, bade me good night.

"Do not be troubled," she said, giving me her hand, "by our misfortunes and anxieties. I can be happier in nothing than in your happiness. If you can ever give me help, rely upon it I will ask you for it. God bless you always!"

In her beaming smile, and in these last tones of her cheerful voice, I seemed again to see and hear my little Dora in her company. I stood awhile, looking through the porch at the stars, with a heart full of love and gratitude, and then walked slowly forth. I had engaged a bed at a decent alehouse close by, and was going out at the gate, when, happening to turn my head, I saw a light in the Doctor's study. A half-reproachful fancy came into my mind, that he had been working at the Dictionary without my help. With the view of seeing if this were so, and, in any case, of bidding him good night, if he were yet sitting among his books, I turned back, and going softly across the hall, and gently opening the door, looked in.

The first person whom I saw, to my surprise, by the sober light of the shaded lamp, was Uriah. He was standing close beside it, with one of his skeleton hands over his mouth, and the other resting on the Doctor's table. The Doctor sat in his study chair, covering his face with his hands. Mr. Wickfield, sorely troubled and distressed, was leaning forward, irresolutely touching the Doctor's arm.

For an instant, I supposed that the Doctor was ill. I hastily advanced a step under that impression, when I met Uriah's eye, and saw what was the matter. I would have withdrawn, but the Doctor made a gesture to detain me, and I remained.

"At any rate," observed Uriah, with a writhe of his ungainly person, "we may keep the door shut. We needn't make it known to ALL the town."

Saying which, he went on his toes to the door, which I had left open, and carefully closed it. He then came back, and took up his former position. There was an obtrusive show of compassionate zeal in his voice and manner, more intolerable—at least to me—than any demeanour he could have assumed.

"I have felt it incumbent upon me, Master Copperfield," said Uriah, "to point out to Doctor Strong what you and me have already talked about. You didn't exactly understand me, though?"

I gave him a look, but no other answer; and, going to my good old master, said a few words that I meant to be words of comfort and encouragement. He put his hand upon my shoulder, as it had been his custom to do when I was quite a little fellow, but did not lift his grey head.

"As you didn't understand me, Master Copperfield," resumed Uriah in the same officious manner, "I may take the liberty of umbly mentioning, being among friends, that I have called Doctor Strong's attention to the goings-on of Mrs. Strong. It's much against the grain with me, I assure you, Copperfield, to be concerned in anything so unpleasant; but really, as it is, we're all mixing ourselves up with what oughtn't to be. That was what my meaning was, Sir, when you didn't understand me."

I wonder now, when I recall his leer, that I did not collar him, and try to shake the breath out of his body.

"I dare say I didn't make myself very clear," he went on, "nor you neither. Naturally, we was both of us inclined to give such a subject a wide berth. Hows'ever, at last I have made up my mind to speak plain; and I have mentioned to Doctor Strong that—did you speak, Sir?"

This was to the Doctor, who had moaned. The sound might have touched any heart, I thought, but it had no effect upon Uriah's.

"—mentioned to Doctor Strong," he proceeded, "that anyone may see that Mr. Maldon, and the lovely and agreeable lady as is Doctor Strong's wife, are too sweet on one another. Really the time is come (we being at present all mixing ourselves up with what oughtn't to be), when Doctor Strong must be told that this was full as plain to everybody as the sun, before Mr. Maldon went to India; that Mr. Maldon made excuses to come back, for nothing else; and that he's always here, for nothing else. When you come in, Sir, I was just putting it to my fellow-partner," towards whom he turned, "to say to Doctor Strong upon his word and honour, whether he'd ever been of this opinion long ago, or not. Come, Mr. Wickfield, Sir! Would you be so good as tell us? Yes or no, Sir? Come, partner!"

"For God's sake, my dear Doctor," said Mr. Wickfield, again laying his irresolute hand upon the Doctor's arm, "don't attach too much weight to any suspicions I may have entertained."

"There!" cried Uriah, shaking his head. "What a melancholy confirmation; ain't it? Him! Such an old friend! Bless your soul, when I was nothing but a clerk in his office, Copperfield, I've seen him twenty times, if I've seen him once, quite in a taking about it—quite put out, you know (and very proper in him as a father; I'm sure *I* can't blame him), to think that Miss Agnes was mixing herself up with what oughtn't to be."

"My dear Strong," said Mr. Wickfield in a tremulous voice, "my good friend, I needn't tell you that it has been my vice to look for some one master motive in everybody, and to try all actions by one narrow test. I may have fallen into such doubts as I have had, through this mistake."

"You have had doubts, Wickfield," said the Doctor, without lifting up his head. "You have had doubts."

"Speak up, fellow-partner," urged Uriah.

"I had, at one time, certainly," said Mr. Wickfield. "I —God forgive me—I thought *you* had."

"No, no, no!" returned the Doctor, in a tone of most pathetic grief.

"I thought, at one time," said Mr. Wickfield, "that you wished to send Maldon abroad to effect a desirable separation."

"No, no, no!" returned the Doctor. "To give Annie pleasure, by making some provision for the companion of her childhood. Nothing else."

"So I found," said Mr. Wickfield. "I couldn't doubt it, when you told me so. But I thought—I implore you to remember the narrow construction which has been my besetting sin—that, in a case where there was so much disparity in point of years——"

"That's the way to put it, you see, Master Copperfield!" observed Uriah, with fawning and offensive pity.

"—a lady of such youth, and such attractions, however real her respect for you, might have been influenced in marrying, by worldly considerations only. I made no allowance for innumerable feelings and circumstances that may have all tended to good. For Heaven's sake remember that!"

"How kind he puts it!" said Uriah, shaking his head.

"Always observing her from one point of view," said Mr. Wickfield; "but by all that is dear to you, my old friend, I entreat you to consider what it was; I am forced to confess now, having no escape——"

"No! There's no way out of it, Mr. Wickfield, Sir," observed Uriah, "when it's got to this."

"—that I did," said Mr. Wickfield, glancing helplessly and distractedly at his partner, "that I did doubt her, and think her wanting in her duty to you; and that I did sometimes, if I must say all, feel averse to Agnes being in such a familiar relation towards her, as to see what I saw, or in my diseased theory fancied that I saw. I never mentioned this to anyone. I never meant it to be known to anyone. And though it is terrible to you to hear," said Mr. Wickfield, quite subdued, "if you knew how terrible it is for me to tell, you would feel compassion for me!"

The Doctor, in the perfect goodness of his nature, put out his hand. Mr. Wickfield held it for a little while in his, with his head bowed down.

"I am sure," said Uriah, writhing himself into the silence like a conger-eel, "that this is a subject full of unpleasantness to everybody. But since we have got so far, I ought to take the liberty of mentioning that Copperfield has noticed it too."

I turned upon him, and asked him how he dared refer to me!

"Oh! it's very kind of you, Copperfield," returned Uriah, undulating all over, "and we all know what an amiable character yours is; but you know that the moment I spoke to you the other night, you knew what I meant. You know you knew what I meant, Copperfield. Don't deny it! You deny it with the best intentions; but don't do it, Copperfield!"

I saw the mild eye of the good old Doctor turned upon me for a moment, and I felt that the confession of my old misgivings and remembrances was too plainly written in my face to be overlooked. It was of no use raging. I could not undo that. Say what I would, I could not unsay it.

We were silent again, and remained so, until the Doctor rose and walked twice or thrice across the room. Presently he returned to where his chair stood; and, leaning on the back of it, and occasionally putting his handkerchief to his eyes, with a simple honesty that did him more honour, to my thinking, than any disguise he could have affected, said:

"I have been much to blame. I believe I have been very much to blame. I have exposed one whom I hold in my heart, to trials and aspersions—I call them aspersions, even to have been conceived in anybody's inmost mind—of which she never, but for me, could have been the object."

Uriah Heep gave a kind of snivel. I think to express sympathy.

"Of which my Annie," said the Doctor, "never, but for me, could have been the object. Gentlemen, I am old now, as you know; I do not feel, to-night, that I have much to live for. But my life—my life—upon the truth and honour of the dear lady who has been the subject of this conversation!"

I do not think that the best embodiment of chivalry, the realisation of the handsomest and most romantic figure ever imagined by painter, could have said this with a more impressive and affecting dignity than the plain old Doctor did.

"But I am not prepared," he went on, "to deny—perhaps I may have been, without knowing it, in some degree prepared to admit—that I may have unwittingly ensnared that lady into an unhappy marriage. I am a man quite unaccustomed to observe; and I cannot but believe that the observation of several people, of different ages and positions, all too plainly tending in one direction (and that so natural), is better than mine."

I had often admired, as I have elsewhere described, his benignant manner towards his youthful wife; but the respectful tenderness he manifested in every reference to her on this occasion, and the almost reverential manner in which he put away from him the lightest doubt of her integrity, exalted him, in my eyes, beyond description.

"I married that lady," said the Doctor, "when she was extremely young. I took her to myself when her character was scarcely formed. So far as it was developed, it had been my happiness to form it. I knew her father well. I knew her well. I had taught her what I could, for the love of all her beautiful and virtuous qualities. If I did her wrong; as I fear I did, in taking advantage (but I never meant it) of her gratitude and her affection; I ask pardon of that lady, in my heart!"

He walked across the room, and came back to the same place; holding the chair with a grasp that trembled, like his subdued voice, in its earnestness.

"I regarded myself as a refuge, for her, from the dangers and vicissitudes of life. I persuaded myself that, unequal though we were in years, she would live tranquilly and contentedly with me. I did not shut out of my consideration the time when I should leave her free, and still young and still beautiful, but with her judgment more matured—no, gentlemen—upon my truth!"

His homely figure seemed to be lightened up by his fidelity and generosity. Every word he uttered had a force that no other grace could have imparted to it.

"My life with this lady has been very happy. Until to-night, I have had uninterrupted occasion to bless the day on which I did her great injustice."

His voice, more and more faltering in the utterance of these words, stopped for a few moments; then he went on:

"Once awakened from my dream—I have been a poor dreamer, in one way or other, all my life—I see how natural it is that she should have some regretful feeling towards her old companion. and her equal. That she does regard him with some innocent regret, with some blameless thoughts of what might have been, is, I fear, too true. Much that I have seen, but not noted, has come back upon me with new meaning, during this last trying hour. But, beyond this, gentlemen, the dear lady's name never must be coupled with a word, a breath, of doubt."

For a little while, his eye kindled and his voice was firm; for a little while he was again silent. Presently, he proceeded as before:

"It only remains for me, to bear the knowledge of the unhappiness I have occasioned, as submissively as I can. It is she who should reproach; not I. To save her from misconstruction, cruel misconstruction, that even my friends have not been able to avoid, becomes my duty. The more retired we live, the better I shall discharge it. And when the time comes—may it come soon, if it be His merciful pleasure!—when my death shall release her from constraint, I shall close my eyes upon her honoured face, with unbounded confidence and love; and leave her, with no sorrow then, to happier and brighter days." ·

I could not see him for the tears which his earnestness and goodness, so adorned by, and so adorning, the perfect

simplicity of his manner, brought into my eyes. He had moved to the door, when he added:

"Gentlemen, I have shown you my heart. I am sure you will respect it. What we have said to-night is never to be said more. Wickfield, give me an old friend's arm up-stairs!"

Mr. Wickfield hastened to him. Without interchanging a word they went slowly out of the room together, Uriah looking after them.

"Well, Master Copperfield!" said Uriah, meekly turning to me. "The thing hasn't took quite the turn that might have been expected, for the old Scholar—what an excellent man!—is as blind as a brick-bat; but *this* family's out of the cart, I think!"

I needed but the sound of his voice to be so madly enraged as I never was before, and never have been since.

"You villain," said I, "what do you mean by entrapping me into your schemes? How dare you appeal to me just now, you false rascal, as if we had been in discussion together?"

As we stood, front to front, I saw so plainly, in the stealthy exultation of his face, what I already so plainly knew; I mean that he forced his confidence upon me, expressly to make me miserable, and had set a deliberate trap for me in this very matter; that I couldn't bear it. The whole of his lank cheek was invitingly before me, and I struck it with my open hand with that force that my fingers tingled as if I had burnt them.

He caught the hand in his, and we stood, in that connexion, looking at each other. We stood so, a long time; long enough for me to see the white marks of my fingers die out of the deep red of his cheek, and leave it a deeper red.

"Copperfield," he said at length, in a breathless voice, "have you taken leave of your senses?"

"I have taken leave of you," said I, wresting my hand away. "You dog, I'll know no more of you."

"Won't you?" said he, constrained by the pain of his cheek to put his hand there. "Perhaps you won't be able to help it. Isn't this ungrateful of you, now?"

"I have shown you often enough," said I, "that I despise you. I have shown you now, more plainly, that I do. Why should I dread your doing your worst to all about you? What else do you ever do?"

He perfectly understood this allusion to the considerations that had hitherto restrained me in my communications with him. I rather think that neither the blow, nor the allusion, would have escaped me, but for the assurance I had had from Agnes that night. It is no matter.

There was another long pause. His eyes, as he looked at me, seemed to take every shade of colour that could make eyes ugly.

"Copperfield," he said, removing his hand from his cheek, "you have always gone against me. I know you always used to be against me at Mr. Wickfield's."

"You may think what you like," said I, still in a towering rage. "If it is not true, so much the worthier you."

"And yet I always liked you, Copperfield!" he rejoined.

I deigned to make him no reply; and, taking up my hat, was going out to bed, when he came between me and the door.

"Copperfield," he said, "there must be two parties to a quarrel. I won't be one."

"You may go to the devil!" said I.

"Don't say that!" he replied. "I know you'll be sorry afterwards. How can you make yourself so inferior to me, as to show such a bad spirit? But I forgive you."

"You forgive me!" I repeated disdainfully.

"I do, and you can't help yourself," replied Uriah. "To think of your going and attacking *me*, that have always been a friend to you! But there can't be a quarrel without two parties, and I won't be one. I will be a friend to you, in spite of you. So now you know what you've got to expect."

The necessity of carrying on this dialogue (his part in which was very slow; mine very quick) in a low tone, that the house might not be disturbed at an unseasonable hour, did not improve my temper; though my passion was cooling down. Merely telling him that I should expect from him what I always had expected, and had never yet been disappointed in, I opened the door upon him, as if he had been a great walnut put there to be cracked, and went out of the house. But he slept out of the house too, at his mother's lodging; and before I had gone many hundred yards, came up with me.

"You know, Copperfield," he said, in my ear (I did not turn my head), "you're in quite a wrong position;" which I felt to be true, and that made me chafe the more; "you can't make this a brave thing, and you can't help being forgiven. I don't intend to mention it to mother, nor to any living soul. I'm determined to forgive you. But I do wonder that you should lift your hand against a person that you knew to be so umble!"

I felt only less mean than he. He knew me better than I knew myself. If he had retorted, or openly exasperated me, it would have been a relief and a justification; but he had put me on a slow fire, on which I lay tormented half the night.

In the morning, when I came out, the early church bell was ringing, and he was walking up and down with his mother. He addressed me as if nothing had happened, and I could do no less than reply. I had struck him hard enough to give him the toothache, I suppose. At all events his face was tied up in a black silk handkerchief, which, with his hat perched on the top of it, was far from improving his appearance. I heard that he went to a dentist's in London on the Monday morning, and had a tooth out. I hope it was a double one.

The Doctor gave out that he was not quite well; and remained alone, for a considerable part of every day, during the remainder of the visit. Agnes and her father had been gone a week, before we resumed our usual work. On the day preceding its resumption, the Doctor gave me with his own hands a folded note, not sealed. It was addressed to myself, and laid an injunction on me, in a few affectionate words, never to refer to the subject of that evening. I had confided it to my aunt, but to no one else. It was not a subject I could discuss with Agnes, and Agnes certainly had not the least suspicion of what had passed.

Neither, I felt convinced, had Mrs. Strong then. Several weeks elapsed before I saw the least change in her. It came on slowly, like a cloud when there is no wind. At first, she seemed to wonder at the gentle compassion with which the Doctor spoke to her, and at his wish that she should have her mother with her, to relieve the dull monotony of her life. Often, when we were at work, and she was sitting by, I would see her pausing and looking at him with that memorable face. Afterwards, I sometimes observed her rise, with her eyes full of tears, and go out of the room. Gradually, an unhappy shadow fell upon her beauty, and deepened every day. Mrs. Markleham was a regular inmate of the cottage then; but she talked and talked, and saw nothing.

As this change stole on Annie, once like sunshine in the Doctor's house, the Doctor became older in appearance, and more grave; but the sweetness of his temper, the placid kindness of his manner, and his benevolent solicitude for her, if they were capable of any increase, were increased. I saw him once, early on the morning of her birthday, when she came to sit in the window while we were at work (which she had always done, but now began to do with a timid and uncertain air that I thought very touching), take her forehead between his hands, kiss it, and go hurriedly away, too much moved to remain. I saw her stand where he had left her, like a statue; and then bend down her head, and clasp her hands, and weep, I cannot say how sorrowfully.

Sometimes, after that, I fancied that she tried to speak even to me, in intervals when we were left alone. But she never uttered word. The Doctor always had some new project for her participating in amusements away from home, with her mother; and Mrs. Markleham, who was very fond of amusements, and very easily dissatisfied with anything else, entered into them with great good-will, and was loud in her commendations. But Annie, in a spiritless, unhappy way, only went whither she was led, and seemed to have no care for anything.

I did not know what to think. Neither did my aunt; who must have walked, at various times, a hundred miles in her uncertainty. What was strangest of all was, that the only real relief which seemed to make its way into the secret region of this domestic unhappiness, made its way there in the person of Mr. Dick.

What his thoughts were on the subject, or what his observation was, I am as unable to explain, as I dare say he would have been to assist me in the task. But, as I have recorded in the narrative of my schooldays, his veneration for the Doctor was unbounded; and there is a subtlety of perception in real attachment, even when it is borne towards man by one of the lower animals, which leaves the highest intellect behind. To this mind of the heart, if I may call it so, in Mr. Dick, some bright ray of the truth shot straight.

He had proudly resumed his privilege, in many of his spare hours, of walking up and down the garden with the Doctor; as he had been accustomed to pace up and down The Doctor's Walk at Canterbury. But matters were no sooner in this state, than he devoted all his spare time (and got up earlier to make it more) to these perambulations. If he had never been so happy as when the Doctor read that marvellous performance, the Dictionary, to him; he was now quite miserable unless the Doctor pulled it out of his pocket, and began. When the Doctor and I were engaged, he now fell into the custom of walking up and down with Mrs. Strong, and helping her to trim her favourite flowers, or weed the beds. I dare say he rarely spoke a dozen words in an hour: but his quiet interest, and his wistful face, found immediate response in both their breasts; each knew that the other liked him, and that he loved both; and he became what no one else could be—a link between them.

When I think of him, with his impenetrably wise face, walking up and down with the Doctor, delighted to be battered by the hard words in the Dictionary; when I think of him carrying huge watering-pots after Annie; kneeling down, in very paws of gloves, at patient microscopic work among the little leaves; expressing as no philosopher could have expressed, in everything he did, a delicate desire to be her friend; showering sympathy, trustfulness, and affection, out of every hole in the watering-pot; when I think of him never wandering in that better mind of his to which unhappiness addressed itself, never bringing the unfortunate King Charles into the garden, never wavering in his grateful service, never diverted from his knowledge that there was something wrong, or from his wish to set it right—I really feel almost ashamed of having known that he was not quite in his wits, taking account of the utmost I have done with mine.

"Nobody but myself, Trot, knows what that man is!" my aunt would proudly remark, when we conversed about it. "Dick will distinguish himself yet!"

I must refer to one other topic before I close this chapter. While the visit at the Doctor's was still in progress, I observed that the postman brought two or three letters every morning for Uriah Heep, who remained at Highgate until the rest went back, it being a leisure time; and that these were always directed in a business-like manner by Mr. Micawber, who now assumed a round legal hand. I was glad to infer, from these slight premises, that Mr. Micawber was doing well; and consequently was much surprised to receive, about this time, the following letter from his amiable wife:—

"CANTERBURY, *Monday Evening.*

"You will doubtless be surprised, my dear Mr. Copperfield, to receive this communication. Still more so, by its contents. Still more so, by the stipulation of implicit confidence which I beg to impose. But my feelings as a wife and mother require relief; and as I do not wish to consult my family (already obnoxious to the feelings of Mr. Micawber), I know no one of whom I can better ask advice than my friend and former lodger.

"You may be aware, my dear Mr. Copperfield, that between myself and Mr. Micawber (whom I will never desert), there has always been preserved a spirit of mutual confidence. Mr. Micawber may have occasionally given a bill without consulting me, or he may have misled me as to the period when that obligation would become due. This has actually happened. But, in general, Mr. Micawber has had no secrets from the bosom of affection—I allude to his wife—and has invariably, on our retirement to rest, recalled the events of the day.

"You will picture to yourself, my dear Mr. Copperfield, what the poignancy of my feelings must be, when I inform you that Mr. Micawber is entirely changed. He is reserved. He is secret. His life is a mystery to the partner of his joys and sorrows—I again allude to his wife—and if I should assure you that beyond knowing that it is passed from morning to night at the office, I now know less of it than I do of the man in the south, connected with whose mouth the thoughtless children repeat an idle tale respecting cold plum porridge, I should adopt a popular fallacy to express an actual fact.

"But this is not all. Mr. Micawber is morose. He is severe. He is estranged from our eldest son and daughter, he has no pride in his twins, he looks with an eye of coldness even on the unoffending stranger who last became a member of our circle. The pecuniary means of meeting our expenses, kept down to the utmost farthing, are obtained from him with great difficulty, and even under fearful threats that he will Settle himself (the exact expression); and he inexorably refuses to give any explanation whatever of this distracting policy.

"This is hard to bear. This is heart-breaking. If you will advise me, knowing my feeble powers such as they are, how you think it will be best to exert them in a dilemma so unwonted, you will add another friendly obligation to the many you have already rendered me. With loves from the children, and a smile from the happily-unconscious stranger, I remain, dear Mr. Copperfield,

"Your afflicted
"EMMA MICAWBER."

I did not feel justified in giving a wife of Mrs. Micawber's experience any other recommendation, than that she should try to reclaim Mr. Micawber by patience and kindness (as I knew she would in any case); but the letter set me thinking about him very much.

CHAPTER XLIII.

ANOTHER RETROSPECT.

ONCE again, let me pause upon a memorable period of my life. Let me stand aside, to see the phantoms of those days go by me, accompanying the shadow of myself, in dim procession.

Weeks, months, seasons, pass along. They seem little more than a summer day and a winter evening. Now, the Common where I walk with Dora is all in bloom, a field of bright gold; and now the unseen heather lies in mounds and bunches underneath a covering of snow. In a breath, the river that flows through our Sunday walks is sparkling in the summer sun, is ruffled by the winter wind, or thickened with drifting heaps of ice. Faster than ever river ran towards the sea, it flashes, darkens, and rolls away.

Not a thread changes, in the house of the two little bird-like ladies. The clock ticks over the fireplace, the weather-glass hangs in the hall. Neither clock nor weather-glass is ever right; but we believe in both, devoutly.

I have come legally to man's estate. I have attained the dignity of twenty-one. But this is a sort of dignity that may be thrust upon one. Let me think what I have achieved.

I have tamed that savage stenographic mystery. I make a respectable income by it. I am in high repute for my accomplishment in all pertaining to the art, and am joined with eleven others in reporting the debates in Parliament for a Morning Newspaper. Night after night, I record predictions that never come to pass, professions that are never fulfilled, explanations that are only meant to mystify. I wallow in words. Britannia, that unfortunate female, is always before me, like a trussed fowl: skewered through and through with office-pens, and bound hand and foot with red tape. I am sufficiently behind the scenes to know the worth of political life. I am quite an Infidel about it, and shall never be converted.

My dear old Traddles has tried his hand at the same pursuit, but it is not in Traddles's way. He is perfectly good-humoured respecting his failure, and reminds me that he always did consider himself slow. He has occasional employment on the same newspaper, in getting up the facts of dry subjects, to be written about and embellished by more fertile minds. He is called to the Bar; and with admirable industry and self-denial has scraped another hundred pounds together, to fee a conveyancer whose chambers he attends. A great deal of very hot port wine was consumed at his call; and, considering the figure, I should think the Inner Temple must have made a profit by it.

I have come out in another way. I have taken with fear and trembling to authorship. I wrote a little something, in secret, and sent it to a magazine, and it was published in the magazine. Since then, I have taken heart to write a good many trifling pieces. Now, I am regularly paid for them. Altogether, I am well off; when I tell my income on the fingers of my left hand, I pass the third finger and take in the fourth to the middle joint.

We have removed from Buckingham Street, to a pleasant little cottage very near the one I looked at, when my enthusiasm first came on. My aunt, however (who has sold the house at Dover, to good advantage), is not going to remain here, but intends removing herself to a still more tiny cottage close at hand. What does this portend? My marriage! Yes!

Yes! I am going to be married to Dora! Miss Lavinia and Miss Clarissa have given their consent; and if ever canary-birds were in a flutter, they are. Miss Lavinia, self-charged with the superintendence of my darling's wardrobe, is constantly cutting out brown-paper cuirasses, and differing in opinion from a highly respectable young man, with a long bundle, and a yard measure under his arm. A dressmaker, always stabbed in the breast with a needle and thread, boards and lodges in the house; and seems to me, eating, drinking, or sleeping, never to take her thimble off. They make a lay-figure of my dear. They are always sending for her to come and try something on. We can't be happy together for five minutes in the evening, but some intrusive female knocks at the door, and says, "Oh, if you please, Miss Dora, would you step up-stairs!"

Miss Clarissa and my aunt roam all over London, to find out articles of furniture for Dora and me to look at. It would be better for them to buy the goods at once, without this ceremony of inspection; for, when we go to see a kitchen fender and meat-screen, Dora sees a Chinese house for Jip, with little bells on the top, and prefers that. And it takes a long time to accustom Jip to his new residence, after we have bought it; whenever he goes in or out, he makes all the little bells ring, and is horribly frightened.

Peggotty comes up to make herself useful, and falls to work immediately. Her department appears to be, to clean everything over and over again. She rubs everything that can be rubbed, until it shines, like her own honest forehead, with perpetual friction. And now it is, that I begin to see her solitary brother passing through the dark streets at night, and looking, as he goes, among the wandering faces. I never speak to him at such an hour. I know too well, as his grave figure passes onward, what he seeks, and what he dreads.

Why does Traddles look so important when he calls upon me this afternoon in the Commons—where I still occasionally attend, for form's sake, when I have time? The realisation of my boyish day-dreams is at hand. I am going to take out the licence.

It is a little document to do so much; and Traddles contemplates it, as it lies upon my desk, half in admiration,

half in awe. There are the names in the sweet old visionary connexion, David Copperfield and Dora Spenlow; and there, in the corner, is that Parental Institution, the Stamp Office, which is so benignantly interested in the various transactions of human life, looking down upon our Union; and there is the Archbishop of Canterbury invoking a blessing on us in print, and doing it as cheap as could possibly be expected.

Nevertheless, I am in a dream, a flustered, happy, hurried dream. I can't believe that it is going to be; and yet I can't believe but that every one I pass in the street, must have some kind of perception, that I am to be married the day after to-morrow. The Surrogate knows me, when I go down to be sworn; and disposes of me easily, as if there were a Masonic understanding between us. Traddles is not at all wanted, but is in attendance as my general backer.

"I hope the next time you come here, my dear fellow," I say to Traddles, "it will be on the same errand for yourself. And I hope it will be soon."

"Thank you for your good wishes, my dear Copperfield," he replies. "I hope so too. It's a satisfaction to know that she'll wait for me any length of time, and that she really is the dearest girl——"

"When are you to meet her at the coach?" I ask.

"At seven," says Traddles, looking at his plain old silver watch—the very watch he once took a wheel out of, at school, to make a water-mill. "That is about Miss Wickfield's time; is it not?"

"A little earlier. Her time is half-past eight."

"I assure you, my dear boy," says Traddles, "I am almost as pleased as if I were going to be married myself, to think that this event is coming to such a happy termination. And really the great friendship and consideration of personally associating Sophy with the joyful occasion, and inviting her to be a bridesmaid in conjunction with Miss Wickfield, demands my warmest thanks. I am extremely sensible of it."

I hear him, and shake hands with him; and we talk, and walk, and dine, and so on; but I don't believe it. Nothing is real.

Sophy arrives at the house of Dora's aunts, in due course. She has the most agreeable of faces,—not absolutely beautiful, but extraordinarily pleasant,—and is one of the most genial, unaffected, frank, engaging creatures I have ever seen. Traddles presents her to us with great pride; and rubs his hands for ten minutes by the clock, with every individual hair upon his head standing on tiptoe, when I congratulate him in a corner on his choice.

I have brought Agnes from the Canterbury coach, and her cheerful and beautiful face is among us for the second time. Agnes has a great liking for Traddles, and it is capital to see them meet, and to observe the glory of Traddles as he commends the dearest girl in the world to her acquaintance.

Still I don't believe it. We have a delightful evening, and are supremely happy; but I don't believe it yet. I can't collect myself. I can't check off my happiness as it takes place. I feel in a misty and unsettled kind of state; as if I had got up very early in the morning a week or two ago, and had never been to bed since. I can't make out when yesterday was. I seem to have been carrying the licence about, in my pocket, many months.

Next day, too, when we all go in a flock to see the house

—our house—Dora's and mine—I am quite unable to regard myself as its master. I seem to be there, by permission of somebody else. I half expect the real master to come home presently, and say he is glad to see me. Such a beautiful little house as it is, with everything so bright and new; with the flowers on the carpets looking as if freshly gathered, and the green leaves on the paper as if they had just come out; with the spotless muslin curtains, and the blushing rose-coloured furniture, and Dora's garden hat with the blue ribbon—do I remember, now, how I loved her in such another hat when I first knew her!—already hanging on its little peg; the guitar-case quite at home on its heels in a corner; and everybody tumbling over Jip's pagoda, which is much too big for the establishment.

Another happy evening, quite as unreal as all the rest of it, and I steal into the usual room before going away. Dora is not there. I suppose they have not done trying on yet. Miss Lavinia peeps in, and tells me mysteriously that she will not be long. She is rather long, notwithstanding; but by-and-by I hear a rustling at the door, and some one taps.

I say, "Come in!" but some one taps again.

I go to the door, wondering who it is; there, I meet a pair of bright eyes, and a blushing face; they are Dora's eyes and face, and Miss Lavinia has dressed her in to-morrow's dress, bonnet and all, for me to see. I take my little wife to my heart; and Miss Lavinia gives a little scream because I tumble the bonnet, and Dora laughs and cries at once, because I am so pleased; and I believe it less than ever.

"Do you think it pretty, Doady?" says Dora.

Pretty! I should rather think I did.

"And are you sure you like me very much?" says Dora.

The topic is fraught with such danger to the bonnet, that Miss Lavinia gives another little scream, and begs me to understand that Dora is only to be looked at, and on no account to be touched. So Dora stands in a delightful state of confusion for a minute or two, to be admired; and then takes off her bonnet—looking so natural without it!—and runs away with it in her hand; and comes dancing down again in her own familiar dress, and asks Jip if I have got a beautiful little wife, and whether he'll forgive her for being married, and kneels down to make him stand upon the Cookery Book, for the last time in his single life.

I go home, more incredulous than ever, to a lodging that I have hard by; and get up very early in the morning, to ride to the Highgate road and fetch my aunt.

I have never seen my aunt in such state. She is dressed in lavender-coloured silk, and has a white bonnet on, and is amazing. Janet has dressed her, and is there to look at me. Peggotty is ready to go to church, intending to behold the ceremony from the gallery. Mr. Dick, who is to give my darling to me at the altar, has had his hair curled. Traddles, whom I have taken up by appointment at the turnpike, presents a dazzling combination of cream colour and light blue; and both he and Mr. Dick have a general effect about them of being all gloves.

No doubt I see this, because I know it is so; but I am astray, and seem to see nothing. Nor do I believe anything whatever. Still, as we drive along in an open carriage, this fairy marriage is real enough to fill me with a sort of wondering pity for the unfortunate people who have no part in it, but are sweeping out the shops, and going to their daily occupations.

My aunt sits with my hand in hers all the way. When we stop a little way short of the church, to put down Peggotty, whom we have brought on the box, she gives it a squeeze, and me a kiss.

"God bless you, Trot! My own boy never could be dearer. I think of poor dear Baby this morning."

"So do I. And of all I owe to you, dear aunt."

"Tut, child!" says my aunt; and gives her hand in overflowing cordiality to Traddles, who then gives his to Mr. Dick, who then gives his to me, who then give mine to Traddles, and then we come to the church door.

The church is calm enough, I am sure; but it might be a steam-power loom in full action, for any sedative effect it has on me. I am too far gone for that.

The rest is all a more or less incoherent dream.

A dream of their coming in with Dora; of the pew-opener arranging us, like a drill-serjeant, before the altar rails; of my wondering, even then, why pew-openers must always be the most disagreeable females procurable, and whether there is any religious dread of a disastrous infection of good-humour which renders it indispensable to set those vessels of vinegar upon the road to Heaven.

Of the clergyman and clerk appearing; of a few boatmen and some other people strolling in; of an ancient mariner behind me, strongly flavouring the church with rum; of the service beginning in a deep voice, and our all being very attentive.

Of Miss Lavinia, who acts as a semi-auxiliary bridesmaid, being the first to cry, and of her doing homage (as I take it) to the memory of Pidger, in sobs; of Miss Clarissa applying a smelling-bottle; of Agnes taking care of Dora; of my aunt endeavouring to represent herself as a model of sternness, with tears rolling down her face; of little Dora trembling very much, and making her responses in faint whispers.

Of our kneeling down together, side by side; of Dora's trembling less and less, but always clasping Agnes by the hand; of the service being got through, quietly and gravely; of our all looking at each other in an April state of smiles and tears, when it is over; of my young wife being hysterical in the vestry, and crying for her poor papa, her dear papa.

Of her soon cheering up again, and our signing the register all round. Of my going into the gallery for Peggotty to bring her to sign it; of Peggotty's hugging me in a corner, and telling me she saw my own dear mother married; of its being over, and our going away.

Of my walking so proudly and lovingly down the aisle with my sweet wife upon my arm, through a mist of half-seen people, pulpits, monuments, pews, fonts, organs, and church-windows, in which there flutter faint airs of association with my childish church at home, so long ago.

Of their whispering, as we pass, what a youthful couple we are, and what a pretty little wife she is. Of our all being so merry and talkative in the carriage going back. Of Sophy telling us that when she saw Traddles (whom I had entrusted with the licence) asked for it, she almost fainted, having been convinced that he would contrive to lose it, or to have his pocket picked. Of Agnes laughing gaily; and of Dora being so fond of Agnes that she will not be separated from her, but still keeps her hand.

Of there being a breakfast, with abundance of things, pretty and substantial, to eat and drink, whereof I partake, as I should do in any other dream, without the least perception of their flavour; eating and drinking, as I may say, nothing but love and marriage, and no more believing in the viands than in anything else.

Of my making a speech in the same dreamy fashion, without having an idea of what I want to say, beyond such as may be comprehended in the full conviction that I haven't said it. Of our being very sociably and simply happy (always in a dream though); and of Jip's having wedding cake, and its not agreeing with him afterwards.

Of the pair of hired post-horses being ready, and of Dora's going away to change her dress. Of my aunt and Miss Clarissa remaining with us; and our walking in the garden; and my aunt, who has made quite a speech at breakfast touching Dora's aunts, being mightily amused with herself, but a little proud of it too.

Of Dora's being ready, and of Miss Lavinia's hovering about her, loth to lose the pretty toy that has given her so much pleasant occupation. Of Dora's making a long series of surprised discoveries that she has forgotten all sorts of little things; and of everybody's running everywhere to fetch them.

Of their all closing about Dora, when at last she begins to say good-bye, looking, with their bright colours and ribbons, like a bed of flowers. Of my darling being almost smothered among the flowers, and coming out, laughing and crying both together, to my jealous arms.

Of my wanting to carry Jip (who is to go along with us), and Dora's saying No, that she must carry him, or else he'll think she don't like him any more, now she is married, and will break his heart. Of our going, arm in arm, and Dora stopping and looking back, and saying, "If I have ever been cross or ungrateful to anybody, don't remember it!" and bursting into tears.

Of her waving her little hand, and our going away once more. Of her once more stopping and looking back, and hurrying to Agnes, and giving Agnes, above all the others, her last kisses and farewells.

We drive away together, and I awake from the dream. I believe it at last. It is my dear, dear, little wife beside me, whom I love so well!

"Are you happy now, you foolish boy?" says Dora, "and sure you don't repent?"

I have stood aside to see the phantoms of those days go by me. They are gone, and I resume the journey of my story.

CHAPTER XLIV.

OUR HOUSEKEEPING.

It was a strange condition of things, the honeymoon being over, and the bridesmaids gone home, when I found myself sitting down in my own small house with Dora; quite thrown out of employment, as I may say, in respect of the delicious old occupation of making love.

It seemed such an extraordinary thing to have Dora always there. It was so unaccountable not to be obliged to go out to see her, not to have any occasion to be tormenting myself about her, not to have to write to her, not to be scheming and devising opportunities of being alone with her. Sometimes of an evening, when I looked up from my writ-ing, and saw her seated opposite, I would lean back in my chair, and think how queer it was that there we were, alone together as a matter of course—nobody's business any more—all the romance of our engagement put away upon a shelf, to rust—no one to please but one another—one another to please, for life.

When there was a debate, and I was kept out very late, it seemed so strange to me, as I was walking home, to think that Dora was at home! It was such a wonderful thing, at first, to have her coming softly down to talk to me as I ate my supper. It was such a stupendous thing to know for certain that she put her hair in papers. It was altogether such an astonishing event to see her do it!

I doubt whether two young birds could have known less about keeping house than I and my pretty Dora did. We had a servant, of course. She kept house for us. I have still a latent belief that she must have been Mrs. Crupp's daughter in disguise, we had such an awful time of it with Mary Anne.

Her name was Paragon. Her nature was represented to us, when we engaged her, as being feebly expressed in her name. She had a written character, as large as a Proclamation; and, according to this document, could do everything of a domestic nature that ever I heard of, and a great many things that I never did hear of. She was a woman in the prime of life; of a severe countenance; and subject (particularly in the arms) to a sort of perpetual measles or fiery rash. She had a cousin in the Life Guards, with such long legs that he looked like the afternoon shadow of somebody else. His shell-jacket was as much too little for him as he was too big for the premises. He made the cottage smaller than it need have been, by being so very much out of proportion to it. Besides which, the walls were not thick, and whenever he passed the evening at our house, we always knew of it by hearing one continual growl in the kitchen.

Our treasure was warranted sober and honest. I am therefore willing to believe that she was in a fit when we found her under the boiler; and that the deficient teaspoons were attributable to the dustman.

But she preyed upon our minds dreadfully. We felt our inexperience, and were unable to help ourselves. We should have been at her mercy, if she had had any; but she was a remorseless woman, and had none. She was the cause of our first little quarrel.

"My dearest life," I said one day to Dora, "do you think Mary Anne has any idea of time?"

"Why, Doady?" inquired Dora, looking up, innocently, from her drawing.

"My love, because it's five, and we were to have dined at four."

Dora glanced wistfully at the clock, and hinted that she thought it was too fast.

"On the contrary, my love," said I, referring to my watch, "it's a few minutes too slow."

My little wife came and sat upon my knee, to coax me to be quiet, and drew a line with her pencil down the middle of my nose; but I couldn't dine off that, though it was very agreeable.

"Don't you think, my dear," said I, "it would be better for you to remonstrate with Mary Anne?"

"Oh no, please! I couldn't, Doady!" said Dora.

"Why not, my love?" I gently asked.

"Oh, because I am such a little goose," said Dora, "and she knows I am!"

I thought this sentiment so incompatible with the establishment of any system of check on Mary Anne, that I frowned a little.

"Oh, what ugly wrinkles in my bad boy's forehead!" said Dora, and still being on my knee, she traced them with her pencil; putting it to her rosy lips to make it mark blacker, and working at my forehead with a quaint little mockery of being industrious, that quite delighted me in spite of myself.

"There's a good child," said Dora, "it makes its face so much prettier to laugh."

"But, my love," said I.

"No, no! please!" cried Dora, with a kiss, "don't be a naughty Blue Beard! Don't be serious!"

"My precious wife," said I, "we must be serious sometimes. Come! Sit down on this chair, close beside me! Give me the pencil! There! Now let us talk sensibly. You know, dear;" what a little hand it was to hold, and what a tiny wedding-ring it was to see! "You know, my love, it is not exactly comfortable to have to go out without one's dinner. Now, is it?"

"N—n—no!" replied Dora, faintly.

"My love, how you tremble!"

"Because I KNOW you're going to scold me," exclaimed Dora, in a piteous voice.

"My sweet, I am only going to reason."

"Oh, but reasoning is worse than scolding!" exclaimed Dora, in despair. "I didn't marry to be reasoned with. If you meant to reason with such a poor little thing as I am, you ought to have told me so, you cruel boy!"

I tried to pacify Dora, but she turned away her face, and shook her curls from side to side, and said "You cruel, cruel boy!" so many times, that I really did not exactly know what to do: so I took a few turns up and down the room in my uncertainty, and came back again.

"Dora, my darling!"

"No, I am not your darling. Because you *must* be sorry that you married me, or else you wouldn't reason with me!" returned Dora.

I felt so injured by the inconsequential nature of this charge, that it gave me courage to be grave.

"Now, my own Dora," said I, "you are very childish, and are talking nonsense. You must remember, I am sure, that I was obliged to go out yesterday when dinner was half over; and that, the day before, I was made quite unwell by being obliged to eat underdone veal in a hurry; today, I don't dine at all—and I am afraid to say how long we waited for breakfast—and *then* the water didn't boil. I don't mean to reproach you, my dear, but this is not comfortable."

"Oh, you cruel, cruel boy, to say I am a disagreeable wife!" cried Dora.

"Now, my dear Dora, you must know that I never said that!"

"You said I wasn't comfortable!" said Dora.

"I said the housekeeping was not comfortable!"

"It's exactly the same thing!" cried Dora. And she evidently thought so, for she wept most grievously.

I took another turn across the room, full of love for my pretty wife, and distracted by self-accusatory inclinations to knock my head against the door. I sat down again, and said:

"I am not blaming you, Dora. We have both a great deal to learn. I am only trying to show you, my dear, that you must—you really must" (I was resolved not to give this up) "accustom yourself to look after Mary Anne. Likewise to act a little for yourself, and me."

"I wonder, I do, at your making such ungrateful speeches," sobbed Dora. "When you know that the other day, when you said you would like a little bit of fish, I went out myself, miles and miles, and ordered it, to surprise you."

"And it was very kind of you, my own darling," said I. "I felt it so much that I wouldn't on any account have even mentioned that you bought a Salmon—which was too much for two. Or that it cost one pound six—which was more than we can afford."

"You enjoyed it very much," sobbed Dora. "And you said I was a Mouse."

"And I'll say so again, my love," I returned, "a thousand times!"

But I had wounded Dora's soft little heart, and she was not to be comforted. She was so pathetic in her sobbing and bewailing, that I felt as if I had said I don't know what to hurt her. I was obliged to hurry away; I was kept out late; and I felt all night such pangs of remorse as made me miserable. I had the conscience of an assassin, and was haunted by a vague sense of enormous wickedness.

It was two or three hours past midnight when I got home. I found my aunt, in our house, sitting up for me.

"Is anything the matter, aunt?" said I, alarmed.

"Nothing, Trot," she replied. "Sit down, sit down. Little Blossom has been rather out of spirits, and I have been keeping her company. That's all."

I leaned my head upon my hand; and felt more sorry and downcast, as I sat looking at the fire, than I could have supposed possible so soon after the fulfilment of my brightest hopes. As I sat thinking, I happened to meet my aunt's eyes, which were resting on my face. There was an anxious expression in them, but it cleared directly.

"I assure you, aunt," said I, "I have been quite unhappy myself all night, to think of Dora's being so. But I had no other intention than to speak to her tenderly and lovingly about our home-affairs."

My aunt nodded encouragement.

"You must have patience, Trot," said she.

"Of course. Heaven knows I don't mean to be unreasonable, aunt!"

"No, no," said my aunt. "But Little Blossom is a very tender little blossom, and the wind must be gentle with her."

I thanked my good aunt, in my heart, for her tenderness towards my wife; and I was sure that she knew I did.

"Don't you think, aunt," said I, after some further contemplation of the fire, "that you could advise and counsel Dora a little, for our mutual advantage, now and then?"

"Trot," returned my aunt, with some emotion, "no! Don't ask me such a thing!"

Her tone was so very earnest that I raised my eyes in surprise.

"I look back on my life, child," said my aunt, "and I think of some who are in their graves, with whom I might have been on kinder terms. If I judged harshly of other people's mistakes in marriage, it may have been because I had bitter reason to judge harshly of my own. Let that pass. I have been a grumpy, frumpy, wayward sort of a woman, a good many years. I am still, and I always shall be. But you and I have done one another some good, Trot—at all events, you have done me good, my dear;

and division must not come between us, at this time of day."

"Division between *us!*" cried I.

"Child, child!" said my aunt, smoothing her dress, "how soon it might come between us, or how unhappy I might make our Little Blossom, if I meddled in anything, a prophet couldn't say. I want our pet to like me, and be as gay as a butterfly. Remember your own home, in that second marriage; and never do both me and her the injury you have hinted at!"

I comprehended, at once, that my aunt was right; and I comprehended the full extent of her generous feeling towards my dear wife.

"These are early days, Trot," she pursued, "and Rome was not built in a day, nor in a year. You have chosen freely for yourself;" a cloud passed over her face for a moment, I thought; "and you have chosen a very pretty and a very affectionate creature. It will be your duty, and it will be your pleasure too—of course I know that; I am not delivering a lecture—to estimate her (as you chose her) by the qualities she has, and not by the qualities she may not have. The latter you must develop in her, if you can. And if you cannot, child," here my aunt rubbed her nose, "you must just accustom yourself to do without 'em. But remember, my dear, your future is between you two. No one can assist you; you are to work it out for yourselves. This is marriage, Trot; and Heaven bless you both, in it, for a pair of babes in the wood as you are!"

My aunt said this in a sprightly way, and gave me a kiss to ratify the blessing.

"Now," said she, "light my little lantern, and see me into my band-box by the garden path;" for there was a communication between our cottages in that direction. "Give Betsey Trotwood's love to Blossom, when you come back; and whatever you do, Trot, never dream of setting Betsey up as a scarecrow, for if *I* ever saw her in the glass, she's quite grim enough and gaunt enough in her private capacity!"

With this my aunt tied her head up in a handkerchief, with which she was accustomed to make a bundle of it on such occasions; and I escorted her home. As she stood in her garden, holding up her little lantern to light me back, I thought her observation of me had an anxious air again; but I was too much occupied in pondering on what she had said, and too much impressed—for the first time, in reality —by the conviction that Dora and I had indeed to work out our future for ourselves, and that no one could assist us, to take much notice of it.

Dora came stealing down in her little slippers, to meet me, now that I was alone; and cried upon my shoulder, and said I had been hard-hearted and she had been naughty; and I said much the same thing in effect, I believe; and we made it up, and agreed that our first little difference was to be our last, and that we were never to have another if we lived a hundred years.

The next domestic trial we went through, was the Ordeal of Servants. Mary Anne's cousin deserted into our coal-hole, and was brought out, to our great amazement, by a piquet of his companions in arms, who took him away handcuffed in a procession that covered our front-garden with ignominy. This nerved me to get rid of Mary Anne, who went so mildly, on receipt of wages, that I was surprised, until I found out about the teaspoons, and also about the little sums she had borrowed in my name of the tradespeople without authority. After an interval of Mrs. Kidger-

bury—the oldest inhabitant of Kentish Town, I believe, who went out charing, but was too feeble to execute her conceptions of that art—we found another treasure, who was one of the most amiable of women, but who generally made a point of falling either up or down the kitchen stairs with the tray, and almost always plunged into the parlour, as into a bath, with the tea-things. The ravages committed by this unfortunate rendering her dismissal necessary, she was succeeded (with intervals of Mrs. Kidgerbury) by a long line of Incapables; terminating in a young person of genteel appearance, who went to Greenwich Fair in Dora's bonnet. After whom I remember nothing but an average equality of failure.

Everybody we had anything to do with seemed to cheat us. Our appearance in a shop was a signal for the damaged goods to be brought out immediately. If we bought a lobster, it was full of water. All our meat turned out to be tough, and there was hardly any crust to our loaves. In search of the principle on which joints ought to be roasted, to be roasted enough, and not too much, I myself referred to the Cookery Book, and found it there established as the allowance of a quarter of an hour to every pound, and say a quarter over. But the principle always failed us by some curious fatality, and we never could hit any medium between redness and cinders.

I had reason to believe that in accomplishing these failures we incurred a far greater expense than if we had achieved a series of triumphs. It appeared to me, on looking over the tradesmen's books, as if we might have kept the basement story paved with butter, such was the extensive scale of our consumption of that article. I don't know whether the Excise returns of the period may have exhibited any increase in the demand for pepper; but if our performances did not affect the market, I should say several families must have left off using it. And the most wonderful fact of all was, that we never had anything in the house.

As to the washerwoman pawning the clothes, and coming in a state of penitent intoxication to apologise, I suppose that might have happened several times to anybody. Also the chimney on fire, the parish engine, and perjury on the part of the Beadle. But I apprehend that we were personally unfortunate in engaging a servant with a taste for cordials, who swelled our running account for porter at the public-house by such inexplicable items as "quartern rum shrub (Mrs. C.);" "Half-quartern gin and cloves (Mrs. C.);" "Glass rum and peppermint (Mrs. C.)"—the parentheses always referring to Dora, who was supposed, it appeared on explanation, to have imbibed the whole of these refreshments.

One of our first feats in the housekeeping way was a little dinner to Traddles. I met him in town, and asked him to walk out with me that afternoon. He readily consenting, I wrote to Dora, saying I would bring him home. It was pleasant weather, and on the road we made my domestic happiness the theme of conversation. Traddles was very full of it; and said, that, picturing himself with such a home, and Sophy waiting and preparing for him, he could think of nothing wanting to complete his bliss.

I could not have wished for a prettier little wife at the opposite end of the table, but I certainly could have wished, when we sate down, for a little more room. I did not know how it was, but though there were only two of us, we were at once always cramped for room, and yet had always room enough to lose everything in. I suspect it may have been because nothing had a place of its own, except Jip's pagoda, which invariably blocked up the main thoroughfare. On the present occasion, Traddles was so hemmed in by the pagoda and the guitar-case, and Dora's flower-painting, and my writing-table, that I had serious doubts of the possibility of his using his knife and fork; but he protested, with his own good-humour, "Oceans of room, Copperfield! I assure you, Oceans."

There was another thing I could have wished, namely, that Jip had never been encouraged to walk about the table-cloth during dinner. I began to think there was something disorderly in his being there at all, even if he had not been in the habit of putting his foot in the salt or the melted butter. On this occasion he seemed to think he was introduced expressly to keep Traddles at bay; and he barked at my old friend, and made short runs at his plate, with such undaunted pertinacity, that he may be said to have engrossed the conversation.

However, as I knew how tender-hearted my dear Dora was, and how sensitive she would be to any slight upon her favourite, I hinted no objection. For similar reasons I made no allusion to the skirmishing plates upon the floor; or to the disreputable appearance of the castors, which were all at sixes and sevens, and looked drunk; or to the further blockade of Traddles by wandering vegetable-dishes and jugs. I could not help wondering in my own mind, as I contemplated the boiled leg of mutton before me, previous to carving it, how it came to pass that our joints of meat were of such extraordinary shapes—and whether our butcher contracted for all the deformed sheep that came into the world; but I kept my reflections to myself.

"My love," said I to Dora, "what have you got in that dish?"

I could not imagine why Dora had been making tempting little faces at me, as if she wanted to kiss me.

"Oysters, dear," said Dora, timidly.

"Was that *your* thought?" said I, delighted.

"Ye-yes, Doady," said Dora.

"There never was a happier one!" I exclaimed, laying down the carving-knife and fork. "There is nothing Traddles likes so much!"

"Ye-yes, Doady," said Dora, "and so I bought a beautiful little barrel of them, and the man said they were very good. But I—I am afraid there's something the matter with them. They don't seem right." Here Dora shook her head, and diamonds twinkled in her eyes.

"They are only opened in both shells," said I. "Take the top one off, my love."

"But it won't come off," said Dora, trying very hard, and looking very much distressed.

"Do you know, Copperfield," said Traddles, cheerfully examining the dish, "I think it is in consequence—they are capital oysters, but I *think* it is in consequence—of their never having been opened."

They never had been opened; and we had no oyster-knives—and couldn't have used them if we had; so we looked at the oysters and ate the mutton. At least we ate as much of it as was done, and made up with capers. If I had permitted him, I am satisfied that Traddles would have made a perfect savage of himself, and eaten a plateful of raw meat, to express enjoyment of the repast; but I would hear of no such immolation on the altar of friendship; and we had a course of bacon instead; there happening, by good fortune, to be cold bacon in the larder.

My poor little wife was in such affliction when she thought

I should be annoyed, and in such a state of joy when she found I was not, that the discomfiture I had subdued very soon vanished, and we passed a happy evening; Dora sitting with her arm on my chair while Traddles and I discussed a glass of wine, and taking every opportunity of whispering in my ear that it was so good of me not to be a cruel, cross old boy. By-and-by she made tea for us; which it was so pretty to see her do, as if she was busying herself with a set of doll's tea-things, that I was not particular about the quality of the beverage. Then Traddles and I played a game or two at cribbage; and Dora singing to the guitar the while, it seemed to me as if our courtship and marriage were a tender dream of mine, and the night when I first listened to her voice were not yet over.

When Traddles went away, and I came back into the parlour from seeing him out, my wife planted her chair close to mine, and sat down by my side.

"I am very sorry," she said. "Will you try to teach me, Doady?"

"I must teach myself first, Dora," said I. "I am as bad as you, love."

"Ah! But you can learn," she returned; "and you are a clever, clever man!"

"Nonsense, Mouse!" said I.

"I wish," resumed my wife, after a long silence, "that I could have gone down into the country for a whole year, and lived with Agnes!"

Her hands were clasped upon my shoulder, and her chin rested on them, and her blue eyes looked quietly into mine.

"Why so?" I asked.

"I think she might have improved me, and I think I might have learned from *her*," said Dora.

"All in good time, my love. Agnes has had her father to take care of for these many years, you should remember. Even when she was quite a child, she was the Agnes whom we know," said I.

"Will you call me a name I want you to call me?" inquired Dora, without moving.

"What is it?" I asked with a smile.

"It's a stupid name," she said, shaking her curls for a moment. "Child-wife."

I laughingly asked my child-wife what her fancy was in desiring to be so called. She answered without moving, otherwise than as the arm I twined about her may have brought her blue eyes nearer to me:

"I don't mean, you silly fellow, that you should use the name instead of Dora. I only mean that you should think of me that way. When you are going to be angry with me, say to yourself, 'it's only my child-wife!' When I am very disappointing, say, 'I knew, a long time ago, that she would make but a child-wife!' When you miss what I should like to be, and I think can never be, say, 'still my foolish child-wife loves me!' For indeed I do."

I had not been serious with her; having no idea, until now, that she was serious herself. But her affectionate nature was so happy in what I now said to her with my whole heart, that her face became a laughing one before her glittering eyes were dry. She was soon my child-wife indeed; sitting down on the floor outside the Chinese house, ringing all the little bells one after another, to punish Jip for his recent bad behaviour; while Jip lay blinking in the doorway with his head out, even too lazy to be teased.

This appeal of Dora's made a strong impression on me. I look back on the time I write of; I invoke the innocent

OUR HOUSEKEEPING.

figure that I dearly loved, to come out from the mists and shadows of the past, and turn its gentle head towards me once again; and I can still declare that this one little speech was constantly in my memory. I may not have used it to the best account; I was young and inexperienced; but I never turned a deaf ear to its artless pleading.

Dora told me, shortly afterwards, that she was going to be a wonderful housekeeper. Accordingly, she polished the tablets, pointed the pencil, bought an immense account-book, carefully stitched up with a needle and thread all the leaves of the Cookery Book which Jip had torn, and made quite a desperate little attempt " to be good," as she called it. But the figures had the old obstinate propensity—they *would not* add up. When she had entered two or three laborious items in the account-book, Jip would walk over the page, wagging his tail, and smear them all out. Her own little right-hand middle finger got steeped to the very bone in ink; and I think that was the only decided result attained.

Sometimes, of an evening, when I was at home and at work—for I wrote a good deal now, and was beginning in a small way to be known as a writer—I would lay down my pen, and watch my child-wife trying to be good. First of all, she would bring out the immense account-book, and lay it down upon the table, with a deep sigh. Then she would open it at the place where Jip had made it illegible last night, and call Jip up, to look at his misdeeds. This would occasion a diversion in Jip's favour, and some inking of his nose, perhaps, as a penalty. Then she would tell Jip to lie down on the table instantly, "like a lion"—which was one of his tricks, though I cannot say the likeness was striking—and, if he were in an obedient humour, he would obey. Then she would take up a pen, and begin to write, and find a hair in it. Then she would take up another pen, and begin to write, and find that it spluttered. Then she would take up another pen, and begin to write, and say in a low voice, "Oh, it's a talking pen, and will disturb Doady!" And then she would give it up as a bad job, and put the account-book away, after pretending to crush the lion with it.

Or, if she were in a very sedate and serious state of mind, she would sit down with the tablets, and a little basket of bills, and other documents, which looked more like curl-papers than anything else, and endeavour to get some result out of them. After severely comparing one with another, and making entries on the tablets, and blotting them out, and counting all the fingers of her left hand over and over again, backwards and forwards, she would be so vexed and discouraged, and would look so unhappy, that it gave me pain to see her bright face clouded—and for me!—and I would go softly to her, and say:

"What's the matter, Dora?"

Dora would look up hopelessly, and reply, "They won't come right. They make my head ache so. And they won't do anything I want!"

Then I would say, "Now let us try together. Let me show you, Dora."

Then I would commence a practical demonstration, to which Dora would pay profound attention, perhaps for five minutes; when she would begin to be dreadfully tired, and would lighten the subject by curling my hair, or trying the effect of my face with my shirt-collar turned down. If I tacitly checked this playfulness, and persisted, she would look so scared and disconsolate, as she became more and more bewildered, that the remembrance of her natural gaiety when I first strayed into her path, and of her being my child-wife, would come reproachfully upon me; and I would lay the pencil down, and call for the guitar.

I had a great deal of work to do, and had many anxieties, but the same considerations made me keep them to myself. I am far from sure, now, that it was right to do this, but I did it for my child-wife's sake. I search my breast, and I commit its secrets, if I know them, without any reservation to this paper. The old unhappy loss or want of something had, I am conscious, some place in my heart; but not to the embitterment of my life. When I walked alone in the fine weather, and thought of the summer days when all the air had been filled with my boyish enchantment, I did miss something of the realisation of my dreams; but I thought it was a softened glory of the Past, which nothing could have thrown upon the present time. I did feel, sometimes, for a little while, that I could have wished my wife had been my counsellor; had had more character and purpose, to sustain me, and improve me by; had been endowed with power to fill up the void which somewhere seemed to be about me; but I felt as if this were an unearthly consummation of my happiness, that never had been meant to be, and never could have been.

I was a boyish husband as to years. I had known the softening influence of no other sorrows or experiences than those recorded in these leaves. If I did any wrong, as I may have done much, I did it in mistaken love, and in my want of wisdom. I write the exact truth. It would avail me nothing to extenuate it now.

Thus it was that I took upon myself the toils and cares of our life, and had no partner in them. We lived much as before, in reference to our scrambling household arrangements; but I had got used to those, and Dora I was pleased to see was seldom vexed now. She was bright and cheerful in the old childish way, loved me dearly, and was happy with her old trifles.

When the debates were heavy—I mean as to length, not quality, for in the last respect they were not often otherwise—and I went home late, Dora would never rest when she heard my footsteps, but would always come down stairs to meet me. When my evenings were unoccupied by the pursuit for which I had qualified myself with so much pains, and I was engaged in writing at home, she would sit quietly near me, however late the hour, and be so mute, that I would often think she had dropped asleep. But generally, when I raised my head, I saw her blue eyes looking at me with the quiet attention of which I have already spoken.

"Oh, what a weary boy!" said Dora one night, when I met her eyes as I was shutting up my desk.

"What a weary girl!" said I. "That's more to the purpose. You must go to bed another time, my love. It's far too late for you."

"No, don't send me to bed!" pleaded Dora, coming to my side. "Pray don't do that!"

"Dora!"

To my amazement she was sobbing on my neck.

"Not well, my dear? not happy?"

"Yes! quite well, and very happy!" said Dora. "But say you'll let me stop, and see you write."

"Why, what a sight for such bright eyes at midnight!" I replied.

"Are they bright, though?" returned Dora, laughing. "I'm so glad they're bright."

"Little Vanity!" said I.

But it was not vanity; it was only harmless delight in my admiration. I knew that very well, before she told me so.

"If you think them pretty, say I may always stop, and see you write!" said Dora. "*Do* you think them pretty?"

"Very pretty."

"Then let me always stop and see you write."

"I am afraid that won't improve their brightness, Dora."

"Yes, it will! Because, you clever boy, you'll not forget me then, while you are full of silent fancies. Will you mind it, if I say something very, very silly?—more than usual?" inquired Dora, peeping over my shoulder into my face.

"What wonderful thing is that?" said I.

"Please let me hold the pens," said Dora. "I want to have something to do with all those many hours when you are so industrious. May I hold the pens?"

The remembrance of her pretty joy when I said Yes, brings tears into my eyes. The next time I sat down to write, and regularly afterwards, she sat in her old place, with a spare bundle of pens at her side. Her triumph in this connexion with my work, and her delight when I wanted a new pen—which I very often feigned to do—suggested to me a new way of pleasing my child-wife. I occasionally made a pretence of wanting a page or two of manuscript copied. Then Dora was in her glory. The preparations she made for this great work, the aprons she put on, the bibs she borrowed from the kitchen to keep off the ink, the time she took, the innumerable stoppages she made to have a laugh with Jip as if he understood it all, her conviction that her work was incomplete unless she signed her name at the end, and the way in which she would bring it to me, like a school-copy, and then, when I praised it, clasp me round the neck, are touching recollections to me, simple as they might appear to other men.

She took possession of the keys soon after this, and went jingling about the house with the whole bunch in a little basket, tied to her slender waist. I seldom found that the places to which they belonged were locked, or that they were of any use except as a plaything for Jip—but Dora was pleased, and that pleased me. She was quite satisfied that a good deal was effected by this make-belief of housekeeping; and was as merry as if we had been keeping a baby-house, for a joke.

So we went on. Dora was hardly less affectionate to my aunt than to me, and often told her of the time when she was afraid she was "a cross old thing." I never saw my aunt unbend more systematically to any one. She courted Jip, though Jip never responded; listened, day after day, to the guitar, though I am afraid she had no taste for music; never attacked the Incapables, though the temptation must have been severe; went wonderful distances on foot to purchase, as surprises, any trifles that she found out Dora wanted; and never came in by the garden, and missed her from the room, but she would call out, at the foot of the stairs, in a voice that sounded cheerfully all over the house:

"Where's Little Blossom!"

CHAPTER XLV.

MR. DICK FULFILS MY AUNT'S PREDICTIONS.

It was some time now, since I had left the Doctor. Living in his neighbourhood, I saw him frequently; and we all went to his house on two or three occasions to dinner or tea. The Old Soldier was in permanent quarters under the Doctor's roof. She was exactly the same as ever, and the same immortal butterflies hovered over her cap.

Like some other mothers, whom I have known in the course of my life, Mrs. Markleham was far more fond of pleasure than her daughter was. She required a great deal of amusement, and, like a deep old soldier, pretended, in consulting her own inclinations, to be devoting herself to her child. The Doctor's desire that Annie should be entertained, was therefore particularly acceptable to this excellent parent; who expressed unqualified approval of his discretion.

I have no doubt, indeed, that she probed the Doctor's wound without knowing it. Meaning nothing but a certain matured frivolity and selfishness, not always inseparable from full-blown years, I think she confirmed him in his fear that he was a constraint upon his young wife, and that there was no congeniality of feeling between them, by so strongly commending his design of lightening the load of her life.

"My dear soul," she said to him one day when I was present, "you know there is no doubt it would be a little pokey for Annie to be always shut up here."

The Doctor nodded his benevolent head.

"When she comes to her mother's age," said Mrs. Markleham, with a flourish of her fan, "then it'll be another thing. You might put ME into a jail, with genteel society and a rubber, and I should never care to come out. But I am not Annie, you know; and Annie is not her mother."

"Surely, surely," said the Doctor.

"You are the best of creatures—no, I beg your pardon!" for the Doctor made a gesture of depreciation, "I must say before your face, as I always say behind your back, you are the best of creatures; but of course you don't—now do you?—enter into the same pursuits and fancies as Annie?"

"No," said the Doctor, in a sorrowful tone.

"No, of course not," retorted the Old Soldier. "Take your Dictionary, for example. What a useful work a Dictionary is! What a necessary work! The meanings of words! Without Doctor Johnson, or somebody of that sort, we might have been at this present moment calling an Italian-iron a bedstead. But we can't expect a Dictionary—especially when it's making—to interest Annie, can we?"

The Doctor shook his head.

"And that's why I *so* much approve," said Mrs. Markleham, tapping him on the shoulder with her shut-up fan, "of your thoughtfulness. It shows that you don't expect, as many elderly people do expect, old heads on young shoulders. You have studied Annie's character, and you understand it. *That's* what I find so charming!"

Even the calm and patient face of Doctor Strong expressed some little sense of pain, I thought, under the infliction of these compliments.

"Therefore, my dear Doctor," said the Soldier, giving him several affectionate taps, "you may command me, at all times and seasons. Now, do understand that I am entirely at your service. I am ready to go with Annie to operas, concerts, exhibitions, all kinds of places; and you shall never find that I am tired. Duty, my dear Doctor, before every consideration in the universe!"

She was as good as her word. She was one of those people who can bear a great deal of pleasure, and she never flinched in her perseverance in the cause. She seldom got hold of the newspaper (which she settled herself down in the softest chair in the house to read through an eye-glass, every day, for two hours), but she found out something that she was certain Annie would like to see. It was in vain for Annie to protest that she was weary of such things. Her mother's remonstrance always was, "Now, my dear Annie, I am sure you know better; and I must tell you, my love, that you are not making a proper return for the kindness of Doctor Strong."

This was usually said in the Doctor's presence, and appeared to me to constitute Annie's principal inducement for withdrawing her objections when she made any. But in general she resigned herself to her mother, and went where the Old Soldier would.

It rarely happened now that Mr. Maldon accompanied them. Sometimes my aunt and Dora were invited to do so, and accepted the invitation. Sometimes Dora only was asked. The time had been, when I should have been uneasy in her going; but reflection on what had passed that former night in the Doctor's study, had made a change in my mistrust. I believed that the Doctor was right, and I had no worse suspicions.

My aunt rubbed her nose sometimes when she happened to be alone with me, and said she couldn't make it out; she wished they were happier; she didn't think our military friend (so she always called the Old Soldier) mended the matter at all. My aunt further expressed her opinion, "that if our military friend would cut off those butterflies, and give 'em to the chimney-sweepers for May Day, it would look like the beginning of something sensible on her part."

But her abiding reliance was on Mr. Dick. That man had evidently an idea in his head, she said; and if he could only once pen it up into a corner, which was his great difficulty, he would distinguish himself in some extraordinary manner.

Unconscious of this prediction, Mr. Dick continued to occupy precisely the same ground in reference to the Doctor and to Mrs. Strong. He seemed neither to advance nor to recede. He appeared to have settled into his original foundation, like a building; and I must confess that my faith in his ever moving, was not much greater than if he had been a building.

But one night, when I had been married some months, Mr. Dick put his head into the parlour, where I was writing alone (Dora having gone out with my aunt to take tea with the two little birds), and said, with a significant cough:

"You couldn't speak to me without inconveniencing yourself, Trotwood, I am afraid?"

"Certainly, Mr. Dick," said I; "come in!"

"Trotwood," said Mr. Dick, laying his finger on the side of his nose, after he had shaken hands with me. "Before I sit down, I wish to make an observation. You know your aunt?"

"A little," I replied.

"She is the most wonderful woman in the world, Sir!"

After the delivery of this communication, which he shot out of himself as if he were loaded with it, Mr. Dick sat down with greater gravity than usual, and looked at me.

"Now, boy," said Mr. Dick, "I am going to put a question to you."

"As many as you please," said I.

"What do you consider me, Sir?" asked Mr. Dick, folding his arms.

"A dear old friend," said I.

"Thank you, Trotwood," returned Mr. Dick, laughing, and reaching across in high glee to shake hands with me. "But I mean, boy," resuming his gravity, "what do you consider me in this respect?" touching his forehead.

I was puzzled how to answer, but he helped me with a word.

"Weak?" said Mr. Dick.

"Well," I replied, dubiously. "Rather so."

"Exactly!" cried Mr. Dick, who seemed quite enchanted by my reply. "That is, Trotwood, when they took some of the trouble out of you-know-who's head, and put it you know where, there was a——" Mr. Dick made his two hands revolve very fast about each other a great number of times, and then brought them into collision, and rolled them over and over one another, to express confusion. "There was that sort of thing done to me somehow? Eh?"

I nodded at him, and he nodded back again.

"In short, boy," said Mr. Dick, dropping his voice to a whisper, "I am simple."

I would have qualified that conclusion, but he stopped me.

"Yes, I am! She pretends I am not. She won't hear of it; but I am. I know I am. If she hadn't stood my friend, Sir, I should have been shut up, to lead a dismal life these many years. But I'll provide for her! I never spend the copying money. I put it in a box. I have made a will. I'll leave it all to her. She shall be rich—noble!"

Mr. Dick took out his pocket-handkerchief, and wiped his eyes. He then folded it up with great care, pressed it smooth between his two hands, put it in his pocket, and seemed to put my aunt away with it.

"Now you are a scholar, Trotwood," said Mr. Dick. "You are a fine scholar. You know what a learned man, what a great man, the Doctor is. You know what honour he has always done me. Not proud in his wisdom. Humble, humble—condescending even to poor Dick, who is simple and knows nothing. I have sent his name up, on a scrap of paper, to the kite, along the string, when it has been in the sky, among the larks. The kite has been glad to receive it, Sir, and the sky has been brighter with it."

I delighted him by saying, most heartily, that the Doctor was deserving of our best respect and highest esteem.

"And his beautiful wife is a star," said Mr. Dick. "A shining star. I have seen her shine, Sir. But," bringing his chair nearer, and laying one hand upon my knee—"clouds, Sir—clouds."

I answered the solicitude which his face expressed, by conveying the same expression into my own, and shaking my head.

"What clouds?" said Mr. Dick.

He looked so wistfully into my face, and was so anxious to understand, that I took great pains to answer him slowly and distinctly, as I might have entered on an explanation to a child.

"There is some unfortunate division between them," I replied. "Some unhappy cause of separation. A secret. It may be inseparable from the discrepancy in their years. It may have grown up out of almost nothing."

Mr. Dick, who told off every sentence with a thoughtful nod, paused when I had done, and sat considering, with his eyes upon my face, and his hand upon my knee.

"Doctor not angry with her, Trotwood?" he said, after some time.

"No. Devoted to her."

"Then, I have got it, boy!" said Mr. Dick.

The sudden exultation with which he slapped me on the knee, and leaned back in his chair, with his eyebrows lifted up as high as he could possibly lift them, made me think him farther out of his wits than ever. He became as suddenly grave again, and leaning forward as before, said—first respectfully taking out his pocket-handkerchief, as if it really did represent my aunt:

"Most wonderful woman in the world, Trotwood. Why has *she* done nothing to set things right?"

"Too delicate and difficult a subject for such interference," I replied.

"Fine scholar," said Mr. Dick, touching me with his finger. "Why has *he* done nothing?"

"For the same reason," I returned.

"Then, I have got it, boy!" said Mr. Dick. And he stood up before me, more exultingly than before, nodding his head, and striking himself repeatedly upon the breast, until one might have supposed that he had nearly nodded and struck all the breath out of his body.

"A poor fellow with a craze, Sir," said Mr. Dick, "a simpleton, a weak-minded person—present company, you know!" striking himself again, "may do what wonderful people may not do. I'll bring them together, boy. I'll try. They'll not blame *me*. They'll not object to *me*. They'll not mind what *I* do, if it's wrong. I'm only Mr. Dick. And who minds Dick? Dick's nobody! Whoo!" He blew a slight, contemptuous breath, as if he blew himself away.

It was fortunate he had proceeded so far with his mystery, for we heard the coach stop at the little garden-gate, which brought my aunt and Dora home.

"Not a word, boy!" he pursued in a whisper; "leave all the blame with Dick—simple Dick—mad Dick. I have been thinking, Sir, for some time, that I was getting it, and now I have got it. After what you have said to me, I am sure I have got it. All right!"

Not another word did Mr. Dick utter on the subject; but he made a very telegraph of himself for the next half-hour (to the great disturbance of my aunt's mind), to enjoin inviolable secrecy on me.

To my surprise, I heard no more about it for some two or three weeks, though I was sufficiently interested in the result of his endeavours; descrying a strange gleam of good sense—I say nothing of good feeling, for that he always exhibited—in the conclusion to which he had come. At last I began to believe, that, in the flighty and unsettled state of his mind, he had either forgotten his intention or abandoned it.

One fair evening, when Dora was not inclined to go out, my aunt and I strolled up to the Doctor's cottage. It was autumn, when there were no debates to vex the evening air; and I remember how the leaves smelt like our garden at Blunderstone as we trod them underfoot, and how the old, unhappy feeling seemed to go by, on the sighing wind.

It was twilight when we reached the cottage. Mrs. Strong was just coming out of the garden, where Mr. Dick yet lingered, busy with his knife, helping the gardener to point some stakes. The Doctor was engaged with some one in his study; but the visitor would be gone directly, Mrs. Strong said, and begged us to remain and see him. We went into the drawing-room with her, and sat down by the darkening window. There was never any ceremony about the visits of such old friends and neighbours as we were.

We had not sat here many minutes, when Mrs. Markleham, who usually contrived to be in a fuss about something, came bustling in, with her newspaper in her hand, and said, out of breath, "My goodness gracious, Annie, why didn't you tell me there was some one in the Study!"

"My dear mama," she quietly returned, "how could I know that you desired the information!"

"Desired the information!" said Mrs. Markleham, sinking on the sofa. "I never had such a turn in all my life!"

"Have you been to the Study, then, mama?" asked Annie.

"*Been* to the Study, my dear!" she returned emphatically. "Indeed I have! I came upon the amiable creature—if you'll imagine my feelings, Miss Trotwood and David—in the act of making his will."

Her daughter looked round from the window quickly.

"In the act, my dear Annie," repeated Mrs. Markleham, spreading the newspaper on her lap like a table-cloth, and patting her hands upon it, "of making his last Will and Testament. The foresight and affection of the dear! I must tell you how it was. I really must, in justice to the darling—for he is nothing less!—tell you how it was. Perhaps you know, Miss Trotwood, that there is never a candle lighted in this house, until one's eyes are literally falling out of one's head with being stretched to read the paper. And that there is not a chair in this house, in which a paper can be what *I* call, read, except one in the Study. This took me to the Study, where I saw a light. I opened the door. In company with the dear Doctor were two professional people, evidently connected with the law, and they were all three standing at the table: the darling Doctor pen in hand. 'This simply expresses then,' said the Doctor—Annie, my love, attend to the very words—'this simply expresses then, gentlemen, the confidence I have in Mrs. Strong, and gives her all unconditionally?' One of the professional people replied, 'And gives her all unconditionally.' Upon that, with the natural feelings of a mother, I said, 'Good God, I beg your pardon!' fell over the doorstep, and came away through the little back-passage where the pantry is."

Mrs. Strong opened the window, and went out into the verandah, where she stood leaning against a pillar.

"But now isn't it, Miss Trotwood, isn't it, David, invigorating," said Mrs. Markleham, mechanically following her with her eyes, "to find a man at Doctor Strong's time of life, with the strength of mind to do this kind of thing? It only shows how right I was. I said to Annie, when Doctor Strong paid a very flattering visit to myself, and made her the subject of a declaration and an offer, I said, 'My dear, there is no doubt whatever, in my opinion, with reference to a suitable provision for you, that Doctor Strong will do more than he binds himself to do.'"

Here the bell rang, and we heard the sound of the visitors' feet as they went out.

"It's all over, no doubt," said the old Soldier, after listening; "the dear creature has signed, sealed, and delivered, and his mind's at rest. Well it may be! What a mind! Annie, my love, I am going to the Study with my paper, for I am a poor creature without news. Miss Trotwood, David, pray come and see the Doctor."

I was conscious of Mr. Dick's standing in the shadow of the room, shutting up his knife, when we accompanied her to the Study; and of my aunt's rubbing her nose violently, by the way, as a mild vent for her intolerance of our military friend; but who got first into the Study, or how Mrs. Markleham settled herself in a moment in her easy-chair, or how my aunt and I came to be left together near the door (unless her eyes were quicker than mine, and she held me back), I have forgotten, if I ever knew. But this I know,—that we saw the Doctor before he saw us, sitting at his table, among the folio volumes in which he delighted, resting his head calmly on his hand. That, in the same moment, we saw Mrs. Strong glide in, pale and trembling. That Mr. Dick supported her on his arm. That he laid his other hand upon the Doctor's arm, causing him to look up with an abstracted air. That, as the Doctor moved his head, his wife dropped down on one knee at his feet, and, with her hands imploringly lifted, fixed upon his face the memorable look I had never forgotten. That at this sight Mrs. Markleham dropped the newspaper, and stared more like a figure-head intended for a ship to be called The Astonishment, then anything else I can think of.

The gentleness of the Doctor's manner and surprise, the dignity that mingled with the supplicating attitude of his wife, the amiable concern of Mr. Dick, and the earnestness with which my aunt said to herself, "*That* man mad!" (triumphantly expressive of the misery from which she had saved him), I see and hear, rather than remember, as I write about it.

"Doctor!" said Mr. Dick. "What is it that's amiss? Look here!"

"Annie!" cried the Doctor. "Not at my feet, my dear!"

"Yes!" she said. "I beg and pray that no one will leave the room! Oh, my husband and father, break this long silence. Let us both know what it is that has come between us!"

Mrs. Markleham, by this time recovering the power of speech, and seeming to swell with family pride and motherly indignation, here exclaimed, "Annie, get up immediately, and don't disgrace everybody belonging to you by humbling yourself like that, unless you wish to see me go out of my mind on the spot!"

"Mama!" returned Annie. "Waste no words on me, for my appeal is to my husband, and even you are nothing here."

"Nothing!" exclaimed Mrs. Markleham. "Me, nothing! The child has taken leave of her senses. Please to get me a glass of water!"

I was too attentive to the Doctor and his wife, to give any heed to this request; and it made no impression on anybody else; so Mrs. Markleham panted, stared, and fanned herself.

"Annie!" said the Doctor, tenderly taking her in his hands. "My dear! If any unavoidable change has come, in the sequence of time, upon our married life, you are not to blame. The fault is mine, and only mine. There is no change in my affection, admiration, and respect. I wish to make you happy. I truly love and honour you. Rise, Annie, pray!"

But she did not rise. After looking at him for a little while, she sank down closer to him, laid her arm across his knee, and dropping her head upon it, said:

"If I have any friend here, who can speak one word for me, or for my husband, in this matter; if I have any friend here, who can give a voice to any suspicion that my heart has sometimes whispered to me; if I have any friend here, who honours my husband, or has ever cared for me, and has anything within his knowledge, no matter what it is, that

may help to mediate between us,—I implore that friend to speak!"

There was a profound silence. After a few moments of painful hesitation, I broke the silence.

"Mrs. Strong," I said, "there is something within my knowledge, which I have been earnestly entreated by Doctor Strong to conceal, and have concealed until to-night. But, I believe the time has come when it would be mistaken faith and delicacy to conceal it any longer, and when your appeal absolves me from this injunction."

She turned her face towards me for a moment, and I knew that I was right. I could not have resisted its entreaty, if the assurance that it gave me had been less convincing.

"Our future peace," she said, "may be in your hands. I trust it confidently to your not suppressing anything. I know beforehand that nothing you, or anyone, can tell me, will show my husband's noble heart in any other light than one. Howsoever it may seem to you to touch me, disregard that. I will speak for myself, before him, and before God afterwards."

Thus earnestly besought, I made no reference to the Doctor for his permission, but, without any other compromise of the truth than a little softening of the coarseness of Uriah Heep, related plainly what had passed in that same room that night. The staring of Mrs. Markleham during the whole narration, and the shrill, sharp interjections with which she occasionally interrupted it, defy description.

When I had finished, Annie remained, for some few moments, silent, with her head bent down, as I have described. Then, she took the Doctor's hand (he was sitting in the same attitude as when we had entered the room), and pressed it to her breast, and kissed it. Mr. Dick softly raised her; and she stood, when she began to speak, leaning on him, and looking down upon her husband—from whom she never turned her eyes.

"All that has ever been in my mind, since I was married," she said, in a low, submissive, tender voice, "I will lay bare before you. I could not live and have one reservation, knowing what I know now."

"Nay, Annie," said the Doctor, mildly, "I have never doubted you, my child. There is no need; indeed there is no need, my dear."

"There is great need," she answered, in the same way, "that I should open my whole heart before the soul of generosity and truth, whom, year by year, and day by day, I have loved and venerated more and more, as Heaven knows!"

"Really," interrupted Mrs. Markleham, "if I have any discretion at all——"

("Which you haven't, you Marplot," observed my aunt, in an indignant whisper.)

—"I must be permitted to observe that it cannot be requisite to enter into these details."

"No one but my husband can judge of that, mama," said Annie, without removing her eyes from his face, "and he will hear me. If I say anything to give you pain, mama, forgive me. I have borne pain first, often and long, myself."

"Upon my word!" gasped Mrs. Markleham.

"When I was very young," said Annie, "quite a little child, my first associations with knowledge of any kind were inseparable from a patient friend and teacher—the friend of my dead father—who was always dear to me. I can remember nothing that I know, without remembering him. He stored my mind with its first treasures, and stamped his character upon them all. They never could have been, I think, as good as they have been to me, if I had taken them from any other hands."

"Makes her mother nothing!" exclaimed Mrs. Markleham.

"Not so, mama," said Annie; "but I make him what he was. I must do that. As I grew up, he occupied the same place still. I was proud of his interest: deeply, fondly, gratefully attached to him. I looked up to him I can hardly describe how—as a father, as a guide, as one whose praise was different from all other praise, as one in whom I could have trusted and confided, if I had doubted all the world. You know, mama, how young and inexperienced I was, when you presented him before me, of a sudden, as a lover."

"I have mentioned the fact, fifty times at least, to everybody here!" said Mrs. Markleham.

("Then hold your tongue, for the Lord's sake, and don't mention it any more!" muttered my aunt.)

"It was so great a change: so great a loss, I felt it at first," said Annie, still preserving the same look and tone, "that I was agitated and distressed. I was but a girl; and when so great a change came in the character in which I had so long looked up to him, I think I was sorry. But nothing could have made him what he used to be again; and I was proud that he should think me so worthy, and we were married."

"—At Saint Alphage, Canterbury," observed Mrs. Markleham.

("Confound the woman!" said my aunt, "she won't be quiet!")

"I never thought," proceeded Annie, with a heightened colour, "of any worldly gain that my husband would bring to me. My young heart had no room in its homage for any such poor reference. Mama, forgive me when I say that it was you who first presented to my mind the thought that anyone could wrong me, and wrong him, by such a cruel suspicion."

"Me!" cried Mrs. Markleham.

("Ah! You, to be sure!" observed my aunt, "and you can't fan it away, my military friend!")

"It was the first unhappiness of my new life," said Annie. "It was the first occasion of every unhappy moment I have known. Those moments have been more, of late, than I can count; but not—my generous husband!—not for the reason you suppose; for in my heart there is not a thought, a recollection, or a hope, that any power could separate from you!"

She raised her eyes, and clasped her hands, and looked as beautiful and true, I thought, as any Spirit. The Doctor looked on her, henceforth, as steadfastly as she on him.

"Mama is blameless," she went on, "of having ever urged you for herself, and she is blameless in intention every way, I am sure,—but when I saw how many importunate claims were pressed upon you in my name; how you were traded on in my name; how generous you were, and how Mr. Wickfield, who had your welfare very much at heart, resented it; the first sense of my exposure to the mean suspicion that my tenderness was bought—and sold to you, of all men, on earth—fell upon me, like unmerited disgrace, in which I forced you to participate. I cannot

tell you what it was—mama cannot imagine what it was—to have this dread and trouble always on my mind, yet know in my own soul that on my marriage-day I crowned the love and honour of my life!"

"A specimen of the thanks one gets," cried Mrs. Markleham, in tears, "for taking care of one's family! I wish I was a Turk!"

("I wish you were, with all my heart—and in your native country!" said my aunt.)

"It was at that time that mama was most solicitous about my cousin Maldon. I had liked him:" she spoke softly, but without any hesitation: "very much. We had been little lovers once. If circumstances had not happened otherwise, I might have come to persuade myself that I really loved him, and might have married him, and been most wretched. There can be no disparity in marriage like unsuitability of mind and purpose."

I pondered on those words, even while I was studiously attending to what followed, as if they had some particular interest, or some strange application that I could not divine. "There can be no disparity in marriage like unsuitability of mind and purpose"—"no disparity in marriage like unsuitability of mind and purpose."

"There is nothing," said Annie, "that we have in common. I have long found that there is nothing. If I were thankful to my husband for no more, instead of for so much, I should be thankful to him for having saved me from the first mistaken impulse of my undisciplined heart."

She stood quite still, before the Doctor, and spoke with an earnestness that thrilled me. Yet her voice was just as quiet as before.

"When he was waiting to be the object of your munificence, so freely bestowed for my sake, and when I was unhappy in the mercenary shape I was made to wear, I thought it would have become him better to have worked his own way on. I thought that if I had been he, I would have tried to do it, at the cost of almost any hardship. But I thought no worse of him, until the night of his departure for India. That night I knew he had a false and thankless heart. I saw a double meaning, then, in Mr. Wickfield's scrutiny of me. I perceived, for the first time, the dark suspicion that shadowed my life."

"Suspicion, Annie!" said the Doctor. "No, no, no!"

"In your mind there was none, I know, my husband!" she returned. "And when I came to you, that night, to lay down all my load of shame and grief, and knew that I had to tell, that, underneath your roof, one of my own kindred, to whom you had been a benefactor, for the love of me, had spoken to me words that should have found no utterance, even if I had been the weak and mercenary wretch he thought me—my mind revolted from the taint the very tale conveyed. It died upon my lips, and from that hour till now has never passed them."

Mrs. Markleham, with a short groan, leaned back in her easy-chair; and retired behind her fan, as if she were never coming out any more.

"I have never, but in your presence, interchanged a word with him from that time; then, only when it has been necessary for the avoidance of this explanation. Years have passed since he knew, from me, what his situation here was. The kindnesses you have secretly done for his advancement, and then disclosed to me, for my surprise and pleasure, have been, you will believe, but aggravations of the unhappiness and burden of my secret."

She sank down gently at the Doctor's feet, though he did his utmost to prevent her; and said, looking up, tearfully, into his face:

"Do not speak to me yet! Let me say a little more! Right or wrong, if this were to be done again, I think I should do just the same. You never can know what it was to be devoted to you, with those old associations; to find that anyone could be so hard as to suppose that the truth of my heart was bartered away, and to be surrounded by appearances confirming that belief. I was very young, and had no adviser. Between mama and me, in all relating to you, there was a wide division. If I shrank into myself, hiding the disrespect I had undergone, it was because I honoured you so much, and so much wished that you should honour me!"

"Annie, my pure heart!" said the Doctor, "my dear girl!"

"A little more! a very few words more! I used to think there were so many whom you might have married, who would not have brought such charge and trouble on you, and who would have made your home a worthier home. I used to be afraid that I had better have remained your pupil, and almost your child. I used to fear that I was so unsuited to your learning and wisdom. If all this made me shrink within myself (as indeed it did), when I had that to tell, it was still because I honoured you so much, and hoped that you might one day honour me."

"That day has shone this long time, Annie," said the Doctor, "and can have but one long night, my dear."

"Another word! I afterwards meant—steadfastly meant, and purposed to myself—to bear the whole weight of knowing the unworthiness of one to whom you had been so good. And now a last word, dearest and best of friends! The cause of the late change in you, which I have seen with so much pain and sorrow, and have sometimes referred to my old apprehension—at other times to lingering suppositions nearer to the truth—has been made clear to-night; and by an accident I have also come to know, to-night, the full measure of your noble trust in me, even under that mistake. I do not hope that any love and duty I may render in return, will ever make me worthy of your priceless confidence; but with all this knowledge fresh upon me, I can lift my eyes to this dear face, revered as a father's, loved as a husband's, sacred to me in my childhood as a friend's, and solemnly declare that in my lightest thought I had never wronged you; never wavered in the love and the fidelity I owe you!"

She had her arms around the Doctor's neck, and he leant his head down over her, mingling his grey hair with her dark brown tresses.

"Oh, hold me to your heart, my husband! Never cast me out! Do not think or speak of disparity between us, for there is none, except in all my many imperfections. Every succeeding year I have known this better, as I have esteemed you more and more. Oh, take me to your heart, my husband, for my love was founded on a rock, and it endures!"

In the silence that ensued, my aunt walked gravely up to Mr. Dick, without at all hurrying herself, and gave him a hug and a sounding kiss. And it was very fortunate, with a view to his credit, that she did so; for I am confident that I detected him at that moment in the act of making preparations to stand on one leg, as an appropriate expression of delight.

"You are a very remarkable man, Dick!" said my aunt, with an air of unqualified approbation; "and never pretend to be anything else, for I know better!"

With that, my aunt pulled him by the sleeve, and nodded to me; and we three stole quietly out of the room, and came away.

"That's a settler for our military friend, at any rate," said my aunt, on the way home. "I should sleep the better for that, if there was nothing else to be glad of!"

"She was quite overcome, I am afraid," said Mr. Dick, with great commiseration.

"What? Did you ever see a crocodile overcome?" inquired my aunt.

"I don't think I ever saw a crocodile," returned Mr. Dick, mildly.

"There never would have been anything the matter, if it hadn't been for that old Animal," said my aunt, with strong emphasis. "It's very much to be wished that some mothers would leave their daughters alone after marriage, and not be so violently affectionate. They seem to think the only return that can be made them for bringing an unfortunate young woman into the world—God bless my soul, as if she asked to be brought, or wanted to come!—is full liberty to worry her out of it again. What are you thinking of, Trot?"

I was thinking of all that had been said. My mind was still running on some of the expressions used. "There can be no disparity in marriage like unsuitability of mind and purpose." "The first mistaken impulse of an undisciplined heart." "My love was founded on a rock." But we were at home; and the trodden leaves were lying underfoot, and the autumn wind was blowing.

CHAPTER XLVI.

INTELLIGENCE.

I MUST have been married, if I may trust to my imperfect memory for dates, about a year or so, when one evening, as I was returning from a solitary walk, thinking of the book I was then writing—for my success had steadily increased with my steady application, and I was engaged at that time upon my first work of fiction—I came past Mrs. Steerforth's house. I had often passed it before, during my residence in that neighbourhood, though never when I could choose another road. Howbeit, it did sometimes happen that it was not easy to find another, without making a long circuit; and so I had passed that way, upon the whole, pretty often.

I had never done more than glance at the house, as I went by with a quickened step. It had been uniformly gloomy and dull. None of the best rooms abutted on the road; and the narrow, heavily-framed old-fashioned windows, never cheerful under any circumstances, looked very dismal, close shut, and with their blinds always drawn down. There was a covered way across a little paved court, to an entrance that was never used; and there was one round staircase window, at odds with all the rest, and the only one unshaded by a blind, which had the same unoccupied blank look. I do not remember that I ever saw a light in all the house. If I had been a casual passer-by, I should have probably supposed that some childless person lay dead in it. If I had happily possessed no knowledge of the place, and had seen it often in that changeless state, I should have pleased my fancy with many ingenious speculations, I dare say.

As it was, I thought as little of it as I might. But my mind could not go by it and leave it, as my body did; and it usually awakened a long train of meditations. Coming before me, on this particular evening that I mention, mingled with the childish recollections and later fancies, the ghosts of half-formed hopes, the broken shadows of disappointments dimly seen and understood, the blending of experience and imagination, incidental to the occupation with which my thoughts had been busy, it was more than commonly suggestive. I fell into a brown study as I walked on, and a voice at my side made me start.

It was a woman's voice, too. I was not long in recollecting Mrs. Steerforth's little parlour-maid, who had formerly worn blue ribbons in her cap. She had taken them out now, to adapt herself, I suppose, to the altered character of the house; and wore but one or two disconsolate bows of sober brown.

"If you please, Sir, would you have the goodness to walk in, and speak to Miss Dartle?"

"Has Miss Dartle sent you for me?" I inquired.

"Not to-night, Sir, but it's just the same. Miss Dartle saw you pass a night or two ago; and I was to sit at work on the staircase, and when I saw you pass again, to ask you to step in and speak to her."

I turned back, and inquired of my conductor, as we went along, how Mrs. Steerforth was. She said her lady was but poorly, and kept her own room a good deal.

When we arrived at the house, I was directed to Miss Dartle in the garden, and left to make my presence known to her myself. She was sitting on a seat at one end of a kind of terrace, overlooking the great city. It was a sombre evening, with a lurid light in the sky; and as I saw the prospect scowling in the distance, with here and there some larger object starting up into the sullen glare, I fancied it was no inapt companion to the memory of this fierce woman.

She saw me as I advanced, and rose for a moment to receive me. I thought her, then, still more colourless and thin than when I had seen her last; the flashing eyes still brighter, and the scar still plainer.

Our meeting was not cordial. We had parted angrily on the last occasion; and there was an air of disdain about her, which she took no pains to conceal.

"I am told you wish to speak to me, Miss Dartle;" said I, standing near her, with my hand upon the back of the seat, and declining her gesture of invitation to sit down.

"If you please," said she. "Pray has this girl been found?"

"No."

"And yet she has run away!"

I saw her thin lips working while she looked at me, as if they were eager to load her with reproaches.

"Run away?" I repeated.

"Yes! From him," she said, with a laugh. "If she is not found, perhaps she never will be found. She may be dead!"

The vaunting cruelty with which she met my glance, I never saw expressed in any other face that ever I have seen.

"To wish her dead," said I, "may be the kindest wish that one of her own sex could bestow upon her. I am glad that time has softened you so much, Miss Dartle."

She condescended to make no reply, but, turning on me with another scornful laugh, said:

"The friends of this excellent and much-injured young lady are friends of yours. You are their champion, and assert their rights. Do you wish to know what is known of her?"

"Yes," said I.

She rose with an ill-favoured smile, and taking a few steps towards a wall of holly that was near at hand, dividing the lawn from a kitchen-garden, said, in a louder voice, "Come here!"—as if she were calling to some unclean beast.

"You will restrain any demonstrative championship or vengeance in this place, of course, Mr. Copperfield?" said she, looking over her shoulder at me with the same expression.

I inclined my head, without knowing what she meant; and she said, "Come here!" again; and returned, followed by the respectable Mr. Littimer, who, with undiminished respectability, made me a bow, and took up his position behind her. The air of wicked grace: of triumph, in which, strange to say, there was yet something feminine and alluring: with which she reclined upon the seat between us, and looked at me, was worthy of a cruel princess in a legend.

"Now," said she, imperiously, without glancing at him, and touching the old wound as it throbbed: perhaps, in this instance, with pleasure rather than pain. "Tell Mr. Copperfield about the flight."

"Mr. James and myself, ma'am——"

"Don't address yourself to me!" she interrupted with a frown.

"Mr. James and myself, Sir——"

"Nor to me, if you please," said I.

Mr. Littimer, without being at all discomposed, signified by a slight obeisance, that anything that was most agreeable to us was most agreeable to him; and began again:

"Mr. James and myself have been abroad with the young woman, ever since she left Yarmouth under Mr. James's protection. We have been in a variety of places, and seen a deal of foreign country. We have been in France, Switzerland, Italy—in fact, almost all parts."

He looked at the back of the seat; as if he were addressing himself to that; and softly played upon it with his hands, as if he were striking chords upon a dumb piano.

"Mr. James took uncommonly to the young woman; and was more settled, for a length of time, than I have known him to be since I have been in his service. The young woman was very improvable, and spoke the languages; and wouldn't have been known for the same country-person. I noticed that she was much admired wherever we went."

Miss Dartle put her hand upon her side. I saw him steal a glance at her, and slightly smile to himself.

"Very much admired, indeed, the young woman was. What with her dress; what with the air and sun; what with being made so much of; what with this, that, and the other; her merits really attracted general notice."

He made a short pause. Her eyes wandered restlessly over the distant prospect, and she bit her nether lip to stop that busy mouth.

Taking his hands from the seat, and placing one of them within the other, as he settled himself on one leg, Mr. Littimer proceeded, with his eyes cast down, and his respectable head a little advanced, and a little on one side:

"The young woman went on in this manner for some time, being occasionally low in her spirits, until I think she began to weary Mr. James by giving way to her low spirits and tempers of that kind; and things were not so comfortable. Mr. James he began to be restless again. The more restless he got, the worse she got; and I must say, for myself, that I had a very difficult time of it indeed between the two. Still matters were patched up here, and made good there, over and over again; and altogether lasted, I am sure, for a longer time than anybody could have expected."

Recalling her eyes from the distance, she looked at me again now, with her former air. Mr. Littimer, clearing his throat behind his hand with a respectable short cough, changed legs, and went on:

"At last, when there had been, upon the whole, a good many words and reproaches, Mr. James he set off one morning, from the neighbourhood of Naples, where we had a villa (the young woman being very partial to the sea), and, under pretence of coming back in a day or so, left it in charge with me to break it out, that, for the general happiness of all concerned, he was"—here an interruption of the short cough—"gone. But Mr. James, I must say, certainly did behave extremely honourable; for he proposed that the young woman should marry a very respectable person, who was fully prepared to overlook the past, and who was, at least, as good as anybody the young woman could have aspired to in a regular way: her connexions being very common."

He changed legs again, and wetted his lips. I was convinced that the scoundrel spoke of himself, and I saw my conviction reflected in Miss Dartle's face.

"This I also had it in charge to communicate. I was willing to do anything to relieve Mr. James from his difficulty, and to restore harmony between himself and an affectionate parent, who has undergone so much on his account. Therefore I undertook the commission. The young woman's violence when she came to, after I broke the fact of his departure, was beyond all expectations. She was quite mad, and had to be held by force; or, if she couldn't have got to a knife, or got to the sea, she'd have beaten her head against the marble floor."

Miss Dartle, leaning back upon the seat, with a light of exultation in her face, seemed almost to caress the sounds this fellow had uttered.

"But when I came to the second part of what had been entrusted to me," said Mr. Littimer, rubbing his hands, uneasily, "which anybody might have supposed would have been, at all events, appreciated as a kind intention, then the young woman came out in her true colours. A more outrageous person I never did see. Her conduct was surprisingly bad. She had no more gratitude, no more feeling, no more patience, no more reason in her, than a stock or a stone. If I hadn't been upon my guard, I am convinced she would have had my blood."

"I think the better of her for it," said I, indignantly.

Mr. Littimer bent his head, as much as to say, "Indeed, Sir? But you're young!" and resumed his narrative.

"It was necessary, in short, for a time, to take away everything nigh her, that she could do herself, or anybody else, an injury with, and to shut her up close. Notwithstanding which, she got out in the night; forced the lattice of a window, that I had nailed up myself; dropped on a vine that was trailed below; and never has been seen or heard of, to my knowledge, since."

"She is dead, perhaps," said Miss Dartle, with a smile, as if she could have spurned the body of the ruined girl.

"She may have drowned herself, miss," returned Mr. Littimer, catching at an excuse for addressing himself to somebody. "It's very possible. Or, she may have had assistance from the boatmen, and the boatmen's wives and children. Being given to low company, she was very much in the habit of talking to them on the beach, Miss Dartle, and sitting by their boats. I have known her do it, when Mr. James has been away, whole days. Mr. James was far from pleased to find out, once, that she had told the children she was a boatman's daughter, and that in her own country, long ago, she had roamed about the beach like them."

Oh, Emily! Unhappy beauty! What a picture rose before me of her sitting on the far-off shore, among the children like herself when she was innocent, listening to little voices such as might have called her Mother had she been a poor man's wife; and to the great voice of the sea, with its eternal "Never more!"

"When it was clear that nothing could be done, Miss Dartle——"

"Did I tell you not to speak to me?" she said, with stern contempt.

"You spoke to me, miss," he replied. "I beg your pardon. But it is my service to obey."

"Do your service," she returned. "Finish your story, and go!"

"When it was clear," he said, with infinite respectability, and an obedient bow, "that she was not to be found, I went to Mr. James, at the place where it had been agreed that I should write to him, and informed him of what had occurred. Words passed between us in consequence, and I felt it due to my character to leave him. I could bear, and I have borne, a great deal from Mr. James; but he insulted me too far. He hurt me. Knowing the unfortunate difference between himself and his mother, and what her anxiety of mind was likely to be, I took the liberty of coming home to England, and relating——"

"For money which I paid him," said Miss Dartle to me.

"Just so, ma'am—and relating what I knew. I am not aware," said Mr. Littimer, after a moment's reflection, "that there is anything else. I am at present out of employment, and should be happy to meet with a respectable situation."

Miss Dartle glanced at me, as though she would inquire if there were anything that I desired to ask. As there was something which had occurred to my mind, I said in reply:

"I could wish to know from this—creature," I could not bring myself to utter any more conciliatory word, "whether they intercepted a letter that was written to her from home, or whether he supposes that she received it."

He remained calm and silent, with his eyes fixed on the ground, and the tip of every finger of his right hand delicately poised against the tip of every finger of his left.

Miss Dartle turned her head disdainfully towards him.

"I beg your pardon, miss," he said, awakening from his abstraction, "but, however submissive to you, I have my position, though a servant. Mr. Copperfield and you, miss, are different people. If Mr. Copperfield wishes to know anything from me, I take the liberty of reminding Mr. Copperfield that he can put a question to me. I have a character to maintain."

After a momentary struggle with myself, I turned my eyes upon him, and said, "You have heard my question. Consider it addressed to yourself, if you choose. What answer do you make?"

"Sir," he rejoined, with an occasional separation and reunion of those delicate tips, "my answer must be qualified; because, to betray Mr. James's confidence to his mother, and to betray it to you, are two different actions. It is not probable, I consider, that Mr. James would encourage the receipt of letters likely to increase low spirits and unpleasantness; but further than that, Sir, I should wish to avoid going."

"Is that all?" inquired Miss Dartle of me.

I indicated that I had nothing more to say. "Except," I added, as I saw him moving off, "that I understand this fellow's part in the wicked story, and that, as I shall make it known to the honest man who has been her father from her childhood, I would recommend him to avoid going too much into public."

He had stopped the moment I began, and had listened with his usual repose of manner.

"Thank you, Sir. But you'll excuse me if I say, Sir, that there are neither slaves nor slave-drivers in this country, and that people are not allowed to take the law into their own hands. If they do, it is more to their own peril, I believe, than to other people's. Consequently speaking, I am not at all afraid of going wherever I may wish, Sir."

With that, he made a polite bow; and, with another to Miss Dartle, went away through the arch in the wall of holly by which he had come. Miss Dartle and I regarded each other for a little while in silence; her manner being exactly what it was, when she had produced the man.

"He says besides," she observed, with a slow curling of her lip, "that his master, as he hears, is coasting Spain; and this done, is away to gratify his seafaring tastes till he is weary. But that is of no interest to you. Between these two proud persons, mother and son, there is a wider breach than before, and little hope of its healing, for they are one at heart, and time makes each more obstinate and imperious. Neither is this of any interest to you; but it introduces what I wish to say. This devil whom you make an angel of, I mean this low girl whom he picked out of the tide-mud," with her black eyes full upon me, and her passionate finger up, "may be alive,—for I believe some common things are hard to die. If she is, you will desire to have a pearl of such price found and taken care of. We desire that, too; that he may not by any chance be made her prey again. So far, we are united in one interest; and that is why I, who would do her any mischief that so coarse a wretch is capable of feeling, have sent for you to hear what you have heard."

I saw, by the change of her face, that some one was advancing behind me. It was Mrs. Steerforth, who gave me her hand more coldly than of yore, and with an augmentation of her former stateliness of manner; but still, I perceived—and I was touched by it—with an ineffaceable remembrance of my old love for her son. She was greatly altered. Her fine figure was far less upright, her handsome face was deeply marked, and her hair was almost white. But when she sat down on the seat, she was a handsome lady still; and well I knew the bright eye with its lofty look, that had been a light in my very dreams at school.

"Is Mr. Copperfield informed of everything, Rosa?"

"Yes."

"And has he heard Littimer himself?"

"Yes; I have told him why you wished it."

"You are a good girl. I have had some slight correspondence with your former friend, Sir," addressing me, "but it has not restored his sense of duty or natural obliga-

tion. Therefore I have no other object in this, than what Rosa has mentioned. If, by the course which may relieve the mind of the decent man you brought here (for whom I am sorry—I can say no more), my son may be saved from again falling into the snares of a designing enemy, well!"

She drew herself up, and sat looking straight before her, far away.

"Madam," I said respectfully, "I understand. I assure you I am in no danger of putting any strained construction on your motives. But I must say, even to you, having known this injured family from childhood, that if you suppose the girl, so deeply wronged, has not been cruelly deluded, and would not rather die a hundred deaths than take a cup of water from your son's hand now, you cherish a terrible mistake."

"Well, Rosa, well!" said Mrs. Steerforth, as the other was about to interpose, "it is no matter. Let it be. You are married, Sir, I am told?"

I answered that I had been some time married.

"And are doing well? I hear little in the quiet life I lead, but I understand you are beginning to be famous."

"I have been very fortunate," I said, "and find my name connected with some praise."

"You have no mother?"—in a softened voice.

"No."

"It is a pity," she returned. "She would have been proud of you. Good night!"

I took the hand she held out with a dignified, unbending air, and it was as calm in mine as if her breast had been at peace. Her pride could still its very pulses, it appeared, and draw the placid veil before her face, through which she sat looking straight before her on the far distance.

As I moved away from them along the terrace, I could not help observing how steadily they both sat gazing on the prospect, and how it thickened and closed around them. Here and there, some early lamps were seen to twinkle in the distant city; and in the eastern quarter of the sky the lurid light still hovered. But, from the greater part of the broad valley interposed, a mist was rising like a sea, which, mingling with the darkness, made it seem as if the gathering waters would encompass them. I have reason to remember this, and think of it with awe; for before I looked upon those two again, a stormy sea had risen to their feet.

Reflecting on what had been thus told me, I felt it right that it should be communicated to Mr. Peggotty. On the following evening I went into London in quest of him. He was always wandering about from place to place, with his one object of recovering his niece before him; but was more in London than elsewhere. Often and often, now, had I seen him in the dead of night passing along the streets, searching, among the few who loitered out of doors at those untimely hours, for what he dreaded to find.

He kept a lodging over the little chandler's shop in Hungerford Market, which I have had occasion to mention more than once, and from which he first went forth upon his errand of mercy. Hither I directed my walk. On making inquiry for him, I learned from the people of the house that he had not gone out yet, and I should find him in his room up-stairs.

He was sitting reading by a window in which he kept a few plants. The room was very neat and orderly. I saw in a moment that it was always kept prepared for her reception, and that he never went out but he thought it possible he might bring her home. He had not heard my tap at the door, and only raised his eyes when I laid my hand upon his shoulder.

"Mas'r Davy! Thank'ee, Sir! thank'ee hearty, for this visit! Sit ye down. You're kindly welcome, Sir!"

"Mr. Peggotty," said I, taking the chair he handed me, "don't expect much! I have heard some news."

"Of Em'ly!"

He put his hand, in a nervous manner, on his mouth, and turned pale, as he fixed his eyes on mine.

"It gives no clue to where she is; but she is not with him."

He sat down, looking intently at me, and listened in profound silence to all I had to tell. I well remember the sense of dignity, beauty even, with which the patient gravity of his face impressed me, when, having gradually removed his eyes from mine, he sat looking downward, leaning his forehead on his hand. He offered no interruption, but remained throughout perfectly still. He seemed to pursue her figure through the narrative, and to let every other shape go by him, as if it were nothing.

When I had done, he shaded his face, and continued silent. I looked out of the window for a little while, and occupied myself with the plants.

"How do you fare to feel about it, Mas'r Davy?" he inquired at length.

"I think that she is living," I replied.

"I doen't know. Maybe the first shock was too rough, and in the wildness of her 'art——! That there blue water as she used to speak on. Could she have thowt o' that so many year, because it was to be her grave!"

He said this, musing, in a low, frightened voice; and walked across the little room.

"And yet," he added, "Mas'r Davy, I have felt so sure as she was living—I know'd, awake and sleeping, as it was so trew that I should find her—I have been so led on by it, and held up by it—that I doen't believe I can have been deceived. No! Em'ly's alive!"

He put his hand down firmly on the table, and set his sunburnt face into a resolute expression.

"My niece, Em'ly, is alive, Sir!" he said steadfastly. "I doen't know wheer it comes from, or how 'tis, but *I am told* as she's alive!"

He looked almost like a man inspired, as he said it. I waited for a few moments, until he could give me his undivided attention; and then proceeded to explain the precaution, that, it had occurred to me last night, it would be wise to take.

"Now, my dear friend——" I began.

"Thank'ee, thank'ee, kind Sir," he said, grasping my hand in both of his.

"If she should make her way to London, which is likely —for where could she lose herself so readily as in this vast city; and what would she wish to do, but lose and hide herself, if she does not go home?——"

"And she won't go home," he interposed, shaking his head mournfully. "If she had left of her own accord, she might; not as 'twas, Sir."

"If she should come here," said I, "I believe there is one person, here, more likely to discover her than any other in the world. Do you remember—hear what I say, with fortitude—think of your great object!—do you remember Martha?"

"Of our town?"

I needed no other answer than his face.

"Do you know that she is in London?"

"I have seen her in the streets," he answered with a shiver.

"But you don't know," said I, "that Emily was charitable to her, with Ham's help, long before she fled from home. Nor, that, when we met one night, and spoke together in the room yonder, over the way, she listened at the door."

"Mas'r Davy?" he replied in astonishment. "That night when it snew so hard?"

"That night. I have never seen her since. I went back, after parting from you, to speak to her, but she was gone. I was unwilling to mention her to you then, and I am now; but she is the person of whom I speak, and with whom I think we should communicate. Do you understand?"

"Too well, Sir," he replied. We had sunk our voices, almost to a whisper, and continued to speak in that tone.

"You say you have seen her. Do you think that you could find her? I could only hope to do so by chance."

"I think, Mas'r Davy, I know wheer to look."

"It is dark. Being together, shall we go out now, and try to find her to-night?"

He assented, and prepared to accompany me. Without appearing to observe what he was doing, I saw how carefully he adjusted the little room, put a candle ready and the means of lighting it, arranged the bed, and finally took out of a drawer one of her dresses (I remembered to have seen her wear it), neatly folded with some other garments, and a bonnet, which he placed upon a chair. He made no allusion to these clothes, neither did I. There they had been waiting for her, many and many a night, no doubt.

"The time was, Mas'r Davy," he said, as we came down stairs, "when I thowt this girl, Martha, a'most like the dirt underneath my Em'ly's feet. God forgive me, there's a difference now!"

As we went along, partly to hold him in conversation, and partly to satisfy myself, I asked him about Ham. He said, almost in the same words as formerly, that Ham was just the same, "wearing away his life with kiender no care nohow for't; but never murmuring, and liked by all."

I asked him what he thought Ham's state of mind was, in reference to the cause of their misfortunes? Whether he believed it was dangerous? What he supposed, for example, Ham would do, if he and Steerforth ever should encounter?

"I doen't know, Sir," he replied. "I have thowt of it oftentimes, but I can't arrize myself of it, no matters."

I recalled to his remembrance the morning after her departure, when we were all three on the beach. "Do you recollect," said I, "a certain wild way in which he looked out to sea, and spoke about 'the end of it?'"

"Sure I do!" said he.

"What do you suppose he meant?"

"Mas'r Davy," he replied, "I've put the question to myself a mort o' times, and never found no answer. And theer's one curous thing—that, though he is so pleasant, I wouldn't fare to feel comfortable to try and get his mind upon't. He never said a wured to me as warn't as dootiful as dootiful could be, and it ain't likely as he'd begin to speak any other ways now; but it's fur from being fleet water in his mind, where them thowts lay. It's deep, Sir, and I can't see down."

"You are right," said I, "and that has sometimes made me anxious."

"And me too, Mas'r Davy," he rejoined. "Even more so, I do assure you, than his ventersome ways, though both belongs to the alteration in him. I doen't know as he'd do violence under any circumstances, but I hope as them two may be kep asunders."

We had come, through Temple Bar, into the City. Conversing no more now, and walking at my side, he yielded himself up to the one aim of his devoted life, and went on, with that hushed concentration of his faculties which would have made his figure solitary in a multitude. We were not far from Blackfriars Bridge, when he turned his head and pointed to a solitary female figure flitting along the opposite side of the street. I knew it, readily, to be the figure that we sought.

We crossed the road, and were pressing on towards her, when it occurred to me that she might be more disposed to feel a woman's interest in the lost girl, if we spoke to her in a quieter place, aloof from the crowd, and where we should be less observed. I advised my companion, therefore, that we should not address her yet, but follow her; consulting in this, likewise, an indistinct desire I had, to know where she went.

He acquiescing, we followed at a distance: never losing sight of her, but never caring to come very near, as she frequently looked about. Once she stopped to listen to a band of music; and then we stopped too.

She went on a long way. Still we went on. It was evident, from the manner in which she held her course, that she was going to some fixed destination; and this, and her keeping in the busy streets, and I suppose the strange fascination in the secrecy and mystery of so following anyone, made me adhere to my first purpose. At length she turned into a dull, dark street, where the noise and crowd were lost; and I said, "We may speak to her now;" and, mending our pace, we went after her.

CHAPTER XLVII.

MARTHA.

WE were now down in Westminster. We had turned back to follow her, having encountered her coming towards us; and Westminster Abbey was the point at which she passed from the lights and noise of the leading streets. She proceeded so quickly, when she got free of the two currents of passengers setting towards and from the bridge, that, between this and the advance she had of us when she struck off, we were in the narrow water-side street by Millbank before we came up with her. At that moment she crossed the road, as if to avoid the footsteps that she heard so close behind; and, without looking back, passed on even more rapidly.

A glimpse of the river through a dull gateway, where some waggons were housed for the night, seemed to arrest my feet. I touched my companion without speaking, and we both forbore to cross after her, and both followed on that opposite side of the way; keeping as quietly as we could in the shadow of the houses, but keeping very near her.

There was, and is when I write, at the end of that low-lying street, a dilapidated little wooden building, probably an obsolete old ferry-house. Its position is just at that point where the street ceases, and the road begins to lie between a row of houses and the river. As soon as she came here, and saw the water, she stopped as if she had

come to her destination; and presently went slowly along by the brink of the river, looking intently at it.

All the way here, I had supposed that she was going to some house; indeed, I had vaguely entertained the hope that the house might be in some way associated with the lost girl. But that one dark glimpse of the river, through the gateway, had instinctively prepared me for her going no farther.

The neighbourhood was a dreary one at that time; as oppressive, sad, and solitary by night, as any about London. There were neither wharves nor houses on the melancholy waste of road near the great blank prison. A sluggish ditch deposited its mud at the prison walls. Coarse grass and rank weeds straggled over all the marshy land in the vicinity. In one part, carcases of houses, inauspiciously begun and never finished, rotted away. In another, the ground was cumbered with rusty iron monsters of steam-boilers, wheels, cranks, pipes, furnaces, paddles, anchors, diving-bells, windmill-sails, and I know not what strange objects, accumulated by some speculator, and grovelling in the dust, underneath which—having sunk into the soil of their own weight in wet weather—they had the appearance of vainly trying to hide themselves. The clash and glare of sundry fiery Works upon the river-side, arose by night to disturb everything except the heavy and unbroken smoke that poured out of their chimneys. Slimy gaps and causeways, winding among old wooden piles, with a sickly substance clinging to the latter, like green hair, and the rags of last year's handbills offering rewards for drowned men fluttering above high-water-mark, led down through the ooze and slush to the ebb-tide. There was a story that one of the pits dug for the dead in the time of the Great Plague was hereabout; and a blighting influence seemed to have proceeded from it over the whole place. Or else it looked as if it had gradually decomposed into that nightmare condition, out of the overflowings of the polluted stream.

As if she were a part of the refuse it had cast out, and left to corruption and decay, the girl we had followed strayed down to the river's brink, and stood in the midst of this night-picture, lonely and still, looking at the water.

There were some boats and barges astrand in the mud, and these enabled us to come within a few yards of her without being seen. I then signed to Mr. Peggotty to remain where he was, and emerged from their shade to speak to her. I did not approach her solitary figure without trembling; for this gloomy end to her determined walk, and the way in which she stood, almost within the cavernous shadow of the iron bridge, looking at the lights crookedly reflected in the strong tide, inspired a dread within me.

I think she was talking to herself. I am sure, although absorbed in gazing at the water, that her shawl was off her shoulders, and that she was muffling her hands in it, in an unsettled and bewildered way, more like the action of a sleep-walker than a waking person. I know, and never can forget, that there was that in her wild manner which gave me no assurance but that she would sink before my eyes, until I had her arm within my grasp.

At the same moment I said "Martha!"

She uttered a terrified scream, and struggled with me with such strength that I doubt if I could have held her alone. But a stronger hand than mine was laid upon her; and when she raised her frightened eyes and saw whose it was, she made but one more effort and dropped down between us. We carried her away from the water to where there were some dry stones, and there laid her down, crying and moaning. In a little while she sat among the stones, holding her wretched head with both her hands.

"Oh, the river!" she cried passionately. "Oh, the river!"

"Hush, hush!" said I. "Calm yourself."

But she still repeated the same words, continually exclaiming, "Oh, the river!" over and over again.

"I know it's like me!" she exclaimed. "I know that I belong to it. I know that it's the natural company of such as I am! It comes from country places, where there was once no harm in it—and it creeps through the dismal streets, defiled and miserable—and it goes away, like my life, to a great sea, that is always troubled—and I feel that I must go with it!"

I have never known what despair was, except in the tone of those words.

"I can't keep away from it. I can't forget it. It haunts me day and night. It's the only thing in all the world that I am fit for, or that's fit for me. Oh, the dreadful river!"

The thought passed through my mind that in the face of my companion, as he looked upon her without speech or motion, I might have read his niece's history, if I had known nothing of it. I never saw, in any painting or reality, horror and compassion so impressively blended. He shook as if he would have fallen; and his hand—I touched it with my own, for his appearance alarmed me—was deadly cold.

"She is in a state of frenzy," I whispered to him. "She will speak differently in a little time."

I don't know what he would have said in answer. He made some motion with his mouth, and seemed to think he had spoken; but he had only pointed to her with his outstretched hand.

A new burst of crying came upon her now, in which she once more hid her face among the stones, and lay before us, a prostrate image of humiliation and ruin. Knowing that this state must pass, before we could speak to her with any hope, I ventured to restrain him when he would have raised her, and we stood by in silence until she became more tranquil.

"Martha," said I then, leaning down, and helping her to rise—she seemed to want to rise as if with the intention of going away, but she was weak, and leaned against a boat. "Do you know who this is, who is with me?"

She said faintly, "Yes."

"Do you know that we have followed you a long way to-night?"

She shook her head. She looked neither at him nor at me, but stood in a humble attitude, holding her bonnet and shawl in one hand, without appearing conscious of them, and pressing the other, clenched, against her forehead.

"Are you composed enough," said I, "to speak on the subject which so interested you—I hope Heaven may remember it!—that snowy night?"

Her sobs broke out afresh, and she murmured some inarticulate thanks to me for not having driven her away from the door.

"I want to say nothing for myself," she said, after a few moments. "I am bad, I am lost. I have no hope at all. But tell him, Sir," she had shrunk away from him, "if you don't feel too hard to me to do it, that I never was in any way the cause of his misfortune."

"It has never been attributed to you," I returned, earnestly responding to her earnestness.

"It was you, if I don't deceive myself," she said, in a broken voice, "that came into the kitchen, the night she took such pity on me; was so gentle to me; didn't shrink away from me like all the rest, and gave me such kind help! Was it you, Sir?"

"It was," said I.

"I should have been in the river long ago," she said, glancing at it with a terrible expression, "if any wrong to her had been upon my mind. I never could have kept out of it a single winter's night, if I had not been free of any share in that!"

"The cause of her flight is too well understood," I said. "You are innocent of any part in it, we thoroughly believe,—we know."

"Oh, I might have been much the better for her, if I had had a better heart!" exclaimed the girl, with most forlorn regret; "for she was always good to me! She never spoke a word to me but what was pleasant and right. Is it likely I would try to make her what I am myself, knowing what I am myself so well! When I lost everything that makes life dear, the worst of all my thoughts was that I was parted for ever from her!"

Mr. Peggotty, standing with one hand on the gunwale of the boat, and his eyes cast down, put his disengaged hand before his face.

"And when I heard what had happened before that snowy night, from some belonging to our town," cried Martha, "the bitterest thought in all my mind was, that the people would remember she once kept company with me, and would say I had corrupted her! When, Heaven knows, I would have died to have brought back her good name!"

Long unused to any self-control, the piercing agony of her remorse and grief was terrible.

"To have died, would not have been much—what can I say?—I would have lived!" she cried. "I would have lived to be old, in the wretched streets—and to wander about, avoided, in the dark—and to see the day break on the ghastly line of houses, and remember how the same sun used to shine into my room, and wake me once—I would have done even that to save her!"

Sinking on the stones, she took some in each hand, and clenched them up, as if she would have ground them. She writhed into some new posture constantly: stiffening her arms, twisting them before her face, as though to shut out from her eyes the little light there was, and drooping her head, as if it were heavy with insupportable recollections.

"What shall I ever do!" she said, fighting thus with her despair. "How can I go on as I am, a solitary curse to myself, a living disgrace to everyone I come near!" Suddenly she turned to my companion. "Stamp upon me, kill me! When she was your pride, you would have thought I had done her harm if I had brushed against her in the street. You can't believe—why should you?—a syllable that comes out of my lips. It would be a burning shame upon you, even now, if she and I exchanged a word. I don't complain. I don't say she and I are alike. I know there is a long, long way between us. I only say, with all my guilt and wretchedness upon my head, that I am grateful to her from my soul, and love her. Oh don't think that all the power I had of loving anything is quite worn out! Throw me away, as all the world does. Kill me for being what I am, and having ever known her; but don't think that of me!"

He looked upon her, while she made this supplication in a wild distracted manner; and, when she was silent, gently raised her.

"Martha," said Mr. Peggotty, "God forbid as I should judge you. Forbid as I, of all men, should do that, my girl! You don't know half the change that's come, in course of time, upon me, when you think it likely. Well!" he paused a moment, then went on. "You don't understand how 'tis that this here gentleman and me has wished to speak to you. You don't understand what 'tis he has afore us. Listen now!"

His influence upon her was complete. She stood, shrinkingly, before him, as if she were afraid to meet his eyes; but her passionate sorrow was quite hushed and mute.

"If you heerd," said Mr. Peggotty, "owt of what passed between Mas'r Davy and me, th' night when it snew so hard, you know as I have been—wheer not—fur to seek my dear niece. My dear niece," he repeated steadily. "Fur she's more dear to me now, Martha, than ever she was dear afore."

She put her hands before her face; but otherwise remained quiet.

"I have heerd her tell," said Mr. Peggotty, "as you was early left fatherless and motherless, with no friend fur to take, in a rough seafaring way, their place. Maybe you can guess that if you'd had such a friend, you'd have got into a way of being fond of him in course of time, and that my niece was kiender daughter-like to me."

As she was silently trembling, he put her shawl carefully about her, taking it up from the ground for that purpose.

"Whereby," said he, "I know, both as she would go to the wureld's furdest end with me, if she could once see me again; and that she would fly to the wureld's furdest end to keep off seeing me. For though she ain't no call to doubt my love, and doen't—and doen't," he repeated, with a quiet assurance of the truth of what he said, "there's shame steps in, and keeps betwixt us."

I read, in every word of his plain impressive way of delivering himself, new evidence of his having thought of this one topic, in every feature it presented.

"According to our reckoning," he proceeded, "Mas'r Davy's here, and mine, she is like, one day, to make her own poor solitary course to London. We believe—Mas'r Davy, me, and all of us—that you are as innocent of everything that has befel her, as the unborn child. You've spoke of her being pleasant, kind, and gentle to you. Bless her, I knew she was! I knew she always was, to all. You're thankful to her, and you love her. Help us all you can to find her, and may Heaven reward you!"

She looked at him hastily, and for the first time, as if she were doubtful of what he had said.

"Will you trust me?" she asked, in a low voice of astonishment.

"Full and free!" said Mr. Peggotty.

"To speak to her, if I should ever find her; shelter her, if I have any shelter to divide with her; and then, without her knowledge, come to you, and bring you to her?" she asked hurriedly.

We both replied together, "Yes!"

She lifted up her eyes, and solemnly declared that she would devote herself to this task, fervently and faithfully. That she would never waver in it, never be diverted from it, never relinquish it, while there was any chance of hope. If she were not true to it, might the object she now had in life, which bound her to something devoid of evil, in its passing away from her, leave her more forlorn and more despairing, if that were possible, than she had been upon the river's brink that night; and then might all help, human and Divine, renounce her evermore!

She did not raise her voice above her breath, or address us, but said this to the night sky; then stood profoundly quiet, looking at the gloomy water.

We judged it expedient, now, to tell her all we knew; which I recounted at length. She listened with great attention, and with a face that often changed, but had the same purpose in all its varying expressions. Her eyes occasionally filled with tears, but those she repressed. It seemed as if her spirit were quite altered, and she could not be too quiet.

She asked, when all was told, where we were to be communicated with, if occasion should arise. Under a dull lamp in the road, I wrote our two addresses on a leaf of my pocket-book, which I tore out and gave to her, and which she put in her poor bosom. I asked her where she lived herself. She said, after a pause, in no place long. It were better not to know.

Mr. Peggotty suggesting to me, in a whisper, what had already occurred to myself, I took out my purse; but I could not prevail upon her to accept any money, nor could I exact any promise from her that she would do so at another time. I represented to her that Mr. Peggotty could not be called, for one in his condition, poor; and that the idea of her engaging in this search, while depending on her own resources, shocked us both. She continued steadfast. In this particular, his influence upon her was equally powerless with mine. She gratefully thanked him, but remained inexorable.

"There may be work to be got," she said. "I'll try."

"At least take some assistance," I returned, "until you have tried."

"I could not do what I have promised, for money," she replied. "I could not take it, if I was starving. To give me money would be to take away your trust, to take away the object that you have given me, to take away the only certain thing that saves me from the river."

"In the name of the great Judge," said I, "before whom you and all of us must stand at His dread time, dismiss that terrible idea! We can all do some good, if we will."

She trembled, and her lip shook, and her face was paler, as she answered:

"It has been put in your hearts, perhaps, to save a wretched creature for repentance. I am afraid to think so; it seems too bold. If any good should come of me, I might begin to hope; for nothing but harm has ever come of my deeds yet. I am to be trusted, for the first time in a long while, with my miserable life, on account of what you have given me to try for. I know no more, and I can say no more."

Again she repressed the tears that had begun to flow; and, putting out her trembling hand, and touching Mr. Peggotty, as if there were some healing virtue in him, went away along the desolate road. She had been ill, probably for a long time. I observed, upon that closer opportunity of observation, that she was worn and haggard, and that her sunken eyes expressed privation and endurance.

We followed her at a short distance, our way lying in the same direction, until we came back into the lighted and populous streets. I had such implicit confidence in her declaration, that I then put it to Mr. Peggotty, whether it would not seem, in the onset, like distrusting her, to follow her any further. He being of the same mind, and equally reliant on her, we suffered her to take her own road, and took ours, which was towards Highgate. He accompanied me a good part of the way; and when we parted, with a prayer for the success of this fresh effort, there was a new and thoughtful compassion in him that I was at no loss to interpret.

It was midnight when I arrived at home. I had reached my own gate, and was standing listening for the deep bell of Saint Paul's, the sound of which I thought had been borne towards me among the multitude of striking clocks, when I was rather surprised to see that the door of my aunt's cottage was open, and that a faint light in the entry was shining out across the road.

Thinking that my aunt might have relapsed into one of her old alarms, and might be watching the progress of some imaginary conflagration in the distance, I went to speak to her. It was with very great surprise that I saw a man standing in her little garden.

He had a glass and bottle in his hand, and was in the act of drinking. I stopped short, among the thick foliage outside, for the moon was up now, though obscured; and I recognised the man whom I had once supposed to be a delusion of Mr. Dick's, and had once encountered with my aunt in the streets of the City.

He was eating as well as drinking, and seemed to eat with a hungry appetite. He seemed curious regarding the cottage, too, as if it were the first time he had seen it. After stooping to put the bottle on the ground, he looked up at the windows, and looked about; though with a covert and impatient air, as if he was anxious to be gone.

The light in the passage was obscured for a moment, and my aunt came out. She was agitated, and told some money into his hand. I heard it chink.

"What's the use of this?" he demanded.

"I can spare no more," returned my aunt.

"Then I can't go," said he. "Here! You may take it back!"

"You bad man," returned my aunt, with great emotion; "how can you use me so? But why do I ask? It is because you know how weak I am! What have I to do, to free myself for ever of your visits, but to abandon you to your deserts?"

"And why don't you abandon me to my deserts?" said he.

"*You* ask me why!" returned my aunt. "What a heart you must have!"

He stood moodily rattling the money, and shaking his head, until at length he said:

"Is this all you mean to give me, then?"

"It is all I *can* give you," said my aunt. "You know I have had losses, and am poorer than I used to be. I have told you so. Having got it, why do you give me the pain of looking at you for another moment, and seeing what you have become?"

"I have become shabby enough, if you mean that," he said. "I lead the life of an owl."

"You stripped me of the greater part of all I ever had," said my aunt. "You closed my heart against the whole world, years and years. You treated me falsely, ungratefully, and cruelly. Go, and repent of it. Don't add new injuries to the long, long list of injuries you have done me!"

"Ay!" he returned. "It's all very fine!—Well! I must do the best I can, for the present, I suppose."

In spite of himself, he appeared abashed by my aunt's indignant tears, and came slouching out of the garden. Taking two or three quick steps, as if I had just come up,

I met him at the gate, and went in as he came out. We eyed one another narrowly in passing, and with no favour.

"Aunt," said I, hurriedly. "This man alarming you again! Let me speak to him. Who is he?"

"Child," returned my aunt, taking my arm, "come in, and don't speak to me for ten minutes."

We sat down in her little parlour. My aunt retired behind the round green fan of former days, which was screwed on the back of a chair, and occasionally wiped her eyes, for about a quarter of an hour. Then she came out, and took a seat beside me.

"Trot," said my aunt, calmly, "it's my husband."

"Your husband, aunt? I thought he had been dead!"

"Dead to me," returned my aunt, "but living."

I sat in silent amazement.

"Betsey Trotwood don't look a likely subject for the tender passion," said my aunt, composedly, "but the time was, Trot, when she believed in that man most entirely. When she loved him, Trot, right well. When there was no proof of attachment and affection that she would not have given him. He repaid her by breaking her fortune, and nearly breaking her heart. So she put all that sort of sentiment, once and for ever, in a grave, and filled it up, and flattened it down."

"My dear, good aunt!"

"I left him," my aunt proceeded, laying her hand as usual on the back of mine, "generously. I may say at this distance of time, Trot, that I left him generously. He had been so cruel to me, that I might have effected a separation on easy terms for myself; but I did not. He soon made ducks and drakes of what I gave him, sank lower and lower, married another woman, I believe, became an adventurer, a gambler, and a cheat. What he is now, you see. But he was a fine-looking man when I married him," said my aunt, with an echo of her old pride and admiration in her tone; "and I believed him—I was a fool!—to be the soul of honour!"

She gave my hand a squeeze, and shook her head.

"He is nothing to me now, Trot,—less than nothing. But, sooner than have him punished for his offences (as he would be if he prowled about in this country), I give him more money than I can afford, at intervals when he reappears, to go away. I was a fool when I married him; and I am so far an incurable fool on that subject, that, for the sake of what I once believed him to be, I wouldn't have even this shadow of my idle fancy hardly dealt with. For I was in earnest, Trot, if ever a woman was."

My aunt dismissed the matter with a heavy sigh, and smoothed her dress.

"There, my dear!" she said. "Now, you know the beginning, middle, and end, and all about it. We won't mention the subject to one another any more; neither, of course, will you mention it to anybody else. This is my grumpy, frumpy story, and we'll keep it to ourselves, Trot!"

CHAPTER XLVIII.

DOMESTIC.

I LABOURED hard at my book, without allowing it to interfere with the punctual discharge of my newspaper duties; and it came out and was very successful. I was not stunned by the praise which sounded in my ears, notwithstanding that I was keenly alive to it, and thought better of my own performance, I have little doubt, than anybody else did. It has always been in my observation of human nature, that a man who has any good reason to believe in himself never flourishes himself before the faces of other people in order that they may believe in him. For this reason, I retained my modesty in very self-respect; and the more praise I got, the more I tried to deserve.

It is not my purpose, in this record, though in all other essentials it is my written memory, to pursue the history of my own fictions. They express themselves, and I leave them to themselves. When I refer to them, incidentally, it is only as a part of my progress.

Having some foundation for believing, by this time, that nature and accident had made me an author, I pursued my vocation with confidence. Without such assurance I should certainly have left it alone, and bestowed my energy on some other endeavour. I should have tried to find out what nature and accident really had made me, and to be that, and nothing else.

I had been writing, in the newspaper and elsewhere, so prosperously, that when my new success was achieved, I considered myself reasonably entitled to escape from the dreary debates. One joyful night, therefore, I noted down the music of the parliamentary bagpipes for the last time, and I have never heard it since; though I still recognise the old drone in the newspapers, without any substantial variation (except, perhaps, that there is more of it) all the livelong session.

I now write of the time when I had been married, I suppose, about a year and a half. After several varieties of experiment, we had given up the housekeeping as a bad job. The house kept itself, and we kept a page. The principal function of this retainer was to quarrel with the cook; in which respect he was a perfect Whittington, without his cat, or the remotest chance of being made Lord Mayor.

He appears to me to have lived in a hail of saucepan-lids. His whole existence was a scuffle. He would shriek for help on the most improper occasions,—as, when we had a little dinner-party, or a few friends in the evening,—and would come tumbling out of the kitchen, with iron missiles flying after him. We wanted to get rid of him, but he was very much attached to us, and wouldn't go. He was a tearful boy, and broke into such deplorable lamentations, when a cessation of our connexion was hinted at, that we were obliged to keep him. He had no mother—no anything in the way of a relative, that I could discover, except a sister, who fled to America the moment we had taken him off her hands; and he became quartered on us like a horrible young changeling. He had a lively perception of his own unfortunate state, and was always rubbing his eyes with the sleeve of his jacket, or stooping to blow his nose on the extreme corner of a little pocket-handkerchief, which he never *would* take completely out of his pocket, but always economised and secreted.

This unlucky page, engaged in an evil hour, at six pounds ten per annum, was a source of continual trouble to me. I watched him as he grew—and he grew like scarlet beans—with painful apprehensions of the time when he would begin to shave; even of the days when he would be bald or grey. I saw no prospect of ever getting rid of him; and, projecting myself into the future, used to think what an inconvenience he would be when he was an old man.

I never expected anything less, than this unfortunate's manner of getting me out of my difficulty. He stole Dora's watch, which, like everything else belonging to us, had no particular place of its own; and, converting it into money, spent the produce (he was always a weak-minded boy) in incessantly riding up and down between London and Uxbridge outside the coach. He was taken to Bow Street, as well as I remember, on the completion of his fifteenth journey; when four-and-sixpence, and a second-hand fife which he couldn't play, were found upon his person.

The surprise and its consequences would have been much less disagreeable to me if he had not been penitent. But he was very penitent indeed, and in a peculiar way—not in the lump, but by instalments. For example; the day after that on which I was obliged to appear against him, he made certain revelations touching a hamper in the cellar, which we believed to be full of wine, but which had nothing in it except bottles and corks. We supposed he had now eased his mind, and told the worst he knew of the cook; but, a day or two afterwards, his conscience sustained a new twinge, and he disclosed how she had a little girl, who, early every morning, took away our bread; and also how he himself had been suborned to maintain the milkman in coals. In two or three days more, I was informed by the authorities of his having led to the discovery of sirloins of beef among the kitchen-stuff, and sheets in the rag-bag. A little while afterwards, he broke out in an entirely new direction, and confessed to a knowledge of burglarious intentions as to our premises, on the part of the pot-boy, who was immediately taken up. I got to be so ashamed of being such a victim, that I would have given him any money to hold his tongue, or would have offered a round bribe for his being permitted to run away. It was an aggravating circumstance in the case that he had no idea of this, but conceived that he was making me amends in every new discovery: not to say, heaping obligations on my head.

At last I ran away myself, whenever I saw an emissary of the police approaching with some new intelligence; and lived a stealthy life until he was tried and ordered to be transported. Even then he couldn't be quiet, but was always writing us letters; and wanted so much to see Dora before he went away, that Dora went to visit him, and fainted when she found herself inside the iron bars. In short, I had no peace of my life until he was expatriated, and made (as I afterwards heard) a shepherd of, "up the country" somewhere; I have no geographical idea where.

All this led me into some serious reflections, and presented our mistakes in a new aspect; as I could not help communicating to Dora one evening, in spite of my tenderness for her.

"My love," said I, "it is very painful to me to think that our want of system and management, involves not only ourselves (which we have got used to), but other people."

"You have been silent for a long time, and now you are going to be cross!" said Dora.

"No, my dear, indeed! Let me explain to you what I mean."

"I think I don't want to know," said Dora.

"But I want you to know, my love. Put Jip down."

Dora put his nose to mine, and said "Boh!" to drive my seriousness away; but, not succeeding, ordered him into his pagoda, and sat looking at me, with her hands folded, and a most resigned little expression of countenance.

"The fact is, my dear," I began, "there is contagion in us. We infect everyone about us."

I might have gone on in this figurative manner, if Dora's face had not admonished me that she was wondering with all her might whether I was going to propose any new kind of vaccination, or other medical remedy, for this unwholesome state of ours. Therefore I checked myself, and made my meaning plainer.

"It is not merely, my pet," said I, "that we lose money and comfort, and even temper sometimes, by not learning to be more careful; but that we incur the serious responsibility of spoiling everyone who comes into our service, or has any dealings with us. I begin to be afraid that the fault is not entirely on one side, but that these people all turn out ill because we don't turn out very well ourselves."

"Oh, what an accusation," exclaimed Dora, opening her eyes wide; "to say that you ever saw me take gold watches! Oh!"

"My dearest," I remonstrated, "don't talk preposterous nonsense! Who has made the least allusion to gold watches?"

"You did," returned Dora. "You know you did. You said I hadn't turned out well, and compared me to him."

"To whom?" I asked.

"To the page," sobbed Dora. "Oh, you cruel fellow, to compare your affectionate wife to a transported page! Why didn't you tell me your opinion of me before we were married? Why didn't you say, you hard-hearted thing, that you were convinced I was worse than a transported page? Oh, what a dreadful opinion to have of me! Oh, my goodness!"

"Now, Dora, my love," I returned, gently trying to remove the handkerchief she pressed to her eyes, "this is not only very ridiculous of you, but very wrong. In the first place, it's not true."

"You always said he was a story-teller," sobbed Dora. "And now you say the same of me! Oh, what shall I do! What shall I do!"

"My darling girl," I retorted, "I really must entreat you to be reasonable, and listen to what I did say, and do say. My dear Dora, unless we learn to do our duty to those whom we employ, they will never learn to do their duty to us. I am afraid we present opportunities to people to do wrong, that never ought to be presented. Even if we were as lax as we are, in all our arrangements, by choice—which we are not—even if we liked it, and found it agreeable to be so—which we don't—I am persuaded we should have no right to go on in this way. We are positively corrupting people. We are bound to think of that. I can't help thinking of it, Dora. It is a reflection I am unable to dismiss, and it sometimes makes me very uneasy. There, dear, that's all. Come now! Don't be foolish!"

Dora would not allow me, for a long time, to remove the handkerchief. She sat sobbing and murmuring behind it, that, if I was uneasy, why had I ever been married? Why hadn't I said, even the day before we went to church, that I knew I should be uneasy, and I would rather not? If I couldn't bear her, why didn't I send her away to her aunts at Putney, or to Julia Mills in India? Julia would be glad to see her, and would not call her a transported page; Julia never had called her anything of the sort. In short, Dora was so afflicted, and so afflicted me by being in that condition, that I felt it was of no use repeating this kind of effort, though never so mildly, and I must take some other course.

What other course was left to take? To "form her mind?" This was a common phrase of words which had a fair and promising sound, and I resolved to form Dora's mind.

I began immediately. When Dora was very childish,

and I would have infinitely preferred to humour her, I tried to be grave—and disconcerted her, and myself too. I talked to her on the subjects which occupied my thoughts; and I read Shakespeare to her—and fatigued her to the last degree. I accustomed myself to giving her, as it were quite casually, little scraps of useful information, or sound opinion—and she started from them when I let them off, as if they had been crackers. No matter how incidentally or naturally I endeavoured to form my little wife's mind, I could not help seeing that she always had an instinctive perception of what I was about, and became a prey to the keenest apprehension. In particular, it was clear to me, that she thought Shakespeare a terrible fellow. The formation went on very slowly.

I pressed Traddles into the service without his knowledge; and whenever he came to see us, exploded my mines upon him for the edification of Dora at second hand. The amount of practical wisdom I bestowed upon Traddles in this manner was immense, and of the best quality; but it had no other effect upon Dora than to depress her spirits, and make her always nervous with the dread that it would be her turn next. I found myself in the condition of a schoolmaster, a trap, a pitfall; of always playing spider to Dora's fly, and always pouncing out of my hole to her infinite disturbance.

Still, looking forward through this intermediate stage, to the time when there should be a perfect sympathy between Dora and me, and when I should have "formed her mind" to my entire satisfaction, I persevered, even for months. Finding at last, however, that, although I had been all this time a very porcupine or hedgehog, bristling all over with determination, I had effected nothing, it began to occur to me that perhaps Dora's mind was already formed.

On farther consideration this appeared so likely, that I abandoned my scheme, which had had a more promising appearance in words than in action; resolving henceforth to be satisfied with my child-wife, and to try to change her into nothing else by any process. I was heartily tired of being sagacious and prudent by myself, and of seeing my darling under restraint; so, I bought a pretty pair of ear-rings for her, and a collar for Jip, and went home one day to make myself agreeable.

Dora was delighted with the little presents, and kissed me joyfully; but, there was a shadow between us, however slight, and I had made up my mind that it should not be there. If there must be such a shadow anywhere, I would keep it for the future in my own breast.

I sat down by my wife on the sofa, and put the ear-rings in her ears; and then I told her that I feared we had not been quite as good company lately, as we used to be, and that the fault was mine. Which I sincerely felt, and which indeed it was.

"The truth is, Dora, my life," I said; "I have been trying to be wise."

"And to make me wise too," said Dora, timidly. "Haven't you, Doady?"

I nodded assent to the pretty inquiry of the raised eyebrows, and kissed the parted lips.

"It's of not a bit of use," said Dora, shaking her head, until the ear-rings rang again. "You know what a little thing I am, and what I wanted you to call me from the first. If you can't do so, I am afraid you'll never like me. Are you sure you don't think, sometimes, it would have been better to have——"

"Done what, my dear?" For she made no effort to proceed.

743

"Nothing!" said Dora.

"Nothing?" I repeated.

She put her arms round my neck, and laughed, and called herself by her favourite name of a goose, and hid her face on my shoulder in such a profusion of curls that it was quite a task to clear them away and see it.

"Don't I think it would have been better to have done nothing, than to have tried to form my little wife's mind?" said I, laughing at myself. "Is that the question? Yes, indeed, I do."

"Is that what you have been trying?" cried Dora. "Oh, what a shocking boy!"

"But I shall never try any more," said I. "For I love her dearly as she is."

"Without a story—really?" inquired Dora, creeping closer to me.

"Why should I seek to change," said I, "what has been so precious to me for so long? You never can show better than as your own natural self, my sweet Dora; and we'll try no conceited experiments, but go back to our old way, and be happy."

"And be happy!" returned Dora. "Yes! All day! And you won't mind things going a tiny morsel wrong, sometimes?"

"No, no," said I. "We must do the best we can."

"And you won't tell me, any more, that we make other people bad," coaxed Dora; "will you? Because you know it's so dreadfully cross."

"No, no," said I.

"It's better for me to be stupid than uncomfortable, isn't it?" said Dora.

"Better to be naturally Dora than anything else in the world."

"In the world! Ah, Doady, it's a large place!"

She shook her head, turned her delighted bright eyes up to mine, kissed me, broke into a merry laugh, and sprang away to put on Jip's new collar.

So ended my last attempt to make any change in Dora. I had been unhappy in trying it; I could not endure my own solitary wisdom; I could not reconcile it with her former appeal to me as my child-wife. I resolved to do what I could, in a quiet way, to improve our proceedings myself; but, I foresaw that my utmost would be very little, or I must degenerate into the spider again, and be for ever lying in wait.

And the shadow I have mentioned, that was not to be between us any more, but was to rest wholly on my own heart? How did that fall?

The old unhappy feeling pervaded my life. It was deepened, if it were changed at all; but it was as undefined as ever, and addressed me like a strain of sorrowful music faintly heard in the night. I loved my wife dearly, and I was happy; but the happiness I had vaguely anticipated, once, was not the happiness I enjoyed, and there was always something wanting.

In fulfilment of the compact I have made with myself, to reflect my mind on this paper, I again examine it, closely, and bring its secrets to the light. What I missed, I still regarded—I always regarded—as something that had been a dream of my youthful fancy; that was incapable of realisation; that I was now discovering to be so, with some natural pain, as all men did. But, that it would have been better for me if my wife could have helped me more, and shared the many thoughts in which I had no partner; and that this might have been; I knew.

Between these two irreconcilable conclusions: the one, that what I felt was general and unavoidable; the other, that it was particular to me, and might have been different: I balanced curiously, with no distinct sense of their opposition to each other. When I thought of the airy dreams of youth that are incapable of realisation, I thought of the better state preceding manhood that I had outgrown; and then the contented days with Agnes, in the dear old house, arose before me, like spectres of the dead, that might have some renewal in another world, but never, never more could be reanimated here.

Sometimes, the speculation came into my thoughts, What might have happened, or what would have happened, if Dora and I had never known each other? But, she was so incorporated with my existence, that it was the idlest of all fancies, and would soon rise out of my reach and sight, like gossamer floating in the air.

I always loved her. What I am describing, slumbered, and half awoke, and slept again, in the innermost recesses of my mind. There was no evidence of it in me; I know of no influence it had in anything I said or did. I bore the weight of all our little cares, and all my projects; Dora held the pens; and we both felt that our shares were adjusted as the case required. She was truly fond of me, and proud of me; and when Agnes wrote a few earnest words in her letters to Dora, of the pride and interest with which my old friends heard of my growing reputation, and read my book as if they heard me speaking its contents, Dora read them out to me with tears of joy in her bright eyes, and said I was a dear old clever, famous boy.

"The first mistaken impulse of an undisciplined heart." Those words of Mrs. Strong's were constantly recurring to me, at this time; were almost always present to my mind. I awoke with them, often, in the night; I remember to have even read them, in dreams, inscribed upon the walls of houses. For I knew, now, that my own heart was undisciplined when it first loved Dora; and that if it had been disciplined, it never could have felt, when we were married, what it had felt in its secret experience.

"There can be no disparity in marriage, like unsuitability of mind and purpose." Those words I remembered too. I had endeavoured to adapt Dora to myself, and found it impracticable. It remained for me to adapt myself to Dora; to share with her what I could, and be happy; to bear on my own shoulders what I must, and be happy still. This was the discipline to which I tried to bring my heart, when I began to think. It made my second year much happier than my first; and, what was better still, made Dora's life all sunshine.

But, as that year wore on, Dora was not strong. I had hoped that lighter hands than mine would help to mould her character, and that a baby-smile upon her breast might change my child-wife to a woman. It was not to be. The spirit fluttered for a moment on the threshold of its little prison, and, unconscious of captivity, took wing.

"When I can run about again, as I used to do, aunt," said Dora, "I shall make Jip race. He is getting quite slow and lazy."

"I suspect, my dear," said my aunt, quietly working by her side, "he has a worse disorder than that. Age, Dora."

"Do you think he is old?" said Dora, astonished. "Oh, how strange it seems that Jip should be old!"

"It's a complaint we are all liable to, Little One, as we get on in life," said my aunt, cheerfully; "I don't feel more free from it than I used to be, I assure you."

"But Jip," said Dora, looking at him with compassion, "even little Jip! Oh, poor fellow!"

"I dare say he'll last a long time yet, Blossom," said my aunt, patting Dora on the cheek, as she leaned out of her couch to look at Jip, who responded by standing on his hind-legs, and baulking himself in various asthmatic attempts to scramble up by the head and shoulders. "He must have a piece of flannel in his house this winter, and I shouldn't wonder if he came out quite fresh again, with the flowers in the spring. Bless the little dog!" exclaimed my aunt, "if he had as many lives as a cat, and was on the point of losing 'em all, he'd bark at me with his last breath, I believe!"

Dora had helped him up on the sofa; where he really was defying my aunt to such a furious extent, that he couldn't keep straight, but barked himself sideways. The more my aunt looked at him, the more he reproached her; for, she had lately taken to spectacles, and for some inscrutable reason he considered the glasses personal.

Dora made him lie down by her, with a good deal of persuasion; and when he was quiet, drew one of his long ears through and through her hand, repeating thoughtfully, "Even little Jip! Oh, poor fellow!"

"His lungs are good enough," said my aunt, gaily, "and his dislikes are not at all feeble. He has a good many years before him, no doubt. But if you want a dog to race with, Little Blossom, he has lived too well for that, and I'll give you one."

"Thank you, aunt," said Dora, faintly. "But don't, please!"

"No?" said my aunt, taking off her spectacles.

"I couldn't have any other dog but Jip," said Dora. "It would be so unkind to Jip! Besides, I couldn't be such friends with any other dog but Jip; because he wouldn't have known me before I was married, and wouldn't have barked at Doady when he first came to our house. I couldn't care for any other dog but Jip, I am afraid, aunt."

"To be sure!" said my aunt, patting her cheek again. "You are right."

"You are not offended," said Dora. "Are you?"

"Why, what a sensitive pet it is!" cried my aunt, bending over her affectionately. "To think that I could be offended!"

"No, no, I didn't really think so," returned Dora; "but I am a little tired, and it made me silly for a moment—I am always a silly little thing, you know; but it made me more silly—to talk about Jip. He has known me in all that has happened to me, haven't you, Jip? And I couldn't bear to slight him, because he was a little altered—could I, Jip?"

Jip nestled closer to his mistress, and lazily licked her hand.

"You are not so old, Jip, are you, that you'll leave your mistress yet?" said Dora. "We may keep one another company a little longer!"

My pretty Dora! When she came down to dinner on the ensuing Sunday, and was so glad to see old Traddles (who always dined with us on Sunday), we thought she would be "running about as she used to do," in a few days. But they said, wait a few days more; and then, wait a few days more; and still she neither ran nor walked. She looked very pretty, and was very merry; but the little feet that used to be so nimble when they danced round Jip, were dull and motionless.

I began to carry her downstairs every morning, and upstairs every night. She would clasp me round the neck and laugh, the while, as if I did it for a wager. Jip would bark and caper round us, and go on before, and look back on the landing, breathing short, to see that we were coming. My aunt, the best and most cheerful of nurses, would trudge after us, a moving mass of shawls and pillows. Mr. Dick would not have relinquished his post of candle-bearer to any one alive. Traddles would be often at the bottom of the staircase, looking on, and taking charge of sportive messages from Dora to the dearest girl in the world. We made quite a gay procession of it, and my child-wife was the gayest there.

But, sometimes, when I took her up, and felt that she was lighter in my arms, a dead blank feeling came upon me, as if I were approaching to some frozen region yet unseen, that numbed my life. I avoided the recognition of this feeling by any name, or by any communing with myself; until one night, when it was very strong upon me, and my aunt had left her with a parting cry of "Good night, Little Blossom," I sat down at my desk alone, and cried to think, Oh what a fatal name it was, and how the blossom withered in its bloom upon the tree!

CHAPTER XLIX.

I AM INVOLVED IN MYSTERY.

I RECEIVED one morning by the post, the following letter, dated Canterbury, and addressed to me at Doctors' Commons; which I read with some surprise:—

"MY DEAR SIR,

"Circumstances beyond my individual control have, for a considerable lapse of time, effected a severance of that intimacy which, in the limited opportunities conceded to me in the midst of my professional duties, of contemplating the scenes and events of the past, tinged by the prismatic hues of memory, has ever afforded me, as it ever must continue to afford, gratifying emotions of no common description. This fact, my dear Sir, combined with the distinguished elevation to which your talents have raised you, deters me from presuming to aspire to the liberty of addressing the companion of my youth, by the familiar appellation of Copperfield! It is sufficient to know that the name to which I do myself the honour to refer will ever be treasured among the muniments of our house (I allude to the archives connected with our former lodgers, preserved by Mrs. Micawber), with sentiments of personal esteem amounting to affection.

"It is not for one situated, through his original errors and a fortuitous combination of unpropitious events, as is the foundered Bark (if he may be allowed to assume so maritime a denomination), who now takes up the pen to address you—it is not, I repeat, for one so circumstanced, to adopt the language of compliment, or of congratulation. That, he leaves to abler and to purer hands.

"If your more important avocations should admit of your ever tracing these imperfect characters thus far—which may be, or may not be, as circumstances arise—you will naturally inquire by what object am I influenced, then, in inditing the present missive? Allow me to say that I fully defer to the reasonable character of that inquiry, and proceed to develop it; premising that it is *not* an object of a pecuniary nature.

"Without more directly referring to any latent ability that may possibly exist on my part, of wielding the thunderbolt, or directing the devouring and avenging flame in any quarter, I may be permitted to observe, in passing, that my brightest visions are for ever dispelled—that my peace is shattered and my power of enjoyment destroyed—that my heart is no longer in the right place—and that I no more walk erect before my fellow-man. The canker is in the flower. The cup is bitter to the brim. The worm is at his work, and will soon dispose of his victim. The sooner the better. But I will not digress.

"Placed in a mental position of peculiar painfulness, beyond the assuaging reach even of Mrs. Micawber's influence, though exercised in the tripartite character of woman, wife, and mother, it is my intention to fly from myself for a short period, and devote a respite of eight-and-forty hours to revisiting some metropolitan scenes of past enjoyment. Among other havens of domestic tranquillity and peace of mind, my feet will naturally tend towards the King's Bench Prison. In stating that I shall be (D.V.) on the outside of the south wall of that place of incarceration on civil process, the day after to-morrow, at seven in the evening, precisely, my object in this epistolary communication is accomplished.

"I do not feel warranted in soliciting my former friend Mr. Copperfield, or my former friend Mr. Thomas Traddles of the Inner Temple, if that gentleman is still existent and forthcoming, to condescend to meet me, and renew (so far as may be) our past relations of the olden time. I confine myself to throwing out the observation, that, at the hour and place I have indicated, may be found such ruined vestiges as yet

"Remain,
"Of
"A
"Fallen Tower,
"WILKINS MICAWBER.

"P.S. It may be advisable to superadd to the above, the statement that Mrs. Micawber is *not* in confidential possession of my intentions."

I read the letter over, several times. Making due allowance for Mr. Micawber's lofty style of composition, and for the extraordinary relish with which he sat down and wrote long letters on all possible and impossible occasions, I still believed that something important lay hidden at the bottom of this roundabout communication. I put it down, to think about it; and took it up again, to read it once more; and was still pursuing it, when Traddles found me in the height of my perplexity.

"My dear fellow, said I, "I never was better pleased to see you. You come to give me the benefit of your sober judgment at a most opportune time. I have received a very singular letter, Traddles, from Mr. Micawber."

"No?" cried Traddles. "You don't say so? And I have received one from Mrs. Micawber!"

With that, Traddles, who was flushed with walking, and whose hair, under the combined effects of exercise and excitement, stood on end as if he saw a cheerful ghost, produced his letter and made an exchange with me. I watched him into the heart of Mr. Micawber's letter, and returned the elevation of eyebrows with which he said "'Wielding the thunderbolt, or directing the devouring and avenging flame!' Bless me, Copperfield!"—and then entered on the perusal of Mrs. Micawber's epistle.

It ran thus:—

"My best regards to Mr. Thomas Traddles, and if he should still remember one who formerly had the happiness of being well acquainted with him, may I beg a few moments of his leisure time? I assure Mr. T. T. that I would not intrude upon his kindness, were I in any other position than on the confines of distraction.

"Though harrowing to myself to mention, the alienation of Mr. Micawber (formerly so domesticated) from his wife and family, is the cause of my addressing my unhappy appeal to Mr. Traddles, and soliciting his best indulgence. Mr. T. can form no adequate idea of the change in Mr. Micawber's conduct, of his wildness, of his violence. It has gradually augmented, until it assumes the appearance of aberration of intellect. Scarcely a day passes, I assure Mr. Traddles, on which some paroxysm does not take place. Mr. T. will not require me to depict my feelings, when I inform him that I have become accustomed to hear Mr. Micawber assert that he has sold himself to the D. Mystery and secrecy have long been his principal characteristic, have long replaced unlimited confidence. The slightest provocation, even being asked if there is anything he would prefer for dinner, causes him to express a wish for a separation. Last night, on being childishly solicited for two-pence, to buy 'lemon-stunners'—a local sweetmeat—he presented an oyster-knife at the twins!

"I entreat Mr. Traddles to bear with me in entering into these details. Without them, Mr. T. would indeed find it difficult to form the faintest conception of my heartrending situation.

"May I now venture to confide to Mr. T. the purport of my letter? Will he now allow me to throw myself on his friendly consideration? Oh yes, for I know his heart!

"The quick eye of affection is not easily blinded, when of the female sex. Mr. Micawber is going to London. Though he studiously concealed his hand, this morning before breakfast, in writing the direction-card which he attached to the little brown valise of happier days, the eagle-glance of matrimonial anxiety detected d, o, n, distinctly traced. The West-End destination of the coach, is the Golden Cross. Dare I fervently implore Mr. T. to see my misguided husband, and to reason with him? Dare I ask Mr. T. to endeavour to step in between Mr. Micawber and his agonised family? Oh no, for that would be too much!

"If Mr. Copperfield should yet remember one unknown to fame, will Mr. T. take charge of my unalterable regards and similar entreaties? In any case, he will have the benevolence *to consider this communication strictly private, and on no account whatever to be alluded to, however distantly, in the presence of Mr. Micawber.* If Mr. T. should ever reply to it (which I cannot but feel to be *most* improbable), a letter addressed to M. E., Post Office, Canterbury, will be fraught with less painful consequences than any addressed immediately to one who subscribes herself, in extreme distress,

"Mr. Thomas Traddles's respectful friend and suppliant,
"EMMA MICAWBER."

"What do you think of that letter?" said Traddles, casting his eyes upon me, when I had read it twice.

"What do you think of the other?" said I. For he was still reading it with knitted brows.

"I think that the two together, Copperfield," replied Traddles, "mean more than Mr. and Mrs. Micawber usually mean in their correspondence—but I don't know what. They are both written in good faith, I have no doubt, and without any collusion. Poor thing!" he was now alluding to Mrs. Micawber's letter, and we were standing side by side comparing the two; "it will be a charity to write to her, at all events, and tell her that we will not fail to see Mr. Micawber."

I acceded to this, the more readily, because I now reproached myself with having treated her former letter rather lightly. It had set me thinking a good deal at the time, as I have mentioned in its place; but my absorption in my own affairs, my experience of the family, and my hearing nothing more, had gradually ended in my dismissing the subject. I had often thought of the Micawbers, but chiefly to wonder what "pecuniary liabilities" they were establishing in Canterbury, and to recall how shy Mr. Micawber was of me when he became clerk to Uriah Heep.

However, I now wrote a comforting letter to Mrs. Micawber, in our joint names, and we both signed it. As we walked into town to post it, Traddles and I held a long conference, and launched into a number of speculations, which I need not repeat. We took my aunt into our counsels in the afternoon; but our only decided conclusion was, that we would be very punctual in keeping Mr. Micawber's appointment.

Although we appeared at the stipulated place a quarter of an hour before the time, we found Mr. Micawber already there. He was standing with his arms folded, over against the wall, looking at the spikes on the top, with a sentimental expression, as if they were the interlacing boughs of trees that had shaded him in his youth.

When we accosted him, his manner was something more confused, and something less genteel, than of yore. He had relinquished his legal suit of black for the purposes of this excursion, and wore the old surtout and tights, but not quite with the old air. He gradually picked up more and more of it as we conversed with him; but, his very eyeglass seemed to hang less easily, and his shirt-collar, though still of the old formidable dimensions, rather drooped.

"Gentlemen!" said Mr. Micawber, after the first salutations, "you are friends in need, and friends indeed. Allow me to offer my inquiries with reference to the physical welfare of Mrs. Copperfield in esse, and Mrs. Traddles in posse,—presuming, that is to say, that my friend Mr. Traddles is not yet united to the object of his affections, for weal and for woe."

We acknowledged his politeness, and made suitable replies. He then directed our attention to the wall, and was beginning, "I assure you, gentlemen," when I ventured to object to that ceremonious form of address, and to beg that he would speak to us in the old way.

"My dear Copperfield," he returned, pressing my hand, "your cordiality overpowers me. This reception of a shattered fragment of the Temple once called Man—if I may be permitted so to express myself—bespeaks a heart that is an honour to our common nature. I was about to observe that I again behold the serene spot where some of the happiest hours of my existence fleeted by."

"Made so, I am sure, by Mrs. Micawber," said I. "I hope she is well?"

"Thank you," returned Mr. Micawber, whose face clouded at this reference, "she is but so-so. And this," said Mr. Micawber, nodding his head sorrowfully, "is the Bench! Where, for the first time in many revolving years, the overwhelming pressure of pecuniary liabilities was not proclaimed, from day to day, by importunate voices declining to vacate the passage; where there was no knocker on the door for any creditor to appeal to; where personal service of process was not required, and detainers were merely lodged at the gate! Gentlemen," said Mr. Micawber, "when the shadow of that ironwork on the summit of the brick structure has been reflected on the gravel of the Parade, I have seen my children thread the mazes of the intricate pattern, avoiding the dark marks. I have been familiar with every stone in the place. If I betray weakness, you will know how to excuse me."

"We have all got on in life since then, Mr. Micawber," said I.

"Mr. Copperfield," returned Mr. Micawber, bitterly, "when I was an inmate of that retreat I could look my fellow-man in the face, and punch his head if he offended me. My fellow-man and myself are no longer on those glorious terms!"

Turning from the building in a downcast manner, Mr. Micawber accepted my proffered arm on one side, and the proffered arm of Traddles on the other, and walked away between us.

"There are some landmarks," observed Mr. Micawber, looking fondly back over his shoulder, "on the road to the tomb, which, but for the impiety of the aspiration, a man would wish never to have passed. Such is the Bench in my chequered career."

"Oh, you are in low spirits, Mr. Micawber," said Traddles.

"I am, Sir," interposed Mr. Micawber.

"I hope," said Traddles, "it is not because you have conceived a dislike to the law—for I am a lawyer myself, you know."

Mr. Micawber answered not a word.

"How is our friend Heep, Mr. Micawber?" said I, after a silence.

"My dear Copperfield," returned Mr. Micawber, bursting into a state of much excitement, and turning pale, "if you ask after my employer as your friend, I am sorry for it; if you ask after him as my friend, I sardonically smile at it. In whatever capacity you ask after my employer, I beg, without offence to you, to limit my reply to this—that whatever his state of health may be, his appearance is foxy: not to say diabolical. You will allow me, as a private individual, to decline pursuing a subject which has lashed me to the utmost verge of desperation in my professional capacity."

I expressed my regret for having innocently touched upon a theme that roused him so much. "May I ask," said I, "without any hazard of repeating the mistake, how my old friends Mr. and Miss Wickfield are?"

"Miss Wickfield," said Mr. Micawber, now turning red, "is, as she always is, a pattern, and a bright example. My dear Copperfield, she is the only starry spot in a miserable existence. My respect for that young lady, my admiration of her character, my devotion to her for her love and truth, and goodness!—Take me," said Mr. Micawber, "down a turning, for, upon my soul, in my present state of mind I am not equal to this!"

We wheeled him off into a narrow street, where he took out his pocket-handkerchief, and stood with his back to a wall. If I looked as gravely at him as Traddles did, he must have found our company by no means inspiriting.

"It is my fate," said Mr. Micawber, unfeignedly sobbing, but doing even that, with a shadow of the old expression of doing something genteel; "it is my fate, gentlemen, that the finer feelings of our nature have become reproaches to me. My homage to Miss Wickfield, is a flight of arrows in my bosom. You had better leave me, if you please, to walk the earth as a vagabond. The worm will settle *my* business in double-quick time."

Without attending to this invocation, we stood by, until he put up his pocket-handkerchief, pulled up his shirt-collar, and, to delude any person in the neighbourhood who might have been observing him, hummed a tune with his hat very much on one side. I then mentioned—not knowing what might be lost, if we lost sight of him yet—that it would give me great pleasure to introduce him to my aunt, if he would ride out to Highgate, where a bed was at his service.

"You shall make us a glass of your own punch, Mr. Micawber," said I, "and forget whatever you have on your mind, in pleasanter reminiscences."

"Or, if confiding anything to friends will be more likely to relieve you, you shall impart it to us, Mr. Micawber," said Traddles, prudently.

"Gentlemen," returned Mr. Micawber, "do with me as you will! I am a straw upon the surface of the deep, and am tossed in all directions by the elephants—I beg your pardon; I should have said the elements."

We walked on, arm-in-arm, again; found the coach in the act of starting; and arrived at Highgate without encountering any difficulties by the way. I was very uneasy and very uncertain in my mind what to say or do for the best—so was Traddles, evidently. Mr. Micawber was for the most part plunged into deep gloom. He occasionally made an attempt to smarten himself, and hum the fag-end of a tune; but his relapses into profound melancholy were only made the more impressive by the mockery of a hat exceedingly much on one side, and a shirt-collar pulled up to his eyes.

We went to my aunt's house rather than to mine, because of Dora's not being well. My aunt presented herself on being sent for, and welcomed Mr. Micawber with gracious cordiality. Mr. Micawber kissed her hand, retired to the window, and pulling out his pocket-handkerchief, had a mental wrestle with himself.

Mr. Dick was at home. He was by nature so exceedingly compassionate of anyone who seemed to be ill at ease, and was so quick to find any such person out, that he shook hands with Mr. Micawber, at least half-a-dozen times in five minutes. To Mr. Micawber, in his trouble, this warmth, on the part of a stranger, was so extremely touching, that he could only say, on the occasion of each successive shake, "My dear sir, you overpower me!" Which gratified Mr. Dick so much, that he went at it again with greater vigour than before.

"The friendliness of this gentleman," said Mr. Micawber to my aunt, "if you will allow me, ma'am, to cull a figure of speech from the vocabulary of our coarser national sports —floors me. To a man who is struggling with a complicated burden of perplexity and disquiet, such a reception is trying, I assure you."

"My friend Mr. Dick," replied my aunt, proudly, "is not a common man."

"That I am convinced of," said Mr. Micawber. "My dear Sir!" for Mr. Dick was shaking hands with him again; "I am deeply sensible of your cordiality!"

"How do you find yourself?" said Mr. Dick, with an anxious look.

"Indifferent, my dear Sir," returned Mr. Micawber, sighing.

"You must keep up your spirits," said Mr. Dick, "and make yourself as comfortable as possible."

Mr. Micawber was quite overcome by these friendly words, and by finding Mr. Dick's hand again within his own. "It has been my lot," he observed, "to meet in the diversified panorama of human existence, with an occasional oasis, but never with one so green, so gushing, as the present!"

At another time I should have been amused by this; but I felt that we were all constrained and uneasy, and I watched Mr. Micawber so anxiously, in his vacillations between an evident disposition to reveal something, and a counter-disposition to reveal nothing, that I was in a perfect fever. Traddles, sitting on the edge of his chair, with his eyes wide open, and his hair more emphatically erect than ever, stared by turns at the ground and at Mr. Micawber, without so much as attempting to put in a word. My aunt, though I saw that her shrewdest observation was concentrated on her new guest, had more useful possession of her wits than either of us; for she held him in conversation, and made it necessary for him to talk, whether he liked it or not.

"You are a very old friend of my nephew's, Mr. Micawber," said my aunt. "I wish I had had the pleasure of seeing you before."

"Madam," returned Mr. Micawber, "I wish I had had the honour of knowing you at an earlier period. I was not always the wreck you at present behold."

"I hope Mrs. Micawber and your family are well, Sir," said my aunt.

Mr. Micawber inclined his head. "They are as well, ma'am," he desperately observed, after a pause, "as Aliens and Outcasts can ever hope to be."

"Lord bless you, Sir!" exclaimed my aunt in her abrupt way. "What are you talking about?"

"The subsistence of my family, ma'am," returned Mr. Micawber, "trembles in the balance. My employer——"

Here Mr. Micawber provokingly left off; and began to peel the lemons that had been under my directions set before him, together with all the other appliances he used in making punch.

"Your employer, you know," said Mr. Dick, jogging his arm as a gentle reminder.

"My good Sir," returned Mr. Micawber, "you recall me. I am obliged to you." They shook hands again. "My employer, ma'am—Mr. Heep—once did me the favour to observe to me, that if I were not in the receipt of the stipendiary emoluments appertaining to my engagement with him, I should probably be a mountebank about the country, swallowing a sword-blade, and eating the devouring element. For anything that I can perceive to the contrary, it is still probable that my children may be reduced to seek a livelihood by personal contortion, while Mrs. Micawber abets their unnatural feats, by playing the barrel-organ."

Mr. Micawber, with a random but expressive flourish of his knife, signified that these performances might be expected to take place after he was no more; then resumed his peeling with a desperate air.

My aunt leaned her elbow on the little round table that she usually kept beside her, and eyed him attentively. Notwithstanding the aversion with which I regarded the idea of entrapping him into any disclosure he was not prepared to make voluntarily, I should have taken him up at this point, but for the strange proceedings in which I saw him engaged; whereof his putting the lemon-peel into the kettle, the sugar into the snuffer-tray, the spirit into the empty jug, and confidently attempting to pour boiling water out of a candlestick, were among the most remarkable. I saw that a crisis was at hand, and it came. He clattered all his means and implements together, rose from his chair, pulled out his pocket-handkerchief, and burst into tears.

"My dear Copperfield," said Mr. Micawber, behind his handkerchief, "this is an occupation, of all others, requiring an untroubled mind, and self-respect. I cannot perform it. It is out of the question."

"Mr. Micawber," said I, "what is the matter? Pray speak out. You are among friends."

"Among friends, Sir?" repeated Mr. Micawber; and all he had reserved came breaking out of him. "Good Heavens, it is principally because I *am* among friends that my state of mind is what it is. What is the matter, gentlemen? What is *not* the matter? Villiany is the matter; baseness is the matter; deception, fraud, conspiracy, are the matter; and the name of the whole atrocious mass is—HEEP!"

My aunt clapped her hands, and we all started up as if we were possessed.

"The struggle is over!" said Mr. Micawber, violently gesticulating with his pocket-handkerchief, and fairly striking out from time to time with both arms, as if he were swimming under superhuman difficulties. "I will lead this life no longer. I am a wretched being, cut off from everything that makes life tolerable. I have been under a Taboo in that infernal scoundrel's service. Give me back my wife, give me back my family, substitute Micawber for the petty wretch who walks about in the boots at present on my feet, and call upon me to swallow a sword to-morrow, and I'll do it. With an appetite!"

I never saw a man so hot in my life. I tried to calm him, that we might come to something rational; but he got hotter and hotter, and wouldn't hear a word.

"I'll put my hand in no man's hand," said Mr. Micawber, gasping, puffing, and sobbing, to that degree that he was like a man fighting with cold water, "until I have—blown to fragments—the—a—detestable—serpent—HEEP! I'll partake of no one's hospitality, until I have—a—moved Mount Vesuvius—to eruption—on—a—the abandoned rascal—HEEP! Refreshment—a—underneath this roof—particularly punch—would—a—choke me—unless—I had—previously—choked the eyes—out of the head—a—of—interminable cheat, and liar—HEEP! I—a—I'll know nobody—and—a—say nothing—and—a—live nowhere—until I have crushed—to—a—undiscoverable atoms—the—transcendent and immortal hypocrite and perjurer—HEEP!"

I really had some fear of Mr. Micawber's dying on the spot. The manner in which he struggled through these inarticulate sentences, and, whenever he found himself getting near the name of Heep, fought his way on to it, dashed at it in a fainting state, and brought it out with a vehemence little less than marvellous, was frightful; but now, when he sank into a chair, steaming, and looked at us, with every possible colour in his face that had no business there, and an endless procession of lumps following one another in hot haste up his throat, whence they seemed to shoot into his forehead, he had the appearance of being in the last extremity. I would have gone to his assistance, but he waved me off, and wouldn't hear a word.

"No, Copperfield!—No communication—a—until—Miss Wickfield—a—redress from wrongs inflicted by consummate scoundrel—HEEP!" (I am quite convinced he could not have uttered three words, but for the amazing energy with which this word inspired him when he felt it coming.) "Inviolable secret—a—from the whole world—a—no exceptions—this day week—a—at breakfast time—a—everybody present—including aunt—a—and extremely friendly gentleman—to be at the hotel at Canterbury—a—where—Mrs. Micawber and myself—Auld Lang Syne in chorus—and—a—will expose intolerable ruffian—HEEP! No more to say—a—or listen to persuasion—go immediately—not capable—a—bear society—upon the track of devoted and doomed traitor—HEEP!"

With this last repetition of the magic word that had kept him going at all, and in which he surpassed all his previous efforts, Mr. Micawber rushed out of the house; leaving us in a state of excitement, hope, and wonder, that reduced us to a condition little better than his own. But even then his passion for writing letters was too strong to be resisted; for while we were yet in the height of our excitement, hope, and wonder, the following pastoral note was brought to me from a neighbouring tavern, at which he had called to write it:—

"Most secret and confidential.

"MY DEAR SIR,

"I beg to be allowed to convey, through you, my apologies to your excellent aunt for my late excitement. An explosion of a smouldering volcano long suppressed, was the result of an internal contest more easily conceived than described.

"I trust I rendered tolerably intelligible my appointment for the morning of this day week, at the house of public entertainment at Canterbury, where Mrs. Micawber and myself had once the honour of uniting our voices to yours, in the well-known strain of the Immortal exciseman nurtured beyond the Tweed.

"The duty done, and act of reparation performed, which can alone enable me to contemplate my fellow-mortal, I shall be known no more. I shall simply require to be deposited in that place of universal resort, where

"'Each in his narrow cell for ever laid,
"'The rude forefathers of the hamlet sleep,'

"—With the plain Inscription,
"WILKINS MICAWBER."

CHAPTER L.

MR. PEGGOTTY'S DREAM COMES TRUE.

By this time, some months had passed, since our interview on the bank of the river with Martha. I had never seen her since, but she had communicated with Mr. Peggotty on several occasions. Nothing had come of her zealous intervention; nor could I infer, from what he told me, that any clue had ever been obtained, for a moment, to Emily's fate. I began to despair of her recovery, and gradually to sink deeper and deeper into the belief that she was dead.

His conviction remained unchanged. So far as I know —and I believe his honest heart was transparent to me—he never wavered again, in his solemn certainty of finding her. His patience never tired. And, although I trembled for the agony it might one day be to him to have his strong assurance shivered at a blow, there was something so religious in it, so affectingly expressive of its anchor being in the purest depths of his fine nature, that the respect and honour in which I held him were exalted every day.

His was not a lazy trustfulness that hoped, and did no more. He had been a man of sturdy action all his life, and he knew that in all things wherein he wanted help he must do his own part faithfully, and help himself. I have known him set out in the night, on a misgiving that the light might not be, by some accident, in the window of the old boat, and walk to Yarmouth. I have known him, on reading something in the newspaper that might apply to her, take up his stick, and go forth on a journey of three or four score miles. He made his way by sea to Naples, and back, after hearing the narrative to which Miss Dartle had assisted me. All his journeys were ruggedly performed; for he was always steadfast in a purpose of saving money for Emily's sake, when she should be found. In all this long pursuit, I never heard him repine; I never heard him say he was fatigued, or out of heart.

Dora had often seen him since our marriage, and was quite fond of him. I fancy his figure before me now, standing near her sofa, with his rough cap in his hand, and the blue eyes of my child-wife raised, with a timid wonder, to his face. Sometimes of an evening, about twilight, when he came to talk with me, I would induce him to smoke his pipe in the garden, as we slowly paced to and fro together; and then, the picture of his deserted home, and the comfortable air it used to have in my childish eyes of an evening when the fire was burning, and the wind moaning round it, came most vividly into my mind.

One evening, at this hour, he told me that he had found Martha waiting near his lodging on the preceding night when he came out, and that she had asked him not to leave London on any account, until he should have seen her again.

"Did she tell you why?" I inquired.

"I asked her, Mas'r Davy," he replied, "but it is but few words as she ever says, and she on'y got my promise and so went away."

"Did she say when you might expect to see her again?" I demanded.

"No, Mas'r Davy," he returned, drawing his hand thoughtfully down his face. "I asked that too: but it was more (she said) than she could tell."

As I had long forborne to encourage him with hopes that hung on threads, I made no other comment on this information than that I supposed he would see her soon. Such speculations as it engendered within me I kept to myself, and those were faint enough.

I was walking alone in the garden, one evening, about a fortnight afterwards. I remember that evening well. It was the second in Mr. Micawber's week of suspense. There had been rain all day, and there was a damp feeling in the air. The leaves were thick upon the trees, and heavy with wet; but the rain had ceased, though the sky was still dark; and the hopeful birds were singing cheerfully. As I walked to and fro in the garden, and the twilight began to close around me, their little voices were hushed; and that peculiar silence which belongs to such an evening in the country when the lightest trees are quite still, save for the occasional droppings from their boughs, prevailed.

There was a little green perspective of trellis-work and ivy at the side of our cottage, through which I could see, from the garden where I was walking, into the road before the house. I happened to turn my eyes towards this place, as I was thinking of many things; and I saw a figure beyond, dressed in a plain cloak. It was bending eagerly towards me, and beckoning.

"Martha!" said I, going to it.

"Can you come with me?" she inquired, in an agitated whisper. "I have been to him, and he is not at home. I wrote down where he was to come, and left it on his table with my own hand. They said he would not be out long. I have tidings for him. Can you come directly?"

My answer was, to pass out at the gate immediately. She made a hasty gesture with her hand, as if to entreat my patience and my silence, and turned towards London, whence, as her dress betokened, she had come expeditiously on foot.

I asked her if that were not our destination? On her motioning Yes, with the same hasty gesture as before, I stopped an empty coach that was coming by, and we got into it. When I asked her where I should tell the coachman to drive, she answered "Anywhere near Golden Square! And quick!"—then shrank into a corner, with one trembling hand before her face, and the other making the former gesture, as if she could not bear a voice.

Now much disturbed, and dazzled with conflicting gleams of hope and dread, I looked at her for some explanation. But, seeing how strongly she desired to remain quiet, and feeling that it was my own natural inclination too, at such a time, I did not attempt to break the silence. We proceeded without a word being spoken. Sometimes she glanced out of the window, as though she thought we were going slowly, though indeed we were going fast; but otherwise remained exactly as at first.

We alighted at one of the entrances to the square she had mentioned, where I directed the coach to wait, not knowing but that we might have some occasion for it. She laid her hand on my arm, and hurried me on to one of the sombre streets, of which there are several in that part, where the houses were once fair dwellings in the occupation of single families, but have, and had, long degenerated into poor lodgings let off in rooms. Entering at the open door of one of these, and releasing my arm, she beckoned me to follow her up the common staircase, which was like a tributary channel to the street.

The house swarmed with inmates. As we went up, doors of rooms were opened and people's heads put out; and we passed other people on the stairs, who were coming down. In glancing up from the outside, before we entered, I had seen women and children lolling at the windows over flower-pots; and we seemed to have attracted their curiosity, for these were principally the observers who looked out of their doors. It was a broad panelled staircase, with massive balustrades of some dark wood; cornices above the doors, ornamented with carved fruit and flowers; and board seats in the windows. But all these tokens of past grandeur were miserably decayed and dirty; rot, damp, and age, had weakened the flooring, which in many places was unsound and even unsafe. Some attempts had been made, I noticed, to infuse new blood into this dwindling frame, by repairing the costly old woodwork here and there with common deal; but it was like the marriage of a reduced old noble to a plebeian pauper, and each party to the ill-assorted union shrank away from the other. Several of the back windows on the staircase had been darkened or wholly blocked up. In those that remained, there was scarcely any glass; and, through the crumbling frames by which the bad air seemed always to come in, and never to go out, I saw, through other glassless windows, into other houses in a similar condition, and looked giddily down into a wretched yard which was the common dust-heap of the mansion.

We proceeded to the top-story of the house. Two or three times, by the way, I thought I observed in the indistinct light the skirts of a female figure going up before us. As we turned to ascend the last flight of stairs between us and the roof, we caught a full view of this figure pausing for a moment, at a door. Then it turned the handle, and went in.

"What's this!" said Martha, in a whisper. "She has gone into my room. I don't know her!"

I knew her. I had recognised her with amazement, for Miss Dartle.

I said something to the effect that it was a lady whom I had seen before, in a few words, to my conductress; and had scarcely done so when we heard her voice in the room, though not, from where we stood, what she was saying. Martha, with an astonished look, repeated her former action, and softly led me up the stairs; and then, by a little back door which seemed to have no lock, and which she pushed open with a touch, into a small empty garret with a low sloping roof: little better than a cupboard. Between this, and the room she had called hers, there was a small door of communication, standing partly open. Here we stopped, breathless with our ascent, and she placed her hand lightly on my lips. I could only see, of the room beyond, that it was pretty large; that there was a bed in it; and that there were some common pictures of ships upon the walls. I could not see Miss Dartle, or the person whom we had heard her address. Certainly, my companion could not, for my position was the best.

A dead silence prevailed for some moments. Martha kept one hand on my lips, and raised the other in a listening attitude.

"It matters little to me her not being at home," said

Rosa Dartle, haughtily, "I know nothing of her. It is you I come to see."

"Me?" replied a soft voice.

At the sound of it, a thrill went through my frame. For it was Emily's!

"Yes," returned Miss Dartle, "I have come to look at you. What? You are not ashamed of the face that has done so much?"

The resolute and unrelenting hatred of her tone, its cold stern sharpness and its mastered rage, presented her before me, as if I had seen her standing in the light. I saw the flashing black eyes, and the passion-wasted figure; and I saw the scar, with its white track cutting through her lips quivering and throbbing as she spoke.

"I have come to see," she said, "James Steerforth's fancy; the girl who ran away with him, and is the town-talk of the commonest people of her native place; the bold, flaunting, practised companion of persons like James Steerforth. I want to know what such a thing is like."

There was a rustle, as if the unhappy girl, on whom she heaped these taunts, ran towards the door, and the speaker swiftly interposed herself before it. It was succeeded by a moment's pause.

When Miss Dartle spoke again, it was through her set teeth, and with a stamp upon the ground.

"Stay there!" she said, "or I'll proclaim you to the house, and the whole street! If you try to evade *me*, I'll stop you, if it's by the hair, and raise the very stones against you!"

A frightened murmur was the only reply that reached my ears. A silence succeeded. I did not know what to do. Much as I desired to put an end to the interview, I felt that I had no right to present myself; that it was for Mr. Peggotty alone to see her and recover her. Would he never come? I thought impatiently.

"So!" said Rosa Dartle, with a contemptuous laugh, "I see her at last! Why, he was a poor creature to be taken by that delicate mock-modesty, and that hanging head!"

"Oh, for Heaven's sake, spare me!" exclaimed Emily. "Whoever you are, you know my pitiable story, and for Heaven's sake spare me, if you would be spared yourself!"

"If *I* would be spared!" returned the other fiercely; "what is there in common between *us*, do you think?"

"Nothing but our sex," said Emily, with a burst of tears.

"And that," said Rosa Dartle, "is so strong a claim, preferred by one so infamous, that if I had any feeling in my breast but scorn and abhorrence of you, it would freeze it up. Our sex! You are an honour to our sex!"

"I have deserved this," cried Emily, "but it's dreadful! Dear, dear lady, think what I have suffered, and how I am fallen! Oh, Martha, come back! Oh, home, home!"

Miss Dartle placed herself in a chair, within view of the door, and looked downward, as if Emily were crouching on the floor before her. Being now between me and the light, I could see her curled lip, and her cruel eyes intently fixed on one place, with a greedy triumph.

"Listen to what I say!" she said; "and reserve your false arts for your dupes. Do you hope to move *me* by your tears? No more than you could charm me by your smiles, you purchased slave."

"Oh, have some mercy on me!" cried Emily. "Show me some compassion, or I shall die mad!"

"It would be no great penance," said Rosa Dartle, "for your crimes. Do you know what you have done? Do you ever think of the home you have laid waste?"

"Oh, is there ever night or day, when I don't think of it!" cried Emily; and now I could just see her, on her knees, with her head thrown back, her pale face looking upward, her hands wildly clasped and held out, and her hair streaming about her. "Has there ever been a single minute, waking or sleeping, when it hasn't been before me, just as it used to be in the lost days when I turned my back upon it for ever and for ever? Oh, home, home! Oh dear, dear uncle, if you ever could have known the agony your love would cause me when I fell away from good, you never would have shown it to me so constant, much as you felt it; but would have been angry to me, at least once in my life, that I might have had some comfort! I have none, none, no comfort upon earth, for all of them were always fond of me!" She dropped on her face, before the imperious figure in the chair, with an imploring effort to clasp the skirt of her dress.

Rosa Dartle sat looking down upon her, as inflexible as a figure of brass. Her lips were tightly compressed, as if she knew that she must keep a strong constraint upon herself—I write what I sincerely believe—or she would be tempted to strike the beautiful form with her foot. I saw her, distinctly, and the whole power of her face and character seemed forced into that expression.—Would he never come?

"The miserable vanity of these earthworms!" she said, when she had so far controlled the angry heavings of her breast, that she could trust herself to speak. "*Your* home! Do you imagine that I bestow a thought on it, or suppose you could do any harm to that low place, which money would not pay for, and handsomely? *Your* home! You were a part of the trade of your home, and were bought and sold like any other vendible thing your people dealt in."

"Oh not that!" cried Emily. "Say anything of me; but don't visit my disgrace and shame, more than I have done, on folks who are as honourable as you! Have some respect for them, as you are a lady, if you have no mercy for me."

"I speak," she said, not deigning to take any heed of this appeal, and drawing away her dress from the contamination of Emily's touch, "I speak of *his* home—where I live. Here," she said, stretching out her hand with her contemptuous laugh, and looking down upon the prostrate girl, "is a worthy cause of division between lady-mother and gentleman-son; of grief in a house where she wouldn't have been admitted as a kitchen-girl; of anger, and repining, and reproach. This piece of pollution, picked up from the water-side, to be made much of for an hour, and then tossed back to her original place!"

"No! no!" cried Emily, clasping her hands together. "When he first came into my way—that the day had never dawned upon me, and he had met me being carried to my grave!—I had been brought up as virtuous as you or any lady, and was going to be the wife of as good a man as you or any lady in the world can ever marry. If you live in his home and know him, you know, perhaps, what his power with a weak, vain girl might be. I don't defend myself, but I know well, and he knows well, or he will know when he comes to die, and his mind is troubled with

it, that he used all his power to deceive me, and that I believed him, trusted him, and loved him!"

Rosa Dartle sprang up from her seat; recoiled; and in recoiling struck at her, with a face of such malignity, so darkened and disfigured by passion, that I had almost thrown myself between them. The blow, which had no aim, fell upon the air. As she now stood panting, looking at her with the utmost detestation that she was capable of expressing, and trembling from head to foot with rage and scorn, I thought I had never seen such a sight, and never could see such another.

"*You* love him? *You?*" she cried, with her clenched hand, quivering as if it only wanted a weapon to stab the object of her wrath.

Emily had shrunk out of my view. There was no reply.

"And tell that to *me*," she added, "with your shameful lips? Why don't they whip these creatures? If I could order it to be done, I would have this girl whipped to death."

And so she would, I have no doubt. I would not have trusted her with the rack itself, while that furious look lasted.

She slowly, very slowly, broke into a laugh, and pointed at Emily with her hand, as if she were a sight of shame for gods and men.

"*She* love!" she said. "That carrion! And he ever cared for her, she'd tell me. Ha, ha! The liars that these traders are!"

Her mockery was worse than her undisguised rage. Of the two, I would have much preferred to be the object of the latter. But, when she suffered it to break loose, it was only for a moment. She had chained it up again, and however it might tear her within, she subdued it to herself.

"I came here, you pure fountain of love," she said, "to see—as I began by telling you—what such a thing as you was like. I was curious. I am satisfied. Also to tell you, that you had best seek that home of yours, with all speed, and hide your head among those excellent people who are expecting you, and whom your money will console. When it's all gone, you can believe, and trust, and love again, you know! I thought you a broken toy that had lasted its time; a worthless spangle that was tarnished, and thrown away. But, finding you true gold, a very lady, and an ill-used innocent, with a fresh heart full of love and trustfulness—which you look like, and is quite consistent with your story!—I have something more to say. Attend to it; for what I say I'll do. Do you hear me, you fair spirit? What I say, I mean to do!"

Her rage got the better of her again, for a moment; but it passed over her face like a spasm, and left her smiling.

"Hide yourself," she pursued, "if not at home, somewhere. Let it be somewhere beyond reach; in some obscure life—or, better still, in some obscure death. I wonder, if your loving heart will not break, you have found no way of helping it to be still! I have heard of such means sometimes. I believe they may be easily found."

A low crying, on the part of Emily, interrupted her here. She stopped, and listened to it as if it were music.

"I am of a strange nature, perhaps," Rosa Dartle went on; "but I can't breathe freely in the air you breathe. I find it sickly. Therefore, I will have it cleared; I will have it purified of you. If you live here to-morrow, I'll have your story and your character proclaimed on the common stair; and it is a pity such a light as you should be among them, and concealed. If, leaving here, you seek any refuge in this town in any character but your true one (which you are welcome to bear, without molestation from me), the same service shall be done you, if I hear of your retreat. Being assisted by a gentleman who not long ago aspired to the favour of your hand, I am sanguine as to that."

Would he never, never come? How long was I to bear this? How long could I bear it?

"Oh me, oh me!" exclaimed the wretched Emily, in a tone that might have touched the hardest heart, I should have thought; but there was no relenting in Rosa Dartle's smile. "What, what shall I do!"

"Do?" returned the other. "Live happy in your own reflections! Consecrate your existence to the recollection of James Steerforth's tenderness—he would have made you his serving-man's wife, would he not?—or to feeling grateful to the upright and deserving creature who would have taken you as his gift. Or, if those proud remembrances, and the consciousness of your own virtues, and the honourable position to which they have raised you in the eyes of everything that wears the human shape, will not sustain you, marry that good man, and be happy in his condescension. If this will not do either, die! There are doorways and dust-heaps for such deaths, and such despair—find one, and take your flight to Heaven!"

I heard a distant foot upon the stairs. I knew it, I was certain. It was his, thank God!

She moved slowly from before the door when she said this, and passed out of my sight.

"But mark!" she added, slowly and sternly, opening the other door to go away, "I am resolved, for reasons that I have and hatreds that I entertain, to cast you out, unless you withdraw from my reach altogether, or drop your pretty mask. This is what I had to say; and what I say, I mean to do!"

The foot upon the stairs came nearer—nearer—passed her as she went down—rushed into the room!

"Uncle!"

A fearful cry followed the word. I paused a moment, and looking in, saw him supporting her insensible figure in his arms. He gazed for a few seconds in the face; then stooped to kiss it—oh, how tenderly! and drew a handkerchief before it.

"Mas'r Davy," he said, in a low tremulous voice, when it was covered, "I thank my Heav'nly Father, as my dream's come true! I thank Him hearty for having guided of me, in His own ways, to my darling!"

With those words he took her up in his arms; and, with the veiled face lying on his bosom, and addressed towards his own, carried her, motionless and unconscious, down the stairs.

CHAPTER LI.

THE BEGINNING OF A LONGER JOURNEY.

It was yet early in the morning of the following day, when, as I was walking in my garden with my aunt (who took little other exercise now, being so much in attendance on my dear Dora), I was told that Mr. Peggotty desired to speak with me. He came into the garden to meet me half-way, on my going towards the gate; and bared his head, as it was always his custom to do when he saw my aunt, for whom he had a high respect. I had been telling her all

that had happened overnight. Without saying a word, she walked up with a cordial face, shook hands with him, and patted him on the arm. It was so expressively done, that she had no need to say a word. Mr. Peggotty understood her quite as well as if she had said a thousand.

"I'll go in now, Trot," said my aunt, "and look after Little Blossom, who will be getting up presently."

"Not along of my being heer, ma'am, I hope?" said Mr. Peggotty. "Unless my wits is gone a bahd's neezing"—by which Mr. Peggotty meant to say, bird's-nesting—"this morning, 'tis along of me as you're a going to quit us?"

"You have something to say, my good friend," returned my aunt, "and will do better without me."

"By your leave, ma'am," returned Mr. Peggotty, "I should take it kind, pervising you doen't mind my clicketten, if you'd bide heer."

"Would you?" said my aunt, with short good-nature. "Then I am sure I will!"

So, she drew her arm through Mr. Peggotty's, and walked with him to a leafy little summer-house there was at the bottom of the garden, where she sat down on a bench, and I beside her. There was a seat for Mr. Peggotty too, but he preferred to stand, leaning his hand on the small rustic table. As he stood, looking at his cap for a little while before beginning to speak, I could not help observing what power and force of character his sinewy hand expressed, and what a good and trusty companion it was to his honest brow and iron-grey hair.

"I took my dear child away last night," Mr. Peggotty began, as he raised his eyes to ours, "to my lodging, wheer I have a long time been expecting of her and preparing fur her. It was hours afore she knowed me right; and when she did, she kneeled down at my feet, and kiender said to me, as if it was her prayers, how it all come to be. You may believe me, when I heerd her voice, as I had heerd at home so playful—and see her humbled, as it might be in the dust our Saviour wrote in with His blessed hand—I felt a wownd go to my 'art, in the midst of all its thankfulness."

He drew his sleeve across his face, without any pretence of concealing why; and then cleared his voice.

"It warn't for long as I felt that; for she was found. I had on'y to think as she was found, and it was gone. I doen't know why I do so much as mention it now, I'm sure. I didn't have it in my mind a minute ago, to say a word about myself; but it come up so nat'ral, that I yielded to it afore I was aweer."

"You are a self-denying soul," said my aunt, "and will have your reward."

Mr. Peggotty, with the shadows of the leaves playing athwart his face, made a surprised inclination of the head towards my aunt, as an acknowledgment of her good opinion; then, took up the thread he had relinquished.

"When my Em'ly took flight," he said, in stern wrath for the moment, "from the house wheer she was made a pris'-ner by that theer spotted snake as Mas'r Davy see,—and his story's trew, and may GOD confound him!—she took flight in the night. It was a dark night, with a many stars a shining. She was wild. She ran along the sea beach, believing the old boat was theer; and calling out to us to turn away our faces, for she was a coming by. She heerd herself a crying out, like as if it was another person; and cut herself on them sharp-pinted stones and rocks, and felt it no more than if she had been rock herself. Ever so fur

MR. PEGGOTTY'S DREAM COMES TRUE.

she run, and there was fire afore her eyes, and roarings in her ears. Of a sudden—or so she thowt, you unnerstand—the day broke, wet and windy, and she was lying b'low a heap of stone upon the shore, and a woman was a speaking to her, saying, in the language of that country, what was it as had gone so much amiss?"

He saw everything he related. It passed before him, as he spoke, so vividly, that, in the intensity of his earnestness, he presented what he described to me, with greater distinctness than I can express. I can hardly believe, writing now long afterwards, but that I was actually present in these scenes; they are impressed upon me with such an astonishing air of fidelity.

"As Em'ly's eyes—which was heavy—see this woman better," Mr. Peggotty went on, "she know'd as she was one of them as she had often talked to on the beach. Fur, though she had run (as I have said) ever so fur in the night, she had oftentimes wandered long ways, partly afoot, partly in boats and carriages, and know'd all that country, 'long the coast, miles and miles. She hadn't no children of her own, this woman, being a young wife; but she was a looking to have one afore long. And may my prayers go up to Heaven that 'twill be a happ'ness to her, and a comfort, and a honour, all her life! May it love her and be dootiful to her, in her old age; helpful of her at the last; a Angel to her heer, and heerafter!"

"Amen!" said my aunt.

"She had been summat timorous and down," said Mr. Peggotty, "and had sat, at first, a little way off, at her spinning, or such work as it was, when Em'ly talked to the children. But Em'ly had took notice of her, and had gone and spoke to her; and as the young woman was partial to the children herself, they had soon made friends. Sermuchser, that when Em'ly went that way, she always giv Em'ly flowers. This was her as now asked what it was that had gone so much amiss. Em'ly told her, and she—took her home. She did indeed. She took her home," said Mr. Peggotty, covering his face.

He was more affected by this act of kindness, than I had ever seen him affected by anything since the night she went away. My aunt and I did not attempt to disturb him.

"It was a little cottage, you may suppose," he said, presently, "but she found space for Em'ly in it,—her husband was away at sea,—and she kep it secret, and prevailed upon such neighbours as she had (they was not many near) to keep it secret too. Em'ly took bad with fever, and, what is very strange to me is,—maybe 'tis not so strange to scholars,—the language of that country went out of her head, and she could only speak her own, that no one unnerstood. She recollects, as if she had dreamed it, that she lay there, always a talking her own tongue, always believing as the old boat was round the next pint in the bay, and begging and imploring of 'em to send theer and tell how she was dying, and bring back a message of forgiveness, if it was on'y a wured. A'most the whole time, she thowt,—now, that him as I made mention on just now was lurking for her unnerneath the winder: now, that him as had brought her to this was in the room,—and cried to the good young woman not to give her up, and know'd, at the same time, that she couldn't unnerstand, and dreaded that she must be took away. Likewise the fire was afore

her eyes, and the roarings in her ears; and there was no to-day, nor yesterday, nor yet to-morrow; but everything in her life as ever had been, or as ever could be, and everything as never had been, and as never could be, was a crowding on her all at once, and nothing clear nor welcome, and yet she sang and laughed about it! How long this lasted, I doen't know; but then there come a sleep; and in that sleep, from being a many times stronger than her own self, she fell into the weakness of the littlest child."

Here he stopped, as if for relief from the terrors of his own description. After being silent for a few moments, he pursued his story.

"It was a pleasant arternoon when she awoke; and so quiet, that there warn't a sound but the rippling of that blue sea without a tide, upon the shore. It was her belief, at first, that she was at home upon a Sunday morning; but, the vine leaves as she see at the winder, and the hills beyond, warn't home, and contradicted of her. Then, come in her friend, to watch alongside of her bed; and then she know'd as the old boat warn't round that next pint in the bay no more, but was fur off; and know'd where she was, and why; and broke out a crying on that good young woman's bosom, wheer I hope her baby is a lying now, a cheering of her with its pretty eyes!"

He could not speak of this good friend of Emily's without a flow of tears. It was in vain to try. He broke down again, endeavouring to bless her!

"That done my Em'ly good," he resumed, after such emotion as I could not behold without sharing in; and as to my aunt, she wept with all her heart; "that done Em'ly good, and she begun to mend. But, the language of that country was quite gone from her, and she was forced to make signs. So she went on, getting better from day to day, slow, but sure, and trying to learn the names of common things—names as she seemed never to have heerd in all her life—till one evening come, when she was a setting at her window, looking at a little girl at play upon the beach. And of a sudden this child held out her hand, and said, what would be in English, 'Fisherman's daughter, here's a shell!'—for you are to unnerstand that they used at first to call her 'Pretty lady,' as the general way in that country is, and that she had taught 'em to call her 'Fisherman's daughter,' instead. The child says of a sudden, 'Fisherman's daughter, here's a shell!' Then Em'ly unnerstands her; and she answers, bursting out a crying; and it all comes back!

"When Em'ly got strong again," said Mr. Peggotty, after another short interval of silence, "she cast about to leave that good young creetur, and get to her own country. The husband was come home, then; and the two together put her aboard a small trader bound to Leghorn, and from that to France. She had a little money, but it was less than little as they would take for all they done. I'm a'most glad on it, though they was so poor! What they done, is laid up wheer neither moth nor rust doth corrupt, and wheer thieves do not break through nor steal. Mas'r Davy, it'll outlast all the treasure in the wureld.

"Em'ly got to France, and took service to wait on travelling ladies at a inn in the port. Theer, theer come, one day, that snake.—Let him never come nigh me. I doen't know what hurt I might do him!—Soon as she see him, without him seeing her, all her fear and wildness returned, and she fled afore the very breath he draw'd. She come to England, and was set ashore at Dover.

"I doen't know," said Mr. Peggotty, "for sure, when her 'art begun to fail her; but all the way to England she had thowt to come to her dear home. Soon as she got to England she turned her face tow'rds it. But, fear of not being forgiv, fear of being pinted at, fear of some of us being dead along of her, fear of many things, turned her from it, kiender by force, upon the road: 'Uncle, uncle,' she says to me, 'the fear of not being worthy to do, what my torn and bleeding breast so longed to do, was the most fright'ning fear of all! I turned back, when my 'art was full of prayers that I might crawl to the old doorstep, in the night, kiss it, lay my wicked face upon it, and theer be found dead in the morning.'

"She come," said Mr. Peggotty, dropping his voice to an awe-stricken whisper, "to London. She—as had never seen it in her life—alone—without a penny—young—so pretty—come to London. A'most the moment as she lighted heer, all so desolate, she found (as she believed) a friend; a decent woman as spoke to her about the needle-work as she had brought up to do, about finding plenty of it fur her, about a lodging for the night, and making secret inquiration concerning of me and all at home, to-morrow. When my child," he said aloud, and with an energy of gratitude that shook him from head to foot, "stood upon the brink of more than I can say or think on—Martha, trew to her promise, saved her!"

I could not repress a cry of joy.

"Mas'r Davy!" he said, gripping my hand in that strong hand of his, "it was you as first made mention of her to me. I thank'ee, Sir! She was arnest. She had know'd of her bitter knowledge wheer to watch and what to do. She had done it. And the Lord was above all! She come, white and hurried, upon Em'ly in her sleep. She says to her, 'Rise up from worse than death, and come with me!' Them belonging to the house would have stopped her, but they might as soon have stopped the sea. 'Stand away from me,' she says, 'I am a ghost that calls her from beside her open grave!' She told Em'ly she had seen me, and know'd I loved her, and forgiv her. She wrapped her, hasty, in her clothes. She took her, faint and trembling, on her arm. She heeded no more what they said, than if she had had no ears. She walked among 'em with my child, minding only her; and brought her safe out, in the dead of the night, from that black pit of ruin!

"She attended on Em'ly," said Mr. Peggotty, who had released my hand, and put his own hand on his heaving chest; "she attended to my Em'ly, lying wearied out, and wandering betwixt whiles, till late next day. Then she went in search of me; then in search of you, Mas'r Davy. She didn't tell Em'ly what she come out fur, lest her 'art should fail, and she should think of hiding of herself. How the cruel lady know'd of her being theer, I can't say. Whether him as I have spoke so much of, chanced to see 'em going theer, or whether (which is most like, to my thinking) he had heerd it from the woman, I doen't greatly ask myself. My niece is found.

"All night long," said Mr. Peggotty, "we have been together, Em'ly and me. 'Tis little (considering the time) as she has said, in wureds, through them broken-hearted tears; 'tis less as I have seen of her dear face, as grow'd into a woman's at my hearth. But, all night long, her arms has been about my neck; and her head has laid heer;

and we knows full well, as we can put our trust in one another, ever more."

He ceased to speak, and his hand upon the table rested there in perfect repose, with a resolution in it that might have conquered lions.

"It was a gleam of light upon me, Trot," said my aunt, drying her eyes, "when I formed the resolution of being godmother to your sister Betsey Trotwood, who disappointed me; but, next to that, hardly anything would have given me greater pleasure, than to be godmother to that good young creature's baby!"

Mr. Peggotty nodded his understanding of my aunt's feelings, but could not trust himself with any verbal reference to the subject of her commendation. We all remained silent, and occupied with our own reflections (my aunt drying her eyes, and now sobbing convulsively, and now laughing and calling herself a fool); until I spoke.

"You have quite made up your mind," said I to Mr. Peggotty, "as to the future, good friend? I need scarcely ask you."

"Quite, Mas'r Davy," he returned; "and told Em'ly. Theer's mighty countries, fur from heer. Our future life lays over the sea."

"They will emigrate together, aunt," said I.

"Yes!" said Mr. Peggotty, with a hopeful smile. "No one can't reproach my darling in Australia. We will begin a new life over theer!"

I asked him if he yet proposed to himself any time for going away.

"I was down at the Docks early this morning, Sir," he returned, "to get information concerning of them ships. In about six weeks or two months from now, there'll be one sailing—I see her this morning—went aboard—and we shall take our passage in her."

"Quite alone?" I asked.

"Ay, Mas'r Davy!" he returned. "My sister, you see, she's that fond of you and yourn, and that accustomed to think on'y of her own country, that it wouldn't be hardly fair to let her go. Besides which, theer's one she has in charge, Mas'r Davy, as doen't ought to be forgot."

"Poor Ham!" said I.

"My good sister takes care of his house, you see, ma'am, and he takes kindly to her," Mr. Peggotty explained for my aunt's better information. "He'll set and talk to her, with a calm spirit, wen it's like he couldn't bring himself to open his lips to another. Poor fellow!" said Mr. Peggotty, shaking his head, "theer's not so much left him, that he could spare the little as he has!"

"And Mrs. Gummidge?" said I.

"Well, I've had a mort of con-sideration, I do tell you," returned Mr. Peggotty, with a perplexed look which gradually cleared as he went on, "concerning of Missis Gummidge. You see, wen Missis Gummidge falls a thinking of the old 'un, she an't what you may call good company. Betwixt you and me, Mas'r Davy—and you, ma'am—wen Missis Gummidge takes to wimicking,"—our old county word for crying,—"she's liable to be considered to be, by them as didn't know the old 'un, peevish-like. Now I did know the old 'un," said Mr. Peggotty, "and I know'd his merits, so I unnerstan' her; but 'tan't entirely so, you see, with others—nat'rally can't be!"

My aunt and I both acquiesced.

"Wheerby," said Mr. Peggotty, "my sister might—I doen't say she would, but might—find Missis Gummidge give her a leetle trouble now-and-again. Theerfur 'tan't my intentions to moor Missis Gummidge 'long with them, but to find a Bein' fur her wheer she can fisherate for herself." (A Bein' signifies, in that dialect, a home, and to fisherate is to provide.) "Fur which purpose," said Mr. Peggotty, "I means to make her a 'lowance afore I go, as'll leave her pretty comfort'ble. She's the faithfullest of creeturs. 'Tan't to be expected, of course, at her time of life, and being lone and lorn, as the good old mawther is to be knocked about aboardship, and in the woods and wilds of a new and fur-away country. So that's what I'm a going to do with *her*."

He forgot nobody. He thought of everybody's claims and strivings, but his own.

"Em'ly," he continued, "will keep along with me—poor child, she's sore in need of peace and rest!—until such time as we goes upon our voyage. She'll work at them clothes, as must be made; and I hope her troubles will begin to seem longer ago than they was, wen she finds herself once more by her rough but loving uncle."

My aunt nodded confirmation of this hope, and imparted great satisfaction to Mr. Peggotty.

"Theer's one thing furder, Mas'r Davy," said he, putting his hand in his breast-pocket, and gravely taking out the little paper bundle I had seen before, which he unrolled on the table. "Theer's these heer bank-notes—fifty pound, and ten. To them I wish to add the money as she come away with. I've asked her about that (but not saying why), and have added of it up; I an't a scholar. Would you be so kind as see how 'tis?"

He handed me, apologetically for his scholarship, a piece of paper, and observed me while I looked it over. It was quite right.

"Thank'ee, Sir," he said, taking it back. "This money, if you don't see objections, Mas'r Davy, I shall put up jest afore I go, in a cover d'rected to him; and put that up in another, d'rected to his mother. I shall tell her, in no more wureds than I speak to you, what it's the price on; and that I'm gone, and past receiving of it back."

I told him that I thought it would be right to do so— that I was thoroughly convinced it would be, since he felt it to be right.

"I said that theer was on'y one thing furder," he proceeded with a grave smile, when he had made up his little bundle again, and put it in his pocket; "but theer was two. I warn't sure in my mind, wen I come out this morning, as I could go and break to Ham, of my own self, what had so thankfully happened. So I writ a letter while I was out, and put it in the post-office, telling of 'em how all was as 'tis, and that I should come down to-morrow to unload my mind of what little needs a doing of down theer, and, most-like, take my farewell leave of Yarmouth."

"And do you wish me to go with you?" said I, seeing that he left something unsaid.

"If you could do me that kind favour, Mas'r Davy," he replied, "I know the sight on you would cheer 'em up a bit."

My little Dora being in good spirits, and very desirous that I should go—as I found on talking it over with her— I readily pledged myself to accompany him in accordance with his wish. Next morning, consequently, we were on the Yarmouth coach, and again travelling over the old ground.

As we passed along the familiar street at night—Mr. Peggotty, in despite of all my remonstrances, carrying my bag—I glanced into Omer and Joram's shop, and saw my old friend Mr. Omer there, smoking his pipe. I felt reluctant to be present, when Mr. Peggotty first met his sister

and Ham; and made Mr. Omer my excuse for lingering behind.

"How is Mr. Omer, after this long time?" said I, going in.

He fanned away the smoke of his pipe, that he might get a better view of me, and soon recognised me with great delight.

"I should get up, Sir, to acknowledge such an honour as this visit," said he, "only my limbs are rather out of sorts, and I am wheeled about. With the exception of my limbs and my breath, hows'ever, I am as hearty as a man can be, I'm thankful to say."

I congratulated him on his contented looks and his good spirits, and saw, now, that his easy-chair went on wheels.

"It's an ingenious thing, ain't it?" he inquired, following the direction of my glance, and polishing the elbow with his arm. "It runs as light as a feather, and tracks as true as a mail-coach. Bless you, my little Minnie—my grand-daughter you know, Minnie's child—puts her little strength against the back, gives it a shove, and away we go, as clever and merry as ever you see anything! And I tell you what—it's a most uncommon chair to smoke a pipe in."

I never saw such a good old fellow to make the best of a thing, and find out the enjoyment of it, as Mr. Omer. He was as radiant, as if his chair, his asthma, and the failure of his limbs, were the various branches of a great invention for enhancing the luxury of a pipe.

"I see more of the world, I can assure you," said Mr. Omer, "in this chair, than ever I see out of it. You'd be surprised at the number of people that looks in of a day to have a chat. You really would! There's twice as much in the newspaper, since I've taken to this chair, as there used to be. As to general reading, dear me, what a lot of it I do get through! That's what I feel so strong, you know! If it had been my eyes, what should I have done? If it had been my ears, what should I have done? Being my limbs, what does it signify? Why, my limbs only made my breath shorter when I used 'em. And now, if I want to go out into the street or down to the sands, I've only got to call Dick, Joram's youngest 'prentice, and away I go in my own carriage, like the Lord Mayor of London."

He half suffocated himself with laughing here.

"Lord bless you!" said Mr. Omer, resuming his pipe, "a man must take the fat with the lean; that's what he must make up his mind to, in this life. Joram does a fine business. Ex-cellent business!"

"I am very glad to hear it," said I.

"I knew you would be," said Mr. Omer. "And Joram and Minnie are like valentines. What more can a man expect? What's his limbs to *that?*"

His supreme contempt for his own limbs, as he sat smoking, was one of the pleasantest oddities I have ever encountered.

"And since I've took to general reading, you've took to general writing, eh, Sir?" said Mr. Omer, surveying me admiringly. "What a lovely work that was of yours! What expressions in it! I read it every word—every word. And as to feeling sleepy! Not at all!"

I laughingly expressed my satisfaction, but I must confess that I thought this association of ideas significant.

"I give you my word and honour, Sir," said Mr. Omer, "that when I lay that book upon the table, and look at it outside; compact in three separate and individual wollumes—one, two, three; I am as proud as Punch to think that I once had the honour of being connected with your family. And dear me, it's a long time ago, now, ain't it? Over at Blunderstone. With a pretty little party laid along with the other party. And you quite a small party then, yourself. Dear, dear!"

I changed the subject by referring to Emily. After assuring him that I did not forget how interested he had always been in her, and how kindly he had always treated her, I gave him a general account of her restoration to her uncle by the aid of Martha; which I knew would please the old man. He listened with the utmost attention, and said, feelingly, when I had done:

"I am rejoiced at it, Sir! It's the best news I have heard for many a day. Dear, dear, dear! And what's going to be undertook for that unfortunate young woman, Martha, now?"

"You touch a point that my thoughts have been dwelling on since yesterday," said I, "but on which I can give you no information yet, Mr. Omer. Mr. Peggotty has not alluded to it, and I have a delicacy in doing so. I am sure he has not forgotten it. He forgets nothing that is disinterested and good."

"Because you know," said Mr. Omer, taking himself up, where he had left off, "whatever *is* done, I should wish to be a member of. Put me down for anything you may consider right, and let me know. I never could think the girl all bad, and I am glad to find she's not. So will my daughter Minnie be. Young women are contradictory creatures in some things—her mother was just the same as her—but their hearts are soft and kind. It's all show with Minnie, about Martha. Why she should consider it necessary to make any show, I don't undertake to tell you. But it's all show, bless you. She'd do her any kindness in private. So, put me down for whatever you may consider right, will you be so good? and drop me a line where to forward it. Dear me!" said Mr. Omer, "when a man is drawing on to a time of life, where the two ends of life meet; when he finds himself, however hearty he is, being wheeled about for the second time, in a speeches of go-cart; he should be over-rejoiced to do a kindness if he can. He wants plenty. And I don't speak of myself, particular," said Mr. Omer, "because, Sir, the way I look at it is, that we are all drawing on to the bottom of the hill, whatever age we are, on account of time never standing still for a single moment. So let us always do a kindness, and be over-rejoiced. To be sure!"

He knocked the ashes out of his pipe, and put it on a ledge in the back of his chair, expressly made for its reception.

"There's Em'ly's cousin, him that she was to have been married to," said Mr. Omer, rubbing his hands feebly, "as fine a fellow as there is in Yarmouth! He'll come and talk or read to me, in the evening, for an hour together sometimes. That's a kindness, I should call it! All his life's a kindness."

"I am going to see him now," said I.

"Are you?" said Mr. Omer. "Tell him I was hearty, and sent my respects. Minnie and Joram's at a ball. They would be as proud to see you as I am, if they was at home. Minnie won't hardly go out at all, you see, 'on account of father,' as she says. So I swore to-night, that if she didn't go, I'd go to bed at six. In consequence of which," Mr. Omer shook himself and his chair, with laughter at the success of his device, "she and Joram's at a ball."

I shook hands with him, and wished him good night.

"Half a minute, Sir," said Mr. Omer. "If you was to go without seeing my little elephant, you'd lose the best of sights. You never see such a sight! Minnie!"

A musical little voice answered, from somewhere upstairs, "I am coming, grandfather!" and a pretty little girl with long, flaxen, curling hair, soon came running into the shop.

"This is my little elephant, Sir," said Mr. Omer, fondling the child. "Siamese breed, Sir. Now, little elephant!"

The little elephant set the door of the parlour open, enabling me to see that, in these latter days, it was converted into a bedroom for Mr. Omer, who could not be easily conveyed upstairs; and then hid her pretty forehead, and tumbled her long hair, against the back of Mr. Omer's chair.

"The elephant butts, you know, Sir," said Mr. Omer, winking, "when he goes at a object. Once, elephant. Twice. Three times!"

At this signal, the little elephant, with a dexterity that was next to marvellous in so small an animal, whisked the chair round with Mr. Omer in it, and rattled it off, pell-mell, into the parlour, without touching the doorpost: Mr. Omer indescribably enjoying the performance, and looking back at me on the road as if it were the triumphant issue of his life's exertions.

After a stroll about the town, I went to Ham's house. Peggotty had now removed here for good; and had let her own house to the successor of Mr. Barkis in the carrying business, who had paid her very well for the good-will, cart, and horse. I believe the very same slow horse that Mr. Barkis drove, was still at work.

I found them in the neat kitchen, accompanied by Mrs. Gummidge, who had been fetched from the old boat by Mr. Peggotty himself. I doubt if she could have been induced to desert her post, by anyone else. He had evidently told them all. Both Peggotty and Mrs. Gummidge had their aprons to their eyes, and Ham had just stepped out "to take a turn on the beach." He presently came home, very glad to see me; and I hope they were all the better for my being there. We spoke, with some approach to cheerfulness, of Mr. Peggotty's growing rich in a new country, and of the wonders he would describe in his letters. We said nothing of Emily by name, but distantly referred to her more than once. Ham was the serenest of the party.

But, Peggotty told me, when she lighted me to a little chamber where the Crocodile Book was lying ready for me on the table, that he always was the same. She believed (she told me, crying) that he was broken-hearted; though he was as full of courage as of sweetness, and worked harder and better than any boat-builder in any yard in all that part. There were times, she said, of an evening, when he talked of their old life in the boat-house; and then he mentioned Emily as a child. But, he never mentioned her as a woman.

I thought I had read in his face that he would like to speak to me alone. I therefore resolved to put myself in his way next evening, as he came home from his work. Having settled this with myself, I fell asleep. That night, for the first time in all those many nights, the candle was taken out of the window, Mr. Peggotty swung in his old hammock in the old boat, and the wind murmured with the old sound round his head.

All next day, he was occupied in disposing of his fishing-boat and tackle; in packing up, and sending to London by waggon, such of his little domestic possessions as he thought would be useful to him; and in parting with the rest, or bestowing them on Mrs. Gummidge. She was with him all day. As I had a sorrowful wish to see the old place once more, before it was locked up, I engaged to meet them there in the evening. But I so arranged it, as that I should meet Ham first.

It was easy to come in his way, as I knew where he worked. I met him at a retired part of the sands, which I knew he would cross, and turned back with him, that he might have leisure to speak to me if he really wished. I had not mistaken the expression of his face. We had walked but a little way together, when he said, without looking at me:

"Mas'r Davy, have you seen her?"

"Only for a moment, when she was in a swoon," I softly answered.

We walked a little farther, and he said:

"Mas'r Davy, shall you see her, d'ye think?"

"It would be too painful to her, perhaps," said I.

"I have thowt of that," he replied. "So 'twould, Sir, so 'twould."

"But, Ham," said I, gently, "if there is anything that I could write to her, for you, in case I could not tell it; if there is anything you would wish to make known to her through me; I should consider it a sacred trust."

"I am sure on't. I thank'ee, Sir, most kind! I think theer is something I could wish said or wrote."

"What is it?"

We walked a little farther in silence, and then he spoke.

"'Tan't that I forgive her. 'Tan't that so much. 'Tis more as I beg of her to forgive me, for having pressed my affections upon her. Odd times, I think that if I hadn't had her promise fur to marry me, Sir, she was that trustful of me, in a friendly way, that she'd have told me what was struggling in her mind, and would have counselled with me, and I might have saved her."

I pressed his hand. "Is that all?"

"Theer's yet a something else," he returned, "if I can say it, Mas'r Davy."

We walked on, farther than we had walked yet, before he spoke again. He was not crying when he made the pauses I shall express by lines. He was merely collecting himself to speak very plainly.

"I loved her—and I love the mem'ry of her—too deep—to be able to lead her to believe of my own self as I'm a happy man. I could only be happy—by forgetting of her —and I'm afeerd I couldn't hardly bear as she should be told I done that. But if you, being so full of learning, Mas'r Davy, could think of anything to say as might bring her to believe I wasn't greatly hurt: still loving of her, and mourning for her: anything as might bring her to believe as I was not tired of my life, and yet was hoping fur to see her without blame, wheer the wicked cease from troubling and the weary are at rest—anything as would ease her sorrowful mind, and yet not make her think as I could ever marry, or as 'twas possible that anyone could ever be to me what she was—I should ask of you to say that—with my prayers for her—that was so dear."

I pressed his manly hand again, and told him I would charge myself to do this as well as I could.

"I thank'ee, Sir," he answered. "'Twas kind of you to meet me. 'Twas kind of you to bear him company down. Mas'r Davy, I unnerstan' very well, though my aunt will come to Lon'on afore they sail, and they'll unite once more, that I am not like to see him agen. I fare to feel sure on't. We doen't say so, but so 'twill be, and better so. The last

you see on him—the very last—will you give him the lovingest duty and thanks of the orphan, as he was ever more than a father to?"

This I also promised, faithfully.

"I thank'ee agen, Sir," he said, heartily shaking hands. "I know where you're a going. Good bye!"

With a slight wave of his hand, as though to explain to me that he could not enter the old place, he turned away. As I looked after his figure, crossing the waste in the moon light, I saw him turn his face towards a strip of silvery light upon the sea, and pass on, looking at it, until he was a shadow in the distance.

The door of the boat-house stood open when I approached; and, on entering, I found it emptied of all its furniture, saving one of the old lockers, on which Mrs. Gummidge, with a basket on her knee, was seated, looking at Mr. Peggotty. He leaned his elbow on the rough chimney-piece, and gazed upon a few expiring embers in the grate; but he raised his head, hopefully, on my coming in, and spoke in a cheery manner.

"Come, according to promise, to bid farewell to't, eh, Mas'r Davy?" he said, taking up the candle. "Bare enough now, an't it?"

"Indeed you have made good use of the time," said I.

"Why, we have not been idle, Sir. Missis Gummidge has worked like a—I doen't know what Missis Gummidge ain't worked like," said Mr. Peggotty, looking at her, at a loss for a sufficiently-approving simile.

Mrs. Gummidge, leaning on her basket, made no observation.

"Theer's the very locker that you used to sit on, 'long with Em'ly!" said Mr. Peggotty, in a whisper. "I'm a going to carry it away with me, last of all. And heer's your old little bedroom, see, Mas'r Davy! A'most as bleak to-night, as 'art could wish!"

In truth, the wind, though it was low, had a solemn sound, and crept around the deserted house with a whispered wailing that was very mournful. Everything was gone, down to the little mirror with the oyster-shell frame. I thought of myself, lying here, when that first great change was being wrought at home. I thought of the blue-eyed child who had enchanted me. I thought of Steerforth: and a foolish, fearful fancy came upon me of his being near at hand, and liable to be met at any turn.

"'Tis like to be long," said Mr. Peggotty, in a low voice, "afore the boat finds new tenants. They look upon't, down heer, as being unfort'nate now!"

"Does it belong to anybody in the neighbourhood?" I asked.

"To a mast-maker up town," said Mr. Peggotty. "I'm a going to give the key to him to-night."

We looked into the other little room, and came back to Mrs. Gummidge, sitting on the locker, whom Mr. Peggotty, putting the light on the chimney-piece, requested to rise, that he might carry it outside the door before extinguishing the candle.

"Dan'l," said Mrs. Gummidge, suddenly deserting her basket, and clinging to his arm, "my dear Dan'l, the parting words I speak in this house is, I mustn't be left behind. Doen't ye think of leaving me behind, Dan'l! Oh, doen't ye ever do it!"

Mr. Peggotty, taken aback, looked from Mrs. Gummidge to me, and from me to Mrs. Gummidge, as if he had been awakened from a sleep.

"Doen't ye, dearest Dan'l, doen't ye!" cried Mrs. Gummidge, fervently. "Take me 'long with you, Dan'l, take me 'long with you and Em'ly! I'll be your servant, constant and trew. If there's slaves in them parts where you're a going, I'll be bound to you for one, and happy, but doen't ye leave me behind, Dan'l, that's a deary dear!"

"My good soul," said Mr. Peggotty, shaking his head, "you doen't know what a long voyage, and what a hard life 'tis."

"Yes I do, Dan'l! I can guess!" cried Mrs. Gummidge. "But my parting words under this roof is, I shall go into the house and die, if I am not took. I can dig, Dan'l. I can work. I can live hard. I can be loving and patient now—more than you think, Dan'l, if you'll on'y try me. I wouldn't touch the 'lowance, not if I was dying of want, Dan'l Peggotty; but I'll go with you and Em'ly, if you'll on'y let me, to the world's end! I know how 'tis; I know you think that I am lone and lorn; but, deary love, t'an't so no more! I ain't sat here, so long, a watching, and a thinking of your trials, without some good being done me. Mas'r Davy, speak to him for me! I knows his ways, and Em'ly's, and I knows their sorrows, and can be a comfort to 'em, some odd times, and labour for 'em allus! Dan'l, deary Dan'l, let me go 'long with you!"

And Mrs. Gummidge took his hand, and kissed it with a homely pathos and affection, in a homely rapture of devotion and gratitude, that he well deserved.

We brought the locker out, extinguished the candle, fastened the door on the outside, and left the old boat close shut up, a dark speck in the cloudy night. Next day, when we were returning to London outside the coach, Mrs. Gummidge and her basket were on the seat behind, and Mrs. Gummidge was happy.

CHAPTER LII.

I ASSIST AT AN EXPLOSION.

When the time Mr. Micawber had appointed so mysteriously, was within four-and-twenty hours of being come, my aunt and I consulted how we should proceed; for my aunt was very unwilling to leave Dora. Ah! how easily I carried Dora up and down stairs, now!

We were disposed, notwithstanding Mr. Micawber's stipulation for my aunt's attendance, to arrange that she should stay at home, and be represented by Mr. Dick and me. In short, we had resolved to take this course, when Dora again unsettled us by declaring that she never would forgive herself, and never would forgive her bad boy, if my aunt remained behind, on any pretence.

"I won't speak to you," said Dora, shaking her curls at my aunt. "I'll be disagreeable! I'll make Jip bark at you all day. I shall be sure that you really are a cross old thing, if you don't go!"

"Tut, Blossom!" laughed my aunt. "You know you can't do without me!"

"Yes, I can," said Dora. "You are no use to me at all. You never run up and down stairs for me, all day long. You never sit and tell me stories about Doady, when his shoes were worn out, and he was covered with dust—oh, what a poor little mite of a fellow! You never do anything at all to please me, do you, dear?" Dora made haste to kiss my aunt, and say, "Yes, you do! I'm only joking!" —lest my aunt should think she really meant it.

"But, aunt," said Dora, coaxingly, "now listen. You must go. I shall tease you, till you let me have my own way about it. I shall lead my naughty boy such a life, if he don't make you go. I shall make myself so disagreeable —and so will Jip! You'll wish you had gone, like a good thing, for ever and ever so long, if you don't go. Besides," said Dora, putting back her hair, and looking wonderingly at my aunt and me, "why shouldn't you both go? I am not very ill indeed. Am I?"

"Why, what a question!" cried my aunt.

"What a fancy!" said I.

"Yes! I know I am a silly little thing!" said Dora, slowly looking from one of us to the other, and then putting up her pretty lips to kiss us as she lay upon her couch. "Well, then, you must both go, or I shall not believe you; and then I shall cry!"

I saw, in my aunt's face, that she began to give way now, and Dora brightened again, as she saw it too.

"You'll come back with so much to tell me, that it'll take at least a week to make me understand!" said Dora. "Because I know I shan't understand, for a length of time, if there's any business in it. And there's sure to be some business in it! If there's anything to add up, besides, I don't know when I shall make it out; and my bad boy will look so miserable all the time. There! Now you'll go, won't you? You'll only be gone one night, and Jip will take care of me while you are gone. Doady will carry me up-stairs before you go, and I won't come down again till you come back; and you shall take Agnes a dreadfully scolding letter from me, because she has never been to see us!"

We agreed, without any more consultation, that we would both go, and that Dora was a little Impostor, who feigned to be rather unwell, because she liked to be petted. She was greatly pleased, and very merry; and we four, that is to say, my aunt, Mr. Dick, Traddles, and I, went down to Canterbury by the Dover mail that night.

At the hotel where Mr. Micawber had requested us to await him, which we got into, with some trouble, in the middle of the night, I found a letter, importing that he would appear in the morning punctually at half-past nine. After which, we went shivering, at that uncomfortable hour, to our respective beds, through various close passages; which smelt as if they had been steeped, for ages, in a solution of soup and stables.

Early in the morning, I sauntered through the dear old tranquil streets, and again mingled with the shadows of the venerable gateways and churches. The rooks were sailing about the Cathedral towers; and the towers themselves, overlooking many a long unaltered mile of the rich country and its pleasant streams, were cutting the bright morning air, as if there were no such thing as change on earth. Yet the bells, when they sounded, told me sorrowfully of change in everything; told me of their own age, and my pretty Dora's youth; and of the many, never old, who had lived and loved and died, while the reverberations of the bells had hummed through the rusty armour of the Black Prince hanging up within, and, motes upon the deep of Time, had lost themselves in air, as circles do in water.

I looked at the old house from the corner of the street, but did not go nearer to it, lest, being observed, I might unwittingly do any harm to the design I had come to aid. The early sun was striking edgewise on its gables and lattice-windows, touching them with gold; and some beams of its old peace seemed to touch my heart.

I strolled into the country for an hour or so, and then returned by the main street, which in the interval had shaken off its last night's sleep. Among those who were stirring in the shops, I saw my ancient enemy the butcher, now advanced to top-boots and a baby, and in business for himself. He was nursing the baby, and appeared to be a benignant member of society.

We all became very anxious and impatient, when we sat down to breakfast. As it approached nearer and nearer to half-past nine o'clock, our restless expectation of Mr. Micawber increased. At last we made no more pretence of attending to the meal, which, except with Mr. Dick, had been a mere form from the first; but my aunt walked up and down the room, Traddles sat upon the sofa affecting to read the paper with his eyes on the ceiling; and I looked out of the window to give early notice of Mr. Micawber's coming. Nor had I long to watch, for, at the first chime of the half-hour, he appeared in the street.

"Here he is," said I, "and not in his legal attire!"

My aunt tied the strings 'of her bonnet (she had come down to breakfast in it), and put on her shawl, as if she were ready for anything that was resolute and uncompromising. Traddles buttoned his coat with a determined air. Mr. Dick, disturbed by these formidable appearances, but feeling it necessary to imitate them, pulled his hat, with both hands, as firmly over his ears as he possibly could; and instantly took it off again, to welcome Mr. Micawber.

"Gentlemen, and madam," said Mr. Micawber, "good morning! My dear Sir," to Mr. Dick, who shook hands with him violently, "you are extremely good."

"Have you breakfasted?" said Mr. Dick. "Have a chop!"

"Not for the world, my good Sir!" cried Mr. Micawber, stopping him on his way to the bell; "appetite and myself, Mr. Dixon, have long been strangers."

Mr. Dixon was so pleased with his new name, and appeared to think it so very obliging in Mr. Micawber to confer it upon him, that he shook hands with him again, and laughed rather childishly.

"Dick," said my aunt, "attention!"

Mr. Dick recovered himself, with a blush.

"Now, Sir," said my aunt to Mr. Micawber, as she put on her gloves, "we are ready for Mount Vesuvius, or anything else, as soon as you please."

"Madam," returned Mr. Micawber, "I trust you will shortly witness an eruption. Mr. Traddles, I have your permission, I believe, to mention here that we have been in communication together?"

"It is undoubtedly the fact, Copperfield," said Traddles, to whom I looked in surprise. "Mr. Micawber has consulted me, in reference to what he has in contemplation; and I have advised him to the best of my judgment."

"Unless I deceive myself, Mr. Traddles," pursued Mr. Micawber, "what I contemplate is a disclosure of an important nature."

"Highly so," said Traddles.

"Perhaps, under such circumstances, madam and gentlemen," said Mr. Micawber, "you will do me the favour to submit yourselves, for the moment, to the direction of one, who, however unworthy to be regarded in any other light but as a Waif and Stray upon the shore of human nature, is still your fellow-man, though crushed out of his original form by individual errors, and the accumulative force of a combination of circumstances?"

"We have perfect confidence in you, Mr. Micawber," said I, "and will do what you please."

"Mr. Copperfield," returned Mr. Micawber, "your confidence is not, at the existing juncture, ill-bestowed. I would beg to be allowed a start of five minutes by the clock; and then to receive the present company, inquiring for Miss Wickfield, at the office of Wickfield and Heep, whose Stipendiary I am."

My aunt and I looked at Traddles, who nodded his approval.

"I have no more," observed Mr. Micawber, "to say at present."

With which, to my infinite surprise, he included us all in a comprehensive bow, and disappeared; his manner being extremely distant, and his face extremely pale.

Traddles only smiled, and shook his head (with his hair standing upright on the top of it), when I looked to him for an explanation; so I took out my watch, and, as a last resource, counted off the five minutes. My aunt, with her own watch in her hand, did the like. When the time was expired, Traddles gave her his arm; and we all went out together to the old house, without saying one word on the way.

We found Mr. Micawber at his desk, in the turret office on the ground floor, either writing, or pretending to write, hard. The large office-ruler was stuck into his waistcoat, and was not so well concealed but that a foot or more of that instrument protruded from his bosom, like a new kind of shirt-frill.

As it appeared to me that I was expected to speak, I said aloud:

"How do you do, Mr. Micawber?"

"Mr. Copperfield," said Mr. Micawber, gravely, "I hope I see you well?"

"Is Miss Wickfield at home?" said I.

"Mr. Wickfield is unwell in bed, Sir, of a rheumatic fever," he returned; "but Miss Wickfield, I have no doubt, will be happy to see old friends. Will you walk in, Sir?"

He preceded us to the dining-room—the first room I had entered in that house—and flinging open the door of Mr. Wickfield's former office, said, in a sonorous voice:

"Miss Trotwood, Mr. David Copperfield, Mr. Thomas Traddles, and Mr. Dixon!"

I had not seen Uriah Heep since the time of the blow. Our visit astonished him, evidently; not the less, I dare say, because it astonished ourselves. He did not gather his eyebrows together, for he had none worth mentioning; but he frowned to that degree that he almost closed his small eyes, while the hurried raising of his grisly hand to his chin betrayed some trepidation or surprise. This was only when we were in the act of entering his room, and when I caught a glance at him over my aunt's shoulder. A moment afterwards, he was as fawning and as humble as ever.

"Well, I am sure," he said. "This is indeed an unexpected pleasure! To have, as I may say, all friends round Saint Paul's, at once, is a treat unlooked for! Mr. Copperfield, I hope I see you well, and—if I may umbly express self so—friendly towards them as is ever your friends, whether or not. Mrs. Copperfield, Sir, I hope she's getting on. We have been made quite uneasy by the poor accounts we have had of her state, lately, I do assure you."

I felt ashamed to let him take my hand, but I did not know yet what else to do.

"Things are changed in this office, Miss Trotwood, since I was a numble clerk, and held your pony; ain't they?" said Uriah, with his sickliest smile. "But I am not changed, Miss Trotwood."

"Well, Sir," returned my aunt, "to tell you the truth, I

think you are pretty constant to the promise of your youth; if that's any satisfaction to you."

"Thank you, Miss Trotwood," said Uriah, writhing in his ungainly manner, "for your good opinion! Micawber, tell 'em to let Miss Agnes know—and mother. Mother will be quite in a state, when she sees the present company!" said Uriah, setting chairs.

"You are not busy, Mr. Heep?" said Traddles, whose eye the cunning red eye accidentally caught, as it at once scrutinised and evaded us.

"No, Mr. Traddles," replied Uriah, resuming his official seat, and squeezing his bony hands, laid palm to palm, between his bony knees. "Not so much so, as I could wish. But lawyers, sharks, and leeches, are not easily satisfied, you know! Not but what myself and Micawber have our hands pretty full, in general, on account of Mr. Wickfield's being hardly fit for any occupation, Sir. But it's a pleasure as well as a duty, I am sure, to work for *him.* You've not been intimate with Mr. Wickfield, I think, Mr. Traddles? I believe I've only had the honour of seeing you once myself?"

"No, I have not been intimate with Mr. Wickfield," returned Traddles; "or I might perhaps have waited on you long ago, Mr. Heep."

There was something in the tone of this reply, which made Uriah look at the speaker again, with a very sinister and suspicious expression. But, seeing only Traddles, with his good-natured face, simple manner, and hair on end, he dismissed it as he replied, with a jerk of his whole body, but especially his throat:

"I am sorry for that, Mr. Traddles. You would have admired him as much as we all do. His little failings would only have endeared him to you the more. But if you would like to hear my fellow-partner eloquently spoken of, I should refer you to Copperfield. The family is a subject he's very strong upon, if you never heard him."

I was prevented from disclaiming the compliment (if I should have done so, in any case), by the entrance of Agnes, now ushered in by Mr. Micawber. She was not quite so self-possessed as usual, I thought; and had evidently undergone anxiety and fatigue. But her earnest cordiality, and her quiet beauty, shone with the gentler lustre for it.

I saw Uriah watch her while she greeted us; and he reminded me of an ugly and rebellious genie watching a good spirit. In the meanwhile, some slight sign passed between Mr. Micawber and Traddles; and Traddles, unobserved except by me, went out.

"Don't wait, Micawber," said Uriah.

Mr. Micawber, with his hand upon the ruler in his breast, stood erect before the door, most unmistakably contemplating one of his fellow-men, and that man his employer.

"What are you waiting for?" said Uriah. "Micawber! did you hear me tell you not to wait?"

"Yes!" replied the immovable Mr. Micawber.

"Then why *do* you wait?" said Uriah.

"Because I—in short choose," replied Mr. Micawber, with a burst.

Uriah's cheeks lost colour, and an unwholesome paleness, still faintly tinged by his pervading red, overspread them. He looked at Mr. Micawber attentively, with his whole face breathing short and quick in every feature.

"You are a dissipated fellow, as all the world knows," he said, with an effort at a smile, "and I am afraid you'll oblige me to get rid of you. Go along! I'll talk to you presently."

"If there is a scoundrel on this earth," said Mr. Micaw-

ber, suddenly breaking out again with the utmost vehemence, "with whom I have already talked too much, that scoundrel's name is—HEEP!"

Uriah fell back, as if he had been struck or stung. Looking slowly round upon us with the darkest and wickedest expression that his face could wear, he said, in a lower voice:

"Oho! This is a conspiracy! You have met here, by appointment! You are playing Booty with my clerk, are you, Copperfield? Now, take care. You'll make nothing of this. We understand each other, you and me. There's no love between us. You were always a puppy with a proud stomach, from your first coming here; and you envy me my rise, do you? None of your plots against me; I'll counterplot you! Micawber, you be off. I'll talk to you presently."

"Mr. Micawber," said I, "there is a sudden change in this fellow, in more respects than the extraordinary one of his speaking the truth in one particular, which assures me that he is brought to bay Deal with him as he deserves!"

"You are a precious set of people, ain't you?" said Uriah, in the same low voice, and breaking out into a clammy heat, which he wiped from his forehead, with his long lean hand, "to buy over my clerk, who is the very scum of society,—as you yourself were, Copperfield, you know it, before any one had charity on you,—to defame me with his lies? Miss Trotwood, you had better stop this; or I'll stop your husband shorter than will be pleasant to you. I won't know your story professionally, for nothing, old lady! Miss Wickfield, if you have any love for your father, you had better not join that gang. I'll ruin him, if you do. Now, come! I have got some of you under the harrow. Think twice, before it goes over you. Think twice, you, Micawber, if you don't want to be crushed. I recommend you to take yourself off, and be talked to presently, you fool! while there's time to retreat. Where's mother?" he said, suddenly appearing to notice, with alarm, the absence of Traddles, and pulling down the bell-rope. "Fine doings in a person's own house!"

"Mrs. Heep is here, Sir," said Traddles, returning with that worthy mother of a worthy son. "I have taken the liberty of making myself known to her."

"Who are you to make yourself known?" retorted Uriah. "And what do you want here?"

"I am the agent and friend of Mr. Wickfield, Sir," said Traddles, in a composed business-like way. "And I have a power of attorney from him in my pocket, to act for him in all matters."

"The old ass has drunk himself into a state of dotage," said Uriah, turning uglier than before, "and it has been got from him by fraud!"

"Something has been got from him by fraud, I know," returned Traddles quietly; "and so do you, Mr. Heep. We will refer that question, if you please, to Mr. Micawber."

"Ury——!" Mrs. Heep began, with an anxious gesture.

"You hold your tongue, mother," he returned; "least said, soonest mended."

"But my Ury——"

"Will you hold your tongue, mother, and leave it to me?"

Though I had long known that his servility was false, and all his pretences knavish and hollow, I had had no adequate conception of the extent of his hypocrisy, until I now saw him with his mask off. The suddenness with which he dropped it, when he perceived that it was useless to him; the malice, insolence, and hatred, he revealed; the leer with which he exulted, even at this moment, in the evil he had done—all this time being desperate too, and at his wits' end for the means of getting the better of us—though perfectly consistent with the experience I had of him, at first took even me by surprise, who had known him so long, and disliked him so heartily.

I say nothing of the look he conferred on me, as he stood eyeing us, one after another; for I had always understood that he hated me, and I remembered the marks of my hand upon his cheek. But when his eyes passed on to Agnes, and I saw the rage with which he felt his power over her slipping away, and the exhibition, in their disappointment, of the odious passions that had led him to aspire to one whose virtues he could never appreciate or care for, I was shocked by the mere thought of her having lived, an hour, within sight of such a man.

After some rubbing of the lower part of his face, and some looking at us with those bad eyes, over his grisly fingers, he made one more address to me, half whining, and half abusive.

"You think it justifiable, do you, Copperfield, you who pride yourself so much on your honour and all the rest of it, to sneak about my place, eavesdropping with my clerk? If it had been *me*, I shouldn't have wondered; for I don't make myself out a gentleman (though I never was in the streets either, as you were, according to Micawber), but being *you!*—And you're not afraid of doing this, either? You don't think at all of what I shall do, in return; or of getting yourself into trouble for conspiracy and so forth? Very well. We shall see! Mr. What's-your-name, you were going to refer some question to Micawber. There's your referee. Why don't you make him speak? He has learned his lesson, I see."

Seeing that what he said had no effect on me or any of us, he sat on the edge of his table with his hands in his pockets, and one of his splay feet twisted round the other leg, waiting doggedly for what might follow.

Mr. Micawber, whose impetuosity I had restrained thus far with the greatest difficulty, and who had repeatedly interposed with the first syllable of SCOUN-drel! without getting to the second, now burst forward, drew the ruler from his breast (apparently as a defensive weapon), and produced from his pocket a foolscap document, folded in the form of a large letter. Opening this packet, with his old flourish, and glancing at the contents, as if he cherished an artistic admiration of their style of composition, he began to read as follows:

"'Dear Miss Trotwood and gentlemen——'"

"Bless and save the man!" exclaimed my aunt in a low voice. "He'd write letters by the ream, if it was a capital offence!"

Mr. Micawber, without hearing her, went on.

"'In appearing before you to denounce probably the most consummate Villain that has ever existed,'" Mr. Micawber, without looking off the letter, pointed the ruler, like a ghostly truncheon, at Uriah Heep, "'I ask no consideration for myself. The victim, from my cradle, of pecuniary liabilities to which I have been unable to respond, I have ever been the sport and toy of debasing circumstances. Ignominy, Want, Despair, and Madness, have, collectively or separately, been the attendants of my career.'"

The relish with which Mr. Micawber described himself, as a prey to these dismal calamities, was only to be equalled by the emphasis with which he read his letter; and the kind of homage he rendered to it with a roll of his head, when he thought he had hit a sentence very hard indeed.

"'In an accumulation of Ignominy, Want, Despair, and Madness, I entered the office—or, as our lively neighbour the Gaul would term it, the Bureau—of the Firm, nominally conducted under the appellation of Wickfield and—HEEP, but, in reality, wielded by HEEP alone. HEEP, and only HEEP, is the mainspring of that machine. HEEP, and only HEEP, is the Forger and the Cheat.'"

Uriah, more blue than white at these words, made a dart at the letter, as if to tear it in pieces. Mr. Micawber, with a perfect miracle of dexterity or luck, caught his advancing knuckles with the ruler, and disabled his right hand. It dropped at the wrist, as if it were broken. The blow sounded as if it had fallen on wood.

"The Devil take you!" said Uriah, writhing in a new way with pain. "I'll be even with you."

"Approach me again, you—you—you HEEP of infamy," gasped Mr. Micawber, "and if your head is human, I'll break it. Come on, come on!"

I think I never saw anything more ridiculous—I was sensible of it, even at the time—than Mr. Micawber making broadsword guards with the ruler, and crying, "Come on!" while Traddles and I pushed him back into a corner, from which, as often as we got him into it, he persisted in emerging again.

His enemy, muttering to himself, after wringing his wounded hand for some time, slowly drew off his neckkerchief and bound it up; then, held it in his other hand, and sat upon his table with his sullen face looking down.

Mr. Micawber, when he was sufficiently cool, proceeded with his letter.

"'The stipendiary emoluments in consideration of which I entered into the service of—HEEP,'" always pausing before that word and uttering it with astonishing vigour, "'were not defined, beyond the pittance, of twenty-two shillings and six per week. The rest was left contingent on the value of my professional exertions; in other and more expressive words, on the baseness of my nature, the cupidity of my motives, the poverty of my family, the general moral (or rather immoral) resemblance between myself and—HEEP. Need I say, that it soon became necessary for me to solicit from—HEEP—pecuniary advances towards the support of Mrs. Micawber, and our blighted but rising family? Need I say that this necessity had been foreseen by—HEEP? That those advances were secured by I O U's and other similar acknowledgments, known to the legal institutions of this country? And that I thus became immeshed in the web he had spun for my reception?'"

Mr. Micawber's enjoyment of his epistolary powers, in describing this unfortunate state of things, really seemed to outweigh any pain or anxiety that the reality could have caused him. He read on:

"'Then it was that—HEEP—began to favour me with just so much of his confidence, as was necessary to the discharge of his infernal business. Then it was that I began, if I may so Shakespearianly express myself, to dwindle, peak, and pine. I found that my services were constantly called into requisition for the falsification of business, and the mystification of an individual whom I will designate as Mr. W. That Mr. W. was imposed upon, kept in ignorance, and deluded, in every possible way; yet, that all this while, the ruffian—HEEP—was professing unbounded gratitude to, and unbounded friendship for, that much-abused gentleman. This was bad enough; but, as the philosophic Dane observes, with that universal applicability which distinguishes the illustrious ornament of the Elizabethan Era, worse remains behind!'"

Mr. Micawber was so very much struck by this happy rounding off with a quotation, that he indulged himself, and us, with a second reading of the sentence, under pretence of having lost his place.

"'It is not my intention,'" he continued, reading on, "'to enter on a detailed list, within the compass of the present epistle (though it is ready elsewhere), of the various malpractices of a minor nature, affecting the individual whom I have denominated Mr. W., to which I have been a tacitly consenting party. My object, when the contest within myself between stipend and no stipend, baker and no baker, existence and non-existence, ceased, was to take advantage of my opportunities to discover and expose the major malpractices committed, to that gentleman's grievous wrong and injury, by—HEEP. Stimulated by the silent monitor within, and by a no less touching and appealing monitor without—to whom I will briefly refer as Miss W. —I entered on a not unlaborious task of clandestine investigation, protracted now, to the best of my knowledge, information, and belief, over a period exceeding twelve calendar months.'"

He read this passage, as if it were from an Act of Parliament; and appeared majestically refreshed by the sound of the words.

"'My charges against—HEEP,'" he read on, glancing at him, and drawing the ruler into a convenient position under his left arm, in case of need, "'are as follows.'"

We all held our breath, I think. I am sure Uriah held his.

"'First,'" said Mr. Micawber. "When Mr. W.'s faculties and memory for business became, through causes into which it is not necessary or expedient for me to enter, weakened and confused,—HEEP—designedly perplexed and complicated the whole of the official transactions. When Mr. W. was least fit to enter on business,—HEEP—was always at hand to force him to enter on it. He obtained Mr. W.'s signature under such circumstances to documents of importance, representing them to be other documents of no importance. He induced Mr. W. to empower him to draw out, thus, one particular sum of trust-money, amounting to twelve six fourteen, two and nine, and employed it to meet pretended business charges and deficiencies which were either already provided for, or had never really existed. He gave this proceeding, throughout, the appearance of having originated in Mr. W.'s own dishonest intention, and of having been accomplished by Mr. W.'s own dishonest act; and has used it, ever since, to torture and constrain him.'"

"You shall prove this, you Copperfield!" said Uriah, with a threatening shake of the head. "All in good time!"

"Ask—HEEP—Mr. Traddles, who lived in his house after him," said Mr. Micawber, breaking off from the letter; "will you?"

"The fool himself—and lives there now," said Uriah, disdainfully.

"Ask—HEEP—if he ever kept a pocket-book in that house," said Mr. Micawber; "will you?"

I saw Uriah's lank hand stop, involuntarily, in the scraping of his chin.

"Or ask him," said Mr. Micawber, "if he ever burnt one there. If he says Yes, and asks you where the ashes are, refer him to Wilkins Micawber, and he will hear of something not at all to his advantage!"

The triumphant flourish with which Mr. Micawber delivered himself of these words, had a powerful effect in alarming the mother; who cried out in much agitation:

"Ury, Ury! Be umble, and make terms, my dear!"

"Mother!" he retorted, "will you keep quiet? You're in a fright, and don't know what you say or mean. Umble!" he repeated, looking at me, with a snarl; "I've umbled some of 'em for a pretty long time back, umble as I was!"

Mr. Micawber, genteelly adjusting his chin in his cravat, presently proceeded with his composition.

"'Second. HEEP has, on several occasions, to the best of my knowledge, information, and belief——'"

"But *that* won't do," muttered Uriah, relieved. "Mother, you keep quiet."

"We will endeavour to provide something that WILL do, and do for you finally, Sir, very shortly," replied Mr. Micawber.

"'Second. HEEP has, on several occasions, to the best of my knowledge, information, and belief, systematically forged, to various entries, books, and documents, the signature of Mr. W.; and has distinctly done so in one instance, capable of proof by me. To wit, in manner following, that is to say:'"

Again, Mr. Micawber had a relish in this formal piling up of words, which, however ludicrously displayed in his case, was, I must say, not at all peculiar to him. I have observed it, in the course of my life, in numbers of men. It seems to me to be a general rule. In the taking of legal oaths, for instance, deponents seem to enjoy themselves mightily when they come to several good words in succession, for the expression of one idea; as, that they utterly detest, abominate, and abjure, or so forth; and the old anathemas were made relishing on the same principle. We talk about the tyranny of words, but we like to tyrannise over them too; we are fond of having a large superfluous establishment of words to wait upon us on great occasions; we think it looks important, and sounds well. As we are not particular about the meaning of our liveries on state occasions, if they be but fine and numerous enough, so, the meaning or necessity of our words is a secondary consideration, if there be but a great parade of them. And as individuals get into trouble by making too great a show of liveries, or as slaves when they are too numerous rise against their masters, so I think I could mention a nation that has got into many great difficulties, and will get into many greater, from maintaining too large a retinue of words.

Mr. Micawber read on, almost smacking his lips:

"'To wit, in manner following, that is to say. Mr. W. being infirm, and it being within the bounds of probability that his decease might lead to some discoveries, and to the downfall of—HEEP's—power over the W. family,—as I, Wilkins Micawber, the undersigned, assume—unless the filial affection of his daughter could be secretly influenced from allowing any investigation of the partnership affairs to be ever made, the said—HEEP—deemed it expedient to have a bond ready by him, as from Mr. W., for the beforementioned sum of twelve six fourteen, two and nine, with interest, stated therein to have been advanced by—HEEP— to Mr. W. to save Mr. W. from dishonour; though really the sum was never advanced by him, and has long been replaced. The signatures to this instrument, purporting to be executed by Mr. W. and attested by Wilkins Micawber, are forgeries by—HEEP. I have, in my possession, in his hand and pocket-book, several similar imitations of Mr. W.'s signature, here and there defaced by fire, but legible to any one. I never attested any such document. And I have the document itself, in my possession.'"

Uriah Heep, with a start, took out of his pocket a bunch of keys, and opened a certain drawer; then, suddenly bethought himself of what he was about, and turned again towards us, without looking in it.

"'And I have the document,'" Mr. Micawber read again, looking about as if it were the text of a sermon, "' in my possession,'—that is to say, I had, early this morning, when this was written, but have since relinquished it to Mr. Traddles."

"It is quite true," assented Traddles.

"Ury, Ury!" cried the mother, "be umble and make terms. I know my son will be umble, gentlemen, if you'll give him time to think. Mr. Copperfield, I'm sure you know that he was always very umble, Sir!"

It was singular to see how the mother still held to the old trick, when the son had abandoned it as useless.

"Mother," he said, with an impatient bite at the handkerchief in which his hand was wrapped, "you had better take and fire a loaded gun at me."

"But I love you, Ury," cried Mrs. Heep. And I have no doubt she did; or that he loved her, however strange it may appear; though, to be sure, they were a congenial couple. "And I can't bear to hear you provoking the gentleman, and endangering of yourself more. I told the gentleman at first, when he told me up-stairs it was come to light, that I would answer for your being umble, and making amends. Oh, see how umble *I* am, gentlemen, and don't mind him!"

"Why, there's Copperfield, mother," he angrily retorted, pointing his lean finger at me, against whom all his animosity was levelled, as the prime mover in the discovery; and I did not undeceive him; "there's Copperfield, would have given you a hundred pound to say less than you've blurted out!"

"I can't help it, Ury," cried his mother. "I can't see you running into danger, through carrying your head so high. Better be umble, as you always was."

He remained for a little, biting the handkerchief, and then said to me with a scowl:

"What more have you got to bring forward? If anything, go on with it. What do you look at me for?"

Mr. Micawber promptly resumed his letter, only too glad to revert to a performance with which he was so highly satisfied.

"'Third. And last. I am now in a condition to show, by—HEEP's—false books, and—HEEP's—real memoranda, beginning with the partially destroyed pocket-book (which I was unable to comprehend, at the time of its accidental discovery by Mrs. Micawber, on our taking possession of our present abode, in the locker or bin devoted to the reception of the ashes calcined on our domestic hearth), that the weaknesses, the faults, the very virtues, the parental affections, and the sense of honour, of the unhappy Mr. W. have been for years acted on by, and warped to the base purposes of—HEEP. That Mr. W. has been for years deluded and plundered, in every conceivable manner, to the pecuniary aggrandisement of the avaricious, false, and grasping—HEEP. That the engrossing object of—HEEP—was, next to gain, to subdue Mr. and Miss W. (of his ulterior views in reference to the latter I say nothing) entirely to himself. That his last act, completed but a few months since, was to induce Mr. W. to execute a relinquishment of his share in the partnership, and even a bill of sale on the very furniture of his house, in consideration of a certain annuity, to be well and truly paid by—HEEP—on the four common quarter-days in each and every year. That these meshes; beginning with alarming and falsified accounts of the estate of which Mr. W. is the receiver, at a period when Mr. W. had launched into imprudent and ill-judged speculations, and may not have had the money, for which he was morally and legally responsible, in hand; going on with pretended borrowings of money at enormous interest, really coming from—HEEP—and by—HEEP—fraudulently obtained or withheld from Mr. W. himself, on pretence of such speculations or otherwise; perpetuated by a miscellaneous catalogue of unscrupulous chicaneries—gradually thickened, until the unhappy Mr. W. could see no world beyond. Bankrupt, as he believed, alike in circumstances, in all other hope, and in honour, his sole reliance was upon the monster in the garb of man,'"—Mr. Micawber made a good deal of this, as a new turn of expression,—"'who, by making himself necessary to him, had achieved his destruction. All this I undertake to show. Probably much more!'"

I whispered a few words to Agnes, who was weeping, half joyfully, half sorrowfully, at my side; and there was a movement among us, as if Mr. Micawber had finished. He said, with exceeding gravity, "Pardon me," and proceeded, with a mixture of the lowest spirits and the most intense enjoyment, to the peroration of his letter.

"'I have now concluded. It merely remains for me to substantiate these accusations; and then, with my ill-starred family, to disappear from the landscape on which we appear to be an incumbrance. That is soon done. It may be reasonably inferred that our baby will first expire of inanition, as being the frailest member of our circle; and that our twins will follow next in order. So be it! For myself, my Canterbury Pilgrimage has done much; imprisonment on civil process, and want, will soon do more. I trust that the labour and hazard of an investigation—of which the smallest results have been slowly pieced together, in the pressure of arduous avocations, under grinding penurious apprehensions, at rise of morn, at dewy eve, in the shadows of night, under the watchful eye of one whom it were superfluous to call Demon—combined with the struggle of parental Poverty to turn it, when completed, to the right account, may be as the sprinkling of a few drops of sweet water on my funereal pyre. I ask no more. Let it be, in justice, merely said of me, as of a gallant and eminent naval Hero, with whom I have no pretensions to cope, that what I have done, I did, in despite of mercenary and selfish objects,

"'For England, home, and beauty.'

"'Remaining always, &c., &c., WILKINS MICAWBER.'"

Much affected, but still intensely enjoying himself, Mr. Micawber folded up his letter, and handed it with a bow to my aunt, as something she might like to keep.

There was, as I had noticed on my first visit long ago, an iron safe in the room. The key was in it. A hasty suspicion seemed to strike Uriah; and, with a glance at Mr. Micawber, he went to it, and threw the doors clanking open. It was empty.

"Where are the books?" he cried, with a frightful face. "Some thief has stolen the books!"

Mr. Micawber tapped himself with the ruler. "*I* did, when I got the key from you as usual—but a little earlier—and opened it this morning."

"Don't be uneasy," said Traddles. "They have come into my possession. I will take care of them, under the authority I mentioned."

"You receive stolen goods, do you?" cried Uriah.

"Under such circumstances," answered Traddles, "yes."

What was my astonishment when I beheld my aunt, who had been profoundly quiet and attentive, make a dart at Uriah Heep, and seize him by the collar with both hands!

"You know what *I* want?" said my aunt.

"A strait-waistcoat," said he.

"No. My property!" returned my aunt. "Agnes, my dear, as long as I believed it had been really made away with by your father, I wouldn't—and, my dear, I didn't, even to Trot, as he knows—breathe a syllable of its having been placed here for investment. But, now I know this fellow's answerable for it, and I'll have it! Trot, come and take it away from him!"

Whether my aunt supposed, for the moment, that he kept her property in his neck-kerchief, I am sure I don't know; but she certainly pulled at it as if she thought so. I hastened to put myself between them, and to assure her that we would all take care that he should make the utmost restitution of everything he had wrongly got. This, and a few moments' reflection, pacified her; but she was not at all disconcerted by what she had done (though I cannot say as much for her bonnet), and resumed her seat composedly.

During the last few minutes, Mrs. Heep had been clamouring to her son to be "umble;" and had been going down on her knees to all of us in succession, and making the wildest promises. Her son sat her down in his chair; and, standing sulkily by her, holding her arm with his hand, but not rudely, said to me, with a ferocious look:

"What do you want done?"

"I will tell you what must be done," said Traddles.

"Has that Copperfield no tongue?" muttered Uriah. "I would do a good deal for you if you could tell me, without lying, that somebody had cut it out."

"My Uriah means to be umble!" cried his mother. "Don't mind what he says, good gentlemen!"

"What must be done," said Traddles, "is this. First, the deed of relinquishment, that we have heard of, must be given over to me now—here."

"Suppose I haven't got it," he interrupted.

"But you have," said Traddles; "therefore, you know, we won't suppose so." And I cannot help avowing that this was the first occasion on which I really did justice to the clear head, and the plain, patient, practical good sense, of my old schoolfellow. "Then," said Traddles, "you must prepare to disgorge all that your rapacity has become possessed of, and to make restoration to the last farthing. All the partnership books and papers must remain in our possession; all your books and papers; all money accounts and securities, of both kinds. In short, everything here."

"Must it? I don't know that," said Uriah. "I must have time to think about that."

"Certainly," replied Traddles; "but, in the meanwhile, and until everything is done to our satisfaction, we shall maintain possession of these things; and beg you—in short, compel you—to keep your own room, and hold no communication with any one."

"I won't do it!" said Uriah, with an oath.

"Maidstone Jail is a safer place of detention," observed Traddles; "and though the law may be longer in righting us, and may not be able to right us so completely as you can, there is no doubt of its punishing *you*. Dear me, you know that quite as well as I! Copperfield, will you go round to the Guildhall, and bring a couple of officers?"

Here, Mrs. Heep broke out again, crying on her knees to Agnes to interfere in their behalf, exclaiming that he was very humble, and it was all true, and if he didn't do what we wanted, she would, and much more to the same purpose; being half frantic with fears for her darling. To inquire what he might have done, if he had had any boldness, would be like inquiring what a mongrel cur might do, if it had the spirit of a tiger. He was a coward, from head to foot; and showed his dastardly nature through his sullenness and mortification, as much as at any time of his mean life.

"Stop!" he growled to me; and wiped his hot face with his hand. "Mother, hold your noise. Well! Let 'em have that deed. Go and fetch it!"

"Do you help her, Mr. Dick," said Traddles, "if you please."

Proud of his commission, and understanding it, Mr. Dick accompanied her as a shepherd's dog might accompany a sheep. But, Mrs. Heep gave him little trouble; for she not only returned with the deed, but with the box in which it was, where we found a banker's book and some other papers that were afterwards serviceable.

"Good!" said Traddles, when this was brought. "Now, Mr. Heep, you can retire to think: particularly observing, if you please, that I declare to you, on the part of all present, that there is only one thing to be done; that it is what I have explained; and that it must be done without delay."

Uriah, without lifting his eyes from the ground, shuffled across the room with his hand to his chin, and pausing at the door, said:

"Copperfield, I have always hated you. You've always been an upstart, and you've always been against me."

"As I think I told you once before," said I, "it is you who have been, in your greed and cunning, against all the world. It may be profitable to you to reflect, in future, that there never were greed and cunning in the world yet, that did not do too much, and overreach themselves. It is as certain as death."

"Or as certain as they used to teach at school (the same school where I picked up so much umbleness), from nine o'clock to eleven, that labour was a curse; and from eleven o'clock to one, that it was a blessing and a cheerfulness, and a dignity, and I don't know what all, eh?" said he with a sneer. "You preach, about as consistent as they did. Won't umbleness go down? I shouldn't have got round my gentleman fellow-partner without it, I think.—Micawber, you old bully, I'll pay *you!*"

Mr. Micawber, supremely defiant of him and his extended finger, and making a great deal of his chest until he had slunk out at the door, then addressed himself to me, and proffered me the satisfaction of "witnessing the re-establishment of mutual confidence between himself and Mrs. Micawber." After which, he invited the company generally to the contemplation of that affecting spectacle.

"The veil that has long been interposed between Mrs. Micawber and myself, is now withdrawn," said Mr. Micawber; "and my children and the Author of their Being can once more come in contact on equal terms."

As we were all very grateful to him, and all desirous to show that we were, as well as the hurry and disorder of our spirits would permit, I dare say we should all have gone, but that it was necessary for Agnes to return to her father, as yet unable to bear more than the dawn of hope; and for some one else to hold Uriah in safe keeping. So, Traddles remained for the latter purpose, to be presently relieved by Mr. Dick; and Mr. Dick, my aunt, and I, went home with Mr. Micawber. As I parted hurriedly from the dear girl to whom I owed so much, and thought from what she had been saved, perhaps, that morning—her better resolution notwithstanding—I felt devoutly thankful for the miseries of my younger days which had brought me to the knowledge of Mr. Micawber.

His house was not far off; and as the street-door opened into the sitting-room, and he bolted in with a precipitation quite his own, we found ourselves at once in the bosom of the family. Mr. Micawber exclaiming, "Emma! my life!" rushed into Mrs. Micawber's arms. Mrs. Micawber shrieked, and folded Mr. Micawber in her embrace. Miss Micawber, nursing the unconscious stranger of Mrs. Micawber's last letter to me, was sensibly affected. The stranger leaped. The twins testified their joy by several inconvenient but innocent demonstrations. Master Micawber, whose disposition appeared to have been soured by early disappointment, and whose aspect had become morose, yielded to his better feelings, and blubbered.

"Emma!" said Mr. Micawber. "The cloud is past from my mind. Mutual confidence, so long preserved between us once, is restored, to know no farther interruption. Now, welcome poverty!" cried Mr. Micawber, shedding tears. "Welcome misery, welcome houselessness, welcome hunger, rags, tempest, and beggary! Mutual confidence will sustain us to the end!"

With these expressions, Mr. Micawber placed Mrs. Micawber in a chair, and embraced the family all round; welcoming a variety of bleak prospects, which appeared, to the best of my judgment, to be anything but welcome to them; and calling upon them to come out into Canterbury and sing a chorus, as nothing else was left for their support.

But Mrs. Micawber having, in the strength of her emotions, fainted away, the first thing to be done, even before the chorus could be considered complete, was to recover her. This, my aunt and Mr. Micawber did; and then my aunt was introduced, and Mrs. Micawber recognised me.

"Excuse me, dear Mr. Copperfield," said the poor lady, giving me her hand, "but I am not strong; and the removal of the late misunderstanding between Mr. Micawber and myself was at first too much for me."

"Is this all your family, ma'am?" said my aunt.

"There are no more at present," returned Mrs. Micawber.

"Good gracious, I didn't mean that, ma'am," said my aunt. "I mean, are all these yours?"

"Madam," replied Mr. Micawber, "it is a true bill."

"And that eldest young gentleman, now," said my aunt, musing. "What has he been brought up to?"

"It was my hope when I came here," said Mr. Micawber, "to have got Wilkins into the Church: or perhaps I shall express my meaning more strictly, if I say the Choir. But there was no vacancy for a tenor in the venerable Pile for which this city is so justly eminent; and he has—in short, he has contracted a habit of singing in public-houses, rather than in sacred edifices."

"But he means well," said Mrs. Micawber, tenderly.

"I dare say, my love," rejoined Mr. Micawber, "that he means particularly well; but I have not yet found that he carries out his meaning, in any given direction whatsoever."

Master Micawber's moroseness of aspect returned upon him again, and he demanded, with some temper, what he was to do? Whether he had been born a carpenter, or a coach-painter, any more than he had been born a bird? Whether he could go into the next street, and open a chemist's shop? Whether he could rush to the next assizes, and proclaim himself a lawyer? Whether he could come out by force at the opera, and succeed by violence? Whether he

could do anything, without being brought up to something?

My aunt mused a little while, and then said:

"Mr. Micawber, I wonder you have never turned your thoughts to emigration."

"Madam," returned Mr. Micawber, "it was the dream of my youth, and the fallacious aspiration of my riper years." I am thoroughly persuaded, by the bye, that he had never thought of it in his life.

"Ay?" said my aunt, with a glance at me. "Why, what a thing it would be for yourselves and your family, Mr. and Mrs. Micawber, if you were to emigrate now."

"Capital, madam, capital," urged Mr. Micawber, gloomily.

"That is the principal, I may say the only difficulty, my dear Mr. Copperfield," assented his wife.

"Capital?" cried my aunt. "But you are doing us a great service—have done us a great service, I may say, for surely much will come out of the fire—and what could we do for you, that would be half so good as to find the capital?"

"I could not receive it as a gift," said Mr. Micawber, full of fire and animation, "but if a sufficient sum could be advanced, say at five per cent. interest, per annum, upon my personal liability—say my notes of hand, at twelve, eighteen, and twenty-four months, respectively, to allow time for something to turn up——"

"Could be? Can be, and shall be, on your own terms," returned my aunt, "if you say the word. Think of this now, both of you. Here are some people David knows, going out to Australia shortly. If you decide to go, why shouldn't you go in the same ship? You may help each other. Think of this now, Mr. and Mrs. Micawber. Take your time, and weigh it well."

"There is but one question, my dear ma'am, I could wish to ask," said Mrs. Micawber. "The climate, I believe, is healthy."

"Finest in the world!" said my aunt.

"Just so," returned Mrs. Micawber. "Then my question arises. Now, are the circumstances of the country such, that a man of Mr. Micawber's abilities would have a fair chance of rising in the social scale? I will not say, at present, might he aspire to be Governor, or anything of that sort; but would there be a reasonable opening for his talents to develop themselves—that would be amply sufficient—and find their own expansion?"

"No better opening anywhere," said my aunt, "for a man who conducts himself well, and is industrious."

"For a man who conducts himself well," repeated Mrs. Micawber, with her clearest business manner, "and is industrious. Precisely. It is evident to me that Australia is the legitimate sphere of action for Mr. Micawber!"

"I entertain the conviction, my dear madam," said Mr. Micawber, "that it is, under existing circumstances, the land, the only land, for myself and family; and that something of an extraordinary nature will turn up on that shore. It is no distance—comparatively speaking; and though consideration is due to the kindness of your proposal, I assure you that is a mere matter of form."

Shall I ever forget how, in a moment, he was the most sanguine of men, looking on to fortune; or how Mrs. Micawber presently discoursed about the habits of the kangaroo! Shall I ever recall that street of Canterbury on a market-day, without recalling him, as he walked back with us; expressing, in the hardy roving manner he assumed, the unsettled habits of a temporary sojourner in the land; and looking at the bullocks, as they came by, with the eye of an Australian farmer!

RESTORATION OF MUTUAL CONFIDENCE BETWEEN MR. AND MRS. MICAWBER.

CHAPTER LIII.

ANOTHER RETROSPECT.

I MUST pause yet once again. Oh, my child-wife, there is a figure in the moving crowd before my memory, quiet and still, saying in its innocent love and childish beauty, Stop to think of me—turn to look upon the Little Blossom, as it flutters to the ground!

I do. All else grows dim, and fades away. I am again with Dora, in our cottage. I do not know how long she has been ill. I am so used to it in feeling, that I cannot count the time. It is not really long, in weeks or months; but, in my usage and experience, it is a weary, weary while.

They have left off telling me to "wait a few days more." I have begun to fear, remotely, that the day may never shine, when I shall see my child-wife running in the sunlight with her old friend Jip.

He is, as it were suddenly, grown very old. It may be, that he misses in his mistress, something that enlivened him and made him younger; but he mopes, and his sight is weak, and his limbs are feeble, and my aunt is sorry that he objects to her no more, but creeps near her as he lies on Dora's bed—she sitting at the bedside—and mildly licks her hand.

Dora lies smiling on us, and is beautiful, and utters no hasty or complaining word. She says that we are very good to her; that her dear old careful boy is tiring himself out, she knows; that my aunt has no sleep, yet is always wakeful, active, and kind. Sometimes, the little bird-like ladies come to see her; and then we talk about our wedding-day, and all that happy time.

What a strange rest and pause in my life there seems to be—and in all life, within doors and without—when I sit in the quiet, shaded, orderly room, with the blue eyes of my child-wife turned towards me, and her little fingers twining round my hand! Many and many an hour I sit thus; but, of all those times, three times come the freshest on my mind.

It is morning; and Dora, made so trim by my aunt's hands, shows me how her pretty hair *will* curl upon the pillow yet, and how long and bright it is, and how she likes to have it loosely gathered in that net she wears.

"Not that I am vain of it, now, you mocking boy," she says, when I smile; "but because you used to say you thought it so beautiful; and because, when I first began to think about you, I used to peep in the glass, and wonder whether you would like very much to have a lock of it. Oh what a foolish fellow you were, Doady, when I gave you one!"

"That was on the day when you were painting the flowers I had given you, Dora, and when I told you how much in love I was."

"Ah! but I didn't like to tell *you*," says Dora, "*then*, how I had cried over them, because I believed you really liked me! When I can run about again as I used to do, Doady, let us go and see those places where we were such a silly couple, shall we? And take some of the old walks? And not forget poor papa?"

"Yes, we will, and have some happy days. So you must make haste to get well, my dear."

"Oh, I shall soon do that! I am so much better, you don't know!"

It is evening; and I sit in the same chair, by the same bed, with the same face turned towards me. We have been silent, and there is a smile upon her face. I have ceased to carry my light burden up and down stairs now. She lies here all the day.

"Doady!"

"My dear Dora!"

"You won't think what I am going to say, unreasonable, after what you told me, such a little while ago, of Mr. Wickfield's not being well? I want to see Agnes. Very much I want to see her."

"I will write to her, my dear."

"Will you?"

"Directly."

"What a good, kind boy! Doady, take me on your arm. Indeed, my dear, it's not a whim. It's not a foolish fancy. I want, very much indeed, to see her!"

"I am certain of it. I have only to tell her so, and she is sure to come."

"You are very lonely when you go down stairs, now?" Dora whispers, with her arm about my neck.

"How can I be otherwise, my own love, when I see your empty chair?"

"My empty chair!" She clings to me for a little while, in silence. "And you really miss me, Doady?" looking up, and brightly smiling. "Even poor, giddy, stupid me?"

"My heart, who is there upon earth that I could miss so much?"

"Oh, husband! I am so glad, yet so sorry!" creeping closer to me, and folding me in both her arms. She laughs and sobs, and then is quiet, and quite happy.

"Quite!" she says. "Only give Agnes my dear love, and tell her that I want very, very much to see her; and I have nothing left to wish for."

"Except to get well again, Dora."

"Ah, Doady! Sometimes I think—you know I always was a silly little thing!—that that will never be!"

"Don't say so, Dora! Dearest love, don't think so!"

"I won't, if I can help it, Doady. But I am very happy; though my dear boy is so lonely by himself, before his child-wife's empty chair!"

It is night; and I am with her still. Agnes has arrived; has been among us, for a whole day and an evening. She, my aunt, and I, have sat with Dora since the morning, all together. We have not talked much, but Dora has been perfectly contented and cheerful. We are now alone.

Do I know, now, that my child-wife will soon leave me? They have told me so; they have told me nothing new to my thoughts; but I am far from sure that I have taken that truth to heart. I cannot master it. I have withdrawn by myself, many times to-day, to weep. I have remembered Who wept for a parting between the living and the dead. I have bethought me of all that gracious and compassionate history. I have tried to resign myself, and to console myself; and that, I hope, I may have done imperfectly; but what I cannot firmly settle in my mind is, that the end will absolutely come. I hold her hand in mine, I hold her heart in mine, I see her love for me, alive in all its strength. I cannot shut out a pale lingering shadow of belief that she will be spared.

"I am going to speak to you, Doady. I am going to say something I have often thought of saying, lately. You won't mind?" with a gentle look.

"Mind, my darling?"

"Because I don't know what you will think, or what you may have thought sometimes. Perhaps you have often thought the same. Doady, dear, I am afraid I was too young."

I lay my face upon the pillow by her, and she looks into my eyes, and speaks very softly. Gradually, as she goes on, I feel, with a stricken heart, that she is speaking of herself as past.

"I am afraid, dear, I was too young. I don't mean in years only, but in experience, and thoughts, and everything. I was such a silly little creature! I am afraid it would have been better, if we had only loved each other as a boy and girl, and forgotten it. I have begun to think I was not fit to be a wife."

I try to stay my tears, and to reply, "Oh, Dora, love, as fit as I to be a husband!"

"I don't know," with the old shake of her curls. "Perhaps! But, if I had been more fit to be married, I might have made you more so, too. Besides, you are very clever, and I never was."

"We have been very happy, my sweet Dora."

"I was very happy, very. But, as years went on, my dear boy would have wearied of his child-wife. She would have been less and less a companion for him. He would have been more and more sensible of what was wanting in his home. She wouldn't have improved. It is better as it is."

"Oh, Dora, dearest, dearest, do not speak to me so. Every word seems a reproach!"

"No, not a syllable!" she answers, kissing me. "Oh, my dear, you never deserved it, and I loved you far too well, to say a reproachful word to you, in earnest—it was all the merit I had, except being pretty—or you thought me so. Is it lonely, down stairs, Doady?"

"Very! Very!"

"Don't cry! Is my chair there?"

"In its old place."

"Oh, how my poor boy cries! Hush, hush! Now, make me one promise. I want to speak to Agnes. When you go down stairs, tell Agnes so, and send her up to me; and while I speak to her, let no one come—not even aunt. I want to speak to Agnes by herself. I want to speak to Agnes, quite alone."

I promise that she shall, immediately; but I cannot leave her, for my grief.

"I said that it was better as it is!" she whispers, as she holds me in her arms. "Oh, Doady, after more years, you never could have loved your child-wife better than you do; and, after more years, she would so have tried and disappointed you, that you might not have been able to love her half so well! I know I was too young and foolish. It is much better as it is!"

Agnes is down stairs, when I go into the parlour; and I give her the message. She disappears, leaving me alone with Jip.

His Chinese house is by the fire; and he lies within it, on his bed of flannel, querulously trying to sleep. The bright moon is high and clear. As I look out on the night, my tears fall fast, and my undisciplined heart is chastened heavily—heavily.

I sit down by the fire, thinking with a blind remorse of all those secret feelings I have nourished since my marriage. I think of every little trifle between me and Dora, and feel the truth, that trifles make the sum of life. Ever rising from the sea of my remembrance, is the image of the dear child as I knew her first, graced by my young love, and by her own, with every fascination wherein such love is rich. Would it, indeed, have been better if we had loved each other as a boy and girl, and forgotten it? Undisciplined heart, reply!

How the time wears, I know not; until I am recalled by my child-wife's old companion. More restless than he was, he crawls out of his house, and looks at me, and wanders to the door, and whines to go up-stairs.

"Not to-night, Jip! Not to-night!"

He comes very slowly back to me, licks my hand, and lifts his dim eyes to my face.

"Oh, Jip! It may be, never again!"

He lies down at my feet, stretches himself out as if to sleep, and with a plaintive cry, is dead.

"Oh, Agnes! Look, look, here!"

—That face, so full of pity and of grief, that rain of tears, that awful mute appeal to me, that solemn hand upraised towards Heaven!

"Agnes?"

It is over. Darkness comes before my eyes; and, for a time, all things are blotted out of my remembrance.

CHAPTER LIV.

MR. MICAWBER'S TRANSACTIONS.

THIS is not the time at which I am to enter on the state of my mind beneath its load of sorrow. I came to think that the Future was walled up before me, that the energy and action of my life were at an end, that I never could find any refuge but in the grave. I came to think so, I say, but not in the first shock of my grief. It slowly grew to that. If the events I go on to relate, had not thickened around me, in the beginning to confuse, and in the end to augment, my affliction, it is possible (though I think not probable), that I might have fallen at once into this condition. As it was, an interval occurred before I fully knew my own distress; an interval, in which I even supposed that its sharpest pangs were past; and when my mind could soothe itself by resting on all that was most innocent and beautiful, in the tender story that was closed for ever.

When it was first proposed that I should go abroad, or how it came to be agreed among us that I was to seek the restoration of my peace in change and travel, I do not, even now, distinctly know. The spirit of Agnes so pervaded all we thought, and said, and did, in that time of sorrow, that I assume I may refer the project to her influence. But her influence was so quiet that I know no more.

And now, indeed, I began to think that in my old association of her with the stained-glass window in the church, a prophetic foreshadowing of what she would be to me, in the calamity that was to happen in the fulness of time, had found a way into my mind. In all that sorrow, from the moment, never to be forgotten, when she stood before me with her upraised hand, she was like a sacred presence in my lonely house. When the Angel of Death alighted there, my child-wife fell asleep—they told me so when I could bear to hear it—on her bosom, with a smile. From my swoon, I first awoke to a consciousness of her compassionate tears, her words of hope and peace, her gentle face bending down as from a purer region nearer Heaven, over my undisciplined heart, and softening its pain.

Let me go on.

I was to go abroad. That seemed to have been determined among us from the first. The ground now covering all that could perish of my departed wife, I waited only for what Mr. Micawber called the "final pulverisation of Heep," and for the departure of the emigrants.

At the request of Traddles, most affectionate and devoted of friends in my trouble, we returned to Canterbury: I mean my aunt, Agnes, and I. We proceeded by appointment straight to Mr. Micawber's house; where, and at Mr. Wickfield's, my friend had been labouring ever since our explosive meeting. When poor Mrs. Micawber saw me come in, in my black clothes, she was sensibly affected. There was a great deal of good in Mrs. Micawber's heart, which had not been dunned out of it in all those many years.

"Well, Mr. and Mrs. Micawber," was my aunt's first salutation after we were seated. "Pray, have you thought about that emigration proposal of mine?"

"My dear madam," returned Mr. Micawber, "perhaps I cannot better express the conclusion at which Mrs. Micawber, your humble servant, and I may add our children, have jointly and severally arrived, than by borrowing the language of an illustrious poet, to reply that our Boat is on the shore, and our Bark is on the sea."

"That's right," said my aunt. "I augur all sorts of good from your sensible decision."

"Madam, you do us a great deal of honour," he rejoined. He then referred to a memorandum. "With respect to the pecuniary assistance enabling us to launch our frail canoe on the ocean of enterprise, I have reconsidered that important business point; and would beg to propose my notes of hand—drawn, it is needless to stipulate, on stamps of the amounts respectively required by the various Acts of Parliament applying to such securities—at eighteen, twenty-four, and thirty months. The proposition I originally submitted, was twelve, eighteen, and twenty-four; but I am apprehensive that such an arrangement might not allow sufficient time for the requisite amount of—Something—to turn up. We might not," said Mr. Micawber, looking round the room as if it represented several hundred acres of highly-cultivated land, "on the first responsibility becoming due, have been successful in our harvest, or we might not have got our harvest in. Labour, I believe, is sometimes difficult to obtain in that portion of our colonial possessions where it will be our lot to combat with the teeming soil."

"Arrange it in any way you please, Sir," said my aunt.

"Madam," he replied, "Mrs. Micawber and myself are deeply sensible of the very considerate kindness of our friends and patrons. What I wish is, to be perfectly business-like, and perfectly punctual. Turning over, as we are about to turn over, an entirely new leaf; and falling back, as we are now in the act of falling back, for a Spring of no common magnitude; it is important to my sense of self-respect, besides being an example to my son, that these arrangements should be concluded as between man and man."

I don't know that Mr. Micawber attached any meaning to this last phrase; I don't know that anybody ever does, or did; but he appeared to relish it uncommonly, and repeated, with an impressive cough, "as between man and man."

"I propose," said Mr. Micawber, "Bills—a convenience to the mercantile world, for which, I believe, we are originally indebted to the Jews, who appear to me to have had a devilish deal too much to do with them ever since—because they are negotiable. But if a Bond, or any other description of security, would be preferred, I should be happy to execute any such instrument. As between man and man."

My aunt observed, that in a case where both parties were willing to agree to anything, she took it for granted there would be no difficulty in settling this point. Mr. Micawber was of her opinion.

"In reference to our domestic preparations, madam," said Mr. Micawber, with some pride, "for meeting the destiny to which we are now understood to be self-devoted, I beg to report them. My eldest daughter attends at five every morning in a neighbouring establishment, to acquire the process—if process it may be called—of milking cows. My younger children are instructed to observe, as closely as circumstances will permit, the habits of the pigs and poultry maintained in the poorer parts of this city: a pursuit from which they have, on two occasions, been brought home, within an inch of being run over. I have myself directed some attention, during the past week, to the art of baking; and my son Wilkins has issued forth with a walking-stick and driven cattle, when permitted, by the rugged hirelings who had them in charge, to render any voluntary service in that direction—which I regret to say, for the credit of our nature, was not often; he being generally warned, with imprecations, to desist."

"All very right, indeed," said my aunt, encouragingly. "Mrs. Micawber has been busy, too, I have no doubt."

"My dear madam," returned Mrs. Micawber, with her business-like air, "I am free to confess, that I have not been actively engaged in pursuits immediately connected with cultivation or with stock, though well aware that both will claim my attention on a foreign shore. Such opportunities as I have been enabled to alienate from my domestic duties, I have devoted to corresponding at some length with my family. For I own it seems to me, my dear Mr. Copperfield," said Mrs. Micawber, who always fell back on me, I suppose from old habit, to whomsoever else she might address her discourse at starting, "that the time is come when the past should be buried in oblivion; when my family should take Mr. Micawber by the hand, and Mr. Micawber should take my family by the hand; when the lion should lie down with the lamb, and my family be on terms with Mr. Micawber."

I said I thought so too.

"This, at least, is the light, my dear Mr. Copperfield," pursued Mrs. Micawber, "in which *I* view the subject. When I lived at home with my papa and mama, my papa was accustomed to ask, when any point was under discussion in our limited circle, 'In what light does my Emma view the subject?' That my papa was too partial, I know; still, on such a point as the frigid coldness which has ever subsisted between Mr. Micawber and my family, I necessarily have formed an opinion, delusive though it may be."

"No doubt. Of course you have, ma'am," said my aunt.

"Precisely so," assented Mrs. Micawber. "Now, I may be wrong in my conclusions; it is very likely that I am; but my individual impression is, that the gulf between my family and Mr. Micawber may be traced to an apprehension, on the part of my family, that Mr. Micawber would require pecuniary accommodation. I cannot help thinking," said Mrs. Micawber, with an air of deep sagacity, "that there are members of my family who have been apprehensive that Mr. Micawber would solicit them for their names.—I do not mean to be conferred in Baptism upon our children, but to be inscribed on Bills of Exchange, and negotiated in the Money Market."

The look of penetration with which Mrs. Micawber announced this discovery, as if no one had ever thought of it before, seemed rather to astonish my aunt; who abruptly replied, "Well, ma'am, upon the whole, I shouldn't wonder if you were right!"

"Mr. Micawber being now on the eve of casting off the pecuniary shackles that have so long enthralled him," said Mrs. Micawber, "and of commencing a new career in a country where there is sufficient range for his abilities,—which, in my opinion, is exceedingly important; Mr. Micawber's abilities peculiarly requiring space,—it seems to me that my family should signalise the occasion by coming forward. What I could wish to see, would be a meeting between Mr. Micawber and my family at a festive entertainment, to be given at my family's expense; where Mr. Micawber's health and prosperity being proposed, by some leading member of my family, Mr. Micawber might have an opportunity of developing his views."

"My dear," said Mr. Micawber, with some heat, "it may be better for me to state distinctly, at once, that if I were to develop my views to that assembled group, they would possibly be found of an offensive nature: my impression being that your family are, in the aggregate, impertinent Snobs; and, in detail, unmitigated Ruffians."

"Micawber," said Mrs. Micawber, shaking her head, "no! You have never understood them, and they have never understood you."

Mr. Micawber coughed.

"They have never understood you, Micawber," said his wife. "They may be incapable of it. If so, that is their misfortune. I can pity their misfortune."

"I am extremely sorry, my dear Emma," said Mr. Micawber, relenting, "to have been betrayed into any expressions that might, even remotely, have the appearance of being strong expressions. All I would say, is, that I can go abroad without your family coming forward to favour me,—in short, with a parting Shove of their cold shoulders; and that, upon the whole, I would rather leave England with such impetus as I possess, than derive any acceleration of it from that quarter. At the same time, my dear, if they should condescend to reply to your communications—which our joint experience renders most improbable—far be it from me to be a barrier to your wishes."

The matter being thus amicably settled, Mr. Micawber gave Mrs. Micawber his arm, and glancing at the heap of books and papers lying before Traddles on the table, said they would leave us to ourselves; which they ceremoniously did.

"My dear Copperfield," said Traddles, leaning back in his chair when they were gone, and looking at me with an affection that made his eyes red, and his hair all kinds of shapes, "I don't make any excuse for troubling you with business, because I know you are deeply interested in it, and it may divert your thoughts. My dear boy, I hope you are not worn out?"

"I am quite myself," said I, after a pause. "We have more cause to think of my aunt than of anyone. You know how much she has done."

"Surely, surely," answered Traddles. "Who can forget it!"

"But even that is not all," said I. "During the last fortnight, some new trouble has vexed her; and she has been in and out of London every day. Several times she has gone out early, and been absent until evening. Last night, Traddles, with this journey before her, it was almost midnight before she came home. You know what her consideration for others is. She will not tell me what has happened to distress her."

My aunt, very pale, and with deep lines in her face, sat immovable until I had finished; when some stray tears found their way to her cheeks, and she put her hand on mine.

"It's nothing, Trot; it's nothing. There will be no more of it. You shall know by-and-by. Now, Agnes, my dear, let us attend to these affairs."

"I must do Mr. Micawber the justice to say," Traddles began, "that although he would appear not to have worked to any good account for himself, he is a most untiring man when he works for other people. I never saw such a fellow. If he always goes on in the same way, he must be, virtually, about two hundred years old, at present. The heat into which he has been continually putting himself; and the distracted and impetuous manner in which he has been diving, day and night, among papers and books; to say nothing of the immense number of letters he has written me between this house and Mr. Wickfield's, and often across the table when he has been sitting opposite, and might much more easily have spoken; is quite extraordinary."

"Letters!" cried my aunt. "I believe he dreams in letters!"

"There's Mr. Dick, too," said Traddles, "has been doing wonders! As soon as he was released from overlooking Uriah Heep, whom he kept in such charge as I never saw exceeded, he began to devote himself to Mr. Wickfield. And really his anxiety to be of use in the investigations we have been making, and his real usefulness in extracting, and copying, and fetching, and carrying, have been quite stimulating to us."

"Dick is a very remarkable man," exclaimed my aunt; "and I always said he was. Trot, you know it!"

"I am happy to say, Miss Wickfield," pursued Traddles, at once with great delicacy and with great earnestness, "that in your absence Mr. Wickfield has considerably improved. Relieved of the incubus that had fastened upon him for so long a time, and of the dreadful apprehensions under which he had lived, he is hardly the same person. At times, even his impaired power of concentrating his memory and attention on particular points of business, has recovered itself very much; and he has been able to assist us in making some things clear, that we should have found very difficult indeed, if not hopeless, without him. But, what I have to do is to come to results; which are short enough; not to gossip on all the hopeful circumstances I have observed, or I shall never have done."

His natural manner and agreeable simplicity made it transparent that he said this to put us in good heart, and to enable Agnes to hear her father mentioned with greater confidence; but it was not the less pleasant for that.

"Now, let me see," said Traddles, looking among the papers on the table. "Having counted our funds, and reduced to order a great mass of unintentional confusion in the first place, and of wilful confusion and falsification in the second, we take it to be clear that Mr. Wickfield might now wind up his business, and his agency-trust, and exhibit no deficiency or defalcation whatever."

"Oh, thank Heaven!" cried Agnes, fervently.

"But," said Traddles, "the surplus that would be left as his means of support—and I suppose the house to be sold, even in saying this—would be so small, not exceeding in all probability some hundreds of pounds, that perhaps, Miss Wickfield, it would be best to consider whether he might not retain his agency of the estate to which he has so long been receiver. His friends might advise him, you know; now he is free. You yourself, Miss Wickfield—Copperfield—I——"

"I have considered it, Trotwood," said Agnes, looking to me, "and I feel that it ought not to be, and must not be; even on the recommendation of a friend to whom I am so grateful, and owe so much."

"I will not say that I recommend it," observed Traddles. "I think it right to suggest it. No more."

"I am happy to hear you say so," answered Agnes, steadily, "for it gives me hope, almost assurance, that we think alike. Dear Mr. Traddles and dear Trotwood, papa once free with honour, what could I wish for! I have always aspired, if I could have released him from the toils in which he was held, to render back some little portion of the love and care I owe him, and to devote my life to him. It has been, for years, the utmost height of my hopes. To take our future on myself, will be the next great happiness—the next to his release from all trust and responsibility—that I can know."

"Have you thought how, Agnes?"

"Often! I am not afraid, dear Trotwood. I am certain of success. So many people know me here, and think kindly of me, that I am certain. Don't mistrust me. Our wants are not many. If I rent the dear old house, and keep a school, I shall be useful and happy."

The calm fervour of her cheerful voice brought back so vividly, first the dear old house itself, and then my solitary home, that my heart was too full for speech. Traddles pretended for a little while to be busily looking among the papers.

"Next, Miss Trotwood," said Traddles, "that property of yours."

"Well, Sir," sighed my aunt. "All I have got to say about it, is, that if it's gone, I can bear it; and if it's not gone, I shall be glad to get it back."

"It was originally, I think, eight thousand pounds, Consols?" said Traddles.

"Right!" replied my aunt.

"I can't account for more than five," said Traddles, with an air of perplexity.

"—Thousand, do you mean?" inquired my aunt, with uncommon composure, "or pounds?"

"Five thousand pounds," said Traddles.

"It was all there was," returned my aunt. "I sold three, myself. One, I paid for your articles, Trot, my dear; and the other two I have by me. When I lost the rest, I thought it wise to say nothing about that sum, but to keep it secretly for a rainy day. I wanted to see how you would come out of the trial, Trot; and you came out nobly—persevering, self-reliant, self-denying! So did Dick. Don't speak to me, for I find my nerves a little shaken!"

Nobody would have thought so, to see her sitting upright, with her arms folded; but she had wonderful self-command.

"Then I am delighted to say," cried Traddles, beaming with joy, "that we have recovered the whole money!"

"Don't congratulate me, anybody!" exclaimed my aunt. "How so, Sir?"

"You believed it had been misappropriated by Mr. Wickfield?" said Traddles.

"Of course I did," said my aunt, "and was therefore easily silenced. Agnes, not a word!"

"And indeed," said Traddles, "it was sold, by virtue of the power of management he held from you; but I needn't say by whom sold, or on whose actual signature. It was afterwards pretended to Mr. Wickfield, by that rascal,—

and proved, too, by figures,—that he had possessed himself of the money (on general instructions, *he* said) to keep other deficiencies and difficulties from the light. Mr. Wickfield, being so weak and helpless in his hands as to pay you, afterwards, several sums of interest on a pretended principal which he knew did not exist, made himself, unhappily, a party to the fraud."

"And at last took the blame upon himself," added my aunt; "and wrote me a mad letter, charging himself with robbery, and wrong unheard of. Upon which I paid him a visit early one morning, called for a candle, burnt the letter, and told him if he ever could right me and himself, to do it; and if he couldn't, to keep his own counsel for his daughter's sake.—If anybody speaks to me, I'll leave the house!"

We all remained quiet; Agnes covering her face.

"Well, my dear friend," said my aunt, after a pause, "and you have really extorted the money back from him?"

"Why, the fact is," returned Traddles, "Mr. Micawber had so completely hemmed him in, and was always ready with so many new points if an old one failed, that he could not escape from us. A most remarkable circumstance is, that I really don't think he grasped this sum even so much for the gratification of his avarice, which was inordinate, as in the hatred he felt for Copperfield. He said so to me, plainly. He said he would even have spent as much, to baulk or injure Copperfield."

"Ha!" said my aunt, knitting her brows thoughtfully, and glancing at Agnes. "And what's become of him?"

"I don't know. He left here," said Traddles, "with his mother, who had been clamouring, and beseeching, and disclosing, the whole time. They went away by one of the London night coaches, and I know no more about him; except that his malevolence to me at parting was audacious. He seemed to consider himself hardly less indebted to me, than to Mr. Micawber; which I consider (as I told him) quite a compliment."

"Do you suppose he has any money, Traddles?" I asked.

"Oh dear, yes, I should think so," he replied, shaking his head, seriously. "I should say he must have pocketed a good deal, in one way or other. But, I think you would find, Copperfield, if you had an opportunity of observing his course, that money would never keep that man out of mischief. He is such an incarnate hypocrite, that whatever object he pursues, he must pursue crookedly. It's his only compensation for the outward restraints he puts upon himself. Always creeping along the ground to some small end or other, he will always magnify every object in the way; and consequently will hate and suspect everybody that comes, in the most innocent manner, between him and it. So, the crooked courses will become crookeder, at any moment, for the least reason, or for none. It's only necessary to consider his history here," said Traddles, "to know that."

"He's a monster of meanness!" said my aunt.

"Really I don't know about that," observed Traddles, thoughtfully. "Many people can be very mean, when they give their minds to it."

"And now, touching Mr. Micawber," said my aunt.

"Well, really," said Traddles, cheerfully, "I must, once more, give Mr. Micawber high praise. But for his having been so patient and persevering for so long a time, we never could have hoped to do anything worth speaking of. And I think we ought to consider that Mr. Micawber did right, for right's sake, when we reflect what terms he might have made with Uriah Heep himself, for his silence."

"I think so too," said I.

"Now, what would you give him?" inquired my aunt.

"Oh! Before you come to that," said Traddles, a little disconcerted, "I am afraid I thought it discreet to omit (not being able to carry everything before me) two points, in making this lawless adjustment—for it's perfectly lawless from beginning to end—of a difficult affair. Those I O U's, and so forth, which Mr. Micawber gave him for the advances he had——"

"Well! They must be paid," said my aunt.

"Yes, but I don't know when they may be proceeded on, or where they are," rejoined Traddles, opening his eyes; "and I anticipate, that, between this time and his departure, that, Mr. Micawber will be constantly arrested, or taken in execution."

"Then he must be constantly set free again, and taken out of execution," said my aunt. "What's the amount altogether?"

"Why, Mr. Micawber has entered the transactions—he calls them transactions—with great form, in a book," rejoined Traddles, smiling; "and he makes the amount a hundred and three pounds, five."

"Now, what shall we give him, that sum included?" said my aunt. "Agnes, my dear, you and I can talk about division of it afterwards. What should it be? Five hundred pounds?"

Upon this, Traddles and I both struck in at once. We both recommended a small sum in money, and the payment, without stipulation to Mr. Micawber, of the Uriah claims as they came in. We proposed that the family should have their passage and their outfit, and a hundred pounds; and that Mr. Micawber's arrangement for the repayment of the advances should be gravely entered into, as it might be wholesome for him to suppose himself under that responsibility. To this, I added the suggestion, that I should give some explanation of his character and history to Mr. Peggotty, who I knew could be relied on; and that to Mr. Peggotty should be quietly entrusted the discretion of advancing another hundred. I further proposed to interest Mr. Micawber in Mr. Peggotty, by confiding so much of Mr. Peggotty's story to him as I might feel justified in relating, or might think expedient; and to endeavour to bring each of them to bear upon the other, for the common advantage. We all entered warmly into these views; and I may mention at once, that the principals themselves did so, shortly afterwards, with perfect good-will and harmony.

Seeing that Traddles now glanced anxiously at my aunt again, I reminded him of the second and last point to which he had adverted.

"You and your aunt will excuse me, Copperfield, if I touch upon a painful theme, as I greatly fear I shall," said Traddles, hesitating; "but I think it necessary to bring it to your recollection. On the day of Mr. Micawber's memorable denunciation, a threatening allusion was made by Uriah Heep to your aunt's—husband."

My aunt, retaining her stiff position, and apparent composure, assented with a nod.

"Perhaps," observed Traddles, "it was mere purposeless impertinence?"

"No," returned my aunt.

"There was—pardon me—really such a person, and at all in his power?" hinted Traddles.

"Yes, my good friend," said my aunt.

Traddles, with a perceptible lengthening of his face,

explained that he had not been able to approach this subject; that it had shared the fate of Mr. Micawber's liabilities, in not being comprehended in the terms he had made; that we were no longer of any authority with Uriah Heep; and that if he could do us, or any of us, any injury or annoyance, no doubt he would.

My aunt remained quiet; until again some stray tears found their way to her cheeks.

"You are quite right," she said. "It was very thoughtful to mention it."

"Can I—or Copperfield—do anything?" asked Traddles gently.

"Nothing," said my aunt. "I thank you many times. Trot, my dear, a vain threat! Let us have Mr. and Mrs. Micawber back. And don't any of you speak to me!" With that, she smoothed her dress, and sat, with her upright carriage, looking at the door.

"Well, Mr. and Mrs. Micawber!" said my aunt, when they entered. "We have been discussing your emigration, with many apologies to you for keeping you out of the room so long; and I'll tell you what arrangements we propose."

These she explained, to the unbounded satisfaction of the family,—children and all being then present,—and so much to the awakening of Mr. Micawber's punctual habits in the opening stage of all bill transactions, that he could not be dissuaded from immediately rushing out, in the highest spirits, to buy the stamps for his notes of hand. But, his joy received a sudden check; for within five minutes, he returned in the custody of a sheriff's officer, informing us, in a flood of tears, that all was lost. We, being quite prepared for this event, which was of course a proceeding of Uriah Heep's, soon paid the money; and in five minutes more Mr. Micawber was seated at the table, filling up the stamps with an expression of perfect joy, which only that congenial employment, or the making of punch, could impart in full completeness to his shining face. To see him at work on the stamps, with the relish of an artist, touching them like pictures, looking at them sideways, taking weighty notes of dates and amounts in his pocket-book, and contemplating them when finished, with a high sense of their precious value, was a sight indeed.

"Now, the best thing you can do, Sir, if you'll allow me to advise you," said my aunt, after silently observing him, "is to abjure that occupation for evermore."

"Madam," replied Mr. Micawber, "it is my intention to register such a vow on the virgin page of the future. Mrs. Micawber will attest it. I trust," said Mr. Micawber, solemnly, "that my son Wilkins will ever bear in mind, that he had infinitely better put his fist in the fire, than use it to handle the serpents that have poisoned the life-blood of his unhappy parent!" Deeply affected, and changed in a moment to the image of despair, Mr. Micawber regarded the serpents with a look of gloomy abhorrence (in which his late admiration of them was not quite subdued), folded them up, and put them in his pocket.

This closed the proceedings of the evening. We were weary with sorrow and fatigue, and my aunt and I were to return to London on the morrow. It was arranged that the Micawbers should follow us, after effecting a sale of their goods to a broker; that Mr. Wickfield's affairs should be brought to a settlement, with all convenient speed, under the direction of Traddles; and that Agnes should also come to London, pending those arrangements. We passed the night at the old house, which, freed from the presence of the Heeps, seemed purged of a disease; and I lay in my old room, like a shipwrecked wanderer come home.

We went back next day to my aunt's house—not to mine; and when she and I sat alone, as of old, before going to bed, she said:

"Trot, do you really wish to know what I have had upon my mind lately?"

"Indeed I do, aunt. If there ever was a time when I felt unwilling that you should have a sorrow or anxiety which I could not share, it is now."

"You have had sorrow enough, child," said my aunt, affectionately, "without the addition of *my* little miseries. I could have no other motive, Trot, in keeping anything from you."

"I know that well," said I. "But tell me now."

'Would you ride with me a little way to-morrow morning?' asked my aunt.

"Of course."

"At nine," said she. "I'll tell you then, my dear."

At nine, accordingly, we went out in a little chariot, and drove to London. We drove a long way through the streets, until we came to one of the large hospitals. Standing hard by the building was a plain hearse. The driver recognised my aunt, and, in obedience to a motion of her hand at the window, drove slowly off; we following.

"You understand it now, Trot," said my aunt. "He is gone!"

"Did he die in the hospital?"

"Yes."

She sat immovable beside me; but, again I saw the stray tears on her face.

"He was there once before," said my aunt presently. "He was ailing a long time—a shattered, broken man, these many years. When he knew his state in this last illness, he asked them to send for me. He was sorry then. Very sorry."

"You went, I know, aunt."

"I went. I was with him a good deal afterwards."

"He died the night before we went to Canterbury?" said I.

My aunt nodded. "No one can harm him now," she said. "It was a vain threat."

We drove away, out of town, to the churchyard at Hornsey. "Better here than in the streets," said my aunt. "He was born here."

We alighted; and followed the plain coffin to a corner I remember well, where the service was read consigning it to the dust.

"Six-and-thirty years ago, this day, my dear," said my aunt, as we walked back to the chariot, "I was married. God forgive us all!"

We took our seats in silence; and so she sat beside me for a long time, holding my hand. At length she suddenly burst into tears, and said:

"He was a fine-looking man when I married him, Trot—and he was sadly changed!"

It did not last long. After the relief of tears, she soon became composed, and even cheerful. Her nerves were a little shaken, she said, or she would not have given way to it. God forgive us all!

So we rode back to her little cottage at Highgate, where we found the following short note, which had arrived by that morning's post from Mr. Micawber:—

"Canterbury,
"Friday.

"My dear Madam, and Copperfield,

"The fair land of promise lately looming on the horizon is again enveloped in impenetrable mists, and for ever withdrawn from the eyes of a drifting wretch whose Doom is sealed!

"Another writ has been issued (in His Majesty's High Court of King's Bench at Westminster), in another cause of HEEP *v.* MICAWBER, and the defendant in that cause is the prey of the sheriff having legal jurisdiction in this bailiwick.

"'Now's the day, and now's the hour,
See the front of battle lower,
See approach proud EDWARD's power—
Chains and slavery!'

"Consigned to which, and to a speedy end (for mental torture is not supportable beyond a certain point, and that point I feel I have attained), my course is run. Bless you, bless you! Some future traveller, visiting, from motives of curiosity, not unmingled, let us hope, with sympathy, the place of confinement allotted to debtors in this city, may, and I trust will, Ponder, as he traces on its wall, inscribed with a rusty nail,

"The obscure initials
"W. M.

"P.S. I re-open this to say that our common friend, Mr. Thomas Traddles (who has not yet left us, and is looking extremely well), has paid the debt and costs, in the noble name of Miss Trotwood; and that myself and family are at the height of earthly bliss."

CHAPTER LV.

TEMPEST.

I NOW approach an event in my life, so indelible, so awful, so bound by an infinite variety of ties to all that has preceded it, in these pages, that, from the beginning of my narrative, I have seen it growing larger and larger as I advanced, like a great tower in a plain, and throwing its fore-cast shadow even on the incidents of my childish days.

For years after it occurred, I dreamed of it often. I have started up so vividly impressed by it, that its fury has yet seemed raging in my quiet room, in the still night. I dream of it sometimes, though at lengthened and uncertain intervals, to this hour. I have an association between it and a stormy wind, or the lightest mention of a sea-shore, as strong as any of which my mind is conscious. As plainly as I behold what happened, I will try to write it down. I do not recall it, but see it done; for it happens again before me.

The time drawing on rapidly for the sailing of the emigrant-ship, my good old nurse (almost broken-hearted for me, when we first met) came up to London. I was constantly with her, and her brother, and the Micawbers (they being very much together); but Emily I never saw.

One evening when the time was close at hand, I was alone with Peggotty and her brother. Our conversation turned on Ham. She described to us how tenderly he had taken leave of her, and how manfully and quietly he had borne himself. Most of all, of late, when she believed he was most tried. It was a subject of which the affectionate creature never tired; and our interest in hearing the many examples which she, who was so much with him, had to relate, was equal to hers in relating them.

My aunt and I were at that time vacating the two cottages at Highgate; I intending to go abroad, and she to return to her house at Dover. We had a temporary lodging in Covent Garden. As I walked home to it, after this evening's conversation, reflecting on what had passed between Ham and myself when I was last at Yarmouth, I wavered in the original purpose I had formed, of leaving a letter for Emily when I should take leave of her uncle on board the ship, and thought it would be better to write to her now. She might desire, I thought, after receiving my communication, to send some parting word by me to her unhappy lover. I ought to give her the opportunity.

I therefore sat down in my room, before going to bed, and wrote to her. I told her that I had seen him, and that he had requested me to tell her what I have already written in its place in these sheets. I faithfully repeated it. I had no need to enlarge upon it, if I had had the right. Its deep fidelity and goodness were not to be adorned by me or any man. I left it out, to be sent round in the morning; with a line to Mr. Peggotty, requesting him to give it to her; and went to bed at daybreak.

I was weaker than I knew then; and, not falling asleep until the sun was up, lay late, and unrefreshed, next day. I was roused by the silent presence of my aunt at my bedside. I felt it in my sleep, as I suppose we all do feel such things.

"Trot, my dear," she said, when I opened my eyes, "I couldn't make up my mind to disturb you. Mr. Peggotty is here; shall he come up?"

I replied yes, and he soon appeared.

"Mas'r Davy," he said, when we had shaken hands, "I giv Em'ly your letter, Sir, and she writ this heer; and begged of me fur to ask you to read it, and if you see no hurt in't, to be so kind as take charge on't."

"Have you read it?" said I.

He nodded sorrowfully. I opened it, and read as follows:—

"I have got your message. Oh, what can I write, to thank you for your good and blessed kindness to me!

"I have put the words close to my heart. I shall keep them till I die. They are sharp thorns, but they are such comfort. I have prayed over them, oh, I have prayed so much. When I find what you are, and what uncle is, I think what God must be, and can cry to Him.

"Good bye for ever. Now, my dear, my friend, good bye for ever in this world. In another world, if I am forgiven, I may wake a child and come to you. All thanks and blessings. Farewell, evermore!"

This, blotted with tears, was the letter.

"May I tell her as you don't see no hurt in't, and as you'll be so kind as take charge on't, Mas'r Davy?" said Mr. Peggotty, when I had read it.

"Unquestionably," said I—"but I am thinking——"

"Yes, Mas'r Davy?"

"I am thinking," said I, "that I'll go down again to Yarmouth. There's time, and to spare, for me to go and come back before the ship sails. My mind is constantly running on him, in his solitude; to put this letter of her writing in his hand at this time, and to enable you to tell her, in the moment of parting, that he has got it, will be a kindness to both of them. I solemnly accepted his commission, dear good fellow, and cannot discharge it too completely. The journey is nothing to me. I am restless, and shall be better in motion. I'll go down to-night."

Though he anxiously endeavoured to dissuade me, I saw that he was of my mind; and this, if I had required to be confirmed in my intention, would have had the effect. He went round to the coach-office, at my request, and took the box-seat for me on the mail. In the evening I started, by that conveyance, down the road I had traversed under so many vicissitudes.

"Don't you think that," I asked the coachman, in the first stage out of London, "a very remarkable sky? I don't remember to have seen one like it."

"Nor I—not equal to it," he replied. "That's wind, Sir. There'll be mischief done at sea, I expect, before long."

It was a murky confusion—here and there blotted with a colour like the colour of the smoke from damp fuel—of flying clouds tossed up into most remarkable heaps, suggesting greater heights in the clouds than there were depths below them to the bottom of the deepest hollows in the earth, through which the wild moon seemed to plunge headlong, as if, in a dread disturbance of the laws of nature, she had lost her way and were frightened. There had been a wind all day; and it was rising then, with an extraordinary great sound. In another hour it had much increased, and the sky was more overcast, and blew hard.

But as the night advanced, the clouds closing in and densely overspreading the whole sky, then very dark, it came on to blow, harder and harder. It still increased, until our horses could scarcely face the wind. Many times, in the dark part of the night (it was then late in September, when the nights were not short), the leaders turned about, or came to a dead stop; and we were often in serious apprehension that the coach would be blown over. Sweeping gusts of rain came up before this storm, like showers of steel; and, at those times, when there was any shelter of trees or lee walls to be got, we were fain to stop, in a sheer impossibility of continuing the struggle.

When the day broke, it blew harder and harder. I had been in Yarmouth when the seamen said it blew great guns, but I had never known the like of this, or anything approaching to it. We came to Ipswich—very late, having had to fight every inch of ground since we were ten miles out of London; and found a cluster of people in the market-place, who had risen from their beds in the night, fearful of falling chimneys. Some of these, congregating about the inn-yard while we changed horses, told us of great sheets of lead having been ripped off a high church-tower, and flung into a by-street, which they then blocked up. Others had to tell of country people, coming in from neighbouring villages, who had seen great trees lying torn out of the earth, and whole ricks scattered about the roads and fields. Still, there was no abatement in the storm, but it blew harder.

As we struggled on, nearer and nearer to the sea, from which this mighty wind was blowing dead on shore, its force became more and more terrific. Long before we saw the sea, its spray was on our lips, and showered salt rain upon us. The water was out, over miles and miles of the flat country adjacent to Yarmouth; and every sheet and puddle lashed its banks, and had its stress of little breakers setting heavily towards us. When we came within sight of the sea, the waves on the horizon, caught at intervals above the rolling abyss, were like glimpses of another shore with towers and buildings. When at last we got into the town, the people came out to their doors, all aslant, and with streaming hair, making a wonder of the mail that had come through such a night.

I put up at the old inn, and went down to look at the sea; staggering along the street, which was strewn with sand and sea-weed, and with flying blotches of sea-foam; afraid of falling slates and tiles; and holding by people I met, at angry corners. Coming near the beach, I saw, not only the boatmen, but half the people of the town, lurking behind buildings; some, now and then braving the fury of the storm to look away to sea, and blown sheer out of their course in trying to get zigzag back.

Joining these groups, I found bewailing women whose husbands were away in herring or oyster boats, which there was too much reason to think might have foundered before they could run in anywhere for safety. Grizzled old sailors were among the people, shaking their heads, as they looked from water to sky, and muttering to one another; shipowners, excited and uneasy; children, huddling together, and peering into older faces; even stout mariners, disturbed and anxious, levelling their glasses at the sea from behind places of shelter, as if they were surveying an enemy.

The tremendous sea itself, when I could find sufficient pause to look at it, in the agitation of the blinding wind, the flying stones and sand, and the awful noise, confounded me. As the high watery walls came rolling in, and, at their highest, tumbled into surf, they looked as if the least would engulf the town. As the receding wave swept back with a hoarse roar, it seemed to scoop out deep caves in the beach, as if its purpose were to undermine the earth. When some white-headed billows thundered on, and dashed themselves to pieces before they reached the land, every fragment of the late whole seemed possessed by the full might of its wrath, rushing to be gathered to the composition of another monster. Undulating hills were changed to valleys, undulating valleys (with a solitary storm-bird sometimes skimming through them) were lifted up to hills; masses of water shivered and shook the beach with a booming sound; every shape tumultuously rolled on, as soon as made, to change its shape and place, and beat another shape and place away; the ideal shore on the horizon, with its towers and buildings, rose and fell; the clouds flew fast and thick; I seemed to see a rending and upheaving of all nature.

Not finding Ham among the people whom this memorable wind—for it is still remembered down there, as the greatest ever known to blow upon that coast—had brought together, I made my way to his house. It was shut; and as no one answered to my knocking, I went, by back ways and by-lanes, to the yard where he worked. I learned, there, that he had gone to Lowestoft, to meet some sudden exigency of ship-repairing in which his skill was required; but that he would be back to-morrow morning, in good time.

I went back to the inn; and when I had washed and dressed, and tried to sleep, but in vain, it was five o'clock in the afternoon. I had not sat five minutes by the coffee-room fire, when the waiter coming to stir it, as an excuse for talking, told me that two colliers had gone down, with all hands, a few miles away; and that some other ships had been seen labouring hard in the Roads, and trying, in great distress, to keep off shore. Mercy on them, and on all poor sailors, said he, if we had another night like the last!

I was very much depressed in spirits; very solitary; and felt an uneasiness in Ham's not being there, disproportionate to the occasion. I was seriously affected, without knowing how much, by late events; and my long exposure to the fierce wind had confused me. There was that jumble in my thoughts and recollections, that I had lost the clear arrangement of time and distance. Thus, if I had gone out into the town, I should not have been surprised, I think, to encounter some one who I knew must be then in London. So to speak, there was in these respects a curious inattention in my mind. Yet it was busy, too, with all the remembrances the place naturally awakened; and they were particularly distinct and vivid.

In this state, the waiter's dismal intelligence about the ships immediately connected itself, without any effort of my volition, with my uneasiness about Ham. I was persuaded that I had an apprehension of his returning from Lowestoft by sea, and being lost. This grew so strong with me, that I resolved to go back to the yard before I took my dinner, and ask the boat-builder if he thought his attempting to return by sea at all likely? If he gave me the least reason to think so, I would go over to Lowestoft and prevent it by bringing him with me.

I hastily ordered my dinner, and went back to the yard. I was none too soon; for the boat-builder, with a lantern in his hand, was locking the yard-gate. He quite laughed, when I asked him the question, and said there was no fear; no man in his senses, or out of them, would put off in such a gale of wind, least of all Ham Peggotty, who had been born to seafaring.

So sensible of this, beforehand, that I had really felt ashamed of doing what I was nevertheless impelled to do, I went back to the inn. If such a wind could rise, I think it was rising. The howl and roar, the rattling of the doors and windows, the rumbling in the chimneys, the apparent rocking of the very house that sheltered me, and the prodigious tumult of the sea, were more fearful than in the morning. But there was now a great darkness besides; and that invested the storm with new terrors, real and fanciful.

I could not eat, I could not sit still, I could not continue steadfast to anything. Something within me, faintly answering to the storm without, tossed up the depths of my memory, and made a tumult in them. Yet, in all the hurry of my thoughts, wild running with the thundering sea,—the storm, and my uneasiness regarding Ham, were always in the foreground.

My dinner went away almost untasted, and I tried to refresh myself with a glass or two of wine. In vain. I fell into a dull slumber before the fire, without losing my consciousness, either of the uproar out of doors, or of the place in which I was. Both became overshadowed by a new and indefinable horror; and when I awoke—or rather when I shook off the lethargy that bound me in my chair—my whole frame thrilled with objectless and unintelligible fear.

I walked to and fro, tried to read an old gazetteer, listened to the awful noises: looked at faces, scenes, and figures in the fire. At length, the steady ticking of the undisturbed clock on the wall tormented me to that degree that I resolved to go to bed.

It was reassuring, on such a night, to be told that some of the inn-servants had agreed together to sit up until morning. I went to bed, exceedingly weary and heavy; but, on my lying down, all such sensations vanished, as if by magic, and I was broad awake, with every sense refined.

For hours I lay there, listening to the wind and water; imagining, now, that I heard shrieks out at sea; now, that I distinctly heard the firing of signal guns; and now, the fall of houses in the town. I got up, several times, and looked out; but could see nothing, except the reflection in the window-panes of the faint candle I had left burning, and of my own haggard face looking in at me from the black void.

At length, my restlessness attained to such a pitch, that I hurried on my clothes, and went down stairs. In the large kitchen, where I dimly saw bacon and ropes of onions hanging from the beams, the watchers were clustered together, in various attitudes, about a table, purposely moved away from the great chimney, and brought near the door. A pretty girl, who had her ears stopped with her apron, and her eyes upon the door, screamed when I appeared, supposing me to be a spirit; but the others had more presence of mind, and were glad of an addition to their company. One man, referring to the topic they had been discussing, asked me whether I thought the souls of the collier-crews who had gone down, were out in the storm?

I remained there, I dare say, two hours. Once, I opened the yard-gate, and looked into the empty street. The sand, the sea-weed, and the flakes of foam, were driving by; and I was obliged to call for assistance before I could shut the gate again, and make it fast against the wind.

There was a dark gloom in my solitary chamber, when I at length returned to it; but I was tired now, and, getting into bed again, fell—off a tower and down a precipice—into the depths of sleep. I have an impression that for a long time, though I dreamed of being elsewhere and in a variety of scenes, it was always blowing in my dream. At length, I lost that feeble hold upon reality, and was engaged with two dear friends, but who they were I don't know, at the siege of some town in a roar of cannonading.

The thunder of the cannon was so loud and incessant, that I could not hear something I much desired to hear, until I made a great exertion and awoke. It was broad day—eight or nine o'clock; the storm raging, in lieu of the batteries; and some one knocking and calling at my door.

"What is the matter?" I cried.

"A wreck! Close by!"

I sprang out of bed, and asked, what wreck?

"A schooner, from Spain or Portugal, laden with fruit and wine. Make haste, Sir, if you want to see her! It's thought, down on the beach, she'll go to pieces every moment."

The excited voice went clamouring along the staircase; and I wrapped myself in my clothes as quickly as I could, and ran into the street.

Numbers of people were there before me, all running in one direction, to the beach. I ran the same way, outstripping a good many, and soon came facing the wild sea.

The wind might by this time have lulled a little, though not more sensibly than if the cannonading I had dreamed of, had been diminished by the silencing of half-a-dozen guns out of hundreds. But, the sea, having upon it the additional agitation of the whole night, was infinitely more terrific than when I had seen it last. Every appearance it had then presented, bore the expression of being *swelled*; and the height to which the breakers rose, and, looking over one another, bore one another down, and rolled in, in interminable hosts, was most appalling.

In the difficulty of hearing anything but wind and wave, and in the crowd, and the unspeakable confusion, and my first breathless efforts to stand against the weather, I was so confused that I looked out to sea for the wreck, and saw nothing but the foaming heads of the great waves. A half-dressed boatman, standing next me, pointed with his bare arm (a tattoo'd arrow on it, pointing in the same direction) to the left. Then, O great Heaven, I saw it, close in upon us!

One mast was broken short off, six or eight feet from the deck, and lay over the side, entangled in a maze of sail and rigging; and all that ruin, as the ship rolled and beat—which she did without a moment's pause, and with a violence quite inconceivable—beat the side as if it would stave it in. Some efforts were even then being made, to cut this portion of the wreck away; for, as the ship, which was broadside on, turned towards us in her rolling, I plainly descried her people at work with axes, especially one active figure with long curling hair, conspicuous among the rest.

But, a great cry, which was audible even above the wind and water, rose from the shore at this moment; the sea, sweeping over the rolling wreck, made a clean breach, and carried men, spars, casks, planks, bulwarks, heaps of such toys, into the boiling surge.

The second mast was yet standing, with the rags of a rent sail, and a wild confusion of broken cordage flapping to and fro. The ship had struck once, the same boatman hoarsely said in my ear, and then lifted in and struck again. I understood him to add that she was parting amidships, and I could readily suppose so, for the rolling and beating were too tremendous for any human work to suffer long. As he spoke, there was another great cry of pity from the beach; four men arose with the wreck out of the deep, clinging to the rigging of the remaining mast; uppermost, the active figure with the curling hair.

There was a bell on board; and as the ship rolled and dashed, like a desperate creature driven mad, now showing us the whole sweep of her deck, as she turned on her beam-ends towards the shore, now nothing but her keel, as she sprang wildly over and turned towards the sea, the bell rang; and its sound, the knell of those unhappy men, was borne towards us on the wind. Again we lost her, and again she rose. Two men were gone. The agony on shore increased. Men groaned, and clasped their hands; women shrieked, and turned away their faces. Some ran wildly up and down along the beach, crying for help where no help could be. I found myself one of these, frantically imploring a knot of sailors whom I knew, not to let those two lost creatures perish before our eyes.

They were making out to me, in an agitated way—I don't know how, for the little I could hear I was scarcely composed enough to understand—that the life-boat had been bravely manned an hour ago, and could do nothing; and that as no man would be so desperate as to attempt to wade off with a rope, and establish a communication with the shore, there was nothing left to try; when I noticed that some new sensation moved the people on the beach, and saw them part, and Ham come breaking through them to the front.

I ran to him—as well as I know, to repeat my appeal for help. But, distracted though I was, by a sight so new to me and terrible, the determination in his face, and his look, out to sea—exactly the same look as I remembered in connexion with the morning after Emily's flight—awoke me to a knowledge of his danger. I held him back with both arms; and implored the men with whom I had been speaking, not to listen to him, not to do murder, not to let him stir from off that sand!

Another cry arose on shore; and looking to the wreck, we saw the cruel sail, with blow on blow, beat off the lower of the two men, and fly up in triumph round the active figure left alone upon the mast.

Against such a sight, and against such determination as that of the calmly desperate man who was already accustomed to lead half the people present, I might as hopefully have entreated the wind. "Mas'r Davy," he said, cheerily grasping me by both hands, "if my time is come, 'tis come. If 'tan't, I'll bide it. Lord above bless you, and bless all! Mates, make me ready! I'm a going off!"

I was swept away, but not unkindly, to some distance, where the people around me made me stay; urging, as I confusedly perceived, that he was bent on going, with help or without, and that I should endanger the precautions for his safety by troubling those with whom they rested. I don't know what I answered, or what they rejoined; but,

I saw hurry on the beach, and men running with ropes from a capstan that was there, and penetrating into a circle of figures that hid him from me. Then, I saw him standing alone, in a seaman's frock and trowsers: a rope in his hand, or slung to his wrist: another round his body: and several of the best men holding, at a little distance, to the latter, which he laid out himself, slack upon the shore, at his feet.

The wreck, even to my unpractised eye, was breaking up. I saw that she was parting in the middle, and that the life of the solitary man upon the mast hung by a thread. Still, he clung to it. He had a singular red cap on,—not like a sailor's cap, but of a finer colour; and as the few yielding planks between him and destruction rolled and bulged, and his anticipative death-knell rang, he was seen by all of us to wave it. I saw him do it now, and thought I was going distracted, when his action brought an old remembrance to my mind of a once dear friend.

Ham watched the sea, standing alone, with the silence of suspended breath behind him, and the storm before, until there was a great retiring wave, when, with a backward glance at those who held the rope which was made fast round his body, he dashed in after it, and in a moment was buffeting with the water; rising with the hills, falling with the valleys, lost beneath the foam; then drawn again to land. They hauled in hastily.

He was hurt. I saw blood on his face, from where I stood; but he took no thought of that. He seemed hurriedly to give them some directions for leaving him more free—or so I judged from the motion of his arm—and was gone as before.

And now he made for the wreck, rising with the hills, falling with the valleys, lost beneath the rugged foam, borne in towards the shore, borne on towards the ship, striving hard and valiantly. The distance was nothing, but the power of the sea and wind made the strife deadly. At length he neared the wreck. He was so near, that with one more of his vigorous strokes he would be clinging to it, —when, a high, green, vast hill-side of water, moving on shoreward, from beyond the ship, he seemed to leap up into it with a mighty bound, and the ship was gone!

Some eddying fragments I saw in the sea, as if a mere cask had been broken, in running to the spot where they were hauling in. Consternation was in every face. They drew him to my very feet—insensible—dead. He was carried to the nearest house; and, no one preventing me now, I remained near him, busy, while every means of restoration were tried; but he had been beaten to death by the great wave, and his generous heart was stilled for ever.

As I sat beside the bed, when hope was abandoned and all was done, a fisherman, who had known me when Emily and I were children, and ever since, whispered my name at the door.

"Sir," said he, with tears starting to his weather-beaten face, which, with his trembling lips, was ashy pale, "will you come over yonder?"

The old remembrance that had been recalled to me, was in his look. I asked him, terror-stricken, leaning on the arm he held out to support me:

"Has a body come ashore?"

He said, "Yes."

"Do I know it?" I asked then.

He answered nothing.

But, he led me to the shore. And on that part of it where she and I had looked for shells, two children—on that part of it where some lighter fragments of the old boat, blown down last night, had been scattered by the wind—

among the ruins of the home he had wronged—I saw him lying with his head upon his arm, as I had often seen him lie at school.

CHAPTER LVI.

THE NEW WOUND, AND THE OLD.

No need, O Steerforth, to have said, when we last spoke together, in that hour which I so little deemed to be our parting-hour—no need to have said, "Think of me at my best!" I had done that ever; and could I change now, looking on this sight!

They brought a hand-bier, and laid him on it, and covered him with a flag, and took him up and bore him on towards the houses. All the men who carried him had known him, and gone sailing with him, and seen him merry and bold. They carried him through the wild roar, a hush in the midst of all the tumult; and took him to the cottage where Death was already.

But, when they set the bier down on the threshold, they looked at one another, and at me, and whispered. I knew why. They felt as if it were not right to lay him down in the same quiet room.

We went into the town, and took our burden to the inn. So soon as I could at all collect my thoughts, I sent for Joram, and begged him to provide me a conveyance in which it could be got to London in the night. I knew that the care of it, and the hard duty of preparing his mother to receive it, could only rest with me; and I was anxious to discharge that duty as faithfully as I could.

I chose the night for the journey, that there might be less curiosity when I left the town. But, although it was nearly midnight when I came out of the yard in a chaise, followed by what I had in charge, there were many people waiting. At intervals, along the town, and even a little way out upon the road, I saw more; but at length only the bleak night and the open country were around me, and the ashes of my youthful friendship.

Upon a mellow autumn day, about noon, when the ground was perfumed by fallen leaves, and many more, in beautiful tints of yellow, red, and brown, yet hung upon the trees, through which the sun was shining, I arrived at Highgate. I walked the last mile, thinking as I went along of what I had to do; and left the carriage that had followed me all through the night, awaiting orders to advance.

The house, when I came up to it, looked just the same. Not a blind was raised; no sign of life was in the dull paved court, with its covered way leading to the disused door. The wind had quite gone down, and nothing moved.

I had not, at first, the courage to ring at the gate; and when I did ring, my errand seemed to me to be expressed in the very sound of the bell. The little parlour-maid came out, with the key in her hand; and looking earnestly at me as she unlocked the gate, said:

"I beg your pardon, Sir. Are you ill?"

"I have been much agitated, and am fatigued."

"Is anything the matter, Sir?—Mr. James——?"

"Hush!" said I. "Yes, something has happened, that I have to break to Mrs. Steerforth. She is at home?"

The girl anxiously replied that her mistress was very seldom out now, even in a carriage; that she kept her room; that she saw no company, but would see me. Her mistress was up, she said, and Miss Dartle was with her. What message should she take up stairs?

Giving her a strict charge to be careful of her manner, and only to carry in my card and say I waited, I sat down in the drawing-room (which we had now reached) until she should come back. Its former pleasant air of occupation was gone, and the shutters were half closed. The harp had not been used for many and many a day. His picture, as a boy, was there. The cabinet in which his mother had kept his letters was there. I wondered if she ever read them now; if she would ever read them more!

The house was so still that I heard the girl's light step up stairs. On her return, she brought a message, to the effect that Mrs. Steerforth was an invalid and could not come down; but, that if I would excuse her being in her chamber, she would be glad to see me. In a few moments I stood before her.

She was in his room; not in her own. I felt, of course, that she had taken to occupy it, in remembrance of him; and that the many tokens of his old sports and accomplishments, by which she was surrounded, remained there, just as he had left them, for the same reason. She murmured, however, even in her reception of me, that she was out of her own chamber because its aspect was unsuited to her infirmity; and with her stately look repelled the least suspicion of the truth.

At her chair, as usual, was Rosa Dartle. From the first moment of her dark eyes resting on me, I saw she knew I was the bearer of evil tidings. The scar sprang into view that instant. She withdrew herself a step behind the chair to keep her own face out of Mrs. Steerforth's observation; and scrutinised me with a piercing gaze that never faltered, never shrank.

"I am sorry to observe you are in mourning, Sir," said Mrs. Steerforth.

"I am unhappily a widower," said I.

"You are very young to know so great a loss," she returned. "I am grieved to hear it. I am grieved to hear it. I hope Time will be good to you."

"I hope Time," said I, looking at her, "will be good to all of us. Dear Mrs. Steerforth, we must all trust to that, in our heaviest misfortunes."

The earnestness of my manner, and the tears in my eyes, alarmed her. The whole course of her thoughts appeared to stop, and change.

I tried to command my voice in gently saying his name, but it trembled. She repeated it to herself, two or three times, in a low tone. Then, addressing me, she said, with enforced calmness:

"My son is ill."

"Very ill."

"You have seen him?"

"I have."

"Are you reconciled?"

I could not say Yes, I could not say No. She slightly turned her head towards the spot where Rosa Dartle had been standing at her elbow, and in that moment I said, by the motion of my lips, to Rosa, "Dead!"

That Mrs. Steerforth might not be induced to look behind her, and read, plainly written, what she was not yet prepared to know, I met her look quickly; but I had seen Rosa Dartle throw her hands up in the air with vehemence of despair and horror, and then clasp them on her face.

The handsome lady—so like, Oh so like!—regarded me with a fixed look, and put her hand to her forehead. I besought her to be calm, and prepare herself to bear what I had to tell; but I should rather have entreated her to weep, for she sat like a stone figure.

"When I was last here," I faltered, "Miss Dartle told me he was sailing here and there. The night before last was a dreadful one at sea. If he were at sea that night, and near a dangerous coast, as it is said he was; and if the vessel that was seen should really be the ship which——"

"Rosa!" said Mrs. Steerforth, "come to me!"

She came, but with no sympathy or gentleness. Her eyes gleamed like fire as she confronted his mother, and broke into a frightful laugh.

"Now," she said, "is your pride appeased, you mad woman? *Now* has he made atonement to you——with his life? Do you hear?—His life!"

Mrs. Steerforth, fallen back stiffly in her chair, and making no sound but a moan, cast her eyes upon her with a wide stare.

"Ay!" cried Rosa, smiting herself passionately on the breast, "look at me! Moan, and groan, and look at me! Look here!" striking the scar, "at your dead child's handiwork!"

The moan the mother uttered, from time to time, went to my heart. Always the same. Always inarticulate and stifled. Always accompanied with an incapable motion of the head, but with no change of face. Always proceeding from a rigid mouth and closed teeth, as if the jaw were locked and the face frozen up in pain.

"Do you remember when he did this?" she proceeded. "Do you remember when, in his inheritance of your nature, and in your pampering of his pride and passion, he did this, and disfigured me for life? Look at me, marked until I die with his high displeasure; and moan and groan for what you made him!"

"Miss Dartle," I entreated her. "For Heaven's sake——"

"I *will* speak!" she said, turning on me with her lightning eyes. "Be silent, you! Look at me, I say, proud mother of a proud false son! Moan for your nurture of him, moan for your corruption of him, moan for your loss of him, moan for mine!"

She clenched her hand, and trembled through her spare, worn figure, as if her passion were killing her by inches.

"You, resent his self-will!" she exclaimed. "You, injured by his haughty temper! You, who opposed to both, when your hair was grey, the qualities which made both when you gave him birth! You, who from his cradle reared him to be what he was, and stunted what he should have been! Are you rewarded, *now*, for your years of trouble?"

"O, Miss Dartle, shame! O cruel!"

"I tell you," she returned, "I *will* speak to her. No power on earth should stop me, while I was standing here! Have I been silent all these years, and shall I not speak now? I loved him better than you ever loved him!" turning on her fiercely. "I could have loved him, and asked no return. If I had been his wife, I could have been the slave of his caprices for a word of love a-year. I should have been. Who knows it better than I? You were exacting, proud, punctilious, selfish. My love would have been devoted—would have trod your paltry whimpering underfoot!"

With flashing eyes, she stamped upon the ground as if she actually did it.

"Look here!" she said, striking the scar again, with a

relentless hand. "When he grew into the better understanding of what he had done, he saw it, and repented of it! I could sing to him, and talk to him, and show the ardour that I felt in all he did, and attain with labour to such knowledge as most interested him; and I attracted him. When he was freshest and truest, he loved *me*. Yes, he did! Many a time, when you were put off with a slight word, he has taken Me to his heart!"

She said it with a taunting pride in the midst of her frenzy—for it was little less—yet with an eager remembrance of it, in which the smouldering embers of a gentler feeling kindled for the moment.

"I descended—as I might have known I should, but that he fascinated me with his boyish courtship—into a doll, a trifle for the occupation of an idle hour, to be dropped, and taken up, and trifled with, as the inconstant humour took him. When he grew weary, I grew weary. As his fancy died out, I would no more have tried to strengthen any power I had, than I would have married him on his being forced to take me for his wife. We fell away from one another without a word. Perhaps you saw it, and were not sorry. Since then, I have been a mere disfigured piece of furniture between you both; having no eyes, no ears, no feelings, no remembrances. Moan? Moan for what you made him; not for your love. I tell you that the time was, when I loved him better than you ever did!"

She stood with her bright angry eyes confronting the wide stare, and the set face; and softened no more, when the moaning was repeated, than if the face had been a picture.

"Miss Dartle," said I, "if you can be so obdurate as not to feel for this afflicted mother——"

"Who feels for me?" she sharply retorted. "She has sown this. Let her moan for the harvest that she reaps to-day!"

"And if his faults——" I began.

"Faults!" she cried, bursting into passionate tears. "Who dares malign him? He had a soul worth millions of the friends to whom he stooped!"

"No one can have loved him better, no one can hold him in dearer remembrance, than I," I replied. "I meant to say, if you have no compassion for his mother; or if his faults—you have been bitter on them——"

"It's false," she cried, tearing her black hair; "I loved him!"

"—cannot," I went on, "be banished from your remembrance, in such an hour; look at that figure, even as one you have never seen before, and render it some help!"

All this time, the figure was unchanged, and looked unchangeable. Motionless, rigid, staring; moaning in the same dumb way from time to time, with the same helpless motion of the head; but giving no other sign of life. Miss Dartle suddenly kneeled down before it, and began to loosen the dress.

"A curse upon you!" she said, looking round at me, with a mingled expression of rage and grief. "It was in an evil hour that you ever came here! A curse upon you! Go!"

After passing out of the room, I hurried back to ring the bell, the sooner to alarm the servants. She had then taken the impassive figure in her arms, and, still upon her knees, was weeping over it, kissing it, calling to it, rocking it to and fro upon her bosom like a child, and trying every tender means to rouse the dormant senses. No longer afraid of leaving her, I noiselessly turned back again; and alarmed the house as I went out.

Later in the day, I returned, and we laid him in his mother's room. She was just the same, they told me; Miss Dartle never left her; doctors were in attendance, many things had been tried; but she lay like a statue, except for the low sound now and then.

I went through the dreary house, and darkened the windows. The windows of the chamber where he lay, I darkened last. I lifted up the leaden hand, and held it to my heart; and all the world seemed death and silence, broken only by his mother's moaning.

CHAPTER LVII.
THE EMIGRANTS.

ONE thing more, I had to do, before yielding myself to the shock of these emotions. It was, to conceal what had occurred from those who were going away; and to dismiss them on their voyage in happy ignorance. In this, no time was to be lost.

I took Mr. Micawber aside that same night, and confided to him the task of standing between Mr. Peggotty and intelligence of the late catastrophe. He zealously undertook to do so, and to intercept any newspaper through which it might, without such precautions, reach him.

"If it penetrates to him, Sir," said Mr. Micawber, striking himself on the breast, "it shall first pass through this body!"

Mr. Micawber, I must observe, in his adaptation of himself to a new state of society, had acquired a bold buccaneering air, not absolutely lawless, but defensive and prompt. One might have supposed him a child of the wilderness, long accustomed to live out of the confines of civilisation, and about to return to his native wilds.

He had provided himself, among other things, with a complete suit of oil-skin, and a straw hat with a very low crown, pitched or caulked on the outside. In this rough clothing, with a common mariner's telescope under his arm, and a shrewd trick of casting up his eye at the sky as looking out for dirty weather, he was far more nautical, after his manner, than Mr. Peggotty. His whole family, if I may so express it, were cleared for action. I found Mrs. Micawber in the closest and most uncompromising of bonnets, made fast under the chin; and in a shawl which tied her up (as I had been tied up, when my aunt first received me) like a bundle, and was secured behind at the waist, in a strong knot. Miss Micawber I found made snug for stormy weather, in the same manner; with nothing superfluous about her. Master Micawber was hardly visible in a Guernsey shirt, and the shaggiest suit of slops I ever saw; and the children were done up, like preserved meats, in impervious cases. Both Mr. Micawber and his eldest son wore their sleeves loosely turned back at the wrists, as being ready to lend a hand in any direction, and to "tumble up," or sing out, "Yeo—Heave—Yeo!" on the shortest notice.

Thus Traddles and I found them at nightfall, assembled on the wooden steps, at that time known as Hungerford Stairs, watching the departure of a boat with some of their property on board. I had told Traddles of the terrible event, and it had greatly shocked him; but there could be no doubt of the kindness of keeping it a secret, and he had come to help me in this last service. It was here that I took Mr. Micawber aside, and received his promise.

The Micawber family were lodged in a little, dirty, tumble-down public-house, which in those days was close to the stairs, and whose protruding wooden rooms overhung the river. The family, as emigrants, being objects of some interest in and about Hungerford, attracted so many beholders, that we were glad to take refuge in their room. It was one of the wooden chambers up-stairs, with the tide flowing underneath. My aunt and Agnes were there, busily making some little extra comforts, in the way of dress, for the children. Peggotty was quietly assisting, with the old insensible work-box, yard measure, and bit of wax-candle before her, that had now outlived so much.

It was not easy to answer her inquiries; still less to whisper Mr. Peggotty, when Mr. Micawber brought him in, that I had given the letter, and all was well. But I did both, and made them happy. If I showed any trace of what I felt, my own sorrows were sufficient to account for it.

"And when does the ship sail, Mr. Micawber?" asked my aunt.

Mr. Micawber considered it necessary to prepare either my aunt or his wife, by degrees, and said, sooner than he had expected yesterday.

"The boat brought you word, I suppose?" said my aunt.

"It did, ma'am," he returned.

"Well?" said my aunt. "And she sails——"

"Madam," he replied, "I am informed that we must positively be on board before seven to-morrow morning."

"Heyday!" said my aunt, "that's soon. Is it a sea-going fact, Mr. Peggotty?"

"'Tis so, ma'am. She'll drop down the river with that theer tide. If Mas'r Davy and my sister comes aboard at Gravesen', arternoon o' next day, they'll see the last on us."

"And that we shall do," said I, "be sure!"

"Until then, and until we are at sea," observed Mr. Micawber, with a glance of intelligence at me, "Mr. Peggotty and myself will constantly keep a double look-out together, on our goods and chattels. Emma, my love," said Mr. Micawber, clearing his throat in his magnificent way, "my friend Mr. Thomas Traddles is so obliging as to solicit, in my ear, that he should have the privilege of ordering the ingredients necessary to the composition of a moderate portion of that Beverage which is peculiarly associated, in our minds, with the Roast Beef of Old England. I allude to—in short, Punch. Under ordinary circumstances, I should scruple to entreat the indulgence of Miss Trotwood and Miss Wickfield, but——"

"I can only say for myself," said my aunt, "that I will drink all happiness and success to you, Mr. Micawber, with the utmost pleasure."

"And I too!" said Agnes, with a smile.

Mr. Micawber immediately descended to the bar, where he appeared to be quite at home; and in due time returned with a steaming jug. I could not but observe that he had been peeling the lemons with his own clasp-knife, which, as became the knife of a practical settler, was about a foot long; and which he wiped, not wholly without ostentation, on the sleeve of his coat. Mrs. Micawber and the two elder members of the family I now found to be provided with similar formidable instruments, while every child had its own wooden spoon attached to its body by a strong line. In a similar anticipation of life afloat, and in the Bush, Mr. Micawber, instead of helping Mrs. Micawber and his eldest son and daughter to punch, in wine-glasses, which he might easily have done, for there was a shelf-full in the room,

served it out to them in a series of villainous little tin pots; and I never saw him enjoy anything so much as drinking out of his own particular pint pot, and putting it in his pocket at the close of the evening.

"The luxuries of the old country," said Mr. Micawber, with an intense satisfaction in their renouncement, "we abandon. The denizens of the forest cannot, of course, expect to participate in the refinements of the land of the Free."

Here, a boy came in to say that Mr. Micawber was wanted down-stairs.

"I have a presentiment," said Mrs. Micawber, setting down her tin pot, "that it is a member of my family."

"If so, my dear," observed Mr. Micawber, with his usual suddenness of warmth on that subject, "as the member of your family—whoever he, she, or it, may be—has kept us waiting for a considerable period, perhaps the Member may now wait my convenience."

"Micawber," said his wife, in a low tone, "at such a time as this——"

"'It is not meet,'" said Mr. Micawber, rising, "'that every nice offence should bear its comment!' Emma, I stand reproved."

"The loss, Micawber," observed his wife, "has been my family's, not yours. If my family are at length sensible of the deprivation to which their own conduct has, in the past, exposed them, and now desire to extend the hand of fellowship, let it not be repulsed."

"My dear," he returned, "so be it!"

"If not for their sakes; for mine, Micawber," said his wife.

"Emma," he returned, "that view of the question is, at such a moment, irresistible. I cannot, even now, distinctly pledge myself to fall upon your family's neck; but the member of your family, who is now in attendance, shall have no genial warmth frozen by me."

Mr. Micawber withdrew, and was absent some little time; in the course of which Mrs. Micawber was not wholly free from an apprehension that words might have arisen between him and the Member. At length the same boy re-appeared, and presented me with a note written in pencil, and headed, in a legal manner, "Heep v. Micawber." From this document, I learned that Mr. Micawber being again arrested, was in a final paroxysm of despair; and that he begged me to send him his knife and pint pot, by bearer, as they might prove serviceable during the brief remainder of his existence, in jail. He also requested, as a last act of friendship, that I would see his family to the Parish Workhouse, and forget that such a Being ever lived.

Of course I answered this note by going down with the boy to pay the money, where I found Mr. Micawber sitting in a corner, looking darkly at the sheriff's officer who had effected the capture. On his release, he embraced me with the utmost fervour; and made an entry of the transaction in his pocket-book—being very particular, I recollect, about a halfpenny I inadvertently omitted from my statement of the total.

This momentous pocket-book was a timely reminder to him of another transaction. On our return to the room upstairs (where he accounted for his absence by saying that it had been occasioned by circumstances over which he had no control), he took out of it a large sheet of paper, folded small, and quite covered with long sums, carefully worked. From the glimpse I had of them, I should say that I never saw such sums out of a school ciphering-book. These, it seemed, were calculations of compound interest on what he called "the principal amount of forty-one, ten, eleven, and a half," for various periods. After a careful consideration of these, and an elaborate estimate of his resources, he had come to the conclusion to select that sum which represented the amount with compound interest to two years, fifteen calendar months, and fourteen days, from that date. For this he had drawn a note-of-hand with great neatness, which he handed over to Traddles on the spot, a discharge of his debt in full (as between man and man), with many acknowledgments.

"I have still a presentiment," said Mrs. Micawber, pensively shaking her head, "that my family will appear on board, before we finally depart."

Mr. Micawber evidently had his presentiment on the subject too, but he put it in his tin pot and swallowed it.

"If you have any opportunity of sending letters home, on your passage, Mrs. Micawber," said my aunt, "you must let us hear from you, you know."

"My dear Miss Trotwood," she replied, "I shall only be too happy to think that anyone expects to hear from us. I shall not fail to correspond. Mr. Copperfield, I trust, as an old and familiar friend, will not object to receive occasional intelligence, himself, from one who knew him when the twins were yet unconscious?"

I said that I should hope to hear, whenever she had an opportunity of writing.

"Please Heaven, there will be many such opportunities," said Mr. Micawber. "The ocean, in these times, is a perfect fleet of ships; and we can hardly fail to encounter many, in running over. It is merely crossing," said Mr. Micawber, trifling with his eye-glass, "merely crossing. The distance is quite imaginary."

I think, now, how odd it was, but how wonderfully like Mr. Micawber, that, when he went from London to Canterbury, he should have talked as if he were going to the farthest limits of the earth; and, when he went from England to Australia, as if he were going for a little trip across the Channel.

"On the voyage, I shall endeavour," said Mr. Micawber, "occasionally to spin them a yarn; and the melody of my son Wilkins will, I trust, be acceptable at the galley-fire. When Mrs. Micawber has her sea-legs on—an expression in which I hope there is no conventional impropriety—she will give them, I dare say, Little Tafflin. Porpoises and dolphins, I believe, will be frequently observed athwart our Bows, and, either on the Starboard or the Larboard Quarter, objects of interest will be continually descried. In short," said Mr. Micawber, with the old genteel air, "the probability is, all will be found so exciting, alow and aloft, that when the look-out, stationed in the maintop, cries Land-oh! we shall be very considerably astonished!"

With that he flourished off the contents of his little tin pot, as if he had made the voyage, and had passed a first-class examination before the highest naval authorities.

"What I chiefly hope, my dear Mr. Copperfield," said Mrs. Micawber, "is, that in some branches of our family we may live again in the old country. Do not frown, Micawber! I do not now refer to my own family, but to our children's children. However vigorous the sapling," said Mrs. Micawber, shaking her head, "I cannot forget the parent-tree; and when our race attains to eminence and fortune, I own I should wish that fortune to flow into the coffers of Britannia."

"My dear," said Mr. Micawber, "Britannia must take her chance. I am bound to say that she has never done much for me, and that I have no particular wish upon the subject."

"Micawber," returned Mrs. Micawber, "there you are wrong. You are going out, Micawber, to this distant clime, to strengthen, not to weaken, the connexion between yourself and Albion."

"The connexion in question, my love," rejoined Mr. Micawber, "has not laid me, I repeat, under that load of personal obligation, that I am at all sensitive as to the formation of another connexion."

"Micawber," returned Mrs. Micawber. "There, I again say, you are wrong. You do not know your power, Micawber. It is that which will strengthen, even in this step you are about to take, the connexion between yourself and Albion."

Mr. Micawber sat in his elbow-chair, with his eyebrows raised; half receiving and half repudiating Mrs. Micawber's views as they were stated, but very sensible of their foresight.

"My dear Mr. Copperfield," said Mrs. Micawber, "I wish Mr. Micawber to feel his position. It appears to me highly important that Mr. Micawber should, from the hour of his embarkation, feel his position. Your old knowledge of me, my dear Mr. Copperfield, will have told you that I have not the sanguine disposition of Mr. Micawber. My disposition is, if I may say so, eminently practical. I know that this is a long voyage. I know that it will involve many privations and inconveniences. I cannot shut my eyes to those facts. But, I also know what Mr. Micawber is. I know the latent power of Mr. Micawber. And therefore I consider it vitally important that Mr. Micawber should feel his position."

"My love," he observed, "perhaps you will allow me to remark that it is barely possible that I *do* feel my position at the present moment."

"I think not, Micawber," she rejoined. "Not fully. My dear Mr. Copperfield, Mr. Micawber's is not a common case. Mr. Micawber is going to a distant country, expressly in order that he may be fully understood and appreciated for the first time. I wish Mr. Micawber to take his stand upon that vessel's prow, and firmly say, 'This country I am come to conquer! Have you honours? Have you riches? Have you posts of profitable pecuniary emolument? Let them be brought forward. They are mine!'"

Mr. Micawber, glancing at us all, seemed to think there was a good deal in this idea.

"I wish Mr. Micawber, if I make myself understood," said Mrs. Micawber, in her argumentative tone, "to be the Cæsar of his own fortunes. That, my dear Mr. Copperfield, appears to me to be his true position. From the first moment of this voyage, I wish Mr. Micawber to stand upon that vessel's prow and say, 'Enough of delay: enough of disappointment: enough of limited means. That was in the old country. This is the new. Produce your reparation. Bring it forward!'"

Mr. Micawber folded his arms, in a resolute manner, as if he were then stationed on the figure-head.

"And doing that," said Mrs. Micawber, "—feeling his position—am I not right in saying that Mr. Micawber will strengthen, and not weaken, his connexion with Britain? An important public character arising in that hemisphere, shall I be told that its influence will not be felt at home? Can I be so weak as to imagine that Mr. Micawber, wielding the rod of talent and of power in Australia, will be nothing in England? I am but a woman; but I should be unworthy of myself, and of my papa, if I were guilty of such absurd weakness."

Mrs. Micawber's conviction that her arguments were unanswerable, gave a moral elevation to her tone which I think I had never heard in it before.

"And therefore it is," said Mrs. Micawber, "that I the more wish, that, at a future period, we may live again on the parent soil. Mr. Micawber may be—I cannot disguise from myself that the probability is, Mr. Micawber will be—a page of History; and he ought then to be represented in the country which gave him birth, and did *not* give him employment!"

"My love," observed Mr. Micawber, "it is impossible for me not to be touched by your affection. I am always willing to defer to your good sense. What will be—will be. Heaven forbid that I should grudge my native country any portion of the wealth that may be accumulated by our descendants!"

"That's well," said my aunt, nodding towards Mr. Peggotty, "and I drink my love to you all, and every blessing and success attend you!"

Mr. Peggotty put down the two children he had been nursing, one on each knee, to join Mr. and Mrs. Micawber in drinking to all of us in return; and when he and the Micawbers cordially shook hands as comrades, and his brown face brightened with a smile, I felt that he would make his way, establish a good name, and be beloved, go where he would.

Even the children were instructed, each to dip a wooden spoon into Mr. Micawber's pot, and pledge us in its contents. When this was done, my aunt and Agnes rose, and parted from the emigrants. It was a sorrowful farewell. They were all crying; the children hung about Agnes to the last; and we left poor Mrs. Micawber in a very distressed condition, sobbing and weeping by a dim candle, that must have made the room look, from the river, like a miserable lighthouse.

I went down again next morning to see that they were away. They had departed, in a boat, as early as five o'clock. It was a wonderful instance to me of the gap such partings make, that although my association of them with the tumble-down public-house and the wooden stairs dated only from last night, both seemed dreary and deserted, now that they were gone.

In the afternoon of the next day, my old nurse and I went down to Gravesend. We found the ship in the river, surrounded by a crowd of boats; a favourable wind blowing; the signal for sailing at her mast-head. I hired a boat directly, and we put off to her; and getting through the little vortex of confusion of which she was the centre, went on board.

Mr. Peggotty was waiting for us on deck. He told me that Mr. Micawber had just now been arrested again (and for the last time) at the suit of Heep, and that, in compliance with a request I had made to him, he had paid the money: which I repaid him. He then took us down between decks; and there, any lingering fears I had of his having heard any rumours of what had happened, were dispelled by Mr. Micawber's coming out of the gloom, taking his arm with an air of friendship and protection, and telling me that they had scarcely been asunder for a moment, since the night before last.

It was such a strange scene to me, and so confined and dark, that, at first, I could make out hardly anything; but, by degrees, it cleared, as my eyes became more accustomed to the gloom, and I seemed to stand in a picture by OSTADE.

Among the great beams, bulks, and ringbolts of the ship, and the emigrant-berths, and chests, and bundles, and barrels, and heaps of miscellaneous baggage—lighted up, here and there, by dangling lanterns; and elsewhere by the yellow daylight straying down a windsail or a hatchway—were crowded groups of people, making new friendships, taking leave of one another, talking, laughing, crying, eating and drinking; some, already settled down into the possession of their few feet of space, with their little households arranged, and tiny children established on stools, or in dwarf elbow-chairs; others, despairing of a resting-place, and wandering disconsolately. From babies who had but a week or two of life behind them, to crooked old men and women who seemed to have but a week or two of life before them; and from ploughmen bodily carrying out soil of England on their boots, to smiths taking away samples of its soot and smoke upon their skins; every age and occupation appeared to be crammed into the narrow compass of the 'tween decks.

As my eye glanced round this place, I thought I saw sitting, by an open port, with one of the Micawber children near her, a figure like Emily's; it first attracted my attention, by another figure parting from it with a kiss; and as it glided calmly away through the disorder, reminding me of—Agnes! But in the rapid motion and confusion, and in the unsettlement of my own thoughts, I lost it again; and only knew that the time was come when all visitors were being warned to leave the ship; that my nurse was crying on a chest beside me; and that Mrs. Gummidge, assisted by some younger stooping woman in black, was busily arranging Mr. Peggotty's goods.

"Is there any last wured, Mas'r Davy?" said he. "Is there any one forgotten thing afore we parts?"

"One thing!" said I. "Martha!"

He touched the younger woman I have mentioned on the shoulder, and Martha stood before me.

"Heaven bless you, you good man!" cried I. "You take her with you!"

She answered for him, with a burst of tears. I could speak no more, at that time, but I wrung his hand; and if ever I have loved and honoured any man, I loved and honoured that man in my soul.

The ship was clearing fast of strangers. The greatest trial that I had, remained. I told him what the noble spirit that was gone, had given me in charge to say at parting. It moved him deeply. But when he charged me, in return, with many messages of affection and regret for those deaf ears, he moved me more.

The time was come. I embraced him, took my weeping nurse upon my arm, and hurried away. On deck, I took leave of poor Mrs. Micawber. She was looking distractedly about for her family, even then; and her last words to me were, that she never would desert Mr. Micawber.

We went over the side into our boat, and lay at a little distance to see the ship wafted on her course. It was then calm, radiant sunset. She lay between us and the red light; and every taper line and spar was visible against the glow. A sight at once so beautiful, so mournful, and so hopeful, as the glorious ship, lying still, on the flushed water, with all the life on board her crowded at the bulwarks, and there clustering, for a moment, bare-headed and silent, I never saw.

Silent, only for a moment. As the sails rose to the wind, and the ship began to move, there broke from all the boats three resounding cheers, which those on board her took up, and echoed back, and which were echoed and re-echoed. My heart burst out when I heard the sound, and beheld the waving of the hats and handkerchiefs—and then I saw her!

Then I saw her, at her uncle's side, and trembling on his shoulder. He pointed to us with an eager hand; and she saw us, and waved her last good-bye to me. Ay, Emily, beautiful and drooping, cling to him with the utmost trust of thy bruised heart; for he has clung to thee, with all the might of his great love!

Surrounded by the rosy light, and standing high upon the deck, apart together, she clinging to him, and he holding her, they solemnly passed away. The night had fallen on the Kentish hills when we were rowed ashore—and fallen darkly upon me.

CHAPTER LVIII.

ABSENCE.

It was a long and gloomy night that gathered on me, haunted by the ghosts of many hopes, of many dear remembrances, many errors, many unavailing sorrows and regrets.

I went away from England; not knowing, even then, how great the shock was, that I had to bear. I left all who were dear to me, and went away; and believed that I had borne it, and it was past. As a man upon a field of battle will receive a mortal hurt, and scarcely know that he is struck, so I, when I was left alone with my undisciplined heart, had no conception of the wound with which it had to strive.

The knowledge came upon me, not quickly, but little by little, and grain by grain. The desolate feeling with which I went abroad, deepened and widened hourly. At first it was a heavy sense of loss and sorrow, wherein I could distinguish little else. By imperceptible degrees, it became a hopeless consciousness of all that I had lost—love, friendship, interest; of all that had been shattered—my first trust, my first affection, the whole airy castle of my life; of all that remained—a ruined blank and waste, lying wide around me, unbroken, to the dark horizon.

If my grief were selfish, I did not know it to be so. I mourned for my child-wife, taken from her blooming world so young. I mourned for him who might have won the love and admiration of thousands, as he had won mine long ago. I mourned for the broken heart that had found rest in the stormy sea; and for the wandering remnants of the simple home, where I had heard the night-wind blowing, when I was a child.

From the accumulated sadness into which I fell, I had at length no hope of ever issuing again. I roamed from place to place, carrying my burden with me everywhere. I felt its whole weight now; and I drooped beneath it, and I said in my heart that it could never be lightened.

When this despondency was at its worst, I believed that I should die. Sometimes, I thought that I would like to die at home; and actually turned back on my road, that I might get there soon. At other times, I passed on farther away, from city to city, seeking I know not what, and trying to leave I know not what behind.

It is not in my power to retrace, one by one, all the weary phases of distress of mind through which I passed. There are some dreams that can only be imperfectly and vaguely described; and when I oblige myself to look back on this time of my life, I seem to be recalling such a dream. I see myself passing on among the novelties of foreign towns, palaces, cathedrals, temples, pictures, castles, tombs, fantastic streets—the old abiding places of History and Fancy—as a dreamer might; bearing my painful load through all, and hardly conscious of the objects as they fade before me. Listlessness to everything, but brooding sorrow, was the night that fell on my undisciplined heart. Let me look up from it—as at last I did, thank Heaven!—and from its long, sad, wretched dream, to dawn.

For many months I travelled with this ever-darkening cloud upon my mind. Some blind reasons that I had for not returning home—reasons then struggling within me, vainly, for more distinct expression—kept me on my pilgrimage. Sometimes, I had proceeded restlessly from place to place, stopping nowhere; sometimes, I had lingered long in one spot. I had had no purpose, no sustaining soul within me, anywhere.

I was in Switzerland. I had come out of Italy, over one of the great passes of the Alps, and had since wandered with a guide among the by-ways of the mountains. If those awful solitudes had spoken to my heart, I did not know it. I had found sublimity and wonder in the dread heights and precipices, in the roaring torrents, and the wastes of ice and snow; but as yet, they had taught me nothing else.

I came, one evening before sunset, down into a valley, where I was to rest. In the course of my descent to it, by the winding track along the mountain-side, from which I saw it shining far below, I think some long-unwonted sense of beauty and tranquillity, some softening influence awakened by its peace, moved faintly in my breast. I remember pausing once, with a kind of sorrow that was not all oppressive, not quite despairing. I remember almost hoping that some better change was possible within me.

I came into the valley, as the evening sun was shining on the remote heights of snow, that closed it in, like eternal clouds. The bases of the mountains forming the gorge in which the little village lay, were richly green; and high above this gentler vegetation, grew forests of dark fir, cleaving the wintry snow-drift, wedge-like, and stemming the avalanche. Above these, were range upon range of craggy steeps, grey rock, bright ice, and smooth verdure-specks of pasture, all gradually blending with the crowning snow. Dotted here and there on the mountain's-side, each tiny dot a home, were lonely wooden cottages, so dwarfed by the towering heights that they appeared too small for toys. So did even the clustered village in the valley, with its wooden bridge across the stream, where the stream tumbled over broken rocks, and roared away among the trees. In the quiet air, there was a sound of distant singing—shepherd voices; but, as one bright evening cloud floated midway along the mountain's-side, I could almost have believed it came from there, and was not earthly music. All at once, in this serenity, great Nature spoke to me; and soothed me to lay down my weary head upon the grass, and weep as I had not wept yet, since Dora died!

I had found a packet of letters awaiting me but a few minutes before, and had strolled out of the village to read them while my supper was making ready. Other packets had missed me, and I had received none for a long time. Beyond a line or two, to say that I was well, and had arrived at such a place, I had not had fortitude or constancy to write a letter since I left home.

The packet was in my hand. I opened it, and read the writing of Agnes.

She was happy and useful, was prospering as she had

hoped. That was all she told me of herself. The rest referred to me.

She gave me no advice; she urged no duty on me; she only told me, in her own fervent manner, what her trust in me was. She knew (she said) how such a nature as mine would turn affliction to good. She knew how trial and emotion would exalt and strengthen it. She was sure that in my every purpose I should gain a firmer and a higher tendency, through the grief I had undergone. She, who so gloried in my fame, and so looked forward to its augmentation, well knew that I would labour on. She knew that in me, sorrow could not be weakness, but must be strength. As the endurance of my childish days had done its part to make me what I was, so greater calamities would nerve me on, to be yet better than I was; and so, as they had taught me, would I teach others. She commended me to God, who had taken my innocent darling to His rest; and in her sisterly affection cherished me always, and was always at my side go where I would; proud of what I had done, but infinitely prouder yet of what I was reserved to do.

I put the letter in my breast, and thought what had I been an hour ago! When I heard the voices die away, and saw the quiet evening cloud grow dim, and all the colours in the valley fade, and the golden snow upon the mountaintops become a remote part of the pale night sky, yet felt that the night was passing from my mind, and all its shadows clearing, there was no name for the love I bore her, dearer to me, henceforward, than ever until then.

I read her letter, many times. I wrote to her before I slept. I told her that I had been in sore need of her help; that without her I was not, and I never had been, what she thought me; but, that she inspired me to be that, and I would try.

I did try. In three months more, a year would have passed since the beginning of my sorrow. I determined to make no resolutions until the expiration of those three months, but to try. I lived in that valley, and its neighbourhood, all the time.

The three months gone, I resolved to remain away from home for some time longer; to settle myself for the present in Switzerland, which was growing dear to me in the remembrance of that evening; to resume my pen; to work.

I resorted humbly whither Agnes had commended me; I sought out Nature, never sought in vain; and I admitted to my breast the human interest I had lately shrunk from. It was not long, before I had almost as many friends in the valley as in Yarmouth; and when I left it, before the winter set in, for Geneva, and came back in the spring, their cordial greetings had a homely sound to me, although they were not conveyed in English words.

I worked early and late, patiently and hard. I wrote a Story, with a purpose growing, not remotely, out of my experience, and sent it to Traddles, and he arranged for its publication very advantageously for me; and the tidings of my growing reputation began to reach me from travellers whom I encountered by chance. After some rest and change, I fell to work, in my old ardent way, on a new fancy, which took strong possession of me. As I advanced in the execution of this task, I felt it more and more, and roused my utmost energies to do it well. This was my third work of fiction. It was not half written, when, in an interval of rest, I thought of returning home.

For a long time, though studying and working patiently, I had accustomed myself to robust exercise. My health, severely impaired when I left England, was quite restored.

I had seen much. I had been in many countries, and I hope I had improved my store of knowledge.

I have now recalled all that I think it needful to recall here, of this term of absence—with one reservation. I have made it, thus far, with no purpose of suppressing any of my thoughts; for, as I have elsewhere said, this narrative is my written memory. I have desired to keep the most secret current of my mind apart, and to the last. I enter on it now.

I cannot so completely penetrate the mystery of my own heart, as to know when I began to think that I might have set its earliest and brightest hopes on Agnes. I cannot say at what stage of my grief it first became associated with the reflection, that, in my wayward boyhood, I had thrown away the treasure of her love. I believe I may have heard some whisper of that distant thought, in the old unhappy loss or want of something never to be realised, of which I had been sensible. But the thought came into my mind as a new reproach and new regret, when I was left so sad and lonely in the world.

If, at that time, I had been much with her, I should, in the weakness of my desolation, have betrayed this. It was what I remotely dreaded when I was first impelled to stay away from England. I could not have borne to lose the smallest portion of her sisterly affection; yet, in that betrayal, I should have set a constraint between us hitherto unknown.

I could not forget that the feeling with which she now regarded me had grown up in my own free choice and course. That if she had ever loved me with another love—and I sometimes thought the time was when she might have done so—I had cast it away. It was nothing, now, that I had accustomed myself to think of her, when we were both mere children, as one who was far removed from my wild fancies. I had bestowed my passionate tenderness upon another object; and what I might have done, I had not done; and what Agnes was to me, I and her own noble heart had made her.

In the beginning of the change that gradually worked in me, when I tried to get a better understanding of myself and be a better man, I did glance, through some indefinite probation, to a period when I might possibly hope to cancel the mistaken past, and to be so blessed as to marry her. But, as time wore on, this shadowy prospect faded, and departed from me. If she had ever loved me, then, I should hold her the more sacred; remembering the confidences I had reposed in her, her knowledge of my errant heart, the sacrifice she must have made to be my friend and sister, and the victory she had won. If she had never loved me, could I believe that she would love me now?

I had always felt my weakness, in comparison with her constancy and fortitude; and now I felt it more and more. Whatever I might have been to her, or she to me, if I had been more worthy of her long ago, I was not now, and she was not. The time was past. I had let it go by, and had deservedly lost her.

That I suffered much in these contentions, that they filled me with unhappiness and remorse, and yet that I had a sustaining sense that it was required of me, in right and honour, to keep away from myself, with shame, the thought of turning to the dear girl in the withering of my hopes, from whom I had frivolously turned when they were bright and fresh—which consideration was at the root of every thought I had concerning her—is all equally true. I made no effort to conceal from myself, now, that I loved her, that I was devoted to her; but I brought the assurance home to myself, that it was now too late, and that our long-subsisting relation must be undisturbed.

I had thought, much and often, of my Dora's shadowing out to me what might have happened, in those years that were destined not to try us; I had considered how the things that never happen, are often as much realities to us, in their effects, as those that are accomplished. The very years she spoke of, were realities now, for my correction; and would have been, one day, a little later perhaps, though we had parted in our earliest folly. I endeavoured to convert what might have been between myself and Agnes, into a means of making me more self-denying, more resolved, more conscious of myself, and my defects and errors. Thus, through the reflection that it might have been, I arrived at the conviction that it could never be.

These, with their perplexities and inconsistencies, were the shifting quicksands of my mind, from the time of my departure to the time of my return home, three years afterwards. Three years had elapsed since the sailing of the emigrant ship; when, at that same hour of sunset, and in the same place, I stood on the deck of the packet vessel that brought me home, looking on the rosy water where I had seen the image of that ship reflected.

Three years. Long in the aggregate, though short as they went by. And home was very dear to me, and Agnes too—but she was not mine—she was never to be mine. She might have been, but that was past!

CHAPTER LIX.
RETURN.

I LANDED in London on a wintry autumn evening. It was dark and raining, and I saw more fog and mud in a minute than I had seen in a year. I walked from the Custom House to the Monument before I found a coach; and although the very house-fronts, looking on the swollen gutters, were like old friends to me, I could not but admit that they were very dingy friends.

I have often remarked—I suppose everybody has—that one's going away from a familiar place, would seem to be the signal for change in it. As I looked out of the coach-window, and observed that an old house on Fish Street Hill, which had stood untouched by painter, carpenter, or bricklayer, for a century, had been pulled down in my absence; and that a neighbouring street, of time-honoured insalubrity and inconvenience, was being drained and widened; I half expected to find St. Paul's Cathedral looking older.

For some changes in the fortunes of my friends, I was prepared. My aunt had long been re-established at Dover, and Traddles had begun to get into some little practice at the Bar, in the very first term after my departure. He had chambers in Gray's Inn, now; and had told me, in his last letters, that he was not without hopes of being soon united to the dearest girl in the world.

They expected me home before Christmas; but had no idea of my returning so soon. I had purposely misled them, that I might have the pleasure of taking them by surprise. And yet, I was perverse enough to feel a chill and disappointment in receiving no welcome, and rattling, alone and silent, through the misty streets.

The well-known shops, however, with their cheerful lights, did something for me; and when I alighted at the door of the Gray's Inn Coffee-house, I had recovered my spirits. It recalled, at first, that so-different time when I had put up at the Golden Cross, and reminded me of the changes that had come to pass since then; but that was natural.

"Do you know where Mr. Traddles lives in the Inn?" I asked the waiter, as I warmed myself by the coffee-room fire.

"Holborn Court, Sir. Number two."

"Mr. Traddles has a rising reputation among the lawyers, I believe?" said I.

"Well, Sir," returned the waiter, "probably he has, Sir; but I am not aware of it myself."

This waiter, who was middle-aged and spare, looked for help to a waiter of more authority—a stout, potential old man, with a double-chin, in black breeches and stockings, who came out of a place like a churchwarden's pew, at the end of the coffee-room, where he kept company with a cash-box, a Directory, a Law-list, and other books and papers.

"Mr. Traddles," said the spare waiter. "Number two in the Court."

The potential waiter waved him away, and turned, gravely, to me.

"I was inquiring," said I, "whether Mr. Traddles, at number two in the Court, has not a rising reputation among the lawyers?"

"Never heard his name," said the waiter, in a rich husky voice.

I felt quite apologetic for Traddles.

"He's a young man, sure?" said the portentous waiter, fixing his eyes severely on me. "How long has he been in the Inn?"

"Not above three years," said I.

The waiter, whom I supposed had lived in his churchwarden's pew for forty years, could not pursue such an insignificant subject. He asked me what I would have for dinner?

I felt I was in England again, and really was quite cast down on Traddles's account. There seemed to be no hope for him. I meekly ordered a bit of fish and a steak, and stood before the fire musing on his obscurity.

As I followed the chief waiter with my eyes, I could not help thinking that the garden in which he had gradually blown to be the flower he was, was an arduous place to rise in. It had such a prescriptive, stiff-necked, long-established, solemn, elderly air. I glanced about the room, which had had its sanded floor sanded, no doubt, in exactly the same manner when the chief waiter was a boy—if he ever was a boy, which appeared improbable; and at the shining tables, where I saw myself reflected, in unruffled depths of old mahogany; and at the lamps, without a flaw in their trimming or cleaning; and at the comfortable green curtains, with their pure brass rods, snugly enclosing the boxes; and at the two large coal fires, brightly burning; and at the rows of decanters, burly as if with the consciousness of pipes of expensive old port-wine below; and both England, and the law, appeared to me to be very difficult indeed to be taken by storm. I went up to my bedroom to change my wet clothes; and the vast extent of that old-wainscoted apartment (which was over the archway leading to the Inn, I remember), and the sedate immensity of the four-post bedstead, and the indomitable gravity of the chests of drawers, all seemed to unite in sternly frowning on the fortunes of Traddles, or on any such daring youth. I came down again to my dinner; and even the slow comfort of the meal, and the orderly silence of the place—which was bare of guests, the Long Vacation not yet being over—were eloquent on the audacity of Traddles, and his small hopes of a livelihood for twenty years to come.

I had seen nothing like this since I went away, and it

quite dashed my hopes for my friend. The chief waiter had had enough of me. He came near me no more; but devoted himself to an old gentleman in long gaiters, to meet whom a pint of special port seemed to come out of the cellar of its own accord, for he gave no order. The second waiter informed me, in a whisper, that this old gentleman was a retired conveyancer living in the Square, and worth a mint of money, which it was expected he would leave to his laundress's daughter; likewise that it was rumoured that he had a service of plate in a bureau, all tarnished with lying by, though more than one spoon and a fork had never yet been beheld in his chambers by mortal vision. By this time, I quite gave Traddles up for lost; and settled in my own mind that there was no hope for him.

Being very anxious to see the dear old fellow, nevertheless, I despatched my dinner, in a manner not at all calculated to raise me in the opinion of the chief waiter, and hurried out by the back-way. Number two in the Court was soon reached; and an inscription on the door-post informing me that Mr. Traddles occupied a set of chambers on the top story, I ascended the staircase. A crazy old staircase I found it to be, feebly lighted on each landing by a club-headed little oil wick, dying away in a little dungeon of dirty glass.

In the course of my stumbling up-stairs, I fancied I heard a pleasant sound of laughter; and not the laughter of an attorney or barrister, or attorney's clerk or barrister's clerk, but of two or three merry girls. Happening, however, as I stopped to listen, to put my foot in a hole where the Honourable Society of Gray's Inn had left a plank deficient, I fell down with some noise, and when I recovered my footing all was silent.

Groping my way more carefully, for the rest of the journey, my heart beat high when I found the outer door, which had MR. TRADDLES painted on it, open. I knocked. A considerable scuffling within ensued, but nothing else. I therefore knocked again.

A small sharp-looking lad, half-footboy and half-clerk, who was very much out of breath, but who looked at me as if he defied me to prove it legally, presented himself.

"Is Mr. Traddles within?" I said.

"Yes, Sir, but he's engaged."

"I want to see him."

After a moment's survey of me, the sharp-looking lad decided to let me in; and opening the door wider for that purpose, admitted me, first, into a little closet of a hall, and next into a little sitting-room; where I came into the presence of my old friend (also out of breath), seated at a table, and bending over papers.

"Good God!" cried Traddles, looking up. "It's Copperfield!" and rushed into my arms, where I held him tight.

"All well, my dear Traddles?"

"All well, my dear, dear Copperfield, and nothing but good news!"

We cried with pleasure, both of us.

"My dear fellow," said Traddles, rumpling his hair in his excitement, which was a most unnecessary operation, "my dearest Copperfield, my long-lost and most welcome friend, how glad I am to see you! How brown you are! How glad I am! Upon my life and honour, I never was so rejoiced, my beloved Copperfield, never!"

I was equally at a loss to express my emotions. I was quite unable to speak, at first.

"My dear fellow!" said Traddles. "And grown so famous! My glorious Copperfield! Good gracious me, *when* did you come, *where* have you come from, *what* have you been doing?"

Never pausing for an answer to anything he said, Traddles, who had clapped me into an easy-chair by the fire, all this time impetuously stirred the fire with one hand, and pulled at my neck-kerchief with the other, under some wild delusion that it was a great-coat. Without putting down the poker, he now hugged me again; and I hugged him; and, both laughing, and both wiping our eyes, we both sat down, and shook hands across the hearth.

"To think," said Traddles, "that you should have been so nearly coming home as you must have been, my dear old boy, and not at the ceremony!"

"What ceremony, my dear Traddles?"

"Good gracious me!" cried Traddles, opening his eyes in his old way. "Didn't you get my last letter?"

"Certainly not, if it referred to any ceremony."

"Why, my dear Copperfield," said Traddles, sticking his hair upright with both hands, and then putting his hands on my knees, "I am married!"

"Married!" I cried, joyfully.

"Lord bless me, yes!" said Traddles—"by the Rev. Horace—to Sophy—down in Devonshire. Why, my dear boy, she's behind the window-curtain! Look here!"

To my amazement, the dearest girl in the world came at that same instant, laughing and blushing, from her place of concealment. And a more cheerful, amiable, honest, happy, bright-looking bride I believe (as I could not help saying on the spot) the world never saw. I kissed her as an old acquaintance should, and wished them joy with all my might of heart.

"Dear me," said Traddles, "what a delightful re-union this is! You are so extremely brown, my dear Copperfield! God bless my soul, how happy I am!"

"And so am I," said I.

"And I am sure I am!" said the blushing and laughing Sophy.

"We are all as happy as possible!" said Traddles. "Even the girls are happy. Dear me, I declare I forgot them!"

"Forgot?" said I.

"The girls," said Traddles. "Sophy's sisters. They are staying with us. They have come to have a peep at London. The fact is, when—was it you that tumbled up stairs, Copperfield?"

"It was," said I, laughing.

"Well then, when you tumbled up stairs," said Traddles, "I was romping with the girls. In point of fact, we were playing at Puss in the Corner. But as that wouldn't do in Westminster Hall, and as it wouldn't look quite professional if they were seen by a client, they decamped. And they are now—listening, I have no doubt," said Traddles, glancing at the door of another room.

"I am sorry," said I, laughing afresh, "to have occasioned such a dispersion."

"Upon my word," rejoined Traddles, greatly delighted, "if you had seen them running away, and running back again, after you had knocked, to pick up the combs they had dropped out of their hair, and going on in the maddest manner, you wouldn't have said so. My love, will you fetch the girls?"

Sophy tripped away, and we heard her received in the adjoining room with a peal of laughter.

"Really musical, isn't it, my dear Copperfield?" said

Traddles. "It's very agreeable to hear. It quite lights up these old rooms. To an unfortunate bachelor of a fellow who has lived alone all his life, you know, it's positively delicious. It's charming. Poor things, they have had a great loss in Sophy—who, I do assure you, Copperfield, is, and ever was, the dearest girl!—and it gratifies me beyond expression to find them in such good spirits. The society of girls is a very delightful thing, Copperfield. It's not professional, but it's very delightful."

Observing that he slightly faltered, and comprehending that in the goodness of his heart he was fearful of giving me some pain by what he had said, I expressed my concurrence with a heartiness that evidently relieved and pleased him greatly.

"But then," said Traddles, "our domestic arrangements are, to say the truth, quite unprofessional altogether, my dear Copperfield. Even Sophy's being here, is unprofessional. And we have no other place of abode. We have put to sea in a cockboat, but we are quite prepared to rough it. And Sophy's an extraordinary manager! You'll be surprised how those girls are stowed away. I am sure I hardly know how it's done."

"Are many of the young ladies with you?" I inquired.

"The eldest, the Beauty is here," said Traddles, in a low confidential voice, "Caroline. And Sarah's here—the one I mentioned to you as having something the matter with her spine, you know. Immensely better! And the two youngest that Sophy educated are with us. And Louisa's here."

"Indeed!" cried I.

"Yes," said Traddles. "Now the whole set—I mean the chambers—is only three rooms; but Sophy arranges for the girls in the most wonderful way, and they sleep as comfortably as possible. Three in that room," said Traddles, pointing. "Two in that."

I could not help glancing round, in search of the accommodation remaining for Mr. and Mrs. Traddles. Traddles understood me.

"Well!" said Traddles, "we are prepared to rough it, as I said just now; and we *did* improvise a bed last week, upon the floor here. But there's a little room in the roof —a very nice room, when you're up there—which Sophy papered herself, to surprise me; and that's our room at present. It's a capital little gipsy sort of place. There's quite a view from it."

"And you are happily married at last, my dear Traddles!" said I. "How rejoiced I am!"

"Thank you, my dear Copperfield," said Traddles, as we shook hands once more. "Yes, I am as happy as it's possible to be. There's your old friend, you see," said Traddles, nodding triumphantly at the flower-pot and stand; "and there's the table with the marble top! All the other furniture is plain and serviceable, you perceive. And as to plate, Lord bless you, we haven't so much as a tea-spoon."

"All to be earned?" said I, cheerfully.

"Exactly so," replied Traddles, "all to be earned. Of course we have something in the shape of teaspoons, because we stir our tea. But they're Britannia metal."

"The silver will be the brighter when it comes," said I.

"The very thing we say!" cried Traddles. "You see, my dear Copperfield," falling again into the low confidential tone, "after I had delivered my argument in Doe dem. Jipes *versus* Wigzell, which did me great service with the profession, I went down into Devonshire, and had some serious conversation in private with the Reverend Horace.

I dwelt upon the fact that Sophy—who I do assure you, Copperfield, is the dearest girl!——"

"I am certain she is!" said I.

"She is indeed!" rejoined Traddles. "But I am afraid, I am wandering from the subject. Did I mention the Reverend Horace?"

"You said that you dwelt upon the fact——"

"True! Upon the fact that Sophy and I had been engaged for a long period, and that Sophy, with the permission of her parents, was more than content to take me—in short," said Traddles, with his old frank smile, "on our present Britannia-metal footing. Very well. I then proposed to the Reverend Horace—who is a most excellent clergyman, Copperfield, and ought to be a Bishop; or at least ought to have enough to live upon, without pinching himself—that if I could turn the corner, say of two hundred and fifty pounds, in one year; and could see my way pretty clearly to that, or something better, next year; and could plainly furnish a little place like this, besides; then, and in that case, Sophy and I should be united. I took the liberty of representing that we had been patient for a good many years; and that the circumstance of Sophy's being extraordinarily useful at home, ought not to operate, with her affectionate parents, against her establishment in life—don't you see?"

"Certainly it ought not," said I.

"I am glad you think so, Copperfield," rejoined Traddles, "because, without any imputation on the Reverend Horace, I do think parents, and brothers, and so forth, are sometimes rather selfish in such cases. Well! I also pointed out, that my most earnest desire was, to be useful to the family; and that if I got on in the world, and anything should happen to him—I refer to the Reverend Horace——"

"I understand," said I.

"—Or to Mrs. Crewler—it would be the utmost gratification of my wishes, to be a parent to the girls. He replied in a most admirable manner, exceedingly flattering to my feelings, and undertook to obtain the consent of Mrs. Crewler to this arrangement. They had a dreadful time of it with her. It mounted from her legs into her chest, and then into her head——"

"What mounted?" I asked.

"Her grief," replied Traddles, with a serious look. "Her feelings generally. As I mentioned on a former occasion, she is a very superior woman, but has lost the use of her limbs. Whatever occurs to harass her, usually settles in her legs; but on this occasion it mounted to the chest, and then to the head, and, in short, pervaded the whole system in a most alarming manner. However, they brought her through it by unremitting and affectionate attention; and we were married yesterday six weeks. You have no idea what a Monster I felt, Copperfield, when I saw the whole family crying and fainting away in every direction! Mrs. Crewler couldn't see me before we left— couldn't forgive me, then, for depriving her of her child --but she is a good creature, and has done so since. I had a delightful letter from her, only this morning."

"And in short, my dear friend," said I, "you feel as blest as you deserve to feel!"

"Oh! That's your partiality!" laughed Traddles. "But, indeed, I am in a most enviable state. I work hard, and read Law insatiably. I get up at five every morning, and don't mind it at all. I hide the girls in the daytime, and make merry with them in the evening. And I assure you I am quite sorry that they are going home on

Tuesday, which is the day before the first day of Michaelmas Term. But here," said Traddles, breaking off in his confidence, and speaking aloud, "*are* the girls! Mr. Copperfield, Miss Crewler—Miss Sarah—Miss Louisa—Margaret and Lucy!"

They were a perfect nest of roses; they looked so wholesome and fresh. They were all pretty, and Miss Caroline was very handsome; but there was a loving, cheerful, fireside quality in Sophy's bright looks, which was better than that, and which assured me that my friend had chosen well. We all sat round the fire; while the sharp boy, who I now divined had lost his breath in putting the papers out, cleared them away again, and produced the tea-things. After that, he retired for the night, shutting the outer door upon us with a bang. Mrs. Traddles, with perfect pleasure and composure beaming from her household eyes, having made the tea, then quietly made the toast as she sat in a corner by the fire.

She had seen Agnes, she told me, while she was toasting. "Tom" had taken her down into Kent for a wedding trip, and there she had seen my aunt, too; and both my aunt and Agnes were well, and they had all talked of nothing but me. "Tom" had never had me out of his thoughts, she really believed, all the time I had been away. "Tom" was the authority for everything. "Tom" was evidently the idol of her life; never to be shaken on his pedestal by any commotion; always to be believed in, and done homage to with the whole faith of her heart, come what might.

The deference which both she and Traddles showed towards the Beauty, pleased me very much. I don't know that I thought it very reasonable; but I thought it very delightful, and essentially a part of their character. If Traddles ever for an instant missed the teaspoons that were still to be won, I have no doubt it was when he handed the Beauty her tea. If his sweet-tempered wife could have got up any self-assertion against anyone, I am satisfied it could only have been because she was the Beauty's sister. A few slight indications of a rather petted and capricious manner, which I observed in the Beauty, were manifestly considered, by Traddles and his wife, as her birthright and natural endowment. If she had been born a Queen Bee, and they labouring Bees, they could not have been more satisfied of that.

But their self-forgetfulness charmed me. Their pride in these girls, and their submission of themselves to all their whims, was the pleasantest little testimony to their own worth I could have desired to see. If Traddles were addressed as "a darling," once in the course of that evening; and besought to bring something here, or carry something there, or take something up, or put something down, or find something, or fetch something; he was so addressed, by one or other of his sisters-in-law, at least twelve times in an hour. Neither could they do anything without Sophy. Somebody's hair fell down, and nobody but Sophy could put it up. Somebody forgot how a particular tune went, and nobody but Sophy could hum that tune right. Somebody wanted to recall the name of a place in Devonshire, and only Sophy knew it. Something was wanted to be written home, and Sophy alone could be trusted to write before breakfast in the morning. Somebody broke down in a piece of knitting, and no one but Sophy was able to put the defaulter in the right direction. They were entire mistresses of the place, and Sophy and Traddles waited on them. How many children Sophy could have taken care

of in her time, I can't imagine; but she seemed to be famous for knowing every sort of song that ever was addressed to a child in the English tongue; and she sang dozens to order with the clearest little voice in the world, one after another (every sister issuing directions for a different tune, and the Beauty generally striking in last), so that I was quite fascinated. The best of all was, that, in the midst of their exactions, all the sisters had a great tenderness and respect both for Sophy and Traddles. I am sure, when I took my leave, and Traddles was coming out to walk with me to the coffee-house, I thought I had never seen an obstinate head of hair, or any other head of hair, rolling about in such a shower of kisses.

Altogether, it was a scene I could not help dwelling on with pleasure, for a long time after I got back and had wished Traddles good night. If I had beheld a thousand roses blowing in a top set of chambers, in that withered Gray's Inn, they could not have brightened it half so much. The idea of those Devonshire girls, among the dry law-stationers and the attorneys' offices; and of the tea and toast, and children's songs, in that grim atmosphere of pounce and parchment, red tape, dusty wafers, ink-jars, brief and draft paper, law reports, writs, declarations, and bills of costs; seemed almost as pleasantly fanciful as if I had dreamed that the Sultan's famous family had been admitted on the roll of attorneys, and had brought the talking bird, the singing tree, and the golden water into Gray's Inn Hall. Somehow, I found that I had taken leave of Traddles for the night, and come back to the coffee-house, with a great change in my despondency about him. I began to think he would get on, in spite of all the many orders of chief waiters in England.

Drawing a chair before one of the coffee-room fires to think about him at my leisure, I gradually fell from the consideration of his happiness to tracing prospects in the live coals, and to thinking, as they broke and changed, of the principal vicissitudes and separations that had marked my life. I had not seen a coal fire, since I had left England three years ago: though many a wood fire had I watched, as it crumbled into hoary ashes, and mingled with the feathery heap upon the hearth, which not inaptly figured to me, in my despondency, my own dead hopes.

I could think of the past now, gravely, but not bitterly; and could contemplate the future in a brave spirit. Home, in its best sense, was for me no more. She in whom I might have inspired a dearer love, I had taught to be my sister. She would marry, and would have new claimants on her tenderness: and in doing it, would never know the love for her that had grown up in my heart. It was right that I should pay the forfeit of my headlong passion. What I reaped, I had sown.

I was thinking, And had I truly disciplined my heart to this, and could I resolutely bear it, and calmly hold the place in her home which she had calmly held in mine,—when I found my eyes resting on a countenance that might have arisen out of the fire, in its association with my early remembrances.

Little Mr. Chillip the Doctor, to whose good offices I was indebted in the very first chapter of this history, sat reading a newspaper in the shadow of an opposite corner. He was tolerably stricken in years by this time; but, being a mild, meek, calm little man, had worn so easily, that I thought he looked at that moment just as he might have looked when he sat in our parlour, waiting for me to be born.

Mr. Chillip had left Blunderstone six or seven years ago, and I had never seen him since. He sat placidly perusing the newspaper, with his little head on one side, and a glass of warm sherry negus at his elbow. He was so extremely conciliatory in his manner that he seemed to apologise to the very newspaper for taking the liberty of reading it.

I walked up to where he was sitting, and said, "How do you do, Mr. Chillip?"

He was greatly fluttered by this unexpected address from a stranger, and replied, in his slow way, "I thank you, Sir, you are very good. Thank you, Sir. I hope *you* are well."

"You don't remember me?" said I.

"Well, Sir," returned Mr. Chillip, smiling very meekly, and shaking his head as he surveyed me, "I have a kind of an impression that something in your countenance is familiar to me, Sir; but I couldn't lay my hand upon your name, really."

"And yet you knew it, long before I knew it myself," I returned.

"Did I indeed, Sir?" said Mr. Chillip. "Is it possible that I had the honour, Sir, of officiating when——?"

"Yes," said I.

"Dear me!" cried Mr. Chillip. "But no doubt you are a good deal changed since then, Sir?"

"Probably," said I.

"Well, Sir," observed Mr. Chillip, "I hope you'll excuse me, if I am compelled to ask the favour of your name?"

On my telling him my name, he was really moved. He quite shook hands with me—which was a violent proceeding for him, his usual course being to slide a tepid little fish-slice, an inch or two in advance of his hip, and evince the greatest discomposure when anybody grappled with it. Even now, he put his hand in his coat-pocket as soon as he could disengage it, and seemed relieved when he had got it safe back.

"Dear me, Sir!" said Mr. Chillip, surveying me with his head on one side. "And it's Mr. Copperfield, is it? Well, Sir, I think I should have known you, if I had taken the liberty of looking more closely at you. There's a strong resemblance between you and your poor father, Sir."

"I never had the happiness of seeing my father," I observed.

"Very true, Sir," said Mr. Chillip, in a soothing tone. "And very much to be deplored it was, on all accounts! We are not ignorant, Sir," said Mr. Chillip, slowly shaking his little head again, "down in our part of the country, of your fame. There must be great excitement here, Sir," said Mr. Chillip, tapping himself on the forehead with his forefinger. "You must find it a trying occupation, Sir!"

"What is your part of the country now?" I asked, seating myself near him.

"I am established within a few miles of Bury St. Edmund's, Sir," said Mr. Chillip. "Mrs. Chillip coming into a little property in that neighbourhood, under her father's will, I bought a practice down there, in which you will be glad to hear I am doing well. My daughter is growing quite a tall lass now, Sir," said Mr. Chillip, giving his little head another little shake. "Her mother let down two tucks in her frocks only last week. Such is time, you see, Sir!"

As the little man put his now empty glass to his lips, when he made this reflection, I proposed to him to have it refilled, and I would keep him company with another. "Well, Sir," he returned, in his slow way, "it's more than

I am accustomed to; but I can't deny myself the pleasure of your conversation. It seems but yesterday that I had the honour of attending you in the measles. You came through them charmingly, Sir!"

I acknowledged this compliment, and ordered the negus, which was soon produced. "Quite an uncommon dissipation!" said Mr. Chillip, stirring it, "but I can't resist so extraordinary an occasion. You have no family, Sir?"

I shook my head.

"I was aware that you sustained a bereavement, Sir, some time ago," said Mr. Chillip. "I heard it from your father-in-law's sister. Very decided character there, Sir?"

"Why, yes," said I, "decided enough. Where did you see her, Mr. Chillip?"

"Are you not aware, Sir," returned Mr. Chillip, with his placidest smile, "that your father-in-law is again a neighbour of mine?"

"No," said I.

"He is indeed, Sir!" said Mr. Chillip. "Married a young lady of that part, with a very good little property, poor thing.—And this action of the brain now, Sir? Don't you find it fatigue you?" said Mr. Chillip, looking at me like an admiring Robin.

I waived that question, and returned to the Murdstones. "I was aware of his being married again. Do you attend the family?" I asked.

"Not regularly. I have been called in," he replied. "Strong phrenological development of the organ of firmness, in Mr. Murdstone and his sister, Sir."

I replied with such an expressive look, that Mr. Chillip was emboldened by that, and the negus together, to give his head several short shakes, and thoughtfully exclaim, "Ah, dear me! We remember old times, Mr. Copperfield!"

"And the brother and sister are pursuing their old course, are they?" said I.

"Well, Sir," replied Mr. Chillip, "a medical man, being so much in families, ought to have neither eyes nor ears for anything but his profession. Still, I must say, they are very severe, Sir; both as to this life and the next."

"The next will be regulated without much reference to them, I dare say," I returned: "what are they doing as to this?"

Mr. Chillip shook his head, stirred his negus, and sipped it.

"She was a charming woman, Sir!" he observed in a plaintive manner.

"The present Mrs. Murdstone?"

"A charming woman indeed, Sir," said Mr. Chillip; "as amiable, I am sure, as it was possible to be! Mrs. Chillip's opinion is, that her spirit has been entirely broken since her marriage, and that she is all but melancholy mad. And the ladies," observed Mr. Chillip, timorously, "are great observers, Sir."

"I suppose she was to be subdued and broken to their detestable mould, Heaven help her!" said I. "And she has been."

"Well, Sir, there were violent quarrels at first, I assure you," said Mr. Chillip; "but she is quite a shadow now. Would it be considered forward if I was to say to you, Sir, in confidence, that since the sister came to help, the brother and sister between them have nearly reduced her to a state of imbecility."

I told him I could easily believe it.

"I have no hesitation in saying," said Mr. Chillip, fortifying himself with another sip of negus, "between you and me, Sir, that her mother died of it—or that tyranny, gloom, and worry have made Mrs. Murdstone nearly imbecile. She was a lively young woman, Sir, before marriage, and their gloom and austerity destroyed her. They go about with her, now, more like her keepers than her husband and sister-in-law. That was Mrs. Chillip's remark to me, only last week. And I assure you, Sir, the ladies are great observers. Mrs. Chillip herself is a *great* observer!"

"Does he gloomily profess to be (I am ashamed to use the word in such association) religious still?" I inquired.

"You anticipate, Sir," said Mr. Chillip, his eyelids getting quite red with the unwonted stimulus in which he was indulging. "One of Mrs. Chillip's most impressive remarks. Mrs. Chillip," he proceeded, in the calmest and slowest manner, "quite electrified me, by pointing out that Mr. Murdstone sets up an image of himself, and calls it the Divine Nature. You might have knocked me down on the flat of my back, Sir, with the feather of a pen, I assure you, when Mrs. Chillip said so. The ladies are great observers, Sir?"

"Intuitively," said I, to his extreme delight.

"I am very happy to receive such support in my opinion, Sir," he rejoined. "It is not often that I venture to give a non-medical opinion, I assure you. Mr. Murdstone delivers public addresses sometimes, and it is said,—in short, Sir, it is said by Mrs. Chillip,—that the darker tyrant he has lately been, the more ferocious is his doctrine."

"I believe Mrs. Chillip to be perfectly right," said I.

"Mrs. Chillip does go so far as to say," pursued the meekest of little men, much encouraged, "that what such people miscall their religion, is a vent for their bad humours and arrogance. And do you know I must say, Sir," he continued, mildly laying his head on one side, "that I *don't* find authority for Mr. and Miss Murdstone in the New Testament?"

"I never found it either!" said I.

"In the meantime, Sir," said Mr. Chillip, "they are much disliked; and as they are very free in consigning everybody who dislikes them to perdition, we really have a good deal of perdition going on in our neighbourhood! However, as Mrs. Chillip says, Sir, they undergo a continual punishment; for they are turned inward, to feed upon their own hearts, and their own hearts are very bad feeding. Now, Sir, about that brain of yours, if you'll excuse my returning to it. Don't you expose it to a good deal of excitement, Sir?"

I found it not difficult, in the excitement of Mr. Chillip's own brain, under his potations of negus, to divert his attention from this topic to his own affairs, on which, for the next half-hour, he was quite loquacious; giving me to understand, among other pieces of information, that he was then at the Gray's Inn Coffee-house to lay his professional evidence before a Commission of Lunacy, touching the state of mind of a patient who had become deranged from excessive drinking.

"And I assure you, Sir," he said, "I am extremely nervous on such occasions. I could not support being what is called Bullied, Sir. It would quite unman me. Do you know it was some time before I recovered the conduct of that alarming lady, on the night of your birth, Mr. Copperfield?"

I told him that I was going down to my aunt, the Dragon of that night, early in the morning; and that she was one of the most tender-hearted and excellent of women, as he would know full well if he knew her better. The mere notion of the possibility of his ever seeing her again, appeared to terrify him. He replied with a small pale smile, "Is she so, indeed, Sir? Really?" and almost immediately called for a candle, and went to bed, as if he were not quite safe anywhere else. He did not actually stagger under the negus; but I should think his placid little pulse must have made two or three more beats in a minute, than it had done since the great night of my aunt's disappointment, when she struck at him with her bonnet.

Thoroughly tired, I went to bed too, at midnight; passed the next day on the Dover coach; burst safe and sound into my aunt's old parlour while she was at tea (she wore spectacles now); and was received by her, and Mr. Dick, and dear old Peggotty, who acted as housekeeper, with open arms and tears of joy. My aunt was mightily amused, when we began to talk composedly, by my account of my meeting with Mr. Chillip, and of his holding her in such dread remembrance; and both she and Peggotty had a great deal to say about my poor mother's second husband, and "that murdering woman of a sister,"—on whom I think no pain or penalty would have induced my aunt to bestow any Christian or Proper Name, or any other designation.

CHAPTER LX.

AGNES.

MY aunt and I, when we were left alone, talked far into the night. How the emigrants never wrote home, otherwise than cheerfully and hopefully; how Mr. Micawber had actually remitted divers small sums of money, on account of those "pecuniary liabilities," in reference to which he had been so business-like as between man and man; how Janet, returning into my aunt's service when she came back to Dover, had finally carried out her renunciation of mankind by entering into wedlock with a thriving tavern-keeper; and how my aunt had finally set *her* seal on the same great principle, by aiding and abetting the bride, and crowning the marriage-ceremony with her presence; were among our topics—already more or less familiar to me through the letters I had had. Mr. Dick, as usual, was not forgotten. My aunt informed me how he incessantly occupied himself in copying everything he could lay his hands on, and kept King Charles the First at a respectful distance by that semblance of employment; how it was one of the main joys and rewards of her life that he was free and happy, instead of pining in monotonous restraint; and how (as a novel general conclusion) nobody but she could ever fully know what he was.

"And when, Trot," said my aunt, patting the back of my hand, as we sat in our old way before the fire, "when are you going over to Canterbury?"

"I shall get a horse, and ride over to-morrow morning, aunt, unless you will go with me?"

"No!" said my aunt, in her short abrupt way. "I mean to stay where I am."

Then, I should ride, I said. I could not have come through Canterbury to-day without stopping, if I had been coming to anyone but her.

She was pleased, but answered, "Tut, Trot; *my* old bones would have kept till to-morrow!" and softly patted my hand again, as I sat looking thoughtfully at the fire.

Thoughtfully, for I could not be here once more, and so near Agnes, without the revival of those regrets with which I had so long been occupied. Softened regrets they might be, teaching me what I had failed to learn when my younger life was all before me, but not the less regrets. "Oh, Trot," I seemed to hear my aunt say once more; and I understood her better now—"Blind, blind, blind!"

We both kept silence for some minutes. When I raised my eyes, I found that she was steadily observant of me. Perhaps she had followed the current of my mind; for it seemed to me an easy one to track now, wilful as it had been once.

"You will find her father a white-haired old man," said my aunt, "though a better man in all other respects—a reclaimed man. Neither will you find him measuring all human interests, and joys, and sorrows, with his one poor little inch-rule now. Trust me, child, such things must shrink very much, before they can be measured off in *that* way."

"Indeed they must," said I.

"You will find her," pursued my aunt, "as good, as beautiful, as earnest, as disinterested, as she has always been. If I knew higher praise, Trot, I would bestow it on her."

There was no higher praise for her; no higher reproach for me. Oh, how had I strayed so far away!

"If she trains the young girls whom she has about her, to be like herself," said my aunt, earnest even to the filling of her eyes with tears, "Heaven knows, her life will be well employed! Useful and happy, as she said that day! How could she be otherwise than useful and happy!"

"Has Agnes any——" I was thinking aloud, rather than speaking.

"Well? Hey? Any what?" said my aunt, sharply.

"Any lover," said I.

"A score," cried my aunt, with a kind of indignant pride. "She might have married twenty times, my dear, since you have been gone!"

"No doubt," said I. "No doubt. But has she any lover who is worthy of her? Agnes could care for no other."

My aunt sat musing for a little while, with her chin upon her hand. Slowly raising her eyes to mine, she said:

"I suspect she has an attachment, Trot."

"A prosperous one?" said I.

"Trot," returned my aunt gravely, "I can't say. I have no right to tell you even so much. She has never confided it to me, but I suspect it."

She looked so attentively and anxiously at me (I even saw her tremble), that I felt now, more than ever, that she had followed my late thoughts. I summoned all the resolutions I had made, in all those many days and nights, and all those many conflicts of my heart.

"If it should be so," I began, "and I hope it is——"

"I don't know that it is," said my aunt curtly. "You must not be ruled by my suspicions. You must keep them secret. They are very slight, perhaps. I have no right to speak."

"If it should be so," I repeated, "Agnes will tell me at her own good time. A sister to whom I have confided so much, aunt, will not be reluctant to confide in me."

My aunt withdrew her eyes from mine, as slowly as she had turned them upon me; and covered them thoughtfully with her hand. By-and-by she put her other hand on my shoulder; and so we both sat, looking into the past, without saying another word, until we parted for the night.

I rode away, early in the morning, for the scene of my old school days. I cannot say that I was yet quite happy, in the hope that I was gaining a victory over myself; even in the prospect of so soon looking on her face again.

The well-remembered ground was soon traversed, and I came into the quiet streets, where every stone was a boy's book to me. I went on foot to the old house, and went away with a heart too full to enter. I returned; and looking, as I passed, through the low window of the turret-room where first Uriah Heep, and afterwards Mr. Micawber, had been wont to sit, saw that it was a little parlour now, and that there was no office. Otherwise the staid old house was, as to its cleanliness and order, still just as it had been when I first saw it. I requested the new maid who admitted me, to tell Miss Wickfield that a gentleman who waited on her from a friend abroad, was there; and I was shown up the grave old staircase (cautioned of the steps I knew so well), into the unchanged drawing-room. The books that Agnes and I had read together, were on their shelves; and the desk where I had laboured at my lessons, many a night, stood yet at the same old corner of the table. All the little changes that had crept in when the Heeps were there, were changed again. Everything was as it used to be, in the happy time.

I stood in the window, and looked across the ancient street at the opposite houses, recalling how I had watched them on wet afternoons, when I first came there; and how I had used to speculate about the people who appeared at any of the windows, and had followed them with my eyes up and down stairs, while women went clicking along the pavement in pattens, and the dull rain fell in slanting lines, and poured out of the waterspout yonder, and flowed into the road. The feeling with which I used to watch the tramps, as they came into the town on those wet evenings, at dusk, and limped past, with their bundles drooping over their shoulders at the ends of sticks, came freshly back to me; fraught, as then, with the smell of damp earth, and wet leaves and briar, and the sensation of the very airs that blew upon me in my own toilsome journey.

The opening of the little door in the panelled wall made me start and turn. Her beautiful serene eyes met mine as she came towards me. She stopped and laid her hand upon her bosom, and I caught her in my arms.

"Agnes! my dear girl! I have come too suddenly upon you."

"No, no! I am so rejoiced to see you, Trotwood!"

"Dear Agnes, the happiness it is to me, to see you once again!"

I folded her to my heart, and, for a little while, we were both silent. Presently we sat down, side by side; and her angel-face was turned upon me with the welcome I had dreamed of, waking and sleeping, for whole years.

She was so true, she was so beautiful, she was so good, —I owed her so much gratitude, she was so dear to me, that I could find no utterance for what I felt. I tried to bless her, tried to thank her, tried to tell her (as I had often done in letters) what an influence she had upon me; but all my efforts were in vain. My love and joy were dumb.

With her own sweet tranquillity, she calmed my agitation; led me back to the time of our parting; spoke to me of Emily, whom she had visited, in secret, many times; spoke to me tenderly of Dora's grave. With the unerring instinct of her noble heart, she touched the chords of my memory so softly and harmoniously, that not one jarred within me; I could listen to the sorrowful, distant music, and desire to shrink from nothing it awoke. How could I, when, blended with it all, was her dear self, the better angel of my life?

"And you, Agnes," I said, by-and-by. "Tell me of yourself. You have hardly ever told me of your own life, in all this lapse of time!"

"What should I tell?" she answered, with her radiant smile. "Papa is well. You see us here, quiet in our own home; our anxieties set at rest, our home restored to us; and knowing that, dear Trotwood, you know all."

"All, Agnes?" said I.

She looked at me, with some fluttering wonder in her face.

"Is there nothing else, Sister?" I said.

Her colour, which had just now faded, returned, and faded again. She smiled; with a quiet sadness, I thought; and shook her head.

I had sought to lead her to what my aunt had hinted at; for, sharply painful to me as it must be to receive that confidence, I was to discipline my heart, and do my duty to her. I saw, however, that she was uneasy, and I let it pass.

"You have much to do, dear Agnes?"

"With my school?" said she, looking up again, in all her bright composure.

"Yes. It is laborious, is it not?"

"The labour is so pleasant," she returned, "that it is scarcely grateful to me to call it by that name."

"Nothing good is difficult to you," said I.

Her colour came and went once more; and once more, as she bent her head, I saw the same sad smile.

"You will wait and see papa," said Agnes, cheerfully, "and pass the day with us? Perhaps you will sleep in your own room? We always call it yours."

I could not do that, having promised to ride back to my aunt's, at night; but I would pass the day there, joyfully.

"I must be a prisoner for a little while," said Agnes, "but here are the old books, Trotwood, and the old music."

"Even the old flowers are here," said I, looking round; "or the old kinds."

"I have found a pleasure," returned Agnes, smiling, "while you have been absent, in keeping everything as it used to be when we were children. For we were very happy then, I think."

"Heaven knows we were!" said I.

"And every little thing that has reminded me of my brother," said Agnes, with her cordial eyes turned cheerfully upon me, "has been a welcome companion. Even this," showing me the basket-trifle, full of keys, still hanging at her side, "seems to jingle a kind of old tune!"

She smiled again, and went out at the door by which she had come.

It was for me to guard this sisterly affection with religious care. It was all that I had left myself, and it was a treasure. If I once shook the foundations of the sacred confidence and usage, in virtue of which it was given to me, it was lost, and could never be recovered. I set this steadily before myself. The better I loved her, the more it behoved me never to forget it.

I walked through the streets; and, once more seeing my old adversary the butcher—now a constable, with his staff hanging up in the shop—went down to look at the place where I had fought him; and there meditated on Miss Shepherd and the eldest Miss Larkins, and all the idle loves and likings, and dislikings, of that time. Nothing seemed to have survived that time but Agnes; and she, ever a star above me, was brighter and higher.

When I returned, Mr. Wickfield had come home, from a garden he had a couple of miles or so out of town, where he now employed himself almost every day. I found him as my aunt had described him. We sat down to dinner, with some half-dozen little girls; and he seemed but the shadow of his handsome picture on the wall.

The tranquillity and peace belonging, of old, to that quiet ground in my memory, pervaded it again. When dinner was done, Mr. Wickfield taking no wine, and I desiring none, we went up stairs; where Agnes and her little charges sang and played, and worked. After tea the children left us; and we three sat together, talking of the bygone days.

"My part in them," said Mr. Wickfield, shaking his white head, "has much matter for regret—for deep regret, and deep contrition, Trotwood, you well know. But I would not cancel it, if it were in my power."

I could readily believe that, looking at the face beside him.

"I should cancel with it," he pursued, "such patience and devotion, such fidelity, such a child's love, as I must not forget, no! even to forget myself."

"I understand you, Sir," I softly said. "I hold it—I have always held it—in veneration."

"But no one knows, not even you," he returned, "how much she has done, how much she has undergone, how hard she has striven. Dear Agnes!"

She had put her hand entreatingly on his arm, to stop him; and was very, very pale.

"Well, well!" he said with a sigh, dismissing, as I then saw, some trial she had borne, or was yet to bear, in connexion with what my aunt had told me. "Well! I have never told you, Trotwood, of her mother. Has any one?"

"Never, Sir."

"It's not much—though it was much to suffer. She married me in opposition to her father's wish, and he renounced her. She prayed him to forgive her, before my Agnes came into this world. He was a very hard man, and her mother had long been dead. He repulsed her. He broke her heart."

Agnes leaned upon his shoulder, and stole her arm about his neck.

"She had an affectionate and gentle heart," he said; "and it was broken. I knew its tender nature very well.

No one could, if I did not. She loved me dearly, but was never happy. She was always labouring, in secret, under this distress; and being delicate and downcast at the time of his last repulse—for it was not the first, by many—pined away and died. She left me Agnes, two weeks old; and the grey hair that you recollect me with, when you first came."

He kissed Agnes on her cheek.

"My love for my dear child was a diseased love, but my mind was all unhealthy then. I say no more of that. I am not speaking of myself, Trotwood, but of her mother, and of her. If I give you any clue to what I am, or to what I have been, you will unravel it, I know. What Agnes is, I need not say. I have always read something of her poor mother's story, in her character; and so I tell it you to-night, when we three are again together, after such great changes. I have told it all."

His bowed head, and her angel face and filial duty, derived a more pathetic meaning from it than they had had before. If I had wanted anything by which to mark this night of our reunion, I should have found it in this.

Agnes rose up from her father's side, before long; and going softly to her piano, played some of the old airs to which we had often listened in that place.

"Have you any intention of going away again?" Agnes asked me, as I was standing by.

"What does my sister say to that?"

"I hope not."

"Then I have no such intention, Agnes."

"I think you ought not, Trotwood, since you ask me," she said, mildly. "Your growing reputation and success enlarge your power of doing good; and if I could spare my brother," with her eyes upon me, "perhaps the time could not."

"What I am, you have made me, Agnes. You should know best."

"I made you, Trotwood?"

"Yes! Agnes, my dear girl!" I said, bending over her. "I tried to tell you, when we met to-day, something that has been in my thoughts since Dora died. You remember, when you came down to me in our little room—pointing upward, Agnes?"

"Oh, Trotwood!" she returned, her eyes filled with tears. "So loving, so confiding, and so young! Can I ever forget?"

"As you were then, my sister, I have often thought since, you have ever been to me. Ever pointing upward, Agnes; ever leading me to something better; ever directing me to higher things!"

She only shook her head; through her tears I saw the same sad quiet smile.

"And I am so grateful to you for it, Agnes, so bound to you, that there is no name for the affection of my heart. I want you to know, yet don't know how to tell you, that all my life long I shall look up to you, and be guided by you, as I have been through the darkness that is past. Whatever betides, whatever new ties you may form, whatever changes may come between us, I shall always look to you, and love you, as I do now, and have always done. You will always be my solace and resource as you have always been. Until I die, my dearest sister, I shall see you always before me, pointing upward!"

She put her hand in mine, and told me she was proud of me, and of what I said; although I praised her very far beyond her worth. Then she went on softly playing, but without removing her eyes from me.

"Do you know, what I have heard to-night, Agnes," said I, "strangely seems to be a part of the feeling with which I regarded you when I saw you first—with which I sat beside you in my rough school-days?"

"You knew I had no mother," she replied with a smile, "and felt kindly towards me."

"More than that, Agnes, I knew, almost as if I had known this story, that there was something inexplicably gentle and softened, surrounding you; something that might have been sorrowful in someone else (as I can now understand it was), but was not so in you."

She softly played on, looking at me still.

"Will you laugh at my cherishing such fancies, Agnes?"

"No!"

"Or at my saying that I really believe I felt, even then, that you could be faithfully affectionate against all discouragement, and never cease to be so, until you ceased to live?—Will you laugh at such a dream?"

"Oh, no! Oh, no!"

For an instant, a distressful shadow crossed her face; but, even in the start it gave me, it was gone; and she was playing on, and looking at me with her own calm smile.

As I rode back in the lonely night, the wind going by me like a restless memory, I thought of this, and feared she was not happy. I was not happy; but, thus far, I had faithfully set the seal upon the Past, and, thinking of her, pointing upward, thought of her as pointing to that sky above me, where, in the mystery to come, I might yet love her with a love unknown on earth, and tell her what the strife had been within me when I loved her here.

CHAPTER LXI.

I AM SHOWN TWO INTERESTING PENITENTS.

For a time—at all events until my book should be completed, which would be the work of several months—I took up my abode in my aunt's house at Dover; and there, sitting in the window from which I had looked out at the moon upon the sea, when that roof first gave me shelter, I quietly pursued my task.

In pursuance of my intention of referring to my own fictions only when their course should incidentally connect itself with the progress of my story, I do not enter on the aspirations, the delights, anxieties, and triumphs, of my art. That I truly devoted myself to it with my strongest earnestness, and bestowed upon it every energy of my soul, I have already said. If the books I have written be of any worth, they will supply the rest. I shall otherwise have written to poor purpose, and the rest will be of interest to no one.

Occasionally, I went to London; to lose myself in the swarm of life there, or to consult with Traddles on some business point. He had managed for me, in my absence, with the soundest judgment; and my worldly affairs were prospering. As my notoriety began to bring upon me an enormous quantity of letters from people of whom I had no knowledge—chiefly about nothing, and extremely difficult to answer—I agreed with Traddles to have my name painted up on his door. There, the devoted postman on that beat delivered bushels of letters for me; and there, at intervals, I laboured through them, like a Home Secretary of State without the salary.

Among this correspondence, there dropped in, every now and then, an obliging proposal from one of the numerous outsiders always lurking about the Commons, to practise under cover of my name (if I would take the necessary steps remaining to make a proctor of myself), and pay me a percentage on the profits. But I declined these offers; being already aware that there were plenty of such covert practitioners in existence, and considering the Commons quite bad enough, without my doing anything to make it worse.

The girls had gone home, when my name burst into bloom on Traddles's door; and the sharp boy looked, all day, as if he had never heard of Sophy, shut up in a back room, glancing down from her work into a sooty little strip of garden with a pump in it. But, there I always found her, the same bright housewife; often humming her Devonshire ballads when no strange foot was coming up the stairs, and blunting the sharp boy in his official closet with melody.

I wondered, at first, why I so often found Sophy writing in a copy-book; and why she always shut it up when I appeared, and hurried it into the table-drawer. But the secret soon came out. One day, Traddles (who had just come home through the drizzling sleet from Court) took a paper out of his desk, and asked me what I thought of that handwriting?

"Oh, *don't*, Tom!" cried Sophy, who was warming his slippers before the fire.

"My dear," returned Tom, in a delighted state, "why not? What do you say to that writing, Copperfield?"

"It's extraordinarily legal and formal," said I. "I don't think I ever saw such a stiff hand."

"Not like a lady's hand, is it?" said Traddles.

"A lady's!" I repeated. "Bricks and mortar are more like a lady's hand!"

Traddles broke into a rapturous laugh, and informed me that it was Sophy's writing; that Sophy had vowed and declared he would need a copying-clerk soon, and she would be that clerk; that she had acquired his hand from a pattern; and that she could throw off—I forget how many folios an hour. Sophy was very much confused by my being told all this, and said that when "Tom" was made a judge he wouldn't be so ready to proclaim it. Which "Tom" denied; averring that he should always be equally proud of it, under all circumstances.

"What a thoroughly good and charming wife she is, my dear Traddles!" said I, when she had gone away, laughing.

"My dear Copperfield," returned Traddles, "she is, without any exception, the dearest girl! The way she manages this place; her punctuality, domestic knowledge, economy, and order; her cheerfulness, Copperfield!"

"Indeed, you have reason to commend her!" I returned. "You are a happy fellow. I believe you make yourselves, and each other, two of the happiest people in the world."

"I am sure we *are* two of the happiest people," returned Traddles. "I admit that, at all events. Bless my soul, when I see her getting up by candle-light on these dark mornings, busying herself in the day's arrangements, going out to market before the clerks come into the Inn, caring for no weather, devising the most capital little dinners out of the plainest materials, making puddings and pies, keeping everything in its right place, always so neat and ornamental herself, sitting up at night with me if it's ever so late, sweet-tempered and encouraging always, and all for me, I positively sometimes can't believe it, Copperfield!"

He was tender of the very slippers she had been warming, as he put them on, and stretched his feet enjoyingly upon the fender.

"I positively sometimes can't believe it," said Traddles. "Then, our pleasures! Dear me, they are inexpensive, but they are quite wonderful! When we are at home here, of an evening, and shut the outer door, and draw those curtains—which she made—where could we be more snug? When it's fine, and we go out for a walk in the evening, the streets abound in enjoyment for us. We look into the glittering windows of the jewellers' shops; and I show Sophy which of the diamond-eyed serpents, coiled up on white satin rising grounds, I would give her if I could afford it; and Sophy shows me which of the gold watches that are capped and jewelled and engine-turned, and possessed of the horizontal lever-escape-movement, and all sorts of things, she would buy for me if *she* could afford it; and we pick out the spoons and forks, fish-slices, butter-knives, and sugar-tongs, we should both prefer if we could both afford it; and really we go away as if we had got them! Then, when we stroll into the squares, and great streets, and see a house to let, sometimes we look up at it, and say, how would *that* do, if I was made a judge? And we parcel it out—such a room for us, such rooms for the girls, and so forth; until we settle to our satisfaction that it would do, or it wouldn't do, as the case may be. Sometimes, we go at half-price to the pit of the theatre—the very smell of which is cheap, in my opinion, at the money—and there we thoroughly enjoy the play: which Sophy believes every word of, and so do I. In walking home, perhaps we buy a little bit of something at a cook's-shop, or a little lobster at the fishmonger's, and bring it here, and make a splendid supper, chatting about what we have seen. Now, you know, Copperfield, if I was Lord Chancellor, we couldn't do this!"

"You would do something, whatever you were, my dear Traddles," thought I, "that would be pleasant and amiable! And by the way," I said aloud, "I suppose you never draw any skeletons now?"

"Really," replied Traddles, laughing, and reddening, "I can't wholly deny that I do, my dear Copperfield. For, being in one of the back rows of the King's Bench the other day, with a pen in my hand, the fancy came into my head to try how I had preserved that accomplishment. And I am afraid there's a skeleton—in a wig—on the ledge of the desk."

After we had both laughed heartily, Traddles wound up by looking with a smile at the fire, and saying, in his forgiving way, "Old Creakle!"

"I have a letter from that old—Rascal here," said I. For I never was less disposed to forgive him the way he used to batter Traddles, than when I saw Traddles so ready to forgive him himself.

"From Creakle the schoolmaster?" exclaimed Traddles. "No!"

"Among the persons who are attracted to me in my rising fame and fortune," said I, looking over my letters, "and who discover that they were always much attached to me, is the self-same Creakle. He is not a schoolmaster now, Traddles. He is retired. He is a Middlesex magistrate."

I thought Traddles might be surprised to hear it, but he was not so at all.

"How do you suppose he comes to be a Middlesex magistrate?" said I.

"Oh dear me!" replied Traddles, "it would be very difficult to answer that question. Perhaps he voted for somebody, or lent money to somebody, or bought something of somebody, or otherwise obliged somebody, or jobbed for somebody, who knew somebody who got the lieutenant of the county to nominate him for the commission."

"On the commission he is, at any rate," said I. "And he writes to me here, that he will be glad to show me, in operation, the only true system of prison discipline; the only unchallengeable way of making sincere and lasting converts and penitents—which, you know, is by solitary confinement. What do you say?"

"To the system?" inquired Traddles, looking grave.

"No. To my accepting the offer, and your going with me?"

"I don't object," said Traddles.

"Then I'll write to say so. You remember (to say nothing of our treatment) this same Creakle turning his son out of doors, I suppose, and the life he used to lead his wife and daughter?"

"Perfectly," said Traddles.

"Yet, if you'll read his letter, you'll find he is the tenderest of men to prisoners convicted of the whole calendar of felonies," said I; "though I can't find that his tenderness extends to any other class of created beings."

Traddles shrugged his shoulders, and was not at all surprised. I had not expected him to be, and was not surprised myself; or my observation of similar practical satires would have been but scanty. We arranged the time of our visit, and I wrote accordingly to Mr. Creakle that evening.

On the appointed day—I think it was the next day, but no matter—Traddles and I repaired to the prison where Mr. Creakle was powerful. It was an immense and solid building, erected at a vast expense. I could not help thinking, as we approached the gate, what an uproar would have been made in the country, if any deluded man had proposed to spend one half the money it had cost, on the erection of an industrial school for the young, or a house of refuge for the deserving old.

In an office that might have been on the ground-floor of the Tower of Babel, it was so massively constructed, we were presented to our old schoolmaster; who was one of a group, composed of two or three of the busier sort of magistrates, and some visitors they had brought. He received me, like a man who had formed my mind in bygone years, and had always loved me tenderly. On my introducing Traddles, Mr. Creakle expressed, in like manner, but in an inferior degree, that he had always been Traddles's guide,

philosopher, and friend. Our venerable instructor was a great deal older, and not improved in appearance. His face was as fiery as ever; his eyes were as small, and rather deeper set. The scanty, wet-looking grey hair, by which I remembered him, was almost gone; and the thick veins in his bald head were none the more agreeable to look at.

After some conversation among these gentlemen, from which I might have supposed that there was nothing in the world to be legitimately taken into account but the supreme comfort of prisoners, at any expense, and nothing on the wide earth to be done outside prison doors, we began our inspection. It being then just dinner-time, we went, first into the great kitchen, where every prisoner's dinner was in course of being set out separately (to be handed to him in his cell), with the regularity and precision of clockwork. I said aside, to Traddles, that I wondered whether it occurred to anybody, that there was a striking contrast between these plentiful repasts of choice quality, and the dinners, not to say of paupers, but of soldiers, sailors, labourers, the great bulk of the honest, working community; of whom not one man in five hundred ever dined half so well. But I learned that "the system" required high living; and, in short, to dispose of the system, once for all, I found that on that head and on all others, "the system" put an end to all doubts, and disposed of all anomalies. Nobody appeared to have the least idea that there was any other system, but *the* system, to be considered.

As we were going through some of the magnificent passages, I inquired of Mr. Creakle and his friends what were supposed to be the main advantages of this all-governing and universally overriding system? I found them to be the perfect isolation of prisoners—so that no one man in confinement there, knew anything about another; and the reduction of prisoners to a wholesome state of mind, leading to sincere contrition and repentance.

Now, it struck me, when we began to visit individuals in their cells, and to traverse the passages in which those cells were, and to have the manner of the going to chapel and so forth, explained to us, that there was a strong probability of the prisoners knowing a good deal about each other, and of their carrying on a pretty complete system of intercourse. This, at the time I write, has been proved, I believe, to be the case; but, as it would have been flat blasphemy against the system to have hinted such a doubt then, I looked out for the penitence as diligently as I could.

And here again, I had great misgivings. I found as prevalent a fashion in the form of the penitence, as I had left outside in the forms of the coats and waistcoats in the windows of the tailors' shops. I found a vast amount of profession, varying very little in character: varying very little (which I thought exceedingly suspicious), even in words. I found a great many foxes, disparaging whole vineyards of inaccessible grapes; but I found very few foxes whom I would have trusted within reach of a bunch. Above all, I found that the most professing men were the greatest objects of interest; and that their conceit, their vanity, their want of excitement, and their love of deception (which many of them possessed to an almost incredible extent, as their histories showed), all prompted to these professions, and were all gratified by them.

However, I heard so repeatedly, in the course of our goings to and fro, of a certain Number Twenty Seven, who was the Favourite, and who really appeared to be a Model Prisoner, that I resolved to suspend my judgment until I should see Twenty Seven. Twenty Eight, I understood, was also a bright particular star; but it was his misfortune to have his glory a little dimmed by the extraordinary lustre of Twenty Seven. I heard so much of Twenty Seven, of his pious admonitions to everybody around him, and of the beautiful letters he constantly wrote to his mother (whom he seemed to consider in a very bad way), that I became quite impatient to see him.

I had to restrain my impatience for some time, on account of Twenty Seven being reserved for a concluding effect. But, at last, we came to the door of his cell; and Mr. Creakle, looking through a little hole in it, reported to us, in a state of the greatest admiration, that he was reading a Hymn Book.

There was such a rush of heads immediately, to see Number Twenty Seven reading his Hymn Book, that the little hole was blocked up, six or seven heads deep. To remedy this inconvenience, and give us an opportunity of conversing with Twenty Seven in all his purity, Mr. Creakle directed the door of the cell to be unlocked, and Twenty Seven to be invited out into the passage. This was done; and whom should Traddles and I then behold, to our amazement, in this converted Number Twenty Seven, but Uriah Heep!

He knew us directly; and said, as he came out—with the old writhe—

"How do you do, Mr. Copperfield? How do you do, Mr. Traddles?"

This recognition caused a general admiration in the party. I rather thought that everyone was struck by his not being proud, and taking notice of us.

"Well, Twenty Seven," said Mr. Creakle, mournfully admiring him. "How do you find yourself to-day?"

"I am very umble, Sir!" replied Uriah Heep.

"You are always so, Twenty Seven," said Mr. Creakle.

Here, another gentleman asked, with extreme anxiety: "Are you quite comfortable?"

"Yes, I thank you, Sir!" said Uriah Heep, looking in that direction. "Far more comfortable here, than ever I was outside. I see my follies now, Sir. That's what makes me comfortable."

Several gentlemen were much affected; and a third questioner, forcing himself to the front, inquired with extreme feeling: "How do you find the beef?"

"Thank you, Sir," replied Uriah, glancing in the new direction of this voice, "it was tougher yesterday than I could wish; but it's my duty to bear. I have committed follies, gentlemen," said Uriah, looking round with a meek smile, "and I ought to bear the consequences without repining."

A murmur, partly of gratification at Twenty Seven's celestial state of mind, and partly of indignation against the Contractor who had given him any cause of complaint (a note of which was immediately made by Mr. Creakle), having subsided, Twenty Seven stood in the midst of us, as if he felt himself the principal object of merit in a highly meritorious museum. That we, the neophytes, might have an excess of light shining upon us all at once, orders were given to let out Twenty Eight.

I had been so much astonished already, that I only felt a kind of resigned wonder when Mr. Littimer walked forth, reading a good book!

"Twenty Eight," said a gentleman in spectacles, who had not yet spoken, "you complained last week, my good fellow, of the cocoa. How has it been since?"

"I thank you, Sir," said Mr. Littimer, "it has been better made. If I might take the liberty of saying so, Sir, I don't think the milk which is boiled with it is quite genuine; but I am aware, Sir, that there is great adulteration of milk, in London, and that the article in a pure state is difficult to be obtained."

It appeared to me that the gentleman in spectacles backed his Twenty Eight against Mr. Creakle's Twenty Seven, for each of them took his own man in hand.

"What is your state of mind, Twenty Eight?" said the questioner in spectacles.

"I thank you, Sir," returned Mr. Littimer; "I see my follies now, Sir. I am a good deal troubled when I think of the sins of my former companions, Sir; but I trust they may find forgiveness."

"You are quite happy yourself?" said the questioner, nodding encouragement.

"I am much obliged to you, Sir," returned Mr. Littimer. "Perfectly so."

"Is there anything at all on your mind, now?" said the questioner. "If so, mention it, Twenty Eight."

"Sir," said Mr. Littimer, without looking up, "if my eyes have not deceived me, there is a gentleman present who was acquainted with me in my former life. It may be profitable to that gentleman to know, Sir, that I attribute my past follies, entirely to having lived a thoughtless life in the service of young men; and to having allowed myself to be led by them into weaknesses, which I had not the strength to resist. I hope that gentleman will take warning, Sir, and will not be offended at my freedom. It is for his good. I am conscious of my own past follies. I hope he may repent of all the wickedness and sin, to which he has been a party."

I observed that several gentlemen were shading their eyes, each, with one hand, as if they had just come into church.

"This does you credit, Twenty Eight," returned the questioner. "I should have expected it of you. Is there anything else?"

"Sir," returned Mr. Littimer, slightly lifting up his eyebrows, but not his eyes, "there was a young woman who fell into dissolute courses, that I endeavoured to save, Sir, but could not rescue. I beg that gentleman, if he has it in his power, to inform that young woman from me that I forgive her her bad conduct towards myself; and that I call her to repentance—if he will be so good."

"I have no doubt, Twenty Eight," returned the questioner, "that the gentleman you refer to feels very strongly —as we all must—what you have so properly said. We will not detain you."

"I thank you, Sir," said Mr. Littimer. "Gentlemen, I wish you a good day, and hoping you and your families will also see your wickedness, and amend!"

With this, Number Twenty Eight retired, after a glance between him and Uriah; as if they were not altogether unknown to each other, through some medium of communication; and a murmur went round the group, as his door shut upon him, that he was a most respectable man, and a beautiful case.

"Now, Twenty Seven," said Mr. Creakle, entering on a clear stage with *his* man, "is there anything that anyone can do for you? If so, mention it."

"I would umbly ask, Sir," returned Uriah, with a jerk of his malevolent head, "for leave to write again to mother."

"It shall certainly be granted," said Mr. Creakle.

"Thank you, Sir! I am anxious about mother. I am afraid she ain't safe."

Somebody incautiously asked, what from? But there was a scandalised whisper of "Hush!"

"Immortally safe, Sir," returned Uriah, writhing in the direction of the voice. "I should wish mother to be got into my state. I never should have been got into my present state if I hadn't come here. I wish mother had come here. It would be better for everybody, if they got took up, and was brought here."

This sentiment gave unbounded satisfaction—greater satisfaction, I think, than anything that had passed yet.

"Before I come here," said Uriah, stealing a look at us, as if he would have blighted the outer world to which he belonged, if he could, "I was given to follies; but now I am sensible of my follies. There's a deal of sin outside. There's a deal of sin in mother. There's nothing but sin everywhere—except here."

"You are quite changed?" said Mr. Creakle.

"Oh dear, yes, Sir!" cried this hopeful penitent.

"You wouldn't relapse, if you were going out?" asked somebody else.

"Oh de-ar no, Sir!"

"Well!" said Mr. Creakle, "this is very gratifying. You have addressed Mr. Copperfield, Twenty Seven. Do you wish to say anything further to him?"

"You knew me, a long time before I came here and was changed, Mr. Copperfield," said Uriah, looking at me; and a more villainous look I never saw, even on his visage. "You knew me when, in spite of my follies, I was umble among them that was proud, and meek among them that was violent—you was violent to me yourself, Mr. Copperfield. Once, you struck me a blow in the face, you know."

General commiseration. Several indignant glances directed at me.

"But I forgive you, Mr. Copperfield," said Uriah, making his forgiving nature the subject of a most impious and awful parallel, which I shall not record. "I forgive everybody. It would ill become me to bear malice. I freely forgive you, and I hope you'll curb your passions in future. I hope Mr. W. will repent, and Miss W., and all of that sinful lot. You've been visited with affliction, and I hope it may do you good; but you'd better have come here. Mr. W. had better have come here, and Miss W. too. The best wish I could give you, Mr. Copperfield, and give all of you gentlemen, is, that you could be took up and brought here. When I think of my past follies, and my present state, I am sure it would be best for you. I pity all who ain't brought here!"

He sneaked back into his cell, amidst a little chorus of approbation; and both Traddles and I experienced a great relief when he was locked in.

It was a characteristic feature in this repentance, that I was fain to ask what these two men had done, to be there at all. That appeared to be the last thing about which they had anything to say. I addressed myself to one of the two warders, who, I suspected, from certain latent indications in their faces, knew pretty well what all this stir was worth.

"Do you know," said I, as we walked along the passage, "what felony was Number Twenty Seven's last 'folly'?"

The answer was that it was a Bank case.

"A fraud on the Bank of England?" I asked.

"Yes, Sir. Fraud, forgery, and conspiracy. He and some others. He set the others on. It was a deep plot for a large sum. Sentence, transportation for life. Twenty Seven was the knowingest bird of the lot, and had very nearly kept himself safe; but not quite. The Bank was just able to put salt upon his tail—and only just."

"Do you know Twenty Eight's offence?"

"Twenty Eight," returned my informant, speaking throughout in a low tone, and looking over his shoulder as we walked along the passage, to guard himself from being overheard, in such an unlawful reference to these Immaculates, by Creakle and the rest; "Twenty Eight (also transportation) got a place, and robbed a young master of a matter of two hundred and fifty pounds in money and valuables, the night before they were going abroad. I particularly recollect his case, from his being took by a dwarf."

"A what?"

"A little woman. I have forgot her name."

"Not Mowcher?"

"That's it! He had eluded pursuit, and was going to America in a flaxen wig and whiskers, and such a complete disguise as never you see in all your born days; when the little woman, being in Southampton, met him walking along the street—picked him out with her sharp eye in a moment—ran betwixt his legs to upset him—and held on to him like grim Death."

"Excellent Miss Mowcher!" cried I.

"You'd have said so, if you had seen her, standing on a chair in the witness-box at his trial, as I did," said my friend. "He cut her face right open, and pounded her in the most brutal manner, when she took him; but she never loosed her hold till he was locked up. She held so tight to him, in fact, that the officers were obliged to take 'em both together. She gave her evidence in the gamest way, and was highly complimented by the Bench, and cheered right home to her lodgings. She said in Court that she'd have took him single-handed (on account of what she knew concerning him), if he had been Samson. And it's my belief she would!"

It was mine too, and I highly respected Miss Mowcher for it.

We had now seen all there was to see. It would have been in vain to represent to such a man as the worshipful Mr. Creakle, that Twenty Seven and Twenty Eight were perfectly consistent and unchanged; that exactly what they were then, they had always been; that the hypocritical knaves were just the subjects to make that sort of profession in such a place; that they knew its market-value at least as well as we did, in the immediate service it would do them when they were expatriated; in a word, that it was a rotten, hollow, painfully suggestive piece of business altogether. We left them to their system and themselves, and went home wondering.

"Perhaps it's a good thing, Traddles," said I, "to have an unsound Hobby ridden hard; for it's the sooner ridden to death."

"I hope so," replied Traddles.

CHAPTER LXII.

A LIGHT SHINES ON MY WAY.

THE year came round to Christmas-time, and I had been at home above two months. I had seen Agnes frequently. However loud the general voice might be in giving me encouragement, and however fervent the emotions and endeavours to which it roused me, I heard her lightest word of praise as I heard nothing else.

At least once a week, and sometimes oftener, I rode over there, and passed the evening. I usually rode back at night; for the old unhappy sense was always hovering about me now—most sorrowfully when I left her—and I was glad to be up and out, rather than wandering over the past in weary wakefulness or miserable dreams. I wore away the longest part of many wild sad nights, in those rides; reviving, as I went, the thoughts that had occupied me in my long absence.

Or, if I were to say rather that I listened to the echoes of those thoughts, I should better express the truth. They spoke to me from afar off. I had put them at a distance, and accepted my inevitable place. When I read to Agnes what I wrote; when I saw her listening face; moved her to smiles or tears; and heard her cordial voice so earnest on the shadowy events of that imaginative world in which I lived; I thought what a fate mine might have been—but only thought so, as I had thought after I was married to Dora, what I could have wished my wife to be.

My duty to Agnes, who loved me with a love, which, if I disquieted, I wronged most selfishly and poorly, and could never restore; my matured assurance that I, who had worked out my own destiny, and won what I had impetuously set my heart on, had no right to murmur, and must bear; comprised what I felt and what I had learned. But I loved her: and now it even became some consolation to me, vaguely to conceive a distant day when I might blamelessly avow it; when all this should be over; when I could say "Agnes, so it was when I came home; and now I am old, and I never have loved since!"

She did not once show me any change in herself. What she always had been to me, she still was; wholly unaltered.

Between my aunt and me there had been something, in this connexion, since the night of my return, which I cannot call a restraint, or an avoidance of the subject, so much as an implied understanding that we thought of it together, but did not shape our thoughts into words. When, according to our old custom, we sat before the fire at night, we often fell into this train; as naturally, and as consciously to each other, as if we had unreservedly said so. But we preserved an unbroken silence. I believed that she had read, or partly read, my thoughts that night; and that she fully comprehended why I gave mine no more distinct expression.

This Christmas-time being come, and Agnes having reposed no new confidence in me, a doubt that had several times arisen in my mind—whether she could have that perception of the true state of my breast, which restrained her with the apprehension of giving me pain—began to oppress me heavily. If that were so, my sacrifice was nothing; my plainest obligation to her unfulfilled; and every poor action I had shrunk from, I was hourly doing. I resolved to set this right beyond all doubt;—if such a barrier were between us, to break it down at once with a determined hand.

It was—what lasting reason have I to remember it!—a cold, harsh, winter day. There had been snow, some hours before; and it lay, not deep, but hard-frozen on the ground. Out at sea, beyond my window, the wind blew ruggedly from the north. I had been thinking of it, sweeping over those mountain wastes of snow in Switzerland, then inaccessible to any human foot; and had been speculating which was the lonelier, those solitary regions, or a deserted ocean.

"Riding to-day, Trot?" said my aunt, putting her head in at the door.

"Yes," said I, "I am going over to Canterbury. It's a good day for a ride."

"I hope your horse may think so too," said my aunt; "but at present he is holding down his head and his ears, standing before the door there, as if he thought his stable preferable."

My aunt, I may observe, allowed my horse on the forbidden ground, but had not at all relented toward the donkeys.

"He will be fresh enough, presently!" said I.

"The ride will do his master good, at all events," observed my aunt, glancing at the papers on my table. "Ah, child, you pass a good many hours here! I never thought, when I used to read books, what work it was to write them."

"It's work enough to read them, sometimes," I returned. "As to the writing, it has its own charms, aunt."

"Ah! I see!" said my aunt. "Ambition, love of approbation, sympathy, and much more, I suppose? Well: go along with you!"

"Do you know anything more," said I, standing composedly before her—she had patted me on the shoulder, and sat down in my chair, "of that attachment of Agnes?"

She looked up in my face a little while, before replying:

"I think I do, Trot."

"Are you confirmed in your impression?" I inquired.

"I think I am, Trot."

She looked so steadfastly at me: with a kind of doubt, or pity, or suspense in her affection: that I summoned the stronger determination to show her a perfectly cheerful face.

"And what is more, Trot——" said my aunt.

"Yes!"

"I think Agnes is going to be married."

"God bless her!" said I, cheerfully.

"God bless her!" said my aunt, "and her husband too!"

I echoed it, parted from my aunt, went lightly down stairs, mounted, and rode away. There was greater reason than before to do what I had resolved to do.

How well I recollect the wintry ride! The frozen particles of ice, brushed from the blades of grass by the wind, and borne across my face; the hard clatter of the horse's hoofs, beating a tune upon the ground; the stiff-tilled soil; the snow-drift, lightly eddying in the chalk-pit as the breeze ruffled it; the smoking team with the waggon of old hay, stopping to breathe on the hill-top, and shaking their bells musically; the whitened slopes and sweeps of Downland lying against the dark sky, as if they were drawn on a huge slate!

I found Agnes alone. The little girls had gone to their own homes now, and she was alone by the fire, reading. She put down her book on seeing me come in; and having welcomed me as usual, took her work-basket and sat in one of the old-fashioned windows.

I sat beside her on the window-seat, and we talked of what I was doing, and when it would be done, and of the progress I had made since my last visit. Agnes was very cheerful; and laughingly predicted that I should soon become too famous to be talked to, on such subjects.

"So I make the most of the present time, you see," said Agnes, "and talk to you while I may."

As I looked at her beautiful face, observant of her work, she raised her mild clear eyes, and saw that I was looking at her.

"You are thoughtful to-day, Trotwood!"

"Agnes, shall I tell you what about? I came to tell you."

She put aside her work, as she was used to do when we were seriously discussing anything; and gave me her whole attention.

"My dear Agnes, do you doubt my being true to you?"

"No!" she answered, with a look of astonishment.

"Do you doubt my being what I always have been to you?"

"No!" she answered, as before.

"Do you remember that I tried to tell you, when I came home, what a debt of gratitude I owed you, dearest Agnes, and how fervently I felt towards you?"

"I remember it," she said, gently, "very well."

"You have a secret," said I. "Let me share it, Agnes." She cast down her eyes, and trembled.

"I could hardly fail to know, even if I had not heard—but from other lips than yours, Agnes, which seems strange—that there is some one upon whom you have bestowed the treasure of your love. Do not shut me out of what concerns your happiness so nearly! If you can trust me, as you say you can, and as I know you may, let me be your friend, your brother, in this matter, of all others!"

With an appealing, almost a reproachful glance, she rose from the window; and hurrying across the room as if without knowing where, put her hands before her face, and burst into such tears as smote me to the heart.

And yet they awakened something in me, bringing promise to my heart. Without my knowing why, these tears allied themselves with the quietly sad smile which was so fixed in my remembrance, and shook me more with hope than fear or sorrow.

"Agnes! Sister! Dearest! What have I done!"

"Let me go away, Trotwood. I am not well. I am not myself. I will speak to you by-and-by—another time. I will write to you. Don't speak to me now. Don't! don't!"

I sought to recollect what she had said, when I had spoken to her on that former night, of her affection needing no return. It seemed a very world that I must search through in a moment.

"Agnes, I cannot bear to see you so, and think that I have been the cause. My dearest girl, dearer to me than anything in life, if you are unhappy, let me share your unhappiness. If you are in need of help or counsel, let me try to give it to you. If you have indeed a burden on your heart, let me try to lighten it. For whom do I live now, Agnes, if it is not for you!"

"Oh, spare me! I am not myself! Another time!" was all I could distinguish.

Was it a selfish error that was leading me away? Or, having once a clue to hope, was there something opening to me that I had not dared to think of?

"I must say more. I cannot let you leave me so! For Heaven's sake, Agnes, let us not mistake each other after all these years, and all that has come and gone with them! I must speak plainly. If you have any lingering thought that I could envy the happiness you will confer; that I could not resign you to a dearer protector, of your own choosing; that I could not, from my removed place, be a contented witness of your joy; dismiss it, for I don't deserve it! I have not suffered quite in vain. You have not taught me quite in vain. There is no alloy of self in what I feel for you."

She was quiet now. In a little time, she turned her pale face towards me, and said in a low voice, broken here and there, but very clear:

"I owe it to your pure friendship for me, Trotwood—which, indeed, I do not doubt—to tell you, you are mistaken. I can do no more. If I have sometimes, in the course of years, wanted help and counsel, they have come to me. If I have sometimes been unhappy, the feeling has passed away. If I have ever had a burden on my heart, it has been lightened for me. If I have any secret, it is—no new one; and is—not what you suppose. I cannot reveal it, or divide it. It has long been mine, and must remain mine."

"Agnes! Stay! A moment!"

She was going away, but I detained her. I clasped my arm about her waist. "In the course of years!" "It is not a new one!" New thoughts and hopes were whirling through my mind, and all the colours of my life were changing.

"Dearest Agnes! Whom I so respect and honour—whom I so devotedly love! When I came here to-day, I thought that nothing could have wrested this confession from me. I thought I could have kept it in my bosom all our lives, till we were old. But, Agnes, if I have indeed any new-born hope that I may ever call you something more than Sister, widely different from Sister!——"

Her tears fell fast; but they were not like those she had lately shed, and I saw my hope brighten in them.

"Agnes! Ever my guide, and best support! If you had been more mindful of yourself, and less of me, when we grew up here together, I think my heedless fancy never would have wandered from you. But you were so much better than I, so necessary to me in every boyish hope and disappointment, that to have you to confide in, and rely upon in everything, became a second nature, supplanting for the time the first and greater one of loving you as I do!"

Still weeping, but not sadly—joyfully! And clasped in my arms as she had never been, as I had thought she never was to be!

"When I loved Dora—fondly, Agnes, as you know——"

"Yes!" she cried, earnestly. "I am glad to know it!"

"When I loved her—even then, my love would have been incomplete, without your sympathy. I had it, and it was perfected. And when I lost her, Agnes, what should I have been without you, still!"

Closer in my arms, nearer to my heart, her trembling hand upon my shoulder, her sweet eyes shining through her tears, on mine!

"I went away, dear Agnes, loving you. I stayed away, loving you. I returned home, loving you!"

And now, I tried to tell her of the struggle I had had, and the conclusion I had come to. I tried to lay my mind before her, truly and entirely. I tried to show her, how I had hoped I had come into the better knowledge of myself and of her; how I had resigned myself to what that better knowledge brought; and how I had come there, even that day, in my fidelity to this. If she did so love me (I said) that she could take me for her husband, she could do so, on no deserving of mine, except upon the truth of my love for her, and the trouble in which it had ripened to be what it was; and hence it was that I revealed it. And O, Agnes, even out of thy true eyes, in that same time, the spirit of my child-wife looked upon me, saying it was well; and winning me, through thee, to tenderest recollections of the Blossom that had withered in its bloom!

"I am so blest, Trotwood—my heart is so overcharged—but there is one thing I must say."

"Dearest, what?"

She laid her gentle hands upon my shoulders, and looked calmly in my face.

"Do you know, yet, what it is?"

"I am afraid to speculate on what it is. Tell me, my dear."

"I have loved you all my life!"

Oh, we were happy, we were happy! Our tears were not for the trials (hers so much the greater), through which we had come to be thus, but for the rapture of being thus, never to be divided more!

We walked, that winter evening, in the fields together; and the blessed calm within us seemed to be partaken by the frosty air. The early stars began to shine while we were lingering on, and looking up to them we thanked our GOD for having guided us to this tranquillity.

We stood together in the same old-fashioned window at night, when the moon was shining; Agnes with her quiet eyes raised up to it; I following her glance. Long miles of road then opened out before my mind; and, toiling on, I saw a ragged wayworn boy forsaken and neglected, who should come to call even the heart now beating against mine, his own.

It was nearly dinner-time next day when we appeared before my aunt. She was up in my study, Peggotty said: which it was her pride to keep in readiness and order for me. We found her, in her spectacles, sitting by the fire.

"Goodness me!" said my aunt, peering through the dusk, "who's this you're bringing home?"

"Agnes," said I.

As we had arranged to say nothing at first, my aunt was not a little discomfited. She darted a hopeful glance at me, when I said "Agnes;" but seeing that I looked as usual, she took off her spectacles in despair, and rubbed her nose with them.

She greeted Agnes heartily, nevertheless; and we were soon in the lighted parlour down stairs, at dinner. My aunt put on her spectacles twice or thrice, to take another look at me, but as often took them off again, disappointed, and rubbed her nose with them. Much to the discomfiture of Mr. Dick, who knew this to be a bad symptom.

"By-the-by, aunt," said I, after dinner; "I have been speaking to Agnes about what you told me."

"Then, Trot," said my aunt, turning scarlet, "you did wrong, and broke your promise."

"You are not angry, aunt, I trust? I am sure you won't be, when you learn that Agnes is not unhappy in any attachment."

"Stuff and nonsense!" said my aunt.

As my aunt appeared to be annoyed, I thought the best way was to cut her annoyance short. I took Agnes in my arm to the back of her chair, and we both leaned over her. My aunt, with one clap of her hands, and one look through her spectacles, immediately went into hysterics, for the first and only time in all my knowledge of her.

The hysterics called up Peggotty. The moment my aunt was restored, she flew at Peggotty, and calling her a silly old creature, hugged her with all her might. After that, she hugged Mr. Dick (who was highly honoured, but a good deal surprised); and after that, told them why. Then, we were all happy together.

I could not discover whether my aunt, in her last short conversation with me, had fallen on a pious fraud, or had really mistaken the state of my mind. It was quite enough, she said, that she had told me Agnes was going to be married; and that I now knew better than any one how true it was.

We were married within a fortnight. Traddles and Sophy, and Doctor and Mrs. Strong, were the only guests at our quiet wedding. We left them full of joy; and drove away together. Clasped in my embrace, I held the source of every worthy aspiration I had ever had; the centre of myself, the circle of my life, my own, my wife; my love of whom was founded on a rock!

"Dearest husband!" said Agnes. "Now that I may call you by that name, I have one thing more to tell you."

"Let me hear it, love."

"It grows out of the night when Dora died. She sent you for me."

"She did."

"She told me that she left me something. Can you think what it was?"

I believed I could. I drew the wife who had so long loved me, closer to my side.

"She told me that she made a last request to me, and left me a last charge."

"And it was——"

"That only I would occupy this vacant place."

And Agnes laid her head upon my breast, and wept; and I wept with her, though we were so happy.

CHAPTER LXIII

A VISITOR.

WHAT I have purposed to record is nearly finished; but there is yet an incident conspicuous in my memory, on which it often rests with delight, and without which one thread in the web I have spun, would have a ravelled end.

I had advanced in fame and fortune, my domestic joy was perfect, I had been married ten happy years. Agnes and I were sitting by the fire, in our house in London, one night in spring, and three of our children were playing in the room, when I was told that a stranger wished to see me.

He had been asked if he came on business, and had answered No; he had come for the pleasure of seeing me, and had come a long way. He was an old man, my servant said, and looked like a farmer.

As this sounded mysterious to the children, and moreover was like the beginning of a favourite story Agnes used to tell them, introductory to the arrival of a wicked old Fairy in a cloak who hated everybody, it produced some commotion. One of our boys laid his head in his mother's lap to be out of harm's way, and little Agnes (our eldest child) left her doll in a chair to represent her, and thrust out her little heap of golden curls from between the window-curtains, to see what happened next.

"Let him come in here!" said I.

There soon appeared, pausing in the dark doorway as he entered, a hale, grey-haired old man. Little Agnes, attracted by his looks, had run to bring him in, and I had not yet clearly seen his face, when my wife, starting up, cried out to me, in a pleased and agitated voice, that it was Mr. Peggotty!

It *was* Mr. Peggotty. An old man now, but in a ruddy, hearty, strong old age. When our first emotion was over, and he sat before the fire with the children on his knees, and the blaze shining on his face, he looked, to me, as vigorous and robust, withal as handsome, an old man, as ever I had seen.

"Mas'r Davy," said he. And the old name in the old tone fell so naturally on my ear! "Mas'r Davy, 'tis a joyful hour as I see you, once more, 'long with your own trew wife!"

"A joyful hour indeed, old friend!" cried I.

"And these heer pretty ones," said Mr. Peggotty. "To look at these heer flowers! Why, Mas'r Davy, you was but the heighth of the littlest of these when I first see you! When Em'ly warn't no bigger, and our poor lad were *but* a lad!"

"Time has changed me more than it has changed you since then," said I. "But let these dear rogues go to bed; and as no house in England but this must hold you, tell me where to send for your luggage (is the old black bag among it, that went so far, I wonder!), and then, over a glass of Yarmouth grog, we will have the tidings of ten years!"

"Are you alone?" asked Agnes.

"Yes, ma'am," he said, kissing her hand, "quite alone."

We sat him between us, not knowing how to give him welcome enough; and as I began to listen to his old familiar voice, I could have fancied he was still pursuing his long journey in search of his darling niece.

"It's a mort of water," said Mr. Peggotty, "fur to come across, and on'y stay a matter of fower weeks. But water ('specially when 'tis salt) comes nat'ral to me; and friends is dear, and I am heer.—Which is verse," said Mr. Peggotty, surprised to find it out, "though I hadn't such intentions."

"Are you going back those many thousand miles, so soon?" asked Agnes.

"Yes, ma'am," he returned. "I giv the promise to Em'ly, afore I come away. You see, I doen't grow younger as the years comes round, and if I hadn't sailed as 'twas, most like I shouldn't never have done't. And it's allus been on my mind, as I *must* come and see Mas'r Davy and your own sweet blooming self, in your wedded happiness, afore I got to be too old."

He looked at us, as if he could never feast his eyes on us sufficiently. Agnes laughingly put back some scattered locks of his grey hair, that he might see us better.

"And now tell us," said I, "everything relating to your fortunes."

"Our fortuns, Mas'r Davy," he rejoined, "is soon told. We haven't fared nohows, but fared to thrive. We've allus thrived. We've worked as we ought to't, and maybe we lived a lettle hard at first or so, but we have allus thrived. What with sheep-farming, and what with stock-farming, and what with one thing and what with t'other, we are as well to do, as well could be. Theer's been kiender a blessing fell upon us," said Mr. Peggotty, reverentially inclining his head, "and we've done nowt but prosper. That is, in the long run. If not yesterday, why then to-day. If not to-day, why then to-morrow."

"And Emily?" said Agnes and I, both together.

"Em'ly," said he, "arter you left her, ma'am—and I never heerd her saying of her prayers at night, t'other side the canvas screen, when we was settled in the Bush, but what I heerd your name—and arter she and me lost sight of Mas'r Davy, that theer shining sundown—was that low, at first, that, if she had know'd then what Mas'r Davy kep from us so kind and thowtful, 'tis my opinion she'd have drooped away. But theer was some poor folks aboard as had illness among 'em, and she took care of *them;* and there was the children in our company, and she took care of *them;* and so she got to be busy, and to be doing good, and that helped her."

"When did she first hear of it?" I asked.

"I kep it from her arter I heerd on't," said Mr. Peggotty, "going on nigh a year. We was living then in a solitary place, but among the beautifullest trees, and with the roses a covering our Beein' to the roof. Theer come along one day, when I was out a working on the land, a traveller from our own Norfolk or Suffolk in England (I doen't rightly mind which), and of course we took him in, and giv him to eat and drink, and made him welcome. We all do that, all the colony over. He'd got an old newspaper with him, and some other account in print of the storm. That's how she know'd it. When I come home at night, I found she know'd it."

He dropped his voice as he said these words, and the gravity I so well remembered overspread his face.

"Did it change her much?" we asked.

"Ay, for a good long time," he said, shaking his head; "if not to this present hour. But I think the solitoode done her good. And she had a deal to mind in the way of poultry and the like, and minded of it, and come through. I wonder," he said thoughtfully, "if you could see my Em'ly now, Mas'r Davy, whether you'd know her!"

"Is she so altered?" I inquired.

"I doen't know. I see her ev'ry day, and doen't know; but, odd-times, I have thowt so. A slight figure," said Mr. Peggotty, looking at the fire, "kiender worn; soft, sorrowful, blue eyes; a delicate face; a pritty head, leaning a little down; a quiet voice and way—timid a'most. That's Em'ly!"

We silently observed him as he sat, still looking at the fire.

"Some thinks," he said, "as her affection was ill-bestowed; some, as her marriage was broke off by death. No one knows how 'tis. She might have married well, a mort of times, 'But, uncle,' she says to me, 'that's gone for ever.' Cheerful along with me; retired when others is by; fond of going any distance fur to teach a child, or fur to tend a sick person, or fur to do some kindness tow'rds a young girl's wedding (and she's done a many, but has never seen one); fondly loving of her uncle; patient; liked by young and old; sowt out by all that has any trouble. That's Em'ly!"

He drew his hand across his face, and with a half-suppressed sigh looked up from the fire.

"Is Martha with you yet?" I asked.

"Martha," he replied, "got married, Mas'r Davy, in the second year. A young man, a farm-labourer, as come by us on his way to market with his mas'r's drays—a journey of over five hundred mile, theer and back—made offers fur to take her fur his wife (wives is very scarce theer), and then to set up fur their two selves in the Bush. She spoke to me fur to tell him her trew story. I did. They was married, and they live fower hundred mile away from any voices but their own and the singing birds."

"Mrs. Gummidge?" I suggested.

It was a pleasant key to touch, for Mr. Peggotty suddenly burst into a roar of laughter, and rubbed his hands up and down his legs, as he had been accustomed to do when he enjoyed himself in the long-shipwrecked boat.

"Would you believe it!" he said. "Why, someun even made offers fur to marry *her!* If a ship's cook that was turning settler, Mas'r Davy, didn't make offers fur to marry Missis Gummidge, I'm Gormed—and I can't say no fairer than that!"

I never saw Agnes laugh so. This sudden ecstasy on the part of Mr. Peggotty was so delightful to her, that she could not leave off laughing; and the more she laughed the more she made me laugh, and the greater Mr. Peggotty's ecstasy became, and the more he rubbed his legs.

"And what did Mrs. Gummidge say?" I asked, when I was grave enough.

"If you'll believe me," returned Mr. Peggotty, "Missis Gummidge, 'stead of saying 'thank you, I'm much obleeged to you, I ain't a going fur to change my condition at my time of life,' up'd with a bucket as was standing by, and laid it over that theer ship's cook's head till he sung out fur help, and I went in and reskied of him."

Mr. Peggotty burst into a great roar of laughter, and Agnes and I both kept him company.

"But I must say this, for the good creetur," he resumed, wiping his face when we were quite exhausted; "she has been all she said she'd be to us, and more. She's the willingest, the trewest, the honestest-helping woman, Mas'r Davy, as ever draw'd the breath of life. I have never known her to be lone and lorn, for a single minute, not even when the colony was all afore us, and we was new to it. And thinking of the old 'un is a thing she never done, I do assure you, since she left England!"

"Now, last, not least, Mr. Micawber," said I. "He has paid off every obligation he incurred here—even to Traddles's bill, you remember, my dear Agnes—and therefore we may take it for granted that he is doing well. But what is the latest news of him?"

Mr. Peggotty, with a smile, put his hand in his breast-pocket, and produced a flat-folded, paper parcel, from which he took out, with much care, a little odd-looking newspaper.

"You are to unnerstan', Mas'r Davy," said he, "as we have left the Bush now, being so well to do; and have gone right away round to Port Middlebay Harbour, wheer theer's what *we* call a town."

"Mr. Micawber was in the Bush near you," said I.

"Bless you, yes," said Mr. Peggotty, "and turned to with a will. I never wish to meet a better gen'l'man for turning to, with a will. I've seen that theer bald head of his, a perspiring in the sun, Mas'r Davy, till I a'most thowt it would have melted away. And now he's a magistrate."

"A magistrate, eh?" said I.

Mr. Peggotty pointed to a certain paragraph in the newspaper, where I read aloud as follows, from the "Port Middlebay Times:"

"☞ The public dinner to our distinguished fellow-colonist and townsman, WILKINS MICAWBER, ESQUIRE, Port Middlebay District Magistrate, came off yesterday in the large room of the Hotel, which was crowded to suffocation. It is estimated that not fewer than forty-seven persons must have been accommodated with dinner at one time, exclusive of the company in the passage and on the stairs. The beauty, fashion, and exclusiveness of Port Middlebay flocked to do honour to one so deservedly esteemed, so highly talented, and so widely popular. Doctor Mell (of Colonial Salem-House Grammar School, Port Middlebay) presided, and on his right sat the distinguished guest. After the removal of the cloth, and the singing of Non Nobis (beautifully executed, and in which we were at no loss to distinguish the bell-like notes of that gifted amateur, WILKINS MICAWBER, ESQUIRE, JUNIOR), the usual loyal and patriotic toasts were severally given and rapturously received. Dr. Mell, in a speech replete with feeling, then proposed 'Our distinguished Guest, the ornament of our town. May he never leave us but to better himself, and may his success among us be such as to render his bettering himself impossible!' The cheering with which the toast was received defies description. Again and again it rose and fell, like the waves of ocean. At length all was hushed, and WILKINS MICAWBER, ESQUIRE, presented himself to return thanks. Far be it from us, in the present comparatively

A STRANGER CALLS TO SEE ME.

imperfect state of the resources of our establishment, to endeavour to follow our distinguished townsman through the smoothly-flowing periods of his polished and highly-ornate address! Suffice it to observe, that it was a master-piece of eloquence; and that those passages in which he more particularly traced his own successful career to its source, and warned the younger portion of his auditory from the shoals of ever incurring pecuniary liabilities which they were unable to liquidate, brought a tear into the manliest eye present. The remaining toasts were DOCTOR MELL; MRS. MICAWBER (who gracefully bowed her acknowledgments from the side-door, where a galaxy of beauty was elevated on chairs, at once to witness and adorn the gratifying scene); MRS. RIDGER BEGS (late Miss Micawber); MRS. MELL; WILKINS MICAWBER, ESQUIRE, JUNIOR (who convulsed the assembly by humorously remarking that he found himself unable to return thanks in a speech, but would do so, with their permission, in a song); MRS. MICAWBER'S FAMILY (well known, it is needless to remark, in the mother-country), &c., &c., &c. At the conclusion of the proceedings the tables were cleared as if by art-magic for dancing. Among the votaries of TERPSICHORE, who disported themselves until Sol gave warning for departure, Wilkins Micawber, Esquire, Junior, and the lovely and accomplished Miss Helena, fourth daughter of Doctor Mell, were particularly remarkable."

I was looking back to the name of Doctor Mell, pleased to have discovered, in these happier circumstances, Mr. Mell, formerly poor pinched usher to my Middlesex magistrate, when Mr. Peggotty pointing to another part of the paper, my eyes rested on my own name, and I read thus:—

"TO DAVID COPPERFIELD, ESQUIRE,

"THE EMINENT AUTHOR.

"MY DEAR SIR,

"Years have elapsed, since I had an opportunity of ocularly perusing the lineaments, now familiar to the imaginations of a considerable portion of the civilised world.

"But, my dear Sir, though estranged (by the force of circumstances over which I have had no control) from the personal society of the friend and companion of my youth, I have not been unmindful of his soaring flight. Nor have I been debarred,

'Though seas between us braid ha' roared,'

(BURNS) from participating in the intellectual feasts he has spread before us.

"I cannot, therefore, allow of the departure from this place of an individual whom we mutually respect and esteem, without, my dear Sir, taking this public opportunity of thanking you, on my own behalf, and, I may undertake to add, on that of the whole of the Inhabitants of Port Middlebay, for the gratification of which you are the ministering agent.

"Go on, my dear Sir! You are not unknown here, you are not unappreciated. Though 'remote,' we are neither 'unfriended,' 'melancholy,' nor (I may add) 'slow.' Go on, my dear Sir, in your Eagle course! The Inhabitants of Port Middlebay may at least aspire to watch it, with delight, with entertainment, with instruction!

"Among the eyes elevated towards you from this portion of the globe, will ever be found, while it has light and life,

"The
"Eye
"Appertaining to
"WILKINS MICAWBER,
"Magistrate."

I found, on glancing at the remaining contents of the newspaper, that Mr. Micawber was a diligent and esteemed correspondent of that journal. There was another letter from him in the same paper, touching a bridge; there was an advertisement of a collection of similar letters by him, to be shortly republished, in a neat volume, "with considerable additions;" and, unless I am very much mistaken, the Leading Article was his also.

We talked much of Mr. Micawber, on many other evenings while Mr. Peggotty remained with us. He lived with us during the whole term of his stay,—which, I think, was something less than a month,—and his sister and my aunt came to London to see him. Agnes and I parted from him aboard ship, when he sailed; and we shall never part from him more, on earth.

But before he left, he went with me to Yarmouth, to see a little tablet I had put up in the churchyard to the memory of Ham. While I was copying the plain inscription for him at his request, I saw him stoop, and gather a tuft of grass from the grave, and a little earth.

"For Em'ly," he said, as he put it in his breast. "I promised, Mas'r Davy."

CHAPTER LXIV.

A LAST RETROSPECT.

AND now my written story ends. I look back, once more—for the last time—before I close these leaves.

I see myself, with Agnes at my side, journeying along the road of life. I see our children and our friends around us; and I hear the roar of many voices, not indifferent to me as I travel on.

What faces are the most distinct to me in the fleeting crowd? Lo, these; all turning to me as I ask my thoughts the question!

Here is my aunt, in stronger spectacles, an old woman of four-score years and more, but upright yet, and a steady walker of six miles at a stretch in winter weather.

Always with her, here comes Peggotty, my good old nurse, likewise in spectacles, accustomed to do needlework at night very close to the lamp, but never sitting down to it without a bit of wax-candle, a yard measure in a little house, and a work-box with a picture of St. Paul's upon the lid.

The cheeks and arms of Peggotty, so hard and red in my childish days, when I wondered why the birds didn't peck her in preference to apples, are shrivelled now; and her eyes, that used to darken their whole neighbourhood in her face, are fainter (though they glitter still); but her rough forefinger, which I once associated with a pocket nutmeg-grater, is just the same, and when I see my least child catching at it as it totters from my aunt to her, I think of our little parlour at home, when I could scarcely walk. My aunt's old disappointment is set right, now.

She is godmother to a real living Betsey Trotwood; and Dora (the next in order) says she spoils her.

There is something bulky in Peggotty's pocket. It is nothing smaller than the Crocodile-Book, which is in rather a dilapidated condition by this time, with divers of the leaves torn and stitched across, but which Peggotty exhibits to the children as a precious relic. I find it very curious to see my own infant face, looking up at me from the crocodile stories; and to be reminded by it of my old acquaintance Brooks of Sheffield.

Among my boys, this summer holiday time, I see an old man making giant kites, and gazing at them in the air, with a delight for which there are no words. He greets me rapturously, and whispers, with many nods and winks, "Trotwood, you will be glad to hear that I shall finish the Memorial when I have nothing else to do, and that your aunt's the most extraordinary woman in the world, Sir!"

Who is this bent lady, supporting herself by a stick, and showing me a countenance in which there are some traces of old pride and beauty, feebly contending with a querulous, imbecile, fretful wandering of the mind? She is in a garden; and near her stands a sharp, dark, withered woman, with a white scar on her lip. Let me hear what they say.

"Rosa, I have forgotten this gentleman's name."

Rosa bends over her, and calls to her, "Mr. Copperfield."

"I am glad to see you, Sir. I am sorry to observe you are in mourning. I hope Time will be good to you!"

Her impatient attendant scolds her, tells her I am not in mourning, bids her look again, tries to rouse her.

"You have seen my son, Sir," says the elderly lady. "Are you reconciled?"

Looking fixedly at me, she puts her hand to her forehead, and moans. Suddenly, she cries, in a terrible voice, "Rosa, come to me. He is dead!" Rosa, kneeling at her feet, by turns caresses her, and quarrels with her; now fiercely telling her, "I loved him better than you ever did!" —now soothing her to sleep on her breast, like a sick child. Thus I leave them; thus I always find them; thus they wear their time away, from year to year.

What ship comes sailing home from India, and what English lady is this, married to a growling old Scotch Crœsus with great flaps of ears? Can this be Julia Mills?

Indeed it is Julia Mills, peevish and fine, with a black man to carry cards and letters to her on a golden salver, and a copper-coloured woman in linen, with a bright handkerchief round her head, to serve her Tiffin in her dressing-room. But Julia keeps no diary in these days; never sings Affection's Dirge; eternally quarrels with the old Scotch Crœsus, who is a sort of yellow bear with a tanned hide. Julia is steeped in money to the throat, and talks and thinks of nothing else. I liked her better in the Desert of Sahara.

Or perhaps this *is* the Desert of Sahara! For, though Julia has a stately house, and mighty company, and sumptuous dinners every day, I see no green growth near her; nothing that can ever come to fruit or flower. What Julia calls "society," I see; among it Mr. Jack Maldon, from his Patent Place, sneering at the hand that gave it him, and speaking to me, of the Doctor, as "so charmingly antique." But when society is the name for such hollow gentlemen and ladies, Julia, and when its breeding is professed indifference to everything that can advance or can retard mankind,

I think we must have lost ourselves in that same Desert of Sahara, and had better find the way out.

And lo, the Doctor, always our good friend, labouring at his Dictionary (somewhere about the letter D), and happy in his home and wife. Also the Old Soldier, on a considerably reduced footing, and by no means so influential as in days of yore!

Working at his chambers in the Temple, with a busy aspect, and his hair (where he is not bald) made more rebellious than ever by the constant friction of his lawyer's wig, I come, in a later time, upon my dear old Traddles. His table is covered with thick piles of papers; and I say, as I look around me:

"If Sophy were your clerk, now, Traddles, she would have enough to do!"

"You may say that, my dear Copperfield! But those were capital days, too, in Holborn Court! Were they not?"

"When she told you you would be a Judge? But it was not the town talk *then!*"

"At all events," says Traddles, "if I ever am one——"

"Why, you know you will be."

"Well, my dear Copperfield, *when* I am one, I shall tell the story, as I said I would."

We walk away, arm in arm. I am going to have a family dinner with Traddles. It is Sophy's birthday; and, on our road, Traddles discourses to me of the good fortune he has enjoyed.

"I really have been able, my dear Copperfield, to do all that I had most at heart. There's the Reverend Horace promoted to that living at four hundred and fifty pounds a year; there are our two boys receiving the very best education, and distinguishing themselves as steady scholars and good fellows; there are three of the girls married very comfortably; there are three more living with us; there are three more keeping house for the Reverend Horace since Mrs. Crewler's decease; and all of them happy."

"Except——" I suggest.

"Except the Beauty," says Traddles. "Yes. It was very unfortunate that she should marry such a vagabond. But there was a certain dash and glare about him that caught her. However, now we have got her safe at our house, and got rid of him, we must cheer her up again."

Traddles's house is one of the very houses—or it easily may have been—which he and Sophy used to parcel out, in their evening walks. It is a large house; but Traddles keeps his papers in his dressing-room, and his boots with his papers; and he and Sophy squeeze themselves into upper rooms, reserving the best bedrooms for the Beauty and the girls. There is no room to spare in the house; for more of "the girls" are here, and always are here, by some accident or other, than I know how to count. Here, when we go in, is a crowd of them, running down to the door, and handing Traddles about to be kissed, until he is out of breath. Here, established in perpetuity, is the poor Beauty, a widow with a little girl; here, at dinner on Sophy's birthday, are the three married girls with their three husbands, and one of the husband's brothers, and another husband's cousin, and another husband's sister, who appears to me to be engaged to the cousin. Traddles, exactly the same simple, unaffected fellow as he ever was, sits at the foot of the large table like a Patriarch; and Sophy beams upon him, from the head, across a cheerful space that is certainly not glittering with Britannia metal.

And now, as I close my task, subduing my desire to linger yet, these faces fade away. But, one face, shining on me like a heavenly light by which I see all other objects, is above them and beyond them all. And that remains.

I turn my head, and see it, in its beautiful serenity, beside me. My lamp burns low, and I have written far into the night; but the dear presence, without which I were nothing, bears me company.

O Agnes, O my soul, so may thy face be by me when I close my life indeed; so may I, when realities are melting from me like the shadows which I now dismiss, still find thee near me, pointing upward!

Great Expectations

"TELL US YOUR NAME!" SAID THE MAN, "QUICK!"

Great Expectations

by

Charles Dickens

With Illustrations

CONTENTS

ILLUSTRATIONS

TO

GREAT EXPECTATIONS

———

GREAT EXPECTATIONS.

CHAPTER I.

My father's family name being Pirrip, and my Christian name Philip, my infant tongue could make of both names nothing longer or more explicit than Pip. So, I called myself Pip, and came to be called Pip.

I give Pirrip as my father's family name, on the authority of his tombstone and my sister—Mrs. Joe Gargery, who married the blacksmith. As I never saw my father or my mother, and never saw any likeness of either of them (for their days were long before the days of photographs), my first fancies regarding what they were like, were unreasonably derived from their tombstones. The shape of the letters on my father's gave me an odd idea that he was a square, stout, dark man, with curly black hair. From the character and turn of the inscription, "*Also Georgiana Wife of the Above*," I drew a childish conclusion that my mother was freckled and sickly. To five little stone lozenges, each about a foot and a half long, which were arranged in a neat row beside their grave, and were sacred to the memory of five little brothers of mine—who gave up trying to get a living exceedingly early in that universal struggle—I am indebted for a belief I religiously entertained that they had all been born on their backs with their hands in their trousers-pockets, and had never taken them out in this state of existence.

Ours was the marsh country, down by the river, within, as the river wound, twenty miles of the sea. My first most vivid and broad impression of the identity of things, seems to me to have been gained on a memorable raw afternoon towards evening. At such a time I found out for certain, that this bleak place overgrown with nettles was the churchyard; and that Philip Pirrip, late of this parish, and also Georgiana wife of the above, were dead and buried; and that Alexander, Bartholomew, Abraham, Tobias, and Roger, infant children of the aforesaid, were also dead and buried; and that the dark flat wilderness beyond the churchyard, intersected with dykes and mounds and gates, with scattered cattle feeding on it, was the marshes; and that the low leaden line beyond was the river; and that the distant savage lair from which the wind was rushing, was the sea; and that the small bundle of shivers growing afraid of it all and beginning to cry, was Pip.

"Hold your noise!" cried a terrible voice, as a man started up from among the graves at the side of the church porch. "Keep still, you little devil, or I'll cut your throat!"

A fearful man, all in coarse grey, with a great iron on his leg. A man with no hat, and with broken shoes, and with an old rag tied round his head. A man who had been soaked in water, and smothered in mud, and lamed by stones, and cut by flints, and stung by nettles, and torn by briars; who limped, and shivered, and glared and growled; and whose teeth chattered in his head as he seized me by the chin.

"O! Don't cut my throat, sir," I pleaded in terror. "Pray don't do it, sir."

"Tell us your name!" said the man. "Quick!"

"Pip, sir."

"Once more," said the man, staring at me. "Give it mouth!"

"Pip. Pip, sir."

"Show us where you live," said the man. "Pint out the place!"

I pointed to where our village lay, on the flat in-shore among the alder-trees and pollards, a mile or more from the church.

The man, after looking at me for a moment, turned me upside down, and emptied my pockets. There was nothing in them but a piece of bread. When the church came to itself—for he was so sudden and strong that he made it go head over heels before me, and I saw the steeple under my feet—when the church came to itself, I say, I was seated on a high tombstone, trembling, while he ate the bread ravenously.

"You young dog," said the man, licking his lips, "what fat cheeks you ha' got."

I believe they were fat, though I was at that time under-sized, for my years, and not strong.

"Darn Me if I couldn't eat 'em," said the man, with a threatening shake of his head, "and if I han't half a mind to't!"

I earnestly expressed my hope that he wouldn't, and held tighter to the tombstone on which he had put me; partly, to keep myself upon it; partly, to keep myself from crying.

"Now lookee here!" said the man. "Where's your mother?"

"There, sir!" said I.

He started, made a short run, and stopped and looked over his shoulder.

"There, sir!" I timidly explained. "Also Georgiana. That's my mother."

"Oh!" said he, coming back. "And is that your father alonger your mother?"

"Yes, sir," said I; "him too; late of this parish."

"Ha!" he muttered then, considering. "Who d'ye live with—supposin' you're kindly let to live, which I han't made up my mind about?"

"My sister, sir—Mrs. Joe Gargery—wife of Joe Gargery, the blacksmith, sir."

"Blacksmith, eh?" said he. And looked down at his leg.

After darkly looking at his leg and at me several times, he came closer to my tombstone, took me by both arms, and tilted me back as far as he could hold me; so that his eyes looked most powerfully down into mine, and mine looked most helplessly up into his.

"Now lookee here," he said, "the question being whether you're to be let to live. You know what a file is?"

"Yes, sir."

"And you know what wittles is?"

"Yes, sir."

After each question he tilted me over a little more, so as to give me a greater sense of helplessness and danger.

"You get me a file." He tilted me again. "And you get me wittles." He tilted me again. "You bring 'em both to me." He tilted me again. "Or I'll have your heart and liver out." He tilted me again.

I was dreadfully frightened, and so giddy that I clung

to him with both hands, and said, "If you would kindly please to let me keep upright, sir, perhaps I shouldn't be sick, and perhaps I could attend more."

He gave me a most tremendous dip and roll, so that the church jumped over its own weather-cock. Then, he held me by the arms in an upright position on the top of the stone, and went on in these fearful terms:

"You bring me, to-morrow morning early, that file and them wittles. You bring the lot to me, at that old Battery over yonder. You do it, and you never dare to say a word or dare to make a sign concerning your having seen such a person as me, or any person sumever, and you shall be let to live. You fail, or you go from my words in any particler, no matter how small it is, and your heart and your liver shall be tore out, roasted and ate. Now, I ain't alone, as you may think I am. There's a young man hid with me, in comparison with which young man I am a Angel. That young man hears the words I speak. That young man has a secret way pecooliar to himself, of getting at a boy, and at his heart, and at his liver. It is in wain for a boy to attempt to hide himself from that young man. A boy may lock his door, may be warm in bed, may tuck himself up, may draw the clothes over his head, may think himself comfortable and safe, but that young man will softly creep and creep his way to him and tear him open. I am a keeping that young man from harming of you at the present moment, with great difficulty. I find it wery hard to hold that young man off of your inside. Now, what do you say?"

I said that I would get him the file, and I would get him what broken bits of food I could, and I would come to him at the Battery, early in the morning.

"Say, Lord strike you dead if you don't!" said the man.

I said so, and he took me down.

"Now," he pursued, "you remember what you've undertook, and you remember that young man, and you get home!"

"Goo-good night, sir," I faltered.

"Much of that!" said he, glancing about him over the cold wet flat. "I wish I was a frog. Or a eel!"

At the same time, he hugged his shuddering body in both his arms—clasping himself, as if to hold himself together—and limped towards the low church wall. As I saw him go, picking his way among the nettles, and among the brambles that bound the green mounds, he looked in my young eyes as if he were eluding the hands of the dead people, stretching up cautiously out of their graves, to get a twist upon his ankle and pull him in.

When he came to the low church wall, he got over it, like a man whose legs were numbed and stiff, and then turned round to look for me. When I saw him turning, I set my face towards home, and made the best use of my legs. But presently I looked over my shoulder, and saw him going on again towards the river, still hugging himself in both arms, and picking his way with his sore feet among the great stones dropped into the marshes here and there, for stepping-places when the rains were heavy, or the tide was in.

The marshes were just a long black horizontal line then, as I stopped to look after him; and the river was just another horizontal line, not nearly so broad nor yet so black; and the sky was just a row of long angry red lines and dense black lines intermixed. On the edge of the river I could faintly make out the only two black things in all the prospect that seemed to be standing upright; one of these

was the beacon by which the sailors steered—like an unhooped cask upon a pole—an ugly thing when you were near it; the other a gibbet, with some chains hanging to it which had once held a pirate. The man was limping on towards this latter, as if he were the pirate come to life, and come down, and going back to hook himself up again. It gave me a terrible turn when I thought so; and as I saw the cattle lifting their heads to gaze after him, I wondered whether they thought so too. I looked all round for the horrible young man, and could see no signs of him. But now I was frightened again, and ran home without stopping.

CHAPTER II.

My sister, Mrs. Joe Gargery, was more than twenty years older than I, and had established a great reputation with herself and the neighbours because she had brought me up "by hand." Having at that time to find out for myself what the expression meant, and knowing her to have a hard and heavy hand, and to be much in the habit of laying it upon her husband as well as upon me, I supposed that Joe Gargery and I were both brought up by hand.

She was not a good-looking woman, my sister; and I had a general impression that she must have made Joe Gargery marry her by hand. Joe was a fair man, with curls of flaxen hair on each side of his smooth face, and with eyes of such a very undecided blue that they seemed to have somehow got mixed with their own whites. He was a mild, good-natured, sweet-tempered, easy-going, foolish, dear fellow—a sort of Hercules in strength, and also in weakness.

My sister, Mrs. Joe, with black hair and eyes, had such a prevailing redness of skin, that I sometimes used to wonder whether it was possible she washed herself with a nutmeg-grater instead of soap. She was tall and bony, and almost always wore a coarse apron, fastened over her figure behind with two loops, and having a square impregnable bib in front, that was stuck full of pins and needles. She made it a powerful merit in herself, and a strong reproach against Joe, that she wore this apron so much. Though I really see no reason why she should have worn it at all; or why, if she did wear it at all, she should not have taken it off every day of her life.

Joe's forge adjoined our house, which was a wooden house, as many of the dwellings in our country were—most of them, at that time. When I ran home from the churchyard, the forge was shut up, and Joe was sitting alone in the kitchen. Joe and I being fellow-sufferers, and having confidences as such, Joe imparted a confidence to me, the moment I raised the latch of the door and peeped in at him opposite to it, sitting in the chimney corner.

"Mrs. Joe has been out a dozen times, looking for you, Pip. And she's out now, making it a baker's dozen."

"Is she?"

"Yes, Pip," said Joe; "and what's worse, she's got Tickler with her."

At this dismal intelligence, I twisted the only button on my waistcoat round and round, and looked in great depression at the fire. Tickler was a wax-ended piece of cane, worn smooth by collision with my tickled frame.

"She sot down," said Joe, "and she got up, and she made a grab at Tickler, and she Ram-paged out. That's what she did," said Joe, slowly clearing the fire between the lower bars with the poker, and looking at it: "she Ram-paged out, Pip."

"Has she been gone long, Joe?" I always treated him as a larger species of child, and as no more than my equal.

"Well," said Joe, glancing up at the Dutch clock, "she's been on the Ram-page, this last spell, about five minutes, Pip. She's a coming! Get behind the door, old chap, and have the jack-towel betwixt you."

I took the advice. My sister, Mrs. Joe, throwing the door wide open, and finding an obstruction behind it, immediately divined the cause, and applied Tickler to its further investigation. She concluded by throwing me—I often served as a connubial missile—at Joe, who, glad to get hold of me on any terms, passed me on into the chimney and quietly fenced me up there with his great leg.

"Where have you been, you young monkey?" said Mrs. Joe, stamping her foot. "Tell me directly what you've been doing to wear me away with fret and fright and worrit, or I'd have you out of that corner if you was fifty Pips, and he was five hundred Gargerys."

"I have only been to the churchyard," said I, from my stool, crying and rubbing myself.

"Churchyard!" repeated my sister. "If it warn't for me you'd have been to the churchyard long ago, and stayed there. Who brought you up by hand?"

"You did," said I.

"And why did I do it, I should like to know?" exclaimed my sister.

I whimpered, "I don't know."

"*I* don't!" said my sister. "I'd never do it again! I know that. I may truly say I've never had this apron of mine off, since born you were. It's bad enough to be a blacksmith's wife, and him a Gargery, without being your mother."

My thoughts strayed from that question as I looked disconsolately at the fire. For, the fugitive out on the marshes with the ironed leg, the mysterious young man, the file, the food, and the dreadful pledge I was under to commit a larceny on those sheltering premises, rose before me in the avenging coals.

"Hah!" said Mrs. Joe, restoring Tickler to his station. "Churchyard, indeed! You may well say churchyard, you two." One of us, by-the-bye, had not said it at all. "You'll drive *me* to the churchyard betwixt you, one of these days, and oh, a pr-r-recious pair you'd be without me!"

As she applied herself to set the tea-things, Joe peeped down at me over his leg, as if he were mentally casting me and himself up, and calculating what kind of pair we practically should make, under the grievous circumstances foreshadowed. After that, he sat feeling his right-side flaxen curls and whisker, and following Mrs. Joe about with his blue eye, as his manner always was at squally times.

My sister had a trenchant way of cutting our bread-and-butter for us, that never varied. First, with her left hand she jammed the loaf hard and fast against her bib—where it sometimes got a pin into it, and sometimes a needle, which we afterwards got into our mouths. Then she took some butter (not too much) on a knife and spread it on the loaf, in an apothecary kind of way, as if she were making a plaister—using both sides of the knife with a slapping dexterity, and trimming and moulding the butter off round the crust. Then, she gave the knife a final smart wipe on the edge of the plaister, and then sawed a very thick round off the loaf: which she finally, before separating from the loaf, hewed into two halves, of which Joe got one, and I the other.

On the present occasion, though I was hungry, I dared not eat my slice. I felt that I must have something in reserve for my dreadful acquaintance, and his ally the still more dreadful young man. I knew Mrs. Joe's housekeeping to be of the strictest kind, and that my larcenous researches might find nothing available in the safe. Therefore I resolved to put my hunk of bread-and-butter down the leg of my trousers.

The effort of resolution necessary to the achievement of this purpose, I found to be quite awful. It was as if I had to make up my mind to leap from the top of a high house, or plunge into a great depth of water. And it was made the more difficult by the unconscious Joe. In our already-mentioned freemasonry as fellow-sufferers, and in his good-natured companionship with me, it was our evening habit to compare the way we bit through our slices, by silently holding them up to each other's admiration now and then—which stimulated us to new exertions. To-night, Joe several times invited me, by the display of his fast-diminishing slice, to enter upon our usual friendly competition; but he found me, each time, with my yellow mug of tea on one knee, and my untouched bread-and-butter on the other. At last, I desperately considered that the thing I contemplated must be done, and that it had best be done in the least improbable manner consistent with the circumstances. I took advantage of a moment when Joe had just looked at me, and got my bread-and-butter down my leg.

Joe was evidently made uncomfortable by what he supposed to be my loss of appetite, and took a thoughtful bite out of his slice, which he didn't seem to enjoy. He turned it about in his mouth much longer than usual, pondering over it a good deal, and after all gulped it down like a pill. He was about to take another bite, and had just got his head on one side for a good purchase on it, when his eye fell on me, and he saw that my bread-and-butter was gone.

The wonder and consternation with which Joe stopped on the threshold of his bite and stared at me, were too evident to escape my sister's observation.

"What's the matter now?" said she, smartly, as she put down her cup.

"I say, you know!" muttered Joe, shaking his head at me in a very serious remonstrance. "Pip, old chap! You'll do yourself a mischief. It'll stick somewhere. You can't have chawed it, Pip."

"What's the matter *now?*" repeated my sister, more sharply than before.

"If you can cough any trifle on it up, Pip, I'd recommend you to do it," said Joe, all aghast. "Manners is manners, but still your elth's your elth."

By this time, my sister was quite desperate, so she pounced on Joe, and, taking him by the two whiskers, knocked his head for a little while against the wall behind him: while I sat in the corner, looking guiltily on.

"Now, perhaps you'll mention what's the matter," said my sister, out of breath, "you staring great stuck pig."

Joe looked at her in a helpless way; then took a helpless bite, and looked at me again.

"You know, Pip," said Joe, solemnly, with his last bite in his cheek, and speaking in a confidential voice, as if we two were quite alone, "you and me is always friends, and I'd be the last to tell upon you, any time. But such a—"

he moved his chair, and looked about the floor between us, and then again at me—"such a most uncommon bolt as that!"

"Been bolting his food, has he?" cried my sister.

"You know, old chap," said Joe, looking at me, and not at Mrs. Joe, with his bite still in his cheek, "I Bolted, myself, when I was your age—frequent—and as a boy I've been among a many Bolters; but I never see your bolting equal yet, Pip, and it's a mercy you ain't Bolted dead."

My sister made a dive at me, and fished me up by the hair: saying nothing more than the awful words, "You come along and be dosed."

Some medical beast had revived Tar-water in those days as a fine medicine, and Mrs. Joe always kept a supply of it in the cupboard; having a belief in its virtues correspondent to its nastiness.. At the best of times, so much of this elixir was administered to me as a choice restorative, that I was conscious of going about, smelling like a new fence. On this particular evening, the urgency of my case demanded a pint of this mixture, which was poured down my throat, for my greater comfort, while Mrs. Joe held my head under her arm, as a boot would be held in a boot-jack. Joe got off with half a pint; but was made to swallow that (much to his disturbance, as he sat slowly munching and meditating before the fire), "because he had had a turn." Judging from myself, I should say he certainly had a turn afterwards, if he had had none before.

Conscience is a dreadful thing when it accuses man or boy; but when, in the case of a boy, that secret burden co-operates with another secret burden down the leg of his trousers, it is (as I can testify) a great punishment. The guilty knowledge that I was going to rob Mrs. Joe—I never thought I was going to rob Joe, for I never thought of any of the housekeeping property as his—united to the necessity of always keeping one hand on my bread-and-butter as I sat, or when I was ordered about the kitchen on any small errand, almost drove me out of my mind. Then, as the marsh winds made the fire glow and flare, I thought I heard the voice outside, of the man with the iron on his leg who had sworn me to secrecy, declaring that he couldn't and wouldn't starve until to-morrow, but must be fed now. At other times, I thought, What if the young man who was with so much difficulty restrained from imbruing his hands in me, should yield to a constitutional impatience, or should mistake the time, and should think himself accredited to my heart and liver to-night, instead of to-morrow! If ever anybody's hair stood on end with terror, mine must have done so then. But, perhaps, nobody's ever did?

It was Christmas Eve, and I had to stir the pudding for next day, with a copper-stick, from seven to eight by the Dutch clock. I tried it with the load upon my leg (and that made me think afresh of the man with the load on *his* leg), and found the tendency of exercise to bring the bread-and-butter out at my ankle, quite unmanageable. Happily I slipped away, and deposited that part of my conscience in my garret bedroom.

"Hark!" said I, when I had done my stirring, and was taking a final warm in the chimney corner before being sent up to bed; "was that great guns, Joe?"

"Ah!" said Joe. "There's another convict off."

"What does that mean, Joe?" said I.

Mrs. Joe, who always took explanations upon herself, said snappishly, "Escaped. Escaped." Administering the definition like Tar-water.

While Mrs. Joe sat with her head bending over her needlework, I put my mouth into the forms of saying to Joe, "What's a convict?" Joe put *his* mouth into the forms of returning such a highly elaborate answer, that I could make out nothing of it but the single word, "Pip."

"There was a convict off last night," said Joe, aloud, "after sunset-gun. And they fired warning of him. And now it appears they're firing warning of another."

"*Who's* firing?" said I.

"Drat that boy," interposed my sister, frowning at me over her work, "what a questioner he is. Ask no questions, and you'll be told no lies."

It was not very polite to herself, I thought, to imply that I should be told lies by her, even if I did ask questions. But she never was polite, unless there was company.

At this point, Joe greatly augmented my curiosity by taking the utmost pains to open his mouth very wide, and to put it into the form of a word that looked to me like "sulks." Therefore, I naturally pointed to Mrs. Joe, and put my mouth into the form of saying "her?" But Joe wouldn't hear of that at all, and opened his mouth very wide, and shook the form of a most emphatic word out of it. But I could make nothing of the word.

"Mrs. Joe," said I, as a last resort, "I should like to know—if you wouldn't much mind—where the firing comes from?"

"Lord bless the boy!" exclaimed my sister, as if she didn't quite mean that, but rather the contrary. "From the Hulks!"

"Oh-h!" said I looking at Joe. "Hulks!"

Joe gave a reproachful cough, as much as to say, "Well, I told you so."

"And please what's Hulks?" said I.

"That's the way with this boy!" exclaimed my sister, pointing me out with her needle and thread, and shaking her head at me. "Answer him one question, and he'll ask you a dozen directly. Hulks are prison-ships, right 'cross th' meshes." We always used that name for marshes in our country.

"I wonder who's put into prison-ships, and why they're put there?" said I, in a general way, and with quiet desperation.

It was too much for Mrs. Joe, who immediately rose. "I tell you what, young fellow," said she, "I didn't bring you up by hand to badger people's lives out. It would be blame to me, and not praise, if I had. People are put in the Hulks because they murder, and because they rob, and forge, and do all sorts of bad; and they always begin by asking questions. Now, you get along to bed!"

I was never allowed a candle to light me to bed, and, as I went upstairs in the dark, with my head tingling—from Mrs. Joe's thimble having played the tambourine upon it, to accompany her last words—I felt fearfully sensible of the great convenience that the hulks were handy for me. I was clearly on my way there. I had begun by asking questions, and I was going to rob Mrs. Joe.

Since that time, which is far enough away now, I have often thought that few people know what secrecy there is in the young, under terror. No matter how unreasonable the terror, so that it be terror. I was in mortal terror of the young man who wanted my heart and liver; I was in mortal terror of my interlocutor with the iron leg; I was in mortal terror of myself, from whom an awful promise had been extracted; I had no hope of deliverance through my all-powerful sister, who repulsed me at every turn; I am afraid to think of what I might have done on requirement, in the secrecy of my terror.

If I slept at all that night, it was only to imagine myself drifting down the river on a strong spring-tide, to the Hulks; a ghostly pirate calling out to me through a speaking-trumpet, as I passed the gibbet-station, that I had better come ashore and be hanged there at once, and not put it off. I was afraid to sleep, even if I had been inclined, for I knew that at the first faint dawn of morning I must rob the pantry. There was no doing it in the night, for there was no getting a light by easy friction then; to have got one, I must have struck it out of flint and steel, and have made a noise like the very pirate himself rattling his chains.

As soon as the great black velvet pall outside my little window was shot with grey, I got up and went downstairs; every board upon the way, and every crack in every board, calling after me, "Stop thief!" and "Get up, Mrs. Joe!" In the pantry, which was far more abundantly supplied than usual, owing to the season, I was very much alarmed, by a hare hanging up by the heels, whom I rather thought I caught, when my back was half turned, winking. I had no time for verification, no time for selection, no time for anything, for I had no time to spare. I stole some bread, some rind of cheese, about half a jar of mincemeat (which I tied up in my pocket-handkerchief with my last night's slice), some brandy from a stone bottle (which I decanted into a glass bottle I had secretly used for making that intoxicating-fluid, Spanish-liquorice-water, up in my room; diluting the stone bottle from a jug in the kitchen cupboard), a meat bone with very little on it, and a beautiful round compact pork pie. I was nearly going away without the pie, but I was tempted to mount upon a shelf, to look what it was that was put away so carefully in a covered earthenware dish in a corner, and I found it was the pie, and I took it, in the hope that it was not intended for early use, and would not be missed for some time.

There was a door in the kitchen communicating with the forge; I unlocked and unbolted that door, and got a file from among Joe's tools. Then I put the fastenings as I had found them, opened the door at which I had entered when I ran home last night, shut it, and ran for the misty marshes.

CHAPTER III.

It was a rimy morning, and very damp. I had seen the damp lying on the outside of my little window, as if some goblin had been crying there all night, and using the window for a pocket-handkerchief. Now I saw the damp lying on the bare hedges and spare grass, like a coarser sort of spiders' webs; hanging itself from twig to twig and blade to blade. On every rail and gate, wet lay clammy, and the marsh-mist was so thick, that the wooden finger on the post directing people to our village—a direction which they never accepted, for they never came there—was invisible to me until I was quite close under it. Then, as I looked up at it, while it dripped, it seemed to my oppressed conscience like a phantom devoting me to the Hulks.

The mist was heavier yet when I got out upon the marshes, so that instead of my running at everything, everything seemed to run at me. This was very disagreeable to a guilty mind. The gates and dykes and banks came bursting at me through the mist, as if they cried as plainly as could be, "A boy with Somebody-else's pork pie! Stop him!" The cattle came upon me with like suddenness, staring out of their eyes, and steaming out of their nostrils, "Holloa, young thief!" One black ox, with a white cravat on—who even had to my awakened conscience something of a clerical air—fixed me so obstinately with his eyes, and moved his blunt head round in such an accusatory manner as I moved round, that I blubbered out to him, "I couldn't help it, sir! It wasn't for myself I took it!" Upon which he put down his head, blew a cloud of smoke out of his nose, and vanished with a kick-up of his hind-legs and a flourish of his tail.

All this time I was getting on towards the river; but however fast I went, I couldn't warm my feet, to which the damp cold seemed riveted, as the iron was riveted to the leg of the man I was running to meet. I knew my way to the Battery, pretty straight, for I had been down there on a Sunday with Joe, and Joe, sitting on an old gun, had told me that when I was 'prentice to him, regularly bound, we would have such Larks there! However, in the confusion of the mist, I found myself at last too far to the right, and consequently had to try back along the river-side, on the bank of loose stones above the mud and the stakes that staked the tide out. Making my way along here with all dispatch, I had just crossed a ditch which I knew to be very near the Battery, and had just scrambled up the mound beyond the ditch, when I saw the man sitting before me. His back was towards me, and he had his arms folded, and was nodding forward, heavy with sleep.

I thought he would be more glad if I came upon him with his breakfast, in that unexpected manner, so I went forward softly and touched him on the shoulder. He instantly jumped up, and it was not the same man, but another man!

And yet this man was dressed in coarse grey, too, and had a great iron on his leg, and was lame, and hoarse, and cold, and was everything that the other man was; except that he had not the same face, and had a flat, broad-brimmed, low-crowned felt hat on. All this I saw in a moment, for I had only a moment to see it in: he swore an oath at me, made a hit at me—it was a round, weak blow that missed me and almost knocked himself down, for it made him stumble—and then he ran into the mist, stumbling twice as he went, and I lost him.

"It's the young man!" I thought, feeling my heart shoot as I identified him. I dare say I should have felt a pain in my liver, too, if I had known where it was.

I was soon at the Battery, after that, and there was the right man—hugging himself and limping to and fro, as if he had never all night left off hugging and limping—waiting for me. He was awfully cold, to be sure. I half expected to see him drop down before my face and die of deadly cold. His eyes looked so awfully hungry, too, that when I handed him the file and he laid it down on the grass, it occurred to me he would have tried to eat it, if he had not seen my bundle. He did not turn me upside down, this time, to get at what I had, but left me right side upwards while I opened the bundle and emptied my pockets.

"What's in the bottle, boy?" said he.

"Brandy," said I.

He was already handing mincemeat down his throat in the most curious manner—more like a man who was putting it away somewhere in a violent hurry, than a man who was eating it—but he left off to take some of the liquor. He shivered all the while so violently, that it was quite as much as he could do to keep the neck of the bottle between his teeth, without biting it off.

"I think you have got the ague," said I.

"I'm much of your opinion, boy," said he.

"It's bad about here," I told him. "You've been lying out on the meshes and they're dreadful aguish. Rheumatic too."

"I'll eat my breakfast afore they're the death of me," said he. "I'd do that if I was going to be strung up to that there gallows as there is over there, directly arterwards. I'll beat the shivers so far, I'll bet you."

He was gobbling mincemeat, meat bone, bread, cheese, and pork pie, all at once: staring distrustfully while he did so at the mist all round us, and often stopping—even stopping his jaws—to listen. Some real or fancied sound, some clink upon the river or breathing of beast upon the marsh, now gave him a start, and he said, suddenly:

"You're not a deceiving imp? You brought no one with you?"

"No, sir! No!"

"Nor giv' no one the office to follow you?"

"No!"

"Well," said he, "I believe you. You'd be but a fierce young hound indeed, if at your time of life you could help to hunt a wretched warmint, hunted as near death and dunghill as this poor wretched warmint is!"

Something clicked in his throat as if he had works in him like a clock, and was going to strike. And he smeared his ragged rough sleeve over his eyes.

Pitying his desolation, and watching him as he gradually settled down upon the pie, I made bold to say, "I am glad you enjoy it."

"Did you speak?"

"I said, I was glad you enjoyed it."

"Thankee, my boy. I do."

I had often watched a large dog of ours eating his food; and I now noticed a decided similarity between the dog's way of eating, and the man's. The man took strong sharp sudden bites, just like the dog. He swallowed, or rather snapped up, every mouthful, too soon and too fast; and he looked sideways here and there while he ate, as if he thought there was danger in every direction of somebody's coming to take the pie away. He was altogether too unsettled in his mind over it, to appreciate it comfortably, I thought, or to have anybody to dine with him, without making a chop with his jaws at the visitor. In all of which particulars he was very like the dog.

"I am afraid you won't leave any of it for him," said I, timidly; after a silence during which I had hesitated as to the politeness of making the remark. "There's no more to be got where that came from." It was the certainty of this fact that impelled me to offer the hint.

"Leave any for him? Who's him?" said my friend, stopping in his crunching of pie-crust.

"The young man. That you spoke of. That was hid with you."

"Oh ah!" he returned, with something like a gruff laugh. "Him? Yes, yes! *He* don't want no wittles."

"I thought he looked as if he did," said I.

The man stopped eating, and regarded me with the keenest scrutiny and the greatest surprise.

"Looked? When?"

"Just now."

"Where?"

"Yonder," said I, pointing; "over there, where I found him nodding asleep, and thought it was you."

He held me by the collar and stared at me so, that I began to think his first idea about cutting my throat had revived.

"Dressed like you, you know, only with a hat," I explained, trembling; "and—and "—I was very anxious to put this delicately—"and with—the same reason for wanting to borrow a file. Didn't you hear the cannon last night?"

"Then, there *was* firing!" he said to himself.

"I wonder you shouldn't have been sure of that," I returned, "for we heard it up at home, and that's further away, and we were shut in besides."

"Why, see now!" said he. "When a man's alone on these flats, with a light head and a light stomach, perishing of cold and want, he hears nothin' all night, but guns firing, and voices calling. Hears? He sees the soldiers, with their red coats lighted up by the torches carried afore, closing in round him. Hears his number called, hears himself challenged, hears the rattle of the muskets, hears the orders 'Make ready! Present! Cover him steady, men!' and is laid hands on—and there's nothin'! Why, if I see one pursuing party last night—coming up in order, Damn 'em, with their tramp, tramp—I see a hundred. And as to firing! Why, I see the mist shake with the cannon, arter it was broad day.—But this man;" he had said all the rest as if he had forgotten my being there; "did you notice anything in him?"

"He had a badly bruised face," said I, recalling what I hardly knew I knew.

"Not here?" exclaimed the man, striking his left cheek mercilessly, with the flat of his hand.

"Yes, there!"

"Where is he?" He crammed what little food was left, into the breast of his grey jacket. "Show me the way he went. I'll pull him down, like a bloodhound. Curse this iron on my sore leg! Give us hold of the file, boy."

I indicated in what direction the mist had shrouded the other man, and he looked up at it for an instant. But he was down on the rank wet grass, filing at his iron like a madman, and not minding me or minding his own leg, which had an old chafe upon it and was bloody, but which he handled as roughly as if it had no more feeling in it than the file. I was very much afraid of him again, now that he had worked himself into this fierce hurry, and I was likewise very much afraid of keeping away from home any longer. I told him I must go, but he took no notice, so I thought the best thing I could do was to slip off. The last I saw of him, his head was bent over his knee and he was working hard at his fetter, muttering impatient imprecations at it and his leg. The last I heard of him, I stopped in the mist to listen, and the file was still going.

CHAPTER IV.

I FULLY expected to find a Constable in the kitchen, waiting to take me up. But not only was there no Constable there, but no discovery had yet been made of the robbery. Mrs. Joe was prodigiously busy in getting the house ready for the festivities of the day, and Joe had been put upon the kitchen door-step to keep him out of the dust-pan—an article into which his destiny always led him, sooner or later, when my sister was vigorously reaping the floors of her establishment.

"And where the deuce ha' *you* been?" was Mrs. Joe's Christmas salutation, when I and my conscience showed ourselves.

I said I had been down to hear the Carols. "Ah! well!" observed Mrs. Joe. "You might ha' done worse." Not a doubt of that I thought.

"Perhaps if I warn't a blacksmith's wife, and (what's the same thing) a slave with her apron never off, *I* should have been to hear the Carols," said Mrs. Joe. "I'm rather partial to Carols myself, and that's the best of reasons for my never hearing any."

Joe, who had ventured into the kitchen after me as the dust-pan had retired before us, drew the back of his hand across his nose with a conciliatory air, when Mrs. Joe darted a look at him, and, when her eyes were withdrawn, secretly crossed his two forefingers, and exhibited them to me, as our token that Mrs. Joe was in a cross temper. This was so much her normal state, that Joe and I would often, for weeks together, be, as to our fingers, like monumental Crusaders as to their legs.

We were to have a superb dinner, consisting of a leg of pickled pork and greens, and a pair of roast stuffed fowls. A handsome mince-pie had been made yesterday morning (which accounted for the mincemeat not being missed), and the pudding was already on the boil. These extensive arrangements occasioned us to be cut off unceremoniously in respect of breakfast; "for I ain't," said Mrs. Joe, "I ain't a going to have no formal cramming and busting and washing up now, with what I've got before me, I promise you!"

So, we had our slices served out, as if we were two thousand troops on a forced march instead of a man and boy at home; and we took gulps of milk and water, with apologetic countenances, from a jug on the dresser. In the meantime, Mrs. Joe put clean white curtains up, and tacked a new flowered-flounce across the wide chimney to replace the old one, and uncovered the little state parlour across the passage, which was never uncovered at any other time, but passed the rest of the year in a cool haze of silver paper, which even extended to the four little white crockery poodles on the mantelshelf, each with a black nose and a basket of flowers in his mouth, and each the counterpart of the other. Mrs. Joe was a very clean housekeeper, but had an exquisite art of making her cleanliness more uncomfortable and unacceptable than dirt itself. Cleanliness is next to Godliness, and some people do the same by their religion.

My sister having so much to do, was going to church vicariously; that is to say, Joe and I were going. In his working clothes, Joe was a well-knit characteristic-looking blacksmith; in his holiday clothes, he was more like a scarecrow in good circumstances, than anything else. Nothing that he wore then, fitted him or seemed to belong to him; and everything that he wore then, grazed him. On the present festive occasion he emerged from his room, when the blithe bells were going, the picture of misery, in a full suit of Sunday penitentials. As to me, I think my sister must have had some general idea that I was a young offender whom an Accoucheur Policeman had taken up (on my birthday) and delivered over to her, to be dealt with according to the outraged majesty of the law. I was always treated as if I had insisted on being born in opposition to the dictates of reason, religion, and morality, and against the dissuading arguments of my best friends. Even when I was taken to have a new suit of clothes, the tailor

had orders to make them like a kind of Reformatory, and on no account to let me have the free use of my limbs.

Joe and I going to church, therefore, must have been a moving spectacle for compassionate minds. Yet, what I suffered outside, was nothing to what I underwent within. The terrors that had assailed me whenever Mrs. Joe had gone near the pantry, or out of the room, were only to be equalled by the remorse with which my mind dwelt on what my hands had done. Under the weight of my wicked secret, I pondered whether the Church would be powerful enough to shield me from the vengeance of the terrible young man, if I divulged to that establishment. I conceived the idea that the time when the banns were read and when the clergyman said, "Ye are now to declare it!" would be the time for me to rise and propose a private conference in the vestry. I am far from being sure that I might not have astonished our small congregation by resorting to this extreme measure, but for its being Christmas Day and no Sunday.

Mr. Wopsle, the clerk at church, was to dine with us; and Mr. Hubble, the wheelwright, and Mrs. Hubble; and Uncle Pumblechook (Joe's uncle, but Mrs. Joe appropriated him), who was a well-to-do cornchandler in the nearest town, and drove his own chaise-cart. The dinner hour was half-past one. When Joe and I got home, we found the table laid, and Mrs. Joe dressed, and the dinner dressing, and the front door unlocked (it never was at any other time) for the company to enter by, and everything most splendid. And still, not a word of the robbery.

The time came, without bringing with it any relief to my feelings, and the company came. Mr. Wopsle, united to a Roman nose and a large shining bald forehead, had a deep voice which he was uncommonly proud of, indeed it was understood among his acquaintance that if you could only give him his head, he would read the clergyman into fits; he himself confessed that if the Church was "thrown open," meaning to competition, he would not despair of making his mark in it. The Church not being "thrown open," he was, as I have said, our clerk. But he punished the Amens tremendously; and when he gave out the psalm —always giving the whole verse—he looked all around the congregation first, as much as to say, "You have heard our friend overhead; oblige me with your opinion of this style!"

I opened the door to the company—making believe that it was a habit of ours to open that door—and I opened it first to Mr. Wopsle, next to Mr. and Mrs. Hubble, and last of all to Uncle Pumblechook. N.B. *I* was not allowed to call him uncle, under the severest penalties.

"Mrs. Joe," said Uncle Pumblechook; a large hard-breathing middle-aged slow man, with a mouth like a fish, dull staring eyes, and sandy hair standing upright on his head, so that he looked as if he had just been all but choked, and had that moment come to; "I have brought you as the compliments of the season—I have brought you, Mum, a bottle of sherry wine—and I have brought you, Mum, a bottle of port wine."

Every Christmas Day he presented himself, as a profound novelty, with exactly the same words, and carrying the two bottles like dumb-bells. Every Christmas Day, Mrs. Joe replied, as she now replied, "Oh, Un—cle Pumble—chook! This is kind!" Every Christmas Day, he retorted, as he now retorted, "It's no more than your merits. And now are you all bobbish, and how's Sixpennorth of halfpence?" meaning me.

We dined on these occasions in the kitchen, and adjourned, for the nuts and oranges and apples, to the parlour; which was a change very like Joe's change from his working clothes to his Sunday dress. My sister was uncommonly lively on the present occasion, and indeed was generally more gracious in the society of Mrs. Hubble than in other company. I remember Mrs. Hubble as a little curly sharp-edged person in sky-blue, who held a conventionally juvenile position, because she had married Mr. Hubble—I don't know at what remote period—when she was much younger than he. I remember Mr. Hubble as a tough high-shouldered stooping old man, of a sawdusty fragrance, with his legs extraordinarily wide apart: so that in my short days I always saw some miles of open country between them when I met him coming up the lane.

Among this good company I should have felt myself, even if I hadn't robbed the pantry, in a false position. Not because I was squeezed in at an acute angle of the table-cloth, with the table in my chest, and the Pumblechookian elbow in my eye, nor because I was not allowed to speak (I didn't want to speak), nor because I was regaled with the scaly tips of the drumsticks of the fowls, and with those obscure corners of pork of which the pig, when living, had had the least reason to be vain. No; I should not have minded that if they would only have left me alone. But they wouldn't leave me alone. They seemed to think the opportunity lost, if they failed to point the conversation at me, every now and then, and stick the point into me. I might have been an unfortunate little bull in a Spanish arena, I got so smartingly touched up by these moral goads.

It began the moment we sat down to dinner. Mr. Wopsle said grace with theatrical declamation—as it now appears to me, something like a religious cross of the Ghost in Hamlet with Richard the Third—and ended with the very proper aspiration that we might be truly grateful. Upon which my sister fixed me with her eye, and said, in a low reproachful voice, "Do you hear that? Be grateful."

"Especially," said Mr. Pumblechook, "be grateful, boy, to them which brought you up by hand."

Mrs. Hubble shook her head, and contemplating me with a mournful presentiment that I should come to no good, asked, "Why is it that the young are never grateful?" This moral mystery seemed too much for the company until Mr. Hubble tersely solved it by saying, "Naterally wicious." Everybody then murmured "True!" and looked at me in a particularly unpleasant and personal manner.

Joe's station and influence were something feebler (if possible) when there was company, than when there was none. But he always aided and comforted me when he could, in some way of his own, and he always did so at dinner-time by giving me gravy, if there were any. There being plenty of gravy to-day, Joe spooned into my plate, at this point, about half a pint.

A little later on in the dinner, Mr. Wopsle reviewed the sermon with some severity, and intimated—in the usual hypothetical case of the Church being "thrown open"—what kind of sermon he would have given them. After favouring them with some heads of that discourse, he remarked that he considered the subject of the day's homily, ill-chosen; which was the less excusable, he added, when there were so many subjects "going about."

"True again," said Uncle Pumblechook. "You've hit it, sir! Plenty of subjects going about, for them that know how to put salt upon their tails. That's what's wanted. A man needn't go far to find a subject, if he's ready with his salt-box." Mr. Pumblechook added, after a short interval of reflection, "Look at Pork alone. There's a subject! If you want a subject, look at Pork!"

"True, sir. Many a moral for the young," returned Mr. Wopsle; and I knew he was going to lug me in, before he said it; "might be deduced from that text."

("You listen to this," said my sister to me, in a severe parenthesis.)

Joe gave me some more gravy.

"Swine," pursued Mr. Wopsle, in his deepest voice, and pointing his fork at my blushes, as if he were mentioning my Christian name; "Swine were the companions of the prodigal. The gluttony of Swine is put before us, as an example to the young." (I thought this pretty well in him who had been praising up the pork for being so plump and juicy.) "What is detestable in a pig, is more detestable in a boy."

"Or girl," suggested Mr. Hubble.

"Of course, or girl, Mr. Hubble," assented Mr. Wopsle, rather irritably, "but there is no girl present."

"Besides," said Mr. Pumblechook, turning sharp on me, "think what you've got to be grateful for. If you'd been born a Squeaker——"

"He was, if ever a child was," said my sister, most emphatically.

Joe gave me some more gravy.

"Well, but I mean a four-footed Squeaker," said Mr. Pumblechook. "If you had been born such, would you have been here now? Not you——"

"Unless in that form," said Mr. Wopsle, nodding towards the dish.

"But I don't mean in that form, sir," returned Mr. Pumblechook, who had an objection to being interrupted; "I mean, enjoying himself with his elders and betters, and improving himself with their conversation, and rolling in the lap of luxury. Would he have been doing that? No, he wouldn't. And what would have been your destination?" turning on me again. "You would have been disposed of for so many shillings according to the market price of the article, and Dunstable the butcher would have come up to you as you lay in your straw, and he would have whipped you under his left arm, and with his right he would have tucked up his frock to get a penknife from out of his waistcoat-pocket, and he would have shed your blood and had your life. No bringing up by hand then. Not a bit of it!"

Joe offered me more gravy, which I was afraid to take.

"He was a world of trouble to you, ma'am," said Mrs. Hubble, commiserating my sister.

"Trouble?" echoed my sister, "trouble?" And then entered on a fearful catalogue of all the illnesses I had been guilty of, and all the acts of sleeplessness I had committed, and all the high places I had tumbled from, and all the low places I had tumbled into, and all the injuries I had done myself, and all the times she had wished me in my grave, and I had contumaciously refused to go there.

I think the Romans must have aggravated one another very much, with their noses. Perhaps, they became the restless people they were, in consequence. Anyhow, Mr. Wopsle's Roman nose so aggravated me, during the recital of my misdemeanours, that I should have liked to pull it until he howled. But, all I had endured up to this time, was nothing in comparison with the awful feelings that took possession of me when the pause was broken which ensued upon my sister's recital, and in which pause everybody had looked at me (as I felt painfully conscious) with indignation and abhorrence.

"Yet," said Mr. Pumblechook, leading the company gently back to the theme from which they had strayed, "Pork—regarded as biled—is rich, too; ain't it?"

"Have a little brandy, uncle," said my sister.

O Heavens, it had come at last! He would find it was weak, he would say it was weak, and I was lost! I held tight to the leg of the table, under the cloth, with both hands, and awaited my fate.

My sister went for the stone bottle, came back with the stone bottle, and poured his brandy out: no one else taking any. The wretched man trifled with his glass—took it up, looked at it through the light, put it down—prolonged my misery. All this time Mrs. Joe and Joe were briskly clearing the table for the pie and pudding.

I couldn't keep my eyes off him. Always holding tight by the leg of the table with my hands and feet, I saw the miserable creature finger his glass playfully, take it up, smile, throw his head back, and drink the brandy off. Instantly afterwards, the company were seized with unspeakable consternation, owing to his springing to his feet, turning round several times in an appalling spasmodic whooping-cough dance, and rushing out at the door; he then became visible through the window, violently plunging and expectorating, making the most hideous faces, and apparently out of his mind.

I held on tight, while Mrs. Joe and Joe ran to him. I didn't know how I had done it, but I had no doubt I had murdered him somehow. In my dreadful situation, it was a relief when he was brought back, and, surveying the company all round as if *they* had disagreed with him, sank down into his chair with the one significant gasp, "Tar!"

I had filled up the bottle from the tar-water jug. I knew he would be worse by-and-bye. I moved the table, like a Medium of the present day, by the vigour of my unseen hold upon it.

"Tar!" cried my sister, in amazement. "Why, how ever could Tar come there?"

But, Uncle Pumblechook, who was omnipotent in that kitchen, wouldn't hear the word, wouldn't hear of the subject, imperiously waved it all away with his hand, and asked for hot gin-and-water. My sister, who had begun to be alarmingly meditative, had to employ herself actively in getting the gin, the hot water, the sugar, and the lemon-peel, and mixing them. For the time at least, I was saved. I still held on to the leg of the table, but clutched it now with the fervour of gratitude.

By degrees, I became calm enough to release my grasp, and partake of pudding. Mr. Pumblechook partook of pudding. All partook of pudding. The course terminated, and Mr. Pumblechook had begun to beam under the genial influence of gin-and-water. I began to think I should get over the day, when my sister said to Joe, "Clean plates—cold."

I clutched the leg of the table again immediately, and pressed it to my bosom as if it had been the companion of my youth and friend of my soul. I foresaw what was coming, and I felt that this time I really was gone.

"You must taste," said my sister, addressing the guests with her best grace, "you must taste, to finish with, such a delightful and delicious present of Uncle Pumblechook's!"

Must they! Let them not hope to taste it!

"You must know," said my sister, rising, "it's a pie; a savoury pork pie."

The company murmured their compliments. Uncle Pumblechook, sensible of having deserved well of his fellow-creatures, said—quite vivaciously, all things considered—"Well, Mrs. Joe, we'll do our best endeavours; let us have a cut at this same pie."

My sister went out to get it. I heard her steps proceed to the pantry. I saw Mr. Pumblechook balance his knife. I saw reawakening appetite in the Roman nostrils of Mr. Wopsle. I heard Mr. Hubble remark that "a bit of savoury pork pie would lay atop of anything you could mention, and do no harm," and I heard Joe say, "You shall have some, Pip." I have never been absolutely certain whether I uttered a shrill yell of terror, merely in spirit, or in the bodily hearing of the company. I felt that I could hear no more, and that I must run away. I released the leg of the table, and ran for my life.

But I ran no further than the house door, for there I ran head foremost into a party of soldiers with their muskets: one of whom held out a pair of handcuffs to me, saying, "Here you are, look sharp, come on!"

CHAPTER V.

THE apparition of a file of soldiers ringing down the butt-ends of their loaded muskets on our door-step, caused the dinner-party to rise from the table in confusion, and caused Mrs. Joe, re-entering the kitchen empty-handed, to stop short and stare, in her wondering lament of "Gracious goodness gracious me, what's gone—with the—pie!"

The sergeant and I were in the kitchen when Mrs. Joe stood staring; at which crisis I partially recovered the use of my senses. It was the sergeant who had spoken to me, and he was now looking round at the company, with his handcuffs invitingly extended towards them in his right hand, and his left on my shoulder.

"Excuse me, ladies and gentlemen," said the sergeant, "but as I have mentioned at the door to this smart young shaver" (which he hadn't), "I am on a chase in the name of the king, and I want the blacksmith."

"And pray, what might you want with *him?*" retorted my sister, quick to resent his being wanted at all.

"Missis," returned the gallant sergeant, "speaking for myself, I should reply, the honour and pleasure of his fine wife's acquaintance; speaking for the king, I answer, a little job done."

This was received as rather neat in the sergeant; insomuch that Mr. Pumblechook cried audibly, "Good again!"

"You see, blacksmith," said the sergeant, who had by this time picked out Joe with his eye, "we have had an accident with these, and I find the lock of one of 'em goes wrong, and the coupling don't act pretty. As they are wanted for immediate service, will you throw your eye over them?"

Joe threw his eye over them and pronounced that the job would necessitate the lighting of his forge fire, and would take nearer two hours than one. "Will it? Then will you set about it at once, blacksmith?" said the off-hand sergeant, "as it's on his Majesty's service. And if my men can bear a hand anywhere, they'll make themselves useful." With that he called to his men, who came trooping into the kitchen one after another, and piled their arms in a corner. And then they stood about, as soldiers do; now, with their hands loosely clasped before them; now, resting a knee or a shoulder; now, easing a belt or a pouch; now, opening the door to spit stiffly over their high stocks, out into the yard.

All these things I saw without then knowing that I saw them, for I was in an agony of apprehension. But, beginning to perceive that the handcuffs were not for me, and that the military had so far got the better of the pie as to put it in the background, I collected a little more of my scattered wits.

"Would you give me the Time?" said the sergeant, addressing himself to Mr. Pumblechook, as to a man whose appreciative powers justified the inference that he was equal to the time.

"It's just gone half-past two."

"That's not so bad," said the sergeant, reflecting; "even if I was forced to halt here nigh two hours, that'll do. How far might you call yourselves from the marshes, hereabouts? Not above a mile, I reckon?"

"Just a mile," said Mrs. Joe.

"That'll do. We begin to close in upon 'em about dusk. A little before dusk, my orders are. That'll do."

"Convicts, sergeant?" asked Mr. Wopsle, in a matter-of-course way.

"Ay!" returned the sergeant, "two. They're pretty well known to be out on the marshes still, and they won't try to get clear of 'em before dusk. Anybody here seen anything of any such game?"

Everybody, myself excepted, said no, with confidence. Nobody thought of me.

"Well," said the sergeant, "they'll find themselves trapped in a circle, I expect, sooner than they count on. Now, blacksmith! If you're ready, his Majesty the King is."

Joe had got his coat and waistcoat and cravat off, and his leather apron on, and passed into the forge. One of the soldiers opened its wooden windows, another lighted the fire, another turned to at the bellows, the rest stood round the blaze, which was soon roaring. Then Joe began to hammer and clink, hammer and clink, and we all looked on.

The interest of the impending pursuit not only absorbed the general attention, but even made my sister liberal. She drew a pitcher of beer from the cask, for the soldiers, and invited the sergeant to take a glass of brandy. But Mr. Pumblechook said sharply, "Give him wine, Mum. I'll engage there's no Tar in that:" so, the sergeant thanked him and said that, as he preferred his drink without tar, he would take wine, if it was equally convenient. When it was given him, he drank his Majesty's health and compliments of the season, and took it all at a mouthful and smacked his lips.

"Good stuff, eh, sergeant?" said Mr. Pumblechook.

"I'll tell you something," returned the sergeant; "I suspect that stuff's of your providing."

Mr. Pumblechook, with a fat sort of laugh, said, "Ay, ay? Why?"

"Because," returned the sergeant, clapping him on the shoulder, "you're a man that knows what's what."

"D'ye think so?" said Mr. Pumblechook, with his former laugh. "Have another glass!"

"With you. Hob and nob," returned the sergeant. "The top of mine to the foot of yours—the foot of yours to the top of mine—Ring once, ring twice—the best tune on the Musical Glasses! Your health. May you live a thousand years, and never be a worse judge of the right sort than you are at the present moment of your life!"

The sergeant tossed off his glass again and seemed quite ready for another glass. I noticed that Mr. Pumblechook in his hospitality appeared to forget that he had made a present of the wine, but took the bottle from Mrs. Joe and had all the credit of handing it about in a gush of joviality. Even I got some. And he was so very free of the wine that he even called for the other bottle, and handed that about with the same liberality, when the first was gone.

As I watched them while they all stood clustering about the forge, enjoying themselves so much, I thought what terrible good sauce for a dinner my fugitive friend on the marshes was. They had not enjoyed themselves a quarter so much, before the entertainment was brightened with the excitement he furnished. And now, when they were all in lively anticipation of "the two villains" being taken, and when the bellows seemed to roar for the fugitives, the fire to flare for them, the smoke to hurry away in pursuit of them, Joe to hammer and clink for them, and all the murky shadows on the wall to shake at them in menace as the blaze rose and sank and the red-hot sparks dropped and died, the pale afternoon outside almost seemed in my pitying young fancy to have turned pale on their account, poor wretches.

At last, Joe's job was done, and the ringing and roaring stopped. As Joe got on his coat, he mustered courage to propose that some of us should go down with the soldiers and see what came of the hunt. Mr. Pumblechook and Mr. Hubble declined, on the plea of a pipe and ladies' society; but Mr. Wopsle said he would go, if Joe would. Joe said he was agreeable, and would take me, if Mrs. Joe approved. We never should have got leave to go, I am sure, but for Mrs. Joe's curiosity to know all about it and how it ended. As it was, she merely stipulated, "If you bring the boy back with his head blown to bits by a musket, don't look to me to put it together again."

The sergeant took a polite leave of the ladies, and parted from Mr. Pumblechook as from a comrade; though I doubt if he were quite as fully sensible of that gentleman's merits under arid conditions, as when something moist was going. His men resumed their muskets and fell in. Mr. Wopsle, Joe, and I, received strict charge to keep in the rear, and to speak no word after we reached the marshes. When we were all out in the raw air and were steadily moving towards our business, I treasonably whispered to Joe, "I hope, Joe, we shan't find them." And Joe whispered to me, "I'd give a shilling if they had cut and run, Pip."

We were joined by no stragglers from the village, for the weather was cold and threatening, the way dreary, the footing bad, darkness coming on, and the people had good fires in-doors and were keeping the day. A few faces hurried to glowing windows and looked after us, but none came out. We passed the finger-post, and held straight on to the churchyard. There, we were stopped a few minutes by a signal from the sergeant's hand, while two or three of his men dispersed themselves among the graves, and also examined the porch. They came in again without finding anything, and then we struck out on the open marshes, through the gate at the side of the churchyard. A bitter sleet came rattling against us here on the east wind, and Joe took me on his back.

Now that we were out upon the dismal wilderness where they little thought I had been within eight or nine hours, and had seen both men hiding, I considered for the first time, with great dread, if we should come upon them, would my particular convict suppose that it was I who had brought the soldiers there? He had asked me if I was a deceiving imp, and he said I should be a fierce young hound if I joined the hunt against him. Would he believe that I was both imp and hound in treacherous earnest, and had betrayed him?

It was of no use asking myself this question now. There I was, on Joe's back, and there was Joe beneath me, charging at the ditches like a hunter, and stimulating Mr. Wopsle not to tumble on his Roman nose, and to keep up with us. The soldiers were in front of us, extending into a pretty wide line with an interval between man and man. We were taking the course I had begun with, and from which I had diverged into the mist. Either the mist was not out again yet, or the wind had dispelled it. Under the low red glare of sunset, the beacon, and the gibbet, and the mound of the Battery, and the opposite shore of the river, were plain, though all of a watery lead colour.

With my heart thumping like a blacksmith at Joe's broad shoulder, I looked all about for any sign of the convicts. I could see none, I could hear none. Mr. Wopsle had greatly alarmed me more than once, by his blowing and hard breathing; but I knew the sounds by this time, and could dissociate them from the object of pursuit. I got a dreadful start, when I thought I heard the file still going; but it was only a sheep bell. The sheep stopped in their eating and looked timidly at us; and the cattle, their heads turned from the wind and sleet, stared angrily as if they held us responsible for both annoyances; but, except these things, and the shudder of the dying day in every blade of grass, there was no break in the bleak stillness of the marshes.

The soldiers were moving on in the direction of the old Battery, and we were moving on a little way behind them, when, all of a sudden, we all stopped. For, there had reached us, on the wings of the wind and rain, a long shout. It was repeated. It was at a distance towards the east, but it was long and loud. Nay, there seemed to be two or more shouts raised together—if one might judge from a confusion in the sound.

To this effect the sergeant and the nearest men were speaking under their breath, when Joe and I came up. After another moment's listening Joe (who was a good judge) agreed, and Mr. Wopsle (who was a bad judge) agreed. The sergeant, a decisive man, ordered that the sound should not be answered, but that the course should be changed, and that his men should make towards it "at the double." So we started to the right (where the East was), and Joe pounded away so wonderfully, that I had to hold on tight to keep my seat.

It was a run indeed now, and what Joe called, in the only two words he spoke all the time, "a Winder." Down banks and up banks, and over gates, and splashing into dykes, and breaking among coarse rushes: no man cared where he went. As we came nearer to the shouting, it became more and more apparent that it was made by more than one voice. Sometimes, it seemed to stop altogether, and then the soldiers stopped. When it broke out again, the soldiers made for it at a greater rate than ever, and we after them. After a while, we had so run it down, that we could hear one voice calling "Murder!" and another voice, "Convicts! Runaways! Guard! This way for the runaway convicts!" Then both voices would seem to be stifled in a struggle, and then would break out again. And when it had come to this, the soldiers ran like deer, and Joe too.

The sergeant ran in first, when we had run the noise quite down, and two of his men ran in close upon him. Their pieces were cocked and levelled when we all ran in.

"Here are ooth men!" panted the sergeant, struggling at the bottom of a ditch. "Surrender, you two! and confound you for two wild beasts! Come asunder!"

Water was splashing, and mud was flying, and oaths were being sworn, and blows were being struck, when some more men went down into the ditch to help the sergeant, and dragged out, separately, my convict and the other one. Both were bleeding and panting and execrating and struggling; but of course I knew them both directly.

"Mind!" said my convict, wiping blood from his face with his ragged sleeves, and shaking torn hair from his fingers; "*I* took him! *I* give him up to you! Mind that!"

"It's not much to be particular about," said the sergeant; "it'll do you small good, my man, being in the same plight yourself. Handcuffs there!"

"I don't expect it to do me any good. I don't want it to do me more good than it does now," said my convict, with a greedy laugh. "I took him. He knows it. That's enough for me."

The other convict was livid to look at, and, in addition to the old bruised left side of his face, seemed to be bruised and torn all over. He could not so much as get his breath to speak, until they were both separately handcuffed, but leaned upon a soldier to keep himself from falling.

"Take notice, guard—he tried to murder me," were his first words.

"Tried to murder him?" said my convict, disdainfully. "Try, and not do it? I took him, and giv' him up; that's what I done. I not only prevented him getting off the marshes, but I dragged him here—dragged him this far on his way back. He's a gentleman, if you please, this villain. Now, the Hulks has got its gentleman again, through me. Murder him? Worth my while, too, to murder him, when I could do worse and drag him back!"

The other one still gasped, "He tried—he tried—to—murder me. Bear—bear witness."

"Lookee here!" said my convict to the sergeant. "Single-handed I got clear of the prison-ship; I made a dash and I done it. I could ha' got clear of these death-cold flats likewise—look at my leg: you won't find much iron on it—if I hadn't made discovery that *he* was here. Let *him* go free? Let *him* profit by the means as I found out? Let *him* make a tool of me afresh and again? Once more? No, no, no. If I had died at the bottom there;" and he made an emphatic swing at the ditch with his manacled hands; "I'd have held to him with that grip, that you should have been safe to find him in my hold."

The other fugitive, who was evidently in extreme horror of his companion, repeated, "He tried to murder me. I should have been a dead man if you had not come up."

"He lies!" said my convict, with fierce energy. "He's a liar born, and he'll die a liar. Look at his face; ain't it written there? Let him turn those eyes of his on me. I defy him to do it."

The other, with an effort at a scornful smile—which could not, however, collect the nervous working of his mouth into any set expression, looked at the soldiers, and looked about at the marshes and at the sky, but certainly did not look at the speaker.

"Do you see him?" pursued my convict. "Do you see what a villain he is? Do you see those grovelling and wandering eyes? That's how he looked when we were tried together. He never looked at me."

The other, always working and working his dry lips and turning his eyes restlessly about him far and near, did at last turn them for a moment on the speaker, with the words, "You are not much to look at," and with a half-taunting glance at the bound hands. At that point, my convict became so frantically exasperated, that he would have rushed upon him but for the interposition of the soldiers. "Didn't I tell you," said the other convict then, "that he would murder me, if he could?" And any one could see that he shook with fear, and that there broke out upon his lips curious white flakes, like thin snow.

"Enough of this parley," said the sergeant. "Light those torches."

As one of the soldiers, who carried a basket in lieu of a gun, went down on his knee to open it, my convict looked round him for the first time, and saw me. I had alighted from Joe's back on the brink of the ditch when we came up, and had not moved since. I looked at him eagerly when he looked at me, and slightly moved my hands and shook my head. I had been waiting for him to see me, that I might try to assure him of my innocence. It was not at all expressed to me that he even comprehended my intention, for he gave me a look that I did not understand, and it all passed in a moment. But if he had looked at me for an hour or for a day, I could not have remembered his face ever afterwards, as having been more attentive.

The soldier with the basket soon got a light, and lighted three or four torches, and took one himself and distributed the others. It had been almost dark before, but now it seemed quite dark, and soon afterwards very dark. Before we departed from that spot, four soldiers standing in a ring, fired twice into the air. Presently we saw other torches kindled at some distance behind us, and others on the marshes on the opposite bank of the river. "All right," said the sergeant. "March."

We had not gone far when three cannon were fired ahead of us with a sound that seemed to burst something inside my ear. "You are expected on board," said the sergeant to my convict; "they know you are coming. Don't straggle, my man. Close up here."

The two were kept apart, and each walked surrounded by a separate guard. I had hold of Joe's hand now, and Joe carried one of the torches. Mr. Wopsle had been for going back, but Joe was resolved to see it out, so we went on with the party. There was a reasonably good path now, mostly on the edge of the river, with a divergence here and there where a dyke came, with a miniature windmill on it and a muddy sluice-gate. When I looked round, I could see the other lights coming in after us. The torches we carried, dropped great blotches of fire upon the track, and I could see those, too, lying smoking and flaring. I could see nothing else but black darkness. Our lights warmed the air about us with their pitchy blaze, and the two prisoners seemed rather to like that, as they limped along in the midst of the muskets. We could not go fast, because of their lameness; and they were so spent, that two or three times we had to halt while they rested.

After an hour or so of this travelling, we came to a rough wooden hut and a landing-place. There was a guard in the hut, and they challenged, and the sergeant answered. Then, we went into the hut, where there was a smell of tobacco and whitewash, and a bright fire, and a lamp, and a stand of muskets, and a drum, and a low wooden bedstead, like an overgrown mangle without the machinery, capable of holding about a dozen soldiers all at once. Three or four soldiers who lay upon it in their great-coats, were not much interested in us, but just lifted their heads and took a sleepy stare, and then lay down again. The sergeant made some kind of report, and some entry in a book, and

then the convict whom I call the other convict was drafted off with his guard, to go on board first.

My convict never looked at me, except that once. While we stood in the hut, he stood before the fire looking thoughtfully at it, or putting up his feet by turns upon the hob, and looking thoughtfully at them as if he pitied them for their recent adventures. Suddenly, he turned to the sergeant, and remarked:

"I wish to say something respecting this escape. It may prevent some persons laying under suspicion alonger me."

"You can say what you like," returned the sergeant, standing coolly looking at him with his arms folded, "but you have no call to say it here. You'll have opportunity enough to say about it, and hear about it, before it's done with, you know."

"I know, but this is another pint, a separate matter. A man can't starve; at least *I* can't. I took some wittles, up at the willage over yonder—where the church stands a'most out on the marshes."

"You mean stole," said the sergeant.

"And I'll tell you where from. From the blacksmith's."

"Halloa!" said the sergeant, staring at Joe.

"Halloa, Pip!" said Joe, staring at me.

"It was some broken wittles—that's what it was—and a dram of liquor, and a pie."

"Have you happened to miss such an article as a pie, blacksmith?" asked the sergeant, confidentially.

"My wife did, at the very moment when you came in. Don't you know, Pip?"

"So," said my convict, turning his eyes on Joe in a moody manner, and without the least glance at me; "so you're the blacksmith, are you? Then I'm sorry to say, I've eat your pie."

"God knows you're welcome to it—so far as it was ever mine," returned Joe, with a saving remembrance of Mrs. Joe. "We don't know what you have done, but we wouldn't have you starved to death for it, poor miserable fellow-creatur.—Would us, Pip?"

The something that I had noticed before, clicked in the man's throat again, and he turned his back. The boat had returned, and his guard were ready, so we followed him to the landing-place made of rough stakes and stones, and saw him put into the boat, which was rowed by a crew of convicts like himself. No one seemed surprised to see him, or interested in seeing him, or glad to see him, or sorry to see him, or spoke a word, except that somebody in the boat growled as if to dogs, "Give way, you!" which was the signal for the dip of the oars. By the light of the torches, we saw the black Hulk lying out a little way from the mud of the shore, like a wicked Noah's ark. Cribbed and barred and moored by massive rusty chains, the prison-ship seemed in my young eyes to be ironed like the prisoners. We saw the boat go alongside, and we saw him taken up the side and disappear. Then, the ends of the torches were flung hissing into the water, and went out, as if it were all over with him.

CHAPTER VI.

My state of mind regarding the pilfering from which I had been so unexpectedly exonerated, did not impel me to frank disclosure; but I hope it had some dregs of good at the bottom of it.

I do not recall that I felt any tenderness of conscience

in reference to Mrs. Joe, when the fear of being found out was lifted off me. But I loved Joe—perhaps for no better reason in those early days than because the dear fellow let me love him—and, as to him, my inner self was not so easily composed. It was much upon my mind (particularly when I first saw him looking about for his file) that I ought to tell Joe the whole truth. Yet I did not, and for the reason that I mistrusted that if I did, he would think me worse than I was. The fear of losing Joe's confidence, and of thenceforth sitting in the chimney-corner at night staring drearily at my for ever lost companion and friend, tied up my tongue. I morbidly represented to myself that if Joe knew it, I never afterwards could see him at the fireside feeling his fair whisker, without thinking that he was meditating on it. That, if Joe knew it, I never afterwards could see him glance, however casually, at yesterday's meat or pudding when it came on to-day's table, without thinking that he was debating whether I had been in the pantry. That, if Joe knew it, and at any subsequent period of our joint domestic life remarked that his beer was flat or thick, the conviction that he suspected Tar in it, would bring a rush of blood to my face. In a word, I was too cowardly to do what I knew to be right, as I had been too cowardly to avoid doing what I knew to be wrong. I had had no intercourse with the world at that time, and I imitated none of its many inhabitants who act in this manner. Quite an untaught genius, I made the discovery of the line of action for myself.

As I was sleepy before we were far away from the prison-ship, Joe took me on his back again and carried me home. He must have had a tiresome journey of it, for Mr. Wopsle, being knocked up, was in such a very bad temper that if the Church had been thrown open, he would probably have ex-communicated the whole expedition, beginning with Joe and myself. In his lay capacity, he persisted in sitting down in the damp to such an insane extent, that when his coat was taken off to be dried at the kitchen fire, the circumstantial evidence on his trousers would have hanged him if it had been a capital offence.

By that time, I was staggering on the kitchen floor like a little drunkard, through having been newly set upon my feet, and through having been fast asleep, and through waking in the heat and lights and noise of tongues. As I came to myself (with the aid of a heavy thump between the shoulders, and the restorative exclamation "Yah! Was there ever such a boy as this!" from my sister), I found Joe telling them about the convict's confession, and all the visitors suggesting different ways by which he had got into the pantry. Mr. Pumblechook made out, after carefully surveying the premises, that he had first got upon the roof of the forge, and had then got upon the roof of the house, and had then let himself down the kitchen chimney by a rope made of his bedding cut into strips; and as Mr. Pumblechook was very positive and drove his own chaise-cart—over everybody—it was agreed that it must be so. Mr. Wopsle, indeed, wildly cried out "No!" with the feeble malice of a tired man; but, as he had no theory, and no coat on, he was unanimously set at nought—not to mention his smoking hard behind, as he stood with his back to the kitchen fire to draw the damp out: which was not calculated to inspire confidence.

This was all I heard that night before my sister clutched me, as a slumberous offence to the company's eyesight, and assisted me up to bed with such a strong hand that I seemed to have fifty boots on, and to be dangling them all against the edges of the stairs. My state of mind, as I have described it, began before I was up in the morning, and lasted long after the subject had died out, and had ceased to be mentioned saving on exceptional occasions.

CHAPTER VII.

AT the time when I stood in the churchyard, reading the family tombstones, I had just enough learning to be able to spell them out. My construction even of their simple meaning was not very correct, for I read "wife of the Above" as a complimentary reference to my father's exaltation to a better world; and if any one of my deceased relations had been referred to as "Below," I have no doubt I should have formed the worst opinions of that member of the family. Neither were my notions of the theological positions to which my Catechism bound me, at all accurate; for, I have a lively remembrance that I supposed my declaration that I was to "walk in the same all the days of my life," laid me under an obligation always to go through the village from our house in one particular direction, and never to vary it by turning down by the wheelwright's or up by the mill.

When I was old enough, I was to be apprenticed to Joe, and until I could assume that dignity I was not to be what Mrs. Joe called "Pompeyed," or (as I render it) pampered. Therefore, I was not only odd-boy about the forge, but if any neighbour happened to want an extra boy to frighten birds, or pick up stones, or do any such job, I was favoured with the employment. In order, however, that our superior position might not be compromised thereby, a money-box was kept on the kitchen mantel-shelf, into which it was publicly made known that all my earnings were dropped. I have an impression that they were to be contributed eventually towards the liquidation of the National Debt, but I know I had no hope of any personal participation in the treasure.

Mr. Wopsle's great-aunt kept an evening school in the village; that is to say, she was a ridiculous old woman of limited means and unlimited infirmity, who used to go to sleep from six to seven every evening, in the society of youth who paid twopence per week each, for the improving opportunity of seeing her do it. She rented a small cottage, and Mr. Wopsle had the room upstairs, where we students used to overhear him reading aloud in a most dignified and terrific manner, and occasionally bumping on the ceiling. There was a fiction that Mr. Wopsle "examined" the scholars once a quarter. What he did on those occasions was to turn up his cuffs, stick up his hair, and give us Mark Antony's oration over the body of Cæsar. This was always followed by Collins's Ode on the Passions, wherein I particularly venerated Mr. Wopsle as Revenge, throwing his blood-stained sword in thunder down, and taking the War-denouncing trumpet with a withering look. It was not with me then, as it was in later life, when I fell into the society of the Passions, and compared them with Collins and Wopsle, rather to the disadvantage of both gentlemen.

Mr. Wopsle's great-aunt, besides keeping this Educational Institution, kept in the same room—a little general shop. She had no idea what stock she had, or what the price of anything in it was; but there was a little greasy memorandum-book kept in a drawer, which served as a Catalogue of Prices, and by this oracle Biddy arranged all the shop transactions. Biddy was Mr. Wopsle's great-aunt's granddaughter; I confess myself quite unequal to the working out of the problem, what relation she was to Mr. Wopsle. She was an orphan like myself; like me, too, had been brought up by hand. She was most noticeable, I thought, in respect of her extremities; for, her hair always wanted brushing, her hands always wanted washing, and her shoes always wanted mending and pulling up at heel. This description must be received with a week-day limitation. On Sundays she went to church elaborated.

Much of my unassisted self, and more by the help of Biddy than of Mr. Wopsle's great-aunt, I struggled through the alphabet as if it had been a bramble-bush; getting considerably worried and scratched by every letter. After that, I fell among those thieves, the nine figures, who seemed every evening to do something new to disguise themselves and baffle recognition. But, at last I began, in a purblind groping way, to read, write, and cipher, on the very smallest scale.

One night, I was sitting in the chimney-corner with my slate, expending great efforts on the production of a letter to Joe. I think it must have been a full year after our hunt upon the marshes, for it was a long time after, and it was winter and a hard frost. With an alphabet on the hearth at my feet for reference, I contrived in an hour or two to print and smear this epistle:

"mI deEr JO i opE U r krWitE wEll i opE i shAl soN B haBell 4 2 teeDge U JO aN theN wE shOrl b sO glOdd aN wEn i M prenGtD 2 u JO woT larX an blEvE ME inF xn PiP."

There was no indispensable necessity for my communicating with Joe by letter, inasmuch as he sat beside me and we were alone. But, I delivered this written communication (slate and all) with my own hand, and Joe received it, as a miracle of erudition.

"I say, Pip, old chap!" cried Joe, opening his blue eyes wide, "what a scholar you are! Ain't you?"

"I should like to be," said I, glancing at the slate as he held it: with a misgiving that the writing was rather hilly.

"Why, here's a J," said Joe, "and a O equal to anythink! Here's a J and a O, Pip, and a J-O, Joe."

I had never heard Joe read aloud to any greater extent than this monosyllable, and I had observed at church last Sunday, when I accidentally held our Prayer-Book upside down, that it seemed to suit his convenience quite as well as if it had been all right. Wishing to embrace the present occasion of finding out whether in teaching Joe, I should have to begin quite at the beginning, I said, "Ah! But read the rest, Joe."

"The rest, eh, Pip?" said Joe, looking at it with a slowly searching eye, "One, two, three. Why, here's three J's, and three O's, and three J-O, Joes, in it, Pip!"

I leaned over Joe, and, with the aid of my forefinger, read him the whole letter.

"Astonishing!" said Joe, when I had finished. "You ARE a scholar."

"How do you spell Gargery, Joe?" I asked him, with a modest patronage.

"I don't spell it at all," said Joe.

"But supposing you did?"

"It *can't* be supposed," said Joe. "Tho' I'm uncommon fond of reading, too."

"Are you, Joe?"

"On-common. Give me," said Joe, "a good book, or a good newspaper, and sit me down afore a good fire, and I ask no better. Lord!" he continued, after rubbing his knees a little, "when you *do* come to a J and a O, and says you, 'Here, at last, is a J-O, Joe,' how interesting reading is!"

I derived from this last, that Joe's education, like Steam, was yet in its infancy. Pursuing the subject, I inquired:

"Didn't you ever go to school, Joe, when you were as little as me?"

"No, Pip."

"Why didn't you ever go to school, Joe, when you were as little as me?"

"Well, Pip," said Joe, taking up the poker, and settling himself to his usual occupation when he was thoughtful, of slowly raking the fire between the lower bars: "I'll tell you. My father, Pip, he were given to drink, and when he were overtook with drink, he hammered away at my mother most onmerciful. It were a'most the only hammering he did, indeed, 'xcepting at myself. And he hammered at me with a wigour only to be equalled by the wigour with which he didn't hammer at his anwil.—You're a listening and understanding, Pip?"

"Yes, Joe."

"'Consequence, my mother and me we ran away from my father several times; and then my mother she'd go out to work, and she'd say, 'Joe,' she'd say, 'now, please God, you shall have some schooling, child,' and she'd put me to school. But my father were that good in his hart that he couldn't abear to be without us. So, he'd come with a most tremenjous crowd and make such a row at the doors of the houses where we was, that they used to be obligated to have no more to do with us and to give us up to him. And then he took us home and hammered us. Which, you see, Pip," said Joe, pausing in his meditative raking of the fire, and looking at me, "were a drawback on my learning."

"Certainly, poor Joe!"

"Though mind you, Pip," said Joe, with a judicial touch or two of the poker on the top bar, "rendering unto all their doo, and maintaining equal justice betwixt man and man, my father were that good in his hart, don't you see?"

I didn't see; but I didn't say so.

"Well!" Joe pursued, "somebody must keep the pot a biling, Pip, or the pot won't bile, don't you know?"

I saw that, and said so.

"'Consequence, my father didn't make objections to my going to work; so I went to work at my present calling, which were his too, if he would have followed it, and I worked tolerable hard, I assure *you*, Pip. In time I were able to keep him, and I kep him till he went off in a purple leptic fit. And it were my intentions to have had put upon his tombstone that Whatsume'er the failings on his part, Remember reader he were that good in his hart."

Joe recited this couplet with such manifest pride and careful perspicuity, that I asked him if he had made it himself.

"I made it," said Joe, "my own self. I made it in a moment. It was like striking out a horseshoe complete, in a single blow. I never was so much surprised in all my life—couldn't credit my own ed—to tell you the truth, hardly believed it were *my* own ed. As I was saying, Pip, it were my intentions to have had it cut over him; but poetry costs money, cut it how you will, small or large, and it were not done. Not to mention bearers, all the money that could be spared were wanted for my mother. She were in poor elth, and quite broke. She waren't long of following, poor soul, and her share of peace come round at last."

Joe's blue eyes turned a little watery; he rubbed, first one of them, and then the other, in a most uncongenial and uncomfortable manner, with the round knob on the top of the poker.

"It were but lonesome then," said Joe, "living here alone, and I got acquainted with your sister. Now, Pip;" Joe looked firmly at me, as if he knew I was not going to agree with him; "your sister is a fine figure of a woman."

I could not help looking at the fire, in an obvious state of doubt.

"Whatever family opinions, or whatever the world's opinions, on that subject may be, Pip, your sister is," Joe tapped the top bar with the poker after every word following, "a—fine—figure—of—a—woman!"

I could think of nothing better to say than "I am glad you think so, Joe."

"So am I," returned Joe, catching me up. "*I* am glad I think so, Pip. A little redness, or a little matter of Bone, here or there, what does it signify to Me?"

I sagaciously observed, if it didn't signify to him, to whom did it signify?

"Certainly!" assented Joe. "That's it. You're right, old chap! When I got acquainted with your sister, it were the talk how she was bringing you up by hand. Very kind of her too, all the folks said, and I said, along with all the folks. As to you," Joe pursued, with a countenance expressive of seeing something very nasty indeed: "if you could have been aware how small and flabby and mean you was, dear me, you'd have formed the most contemptible opinions of yourself!"

Not exactly relishing this, I said, "Never mind me, Joe."

"But I did mind you, Pip," he returned, with tender simplicity. "When I offered to your sister to keep company, and to be asked in church, at such times as she was willing and ready to come to the forge, I said to her, 'And bring the poor little child. God bless the poor little child,' I said to your sister, 'there's room for *him* at the forge!'"

I broke out crying and begging pardon, and hugged Joe round the neck: who dropped the poker to hug me, and to say, "Ever the best of friends; ain't us, Pip? Don't cry, old chap!"

When this little interruption was over, Joe resumed:

"Well, you see, Pip, and here we are! That's about where it lights; here we are! Now, when you take me in hand in my learning, Pip (and I tell you beforehand I am awful dull, most awful dull), Mrs. Joe mustn't see too much of what we're up to. It must be done, as I may say, on the sly. And why on the sly? I'll tell you why, Pip."

He had taken up the poker again; without which, I doubt if he could have proceeded in his demonstration.

"Your sister is given to government."

"Given to government, Joe?" I was startled, for I had some shadowy idea (and I am afraid I must add, hope) that Joe had divorced her in favour of the Lords of the Admiralty, or Treasury.

"Given to government," said Joe. "Which I meantersay the government of you and myself."

"Oh!"

"And she ain't over partial to having scholars on the premises," Joe continued, "and in partickler would not be over partial to my being a scholar, for fear as I might rise. Like a sort of rebel, don't you see?"

I was going to retort with an inquiry, and had got as far as "Why——" when Joe stopped me.

"Stay a bit. I know what you're a going to say, Pip; stay a bit! I don't deny that your sister comes the Mo-gul over us, now and again. I don't deny that she do throw us back-falls, and that she do drop down upon us heavy. At such times as when your sister is on the Ram-page, Pip," Joe sank his voice to a whisper and glanced at the door, "candour compels fur to admit that she is a Buster."

Joe pronounced this word, as if it began with at least twelve capital B's.

"Why don't I rise? That were your observation when I broke it off, Pip?"

"Yes, Joe."

"Well," said Joe, passing the poker into his left hand, that he might feel his whisker; and I had no hope of him whenever he took to that placid occupation; "your sister's a master-mind. A master-mind."

"What's that?" I asked, in some hope of bringing him to a stand. But, Joe was readier with his definition than I had expected, and completely stopped me by arguing circularly, and answering with a fixed look, "Her."

"And I ain't a master-mind," Joe resumed, when he had unfixed his look, and got back to his whisker. "And last of all, Pip—and this I want to say very serous to you, old chap—I see so much in my poor mother, of a woman drudging and slaving and breaking her honest hart and never getting no peace in her mortal days, that I'm dead afeerd of going wrong in the way of not doing what's right by a woman, and I'd fur rather of the two go wrong the t'other way, and be a little ill-conwenienced myself. I wish it was only me that got put out, Pip; I wish there warn't no Tickler for you, old chap; I wish I could take it all on myself; but this is the up-and-down-and-straight on it, Pip, and I hope you'll overlook shortcomings."

Young as I was, I believe that I dated a new admiration of Joe from that night. We were equals afterwards, as we had been before; but, afterwards at quiet times when I sat looking at Joe and thinking about him, I had a new sensation of feeling conscious that I was looking up to Joe in my heart.

"However," said Joe, rising to replenish the fire; "here's the Dutch-clock a working himself up to being equal to strike Eight of 'em, and she's not come home yet! I hope Uncle Pumblechook's mare mayn't have set a forefoot on a piece o' ice, and gone down."

Mrs. Joe made occasional trips with Uncle Pumblechook on market-days, to assist him in buying such household stuffs and goods as required a woman's judgment; Uncle Pumblechook being a bachelor and reposing no confidences in his domestic servant. This was market-day, and Mrs. Joe was out on one of these expeditions.

Joe made the fire and swept the hearth, and then we went to the door to listen for the chaise-cart. It was a dry cold night, and the wind blew keenly, and the frost was white and hard. A man would die to-night of lying out on the marshes, I thought. And then I looked at the stars, and considered how awful it would be for a man to turn his face up to them as he froze to death, and see no help or pity in all the glittering multitude.

"Here comes the mare," said Joe, "ringing like a peal of bells!"

The sound of her iron shoes upon the hard road was quite musical, as she came along at a much brisker trot than usual. We got a chair out, ready for Mrs. Joe's alighting, and stirred up the fire that they might see a bright window, and took a final survey of the kitchen that nothing might be out of its place. When we had completed these preparations, they drove up, wrapped to the eyes. Mrs. Joe was soon landed, and Uncle Pumblechook was soon down too, covering the mare with a cloth, and we were soon all in the kitchen, carrying so much cold air with us that it seemed to drive all the heat out of the fire.

"Now," said Mrs. Joe, unwrapping herself with haste and excitement, and throwing her bonnet back on her shoulders where it hung by the strings: "if this boy ain't grateful this night, he never will be!"

I looked as grateful as any boy could, who was wholly uninformed why he ought to assume that expression.

"It's only to be hoped," said my sister, "that he won't be Pompeyed. But I have my fears."

"She ain't in that line, Mum," said Mr. Pumblechook. "She knows better."

She? I looked at Joe, making the motion with my lips and eyebrows, "She?" Joe looked at me, making the motion with *his* lips and eyebrows, "She?" My sister catching him in the act, he drew the back of his hand across his nose with his usual conciliatory air on such occasions, and looked at her.

"Well?" said my sister, in her snappish way. "What are you staring at? Is the house afire?"

"—Which some individual," Joe politely hinted, "mentioned she."

"And she is a she, I suppose?" said my sister. "Unless you call Miss Havisham a he. And I doubt if even you'll go so far as that."

"Miss Havisham up town?" said Joe.

"Is there any Miss Havisham down town?" returned my sister. "She wants this boy to go and play there. And of course he's going. And he had better play there," said my sister, shaking her head at me as an encouragement to be extremely light and sportive, "or I'll work him."

I had heard of Miss Havisham up town—everybody for miles round had heard of Miss Havisham up town—as an immensely rich and grim lady who lived in a large and dismal house barricaded against robbers, and who led a life of seclusion.

"Well to be sure!" said Joe, astounded. "I wonder how she comes to know Pip!"

"Noodle!" cried my sister. "Who said she knew him?"

"—Which some individual," Joe again politely hinted, "mentioned that she wanted him to go and play there."

"And couldn't she ask Uncle Pumblechook if he knew of a boy to go and play there? Isn't it just barely possible that Uncle Pumblechook may be a tenant of hers, and that he may sometimes—we won't say quarterly or half-yearly, for that would be requiring too much of you—but sometimes—go there to pay his rent? And couldn't she then ask Uncle Pumblechook if he knew of a boy to go and play there? And couldn't Uncle Pumblechook, being always considerate and thoughtful for us—though you may not think it, Joseph," in a tone of the deepest reproach, as if he were the most callous of nephews, "then mention this boy, standing Prancing here"—which I solemnly declare I

was not doing—"that I have for ever been a willing slave to?"

"Good again!" cried Uncle Pumblechook. "Well put! Prettily pointed! Good indeed! Now, Joseph, you know the case."

"No, Joseph," said my sister, still in a reproachful manner, while Joe apologetically drew the back of his hand across and across his nose, "you do not yet—though you may not think it—know the case. You may consider that you do, but you do *not*, Joseph. For you do not know that Uncle Pumblechook, being sensible that for anything we can tell, this boy's fortune may be made by his going to Miss Havisham's, has offered to take him into town to-night in his own chaise-cart, and to keep him to-night, and to take him with his own hands to Miss Havisham's to-morrow morning. And Lor-a-mussy me!" cried my sister, casting off her bonnet in sudden desperation, "here I stand talking to mere Mooncalfs, with Uncle Pumblechook waiting, and the mare catching cold at the door, and the boy grimed with crock and dirt from the hair of his head to the sole of his foot!"

With that, she pounced on me, like an eagle on a lamb, and my face was squeezed into wooden bowls in sinks, and my head was put under taps of water-butts, and I was soaped, and kneaded, and towelled, and thumped, and harrowed, and rasped, until I really was quite beside myself. (I may here remark that I suppose myself to be better acquainted than any living authority, with the ridgy effect of a wedding-ring, passing unsympathetically over the human countenance.)

When my ablutions were completed, I was put into clean linen of the stiffest character, like a young penitent into sackcloth, and was trussed up in my tightest and fearfullest suit. I was then delivered over to Mr. Pumblechook, who formally received me as if he were the Sheriff, and who let off upon me the speech that I knew he had been dying to make all along: "Boy, be for ever grateful to all friends, but especially unto them which brought you up by hand!"

"Good-bye, Joe!"

"God bless you, Pip, old chap!"

I had never parted from him before, and what with my feelings and what with soap-suds, I could at first see no stars from the chaise-cart. But they twinkled out one by one, without throwing any light on the questions why on earth I was going to play at Miss Havisham's, and what on earth I was expected to play at.

CHAPTER VIII.

Mr. Pumblechook's premises in the High-street of the market town, were of a peppercorny and farinaceous character, as the premises of a corn-chandler and seedsman should be. It appeared to me that he must be a very happy man indeed, to have so many little drawers in his shop: and I wondered when I peeped into one or two on the lower tiers, and saw the tied-up brown paper packets inside, whether the flower-seeds and bulbs ever wanted of a fine day to break out of those jails, and bloom.

It was in the early morning after my arrival that I entertained this speculation. On the previous night, I had been sent straight to bed in an attic with a sloping roof, which was so low in the corner where the bedstead was, that I calculated the tiles as being within a foot of my eyebrows. In the same early morning, I discovered a singular affinity between seeds and corduroys. Mr. Pumblechook wore corduroys, and so did his shopman; and somehow, there was a general air and flavour about the corduroys, so much in the nature of seeds, and a general air and flavour about the seeds, so much in the nature of corduroys, that I hardly knew which was which. The same opportunity served me for noticing that Mr. Pumblechook appeared to conduct his business by looking across the street at the saddler, who appeared to transact *his* business by keeping his eye on the coach-maker, who appeared to get on in life by putting his hands in his pockets and contemplating the baker, who in his turn folded his arms and stared at the grocer, who stood at his door and yawned at the chemist. The watchmaker, always poring over a little desk with a magnifying glass at his eye, and always inspected by a group in smock-frocks poring over him through the glass of his shop-window, seemed to be about the only person in the High-street whose trade engaged his attention.

Mr. Pumblechook and I breakfasted at eight o'clock in the parlour behind the shop, while the shopman took his mug of tea and hunch of bread-and-butter on a sack of peas in the front premises. I considered Mr. Pumblechook wretched company. Besides being possessed by my sister's idea that a mortifying and penitential character ought to be imparted to my diet—besides giving me as much crumb as possible in combination with as little butter, and putting such a quantity of warm water into my milk that it would have been more candid to have left the milk out altogether—his conversation consisted of nothing but arithmetic. On my politely bidding him Good morning, he said, pompously, "Seven times nine, boy?" And how should *I* be able to answer, dodged in that way, in a strange place, on an empty stomach! I was hungry, but before I had swallowed a morsel, he began a running sum that lasted all through the breakfast. "Seven?" "And four?" "And eight?" "And six?" "And two?" "And ten?" And so on. And after each figure was disposed of, it was as much as I could do to get a bite or a sup, before the next came; while he sat at his ease guessing nothing, and eating bacon and hot roll, in (if I may be allowed the expression) a gorging and gormandising manner.

For such reasons I was very glad when ten o'clock came and we started for Miss Havisham's; though I was not at all at my ease regarding the manner in which I should acquit myself under that lady's roof. Within a quarter of an hour we came to Miss Havisham's house, which was of old brick, and dismal, and had a great many iron bars to it. Some of the windows had been walled up; of those that remained, all the lower were rustily barred. There was a courtyard in front, and that was barred; so, we had to wait, after ringing the bell, until some one should come to open it. While we waited at the gate, I peeped in (even then Mr. Pumblechook said, "And fourteen?" but I pretended not to hear him), and saw that at the side of the house there was a large brewery. No brewing was going on in it, and none seemed to have gone on for a long time.

A window was raised, and a clear voice demanded "What name?" To which my conductor replied "Pumblechook." The voice returned, "Quite right," and the window was

shut again, and a young lady came across the courtyard, with keys in her hand.

"This," said Mr. Pumblechook, "is Pip."

"This is Pip, is it?" returned the young lady, who was very pretty and seemed very proud; "come in, Pip."

Mr. Pumblechook was coming in also, when she stopped him with the gate.

"Oh!" she said. "Did you wish to see Miss Havisham?"

"If Miss Havisham wished to see me," returned Mr. Pumblechook, discomfited.

"Ah!" said the girl; "but you see she don't."

She said it so finally, and in such an undiscussable way, that Mr. Pumblechook, though in a condition of ruffled dignity, could not protest. But he eyed me severely—as if *I* had done anything to him!—and departed with the words reproachfully delivered: "Boy! Let your behaviour here be a credit unto them which brought you up by hand!" I was not free from apprehension that he would come back to propound through the gate, "And sixteen?" But he didn't.

My young conductress locked the gate, and we went across the courtyard. It was paved and clean, but grass was growing in every crevice. The brewery buildings had a little lane of communication with it; and the wooden gates of that lane stood open, and all the brewery beyond stood open, away to the high enclosing wall; and all was empty and disused. The cold wind seemed to blow colder there, than outside the gate; and it made a shrill noise in howling in and out at the open sides of the brewery, like the noise of wind in the rigging of a ship at sea.

She saw me looking at it, and she said, "You could drink without hurt all the strong beer that's brewed there now, boy."

"I should think I could, miss," said I, in a shy way.

"Better not try to brew beer there now, or it would turn out sour, boy; don't you think so?"

"It looks like it, miss."

"Not that anybody means to try," she added, "for that's all done with, and the place will stand as idle as it is, till it falls. As to strong beer, there's enough of it in the cellars already, to drown the Manor House."

"Is that the name of this house, miss?"

"One of its names, boy."

"It has more than one, then, miss?"

"One more. Its other name was Satis; which is Greek, or Latin, or Hebrew, or all three—or all one to me—for enough."

"Enough House!" said I: "that's a curious name, miss."

"Yes," she replied; "but it meant more than it said. It meant, when it was given, that whoever had this house, could want nothing else. They must have been easily satisfied in those days, I should think. But don't loiter, boy."

Though she called me "boy" so often, and with a carelessness that was far from complimentary, she was of about my own age. She seemed much older than I, of course, being a girl, and beautiful and self-possessed; and she was as scornful of me as if she had been one-and-twenty, and a queen.

We went into the house by a side door—the great front entrance had two chains across it outside—and the first thing I noticed was, that the passages were all dark, and that she had left a candle burning there. She took it up, and we went through more passages and up a staircase, and still it was all dark, and only the candle lighted us.

At last we came to the door of a room, and she said, "Go in."

I answered, more in shyness than politeness, "After you, miss."

To this, she returned : "Don't be ridiculous, boy; I am not going in." And scornfully walked away, and—what was worse—took the candle with her.

This was very uncomfortable, and I was half afraid. However, the only thing to be done being to knock at the door, I knocked, and was told from within to enter. I entered, therefore, and found myself in a pretty large room, well lighted with wax candles. No glimpse of daylight was to be seen in it. It was a dressing-room, as I supposed from the furniture, though much of it was of forms and uses then quite unknown to me. But prominent in it was a draped table with a gilded looking-glass, and that I made out at first sight to be a fine lady's dressing-table.

Whether I should have made out this object so soon, if there had been no fine lady sitting at it, I cannot say. In an arm-chair, with an elbow resting on the table and her head leaning on that hand, sat the strangest lady I have ever seen, or shall ever see.

She was dressed in rich materials—satins, and lace, and silks—all of white. Her shoes were white. And she had a long white veil dependent from her hair, and she had bridal flowers in her hair, but her hair was white. Some bright jewels sparkled on her neck and on her hands, and some other jewels lay sparkling on the table. Dresses, less splendid than the dress she wore, and half-packed trunks, were scattered about. She had not quite finished dressing, for she had but one shoe on—the other was on the table near her hand—her veil was but half-arranged, her watch and chain were not put on, and some lace for her bosom lay with those trinkets, and with her handkerchief, and gloves, and some flowers, and a Prayer-book, all confusedly heaped about the looking-glass.

It was not in the first few moments that I saw all these things, though I saw more of them in the first moments than might be supposed. But, I saw that everything within my view which ought to be white, had been white long ago, and had lost its lustre, and was faded and yellow. I saw that the bride within the bridal dress had withered like the dress, and like the flowers, and had no brightness left but the brightness of her sunken eyes. I saw that the dress had been put upon the rounded figure of a young woman, and that the figure upon which it now hung loose, had shrunk to skin and bone. Once, I had been taken to see some ghastly waxwork at the Fair, representing I know not what impossible personage lying in state. Once, I had been taken to one of our old marsh churches to see a skeleton in the ashes of a rich dress, that had been dug out of a vault under the church pavement. Now, waxwork and skeleton seemed to have dark eyes that moved and looked at me. I should have cried out, if I could.

"Who is it?" said the lady at the table.

"Pip, ma'am."

"Pip?"

"Mr. Pumblechook's boy, ma'am. Come—to play."

"Come nearer; let me look at you. Come close."

It was when I stood before her, avoiding her eyes, that I took note of the surrounding objects in detail, and saw that her watch had stopped at twenty minutes to nine, and that a clock in the room had stopped at twenty minutes to nine.

"Look at me," said Miss Havisham. "You are not afraid of a woman who has never seen the sun since you were born?"

I regret to state that I was not afraid of telling the enormous lie comprehended in the answer "No."

"Do you know what I touch here?" she said, laying her hands, one upon the other, on her left side.

"Yes, ma'am." (It made me think of the young man.)

"What do I touch?"

"Your heart."

"Broken!"

She uttered the word with an eager look, and with strong emphasis, and with a weird smile that had a kind of boast in it. Afterwards, she kept her hands there for a little while, and slowly took them away as if they were heavy.

"I am tired," said Miss Havisham. "I want diversion, and I have done with men and women. Play."

I think it will be conceded by my most disputatious reader, that she could hardly have directed an unfortunate boy to do anything in the wide world more difficult to be done under the circumstances.

"I sometimes have sick fancies," she went on, "and I have a sick fancy that I want to see some play. There, there!" with an impatient movement of the fingers of her right hand; "play, play, play!"

For a moment, with the fear of my sister's working me before my eyes, I had a desperate idea of starting round the room in the assumed character of Mr. Pumblechook's chaise-cart. But, I felt myself so unequal to the performance that I gave it up, and stood looking at Miss Havisham in what I suppose she took for a dogged manner, inasmuch as she said, when we had taken a good look at each other:

"Are you sullen and obstinate?"

"No, ma'am, I am very sorry for you, and very sorry I can't play just now. If you complain of me I shall get into trouble with my sister, so I would do it if I could; but it's so new here, and so strange, and so fine—and melancholy——" I stopped, fearing I might say too much, or had already said it, and we took another look at each other.

Before she spoke again, she turned her eyes from me, and looked at the dress she wore, and at the dressing-table, and finally at herself in the looking-glass.

"So new to him," she muttered, "so old to me; so strange to him, so familiar to me; so melancholy to both of us! Call Estella."

As she was still looking at the reflection of herself, I thought she was still talking to herself, and kept quiet.

"Call Estella," she repeated, flashing a look at me. "You can do that. Call Estella. At the door."

To stand in the dark in a mysterious passage of an unknown house, bawling Estella to a scornful young lady neither visible nor responsive, and feeling it a dreadful liberty so to roar out her name, was almost as bad as playing to order. But, she answered at last, and her light came along the dark passage like a star.

Miss Havisham beckoned her to come close, and took up a jewel from the table, and tried its effect upon her fair young bosom and against her pretty brown hair.

"Your own, one day, my dear, and you will use it well. Let me see you play cards with this boy."

"With this boy! Why, he is a common labouring-boy!"

I thought I overheard Miss Havisham answer—only it seemed so unlikely—"Well? You can break his heart."

"What do you play, boy?" asked Estella of myself, with the greatest disdain.

"Nothing but beggar my neighbour, miss."

"Beggar him," said Miss Havisham to Estella. So we sat down to cards.

It was then I began to understand that everything in the room had stopped, like the watch and the clock, a long time ago. I noticed that Miss Havisham put down the jewel exactly on the spot from which she had taken it up. As Estella dealt the cards, I glanced at the dressing-table again, and saw that the shoe upon it, once white, now yellow, had never been worn. I glanced down at the foot from which the shoe was absent, and saw that the silk stocking on it, once white, now yellow, had been trodden ragged. Without this arrest of everything, this standing still of all the pale decayed objects, not even the withered bridal dress on the collapsed form could have looked so like grave-clothes, or the long veil so like a shroud.

So she sat, corpse-like, as we played at cards; the frillings and trimmings on her bridal dress, looking like earthy paper. I knew nothing then of the discoveries that are occasionally made of bodies buried in ancient times, which fall to powder in the moment of being distinctly seen; but, I have often thought since, that she must have looked as if the admission of the natural light of day would have struck her to dust.

"He calls the knaves, Jacks, this boy!" said Estella with disdain, before our first game was out. "And what coarse hands he has! And what thick boots!"

I had never thought of being ashamed of my hands before; but I began to consider them a very indifferent pair. Her contempt for me was so strong, that it became infectious, and I caught it.

She won the game, and I dealt. I misdealt, as was only natural, when I knew she was lying in wait for me to do wrong; and she denounced me for a stupid, clumsy labouring-boy.

"You say nothing of her," remarked Miss Havisham to me, as she looked on. "She says many hard things of you, yet you say nothing of her. What do you think of her?"

"I don't like to say," I stammered.

"Tell me in my ear," said Miss Havisham, bending down.

"I think she is very proud," I replied, in a whisper.

"Anything else?"

"I think she is very pretty."

"Anything else?"

"I think she is very insulting." (She was looking at me then with a look of supreme aversion.)

"Anything else?"

"I think I should like to go home."

"And never see her again, though she is so pretty?"

"I am not sure that I shouldn't like to see her again, but I should like to go home now."

"You shall go soon," said Miss Havisham aloud. "Play the game out."

Saving for the one weird smile at first, I should have felt almost sure that Miss Havisham's face could not smile. It had dropped into a watchful and brooding expression—most likely when all the things about her had become transfixed—and it looked as if nothing could ever lift it up again. Her chest had dropped, so that she stooped; and her voice had dropped, so that she spoke low, and with a dead lull upon her; altogether, she had the appearance of having dropped, body and soul, within and without, under the weight of a crushing blow.

I played the game to an end with Estella, and she beggared me. She threw the cards down on the table when she had won them all, as if she despised them for having been won of me.

"When shall I have you here again?" said Miss Havisham. "Let me think."

I was beginning to remind her that to-day was Wednesday, when she checked me with her former impatient movement of the fingers of her right hand.

"There, there! I know nothing of days of the week; I know nothing of weeks of the year. Come again after six days. You hear?"

"Yes, ma'am."

"Estella, take him down. Let him have something to eat, and let him roam and look about him while he eats. Go, Pip."

I followed the candle down, as I had followed the candle up, and she stood it in the place where we had found it. Until she opened the side entrance, I had fancied, without thinking about it, that it must necessarily be night-time. The rush of the daylight quite confounded me, and made me feel as if I had been in the candlelight of the strange room many hours.

"You are to wait here, you boy," said Estella; and disappeared and closed the door.

I took the opportunity of being alone in the courtyard, to look at my coarse hands and my common boots. My opinion of those accessories was not favourable. They had never troubled me before, but they troubled me now, as vulgar appendages. I determined to ask Joe why he had ever taught me to call those picture-cards, Jacks, which ought to be called knaves. I wished Joe had been rather more genteelly brought up, and then I should have been so too.

She came back, with some bread and meat and a little mug of beer. She put the mug down on the stones of the yard, and gave me the bread and meat without looking at me, as insolently as if I were a dog in disgrace. I was so humiliated, hurt, spurned, offended, angry, sorry—I cannot hit upon the right name for the smart—God knows what its name was—that tears started to my eyes. The moment they sprang there, the girl looked at me with a quick delight in having been the cause of them. This gave me power to keep them back and to look at her: so, she gave a contemptuous toss—but with a sense, I thought, of having made too sure that I was so wounded—and left me.

But, when she was gone, I looked about me for a place to hide my face in, and got behind one of the gates in the brewery-lane, and leaned my sleeve against the wall there, and leaned my forehead on it and cried. As I cried, I kicked the wall, and took a hard twist at my hair; so bitter were my feelings, and so sharp was the smart without a name, that needed counteraction.

My sister's bringing up had made me sensitive. In the little world in which children have their existence, whosoever brings them up, there is nothing so finely perceived and so finely felt, as injustice. It may be only small injustice that the child can be exposed to; but the child is small, and its world is small, and its rocking-horse stands as many hands high, according to scale, as a big-boned Irish hunter. Within myself, I had sustained, from my baby-hood, a perpetual conflict with injustice. I had known, from the time when I could speak, that my sister, in her capricious and violent coercion, was unjust to me. I had cherished a profound conviction that her bringing me up by hand, gave her no right to bring me up by jerks. Through all my punishments, disgraces, fasts and vigils, and other penitential performances, I had nursed this assurance; and to my communing so much with it, in a solitary and unpro-tected way, I in great part refer the fact that I was morally timid and very sensitive.

I got rid of my injured feelings for the time, by kicking them into the brewery-wall, and twisting them out of my hair, and then I smoothed my face with my sleeve, and came from behind the gate. The bread and meat were ac-ceptable, and the beer was warming and tingling, and I was soon in spirits to look about me.

To be sure, it was a deserted place, down to the pigeon-house in the brewery-yard, which had been blown crooked on its pole by some high wind, and would have made the pigeons think themselves at sea, if there had been any pig-eons there to be rocked by it. But, there were no pigeons in the dove-cot, no horses in the stable, no pigs in the sty, no malt in the store-house, no smells of grains and beer in the copper or the vat. All the uses and scents of the brewery might have evaporated with its last reek of smoke. In a bye-yard, there was a wilderness of empty casks, which had a certain sour remembrance of better days lingering about them; but it was too sour to be ac-cepted as a sample of the beer that was gone—and in this respect I remember those recluses as being like most others.

Behind the furthest end of the brewery, was a rank gar-den with an old wall: not so high but that I could struggle up and hold on long enough to look over it, and see that the rank garden was the garden of the house, and that it was overgrown with tangled weeds, but that there was a track upon the green and yellow paths, as if some one sometimes walked there, and that Estella was walking away from me even then. But she seemed to be every-where. For, when I yielded to the temptation presented by the casks, and began to walk on them, I saw her walk-ing on them at the end of the yard of casks. She had her back towards me, and held her pretty brown hair spread out in her two hands, and never looked round, and passed out of my view directly. So, in the brewery itself—by which I mean the large paved lofty place in which they used to make the beer, and where the brewing utensils still were. When I first went into it, and, rather oppressed by its gloom, stood near the door looking about me, I saw her pass among the extinguished fires, and ascend some light iron stairs, and go out by a gallery high overhead, as if she were going out into the sky.

It was in this place, and at this moment, that a strange thing happened to my fancy. I thought it a strange thing then, and I thought it a stranger thing long afterwards. I turned my eyes—a little dimmed by looking up at the frosty light—towards a great wooden beam in a low nook of the building near me on my right hand, and I saw a figure hanging there by the neck. A figure all in yellow white, with but one shoe to the feet; and it hung so, that I could see that the faded trimmings of the dress were like earthy paper, and that the face was Miss Havisham's, with a

movement going over the whole countenance as if she were trying to call to me. In the terror of seeing the figure, and in the terror of being certain that it had not been there a moment before, I at first ran from it, and then ran towards it. And my terror was greatest of all when I found no figure there.

Nothing less than the frosty light of the cheerful sky, the sight of people passing beyond the bars of the court-yard gate, and the reviving influence of the rest of the bread and meat and beer, could have brought me round. Even with those aids, I might not have come to myself as soon as I did, but that I saw Estella approaching with the keys, to let me out. She would have some fair reason for looking down upon me, I thought, if she saw me fright-ened; and she should have no fair reason.

She gave me a triumphant glance in passing me, as if she rejoiced that my hands were so coarse and my boots were so thick, and she opened the gate, and stood holding it. I was passing out without looking at her, when she touched me with a taunting hand.

"Why don't you cry?"

"Because I don't want to."

"You do," said she. "You have been crying till you are half blind, and you are near crying again now."

She laughed contemptuously, pushed me out, and locked the gate upon me. I went straight to Mr. Pumblechook's, and was immensely relieved to find him not at home. So, leaving word with the shopman on what day I was wanted at Miss Havisham's again, I set off on the four-mile walk to our forge; pondering, as I went along, on all I had seen, and deeply revolving that I was a common labouring-boy; that my hands were coarse; that my boots were thick; that I had fallen into a despicable habit of calling knaves Jacks; that I was much more ignorant than I had considered myself last night, and generally that I was in a low-lived bad way.

CHAPTER IX.

WHEN I reached home, my sister was very curious to know all about Miss Havisham's, and asked a number of questions. And I soon found myself getting heavily bumped from behind in the nape of the neck and the small of the back, and having my face ignominiously shoved against the kitchen wall, because I did not answer those questions at sufficient length.

If a dread of not being understood be hidden in the breasts of other young people to anything like the extent to which it used to be hidden in mine—which I consider probable, as I have no particular reason to suspect myself of having been a monstrosity—it is the key to many reser-vations. I felt convinced that if I described Miss Havis-ham's as my eyes had seen it, I should not be understood. Not only that, but I felt convinced that Miss Havisham too would not be understood; and although she was perfectly incomprehensible to me, I entertained an impression that there would be something coarse and treacherous in my dragging her as she really was (to say nothing of Miss Estella) before the contemplation of Mrs. Joe. Conse-quently, I said as little as I could, and had my face shoved against the kitchen wall.

The worst of it was that that bullying old Pumblechook,

preyed upon by a devouring curiosity to be informed of all I had seen and heard, came gaping over in his chaise-cart at tea-time, to have the details divulged to him. And the mere sight of the torment, with his fishy eyes and mouth open, his sandy hair inquisitively cn end, and his waistcoat heaving with windy arithmetic, made me vicious in my reticence.

"Well, boy," Uncle Pumblechook began, as soon as he was seated in the chair of honour by the fire. "How did you get on up town?"

I answered, "Pretty well, sir," and my sister shook her fist at me.

"Pretty well?" Mr. Pumblechook repeated. "Pretty well is no answer. Tell us what you mean by pretty well, boy?"

Whitewash on the forehead hardens the brain into a state of obstinacy perhaps. Anyhow, with whitewash from the wall on my forehead, my obstinacy was adamantine. I reflected for some time, and then answered as if I had discovered a new idea, "I mean pretty well."

My sister with an exclamation of impatience was going to fly at me—I had no shadow of defence, for Joe was busy in the forge—when Mr. Pumblechook interposed with "No! Don't lose your temper. Leave this lad to me, ma'am; leave this lad to me." Mr. Pumblechook then turned me towards him, as if he were going to cut my hair, and said:

"First (to get our thoughts in order): Forty-three pence?"

I calculated the consequences of replying "Four Hundred Pound," and finding them against me, went as near the answer as I could—which was somewhere about eight-pence off. Mr. Pumblechook then put me through my pence-table from "twelve pence make one shilling," up to "forty pence make three and fourpence," and then triumphantly demanded, as if he had done for me, "*Now!* How much is forty-three pence?" To which I replied, after a long interval of reflection, "I don't know." And I was so aggravated that I almost doubt if I did know.

Mr. Pumblechook worked his head like a screw to screw it out of me, and said, "Is forty-three pence seven and six pence three fardens, for instance?"

"Yes!" said I. And although my sister instantly boxed my ears, it was highly gratifying to me to see that the answer spoilt his joke, and brought him to a dead stop.

"Boy! What like is Miss Havisham?" Mr. Pumblechook began again when he had recovered; folding his arms tight on his chest and applying the screw.

"Very tall and dark," I told him.

"Is she, uncle?" asked my sister.

Mr. Pumblechook winked assent; from which I at once inferred that he had never seen Miss Havisham, for she was nothing of the kind.

"Good!" said Mr. Pumblechook, conceitedly. ("This is the way to have him! We are beginning to hold our own, I think, Mum?")

"I am sure, uncle," returned Mrs. Joe, "I wish you had him always: you know so well how to deal with him."

"Now, boy! What was she a doing of, when you went in to-day?" asked Mr. Pumblechook.

"She was sitting," I answered, "in a black velvet coach."

Mr. Pumblechook and Mrs. Joe stared at one another—as they well might—and both repeated, "In a black velvet coach?"

"Yes," said I. "And Miss Estella—that's her niece, I

think—handed her in cake and wine at the coach-window, on a gold plate. And we all had cake and wine on gold plates. And I got up behind the coach to eat mine, because she told me to."

"Was anybody else there?" asked Mr. Pumblechook.

"Four dogs," said I.

"Large or small?"

"Immense," said I. "And they fought for veal-cutlets out of a silver basket."

Mr. Pumblechook and Mrs. Joe stared at one another again, in utter amazement. I was perfectly frantic—a reckless witness under the torture—and would have told them anything.

"Where *was* this coach, in the name of gracious?" asked my sister.

"In Miss Havisham's room." They stared again. "But there weren't any horses to it." I added this saving clause, in the moment of rejecting four richly caparisoned coursers, which I had had wild thoughts of harnessing.

"Can this be possible, uncle?" asked Mrs. Joe. "What can the boy mean?"

"I'll tell you, Mum," said Mr. Pumblechook. "My opinion is, it's a sedan-chair. She's flighty, you know—very flighty—quite flighty enough to pass her days in a sedan-chair."

"Did you ever see her in it, uncle?" asked Mrs. Joe.

"How could I," he returned, forced to the admission, "when I never see her in my life? Never clapped eyes upon her!"

"Goodness, uncle! And yet you have spoken to her?"

"Why, don't you know," said Mr. Pumblechook, testily, "that when I have been there, I have been took up to the outside of her door, and the door has stood ajar, and she has spoken to me that way. Don't say you don't know *that*, Mum. Howsever, the boy went there to play. What did you play at, boy?"

"We played with flags," I said. (I beg to observe that I think of myself with amazement, when I recall the lies I told on this occasion.)

"Flags!" echoed my sister.

"Yes," said I. "Estella waved a blue flag, and I waved a red one, and Miss Havisham waved one sprinkled all over with little gold stars, out at the coach-window. And then we all waved our swords and hurrahed."

"Swords!" repeated my sister. "Where did you get swords from?"

"Out of a cupboard," said I. "And I saw pistols in it—and jam—and pills. And there was no daylight in the room, but it was all lighted up with candles."

"That's true, Mum," said Mr. Pumblechook, with a grave nod. "That's the state of the case, for that much I've seen myself." And then they both stared at me, and I, with an obtrusive show of artlessness on my countenance, stared at them, and plaited the right leg of my trousers with my right hand.

If they had asked me any more questions I should undoubtedly have betrayed myself, for I was even then on the point of mentioning that there was a balloon in the yard, and should have hazarded the statement but for my invention being divided between that phenomenon and a bear in the brewery. They were so much occupied, however, in discussing the marvels I had already presented for their consideration, that I escaped. The subject still held them when Joe came in from his work to have a cup of tea. To whom my sister, more for the relief of her own mind than for the gratification of his, related my pretended experiences.

Now, when I saw Joe open his blue eyes and roll them all round the kitchen in helpless amazement, I was overtaken by penitence; but only as regarded him—not in the least as regarded the other two. Towards Joe, and Joe only, I considered myself a young monster, while they sat debating what results would come to me from Miss Havisham's acquaintance and favour. They had no doubt that Miss Havisham would "do something" for me; their doubts related to the form that something would take. My sister stood out for "property." Mr. Pumblechook was in favour of a handsome premium for binding me apprentice to some genteel trade—say, the corn and seed trade, for instance. Joe fell into the deepest disgrace with both, for offering the bright suggestion that I might only be presented with one of the dogs who had fought for the vealcutlets. "If a fool's head can't express better opinions than that," said my sister, "and you have got any work to do, you had better go and do it." So he went.

After Mr. Pumblechook had driven off, and when my sister was washing up, I stole into the forge to Joe, and remained by him until he had done for the night. Then I said, "Before the fire goes out, Joe, I should like to tell you something."

"Should you, Pip?" said Joe, drawing his shoeing-stool near the forge. "Then tell us. What is it, Pip?"

"Joe," said I, taking hold of his rolled-up shirt sleeve, and twisting it between my finger and thumb, "you remember all that about Miss Havisham's?"

"Remember?" said Joe. "I believe you! Wonderful!"

"It's a terrible thing, Joe; it ain't true."

"What are you telling of, Pip?" cried Joe, falling back in the greatest amazement. "You don't mean to say it's——"

"Yes, I do; it's lies, Joe."

"But not all of it? Why sure you don't mean to say, Pip, that there was no black welwet co——ch?" For, I stood shaking my head. "But at least there was dogs, Pip? Come, Pip," said Joe persuasively, "if there warn't no weal-cutlets, at least there was dogs?"

"No, Joe."

"A dog?" said Joe. "A puppy? Come!"

"No, Joe, there was nothing at all of the kind."

As I fixed my eyes hopelessly on Joe, Joe contemplated me in dismay. "Pip, old chap! This won't do, old fellow! I say! Where do you expect to go to?"

"It's terrible, Joe; ain't it?"

"Terrible?" cried Joe. "Awful! What possessed you?"

"I don't know what possessed me, Joe," I replied, letting his shirt sleeve go, and sitting down in the ashes at his feet, hanging my head; "but I wish you hadn't taught me to call knaves at cards, Jacks; and I wish my boots weren't so thick nor my hands so coarse."

And then I told Joe that I felt very miserable, and that I hadn't been able to explain myself to Mrs. Joe and Pumblechook, who were so rude to me, and that there had been a beautiful young lady at Miss Havisham's who was dreadfully proud, and that she had said I was common, and that I knew I was common, and that I wished I was not common, and that the lies had come of it somehow, though I didn't know how.

This was a case of metaphysics, at least as difficult for Joe to deal with, as for me. But Joe took the case altogether out of the region of metaphysics, and by that means vanquished it.

"There's one thing you may be sure of, Pip," said Joe, after some rumination, "namely, that lies is lies. Howsever they come, they didn't ought to come, and they come from the father of lies, and work round to the same. Don't you tell no more of 'em, Pip. *That* ain't the way to get out of being common, old chap. And as to being common, I don't make it out at all clear. You are oncommon in some things. You're oncommon small. Likewise you're a oncommon scholar."

"No, I am ignorant and backward, Joe."

"Why, see what a letter you wrote last night! Wrote in print even! I've seen letters—Ah! and from gentlefolks!—that I'll swear weren't wrote in print," said Joe.

"I have learnt next to nothing, Joe. You think much of me. It's only that."

"Well, Pip," said Joe, "be it so, or be it son't, you must be a common scholar afore you can be a oncommon one, I should hope! The king upon his throne, with his crown upon his 'ed, can't sit and write his acts of Parliament in print, without having begun, when he were a unpromoted Prince, with the alphabet—Ah!" added Joe, with a shake of the head that was full of meaning, "and begun at A too, and worked his way to Z. And *I* know what that is to do, though I can't say I've exactly done it."

There was some hope in this piece of wisdom, and it rather encouraged me.

"Whether common ones as to callings and earnings," pursued Joe, reflectively, "mightn't be the better of continuing for to keep company with common ones, instead of going out to play with oncommon ones—which reminds me to hope that there were a flag, perhaps?"

"No, Joe."

"(I'm sorry there weren't a flag, Pip.) Whether that might be, or mightn't be, is a thing as can't be looked into now, without putting your sister on the Rampage; and that's a thing not to be thought of, as being done intentional. Lookee here, Pip, at what is said to you by a true friend. Which this to you the true friend say. If you can't get to be oncommon through going straight, you'll never get to do it through going crooked. So don't tell no more on 'em, Pip, and live well and die happy."

"You are not angry with me, Joe?"

"No, old chap. But bearing in mind that them were which I meantersay of a stunning and outdacious sort—alluding to them which bordered on weal-cutlets and dog fighting—a sincere well-wisher would adwise, Pip, their being dropped into your meditations, when you go upstairs to bed. That's all, old chap, and don't never do it no more."

When I got up to my little room and said my prayers, I did not forget Joe's recommendation, and yet my young mind was in that disturbed and unthankful state, that I thought long after I laid me down, how common Estella would consider Joe, a mere blacksmith: how thick his boots, and how coarse his hands. I thought how Joe and my sister were then sitting in the kitchen, and how I had come up to bed from the kitchen, and how Miss Havisham and Estella never sat in a kitchen, but were far above the level of such common doings. I fell asleep recalling what I "used to do" when I was at Miss Havisham's; as though I had been there weeks or months, instead of hours: and as though it were quite an old subject of remembrance, instead of one that had risen only that day.

That was a memorable day to me, for it made great changes in me. But it is the same with any life. Imagine one selected day struck out of it, and think how different its course would have been. Pause you who read this, and think for a moment of the long chain of iron or gold, of thorns or flowers, that would never have bound you, but for the formation of the first link on one memorable day.

CHAPTER X.

THE felicitous idea occurred to me a morning or two later when I woke, that the best step I could take towards making myself uncommon was to get out of Biddy everything she knew. In pursuance of this luminous conception, I mentioned to Biddy when I went to Mr. Wopsle's great-aunt's at night, that I had a particular reason for wishing to get on in life, and that I should feel very much obliged to her if she would impart all her learning to me. Biddy, who was the most obliging of girls, immediately said she would, and indeed began to carry out her promise within five minutes.

The Educational scheme or Course established by Mr. Wopsle's great-aunt may be resolved into the following synopsis. The pupils ate apples and put straws down one another's backs, until Mr. Wopsle's great-aunt collected her energies, and made an indiscriminate totter at them with a birch-rod. After receiving the charge with every mark of derision, the pupils formed in line and buzzingly passed a ragged book from hand to hand. The book had an alphabet in it, some figures and tables, and a little spelling—that is to say, it had had once. As soon as this volume began to circulate, Mr. Wopsle's great-aunt fell into a state of coma; arising either from sleep or a rheumatic paroxysm. The pupils then entered among themselves upon a competitive examination on the subject of Boots, with the view of ascertaining who could tread the hardest upon whose toes. This mental exercise lasted until Biddy made a rush at them and distributed three defaced Bibles (shaped as if they had been unskilfully cut off the chump-end of something), more illegibly printed at the best than any curiosities of literature I have since met with, speckled all over with ironmould, and having various specimens of the insect world smashed between their leaves. This part of the Course was usually lightened by several single combats between Biddy and refractory students. When the fights were over, Biddy gave out the number of a page, and then we all read aloud what we could—or what we couldn't—in a frightful chorus; Biddy leading with a high shrill monotonous voice, and none of us having the least notion of, or reverence for, what we were reading about. When this horrible din had lasted a certain time, it mechanically awoke Mr. Wopsle's great-aunt, who staggered at a boy fortuitously, and pulled his ears. This was understood to terminate the Course for the evening, and we emerged into the air with shrieks of intellectual victory. It is fair to remark that there was no prohibition against any pupil's entertaining himself with a slate or even with the ink (when there was any), but that it was not easy to pursue that branch of study in the winter season, on account of the little general shop in which the classes were holden—and which was also Mr. Wopsle's great-aunt's sitting-room and bed-chamber—being but faintly illuminated through the agency of one low-spirited dip-candle and no snuffers.

It appeared to me that it would take time to become uncommon under these circumstances: nevertheless, I resolved to try it, and that very evening Biddy entered on our special agreement, by imparting some information from her little catalogue of Prices, under the head of moist sugar, and lending me, to copy at home, a large old English D which she had imitated from the heading of some newspaper, and which I supposed, until she told me what it was, to be a design for a buckle.

Of course there was a public-house in the village, and of course Joe liked sometimes to smoke his pipe there. I had received strict orders from my sister to call for him at the Three Jolly Bargemen, that evening, on my way from school, and bring him home at my peril. To the Three Jolly Bargemen, therefore, I directed my steps.

There was a bar at the Jolly Bargemen, with some alarmingly long chalk scores in it on the wall at the side of the door, which seemed to me to be never paid off. They had been there ever since I could remember, and had grown more than I had. But there was a quantity of chalk about our country, and perhaps the people neglected no opportunity of turning it to account.

It being Saturday night, I found the landlord looking rather grimly at these records, but as my business was with Joe and not with him, I merely wished him good evening, and passed into the common room at the end of the passage, where there was a bright large kitchen fire, and where Joe was smoking his pipe in company with Mr. Wopsle and a stranger. Joe greeted me as usual with "Halloa, Pip, old chap!" and the moment he said that, the stranger turned his head and looked at me.

He was a secret-looking man whom I had never seen before. His head was all on one side, and one of his eyes was half shut up, as if he were taking aim at something with an invisible gun. He had a pipe in his mouth, and he took it out, and, after slowly blowing all his smoke away and looking hard at me all the time, nodded. So, I nodded, and then he nodded again, and made room on the settle beside him that I might sit down there.

But, as I was used to sit beside Joe whenever I entered that place of resort, I said "No, thank you, sir," and fell into the space Joe made for me on the opposite settle. The strange man, after glancing at Joe, and seeing that his attention was otherwise engaged, nodded to me again when I had taken my seat, and then rubbed his leg—in a very odd way, as it struck me.

"You was saying," said the strange man, turning to Joe, "that you was a blacksmith."

"Yes. I said it, you know," said Joe.

"What'll you drink, Mr. ——? You didn't mention your name, by-the-bye."

Joe mentioned it now, and the strange man called him by it.

"What'll you drink, Mr. Gargery? At my expense? To top up with?"

"Well," said Joe, "to tell you the truth, I ain't much in the habit of drinking at anybody's expense but my own."

"Habit? No," returned the stranger, "but once and away, and on a Saturday night too. Come! Put a name to it, Mr. Gargery."

"I wouldn't wish to be stiff company," said Joe. "Rum."

"Rum," repeated the stranger. "And will the other gentleman originate a sentiment."

"Rum," said Mr. Wopsle.

"Three Rums!" cried the stranger, calling to the landlord. "Glasses round!"

"This other gentleman," observed Joe, by way of introducing Mr. Wopsle, "is a gentleman that you would like to hear give it out. Our clerk at church."

"Aha!" said the stranger, quickly, and cocking his eye at me. "The lonely church, right out on the marshes, with the graves round it!"

"That's it," said Joe.

The stranger, with a comfortable kind of grunt over his pipe, put his legs up on the settle that he had to himself. He wore a flapping broad-brimmed traveller's hat, and under it a handkerchief tied over his head in the manner of a cap: so that he showed no hair. As he looked at the fire, I thought I saw a cunning expression, followed by a half-laugh, come into his face.

"I am not acquainted with this country, gentlemen, but it seems a solitary country towards the river."

"Most marshes is solitary," said Joe.

"No doubt, no doubt. Do you find any gipsies, now, or tramps, or vagrants of any sort, out there?"

"No," said Joe; "none but a runaway convict now and then. And we don't find *them*, easy. Eh, Mr. Wopsle?"

Mr. Wopsle, with a majestic remembrance of old discomfiture, assented; but not warmly.

"Seems you have been out after such?" asked the stranger.

"Once," returned Joe. "Not that we wanted to take them, you understand; we went out as lookers on; me and Mr. Wopsle, and Pip. Didn't us, Pip?"

"Yes, Joe."

The stranger looked at me again—still cocking his eye, as if he were expressly taking aim at me with his invisible gun—and said, "He's a likely young parcel of bones that. What is it you call him?"

"Pip," said Joe.

"Christened Pip?"

"No, not christened Pip."

"Surname Pip?"

"No," said Joe; "it's a kind of a family name what he gave himself when an infant, and is called by."

"Son of yours?"

"Well," said Joe, meditatively—not, of course, that it could be in anywise necessary to consider about it, but because it was the way at the Jolly Bargemen to seem to consider deeply about everything that was discussed over pipes; "well—no. No, he ain't."

"Nevvy?" said the strange man.

"Well," said Joe, with the same appearance of profound cogitation, "he is not—no, not to deceive you, he is *not*—my nevvy."

"What the Blue Blazes is he?" asked the stranger. Which appeared to me to be an inquiry of unnecessary strength.

Mr. Wopsle struck in upon that; as one who knew all about relationships, having professional occasion to bear in mind what female relations a man might not marry; and expounded the ties between me and Joe. Having his hand in, Mr. Wopsle finished off with a most terrifically snarling passage from Richard the Third, and seemed to think he had done quite enough to account for it when he added,— "as the poet says."

And here I may remark that when Mr. Wopsle referred to me, he considered it a necessary part of such reference to rumple my hair and poke it into my eyes. I cannot conceive why everybody of his standing who visited at our house should always have put me through the same inflammatory process under similar circumstances. Yet I do not call to mind that I was ever in my earlier youth the subject of remark in our social family circle, but some large-handed person took some such ophthalmic steps to patronise me.

All this while, the strange man looked at nobody but me, and looked at me as if he were determined to have a shot at me at last, and bring me down. But he said nothing after offering his Blue Blazes observation, until the glasses of rum-and-water were brought: and then he made his shot, and a most extraordinary shot it was.

It was not a verbal remark, but a proceeding in dumb show, and was pointedly addressed to me. He stirred his rum-and-water pointedly at me, and he tasted his rum-and-water pointedly at me. And he stirred it and he tasted it: not with a spoon that was brought to him, but *with a file.*

He did this so that nobody but I saw the file; and when he had done it, he wiped the file and put it in a breast-pocket. I knew it to be Joe's file, and I knew that he knew my convict, the moment I saw the instrument. I sat gazing at him, spellbound. But he now reclined on his settle, taking very little notice of me, and talking principally about turnips.

There was a delicious sense of cleaning-up and making a quiet pause before going on in life afresh, in our village on Saturday nights, which stimulated Joe to dare to stay out half an hour longer on Saturdays than at other times. The half hour and the rum-and-water running out together, Joe got up to go, and took me by the hand.

"Stop half a moment, Mr. Gargery," said the strange man. "I think I've got a bright new shilling somewhere in my pocket, and if I have, the boy shall have it."

He looked it out from a handful of small change, folded it in some crumpled paper, and gave it to me. "Yours!" said he. "Mind! Your own."

I thanked him, staring at him far beyond the bounds of good manners, and holding tight to Joe. He gave Joe good night, and he gave Mr. Wopsle good night (who went out with us), and he gave me only a look with his aiming eye—no, not a look, for he shut it up, but wonders may be done with an eye by hiding it.

On the way home, if I had been in the humour for talking, the talk must have been all on my side, for Mr. Wopsle parted from us at the door of the Jolly Bargemen, and Joe went all the way home with his mouth wide open, to rinse the rum out with as much air as possible. But I was in a manner stupefied by this turning up of my old misdeed and old acquaintance, and could think of nothing else.

My sister was not in a very bad temper when we presented ourselves in the kitchen, and Joe was encouraged by that unusual circumstance to tell her about the bright shilling. "A bad un, I'll be bound," said Mrs. Joe, triumphantly, "or he wouldn't have given it to the boy! Let's look at it."

I took it out of the paper, and it proved to be a good one. "But what's this?" said Mrs. Joe, throwing down the shilling and catching up the paper. "Two One-Pound notes?"

Nothing less than two fat sweltering one-pound notes

that seemed to have been on terms of the warmest intimacy with all the cattle markets in the county. Joe caught up his hat again, and ran with them to the Jolly Bargemen to restore them to their owner. While he was gone I sat down on my usual stool and looked vacantly at my sister, feeling pretty sure that the man would not be there.

Presently, Joe came back, saying that the man was gone, but that he, Joe, had left word at the Three Jolly Bargemen concerning the notes. Then my sister sealed them up in a piece of paper, and put them under some dried rose-leaves in an ornamental teapot on the top of a press in the state parlour. There they remained a nightmare to me many and many a night and day.

I had sadly broken sleep when I got to bed, through thinking of the strange man taking aim at me with his invisible gun, and of the guiltily coarse and common thing it was, to be on secret terms of conspiracy with convicts—a feature in my low career that I had previously forgotten. I was haunted by the file too. A dread possessed me that when I least expected it, the file would reappear. I coaxed myself to sleep by thinking of Miss Havisham's next Wednesday; and in my sleep I saw the file coming at me out of a door, without seeing who held it, and I screamed myself awake.

CHAPTER XI.

AT the appointed time I returned to Miss Havisham's, and my hesitating ring at the gate brought out Estella. She locked it after admitting me, as she had done before, and again preceded me into the dark passage where her candle stood. She took no notice of me until she had the candle in her hand, when she looked over her shoulder, superciliously saying, "You are to come this way to-day," and took me to quite another part of the house.

The passage was a long one, and seemed to pervade the whole square basement of the Manor House. We traversed but one side of the square, however, and at the end of it she stopped and put her candle down and opened a door. Here, the daylight reappeared, and I found myself in a small paved courtyard, the opposite side of which was formed by a detached dwelling-house, that looked as if it had once belonged to the manager or head clerk of the extinct brewery. There was a clock in the outer wall of this house. Like the clock in Miss Havisham's room, and like Miss Havisham's watch, it had stopped at twenty minutes to nine.

We went in at the door, which stood open, and into a gloomy room with a low ceiling, on the ground floor at the back. There was some company in the room, and Estella said to me as she joined it, "You are to go and stand there, boy, till you are wanted." "There" being the window, I crossed to it, and stood "there," in a very uncomfortable state of mind, looking out.

It opened to the ground, and looked into a most miserable corner of the neglected garden, upon a rank ruin of cabbage-stalks, and one box-tree that had been clipped round long ago, like a pudding, and had a new growth at the top of it, out of shape and of a different colour, as if that part of the pudding had stuck to the saucepan and got burnt. This was my homely thought, as I contemplated the box-tree. There had been some light snow, overnight, and it lay nowhere else to my knowledge; but, it had not quite melted from the cold shadow of this bit of garden,

and the wind caught it up in little eddies and threw it at the window, as if it pelted me for coming there.

I divined that my coming had stopped conversation in the room, and that its other occupants were looking at me. I could see nothing of the room except the shining of the fire in the window glass, but I stiffened in all my joints with the consciousness that I was under close inspection.

There were three ladies in the room and one gentleman. Before I had been standing at the window five minutes, they somehow conveyed to me that they were all toadies and humbugs, but that each of them pretended not to know that the others were toadies and humbugs: because the admission that he or she did know it, would have made him or her out to be a toady and humbug.

They all had a listless and dreary air of waiting somebody's pleasure, and the most talkative of the ladies had to speak quite rigidly to suppress a yawn. This lady, whose name was Camilla, very much reminded me of my sister, with the difference that she was older, and (as I found when I caught sight of her) of a blunter cast of features. Indeed, when I knew her better I began to think it was a mercy she had any features at all, so very blank and high was the dead wall of her face.

"Poor dear soul!" said this lady, with an abruptness of manner quite my sister's. "Nobody's enemy but his own!"

"It would be much more commendable to be somebody else's enemy," said the gentleman; "far more natural."

"Cousin Raymond," observed another lady, "we are to love our neighbour."

"Sarah Pocket," returned Cousin Raymond, "if a man is not his own neighbour, who is?"

Miss Pocket laughed, and Camilla laughed and said (checking a yawn), "The idea!" But I thought they seemed to think it rather a good idea too. The other lady, who had not spoken yet, said gravely and emphatically, "*Very* true!"

"Poor soul!" Camilla presently went on (I knew they had all been looking at me in the mean time), "he is so very strange! Would any one believe that when Tom's wife died, he actually could not be induced to see the importance of the children's having the deepest of trimmings to their mourning? 'Good Lord!' says he, 'Camilla, what can it signify so long as the poor bereaved little things are in black?' So like Matthew! The idea!"

"Good points in him, good points in him," said Cousin Raymond; "Heaven forbid I should deny good points in him; but he never had, and he never will have, any sense of the proprieties."

"You know I was obliged," said Camilla, "I was obliged to be firm. I said, 'It WILL NOT DO, for the credit of the family.' I told him that, without deep trimmings, the family was disgraced. I cried about it from breakfast till dinner. I injured my digestion. And at last he flung out in his violent way, and said, with a D, 'Then do as you like.' Thank Goodness it will always be a consolation to me to know that I instantly went out in a pouring rain and bought the things."

"*He* paid for them, did he not?" asked Estella.

"It's not the question, my dear child, who paid for them," returned Camilla. "*I* bought them. And I shall often think of that with peace, when I wake up in the night."

The ringing of a distant bell, combined with the echoing of some cry or call along the passage by which I had come, interrupted the conversation and caused Estella to say to me, "Now, boy!" On my turning round, they all looked at me with the utmost contempt, and, as I went out, I heard Sarah Pocket say, "Well I am sure! What next!" and Camilla add, with indignation, "Was there ever such a fancy! The i-de-a!"

As we were going with our candle along the dark passage, Estella stopped all of a sudden, and, facing round, said in her taunting manner, with her face quite close to mine:

"Well?"

"Well, miss," I answered, almost falling over her and checking myself.

She stood looking at me, and of course I stood looking at her.

"Am I pretty?"

"Yes; I think you are very pretty."

"Am I insulting?"

"Not so much so as you were last time," said I.

"Not so much so?"

"No."

She fired when she asked the last question, and she slapped my face with such force as she had, when I answered it.

"Now?" said she. "You little coarse monster, what do you think of me now?"

"I shall not tell you."

"Because you are going to tell upstairs. Is that it?"

"No," said I, "that's not it."

"Why don't you cry again, you little wretch?"

"Because I'll never cry for you again," said I. Which was, I suppose, as false a declaration as ever was made; for I was inwardly crying for her then, and I know what I know of the pain she cost me afterwards.

We went on our way upstairs after this episode; and, as we were going up, we met a gentleman groping his way down.

"Whom have we here?" asked the gentleman, stopping and looking at me.

"A boy," said Estella.

He was a burly man of an exceedingly dark complexion, with an exceedingly large head, and a corresponding large hand. He took my chin in his large hand and turned up my face to have a look at me by the light of the candle. He was prematurely bald on the top of his head, and had bushy black eyebrows that wouldn't lie down, but stood up bristling. His eyes were set very deep in his head, and were disagreeably sharp and suspicious. He had a large watch-chain, and strong black dots where his beard and whiskers would have been if he had let them. He was nothing to me, and I could have had no foresight then, that he ever would be anything to me, but it happened that I had this opportunity of observing him well.

"Boy of the neighbourhood? Hey?" said he.

"Yes, sir," said I.

"How do you come here?"

"Miss Havisham sent for me, sir," I explained.

"Well! Behave yourself. I have a pretty large experience of boys, and you're a bad set of fellows. Now mind!" said he, biting the side of his great forefinger as he frowned at me, "you behave yourself!"

With these words he released me—which I was glad of, for his hand smelt of scented soap—and went his way downstairs. I wondered whether he could be a doctor; but no, I thought; he couldn't be a doctor, or he would have a quieter and more persuasive manner. There was not much time to consider the subject, for we were soon in Miss Havisham's room, where she and everything else were just as I had left them. Estella left me standing near the door, and I stood there until Miss Havisham cast her eyes upon me from the dressing-table.

"So!" she said, without being startled or surprised; "the days have worn away, have they?"

"Yes, ma'am. To-day is——"

"There, there, there!" with the impatient movement of her fingers. "I don't want to know. Are you ready to play?"

I was obliged to answer in some confusion, "I don't think I am, ma'am."

"Not at cards again?" she demanded with a searching look.

"Yes, ma'am; I could do that, if I was wanted."

"Since this house strikes you old and grave, boy," said Miss Havisham, impatiently, "and you are unwilling to play, are you willing to work?"

I could answer this inquiry with a better heart than I had been able to find for the other question, and I said I was quite willing.

"Then go into that opposite room," said she, pointing at the door behind me with her withered hand, "and wait there till I come."

I crossed the staircase landing, and entered the room she indicated. From that room, too, the daylight was completely excluded, and it had an airless smell that was oppressive. A fire had been lately kindled in the damp old-fashioned grate, and it was more disposed to go out than to burn up, and the reluctant smoke which hung in the room seemed colder than the clearer air—like our own marsh mist. Certain wintry branches of candles on the high chimneypiece faintly lighted the chamber; or, it would be more expressive to say, faintly troubled its darkness. It was spacious, and I dare say had once been handsome, but every discernible thing in it was covered with dust and mould, and dropping to pieces. The most prominent object was a long table with a tablecloth spread on it, as if a feast had been in preparation when the house and the clocks all stopped together. An épergne or centre-piece of some kind was in the middle of this cloth; it was so heavily overhung with cobwebs that its form was quite undistinguishable; and, as I looked along the yellow expanse out of which I remember its seeming to grow, like a black fungus, I saw speckled-legged spiders with blotchy bodies running home to it, and running out from it, as if some circumstance of the greatest public importance had just transpired in the spider community.

I heard the mice too, rattling behind the panels, as if the same occurrence were important to their interests. But, the blackbeetles took no notice of the agitation, and groped about the hearth in a ponderous elderly way, as if they were shortsighted and hard of hearing, and not on terms with one another.

These crawling things had fascinated my attention, and I was watching them from a distance, when Miss Havisham laid a hand upon my shoulder. In her other hand she had a crutch-headed stick on which she leaned, and she looked like the Witch of the place.

"This," said she, pointing to the long table with her stick, "is where I will be laid when I am dead. They shall come and look at me here."

With some vague misgiving that she might get upon the table then and there and die at once, the complete realisation of the ghastly waxwork at the Fair, I shrank under her touch.

"What do you think that is?" she asked me, again

pointing with her stick; "that, where those cobwebs are?"

"I can't guess what it is, ma'am."

"It's a great cake. A bride-cake. Mine!"

She looked all round the room in a glaring manner, and then said, leaning on me while her hand twitched my shoulder, "Come, come, come! Walk me, walk me!"

I made out from this, that the work I had to do, was to walk Miss Havisham round and round the room. Accordingly, I started at once, and she leaned upon my shoulder, and we went away at a pace that might have been an imitation (founded on my first impulse under that roof) of Mr. Pumblechook's chaise-cart.

She was not physically strong, and after a little time said, "Slower!" Still, we went at an impatient fitful speed, and as we went, she twitched the hand upon my shoulder, and worked her mouth, and led me to believe that we were going fast because her thoughts went fast. After a while she said, "Call Estella!" so I went out on the landing and roared that name as I had done on the previous occasion. When her light appeared, I returned to Miss Havisham, and we started away again round and round the room.

If only Estella had come to be a spectator of our proceedings, I should have felt sufficiently discontented; but, as she brought with her the three ladies and the gentleman whom I had seen below, I didn't know what to do. In my politeness I would have stopped; but, Miss Havisham twitched my shoulder, and we posted on—with a shame-faced consciousness on my part that they would think it was all my doing.

"Dear Miss Havisham," said Miss Sarah Pocket. "How well you look!"

"I do not," returned Miss Havisham. "I am yellow skin and bone."

Camilla brightened when Miss Pocket met with this rebuff; and she murmured, as she plaintively contemplated Miss Havisham, "Poor dear soul! Certainly not to be expected to look well, poor thing. The idea!"

"And how are *you?*" said Miss Havisham to Camilla. As we were close to Camilla then, I would have stopped as a matter of course, only Miss Havisham wouldn't stop. We swept on, and I felt that I was highly obnoxious to Camilla.

"Thank you, Miss Havisham," she returned, "I am as well as can be expected."

"Why, what's the matter with you?" asked Miss Havisham, with exceeding sharpness.

"Nothing worth mentioning," replied Camilla. "I don't wish to make a display of my feelings, but I have habitually thought of you more in the night than I am quite equal to."

"Then don't think of me," retorted Miss Havisham.

"Very easily said!" remarked Camilla, amiably repressing a sob, while a hitch came into her upper lip, and her tears overflowed. "Raymond is a witness what ginger and sal volatile I am obliged to take in the night. Raymond is a witness what nervous jerkings I have in my legs. Chokings and nervous jerkings, however, are nothing new to me when I think with anxiety of those I love. If I could be less affectionate and sensitive, I should have a better digestion and an iron set of nerves. I am sure I wish it could be so. But as to not thinking of you in the night—the idea!" Here, a burst of tears.

The Raymond referred to, I understood to be the gentleman present, and him I understood to be Mr. Camilla. He came to the rescue at this point, and said in a consolatory and complimentary voice, "Camilla, my dear, it is well known that your family feelings are gradually undermining

you to the extent of making one of your legs shorter than the other."

"I am not aware," observed the grave lady whose voice I had heard but once, "that to think of any person is to make a great claim upon that person, my dear."

Miss Sarah Pocket, whom I now saw to be a little dry brown corrugated old woman, with a small face that might have been made of walnut shells, and a large mouth like a cat's without the whiskers, supported this position by saying, "No, indeed, my dear. Hem!"

"Thinking is easy enough," said the grave lady.

"What is easier, you know?" assented Miss Sarah Pocket.

"Oh, yes, yes!" cried Camilla, whose fermenting feelings appeared to rise from her legs to her bosom. "It's all very true! It's a weakness to be so affectionate, but I can't help it. No doubt my health would be much better if it was otherwise, still I wouldn't change my disposition if I could. It's the cause of much suffering, but it's a consolation to know I possess it, when I wake up in the night." Here another burst of feeling.

Miss Havisham and I had never stopped all this time, but kept going round and round the room: now, brushing against the skirts of the visitors: now, giving them the whole length of the dismal chamber.

"There's Matthew!" said Camilla. "Never mixing with any natural ties, never coming here to see how Miss Havisham is! I have taken to the sofa with my stay-lace cut, and have lain there hours, insensible, with my head over the side, and my hair all down, and my feet I don't know where——"

("Much higher than your head, my love," said Mr. Camilla.)

"I have gone off into that state, hours and hours, on account of Matthew's strange and inexplicable conduct, and nobody has thanked me."

"Really I must say I should think not!" interposed the grave lady.

"You see, my dear," added Miss Sarah Pocket (a blandly vicious personage), "the question to put to yourself is, who did you expect to thank you, my love?"

"Without expecting any thanks, or anything of the sort," resumed Camilla, "I have remained in that state hours and hours, and Raymond is a witness of the extent to which I have choked, and what the total inefficacy of ginger has been, and I have been heard at the pianoforte-tuner's across the street, where the poor mistaken children have even supposed it to be pigeons cooing at a distance—and now to be told——" Here Camilla put her hand to her throat, and began to be quite chemical as to the formation of new combinations there.

When this same Matthew was mentioned, Miss Havisham stopped me and herself, and stood looking at the speaker. This change had a great influence in bringing Camilla's chemistry to a sudden end.

"Matthew will come and see me at last," said Miss Havisham, sternly, "when I am laid on that table. That will be his place—there," striking the table with her stick, "at my head! And yours will be there! And your husband's there! And Sarah Pocket's there! And Georgiana's there! Now you all know where to take your stations when you come to feast upon me. And now go!"

At the mention of each name, she had struck the table with her stick in a new place. She now said, "Walk me, walk me!" and we went on again.

"I suppose there's nothing to be done," exclaimed Camilla, "but comply and depart. It's something to have seen the object of one's love and duty, even for so short a time. I shall think of it with a melancholy satisfaction when I wake up in the night. I wish Matthew could have that comfort, but he sets it at defiance. I am determined not to make a display of my feelings, but it's very hard to be told one wants to feast on one's relations—as if one was a Giant—and to be told to go. The bare idea!"

Mr. Camilla interposing, as Mrs. Camilla laid her hand upon her heaving bosom, that lady assumed an unnatural fortitude of manner which I supposed to be expressive of an intention to drop and choke when out of view, and kissing her hand to Miss Havisham, was escorted forth. Sarah Pocket and Georgiana contended who should remain last; but, Sarah was too knowing to be outdone, and ambled round Georgiana with that artful slipperiness, that the latter was obliged to take precedence. Sarah Pocket then made her separate effect of departing with "Bless you, Miss Havisham dear!" and with a smile of forgiving pity on her walnut-shell countenance for the weaknesses of the rest.

While Estella was away lighting them down, Miss Havisham still walked with her hand on my shoulder, but more and more slowly. At last she stopped before the fire, and said, after muttering and looking at it some seconds:

"This is my birthday, Pip."

I was going to wish her many happy returns, when she lifted her stick.

"I don't suffer it to be spoken of. I don't suffer those who were here just now, or any one, to speak of it. They come here on the day, but they dare not refer to it."

Of course I made no further effort to refer to it.

"On this day of the year, long before you were born, this heap of decay," stabbing with her crutched stick at the pile of cobwebs on the table, but not touching it, "was brought here. It and I have worn away together. The mice have gnawed at it, and sharper teeth than teeth of mice have gnawed at me."

She held the head of her stick against her heart as she stood looking at the table; she in her once white dress, all yellow and withered; the once white cloth all yellow and withered; everything around, in a state to crumble under a touch.

"When the ruin is complete," said she, with a ghastly look, "and when they lay me dead, in my bride's dress on the bride's table—which shall be done, and which will be the finished curse upon him—so much the better if it is done on this day!"

She stood looking at the table as if she stood looking at her own figure lying there. I remained quiet. Estella returned, and she too remained quiet. It seemed to me that we continued thus a long time. In the heavy air of the room, and the heavy darkness that brooded in its remoter corners, I even had an alarming fancy that Estella and I might presently begin to decay.

At length, not coming out of her distraught state by degrees, but in an instant, Miss Havisham said, "Let me see you two play at cards; why have you not begun?" With that, we returned to her room, and sat down as before; I was beggared, as before; and again, as before, Miss Havisham watched us all the time, directed my attention to Estella's beauty, and made me notice it the more by trying her jewels on Estella's breast and hair.

Estella, for her part, likewise treated me as before; except that she did not condescend to speak. When we had played some half-dozen games, a day was appointed for my return, and I was taken down into the yard to be fed in the former dog-like manner. There, too, I was again left to wander about as I liked.

It is not much to the purpose whether a gate in that garden wall which I had scrambled up to peep over on the last occasion was, on that last occasion, open or shut. Enough that I saw no gate then, and that I saw one now. As it stood open, and as I knew that Estella had let the visitors out—for, she had returned with the keys in her hand—I strolled into the garden, and strolled all over it. It was quite a wilderness, and there were old melon-frames and cucumber-frames in it, which seemed in their decline to have produced a spontaneous growth of weak attempts at pieces of old hats and boots, with now and then a weedy offshoot into the likeness of a battered saucepan.

When I had exhausted the garden and a greenhouse with nothing in it but a fallen-down grape-vine and some bottles, I found myself in the dismal corner upon which I had looked out of window. Never questioning for a moment that the house was now empty, I looked in at another window, and found myself, to my great surprise, exchanging a broad stare with a pale young gentleman with red eyelids and light hair.

This pale young gentleman quickly disappeared, and reappeared beside me. He had been at his books when I had found myself staring at him, and I now saw that he was inky.

"Halloa!" said he, "young fellow!"

Halloa being a general observation which I had usually observed to be best answered by itself, I said "Halloa!" politely omitting young fellow.

"Who let you in?" said he.

"Miss Estella."

"Who gave you leave to prowl about?"

"Miss Estella."

"Come and fight," said the pale young gentleman.

What could I do but follow him? I have often asked myself the question since: but, what else could I do? His manner was so final and I was so astonished, that I followed where he led, as if I had been under a spell.

"Stop a minute, though," he said, wheeling round before we had gone many paces. "I ought to give you a reason for fighting, too. There it is!" In a most irritating manner he instantly slapped his hands against one another, daintily flung one of his legs up behind him, pulled my hair, slapped his hands again, dipped his head, and butted it into my stomach.

The bull-like proceeding last mentioned, besides that it was unquestionably to be regarded in the light of a liberty, was particularly disagreeable just after bread and meat. I therefore hit out at him, and was going to hit out again, when he said, "Aha! Would you?" and began dancing backwards and forwards in a manner quite unparalleled within my limited experience.

"Laws of the game!" said he. Here, he skipped from his left leg on to his right. "Regular rules!" Here, he skipped from his right leg on to his left. "Come to the ground, and go through the preliminaries!" Here, he dodged backwards and forwards, and did all sorts of things while I looked helplessly at him.

I was secretly afraid of him when I saw him so dexterous; but, I felt morally and physically convinced that his light head of hair could have had no business in the pit of my stomach, and that I had a right to consider it irrelevant when so obtruded on my attention. Therefore, I followed him without a word, to a retired nook of the garden, formed by the junction of two walls and screened by some rubbish. On his asking me if I was satisfied with the ground, and on my replying Yes, he begged my leave to absent himself for a moment, and quickly returned with a bottle of water and a sponge dipped in vinegar. "Available for both," he said, placing these against the wall. And then fell to pulling off, not only his jacket and waistcoat, but his shirt too, in a manner at once light-hearted, business-like, and bloodthirsty.

Although he did not look very healthy—having pimples on his face, and a breaking out on his mouth—these dreadful preparations quite appalled me. I judged him to be about my own age, but he was much taller, and he had a way of spinning himself about that was full of appearance. For the rest, he was a young gentleman in a grey suit (when not denuded for battle), with his elbows, knees, wrists, and heels considerably in advance of the rest of him as to development.

My heart failed me when I saw him squaring at me with every demonstration of mechanical nicety, and eyeing my anatomy as if he were minutely choosing my bone. I never have been so surprised in my life, as I was when I let out the first blow, and saw him lying on his back, looking up at me with a bloody nose and his face exceedingly foreshortened.

But, he was on his feet directly, and after sponging himself with a great show of dexterity began squaring again. The second greatest surprise I have ever had in my life was seeing him on his back again, looking up at me out of a black eye.

His spirit inspired me with great respect. He seemed to have no strength, and he never once hit me hard, and he was always knocked down; but, he would be up again in a moment, sponging himself or drinking out of the water-bottle, with the greatest satisfaction in seconding himself according to form, and then came at me with an air and a show that made me believe he really was going to do for me at last. He got heavily bruised, for I am sorry to record that the more I hit him, the harder I hit him; but, he came up again and again and again, until at last he got a bad fall with the back of his head against the wall. Even after that crisis in our affairs, he got up and turned round and round confusedly a few times, not knowing where I was; but finally went on his knees to his sponge and threw it up: at the same time panting out, "That means you have won."

He seemed so brave and innocent, that although I had not proposed the contest, I felt but a gloomy satisfaction in my victory. Indeed, I go so far as to hope that I regarded myself while dressing, as a species of savage young wolf, or other wild beast. However, I got dressed, darkly wiping my sanguinary face at intervals, and I said, "Can I help you?" and he said, "No thankee," and I said, "Good afternoon," and he said, "Same to you."

When I got into the courtyard, I found Estella waiting with the keys. But, she neither asked me where I had been, nor why I had kept her waiting; and there was a bright flush upon her face, as though something had happened to delight her. Instead of going straight to the gate, too, she stepped back into the passage, and beckoned me.

"Come here! You may kiss me if you like."

I kissed her cheek as she turned it to me. I think I would have gone through a great deal to kiss her cheek.

But, I felt that the kiss was given to the coarse common boy as a piece of money might have been, and that it was worth nothing.

What with the birthday visitors, and what with the cards, and what with the fight, my stay had lasted so long, that when I neared home the light on the spit of sand off the point on the marshes was gleaming against a black night-sky, and Joe's furnace was flinging a path of fire across the road.

CHAPTER XII.

My mind grew very uneasy on the subject of the pale young gentleman. The more I thought of the fight, and recalled the pale young gentleman on his back in various stages of puffy and incrimsoned countenance, the more certain it appeared that something would be done to me. I felt that the pale young gentleman's blood was on my head, and that the Law would avenge it. Without having any definite idea of the penalties I had incurred, it was clear to me that village boys could not go stalking about the country, ravaging the houses of gentlefolks and pitching into the studious youth of England, without laying themselves open to severe punishment. For some days, I even kept close at home, and looked out at the kitchen door with the greatest caution and trepidation before going on an errand, lest the officers of the County Jail should pounce upon me. The pale young gentleman's nose had stained my trousers, and I tried to wash out that evidence of my guilt in the dead of night. I had cut my knuckles against the pale young gentleman's teeth, and I twisted my imagination into a thousand tangles, as I devised incredible ways of accounting for that damnatory circumstance when I should be haled before the Judges.

When the day came round for my return to the scene of the deed of violence, my terrors reached their height. Whether myrmidons of Justice, specially sent down from London, would be lying in ambush behind the gate? Whether Miss Havisham, preferring to take personal vengeance for an outrage done to her house, might rise in those grave-clothes of hers, draw a pistol, and shoot me dead? Whether suborned boys—a numerous band of mercenaries—might be engaged to fall upon me in the brewery, and cuff me until I was no more? It was high testimony to my confidence in the spirit of the pale young gentleman, that I never imagined *him* accessory to these retaliations; they always came into my mind as the acts of injudicious relatives of his, goaded on by the state of his visage and an indignant sympathy with the family features.

However, go to Miss Havisham's I must, and go I did. And behold! nothing came of the late struggle. It was not alluded to in any way, and no pale young gentleman was to be discovered on the premises. I found the same gate open, and I explored the garden, and even looked in at the windows of the detached house; but, my view was suddenly stopped by the closed shutters within, and all was lifeless. Only in the corner where the combat had taken place, could I detect any evidence of the young gentleman's existence. There were traces of his gore in that spot, and I covered them with garden-mould from the eye of man.

On the broad landing between Miss Havisham's own room and that other room in which the long table was laid out, I saw a garden-chair—a light chair on wheels, that you pushed from behind. It had been placed there since my last visit, and I entered, that same day, on a regular occupation of pushing Miss Havisham in this chair (when she was tired of walking with her hand upon my shoulder) round her own room, and across the landing, and round the other room. Over and over and over again, we would make these journeys, and sometimes they would last as long as three hours at a stretch. I insensibly fall into a general mention of these journeys as numerous, because it was at once settled that I should return every alternate day at noon for these purposes, and because I am now going to sum up a period of at least eight or ten months.

As we began to be more used to one another, Miss Havisham talked more to me, and asked me such questions as what had I learnt and what was I going to be? I told her I was going to be apprenticed to Joe, I believed; and I enlarged upon my knowing nothing and wanting to know everything, in the hope that she might offer some help towards that desirable end. But, she did not; on the contrary, she seemed to prefer my being ignorant. Neither did she ever give me any money or anything but my daily dinner—nor even stipulate that I should be paid for my services.

Estella was always about, and always let me in and out, but never told me I might kiss her again. Sometimes, she would coldly tolerate me; sometimes, she would condescend to me; sometimes, she would be quite familiar with me; sometimes, she would tell me energetically that she hated me. Miss Havisham would often ask me in a whisper, or when we were alone, "Does she grow prettier and prettier, Pip?" And when I said Yes (for indeed she did), would seem to enjoy it greedily. Also, when we played at cards Miss Havisham would look on, with a miserly relish of Estella's moods, whatever they were. And sometimes, when her moods were so many and so contradictory of one another that I was puzzled what to say or do, Miss Havisham would embrace her with lavish fondness, murmuring something in her ear that sounded like "Break their hearts, my pride and hope, break their hearts and have no mercy!"

There was a song Joe used to hum fragments of at the forge, of which the burden was Old Clem. This was not a very ceremonious way of rendering homage to a patron saint; but I believe Old Clem stood in that relation toward smiths. It was a song that imitated the measure of beating upon iron, and was a mere lyrical excuse for the introduction of Old Clem's respected name. Thus, you were to hammer boys round—Old Clem! With a thump and a sound—Old Clem! Beat it out, beat it out—Old Clem! With a clink for the stout—Old Clem! Blow the fire, blow the fire—Old Clem! Roaring dryer, soaring higher—Old Clem! One day soon after the appearance of the chair, Miss Havisham suddenly saying to me, with the impatient movement of her fingers, "There, there, there! Sing!" I was surprised into crooning this ditty as I pushed her over the floor. It happened so to catch her fancy that she took it up in a low brooding voice as if she were singing in her sleep. After that, it became customary with us to have it as we moved about, and Estella would often join in; though the whole strain was so subdued, even when there were three of us, that it made less noise in the grim old house than the lightest breath of wind.

What could I become with these surroundings? How could my character fail to be influenced by them? Is it to be wondered at if my thoughts were dazed, as my eyes were, when I came out into the natural light from the misty yellow rooms?

Perhaps I might have told Joe about the pale young gentleman, if I had not previously been betrayed into those enormous inventions to which I had confessed. Under the circumstances, I felt that Joe could hardly fail to discern in the pale young gentleman, an appropriate passenger to be put into the black velvet coach; therefore, I said nothing of him. Besides: that shrinking from having Miss Havisham and Estella discussed, which had come upon me in the beginning, grew much more potent as time went on. I reposed complete confidence in no one but Biddy: but, I told poor Biddy everything. Why it came natural for me to do so, and why Biddy had a deep concern in everything I told her, I did not know then, though I think I know now.

Meanwhile, councils went on in the kitchen at home, fraught with almost insupportable aggravation to my exasperated spirit. That ass, Pumblechook, used often to come over of a night for the purpose of discussing my prospects with my sister; and I really do believe (to this hour with less penitence than I ought to feel), that if these hands could have taken a linchpin out of his chaise-cart, they would have done it. The miserable man was a man of that confined stolidity of mind, that he could not discuss my prospects without having me before him—as it were, to operate upon—and he would drag me up from my stool (usually by the collar) where I was quiet in a corner, and, putting me before the fire as if I were going to be cooked, would begin by saying, "Now, Mum, here is this boy! Here is this boy which you brought up by hand. Hold up your head, boy, and be for ever grateful unto them which so did do. Now, Mum, with respections to this boy!" And then he would rumple my hair the wrong way—which from my earliest remembrance, as already hinted, I have in my soul denied the right of any fellow-creature to do—and would hold me before him by the sleeve: a spectacle of imbecility only to be equalled by himself.

Then, he and my sister would pair off in such nonsensical speculations about Miss Havisham, and about what she would do with me and for me, that I used to want—quite painfully—to burst into spiteful tears, fly at Pumblechook, and pummel him all over. In these dialogues, my sister spoke to me as if she were morally wrenching one of my teeth out at every reference; while Pumblechook himself, self-constituted my patron, would sit supervising me with a depreciatory eye, like the architect of my fortunes who thought himself engaged in a very unremunerative job.

In these discussions, Joe bore no part. But he was often talked at, while they were in progress, by reason of Mrs. Joe's perceiving that he was not favourable to my being taken from the forge. I was fully old enough now, to be apprenticed to Joe; and when Joe sat with the poker on his knees thoughtfully raking out the ashes between the lower bars, my sister would so distinctly construe that innocent action into opposition on his part, that she would dive at him, take the poker out of his hands, shake him, and put it away. There was a most irritating end to every one of these debates. All in a moment, with nothing to lead up to it, my sister would stop herself in a yawn, and catching sight of me as it were incidentally, would swoop upon me with "Come! there's enough of you! You get along to bed; you've given trouble enough for one night, I hope!" As if I had besought them as a favour to bother my life out.

We went on in this way for a long time, and it seemed

likely that we should continue to go on in this way for a long time, when, one day, Miss Havisham stopped short as she and I were walking, she leaning on my shoulder; and said with some displeasure:

"You are growing tall, Pip!"

I thought it best to hint, through the medium of a meditative look, that this might be occasioned by circumstances over which I had no control.

She said no more at the time; but, she presently stopped and looked at me again; and presently again; and after that, looked frowning and moody. On the next day of my attendance, when our usual exercise was over, and I had landed her at her dressing-table, she stayed me with a movement of her impatient fingers:

"Tell me the name again of that blacksmith of yours."

"Joe Gargery, ma'am."

"Meaning the master you were to be apprenticed to?"

"Yes, Miss Havisham."

"You had better be apprenticed at once. Would Gargery come here with you, and bring your indentures, do you think?"

I signified that I had no doubt he would take it as an honour to be asked.

"Then let him come."

"At any particular time, Miss Havisham?"

"There, there! I know nothing about times. Let him come soon, and come alone with you."

When I got home at night, and delivered this message for Joe, my sister "went on the Rampage," in a more alarming degree than at any previous period. She asked me and Joe whether we supposed she was door-mats under our feet, and how we dared to use her so, and what company we graciously thought she *was* fit for? When she had exhausted a torrent of such inquiries, she threw a candlestick at Joe, burst into a loud sobbing, got out the dustpan—which was always a very bad sign—put on her coarse apron, and began cleaning up to a terrible extent. Not satisfied with a dry cleaning, she took to a pail and scrubbing-brush, and cleaned us out of house and home, so that we stood shivering in the backyard. It was ten o'clock at night before we ventured to creep in again, and then she asked Joe why he had not married a Negress Slave at once? Joe offered no answer, poor fellow, but stood feeling his whiskers and looking dejectedly at me, as if he thought it really might have been a better speculation.

CHAPTER XIII.

It was a trial to my feelings, on the next day but one, to see Joe arraying himself in his Sunday clothes to accompany me to Miss Havisham's. However, as he thought his court-suit necessary to the occasion, it was not for me to tell him that he looked far better in his working dress; the rather, because I knew he made himself so dreadfully uncomfortable, entirely on my account, and that it was for me he pulled up his shirt-collar so very high behind, that it made the hair on the crown of his head stand up like a tuft of feathers.

At breakfast-time, my sister declared her intention of going to town with us, and being left at Uncle Pumblechook's, and called for "when we had done with our fine ladies"—a way of putting the case, from which Joe appeared inclined to augur the worst. The forge was shut up

for the day, and Joe inscribed in chalk upon the door (as it was his custom to do on the very rare occasions when he was not at work) the monosyllable HOUT, accompanied by a sketch of an arrow supposed to be flying in the direction he had taken.

We walked to town, my sister leading the way in a very large beaver bonnet, and carrying a basket like the Great Seal of England in plaited straw, a pair of pattens, a spare shawl, and an umbrella, though it was a fine bright day. I am not quite clear whether these articles were carried penitentially or ostentatiously; but, I rather think they were displayed as articles of property—much as Cleopatra or any other sovereign lady on the Rampage might exhibit her wealth in a pageant or procession.

When we came to Pumblechook's, my sister bounced in and left us. As it was almost noon, Joe and I held straight on to Miss Havisham's house. Estella opened the gate as usual, and, the moment she appeared, Joe took his hat off and stood weighing it by the brim in both his hands: as if he had some urgent reason in his mind for being particular to half a quarter of an ounce.

Estella took no notice of either of us, but led us the way that I knew so well. I followed next to her, and Joe came last. When I looked back at Joe in the long passage, he was still weighing his hat with the greatest care, and was coming after us in long strides on the tips of his toes.

Estella told me we were both to go in, so I took Joe by the coat-cuff and conducted him into Miss Havisham's presence. She was seated at her dressing-table, and looked round at us immediately.

"Oh!" said she to Joe. "You are the husband of the sister of this boy?"

I could hardly have imagined dear old Joe looking so unlike himself or so like some extraordinary bird; standing, as he did, speechless, with his tuft of feathers ruffled, and his mouth open as if he wanted a worm.

"You are the husband," repeated Miss Havisham, "of the sister of this boy?"

It was very aggravating; but, throughout the interview, Joe persisted in addressing Me instead of Miss Havisham.

"Which I meantersay, Pip," Joe now observed, in a manner that was at once expressive of forcible argumentation, strict confidence, and great politeness, "as I hup and married your sister, and I were at the time what you might call (if you was any ways inclined) a single man."

"Well!" said Miss Havisham. "And you have reared the boy, with the intention of taking him for your apprentice; is that so, Mr. Gargery?"

"You know, Pip," replied Joe, "as you and me were ever friends, and it were looked for'ard to betwixt us, as being calc'lated to lead to larks. Not but what, Pip, if you had ever made objections to the business—such as its being open to black and sut, or such-like—not but what they would have been attended to, don't you see?"

"Has the boy," said Miss Havisham, "ever made any objection? Does he like the trade?"

"Which it is well beknown to yourself, Pip," returned Joe, strengthening his former mixture of argumentation, confidence, and politeness, "that it were the wish of your own hart." (I saw the idea suddenly break upon him that he would adapt his epitaph to the occasion, before he went on to say) "And there weren't no objection on your part, and Pip it were the great wish of your hart!"

It was quite in vain for me to endeavour to make him sensible that he ought to speak to Miss Havisham. The more I made faces and gestures to him to do it, the more confidential, argumentative, and polite, he persisted in being to Me.

"Have you brought his indentures with you?" asked Miss Havisham.

"Well, Pip, you know," replied Joe, as if that were a little unreasonable, "you yourself see me put 'em in my 'at, and therefore you know as they are here." With which he took them out, and gave them, not to Miss Havisham, but to me. I am afraid I was ashamed of the dear good fellow—I *know* I was ashamed of him—when I saw that Estella stood at the back of Miss Havisham's chair, and that her eyes laughed mischievously. I took the indentures out of his hand and gave them to Miss Havisham.

"You expected," said Miss Havisham, as she looked them over, "no premium with the boy?"

"Joe!" I remonstrated; for he made no reply at all. "Why don't you answer——"

"Pip," returned Joe, cutting me short as if he were hurt, "which I meantersay that were not a question requiring a answer betwixt yourself and me, and which you know the answer to be full well No. You know it to be No, Pip, and wherefore should I say it?"

Miss Havisham glanced at him as if she understood what he really was, better than I had thought possible, seeing what he was there; and took up a little bag from the table beside her.

"Pip has earned a premium here," she said, "and here it is. There are five-and-twenty guineas in this bag. Give it to your master, Pip!"

As if he were absolutely out of his mind with the wonder awakened in him by her strange figure and the strange room, Joe, even at this pass, persisted in addressing me.

"This is very liberal on your part, Pip," said Joe, "and it is as such received and grateful welcome, though never looked for, far nor near nor nowheres. And now, old chap," said Joe, conveying to me a sensation, first of burning and then of freezing, for I felt as if that familiar expression were applied to Miss Havisham; "and now, old chap, may we do our duty! May you and me do our duty, both on us by one and another, and by them which your liberal present —have—conweyed—to be—for the satisfaction of mind— of—them as never—" here Joe showed that he felt he had fallen into frightful difficulties, until he triumphantly rescued himself with the words, "and from myself far be it!" These words had such a round and convincing sound for him that he said them twice.

"Good bye, Pip!" said Miss Havisham. "Let them out, Estella."

"Am I to come again, Miss Havisham?" I asked.

"No. Gargery is your master now. Gargery! One word!"

Thus calling him back as I went out of the door, I heard her say to Joe, in a distinct emphatic voice, "The boy has been a good boy here, and that is his reward. Of course, as an honest man, you will expect no other and no more."

How Joe got out of the room, I have never been able to determine; but, I know that when he did get out he was steadily proceeding upstairs instead of coming down, and was deaf to all remonstrances until I went after him and laid hold of him. In another minute we were outside the gate, and it was locked, and Estella was gone. When we stood in the daylight alone again, Joe backed up against a wall, and said to me, "Astonishing!" And there he remained so long, saying "Astonishing" at intervals, so often, that I began to think his senses were never coming

back. At length, he prolonged his remark into "Pip, I do assure *you* this is as-ton-ishing!" and so, by degrees, became conversational and able to walk away.

I have reason to think that Joe's intellects were brightened by the encounter they had passed through, and that on our way to Pumblechook's, he invented a subtle and deep design. My reason is to be found in what took place in Mr. Pumblechook's parlour: where, on our presenting ourselves, my sister sat in conference with that detested seedsman.

"Well!" cried my sister, addressing us both at once. "And what's happened to *you*? I wonder you condescended to come back to such poor society as this, I am sure I do!"

"Miss Havisham," said Joe, with a fixed look at me, like an effort of remembrance, "made it wery partick'ler that we should give her—were it compliments or respects, Pip?"

"Compliments," I said.

"Which that were my own belief," answered Joe—"her compliments to Mrs. J. Gargery——"

"Much good they'll do me!" observed my sister: but rather gratified too.

"And wishing," pursued Joe, with another fixed look at me, like another effort of remembrance, "that the state of Miss Havisham's elth were sitch as would have—allowed, were it, Pip?"

"Of her having the pleasure," I added.

"Of ladies' company," said Joe. And drew a long breath

"Well!" cried my sister, with a mollified glance at Mr. Pumblechook. "She might have had the politeness to send that message at first, but it's better late than never. And what did she give young Rantipole here?"

"She giv' him," said Joe, "nothing."

Mrs. Joe was going to break out, but Joe went on.

"What she giv'," said Joe, "she giv' to his friends. 'And by his friends,' were her explanation, 'I mean into the hands of his sister, Mrs. J. Gargery.' Them were her words; 'Mrs. J. Gargery.' She mayn't have know'd," added Joe, with an appearance of reflection, "whether it were Joe or Jorge."

My sister looked at Pumblechook: who smoothed the elbows of his wooden arm-chair, and nodded at her and at the fire as if he had known all about it beforehand.

"And how much have you got?" asked my sister, laughing. Positively, laughing!

"What would present company say to ten pound?" demanded Joe.

"They'd say," returned my sister curtly, "pretty well. Not too much, but pretty well."

"It's more than that, then," said Joe.

That fearful impostor, Pumblechook, immediately nodded, and said, as he rubbed the arms of his chair: "It's more than that, Mum."

"Why, you don't mean to say——" began my sister.

"Yes I do, Mum," said Pumblechook; "but wait a bit. Go on, Joseph. Good in you! Go on!"

"What would present company say," proceeded Joe, "to twenty pound?"

"Handsome would be the word," returned my sister.

"Well then," said Joe, "it's more than twenty pound."

That abject hypocrite, Pumblechook, nodded again, and said with a patronising laugh, "It's more than that, Mum. Good again! Follow her up, Joseph!"

"Then to make an end of it," said Joe, delightedly handing the bag to my sister. "It is five-and-twenty pound."

"It's five-and-twenty pound, Mum," echoed that basest of swindlers, Pumblechook, rising to shake hands with her; "and it's no more than your merits (as I said when my opinion was asked), and I wish you joy of the money!"

If the villain had stopped here, his case would have been sufficiently awful, but he blackened his guilt by proceeding to take me into custody, with a right of patronage that left all his former criminality far behind.

"Now you see, Joseph and wife," said Mr. Pumblechook, as he took me by the arm above the elbow, "I am one of them that always go right through with what they've begun. This boy must be bound out of hand. That's my way. Bound out of hand."

"Goodness knows, Uncle Pumblechook," said my sister (grasping the money), "we're deeply beholden to you."

"Never mind me, Mum," returned that diabolical corn-chandler. "A pleasure's a pleasure all the world over. But this boy, you know; we must have him bound. I said I'd see to it—to tell you the truth."

The Justices were sitting in the Town Hall near at hand, and we at once went over to have me bound apprentice to Joe in the Magisterial presence. I say, we went over, but I was pushed over by Pumblechook, exactly as if I had that moment picked a pocket or fired a rick; indeed, it was the general impression in Court that I had been taken red-handed; for, as Pumblechook shoved me before him through the crowd, I heard some people say, "What's he done?" and others, "He's a young 'un, too, but looks bad, don't he?" One person of mild and benevolent aspect even gave me a tract ornamented with a woodcut of a malevolent young man fitted up with a perfect sausage-shop of fetters, and entitled, TO BE READ IN MY CELL.

The Hall was a queer place, I thought, with higher pews in it than a church—and with people hanging over the pews looking on—and with mighty Justices (one with a powdered head) leaning back in chairs, with folded arms, or taking snuff, or going to sleep, or writing, or reading the newspapers—and with some shining black portraits on the walls, which my unartistic eye regarded as a composition of hardbake and sticking-plaister. Here, in a corner, my indentures were duly signed and attested, and I was "bound;" Mr. Pumblechook holding me all the while as if we had looked in on our way to the scaffold to have those little preliminaries disposed of.

When we had come out again, and had got rid of the boys who had been put into great spirits by the expectation of seeing me publicly tortured, and who were much disappointed to find that my friends were merely rallying round me, we went back to Pumblechook's. And there my sister became so excited by the twenty-five guineas, that nothing would serve her but we must have a dinner out of that windfall, at the Blue Boar, and that Mr. Pumblechook must go over in his chaise-cart, and bring the Hubbles and Mr. Wopsle.

It was agreed to be done; and a most melancholy day I passed. For, it inscrutably appeared to stand to reason, in the minds of the whole company, that I was an excrescence on the entertainment. And to make it worse, they all asked me from time to time—in short, whenever they had nothing else to do—why I didn't enjoy myself? And what could I possibly do then, but say that I was enjoying myself—when I wasn't!

However, they were grown up and had their own way, and made the most of it. That swindling Pumblechook, exalted into the beneficent contriver of the whole occasion, actually took the top of the table; and, when he addressed them on the subject of my being bound, and had fiendishly congratulated them on my being liable to imprisonment if I played at cards, drank strong liquors, kept late hours or bad company, or indulged in other vagaries which the form of my indentures appeared to contemplate as next to inevitable, he placed me standing on a chair beside him to illustrate his remarks.

My only other remembrances of the great festival are, That they wouldn't let me go to sleep, but whenever they saw me dropping off, woke me up and told me to enjoy myself. That, rather late in the evening Mr. Wopsle gave us Collins's ode, and threw his blood-stain'd sword in thunder down, with such effect that a waiter came in and said, "The Commercials underneath sent up their compliments, and it wasn't the Tumblers' Arms." That, they were all in excellent spirits on the road home, and sang O Lady Fair! Mr. Wopsle taking the bass, and asserting with a tremendously strong voice (in reply to the inquisitive bore who leads that piece of music in a most impertinent manner, by wanting to know all about everybody's private affairs) that he was the man with his white locks flowing, and that he was upon the whole the weakest pilgrim going.

Finally, I remember that when I got into my little bed-room, I was truly wretched, and had a strong conviction on me that I should never like Joe's trade. I had liked it once, but once was not now.

CHAPTER XIV.

It is a most miserable thing to feel ashamed of home. There may be black ingratitude in the thing, and the punishment may be retributive and well deserved; but, that it is a miserable thing, I can testify.

Home had never been a very pleasant place to me, because of my sister's temper. But, Joe had sanctified it, and I believed in it. I had believed in the best parlour as a most elegant saloon; I had believed in the front door, as a mysterious portal of the Temple of State whose solemn opening was attended with a sacrifice of roast fowls; I had believed in the kitchen as a chaste though not magnificent apartment; I had believed in the forge as the glowing road to manhood and independence. Within a single year all this was changed. Now, it was all coarse and common, and I would not have had Miss Havisham and Estella see it on any account.

How much of my ungracious condition of mind may have been my own fault, how much Miss Havisham's, how much my sister's, is now of no moment to me or to any one. The change was made in me; the thing was done. Well or ill done, excusably or inexcusably, it was done.

Once, it had seemed to me that when I should at last roll up my shirt-sleeves and go into the forge, Joe's 'prentice, I should be distinguished and happy. Now the reality was in my hold, I only felt that I was dusty with the dust of the small coal, and that I had a weight upon my daily remembrance to which the anvil was a feather. There have been occasions in my later life (I suppose as in most lives) when I have felt for a time as if a thick curtain had fallen on all its interest and romance, to shut me out from anything save dull endurance any more. Never has that curtain dropped so heavy and blank, as when my way in life lay stretched out straight before me through the newly-entered road of apprenticeship to Joe.

I remember that at a later period of my "time," I used to stand about the churchyard on Sunday evenings, when night was falling, comparing my own perspective with the windy marsh view, and making out some likeness between them by thinking how flat and low both were, and how on both there came an unknown way and a dark mist and then the sea. I was quite as dejected on the first working-day of my apprenticeship as in that after-time; but I am glad to know that I never breathed a murmur to Joe while my indentures lasted. It is about the only thing I *am* glad to know of myself in that connection.

For, though it includes what I proceed to add, all the merit of what I proceed to add was Joe's. It was not because I was faithful, but because Joe was faithful, that I never ran away and went for a soldier or a sailor. It was not because I had a strong sense of the virtue of industry, but because Joe had a strong sense of the virtue of industry, that I worked with tolerable zeal against the grain. It is not possible to know how far the influence of any amiable honest-hearted duty-doing man flies out into the world; but it is very possible to know how it has touched one's self in going by, and I know right well that any good that intermixed itself with my apprenticeship came of plain contented Joe, and not of restless aspiring discontented me.

What I wanted, who can say? How can *I* say, when I never knew? What I dreaded was, that in some unlucky hour I, being at my grimiest and commonest, should lift up my eyes and see Estella looking in at one of the wooden windows of the forge. I was haunted by the fear that she would, sooner or later, find me out, with a black face and hands, doing the coarsest part of my work, and would exult over me and despise me. Often after dark, when I was pulling the bellows for Joe, and we were singing Old Clem, and when the thought how we used to sing it at Miss Havisham's would seem to show me Estella's face in the fire, with her pretty hair fluttering in the wind and her eyes scorning me,—often at such a time I would look towards those panels of black night in the wall which the wooden windows then were, and would fancy that I saw her just drawing her face away, and would believe that she had come at last.

After that, when we went in to supper, the place and the meal would have a more homely look than ever, and I would feel more ashamed of home than ever, in my own ungracious breast.

CHAPTER XV.

As I was getting too big for Mr. Wopsle's great-aunt's room, my education under that preposterous female terminated. Not, however, until Biddy had imparted to me everything she knew, from the little catalogue of prices, to a comic song she had once bought for a halfpenny. Although the only coherent part of the latter piece of literature were the opening lines,

When I went to Lunnon town sirs,
  Too rul loo rul
  Too rul loo rul
Wasn't I done very brown sirs?
  Too rul loo rul
  Too rul loo rul

—still, in my desire to be wiser, I got this composition by heart with the utmost gravity; nor do I recollect that I questioned its merit, except that I thought (as I still do) the amount of Too rul somewhat in excess of the poetry. In my hunger for information, I made proposals to Mr. Wopsle to bestow some intellectual crumbs upon me; with which he kindly complied. As it turned out, however, that he only wanted me for a dramatic lay-figure, to be contradicted and embraced and wept over and bullied and clutched and stabbed and knocked about in a variety of ways, I soon declined that course of instruction; though not until Mr. Wopsle in his poetic fury had severely mauled me.

Whatever I acquired, I tried to impart to Joe. This statement sounds so well, that I cannot in my conscience let it pass unexplained. I wanted to make Joe less ignorant and common, that he might be worthier of my society and less open to Estella's reproach.

The old Battery out on the marshes was our place of study, and a broken slate and a short piece of slate pencil were our educational implements: to which Joe always added a pipe of tobacco. I never knew Joe to remember anything from one Sunday to another, or to acquire, under my tuition, any piece of information whatever. Yet he would smoke his pipe at the Battery with a far more sagacious air than anywhere else—even with a learned air—as if he considered himself to be advancing immensely. Dear fellow, I hope he did.

It was pleasant and quiet, out there with the sails on the river passing beyond the earthwork, and sometimes, when the tide was low, looking as if they belonged to sunken ships that were still sailing on at the bottom of the water. Whenever I watched the vessels standing out to sea with their white sails spread, I somehow thought of Miss Havisham and Estella; and whenever the light struck aslant, afar off, upon a cloud or sail or green hill-side or water-line, it was just the same.—Miss Havisham and Estella and the strange house and the strange life appeared to have something to do with everything that was picturesque.

One Sunday when Joe, greatly enjoying his pipe, had so plumed himself on being "most awful dull," that I had given him up for the day, I lay on the earthwork for some time with my chin on my hand, descrying traces of Miss Havisham and Estella all over the prospect, in the sky and in the water, until at last I resolved to mention a thought concerning them that had been much in my head.

"Joe," said I; "don't you think I ought to pay Miss Havisham a visit?"

"Well, Pip," returned Joe, slowly considering. "What for?"

"What for, Joe? What is any visit made for?"

"There is some wisits p'r'aps," said Joe, "as for ever remains open to the question, Pip. But in regard to visiting Miss Havisham. She might think you wanted something—expected something of her."

"Don't you think I might say that I did not, Joe?"

"You might, old chap," said Joe. "And she might credit it. Similarly, she mightn't."

Joe felt, as I did, that he had made a point there, and he pulled hard at his pipe to keep himself from weakening it by repetition.

"You see, Pip," Joe pursued, as soon as he was past that danger, "Miss Havisham done the handsome thing by you. When Miss Havisham done the handsome thing by you, she called me back to say to me as that were all."

"Yes, Joe. I heard her."

"ALL," Joe repeated, very emphatically.

"Yes, Joe. I tell you, I heard her."

"Which I meantersay, Pip, it might be that her meaning were—Make a end on it!—As you was!—Me to the North, and you to the South!—Keep in sunders!"

I had thought of that too, and it was very far from comforting to me to find that he had thought of it; for it seemed to render it more probable.

"But, Joe."

"Yes, old chap."

"Here am I, getting on in the first year of my time, and, since the day of my being bound I have never thanked Miss Havisham, or asked after her, or shown that I remember her."

"That's true, Pip; and unless you was to turn her out a set of shoes all four round—and which I meantersay as even a set of shoes all four round might not act acceptable as a present in a total wacancy of hoofs——"

"I don't mean that sort of remembrance, Joe; I don't mean a present."

But Joe had got the idea of a present in his head and must harp upon it. "Or even," said he, "if you was helped to knocking her up a new chain for the front door—or say a gross or two of shark-headed screws for general use—or some light fancy article, such as a toasting-fork when she took her muffins—or a gridiron when she took a sprat or such like——"

"I don't mean any present at all, Joe," I interposed.

"Well," said Joe, still harping on it as though I had particularly pressed it, "if I was yourself, Pip, I wouldn't. No, I would not. For what's a door-chain when she's got one always up? And shark-headers is open to misrepresentations. And if it was a toasting-fork, you'd go into brass and do yourself no credit. And the oncommonest workman can't show himself oncommon in a gridiron—for a gridiron IS a gridiron," said Joe, steadfastly impressing it upon me, as if he were endeavouring to rouse me from a fixed delusion, "and you may haim at what you like, but a gridiron it will come out, either by your leave or again your leave, and you can't help yourself——"

"My dear Joe," I cried in desperation, taking hold of his coat, "don't go on in that way. I never thought of making Miss Havisham any present."

"No, Pip," Joe assented, as if he had been contending for that all along; "and what I say to you is, you are right, Pip."

"Yes, Joe; but what I wanted to say, was, that as we are rather slack just now, if you would give me a half-holiday to-morrow, I think I would go up-town and make a call on Miss Est—Havisham."

"Which her name," said Joe, gravely, "ain't Estavisham, Pip, unless she have been rechris'ened."

"I know, Joe, I know. It was a slip of mine. What do you think of it, Joe?"

In brief, Joe thought that if I thought well of it, he thought well of it. But, he was particular in stipulating

that if I were not received with cordiality, or if I were not encouraged to repeat my visit as a visit which had no ulterior object, but was simply one of gratitude for a favour received, then this experimental trip should have no successor. By these conditions I promised to abide.

Now, Joe kept a journeyman at weekly wages whose name was Orlick. He pretended that his Christian name was Dolge—a clear impossibility—but he was a fellow of that obstinate disposition that I believe him to have been the prey of no delusion in this particular, but wilfully to have imposed that name upon the village as an affront to its understanding. He was a broad-shouldered loose-limbed swarthy fellow of great strength, never in a hurry, and always slouching. He never even seemed to come to his work on purpose, but would slouch in as if by mere accident; and when he went to the Jolly Bargemen to eat his dinner, or went away at night, he would slouch out, like Cain or the Wandering Jew, as if he had no idea where he was going, and no intention of ever coming back. He lodged at a sluice-keeper's out on the marshes, and on working-days would come slouching from his hermitage, with his hands in his pockets and his dinner loosely tied in a bundle round his neck and dangling on his back. On Sundays he mostly lay all day on sluice-gates, or stood against ricks and barns. He always slouched, locomotively, with his eyes on the ground; and, when accosted or otherwise required to raise them, he looked up in a half resentful, half puzzled way, as though the only thought he ever had, was, that it was rather an odd and injurious fact that he should never be thinking.

This morose journeyman had no liking for me. When I was very small and timid, he gave me to understand that the Devil lived in a black corner of the forge, and that he knew the fiend very well: also that it was necessary to make up the fire, once in seven years, with a live boy, and that I might consider myself fuel. When I became Joe's 'prentice, Orlick was perhaps confirmed in some suspicion that I should displace him; howbeit, he liked me still less. Not that he ever said anything, or did anything, openly importing hostility; I only noticed that he always beat his sparks in my direction, and that whenever I sang Old Clem, he came in out of time.

Dolge Orlick was at work and present, next day, when I reminded Joe of my half-holiday. He said nothing at the moment, for he and Joe had just got a piece of hot iron between them, and I was at the bellows; but by-and-bye he said, leaning on his hammer:

"Now, master! Sure you're not going to favour only one of us. If Young Pip has a half-holiday, do as much for Old Orlick." I suppose he was about five-and-twenty, but he usually spoke of himself as an ancient person.

"Why, what'll you do with a half-holiday, if you get it?" said Joe.

"What'll *I* do with it? What'll *he* do with it? I'll do as much with it as *him*," said Orlick.

"As to Pip, he's going up-town," said Joe.

"Well then, as to Old Orlick, *he's* a going up-town," retorted that worthy. "Two can go up-town. Tain't only one wot can go up-town."

"Don't lose your temper," said Joe.

"Shall if I like," growled Orlick. "Some and their up-towning! Now, master! Come. No favouring in this shop. Be a man!"

The master refusing to entertain the subject until the

journeyman was in a better temper, Orlick plunged at the furnace, drew out a red-hot bar, made at me with it as if he were going to run it through my body, whisked it round my head, laid it on the anvil, hammered it out—as if it were I, I thought, and the sparks were my spirting blood—and finally said, when he had hammered himself hot and the iron cold, and he again leaned on his hammer:

"Now, master!"

"Are you all right now?" demanded Joe.

"Ah! I am all right," said gruff Old Orlick.

"Then, as in general you stick to your work as well as most men," said Joe, "let it be a half-holiday for all."

My sister had been standing silent in the yard, within hearing—she was a most unscrupulous spy and listener—and she instantly looked in at one of the windows.

"Like you, you fool!" said she to Joe, "giving holidays to great idle hulkers like that. You are a rich man, upon my life, to waste wages in that way. I wish *I* was his master!"

"You'd be everybody's master if you durst," retorted Orlick, with an ill-favoured grin.

("Let her alone," said Joe.)

"I'd be a match for all noodles and all rogues," returned my sister, beginning to work herself into a mighty rage. "And I couldn't be a match for the noodles, without being a match for your master, who's the dunder-headed king of the noodles. And I couldn't be a match for the rogues, without being a match for you, who are the blackest-looking and the worst rogue between this and France. Now!"

"You're a foul shrew, Mother Gargery," growled the journeyman. "If that makes a judge of rogues, you ought to be a good'un."

("Let her alone, will you?" said Joe.)

"What did you say?" cried my sister, beginning to scream. "What did you say? What did that fellow Orlick say to me, Pip? What did he call me, with my husband standing by? O! O! O!" Each of these exclamations was a shriek; and I must remark of my sister, what is equally true of all the violent women I have ever seen, that passion was no excuse for her, because it is undeniable that instead of lapsing into passion, she consciously and deliberately took extraordinary pains to force herself into it, and became blindly furious by regular stages; "what was the name that he gave me before the base man who swore to defend me? O! Hold me! O!"

"Ah-h-h!" growled the journeyman, between his teeth, "I'd hold you, if you was my wife. I'd hold you under the pump, and choke it out of you."

("I tell you, let her alone," said Joe.)

"O! To hear him!" cried my sister, with a clap of her hands and a scream together—which was her next stage. "To hear the names he's giving me! That Orlick! In my own house! Me, a married woman! With my husband standing by! O! O!" Here my sister, after a fit of clappings and screamings, beat her hands upon her bosom and upon her knees, and threw her cap off, and pulled her hair down—which were the last stages on her road to frenzy. Being by this time a perfect Fury and a complete success, she made a dash at the door, which I had fortunately locked.

What could the wretched Joe do now, after his disregarded parenthetical interruptions, but stand up to his journeyman, and ask him what he meant by interfering betwixt himself and Mrs. Joe; and further whether he was man enough to come on? Old Orlick felt that the situation admitted of nothing less than coming on, and was on his defence straightway; so, without so much as pulling off their singed and burnt aprons, they went at one another, like two giants. But, if any man in that neighbourhood could stand up long against Joe, I never saw the man. Orlick, as if he had been of no more account than the pale young gentleman, was very soon among the coal-dust, and in no hurry to come out of it. Then, Joe unlocked the door and picked up my sister, who had dropped insensible at the window (but who had seen the fight first I think) and who was carried into the house and laid down, and who was recommended to revive, and would do nothing but struggle and clench her hands in Joe's hair. Then came that singular calm and silence which succeed all uproars; and then with the vague sensation which I have always connected with such a lull—namely, that it was Sunday, and somebody was dead—I went upstairs to dress myself.

When I came down again, I found Joe and Orlick sweeping up, without any other traces of discomposure than a slit in one of Orlick's nostrils, which was neither expressive nor ornamental. A pot of beer had appeared from the Jolly Bargemen, and they were sharing it by turns in a peaceable manner. The lull had a sedative and philosophical influence on Joe, who followed me out into the road to say, as a parting observation that might do me good, "On the Rampage, Pip, and off the Rampage, Pip;—such is Life!"

With what absurd emotions (for, we think the feelings that are very serious in a man quite comical in a boy) I found myself again going to Miss Havisham's, matters little here. Nor, how I passed and repassed the gate many times before I could make up my mind to ring. Nor, how I debated whether I should go away without ringing; nor, how I should undoubtedly have gone, if my time had been my own, to come back.

Miss Sarah Pocket came to the gate. No Estella.

"How, then? You here again?" said Miss Pocket. "What do you want?"

When I said that I only came to see how Miss Havisham was, Sarah evidently deliberated whether or no she should send me about my business. But, unwilling to hazard the responsibility, she let me in, and presently brought the sharp message that I was to "come up."

Everything was unchanged, and Miss Havisham was alone. "Well!" said she, fixing her eyes upon me. "I hope you want nothing? You'll get nothing."

"No indeed, Miss Havisham. I only wanted you to know that I am doing very well in my apprenticeship, and am always much obliged to you."

"There, there!" with the old restless fingers. "Come now and then; come on your birthday.—Ay!" she cried suddenly, turning herself and her chair towards me, "You are looking round for Estella? Hey?"

I had been looking round—in fact, for Estella—and I stammered that I hoped she was well.

"Abroad," said Miss Havisham; "educating for a lady; far out of reach; prettier than ever; admired by all who see her. Do you feel that you have lost her?"

There was such a malignant enjoyment in her utterance of the last words, and she broke into such a disagreeable laugh, that I was at a loss what to say. She spared me the trouble of considering, by dismissing me. When the gate was closed upon me by Sarah of the walnut-shell countenance, I felt more than ever dissatisfied with my home and with my trade and with everything; and that was all I took by *that* motion.

As I was loitering along the High-street, looking in disconsolately at the shop windows, and thinking what I would buy if I were a gentleman, who should come out of the bookshop but Mr. Wopsle. Mr. Wopsle had in his hand the affecting tragedy of George Barnwell, in which he had that moment invested sixpence, with the view of heaping every word of it on the head of Pumblechook, with whom he was going to drink tea. No sooner did he see me, than he appeared to consider that a special Providence had put a 'prentice in his way to be read at; and he laid hold of me, and insisted on my accompanying him to the Pumblechookian parlour. As I knew it would be miserable at home, and as the nights were dark and the way was dreary, and almost any companionship on the road was better than none, I made no great resistance; consequently, we turned into Pumblechook's just as the street and the shops were lighting up.

As I never assisted at any other representation of George Barnwell, I don't know how long it may usually take; but I know very well that it took until half-past nine o'clock that night, and that when Mr. Wopsle got into Newgate, I thought he never would go to the scaffold, he became so much slower than at any former period of his disgraceful career. I thought it a little too much that he should complain of being cut short in his flower after all, as if he had not been running to seed, leaf after leaf, ever since his course began. This, however, was a mere question of length and wearisomeness. What stung me, was the identification of the whole affair with my unoffending self. When Barnwell began to go wrong, I declare I felt positively apologetic, Pumblechook's indignant stare so taxed me with it. Wopsle, too, took pains to present me in the worst light. At once ferocious and maudlin, I was made to murder my uncle with no extenuating circumstances whatever; Millwood put me down in argument, on every occasion; it became sheer monomania in my master's daughter to care a button for me; and all I can say for my gasping and procrastinating conduct on the fatal morning, is, that it was worthy of the general feebleness of my character. Even after I was happily hanged and Wopsle had closed the book, Pumblechook sat staring at me, and shaking his head, and saying, "Take warning, boy, take warning!" as if it were a well-known fact that I contemplated murdering a near relation, provided I could only induce one to have the weakness to become my benefactor.

It was a very dark night when it was all over, and when I set out with Mr. Wopsle on the walk home. Beyond town, we found a heavy mist out, and it fell wet and thick. The turnpike lamp was a blur, quite out of the lamp's usual place apparently, and its rays looked solid substance on the fog. We were noticing this, and saying how that the mist rose with a change of wind from a certain quarter of our marshes, when we came upon a man, slouching under the lee of the turnpike house.

"Halloa!" we said, stopping. "Orlick there?"

"Ah!" he answered, slouching out. "I was standing by, a minute, on the chance of company."

"You are late," I remarked.

Orlick not unnaturally answered, "Well? And *you're* late."

"We have been," said Mr. Wopsle, exalted with his late performance, "we have been indulging, Mr. Orlick, in an intellectual evening."

Old Orlick growled, as if he had nothing to say about that, and we all went on together. I asked him presently whether he had been spending his half-holiday up and down town?

"Yes," said he, "all of it. I come in behind yourself. I didn't see you, but I must have been pretty close behind you. By-the-bye, the guns is going again."

"At the Hulks?" said I.

"Ay! There's some of the birds flown from the cages. The guns have been going since dark, about. You'll hear one presently."

In effect, we had not walked many yards further, when the well-remembered boom came towards us, deadened by the mist, and heavily rolled away along the low grounds by the river, as if it were pursuing and threatening the fugitives.

"A good night for cutting off in," said Orlick. "We'd be puzzled how to bring down a jail-bird on the wing, to-night."

The subject was a suggestive one to me, and I thought about it in silence. Mr. Wopsle, as the ill-requited uncle of the evening's tragedy, fell to meditating aloud in his garden at Camberwell. Orlick, with his hands in his pockets, slouched heavily at my side. It was very dark, very wet, very muddy, and so we splashed along. Now and then, the sound of the signal cannon broke upon us again, and again rolled sulkily along the course of the river. I kept myself to myself and my thoughts. Mr. Wopsle died amiably at Camberwell, and exceedingly game on Bosworth Field, and in the greatest agonies at Glastonbury. Orlick sometimes growled, "Beat it out, beat it out—Old Clem! With a clink for the stout—Old Clem!" I thought he had been drinking, but he was not drunk.

Thus, we came to the village. The way by which we approached it, took us past the Three Jolly Bargemen, which we were surprised to find—it being eleven o'clock—in a state of commotion, with the door wide open, and unwonted lights that had been hastily caught up and put down, scattered about. Mr. Wopsle dropped in to ask what was the matter (surmising that a convict had been taken), but came running out in a great hurry.

"There's something wrong," said he, without stopping, "up at your place, Pip. Run all!"

"What is it?" I asked, keeping up with him. So did Orlick, at my side.

"I can't quite understand. The house seems to have been violently entered when Joe Gargery was out. Supposed by convicts. Somebody has been attacked and hurt."

We were running too fast to admit of more being said, and we made no stop until we got into our kitchen. It was full of people; the whole village was there, or in the yard; and there was a surgeon, and there was Joe, and there was a group of women, all on the floor in the midst of the kitchen. The unemployed bystanders drew back when they saw me, and so I became aware of my sister—lying without sense or movement on the bare boards where she had been knocked down by a tremendous blow on the back of the head, dealt by some unknown hand when her face was turned towards the fire—destined never to be on the Rampage again, while she was the wife of Joe.

CHAPTER XVI.

WITH my head full of George Barnwell, I was at first disposed to believe that *I* must have had some hand in the attack upon my sister, or at all events that as her near relation, popularly known to be under obligations to her, I was a more legitimate object of suspicion than any one else.

But when, in the clearer light of next morning, I began to reconsider the matter and to hear it discussed around me on all sides, I took another view of the case, which was more reasonable.

Joe had been at the Three Jolly Bargemen, smoking his pipe, from a quarter after eight o'clock to a quarter before ten. While he was there, my sister had been seen standing at the kitchen door and had exchanged Good Night with a farm-labourer going home. The man could not be more particular as to the time at which he saw her (he got into dense confusion when he tried to be) than that it must have been before nine. When Joe went home at five minutes before ten, he found her struck down on the floor, and promptly called in assistance. The fire had not then burnt unusually low, nor was the snuff of the candle very long; the candle, however, had been blown out.

Nothing had been taken away from any part of the house. Neither, beyond the blowing out of the candle—which stood on a table between the door and my sister, and was behind her when she stood facing the fire and was struck—was there any disarrangement of the kitchen, excepting such as she herself had made, in falling and bleeding. But, there was one remarkable piece of evidence on the spot. She had been struck with something blunt and heavy, on the head and spine; after the blows were dealt, something heavy had been thrown down at her with considerable violence, as she lay on her face. And on the ground beside her, when Joe picked her up, was a convict's leg-iron which had been filed asunder.

Now, Joe, examining this iron with a smith's eye, declared it to have been filed asunder some time ago. The hue and cry going off to the Hulks, and people coming thence to examine the iron, Joe's opinion was corroborated. They did not undertake to say when it had left the prison-ships to which it undoubtedly had once belonged; but they claimed to know for certain that that particular manacle had not been worn by either of two convicts who had escaped last night. Further, one of those two was already re-taken, and had not freed himself of his iron.

Knowing what I knew, I set up an inference of my own here. I believed the iron to be my convict's iron—the iron I had seen and heard him filing at, on the marshes—but my mind did not accuse him of having put it to its latest use. For, I believed one of two other persons to have become possessed of it, and to have turned it to this cruel account. Either Orlick, or the strange man who had shown me the file.

Now, as to Orlick; he had gone to town exactly as he told us when we picked him up at the turnpike, he had been seen about town all the evening, he had been in divers companies in several public-houses, and he had come back with myself and Mr. Wopsle. There was nothing against him, save the quarrel; and my sister had quarrelled with him, and with everybody else about her, ten thousand times. As to the strange man; if he had come back for his two bank-notes there could have been no dispute about them, because my sister was fully prepared to restore them. Besides, there had been no altercation; the assailant had come in so silently and suddenly, that she had been felled before she could look round.

It was horrible to think that I had provided the weapon, however undesignedly, but I could hardly think otherwise. I suffered unspeakable trouble while I considered and reconsidered whether I should at last dissolve that spell of my childhood and tell Joe all the story. For months after-wards, I every day settled the question finally in the negative, and reopened and reargued it next morning. The contention came, after all, to this;—the secret was such an old one now, had so grown into me and become a part of myself, that I could not tear it away. In addition to the dread that, having led up to so much mischief, it would be now more likely than ever to alienate Joe from me if he believed it, I had a further restraining dread that he would not believe it, but would assert it with the fabulous dogs and veal-cutlets as a monstrous invention. However, I temporised with myself, of course—for, was I not wavering between right and wrong, when the thing is always done?—and resolved to make a full disclosure if I should see any such new occasion as a new chance of helping in the discovery of the assailant.

The Constables, and the Bow Street men from London—for, this happened in the days of the extinct red-waist-coated police—were about the house for a week or two, and did pretty much what I have heard and read of like authorities doing in other such cases. They took up several obviously wrong people, and they ran their heads very hard against wrong ideas, and persisted in trying to fit the circumstances to the ideas, instead of trying to extract ideas from the circumstances. Also, they stood about the door of the Jolly Bargemen, with knowing and reserved looks that filled the whole neighbourhood with admiration; and they had a mysterious manner of taking their drink, that was almost as good as taking the culprit. But not quite, for they never did it.

Long after these constitutional powers had dispersed, my sister lay very ill in bed. Her sight was disturbed, so that she saw objects multiplied, and grasped at visionary tea-cups and wine-glasses instead of the realities; her hearing was greatly impaired; her memory also; and her speech was unintelligible. When, at last, she came round so far as to be helped downstairs, it was still necessary to keep my slate always by her, that she might indicate in writing what she could not indicate in speech. As she was (very bad handwriting apart) a more than indifferent speller, and as Joe was a more than indifferent reader, extraordinary complications arose between them, which I was always called in to solve. The administration of mutton instead of medicine, the substitution of Tea for Joe, and the baker for bacon, were among the mildest of my own mistakes.

However, her temper was greatly improved, and she was patient. A tremulous uncertainty of the action of all her limbs soon became a part of her regular state, and afterwards, at intervals of two or three months, she would often put her hands to her head, and would then remain for about a week at a time in some gloomy aberration of mind. We were at a loss to find a suitable attendant for her, until a circumstance happened conveniently to relieve us. Mr. Wopsle's great-aunt conquered a confirmed habit of living into which she had fallen, and Biddy became a part of our establishment.

It may have been a month after my sister's reappearance in the kitchen, when Biddy came to us with a small speckled box containing the whole of her worldly effects, and became a blessing to the household. Above all she was a blessing to Joe, for the dear old fellow was sadly cut up by the constant contemplation of the wreck of his wife, and had been accustomed, while attending on her of an evening, to turn to me every now and then and say, with his blue eyes moistened, "Such a fine figure of a woman as she once were, Pip!" Biddy instantly taking the cleverest charge of her as though she had studied her from infancy, Joe became able in some sort to appreciate the greater quiet of his life, and to get down to the Jolly Bargemen now and then for a change that did him good. It was characteristic of the police people that they had all more or less suspected poor Joe (though he never knew it), and that they had to a man concurred in regarding him as one of the deepest spirits they had ever encountered.

Biddy's first triumph in her new office, was to solve a difficulty that had completely vanquished me. I had tried hard at it, but had made nothing of it. Thus it was:

Again and again and again, my sister had traced upon the slate, a character that looked like a curious T, and then with the utmost eagerness had called our attention to it as something she particularly wanted. I had in vain tried everything producible that began with a T, from tar to toast and tub. At length it had come into my head that the sign looked like a hammer, and on my lustily calling that word in my sister's ear, she had begun to hammer on the table and had expressed a qualified assent. Thereupon, I had brought in all our hammers, one after another, but without avail. Then I bethought me of a crutch, the shape being much the same, and I borrowed one in the village, and displayed it to my sister with considerable confidence. But she shook her head to that extent when she was shown it, that we were terrified lest in her weak and shattered state she should dislocate her neck.

When my sister found that Biddy was very quick to understand her, this mysterious sign reappeared on the slate. Biddy looked thoughtfully at it, heard my explanation, looked thoughtfully at my sister, looked thoughtfully at Joe (who was always represented on the slate by his initial letter), and ran into the forge, followed by Joe and me.

"Why, of course!" cried Biddy, with an exultant face. "Don't you see? It's *him!*"

Orlick, without a doubt! She had lost his name, and could only signify him by his hammer. We told him why we wanted him to come into the kitchen, and he slowly laid down his hammer, wiped his brow with his arm, took another wipe at it with his apron, and came slouching out, with a curious loose vagabond bend in the knees that strongly distinguished him.

I confess that I expected to see my sister denounce him, and that I was disappointed by the different result. She manifested the greatest anxiety to be on good terms with him, was evidently much pleased by his being at length produced, and motioned that she would have him given something to drink. She watched his countenance as if she were particularly wishful to be assured that he took kindly to his reception, and there were an air of humble propitiation in all she did, such as I have seen pervade the bearing of a child towards a hard master. After that day, a day rarely passed without her drawing the hammer on her slate, and without Orlick's slouching in and standing doggedly before her, as if he knew no more than I did what to make of it.

CHAPTER XVII.

I now fell into a regular routine of apprenticeship life, which was varied, beyond the limits of the village and the marshes, by no more remarkable circumstance than the arrival of my birthday and my paying another visit to Miss Havisham. I found Miss Sarah Pocket still on duty at the gate, I found Miss Havisham just as I had left her, and she spoke of Estella in the very same way, if not in the very same words. The interview lasted but a few minutes, and she gave me a guinea when I was going, and told me to come again on my next birthday. I may mention at once that this became an annual custom. I tried to decline taking the guinea on the first occasion, but with no better effect than causing her to ask me very angrily, if I expected more? Then, and after that, I took it.

So unchanging was the dull old house, the yellow light in the darkened room, the faded spectre in the chair by the dressing-table glass, that I felt as if the stopping of the clocks had stopped Time in that mysterious place, and, while I and everything else outside it grew older, it stood still. Daylight never entered the house, as to my thoughts and remembrances of it, any more than as to the actual fact. It bewildered me, and under its influence I continued at heart to hate my trade and to be ashamed of home.

Imperceptibly I became conscious of a change in Biddy, however. Her shoes came up at the heel, her hair grew bright and neat, her hands were always clean. She was not beautiful—she was common, and could not be like Estella—but she was pleasant and wholesome and sweet-tempered. She had not been with us more than a year (I remember her being newly out of mourning at the time it struck me), when I observed to myself one evening that she had curiously thoughtful and attentive eyes; eyes that were very pretty and very good.

It came of my lifting up my own eyes from a task I was poring at—writing some passages from a book, to improve myself in two ways at once by a sort of stratagem—and seeing Biddy observant of what I was about. I laid down my pen, and Biddy stopped in her needlework without laying it down.

"Biddy," said I, "how do you manage it? Either I am very stupid, or you are very clever."

"What is it that I manage? I don't know," returned Biddy, smiling.

She managed her whole domestic life, and wonderfully too; but I did not mean that, though that made what I did mean, more surprising.

"How do you manage, Biddy," said I, "to learn everything that I learn, and always to keep up with me?" I was beginning to be rather vain of my knowledge, for I spent my birthday guineas on it, and set aside the greater part of my pocket-money for similar investment; though I have no doubt, now, that the little I knew was extremely dear at the price.

"I might as well ask you," said Biddy, "how *you* manage?"

"No; because when I come in from the forge of a night, any one can see me turning to at it. But you never turn to at it, Biddy."

"I suppose I must catch it—like a cough," said Biddy, quietly; and went on with her sewing.

Pursuing my idea as I leaned back in my wooden chair and looked at Biddy sewing away with her head on one side, I began to think her rather an extraordinary girl. For, I called to mind now, that she was equally accomplished in the terms of our trade, and the names of our different sorts of work, and our various tools. In short, whatever I knew, Biddy knew. Theoretically, she was already as good a blacksmith as I, or better.

"You are one of those, Biddy," said I, "who make the most of every chance. You never had a chance before you came here, and see how improved you are!"

Biddy looked at me for an instant, and went on with her sewing.

"I was your first teacher though; wasn't I?" said she, as she sewed.

"Biddy!" I exclaimed, in amazement. "Why, you are crying!"

"No I am not," said Biddy, looking up and laughing. "What put that in your head?"

What could have put it in my head, but the glistening of a tear as it dropped on her work? I sat silent, recalling what a drudge she had been until Mr. Wopsle's great-aunt successfully overcame that bad habit of living, so highly desirable to be got rid of by some people. I recalled the hopeless circumstances by which she had been surrounded in the miserable little shop and the miserable little noisy evening school, with that miserable old bundle of incompetence always to be dragged and shouldered. I reflected that even in those untoward times there must have been latent in Biddy what was now developing, for, in my first uneasiness and discontent I had turned to her for help, as a matter of course. Biddy sat quietly sewing, shedding no more tears, and while I looked at her and thought about it all, it occurred to me that perhaps I had not been sufficiently grateful to Biddy. I might have been too reserved, and should have patronised her more (though I did not use that precise word in my meditations), with my confidence.

"Yes, Biddy," I observed, when I had done turning it over, "you were my first teacher, and that at a time when we little thought of ever being together like this, in this kitchen."

"Ah, poor thing!" replied Biddy. It was like her self-forgetfulness, to transfer the remark to my sister, and to get up and be busy about her, making her more comfortable: "that's sadly true!"

"Well," said I, "we must talk together a little more, as we used to do. And I must consult you a little more, as I used to do. Let us have a quiet walk on the marshes next Sunday, Biddy, and a long chat."

My sister was never left alone now; but Joe more than readily undertook the care of her on that Sunday afternoon, and Biddy and I went out together. It was summer-time and lovely weather. When we had passed the village and the church and the church-yard, and were out on the marshes, and began to see the sails of the ships as they sailed on, I began to combine Miss Havisham and Estella with the prospect, in my usual way. When we came to the river-side and sat down on the bank, with the water rippling at our feet, making it all more quiet than it would have been without that sound, I resolved that it was a good time and place for the admission of Biddy into my inner confidence.

"Biddy," said I, after binding her to secrecy, "I want to be a gentleman."

"Oh, I wouldn't, if I was you!" she returned. "I don't think it would answer."

"Biddy," said I, with some severity, "I have particular reasons for wanting to be a gentleman."

"You know best, Pip; but don't you think you are happier as you are?"

"Biddy," I exclaimed, impatiently, "I am not at all happy as I am. I am disgusted with my calling and with

my life. I have never taken to either since I was bound. Don't be absurd."

"Was I absurd?" said Biddy, quietly raising her eyebrows; "I am sorry for that; I didn't mean to be. I only want you to do well, and be comfortable "

"Well, then, understand once for all that I never shall or can be comfortable—or anything but miserable—there, Biddy!—unless I can lead a very different sort of life from the life I lead now."

"That's a pity!" said Biddy, shaking her head with a sorrowful air.

Now, I too had so often thought it a pity, that, in the singular kind of quarrel with myself which I was always carrying on, I was half inclined to shed tears of vexation and distress when Biddy gave utterance to her sentiment and my own. I told her she was right, and I knew it was much to be regretted, but still it was not to be helped.

"If I could have settled down," I said to Biddy, plucking up the short grass within reach, much as I had once upon a time pulled my feelings out of my hair and kicked them into the brewery well: "if I could have settled down and been but half as fond of the forge as I was when I was little, I know it would have been much better for me. You and I and Joe would have wanted nothing then, and Joe and I would perhaps have gone partners when I was out of my time, and I might even have grown up to keep company with you, and we might have sat on this very bank on a fine Sunday, quite different people. I should have been good enough for _you;_ shouldn't I, Biddy?"

Biddy sighed as she looked at the ships sailing on, and returned for answer, "Yes; I am not over-particular." It scarcely sounded flattering but I knew she meant well.

"Instead of that," said I, plucking up more grass and chewing a blade or two, "see how I am going on. Dissatisfied, and uncomfortable, and—what would it signify to me, being coarse and common, if nobody had told me so!"

Biddy turned her face suddenly towards mine, and looked far more attentively at me than she had looked at the sailing ships.

"It was neither a very true nor a very polite thing to say," she remarked, directing her eyes to the ships again. "Who said it?"

I was disconcerted, for I had broken away without quite seeing where I was going to. It was not to be shuffled off, now, however, and I answered, "The beautiful young lady at Miss Havisham's, and she's more beautiful than anybody ever was, and I admire her dreadfully, and I want to be a gentleman on her account." Having made this lunatic confession, I began to throw my torn-up grass into the river, as if I had some thoughts of following it.

"Do you want to be a gentleman, to spite her or to gain her over?" Biddy quietly asked me, after a pause.

"I don't know," I moodily answered.

"Because, if it is to spite her," Biddy pursued, "I should think—but you know best—that might be better and more independently done by caring nothing for her words. And if it is to gain her over, I should think—but you know best —she was not worth gaining over."

Exactly what I myself had thought, many times. Exactly what was perfectly manifest to me at the moment. But how could I, a poor dazed village lad, avoid that wonderful inconsistency into which the best and wisest of men fall every day?

"It may be all quite true," said I to Biddy, "but I admire her dreadfully."

In short, I turned over on my face when I came to that,

THEN SHE SOFTLY PATTED MY SHOULDER IN A SOOTHING WAY.

and got a good grasp on the hair, on each side of my head, and wrenched it well. All the while knowing the madness of my heart to be so very mad and misplaced, that I was quite conscious it would have served my face right, if I had lifted it up by my hair, and knocked it against the pebbles as a punishment for belonging to such an idiot.

Biddy was the wisest of girls, and she tried to reason no more with me. She put her hand, which was a comfortable hand though roughened by work, upon my hands, one after another, and gently took them out of my hair. Then she softly patted my shoulder in a soothing way, while with my face upon my sleeve I cried a little—exactly as I had done in the brewery yard—and felt vaguely convinced that I was very much ill-used by somebody, or by everybody; I can't say which.

"I am glad of one thing," said Biddy, "and that is, that you have felt you could give me your confidence, Pip. And I am glad of another thing, and that is, that of course you know you may depend upon my keeping it and always so far deserving it. If your first teacher (dear! such a poor one, and so much in need of being taught herself!) had been your teacher at the present time, she thinks she knows what lesson she would set. But it would be a hard one to learn, and you have got beyond her, and it's of no use now." So, with a quiet sigh for me, Biddy rose from the bank, and said, with a fresh and pleasant change of voice, "Shall we walk a little further, or go home?"

"Biddy," I cried, getting up, putting my arm around her neck, and giving her a kiss, "I shall always tell you everything."

"Till you're a gentleman," said Biddy.

"You know I never shall be, so that's always. Not that I have any occasion to tell you anything, for you know everything I know—as I told you at home the other night."

"Ah!" said Biddy, quite in a whisper, as she looked away at the ships. And then repeated, with her former pleasant change; "shall we walk a little further, or go home?"

I said to Biddy we would walk a little further, and we did so, and the summer afternoon toned down into the summer evening, and it was very beautiful. I began to consider whether I was not more naturally and wholesomely situated, after all, in these circumstances, than playing beggar my neighbour by candlelight in the room with the stopped clocks, and being despised by Estella. I thought it would be very good for me if I could get her out of my head with all the rest of those remembrances and fancies, and could go to work determined to relish what I had to do, and stick to it, and make the best of it. I asked myself the question whether I did not surely know that if Estella were beside me at that moment instead of Biddy, she would make me miserable? I was obliged to admit that I did know it for a certainty, and I said to myself, "Pip, what a fool you are!"

We talked a good deal as we walked, and all that Biddy said seemed right. Biddy was never insulting, or capricious, or Biddy to-day and somebody else to-morrow; she would have derived only pain, and no pleasure, from giving me pain; she would far rather have wounded her own breast than mine. How could it be, then, that I did not like her much the better of the two?

"Biddy," said I, when we were walking homeward, "I wish you could put me right."

"I wish I could!" said Biddy.

"If I could only get myself to fall in love with you— you don't mind my speaking so openly to such an old acquaintance?"

"Oh dear, not at all!" said Biddy. "Don't mind me."

"If I could only get myself to do it, *that* would be the thing for me."

"But you never will, you see," said Biddy.

It did not appear quite so unlikely to me that evening, as it would have done if we had discussed it a few hours before. I therefore observed I was not quite sure of that. But Biddy said she *was*, and she said it decisively. In my heart I believed her to be right; and yet I took it rather ill, too, that she should be so positive on the point.

When we came near the churchyard, we had to cross an embankment, and get over a stile near a sluice-gate. There started up, from the gate, or from the rushes, or from the ooze (which was quite in his stagnant way), Old Orlick.

"Halloa!" he growled, "where are you two going?"

"Where should we be going, but home?"

"Well, then," said he, "I'm jiggered if I don't see you home!"

This penalty of being jiggered was a favourite suppositious case of his. He attached no definite meaning to the word that I am aware of, but used it, like his own pretended Christian name, to affront mankind, and convey an idea of something savagely damaging. When I was younger, I had had a general belief that if he had jiggered me personally, he would have done it with a sharp and twisted hook.

Biddy was much against his going with us, and said to me in a whisper, "Don't let him come; I don't like him." As I did not like him either, I took the liberty of saying that we thanked him, but we didn't want seeing home. He received that piece of information with a yell of laughter, and dropped back, but came slouching after us at a little distance.

Curious to know whether Biddy suspected him of having had a hand in that murderous attack of which my sister had never been able to give any account, I asked her why she did not like him.

"Oh!" she replied, glancing over her shoulder as he slouched after us, "because I—I am afraid he likes me."

"Did he ever tell you he liked you?" I asked, indignantly.

"No," said Biddy, glancing over her shoulder again, "he never told me so; but he dances at me, whenever he can catch my eye."

However novel and peculiar this testimony of attachment, I did not doubt the accuracy of the interpretation. I was very hot indeed upon Old Orlick's daring to admire her; as hot if it were an outrage on myself.

"But it makes no difference to you, you know," said Biddy, calmly.

"No, Biddy, it makes no difference to me; only I don't like it; I don't approve of it."

"Nor I neither," said Biddy. "Though *that* makes no difference to you."

"Exactly," said I; "but I must tell you I should have no opinion of you, Biddy, if he danced at you with your own consent."

I kept an eye on Orlick after that night, and whenever circumstances were favourable to his dancing at Biddy, got before him, to obscure that demonstration. He had struck root in Joe's establishment, by reason of my sister's sudden fancy for him, or I should have tried to get him dismissed. He quite understood and reciprocated my good intentions, as I had reason to know thereafter.

And now, because my mind was not confused enough before, I complicated its confusion fifty thousand-fold, by having states and seasons when I was clear that Biddy was immeasurably better than Estella, and that the plain honest working life to which I was born had nothing in it to be ashamed of, but offered me sufficient means of self-respect and happiness. At those times, I would decide conclusively that my disaffection to dear old Joe and the forge, was gone, and that I was growing up in a fair way to be partners with Joe and to keep company with Biddy—when all in a moment some confounding remembrance of the Havisham days would fall upon me, like a destructive missile, and scatter my wits again. Scattered wits take a long time picking up; and often, before I had got them well together, they would be dispersed in all directions by one stray thought, that perhaps after all Miss Havisham was going to make my fortune when my time was out.

If my time had run out, it would have left me still at the height of my perplexities, I dare say. It never did run out, however, but was brought to a premature end, as I proceed to relate.

CHAPTER XVIII

It was in the fourth year of my apprenticeship to Joe, and it was a Saturday night. There was a group assembled round the fire at the Three Jolly Bargemen, attentive to Mr. Wopsle as he read the newspaper aloud. Of that group I was one.

A highly popular murder had been committed, and Mr. Wopsle was imbrued in blood to the eyebrows. He gloated over every abhorrent adjective in the description, and identified himself with every witness at the Inquest. He faintly moaned, "I am done for," as the victim, and he barbarously bellowed, "I'll serve you out," as the murderer. He gave the medical testimony, in pointed imitation of our local practitioner; and he piped and shook, as the aged turnpike-keeper who had heard blows, to an extent so very paralytic as to suggest a doubt regarding the mental competency of that witness. The coroner, in Mr. Wopsle's hands, became Timon of Athens; the beadle, Coriolanus. He enjoyed himself thoroughly, and we all enjoyed ourselves, and were delightfully comfortable. In this cozy state of mind we came to the verdict of Wilful Murder.

Then, and not sooner, I became aware of a strange gentleman leaning over the back of the settle opposite me, looking on. There was an expression of contempt on his face, and he bit the side of a great forefinger as he watched the group of faces.

"Well!" said the stranger to Mr. Wopsle, when the reading was done, "you have settled it all to your own satisfaction, I have no doubt?"

Everybody started and looked up, as if it were the murderer. He looked at everybody coldly and sarcastically.

"Guilty, of course?" said he. "Out with it. Come!"

"Sir," returned Mr. Wopsle, "without having the honour of your acquaintance, I do say Guilty." Upon this we all took courage to unite in a confirmatory murmur.

"I know you do," said the stranger; "I knew you would.

I told you so. But now I'll ask you a question. Do you know, or do you not know, that the law of England supposes every man to be innocent, until he is proved—proved—to be guilty?"

"Sir," Mr. Wopsle began to reply, "as an Englishman myself, I——"

"Come!" said the stranger, biting his forefinger at him. "Don't evade the question. Either you know it, or you don't know it. Which is it to be?"

He stood with his head on one side and himself on one side, in a bullying interrogative manner, and he threw his forefinger at Mr. Wopsle—as it were to mark him out—before biting it again.

"Now!" said he. "Do you know it, or don't you know it?"

"Certainly I know it," replied Mr. Wopsle.

"Certainly you know it. Then why didn't you say so at first? Now, I'll ask you another question;" taking possession of Mr. Wopsle, as if he had a right to him. "Do you know that none of these witnesses have yet been cross-examined?"

Mr. Wopsle was beginning, "I can only say——" when the stranger stopped him.

"What? You won't answer the question, yes or no? Now, I'll try you again." Throwing his finger at him again. "Attend to me. Are you aware, or are you not aware, that none of these witnesses have yet been cross-examined? Come, I only want one word from you. Yes, or no?"

Mr. Wopsle hesitated, and we all began to conceive rather a poor opinion of him.

"Come!" said the stranger, "I'll help you. You don't deserve help, but I'll help you. Look at that paper you hold in your hand. What is it?"

"What is it?" repeated Mr. Wopsle, eyeing it much at a loss.

"Is it," pursued the stranger in his most sarcastic and suspicious manner, "the printed paper you have just been reading from?"

"Undoubtedly."

"Undoubtedly. Now, turn to that paper, and tell me whether it distinctly states that the prisoner expressly said that his legal advisers instructed him altogether to reserve his defence?"

"I read that just now," Mr. Wopsle pleaded.

"Never mind what you read just now, sir; I don't ask you what you read just now. You may read the Lord's Prayer backwards, if you like—and, perhaps, have done it before to-day. Turn to the paper. No, no, no, my friend; not to the top of the column; you know better than that; to the bottom, to the bottom." (We all began to think Mr. Wopsle full of subterfuge.) "Well? Have you found it?"

"Here it is," said Mr. Wopsle.

"Now, follow that passage with your eye, and tell me whether it distinctly states that the prisoner expressly said that he was instructed by his legal advisers wholly to reserve his defence? Come! Do you make that of it?"

Mr. Wopsle answered, "Those are not the exact words."

"Not the exact words!" repeated the gentleman, bitterly. "Is that the exact substance?"

"Yes," said Mr. Wopsle.

"Yes," repeated the stranger, looking round at the rest of the company with his right hand extended towards the witness, Wopsle. "And now I ask you what you say to the conscience of that man who, with that passage before his eyes, can lay his head upon his pillow after having pronounced a fellow-creature guilty, unheard?"

We all began to suspect that Mr. Wopsle was not the man we had thought him, and that he was beginning to be found out.

"And that same man, remember," pursued the gentleman, throwing his finger at Mr. Wopsle heavily; "that same man might be summoned as a juryman upon this very trial, and having thus deeply committed himself, might return to the bosom of his family and lay his head upon his pillow, after deliberately swearing that he would well and truly try the issue joined between Our Sovereign Lord the King and the prisoner at the bar, and would a true verdict give according to the evidence, so help him God!"

We were all deeply persuaded that the unfortunate Wopsle had gone too far, and had better stop in his reckless career while there was yet time.

The strange gentleman, with an air of authority not to be disputed, and with a manner expressive of knowing something secret about every one of us that would effectually do for each individual if he chose to disclose it, left the back of the settle, and came into the space between the two settles, in front of the fire, where he remained standing: his left hand in his pocket, and he biting the forefinger of his right.

"From information I have received," said he, looking round at us as we all quailed before him, "I have reason to believe there is a blacksmith among you, by name Joseph —or Joe—Gargery. Which is the man?"

"Here is the man," said Joe.

The strange gentleman beckoned him out of his place, and Joe went.

"You have an apprentice," pursued the stranger, "commonly known as Pip? Is he here?"

"I am here!" I cried.

The stranger did not recognise me, but I recognised him as the gentleman I had met on the stairs, on the occasion of my second visit to Miss Havisham. I had known him the moment I saw him looking over the settle, and now that I stood confronting him with his hand upon my shoulder, I checked off again in detail, his large head, his dark complexion, his deep-set eyes, his bushy black eyebrows, his large watch-chain, his strong black dots of beard and whisker, and even the smell of scented soap on his great hand.

"I wish to have a private conference with you two," said he, when he had surveyed me at his leisure. "It will take a little time. Perhaps we had better go to your place of residence. I prefer not to anticipate my communication here; you will impart as much or as little of it as you please to your friends afterwards; I have nothing to do with that."

Amidst a wondering silence, we three walked out of the Jolly Bargemen, and in a wondering silence walked home. While going along, the strange gentleman occasionally looked at me, and occasionally bit the side of his finger. As we neared home, Joe vaguely acknowledging the occasion as an impressive and ceremonious one, went on ahead to open the front door. Our conference was held in the state parlour, which was feebly lighted by one candle.

It began with the strange gentleman's sitting down at the table, drawing the candle to him, and looking over some entries in his pocket-book. He then put up the pocket-book and set the candle a little aside: after peering round it into the darkness at Joe and me, to ascertain which was which.

"My name," he said, "is Jaggers, and I am a lawyer in London. I am pretty well known. I have unusual business to transact with you, and I commence by explaining that it is not of my originating. If my advice had been asked, I should not have been here. It was not asked, and you see me here. What I have to do as the confidential agent of another, I do. No less, no more."

Finding that he could not see us very well from where he sat, he got up, and threw one leg over the back of a chair and leaned upon it; thus having one foot on the seat of a chair, and one foot on the ground.

"Now, Joseph Gargery, I am the bearer of an offer to relieve you of this young fellow, your apprentice. You would not object to cancel his indentures at his request and for his good? You would want nothing for so doing?"

"Lord forbid that I should want anything for not standing in Pip's way," said Joe, staring.

"Lord forbidding is pious, but not to the purpose," returned Mr. Jaggers. "The question is, Would you want anything? Do you want anything?"

"The answer is," returned Joe, sternly, "No."

I thought Mr. Jaggers glanced at Joe, as if he considered him a fool for his disinterestedness. But I was too much bewildered between breathless curiosity and surprise, to be sure of it.

"Very well," said Mr. Jaggers. "Recollect the admission you have made, and don't try to go from it presently."

"Who's a going to try?" retorted Joe.

"I don't say anybody is. Do you keep a dog?"

"Yes, I do keep a dog."

"Bear in mind then, that Brag is a good dog, but that Holdfast is a better. Bear that in mind, will you?" repeated Mr. Jaggers, shutting his eyes and nodding his head at Joe, as if he were forgiving him something. "Now, I return to this young fellow. And the communication I have got to make is, that he has Great Expectations."

Joe and I gasped, and looked at one another.

"I am instructed to communicate to him," said Mr. Jaggers, throwing his finger at me sideways, "that he will come into a handsome property. Further, that it is the desire of the present possessor of that property, that he be immediately removed from his present sphere of life and from this place, and be brought up as a gentleman—in a word, as a young fellow of great expectations."

My dream was out; my wild fancy was surpassed by sober reality; Miss Havisham was going to make my fortune on a grand scale.

"Now, Mr. Pip," pursued the lawyer, "I address the rest of what I have to say, to you. You are to understand, first, that it is the request of the person from whom I take my instructions, that you always bear the name of Pip. You will have no objection, I dare say, to your great expectations being encumbered with that easy condition. But if you have any objection, this is the time to mention it."

My heart was beating so fast, and there was such a singing in my ears, that I could scarcely stammer I had no objection.

"I should think not! Now you are to understand, secondly, Mr. Pip, that the name of the person who is your liberal benefactor remains a profound secret, until the person chooses to reveal it. I am empowered to mention that it is the intention of the person to reveal it at first hand by word of mouth to yourself. When or where that intention may be carried out, I cannot say; no one can say. It may be years hence. Now, you are distinctly to understand that you are most positively prohibited from making any inquiry on this head, or any allusion or reference, however distant, to any individual whomsoever as *the* individual, in all the communications you may have with me. If you have a suspicion in your own breast, keep that suspicion in your own breast. It is not the least to the purpose what the reasons of this prohibition are; they may be the strongest and gravest reasons, or they may be a mere whim. This is not for you to inquire into. The condition is laid down. Your acceptance of it, and your observance of it as binding, is the only remaining condition that I am charged with, by the person from whom I take my instructions, and for whom I am not otherwise responsible. That person is the person from whom you derive your expectations, and the secret is solely held by that person and by me. Again, not a very difficult condition with which to encumber such a rise in fortune; but if you have any objection to it, this is the time to mention it. Speak out."

Once more, I stammered with difficulty that I had no objection.

"I should think not! Now, Mr. Pip, I have done with stipulations." Though he called me Mr. Pip, and began rather to make up to me, he still could not get rid of a certain air of bullying suspicion; and even now he occasionally shut his eyes and threw his finger at me while he spoke, as much as to express that he knew all kinds of things to my disparagement, if he only chose to mention them. "We come next, to mere details of arrangement. You must know that although I use the term 'expectations' more than once, you are not endowed with expectations only. There is already lodged in my hands, a sum of money amply sufficient for your suitable education and maintenance. You will please consider me your guardian. Oh!" for I was going to thank him, "I tell you at once, I am paid for my services, or I shouldn't render them. It is considered that you must be better educated, in accordance with your altered position, and that you will be alive to the importance and necessity of at once entering on that advantage."

I said I had always longed for it.

"Never mind what you have always longed for, Mr. Pip," he retorted; "keep to the record. If you long for it now, that's enough. Am I answered that you are ready to be placed at once, under some proper tutor? Is that it?"

I stammered yes, that was it.

"Good. Now, your inclinations are to be consulted. I don't think that wise, mind, but it's my trust. Have you ever heard of any tutor whom you would prefer to another?"

I had never heard of any tutor but Biddy, and Mr. Wopsle's great-aunt; so, I replied in the negative.

"There is a certain tutor, of whom I have some knowledge, who I think might suit the purpose," said Mr. Jaggers. "I don't recommend him, observe; because I never recommend anybody. The gentleman I speak of is one Mr. Matthew Pocket."

Ah! I caught at the name directly. Miss Havisham's relation. The Matthew whom Mr. and Mrs. Camilla had spoken of. The Matthew whose place was to be at Miss Havisham's head, when she lay dead, in her bride's dress on the bride's table.

"You know the name?" said Mr. Jaggers, looking shrewdly at me, and then shutting up his eyes while he waited for my answer.

My answer was, that I had heard of the name.

"Oh!" said he. "You have heard of the name! But the question is, what do you say of it?"

I said, or tried to say, that I was much obliged to him for his recommendation——

"No, my young friend!" he interrupted, shaking his great head very slowly. "Recollect yourself!"

Not recollecting myself, I began again that I was much obliged to him for his recommendation——

"No, my young friend," he interrupted, shaking his head and frowning and smiling both at once; "no, no, no; it's very well done, but it won't do; you are too young to fix me with it. Recommendation is not the word, Mr. Pip. Try another."

Correcting myself, I said that I was much obliged to him for his mention of Mr. Matthew Pocket——

"*That's* more like it!" cried Mr. Jaggers.

—And (I added) I would gladly try that gentleman.

"Good. You had better try him in his own house. The way shall be prepared for you, and you can see his son first, who is in London. When will you come to London?"

I said (glancing at Joe, who stood looking on, motionless), that I supposed I could come directly.

"First," said Mr. Jaggers, "you should have some new clothes to come in, and they should not be working clothes. Say this day week. You'll want some money. Shall I leave you twenty guineas?"

He produced a long purse, with the greatest coolness, and counted them out on the table and pushed them over to me. This was the first time he had taken his leg from the chair. He sat astride of the chair when he had pushed the money over, and sat swinging his purse and eyeing Joe.

"Well, Joseph Gargery? You look dumbfoundered?"

"I *am* I" said Joe, in a very decided manner.

"It was understood that you wanted nothing for yourself, remember?"

"It were understood," said Joe. "And it are understood. And it ever will be similar according."

"But what," said Mr. Jaggers, swinging his purse, "what if it was in my instructions to make you a present, as compensation?"

"As compensation what for?" Joe demanded.

"For the loss of his services."

Joe laid his hand upon my shoulder with the touch of a woman. I have often thought him since, like the steam-hammer, that can crush a man or pat an egg-shell, in his combination of strength with gentleness. "Pip is that hearty welcome," said Joe, "to go free with his services, to honour and fortun', as no words can tell him. But if you think as Money can make compensation to me for the loss of the little child—what come to the forge—and ever the best of friends!—"

O dear good Joe, whom I was so ready to leave and so unthankful to, I see you again, with your muscular blacksmith's arm before your eyes, and your broad chest heaving, and your voice dying away. O dear good faithful tender Joe, I feel the loving tremble of your hand upon my arm, as solemnly this day as if it had been the rustle of an angel's wing!

But I encouraged Joe at the time. I was lost in the mazes of my future fortunes, and could not retrace the bye-paths we had trodden together. I begged Joe to be comforted, for (as he said) we had ever been the best of friends, and (as I said) we ever would be so. Joe scooped his eyes with his disengaged wrist, as if he were bent on gouging himself, but said not another word.

Mr. Jaggers had looked on at this, as one who recognized in Joe the village idiot, and in me his keeper. When it was over, he said, weighing in his hand the purse he had ceased to swing:

"Now, Joseph Gargery, I warn you this is your last chance. No half measures with me. If you mean to take a present that I have it in charge to make you, speak out, and you shall have it. If on the contrary you mean to say——" Here, to his great amazement, he was stopped by Joe's suddenly working round him with every demonstration of a fell pugilistic purpose.

"Which I meantersay," cried Joe, "that if you come into my place bull-baiting and badgering me, come out! Which I meantersay as sech if you're a man, come on! Which I meantersay that what I say, I meantersay and stand or fall by!"

I drew Joe away, and he immediately became placable: merely stating to me, in an obliging manner and as a polite expostulatory notice to any one whom it might happen to concern, that he were not a going to be bull-baited and badgered in his own place. Mr. Jaggers had risen when Joe demonstrated, and had backed near the door. Without evincing any inclination to come in again, he there delivered his valedictory remarks. They were these:

"Well, Mr. Pip, I think the sooner you leave here—as you are to be a gentleman—the better. Let it stand for this day week, and you shall receive my printed address in the meantime. You can take a hackney-coach at the stage-coach office in London, and come straight to me. Understand that I express no opinion, one way or other, on the trust I undertake. I am paid for undertaking it, and I do so. Now, understand that finally. Understand that!"

He was throwing his finger at both of us, and I think would have gone on, but for his seeming to think Joe dangerous, and going off.

Something came into my head which induced me to run after him as he was going down to the Jolly Bargemen, where he had left a hired carriage.

"I beg your pardon, Mr. Jaggers."

"Halloa!" said he, facing round, "what's the matter?"

"I wish to be quite right, Mr. Jaggers, and to keep to your directions; so I thought I had better ask. Would there be any objection to my taking leave of any one I know, about here, before I go away?"

"No," said he, looking as if he hardly understood me.

"I don't mean in the village only, but up-town?"

"No," said he. "No objection."

I thanked him and ran home again, and there I found that Joe had already locked the front door and vacated the state parlour, and was seated by the kitchen fire with a hand on each knee, gazing intently at the burning coals. I too sat down before the fire and gazed at the coals, and nothing was said for a long time.

My sister was in her cushioned chair in her corner, and Biddy sat at her needle-work before the fire, and Joe sat next Biddy, and I sat next Joe in the corner opposite my sister. The more I looked into the glowing coals, the more incapable I became of looking at Joe; the longer the silence lasted, the more unable I felt to speak.

At length I got out, "Joe, have you told Biddy?"

"No, Pip," returned Joe, still looking at the fire, and holding his knees tight, as if he had private information that they intended to make off somewhere, "which I left it to yourself, Pip."

"I would rather you told, Joe."

"Pip's a gentleman of fortun' then," said Joe, "and God bless him in it!"

Biddy dropped her work, and looked at me. Joe held his knees and looked at me. I looked at both of them. After a pause they both heartily congratulated me; but there was a certain touch of sadness in their congratulations that I rather resented.

I took it upon myself to impress Biddy (and through Biddy, Joe) with the grave obligation I considered my friends under, to know nothing and say nothing about the maker of my fortune. It would all come out in good time, I observed, and in the meanwhile nothing was to be said, save that I had come into great expectations from a mysterious patron. Biddy nodded her head thoughtfully at the fire as she took up her work again, and said she would be very particular; and Joe, still detaining his knees, said, "Ay, ay, I'll be ekervally partickler, Pip;" and then they congratulated me again, and went on to express so much wonder at the notion of my being a gentleman, that I didn't half like it.

Infinite pains were then taken by Biddy to convey to my sister some idea of what had happened. To the best of my belief, those efforts entirely failed. She laughed and nodded her head a great many times, and even repeated after Biddy, the words "Pip" and "Property." But I doubt if they had more meaning in them than an election cry, and I cannot suggest a darker picture of her state of mind.

I never could have believed it without experience, but as Joe and Biddy became more at their cheerful ease again, I became quite gloomy. Dissatisfied with my fortune, of course I could not be; but it is possible that I may have been, without quite knowing it, dissatisfied with myself.

Anyhow, I sat with my elbow on my knee and my face upon my hand, looking into the fire, as those two talked about my going away, and about what they should do without me, and all that. And whenever I caught one of them looking at me, though never so pleasantly (and they often looked at me—particularly Biddy), I felt offended: as if they were expressing some mistrust of me. Though Heaven knows they never did by word or sign.

At those times I would get up and look out at the door; for our kitchen door opened at once upon the night, and stood open on summer evenings to air the room. The very stars to which I then raised my eyes, I am afraid I took to be but poor and humble stars for glittering on the rustic objects among which I had passed my life.

"Saturday night," said I, when we sat at our supper of bread-and-cheese and beer. "Five more days, and then the day before *the* day! They'll soon go."

"Yes, Pip," observed Joe, whose voice sounded hollow in his beer mug. "They'll soon go."

"Soon, soon go," said Biddy.

"I have been thinking, Joe, that when I go down-town on Monday, and order my new clothes, I shall tell the tailor that I'll come and put them on there, or that I'll have them sent to Mr. Pumblechook's. It would be very disagreeable to be stared at by all the people here."

"Mr. and Mrs. Hubble might like to see you in your new genteel figure too, Pip," said Joe, industriously cutting his bread with his cheese on it, in the palm of his left hand, and glancing at my untasted supper as if he thought of the time when we used to compare slices. "So might Wopsle. And the Jolly Bargemen might take it as a compliment."

"That's just what I don't want, Joe. They would make such a business of it—such a coarse and common business —that I couldn't bear myself."

"Ah, that indeed, Pip!" said Joe. "If you couldn't abear yourself——"

Biddy asked me here, as she sat holding my sister's plate, "Have you thought about when you'll show yourself to Mr. Gargery, and your sister, and me? You will show yourself to us; won't you?"

"Biddy," I returned with some resentment, "you are so exceedingly quick that it's difficult to keep up with you."

("She always were quick," observed Joe.)

"If you had waited another moment, Biddy, you would have heard me say that I shall bring my clothes here in a bundle one evening—most likely on the evening before I go away."

Biddy said no more. Handsomely forgiving her, I soon exchanged an affectionate good night with her and Joe, and went up to bed. When I got into my little room, I sat down and took a long look at it, as a mean little room that I should soon be parted from and raised above, for ever. It was furnished with fresh young remembrances too, and even at the same moment I fell into much the same confused division of mind between it and the better rooms to which I was going, as I had been in so often between the forge and Miss Havisham's, and Biddy and Estella.

The sun had been shining brightly all day on the roof of my attic, and the room was warm. As I put the window open and stood looking out, I saw Joe come slowly forth at the dark door below, and take a turn or two in the air; and then I saw Biddy come, and bring him a pipe and light it for him. He never smoked so late, and it seemed to hint to me that he wanted comforting, for some reason or other.

He presently stood at the door immediately beneath me, smoking his pipe, and Biddy stood there too, quietly talking to him, and I knew that they talked of me, for I heard my name mentioned in an endearing tone by both of them more than once. I would not have listened for more, if I could have heard more: so, I drew away from the window, and sat down in my one chair by the bedside, feeling it very sorrowful and strange that this first night of my bright fortunes should be the loneliest I had ever known.

Looking towards the open window, I saw light wreaths from Joe's pipe floating there, and I fancied it was like a blessing from Joe—not obtruded on me or paraded before me, but pervading the air we shared together. I put my light out, and crept into bed; and it was an uneasy bed now, and I never slept the old sound sleep in it any more.

CHAPTER XIX.

MORNING made a considerable difference in my general prospect of Life, and brightened it so much that it scarcely seemed the same. What lay heaviest on my mind, was, the consideration that six days intervened between me and

the day of departure; for, I could not divest myself of a misgiving that something might happen to London in the meanwhile, and that, when I got there, it might be either greatly deteriorated or clean gone.

Joe and Biddy were very sympathetic and pleasant when I spoke of our approaching separation; but they only referred to it when I did. After breakfast, Joe brought out my indentures from the press in the best parlour, and we put them in the fire, and I felt that I was free. With all the novelty of my emancipation on me, I went to church with Joe, and thought, perhaps the clergyman wouldn't have read that about the rich man and the kingdom of Heaven, if he had known all.

After our early dinner, I strolled out alone, proposing to finish off the marshes at once, and get them done with. As I passed the church, I felt (as I had felt during service in the morning) a sublime compassion for the poor creatures who were destined to go there, Sunday after Sunday, all their lives through, and to lie obscurely at last among the low green mounds. I promised myself that I would do something for them one of these days, and formed a plan in outline for bestowing a dinner of roast-beef and plum-pudding, a pint of ale, and a gallon of condescension, upon everybody in the village.

If I had often thought before, with something allied to shame, of my companionship with the fugitive whom I had once seen limping among those graves, what were my thoughts on this Sunday, when the place recalled the wretch, ragged and shivering, with his felon iron and badge! My comfort was, that it happened a long time ago, and that he had doubtless been transported a long way off, and that he was dead to me, and might be veritably dead into the bargain.

No more low wet grounds, no more dykes and sluices, no more of these grazing cattle—though they seemed, in their dull manner, to wear a more respectful air now, and to face round, in order that they might stare as long as possible at the possessor of such great expectations—farewell, monotonous acquaintances of my childhood, henceforth I was for London and greatness; not for smith's work in general and for you! I made my exultant way to the old Battery, and, lying down there to consider the question whether Miss Havisham intended me for Estella, fell asleep.

When I awoke, I was much surprised to find Joe sitting beside me, smoking his pipe. He greeted me with a cheerful smile on my opening my eyes, and said:

"As being the last time, Pip, I thought I'd foller."

"And Joe, I am very glad you did so."

"Thankee, Pip."

"You may be sure, dear Joe," I went on, after we had shaken hands, "that I shall never forget you."

"No, no, Pip!" said Joe, in a comfortable tone, "I'm sure of that. Ay, ay, old chap! Bless you, it were only necessary to get it well round in a man's mind, to be certain on it. But it took a bit of time to get it well round, the change come so oncommon plump; didn't it?"

Somehow, I was not best pleased with Joe's being so mightily secure of me. I should have liked him to have betrayed emotion, or to have said, "It does you credit, Pip," or something of that sort. Therefore, I made no remark on Joe's first head: merely saying as to his second, that the tidings had indeed come suddenly, but that I had always wanted to be a gentleman, and had often and often speculated on what I would do, if I were one.

"Have you though?" said Joe. "Astonishing!"

"It's a pity now, Joe," said I, "that you did not get on a little more, when we had our lessons here; isn't it?"

"Well, I don't know," returned Joe. "I'm so awful dull. I'm only master of my own trade. It were always a pity as I was so awful dull; but it's no more of a pity now, than it was—this day twelvemonth—don't you see!"

What I had meant was, that when I came into my property and was able to do something for Joe, it would have been much more agreeable if he had been better qualified for a rise in station. He was so perfectly innocent of my meaning, however, that I thought I would mention it to Biddy in preference.

So, when we had walked home and had had tea, I took Biddy into our little garden by the side of the lane, and, after throwing out in a general way for the elevation of her spirits, that I should never forget her, said I had a favour to ask of her.

"And it is, Biddy," said I, "that you will not omit any opportunity of helping Joe on, a little."

"How helping him on?" asked Biddy, with a steady sort of glance.

"Well! Joe is a dear good fellow—in fact, I think he is the dearest fellow that ever lived—but he is rather backward in some things. For instance, Biddy, in his learning and his manners."

Although I was looking at Biddy as I spoke, and although she opened her eyes very wide when I had spoken, she did not look at me.

"Oh, his manners! won't his manners do, then?" asked Biddy, plucking a black-currant leaf.

"My dear Biddy, they do very well here——"

"Oh! they *do* very well here?" interrupted Biddy, looking closely at the leaf in her hand.

"Hear me out—but if I were to remove Joe into a higher sphere, as I shall hope to remove him when I fully come into my property, they would hardly do him justice."

"And don't you think he knows that?" asked Biddy.

It was such a provoking question (for it had never in the most distant manner occurred to me), that I said, snappishly, "Biddy, what do you mean?"

Biddy having rubbed the leaf to pieces between her hands—and the smell of a black-currant bush has ever since recalled to me that evening in the little garden by the side of the lane—said, "Have you never considered that he may be proud?"

"Proud?" I repeated, with disdainful emphasis.

"Oh! there are many kinds of pride," said Biddy, looking full at me and shaking her head; "pride is not all of one kind——"

"Well? What are you stopping for?" said I.

"Not all of one kind," resumed Biddy. "He may be too proud to let any one take him out of a place that he is competent to fill, and fills well and with respect. To tell you the truth, I think he is: though it sounds bold in me to say so, for you must know him far better than I do."

"Now, Biddy," said I, "I am very sorry to see this in you. I did not expect to see this in you. You are envious, Biddy, and grudging. You are dissatisfied on account of my rise in fortune, and you can't help showing it."

"If you have the heart to think so," returned Biddy, "say so. Say so over and over again, if you have the heart to think so."

"If you have the heart to be so, you mean, Biddy," said I, in a virtuous and superior tone; "don't put it off upon me. I am very sorry to see it, and it's a—it's a bad side of human nature. I did intend to ask you to use any little opportunities you might have after I was gone, of improving dear Joe. But after this, I ask you nothing. I am extremely sorry to see this in you, Biddy," I repeated. "It's a—it's a bad side of human nature."

"Whether you scold me or approve of me," returned poor Biddy, "you may equally depend upon my trying to do all that lies in my power, here, at all times. And whatever opinion you take away of me, shall make no difference in my remembrance of you. Yet a gentleman should not be unjust neither," said Biddy, turning away her head.

I again warmly repeated that it was a bad side of human nature (in which sentiment, waiving its application, I have since seen reason to think I was right), and I walked down the little path away from Biddy, and Biddy went into the house, and I went out at the garden gate and took a dejected stroll until supper-time; again feeling it very sorrowful and strange that this, the second night of my bright fortunes, should be as lonely and unsatisfactory as the first.

But, morning once more brightened my view, and I extended my clemency to Biddy, and we dropped the subject. Putting on the best clothes I had, I went into town as early as I could hope to find the shops open, and presented myself before Mr. Trabb, the tailor; who was having his breakfast in the parlour behind his shop, and who did not think it worth his while to come out to me, but called me in to him.

"Well!" said Mr. Trabb, in a hail-fellow-well-met kind of way. "How are you, and what can I do for you?"

Mr. Trabb had sliced his hot roll into three feather beds, and was slipping butter in between the blankets, and covering it up. He was a prosperous old bachelor, and his open window looked into a prosperous little garden and orchard, and there was a prosperous iron safe let into the wall at the side of his fireplace, and I did not doubt that heaps of his prosperity were put away in it in bags.

"Mr. Trabb," said I, "it's an unpleasant thing to have to mention, because it looks like boasting; but I have come into a handsome property."

A change passed over Mr. Trabb. He forgot the butter in bed, got up from the bedside, and wiped his fingers on the table-cloth, exclaiming, "Lord bless my soul!"

"I am going up to my guardian in London," said I, casually drawing some guineas out of my pocket and looking at them; "and I want a fashionable suit of clothes to go in. I wish to pay for them," I added—otherwise I thought he might only pretend to make them—"with ready money."

"My dear sir," said Mr. Trabb, as he respectfully bent his body, opened his arms, and took the liberty of touching me on the outside of each elbow, "don't hurt me by mentioning that. May I venture to congratulate you? Would you do me the favour of stepping into the shop?"

Mr. Trabb's boy was the most audacious boy in all that country-side. When I had entered he was sweeping the shop, and he had sweetened his labours by sweeping over me. He was still sweeping when I came out into the shop with Mr. Trabb, and he knocked the broom against all possible corners and obstacles, to express (as I understood it) equality with any blacksmith, alive or dead.

"Hold that noise," said Mr. Trabb, with the greatest sternness, "or I'll knock your head off! Do me the favour to be seated, sir. Now, this," said Mr. Trabb, taking down a roll of cloth, and tiding it out in a flowing manner over the counter, preparatory to getting his hand under it to show the gloss, "is a very sweet article. I can recommend it for your purpose, sir, because it really is extra super. But you shall see some others. Give me Number Four, you!" (To the boy, and with a dreadfully severe stare; foreseeing the danger of that miscreant's brushing me with it, or making some other sign of familiarity.)

Mr. Trabb never removed his stern eye from the boy until he had deposited number four on the counter and was at a safe distance again. Then, he commanded him to bring number five, and number eight. "And let me have none of your tricks here," said Mr. Trabb, "or you shall repent it, you young scoundrel, the longest day you have to live."

Mr. Trabb then bent over number four, and in a sort of deferential confidence recommended it to me as a light article for summer wear, an article much in vogue among the nobility and gentry, an article that it would ever be an honour to him to reflect upon a distinguished fellow-townsman's (if he might claim me for a fellow-townsman) having worn. "Are you bringing numbers five and eight, you vagabond," said Mr. Trabb to the boy after that, "or shall I kick you out of the shop and bring them myself?"

I selected the materials for a suit, with the assistance of Mr. Trabb's judgment, and re-entered the parlour to be measured. For, although Mr. Trabb had my measure already, and had previously been quite contented with it, he said apologetically that it "wouldn't do under existing circumstances, sir—wouldn't do at all." So, Mr. Trabb measured and calculated me in the parlour, as if I were an estate and he the finest species of surveyor, and gave himself such a world of trouble that I felt that no suit of clothes could possibly remunerate him for his pains. When he had at last done and had appointed to send the articles to Mr. Pumblechook's on the Thursday evening, he said, with his hand upon the parlour lock, "I know, sir, that London gentlemen cannot be expected to patronise local work, as a rule; but if you would give me a turn now and then in the quality of a townsman, I should greatly esteem it. Good morning, sir, much obliged.—Door!"

The last word was flung at the boy, who had not the least notion what it meant. But I saw him collapse as his master rubbed me out with his hands, and my first decided experience of the stupendous power of money, was, that it had morally laid upon his back, Trabb's boy.

After this memorable event, I went to the hatter's, and the bootmaker's, and the hosier's, and felt rather like Mother Hubbard's dog whose outfit required the services of so many trades. I also went to the coach-office and took my place for seven o'clock on Saturday morning. It was not necessary to explain everywhere that I had come into a handsome property; but whenever I said anything to that effect, it followed that the officiating tradesman ceased to have his attention diverted through the window by the High-street, and concentrated his mind upon me. When I had ordered everything I wanted, I directed my steps towards Pumblechook's, and, as I approached that gentleman's place of business, I saw him standing at his door.

He was waiting for me with great impatience. He had been out early with the chaise-cart, and had called at the forge and heard the news. He had prepared a collation for me in the Barnwell parlour, and he too ordered his shopman to "come out of the gangway" as my sacred person passed.

"My dear friend," said Mr. Pumblechook, taking me by both hands, when he and I and the collation were alone,

"I give you joy of your good fortune. Well deserved, well deserved!"

This was coming to the point, and I thought it a sensible way of expressing himself.

"To think," said Mr. Pumblechook, after snorting admiration at me for some moments, "that I should have been the humble instrument of leading up to this, is a proud reward."

I begged Mr. Pumblechook to remember that nothing was to be ever said or hinted, on that point.

"My dear young friend," said Mr. Pumblechook; "if you will allow me to call you so——"

I murmured "Certainly," and Mr. Pumblechook took me by both hands again, and communicated a movement to his waistcoat, which had an emotional appearance, though it was rather low down, "My dear young friend, rely upon my doing my little all in your absence, by keeping the fact before the mind of Joseph—Joseph!" said Mr. Pumblechook, in the way of a compassionate adjuration. "Joseph!! Joseph!!!" Thereupon he shook his head and tapped it, expressing his sense of deficiency in Joseph.

"But my dear young friend," said Mr. Pumblechook, "you must be hungry, you must be exhausted. Be seated. Here is a chicken had round from the Boar, here is a tongue had round from the Boar, here's one or two little things had round from the Boar, that I hope you may not despise. But do I," said Mr. Pumblechook, getting up again the moment after he had sat down, "see afore me, him as I ever sported with in his times of happy infancy? And may I——?"

This May I, meant might he shake hands? I consented, and he was fervent, and then sat down again.

"Here is wine," said Mr. Pumblechook. "Let us drink, Thanks to Fortune, and may she ever pick out her favourites with equal judgment! And yet I cannot," said Mr. Pumblechook, getting up again, "see afore me One—and likewise drink to One—without again expressing—May I—*may* I——?"

I said he might, and he shook hands with me again, and emptied his glass and turned it upside down. I did the same; and if I had turned myself upside down before drinking, the wine could not have gone more direct to my head.

Mr. Pumblechook helped me to the liver wing, and to the best slice of tongue (none of those out-of-the-way No Thoroughfares of Pork now), and took, comparatively speaking, no care of himself at all. "Ah! poultry, poultry! You little thought," said Mr. Pumblechook, apostrophising the fowl in the dish, "when you was a young fledgeling, what was in store for you. You little thought you was to be refreshment beneath this humble roof for one as—Call it a weakness, if you will," said Mr. Pumblechook, getting up again, "but may I? *may* I——?"

It began to be unnecessary to repeat the form of saying he might, so he did it at once. How he ever did it so often without wounding himself with my knife, I don't know.

"And your sister," he resumed, after a little steady eating, "which had the honour of bringing you up by hand! It's a sad picter, to reflect that she's no longer equal to fully understanding the honour. May——"

I saw he was about to come at me again, and I stopped him.

"We'll drink her health," said I.

"Ah!" cried Mr. Pumblechook, leaning back in his chair, quite flaccid with admiration, "that's the way you know 'em, sir!" (I don't know who Sir was, but he certainly was not I, and there was no third person present); "that's the way you know the noble-minded, sir! Ever forgiving and ever affable. It might," said the servile Pumblechook, putting down his untasted glass in a hurry and getting up again, "to a common person, have the appearance of repeating—but may I——?"

When he had done it, he resumed his seat and drank to my sister. "Let us never be blind," said Mr. Pumblechook, "to her faults of temper, but it is to be hoped she meant well."

At about this time, I began to observe that he was getting flushed in the face; as to myself, I felt all face, steeped in wine and smarting.

I mentioned to Mr. Pumblechook that I wished to have my new clothes sent to his house, and he was ecstatic on my so distinguishing him. I mentioned my reason for desiring to avoid observation in the village, and he lauded it to the skies. There was nobody but himself, he intimated, worthy of my confidence, and—in short, might he? Then he asked me tenderly if I remembered our boyish games at sums, and how we had gone together to have me bound apprentice, and, in effect, how he had ever been my favourite fancy and my chosen friend? If I had taken ten times as many glasses of wine as I had, I should have known that he never had stood in that relation towards me, and should in my heart of hearts have repudiated the idea. Yet for all that, I remember feeling convinced that I had been much mistaken in him, and that he was a sensible practical good-hearted prime fellow.

By degrees he fell to reposing such great confidence in me, as to ask my advice in reference to his own affairs. He mentioned that there was an opportunity for a great amalgamation and monopoly of the corn and seed trade on those premises, if enlarged, such as had never occurred before in that, or any other neighbourhood. What alone was wanting to the realisation of a vast fortune, he considered to be More Capital. Those were the two little words, more capital. Now it appeared to him (Pumblechook) that if that capital were got into the business, through a sleeping partner, sir—which sleeping partner would have nothing to do but walk in, by self or deputy, whenever he pleased, and examine the books—and walk in twice a year and take his profits away in his pocket, to the tune of fifty per cent. —it appeared to him that that might be an opening for a young gentleman of spirit combined with property, which would be worthy of his attention. But what did I think? He had great confidence in my opinion, and what did I think? I gave it as my opinion. "Wait a bit!" The united vastness and distinctness of this view so struck him, that he no longer asked me if he might shake hands with me, but said he really must—and did.

We drank all the wine, and Mr. Pumblechook pledged himself over and over again to keep Joseph up to the mark (I don't know what mark), and to render me efficient and constant service (I don't know what service). He also made known to me for the first time in my life, and certainly after having kept his secret wonderfully well, that he had always said of me, "That boy is no common boy, and mark me, his fortun' will be no common fortun'." He said with a tearful smile that it was a singular thing to think of now, and I said so too. Finally, I went out into the air, with a dim perception that there was something unwonted in the conduct of the sunshine, and found that I had slumberously got to the turnpike without having taken any account of the road.

There, I was roused by Mr. Pumblechook's hailing me. He was a long way down the sunny street, and was making expressive gestures for me to stop. I stopped, and he came up breathless.

"No, my dear friend," said he, when he had recovered wind for speech. "Not if I can help it. This occasion shall not entirely pass without that affability on your part. —May I, as an old friend and well-wisher? May I?"

We shook hands for the hundredth time at least, and he ordered a young carter out of my way with the greatest indignation. Then, he blessed me, and stood waving his hand to me until I had passed the crook in the road; and then I turned into a field and had a long nap under a hedge before I pursued my way home.

I had scant luggage to take with me to London, for little of the little I possessed was adapted to my new station. But, I began packing that same afternoon, and wildly packed up things that I knew I should want next morning, in a fiction that there was not a moment to be lost.

So, Tuesday, Wednesday, and Thursday, passed; and on Friday morning I went to Mr. Pumblechook's, to put on my new clothes and pay my visit to Miss Havisham. Mr. Pumblechook's own room was given up to me to dress in, and was decorated with clean towels expressly for the event. My clothes were rather a disappointment, of course. Probably every new and eagerly expected garment ever put on since clothes came in, fell a trifle short of the wearer's expectation. But after I had had my new suit on, some half an hour, and had gone through an immensity of posturing with Mr. Pumblechook's very limited dressing-glass, in the futile endeavour to see my legs, it seemed to fit me better. It being market morning at a neighbouring town some ten miles off, Mr. Pumblechook was not at home. I had not told him exactly when I meant to leave, and was not likely to shake hands with him again before departing. This was all as it should be, and I went out in my new array: fearfully ashamed of having to pass the shopman, and suspicious after all that I was at a personal disadvantage, something like Joe's in his Sunday suit.

I went circuitously to Miss Havisham's by all the back ways, and rang at the bell constrainedly, on account of the stiff long fingers of my gloves. Sarah Pocket came to the gate, and positively reeled back when she saw me so changed; her walnut-shell countenance likewise, turned from brown to green and yellow.

"You?" said she. "You? Good gracious! What do you want?"

"I am going to London, Miss Pocket," said I, "and want to say good bye to Miss Havisham."

I was not expected, for she left me locked in the yard, while she went to ask if I were to be admitted. After a very short delay, she returned and took me up, staring at me all the way.

Miss Havisham was taking exercise in the room with the long spread table, leaning on her crutch stick. The room was lighted as of yore, and at the sound of her entrance, she stopped and turned. She was then just abreast of the rotted bride-cake.

"Don't go, Sarah," she said. "Well, Pip?"

"I start for London, Miss Havisham, to-morrow," I was exceedingly careful what I said, "and I thought you would kindly not mind my taking leave of you."

"This is a gay figure, Pip," said she, making her crutch stick play round me, as if she, the fairy godmother who had changed me, were bestowing the finishing gift.

"I have come into such good fortune since I saw you

last, Miss Havisham," I murmured. "And I am so grateful for it, Miss Havisham!"

"Ay, ay!" said she, looking at the discomfited and envious Sarah, with delight. "I have seen Mr. Jaggers. *I* have heard about it, Pip. So you go to-morrow?"

"Yes, Miss Havisham."

"And you are adopted by a rich person?"

"Yes, Miss Havisham."

"Not named?"

"No, Miss Havisham."

"And Mr. Jaggers is made your guardian?"

"Yes, Miss Havisham."

She quite gloated on these questions and answers, so keen was her enjoyment of Sarah Pocket's jealous dismay. "Well!" she went on; "you have a promising career before you. Be good—deserve it—and abide by Mr. Jaggers's instructions." She looked at me, and looked at Sarah, and Sarah's countenance wrung out of her watchful face a cruel smile. "Good bye, Pip!—you will always keep the name of Pip, you know."

"Yes, Miss Havisham."

"Good bye, Pip!"

She stretched out her hand, and I went down on my knee and put it to my lips. I had not considered how I should take leave of her; it came naturally to me at the moment, to do this. She looked at Sarah Pocket with triumph in her weird eyes, and so I left my fairy godmother, with both her hands on her crutch stick, standing in the midst of the dimly lighted room beside the rotten bride-cake that was hidden in cobwebs.

Sarah Pocket conducted me down, as if I were a host who must be seen out. She could not get over my appearance, and was in the last degree confounded. I said "Good bye, Miss Pocket;" but she merely stared, and did not seem collected enough to know that I had spoken. Clear of the house, I made the best of my way back to Pumblechook's, took off my new clothes, made them into a bundle, and went back home in my older dress, carrying it—to speak the truth—much more at my ease too, though I had the bundle to carry.

And now, those six days which were to have run out so slowly, had run out fast and were gone, and to-morrow looked me in the face more steadily than I could look at it. As the six evenings had dwindled away to five, to four, to three, to two, I had become more and more appreciative of the society of Joe and Biddy. On this last evening, I dressed myself out in my new clothes, for their delight, and sat in my splendour until bedtime. We had a hot supper on the occasion, graced by the inevitable roast fowl, and we had some flip to finish with. We were all very low, and none the higher for pretending to be in spirits.

I was to leave our village at five in the morning, carrying my little hand-portmanteau, and I had told Joe that I wished to walk away all alone. I am afraid—sore afraid—that this purpose originated in my sense of the contrast there would be between me and Joe, if we went to the coach together. I had pretended with myself that there was nothing of this taint in the arrangement; but when I went up to my little room on this last night, I felt compelled to admit that it might be done so, and had an impulse upon me to go down again and entreat Joe to walk with me in the morning. I did not.

All night there were coaches in my broken sleep, going to wrong places instead of to London, and having in the traces, now dogs, now cats, now pigs, now men—never horses. Fantastic failures of journeys occupied me until the day dawned and the birds were singing. Then, I got up and partly dressed, and sat at the window to take a last look out, and in taking it fell asleep.

Biddy was astir so early to get my breakfast, that, although I did not sleep at the window an hour, I smelt the smoke of the kitchen fire when I started up with a terrible idea that it must be late in the afternoon. But long after that, and long after I heard the clinking of the teacups and was quite ready, I wanted the resolution to go downstairs. After all, I remained up there, repeatedly unlocking and unstrapping my small portmanteau and locking and strapping it up again, until Biddy called to me that I was late.

It was a hurried breakfast with no taste in it. I got up from the meal, saying with a sort of briskness, as if it had only just occurred to me, "Well! I suppose I must be off!" and then I kissed my sister, who was laughing, and nodding and shaking in her usual chair, and kissed Biddy, and threw my arms around Joe's neck. Then I took up my little portmanteau and walked out. The last I saw of them was, when I presently heard a scuffle behind me, and looking back, saw Joe throwing an old shoe after me and Biddy throwing another old shoe. I stopped then, to wave my hat, and dear old Joe waved his strong right arm above his head, crying huskily, "Hooroar!" and Biddy put her apron to her face.

I walked away at a good pace, thinking it was easier to go than I had supposed it would be, and reflecting that it would never have done to have an old shoe thrown after the coach, in sight of all the High-street. I whistled and made nothing of going. But the village was very peaceful and quiet, and the light mists were solemnly rising, as if to show me the world, and I had been so innocent and little there, and all beyond was so unknown and great, that in a moment with a strong heave and sob I broke into tears. It was by the finger-post at the end of the village, and I laid my hand upon it, and said, "Good bye, O my dear, dear friend!"

Heaven knows we need never be ashamed of our tears, for they are rain upon the blinding dust of earth, overlying our hard hearts. I was better after I had cried, than before—more sorry, more aware of my own ingratitude, more gentle. If I had cried before, I should have had Joe with me then.

So subdued I was by those tears, and by their breaking out again in the course of the quiet walk, that when I was on the coach, and it was clear of the town, I deliberated with an aching heart whether I would not get down when we changed horses and walk back, and have another evening at home, and a better parting. We changed, and I had not made up my mind, and still reflected for my comfort that it would be quite practicable to get down and walk back, when we changed again. And while I was occupied with those deliberations, I would fancy an exact resemblance to Joe in some man coming along the road towards us, and my heart would beat high.—As if he could possibly be there!

We changed again, and yet again, and it was now too late and too far to go back, and I went on. And the mists had all solemnly risen now, and the world lay spread before me.

THIS IS THE END OF THE FIRST STAGE OF PIP'S EXPECTATIONS.

CHAPTER XX.

The journey from our town to the metropolis, was a journey of about five hours. It was a little past mid-day when the four-horse stage-coach by which I was a passenger, got into the ravel of traffic frayed out by the Cross Keys, Wood-street, Cheapside, London.

We Britons had at that time particularly settled that it was treasonable to doubt our having and our being the best of everything: otherwise, while I was scared by the immensity of London, I think I might have had some faint doubts whether it was not rather ugly, crooked, narrow, and dirty.

Mr. Jaggers had duly sent me his address; it was Little Britain, and he had written after it on his card, "just out of Smithfield, and close by the coach-office." Nevertheless, a hackney-coachman, who seemed to have as many capes to his greasy great-coat as he was years old, packed me up in his coach and hemmed me in with a folding and jingling barrier of steps, as if he were going to take me fifty miles. His getting on his box, which I remember to have been decorated with an old weather-stained pea-green hammercloth, moth-eaten into rags, was quite a work of time. It was a wonderful equipage, with six great coronets outside, and ragged things behind for I don't know how many footmen to hold on by, and a harrow below them, to prevent amateur footmen from yielding to the temptation.

I had scarcely had time to enjoy the coach and to think how like a straw-yard it was, and yet how like a rag-shop, and to wonder why the horses' nose-bags were kept inside, when I observed the coachman beginning to get down, as if we were going to stop presently. And stop we presently did, in a gloomy street, at certain offices with an open door, whereon was painted Mr. Jaggers.

"How much?" I asked the coachman.

The coachman answered, "A shilling—unless you wish to make it more."

I naturally said I had no wish to make it more.

"Then it must be a shilling," observed the coachman. "I don't want to get into trouble. I know him!" He darkly closed an eye at Mr. Jaggers's name, and shook his head.

When he had got his shilling, and had in course of time completed the ascent to his box, and had got away (which appeared to relieve his mind), I went into the front office with my little portmanteau in my hand, and asked, was Mr. Jaggers at home?

"He is not," returned the clerk. "He is in Court at present. Am I addressing Mr. Pip?"

I signified that he was addressing Mr. Pip.

"Mr. Jaggers left word would you wait in his room. He couldn't say how long he might be, having a case on. But it stands to reason, his time being valuable, that he won't be longer than he can help."

With those words, the clerk opened a door, and ushered me into an inner chamber at the back. Here we found a gentleman with one eye, in a velveteen suit and knee-breeches, who wiped his nose with his sleeve on being interrupted in the perusal of the newspaper.

"Go and wait outside, Mike," said the clerk.

I began to say that I hoped I was not interrupting—when the clerk shoved this gentleman out with as little ceremony as I ever saw used, and tossing his fur cap out after him, left me alone.

Mr. Jaggers's room was lighted by a skylight only, and was a most dismal place; the skylight, eccentrically patched like a broken head, and the distorted adjoining houses looking as if they had twisted themselves to peep down at me through it. There were not so many papers about, as I should have expected to see; and there were some odd objects about, that I should not have expected to see—such as an old rusty pistol, a sword in a scabbard, several strange-looking boxes and packages, and two dreadful casts on a shelf, of faces peculiarly swollen, and twitchy about the nose. Mr. Jaggers's own high-backed chair was of deadly black horse-hair, with rows of brass nails round it, like a coffin; and I fancied I could see how he leaned back in it, and bit his forefinger at the clients. The room was but small, and the clients seemed to have had a habit of backing up against the wall: the wall, especially opposite to Mr. Jaggers's chair, being greasy with shoulders. I recalled, too, that the one-eyed gentleman had shuffled forth against the wall when I was the innocent cause of his being turned out.

I sat down in the cliental chair placed over against Mr. Jaggers's chair, and became fascinated by the dismal atmosphere of the place. I called to mind that the clerk had the same air of knowing something to everybody else's disadvantage, as his master had. I wondered how many other clerks there were upstairs, and whether they all claimed to have the same detrimental mastery of their fellow-creatures. I wondered what was the history of all the odd litter about the room, and how it came there. I wondered whether the two swollen faces were of Mr. Jaggers's family, and, if he were so unfortunate as to have had a pair of such ill-looking relations, why he stuck them on that dusty perch for the blacks and flies to settle on, instead of giving them a place at home. Of course I had no experience of a London summer day, and my spirits may have been oppressed by the hot exhausted air, and by the dust and grit that lay thick on everything. But I sat wondering and waiting in Mr. Jaggers's close room, until I really could not bear the two casts on the shelf above Mr. Jaggers's chair, and got up and went out.

When I told the clerk that I would take a turn in the air while I waited, he advised me to go round the corner and I should come into Smithfield. So, I came into Smithfield; and the shameful place, being all asmear with filth and fat and blood and foam, seemed to stick to me. So I rubbed it off with all possible speed by turning into a street where I saw the great black dome of Saint Paul's bulging at me from behind a grim stone building which a bystander said was Newgate Prison. Following the wall of the jail, I found the roadway covered with straw to deaden the noise of passing vehicles; and from this, and from the quantity of people standing about, smelling strongly of spirits and beer, I inferred that the trials were on.

While I looked about me here, an exceedingly dirty and partially drunk minister of justice asked me if I would like to step in and hear a trial or so: informing me that he could give me a front place for half-a-crown, whence I should command a full view of the Lord Chief Justice in his wig and robes—mentioning that awful personage like waxwork, and presently offering him at the reduced price of eighteen-pence. As I declined the proposal on the plea of an appointment, he was so good as to take me into a yard and show me where the gallows was kept, and also where people were publicly whipped, and then he showed me the Debtors' Door, out of which culprits came to be hanged; heightening the interest of that dreadful portal by giving me to understand that "four on 'em" would come out at that door the day after to-morrow at eight in the morning to be killed in a row. This was horrible, and gave me a sickening idea of London: the more so as the Lord Chief Justice's proprietor wore (from his hat down to his boots and up again to his pocket-handkerchief inclusive) mildewed clothes, which had evidently not belonged to him originally, and which, I took it into my head, he had bought cheap of the executioner. Under these circumstances I thought myself well rid of him for a shilling.

I dropped into the office to ask if Mr. Jaggers had come in yet, and I found he had not, and I strolled out again. This time, I made the tour of Little Britain, and turned into Bartholomew Close; and now I became aware that other people were waiting about for Mr. Jaggers, as well as I. There were two men of secret appearance lounging in Bartholomew Close, and thoughtfully fitting their feet into the cracks of the pavement as they talked together, one of whom said to the other when they first passed me, that "Jaggers would do it if it was to be done." There was a knot of three men and two women standing at a corner, and one of the women was crying on her dirty shawl, and the other comforted her by saying, as she pulled her own shawl over her shoulders, "Jaggers is for him, 'Melia, and what more *could* you have?" There was a red-eyed little Jew who came into the Close while I was loitering there, in company with a second little Jew whom he sent upon an errand; and while the messenger was gone, I remarked this Jew, who was of a highly excitable temperament, performing a jig of anxiety under a lamp-post, and accompanying himself, in a kind of frenzy, with the words, "Oh Jaggerth, Jaggerth, Jaggerth! all otherth ith Cag-Maggerth, give me Jaggerth!" These testimonies to the popularity of my guardian made a deep impression on me, and I admired and wondered more than ever.

At length, as I was looking out at the iron gate of Bartholomew Close into Little Britain, I saw Mr. Jaggers coming across the road towards me. All the others who were waiting, saw him at the same time, and there was quite a rush at him. Mr. Jaggers, putting a hand on my shoulder and walking me on at his side without saying anything to me, addressed himself to his followers.

First, he took the two secret men.

"Now, I have nothing to say to *you*," said Mr. Jaggers, throwing his finger at them. "I want to know no more than I know. As to the result, it's a toss-up. I told you from the first it was a toss-up. Have you paid Wemmick?"

"We made the money up this morning, sir," said one of the men submissively, while the other perused Mr. Jaggers's face.

"I don't ask you when you made it up, or where, or whether you made it up at all. Has Wemmick got it?"

"Yes, sir," said both the men together.

"Very well; then you may go. Now, I won't have it!" said Mr. Jaggers, waving his hand at them to put them behind him. "If you say a word to me, I'll throw up the case."

"We thought, Mr. Jaggers——" one of the men began, pulling off his hat.

"That's what I told you not to do," said Mr. Jaggers. "*You* thought! I think for you; that's enough for you. If I want you, I know where to find you; I don't want you to find me. Now I won't have it. I won't hear a word."

The two men looked at one another as Mr. Jaggers waved them behind again, and humbly fell back and were heard no more.

"And now *you!*" said Mr. Jaggers, suddenly stopping, and turning on the two women with the shawls, from whom the three men had meekly separated—"Oh! Amelia, is it?"

"Yes, Mr. Jaggers."

"And do you remember," retorted Mr. Jaggers, "that but for me you wouldn't be here and couldn't be here?"

"Oh yes, sir!" exclaimed both women together. "Lord bless you, sir, well we knows that!"

"Then why," said Mr. Jaggers, "do you come here?"

"My Bill, sir!" the crying woman pleaded.

"Now, I tell you what!" said Mr. Jaggers. "Once for all. If you don't know that your Bill's in good hands, I know it. And if you come here, bothering about your Bill, I'll make an example of both your Bill and you, and let him slip through my fingers. Have you paid Wemmick?"

"Oh yes, sir! Every farden."

"Very well. Then you have done all you have got to do. Say another word—one single word—and Wemmick shall give you your money back."

This terrible threat caused the two women to fall off immediately. No one remained now but the excitable Jew, who had already raised the skirts of Mr. Jaggers's coat to his lips several times.

"I don't know this man?" said Mr. Jaggers, in the most devastating strain. "What does this fellow want?"

"Ma thear Mithter Jaggerth. Hown brother to Habraham Latharuth?"

"Who's he?" said Mr. Jaggers. "Let go of my coat."

The suitor, kissing the hem of the garment again before relinquishing it, replied, "Habraham Latharuth, on thuthpithion of plate."

"You're too late," said Mr. Jaggers. "I am over the way."

"Holy father, Mithter Jaggerth!" cried my excitable acquaintance, turning white, "don't thay you're again Habraham Latharuth!"

"I am," said Mr. Jaggers, "and there's an end of it. Get out of the way."

"Mithter Jaggerth! Half a moment! My hown cuthen'th gone to Mithter Wemmick at thith prethenth minute to hoffer him hany termth. Mithter Jaggerth! Half a quarter of a moment! If you'd have the condethenthun to be brought off from the t'other thide—at any thuperior prithe!—money no object!—Mithter Jaggerth—Mithter——!"

My guardian threw his supplicant off with supreme indifference, and left him dancing on the pavement as if it were red-hot. Without further interruption, we reached the front office, where we found the clerk and the man in velveteen with the fur cap.

"Here's Mike," said the clerk, getting down from his stool, and approaching Mr. Jaggers confidentially.

"Oh!" said Mr. Jaggers, turning to the man, who was pulling a lock of hair in the middle of his forehead, like the Bull in Cock Robin pulling at the bell-rope; "your man comes on this afternoon. Well?"

"Well, Mas'r Jaggers," returned Mike, in the voice of a sufferer from a constitutional cold; "arter a deal o' trouble, I've found one, sir, as might do."

"What is he prepared to swear?"

"Well, Mas'r Jaggers," said Mike, wiping his nose on his fur cap this time; "in a general way, anythink."

Mr. Jaggers suddenly became most irate. "Now, I warned you before," said he, throwing his forefinger at the terrified client, "that if ever you presumed to talk in that way here, I'd make an example of you. You infernal scoundrel, how dare you tell ME that?"

The client looked scared, but bewildered too, as if he were unconscious what he had done.

"Spooney!" said the clerk, in a low voice, giving him a stir with his elbow. "Soft Head! Need you say it face to face?"

"Now, I ask you, you blundering booby," said my guardian, very sternly, "once more and for the last time, what the man you have brought here is prepared to swear?"

Mike looked hard at my guardian, as if he were trying to learn a lesson from his face, and slowly replied, "Ayther to character, or to having been in his company and never left him all the night in question."

"Now, be careful. In what station of life is this man?"

Mike looked at his cap, and looked at the floor, and looked at the ceiling, and looked at the clerk, and even looked at me, before beginning to reply in a nervous manner, "We've dressed him up like——" when my guardian blustered out:

"What? You WILL, will you?"

("Spooney!" added the clerk again, with another stir.)

After some helpless casting about, Mike brightened and began again:

"He is dressed like a 'spectable pieman. A sort of a pastry-cook."

"Is he here?" asked my guardian.

"I left him," said Mike, "a setting on some doorsteps round the corner."

"Take him past that window, and let me see him."

The window indicated, was the office window. We all three went to it, behind the wire blind, and presently saw the client go by in an accidental manner, with a murderous-looking tall individual, in a short suit of white linen and a paper cap. This guileless confectioner was not by any means sober, and had a black eye in the green stage of recovery, which was painted over.

"Tell him to take his witness away directly," said my guardian to the clerk, in extreme disgust, "and ask him what he means by bringing such a fellow as that."

My guardian then took me into his own room, and while he lunched, standing, from a sandwich-box and a pocket flask of sherry (he seemed to bully his very sandwich as he ate it), informed me what arrangements he had made for me. I was to go to "Barnard's Inn," to young Mr. Pocket's rooms, where a bed had been sent in for my accommodation; I was to remain with young Mr. Pocket until Monday; on Monday I was to go with him to his father's house on a visit, that I might try how I liked it. Also, I was told what my allowance was to be—it was a very liberal one—and had handed to me from one of my guardian's drawers, the cards of certain tradesmen with whom I was to deal for all kinds of clothes, and such other things as I could in reason want. "You will find your credit good, Mr. Pip," said my guardian, whose flask of sherry smelt like a whole cask-full, as he hastily refreshed himself, "but I shall by this means be able to check your bills, and to pull you up if I find you outrunning the constable. Of course you'll go wrong somehow, but that's no fault of mine."

After I had pondered a little over this encouraging sentiment, I asked Mr. Jaggers if I could send for a coach? He said it was not worth while, I was so near my destination; Wemmick should walk round with me, if I pleased.

I then found that Wemmick was the clerk in the next room. Another clerk was rung down from upstairs to take his place while he was out, and I accompanied him into the street, after shaking hands with my guardian. We found a new set of people lingering outside, but Wemmick made a way among them by saying coolly yet decisively, "I tell you it's no use; he won't have a word to say to one of you;" and we soon got clear of them, and went on side by side.

CHAPTER XXI.

CASTING my eyes on Mr. Wemmick as we went along, to see what he was like in the light of day, I found him to be a dry man, rather short in stature, with a square wooden face, whose expression seemed to have been imperfectly chipped out with a dull-edged chisel. There were some marks in it that might have been dimples, if the material had been softer and the instrument finer, but which, as it was, were only dints. The chisel had made three or four of these attempts at embellishment over his nose, but had given them up without an effort to smooth them off. I judged him to be a bachelor from the frayed condition of his linen, and he appeared to have sustained a good many bereavements; for he wore at least four mourning rings, besides a brooch representing a lady and a weeping willow at a tomb with an urn on it. I noticed, too, that several rings and seals hung at his watch chain, as if he were quite laden with remembrances of departed friends. He had glittering eyes—small, keen, and black—and thin wide mottled lips. He had had them, to the best of my belief, from forty to fifty years.

"So you were never in London before?" said Mr. Wemmick to me.

"No," said I.

"I was new here once," said Mr. Wemmick. "Rum to think of now!"

"You are well acquainted with it now?"

"Why, yes," said Mr. Wemmick. "I know the moves of it."

"Is it a very wicked place?" I asked, more for the sake of saying something than for information.

"You may get cheated, robbed, and murdered, in London. But there are plenty of people anywhere, who'll do that for you."

"If there is bad blood between you and them," said I, to soften it off a little.

"Oh! I don't know about bad blood," returned Mr. Wemmick. "There's not much bad blood about. They'll do it, if there's anything to be got by it."

"That makes it worse."

"You think so?" returned Mr. Wemmick. "Much about the same, I should say."

He wore his hat on the back of his head, and looked straight before him: walking in a self-contained way as if there were nothing in the streets to claim his attention. His mouth was such a post-office of a mouth that he had a mechanical appearance of smiling. We had got to the top of

Holborn Hill before I knew that it was merely a mechanical appearance, and that he was not smiling at all.

"Do you know where Mr. Matthew Pocket lives?" I asked Mr. Wemmick.

"Yes," said he, nodding in the direction. "At Hammersmith, west of London."

"Is that far?"

"Well! Say five miles."

"Do you know him?"

"Why, you are a regular cross-examiner!" said Mr. Wemmick, looking at me with an approving air. "Yes. I know him. I know him!"

There was an air of toleration or depreciation about his utterance of these words, that rather depressed me; and I was still looking sideways at his block of a face in search of any encouraging note to the text, when he said here we were at Barnard's Inn. My depression was not alleviated by the announcement, for, I had supposed that establishment to be an hotel kept by Mr. Barnard, to which the Blue Boar in our town was a mere public-house. Whereas I now found Barnard to be a disembodied spirit, or a fiction, and his inn the dingiest collection of shabby buildings ever squeezed together in a rank corner as a club for Tomcats.

We entered this haven through a wicket-gate, and were disgorged by an introductory passage into a melancholy little square that looked to me like a flat burying-ground. I thought it had the most dismal trees in it, and the most dismal sparrows, and the most dismal cats, and the most dismal houses (in number half a dozen or so), that I had ever seen. I thought the windows of the sets of chambers into which those houses were divided, were in every stage of dilapidated blind and curtain, crippled flower-pot, cracked glass, dusty decay, and miserable makeshift; while To Let To Let To Let, glared at me from empty rooms, as if no new wretches ever came there, and the vengeance of the soul of Barnard were being slowly appeased by the gradual suicide of the present occupants and their unholy interment under the gravel. A frouzy morning of soot and smoke attired this forlorn creation of Barnard, and it had strewed ashes on its head, and was undergoing penance and humiliation as a mere dust-hole. Thus far my sense of sight; while dry rot and wet rot and all the silent rots that rot in neglected roof and cellar—rot of rat and mouse and bug and coaching-stables near at hand besides—addressed themselves faintly to my sense of smell, and moaned, "Try Barnard's Mixture."

So imperfect was this realisation of the first of my great expectations, that I looked in dismay at Mr. Wemmick. "Ah!" said he, mistaking me; "the retirement reminds you of the country. So it does me."

He led me into a corner and conducted me up a flight of stairs—which appeared to me to be slowly collapsing into sawdust, so that one of those days the upper lodgers would look out at their doors and find themselves without the means of coming down—to a set of chambers on the top floor. MR. POCKET, JUN., was painted on the door, and there was a label on the letter-box, "Return shortly."

"He hardly thought you'd come so soon," Mr. Wemmick explained. "You don't want me any more?"

"No, thank you," said I.

"As I keep the cash," Mr. Wemmick observed, "we shall most likely meet pretty often. Good day."

"Good day."

I put out my hand, and Mr. Wemmick at first looked at it as if he thought I wanted something. Then he looked at me, and said, correcting himself,

"To be sure! Yes. You're in the habit of shaking hands?"

I was rather confused, thinking it must be out of the London fashion, but said yes.

"I have got so out of it!" said Mr. Wemmick—"except at last. Very glad, I'm sure, to make your acquaintance. Good day!"

When we had shaken hands and he was gone, I opened the staircase window and had nearly beheaded myself, for, the lines had rotted away, and it came down like the guillotine. Happily it was so quick that I had not put my head out. After this escape, I was content to take a foggy view of the Inn through the window's encrusting dirt, and to stand dolefully looking out, saying to myself that London was decidedly overrated.

Mr. Pocket, Junior's, idea of Shortly was not mine, for I had nearly maddened myself with looking out for half an hour, and had written my name with my finger several times in the dirt of every pane in the window, before I heard footsteps on the stairs. Gradually there arose before me the hat, head, neckcloth, waistcoat, trousers, boots, of a member of society of about my own standing. He had a paper-bag under each arm and a pottle of strawberries in one hand, and was out of breath.

"Mr. Pip?" said he.

"Mr. Pocket?" said I.

"Dear me!" he exclaimed. "I am extremely sorry; but I knew there was a coach from your part of the country at midday, and I thought you would come by that one. The fact is, I have been out on your account—not that that is any excuse—for I thought, coming from the country, you might like a little fruit after dinner, and I went to Covent Garden Market to get it good."

For a reason that I had, I felt as if my eyes would start out of my head. I acknowledged his attention incoherently, and began to think this was a dream.

"Dear me!" said Mr. Pocket, Junior. "This door sticks so!"

As he was fast making jam of his fruit by wrestling with the door while the paper-bags were under his arms, I begged him to allow me to hold them. He relinquished them with an agreeable smile, and combated with the door as if it were a wild beast. It yielded so suddenly at last, that he staggered back upon me, and I staggered back upon the opposite door, and we both laughed. But still I felt as if my eyes must start out of my head, and as if this must be a dream.

"Pray come in," said Mr. Pocket, Junior. "Allow me to lead the way. I am rather bare here, but I hope you'll be able to make out tolerably well till Monday. My father thought you would get on more agreeably through to-morrow with me than with him, and might like to take a walk about London. I am sure I shall be very happy to show London to you. As to our table, you won't find that bad, I hope, for it will be supplied from our coffee-house here, and (it is only right I should add) at your expense, such being Mr. Jaggers's directions. As to our lodging, it's not by any means splendid, because I have my own bread to earn, and my father hasn't anything to give me, and I shouldn't be willing to take it, if he had. This is our sitting-room—just such chairs and tables and carpet and so forth, you see, as they could spare from home. You mustn't give me credit for the table-cloth and spoons and castors, because they come for you from the coffee-house. This is my little bedroom; rather musty, but Barnard's *is* musty. This is your bedroom; the furniture's hired for the occasion, but I trust it will answer the purpose; if you should want anything, I'll go and fetch it. The chambers are retired, and we shall be alone together, but we shan't fight, I dare say. But, dear me, I beg your pardon, you're holding the fruit all this time. Pray let me take these bags from you. I am quite ashamed."

As I stood opposite to Mr. Pocket, Junior, delivering him the bags, One, Two, I saw the starting appearance come into his own eyes that I knew to be in mine, and he said, falling back:

"Lord bless me, you're the prowling boy!"

"And you," said I, "are the pale young gentleman!"

CHAPTER XXII.

THE pale young gentleman and I stood contemplating one another in Barnard's Inn, until we both burst out laughing. "The idea of its being you!" said he. "The idea of its being *you!*" said I. And then we contemplated one another afresh, and laughed again. "Well!" said the pale young gentleman, reaching out his hand good-humouredly, "it's all over now, I hope, and it will be magnanimous in you if you'll forgive me for having knocked you about so."

I derived from this speech that Mr. Herbert Pocket (for Herbert was the pale young gentleman's name) still rather confounded his intention with his execution. But I made a modest reply, and we shook hands warmly.

"You hadn't come into your good fortune at that time?" said Herbert Pocket.

"No," said I.

"No," he acquiesced: "I heard it had happened very lately. *I* was rather on the look-out for good fortune then."

"Indeed?"

"Yes. Miss Havisham had sent for me, to see if she could take a fancy to me. But she couldn't—at all events, she didn't."

I thought it polite to remark that I was surprised to hear that.

"Bad taste," said Herbert, laughing, "but a fact. Yes, she had sent for me on a trial visit, and if I had come out of it successfully. I suppose I should have been provided for; perhaps I should have been what-you-may-called it to Estella."

"What's that?" I asked, with sudden gravity.

He was arranging his fruit in plates while we talked, which divided his attention, and was the cause of his having made this lapse of a word. "Affianced," he explained, still busy with the fruit. "Betrothed. Engaged. What's-his-named. Any word of that sort."

"How did you bear your disappointment?" I asked.

"Pooh!" said he, "I didn't care much for it. *She's* a Tartar."

"Miss Havisham?"

"I don't say no to that, but I meant Estella. That girl's hard and haughty and capricious to the last degree, and has been brought up by Miss Havisham to wreak revenge on all the male sex."

"What relation is she to Miss Havisham?"

"None," said he. "Only adopted."

"Why should she wreak revenge on all the male sex? What revenge?"

"Lord, Mr. Pip!" said he. "Don't you know?"

"No," said I.

"Dear me! It's quite a story, and shall be saved till dinner time. And now let me take the liberty of asking you a question. How did you come there, that day?"

I told him, and he was attentive until I had finished, and then burst out laughing again, and asked me if I was sore afterwards? I didn't ask him if *he* was, for my conviction on that point was perfectly established.

"Mr. Jaggers is your guardian, I understand?" he went on.

"Yes."

"You know he is Miss Havisham's man of business and solicitor, and has her confidence when nobody else has?"

This was bringing me (I felt) towards dangerous ground. I answered with a constraint I made no attempt to disguise, that I had seen Mr. Jaggers in Miss Havisham's house on the very day of our combat, but never at any other time, and that I believed he had no recollection of having ever seen me there.

"He was so obliging as to suggest my father for your tutor, and he called on my father to propose it. Of course he knew about my father from his connection with Miss Havisham. My father is Miss Havisham's cousin; not that that implies familiar intercourse between them, for he is a bad courtier and will not propitiate her."

Herbert Pocket had a frank and easy way with him that was very taking. I had never seen any one then, and I have never seen any one since, who more strongly expressed to me, in every look and tone, a natural incapacity to do anything secret and mean. There was something wonderfully hopeful about his general air, and something that at the same time whispered to me he would never be very successful or rich. I don't know how this was. I became imbued with the notion on that first occasion before we sat down to dinner, but I cannot define by what means.

He was still a pale young gentleman, and had a certain conquered languor about him in the midst of his spirits and briskness, that did not seem indicative of natural strength. He had not a handsome face, but it was better than handsome: being extremely amiable and cheerful. His figure was a little ungainly, as in the days when my knuckles had taken such liberties with it, but it looked as if it would always be light and young. Whether Mr. Trabb's local work would have sat more gracefully on him than on me, may be a question; but I am conscious that he carried off his rather old clothes, much better than I carried off my new suit.

As he was so communicative, I felt that reserve on my part would be a bad return unsuited to our years. I therefore told him my small story, and laid stress on my being forbidden to inquire who my benefactor was. I further mentioned that as I had been brought up a blacksmith in a country place, and knew very little of the ways of politeness, I would take it as a great kindness in him if he would give me a hint whenever he saw me at a loss or going wrong.

"With pleasure," said he, "though I venture to prophesy that you'll want very few hints. I dare say we shall be often together, and I should like to banish any needless restraint between us. Will you do me the favour to begin at once to call me by my Christian name, Herbert?"

I thanked him, and said I would. I informed him in exchange that my Christian name was Philip.

"I don't take to Philip," said he, smiling, "for it sounds like a moral boy out of the spelling-book, who was so lazy that he fell into a pond, or so fat that he couldn't see out of his eyes, or so avaricious that he locked up his cake till the mice ate it, or so determined to go a bird's-nesting that he got himself eaten by bears who lived handy in the neighbourhood. I tell you what I should like. We are so harmonious, and you have been a blacksmith—would you mind it?"

"I shouldn't mind anything that you propose," I answered, "but I don't understand you."

"Would you mind Handel for a familiar name? There's a charming piece of music by Handel, called the Harmonious Blacksmith."

"I should like it very much."

"Then, my dear Handel," said he, turning round as the door opened, "here is the dinner, and I must beg of you to take the top of the table, because the dinner is of your providing."

This I would not hear of, so he took the top, and I faced him. It was a nice little dinner—seemed to me then, a very Lord Mayor's Feast—and it acquired additional relish from being eaten under those independent circumstances, with no old people by, and with London all around us. This again was heightened by a certain gipsy character that set the banquet off; for, while the table was, as Mr. Pumblechook might have said, the lap of luxury—being entirely furnished forth from the coffee-house—the circumjacent region of sitting-room was of a comparatively pastureless and shifty character: imposing on the waiter the wandering habits of putting the covers on the floor (where he fell over them), the melted butter in the armchair, the bread on the bookshelves, the cheese in the coalscuttle, and the boiled fowl into my bed in the next room—where I found much of its parsley and butter in a state of congelation when I retired for the night. All this made the feast delightful, and when the waiter was not there to watch me, my pleasure was without alloy.

We had made some progress in the dinner, when I reminded Herbert of his promise to tell me about Miss Havisham.

"True," he replied. "I'll redeem it at once. Let me introduce the topic, Handel, by mentioning that in London it is not the custom to put the knife in the mouth—for fear of accidents—and that while the fork is reserved for that use, it is not put further in than necessary. It is scarcely worth mentioning, only it's as well to do as other people do. Also, the spoon is not generally used over-hand, but under. This has two advantages. You get at your mouth better (which after all is the object), and you save a good deal of the attitude of opening oysters, on the part of the right elbow."

He offered these friendly suggestions in such a lively way, that we both laughed and I scarcely blushed.

"Now," he pursued, "concerning Miss Havisham. Miss Havisham, you must know, was a spoilt child. Her mother died when she was a baby, and her father denied her nothing. Her father was a country gentleman down in your part of the world, and was a brewer. I don't know why it should be a crack thing to be a brewer; but it is indisputable that while you cannot possibly be genteel and bake, you may be as genteel as never was and brew. You see it every day."

"Yet a gentleman may not keep a public-house; may he?" said I.

"Not on any account," returned Herbert; "but a public-house may keep a gentleman. Well! Mr. Havisham was very rich and very proud. So was his daughter."

"Miss Havisham was an only child?" I hazarded.

"Stop a moment, I am coming to that. No, she was not an only child; she had a half-brother. Her father privately married again—his cook, I rather think."

"I thought he was proud," said I.

"My good Handel, so he was. He married his second wife privately, because he was proud, and in course of time *she* died. When she was dead, I apprehend he first told his daughter what he had done, and then the son became a part of the family, residing in the house you are acquainted with. As the son grew a young man, he turned out riotous, extravagant, undutiful—altogether bad. At last his father disinherited him; but he softened when he was dying, and left him well off, though not nearly so well off as Miss Havisham.—Take another glass of wine, and excuse my mentioning that society as a body does not expect one to be so strictly conscientious in emptying one's glass, as to turn it bottom upwards with the rim on one's nose."

I had been doing this, in an excess of attention to his recital. I thanked him and apologised. He said, "Not at all," and resumed.

"Miss Havisham was now an heiress, and you may suppose was looked after as a great match. Her half-brother had now ample means again, but what with debts and what with new madness wasted them most fearfully again. There were stronger differences between him and her, than there had been between him and his father, and it is suspected that he cherished a deep and mortal grudge against her as having influenced the father's anger. Now, I come to the cruel part of the story—merely breaking off, my dear Handel, to remark that a dinner-napkin will not go into a tumbler."

Why I was trying to pack mine into my tumbler, I am wholly unable to say. I only know that I found myself, with a perseverance worthy of a much better cause, making the most strenuous exertions to compress it within those limits. Again I thanked him and apologised, and again he said in the cheerfullest manner, "Not at all, I am sure!" and resumed.

"There appeared upon the scene—say at the races, or the public balls, or anywhere else you like—a certain man, who made love to Miss Havisham. I never saw him (for this happened five-and-twenty years ago, before you and I were, Handel), but I have heard my father mention that he was a showy man, and the kind of man for the purpose. But that he was not to be, without ignorance or prejudice, mistaken for a gentleman, my father most strongly asseverates; because it is a principle of his that no man who was not a true gentleman at heart, ever was, since the world began, a true gentleman in manner. He says, no varnish can hide the grain of the wood; and that the more varnish you put on, the more the grain will express itself. Well! This man pursued Miss Havisham closely, and professed to be devoted to her. I believe she had not shown much susceptibility up to that time; but all the susceptibility she possessed, certainly came out then, and she passionately loved him. There is no doubt that she perfectly idolized him. He practised on her affection in that systematic way, that he got great sums of money from her, and he induced her to buy her brother out of a share in the brewery (which had been weakly left him by his father) at an immense price, on the plea that when he was her husband he must hold and manage it all. Your guardian was not at that time in Miss Havisham's councils, and she was too haughty and too much in love, to be advised by any one. Her relations were poor and scheming, with the exception of my father; he was poor enough, but not timeserving or jealous. The only independent one among them, he warned her that she was doing too much for this man, and was placing herself too unreservedly in his power. She took the first opportunity of angrily ordering my father out of the house, in his presence, and my father has never seen her since."

I thought of her having said, "Matthew will come and see me at last when I am laid dead upon that table;" and I asked Herbert whether his father was so inveterate against her?

"It's not that," said he, "but she charged him, in the presence of her intended husband, with being disappointed in the hope of fawning upon her for his own advancement, and, if he were to go to her now, it would look true—even to him—and even to her. To return to the man and make an end of him. The marriage day was fixed, the wedding dresses were bought, the wedding tour was planned out, the wedding guests were invited. The day came, but not the bridegroom. He wrote a letter——"

"Which she received," I struck in, "when she was dressing for her marriage? At twenty minutes to nine?"

"At the hour and minute," said Herbert, nodding, "at which she afterwards stopped all the clocks. What was in it, further than that it most heartlessly broke the marriage off, I can't tell you, because I don't know. When she recovered from a bad illness that she had, she laid the whole place waste, as you have seen it, and she has never since looked upon the light of day."

"Is that all the story?" I asked, after considering it.

"All I know of it; and indeed I only know so much, through piecing it out for myself; for my father always avoids it, and, even when Miss Havisham invited me to go there, told me no more of it than it was absolutely requisite I should understand. But I have forgotten one thing. It has been supposed that the man to whom she gave her misplaced confidence, acted throughout in concert with her halfbrother; that it was a conspiracy between them; and that they shared the profits."

"I wonder he didn't marry her and get all the property," said I.

"He may have been married already, and her cruel mortification may have been a part of her half-brother's scheme," said Herbert. "Mind! I don't know that."

"What became of the two men?" I asked, after again considering the subject.

"They fell into deeper shame and degradation—if there can be deeper—and ruin."

"Are they alive now?"

"I don't know."

"You said just now that Estella was not related to Miss Havisham, but adopted. When adopted?"

Herbert shrugged his shoulders. "There has always been an Estella, since I have heard of a Miss Havisham. I know no more. And now, Handel," said he, finally throwing off the story as it were, "there is a perfectly open understanding between us. All I know about Miss Havisham, you know."

"And all I know," I retorted, "you know."

"I fully believe it. So there can be no competition or perplexity between you and me. And as to the condition on which you hold your advancement in life—namely, that you are not to inquire or discuss to whom you owe it—you may be very sure that it will never be encroached upon, or even approached, by me, or by any one belonging to me."

In truth, he said this with so much delicacy, that I felt the subject done with, even though I should be under his father's roof for years and years to come. Yet he said it with so much meaning, too, that I felt he as perfectly understood Miss Havisham to be my benefactress, as I understood the fact myself.

It had not occurred to me before, that he had led up to the theme for the purpose of clearing it out of our way; but we were so much the lighter and easier for having broached it, that I now perceived this to be the case. We were very gay and sociable, and I asked him, in the course of conversation, what he was? He replied, "A capitalist —an Insurer of Ships." I suppose he saw me glancing about the room in search of some tokens of Shipping, or capital, for he added, "In the City."

I had grand ideas of the wealth and importance of Insurers of Ships in the City, and I began to think with awe, of having laid a young Insurer on his back, blackened his enterprising eye, and cut his responsible head open. But, again, there came upon me, for my relief, that odd impression that Herbert Pocket would never be very successful or rich.

"I shall not rest satisfied with merely employing my capital in insuring ships. I shall buy up some good Life Assurance shares, and cut into the Direction. I shall also do a little in the mining way. None of these things will interfere with my chartering a few thousand tons on my own account. I think I shall trade," said he, leaning back in his chair, "to the East Indies, for silks, shawls, spices, dyes, drugs, and precious woods. It's an interesting trade."

"And the profits are large?" said I.

"Tremendous!" said he.

I wavered again, and began to think here were greater expectations than my own.

"I think I shall trade, also," said he, putting his thumbs in his waistcoat pockets, "to the West Indies, for sugar, tobacco, and rum. Also to Ceylon, especially for elephants' tusks."

"You will want a good many ships," said I.

"A perfect fleet," said he.

Quite overpowered by the magnificence of these transactions, I asked him where the ships he insured mostly traded to at present?

"I haven't begun insuring yet," he replied. "I am looking about me."

Somehow, that pursuit seemed more in keeping with Barnard's Inn. I said (in a tone of conviction), "Ah-h!"

"Yes. I am in a counting-house, and looking about me."

"Is a counting-house profitable?" I asked.

"To——do you mean to the young fellow who's in it?" he asked, in reply.

"Yes; to you."

"Why, n-no; not to me." He said this with the air of one carefully reckoning up and striking a balance. "Not directly profitable. That is, it doesn't pay me anything, and I have to ——keep myself."

This certainly had not a profitable appearance, and I

shook my head as if I would imply that it would be difficult to lay by much accumulative capital from such a source
of income.

"But the thing is," said Herbert Pocket, "that you look
about you. *That's* the grand thing. You are in a counting-house, you know, and you look about you."

It struck me as a singular implication that you couldn't
be out of a counting-house, you know, and look about you;
but I silently deferred to his experience.

"Then the time comes," said Herbert, "when you see
your opening. And you go in, and you swoop upon it and
you make your capital, and then there you are! When
you have once made your capital, you have nothing to do
but employ it."

This was very like his way of conducting that encounter
in the garden; very like. His manner of bearing his poverty, too, exactly corresponded to his manner of bearing
that defeat. It seemed to me that he took all blows and
buffets now, with just the same air as he had taken mine
then. It was evident that he had nothing around him but
the simplest necessaries, for everything that I remarked
upon turned out to have been sent in on my account from
the coffee-house or somewhere else.

Yet, having already made his fortune in his own mind,
he was so unassuming with it that I felt quite grateful to
him for not being puffed up. It was a pleasant addition
to his naturally pleasant ways, and we got on famously.
In the evening we went out for a walk in the streets, and
went half-price to the Theatre; and next day we went to
church at Westminster Abbey, and in the afternoon we
walked in the Parks; and I wondered who shod all the
horses there, and wished Joe did.

On a moderate computation, it was many months, that
Sunday, since I had left Joe and Biddy. The space interposed between myself and them, partook of that expansion, and our marshes were any distance off. That I could
have been at our old church in my old church-going clothes,
on the very last Sunday that ever was, seemed a combination of impossibilities, geographical and social, solar and
lunar. Yet in the London streets, so crowded with people
and so brilliantly lighted in the dusk of evening, there
were depressing hints of reproaches for that I had put the
poor old kitchen at home so far away; and in the dead of
night, the footsteps of some incapable impostor of a porter
mooning about Barnard's Inn, under pretence of watching
it, fell hollow on my heart.

On the Monday morning at a quarter before nine, Herbert went to the counting-house to report himself—to look
about him, too, I suppose—and I bore him company. He
was to come away in an hour or two to attend me to Hammersmith, and I was to wait about for him. It appeared to
me that the eggs from which young Insurers were hatched,
were incubated in dust and heat, like the eggs of ostriches,
judging from the places to which those incipient giants repaired on a Monday morning. Nor did the counting-house
where Herbert assisted, show in my eyes as at all a good
Observatory; being a back second floor up a yard, of a
grimy presence in all particulars, and with a look into another back second floor, rather than a look out.

I waited about until it was noon, and I went upon 'Change,
and I saw fluey men sitting there under the bills about
shipping, whom I took to be great merchants, though I
couldn't understand why they should all be out of spirits.
When Herbert came, we went and had lunch at a celebrated
house which I then quite venerated, but now believe to
have been the most abject superstition in Europe, and

where I could not help noticing, even then, that there was
much more gravy on the table-cloths and knives and waiters' clothes, than in the steaks. This collation disposed
of at a moderate price (considering the grease, which was not
charged for), we went back to Barnard's Inn and got my
little portmanteau, and then took coach for Hammersmith.
We arrived there at two or three o'clock in the afternoon,
and had very little way to walk to Mr. Pocket's house.
Lifting the latch of a gate, we passed direct into a little
garden overlooking the river, where Mr. Pocket's children
were playing about. And, unless I deceive myself on a
point where my interests or prepossessions are certainly not
concerned, I saw that Mr. and Mrs. Pocket's children were
not growing up or being brought up, but were tumbling up.

Mrs. Pocket was sitting on a garden chair under a tree,
reading, with her legs upon another garden chair; and
Mrs. Pocket's two nursemaids were looking about them
while the children played. "Mama," said Herbert, "this
is young Mr. Pip." Upon which Mrs. Pocket received me
with an appearance of amiable dignity.

"Master Alick and Miss Jane," cried one of the nurses
to two of the children, "if you go a bouncing up against
them bushes you'll fall over into the river and be drownded,
and what'll your pa say then?"

At the same time this nurse picked up Mrs. Pocket's
handkerchief, and said, "If that don't make six times
you've dropped it, Mum!" Upon which Mrs. Pocket
laughed and said, "Thank you, Flopson," and settling herself in one chair only, resumed her book. Her countenance
immediately assumed a knitted and intent expression as if
she had been reading for a week, but before she could have
read half a dozen lines, she fixed her eyes upon me, and
said, "I hope your mama is quite well?" ·This unexpected
inquiry put me into such a difficulty that I began saying in
the absurdest way that if there had been any such person
I had no doubt she would have been quite well and would
have been very much obliged and would have sent her compliments, when the nurse came to my rescue.

"Well!" she cried, picking up the pocket-handkerchief,
"if that don't make seven times! What ARE you a doing
of this afternoon, Mum!" Mrs. Pocket received her property, at first with a look of unutterable surprise as if she
had never seen it before, and then with a laugh of recognition, and said, "Thank you, Flopson," and forgot me, and
went on reading.

I found, now I had leisure to count them, that there were
no fewer than six little Pockets present, in various stages of
tumbling up. I had scarcely arrived at the total when a
seventh was heard, as in the region of air, wailing dolefully.

"If there ain't Baby!" said Flopson, appearing to think
it most surprising. "Make haste up, Millers!"

Millers, who was the other nurse, retired into the house,
and by degrees the child's wailing was hushed and stopped,
as if it were a young ventriloquist with something in its
mouth. Mrs. Pocket read all the time, and I was curious
to know what the book could be.

We were waiting, I suppose, for Mr. Pocket to come out
to us; at any rate we waited there, and so I had an opportunity of observing the remarkable family phenomenon that
whenever any of the children strayed near Mrs. Pocket in
their play, they always tripped themselves up and tumbled
over her—always very much to her momentary astonishment, and their own more enduring lamentation. I was at
a loss to account for this surprising circumstance, and
could not help giving my mind to speculations about it,

until by-and-bye Millers came down with the baby, which Baby was handed to Flopson, which Flopson was handing it to Mrs. Pocket, when she too went fairly head foremost over Mrs. Pocket, baby and all, and was caught by Herbert and myself.

"Gracious me, Flopson!" said Mrs. Pocket, looking off her book for a moment, "everybody's tumbling!"

"Gracious you, indeed, Mum!" returned Flopson, very red in the face; "what have you got there?"

"I got here, Flopson?" asked Mrs. Pocket.

"Why, if it ain't your footstool!" cried Flopson. "And if you keep it under your skirts like that, who's to help tumbling? Here! Take the baby, Mum, and give me your book."

Mrs. Pocket acted on the advice, and inexpertly danced the infant a little in her lap, while the other children played about it. This had lasted but a very short time, when Mrs. Pocket issued summary orders that they were all to be taken into the house for a nap. Thus I made the second discovery on that first occasion, that the nurture of the little Pockets consisted of alternately tumbling up and lying down.

Under these circumstances, when Flopson and Millers had got the children into the house, like a little flock of sheep, and Mr. Pocket came out of it to make my acquaintance, I was not much surprised to find that Mr. Pocket was a gentleman with a rather perplexed expression of face, and with his very grey hair disordered on his head, as if he didn't quite see his way to putting anything straight.

CHAPTER XXIII.

Mr. Pocket said he was glad to see me, and he hoped I was not sorry to see him. "For, I really am not," he added, with his son's smile, "an alarming personage." He was a young-looking man, in spite of his perplexities and his very grey hair, and his manner seemed quite natural. I use the word natural, in the sense of its being unaffected; there was something comic in his distraught way, as though it would have been downright ludicrous but for his own perception that it was very near being so. When he had talked with me a little, he said to Mrs. Pocket, with a rather anxious contraction of his eyebrows, which were black and handsome, "Belinda, I hope you have welcomed Mr. Pip?" And she looked up from her book, and said, "Yes." She then smiled upon me in an absent state of mind, and asked me if I liked the taste of orange-flower water? As the question had no bearing, near or remote, on any foregone or subsequent transactions, I considered it to have been thrown out, like her previous approaches, in general conversational condescension.

I found out within a few hours, and may mention at once, that Mrs. Pocket was the only daughter of a certain quite accidental deceased Knight, who had invented for himself a conviction that his deceased father would have been made a Baronet but for somebody's determined opposition arising out of entirely personal motives—I forget whose, if I ever knew—the Sovereign's, the Prime Minister's, the Lord Chancellor's, the Archbishop of Canterbury's, anybody's—and had tacked himself on to the nobles of the earth in right of this quite supposititious fact. I believe he had been knighted himself for storming the English grammar at the point of the pen, in a desperate address engrossed on vellum, on the occasion of the laying of the first stone of some building or other, and for handing some Royal Personage either the trowel or the mortar. Be that as it may, he had directed Mrs. Pocket to be brought up from her cradle as one who in the nature of things must marry a title, and who was to be guarded from the acquisition of plebeian domestic knowledge.

So successful a watch and ward had been established over the young lady by this judicious parent, that she had grown up highly ornamental, but perfectly helpless and useless. With her character thus happily formed, in the first bloom of her youth she had encountered Mr. Pocket: who was also in the first bloom of youth, and not quite decided whether to mount to the Woolsack, or to roof himself in with a mitre. As his doing the one or the other was a mere question of time, he and Mrs. Pocket had taken Time by the forelock (when, to judge from its length, it would seem to have wanted cutting), and had married without the knowledge of the judicious parent. The judicious parent, having nothing to bestow or withhold but his blessing, had handsomely settled that dower upon them after a short struggle, and had informed Mr. Pocket that his wife was "a treasure for a Prince." Mr. Pocket had invested the Prince's treasure in the ways of the world ever since, and it was supposed to have brought him in but indifferent interest. Still, Mrs. Pocket was in general the object of a queer sort of respectful pity, because she had not married a title; while Mr. Pocket was the object of a queer sort of forgiving reproach, because he had never got one.

Mr. Pocket took me into the house and showed me my room; which was a pleasant one, and so furnished as that I could use it with comfort for my own private sitting-room. He then knocked at the doors of two other similar rooms, and introduced me to their occupants, by name Drummle and Startop. Drummle, an old-looking young man of a heavy order of architecture, was whistling. Startop, younger in years and appearance, was reading and holding his head, as if he thought himself in danger of exploding it with too strong a charge of knowledge.

Both Mr. and Mrs. Pocket had such a noticeable air of being in somebody else's hands, that I wondered who really was in possession of the house and let them live there, until I found this unknown power to be the servants. It was a smooth way of going on, perhaps, in respect of saving trouble; but it had the appearance of being expensive, for the servants felt it a duty they owed to themselves to be nice in their eating and drinking, and to keep a deal of company downstairs. They allowed a very liberal table to Mr. and Mrs. Pocket, yet it always appeared to me that by far the best part of the house to have boarded in, would have been the kitchen—always supposing the boarder capable of self-defence, for, before I had been there a week, a neighbouring lady with whom the family were personally unacquainted, wrote in to say that she had seen Millers slapping the baby. This greatly distressed Mrs. Pocket, who burst into tears on receiving the note, and said that it was an extraordinary thing that the neighbours couldn't mind their own business.

By degrees I learnt, and chiefly from Herbert, that Mr. Pocket had been educated at Harrow and at Cambridge, where he had distinguished himself; but that when he had had the happiness of marrying Mrs. Pocket very early in life, he had impaired his prospects and taken up the calling of a Grinder. After grinding a number of dull blades—of whom it was remarkable that their fathers, when influential, were always going to help him to preferment, but always forgot to do it when the blades had left the Grindstone—he had wearied of that poor work and had come to London. Here, after gradually failing in loftier hopes, he had "read" with divers who had lacked opportunities or neglected them, and had refurbished divers others for special occasions, and had turned his acquirements to the account of literary compilation and correction, and on such means, added to some very moderate private resources, still maintained the house I saw.

Mr. and Mrs. Pocket had a toady neighbour; a widow lady of that highly sympathetic nature that she agreed with everybody, blessed everybody, and shed smiles and tears on everybody, according to circumstances. This lady's name was Mrs. Coiler, and I had the honour of taking her down to dinner on the day of my installation. She gave me to understand on the stairs, that it was a blow to dear Mrs. Pocket that dear Mr. Pocket should be under the necessity of receiving gentlemen to read with him. That did not extend to me, she told me in a gush of love and confidence (at that time, I had known her something less than five minutes); if they were all like Me, it would be quite another thing.

"But dear Mrs. Pocket," said Mrs. Coiler, "after her early disappointment (not that dear Mr. Pocket was to blame in that), requires so much luxury and elegance——"

"Yes, ma'am," I said, to stop her, for I was afraid she was going to cry.

"And she is of so aristocratic a disposition——"

"Yes, ma'am," I said again, with the same object as before.

"—that it *is* hard," said Mrs. Coiler, "to have dear Mr. Pocket's time and attention diverted from dear Mrs. Pocket."

I could not help thinking that it might be harder if the butcher's time and attention were diverted from dear Mrs. Pocket; but I said nothing, and indeed had enough to do in keeping a bashful watch upon my company-manners.

It came to my knowledge, through what passed between Mrs. Pocket and Drummle, while I was attentive to my knife and fork, spoon, glasses, and other instruments of self-destruction, that Drummle, whose Christian name was Bentley, was actually the next heir but one to a baronetcy. It further appeared that the book I had seen Mrs. Pocket reading in the garden, was all about titles, and that she knew the exact date at which her grandpapa would have come into the book, if he ever had come into it at all. Drummle didn't say much, but in his limited way (he struck me as a sulky kind of fellow) he spoke as one of the elect, and recognised Mrs. Pocket as a woman and a sister. No one but themselves and Mrs. Coiler the toady neighbour showed any interest in this part of the conversation, and it appeared to me that it was painful to Herbert; but it promised to last a long time, when the page came in with the announcement of a domestic affliction. It was, in effect, that the cook had mislaid the beef. To my unutterable amazement, I now, for the first time, saw Mr. Pocket relieve his mind by going through a performance that struck me as very extraordinary, but which made no impression on anybody else, and with which I soon became as familiar as the rest. He laid down the carving-knife and fork—being engaged in carving at the moment—put his two hands into his disturbed hair, and appeared to make an extraordinary effort to lift himself up by it. When he had done this, and had not lifted himself up at all, he quietly went on with what he was about.

Mrs. Coiler then changed the subject and began to flatter me. I liked it for a few moments, but she flattered me so very grossly that the pleasure was soon over. She had a serpentine way of coming close at me when she pretended to be vitally interested in the friends and localities I had left, which was altogether snaky and fork-tongued; and when she made an occasional bounce upon Startop (who said very little to her), or upon Drummle (who said less), I rather envied them for being on the opposite side of the table.

After dinner the children were introduced, and Mrs. Coiler made admiring comments on their eyes, noses, and legs—a sagacious way of improving their minds. There were four little girls, and two little boys, besides the baby who might have been either, and the baby's next successor who was as yet neither. They were brought in by Flopson and Millers, much as though those two non-commissioned officers had been recruiting somewhere for children and had enlisted these: while Mrs. Pocket looked at the young Nobles that ought to have been, as if she rather thought she had had the pleasure of inspecting them before, but didn't quite know what to make of them.

"Here! Give me your fork, Mum, and take the baby," said Flopson. "Don't take it that way, or you'll get its head under the table."

Thus advised, Mrs. Pocket took it the other way, and got its head upon the table; which was announced to all present by a prodigious concussion.

"Dear, dear! give it me back, Mum," said Flopson; "and Miss Jane, come and dance the baby, do!"

One of the little girls, a mere mite who seemed to have prematurely taken upon herself some charge of the others, stepped out of her place by me, and danced to and from the baby until it left off crying, and laughed. Then all the children laughed, and Mr. Pocket (who in the meantime had twice endeavoured to lift himself up by the hair) laughed, and we all laughed and were glad.

Flopson, by dint of doubling the baby at the joints like a Dutch doll, then got it safely into Mrs. Pocket's lap, and gave it the nutcrackers to play with: at the same time recommending Mrs. Pocket to take notice that the handles of that instrument were not likely to agree with its eyes, and sharply charging Miss Jane to look after the same. Then, the two nurses left the room, and had a lively scuffle on the staircase with a dissipated page who had waited at dinner, and who had clearly lost half his buttons at the gaming-table.

I was made very uneasy in my mind by Mrs. Pocket falling into a discussion with Drummle respecting two baronetcies while she ate a sliced orange steeped in sugar and wine, and forgetting all about the baby on her lap: who did most appalling things with the nutcrackers. At length little Jane perceived its young brains to be imperilled, softly left her place, and with many small artifices coaxed the dangerous weapon away. Mrs. Pocket finishing her orange at about the same time, and not approving of this, said to Jane:

"You naughty child, how dare you? Go and sit down this instant!"

"Mama, dear," lisped the little girl, "baby ood have put hith eyeth out."

"How dare you tell me so!" retorted Mrs. Pocket. "Go and sit down in your chair this moment!"

Mrs. Pocket's dignity was so crushing, that I felt quite abashed: as if I myself had done something to rouse it.

"Belinda," remonstrated Mr. Pocket, from the other end of the table, "how can you be so unreasonable? Jane only interfered for the protection of baby."

"I will not allow anybody to interfere," said Mrs. Pocket. "I am surprised, Matthew, that you should expose me to the affront of interference."

"Good God!" cried Mr. Pocket, in an outbreak of desolate desperation. "Are infants to be nutcrackered into their tombs, and is nobody to save them?"

"I will not be interfered with by Jane," said Mrs. Pocket, with a majestic glance at that innocent little offender. "I hope I know my poor grandpapa's position. Jane, indeed!"

Mr. Pocket got his hands in his hair again, and this time really did lift himself some inches out of his chair. "Hear this!" he helplessly exclaimed to the elements. "Babies are to be nutcrackered dead, for people's poor grandpapa's positions!" Then he let himself down again, and became silent.

We all looked awkwardly at the table-cloth while this was going on. A pause succeeded, during which the honest and irrepressible baby made a series of leaps and crows at little Jane, who appeared to me to be the only member of the family (irrespective of the servants) with whom it had any decided acquaintance.

"Mr. Drummle," said Mrs. Pocket, "will you ring for Flopson? Jane, you undutiful little thing, go and lie down. Now, baby darling, come with ma!"

The baby was the soul of honour, and protested with all its might. It doubled itself up the wrong way over Mrs. Pocket's arm, exhibited a pair of knitted shoes and dimpled ankles to the company in lieu of its soft face, and was carried out in the highest state of mutiny. And it gained its point after all, for I saw it through the window within a few minutes, being nursed by little Jane.

It happened that the other five children were left behind at the dinner-table, through Flopson's having some private engagement, and their not being anybody else's business. I thus became aware of the mutual relations between them and Mr. Pocket, which were exemplified in the following manner. Mr. Pocket, with the normal perplexity of his face heightened, and his hair rumpled, looked at them for some minutes, as if he couldn't make out how they came to be boarding and lodging in that establishment, and why they hadn't been billeted by Nature on somebody else. Then, in a distant, Missionary way he asked them certain questions—as why little Joe had that hole in his frill: who said, Pa, Flopson was going to mend it when she had time—and how little Fanny came by that whitlow: who said, Pa, Millers was going to poultice it when she didn't forget. Then he melted into parental tenderness, and gave them a shilling apiece and told them to go and play; and then as they went out, with one very strong effort to lift himself up by the hair he dismissed the hopeless subject.

In the evening there was rowing on the river. As Drummle and Startop had each a boat, I resolved to set up mine, and to cut them both out. I was pretty good at most exercises in which country-boys are adepts, but, as I was conscious of wanting elegance of style for the Thames—not to say for other waters—I at once engaged to place myself under the tuition of the winner of a prize-wherry who plied at our stairs, and to whom I was introduced by my new allies. This practical authority confused me very much, by saying I had the arm of a blacksmith. If he

could have known how nearly the compliment had lost him his pupil, I doubt if he would have paid it.

There was a supper-tray after we got home at night, and I think we should all have enjoyed ourselves, but for a rather disagreeable domestic occurrence. Mr. Pocket was in good spirits, when a housemaid came in, and said, "If you please, sir, I should wish to speak to you."

"Speak to your master?" said Mrs. Pocket, whose dignity was roused again. "How can you think of such a thing? Go and speak to Flopson. Or speak to me—at some other time."

"Begging your pardon, ma'am," returned the housemaid, "I should wish to speak at once, and to speak to master."

Hereupon Mr. Pocket went out of the room, and we made the best of ourselves until he came back.

"This is a pretty thing, Belinda!" said Mr. Pocket, returning with a countenance expressive of grief and despair. "Here's the cook lying insensibly drunk on the kitchen floor, with a large bundle of fresh butter made up in the cupboard ready to sell for grease!"

Mrs. Pocket instantly showed much amiable emotion, and said, "This is that odious Sophia's doing!"

"What do you mean, Belinda?" demanded Mr. Pocket.

"Sophia has told you," said Mrs. Pocket. "Did I not see her, with my own eyes, and hear her with my own ears, come into the room just now and ask to speak to you?"

"But has she not taken me downstairs, Belinda," returned Mr. Pocket, "and shown me the woman, and the bundle too?"

"And do you defend her, Matthew," said Mrs. Pocket, "for making mischief?"

Mr. Pocket uttered a dismal groan.

"Am I, grandpapa's granddaughter, to be nothing in the house?" said Mrs. Pocket. "Besides, the cook has always been a very nice respectful woman, and said in the most natural manner when she came to look after the situation, that she felt I was born to be a Duchess."

There was a sofa where Mr. Pocket stood, and he dropped upon it in the attitude of a Dying Gladiator. Still in that attitude he said, with a hollow voice, "Good night, Mr. Pip," when I deemed it advisable to go to bed and leave him.

CHAPTER XXIV.

AFTER two or three days, when I had established myself in my room and had gone backwards and forwards to London several times, and had ordered all I wanted of my tradesmen, Mr. Pocket and I had a long talk together. He knew more of my intended career than I knew myself, for he referred to his having been told by Mr. Jaggers that I was not designed for any profession, and that I should be well enough educated for my destiny if I could "hold my own" with the average of young men in prosperous circumstances. I acquiesced, of course, knowing nothing to the contrary.

He advised my attending certain places in London, for the acquisition of such mere rudiments as I wanted, and my investing him with the functions of explainer and director of all my studies. He hoped that with intelligent assistance I should meet with little to discourage me, and should soon be able to dispense with any aid but his. Through his way of saying this, and much more to similar purpose, he placed himself on confidential terms with me in an admirable manner: and I may state at once that he was always so zealous and honourable in fulfilling his compact with me, that he made me zealous and honourable in fulfilling mine with him. If he had shown indifference as a master, I have no doubt I should have returned the compliment as a pupil; he gave me no such excuse, and each of us did the other justice. Nor, did I ever regard him as having anything ludicrous about him—or anything but what was serious, honest, and good—in his tutor communication with me.

When these points were settled, and so far carried out as that I had begun to work in earnest, it occurred to me that if I could retain my bedroom in Barnard's Inn, my life would be agreeably varied, while my manners would be none the worse for Herbert's society. Mr. Pocket did not object to this arrangement, but urged that before any step could possibly be taken in it, it must be submitted to my guardian. I felt that his delicacy arose out of the consideration that the plan would save Herbert some expense, so I went off to Little Britain and imparted my wish to Mr. Jaggers.

"If I could buy the furniture now hired for me," said I, "and one or two other little things, I should be quite at home there."

"Go it!" said Mr. Jaggers, with a short laugh. "I told you you'd get on. Well! How much do you want?"

I said I didn't know how much.

"Come!" retorted Mr. Jaggers. "How much? Fifty pounds?"

"Oh, not nearly so much."

"Five pounds?" said Mr. Jaggers.

This was such a great fall, that I said in discomfiture, "Oh! more than that."

"More than that, eh!" retorted Mr. Jaggers, lying in wait for me, with his hands in his pockets, his head on one side, and his eyes on the wall behind me; "how much more?"

"It is so difficult to fix a sum," said I, hesitating.

"Come!" said Mr. Jaggers. "Let's get at it. Twice five; will that do? Three times five; will that do? Four times five; will that do?"

I said I thought that would do handsomely.

"Four times five will do handsomely, will it?" said Mr. Jaggers, knitting his brows. "Now, what do you make of four times five?"

"What do I make of it!"

"Ah!" said Mr. Jaggers; "how much?"

"I suppose you make it twenty pounds," said I, smiling.

"Never mind what I make it, my friend," observed Mr. Jaggers, with a knowing and contradictory toss of the head. "I want to know what you make it?"

"Twenty pounds, of course."

"Wemmick!" said Mr. Jaggers, opening his office door. "Take Mr. Pip's written order, and pay him twenty pounds."

This strongly marked way of doing business made a strongly marked impression on me, and that not of an agreeable kind. Mr. Jaggers never laughed; but he wore great bright creaking boots; and, in poising himself on those boots, with his large head bent down and his eyebrows joined together, awaiting an answer, he sometimes caused the boots to creak, as if they laughed in a dry and suspicious way. As he happened to go out now, and as

Wemmick was brisk and talkative, I said to Wemmick that I hardly knew what to make of Mr. Jaggers's manner.

"Tell him that, and he'll take it as a compliment," answered Wemmick; "he don't mean that you should know what to make of it.—Oh!" for I looked surprised, "it's not personal; it's professional: only professional."

Wemmick was at his desk, lunching—and crunching—on a dry hard biscuit; pieces of which he threw from time to time into his slit of a mouth, as if he were posting them.

"Always seems to me," said Wemmick, "as if he had set a man-trap and was watching it. Suddenly—click—you're caught!"

Without remarking that man-traps were not among the amenities of life, I said I supposed he was very skilful?

"Deep," said Wemmick, "as Australia." Pointing with his pen at the office floor, to express that Australia was understood, for the purposes of the figure, to be symmetrically on the opposite spot of the globe. "If there was anything deeper," added Wemmick, bringing his pen to paper, "he'd be it."

Then, I said I supposed he had a fine business and Wemmick said, "Ca-pi-tal!" Then I asked if there were many clerks? to which he replied:

"We don't run much into clerks, because there's only one Jaggers, and people won't have him at second-hand. There are only four of us. Would you like to see 'em? You are one of us, as I may say."

I accepted the offer. When Mr. Wemmick had put all the biscuit into the post, and had paid me my money from a cash-box in a safe, the key of which safe he kept somewhere down his back, and produced from his coat-collar like an iron pigtail, we went upstairs. The house was dark and shabby, and the greasy shoulders that had left their mark in Mr. Jaggers's room seemed to have been shuffling up and down the staircase for years. In the front first floor, a clerk who looked something between a publican and a rat-catcher—a large pale puffed swollen man—was attentively engaged with three or four people of shabby appearance, whom he treated as unceremoniously as everybody seemed to be treated who contributed to Mr. Jaggers's coffers. "Getting evidence together," said Mr. Wemmick, as we came out, "for the Bailey." In the room over that, a little flabby terrier of a clerk with dangling hair (his cropping seemed to have been forgotten when he was a puppy) was similarly engaged with a man with weak eyes, whom Mr. Wemmick presented to me as a smelter who kept his pot always boiling, and who would melt me anything I pleased—and who was in an excessive white-perspiration, as if he had been trying his art on himself. In a back room, a high-shouldered man with a face-ache tied up in dirty flannel, who was dressed in old black clothes that bore the appearance of having been waxed, was stooping over his work of making fair copies of the notes of the other two gentlemen, for Mr. Jaggers's own use.

This was all the establishment. When we went downstairs again, Wemmick led me into my guardian's room, and said, "This you've seen already."

"Pray," said I, as the two odious casts with the twitchy leer upon them caught my sight again, "whose likenesses are those?"

"These?" said Wemmick, getting upon a chair, and blowing the dust off the horrible heads before bringing them down. "These are two celebrated ones. Famous clients of ours that got us a world of credit. This chap (why you must have come down in the night and been peeping into the inkstand, to get this blot upon your eyebrow, you old rascal!) murdered his master, and, considering that he wasn't brought up to evidence, didn't plan it badly."

"Is it like him?" I asked, recoiling from the brute, as Wemmick spat upon his eyebrow, and gave it a rub with his sleeve.

"Like him? It's himself, you know. The cast was made in Newgate, directly after he was taken down. You had a particular fancy for me, hadn't you, Old Artful?" said Wemmick. He then explained this affectionate apostrophe, by touching his brooch representing the lady and the weeping willow at the tomb with the urn upon it, and said, "Had it made for me express!"

"Is the lady anybody?" said I.

"No," returned Wemmick. "Only his game. (You liked your bit of game, didn't you?) No; deuce a bit of a lady in the case, Mr. Pip, except one—and she wasn't of this slender ladylike sort, and you wouldn't have caught *her* looking after this urn—unless there was something to drink in it." Wemmick's attention being thus directed to his brooch, he put down the cast, and polished the brooch with his pocket-handkerchief.

"Did that other creature come to the same end?" I asked. "He has the same look."

"You're right," said Wemmick; "it's the genuine look. Much as if one nostril was caught up with a horsehair and a little fish-hook. Yes, he came to the same end; quite the natural end here, I assure you. He forged wills, this blade did, if he didn't also put the supposed testators to sleep too. You were a gentlemanly Cove, though" (Mr. Wemmick was again apostrophising), "and you said you could write Greek. Yah, Bounceable! What a liar you were! I never met such a liar as you!" Before putting his late friend on his shelf again, Wemmick touched the largest of his mourning rings, and said, "Sent out to buy it for me, only the day before."

While he was putting up the other cast and coming down from the chair, the thought crossed my mind that all his personal jewellery was derived from like sources. As he had shown no diffidence on the subject, I ventured on the liberty of asking him the question, when he stood before me, dusting his hands.

"Oh yes," he returned, "these are all gifts of that kind. One brings another, you see; that's the way of it. I always take 'em. They're curiosities. And they're property. They may not be worth much, but, after all, they're property and portable. It don't signify to you with your brilliant look-out, but as to myself, my guiding-star always is, Get hold of portable property."

When I had rendered homage to this light, he went on to say in a friendly manner:

"If at any odd time when you have nothing better to do, you wouldn't mind coming over to see me at Walworth, I could offer you a bed, and I should consider it an honour. I have not much to show you; but such two or three curiosities as I have got, you might like to look over; and I am fond of a bit of garden and a summer-house."

I said I should be delighted to accept his hospitality.

"Thankee," said he: "then we'll consider that it's to come off, when convenient to you. Have you dined with Mr. Jaggers yet?"

"Not yet."

"Well," said Wemmick, "he'll give you wine, and good wine. I'll give you punch, and not bad punch. And now I'll tell you something. When you go to dine with Mr. Jaggers, look at his housekeeper."

"Shall I see something very uncommon?"

"Well," said Wemmick, "you'll see a wild beast tamed. Not so very uncommon, you'll tell me. I reply, that depends on the original wildness of the beast, and the amount of taming. It won't lower your opinion of Mr. Jaggers's powers. Keep your eye on it."

I told him I would do so, with all the interest and curiosity that his preparation awakened. As I was taking my departure, he asked me if I would like to devote five minutes to seeing Mr. Jaggers "at it?"

For several reasons, and not least because I didn't clearly know what Mr. Jaggers would be found to be "at," I replied in the affirmative. We dived into the City, and came up in a crowded police-court, where a blood-relation (in the murderous sense) of the deceased with the fanciful taste in brooches, was standing at the bar, uncomfortably chewing something; while my guardian had a woman under examination or cross-examination—I don't know which—and was striking her, and the bench, and everybody with awe. If anybody, of whatsoever degree, said a word that he didn't approve of, he instantly required to have it "taken down." If anybody wouldn't make an admission, he said, "I'll have it out of you!" and if anybody made an admission, he said, "Now I have got you!" The magistrates shivered under a single bite of his finger. Thieves and thieftakers hung in dread rapture on his words, and shrank when a hair of his eyebrows turned in their direction. Which side he was on, I couldn't make out, for he seemed to me to be grinding the whole place in a mill; I only know that when I stole out on tiptoe, he was not on the side of the bench; for, he was making the legs of the old gentleman who presided, quite convulsive under the table, by his denunciations of his conduct as the representative of British law and justice in that chair that day.

CHAPTER XXV.

BENTLEY DRUMMLE, who was so sulky a fellow that he even took up a book as if its writer had done him an injury, did not take up an acquaintance in a more agreeable spirit. Heavy in figure, movement, and comprehension—in the sluggish complexion of his face, and in the large awkward tongue that seemed to loll about in his mouth as he himself lolled about in a room—he was idle, proud, niggardly, reserved, and suspicious. He came of rich people down in Somersetshire, who had nursed this combination of qualities until they made the discovery that it was just of age and a blockhead. Thus, Bentley Drummle had come to Mr. Pocket when he was a head taller than that gentleman, and half a dozen heads thicker than most gentlemen.

Startop had been spoiled by a weak mother, and kept at home when he ought to have been at school, but he was devotedly attached to her, and admired her beyond measure. He had a woman's delicacy of feature, and was—"as you may see, though you never saw her," said Herbert to me—"exactly like his mother." It was but natural that I should take to him much more kindly than to Drummle, and that, even in the earliest evenings of our boating, he and I should pull homeward abreast of one another, conversing from boat to boat, while Bentley Drummle came up in our wake alone, under the overhanging banks and among the rushes. He would always creep in-shore like some uncomfortable amphibious creature, even when the

GREAT EXPECTATIONS

tide would have sent him fast upon his way; and I always think of him as coming after us in the dark or by the backwater, when our own two boats were breaking the sunset or the moonlight in mid-stream.

Herbert was my intimate companion and friend. I presented him with a half-share in my boat, which was the occasion of his often coming down to Hammersmith; and my possession of a half-share in his chambers often took me up to London. We used to walk between the two places at all hours. I have an affection for the road yet (though it is not so pleasant a road as it was then), formed in the impressibility of untried youth and hope.

When I had been in Mr. Pocket's family a month or two, Mr. and Mrs. Camilla turned up. Camilla was Mr. Pocket's sister. Georgiana, whom I had seen at Miss Havisham's on the same occasion, also turned up. She was a cousin—an indigestive single woman, who called her rigidity religion, and her liver love. These people hated me with the hatred of cupidity and disappointment. As a matter of course, they fawned upon me in my prosperity with the basest meanness. Towards Mr. Pocket, as a grown-up infant with no notion of his own interests, they showed the complacent forbearance I had heard them express. Mrs. Pocket they held in contempt; but they allowed the poor soul to have been heavily disappointed in life, because that shed a feeble reflected light upon themselves.

These were the surroundings among which I settled down, and applied myself to my education. I soon contracted expensive habits, and began to spend an amount of money that within a few short months I should have thought almost fabulous; but through good and evil I stuck to my books. There was no other merit in this, than my having sense enough to feel my deficiencies. Between Mr. Pocket and Herbert I got on fast; and, with one or the other always at my elbow to give me the start I wanted, and clear obstructions out of my road, I must have been as great a dolt as Drummle if I had done less.

I had not seen Mr. Wemmick for some weeks, when I thought I would write him a note and propose to go home with him on a certain evening. He replied that it would give him much pleasure, and that he would expect me at the office at six o'clock. Thither I went, and there I found him, putting the key of his safe down his back as the clock struck.

"Did you think of walking down to Walworth?" said he.

"Certainly," said I, "if you approve."

"Very much," was Wemmick's reply, "for I have had my legs under the desk all day, and shall be glad to stretch them. Now I'll tell you what I've got for supper, Mr. Pip. I have got a stewed steak—which is of home preparation—and a cold roast fowl—which is from the cook's-shop. I think it's tender, because the master of the shop was a Juryman in some cases of ours the other day, and we let him down easy. I reminded him of it when I bought the fowl, and I said, 'Pick us out a good one, old Briton, because if we had chosen to keep you in the box another day or two, we could have done it.' He said to that, 'Let me make you a present of the best fowl in the shop.' I let him of course. As far as it goes, it's property and portable. You don't object to an aged parent, I hope?"

I really thought he was still speaking of the fowl, until he added, "Because I have got an aged parent at my place." I then said what politeness required.

"So you haven't dined with Mr. Jaggers yet?" he pursued, as we walked along.

"Not yet."

"He told me so this afternoon when he heard you were coming. I expect you'll have an invitation to-morrow. He's going to ask your pals, too. Three of 'em; ain't there?"

Although I was not in the habit of counting Drummle as one of my intimate associates, I answered, "Yes."

"Well, he's going to ask the whole gang;" I hardly felt complimented by the word; "and whatever he gives you, he'll give you good. Don't look forward to variety, but you'll have excellence. And there's another rum thing in his house," proceeded Wemmick after a moment's pause, as if the remark followed on the housekeeper understood; "he never lets a door or window be fastened at night."

"Is he never robbed?"

"That's it!" returned Wemmick. "He says, and gives it out publicly, 'I want to see the man who'll rob me.' Lord bless you, I have heard him, a hundred times if I have heard once, say to regular cracksmen in our front office, 'You know where I live; now no bolt is ever drawn there; why don't you do a stroke of business with me? Come; can't I tempt you?' Not a man of them, sir, would be bold enough to try it on, for love or money."

"They dread him so much?" said I.

"Dread him," said Wemmick. "I believe you they dread him. Not but what he's artful, even in his defiance of them. No silver, sir. Britannia metal, every spoon."

"So they wouldn't have much," I observed, "even if they——"

"Ah! But he would have much," said Wemmick, cutting me short, "and they know it. He'd have their lives, and the lives of scores of 'em. He'd have all he could get. And it's impossible to say what he couldn't get, if he gave his mind to it."

I was falling into meditation on my guardian's greatness, when Wemmick remarked:

"As to the absence of plate, that's only his natural depth, you know. A river's its natural depth, and he's his natural depth. Look at his watch-chain. That's real enough."

"It's very massive," said I.

"Massive?" repeated Wemmick. "I think so. And his watch is a gold repeater, and worth a hundred pound if it's worth a penny. Mr. Pip, there are about seven hundred thieves in this town who know all about that watch; there's not a man, a woman, or a child, among them, who wouldn't identify the smallest link in that chain, and drop it as if it was red-hot, if inveigled into touching it."

At first with such discourse, and afterwards with conversation of a more general nature, did Mr. Wemmick and I beguile the time and the road, until he gave me to understand that we had arrived in the district of Walworth.

It appeared to be a collection of black lanes, ditches, and little gardens, and to present the aspect of a rather dull retirement. Wemmick's house was a little wooden cottage in the midst of plots of garden, and the top of it was cut out and painted like a battery mounted with guns.

"My own doing," said Wemmick. "Looks pretty; don't it?"

I highly commended it. I think it was the smallest house I ever saw; with the queerest Gothic windows (by far the greater part of them sham), and a Gothic door, almost too small to get in at.

"That's a real flagstaff, you see," said Wemmick, "and on Sundays I run up a real flag. Then look here. After I have crossed this bridge, I hoist it up—so—and cut off the communication."

The bridge was a plank, and it crossed a chasm four feet wide and two deep. But it was very pleasant to see the pride with which he hoisted it up, and made it fast; smiling as he did so, with a relish, and not merely mechanically.

"At nine o'clock every night, Greenwich time," said Wemmick, "the gun fires. There he is, you see! And when you hear him go, I think you'll say he's a Stinger."

The piece of ordnance referred to, was mounted in a separate fortress, constructed of lattice-work. It was protected from the weather by an ingenious little tarpaulin contrivance in the nature of an umbrella.

"Then, at the back," said Wemmick, "out of sight, so as not to impede the idea of fortifications—for it's a principle with me, if you have an idea, carry it out and keep it up—I don't know whether that's your opinion——"

I said, decidedly.

"—At the back, there's a pig, and there are fowls and rabbits; then I knock together my own little frame, you see, and grow cucumbers; and you'll judge at supper what sort of a salad I can raise. So, sir," said Wemmick, smiling again, but seriously, too, as he shook his head, "if you can suppose the little place besieged, it would hold out a devil of a time in point of provisions."

Then, he conducted me to a bower about a dozen yards off, but which was approached by such ingenious twists of path that it took quite a long time to get at; and in this retreat our glasses were already set forth. Our punch was cooling in an ornamental lake, on whose margin the bower was raised. This piece of water (with an island in the middle which might have been the salad for supper) was of a circular form, and he had constructed a fountain in it, which, when you set a little mill going and took a cork out of a pipe, played to that powerful extent that it made the back of your hand quite wet.

"I am my own engineer, and my own carpenter, and my own plumber, and my own gardener, and my own Jack of all Trades," said Wemmick, in acknowledging my compliments. "Well, it's a good thing, you know. It brushes the Newgate cobwebs away, and pleases the Aged. You wouldn't mind being at once introduced to the Aged, would you? It wouldn't put you out?"

I expressed the readiness I felt, and we went into the castle. There, we found, sitting by a fire, a very old man in a flannel coat: clean, cheerful, comfortable, and well cared for, but intensely deaf.

"Well, aged parent," said Wemmick, shaking hands with him in a cordial and jocose way, "how are you?"

"All right, John; all right!" replied the old man.

"Here's Mr. Pip, aged parent," said Wemmick, "and I wish you could hear his name. Nod away at him, Mr. Pip; that's what he likes. Nod away at him, if you please, like winking!"

"This is a fine place of my son's, sir," cried the old man, while I nodded as hard as I possibly could. "This is a pretty pleasure-ground, sir. This spot and these beautiful works upon it ought to be kept together by the Nation, after my son's time, for the people's enjoyment."

"You're as proud of it as Punch; ain't you, Aged?" said Wemmick, contemplating the old man, with his hard face really softened; "there's a nod for you;" giving him a tremendous one; "there's another for you;" giving him a still more tremendous one; "you like that, don't you? If you're not tired, Mr. Pip—though I know it's tiring to strangers—will you tip him one more? You can't think how it pleases him."

I tipped him several more, and he was in great spirits.

We left him bestirring himself to feed the fowls, and we sat down to our punch in the arbour; where Wemmick told me as he smoked a pipe, that it had taken him a good many years to bring the property up to its present pitch of perfection.

"Is it your own, Mr. Wemmick?"

"O yes," said Wemmick, "I have got hold of it, a bit at a time. It's a freehold, by George!"

"Is it, indeed? I hope Mr. Jaggers admires it."

"Never seen it," said Wemmick. "Never heard of it. Never seen the Aged. Never heard of him. No; the office is one thing, and private life is another. When I go into the office, I leave the Castle behind me, and when I come into the Castle, I leave the office behind me. If it's not in any way disagreeable to you, you'll oblige me by doing the same. I don't wish it professionally spoken about."

Of course I felt my good faith involved in the observance of his request. The punch being very nice, we sat there drinking it and talking, until it was almost nine o'clock. "Getting near gun-fire," said Wemmick then, as he laid down his pipe; "it's the Aged's treat."

Proceeding into the Castle again, we found the Aged heating the poker, with expectant eyes, as a preliminary to the performance of this great nightly ceremony. Wemmick stood with his watch in his hand until the moment was come for him to take the red-hot poker from the Aged, and repair to the battery. He took it, and went out, and presently the Stinger went off with a bang that shook the crazy little box of a cottage as if it must fall to pieces, and made every glass and teacup in it ring. Upon this the Aged—who I believe would have been blown out of his arm-chair but for holding on by the elbows—cried out exultingly, "He's fired! I heerd him!" and I nodded at the old gentleman until it is no figure of speech to declare that I absolutely could not see him.

The interval between that time and supper, Wemmick devoted to showing me his collection of curiosities. They were mostly of a felonious character; comprising the pen with which a celebrated forgery had been committed, a distinguished razor or two, some locks of hair, and several manuscript confessions written under condemnation—upon which Mr. Wemmick set particular value as being, to use his own words, "every one of 'em Lies, sir." These were agreeably dispersed among small specimens of china and glass, various neat trifles made by the proprietor of the museum, and some tobacco-stoppers carved by the Aged. They were all displayed in that chamber of the Castle into which I had been first inducted, and which served, not only as the general sitting-room, but as the kitchen too, if I might judge from a saucepan on the hob, and a brazen bijou over the fireplace designed for the suspension of a roasting-jack.

There was a neat little girl in attendance, who looked after the Aged in the day. When she had laid the supper-cloth, the bridge was lowered to give her the means of egress, and she withdrew for the night. The supper was excellent; and though the Castle was rather subject to dry-rot, insomuch that it tasted like a bad nut, and though the pig might have been farther off, I was heartily pleased with my whole entertainment. Nor was there any draw-back on my little turret bedroom, beyond there being such a very thin ceiling between me and the flagstaff, that when I lay down on my back in bed, it seemed as if I had to balance that pole on my forehead all night.

Wemmick was up early in the morning, and I am afraid

I heard him cleaning my boots. After that, he fell to gardening, and I saw him from my Gothic window pretending to employ the Aged, and nodding at him in a most devoted manner. Our breakfast was as good as the supper, and at half-past eight precisely we started for Little Britain. By degrees, Wemmick got dryer and harder as we went along, and his mouth tightened into a post-office again. At last, when we got to his place of business and he pulled out his key from his coat-collar, he looked as unconscious of his Walworth property as if the Castle and the drawbridge and the arbour and the lake and the fountain and the Aged, had all been blown into space together by the last discharge of the Stinger.

CHAPTER XXVI.

IT fell out as Wemmick had told me it would, that I had an early opportunity of comparing my guardian's establishment with that of his cashier and clerk. My guardian was in his room, washing his hands with his scented soap, when I went into the office from Walworth; and he called me to him, and gave me the invitation for myself and friends which Wemmick had prepared me to receive. "No ceremony," he stipulated, "and no dinner dress, and say to-morrow." I asked him where we should come to (for I had no idea where he lived), and I believe it was in his general objection to make anything like an admission, that he replied, "Come here, and I'll take you home with me." I embrace this opportunity of remarking that he washed his clients off, as if it were a surgeon or a dentist. He had a closet in his room, fitted up for the purpose, which smelt of the scented soap like a perfumer's shop. It had an unusually large jack-towel on a roller inside the door, and he would wash his hands, and wipe them and dry them all over this towel, whenever he came in from a police-court or dismissed a client from his room. When I and my friends repaired to him at six o'clock next day, he seemed to have been engaged on a case of a darker complexion than usual, for, we found him with his head butted into this closet, not only washing his hands, but laving his face and gargling his throat. And even when he had done all that, and had gone all round the jack-towel, he took out his penknife and scraped the case out of his nails before he put his coat on.

There were some people slinking about as usual when we passed out into the street, who were evidently anxious to speak with him; but there was something so conclusive in the halo of scented soap which encircled his presence, that they gave it up for that day. As we walked along westward, he was recognised ever and again by some face in the crowd of the streets, and whenever that happened he talked louder to me; but he never otherwise recognised anybody, or took notice that anybody recognised him.

He conducted us to Gerrard-street, Soho, to a house on the south side of that street, rather a stately house of its kind, but dolefully in want of painting, and with dirty windows. He took out his key and opened the door, and we all went into a stone hall, bare, gloomy, and little used. So, up a dark brown staircase into a series of three dark brown rooms on the first floor. There were carved garlands on the panelled walls, and as he stood among them giving us welcome, I know what kind of loops I thought they looked like.

Dinner was laid in the best of these rooms; the second was his dressing-room; the third, his bedroom. He told us that he held the whole house, but rarely used more of it than we saw. The table was comfortably laid—no silver in the service, of course—and at the side of his chair was a capacious dumb-waiter, with a variety of bottles and decanters on it, and four dishes of fruit for desert. I noticed throughout, that he kept everything under his own hand, and distributed everything himself.

There was a bookcase in the room; I saw from the backs of the books, that they were about evidence, criminal law, criminal biography, trials, acts of parliament, and such things. The furniture was all very solid and good, like his watch-chain. It had an official look, however, and there was nothing merely ornamental to be seen. In a corner, was a little table of papers with a shaded lamp; so that he seemed to bring the office home with him in that respect too, and to wheel it out of an evening and fall to work.

As he had scarcely seen my three companions until now—for, he and I had walked together—he stood on the hearth-rug, after ringing the bell, and took a searching look at them. To my surprise, he seemed at once to be principally, if not solely, interested in Drummle.

"Pip," said he, putting his large hand on my shoulder and moving me to the window, "I don't know one from the other. Who's the Spider?"

"The spider?" said I.

"The blotchy, sprawly, sulky fellow."

"That's Bentley Drummle," I replied; "the one with the delicate face is Startop."

Not making the least account of "the one with the delicate face," he returned, "Bentley Drummle is his name, is it? I like the look of that fellow."

He immediately began to talk to Drummle: not at all deterred by his replying in his heavy reticent way, but apparently led on by it to screw discourse out of him. I was looking at the two, when there came between me and them, the housekeeper, with the first dish for the table.

She was a woman of about forty, I supposed—but I may have thought her younger than she was. Rather tall, of a lithe nimble figure, extremely pale, with large faded eyes, and a quantity of streaming hair. I cannot say whether any diseased affection of the heart caused her lips to be parted as if she were panting, and her face to bear a curious expression of suddenness and flutter; but I know that I had been to see Macbeth at the theatre, a night or two before, and that her face looked to me as if it were all disturbed by fiery air, like the faces I had seen rise out of the Witches' caldron.

She set the dish on, touched my guardian quietly on the arm with a finger to notify that dinner was ready, and vanished. We took our seats at the round table, and my guardian kept Drummle on one side of him, while Startop sat on the other. It was a noble dish of fish that the housekeeper had put on table, and we had a joint of equally choice mutton afterwards, and then an equally choice bird. Sauces, wines, all the accessories we wanted, and all of the best, were given out by our host from his dumb-waiter; and when they had made the circuit of the table, he always put them back again. Similarly, he dealt us clean plates and knives and forks, for each course, and dropped those just disused into two baskets on the ground by his chair. No other attendant than the housekeeper appeared. She set on every dish; and I always saw in her face, a face rising out of the caldron. Years afterwards, I made a dreadful likeness of that woman, by causing a face that had no other natural resemblance to it than it derived from flowing hair, to pass behind a bowl of flaming spirits in a dark room.

Induced to take particular notice of the housekeeper, both by her own striking appearance and by Wemmick's preparation, I observed that whenever she was in the room, she kept her eyes attentively on my guardian, and that she would remove her hands from any dish she put before him, hesitatingly, as if she dreaded his calling her back, and wanted him to speak when she was nigh, if he had anything to say. I fancied that I could detect in his manner a consciousness of this, and a purpose of always holding her in suspense.

Dinner went off gaily, and, although my guardian seemed to follow rather than originate subjects, I knew that he wrenched the weakest part of our dispositions out of us. For myself, I found that I was expressing my tendency to lavish expenditure, and to patronise Herbert, and to boast of my great prospects, before I quite knew that I had opened my lips. It was so with all of us, but with no one more than Drummle: the development of whose inclination to gird in a grudging and suspicious way at the rest, was screwed out of him before the fish was taken off.

It was not then, but when we had got to the cheese, that our conversation turned upon our rowing feats, and that Drummle was rallied for coming up behind of a night in that slow amphibious way of his. Drummle, upon this, informed our host that he much preferred our room to our company, and that as to skill he was more than our master, and that as to strength he could scatter us like chaff. By some invisible agency, my guardian wound him up to a pitch little short of ferocity about this trifle; and he fell to baring and spanning his arm to show how muscular it was, and we all fell to baring and spanning our arms in a ridiculous manner.

Now, the housekeeper was at that time clearing the table; my guardian, taking no heed of her, but with the side of his face turned from her, was leaning back in his chair biting the side of his forefinger and showing an interest in Drummle, that, to me, was quite inexplicable. Suddenly, he clapped his large hand on the housekeeper's, like a trap, as she stretched it across the table. So suddenly and smartly did he do this, that we all stopped in our foolish contention.

"If you talk of strength," said Mr. Jaggers, "*I*'ll show you a wrist. Molly, let them see your wrist."

Her entrapped hand was on the table, but she had already put her other hand behind her waist. "Master," she said, in a low voice, with her eyes attentively and entreatingly fixed upon him, "Don't."

"*I*'ll show you a wrist," repeated Mr. Jaggers, with an immovable determination to show it. "Molly, let them see your wrist."

"Master," she again murmured. "Please!"

"Molly," said Mr. Jaggers, not looking at her, but obstinately looking at the opposite side of the room, "let them see *both* your wrists. Show them. Come!"

He took his hand from hers, and turned that wrist up on the table. She brought her other hand from behind her, and held the two out side by side. The last wrist was much disfigured—deeply scarred and scarred across and across. When she held her hands out, she took her eyes from Mr. Jaggers, and turned them watchfully on every one of the rest of us in succession.

"There's power here," said Mr. Jaggers, coolly tracing out the sinews with his forefinger. "Very few men have the power of wrist that this woman has. It's remarkable what mere force of grip there is in these hands. I have had occasion to notice many hands; but I never saw stronger in that respect, man's or woman's, than these."

While he said these words in a leisurely critical style, she continued to look at every one of us in regular succession as we sat. The moment he ceased, she looked at him again. "That'll do, Molly," said Mr. Jaggers, giving her a slight nod; "you have been admired, and can go." She withdrew her hands and went out of the room, and Mr. Jaggers, putting the decanters on from his dumb-waiter, filled his glass and passed round the wine.

"At half-past nine, gentlemen," said he, "we must break up. Pray make the best use of your time. I am glad to see you all. Mr. Drummle, I drink to you."

If his object in singling out Drummle were to bring him out still more, it perfectly succeeded. In a sulky triumph, Drummle showed his morose depreciation of the rest of us, in a more and more offensive degree, until he became downright intolerable. Through all his stages, Mr. Jaggers followed him with the same strange interest. He actually seemed to serve as a zest to Mr. Jaggers's wine.

In our boyish want of discretion I dare say we took too much to drink, and I know we talked too much. We became particularly hot upon some boorish sneer of Drummle's, to the effect that we were too free with our money. It led to my remarking, with more zeal than discretion, that it came with a bad grace from him, to whom Startop had lent money in my presence but a week or so before.

"Well," retorted Drummle, "he'll be paid."

"I don't mean to imply that he won't," said I, "but it might make you hold your tongue about us and our money, I should think."

"*You* should think!" retorted Drummle. "Oh Lord!"

"I dare say," I went on, meaning to be very severe, "that you wouldn't lend money to any of us if we wanted it."

"You are right," said Drummle. "I wouldn't lend one of you a sixpence. I wouldn't lend anybody a sixpence."

"Rather mean to borrow under those circumstances, I should say."

"*You* should say," repeated Drummle. "Oh Lord!"

This was so very aggravating—the more especially as I found myself making no way against his surly obtuseness—that I said, disregarding Herbert's efforts to check me:

"Come, Mr. Drummle, since we are on the subject, I'll tell you what passed between Herbert here and me, when you borrowed that money."

"*I* don't want to know what passed between Herbert there and you," growled Drummle. And I think he added in a lower growl, that we might both go to the devil and shake ourselves.

"I'll tell you, however," said I, "whether you want to know or not. We said that as you put it into your pocket very glad to get it, you seemed to be immensely amused at his being so weak as to lend it."

Drummle laughed outright, and sat laughing in our faces, with his hands in his pockets and his round sholders raised; plainly signifying that it was quite true, and that he despised us as asses all.

Hereupon Startop took him in hand, though with a much better grace than I had shown, and exhorted him to be a little more agreeable. Startop being a lively bright young fellow, and Drummle being the exact opposite, the latter was always disposed to resent him as a direct personal affront. He now retorted in a coarse lumpish way, and Startop tried to turn the discussion aside with some small pleasantry that made us all laugh. Resenting this little success more than anything, Drummle, without any threat or warning, pulled his hands out of his pockets, dropped his round shoulders, swore, took up a large glass, and would have flung it at his adversary's head, but for our entertainer's dexterously seizing it at the instant when it was raised for that purpose.

"Gentlemen," said Mr. Jaggers, deliberately putting down the glass, and hauling out his gold repeater by its massive chain, "I am exceedingly sorry to announce that it's half-past nine."

On this hint we all rose to depart. Before we got to the street door, Startop was cheerily calling Drummle "old boy," as if nothing had happened. But the old boy was so far from responding, that he would not even walk to Hammersmith on the same side of the way; so, Herbert and I, who remained in town, saw them going down the street on opposite sides; Startop leading, and Drummle lagging behind in the shadow of the houses, much as he was wont to follow in his boat.

As the door was not yet shut, I thought I would leave Herbert there for a moment, and run upstairs again to say a word to my guardian. I found him in his dressing-room surrounded by his stock of boots, already hard at it, washing his hands of us.

I told him I had come up again to say how sorry I was that anything disagreeable should have occurred, and that I hoped he would not blame me much.

"Pooh!" said he, sluicing his face, and speaking through the water-drops; "it's nothing, Pip. I like that Spider though."

He had turned towards me now, and was shaking his head, and blowing, and towelling himself.

"I am glad you like him, sir," said I—"but I don't."

"No, no," my guardian assented; "don't have too much to do with him. Keep as clear of him as you can. But I like the fellow, Pip; he is one of the true sort. Why, if I was a fortune-teller——"

Looking out of the towel, he caught my eye.

"But I am not a fortune-teller," he said, letting his head drop into a festoon of towel, and towelling away at his two ears. "You know what I am, don't you? Good night, Pip."

"Good night, sir."

In about a month after that, the Spider's time with Mr. Pocket was up for good, and, to the great relief of all the house but Mrs. Pocket, he went home to the family hole.

CHAPTER XXVII.

"MY DEAR MR. PIP,

"I write this by request of Mr. Gargery, for to let you know that he is going to London in company with Mr. Wopsle and would be glad if agreeable to be allowed to see you. He would call at Barnard's Hotel Tuesday morning at nine o'clock, when if not agreeable please leave word. Your poor sister is much the same as when you left. We talk of you in the kitchen every night, and wonder what you are saying and doing. If now considered in the light of a liberty, excuse it for the love of poor old days. No more, dear Mr. Pip, from

"Your ever obliged, and affectionate servant,
"BIDDY."

"P.S. He wishes me most particular to write *what larks*. He says you will understand. I hope and do not doubt it will be agreeable to see him even though a gentleman, for you had ever a good heart, and he is a worthy worthy man. I have read him all excepting only the last little sentence, and he wishes me most particular to write again *what larks*."

I received this letter by post on Monday morning, and therefore its appointment was for next day. Let me confess exactly, with what feelings I looked forward to Joe's coming.

Not with pleasure, though I was bound to him by so many ties; no; with considerable disturbance, some mortification, and a keen sense of incongruity. If I could have kept him away by paying money, I certainly would have paid money. My greatest reassurance was, that he was coming to Barnard's Inn, not to Hammersmith, and consequently would not fall in Bentley Drummle's way. I had little objection to his being seen by Herbert or his father, for both of whom I had a respect; but I had the sharpest sensitiveness as to his being seen by Drummle, whom I held in contempt. So, throughout life, our worst weaknesses and meannesses are usually committed for the sake of the people whom we most despise.

I had begun to be always decorating the chambers in some quite unnecessary and inappropriate way or other, and very expensive those wrestles with Barnard proved to be. By this time, the rooms were vastly different from what I had found them, and I enjoyed the honour of occupying a few prominent pages in the books of a neighbouring upholsterer. I had got on so fast of late, that I had even started a boy in boots—top boots—in bondage and slavery to whom I might be said to pass my days. For, after I had made this monster (out of the refuse of my washerwoman's family) and had clothed him with a blue coat, canary waistcoat, white cravat, creamy breeches, and the boots already mentioned, I had to find him a little to do and a great deal to eat; and with both of these horrible requirements he haunted my existence.

This avenging phantom was ordered to be on duty at eight on Tuesday morning in the hall (it was two feet square, as charged for floorcloth), and Herbert suggested certain things for breakfast that he thought Joe would like. While I felt sincerely obliged to him for being so interested and considerate, I had an odd half-provoked sense of suspicion upon me, that if Joe had been coming to see *him*, he wouldn't have been quite so brisk about it.

However, I came into town on the Monday night to be ready for Joe, and I got up early in the morning, and caused the sitting-room and breakfast-table to assume their most splendid appearance. Unfortunately the morning was drizzly, and an angel could not have concealed the fact that Barnard was shedding sooty tears outside the window, like some weak giant of a Sweep.

As the time approached I should have liked to run away, but the Avenger pursuant to orders was in the hall, and presently I heard Joe, on the staircase. I knew it was Joe, by his clumsy manner of coming upstairs—his state boots being always too big for him—and by the time it took him to read the names on the other floors in the course of his ascent. When at last he stopped outside our door, I could hear his finger tracing over the painted letters of my name, and I afterwards distinctly heard him breathing in at the keyhole. Finally he gave a faint single rap, and Pepper—such was the compromising name of the avenging boy—announced "Mr. Gargery!" I thought he never would have done wiping his feet, and that I must have gone out to lift him off the mat, but at last he came in.

"Joe, how are you, Joe?"

"Pip, how AIR you, Pip?"

With his good honest face all glowing and shining, and his hat put down on the floor between us, he caught both my hands and worked them straight up and down, as if I had been the last-patented Pump.

"I am glad to see you, Joe. Give me your hat."

But Joe, taking it up carefully with both hands, like a bird's-nest with eggs in it, wouldn't hear of parting with that piece of property, and persisted in standing talking over it in a most uncomfortable way.

"Which you have that growed," said Joe, "and that swelled, and that gentle-folked;" Joe considered a little before he discovered this word; "as to besure you are a honour to your king and country."

"And you, Joe, look wonderfully well."

"Thank God," said Joe, "I'm ekerval to most. And your sister, she's no worse than she were. And Biddy, she's ever right and ready. And all friends is no backerder, if not no forarder. 'Ceptin' Wopsle: he's had a drop."

All this time (still with both hands taking great care of the bird's-nest), Joe was rolling his eyes round and round the room, and round and round the flowered pattern of my dressing-gown.

"Had a drop, Joe?"

"Why yes," said Joe, lowering his voice, "he's left the Church and went into the playacting. Which the playacting have likewise brought him to London along with me. And his wish were," said Joe, getting the bird's-nest under his left arm for the moment, and groping in it for an egg with his right; "if no offence, as I would 'and you that."

I took what Joe gave me, and found it to be the crumpled playbill of a small metropolitan theatre, announcing the first appearance, in that very week, of "the celebrated Provincial Amateur of Roscian renown, whose unique performance in the highest tragic walk of our National Bard has lately occasioned so great a sensation in local dramatic circles."

"Were you at his performance, Joe?" I inquired.

"I were," said Joe, with emphasis and solemnity.

"Was there a great sensation?"

"Why," said Joe, "yes, there certainly were a peck of orange-peel. Partickler when he see the ghost. Though I put it to yourself, sir, whether it were calc'lated to keep a man up to his work with a good hart, to be continivally cutting in betwixt him and the Ghost with 'Amen!' A man may have had a misfortun' and been in the Church," said Joe, lowering his voice to an argumentative and feeling tone, "but that is no reason why you should put him out at such a time. Which I meantersay, if the ghost of a man's own father cannot be allowed to claim his attention, what can, Sir? Still more, when his mourning 'at is unfortunately made so small as that the weight of the black feathers brings it off, try to keep it on how you may."

A ghost-seeing effect in Joe's own countenance informed me that Herbert had entered the room. So, I presented Joe to Herbert, who held out his hand; but Joe backed from it, and held on by the bird's-nest.

"Your servant, Sir," said Joe, "which I hope as you and Pip"—here his eye fell on the Avenger, who was putting some toast on table, and so plainly denoted an intention to make that young gentleman one of the family, that I frowned it down and confused him more—"I meantersay, you two gentlemen—which I hope as you gets your elths in this close spot? For the present may be a wery good inn, according to London opinions," said Joe, confidentially, "and I believe its character do stand i; but I wouldn't keep a pig in it myself—not in the case that I wished him to fatten wholesome and to eat with a meller flavour on him."

Having borne this flattering testimony to the merits of our dwelling-place, and having incidentally shown this tendency to call me "sir," Joe, being invited to sit down to table, looked all round the room for a suitable spot on which to deposit his hat—as if it were only on some few very rare substances in nature that it could find a resting-place—and ultimately stood it on an extreme corner of the chimney-piece, from which it ever afterwards fell off at intervals.

"Do you take tea, or coffee, Mr. Gargery?" asked Herbert, who always presided of a morning.

"Thankee, Sir," said Joe, stiff from head to foot, "I'll take whichever is most agreeable to yourself."

"What do you say to coffee?"

"Thankee, Sir," returned Joe, evidently dispirited by the proposal, "since you are so kind as to make chice of coffee, I will not run contrairy to your own opinions. But don't you never find it a little 'eating?"

"Say tea, then," said Herbert, pouring it out.

Here Joe's hat tumbled off the mantel-piece, and he started out of his chair and picked it up, and fitted it to the same exact spot. As if it were an absolute point of good breeding that it should tumble off again soon.

"When did you come to town, Mr. Gargery?"

"Were it yesterday afternoon?" said Joe, after coughing behind his hand as if he had had time to catch the whooping-cough since he came. "No it were not. Yes it were. Yes. It were yesterday afcernoon" (with an appearance of mingled wisdom, relief, and strict impartiality).

"Have you seen anything of London, yet?"

"Why, yes, Sir," said Joe, "me and Wopsle went off straight to look at the Blacking Ware'us. But we didn't find that it come up to its likeness in the red bills at the shop doors: which I meantersay," added Joe, in an explanatory manner, "as it is there drawd too architectooral-ooral."

I really believe Joe would have prolonged this word (mightily expressive to my mind of some architecture that I know) into a perfect Chorus, but for his attention being providentially attracted by his hat, which was toppling. Indeed, it demanded from him a constant attention, and a quickness of eye and hand, very like that exacted by wicket-keeping. He made extraordinary play with it, and showed the greatest skill; now, rushing at it and catching it neatly as it dropped; now, merely stopping it midway, beating it up, and humouring it in various parts of the room and against a good deal of the pattern of the paper on the wall, before he felt it safe to close with it; finally splashing it into the slop-basin, where I took the liberty of laying hands upon it.

As to his shirt-collar, and his coat-collar, they were perplexing to reflect upon—insoluble mysteries both. Why should a man scrape himself to that extent, before he could consider himself full dressed? Why should he suppose it necessary to be purified by suffering for his holiday clothes? Then he fell into such unaccountable fits of meditation, with his fork midway between his plate and his mouth; had his eyes attracted in such strange directions; was afflicted with such remarkable coughs; sat so far from the table, and dropped so much more than he ate, and pretended that he hadn't dropped it; that I was heartily glad when Herbert left us for the city.

I had neither the good sense nor the good feeling to know that this was all my fault, and that if I had been easier with Joe, Joe would have been easier with me. I felt impatient of him and out of temper with him; in which condition he heaped coals of fire on my head.

"Us two being now alone, Sir"—began Joe.

"Joe," I interrupted, pettishly, "how can you call me Sir?"

Joe looked at me for a single instant with something faintly like reproach. Utterly preposterous as his cravat was, and as his collars were, I was conscious of a sort of dignity in the look.

"Us two being now alone," resumed Joe, "and me having the intentions and abilities to stay not many minutes more, I will now conclude—leastways begin—to mention what have led to my having had the present honour. For was it not," said Joe, with his old air of lucid exposition, "that my only wish were to be useful to you, I should not have had the honour of breaking wittles in the company and abode of gentlemen."

I was so unwilling to see the look again, that I made no remonstrance against this tone.

"Well, Sir," pursued Joe, "this is how it were. I were at the Bargemen t'other night, Pip; " whenever he subsided into affection, he called me Pip, and whenever he relapsed into politeness he called me Sir; "when there come up in his shay-cart Pumblechook. Which that same identical," said Joe, going down a new track, "do comb my 'air the wrong way sometimes, awful, by giving out up and down town as it were him which ever had your infant companionation and were looked upon as a playfellow by yourself."

"Nonsense. It was you, Joe."

"Which I fully believed it were, Pip," said Joe, slightly tossing his head, "though it signify little now, Sir. Well, Pip; this same identical, which his manners is given to blusterous, come to me at the Bargemen (wot a pipe and a pint of beer do give refreshment to the working-man, Sir, and do not over stimulate), and his word were, 'Joseph, Miss Havisham she wish to speak to you.'"

"Miss Havisham, Joe?"

"'She wished,' were Pumblechook's word, 'to speak to you.'" Joe sat and rolled his eyes at the ceiling.

"Yes, Joe? Go on, please."

"Next day, Sir," said Joe, looking at me as if I were a long way off, "having cleaned myself, I go and I see Miss A."

"Miss A., Joe? Miss Havisham?"

"Which I say, Sir," replied Joe, with an air of legal formality, as if he were making his will, "Miss A., or otherways Havisham. Her expression air then as follering: 'Mr. Gargery. You air in correspondence with Mr. Pip?' Having had a letter from you, I were able to say 'I am.' (When I married your sister, Sir, I said 'I will;' and when I answered your friend, Pip, I said, 'I am.') 'Would you tell him, then,' said she, 'that which Estella has come home, and would be glad to see him.'"

I felt my face fire up as I looked at Joe. I hope one remote cause of its firing, may have been my consciousness that if I had known his errand, I should have given him more encouragement.

"Biddy," pursued Joe, "when I got home and asked her fur to write the message to you, a little hung back. Biddy says, 'I know he will be very glad to have it by word of mouth, it is holiday-time, you want to see him, go!' I have now concluded, Sir," said Joe, rising from his chair, "and, Pip, I wish you ever well and ever prospering to a greater and greater height."

"But you are not going now, Joe?"

"Yes I am," said Joe.

"But you are coming back to dinner, Joe?"

"No I am not," said Joe.

Our eyes met, and all the "Sir" melted out of that manly heart as he gave me his hand.

"Pip, dear old chap, life is made of ever so many partings welded together, as I may say, and one man's a blacksmith, and one's a whitesmith, and one's a goldsmith, and one's a coppersmith. Diwisions among such must come, and must be met as they come. If there's been any fault at all to-day, it's mine. You and me is not two figures to be together in London; nor yet anywheres else but what is private, and beknown, and understood among friends. It ain't that I am proud, but that I want to be right, as you shall never see me no more in these clothes. I'm wrong in these clothes. I'm wrong out of the forge, the kitchen, or off th' meshes. You won't find half so much fault in me if you think of me in my forge dress, with my hammer in my hand, or even my pipe. You won't find half so much fault in me if, supposing as you should ever wish to see me, you come and put your head in at the forge window and see Joe the blacksmith, there, at the old anvil, in the old burnt apron, sticking to the old work. I'm awful dull, but I hope I've beat out something nigh the rights of this at last. And so GOD bless you, dear old Pip, old chap, GOD bless you!"

I had not been mistaken in my fancy that there was a simple dignity in him. The fashion of his dress could no more come in its way when he spoke these words, than it could come in its way in Heaven. He touched me gently on the forehead, and went out. As soon as I could recover myself sufficiently, I hurried out after him and looked for him in the neighbouring streets; but he was gone.

CHAPTER XXVIII.

IT was clear that I must repair to our town next day, and in the first flow of my repentance it was equally clear that I must stay at Joe's. But, when I had secured my box-place by to-morrow's coach, and had been down to Mr. Pocket's and back, I was not by any means convinced on the last point, and began to invent reasons and make excuses for putting up at the Blue Boar. I should be an inconvenience at Joe's; I was not expected, and my bed would not be ready; I should be too far from Miss Havisham's, and she was exacting and mightn't like it. All other swindlers upon earth are nothing to the self-swindlers, and with such pretences did I cheat myself. Surely a curious thing. That I should innocently take a bad half-crown of somebody else's manufacture, is reasonable enough; but that I should knowingly reckon the spurious coin of my own make, as good money! An obliging stranger, under pretence of compactly folding up my bank-notes for security's sake, abstracts the notes and gives me nutshells; but what is his sleight of hand to mine, when I fold up my own nutshells and pass them on myself as notes!

Having settled that I must go to the Blue Boar, my mind was much disturbed by indecision whether or no to take the Avenger. It was tempting to think of that expensive Mercenary publicly airing his boots in the archway of the Blue Boar's posting-yard: it was almost solemn to imagine him casually produced in the tailor's shop and confounding the disrespectful senses of Trabb's boy. On the other hand, Trabb's boy might worm himself into my intimacy and tell him things; or, reckless and desperate wretch as I knew he could be, might hoot him in the High-street. My patroness, too, might hear of him, and not approve. On the whole, I resolved to leave the Avenger behind.

It was the afternoon coach by which I had taken my place, and, as winter had now come round, I should not arrive at my destination until two or three hours after dark. Our time of starting from the Cross Keys was two o'clock. I arrived on the ground with a quarter of an hour to spare, attended by the Avenger—if I may connect that expression with one who never attended on me if he could possibly help it.

At that time it was customary to carry convicts down to the dockyards by stage-coach. As I had often heard of them in the capacity of outside passengers, and had more than once seen them on the high road dangling their ironed legs over the coach roof, I had no cause to be surprised when Herbert, meeting me in the yard, came up and told me there were two convicts going down with me. But I had a reason that was an old reason now, for constitutionally faltering whenever I heard the word convict.

"You don't mind them, Handel?" said Herbert.

"Oh no!"

"I thought you seemed as if you didn't like them?"

"I can't pretend that I do like them, and I suppose you don't particularly. But I don't mind them."

"See! There they are," said Herbert, "coming out of the Tap. What a degraded and vile sight it is!"

They had been treating their guard, I suppose, for they had a gaoler with them, and all three came out wiping their mouths on their hands. The two convicts were handcuffed together, and had irons on their legs—irons of a pattern that I knew well. They wore the dress that I likewise knew well. Their keeper had a brace of pistols, and carried a thick-knobbed bludgeon under his arm; but he was on terms of good understanding with them, and stood, with them beside him, looking on at the putting-to of the horses, rather with an air as if the convicts were an interesting Exhibition not formally open at the moment, and he the Curator. One was a taller and stouter man than the other, and appeared as a matter of course, according to the mysterious ways of the world both convict and free, to have had allotted to him the smaller suit of clothes. His arms and legs were like great pincushions of those shapes, and his attire disguised him absurdly; but I knew his half-closed eye at one glance. There stood the man whom I had seen on the settle at the Three Jolly Barge-men on a Saturday night, and who had brought me down with his invisible gun!

It was easy to make sure that as yet he knew me no more than if he had never seen me in his life. He looked across at me, and his eye appraised my watch-chain, and then he incidentally spat and said something to the other convict, and they laughed and slued themselves round with a clink of their coupling manacle, and looked at something else. The great numbers on their backs, as if they were street doors; their coarse mangy ungainly outer surface, as if they were lower animals; their ironed legs, apologetically garlanded with pocket-handkerchiefs; and the way in which all present looked at them and kept from them; made them (as Herbert had said) a most disagreeable and degraded spectacle.

But this was not the worst of it. It came out that the whole of the back of the coach had been taken by a family removing from London, and that there were no places for the two prisoners but on the seat in front, behind the coachman. Hereupon, a choleric gentleman, who had taken the fourth place on that seat, flew into a most violent passion, and said that it was a breach of contract to mix him up with such villainous company, and that it was poisonous and pernicious and infamous and shameful, and I don't know what else. At this time the coach was ready and the coachman impatient, and we were all preparing to get up, and the prisoners had come over with their keeper—bringing with them that curious flavour of bread-poultice, baize, rope-yarn, and hearth-stone, which attends the convict presence.

"Don't take it so much amiss, sir," pleaded the keeper to the angry passenger; "I'll sit next you myself. I'll put 'em on the outside of the row. They won't interfere with you, sir. You needn't know they're there."

"And don't blame *me*," growled the convict I had recognised. "*I* don't want to go. *I* am quite ready to stay behind. As fur as I am concerned any one's welcome to *my* place."

"Or mine," said the other, gruffly. "*I* wouldn't have incommoded none of you, if I'd a had *my* way." Then, they both laughed, and began cracking nuts, and spitting the shells about.—As I really think I should have liked to do myself, if I had been in their place and so despised.

At length, it was voted that there was no help for the angry gentleman, and that he must either go in his chance company or remain behind. So, he got into his place, still making complaints, and the keeper got into the place next him, and the convicts hauled themselves up as well as they could, and the convict I had recognised sat behind me with his breath on the hair of my head.

"Good bye, Handel!" Herbert called out as we started. I thought what a blessed fortune it was, that he had found another name for me than Pip.

It is impossible to express with what acuteness I felt the convict's breathing, not only on the back of my head, but all along my spine. The sensation was like being touched in the marrow with some pungent and searching acid, and it set my very teeth on edge. He seemed to have more breathing business to do than another man, and to make more noise in doing it; and I was conscious of growing high-shouldered on one side, in my shrinking endeavours to fend him off.

The weather was miserably raw, and the two cursed the cold. It made us all lethargic before we had gone far, and when we had left the Half-way House behind, we habitually dozed and shivered and were silent. I dozed off, myself, in considering the question whether I ought to restore a couple of pounds sterling to this creature before losing sight of him, and how it could best be done. In the act of dipping forward as if I were going to bathe among the horses, I woke in a fright and took the question up again.

But I must have lost it longer than I had thought, since, although I could recognise nothing in the darkness and the fitful lights and shadows of our lamps, I traced marsh country in the cold damp wind that blew at us. Cowering forward for warmth and to make me a screen against the wind, the convicts were closer to me than before. The very first words I heard them interchange as I became conscious, were the words of my own thought, "Two One Pound notes."

"How did he get 'em?" said the convict I had never seen.

"How should I know?" returned the other. "He had 'em stowed away somehows. Giv him by friends, I expect."

"I wish," said the other, with a bitter curse upon the cold, "that I had 'em here."

"Two one pound notes, or friends?"

"Two one pound notes. I'd sell all the friends I ever had, for one, and think it a blessed good bargain. Well? So he says——?"

"So he says," resumed the convict I had recognised— "it was all said and done in half a minute, behind a pile of timber in the Dockyard—'You're a going to be discharged!' Yes, I was. Would I find out that boy that had fed him and kep his secret, and give him them two one pound notes? Yes I would. And I did."

"More fool you," growled the other. "I'd have spent 'em on a Man, in wittles and drink. He must have been a green one. Mean to say he knowed nothing of you?"

"Not a ha'porth. Different gangs and different ships. He was tried again for prison breaking, and got made a Lifer."

"And was that—Honour!—the only time you worked out, in this part of the country?"

"The only time."

"What might have been your opinion of the place?"

"A most beastly place. Mudbank, mist, swamp, and work: work, swamp, mist, and mudbank."

They both execrated the place in very strong language, and gradually growled themselves out, and had nothing left to say.

After overhearing this dialogue, I should assuredly have got down and been left in the solitude and darkness of the highway, but for feeling certain that the man had no suspicion of my identity. Indeed, I was not only so changed in the course of nature, but so differently dressed and so differently circumstanced, that it was not at all likely he could have known me without accidental help. Still, the coincidence of our being together on the coach, was sufficiently strange to fill me with a dread that some other coincidence might at any moment connect me, in his hearing, with my name. For this reason, I resolved to alight as soon as we touched the town, and put myself out of his hearing. This device I executed successfully. My little portmanteau was in the boot under my feet; I had but to turn a hinge to get it out; I threw it down before me, got down after it, and was left at the first lamp on the first

stones of the town pavement. As to the convicts, they went their way with the coach, and I knew at what point they would be spirited off to the river. In my fancy, I saw the boat with its convict crew waiting for them at the slime-washed stairs,—again heard the gruff "Give way, you!" like an order to dogs—again saw the wicked Noah's Ark lying out on the black water.

I could not have said what I was afraid of, for my fear was altogether undefined and vague, but there was great fear upon me. As I walked on to the hotel, I felt that a dread, much exceeding the mere apprehension of a painful or disagreeable recognition, made me tremble. I am confident that it took no distinctness of shape, and that it was the revival for a few minutes of the terror of childhood.

The coffee-room at the Blue Boar was empty, and I had not only ordered my dinner there, but had sat down to it, before the waiter knew me. As soon as he had apologised for the remissness of his memory, he asked me if he should send Boots for Mr. Pumblechook?

"No," said I, "certainly not."

The waiter (it was he who had brought up the Great Remonstrance from the Commercials on the day when I was bound) appeared surprised, and took the earliest opportunity of putting a dirty old copy of a local newspaper so directly in my way, that I took it up and read this paragraph:

"Our readers will learn, not altogether without interest, in reference to the recent romantic rise in fortune of a young artificer in iron of this neighbourhood (what a theme, by the way, for the magic pen of our as yet not universally acknowledged townsman TOOBY, the poet of our columns!) that the youth's earliest patron, companion, and friend, was a highly-respected individual not entirely unconnected with the corn and seed trade, and whose eminently convenient and commodious business premises are situate within a hundred miles of the High-street. It is not wholly irrespective of our personal feelings that we record HIM as the Mentor of our young Telemachus, for it is good to know that our town produced the founder of the latter's fortunes. Does the thought-contracted brow of the local Sage or the lustrous eye of local Beauty inquire whose fortunes? We believe that Quintin Matsys was the BLACKSMITH of Antwerp. VERB. SAP."

I entertain a conviction, based upon large experience, that if in the days of my prosperity I had gone to the North Pole, I should have met somebody there, wandering Esquimaux or civilised man, who would have told me that Pumblechook was my earliest patron and the founder of my fortunes.

CHAPTER XXIX.

BETIMES in the morning I was up and out. It was too early yet to go to Miss Havisham's, so I loitered into the country on Miss Havisham's side of town—which was not Joe's side; I could go there to-morrow—thinking about my patroness, and painting brilliant pictures of her plans for me.

She had adopted Estella, she had as good as adopted me, and it could not fail to be her intention to bring us together. She reserved it for me to restore the desolate house, admit the sunshine into the dark rooms, set the clocks a going and the cold hearths a blazing, tear down the cobwebs, destroy the vermin—in short, do all the shining deeds of the young Knight of romance, and marry the Princess. I had stopped to look at the house as I passed; and its seared red brick walls, blocked windows, and strong green ivy clasping even the stacks of chimneys with its twigs and tendons, as if with sinewy old arms, had made up a rich attractive mystery, of which I was the hero. Estella was the inspiration of it, and the heart of it, of course. But, though she had taken such a strong possession of me, though my fancy and my hope were so set upon her, though her influence on my boyish life and character had been all-powerful, I did not, even that romantic morning, invest her with any attributes save those she possessed. I mention this in this place, of a fixed purpose, because it is the clue by which I am to be followed into my poor labyrinth. According to my experience, the conventional notion of a lover cannot be always true. The unqualified truth is, that when I loved Estella with the love of a man, I loved her simply because I found her irresistible. Once for all; I knew to my sorrow, often and often, if not always, that I loved her against reason, against promise, against peace, against hope, against happiness, against all discouragement that could be. Once for all; I loved her none the less because I knew it, and it had no more influence in restraining me, than if I had devoutly believed her to be human perfection.

I so shaped out my walk as to arrive at the gate at my old time. When I had rung at the bell with an unsteady hand, I turned my back upon the gate, while I tried to get my breath and keep the beating of my heart moderately quiet. I heard the side door open, and steps came across the courtyard; but I pretended not to hear, even when the gate swung on its rusty hinges.

Being at last touched on the shoulder, I started and turned. I started much more naturally then, to find myself confronted by a man in a sober grey dress. The last man I should have expected to see in that place of porter at Miss Havisham's door.

"Orlick!"

"Ah, young master, there's more changes than yours. But come in, come in. It's opposed to my orders to hold the gate open."

I entered and he swung it, and locked it, and took the key out. "Yes!" said he, facing round, after doggedly preceding me a few steps towards the house. "Here I am!"

"How did you come here?"

"I come here," he retorted, "on my legs. I had my box brought alongside me in a barrow."

"Are you here for good?"

"I ain't here for harm, young master, I suppose."

I was not so sure of that. I had leisure to entertain the retort in my mind, while he slowly lifted his heavy glance from the pavement, up my legs and arms to my face.

"Then you have left the forge?" I said.

"Do this look like a forge?" replied Orlick, sending his glance all round him with an air of injury. "Now, do it look like it?"

I asked him how long he had left Gargery's forge?

"One day is so like another here," he replied, "that I don't know without casting it up. However, I come here some time since you left."

"I could have told you that, Orlick."

"Ah!" said he, drily. "But then you've got to be a scholar."

By this time we had come to the house, where I found his room to be one just within the side door, with a little window in it looking on the courtyard. In its small proportions, it was not unlike the kind of place usually assigned to a gate-porter in Paris. Certain keys were hanging on the wall, to which he now added the gate-key; and his patchwork-covered bed was in a little inner division or recess. The whole had a slovenly, confined and sleepy look, like a cage for a human dormouse: while he, looming dark and heavy in the shadow of a corner by the window, looked like the human dormouse for whom it was fitted up —as indeed he was.

"I never saw this room before," I remarked; "but there used to be no Porter here."

"No," said he; "not till it got about that there was no protection on the premises, and it come to be considered dangerous, with convicts and Tag and Rag and Bobtail going up and down. And then I was recommended to the place as a man who could give another man as good as he brought, and I took it. It's easier than bellowing and hammering.—That's loaded, that is."

My eye had been caught by a gun with a brass-bound stock over the chimney-piece, and his eye had followed mine.

"Well," said I, not desirous of more conversation, "shall I go up to Miss Havisham?"

"Burn me, if I know!" he retorted, first stretching himself and then shaking himself; "my orders ends here, young master. I give this here bell a rap with this here hammer, and you go on along the passage till you meet somebody."

"I am expected, I believe?"

"Burn me twice over, if I can say!" said he.

Upon that I turned down the long passage which I had first trodden in my thick boots, and he made his bell sound. At the end of the passage, while the bell was still reverberating, I found Sarah Pocket: who appeared to have now become constitutionally green and yellow by reason of me.

"Oh!" said she. "You, is it, Mr. Pip?"

"It is, Miss Pocket. I am glad to tell you that Mr. Pocket and family are all well."

"Are they any wiser?" said Sarah, with a dismal shake of the head; "they had better be wiser than well. Ah, Matthew, Matthew! You know your way, sir?"

Tolerably, for I had gone up the staircase in the dark, many a time. I ascended it now, in lighter boots than of yore, and tapped in my old way at the door of Miss Havisham's room. "Pip's rap," I heard her say, immediately; "come in, Pip."

She was in her chair near the old table, in the old dress, with her two hands crossed on her stick, her chin resting on them, and her eyes on the fire. Sitting near her, with the white shoe, that had never been worn, in her hand, and her head bent as she looked at it, was an elegant lady whom I had never seen.

"Come in, Pip," Miss Havisham continued to mutter, without looking round or up; "come in, Pip; how do you do, Pip? so you kiss my hand as if I were a queen, eh?—— Well?"

She looked up at me suddenly, only moving her eyes, and repeated in a grimly playful manner,

"Well?"

"I heard, Miss Havisham," said I, rather at a loss, "that you were so kind as to wish me to come and see you, and I came directly."

"Well?"

The lady whom I had never seen before, lifted up her eyes and looked archly at me, and then I saw that the eyes were Estella's eyes. But she was so much changed, was so much more beautiful, so much more womanly, in all things winning admiration had made such wonderful advance, that I seemed to have made none. I fancied, as I looked at her, that I slipped hopelessly back into the coarse and common boy again. O the sense of distance and disparity that came upon me, and the inaccessibility that came about her!

She gave me her hand. I stammered something about the pleasure I felt in seeing her again, and about my having looked forward to it for a long, long time.

"Do you find her much changed, Pip?" asked Miss Havisham, with her greedy look, and striking her stick upon a chair that stood between them, as a sign to me to sit down there.

"When I came in, Miss Havisham, I thought there was nothing of Estella in the face or figure; but now it all settles down so curiously into the old——"

"What? You are not going to say into the old Estella?" Miss Havisham interrupted. "She was proud and insulting, and you wanted to go away from her. Don't you remember?"

I said confusedly that that was long ago, and that I knew no better then, and the like. Estella smiled with perfect composure, and said she had no doubt of my having been quite right, and of her having been very disagreeable.

"Is _he_ changed?" Miss Havisham asked her.

"Very much," said Estella, looking at me.

"Less coarse and common?" said Miss Havisham, playing with Estella's hair.

Estella laughed, and looked at the shoe in her hand, and laughed again and looked at me, and put the shoe down. She treated me as a boy still, but she lured me on.

We sat in the dreamy room among the old strange influences which had so wrought upon me, and I learnt that she had but just come home from France, and that she was going to London. Proud and wilful as of old, she had brought those qualities into such subjection to her beauty that it was impossible and out of nature—or I thought so —to separate them from her beauty. Truly it was impossible to dissociate her presence from all those wretched hankerings after money and gentility that had disturbed my boyhood—from all those ill-regulated aspirations that had first made me ashamed of home and Joe—from all those visions that had raised her face in the glowing fire, struck it out of the iron on the anvil, extracted it from the darkness of night to look in at the wooden window of the forge and flit away. In a word, it was impossible for me to separate her, in the past or in the present, from the innermost life of my life.

It was settled that I should stay there all the rest of the day, and return to the hotel at night, and to London tomorrow. When we had conversed for a while, Miss Havisham sent us two out to walk in the neglected garden: on our coming in by-and-bye, she said I should wheel her about a little, as in times of yore.

So, Estella and I went out into the garden by the gate through which I had strayed to my encounter with the pale young gentleman, now Herbert; I, trembling in spirit and worshipping the very hem of her dress; she, quite composed and most decidedly not worshipping the hem of mine. As we drew near to the place of encounter, she stopped, and said:

"I must have been a singular little creature to hide and see that fight that day: but I did, and I enjoyed it very much."

"You rewarded me very much."

"Did I?" she replied, in an incidental and forgetful way. "I remember I entertained a great objection to your adversary, because I took it ill that he should be brought here to pester me with his company."

"He and I are great friends now."

"Are you? I think I recollect though, that you read with his father?"

"Yes."

I made the admission with reluctance, for it seemed to have a boyish look, and she already treated me more than enough like a boy.

"Since your change of fortune and prospects, you have changed your companions," said Estella.

"Naturally," said I.

"And necessarily," she added, in a haughty tone; "what was fit company for you once, would be quite unfit company for you now."

In my conscience, I doubt very much whether I had any lingering intention left of going to see Joe; but if I had, this observation put it to flight.

"You had no idea of your impending good fortune, in those times?" said Estella, with a slight wave of her hand, signifying the fighting times.

"Not the least."

The air of completeness and superiority with which she walked at my side, and the air of youthfulness and submission with which I walked at hers, made a contrast that I strongly felt. It would have rankled in me more than it did, if I had not regarded myself as eliciting it by being so set apart for her and assigned to her.

The garden was too overgrown and rank for walking in with ease, and after we had made the round of it twice or thrice, we came out again into the brewery yard. I showed her to a nicety where I had seen her walking on the casks, that first old day, and she said with a cold and careless look in that direction, "Did I?" I reminded her where she had come out of the house and given me my meat and drink, and she said, "I don't remember." "Not remember that you made me cry?" said I. "No," said she, and shook her head and looked about her. I verily believe that her not remembering and not minding in the least, made me cry again, inwardly—and that is the sharpest crying of all.

"You must know," said Estella, condescending to me as a brilliant and beautiful woman might, "that I have no heart—if that has anything to do with my memory."

I got through some jargon to the effect that I took the liberty of doubting that. That I knew better. That there could be no beauty without it.

"Oh! I have a heart to be stabbed in or shot in, I have no doubt," said Estella, "and, of course, if it ceased to beat I should cease to be. But you know what I mean. I have no softness there, no—sympathy—sentiment—nonsense."

What _was_ it that was borne in upon my mind when she stood still and looked attentively at me? Anything that I had seen in Miss Havisham? No. In some of her looks and gestures there was that tinge of resemblance to Miss Havisham which may often be noticed to have been acquired by children, from grown persons with whom they have been much associated and secluded, and which, when childhood is past, will produce a remarkable occasional likeness of expression between faces that are otherwise quite different. And yet I could not trace this to Miss Havisham. I looked again, and though she was still looking at me, the suggestion was gone.

What *was* it?

"I am serious," said Estella, not so much with a frown (for her brow was smooth) as with a darkening of her face; "if we are to be thrown much together, you had better believe it at once. No!" imperiously stopping me as I opened my lips. "I have not bestowed my tenderness anywhere. I have never had any such thing."

In another moment we were in the brewery so long disused, and she pointed to the high gallery where I had seen her going out on that same first day, and told me she remembered to have been up there, and to have seen me standing scared below. As my eyes followed her white hand, again the same dim suggestion that I could not possibly grasp, crossed me. My involuntary start occasioned her to lay her hand upon my arm. Instantly the ghost passed once more and was gone.

What *was* it?

"What is the matter?" asked Estella. "Are you scared again?"

"I should be if I believed what you said just now," I replied, to turn it off.

"Then you don't? Very well. It is said, at any rate. Miss Havisham will soon be expecting you at your old post, though I think that might be laid aside now, with other old belongings. Let us make one more round of the garden, and then go in. Come! You shall not shed tears for my cruelty to-day; you shall be my Page, and give me your shoulder."

Her handsome dress had trailed upon the ground. She held it in one hand now, and with the other lightly touched my shoulder as we walked.

We walked about the ruined garden twice or thrice more, and it was all in bloom for me. If the green and yellow growth of weed in the chinks of the old wall had been the most precious flowers that ever blew, it could not have been more cherished in my remembrance.

There was no discrepancy of years between us, to remove her far from me; we were of nearly the same age, though of course the age told for more in her case than in mine; but the air of inaccessibility which her beauty and her manner gave her, tormented me in the midst of my delight, and at the height of the assurance I felt that our patroness had chosen us for one another. Wretched boy!

At last we went back into the house, and there I heard, with surprise, that my guardian had come down to see Miss Havisham on business, and would come back to dinner. The old wintry branches of chandeliers in the room where the mouldering table was spread, had been lighted while we were out, and Miss Havisham was in her chair and waiting for me.

It was like pushing the chair itself back into the past, when we began the old slow circuit round about the ashes of the bridal feast. But, in the funereal room, with that figure of the grave fallen back in the chair fixing its eyes upon her, Estella looked more bright and beautiful than before, and I was under stronger enchantment.

The time so melted away, that our early dinner-hour drew close at hand, and Estella left us to prepare herself. We had stopped near the centre of the long table, and Miss Havisham, with one of her withered arms stretched out of the chair, rested that clenched hand upon the yellow cloth. As Estella looked back over her shoulder before going out at the door, Miss Havisham kissed that hand to her, with a ravenous intensity that was of its kind quite dreadful.

Then, Estella being gone and we two left alone, she turned to me and said in a whisper:

"Is she beautiful, graceful, well-grown? Do you admire her?"

"Everybody must who sees her, Miss Havisham."

She drew an arm round my neck, and drew my head close down to hers as she sat in the chair. "Love her, love her, love her! How does she use you?"

Before I could answer (if I could have answered so difficult a question at all), she repeated, "Love her, love her, love her! If she favours you, love her. If she wounds you, love her. If she tears your heart to pieces—and as it gets older and stronger it will tear deeper—love her, love her, love her!"

Never had I seen such passionate eagerness as was joined to her utterance of these words. I could feel the muscles of the thin arm round my neck, swell with the vehemence that possessed her.

"Hear me, Pip! I adopted her to be loved. I bred her and educated her, to be loved. I developed her into what she is, that she might be loved. Love her!"

She said the word often enough, and there could be no doubt that she meant to say it; but if the often repeated word had been hate instead of love—despair—revenge—dire death—it could not have sounded from her lips more like a curse.

"I'll tell you," said she, in the same hurried passionate whisper, "what real love is. It is blind devotion, unquestioning self-humiliation, utter submission, trust and belief against yourself and against the whole world, giving up your whole heart and soul to the smiter—as I did!"

When she came to that, and to a wild cry that followed that, I caught her round the waist. For she rose up in the chair, in her shroud of a dress, and struck at the air as if she would as soon have struck herself against the wall and fallen dead.

All this passed in a few seconds. As I drew her down into her chair, I was conscious of a scent that I knew, and turning, saw my guardian in the room.

He always carried (I have not yet mentioned it, I think) a pocket-handkerchief of rich silk and of imposing proportions, which was of great value to him in his profession. I have seen him so terrify a client or a witness by ceremoniously unfolding this pocket-handkerchief as if he were immediately going to blow his nose, and then pausing, as if he knew he should not have time to do it, before such client or witness committed himself, that the self-committal has followed directly, quite as a matter of course. When I saw him in the room he had this expressive pocket-handkerchief in both hands, and was looking at us. On meeting my eye, he said plainly, by a momentary and silent pause in that attitude, "Indeed? Singular!" and then put the handkerchief to its right use with wonderful effect. Miss Havisham had seen him as soon as I, and was (like everybody else) afraid of him. She made a strong attempt to compose herself, and stammered that he was as punctual as ever.

"As punctual as ever," he repeated, coming up to us.

"(How do you do, Pip? Shall I give you a ride, Miss Havisham? Once round?) And so you are here, Pip?"

I told him when I had arrived, and how Miss Havisham wished me to come and see Estella. To which he replied, "Ah! Very fine young lady!" Then he pushed Miss Havisham in her chair before him, with one of his large hands, and put the other in his trousers-pocket as if the pocket were full of secrets.

"Well, Pip! How often have you seen Miss Estella before?" said he, when he came to a stop.

"How often?"

"Ah! How many times? Ten thousand times?"

"Oh! Certainly not so many."

"Twice?"

"Jaggers," interposed Miss Havisham, much to my relief; "leave my Pip alone, and go with him to your dinner."

He complied, and we groped our way down the dark stairs together. While we were still on our way to those detached apartments across the paved yard at the back, he asked me how often I had seen Miss Havisham eat and drink; offering me a breadth of choice, as usual, between a hundred times and once.

I considered, and said, "Never."

"And never will, Pip," he retorted, with a frowning smile. "She has never allowed herself to be seen doing either, since she lived this present life of hers. She wanders about in the night, and then lays hands on such food as she takes."

"Pray, sir," said I, "may I ask you a question?"

"You may," said he, "and I may decline to answer it. Put your question."

"Estella's name, is it Havisham or ——?" I had nothing to add.

"Or what?" said he.

"Is it Havisham?"

"It is Havisham."

This brought us to the dinner-table, where she and Sarah Pocket awaited us. Mr. Jaggers presided, Estella sat opposite to him, I faced my green and yellow friend. We dined very well, and were waited on by a maid-servant whom I had never seen in all my comings and goings, but who, for anything I know, had been in that mysterious house the whole time. After dinner a bottle of choice old port was placed before my guardian (he was evidently well acquainted with the vintage), and the two ladies left us.

Anything to equal the determined reticence of Mr. Jaggers under that roof I never saw elsewhere, even in him. He kept his very looks to himself, and scarcely directed his eyes to Estella's face once during dinner. When she spoke to him, he listened, and in due course, answered, but never looked at her that I could see. On the other hand, she often looked at him, with interest and curiosity, if not distrust, but his face never showed the least consciousness. Throughout dinner he took a dry delight in making Sarah Pocket greener and yellower, by often referring in conversation with me to my expectations: but here, again, he showed no consciousness, and even made it appear that he extorted—and even did extort, though I don't know how—those references out of my innocent self.

And when he and I were left alone together, he sat with an air upon him of general lying by in consequence of information he possessed, that really was too much for me. He cross-examined his very wine when he had nothing else in hand. He held it between himself and the candle, tasted the port, rolled it in his mouth, swallowed it, looked at his glass again, smelt the port, tried it, drank it, filled again, and cross-examined the glass again, until I was as nervous as if I had known the wine to be telling him something to my disadvantage. Three or four times I feebly thought I would start conversation; but whenever he saw me going to ask him anything, he looked at me with his glass in his hand, and rolling his wine about in his mouth, as if requesting me to take notice that it was of no use, for he couldn't answer.

I think Miss Pocket was conscious that the sight of me involved her in the danger of being goaded to madness, and perhaps tearing off her cap—which was a very hideous one, in the nature of a muslin mop—and strewing the ground with her hair—which assuredly had never grown on *her* head. She did not appear when we afterwards went up to Miss Havisham's room, and we four played at whist. In the interval, Miss Havisham, in a fantastic way, had put some of the most beautiful jewels from her dressing-table into Estella's hair, and about her bosom and arms; and I saw even my guardian look at her from under his thick eyebrows, and raise them a little when her loveliness was before him, with those rich flushes of glitter and colour in it.

Of the manner and extent to which he took our trumps into custody, and came out with mean little cards at the ends of hands, before which the glory of our Kings and Queens was utterly abased, I say nothing; nor, of the feeling that I had, respecting his looking upon us personally in the light of three very obvious and poor riddles that he had found out long ago. What I suffered from, was the incompatibility between his cold presence and my feelings towards Estella. It was not that I knew I could never bear to speak to him about her, that I knew I could never bear to hear him creak his boots at her, that I knew I could never bear to see him wash his hands of her; it was, that my admiration should be within a foot or two of him—it was, that my feelings should be in the same place with him—*that*, was the agonising circumstance.

We played until nine o'clock, and then it was arranged that when Estella came to London I should be forewarned of her coming and should meet her at the coach; and then I took leave of her, and touched her and left her.

My guardian lay at the Boar in the next room to mine. Far into the night, Miss Havisham's words, "Love her, love her, love her!" sounded in my ears. I adapted them for my own repetition, and said to my pillow, "I love her, I love her, I love her!" hundreds of times. Then, a burst of gratitude came upon me, that she should be destined for me, once the blacksmith's boy. Then, I thought if she were, as I feared, by no means rapturously grateful for that destiny yet, when would she begin to be interested in me? When should I awaken the heart within her, that was mute and sleeping now?

Ah me! I thought those were high and great emotions. But I never thought there was anything low and small in my keeping away from Joe, because I knew she would be contemptuous of him. It was but a day gone, and Joe had brought the tears into my eyes; they had soon dried, God forgive me! soon dried.

CHAPTER XXX.

AFTER well considering the matter while I was dressing at the Blue Boar in the morning, I resolved to tell my guardian that I doubted Orlick's being the right sort of man to fill a post of trust at Miss Havisham's. "Why, of course he is not the right sort of man, Pip," said my guardian, comfortably satisfied beforehand on the general head, "because the man who fills the post of trust never is the right sort of man." It seemed quite to put him in spirits, to find that this particular post was not exceptionally held by the right sort of man, and he listened in a satisfied manner while I told him what knowledge I had of Orlick. "Very good, Pip," he observed, when I concluded, "I'll go round presently, and pay our friend off." Rather alarmed by this summary action, I was for a little delay, and even hinted that our friend himself might be difficult to deal with. "Oh no, he won't," said my guardian, making his pocket-handkerchief-point, with perfect confidence; "I should like to see him argue the question with *me*."

As we were going back together to London by the mid-day coach, and as I breakfasted under such terrors of Pumblechook that I could scarcely hold my cup, this gave me an opportunity of saying that I wanted a walk, and that I would go on along the London-road while Mr. Jaggers was occupied, if he would let the coachman know that I would get into my place when overtaken. I was thus enabled to fly from the Blue Boar immediately after breakfast. By then making a loop of about a couple of miles into the open country at the back of Pumblechook's premises, I got round into High-street again, a little beyond that pitfall, and felt myself in comparative security.

It was interesting to be in the quiet old town once more, and it was not disagreeable to be here and there suddenly recognised and stared after. One or two of the tradespeople even darted out of their shops, and little way down the street before me, that they might turn, as if they had forgotten something, and pass me face to face—on which occasion I don't know whether they or I made the worst pretence; they of not doing it, or I of not seeing it. Still my position was a distinguished one, and I was not at all dissatisfied with it, until Fate threw me in the way of that unlimited miscreant, Trabb's boy.

Casting my eyes along the street at a certain point of my progress, I beheld Trabb's boy approaching, lashing himself with an empty blue bag. Deeming that a serene and unconscious contemplation of him would best beseem me, and would be most likely to quell his evil mind, I advanced with that expression of countenance, and was rather congratulating myself on my success, when suddenly the knees of Trabb's boy smote together, his hair uprose, his cap fell off, he trembled violently in every limb, staggered out into the road and crying to the populace, "Hold me! I'm so frightened!" feigned to be in a paroxysm of terror and contrition, occasioned by the dignity of my appearance. As I passed him, his teeth loudly chattered in his head, and with every mark of extreme humiliation, he prostrated himself in the dust.

This was a hard thing to bear, but this was nothing. I had not advanced another two hundred yards, when, to my inexpressible terror, amazement, and indignation, I again beheld Trabb's boy approaching. He was coming round a narrow corner. His blue bag was slung over his shoulder, honest industry beamed in his eyes, a determination to proceed to Trabb's with cheerful briskness was indicated in his gait. With a shock he became aware of me, and was severely visited as before; but this time his motion was rotatory, and he staggered round and round me with knees more afflicted, and with uplifted hands as if beseeching for mercy. His sufferings were hailed with the great-

est joy by a knot of spectators, and I felt utterly confounded.

I had not got as much further down the street as the post-office, when I again beheld Trabb's boy shooting round by a back way. This time he was entirely changed. He wore the blue bag in the manner of my great-coat, and was strutting along the pavement towards me on the opposite side of the street, attended by a company of delighted young friends to whom he from time to time exclaimed, with a wave of his hand, "Don't know yah!" Words cannot state the amount of aggravation and injury wreaked upon me by Trabb's boy, when, passing abreast of me, he pulled up his shirt collar, twined his side-hair, stuck an arm akimbo, and smirked extravagantly by, wriggling his elbows and body, and drawling to his attendants, "Don't know yah, don't know yah, pon my soul don't know yah!" The disgrace attendant on his immediately afterwards taking to crowing and pursuing me across the bridge with crows, as from an exceedingly dejected fowl who had known me when I was a blacksmith, culminated the disgrace with which I left the town, and was, so to speak, ejected by it into the open country.

But unless I had taken the life of Trabb's boy on that occasion, I really do not even now see what I could have done save endure. To have struggled with him in the street, or to have exacted any lower recompense from him than his heart's best blood, would have been futile and degrading. Moreover, he was a boy whom no man could hurt; an invulnerable and dodging serpent who, when chased into a corner, flew out again between his captor's legs, scornfully yelping. I wrote, however, to Mr. Trabb by next day's post, to say that Mr. Pip must decline to deal further with one who could so far forget what he owed to the best interests of society, as to employ a boy who excited Loathing in every respectable mind.

The coach, with Mr. Jaggers inside, came up in due time, and I took my box-seat again, and arrived in London safe—but not sound, for my heart was gone. As soon as I arrived, I sent a penitential codfish and a barrel of oysters to Joe (as reparation for not having gone myself), and then went on to Barnard's Inn.

I found Herbert dining on cold meat, and delighted to welcome me back. Having despatched the Avenger to the coffee-house for an addition to the dinner, I felt that I must open my breast that very evening to my friend and chum. As confidence was out of the question with the Avenger in the hall, which could merely be regarded in the light of an ante-chamber to the keyhole, I sent him to the Play. A better proof of the severity of my bondage to that taskmaster could scarcely be afforded, than the degrading shifts to which I was constantly driven to find him employment. So mean is extremity, that I sometimes sent him to Hyde Park Corner to see what o'clock it was.

Dinner done and we sitting with our feet upon the fender, I said to Herbert, "My dear Herbert, I have something very particular to tell you."

"My dear Handel," he returned, "I shall esteem and respect your confidence."

"It concerns myself, Herbert," said I, "and one other person."

Herbert crossed his feet, looked at the fire with his head on one side, and having looked at it in vain for some time, looked at me because I didn't go on.

"Herbert," said I, laying my hand upon his knee, "I love—I adore—Estella."

Instead of being transfixed, Herbert replied in an easy matter-of-course way, "Exactly. Well?"

"Well, Herbert. Is that all you say? Well?"

"What next, I mean?" said Herbert. "Of course I know *that*."

"How do you know it?" said I.

"How do I know it, Handel? Why, from you."

"I never told you."

"Told me! You have never told me when you have got your hair cut, but I have had senses to perceive it. You have always adored her, ever since I have known you. You brought your adoration and your portmanteau here, together. Told me! Why, you have always told me all day long. When you told me your own story, you told me plainly that you began adoring her the first time you saw her, when you were very young indeed."

"Very well, then," said I, to whom this was a new and not unwelcome light, "I have never left off adoring her. And she has come back, a most beautiful and most elegant creature. And I saw her yesterday. And if I adored her before, I now doubly adore her."

"Lucky for you then, Handel," said Herbert, "that you are picked out for her and allotted to her. Without encroaching on forbidden ground, we may venture to say, that there can be no doubt between ourselves of that fact. Have you any idea yet, of Estella's views on the adoration question?"

I shook my head gloomily. "Oh! She is thousands of miles away, from me," said I.

"Patience, my dear Handel: time enough, time enough. But you have something more to say?"

"I am ashamed to say it," I returned, "and yet it's no worse to say it than to think it. You call me a lucky fellow. Of course, I am. I was a blacksmith's boy but yesterday; I am—what shall I say I am—to-day?"

"Say, a good fellow, if you want a phrase," returned Herbert, smiling, and clapping his hand on the back of mine: "a good fellow, with impetuosity and hesitation, boldness and diffidence, action and dreaming, curiously mixed in him."

I stopped for a moment to consider whether there really was this mixture in my character. On the whole, I by no means recognised the analysis, but thought it not worth disputing.

"When I ask what I am to call myself to-day, Herbert," I went on, "I suggest what I have in my thoughts. You say I am lucky. I know I have done nothing to raise myself in life, and that Fortune alone has raised me; that is being very lucky. And yet, when I think of Estella——"

("And when don't you, you know!" Herbert threw in, with his eyes on the fire; which I thought kind and sympathetic of him.)

"—Then, my dear Herbert, I cannot tell you how dependent and uncertain I feel, and how exposed to hundreds of chances. Avoiding forbidden ground, as you did just now, I may still say that on the constancy of one person (naming no person) all my expectations depend. And at the best, how indefinite and unsatisfactory, only to know so vaguely what they are!" In saying this, I relieved my mind of what had always been there, more or less, though no doubt most since yesterday.

"Now, Handel," Herbert replied, in his gay hopeful way, "it seems to me that in the despondency of the tender passion, we are looking into our gift-horse's mouth with a magnifying-glass. Likewise, it seems to me that, concentrating our attention on the examination, we altogether overlook one of the best points of the animal. Didn't you tell me that your guardian, Mr. Jaggers, told you in the beginning, that you were not endowed with expectations only? And even if he had not told you so—though that is a very large If, I grant—could you believe that of all men in London, Mr. Jaggers is the man to hold his present relations towards you unless he were sure of his ground?"

I said I could not deny that this was a strong point. I said it (people often do so in such cases) like a rather reluctant concession to truth and justice;—as if I wanted to deny it!

"I should think it *was* a strong point," said Herbert, "and I should think you would be puzzled to imagine a stronger; as to the rest, you must bide your guardian's time, and he must bide his client's time. You'll be one-and-twenty before you know where you are, and then perhaps you'll get some further enlightenment. At all events, you'll be nearer getting it, for it must come at last."

"What a hopeful disposition you have!" said I, gratefully admiring his cheery ways.

"I ought to have," said Herbert, "for I have not much else. I must acknowledge, by-the-bye, that the good sense of what I have just said is not my own, but my father's. The only remark I ever heard him make on your story, was the final one: 'The thing is settled and done, or Mr. Jaggers would not be in it.' And now, before I say anything more about my father, or my father's son, and repay confidence with confidence, I want to make myself seriously disagreeable to you for a moment—positively repulsive."

"You won't succeed," said I.

"Oh yes I shall!" said he. "One, two, three, and now I am in for it. Handel, my good fellow:" though he spoke in this light tone, he was very much in earnest: "I have been thinking since we have been talking with our feet on this fender, that Estella cannot surely be a condition of your inheritance, if she was never referred to by your guardian. Am I right in so understanding what you have told me, as that he never referred to her, directly or indirectly, in any way? Never even hinted, for instance, that your patron might have views as to your marriage ultimately?"

"Never."

"Now, Handel, I am quite free from the flavour of sour grapes, upon my soul and honour! Not being bound to her, can you not detach yourself from her?—I told you I should be disagreeable."

I turned my head aside, for, with a rush and a sweep, like the old marsh winds coming up from the sea, a feeling like that which had subdued me on the morning when I left the forge, when the mists were solemnly rising, and when I laid my hand upon the village finger-post, smote upon my heart again. There was silence between us for a little while.

"Yes; but my dear Handel," Herbert went on, as if we had been talking instead of silent, "its having been so strongly rooted in the breast of a boy whom nature and circumstances made so romantic, renders it very serious. Think of her bringing-up, and think of Miss Havisham. Think of what she is herself (now I am repulsive and you abominate me). This may lead to miserable things."

"I know it, Herbert," said I, with my head still turned away, "but I can't help it."

"You can't detach yourself?"

"No. Impossible!"

"You can't try, Handel?"

"No. Impossible!"

"Well!" said Herbert, getting up with a lively shake as if he had been asleep, and stirring the fire; "now I'll endeavour to make myself agreeable again!"

So, he went round the room and shook the curtains out, put the chairs in their places, tidied the books and so forth that were lying about, looked into the hall, peeped into the letter-box, shut the door, and came back to his chair by the fire; when he sat down, nursing his left leg in both arms.

"I was going to say a word or two, Handel, concerning my father and my father's son. I am afraid it is scarcely necessary for my father's son to remark that my father's establishment is not particularly brilliant in its house-keeping."

"There is always plenty, Herbert," said I, to say something encouraging.

"Oh yes! and so the dustman says, I believe, with the strongest approval, and so does the marine-store shop in the back street. Gravely, Handel, for the subject is grave enough, you know how it is, as well as I do. I suppose there was a time once, when my father had not given matters up; but if ever there was, the time is gone. May I ask you if you have ever had an opportunity of remarking, down in your part of the country, that the children of not exactly suitable marriages, are always most particularly anxious to be married?"

This was such a singular question, that I asked him, in return, "Is it so?"

"I don't know," said Herbert; "that's what I want to know. Because it is decidedly the case with us. My poor sister Charlotte, who was next me and died before she was fourteen, was a striking example. Little Jane is the same. In her desire to be matrimonially established, you might suppose her to have passed her short existence in the perpetual contemplation of domestic bliss. Little Alick in a frock has already made arrangements for his union with a suitable young person at Kew. And, indeed, I think we are all engaged, except the baby."

"Then you are?" said I.

"I am," said Herbert; "but it's a secret."

I assured him of my keeping the secret, and begged to be favoured with further particulars. He had spoken so sensibly and feelingly of my weakness, that I wanted to know something about his strength.

"May I ask the name?" I said.

"Name of Clara," said Herbert.

"Live in London?"

"Yes. Perhaps I ought to mention," said Herbert, who had become curiously crestfallen and meek, since we entered on the interesting theme, "that she is rather below my mother's nonsensical family notions. Her father had to do with the victualling of passenger-ships. I think he was a species of purser."

"What is he now?" said I.

"He's an invalid now," replied Herbert.

"Living on ——?"

"On the first floor," said Herbert. Which was not at all what I meant, for I had intended my question to apply to his means. "I have never seen him, for he has always kept his room overhead, since I have known Clara. But I have heard him constantly. He makes tremendous rows—roars, and pegs at the floor with some frightful instru-

ment." In looking at me and then laughing heartily, Herbert for the time recovered his usual lively manner.

"Don't you expect to see him?" said I.

"Oh yes, I constantly expect to see him," returned Herbert, "because I never hear him, without expecting him to come tumbling through the ceiling. But I don't know how long the rafters may hold."

When he had once more laughed heartily, he became meek again, and told me that the moment he began to realise Capital, it was his intention to marry this young lady. He added as a self-evident proposition, engendering low spirits, "But you *can't* marry, you know, while you're looking about you."

As we contemplated the fire, and as I thought what a difficult vision to realise this same Capital sometimes was, I put my hands in my pockets. A folded piece of paper in one of them attracting my attention, I opened it and found it to be the playbill I had received from Joe, relative to the celebrated provincial amateur of Roscian renown. "And bless my heart," I involuntarily added aloud, "it's to-night!"

This changed the subject in an instant, and made us hurriedly resolve to go to the play. So, when I had pledged myself to comfort and abet Herbert in the affair of his heart by all practicable and impracticable means, and when Herbert had told me that his affianced already knew me by reputation, and that I should be presented to her, and when we had warmly shaken hands upon our mutual confidence, we blew out our candles, made up our fire, locked our door, and issued forth in quest of Mr. Wopsle and Denmark.

CHAPTER XXXI.

On our arrival in Denmark, we found the king and queen of that country elevated in two arm-chairs on a kitchen-table, holding a Court. The whole of the Danish nobility were in attendance; consisting of a noble boy in the wash-leather boots of a gigantic ancestor, a venerable Peer with a dirty face, who seemed to have risen from the people late in life, and the Danish chivalry with a comb in its hair and a pair of white silk legs, and presenting on the whole a feminine appearance. My gifted townsman stood gloomily apart, with folded arms, and I could have wished that his curls and forehead had been more probable.

Several curious little circumstances transpired as the action proceeded. The late king of the country not only appeared to have been troubled with a cough at the time of his decease, but to have taken it with him to the tomb, and to have brought it back. The royal phantom also carried a ghostly manuscript round its truncheon, to which it had the appearance of occasionally referring, and that, too, with an air of anxiety and a tendency to lose the place of reference which were suggestive of a state of mortality. It was this, I conceive, which led to the Shade's being advised by the gallery to "turn over!"—a recommendation which it took extremely ill. It was likewise to be noted of this majestic spirit that whereas it always appeared with an air of having been out a long time and walked an immense distance, it perceptibly came from a closely-contiguous wall. This occasioned its terrors to be received derisively. The Queen of Denmark, a very buxom lady, though no doubt historically brazen, was considered by the public to have too much brass about her; her chin being attached to her diadem by a broad band of that metal (as if she had a gorgeous toothache), her waist being encircled by another, and each of her arms by another, so that she was openly mentioned as "the kettledrum." The noble boy in the ancestral boots, was inconsistent; representing himself, as it were in one breath, as an able seaman, a strolling actor, a gravedigger, a clergyman, and a person of the utmost importance at a Court fencing-match, on the authority of whose practised eye and nice discrimination the finest strokes were judged. This gradually led to a want of toleration for him, and even—on his being detected in holy orders, and declining to perform the funeral service—to the general indignation taking the form of nuts. Lastly, Ophelia was a prey to such slow musical madness, that when, in course of time, she had taken off her white muslin scarf, folded it up, and buried it, a sulky man who had been long cooling his impatient nose against an iron bar in the front row of the gallery, growled, "Now the baby's put to bed, let's have supper!" Which, to say the least of it, was out of keeping.

Upon my unfortunate townsman all these incidents accumulated with playful effect. Whenever that undecided Prince had to ask a question or state a doubt, the public helped him out with it. As for example; on the question whether 'twas nobler in the mind to suffer, some roared yes, and some no, and some inclining to both opinions said "toss up for it;" and quite a Debating Society arose. When he asked what should such fellows as he do crawling between earth and heaven, he was encouraged with loud cries of "Hear, hear!" When he appeared with his stocking disordered (its disorder expressed, according to usage, by one very neat fold in the top, which I suppose to be always got up with a flat iron), a conversation took place in the gallery respecting the paleness of his leg, and whether it was occasioned by the turn the ghost had given him. On his taking the recorders—very like a little black flute that had just been played in the orchestra and handed out at the door—he was called upon unanimously for Rule Britannia. When he recommended the player not to saw the air thus, the sulky man said, "And don't *you* do it, neither; you're a deal worse than *him!*" And I grieve to add that peals of laughter greeted Mr. Wopsle on every one of these occasions.

But his greatest trials were in the churchyard: which had the appearance of a primeval forest, with a kind of small ecclesiastical wash-house on one side, and a turnpike gate on the other. Mr. Wopsle, in a comprehensive black cloak, being descried entering at the turnpike, the grave-digger was admonished in a friendly way, "Look out! Here's the undertaker a coming, to see how you're getting on with your work!" I believe it is well known in a constitutional country that Mr. Wopsle could not possibly have returned the skull, after moralising over it, without dusting his fingers on a white napkin taken from his breast; but even that innocent and indispensable action did not pass without the comment "Wai-ter!" The arrival of the body for interment (in an empty black box with the lid tumbling open), was the signal for a general joy which was much enhanced by the discovery, among the bearers, of an individual obnoxious to identification. The joy attended Mr. Wopsle through his struggle with Laertes on the brink of the orchestra and the grave, and slackened no more until he had tumbled the king off the kitchen-table, and had died by inches from the ankles upward.

We had made some pale efforts in the beginning to applaud Mr. Wopsle; but they were too hopeless to be persisted in. Therefore we had sat, feeling keenly for him, but laughing, nevertheless, from ear to ear. I laughed in spite of myself all the time, the whole thing was so droll; and yet I had a latent impression that there was something decidedly fine in Mr. Wopsle's elocution—not for old associations' sake, I am afraid, but because it was very slow, very dreary, very up-hill and down-hill, and very unlike any way in which any man in any natural circumstances of life or death ever expressed himself about anything. When the tragedy was over, and he had been called for and hooted, I said to Herbert, "Let us go at once, or perhaps we shall meet him."

We made all the haste we could downstairs, but we were not quick enough either. Standing at the door was a Jewish man with an unnatural heavy smear of eyebrow, who caught my eyes as we advanced, and said, when we came up with him:

"Mr. Pip and friend?"

Identity of Mr. Pip and friend confessed.

"Mr. Waldengarver," said the man, "would be glad to have the honour."

"Waldengarver?" I repeated—when Herbert murmured in my ear, "Probably Wopsle."

"Oh!" said I. "Yes. Shall we follow you?"

"A few steps, please." When we were in a side alley, he turned and asked, "How do you think he looked?—*I* dressed him."

I don't know what he had looked like, except a funeral; with the addition of a large Danish sun or star hanging round his neck by a blue ribbon, that had given him the appearance of being insured in some extraordinary Fire Office. But I said he had looked very nice.

"When he come to the grave," said our conductor, "he showed his cloak beautiful. But, judging from the wing, it looked to me that when he see the ghost in the queen's apartment, he might have made more of his stockings."

I modestly assented, and we all fell through a little dirty swing door, into a sort of hot packing-case immediately behind it. Here Mr. Wopsle was divesting himself of his Danish garments, and here there was just room for us to look at him over one another's shoulders by keeping the packing-case door, or lid, wide open.

"Gentlemen," said Mr. Wopsle, "I am proud to see you. I hope, Mr. Pip, you will excuse my sending round. I had the happiness to know you in former times, and the Drama has ever had a claim which has ever been acknowledged, on the noble and the affluent."

Meanwhile, Mr. Waldengarver, in a frightful perspiration, was trying to get himself out of his princely sables.

"Skin the stockings off, Mr. Waldengarver," said the owner of that property, "or you'll bust 'em. Bust 'em and you'll bust five-and-thirty shillings. Shakspeare never was complimented with a finer pair. Keep quiet in your chair now, and leave 'em to me."

With that, he went upon his knees, and began to flay his victim; who, on the first stocking coming off, would certainly have fallen over backward with his chair, but for there being no room to fall anyhow.

I had been afraid until then to say a word about the play. But then, Mr. Waldengarver looked up at us complacently, and said:

"Gentlemen, how did it seem to you, to go, in front?"

Herbert said from behind (at the same time poking me), "capitally." So I said "capitally."

"How did you like my reading of the character, gentlemen?" said Mr. Waldengarver, almost, if not quite, with patronage.

Herbert said from behind (again poking me), "massive and concrete." So I said boldly, as if I had originated it, and must beg to insist upon it, "massive and concrete."

"I am glad to have your approbation, gentlemen," said Mr. Waldengarver, with an air of dignity, in spite of his being ground against the wall at the time, and holding on by the seat of the chair.

"But I'll tell you one thing, Mr. Waldengarver," said the man who was on his knees, "in which you're out in your reading. Now mind! I don't care who says contrary; I tell you so. You're out in your reading of Hamlet when you get your legs in profile. The last Hamlet as I dressed, made the same mistakes in his reading at rehearsal, till I got him to put a large red wafer on each of his shins, and then at that rehearsal (which was the last) I went in front, sir, to the back of the pit, and whenever his reading brought him into profile, I called out 'I don't see no wafers!' And at night his reading was lovely."

Mr. Waldengarver smiled at me, as much as to say "a faithful dependent—I overlook his folly;" and then said aloud, "My view is a little classic and thoughtful for them here; but they will improve, they will improve."

Herbert and I said together, Oh, no doubt they would improve.

"Did you observe, gentlemen," said Mr. Waldengarver, "that there was a man in the gallery who endeavoured to cast derision on the service—I mean, the representation?"

We basely replied that we rather thought we had noticed such a man. I added, "He was drunk, no doubt."

"Oh dear no, sir," said Mr. Wopsle, "not drunk. His employer would see to that, sir. His employer would not allow him to be drunk."

"You know his employer?" said I.

Mr. Wopsle shut his eyes, and opened them again; performing both ceremonies very slowly. "You must have observed, gentlemen," said he, "an ignorant and a blatant ass, with a rasping throat and a countenance expressive of low malignity, who went through—I will not say sustained—the rôle (if I may use a French expression) of Claudius King of Denmark. That is his employer, gentlemen. Such is the profession!"

Without distinctly knowing whether I should have been more sorry for Mr. Wopsle if he had been in despair, I was so sorry for him as it was, that I took the opportunity of his turning round to have his braces put on—which jostled us out at the doorway—to ask Herbert what he thought of having him home to supper? Herbert said he thought it would be kind to do so; therefore I invited him, and he went to Barnard's with us, wrapped up to the eyes, and we did our best for him, and he sat until two o'clock in the morning, reviewing his success and developing his plans. I forget in detail what they were, but I have a general recollection that he was to begin with reviving the Drama, and to end with crushing it; inasmuch as his decease would leave it utterly bereft and without a chance or hope.

Miserably I went to bed after all, and miserably thought of Estella, and miserably dreamed that my expectations were all cancelled, and that I had to give my hand in marriage to Herbert's Clara, or play Hamlet to Miss Havisham's Ghost, before twenty thousand people, without knowing twenty words of it.

CHAPTER XXXII.

One day when I was busy with my books and Mr. Pocket, I received a note by the post, the mere outside of which threw me into a great flutter; for, though I had never seen the handwriting in which it was addressed, I divined whose hand it was. It had no set beginning, as Dear Mr. Pip, or Dear Pip, or Dear Sir, or Dear Anything, but ran thus:

"I am to come to London the day after to-morrow by the mid-day coach. I believe it was settled you should meet me? At all events Miss Havisham has that impression, and I write in obedience to it. She sends you her regard. —Yours, Estella."

If there had been time, I should probably have ordered several suits of clothes for this occasion; but as there was not, I was fain to be content with those I had. My appetite vanished instantly, and I knew no peace or rest until the day arrived. Not that its arrival brought me either; for, then I was worse than ever, and began haunting the coach-office in Wood-street, Cheapside, before the coach had left the Blue Boar in our town. For all that I knew this perfectly well, I still felt as if it were not safe to let the coach-office be out of my sight longer than five minutes at a time; and in this condition of unreason I had performed the first half-hour of a watch of four or five hours, when Wemmick ran against me.

"Halloa, Mr. Pip," said he, "how do you do? I should hardly have thought this was your beat."

I explained that I was waiting to meet somebody who was coming up by coach, and I inquired after the Castle and the Aged.

"Both flourishing, thankye," said Wemmick, "and particularly the Aged. He's in wonderful feather. He'll be eighty-two next birthday. I have a notion of firing eighty-two times, if the neighbourhood shouldn't complain, and that cannon of mine should prove equal to the pressure. However, this is not London talk. Where do you think I am going to?"

"To the office," said I, for he was tending in that direction.

"Next thing to it," returned Wemmick, "I am going to Newgate. We are in a banker's-parcel case just at present, and I have been down the road taking a squint at the scene of action, and thereupon must have a word or two with our client."

"Did your client commit the robbery?" I asked.

"Bless your soul and body, no," answered Wemmick, very drily. "But he is accused of it. So might you or I be. Either of us might be accused of it, you know."

"Only neither of us is," I remarked.

"Yah!" said Wemmick, touching me on the breast with his forefinger; "you're a deep one, Mr. Pip! Would you like to have a look at Newgate? Have you time to spare?"

I had so much time to spare that the proposal came as a relief, notwithstanding its irreconcilability with my latent desire to keep my eye on the coach-office. Muttering that I would make the inquiry whether I had time to walk with him, I went into the office, and ascertained from the clerk with the nicest precision and much to the trying of his temper, the earliest moment at which the coach could be expected—which I knew beforehand, quite as well as he. I then rejoined Mr. Wemmick, and affecting to consult my watch and to be surprised by the information I had received, accepted his offer.

We were at Newgate in a few minutes, and we passed through the lodge where some fetters were hanging up on the bare walls among the prison rules, into the interior of the jail. At that time, jails were much neglected, and the period of exaggerated reaction consequent on all public wrong-doing—and which is always its heaviest and longest punishment—was still far off. So, felons were not lodged and fed better than soldiers (to say nothing of paupers), and seldom set fire to their prisons with the excusable object of improving the flavour of their soup. It was visiting time when Wemmick took me in; and a potman was going his rounds with beer; and the prisoners, behind bars in yards, were buying beer, and talking to friends; and a frouzy, ugly, disorderly, depressing scene it was.

It struck me that Wemmick walked among the prisoners, much as a gardener might walk among his plants. This was first put into my head by his seeing a shoot that had come up in the night, and saying, "What, Captain Tom? Are *you* there? Ah, indeed?" and also, "Is that Black Bill behind the cistern? Why I didn't look for you these two months; how do you find yourself?" Equally in his stopping at the bars and attending to anxious whisperers—always singly—Wemmick, with his post-office in an immovable state, looked at them while in conference, as if he were taking particular notice of the advance they had made, since last observed, towards coming out in full blow at their trial.

He was highly popular, and I found that he took the familiar department of Mr. Jaggers's business: though something of the state of Mr. Jaggers hung about him too, forbidding approach beyond certain limits. His personal recognition of each successive client was comprised in a nod, and in his settling his hat a little easier on his head with both hands, and then tightening the post-office, and putting his hands in his pockets. In one or two instances, there was a difficulty respecting the raising of fees, and then Mr. Wemmick, backing as far as possible from the insufficient money produced, said, "It's no use, my boy. I am only a subordinate. I can't take it. Don't go on in that way with a subordinate. If you are unable to make up your quantum, my boy, you had better address yourself to a principal; there are plenty of principals in the profession, you know, and what is not worth the while of one, may be worth the while of another; that's my recommendation to you, speaking as a subordinate. Don't try on useless measures. Why should you? Now who's next?"

Thus, we walked through Wemmick's greenhouse, until he turned to me and said, "Notice the man I shall shake hands with." I should have done so, without the preparation, as he had shaken hands with no one yet.

Almost as soon as he had spoken, a portly upright man (whom I can see now, as I write) in a well-worn olive-coloured frock-coat, with a peculiar pallor overspreading the red in his complexion, and eyes that went wandering about when he tried to fix them, came up to a corner of the bars, and put his hand to his hat—which had a greasy and fatty surface like cold broth—with a half-serious and half-jocose military salute.

"Colonel, to you!" said Wemmick; "how are you, Colonel?"

"All right, Mr. Wemmick."

"Everything was done that could be done, but the evidence was too strong for us, Colonel."

"Yes, it was too strong, sir—but *I* don't care."

"No, no," said Wemmick, coolly, "*you* don't care." Then, turning to me, "Served His Majesty, this man. Was a soldier in the line and bought his discharge."

I said, "Indeed?" and the man's eyes looked at me, and then looked over my head, and then looked all round me, and then he drew his hand across his lips and laughed.

"I think I shall be out of this on Monday, sir," he said to Wemmick.

"Perhaps," returned my friend, "but there's no knowing."

"I am glad to have the chance of bidding you good bye, Mr. Wemmick," said the man, stretching out his hand between two bars.

"Thankye," said Wemmick, shaking hands with him. "Same to you, Colonel."

"If what I had upon me when taken, had been real, Mr. Wemmick," said the man, unwilling to let his hand go, "I should have asked the favour of your wearing another ring —in acknowledgment of your attentions."

"I'll accept the will for the deed," said Wemmick. "By-the-bye; you were quite a pigeon-fancier." The man looked up at the sky. "I am told you had a remarkable breed of tumblers. *Could* you commission any friend of yours to bring me a pair, if you've no further use for 'em?"

"It shall be done, sir."

"All right," said Wemmick, "they shall be taken care of. Good afternoon, Colonel. Good bye!" They shook hands again, and as we walked away Wemmick said to me, "A Coiner, a very good workman. The Recorder's report is made to-day, and he is sure to be executed on Monday. Still you see, as far as it goes, a pair of pigeons are portable property, all the same." With that he looked back, and nodded at his dead plant, and then cast his eyes about him in walking out of the yard, as if he were considering what other pot would go best in its place.

As we came out of the prison through the lodge, I found that the great importance of my guardian was appreciated by the turnkeys, no less than by those whom they held in charge. "Well, Mr. Wemmick," said the turnkey, who kept us between the two studded and spiked lodge gates, and who carefully locked one before he unlocked the other, "What's Mr. Jaggers going to do with that Waterside murder? Is he going to make it manslaughter, or what is he going to make of it?"

"Why don't you ask him?" returned Wemmick.

"Oh, yes, I dare say!" said the turnkey.

"Now, that's the way with them here, Mr. Pip," remarked Wemmick, turning to me with his post-office elongated. "They don't mind what they ask of me, the subordinate; but you'll never catch 'em asking any questions of my principal."

"Is this young gentleman one of the 'prentices or articled ones of your office?" asked the turnkey, with a grin at Mr. Wemmick's humour.

"There he goes again, you see!" cried Wemmick, "I told you so! Asks another question of the subordinate before the first is dry! Well, supposing Mr. Pip is one of them?"

"Why then," said the turnkey, grinning again, "he knows what Mr. Jaggers is."

"Yah!" cried Wemmick, suddenly hitting out at the turnkey in a facetious way, "you're as dumb as one of your own keys when you have to do with my principal, you know you are. Let us out, you old fox, or I'll get him to bring an action against you for false imprisonment."

The turnkey laughed, and gave us good day, and stood laughing at us over the spikes of the wicket when we descended the steps into the street.

"Mind you, Mr. Pip," said Wemmick, gravely in my ear; as he took my arm to be more confidential; "I don't know that Mr. Jaggers does a better thing than the way in which he keeps himself so high. He's always so high. His constant height is of a piece with his immense abilities. That Colonel durst no more take leave of *him*, than that turnkey durst ask him his intentions respecting a case. Then, between his height and them, he slips in his subordinate—don't you see?—and so he has 'em, soul and body."

I was very much impressed, and not for the first time, by my guardian's subtlety. To confess the truth, I very heartily wished, and not for the first time, that I had had some other guardian of minor abilities.

Mr. Wemmick and I parted at the office in Little Britain, where suppliants for Mr. Jaggers's notice were lingering about as usual, and I returned to my watch in the street of the coach-office, with some three hours on hand. I consumed the whole time in thinking how strange it was that I should be encompassed by all this taint of prison and crime; that, in my childhood out on our lonely marshes on a winter evening I should have first encountered it; that, it should have reappeared on two occasions, starting out like a stain that was faded but not gone; that, it should in this new way pervade my fortune and advancement. While my mind was thus engaged, I thought of the beautiful young Estella, proud and refined, coming towards me, and I thought with absolute abhorrence of the contrast between the jail and her. I wished that Wemmick had not met me, or that I had not yielded to him and gone with him, so that, of all days in the year, on this day I might not have had Newgate in my breath and on my clothes. I beat the prison dust off my feet as I sauntered to and fro, and I shook it out of my dress, and I exhaled its air from my lungs. So contaminated did I feel, remembering who was coming, that the coach came quickly after all, and I was not yet free from the soiling consciousness of Mr. Wemmick's conservatory, when I saw her face at the coach window and her hand waving to me.

What *was* the nameless shadow which again in that one instant had passed?

CHAPTER XXXIII.

In her furred travelling-dress, Estella seemed more delicately beautiful than she had ever seemed yet, even in my eyes. Her manner was more winning than she had cared to let it be to me before, and I thought I saw Miss Havisham's influence in the change.

We stood in the Inn Yard while she pointed out her luggage to me, and when it was all collected I remembered—having forgotten everything but herself in the meanwhile—that I knew nothing of her destination.

"I am going to Richmond," she told me. "Our lesson is, that there are two Richmonds, one in Surrey and one in Yorkshire, and that mine is the Surrey Richmond. The distance is ten miles. I am to have a carriage, and you are to take me. This is my purse, and you are to pay my charges out of it. Oh, you must take the purse! We have no choice, you and I, but to obey our instructions. We are not free to follow our own devices, you and I."

As she looked at me in giving me the purse, I hoped there was an inner meaning in her words. She said them slightingly, but not with displeasure.

"A carriage will have to be sent for, Estella. Will you rest here a little?"

"Yes, I am to rest here a little, and I am to drink some tea, and you are to take care of me the while."

She drew her arm through mine, as if it must be done, and I requested a waiter who had been staring at the coach like a man who had never seen such a thing in his life, to show us a private sitting-room. Upon that, he pulled out a napkin, as if it were a magic clue without which he couldn't find the way upstairs, and led us to the black hole of the establishment: fitted up with a diminishing mirror) quite a superfluous article considering the hole's proportions), an anchovy sauce-cruet, and somebody's pattens. On my objecting to this retreat, he took us into another room with a dinner-table for thirty, and in the grate a scorched leaf of a copy-book under a bushel of coal-dust. Having looked at this extinct conflagration and shaken his head, he took my order: which, proving to be merely "Some tea for the lady," sent him out of the room in a very low state of mind.

I was, and I am, sensible that the air of this chamber, in its strong combination of stable with soup-stock, might have led one to infer that the coaching department was not doing well, and that the enterprising proprietor was boiling down the horses for the refreshment department. Yet the room was all in all to me, Estella being in it. I thought that with her I could have been happy here for life. (I was not at all happy there at the time, observe, and I knew it well.)

"Where are you going to, at Richmond?" I asked Estella.

"I am going to live," said she, "at a great expense, with a lady there, who has the power—or says she has—of taking me about, and introducing me, and showing people to me and showing me to people."

"I suppose you will be glad of variety and admiration?"

"Yes, I suppose so."

She answered so carelessly, that I said, "You speak of yourself as if you were some one else."

"Where did you learn how I speak of others? Come, come," said Estella, smiling delightfully, "you must not expect me to go to school to *you*; I must talk in my own way. How do you thrive with Mr. Pocket?"

"I live quite pleasantly there; at least——" It appeared to me that I was losing a chance.

"At least?" repeated Estella.

"As pleasantly as I could anywhere, away from you."

"You silly boy," said Estella, quite composedly, "how can you talk such nonsense? Your friend Mr. Matthew, I believe, is superior to the rest of his family?"

"Very superior indeed. He is nobody's enemy——"

"—Don't add but his own," interposed Estella, "for I hate that class of man. But he really is disinterested, and above small jealousy and spite, I have heard?"

"I am sure I have every reason to say so."

"You have not every reason to say so of the rest of his

"OH, YOU MUST TAKE THE PURSE!"

people," said Estella, nodding at me with an expression of face that was at once grave and rallying, "for they beset Miss Havisham with reports and insinuations to your disadvantage. They watch you, misrepresent you, write letters about you (anonymous sometimes), and you are the torment and occupation of their lives. You can scarcely realise to yourself the hatred those people feel for you."

"They do me no harm, I hope?"

Instead of answering, Estella burst out laughing. This was very singular to me, and I looked at her in considerable perplexity. When she left off—and she had not laughed languidly, but with real enjoyment—I said, in my diffident way with her:

"I hope I may suppose that you would not be amused if they did me any harm?"

"No, no, you may be sure of that," said Estella. "You may be certain that I laugh because they fail. Oh, those people with Miss Havisham, and the tortures they undergo!" She laughed again, and even now, when she had told me why, her laughter was very singular to me, for I could not doubt its being genuine, and yet it seemed too much for the occasion. I thought there must really be something more here than I knew; she saw the thought in my mind and answered it.

"It is not easy for even you," said Estella, "to know what satisfaction it gives me to see those people thwarted, or what an enjoyable sense of the ridiculous I have when they are made ridiculous. For you were not brought up in that strange house from a mere baby.—I was. You had not your little wits sharpened by their intriguing against you, suppressed and defenceless, under the mask of sympathy and pity and what not, that is soft and soothing.—I had. You did not gradually open your round childish eyes wider and wider to the discovery of that impostor of a woman who calculates her stores of peace of mind for when she wakes up in the night.—I did."

It was no laughing matter with Estella now, nor was she summoning these remembrances from any shallow place. I would not have been the cause of that look of hers, for all my expectations in a heap.

"Two things I can tell you," said Estella. "First, notwithstanding the proverb, that constant dropping will wear away a stone, you may set your mind at rest that these people never will—never would in a hundred years—impair your ground with Miss Havisham, in any particular, great or small. Second, I am beholden to you as the cause of their being so busy and so mean in vain, and there is my hand upon it."

As she gave it me playfully—for her darker mood had been but momentary—I held it and put it to my lips. "You ridiculous boy," said Estella, "will you never take warning? Or do you kiss my hand in the same spirit in which I once let you kiss my cheek?"

"What spirit was that?" said I.

"I must think a moment. A spirit of contempt for the fawners and plotters."

"If I say yes, may I kiss the cheek again?"

"You should have asked before you touched the hand. But, yes, if you like."

I leaned down, and her calm face was like a statue's. "Now," said Estella, gliding away the instant I touched her cheek, "you are to take care that I have some tea, and you are to take me to Richmond."

Her reverting to this tone as if our association were forced upon us and we were mere puppets, gave me pain; but everything in our intercourse did give me pain. Whatever her tone with me happened to be, I could put no trust in it, and build no hope on it; and yet I went on against trust and against hope. Why repeat it a thousand times? So it always was.

I rang for the tea, and the waiter, reappearing with his magic clue, brought in by degrees some fifty adjuncts to that refreshment, but of tea not a glimpse. A teaboard, cups and saucers, plates, knives and forks (including carvers), spoons (various), salt-cellars, a meek little muffin confined with the utmost precaution under a strong iron cover, Moses in the bulrushes typified by a soft bit of butter in a quantity of parsley, a pale loaf with a powdered head, two proof impressions of the bars of the kitchen fireplace on triangular bits of bread, and ultimately a fat family urn: which the waiter staggered in with, expressing in his countenance burden and suffering. After a prolonged absence at this stage of the entertainment, he at length came back with a casket of precious appearance containing twigs. These I steeped in hot water, and so from the whole of these appliances extracted one cup of I don't know what, for Estella.

The bill paid, and the waiter remembered, and the ostler not forgotten, and the chambermaid taken into consideration—in a word, the whole house bribed into a state of contempt and animosity, and Estella's purse much lightened—we got into our post-coach and drove away. Turning into Cheapside and rattling up Newgate-street, we were soon under the walls of which I was so ashamed.

"What place is that?" Estella asked me.

I made a foolish pretence of not at first recognising it, and then told her. As she looked at it, and drew in her head again, murmuring "Wretches!" I would not have confessed to my visit for any consideration.

"Mr. Jaggers," said I, by way of putting it neatly on somebody else, "has the reputation of being more in the secrets of that dismal place than any man in London."

"He is more in the secrets of every place, I think," said Estella, in a low voice.

"You have been accustomed to see him often, I suppose?"

"I have been accustomed to see him at uncertain intervals, ever since I can remember. But I know him no better now, than I did before I could speak plainly. What is your own experience of him? Do you advance with him?"

"Once habituated to his distrustful manner," said I, "I have done very well."

"Are you intimate?"

"I have dined with him at his private house."

"I fancy," said Estella, shrinking, "that must be a curious place."

"It is a curious place."

I should have been chary of discussing my guardian too freely even with her; but I should have gone on with the subject so far as to describe the dinner in Gerrard-street, if we had not then come into a sudden glare of gas. It seemed, while it lasted, to be all alight and alive with that inexplicable feeling I had had before; and when we were out of it, I was as much dazed for a few moments as if I had been in Lightning.

So, we fell into other talk, and it was principally about the way by which we were travelling, and about what parts of London lay on this side of it, and what on that. The great city was almost new to her, she told me, for she had never left Miss Havisham's neighbourhood until she had gone to France, and she had merely passed through London then in going and returning. I asked her if my guardian had any charge of her while she remained here? To that she emphatically said, "God forbid!" and no more.

It was impossible for me to avoid seeing that she cared to attract me; that she made herself winning; and would have won me even if the task had needed pains. Yet this made me none the happier, for, even if she had not taken that tone of our being disposed of by others, I should have felt that she held my heart in her hand because she wilfully chose to do it, and not because it would have wrung any tenderness in her, to crush it and throw it away.

When we passed through Hammersmith, I showed her where Mr. Matthew Pocket lived, and said it was no great way from Richmond, and that I hoped I should see her sometimes.

"Oh yes, you are to see me; you are to come when you think proper; you are to be mentioned to the family; indeed you are already mentioned."

I inquired was it a large household she was going to be a member of?

"No; there are only two; mother and daughter. The mother is a lady of some station, though not averse to increasing her income."

"I wonder Miss Havisham could part with you again so soon."

"It is part of Miss Havisham's plans for me, Pip," said Estella, with a sigh, as if she were tired; "I am to write to her constantly and see her regularly, and report how I go on—I and the jewels—for they are nearly all mine now."

It was the first time she had ever called me by my name. Of course she did so purposely, and knew that I should treasure it up.

We came to Richmond all too soon, and our destination there was a house by the Green: a staid old house, where hoops and powder and patches, embroidered coats, rolled stockings, ruffles, and swords, had had their court days many a time. Some ancient trees before the house were still cut into fashions as formal and unnatural as the hoops and wigs and stiff skirts; but their own allotted places in the great procession of the dead were not far off, and they would soon drop into them and go the silent way of the rest.

A bell with an old voice—which I dare say in its time had often said to the house, Here is the green farthingale, Here is the diamond-hilted sword, Here are the shoes with red heels and the blue solitaire,—sounded gravely in the moonlight, and two cherry-coloured maids came fluttering out to receive Estella. The doorway soon absorbed her boxes, and she gave me her hand and a smile, and said good night, and was absorbed likewise. And still I stood looking at the house, thinking how happy I should be if I lived there with her, and knowing that I never was happy with her, but always miserable.

I got into the carriage to be taken back to Hammersmith, and I got in with a bad heart-ache, and I got out with a worse heart-ache. At our own door I found little Jane Pocket coming home from a little party, escorted by her little lover; and I envied her little lover, in spite of his being subject to Flopson.

Mr. Pocket was out lecturing; for he was a most delightful lecturer on domestic economy, and his treatises on the management of children and servants were considered the very best text-books on those themes. But Mrs. Pocket was at home, and was in a little difficulty, on account of the baby's having been accommodated with a needle-case to keep him quiet during the unaccountable absence (with a relative in the Foot Guards) of Millers. And more needles were missing than it could be regarded as quite wholesome for a patient of such tender years either to apply externally or to take as a tonic.

Mr. Pocket being justly celebrated for giving most excellent practical advice, and for having a clear and sound perception of things and a highly judicious mind, I had some notion in my heart-ache of begging him to accept my confidence. But happening to look up at Mrs. Pocket as she sat reading her book of dignities after prescribing Bed as a sovereign remedy for baby, I thought—Well—No, I wouldn't.

CHAPTER XXXIV.

As I had grown accustomed to my expectations, I had insensibly begun to notice their effect upon myself and those around me. Their influence on my own character I disguised from my recognition as much as possible, but I knew very well that it was not all good. I lived in a state of chronic uneasiness respecting my behaviour to Joe. My conscience was not by any means comfortable about Biddy. When I woke up in the night—like Camilla—I used to think, with a weariness on my spirits, that I should have been happier and better if I had never seen Miss Havisham's face, and had risen to manhood content to be partners with Joe in the honest old forge. Many a time of an evening, when I sat alone looking at the fire, I thought, after all, there was no fire like the forge fire and the kitchen fire at home.

Yet Estella was so inseparable from all my restlessness and disquiet of mind, that I really fell into confusion as to the limits of my own part in its production. That is to say, supposing I had had no expectations, and yet had had Estella to think of, I could not make out to my satisfaction that I should have done much better. Now, concerning the influence of my position on others, I was in no such difficulty, and so I perceived—though dimly enough perhaps—that it was not beneficial to anybody, and, above all, that it was not beneficial to Herbert. My lavish habits led his easy nature into expenses that he could not afford, corrupted the simplicity of his life, and disturbed his peace with anxieties and regrets. I was not at all remorseful for having unwittingly set those other branches of the Pocket family to the poor arts they practised: because such littlenesses were their natural bent, and would have been evoked by anybody else, if I had left them slumbering. But Herbert's was a very different case, and it often caused me a twinge to think that I had done him evil service in crowding his sparsely-furnished chambers with incongruous upholstery work, and placing the canary-breasted Avenger at his disposal.

So now, as an infallible way of making little ease great ease, I began to contract a quantity of debt. I could hardly begin but Herbert must begin too, so he soon followed. At Startop's suggestion, we put ourselves down for election into a club called the Finches of the Grove: the object of which institution I have never divined, if it were not that the members should dine expensively once a fortnight, to quarrel among themselves as much as possible after dinner, and to cause six waiters to get drunk on the stairs. I know that these gratifying social ends were so invariably accomplished, that Herbert and I understood nothing else to be referred to in the first standing toast of the society: which ran, "Gentlemen, may the present promotion of good feeling ever reign predominant among the Finches of the Grove."

The Finches spent their money foolishly (the Hotel we dined at was in Covent Garden), and the first Finch I saw when I had the honour of joining the Grove was Bentley Drummle: at that time floundering about town in a cab of his own, and doing a great deal of damage to the posts at the street corners. Occasionally, he shot himself out of his equipage head-foremost over the apron; and I saw him on one occasion deliver himself at the door of the Grove in this unintentional way—like coals. But here I anticipate a little, for I was not a Finch, and could not be, according to the sacred laws of the society, until I came of age.

In my confidence in my own resources, I would willingly have taken Herbert's expenses on myself; but Herbert was proud, and I could make no such proposal to him. So, he got into difficulties in every direction, and continued to look about him. When we gradually fell into keeping late hours and late company, I noticed that he looked about him with a desponding eye at breakfast-time; that he began to look about him more hopefully about mid-day; that he drooped when he came in to dinner; that he seemed to descry Capital in the distance, rather clearly, after dinner; that he all but realised Capital towards midnight; and that about two o'clock in the morning, he became so deeply despondent again as to talk of buying a rifle and going to America, with a general purpose of compelling buffaloes to make his fortune.

I was usually at Hammersmith about half the week, and when I was at Hammersmith I haunted Richmond: whereof separately by-and-bye. Herbert would often come to Hammersmith when I was there, and I think at those seasons his father would occasionally have some passing perception that the opening he was looking for had not appeared yet. But in the general tumbling up of the family, his tumbling out in life somewhere, was a thing to transact itself somehow. In the meantime Mr. Pocket grew greyer, and tried oftener to lift himself out of his perplexities by the hair. While Mrs. Pocket tripped up the family with her footstool, read her book of dignities, lost her pocket-handkerchief, told us about her grandpapa, and taught the young idea how to shoot, by shooting it into bed whenever it attracted her notice.

As I am now generalising a period of my life with the object of clearing my way before me, I can scarcely do so better than by at once completing the description of our usual manners and customs at Barnard's Inn.

We spent as much money as we could, and got as little for it as people could make up their minds to give us. We were always more or less miserable, and most of our acquaintance were in the same condition. There was a gay fiction among us that we were constantly enjoying ourselves, and a skeleton truth that we never did. To the best of my belief, our case was in the last aspect a rather common one.

Every morning, with an air ever new, Herbert went into the City to look about him. I often paid him a visit in the dark back-room in which he consorted with an ink-jar, a hat-peg, a coal-box, a string-box, an almanack, a desk and stool, and a ruler; and I do not remember that I ever saw him do anything else but look about him. If we all did what we undertake to do, as faithfully as Herbert did, we might live in a Republic of the Virtues. He had nothing else to do, poor fellow, except at a certain hour of every afternoon to "go to Lloyd's"—in observance of a ceremony of seeing his principal, I think. He never did anything else in connection with Lloyd's that I could find out, except come back again. When he felt his case unusually serious, and that he positively must find an opening, he would go on 'Change at a busy time, and walk in and out, in a kind of gloomy country dance figure, among the assembled magnates. "For," says Herbert to me, coming home to dinner on one of those special occasions, "I find the truth to be, Handel, that an opening won't come to one, but one must go to it——so I have been."

If we had been less attached to one another, I think we must have hated one another regularly every morning. I detested the chambers beyond expression at that period of repentance, and could not endure the sight of the Avenger's livery: which had a more expensive and a less remunerative appearance then, than at any other time in the four-and-twenty hours. As we got more and more into debt, breakfast became a hollower and hollower form, and being on one occasion at breakfast-time threatened (by letter) with legal proceedings, "not unwholly unconnected," as my local paper might put it, "with jewellery," I went so far as to seize the Avenger by his blue collar and shake him off his feet—so that he was actually in the air, like a booted Cupid—for presuming to suppose that we wanted a roll.

At certain times—meaning at uncertain times, for they depended on our humour—I would say to Herbert, as if it were a remarkable discovery:

"My dear Herbert, we are getting on badly."

"My dear Handel," Herbert would say to me, in all sincerity, "if you will believe me, those very words were on my lips, by a strange coincidence."

"Then, Herbert," I would respond, "let us look into our affairs."

We always derived profound satisfaction from making an appointment for this purpose. I always thought this was business, this was the way to confront the thing, this was the way to take the foe by the throat. And I know Herbert thought so too.

We ordered something rather special for dinner, with a bottle of something similarly out of the common way, in order that our minds might be fortified for the occasion, and we might come well up to the mark. Dinner over, we produced a bundle of pens, a copious supply of ink, and a goodly show of writing and blotting paper. For, there was something very comfortable in having plenty of stationery.

I would then take a sheet of paper, and write across the top of it, in a neat hand, the heading, "Memorandum of Pip's debts;" with Barnard's Inn and the date very carefully added. Herbert would also take a sheet of paper, and write across it with similar formalities, "Memorandum of Herbert's debts."

Each of us would then refer to a confused heap of papers at his side, which had been thrown into drawers, worn into holes in pockets, half-burnt in lighting candles, stuck for weeks into the looking-glass, and otherwise damaged. The sound of our pens going refreshed us exceedingly, insomuch that I sometimes found it difficult to distinguish between this edifying business proceeding and actually paying the money. In point of meritorious character, the two things seemed about equal.

When we had written a little while, I would ask Herbert how he got on? Herbert probably would have been scratching his head in a most rueful manner at the sight of his accumulating figures.

"They are mounting up, Handel," Herbert would say; "upon my life they are mounting up."

"Be firm, Herbert," I would retort, plying my own pen with great assiduity. "Look the thing in the face. Look into your affairs. Stare them out of countenance."

"So I would, Handel, only they are staring *me* out of countenance."

However, my determined manner would have its effect, and Herbert would fall to work again. After a time he would give up once more, on the plea that he had not got Cobbs's bill, or Lobbs's, or Nobbs's, as the case might be.

"Then, Herbert, estimate; estimate it in round numbers, and put it down."

"What a fellow of resource you are!" my friend would reply, with admiration. "Really your business powers are very remarkable."

I thought so too. I established with myself, on these occasions, the reputation of a first-rate man of business—prompt, decisive, energetic, clear, cool-headed. When I had got all my responsibilities down upon my list, I compared each with the bill, and ticked it off. My self-approval when I ticked an entry was quite a luxurious sensation. When I had no more ticks to make, I folded all my bills up uniformly, docketed each on the back, and tied the whole into a symmetrical bundle. Then I did the same for Herbert (who modestly said he had not my administrative genius), and felt that I had brought his affairs into a focus for him.

My business habits had one other bright feature, which I called "leaving a Margin." For example; supposing Herbert's debts to be one hundred and sixty-four pounds four-and-twopence, I would say, "Leave a margin, and put them down at two hundred." Or, supposing my own to be four times as much, I would leave a margin, and put them down at seven hundred. I had the highest opinion of the wisdom of this same Margin, but I am bound to acknowledge that on looking back, I deem it to have been an expensive device. For, we always ran into new debt immediately, to the full extent of the margin, and sometimes, in the sense of freedom and solvency it imparted, got pretty far on into another margin.

But there was a calm, a rest, a virtuous hush, consequent on these examinations of our affairs, that gave me, for the time, an admirable opinion of myself. Soothed by my exertions, my method, and Herbert's compliments, I would sit with his symmetrical bundle and my own on the table before me among the stationery, and feel like a Bank of some sort, rather than a private individual.

We shut our outer door on these solemn occasions in order that we might not be interrupted. I had fallen into my serene state one evening, when we heard a letter dropped through the slit in the said door, and fall on the ground. "It's for you, Handel," said Herbert, going out and coming back with it, "and I hope there is nothing the matter." This was in allusion to its heavy black seal and border.

The letter was signed TRABB & Co., and its contents were simply, that I was an honoured sir, and that they begged to inform me that Mrs. J. Gargery had departed this life on Monday last at twenty minutes past six in the evening, and that my attendance was requested at the interment on Monday next at three o'clock in the afternoon.

CHAPTER XXXV.

IT was the first time that a grave had opened in my road of life, and the gap it made in the smooth ground was wonderful. The figure of my sister in her chair by the kitchen fire, haunted me night and day. That the place could possibly be, without her, was something my mind seemed unable to compass; and whereas she had seldom or never been in my thoughts of late, I had now the strangest idea that she was coming towards me in the street, or that she would presently knock at the door. In my rooms too, with which she had never been at all associated, there was at once the blankness of death and a perpetual suggestion of the sound of her voice or the turn of her face or figure, as if she were still alive and had been often there.

Whatever my fortunes might have been, I could scarcely have recalled my sister with much tenderness. But I suppose there is a shock of regret which may exist without much tenderness. Under its influence (and perhaps to make up for the want of the softer feeling) I was seized with a violent indignation against the assailant from whom she had suffered so much; and I felt that on sufficient proof I could have revengefully pursued Orlick, or any one else, to the last extremity.

Having written to Joe, to offer him consolation, and to assure him that I would come to the funeral, I passed the intermediate days in the curious state of mind I have glanced at. I went down early in the morning, and alighted at the Blue Boar, in good time to walk over to the forge.

It was fine summer weather again, and, as I walked along, the times when I was a little helpless creature, and my sister did not spare me, vividly returned. But they returned with a gentle tone upon them, that softened even the edge of Tickler. For now, the very breath of the beans and clover whispered to my heart that the day must come when it would be well for my memory that others walking in the sunshine should be softened as they thought of me.

At last I came within sight of the house, and saw that Trabb and Co. had put in a funeral execution and taken possession. Two dismally absurd persons, each ostentatiously exhibiting a crutch done up in a black bandage—as if that instrument could possibly communicate any comfort to anybody—were posted at the front door; and in one of them I recognised a postboy discharged from the Boar for turning a young couple into a sawpit on their bridal morning, in consequence of intoxication rendering it necessary for him to ride his horse clasped round the neck with both arms. All the children of the village, and most of the women, were admiring these sable warders and the closed windows of the house and forge; and as I came up, one of the two warders (the postboy) knocked at the door—implying that I was far too much exhausted by grief, to have strength remaining to knock for myself.

Another sable warder (a carpenter, who had once eaten two geese for a wager) opened the door, and showed me into the best parlour. Here, Mr. Trabb had taken unto himself the best table, and had got all the leaves up, and was holding a kind of black Bazaar, with the aid of a quantity of black pins. At the moment of my arrival, he had just finished putting somebody's hat into black long-clothes, like an African baby; so he held out his hand for mine. But I, misled by the action, and confused by the occasion, shook hands with him with every testimony of warm affection.

Poor dear Joe, entangled in a little black cloak tied in a large bow under his chin, was seated apart at the upper end of the room; where, as chief mourner, he had evidently been stationed by Trabb. When I bent down and said to him, "Dear Joe, how are you?" he said, "Pip, old chap, you know'd her when she were a fine figure of a——" and clasped my hand and said no more.

Biddy, looking very neat and modest in her black dress, went quietly here and there, and was very helpful. When I had spoken to Biddy, as I thought it not a time for talking, I went and sat down near Joe, and there began to wonder in what part of the house it—she—my sister—was. The air of the parlour being faint with the smell of sweet cake, I looked about for the table of refreshments; it was scarcely visible until one had got accustomed to the gloom, but there was a cut-up plum-cake upon it, and there were cut-up oranges, and sandwiches, and biscuits, and two decanters that I knew very well as ornaments, but had never seen used in all my life: one full of port, and one of sherry. Standing at this table, I became conscious of the servile Pumblechook in a black cloak and several yards of hatband, who was alternately stuffing himself, and making obsequious movements to catch my attention. The moment he succeeded, he came over to me (breathing sherry and crumbs), and said in a subdued voice, "May I, dear sir?" and did. I then descried Mr. and Mrs. Hubble; the last-named in a decent speechless paroxysm in a corner. We were all going to "follow," and were all in course of being tied up separately (by Trabb) into ridiculous bundles.

"Which I meantersay, Pip," Joe whispered me, as we were being what Mr. Trabb called "formed" in the parlour, two and two—and it was dreadfully like a preparation for some grim kind of dance; "which I meantersay, sir, as I would in preference have carried her to the church myself, along with three or four friendly ones wot come to it with willing harts and arms, but it were considered wot the neighbours would look down on such and would be of opinions as it were wanting in respect."

"Pocket-handkerchiefs out, all!" cried Mr. Trabb at this point, in a depressed business-like voice—"Pocket-handkerchiefs out! We are ready!"

So, we all put our pocket-handkerchiefs to our faces, as if our noses were bleeding, and filed out two and two; Joe and I; Biddy and Pumblechook; Mr. and Mrs. Hubble. The remains of my poor sister had been brought round by the kitchen door, and, it being a point of Undertaking ceremony that the six bearers must be stifled and blinded under a horrible black velvet housing with a white border, the whole looked like a blind monster with twelve human legs, shuffling and blundering along under the guidance of two keepers—the postboy and his comrade.

The neighbourhood, however, highly approved of these arrangements, and we were much admired as we went through the village; the more youthful and vigorous part of the community making dashes now and then to cut us off, and lying in wait to intercept us at points of vantage. At such times the more exuberant among them called out in an excited manner on our emergency round some corner of expectancy, "*Here* they come!" "*Here* they are!" and we were all but cheered. In this progress I was much annoyed by the abject Pumblechook, who, being behind me, persisted all the way, as a delicate attention, in arranging my streaming hatband, and smoothing my cloak. My thoughts were further distracted by the excessive pride of Mr. and Mrs. Hubble, who were surpassingly conceited and vainglorious in being members of so distinguished a procession.

And now the range of marshes lay clear before us, with the sails of the ships on the river growing out of it; and we went into the churchyard, close to the graves of my unknown parents, Philip Pirrip, late of this parish, and Also Georgiana, Wife of the Above. And there, my sister was laid quietly in the earth while the larks sang high above it, and the light wind strewed it with beautiful shadows of clouds and trees.

Of the conduct of the worldly-minded Pumblechook while this was doing, I desire to say no more than it was all addressed to me; and that even when those noble passages were read which reminded humanity how it brought nothing into the world and can take nothing out, and how it fleeth like a shadow and never continueth long in one stay, I heard him cough a reservation of the case of a young gentleman who came unexpectedly into large property. When we got back, he had the hardihood to tell me that he wished my sister could have known I had done her so much honour, and to hint that she would have considered it reasonably purchased at the price of her death. After that, he drank all the rest of the sherry, and Mr. Hubble drank the port, and the two talked (which I have since observed to be customary in such cases) as if they were of quite another race from the deceased, and were notoriously immortal. Finally, he went away with Mr. and Mrs. Hubble—to make an evening of it, I felt sure, and to tell the Jolly Bargemen that he was the founder of my fortunes and my earliest benefactor.

When they were all gone, and when Trabb and his men —but not his boy: I looked for him—had crammed their mummery into bags, and were gone too, the house felt wholesomer. Soon afterwards, Biddy, Joe, and I, had a cold dinner together; but we dined in the best parlour, not in the old kitchen, and Joe was so exceedingly particular what he did with his knife and fork and the salt-cellar and what not, that there was great restraint upon us. But after dinner, when I made him take his pipe, and when I had loitered with him about the forge, and when we sat down together on the great block of stone outside it, we got on better. I noticed that after the funeral Joe changed his clothes so far, as to make a compromise between his Sunday dress and working dress: in which the dear fellow looked natural, and like the Man he was.

He was very much pleased by my asking if I might sleep in my own little room, and I was pleased too; for, I felt that I had done rather a great thing in making the request. When the shadows of evening were closing in, I took an opportunity of getting into the garden with Biddy for a little talk. "Biddy," said I, "I think you might have written to me about these sad matters."

"Do you, Mr. Pip?" said Biddy. "I should have written if I had thought that."

"Don't suppose that I mean to be unkind, Biddy, when I say I consider that you ought to have thought that."

"Do you, Mr. Pip?"

She was so quiet, and had such an orderly, good, and pretty way with her, that I did not like the thought of making her cry again. After looking a little at her downcast eyes as she walked beside me, I gave up that point.

"I suppose it will be difficult for you to remain here now, Biddy, dear?"

"Oh! I can't do so, Mr. Pip," said Biddy, in a tone of regret, but still of quiet conviction. "I have been speaking to Mrs. Hubble, and I am going to her to-morrow. I hope we shall be able to take some care of Mr. Gargery, together, until he settles down."

"How are you going to live, Biddy? If you want any mo—"

"How am I going to live?" repeated Biddy, striking in, with a momentary flush upon her face. "I'll tell you, Mr. Pip. I am going to try to get the place of mistress in the new school nearly finished here. I can be well recommended by all the neighbours, and I hope I can be industrious and patient, and teach myself while I teach others. You know, Mr. Pip," pursued Biddy, with a smile, as she raised her eyes to my face, "the new schools are not like the old, but I learnt a good deal from you after that time, and have had time since then to improve."

"I think you would always improve, Biddy, under any circumstances."

"Ah! Except in my bad side of human nature," murmured Biddy.

It was not so much a reproach, as an irresistible thinking aloud. Well! I thought I would give up that point too. So, I walked a little further with Biddy, looking silently at her downcast eyes.

"I have not heard the particulars of my sister's death, Biddy."

"They are very slight, poor thing. She had been in one of her bad states—though they had got better of late, rather than worse—for four days, when she came out of it in the evening, just at tea-time, and said quite plainly, 'Joe.' As she had never said any word for a long while, I ran and fetched in Mr. Gargery from the forge. She made signs to me that she wanted him to sit down close to her, and wanted me to put her arms round his neck. So I put them round his neck, and she laid her head down on his shoulder quite content and satisfied. And so she presently said 'Joe' again, and once 'Pardon,' and once 'Pip.' And so she never lifted her head up any more, and it was just an hour later when we laid it down on her own bed, because we found she was gone."

Biddy cried; the darkening garden, and the lane, and the stars that were coming out, were blurred in my own sight.

"Nothing was ever discovered, Biddy?"

"Nothing."

"Do you know what is become of Orlick?"

"I should think from the colour of his clothes that he is working in the quarries."

"Of course you have seen him then?—Why are you looking at that dark tree in the lane?"

"I saw him there, on the night she died."

"That was not the last time either, Biddy?"

"No; I have seen him there since we have been walking here.—It is of no use," said Biddy, laying her hand upon my arm, as I was for running out, "you know I would not deceive you; he was not there a minute, and he is gone."

It revived my utmost indignation to find that she was still pursued by this fellow, and I felt inveterate against him.

I told her so, and told her that I would spend any money or take any pains to drive him out of that country. By degrees she led me into more temperate talk, and she told me how Joe loved me, and how Joe never complained of anything—she didn't say, of me; she had no need; I knew what she meant—but ever did his duty in his way of life, with a strong hand, a quiet tongue, and a gentle heart.

"Indeed, it would be hard to say too much for him," said I; "and, Biddy, we must often speak of these things, for of course I shall be often down here now. I am not going to leave poor Joe alone."

Biddy said never a single word.

"Biddy, don't you hear me?"

"Yes, Mr. Pip."

"Not to mention your calling me Mr. Pip—which appears to me to be in bad taste, Biddy—what do you mean?"

"What do I mean?" asked Biddy, timidly.

"Biddy," said I, in a virtuously self-asserting manner, "I must request to know what you mean by this?"

"By this?" said Biddy.

"No, don't echo," I retorted. "You used not to echo, Biddy."

"Used not!" said Biddy. "O Mr. Pip! Used!"

Well! I rather thought I would give up that point too. After another silent turn in the garden, I fell back on the main position.

"Biddy," said I, "I made a remark respecting my coming down here often, to see Joe, which you received with a marked silence. Have the goodness, Biddy, to tell me why."

"Are you quite sure, then, that you WILL come to see him often?" asked Biddy, stopping in the narrow garden walk, and looking at me under the stars, with a clear and honest eye.

"Oh dear me!" said I, as I found myself compelled to give up Biddy in despair. "This really is a very bad side of human nature! Don't say any more, if you please, Biddy. This shocks me very much."

For which cogent reason I kept Biddy at a distance during supper, and when I went up to my own old little room, took as stately a leave of her as I could, in my murmuring soul, deem reconcilable with the churchyard and the event of the day. As often as I was restless in the night, and that was every quarter of an hour, I reflected what an unkindness, what an injury, what an injustice, Biddy had done me.

Early in the morning, I was to go. Early in the morning, I was out, and looking in, unseen, at one of the wooden windows of the forge. There I stood, for minutes, looking at Joe, already at work with a glow of health and strength upon his face that made it show as if the bright sun of the life in store for him were shining on it.

"Good bye, dear Joe!—No, don't wipe it off—for God's sake, give me your blackened hand!—I shall be down soon and often."

"Never too soon, sir," said Joe, "and never too often, Pip!"

Biddy was waiting for me at the kitchen door, with a mug of new milk and a crust of bread. "Biddy," said I, when I gave her my hand at parting, "I am not angry, but I am hurt."

"No, don't be hurt," she pleaded quite pathetically; "let only me be hurt, if I have been ungenerous."

Once more, the mists were rising as I walked away. If they disclosed to me, as I suspect they did, that I should *not* come back, and that Biddy was quite right, all I can say is—they were quite right too.

CHAPTER XXXVI.

HERBERT and I went on from bad to worse, in the way of increasing our debts, looking into our affairs, leaving Margins, and the like exemplary transactions; and Time went on, whether or no, as he has a way of doing; and I came of age—in fulfilment of Herbert's prediction, that I should do so before I knew where I was.

Herbert himself had come of age, eight months before me. As he had nothing else than his majority to come into, the event did not make a profound sensation in Barnard's Inn. But we had looked forward to my one-and-twentieth birthday, with a crowd of speculations and anticipations, for we had both considered that my guardian could hardly help saying something definite on that occasion.

I had taken care to have it well understood in Little Britain when my birthday was. On the day before it, I received an official note from Wemmick, informing me that Mr. Jaggers would be glad if I would call upon him at five in the afternoon of the auspicious day. This convinced us that something great was to happen, and threw me into an unusual flutter when I repaired to my guardian's office, a model of punctuality.

In the outer office Wemmick offered me his congratulations, and incidentally rubbed the side of his nose with a folded piece of tissue-paper that I liked the look of. But he said nothing respecting it, and motioned me with a nod into my guardian's room. It was November, and my guardian was standing before his fire leaning his back against the chimney-piece, with his hands under his coat-tails.

"Well, Pip," said he, "I must call you Mr. Pip to-day. Congratulations, Mr. Pip."

We shook hands—he was always a remarkably short shaker—and I thanked him.

"Take a chair, Mr. Pip," said my guardian.

As I sat down, and he preserved his attitude and bent his brows at his boots, I felt at a disadvantage, which reminded me of that old time when I had been put upon a tombstone. The two ghastly casts on the shelf were not far from him, and their expression was as if they were making a stupid apoplectic attempt to attend to the conversation.

"Now, my young friend," my guardian began, as if I were a witness in the box, "I am going to have a word or two with you."

"If you please, sir."

"What do you suppose," said Mr. Jaggers, bending forward to look at the ground, and then throwing his head back to look at the ceiling, "what do you suppose you are living at the rate of?"

"At the rate of, sir?"

"At," repeated Mr. Jaggers, still looking at the ceiling, "the—rate—of?" And then looked all round the room, and paused with his pocket-handkerchief in his hand, half way to his nose.

I had looked into my affairs so often, that I had thoroughly destroyed any slight notion I might ever have had of their bearings. Reluctantly, I confessed myself quite unable to answer the question. This reply seemed agreeable to Mr. Jaggers, who said, "I thought so!" and blew his nose with an air of satisfaction.

"Now, I have asked *you* a question, my friend," said Mr. Jaggers. "Have you anything to ask *me?*"

"Of course it would be a great relief to me to ask you several questions, sir; but I remember your prohibition."

"Ask one," said Mr. Jaggers.

"Is my benefactor to be made known to me to-day?"

"No. Ask another."

"Is that confidence to be imparted to me soon?"

"Waive that, a moment," said Mr. Jaggers, "and ask another."

I looked about me, but there appeared to be now no possible escape from the inquiry, "Have—I—anything to receive, sir?" On that, Mr. Jaggers said, triumphantly, "I thought we should come to it!" and called to Wemmick to give him that piece of paper. Wemmick appeared, handed it in, and disappeared.

"Now, Mr. Pip," said Mr. Jaggers, "attend if you please. You have been drawing pretty freely here; your name occurs pretty often in Wemmick's cash book: but you are in debt, of course?"

"I am afraid I must say yes, sir."

"You know you must say yes; don't you?" said Mr. Jaggers.

"Yes, sir."

"I don't ask you what you owe because you don't know; and if you did know, you wouldn't tell me; you would say less. Yes, yes, my friend," cried Mr. Jaggers, waving his forefinger to stop me, as I made a show of protesting: "it's likely enough that you think you wouldn't, but you would. You'll excuse me, but I know better than you. Now, take this piece of paper in your hand. You have got it? Very good. Now, unfold it and tell me what it is."

"This is a bank-note," said I, "for five hundred pounds."

"That is a bank-note," repeated Mr. Jaggers, "for five hundred pounds. And a very handsome sum of money too, I think. You consider it so?"

"How could I do otherwise!"

"Ah! But answer the question," said Mr. Jaggers.

"Undoubtedly."

"You consider it, undoubtedly, a handsome sum of money. Now, that handsome sum of money, Pip, is your own. It is a present to you on this day, in earnest of your expectations. And at the rate of that handsome sum of money per annum, and at no higher rate, you are to live until the donor of the whole appears. That is to say, you will now take your money affairs entirely into your own hands, and you will draw from Wemmick one hundred and twenty-five pounds per quarter, until you are in communication with the fountain-head, and no longer with the mere agent. As I have told you before, I am the mere agent. I execute my instructions, and I am paid for doing so. I think them injudicious, but I am not paid for giving any opinion on their merits."

I was beginning to express my gratitude to my benefactor for the great liberality with which I was treated, when Mr. Jaggers stopped me. "I am not paid, Pip," said he, coolly, "to carry your words to any one;" and then gathered up his coat-tails, as he had gathered up the subject, and stood frowning at his boots as if he suspected them of designs against him.

After a pause, I hinted:

"There was a question just now, Mr. Jaggers, which you desired me to waive for a moment. I hope I am doing nothing wrong in asking it again?"

"What is it?" said he.

I might have known that he would never help me out; but it took me aback to have to shape the question afresh, as if it were quite new. "Is it likely," I said, after hesitating, "that my patron, the fountain-head you have spoken of, Mr. Jaggers, will soon——" there I delicately stopped.

"Will soon what?" asked Mr. Jaggers. "That's no question as it stands, you know."

"Will soon come to London," said I, after casting about for a precise form of words, "or summon me anywhere else?"

"Now here," replied Mr. Jaggers, fixing me for the first time with his dark deep-set eyes, "we must revert to the evening when we first encountered one another in your village. What did I tell you then, Pip?"

"You told me, Mr. Jaggers, that it might be years hence when that person appeared."

"Just so," said Mr. Jaggers; "that's my answer."

As we looked full at one another, I felt my breath come quicker in my strong desire to get something out of him. And as I felt that it came quicker, and as I felt that he saw that it came quicker, I felt that I had less chance than ever of getting anything out of him.

"Do you suppose it will still be years hence, Mr. Jaggers?"

Mr. Jaggers shook his head—not in negativing the question, but in altogether negativing the notion that he could anyhow be got to answer it—and the two horrible casts of the twitched faces looked, when my eyes strayed up to them, as if they had come to a crisis in their suspended attention, and were going to sneeze.

"Come!" said Mr. Jaggers, warming the backs of his legs with the backs of his warmed hands, "I'll be plain with you, my friend Pip. That's a question I must not be asked. You'll understand that, better, when I tell you it's a question that might compromise *me*. Come! I'll go a little further with you; I'll say something more."

He bent down so low to frown at his boots, that he was able to rub the calves of his legs in the pause he made.

"When that person discloses," said Mr. Jaggers, straightening himself, "you and that person will settle your own affairs. When that person discloses, my part in this business will cease and determine. When that person discloses, it will not be necessary for me to know anything about it. And that's all I have got to say."

We looked at one another until I withdrew my eyes, and looked thoughtfully at the floor. From this last speech I derived the notion that Miss Havisham, for some reason or no reason, had not taken him into her confidence as to her designing me for Estella; that he resented this, and felt a jealousy about it; or that he really did object to that scheme, and would have nothing to do with it. When I raised my eyes again, I found that he had been shrewdly looking at me all the time, and was doing so still.

"If that is all you have to say, sir," I remarked, "there can be nothing left for me to say."

He nodded assent, and pulled out his thief-dreaded watch, and asked me where I was going to dine? I replied, at my own chambers, with Herbert. As a necessary sequence, I asked him if he would favour us with his company, and he promptly accepted the invitation. But he insisted on walking home with me, in order that I might

make no extra preparation for him, and first he had a letter or two to write, and (of course) had his hands to wash. So, I said I would go into the outer office and talk to Wemmick.

The fact was, that when the five hundred pounds had come into my pocket, a thought had come into my head which had been often there before; and it appeared to me that Wemmick was a good person to advise with, concerning such thought.

He had already locked up his safe, and made preparations for going home. He had left his desk, brought out his two greasy office candlesticks and stood them in line with the snuffers on a slab near the door, ready to be extinguished; he had raked his fire low, put his hat and greatcoat ready, and was beating himself all over the chest with his safe-key as an athletic exercise after business.

"Mr. Wemmick," said I, "I want to ask your opinion. I am very desirous to serve a friend."

Wemmick tightened his post-office and shook his head, as if his opinion were dead against any fatal weakness of that sort.

"This friend," I pursued, "is trying to get on in commercial life, but has no money, and finds it difficult and disheartening to make a beginning. Now, I want somehow to help him to a beginning."

"With money down?" said Wemmick, in a tone drier than any sawdust.

"With *some* money down," I replied, for an uneasy remembrance shot across me of that symmetrical bundle of papers at home; "with *some* money down, and perhaps some anticipation of my expectations."

"Mr. Pip," said Wemmick, "I should like just to run over with you on my fingers, if you please, the names of the various bridges up as high as Chelsea Reach. Let's see; there's London, one; Southwark, two; Blackfriars, three; Waterloo, four; Westminster, five; Vauxhall, six." He had checked off each bridge in its turn, with the handle of his safe-key on the palm of his hand. "There's as many as six, you see, to choose from."

"I don't understand you," said I.

"Choose your bridge, Mr. Pip," returned Wemmick, "and take a walk upon your bridge, and pitch your money into the Thames over the centre arch of your bridge, and you know the end of it. Serve a friend with it, and you may know the end of it too—but it's a less pleasant and profitable end."

I could have posted a newspaper in his mouth, he made it so wide after saying this.

"This is very discouraging," said I.

"Meant to be so," said Wemmick.

"Then is it your opinion," I inquired, with some little indignation, "that a man should never——"

"—Invest portable property in a friend?" said Wemmick. "Certainly he should not. Unless he wants to get rid of the friend—and then it becomes a question how much portable property it may be worth to get rid of him."

"And that," said I, "is your deliberate opinion, Mr. Wemmick?"

"That," he returned, "is my deliberate opinion in this office."

"Ah!" said I, pressing him, for I thought I saw him near a loophole here; "but would that be your opinion at Walworth?"

"Mr. Pip," he replied with gravity, "Walworth is one

WORKS OF CHARLES DICKENS

place, and this office is another. Much as the Aged is one person, and Mr. Jaggers is another. They must not be confounded together. My Walworth sentiments must be taken at Walworth; none but my official sentiments can be taken in this office."

"Very well," said I, much relieved, "then I shall look you up at Walworth, you may depend upon it."

"Mr. Pip," he returned, "you will be welcome there, in a private and personal capacity."

We had held this conversation in a low voice, well knowing my guardian's ears to be the sharpest of the sharp. As he now appeared in his doorway, towelling his hands, Wemmick got on his great-coat and stood by to snuff out the candles. We all three went into the street together, and from the door-step Wemmick turned his way, and Mr. Jaggers and I turned ours.

I could not help wishing more than once that evening, that Mr. Jaggers had had an Aged in Gerrard-street, or a Stinger, or a Something, or a Somebody, to unbend his brows a little. It was an uncomfortable consideration on a twenty-first birthday, that coming of age at all seemed hardly worth while in such a guarded and suspicious world as he made of it. He was a thousand times better informed and cleverer than Wemmick, and yet I would a thousand times rather have had Wemmick to dinner. And Mr. Jaggers made not me alone intensely melancholy, because, after he was gone, Herbert said of himself, with his eyes fixed on the fire, that he thought he must have committed a felony and forgotten the details of it, he felt so dejected and guilty.

CHAPTER XXXVII.

DEEMING Sunday the best day for taking Mr. Wemmick's Walworth sentiments, I devoted the next ensuing Sunday afternoon to a pilgrimage to the Castle. On arriving before the battlements, I found the Union Jack flying and the drawbridge up, but undeterred by this show of defiance and resistance, I rang at the gate, and was admitted in a most pacific manner by the Aged.

"My son, sir," said the old man, after securing the drawbridge, "rather had it in his mind that you might happen to drop in, and he left word that he would soon be home from his afternoon's walk. He is very regular in his walks, is my son. Very regular in everything, is my son."

I nodded at the old gentleman as Wemmick himself might have nodded, and we went in and sat down by the fireside.

"You made acquaintance with my son, sir," said the old man, in his chirping way, while he warmed his hands at the blaze, "at his office, I expect?" I nodded. "Hah! I have heerd that my son is a wonderful hand at his business, sir?" I nodded hard. "Yes; so they tell me. His business is the Law?" I nodded harder. "Which makes it more surprising in my son," said the old man, "for he was not brought up to the Law, but to the Wine-Coopering."

Curious to know how the old gentleman stood informed concerning the reputation of Mr. Jaggers, I roared that name at him. He threw me into the greatest confusion by laughing heartily and replying in a very sprightly manner, "No, to be sure; you're right." And to this hour I have not the faintest notion of what he meant, or what joke he thought I had made.

As I could not sit there nodding at him perpetually, without making some other attempt to interest him, I shouted an inquiry whether his own calling in life had been "the Wine-Coopering." By dint of straining that term out of myself several times and tapping the old gentleman on the chest to associate it with him, I at last succeeded in making my meaning understood.

"No," said the old gentleman; "the warehousing, the warehousing. First, over yonder;" he appeared to mean up the chimney, but I believe he intended to refer me to Liverpool; "and then in the City of London here. However, having an infirmity—for I am hard of hearing, sir—"

I expressed in pantomime the greatest astonishment.

"—Yes, hard of hearing; having that infirmity coming upon me, my son he went into the Law, and he took charge of me, and he by little and little made out this elegant and beautiful property. But returning to what you said, you know," pursued the old man, again laughing heartily, "what I say is, No, to be sure; you're right."

I was modestly wondering whether my utmost ingenuity would have enabled me to say anything that would have amused him half as much as this imaginary pleasantry, when I was startled by a sudden click in the wall on one side of the chimney, and the ghostly tumbling open of a little wooden flap with "JOHN" upon it. The old man, following my eyes, cried with great triumph, "My son's come home!" and we both went out to the drawbridge.

It was worth any money to see Wemmick waving a salute to me from the other side of the moat, when we might have shaken hands across it with the greatest ease. The Aged was so delighted to work the drawbridge, that I made no offer to assist him, but stood quiet until Wemmick had come across, and had presented me to Miss Skiffins: a lady by whom he was accompanied.

Miss Skiffins was of a wooden appearance, and was, like her escort, in the post-office branch of the service. She might have been some two or three years younger than Wemmick, and I judged her to stand possessed of portable property. The cut of her dress from the waist upward, both before and behind, made her figure very like a boy's kite; and I might have pronounced her gown a little too decidedly orange, and her gloves a little too intensely green. But she seemed to be a good sort of fellow, and showed a high regard for the Aged. I was not long in discovering that she was a frequent visitor at the Castle; for, on our going in, and my complimenting Wemmick on his ingenious contrivance for announcing himself to the Aged, he begged me to give my attention for a moment to the other side of the chimney, and disappeared. Presently another click came, and another little door tumbled open with "Miss Skiffins" on it; then Miss Skiffins shut up and John tumbled open; then Miss Skiffins and John both tumbled open together, and finally shut up together. On Wemmick's return from working these mechanical appliances, I expressed the great admiration with which I regarded them, and he said, "Well, you know, they're both pleasant and useful to the Aged. And by George, sir, it's a thing worth mentioning, that of all the people who come to this gate, the secret of those pulls is only known to the Aged, Miss Skiffins, and me!"

"And Mr. Wemmick made them," added Miss Skiffins, "with his own hands out of his own head."

While Miss Skiffins was taking off her bonnet (she retained her green gloves during the evening as an outward and visible sign that there was company), Wemmick invited me to take a walk with him round the property, and see how the island looked in winter-time. Thinking that he did this to give me an opportunity of taking his Walworth sentiments, I seized the opportunity as soon as we were out of the Castle.

Having thought of the matter with care, I approached my subject as if I had never hinted at it before. I informed Wemmick that I was anxious in behalf of Herbert Pocket, and I told him how we had first met, and how we had fought. I glanced at Herbert's home, and at his character, and at his having no means but such as he was dependent on his father for: those, uncertain and unpunctual. I alluded to the advantages I had derived in my first rawness and ignorance from his society, and I confessed that I feared I had but ill repaid them, and that he might have done better without me and my expectations. Keeping Miss Havisham in the background at a great distance, I still hinted at the possibility of my having competed with him in his prospects, and at the certainty of his possessing a generous soul, and being far above any mean distrusts, retaliations, or designs. For all these reasons (I told Wemmick), and because he was my young companion and friend, and I had a great affection for him, I wished my own good fortune to reflect some rays upon him, and therefore I sought advice from Wemmick's experience and knowledge of men and affairs, how I could best try with my resources to help Herbert to some present income—say of a hundred a year, to keep him in good hope and heart—and gradually to buy him on to some small partnership. I begged Wemmick, in conclusion, to understand that my help must always be rendered without Herbert's knowledge or suspicion, and that there was no one else in the world with whom I could advise. I wound up by laying my hand upon his shoulder, and saying "I can't help confiding in you; though I know it must be troublesome to you; but that is your fault; in having ever brought me here."

Wemmick was silent for a little while, and then said with a kind of start, "Well, you know, Mr. Pip, I must tell you one thing. This is devilish good of you."

"Say you'll help me to be good then," said I.

"Ecod," replied Wemmick, shaking his head, "that's not my trade."

"Nor is this your trading-place," said I.

"You are right," he returned. "You hit the nail on the head. Mr. Pip, I'll put on my considering cap, and I think all you want to do may be done by degrees. Skiffins (that's her brother) is an accountant and agent. I'll look him up and go to work for you."

"I thank you ten thousand times."

"On the contrary," said he, "I thank you, for though we are strictly in our private and personal capacity, still it may be mentioned that there *are* Newgate cobwebs about, and it brushes them away."

After a little further conversation to the same effect, we returned into the Castle where we found Miss Skiffins preparing tea. The responsible duty of making the toast was delegated to the Aged, and that excellent old gentleman was so intent upon it that he seemed to be in some danger of melting his eyes. It was no nominal meal that we were going to make, but a vigorous reality. The Aged prepared such a haystack of buttered toast, that I could scarcely see him over it as it simmered on an iron stand hooked on to the top-bar; while Miss Skiffins brewed such a jorum of tea, that the pig in the back premises became strongly excited, and repeatedly expressed his desire to participate in the entertainment.

The flag had been struck, and the gun had been fired, at the right moment of time, and I felt as snugly cut off from the rest of Walworth as if the moat were thirty feet wide by as many deep. Nothing disturbed the tranquillity of the Castle, but the occasional tumbling open of John and Miss Skiffins: which little doors were a prey to some spasmodic infirmity that made me sympathetically uncomfortable until I got used to it. I inferred from the methodical nature of Miss Skiffins's arrangements that she made tea there every Sunday night; and I rather suspected that a classic brooch she wore, representing the profile of an undesirable female with a very straight nose and a very new moon, was a piece of portable property that had been given her by Wemmick.

We ate the whole of the toast, and drank tea in proportion, and it was delightful to see how warm and greasy we all got after it. The Aged, especially, might have passed for some clean old chief of a savage tribe, just oiled. After a short pause of repose, Miss Skiffins—in the absence of the little servant, who, it seemed, retired to the bosom of her family on Sunday afternoons—washed up the tea-things, in a trifling lady-like amateur manner that compromised none of us. Then, she put on her gloves again, and we drew round the fire, and Wemmick said, "Now, Aged Parent, tip us the paper."

Wemmick explained to me while the Aged got his spectacles out, that this was according to custom, and that it gave the old gentleman infinite satisfaction to read the news aloud. "I won't offer an apology," said Wemmick, "for he isn't capable of many pleasures—are you, Aged P.?"

"All right, John, all right," returned the old man, seeing himself spoken to.

"Only tip him a nod every now and then when he looks off his paper," said Wemmick, "and he'll be as happy as a king. We are all attention, Aged One."

"All right, John, all right!" returned the cheerful old man: so busy and so pleased, that it really was quite charming.

The Aged's reading reminded me of the classes at Mr. Wopsle's great-aunt's, with the pleasanter peculiarity that it seemed to come through a keyhole. As he wanted the candles close to him, and as he was always on the verge of putting either his head or the newspaper into them, he required as much watching as a powder-mill. But Wemmick was equally untiring and gentle in his vigilance, and the Aged read on, quite unconscious of his many rescues. Whenever he looked at us, we all expressed the greatest interest and amazement, and nodded until he resumed again.

As Wemmick and Miss Skiffins sat side by side, and as I sat in a shadowy corner, I observed a slow and gradual elongation of Mr. Wemmick's mouth, powerfully suggestive of his slowly and gradually stealing his arm round Miss Skiffins's waist. In course of time I saw his hand appear on the other side of Miss Skiffins; but at that moment Miss Skiffins neatly stopped him with the green glove, unwound his arm again as if it were an article of dress, and with the greatest deliberation laid it on the table before her. Miss Skiffins's composure while she did this was one of the most remarkable sights I have ever seen, and if I could have thought the act consistent with abstraction of mind, I should have deemed that Miss Skiffins performed it mechanically.

By-and-bye, I noticed Wemmick's arm beginning to disappear again, and gradually fading out of view. Shortly afterwards, his mouth began to widen again. After an interval of suspense on my part that was quite enthralling and almost painful, I saw his hand appear on the other side of Miss Skiffins. Instantly, Miss Skiffins stopped it with the neatness of a placid boxer, took off that girdle or cestus as before, and laid it on the table. Taking the table to represent the path of virtue, I am justified in stating that during the whole time of the Aged's reading, Wemmick's arm was straying from the path of virtue and being recalled to it by Miss Skiffins.

At last the Aged read himself into a light slumber. This was the time for Wemmick to produce a little kettle, a tray of glasses, and a black bottle with a porcelain-topped cork, representing some clerical dignitary of a rubicund and social aspect. With the aid of these appliances we all had something warm to drink: including the Aged, who was soon awake again. Miss Skiffins mixed, and I observed that she and Wemmick drank out of one glass. Of course I knew better than to offer to see Miss Skiffins home, and under the circumstances I thought I had best go first: which I did, taking a cordial leave of the Aged, and having passed a pleasant evening.

Before a week was out, I received a note from Wemmick, dated Walworth, stating that he hoped he had made some advance in that matter appertaining to our private and personal capacities, and that he would be glad if I could come and see him again upon it. So, I went out to Walworth again, and yet again, and yet again, and I saw him by appointment in the City several times, but never held any communication with him on the subject in or near Little Britain. The upshot was, that we found a worthy young merchant or shipping-broker, not long established in business, who wanted intelligent help, and who wanted capital, and who in due course of time and receipt would want a partner. Between him and me, secret articles were signed of which Herbert was the subject, and I paid him half of my five hundred pounds down, and engaged for sundry other payments: some, to fall due at certain dates out of my income: some contingent on my coming into my property. Miss Skiffins's brother conducted the negotiation. Wemmick pervaded it throughout, but never appeared in it.

The whole business was so cleverly managed, that Herbert had not the least suspicion of my hand being in it. I never shall forget the radiant face with which he came home one afternoon, and told me as a mighty piece of news, of his having fallen in with one Clarriker (the young merchant's name), and of Clarriker's having shown an extraordinary inclination towards him, and of his belief that the opening had come at last. Day by day as his hopes grew stronger and his face brighter, he must have thought me a more and more affectionate friend, for I had the greatest difficulty in restraining my tears of triumph when I saw him so happy.

At length, the thing being done, and he having that day entered Clarriker's House, and he having talked to me for a whole evening in a flush of pleasure and success, I did really cry in good earnest when I went to bed, to think that my expectations had done some good to somebody.

A great event in my life, the turning point of my life, now opens on my view. But, before I proceed to narrate it, and before I pass on to all the changes it involved, I must give one chapter to Estella. It is not much to give to the theme that so long filled my heart.

CHAPTER XXXVIII.

IF that staid old house near the Green at Richmond should ever come to be haunted when I am dead, it will be haunted, surely, by my ghost. O the many, many nights and days through which the unquiet spirit within me haunted that house when Estella lived there! Let my body be where it would, my spirit was always wandering, wandering, wandering about that house.

The lady with whom Estella was placed, Mrs. Brandley by name, was a widow, with one daughter several years older than Estella. The mother looked young and the daughter looked old; the mother's complexion was pink, and the daughter's was yellow; the mother set up for frivolity, and the daughter for theology. They were in what is called a good position, and visited, and were visited by, numbers of people. Little, if any, community of feeling subsisted between them and Estella, but the understanding was established that they were necessary to her, and that she was necessary to them. Mrs. Brandley had been a friend of Miss Havisham's before the time of her seclusion.

In Mrs. Brandley's house and out of Mrs. Brandley's house, I suffered every kind and degree of torture that Estella could cause me. The nature of my relations with her, which placed me on terms of familiarity without placing me on terms of favour, conduced to my distraction. She made use of me to tease other admirers, and she turned the very familiarity between herself and me, to the account of putting a constant slight on my devotion to her. If I had been her secretary, steward, half-brother, poor relation —if I had been a younger brother of her appointed husband—I could not have seemed to myself, further from my hopes when I was nearest to her. The privilege of calling her by her name and hearing her call me by mine, became under the circumstances an aggravation of my trials; and while I think it likely that it almost maddened her other lovers, I knew too certainly that it almost maddened me.

She had admirers without end. No doubt my jealousy made an admirer of every one who went near her; but there were more than enough of them without that.

I saw her often at Richmond, I heard of her often in town, and I used often to take her and the Brandleys on the water; there were picnics, fête days, plays, operas, concerts, parties, all sorts of pleasures, through which I pursued her—and they were all miseries to me. I never had one hour's happiness in her society, and yet my mind all round the four-and-twenty hours was harping on the happiness of having her with me unto death.

Throughout this part of our intercourse—and it lasted, as will presently be seen, for what I then thought a long time—she habitually reverted to that tone which expressed that our association was forced upon us. There were other times when she would come to a sudden check in this tone and in all her many tones, and would seem to pity me.

"Pip, Pip," she said one evening, coming to such a

check, when we sat apart at a darkening window of the house in Richmond; "will you never take warning?"

"Of what?"

"Of me."

"Warning not to be attracted by you, do you mean, Estella?"

"Do I mean! If you don't know what I mean, you are blind."

I should have replied that Love was commonly reputed blind, but for the reason that I always was restrained—and this was not the least of my miseries—by a feeling that it was ungenerous to press myself upon her, when she knew that she could not choose but obey Miss Havisham. My dread always was, that this knowledge on her part laid me under a heavy disadvantage with her pride, and made me the subject of a rebellious struggle in her bosom.

"At any rate," said I, "I have no warning given me just now, for you wrote to me to come to you, this time."

"That's true," said Estella, with a cold careless smile that always chilled me.

After looking at the twilight without, for a little while, she went on to say:

"The time has come round when Miss Havisham wishes to have me for a day at Satis. You are to take me there, and bring me back, if you will. She would rather I did not travel alone, and objects to receiving my maid, for she has a sensitive horror of being talked of by such people. Can you take me?"

"Can I take you, Estella!"

"You can then? The day after to-morrow, if you please. You are to pay all charges out of my purse. You hear the condition of your going?"

"And must obey," said I.

This was all the preparation I received for that visit, or for others like it: Miss Havisham never wrote to me, nor had I ever so much as seen her handwriting. We went down on the next day but one, and we found her in the room where I had first beheld her, and it is needless to add that there was no change in Satis House.

She was even more dreadfully fond of Estella than she had been when I last saw them together; I repeat the word advisedly, for there was something positively dreadful in the energy of her looks and embraces. She hung upon Estella's beauty, hung upon her words, hung upon her gestures, and sat mumbling her own trembling fingers while she looked at her, as though she were devouring the beautiful creature she had reared.

From Estella she looked at me, with a searching glance that seemed to pry into my heart and probe its wounds. "How does she use you, Pip, how does she use you?" she asked me again, with her witch-like eagerness, even in Estella's hearing. But, when we sat by her flickering fire at night, she was most weird; for then, keeping Estella's hand drawn through her arm and clutched in her own hand, she extorted from her by dint of referring back to what Estella had told her in her regular letters, the names and conditions of the men whom she had fascinated; and as Miss Havisham dwelt upon this roll, with the intensity of a mind mortally hurt and diseased, she sat with her other hand on her crutch stick, and her chin on that, and her wan bright eyes glaring at me, a very spectre.

I saw in this, wretched though it made me, and bitter the sense of dependence, even of degradation, that it awakened—I saw in this, that Estella was set to wreak Miss Havisham's revenge on men, and that she was not to be given to me until she had gratified it for a term. I saw in this, a reason for her being beforehand assigned to me. Sending her out to attract and torment and do mischief, Miss Havisham sent her with the malicious assurance that she was beyond the reach of all admirers, and that all who staked upon that cast were secured to lose. I saw in this, that I, too, was tormented by a perversion of ingenuity, even while the prize was reserved for me. I saw in this, the reason for my being staved off so long, and the reason for my late guardian's declining to commit himself to the formal knowledge of such a scheme. In a word, I saw in this, Miss Havisham as I had her then and there before my eyes, and always had had her before my eyes; and I saw in this, the distinct shadow of the darkened and unhealthy house in which her life was hidden from the sun.

The candles that lighted that room of hers were placed in sconces on the wall. They were high from the ground, and they burnt with the steady dulness of artificial light in air that is seldom renewed. As I looked round at them, and at the pale gloom they made, and at the stopped clock, and at the withered articles of bridal dress upon the table and the ground, and at her own awful figure with its ghostly reflection thrown large by the fire upon the ceiling and the wall, I saw in everything the construction that my mind had come to, repeated and thrown back to me. My thoughts passed into the great room across the landing where the table was spread, and I saw it written, as it were, in the falls of the cobwebs from the centre-piece, in the crawlings of the spiders on the cloth, in the tracks of the mice as they betook their little quickened hearts behind the panels, and in the gropings and pausings of the beetles on the floor.

It happened on the occasion of this visit that some sharp words arose between Estella and Miss Havisham. It was the first time I had ever seen them opposed.

We were seated by the fire, as just now described, and Miss Havisham still had Estella's arm drawn through her own, and still clutched Estella's hand in hers, when Estella gradually began to detach herself. She had shown a proud impatience more than once before, and had rather endured that fierce affection than accepted or returned it.

"What!" said Miss Havisham, flashing her eyes upon her, "are you tired of me?"

"Only a little tired of myself," replied Estella, disengaging her arm, and moving to the great chimney-piece, where she stood looking down at the fire.

"Speak the truth, you ingrate!" cried Miss Havisham, passionately striking her stick upon the floor; "you are tired of me."

Estella looked at her with perfect composure, and again looked down at the fire. Her graceful figure and her beautiful face expressed a self-possessed indifference to the wild heat of the other, that was almost cruel.

"You stock and stone!" exclaimed Miss Havisham. "You cold, cold heart!"

"What!" said Estella, preserving her attitude of indifference as she leaned against the great chimney-piece and only moving her eyes; "do you reproach me for being cold? You?"

"Are you not?" was the fierce retort.

"You should know," said Estella. "I am what you have made me. Take all the praise, take all the blame; take all the success, take all the failure; in short, take me."

"O, look at her, look at her!" cried Miss Havisham, bitterly; "look at her, so hard and thankless, on the hearth where she was reared! Where I took her into this wretched breast when it was first bleeding from its stabs, and where I have lavished years of tenderness upon her!"

"At least I was no party to the compact," said Estella, "for if I could walk and speak, when it was made, it was as much as I could do. But what would you have? You have been very good to me, and I owe everything to you. What would you have?"

"Love," replied the other.

"You have it."

"I have not," said Miss Havisham.

"Mother by adoption," retorted Estella, never departing from the easy grace of her attitude, never raising her voice as the other did, never yielding either to anger or tenderness, "Mother by adoption, I have said that I owe everything to you. All I possess is freely yours. All that you have given me, is at your command to have again. Beyond that, I have nothing. And if you ask me to give you what you never gave me, my gratitude and duty cannot do impossibilities."

"Did I never give her love!" cried Miss Havisham, turning wildly to me. "Did I never give her a burning love, inseparable from jealousy at all times, and from sharp pain, while she speaks thus to me! Let her call me mad, let her call me mad!"

"Why should I call you mad," returned Estella, "I, of all people? Does any one live, who knows what set purposes you have, half as well as I do? Does any one live, who knows what a steady memory you have, half as well as I do? I who have sat on this same hearth on the little stool that is even now beside you there, learning your lessons and looking up into your face, when your face was strange and frightened me!"

"Soon forgotten!" moaned Miss Havisham. "Times soon forgotten!"

"No, not forgotten," retorted Estella. "Not forgotten, but treasured up in my memory. When have you found me false to your teaching? When have you found me unmindful of your lessons? When have you found me giving admission here," she touched her bosom with her hand, "to anything that you excluded? Be just to me."

"So proud, so proud!" moaned Miss Havisham, pushing away her grey hair with both her hands.

"Who taught me to be proud?" returned Estella. "Who praised me when I learnt my lesson?"

"So hard, so hard!" moaned Miss Havisham, with her former action.

"Who taught me to be hard?" returned Estella. "Who praised me when I learnt my lesson?"

"But to be proud and hard to *me!*" Miss Havisham quite shrieked, as she stretched out her arms. "Estella, Estella, Estella, to be proud and hard to *me!*"

Estella looked at her for a moment with a kind of calm wonder, but was not otherwise disturbed; when the moment was past, she looked down at the fire again.

"I cannot think," said Estella, raising her eyes after a silence, "why you should be so unreasonable when I come to see you after a separation. I have never forgotten your wrongs and their causes. I have never been unfaithful to you or your schooling. I have never shown any weakness that I can charge myself with."

"Would it be weakness to return my love?" exclaimed Miss Havisham. "But yes, yes, she would call it so!"

"I begin to think," said Estella, in a musing way, after another moment of calm wonder, "that I almost understand how this comes about. If you had brought up your adopted daughter wholly in the dark confinement of these rooms, and had never let her know that there was such a thing as the daylight by which she has never once seen your face—if you had done that, and then, for a purpose, had wanted her to understand the daylight and know all about it, you would have been disappointed and angry?"

Miss Havisham, with her head in her hands, sat making a low moaning, and swaying herself on her chair, but gave no answer.

"Or," said Estella, "—which is a nearer case—if you had taught her, from the dawn of her intelligence, with your utmost energy and might, that there was such a thing as daylight, but that it was made to be her enemy and destroyer, and she must always turn against it, for it had blighted you and would else blight her;—if you had done this, and then, for a purpose, had wanted her to take naturally to the daylight and she could not do it, you would have been disappointed and angry?"

Miss Havisham sat listening (or it seemed so, for I could not see her face), but still made no answer.

"So," said Estella, "I must be taken as I have been made. The success is not mine, the failure is not mine, but the two together make me."

Miss Havisham had settled down, I hardly knew how, upon the floor, among the faded bridal relics with which it was strewn. I took advantage of the moment—I had sought one from the first—to leave the room, after beseeching Estella's attention to her with a movement of my hand. When I left, Estella was yet standing by the great chimney-piece, just as she had stood throughout. Miss Havisham's grey hair was all adrift upon the ground, among the other bridal wrecks, and was a miserable sight to see.

It was with a depressed heart that I walked in the starlight for an hour and more, about the courtyard, and about the brewery, and about the ruined garden. When I at last took courage to return to the room, I found Estella sitting at Miss Havisham's knee, taking up some stitches in one of those old articles of dress that were dropping to pieces, and of which I have often been reminded since by the faded tatters of old banners that I have seen hanging up in cathedrals. Afterwards, Estella and I played at cards, as of yore—only we were skilful now, and played French games—and so the evening wore away, and I went to bed.

I lay in that separate building across the courtyard. It was the first time I had ever lain down to rest in Satis House, and sleep refused to come near me. A thousand Miss Havishams haunted me. She was on this side of my pillow, on that, at the head of the bed, at the foot, behind the half-opened door of the dressing-room, in the dressing-room, in the room overhead, in the room beneath—everywhere. At last, when the night was slow to creep on towards two o'clock, I felt that I absolutely could no longer bear the place as a place to lie down in, and that I must get up. I therefore got up and put on my clothes, and went out across the yard into the long stone passage, designing to gain the outer courtyard and walk there for the relief of my mind. But, I was no sooner in the passage than I extinguished my candle; for, I saw Miss Havisham going along it in a ghostly manner, making a low cry. I followed her at a distance, and saw her go up the staircase. She carried a bare candle in her hand, which she had probably taken from one of the sconces in her own room, and was a most unearthly object by its light. Standing at the bottom of the staircase, I felt the mildewed air of the feast chamber, without seeing her open the door, and I heard her walking there, and so across into her own room, and so across again into that, never ceasing the low cry. After a time, I tried in the dark both to get out and to go back, but I could do neither until some streaks of day strayed in and showed me where to lay my hands. During the whole interval, whenever I went to the bottom of the staircase, I heard her footstep, saw her candle pass above, and heard her ceaseless low cry.

Before we left next day, there was no revival of the difference between her and Estella, nor was it ever revived on any similar occasion; and there were four similar occasions, to the best of my remembrance. Nor, did Miss Havisham's manner towards Estella, in anywise change, except that I believed it to have something like fear infused among its former characteristics.

It is impossible to turn this leaf of my life without putting Bentley Drummle's name upon it; or I would, very gladly.

On a certain occasion when the Finches were assembled in force, and when good feeling was being promoted in the usual manner by nobody's agreeing with anybody else, the presiding Finch called the Grove to order, forasmuch as Mr. Drummle had not yet toasted a lady; which, according to the solemn constitution of the society, it was the brute's turn to do that day. I thought I saw him leer in an ugly way at me while the decanters were going round, but as there was no love lost between us, that might easily be. What was my indignant surprise when he called upon the company to pledge him to "Estella!"

"Estella who?" said I.

"Never you mind," retorted Drummle.

"Estella of where?" said I. "You are bound to say of where." Which he was, as a Finch.

"Of Richmond, gentlemen," said Drummle, putting me out of the question, "and a peerless beauty."

Much he knew about peerless beauties, a mean miserable idiot! I whispered Herbert.

"I know that lady," said Herbert, across the table, when the toast had been honoured.

"_Do_ you?" said Drummle.

"And so do I," I added with a scarlet face.

"_Do_ you?" said Drummle. "_Oh_, Lord!"

This was the only retort—except glass or crockery—that the heavy creature was capable of making; but, I became as highly incensed by it as if it had been barbed with wit, and I immediately rose in my place and said that I could not but regard it as being like the honourable Finch's impudence to come down to that Grove—we always talked about coming down to that Grove, as a neat Parliamentary turn of expression—down to that Grove, proposing a lady of whom he knew nothing. Mr. Drummle upon this, starting up, demanded what I meant by that? Whereupon, I made him the extreme reply that I believed he knew where I was to be found.

Whether it was possible in a Christian country to get on without blood, after this, was a question on which the Finches were divided. The debate upon it grew so lively, indeed, that at least six more honourable members told six more, during the discussion, that they believed _they_ knew where _they_ were to be found. However, it was decided at last (the Grove being a Court of Honour) that if Mr. Drummle would bring never so slight a certificate from the lady, importing that he had the honour of her acquaintance, Mr. Pip must express his regret, as a gentleman and a Finch, for "having been betrayed into a warmth which."

Next day was appointed for the production (lest our honour should take cold from delay), and next day Drummle appeared with a polite little avowal in Estella's hand, that she had had the honour of dancing with him several times. This left me no course but to regret that I had been "betrayed into a warmth which," and on the whole to repudiate, as untenable, the idea that I was to be found anywhere. Drummle and I then sat snorting at one another for an hour, while the Grove engaged in indiscriminate contradiction, and finally the promotion of good feeling was declared to have gone ahead at an amazing rate.

I tell this lightly, but it was no light thing to me. For, I cannot adequately express what pain it gave me to think that Estella should show any favour to a contemptible, clumsy, sulky booby, so very far below the average. To the present moment, I believe it to have been referable to some pure fire of generosity and disinterestedness in my love for her, that I could not endure the thought of her stooping to that hound. No doubt I should have been miserable whomsoever she had favoured; but a worthier object would have caused me a different kind and degree of distress.

It was easy for me to find out, and I did soon find out, that Drummle had begun to follow her closely, and that she allowed him to do it. A little while, and he was always in pursuit of her, and he and I crossed one another every day. He held on, in a dull persistent way, and Estella held him on; now with encouragement, now with discouragement, now almost flattering him, now openly despising him, now knowing him very well, now scarcely remembering who he was.

The Spider, as Mr. Jaggers had called him, was used to lying in wait, however, and had the patience of his tribe. Added to that, he had a blockhead confidence in his money and in his family greatness, which sometimes did him good service—almost taking the place of concentration and determined purpose. So, the Spider, doggedly watching Estella, outwatched many brighter insects, and would often uncoil himself and drop at the right nick of time.

At a certain Assembly Ball at Richmond (there used to be Assembly Balls at most places then), where Estella had outshone all other beauties, this blundering Drummle so hung about her, and with so much toleration on her part, that I resolved to speak to her concerning him. I took the next opportunity: which was when she was waiting for Mrs. Brandley to take her home, and was sitting apart among some flowers, ready to go. I was with her, for I almost always accompanied them to and from such places.

"Are you tired, Estella?"

"Rather, Pip."

"You should be."

"Say, rather, I should not be; for I have my letter to Satis House to write, before I go to sleep."

"Recounting to-night's triumph?" said I. "Surely a very poor one, Estella."

"What do you mean? I didn't know there had been any."

"Estella," said I, "do look at that fellow in the corner yonder, who is looking over here at us."

"Why should I look at him?" returned Estella, with her eyes on me, instead. "What is there in that fellow in the corner yonder—to use your words—that I need look at?"

"Indeed, that is the very question I want to ask you," said I. "For he has been hovering about you all night."

"Moths, and all sorts of ugly creatures," replied Estella,

with a glance towards him, "hover about a lighted candle. Can the candle help it?"

"No," I returned: "but cannot the Estella help it?"

"Well!" said she, laughing after a moment, "perhaps. Yes. Anything you like."

"But, Estella, do hear me speak. It makes me wretched that you should encourage a man so generally despised as Drummle. You know he is despised."

"Well?" said she.

"You know he is as ungainly within as without. A deficient, ill-tempered, lowering, stupid fellow."

"Well?" said she.

"You know he has nothing to recommend him but money, and a ridiculous roll of addle-headed predecessors; now, don't you?"

"Well?" said she again; and each time she said it, she opened her lovely eyes the wider.

To overcome the difficulty of getting past that monosyllable, I took it from her, and said, repeating it with emphasis, "Well! Then, that is why it makes me wretched."

Now, if I could have believed that she favoured Drummle with any idea of making me—me—wretched, I should have been in better heart about it; but in that habitual way of hers, she put me so entirely out of the question, that I could believe nothing of the kind.

"Pip," said Estella, casting her glance over the room, "don't be foolish about its effect on you. It may have its effect on others, and may be meant to have. It's not worth discussing."

"Yes, it is," said I, "because I cannot bear that people should say, 'she throws away her graces and attractions on a mere boor, the lowest in the crowd.'"

"I can bear it," said Estella.

"Oh! don't be so proud, Estella, and so inflexible."

"Calls me proud and inflexible in this breath!" said Estella, opening her hands. "And in his last breath reproached me for stooping to a boor!"

"There is no doubt you do," said I, something hurriedly, "for I have seen you give him looks and smiles this very night, such as you never give to—me."

"Do you want me then," said Estella, turning suddenly with a fixed and serious, if not angry look, "to deceive and entrap you?"

"Do you deceive and entrap him, Estella?"

"Yes, and many others—all of them but you. Here is Mrs. Brandley. I'll say no more."

And now that I have given the one chapter to the theme that so filled my heart, and so often made it ache and ache again, I pass on, unhindered, to the event that had impended over me longer yet; the event that had begun to be prepared for, before I knew that the world held Estella, and in the days when her baby intelligence was receiving its first distortions from Miss Havisham's wasting hands.

In the Eastern story, the heavy slab that was to fall on the bed of state in the flush of conquest was slowly wrought out of the quarry, the tunnel for the rope to hold it in its place was slowly carried through the leagues of rock, the slab was slowly raised and fitted in the roof, the rope was rove to it and slowly taken through the miles of hollow to the great iron ring. All being made ready with much labour, and the hour come, the sultan was aroused in the dead of the night, and the sharpened axe that was to sever the rope from the great iron ring was put into his hand,

and he struck with it, and the rope parted and rushed away, and the ceiling fell. So, in my case; all the work, near and afar, that tended to the end, had been accomplished; and in an instant the blow was struck, and the roof of my stronghold dropped upon me.

CHAPTER XXXIX.

I was three-and-twenty years of age. Not another word had I heard to enlighten me on the subject of my expectations, and my twenty-third birthday was a week gone. We had left Barnard's Inn more than a year, and lived in the Temple. Our chambers were in Garden-court, down by the river.

Mr. Pocket and I had for some time parted company as to our original relations, though we continued on the best terms. Notwithstanding my inability to settle to anything—which I hope arose out of the restless and incomplete tenure on which I held my means—I had a taste for reading, and read regularly so many hours a day. That matter of Herbert's was still progressing, and everything with me was as I have brought it down to the close of the last preceding chapter.

Business had taken Herbert on a journey to Marseilles. I was alone, and had a dull sense of being alone. Dispirited and anxious, long hoping that to-morrow or next week would clear my way, and long disappointed, I sadly missed the cheerful face and ready response of my friend.

It was wretched weather; stormy and wet, stormy and wet; mud, mud, mud, deep in all the streets. Day after day, a vast heavy veil had been driving over London from the East, and it drove still, as if in the East there were an eternity of cloud and wind. So furious had been the gusts, that high buildings in town had had the lead stripped off their roofs; and in the country, trees had been torn up, and sails of windmills carried away; and gloomy accounts had come in from the coast, of shipwreck and death. Violent blasts of rain had accompanied these rages of wind, and the day just closed as I sat down to read had been the worst of all.

Alterations have been made in that part of the Temple since that time, and it has not now so lonely a character as it had then, nor is it so exposed to the river. We lived at the top of the last house, and the wind rushing up the river shook the house that night, like discharges of cannon, or breakings of a sea. When the rain came with it and dashed against the windows, I thought, raising my eyes to them as they rocked, that I might have fancied myself in a storm-beaten light-house. Occasionally, the smoke came rolling down the chimney as though it could not bear to go out into such a night; and when I set the doors open and looked down the staircase, the staircase lamps were blown out; and when I shaded my face with my hands and looked through the black windows (opening them ever so little, was out of the question in the teeth of such wind and rain) I saw that the lamps in the court were blown out, and that the lamps on the bridges and the shore were shuddering, and that the coal fires in barges on the river were being carried away before the wind like red-hot splashes in the rain.

I read with my watch upon the table, purposing to close my book at eleven o'clock. As I shut it, Saint Paul's, and all the many church-clocks in the City—some leading, some accompanying, some following—struck that hour. The sound was curiously flawed by the wind; and I was listening, and thinking how the wind assailed and tore it, when I heard a footstep on the stair.

What nervous folly made me start, and awfully connect it with the footstep of my dead sister, matters not. It was past in a moment, and I listened again, and heard the footstep stumble in coming on. Remembering then, that the staircase-lights were blown out, I took up my reading-lamp and went out to the stair-head. Whoever was below had stopped on seeing my lamp, for all was quiet.

"There is some one down there, is there not?" I called out, looking down.

"Yes," said a voice from the darkness beneath.

"What floor do you want?"

"The top. Mr. Pip."

"That is my name.—There is nothing the matter?"

"Nothing the matter," returned the voice. And the man came on.

I stood with my lamp held out over the stair-rail, and he came slowly within its light. It was a shaded lamp, to shine upon a book, and its circle of light was very contracted; so that he was in it for a mere instant, and then out of it. In the instant I had seen a face that was strange to me, looking up with an incomprehensible air of being touched and pleased by the sight of me.

Moving the lamp as the man moved, I made out that he was substantially dressed, but roughly; like a voyager by sea. That he had long iron-grey hair. That his age was about sixty. That he was a muscular man, strong on his legs, and that he was browned and hardened by exposure to weather. As he ascended the last stair or two, and the light of my lamp included us both, I saw, with a stupid kind of amazement, that he was holding out both his hands to me.

"Pray what is your business?" I asked him.

"My business?" he repeated, pausing. "Ah! Yes. I will explain my business, by your leave."

"Do you wish to come in?"

"Yes," he replied; "I wish to come in, Master."

I had asked him the question inhospitably enough, for I resented the sort of bright and gratified recognition that still shone in his face. I resented it, because it seemed to imply that he expected me to respond to it. But, I took him into the room I had just left, and, having set the lamp on the table, asked him as civilly as I could to explain himself.

He looked about him with the strangest air—an air of wondering pleasure, as if he had some part in the things he admired—and he pulled off a rough outer coat, and his hat. Then, I saw that his head was furrowed and bald, and that the long iron-grey hair grew only on its sides. But, I saw nothing that in the least explained him. On the contrary, I saw him next moment, once more holding out both his hands to me.

"What do you mean?" said I, half suspecting him to be mad.

He stopped in his looking at me, and slowly rubbed his right hand over his head. "It's disappinting to a man," he said, in a coarse broken voice, "arter having looked for'ard so distant, and come so fur; but you're not to blame for that—neither on us is to blame for that. I'll speak in half a minute. Give me half a minute, please."

He sat down on a chair that stood before the fire, and covered his forehead with his large brown veinous hands. I looked at him attentively then, and recoiled a little from him; but I did not know him.

"There's no one nigh," said he, looking over his shoulder; "is there?"

"Why do you, a stranger coming into my rooms at this time of the night, ask that question?" said I.

"You're a game one," he returned, shaking his head at me with a deliberate affection, at once most unintelligible and most exasperating; "I'm glad you've grow'd up, a game one! But don't catch hold of me. You'd be sorry arterwards to have done it."

I relinquished the intention he had detected, for I knew him! Even yet I could not recall a single feature, but I knew him! If the wind and the rain had driven away the intervening years, had scattered all the intervening objects, had swept us to the church-yard where we first stood face to face on such different levels, I could not have known my convict more distinctly than I knew him now, as he sat in the chair before the fire. No need to take a file from his pocket and show it to me; no need to take the handkerchief from his neck and twist it round his head; no need to hug himself with both his arms, and take a shivering turn across the room, looking back at me for recognition. I knew him before he gave me one of those aids, though, a moment before, I had not been conscious of remotely suspecting his identity.

He came back to where I stood, and again held out both his hands. Not knowing what to do—for, in my astonishment I had lost my self-possession—I reluctantly gave him my hands. He grasped them heartily, raised them to his lips, kissed them, and still held them.

"You acted nobly, my boy," said he. "Noble Pip! And I have never forgot it!"

At a change in his manner as if he were even going to embrace me, I laid a hand upon his breast and put him away.

"Stay!" said I. "Keep off! If you are grateful to me for what I did when I was a little child, I hope you have shown your gratitude by mending your way of life. If you have come here to thank me, it was not necessary. Still, however, you have found me out, there must be something good in the feeling that has brought you here, and I will not repulse you; but surely you must understand—I——"

My attention was so attracted by the singularity of his fixed look at me, that the words died away on my tongue.

"You was a saying," he observed, when we had confronted one another in silence, "that surely I must understand. What, surely must I understand?"

"That I cannot wish to renew that chance intercourse with you of long ago, under these different circumstances. I am glad to believe you have repented and recovered yourself. I am glad to tell you so. I am glad that, thinking I deserve to be thanked, you have come to thank me. But our ways are different ways, none the less. You are wet, and you look weary. Will you drink something before you go?"

He had replaced his neckerchief loosely, and had stood, keenly observant of me, biting a long end of it. "I think," he answered, still with the end at his mouth and still observant of me, "that I *will* drink (I thank you) afore I go."

There was a tray ready on a side-table. I brought it to the table near the fire, and asked him what he would have? He touched one of the bottles without looking at it or speaking, and I made him some hot rum-and-water. I tried to keep my hand steady while I did so, but his look at me as he leaned back in his chair with the long draggled end of his neckerchief between his teeth—evidently forgotten—made my hand very difficult to master. When at last I put the glass to him, I saw with amazement that his eyes were full of tears.

Up to this time I had remained standing, not to disguise that I wished him gone. But I was softened by the softened aspect of the man, and felt a touch of reproach. "I hope," said I, hurriedly putting something into a glass for myself, and drawing a chair to the table, "that you will not think I spoke harshly to you just now. I had no intention of doing it, and I am sorry for it if I did. I wish you well, and happy!"

As I put my glass to my lips, he glanced with surprise at the end of his neckerchief, dropping from his mouth when he opened it, and stretched out his hand. I gave him mine, and then he drank, and drew his sleeve across his eyes and forehead.

"How are you living?" I asked him.

"I've been a sheep-farmer, stock-breeder, other trades besides, away in the new world," said he: "many a thousand mile of stormy water off from this."

"I hope you have done well?"

"I've done wonderful well. There's others went out alonger me as has done well too, but no man has done nigh as well as me. I'm famous for it."

"I am glad to hear it."

"I hope to hear you say so, my dear boy."

Without stopping to try to understand those words or the tone in which they were spoken, I turned off to a point that had just come into my mind.

"Have you ever seen a messenger you once sent to me," I inquired, "since he undertook that trust?"

"Never set eyes upon him. I warn't likely to it."

"He came faithfully, and brought me the two one-pound notes. I was a poor boy then, as you know, and to a poor boy they were a little fortune. But, like you, I have done well since, and you must let me pay them back. You can put them to some other poor boy's use." I took out my purse.

He watched me as I laid my purse upon the table and opened it, and he watched me as I separated two one-pound notes from its contents. They were clean and new, and I spread them out and handed them over to him. Still watching me, he laid them one upon the other, folded them long-wise, gave them a twist, set fire to them at the lamp, and dropped the ashes into the tray.

"May I make so bold," he said then, with a smile that was like a frown, and with a frown that was like a smile, "as ask you *how* you have done well, since you and me was out on them lone shivering marshes?"

"How?"

"Ah!"

He emptied his glass, got up, and stood at the side of the fire, with his heavy brown hand on the mantel-shelf. He put a foot up to the bars, to dry and warm it, and the wet boot began to steam; but, he neither looked at it, nor at the fire, but steadily looked at me. It was only now that I began to tremble.

When my lips had parted, and had shaped some words that were without sound, I forced myself to tell him (though I could not do it distinctly), that I had been chosen to succeed to some property.

"Might a mere warmint ask what property?" said he.

I faltered, "I don't know."

"Might a mere warmint ask whose property?" said he.

I faltered again, "I don't know."

"Could I make a guess, I wonder," said the Convict, "at your income since you come of age! As to the first figure, now. Five?"

With my heart beating like a heavy hammer of disordered action, I rose out of my chair, and stood with my hand upon the back of it, looking wildly at him.

"Concerning a guardian," he went on. "There ought to have been some guardian, or such-like, whiles you was a minor. Some lawyer, maybe. As to the first letter of that lawyer's name, now. Would it be J?"

All the truth of my position came flashing on me; and its disappointments, dangers, disgraces, consequences of all kinds, rushed in in such a multitude that I was borne down by them and had to struggle for every breath I drew. "Put it," he resumed, "as the employer of that lawyer whose name begun with a J, and might be Jaggers—put it as he had come over sea to Portsmouth, and had landed there, and had wanted to come on to you. 'However, you have found me out,' you says just now. Well! however did I find you out? Why, I wrote from Portsmouth to a person in London, for particulars of your address. That person's name? Why, Wemmick."

I could not have spoken one word, though it had been to save my life. I stood, with a hand on the chair-back and a hand on my breast, where I seemed to be suffocating—I stood so, looking wildly at him, until I grasped at the chair, when the room began to surge and turn. He caught me, drew me to the sofa, put me up against the cushions, and bent on one knee before me: bringing the face that I now well remembered, and that I shuddered at, very near to mine.

"Yes, Pip, dear boy, I've made a gentleman on you! It's me wot has done it! I swore that time, sure as ever I earned a guinea, that guinea should go to you. I swore arterwards, sure as ever I spec'lated and got rich, you should get rich. I lived rough, that you should live smooth; I worked hard that you should be above work. What odds, dear boy? Do I tell it fur you to feel a obligation? Not a bit. I tell it, fur you to know as that there hunted dunghill dog wot you kep life in, got his head so high that he could make a gentleman—and, Pip, you're him!"

The abhorrence in which I held the man, the dread I had of him, the repugnance with which I shrank from him, could not have been exceeded if he had been some terrible beast.

"Look'ee here, Pip. I'm your second father. You're my son—more to me nor any son. I've put away money, only for you to spend. When I was a hired-out shepherd in a solitary hut, not seeing no faces but faces of sheep till I half forgot wot men's and women's faces wos like, I see yourn. I drops my knife many a time in that hut when I was a eating my dinner or my supper, and I says, 'Here's the boy again, a looking at me whiles I eats and drinks!' I see you there a many times as plain as ever I see you on them misty marshes. 'Lord strike me dead!' I says each time—and I goes out in the open air to say it under the open heavens—'but wot, if I gets liberty and money, I'll make that boy a gentleman!' And I done it. Why, look at you, dear boy! Look at these here lodgings of yourn, fit for a lord! A lord? Ah! You shall show money with lords for wagers, and beat 'em!"

I ROSE OUT OF MY CHAIR, AND STOOD WITH MY HAND UPON THE BACK OF IT, LOOKING
MILDLY AT HIM.

In his heat and triumph, and in his knowledge that I had been nearly fainting, he did not remark on my reception of all this. It was the one grain of relief I had.

"Look'ee here!" he went on, taking my watch out of my pocket and turning towards him a ring on my finger, while I recoiled from his touch as if he had been a snake, "a gold 'un and a beauty: *that's* a gentleman's, I hope! A diamond all set round with rubies; *that's* a gentleman's, I hope! Look at your linen; fine and beautiful! Look at your clothes; better ain't to be got! And your books too," turning his eyes round the room, "mounting up, on their shelves, by hundreds! And you read 'em; don't you? I see you'd been a reading of 'em when I come in. Ha, ha, ha! You shall read 'em to me, dear boy! And if they're in foreign languages wot I don't understand, I shall be just as proud as if I did."

Again he took both my hands and put them to his lips, while my blood ran cold within me.

"Don't you mind talking, Pip," said he, after again drawing his sleeve over his eyes and forehead, as the click came in his throat which I well remembered—and he was all the more horrible to me that he was so much in earnest; "you can't do better nor keep quiet, dear boy. You ain't looked slowly forward to this as I have; you wosn't prepared for this, as I wos. But didn't you never think it might be me?"

"O no, no, no," I returned. "Never, never!"

"Well, you see it *wos* me, and single-handed. Never a soul in it but my own self and Mr. Jaggers."

"Was there no one else?" I asked.

"No," said he, with a glance of surprise: "who else should there be? And, dear boy, how good-looking you have growed! There's bright eyes somewheres—eh? Isn't there bright eyes somewheres, wot you love the thoughts on?"

O Estella, Estella!

"They shall be yourn, dear boy, if money can buy 'em. Not that a gentleman like you, so well set up as you, can't win 'em off of his own game; but money shall back you! Let me finish wot I was a telling you, dear boy. From that there hut and that there hiring-out, I got money left me by my master (which died, and had been the same as me), and got my liberty and went for myself. In every single thing I went for, I went for you. 'Lord strike a blight upon it,' I says, wotever it was I went for, 'if it ain't for him!' It all prospered wonderful. As I give you to understand just now, I'm famous for it. It was the money left me, and the gains of the first few year, wot I sent home to Mr. Jaggers—all for you—when he first come arter you, agreeable to my letter."

O, that he had never come! That he had left me at the forge—far from contented, yet, by comparison, happy!

"And then, dear boy, it was a recompense to me, look'ee here, to know in secret that I was making a gentleman. The blood horses of them colonists might fling up the dust over me as I was walking; what do I say? I says to myself, 'I'm making a better gentleman nor ever *you*'ll be!' When one of 'em says to another, 'He was a convict, a few years ago, and is a ignorant common fellow now, for all he's lucky,' what do I say? I says to myself, 'If I ain't a gentleman, nor yet ain't got no learning, I'm the owner of such. All on you owns stock and land; which on you owns a brought-up London gentleman?' This way I kept myself a going. And this way I held steady afore my mind that I would for certain come one day and see my boy, and make myself known to him, on his own ground."

He laid his hand on my shoulder. I shuddered at the thought that for anything I knew, his hand might be stained with blood.

"It warn't easy, Pip, for me to leave them parts, nor yet it warn't safe. But I held to it, and the harder it was, the stronger I held, for I was determined, and my mind firm made up. At last I done it. Dear boy, I done it!"

I tried to collect my thoughts, but I was stunned. Throughout, I had seemed to myself to attend more to the wind and the rain than to him; even now, I could not separate his voice from those voices, though those were loud and his was silent.

"Where will you put me?" he asked, presently. "I must be put somewheres, dear boy."

"To sleep?" said I.

"Yes. And to sleep long and sound," he answered; "for I've been sea-tossed and sea-washed, months and months."

"My friend and companion," said I, rising from the sofa, "is absent; you must have his room."

"He won't come back to-morrow; will he?"

"No," said I, answering almost mechanically, in spite of my utmost efforts; "not to-morrow."

"Because look'ee here, dear boy," he said, dropping his voice, and laying a long finger on my breast in an impressive manner, "caution is necessary."

"How do you mean? Caution?"

"By G—, it's Death!"

"What's death?"

"I was sent for life. It's death to come back. There's been overmuch coming back of late years, and I should of a certainty be hanged if took."

Nothing was needed but this; the wretched man, after loading me with his wretched gold and silver chains for years, had risked his life to come to me, and I held it there in my keeping! If I had loved him instead of abhorring him; if I had been attracted to him by the strongest admiration and affection, instead of shrinking from him with the strongest repugnance; it could not have been no worse. On the contrary, it would have been better, for his preservation would then have naturally and tenderly addressed my heart.

My first care was to close the shutters, so that no light might be seen from without, and then to close and make fast the doors. While I did so, he stood at the table drinking rum and eating biscuit; and when I saw him thus engaged, I saw my convict on the marshes at his meal again. It almost seemed to me as if he must stoop down presently, to file at his leg.

When I had gone into Herbert's room, and shut off any other communication between it and the staircase than through the room in which our conversation had been held, I asked him if he would go to bed? He said yes, but asked me for some of my "gentleman's linen" to put on in the morning. I brought it out, and laid it ready for him, and my blood again ran cold when he again took me by both hands to give me good night.

I got away from him, without knowing how I did it, and mended the fire in the room where we had been together, and sat down by it, afraid to go to bed. For an hour or more, I remained too stunned to think; and it was not until I began to think, that I began fully to know how wrecked I was, and how the ship in which I had sailed was gone to pieces.

Miss Havisham's intentions towards me, all a mere dream; Estella not designed for me; I only suffered in Satis House as a convenience, a sting for the greedy relations, a model with a mechanical heart to practise on when no other practice was at hand; those were the first smarts I had. But, sharpest and deepest pain of all—it was for the convict, guilty of I knew not what crimes, and liable to be taken out of those rooms where I sat thinking, and hanged at the Old Bailey door, that I had deserted Joe.

I would not have gone back to Joe now, I would not have gone back to Biddy now, for any consideration: simply, I suppose, because my sense of my own worthless conduct to them was greater than every consideration. No wisdom on earth could have given me the comfort that I should have derived from their simplicity and fidelity; but I could never, never, never, undo what I had done.

In every rage of wind and rush of rain, I heard pursuers. Twice, I could have sworn there was a knocking and whispering at the outer door. With these fears upon me, I began either to imagine or recall that I had had mysterious warnings of this man's approach. That, for weeks gone by, I had passed faces in the streets which I had thought like his. That, these likenesses had grown more numerous, as he, coming over the sea, had drawn nearer. That, his wicked spirit had somehow sent these messengers to mine, and that now on this stormy night he was as good as his word, and with me.

Crowding up with these reflections came the reflection that I had seen him with my childish eyes to be a desperately violent man; that I had heard that other convict reiterate that he had tried to murder him; that I had seen him down in the ditch, tearing and fighting like a wild beast. Out of such remembrances I brought into the light of the fire, a half-formed terror that it might not be safe to be shut up there with him in the dead of the wild solitary night. This dilated until it filled the room, and impelled me to take a candle and go in and look at my dreadful burden.

He had rolled a handkerchief round his head, and his face was set and lowering in his sleep. But he was asleep, and quietly too, though he had a pistol lying on the pillow. Assured of this, I softly removed the key to the outside of his door, and turned it on him before I again sat down by the fire. Gradually I slipped from the chair and lay on the floor. When I awoke without having parted in my sleep with the perception of my wretchedness, the clocks of the Eastward churches were striking five, the candles were wasted out, the fire was dead, and the wind and rain intensified the thick black darkness.

THIS IS THE END OF THE SECOND STAGE OF PIP'S EXPECTATIONS.

CHAPTER XL.

It was fortunate for me that I had to take precautions to ensure (so far as I could) the safety of my dreaded visitor; for, this thought pressing on me when I awoke, held other thoughts in a confused concourse at a distance.

The impossibility of keeping him concealed in the chambers was self-evident. It could not be done, and the attempt to do it would inevitably engender suspicion. True, I had no Avenger in my service now, but I was looked after by an inflammatory old female, assisted by an animated rag-bag whom she called her niece; and to keep a room secret from them would be to invite curiosity and ex-

aggeration. They both had weak eyes, which I had long attributed to their chronically looking in at keyholes, and they were always at hand when not wanted, indeed that was their only reliable quality besides larceny. Not to get up a mystery with these people, I resolved to announce in the morning that my uncle had unexpectedly come from the country.

This course I decided on while I was yet groping about in the darkness for the means of getting a light. Not stumbling on the means after all, I was fain to go out to the adjacent Lodge and get the watchman there to come with his lantern. Now, in groping my way down the black staircase I fell over something, and that something was a man crouching in a corner.

As the man made no answer when I asked him what he did there, but eluded my touch in silence, I ran to the Lodge and urged the watchman to come quickly: telling him of the incident on the way back. The wind being as fierce as ever, we did not care to endanger the light in the lantern by rekindling the extinguished lamps on the staircase, but we examined the staircase from the bottom to the top and found no one there. It then occurred to me as possible that the man might have slipped into my rooms; so, lighting my candle at the watchman's, and leaving him standing at the door, I examined them carefully, including the room in which my dreaded guest lay asleep. All was quiet, and assuredly no other man was in those chambers.

It troubled me that there should have been a lurker on the stairs, on that night of all nights in the year, and I asked the watchman, on the chance of eliciting some hopeful explanation as I handed him a dram at the door, whether he had admitted at his gate any gentleman who had perceptibly been dining out? Yes, he said; at different times of the night, three. One lived in Fountain Court, and the other two lived in the Lane, and he had seen them all go home. Again, the only other man who dwelt in the house of which my chambers formed a part, had been in the country for some weeks; and he certainly had not returned in the night, because we had seen his door with his seal on it as we came upstairs.

"The night being so bad, sir," said the watchman, as he gave me back my glass, "uncommon few have come in at my gate. Besides them three gentlemen that I have named, I don't call to mind another since about eleven o'clock, when a stranger asked for you."

"My uncle," I muttered "Yes."

"You saw him, sir?"

"Yes. Oh yes."

"Likewise the person with him?"

"Person with him?" I repeated.

"I judged the person to be with him," returned the watchman. "The person stopped, when he stopped to make inquiry of me, and the person took this way when he took this way."

"What sort of person?"

The watchman had not particularly noticed; he should say a working person; to the best of his belief, he had a dust-coloured kind of clothes on, under a dark coat. The watchman made more light of the matter than I did, and naturally; not having my reason for attaching weight to it.

When I had got rid of him, which I thought it well to do without prolonging explanations, my mind was much troubled by these two circumstances taken together. Whereas they were easy of innocent solution apart—as, for instance, some diner-out or diner-at-home, who had not gone near this watchman's gate, might have strayed to my staircase and dropped asleep there—and my nameless visitor might have brought some one with him to show him the way—still, joined, they had an ugly look to one as prone to distrust and fear as the changes of a few hours had made me.

I lighted my fire, which burnt with a raw pale flare at that time of the morning, and fell into a doze before it. I seemed to have been dozing a whole night when the clock struck six. As there was full an hour and a half between me and daylight, I dozed again; now, waking up uneasily, with prolix conversations about nothing, in my ears; now, making thunder of the wind in the chimney; at length, falling off into a profound sleep from which the daylight woke me with a start.

All this time I had never been able to consider my own situation, nor could I do so yet. I had not the power to attend to it. I was greatly dejected and distressed, but in an incoherent wholesale sort of way. As to forming any plan for the future, I could as soon have formed an elephant. When I opened the shutters and looked out at the wet wild morning, all of a leaden hue; when I walked from room to room; when I sat down again shivering, before the fire, waiting for my laundress to appear; I thought how miserable I was, but hardly knew why, or how long I had been so, or on what day of the week I made the reflection, or even who I was that made it.

At last the old woman and the niece came in—the latter with a head not easily distinguishable from her dusty broom—and testified surprise at sight of me and the fire. To whom I imparted how my uncle had come in the night and was then asleep, and how the breakfast preparations were to be modified accordingly. Then, I washed and dressed while they knocked the furniture about and made a dust; and so, in a sort of dream or sleep-waking, I found myself sitting by the fire again, waiting for—Him—to come to breakfast.

By-and-bye, his door opened and he came out. I could not bring myself to bear the sight of him, and I thought he had a worse look by daylight.

"I do not even know," said I, speaking low as he took his seat at the table, "by what name to call you. I have given out that you are my uncle."

"That's it, dear boy! Call me uncle."

"You assumed some name, I suppose, on board ship?"

"Yes, dear boy. I took the name of Provis."

"Do you mean to keep that name?"

"Why, yes, dear boy, it's as good as another—unless you'd like another."

"What is your real name?" I asked him in a whisper.

"Magwitch," he answered, in the same tone; "chrisen'd Abel."

"What were you brought up to be?"

"A warmint, dear boy."

He answered quite seriously, and used the word as if it denoted some profession.

"When you came into the Temple last night—" said I, pausing to wonder whether that could really have been last night, which seemed so long ago.

"Yes, dear boy?"

"When you came in at the gate and asked the watchman the way here, had you any one with you?"

"With me? No, dear boy."

"But there was some one there?"

"I didn't take particular notice," he said, dubiously,

"not knowing the ways of the place. But I think there *was* a person, too, come in alonger me."

"Are you known in London?"

"I hope not!" said he, giving his neck a jerk with his forefinger that made me turn hot and sick.

"Were you known in London, once?"

"Not over and above, dear boy. I was in the provinces mostly."

"Were you—tried—in London?"

"Which time?" said he, with a sharp look.

"The last time."

He nodded. "First knowed Mr. Jaggers that way. Jaggers was for me."

It was on my lips to ask him what he was tried for, but he took up a knife, gave it a flourish, and with the words, "And what I done is worked out and paid for!" fell to at his breakfast.

He ate in a ravenous way that was very disagreeable, and all his actions were uncouth, noisy, and greedy. Some of his teeth had failed him since I saw him eat on the marshes, and as he turned his food in his mouth, and turned his head sideways to bring his strongest fangs to bear upon it, he looked terribly like a hungry old dog.

If I had begun with any appetite, he would have taken it away, and I should have sat much as I did—repelled from him by an insurmountable aversion, and gloomily looking at the cloth.

"I'm a heavy grubber, dear boy," he said, as a polite kind of apology when he had made an end of his meal, "but I always was. If it had been in my constitution to be a lighter grubber I might ha' got into lighter trouble. Similarly I must have my smoke. When I was first hired out as a shepherd t'other side the world, it's my belief I should ha' turned into a molloncolly-mad sheep myself, if I hadn't a had my smoke."

As he said so he got up from table, and putting his hand into the breast of the pea-coat he wore, brought out a short black pipe, and a handful of loose tobacco of the kind that is called negro-head. Having filled his pipe, he put the surplus tobacco back again, as if his pocket were a drawer. Then, he took a live coal from the fire with the tongs, and lighted his pipe at it, and then turned round on the hearth-rug with his back to the fire, and went through his favourite action of holding out both his hands for mine.

"And this," said he, dandling my hands up and down in his, as he puffed at his pipe; "and this is the gentleman what I made! The real genuine One! It does me good fur to look at you, Pip. All I stip'late, is, to stand by and look at you, dear boy!"

I released my hands as soon as I could, and found that I was beginning slowly to settle down to the contemplation of my condition. What I was chained to, and how heavily, became intelligible to me, as I heard his hoarse voice, and sat looking up at his furrowed bald head with its iron grey hair at the sides.

"I mustn't see my gentleman a footing it in the mire of the streets; there mustn't be no mud on *his* boots. My gentleman must have horses, Pip! Horses to ride, and horses to drive, and horses for his servant to ride and drive as well. Shall colonists have their horses (and blood-'uns, if you please, good Lord!) and not my London gentleman? No, no. We'll show 'em another pair of shoes than that, Pip; won't us?"

He took out of his pocket a great thick pocket-book, bursting with papers, and tossed it on the table.

"There's something worth spending in that there book, dear boy. It's yourn. All I've got ain't mine; it's yourn. Don't you be afeered on it. There's more where that come from. I've come to the old country for to see my gentleman spend his money *like* a gentleman. That'll be *my* pleasure. *My* pleasure 'ull be fur to see him do it. And blast you all!" he wound up, looking round the room and snapping his fingers once with a loud snap, "blast you every one, from the judge in his wig, to the colonist a stirring up the dust, I'll show a better gentleman than the whole kit on you put together!"

"Stop!" said I, almost in a frenzy of fear and dislike, "I want to speak to you. I want to know what is to be done. I want to know how you are to be kept out of danger, how long you are going to stay, what projects you have."

"Look'ee here, Pip," said he, laying his hand on my arm in a suddenly altered and subdued manner; "first of all, look'ee here. I forgot myself half a minute ago. What I said was low; that's what it was; low. Look'ee here, Pip. Look over it. I ain't a going to be low."

"First," I resumed, half-groaning, "what precautions can be taken against your being recognised and seized?"

"No, dear boy," he said, in the same tone as before, "that don't go first. Lowness goes first. I ain't took so many year to make a gentleman, not without knowing what's due to him. Look'ee here, Pip. I was low; that's what I was; low. Look over it, dear boy."

Some sense of the grimly-ludicrous moved me to a fretful laugh, as I replied, "I *have* looked over it. In Heaven's name, don't harp upon it!"

"Yes, but look'ee here," he persisted. "Dear boy, I ain't come so fur, not fur to be low. Now, go on, dear boy. You was a saying——"

"How are you to be guarded from the danger you have incurred?"

"Well, dear boy, the danger ain't so great. Without I was informed agen, the danger ain't so much to signify. There's Jaggers, and there's Wemmick, and there's you. Who else is there to inform?"

"Is there no chance person who might identify you in the street?" said I.

"Well," he returned, "there ain't many. Nor yet I don't intend to advertise myself in the newspapers by the name of A. M. come back from Botany Bay; and years have rolled away and who's to gain by it? Still, look'ee here, Pip. If the danger had been fifty times as great, I should ha' come to see you, mind you, just the same."

"And how long do you remain?"

"How long?" said he, taking his black pipe from his mouth, and dropping his jaw as he stared at me. "I'm not a going back. I've come for good."

"Where are you to live?" said I. "What is to be done with you? Where will you be safe?"

"Dear boy," he returned, "there's disguising wigs can be bought for money, and there's hair powder, and spectacles, and black clothes—shorts and what not. Others has done it safe afore, and what others has done afore, others can do agen. As to the where and how of living, dear boy, give me your own opinions on it."

"You take it smoothly now," said I, "but you were very serious last night, when you swore it was Death."

"And so I swear it is Death," said he, putting his pipe back in his mouth, "and Death by the rope, in the open street not fur from this, and it's serious that you should fully understand it to be so. What then, when that's once done? Here I am. To go back now, 'ud be as bad as to stand ground—worse. Besides, Pip, I'm here, because I've meant it by you, years and years. As to what I dare, I'm a old bird now, as has dared all manner of traps since first he was fledged, and I'm not afeerd to perch upon a scarecrow. If there's Death hid inside of it, there is, and let him come out, and I'll face him, and then I'll believe in him and not afore. And now let me have a look at my gentleman agen."

Once more he took me by both hands and surveyed me with an air of admiring proprietorship, smoking with great complacency all the while.

It appeared to me that I could do no better than secure him some quiet lodging hard by, of which he might take possession when Herbert returned: whom I expected in two or three days. That the secret must be confided to Herbert as a matter of unavoidable necessity, even if I could have put the immense relief I should derive from sharing it with him out of the question, was plain to me. But it was by no means so plain to Mr. Provis (I resolved to call him by that name), who reserved his consent to Herbert's participation until he should have seen him and formed a favourable judgment of his physiognomy. "And even then, dear boy," said he, pulling a greasy little clasped black Testament out of his pocket, "we'll have him on his oath."

To state that my terrible patron carried this little black book about the world solely to swear people on in cases of emergency, would be to state what I never quite established—but this I can say, that I never knew him put it to any other use. The book itself had the appearance of having been stolen from some court of justice, and perhaps his knowledge of its antecedents, combined with his own experience in that wise, gave him a reliance on its powers as a sort of legal spell or charm. On this first occasion of his producing it, I recalled how he had made me swear fidelity in the churchyard long ago, and how he had described himself last night as always swearing to his resolutions in his solitude.

As he was at present dressed in a seafaring slop suit, in which he looked as if he had some parrots and cigars to dispose of, I next discussed with him what dress he should wear. He cherished an extraordinary belief in the virtues of "shorts" as a disguise, and had in his own mind sketched a dress for himself that would have made him something between a dean and a dentist. It was with considerable difficulty that I won him over to the assumption of a dress more like a prosperous farmer's; and we arranged that he should cut his hair close, and wear a little powder. Lastly, as he had not yet been seen by the laundress or her niece, he was to keep himself out of their view until his change of dress was made.

It would seem a simple matter to decide on these precautions; but in my dazed, not to say distracted, state, it took so long, that I did not get out to further them until two or three in the afternoon. He was to remain shut up in the chambers while I was gone, and was on no account to open the door.

There being to my knowledge a respectable lodging-house in Essex-street, the back of which looked into the Temple, and was almost within hail of my windows, I first of all repaired to that house, and was so fortunate as to secure the second floor for my uncle, Mr. Provis. I then went from shop to shop, making such purchases as were necessary to the change in his appearance. This business transacted, I turned my face, on my own account, to Little Britain. Mr. Jaggers was at his desk, but, seeing me enter, got up immediately and stood before his fire.

"Now, Pip," said he, "be careful."

"I will, sir," I returned. For, coming along I had thought well of what I was going to say.

"Don't commit yourself," said Mr. Jaggers, "and don't commit any one. You understand—any one. Don't tell me anything: I don't want to know anything: I am not curious."

Of course I saw that he knew the man was come.

"I merely want, Mr. Jaggers," said I, "to assure myself what I have been told, is true. I have no hope of its being untrue, but at least I may verify it."

Mr. Jaggers nodded. "But did you say 'told' or 'informed'?" he asked me, with his head on one side, and not looking at me, but looking in a listening way at the floor. "Told would seem to imply verbal communication. You can't have verbal communication with a man in New South Wales, you know."

"I will say, informed, Mr. Jaggers."

"Good."

"I have been informed by a person named Abel Magwitch, that he is the benefactor so long unknown to me."

"That is the man," said Mr. Jaggers, "—in New South Wales."

"And only he?" said I.

"And only he," said Mr. Jaggers.

"I am not so unreasonable, sir, as to think you at all responsible for my mistakes and wrong conclusions; but I always supposed it was Miss Havisham."

"As you say, Pip," returned Mr. Jaggers,, turning his eyes upon me coolly, and taking a bite at his forefinger, "I am not at all responsible for that."

"And yet it looked so like it, sir," I pleaded with a downcast heart.

"Not a particle of evidence, Pip," said Mr. Jaggers, shaking his head and gathering up his skirts. "Take nothing on its looks; take everything on evidence. There's no better rule."

"I have no more to say," said I, with a sigh, after standing silent for a little while. "I have verified my information, and there's an end."

"And Magwitch—in New South Wales—having at last disclosed himself," said Mr. Jaggers, "you will comprehend, Pip, how rigidly throughout my communication with you, I have always adhered to the strict line of fact. There has never been the least departure from the strict line of fact. You are quite aware of that?"

"Quite, sir."

"I communicated to Magwitch—in New South Wales—when he first wrote to me—from New South Wales—the caution that he must not expect me ever to deviate from the strict line of fact. I also communicated to him another caution. He appeared to me to have obscurely hinted in his letter at some distant idea of seeing you in England here. I cautioned him that I must hear no more of that; that he was not at all likely to obtain a pardon; that he was expatriated for the term of his natural life; and that his presenting himself in this country would be an act of felony, rendering him liable to the extreme penalty of the law. I gave Magwitch that caution," said Mr. Jaggers, looking hard at me; "I wrote it to New South Wales. He guided himself by it, no doubt."

"No doubt," said I.

"I have been informed by Wemmick," pursued Mr. Jaggers, still looking hard at me, "that he has received a letter, under date Portsmouth, from a colonist of the name of Purvis, or——"

"Or Provis," I suggested.

"Or Provis—thank you, Pip. Perhaps it *is* Provis? Perhaps you know it's Provis?"

"Yes," said I.

"You know it's Provis. A letter, under date Portsmouth, from a colonist of the name of Provis, asking for the particulars of your address, on behalf of Magwitch. Wemmick sent him the particulars, I understand, by return of post. Probably it is through Provis that you have received the explanation of Magwitch—in New South Wales?"

"It came through Provis," I replied.

"Good day, Pip," said Mr. Jaggers, offering his hand; "glad to have seen you. In writing by post to Magwitch —in New South Wales—or in communicating with him through Provis, have the goodness to mention that the particulars and vouchers of our long account shall be sent to you, together with the balance; for there is still a balance remaining. Good day, Pip!"

We shook hands, and he looked hard at me as long as he could see me. I turned at the door, and he was still looking hard at me, while the two vile casts on the shelf seemed to be trying to get their eyelids open, and to force out of their swollen throats, "O, what a man he is!"

Wemmick was out, and though he had been at his desk he could have done nothing for me. I went straight back to the Temple, where I found the terrible Provis drinking rum-and-water, and smoking negro-head, in safety.

Next day the clothes I had ordered all came home, and he put them on. Whatever he put on, became him less (it dismally seemed to me) than what he had worn before. To my thinking there was something in him that made it hopeless to attempt to disguise him. The more I dressed him, and the better I dressed him, the more he looked like the slouching fugitive on the marshes. This effect on my anxious fancy was partly referable, no doubt, to his old face and manner growing more familiar to me: but I believed too that he dragged one of his legs as if there were still a weight of iron on it, and that from head to foot there was Convict in the very grain of the man.

The influences of his solitary hut-life were upon him besides, and gave him a savage air that no dress could tame; added to these were the influences of his subsequent branded life among men, and, crowning all, his consciousness that he was dodging and hiding now. In all his ways of sitting and standing, and eating and drinking—of brooding about, in a high-shouldered reluctant style—of taking out his great horn-handled jack-knife and wiping it on his legs and cutting his food—of lifting light glasses and cups to his lips, as if they were clumsy pannikins—of chopping a wedge off his bread, and soaking up with it the last fragments of gravy round and round his plate, as if to make the most of an allowance, and then drying his fingers on it, and then swallowing it—in these ways and a thousand other small nameless instances arising every minute in the day, there was Prisoner, Felon, Bondsman, plain as plain could be.

It had been his own idea to wear that touch of powder, and I conceded the powder after overcoming the shorts. But I can compare the effect of it, when on, to nothing but the probable effect of rouge upon the dead; so awful was the manner in which everything in him that it was most desirable to repress, started through that thin layer of pretence, and seemed to come blazing out at the crown of his head. It was abandoned as soon as tried, and he wore his grizzled hair cut short.

Words cannot tell what a sense I had, at the same time, of the dreadful mystery that he was to me. When he fell asleep of an evening, with his knotted hands clutching the sides of the easy-chair, and his bald head tattooed with deep wrinkles falling forward on his breast, I would sit and look at him, wondering what he had done, and loading him with all the crimes in the Calendar, until the impulse was powerful on me to start up and fly from him. Every hour so increased my abhorrence of him, that I even think I might have yielded to this impulse in the first agonies of being so haunted, notwithstanding all he had done for me and the risk he ran, but for the knowledge that Herbert must soon come back. Once, I actually did start out of bed in the night, and begin to dress myself in my worst clothes, hurriedly intending to leave him there with everything else I possessed, and enlist for India, as a private soldier.

I doubt if a ghost could have been more terrible to me, up in those lonely rooms in the long evenings and long nights, with the wind and the rain always rushing by. A ghost could not have been taken and hanged on my account, and the consideration that he could be, and the dread that he would be, were no small addition to my horrors. When he was not asleep, or playing a complicated kind of Patience with a ragged pack of cards of his own— a game that I never saw before or since, and in which he recorded his winnings by sticking his jack-knife into the table—when he was not engaged in either of these pursuits, he would ask me to read to him—" Foreign language, dear boy!" While I complied, he, not comprehending a single word, would stand before the fire surveying me with the air of an Exhibitor, and I would see him, between the fingers of the hand with which I shaded my face, appealing in dumb show to the furniture to take notice of my proficiency. The imaginary student pursued by the misshapen creature he had impiously made, was not more wretched than I, pursued by the creature who had made me, and recoiling from him with a stronger repulsion, the more he admired me and the fonder he was of me.

This is written, as if it had lasted a year. It lasted about five days. Expecting Herbert all the time, I dared not go out, except when I took Provis for an airing after dark. At length, one evening when dinner was over and I had dropped into a slumber quite worn out —for my nights had been agitated and my rest broken by fearful dreams—I was roused by the welcome footstep on the staircase. Provis, who had been asleep too, staggered up at the noise I made, and in an instant I saw his jack-knife shining in his hand.

"Quiet! It's Herbert!" I said; and Herbert came bursting in, with the airy freshness of six hundred miles of France upon him.

"Handel, my dear fellow, how are you, and again how are you, and again how are you? I seem to have been gone a twelvemonth! Why, so I must have been, for you have grown quite thin and pale! Handel, my——Halloa! I beg your pardon."

He was stopped in his running on and in his shaking hands with me, by seeing Provis. Provis, regarding him

with a fixed attention, was slowly putting up his jack-knife, and groping in another pocket for something else.

"Herbert, my dear friend," said I, shutting the double doors, while Herbert stood staring and wondering, "something very strange has happened. This is—a visitor of mine."

"It's all right, dear boy!" said Provis, coming forward, with his little clasped black book, and then addressing himself to Herbert. "Take it in your right hand. Lord strike you dead on the spot, if ever you split in any way sumever. Kiss it!"

"Do so, as he wishes it," I said to Herbert. So Herbert, looking at me with a friendly uneasiness and amazement, complied, and Provis immediately shaking hands with him, said, "Now, you're on your oath, you know. And never believe me on mine, if Pip shan't make a gentleman on you!"

CHAPTER XLI.

In vain should I attempt to describe the astonishment and disquiet of Herbert, when he and I and Provis sat down before the fire, and I recounted the whole of the secret. Enough that I saw my own feelings reflected in Herbert's face, and, not least among them, my repugnance towards the man who had done so much for me.

What would alone have set a division between that man and us, if there had been no other dividing circumstance, was his triumph in my story. Saving his troublesome sense of having been "low" on one occasion since his return—on which point he began to hold forth to Herbert, the moment my revelation was finished—he had no perception of the possibility of my finding any fault with my good fortune. His boast that he had made me a gentleman, and that he had come to see me support the character on his ample resources, was made for me quite as much as for himself. And that it was a highly agreeable boast to both of us, and that we must both be very proud of it, was a conclusion quite established in his own mind.

"Though, look'ee here, Pip's comrade," he said to Herbert, after having discoursed for some time, "I know very well that once since I come back—for half a minute—I've been low. I said to Pip, I knowed as I had been low. But don't you fret yourself on that score. I ain't made Pip a gentleman, and Pip ain't a going to make you a gentleman, not fur me not to know what's due to ye both. Dear boy, and Pip's comrade, you two may count upon me always having a genteel muzzle on. Muzzled I have been since that half a minute when I was betrayed into lowness, muzzled I am at the present time, muzzled I ever will be."

Herbert said "Certainly," but looked as if there were no specific consolation in this, and remained perplexed and dismayed. We were anxious for the time when he would go to his lodging, and leave us together, but he was evidently jealous of leaving us together, and sat late. It was midnight before I took him round to Essex-street, and saw him safely in at his own dark door. When it closed upon him, I experienced the first moment of relief I had known since the night of his arrival.

Never quite free from an uneasy remembrance of the man on the stairs, I had always looked about me in taking my guest out after dark, and in bringing him back; and I looked about me now. Difficult as it is in a large city to avoid the suspicion of being watched when the mind is conscious of danger in that regard, I could not persuade myself that any of the people within sight cared about my movements. The few who were passing, passed on their several ways, and the street was empty when I turned back into the Temple. Nobody had come out at the gate with us, nobody went in at the gate with me. As I crossed by the fountain, I saw his lighted back windows looking bright and quiet, and, when I stood for a few minutes in the doorway of the building where I lived, before going up the stairs, Garden-court was as still and lifeless as the staircase was when I ascended it.

Herbert received me with open arms, and I had never felt before so blessedly, what it is to have a friend. When he had spoken some sound words of sympathy and encouragement, we sat down to consider the question, What was to be done?

The chair that Provis had occupied still remaining where it had stood—for he had a barrack way with him of hanging about one spot, in one unsettled manner, and going through one round of observances with his pipe and his negro-head and his jack-knife and his pack of cards, and what not, as if it were all put down for him on a slate—I say, his chair remaining where it had stood, Herbert unconsciously took it, but next moment started out of it, pushed it away, and took another. He had no occasion to say, after that, that he had conceived an aversion for my patron, neither had I occasion to confess my own. We interchanged that confidence without shaping a syllable.

"What," said I to Herbert, when he was safe in another chair, "what is to be done?"

"My poor dear Handel," he replied, holding his head, "I am too stunned to think."

"So was I, Herbert, when the blow first fell. Still, something must be done. He is intent upon various new expenses—horses, and carriages, and lavish appearances of all kinds. He must be stopped somehow."

"You mean that you can't accept——"

"How can I?" I interposed, as Herbert paused. "Think of him! Look at him!"

An involuntary shudder passed over both of us.

"Yet I am afraid the dreadful truth is, Herbert, that he is attached to me, strongly attached to me. Was there ever such a fate!"

"My poor dear Handel," Herbert repeated.

"Then," said I, "after all, stopping short here, never taking another penny from him, think what I owe him already! Then again: I am heavily in debt—very heavily for me, who have now no expectations—and I have been bred to no calling, and I am fit for nothing."

"Well, well, well!" Herbert remonstrated. "Don't say fit for nothing."

"What am I fit for? I know only one thing that I am fit for, and that is, to go for a soldier. And I might have gone, my dear Herbert, but for the prospect of taking counsel with your friendship and affection."

Of course I broke down there; and of course Herbert, beyond seizing a warm grip of my hand, pretended not to know it.

"Anyhow, my dear Handel," said he presently, "soldiering won't do. If you were to renounce this patronage and these favours, I suppose you would do so with some faint hope of one day repaying what you have already had. Not very strong, that hope, if you went soldiering. Besides, it's absurd. You would be infinitely better in Clarriker's

house, small as it is. I am working up towards a partnership, you know."

Poor fellow! He little suspected with whose money.

"But there is another question," said Herbert. "This is an ignorant determined man, who has long had one fixed idea. More than that, he seems to me (I may misjudge him) to be a man of a desperate and fierce character."

"I know he is," I returned. "Let me tell you what evidence I have seen of it." And I told him what I had not mentioned in my narrative; of that encounter with the other convict.

"See, then," said Herbert; "think of this! He comes here at the peril of his life, for the realisation of his fixed idea. In the moment of realisation, after all his toil and waiting, you cut the ground from under his feet, destroy his idea, and make his gains worthless to him. Do you see nothing that he might do under the disappointment?"

"I have seen it, Herbert, and dreamed of it ever since the fatal night of his arrival. Nothing has been in my thoughts so distinctly as his putting himself in the way of being taken."

"Then you may rely upon it," said Herbert, "that there would be great danger of his doing it. That is his power over you as long as he remains in England, and that would be his reckless course if you forsook him."

I was so struck by the horror of this idea, which had weighed upon me from the first, and the working out of which would make me regard myself, in some sort, as his murderer, that I could not rest in my chair, but began pacing to and fro. I said to Herbert, meanwhile, that even if Provis were recognised and taken, in spite of himself, I should be wretched as the cause, however innocently. Yes; even though I was so wretched in having him at large and near me, and even though I would far rather have worked at the forge all the days of my life than I would ever have come to this!

But there was no raving off the question, What was to be done?

"The first and the main thing to be done," said Herbert, "is to get him out of England. You will have to go with him, and then he may be induced to go."

"But get him where I will, could I prevent his coming back?"

"My good Handel, is it not obvious that with Newgate in the next street, there must be far greater hazard in your breaking your mind to him and making him reckless, here, than elsewhere. If a pretext to get him away could be made out of that other convict, or out of anything else in his life, now."

"There again!" said I, stopping before Herbert, with my open hands held out, as if they contained the desperation of the case. "I know nothing of his life. It has almost made me mad to sit here of a night and see him before me, so bound up with my fortunes and misfortunes, and yet so unknown to me, except as the miserable wretch who terrified me two days in my childhood!"

Herbert got up, and linked his arm in mine, and we slowly walked to and fro together, studying the carpet.

"Handel," said Herbert, stopping, "you feel convinced that you can take no further benefits from him; do you?"

"Fully. Surely you would, too, if you were in my place?"

"And you feel convinced that you must break with him!"

"Herbert, can you ask me?"

"And you have, and are bound to have, that tenderness for the life he has risked on your account, that you must save him, if possible, from throwing it away. Then you must get him out of England before you stir a finger to extricate yourself. That done, extricate yourself, in Heaven's name, and we'll see it out together, dear old boy."

It was a comfort to shake hands upon it, and walk up and down again, with only that done.

"Now, Herbert," said I, "with reference to gaining some knowledge of his history. There is but one way that I know of. I must ask him point-blank."

"Yes. Ask him," said Herbert, "when we sit at breakfast in the morning." For, he had said, on taking leave of Herbert, that he would come to breakfast with us.

With this project formed, we went to bed. I had the wildest dreams concerning him, and woke unrefreshed; I woke, too, to recover the fear which I had lost in the night, of his being found out as a returned transport. Waking, I never lost that fear.

He came round at the appointed time, took out his jack-knife, and sat down to his meal. He was full of plans "for his gentleman's coming out strong, and like a gentleman," and urged me to begin speedily upon the pocket-book, which he had left in my possession. He considered the chambers and his own lodging as temporary residences, and advised me to look out at once for a "fashionable crib" near Hyde Park, in which he could have "a shake-down." When he had made an end of his breakfast, and was wiping his knife on his leg, I said to him, without a word of preface:

"After you were gone last night, I told my friend of the struggle that the soldiers found you engaged in on the marshes, when we came up. You remember?"

"Remember!" said he. "I think so!"

"We want to know something about that man—and about you. It is strange to know no more about either, and particularly you, than I was able to tell last night. Is not this as good a time as another for our knowing more?"

"Well!" he said, after consideration. "You're on your oath, you know, Pip's comrade?"

"Assuredly," replied Herbert.

"As to anything I say, you know," he insisted. "The oath applies to all."

"I understand it to do so."

"And look'ee here! Wotever I done, is worked out and paid for," he insisted again.

"So be it."

He took out his black pipe and was going to fill it with negro-head, when, looking at the tangle of tobacco in his hand, he seemed to think it might perplex the thread of his narrative. He put it back again, stuck his pipe in a buttonhole of his coat, spread a hand on each knee, and, after turning an angry eye on the fire for a few silent moments, looked around at us and said what follows.

CHAPTER XLII.

"DEAR boy and Pip's comrade. I am not a going fur to tell you my life, like a song or a story-book. But to give it you short and handy, I'll put it at once into a mouthful of English. In jail and out of jail, in jail and out of jail, in jail and out of jail. There, you've got it That's *my* life pretty much, down to such times as I got shipped off, arter Pip stood my friend.

"I've been done everything to, pretty well—except hanged. I've been locked up, as much as a silver tea-kettle. I've been carted here and carted there, and put out of this town and put out of that town, and stuck in the stocks, and whipped and worried and drove. I've no more notion where I was born, than you have—if so much. I first became aware of myself, down in Essex, a thieving turnips for my living. Summun had run away from me—a man—a tinker—and he'd took the fire with him, and left me wery cold.

"I know'd my name to be Magwitch, chrisen'd Abel. How did I know it? Much as I know'd the birds' names in the hedges to be chaffinch, sparrer, thrush. I might have thought it was all lies together, only as the birds' names come out true, I supposed mine did.

"So fur as I could find, there warn't a soul that see young Abel Magwitch, with as little on him as in him, but wot caught fright at him, and either drove him off, or took him up. I was took up, took up, took up, to that extent that I reg'larly grow'd up took up.

"This is the way it was, that when I was a ragged little creetur as much to be pitied as ever I see (not that I looked in the glass, for there warn't many insides of furnished houses known to me), I got the name of being hardened. 'This is a terrible hardened one,' they says to prison wisitors, picking out me. 'May be said to live in jails, this boy.' Then they looked at me, and I looked at them, and they measured my head, some on 'em—they had better a measured my stomach—and others on 'em giv me tracts what I couldn't read, and made me speeches what I couldn't unnerstand. They always went on agen me about the Devil. But what the devil was I to do? I must put something into my stomach, mustn't I?—Howsomever, I'm a getting low, and I know what's due. Dear boy and Pip's comrade, don't you be afeered of me being low.

"Tramping, begging, thieving, working sometimes when I could—though that warn't as often as you may think, till you put the question whether you would ha' been overready to give me work yourselves—a bit of a poacher, a bit of a labourer, a bit of a waggoner, a bit of a haymaker, a bit of a hawker, a bit of most things that don't pay and lead to trouble, I got to be a man. A deserting soldier in a Traveller's Rest, what lay hid up to the chin under a lot of taturs, learnt me to read; and a travelling Giant what signed his name at a penny a time learnt me to write. I warn't locked up as often now as formerly, but I wore out my good share of key-metal still.

"At Epsom races, a matter of over twenty year ago, I got acquainted wi' a man whose skull I'd crack wi' this poker, like the claw of a lobster, if I'd got it on this hob. His right name was Compeyson; and that's the man, dear boy, what you see me a pounding in the ditch, according to what you truly told your comrade arter I was gone last night.

"He set up fur a gentleman, this Compeyson, and he'd been to a public boarding-school and had learning. He was a smooth one to talk, and was a dab at the ways of gentlefolks. He was good-looking too. It was the night afore the great race, when I found him on the heath, in a booth that I know'd on. Him and some more was a sitting among the tables when I went in, and the landlord (which had a knowledge of me, and was a sporting one) called him out, and said, ' I think this is a man that might suit you '—meaning I was.

"Compeyson, he looks at me very noticing, and I look at him. He has a watch and a chain and a ring and a breast-pin and a handsome suit of clothes.

"'To judge from appearances, you're out of luck,' says Compeyson to me.

"'Yes, master, and I've never been in it much.' (I had come out of Kingston Jail last on a vagrancy committal. Not but what it might have been for something else; but it warn't.)

"'Luck changes,' says Compeyson, 'perhaps yours is going to change.'

"I says, 'I hope it may be so. There's room.'

"'What can you do?' says Compeyson.

"'Eat and drink,' I says; 'if you'll find the materials.'

"Compeyson laughed, looked at me again very noticing, giv me five shillings, and appointed me for next night. Same place.

"I went to Compeyson next night, same place, and Compeyson took me on to be his man and pardner. And what was Compeyson's business in which we was to go pardners? Compeyson's business was the swindling, handwriting forging, stolen bank-note passing, and such-like. All sorts of traps as Compeyson could set with his head, and keep his own legs out of and get the profits from and let another man in for, was Compeyson's business. He'd no more heart than a iron file, he was as cold as death, and he had the head of the Devil afore mentioned.

"There was another in with Compeyson, as was called Arthur—not as being so chrisen'd, but as a surname. He was in a Decline, and was a shadow to look at. Him and Compeyson had been in a bad thing with a rich lady some years afore, and they'd made a pot of money by it; but Compeyson betted and gamed, and he'd have run through the king's taxes. So, Arthur was a dying and a dying poor and with the horrors on him, and Compeyson's wife (which Compeyson kicked mostly) was a having pity on him when she could, and Compeyson was a having pity on nothing and nobody.

"I might a took warning by Arthur, but I didn't; and I won't pretend I was partick'ler—for where 'ud be the good on it, dear boy and comrade? So I begun wi' Compeyson, and a poor tool I was in his hands. Arthur lived at the top of Compeyson's house (over nigh Brentford it was), and Compeyson kept a careful account agen him for board and lodging, in case he should ever get better to work it out. But Arthur soon settled the account. The second or third time as ever I see him, he come a tearing down into Compeyson's parlour late at night, in only a flannel gown, with his hair all in a sweat, and he says to Compeyson's wife, 'Sally, she really is upstairs alonger me, now, and I can't get rid of her. She's all in white,' he says, 'wi' white flowers in her hair, and she's awful mad, and she's got a shroud hanging over her arm, and she says she'll put it on me at five in the morning.'

"Says Compeyson: 'Why, you fool, don't you know she's got a living body? And how should she be up there, without coming through the door, or in at the window, and up the stairs?'

"'I don't know how she's there,' says Arthur, shivering dreadful with the horrors, 'but she's standing in the corner at the foot of the bed, awful mad. And over where her heart's broke—you broke it!—there's drops of blood.'

"Compeyson spoke hardy, but he was always a coward.

'Go up alonger this drivelling sick man,' he says to his wife, 'and, Magwitch, lend her a hand, will you?' But he never come nigh himself.

"Compeyson's wife and me took him up to bed agen, and he raved most dreadful. 'Why look at her!' he cries out. 'She's a shaking the shroud at me! Don't you see her? Look at her eyes! Ain't it awful to see her so mad?' Next, he cries, 'She'll put it on me, and then I'm done for! Take it away from her, take it away!' And then he catched hold of us, and kep on a talking to her, and answering of her, till I half-believed I see her myself.

"Compeyson's wife, being used to him, give him some liquor to get the horrors off, and by-and-bye he quieted. 'Oh, she's gone! Has her keeper been for her?' he says. 'Yes,' says Compeyson's wife. 'Did you tell him to lock and bar her in?' 'Yes.' 'And to take that ugly thing away from her?' 'Yes, yes, all right.' 'You're a good creetur,' he says, 'don't leave me, whatever you do, and thank you!'

"He rested pretty quiet till it might want a few minutes of five, and then he starts up with a scream, and screams out, 'Here she is! She's got the shroud again. She's unfolding it. She's coming out of the corner. She's coming to the bed. Hold me, both on you—one of each side—don't let her touch me with it. Hah! She missed me that time. Don't let her throw it over my shoulders. Don't let her lift me up to get it round me. She's lifting me up. Keep me down!' Then he lifted himself up hard, and was dead.

"Compeyson took it easy as a good riddance for both sides. Him and me was soon busy, and first he swore me (being ever artful) on my own book—this here little black book, dear boy, what I swore your comrade on.

"Not to go into the things that Compeyson planned, and I done—which 'ud take a week—I'll simply say to you, dear boy, and Pip's comrade, that that man got me into such nets as made me his black slave. I was always in debt to him, always under his thumb, always a working, always a getting into danger. He was younger than me, but he'd got craft, and he'd got learning, and he overmatched me five hundred times told and no mercy. My Missis as I had the hard time wi'——Stop though! I ain't brought her in——"

He looked about him in a confused way, as if he had lost his place in the book of his remembrance; and he turned his face to the fire, and spread his hands broader on his knees, and lifted them off and put them on again.

"There ain't no need to go into it," he said, looking round once more. "The time wi' Compeyson was a'most as hard a time as ever I had; that said, all's said. Did I tell you as I was tried, alone, for misdemeanour, while with Compeyson?"

I answered, No.

"Well!" he said, "I *was*, and got convicted. As to took up on suspicion, that twice or three times in the four or five year that it lasted; but evidence was wanting. At last, me and Compeyson was both committed for felony —on a charge of putting stolen notes in circulation—and there was other charges behind. Compeyson says to me, 'Separate defences, no communication,' and that was all. And I was so miserable poor, that I sold all the clothes I had, except what hung on my back, afore I could get Jaggers.

"When we was put in the dock, I noticed first of all what a gentleman Compeyson looked, wi' his curly hair and his black clothes and his white pocket-handkercher, and what a common sort of a wretch I looked. When the prosecution opened and the evidence was put short, aforehand, I noticed how heavy it all bore on me, and how light on him. When the evidence was giv in the box, I noticed how it was always me that had come for'ard, and could be swore to, how it was always me that the money had been paid to, how it was always me that had seemed to work the thing and get the profit. But, when the defence come on, then I see the plan plainer; for, says the counsellor for Compeyson, 'My lord and gentlemen, here you has afore you, side by side, two persons as your eyes can separate wide; one, the younger, well brought up, who will be spoke to as such; one, the elder, ill brought up, who will be spoke to as such; one, the younger, seldom if ever seen in these here transactions, and only suspected; t'other, the elder, always seen in 'em and always wi' his guilt brought home. Can you doubt, if there is but one in it, which is the one, and if there is two in it, which is much the worst one?' And such-like. And when it come to character, warn't it Compeyson as had been to school, and warn't it his schoolfellows as was in this position and in that, and warn't it him as had been know'd by witnesses in such clubs and societies, and nowt to his disadvantage? And warn't it me as had been tried afore, and as had been know'd up hill and down dale in Bridewells and Lock-Ups? And when it comes to speech-making, warn't it Compeyson as could speak to 'em wi' his face dropping every now and then into his white pocket-handkercher—ah! and wi' verses in his speech, too—and warn't it me as could only say, 'Gentlemen, this man at my side is a most precious rascal'? And when the verdict come, warn't it Compeyson as was recommended to mercy on account of good character and bad company, and giving up all the information he could agen me, and warn't it me as got never a word but Guilty? And when I says to Compeyson, 'Once out of this court, I'll smash that face of yourn!' ain't it Compeyson as prays the Judge to be protected, and gets two turnkeys stood betwixt us? And when we're sentenced, ain't it him as gets seven year, and me fourteen, and ain't it him as the Judge is sorry for, because he might a done so well, and ain't it me as the Judge perceives to be a old offender of wiolent passion, likely to come to worse?"

He had worked himself into a state of great excitement, but he checked it, took two or three short breaths, swallowed as often, and stretching out his hand towards me, said, in a reassuring manner, "I ain't a going to be low, dear boy!"

He had so heated himself that he took out his handkerchief and wiped his face and head and neck and hands, before he could go on.

"I had said to Compeyson that I'd smash that face of his, and I swore Lord smash mine! to do it. We was in the same prison-ship, but I couldn't get at him for long, though I tried. At last I come behind him and hit him on the cheek to turn him round and get a smashing one at him, when I was seen and seized. The black-hole of that ship warn't a strong one, to a judge of black-holes that could swim and dive. I escaped to the shore, and I was a hiding among the graves there, envying them as was in 'em and all over, when I first see my boy!"

He regarded me with a look of affection that made him almost abhorrent to me again, though I had felt great pity for him.

"By my boy, I was giv to understand as Compeyson was out on them marshes too. Upon my soul, I half believe he escaped in his terror, to get quit of me, not knowing it was me as had got ashore. I hunted him down. I smashed his face. 'And now,' says I, 'as the worse thing I can do, caring nothing for myself, I'll drag you back.' And I'd have swum off, towing him by the hair, if it had come to that, and I'd a got him aboard without the soldiers.

"Of course he'd much the best of it to the last—his character was so good. He had escaped when he was made half-wild by me and my murderous intentions; and his punishment was light. I was put in irons, brought to trial again, and sent for life. I didn't stop for life, dear boy and Pip's comrade, being here."

He wiped himself again, as he had done before, and then slowly took his tangle of tobacco from his pocket, and plucked his pipe from his buttonhole, and slowly filled it, and began to smoke.

"Is he dead?" I asked after a silence.

"Is who dead, dear boy?"

"Compeyson."

"He hopes *I* am, if he's alive, you may be sure," with a fierce look. "I never heard no more of him."

Herbert had been writing with his pencil in the cover of a book. He softly pushed the book over to me, as Provis stood smoking with his eyes on the fire, and I read in it:

"Young Havisham's name was Arthur. Compeyson is the man who professed to be Miss Havisham's lover."

I shut the book and nodded slightly to Herbert, and put the book by; but we neither of us said anything, and both looked at Provis as he stood smoking by the fire.

CHAPTER XLIII.

WHY should I pause to ask how much of my shrinking from Provis might be traced to Estella? Why should I loiter on my road, to compare the state of mind in which I had tried to rid myself of the stain of the prison before meeting her at the coach-office, with the state of mind in which I now reflected on the abyss between Estella in her pride and beauty, and the returned transport whom I harboured? The road would be none the smoother for it, the end would be none the better for it; he would not be helped, nor I extenuated.

A new fear had been engendered in my mind by his narrative; or rather, his narrative had given form and purpose to the fear that was already there. If Compeyson were alive and should discover his return, I could hardly doubt the consequence. That Compeyson stood in mortal fear of him, neither of the two could know much better than I; and that any such man as that man had been described to be, would hesitate to release himself for good from a dreaded enemy by the safe means of becoming an informer, was scarcely to be imagined.

Never had I breathed, and never would I breathe—or so I resolved—a word of Estella to Provis. But, I said to Herbert that before I could go abroad, I must see both Estella and Miss Havisham. This was when we were left alone on the night of the day when Provis told us his story. I resolved to go out to Richmond next day, and I went.

On my presenting myself at Mrs. Brandley's, Estella's maid was called to tell me that Estella had gone into the country. Where? To Satis House, as usual. Not as usual, I said, for she had never yet gone there without me; when was she coming back? There was an air of reservation in the answer which increased my perplexity, and the answer was that her maid believed she was only coming back at all for a little while. I could make nothing of this, except that it was meant that I should make nothing of it, and I went home again in complete discomfiture.

Another night-consultation with Herbert after Provis was gone home (I always took him home, and always looked well about me), led us to the conclusion that nothing should be said about going abroad until I came back from Miss Havisham's. In the meantime Herbert and I were to consider separately what it would be best to say; whether we should devise any pretence of being afraid that he was under suspicious observation; or whether I, who had never yet been abroad, should propose an expedition. We both knew that I had but to propose anything, and he would consent. We agreed that his remaining many days in his present hazard was not to be thought of.

Next day, I had the meanness to feign that I was under a binding promise to go down to Joe; but I was capable of almost any meanness towards Joe or his name. Provis was to be strictly careful while I was gone, and Herbert was to take the charge of him that I had taken. I was to be absent only one night, and, on my return, the gratification of his impatience for my starting as a gentleman on a greater scale, was to be begun. It occurred to me then, and as I afterwards found to Herbert also, that he might be best got away across the water, on that pretence—as, to make purchases, or the like.

Having thus cleared the way for my expedition to Miss Havisham's, I set off by the early morning coach before it was yet light, and was out in the open country-road when the day came creeping on, halting and whimpering and shivering, and wrapped in patches of cloud and rags of mist, like a beggar. When we drove up to the Blue Boar after a drizzly ride, whom should I see come out under the gateway, toothpick in hand, to look at the coach, but Bentley Drummle!

As he pretended not to see me, I pretended not to see him. It was a very lame pretence on both sides; the lamer, because we both went into the coffee-room, where he had just finished his breakfast, and where I had ordered mine. It was poisonous to me to see him in the town, for I very well knew why he had come there.

Pretending to read a smeary newspaper long out of date, which had nothing half so legible in its local news, as the foreign matter of coffee, pickles, fish-sauces, gravy, melted butter, and wine, with which it was sprinkled all over, as if it had taken the measles in a highly irregular form, I sat at my table while he stood before the fire. By degrees it became an enormous injury to me that he stood before the fire. And I got up, determined to have my share of it. I had to put my hands behind his legs for the poker when I went to the fireplace to stir the fire, but still pretended not to know him.

"Is this a cut?" said Mr. Drummle.

"Oh?" said I, poker in hand; "it's you, is it? How do you do? I was wondering who it was, who kept the fire off."

With that I poked tremendously, and having done so, planted myself side by side with Mr. Drummle, my shoulders squared, and my back to the fire.

"You have just come down?" said Mr. Drummle, edging me a little away with his shoulder.

"Yes," said I, edging *him* a little away with *my* shoulder.

"Beastly place," said Drummle—"Your part of the country, I think?"

"Yes," I assented. "I am told it's very like your Shropshire."

"Not in the least like it," said Drummle.

Here Mr. Drummle looked at his boots and I looked at mine, and then Mr. Drummle looked at my boots and I looked at his.

"Have you been here long?" I asked, determined not to yield an inch of the fire.

"Long enough to be tired of it," returned Drummle, pretending to yawn, but equally determined.

"Do you stay here long?"

"Can't say," answered Mr. Drummle. "Do you?"

"Can't say," said I.

I felt here, through a tingling in my blood, that if Mr. Drummle's shoulder had claimed another hair's breadth of room, I should have jerked him into the window; equally, that if my shoulder had urged a similar claim, Mr. Drummle would have jerked me into the nearest box. He whistled a little. So did I.

"Large tract of marshes about here, I believe?" said Drummle.

"Yes. What of that?" said I.

Mr. Drummle looked at me, and then at my boots, and then said, "Oh!" and laughed.

"Are you amused, Mr. Drummle?"

"No," said he, "not particularly. I am going out for a ride in the saddle. I mean to explore those marshes for amusement. Out-of-the-way villages there, they tell me. Curious little public-houses — and smithies — and that. Waiter!"

"Yes, sir."

"Is that horse of mine ready?"

"Brought round to the door, sir."

"I say. Look here, you sir. The lady won't ride to-day; the weather won't do."

"Very good, sir."

"And I don't dine, because I am going to dine at the lady's."

"Very good, sir."

Then, Drummle glanced at me, with an insolent triumph on his great-jowled face that cut me to the heart, dull as he was, and so exasperated me, that I felt inclined to take him in my arms (as the robber in the story-book is said to have taken the old lady) and seat him on the fire.

One thing was manifest to both of us, and that was, that until relief came, neither of us could relinquish the fire. There we stood, well squared up before it, shoulder to shoulder and foot to foot, with our hands behind us, not budging an inch. The horse was visible outside in the drizzle at the door, my breakfast was put on table, Drummle's was cleared away, the waiter invited me to begin, I nodded, we both stood our ground.

"Have you been to the Grove since?" said Drummle.

"No," said I, "I had quite enough of the Finches the last time I was there."

"Was that when we had the difference of opinion?"

"Yes," I replied, very shortly.

"Come, come! they let you off easily enough," sneered Drummle. "You shouldn't have lost your temper."

"Mr. Drummle," said I, "you are not competent to give

advice on that subject. When I lose my temper (not that I admit having done so on that occasion), I don't throw glasses."

"I do," said Drummle.

After glancing at him once or twice, in an increased state of smouldering ferocity, I said:

"Mr. Drummle, I did not seek this conversation, and I don't think it's an agreeable one."

"I am sure it's not," said he, superciliously over his shoulder, "I don't think anything about it."

"And therefore," I went on, "with your leave, I will suggest that we hold no kind of communication in future."

"Quite my opinion," said Drummle, "and what I should have suggested myself, or done—more likely—without suggesting. But don't lose your temper. Haven't you lost enough without that?"

"What do you mean, sir?"

"Waiter," said Drummle, by way of answering me.

The waiter reappeared.

"Look here, you sir. You quite understand that the young lady don't ride to-day, and that I dine at the young lady's?"

"Quite so, sir!"

When the waiter had felt my fast cooling tea-pot with the palm of his hand, and looked imploringly at me, and had gone out, Drummle, careful not to move the shoulder next me, took a cigar from his pocket and bit the end off, but showed no sign of stirring. Choking and boiling as I was, I felt that we could not go a word further, without introducing Estella's name, which I could not endure to hear him utter; and therefore I looked stonily at the opposite wall, as if there were no one present, and forced myself to silence. How long we might have remained in this ridiculous position it is impossible to say, but for the incursion of three thriving farmers—laid on by the waiter, I think—who came into the coffee-room unbuttoning their great-coats and rubbing their hands, and before whom, as they charged at the fire, we were obliged to give way.

I saw him through the window, seizing his horse's mane, and mounting in his blundering brutal manner, and sidling and backing away. I thought he was gone, when he came back, calling for a light for the cigar in his mouth, which he had forgotten. A man in a dust-coloured dress appeared with what was wanted—I could not have said from where: whether from the inn yard, or the street, or where not—and as Drummle leaned down from his saddle and lighted his cigar and laughed, with a jerk of his head towards the coffee-room windows, the slouching shoulders, and ragged hair, of this man, whose back was towards me, reminded me of Orlick.

Too heavily out of sorts to care much at the time whether it were he or no, or after all to touch the breakfast, I washed the weather and the journey from my face and hands, and went out to the memorable old house that it would have been so much the better for me never to have entered, never to have seen.

CHAPTER XLIV.

In the room where the dressing-table stood, and where the wax candles burnt on the wall, I found Miss Havisham and Estella; Miss Havisham seated on a settee near the fire, and Estella on a cushion at her feet. Estella was knitting, and Miss Havisham was looking on. They both raised their eyes as I went in, and both saw an alteration in me. I derived that from the look they interchanged.

"And what wind," said Miss Havisham, "blows you here, Pip?"

Though she looked steadily at me, I saw that she was rather confused. Estella, pausing a moment in her knitting with her eyes upon me, and then going on, I fancied that I read in the action of her fingers, as plainly as if she had told me in the dumb alphabet, that she perceived I had discovered my real benefactor.

"Miss Havisham," said I, "I went to Richmond yesterday, to speak to Estella; and finding that some wind had blown *her* here, I followed."

Miss Havisham motioning to me for the third or fourth time to sit down, I took the chair by the dressing-table, which I had often seen her occupy. With all that ruin at my feet and about me, it seemed a natural place for me, that day.

"What I had to say to Estella, Miss Havisham, I will say before you, presently—in a few moments. It will not surprise you, it will not displease you. I am as unhappy as you can ever have meant me to be."

Miss Havisham continued to look steadily at me. I could see in the action of Estella's fingers as they worked, that she attended to what I said: but she did not look up.

"I have found out who my patron is. It is not a fortunate discovery, and is not likely ever to enrich me in reputation, station, fortune, anything. There are reasons why I must say no more of that. It is not my secret, but another's."

As I was silent for a while, looking at Estella and considering how to go on, Miss Havisham repeated, "It is not your secret, but another's. Well?"

"When you first caused me to be brought here, Miss Havisham; when I belonged to the village over yonder, that I wish I had never left; I suppose I did really come here, as any other chance boy might have come—as a kind of servant, to gratify a want or a whim, and to be paid for it?"

"Ay, Pip," replied Miss Havisham, steadily nodding her head; "you did."

"And that Mr. Jaggers——"

"Mr. Jaggers," said Miss Havisham, taking me up in a firm tone, "had nothing to do with it, and knew nothing of it. His being my lawyer, and his being the lawyer of your patron, is a coincidence. He holds the same relation towards numbers of people, and it might easily arise. Be that as it may, it did arise, and was not brought about by any one."

Any one might have seen in her haggard face that there was no suppression or evasion so far.

"But when I fell into the mistake I have so long remained in, at least you led me on?" said I.

"Yes," she returned, again nodding steadily, "I let you go on."

"Was that kind?"

"Who am I," cried Miss Havisham, striking her stick upon the floor and flashing into wrath so suddenly that Estella glanced up at her in surprise, "who am I, for God's sake, that I should be kind?"

It was a weak complaint to have made, and I had not meant to make it. I told her so, as she sat brooding over this outburst.

"Well, well, well!" she said. "What else?"

"I was liberally paid for my old attendance here," I said, to soothe her, "in being apprenticed, and I have asked these questions only for my own information. What follows has another (and I hope more disinterested) purpose. In humouring my mistake, Miss Havisham, you punished—practised on—perhaps you will supply whatever term expresses your intention, without offence—your self-seeking relations?"

"I did. Why, they would have it so! So would you. What has been my history, that I should be at the pains of entreating either them or you not to have it so! You made your own snares. I never made them."

Waiting until she was quiet again—for this, too, flashed out of her in a wild and sudden way—I went on.

"I have been thrown among one family of your relations, Miss Havisham, and have been constantly among them since I went to London. I know them to have been as honestly under my delusion as I myself. And I should be false and base if I did not tell you, whether it is acceptable to you or no, and whether you are inclined to give credence to it or no, that you deeply wrong both Mr. Matthew Pocket and his son Herbert, if you suppose them to be otherwise than generous, upright, open, and incapable of anything designing or mean."

"They are your friends," said Miss Havisham.

"They made themselves my friends," said I, "when they supposed me to have superseded them; and when Sarah Pocket, Miss Georgiana, and Mistress Camilla, were not my friends, I think."

This contrasting of them with the rest seemed, I was glad to see, to do them good with her. She looked at me keenly for a little while, and then said quietly:

"What do you want for them?"

"Only," said I, "that you would not confound them with the others. They may be of the same blood, but, believe me, they are not of the same nature."

Still looking at me keenly, Miss Havisham repeated:

"What do you want for them?"

"I am not so cunning, you see," I said in answer, conscious that I reddened a little, "as that I could hide from you, even if I desired, that I do want something. Miss Havisham, if you could spare the money to do my friend Herbert a lasting service in life, but which from the nature of the case must be done without his knowledge, I could show you how."

"Why must it be done without his knowledge?" she asked, settling her hands upon her stick, that she might regard me the more attentively.

"Because," said I, "I began the service myself, more than two years ago, without his knowledge, and I don't want to be betrayed. Why I fail in my ability to finish it, I cannot explain. It is a part of the secret which is another person's and not mine."

She gradually withdrew her eyes from me, and turned them on the fire. After watching it for what appeared in the silence and by the light of the slowly wasting candles to be a long time, she was roused by the collapse of some of the red coals, and looked towards me again—at first, vacantly—then, with a gradually concentrating attention. All this time, Estella knitted on. When Miss Havisham had fixed her attention on me, she said, speaking as if there had been no lapse in our dialogue:

"What else?"

"Estella," said I, turning to her now, and trying to command my trembling voice, "you know I love you. You know that I have loved you long and dearly."

She raised her eyes to my face, on being thus addressed, and her fingers plied their work, and she looked at me with an unmoved countenance. I saw that Miss Havisham glanced from me to her, and from her to me.

"I should have said this sooner, but for my long mistake. It induced me to hope that Miss Havisham meant us for one another. While I thought you could not help yourself, as it were, I refrained from saying it. But I must say it now."

Preserving her unmoved countenance, and with her fingers still going, Estella shook her head.

"I know," said I, in answer to that action; "I know. I have no hope that I shall ever call you mine, Estella. I am ignorant what may become of me very soon, how poor I may be, or where I may go. Still, I love you. I have loved you ever since I first saw you in this house."

Looking at me perfectly unmoved and with her fingers busy, she shook her head again.

"It would have been cruel in Miss Havisham, horribly cruel, to practise on the susceptibility of a poor boy, and to torture me through all these years with a vain hope and an idle pursuit, if she had reflected on the gravity of what she did. But I think she did not. I think that in the endurance of her own trial, she forgot mine, Estella."

I saw Miss Havisham put her hand to her heart and hold it there, as she sat looking by turns at Estella and at me.

"It seems," said Estella, very calmly, "that there are sentiments, fancies—I don't know how to call them—which I am not able to comprehend. When you say you love me, I know what you mean, as a form of word; but nothing more. You address nothing in my breast, you touch nothing there. I don't care for what you say at all. I have tried to warn you of this; now, have I not?"

I said in a miserable manner, "Yes."

"Yes. But you would not be warned, for you thought I did not mean it. Now, did you not think so?"

"I thought and hoped you could not mean it. You, so young, untried, and beautiful, Estella! Surely it is not in Nature."

"It is in my nature," she returned. And then she added, with a stress upon the words, "It is in the nature formed within me. I make a great difference between you and all other people when I say so much. I can do no more."

"Is it not true," said I, "that Bentley Drummle is in town here, and pursuing you?"

"It is quite true," she replied, referring to him with the indifference of utter contempt.

"That you encourage him, and ride out with him, and that he dines with you this very day?"

She seemed a little surprised that I should know it, but again replied, "Quite true."

"You cannot love him, Estella?"

Her fingers stopped for the first time, as she retorted rather angrily, "What have I told you? Do you still think, in spite of it, that I do not mean what I say?"

"You would never marry him, Estella?"

She looked towards Miss Havisham, and considered for a moment with her work in her hands. Then she said, "Why not tell you the truth? I am going to be married to him."

I dropped my face into my hands, but was able to control myself better than I could have expected, considering what agony it gave me to hear her say those words. When I raised my face again, there was such a ghastly look upon Miss Havisham's, that it impressed me, even in my passionate hurry and grief.

"Estella, dearest, dearest Estella, do not let Miss Havisham lead you into this fatal step. Put me aside for ever —you have done so, I well know—but bestow yourself on some worthier person than Drummle. Miss Havisham gives you to him, as the greatest slight and injury that could be done to the many far better men who admire you, and to the few who truly love you. Among those few there may be one who loves you even as dearly, though he has not loved you as long, as I. Take him, and I can bear it better for your sake!"

My earnestness awoke a wonder in her that seemed as if it would have been touched with compassion, if she could have rendered me at all intelligible to her own mind.

"I am going," she said again, in a gentler voice, "to be married to him. The preparations for my marriage are making, and I shall be married soon. Why do you injuriously introduce the name of my mother by adoption? It is my own act."

"Your own act, Estella, to fling yourself away upon a brute?"

"On whom should I fling myself away?" she retorted, with a smile. "Should I fling myself away upon the man who would the soonest feel (if people do feel such things) that I took nothing to him? There! It is done. I shall do well enough, and so will my husband. As to leading me into what you call this fatal step, Miss Havisham would have had me wait, and not marry yet; but I am tired of the life I have led, which has very few charms for me, and I am willing enough to change it. Say no more. We shall never understand each other."

"Such a mean brute, such a stupid brute!" I urged in despair.

"Don't be afraid of my being a blessing to him," said Estella; "I shall not be that. Come! Here is my hand. Do we part on this, you visionary boy——or man?"

"O Estella!" I answered, as my bitter tears fell fast on her hand, do what I would to restrain them; "even if I remained in England and could hold my head up with the rest, how could I see you Drummle's wife?"

"Nonsense," she returned, "nonsense. This will pass in no time."

"Never, Estella!"

"You will get me out of your thoughts in a week."

"Out of my thoughts! You are part of my existence, part of myself. You have been in every line I have ever read, since I first came here, the rough common boy whose poor heart you wounded even then. You have been in every prospect I have ever seen since—on the river, on the sails of the ships, on the marshes, in the clouds, in the light, in the darkness, in the wind, in the woods, in the sea, in the streets. You have been the embodiment of every graceful fancy that my mind has ever become acquainted with. The stones of which the strongest London buildings are made, are not more real, or more impossible to be displaced by your hands, than your presence and influence have been to me, there and everywhere, and will be. Estella, to the last hour of my life, you cannot choose but remain part of my character, part of the little good in me, part of the evil. But, in this separation I associate you only with the good, and I will faithfully hold you to that always, for you must have done me far more good than harm, let me feel now what sharp distress I may. O God bless you, God forgive you!"

In what ecstasy of unhappiness I got these broken words out of myself, I don't know. The rhapsody welled up within me, like blood from an inward wound, and gushed out. I held her hand to my lips some lingering moments, and so I left her. But ever afterwards, I remembered—and soon afterwards with stronger reason—that while Estella looked at me merely with incredulous wonder, the spectral figure of Miss Havisham, her hand still covering her heart, seemed all resolved into a ghastly stare of pity and remorse.

All done, all gone! So much was done and gone, that when I went out at the gate, the light of day seemed of a darker colour than when I went in. For a while, I hid myself among some lanes and bye-paths, and then struck off to walk all the way to London. For, I had by that time come to myself so far, as to consider that I could not go back to the inn and see Drummle there; that I could not bear to sit upon the coach and be spoken to; that I could do nothing half so good for myself as tire myself out.

It was past midnight when I crossed London Bridge. Pursuing the narrow intricacies of the streets which at that time tended westward near the Middlesex shore of the river, my readiest access to the Temple was close by the river-side, through Whitefriars. I was not expected till to-morrow, but I had my keys, and, if Herbert were gone to bed, could get to bed myself without disturbing him.

As it seldom happened that I came in at that Whitefriars gate after the Temple was closed, and as I was very muddy and weary, I did not take it ill that the night-porter examined me with much attention as he held the gate a little way open for me to pass in. To help his memory I mentioned my name.

"I was not quite sure, sir, but I thought so. Here's a note, sir. The messenger that brought it, said would you be so good as read it by my lantern?"

Much surprised by the request, I took the note. It was directed to Philip Pip, Esquire, and on the top of the superscription were the words, "PLEASE READ THIS HERE." I opened it, the watchman holding up his light, and read inside, in Wemmick's writing:

"DON'T GO HOME."

CHAPTER XLV.

TURNING from the Temple gate as soon as I had read the warning, I made the best of my way to Fleet-street, and there got a late hackney chariot and drove to the Hummums in Covent Garden. In those times a bed was always to be got there at any hour of the night, and the chamberlain, letting me in at his ready wicket, lighted the candle next in order on his shelf, and showed me straight into the bedroom next in order on his list. It was a sort of vault on the ground floor at the back, with a despotic monster of a four-post bedstead in it, straddling over the whole place, putting one of his arbitrary legs into the fireplace, and another into the doorway, and squeezing the wretched little washing-stand in quite a Divinely Righteous manner.

As I had asked for a night-light, the chamberlain had brought me in, before he left me, the good old constitutional rush-light of those virtuous days—an object like the ghost of a walking-cane, which instantly broke its back if it were touched, which nothing could ever be lighted at, and which was placed in solitary confinement at the bottom of a high tin tower, perforated with round holes that made a staringly wide-awake pattern on the walls. When I had got into bed, and lay there, footsore, weary, and wretched, I found that I could no more close my own eyes than I could close the eyes of this foolish Argus. And thus, in the gloom and death of night, we stared at one another.

What a doleful night! How anxious, how dismal, how long! There was an inhospitable smell in the room, of cold soot and hot dust; and, as I looked up into the corners of the tester over my head, I thought what a number of blue-bottle flies from the butcher's, and earwigs from the market, and grubs from the country, must be holding on up there, lying by for next summer. This led me to speculate whether any of them ever tumbled down, and then I fancied that I felt light falls on my face—a disagreeable turn of thought, suggesting other and more objectionable approaches up my back. When I had lain awake a little while, those extraordinary voices with which silence teems, began to make themselves audible. The closet whispered, the fireplace sighed, the little washing-stand ticked, and one guitar-string played occasionally in the chest of drawers. At about the same time, the eyes on the wall acquired a new expression, and in every one of those staring rounds I saw written, Don't go Home.

Whatever night-fancies and night-noises crowded on me, they never warded off this Don't go Home. It plaited itself into whatever I thought of, as a bodily pain would have done. Not long before, I had read in the newspapers how a gentleman unknown had come to the Hummums in the night, and had gone to bed, and had destroyed himself, and had been found in the morning weltering in blood. It came into my head that he must have occupied this very vault of mine, and I got out of bed to assure myself that there were no red marks about; then opened the door to look out into the passages, and cheer myself with the companionship of a distant light, near which I knew the chamberlain to be dozing. But all this time, why I was not to go home, and what had happened at home, and whether I should go home, and whether Provis was safe at home, were questions occupying my mind so busily, that one might have supposed there could be no more room in it for any other theme. Even when I thought of Estella, and how we had parted that day for ever, and when I recalled all the circumstances of our parting, and all her looks and tones, and the action of her fingers while she knitted—even then I was pursuing, here and there and everywhere, the caution Don't go home. When at last I dozed, in sheer exhaustion of mind and body, it became a vast shadowy verb which I had to conjugate, Imperative mood, present tense: Do not thou go home, let him not go home, let us not go home, do not ye or you go home, let not them go home. Then, potentially: I may not and I cannot go home; and I might not, could not, would not, and should not go home; until I felt that I was going distracted, and rolled over on the pillow, and looked at the staring rounds upon the wall again.

I had left directions that I was to be called at seven; for it was plain that I must see Wemmick before seeing any one else, and equally plain that this was a case in which his Walworth sentiments, only, could be taken. It was a relief to get out of the room where the night had been so miserable, and I needed no second knocking at the door to startle me from my uneasy bed.

The Castle battlements arose upon my view at eight o'clock. The little servant happening to be entering the fortress with two hot rolls, I passed through the postern and crossed the drawbridge, in her company, and so came without announcement into the presence of Wemmick as he was making tea for himself and the Aged. An open door afforded a perspective view of the Aged in bed.

"Halloa, Mr. Pip!" said Wemmick. "You did come home, then?"

"Yes," I returned; "but I didn't go home."

"That's all right," said he, rubbing his hands. "I left a note for you at each of the Temple gates, on the chance. Which gate did you come to?"

I told him.

"I'll go round to the others in the course of the day and destroy the notes," said Wemmick; "it's a good rule never to leave documentary evidence if you can help it, because you don't know when it may be put in. I'm going to take a liberty with you—Would you mind toasting this sausage for the Aged P.?"

I said I should be delighted to do it.

"Then you can go about your work, Mary Anne," said Wemmick to the little servant; "which leaves us to ourselves, don't you see, Mr. Pip?" he added, winking, as she disappeared.

I thanked him for his friendship and caution, and our discourse proceeded in a low tone, while I toasted the Aged's sausage and he buttered the crumb of the Aged's roll.

"Now, Mr. Pip, you know," said Wemmick, "you and I understand one another. We are in our private and personal capacities, and we have been engaged in a confidential transaction before to-day. Official sentiments are one thing. We are extra official."

I cordially assented. I was so very nervous, that I had already lighted the Aged's sausage like a torch, and been obliged to blow it out.

"I accidentally heard, yesterday morning," said Wemmick, "being in a certain place where I once took you—even between you and me, it's as well not to mention names when avoidable——"

"Much better not," said I. "I understand you."

"I heard there by chance, yesterday morning," said Wemmick, "that a certain person not altogether of uncolonial pursuits, and not unpossessed of portable property—I don't know who it may really be—we won't name this person——"

"Not necessary," said I.

"—had made some little stir in a certain part of the world where a good many people go, not always in gratification of their own inclinations, and not quite irrespective of the government expense——"

In watching his face, I made quite a firework of the Aged's sausage, and greatly discomposed both my own attention and Wemmick's; for which I apologised.

"—by disappearing from such place, and being no more heard of thereabouts. From which," said Wemmick, "conjectures had been raised and theories formed. I also heard that you at your chambers in Garden-court, Temple, had been watched. and might be watched again."

"By whom?" said I.

"I wouldn't go into that," said Wemmick, evasively, "it might clash with official responsibilities. I heard it, as I have in my time heard other curious things in the same place. I don't tell it you on information received. I heard it."

He took the toasting-fork and sausage from me as he spoke, and set forth the Aged's breakfast neatly on a little tray. Previous to placing it before him, he went into the Aged's room with a clean white cloth, and tied the same under the old gentleman's chin, and propped him up, and put his nightcap on one side, and gave him quite a rakish air. Then he placed his breakfast before him with great care, and said, "All right, ain't you, Aged P.?" To which the cheerful Aged replied, "All right, John, my boy, all right!" As there seemed to be a tacit understanding that the Aged was not in a presentable state, and was therefore to be considered invisible, I made a pretence of being in complete ignorance of these proceedings

"This watching of me at my chambers (which I have once had reason to suspect)," I said to Wemmick when he came back, "is inseparable from the person to whom you have adverted; is it?"

Wemmick looked very serious. "I couldn't undertake to say that, of my own knowledge. I mean, I couldn't undertake to say it was at first. But it either is, or it will be, or it's in great danger of being."

As I saw that he was restrained by fealty to Little Britain from saying as much as he could, and as I knew with thankfulness to him how far out of his way he went to say what he did, I could not press him. But I told him, after a little meditation over the fire, that I would like to ask him a question, subject to his answering or not answering, as he deemed right, and sure that his course would be right He paused in his breakfast, and crossing his arms, and pinching his shirt-sleeves (his notion of indoor comfort was to sit without any coat), he nodded to me once, to put my question.

"You have heard of a man of bad character, whose true name is Compeyson?"

He answered with one other nod.

"Is he living?"

One other nod.

"Is he in London?"

He gave me one other nod, compressed the post-office exceedingly, gave me one last nod, and went on with his breakfast.

"Now," said Wemmick, "questioning being over;" which he emphasised and repeated for my guidance; "I come to what I did, after hearing what I heard. I went to Garden-court to find you; not finding you, I went to Clarriker's to find Mr. Herbert."

"And him you found?" said I, with great anxiety.

"And him I found. Without mentioning any names or going into any details, I gave him to understand that if he was aware of anybody—Tom, Jack, or Richard—being about the chambers, or about the immediate neighbourhood, he had better get Tom, Jack, or Richard, out of the way while you were out of the way."

"He would be greatly puzzled what to do?"

"He *was* puzzled what to do; not the less, because I gave him my opinion that it was not safe to try to get Tom, Jack, or Richard, too far out of the way at present. Mr. Pip, I'll tell you something. Under existing circumstances there is no place like a great city when you are once in it. Don't break cover too soon. Lie close. Wait till things slacken, before you try the open, even for foreign air."

I thanked him for his valuable advice, and asked him

what Herbert had done?

"Mr. Herbert," said Wemmick, "after being all of a heap for half an hour, struck out a plan. He mentioned to me as a secret, that he is courting a young lady who has, as no doubt you are aware, a bedridden Pa. Which Pa, having been in the Purser line of life, lies abed in a bow-window where he can see the ships sail up and down the river. You are acquainted with the young lady, most probably?"

"Not personally," said I.

The truth was, that she had objected to me as an expensive companion who did Herbert no good, and that, when Herbert had first proposed to present me to her, she had received the proposal with such very moderate warmth, that Herbert had felt himself obliged to confide the state of the case to me, with a view to the lapse of a little time before I made her acquaintance. When I had begun to advance Herbert's prospects by stealth, I had been able to bear this with cheerful philosophy; he and his affianced, for their part, had naturally not been very anxious to introduce a third person into their interviews; and thus, although I was assured that I had risen in Clara's esteem, and although the young lady and I had long regularly interchanged messages and remembrances by Herbert, I had never seen her. However, I did not trouble Wemmick with those particulars.

"The house with the bow-window," said Wemmick, "being all of it by the river-side, down the Pool there between Limehouse and Greenwich, and being kept, it seems, by a very respectable widow, who has a furnished upper floor to let, Mr. Herbert put it to me, what did I think of that as a temporary tenement for Tom, Jack, or Richard? Now, I thought very well of it, for three reasons I'll give you. That is to say. Firstly. It's altogether out of all your beats, and is well away from the usual heap of streets great and small. Secondly. Without going near it yourself, you could always hear of the safety of Tom, Jack, or Richard, through Mr. Herbert. Thirdly. After a while and when it might be prudent, if you should want to slip Tom, Jack, or Richard, on board a foreign packet-boat, there he is—ready."

Much comforted by these considerations, I thanked Wemmick again and again, and begged him to proceed.

"Well, sir! Mr. Herbert threw himself into the business with a will, and by nine o'clock last night he housed Tom, Jack, or Richard—whichever it may be—you and I don't want to know—quite successfully. At the old lodgings it was understood that he was summoned to Dover, and in fact he was taken down the Dover road and cornered out of it. Now, another great advantage of all this is, that it was done without you, and when, if any one was concerning himself about your movements, you must be known to be ever so many miles off, and quite otherwise engaged. This diverts suspicion and confuses it; and for the same reason I recommended that even if you came back last night, you should not go home. It brings in more confusion, and you want confusion."

Wemmick, having finished his breakfast, here looked at his watch, and began to get his coat on.

"And now, Mr. Pip," said he, with his hands still in the sleeves, "I have probably done the most I can do; but if I can ever do more—from a Walworth point of view, and in a strictly private and personal capacity—I shall be glad to do it. Here's the address. There can be no harm in your going here to-night and seeing for yourself that all is well with Tom, Jack, or Richard, before you go home—which is another reason for your not going home last night. But after you have gone home, don't go back here. You are very welcome, I am sure, Mr. Pip;" his hands were now out of his sleeves, and I was shaking them; "and let me finally impress one important point upon you." He laid his hands upon my shoulders, and added in a solemn whisper: "Avail yourself of this evening to lay hold of his portable property. You don't know what may happen to him. Don't let anything happen to the portable property."

Quite despairing of making my mind clear to Wemmick on this point, I forbore to try.

"Time's up," said Wemmick, "and I must be off. If you had nothing more pressing to do than to keep here till dark, that's what I should advise. You look very much worried, and it would do you good to have a perfectly quiet day with the Aged—he'll be up presently—and a little bit of——you remember the pig?"

"Of course," said I.

"Well; and a little bit of *him*. That sausage you toasted was his, and he was in all respects a first-rater. Do try him, if it is only for old acquaintance' sake. Good bye, Aged Parent!" in a cheery shout.

"All right, John; all right, my boy!" piped the old man from within.

I soon fell asleep before Wemmick's fire, and the Aged and I enjoyed one another's society by falling asleep before it more or less all day. We had loin of pork for dinner, and greens grown on the estate, and I nodded at the Aged with a good intention whenever I failed to do it drowsily. When it was quite dark, I left the Aged preparing the fire for toast; and I inferred from the number of tea-cups, as well as from his glances at the two little doors in the wall, that Miss Skiffins was expected.

CHAPTER XLVI.

Eight o'clock had struck before I got into the air that was scented, not disagreeably, by the chips and shavings of the longshore boat-builders, and mast, oar, and block makers. All that water-side region of the upper and lower Pool below Bridge, was unknown ground to me, and when I struck down by the river, I found that the spot I wanted was not where I had supposed it to be, and was anything but easy to find. It was called Mill Pond Bank, Chinks's Basin; and I had no other guide to Chinks's Basin than the Old Green Copper Rope-Walk.

It matters not what stranded ships repairing in dry docks I lost myself among, what old hulls of ships in course of being knocked to pieces, what ooze and slime and other dregs of tide, what yards of ship-builders and ship-breakers, what rusty anchors blindly biting into the ground though for years off duty, what mountainous country of accumulated casks and timber, how many rope-walks that were not the Old Green Copper. After several times falling short of my destination and as often overshooting it, I came unexpectedly round a corner, upon Mill Pond Bank. It was a fresh kind of place, all circumstances considered, where the wind from the river had room to turn itself round; and there were two or three trees in it, and there

was the stump of a ruined windmill, and there was the Old Green Copper Rope-Walk—whose long and narrow vista I could trace in the moonlight, along a series of wooden frames set in the ground, that looked like superannuated haymaking-rakes which had grown old and lost most of their teeth.

Selecting from the few queer houses upon Mill Pond Bank, a house with a wooden front and three stories of bow-window (not bay-window, which is another thing), I looked at the plate upon the door, and read there Mrs. Whimple. That being the name I wanted, I knocked, and an elderly woman of a pleasant and thriving appearance responded. She was immediately deposed, however, by Herbert, who silently led me into the parlour and shut the door. It was an odd sensation to see his very familiar face established quite at home in that very unfamiliar room and region; and I found myself looking at him, much as I looked at the corner cupboard with the glass and china, the shells upon the chimney-piece, and the coloured engravings on the wall, representing the death of Captain Cook, a ship-launch, and his Majesty King George the Third in a state coachman's wig, leather breeches, and top-boots, on the terrace at Windsor.

"All is well, Handel," said Herbert, "and he is quite satisfied, though eager to see you. My dear girl is with her father; and if you'll wait till she comes down, I'll make you known to her, and then we'll go upstairs.——*That's* her father"

I had become aware of an alarming growling overhead, and had probably expressed the fact in my countenance.

"I am afraid he is a sad old rascal," said Herbert, smiling, "but I have never seen him. Don't you smell rum? He is always at it."

"At rum?" said I.

"Yes," returned Herbert, "and you may suppose how mild it makes his gout. He persists, too, in keeping all the provisions upstairs in his room, and serving them out. He keeps them on shelves over his head, and *will* weigh them all. His room must be like a chandler's shop."

While he thus spoke, the growling noise became a prolonged roar, and then died away.

"What else can be the consequence," said Herbert, in explanation, "if he *will* cut the cheese? A man with the gout in his right hand—and everywhere else—can't expect to get through a Double Gloucester without hurting himself."

He seemed to have hurt himself very much, for he gave another furious roar.

"To have Provis for an upper lodger is quite a godsend to Mrs. Whimple," said Herbert, "for of course people in general won't stand that noise. A curious place, Handel; isn't it?"

It was a curious place, indeed; but remarkably well kept and clean.

"Mrs. Whimple," said Herbert, when I told him so, "is the best of housewives, and I really do not know what my Clara would do without her motherly help. For, Clara has no mother of her own, Handel, and no relation in the world but old Gruffandgrim."

"Surely that's not his name, Herbert?"

"No, no," said Herbert, "that's my name for him. His name is Mr. Barley. But what a blessing it is for the son of my father and mother, to love a girl who has no relations, and who can never bother herself, or anybody else, about her family?"

Herbert had told me on former occasions, and now reminded me, that he first knew Miss Clara Barley when she was completing her education at an establishment at Hammersmith, and that on her being recalled home to nurse her father, he and she had confided their affection to the motherly Mrs. Whimple, by whom it had been fostered and regulated with equal kindness and discretion ever since. It was understood that nothing of a tender nature could possibly be confided to Old Barley, by reason of his being totally unequal to the consideration of any subject more psychological than Gout, Rum, and Purser's stores.

As we were thus conversing in a low tone while Old Barley's sustained growl vibrated in the beam that crossed the ceiling, the room door opened, and a very pretty, slight, dark-eyed girl of twenty or so, came in with a basket in her hand: whom Herbert tenderly relieved of the basket, and presented blushing, as "Clara." She really was a most charming girl, and might have passed for a captive fairy, whom that truculent Ogre, Old Barley, had pressed into his service.

"Look here," said Herbert, showing me the basket, with a compassionate and tender smile after we had talked a little; "here's poor Clara's supper, served out every night. Here's her allowance of bread, and here's her slice of cheese, and here's her rum—which I drink. This is Mr. Barley's breakfast for to-morrow, served out to be cooked. Two mutton chops, three potatoes, some split peas, a little flour, two ounces of butter, a pinch of salt, and all this black pepper. It's stewed up together, and taken hot, and it's a nice thing for the gout, I should think!"

There was something so natural and winning in Clara's resigned way of looking at these stores in detail, as Herbert pointed them out,—something so confiding, loving and innocent, in her modest manner of yielding herself to Herbert's embracing arm—and something so gentle in her, so much needing protection on Mill Pond Bank, by Chinks's Basin, and the Old Green Copper Rope-Walk, with Old Barley growling in the beam—that I would not have undone the engagement between her and Herbert, for all the money in the pocket-book I had never opened.

I was looking at her with pleasure and admiration, when suddenly the growl swelled into a roar again, and a frightful bumping noise was heard above, as if a giant with a wooden leg were trying to bore it through the ceiling to come at us. Upon this Clara said to Herbert, "Papa wants me, darling!" and ran away.

"There is an unconscionable old shark for you!" said Herbert. "What do you suppose he wants now, Handel?"

"I don't know," said I. "Something to drink?"

"That's it!" cried Herbert, as if I had made a guess of extraordinary merit. "He keeps his grog ready-mixed in a little tub on the table. Wait a moment, and you'll hear Clara lift him up to take some.—There he goes!" Another roar, with a prolonged shake at the end. "Now," said Herbert, as it was succeeded by silence, "he's drinking. Now," said Herbert, as the growl resounded in the beam once more, "he's down again on his back!"

Clara returned soon afterwards, and Herbert accompanied me upstairs to see our charge. As we passed Mr. Barley's door, he was heard hoarsely muttering within, in a strain that rose and fell like wind, the following refrain; in which I substitute good wishes for something quite the reverse.

"Ahoy! Bless your eyes, here's old Bill Barley. Here's old Bill Barley, bless your eyes. Here's old Bill Barley on the flat of his back, by the Lord. Lying on the flat of his back, like a drifting old dead flounder, here's your old Bill Barley, bless your eyes. Ahoy! Bless you."

In this strain of consolation, Herbert informed me the invisible Barley would commune with himself by the day and night together; often while it was light, having, at the same time, one eye at a telescope which was fitted on his bed for the convenience of sweeping the river.

In his two cabin rooms at the top of the house, which were fresh and airy, and in which Mr. Barley was less audible than below, I found Provis comfortably settled. He expressed no alarm, and seemed to feel none that was worth mentioning; but it struck me that he was softened —indefinably, for I could not have said how, and could never afterwards recall how when I tried; but certainly.

The opportunity that the day's rest had given me for reflection had resulted in my fully determining to say nothing to him respecting Compeyson. For anything I knew, his animosity towards the man might otherwise lead to his seeking him out and rushing on his own destruction. Therefore, when Herbert and I sat down with him by his fire, I asked him first of all whether he relied on Wemmick's judgment and sources of information?

"Ay, ay, dear boy!" he answered, with a grave nod, "Jaggers knows."

"Then, I have talked with Wemmick," said I, "and have come to tell you what caution he gave me and what advice."

This I did accurately, with the reservation just mentioned; and I told him how Wemmick had heard, in Newgate prison (whether from officers or prisoners I could not say), that he was under some suspicion, and that my chambers had been watched; how Wemmick had recommended his keeping close for a time, and my keeping away from him; and what Wemmick had said about getting him abroad. I added, that of course, when the time came, I should go with him, or should follow close upon him, as might be safest in Wemmick's judgment. What was to follow that, I did not touch upon; neither indeed was I at all clear or comfortable about it in my own mind, now that I saw him in that softer condition, and in declared peril for my sake. As to altering my way of living, by enlarging my expenses, I put it to him whether in our present unsettled and difficult circumstances, it would not be simply ridiculous, if it were no worse?

He could not deny this, and indeed was very reasonable throughout. His coming back was a venture, he said, and he had always known it to be a venture. He would do nothing to make it a desperate venture, and he had very little fear of his safety with such good help.

Herbert, who had been looking at the fire and pondering, here said that something had come into his thoughts arising out of Wemmick's suggestion, which it might be worth while to pursue. "We are both good watermen, Handel, and could take him down the river ourselves when the right time comes. No boat would then be hired for the purpose, and no boatmen; that would save at least a chance of suspicion, and any chance is worth saving. Never mind the season; don't you think it might be a good thing if you began at once to keep a boat at the Temple stairs, and were in the habit of rowing up and down the river? You fall into that habit, and then who notices or minds? Do it twenty or fifty times, and there is nothing special in your doing it the twenty-first or fifty-first."

I liked this scheme, and Provis was quite elated by it. We agreed that it should be carried into execution, and that Provis should never recognise us if we came below Bridge and rode past Mill Pond Bank. But, we further agreed that he should pull down the blind in that part of his window which gave upon the east, whenever he saw us and all was right.

Our conference being now ended, and everything arranged, I rose to go; remarking to Herbert that he and I had better not go home together, and that I would take half an hour's start of him. "I don't like to leave you here," I said to Provis, "though I cannot doubt your being safer here than near me. Good bye!"

"Dear boy," he answered, clasping my hands, "I don't know when we may meet again, and I don't like Good bye. Say Good Night!"

"Good night! Herbert will go regularly between us, and when the time comes you may be certain I shall be ready. Good night, Good night!"

We thought it best that he should stay in his own rooms, and we left him on the landing outside his door, holding a light over the stair-rail to light us downstairs. Looking back at him, I thought of the first night of his return when our positions were reversed, and when I little supposed my heart could ever be as heavy and anxious at parting from him as it was now.

Old Barley was growling and swearing when we repassed his door, with no appearance of having ceased or of meaning to cease. When we got to the foot of the stairs, I asked Herbert whether he had preserved the name of Provis? He replied, certainly not, and that the lodger was Mr. Campbell. He also explained that the utmost known of Mr. Campbell there, was, that he (Herbert) had Mr. Campbell consigned to him, and felt a strong personal interest in his being well cared for, and living a secluded life. So, when we went into the parlour where Mrs. Whimple and Clara were seated at work, I said nothing of my own interest in Mr. Campbell, but kept it to myself.

When I had taken leave of the pretty gentle dark-eyed girl, and of the motherly woman who had not outlived her honest sympathy with a little affair of true love, I felt as if the Old Green Copper Rope-Walk had grown quite a different place. Old Barley might be as old as the hills, and might swear like a whole field of troopers, but there were redeeming youth and trust and hope enough in Chinks's Basin to fill it to overflowing. And then I thought of Estella, and of our parting, and went home very sadly.

All things were as quiet in the Temple as ever I had seen them. The windows of the rooms of that side, lately occupied by Provis, were dark and still, and there was no lounger in Garden-court. I walked past the fountain twice or thrice before I descended the steps that were between me and my rooms, but I was quite alone. Herbert coming to my bedside when he came in—for I went straight to bed, dispirited and fatigued—made the same report. Opening one of the windows after that, he looked out into the moonlight, and told me that the pavement was as solemnly empty as the pavement of any Cathedral at that same hour.

Next day, I set myself to get the boat. It was soon done, and the boat was brought round to the Temple stairs, and lay where I could reach her within a minute or two. Then, I began to go out as for training and practice: sometimes alone, sometimes with Herbert. I was often out in cold, rain, and sleet, but nobody took much note of me after I had been out a few times. At first, I kept above Blackfriars Bridge; but as the hours of the tide changed, I took towards London Bridge. It was Old London Bridge in those days, and at certain states of the tide there was a race and fall of water there which gave it a bad reputation. But I knew well enough how to "shoot" the bridge after seeing it done, and so began to row about among the shipping in the Pool, and down to Erith. The first time I passed Mill Pond Bank, Herbert and I were pulling a pair of oars; and, both in going and returning, we saw the blind towards the east come down. Herbert was rarely there less frequently than three times in a week, and he never brought me a single word of intelligence that was at all alarming. Still, I knew that there was cause for alarm, and I could not get rid of the notion of being watched. Once received, it is a haunting idea; how many undesigning persons I suspected of watching me, it would be hard to calculate.

In short, I was always full of fears for the rash man who was in hiding. Herbert had sometimes said to me that he found it pleasant to stand at one of our windows after dark, when the tide was running down, and to think that it was flowing, with everything it bore, towards Clara. But I thought with dread that it was flowing towards Magwitch, and that any black mark on its surface might be his pursuers, going swiftly, silently and surely, to take him.

CHAPTER XLVII.

SOME weeks passed without bringing any change. We waited for Wemmick, and he made no sign. If I had never known him out of Little Britain, and had never enjoyed the privilege of being on a familiar footing at the Castle, I might have doubted him; not so for a moment, knowing him as I did.

My worldly affairs began to wear a gloomy appearance, and I was pressed for money by more than one creditor. Even I myself began to know the want of money (I mean of ready money in my own pocket), and to relieve it by converting some easily spared articles of jewellery into cash. But I had quite determined that it would be a heartless fraud to take more money from my patron in the existing state of my uncertain thoughts and plans. Therefore, I had sent him the unopened pocket-book by Herbert, to hold in his own keeping, and I felt a kind of satisfaction—whether it was a false kind or a true, I hardly know—in not having profited by his generosity since his revelation of himself.

As the time wore on, an impression settled heavily upon me that Estella was married. Fearful of having it confirmed, though it was all but a conviction, I avoided the newspapers, and begged Herbert (to whom I had confided the circumstances of our last interview) never to speak of her to me. Why I hoarded up this last wretched little rag of the robe of hope that was rent and given to the winds, how do I know! Why did you who read this, commit that not dissimilar inconsistency of your own, last year, last month, last week?

It was an unhappy life that I lived, and its one dominant anxiety, towering over all its other anxieties like a high mountain above a range of mountains, never disappeared from my view. Still, no new cause for fear arose. Let me start from my bed as I would, with the terror fresh upon me that he was discovered; let me sit listening as I would, with dread for Herbert's returning step at night, lest it should be fleeter than ordinary, and winged with evil news; for all that, and much more to like purpose, the round of things went on. Condemned to inaction and a state of constant restlessness and suspense, I rowed about in my boat, and waited, waited, waited, as I best could.

There were states of the tide when, having been down the river, I could not get back through the eddy-chafed arches and starlings of Old London Bridge; then, I left my boat at a wharf near the Custom House, to be brought up afterwards to the Temple stairs. I was not averse to doing this, as it served to make me and my boat a commoner incident among the water-side people there. From this slight occasion, sprang two meetings that I have now to tell of.

One afternoon, late in the month of February, I came ashore at the wharf at dusk. I had pulled down as far as Greenwich with the ebb tide, and had turned with the tide. It had been a fine bright day, but had become foggy as the sun dropped, and I had had to feel my way back among the shipping pretty carefully. Both in going and returning, I had seen the signal in his window, All well.

As it was a raw evening and I was cold, I thought I would comfort myself with dinner at once; and as I had hours of dejection and solitude before me if I went home to the Temple, I thought I would afterwards go to the play. The theatre where Mr. Wopsle had achieved his questionable triumph, was in that water-side neighbourhood (it is nowhere now), and to that theatre I resolved to go.

I was aware that Mr. Wopsle had not succeeded in reviving the drama, but, on the contrary, had rather partaken of its decline. He had been ominously heard of, through the playbills, as a faithful Black, in connection with a little girl of noble birth, and a monkey. And Herbert had seen him as a predatory Tartar, of comic propensities, with a face like a red brick, and an outrageous hat all over bells.

I dined at what Herbert and I used to call a Geographical chop-house—where there were maps of the world in porter-pot rims on every half-yard of the table-cloths, and charts of gravy on every one of the knives—to this day there is scarcely a single chop-house within the Lord Mayor's dominions which is not Geographical—and wore out the time in dozing over crumbs, staring at gas, and baking in a hot blast of dinners. By-and-bye, I roused myself and went to the play.

There I found a virtuous boatswain in his Majesty's service—a most excellent man, though I could have wished his trousers not quite so tight in some places and not quite so loose in others—who knocked all the little men's hats over their eyes, though he was very generous and brave, and who wouldn't hear of anybody's paying taxes, though he was very patriotic. He had a bag of money in his pocket, like a pudding in the cloth, and on that property married a young person in bed-furniture, with great rejoicings; the whole population of Portsmouth (nine in number at the last Census) turning out on the beach, to rub their own hands, and shake everybody else's, and sing, "Fill, fill!" A certain dark-complexioned Swab, however, who wouldn't fill, or do anything else that was proposed to him, and whose heart was openly stated (by the boatswain) to be as black as his figure-head, proposed to two other Swabs to get all mankind into difficulties; which was so effectually done (the Swab family having considerable political influence) that it took half the evening to set things right, and then it

was only brought about through an honest little grocer with a white hat, black gaiters, and red nose, getting into a clock, with a gridiron, and listening, and coming out, and knocking everybody down from behind with the gridiron whom he couldn't confute with what he had overheard. This led to Mr. Wopsle's (who had never been heard of before) coming in with a star and garter on, as a plenipotentiary of great power direct from the Admiralty, to say that the Swabs were all to go to prison on the spot, and that he had brought the boatswain down the Union Jack, as a slight acknowledgment of his public services. The boatswain, unmanned for the first time, respectfully dried his eyes on the Jack, and then cheering up and addressing Mr. Wopsle as Your Honour, solicited permission to take him by the fin. Mr. Wopsle conceding his fin with a gracious dignity, was immediately shoved into a dusty corner, while everybody danced a hornpipe; and from that corner, surveying the public with a discontented eye, became aware of me.

The second piece was the last new grand comic Christmas pantomime, in the first scene of which, it pained me to suspect that I detected Mr. Wopsle with red worsted legs under a highly magnified phosphoric countenance and a shock of red curtain-fringe for his hair, engaged in the manufacture of thunderbolts in a mine, and displaying great cowardice when his gigantic master came home (very hoarse) to dinner. But he presently presented himself under worthier circumstances; for, the Genius of Youthful Love being in want of assistance—on account of the parental brutality of an ignorant farmer who opposed the choice of his daughter's heart, by purposely falling upon the object in a flour sack, out of the first-floor window—summoned a sententious Enchanter; and he, coming up from the antipodes rather unsteadily, after an apparently violent journey, proved to be Mr. Wopsle in a high-crowned hat, with a necromantic work in one volume under his arm. The business of this enchanter on earth being principally to be talked at, sung at, butted at, danced at, and flashed at with fires of various colours, he had a good deal of time on his hands. And I observed with great surprise, that he devoted it to staring in my direction as if he were lost in amazement.

There was something so remarkable in the increasing glare of Mr. Wopsle's eye, and he seemed to be turning so many things over in his mind and to grow so confused, that I could not make it out. I sat thinking of it, long after he had ascended to the clouds in a large watch-case, and still I could not make it out. I was still thinking of it when I came out of the theatre an hour afterwards, and found him waiting for me near the door.

"How do you do?" said I, shaking hands with him as we turned down the street together. "I saw that you saw me."

"Saw you, Mr. Pip!" he returned. "Yes, of course I saw you. But who else was there?"

"Who else?"

"It is the strangest thing," said Mr. Wopsle, drifting into his lost look again; "and yet I could swear to him."

Becoming alarmed, I entreated Mr. Wopsle to explain his meaning.

"Whether I should have noticed him at first but for your being there," said Mr. Wopsle, going on in the same lost way, "I can't be positive; yet I think I should."

Involuntarily I looked round me, as I was accustomed to look round me when I went home; for, these mysterious words gave me a chill.

"Oh! He can't be in sight," said Mr. Wopsle. "He went out, before I went off; I saw him go."

Having the reason that I had for being suspicious, I even suspected this poor actor. I mistrusted a design to entrap me into some admission. Therefore, I glanced at him as we walked on together, but said nothing.

"I had a ridiculous fancy that he must be with you, Mr. Pip, till I saw that you were quite unconscious of him, sitting behind you there like a ghost."

My former chill crept over me again, but I was resolved not to speak yet, for it was quite consistent with his words that he might be set on to induce me to connect these references with Provis. Of course, I was perfectly sure and safe that Provis had not been there.

"I dare say you wonder at me, Mr. Pip; indeed, I see you do. But it is so very strange! You'll hardly believe what I am going to tell you. I could hardly believe it myself, if you told me."

"Indeed?" said I.

"No, indeed. Mr. Pip, you remember in old times a certain Christmas Day, when you were quite a child, and I dined at Gargery's, and some soldiers came to the door to get a pair of handcuffs mended?"

"I remember it very well."

"And you remember that there was a chase after two convicts, and that we joined in it, and that Gargery took you on his back, and that I took the lead and you kept up with me as well as you could?"

"I remember it all very well." Better than he thought —except that last clause.

"And you remember that we came up with the two in a ditch, and that there was a scuffle between them, and that one of them had been severely handled and much mauled about the face, by the other?"

"I see it all before me."

"And that the soldiers lighted torches, and put the two in the centre, and that we went on to see the last of them, over the black marshes, with the torchlight shining on their faces—I am particular about that; with the torchlight shining on their faces, when there was an outer ring of dark night all about us?"

"Yes," said I. "I remember all that."

"Then, Mr. Pip, one of those two prisoners sat behind you to-night. I saw him over your shoulder."

"Steady!" I thought. I asked him then, "Which of the two do you suppose you saw?"

"The one who had been mauled," he answered readily, "and I'll swear I saw him! The more I think of him, the more certain I am of him."

"This is very curious!" said I, with the best assumption I could put on, of its being nothing more to me. "Very curious indeed!"

I cannot exaggerate the enhanced disquiet into which this conversation threw me, or the special and peculiar terror I felt at Compeyson's having been behind me "like a ghost." For, if he had ever been out of my thoughts for a few moments together since the hiding had begun, it was in those very moments when he was closest to me; and to think that I should be so unconscious and off my guard after all my care, was as if I had shut an avenue of a hundred doors to keep him out, and then had found him at my elbow. I could not doubt either that he was there, because I was there, and that however slight an appearance of danger there might be about us, danger was always near and active.

I put such questions to Mr. Wopsle as, When did the man come in? He could not tell me that; he saw me, and over my shoulder he saw the man. It was not until he had seen him for some time that he began to identify him; but he had from the first vaguely associated him with me, and known him as somehow belonging to me in the old village time. How was he dressed? Prosperously, but not noticeably otherwise; he thought, in black. Was his face at all disfigured? No, he believed not. I believed not, too, for although in my brooding state I had taken no especial notice of the people behind me, I thought it likely that a face at all disfigured would have attracted my attention.

When Mr. Wopsle had imparted to me all that he could recall or I extract, and when I had treated him to a little appropriate refreshment after the fatigues of the evening, we parted. It was between twelve and one o'clock when I reached the Temple, and the gates were shut. No one was near me when I went in and went home.

Herbert had come in, and we held a very serious council by the fire. But there was nothing to be done, saving to communicate to Wemmick what I had that night found out, and to remind him that we waited for his hint. As I thought that I might compromise him if I went too often to the Castle, I made this communication by letter. I wrote it before I went to bed and went out and posted it; and again no one was near me. Herbert and I agreed that we could do nothing else but be very cautious. And we were very cautious indeed—more cautious than before, if that were possible—and I for my part never went near Chinks's Basin, except when I rowed by, and then I only looked at Mill Pond Bank as I looked at anything else.

CHAPTER XLVIII.

THE second of the two meetings referred to in the last chapter, occurred about a week after the first. I had again left my boat at the wharf below Bridge; the time was an hour earlier in the afternoon; and, undecided where to dine, I had strolled up into Cheapside, and was strolling along it, surely the most unsettled person in all the busy concourse, when a large hand was laid upon my shoulder, by some one overtaking me. It was Mr. Jaggers's hand, and he passed it through my arm.

"As we are going in the same direction, Pip, we may walk together. Where are you bound for?"

"For the Temple, I think," said I.

"Don't you know?" said Mr. Jaggers.

"Well," I returned, glad for once to get the better of him in cross-examination, "I do not know, for I have not made up my mind."

"You are going to dine?" said Mr. Jaggers. "You don't mind admitting that, I suppose?"

"No," I returned, "I don't mind admitting that."

"And are not engaged?"

"I don't mind admitting also, that I am not engaged."

"Then," said Mr Jaggers, "come and dine with me."

I was going to excuse myself, when he added, "Wemmick's coming." So I changed my excuse into an acceptance—the few words I had uttered serving for the beginning of either—and we went along Cheapside and slanted off to Little Britain, while the lights were springing up brilliantly in the shop windows, and the street lamplighters, scarcely finding ground enough to plant their ladders on in the midst of the afternoon's bustle, were skipping up and down and running in and out, opening more red eyes in the gathering fog than my rushlight tower at the Hummums had opened white eyes in the ghostly wall.

At the office in Little Britain there was the usual letter-writing, hand-washing, candle-snuffing, and safe-locking, that closed the business of the day. As I stood idle by Mr. Jaggers's fire, its rising and falling flame made the two casts on the shelf look as if they were playing a diabolical game at bo-peep with me; while the pair of coarse fat office candles that dimly lighted Mr. Jaggers as he wrote in a corner, were decorated with dirty winding-sheets, as if in remembrance of a host of hanged clients.

We went to Gerrard-street, all three together, in a hackney-coach: and as soon as we got there, dinner was served. Although I should not have thought of making, in that place, the most distant reference by so much as a look to Wemmick's Walworth sentiments, yet I should have had no objection to catching his eye now and then in a friendly way. But it was not to be done. He turned his eyes on Mr. Jaggers whenever he raised them from the table, and was as dry and distant to me as if there were twin Wemmicks and this was the wrong one.

"Did you send that note of Miss Havisham's to Mr. Pip, Wemmick?" Mr. Jaggers asked, soon after we began dinner.

"No, sir," returned Wemmick; "it was going by post, when you brought Mr. Pip into the office. Here it is." He handed it to his principal, instead of to me.

"It's a note of two lines, Pip," said Mr. Jaggers, handing it on, "sent up to me by Miss Havisham, on account of her not being sure of your address. She tells me that she wants to see you on a little matter of business you mentioned to her. You'll go down?"

"Yes," said I, casting my eyes over the note, which was exactly in those terms.

"When do you think of going down?"

"I have an impending engagement," said I, glancing at Wemmick, who was putting fish into the post-office, "that renders me rather uncertain of my time. At once, I think."

"If Mr. Pip has the intention of going at once," said Wemmick to Mr. Jaggers, "he needn't write an answer, you know."

Receiving this as an intimation that it was best not to delay, I settled that I would go to-morrow, and said so. Wemmick drank a glass of wine and looked with a grimly satisfied air at Mr. Jaggers, but not at me.

"So, Pip! Our friend the Spider," said Mr. Jaggers, "has played his cards. He has won the pool."

It was as much as I could do to assent.

"Hah! He is a promising fellow—in his way—but he may not have it all his own way. The stronger will win in the end, but the stronger has to be found out first. If he should turn to, and beat her—"

"Surely," I interrupted, with a burning face and heart, "you do not seriously think that he is scoundrel enough for that, Mr. Jaggers?"

"I didn't say so, Pip. I am putting a case. If he should turn to and beat her, he may possibly get the strength on his side; if it should be a question of intellect, he certainly will not. It would be chance work to give an opinion how a fellow of that sort will turn out in such circumstances, because it's a toss-up between two results."

"May I ask what they are?"

"A fellow like our friend the Spider," answered Mr.

Jaggers, "either beats, or cringes. He may cringe and growl, or cringe and not growl; but he either beats or cringes. Ask Wemmick his opinion."

"Either beats or cringes," said Wemmick, not at all addressing himself to me.

"So, here's to Mrs. Bentley Drummle," said Mr. Jaggers, taking a decanter of choicer wine from his dumb-waiter, and filling for each of us and for himself, "and may the question of supremacy be settled to the lady's satisfaction! To the satisfaction of the lady *and* the gentleman, it never will be. Now, Molly, Molly, Molly, Molly, how slow you are to-day!"

She was at his elbow when he addressed her, putting a dish upon the table. As she withdrew her hands from it, she fell back a step or two, nervously muttering some excuse. And a certain action of her fingers as she spoke arrested my attention.

"What's the matter?" said Mr. Jaggers.

"Nothing. Only the subject we were speaking of," said I, "was rather painful to me."

The action of her fingers was like the action of knitting. She stood looking at her master, not understanding whether she was free to go, or whether he had more to say to her and would call her back if she did go. Her look was very intent. Surely, I had seen exactly such eyes and such hands, on a memorable occasion very lately!

He dismissed her, and she glided out of the room. But she remained before me, as plainly as if she were still there. I looked at those hands, I looked at those eyes, I looked at that flowing hair; and I compared them with other hands, other eyes, other hair, that I knew of, and with what those might be after twenty years of a brutal husband and a stormy life. I looked again at those hands and eyes of the housekeeper, and thought of the inexplicable feeling that had come over me when I last walked—not alone—in the ruined garden, and through the deserted brewery. I thought how the same feeling had come back when I saw a face looking at me, and a hand waving to me from a stage-coach window; and how it had come back again and had flashed about me like lightning, when I had passed in a carriage—not alone—through a sudden glare of light in a dark street. I thought how one link of association had helped that identification in the theatre, and how such a link, wanting before, had been riveted for me now, when I had passed by a chance swift from Estella's name to the fingers with their knitting action, and the attentive eyes. And I felt absolutely certain that this woman was Estella's mother.

Mr. Jaggers had seen me with Estella, and was not likely to have missed the sentiments I had been at no pains to conceal. He nodded when I said the subject was painful to me, clapped me on the back, put round the wine again, and went on with his dinner.

Only twice more did the housekeeper reappear, and then her stay in the room was very short, and Mr. Jaggers was sharp with her. But her hands were Estella's hands, and her eyes were Estella's eyes, and if she had reappeared a hundred times I could have been neither more sure nor less sure that my conviction was the truth.

It was a dull evening, for Wemmick drew his wine when it came round, quite as a matter of business—just as he might have drawn his salary when that came round—and with his eyes on his chief, sat in a state of perpetual readiness for cross-examination. As to the quantity of wine, his post-office was as indifferent and ready as any other post-office for its quantity of letters. From my point of view, he was the wrong twin all the time, and only externally like the Wemmick of Walworth.

We took our leave early, and left together. Even when we were groping among Mr. Jaggers's stock of boots for our hats, I felt that the right twin was on his way back; and we had not gone half a dozen yards down Gerrard-street in the Walworth direction before I found that I was walking arm-in-arm with the right twin, and that the wrong twin had evaporated into the evening air.

"Well!" said Wemmick, "that's over! He's a wonderful man, without his living likeness; but I feel that I have to screw myself up when I dine with him—and I dine more comfortably unscrewed."

I felt that this was a good statement of the case, and told him so.

"Wouldn't say it to anybody but yourself," he answered. "I know that what is said between you and me, goes no further."

I asked him if he had ever seen Miss Havisham's adopted daughter, Mrs. Bentley Drummle? He said no. To avoid being too abrupt, I then spoke of the Aged, and of Miss Skiffins. He looked rather sly when I mentioned Miss Skiffins, and stopped in the street to blow his nose, with a roll of the head and a flourish not quite free from latent boastfulness.

"Wemmick," said I, "do you remember telling me, before I first went to Mr. Jaggers's private house, to notice that housekeeper?"

"Did I?" he replied. "Ah, I dare say I did. Deuce take me," he added sullenly, "I know I did. I find I am not quite unscrewed yet."

"A wild beast tamed, you called her?"

"And what did *you* call her?"

"The same. How did Mr. Jaggers tame her, Wemmick?"

"That's his secret. She has been with him many a long year."

"I wish you would tell me her story. I feel a particular interest in being acquainted with it. You know that what is said between you and me goes no further."

"Well!" Wemmick replied, "I don't know her story—that is, I don't know all of it. But what I do know, I'll tell you. We are in our private and personal capacities, of course."

"Of course."

"A score or so of years ago, that woman was tried at the Old Bailey for murder and was acquitted. She was a very handsome young woman, and I believe had some gipsy blood in her. Anyhow, it was hot enough when it was up, as you may suppose."

"But she was acquitted."

"Mr. Jaggers was for her," pursued Wemmick, with a look full of meaning, "and worked the case in a way quite astonishing. It was a desperate case, and it was comparatively early days with him then, and he worked it to general admiration; in fact, it may almost be said to have made him. He worked it himself at the police-office, day after day for many days, contending against even a committal; and at the trial where he couldn't work it himself, sat under counsel, and—every one knew—put in all the salt and pepper. The murdered person was a woman; a woman, a good ten years older, very much larger, and very much stronger. It was a case of jealousy. They both led tramping lives, and this woman in Gerrard-street here, had

been married very young, over the broomstick (as we say), to a tramping man, and was a perfect fury in point of jealousy. The murdered woman—more a match for the man, certainly, in point of years—was found dead in a barn near Hounslow Heath. There had been a violent struggle, perhaps a fight. She was bruised and scratched and torn, and had been held by the throat at last and choked. Now, there was no reasonable evidence to implicate any person but this woman, and, on the improbabilities of her having been able to do it, Mr. Jaggers principally rested his case. You may be sure," said Wemmick, touching me on the sleeve, "that he never dwelt upon the strength of her hands then, though he sometimes does now."

I had told Wemmick of his showing us her wrists, that day of the dinner party.

"Well, sir!" Wemmick went on; "it happened—happened, don't you see?—that this woman was so very artfully dressed from the time of her apprehension, that she looked much slighter than she really was; in particular, her sleeves are always remembered to have been so skilfully contrived that her arms had quite a delicate look. She had only a bruise or two about her—nothing for a tramp—but the backs of her hands were lacerated, and the question was, was it with finger-nails? Now, Mr. Jaggers showed that she had struggled through a great lot of brambles which were not as high as her face; but which she could not have got through and kept her hands out of; and bits of those brambles were actually found in her skin and put in evidence, as well as the fact that the brambles in question were found on examination to have been broken through, and to have little shreds of her dress and little spots of blood upon them here and there. But the boldest point he made, was this. It was attempted to be set up in proof of her jealousy that she was under strong suspicion of having, at about the time of the murder, frantically destroyed her child by this man—some three years old—to revenge herself upon him. Mr. Jaggers worked that, in this way. 'We say these are not marks of finger-nails, but marks of brambles, and we show you the brambles. You say they are marks of finger-nails, and you set up the hypothesis that she destroyed her child. You must accept all consequences of that hypothesis. For anything we know, she may have destroyed her child, and the child in clinging to her may have scratched her hands. What then? You are not trying her for the murder of her child; why don't you? As to this case, if you *will* have scratches, we say that, for anything we know, you may have accounted for them, assuming for the sake of argument that you have not invented them?' To sum up, sir," said Wemmick, "Mr. Jaggers was altogether too many for the Jury, and they gave in."

"Has she been in his service ever since?"

"Yes; but not only that," said Wemmick, "she went into his service immediately after her acquittal, tamed as she is now. She has since been taught one thing and another in the way of her duties, but she was tamed from the beginning."

"Do you remember the sex of the child?"

"Said to have been a girl."

"You have nothing more to say to me to-night?"

"Nothing. I got your letter and destroyed it. Nothing."

We exchanged a cordial Good Night, and I went home, with new matter for my thoughts, though with no relief from the old.

CHAPTER XLIX.

PUTTING Miss Havisham's note in my pocket, that it might serve as my credentials for so soon reappearing at Satis House, in case her waywardness should lead her to express any surprise at seeing me, I went down again by the coach next day. But, I alighted at the Halfway House, and breakfasted there, and walked the rest of the distance; for, I sought to get into the town quietly by the unfrequented ways, and to leave it in the same manner.

The best light of the day was gone when I passed along the quiet echoing courts behind the High-street. The nooks of ruin where the old monks had once had their refectories and gardens, and where the strong walls were now pressed into the service of humble sheds and stables, were almost as silent as the old monks in their graves. The cathedral chimes had at once a sadder and a more remote sound to me, as I hurried on avoiding observation, than they had ever had before; so, the swell of the old organ was borne to my ears like funeral music; and the rooks, as they hovered about the grey tower and swung in the bare high trees of the priory-garden, seemed to call to me that the place was changed, and that Estella was gone out of it for ever.

An elderly woman whom I had seen before as one of the servants who lived in the supplementary house across the back court-yard, opened the gate. The lighted candle stood in the dark passage within, as of old, and I took it up and ascended the staircase alone. Miss Havisham was not in her own room, but was in the larger room across the landing. Looking in at the door, after knocking in vain, I saw her sitting on the hearth in a ragged chair, close before, and lost in the contemplation of, the ashy fire.

Doing as I had often done, I went in, and stood, touching the old chimney-piece, where she could see me when she raised her eyes. There was an air of utter loneliness upon her, that would have moved me to pity though she had wilfully done me a deeper injury than I could charge her with. As I stood compassionating her, and thinking how in the progress of time I too had come to be a part of the wrecked fortunes of that house, her eyes rested on me. She stared, and said in a low voice, "Is it real?"

"It is I, Pip. Mr. Jaggers gave me your note yesterday, and I have lost no time."

"Thank you. Thank you."

As I brought another of the ragged chairs to the hearth and sat down, I remarked a new expression on her face, as if she were afraid of me.

"I want," she said, "to pursue that subject you mentioned to me when you were last here, and to show you that I am not all stone. But perhaps you can never believe, now, that there is anything human in my heart?"

When I said some reassuring words, she stretched out her tremulous right hand, as though she was going to touch me; but she recalled it again before I understood the action, or knew how to receive it.

"You said, speaking for your friend, that you could tell me how to do something useful and good. Something that you would like done, is it not?"

"Something that I would like done very, very much."

"What is it?"

I began explaining to her that secret history of the partnership. I had not got far into it, when I judged from her looks that she was thinking in a discursive way of me, rather than of what I said. It seemed to be so, for, when I stopped speaking, many moments passed before she showed that she was conscious of the fact.

"Do you break off," she asked then, with her former air of being afraid of me, "because you hate me too much to bear to speak to me?"

"No, no," I answered, "how can you think so, Miss Havisham! I stopped because I thought you were not following what I said."

"Perhaps I was not," she answered, putting a hand to her head. "Begin again, and let me look at something else. Stay! Now tell me."

She set her hand upon her stick, in the resolute way that sometimes was habitual to her, and looked at the fire with a strong expression of forcing herself to attend. I went on with my explanation, and told her how I had hoped to complete the transaction out of my means, but how in this I was disappointed. That part of the subject (I reminded her) involved matters which could form no part of my explanation, for they were the weighty secrets of another.

"So!" said she, assenting with her head, but not looking at me. "And how much money is wanting to complete the purchase?"

I was rather afraid of stating it, for it sounded a large sum. "Nine hundred pounds."

"If I give you the money for this purpose, will you keep my secret as you have kept your own?"

"Quite as faithfully."

"And your mind will be more at rest?"

"Much more at rest."

"Are you very unhappy now?"

She asked this question, still without looking at me, but in an unwonted tone of sympathy. I could not reply at the moment for my voice failed me. She put her left arm across the head of her stick, and softly laid her forehead on it.

"I am far from happy, Miss Havisham; but I have other causes of disquiet than any you know of. They are the secrets I have mentioned."

After a little while, she raised her head, and looked at the fire again.

"'Tis noble in you to tell me that you have other causes of unhappiness. Is it true?"

"Too true."

"Can I only serve you, Pip, by serving your friend? Regarding that as done, is there nothing I can do for you yourself?"

"Nothing. I thank you for the question. I thank you even more for the tone of the question. But, there is nothing."

She presently rose from her seat, and looked about the blighted room for the means of writing. There were none there, and she took from her pocket a yellow set of ivory tablets, mounted in tarnished gold, and wrote upon them with a pencil in a case of tarnished gold that hung from her neck.

"You are still on friendly terms with Mr. Jaggers?"

"Quite. I dined with him yesterday."

"This is an authority to him to pay you that money, to lay out at your irresponsible discretion for your friend. I keep no money here; but if you would rather Mr. Jaggers knew nothing of the matter, I will send it to you."

"Thank you, Miss Havisham; I have not the least objection to receiving it from him."

She read me what she had written, and it was direct and clear, and evidently intended to absolve me from any suspicion of profiting by the receipt of the money. I took the tablets from her hand, and it trembled again, and it trembled more as she took off the chain to which the pencil was attached, and put it in mine. All this she did, without looking at me.

"My name is on the first leaf. If you can ever write under my name, 'I forgive her,' though ever so long after my broken heart is dust—pray do it!"

"O Miss Havisham," said I, "I can do it now. There have been sore mistakes; and my life has been a blind and thankless one; and I want forgiveness and direction far too much, to be bitter with you."

She turned her face to me for the first time since she had averted it, and to my amazement, I may even add to my terror, dropped on her knees at my feet; with her folded hands raised to me in the manner in which, when her poor heart was young and fresh and whole, they must often have been raised to Heaven from her mother's side.

To see her with her white hair and her worn face, kneeling at my feet, gave me a shock through all my frame. I entreated her to rise, and got my arms about her to help her up; but she only pressed that hand of mine which was nearest to her grasp, and hung her head over it and wept. I had never seen her shed a tear before, and in the hope that the relief might do her good, I bent over her without speaking. She was not kneeling now, but was down upon the ground.

"O!" she cried, despairingly. "What have I done? What have I done!"

"If you mean, Miss Havisham, what have you done to injure me, let me answer. Very little. I should have loved her under any circumstances.—Is she married?"

"Yes!"

It was a needless question, for a new desolation in the desolate house had told me so.

"What have I done! What have I done!" She wrung her hands, and crushed her white hair, and returned to this cry over and over again. "What have I done!"

I knew not how to answer, or how to comfort her. That she had done a grievous thing in taking an impressionable child to mould into the form that her wild resentment, spurned affection, and wounded pride, found vengeance in, I knew full well. But that, in shutting out the light of day, she had shut out infinitely more; that, in seclusion she had secluded herself from a thousand natural and healing influences; that, her mind, brooding solitary, had grown diseased, as all minds do and must and will that reverse the appointed order of their Maker; I knew equally well. And could I look upon her without compassion, seeing her punishment in the ruin she was, in her profound unfitness for this earth on which she was placed, in the vanity of sorrow which had become a master mania, like the vanity of penitence, the vanity of remorse, the vanity of unworthiness, and other monstrous vanities that have been curses in this world?

"Until you spoke to her the other day, and until I saw in you a looking-glass that showed me what I once felt myself, I did not know what I had done. What have I done! What have I done!" And so again, twenty, fifty times over, What had she done!

"Miss Havisham," I said, when her cry had died away, "you may dismiss me from your mind and conscience. But Estella is a different case, and if you can ever undo any scrap of what you have done amiss in keeping a part

of her right nature away from her, it will be better to do that, than to bemoan the past through a hundred years."

"Yes, yes, I know it. But, Pip—my Dear!" There was an earnest womanly compassion for me in her new affection. "My dear! Believe this: when she first came to me, I meant to save her from misery like my own. At first I meant no more."

"Well, well!" said I. "I hope so."

"But as she grew, and promised to be very beautiful, I gradually did worse, and with my praises, and with my jewels, and with my teachings, and with this figure of myself always before her, a warning to back and point my lessons, I stole her heart away and put ice in its place."

"Better," I could not help saying, "to have left her a natural heart, even to be bruised or broken."

With that, Miss Havisham looked distractedly at me for a while, and then burst out again, What had she done!

"If you knew all my story," she pleaded, "you would have some compassion for me and a better understanding of me."

"Miss Havisham," I answered, as delicately as I could, "I believe I may say that I do know your story, and have known it ever since I first left this neighbourhood. It has inspired me with great commiseration, and I hope I understand it and its influences. Does what has passed between us give me any excuse for asking you a question relative to Estella? Not as she is, but as she was when she first came here?"

She was seated on the ground, with her arms on the ragged chair, and her head leaning on them. She looked full at me when I said this, and replied, "Go on."

"Whose child was Estella?"

She shook her head.

"You don't know?"

She shook her head again.

"But Mr. Jaggers brought her here, or sent her here?"

"Brought her here."

"Will you tell me how that came about?"

She answered in a low whisper and with caution: "I had been shut up in these rooms a long time (I don't know how long; you know what time the clocks keep here), when I told him that I wanted a little girl to rear and love, and save from my fate. I had first seen him when I sent for him to lay this place waste for me; having read of him in the newspapers before I and the world parted. He told me that he would look about him for such an orphan child. One night he brought her here asleep, and I called her Estella."

"Might I ask her age then?"

"Two or three. She herself knows nothing, but that she was left an orphan and I adopted her."

So convinced I was of that woman's being her mother, that I wanted no evidence to establish the fact in my mind. But, to any mind, I thought, the connection here was clear and straight.

What more could I hope to do by prolonging the interview? I had succeeded on behalf of Herbert, Miss Havisham had told me all she knew of Estella, I had said and done what I could to ease her mind. No matter with what other words we parted; we parted.

Twilight was closing in when I went downstairs into the natural air. I called to the woman who had opened the

I ENTREATED HER TO RISE.

gate when I entered, that I would not trouble her just yet, but would walk round the place before leaving. For, I had a presentiment that I should never be there again, and I felt that the dying light was suited to my last view of it.

By the wilderness of casks that I had walked on long ago, and on which the rain of years had fallen since, rotting them in many places, and leaving miniature swamps and pools of water upon those that stood on end, I made my way to the ruined garden. I went all round it; round by the corner where Herbert and I had fought our battle; round by the paths where Estella and I had walked. So cold, so lonely, so dreary all!

Taking the brewery on my way back, I raised the rusty latch of a little door at the garden end of it, and walked through. I was going out at the opposite door—not easy to open now, for the damp wood had started and swelled, and the hinges were yielding, and the threshold was encumbered with a growth of fungus—when I turned my head to look back. A childish association revived with wonderful force in the moment of the slight action, and I fancied that I saw Miss Havisham hanging to the beam. So strong was the impression, that I stood under the beam shuddering from head to foot before I knew it was a fancy —though to be sure I was there in an instant.

The mournfulness of the place and time, and the great terror of this illusion, though it was but momentary, caused me to feel an indescribable awe as I came out between the open wooden gates where I had once wrung my hair after Estella had wrung my heart. Passing on into the front courtyard, I hesitated whether to call the woman to let me out at the locked gate, of which she had the key, or first to go upstairs and assure myself that Miss Havisham was as safe and well as I had left her. I took the latter course and went up.

I looked into the room where I had left her, and I saw her seated in the ragged chair upon the hearth close to the fire, with her back towards me. In the moment when I was withdrawing my head to go quietly away, I saw a great flaming light spring up. In the same moment I saw her running at me, shrieking, with a whirl of fire blazing all about her, and soaring at least as many feet above her head as she was high.

I had a double-caped great-coat on, and over my arm another thick coat. That I got them off, closed with her, threw her down, and got them over her; that I dragged the great cloth from the table for the same purpose, and with it dragged down the heap of rottenness in the midst, and all the ugly things that sheltered there; that we were on the ground struggling like desperate enemies, and that the closer I covered her, the more wildly she shrieked and tried to free herself; that this occurred I knew through the result, but not through anything I felt, or thought, or knew I did. I knew nothing until I knew that we were on the floor by the great table, and that patches of tinder yet alight were floating in the smoky air, which a moment ago had been her faded bridal dress.

Then, I looked round and saw the disturbed beetles and spiders running away over the floor, and the servants coming in with breathless cries at the door. I still held her forcibly down with all my strength, like a prisoner who might escape; and I doubt if I even knew who she was, or why we had struggled, or that she had been in flames, or that the flames were out, until I saw the patches of tinder that had been her garments, no longer alight, but falling in a black shower around us.

She was insensible, and I was afraid to have her moved, or even touched. Assistance was sent for, and I held her until it came, as if I unreasonably fancied (I think I did) that if I let her go, the fire would break out again and consume her. When I got up, on the surgeon's coming to her with other aid, I was astonished to see that both my hands were burnt; for, I had no knowledge of it through the sense of feeling.

On examination it was pronounced that she had received serious hurts, but that they of themselves were far from hopeless; the danger lay mainly in the nervous shock. By the surgeon's directions, her bed was carried into that room and laid upon the great table: which happened to be well suited to the dressing of her injuries. When I saw her again, an hour afterwards, she lay indeed where I had seen her strike her stick, and had heard her say she would lie one day.

Though every vestige of her dress was burnt, as they told me, she still had something of her old ghastly bridal appearance; for, they had covered her to the throat with white cotton-wool, and as she lay with a white sheet loosely overlying that, the phantom air of something that had been and was changed was still upon her.

I found, on questioning the servants, that Estella was in Paris, and I got a promise from the surgeon that he would write by the next post. Miss Havisham's family I took upon myself; intending to communicate with Matthew Pocket only, and leave him to do as he liked about informing the rest. This I did next day, through Herbert, as soon as I returned to town.

There was a stage, that evening, when she spoke collectedly of what had happened, though with a certain terrible vivacity. Towards midnight she began to wander in her speech, and after that it gradually set in that she said innumerable times in a low solemn voice, "What have I done!" And then, "When she first came, I meant to save her from misery like mine." And then, "Take the pencil and write under my name, 'I forgive her!'" She never changed the order of these three sentences, but she sometimes left out a word in one or other of them; never putting in another word, but always leaving a blank and going on to the next word.

As I could do no service there, and as I had, nearer home, that pressing reason for anxiety and fear which even her wanderings could not drive out of my mind, I decided in the course of the night that I would return by the early morning coach: walking on a mile or so, and being taken up clear of the town. At about six o'clock of the morning, therefore, I leaned over her and touched her lips with mine, just as they said, not stopping for being touched, "Take the pencil and write under my name, 'I forgive her.'"

CHAPTER L.

My hands had been dressed twice or thrice in the night, and again in the morning. My left arm was a good deal burned to the elbow, and, less severely, as high as the shoulder; it was very painful, but the flames had set in that direction, and I felt thankful it was no worse. My right hand was not so badly burnt but that I could move the fingers. It was bandaged, of course, but much less in-

GREAT EXPECTATIONS

conveniently than my left hand and arm; those I carried in a sling; and I could only wear my coat like a cloak, loose over my shoulders and fastened at the neck. My hair had been caught by the fire, but not my head or face.

When Herbert had been down to Hammersmith and had seen his father, he came back to me at our chambers, and devoted the day to attending on me. He was the kindest of nurses, and at stated times took off the bandages, and steeped them in the cooling liquid that was kept ready, and put them on again, with a patient tenderness that I was deeply grateful for.

At first, as I lay quiet on the sofa, I found it painfully difficult, I might say impossible, to get rid of the impression of the glare of the flames, their hurry and noise, and the fierce burning smell. If I dozed for a minute, I was awakened by Miss Havisham's cries, and by her running at me with all that height of fire above her head. This pain of the mind was much harder to strive against than any bodily pain I suffered; and Herbert, seeing that, did his utmost to hold my attention engaged.

Neither of us spoke of the boat, but we both thought of it. That was made apparent by our avoidance of the subject, and by our agreeing—without agreement—to make my recovery of the use of my hands, a question of so many hours, not of so many weeks.

My first question when I saw Herbert had been, of course, whether all was well down the river? As he replied in the affirmative, with perfect confidence and cheerfulness, we did not resume the subject until the day was wearing away. But then, as Herbert changed the bandages, more by the light of the fire than by the outer light, he went back to it spontaneously.

"I sat with Provis last night, Handel, two good hours."

"Where was Clara?"

"Dear little thing!" said Herbert. "She was up and down with Gruffandgrim all the evening. He was perpetually pegging at the floor, the moment she left his sight. I doubt if he can hold out long though. What with rum and pepper—and pepper and rum—I should think his pegging must be nearly over."

"And then you will be married, Herbert?"

"How can I take care of the dear child otherwise?—Lay your arm out upon the back of the sofa, my dear boy, and I'll sit down here, and get the bandage off so gradually that you shall not know when it comes. I was speaking of Provis. Do you know, Handel, he improves?"

"I said to you I thought he was softened when I last saw him."

"So you did. And so he is. He was very communicative last night, and told me more of his life. You remember his breaking off here about some woman that he had had great trouble with.—Did I hurt you?"

I had started, but not under his touch. His words had given me a start.

"I had forgotten that, Herbert, but I remember it now you speak of it."

"Well! He went into that part of his life, and a dark wild part it is. Shall I tell you? Or would it worry you just now?"

"Tell me by all means. Every word."

Herbert bent forward to look at me more nearly, as if my reply had been rather more hurried or more eager than he could quite account for. "Your head is cool?" he said, touching it.

"Quite," said I. "Tell me what Provis said, my dear Herbert."

"It seems," said Herbert, "—there's a bandage off most charmingly, and now comes the cool one—makes you shrink at first, my poor dear fellow, don't it? but it will be comfortable presently—it seems that the woman was a young woman, and a jealous woman, and a revengeful woman; revengeful, Handel, to the last degree."

"To what last degree?"

"Murder.—Does it strike too cold on that sensitive place?"

"I don't feel it. How did she murder? Whom did she murder?"

"Why, the deed may not have merited quite so terrible a name," said Herbert, "but she was tried for it, and Mr. Jaggers defended her, and the reputation of that defence first made his name known to Provis. It was another and a stronger woman who was the victim, and there had been a struggle—in a barn. Who began it, or how fair it was, or how unfair, may be doubtful; but how it ended is certainly not doubtful, for the victim was found throttled."

"Was the woman brought in guilty?"

"No; she was acquitted.—My poor Handel, I hurt you!"

"It is impossible to be gentler, Herbert. Yes? What else?"

"This acquitted young woman and Provis had a little child: a little child of whom Provis was exceedingly fond. On the evening of the very night when the object of her jealousy was strangled as I tell you, the young woman presented herself before Provis for one moment, and swore that she would destroy the child (which was in her possession), and he should never see it again; then, she vanished.—There's the worst arm comfortably in the sling once more, and now there remains but the right hand, which is a far easier job. I can do it better by this light than by a stronger, for my hand is steadiest when I don't see the poor blistered patches too distinctly.—You don't think your breathing is affected, my dear boy? You seem to breathe quickly."

"Perhaps I do, Herbert. Did the woman keep her oath?"

"There comes the darkest part of Provis's life. She did."

"That is, he says she did."

"Why, of course, my dear boy," returned Herbert, in a tone of surprise, and again bending forward to get a nearer look at me. "He says it all. I have no other information."

"No, to be sure."

"Now, whether," pursued Herbert, "he had used the child's mother ill, or whether he had used the child's mother well, Provis doesn't say; but, she had shared some four or five years of the wretched life he described to us at this fireside, and he seems to have felt pity for her, and forbearance towards her. Therefore, fearing he should be called upon to depose about this destroyed child, and so be the cause of her death, he hid himself (much as he grieved for the child), kept himself dark, as he says, out of the way and out of the trial, and was only vaguely talked of as a certain man called Abel, out of whom the jealousy arose. After the acquittal she disappeared, and thus he lost the child and the child's mother."

"I want to ask—"

"A moment, my dear boy, and I have done. That evil genius, Compeyson, the worst of scoundrels, knowing of his keeping out of the way at that time, and of his reasons for doing so, of course afterwards held the knowledge over his head as a means of keeping him poorer, and working him harder. It was clear last night that this barbed the point of Provis's animosity."

"I want to know," said I, "and particularly, Herbert, whether he told you when this happened?"

"Particularly? Let me remember, then, what he said as to that. His expression was, 'a round score o' year ago, and a'most directly after I took up wi' Compeyson.' How old were you when you came upon him in the little church-yard?"

"I think in my seventh year."

"Ay. It had happened some three or four years then, he said, and you brought into his mind the little girl so tragically lost, who would have been about your age."

"Herbert," said I, after a short silence, in a hurried way, "can you see me best by the light of the window, or the light of the fire?"

"By the firelight," answered Herbert, coming close again.

"Look at me."

"I do look at you, my dear boy."

"Touch me."

"I do touch you, my dear boy."

"You are not afraid that I am in any fever, or that my head is much disordered by the accident of last night?"

"N-no, my dear boy," said Herbert, after taking time to examine me. "You are rather excited, but you are quite yourself."

"I know I am quite myself. And the man we have in hiding down the river, is Estella's Father."

CHAPTER LI.

WHAT purpose I had in view when I was hot on tracing out and proving Estella's parentage, I cannot say. It will presently be seen that the question was not before me in distinct shape, until it was put before me by a wiser head than my own.

But, when Herbert and I had held our momentous conversation, I was seized with a feverish conviction that I ought to hunt the matter down—that I ought not to let it rest, but that I ought to see Mr. Jaggers, and come at the bare truth. I really do not know whether I felt that I did this for Estella's sake, or whether I was glad to transfer to the man in whose preservation I was so much concerned, some rays of the romantic interest that had so long surrounded me. Perhaps the latter possibility may be the nearer to the truth.

Anyway, I could scarcely be withheld from going out to Gerrard-street that night. Herbert's representations, that if I did, I should probably be laid up and stricken useless, when our fugitive's safety would depend upon me, alone restrained my impatience. On the understanding, again and again reiterated, that come what would, I was to go to Mr. Jaggers to-morrow, I at length submitted to keep quiet, and to have my hurts looked after, and to stay at home. Early next morning we went out together, and at the corner of Giltspur-street by Smithfield, I left Herbert to go his way into the city, and took my way to Little Britain.

There were periodical occasions when Mr. Jaggers and Mr. Wemmick went over the office accounts, and checked off the vouchers, and put all things straight. On these occasions Wemmick took his books and papers into Mr. Jaggers's room, and one of the upstairs clerks came down into the outer office. Finding such clerk on Wemmick's post that morning, I knew what was going on; but I was not sorry to have Mr. Jaggers and Wemmick together, as Wemmick would then hear for himself that I said nothing to compromise him.

My appearance with my arm bandaged and my coat loose over my shoulders, favoured my object. Although I had sent Mr. Jaggers a brief account of the accident as soon as I had arrived in town, yet I had to give him all the details now; and the specialty of the occasion caused our talk to be less dry and hard, and less strictly regulated by the rules of evidence, than it had been before. While I described the disaster, Mr. Jaggers stood, according to his wont, before the fire. Wemmick leaned back in his chair, staring at me, with his hands in the pockets of his trousers, and his pen put horizontally into the post. The two brutal casts, always inseparable in my mind from official proceedings, seemed to be congestively considering whether they didn't smell fire at the present moment.

My narrative finished, and their questions exhausted, I then produced Miss Havisham's authority to receive the nine hundred pounds for Herbert. Mr. Jaggers's eyes retired a little deeper into his head when I handed him the tablets, but he presently handed them over to Wemmick, with instructions to draw the cheque for his signature. While that was in course of being done, I looked on at Wemmick as he wrote, and Mr. Jaggers, poising and swaying himself on his well-polished boots, looked on at me. "I am sorry, Pip," said he, as I put the cheque in my pocket, when he had signed it, "that we do nothing for *you*."

"Miss Havisham was good enough to ask me," I returned, "whether she could do nothing for me, and I told her No."

"Everybody should know his own business," said Mr. Jaggers. And I saw Wemmick's lips form the word "portable property."

"I should *not* have told her No, if I had been you," said Mr. Jaggers; "but every man ought to know his own business best."

"Every man's business," said Wemmick, rather reproachfully towards me, "is 'portable property.'"

As I thought the time was now come for pursuing the theme I had at heart, I said, turning on Mr. Jaggers:

"I did ask something of Miss Havisham, however, sir. I asked her to give me some information relative to her adopted daughter, and she gave me all she possessed."

"Did she?" said Mr. Jaggers, bending forward to look at his boots and then straightening himself. "Hah! I don't think I should have done so, if I had been Miss Havisham. But *she* ought to know her own business best."

"I know more of the history of Miss Havisham's adopted child, than Miss Havisham herself does, sir. I know her mother."

Mr. Jaggers looked at me inquiringly, and repeated, "Mother?"

"I have seen her mother within these three days."

"Yes?" said Mr. Jaggers.

"And so have you, sir. And you have seen her still more recently."

"Yes?" said Mr. Jaggers.

"Perhaps I know more of Estella's history, than even you do," said I. "I know her father, too."

A certain stop that Mr. Jaggers came to in his manner—he was too self-possessed to change his manner, but he could not help its being brought to an indefinably attentive stop—assured me that he did not know who her father was. This I had strongly suspected from Provis's account (as Herbert had repeated it) of his having kept himself dark; which I pieced on to the fact that he himself was not Mr. Jaggers's client until some four years later, and when he could have no reason for claiming his identity. But, I could not be sure of this unconsciousness on Mr. Jaggers's part before, though I was quite sure of it now.

"So! You know the young lady's father, Pip?" said Mr. Jaggers.

"Yes," I replied, "and his name is Provis—from New South Wales."

Even Mr. Jaggers started when I said those words. It was the slightest start that could escape a man, the most carefully repressed and the sooner checked, but he did start, though he made it a part of the action of taking out his pocket-handkerchief. How Wemmick received the announcement I am unable to say, for I was afraid to look at him just then, lest Mr. Jaggers's sharpness should detect that there had been some communication unknown to him between us.

"And on what evidence, Pip," asked Mr. Jaggers, very coolly, as he paused with his handkerchief half way to his nose, "does Provis make this claim?"

"He does not make it," said I, "and has never made it, and has no knowledge or belief that his daughter is in existence."

For once, the powerful pocket-handkerchief failed. My reply was so unexpected that Mr. Jaggers put the handkerchief back into his pocket without completing the usual performance, folded his arms, and looked with stern attention at me, though with an immovable face.

Then I told him all I knew, and how I knew it; with the one reservation that I left him to infer that I knew from Miss Havisham what I in fact knew from Wemmick. I was very careful indeed as to that. Nor, did I look towards Wemmick until I had finished all I had to tell, and had been for some time silently meeting Mr. Jaggers's look. When I did at last turn my eyes in Wemmick's direction, I found that he had unposted his pen, and was intent upon the table before him.

"Hah!" said Mr. Jaggers at last, as he moved towards the papers on the table. "—What item was it you were at, Wemmick, when Mr. Pip came in?"

But I could not submit to be thrown off in that way, and I made a passionate, almost an indignant appeal to him to be more frank and manly with me. I reminded him of the false hopes into which I had lapsed, the length of time they had lasted, and the discovery I had made: and I hinted at the danger that weighed upon my spirits. I represented myself as being surely worthy of some little confidence from him, in return for the confidence I had just now imparted. I said that I did not blame him, or suspect him, or mistrust him, but I wanted assurance of the truth from him. And if he asked me why I wanted it and why I thought I had any right to it, I would tell him, little as he cared for such poor dreams, that I had loved Estella dearly and long, and that, although I had lost her and must live a bereaved life, whatever concerned her was still nearer and dearer to me than anything else in the world. And

seeing that Mr. Jaggers stood quite still and silent, and apparently quite obdurate, under this appeal, I turned to Wemmick, and said, "Wemmick, I know you to be a man with a gentle heart. I have seen your pleasant home, and your old father, and all the innocent cheerful playful ways with which you refresh your business life. And I entreat you to say a word for me to Mr. Jaggers, and to represent to him that, all circumstances considered, he ought to be more open with me!"

I have never seen two men look more oddly at one another than Mr. Jaggers and Wemmick did after this apostrophe. At first, a misgiving crossed me that Wemmick would be instantly dismissed from his employment; but, it melted as I saw Mr. Jaggers relax into something like a smile, and Wemmick become bolder.

"What's all this?" said Mr. Jaggers. "You with an old father, and you with pleasant and playful ways?"

"Well!" returned Wemmick. "If I don't bring 'em here, what does it matter?"

"Pip," said Mr. Jaggers, laying his hand upon my arm, and smiling openly, "this man must be the most cunning impostor in all London."

"Not a bit of it," returned Wemmick, growing bolder and bolder. "I think you're another."

Again they exchanged their former odd looks, each apparently still distrustful that the other was taking him in.

"You with a pleasant home?" said Mr. Jaggers.

"Since it don't interfere with business," returned Wemmick, "let it be so. Now, I look at you, sir, I shouldn't wonder if you might be planning and contriving to have a pleasant home of your own, one of these days, when you're tired of all this work."

Mr. Jaggers nodded his head retrospectively two or three times, and actually drew a sigh. "Pip," said he, "we won't talk about 'poor dreams;' you know more about such things than I, having much fresher experience of that kind. But now, about this other matter. I'll put a case to you. Mind! I admit nothing."

He waited for me to declare that I quite understood that he expressly said that he admitted nothing.

"Now, Pip," said Mr. Jaggers, "put this case. Put the case that a woman, under such circumstances as you have mentioned, held her child concealed, and was obliged to communicate the fact to her legal adviser, on his representing to her that he must know, with an eye to the latitude of his defence, how the fact stood about that child. Put the case that at the same time he held a trust to find a child for an eccentric rich lady to adopt and bring up."

"I follow you, sir."

"Put the case that he lived in an atmosphere of evil, and that all he saw of children was, their being generated in great numbers for certain destruction. Put the case that he often saw children solemnly tried at a criminal bar, where they were held up to be seen; put the case that he habitually knew of their being imprisoned, whipped, transported, neglected, cast out, qualified in all ways for the hangman, and growing up to be hanged. Put the case that pretty nigh all the children he saw in his daily business life, he had reason to look upon as so much spawn, to develop into the fish that were to come to his net—to be prosecuted, defended, forsworn, made orphans, bedevilled somehow."

"I follow you, sir."

"Put the case, Pip, that here was one pretty little child out of the heap who could be saved; whom the father believed dead, and dared make no stir about; as to whom, over the mother, the legal adviser had this power: 'I know what you did, and how you did it. You came so and so, you did such and such things to divert suspicion. I have tracked you through it all, and I tell it you all. Part with the child, unless it should be necessary to produce it to clear you, and then it shall be produced. Give the child into my hands, and I will do my best to bring you off. If you are saved, your child will be saved too; if you are lost, your child is still saved.' Put the case that this was done, and that the woman was cleared."

"I understand you perfectly."

"But that I make no admissions?"

"But that you make no admissions." And Wemmick repeated, "No admissions."

"Put the case, Pip, that passion and the terror of death had a little shaken the woman's intellects, and that when she was set at liberty, she was scared out of the ways of the world and went to him to be sheltered. Put the case that he took her in, and that he kept down the old wild violent nature, whenever he saw an inkling of its breaking out, by asserting his power over her in the old way. Do you comprehend the imaginary case?"

"Quite."

"Put the case that the child grew up, and was married for money. That the mother was still living. That the father was still living. That the mother and father, unknown to one another, were dwelling within so many miles, furlongs, yards if you like, of one another. That the secret was still a secret, except that you had got wind of it. Put that last case to yourself very carefully."

"I do."

"I ask Wemmick to put it to *him*self very carefully." And Wemmick said, "I do."

"For whose sake would you reveal the secret? For the father's? I think he would not be much the better for the mother. For the mother's? I think if she had done such a deed she would be safer where she was. For the daughter's? I think it would hardly serve her, to establish her parentage for the information of her husband, and to drag her back to disgrace, after an escape of twenty years, pretty secure to last for life. But, add the case that you had loved her, Pip, and had made her the subject of those 'poor dreams' which have, at one time or another, been in the heads of more men than you think likely, then I tell you that you had better—and would much sooner when you had thought well of it—chop off that bandaged left hand of yours with your bandaged right hand, and then pass the chopper on to Wemmick there, to cut *that* off, too."

I looked at Wemmick, whose face was very grave. He gravely touched his lips with his forefinger. I did the same. Mr. Jaggers did the same. "Now, Wemmick," said the latter then, resuming his usual manner, "what item was it you were at, when Mr. Pip came in?"

Standing by for a little, while they were at work, I observed that the odd looks they had cast at one another were repeated several times: with this difference now, that each of them seemed suspicious, not to say conscious, of having shown himself in a weak and unprofessional light to the other. For this reason, I suppose, they were now inflexible with one another; Mr. Jaggers being highly dictatorial, and Wemmick obstinately justifying himself whenever there was the smallest point in abeyance for a moment. I had never seen them on such ill terms; for generally they got on very well indeed together.

But, they were both happily relieved by the opportune appearance of Mike, the client with the fur cap, and the habit of wiping his nose on his sleeve, whom I had seen on the very first day of my appearance within those walls. This individual, who, either in his own person or in that of some member of his family, seemed to be always in trouble (which in that place meant Newgate), called to announce that his eldest daughter was taken up on suspicion of shop-lifting. As he imparted this melancholy circumstance to Wemmick, Mr. Jaggers standing magisterially before the fire and taking no share in the proceedings, Mike's eye happened to twinkle with a tear.

"What are you about?" demanded Wemmick, with the utmost indignation. "What do you come snivelling here for?"

"I didn't go to do it, Mr. Wemmick."

"You did," said Wemmick. "How dare you? You're not in a fit state to come here, if you can't come here without spluttering like a bad pen. What do you mean by it?"

"A man can't help his feelings, Mr. Wemmick," pleaded Mike.

"His what?" demanded Wemmick, quite savagely. "Say that again!"

"Now look here, my man," said Mr. Jaggers, advancing a step, and pointing to the door. "Get out of this office. I'll have no feelings here. Get out."

"It serves you right," said Wemmick. "Get out."

So the unfortunate Mike very humbly withdrew, and Mr. Jaggers and Wemmick appeared to have re-established their good understanding, and went to work again with an air of refreshment upon them as if they had just had lunch.

CHAPTER LII.

FROM Little Britain, I went, with my cheque in my pocket, to Miss Skiffins's brother, the accountant; and Miss Skiffins's brother, the accountant, going straight to Clarriker's and bringing Clarriker to me, I had the great satisfaction of concluding that arrangement. It was the only good thing I had done, and the only completed thing I had done, since I was first apprised of my great expectations.

Clarriker informing me on that occasion that the affairs of the House were steadily progressing, that he would now be able to establish a small branch-house in the East which was much wanted for the extension of the business, and that Herbert in his new partnership capacity would go out and take charge of it, I found that I must have prepared for a separation from my friend, even though my own affairs had been more settled. And now indeed I felt as if my last anchor were loosening its hold, and I should soon be driving with the winds and waves.

But, there was recompense in the joy with which Herbert would come home of a night and tell me of these changes, little imagining that he told me no news, and would sketch airy pictures of himself conducting Clara Barley to the land of the Arabian Nights, and of me going out to join them (with a caravan of camels, I believe), and of our all going up the Nile and seeing wonders. Without being sanguine as to my own part in those bright plans, I felt that Herbert's way was clearing fast, and that old Bill Barley had but to stick to his pepper and rum, and his daughter would soon be happily provided for.

We had now got into the month of March. My left arm,

though it presented no bad symptoms, took in the natural course so long to heal that I was still unable to get a coat on. My right arm was tolerably restored;—disfigured, but fairly serviceable.

On a Monday morning, when Herbert and I were at breakfast, I received the following letter from Wemmick by the post.

"Walworth. Burn this as soon as read. Early in the week, or say Wednesday, you might do what you know of, if you felt disposed to try it. Now burn."

When I had shown this to Herbert and had put it in the fire—but not before we had both got it by heart—we considered what to do. For, of course, my being disabled could now be no longer kept out of view.

"I have thought it over again and again," said Herbert, "and I think I know a better course than taking a Thames waterman. Take Startop. A good fellow, a skilled hand, fond of us, and enthusiastic and honourable."

I had thought of him, more than once.

"But how much would you tell him, Herbert?"

"It is necessary to tell him very little. Let him suppose it a mere freak, but a secret one, until the morning comes: then let him know that there is urgent reason for your getting Provis aboard and away. You go with him?"

"No doubt."

"Where?"

It had seemed to me, in the many anxious considerations I had given the point, almost indifferent what port we made for—Hamburg, Rotterdam, Antwerp—the place signified little, so that he was out of England. Any foreign steamer that fell in our way and would take us up would do. I had always proposed to myself to get him well down the river in the boat; certainly well beyond Gravesend, which was a critical place for search or inquiry if suspicion were afoot. As foreign steamers would leave London at about the time of high-water, our plan would be to get down the river by a previous ebb-tide, and lie by in some quiet spot until we could pull off to one. The time when one would be due where we lay, wherever that might be, could be calculated pretty nearly, if we made inquiries beforehand.

Herbert assented to all this, and we went out immediately after breakfast to pursue our investigations. We found that a steamer for Hamburg was likely to suit our purpose best, and we directed our thoughts chiefly to that vessel. But we noted down what other foreign steamers would leave London with the same tide, and we satisfied ourselves that we knew the build and colour of each. We then separated for a few hours; I to get at once such passports as were necessary; Herbert, to see Startop at his lodgings. We both did what we had to do without any hindrance, and when we met again at one o'clock reported it done. I, for my part, was prepared with passports; Herbert had seen Startop, and he was more than ready to join.

Those two would pull a pair of oars, we settled, and I would steer: our charge would be sitter, and keep quiet; as speed was not our object, we should make way enough. We arranged that Herbert should not come home to dinner before going to Mill Pond Bank that evening; that he should not go there at all, to-morrow evening, Tuesday; that he should prepare Provis to come down to some Stairs hard by the house, on Wednesday, when he saw us approach, and not sooner; that all the arrangements with him should be concluded that Monday night; and that he should be communicated with no more in any way, until we took him on board.

These precautions well understood by both of us, I went home.

On opening the outer door of our chambers with my key, I found a letter in the box, directed to me; a very dirty letter, though not ill-written. It had been delivered by hand (of course since I left home), and its contents were these:

"If you are not afraid to come to the old marshes to-night or to-morrow night at Nine, and to come to the little sluice-house by the lime-kiln, you had better come. If you want information regarding *your uncle Provis* you had much better come and tell no one and lose no time. *You must come alone.* Bring this with you."

I had had load enough upon my mind before the receipt of this strange letter. What to do now, I could not tell. And the worst was, that I must decide quickly, or I should miss the afternoon coach, which would take me down in time for to-night. To-morrow night I could not think of going, for it would be too close upon the time of the flight. And again, for anything I knew, the proffered information might have some important bearing on the flight itself.

If I had had ample time for consideration, I believe I should still have gone. Having hardly any time for consideration—my watch showing me that the coach started within half an hour—I resolved to go. I should certainly not have gone, but for the reference to my Uncle Provis. That, coming on Wemmick's letter and the morning's busy preparation, turned the scale.

It is so difficult to become clearly possessed of the contents of almost any letter, in a violent hurry, that I had to read this mysterious epistle again, twice, before its injunction to me to be secret got mechanically into my mind. Yielding to it in the same mechanical kind of way, I left a note in pencil for Herbert, telling him that as I should be so soon going away, I knew not for how long, I had decided to hurry down and back, to ascertain for myself how Miss Havisham was faring. I had then barely time to get my great-coat, lock up the chambers, and make for the coach-office by the short byeways. If I had taken a hackney-chariot and gone by the streets, I should have missed my aim; going as I did, I caught the coach just as it came out of the yard. I was the only inside passenger, jolting away knee-deep in straw, when I came to myself.

For, I really had not been myself since the receipt of the letter; it had so bewildered me, ensuing on the hurry of the morning. The morning hurry and flutter had been great, for, long and anxiously as I had waited for Wemmick, his hint had come like a surprise at last. And now, I began to wonder at myself for being in the coach, and to doubt whether I had sufficient reason for being there, and to consider whether I should get out presently and go back, and to argue against ever heeding an anonymous communication, and, in short, to pass through all those phases of contradiction and indecision to which I suppose very few hurried people are strangers. Still, the reference to Provis by name, mastered everything. I reasoned as I had reasoned already without knowing it—if that be reasoning—in case any harm should befall him through my not going, how could I ever forgive myself!

It was dark before we got down, and the journey seemed long and dreary to me who could see little of it inside, and who could not go outside in my disabled state. Avoiding the Blue Boar, I put up at an inn of minor reputation down the town, and ordered some dinner. While it was preparing, I went to Satis House and inquired for Miss Havisham; she was still very ill, though considered something better.

My inn had once been a part of an ancient ecclesiastical house, and I dined in a little octagonal common-room, like a font. As I was not able to cut my dinner, the old landlord with a shining bald head did it for me. This bringing us into conversation, he was so good as to entertain me with my own story—of course with the popular feature that Pumblechook was my earliest benefactor and the founder of my fortunes.

"Do you know the young man?" said I.

"Know him?" repeated the landlord. "Ever since he was—no height at all."

"Does he ever come back to this neighbourhood?"

"Ay, he comes back," said the landlord, "to his great friends, now and again, and gives the cold shoulder to the man that made him."

"What man is that?"

"Him that I speak of," said the landlord. "Mr. Pumblechook."

"Is he ungrateful to no one else?"

"No doubt he would be, if he could," returned the landlord, "but he can't. And why? Because Pumblechook done everything for him."

"Does Pumblechook say so?"

"Say so!" replied the landlord. "He han't no call to say so."

"But does he say so?"

"It would turn a man's blood to white wine winegar, to hear him tell of it, sir," said the landlord.

I thought, "Yet Joe, dear Joe, *you* never tell of it. Long-suffering and loving Joe, *you* never complain. Nor you, sweet-tempered Biddy!"

"Your appetite's been touched like, by your accident," said the landlord, glancing at the bandaged arm under my coat. "Try a tenderer bit."

"No thank you," I replied, turning from the table to brood over the fire. "I can eat no more. Please take it away."

I had never been struck at so keenly, for my thanklessness to Joe, as through the brazen impostor Pumblechook. The falser he, the truer Joe; the meaner he, the nobler Joe.

My heart was deeply and most deservedly humbled as I mused over the fire for an hour or more. The striking of the clock aroused me, but not from my dejection or remorse, and I got up and had my coat fastened round my neck, and went out. I had previously sought in my pockets for the letter, that I might refer to it again, but I could not find it, and was uneasy to think that it must have been dropped in the straw of the coach. I knew very well, however, that the appointed place was the little sluice-house by the lime-kiln on the marshes, and the hour nine. Towards the marshes I now went straight, having no time to spare.

CHAPTER LIII.

It was a dark night, though the full moon rose as I left the enclosed lands, and passed out upon the marshes. Beyond their dark line there was a ribbon of clear sky, hardly broad enough to hold the red large moon. In a few minutes she had ascended out of that clear field, in among the piled mountains of cloud.

There was a melancholy wind, and the marshes were very dismal. A stranger would have found them insupportable, and even to me they were so oppressive that I hesitated, half inclined to go back. But, I knew them, and could have found my way on a far darker night, and had no excuse for returning, being there. So, having come there against my inclination, I went on against it.

The direction that I took, was not that in which my old home lay, nor that in which we had pursued the convicts. My back was turned towards the distant Hulks as I walked on, and, though I could see the old lights away on the spits of sand, I saw them over my shoulder. I knew the lime-kiln as well as I knew the old Battery, but they were miles apart; so that if a light had been burning at each point that night, there would have been a long strip of the blank horizon between the two bright specks.

At first, I had to shut some gates after me, and now and then to stand still while the cattle that were lying in the banked-up pathway, arose and blundered down among the grass and reeds. But after a little while, I seemed to have the whole flats to myself.

It was another half-hour before I drew near to the kiln. The lime was burning with a sluggish stifling smell, but the fires were made up and left, and no workmen were visible. Hard by was a small stone-quarry. It lay directly in my way, and had been worked that day, as I saw by the tools and barrows that were lying about.

Coming up again to the marsh level out of this excavation—for the rude path lay through it—I saw a light in the old sluice-house. I quickened my pace, and knocked at the door with my hand. Waiting for some reply, I looked about me, noticing how the sluice was abandoned and broken, and how the house—of wood with a tiled roof —would not be proof against the weather much longer, if it were so even now, and how the mud and ooze were coated with lime, and how the choking vapour of the kiln crept in a ghostly way towards me. Still there was no answer, and I knocked again. No answer still, and I tried the latch.

It rose under my hand, and the door yielded. Looking in, I saw a lighted candle on a table, a bench, and a mattress on a truckle bedstead. As there was a loft above, I called, "Is there any one here?" but no voice answered. Then, I looked at my watch, and, finding it was past nine, called again, "Is there any one here?" There being still no answer, I went out at the door, irresolute what to do.

It was beginning to rain fast. Seeing nothing save what I had seen already, I turned back into the house, and stood just within the shelter of the doorway, looking out into the night. While I was considering that some one must have been there lately and must soon be coming back, or the candle would not be burning, it came into my head to look if the wick were long. I turned round to do so, and had taken up the candle in my hand, when it was extinguished by some violent shock, and the next thing I comprehended was, that I had been caught in a strong running noose, thrown over my head from behind.

"Now," said a suppressed voice with an oath, "I've got you!"

"What is this?" I cried, struggling. "Who is it? Help, help, help!"

Not only were my arms pulled close to my sides, but the pressure on my bad arm caused me exquisite pain. Sometimes a strong man's hand, sometimes a strong man's breast, was set against my mouth to deaden my cries, and with a hot breath always close to me, I struggled ineffectually in the dark, while I was fastened tight to the wall. "And now," said the suppressed voice with another oath, "call out again, and I'll make short work of you!"

Faint and sick with the pain of my injured arm, bewildered by the surprise, and yet conscious how easily this threat could be put in execution, I desisted, and tried to ease my arm were it ever so little. But it was bound too tight for that. I felt as if, having been burnt before, it were now being boiled.

The sudden exclusion of the night and the substitution of black darkness in its place, warned me that the man had closed a shutter. After groping about for a little, he found the flint and steel he wanted, and began to strike a light. I strained my sight upon the sparks that fell among the tinder, and upon which he breathed and breathed, match in hand, but I could only see his lips, and the blue point of the match; even those but fitfully. The tinder was damp—no wonder there—and one after another the sparks died out.

The man was in no hurry, and struck again with the flint and steel. As the sparks fell thick and bright about him, I could see his hands and touches of his face, and could make out that he was seated and bending over the table; but nothing more. Presently I saw his blue lips again, breathing on the tinder, and then a flare of light flashed up, and showed me Orlick.

Whom I had looked for, I don't know. I had not looked for him. Seeing him, I felt that I was in a dangerous strait indeed, and I kept my eyes upon him.

He lighted the candle from the flaring match with great deliberation, and dropped the match, and trod it out. Then, he put the candle away from him on the table, so that he could see me, and sat with his arms folded on the table and looked at me. I made out that I was fastened to a stout perpendicular ladder a few inches from the wall —a fixture there—the means of ascent to the loft above.

"Now," said he, when we had surveyed one another for some time, "I've got you."

"Unbind me. Let me go!"

"Ah!" he returned, "I'll let you go. I'll let you go to the moon, I'll let you go to the stars. All in good time."

"Why have you lured me here?"

"Don't you know?" said he, with a deadly look.

"Why have you set upon me in the dark?"

"Because I mean to do it all myself. One keeps a secret better than two. Oh, you enemy, you enemy!"

His enjoyment of the spectacle I furnished, as he sat with his arms folded on the table, shaking his head at me and hugging himself, had a malignity in it that made me tremble. As I watched him in silence, he put his hand into the corner at his side, and took up a gun with a brass-bound stock.

"Do you know this?" said he, making as if he would take aim at me. "Do you know where you saw it afore? Speak, wolf!"

"Yes," I answered.

"You cost me that place. You did. Speak!"

"What else could I do?"

"You did that, and that would be enough, without more. How dared you come betwixt me and a young woman I liked?"

"When did I?"

"When didn't you? It was you as always give Old Orlick a bad name to her."

"You gave it to yourself; you gained it for yourself. I could have done you no harm, if you had done yourself none."

"You're a liar. And you'll take any pains, and spend any money, to drive me out of this country, will you?" said he, repeating my words to Biddy, in the last interview I had with her. "Now, I'll tell you a piece of information. It was never so worth your while to get me out of this country, as it is to-night. It was never so worth your money twenty times told, to the last brass farden!" As he shook his heavy hand at me, with his mouth snarling like a tiger's, I felt that it was true.

"What are you going to do to me?"

"I'm a going," said he, bringing his fist down upon the table with a heavy blow, and rising as the blow fell, to give it greater force, "I'm a going to have your life!"

He leaned forward staring at me, slowly unclenched his hand and drew it across his mouth as if his mouth watered for me, and sat down again.

"You was always in Old Orlick's way since ever you was a child. You goes out of his way this present night. He'll have no more on you. You're dead."

I felt that I had come to the brink of my grave. For a moment I looked wildly round my trap for any chance of escape; but there was none.

"More than that," said he, folding his arms on the table again, "I won't have a rag of you, I won't have a bone of you, left on earth. I'll put your body in the kiln—I'd carry two such to it, on my shoulders—and, let people suppose what they may of you, they shall never know nothing."

My mind, with inconceivable rapidity, followed out all the consequences of such a death. Estella's father would believe I had deserted him, would be taken, would die accusing me; even Herbert would doubt me, when he compared the letter I had left for him, with the fact that I had called at Miss Havisham's gate for only a moment; Joe and Biddy would never know how sorry I had been that night, none would ever know what I had suffered, how true I had meant to be, what an agony I had passed through. The death close before me was terrible, but far more terrible than death was the dread of being misremembered after death. And so quick were my thoughts, that I saw myself despised by unborn generations—Estella's children, and their children—while the wretch's words were yet on his lips.

"Now, wolf," said he, "afore I kill you like any other beast—which is wot I mean to do and wot I have tied you up for—I'll have a good look at you and a good goad at you. Oh, you enemy!"

It had passed through my thoughts to cry out for help again; though few could know better than I, the solitary nature of the spot, and the hopelessness of aid. But as he sat gloating over me, I was supported by a scornful detestation of him that sealed my lips. Above all things, I resolved that I would not entreat him, and that I would die making some last poor resistance to him. Softened as my thoughts of all the rest of men were in that dire extremity; humbly beseeching pardon, as I did, of Heaven; melted at heart, as I was, by the thought that I had taken no farewell, and never now could take farewell, of those who were dear to me, or could explain myself to them, or ask for their compassion on my miserable errors; still, if I could have killed him, even in dying, I would have done it.

"DO YOU KNOW THIS?" SAID HE.

He had been drinking, and his eyes were red and blood-shot. Around his neck was slung a tin bottle, as I had often seen his meat and drink slung about him in other days. He brought the bottle to his lips, and took a fiery drink from it; and I smelt the strong spirits that I saw flash into his face.

"Wolf!" said he, folding his arms again, "Old Orlick's a going to tell you somethink. It was you as did for your shrew sister."

Again my mind, with its former inconceivable rapidity, had exhausted the whole subject of the attack upon my sister, her illness, and her death, before his slow and hesitating speech had formed those words.

"It was you, villain," said I.

"I tell you it was your doing—I tell you it was done through you," he retorted, catching up the gun, and making a blow with the stock at the vacant air between us. "I come upon her from behind, as I come upon you to-night. I giv' it her! I left her for dead, and if there had been a lime-kiln as nigh her as there is now nigh you, she shouldn't have come to life again. But it warn't Old Orlick as did it; it was you. You was favoured, and he was bullied and beat. Old Orlick bullied and beat, eh? Now you pays for it. You done it; now you pays for it."

He drank again, and became more ferocious. I saw by his tilting of the bottle that there was no great quantity left in it. I distinctly understood that he was working himself up with its contents, to make an end of me. I knew that every drop it held, was a drop of my life. I knew that I was changed into a part of the vapour that had crept towards me but a little while before, like my own warning ghost, he would do as he had done in my sister's case—make all haste to the town, and be seen slouching about there, drinking at the ale-houses. My rapid mind pursued him to the town, made a picture of the street with him in it, and contrasted its lights and life with the lonely marsh and the white vapour creeping over it, into which I should have dissolved.

It was not only that I could have summed up years and years and years while he said a dozen words, but that what he did say, presented pictures to me, and not mere words. In the excited and exalted state of my brain, I could not think of a place without seeing it, or of persons without seeing them. It is impossible to over-state the vividness of these images, and yet I was so intent, all the time, upon him himself—who would not be intent on the tiger crouching to spring!—that I knew of the slightest action of his fingers.

When he had drunk this second time, he rose from the bench on which he sat, and pushed the table aside. Then, he took up the candle, and shading it with his murderous hand so as to throw its light on me, stood before me, looking at me and enjoying the sight.

"Wolf, I'll tell you something more. It was Old Orlick as you tumbled over on your stairs that night."

I saw the staircase with its extinguished lamps. I saw the shadows of the heavy stair-rails, thrown by the watchman's lantern on the wall. I saw the rooms that I was never to see again; here, a door half open; there, a door closed; all the articles of furniture around.

"And why was Old Orlick there? I'll tell you something more, wolf. You and her *have* pretty well hunted me out of this country, so far as getting an easy living in it goes, and I've took up with new companions and new masters. Some of 'em writes my letters when I wants 'em wrote—do you mind?—writes my letters, wolf! They

writes fifty hands; they're not like sneaking you, as writes but one. I've had a firm mind and a firm will to have your life, since you was down here at your sister's burying. I han't seen a way to get you safe, and I've looked arter you to know your ins and outs. For, says Old Orlick to himself, 'Somehow or another I'll have him!' What! When I looks for you, I finds your uncle Provis, eh?"

Mill Pond Bank, and Chinks's Basin, and the Old Green Copper Rope-Walk, all so clear and plain! Provis in his rooms, the signal whose use was over, pretty Clara, the good motherly woman, old Bill Barley on his back, all drifting by, as on the swift stream of my life fast running out to sea!

"*You* with a uncle too! Why, I knowed you at Gargery's when you was so small a wolf that I could have took your weazen betwixt this finger and thumb and chucked you away dead (as I'd thoughts o' doing, odd times, when I saw you a loitering among the pollards on a Sunday) and you hadn't found no uncles then. No, not you! But when Old Orlick come for to hear that your uncle Provis had mostlike wore the leg-iron wot Old Orlick had picked up, filed asunder, on these meshes ever so many year ago, and wot he kep by him till he dropped your sister with it, like a bullock, as he means to drop you—hey? —when he come for to hear that—hey?——"

In his savage taunting, he flared the candle so close at me, that I turned my face aside to save it from the flame.

"Ah!" he cried, laughing, after doing it again, "the burnt child dreads the fire! Old Orlick knowed you was burnt, Old Orlick knowed you was a smuggling your uncle Provis away, Old Orlick's a match for you and knowed you'd come to-night! Now I'll tell you something more, wolf, and this ends it. There's them that's as good a match for your uncle Provis as Old Orlick has been for you. Let him 'ware them when he's lost his nevvy. Let him 'ware them when, no man can't find a rag of his dear relation's clothes, nor yet a bone of his body. There's them that can't and won't have Magwitch—yes, *I* know the name!—alive in the same land with them, and that's had such sure information of him when he was alive in another land, as that he couldn't and shouldn't leave it unbeknown and put them in danger. P'raps it's them that writes fifty hands, and that's not like sneaking you as writes but one. 'Ware Compeyson, Magwitch, and the gallows!"

He flared the candle at me again, smoking my face and hair, and for an instant blinding me, and turned his powerful back as he replaced the light on the table. I had thought a prayer, and had been with Joe and Biddy and Herbert, before he turned towards me again.

There was a clear space of a few feet between the table and the opposite wall. Within this space, he now slouched backwards and forwards. His great strength seemed to sit stronger upon him than ever before, as he did this with his hands hanging loose and heavy at his sides, and with his eyes scowling at me. I had no grain of hope left. Wild as my inward hurry was, and wonderful the force of the pictures that rushed by me instead of thoughts, I could yet clearly understand that unless he had resolved that I was within a few moments of surely perishing out of all human knowledge, he would never have told me what he had told.

Of a sudden, he stopped, took the cork out of his bottle, and tossed it away. Light as it was, I heard it fall like a plummet. He swallowed slowly, tilting up the bottle by little and little, and now he looked at me no more. The last few drops of liquor he poured into the palm of his hand, and licked up. Then with a sudden hurry of violence and swearing horribly, he threw the bottle from him, and stooped; and I saw in his hand a stone-hammer with a long heavy handle.

The resolution I had made did not desert me, for, without uttering one vain word of appeal to him, I shouted out with all my might, and struggled with all my might. It was only my head and my legs that I could move, but to that extent I struggled with all the force, until then unknown, that was within me. In the same instant I heard responsive shouts, saw figures and a gleam of light dash in at the door, heard voices and tumult, and saw Orlick emerge from a struggle of men, as if it were tumbling water, clear the table at a leap, and fly out into the night!

After a blank, I found that I was lying unbound, on the floor, in the same place, with my head on some one's knee. My eyes were fixed on the ladder against the wall, when I came to myself—had opened on it before my mind saw it—and thus as I recovered consciousness, I knew that I was in the place where I had lost it.

Too indifferent at first, even to look round and ascertain who supported me, I was lying looking at the ladder, when there came between me and it, a face. The face of Trabb's boy!

"I think he's all right!" said Trabb's boy, in a sober voice; "but ain't he just pale though!"

At these words, the face of him who supported me looked over into mine, and I saw my supporter to be——

"Herbert! Great Heaven!"

"Softly," said Herbert. "Gently, Handel. Don't be too eager."

"And our old comrade, Startop!" I cried, as he too bent over me.

"Remember what he is going to assist us in," said Herbert, "and be calm."

The allusion made me spring up; though I dropped again from the pain in my arm. "The time has not gone by, Herbert, has it? What night is to-night? How long have I been here?" For, I had a strange and strong misgiving that I had been lying there a long time—a day and a night—two days and nights—more.

"The time has not gone by. It is still Monday night."

"Thank God!"

"And you have all to-morrow, Tuesday, to rest in," said Herbert. "But you can't help groaning, my dear Handel. What hurt have you got? Can you stand?"

"Yes, yes," said I, "I can walk. I have no hurt but in this throbbing arm."

They laid it bare, and did what they could. It was violently swollen and inflamed, and I could scarcely endure to have it touched. But, they tore up their handkerchiefs to make fresh bandages, and carefully replaced it in the sling, until we could get to the town and obtain some cooling lotion to put upon it. In a little while we had shut the door of the dark and empty sluice-house, and were passing through the quarry on our way back. Trabb's boy—Trabb's overgrown young man now—went before us with a lantern, which was the light I had seen come in at the door. But, the moon was a good two hours higher than when I had last seen the sky, and the night though rainy was much lighter. The white vapour of the kiln was passing from us as we went by, and, as I had thought a prayer before, I thought a thanksgiving now.

Entreating Herbert to tell me how he had come to my rescue—which at first he had flatly refused to do, but had insisted on my remaining quiet—I learnt that I had in my hurry dropped the letter, open, in our chambers, where he, coming home to bring with him Startop, whom he had met in the street on his way to me, found it, very soon after I was gone. Its tone made him uneasy, and the more so because of the inconsistency between it and the hasty letter I had left for him. His uneasiness increasing instead of subsiding after a quarter of an hour's consideration, he set off for the coach-office, with Startop, who volunteered his company, to make inquiry when the next coach went down. Finding that the afternoon coach was gone, and finding that his uneasiness grew into positive alarm, as obstacles came in his way, he resolved to follow in a post-chaise. So, he and Startop arrived at the Blue Boar, fully expecting there to find me, or tidings of me; but, finding neither, went on to Miss Havisham's, where they lost me. Hereupon they went back to the hotel (doubtless at about the time when I was hearing the popular local version of my own story), to refresh themselves and to get some one to guide them out upon the marshes. Among the loungers under the Boar's archway, happened to be Trabb's boy—true to his ancient habit of happening to be everywhere where he had no business—and Trabb's boy had seen me passing from Miss Havisham's, in the direction of my dining-place. Thus, Trabb's boy became their guide, and with him they went out to the sluice-house: though by the town way to the marshes, which I had avoided. Now, as they went along, Herbert reflected, that I might, after all, have been brought there on some genuine and serviceable errand tending to Provis's safety, and bethinking himself that in that case interruption might be mischievous, left his guide and Startop on the edge of the quarry, and went on by himself, and stole round the house two or three times, endeavouring to ascertain whether all was right within. As he could hear nothing but indistinct sounds of one deep rough voice (this was while my mind was so busy), he even at last began to doubt whether I was there, when suddenly I cried out loudly, and he answered the cries, and rushed in, closely followed by the other two.

When I told Herbert what had passed within the house, he was for our immediately going before a magistrate in the town, late at night as it was, and getting out a warrant. But, I had already considered that such a course, by detaining us there, or binding us to come back, might be fatal to Provis. There was no gainsaying this difficulty, and we relinquished all thoughts of pursuing Orlick at that time. For the present, under the circumstances, we deemed it prudent to make rather light of the matter to Trabb's boy; who I am convinced would have been much affected by disappointment, if he had known that his intervention saved me from the lime-kiln. Not that Trabb's boy was of a malignant nature, but that he had too much spare vivacity, and that it was in his constitution to want variety and excitement at anybody's expense. When we parted, I presented him with two guineas (which seemed to meet his views), and told him that I was sorry ever to have had an ill opinion of him (which made no impression on him at all).

Wednesday being so close upon us, we determined to go back to London that night, three in the post-chaise; the rather, as we should then be clear away, before the night's adventure began to be talked of. Herbert got a large bottle of stuff for my arm, and by dint of having this stuff dropped over it all the night through, I was just able to bear its pain on the journey. It was daylight when we reached the Temple, and I went at once to bed, and lay in bed all day.

My terror, as I lay there, of falling ill and being unfitted for to-morrow, was so besetting, that I wonder it did not disable me of itself. It would have done so, pretty surely, in conjunction with the mental wear and tear I had suffered, but for the unnatural strain upon me that to-morrow was. So anxiously looked forward to, charged with such consequences, its results so impenetrably hidden though so near.

No precaution could have been more obvious than our refraining from communication with him that day; yet this again increased my restlessness. I started at every footstep and every sound, believing that he was discovered and taken, and this was the messenger to tell me so. I persuaded myself that I knew he was taken; that there was something more upon my mind than a fear or a presentiment; that the fact had occurred, and I had a mysterious knowledge of it. As the day wore on and no ill news came, as the day closed in and darkness fell, my overshadowing dread of being disabled by illness before to-morrow morning, altogether mastered me. My burning arm throbbed, and my burning head throbbed, and I fancied I was beginning to wander. I counted up to high numbers, to make sure of myself, and repeated passages that I knew in prose and verse. It happened sometimes that in the mere escape of a fatigued mind, I dozed for some moments or forgot; then I would say to myself with a start, "Now it has come, and I am turning delirious!"

They kept me very quiet all day, and kept my arm constantly dressed, and gave me cooling drinks. Whenever I fell asleep, I awoke with the notion I had had in the sluice-house, that a long time had elapsed and the opportunity to save him was gone. About midnight I got out of bed and went to Herbert, with the conviction that I had been asleep for four-and-twenty hours, and that Wednesday was past. It was the last self-exhausting effort of my fretfulness, for after that, I slept soundly.

Wednesday morning was dawning when I looked out of window. The winking lights upon the bridges were already pale, the coming sun was like a marsh of fire on the horizon. The river, still dark and mysterious, was spanned by bridges that were turning coldly grey, with here and there at top a warm touch from the burning in the sky. As I looked along the clustered roofs, with church towers and spires shooting into the unusually clear air, the sun rose up, and a veil seemed to be drawn from the river, and millions of sparkles burst out upon its waters. From me, too, a veil seemed to be drawn, and I felt strong and well.

Herbert lay asleep in his bed, and our old fellow-student lay asleep on the sofa. I could not dress myself without help, but I made up the fire which was still burning, and got some coffee ready for them. In good time they too started up strong and well, and we admitted the sharp morning air at the windows, and looked at the tide that was still flowing towards us.

"When it turns at nine o'clock," said Herbert, cheerfully, "look out for us, and stand ready, you over there at Mill Pond Bank."

CHAPTER LIV.

It was one of those March days when the sun shines hot and the wind blows cold: when it is summer in the light, and winter in the shade. We had our pea-coats with us, and I took a bag. Of all my worldly possessions I took no more than the few necessaries that filled the bag. Where I might go, what I might do, or when I might return, were questions utterly unknown to me; nor did I vex my mind with them, for it was wholly set on Provis's safety. I only wondered for the passing moment, as I stopped at the door and looked back, under what altered circumstances I should next see those rooms, if ever.

We loitered down to the Temple stairs, and stood loitering there, as if we were not quite decided to go upon the water at all. Of course I had taken care that the boat should be ready, and everything in order. After a little show of indecision, which there were none to see but the two or three amphibious creatures belonging to our Temple stairs, we went on board and cast off; Herbert in the bow, I steering. It was then about high-water—half-past eight.

Our plan was this. The tide, beginning to run down at nine, and being with us until three, we intended still to creep on after it had turned, and row against it until dark. We should then be well in those long reaches below Gravesend, between Kent and Essex, where the river is broad and solitary, where the water-side inhabitants are very few, and where lone public-houses are scattered here and there, of which we could choose one for a resting-place. There, we meant to lie by, all night. The steamer for Hamburg, and the steamer for Rotterdam, would start for London at about nine on Thursday morning. We should know at what time to expect them, according to where we were, and would hail the first; so that if by any accident we were not taken aboard, we should have another chance. We knew the distinguishing marks of each vessel.

The relief of being at last engaged in the execution of the purpose, was so great to me that I felt it difficult to realise the condition which I had been in a few hours before. The crisp air, the sunlight, the movement on the river, and the moving river itself—the road that ran with us, seeming to sympathise with us, animate us, and encourage us on—freshened me with new hope. I felt mortified to be of so little use in the boat; but there were few better oarsmen than my two friends, and they rowed with a steady stroke, that was to last all day.

At that time, the steam-traffic on the Thames was far below its present extent, and watermen's boats were far more numerous. Of barges, sailing colliers, and coasting traders, there were perhaps as many as now; but, of steamships, great and small, not a tithe or a twentieth part so many. Early as it was, there were plenty of scullers going here and there that morning, and plenty of barges dropping down with the tide; the navigation of the river between bridges, in an open boat, was a much easier and commoner matter in those days than it is in these; and we went ahead among many skiffs and wherries, briskly.

Old London Bridge was soon passed, and old Billingsgate market with its oyster-boats and Dutchmen, and the White Tower and Traitor's Gate, and we were in among the tiers of shipping. Here, were the Leith, Aberdeen, and Glasgow steamers, loading and unloading goods, and looking immensely high out of the water as we passed alongside; here, were colliers by the score and score, with the coal-whippers plunging off stages on deck, as counterweights to measures of coal swinging up, which were then rattled over the side into barges; here, at her moorings, was to-morrow's steamer for Rotterdam, of which we took good notice; and here to-morrow's for Hamburg, under whose bowsprit we crossed. And now I, sitting in the stern, could see with a faster beating heart, Mill Pond Bank and Mill Pond stairs.

"Is he there?" said Herbert.

"Not yet."

"Right! He was not to come down till he saw us. Can you see his signal?"

"Not well from here; but I think I see it.—Now I see him! Pull both. Easy, Herbert. Oars!"

We touched the stairs lightly for a single moment, and he was on board and we were off again. He had a boat-cloak with him, and a black canvas bag, and he looked as like a river-pilot as my heart could have wished.

"Dear boy!" he said, putting his arm on my shoulder, as he took his seat. "Faithful dear boy, well done. Thankye, thankye!"

Again among the tiers of shipping, in and out, avoiding rusty chain-cables, frayed hempen hawsers, and bobbing buoys, sinking for the moment floating broken baskets, scattering floating chips of wood and shaving, cleaving floating scum of coal, in and out, under the figure-head of the John of Sunderland making a speech to the winds (as is done by many Johns), and the Betsy of Yarmouth with a firm formality of bosom and her nobby eyes starting two inches out of her head; in and out, hammers going in ship-builders' yards, saws going at timber, clashing engines going at things unknown, pumps going in leaky ships, cap-stans going, ships going out to sea, and unintelligible sea-creatures roaring curses over the bulwarks at respondent lightermen; in and out—out at last upon the clearer river, where the ships' boys might take their fenders in, no longer fishing in troubled waters with them over the side, and where the festooned sails might fly out to the wind.

At the Stairs where we had taken him aboard, and ever since, I had looked warily for any token of our being suspected. I had seen none. We certainly had not been, and at that time as certainly we were not, either attended or followed by any boat. If we had been waited on by any boat, I should have run in to shore, and have obliged her to go on, or to make her purpose evident. But, we held our own, without any appearance of molestation.

He had his boat-cloak on him, and looked, as I have said, a natural part of the scene. It was remarkable (but perhaps the wretched life he had led accounted for it), that he was the least anxious of any of us. He was not indifferent, for he told me that he hoped to live to see his gentleman one of the best of gentlemen in a foreign country; he was not disposed to be passive or resigned, as I understood it; but he had no notion of meeting danger half way. When it came upon him, he confronted it, but it must come before h troubled himself.

"If you knowed, dear boy," he said to me, "what it is to sit here alonger my dear boy and have my smoke, arter having been day by day betwixt four walls, you'd envy me. But you don't know what it is."

"I think I know the delights of freedom," I answered.

"Ah," said he, shaking his head gravely. "But you don't know it equal to me. You must have been under lock and key, dear boy, to know it equal to me—but I ain't a going to be low."

It occurred to me as inconsistent, that for any mastering idea, he should have endangered his freedom and even his life. But I reflected that perhaps freedom without danger

was too much apart from all the habit of his existence to be to him what it would be to another man. I was not far out, since he said, after smoking a little:

"You see, dear boy, when I was over yonder, t'other side the world, I was always a looking to this side; and it come flat to be there, for all I was a growing rich. Everybody knowed Magwitch, and Magwitch could come, and Magwitch could go, and nobody's head would be troubled about him. They ain't so easy concerning me here, dear boy—wouldn't be, leastwise, if they knowed where I was."

"If all goes well," said I, "you will be perfectly free and safe again, within a few hours."

"Well," he returned, drawing a long breath, "I hope so."

"And think so?"

He dipped his hand in the water over the boat's gun-wale, and said, smiling with that softened air upon him which was not new to me:

"Ay, I s'pose I think so, dear boy. We'd be puzzled to be more quiet and easy-going than we are at present. But—it's a flowing so soft and pleasant through the water, p'raps, as makes me think it—I was a thinking through my smoke just then, that we can no more see to the bottom of the next few hours, than we can see to the bottom of this river what I catches hold of. Nor yet we can't no more hold their tide than I can hold this. And it's run through my fingers and gone, you see!" holding up his dripping hand.

"But for your face, I should think you were a little despondent," said I.

"Not a bit on it, dear boy! It comes of flowing on so quiet, and of that there rippling at the boat's head making a sort of a Sunday tune. Maybe I'm a growing a trifle old besides."

He put his pipe back in his mouth with an undisturbed expression of face, and sat as composed and contented as if we were already out of England. Yet he was as submissive to a word of advice as if he had been in constant terror, for, when we ran ashore to get some bottles of beer into the boat, and he was stepping out, I hinted that I thought he would be safest where he was, and he said, "Do you, dear boy?" and quietly sat down again.

The air felt cold upon the river, but it was a bright day, and the sunshine was very cheering. The tide ran strong, I took care to lose none of it, and our steady stroke carried us on thoroughly well. By imperceptible degrees, as the tide ran out we lost more and more of the nearer woods and hills, and dropped lower and lower between the muddy banks, but the tide was yet with us when we were off Gravesend. As our charge was wrapped in his cloak, I purposely passed within a boat or two's length of the floating Custom House, and so out to catch the stream, alongside of two emigrant ships, and under the bows of a large transport with troops on the forecastle looking down at us. And soon the tide began to slacken, and the craft lying at anchor to swing, and presently they had all swung round, and the ships that were taking advantage of the new tide to get up to the Pool, began to crowd upon us in a fleet, and we kept under the shore, as much out of the strength of the tide now as we could, standing carefully off from low shallows and mud-banks.

Our oarsmen were so fresh, by dint of having occasionally let her drive with the tide for a minute or two, that a quarter of an hour's rest proved full as much as they wanted. We got ashore among some slippery stones while we ate and drank what we had with us, and looked about.

It was like my own marsh country, flat and monotonous, and with a dim horizon; while the winding river turned and turned, and the great floating buoys upon it turned and turned, and everything else seemed stranded and still. For now, the last of the fleet of ships was round the last low point we had headed; and the last green barge, straw-laden, with a brown sail, had followed; and some ballast-lighters, shaped like a child's first rude imitation of a boat, lay low in the mud; and a little squat shoal-lighthouse on open piles, stood crippled in the mud on stilts and crutches; and slimy stakes stuck out of the mud, and slimy stones stuck out of the mud, and red landmarks and tidemarks stuck out of the mud, and an old landing-stage and an old roofless building slipped into the mud, and all about us was stagnation and mud.

We pushed off again, and made what way we could. It was much harder work now, but Herbert and Startop persevered, and rowed, and rowed, and rowed, until the sun went down. By that time the river had lifted us a little, so that we could see above the bank. There was the red sun, on the low level of the shore, in a purple haze, fast deepening into black; and there was the solitary flat marsh; and far away there were the rising grounds, between which and us there seemed to be no life, save here and there in the foreground a melancholy gull.

As the night was fast falling, and as the moon, being past the full, would not rise early, we held a little council: a short one, for clearly our course was to lie by at the first lonely tavern we could find. So they plied their oars once more, and I looked out for anything like a house. Thus we held on, speaking little, for four or five dull miles. It was very cold, and a collier coming by us, with her galley-fire smoking and flaring, looked like a comfortable home. The night was dark by this time as it would be until morning; what light we had, seemed to come more from the river than the sky, as the oars in their dipping struck at a few reflected stars.

At this dismal time we were evidently all possessed by the idea that we were followed. As the tide made, it flapped heavily at irregular intervals against the shore; and whenever such a sound came, one or other of us was sure to start and look in that direction. Here and there, the set of the current had worn down the bank into a little creek, and we were all suspicious of such places, and eyed them nervously. Sometimes, "What was that ripple?" one of us would say in a low voice. Or another, "Is that a boat yonder?" And afterwards, we would fall into a dead silence, and I would sit impatiently thinking with what an unusual amount of noise the oars worked in the thowels.

At length we descried a light and a roof, and presently afterwards ran alongside a little causeway made of stones that had been picked up hard by. Leaving the rest in the boat, I stepped ashore, and found the light to be in the window of a public-house. It was a dirty place enough, and I dare say not unknown to smuggling adventurers; but there was a good fire in the kitchen, and there were eggs and bacon to eat, and various liquors to drink. Also, there were two double-bedded rooms—"such as they were," the landlord said. No other company was in the house than the landlord, his wife, and a grizzled male creature, the "Jack" of the little causeway, who was as slimy and smeary as if he had been low-water mark too.

With this assistant, I went down to the boat again, and we all came ashore, and brought out the oars, and rudder, and boat-hook, and all else, and hauled her up for the night.

We made a very good meal by the kitchen fire, and then apportioned the bedrooms: Herbert and Startop were to occupy one; I and our charge the other. We found the air as carefully excluded from both as if air were fatal to life; and there were more dirty clothes and bandboxes under the beds, than I should have thought the family possessed. But, we considered ourselves well off, notwithstanding, for a more solitary place we could not have found.

While we were comforting ourselves by the fire after our meal, the Jack—who was sitting in a corner, and who had a bloated pair of shoes on, which he had exhibited while we were eating our eggs and bacon, as interesting relics that he had taken a few days ago from the feet of a drowned seaman washed ashore—asked me if we had seen a four-oared galley going up with the tide? When I told him No, he said she must have gone down then, and yet she "took up too," when she left there.

"They must ha' thought better on't for some reason or another," said the Jack, "and gone down."

"A four-oared galley did you say?" said I.

"A four," said the Jack, "and two sitters."

"Did they come ashore here?"

"They put in with a stone two-gallon jar, for some beer. I'd ha' been glad to pison the beer myself," said the Jack, "or put some rattling physic in it."

"Why?"

"*I* know why," said the Jack. He spoke in a slushy voice, as if much mud had washed into his throat.

"He thinks," said the landlord: a weakly meditative man with a pale eye, who seemed to rely greatly on his Jack: "he thinks they was, what they wasn't."

"*I* knows what I thinks," observed the Jack.

"*You* thinks Custom 'Us, Jack?" said the landlord.

"I do," said the Jack.

"Then you're wrong, Jack."

"Am I!"

In the infinite meaning of his reply and his boundless confidence in his views, the Jack took one of his bloated shoes off, looked into it, knocked a few stones out of it on the kitchen floor, and put it on again. He did this with the air of a Jack who was so right that he could afford to do anything.

"Why, what do you make out that they done with their buttons, then, Jack?" asked the landlord, vacillating weakly.

"Done with their buttons?" returned the Jack. "Chucked 'em overboard. Swallered 'em. Sowed 'em, to come up small salad. Done with their buttons!"

"Don't be cheeky, Jack," remonstrated the landlord, in a melancholy and pathetic way.

"A Custom 'Us officer knows what to do with his Buttons," said the Jack, repeating the obnoxious word with the greatest contempt, "when they comes betwixt him and his own light. A Four and two sitters don't go hanging and hovering, up with one tide and down with another, and both with and against another, without there being Custom 'Us at the bottom of it." Saying which he went out in disdain; and the landlord, having no one to rely upon, found it impracticable to pursue the subject.

This dialogue made us all uneasy, and me very uneasy. The dismal wind was muttering round the house, the tide was flapping at the shore, and I had a feeling that we were caged and threatened. A four-oared galley hovering about in so unusual a way as to attract this notice, was an ugly circumstance that I could not get rid of. When I had induced Provis to go up to bed, I went outside with my two companions (Startop by this time knew the state of the case), and held another council. Whether we should remain at the house until near the steamer's time, which would be about one in the afternoon; or whether we should put off early in the morning; was the question we discussed. On the whole we deemed it the better course to lie where we were, until within an hour or so of the steamer's time, and then to get out in her track, and drift easily with the tide. Having settled to do this, we returned into the house and went to bed.

I lay down with the greater part of my clothes on, and slept well for a few hours. When I awoke, the wind had risen, and the sign of the house (the Ship) was creaking and banging about, with noises that startled me. Rising softly, for my charge lay fast asleep, I looked out of the window. It commanded the causeway where we had hauled up our boat, and, as my eyes adapted themselves to the light of the clouded moon, I saw two men looking into her. They passed by under the window, looking at nothing else, and they did not go down to the landing-place which I could discern to be empty, but struck across the marsh in the direction of the Nore.

My first impulse was to call up Herbert, and show him the two men going away. But, reflecting before I got into his room, which was at the back of the house and adjoined mine, that he and Startop had had a harder day than I, and were fatigued, I forebore. Going back to my window I could see the two men moving over the marsh. In that light, however, I soon lost them, and feeling very cold, lay down to think of the matter and fell asleep again.

We were up early. As we walked to and fro, all four together, before breakfast, I deemed it right to recount what I had seen. Again our charge was the least anxious of the party. It was very likely that the men belonged to the Custom House, he said quietly, and that they had no thought of us. I tried to persuade myself that it was so— as, indeed, it might easily be. However, I proposed that he and I should walk away together to a distant point we could see, and that the boat should take us aboard there, or as near there as might prove feasible, at about noon. This being considered a good precaution, soon after breakfast he and I set forth, without saying anything at the tavern.

He smoked his pipe as we went along, and sometimes stopped to clap me on the shoulder. One would have supposed that it was I who was in danger, not he, and that he was reassuring me. We spoke very little. As we approached the point, I begged him to remain in a sheltered place, while I went on to reconnoitre; for it was towards it that the men had passed in the night. He complied, and I went on alone. There was no boat off the point, nor any boat drawn up anywhere near it, nor were there any signs of the men having embarked there. But, to be sure the tide was high, and there might have been some footprints under water.

When he looked out from his shelter in the distance, and saw that I waved my hat to him to come up, he rejoined me, and there we waited; sometimes lying on the bank wrapped in our coats, and sometimes moving about to warm ourselves: until we saw our boat coming round. We got aboard easily, and rowed out into the track of the steamer. By that time it wanted but ten minutes of one o'clock, and we began to look out for her smoke.

But, it was half-past one before we saw her smoke, and soon after we saw behind it the smoke of another steamer. As they were coming on at full speed, we got the two bags ready, and took that opportunity of saying good bye to Herbert and Startop. We had all shaken hands cordially, and neither Herbert's eyes nor mine were quite dry, when I saw a four-oared galley shoot out from under the bank but a little way ahead of us, and row out into the same track.

A stretch of shore had been as yet between us and the steamer's smoke, by reason of the bend and wind of the river; but now she was visible coming head on. I called to Herbert and Startop to keep before the tide, that she might see us lying by for her, and adjured Provis to sit quite still, wrapped in his cloak. He answered cheerily, "Trust to me, dear boy," and sat like a statue. Meantime the galley, which was skilfully handled, had crossed us, let us come up with her, and fallen alongside. Leaving just room enough for the play of the oars, she kept alongside, drifting when we drifted, and pulling a stroke or two when we pulled. Of the two sitters, one held the rudder lines, and looked at us attentively—as did all the rowers; the other sitter was wrapped up, much as Provis was, and seemed to shrink, and whisper some instruction to the steerer as he looked at us. Not a word was spoken in either boat.

Startop could make out, after a few minutes, which steamer was first, and gave me the word "Hamburg," in a low voice as we sat face to face. She was nearing us very fast, and the beating of her paddles grew louder and louder. I felt as if her shadow were absolutely upon us, when the galley hailed us. I answered.

"You have a return transport there," said the man who held the lines. "That's the man, wrapped in the cloak. His name is Abel Magwitch, otherwise Provis. I apprehend that man, and call upon him to surrender, and you to assist."

At the same moment, without giving any audible direction to his crew, he ran the galley aboard of us. They had pulled one sudden stroke ahead, had got their oars in, had run athwart us, and were holding on to our gunwale, before we knew what they were doing. This caused great confusion on board of the steamer, and I heard them calling to us, and heard the order given to stop the paddles, and heard them stop, but felt her driving down upon us irresistibly. In the same moment, I saw the steersman of the galley lay his hand on his prisoner's shoulder, and saw that both boats were swinging round with the force of the tide, and saw that all hands on board the steamer were running forward quite frantically. Still in the same moment, I saw the prisoner start up, lean across his captor, and pull the cloak from the neck of the shrinking sitter in the galley. Still in the same moment, I saw that the face disclosed, was the face of the other convict of long ago. Still in the same moment, I saw the face tilt backward with a white terror on it that I shall never forget, and heard a great cry on board the steamer and a loud splash in the water, and felt the boat sink from under me.

It was but for an instant that I seemed to struggle with a thousand mill-weirs and a thousand flashes of light; that instant past, I was taken on board the galley. Herbert was there, and Startop was there; but our boat was gone, and the two convicts were gone.

What with the cries aboard the steamer, and the furious blowing off of her steam, and her driving on, and our driving on, I could not at first distinguish sky from water or shore from shore; but the crew of the galley righted her with great speed, and, pulling certain swift strong strokes ahead, lay upon their oars, every man looking silently and eagerly at the water astern. Presently a dark object was seen in it, bearing towards us on the tide. No man spoke, but the steersman held up his hand, and all softly backed water, and kept the boat straight and true before it. As it came nearer, I saw it to be Magwitch, swimming, but not swimming freely. He was taken on board, and instantly manacled at the wrists and ankles.

The galley was kept steady, and the silent eager look-out at the water was resumed. But the Rotterdam steamer now came up, and apparently not understanding what had happened, came on at speed. By the time she had been hailed and stopped, both steamers were drifting away from us, and we were rising and falling in a troubled wake of water. The look-out was kept, long after all was still again and the two steamers were gone; but everybody knew that it was hopeless now.

At length we gave it up, and pulled under the shore towards the tavern we had lately left, where we were received with no little surprise. Here, I was able to get some comforts for Magwitch—Provis no longer—who had received some very severe injury in the chest and a deep cut in the head.

He told me that he believed himself to have gone under the keel of the steamer, and to have been struck on the head in rising. The injury to his chest (which rendered his breathing extremely painful) he thought he had received against the side of the galley. He added that he did not pretend to say what he might or might not have done to Compeyson, but, that in the moment of his laying his hand on his cloak to identify him, that villain had staggered up and staggered back, and they had both gone overboard together; when the sudden wrenching of him (Magwitch) out of our boat, and the endeavour of his captor to keep him in it, had capsized us. He told me in a whisper that they had gone down, fiercely locked in each other's arms, and that there had been a struggle under water, and that he had disengaged himself, struck out, and swam away.

I never had any reason to doubt the exact truth of what he had told me. The officer who steered the galley gave the same account of their going overboard.

When I asked this officer's permission to change the prisoner's wet clothes by purchasing any spare garments I could get at the public-house, he gave it readily: merely observing that he must take charge of everything his prisoner had about him. So the pocket-book which had once been in my hands, passed into the officer's. He further gave me leave to accompany the prisoner to London; but, declined to accord that grace to my two friends.

The Jack at the Ship was instructed where the drowned man had gone down, and undertook to search for the body in the places where it was likeliest to come ashore. His interest in its recovery seemed to me to be much heightened when he heard that it had stockings on. Probably, it took about a dozen drowned men to fit him out completely; and that may have been the reason why the different articles of his dress were in various stages of decay.

We remained at the public-house until the tide turned, and then Magwitch was carried down to the galley and put on board. Herbert and Startop were to get to London by land, as soon as they could. We had a doleful parting,

and when I took my place by Magwitch's side, I felt that that was my place henceforth while he lived.

For now my repugnance to him had all melted away, and in the hunted wounded shackled creature who held my hand in his, I only saw a man who had meant to be my benefactor, and who had felt affectionately, gratefully, and generously, towards me with great constancy through a series of years. I only saw in him a much better man than I had been to Joe.

His breathing became more difficult and painful as the night drew on, and often he could not repress a groan. I tried to rest him on the arm I could use, in any easy position; but it was dreadful to think that I could not be sorry at heart for his being badly hurt, since it was unquestionably best that he should die. That there were, still living, people enough who were able and willing to identify him, I could not doubt. That he would be leniently treated, I could not hope. He who had been presented in the worst light at his trial, who had since broken prison and been tried again, who had returned from transportation under a life sentence, and who had occasioned the death of the man who was the cause of his arrest.

As we returned towards the setting sun we had yesterday left behind us, and as the stream of our hopes seemed all running back, I told him how grieved I was to think he had come home for my sake.

"Dear boy," he answered, "I'm quite content to take my chance. I've seen my boy, and he can be a gentleman without me."

No. I had thought about that while we had been there side by side. No. Apart from any inclinations of my own, I understand Wemmick's hint now. I foresaw that, being convicted, his possessions would be forfeited to the Crown.

"Lookee here, dear boy," said he. "It's best as a gentleman should not be knowed to belong to me now. Only come to see me as if you come by chance alonger Wemmick. Sit where I can see you when I am swore to, for the last o' many times, and I don't ask no more."

"I will never stir from your side," said I, "when I am suffered to be near you. Please God, I will be as true to you as you have been to me!"

I felt his hand tremble as it held mine, and he turned his face away as he lay in the bottom of the boat, and I heard that old sound in his throat—softened now, like all the rest of him. It was a good thing that he had touched this point, for it put into my mind what I might not otherwise have thought of until too late: that he need never know how his hopes of enriching me had perished.

CHAPTER LV.

He was taken to the Police Court next day, and would have been immediately committed for trial, but that it was necessary to send down for an old officer of the prison-ship from which he had once escaped, to speak to his identity. Nobody doubted it; but, Compeyson, who had meant to depose to it, was tumbling on the tides, dead, and it happened that there was not at that time any prison officer in London who could give the required evidence. I had gone direct to Mr. Jaggers at his private house, on my arrival over night, to retain his assistance, and Mr. Jaggers on the prisoner's behalf would admit nothing. It was the sole resource, for he told me that the case must be over in five minutes when the witness was there, and that no power on earth could prevent its going against us.

I imparted to Mr. Jaggers my design of keeping him in ignorance of the fate of his wealth. Mr. Jaggers was querulous and angry with me for having "let it slip through my fingers," and said we must memorialise by-and-bye, and try at all events for some of it. But he did not conceal from me that although there might be many cases in which forfeiture would not be exacted, there were no circumstances in this case to make it one of them. I understood that very well. I was not related to the outlaw, or connected with him by any recognisable tie; he had put his hand to no writing or settlement in my favour before his apprehension, and to do so now would be idle. I had no claim, and I finally resolved, and ever afterwards abided by the resolution, that my heart should never be sickened with the hopeless task of attempting to establish one.

There appeared to be reason for supposing that the drowned informer had hoped for a reward out of this forfeiture, and had obtained some accurate knowledge of Magwitch's affairs. When his body was found, many miles from the scene of his death, and so horribly disfigured that he was only recognisable by the contents of his pockets, notes were still legible, folded in a case he carried. Among these were the name of a banking-house in New South Wales where a sum of money was, and the designation of certain lands of considerable value. Both those heads of information were in a list that Magwitch, while in prison, gave to Mr. Jaggers, of the possessions he supposed I should inherit. His ignorance, poor fellow, at last served him; he never mistrusted but that my inheritance was quite safe, with Mr. Jaggers's aid.

After three days' delay, during which the crown prosecution stood over for the production of the witness from the prison-ship, the witness came, and completed the easy case. He was committed to take his trial at the next Session, which would come on in a month.

It was at this dark time of my life that Herbert returned home one evening, a good deal cast down, and said:

"My dear Handel, I fear I shall soon have to leave you."

His partner having prepared me for that, I was less surprised than he thought.

"We shall lose a fine opportunity if I put off going to Cairo, and I am very much afraid I must go, Handel, when you most need me."

"Herbert, I shall always need you, because I shall always love you; but my need is no greater now, than at another time."

"You will be so lonely."

"I have not leisure to think of that," said I. "You know that I am always with him to the full extent of the time allowed, and that I should be with him all day long, if I could. And when I come away from him, you know that my thoughts are with him."

The dreadful condition to which he was brought, was so appalling to both of us, that we could not refer to it in plainer words.

"My dear fellow," said Herbert, "let the near prospect of our separation—for, it is very near—be my justification for troubling you about yourself. Have you thought of your future?"

"No, for I have been afraid to think of any future."

"But yours cannot be dismissed; indeed, my dear, dear Handel, it must not be dismissed. I wish you would enter on it now, as far as a few friendly words go, with me."

"I will," said I.

"In this branch house of ours, Handel, we must have a——"

I saw that his delicacy was avoiding the right word, so I said, "A clerk."

"A clerk. And I hope it is not at all unlikely that he may expand (as a clerk of your acquaintance has expanded) into a partner. Now, Handel——in short, my dear boy, will you come to me?"

There was something charmingly cordial and engaging in the manner in which after saying, "Now, Handel," as if it were the grave beginning of a portentous business exordium, he had suddenly given up that tone, stretched out his honest hand, and spoken like a schoolboy.

"Clara and I have talked about it again and again," Herbert pursued, "and the dear little thing begged me only this evening, with tears in her eyes, to say to you that if you will live with us, when we come together, she will do her best to make you happy, and to convince her husband's friend that he is her friend too. We should get on so well, Handel!"

I thanked her heartily, and I thanked him heartily, but said I could not yet make sure of joining him as he so kindly offered. Firstly, my mind was too preoccupied to be able to take in the subject clearly. Secondly——Yes! Secondly, there was a vague something lingering in my thoughts that will come out very near the end of this slight narrative.

"But if you thought, Herbert, that you could, without doing any injury to your business, leave the question open for a little while——"

"For any while," cried Herbert. "Six months, a year!"

"Not so long as that," said I. "Two or three months at most."

Herbert was highly delighted when we shook hands on this arrangement, and said he could now take courage to tell me that he believed he must go away at the end of the week.

"And Clara?" said I.

"The dear little thing," returned Herbert, "holds dutifully to her father as long as he lasts; but he won't last long. Mrs. Whimple confides to me that he is certainly going."

"Not to say an unfeeling thing," said I, "he cannot do better than go."

"I am afraid that must be admitted," said Herbert: "and then I shall come back for the dear little thing, and the dear little thing and I will walk quietly into the nearest church. Remember! The blessed darling comes of no family, my dear Handel, and never looked into the red book, and hasn't a notion about her grandpapa. What a fortune for the son of my mother!"

On the Saturday in that same week, I took my leave of Herbert—full of bright hope, but sad and sorry to leave me—as he sat on one of the seaport mail coaches. I went into a coffee-house to write a little note to Clara, telling her he had gone off, sending his love to her over and over again, and then went to my lonely home—if it deserved the name, for it was now no home to me, and I had no home anywhere.

On the stairs I encountered Wemmick, who was coming down, after an unsuccessful application of his knuckles to my door. I had not seen him alone, since the disastrous issue of the attempted flight; and he had come, in his private and personal capacity, to say a few words of explanation in reference to that failure.

"The late Compeyson," said Wemmick, "had by little and little got at the bottom of half of the regular business now transacted, and it was from the talk of some of his people in trouble (some of his people being always in trouble) that I heard what I did. I kept my ears open, seeming to have them shut, until I heard that he was absent, and I thought that would be the best time for making the attempt. I can only suppose now, that it was part of his policy, as a very clever man, habitually to deceive his own instruments. You don't blame me, I hope, Mr. Pip? I'm sure I tried to serve you, with all my heart."

"I am as sure of that, Wemmick, as you can be, and I thank you most earnestly for all your interest and friendship."

"Thank you, thank you very much. It's a bad job," said Wemmick, scratching his head, "and I assure you I haven't been so cut up for a long time. What I look at is, the sacrifice of so much portable property. Dear me!"

"What *I* think of, Wemmick, is the poor owner of the property."

"Yes, to be sure," said Wemmick. "Of course there can be no objection to your being sorry for him, and I'd put down a five-pound note myself to get him out of it. But what I look at, is this. The late Compeyson having been beforehand with him in intelligence of his return, and being so determined to bring him to book, I do not think he could have been saved. Whereas, the portable property certainly could have been saved. That's the difference between the property and the owner, don't you see?"

I invited Wemmick to come upstairs, and refresh himself with a glass of grog before walking to Walworth. He accepted the invitation. While he was drinking his moderate allowance, he said, with nothing to lead up to it, and after having appeared rather fidgety:

"What do you think of my meaning to take a holiday on Monday, Mr. Pip?"

"Why, I suppose you have not done such a thing these twelve months."

"These twelve years, more likely," said Wemmick. "Yes. I'm going to take a holiday. More than that; I'm going to take a walk. More than that; I'm going to ask you to take a walk with me."

I was about to excuse myself, as being but a bad companion just then, when Wemmick anticipated me.

"I know your engagements," said he, "and I know you are out of sorts, Mr. Pip. But if you *could* oblige me, I should take it as a kindness. It ain't a long walk, and it's an early one. Say it might occupy you (including breakfast on the walk) from eight to twelve. Couldn't you stretch a point and manage it?"

He had done so much for me at various times, that this was very little to do for him. I said I could manage it—would manage it—and he was so very much pleased by my acquiescence, that I was pleased too. At his particular request, I appointed to call for him at the Castle at half-past eight on Monday morning, and so we parted for the time.

Punctual to my appointment, I rang at the Castle gate on the Monday morning, and was received by Wemmick himself: who struck me as looking tighter than usual, and having a sleeker hat on. Within, there were two glasses of rum-and-milk prepared, and two biscuits. The Aged must

have been stirring with the lark, for, glancing into the perspective of his bedroom, I observed that his bed was empty.

When we had fortified ourselves with the rum-and-milk and biscuits, and were going out for the walk with that training preparation on us, I was considerably surprised to see Wemmick take up a fishing-rod, and put it over his shoulder. "Why, we are not going fishing!" said I. "No," returned Wemmick, "but I like to walk with one."

I thought this odd; however, I said nothing, and we set off. We went towards Camberwell Green, and when we were thereabouts, Wemmick said suddenly:

"Halloa! Here's a church!"

There was nothing very surprising in that; but again, I was rather surprised, when he said, as if he were animated by a brilliant idea:

"Let's go in!"

We went in, Wemmick leaving his fishing-rod in the porch, and looked all round. In the mean time, Wemmick was diving into his coat-pockets, and getting something out of paper there.

"Halloa!" said he. "Here's a couple of pair of gloves! Let's put 'em on!"

As the gloves were white kid gloves, and as the post-office was widened to its utmost extent, I now began to have my strong suspicions. They were strengthened into certainty when I beheld the Aged enter at a side door, escorting a lady.

"Halloa!" said Wemmick. "Here's Miss Skiffins! Let's have a wedding."

That discreet damsel was attired as usual, except that she was now engaged in substituting for her green kid gloves, a pair of white. The Aged was likewise occupied in preparing a similar sacrifice for the altar of Hymen. The old gentleman, however, experienced so much difficulty in getting his gloves on, that Wemmick found it necessary to put him with his back against a pillar, and then to get behind the pillar himself and pull away at them, while I for my part held the old gentleman round the waist, that he might present an equal and safe resistance. By dint of this ingenious scheme, his gloves were got on to perfection.

The clerk and clergyman then appearing, we were ranged in order at those fatal rails. True to his notion of seeming to do it all without preparation, I heard Wemmick say to himself as he took something out of his waistcoat-pocket before the service began, "Halloa! Here's a ring!"

I acted in the capacity of backer, or best man, to the bridegroom; while a little limp pew-opener in a soft bonnet like a baby's, made a feint of being the bosom friend of Miss Skiffins. The responsibility of giving the lady away, devolved upon the Aged, which led to the clergyman's being unintentionally scandalised, and it happened thus. When he said, "Who giveth this woman to be married to this man?" the old gentleman, not in the least knowing what point of the ceremony we had arrived at, stood most amiably beaming at the ten commandments. Upon which, the clergyman said again, "WHO giveth this woman to be married to this man?" The old gentleman being still in a state of most estimable unconsciousness, the bridegroom cried out in his accustomed voice, "Now Aged P. you know; who giveth?" To which the Aged replied with great briskness, before saying that *he* gave, "All right, John, all right, my boy!" And the clergyman came to so gloomy a pause upon it, that I had doubts for the moment whether we should get completely married that day.

It was completely done, however, and when we were going out of church, Wemmick took the cover off the font, and put his white gloves in it, and put the cover on again. Mrs. Wemmick, more heedful of the future, put her white gloves in her pocket and assumed her green. "*Now*, Mr. Pip," said Wemmick, triumphantly shouldering the fishing-rod as we came out, "let me ask you whether anybody would suppose this to be a wedding party!"

Breakfast had been ordered at a pleasant little tavern, a mile or so away upon the rising ground beyond the green; and there was a bagatelle board in the room, in case we should desire to unbend our minds after the solemnity. It was pleasant to observe that Mrs. Wemmick no longer unwound Wemmick's arm when it adapted itself to her figure, but sat in the high-backed chair against the wall, like a violoncello in its case, and submitted to be embraced as that melodious instrument might have done.

We had an excellent breakfast, and when any one declined anything on table, Wemmick said, "Provided by contract, you know; don't be afraid of it!" I drank to the new couple, drank to the Aged, drank to the Castle, saluted the bride at parting, and made myself as agreeable as I could.

Wemmick came down to the door with me, and I again shook hands with him, and wished him joy.

"Thank'ee!" said Wemmick, rubbing his hands. "She's such a manager of fowls, you have no idea. You shall have some eggs and judge for yourself. I say, Mr. Pip!" calling me back and speaking low. "This is altogether a Walworth sentiment, please."

"I understand. Not to be mentioned in Little Britain," said I.

Wemmick nodded. "After what you let out the other day, Mr. Jaggers may as well not know of it. He might think my brain was softening, or something of the kind."

CHAPTER LVI.

HE lay in prison very ill, during the whole interval between his committal for trial, and the coming round of the Sessions. He had broken two ribs, they had wounded one of his lungs, and he breathed with great pain and difficulty, which increased daily. It was a consequence of his hurt that he spoke so low as to be scarcely audible; therefore, he spoke very little. But, he was ever ready to listen to me, and it became the first duty of my life to say to him, and to read to him, what I knew he ought to hear.

Being far too ill to remain in the common prison, he was removed, after the first day or so, into the infirmary. This gave me opportunities of being with him that I could not otherwise have had. And but for his illness he would have been put in irons, for he was regarded as a determined prison-breaker, and I know not what else.

Although I saw him every day, it was for only a short time; hence the regularly recurring spaces of our separation were long enough to record on his face any slight changes that occurred in his physical state. I do not recollect that I once saw any change in it for the better; he wasted, and became slowly weaker and worse, day by day from the day when the prison door closed upon him.

The kind of submission or resignation that he showed, was that of a man who was tired out. I sometimes derived an impression, from his manner or from a whispered word

or two which escaped him, that he pondered over the question whether he might have been a better man under better circumstances. But, he never justified himself by a hint tending that way, or tried to bend the past out of its eternal shape.

It happened on two or three occasions in my presence, that his desperate reputation was alluded to by one or other of the people in attendance on him. A smile crossed his face then, and he turned his eyes on me with a trustful look, as if he were confident that I had seen some small redeeming touch in him, even so long ago as when I was a little child. As to all the rest, he was humble and contrite, and I never knew him complain.

When the Sessions came round, Mr. Jaggers caused an application to be made for the postponement of his trial until the following Sessions. It was obviously made with the assurance that he could not live so long, and was refused. The trial came on at once, and when he was put to the bar, he was seated in a chair. No objection was made to my getting close to the dock, on the outside of it, and holding the hand that he stretched forth to me.

The trial was very short and very clear. Such things as could be said for him, were said—how he had taken to industrious habits, and had thriven lawfully and reputably. But, nothing could unsay the fact that he had returned, and was there in presence of the Judge and Jury. It was impossible to try him for that, and do otherwise than find him guilty.

At that time it was the custom (as I learnt from my terrible experience of that Sessions) to devote a concluding day to the passing of Sentences, and to make a finishing effect with the Sentence of Death. But for the indelible picture that my remembrance now holds before me, I could scarcely believe, even as I write these words, that I saw two-and-thirty men and women put before the Judge to receive that sentence together. Foremost among the two-and-thirty was he; seated, that he might get breath enough to keep life in him.

The whole scene starts out again in the vivid colours of the moment, down to the drops of April rain on the windows of the court, glittering in the rays of April sun. Penned in the dock, as I again stood outside it at the corner with his hand in mine, were the two-and-thirty men and women; some defiant, some stricken with terror, some sobbing and weeping, some covering their faces, some staring gloomily about. There had been shrieks from among the women convicts, but they had been stilled, and a hush had succeeded. The sheriffs with their great chains and nosegays, other civic gewgaws and monsters, criers, ushers, a great gallery full of people—a large theatrical audience —looked on, as the two-and-thirty and the Judge were solemnly confronted. Then, the Judge addressed them. Among the wretched creatures before him whom he must single out for special address, was one who almost from his infancy had been an offender against the laws; who, after repeated imprisonments and punishments, had been at length sentenced to exile for a term of years; and who, under circumstances of great violence and daring, had made his escape and been resentenced to exile for life. That miserable man would seem for a time to have become convinced of his errors, when far removed from the scenes of his old offences, and to have lived a peaceable and honest life. But in a fatal moment, yielding to those propensities and passions, the indulgence of which had so long rendered him a scourge to society, he had quitted his haven of rest and repentance, and had come back to the country where he was proscribed. Being here presently denounced, he had for a time succeeded in evading the officers of Justice, but being at length seized while in the act of flight, he had resisted them, and had—he best knew whether by express design, or in the blindness of his hardihood—caused the death of his denouncer, to whom his whole career was known. The appointed punishment for his return to the land that had cast him out being Death, and his case being this aggravated case, he must prepare himself to Die.

The sun was striking in at the great windows of the court, through the glittering drops of rain upon the glass, and it made a broad shaft of light between the two-and-thirty and the Judge, linking both together, and perhaps reminding some among the audience, how both were passing on, with absolute equality, to the greater Judgment that knoweth all things and cannot err. Rising for a moment, a distinct speck of face in this ray of light, the prisoner said, "My Lord, I have received my sentence of Death from the Almighty, but I bow to yours," and sat down again. There was some hushing, and the Judge went on with what he had to say to the rest. Then, they were all formally doomed, and some of them were supported out, and some of them sauntered out with a haggard look of bravery, and a few nodded to the gallery, and two or three shook hands, and others went out chewing the fragments of herb they had taken from the sweet herbs lying about. He went last of all, because of having to be helped from his chair and to go very slowly; and he held my hand while all the others were removed, and while the audience got up (putting their dresses right, as they might at church or elsewhere) and pointed down at this criminal or at that, and most of all at him and me.

I earnestly hoped and prayed that he might die before the Recorder's Report was made, but, in the dread of his lingering on, I began that night to write out a petition to the Home Secretary of State, setting forth my knowledge of him, and how it was that he had come back for my sake. I wrote it as fervently and pathetically as I could, and when I had finished it and sent it in, I wrote out other petitions to such men in authority as I hoped were the most merciful, and drew up one to the Crown itself. For several days and nights after he was sentenced I took no rest, except when I fell asleep in my chair, but was wholly absorbed in these appeals. And after I had sent them in, I could not keep away from the places where they were, but felt as if they were more hopeful and less desperate when I was near them. In this unreasonable restlessness and pain of mind, I would roam the streets of an evening, wandering by those offices and houses where I had left the petitions. To the present hour, the weary western streets of London on a cold dusty spring night, with their ranges of stern shut-up mansions and their long rows of lamps, are melancholy to me from this association.

The daily visits I could make him were shortened now, and he was more strictly kept. Seeing, or fancying, that I was suspected of an intention of carrying poison to him, I asked to be searched before I sat down at his bedside, and told the officer who was always there, that I was willing to do anything that would assure him of the singleness of my designs. Nobody was hard with him or with me. There was duty to be done, and it was done, but not harshly. The officer always gave me the assurance that he was worse, and some other sick prisoners in the room, and

some other prisoners who attended on them as sick nurses (malefactors, but not incapable of kindness, God be thanked!), always joined in the same report.

As the days went on, I noticed more and more that he would lie placidly looking at the white ceiling, with an absence of light in his face, until some word of mine brightened it for an instant, and then it would subside again. Sometimes he was almost, or quite, unable to speak; then, he would answer me with slight pressures on my hand, and I grew to understand his meaning very well.

The number of the days had risen to ten, when I saw a greater change in him than I had seen yet. His eyes were turned towards the door, and lighted up as I entered.

"Dear boy," he said, as I sat down by his bed: "I thought you was late. But I knowed you couldn't be that."

"It is just the time," said I. "I waited for it at the gate."

"You always waits at the gate; don't you, dear boy?"

"Yes. Not to lose a moment of the time."

"Thank'ee, dear boy, thank'ee. God bless you! You've never deserted me, dear boy."

I pressed his hand in silence, for I could not forget that I had once meant to desert him.

"And what's the best of all," he said, "you've been more comfortable alonger me, since I was under a dark cloud, than when the sun shone. That's the best of all."

He lay on his back, breathing with great difficulty. Do what he would, and love me though he did, the light left his face ever and again, and a film came over the placid look at the white ceiling.

"Are you in much pain to-day?"

"I don't complain of none, dear boy."

"You never do complain."

He had spoken his last words. He smiled, and I understood his touch to mean that he wished to lift my hand, and lay it on his breast. I laid it there, and he smiled again, and put both his hands upon it.

The allotted time ran out, while we were thus; but, looking round, I found the governor of the prison standing near me, and he whispered, "You needn't go yet." I thanked him gratefully, and asked, "Might I speak to him, if he can hear me?"

The governor stepped aside, and beckoned the officer away. The change, though it was made without noise, drew back the film from the placid look at the white ceiling, and he looked most affectionately at me.

"Dear Magwitch, I must tell you now, at last. You understand what I say?"

A gentle pressure on my hand.

"You had a child once, whom you loved and lost."

A stronger pressure on my hand.

"She lived and found powerful friends. She is living now. She is a lady and very beautiful. And I love her!"

With a last faint effort, which would have been powerless but for my yielding to it, and assisting it, he raised my hand to his lips. Then he gently let it sink upon his breast again, with his own hands lying on it. The placid look at the white ceiling came back, and passed away, and his head dropped quietly on his breast.

Mindful, then, of what we had read together, I thought of the two men who went up into the Temple to pray, and I knew there were no better words that I could say beside his bed, than "O Lord, be merciful to him a sinner!"

CHAPTER LVII.

Now that I was left wholly to myself I gave notice of my intention to quit the chambers in the Temple as soon as my tenancy could legally determine, and in the meanwhile to underlet them. At once I put bills up in the windows; for, I was in debt, and had scarcely any money, and began to be seriously alarmed by the state of my affairs. I ought rather to write that I should have been alarmed if I had had energy and concentration enough to help me to the clear perception of any truth beyond the fact that I was falling very ill. The late stress upon me had enabled me to put off illness, but not to put it away; I knew that it was coming on me now, and I knew very little else, and was even careless as to that.

For a day or two, I lay on the sofa, or on the floor—anywhere, according as I happened to sink down—with a heavy head and aching limbs, and no purpose, and no power. Then there came one night which appeared of great duration, and which teemed with anxiety and horror; and when in the morning I tried to sit up in my bed and think of it, I found I could not do so.

Whether I really had been down in Garden-court in the dead of the night, groping about for the boat that I supposed to be there; whether I had two or three times come to myself on the staircase with great terror, not knowing how I had got out of bed; whether I had found myself lighting the lamp, possessed by the idea that he was coming up the stairs, and that the lights were blown out; whether I had been inexpressibly harassed by the distracted talking, laughing, and groaning, of some one, and had half suspected those sounds to be of my own making; whether there had been a closed iron furnace in a dark corner of the room, and a voice had called out over and over again that Miss Havisham was consuming within it; these were things that I tried to settle with myself and get into some order, as I lay that morning on my bed. But the vapour of a lime-kiln would come between me and them, disordering them all, and it was through the vapour at last that I saw two men looking at me.

"What do you want?" I asked, starting; "I don't know you."

"Well, sir," returned one of them, bending down and touching me on the shoulder, "this is a matter that you'll soon arrange, I dare say, but you're arrested."

"What is the debt?"

"Hundred and twenty-three pound, fifteen, six. Jeweller's account, I think."

"What is to be done?"

"You had better come to my house," said the man. "I keep a very nice house."

I made some attempt to get up and dress myself. When I next attended to them, they were standing a little off from the bed, looking at me. I still lay there.

"You see my state," said I. "I would come with you if I could; but indeed I am quite unable. If you take me from here, I think I shall die by the way."

Perhaps they replied, or argued the point, or tried to encourage me to believe that I was better than I thought. Forasmuch as they hang in my memory by only this one slender thread, I don't know what they did, except that they forbore to remove me.

That I had a fever and was avoided, that I suffered greatly, that I often lost my reason, that the time seemed interminable, that I confounded impossible existences with

my own identity; that I was a brick in the house wall, and yet entreating to be released from the giddy place where the builders had set me; that I was a steel beam of a vast engine, clashing and whirling over a gulf, and yet that I implored in my own person to have the engine stopped, and my part in it hammered off; that I passed through these phases of disease, I know of my own remembrance, and did in some sort know at the time. That I sometimes struggled with real people, in the belief that they were murderers, and that I would all at once comprehend that they meant to do me good, and would then sink exhausted in their arms, and suffer them to lay me down, I also knew at the time. But, above all, I knew that there was a constant tendency in all these people—who, when I was very ill, would present all kinds of extraordinary transformations of the human face, and would be much dilated in size—above all, I say, I knew that there was an extraordinary tendency in all these people, sooner or later, to settle down into the likeness of Joe.

After I had turned the worst point of my illness, I began to notice that while all its other features changed, this one consistent feature did not change. Whoever came about me, still settled down into Joe. I opened my eyes in the night, and I saw in the great chair at the bedside, Joe. I opened my eyes in the day, and, sitting on the window-seat, smoking his pipe in the shaded open window, still I saw Joe. I asked for cooling drink, and the dear hand that gave it me was Joe's. I sank back on my pillow after drinking, and the face that looked so hopefully and tenderly upon me was the face of Joe.

At last, one day, I took courage, and said, "*Is* it Joe?"

And the dear old home-voice answered, "Which it air, old chap."

"O Joe, you break my heart! Look angry at me, Joe. Strike me, Joe. Tell me of my ingratitude. Don't be so good to me!"

For, Joe had actually laid his head down on the pillow at my side, and put his arm round my neck, in his joy that I knew him.

"Which dear old Pip, old chap," said Joe, "you and me was ever friends. And when you're well enough to go out for a ride—what larks!"

After which, Joe withdrew to the window, and stood with his back towards me, wiping his eyes. And as my extreme weakness prevented me from getting up and going to him, I lay there, penitently whispering, "O God bless him! O God bless this gentle Christian man!"

Joe's eyes were red when I next found him beside me; but, I was holding his hand and we both felt happy.

"How long, dear Joe?"

"Which you meantersay, Pip, how long have your illness lasted, dear old chap?"

"Yes, Joe."

"It's the end of May, Pip. To-morrow is the first of June."

"And have you been here all the time, dear Joe?"

"Pretty nigh, old chap. For, as I says to Biddy when the news of your being ill were brought by letter, which it were brought by the post, and being formerly single he is now married though underpaid for a deal of walking and shoe-leather, but wealth were not a object on his part, and marriage were the great wish of his hart——"

"It is so delightful to hear you, Joe! But I interrupt you in what you said to Biddy."

"Which it were," said Joe, "that how you might be

amongst strangers, and that how you and me having been ever friends, a wisit at such a moment might not prove unacceptabobble. And Biddy, her word were, 'Go to him, without loss of time.' That," said Joe, summing up with his judicial air, "were the word of Biddy. 'Go to him,' Biddy say, 'without loss of time.' In short, I shouldn't greatly deceive you," Joe added, after a little grave reflection, "if I represented to you that the word of that young woman were, 'without a minute's loss of time.' "

There Joe cut himself short, and informed me that I was to be talked to in great moderation, and that I was to take a little nourishment at stated frequent times, whether I felt inclined for it or not, and that I was to submit myself to all his orders. So, I kissed his hand, and lay quiet, while he proceeded to indite a note to Biddy, with my love in it.

Evidently Biddy had taught Joe to write. As I lay in bed looking at him, it made me, in my weak state, cry again with pleasure to see the pride with which he set about his letter. My bedstead, divested of its curtains, had been removed, with me upon it, into the sitting-room, as the airiest and largest, and the carpet had been taken away, and the room kept always fresh and wholesome night and day. At my own writing-table, pushed into a corner and cumbered with little bottles, Joe now sat down to his great work, first choosing a pen from the pen-tray as if it were a chest of large tools, and tucking up his sleeves as if he were going to wield a crowbar or sledge-hammer. It was necessary for Joe to hold on heavily to the table with his left elbow, and to get his right leg well out behind him, before he could begin, and when he did begin he made every down-stroke so slowly that it might have been six feet long, while at every up-stroke I could hear his pen spluttering extensively. He had a curious idea that the inkstand was on the side of him where it was not, and constantly dipped his pen into space, and seemed quite satisfied with the result. Occasionally he was tripped up by some orthographical stumbling-block, but on the whole he got on very well indeed, and when he had signed his name, and had removed a finishing blot from the paper to the crown of his head with his two forefingers, he got up and hovered about the table, trying the effect of his performance from various points of view as it lay there, with unbounded satisfaction.

Not to make Joe uneasy by talking too much, even if I had been able to talk much, I deferred asking him about Miss Havisham until next day. He shook his head when I then asked him if she had recovered.

"Is she dead, Joe?"

"Why, you see, old chap," said Joe, in a tone of remonstrance, and by way of getting at it by degrees, "I wouldn't go so far as to say that, for that's a deal to say; but she ain't——"

"Living, Joe?"

"That's nigher where it is," said Joe; "she ain't living."

"Did she linger long, Joe?"

"Arter you was took ill, pretty much about what you might call (if you was put to it) a week," said Joe; still determined, on my account, to come at everything by degrees.

"Dear Joe, have you heard what becomes of her property?"

"Well, old chap," said Joe, "it do appear that she had settled the most of it, which I meantersay tied it up, on

Miss Estella. But she had wrote out a little coddleshell in her own hand a day or two afore the accident, leaving a cool four thousand to Mr. Matthew Pocket. And why, do you suppose, above all things, Pip, she left that cool four thousand unto him? 'Because of Pip's account of him the said Matthew.' I am told by Biddy, that air the writing," said Joe, repeating the legal term as if it did him infinite good, "'account of him the said Matthew.' And a cool four thousand, Pip!"

I never discovered from whom Joe derived the conventional temperature of the four thousand pounds, but it appeared to make the sum of money more to him, and he had a manifest relish in insisting on its being cool.

This account gave me great joy, as it perfected the only good thing I had done. I asked Joe whether he had heard if any of the other relations had any legacies?

"Miss Sarah," said Joe, "she have twenty-five pound perannium fur to buy pills, on account of being bilious. Miss Georgiana, she have twenty pound down. Mrs.—— what's the name of them wild beasts with humps, old chap?"

"Camels?" said I, wondering why he could possibly want to know.

Joe nodded. "Mrs. Camels," by which I presently understood he meant Camilla, "she have five pound fur to buy rushlights to put her in spirits when she wake up in the night."

The accuracy of these recitals was sufficiently obvious to me, to give me great confidence in Joe's information. "And now," said Joe, "you ain't that strong yet, old chap, that you can take in more nor one additional shovelfull to-day. Old Orlick he's been a bustin' open a dwelling-ouse."

"Whose?" said I.

"Not, I grant you, but what his manners is given to blusterous," said Joe, apologetically; "still, a Englishman's ouse is his Castle, and castles must not be busted 'cept when done in war time. And wotsume'er the failings on his part, he were a corn and seedsman in his hart."

"Is it Pumblechook's house that has been broken into, then?"

"That's it, Pip," said Joe; "and they took his till, and they took his cash-box, and they drinked his wine, and they partook of his wittles, and they slapped his face, and they pulled his nose, and they tied him up to his bedpust, and they giv' him a dozen, and they stuffed his mouth full of flowering annuals to perwent his crying out. But he knowed Orlick, and Orlick's in the county jail."

By these approaches we arrived at unrestricted conversation. I was slow to gain strength, but I did slowly and surely become less weak, and Joe stayed with me, and I fancied I was little Pip again.

For, the tenderness of Joe was so beautifully proportioned to my need, that I was like a child in his hands. He would sit and talk to me in the old confidence, and with the old simplicity, and in the old unassertive protecting way, so that I would half believe that all my life since the days of the old kitchen was one of the mental troubles of the fever that was gone. He did everything for me except the household work, for which he had engaged a very decent woman, after paying off the laundress on his first arrival. "Which I do assure you, Pip," he would often say, in explanation of that liberty; "I found her a tapping the spare bed, like a cask of beer, and drawing off the feathers in a bucket, for sale. Which she would have tapped yourn next, and draw'd it off with you a laying on it, and was then a carrying away the coals gradivally in the soup-tureen and wegetable dishes, and the wine and spirits in your Wellington boots."

We looked forward to the day when I should go out for a ride, as we had once looked forward to the day of my apprenticeship. And when the day came, and an open carriage was got into the Lane, Joe wrapped me up, took me in his arms, carried me down to it, and put me in, as if I were still the small helpless creature to whom he had so abundantly given of the wealth of his great nature.

And Joe got in beside me, and we drove away together into the country, where the rich summer growth was already on the trees and on the grass, and sweet summer scents filled all the air. The day happened to be Sunday, and when I looked on the loveliness around me, and thought how it had grown and changed, and how the little wild flowers had been forming, and the voices of the birds had been strengthened, by day and by night, under the sun and under the stars, while poor I lay burning and tossing on my bed, the mere remembrace of having burned and tossed there, came like a check upon my peace. But, when I heard the Sunday bells, and looked around a little more upon the outspread beauty, I felt that I was not nearly thankful enough—that I was too weak yet, to be even that—and I laid my head on Joe's shoulder, as I had laid it long ago when he had taken me to the Fair or where not, and it was too much for my young senses.

More composure came to me after a while, and we talked as we used to talk, lying on the grass at the old Battery. There was no change whatever in Joe. Exactly what he had been in my eyes then, he was in my eyes still; just as simply faithful, just as simply right.

When we got back again and he lifted me out, and carried me—so easily!—across the court and up the stairs, I thought of that eventful Christmas Day when he had carried me over the marshes. We had not yet made any allusion to my change of fortune, nor did I know how much of my late history he was acquainted with. I was so doubtful of myself now, and put so much trust in him, that I could not satisfy myself whether I ought to refer to it when he did not.

"Have you heard, Joe," I asked him that evening, upon further consideration, as he smoked his pipe at the window, "who my patron was?"

"I heerd," returned Joe, "as it were not Miss Havisham, old chap."

"Did you hear who it was, Joe?"

"Well! I heerd as it were a person what sent the person what giv' you the bank-notes at the Jolly Bargemen, Pip."

"So it was."

"Astonishing!" said Joe, in the placidest way.

"Did you hear that he was dead, Joe?" I presently asked, with increasing diffidence.

"Which? Him as sent the bank-notes, Pip?"

"Yes."

"I think," said Joe, after meditating a long time, and looking rather evasively at the window-seat, "as I did hear tell that how he were something or another in a general way in that direction."

"Did you hear anything of his circumstances, Joe?"

"Not partickler, Pip."

"If you would like to hear, Joe——" I was beginning, when Joe got up and came to my sofa.

"Lookee here, old chap," said Joe, bending over me. "Ever the best of friends; ain't us, Pip?"

I was ashamed to answer him.

"Werry good, then," said Joe, as if I had answered; "that's all right; that's agreed upon. Then why go into subjects, old chap, which as betwixt two sech must be for ever onnecessary? There's subjects enough as betwixt two sech, without onnecessary ones. Lord! To think of your poor sister and her Rampages! And don't you remember Tickler?"

"I do indeed, Joe."

"Lookee here, old chap," said Joe. "I done what I could to keep you and Tickler in sunders, but my power were not always fully equal to my inclinations. For when your poor sister had a mind to drop into you, it were not so much," said Joe, in his favourite argumentative way, "that she dropped into me too, if I put myself in opposition to her, but that she dropped into you always heavier for it. I noticed that. It ain't a grab at a man's whisker, nor yet a shake or two of a man (to which your sister was quite welcome), that 'ud put a man off from getting a little child out of punishment. But when that little child is dropped into, heavier, for that grab of whisker or shaking, then that man naterally up and says to himself, 'Where is the good as you are a doing? I grant you I see the 'arm,' says the man, 'but I don't see the good. I call upon you, sir, therefore, to pint out the good.'"

"The man says?" I observed, as Joe waited for me to speak.

"The man says," Joe assented. "Is he right, that man?"

"Dear Joe, he is always right."

"Well, old chap," said Joe, "then abide by your words. If he's always right (which in general he's more likely wrong), he's right when he says this:—Supposing ever you kep any little matter to yourself, when you was a little child, you kep it mostly because you know'd as J. Gargery's power to part you and Tickler in sunders, were not fully equal to his inclinations. Theerfore, think no more of it as betwixt two sech, and do not let us pass remarks upon onnecessary subjects. Biddy giv' herself a deal o' trouble with me afore I left (for I am most awful dull), as I should view it in this light, and, viewing it in this light, as I should ser put it. Both of which," said Joe, quite charmed with his logical arrangement, "being done, now this to you a true friend, say. Namely. You mustn't go a overdoing on it, but you must have your supper and your wine-and-water, and you must be put betwixt the sheets."

The delicacy with which Joe dismissed this theme, and the sweet tact and kindness with which Biddy—who with her woman's wit had found me out so soon—had prepared him for it, made a deep impression on my mind. But whether Joe knew how poor I was, and how my great expectations had all dissolved, like our own marsh mists before the sun, I could not understand.

Another thing in Joe that I could not understand when it first began to develop itself, but which I soon arrived at a sorrowful comprehension of, was this: As I became stronger and better, Joe became a little less easy with me. In my weakness and entire dependence on him, the dear fellow had fallen into the old tone, and called me by the old names, the dear "old Pip, old chap," that now were music in my ears. I too had fallen into the old ways, only happy and thankful that he let me. But, imperceptibly, though I held by them fast, Joe's hold upon them began to slacken; and whereas I wondered at this, at first, I soon began to understand that the cause of it was in me, and that the fault of it was all mine.

Ah! Had I given Joe no reason to doubt my constancy,

and to think that in prosperity I should grow cold to him and cast him off? Had I given Joe's innocent heart no cause to feel instinctively that as I got stronger, his hold upon me would be weaker, and that he had better loosen it in time and let me go, before I plucked myself away?

It was on the third or fourth occasion of my going out walking in the Temple Gardens, leaning on Joe's arm, that I saw this change in him very plainly. We had been sitting in the bright warm sunlight, looking at the river, and I chanced to say as we got up:

"See, Joe! I can walk quite strongly. Now, you shall see me walk back by myself."

"Which do not overdo it, Pip," said Joe; "but I shall be happy fur to see you able, sir."

The last word grated on me; but how could I remonstrate! I walked no further than the gate of the gardens, and then pretended to be weaker than I was, and asked Joe for his arm. Joe gave it me, but was thoughtful.

I, for my part, was thoughtful too; for how best to check this growing change in Joe, was a great perplexity to my remorseful thoughts. That I was ashamed to tell him exactly how I was placed, and what I had come down to, I do not seek to conceal; but, I hope my reluctance was not quite an unworthy one. He would want to help me out of his little savings, I knew, and I knew that he ought not to help me, and that I must not suffer him to do it.

It was a thoughtful evening with both of us. But, before we went to bed, I had resolved that I would wait over to-morrow, to-morrow being Sunday, and would begin my new course with the new week. On Monday morning I would speak to Joe about this change, I would lay aside this last vestige of reserve, I would tell him what I had in my thoughts (that Secondly, not yet arrived at), and why I had not decided to go out to Herbert, and then the change would be conquered for ever. As I cleared, Joe cleared, and it seemed as though he had sympathetically arrived at a resolution too.

We had a quiet day on the Sunday, and we rode out into the country, and then walked in the fields.

"I feel thankful that I have been ill, Joe," I said.

"Dear old Pip, old chap, you're a'most come round, sir."

"It has been a memorable time for me, Joe."

"Likeways for myself, sir," Joe returned.

"We have had a time together, Joe, that I can never forget. There were days once, I know, that I did for a while forget; but I never shall forget these."

"Pip," said Joe, appearing a little hurried and troubled, "there has been larks. And, dear sir, what have been betwixt us—have been."

At night, when I had gone to bed, Joe came into my room, as he had done all through my recovery. He asked me if I felt sure that I was as well as in the morning?

"Yes, dear Joe, quite."

"And are always a getting stronger, old chap?"

"Yes, dear Joe, steadily."

Joe patted the coverlet on my shoulder with his great good hand, and said, in what I thought a husky voice, "Good night!"

When I got up in the morning, refreshed and stronger yet, I was full of my resolution to tell Joe all, without delay. I would tell him before breakfast. I would dress at once and go to his room and surprise him; for, it was the first day I had been up early. I went to his room, and he was not there. Not only was he not there, but his box was gone.

I hurried then to the breakfast-table, and on it found a letter. These were its brief contents:

"Not wishful to intrude I have departured fur you are well again dear Pip and will do better without "Jo.

"P.S. Ever the best of friends."

Enclosed in the letter, was a receipt for the debt and costs on which I had been arrested. Down to that moment I had vainly supposed that my creditor had withdrawn or suspended proceedings until I should be quite recovered. I had never dreamed of Joe's having paid the money; but, Joe had paid it, and the receipt was in his name.

What remained for me now, but to follow him to the dear old forge, and there to have out my disclosure to him, and my penitent remonstrance with him, and there to relieve my mind and heart of that reserved Secondly, which had begun as a vague something lingering in my thoughts, and had formed into a settled purpose?

The purpose was, that I would go to Biddy, that I would show her how humbled and repentant I came back, that I would tell her how I had lost all I once hoped for, that I would remind her of our old confidences in my first unhappy time. Then, I would say to her, "Biddy, I think you once liked me very well, when my errant heart, even while it strayed away from you, was quieter and better with you than it ever has been since. If you can like me only half as well once more, if you can take me with all my faults and disappointments on my head, if you can receive me like a forgiven child (and indeed I am as sorry, Biddy, and have as much need of a hushing voice and a soothing hand), I hope I am a little worthier of you than I was—not much, but a little. And, Biddy, it shall rest with you to say whether I shall work at the forge with Joe, or whether I shall try for any different occupation down in this country, or whether we shall go away to a distant place where an opportunity awaits me which I set aside when it was offered, until I knew your answer. And now, dear Biddy, if you can tell me that you will go through the world with me, you will surely make it a better world for me, and me a better man for it, and I will try hard to make it a better world for you."

Such was my purpose. After three days more of recovery, I went down to the old place, to put it in execution. And how I sped in it, is all I have left to tell.

CHAPTER LVIII.

The tidings of my high fortunes having had a heavy fall, had got down to my native place and its neighbourhood, before I got there. I found the Blue Boar in possession of the intelligence, and I found that it made a great change in the Boar's demeanour. Whereas the Boar had cultivated my good opinion with warm assiduity when I was coming into property, the Boar was exceedingly cool on the subject now that I was going out of property.

It was evening when I arrived, much fatigued by the journey I had so often made so easily. The Boar could not put me into my usual bedroom, which was engaged (probably by some one who had expectations), and could only assign me a very indifferent chamber among the pigeons and post-chaises up the yard. But, I had as sound a sleep in that lodging as in the most superior accommodations the Boar could have given me, and the quality of my dreams was about the same as in the best bedroom.

Early in the morning while my breakfast was getting ready, I strolled round by Satis House. There were printed

bills on the gate and on bits of carpet hanging out of the
windows, announcing a sale by auction of the Household
Furniture and Effects, next week. The House itself was
to be sold as old building materials, and pulled down.
LOT 1 was marked in whitewashed knock-knee letters on
the brewhouse; LOT 2 on that part of the main building
which had been so long shut up. Other lots were marked
off on other parts of the structure, and the ivy had been
torn down to make room for the inscriptions, and much of
it trailed low in the dust and was withered already. Stepping in for a moment at the open gate and looking around
me with the uncomfortable air of a stranger who had no
business there, I saw the auctioneer's clerk walking on the
casks and telling them off for the information of a catalogue compiler, pen in hand, who made a temporary desk
of the wheeled chair I had so often pushed along to the
tune of Old Clem.

When I got back to my breakfast in the Boar's coffee-
room, I found Mr. Pumblechook conversing with the landlord. Mr. Pumblechook (not improved in appearance by
his late nocturnal adventure) was waiting for me, and addressed me in the following terms.

"Young man, I am sorry to see you brought low. But
what else could be expected! what else could be expected!"

As he extended his hand with a magnificently forgiving
air, and as I was broken by illness and unfit to quarrel, I
took it.

"William," said Mr. Pumblechook to the waiter, "put a
muffin on table. And has it come to this! Has it come to
this!"

I frowningly sat down to my breakfast. Mr. Pumblechook stood over me and poured out my tea—before I could
touch the teapot—with the air of a benefactor who was resolved to be true to the last.

"William," said Mr. Pumblechook, mournfully, "put
the salt on. In happier times," addressing me, "I think
you took sugar? And did you take milk? You did.
Sugar and milk. William, bring a watercress."

"Thank you," said I shortly, "but I don't eat watercresses."

"You don't eat 'em," returned Mr. Pumblechook, sighing and nodding his head several times, as if he might
have expected that, and as if abstinence from watercresses
were consistent with my downfall. "True. The simple
fruits of the earth. No. You needn't bring any, William."

I went on with my breakfast, and Mr. Pumblechook
continued to stand over me, staring fishily and breathing
noisily, as he always did.

"Little more than skin and bone!" mused Mr. Pumblechook, aloud. "And yet when he went away from here
(I may say with my blessing), and I spread afore him
my humble store, like the Bee, he was as plump as a
Peach!"

This reminded me of the wonderful difference between
the servile manner in which he had offered his hand in my
new prosperity, saying, "May I?" and the ostentatious
clemency with which he had just now exhibited the same
fat five fingers.

"Hah!" he went on, handing me the bread-and-butter.
"And air you a going to Joseph?"

"In Heaven's name," said I, firing in spite of myself,
"what does it matter to you where I am going? Leave
that teapot alone."

It was the worst course I could have taken, because it
gave Pumblechook the opportunity he wanted.

"Yes, young man," said he, releasing the handle of the
article in question, retiring a step or two from my table,
and speaking for the behoof of the landlord and waiter at
the door, "I will leave that teapot alone. You are right,
young man. For once, you are right. I forgit myself
when I take such an interest in your breakfast, as to wish
your frame, exhausted by the debilitating effects of pro-
digygality, to be stimulated by the 'olesome nourishment of
your forefathers. And yet," said Pumblechook, turning
to the landlord and waiter, and pointing me out at arm's
length, "this is him as I ever sported with in his days of
happy infancy! Tell me not it cannot be; I tell you this
is him!"

A low murmur from the two replied. The waiter appeared to be particularly affected.

"This is him," said Pumblechook, "as I have rode in
my shay-cart. This is him as I have seen brought up by
hand. This is him untoe the sister of which I was uncle
by marriage, as her name was Georgiana M'ria from her
own mother, let him deny it if he can!"

The waiter seemed convinced that I could not deny it,
and that it gave the case a black look.

"Young man," said Pumblechook, screwing his head at
me in the old fashion, "you air a going to Joseph. What
does it matter to me, you ask me, where you air a going?
I say to you, sir, you air a going to Joseph."

The waiter coughed, as if he modestly invited me to get
over that.

"Now," said Pumblechook, and all this with a most exasperating air of saying in the cause of virtue what was
perfectly convincing and conclusive, "I will tell you what
to say to Joseph. Here is Squires of the Boar present,
known and respected in this town, and here is William,
which his father's name was Potkins if I do not deceive
myself."

"You do not, sir," said William.

"In their presence," pursued Pumblechook, "I will tell
you, young man, what to say to Joseph. Says you, 'Joseph, I have this day seen my earliest benefactor and the
founder of my fortun's. I will name no names, Joseph,
but so they are pleased to call him up-town, and I have
seen that man.'"

"I swear I don't see him here," said I.

"Say that likewise," retorted Pumblechook. "Say you
said that, and even Joseph will probably betray surprise."

"There you quite mistake him," said I. "I know better."

"Says you," Pumblechook went on, "'Joseph, I have
seen that man, and that man bears you no malice and bears
me no malice. He knows your character, Joseph, and is
well acquainted with your pig-headedness and ignorance;
and he knows my character, Joseph, and he knows my
want of gratitoode. Yes, Joseph,' says you," here Pumblechook shook his head and hand at me, "'he knows my
total deficiency of common human gratitoode. He knows
it, Joseph, as none can. You do not know it, Joseph, having no call to know it, but that man do.'"

Windy donkey as he was, it really amazed me that he
could have the face to talk thus to mine.

"Says you, 'Joseph, he gave me a little message, which
I will now repeat. It was, that in my being brought low,
he saw the finger of Providence. He knowed that finger

when he saw it, Joseph, and he saw it plain. It pinted out this writing, Joseph. *Reward of ingratitoode to earliest benefactor, and founder of fortun's.* But that man said that he did not repent of what he had done, Joseph. Not at all. It was right to do it, it was kind to do it, it was benevolent to do it, and he would do it again.'"

"It's a pity," said I, scornfully, as I finished my interrupted breakfast, "that the man did not say what he had done and would do again."

"Squires of the Boar!" Pumblechook was now addressing the landlord, Joseph, "and William! I have no objections to your mentioning, either up-town or down-town, if such should be your wishes, that it was right to do it, kind to do it, benevolent to do it, and that I would do it again."

With those words the Impostor shook them both by the hand, with an air, and left the house; leaving me much more astonished than delighted by the virtues of that same indefinite "it." I was not long after him in leaving the house too, and when I went down the High-street I saw him holding forth (no doubt to the same effect) at his shop door to a select group, who honoured me with very unfavourable glances as I passed on the opposite side of the way.

But, it was only the pleasanter to turn to Biddy and to Joe, whose great forbearance shone more brightly than before, if that could be, contrasted with this brazen pretender. I went towards them slowly, for my limbs were weak, but with a sense of increasing relief as I drew nearer to them, and a sense of leaving arrogance and untruthfulness further and further behind.

The June weather was delicious. The sky was blue, the larks were soaring high over the green corn, I thought all that country-side more beautiful and peaceful by far than I had ever known it to be yet. Many pleasant pictures of the life that I would lead there, and of the change for the better that would come over my character when I had a guiding spirit at my side whose simple faith and clear home-wisdom I had proved, beguiled my way. They awakened a tender emotion in me; for, my heart was softened by my return, and such a change had come to pass that I felt like one who was toiling home barefoot from distant travel, and whose wanderings had lasted many years.

The schoolhouse where Biddy was mistress, I had never seen; but, the little roundabout lane by which I entered the village for quietness' sake, took me past it. I was disappointed to find that the day was a holiday; no children were there, and Biddy's house was closed. Some hopeful notion of seeing her, busily engaged in her daily duties, before she saw me, had been in my mind and was defeated.

But, the forge was a very short distance off, and I went towards it under the sweet green limes, listening for the clink of Joe's hammer. Long after I ought to have heard it, and long after I had fancied I heard it and found it but a fancy, all was still. The limes were there, and the white thorns were there, and the chestnut-trees were there, and the leaves rustled harmoniously when I stopped to listen; but, the clink of Joe's hammer was not in the midsummer wind.

Almost fearing, without knowing why, to come in view of the forge, I saw it at last, and saw that it was closed. No gleam of fire, no glittering shower of sparks, no roar of bellows; all shut up, and still.

But, the house was not deserted, and the best parlour seemed to be in use, for there were white curtains fluttering in its window, and the window was open and gay with flowers. I went softly towards it, meaning to peep over the flowers, when Joe and Biddy stood before me, arm in arm.

At first Biddy gave a cry, as if she thought it was my apparition, but in another moment she was in my embrace. I wept to see her, and she wept to see me; I, because she looked so fresh and pleasant; she, because I looked so worn and white.

"But, dear Biddy, how smart you are!"

"Yes, dear Pip."

"And Joe, how smart *you* are!"

"Yes, dear old Pip, old chap."

I looked at both of them, from one to the other, and then——

"It's my wedding-day," cried Biddy, in a burst of happiness, "and I am married to Joe!"

*   *   *   *   *   *   *   *

They had taken me into the kitchen, and I had laid my head down on the old deal table. Biddy held one of my hands to her lips, and Joe's restoring touch was on my shoulder. "Which he warn't strong enough, my dear, fur to be surprised," said Joe. And Biddy said, "I ought to have thought of it, dear Joe, but I was too happy." They were both so overjoyed to see me, so proud to see me, so touched by my coming to them, so delighted that I should have come by accident to make their day complete!

My first thought was one of great thankfulness that I had never breathed this last baffled hope to Joe. How often, while he was with me in my illness, had it risen to my lips. How irrevocable would have been his knowledge of it, if he had remained with me but another hour!

"Dear Biddy," said I, "you have the best husband in the whole world, and if you could have seen him by my bed you would have——But no, you couldn't love him better than you do."

"No, I couldn't indeed," said Biddy.

"And, dear Joe, you have the best wife in the whole world, and she will make you as happy as even you deserve to be, you dear, good, noble Joe!"

Joe looked at me with a quivering lip, and fairly put his sleeve before his eyes.

"And Joe and Biddy both, as you have been to church to-day and are in charity and love with all mankind, receive my humble thanks for all you have done for me, and all I have so ill repaid! And when I say that I am going away within the hour, for I am soon going abroad, and that I shall never rest until I have worked for the money with which you have kept me out of prison, and have sent it to you, don't think, dear Joe and Biddy, that if I could repay it a thousand times over, I suppose I could cancel a farthing of the debt I owe you, or that I would do so if I could!"

They were both melted by these words, and both entreated me to say no more.

"But I must say more. Dear Joe, I hope you will have children to love, and that some little fellow will sit in this chimney corner of a winter night, who may remind you of another little fellow gone out of it for ever. Don't tell him, Joe, that I was thankless; don't tell him, Biddy, that I was ungenerous and unjust; only tell him that I honoured you both, because you were both so good and true, and that, as your child, I said it would be natural to him to grow up a much better man than I did."

"I ain't a going," said Joe, from behind his sleeve, "to tell him nothink o' that natur, Pip. Nor Biddy ain't. Nor yet no one ain't."

"And now, though I know you have already done it in your own kind hearts, pray tell me, both, that you forgive me! Pray let me hear you say the words, that I may carry the sound of them away with me, and then I shall be able to believe that you can trust me, and think better of me, in the time to come!"

"O dear old Pip, old chap," said Joe. "God knows as I forgive you, if I have anythink to forgive!"

"Amen! And God knows I do!" echoed Biddy.

"Now let me go up and look at my old little room, and rest there a few minutes by myself. And then when I have eaten and drunk with you, go with me as far as the finger-post, dear Joe and Biddy, before we say good bye!"

I sold all I had, and put aside as much as I could, for a composition with my creditors—who gave me ample time to pay them in full—and I went out and joined Herbert. Within a month, I had quitted England, and within two months I was clerk to Clarriker and Co., and within four months I assumed my first undivided responsibility. For, the beam across the parlour ceiling at Mill Pond Bank, had then ceased to tremble under old Bill Barley's growls and was at peace, and Herbert had gone away to marry Clara, and I was left in sole charge of the Eastern Branch until he brought her back.

Many a year went round, before I was a partner in the House; but, I lived happily with Herbert and his wife, and lived frugally, and paid my debts, and maintained a constant correspondence with Biddy and Joe. It was not until I became third in the Firm, that Clarriker betrayed me to Herbert; but, he then declared that the secret of Herbert's partnership had been long enough upon his conscience, and he must tell it. So, he told it, and Herbert was as much moved as amazed, and the dear fellow and I were not the worse friends for the long concealment. I must not leave it to be supposed that we were ever a great House, or that we made mints of money. We were not in a grand way of business, but we had a good name, and worked for our profits, and did very well. We owed so much to Herbert's ever cheerful industry and readiness, that I often wondered how I had conceived that old idea of his inaptitude, until I was one day enlightened by the reflection, that perhaps the inaptitude had never been in him at all, but had been in me.

CHAPTER LIX.

For eleven years I had not seen Joe nor Biddy with my bodily eyes—though they had both been often before my fancy in the East—when, upon an evening in December, an hour or two after dark, I laid my hand softly on the latch of the old kitchen door. I touched it so softly that I was not heard, and I looked in unseen. There, smoking his pipe in the old place by the kitchen firelight, as hale and as strong as ever, though a little grey, sat Joe; and there, fenced in the corner with Joe's leg, and sitting on my own little stool looking at the fire, was——I again!

"We giv' him the name of Pip for your sake, dear old chap," said Joe, delighted when I took another stool by the child's side (but I did not rumple his hair), "and we hoped he might grow a little bit like you, and we think he do."

I thought so too, and I took him out for a walk next morning, and we talked immensely, understanding one another. And I took him down to the churchyard, and set him on a certain tombstone there, and he showed me from that elevation which stone was sacred to the memory of Philip Pirrip, late of this parish, and Also Georgiana, Wife of the Above.

"Biddy," said I, when I talked with her after dinner, as her little girl lay sleeping in her lap, "you must give Pip to me, one of these days; or lend him, at all events."

"No, no," said Biddy, gently. "You must marry."

"So Herbert and Clara say, but I don't think I shall, Biddy. I have so settled down in their home, that it's not at all likely. I am already quite an old bachelor."

Biddy looked down at her child, and put its little hand to her lips, and then put the good matronly hand with which she had touched it into mine. There was something in the action and in the light pressure of Biddy's wedding-ring, that had a very pretty eloquence in it.

"Dear Pip," said Biddy, "you are sure you don't fret for her?"

"O no—I think not, Biddy."

"Tell me as an old friend. Have you quite forgotten her?"

"My dear Biddy, I have forgotten nothing in my life that ever had a foremost place there, and little that ever had any place there. But that poor dream, as I once used to call it, has all gone by, Biddy, all gone by!"

Nevertheless, I knew while I said those words, that I secretly intended to revisit the site of the old house that evening, alone, for her sake. Yes, even so. For Estella's sake.

I had heard of her as leading a most unhappy life, and as being separated from her husband, who had used her with great cruelty, and who had become quite renowned as a compound of pride, avarice, brutality, and meanness. And I had heard of the death of her husband, from an accident consequent on his ill-treatment of a horse. This release had befallen her some two years before; for anything I knew, she was married again.

The early dinner-hour at Joe's left me abundance of time, without hurrying my talk with Biddy, to walk over to the old spot before dark. But, what with loitering on the way, to look at old objects and to think of old times, the day had quite declined when I came to the place.

There was no house now, no brewery, no building whatever left, but the wall of the old garden. The cleared space had been enclosed with a rough fence, and, looking over it, I saw that some of the old ivy had struck root anew, and was growing green on low quiet mounds of ruin. A gate in the fence standing ajar, I pushed it open, and went in.

A cold silvery mist had veiled the afternoon, and the moon was not yet up to scatter it. But, the stars were shining beyond the mist, and the moon was coming, and the evening was not dark. I could trace out where every part of the old house had been, and where the brewery had been, and where the gates, and where the casks. I had done so, and was looking along the desolate garden-walk, when I beheld a solitary figure in it.

The figure showed itself aware of me as I advanced. It

had been moving towards me, but it stood still. As I drew nearer, I saw it to be the figure of a woman. As I drew nearer yet, it was about to turn away, when it stopped, and let me come up with it. Then, it faltered as if much surprised, and uttered my name, and I cried out:

"Estella!"

"I am greatly changed. I wonder you know me."

The freshness of her beauty was indeed gone, but its indescribable majesty and its indescribable charm remained. Those attractions in it, I had seen before; what I had never seen before, was the saddened softened light of the once proud eyes; what I had never felt before, was the friendly touch of the once insensible hand.

We sat down on a bench that was near, and I said, "After so many years, it is strange that we should thus meet again, Estella, here where our first meeting was! Do you often come back?"

"I have never been here since."

"Nor I."

The moon began to rise, and I thought of the placid look at the white ceiling, which had passed away. The moon began to rise, and I thought of the pressure on my hand when I had spoken the last words he had heard on earth.

Estella was the next to break the silence that ensued between us.

"I have very often hoped and intended to come back, but have been prevented by many circumstances. Poor, poor old place!"

The silvery mist was touched with the first rays of the moonlight, and the same rays touched the tears that dropped from her eyes. Not knowing that I saw them and setting herself to get the better of them, she said quietly:

"Were you wondering, as you walked along, how it came to be left in this condition?"

"Yes, Estella."

"The ground belongs to me. It is the only possession I have not relinquished. Everything else has gone from me, little by little, but I have kept this. It was the subject of the only determined resistance I made in all the wretched years."

"Is it to be built on?"

"At last it is. I came here to take leave of it before its change. And you," she said, in a voice of touching interest to a wanderer, "you live abroad still."

"Still."

"And do well, I am sure?"

"I work pretty hard for a sufficient living, and therefore—Yes, I do well!"

"I have often thought of you," said Estella.

"Have you?"

"Of late, very often. There was a long hard time when I kept far from me, the remembrance of what I had thrown away when I was quite ignorant of its worth. But, since my duty has not been incompatible with the admission of that remembrance, I have given it a place in my heart."

"You have always held your place in *my* heart," I answered.

And we were silent again until she spoke.

"I little thought," said Estella, "that I should take leave of you in taking leave of this spot. I am very glad to do so."

"Glad to part again, Estella? To me, parting is a painful thing. To me, the remembrance of our last parting has been ever mournful and painful."

"But you said to me," returned Estella, very earnestly, "'God bless you, God forgive you!' And if you could say that to me then, you will not hesitate to say that to me now—now, when suffering has been stronger than all other teaching, and has taught me to understand what your heart used to be. I have been bent and broken, but—I hope—into a better shape. Be as considerate and good to me as you were, and tell me we are friends."

"We are friends," said I, rising and bending over her, as she rose from the bench.

"And will continue friends apart," said Estella.

I took her hand in mine, and we went out of the ruined place; and, as the morning mists had risen long ago when I first left the forge, so, the evening mists were rising now, and in all the broad expanse of tranquil light they showed to me, I saw no shadow of another parting from her.

Tale of Two Cities

SIDNEY CARTON.

Tale of Two Cities

by

Charles Dickens

With Illustrations by

Barnard, and Others

CONTENTS.

ILLUSTRATIONS

TO

TALE OF TWO CITIES

A TALE OF TWO CITIES.

IN THREE BOOKS.

BOOK THE FIRST.—RECALLED TO LIFE.

CHAPTER I.

THE PERIOD.

IT was the best of times, it was the worst of times, it was the age of wisdom, it was the age of foolishness, it was the epoch of belief, it was the epoch of incredulity, it was the season of Light, it was the season of Darkness, it was the spring of hope, it was the winter of despair, we had everything before us, we had nothing before us, we were all going direct to Heaven, we were all going direct the other way—in short, the period was so far like the present period, that some of its noisiest authorities insisted on its being received, for good or for evil, in the superlative degree of comparison only.

There were a king with a large jaw and a queen with a plain face, on the throne of England; there were a king with a large jaw and a queen with a fair face, on the throne of France. In both countries it was clearer than crystal to the lords of the State preserves of loaves and fishes, that things in general were settled for ever.

It was the year of Our Lord one thousand seven hundred and seventy-five. Spiritual revelations were conceded to England at that favoured period, as at this. Mrs. Southcott had recently attained her five-and-twentieth blessed birthday, of whom a prophetic private in the Life Guards had heralded the sublime appearance by announcing that arrangements were made for the swallowing up of London and Westminster. Even the Cock-lane ghost had been laid only a round dozen of years, after rapping out its messages, as the spirits of this very year last past (supernaturally deficient in originality) rapped out theirs. Mere messages in the earthly order of events had lately come to the English Crown and People, from a congress of British subjects in America: which, strange to relate, have proved more important to the human race than any communications yet received through any of the chickens of the Cock-lane brood.

France, less favoured on the whole as to matters spiritual than her sister of the shield and trident, rolled with exceeding smoothness down hill, making paper money and spending it. Under the guidance of her Christian pastors, she entertained herself, besides, with such humane achievements as sentencing a youth to have his hands cut off, his tongue torn out with pincers, and his body burned alive, because he had not kneeled down in the rain to do honour to a dirty procession of monks which passed within his view, at a distance of some fifty or sixty yards. It is likely enough that, rooted in the woods of France and Norway, there were growing trees, when that sufferer was put to death, already marked by the Woodman, Fate, to come down and be sawn into boards, to make a certain movable framework with a sack and a knife in it, terrible in history. It is likely enough that in the rough outhouses of some tillers of the heavy lands adjacent to Paris, there were sheltered from the weather that very day, rude carts, bespattered with rustic mire, snuffed about by pigs, and roosted in by poultry, which the Farmer, Death, had already set apart to be his tumbrils of the Revolution. But that Woodman and that Farmer, though they work unceasingly, work silently, and no one heard them as they went about with muffled tread: the rather, forasmuch as to entertain any suspicion that they were awake, was to be atheistical and traitorous.

In England, there was scarcely an amount of order and protection to justify much national boasting. Daring burglaries by armed men, and highway robberies, took place in the capital itself every night; families were publicly cautioned not to go out of town without removing their furniture to upholsterers' warehouses for security; the highwayman in the dark was a City tradesman in the light, and, being recognised and challenged by his fellow-tradesman whom he stopped in his character of "the Captain," gallantly shot him through the head and rode away; the mail was waylaid by seven robbers, and the guard shot three dead, and then got shot dead himself by the other four, "in consequence of the failure of his ammunition:" after which the mail was robbed in peace; that magnificent potentate, the Lord Mayor of London, was made to stand and deliver on Turnham Green, by one highwayman, who despoiled the illustrious creature in sight of all his retinue; prisoners in London gaols fought battles with their turnkeys, and the majesty of the law fired blunderbusses in among them, loaded with rounds of shot and ball; thieves snipped off diamond crosses from the necks of noble lords at Court drawing-rooms; musketeers went into St. Giles's, to search for contraband goods, and the mob fired on the musketeers, and the musketeers fired on the mob, and nobody thought any of these occurrences much out of the common way. In the midst of them, the hangman, ever busy and ever worse than useless, was in constant requisition; now, stringing up long rows of miscellaneous criminals; now, hanging a housebreaker on Saturday who had been taken on Tuesday; now, burning people in the hand at Newgate by the dozen, and now burning pamphlets at the door of Westminster Hall; to-day, taking the life of an atrocious murderer, and to-morrow of a wretched pilferer who had robbed a farmer's boy of sixpence.

All these things, and a thousand like them, came to pass in and close upon the dear old year one thousand seven hundred and seventy-five. Environed by them, while the Woodman and the Farmer worked unheeded, those two of the large jaws, and those other two of the plain and the fair faces, trod with stir enough, and carried their divine rights with a high hand. Thus did the year one thousand seven hundred and seventy-five conduct their Greatnesses, and myriads of small creatures—the creatures of this chronicle among the rest—along the roads that lay before them.

GEORGE III.

CHAPTER II.

THE MAIL.

It was the Dover road that lay, on a Friday night late in November, before the first of the persons with whom this history has business. The Dover road lay, as to him, beyond the Dover mail, as it lumbered up Shooter's Hill. He walked up hill in the mire by the side of the mail, as the rest of the passengers did; not because they had the least relish for walking exercise, under the circumstances, but because the hill, and the harness, and the mud, and the mail, were all so heavy, that the horses had three times already come to a stop, besides once drawing the coach across the road, with the mutinous intent of taking it back to Blackheath. Reins and whip and coachman and guard, however, in combination, had read that article of war which forbade a purpose otherwise strongly in favour of the argument, that some brute animals are endued with Reason; and the team had capitulated and returned to their duty.

With drooping heads and tremulous tails, they mashed their way through the thick mud, floundering and stumbling between whiles, as if they were falling to pieces at the larger joints. As often as the driver rested them and brought them to a stand, with a wary "Wo-ho! so-hothen!" the near leader violently shook his head and everything upon it—like an unusually emphatic horse, denying that the coach could be got up the hill. Whenever the leader made this rattle, the passenger started, as a nervous passenger might, and was disturbed in mind.

There was a steaming mist in all the hollows, and it had roamed in its forlornness up the hill, like an evil spirit, seeking rest and finding none. A clammy and intensely cold mist, it made its slow way through the air in ripples that visibly followed and overspread one another, as the waves of an unwholesome sea might do. It was dense enough to shut out everything from the light of the coach-lamps but these its own workings, and a few yards of road; and the reek of the labouring horses steamed into it, as if they had made it all.

Two other passengers, besides the one, were plodding up the hill by the side of the mail. All three were wrapped to the cheek-bones and over the ears, and wore jack-boots. Not one of the three could have said, from anything he saw, what either of the other two was like; and each was hidden under almost as many wrappers from the eyes of the mind, as from the eyes of the body, of his two companions. In those days, travellers were very shy of being confidential on a short notice, for anybody on the road might be a robber or in league with robbers. As to the latter, when every posting-house and ale-house could produce somebody in "the Captain's" pay, ranging from the landlord to the lowest stable nondescript, it was the likeliest thing upon the cards. So the guard of the Dover mail thought to himself, that Friday night in November, one thousand seven hundred and seventy-five, lumbering up Shooter's Hill, as he stood on his own particular perch behind the mail, beating his feet, and keeping an eye and a hand on the arm-chest before him, where a loaded blunderbuss lay at the top of six or eight loaded horse-pistols, deposited on a substratum of cutlass.

The Dover mail was in its usual genial position that the guard suspected the passengers, the passengers suspected one another and the guard, they all suspected everybody else, and the coachman was sure of nothing but the horses; as to which cattle he could with a clear conscience have taken his oath on the Two Testaments that they were not fit for the journey.

"Wo-ho!" said the coachman. "So, then! One more pull and you're at the top and be damned to you, for I have had trouble enough to get you to it!—Joe!"

"Halloa!" the guard replied.

"What o'clock do you make it, Joe?"

"Ten minutes, good, past eleven."

"My blood!" ejaculated the vexed coachman, "and not atop of Shooter's yet! Tst! Yah! Get on with you!"

The emphatic horse, cut short by the whip in a most decided negative, made a decided scramble for it, and the three other horses followed suit. Once more, the Dover mail struggled on, with the jack-boots of its passengers squashing along by its side. They had stopped when the coach stopped, and they kept close company with it. If any one of the three had had the hardihood to propose to another to walk on a little ahead into the mist and darkness, he would have put himself in a fair way of getting shot instantly as a highwayman.

The last burst carried the mail to the summit of the hill. The horses stopped to breathe again, and the guard got down to skid the wheel for the descent, and open the coach-door to let the passengers in.

"Tst! Joe!" cried the coachman in a warning voice, looking down from his box.

"What do you say, Tom?"

They both listened.

"I say a horse at a canter coming up, Joe."

"*I* say a horse at a gallop, Tom," returned the guard, leaving his hold of the door, and mounting nimbly to his place. "Gentlemen! In the king's name, all of you!"

With this hurried adjuration, he cocked his blunderbuss, and stood on the offensive.

The passenger booked by this history, was on the coach-step, getting in; the two other passengers were close behind him, and about to follow. He remained on the step, half in the coach and half out of; they remained in the road below him. They all looked from the coachman to the guard, and from the guard to the coachman, and listened. The coachman looked back and the guard looked back, and even the emphatic leader pricked up his ears and looked back, without contradicting.

The stillness consequent on the cessation of the rumbling and labouring of the coach, added to the stillness of the night, made it very quiet indeed. The panting of the horses communicated a tremulous motion to the coach, as if it were in a state of agitation. The hearts of the passengers beat loud enough perhaps to be heard; but at any rate, the quiet pause was audibly expressive of people out of breath, and holding the breath, and having the pulses quickened by expectation.

The sound of a horse at a gallop came fast and furiously up the hill.

"So-ho!" the guard sang out, as loud as he could roar. "Yo there! Stand! I shall fire!"

The pace was suddenly checked, and, with much splashing and floundering, a man's voice called from the mist, "Is that the Dover mail?"

"Never you mind what it is!" the guard retorted. "What are you?"

"*Is* that the Dover mail?"

"Why do you want to know?"

"I want a passenger, if it is."

"What passenger?"

"Mr. Jarvis Lorry."

Our booked passenger showed in a moment that it was his name. The guard, the coachman, and the two other passengers eyed him distrustfully.

"Keep where you are," the guard called to the voice in the mist, "because, if I should make a mistake, it could never be set right in your lifetime. Gentleman of the name of Lorry answer straight."

"What is the matter?" asked the passenger, then, with mildly quavering speech. "Who wants me? Is it Jerry?"

("I don't like Jerry's voice, if it is Jerry," growled the guard to himself. "He's hoarser than suits me, is Jerry.")

"Yes, Mr. Lorry."

"What is the matter?"

"A despatch sent after you from over yonder. T. and Co."

"I know this messenger, guard," said Mr. Lorry, getting down into the road—assisted from behind more swiftly than politely by the other two passengers, who immediately scrambled into the coach, shut the door, and pulled up the window. "He may come close; there's nothing wrong."

"I hope there ain't, but I can't make so 'Nation sure of that," said the guard, in gruff soliloquy. "Hallo you!"

"Well! And hallo you!" said Jerry, more hoarsely than before.

"Come on at a footpace! d'ye mind me? And if you've got holsters to that saddle o' yourn, don't let me see your hand go nigh' em. For I'm a devil at a quick mistake, and when I make one it takes the form of Lead. So now let's look at you."

The figures of a horse and rider came slowly through the eddying mist, and came to the side of the mail, where the passenger stood. The rider stooped, and, casting up his eyes at the guard, handed the passenger a small folded paper. The rider's horse was blown, and both horse and rider were covered with mud, from the hoofs of the horse to the hat of the man.

"Guard!" said the passenger, in a tone of quiet business confidence.

The watchful guard, with his right hand at the stock of his raised blunderbuss, his left at the barrel, and his eye on the horseman, answered, curtly "Sir."

"There is nothing to apprehend. I belong to Tellson's Bank. You must know Tellson's Bank in London. I am going to Paris on business. A crown to drink. I may read this?"

"If so be as you're quick, sir."

He opened it in the light of the coach-lamp on that side, and read—first to himself and then aloud: "'Wait at Dover for Mam'selle.' It's not long, you see, guard. Jerry, say that my answer was, RECALLED TO LIFE."

Jerry started in his saddle. "That's a Blazing strange answer, too," said he, at his hoarsest.

"Take that message back, and they will know that I received this, as well as if I wrote. Make the best of your way. Good night."

With those words the passenger opened the coach-door and got in; not at all assisted by his fellow-passengers, who had expeditiously secreted their watches and purses in their boots, and were now making a general pretence of being asleep. With no more definite purpose than to escape the hazard of originating any other kind of action.

The coach lumbered on again, with heavier wreaths of mist closing round it as it began the descent. The guard soon replaced his blunderbuss in his arm-chest, and, having looked to the rest of its contents, and having looked to the supplementary pistols that he wore in his belt, looked to a smaller chest beneath his seat, in which there were a few smith's tools, a couple of torches, and a tinder-box. For he was furnished with that completeness that if the coach-lamps had been blown and stormed out, which did occasionally happen, he had only to shut himself up inside, keep the flint and steel sparks well off the straw, and get a light with tolerable safety and ease (if he were lucky) in five minutes.

"Tom!" softly over the coach roof.

"Hallo, Joe."

"Did you hear the message?"

"I did, Joe."

"What did you make of it, Tom?"

"Nothing at all, Joe."

"That's a coincidence, too," the guard mused, "for I made the same of it myself."

Jerry, left alone in the mist and darkness, dismounted meanwhile, not only to ease his spent horse, but to wipe the mud from his face, and shake the wet out of his hat-brim, which might be capable of holding about half a gallon. After standing with the bridle over his heavily-splashed arm, until the wheels of the mail were no longer within hearing and the night was quite still again, he turned to walk down the hill. "After that there gallop from Temple Bar, old lady, I won't trust your fore-legs till I get you on the level," said this hoarse messenger, glancing at his mare. "'Recalled to life.' That's a Blazing strange message. Much of that wouldn't do for you, Jerry! I say, Jerry! You'd be in a Blazing bad way, if recalling to life was to come into fashion, Jerry!"

CHAPTER III

THE NIGHT SHADOWS.

A WONDERFUL fact to reflect upon, that every human creature is constituted to be that profound secret and mystery to every other. A solemn consideration, when I enter a great city by night, that every one of those darkly clustered houses encloses its own secret; that every room in every one of them encloses its own secret; that every beating heart in the hundreds of thousands of breasts there, is, in some of its imaginings, a secret to the heart nearest it! Something of the awfulness, even of Death itself, is referable to this. No more can I turn the leaves of this dear book that I loved, and vainly hope in time to read it all. No more can I look into the depths of this unfathomable water, wherein, as momentary lights glanced into it, I have had glimpses of buried treasure and other things submerged. It was appointed that the book should shut with a spring, for ever and for ever, when I had read but a page. It was appointed that the water should be locked in an eternal frost, when the light was playing on its surface, and I stood in ignorance on the shore. My friend is dead, my neighbour is dead, my love, the darling of my soul, is dead; it is the inexorable consolidation and perpetuation of the secret that was always in that individuality, and which I shall carry in mine to my life's end. In any of the burial-places of this city through which I pass, is there a sleeper more inscrutable than its busy inhabitants are, in their innermost personality, to me, or than I am to them?

As to this, his natural and not to be alienated inheritance, the messenger on horseback had exactly the same possessions as the King, the first Minister of State, or the richest merchant in London. So with the three passengers shut up in the narrow compass of one lumbering old mail coach; they were mysteries to one another, as complete as if each had been in his own coach and six, or his own coach and sixty, with the breadth of a county between him and the next.

The messenger rode back at an easy trot, stopping pretty often at ale-houses by the way to drink, but evincing a tendency to keep his own counsel, and to keep his hat cocked over his eyes. He had eyes that assorted very well with that decoration, being of a surface black, with no depth in the colour or form, and much too near together—as if they were afraid of being found out in something, singly, if they kept too far apart. They had a sinister expression, under an old cocked-hat like a three-cornered spittoon, and over a great muffler for the chin and throat, which descended nearly to the wearer's knees. When he stopped for drink, he moved this muffler with his left hand, only while he poured his liquor in with his right; as soon as that was done, he muffled again.

"No, Jerry, no!" said the messenger, harping on one theme as he rode. "It wouldn't do for you, Jerry. Jerry, you honest tradesman, it wouldn't suit *your* line of business! Recalled—! Bust me if I don't think he'd been a drinking!"

His message perplexed his mind to that degree that he was fain, several times, to take off his hat to scratch his head. Except on the crown, which was raggedly bald, he had stiff, black hair, standing jaggedly all over it, and growing down hill almost to his broad, blunt nose. It was so like Smith's work, so much more like the top of a strongly spiked wall than a head of hair, that the best of players at leap-frog might have declined him, as the most dangerous man in the world to go over.

While he trotted back with the message he was to deliver to the night watchman in his box at the door of Tellson's Bank, by Temple Bar, who was to deliver it to greater authorities within, the shadows of the night took such shapes to him as arose out of the message, and took such shapes to the mare as arose out of *her* private topics of uneasiness. They seemed to be numerous, for she shied at every shadow on the road.

What time, the mail-coach lumbered, jolted, rattled, and bumped upon its tedious way, with its three fellow-inscrutables inside. To whom, likewise, the shadows of the night revealed themselves, in the forms their dozing eyes and wandering thoughts suggested.

Tellson's Bank had a run upon it in the mail. As the bank passenger—with an arm drawn through the leathern strap, which did what lay in it to keep him from pounding against the next passenger, and driving him into his corner, whenever the coach got a special jolt—nodded in his place,

with half-shut eyes, the little coach-windows, and the coach-lamp dimly gleaming through them, and the bulky bundle of opposite passenger, became the bank, and did a great stroke of business. The rattle of the harness was the chink of money, and more drafts were honoured in five minutes than even Tellson's, with all its foreign and home connection, ever paid in thrice the time. Then the strong-rooms underground, at Tellson's, with such of their valuable stores and secrets as were known to the passenger (and it was not a little that he knew about them), opened before him, and he went in among them with the great keys and the feebly-burning candle, and found them safe, and strong, and sound, and still, just as he had last seen them.

But, though the bank was almost always with him, and though the coach (in a confused way, like the presence of pain under an opiate) was always with him, there was another current of impression that never ceased to run, all through the night. He was on his way to dig some one out of a grave.

Now, which of the multitude of faces that showed themselves before him was the true face of the buried person, the shadows of the night did not indicate; but they were all the faces of a man of five-and-forty by years, and they differed principally in the passions they expressed, and in the ghastliness of their worn and wasted state. Pride, contempt, defiance, stubbornness, submission, lamentation, succeeded one another; so did varieties of sunken cheek, cadaverous colour, emaciated hands and figures. But the face was in the main one face, and every head was prematurely white. A hundred times the dozing passenger inquired of this spectre:

"Buried how long?"

The answer was always the same: "Almost eighteen years."

"You had abandoned all hope of being dug out?"

"Long ago."

"You know that you are recalled to life?"

"They tell me so."

"I hope you care to live?"

"I can't say."

"Shall I show her to you? Will you come and see her?"

The answers to this question were various and contradictory. Sometimes the broken reply was, "Wait! It would kill me if I saw her too soon." Sometimes, it was given in a tender rain of tears, and then it was, "Take me to her." Sometimes it was staring and bewildered, and then it was, "I don't know her. I don't understand."

After such imaginary discourse, the passenger in his fancy would dig, and dig, dig—now with a spade, now with a great key, now with his hands—to dig this wretched creature out. Got out at last, with earth hanging about his face and hair, he would suddenly fall away to dust. The passenger would then start to himself, and lower the window, to get the reality of mist and rain on his cheek.

Yet even when his eyes were opened on the mist and rain, on the moving patch of light from the lamps, and the hedge at the roadside retreating by jerks, the night shadows outside the coach would fall into the train of the night shadows within. The real Banking-house by Temple Bar, the real business of the past day, the real strong rooms, the real express sent after him, and the real message returned, would all be there. Out of the midst of them, the ghostly face would rise, and he would accost it again.

"Buried how long?"

"Almost eighteen years."

"I hope you care to live?"

"I can't say."

Dig—dig—dig—until an impatient movement from one of the two passengers would admonish him to pull up the window, draw his arm securely through the leathern strap, and speculate upon the two slumbering forms, until his mind lost its hold of them, and they again slid away into the bank and the grave.

"Buried how long?"

"Almost eighteen years."

"You had abandoned all hope of being dug out?"

"Long ago."

The words were still in his hearing as just spoken—distinctly in his hearing as ever spoken words had been in his life—when the weary passenger started to the consciousness of daylight, and found that the shadows of the night were gone.

He lowered the window, and looked out at the rising sun. There was a ridge of ploughed land, with a plough upon it where it had been left last night when the horses were unyoked; beyond, a quiet coppice-wood, in which many leaves of burning red and golden yellow still remained upon the trees. Though the earth was cold and wet, the sky was clear, and the sun rose bright, placid, and beautiful.

"Eighteen years!" said the passenger, looking at the sun. "Gracious Creator of day! To be buried alive for eighteen years!"

CHAPTER IV.

THE PREPARATION.

WHEN the mail got successfully to Dover, in the course of the forenoon, the head drawer at the Royal George Hotel opened the coach-door as his custom was. He did it with some flourish of ceremony, for a mail journey from London in winter was an achievement to congratulate an adventurous traveller upon.

By that time, there was only one adventurous traveller left to be congratulated: for the two others had been set down at their respective roadside destinations. The mildewy inside of the coach, with its damp and dirty straw, its disagreeable smell, and its obscurity, was rather like a larger dog-kennel. Mr. Lorry, the passenger, shaking himself out of it in chains of straw, a tangle of shaggy wrapper, flapping hat, and muddy legs, was rather like a larger sort of dog.

"There will be a packet to Calais, to-morrow, drawer?"

"Yes, sir, if the weather holds and the wind sets tolerable fair. The tide will serve pretty nicely at about two in the afternoon, sir. Bed, sir?"

"I shall not go to bed till night; but I want a bedroom, and a barber."

"And then breakfast, sir? Yes, sir. That way, sir, if you please. Show Concord! Gentleman's valise and hot water to Concord. Pull off gentleman's boots in Concord. (You will find a fine sea-coal fire, sir.) Fetch barber to Concord. Stir about there, now, for Concord!"

The Concord bed-chamber being always assigned to a passenger by the mail, and passengers by the mail being always heavily wrapped up from head to foot, the room had the odd interest for the establishment of the Royal George, that although but one kind of man was seen to go into it, all kinds and varieties of men came out of it. Consequently, another drawer, and two porters, and several maids and the landlady, were all loitering by accident at various points of the road between the Concord and the coffee-room, when a gentleman of sixty, formally dressed in a brown suit of clothes, pretty well worn, but very well kept, with large square cuffs and large flaps to the pockets, passed along on his way to his breakfast.

The coffee-room had no other occupant, that forenoon, than the gentleman in brown. His breakfast-table was drawn before the fire, and as he sat, with its light shining on him, waiting for the meal, he sat so still, that he might have been sitting for his portrait.

Very orderly and methodical he looked, with a hand on each knee, and a loud watch ticking a sonorous sermon under his flapped waistcoat, as though it pitted its gravity and longevity against the levity and evanescence of the brisk fire. He had a good leg, and was a little vain of it, for his brown stockings fitted sleek and close, and were of a fine texture; his shoes and buckles, too, though plain, were trim. He wore an odd little sleek crisp flaxen wig, setting very close to his head: which wig, it is to be presumed, was made of hair, but which looked far more as though it were spun from filaments of silk or glass. His linen, though not of a fineness in accordance with his stockings, was as white as the tops of the waves that broke upon the neighbouring beach, or the specks of sail that glinted in the sunlight far at sea. A face habitually suppressed and quieted, was still lighted up under the quaint wig by a pair of moist bright eyes that it must have cost their owner, in years gone by, some pains to drill to the composed and reserved expression of Tellson's Bank. He had a healthy colour in his cheeks, and his face, though lined, bore few traces of anxiety. But, perhaps the confidential bachelor clerks in Tellson's Bank were principally occupied with the cares of other people; and perhaps second-hand cares, like second-hand clothes, come easily off and on.

Completing his resemblance to a man who was sitting for his portrait, Mr. Lorry dropped off to sleep. The arrival of his breakfast roused him, and he said to the drawer, as he moved his chair to it:

"I wish accommodation prepared for a young lady who may come here at any time to-day. She may ask for Mr. Jarvis Lorry, or she may only ask for a gentleman from Tellson's Bank. Please to let me know."

"Yes, sir. Tellson's Bank in London, sir?"

"Yes."

"Yes, sir. We have oftentimes the honour to entertain your gentlemen in their travelling backwards and forwards betwixt London and Paris, sir. A vast deal of travelling, sir, in Tellson and Company's House."

"Yes. We are quite a French House, as well as an English one."

"Yes, sir. Not much in the habit of such travelling yourself, I think, sir?"

"Not of late years. It is fifteen years since we—since I—came last from France."

"Indeed, sir? That was before my time here, sir. Before our people's time here, sir. The George was in other hands at that time, sir."

"I believe so."

"But I would hold a pretty wager, sir, that a House like Tellson and Company was flourishing, a matter of fifty, not to speak of fifteen years ago?"

"You might treble that, and say a hundred and fifty, yet not be far from the truth."

"Indeed, sir!"

Rounding his mouth and both his eyes, as he stepped backward from the table, the waiter shifted his napkin from his right arm to his left, dropped into a comfortable attitude, and stood surveying the guest while he ate and drank, as from an observatory or watch-tower. According to the immemorial usage of waiters in all ages.

When Mr. Lorry had finished his breakfast, he went out for a stroll on the beach. The little narrow, crooked town of Dover hid itself away from the beach, and ran its head into the chalk cliffs, like a marine ostrich. The beach was a desert of heaps of sea and stones tumbling wildly about, and the sea did what it liked, and what it liked was destruction. It thundered at the town, and thundered at the cliffs, and brought the coast down, madly. The air among the houses was of so strong a piscatory flavour that one might have supposed sick fish went up to be dipped in it, as sick people went down to be dipped in the sea. A little fishing was done in the port, and a quantity of strolling about by night, and looking seaward: particularly at those times when the tide made, and was near flood. Small tradesmen, who did no business whatever, sometimes unaccountably realised large fortunes, and it was remarkable that nobody in the neighbourhood could endure a lamplighter.

As the day declined into the afternoon, and the air, which had been at intervals clear enough to allow the French coast to be seen, became again charged with mist and vapour, Mr. Lorry's thoughts seemed to cloud too. When it was dark, and he sat before the coffee-room fire, awaiting his dinner as he had awaited his breakfast, his mind was busily digging, digging, digging, in the live red coals.

A bottle of good claret after dinner does a digger in the red coals no harm, otherwise than as it has a tendency to throw him out of work. Mr. Lorry had been idle a long time, and had just poured out his last glassful of wine with as complete an appearance of satisfaction as is ever to be found in an elderly gentleman of a fresh complexion who has got to the end of a bottle, when a rattling of wheels came up the narrow street, and rumbled into the innyard.

He set down his glass untouched. "This is Mam'selle!" said he.

In a very few minutes the waiter came in to announce that Miss Manette had arrived from London, and would be happy to see the gentleman from Tellson's.

"So soon?"

Miss Manette had taken some refreshment on the road, and required none then, and was extremely anxious to see the gentleman from Tellson's immediately, if it suited his pleasure and convenience.

The gentleman from Tellson's had nothing left for it but to empty his glass with an air of stolid desperation, settle his odd little flaxen wig at the ears, and follow the waiter to Miss Manette's apartment. It was a large, dark room,

furnished in a funereal manner with black horsehair, and loaded with heavy dark tables. These had been oiled and oiled, until the two tall candles on the table in the middle of the room were gloomily reflected on every leaf; as if they were buried, in deep graves of black mahogany, and no light to speak of could be expected from them until they were dug out.

The obscurity was so difficult to penetrate that Mr. Lorry, picking his way over the well-worn Turkey carpet, supposed Miss Manette to be, for the moment, in some adjacent room, until, having got past the two tall candles, he saw standing to receive him by the table between them and the fire, a young lady of not more than seventeen, in a riding-cloak, and still holding her straw travelling-hat by its ribbon in her hand. As his eyes rested on a short, slight, pretty figure, a quantity of golden hair, a pair of blue eyes that met his own with an inquiring look, and a forehead with a singular capacity (remembering how young and smooth it was), of lifting and knitting itself into an expression that was not quite one of perplexity, or wonder, or alarm, or merely of a bright fixed attention, though it included all the four expressions—as his eyes rested on these things, a sudden vivid likeness passed before him, of a child whom he had held in his arms on the passage across that very Channel, one cold time, when the hail drifted heavily and the sea ran high. The likeness passed away, like a breath along the surface of the gaunt pier-glass behind her, on the frame of which, a hospital procession of negro cupids, several headless and all cripples, were offering black baskets of Dead Sea fruit to black divinities of the feminine gender—and he made his formal bow to Miss Manette.

"Pray take a seat, sir." In a very clear and pleasant young voice; a little foreign in its accent, but a very little indeed.

"I kiss your hand, miss," said Mr. Lorry, with the manners of an earlier date, as he made his formal bow again, and took his seat.

"I received a letter from the Bank, sir, yesterday, informing me that some intelligence—or discovery——"

"The word is not material, miss; either word will do."

"—respecting the small property of my poor father, whom I never saw—so long dead——"

Mr. Lorry moved in his chair, and cast a troubled look towards the hospital procession of negro cupids. As if they had any help for anybody in their absurd baskets!

"—rendered it necessary that I should go to Paris, there to communicate with a gentleman of the Bank, so good as to be despatched to Paris for the purpose."

"Myself."

"As I was prepared to hear, sir."

She curtseyed to him (young ladies made curtseys in those days), with a pretty desire to convey to him that she felt how much older and wiser he was than she. He made her another bow.

"I replied to the Bank, sir, that as it was considered necessary, by those who know, and who are so kind as to advise me, that I should go to France, and that as I am an orphan and have no friend who could go with me, I should esteem it highly if I might be permitted to place myself, during the journey, under that worthy gentleman's protection. The gentleman had left London, but I think a messenger was sent after him to beg the favour of his waiting for me here."

"I was happy," said Mr. Lorry, "to be entrusted with the charge. I shall be more happy to execute it."

"Sir, I thank you indeed. I thank you very gratefully. It was told me by the Bank that the gentleman would explain to me the details of the business, and that I must prepare myself to find them of a surprising nature. I have done my best to prepare myself, and I naturally have a strong and eager interest to know what they are."

"Naturally," said Mr. Lorry. "Yes—I——"

After a pause, he added, again settling the crisp flaxen wig at the ears,

"It is very difficult to begin."

He did not begin, but, in his indecision, met her glance. The young forehead lifted itself into that singular expression—but it was pretty and characteristic, besides being singular—and she raised her hand, as if with an involuntary action she caught at, or stayed some passing shadow.

"Are you quite a stranger to me, sir?"

"Am I not?" Mr. Lorry opened his hands, and extended them outwards with an argumentative smile.

Between the eyebrows and just over the little feminine nose, the line of which was as delicate and fine as it was possible to be, the expression deepened itself as she took her seat thoughtfully in the chair by which she had hitherto remained standing. He watched her as she mused, and the moment she raised her eyes again, went on:

"In your adopted country, I presume, I cannot do better than address you as a young English lady, Miss Manette?"

"If you please, sir."

"Miss Manette, I am a man of business. I have a business charge to acquit myself of. In your reception of it, don't heed me any more than if I was a speaking machine —truly, I am not much else. I will, with your leave, relate to you, miss, the story of one of our customers."

"Story!"

He seemed wilfully to mistake the word she had repeated, when he added, in a hurry, "Yes, customers; in the banking business we usually call our connection our customers. He was a French gentleman; a scientific gentleman; a man of great acquirements—a Doctor."

"Not of Beauvais?"

"Why, yes, of Beauvais. Like Monsieur Manette, your father, the gentleman was of Beauvais. Like Monsieur Manette, your father, the gentleman was of repute in Paris. I had the honour of knowing him there. Our relations were business relations, but confidential. I was at that time in our French House, and had been—oh! twenty years."

"At that time—I may ask, at what time, sir?"

"I speak, miss, of twenty years ago. He married—an English lady—and I was one of the trustees. His affairs, like the affairs of many other French gentlemen and French families, were entirely in Tellson's hands. In a similar way I am, or I have been, trustee of one kind or other for scores of our customers. These are mere business relations, miss; there is no friendship in them, no particular interest, nothing like sentiment. I have passed from one to another, in the course of my business life, just as I pass from one of our customers to another in the course of my business day; in short, I have no feelings; I am a mere machine. To go on——"

"But this is my father's story, sir; and I begin to think" —the curiously roughened forehead was very intent upon him—"that when I was left an orphan through my moth-er's surviving my father only two years, it was you who brought me to England. I am almost sure it was you."

Mr. Lorry took the hesitating little hand that confidingly advanced to take his, and he put it with some ceremony to his lips. He then conducted the young lady straightway to her chair again, and, holding the chair-back with his left hand, and using his right by turns to rub his chin, pull his wig at the ears, or point what he said, stood looking down into her face while she sat looking up into his.

"Miss Manette, it *was* I. And you will see how truly I spoke of myself just now, in saying I had no feelings, and that all the relations I hold with my fellow-creatures are mere business relations, when you reflect that I have never seen you since. No; you have been the ward of Tellson's House since, and I have been busy with the other business of Tellson's House since. Feelings! I have no time for them, no chance of them. I pass my whole life, miss, in turning an immense pecuniary Mangle."

After this odd description of his daily routine of employment, Mr. Lorry flattened his flaxen wig upon his head with both hands (which was most unnecessary, for nothing could be flatter than its shining surface was before), and resumed his former attitude.

"So far, miss (as you have remarked), this is the story of your regretted father. Now comes the difference. If your father had not died when he did——Don't be frightened! How you start!"

She did, indeed, start. And she caught his wrist with both her hands.

"Pray," said Mr. Lorry, in a soothing tone, bringing his left hand from the back of the chair to lay it on the supplicatory fingers that clasped him in so violent a tremble: "pray control your agitation—a matter of business. As I was saying——"

Her look so discomposed him that he stopped, wandered, and began anew:

"As I was saying; if Monsieur Manette had not died; if he had suddenly and silently disappeared; if he had been spirited away; if it had not been difficult to guess to what dreadful place, though no art could trace him; if he had an enemy in some compatriot who could exercise a privilege that I in my own time have known the boldest people afraid to speak of in a whisper, across the water there; for instance, the privilege of filling up blank forms for the consignment of any one to the oblivion of a prison for any length of time; if his wife had implored the king, the queen, the court, for any tidings of him, and all quite in vain;—then the history of your father would have been the history of this unfortunate gentleman, the Doctor of Beauvais."

"I entreat you to tell me more, sir."

"I will. I am going to. You can bear it?"

"I can bear anything but the uncertainty you leave me in at this moment."

"You speak collectedly, and you—*are* collected. That's good!" (Though his manner was less satisfied than his words.) "A matter of business. Regard it as a matter of business—business that must be done. Now if this doctor's wife, though a lady of great courage and spirit, had suffered so intensely from this cause before her little child was born——"

"The little child was a daughter, sir."

"A daughter. A—a—matter of business—don't be distressed. Miss, if the poor lady had suffered so intensely before her little child was born, that she came to the determination of sparing the poor child the inheritance of any part of the agony she had known the pains of, by rearing her in the belief that her father was dead——No, don't kneel! In Heaven's name why should you kneel to me!"

"For the truth. O dear, good, compassionate sir, for the truth!"

"A—a matter of business. You confuse me, and how can I transact business if I am confused? Let us be clear-headed. If you could kindly mention now, for instance, what nine times ninepence are, or how many shillings in twenty guineas, it would be so encouraging. I should be so much more at my ease about your state of mind."

Without directly answering to this appeal, she sat so still when he had very gently raised her, and the hands that had not ceased to clasp his wrists were so much more steady than they had been, that she communicated some reassurance to Mr. Jarvis Lorry.

"That's right, that's right. Courage! Business! You have business before you; useful business. Miss Manette, your mother took this course with you. And when she died—I believe broken-hearted—having never slackened her unavailing search for your father, she left you, at two years old, to grow to be blooming, beautiful, and happy, without the dark cloud upon you of living in uncertainty whether your father soon wore his heart out in prison, or wasted there through many lingering years."

As he said the words he looked down, with an admiring pity, on the flowing golden hair; as if he pictured to himself that it might have been already tinged with grey.

"You know that your parents had no great possession, and that what they had was secured to your mother and to you. There has been no new discovery, of money, or of any other property; but——"

He felt his wrist held closer, and he stopped. The expression in the forehead, which had so particularly attracted his notice, and which was now immovable, had deepened into one of pain and horror.

"But he has been—been found. He is alive. Greatly changed, it is too probable; almost a wreck, it is possible; though we will hope the best. Still, alive. Your father has been taken to the house of an old servant in Paris, and we are going there: I, to identify him if I can: you, to restore him to life, love, duty, rest, comfort."

A shiver ran through her frame, and from it through his. She said, in a low, distinct, awe-stricken voice, as if she were saying it in a dream,

"I am going to see his Ghost! It will be his Ghost—not him!"

Mr. Lorry quietly chafed the hands that held his arm. "There, there, there! See now, see now! The best and the worst are known to you, now. You are well on your way to the poor wronged gentleman, and, with a fair sea voyage, and a fair land journey, you will be soon at his dear side."

She repeated in the same tone, sunk to a whisper, "I have been free, I have been happy, yet his Ghost has never haunted me!"

"Only one thing more," said Mr. Lorry, laying stress upon it as a wholesome means of enforcing her attention: "he has been found under another name; his own, long forgotten or long concealed. It would be worse than useless now to inquire which; worse than useless to seek to know whether he has been for years overlooked, or always

designedly held prisoner. It would be worse than useless now to make any inquiries, because it would be dangerous. Better not to mention the subject, anywhere or in any way, and to remove him—for a while at all events—out of France. Even I, safe as an Englishman, and even Tellson's, important as they are to French credit, avoid all naming of the matter. I carry about me, not a scrap of writing openly referring to it. This is a secret service altogether. My credentials, entries, and memoranda, are all comprehended in the one line, 'Recalled to Life;' which may mean anything. But what is the matter! She doesn't notice a word! Miss Manette!"

Perfectly still and silent, and not even fallen back in her chair, she sat under his hand, utterly insensible; with her eyes open and fixed upon him, and with that last expression looking as if it were carved or branded into her forehead. So close was her hold upon his arm, that he feared to detach himself lest he should hurt her; therefore he called out loudly for assistance without moving.

A wild-looking woman, whom even in his agitation, Mr. Lorry observed to be all of a red colour, and to have red hair, and to be dressed in some extraordinary tight-fitting fashion, and to have on her head a most wonderful bonnet like a Grenadier wooden measure, and good measure too, or a great Stilton cheese, came running into the room in advance of the inn servants, and soon settled the question of his detachment from the poor young lady, by laying a brawny hand upon his chest, and sending him flying back against the nearest wall.

("I really think this must be a man!" was Mr. Lorry's breathless reflection, simultaneously with his coming against the wall.)

"Why, look at you all!" bawled this figure, addressing the inn servants. "Why don't you go and fetch things, instead of standing there staring at me? I am not so much to look at, am I? Why don't you go and fetch things? I'll let you know, if you don't bring smelling-salts, cold water, and vinegar, quick, I will."

There was an immediate dispersal for these restoratives, and she softly laid the patient on a sofa, and tended her with great skill and gentleness: calling her "my precious!" and "my bird!" and spreading her golden hair aside over her shoulders with great pride and care.

"And you in brown!" she said, indignantly turning to Mr. Lorry; "couldn't you tell her what you had to tell her, without frightening her to death? Look at her, with her pretty pale face and her cold hands. Do you call that being a Banker?"

Mr. Lorry was so exceedingly disconcerted by a question so hard to answer, that he could only look on, at a distance, with much feebler sympathy and humility, while the strong woman, having banished the inn servants under the mysterious penalty of "letting them know" something not mentioned if they stayed there, staring, recovered her charge by a regular series of gradations, and coaxed her to lay her drooping head upon her shoulder.

"I hope she will do well now," said Mr. Lorry.

"No thanks to you in brown, if she does. My darling pretty!"

"I hope," said Mr. Lorry, after another pause of feeble sympathy and humility, "that you accompany Miss Manette to France?"

"A likely thing, too!" replied the strong woman. "If it was ever intended that I should go across salt water, do you suppose Providence would have cast my lot in an island?"

This being another question hard to answer, Mr. Jarvis Lorry withdrew to consider it.

CHAPTER V.

THE WINE-SHOP.

A LARGE cask of wine had been dropped and broken, in the street. The accident had happened in getting it out of a cart; the cask had tumbled out with a run, the hoops had burst, and it lay on the stones just outside the door of the wine-shop, shattered like a walnut-shell.

All the people within reach had suspended their business, or their idleness, to run to the spot and drink the wine. The rough, irregular stones of the street, pointing every way, and designed, one might have thought, expressly to lame all living creatures that approached them, had dammed it into little pools; these were surrounded, each by its own jostling group or crowd, according to its size. Some men kneeled down, made scoops of their two hands joined, and sipped, or tried to help women, who bent over their shoulders, to sip, before the wine had all run out between their fingers. Others, men and women, dipped in the puddles with little mugs of mutilated earthenware, or even with handkerchiefs from women's heads, which were squeezed dry into infants' mouths; others made small mud-embankments, to stem the wine as it ran; others, directed by lookers-on up at high windows, darted here and there, to cut off little streams of wine that started away in new directions; others devoted themselves to the sodden and lee-dyed pieces of the cask, licking, and even champing the moister wine-dotted fragments with eager relish. There was no drainage to carry off the wine, and not only did it all get taken up, but so much mud got taken up along with it, that there might have been a scavenger in the street, if anybody acquainted with it could have believed in such a miraculous presence.

A shrill sound of laughter and of amused voices—voices of men, women, and children—resounded in the street while this wine game lasted. There was little roughness in the sport, and much playfulness. There was a special companionship in it, an observable inclination on the part of every one to join some other one, which led, especially among the luckier or lighter-hearted, to frolicsome embraces, drinking of healths, shaking of hands, and even joining of hands and dancing, a dozen together. When the wine was gone, and the places where it had been most abundant were raked into a gridiron-pattern by fingers, these demonstrations ceased, as suddenly as they had broken out. The man who had left his saw sticking in the firewood he was cutting, set it in motion again; the woman who had left on a door-step the little pot of hot ashes, at which she had been trying to soften the pain in her own starved fingers and toes, or in those of her child, returned to it; men with bare arms, matted locks, and cadaverous faces, who had emerged into the winter light from cellars, moved away, to descend again; and a gloom gathered on the scene that appeared more natural to it than sunshine.

The wine was red wine, and had stained the ground of the narrow street in the suburb of Saint Antoine, in Paris, where it was spilled. It had stained many hands, too, and many faces, and many naked feet, and many wooden shoes. The hands of the man who sawed the wood, left red marks on the billets; and the forehead of the woman who nursed her baby, was stained with the stain of the old rag she wound about her head again. Those who had been greedy with the staves of the cask, had acquired a tigerish smear about the mouth; and one tall joker so besmirched, his head more out of a long squalid bag of a nightcap than in it, scrawled upon a wall with his finger dipped in muddy wine-lees—BLOOD.

The time was to come, when that wine too would be spilled on the street-stones, and when the stain of it would be red upon many there.

And now that the cloud settled on Saint Antoine, which a momentary gleam had driven from his sacred countenance, the darkness of it was heavy—cold, dirt, sickness, ignorance, and want, were the lords in waiting on the saintly presence—nobles of great power all of them; but, most especially the last. Samples of a people that had undergone a terrible grinding and regrinding in the mill, and certainly not in the fabulous mill which ground old people young, shivered at every corner, passed in and out at every doorway, looked from every window, fluttered in every vestige of a garment that the wind shook. The mill which had worked them down, was the mill that grinds young people old; the children had ancient faces and grave voices; and upon them, and upon the grown faces, and ploughed into every furrow of age and coming up afresh, was the sign, Hunger. It was prevalent everywhere. Hunger was pushed out of the tall houses, in the wretched clothing that hung upon poles and lines; Hunger was patched into them with straw and rag and wood and paper; Hunger was repeated in every fragment of the small modicum of firewood that the man sawed off; Hunger stared down from the smokeless chimneys, and started up from the filthy street that had no offal, among its refuse, of anything to eat. Hunger was the inscription on the baker's shelves, written in every small loaf of his scanty stock of bad bread; at the sausage-shop, in every dead-dog preparation that was offered for sale. Hunger rattled its dry bones among the roasting chestnuts in the turned cylinder; Hunger was shred into atomies in every farthing porringer of husky chips of potato, fried with some reluctant drops of oil.

Its abiding place was in all things fitted to it. A narrow winding street, full of offence and stench, with other narrow winding streets diverging, all peopled by rags and nightcaps, and all smelling of rags and nightcaps, and all visible things with a brooding look upon them that looked ill. In the hunted air of the people there was yet some wild-beast thought of the possibility of turning at bay. Depressed and slinking though they were, eyes of fire were not wanting among them; nor compressed lips, white with what they suppressed; nor foreheads knitted into the likeness of the gallows-rope they mused about enduring, or inflicting. The trade signs (and they were almost as many as the shops) were, all, grim illustrations of Want. The butcher and the porkman painted up, only the leanest scrags of meat; the baker, the coarsest of meagre loaves. The people rudely pictured as drinking in the wine-shops, croaked over their scanty measures of thin wine and beer, and were gloweringly confidential together. Nothing was represented in a flourishing condition, save tools and weapons; but, the cutler's knives and axes were sharp and bright, the smith's hammers were heavy, and the gunmaker's stock was murderous. The crippling stones of the pavement, with their many little reservoirs of mud and water, had no footways, but broke off abruptly at the doors. The kennel, to make amends, ran down the middle of the street—when it ran at all: which was only after heavy rains, and then it ran, by many eccentric fits, into the

HE SCRAWLED UPON A WALL WITH HIS FINGERS DIPPED IN MUDDY
WINE-LEES—BLOOD.

houses. Across the streets, at wide intervals, one clumsy lamp was slung by a rope and pulley; at night, when the lamplighter had let these down, and lighted, and hoisted them again, a feeble grove of dim wicks swung in a sickly manner overhead, as if they were at sea. Indeed they were at sea, and the ship and crew were in peril of tempest.

For, the time was to come, when the gaunt scarecrows of that region should have watched the lamplighter, in their idleness and hunger, so long, as to conceive the idea of improving on his method, and hauling up men by those ropes and pulleys, to flare upon the darkness of their condition. But, the time was not come yet; and every wind that blew over France shook the rags of the scarecrows in vain, for the birds, fine of song and feather, took no warning.

The wine-shop was a corner shop, better than most others in its appearance and degree, and the master of the wine-shop had stood outside it, in a yellow waistcoat and green breeches, looking on at the struggle for the lost wine. "It's not my affair," said he, with a final shrug of the shoulders. "The people from the market did it. Let them bring another."

There, his eyes happening to catch the tall joker writing up his joke, he called to him across the way:

"Say, then, my Gaspard, what do you do there?"

The fellow pointed to his joke with immense significance, as is often the way with his tribe. It missed its mark, and completely failed, as is often the way with his tribe too.

"What now? Are you a subject for the mad hospital?" said the wine-shop keeper, crossing the road, and obliterating the jest with a handful of mud, picked up for the purpose, and smeared over it. "Why do you write in the public streets? Is there—tell me thou—is there no other place to write such words in?"

In his expostulation he dropped his cleaner hand (perhaps accidentally, perhaps not) upon the joker's heart. The joker rapped it with his own, took a nimble spring upward, and came down in a fantastic dancing attitude, with one of his stained shoes jerked off his foot into his hand, and held out. A joker of an extremely, not to say wolfishly practical character, he looked, under those circumstances.

"Put it on, put it on," said the other. "Call wine, wine; and finish there." With that advice, he wiped his soiled hand upon the joker's dress, such as it was—quite deliberately, as having dirtied the hand on his account; and then recrossed the road and entered the wine-shop.

This wine-shop keeper was a bull-necked, martial-looking man of thirty, and he should have been of a hot temperament, for, although it was a bitter day, he wore no coat, but carried one slung over his shoulder. His shirt-sleeves were rolled up, too, and his brown arms were bare to the elbows. Neither did he wear anything more on his head than his own crisply-curling short dark hair. He was a dark man altogether, with good eyes and a good bold breadth between them. Good-humoured looking on the whole, but implacable-looking, too; evidently a man of a strong resolution and a set purpose; a man not desirable to be met, rushing down a narrow pass with a gulf on either side, for nothing would turn the man.

Madame Defarge, his wife, sat in the shop behind the counter as he came in. Madame Defarge was a stout woman of about his own age, with a watchful eye that seldom seemed to look at anything, a large hand heavily ringed, a steady face, strong features, and great composure of manner. There was a character about Madame Defarge, from which one might have predicated that she did not often make mistakes against herself in any of the reckonings over which she presided. Madame Defarge being sensitive to cold, was wrapped in fur, and had a quantity of bright shawl twined about her head, though not to the concealment of her large ear-rings. Her knitting was before her, but she had laid it down to pick her teeth with a toothpick. Thus engaged, with her right elbow supported by her left hand, Madame Defarge said nothing when her lord came in, but coughed just one grain of cough. This, in combination with the lifting of her darkly defined eyebrows over her toothpick by the breadth of a line, suggested to her husband that he would do well to look round the shop among the customers, for any new customer who had dropped in while he stepped over the way.

The wine-shop keeper accordingly rolled his eyes about, until they rested upon an elderly gentleman and a young lady, who were seated in a corner. Other company were there: two playing cards, two playing dominoes, three standing by the counter lengthening out a short supply of wine. As he passed behind the counter, he took notice that the elderly gentleman said in a look to the young lady, "This is our man."

"What the devil do *you* do in that galley there?" said Monsieur Defarge to himself; "I don't know you."

But, he feigned not to notice the two strangers, and fell into discourse with the triumvirate of customers who were drinking at the counter.

"How goes it, Jacques?" said one of these three to Monsieur Defarge. "Is all the spilt wine swallowed?"

"Every drop, Jacques," answered Monsieur Defarge.

When this interchange of Christian name was effected, Madame Defarge, picking her teeth with her toothpick, coughed another grain of cough, and raised her eyebrows by the breadth of another line.

"It is not often," said the second of the three, addressing Monsieur Defarge, "that many of these miserable beasts know the taste of wine, or of anything but black bread and death. Is it not so, Jacques?"

"It is so, Jacques," Monsieur Defarge returned.

At this second interchange of the Christian name, Madame Defarge, still using her toothpick with profound composure, coughed another grain of cough, and raised her eyebrows by the breadth of another line.

The last of the three now said his say, as he put down his empty drinking vessel and smacked his lips.

"Ah! So much the worse! A bitter taste it is that such poor cattle always have in their mouths, and hard lives they live, Jacques. Am I right, Jacques?"

"You are right, Jacques," was the response of Monsieur Defarge.

This third interchange of the Christian name was completed at the moment when Madame Defarge put her toothpick by, kept her eyebrows up, and slightly rustled in her seat.

"Hold then! True!" muttered her husband. "Gentlemen—my wife!"

The three customers pulled off their hats to Madame Defarge, with three flourishes. She acknowledged their homage by bending her head, and giving them a quick look. Then she glanced in a casual manner round the wine-shop, took up her knitting with great apparent calmness and repose of spirit, and became absorbed in it.

"Gentlemen," said her husband, who had kept his right eye observantly upon her, "good day. The chamber, furnished bachelor-fashion, that you wished to see, and were inquiring for when I stepped out, is on the fifth floor. The doorway of the staircase gives on the little courtyard close to the left here," pointing with his hand, "near to the window of my establishment. But, now that I remember, one of you has already been there, and can show the way. Gentlemen, adieu!"

They paid for their wine, and left the place. The eyes of Monsieur Defarge were studying his wife at her knitting when the elderly gentleman advanced from his corner, and begged the favour of a word.

"Willingly, sir," said Monsieur Defarge, and quietly stepped with him to the door.

Their conference was very short, but very decided. Almost at the first word, Monsieur Defarge started and became deeply attentive. It had not lasted a minute, when he nodded and went out. The gentleman then beckoned to the young lady, and they, too, went out. Madame Defarge knitted with nimble fingers and steady eyebrows, and saw nothing.

Mr. Jarvis Lorry and Miss Manette, emerging from the wine-shop thus, joined Monsieur Defarge in the doorway to which he had directed his own company just before. It opened from a stinking little black courtyard, and was the general public entrance to a great pile of houses, inhabited by a great number of people. In the gloomy tile-paved entry to the gloomy tile-paved staircase, Monsieur Defarge bent down on one knee to the child of his old master, and put her hand to his lips. It was a gentle action, but not at all gently done; a very remarkable transformation had come over him in a few seconds. He had no good-humour in his face, nor any openness of aspect left, but had become a secret, angry, dangerous man.

"It is very high; it is a little difficult. Better to begin slowly." Thus, Monsieur Defarge, in a stern voice, to Mr. Lorry, as they began ascending the stairs.

"Is he alone?" the latter whispered.

"Alone! God help him, who should be with him!" said the other, in the same low voice.

"Is he always alone, then?"

"Yes."

"Of his own desire?"

"Of his own necessity. As he was, when I first saw him after they found me and demanded to know if I would take him, and, at my peril be discreet—as he was then, so he is now."

"He is greatly changed?"

"Changed!"

The keeper of the wine-shop stopped to strike the wall with his hand, and mutter a tremendous curse. No direct answer could have been half so forcible. Mr. Lorry's spirits grew heavier and heavier, as he and his two companions ascended higher and higher.

Such a staircase, with its accessories, in the older and more crowded parts of Paris, would be bad enough now; but, at that time, it was vile indeed to unaccustomed and unhardened senses. Every little habitation within the great foul nest of one high building—that is to say, the room or rooms within every door that opened on the general staircase—left its own heap of refuse on its own land-

ing, besides flinging other refuse from its own windows. The uncontrollable and hopeless mass of decomposition so engendered, would have polluted the air, even if poverty and deprivation had not loaded it with their intangible impurities; the two bad sources combined made it almost insupportable. Through such an atmosphere, by a steep dark shaft of dirt and poison, the way lay. Yielding to his own disturbance of mind, and to his young companion's agitation, which became greater every instant, Mr. Jarvis Lorry twice stopped to rest. Each of these stoppages was made at a doleful grating, by which any languishing good airs that were left uncorrupted, seemed to escape, and all spoilt and sickly vapours seemed to crawl in. Through the rusted bars, tastes, rather than glimpses, were caught of the jumbled neighbourhood; and nothing within range, nearer or lower than the summits of the two great towers of Notre-Dame, had any promise on it of healthy life or wholesome aspirations.

At last, the top of the staircase was gained, and they stopped for the third time. There was yet an upper staircase, of a steeper inclination and of contracted dimensions, to be ascended, before the garret story was reached. The keeper of the wine-shop, always going a little in advance, and always going on the side which Mr. Lorry took, as though he dreaded to be asked any question by the young lady, turned himself about here, and, carefully feeling in the pockets of the coat he carried over his shoulder, took out a key.

"The door is locked then, my friend?" said Mr. Lorry, surprised.

"Ay. Yes," was the grim reply of Monsieur Defarge.

"You think it necessary to keep the unfortunate gentleman so retired?"

"I think it necessary to turn the key." Monsieur Defarge whispered it closer in his ear, and frowned heavily.

"Why?"

"Why! Because he has lived so long, locked up, that he would be frightened—rave—tear himself to pieces—die—come to I know not what harm—if this door was left open."

"Is it possible!" exclaimed Mr. Lorry.

"Is it possible!" repeated Defarge, bitterly. "Yes. And a beautiful world we live in, when it *is* possible, and when many other such things are possible, and not only possible, but done—done, see you!—under that sky there, every day. Long live the Devil. Let us go on."

This dialogue had been held in so very low a whisper, that not a word of it had reached the young lady's ears. But, by this time she trembled under such strong emotion, and her face expressed such deep anxiety, and, above all, such dread and terror, that Mr. Lorry felt it incumbent on him to speak a word or two of reassurance.

"Courage, dear miss! Courage! Business! The worst will be over in a moment; it is but passing the room-door, and the worst is over. Then, all the good you bring to him, all the relief, all the happiness you bring to him, begin. Let our good friend here, assist you on that side. That's well, friend Defarge. Come, now. Business, business!"

They went up slowly and softly. The staircase was short, and they were soon at the top. There, as it had an abrupt turn in it, they came all at once in sight of three men, whose heads were bent down close together at the side of a door, and who were intently looking into the room to which the door belonged, through some chinks or holes in the wall. On hearing footsteps close at hand, these three turned, and rose, and showed themselves to be the three of one name who had been drinking in the wine-shop.

"I forgot them in the surprise of your visit," explained Monsieur Defarge. "Leave us, good boys; we have business here."

The three glided by, and went silently down.

There appearing to be no other door on that floor, and the keeper of the wine-shop going straight to this one when they were left alone, Mr. Lorry asked him in a whisper, with a little anger:

"Do you make a show of Monsieur Manette?"

"I show him, in the way you have seen, to a chosen few."

"Is that well?"

"*I* think it is well."

"Who are the few? How do you choose them?"

"I choose them as real men, of my name—Jacques is my name—to whom the sight is likely to do good. Enough; you are English; that is another thing. Stay there, if you please, a little moment."

With an admonitory gesture to keep them back, he stooped, and looked in through the crevice in the wall. Soon raising his head again, he struck twice or thrice upon the door—evidently with no other object than to make a noise there. With the same intention, he drew the key across it, three or four times, before he put it clumsily into the lock, and turned it as heavily as he could.

The door slowly opened inward under his hand, and he looked into the room and said something. A faint voice answered something. Little more than a single syllable could have been spoken on either side.

He looked back over his shoulder, and beckoned them to enter. Mr. Lorry got his arm securely round the daughter's waist, and held her; for he felt that she was sinking.

"A—a—a—business, business!" he urged, with a moisture that was not of business shining on his cheek. "Come in, come in!"

"I am afraid of it," she answered, shuddering.

"Of it? What?"

"I mean of him. Of my father."

Rendered in a manner desperate, by her state and by the beckoning of their conductor, he drew over his neck the arm that shook upon his shoulder, lifted her a little, and hurried her into the room. He sat her down just within the door, and held her, clinging to him.

Defarge drew out the key, closed the door, locked it on the inside, took out the key again, and held it in his hand. All this he did, methodically, and with as loud and harsh an accompaniment of noise as he could make. Finally, he walked across the room with a measured tread to where the window was. He stopped there, and faced round.

The garret, built to be a depository for firewood and the like, was dim and dark: for, the window of dormer shape, was in truth a door in the roof, with a little crane over it for the hoisting up of stores from the street: unglazed, and closing up the middle in two pieces, like any other door of French construction. To exclude the cold, one half of this door was fast closed, and the other was opened but a very little way. Such a scanty portion of light was admitted through these means, that it was difficult, on first coming in, to see anything; and long habit alone could have slowly formed in any one, the ability to do any work requiring

nicety in such obscurity. Yet, work of that kind was being done in the garret; for, with his back towards the door, and his face towards the window where the keeper of the wine-shop stood looking at him, a white-haired man sat on a low bench, stooping forward and very busy, making shoes.

CHAPTER VI.

THE SHOEMAKER.

"Good day!" said Monsieur Defarge, looking down at the white head that bent low over the shoemaking.

It was raised for a moment, and a very faint voice responded to the salutation, as if it were at a distance:

"Good day!"

"You are still hard at work, I see?"

After a long silence, the head was lifted for another moment, and the voice replied, "Yes—I am working." This time, a pair of haggard eyes had looked at the questioner, before the face had dropped again.

The faintness of the voice was pitiable and dreadful. It was not the faintness of physical weakness, though confinement and hard fare no doubt had their part in it. Its deplorable peculiarity was, that it was the faintness of solitude and disuse. It was like the last feeble echo of a sound made long and long ago. So entirely had it lost the life and resonance of the human voice, that it affected the senses like a once beautiful colour faded away into a poor weak stain. So sunken and suppressed it was, that it was like a voice underground. So expressive it was, of a hopeless and lost creature, that a famished traveller, wearied out by lonely wandering in a wilderness, would have remembered home and friends in such a tone before lying down to die.

Some minutes of silent work had passed: and the haggard eyes had looked up again: not with any interest or curiosity, but with a dull mechanical perception, beforehand, that the spot where the only visitor they were aware of had stood, was not yet empty.

"I want," said Defarge, who had not removed his gaze from the shoemaker, "to let in a little more light here. You can bear a little more?"

The shoemaker stopped his work; looked with a vacant air of listening, at the floor on one side of him; then similarly, at the floor on the other side of him; then, upward at the speaker.

"What did you say?"

"You can bear a little more light?"

"I must bear it, if you let it in." (Laying the palest shadow of a stress upon the second word.)

The opened half-door was opened a little further, and secured at that angle for the time. A broad ray of light fell into the garret, and showed the workman with an unfinished shoe upon his lap, pausing in his labour. His few common tools and various scraps of leather were at his feet and on his bench. He had a white beard, raggedly cut, but not very long, a hollow face, and exceedingly bright eyes. The hollowness and thinness of his face would have caused them to look large, under his yet dark eyebrows and his confused white hair, though they had been really otherwise, but, they were naturally large, and looked unnaturally so. His yellow rags of shirt lay open at the throat, and showed his body to be withered and worn. He, and his old canvas frock, and his loose stockings, and all his poor tatters of clothes, had, in a long seclusion from direct light and air, faded down to such a dull uniformity of parchment-yellow, that it would have been hard to say which was which.

He had put up a hand between his eyes and the light, and the very bones of it seemed transparent. So he sat, with a steadfastly vacant gaze, pausing in his work. He never looked at the figure before him, without first looking down on this side of himself, then on that, as if he had lost the habit of associating place with sound; he never spoke, without first wandering in this manner, and forgetting to speak.

"Are you going to finish that pair of shoes to-day?" asked Defarge, motioning to Mr. Lorry to come forward.

"What did you say?"

"Do you mean to finish that pair of shoes to-day?"

"I can't say that I mean to. I suppose so. I don't know."

But, the question reminded him of his work, and he bent over it again.

Mr. Lorry came silently forward, leaving the daughter by the door. When he had stood, for a minute or two, by the side of Defarge, the shoemaker looked up. He showed no surprise at seeing another figure, but the unsteady fingers of one of his hands strayed to his lips as he looked at it (his lips and his nails were of the same pale lead-colour), and then the hand dropped to his work, and he once more bent over the shoe. The look and the action had occupied but an instant.

"You have a visitor, you see," said Monsieur Defarge.

"What did you say?"

"Here is a visitor."

The shoemaker looked up as before, but without removing a hand from his work.

"Come!" said Defarge. "Here is monsieur, who knows a well-made shoe when he sees one. Show him that shoe you are working at. Take it, monsieur."

Mr. Lorry took it in his hand.

"Tell monsieur what kind of shoe it is, and the maker's name."

There was a longer pause than usual, before the shoemaker replied:

"I forget what it was you asked me. What did you say?"

"I said, couldn't you describe the kind of shoe, for monsieur's information?"

"It is a lady's shoe. It is a young lady's walking-shoe. It is in the present mode. I never saw the mode. I have had a pattern in my hand." He glanced at the shoe with some little passing touch of pride.

"And the maker's name?" said Defarge.

Now that he had no work to hold, he laid the knuckles of the right hand in the hollow of the left, and then the knuckles of the left hand in the hollow of the right, and then passed a hand across his bearded chin, and so on in regular changes, without a moment's intermission. The task of recalling him from the vagrancy into which he always sank when he had spoken, was like recalling some very weak person from a swoon, or endeavouring, in the hope of some disclosure, to stay the spirit of a fast-dying man.

"Did you ask me for my name?"

"Assuredly I did."

"One Hundred and Five, North Tower."

"Is that all?"

"One Hundred and Five, North Tower."

With a weary sound that was not a sigh, nor a groan, he bent to work again, until the silence was again broken.

"You are not a shoemaker by trade?" said Mr. Lorry, looking steadfastly at him.

His haggard eyes turned to Defarge as if he would have transferred the question to him: but as no help came from that quarter, they turned back on the questioner when they had sought the ground.

"I am not a shoemaker by trade? No, I was not a shoemaker by trade. I—I learnt it here. I taught myself. I asked leave to——"

He lapsed away, even for minutes, ringing those measured changes on his hands the whole time. His eyes came slowly back, at last, to the face from which they had wandered; when they rested on it, he started, and resumed, in the manner of a sleeper that moment awake, reverting to a subject of last night.

"I asked leave to teach myself, and I got it with much difficulty after a long while, and I have made shoes ever since."

As he held out his hand for the shoe that had been taken from him, Mr. Lorry said, still looking steadfastly in his face:

"Monsieur Manette, do you remember nothing of me?"

The shoe dropped to the ground, and he sat looking fixedly at the questioner.

"Monsieur Manette;" Mr. Lorry laid his hand upon Defarge's arm; "do you remember nothing of this man? Look at him. Look at me. Is there no old banker, no old business, no old servant, no old time, rising in your mind, Monsieur Manette?"

As the captive of many years sat looking fixedly, by turns, at Mr. Lorry and at Defarge, some long obliterated marks of an actively intent intelligence in the middle of the forehead, gradually forced themselves through the black mist that had fallen on him. They were overclouded again, they were fainter, they were gone; but they had been there. And so exactly was the expression repeated on the fair young face of her who had crept along the wall to a point where she could see him, and where she now stood looking at him, with hands which at first had been only raised in frightened compassion, if not even to keep him off and shut out the sight of him, but which were now extending towards him, trembling with eagerness to lay the spectral face upon her warm young breast, and love it back to life and hope—so exactly was the expression repeated (though in stronger characters) on her fair young face, that it looked as though it had passed like a moving light, from him to her.

Darkness had fallen on him in its place. He looked at the two, less and less attentively, and his eyes in gloomy abstraction sought the ground and looked about him in the old way. Finally, with a deep long sigh, he took the shoe up, and resumed his work.

"Have you recognised him, monsieur?" asked Defarge in a whisper.

"Yes; for a moment. At first I thought it quite hopeless, but I have unquestionably seen, for a single moment, the face that I once knew so well. Hush! Let us draw further back. Hush!"

She had moved from the wall of the garret, very near to the bench on which he sat. There was something awful in his unconsciousness of the figure that could have put out its hand and touched him as he stooped over his labour.

Not a word was spoken, not a sound was made. She stood, like a spirit, beside him, and he bent over his work.

It happened, at length, that he had occasion to change the instrument in his hand, for his shoemaker's knife. It lay on that side of him which was not the side on which she stood. He had taken it up, and was stooping to work again, when his eyes caught the skirt of her dress. He raised them, and saw her face. The two spectators started forward, but she stayed them with a motion of her hand. She had no fear of his striking at her with the knife, though they had.

He stared at her with a fearful look, and after a while his lips began to form some words, though no sound proceeded from them. By degrees, in the pauses of his quick and laboured breathing, he was heard to say:

"What is this?"

With the tears streaming down her face, she put her two hands to her lips, and kissed them to him; then clasped them on her breast, as if she laid his ruined head there.

"You are not the gaoler's daughter?"

She sighed "No."

"Who are you?"

Not yet trusting the tones of her voice, she sat down on the bench beside him. He recoiled, but she laid her hand upon his arm. A strange thrill struck him when she did so, and visibly passed over his frame; he laid the knife down softly, as he sat staring at her.

Her golden hair, which she wore in long curls, had been hurriedly pushed aside, and fell down over her neck. Advancing his hand by little and little, he took it up and looked at it. In the midst of the action he went astray, and, with another deep sigh, fell to work at his shoemaking.

But not for long. Releasing her arm, she laid her hand upon his shoulder. After looking doubtfully at it, two or three times, as if to be sure that it was really there, he laid down his work, put his hand to his neck, and took off a blackened string with a scrap of folded rag attached to it. He opened this, carefully, on his knee, and it contained a very little quantity of hair: not more than one or two long golden hairs, which he had, in some old day, wound off upon his finger.

He took her hair into his hand again, and looked closely at it. "It is the same. How can it be! When was it! How was it!"

As the concentrated expression returned to his forehead, he seemed to become conscious that it was in hers too. He turned her full to the light, and looked at her.

"She had laid her head upon my shoulder, that night when I was summoned out—she had a fear of my going, though I had none—and when I was brought to the North Tower they found these upon my sleeve. 'You will leave me them? They can never help me to escape in the body, though they may in the spirit.' Those were the words I said. I remember them very well."

He formed this speech with his lips many times before he could utter it. But when he did find spoken words for it, they came to him coherently, though slowly.

"How was this?—*Was it you?*"

Once more, the two spectators started, as he turned upon her with a frightful suddenness. But she sat perfectly still in his grasp, and only said, in a low voice, "I entreat you, good gentlemen, do not come near us, do not speak, do not move!"

"Hark!" he exclaimed. "Whose voice was that?"

His hands released her as he uttered this cry, and went up to his white hair, which they tore in a frenzy. It died out, as everything but his shoemaking did die out of him, and he refolded his little packet and tried to secure it in his breast; but he still looked at her, and gloomily shook his head.

"No, no, no; you are too young, too blooming. It can't be. See what the prisoner is. These are not the hands she knew, this is not the face she knew, this is not a voice she ever heard. No, no. She was—and He was—before the slow years of the North Tower—ages ago. What is your name, my gentle angel?"

Hailing his softened tone and manner, his daughter fell upon her knees before him, with her appealing hands upon his breast.

"O, sir, at another time you shall know my name, and who my mother was, and who my father, and how I never knew their hard, hard history. But I cannot tell you at this time, and I cannot tell you here. All that I may tell you, here and now, is, that I pray to you to touch me and to bless me. Kiss me, kiss me! O my dear, my dear!"

His cold white head mingled with her radiant hair, which warmed and lighted it as though it were the light of Freedom shining on him.

"If you hear in my voice—I don't know that it is so, but I hope it is—if you hear in my voice any resemblance to a voice that once was sweet music in your ears, weep for it, weep for it! If you touch, in touching my hair, anything that recalls a beloved head that lay on your breast when you were young and free, weep for it, weep for it! If, when I hint to you of a Home that is before us, where I will be true to you with all my duty and with all my faithful service, I bring back the remembrance of a Home long desolate, while your poor heart pined away, weep for it, weep for it!"

She held him closer round the neck, and rocked him on her breast like a child.

"If, when I tell you, dearest dear, that your agony is over, and that I have come here to take you from it, and that we go to England to be at peace and at rest, I cause you to think of your useful life laid waste, and of our native France so wicked to you, weep for it, weep for it! And if, when I shall tell you of my name, and of my father who is living, and of my mother who is dead, you learn that I have to kneel to my honoured father, and implore his pardon for having never for his sake striven all day and lain awake and wept all night, because the love of my poor mother hid his torture from me, weep for it, weep for it! Weep for her, then, and for me! Good gentlemen, thank God! I feel his sacred tears upon my face, and his sobs strike against my heart. O, see! Thank God for us, thank God!"

He had sunk in her arms, and his face dropped on her breast: a sight so touching, yet so terrible in the tremendous wrong and suffering which had gone before it, that the two beholders covered their faces.

When the quiet of the garret had been long undisturbed, and his heaving breast and shaken form had long yielded to the calm that must follow all storms—emblem to hu-

"HE HAD SUNK IN HER ARMS, WITH HIS FACE DROPPED ON HER BREAST."

manity, of the rest and silence into which the storm called Life must hush at last—they came forward to raise the father and daughter from the ground. He had gradually dropped to the floor, and lay there in a lethargy, worn out. She had nestled down with him, that his head might lie upon her arm; and her hair drooping over him curtained him from the light.

"If, without disturbing him," she said, raising her hand to Mr. Lorry as he stooped over them, after repeated blowings of his nose, "all could be arranged for our leaving Paris at once, so that, from the very door, he could be taken away——"

"But, consider. Is he fit for the journey?" asked Mr. Lorry.

"More fit for that, I think, than to remain in this city, so dreadful to him."

"It is true," said Defarge, who was kneeling to look on and hear. "More than that; Monsieur Manette is, for all reasons, best out of France. Say, shall I hire a carriage and post-horses?"

"That's business," said Mr. Lorry, resuming on the shortest notice his methodical manners; "and if business is to be done, I had better do it."

"Then be so kind," urged Miss Manette, "as to leave us here. You see how composed he has become, and you cannot be afraid to leave him with me now. Why should you be? If you will lock the door to secure us from interruption, I do not doubt that you will find him, when you come back, as quiet as you leave him. In any case, I will take care of him until you return, and then we will remove him straight."

Both Mr. Lorry and Defarge were rather disinclined to this course, and in favour of one of them remaining. But, as there were not only carriage and horses to be seen to, but travelling papers; and as time pressed, for the day was drawing to an end, it came at last to their hastily dividing the business that was necessary to be done, and hurrying away to do it.

Then, as the darkness closed in, the daughter laid her head down on the hard ground close at the father's side, and watched him. The darkness deepened and deepened, and they both lay quiet, until a light gleamed through the chinks in the wall.

Mr. Lorry and Monsieur Defarge had made all ready for the journey, and had brought with them, besides travelling cloaks and wrappers, bread and meat, wine, and hot coffee. Monsieur Defarge put this provender, and the lamp he carried, on the shoemaker's bench (there was nothing else in the garret but a pallet bed), and he and Mr. Lorry roused the captive, and assisted him to his feet.

No human intelligence could have read the mysteries of his mind, in the scared blank wonder of his face. Whether he knew what had happened, whether he recollected what they had said to him, whether he knew that he was free, were questions which no sagacity could have solved. They tried speaking to him; but, he was so confused, and so very slow to answer, that they took fright at his bewilderment, and agreed for the time to tamper with him no more. He had a wild, lost manner of occasionally clasping his head in his hands, that had not been seen in him before; yet, he had some pleasure in the mere sound of his daughter's voice, and invariably turned to it when she spoke.

In the submissive way of one long accustomed to obey under coercion, he ate and drank what they gave him to eat and drink, and put on the cloak and other wrappings, that they gave him to wear. He readily responded to his daughter's drawing her arm through his, and took—and kept—her hand in both his own.

They began to descend; Monsieur Defarge going first with the lamp, Mr. Lorry closing the little procession. They had not traversed many steps of the long main staircase when he stopped, and stared at the roof and round at the walls.

"You remember the place, my father? You remember coming up here?"

"What did you say?"

But, before she could repeat the question, he murmured an answer as if she had repeated it.

"Remember? No, I don't remember. It was so very long ago."

That he had no recollection whatever of his having been brought from his prison to that house, was apparent to them. They heard him mutter, "One Hundred and Five, North Tower;" and when he looked about him, it evidently was for the strong fortress-walls which had long encompassed him. On their reaching the courtyard he instinctively altered his tread, as being in expectation of a drawbridge; and when there was no drawbridge, and he saw the carriage waiting in the open street, he dropped his daughter's hand and clasped his head again.

No crowd was about the door; no people were discernible at any of the many windows; not even a chance passer-by was in the street. An unnatural silence and desertion reigned there. Only one soul was to be seen, and that was Madame Defarge—who leaned against the door-post, knitting, and saw nothing.

The prisoner had got into a coach, and his daughter had followed him, when Mr. Lorry's feet were arrested on the step by his asking, miserably, for his shoemaking tools and the unfinished shoes. Madame Defarge immediately called to her husband that she would get them, and went, knitting, out of the lamplight, through the courtyard. She quickly brought them down and handed them in;—and immediately afterwards leaned against the door-post, knitting, and saw nothing.

Defarge got upon the box, and gave the word "To the Barrier!" The postilion cracked his whip, and they clattered away under the feeble over-swinging lamps.

Under the over-swinging lamps—swinging ever brighter in the better streets, and ever dimmer in the worse—and by lighted shops, gay crowds, illuminated coffee-houses, and theatre-doors, to one of the city gates. Soldiers with lanterns, at the guard-house there. "Your papers, travellers!" "See here then, Monsieur the Officer," said Defarge, getting down, and taking him gravely apart, "these are the papers of monsieur inside, with the white head. They were consigned to me, with him, at the——" He dropped his voice, there was a flutter among the military lanterns, and one of them being handed into the coach by an arm in uniform, the eyes connected with the arm looked, not an every day or an every night look, at monsieur with the white head. "It is well. Forward!" from the uniform. "Adieu!" from Defarge. And so, under a short grove of feebler and feebler over-swinging lamps, out under the great grove of stars.

Beneath that arch of unmoved and eternal lights; some, so remote from this little earth that the learned tell us it is doubtful whether their rays have even yet discovered it, as a point in space where anything is suffered or done: the shadows of the night were broad and black. All through the cold and restless interval, until dawn, they once more whispered in the ears of Mr. Jarvis Lorry—sitting opposite the buried man who had been dug out, and wondering what subtle powers were for ever lost to him, and what were capable of restoration—the old inquiry:

"I hope you care to be recalled to life?"

And the old answer:

"I can't say."

BOOK THE SECOND.—THE GOLDEN THREAD.

CHAPTER I.

FIVE YEARS LATER.

Tellson's Bank by Temple Bar was an old-fashioned place, even in the year one thousand seven hundred and eighty. It was very small, very dark, very ugly, very incommodious. It was an old-fashioned place, moreover, in the moral attribute that the partners in the House were proud of its smallness, proud of its darkness, proud of its ugliness, proud of its incommodiousness. They were even boastful of its eminence in those particulars, and were fired by an express conviction that, if it were less objectionable, it would be less respectable. This was no passive belief, but an active weapon which they flashed at more convenient places of business. Tellson's (they said) wanted no elbow-room, Tellson's wanted no light, Tellson's wanted no embellishment. Noakes and Co.'s might, or Snooks Brothers' might; but Tellson's, thank Heaven!——

Any one of these partners would have disinherited his son on the question of rebuilding Tellson's. In this respect the House was much on a par with the Country; which did very often disinherit its sons for suggesting improvements in laws and customs that had long been highly objectionable, but were only the more respectable.

Thus it had come to pass, that Tellson's was the triumphant perfection of inconvenience. After bursting open a door of idiotic obstinacy with a weak rattle in its throat, you fell into Tellson's down two steps, and came to your senses in a miserable little shop, with two little counters, where the oldest of men made your cheque shake as if the wind rustled it, while they examined the signature by the dingiest of windows, which were always under a showerbath of mud from Fleet-street, and which were made the dingier by their own iron bars proper, and the heavy shadow of Temple Bar. If your business necessitated your seeing "the House," you were put into a species of Condemned Hold at the back, where you meditated on a misspent life, until the House came with its hands in its pockets, and you could hardly blink at it in the dismal twilight. Your money came out of, or went into, wormy old wooden drawers, particles of which flew up your nose and down your throat when they were opened and shut. Your banknotes had a musty odour, as if they were fast decomposing into rags again. Your plate was stowed away among the neighbouring cesspools, and evil communications corrupted its good polish in a day or two. Your deeds got into extemporised strong-rooms made of kitchens and sculleries, and fretted all the fat out of their parchments into the banking-house air. Your lighter boxes of family papers went up-stairs into a Barmecide room, that always had a great dining-table in it and never had a dinner, and where, even in the year one thousand seven hundred and eighty, the first letters written to you by your old love, or by your little children, were but newly released from the horror of being ogled through the windows, by the heads exposed on Temple Bar with an insensate brutality and ferocity worthy of Abyssinia or Ashantee.

But indeed, at that time, putting to death was a recipe much in vogue with all trades and professions, and not least of all with Tellson's. Death is Nature's remedy for all things, and why not Legislation's? Accordingly, the forger was put to Death; the utterer of a bad note was put to Death; the unlawful opener of a letter was put to Death; the purloiner of forty shillings and sixpence was put to Death; the holder of a horse at Tellson's door, who made off with it, was put to Death; the coiner of a bad shilling was put to Death; the sounders of three-fourths of the notes in the whole gamut of Crime, were put to Death. Not that it did the least good in the way of prevention—it might almost have been worth remarking that the fact was exactly the reverse—but, it cleared off (as to this world) the trouble of each particular case, and left nothing else connected with it to be looked after. Thus, Tellson's, in its day, like greater places of business, its contemporaries, had taken so many lives, that, if the heads laid low before it had been ranged on Temple Bar instead of being privately disposed of, they would probably have excluded what little light the ground floor had, in a rather significant manner.

Cramped in all kinds of dim cupboards and hutches at Tellson's, the oldest of men carried on the business gravely. When they took a young man into Tellson's London house, they hid him somewhere till he was old. They kept him in a dark place, like a cheese, until he had the full Tellson flavour and blue-mould upon him. Then only was he permitted to be seen, spectacularly poring over large books, and casting his breeches and gaiters into the general weight of the establishment.

Outside Tellson's—never by any means in it, unless called in—was an odd-job-man, an occasional porter and messenger, who served as the live sign of the house. He was never absent during business hours, unless upon an errand, and then he was represented by his son: a grisly urchin of twelve, who was his express image. People understood that Tellson's, in a stately way, tolerated the odd-job-man. The house had always tolerated some person in that capacity, and time and tide had drifted this person to the post. His surname was Cruncher, and on the youthful occasion of his renouncing by proxy the works of darkness, in the easterly parish church of Houndsditch, he had received the added appellation of Jerry.

The scene was Mr. Cruncher's private lodging in Hanging-sword-alley, Whitefriars: the time, half-past seven of the clock on a windy March morning, Anno Domini seventeen hundred and eighty. (Mr. Cruncher himself always spoke of the year of our Lord as Anna Dominoes: apparently under the impression that the Christian era dated from the invention of a popular game, by a lady who had bestowed her name upon it.)

Mr. Cruncher's apartments were not in a savoury neighbourhood, and were but two in number, even if a closet with a single pane of glass in it might be counted as one. But they were very decently kept. Early as it was, on the windy March morning, the room in which he lay abed was already scrubbed throughout; and between the cups and saucers arranged for breakfast, and the lumbering deal table, a very clean white cloth was spread.

Mr. Cruncher reposed under a patchwork counterpane, like a Harlequin at home. At first, he slept heavily, but, by degrees, began to roll and surge in bed, until he rose above the surface, with his spiky hair looking as if it must tear the sheets to ribbons. At which juncture, he exclaimed, in a voice of dire exasperation:

"Bust me, if she ain't at it agin!"

A woman of orderly and industrious appearance rose from her knees in a corner, with sufficient haste and trepidation to show that she was the person referred to.

"What!" said Mr. Cruncher, looking out of bed for a boot. "You're at it agin, are you?"

After hailing the morn with this second salutation, he threw a boot at the woman as a third. It was a very muddy boot, and may introduce the odd circumstance connected with Mr. Cruncher's domestic economy, that, whereas he often came home after banking hours with clean boots, he often got up next morning to find the same boots covered with clay.

"What," said Mr. Cruncher, varying his apostrophe after missing his mark—"what are you up to, Aggerawayter?"

"I was only saying my prayers."

"Saying your prayers! You're a nice woman! What do you mean by flopping yourself down and praying agin me?"

"I was not praying against you; I was praying for you."

"You weren't. And if you were, I won't be took the liberty with. Here! your mother's a nice woman, young Jerry, going a praying agin your father's prosperity. You've got a dutiful mother, you have, my son. You've got a religious mother, you have, my boy: going and flopping herself down, and praying that the bread-and-butter may be snatched out of the mouth of her only child."

Master Cruncher (who was in his shirt) took this very ill, and, turning to his mother, strongly deprecated any praying away of his personal board.

"And what do you suppose, you conceited female," said Mr. Cruncher, with unconscious inconsistency, "that the worth of *your* prayers may be? Name the price that you put *your* prayers at!"

"They only come from the heart, Jerry. They are worth no more than that."

"Worth no more than that," repeated Mr. Cruncher. "They ain't worth much, then. Whether or no, I won't be prayed agin, I tell you. I can't afford it. I'm not a going to be made unlucky by *your* sneaking. If you must go flopping yourself down, flop in favour of your husband and child, and not in opposition to 'em. If I had had any but a unnat'ral wife, and this poor boy had had any but a unnat'ral mother, I might have made some money last week instead of being counterprayed and countermined and religiously circumwented into the worst of luck. B-u-u-ust me!" said Mr. Cruncher, who all this time had been putting on his clothes, "if I ain't, what with piety and one blowed thing and another, been choused this last week into as bad luck as ever a poor devil of a honest tradesman met with! Young Jerry, dress yourself, my boy, and while I clean my boots keep a eye upon your mother now and then, and if you see any signs of more flopping, give me a call. For, I tell you," here he addressed his wife once more, "I won't be gone agin, in this manner. I am as rickety as a hackney-coach, I'm as sleepy as laudanum, my lines is strained to that degree that I shouldn't know, if it wasn't for the pain in 'em, which was me and which was somebody else, yet I'm none the better for it in pocket; and it's my suspicion that you've been at it from morning to night to prevent me from being the better for it in pocket, and I won't put up with it, Aggerawayter, and what do you say now!"

Growling, in addition, such phrases as "Ah! yes! You're religious, too. You wouldn't put yourself in opposition to the interests of your husband and child, would you? Not you!" and throwing off other sarcastic sparks form the whirling grindstone of his indignation, Mr. Cruncher betook himself to his boot-cleaning and his general preparation for business. In the meantime, his son, whose head was garnished with tenderer spikes, and whose young eyes stood close by one another, as his father's did, kept the required watch upon his mother. He greatly disturbed that poor woman at intervals, by darting out of his sleeping closet, where he made his toilet, with a suppressed cry of "You are going to flop, mother.—Halloa, father!" and, after raising this fictitious alarm, darting in again with an undutiful grin.

Mr. Cruncher's temper was not at all improved when he came to his breakfast. He resented Mrs. Cruncher's saying grace with particular animosity.

"Now, Aggerawayter! What are you up to? At it again?"

His wife explained that she had merely "asked a blessing."

"Don't do it!" said Mr. Cruncher, looking about, as if he rather expected to see the loaf disappear under the efficacy of his wife's petitions. "I ain't a going to be blest out of house and home. I won't have my wittles blest off my table. Keep still!"

Exceedingly red-eyed and grim, as if he had been up all night at a party which had taken anything but a convivial turn, Jerry Cruncher worried his breakfast rather than ate it, growling over it like any four-footed inmate of a menagerie. Towards nine o'clock he smoothed his ruffled aspect, and, presenting as respectable and business-like an exterior as he could overlay his natural self with, issued forth to the occupation of the day.

It could scarcely be called a trade, in spite of his favourite description of himself as "a honest tradesman." His stock consisted of a wooden stool, made out of a broken-backed chair cut down, which stool, young Jerry, walking at his father's side, carried every morning to beneath the banking-house window that was nearest Temple Bar: where, with the addition of the first handful of straw that could be gleaned from any passing vehicle to keep the cold and wet from the odd-job-man's feet, it formed the encampment for the day. On this post of his, Mr. Cruncher was as well known to Fleet-street and the Temple, as the Bar itself,—and was almost as ill-looking.

Encamped at a quarter before nine, in good time to touch his three-cornered hat to the oldest of men as they passed in to Tellson's, Jerry took up his station on this windy March morning, with young Jerry standing by him, when not engaged in making forays through the Bar, to inflict bodily and mental injuries of an acute description on passing boys who were small enough for his amiable purpose. Father and son, extremely like each other, looking silently on at the morning traffic in Fleet-street, with their two heads as near to one another as the two eyes of each were, bore a considerable resemblance to a pair of monkeys. The

MESSRS. CRUNCHER AND SON.

resemblance was not lessened by the accidental circumstance, that the mature Jerry bit and spat out straw, while the twinkling eyes of the youthful Jerry were as restlessly watchful of him as of everything else in Fleet-street.

The head of one of the regular indoor messengers attached to Tellson's establishment was put through the door, and the word was given:

"Porter wanted!"

"Hooray, father! Here's an early job to begin with!"

Having thus given his parent God speed, young Jerry seated himself on the stool, entered on his reversionary interest in the straw his father had been chewing, and cogitated.

"Al-ways rusty! His fingers is al-ways rusty!" muttered young Jerry. "Where does my father get all that iron rust from? He don't get no iron rust here!"

CHAPTER II.

A SIGHT.

"You know the Old Bailey, well, no doubt?" said one of the oldest of clerks to Jerry the messenger.

"Ye-es, sir," returned Jerry, in something of a dogged manner. "I *do* know the Bailey."

"Just so. And you know Mr. Lorry."

"I know Mr. Lorry, sir, much better than I know the Bailey. Much better," said Jerry, not unlike a reluctant witness at the establishment in question, "than I, as a honest tradesman, wish to know the Bailey."

"Very well. Find the door where the witnesses go in, and show the door-keeper this note for Mr. Lorry. He will then let you in."

"Into the court, sir?"

"Into the court."

Mr. Cruncher's eyes seemed to get a little closer to one another, and to interchange the inquiry, "What do you think of this?"

"Am I to wait in the court, sir?" he asked, as the result of that conference.

"I am going to tell you. The door-keeper will pass the note to Mr. Lorry, and do you make any gesture that will attract Mr. Lorry's attention, and show him where you stand. Then what you have to do, is, to remain there until he wants you."

"Is that all, sir?"

"That's all. He wishes to have a messenger at hand. This is to tell him you are there."

As the ancient clerk deliberately folded and superscribed the note, Mr. Cruncher, after surveying him in silence until he came to the blotting-paper stage, remarked:

"I suppose they'll be trying Forgeries this morning?"

"Treason!"

"That's quartering," said Jerry. "Barbarous!"

"It is the law," remarked the ancient clerk, turning his surprised spectacles upon him. "It is the law."

"It's hard in the law to spile a man, I think. It's hard enough to kill him, but it's wery hard to spile him, sir."

"Not at all," returned the ancient clerk. "Speak well of the law. Take care of your chest and voice, my good friend, and leave the law to take care of itself. I give you that advice."

"It's the damp, sir, what settles on my chest and voice," said Jerry. "I leave you to judge what a damp way of earning a living mine is."

"Well, well," said the old clerk; "we all have our various ways of gaining a livelihood. Some of us have damp ways, and some of us have dry ways. Here is the letter. Go along."

Jerry took the letter, and, remarking to himself with less internal deference than he made an outward show of, "You are a lean old one, too," made his bow, informed his son, in passing, of his destination, and went his way.

They hanged at Tyburn, in those days, so the street outside Newgate had not obtained one infamous notoriety that has since attached to it. But, the gaol was a vile place, in which most kinds of debauchery and villainy were practised, and where dire diseases were bred, that came into court with the prisoners, and sometimes rushed straight from the dock at my Lord Chief Justice himself, and pulled him off the bench. It had more than once happened, that the Judge in the black cap pronounced his own doom as certainly as the prisoner's, and even died before him. For the rest, the Old Bailey was famous as a kind of deadly inn-yard, from which pale travellers set out continually, in carts and coaches, on a violent passage into the other world: traversing some two miles and a half of public street and road, and shaming few good citizens, if any. So powerful is use, and so desirable to be good use in the beginning. It was famous, too, for the pillory, a wise old institution, that inflicted a punishment of which no one could forsee the extent; also, for the whipping-post, another dear old institution, very humanising and softening to behold in action; also, for extensive transactions in blood-money, another fragment of ancestral wisdom, systematically leading to the most frightful mercenary crimes that could be committed under Heaven. Altogether, the Old Bailey, at that date, was a choice illustration of the precept, that "Whatever is is right;" an aphorism that would be as final as it is lazy, did it not include the troublesome consequence, that nothing that ever was, was wrong.

Making his way through the tainted crowd, dispersed up and down this hideous scene of action, with the skill of a man accustomed to make his way quietly, the messenger found out the door he sought, and handed in his letter through a trap in it. For, people then paid to see the play at the Old Bailey, just as they paid to see the play in Bedlam—only the former entertainment was much the dearer. Therefore, all the Old Bailey doors were well guarded—except, indeed, the social doors by which the criminals got there, and those were always left wide open.

After some delay and demur, the door grudgingly turned on its hinges a very little way, and allowed Mr. Jerry Cruncher to squeeze himself into court.

"What's on?" he asked, in a whisper, of the man he found himself next to.

"Nothing yet."

"What's coming on?"

"The Treason case."

"The quartering one, eh?"

"Ah!" returned the man, with a relish; "he'll be drawn on a hurdle to be half hanged, and then he'll be taken down and sliced before his own face, and then his inside will be taken out and burnt while he looks on, and then his head will be chopped off, and he'll be cut into quarters. That's the sentence."

"If he's found Guilty, you mean to say?" Jerry added, by way of proviso.

"Oh! they'll find him guilty," said the other. "Don't you be afraid of that."

Mr. Cruncher's attention was here diverted to the door-keeper, whom he saw making his way to Mr. Lorry, with the note in his hand. Mr. Lorry sat at a table, among the gentlemen in wigs: not far from a wigged gentleman, the prisoner's counsel, who had a great bundle of papers before him: and nearly opposite another wigged gentleman with his hands in his pockets, whose whole attention, when Mr. Cruncher looked at him then or afterwards, seemed to be concentrated on the ceiling of the court. After some gruff coughing and rubbing of his chin and signing with his hand, Jerry attracted the notice of Mr. Lorry, who had stood up to look for him, and who quietly nodded and sat down again.

"What's *he* got to do with the case?" asked the man he had spoken with.

"Blest if I know," said Jerry.

"What have *you* got to do with it, then, if a person may inquire?"

"Blest if I know that either," said Jerry.

The entrance of the Judge, and a consequent great stir and settling down in the court, stopped the dialogue. Presently, the dock became the central point of interest. Two gaolers, who had been standing there, went out, and the prisoner was brought in, and put to the bar.

Everybody present, except the one wigged gentleman who looked at the ceiling, stared at him. All the human breath in the place, rolled at him, like a sea, or a wind, or a fire. Eager faces strained round pillars and corners, to get a sight of him; spectators in back rows stood up, not to miss a hair of him; people on the floor of the court, laid their hands on the shoulders of the people before them, to help themselves, at anybody's cost, to a view of him—stood a-tiptoe, got upon ledges, stood upon next to nothing, to see every inch of him. Conspicuous among these latter, like an animated bit of the spiked wall of Newgate, Jerry stood: aiming at the prisoner the beery breath of a whet he had taken as he came along, and discharging it to mingle with the waves of other beer, and gin, and tea, and coffee, and what not, that flowed at him, and already broke upon the great windows behind him in an impure mist and rain.

The object of all this staring and blaring, was a young man of about five-and-twenty, well-grown and well-looking, with a sunburnt cheek and a dark eye. His condition was that of a young gentleman. He was plainly dressed in black, or very dark grey, and his hair, which was long and dark, was gathered in a ribbon at the back of his neck; more to be out of his way than for ornament. As an emotion of the mind will express itself through any covering of the body, so the paleness which his situation engendered came through the brown upon his cheek, showing the soul to be stronger than the sun. He was otherwise quite self-possessed, bowed to the Judge, and stood quiet.

The sort of interest with which this man was stared and breathed at, was not a sort that elevated humanity. Had he stood in peril of a less horrible sentence—had there been a chance of any one of its savage details being spared—by just so much would he have lost in his fascination. The form that was to be doomed to be so shamefully mangled, was the sight; the immortal creature that was to be so butchered and torn asunder, yielded the sensation. Whatever gloss the various spectators put upon the interest, according to their several arts and powers of self-deceit, the interest was, at the root of it, Ogreish.

Silence in the court! Charles Darnay had yesterday pleaded Not Guilty to an indictment denouncing him (with infinite jingle and jangle) for that he was a false traitor to our serene, illustrious, excellent, and so forth, prince, our Lord the King, by reason of his having, on divers occasions, and by divers means and ways, assisted Lewis, the French King, in his wars against our said serene, illustrious, excellent, and so forth; that was to say, by coming and going, between the dominions of our said serene, illustrious, excellent, and so forth, and those of the said French Lewis, and wickedly, falsely, traitorously, and otherwise evil-adverbiously, revealing to the said French Lewis what forces our said serene, illustrious, excellent, and so forth, had in preparation to send to Canada and North America. This much, Jerry, with his head becoming more and more spiky as the law terms bristled it, made out with huge satisfaction, and so arrived circuitously at the understanding that the aforesaid, and over and over again aforesaid, Charles Darnay, stood there before him upon his trial; that the jury were swearing in; and that Mr. Attorney-General was making ready to speak.

The accused, who was (and who knew he was) being mentally hanged, beheaded, and quartered, by everybody there, neither flinched from the situation, nor assumed any theatrical air in it. He was quiet and attentive; watched the opening proceedings with a grave interest; and stood with his hands resting on the slab of wood before him, so composedly, that they had not displaced a leaf of the herbs with which it was strewn. The court was all bestrewn with herbs and sprinkled with vinegar, as a precaution against gaol air and gaol fever.

Over the prisoner's head there was a mirror, to throw the light down upon him. Crowds of the wicked and the wretched had been reflected in it, and had passed from its surface and this earth's together. Haunted in a most ghastly manner that abominable place would have been, if the glass could ever have rendered back its reflections, as the ocean is one day to give up its dead. Some passing thought of the infamy and disgrace for which it had been reserved, may have struck the prisoner's mind. Be that as it may, a change in his position making him conscious of a bar of light across his face, he looked up; and when he saw the glass his face flushed, and his right hand pushed the herbs away.

It happened, that the action turned his face to that side of the court which was on his left. About on a level with his eyes, there sat, in that corner of the Judge's bench, two persons upon whom his look immediately rested; so immediately, and so much to the changing of his aspect, that all the eyes that were turned upon him, turned to them.

The spectators saw in the two figures, a young lady of little more than twenty, and a gentleman who was evidently her father; a man of a very remarkable appearance in respect of the absolute whiteness of his hair, and a certain indescribable intensity of face: not of an active kind, but pondering and self-communing. When this expression was upon him, he looked as if he were old; but when it was stirred and broken up—as it was now, in a moment, on his speaking to his daughter—he became a handsome man, not past the prime of life.

His daughter had one of her hands drawn through his arm, as she sat by him, and the other pressed upon it. She had drawn close to him, in her dread of the scene, and in her pity for the prisoner. Her forehead had been strikingly expressive of an engrossing terror and compassion that saw nothing but the peril of the accused. This had been so very noticeable, so very powerfully and naturally shown, that starers who had had no pity for him were touched by her; and the whisper went about, "Who are they?"

Jerry, the messenger, who had made his own observations, in his own manner, and who had been sucking the rust off his fingers in his absorption, stretched his neck to hear who they were. The crowd about him had pressed and passed the inquiry on to the nearest attendant, and from him it had been more slowly pressed and passed back; at last it got to Jerry:

"Witnesses."

"For which side?"

"Against."

"Against what side?"

"The prisoner's."

The Judge, whose eyes had gone in the general direction, recalled them, leaned back in his seat, and looked steadily at the man whose life was in his hand, as Mr. Attorney-General rose to spin the rope, grind the axe, and hammer the nails into the scaffold.

CHAPTER III

A DISAPPOINTMENT.

MR. ATTORNEY-GENERAL had to inform the jury, that the prisoner before them, though young in years, was old in the treasonable practices which claimed the forfeit of his life. That this correspondence with the public enemy was not a correspondence of to-day, or of yesterday, or even of last year, or of the year before. That, it was certain the prisoner had, for longer than that, been in the habit of passing and repassing between France and England, on secret business of which he could give no honest account. That, if it were in the nature of traitorous ways to thrive (which happily it never was), the real wickedness and guilt of his business might have remained undiscovered. That Providence, however, had put it into the heart of a person who was beyond fear and beyond reproach, to ferret out the nature of the prisoner's schemes, and, struck with horror, to disclose them to his Majesty's Chief Secretary of State and most honourable Privy Council. That, this patriot would be produced before them. That, his position and attitude were, on the whole, sublime. That, he had been the prisoner's friend, but, at once in an auspicious and an evil hour detecting his infamy, had resolved to immolate the traitor he could no longer cherish in his bosom, on the sacred altar of his country. That, if statues were decreed in Britain, as in ancient Greece and Rome, to public benefactors, this shining citizen would assuredly have had one. That, as they were not so decreed, he probably would not have one. That, Virtue, as had been observed by the poets (in many passages which he well knew the jury would have, word for word, at the tips of their

tongues; whereat the jury's countenances displayed a guilty consciousness that they knew nothing about the passages), was in a manner contagious; more especially the bright virtue known as patriotism, or love of country. That, the lofty example of this immaculate and unimpeachable witness for the Crown, to refer to whom however unworthily was an honour, had communicated itself to the prisoner's servant, and had engendered in him a holy determination to examine his master's table-drawers and pockets, and secrete his papers. That, he (Mr. Attorney-General) was prepared to hear some disparagement attempted of this admirable servant; but that, in a general way, he preferred him to his (Mr. Attorney-General's) brothers and sisters, and honoured him more than his (Mr. Attorney-General's) father and mother. That, he called with confidence on the jury to come and do likewise. That, the evidence of these two witnesses, coupled with the documents of their discovering that would be produced, would show the prisoner to have been furnished with lists of his Majesty's forces, and of their disposition and preparation, both by sea and land, and would leave no doubt that he had habitually conveyed such information to a hostile power. That, these lists could not be proved to be in the prisoner's handwriting; but that it was all the same; that, indeed, it was rather the better for the prosecution, as showing the prisoner to be artful in his precautions. That, the proof would go back five years, and would show the prisoner already engaged in these pernicious missions, within a few weeks before the date of the very first action fought between the British troops and the Americans. That, for these reasons, the jury, being a loyal jury (as he knew they were), and being a responsible jury (as *they* knew they were), must positively find the prisoner Guilty, and make an end of him, whether they liked it or not. That, they never could lay their heads upon their pillows; that, they never could tolerate the idea of their wives laying their heads upon their pillows; that, they never could endure the notion of their children laying their heads upon their pillows; in short, that there never more could be, for them or theirs, any laying of heads upon pillows at all, unless the prisoner's head was taken off. That head Mr. Attorney-General concluded by demanding of them, in the name of everything he could think of with a round turn in it, and on the faith of his solemn asseveration that he already considered the prisoner as good as dead and gone.

When the Attorney-General ceased, a buzz arose in the court as if a cloud of great blue-flies were swarming about the prisoner, in anticipation of what he was soon to become. When toned down again, the unimpeachable patriot appeared in the witness-box.

Mr. Solicitor-General then, following his leader's lead, examined the patriot: John Barsad, gentleman, by name. The story of his pure soul was exactly what Mr. Attorney-General had described it to be—perhaps, if it had a fault, a little too exactly. Having released his noble bosom of its burden, he would have modestly withdrawn himself, but that the wigged gentleman with the papers before him, sitting not far from Mr. Lorry, begged to ask him a few questions. The wigged gentleman sitting opposite, still looking at the ceiling of the court.

Had he ever been a spy himself? No, he scorned the base insinuation. What did he live upon? His property. Where was his property? He didn't precisely remember where it was. What was it? No business of anybody's.

Had he inherited it? Yes, he had. From whom? Distant relation. Very distant? Rather. Ever been in prison? Certainly not. Never in a debtors' prison? Didn't see what that had to do with it. Never in a debtors' prison? —Come, once again. Never? Yes. How many times? Two or three times. Not five or six? Perhaps. Of what profession? Gentleman. Ever been kicked? Might have been. Frequently? No. Ever kicked down-stairs? Decidedly not; once received a kick on the top of a staircase, and fell down-stairs of his own accord. Kicked on that occasion for cheating at dice? Something to that effect was said by the intoxicated liar who committed the assault, but it was not true. Swear it was not true? Positively. Ever live by cheating at play? Never. Ever live by play? Not more than other gentlemen do. Ever borrow money of the prisoner? Yes. Ever pay him? No. Was not this intimacy with the prisoner, in reality a very slight one, forced upon the prisoner in coaches, inns, and packets? No. Sure he saw the prisoner with these lists? Certain. Knew no more about the lists? No. Had not procured them himself, for instance? No. Expect to get anything by this evidence? No. Not in regular government pay and employment, to lay traps? Oh dear no. Or to do anything? Oh dear no. Swear that? Over and over again. No motives but motives of sheer patriotism? None whatever.

The virtuous servant, Roger Cly, swore his way through the case at a great rate. He had taken service with the prisoner, in good faith and simplicity, four years ago. He had asked the prisoner, aboard the Calais packet, if he wanted a handy fellow, and the prisoner had engaged him. He had not asked the prisoner to take the handy fellow as an act of charity—never thought of such a thing. He began to have suspicions of the prisoner, and to keep an eye upon him, soon afterwads. In arranging his clothes, while travelling, he had seen similar lists to these in the prisoner's pockets, over and over again. He had taken these lists from the drawer of the prisoner's desk. He had not put them there first. He had seen the prisoner show these identical lists to French gentlemen at Calais, and similar lists to French gentlemen, both at Calais and Boulogne. He loved his country, and couldn't bear it, and had given information. He had never been suspected of stealing a silver tea-pot; he had been maligned respecting a mustard-pot, but it turned out to be only a plated one. He had known the last witness seven or eight years; that was merely a coincidence. He didn't call it a particularly curious coincidence; most coincidences were curious. Neither did he call it a curious coincidence that true patriotism was *his* only motive too. He was a true Briton, and hoped there were many like him.

The blue-flies buzzed again, and Mr. Attorney-General called Mr. Jarvis Lorry.

"Mr. Jarvis Lorry, are you a clerk in Tellson's bank?"

"I am."

"On a certain Friday night in November one thousand seven hundred and seventy-five, did business occasion you to travel between London and Dover by the mail?"

"It did."

"Were there any other passengers in the mail?"

"Two."

"Did they alight on the road in the course of the night?"

"They did."

"Mr. Lorry, look upon the prisoner. Was he one of those two passengers?"

"I cannot undertake to say that he was."

"Does he resemble either of these two passengers?"

"Both were so wrapped up, and the night was so dark, and we were all so reserved, that I cannot undertake to say even that."

"Mr. Lorry, look again upon the prisoner. Supposing him wrapped up as those two passengers were, is there anything in his bulk and stature to render it unlikely that he was one of them?"

"No."

"You will not swear, Mr. Lorry, that he was not one of them?"

"No."

"So at least you say he may have been one of them?"

"Yes. Except that I remember them both to have been —like myself—timorous of highwaymen, and the prisoner has not a timorous air."

"Did you ever see a counterfeit of timidity, Mr. Lorry?"

"I certainly have seen that."

"Mr. Lorry, look once more upon the prisoner. Have you seen him, to your certain knowledge, before?"

"I have."

"When?"

"I was returning from France a few days afterwards, and, at Calais, the prisoner came on board the packet-ship in which I returned, and made the voyage with me."

"At what hour did he come on board?"

"At a little after midnight."

"In the dead of the night. Was he the only passenger who came on board at that untimely hour?"

"He happened to be the only one."

"Never mind about 'happening,' Mr. Lorry. He was the only passenger who came on board in the dead of the night?"

"He was."

"Were you travelling alone, Mr. Lorry, or with any companion?"

"With two companions. A gentleman and lady. They are here."

"They are here. Had you any conversation with the prisoner?"

"Hardly any. The weather was stormy, and the passage long and rough, and I lay on a sofa, almost from shore to shore."

"Miss Manette!"

The young lady, to whom all eyes had been turned before, and were now turned again, stood up where she had sat. Her father rose with her, and kept her hand drawn through his arm.

"Miss Manette, look upon the prisoner."

To be confronted with such pity, and such earnest youth and beauty, was far more trying to the accused than to be confronted with all the crowd. Standing, as it were, apart with her on the edge of his grave, not all the staring curiosity that looked on, could, for the moment, nerve him to remain quite still. His hurried right hand parcelled out the herbs before him into imaginary beds of flowers in a garden; and his efforts to control and steady his breathing shook the lips from which the colour rushed to his heart. The buzz of the great flies was loud again.

"Miss Manette, have you seen the prisoner before?"

"Yes, sir."

"Where?"

"On board of the packet-ship just now referred to, sir, and on the same occasion."

"You are the young lady just now referred to?"

"O! most unhappily, I am!"

The plaintive tone of her compassion merged into the less musical voice of the Judge, as he said something fiercely: "Answer the questions put to you, and make no remark upon them."

"Miss Manette, had you any conversation with the prisoner on that passage across the Channel?"

"Yes, sir."

"Recall it."

In the midst of a profound stillness, she faintly began:

"When the gentleman came on board——"

"Do you mean the prisoner?" inquired the Judge, knitting his brows.

"Yes, my Lord."

"Then say the prisoner."

"When the prisoner came on board, he noticed that my father," turning her eyes lovingly to him as he stood beside her, "was much fatigued and in a very weak state of health. My father was so reduced that I was afraid to take him out of the air, and I had made a bed for him on the deck near the cabin steps, and I sat on the deck at his side to take care of him. There were no other passengers that night, but we four. The prisoner was so good as to beg permission to advise me how I could shelter my father from the wind and weather, better than I had done. I had not known how to do it well, not understanding how the wind would set when we were out of the harbour. He did it for me. He expressed great gentleness and kindness for my father's state, and I am sure he felt it. That was the manner of our beginning to speak together."

"Let me interrupt you for a moment. Had he come on board alone?"

"No."

"How many were with him?"

"Two French gentlemen."

"Had they conferred together?"

"They had conferred together until the last moment, when it was necessary for the French gentlemen to be landed in their boat."

"Had any papers been handed about among them, similar to these lists?"

"Some papers had been handed about among them, but I don't know what papers."

"Like these in shape and size?"

"Possibly, but indeed I don't know, although they stood whispering very near to me: because they stood at the top of the cabin steps to have the light of the lamp that was hanging there; it was a dull lamp, and they spoke very low, and I did not hear what they said, and saw only that they looked at papers."

"Now, to the prisoner's conversation, Miss Manette."

"The prisoner was as open in his confidence with me—which arose out of my helpless situation—as he was kind, and good, and useful to my father. I hope," bursting into tears, "I may not repay him by doing him harm to-day."

Buzzing from the blue-flies.

"Miss Manette, if the prisoner does not perfectly understand that you give the evidence which it is your duty to give—which you must give—and which you cannot escape from giving—with great unwillingness, he is the only person present in that condition. Please to go on."

"He told me that he was travelling on business of a delicate and difficult nature, which might get people into trouble, and that he was therefore travelling under an assumed name. He said that this business had, within a few days, taken him to France, and might, at intervals, take him backwards and forwards between France and England for a long time to come."

"Did he say anything about America, Miss Manette? Be particular."

"He tried to explain to me how that quarrel had arisen, and he said that, so far as he could judge, it was a wrong and foolish one on England's part. He added, in a jesting way, that perhaps George Washington might gain almost as great a name in history as George the Third. But there was no harm in his way of saying this: it was said laughingly, and to beguile the time."

Any strongly marked expression of face on the part of a chief actor in a scene of great interest to whom many eyes are directed, will be unconsciously imitated by the spectators. Her forehead was painfully anxious and intent as she gave this evidence, and, in the pauses when she stopped for the Judge to write it down, watched its effect upon the counsel for and against. Among the lookers-on there was the same expression in all quarters of the court; insomuch, that a great majority of the foreheads there, might have been mirrors reflecting the witness, when the Judge looked up from his notes to glare at that tremendous heresy about George Washington.

Mr. Attorney-General now signified to my Lord, that he deemed it necessary, as a matter of precaution and form, to call the young lady's father, Doctor Manette. Who was called accordingly.

"Doctor Manette, look upon the prisoner. Have you ever seen him before?"

"Once. When he called at my lodgings in London. Some three years, or three years and a half ago."

"Can you identify him as your fellow-passenger on board the packet, or speak to his conversation with your daughter?"

"Sir, I can do neither."

"Is there any particular and special reason for your being unable to do either?"

He answered, in a low voice, "There is."

"Has it been your misfortune to undergo a long imprisonment, without trial, or even accusation, in your native country, Doctor Manette?"

He answered, in a tone that went to every heart, "A long imprisonment."

"Were you newly released on the occasion in question?"

"They tell me so."

"Have you no remembrance of the occasion?"

"None. My mind is a blank, from some time—I cannot even say what time—when I employed myself, in my captivity, in making shoes, to the time when I found myself living in London with my dear daughter here. She had become familiar to me, when a gracious God restored my faculties; but, I am quite unable even to say how she had become familiar. I have no remembrance of the process."

Mr. Attorney-General sat down, and the father and daughter sat down together.

A singular circumstance then arose in the case. The object in hand being to show that the prisoner went down, with some fellow-plotter untracked, in the Dover mail on that Friday night in November five years ago, and got out of the mail in the night, as a blind, at a place where he did not remain, but from which he travelled back some dozen miles or more, to a garrison and dockyard, and there collected information; a witness was called to identify him as having been at the precise time required, in the coffee-room of an hotel in that garrison-and-dockyard town, waiting for another person. The prisoner's counsel was cross-examining this witness with no result, except that he had never seen the prisoner on any other occasion, when the wigged gentleman who had all this time been looking at the ceiling of the court, wrote a word or two on a little piece of paper, screwed it up, and tossed it to him. Opening this piece of paper in the next pause, the counsel looked with great attention and curiosity at the prisoner.

"You say again you are quite sure that it *was* the prisoner?"

The witness was quite sure.

"Did you ever see anybody very like the prisoner?"

Not so like (the witness said) as that he could be mistaken.

"Look well upon that gentleman, my learned friend there," pointing to him who had tossed the paper over, "and then look well upon the prisoner. How say you? Are they very like each other?"

Allowing for my learned friend's appearance being careless and slovenly if not debauched, they were sufficiently like each other to surprise, not only the witness, but everybody present, when they were thus brought into comparison. My Lord being prayed to bid my learned friend lay aside his wig, and giving no very gracious consent, the likeness became much more remarkable. My Lord inquired of Mr. Stryver (the prisoner's counsel), whether they were next to try Mr. Carton (name of my learned friend) for treason? But, Mr. Stryver replied to my Lord, no; but he would ask the witness to tell him whether what happened once, might happen twice; whether he would have been so confident if he had seen this illustration of his rashness sooner, whether he would be so confident, having seen it; and more. The upshot of which was, to smash this witness like a crockery vessel, and shiver his part of the case to useless lumber.

Mr. Cruncher had by this time taken quite a lunch of rust off his fingers in his following of the evidence. He had now to attend while Mr. Stryver fitted the prisoner's case on the jury, like a compact suit of clothes; showing them how the patriot, Barsad, was a hired spy and traitor, an unblushing trafficker in blood, and one of the greatest scoundrels upon earth since accursed Judas—which he certainly did look rather like. How the virtuous servant, Cly, was his friend and partner, and was worthy to be; how the watchful eyes of those forgers and false swearers had rested on the prisoner as a victim, because some family affairs in France, he being of French extraction, did require his making those passages across the Channel—though what those affairs were, a consideration for others who were near and dear to him, forbade him, even for his life, to disclose. How the evidence that had been warped and wrested from the young lady, whose anguish in giving it they had witnessed, came to nothing, involving the mere little innocent gallantries and politenesses likely to pass between any young gentleman and young lady so thrown together—with the exception of that reference to George Washington, which was altogether too extravagant and impossible to be regarded in any other light than as a monstrous joke. How it would be a weakness in the government to break down in this attempt to practise for popularity on the lowest national antipathies and fears, and therefore Mr. Attorney-General had made the most of it; how, nevertheless, it rested upon nothing, save that vile and infamous character of evidence too often disfiguring such cases, and of which the State Trials of this country were full. But, there my Lord interposed (with as grave a face as if it had not been true), saying that he could not sit upon that Bench and suffer those allusions.

Mr. Stryver then called his few witnesses, and Mr. Cruncher had next to attend while Mr. Attorney-General turned the whole suit of clothes Mr. Stryver had fitted on the jury, inside out; showing how Barsad and Cly were even a hundred times better than he had thought them, and the prisoner a hundred times worse. Lastly, came my Lord himself, turning the suit of clothes, now inside out, now outside in, but on the whole decidedly trimming and shaping them into grave-clothes for the prisoner.

And now, the jury turned to consider, and the great flies swarmed again.

Mr. Carton, who had so long sat looking at the ceiling of the court, changed neither his place nor his attitude, even in this excitement. While his learned friend, Mr. Stryver, massing his papers before him, whispered with those who sat near, and from time to time glanced anxiously at the jury; while all the spectators moved more or less, and grouped themselves anew; while even my Lord himself arose from his seat, and slowly paced up and down his platform, not unattended by a suspicion in the minds of the audience that his state was feverish; this one man sat leaning back, with his torn gown half off him, his untidy wig put on just as it had happened to light on his head after its removal, his hands in his pockets, and his eyes on the ceiling as they had been all day. Something especially reckless in his demeanour, not only gave him a disreputable look, but so diminished the strong resemblance he undoubtedly bore to the prisoner (which his momentary earnestness, when they were compared together, had strengthened), that many of the lookers-on, taking note of him now, said to one another they would hardly have thought the two were so alike. Mr. Cruncher made the observation to his next neighbour, and added, "I'd hold half a guinea that *he* don't get no law-work to do. Don't look like the sort of one to get any, do he?"

Yet, this Mr. Carton took in more of the details of the scene than he appeared to take in; for now, when Miss Manette's head dropped upon her father's breast, he was the first to see it, and to say audibly: "Officer! look to that young lady. Help the gentleman to take her out. Don't you see she will fall!"

There was much commiseration for her as she was removed, and much sympathy with her father. It had evidently been a great distress to him, to have the days of his imprisonment recalled. He had shown strong internal agitation when he was questioned, and that pondering or brooding look which made him old, had been upon him, like a heavy cloud, ever since. As he passed out, the jury, who had turned back and paused a moment, spoke, through their foreman.

They were not agreed, and wished to retire. My Lord (perhaps with George Washington on his mind) showed some surprise that they were not agreed, but signified his pleasure that they should retire under watch and ward, and retired himself. The trial had lasted all day, and the lamps in the court were now being lighted. It began to be rumoured that the jury would be out a long while. The spectators dropped off to get refreshment, and the prisoner withdrew to the back of the dock, and sat down.

Mr. Lorry, who had gone out when the young lady and her father went out, now reappeared, and beckoned to Jerry: who, in the slackened interest, could easily get near him.

"Jerry, if you wish to take something to eat, you can. But, keep in the way. You will be sure to hear when the jury come in. Don't be a moment behind them, for I want you to take the verdict back to the bank. You are the quickest messenger I know, and will get to Temple Bar long before I can."

Jerry had just enough forehead to knuckle, and he knuckled it in acknowledgment of this communication and a shilling. Mr. Carton came up at the moment, and touched Mr. Lorry on the arm.

"How is the young lady?"

"She is greatly distressed; but her father is comforting her, and she feels the better for being out of court."

"I'll tell the prisoner so. It won't do for a respectable bank gentleman like you, to be seen speaking to him publicly, you know."

Mr. Lorry reddened as if he were conscious of having debated the point in his mind, and Mr. Carton made his way to the outside of the bar. The way out of court lay in that direction, and Jerry followed him, all eyes, ears, and spikes.

"Mr. Darnay!"

The prisoner came forward directly.

"You will naturally be anxious to hear of the witness, Miss Manette. She will do very well. You have seen the worst of her agitation."

"I am deeply sorry to have been the cause of it. Could you tell her so for me, with my fervent acknowledgments?"

"Yes, I could. I will, if you ask it."

Mr. Carton's manner was so careless as to be almost insolent. He stood, half turned from the prisoner, lounging with his elbow against the bar.

"I do ask it. Accept my cordial thanks."

"What," said Carton, still only half turned towards him, "do you expect, Mr. Darnay?"

"The worst."

"It's the wisest thing to expect, and the likeliest. But I think their withdrawing is in your favour."

Loitering on the way out of court not being allowed, Jerry heard no more: but left them—so like each other in feature, so unlike each other in manner—standing side by side, both reflected in the glass above them.

An hour and a half limped heavily away in the thief-and-rascal crowded passages below, even though assisted off with mutton pies and ale. The hoarse messenger, uncomfortably seated on a form after taking that refection, had dropped into a doze, when a loud murmur and a rapid tide of people setting up the stairs that led to the court, carried him along with them.

"Jerry! Jerry!" Mr. Lorry was already calling at the door when he got there.

"Here, sir! It's a fight to get back again. Here I am, sir!"

Mr. Lorry handed him a paper through the throng. "Quick! Have you got it?"

"Yes, sir."

Hastily written on the paper was the word "ACQUITTED."

"If you had sent the message, 'Recalled to Life,' again," muttered Jerry, as he turned, "I should have known what you meant, this time."

He had no opportunity of saying, or so much as thinking, anything else, until he was clear of the Old Bailey; for, the crowd came pouring out with a vehemence that nearly took him off his legs, and a loud buzz swept into the street as if the baffled blue-flies were dispersing in search of other carrion.

CHAPTER IV.

CONGRATULATORY.

FROM the dimly-lighted passages of the court, the last sediment of the human stew that had been boiling there all day, was straining off, when Doctor Manette, Lucie Manette, his daughter, Mr. Lorry, the solicitor for the defence, and its counsel, Mr. Stryver, stood gathered round Mr. Charles Darnay—just released—congratulating him on his escape from death.

It would have been difficult by a far brighter light, to recognise in Doctor Manette, intellectual of face and upright of bearing, the shoemaker of the garret in Paris. Yet, no one could have looked at him twice, without looking again: even though the opportunity of observation had not extended to the mournful cadence of his low grave voice, and to the abstraction that overclouded him fitfully, without any apparent reason. While one external cause, and that a reference to his long lingering agony, would always—as on the trial—evoke this condition from the depths of his soul, it was also in its nature to arise of itself, and to draw a gloom over him, as incomprehensible to those unacquainted with his story as if they had seen the shadow of the actual Bastille thrown upon him by a summer sun, when the substance was three hundred miles away.

Only his daughter had the power of charming this black brooding from his mind. She was the golden thread that united him to a Past beyond his misery, and to a Present beyond his misery: and the sound of her voice, the light of her face, the touch of her hand, had a strong beneficial influence with him almost always. Not absolutely always, for she could recall some occasions on which her power had failed; but they were few and slight, and she believed them over.

Mr. Darnay had kissed her hand fervently and gratefully, and had turned to Mr. Stryver, whom he warmly thanked. Mr. Stryver, a man of little more than thirty, but looking twenty years older than he was, stout, loud, red, bluff, and free from any drawback of delicacy, had a pushing way of shouldering himself (morally and physically) into companies and conversations, that argued well for his shouldering his way up in life.

He still had his wig and gown on, and he said, squaring himself at his late client to that degree that he squeezed the innocent Mr. Lorry clean out of the group: "I am glad to have brought you off with honour, Mr. Darnay. It was an infamous prosecution, grossly infamous; but not the less likely to succeed on that account."

"You have laid me under an obligation to you for life—in two senses," said his late client, taking his hand.

"I have done my best for you, Mr. Darnay; and my best is as good as another man's, I believe."

It clearly being incumbent on some one to say, "Much better," Mr. Lorry said it; perhaps not quite disinterestedly, but with the interested object of squeezing himself back again.

"You think so?" said Mr. Stryver. "Well! you have been present all day, and you ought to know. You are a man of business, too."

"And as such," quoth Mr. Lorry, whom the counsel learned in the law had now shouldered back into the group, just as he had previously shouldered him out of it—"as such I will appeal to Doctor Manette, to break up this conference and order us all to our homes. Miss Lucie looks ill, Mr. Darnay has had a terrible day, we are worn out."

"Speak for yourself, Mr. Lorry," said Stryver; "I have a night's work to do yet. Speak for yourself."

"I speak for myself," answered Mr. Lorry, "and for Mr. Darnay, and for Miss Lucie, and——Miss Lucie, do you not think I may speak for us all?" He asked her the question pointedly, and with a glance at her father.

His face had become frozen, as it were, in a very curious look at Darnay: an intent look, deepening into a frown of dislike and distrust, not even unmixed with fear. With this strange expression on him his thoughts had wandered away.

"My father," said Lucie, softly laying her hand on his. He slowly shook the shadow off, and turned to her.

"Shall we go home, my father?"

With a long breath, he answered "Yes."

The friends of the acquitted prisoner had dispersed, under the impression—which he himself had originated—that he would not be released that night. The lights were nearly all extinguished in the passages, the iron gates were being closed with a jar and a rattle, and the dismal place was deserted until to-morrow morning's interest of gallows, pillory, whipping-post, and branding-iron, should repeople it. Walking between her father and Mr. Darnay, Lucie Manette passed into the open air. A hackney-coach was called, and the father and daughter departed in it.

Mr. Stryver had left them in the passages, to shoulder his way back to the robing-room. Another person, who had not joined the group, or interchanged a word with any one of them, but who had been leaning against the wall where its shadow was darkest, had silently strolled out after the rest, and had looked on until the coach drove away. He now stepped up to where Mr. Lorry and Mr. Darnay stood upon the pavement.

"So, Mr. Lorry! Men of business may speak to Mr. Darnay now?"

Nobody had made any acknowledgment of Mr. Carton's part in the day's proceedings; nobody had known of it. He was unrobed, and was none the better for it in appearance.

"If you knew what a conflict goes on in the business mind, when the business mind is divided between good-natured impulse and business appearances, you would be amused, Mr. Darnay."

Mr. Lorry reddened, and said, warmly, "You have mentioned that before, sir. We men of business, who serve a House, are not our own masters. We have to think of the House more than ourselves."

"*I* know, *I* know," rejoined Mr. Carton, carelessly. "Don't be nettled, Mr. Lorry. You are as good as another, I have no doubt: better, I dare say."

"And indeed, sir," pursued Mr. Lorry, not minding him, "I really don't know what you have to do with the matter. If you'll excuse me, as very much your elder, for saying so, I really don't know that it is your business."

"Business! Bless you, *I* have no business," said Mr. Carton.

"It is a pity you have not, sir."

"I think so, too."

"If you had," pursued Mr. Lorry, "perhaps you would attend to it."

"Lord love you, no!—I shouldn't," said Mr. Carton.

"Well, sir!" cried Mr. Lorry, thoroughly heated by his indifference, "business is a very good thing, and a very respectable thing. And, sir, if business imposes its restraints and its silences and impediments, Mr. Darnay as a young gentleman of generosity knows how to make allowance for that circumstance. Mr. Darnay, good night, God bless you, sir! I hope you have been this day preserved for a prosperous and happy life.—Chair there!"

Perhaps a little angry with himself, as well as with the barrister, Mr. Lorry bustled into the chair, and was carried off to Tellson's. Carton, who smelt of port wine, and did not appear to be quite sober, laughed then, and turned to Darnay:

"This is a strange chance that throws you and me together. This must be a strange night to you, standing alone here with your counterpart on these street stones?"

"I hardly seem yet," returned Charles Darnay, "to belong to this world again."

"I don't wonder at it; it's not so long since you were pretty far advanced on your way to another. You speak faintly."

"I begin to think I *am* faint."

"Then why the devil don't you dine? I dined, myself, while those numskulls were deliberating which world you should belong to—this, or some other. Let me show you the nearest tavern to dine well at."

Drawing his arm through his own, he took him down Ludgate-hill to Fleet-street, and so, up a covered way, into a tavern. Here, they were shown into a little room, where Charles Darnay was soon recruiting his strength with a good plain dinner and good wine: while Carton sat opposite to him at the same table, with his separate bottle of port before him, and his fully half-insolent manner upon him.

"Do you feel, yet, that you belong to this terrestrial scheme again, Mr. Darnay?"

"I am frightfully confused regarding time and place; but I am so far mended as to feel that."

"It must be an immense satisfaction!"

He said it bitterly, and filled up his glass again: which was a large one.

"As to me, the greatest desire I have, is to forget that I belong to it. It has no good in it for me—except wine like this—nor I for it. So we are not much alike in that particular. Indeed, I begin to think we are not much alike in any particular, you and I."

Confused by the emotion of the day, and feeling his being there with this Double of coarse deportment, to be like a dream, Charles Darnay was at a loss how to answer; finally, answered not at all.

"Now your dinner is done," Carton presently said, "why don't you call a health, Mr. Darnay; why don't you give your toast?"

"What health? What toast?"

"Why, it's on the tip of your tongue. It ought to be, it must be, I'll swear it's there."

"Miss Manette, then!"

"Miss Manette, then!"

Looking his companion full in the face while he drank the toast, Carton flung his glass over his shoulder against the wall, where it shivered to pieces; then, rang the bell, and ordered in another.

"That's a fair young lady to hand to a coach in the dark, Mr. Darnay!" he said, filling his new goblet.

A slight frown and a laconic "Yes," were the answer.

"That's a fair young lady to be pitied by and wept for by! How does it feel? Is it worth being tried for one's life, to be the object of such sympathy and compassion, Mr. Darnay?"

Again Darnay answered not a word.

"She was mightily pleased to have your message, when I gave it her. Not that she showed she was pleased, but I suppose she was."

The allusion served as a timely reminder to Darnay that this disagreeable companion had, of his own free will, assisted him in the strait of the day. He turned the dialogue to that point, and thanked him for it.

"I neither want any thanks, nor merit any," was the careless rejoinder. "It was nothing to do, in the first place; and I don't know why I did it, in the second. Mr. Darnay, let me ask you a question."

"Willingly, and a small return for your good offices."

"Do you think I particularly like you?"

"Really, Mr. Carton," returned the other, oddly disconcerted, "I have not asked myself the question."

"But ask yourself the question now."

"You have acted as if you do; but I don't think you do."

"*I* don't think I do," said Carton. "I begin to have a very good opinion of your understanding."

"Nevertheless," pursued Darnay, rising to ring the bell, "there is nothing in that, I hope, to prevent my calling the reckoning, and our parting without ill-blood on either side."

Carton rejoining, "Nothing in life!" Darnay rang. "Do you call the whole reckoning?" said Carton. On his answering in the affirmative, "Then bring me another pint of this same wine, drawer, and come and wake me at ten."

The bill being paid, Charles Darnay rose and wished him good night. Without returning the wish, Carton rose too, with something of a threat of defiance in his manner, and said, "A last word, Mr. Darnay: you think I am drunk?"

"I think you have been drinking, Mr. Carton."

"Think? You know I have been drinking."

"Since I must say so, I know it."

"Then you shall likewise know why. I am a disappointed drudge, sir. I care for no man on earth, and no man on earth cares for me."

"Much to be regretted. You might have used your talents better."

"May be so, Mr. Darnay; may be not. Don't let your sober face elate you, however; you don't know what it may come to. Good night!"

When he was left alone, this strange being took up a candle, went to a glass that hung against the wall, and surveyed himself minutely in it.

"Do you particularly like the man?" he muttered, at his own image; "why should you particularly like a man who resembles you? There is nothing in you to like; you

know that. Ah, confound you! What a change you have made in yourself! A good reason for taking to a man, that he shows you what you have fallen away from, and what you might have been! Change places with him, and would you have been looked at by those blue eyes as he was, and commiserated by that agitated face as he was? Come on, and have it out in plain words! You hate the fellow."

He resorted to his pint of wine for consolation, drank it all in a few minutes, and fell asleep on his arms, with his hair straggling over the table, and a long winding-sheet in the candle dripping down upon him.

CHAPTER V.

THE JACKAL.

THOSE were drinking days, and most men drank hard. So very great is the improvement Time has brought about in such habits, that a moderate statement of the quantity of wine and punch which one man would swallow in the course of a night, without any detriment to his reputation as a perfect gentleman, would seem, in these days, a ridiculous exaggeration. The learned profession of the law was certainly not behind any other learned profession in its Bacchanalian propensities; neither was Mr. Stryver, already fast shouldering his way to a large and lucrative practice, behind his compeers in this particular, any more than in the drier parts of the legal race.

A favourite at the Old Bailey, and eke at the Sessions, Mr. Stryver had begun cautiously to hew away the lower staves of the ladder on which he mounted. Sessions and Old Bailey had now to summon their favourite, specially, to their longing arms; and shouldering itself towards the visage of the Lord Chief Justice in the Court of King's Bench, the florid countenance of Mr. Stryver might be daily seen, bursting out of the bed of wigs, like a great sunflower pushing its way at the sun from among a rank garden-full of flaring companions.

It had once been noted at the Bar, that while Mr. Stryver was a glib man, and an unscrupulous, and a ready, and a bold, he had not that faculty of extracting the essence from a heap of statements, which is among the most striking and necessary of the advocate's accomplishments. But, a remarkable improvement came upon him as to this. The more business he got, the greater his power seemed to grow of getting at its pith and marrow; and however late at night he sat carousing with Sydney Carton, he always had his points at his fingers' ends in the morning.

Sydney Carton, idlest and most unpromising of men, was Stryver's great ally. What the two drank together, between Hilary Term and Michaelmas, might have floated a king's ship. Stryver never had a case in hand, anywhere, but Carton was there, with his hands in his pockets, staring at the ceiling of the court; they went the same Circuit, and even there they prolonged their usual orgies late into the night, and Carton was rumoured to be seen at broad day, going home stealthily and unsteadily to his lodgings, like a dissipated cat. At last, it began to get about, among such as were interested in the matter, that although Sydney Carton would never be a lion, he was an amazingly good jackal, and that he rendered suit and service to Stryver in that humble capacity.

"Ten o'clock, sir," said the man at the tavern, whom he had charged to wake him—"ten o'clock, sir."

" *What's* the matter?"

"Ten o'clock, sir."

"What do you mean? Ten o'clock at night?"

"Yes, sir. Your honour told me to call you."

"Oh! I remember. Very well, very well."

After a few dull efforts to get to sleep again, which the man dexterously combated by stirring the fire continuously for five minutes, he got up, tossed his hat on, and walked out. He turned into the Temple, and, having revived himself by twice pacing the pavements of King's Bench-walk and Paper-buildings, turned into the Stryver chambers.

The Stryver clerk, who never assisted at these conferences, had gone home, and the Stryver principal opened the door. He had his slippers on, and a loose bed-gown, and his throat was bare for his greater ease. He had that rather wild, strained, seared marking about the eyes, which may be observed in all free livers of his class, from the portrait of Jeffries downward, and which can be traced, under various disguises of Art, through the portraits of every Drinking Age.

"You are a little late, Memory," said Stryver.

"About the usual time; it may be a quarter of an hour later."

They went into a dingy room lined with books and littered with papers, where there was a blazing fire. A kettle steamed upon the hob, and in the midst of the wreck of papers a table shone, with plenty of wine upon it, and brandy, and rum, and sugar, and lemons.

"You have had your bottle, I perceive, Sydney."

"Two to-night, I think. I have been dining with the day's client; or seeing him dine—it's all one!"

"That was a rare point, Sydney, that you brought to bear upon the identification. How did you come by it? When did it strike you?"

"I thought he was rather a handsome fellow, and I thought I should have been much the same sort of fellow, if I had had any luck."

Mr. Stryver laughed till he shook his precocious paunch.

"You and your luck, Sydney! Get to work, get to work."

Sullenly enough, the jackal loosened his dress, went into an adjoining room, and came back with a large jug of cold water, a basin, and a towel or two. Steeping the towels in the water, and partially wringing them out, he folded them on his head in a manner hideous to behold, sat down at the table, and said, "Now I am ready!"

"Not much boiling down to be done to-night, Memory," said Mr. Stryver, gaily, as he looked among his papers.

"How much?"

"Only two sets of them."

"Give me the worst first."

"There they are, Sydney. Fire away!"

The lion then composed himself on his back on a sofa on one side of the drinking-table, while the jackal sat at his own paper-bestrewn table proper, on the other side of it, with the bottles and glasses ready to his hand. Both resorted to the drinking-table without stint, but each in a different way; the lion for the most part reclining with his hands in his waistband, looking at the fire, or occasionally flirting with some lighter document; the jackal, with knitted brows and intent face, so deep in his task, that his eyes did not even follow the hand he stretched out for his glass—which often groped about, for a minute or more, before it found the glass for his lips. Two or three times, the matter in hand became so knotty, that the jackal found it imperative on him to get up, and steep his towels anew. From these pilgrimages to the jug and basin, he returned with such eccentricities of damp head-gear as no words can describe; which were made the more ludicrous by his anxious gravity.

At length the jackal had got together a compact repast for the lion and proceeded to offer it to him. The lion took it with care and caution, made his selections from it, and his remarks upon it, and the jackal assisted both. When the repast was fully discussed, the lion put his hands in his waistband again, and lay down to meditate. The jackal then invigorated himself with a bumper for his throttle, and a fresh application to his head, and applied himself to the collection of a second meal; this was administered to the lion in the same manner, and was not disposed of until the clocks struck three in the morning.

"And now we have done, Sydney, fill a bumper of punch," said Mr. Stryver.

The jackal removed the towels from his head, which had been steaming again, shook himself, yawned, shivered, and complied.

"You were very sound, Sydney, in the matter of those crown witnesses to-day. Every question told."

"I always am sound; am I not?"

"I don't gainsay it. What has roughened your temper? Put some punch to it and smooth it again."

With a deprecatory grunt, the jackal again complied.

"The old Sydney Carton of old Shrewsbury School," said Stryver, nodding his head over him as he reviewed him in the present and the past, "the old seesaw Sydney. Up one minute and down the next; now in spirits and now in despondency!"

"Ah!" returned the other, sighing: "yes! The same Sydney, with the same luck. Even then, I did exercises for other boys, and seldom did my own."

"And why not?"

"God knows. It was my way, I suppose."

He sat, with his hands in his pockets and his legs stretched out before him, looking at the fire.

"Carton," said his friend, squaring himself at him with a bullying air, as if the fire-grate had been the furnace in which sustained endeavour was forged, and the one delicate thing to be done for the old Sydney Carton of old Shrewsbury School was to shoulder him into it, "your way is, and always was, a lame way. You summon no energy and purpose. Look at me."

"Oh, botheration!" returned Sydney, with a lighter and more good-humoured laugh, "don't *you* be moral!"

"How have I done what I have done?" said Stryver; "how do I do what I do?"

"Partly through paying me to help you, I suppose. But it's not worth your while to apostrophise me, or the air, about it; what you want to do, you do. You were always in the front rank, and I was always behind."

"I had to get into the front rank; I was not born there, was I?"

"I was not present at the ceremony; but my opinion is you were," said Carton. At this, he laughed again, and they both laughed.

"Before Shrewsbury, and at Shrewsbury, and ever since Shrewsbury," pursued Carton, "you have fallen into your rank, and I have fallen into mine. Even when we were fellow-students in the Student-Quarter of Paris, picking up French, and French law, and other French crumbs that we didn't get much good of, you were always somewhere, and I was always—nowhere."

"And whose fault was that?"

"Upon my soul, I am not sure that it was not yours. You were always driving and driving and shouldering and passing, to that restless degree that I had no chance for my life but in rust and repose. It's a gloomy thing, however, to talk about one's own past, with the day breaking. Turn me in some other direction before I go."

"Well then! Pledge me to the pretty witness," said Stryver, holding up his glass. "Are you turned in a pleasant direction?"

Apparently not, for he became gloomy again.

"Pretty witness," he muttered, looking down into his glass. "I have had enough of witnesses to-day and tonight; who's your pretty witness?"

"The picturesque doctor's daughter, Miss Manette."

"*She* pretty?"

"Is she not?"

"No."

"Why, man alive, she was the admiration of the whole Court!"

"Rot the admiration of the whole Court! Who made the Old Bailey a judge of beauty? She was a golden-haired doll!"

"Do you know, Sydney," said Mr. Stryver, looking at him with sharp eyes, and slowly drawing a hand across his florid face: "do you know, I rather thought, at the time, that you sympathised with the golden-haired doll, and were quick to see what happened to the golden-haired doll?"

"Quick to see what happened! If a girl, doll or no doll, swoons within a yard or two of a man's nose, he can see it without a perspective-glass. I pledge you, but I deny the beauty. And now I'll have no more drink; I'll get to bed."

When his host followed him out on the staircase with a candle, to light him down the stairs, the day was coldly looking in through its grimy windows. When he got out of the house, the air was cold and sad, the dull sky overcast, the river dark and dim, the whole scene like a lifeless desert. And wreaths of dust were spinning round and round before the morning blast, as if the desert-sand had risen far away, and the first spray of it in its advance had begun to overwhelm the city.

Waste forces within him, and a desert all around, this man stood still on his way across a silent terrace, and saw for a moment, lying in the wilderness before him, a mirage of honourable ambition, self-denial, and perseverance. In the fair city of this vision, there were airy galleries from which the loves and graces looked upon him, gardens in which the fruits of life hung ripening, waters of Hope that sparkled in his sight. A moment, and it was gone. Climbing to a high chamber in a well of houses, he threw himself down in his clothes on a neglected bed, and its pillow was wet with wasted tears.

Sadly, sadly, the sun rose; it rose upon no sadder sight than the man of good abilities and good emotions, incapable of their directed exercise, incapable of his own help and his own happiness, sensible of the blight on him, and resigning himself to let it eat him away.

CHAPTER VI.
HUNDREDS OF PEOPLE.

THE quiet lodgings of Doctor Manette were in a quiet street-corner not far from Soho-square. On the afternoon of a certain fine Sunday when the waves of four months had rolled over the trial for treason, and carried it, as to the public interest and memory, far out to sea, Mr. Jarvis Lorry walked along the sunny streets from Clerkenwell where he lived, on his way to dine with the Doctor. After several relapses into business-absorption, Mr. Lorry had become the Doctor's friend, and the quiet street-corner was the sunny part of his life.

On this certain fine Sunday, Mr. Lorry walked towards Soho, early in the afternoon, for three reasons of habit. Firstly, because, on fine Sundays, he often walked out, before dinner, with the Doctor and Lucie; secondly, because, on unfavourable Sundays, he was accustomed to be with them as the family friend, talking, reading, looking out of window, and generally getting through the day; thirdly, because he happened to have his own little shrewd doubts to solve, and knew how the ways of the Doctor's household pointed to that time as a likely time for solving them.

A quainter corner than the corner where the Doctor lived, was not to be found in London. There was no way through it, and the front windows of the Doctor's lodgings commanded a pleasant little vista of street that had a congenial air of retirement on it. There were few buildings then, north of the Oxford-road, and forest-trees flourished, and wild flowers grew, and the hawthorn blossomed, in the now vanished fields. As a consequence, country airs circulated in Soho with vigorous freedom, instead of languishing into the parish like stray paupers without a settlement; and there was many a good south wall, not far off, on which the peaches ripened in their season.

The summer light struck into the corner brilliantly in the earlier part of the day; but, when the streets grew hot, the corner was in shadow, though not in shadow so remote but that you could see beyond it into a glare of brightness. It was a cool spot, staid but cheerful, a wonderful place for echoes, and a very harbour from the raging streets.

There ought to have been a tranquil bark in such an anchorage, and there was. The Doctor occupied two floors of a large still house, where several callings purported to be pursued by day, but whereof little was audible any day, and which was shunned by all of them at night. In a building at the back, attainable by a court-yard where a plane-tree rustled its green leaves, church-organs claimed to be made, and silver to be chased, and likewise gold to be beaten by some mysterious giant who had a golden arm starting out of the wall of the front hall—as if he had beaten himself precious, and menaced a similar conversion of all visitors. Very little of these trades, or of a lonely lodger rumoured to live upstairs, or of a dim coach-trimming maker asserted to have a counting-house below, was ever heard or seen. Occasionally, a stray workman putting his coat on, traversed the hall, or a stranger peered about there, or a distant clink was heard across the court-yard, or a thump from the golden giant. These, however, were only the exceptions required to prove the rule that the sparrows in the plane-tree behind the house, and the echoes in the corner before it, had their own way from Sunday morning unto Saturday night.

Doctor Manette received such patients here as his old reputation, and its revival in the floating whispers of his story, brought him. His scientific knowledge, and his vigilance and skill in conducting ingenious experiments, brought him otherwise into moderate request, and he earned as much as he wanted.

These things were within Mr. Jarvis Lorry's knowledge, thoughts, and notice, when he rang the door-bell of the tranquil house in the corner, on the fine Sunday afternoon.

"Doctor Manette at home?"

Expected home.

"Miss Lucie at home?"

Expected home.

"Miss Pross at home?"

Possibly at home, but of a certainty impossible for hand-maid to anticipate intentions of Miss Pross, as to admission or denial of the fact.

"As I am at home myself," said Mr. Lorry, "I'll go up-stairs."

Although the Doctor's daughter had known nothing of the country of her birth, she appeared to have innately de-rived from it that ability to make much of little means, which is one of its most useful and most agreeable charac-teristics. Simple as the furniture was, it was set off by so many little adornments, of no value but for their taste and fancy, that its effect was delightful. The disposition of everything in the rooms, from the largest object to the least; the arrangement of colours, the elegant variety and contrast obtained by thrift in trifles, by delicate hands, clear eyes, and good sense; were at once so pleasant in themselves, and so expressive of their originator, that, as Mr. Lorry stood looking about him, the very chairs and tables seemed to ask him, with something of that peculiar expression which he knew so well by this time, whether he approved?

There were three rooms on a floor, and, the doors by which they communicated being put open that the air might pass freely through them all, Mr. Lorry, smilingly observ-ant of that fanciful resemblance which he detected all around him, walked from one to another. The first was the best room, and in it were Lucie's birds, and flowers, and books, and desk, and work-table, and box of water-colours; the second was the Doctor's consulting-room, used also as the dining-room; the third, changingly speckled by the rustle of the plane-tree in the yard, was the Doctor's bed-room, and there, in a corner, stood the disused shoe-maker's bench and tray of tools, much as it had stood on the fifth floor of the dismal house by the wine-shop, in the suburb of Saint Antoine in Paris.

"I wonder," said Mr. Lorry, pausing in his looking about, "that he keeps that reminder of his sufferings about him!"

"And why wonder at that?" was the abrupt inquiry that made him start.

It proceeded from Miss Pross, the wild red woman, strong of hand, whose acquaintance he had first made at the Royal George Hotel at Dover, and had since improved.

"I should have thought——" Mr. Lorry began.

"Pooh! You'd have thought!" said Miss Pross; and Mr. Lorry left off.

"How do you do?" inquired that lady then—sharply, and yet as if to express that she bore him no malice.

"I am pretty well, I thank you," answered Mr. Lorry, with meekness; "how are you?"

"Nothing to boast of," said Miss Pross.

"Indeed?"

"Ah! indeed!" said Miss Pross. "I am very much put out about my Ladybird."

"Indeed?"

"For gracious sake say something else besides 'indeed,' or you'll fidget me to death," said Miss Pross: whose character (dissociated from stature) was shortness.

"Really, then?" said Mr. Lorry, as an amendment.

"Really, is bad enough," returned Miss Pross, "but bet-ter. Yes, I am very much put out."

"May I ask the cause?"

"I don't want dozens of people who are not at all worthy of Ladybird, to come here looking after her," said Miss Pross.

"Do dozens come for that purpose?"

"Hundreds," said Miss Pross.

It was characteristic of this lady (as of some other peo-ple before her time and since) that whenever her original proposition was questioned, she exaggerated it.

"Dear me!" said Mr. Lorry, as the safest remark he could think of.

"I have lived with the darling—or the darling has lived with me, and paid me for it; which she certainly should never have done, you may take your affidavit, if I could have afforded to keep either myself or her for nothing—since she was ten years old. And it's really very hard," said Miss Pross.

Not seeing with precision what was very hard, Mr. Lorry shook his head; using that important part of himself as a sort of fairy cloak that would fit anything.

"All sorts of people who are not in the least degree worthy of the pet, are always turning up," said Miss Pross. "When you began it——"

"I began it, Miss Pross?"

"Didn't you? Who brought her father to life?"

"Oh! If that was beginning it——" said Mr. Lorry.

"It wasn't ending it, I suppose? I say, when you be-gan it, it was hard enough; not that I have any fault to find with Doctor Manette, except that he is not worthy of such a daughter, which is no imputation on him, for it was not to be expected that anybody should be, under any cir-cumstances. But it really is doubly and trebly hard to have crowds and multitudes of people turning up after him (I could have forgiven him), to take Ladybird's affections away from me."

Mr. Lorry knew Miss Pross to be very jealous, but he also knew her by this time to be, beneath the surface of her eccentricity, one of those unselfish creatures—found only among women—who will, for pure love and admiration, bind themselves willing slaves, to youth when they have lost it, to beauty that they never had, to accomplishments that they were never fortunate enough to gain, to bright hopes that never shone upon their own sombre lives. He knew enough of the world to know that there is nothing in it better than the faithful service of the heart; so rendered and so free from any mercenary taint, he had such an ex-alted respect for it, that in the retributive arrangements made by his own mind—we all make such arrangements, more or less—he stationed Miss Pross much nearer to the lower Angels than many ladies immeasurably better got up both by Nature and Art, who had balances at Tellson's.

"There never was, nor will be, but one man worthy of Ladybird," said Miss Pross; "and that was my brother Solomon, if he hadn't made a mistake in life."

Here again: Mr. Lorry's inquiries into Miss Pross's personal history had established the fact that her brother Solomon was a heartless scoundrel who had stripped her of everything she possessed, as a stake to speculate with, and had abandoned her in her poverty for evermore, with no touch of compunction. Miss Pross's fidelity of belief in Solomon (deducting a mere trifle for this slight mistake) was quite a serious matter with Mr. Lorry, and had its weight in his good opinion of her.

"As we happen to be alone for the moment, and are both people of business," he said, when they had got back to the drawing-room and had sat down there in friendly relations, "let me ask you—does the Doctor, in talking with Lucie, never refer to the shoemaking time, yet?"

"Never."

"And yet keeps that bench and those tools beside him?"

"Ah!" returned Miss Pross, shaking her head. "But I don't say he don't refer to it within himself."

"Do you believe that he thinks of it much?"

"I do," said Miss Pross.

"Do you imagine——" Mr. Lorry had begun, when Miss Pross took him up short with:

"Never imagine anything. Have no imagination at all."

"I stand corrected; do you suppose—you go so far as to suppose, sometimes?"

"Now and then," said Miss Pross.

"Do you suppose," Mr. Lorry went on, with a laughing twinkle in his bright eye, as it looked kindly at her, "that Doctor Manette has any theory of his own, preserved through all those years, relative to the cause of his being so oppressed; perhaps, even to the name of his oppressor?"

"I don't suppose anything about it but what Ladybird tells me."

"And that is——?"

"That she thinks he has."

"Now don't be angry at my asking all these questions; because I am a mere dull man of business, and you are a woman of business."

"Dull?" Miss Pross inquired, with placidity.

Rather wishing his modest adjective away, Mr. Lorry replied, "No, no, no. Surely not. To return to business:— Is it not remarkable that Doctor Manette, unquestionably innocent of any crime as we are all well assured he is, should never touch upon that question? I will not say with me, though he had business relations with me many years ago, and we are now intimate; I will say with the fair daughter to whom he is so devotedly attached, and who is so devotedly attached to him? Believe me, Miss Pross, I don't approach the topic with you, out of curiosity, but out of zealous interest."

"Well! To the best of my understanding, and bad's the best, you'll tell me," said Miss Pross, softened by the tone of the apology, "he is afraid of the whole subject."

"Afraid?"

"It's plain enough, I should think, why he may be. It's a dreadful remembrance. Besides that, his loss of himself grew out of it. Not knowing how he lost himself, or how he recovered himself, he may never feel certain of not losing himself again. That alone wouldn't make the subject pleasant, I should think."

It was a profounder remark than Mr. Lorry had looked for. "True," said he, "and fearful to reflect upon. Yet, a doubt lurks in my mind, Miss Pross, whether it is good for Doctor Manette to have that suppression always shut up within him. Indeed, it is this doubt and the uneasiness it sometimes causes me that has led me to our present confidence."

"Can't be helped," said Miss Pross, shaking her head. "Touch that string, and he instantly changes for the worse. Better leave it alone. In short, must leave it alone, like or no like. Sometimes, he gets up in the dead of the night, and will be heard, by us overhead there, walking up and down, walking up and down, in his room. Ladybird has learnt to know then that his mind is walking up and down, walking up and down, in his old prison. She hurries to him, and they go on together, walking up and down, walking up and down, until he is composed. But he never says a word of the true reason of his restlessness, to her, and she finds it best not to hint at it to him. In silence they go walking up and down together, walking up and down together, till her love and company have brought him to himself."

Notwithstanding Miss Pross's denial of her own imagination, there was a perception of the pain of being monotonously haunted by one sad idea, in her repetition of the phrase, walking up and down, which testified to her possessing such a thing.

The corner has been mentioned as a wonderful corner for echoes; it had begun to echo so resoundingly to the tread of coming feet, that it seemed as though the very mention of that weary pacing to and fro had set it going.

"Here they are!" said Miss Pross, rising to break up the conference; "and now we shall have hundreds of people pretty soon!"

It was such a curious corner in its acoustical properties, such a peculiar Ear of a place, that as Mr. Lorry stood at the open window, looking for the father and daughter whose steps he heard, he fancied they would never approach. Not only would the echoes die away, as though the steps had gone; but, echoes of other steps that never came would be heard in their stead, and would die away for good when they seemed close at hand. However, father and daughter did at last appear, and Miss Pross was ready at the street door to receive them.

Miss Pross was a pleasant sight, albeit wild, and red, and grim, taking off her darling's bonnet when she came up-stairs, and touching it up with the ends of her handkerchief, and blowing the dust off it, and folding her mantle ready for laying by, and smoothing her rich hair with as much pride as she could possibly have taken in her own hair if she had been the vainest and handsomest of women. Her darling was a pleasant sight too, embracing her and thanking her, and protesting against her taking so much trouble for her—which last she only dared to do playfully, or Miss Pross, sorely hurt, would have retired to her own chamber and cried. The Doctor was a pleasant sight too, looking on at them, and telling Miss Pross how she spoilt Lucie, in accents and with eyes that had as much spoiling in them as Miss Pross had, and would have had more if it were possible. Mr. Lorry was a pleasant sight too, beaming at all this in his little wig, and thanking his bachelor stars for having lighted him in his declining years to a Home. But, no Hundreds of people came to see the sights, and Mr. Lorry looked in vain for the fulfilment of Miss Pross's prediction.

Dinner-time, and still no Hundreds of people. In the arrangements of the little household, Miss Pross took charge of the lower regions, and always acquitted herself marvellously. Her dinners, of a very modest quality, were so well-cooked and so well served, and so neat in their contrivances, half English and half French, that nothing could be better. Miss Pross's friendship being of the thoroughly practical kind, she had ravaged Soho and the adjacent provinces, in search of impoverished French, who, tempted by shillings and half-crowns, would impart culinary mysteries to her. From these decayed sons and daughters of Gaul, she had acquired such wonderful arts, that the woman and girl who formed the staff of domestics regarded her as quite a Sorceress, or Cinderella's Godmother: who would send out for a fowl, a rabbit, a vegetable or two from the garden, and change them into anything she pleased.

On Sundays, Miss Pross dined at the Doctor's table, but on other days persisted in taking her meals at unknown periods, either in the lower regions, or in her own room on the second floor—a blue chamber, to which no one but her Ladybird ever gained admittance. On this occasion, Miss Pross, responding to Ladybird's pleasant face and pleasant efforts to please her, unbent exceedingly; so the dinner was very pleasant, too.

It was an oppressive day, and, after dinner, Lucie proposed that the wine should be carried out under the plane-tree, and they should sit there in the air. As everything turned upon her, and revolved about her, they went out under the plane-tree, and she carried the wine down for the special benefit of Mr. Lorry. She had installed herself, some time before, as Mr. Lorry's cup-bearer; and while they sat under the plane-tree, talking, she kept his glass replenished. Mysterious backs and ends of houses peeped at them as they talked, and the plane-tree whispered to them in its own way above their heads.

Still, the Hundreds of people did not present themselves. Mr. Darnay presented himself while they were sitting under the plane-tree, but he was only One.

Doctor Manette received him kindly, and so did Lucie. But, Miss Pross suddenly became afflicted with a twitching in the head and body, and retired into the house. She was not unfrequently the victim of this disorder, and she called it, in familiar conversation, "a fit of the jerks."

The Doctor was in his best condition, and looked specially young. The resemblance between him and Lucie was very strong at such times, and as they sat side by side, she leaning on his shoulder, and he resting his arm on the back of her chair, it was very agreeable to trace the likeness.

He had been talking all day, on many subjects, and with unusual vivacity. "Pray, Doctor Manette," said Mr. Darnay, as they sat under the plane-tree—and he said it in the natural pursuit of the topic in hand, which happened to be the old buildings of London—"have you seen much of the Tower?"

"Lucie and I have been there; but only casually. We have seen enough of it, to know that it teems with interest; little more."

"*I* have been there, as you remember," said Darnay, with a smile, though reddening a little angrily, "in another character, and not in a character that gives facilities for seeing much of it. They told me a curious thing when I was there."

"What was that?" Lucie asked.

"In making some alterations, the workmen came upon an old dungeon, which had been, for many years, built up and forgotten. Every stone of its inner wall was covered by inscriptions which had been carved by prisoners—dates, names, complaints, and prayers. Upon a corner stone in an angle of the wall, one prisoner, who seemed to have

gone to execution, had cut as his last work, three letters. They were done with some very poor instrument, and hurriedly, with an unsteady hand. At first, they were read as D. I. C.; but, on being more carefully examined, the last letter was found to be G. There was no record or legend of any prisoner with those initials, and many fruitless guesses were made what the name could have been. At length, it was suggested that the letters were not initials, but the complete word, Dig. The floor was examined very carefully under the inscription, and, in the earth beneath a stone, or tile, or some fragment of paving, were found the ashes of a paper, mingled with the ashes of a small leathern case or bag. What the unknown prisoner had written will never be read, but he had written something, and hidden it away to keep it from the gaoler."

"My father," exclaimed Lucie, "you are ill!"

He had suddenly started up, with his hand to his head. His manner and his look quite terrified them all.

"No, my dear, not ill. There are large drops of rain falling, and they made me start. We had better go in."

He recovered himself almost instantly. Rain was really falling in large drops, and he showed the back of his hand with rain-drops on it. But, he said not a single word in reference to the discovery that had been told of, and, as they went into the house, the business eye of Mr. Lorry either detected, or fancied it detected, on his face, as it turned towards Charles Darnay, the same singular look that had been upon it when it turned towards him in the passages of the Court House.

He recovered himself so quickly, however, that Mr. Lorry had doubts of his business eye. The arm of the golden giant in the hall was not more steady than he was, when he stopped under it to remark to them that he was not yet proof against slight surprises (if he ever would be), and that the rain had startled him.

Tea-time, and Miss Pross making tea, with another fit of the jerks upon her, and yet no Hundreds of people. Mr. Carton had lounged in, but he made but Two.

The night was so very sultry, that although they sat with doors and windows open, they were overpowered by heat. When the tea-table was done with, they all moved to one of the windows, and looked out into the heavy twilight. Lucie sat by her father; Darnay sat beside her; Carton leaned against a window. The curtains were long and white, and some of the thunder-gusts that whirled into the corner, caught them up to the ceiling and waved them like spectral wings.

"The rain-drops are still falling, large, heavy, and few," said Doctor Manette. "It comes slowly."

"It comes surely," said Carton.

They spoke low, as people watching and waiting mostly do; as people in a dark room, watching and waiting for Lightning, always do.

There was a great hurry in the streets of people speeding away to get shelter before the storm broke; the wonderful corner for echoes resounded with the echoes of footsteps coming and going, yet not a footstep was there.

"A multitude of people, and yet a solitude!" said Darnay, when they had listened for a while.

"Is it not impressive, Mr. Darnay?" asked Lucie. "Sometimes, I have sat here of an evening, until I have fancied—but even the shade of a foolish fancy makes me shudder to-night, when all is so black and solemn——"

"Let us shudder too. We may know what it is."

"It will seem nothing to you. Such whims are only impressive as we originate them, I think; they are not to be communicated. I have sometimes sat alone here of an evening, listening, until I have made the echoes out to be the echoes of all the footsteps that are coming by-and-bye into our lives."

"There is a great crowd coming one day into our lives, if that be so," Sydney Carton struck in, in his moody way.

The footsteps were incessant, and the hurry of them became more and more rapid. The corner echoed and re-echoed with the tread of feet; some, as it seemed, under the windows; some, as it seemed, in the room; some coming, some going, some breaking off, some stopping altogether; all in the distant streets, and not one within sight.

"Are all these footsteps destined to come to all of us, Miss Manette, or are we to divide them among us?"

"I don't know, Mr. Darnay; I told you it was a foolish fancy, but you asked for it. When I have yielded myself to it, I have been alone, and then I have imagined them the footsteps of the people who are to come into my life, and my father's."

"I take them into mine!" said Carton. "I ask no questions and make no stipulations. There is a great crowd bearing down upon us, Miss Manette, and I see them—— by the Lightning." He added the last words, after there had been a vivid flash which had shown him lounging in the window.

"And I hear them!" he added again, after a peal of thunder. "Here they come, fast, fierce, and furious!"

It was the rush and roar of rain that he typefied, and it stopped him, for no voice could be heard in it. A memorable storm of thunder and lightning broke with that sweep of water, and there was not a moment's interval in crash, and fire, and rain, until after the moon rose at midnight.

The great bell of Saint Paul's was striking One in the cleared air, when Mr. Lorry, escorted by Jerry, high-booted and bearing a lantern, set forth on his return-passage to Clerkenwell. There were solitary patches of road on the way between Soho and Clerkenwell, and Mr. Lorry, mindful of footpads, always retained Jerry for this service: though it was usually performed a good two hours earlier.

"What a night it has been! Almost a night, Jerry," said Mr. Lorry, "to bring the dead out of their graves."

"I never see the night myself, master—not yet I don't expect to—what would do that," answered Jerry.

"Good night, Mr. Carton," said the man of business. "Good night, Mr. Darnay. Shall we ever see such a night again, together!"

Perhaps. Perhaps, see the great crowd of people with its rush and roar, bearing down upon them, too.

CHAPTER VII.

MONSEIGNEUR IN TOWN.

MONSEIGNEUR, one of the great lords in power at the Court, held his fortnightly reception in his grand hotel in Paris. Monseigneur was in his inner room, his sanctuary of sanctuaries, the Holiest of Holiests to the crowd of worshippers in the suite of rooms without. Monseigneur was about to take his chocolate. Monseigneur could swallow a great many things with ease, and was by some few sullen minds supposed to be rather rapidly swallowing France; but, his morning's chocolate could not so much as get into the throat of Monseigneur, without the aid of four strong men besides the Cook.

Yes. It took four men, all four ablaze with gorgeous decoration, and the Chief of them unable to exist with fewer than two gold watches in his pocket, emulative of the noble and chaste fashion set by Monseigneur, to conduct the happy chocolate to Monseigneur's lips. One lacquey carried the chocolate-pot into the sacred presence; a second, milled and frothed the chocolate with the little instrument he bore for that function; a third, presented the favoured napkin; a fourth (he of the two gold watches), poured the chocolate out. It was impossible for Monseigneur to dispense with one of these attendants on the chocolate and hold his high place under the admiring Heavens. Deep would have been the blot upon his escutcheon if his chocolate had been ignobly waited on by only three men; he must have died of two.

Monseigneur had been out at a little supper last night, where the comedy and the Grand Opera were charmingly represented. Monseigneur was out at a little supper most nights, with fascinating company. So polite and so impressible was Monseigneur, that the Comedy and the Grand Opera had far more influence with him in the tiresome articles of state affairs and state secrets, than the needs of all France. A happy circumstance for France, as the like always is for all countries similarly favoured!—always was for England (by way of example), in the regretted days of the merry Stuart who sold it.

Monseigneur had one truly noble idea of general public business, which was, to let everything go on in its own way; of particular public business, Monseigneur had the other truly noble idea that it must all go his way—tend to his own power and pocket. Of his pleasures, general and particular, Monseigneur had the other truly noble idea, that the world was made for them. The text of his order (altered from the original by only a pronoun, which is not much) ran: "The earth and the fulness thereof are mine, saith Monseigneur."

Yet, Monseigneur had slowly found that vulgar embarrassments crept into his affairs, both private and public; and he had, as to both classes of affairs, allied himself perforce with a Farmer-General. As to finances public, because Monseigneur could not make anything at all of them, and must consequently let them out to somebody who could; as to finances private, because Farmer-Generals were rich, and Monseigneur, after generations of great luxury and expense, was growing poor. Hence Monseigneur had taken his sister from a convent, while there was yet time to ward off the impending veil, the cheapest garment she could wear, and had bestowed her as a prize upon a very rich Farmer-General, poor in family. Which Farmer-General, carrying an appropriate cane with a golden apple on the top of it, was now among the company in the outer rooms, much prostrated before by mankind—always excepting superior mankind of the blood of Monseigneur, who, his own wife included, looked down upon him with the loftiest contempt.

A sumptuous man was the Farmer-General. Thirty horses stood in his stables, twenty-four male domestics sat in his halls, six body-women waited on his wife. As one who pretended to do nothing but plunder and forage where he could, the Farmer-General—howsoever his matrimonial relations conduced to social morality—was at least the greatest reality among the personages who attended at the hotel of Monseigneur that day.

For, the rooms, though a beautiful scene to look at, and adorned with every device of decoration that the taste and skill of the time could achieve, were, in truth, not a sound business; considered with any reference to the scarecrows in the rags and nightcaps elsewhere (and not so far off, either, but that the watching towers of Notre Dame, almost equi-distant from the two extremes, could see them both), they would have been an exceedingly uncomfortable business—if that could have been anybody's business, at the house of Monseigneur. Military officers destitute of military knowledge; naval officers with no idea of a ship; civil officers without a notion of affairs; brazen ecclesiastics, of the worst world worldly, with sensual eyes, loose tongues, and looser lives; all totally unfit for their several callings, all lying horribly in pretending to belong to them, but all nearly or remotely of the order of Monseigneur, and therefore foisted on all public employments from which anything was to be got; these were to be told off by the score and the score. People not immediately connected with Monseigneur or the State, yet equally unconnected with anything that was real, or with lives passed in travelling by any straight road to any true earthly end, were no less abundant. Doctors who made great fortunes out of dainty remedies for imaginary disorders that never existed, smiled upon their courtly patients in the ante-chambers of Monseigneur. Projectors who had discovered every kind of remedy for the little evils with which the State was touched, except the remedy of setting to work in earnest to root out a single sin, poured their distracting babble into any ears they could lay hold of, at the reception of Monseigneur. Unbelieving Philosophers who were remodelling the world with words, and making card-towers of Babel to scale the skies with, talked with Unbelieving Chemists who had an eye on the transmutation of metals, at this wonderful gathering accumulated by Monseigneur. Exquisite gentlemen of the finest breeding, which was at that remarkable time —and has been since—to be known by its fruits of indifference to every natural subject of human interest, were in the most exemplary state of exhaustion, at the hotel of Monseigneur. Such homes had these various notabilities left behind them in the fine world of Paris, that the spies among the assembled devotees of Monseigneur—forming a goodly half of the polite company—would have found it hard to discover among the angels of that sphere one solitary wife, who, in her manners and appearance, owned to being a Mother. Indeed, except for the mere act of bringing a troublesome creature into this world—which does not go far towards the realisation of the name of mother—there was no such thing known to the fashion. Peasant women kept the unfashionable babies close, and brought them up, and charming grandmammas of sixty dressed and supped as at twenty.

The leprosy of unreality disfigured every human creature in attendance upon Monseigneur. In the outermost room were half a dozen exceptional people who had had, for a few years, some vague misgiving in them that things in general were going rather wrong. As a promising way of setting them right, half of the half-dozen had become members of a fantastic sect of Convulsionists, and were even then considering within themselves whether they should foam, rage, roar, and turn cataleptic on the spot—thereby setting up a highly intelligible finger-post to the Future, for Monseigneur's guidance. Besides these Dervishes, were other three who had rushed into another sect, which mended matters with a jargon about "the Centre of Truth:" holding that Man had got out of the Centre of Truth—which did not need much demonstration—but had not got out of the Circumference, and that he was to be kept from flying out of the Circumference, and was even to be shoved back into the Centre, by fasting and seeing of spirits. Among these, accordingly, much discoursing with spirits went on—and it did a world of good which never became manifest.

But, the comfort was, that all the company at the grand hotel of Monseigneur were perfectly dressed. If the Day of Judgment had only been ascertained to be a dress day, everybody there would have been eternally correct. Such frizzling and powdering and sticking up of hair, such delicate complexions artificially preserved and mended, such gallant swords to look at, and such delicate honour to the sense of smell, would surely keep anything going, for ever and ever. The exquisite gentlemen of the finest breeding wore little pendent trinkets that chinked as they languidly moved; these golden fetters rang like precious little bells; and what with that ringing, and with the rustle of silk and brocade and fine linen, there was a flutter in the air that fanned Saint Antoine and his devouring hunger far away.

Dress was the one unfailing talisman and charm used for keeping all things in their places. Everybody was dressed for a Fancy Ball that was never to leave off. From the Palace of the Tuileries, through Monseigneur and the whole Court, through the Chambers, the Tribunals of Justice, and all society (except the scarecrows), the Fancy Ball descended to the Common Executioner: who, in pursuance of the charm, was required to officiate "frizzled, powdered, in a gold-laced coat, pumps, and white silk stockings." At the gallows and the wheel—the axe was a rarity—Monsieur Paris, as it was the episcopal mode among his brother Professors of the provinces, Monsieur Orleans, and the rest, to call him, presided in this dainty dress. And who among the company at Monseigneur's reception in that seventeen hundred and eightieth year of our Lord, could possibly doubt, that a system rooted in a frizzled hangman, powdered, gold-laced, pumped, and white-silk stockinged, would see the very stars out!

Monseigneur having eased his four men of their burdens and taken his chocolate, caused the doors of the Holiest of Holiests to be thrown open, and issued forth. Then, what submission, what cringing and fawning, what servility, what abject humiliation! As to bowing down in body and spirit, nothing in that way was left for Heaven—which may have been one among other reasons why the worshippers of Monseigneur never troubled it.

Bestowing a word of promise here and a smile there, a whisper on one happy slave and a wave of the hand on another, Monseigneur affably passed through his rooms to the remote region of the Circumference of Truth. There, Monseigneur turned, and came back again, and so in due course of time got himself shut up in his sanctuary by the chocolate sprites, and was seen no more.

The show being over, the flutter in the air became quite a little storm, and the precious little bells went ringing down-stairs. There was soon but one person left of all the crowd, and he, with his hat under his arm and his snuff-box in his hand, slowly passed among the mirrors on his way out.

"I devote you," said this person, stopping at the last door on his way, and turning in the direction of the sanctuary, "to the Devil!"

With that, he shook the snuff from his fingers as if he had shaken the dust from his feet, and quietly walked down-stairs.

He was a man of about sixty, handsomely dressed, haughty in manner, and with a face like a fine mask. A face of a transparent paleness; every feature in it clearly defined; one set expression on it. The nose, beautifully formed otherwise, was very slightly pinched at the top of each nostril. In those two compressions, or dints, the only little change that the face showed, resided. They persisted in changing colour sometimes, and they would be occasionally dilated and contracted by something like a faint pulsation; then, they gave a look of treachery, and cruelty, to the whole countenance. Examined with attention, its capacity of helping such a look was to be found in the line of the mouth, and the lines of the orbits of the eyes, being much too horizontal and thin; still, in the effect of the face made, it was a handsome face, and a remarkable one.

Its owner went down-stairs into the courtyard, got into his carriage, and drove away. Not many people had talked with him at the reception; he had stood in a little space apart, and Monseigneur might have been warmer in his manner. It appeared, under the circumstances, rather agreeable to him to see the common people dispersed before his horses, and often barely escaping from being run down. His man drove as if he were charging an enemy, and the furious recklessness of the man brought no check into the face, or to the lips, of the master. The complaint had sometimes made itself audible, even in that deaf city and dumb age, that, in the narrow streets without footways, the fierce patrician custom of hard driving endangered and maimed the mere vulgar in a barbarous manner. But, few cared enough for that to think of it a second time. and, in this matter, as in all others, the common wretches were left to get out of their difficulties as they could.

With a wild rattle and clatter, and an inhuman abandonment of consideration not easy to be understood in these days, the carriage dashed through streets and swept round corners, with women screaming before it, and men clutching each other and clutching children out of its way. At last, swooping at a street corner by a fountain, one of its wheels came to a sickening little jolt, and there was a loud cry from a number of voices, and the horses reared and plunged.

But for the latter inconvenience, the carriage probably would not have stopped; carriages were often known to drive on, and leave their wounded behind, and why not? But the frightened valet had got down in a hurry, and there were twenty hands at the horses' bridles.

"What has gone wrong?" said Monsieur, calmly looking out.

A tall man in a nightcap had caught up a bundle from among the feet of the horses, and had laid it on the basement of the fountain, and was down in the mud and wet, howling over it like a wild animal.

"Pardon, Monsieur the Marquis!" said a ragged and submissive man, "it is a child."

"Why does he make that abominable noise? Is it his child?"

"Excuse me, Monsieur the Marquis—it is a pity—yes."

The fountain was a little removed; for the street opened, where it was, into a space some ten or twelve yards square. As the tall man suddenly got up from the ground, and came running at the carriage, Monsieur the Marquis clapped his hand for an instant on his sword-hilt.

"Killed!" shrieked the man, in wild desperation, extending both arms at their length above his head, and staring at him. "Dead!"

The people closed round, and looked at Monsieur the Marquis. There was nothing revealed by the many eyes that looked at him but watchfulness and eagerness; there was no visible menacing or anger. Neither did the people say anything; after the first cry, they had been silent, and they remained so. The voice of the submissive man who had spoken, was flat and tame in its extreme submission. Monsieur the Marquis ran his eyes over them all, as if they had been mere rats come out of their holes.

He took out his purse.

"It is extraordinary to me," said he, "that you people cannot take care of yourselves and your children. One or the other of you is for ever in the way. How do I know what injury you have done my horses. See! Give him that."

He threw out a gold coin for the valet to pick up, and all the heads craned forward so that all the eyes might look down at it as it fell. The tall man called out again with a most unearthly cry, "Dead!"

He was arrested by the quick arrival of another man, for whom the rest made way. On seeing him, the miserable creature fell upon his shoulder, sobbing and crying, and pointing to the fountain, where some women were stooping over the motionless bundle, and moving gently about it. They were as silent, however, as the men.

"I know all, I know all," said the last comer. "Be a brave man, my Gaspard! It is better for the poor little plaything to die so, than to live. It has died in a moment without pain. Could it have lived an hour as happily?"

"You are a philosopher, you there," said the Marquis, smiling. "How do they call you?"

"They call me Defarge."

"Of what trade?"

"Monsieur the Marquis, vendor of wine."

"Pick up that, philosopher and vendor of wine," said the Marquis, throwing him another gold coin, "and spend it as you will. The horses there; are they right?"

Without deigning to look at the assemblage a second time, Monsieur the Marquis leaned back in his seat, and was just being driven away with the air of a gentleman who had accidentally broke some common thing, and had paid for it, and could afford to pay for it; when his ease was suddenly disturbed by a coin flying into his carriage, and ringing on its floor.

"Hold!" said Monsieur the Marquis. "Hold the horses! Who threw that?"

He looked to the spot where Defarge the vendor of wine had stood, a moment before; but the wretched father was grovelling on his face on the pavement in that spot, and the figure that stood beside him was the figure of a dark stout woman, knitting.

"You dogs!" said the Marquis, but smoothly, and with an unchanged front, except as to the spots on his nose: "I

"KILLED!" SHRIEKED THE MAN.

would ride over any of you very willingly, and exterminate you from the earth. If I knew which rascal threw at the carriage, and if that brigand were sufficiently near it, he should be crushed under the wheels."

So cowed was their condition, and so long and hard their experience of what such a man could do to them, within the law and beyond it, that not a voice, or a hand, or even an eye was raised. Among the men, not one. But the woman who stood knitting looked up steadily, and looked the Marquis in the face. It was not for his dignity to notice it; his contemptuous eyes passed over her, and over all the other rats; and he leaned back in his seat again, and gave the word "Go on!"

He was driven on, and other carriages came whirling by in quick succession; the Minister, the State-Projector, the Farmer-General, the Doctor, the Lawyer, the Ecclesiastic, the Grand Opera, the Comedy, the whole Fancy Ball in a bright continuous flow, came whirling by. The rats had crept out of their holes to look on, and they remained looking on for hours; soldiers and police often passing between them and the spectacle, and making a barrier behind which they slunk, and through which they peeped. The father had long ago taken up his bundle and hidden himself away with it, when the women who had tended the bundle while it lay on the base of the fountain, sat there watching the running of the water and the rolling of the Fancy Ball—when the one woman who had stood conspicuous, knitting, still knitted on with the steadfastness of Fate. The water of the fountain ran, the swift river ran, the day ran into evening, so much life in the city ran into death according to rule, time and tide waited for no man, the rats were sleeping close together in their dark holes again, the Fancy Ball was lighted up at supper, all things ran their course.

CHAPTER VIII.

MONSEIGNEUR IN THE COUNTRY.

A BEAUTIFUL landscape, with the corn bright in it, but not abundant. Patches of poor rye where corn should have been, patches of poor peas and beans, patches of most coarse vegetable substitutes for wheat. On inanimate nature, as on the men and women who cultivated it, a prevalent tendency towards an appearance of vegetating unwillingly—a dejected disposition to give up, and wither away.

Monsieur the Marquis in his travelling carriage (which might have been lighter), conducted by four post-horses and two postilions, fagged up a steep hill. A blush on the countenance of Monsieur the Marquis was no impeachment of his high breeding; it was not from within; it was occasioned by an external circumstance beyond his control—the setting sun.

The sunset struck so brilliantly into the travelling carriage when it gained the hill-top, that its occupant was steeped in crimson. "It will die out," said Monsieur the Marquis, glancing at his hands, "directly."

In effect, the sun was so low that it dipped at the moment. When the heavy drag had been adjusted to the wheel, and the carriage slid down hill, with a cinderous smell, in a cloud of dust, the red glow departed quickly; the sun and the Marquis going down together, there was no glow left when the drag was taken off.

But, there remained a broken country, bold and open, a little village at the bottom of the hill, a broad sweep and rise beyond it, a church-tower, a windmill, a forest for the chase, and a crag with a fortress on it used as a prison. Round upon all these darkening objects as the night drew on, the Marquis looked, with the air of one who was coming near home.

The village had its one poor street, with its poor brewery, poor tannery, poor tavern, poor stable-yard for relays of post-horses, poor fountain, all usual poor appointments. It had its poor people too. All its people were poor, and many of them were sitting at their doors, shredding spare onions and the like for supper, while many were at the fountain, washing leaves, and grasses, and any such small yieldings of the earth that could be eaten. Expressive signs of what made them poor, were not wanting; the tax for the state, the tax for the church, the tax for the lord, tax local and tax general, were to be paid here and to be paid there, according to solemn inscription in the little village, until the wonder was, that there was any village left unswallowed.

Few children were to be seen, and no dogs. As to the men and women, their choice on earth was stated in the prospect—Life on the lowest terms that could sustain it, down in the little village under the mill; or captivity and Death in the dominant prison on the crag.

Heralded by a courier in advance, and by the cracking of his postilions' whips, which twined snake-like about their heads in the evening air, as if he came attended by the Furies, Monsieur the Marquis drew up in his travelling carriage at the posting-house gate. It was hard by the fountain, and the peasants suspended their operations to look at him. He looked at them, and saw in them, without knowing it, the slow sure filing down of misery-worn face and figure, that was to make the meagreness of Frenchmen an English superstition which should survive the truth through the best part of a hundred years.

Monsieur the Marquis cast his eyes over the submissive faces that drooped before him, as the like of himself had drooped before Monseigneur of the Court—only the difference was, that these faces drooped merely to suffer and not to propitiate—when a grizzled mender of the roads joined the group.

"Bring me hither that fellow!" said the Marquis to the courier.

The fellow was brought, cap in hand, and the other fellows closed round to look and listen, in the manner of the people at the Paris fountain.

"I passed you on the road?"

"Monseigneur, it is true. I had the honour of being passed on the road."

"Coming up the hill, and at the top of the hill, both?"

"Monseigneur, it is true."

"What did you look at, so fixedly?"

"Monseigneur, I looked at the man."

He stooped a little, and with his tattered blue cap pointed under the carriage. All his fellows stooped to look under the carriage.

"What man, pig? And why look there?"

"Pardon, Monseigneur; he swung by the chain of the shoe—the drag."

"Who?" demanded the traveller.

"Monseigneur, the man."

"May the Devil carry away these idiots! How do you call the man? You know all the men of this part of the country. Who was he?"

"Your clemency, Monseigneur! He was not of this part of the country. Of all the days of my life, I never saw him."

"Swinging by the chain? To be suffocated?"

"With your gracious permission, that was the wonder of it, Monseigneur. His head hanging over—like this!"

He turned himself sideways to the carriage, and leaned back, with his face thrown up to the sky, and his head hanging down; then recovered himself, fumbled with his cap, and made a bow.

"What was he like?"

"Monseigneur, he was whiter than the miller. All covered with dust, white as a spectre, tall as a spectre!"

The picture produced an immense sensation in the little crowd; but all eyes, without comparing notes with other eyes, looked at Monsieur the Marquis. Perhaps, to observe whether he had any spectre on his conscience.

"Truly, you did well," said the Marquis, felicitously sensible that such vermin were not to ruffle him, "to see a thief accompanying my carriage, and not open that great mouth of yours. Bah! Put him aside, Monsieur Gabelle!"

Monsieur Gabelle was the Postmaster, and some other taxing functionary united; he had come out with great obsequiousness to assist at this examination, and had held the examined by the drapery of his arm in an official manner.

"Bah! Go aside!" said Monsieur Gabelle.

"Lay hands on this stranger if he seeks to lodge in your village to-night, and be sure that his business is honest, Gabelle."

"Monseigneur, I am flattered to devote myself to your orders."

"Did he run away, fellow?—where is that Accursed?"

The accursed was already under the carriage with some half-dozen particular friends, pointing out the chain with his blue cap. Some half-dozen other particular friends promptly hauled him out, and presented him breathless to Monsieur the Marquis.

"Did the man run away, Dolt, when we stopped for the drag?"

"Monseigneur, he precipitated himself over the hill-side, head first, as a person plunges into the river."

"See to it, Gabelle. Go on!"

The half-dozen who were peering at the chain were still among the wheels, like sheep; the wheels turned so suddenly that they were lucky to save their skins and bones; they had very little else to save, or they might not have been so fortunate.

The burst with which the carriage started out of the village and up the rise beyond, was soon checked by the steepness of the hill. Gradually, it subsided to a foot pace, swinging and lumbering upward among the many sweet scents of a summer night. The postilions, with a thousand gossamer gnats circling about them in lieu of the Furies, quietly mended the points to the lashes of their whips; the valet walked by the horses; the courier was audible, trotting on ahead into the dim distance.

At the steepest point of the hill there was a little burial-ground, with a Cross and a new large figure of Our Saviour on it; it was a poor figure in wood, done by some inexperienced rustic carver, but he had studied the figure from the life—his own life, maybe—for it was dreadfully spare and thin.

To this distressful emblem of a great distress that had long been growing worse, and was not at its worst, a woman was kneeling. She turned her head as the carriage came up to her, rose quickly, and presented herself at the carriage-door.

"It is you, Monseigneur! Monseigneur, a petition."

With an exclamation of impatience, but with his unchangeable face, Monseigneur looked out.

"How, then! What is it? Always petitions!"

"Monseigneur. For the love of the great God! My husband, the forester."

"What of your husband, the forester? Always the same with you people. He cannot pay something?"

"He has paid all, Monseigneur. He is dead."

"Well! He is quiet. Can I restore him to you?"

"Alas, no, Monseigneur! But he lies yonder, under a little heap of poor grass."

"Well?"

"Monseigneur, there are so many little heaps of poor grass?"

"Again, well?"

She looked an old woman, but was young. Her manner was one of passionate grief; by turns she clasped her veinous and knotted hands together with wild energy, and laid one of them on the carriage-door—tenderly, caressingly, as if it had been a human breast, and could be expected to feel the appealing touch.

"Monseigneur, hear me! Monseigneur, hear my petition! My husband died of want; so many die of want; so many more will die of want."

"Again, well? Can I feed them?"

"Monseigneur, the good God knows; but I don't ask it. My petition is, that a morsel of stone or wood, with my husband's name, may be placed over him to show where he lies. Otherwise, the place will be quickly forgotten, it will never be found when I am dead of the same malady, I shall be laid under some other heap of poor grass. Monseigneur, they are so many, they increase so fast, there is so much want. Monseigneur! Monseigneur!"

The valet had put her away from the door, the carriage had broken into a brisk trot, the postilions had quickened the pace, she was left far behind, and Monseigneur, again escorted by the Furies, was rapidly diminishing the league or two of distance that remained between him and his château.

The sweet scents of the summer night rose all around him, and rose, as the rain falls, impartially, on the dusty, ragged, and toil-worn group at the fountain not far away; to whom the mender of roads, with the aid of the blue cap without which he was nothing, still enlarged upon his man like a spectre, as long as they could bear it. By degrees, as they could bear no more, they dropped off one by one, and lights twinkled in little casements; which lights, as the casements darkened, and more stars came out, seemed to have shot up into the sky instead of having been extinguished.

The shadow of a large high-roofed house, and of many overhanging trees, was upon Monsieur the Marquis by that time; and the shadow was exchanged for the light of a flambeau, as his carriage stopped, and the great door of his château was opened to him.

"Monsieur Charles, whom I expect; is he arrived from England?"

"Monseigneur, not yet."

CHAPTER IX.

THE GORGON'S HEAD.

It was a heavy mass of building, that château of Monsieur the Marquis, with a large stone courtyard before it, and two stone sweeps of staircase meeting in a stone terrace before the principal door. A stony business altogether, with heavy stone balustrades, and stone urns, and stone flowers, and stone faces of men, and stone heads of lions, in all directions. As if the Gorgon's head had surveyed it, when it was finished, two centuries ago.

Up the broad flight of shallow steps, Monsieur the Marquis, flambeau preceded, went from his carriage, sufficiently disturbing the darkness to elicit loud remonstrance from an owl in the roof of the great pile of stable building away among the trees. All else was so quiet, that the flambeau carried up the steps, and the other flambeau held at the great door, burnt as if they were in a close room of state, instead of being in the open night-air. Other sound than the owl's voice there was none, save the falling of a fountain into its stone basin; for, it was one of those dark nights that hold their breath by the hour together, and then heave a long low sigh, and hold their breath again.

The great door clanged behind him, and Monsieur the Marquis crossed a hall grim with certain old boar-spears, swords, and knives of the chase; grimmer with certain heavy riding-rods and riding-whips, of which many a peasant, gone to his benefactor Death, had felt the weight when his lord was angry.

Avoiding the larger rooms, which were dark and made fast for the night, Monsieur the Marquis, with his flambeau-bearer going on before, went up the staircase to a door in a corridor. This thrown open, admitted him to his own private apartment of three rooms: his bed-chamber and two others. High vaulted rooms with cool uncarpeted floors, great dogs upon the hearths for the burning of wood in winter time, and all luxuries befitting the state of a marquis in a luxurious age and country. The fashion of the last Louis but one, of the line that was never to break—the fourteenth Louis—was conspicuous in their rich furniture; but, it was diversified by many objects that were illustrations of old pages in the history of France.

A supper-table was laid for two, in the third of the rooms; a round room, in one of the château's four extinguisher-topped towers. A small lofty room, with its window wide open, and the wooden jalousie-blinds closed, so that the dark night only showed in slight horizontal lines of black, alternating with their broad lines of stone colour.

"My nephew," said the Marquis, glancing at the supper preparation; "they said he was not arrived."

Nor was he; but, he had been expected with Monseigneur.

"Ah! It is not probable he will arrive to-night; nevertheless, leave the table as it is. I shall be ready in a quarter of an hour."

In a quarter of an hour Monseigneur was ready, and sat down alone to his sumptuous and choice supper. His chair was opposite to the window, and he had taken his soup, and was raising his glass of Bordeaux to his lips, when he put it down.

"What is that?" he calmly asked, looking with attention at the horizontal lines of black and stone colour.

"Monseigneur? That?"

"Outside the blinds. Open the blinds."

It was done.

"Well?"

"Monseigneur, it is nothing. The trees and the night are all that are here."

The servant who spoke, had thrown the blinds wide, had looked out into the vacant darkness, and stood with that blank behind him, looking round for instructions.

"Good," said the imperturbable master. "Close them again."

That was done too, and the Marquis went on with his supper. He was half way through it, when he again stopped with his glass in his hand, hearing the sound of wheels. It came on briskly, and came up to the front of the château.

"Ask who is arrived?"

It was the nephew of Monseigneur. He had been some few leagues behind Monseigneur, early in the afternoon. He had diminished the distance rapidly, but not so rapidly as to come up with Monseigneur on the road. He had heard of Monseigneur, at the posting-houses, as being before him.

He was to be told (said Monseigneur) that supper awaited him then and there, and that he was prayed to come to it. In a little while he came. He had been known in England as Charles Darnay.

Monseigneur received him in a courtly manner, but they did not shake hands.

"You left Paris yesterday, sir?" he said to Monseigneur, as he took his seat at table.

"Yesterday. And you?"

"I come direct."

"From London?"

"Yes."

"You have been a long time coming," said the Marquis, with a smile.

"On the contrary; I come direct."

"Pardon me! I mean, not a long time on the journey; a long time intending the journey."

"I have been detained by"—the nephew stopped a moment in his answer—"various business."

"Without doubt," said the polished uncle.

So long as a servant was present, no other words passed between them. When coffee had been served and they were alone together, the nephew, looking at the uncle and meeting the eyes of the face that was like a fine mask, opened a conversation.

"I have come back, sir, as you anticipate, pursuing the object that took me away. It carried me into great and unexpected peril; but it is a sacred object, and if it had carried me to death I hope it would have sustained me."

"Not to death," said the uncle; "it is not necessary to say, to death."

"I doubt, sir," returned the nephew, "whether, if it had carried me to the utmost brink of death, you would have cared to stop me there."

The deepened marks in the nose, and the lengthening of the fine straight lines in the cruel face, looked ominous as to that; the uncle made a graceful gesture of protest, which was so clearly a slight form of good breeding that it was not reassuring.

"Indeed, sir," pursued the nephew, "for anything I

know, you may have expressly worked to give a more suspicious appearance to the suspicious circumstances that surrounded me."

"No, no, no," said the uncle, pleasantly.

"But, however that may be," resumed the nephew, glancing at him with deep distrust, "I know that your diplomacy would stop me by any means, and would know no scruple as to means."

"My friend, I told you so," said the uncle, with a fine pulsation in the two marks. "Do me the favour to recall that I told you so, long ago."

"I recall it."

"Thank you," said the Marquis—very sweetly indeed. His tone lingered in the air, almost like the tone of a musical instrument.

"In effect, sir," pursued the nephew, "I believe it to be at once your bad fortune, and my good fortune, that has kept me out of a prison in France here."

"I do not quite understand," returned the uncle, sipping his coffee. "Dare I ask you to explain?"

"I believe that if you were not in disgrace with the Court, and had not been overshadowed by that cloud for years past, a letter *de cachet* would have sent me to some fortress indefinitely."

"It is possible," said the uncle, with great calmness. "For the honour of the family, I could even resolve to incommode you to that extent. Pray excuse me!"

"I perceive that, happily for me, the Reception of the day before yesterday was, as usual, a cold one," observed the nephew.

"I would not say happily, my friend," returned the uncle, with refined politeness; "I would not be sure of that. A good opportunity for consideration, surrounded by the advantages of solitude, might influence your destiny to far greater advantage than you influence it for yourself. But it is useless to discuss the question. I am, as you say, at a disadvantage. These little instruments of correction, these gentle aids to the power and honour of families, these slight favours that might so incommode you, are only to be obtained now by interest and importunity. They are sought by so many, and they are granted (comparatively) to so few! It used not to be so, but France in all such things is changed for the worse. Our not remote ancestors held the right of life and death over the surrounding vulgar. From this room, many such dogs have been taken out to be hanged; in the next room (my bedroom), one fellow, to our knowledge, was poniarded on the spot for professing some insolent delicacy respecting his daughter—*his* daughter? We have lost many privileges; a new philosophy has become the mode; and the assertion of our station in these days, might (I do not go so far as to say would, but might) cause us real inconvenience. All very bad, very bad!"

The Marquis took a gentle little pinch of snuff, and shook his head; as elegantly despondent as he could becomingly be of a country still containing himself, that great means of regeneration.

"We have so asserted our station, both in the old time and in the modern time also," said the nephew, gloomily, "that I believe our name to be more detested than any name in France."

"Let us hope so," said the uncle. "Detestation of the high is the involuntary homage of the low."

"There is not," pursued the nephew, in his former tone, "a face I can look at, in all this country round about us, which looks at me with any deference on it but the dark deference of fear and slavery."

"A compliment," said the Marquis, "to the grandeur of the family, merited by the manner in which the family has sustained its grandeur. Hah!" And he took another gentle little pinch of snuff, and lightly crossed his legs.

But, when his nephew, leaning an elbow on the table, covered his eyes thoughtfully and dejectedly with his hand, the fine mask looked at him sideways with a stronger concentration of keenness, closeness, and dislike, than was comportable with its wearer's assumption of indifference.

"Repression is the only lasting philosophy. The dark deference of fear and slavery, my friend," observed the Marquis, "will keep the dogs obedient to the whip, as long as this roof," looking up to it, "shuts out the sky."

That might not be so long as the Marquis supposed. If a picture of the château as it was to be a very few years hence, and of fifty like it as they too were to be a very few years hence, could have been shown to him that night, he might have been at a loss to claim his own from the ghastly, fire-charred, plunder-wrecked ruins. As for the roof he vaunted, he might have found *that* shutting out the sky in a new way—to wit, for ever, from the eyes of the bodies into which its lead was fired, out of the barrels of a hundred thousand muskets.

"Meanwhile," said the Marquis, "I will preserve the honour and repose of the family, if you will not. But you must be fatigued. Shall we terminate our conference for the night?"

"A moment more."

"An hour, if you please."

"Sir," said the nephew, "we have done wrong, and are reaping the fruits of wrong."

"*We* have done wrong?" repeated the Marquis, with an inquiring smile, and delicately pointing, first to his nephew, then to himself.

"Our family; our honourable family, whose honour is of so much account to both of us, in such different ways. Even in my father's time, we did a world of wrong, injuring every human creature who came between us and our pleasure, whatever it was. Why need I speak of my father's time, when it is equally yours? Can I separate my father's twin-brother, joint inheritor, and next successor, from himself?"

"Death has done that!" said the Marquis.

"And has left me," answered the nephew, "bound to a system that is frightful to me, responsible for it, but powerless in it; seeking to execute the last request of my dear mother's lips, and obey the last look of my dear mother's eyes, which implored me to have mercy and to redress; and tortured by seeking assistance and power in vain."

"Seeking them from me, my nephew," said the Marquis, touching him on the breast with his forefinger—they were now standing by the hearth—"you will for ever seek them in vain, be assured."

Every fine straight line in the clear whiteness of his face, was cruelly, craftily, and closely compressed, while he stood looking quietly at his nephew, with his snuff-box in his hand. Once again he touched him on the breast, as though his finger were the fine point of a small sword, with which, in delicate finesse, he ran him through the body, and said,

"My friend, I will die, perpetuating the system under which I have lived."

When he had said it, he took a culminating pinch of snuff, and put his box in his pocket.

"Better to be a rational creature," he added then, after ringing a small bell on the table, "and accept your natural destiny. But you are lost, Monsieur Charles, I see."

"This property and France are lost to me," said the nephew, sadly; "I renounce them."

"Are they both yours to renounce? France may be, but is the property? It is scarcely worth mentioning; but, is it yet?"

"I had no intention, in the words I used, to claim it yet. If it passed to me from you, to-morrow——"

"Which I have the vanity to hope is not probable."

"—or twenty years hence——"

"You do me too much honour," said the Marquis; "still, I prefer that supposition."

"—I would abandon it, and live otherwise and elsewhere. It is little to relinquish. What is it but a wilderness of misery and ruin!"

"Hah!" said the Marquis, glancing round the luxurious room.

"To the eye it is fair enough, here; but seen in its integrity, under the sky, and by the daylight, it is a crumbling tower of waste, mismanagement, extortion, debt, mortgage, oppression, hunger, nakedness, and suffering."

"Hah!" said the Marquis again, in a well-satisfied manner.

"If it ever becomes mine, it shall be put into some hands better qualified to free it slowly (if such a thing is possible) from the weight that drags it down, so that the miserable people who cannot leave it and who have been long wrung to the last point of endurance, may, in another generation, suffer less; but it is not for me. There is a curse on it, and on all this land."

"And you?" said the uncle. "Forgive my curiosity; do you, under your new philosophy, graciously intend to live?"

"I must do, to live, what others of my countrymen, even with nobility at their backs, may have to do some day—work."

"In England, for example?"

"Yes. The family honour, sir, is safe from me in this country. The family name can suffer from me in no other, for I bear it in no other."

The ringing of the bell had caused the adjoining bedchamber to be lighted. It now shone brightly, through the door of communication. The Marquis looked that way, and listened for the retreating step of his valet.

"England is very attractive to you, seeing how indifferently you have prospered there," he observed then, turning his calm face to his nephew with a smile.

"I have already said, that for my prospering there, I am sensible I may be indebted to you, sir. For the rest, it is my Refuge."

"They say, those boastful English, that it is the Refuge of many. You know a compatriot who has found a Refuge there? A Doctor?"

"Yes."

"With a daughter?"

"Yes."

"Yes," said the Marquis. "You are fatigued. Good night!"

As he bent his head in his most courtly manner, there was a secrecy in his smiling face, and he conveyed an air of mystery to those words, which struck the eyes and ears of his nephew forcibly. At the same time, the thin straight lines of the setting of the eyes, and the thin straight lips, and the markings in the nose, curved with a sarcasm that looked handsomely diabolic.

"Yes," repeated the Marquis. "A Doctor with a daughter. Yes. So commences the new philosophy! You are fatigued. Good night!"

It would have been of as much avail to interrogate any stone face outside the château as to interrogate that face of his. The nephew looked at him, in vain, in passing on to the door.

"Good night!" said the uncle. "I look to the pleasure of seeing you again in the morning. Good repose! Light Monsieur my nephew to his chamber there!—And burn Monsieur my nephew in his bed, if you will," he added to himself, before he rang his little bell again, and summoned his valet to his own bedroom.

The valet come and gone, Monsieur the Marquis walked to and fro in his loose chamber-robe, to prepare himself gently for sleep, that hot still night. Rustling about the room, his softly-slippered feet making no noise on the floor, he moved like a refined tiger:—looked like some enchanted marquis of the impenitently wicked sort, in story, whose periodical change into tiger form was either just going off, or just coming on.

He moved from end to end of his voluptuous bedroom, looking again at the scraps of the day's journey that came unbidden into his mind; the slow toil up the hill at sunset, the setting sun, the descent, the mill, the prison on the crag, the little village in the hollow, the peasants at the fountain, and the mender of roads with his blue cap pointing out the chain under the carriage. That fountain suggested the Paris fountain, the little bundle lying on the step, the women bending over it, and the tall man with his arms up, crying, "Dead!"

"I am cool now," said Monsieur the Marquis, "and may go to bed."

So, leaving only one light burning on the large hearth, he let his thin gauze curtains fall around him, and heard the night break its silence with a long sigh as he composed himself to sleep.

The stone faces on the outer walls stared blindly at the black night for three heavy hours; for three heavy hours, the horses in the stables rattled at their racks, the dogs barked, and the owl made a noise with very little resemblance in it to the noise conventionally assigned to the owl by men-poets. But it is the obstinate custom of such creatures hardly ever to say what is set down for them.

For three heavy hours, the stone faces of the château, lion and human, stared blindly at the night. Dead darkness lay on all the landscape, dead darkness added its own hush to the hushing dust on all the roads. The burial-place had got to the pass that its little heaps of poor grass were undistinguishable from one another; the figure on the Cross might have come down, for anything that could be seen of it. In the village, taxers and taxed were fast asleep. Dreaming, perhaps, of banquets, as the starved usually do, and of ease and rest, as the driven slave and the yoked ox may, its lean inhabitants slept soundly, and were fed and freed.

The fountain in the village flowed unseen and unheard,

and the fountain at the château dropped unseen and unheard—both melting away, like the minutes that were falling from the spring of Time—through three dark hours. Then, the grey water of both began to be ghostly in the light, and the eyes of the stone faces of the château were opened.

Lighter and lighter, until at last the sun touched the tops of the still trees, and poured its radiance over the hill. In the glow, the water of the château fountain seemed to turn to blood, and the stone faces crimsoned. The carol of the birds was loud and high, and, on the weather-beaten sill of the great window of the bed-chamber of Monsieur the Marquis, one little bird sang its sweetest song with all its might. At this, the nearest stone face seemed to stare amazed, and, with open mouth and dropped under-jaw, looked awe-stricken.

Now, the sun was full up, and movement began in the village. Casement windows opened, crazy doors were unbarred, and people came forth shivering—chilled, as yet, by the new sweet air. Then began the rarely lightened toil of the day among the village population. Some, to the fountain; some, to the fields; men and women here, to dig and delve; men and women there, to see to the poor live stock, and lead the bony cows out, to such pasture as could be found by the roadside. In the church and at the Cross, a kneeling figure or two; attendant on the latter prayers, the led cow, trying for a breakfast among the weeds at its foot.

The château awoke later, as became its quality, but woke gradually and surely. First, the lonely boar-spears and knives of the chase had been reddened as of old; then, had gleamed trenchant in the morning sunshine; now, doors and windows were thrown open, horses in their stables looked round over their shoulders at the light and freshness pouring in at doorways, leaves sparkled and rustled at iron-grated windows, dogs pulled hard at their chains, and reared impatient to be loosed.

All these trivial incidents belonged to the routine of life, and the return of morning. Surely, not so the ringing of the great bell of the château, nor the running up and down the stairs; nor the hurried figures on the terrace; nor the booting and tramping here and there and everywhere, nor the quick saddling of horses and riding away?

What winds conveyed this hurry to the grizzled mender of roads, already at work on the hill-top beyond the village, with his day's dinner (not much to carry) lying in a bundle that it was worth no crow's while to peck at, on a heap of stones? Had the birds, carrying some grains of it to a distance, dropped one over him as they sow chance seeds? Whether or no, the mender of roads ran, on the sultry morning, as if for his life, down the hill, knee-high in dust, and never stopped till he got to the fountain.

All the people of the village were at the fountain, standing about in their depressed manner, and whispering low, but showing no other emotions than grim curiosity and surprise. The led cows, hastily brought in and tethered to anything that would hold them, were looking stupidly on, or lying down chewing the cud of nothing particularly repaying their trouble, which they had picked up in their interrupted saunter. Some of the people of the château, and some of those of the posting-house, and all the taxing authorities, were armed more or less, and were crowded on the other side of the little street in a purposeless way, that was highly fraught with nothing. Already, the mender of roads had penetrated into the midst of a group of fifty particular friends, and was smiting himself in the breast with his blue cap. What did all this portend, and what portended the swift hoisting-up of Monsieur Gabelle behind a servant on horseback, and the conveying away of the said Gabelle (double-laden though the horse was), at a gallop, like a new version of the German ballad of Leonora?

It portended that there was one stone face too many, up at the château.

The Gorgon had surveyed the building again in the night, and had added the one stone face wanting; the stone face for which it had waited through about two hundred years.

It lay back on the pillow of Monsieur the Marquis. It was like a fine mask, suddenly startled, made angry, and petrified. Driven home into the heart of the stone figure attached to it, was a knife. Round its hilt was a frill of paper, on which was scrawled:

"*Drive him fast to his tomb. This, from* JACQUES."

CHAPTER X.

TWO PROMISES.

MORE months, to the number of twelve, had come and gone, and Mr. Charles Darnay was established in England as a higher teacher of the French language who was conversant with French literature. In this age, he would have been a Professor; in that age, he was a Tutor. He read with young men who could find any leisure and interest for the study of a living tongue spoken all over the world, and he cultivated a taste for its stores of knowledge and fancy. He could write of them, besides, in sound English, and render them into sound English. Such masters were not at that time easily found; Princes that had been, and Kings that were to be, were not yet of the Teacher class, and no ruined nobility had dropped out of Tellson's ledgers to turn cooks and carpenters. As a tutor, whose attainments made the student's way unusually pleasant and profitable, and as an elegant translator who br ught something to his work besides mere dictionary knowledge, young Mr. Darnay soon became known and encouraged. He was well acquainted, moreover, with the circumstances of his country, and those were of ever-growing interest. So, with great perseverance and untiring industry, he prospered.

In London, he had expected neither to walk on pavements of gold, nor to lie on beds of roses; if he had had any such exalted expectation, he would not have prospered. He had expected labour, and he found it, and did it, and made the best of it. In this, his prosperity consisted.

A certain portion of his time was passed at Cambridge, where he read with undergraduates as a sort of tolerated smuggler who drove a contraband trade in European languages, instead of conveying Greek and Latin through the Custom-house. The rest of his time he passed in London.

Now, from the days when it was always summer in Eden, to these days when it is mostly winter in fallen latitudes, the world of a man has invariably gone one way—Charles Darnay's way—the way of the love of a woman.

He had loved Lucie Manette from the hour of his danger. He had never heard a sound so sweet and dear as the sound of her compassionate voice; he had never seen a face so tenderly beautiful, as hers when it was confronted with his own on the edge of the grave that had been dug for him. But, he had not yet spoken to her on the subject;

the assassination at the deserted château far away beyond the heaving water and the long, long, dusty roads—the solid stone château which had itself become the mere mist of a dream—had been done a year, and he had never yet, by so much as a single spoken word, disclosed to her the state of his heart.

That he had his reasons for this, he knew full well. It was again a summer day when, lately arrived in London from his college occupation, he turned into the quiet corner in Soho, bent on seeking an opportunity of opening his mind to Doctor Manette. It was the close of the summer day, and he knew Lucie to be out with Miss Pross.

He found the Doctor reading in his arm-chair at a window. The energy which had at once supported him under his old sufferings and aggravated their sharpness, had been gradually restored to him. He was now a very energetic man indeed, with great firmness of purpose, strength of resolution, and vigour of action. In his recovered energy he was sometimes a little fitful and sudden, as he had at first been in the exercise of his other recovered faculties; but, this had never been frequently observable, and had grown more and more rare.

He studied much, slept little, sustained a great deal of fatigue with ease, and was equally cheerful. To him, now entered Charles Darnay, at sight of whom he laid aside his book and held out his hand.

"Charles Darnay! I rejoice to see you. We have been counting on your return these three or four days past. Mr. Stryver and Sydney Carton were both here yesterday, and both made you out to be more than due."

"I am obliged to them for their interest in the matter," he answered, a little coldly as to them, though very warmly as to the Doctor. "Miss Manette——"

"Is well," said the Doctor, as he stopped short, "and your return will delight us all. She has gone out on some household matters, but will soon be home."

"Doctor Manette, I knew she was from home. I took the opportunity of her being from home, to beg to speak to you."

There was a blank silence.

"Yes?" said the Doctor, with evident constraint. "Bring your chair here, and speak on."

He complied as to the chair, but appeared to find the speaking on less easy.

"I have had the happiness, Doctor Manette, of being so intimate here," so he at length began, "for some year and a half, that I hope the topic on which I am about to touch may not——"

He was stayed by the Doctor's putting out his hand to stop him. When he had kept it so a little while, he said, drawing it back:

"Is Lucie the topic?"

"She is."

"It is hard for me to speak of her at any time. It is very hard for me to hear her spoken of in that tone of yours, Charles Darnay."

"It is a tone of fervent admiration, true homage, and deep love, Doctor Manette!" he said deferentially.

There was another blank silence before her father rejoined:

"I believe it. I do you justice; I believe it."

His constraint was so manifest, and it was so manifest, too, that it originated in an unwillingness to approach the subject, that Charles Darnay hesitated.

"Shall I go on, sir?"

Another blank.

"Yes, go on."

"You anticipate what I would say, though you cannot know how earnestly I say it, how earnestly I feel it, without knowing my secret heart, and the hopes and fears and anxieties with which it has long been laden. Dear Doctor Manette, I love your daughter fondly, dearly, disinterestedly, devotedly. If ever there were love in the world, I love her. You have loved yourself; let your old love speak for me!"

The Doctor sat with his face turned away, and his eyes bent on the ground. At the last words, he stretched out his hand again, hurriedly, and cried:

"Not that, sir! Let that be! I adjure you, do not recall that!"

His cry was so like a cry of actual pain, that it rang in Charles Darnay's ears long after he had ceased. He motioned with the hand he had extended, and it seemed to be an appeal to Darnay to pause. The latter so received it, and remained silent.

"I ask your pardon," said the Doctor, in a subdued tone, after some moments. "I do not doubt your loving Lucie; you may be satisfied of it."

He turned towards him in his chair, but did not look at him, or raise his eyes. His chin dropped upon his hand, and his white hair overshadowed his face:

"Have you spoken to Lucie?"

"No."

"Nor written?"

"Never."

"It would be ungenerous to affect not to know that your self-denial is to be referred to your consideration for her father. Her father thanks you."

He offered his hand; but his eyes did not go with it.

"I know," said Darnay, respectfully, "how can I fail to know, Doctor Manette, I who have seen you together from day to day, that between you and Miss Manette there is an affection so unusual, so touching, so belonging to the circumstances in which it has been nurtured, that it can have few parallels, even in the tenderness between a father and child. I know, Doctor Manette—how can I fail to know—that, mingled with the affection and duty of a daughter who has become a woman, there is, in her heart, towards you, all the love and reliance of infancy itself. I know that, as in her childhood she had no parent, so she is now devoted to you with all the constancy and fervour of her present years and character, united to the trustfulness and attachment of the early days in which you were lost to her. I know perfectly well that if you had been restored to her from the world beyond this life, you could hardly be invested, in her sight, with a more sacred character than that in which you are always with her. I know that when she is clinging to you, the hands of baby, girl, and woman, all in one, are round your neck. I know that in loving you she sees and loves her mother at her own age, sees and loves you at my age, loves her mother broken-hearted, loves you through your dreadful trial and in your blessed restoration. I have known this, night and day, since I have known you in your home."

Her father sat silent, with his face bent down. His breathing was a little quickened; but he repressed all other signs of agitation.

"Dear Doctor Manette, always knowing this, always seeing her and you with this hallowed light about you, I have forborne, and forborne, as long as it was in the nature of man to do it. I have felt, and do even now feel, that to bring my love—even mine—between you, is to touch your history with something not quite so good as itself. But I love her. Heaven is my witness that I love her!"

"I believe it," answered her father, mournfully. "I have thought so before now. I believe it."

"But, do not believe," said Darnay, upon whose ear the mournful voice struck with a reproachful sound, "that if my fortune were so cast as that, being one day so happy as to make her my wife, I must at any time put any separation between her and you, I could or would breathe a word of what I now say. Besides that I should know it to be hopeless, I should know it to be a baseness. If I had any such possibility, even at a remote distance of years, harboured in my thoughts, and hidden in my heart—if it ever had been there—if it ever could be there—I could not now touch this honoured hand."

He laid his own upon it as he spoke.

"No, dear Doctor Manette. Like you, a voluntary exile from France; like you, driven from it by its distractions, oppressions, and miseries; like you, striving to live away from it by my own exertions, and trusting to a happier future; I look only to sharing your fortunes, sharing your life and home, and being faithful to you to the death. Not to divide with Lucie her privilege as your child, companion, and friend; but to come in aid of it, and bind her closer to you, if such a thing can be."

His touch still lingered on her father's hand. Answering the touch for a moment, but not coldly, her father rested his hands upon the arms of his chair, and looked up for the first time since the beginning of the conference. A struggle was evidently in his face; a struggle with that occasional look which had a tendency in it to dark doubt and dread.

"You speak so feelingly and so manfully, Charles Darnay, that I thank you with all my heart, and will open all my heart—or nearly so. Have you any reason to believe that Lucie loves you?"

"None. As yet, none."

"Is it the immediate object of this confidence, that you may at once ascertain that, with my knowledge?"

"Not even so. I might not have the hopefulness to do it for weeks; I might (mistaken or not mistaken) have that hopefulness to-morrow."

"Do you seek any guidance from me?"

"I ask none, sir. But I have thought it possible that you might have it in your power, if you should deem it right, to give me some."

"Do you seek any promise from me?"

"I do seek that."

"What is it?"

"I well understand that, without you, I could have no hope. I well understand that, even if Miss Manette held me at this moment in her innocent heart—do not think I have the presumption to assume so much—I could retain no place in it against her love for her father."

"If that be so, do you see what, on the other hand, is involved in it?"

"I understand equally well, that a word from her father in any suitor's favour, would outweigh herself and all the world. For which reason, Doctor Manette," said Darnay, modestly but firmly, "I would not ask that word, to save my life."

"I am sure of it. Charles Darnay, mysteries arise out of close love, as well as out of wide division; in the former case, they are subtle and delicate, and difficult to penetrate. My daughter Lucie is, in this one respect, such a mystery to me; I can make no guess at the state of her heart."

"May I ask, sir, if you think she is——" As he hesitated, her father supplied the rest.

"Is sought by any other suitor?"

"It is what I meant to say."

Her father considered a little before he answered:

"You have seen Mr. Carton here, yourself. Mr. Stryver is here too, occasionally. If it be at all, it can only be by one of these."

"Or both," said Darnay.

"I had not thought of both; I should not think either, likely. You want a promise from me. Tell me what it is."

"It is, that if Miss Manette should bring to you at any time, on her own part, such a confidence as I have ventured to lay before you, you will bear testimony to what I have said, and to your belief in it. I hope you may be able to think so well of me, as to urge no influence against me. I say nothing more of my stake in this; this is what I ask. The condition on which I ask it, and which you have an undoubted right to require, I will observe immediately."

"I give the promise," said the Doctor, "without any condition. I believe your object to be, purely and truthfully, as you have stated it. I believe your intention is to perpetuate, and not to weaken, the ties between me and my other and far dearer self. If she should ever tell me that you are essential to her perfect happiness, I will give her to you. If there were—Charles Darnay, if there were——"

The young man had taken his hand gratefully; their hands were joined as the Doctor spoke:

"—any fancies, any reasons, any apprehensions, anything whatsoever, new or old, against the man she really loved—the direct responsibility thereof not lying on his head—they should all be obliterated for her sake. She is everything to me; more to me than suffering, more to me than wrong, more to me——Well! This is idle talk."

So strange was the way in which he faded into silence, and so strange his fixed look when he had ceased to speak, that Darnay felt his own hand turn cold in the hand that slowly released and dropped it.

"You said something to me," said Doctor Manette, breaking into a smile. "What was it you said to me?"

He was at a loss how to answer, until he remembered having spoken of a condition. Relieved as his mind reverted to that, he answered:

"Your confidence in me ought to be returned with full confidence on my part. My present name, though but slightly changed from my mother's, is not, as you will remember, my own. I wish to tell you what that is, and why I am in England."

"Stop!" said the Doctor of Beauvais.

"I wish it, that I may the better deserve your confidence, and have no secret from you."

"Stop!"

For an instant, the Doctor even had his two hands at his ears; for another instant, even had his two hands laid on Darnay's lips.

"Tell me when I ask you, not now. If your suit should prosper, if Lucie should love you, you shall tell me on your marriage morning. Do you promise?"

"Willingly."

"Give me your hand. She will be home directly, and it

is better she should not see us together to-night. Go! God bless you!"

It was dark when Charles Darnay left him, and it was an hour later and darker when Lucie came home; she hurried into the room alone—for Miss Pross had gone straight up-stairs—and was surprised to find his reading-chair empty.

"My father!" she called to him. Father dear!"

Nothing was said in answer, but she heard a low hammering sound in his bedroom. Passing lightly across the intermediate room, she looked in at his door and came running back frightened, crying to herself, with her blood all chilled, "What shall I do! What shall I do!"

Her uncertainty lasted but a moment; she hurried back, and tapped at his door, and softly called to him. The noise ceased at the sound of her voice, and he presently came out to her, and they walked up and down together for a long time.

She came down from her bed, to look at him in his sleep that night. He slept heavily, and his tray of shoemaking tools, and his old unfinished work, were all as usual.

CHAPTER XI.

A COMPANION PICTURE.

"SYDNEY," said Mr. Stryver, on that selfsame night, or morning, to his jackal; "mix another bowl of punch; I have something to say to you."

Sydney had been working double tides that night, and the night before, and the night before that, and a good many nights in succession, making a grand clearance among Mr. Stryver's papers before the setting in of the long vacation. The clearance was effected at last; the Stryver arrears were handsomely fetched up; everything was got rid of until November should come with its fogs atmospheric and fogs legal, and bring grist to the mill again.

Sydney was none the livelier and none the soberer for so much application. It had taken a deal of extra wet-towelling to pull him through the night; a correspondingly extra quantity of wine had preceded the towelling; and he was in a very damaged condition, as he now pulled his turban off and threw it into the basin in which he had steeped it at intervals for the last six hours.

"Are you mixing that other bowl of punch?" said Stryver the portly, with his hands in his waistband, glancing round from the sofa where he lay on his back.

"I am."

"Now, look here! I am going to tell you something that will rather surprise you, and that perhaps will make you think me not quite as shrewd as you usually do think me. I intend to marry."

"*Do* you?"

"Yes. And not for money. What do you say now?"

"I don't feel disposed to say much. Who is she?"

"Guess."

"Do I know her?"

"Guess."

"I am not going to guess, at five o'clock in the morning, with my brains frying and sputtering in my head. If you want me to guess, you must ask me to dinner."

"Well then, I'll tell you," said Stryver, coming slowly into a sitting posture. "Sydney, I rather despair of making myself intelligible to you, because you are such an insensible dog."

"And you," returned Sydney, busy concocting the punch, "are such a sensitive and poetical spirit."

"Come!" rejoined Stryver, laughing boastfully, "though I don't prefer any claim to being the soul of Romance (for I hope I know better), still I am a tenderer sort of fellow than *you*."

"You are a luckier, if you mean that."

"I don't mean that. I mean I am a man of more—more——"

"Say gallantry, while you are about it," suggested Carton.

"Well! I'll say gallantry. My meaning is that I am a man," said Stryver, inflating himself at his friend as he made the punch, "who cares more to be agreeable, who takes more pains to be agreeable, who knows better how to be agreeable, in a woman's society, than you do."

"Go on," said Sydney Carton.

"No; but before I go on," said Stryver, shaking his head in his bullying way, "I'll have this out with you. You've been at Doctor Manette's house as much as I have, or more than I have. Why, I have been ashamed of your moroseness there! Your manners have been of that silent and sullen and hang-dog kind, that, upon my life and soul, I have been ashamed of you, Sydney!"

"It should be very beneficial to a man in your practice at the bar, to be ashamed of anything," returned Sydney; "you ought to be much obliged to me."

"You shall not get off in that way," rejoined Stryver, shouldering the rejoinder at him; "no, Sydney, it's my duty to tell you—and I tell you to your face to do you good—that you are a de-vilish ill-conditioned fellow in that sort of society. You are a disagreeable fellow."

Sydney drank a bumper of the punch he had made, and laughed.

"Look at me!" said Stryver, squaring himself; "I have less need to make myself agreeable than you have, being more independent in circumstances. Why do I do it?"

"I never saw you do it yet," muttered Carton.

"I do it because it's politic; I do it on principle. And look at me! I get on."

"You don't get on with your account of your matrimonial intentions," answered Carton, with a careless air; "I wish you would keep to that. As to me—will you never understand that I am incorrigible?"

He asked the question with some appearance of scorn.

"You have no business to be, incorrigible," was his friend's answer, delivered in no very soothing tone.

I have no business to be, at all, that I know of," said Sydney Carton. "Who is the lady?"

"Now, don't let my announcement of the name make you uncomfortable, Sydney," said Mr. Stryver, preparing him with ostentatious friendliness for the disclosure he was about to make, "because I know you don't mean half you say; and if you meant it all, it would be of no importance. I make this little preface, because you once mentioned the young lady to me in slighting terms."

"I did?"

"Certainly; and in these chambers."

Sydney Carton looked at his punch and looked at his complacent friend; drank his punch and looked at his complacent friend.

"You made mention of the young lady as a golden-haired doll. The young lady is Miss Manette. If you had been a fellow of any sensitiveness or delicacy of feeling in that kind of way, Sydney, I might have been a little resentful of your employing such a designation; but you are not. You want that sense altogether; therefore I am no more annoyed when I think of the expression, than I should be annoyed by a man's opinion of a picture of mine, who had no eye for pictures: or of a piece of music of mine, who had no ear for music."

Sydney Carton drank the punch at a great rate; drank it by bumpers, looking at his friend.

"Now you know all about it, Syd," said Mr. Stryver. "I don't care about fortune: she is a charming creature, and I have made up my mind to please myself: on the whole, I think I can afford to please myself. She will have in me a man already pretty well off, and a rapidly rising man, and a man of some distinction: it is a piece of good fortune for her, but she is worthy of good fortune. Are you astonished?"

Carton, still drinking the punch, rejoined, "Why should I be astonished?"

"You approve?"

Carton, still drinking the punch, rejoined, "Why should I not approve?"

"Well!" said his friend Stryver, "you take it more easily than I fancied you would, and are less mercenary on my behalf than I thought you would be; though, to be sure, you know well enough by this time that your ancient chum is a man of a pretty strong will. Yes, Sydney, I have had enough of this style of life, with no other as a change from it; I feel that it is a pleasant thing for a man to have a home when he feels inclined to go to it (when he doesn't, he can stay away), and I feel that Miss Manette will tell well in any station, and will always do me credit. So I have made up my mind. And now, Sydney, old boy, I want to say a word to *you* about *your* prospects. You are in a bad way, you know; you really are in a bad way. You don't know the value of money, you live hard, you'll knock up one of these days, and be ill and poor; you really ought to think about a nurse."

The prosperous patronage with which he said it, made him look twice as big as he was, and four times as offensive.

"Now, let me recommend you," pursued Stryver, "to look it in the face. I have looked it in the face, in my different way; look it in the face, you, in your different way. Marry. Provide somebody to take care of you. Never mind your having no enjoyment of women's society, nor understanding of it, nor tact for it. Find out some respectable woman with a little property—somebody in the landlady way, or lodging-letting way—and marry her, against a rainy day. That's the kind of thing for *you*. Now think of it, Sydney."

"I'll think of it." said Sydney.

CHAPTER XII.

THE FELLOW OF DELICACY.

MR. STRYVER having made up his mind to that magnanimous bestowal of good fortune on the Doctor's daughter, resolved to make her happiness known to her before he left town for the Long Vacation. After some mental debating of the point, he came to the conclusion that it would be as well to get all the preliminaries done with, and they could then arrange at their leisure whether he should give her his hand a week or two before Michaelmas Term, or in the little Christmas vacation between it and Hilary.

As to the strength of his case, he had not a doubt about it, but clearly saw his way to the verdict. Argued with the jury on substantial worldly grounds—the only grounds ever worth taking into account—it was a plain case, and had not a weak spot in it. He called himself for the plaintiff, there was no getting over his evidence, the counsel for the defendant threw up his brief, and the jury did not even turn to consider. After trying it, Stryver, C. J., was satisfied that no plainer case could be.

Accordingly, Mr. Stryver inaugurated the Long Vacation with a formal proposal to take Miss Manette to Vauxhall Gardens; that failing, to Ranelagh; that unaccountably failing too, it behoved him to present himself in Soho, and there declare his noble mind.

Towards Soho, therefore, Mr. Stryver shouldered his way from the Temple, while the bloom of the Long Vacation's infancy was still upon it. Anybody who had seen him projecting himself into Soho while he was yet on Saint Dunstan's side of Temple Bar, bursting in his full-blown way along the pavement, to the jostlement of all weaker people, might have seen how safe and strong he was.

His way taking him past Tellson's, and he both banking at Tellson's and knowing Mr. Lorry as the intimate friend of the Manettes, it entered Mr. Stryver's mind to enter the bank, and reveal to Mr. Lorry the brightness of the Soho horizon. So, he pushed open the door with the weak rattle in its throat, stumbled down the two steps, got past the two ancient cashiers, and shouldered himself into the musty back closet where Mr. Lorry sat at great books ruled for figures, with perpendicular iron bars to his window as if that were ruled for figures too, and everything under the clouds were a sum.

"Halloa!" said Mr. Stryver. "How do you do? I hope you are well!"

It was Stryver's grand peculiarity that he always seemed too big for any place, or space. He was so much too big for Tellson's, that old clerks in distant corners looked up with looks of remonstrance, as though he squeezed them against the wall. The House itself, magnificently reading the paper quite in the far-off perspective, lowered displeased, as if the Stryver head had been butted into its responsible waistcoat.

The discreet Mr. Lorry said, in a sample tone of the voice he would recommend under the circumstances, "How do you do, Mr. Stryver? How do you do, sir?" and shook hands. There was a peculiarity in his manner of shaking hands, always to be seen in any clerk at Tellson's who shook hands with a customer when the House pervaded the air. He shook in a self-abnegating way, as one who shook for Tellson and Co.

"Can I do anything for you, Mr. Stryver?" asked Mr. Lorry, in his business character.

"Why, no, thank you; this is a private visit to yourself, Mr. Lorry; I have come for a private word."

"Oh indeed!" said Mr. Lorry, bending down his ear, while his eye strayed to the House afar off.

"I am going," said Mr. Stryver, leaning his arms confidentially on the desk: whereupon, although it was a large double one, there appeared to be not half desk enough for him: "I am going to make an offer of myself in marriage to your agreeable little friend, Miss Manette, Mr. Lorry."

"Oh dear me!" cried Mr. Lorry, rubbing his chin, and looking at his visitor dubiously.

"Oh dear me, sir?" repeated Stryver, drawing back. "Oh dear you, sir? What may your meaning be, Mr. Lorry?"

"My meaning," answered the man of business, "is, of course, friendly and appreciative, and that it does you the greatest credit, and—in short, my meaning is everything you could desire. But—really, you know, Mr. Stryver ——" Mr. Lorry paused, and shook his head at him in the oddest manner, as if he were compelled against his will to add, internally, "you know there really is so much too much of you!"

"Well!" said Stryver, slapping the desk with his contentious hand, opening his eyes wider, and taking a long breath, "if I understand you, Mr. Lorry, I'll be hanged!"

Mr. Lorry adjusted his little wig at both ears as a means towards that end, and bit the feather of a pen.

"D—n it all, sir!" said Stryver, staring at him, "am I not eligible?"

"Oh dear yes! Yes. Oh yes, you're eligible!" said Mr. Lorry. "If you say eligible, you are eligible."

"Am I not prosperous?" asked Stryver.

"Oh! if you come to prosperous, you are prosperous," said Mr. Lorry.

"And advancing?"

"If you come to advancing you know," said Mr. Lorry, delighted to be able to make another admission, "nobody can doubt that."

"Then what on earth is your meaning, Mr. Lorry?" demanded Stryver, perceptibly crestfallen.

"Well! I——Were you going there now?" asked Mr. Lorry.

"Straight!" said Stryver, with a plump of his fist on the desk.

"Then I think I wouldn't, if I was you."

"Why?" said Stryver. "Now, I'll put you in a corner," forensically shaking a forefinger at him. "You are a man of business and bound to have a reason. State your reason. Why wouldn't you go?"

"Because," said Mr. Lorry, "I wouldn't go on such an object without having some cause to believe that I should succeed."

"D—n ME!" cried Stryver, "but this beats everything."

Mr. Lorry glanced at the distant House, and glanced at the angry Stryver.

"Here's a man of business—man of years—a man of experience—in a Bank," said Stryver; "and having summed up three leading reasons for complete success, he says there's no reason at all! Says it with his head on!" Mr. Stryver remarked upon the peculiarity as if it would have been infinitely less remarkable if he had said it with his head off.

"When I speak of success, I speak of success with the young lady; and when I speak of causes and reasons to make success probable, I speak of causes and reasons that will tell as such with the young lady. The young lady, my good sir," said Mr. Lorry, mildly tapping the Stryver arm, "the young lady. The young lady goes before all."

"Then you mean to tell me, Mr. Lorry," said Stryver, squaring his elbows, "that it is your deliberate opinion that the young lady at present in question is a mincing Fool?"

"Not exactly so. I mean to tell you, Mr. Stryver," said Mr. Lorry, reddening, "that I will hear no disrespectful word of that young lady from any lips; and that if I knew any man—which I hope I do not—whose taste was so coarse, and whose temper was so overbearing, that he could not restrain himself from speaking disrespectfully of that young lady at this desk, not even Tellson's should prevent my giving him a piece of my mind."

The necessity of being angry in a suppressed tone had put Mr. Stryver's blood-vessels into a dangerous state when it was his turn to be angry; Mr. Lorry's veins, methodical as their courses could usually be, were in no better state now it was his turn.

"That is what I mean to tell you, sir," said Mr. Lorry. "Pray let there be no mistake about it."

Mr. Stryver sucked the end of a ruler for a little while, and then stood hitting a tune out of his teeth with it, which probably gave him the toothache. He broke the awkward silence by saying:

"This is something new to me, Mr. Lorry. You deliberately advise me not to go up to Soho and offer myself—myself, Stryver of the King's Bench bar?"

"Do you ask me for my advice, Mr. Stryver?"

"Yes, I do."

"Very good. Then I give it, and you have repeated it correctly."

"And all I can say of it is," laughed Stryver with a vexed laugh, "that this—ha, ha!—beats everything past, present, and to come."

"Now understand me," pursued Mr. Lorry. "As a man of business, I am not justified in saying anything about this matter, for, as a man of business, I know nothing of it. But, as an old fellow, who has carried Miss Manette in his arms, who is the trusted friend of Miss Manette and of her father too, and who has a great affection for them both, I have spoken. The confidence is not of my seeking, recollect. Now, you think I may not be right?"

"Not I!" said Stryver, whistling. "I can't undertake to find third parties in common sense; I can only find it for myself. I suppose sense in certain quarters; you suppose mincing bread-and-butter nonsense. It's new to me, but you are right, I dare say."

"What I suppose, Mr. Stryver, I claim to characterise for myself. And understand me, sir," said Mr. Lorry, quickly flushing again, "I will not—not even at Tellson's—have it characterised for me by any gentleman breathing."

"There! I beg your pardon!" said Stryver.

"Granted. Thank you. Well, Mr. Stryver, I was about to say:—it might be painful to you to find yourself mistaken, it might be painful to Doctor Manette to have the task of being explicit with you, it might be very painful to Miss Manette to have the task of being explicit with you. You know the terms upon which I have the honour and happiness to stand with the family. If you please, committing you in no way, representing you in no way, I will undertake to correct my advice by the exercise of a little new observation and judgment expressly brought to bear upon it. If you should then be dissatisfied with it, you can but test its soundness for yourself; if, on the other hand, you should be satisfied with it, and it should be what it now is, it may spare all sides what is best spared. What do you say?"

"D—N IT ALL, SIR! AM I NOT ELIGIBLE?"

"How long would you keep me in town?"

"Oh! It is only a question of a few hours. I could go to Soho in the evening, and come to your chambers afterwards."

"Then I say yes," said Stryver: "I won't go up there now, I am not so hot upon it as that comes to; I say yes, and I shall expect you to look in to-night. Good morning."

Then Mr. Stryver turned and burst out of the Bank, causing such a concussion of air on his passage through, that to stand up against it bowing behind the two counters, required the utmost remaining strength of the two ancient clerks. Those venerable and feeble persons were always seen by the public in the act of bowing, and were popularly believed, when they had bowed a customer out, still to keep on bowing in the empty office until they bowed another customer in.

The barrister was keen enough to divine that the banker would not have gone so far in his expression of opinion on any less solid ground than moral certainty. Unprepared as he was for the large pill he had to swallow, he got it down. "And now," said Mr. Stryver, shaking his forensic forefinger at the Temple in general, when it was down, "my way out of this, is, to put you all in the wrong."

It was a bit of the art of an Old Bailey tactician, in which he found great relief. "You shall not put me in the wrong, young lady," said Mr. Stryver; "I'll do that for you."

Accordingly, when Mr. Lorry called that night as late as ten o'clock, Mr. Stryver, among a quantity of books and papers littered out for the purpose, seemed to have nothing less on his mind than the subject of the morning. He even showed surprise when he saw Mr. Lorry, and was altogether in an absent and preoccupied state.

"Well!" said that good-natured emissary, after a full half-hour of bootless attempts to bring him round to the question. "I have been to Soho."

"To Soho?" repeated Mr. Stryver, coldly. "Oh, to be sure! What am I thinking of!"

"And I have no doubt," said Mr. Lorry, "that I was right in the conversation we had. My opinion is confirmed, and I reiterate my advice."

"I assure you," returned Mr. Stryver, in the friendliest way, "that I am sorry for it on your account, and sorry for it on the poor father's account. I know this must always be a sore subject with the family; let us say no more about it."

"I don't understand you," said Mr. Lorry.

"I dare say not," rejoined Stryver, nodding his head in a smoothing and final way; "no matter, no matter."

"But it does matter," Mr. Lorry urged.

"No it doesn't; I assure you it doesn't. Having supposed that there was sense where there is no sense, and a laudable ambition where there is not a laudable ambition, I am well out of my mistake, and no harm is done. Young women have committed similar follies often before, and have repented them in poverty and obscurity often before. In an unselfish aspect, I am sorry that the thing is dropped, because it would have been a bad thing for me in a worldly point of view; in a selfish aspect I am glad that the thing has dropped, because it would have been a bad thing for me in a worldly point of view—it is hardly necessary to say I could have gained nothing by it. There is no harm at all done. I have not proposed to the young lady, and, be-

tween ourselves, I am by no means certain, on reflection, that I ever should have committed myself to that extent. Mr. Lorry, you cannot control the mincing vanities and giddinesses of empty-headed girls; you must not expect to do it, or you will always be disappointed. Now, pray say no more about it. I tell you, I regret it on account of others, but I am satisfied on my own account. And I am really very much obliged to you for allowing me to sound you, and for giving me your advice; you know the young lady better than I do; you were right, it never would have done."

Mr. Lorry was so taken aback, that he looked quite stupidly at Mr. Stryver shouldering him towards the door, with an appearance of showering generosity, forbearance, and good-will, on his erring head. "Make the best of it, my dear sir," said Stryver; "say no more about it; thank you again for allowing me to sound you; good-night!"

Mr. Lorry was out in the night, before he knew where he was. Mr. Stryver was lying back on his sofa, winking at his ceiling.

CHAPTER XIII.

THE FELLOW OF NO DELICACY.

IF Sydney Carton ever shone anywhere, he certainly never shone in the house of Doctor Manette. He had been there often, during a whole year, and had always been the same moody and morose lounger there. When he cared to talk, he talked well; but, the cloud of caring for nothing, which overshadowed him with such a fatal darkness, was very rarely pierced by the light within him.

And yet he did care something for the streets that environed that house, and for the senseless stones that made their pavements. Many a night he vaguely and unhappily wandered there, when wine had brought no transitory gladness to him; many a dreary daybreak revealed his solitary figure lingering there, and still lingering there when the first beams of the sun brought into strong relief, removed beauties of architecture in spires of churches and lofty buildings, as perhaps the quiet time brought some sense of better things, else forgotten and unattainable, into his mind. Of late, the neglected bed in the Temple Court had known him more scantily than ever; and often when he had thrown himself upon it no longer than a few minutes, he had got up again, and haunted that neighbourhood.

On a day in August, when Mr. Stryver (after notifying to his jackal that "he had thought better of that marrying matter") had carried his delicacy into Devonshire, and when the sight and scent of flowers in the City streets had some waifs of goodness in them for the worst, of health for the sickliest, and of youth for the oldest, Sydney's feet still trod those stones. From being irresolute and purposeless, his feet became animated by an intention, and, in the working out of that intention, they took him to the Doctor's door.

He was shown up-stairs, and found Lucie at her work, alone. She had never been quite at her ease with him, and received him with some little embarrassment as he seated himself near her table. But, looking up at his face in the interchange of the first few common-places, she observed a change in it.

"I fear you are not well, Mr. Carton!"

"No. But the life I lead, Miss Manette, is not conducive to health. What is to be expected of, or by, such profligates?"

"Is it not—forgive me; I have begun the question on my lips—a pity to live no better life?"

"God knows it is a shame!"

"Then why not change it?"

Looking gently at him again, she was surprised and saddened to see that there were tears in his eyes. There were tears in his voice too, as he answered:

"It is too late for that. I shall never be better than I am. I shall sink lower, and be worse."

He leaned an elbow on her table, and covered his eyes with his hand. The table trembled in the silence that followed.

She had never seen him softened, and was much distressed. He knew her to be so, without looking at her, and said:

"Pray forgive me, Miss Manette. I break down before the knowledge of what I want to say to you. Will you hear me?"

"If it will do you any good, Mr. Carton, if it would make you happier, it would make me very glad!"

"God bless you for your sweet compassion!"

He unshaded his face after a little while, and spoke steadily.

"Don't be afraid to hear me. Don't shrink from anything I say. I am like one who died young. All my life might have been."

"No, Mr. Carton. I am sure that the best part of it might still be; I am sure that you might be much, much worthier of yourself."

"Say of you, Miss Manette, and although I know better—although in the mystery of my own wretched heart I know better—I shall never forget it!"

She was pale and trembling. He came to her relief with a fixed despair of himself which made the interview unlike any other that could have been holden.

"If it had been possible, Miss Manette, that you could have returned the love of the man you see before you—self-flung away, wasted, drunken, poor creature of misuse as you know him to be—he would have been conscious this day and hour, in spite of his happiness, that he would bring you to misery, bring you to sorrow and repentance, blight you, disgrace you, pull you down with him. I know very well that you can have no tenderness for me; I ask for none; I am even thankful that it cannot be."

"Without it, can I not save you, Mr. Carton? Can I not recall you—forgive me again!—to a better course? Can I in no way repay your confidence? I know this is a confidence," she modestly said, after a little hesitation, and in earnest tears, "I know you would say this to no one else. Can I turn it to no good account for yourself, Mr. Carton?"

He shook his head.

"To none. No, Miss Manette, to none. If you will hear me through a very little more, all you can ever do for me is done. I wish you to know that you have been the last dream of my soul. In my degradation I have not been so degraded but that the sight of you with your father, and of this home made such a home by you, has stirred old shadows that I thought had died out of me. Since I knew you, I have been troubled by a remorse that I thought would never reproach me again, and have heard whispers from old voices impelling me upward, that I thought were silent for ever. I have had unformed ideas of striving

afresh, beginning anew, shaking off sloth and sensuality, and fighting out the abandoned fight. A dream, all a dream, that ends in nothing, and leaves the sleeper where he lay down, but I wish you to know that you inspired it."

"Will nothing of it remain? O Mr. Carton, think again! Try again!"

"No, Miss Manette; all through it, I have known myself to be quite undeserving. And yet I have had the weakness, and have still the weakness, to wish you to know with what a sudden mastery you kindled me, heap of ashes that I am, into fire—a fire, however, inseparable in its nature from myself, quickening nothing, lighting nothing, doing no service, idly burning away."

"Since it is my misfortune, Mr. Carton, to have made you more unhappy than you were before you knew me——"

"Don't say that, Miss Manette, for you would have reclaimed me, if anything could. You will not be the cause of my becoming worse."

"Since the state of your mind that you describe, is, at all events, attributable to some influence of mine—this is what I mean, if I can make it plain—can I use no influence to serve you? Have I no power for good, with you, at all?"

"The utmost good that I am capable of now, Miss Manette, I have come here to realise. Let me carry through the rest of my misdirected life, the remembrance that I opened my heart to you, last of all the world; and that there was something left in me at this time which you could deplore and pity."

"Which I entreated you to believe, again and again, most fervently, with all my heart, was capable of better things, Mr. Carton!"

"Entreat me to believe it no more, Miss Manette. I have proved myself, and I know better. I distress you; I draw fast to an end. Will you let me believe, when I recall this day, that the last confidence of my life was reposed in your pure and innocent breast, and that it lies there alone, and will be shared by no one?"

"If that will be a consolation to you, yes."

"Not even by the dearest one ever to be known to you?"

"Mr. Carton," she answered, after an agitated pause, "the secret is yours, not mine; and I promise to respect it."

"Thank you. And again, God bless you."

He put her hand to his lips, and moved towards the door.

"Be under no apprehension, Miss Manette, of my ever resuming this conversation by so much as a passing word. I will never refer to it again. If I were dead, that could not be surer than it is henceforth. In the hour of my death, I shall hold sacred the one good remembrance—and shall thank and bless you for it—that my last avowal of myself was made to you, and that my name, and faults, and miseries were gently carried in your heart. May it otherwise be light and happy!"

He was so unlike what he had ever shown himself to be, and it was so sad to think how much he had thrown away, and how much he every day kept down and perverted, that Lucie Manette wept mournfully for him as he stood looking back at her.

"Be comforted!" he said, "I am not worth such feeling, Miss Manette. An hour or two hence, and the low companions and low habits that I scorn but yield to, will render me less worth such tears as those, than any wretch who creeps along the streets. Be comforted! But, within myself, I shall always be, towards you, what I am now, though outwardly I shall be what you have heretofore seen me. The last supplication but one I make to you, is, that you will believe this of me."

"I will, Mr. Carton."

"My last supplication of all, is this; and with it, I will relieve you of a visitor with whom I well know you have nothing in unison, and between whom and you there is an impassable space. It is useless to say it, I know, but it rises out of my soul. For you, and for any dear to you, I would do anything. If my career were of that better kind that there was any opportunity or capacity of sacrifice in it, I would embrace any sacrifice for you and for those dear to you. Try to hold me in your mind, at some quiet times, as ardent and sincere in this one thing. The time will come, the time will not be long in coming, when new ties will be formed about you—ties that will bind you yet more tenderly and strongly to the home you so adorn—the dearest ties that will ever grace and gladden you. O Miss Manette, when the little picture of a happy father's face looks up in yours, when you see your own bright beauty springing up anew at your feet, think now and then that there is a man who would give his life, to keep a life you love beside you!"

He said, "Farewell!" said a last "God bless you!" and left her.

CHAPTER XIV.

THE HONEST TRADESMAN.

To the eyes of Mr. Jeremiah Cruncher, sitting on his stool in Fleet Street with his grisly urchin beside him, a vast number and variety of objects in movement were every day presented. Who could sit upon anything in Fleet Street during the busy hours of the day, and not be dazed and deafened by two immense processions, one ever tending westward with the sun, the other ever tending eastward from the sun, both ever tending to the plains beyond the range of red and purple where the sun goes down!

With his straw in his mouth, Mr. Cruncher sat watching the two streams, like the heathen rustic who has for several centuries been on duty watching one stream—saving that Jerry had no expectation of their ever running dry. Nor would it have been an expectation of a hopeful kind, since a small part of his income was derived from the pilotage of timid women (mostly of a full habit and past the middle term of life) from Tellson's side of the tides to the opposite shore. Brief as such companionship was in every separate instance, Mr. Cruncher never failed to become so interested in the lady as to express a strong desire to have the honour of drinking her very good health. And it was from the gifts bestowed upon him towards the execution of this benevolent purpose, that he recruited his finances, as just now observed.

Time was, when a poet sat upon a stool in a public place, and mused in the sight of men. Mr. Cruncher, sitting on a stool in a public place, but not being a poet, mused as little as possible, and looked about him.

It fell out that he was thus engaged in a season when crowds were few, and belated women few, and when his affairs in general were so unprosperous as to awaken a strong suspicion in his breast that Mrs. Cruncher must

have been "flopping" in some pointed manner, when an unusual concourse pouring down Fleet Street westward, attracted his attention. Looking that way, Mr. Cruncher made out that some kind of funeral was coming along, and that there was popular objection to this funeral, which engendered uproar.

"Young Jerry," said Mr. Cruncher, turning to his offspring, "it's a buryin'."

"Hooroar, father!" cried Young Jerry.

The young gentleman uttered this exultant sound with mysterious significance. The elder gentleman took the cry so ill, that he watched his opportunity, and smote the young gentleman on the ear.

"What d'ye mean? What are you hooroaring at? What do you want to conwey to your own father, you young Rip? This boy is a getting too many for *me*!" said Mr. Cruncher, surveying him. "Him and his hooroars! Don't let me hear no more of you, or you shall feel some more of me. D'ye hear?"

"I warn't doing no harm," Young Jerry protested, rubbing his cheek.

"Drop it, then," said Mr. Cruncher; "I won't have none of *your* no harms. Get a top of that there seat, and look at the crowd."

His son obeyed, and the crowd approached; they were bawling and hissing round a dingy hearse and dingy mourning coach, in which mourning coach there was only one mourner, dressed in the dingy trappings that were considered essential to the dignity of the position. The position appeared by no means to please him, however, with an increasing rabble surrounding the coach, deriding him, making grimaces at him, and incessantly groaning and calling out: "Yah! Spies! Tst! Spies!" with many compliments, too numerous and forcible to repeat.

Funerals had at all times a remarkable attraction for Mr. Cruncher; he always pricked up his senses, and became excited, when a funeral passed Tellson's. Naturally, therefore, a funeral with this uncommon attendance excited him greatly, and he asked of the first man who ran against him:

"What is it, brother? What's it about?"

"*I* don't know," said the man. "Spies! Yaha! Tst! Spies!"

He asked another man. "Who is it?"

"*I* don't know," returned the man, clapping his hands to his mouth nevertheless, and vociferating in a surprising heat and with the greatest ardour, "Spies! Yaha! Tst, tst! Spi-ies!"

At length, a person better informed on the merits of the case, tumbled against him, and from this person he learned that the funeral was the funeral of one Roger Cly.

"Was He a spy?" asked Mr. Cruncher.

"Old Bailey spy," returned his informant. "Yaha! Tst! Yah! Old Bailey Spi-i-ies!"

"Why, to be sure!" exclaimed Jerry, recalling the Trial at which he had assisted. "I've seen him. Dead, is he?"

"Dead as mutton," returned the other, "and can't be too dead. Have 'em out, there! Spies! Pull 'em out, there! Spies!"

The idea was so acceptable in the prevalent absence of any idea, that the crowd caught it up with eagerness, and loudly repeating the suggestion to have 'em out, and to pull 'em out, mobbed the two vehicles so closely that they came to a stop. On the crowd's opening the coach doors, the one mourner scuffled out of himself and was in their hands for a moment; but he was so alert, and made such good use of his time, that in another moment he was scouring away up a bye-street, after shedding his cloak, hat, long hatband, white pocket-handkerchief, and other symbolical tears.

These, the people tore to pieces and scattered far and wide with great enjoyment, while the tradesmen hurriedly shut up their shops; for a crowd in those times stopped at nothing, and was a monster much dreaded. They had already got the length of opening the hearse to take the coffin out, when some brighter genius proposed instead, its being escorted to its destination amidst general rejoicing. Practical suggestions being much needed, this suggestion, too, was received with acclamation, and the coach was immediately filled with eight inside and a dozen out, while as many people got on the roof of the hearse as could by any exercise of ingenuity stick upon it. Among the first of these volunteers was Jerry Cruncher himself, who modestly concealed his spiky head from the observation of Tellson's, in the further corner of the mourning coach.

The officiating undertakers made some protest against these changes in the ceremonies; but, the river being alarmingly near, and several voices remarking on the efficacy of cold immersion in bringing refractory members of the profession to reason, the protest was faint and brief. The remodelled procession started, with a chimney-sweep driving the hearse—advised by the regular driver, who was perched beside him, under close inspection, for the purpose —and with a pieman, also attended by his cabinet minister, driving the mourning coach. A bear-leader, a popular street character of the time, was impressed as an additional ornament, before the cavalcade had gone far down the Strand; and his bear, who was black and very mangy, gave quite an Undertaking air to that part of the procession in which he walked.

Thus, with beer-drinking, pipe-smoking, song-roaring, and infinite caricaturing of woe, the disorderly procession went its way, recruiting at every step, and all the shops shutting up before it. Its destination was the old church of Saint Pancras, far off in the fields. It got there in course of time; insisted on pouring into the burial-ground; finally, accomplished the interment of the deceased Roger Cly in its own way, and highly to its own satisfaction.

The dead man disposed of, and the crowd being under the necessity of providing some other entertainment for itself, another brighter genius (or perhaps the same) conceived the humour of impeaching casual passers-by, as Old Bailey spies, and wreaking vengeance on them. Chase was given to some scores of inoffensive persons who had never been near the Old Bailey in their lives, in the realisation of this fancy, and they were roughly hustled and maltreated. The transition to the sport of window-breaking, and thence to the plundering of public-houses, was easy and natural. At last, after several hours, when sundry summer-houses had been pulled down, and some area-railings had been torn up, to arm the more belligerent spirits, a rumour got about that the Guards were coming. Before this rumour, the crowd gradually melted away, and perhaps the Guards came, and perhaps they never came, and this was the usual progress of a mob.

Mr. Cruncher did not assist at the closing sports, but had remained behind in the churchyard, to confer and condole with the undertakers. The place had a soothing influence on him. He procured a pipe from a neighbouring public-house, and smoked it, looking in at the railings and maturely considering the spot.

"Jerry," said Mr. Cruncher, apostrophising himself in his usual way, "you see that there Cly that day, and you see with your own eyes that he was a young 'un and a straight made 'un."

Having smoked his pipe out, and ruminated a little longer, he turned himself about, that he might appear, before the hour of closing, on his station at Tellson's. Whether his meditations on mortality had touched his liver, or whether his general health had been previously at all amiss, or whether he desired to show a little attention to an eminent man, is not so much to the purpose, as that he made a short call upon his medical adviser—a distinguished surgeon—on his way back.

Young Jerry relieved his father with dutiful interest, and reported No job in his absence: The bank closed, the ancient clerks came out, the usual watch was set, and Mr. Cruncher and his son went home to tea.

"Now, I tell you where it is!" said Mr. Cruncher to his wife, on entering. "If, as a honest tradesman, my venturs goes wrong to-night, I shall make sure that you've been praying again me, and I shall work you for it just the same as if I seen you do it."

The dejected Mrs. Cruncher shook her head.

"Why, you're at it afore my face!" said Mr. Cruncher, with signs of angry apprehension.

"I am saying nothing."

"Well, then; don't meditate nothing. You might as well flop as meditate. You may as well go again me one way as another. Drop it altogether."

"Yes, Jerry."

"Yes, Jerry," repeated Mr. Cruncher sitting down to tea. "Ah! It *is* yes, Jerry. That's about it. You may say yes, Jerry."

Mr. Cruncher had no particular meaning in these sulky corroborations, but made use of them, as people not unfrequently do, to express general ironical dissatisfaction.

"You and your yes, Jerry," said Mr. Cruncher, taking a bite out of his bread-and-butter, and seeming to help it down with a large invisible oyster out of his saucer. "Ah! I think so. I believe you."

"You are going out to-night?" asked his decent wife, when he took another bite.

"Yes, I am."

"May I go with you, father?" asked his son, briskly.

"No, you mayn't. I'm a going—as your mother knows —a fishing. That's where I'm a going to. Going a fishing."

"Your fishing-rod gets rayther rusty; don't it, father?"

"Never you mind."

"Shall you bring any fish home, father?"

"If I don't, you'll have short commons, to-morrow," returned that gentleman, shaking his head; "that's questions enough for you; I ain't a going out, till you've been long abed."

He devoted himself during the remainder of the evening to keeping a most vigilant watch on Mrs. Cruncher, and sullenly holding her in conversation that she might be prevented from meditating any petitions to his disadvantage. With this view, he urged his son to hold her in conversation also, and led the unfortunate woman a hard life by dwelling on any causes of complaint he could bring against her, rather than he would leave her for a moment to her own reflections. The devoutest person could have rendered no greater homage to the efficacy of an honest prayer than he did in this distrust of his wife. It was as if a professed unbeliever in ghosts should be frightened by a ghost story.

"And mind you!" said Mr. Cruncher. "No games tomorrow! If I, as a honest tradesman, succeed in providing a jinte of meat or two, none of your not touching of it, and sticking to bread. If I, as a honest tradesman, am able to provide a little beer, none of your declaring on water. When you go to Rome, do as Rome does. Rome will be a ugly customer to you, if you don't. *I*'m your Rome, you know."

Then he began grumbling again:

"With your flying into the face of your own wittles and drink! I don't know how scarce you mayn't make the wittles and drink here, by your flopping tricks and your unfeeling conduct. Look at your boy: he *is* your'n, ain't he? He's as thin as a lath. Do you call yourself a mother, and not know that a mother's first duty is to blow her boy out?"

This touched young Jerry on a tender place; who adjured his mother to perform her first duty, and, whatever else she did or neglected, above all things to lay especial stress on the discharge of that maternal function so affectingly and delicately indicated by his other parent.

Thus the evening wore away with the Cruncher family, until Young Jerry was ordered to bed, and his mother, laid under similar injunctions, obeyed them. Mr. Cruncher beguiled the earlier watches of the night with solitary pipes, and did not start upon his excursion until nearly one o'clock. Towards that small and ghostly hour, he rose up form his chair, took a key out of his pocket, opened a locked cupboard, and brought forth a sack, a crowbar of convenient size, a rope and chain, and other fishing tackle of that nature. Disposing these articles about him in skilful manner, he bestowed a parting defiance on Mrs. Cruncher, extinguished the light, and went out.

Young Jerry, who had only made a feint of undressing when he went to bed, was not long after his father. Under cover of the darkness he followed out of the room, followed down the stairs, followed down the court, followed out into the streets. He was in no uneasiness concerning his getting into the house again, for it was full of lodgers, and the door stood ajar all night.

Impelled by a laudable ambition to study the art and mystery of his father's honest calling, Young Jerry, keeping as close to house fronts, walls, and doorways, as his eyes were close to one another, held his honoured parent in view. The honoured parent steering Northward, had not gone far, when he was joined by another disciple of Izaak Walton, and the two trudged on together.

Within half an hour from the first starting, they were beyond the winking lamps, and the more than winking watchmen, and were out upon a lonely road. Another fisherman was picked up here—and that so silently, that if Young Jerry had been superstitious, he might have supposed the second follower of the gentle craft to have, all of a sudden, split himself into two.

The three went on, and Young Jerry went on, until the three stopped under a bank overhanging the road. Upon the top of the bank was a low brick wall, surmounted by an iron railing. In the shadow of bank and wall the three turned out of the road, and up a blind lane, of which the wall—there, risen to some eight or ten feet high—formed

one side. Crunching down in a corner, peeping up the lane, the next object that Young Jerry saw, was the form of his honoured parent, pretty well defined against a watery and clouded moon, nimbly scaling an iron gate. He was soon over, and then the second fisherman got over, and then the third. They all dropped softly on the ground within the gate, and lay there a little—listening perhaps. Then, they moved away on their hands and knees.

It was now Young Jerry's turn to approach the gate: which he did, holding his breath. Crouching down again in a corner there, and looking in, he made out the three fishermen creeping through some rank grass! and all the gravestones in the churchyard—it was a large churchyard that they were in—looking on like ghosts in white, while the church tower itself looked on like the ghost of a monstrous giant. They did not creep far, before they stopped and stood upright. And then they began to fish.

They fished with a spade, at first. Presently the honoured parent appeared to be adjusting some instrument like a great corkscrew. Whatever tools they worked with, they worked hard, until the awful striking of the church clock so terrified Young Jerry, that he made off, with his hair as stiff as his father's.

But, his long-cherished desire to know more about these matters, not only stopped him in his running away, but lured him back again. They were still fishing perseveringly, when he peeped in at the gate for the second time; but, now they seemed to have got a bite. There was a screwing and complaining sound down below, and their bent figures were strained, as if by a weight. By slow degrees the weight broke away the earth upon it, and came to the surface. Young Jerry very well knew what it would be; but, when he saw it, and saw his honoured parent about to wrench it open, he was so frightened, being new to the sight, that he made off again, and never stopped until he had run a mile or more.

He would not have stopped then, for anything less necessary than breath, it being a spectral sort of race that he ran, and one highly desirable to get to the end of. He had a strong idea that the coffin he had seen was running after him; and, pictured as hopping on behind him, bolt upright, upon its narrow end, always on the point of overtaking him and hopping on at his side—perhaps taking his arm—it was a pursuer to shun. It was an inconsistent and ubiquitous fiend too, for, while it was making the whole night behind him dreadful, he darted out into the roadway to avoid dark alleys, fearful of its coming hopping out of them like a dropsical boy's-Kite without tail and wings. It hid in doorways too, rubbing its horrible shoulders against doors, and drawing them up to its ears, as if it were laughing. It got into shadows on the road, and lay cunningly on its back to trip him up. All this time it was incessantly hopping on behind and gaining on him, so that when the boy got to his own door he had reason for being half dead. And even then it would not leave him, but followed him up-stairs with a bump on every stair, scrambled into bed with him, and bumped down, dead and heavy, on his breast when he fell asleep.

From his oppressed slumber, Young Jerry in his closet was awakened after daybreak and before sunrise, by the presence of his father in the family room. Something had gone wrong with him; at least, so Young Jerry inferred, from the circumstance of his holding Mrs. Cruncher by the ears, and knocking the back of her head against the head-board of the bed.

"I told you I would," said Mr. Cruncher, "and I did."

"Jerry, Jerry, Jerry!" his wife implored.

"You oppose yourself to the profit of the business," said Jerry, "and me and my partners suffer. You was to honour and obey; why the devil don't you?"

"I try to be a good wife, Jerry," the poor woman protested, with tears.

"Is it being a good wife to oppose your husband's business? Is it honouring your husband to dishonour his business? Is it obeying your husband to disobey him on the wital subject of his business?"

"You hadn't taken to the dreadful business then, Jerry."

"It's enough for you," retorted Mr. Cruncher, "to be the wife of a honest tradesman, and not to occupy your female mind with calculations when he took to his trade or when he didn't. A honouring and obeying wife would let his trade alone altogether. Call yourself a religious woman? If you're a religious woman, give me a irreligious one! You have no more nat'ral sense of duty than the bed of this here Thames river has of a pile, and similarly it must be knocked into you."

The altercation was conducted in a low tone of voice, and terminated in the honest tradesman's kicking off his clay-soiled boots, and lying down at his length on the floor. After taking a timid peep at him lying on his back, with his rusty hands under his head for a pillow, his son lay down too, and fell asleep again.

There was no fish for breakfast, and not much of anything else. Mr. Cruncher was out of spirits, and out of temper, and kept an iron pot-lid by him as a projectile for the correction of Mrs. Cruncher, in case he should observe any symptoms of her saying Grace. He was brushed and washed at the usual hour, and set off with his son to pursue his ostensible calling.

Young Jerry, walking with the stool under his arm at his father's side along sunny and crowded Fleet Street, was a very different Young Jerry from him of the previous night, running home through darkness and solitude from his grim pursuer. His cunning was fresh with the day, and his qualms were gone with the night—in which particulars it is not improbable that he had compeers in Fleet Street and the City of London, that fine morning.

"Father," said Young Jerry, as they walked along: taking care to keep at arm's length and to have the stool well between them: "what's a Resurrection-Man?"

Mr. Cruncher came to a stop on the pavement before he answered, "How should I know?"

"I thought you knowed everything, father," said the artless boy.

"Hem! Well," returned Mr. Cruncher, going on again, and lifting off his hat to give his spikes free play, "he's a tradesman."

"What's his goods, father?" asked the brisk Young Jerry.

"His goods," said Mr. Cruncher, after turning it over in his mind, "is a branch of Scientific goods."

"Persons' bodies, ain't it, father?" asked the lively boy.

"I believe it is something of that sort," said Mr. Cruncher.

"Oh, father, I should so like to be a Resurrection-Man when I'm quite growed up!"

Mr. Cruncher was soothed, but shook his head in a dubious and moral way. "It depends upon how you dewelop your talents. Be careful to dewelop your talents, and never to say no more than you can help to nobody, and there's no telling at the present time what you may not come to be fit for." As Young Jerry, thus encouraged, went on a few yards in advance, to plant the stool in the shadow of the Bar, Mr. Cruncher added to himself: "Jerry, you honest tradesman, there's hopes wot that boy will yet be a blessing to you, and a recompense to you for his mother!"

CHAPTER XV.

KNITTING.

THERE had been earlier drinking than usual in the wine-shop of Monsieur Defarge. As early as six o'clock in the morning, sallow faces peeping through its barred windows had descried other faces within, bending over measures of wine. Monsieur Defarge sold a very thin wine at the best of times, but it would seem to have been an unusually thin wine that he sold at this time. A sour wine, moreover, or a souring, for its influence on the mood of those who drank it was to make them gloomy. No vivacious Bacchanalian flame leaped out of the pressed grape of Monsieur Defarge; but, a smouldering fire that burnt in the dark, lay hidden in the dregs of it.

This had been the third morning in succession, on which there had been early drinking at the wine-shop of Monsieur Defarge. It had begun on Monday, and here was Wednesday come. There had been more of early brooding than drinking; for, many men had listened and whispered and slunk about there from the time of the opening of the door, who could not have laid a piece of money on the counter to save their souls. These were to the full as interested in the place, however, as if they could have commanded whole barrels of wine; and they glided from seat to seat, and from corner to corner, swallowing talk in lieu of drink, with greedy looks.

Notwithstanding an unusual flow of company, the master of the wine-shop was not visible. He was not missed; for, nobody who crossed the threshold looked for him, nobody asked for him, nobody wondered to see only Madame Defarge in her seat, presiding over the distribution of wine, with a bowl of battered small coins before her, as much defaced and beaten out of their original impress as the small coinage of humanity from whose ragged pockets they had come.

A suspended interest and a prevalent absence of mind, were perhaps observed by the spies who looked in at the wine-shop, as they looked in at every place, high and low, from the king's palace to the criminal's gaol. Games at cards languished, players at dominoes musingly built towers with them, drinkers drew figures on the tables with spilt drops of wine, Madame Defarge herself picked out the pattern on her sleeve with her toothpick, and saw and heard something inaudible and invisible a long way off.

Thus, Saint Antoine in this vinous feature of his, until mid-day. It was high noontide, when two dusty men passed through his streets and under his swinging lamps: of whom, one was Monsieur Defarge: the other a mender of roads in a blue cap. All adust and athirst, the two entered the wine-shop. Their arrival had lighted a kind of fire in the breast of Saint Antoine, fast spreading as they came along, which stirred and flickered in flames of faces at most doors and windows. Yet, no one had followed them, and no man spoke when they entered the wine-shop, though the eyes of every man there were turned upon them.

"Good day, gentlemen!" said Monsieur Defarge.

It may have been a signal for loosening the general tongue. It elicited an answering chorus of "Good day!"

"It is bad weather, gentlemen," said Defarge, shaking his head.

Upon which, every man looked at his neighbour, and then all cast down their eyes and sat silent. Except one man, who got up and went out.

"My wife," said Defarge aloud, addressing Madame Defarge: "I have travelled certain leagues with this good mender of roads, called Jacques. I met him—by accident—a day and half's journey out of Paris. He is a good child, this mender of roads, called Jacques. Give him to drink, my wife!"

A second man got up and went out. Madame Defarge set wine before the mender of roads called Jacques, who doffed his blue cap to the company, and drank. In the breast of his blouse he carried some coarse dark bread; he ate of this between whiles, and sat munching and drinking near Madame Defarge's counter. A third man got up and went out.

Defarge refreshed himself with a draught of wine—but, he took less than was given to the stranger, as being himself a man to whom it was no rarity—and stood waiting until the countryman had made his breakfast. He looked at no one present, and no one now looked at him; not even Madame Defarge, who had taken up her knitting, and was at work.

"Have you finished your repast, friend?" he asked, in due season.

"Yes, thank you."

"Come, then! You shall see the apartment that I told you you could occupy. It will suit you to a marvel."

Out of the wine-shop into the street, out of the street into a courtyard, out of the courtyard up a steep staircase, out of the staircase into a garret,—formerly the garret where a white-haired man sat on a low bench, stooping forward and very busy, making shoes.

No white-haired man was there now; but, the three men were there who had gone out of the wine-shop singly. And between them and the white-haired man afar off, was the one small link, that they had once looked in at him through the chinks in the wall.

Defarge closed the door carefully, and spoke in a subdued voice:

"Jacques One, Jacques Two, Jacques Three! This is the witness encountered by appointment, by me, Jacques Four. He will tell you all. Speak, Jacques Five!"

The mender of roads, blue cap in hand, wiped his swarthy forehead with it, and said, "Where shall I commence, monsieur?"

"Commence," was Monsieur Defarge's not unreasonable reply, "at the commencement."

"I saw him then, messieurs," began the mender of roads, "a year ago this running summer, underneath the carriage of the Marquis, hanging by the chain. Behold the manner of it. I leaving my work on the road, the sun going to bed, the carriage of the Marquis slowly ascending the hill, he hanging by the chain—like this."

Again the mender of roads went through the whole performance; in which he ought to have been perfect by that time, seeing that it had been the infallible resource and indispensable entertainment of his village during a whole year.

Jacques One struck in, and asked if he had ever seen the man before?

"Never," answered the mender of roads, recovering his perpendicular.

Jacques Three demanded how he afterwards recognised him then?

"By his tall figure," said the mender of roads, softly, and with his finger at his nose. "When Monsieur the Marquis demands that evening, 'Say, what is he like?' I make response, 'Tall as a spectre.'"

"You should have said, short as a dwarf," returned Jacques Two.

"But what did I know? The deed was not then accomplished, neither did he confide in me. Observe! Under those circumstances even, I do not offer my testimony. Monsieur the Marquis indicates me with his finger, standing near our little fountain, and says, 'To me! Bring that rascal!' My faith, messieurs, I offer nothing."

"He is right there, Jacques," murmured Defarge, to him who had interrupted. "Go on!"

"Good!" said the mender of roads, with an air of mystery. "The tall man is lost, and he is sought—how many months? Nine, ten, eleven?"

"No matter, the number," said Defarge. "He is well hidden, but at last he is unluckily found. Go on!"

"I am again at work upon the hill-side, and the sun is again about to go to bed. I am collecting my tools to descend to my cottage down in the village below, where it is already dark, when I raise my eyes, and see coming over the hill six men. In the midst of them is a tall man with his arms bound—tied to his sides—like this!"

With the aid of his indispensable cap, he represented a man with his elbows bound fast at his hips, with cords that were knotted behind him.

"I stand aside, messieurs, by my heap of stones, to see the soldiers and their prisoner pass (for it is a solitary road, that, where any spectacle is well worth looking at), and at first, as they approach, I see no more than that they are six soldiers with a tall man bound, and that they are almost black to my sight—except on the side of the sun going to bed, where they have a red edge, messieurs. Also, I see that their long shadows are on the hollow ridge on the opposite side of the road, and are on the hill above it, and are like the shadows of giants. Also, I see that they are covered with dust, and that the dust moves with them as they come, tramp, tramp! But when they advance quite near to me, I recognise the tall man, and he recognises me. Ah, but he would be well content to precipitate himself over the hill-side once again, as on the evening when he and I first encountered, close to the same spot!"

He described it as if he were there, and it was evident that he saw it vividly; perhaps he had not seen much in his life.

"I do not show the soldiers that I recognise the tall man; he does not show the soldiers that he recognises me; we do it, and we know it, with our eyes. 'Come on!' says the chief of that company, pointing to the village, 'bring him fast to his tomb!' and they bring him faster. I follow. His arms are swelled because of being bound so tight, his wooden shoes are large and clumsy, and he is lame. Because he is lame, and consequently slow, they drive him with their guns—like this!"

He imitated the action of a man's being impelled forward by the butt-ends of muskets.

"As they descend the hill like madmen running a race,

he falls. They laugh and pick him up again. His face is bleeding and covered with dust, but he cannot touch it; thereupon they laugh again. They bring him into the village; all the village runs to look; they take him past the mill, and up to the prison; all the village sees the prison gate open in the darkness of the night, and swallow him—like this!"

He opened his mouth as wide as he could, and shut it with a sounding snap of his teeth. Observant of his unwillingness to mar the effect by opening it again, De.°arge said, "Go on, Jacques."

"All the village," pursued the mender of roads, on tiptoe and in a low voice, "withdraws; all the village whispers by the fountain; all the village sleeps; all the village dreams of that unhappy one, within the locks and bars of the prison on the crag, and never to come out of it except to perish. In the morning, with my tools upon my shoulder, eating my morsel of black bread as I go, I make a circuit by the prison, on my way to my work. There I see him, high up, behind the bars of a lofty iron cage, bloody and dusty as last night, looking through. He has no hand free, to wave to me; I dare not call to him; he regards me like a dead man."

Defarge and the three glanced darkly at one another. The looks of all of them were dark, repressed, and revengeful, as they listened to the countryman's story; the manner of all of them, while it was secret, was authoritative too. They had the air of a rough tribunal; Jacques One and Two sitting on the old pallet-bed, each with his chin resting on his hand, and his eyes intent on the road-mender; Jacques Three, equally intent, on one knee behind them, with his agitated hand always gliding over the network of fine nerves about his mouth and nose; Defarge standing between them and the narrator, whom he had stationed in the light of the window, by turns looking from him to them, and from them to him.

"Go on, Jacques," said Defarge.

"He remains up there in his iron cage some days. The village looks at him by stealth, for it is afraid. But it always looks up, from a distance, at the prison on the crag; and in the evening, when the work of the day is achieved and it assembles to gossip at the fountain, all faces are turned towards the prison. Formerly, they were turned towards the posting-house, now, they are turned towards the prison. They whisper at the fountain, that although condemned to death he will not be executed; they say that petitions have been presented in Paris, showing that he was enraged and made mad by the death of his child; they say that a petition has been presented to the King himself. What do I know? It is possible. Perhaps yes, perhaps no."

"Listen then, Jacques," Number One of that name sternly interposed. "Know that a petition was presented to the King and Queen. All here, yourself excepted, saw the King take it, in his carriage in the street, sitting beside the Queen. It is Defarge whom you see here, who, at the hazard of his life, darted out before the horses, with the petition in his hand."

"And once again listen, Jacques!" said the kneeling Number Three: his fingers ever wandering over and over those fine nerves, with a strikingly greedy air, as if he hungered for something—that was neither food nor drink; "the guard, horse and foot, surrounded the petitioner, and struck him blows. You hear?"

"I hear, messieurs."

"Go on then," said Defarge.

"Again; on the other hand, they whisper at the fountain," resumed the countryman, "that he is brought down into our country to be executed on the spot, and that he will very certainly be executed. They even whisper that because he has slain Monseigneur, and because Monseigneur was the father of his tenants—serfs—what you will—he will be executed as a parricide. One old man says at the fountain, that his right hand, armed with the knife, will be burnt off before his face; that, into wounds which will be made in his arms, his breast, and his legs, there will be poured boiling oil, melted lead, hot resin, wax, and sulphur; finally, that he will be torn limb from limb by four strong horses. That old man says, all this was actually done to a prisoner who made an attempt on the life of the late King, Louis Fifteen. But how do I know if he lies? I am not a scholar."

"Listen once again then, Jacques!" said the man with the restless hand and the craving air. "The name of that prisoner was Damiens, and it was all done in open day, in the open streets of this city of Paris; and nothing was more noticed in the vast concourse that saw it done, than the crowd of ladies of quality and fashion, who were full of eager attention to the last—to the last, Jacques, prolonged until nightfall, when he had lost two legs and an arm, and still breathed! And it was done—why, how old are you?"

"Thirty-five," said the mender of roads, who looked sixty.

"It was done when you were more than ten years old; you might have seen it."

"Enough!" said Defarge, with grim impatience. "Long live the Devil! Go on."

"Well! Some whisper this, some whisper that; they speak of nothing else; even the fountain appears to fall to that tune. At length, on Sunday night when all the village is asleep, come soldiers, winding down from the prison, and their guns ring on the stones of the little street. Workmen dig, workmen hammer, soldiers laugh and sing; in the morning, by the fountain, there is raised a gallows forty feet high, poisoning the water."

The mender of roads looked *through* rather than *at* the low ceiling, and pointed as if he saw the gallows somewhere in the sky.

"All work is stopped, all assemble there, nobody leads the cows out, the cows are there with the rest. At midday, the roll of drums. Soldiers have marched into the prison in the night, and he is in the midst of many soldiers. He is bound as before, and in his mouth there is a gag—tied so, with a tight string, making him look almost as if he laughed." He suggested it, by creasing his face with his two thumbs, from the corners of his mouth to his ears. "On the top of the gallows is fixed the knife, blade upwards, with its point in the air. He is hanged there forty feet high—and is left hanging, poisoning the water."

They looked at one another, as he used his blue cap to wipe his face, on which the perspiration had started afresh while he recalled the spectacle.

"It is frightful, messieurs. How can the women and the children draw water! Who can gossip of an evening, under that shadow! Under it, have I said? When I left the village, Monday evening as the sun was going to bed, and looked back from the hill, the shadow struck across the church, across the mill, across the prison—seemed to strike across the earth, messieurs, to where the sky rests upon it!"

The hungry man gnawed one of his fingers as he looked

at the other three, and his finger quivered with the craving that was on him.

"That's all, messieurs. I left at sunset (as I had been warned to do), and I walked on, that night and half next day, until I met (as I was warned I should) this comrade. With him, I came on, now riding and now walking, through the rest of yesterday and through last night. And here you see me!"

After a gloomy silence, the first Jacques said, "Good! You have acted and recounted faithfully. Will you wait for us a little, outside the door?"

"Very willingly," said the mender of roads. Whom Defarge escorted to the top of the stairs, and, leaving seated there, returned.

The three had risen, and their heads were together when he came back to the garret.

"How say you, Jacques?" demanded Number One. "To be registered?"

"To be registered, as doomed to destruction," returned Defarge.

"Magnificent!" croaked the man with the craving.

"The château, and all the race?" inquired the first.

"The château and all the race," returned Defarge. "Extermination."

The hungry man repeated, in a rapturous croak, "Magnificent!" and began gnawing another finger.

"Are you sure," asked Jacques Two, of Defarge, "that no embarrassment can arise from our manner of keeping the register? Without doubt it is safe, for no one beyond ourselves can decipher it; but shall we always be able to decipher it—or, I ought to say, will she?"

"Jacques," returned Defarge, drawing himself up, "if madame my wife undertook to keep the register in her memory alone, she would not lose a word of it—not a syllable of it. Knitted, in her own stitches and her own symbols, it will always be as plain to her as the sun. Confide in Madame Defarge. It would be easier for the weakest poltroon that lives, to erase himself from existence, than to erase one letter of his name or crimes from the knitted register of Madame Defarge."

There was a murmur of confidence and approval, and then the man who hungered, asked: "Is this rustic to be sent back soon? I hope so. He is very simple; is he not a little dangerous?"

"He knows nothing," said Defarge; "at least nothing more than would easily elevate himself to a gallows of the same height. I charge myself with him; let him remain with me; I will take care of him, and set him on his road. He wishes to see the fine world—the King, the Queen, and Court; let him see them on Sunday."

"What?" exclaimed the hungry man, staring. "Is it a good sign, that he wishes to see Royalty and Nobility?"

"Jacques," said Defarge; "judiciously show a cat milk, if you wish her to thirst for it. Judiciously show a dog his natural prey, if you wish him to bring it down one day."

Nothing more was said, and the mender of roads, being found already dozing on the topmost stair, was advised to lay himself down on the pallet-bed and take some rest. He needed no persuasion, and was soon asleep.

Worse quarters than Defarge's wine-shop, could easily have been found in Paris for a provincial slave of that degree. Saving for a mysterious dread of madame by which he was constantly haunted, his life was very new and agreeable. But, madame sat all day at her counter, so expressly unconscious of him, and so particularly determined not to perceive that his being there had any connection with anything below the surface, that he shook in his wooden shoes whenever his eye lighted on her. For, he contended with himself that it was impossible to foresee what that lady might pretend next; and he felt assured that if she should take it into her brightly ornamented head to pretend that she had seen him do a murder and afterwards flay the victim, she would infallibly go through with it until the play was played out.

Therefore, when Sunday came, the mender of roads was not enchanted (though he said he was) to find that madame was to accompany monsieur and himself to Versailles. It was additionally disconcerting to have madame knitting all the way there, in a public conveyance; it was additionally disconcerting yet, to have madame in the crowd in the afternoon, still with her knitting in her hands as the crowd waited to see the carriage of the King and Queen.

"You work hard, madame," said a man near her.

"Yes," answered Madame Defarge; "I have a good deal to do."

"What do you make, madame?"

"Many things."

"For instance——"

"For instance," returned Madame Defarge, composedly, "shrouds."

The man moved a little further away, as soon as he could, and the mender of roads fanned himself with his blue cap: feeling it mightily close and oppressive. If he needed a King and Queen to restore him, he was fortunate in having his remedy at hand; for, soon the large-faced King and the fair-faced Queen came in their golden coach, attended by the shining Bull's Eye of their Court, a glittering multitude of laughing ladies and fine lords; and in jewels and silks and powder and splendour and elegantly spurning figures and handsomely disdainful faces of both sexes, the mender of roads bathed himself, so much to his temporary intoxication, that he cried Long live the King, Long live the Queen, Long live everybody and everything! as if he had never heard of ubiquitous Jacques in his time. Then, there were gardens, courtyards, terraces, fountains, green banks, more King and Queen, more Bull's Eye, more lords and ladies, more Long live they all! until he absolutely wept with sentiment. During the whole of this scene, which lasted some three hours, he had plenty of shouting and weeping and sentimental company, and throughout Defarge held him by the collar, as if to restrain him from flying at the objects of his brief devotion and tearing them to pieces.

"Bravo!" said Defarge, clapping him on the back when it was over, like a patron; "you are a good boy!"

The mender of roads was now coming to himself, and was mistrustful of having made a mistake in his late demonstrations; but no.

"You are the fellow we want," said Defarge, in his ear; "you make these fools believe that it will last for ever. Then, they are the more insolent, and it is the nearer ended."

"Hey!" cried the mender of roads, reflectively; "that's true."

"These fools know nothing. While they despise your breath, and would stop it for ever and ever, in you or in a hundred like you rather than in one of their own horses or dogs, they only know what your breath tells them. Let it deceive them, then, a little longer; it cannot deceive them too much."

LOUIS XVI.

Madame Defarge looked superciliously at the client, and nodded in confirmation.

"As to you," said she, "you would shout and shed tears for anything, if it made a show and a noise. Say! Would you not?"

"Truly, madame, I think so. For the moment."

"If you were shown a great heap of dolls, and were set upon them to pluck them to pieces and despoil them for your own advantage, you would pick out the richest and gayest. Say! Would you not?"

"Truly yes, madame."

"Yes. And if you were shown a flock of birds, unable to fly, and were set upon them to strip them of their feathers for your own advantage, you would set upon the birds of the finest feathers; would you not?"

"It is true, madame."

"You have seen both dolls and birds to-day," said Madame Defarge, with a wave of her hand towards the place where they had last been apparent; "now, go home!"

CHAPTER XVI.

STILL KNITTING.

MADAME DEFARGE and monsieur her husband returned amicably to the bosom of Saint Antoine, while a speck in a blue cap toiled through the darkness, and through the dust, and down the weary miles of avenue by the wayside, slowly tending towards that point of the compass where the château of Monsieur the Marquis, now in his grave, listened to the whispering trees. Such ample leisure had the stone faces, now, for listening to the trees and to the fountain, that the few village scarecrows who, in their quest for herbs to eat and fragments of dead stick to burn, strayed within sight of the great stone courtyard and terrace staircase, had it borne in upon their starved fancy that the expression of the faces was altered. A rumour just lived in the village—had a faint and bare existence there, as its people had—that when the knife struck home, the faces changed, from faces of pride to faces of anger and pain; also, that when that dangling figure was hauled up forty feet above the fountain, they changed again, and bore a cruel look of being avenged, which they would henceforth bear for ever. In the stone face over the great window of the bedchamber where the murder was done, two fine dints were pointed out in the sculptured nose, which everybody recognised, and which nobody had seen of old; and on the scarce occasions when two or three ragged peasants emerged from the crowd to take a hurried peep at Monsieur the Marquis petrified, a skinny finger would not have pointed to it for a minute, before they all started away among the moss and leaves, like the more fortunate hares who could find a living there.

Château and hut, stone face and dangling figure, the red stain on the stone floor, and the pure water in the village well—thousands of acres of land—a whole province of France—all France itself—lay under the night sky, concentrated into a faint hair-breadth line. So does a whole world, with all its greatnesses and littlenesses, lie in a twinkling star. And as mere human knowledge can split a ray of light and analyse the manner of its composition, so, sublimer intelligences may read in the feeble shining of this earth of ours, every thought and act, every vice and virtue, of every responsible creature on it.

The Defarges, husband and wife, came lumbering under the starlight, in their public vehicle, to that gate of Paris whereunto their journey naturally tended. There was the usual stoppage at the barrier guard-house, and the usual lanterns came glancing forth for the usual examination and inquiry. Monsieur Defarge alighted; knowing one or two of the soldiery there, and one of the police. The latter he was intimate with, and affectionately embraced.

When Saint Antoine had again enfolded the Defarges in his dusky wings, and they, having finally alighted near the Saint's boundaries, were picking their way on foot through the black mud and offal of his streets, Madame Defarge spoke to her husband:

"Say then, my friend; what did Jacques of the police tell thee?"

"Very little to-night, but all he knows. There is another spy commissioned for our quarter. There may be many more, for all that he can say, but he knows of one."

"Eh well!" said Madame Defarge, raising her eyebrows with a cool business air. "It is necessary to register him. How do they call that man?"

"He is English."

"So much the better. His name?"

"Barsad," said Defarge, making it French by pronunciation. But, he had been so careful to get it accurately, that he then spelt it with perfect correctness.

"Barsad," repeated madame. "Good. Christian name?"

"John."

"John Barsad," repeated madame, after murmuring it once to herself. "Good. His appearance; is it known?"

"Age, about forty years; height, about five feet nine; black hair; complexion dark; generally, rather handsome visage; eyes dark, face thin, long, and sallow; nose aquiline, but not straight, having a peculiar inclination towards the left cheek; expression, therefore, sinister."

"Eh my faith. It is a portrait!" said madame, laughing. "He shall be registered to-morrow."

They turned into the wine-shop, which was closed (for it was midnight), and where Madame Defarge immediately took her post at her desk, counted the small moneys that had been taken during her absence, examined the stock, went through the entries in the book, made other entires of her own, checked the serving man in every possible way, and finally dismissed him to bed. Then she turned out the contents of the bowl of money for the second time, and began knotting them up in her handkerchief, in a chain of separate knots, for safe keeping through the night. All this while, Defarge, with his pipe in his mouth, walked up and down, complacently admiring, but never interfering; in which condition, indeed, as to the business and his domestic affairs, he walked up and down through life.

The night was hot, and the shop, close shut and surrounded by so foul a neighbourhood, was ill-smelling. Monsieur Defarge's olfactory sense was by no means delicate, but the stock of wine smelt much stronger than it ever tasted, and so did the stock of rum and brandy and aniseed. He whiffed the compound of scents away, as he put down his smoked-out pipe.

"You are fatigued," said madame, raising her glance as she knotted the money. "There are only the usual odours."

"I am a little tired," her husband acknowledged.

"You are a little depressed, too," said madame, whose

quick eyes had never been so intent on the accounts, but they had had a ray or two for him. "Oh, the men, the men!"

"But my dear!" began Defarge.

"But my dear!" repeated madame, nodding firmly; "but my dear! You are faint of heart to-night, my dear!"

"Well, then," said Defarge, as if a thought were wrung out of his breast, "it *is* a long time."

"It is a long time," repeated his wife; "and when is it not a long time? Vengeance and retribution require a long time; it is the rule."

"It does not take a long time to strike a man with Lightning," said Defarge.

"How long," demanded madame, composedly, "does it take to make and store the lightning? Tell me."

Defarge raised his head thoughtfully, as if there were something in that too.

"It does not take a long time," said madame, "for an earthquake to swallow a town. Eh well! Tell me how long it takes to prepare the earthquake?"

"A long time, I suppose," said Defarge.

"But when it is ready, it takes place, and grinds to pieces everything before it. In the meantime, it is always preparing, though it is not seen or heard. That is your consolation. Keep it."

She tied a knot with flashing eyes, as if it throttled a foe.

"I tell thee," said madame, extending her right hand, for emphasis, "that although it is a long time on the road, it is on the road and coming. I tell thee it never retreats, and never stops. I tell thee it is always advancing. Look around and consider the lives of all the world that we know, consider the faces of all the world that we know, consider the rage and discontent to which the Jacquerie addresses itself with more and more of certainty every hour. Can such things last? Bah! I mock you."

"My brave wife," returned Defarge, standing before her with his head a little bent, and his hands clasped at his back, like a docile and attentive pupil before his catechist, "I do not question all this. But it has lasted a long time, and it is possible—you know well, my wife, it is possible —that it may not come, during our lives."

"Eh well! How then?" demanded madame, tying another knot, as if there were another enemy strangled.

"Well!" said Defarge, with a half complaining and half apologetic shrug. "We shall not see the triumph."

"We shall have helped it," returned madame, with her extended hand in strong action. "Nothing that we do, is done in vain. I believe, with all my soul, that we shall see the triumph. But even if not, even if I knew certainly not, show me the neck of an aristocrat and tyrant, and still I would——"

Then madame, with her teeth set, tied a very terrible knot indeed.

"Hold!" cried Defarge, reddening a little as if he felt charged with cowardice; "I too, my dear, will stop at nothing."

"Yes! But it is your weakness that you sometimes need to see your victim and your opportunity, to sustain you. Sustain yourself without that. When the time comes, let loose a tiger and a devil; but wait for the time with the tiger and the devil chained — not shown — yet always ready."

Madame enforced the conclusion of this piece of advice by striking her little counter with her chain of money as if she knocked its brains out, and then gathering the heavy handkerchief under her arm in a serene manner, and observing that it was time to go to bed.

Next noontide saw the admirable woman in her usual place in the wine-shop, knitting away assiduously. A rose lay beside her, and if she now and then glanced at the flower, it was with no infraction of her usual preoccupied air. There were a few customers, drinking or not drinking, standing or seated, sprinkled about. The day was very hot, and heaps of flies, who were extending their inquisitive and adventurous perquisitions into all the glutinous little glasses near madame, fell dead at the bottom. Their decease made no impression on the other flies out promenading, who looked at them in the coolest manner (as if they themselves were elephants, or something as far removed), until they met the same fate. Curious to consider how heedless flies are!—perhaps they thought as much at Court that sunny summer day.

A figure entering at the door threw a shadow on Madame Defarge which she felt to be a new one. She laid down her knitting, and began to pin her rose in her head-dress, before she looked at the figure.

It was curious. The moment Madame Defarge took up the rose, the customers ceased talking, and began gradually to drop out of the wine-shop.

"Good day, madame," said the new-comer.

"Good day, monsieur."

She said it aloud, but added to herself, as she resumed her knitting: "Hah! Good day, age about forty, height about five feet nine, black hair, generally rather handsome visage, complexion dark, eyes dark, thin, long and sallow face, aquiline nose but not straight, having a peculiar inclination towards the left cheek which imparts a sinister expression! Good day, one and all!"

"Have the goodness to give me a little glass of old cognac, and a mouthful of cool fresh water, madame."

Madame complied with a polite air.

"Marvellous cognac this, madame!"

It was the first time it had ever been so complimented, and Madame Defarge knew enough of its antecedents to know better. She said, however, that the cognac was flattered, and took up her knitting. The visitor watched her fingers for a few moments, and took the opportunity of observing the place in general.

"You knit with great skill, madame."

"I am accustomed to it."

"A pretty pattern too!"

"*You* think so?" said madame, looking at him with a smile.

"Decidedly. May one ask what it is for?"

"Pastime," said madame, still looking at him with a smile, while her fingers moved nimbly.

"Not for use?"

"That depends. I may find a use for it one day. If I do——well," said madame, drawing a breath and nodding her head with a stern kind of coquetry, "I'll use it!"

It was remarkable; but, the taste of Saint Antoine seemed to be decidedly opposed to a rose on the head-dress of Madame Defarge. Two men had entered separately, and had been about to order drink, when, catching sight of that novelty, they faltered, made a pretence of looking about as if for some friend who was not there, and went away. Nor, of those who had been there when this visitor entered, was there one left. They had all dropped off. The spy had kept his eyes open, but and been able to detect no sign. They had lounged away in a poverty-stricken, purposeless, accidental manner, quite natural and unimpeachable.

"JOHN," thought madame, checking off her work as her fingers knitted, and her eyes looked at the stranger. "Stay long enough, and I shall knit 'BARSAD' before you go."

"You have a husband, madame?"

"I have."

"Children?"

"No children."

"Business seems bad?"

"Business is very bad; the people are so poor."

"Ah, the unfortunate, miserable people! So oppressed, too—as you say."

"As *you* say," madame retorted, correcting him, and deftly knitting an extra something into his name that boded him no good.

"Pardon me; certainly it was I who said so, but you naturally think so. Of course."

"*I* think?" returned madame, in a high voice. "I and my husband have enough to do to keep this wine-shop open, without thinking. All we think, here, is how to live. That is the subject *we* think of, and it gives us, from morning to night, enough to think about, without embarrassing our heads concerning others. *I* think for others? No, no."

The spy, who was there to pick up any crumbs he could find or make, did not allow his baffled state to express itself in his sinister face; but, stood with an air of gossiping gallantry, leaning his elbow on Madame Defarge's little counter, and occasionally sipping his cognac.

"A bad business this, madame, of Gaspard's execution. Ah! the poor Gaspard!" With a sigh of great compassion.

"My faith!" returned madame, coolly and lightly, "if people use knives for such purposes, they have to pay for it. He knew beforehand what the price of his luxury was; he has paid the price."

"I believe," said the spy, dropping his soft voice to a tone that invited confidence, and expressing an injured revolutionary susceptibility in every muscle of his wicked face: "I believe there is much compassion and anger in this neighbourhood, touching the poor fellow? Between ourselves."

"Is there?" asked madame, vacantly.

"Is there not?"

"—Here is my husband!" said Madame Defarge.

As the keeper of the wine-shop entered at the door, the spy saluted him by touching his hat, and saying, with an engaging smile, "Good day, Jacques!" Defarge stopped short, and stared at him.

"Good day, Jacques!" the spy repeated; with not quite so much confidence, or quite so easy a smile under the stare.

"You deceive yourself, monsieur," returned the keeper of the wine-shop. "You mistake me for another. That is not my name. I am Ernest Defarge."

"It is all the same," said the spy, airily, but discomfited too: "good day!"

"Good day!" answered Defarge, drily.

"I was saying to madame, with whom I had the pleasure of chatting when you entered, that they tell me there is—and no wonder!—much sympathy and anger in Saint Antoine, touching the unhappy fate of poor Gaspard."

"No one has told me so," said Defarge, shaking his head. "I know nothing of it."

Having said it, he passed behind the little counter, and stood with his hand on the back of his wife's chair, looking over that barrier at the person to whom they were both opposed, and whom either of them would have shot with the greatest satisfaction.

The spy, well used to his business, did not change his unconscious attitude, but drained his little glass of cognac, took a sip of fresh water, and asked for another glass of cognac. Madame Defarge poured it out for him, took to her knitting again, and hummed a little song over it.

"You seem to know this quarter well; that is to say, better than I do?" observed Defarge.

"Not at all, but I hope to know it better. I am so profoundly interested in its miserable inhabitants."

"Hah!" muttered Defarge.

"The pleasure of conversing with you, Monsieur Defarge, recalls to me," pursued the spy, "that I have the honour of cherishing some interesting associations with your name."

"Indeed!" said Defarge, with much indifference.

"Yes, indeed. When Doctor Manette was released, you, his old domestic, had the charge of him, I know. He was delivered to you. You see I am informed of the circumstances?"

"Such is the fact, certainly," said Defarge. He had had it conveyed to him, in an accidental touch of his wife's elbow as she knitted and warbled, that he would do best to answer, but always with brevity.

"It was to you," said the spy, "that his daughter came; and it was from your care that his daughter took him, accompanied by a neat brown monsieur; how is he called?—in a little wig—Lorry—of the bank of Tellson and Company—over to England."

"Such is the fact," repeated Defarge.

"Very interesting remembrances!" said the spy. "I have known Doctor Manette and his daughter, in England."

"Yes?" said Defarge.

"You don't hear much about them now?" said the spy.

"No," said Defarge.

"In effect," madame struck in, looking up from her work and her little song, "we never hear about them. We received the news of their safe arrival, and perhaps another letter, or perhaps two; but, since then, they have gradually taken their road in life—we, ours—and we have held no correspondence."

"Perfectly so, madame," replied the spy. "She is going to be married."

"Going?" echoed madame. "She was pretty enough to have been married long ago. You English are cold, it seems to me."

"Oh! You know I am English."

"I perceive your tongue is," returned madame; "and what the tongue is, I suppose the man is."

He did not take the identification as a compliment; but he made the best of it, and turned it off with a laugh. After sipping his cognac to the end, he added:

"Yes, Miss Manette is going to be married. But not to an Englishman; to one who, like herself, is French by birth. And speaking of Gaspard (ah, poor Gaspard! It was cruel, cruel!), it is a curious thing that she is going to marry the nephew of Monsieur the Marquis, for whom Gaspard was exalted to that height of so many feet; in other words, the present Marquis. But he lives unknown in England, he is no Marquis there; he is Mr. Charles Darnay. D'Aulnais is the name of his mother's family."

Madame Defarge knitted steadily, but the intelligence had a palpable effect upon her husband. Do what he would, behind the little counter, as to the striking of a light and the lighting of his pipe, he was troubled, and his hand was not trustworthy. The spy would have been no spy if he had failed to see it, or to record it in his mind.

Having made, at least, this one hit, whatever it might prove to be worth, and no customers coming in to help him to any other, Mr. Barsad paid for what he had drunk, and took his leave: taking occasion to say, in a genteel manner, before he departed, that he looked forward to the pleasure of seeing Monsieur and Madame Defarge again. For some minutes after he had emerged into the outer presence of Saint Antoine, the husband and wife remained exactly as he had left them, lest he should come back.

"Can it be true," said Defarge, in a low voice, looking down at his wife as he stood smoking with his hand on the back of her chair: "what he has said of Ma'amselle Manette?"

"As he has said it," returned madame, lifting her eyebrows a little, "it is probably false. But it may be true."

"If it is——" Defarge began, and stopped.

"If it is?" repeated his wife.

"——And if it does come, while we live to see it triumph —I hope, for her sake, Destiny will keep her husband out of France."

"Her husband's destiny," said Madame Defarge, with her usual composure, "will take him where he is to go, and will lead him to the end that is to end him. That is all I know."

"But it is very strange—now, at least, is it not very strange"—said Defarge, rather pleading with his wife to induce her to admit it, "that, after all our sympathy for Monsieur her father, and herself, her husband's name should be proscribed under your hand at this moment, by the side of that infernal dog's who has just left us?"

"Stranger things than that will happen when it does come," answered madame. "I have them both here, of a certainty; and they are both here for their merits; that is enough."

She rolled up her knitting when she had said those words, and presently took the rose out of the handkerchief that was wound about her head. Either Saint Antoine had an instinctive sense that the objectionable decoration was gone, or Saint Antoine was on the watch for its disappearance; howbeit, the Saint took courage to lounge in, very shortly afterwards, and the wine-shop recovered its habitual aspect.

In the evening, at which season of all others Saint Antoine turned himself inside out, and sat on door-steps and window-ledges, and came to the corners of vile streets and courts, for a breath of air, Madame Defarge with her work in her hand was accustomed to pass from place to place and form group to group: a Missionary—there were many like her—such as the world will do well never to breed again. All the women knitted. They knitted worthless things; but, the mechanical work was a mechanical substitute for eating and drinking; the hands moved for the jaws and the digestive apparatus: if the bony fingers had been still, the stomachs would have been more famine-pinched.

But, as the fingers went, the eyes went, and the thoughts. And as Madame Defarge moved on from group to group, all three went quicker and fiercer among every little knot of women that she had spoken with, and left behind.

Her husband smoked at his door, looking after her with admiration. "A great woman," said he, "a strong woman, a grand woman, a frightfully grand woman!"

Darkness closed around, and then came the ringing of church bells and the distant beating of the military drums in the Palace Courtyard, as the women sat knitting, knitting. Darkness encompassed them. Another darkness was closing in as surely, when the church bells, then ringing pleasantly in many an airy steeple over France, should be melted into thundering cannon; when the military drums should be beating to drown a wretched voice, that night all potent as the voice of Power and Plenty, Freedom and Life. So much was closing in about the women who sat knitting, knitting, that they their very selves were closing in around a structure yet unbuilt, where they were to sit knitting, knitting, counting dropping heads.

CHAPTER XVII.

ONE NIGHT.

NEVER did the sun go down with a brighter glory on the quiet corner in Soho, than one memorable evening when the Doctor and his daughter sat under the plane-tree together. Never did the moon rise with a milder radiance over great London, than on that night when it found them still seated under the tree, and shone upon their faces through its leaves.

Lucie was to be married to-morrow. She had reserved this last evening for her father, and they sat alone under the plane-tree.

"You are happy, my dear father?"

"Quite, my child."

They had said little, though they had been there a long time. When it was yet light enough to work and read, she had neither engaged herself in her usual work, nor had she read to him. She had employed herself in both ways, at his side under the tree, many and many a time; but, this time was not quite like any other, and nothing could make it so.

"And I am very happy to-night, dear father. I am deeply happy in the love that Heaven has so blessed—my love for Charles, and Charles's love for me. But, if my life were not to be still consecrated to you, or if my marriage were so arranged as that it would part us, even by the length of a few of these streets, I should be more unhappy and self-reproachful now than I can tell you. Even as it is——"

Even as it was, she could not command her voice.

In the sad moonlight, she clasped him by the neck, and laid her face upon his breast. In the moonlight which is always sad, as the light of the sun itself is—as the light called human life is—at its coming and its going.

"Dearest dear! Can you tell me, this last time, that you feel quite, quite sure, no new affections of mine, and no new duties of mine, will ever interpose between us? *I* know it well, but do you know it? In your own heart, do you feel quite certain?"

Her father answered, with a cheerful firmness of conviction he could scarcely have assumed, "Quite sure, my darling! More than that," he added, as he tenderly kissed her: "my future is far brighter, Lucie, seen through your marriage, than it could have been—nay, than it ever was—without it."

"If I could hope *that*, my father!——"

"Believe it, love! Indeed it is so. Consider how natural and how plain it is, my dear, that it should be so. You, devoted and young, cannot fully appreciate the anxiety I have felt that your life should not be wasted——"

She moved her hand towards his lips, but he took it in his, and repeated the word.

"—wasted, my child—should not be wasted, struck aside from the natural order of things—for my sake. Your unselfishness cannot entirely comprehend how much my mind has gone on this; but, only ask yourself, how could my happiness be perfect, while yours was incomplete?"

"If I had never seen Charles, my father, I should have been quite happy with you."

He smiled at her unconscious admission that she would have been unhappy without Charles, having seen him; and replied:

"My child, you did see him, and it is Charles. If it had not been Charles, it would have been another. Or, if it had been no other, I should have been the cause, and then the dark part of my life would have cast its shadow beyond myself, and would have fallen on you."

It was the first time, except at the trial, of her ever hearing him refer to the period of his suffering. It gave her a strange and new sensation while his words were in her ears; and she remembered it long afterwards.

"See!" said the Doctor of Beauvais, raising his hand towards the moon. "I have looked at her from my prison-window, when I could not bear her light. I have looked at her when it has been such torture to me to think of her shining upon what I had lost, that I have beaten my head against my prison-walls. I have looked at her, in a state so dull and lethargic, that I have thought of nothing but the number of horizontal lines I could draw across her at the full, and the number of perpendicular lines with which I could intersect them." He added in his inward and pondering manner, as he looked at the moon, "It was twenty either way, I remember, and the twentieth was difficult to squeeze in."

The strange thrill with which she heard him go back to that time, deepened as he dwelt upon it; but, there was nothing to shock her in the manner of his reference. He only seemed to contrast his present cheerfulness and felicity with the dire endurance that was over.

"I have looked at her, speculating thousands of times upon the unborn child from whom I had been rent. Whether it was alive. Whether it had been born alive, or the poor mother's shock had killed it. Whether it was a son who would some day avenge his father. (There was a time in my imprisonment, when my desire for vengeance was unbearable.) Whether it was a son who would never know his father's story; who might even live to weigh the possibility of his father's having disappeared of his own

will and act. Whether it was a daughter who would grow to be a woman."

She drew closer to him, and kissed his cheek and his hand.

"I have pictured my daughter, to myself, as perfectly forgetful of me—rather, altogether ignorant of me, and unconscious of me. I have cast up the years of her age, year after year. I have seen her married to a man who knew nothing of my fate. I have altogether perished from the remembrance of the living, and in the next generation my place was a blank."

"My father! Even to hear that you had such thoughts of a daughter who never existed, strikes to my heart as if I had been that child."

"You, Lucie? It is out of the consolation and restoration you have brought to me, that these remembrances arise, and pass between us and the moon on this last night. —What did I say just now?"

"She knew nothing of you. She cared nothing for you."

"So! But on other moonlight nights, when the sadness and the silence have touched me in a different way—have affected me with something as like a sorrowful sense of peace, as any emotion that had pain for its foundations could—I have imagined her as coming to me in my cell, and leading me out into the freedom beyond the fortress. I have seen her image in the moonlight often, as I now see you; except that I never held her in my arms; it stood between the little grated window and the door. But, you understand that that was not the child I am speaking of?"

"The figure was not; the—the—image; the fancy?"

"No. That was another thing. It stood before my disturbed sense of sight, but it never moved. The phantom that my mind pursued, was another and more real child. Of her outward appearance I know no more than that she was like her mother. The other had that likeness too—as you have—but was not the same. Can you follow me, Lucie? Hardly, I think? I doubt you must have been a solitary prisoner to understand these perplexed distinctions."

His collected and calm manner could not prevent her blood from running cold, as he thus tried to anatomise his old condition.

"In that more peaceful state, I have imagined her, in the moonlight, coming to me and taking me out to show me that the home of her married life was full of her loving remembrance of her lost father. My picture was in her room, and I was in her prayers. Her life was active, cheerful, useful; but my poor history pervaded it all."

"I was that child, my father, I was not half so good, but in my love that was I."

"And she showed me her children," said the Doctor of Beauvais, "and they had heard of me, and had been taught to pity me. When they passed a prison of the State, they kept far from its frowning walls, and looked up at its bars, and spoke in whispers. She could never deliver me; I imagined that she always brought me back after showing me such things. But then, blessed with the relief of tears, I fell upon my knees, and blessed her."

"I am that child, I hope, my father. O my dear, my dear, will you bless me as fervently to-morrow?"

"Lucie, I recall these old troubles in the reason that I have to-night for loving you better than words can tell, and thanking God for my great happiness. My thoughts, when they were wildest, never rose near the happiness that I have known with you, and that we have before us."

He embraced her, solemnly commended her to Heaven, and humbly thanked Heaven for having bestowed her on him. By-and-bye, they went into the house.

There was no one bidden to the marriage but Mr. Lorry; there was even to be no bridesmaid but the gaunt Miss Pross. The marriage was to make no change in their place of residence; they had been able to extend it, by taking to themselves the upper rooms formerly belonging to the apocryphal invisible lodger, and they desired nothing more.

Doctor Manette was very cheerful at the little supper. They were only three at table, and Miss Pross made the third. He regretted that Charles was not there; was more than half disposed to object to the loving little plot that kept him away; and drank to him affectionately.

So, the time came for him to bid Lucie good night, and they separated. But, in the stillness of the third hour of the morning, Lucie came down-stairs again, and stole into his room; not free from unshaped fears, beforehand.

All things, however, were in their places; all was quiet; and he lay asleep, his white hair picturesque on the untroubled pillow, and his hands lying quiet on the coverlet. She put her needless candle in the shadow at a distance, crept up to his bed, and put her lips to his; then, leaned over him, and looked at him.

Into his handsome face, the bitter waters of captivity had worn; but, he covered up their tracks with a determination so strong, that he held the mastery of them even in his sleep. A more remarkable face in its quiet, resolute, and guarded struggle with an unseen assailant, was not to be beheld in all the wide dominions of sleep, that night.

She timidly laid her hand on his dear breast, and put up a prayer that she might ever be as true to him as her love aspired to be, and as his sorrows deserved. Then, she withdrew her hand, and kissed his lips once more, and went away. So, the sunrise came, and the shadows of the leaves of the plane-tree moved upon his face, as softly as her lips had moved in praying for him.

CHAPTER XVIII.

NINE DAYS.

THE marriage-day was shining brightly, and they were ready outside the closed door of the Doctor's room, where he was speaking with Charles Darnay. They were ready to go to church; the beautiful bride, Mr. Lorry, and Miss Pross—to whom the event, through a gradual process of reconcilement to the inevitable, would have been one of absolute bliss, but for the yet lingering consideration that her brother Solomon should have been the bridegroom.

"And so," said Mr. Lorry, who could not sufficiently admire the bride, and who had been moving round her to take in every point of her quiet, pretty dress; "and so it was for this, my sweet Lucie, that I brought you across the Channel, such a baby! Lord bless me! How little I thought what I was doing! How lightly I valued the obligation I was conferring on my friend Mr. Charles!"

"You didn't mean it," remarked the matter-of-fact Miss Pross, "and therefore how could you know it? Nonsense!"

"Really? Well; but don't cry," said the gentle Mr. Lorry.

"I am not crying," said Miss Pross; "you are."

"I, my Pross?" (By this time, Mr. Lorry dared to be pleasant with her, on occasion.)

"You were, just now; I saw you do it, and I don't wonder at it. Such a present of plate as you have made 'em, is enough to bring tears into anybody's eyes. There's not a fork or a spoon in the collection," said Miss Pross, "that I didn't cry over, last night after the box came, till I couldn't see it."

"I am highly gratified," said Mr. Lorry, "though, upon my honour, I had no intention of rendering those trifling articles of remembrance invisible to any one. Dear me! This is an occasion that makes a man speculate on all he has lost. Dear, dear, dear! To think that there might have been a Mrs. Lorry, any time these fifty years almost!"

"Not at all!" From Miss Pross.

"You think there never might have been a Mrs. Lorry?" asked the gentleman of that name.

"Pooh!" rejoined Miss Pross; "you were a bachelor in your cradle."

"Well!" observed Mr. Lorry, beamingly adjusting his little wig, "that seems probable, too."

"And you were cut out for a bachelor," pursued Miss Pross, "before you were put in your cradle."

"Then, I think," said Mr. Lorry, "that I was very unhandsomely dealt with, and that I ought to have had a voice in the selection of my pattern. Enough! Now, my dear Lucie," drawing his arm soothingly round her waist, "I hear them moving in the next room, and Miss Pross and I, as two formal folks of business, are anxious not to lose the final opportunity of saying something to you that you wish to hear. You leave your good father, my dear, in hands as earnest and as loving as your own; he shall be taken every conceivable care of; during the next fortnight, while you are in Warwickshire and thereabouts, even Tellson's shall go to the wall (comparatively speaking) before him. And when, at the fortnight's end, he comes to join you and your beloved husband, on your other fortnight's trip in Wales, you shall say that we have sent him to you in the best health and in the happiest frame. Now, I hear Somebody's step coming to the door. Let me kiss my dear girl with an old-fashioned bachelor blessing, before Somebody comes to claim his own."

For a moment, he held the fair face from him to look at the well-remembered expression on the forehead, and then laid the bright golden hair against his little brown wig, with a genuine tenderness and delicacy which, if such things be old-fashioned, were as old as Adam.

The door of the Doctor's room opened, and he came out with Charles Darnay. He was so deadly pale—which had not been the case when they went in together—that no vestige of colour was to be seen in his face. But, in the composure of his manner he was unaltered, except that to the shrewd glance of Mr. Lorry it disclosed some shadowy indication that the old air of avoidance and dread had lately passed over him, like a cold wind.

He gave his arm to his daughter, and took her downstairs to the chariot which Mr. Lorry had hired in honour of the day. The rest followed in another carriage, and soon, in a neighbouring church, where no strange eyes looked on, Charles Darnay and Lucie Manette were happily married.

Besides the glancing tears that shone among the smiles of the little group when it was done, some diamonds, very bright and sparkling, glanced on the bride's hand, which were newly released from the dark obscurity of one of Mr. Lorry's pockets. They returned home to breakfast, and all went well, and in due course the golden hair that had mingled with the poor shoemaker's white locks in the Paris garret, were mingled with them again in the morning sunlight, on the threshold of the door at parting.

It was a hard parting, though it was not for long. But her father cheered her, and said at last, gently disengaging himself from her enfolding arms, "Take her, Charles! She is yours!"

And her agitated hand waved to them from a chaise window, and she was gone.

The corner being out of the way of the idle and curious, and the preparations having been very simple and few, the Doctor, Mr. Lorry, and Miss Pross, were left quite alone. It was when they turned into the welcome shade of the cool old hall, that Mr. Lorry observed a great change to have come over the Doctor; as if the golden arm uplifted there, had struck him a poisoned blow.

He had naturally repressed much, and some revulsion might have been expected in him when the occasion for repression was gone. But, it was the old scared lost look that troubled Mr. Lorry; and through his absent manner of clasping his head and drearily wandering away into his own room when they got up-stairs, Mr. Lorry was reminded of Defarge the wine-shop keeper, and the starlight ride.

"I think," he whispered to Miss Pross, after anxious consideration, "I think we had best not speak to him just now, or at all disturb him. I must look in at Tellson's; so I will go there at once and come back presently. Then, we will take him a ride into the country, and dine there, and all will be well."

It was easier for Mr. Lorry to look in at Tellson's, than to look out of Tellson's. He was detained two hours. When he came back, he ascended the old staircase alone, having asked no question of the servant; going thus into the Doctor's rooms, he was stopped by a low sound of knocking.

"Good God!" he said, with a start. "What's that?"

Miss Pross, with a terrified face, was at his ear. "O me, O me! All is lost!" cried she, wringing her hands. "What is to be told to Ladybird? He doesn't know me, and is making shoes!"

Mr. Lorry said what he could to calm her, and went himself into the Doctor's room. The bench was turned towards the light, as it had been when he had seen the shoemaker at his work before, and his head was bent down, and he was very busy.

"Doctor Manette. My dear friend, Doctor Manette!"

The Doctor looked at him for a moment—half inquiringly, half as if he were angry at being spoken to—and bent over his work again.

He had laid aside his coat and waistcoat; his shirt was open at the throat, as it used to be when he did that work; and even the old haggard, faded surface of face had come back to him. He worked hard—impatiently—as if in some sense of having been interrupted.

Mr. Lorry glanced at the work in his hand, and observed that it was a shoe of the old size and shape. He took up another that was lying by him, and asked what it was?

"A young lady's walking shoe," he muttered, without looking up. "It ought to have been finished long ago. Let it be."

"But, Doctor Manette. Look at me!"

He obeyed, in the old mechanically submissive manner, without pausing in his work.

"You know me, my dear friend? Think again. This is not your proper occupation. Think, dear friend!"

Nothing would induce him to speak more. He looked up, for an instant at a time, when he was requested to do so; but, no persuasion would extract a word from him. He worked, and worked, and worked, in silence, and words fell on him as they would have fallen on an echoless wall, or on the air. The only ray of hope that Mr. Lorry could discover, was, that he sometimes furtively looked up without being asked. In that, there seemed a faint expression of curiosity or perplexity—as though he were trying to reconcile some doubts in his mind.

Two things at once impressed themselves on Mr. Lorry, as important above all others; the first, that this must be kept secret from Lucie; the second, that it must be kept secret from all who knew him. In conjunction with Miss Pross, he took immediate steps towards the latter precaution, by giving out that the Doctor was not well, and required a few days of complete rest. In aid of the kind deception to be practised on his daughter, Miss Pross was to write, describing his having been called away professionally, and referring to an imaginary letter of two or three hurried lines in his own hand, represented to have been addressed to her by the same post.

These measures, advisable to be taken in any case, Mr. Lorry took in the hope of his coming to himself. If that should happen soon, he kept another course in reserve; which was, to have a certain opinion that he thought the best, on the Doctor's case.

In the hope of his recovery, and of resort to this third course being thereby rendered practicable, Mr. Lorry resolved to watch him attentively, with as little appearance as possible of doing so. He therefore made arrangements to absent himself from Tellson's for the first time in his life, and took his post by the window in the same room.

He was not long in discovering that it was worse than useless to speak to him, since, on being pressed, he became worried. He abandoned that attempt on the first day, and resolved merely to keep himself always before him, as a silent protest against the delusion into which he had fallen, or was falling. He remained, therefore, in his seat near the window, reading and writing, and expressing in as many pleasant and natural ways as he could think of, that it was a free place.

Doctor Manette took what was given him to eat and drink, and worked on, that first day, until it was too dark to see—worked on, half an hour after Mr. Lorry could not have seen, for his life, to read or write. When he put his tools aside as useless, until morning, Mr. Lorry rose and said to him:

"Will you go out?"

He looked down at the floor on either side of him in the old manner, looked up in the old manner, and repeated in the old low voice:

"Out?"

"Yes; for a walk with me. Why not?"

He made no effort to say why not, and said not a word more. But, Mr. Lorry thought he saw, as he leaned forward on his bench in the dusk, with his elbows on his knees and his head in his hands, that he was in some misty way asking himself, "Why not?" The sagacity of the man of business perceived an advantage here, and determined to hold it.

Miss Pross and he divided the night into two watches, and observed him at intervals from the adjoining room. He paced up and down for a long time before he lay down; but, when he did finally lay himself down, he fell asleep. In the morning, he was up betimes, and went straight to his bench and to work.

On this second day, Mr. Lorry saluted him cheerfully by his name, and spoke to him on topics that had been of late familiar to them. He returned no reply, but it was evident that he heard what was said, and that he thought about it, however confusedly. This encouraged Mr. Lorry to have Miss Pross in with her work, several times during the day; at those times, they quietly spoke of Lucie, and of her father then present, precisely in the usual manner, and as if there were nothing amiss. This was done without any demonstrative accompaniment, not long enough, or often enough to harass him; and it lightened Mr. Lorry's friendly heart to believe that he looked up oftener, and that he appeared to be stirred by some perception of inconsistencies surrounding him.

When it fell dark again, Mr. Lorry asked him as before:

"Dear Doctor, will you go out?"

As before, he repeated, "Out?"

"Yes; for a walk with me. Why not?"

This time, Mr. Lorry feigned to go out when he could extract no answer from him, and, after remaining absent for an hour, returned. In the meanwhile, the Doctor had removed to the seat in the window, and had sat there looking down at the plane-tree; but, on Mr. Lorry's return, he slipped away to his bench.

The time went very slowly on, and Mr. Lorry's hope darkened, and his heart grew heavier again, and grew yet heavier and heavier every day. The third day came and went, the fourth, the fifth. Five days, six days, seven days, eight days, nine days.

With a hope ever darkening, and with a heart always growing heavier and heavier, Mr. Lorry passed through this anxious time. The secret was well kept, and Lucie was unconscious and happy; but he could not fail to observe that the shoemaker, whose hand had been a little out at first, was growing dreadfully skilful, and that he had never been so intent on his work, and that his hands had never been so nimble and expert, as in the dusk of the ninth evening.

CHAPTER XIX.

AN OPINION.

Worn out by anxious watching, Mr. Lorry fell asleep at his post. On the tenth morning of his suspense, he was startled by the shining of the sun into the room where a heavy slumber had overtaken him when it was dark night.

He rubbed his eyes and roused himself; but he doubted, when he had done so, whether he was not still asleep. For, going to the door of the Doctor's room and looking in, he perceived that the shoemaker's bench and tools were put aside again, and that the Doctor himself sat reading at the window. He was in his usual morning dress, and his face (which Mr. Lorry could distinctly see), though still very pale, was calmly studious and attentive.

Even when he had satisfied himself that he was awake, Mr. Lorry felt giddily uncertain for some few moments whether the late shoemaking might not be a disturbed dream of his own; for, did not his eyes show him his friend before him in his accustomed clothing and aspect, and employed as usual; and was there any sign within their range, that the change of which he had so strong an impression had actually happened?

It was but the inquiry of his first confusion and astonishment, the answer being obvious. If the impression were not produced by a real corresponding and sufficient cause, how came he, Jarvis Lorry, there? How came he to have fallen asleep, in his clothes, on the sofa in Doctor Manette's consulting-room, and to be debating these points outside the Doctor's bedroom door in the early morning?

Within a few minutes, Miss Pross stood whispering at his side. If he had had any particle of doubt left, her talk would of necessity have resolved it; but he was by that time clear-headed, and had none. He advised that they should let the time go by until the regular breakfast-hour, and should then meet the Doctor as if nothing unusual had occurred. If he appeared to be in his customary state of mind, Mr. Lorry would then cautiously proceed to seek direction and guidance from the opinion he had been, in his anxiety, so anxious to obtain.

Miss Pross, submitting herself to his judgment, the scheme was worked out with care. Having abundance of time for his usual methodical toilette, Mr. Lorry presented himself at the breakfast-hour in his usual white linen, and with his usual neat leg. The Doctor was summoned in the usual way, and came to breakfast.

So far as it was possible to comprehend him without overstepping those delicate and gradual approaches which Mr. Lorry felt to be the only safe advance, he at first supposed that his daughter's marriage had taken place yesterday. An incidental allusion, purposely thrown out, to the day of the week, and the day of the month, set him thinking and counting, and evidently made him uneasy. In all other respects, however, he was so composedly himself, that Mr. Lorry determined to have the aid he sought. And that aid was his own.

Therefore, when the breakfast was done and cleared away, and he and the Doctor were left together, Mr. Lorry said, feelingly:

"My dear Manette, I am anxious to have your opinion, in confidence, on a very curious case in which I am deeply interested; that is to say, it is very curious to me; perhaps, to your better information it may be less so."

Glancing at his hands, which were discoloured by his late work, the Doctor looked troubled, and listened attentively. He had already glanced at his hands more than once.

"Doctor Manette," said Mr. Lorry, touching him affectionately on the arm, "the case is the case of a particularly dear friend of mine. Pray give your mind to it, and advise me well for his sake—and above all, for his daughter's—his daughter's, my dear Manette."

"If I understand," said the Doctor, in a subdued tone, "some mental shock——?"

"Yes!"

"Be explicit," said the Doctor. "Spare no detail."

Mr. Lorry saw that they understood one another, and proceeded.

"My dear Manette, it is the case of an old and a prolonged shock, of great acuteness and severity to the affections, the feelings, the—the—as you express it—the mind. The mind. It is the case of a shock under which the sufferer was borne down, one cannot say for how long, because I believe he cannot calculate the time himself, and there are no other means of getting at it. It is the case of a shock from which the sufferer recovered, by a process that he cannot trace himself—as I once heard him publicly relate in a striking manner. It is the case of a shock from which he has recovered, so completely, as to be a highly intelligent man, capable of close application of mind, and great exertion of body, and of constantly making fresh additions to his stock of knowledge, which was already very large. But, unfortunately, there has been," he paused and took a deep breath—"a slight relapse."

The Doctor, in a low voice, asked, "Of how long duration?"

"Nine days and nights."

"How did it show itself? I infer," glancing at his hands again, "in the resumption of some old pursuit connected with the shock?"

"That is the fact."

"Now, did you ever see him," asked the Doctor, distinctly and collectedly, though in the same low voice, "engaged in that pursuit originally?"

"Once."

"And when the relapse fell on him, was he in most respects—or in all respects—as he was then?"

"I think in all respects."

"You spoke of his daughter. Does his daughter know of the relapse?"

"No. It has been kept from her, and I hope will always be kept from her. It is known only to myself, and to one other who may be trusted."

The Doctor grasped his hand, and murmured, "That was very kind. That was very thoughtful?" Mr. Lorry grasped his hand in return, and neither of the two spoke for a little while.

"Now, my dear Manette," said Mr. Lorry, at length, in his most considerate and most affectionate way, "I am a mere man of business, and unfit to cope with such intricate and difficult matters. I do not possess the kind of information necessary; I do not possess the kind of intelligence; I want guiding. There is no man in this world on whom I could so rely for right guidance, as on you. Tell me, how does this relapse come about? Is there danger of another? Could a repetition of it be prevented? How should a repetition of it be treated? How does it come about at all? What can I do for my friend? No man ever can have been more desirous in his heart to serve a friend, than I am to serve mine, if I knew how. But I don't know how to originate, in such a case. If your sagacity, knowledge, and experience, could put me on the right track, I might be able to do so much; unenlightened and undirected, I can do so little. Pray discuss it with me; pray enable me to see it a little more clearly, and teach me how to be a little more useful."

Doctor Manette sat meditating after these earnest words were spoken, and Mr. Lorry did not press him.

"I think it probable," said the Doctor, breaking silence with an effort, "that the relapse you have described, my dear friend, was not quite unforeseen by its subject."

"Was it dreaded by him?" Mr. Lorry ventured to ask.

"Very much." He said it with an involuntary shudder.

"You have no idea how such an apprehension weighs on the sufferer's mind, and how difficult—how almost impossible—it is, for him to force himself to utter a word upon the topic that oppresses him."

"Would he," asked Mr. Lorry "be sensibly relieved if he could prevail upon himself to impart that secret brooding to any one when it is on him?"

"I think so. But it is, as I have told you, next to impossible. I even believe it—in some cases—to be quite impossible."

"Now," said Mr. Lorry, gently laying his hand on the Doctor's arm again, after a short silence on both sides, "to what would you refer this attack?"

"I believe," returned Doctor Manette "that there had been a strong and extraordinary revival of the train of thought and remembrance that was the first cause of the malady. Some intense associations of a most distressing nature were vividly recalled, I think. It is probable that there had long been a dread lurking in his mind that those associations would be recalled—say, under certain circumstances—say, on a particular occasion. He tried to prepare himself in vain; perhaps the effort to prepare himself made him less able to bear it."

"Would he remember what took place in the relapse?" asked Mr. Lorry, with natural hesitation.

The Doctor looked desolately round the room, shook his head, and answered, in a low voice, "Not at all."

"Now, as to the future," hinted Mr. Lorry.

"As to the future," said the Doctor, recovering firmness, "I should have great hope. As it pleased Heaven in its mercy to restore him so soon, I should have great hope. He, yielding under the pressure of a complicated something, long dreaded and long vaguely foreseen and contended against, and recovering after the cloud had burst and passed, I should hope that the worst was over."

"Well, well! That's good comfort. I am thankful!" said Mr. Lorry.

"I am thankful!" repeated the Doctor, bending his head with reverence.

"There are two other points," said Mr. Lorry, "on which I am anxious to be instructed. I may go on?"

"You cannot do your friend a better service." The Doctor gave him his hand.

"To the first, then. He is of a studious habit, and unusually energetic; he applies himself with great ardour to the acquisition of professional knowledge, to the conducting of experiments, to many things. Now, does he do too much?"

"I think not. It may be the character of his mind, to be always in singular need of occupation. That may be, in part, natural to it; in part, the result of affliction. The less it was occupied with healthy things, the more it would be in danger of turning in the unhealthy direction. He may have observed himself, and made the discovery."

"You are sure that he is not under too great a strain?"

"I think I am quite sure of it."

"My dear Manette, if he were overworked now——"

"My dear Lorry, I doubt if that could easily be. There has been a violent stress in one direction, and it needs a counterweight."

"Excuse me, as a persistent man of business. Assuming for a moment, that he *was* overworked; it would show itself in some renewal of this disorder?"

"I do not think so. I do not think," said Doctor Manette with the firmness of self-conviction, "that anything but the one train of association would renew it. I think that, henceforth, nothing but some extraordinary jarring of that chord could renew it. After what has happened, and after his recovery, I find it difficult to imagine any such violent sounding of that string again. I trust, and I almost believe, that the circumstances likely to renew it are exhausted."

He spoke with the diffidence of a man who knew how slight a thing would overset the delicate organisation of the mind, and yet with the confidence of a man who had slowly won his assurance out of personal endurance and distress. It was not for his friend to abate that confidence. He professed himself more relieved and encouraged than he really was, and approached his second and last point. He felt it to be the most difficult of all; but, remembering his old Sunday morning conversation with Miss Pross, and remembering what he had seen in the last nine days, he knew that he must face it.

"The occupation resumed under the influence of this passing affliction so happily recovered from," said Mr. Lorry, clearing his throat, "we will call—Blacksmith's work, Blacksmith's work. We will say, to put a case and for the sake of illustration, that he had been used, in his bad time, to work at a little forge. We will say that he was unexpectedly found at his forge again. Is it not a pity that he should keep it by him?"

The Doctor shaded his forehead with his hand, and beat his foot nervously on the ground.

"He has always kept it by him," said Mr. Lorry, with an anxious look at his friend. "Now, would it not be better that he should let it go?"

Still, the Doctor, with shaded forehead, beat his foot nervously on the ground.

"You do not find it easy to advise me?" said Mr. Lorry. "I quite understand it to be a nice question. And yet I think——" And there he shook his head, and stopped.

"You see," said Doctor Manette, turning to him after an uneasy pause, "it is very hard to explain, consistently, the innermost workings of this poor man's mind. He once yearned so frightfully for that occupation, and it was so welcome when it came; no doubt it relieved his pain so much, by substituting the perplexity of the fingers for the perplexity of the brain, and by substituting, as he became more practised, the ingenuity of the hands, for the ingenuity of the mental torture; that he has never been able to bear the thought of putting it quite out of his reach. Even now, when I believe he is more hopeful of himself than he has ever been, and even speaks of himself with a kind of confidence, the idea that he might need that old employment, and not find it, gives him a sudden sense of terror, like that which one may fancy strikes to the heart of a lost child."

He looked like his illustration, as he raised his eyes to Mr. Lorry's face.

"But may not—mind! I ask for information, as a plodding man of business who only deals with such material objects as guineas, shillings, and bank-notes—may not the retention of the thing involve the retention of the idea? If the thing were gone, my dear Manette, might not the fear go with it? In short, is it not a concession to the misgiving, to keep the forge?"

There was another silence.

"You see, too," said the Doctor, tremulously, "it is such an old companion."

"I would not keep it," said Mr. Lorry, shaking his head; for he gained in firmness as he saw the Doctor disquieted. "I would recommend him to sacrifice it. I only want your authority. I am sure it does no good. Come! Give me your authority, like a dear good man. For his daughter's sake, my dear Manette!"

Very strange to see what a struggle there was within him!

"In her name, then, let it be done; I sanction it. But, I would not take it away while he was present. Let it be removed when he is not there; let him miss his old companion after an absence."

Mr. Lorry readily engaged for that, and the conference was ended. They passed the day in the country, and the Doctor was quite restored. On the three following days he remained perfectly well, and on the fourteenth day he went away to join Lucie and her husband. The precaution that had been taken to account for his silence, Mr. Lorry had previously explained to him, and he had written to Lucie in accordance with it, and she had no suspicions.

On the night of the day on which he left the house, Mr. Lorry went into his room with a chopper, saw, chisel, and hammer, attended by Miss Pross carrying a light. There, with closed doors, and in a mysterious and guilty manner, Mr. Lorry hacked the shoemaker's bench to pieces, while Miss Pross held the candle as if she were assisting at a murder—for which, indeed, in her grimness, she was no unsuitable figure. The burning of the body (previously reduced to pieces convenient for the purpose) was commenced without delay in the kitchen fire; and the tools, shoes, and leather, were buried in the garden. So wicked do destruction and secrecy appear to honest minds, that Mr. Lorry and Miss Pross, while engaged in the commission of their deed and in the removal of its traces, almost felt, and almost looked, like accomplices in a horrible crime.

CHAPTER XX.

A PLEA.

WHEN the newly-married pair came home, the first person who appeared, to offer his congratulations, was Sydney Carton. They had not been at home many hours, when he presented himself. He was not improved in habits, or in looks, or in manner; but there was a certain rugged air of fidelity about him, which was new to the observation of Charles Darnay.

He watched his opportunity of taking Darnay aside into a window, and of speaking to him when no one overheard.

"Mr. Darnay," said Carton, "I wish we might be friends."

"We are already friends, I hope."

"You are good enough to say so, as a fashion of speech; but, I don't mean any fashion of speech. Indeed, when I say I wish we might be friends, I scarcely mean quite that, either."

Charles Darnay—as was natural—asked him, in all good-humour and good-fellowship, what he did mean?

"Upon my life," said Carton, smiling, "I find that easier to comprehend in my own mind, than to convey to yours. However, let me try. You remember a certain famous occasion when I was more drunk than—than usual?"

"I remember a certain famous occasion when you forced me to confess that you had been drinking."

"I remember it too. The curse of those occasions is heavy upon me, for I always remember them. I hope it may be taken into account one day, when all days are at an end for me! Don't be alarmed; I am not going to preach."

"I am not at all alarmed. Earnestness in you, is anything but alarming to me."

"Ah!" said Carton, with a careless wave of his hand, as if he waved that away. "On the drunken occasion in question (one of a large number, as you know), I was insufferable about liking you, and not liking you. I wish you would forget it."

"I forgot it long ago."

"Fashion of speech again! But, Mr. Darnay, oblivion is not so easy to me, as you represent it to be to you. I have by no means forgotten it, and a light answer does not help me to forget it."

"If it was a light answer," returned Darnay, "I beg your forgiveness for it. I had no other object than to turn a slight thing, which, to my surprise, seems to trouble you too much, aside. I declare to you, on the faith of a gentleman, that I have long dismissed it from my mind. Good Heaven, what was there to dismiss! Have I had nothing more important to remember, in the great service you rendered me that day?"

"As to the great service," said Carton, "I am bound to avow to you, when you speak of it in that way, that it was mere professional claptrap, I don't know that I cared what became of you, when I rendered it.—Mind! I say when I rendered it; I am speaking of the past."

"You make light of the obligation," returned Darnay, "but I will not quarrel with *your* light answer."

"Genuine truth, Mr. Darnay, trust me! I have gone aside from my purpose; I was speaking about our being friends. Now, you know me; you know I am incapable of all the higher and better flights of men. If you doubt it, ask Stryver, and he'll tell you so."

"I prefer to form my own opinion, without the aid of his."

"Well! At any rate you know me as a dissolute dog, who has never done any good, and never will."

"I don't know that you 'never will.'"

"But I do, and you must take my word for it. Well! If you could endure to have such a worthless fellow, and a fellow of such indifferent reputation, coming and going at odd times, I should ask that I might be permitted to come and go as a privileged person here; that I might be regarded as an useless (and I would add, if it were not for the resemblance I detected between you and me, an unornamental) piece of furniture, tolerated for its old service, and taken no notice of. I doubt if I should abuse the permission. It is a hundred to one if I should avail myself of it four times in a year. It would satisfy me, I dare say, to know that I had it."

"Will you try?"

"That is another way of saying that I am placed on the footing I have indicated. I thank you, Darnay. I may use that freedom with your name?"

"I think so, Carton, by this time."

They shook hands upon it, and Sydney turned away.

Within a minute afterwards, he was, to all outward appearance, as unsubstantial as ever.

When he was gone, and in the course of an evening passed with Miss Pross, the Doctor, and Mr. Lorry, Charles Darnay made some mention of this conversation in general terms, and spoke of Sydney Carton as a problem of carelessness and recklessness. He spoke of him, in short, not bitterly or meaning to bear hard upon him, but as anybody might who saw him as he showed himself.

He had no idea that this could dwell in the thoughts of his fair young wife; but, when he afterwards joined her in their own rooms, he found her waiting for him with the old pretty lifting of the forehead strongly marked.

"We are thoughtful to-night!" said Darnay, drawing his arm about her.

"Yes, dearest Charles," with her hands on his breast, and the inquiring and attentive expression fixed upon him; "we are rather thoughtful to-night, for we have something our our mind to-night."

"What is it, my Lucie?"

"Will you promise not to press one question on me, if I beg you not to ask it?"

"Will I promise? What will I not promise to my Love?"

What, indeed, with his hand putting aside the golden hair from the cheek, and his other hand against the heart that beat for him!

"I think, Charles, poor Mr. Carton deserves more consideration and respect than you expressed for him to-night."

"Indeed, my own? Why so?"

"That is what you are not to ask me. But I think—I know—he does."

"If you know it, it is enough. What would you have me do, my Life?"

"I would ask you, dearest, to be very generous with him always, and very lenient on his faults when he is not by. I would ask you to believe that he has a heart he very, very seldom reveals, and that there are deep wounds in it. My dear, I have seen it bleeding."

"It is a painful reflection to me," said Charles Darnay, quite astounded, "that I should have done him any wrong. I never thought this of him."

"My husband, it is so. I fear he is not to be reclaimed; there is scarcely a hope that anything in his character or fortunes is reparable now. But, I am sure that he is capable of good things, gentle things, even magnanimous things."

She looked so beautiful in the purity of her faith in this lost man, that her husband could have looked at her as she was for hours.

"And, O my dearest Love!" she urged, clinging nearer to him, laying her head upon his breast, and raising her eyes to his, "remember how strong we are in our happiness, and how weak he is in his misery!"

The supplication touched him home. "I will always remember it, dear Heart! I will remember it as long as I live."

He bent over the golden head, and put the rosy lips to his, and folded her in his arms. If one forlorn wanderer then pacing the dark streets, could have heard her innocent disclosure, and could have seen the drops of pity kissed away by her husband from the soft blue eyes so loving of that husband, he might have cried to the night—

and the words would not have parted from his lips for the first time—

"God bless her for her sweet compassion!"

CHAPTER XXI.

ECHOING FOOTSTEPS.

A WONDERFUL corner for echoes, it has been remarked, that corner where the Doctor lived. Ever busily winding the golden thread which bound her husband, and her father, and herself, and her old directress and companion, in a life of quiet bliss, Lucie sat in the still house in the tranquilly resounding corner, listening to the echoing footsteps of years.

At first, there were times, though she was a perfectly happy young wife, when her work would slowly fall from her hands, and her eyes would be dimmed. For, there was something coming in the echoes, something light, afar off, and scarcely audible yet, that stirred her heart too much. Fluttering hopes and doubts—hopes, of a love as yet unknown to her: doubts, of her remaining upon earth, to enjoy that new delight—divided her breast. Among the echoes then, there would arise the sound of footsteps at her own early grave; and thoughts of the husband who would be left so desolate, and who would mourn for her so much, swelled to her eyes, and broke like waves.

That time passed, and her little Lucie lay on her bosom. Then, among the advancing echoes, there was the tread of her tiny feet and the sound of her prattling words. Let greater echoes resound as they would, the young mother at the cradle side could always hear those coming. They came, and the shady house was sunny with a child's laugh, and the Divine friend of children, to whom in her trouble she had confided hers, seemed to take her child in his arms, as He took the child of old, and made it a sacred joy to her.

Ever busily winding the golden thread that bound them all together, weaving the service of her happy influence through the tissue of all their lives, and making it predominate nowhere, Lucie heard in the echoes of years none but friendly and soothing sounds. Her husband's step was strong and prosperous among them; her father's firm and equal. Lo, Miss Pross, in harness of string, awakening the echoes, as an unruly charger, whip-corrected, snorting and pawing the earth under the plane-tree in the garden!

Even when there were sounds of sorrow among the rest, they were not harsh nor cruel. Even when golden hair, like her own, lay in a halo on a pillow round the worn face of a little boy, and he said, with a radiant smile, "Dear papa and mamma, I am very sorry to leave you both, and to leave my pretty sister; but I am called, and I must go!" those were not tears all of agony that wetted his young mother's cheek, as the spirit departed from her embrace that had been entrusted to it. Suffer them and forbid them not. They see my Father's face. O Father, blessed words!

Thus, the rustling of an Angel's wings got blended with the other echoes, and they were not wholly of earth, but had in them that breath of Heaven. Sighs of the winds that blew over a little garden-tomb were mingled with them also, and both were audible to Lucie, in a hushed murmur—like the breathing of a summer sea asleep upon a sandy shore—as the little Lucie, comically studious at the task of the morning, or dressing a doll at her mother's footstool, chattered in the tongues of the Two Cities that were blended in her life.

The echoes rarely answered to the actual tread of Sydney Carton. Some half-dozen times a year, at most, he claimed his privilege of coming in uninvited, and would sit among them through the evening, as he had once done often. He never came there heated with wine. And one other thing regarding him was whispered in the echoes, which has been whispered by all true echoes for ages and ages.

No man ever really loved a woman, lost her, and knew her with a blameless though an unchanged mind, when she was a wife and a mother, but her children had a strange sympathy with him—an instinctive delicacy of pity for him. What fine hidden sensibilities are touched in such a case, no echoes tell; but it is so, and it was so here. Carton was the first stranger to whom little Lucie held out her chubby arms, and he kept his place with her as she grew. The little boy had spoken of him, almost at the last. "Poor Carton! Kiss him for me!"

Mr. Stryver shouldered his way through the law, like some great engine forcing itself through turbid water, and dragged his useful friend in his wake, like a boat towed astern. As the boat so favoured is usually in a rough plight, and mostly under water, so, Sydney had a swamped life of it. But, easy and strong custom, unhappily so much easier and stronger in him than any stimulating sense of desert or disgrace, made it the life he was to lead; and he no more thought of emerging from his state of lion's jackal, than any real jackal may be supposed to think of rising to be a lion. Stryver was rich; had married a florid widow with property and three boys, who had nothing particularly shining about them but the straight hair of their dumpling heads.

These three young gentlemen, Mr. Stryver, exuding patronage of the most offensive quality from every pore, had walked before him like three sheep to the quiet corner in Soho, and had offered as pupils to Lucie's husband: delicately saying "Halloa! here are three lumps of bread-and-cheese towards your matrimonial picnic, Darnay!" The polite rejection of the three lumps of bread-and-cheese had quite bloated Mr. Stryver with indignation, which he afterwards turned to account in the training of the young gentlemen, by directing them to beware of the pride of Beggars, like that tutor-fellow. He was also in the habit of declaiming to Mrs. Stryver, over his full-bodied wine, on the arts Mrs. Darnay had once put in practice to "catch" him, and on the diamond-cut-diamond arts in himself, madam, which had rendered him "not to be caught." Some of his King's Bench familiars, who were occasionally parties to the full-bodied wine and the lie, excused him for the latter by saying that he had told it so often, that he believed it himself—which is surely such an incorrigible aggravation of an originally bad offence, as to justify any such offender's being carried off to some suitably retired spot, and there hanged out of the way.

These were among the echoes to which Lucie, sometimes pensive, sometimes amused and laughing, listened in the echoing corner, until her little daughter was six years old. How near to her heart the echoes of her child's tread came, and those of her own dear father's, always active and self-possessed, and those of her dear husband's, need not be told. Nor, how the lightest echo of their united home, directed by herself with such a wise and elegant thrift that it was more abundant than any waste, was music to her. Nor, how there were echoes all about her, sweet in her ears, of the many times her father had told her that he found her more devoted to him married (if that could be) than single, and of the many times her husband had said to her that no cares and duties seemed to divide her love for him or her help to him, and asked her "What is the magic secret, my darling, of your being everything to all of us, as if there were only one of us, yet never seeming to be hurried, or to have too much to do?"

But, there were other echoes, from a distance, that rumbled menacingly in the corner all through this space of time. And it was now, about little Lucie's sixth birthday, that they began to have an awful sound, as of a great storm in France with a dreadful sea rising.

On a night in mid-July, one thousand seven hundred and eighty-nine, Mr. Lorry came in late, from Tellson's, and sat himself down by Lucie and her husband in the dark window. It was a hot, wild night, and they were all three reminded of the old Sunday night when they had looked at the lightning from the same place.

"I began to think," said Mr. Lorry, pushing his brown wig back, "that I should have to pass the night at Tellson's. We have been so full of business all day, that we have not known what to do first, or which way to turn. There is such an uneasiness in Paris, that we have actually a run of confidence upon us! Our customers over there, seem not to be able to confide their property to us fast enough. There is positively a mania among some of them for sending it to England."

"That has a bad look," said Darnay.

"A bad look, you say, my dear Darnay? Yes, but we don't know what reason there is in it. People are so unreasonable! Some of us at Tellson's are getting old, and we really can't be troubled out of the ordinary course without due occasion."

"Still," said Darnay, "you know how gloomy and threatening the sky is."

"I know that, to be sure," assented Mr. Lorry, trying to persuade himself that his sweet temper was soured, and that he grumbled, "but I am determined to be peevish after my long day's botheration. Where is Manette?"

"Here he is," said the Doctor, entering the dark room at the moment.

"I am quite glad you are at home; for these hurries and forebodings by which I have been surrounded all day long, have made me nervous without reason. You are not going out, I hope?"

"No; I am going to play backgammon with you, if you like," said the Doctor.

"I don't think I do like, if I may speak my mind. I am not fit to be pitted against you to-night. Is the tea-board still there, Lucie? I can't see."

"Of course, it has been kept for you."

"Thank ye, my dear. The precious child is safe in bed?"

"And sleeping soundly."

"That's right; all safe and well! I don't know why anything should be otherwise than safe and well here, thank God; but I have been so put out all day, and I am not as young as I was! My tea, my dear! Thank ye. Now, come and take your place in the circle, and let us sit quiet, and hear the echoes about which you have your theory."

"Not a theory; it was a fancy."

"A fancy, then, my wise pet," said Mr. Lorry, patting her hand. "They are very numerous and very loud, though, are they not? Only hear them!"

Headlong, mad, and dangerous footsteps to force their way into anybody's life, footsteps not easily made clean again if once stained red, the footsteps raging in Saint Antoine afar off, as the little circle sat in the dark London window.

Saint Antoine had been, that morning, a vast dusky mass of scarecrows heaving to and fro, with frequent gleams of light above the billowy heads, where steel blades and bayonets shone in the sun. A tremendous roar arose from the throat of Saint Antoine, and a forest of naked arms struggled in the air like shrivelled branches of trees in a winter wind: all the fingers convulsively clutching at every weapon or semblance of a weapon that was thrown up from the depths below, no matter how far off.

Who gave them out, whence they last came, where they began, through what agency they crookedly quivered and jerked, scores at a time, over the heads of the crowd, like a kind of lightning, no eye in the throng could have told; but, muskets were being distributed—so were cartridges, powder, and ball, bars of iron and wood, knives, axes, pikes, every weapon that distracted ingenuity could discover or devise. People who could lay hold of nothing else, set themselves with bleeding hands to force stones and bricks out of their places in walls. Every pulse and heart in Saint Antoine was on high-fever strain and at high-fever heat. Every living creature there held life as of no account, and was demented with a passionate readiness to sacrifice it.

As a whirlpool of boiling waters has a centre point, so, all this raging circled round Defarge's wine-shop, and every human drop in the caldron had a tendency to be sucked towards the vortex where Defarge himself, already begrimed with gunpowder and sweat, issued orders, issued arms, thrust this man back, dragged that man forward, disarmed one to arm another, laboured and strove in the thickest of the uproar.

"Keep near to me, Jacques Three," cried Defarge; "and do you, Jacques One and Two, separate and put yourselves at the head of as many of these patriots as you can. Where is my wife?"

"Eh, well! Here you see me!" said madame, composed as ever, but not knitting to-day. Madame's resolute right hand was occupied with an axe, in place of the usual softer implements, and in her girdle were a pistol and a cruel knife.

"Where do you go, my wife?"

"I go," said madame, "with you at present. You shall see me at the head of women, by-and-bye."

"Come, then!" cried Defarge, in a resounding voice. "Patriots and friends, we are ready! The Bastille!"

With a roar that sounded as if all the breath in France had been shaped into the detested word, the living sea rose, wave on wave, depth on depth, and overflowed the city to that point. Alarm-bells ringing, drums beating, the sea raging and thundering on its new beach, the attack begun.

Deep ditches, double drawbridge, massive stone walls, eight great towers, cannon, muskets, fire and smoke. Through the fire and through the smoke—in the fire and in the smoke, for the sea cast him up against a cannon, and on the instant he became a cannonier—Defarge of the wine-shop worked like a manful soldier, Two fierce hours.

Deep ditch, single drawbridge, massive stone walls, eight great towers, cannon, muskets, fire and smoke. One drawbridge down! "Work, comrades all, work! Work, Jacques One, Jacques Two, Jacques One Thousand, Jacques Two Thousand, Jacques Five-and-Twenty Thousand; in the name of all the Angles or the Devils—which you prefer—work!" Thus Defarge of the wine-shop, still at his gun, which had long grown hot.

"To me, women!" cried madame his wife. "What! We can kill as well as the men when the place is taken!" And to her, with a shrill thirsty cry, trooping women variously armed, but all armed alike in hunger and revenge.

Cannon, muskets, fire and smoke; but, still the deep ditch, the single drawbridge, the massive stone walls, and the eight great towers. Slight displacements of the raging sea made by the falling wounded. Flashing weapons, blazing, torches smoking waggon-loads of wet straw, hard work at neighbouring barricades in all directions, shrieks, volleys, execrations, bravery without stint, boom smash and rattle, and the furious sounding of the living sea; but, still the deep ditch, and the single drawbridge, and the massive stone walls, and the eight great towers, and still Defarge of the wine-shop at his gun, grown doubly hot by the service of Four fierce hours.

A white flag from within the fortress, and a parley—this dimly perceptible through the raging storm, nothing audible in it—suddenly the sea rose immeasurably wider and higher, and swept Defarge of the wine-shop over the lowered drawbridge, past the massive stone outer walls, in among the eight great towers surrendered!

So resistless was the force of the ocean bearing him on, that even to draw his breath or turn his head was as impracticable as if he had been struggling in the surf at the South Sea, until he was landed in the outer courtyard of the Bastille. There, against an angle of a wall, he made a struggle to look about him. Jacques Three was nearly at his side; Madame Defarge, still heading some of her women, was visible in the inner distance, and her knife was in her hand. Everywhere was tumult, exultation, deafening and maniacal bewilderment, astounding noise, yet furious dumb-show.

"The Prisoners!"
"The Records!"
"The secret cells!"
"The instruments of torture!"
"The Prisoners!"

Of all these cries, and ten thousand incoherences, "The Prisoners!" was the cry most taken up by the sea that rushed in, as if there were an eternity of people, as well as of time and space. When the foremost billows rolled past, bearing the prison officers with them, and threatening them all with instant death if any secret nook remained undisclosed, Defarge laid his strong hand on the breast of one of these men—a man with a grey head, who had a lighted torch in his hand—separated him from the rest, and got him between himself and the wall.

"Show me the North Tower!" said Defarge. "Quick!"

"I will faithfully," replied the man, "if you will come with me. But there is no one there."

"What is the meaning of One Hundred and Five, North Tower?" asked Defarge. "Quick!"

"The meaning, monsieur?"

"Does it mean a captive, or a place of captivity? Or do you mean that I shall strike you dead?"

"Kill him!" croaked Jacques Three, who had come close up.

"Monsieur, it is a cell."

"Show it me!"

"Pass this way, then."

Jacques Three, with his usual craving on him, and evidently disappointed by the dialogue taking a turn that did not seem to promise bloodshed, held by Defarge's arm as he held by the turnkey's. Their three heads had been close together during this brief discourse, and it had been as much as they could do to hear one another, even then: so tremendous was the noise of the living ocean, in its irruption into the Fortress, and its inundation of the courts and passages and staircases. All around outside, too, it beat the walls with a deep, hoarse roar, from which, occasionally, some partial shouts of tumult broke and leaped into the air like spray.

Through gloomy vaults where the light of day had never shone, past hideous doors of dark dens and cages, down cavernous flights of steps, and again up steep rugged ascents of stone and brick, more like dry waterfalls than staircases, Defarge, the turnkey, and Jacques Three, linked hand and arm, went with all the speed they could make. Here and there, especially at first, the inundation started on them and swept by; but when they had done descending, and were winding and climbing up a tower, they were alone. Hemmed in here by the massive thickness of walls and arches, the storm within the fortress and without was only audible to them in a dull, subdued way, as if the noise out of which they had come had almost destroyed their sense of hearing.

The turnkey stopped at a low door, put a key in a clashing lock, swung the door slowly open, and said, as they all bent their heads and passed in:

"One hundred and five, North Tower!"

There was a small heavily-grated, unglazed window high in the wall, with a stone screen before it, so that the sky could be only seen by stooping low and looking up. There was a small chimney, heavily barred across, a few feet within. There was a heap of old feathery wood-ashes on the hearth. There was a stool, and table, and a straw bed. There were the four blackened walls, and a rusted iron ring in one of them.

"Pass that torch slowly along these walls, that I may see them," said Defarge to the turnkey.

The man obeyed, and Defarge followed the light closely with his eyes.

"Stop!—Look here, Jacques!"

"A. M.!" croaked Jacques Three, as he read greedily.

"Alexandre Manette," said Defarge in his ear, following the letters with his swart forefinger, deeply engrained with gunpowder. "And here he wrote 'a poor physician.' And it was he, without doubt, who scratched a calendar on this stone. What is that in your hand? A crowbar? Give it me!"

He had still the linstock of his gun in his own hand. He made a sudden exchange of the two instruments, and turning on the worm-eaten stool and table, beat them to pieces in a few blows.

"Hold the light higher!" he said, wrathfully, to the turnkey. "Look among those fragments with care, Jacques. And see! Here is my knife," throwing it to him; "rip open that bed, and search the straw. Hold the light higher, you!"

With a menacing look at the turnkey he crawled upon the hearth, and, peering up the chimney, struck and prised at its sides with the crowbar, and worked at the iron grating across it. In a few minutes, some mortar and dust came dropping down, which he averted his face to avoid; and in it, and in the old wood-ashes, and in a crevice in the chimney into which his weapon had slipped or wrought itself, he groped with a cautious touch.

"Nothing in the wood, and nothing in the straw, Jacques?"

"Nothing."

"Let us collect them together, in the middle of the cell. So! Light them, you!"

The turnkey fired the little pile, which blazed high and hot. Stooping again to come out at the low-arched door, they left it burning, and retraced their way to the courtyard; seeming to recover their sense of hearing as they came down, until they were in the raging flood once more.

They found it surging and tossing, in quest of Defarge himself. Saint Antoine was clamorous to have its wine-shop keeper foremost in the guard upon the governor who had defended the Bastille and shot the people. Otherwise, the governor would not be marched to the Hôtel de Ville for judgment. Otherwise, the governor would escape, and the people's blood (suddenly of some value, after many years of worthlessness) be unavenged.

In the howling universe of passion and contention that seemed to encompass this grim old officer conspicuous in his grey coat and red decoration, there was but one quite steady figure, and that was a woman's. "See, there is my husband!" she cried, pointing him out. "See Defarge!" She stood immovable close to the grim old officer, and remained immovable close to him; remained immovable close to him through the streets, as Defarge and the rest bore him along; remained immovable close to him when he was got near his destination, and began to be struck at from behind; remained immovable close to him when the long-gathering rain of stabs and blows fell heavy; was so close to him when he dropped dead under it, that, suddenly animated, she put her foot upon his neck, and with her cruel knife—long ready—hewed off his head.

The hour was come, when Saint Antoine was to execute his horrible idea of hoisting up men for lamps to show what he could be and do. Saint Antoine's blood was up, and the blood of tyranny and domination by the iron hand was down—down on the steps of the Hôtel de Ville where the governor's body lay—down on the sole of the shoe of Madame Defarge where she had trodden on the body to steady it for mutilation. "Lower the lamp yonder!" cried Saint Antoine, after glaring round for a new means of death; "here is one of his soldiers to be left on guard!" The swinging sentinel was posted, and the sea rushed on.

The sea of black and threatening waters, and of destructive upheaving of wave against wave, whose depths were yet unfathomed and whose forces were yet unknown. The remorseless sea of turbulently swaying shapes, voices of vengeance, and faces hardened in the furnaces of suffering until the touch of pity could make no mark on them.

But, in the ocean of faces where every fierce and furious expression was in vivid life, there were two groups of faces —each seven in number—so fixedly contrasting with the rest, that never did sea roll which bore more memorable wrecks with it. Seven faces of prisoners, suddenly released by the storm that had burst their tomb, were carried high overhead: all scared, all lost, all wondering and amazed, as if the Last Day were come, and those who rejoiced around them were lost spirits. Other seven faces there were, carried higher, seven dead faces, whose drooping eyelids and half-seen eyes awaited the Last Day. Impassive faces, yet with a suspended—not an abolished—expression on them; faces, rather, in a fearful pause, as having yet to raise the dropped lids of the eyes, and bear witness with the bloodless lips, "THOU DIDST IT!"

Seven prisoners released, seven gory heads on pikes, the keys of the accursed fortress of the eight strong towers, some discovered letters and other memorials of prisoners of old time, long dead of broken hearts,—such, and such-like, the loudly echoing footsteps of Saint Antoine escort through the Paris streets in mid-July, one thousand seven hundred and eighty-nine. Now, Heaven defeat the fancy of Lucie Darnay, and keep these feet far out of her life! For, they are headlong, mad, and dangerous; and in the years so long after the breaking of the cask at Defarge's wine-shop door, they are not easily purified when once stained red.

CHAPTER XXII.

THE SEA STILL RISES.

HAGGARD Saint Antoine had had only one exultant week, in which to soften his modicum of hard and bitter bread to such extent as he could, with the relish of fraternal embraces and congratulations, when Madame Defarge sat at her counter, as usual, presiding over the customers. Madame Defarge wore no rose in her head, for the great brotherhood of Spies had become, even in one short week, extremely chary of trusting themselves to the saint's mercies. The lamps across his streets had a portentously elastic swing with them.

Madame Defarge, with her arms folded, sat in the morning light and heat, contemplating the wine-shop and the street. In both, there were several knots of loungers, squalid and miserable, but now with a manifest sense of power enthroned on their distress. The raggedest night-cap, awry on the wretchedest head, had this crooked significance in it: "I know how hard it has grown for me, the wearer of this, to support life in myself; but do you know how easy it has grown for me, the wearer of this, to destroy life in you?" Every lean bare arm, that had been without work before, had this work always ready for it now, that it could strike. The fingers of the knitting women were vicious, with the experience that they could tear. There was a change in the appearance of Saint Antoine; the image had been hammering into this for hundreds of years, and the last finishing blows had told mightily on the expression.

Madame Defarge sat observing it, with such suppressed approval as was to be desired in the leader of the Saint Antoine women. One of her sisterhood knitted beside her. The short, rather plump wife of a starved grocer, and the mother of two children withal, this lieutenant had already earned the complimentary name of The Vengeance.

1059

"Hark!" said The Vengeance. "Listen, then! Who comes?"

As if a train of powder laid from the outermost bound of Saint Antoine Quarter to the wine-shop door, had been suddenly fired, a fast-spreading murmur came rushing along.

"It is Defarge," said madame. "Silence, patriots!"

Defarge came in breathless, pulled off a red cap he wore, and looked around him! "Listen, everywhere!" said madame again. "Listen to him!" Defarge stood, panting, against a background of eager eyes and open mouths, formed outside the door; all those within the wine-shop had sprung to their feet.

"Say then, my husband. What is it?"

"News from the other world!"

"How, then?" cried madame, contemptuously. "The other world?"

"Does everybody here recall old Foulon, who told the famished people that they might eat grass, and who died, and went to Hell?"

"Everybody!" from all throats.

"The news is of him. He is among us!"

"Among us!" from the universal throat again. "And dead?"

"Not dead! He feared us so much—and with reason—that he caused himself to be represented as dead, and had a grand mock-funeral. But they have found him alive, hiding in the country, and have brought him in. I have seen him but now, on his way to the Hôtel de Ville, a prisoner. I have said that he had reason to fear us. Say all! Had he reason?"

Wretched old sinner of more than threescore years and ten, if he had never known it yet, he would have known it in his heart of hearts if he could have heard the answering cry.

A moment of profound silence followed. Defarge and his wife looked steadfastly at one another. The Vengeance stooped, and the jar of a drum was heard as she moved it at her feet behind the counter.

"Patriots!" said Defarge, in a determined voice, "are we ready?"

Instantly Madame Defarge's knife was in her girdle; the drum was beating in the streets, as if it and a drummer had flown together by magic; and The Vengeance, uttering terrific shrieks, and flinging her arms about her head like all the forty Furies at once, was tearing from house to house, rousing the women.

The men were terrible, in the bloody-minded anger with which they looked from windows, caught up what arms they had, and came pouring down into the streets; but, the women were a sight to chill the boldest. From such household occupations as their bare poverty yielded, from their children, from their aged and their sick crouching on the bare ground famished and naked, they ran out with streaming hair, urging one another, and themselves, to madness with the wildest cries and actions. Villain Foulon taken, my sister! Old Foulon taken, my mother! Miscreant Foulon taken, my daughter! Then, a score of others ran into the midst of these, beating their breasts, tearing their hair, and screaming, Foulon alive! Foulon who told the starving people they might eat grass! Foulon who told my old father that he might eat grass, when I had no bread to give him! Foulon who told my baby it might suck grass, when these breasts were dry with want! O mother of God, this Foulon! O Heaven, our suffering! Hear me, my dead baby and my withered father: I swear on my knees, on these stones, to·avenge you on Foulon! Husbands, and brothers, and young men, Give us the blood of Foulon, Give us the head of Foulon, Give us the heart of Foulon, Give us the body and soul of Foulon, Rend Foulon to pieces, and dig him into the ground, that grass may grow from him! With these cries, numbers of the women, lashed into blind frenzy, whirled about, striking and tearing at their own friends until they dropped into a passionate swoon, and were only saved by the men belonging to them from being trampled under foot.

Nevertheless, not a moment was lost; not a moment! This Foulon was at the Hôtel de Ville, and might be loosed. Never, if Saint Antoine knew his own sufferings, insults, and wrongs! Armed men and women flocked out of the Quarter so fast, and drew even these last dregs after them with such a force of suction, that within a quarter of an hour there was not a human creature in Saint Antoine's bosom but a few old crones and the wailing children.

No. They were all by that time choking the Hall of Examination where this old man, ugly and wicked, was, and overflowing into the adjacent open space and streets. The Defarges, husband and wife, The Vengeance, and Jacques Three, were in the first press, and at no great distance from him in the Hall.

"See!" cried madame, pointing with her knife. "See the old villain bound with ropes. That was well done to tie a bunch of grass upon his back. Ha, ha! That was well done. Let him eat it now!" Madame put her knife under her arm, and clapped her hands as at a play.

The people immediately behind Madame Defarge, explaining the cause of her satisfaction to those behind them, and those again explaining to others, and those to others, the neighbouring streets resounded with the clapping of hands. Similarly, during two or three hours of drawl, and the winnowing of many bushels of words, Madame Defarge's frequent expressions of impatience were taken up, with marvellous quickness, at a distance: the more readily, because certain men who had by some wonderful exercise of agility climbed up the external architecture to look in from the windows, knew Madame Defarge well, and acted as a telegraph between her and the crowd outside the building.

At length the sun rose so high that it struck a kindly ray as of hope or protection, directly down upon the old prisoner's head. The favour was too much to bear; in an instant the barrier of dust and chaff that had stood surprisingly long, went to the winds, and Saint Antoine had got him!

It was known directly, to the furthest confines of the crowd. Defarge had but sprung over a railing and a table, and folded the miserable wretch in a deadly embrace—Madame Defarge had but followed and turned her hand in one of the ropes with which he was tied—The Vengeance and Jacques Three were not yet up with them, and the men at the windows had not yet swooped into the Hall, like birds of prey from their high perches—when the cry seemed to go up, all over the city, "Bring him out! Bring him to the lamp!"

Down, and up, and head foremost on the steps of the building; now, on his knees; now, on his feet; now, on his back; dragged, and struck at, and stifled by the bunches of grass and straw that were thrust into his face by hundreds of hands; torn, bruised, panting, bleeding, yet always entreating and beseeching for mercy; now full of vehement agony of action, with a small clear space about him as the people drew one another back that they might see; now, a log of dead wood drawn through a forest of legs; he was hauled to the nearest street corner where one of the fatal lamps swung, and there Madame Defarge let him go—as a cat might have done to a mouse—and silently and composedly looked at him while they made ready, and while he besought her: the women passionately screeching at him all the time, and the men sternly calling out to have him killed with grass in his mouth. Once, he went aloft, and the rope broke, and they caught him shrieking; twice, he went aloft, and the rope broke, and they caught him shrieking; then, the rope was merciful, and held him, and his head was soon upon a pike, with grass enough in the mouth for all Saint Antoine to dance at the sight of.

Nor was this the end of the day's bad work, for Saint Antoine so shouted and danced his angry blood up, that it boiled again, on hearing when the day closed in that the son-in-law of the despatched, another of the people's enemies and insulters, was coming into Paris under a guard five hundred strong, in cavalry alone. Saint Antoine wrote his crimes on flaring sheets of paper, seized him—would have torn him out of the breast of an army to bear Foulon company—set his head and heart on pikes, and carried the three spoils of the day, in Wolf-procession through the streets.

Not before dark night did the men and women come back to the children, wailing and breadless. Then, the miserable bakers' shops were beset by long files of them, patiently waiting to buy bad bread; and while they waited with stomachs faint and empty, they beguiled the time by embracing one another on the triumphs of the day, and achieving them again in gossip. Gradually, these strings of ragged people shortened and frayed away; and then poor lights began to shine in high windows, and slender fires were made in the streets, at which neighbours cooked in common, afterwards supping at their doors.

Scanty and insufficient suppers those, and innocent of meat, as of most other sauce to wretched bread. Yet, human fellowship infused some nourishment into the flinty viands, and struck some sparks of cheerfulness out of them. Fathers and mothers who had had their full share in the worst of the day, played gently with their meagre children; and lovers, with such a world around them and before them, loved and hoped.

It was almost morning, when Defarge's wine-shop parted with its last knot of customers, and Monsieur Defarge said to madame his wife, in husky tones, while fastening the door:

"At last it is come, my dear!"

"Eh well!" returned madame. "Almost."

Saint Antoine slept, the Defarges slept: even The Vengeance slept with her starved grocer, and the drum was at rest. The drum's was the only voice in Saint Antoine that blood and hurry had not changed. The Vengeance, as custodian of the drum, could have wakened him up and had the same speech out of him as before the Bastille fell, or old Foulon was seized; not so with the hoarse tones of the men and women in Saint Antoine's bosom.

CHAPTER XXIII.

FIRE RISES.

THERE was a change on the village where the fountain fell, and where the mender of roads went forth daily to hammer out of the stones on the highway such morsels of bread as might serve for patches to hold his poor ignorant soul and his poor reduced body together. The prison on the crag was not so dominant as of yore; there were soldiers to guard it, but not many; there were officers to guard the soldiers, but not one of them knew what his men would do—beyond this: that it would probably not be what he was ordered.

Far and wide lay a ruined country, yielding nothing but desolation. Every green leaf, every blade of grass and blade of grain, was as shrivelled and poor as the miserable people. Everything was bowed down, dejected, oppressed, and broken. Habitations, fences, domesticated animals, men, women, children, and the soil that bore them—all worn out.

Monseigneur (often a most worthy individual gentleman) was a national blessing, gave a chivalrous tone to things, was a polite example of luxurious and shining life, and a great deal more to equal purpose; nevertheless, Monseigneur as a class had, somehow or other, brought things to this. Strange that Creation, designed expressly for Monseigneur, should be so soon wrung dry and squeezed out! There must be something short-sighted in the eternal arrangements, surely! Thus it was, however; and the last drop of blood having been extracted from the flints, and the last screw of the rack having been turned so often that its purchase crumbled, and it now turned and turned with nothing to bite, Monseigneur began to run away from a phenomenon so low and unaccountable.

But, this was not the change on the village, and on many a village like it. For scores of years gone by, Monseigneur had squeezed it and wrung it, and had seldom graced it with his presence except for the pleasures of the chase—now, found in hunting the people; now, found in hunting the beasts, for whose preservation Monseigneur made edifying spaces of barbarous and barren wilderness. No. The change consisted in the appearance of strange faces of low caste, rather than in the disappearance of the high caste, chiselled, and otherwise beautified and beautifying features of Monseigneur.

For, in these times, as the mender of roads worked, solitary, in the dust, not often troubling himself to reflect that dust he was and to dust he must return, being for the most part too much occupied in thinking how little he had for supper and how much more he would eat if he had it—in these times, as he raised his eyes from his lonely labour, and viewed the prospect, he would see some rough figure approaching on foot, the like of which was once a rarity in those parts, but was now a frequent presence. As it advanced, the mender of roads would discern without surprise, that it was a shaggy-haired man, of almost barbarian aspect, tall, in wooden shoes that were clumsy even to the eyes of a mender of roads, grim, rough, swart, steeped in the mud and dust of many highways, dank with the marshy moisture of many low grounds, sprinkled with the thorns and leaves and moss of many byways through woods.

Such a man came upon him, like a ghost, at noon in the July weather, as he sat on his heap of stones under a bank,

SAINT ANTOINE RAGING IN "WOLF PROCESSION THROUGH
THE STREETS."

taking such shelter as he could get from a shower of hail.

The man looked at him, looked at the village in the hollow, at the mill, and at the prison on the crag. When he had identified these objects in what benighted mind he had, he said, in a dialect that was just intelligible:

"How goes it, Jacques?"

"All well, Jacques."

"Touch then!"

They joined hands, and the man sat down on the heap of stones.

"No dinner?"

"Nothing but supper now," said the mender of roads, with a hungry face.

"It is the fashion," growled the man. "I meet no dinner anywhere."

He took out a blackened pipe, filled it, lighted it with flint and steel, pulled at it until it was in a bright glow: then, suddenly held it from him and dropped something into it from between his finger and thumb, that blazed and went out in a puff of smoke.

"Touch then." It was the turn of the mender of roads to say it this time, after observing these operations. They again joined hands.

"To-night?" said the mender of roads.

"To-night," said the man, putting the pipe in his mouth.

"Where?"

"Here."

He and the mender of roads sat on the heap of stones looking silently at one another, with the hail driving in between them like a pigmy charge of bayonets, until the sky began to clear over the village.

"Show me!" said the traveller then, moving to the brow of the hill.

"See!" returned the mender of roads, with extended finger. "You go down here, and straight through the street, and past the fountain——"

"To the Devil with all that!" interrupted the other, rolling his eye over the landscape. "I go through no streets and past no fountains. Well?"

"Well! About two leagues beyond the summit of that hill above the village."

"Good. When do you cease to work?"

"At sunset."

"Will you wake me, before departing? I have walked two nights without resting. Let me finish my pipe, and I shall sleep like a child. Will you wake me?"

"Surely."

The wayfarer smoked his pipe out, put it in his breast, slipped off his great wooden shoes, and lay down on his back on the heap of stones. He was fast asleep directly.

As the road-mender plied his dusty labour, and the hail-clouds, rolling away, revealed bright bars and streaks of sky which were responded to by silver gleams upon the landscape, the little man (who wore a red cap now, in place of his blue one) seemed fascinated by the figure on the heap of stones. His eyes were so often turned towards it, that he used his tools mechanically, and, one would have said, to very poor account. The bronze face, the shaggy black hair and beard, the coarse woollen red cap, the rough medley dress of home-spun stuff and hairy skins of beasts, the powerful frame attenuated by spare living, and the sullen and desperate compression of the lips in sleep, inspired the mender of roads with awe. The traveller had travelled far, and his feet were footsore, and his ankles chafed and bleeding; his great shoes, stuffed with leaves and grass, had been heavy to drag over the many long leagues, and his clothes were chafed into holes, as he himself was into sores. Stooping down beside him, the road-mender tried to get a peep at secret weapons in his breast or where not; but, in vain, for he slept with his arms crossed upon him, and set as resolutely as his lips. Fortified towns with their stockades, guard-houses, gates, trenches, and drawbridges, seemed to the mender of roads, to be so much air as against this figure. And when he lifted his eyes from it to the horizon and looked around, he saw in his small fancy similar figures, stopped by no obstacle, tending to centres all over France.

The man slept on, indifferent to showers of hail and intervals of brightness, to sunshine on his face and shadow, to the pattering lumps of dull ice on his body and the diamonds into which the sun changed them, until the sun was low in the west, and the sky was glowing. Then, the mender of roads having got his tools together and all things ready to go down into the village, roused him.

"Good!" said the sleeper, rising on his elbow. "Two leagues beyond the summit of the hill?"

"About."

"About. Good!"

The mender of roads went home, with the dust going on before him according to the set of the wind, and was soon at the fountain, squeezing himself in among the lean kine brought there to drink, and appearing even to whisper to them in his whispering to all the village. When the village had taken its poor supper, it did not creep to bed, as it usually did, but came out of doors again, and remained there. A curious contagion of whispering was upon it, and also, when it gathered together at the fountain in the dark, another curious contagion of looking expectantly at the sky in one direction only. Monsieur Gabelle, chief functionary of the place, became uneasy; went out on his house-top alone, and looked in that direction too; glanced down from behind his chimneys at the darkening faces by the fountain below, and sent word to the sacristan who kept the keys of the church, that there might be need to ring the tocsin by-and-bye.

The night deepened. The trees environing the old château, keeping its solitary state apart, moved in a rising wind, as though they threatened the pile of building massive and dark in the gloom. Up the two terrace flights of steps the rain ran wildly, and beat at the great door, like a swift messenger rousing those within; uneasy rushes of wind went through the hall, among the old spears and knives, and passed lamenting up the stairs, and shook the curtains of the bed where the last Marquis had slept. East, West, North, and South, through the woods, four heavy-treading, unkempt figures crushed the high grass and cracked the branches, striding on cautiously to come together in the courtyard. Four lights broke out there, and moved away in different directions, and all was black again.

But, not for long. Presently, the château began to make itself strangely visible by some light of its own, as though it were growing luminous. Then, a flickering streak played behind the architecture of the front, picking out transparent places, and showing where balustrades, arches, and windows were. Then it soared higher, and grew broader and brighter. Soon, from a score of the great windows, flames burst forth, and the stone faces awakened, stared out of fire.

A faint murmur arose about the house from the few people who were left there, and there was a saddling of a horse and riding away. There was spurring and splashing through the darkness, and bridle was drawn in the space by the village fountain, and the horse in a foam stood at Monsieur Gabelle's door. "Help, Gabelle! Help, every one!" The tocsin rang impatiently, but other help (if that were any) there was none. The mender of roads, and two hundred and fifty particular friends, stood with folded arms at the fountain, looking at the pillar of fire in the sky. "It must be forty feet high," said they, grimly; and never moved.

The rider from the château, and the horse in a foam, clattered away through the village, and galloped up the stony steep, to the prison on the crag. At the gate, a group of officers were looking at the fire; removed from them, a group of soldiers. "Help, gentlemen-officers! The château is on fire; valuable objects may be saved from the flames by timely aid! Help, help!" The officers looked towards the soldiers who looked at the fire; gave no orders; and answered, with shrugs and biting of lips, "It must burn."

As the rider rattled down the hill again and through the street, the village was illuminating. The mender of roads, and the two hundred and fifty particular friends, inspired as one man and woman by the idea of lighting up, had darted into their houses, and were putting candles in every dull little pane of glass. The general scarcity of everything, occasioned candles to be borrowed in a rather peremptory manner of Monsieur Gabelle; and in a moment of reluctance and hesitation on that functionary's part, the mender of roads, once so submissive to authority, had remarked that carriages were good to make bonfires with, and that post-horses would roast.

The château was left to itself to flame and burn. In the roaring and raging of the conflagration, a red-hot wind, driving straight from the infernal regions, seemed to be blowing the edifice away. With the rising and falling of the blaze, the stone faces showed as if they were in torment. When great masses of stone and timber fell, the face with the two dints in the nose became obscured: anon struggled out of the smoke again, as if it were the face of the cruel Marquis, burning at the stake and contending with the fire.

The château burned; the nearest trees, laid hold of by the fire, scorched and shrivelled; trees at a distance, fired by the four fierce figures, begirt the blazing edifice with a new forest of smoke. Molten lead and iron boiled in the marble basin of the fountain; the water ran dry; the extinguisher tops of the towers vanished like ice before the heat, and trickled down into four rugged wells of flame. Great rents and splits branched out in the solid walls, like crystallisation; stupefied birds wheeled about and dropped into the furnace; four fierce figures trudged away, East, West, North, and South, along the night-enshrouded roads, guided by the beacon they had lighted, towards their next destination. The illuminated village had seized hold of the tocsin, and, abolishing the lawful ringer, rang for joy.

Not that only; but the village, light-headed with famine, fire, and bell-ringing, and bethinking itself that Monsieur Gabelle had to do with the collection of rent and taxes—though it was but a small instalment of taxes, and no rent at all, that Gabelle had got in those latter days—became impatient for an interview with him, and, surrounding his house, summoned him to come forth for personal conference. Whereupon, Monsieur Gabelle did heavily bar his

door, and retire to hold counsel with himself. The result of that conference was, that Gabelle again withdrew himself to his house-top behind his stack of chimneys; this time resolved, if his door were broken in (he was a small Southern man of retaliative temperament), to pitch himself head foremost over the parapet, and crush a man or two below.

Probably, Monsieur Gabelle passed a long night up there, with the distant château for fire and candle, and the beating at his door, combined with the joy-ringing, for music; not to mention his having an ill-omened lamp slung across the road before his posting-house gate, which the village showed a lively inclination to displace in his favour. A trying suspense, to be passing a whole summer night on the brink of the black ocean, ready to take that plunge into it upon which Monsieur Gabelle had resolved! But, the friendly dawn appearing at last, and the rush-candles of the village guttering out, the people happily dispersed, and Monsieur Gabelle came down bringing his life with him for that while.

Within a hundred miles, and in the light of other fires, there were other functionaries less fortunate, that night and other nights, whom the rising sun found hanging across once-peaceful streets, where they had been born and bred; also, there were other villagers and townspeople less fortunate than the mender of roads and his fellows, upon whom the functionaries and soldiery turned with success, and whom they strung up in their turn. But, the fierce figures were steadily wending East, West, North, and South, be that as it would; and whosoever hung, fire burned. The altitude of the gallows that would turn to water and quench it, no functionary, by any stretch of mathematics, was able to calculate successfully.

CHAPTER XXIV.

DRAWN TO THE LOADSTONE ROCK.

IN such risings of fire and risings of sea—the firm earth shaken by the rushes of an angry ocean which had now no ebb, but was always on the flow, higher and higher, to the terror and wonder of the beholders on the shore—three years of tempest were consumed. Three more birthdays of little Lucie had been woven by the golden thread into the peaceful tissue of the life of her home.

Many a night and many a day had its inmates listened to the echoes in the corner, with hearts that failed them when they heard the thronging feet. For, the footsteps had become to their minds as the footsteps of a people, tumultuous under a red flag and with their country declared in danger, changed into wild beasts, by terrible enchantment long persisted in.

Monseigneur, as a class, had dissociated himself from the phenomenon of his not being appreciated: of his being so little wanted in France, as to incur considerable danger of receiving his dismissal from it, and this life together. Like the fabled rustic who raised the Devil with infinite pains, and was so terrified at the sight of him that he could ask the Enemy no question, but immediately fled; so, Monseigneur, after boldly reading the Lord's Prayer backwards for a great number of years, and performing many other potent spells for compelling the Evil One, no sooner beheld him in his terrors than he took to his noble heels.

The shining Bull's Eye of the Court was gone, or it would have been the mark for a hurricane of national bul-

TALE OF TWO CITIES

lets. It had never been a good eye to see with—had long had the mote in it of Lucifer's pride, Sardanapalus's luxury, and a mole's blindness—but it had dropped out and was gone. The Court, from that exclusive inner circle to its outermost rotten ring of intrigue, corruption, and dissimulation, was all gone together. Royalty was gone; had been besieged in its Palace and "suspended," when the last tidings came over.

The August of the year one thousand seven hundred and ninety-two was come, and Monseigneur was by this time scattered far and wide.

As was natural, the head-quarters and great gathering-place of Monseigneur, in London, was Tellson's Bank. Spirits are supposed to haunt the places where their bodies most resorted, and Monseigneur without a guinea haunted the spot where his guineas used to be. Moreover, it was the spot to which such French intelligence as was most to be relied upon, came quickest. Again: Tellson's was a munificent house, and extended great liberality to old customers who had fallen from their high estate. Again: those nobles who had seen the coming storm in time, and anticipating plunder or confiscation, had made provident remittances to Tellson's, were always to be heard of there by their needy brethren. To which it must be added that every new-comer from France reported himself and his tidings at Tellson's, almost as a matter of course. For such variety of reasons, Tellson's was at that time, as to French intelligence, a kind of High Exchange; and this was so well known to the public, and the inquiries made there were in consequence so numerous, that Tellson's sometimes wrote the latest news out in a line or so and posted it in the Bank windows, for all who ran through Temple Bar to read.

On a steaming, misty afternoon, Mr. Lorry sat at his desk, and Charles Darnay stood leaning on it, talking with him in a low voice. The penitential den once set apart for interviews with the House, was now the news-Exchange, and was filled to overflowing. It was within half an hour or so of the time of closing.

"But, although you are the youngest man that ever lived," said Charles Darnay, rather hesitating, "I must still suggest to you——"

"I understand. That I am too old?" said Mr. Lorry.

"Unsettled weather, a long journey, uncertain means of travelling, a disorganised country, a city that may not be even safe for you."

"My dear Charles," said Mr. Lorry, with cheerful confidence, "you touch some of the reasons for my going: not for my staying away. It is safe enough for me; nobody will care to interfere with an old fellow of hard upon fourscore when there are so many people there much better worth interfering with. As to its being a disorganised city, if it were not a disorganised city there would be no occasion to send somebody from our House here to our House there, who knows the city and the business, of old, and is in Tellson's confidence. As to the uncertain travelling, the long journey, and the winter weather, if I were not prepared to submit myself to a few inconveniences for the sake of Tellson's, after all these years, who ought to be?"

"I wish I were going myself," said Charles Darnay, somewhat restlessly, and like one thinking aloud.

"Indeed! You are a pretty fellow to object and advise!" exclaimed Mr. Lorry. "You wish you were going yourself? And you a Frenchman born? You are a wise counsellor."

"My dear Mr. Lorry, it is because I am a Frenchman born, that the thought (which I did not mean to utter here, however) has passed through my mind often. One cannot help thinking, having had some sympathy for the miserable people, and having abandoned something to them," he spoke here in his former thoughtful manner, "that one might be listened to, and might have the power to persuade to some restraint. Only last night, after you had left us, when I was talking to Lucie——"

"When you were talking to Lucie," Mr. Lorry repeated. "Yes. I wonder you are not ashamed to mention the name of Lucie! Wishing you were going to France at this time of day!"

"However, I am not going," said Charles Darnay, with a smile. "It is more to the purpose that you say you are."

"And I am, in plain reality. The truth is, my dear Charles," Mr. Lorry glanced at the distant House, and lowered his voice, "you can have no conception of the difficulty with which our business is transacted, and of the peril in which our books and papers over yonder are involved. The Lord above knows what the compromising consequences would be to numbers of people, if some of our documents were seized or destroyed; and they might be, at any time, you know, for who can say that Paris is not set afire to-day, or sacked to-morrow! Now, a judicious selection from these with the least possible delay, and the burying of them, or otherwise getting of them out of harm's way, is within the power (without loss of precious time) of scarcely any one but myself, if any one. And shall I hang back, when Tellson's knows this and says this—Tellson's, whose bread I have eaten these sixty years—because I am a little stiff about the joints? Why, I am a boy, sir, to half a dozen old codgers here!"

"How I admire the gallantry of your youthful spirit, Mr. Lorry."

"Tut! Nonsense, sir!—And, my dear Charles," said Mr. Lorry, glancing at the House again, "you are to remember, that getting things out of Paris at this present time, no matter what things, is next to an impossibility. Papers and precious matters were this very day brought to us here (I speak in strict confidence; it is not business-like to whisper it, even to you,) by the strangest bearers you can imagine, every one of whom had his head hanging on by a single hair as he passed the Barriers. At another time, our parcels would come and go, as easily as in business-like Old England; but now, everything is stopped."

"And do you really go to-night?"

"I really go to-night, for the case has become too pressing to admit of delay."

"And do you take no one with you?"

"All sorts of people have been proposed to me, but I will have nothing to say to any of them. I intend to take Jerry. Jerry has been my body-guard on Sunday nights for a long time past, and I am used to him. Nobody will suspect Jerry of being anything but an English bull-dog, or of having any design in his head but to fly at anybody who touches his master."

"I must say again that I heartily admire your gallantry and youthfulness."

"I must say again, nonsense, nonsense! When I have executed this little commission, I shall, perhaps, accept Tellson's proposal to retire and live at my ease. Time enough, then, to think about growing old."

This dialogue had taken place at Mr. Lorry's usual desk,

1065

with Monseigneur swarming within a yard or two of it, boastful of what he would do to avenge himself on the rascal-people before long. It was too much the way of Monseigneur under his reverses as a refugee, and it was much too much the way of native British orthodoxy, to talk of this terrible Revolution as if it were the only harvest ever known under the skies that had not been sown—as if nothing had ever been done, or omitted to be done, that had led to it—as if observers of the wretched millions in France, and of the misused and perverted resources that should have made them prosperous, had not seen it inevitably coming, years before, and had not in plain words recorded what they saw. Such vapouring, combined with the extravagant plots of Monseigneur for the restoration of a state of things that had utterly exhausted itself, and worn out Heaven and earth as well as itself, was hard to be endured without some remonstrance by any sane man who knew the truth. And it was such vapouring all about his ears, like a troublesome confusion of blood in his own head, added to a latent uneasiness in his mind, which had already made Charles Darnay restless, and which still kept him so.

Among the talkers, was Stryver, of the King's Bench Bar, far on his way to state promotion, and therefore, loud on the theme: broaching to Monseigneur his devices for blowing the people up and exterminating them from the face of the earth, and doing without them: and for accomplishing many similar objects akin in their nature to the abolition of eagles by sprinkling salt on the tails of the race. Him, Darnay heard with a particular feeling of objection; and Darnay stood divided between going away that he might hear no more, and remaining to interpose his word, when the thing that was to be, went on to shape itself out.

The House approached Mr. Lorry, and laying a soiled and unopened letter before him, asked if he had yet discovered any traces of the person to whom it was addressed? The House laid the letter down so close to Darnay that he saw the direction—the more quickly because it was his own right name. The address, turned into English, ran:

"Very pressing. To Monsieur heretofore the Marquis St. Evrémonde, of France. Confided to the cares of Messrs. Tellson and Co., Bankers, London, England."

On the marriage morning, Doctor Manette had made it his one urgent and express request to Charles Darnay, that the secret of this name should be—unless he, the Doctor, dissolved the obligation—kept inviolate between them. Nobody else knew it to be his name; his own wife had no suspicion of the fact; Mr. Lorry could have none.

"No," said Mr. Lorry, in reply to the House; "I have referred it, I think, to everybody now here, and no one can tell me where this gentleman is to be found."

The hands of the clock verging upon the hour of closing the Bank, there was a general set of the current of talkers past Mr. Lorry's desk. He held the letter out inquiringly; and Monseigneur looked at it, in the person of this plotting and indignant refugee; and Monseigneur looked at it in the person of that plotting and indignant refugee; and This, That, and The Other, all had something disparaging to say, in French or in English, concerning the Marquis who was not to be found.

"Nephew, I believe—but in any case degenerate successor—of the polished Marquis who was murdered," said one. "Happy to say, I never knew him."

"A craven who abandoned his post," said another—this

Monseigneur had been got out of Paris, legs uppermost and half suffocated, in a load of hay—"some years ago."

"Infected with the new doctrines," said a third, eyeing the direction through his glass in passing; "set himself in opposition to the last Marquis, abandoned the estates when he inherited them, and left them to the ruffian herd. They will recompense him now, I hope, as he deserves."

"Hey?" cried the blatant Stryver. "Did he though? Is that the sort of fellow? Let us look at his infamous name. D—n the fellow!"

Darnay, unable to restrain himself any longer, touched Mr. Stryver on the shoulder, and said:

"I know the fellow."

"Do you, by Jupiter?" said Stryver. "I am sorry for it."

"Why?"

"Why, Mr. Darnay? D'ye hear what he did? Don't ask, why, in these times."

"But I do ask why?"

"Then I tell you again, Mr. Darnay, I am sorry for it. I am sorry to hear you putting any such extraordinary questions. Here is a fellow, who, infected by the most pestilent and blasphemous code of devilry that ever was known, abandoned his property to the vilest scum of the earth that ever did murder by wholesale, and you ask me why I am sorry that a man who instructs youth knows him? Well, but I'll answer you. I am sorry because I believe there is contamination in such a scoundrel. That's why."

Mindful of the secret, Darnay with great difficulty checked himself, and said: "You may not understand the gentleman."

"I understand how to put *you* in a corner, Mr. Darnay," said Bully Stryver, "and I'll do it. If this fellow is a gentleman, I *don't* understand him. You may tell him so, with my compliments. You may also tell him, from me, that after abandoning his worldly goods and position to this butcherly mob, I wonder he is not at the head of them. But, no, gentlemen," said Stryver, looking all round, and snapping his fingers, "I know something of human nature, and I tell you that you'll never find a fellow like this fellow, trusting himself to the mercies of such precious *protégés*. No, gentlemen; he'll always show 'em a clean pair of heels very early in the scuffle, and sneak away."

With those words, and a final snap of his fingers, Mr. Stryver shouldered himself into Fleet-street, amidst the general approbation of his hearers. Mr. Lorry and Charles Darnay were left alone at the desk, in the general departure from the Bank.

"Will you take charge of the letter?" said Mr. Lorry. "You know where to deliver it?"

"I do."

"Will you undertake to explain, that we suppose it to have been addressed here, on the chance of our knowing where to forward it, and that it has been here some time?"

"I will do so. Do you start for Paris from here?"

"From here, at eight."

"I will come back, to see you off."

Very ill at ease with himself, and with Stryver and most other men, Darnay made the best of his way into the quiet of the Temple, opened the letter, and read it. These were its contents:

"Prison of the Abbaye, Paris.
"June 21, 1792.

"MONSIEUR HERETOFORE THE MARQUIS.

"After having long been in danger of my life at the

hands of the village, I have been seized, with great violence and indignity, and brought a long journey on foot to Paris. On the road I have suffered a great deal. Nor is that all; my house has been destroyed—razed to the ground.

"The crime for which I am imprisoned, Monsieur heretofore the Marquis, and for which I shall be summoned before the tribunal, and shall lose my life (without your so generous help), is, they tell me, treason against the majesty of the people, in that I have acted against them for an emigrant. It is in vain I represent that I have acted for them, and not against, according to your commands. It is in vain I represent that, before the sequestration of emigrant property, I had remitted the imposts they had ceased to pay; that I had collected no rent; that I had had recourse to no process. The only response is, that I have acted for an emigrant, and where is that emigrant?

"Ah! most gracious Monsieur heretofore the Marquis, where is that emigrant? I cry in my sleep where is he? I demand of Heaven, will he not come to deliver me? No answer. Ah Monsieur heretofore the Marquis, I send my desolate cry across the sea, hoping it may perhaps reach your ears through the great bank of Tilson known at Paris!

"For the love of Heaven, of justice, of generosity, of the honour of your noble name, I supplicate you, Monsieur heretofore the Marquis, to succour and release me. My fault is, that I have been true to you. Oh Monsieur heretofore the Marquis, I pray you be you true to me!

"From this prison here of horror, whence I every hour tend nearer and nearer to destruction, I send you, Monsieur heretofore the Marquis, the assurance of my dolorous and unhappy service. "Your afflicted,
"GABELLE."

The latent uneasiness in Darnay's mind was roused to vigorous life by this letter. The peril of an old servant and a good one, whose only crime was fidelity to himself and his family, stared him so reproachfully in the face, that, as he walked to and fro in the Temple considering what to do, he almost hid his face from the passers-by.

He knew very well, that in his horror of the deed which had culminated the bad deeds and bad reputation of the old family house, in his resentful suspicions of his uncle, and in the aversion with which his conscience regarded the crumbling fabric that he was supposed to uphold, he had acted imperfectly. He knew very well, that in his love for Lucie, his renunciation of his social place, though by no means new to his own mind, had been hurried and incomplete. He knew that he ought to have systematically worked it out and supervised it, and that he had meant to do it, and that it had never been done.

The happiness of his own chosen English home, the necessity of being always actively employed, the swift changes and troubles of the time which had followed on one another so fast, that the events of this week annihilated the immature plans of last week, and the events of the week following made all new again; he knew very well, that to the force of these circumstances he had yielded:—not without disquiet, but still without continuous and accumulating resistance. That he had watched the times for a time of action, and that they had shifted and struggled until the time had gone by, and the nobility were trooping from France by every highway and byway, and their property was in course of confiscation and destruction, and their very names were blotting out, was as

well known to himself as it could be to any new authority in France that might impeach him for it.

But, he had oppressed no man, he had imprisoned no man; he was so far from having harshly exacted payment of his dues, that he had relinquished them of his own will, thrown himself on a world with no favour in it, won his own private place there, and earned his own bread. Monsieur Gabelle had held the impoverished and involved estate on written instructions, to spare the people, to give them what little there was to give—such fuel as the heavy creditors would let them have in the winter, and such produce as could be saved from the same grip in the summer—and no doubt he had put the fact in plea and proof, for his own safety, so that it could not but appear now."

This favoured the desperate resolution Charles Darnay had begun to make, that he would go to Paris.

Yes. Like the mariner in the old story, the winds and streams had driven him within the influence of the Loadstone Rock, and it was drawing him to itself, and he must go. Everything that arose before his mind drifted him on, faster and faster, more and more steadily, to the terrible attraction. His latent uneasiness had been, that bad aims were being worked out in his own unhappy land by bad instruments, and that he who could not fail to know that he was better than they, was not there, trying to do something to stay bloodshed, and assert the claims of mercy and humanity. With this uneasiness half stifled, and half reproaching him, he had been brought to the pointed comparison of himself with the brave old gentleman in whom duty was so strong; upon that comparison (injurious to himself) had instantly followed the sneers of Monseigneur, which had stung him bitterly, and those of Stryver, which above all were coarse and galling, for old reasons. Upon those, had followed Gabelle's letter: the appeal of an innocent prisoner, in danger of death, to his justice, honour, and good name.

His resolution was made. He must go to Paris.

Yes. The Loadstone Rock was drawing him, and he must sail on, until he struck. He knew of no rock; he saw hardly any danger. The intention with which he had done what he had done, even although he had left it incomplete, presented it before him in an aspect that would be gratefully acknowledged in France on his presenting himself to assert it. Then, that glorious vision of doing good, which is so often the sanguine mirage of so many good minds, arose before him, and he even saw himself in the illusion with some influence to guide this raging Revolution that was running so fearfully wild.

As he walked to and fro with his resolution made, he considered that neither Lucie nor her father must know of it until he was gone. Lucie should be spared the pain of separation; and her father, always reluctant to turn his thoughts towards the dangerous ground of old, should come to the knowledge of the step, as a step taken, and not in the balance of suspense and doubt. How much of the incompleteness of his situation was referable to her father, through the painful anxiety to avoid reviving old associations of France in his mind, he did not discuss with himself. But, that circumstance too, had had its influence in his course.

He walked to and fro, with thoughts very busy, until it was time to return to Tellson's and take leave of Mr. Lorry. As soon as he arrived in Paris he would present himself to this old friend, but he must say nothing of his intention now.

A carriage with post-horses was ready at the Bank door, and Jerry was booted and equipped.

"I have delivered that letter," said Charles Darnay to Mr. Lorry. "I would not consent to your being charged with any written answer, but perhaps you will take a verbal one?"

"That I will, and readily," said Mr. Lorry, "if it is not dangerous."

"Not at all. Though it is to a prisoner in the Abbaye."

"What is his name?" said Mr. Lorry, with his open pocket-book in his hand.

"Gabelle."

"Gabelle. And what is the message to the unfortunate Gabelle in prison?"

"Simply, 'that he has received the letter, and will come.'"

"Any time mentioned?"

"He will start upon his journey to-morrow night."

"Any person mentioned?"

"No."

He helped Mr. Lorry to wrap himself in a number of coats and cloaks, and went out with him from the warm atmosphere of the old Bank, into the misty air of Fleet-street. "My love to Lucie, and to little Lucie," said Mr. Lorry at parting, "and take precious care of them till I come back." Charles Darnay shook his head and doubtfully smiled, as the carriage rolled away.

That night—it was the fourteenth of August—he sat up late, and wrote two fervent letters; one was to Lucie, explaining the strong obligation he was under to go to Paris, and showing her, at length, the reasons that he had, for feeling confident that he could become involved in no personal danger there; the other was to the Doctor, confiding Lucie and their dear child to his care, and dwelling on the same topics with the strongest assurances. To both, he wrote that he would despatch letters in proof of his safety, immediately after his arrival.

It was a hard day, that day of being among them, with the first reservation of their joint lives on his mind. It was a hard matter to preserve the innocent deceit of which they were profoundly unsuspicious. But, an affectionate glance at his wife, so happy and busy, made him resolute not to tell her what impended (he had been half moved to do it, so strange it was to him to act in anything without her quiet aid), and the day passed quickly. Early in the evening he embraced her, and her scarcely less dear name-sake, pretending that he would return by-and-bye (an imaginary engagement took him out, and he had secreted a valise of clothes ready), and so he emerged into the heavy mist of the heavy streets, with a heavier heart.

The unseen force was drawing him fast to itself, now, and all the tides and winds were setting straight and strong towards it. He left his two letters with a trusty porter, to be delivered half an hour before midnight, and no sooner; took horse for Dover; and began his journey. "For the love of Heaven, of justice, of generosity, of the honour of your noble name!" was the poor prisoner's cry with which he strengthened his sinking heart, as he left all that was dear on earth behind him, and floated away for the Loadstone Rock.

BOOK THE THIRD.—THE TRACK OF A STORM.

CHAPTER I.

IN SECRET.

THE traveller fared slowly on his way, who fared towards Paris from England in the autumn of the year, one thousand seven hundred and ninety-two. More than enough of bad roads, bad equipages, and bad horses, he would have encountered to delay him, though the fallen and unfortunate King of France had been upon his throne in all his glory; but, the changed times were fraught with other obstacles than these. Every town-gate and village taxing-house had its band of citizen-patriots, with their national muskets in a most explosive state of readiness, who stopped all comers and goers, cross-questioned them, inspected their papers, looked for their names in lists of their own, turned them back, or sent them on, or stopped them and laid them in hold, as their capricious judgment or fancy deemed best for the dawning Republic One and Indivisible, of Liberty, Equality, Fraternity, or Death.

A very few French leagues of his journey were accomplished, when Charles Darnay began to perceive that for him along these country roads there was no hope of return until he should have been declared a good citizen at Paris. Whatever might befall now, he must on to his journey's end. Not a mean village closed upon him, not a common barrier dropped across the road behind him, but he knew it to be another iron door in the series that was barred between him and England. The universal watchfulness so encompassed him, that if he had been taken in a net, or were being forwarded to his destination in a cage, he could not have felt his freedom more completely gone.

This universal watchfulness not only stopped him on the highway twenty times in a stage, but retarded his progress twenty times in a day, by riding after him and taking him back, riding before him and stopping him by anticipation, riding with him and keeping him in charge. He had been days upon his journey in France alone, when he went to bed tired out, in a little town on the high road, still a long way from Paris.

Nothing but the production of the afflicted Gabelle's letter from his prison of the Abbaye would have got him on so far. His difficulty at the guard-house in this small place had been such, that he felt his journey to have come to a crisis. And he was, therefore, as little surprised as a man could be, to find himself awakened at the small inn to which he had been remitted until morning, in the middle of the night.

Awakened by a timid local functionary and three armed patriots in rough red caps and with pipes in their mouths, who sat down on the bed.

"Emigrant," said the functionary, "I am going to send you on to Paris, under an escort."

"Citizen, I desire nothing more than to get to Paris, though I could dispense with the escort."

"Silence!" growled a red-cap, striking at the coverlet with the butt-end of his musket. "Peace, aristocrat!"

"It is as the good patriot says," observed the timid functionary. "You are an aristocrat, and must have an escort—and must pay for it."

"I have no choice," said Charles Darnay.

"Choice! Listen to him!" cried the same scowling red-cap. "As if it was not a favour to be protected from the lamp-iron!"

"It is always as the good patriot says," observed the functionary. "Rise and dress yourself, emigrant."

Darnay complied, and was taken back to the guard-house, where other patriots in rough red caps were smoking, drinking, and sleeping, by a watch-fire. Here he paid a heavy price for his escort, and hence he started with it on the wet, wet roads at three o'clock in the morning.

The escort were two mounted patriots in red caps and tricoloured cockades, armed with national muskets and sabres, who rode one on either side of him.

The escorted governed his own horse, but a loose line was attached to his bridle, the end of which one of the patriots kept girded round his wrist. In this state they set forth with the sharp rain driving in their faces: clattering at a heavy dragoon trot over the uneven town pavement, and out upon the mire-deep roads. In this state they traversed without change, except of horses and pace, all the mire-deep leagues that lay between them and the capital.

They travelled in the night, halting an hour or two after daybreak, and lying by until the twilight fell. The escort were so wretchedly clothed, that they twisted straw round their bare legs, and thatched their ragged shoulders to keep the wet off. Apart from the personal discomfort of being so attended, and apart from such considerations of present danger as arose from one of the patriots being chronically drunk, and carrying his musket very recklessly, Charles Darnay did not allow the restraint that was laid upon him to awaken any serious fears in his breast; for, he reasoned with himself that it could have no reference to the merits of an individual case that was not yet stated, and of representations, confirmable by the prisoner in the Abbaye, that were not yet made.

But when they came to the town of Beauvais—which they did at eventide, when the streets were filled with people—he could not conceal from himself that the aspect of affairs was very alarming. An ominous crowd gathered to see him dismount at the posting-yard, and many voices called out loudly, "Down with the emigrant!"

He stopped in the act of swinging himself out of his saddle, and, resuming it as his safest place, said:

"Emigrant, my friends! Do you not see me here, in France, of my own will?"

"You are a cursed emigrant," cried a farrier, making at him in a furious manner through the press, hammer in hand; "and you are a cursed aristocrat!"

The postmaster interposed himself between this man and the rider's bridle (at which he was evidently making), and soothingly said, "Let him be; let him be! He will be judged at Paris."

"Judged!" repeated the farrier, swinging his hammer. "Ay! and condemned as a traitor." At this the crowd roared approval.

Checking the postmaster, who was for turning his horse's head to the yard (the drunken patriot sat composedly in his saddle looking on, with the line round his wrist), Darnay said, as soon as he could make his voice heard:

"Friends, you deceive yourselves, or you are deceived. I am not a traitor."

"He lies!" cried the smith. "He is a 'raitor since the decree. His life is forfeit to the people. His cursed life is not his own!"

At the instant when Darnay saw a rush in the eyes of the crowd, which another instant would have brought upon him, the postmaster turned his horse into the yard, the escort rode in close upon his horse's flanks, and the postmaster shut and barred the crazy double gates. The farrier struck a blow upon them with his hammer, and the crowd groaned; but, no more was done.

"What is this decree that the smith spoke of?" Darnay asked the postmaster, when he had thanked him, and stood beside him in the yard.

"Truly, a decree for selling the property of emigrants."

"When passed?"

"On the fourteenth."

"The day I left England!"

"Everybody says it is but one of several, and that there will be others—if there are not already—banishing all emigrants, and condemning all to death who return. That is what he meant when he said your life was not your own."

"But there are no such decrees yet?"

"What do I know!" said the postmaster, shrugging his shoulders; "there may be, or there will be. It is all the same. What would you have?"

They rested on some straw in a loft until the middle of the night, and then rode forward again when all the town was asleep. Among the many wild changes observable on familiar things which made this wild ride unreal, not the least was the seeming rarity of sleep. After long and lonely spurring over dreary roads, they would come to a cluster of poor cottages, not steeped in darkness, but all glittering with lights, and would find the people, in a ghostly manner in the dead of the night, circling hand in hand round a shrivelled tree of Liberty, or all drawn up together singing a Liberty song. Happily, however, there was sleep in Beauvais that night to help them out of it, and they passed on once more into solitude and loneliness: jingling through the untimely cold and wet, among impoverished fields that had yielded no fruits of the earth that year, diversified by the blackened remains of burnt houses, and by the sudden emergence from ambuscade, and sharp reining up across their way, of patriot patrols on the watch on all the roads.

Daylight at last found them before the wall of Paris. The barrier was closed and strongly guarded when they rode up to it.

"Where are the papers of this prisoner?" demanded a resolute-looking man in authority, who was summoned out by the guard.

Naturally struck by the disagreeable word, Charles Darnay requested the speaker to take notice that he was a free traveller and French citizen, in charge of an escort which the disturbed state of the country had imposed upon him, and which he had paid for.

"Where," repeated the same personage, without taking any heed of him whatever, "are the papers of this prisoner?"

The drunken patriot had them in his cap, and produced them. Casting his eyes over Gabelle's letter, the same personage in authority showed some disorder and surprise, and looked at Darnay with a close attention.

He left escort and escorted without saying a word, however, and went into the guard-room; meanwhile, they sat upon their horses outside the gate. Looking about him while in this state of suspense, Charles Darnay observed that the gate was held by a mixed guard of soldiers and patriots, the latter far outnumbering the former; and that while ingress into the city for peasants' carts bringing in supplies, and for similar traffic and traffickers, was easy enough, egress, even for the homeliest people, was very difficult. A numerous medley of men and women, not to mention beasts and vehicles of various sorts, was waiting to issue forth; but, the previous identification was so strict, that they filtered through the barrier very slowly. Some of these people knew their turn for examination to be so far off, that they lay down on the ground to sleep or smoke, while others talked together, or loitered about. The red cap and tricolour cockade were universal, both among men and women.

When he had sat in his saddle some half-hour, taking note of these things, Darnay found himself confronted by the same man in authority, who directed the guard to open the barrier. Then he delivered to the escort, drunk and sober, a receipt for the escorted, and requested him to dismount. He did so, and the two patriots, leading his tired horse, turned and rode away without entering the city.

He accompanied his conductor into a guard-room, smelling of common wine and tobacco, where certain soldiers and patriots, asleep and awake, drunk and sober, and in various neutral states between sleeping and waking, drunkenness and sobriety, were standing and lying about. The light in the guard-house, half derived from the waning oil-lamps of the night, and half from the overcast day, was in a correspondingly uncertain condition. Some registers were lying open on a desk, and an officer of a coarse, dark aspect, presided over these.

"Citizen Defarge," said he to Darnay's conductor, as he took a slip of paper to write on. "Is this the emigrant Evrémonde?"

"This is the man."

"Your age, Evrémonde?"

"Thirty-seven."

"Married, Evrémonde?"

"Yes."

"Where married?"

"In England."

"Without doubt. Where is your wife, Evrémonde?"

"In England."

"Without doubt. You are consigned, Evrémonde, to the prison of La Force."

"Just Heaven!" exclaimed Darnay. "Under what law, and for what offence?"

The officer looked up from his slip of paper for a moment.

"We have new laws, Evrémonde, and new offences, since you were here." He said it with a hard smile, and went on writing.

"I entreat you to observe that I have come here voluntarily, in response to that written appeal of a fellow-countryman which lies before you. I demand no more than the opportunity to do so without delay. Is not that my right?"

"Emigrants have no rights, Evrémonde," was the stolid reply. The officer wrote until he had finished, read over to himself what he had written, sanded it, and handed it to Defarge, with the words "In secret."

Defarge motioned with the paper to the prisoner that he must accompany him. The prisoner obeyed, and a guard of two armed patriots attended them.

"Is it you," said Defarge, in a low voice, as they went down the guard-house steps and turned into Paris, "who married the daughter of Doctor Manette, once a prisoner in the Bastille that is no more?"

"Yes," replied Darnay, looking at him with surprise.

"My name is Defarge, and I keep a wine-shop in the Quarter Saint Antoine. Possibly you have heard of me."

"My wife came to your house to reclaim her father? Yes!"

The word "wife" seemed to serve as a gloomy reminder to Defarge, to say with sudden impatience, "In the name of that sharp female newly-born, and called La Guillotine, why did you come to France?"

"You heard me say why, a minute ago. Do you not believe it is the truth?"

"A bad truth for you," said Defarge, speaking with knitted brows, and looking straight before him.

"Indeed I am lost here. All here is so unprecedented, so changed, so sudden and unfair, that I am absolutely lost. Will you render me a little help?"

"None." Defarge spoke, always looking straight before him.

"Will you answer me a single question?"

"Perhaps. According to its nature. You can say what it is."

"In this prison that I am going to so unjustly, shall I have some free communication with the world outside?"

"You will see."

"I am not to be buried there, prejudged, and without any means of presenting my case?"

"You will see. But, what then? Other people have been similarly buried in worse prisons, before now."

"But never by me, Citizen Defarge."

Defarge glanced darkly at him for answer, and walked on in a steady and set silence. The deeper he sank into this silence, the fainter hope there was—or so Darnay thought—of his softening in any slight degree. He, therefore, made haste to say:

"It is of the utmost importance to me (you know, Citizen, even better than I, of how much importance), that I should be able to communicate to Mr. Lorry of Tellson's Bank, an English gentleman who is now in Paris, the simple fact, without comment, that I have been thrown into the prison of La Force. Will you cause that to be done for me?"

"I will do," Defarge doggedly rejoined, "nothing for you. My duty is to my country and the People. I am the sworn servant of both, against you. I will do nothing for you."

Charles Darnay felt it hopeless to entreat him further, and his pride was touched besides. As they walked on in silence, he could not but see how used the people were to the spectacle of prisoners passing along the streets. The very children scarcely noticed him. A few passers turned their heads, and a few shook their fingers at him as an aristocrat; otherwise, that a man in good clothes should be going to prison, was no more remarkable than that a labourer in working clothes should be going to work. In one narrow, dark, and dirty street through which they passed, an excited orator, mounted on a stool, was address-

ing an excited audience on the crimes against the people, of the king and the royal family. The few words that he caught from this man's lips, first made it known to Charles Darnay that the king was in prison, and that the foreign ambassadors had one and all left Paris. On the road (except at Beauvais) he had heard absolutely nothing. The escort and the universal watchfulness had completely isolated him.

That he had fallen among far greater dangers than those which had developed themselves when he left England, he of course knew now. That perils had thickened about him fast, and might thicken faster and faster yet, he of course knew now. He could not but admit to himself that he might not have made this journey, if he could have foreseen the events of a few days. And yet his misgivings were not so dark as, imagined by the light of this later time, they would appear. Troubled as the future was, it was the unknown future, and in its obscurity there was ignorant hope. The horrible massacre, days and nights long, which, within a few rounds of the clock, was to set a great mark of blood upon the blessed garnering time of harvest, was as far out of his knowledge as if it had been a hundred thousand years away. The "sharp female newly-born, and called La Guillotine," was hardly known to him, or to the generality of people, by name. The frightful deeds that were to be soon done, were probably unimagined at that time in the brains of the doers. How could they have a place in the shadowy conceptions of a gentle mind?

Of unjust treatment in detention and hardship, and in cruel separation from his wife and child, he foreshadowed the likelihood, or the certainty; but, beyond this, he dreaded nothing distinctly. With this on his mind, which was enough to carry into a dreary prison courtyard, he arrived at the prison of La Force.

A man with a bloated face opened the strong wicket, to whom Defarge presented "The Emigrant Evrémonde."

"What the Devil! How many more of them!" exclaimed the man with the bloated face.

Defarge took his receipt without noticing the exclamation, and withdrew, with his two fellow-patriots.

"What the Devil, I say again!" exclaimed the gaoler, left with his wife. "How many more!"

The gaoler's wife, being provided with no answer to the question, merely replied, "One must have patience, my dear!" Three turnkeys who entered responsive to a bell she rang, echoed the sentiment, and one added, "For the love of Liberty;" which sounded in that place like an inappropriate conclusion.

The prison of La Force was a gloomy prison, dark and filthy, and with a horrible smell of foul sleep in it. Extraordinary how soon the noisome flavour of imprisoned sleep, becomes manifest in all such places that are ill cared for!

"In secret, too," grumbled the gaoler, looking at the written paper. "As if I was not already full to bursting!"

He stuck the paper on a file, in an ill-humour, and Charles Darnay awaited his further pleasure for half an hour: sometimes, pacing to and fro in the strong arched room: sometimes, resting on a stone seat: in either case detained to be imprinted on the memory of the chief and his subordinates.

"Come!" said the chief, at length taking up his keys, "come with me, emigrant."

Through the dismal prison twilight, his new charge accompanied him by corridor and staircase, many doors clanging and locking behind them, until they came into a large, low, vaulted chamber, crowded with prisoners of both sexes. The women were seated at a long table, reading and writing, knitting, sewing, and embroidering; the men were for the most part standing behind their chairs, or lingering up and down the room.

In the instinctive association of prisoners with shameful crime and disgrace, the new comer recoiled from this company. But the crowning unreality of his long unreal ride, was, their all at once rising to receive him, with every refinement of manner known to the time, and with all the engaging graces and courtesies of life.

So strangely clouded were these refinements by the prison manners and gloom, so spectral did they become in the inappropriate squalor and misery through which they were seen, that Charles Darnay seemed to stand in a company of the dead. Ghosts all! The ghost of beauty, the ghost of stateliness, the ghost of elegance, the ghost of pride, the ghost of frivolity, the ghost of wit, the ghost of youth, the ghost of age, all waiting their dismissal from the desolate shore, all turning on him eyes that were changed by the death they had died in coming there.

It struck him motionless. The gaoler standing at his side, and the other gaolers moving about, who would have been well enough as to appearance in the ordinary exercise of their functions, looked so extravagantly coarse contrasted with sorrowing mothers and blooming daughters who were there—with the apparitions of the coquette, the young beauty, and the mature woman delicately bred—that the inversion of all experience and likelihood which the scene of shadows presented, was heightened to its utmost. Surely, ghosts all. Surely, the long unreal ride some progress of disease that had brought him to these gloomy shades!

"In the name of the assembled companions in misfortune," said a gentleman of courtly appearance and address, coming forward, "I have the honour of giving you welcome to La Force, and of condoling with you on the calamity that has brought you among us. May it soon terminate happily! It would be an impertinence elsewhere, but it is not so here, to ask your name and condition?"

Charles Darnay roused himself, and gave the required information, in words as suitable as he could find.

"But I hope," said the gentleman, following the chief gaoler with his eyes, who moved across the room, "that you are not in secret?"

"I do not understand the meaning of the term, but I have heard them say so."

"Ah, what a pity! We so much regret it! But take courage; several members of our society have been in secret, at first, and it has lasted but a short time." Then he added, raising his voice, "I grieve to inform the society—in secret."

There was a murmur of commiseration as Charles Darnay crossed the room to a grated door where the gaoler awaited him, and many voices—among which, the soft and compassionate voices of women were conspicuous—gave him good wishes and encouragement. He turned at the grated door, to render the thanks of his heart; it closed under the gaoler's hand; and the apparitions vanished from his sight for ever.

The wicket opened on a stone staircase, leading upward. When they had ascended forty steps (the prisoner of half an hour already counted them), the gaoler opened a low black door, and they passed into a solitary cell. It struck cold and damp, but was not dark.

"Yours," said the gaoler.

"Why am I confined alone?"

"How do I know!"

"I can buy pen, ink, and paper?"

"Such are not my orders. You will be visited, and can ask then. At present, you may buy your food, and nothing more."

There were in the cell, a chair, a table, and a straw mattress. As the gaoler made a general inspection of these objects, and of the four walls, before going out, a wandering fancy wandered through the mind of the prisoner leaning against the wall opposite to him, that this gaoler was so unwholesomely bloated, both in face and person, as to look like a man who had been drowned and filled with water. When the gaoler was gone, he thought in the same wandering way, "Now am I left, as if I were dead." Stopping then, to look down at the mattress, he turned from it with a sick feeling, and thought, "And here in these crawling creatures is the first condition of the body after death."

"Five paces by four and a half, five paces by four and a half, five paces by four and a half." The prisoner walked to and fro in his cell, counting its measurement, and the roar of the city arose like muffled drums with a wild swell of voices added to them. "He made shoes, he made shoes, he made shoes." The prisoner counted the measurement again, and paced faster, to draw his mind with him from that latter repetition. "The ghosts that vanished when the wicket closed. There was one among them, the appearance of a lady dressed in black, who was leaning in the embrasure of a window, and she had a light shining upon her golden hair, and she looked like * * * * Let us ride on again, for God's sake, through the illuminated villages with the people all awake! * * * * He made shoes, he made shoes, he made shoes. * * * * Five paces by four and a half." With such scraps tossing and rolling upward from the depths of his mind, the prisoner walked faster and faster, obstinately counting and counting; and the roar of the city changed to this extent—that it still rolled in like muffled drums, but with the wail of voices that he knew, in the swell that rose above them.

CHAPTER II.

THE GRINDSTONE.

Tellson's Bank, established in the Saint Germain Quarter of Paris, was in a wing of a large house, approached by a courtyard and shut off from the street by a high wall and a strong gate. The house belonged to a great nobleman who had lived in it until he made a flight from the troubles, in his own cook's dress, and got across the borders. A mere beast of the chase flying from hunters, he was still in his metempsychosis no other than the same Monseigneur, the preparation of whose chocolate for whose lips had once occupied three strong men besides the cook in question.

Monseigneur gone, and the three strong men absolving themselves from the sin of having drawn his high wages, by being more than ready and willing to cut his throat on the altar of the dawning Republic one and indivisible of Liberty, Equality, Fraternity, or Death, Monseigneur's house had been first sequestrated, and then confiscated. For, all things moved so fast, and decree followed decree with that fierce precipitation, that now upon the third night of the autumn month of September, patriot emissaries of the law were in possession of Monseigneur's house, and had marked it with the tricolour, and were drinking brandy in its state apartments.

A place of business in London like Tellson's place of business in Paris, would soon have driven the House out of its mind and into the Gazette. For, what would staid British responsibility and respectability have said to orange-trees in boxes in a Bank courtyard, and even to a Cupid over the counter? Yet such things were. Tellson's had whitewashed the Cupid, but he was still to be seen on the ceiling, in the coolest linen, aiming (as he very often does) at money from morning to night. Bankruptcy must inevitably have come of this young Pagan, in Lombard-street, London, and also of a curtained alcove in the rear of the immortal boy, and also of a looking-glass let into the wall, and also of clerks not at all old, who danced in public on the slightest provocation. Yet, a French Tellson's could get on with these things exceedingly well, and, as long as the times held together, no man had taken fright at them, and drawn out his money.

What money would be drawn out of Tellson's henceforth, and what would lie there, lost and forgotten; what plate and jewels would tarnish in Tellson's hiding-places, while the depositors rusted in prisons, and when they should have violently perished; how many accounts with Tellson's never to be balanced in this world, must be carried over into the next; no man could have said, that night, any more than Mr. Jarvis Lorry could, though he thought heavily of these questions. He sat by a newly-lighted wood fire (the blighted and unfruitful year was prematurely cold), and on his honest and courageous face there was a deeper shade than the pendent lamp could throw, or any object in the room distortedly reflect—a shade of horror.

He occupied rooms in the Bank, in his fidelity to the House of which he had grown to be a part, like strong root-ivy. It chanced that they derived a kind of security from the patriotic occupation of the main building, but the true-hearted old gentleman never calculated about that. All such circumstances were indifferent to him, so that he did his duty. On the opposite side of the courtyard, under a colonnade, was extensive standing for carriages—where, indeed, some carriages of Monseigneur yet stood. Against two of the pillars were fastened two great flaring flambeaux, and in the light of these, standing out in the open air, was a large grindstone: a roughly mounted thing which appeared to have hurriedly been brought there from some neighbouring smithy, or other workshop. Rising and looking out of window at these harmless objects, Mr. Lorry shivered, and retired to his seat by the fire. He had opened, not only the glass window, but the lattice blind outside it, and he had closed both again, and he shivered through his frame.

From the streets beyond the high wall and a strong gate, there came the usual night hum of the city, with now and then an indescribable ring in it, weird and unearthly, as if some unwonted sounds of a terrible nature were going up to Heaven.

"Thank God," said Mr. Lorry, clasping his hands, "that no one near and dear to me is in this dreadful town to-night. May He have mercy on all who are in danger!"

Soon afterwards, the bell at the great gate sounded, and he thought, "They have come back!" and sat listening. But, there was no loud irruption into the courtyard, as he had expected, and he heard the gate clash again, and all was quiet.

The nervousness and dread that were upon him inspired that vague uneasiness respecting the Bank, which a great change would naturally awaken, with such feelings roused. It was well guarded, and he got up to go among the trusty people who were watching it, when his door suddenly opened, and two figures rushed in, at sight of which he fell back in amazement.

Lucie and her father! Lucie with her arms stretched out to him, and with that old look of earnestness so concentrated and intensified, that it seemed as though it had been stamped upon her face expressly to give force and power to it in this one passage of her life.

"What is this?" cried Mr. Lorry, breathless and confused. "What is the matter? Lucie! Manette! What has happened? What has brought you here? What is it?"

With the look fixed upon him, in her paleness and wildness, she panted out in his arms, imploringly, "O my dear friend! My husband!"

"Your husband, Lucie?"

"Charles."

"What of Charles?"

"Here."

"Here, in Paris?"

"Has been here some days—three or four—I don't know how many—I can't collect my thoughts. An errand of generosity brought him here unknown to us; he was stopped at the barrier, and sent to prison."

The old man uttered an irrepressible cry. Almost at the same moment, the bell of the great gate rang again, and a loud noise of feet and voices came pouring into the courtyard.

"What is that noise?" said the Doctor, turning towards the window.

"Don't look!" cried Mr. Lorry. "Don't look out! Manette, for your life, don't touch the blind!"

The Doctor turned, with his hand upon the fastening of the window, and said, with a cool, bold smile:

"My dear friend, I have a charmed life in this city. I have been a Bastille prisoner. There is no patriot in Paris—in Paris? In France—who, knowing me to have been a prisoner in the Bastille, would touch me, except to overwhelm me with embraces, or carry me in triumph. My old pain has given me a power that has brought us through the barrier, and gained us news of Charles there, and brought us here. I knew it would be so; I knew I could help Charles out of all danger; I told Lucie so.—What is that noise?" His hand was again upon the window.

"Don't look!" cried Mr. Lorry, absolutely desperate. "No, Lucie, my dear, nor you!" He got his arm round her, and held her. "Don't be so terrified, my love. I solemnly swear to you that I know of no harm having happened to Charles; that I had no suspicion even of his being in this fatal place. What prison is he in?"

"La Force!"

"La Force! Lucie, my child, if ever you were brave and serviceable in your life—and you were always both—you will compose yourself now, to do exactly as I bid you; for more depends upon it than you can think, or I can say. There is no help for you in any action on your part to-night; you cannot possibly stir out. I say this, because what I must bid you to do for Charles's sake, is the hardest thing to do of all. You must instantly be obedient, still, and quiet. You must let me put you in a room at the back here. You must leave your father and me alone for two minutes, and as there are Life and Death in the world you must not delay."

"I will be submissive to you. I see in your face that you know I can do nothing else than this. I know you are true."

The old man kissed her, and hurried her into his room, and turned the key; then, came hurrying back to the Doctor, and opened the window and partly opened the blind, and put his hand upon the Doctor's arm, and looked out with him into the courtyard.

Looked out upon a throng of men and women: not enough in number, or near enough, to fill the courtyard: not more than forty or fifty in all. The people in possession of the house had let them in at the gate, and they had rushed in to work at the grindstone; it had evidently been set up there for their purpose, as in a convenient and retired spot.

But, such awful workers, and such awful work!

The grindstone had a double handle, and, turning at it madly were two men, whose faces, as their long hair flapped back when the whirlings of the grindstone brought their faces up, were more horrible and cruel than the visages of the wildest savages in their most barbarous disguise. False eyebrows and false moustaches were stuck upon them, and their hideous countenances were all bloody and sweaty, and all awry with howling, and all staring and glaring with beastly excitement and want of sleep. As these ruffians turned and turned, their matted locks now flung forward over their eyes, now flung backward over their necks, some women held wine to their mouths that they might drink; and what with dropping blood, and what with dropping wine, and what with the stream of sparks struck out of the stone, all their wicked atmosphere seemed gore and fire. The eye could not detect one creature in the group free from the smear of blood. Shouldering one another to get next at the sharpening-stone, were men stripped to the waist, with the stain all over their limbs and bodies; men in all sorts of rags, with the stain upon those rags; men devilishly set off with spoils of women's lace and silk and ribbon, with the stain dyeing those trifles through and through. Hatchets, knives, bayonets, swords, all brought to be sharpened, were all red with it. Some of the hacked swords were tied to the wrists of those who carried them, with strips of linen and fragments of dress: ligatures various in kind, but all deep of the one colour. And as the frantic wielders of these weapons snatched them from the stream of sparks and tore away into the streets, the same red hue was red in their frenzied eyes;—eyes which any unbrutalised beholder would have given twenty years of life, to petrify with a well-directed gun.

All this was seen in a moment, as the vision of a drowning man, or of any human creature at any very great pass, could see a world if it were there. They drew back from the window, and the Docter looked for explanation in his friend's ashy face.

"They are," Mr. Lorry whispered the words, glancing fearfully round at the locked room, "murdering the prisoners. If you are sure of what you say; if you really have the power you think you have—as I believe you have—make yourself known to these devils, and get taken to La

Force. It may be too late, I don't know, but let it not be a minute later!"

Doctor Manette pressed his hand, hastened bareheaded out of the room, and was in the courtyard when Mr. Lorry regained the blind.

His streaming white hair, his remarkable face, and the impetuous confidence of his manner, as he put the weapons aside like water, carried him in an instant to the heart of the concourse at the stone. For a few moments there was a pause, and a hurry, and a murmur, and the unintelligible sound of his voice; and then Mr. Lorry saw him, surrounded by all, and in the midst of a line of twenty men long, all linked shoulder to shoulder, and hand to shoulder, hurried out with cries of—"Live the Bastille prisoner! Help for the Bastille prisoner's kindred in La Force! Room for the Bastille prisoner in front there! Save the prisoner Evrémonde at La Force!" and a thousand answering shouts.

He closed the lattice again with a fluttering heart, closed the window and the curtain, hastened to Lucie, and told her that her father was assisted by the people, and gone in search of her husband. He found her child and Miss Pross with her; but, it never occurred to him to be surprised by their appearance until a long time afterwards, when he sat watching them in such quiet as the night knew.

Lucie had, by that time, fallen into a stupor on the floor at his feet, clinging to his hand. Miss Pross had laid the child down on his own bed, and her head had gradually fallen on the pillow beside her pretty charge. O the long, long night, with the moans of the poor wife! And O the long, long night, with no return of her father and no tidings!

Twice more in the darkness the bell at the great gate sounded, and the irruption was repeated, and the grindstone whirled and spluttered. "What is it?" cried Lucie, affrighted. "Hush! The soldiers' swords are sharpened there," said Mr. Lorry. "The place is national property now, and used as a kind of armoury, my love."

Twice more in all; but, the last spell of work was feeble and fitful. Soon afterwards the day began to dawn, and he softly detached himself from the clasping hand, and cautiously looked out again. A man, so besmeared that he might have been a sorely wounded soldier creeping back to consciousness on a field of slain, was rising from the pavement by the side of the grindstone, and looking about him with a vacant air. Shortly, this worn-out murderer descried in the imperfect light one of the carriages of Monseigneur, and, staggering to that gorgeous vehicle, climbed in at the door, and shut himself up to take his rest on its dainty cushions.

The great grindstone, Earth, had turned when Mr. Lorry looked out again, and the sun was red on the courtyard. But, the lesser grindstone stood alone there in the calm morning air, with a red upon it that the sun had never given, and would never take away.

CHAPTER III.

THE SHADOW.

ONE of the first considerations which arose in the business mind of Mr. Lorry when business hours came round, was this:—that he had no right to imperil Tellson's by sheltering the wife of an emigrant prisoner under the Bank roof. His own possessions, safety, life, he would have hazarded for Lucie and her child, without a moment's demur; but the great trust he held was not his own, and as to that business charge he was a strict man of business.

At first, his mind reverted to Defarge, and he thought of finding out the wine-shop again and taking counsel with its master in reference to the safest dwelling-place in the distracted state of the city. But, the same consideration that suggested him, repudiated him; he lived in the most violent Quarter, and doubtless was influential there, and deep in its dangerous workings.

Noon coming, and the Doctor not returning, and every minute's delay tending to compromise Tellson's, Mr. Lorry advised with Lucie. She said that her father had spoken of hiring a lodging for a short term, in that Quarter, near the Banking-house. As there was no business objection to this, and as he foresaw that even if it were all well with Charles, and he were to be released, he could not hope to leave the city, Mr. Lorry went out in quest of such a lodging, and found a suitable one, high up in a removed by-street where the closed blinds in all the other windows of a high melancholy square of buildings marked deserted homes.

To this lodging he at once removed Lucie and her child, and Miss Pross: giving them what comfort he could, and much more than he had himself. He left Jerry with them, as a figure to fill a doorway that would bear considerable knocking on the head, and returned to his own occupations. A disturbed and doleful mind he brought to bear upon them, and slowly and heavily the day lagged on with him.

It wore itself out, and wore him out with it, until the Bank closed. He was again alone in his room of the previous night, considering what to do next, when he heard a foot upon the stair. In a few moments, a man stood in his presence, who, with a keenly observant look at him, addressed him by his name.

"Your servant," said Mr. Lorry. "Do you know me?"

He was a strongly made man with dark curling hair, from forty-five to fifty years of age. For answer he repeated, without any change of emphasis, the words:

"Do you know me?"

"I have seen you somewhere."

"Perhaps at my wine-shop?"

Much interested and agitated, Mr. Lorry said: "You come from Doctor Manette?"

"Yes. I come from Doctor Manette."

"And what says he? What does he send me?"

Defarge gave into his anxious hand, an open scrap of paper. It bore the words in the Doctor's writing:

"Charles is safe, but I cannot safely leave this place yet. I have obtained the favour that the bearer has a short note from Charles to his wife. Let the bearer see his wife."

It was dated from La Force, within an hour.

"Will you accompany me," said Mr. Lorry, joyfully relieved after reading this note aloud, "to where his wife resides?"

"Yes," returned Defarge.

Scarcely noticing as yet, in what a curiously reserved and mechanical way Defarge spoke, Mr. Lorry put on his hat and they went down into the courtyard. There, they found two women; one, knitting.

"Madame Defarge, surely!" said Mr. Lorry, who had left her in exactly the same attitude some seventeen years ago.

"It is she," observed her husband.

"Does Madame go with us?" inquired Mr. Lorry, seeing that she moved as they moved.

"Yes. That she may be able to recognise the faces and know the persons. It is for their safety."

Beginning to be struck by Defarge's manner, Mr. Lorry looked dubiously at him, and led the way. Both the women followed; the second woman being The Vengeance.

They passed through the intervening streets as quickly as they might, ascended the staircase of the new domicile, were admitted by Jerry, and found Lucie weeping, alone. She was thrown into a transport by the tidings Mr. Lorry gave her of her husband, and clasped the hand that delivered his note—little thinking what it had been doing near him in the night, and might, but for a chance, have done to him.

"DEAREST,—Take courage. I am well, and your father has influence around me. You cannot answer this. Kiss our child for me."

That was all the writing. It was so much, however, to her who received it, that she turned from Defarge to his wife, and kissed one of the hands that knitted. It was a passionate, loving, thankful, womanly action, but the hand made no response—dropped cold and heavy, and took to its knitting again.

There was something in its touch that gave Lucie a check. She stopped in the act of putting the note in her bosom, and, with her hands yet at her neck, looked terrified at Madame Defarge. Madame Defarge met the lifted eyebrows and forehead with a cold, impassive stare.

"My dear," said Mr. Lorry, striking in to explain; "there are frequent risings in the streets; and, although it is not likely they will ever trouble you, Madame Defarge wishes to see those whom she has the power to protect at such times, to the end that she may know them—that she may identify them. I believe," said Mr. Lorry, rather halting in his reassuring words, as the stony manner of all the three impressed itself upon him more and more, "I state the case, Citizen Defarge?"

Defarge looked gloomily at his wife, and gave no other answer than a gruff sound of acquiescence.

"You had better, Lucie," said Mr. Lorry, doing all he could to propitiate, by tone and manner, "have the dear child here, and our good Pross. Our good Pross, Defarge, is an English lady, and knows no French."

The lady in question, whose rooted conviction that she was more than a match for any foreigner, was not to be shaken by distress and danger, appeared with folded arms, and observed in English to The Vengeance, whom her eyes first encountered, "Well, I am sure, Boldface! I hope *you* are pretty well!" She also bestowed a British cough on Madame Defarge; but, neither of the two took much heed of her.

"Is that his child?" said Madame Defarge, stopping in her work for the first time, and pointing her knitting-needle at little Lucie as if it were the finger of Fate.

"Yes, madame," answered Mr. Lorry; "this is our poor prisoner's darling daughter, and only child."

The shadow attendant on Madame Defarge and her party seemed to fall so threatening and dark on the child, that her mother instinctively kneeled on the ground beside her, and held her to her breast. The shadow attendant on Madame Defarge and her party seemed then to fall, threatening and dark, on both the mother and the child.

"It is enough, my husband," said Madame Defarge. "I have seen them. We may go."

But, the suppressed manner had enough of menace in it —not visible and presented, but indistinct and withheld— to alarm Lucie into saying, as she laid her appealing hand on Madame Defarge's dress:

"You will be good to my poor husband. You will do him no harm. You will help me to see him if you can?"

"Your husband is not my business here," returned Madame Defarge, looking down at her with perfect composure. "It is the daughter of your father who is my business here."

"For my sake, then, be merciful to my husband. For my child's sake! She will put her hands together and pray you to be merciful. We are more afraid of you than of these others."

Madame Defarge received it as a compliment, and looked at her husband. Defarge, who had been uneasily biting his thumb-nail and looking at her, collected his face into a sterner expression.

"What is it that your husband says in that little letter?" asked Madame Defarge, with a lowering smile. "Influence; he says something touching influence?"

"That my father," said Lucie, hurriedly taking the paper from her breast, but with her alarmed eyes on her questioner and not on it, "has much influence around him."

"Surely it will release him!" said Madame Defarge. "Let it do so."

"As a wife and mother," cried Lucie, most earnestly, "I implore you to have pity on me and not to exercise any power that you possess, against my innocent husband, but to use it in his behalf. O sister-woman, think of me. As a wife and mother!"

Madame Defarge looked, coldly as ever, at the suppliant, and said, turning to her friend The Vengeance:

"The wives and mothers we have been used to see, since we were as little as this child, and much less, have not been greatly considered? We have known *their* husbands and fathers laid in prison and kept from them, often enough? All our lives, we have seen our sister-women suffer, in themselves and in their children, poverty, nakedness, hunger, thirst, sickness, misery, oppression and neglect of all kinds?"

"We have seen nothing else," returned The Vengeance.

"We have borne this a long time," said Madame Defarge, turning her eyes again upon Lucie. "Judge you! Is it likely that the trouble of one wife and mother would be much to us now?"

She resumed her knitting and went out. The Vengeance followed. Defarge went last, and closed the door.

"Courage, my dear Lucie," said Mr. Lorry, as he raised her. "Courage, courage! So far all goes well with us— much, much better than it has of late gone with many poor souls. Cheer up, and have a thankful heart."

"I am not thankless, I hope, but that dreadful woman seems to throw a shadow on me and on all my hopes."

"Tut, tut!" said Mr. Lorry; "what is this despondency in the brave little breast? A shadow indeed! No substance in it, Lucie."

But the shadow of the manner of these Defarges was

dark upon himself, for all that, and in his secret mind it troubled him greatly.

CHAPTER IV.

CALM IN STORM.

DOCTOR MANETTE did not return until the morning of the fourth day of his absence. So much of what had happened in that dreadful time as could be kept from the knowledge of Lucie was so well concealed from her, that not until long afterwards, when France and she were far apart, did she know that eleven hundred defenceless prisoners of both sexes and all ages had been killed by the populace; that four days and nights had been darkened by this deed of horror; and that the air around her had been tainted by the slain. She only knew that there had been an attack upon the prisons, that all political prisoners had been in danger, and that some had been dragged out by the crowd and murdered.

To Mr. Lorry, the Doctor communicated under an injunction of secrecy on which he had no need to dwell, that the crowd had taken him through a scene of carnage to the prison of La Force. That, in the prison he had found a self-appointed Tribunal sitting, before which the prisoners were brought singly, and by which they were rapidly ordered to be put forth to be massacred, or to be released, or (in a few cases) to be sent back to their cells. That, presented by his conductors to this Tribunal, he had announced himself by name and profession as having been for eighteen years a secret and unaccused prisoner in the Bastille; that, one of the body so sitting in judgment had risen and identified him, and that this man was Defarge.

That, hereupon he had ascertained, through the registers on the table, that his son-in-law was among the living prisoners, and had pleaded hard to the Tribunal—of whom some members were asleep and some awake, some dirty with murder and some clean, some sober and some not—for his life and liberty. That, in the first frantic greetings lavished on himself as a notable sufferer under the overthrown system, it had been accorded to him to have Charles Darnay brought before the lawless Court, and examined. That, he seemed on the point of being at once released, when the tide in his favour met with some unexplained check (not intelligible to the Doctor), which led to a few words of secret conference. That, the man sitting as President had then informed Doctor Manette that the prisoner must remain in custody, but should, for his sake, be held inviolate in safe custody. That, immediately, on a signal, the prisoner was removed to the interior of the prison again; but, that he, the Doctor, had then so strongly pleaded for permission to remain and assure himself that his son-in-law was, through no malice or mischance, delivered to the concourse whose murderous yells outside the gate had often drowned the proceedings, that he had obtained the permission, and had remained in that Hall of Blood until the danger was over.

The sights he had seen there, with brief snatches of food and sleep by intervals, shall remain untold. The mad joy over the prisoners who were saved, had astounded him scarcely less than the mad ferocity against those who were cut to pieces. One prisoner there was, he said, who had been discharged into the street free, but at whom a mistaken savage had thrust a pike as he passed out. Being besought to go to him and dress the wound, the Doctor had passed out at the same gate, and had found him in the arms of a company of Samaritans, who were seated on the bodies of their victims. With an inconsistency as monstrous as anything in this awful nightmare, they had helped the healer, and tended the wounded man with the gentlest solicitude—had made a litter for him and escorted him carefully from the spot—had then caught up their weapons and plunged anew into a butchery so dreadful, that the Doctor had covered his eyes with his hands, and swooned away in the midst of it.

As Mr. Lorry received these confidences, and as he watched the face of his friend now sixty-two years of age, a misgiving arose within him that such dread experiences would revive the old danger. But, he had never seen his friend in his present aspect: he had never at all known him in his present character. For the first time the Doctor felt, now, that his suffering was strength and power. For the first time he felt that in that sharp fire, he had slowly forged the iron which could break the prison door of his daughter's husband, and deliver him. " It all tended to a good end, my friend; it was not mere waste and ruin. As my beloved child was helpful in restoring me to myself, I will be helpful now in restoring the dearest part of herself to her; by the aid of Heaven I will do it!" Thus, Doctor Manette. And when Jarvis Lorry saw the kindled eyes, the resolute face, the calm strong look and bearing of the man whose life always seemed to him to have been stopped, like a clock, for so many years, and then going again with an energy which had lain dormant during the cessation of its usefulness, he believed.

Greater things than the Doctor had at that time to contend with, would have yielded before his persevering purpose. While he kept himself in his place, as a physician, whose business was with all degrees of mankind, bond and free, rich and poor, bad and good, he used his personal influence so wisely, that he was soon the inspecting physician of three prisons, and among them of La Force. He could now assure Lucie that her husband was no longer confined alone, but was mixed with the general body of prisoners; he saw her husband weekly, and brought sweet messages to her, straight from his lips; sometimes her husband himself sent a letter to her, though never by the Doctor's hand), but she was not permitted to write to him: for, among the many wild suspicions of plots in the prisons, the wildest of all pointed at emigrants who were known to have made friends or permanent connections abroad.

This new life of the Doctor's was an anxious life, no doubt; still, the sagacious Mr. Lorry saw that there was a new sustaining pride in it. Nothing unbecoming tinged the pride; it was a natural and worthy one; but he observed it as a curiosity. The Doctor knew, that up to that time, his imprisonment had been associated in the minds of his daughter and his friend, with his personal affliction, deprivation, and weakness. Now that this was changed, and he knew himself to be invested through that old trial with forces to which they both looked for Charles's ultimate safety and deliverance, he became so far exalted by the change, that he took the lead and direction, and required them as the weak, to trust to him as the strong. The preceding relative positions of himself and Lucie were reversed, yet only as the liveliest gratitude and affection

could reverse them, for he could have had no pride but in rendering some service to her who had rendered so much to him. " All curious to see," thought Mr. Lorry, in his amiably shrewd way, " but all natural and right; so, take the lead, my dear friend, and keep it; it couldn't be in better hands."

But, though the Doctor tried hard, and never ceased trying, to get Charles Darnay set at liberty, or at least to get him brought to trial, the public current of the time set too strong and fast for him. The new era began; the king was tried, doomed, and beheaded; the Republic of Liberty, Equality, Fraternity, or Death, declared for victory or death against the world in arms; the black flag waved night and day from the great towers of Notre Dame; three hundred thousand men, summoned to rise against the tyrants of the earth, rose from all the varying soils of France, as if the dragon's teeth had been sown broadcast, and had yielded fruit equally on hill and plain, on rock, in gravel, and alluvial mud, under the bright sky of the South and under the clouds of the North, in fell and forest, in the vineyards and the olive-grounds and among the cropped grass and the stubble of the corn, along the fruitful banks of the broad rivers, and in the sand of the sea-shore. What private solicitude could rear itself against the deluge of the Year One of Liberty—the deluge rising from below, not falling from above, and with the windows of Heaven shut, not opened!

There was no pause, no pity, no peace, no interval of relenting rest, no measurement of time. Though days and nights circled as regularly as when time was young, and the evening and morning were the first day, other count of time there was none. Hold of it was lost in the raging fever of a nation, as it is in the fever of one patient. Now, breaking the unnatural silence of a whole city, the executioner showed the people the head of the king—and now, it seemed almost in the same breath, the head of his fair wife which had had eight weary months of imprisoned widowhood and misery, to turn it grey.

And yet, observing the strange law of contradiction which obtains in all such cases, the time was long, while it flamed by so fast. A revolutionary tribunal in the capital, and forty or fifty thousand revolutionary committees all over the land; a law of the Suspected, which struck away all security for liberty or life, and delivered over any good and innocent person to any bad and guilty one; prisons gorged with people who had committed no offence, and could obtain no hearing; these things became the established order and nature of appointed things, and seemed to be ancient usage before they were many weeks old. Above all, one hideous figure grew as familiar as if it had been before the general gaze from the foundations of the world—the figure of the sharp female called La Guillotine.

It was the popular theme for jests; it was the best cure for headache, it infallibly prevented the hair from turning grey, it imparted a peculiar delicacy to the complexion, it was the National Razor which shaved close: who kissed La Guillotine, looked through the little window and sneezed into the sack. It was the sign of the regeneration of the human race. It superseded the Cross. Models of it were worn on breasts from which the Cross was discarded, and it was bowed down to and believed in where the Cross was denied

It sheared off heads so many, that it, and the ground it most polluted, were a rotten red. It was taken to pieces,

THE FIGURE OF THE SHARP FEMALE CALLED LA GUILLOTINE.

like a toy-puzzle for a young Devil, and was put together again when the occasion wanted it. It hushed the eloquent, struck down the powerful, abolished the beautiful and good. Twenty-two friends of high public mark, twenty-one living and one dead, it had lopped the heads off, in one morning, in as many minutes. The name of the strong man of Old Scripture had descended to the chief functionary who worked it; but, so armed, he was stronger than his namesake, and blinder, and tore away the gates of God's own Temple every day.

Among these terrors, and the brood belonging to them, the Doctor walked with a steady head: confident in his power, cautiously persistent in his end, never doubting that he would save Lucie's husband at last. Yet the current of the time swept by, so strong and deep, and carried the time away so fiercely, that Charles had lain in prison one year and three months when the Doctor was thus steady and confident. So much more wicked and distracted had the Revolution grown in that December month, that the rivers of the South were encumbered with the bodies of the violently drowned by night, and prisoners were shot in lines and squares under the southern wintry sun. Still, the Doctor walked among the terrors with a steady head. No man better known than he, in Paris at that day; no man in a stranger situation. Silent, humane, indispensable in hospital and prison, using his art equally among assassins and victims, he was a man apart. In the exercise of his skill, the appearance and the story of the Bastille Captive removed him from all other men. He was not suspected or brought in question, any more than if he had indeed been recalled to life some eighteen years before, or were a Spirit moving among mortals.

CHAPTER V.

THE WOOD-SAWYER.

ONE year and three months. During all that time Lucie was never sure, from hour to hour, but the Guillotine would strike off her husband's head next day. Every day, through the stony streets, the tumbrils now jolted heavily, filled with Condemned. Lovely girls; bright women, brown-haired, black-haired, and grey; youths; stalwart men and old; gentle born and peasant born; all red wine for La Guillotine, all daily brought into light from the dark cellars of the loathsome prisons, and carried to her through the streets to slake her devouring thirst. Liberty, equality, fraternity, or death;—the last, much the easiest to bestow, O Guillotine!

If the suddenness of her calamity, and the whirling wheels of the time, had stunned the Doctor's daughter into awaiting the result in idle despair, it would but have been with her as it was with many. But, from the hour when she had taken the white head to her fresh young bosom in the garret of Saint Antoine, she had been true to her duties. She was truest to them in the season of trial, as all the quietly loyal and good will always be.

As soon as they were established in their new residence, and her father had entered on the routine of his avocations, she arranged the little household as exactly as if her husband had been there. Everything had its appointed place and its appointed time. Little Lucie she taught, as regu-

larly, as if they had all been united in their English home. The slight devices with which she cheated herself into the show of a belief that they would soon be reunited—the little preparations for his speedy return, the setting aside of his chair and his books—these, and the solemn prayer at night for one dear prisoner especially, among the many unhappy souls in prison and the shadow of death—were almost the only outspoken reliefs of her heavy mind.

She did not greatly alter in appearance. The plain dark dresses, akin to mourning dresses, which she and her child wore, were as neat and as well attended to as the brighter clothes of happy days. She lost her colour, and the old and intent expression was a constant, not an occasional, thing; otherwise, she remained very pretty and comely. Sometimes, at night on kissing her father, she would burst into the grief she had repressed all day, and would say that her sole reliance, under Heaven, was on him. He always resolutely answered: "Nothing can happen to him without my knowledge, and I know that I can save him, Lucie."

They had not made the round of their changed life many weeks, when her father said to her, on coming home one evening:

"My dear, there is an upper window in the prison, to which Charles can sometimes gain access at three in the afternoon. When he can get to it—which depends on many uncertainties and incidents—he might see you in the street, he thinks, if you stood in a certain place that I can show you. But you will not be able to see him, my poor child, and even if you could, it would be unsafe for you to make a sign of recognition."

"O show me the place, my father, and I will go there every day."

From that time, in all weathers, she waited there two hours. As the clock struck two, she was there, and at four she turned resignedly away. When it was not too wet or inclement for her child to be with her, they went together; at other times she was alone; but, she never missed a single day.

It was the dark and dirty corner of a small winding street. The hovel of a cutter of wood into lengths for burning, was the only house at that end; all else was wall. On the third day of her being there, he noticed her.

"Good day, citizeness."

"Good day, citizen."

This mode of address was now prescribed by decree. It had been established voluntarily some time ago, among the more thorough patriots; but, was now law for everybody.

"Walking here again, citizeness?"

"You see me, citizen!"

The wood-sawyer, who was a little man with a redundancy of gesture (he had once been a mender of roads), cast a glance at the prison, pointed at the prison, and putting his ten fingers before his face to represent bars, peeped through them jocosely.

"But it's not my business," said he. And went on sawing his wood.

Next day he was looking out for her, and accosted her the moment she appeared.

"What? Walking here again, citizeness?"

"Yes, citizen."

"Ah! A child too! Your mother, is it not, my little citizeness?"

"Do I say yes, mamma?" whispered little Lucie, drawing close to her.

"Yes, dearest."

"Yes, citizen."

"Ah! But it's not my business. My work is my business. See my saw! I call it my Little Guillotine. La, la, la; La, la, la! And off his head comes!"

The billet fell as he spoke, and he threw it into a basket. "I call myself the Samson of the firewood guillotine. See here again! Loo, loo, loo; Loo, loo, loo! And off *her* head comes! Now, a child. Tickle, tickle; Pickle, pickle! And off *its* head comes. All the family!"

Lucie shuddered as he threw two more billets into his basket, but it was impossible to be there while the wood-sawyer was at work, and not be in his sight. Thenceforth, to secure his good will, she always spoke to him first, and often gave him drink-money, which he readily received.

He was an inquisitive fellow, and sometimes when she had quite forgotten him in gazing at the prison roof and grates, and in lifting her heart up to her husband, she would come to herself to find him looking at her, with his knee on his bench and his saw stopped in its work. "But it's not my business!" he would generally say at those times, and would briskly fall to his sawing again.

In all weathers, in the snow and frost of winter, in the bitter winds of spring, in the hot sunshine of summer, in the rains of autumn, and again in the snow and frost of winter, Lucie passed two hours of every day at this place; and every day on leaving it, she kissed the prison w.ll. Her husband saw her (so she learned from her father) it might be once in five or six times: it might be twice or thrice running: it might be, not for a week or a fortnight together. It was enough that he could and did see her when the chances served, and on that possibility she would have waited out the day, seven days a week.

These occupations brought her round to the December month, wherein her father walked among the terrors with a steady head. On a lightly-snowing afternoon she arrived at the usual corner. It was a day of some wild rejoicing, and a festival. She had seen the houses, as she came along, decorated with little pikes, and with little red caps stuck upon them; also, with tricoloured ribbons; also, with the standard inscription (tricoloured letters were the favourite), Republic One and Indivisible. Liberty, Equality, Fraternity, or Death!

The miserable shop of the wood-sawyer was so small, that its whole surface furnished very indifferent space for this legend. He had got somebody to scrawl it up for him, however, who had squeezed Death in with most inappropriate difficulty. On his house-top, he displayed pike and cap, as a good citizen must, and in a window he had stationed his saw inscribed as his "Little Sainte Guillotine" —for the great sharp female was by that time popularly canonised. His shop was shut and he was not there, which was a relief to Lucie, and left her quite alone.

But, he was not far off, for presently she heard a troubled movement and a shouting coming along, which filled her with fear. A moment afterwards, and a throng of people came pouring round the corner by the prison wall, in the midst of whom was the wood-sawyer hand in hand with The Vengeance. There could not be fewer than five hundred people, and they were dancing like five thousand demons. There was no other music than their own singing. They danced to the popular Revolution song, keeping a ferocious time that was like a gnashing of teeth in unison.

Men and women danced together, women danced together, men danced together, as hazard had brought them together. At first, they were a mere storm of coarse red caps and coarse woollen rags; but, as they filled the place, and stopped to dance about Lucie, some ghastly apparition of a dance-figure gone raving mad arose among them. They advanced, retreated, struck at one another's hands, clutched at one another's heads, spun round alone, caught one another and spun round in pairs, until many of them dropped. While those were down, the rest linked hand in hand, and all spun round together: then the ring broke, and in separate rings of two and four they turned and turned until they all stopped at once, began again, struck, clutched, and tore, and then reversed the spin, and all spun round another way. Suddenly they stopped again, paused, struck out the time afresh, formed into lines the width of the public way, and with their heads low down and their hands high up, swooped screaming off. No fight could have been half so terrible as this dance. It was so emphatically a fallen sport—a something, once innocent, delivered over to all devilry—a healthy pastime changed into a means of angering the blood, bewildering the senses, and steeling the heart. Such grace as was visible in it, made it the uglier, showing how warped and perverted all things good by nature were become. The maidenly bosom bared to this, the pretty almost-child's head thus distracted, the delicate foot mincing in this slough of blood and dirt, were types of the disjointed time.

This was the Carmagnole. As it passed, leaving Lucie frightened and bewildered in the doorway of the wood-sawyer's house, the feathery snow fell as quietly and lay as white and soft, as if it had never been.

"O my father!" for he stood before her when she lifted up the eyes she had momentarily darkened with her hand; "such a cruel, bad sight."

"I know, my dear, I know. I have seen it many times. Don't be frightened! Not one of them would harm you."

"I am not frightened for myself, my father. But when I think of my husband, and the mercies of these people ——"

"We will set him above their mercies very soon. I left him climbing to the window, and I came to tell you. There is no one here to see. You may kiss your hand towards that highest shelving roof."

"I do so, father, and I send my Soul with it!"

"You cannot see him, my poor dear?"

"No, father," said Lucie, yearning and weeping as she kissed her hand, "no."

A footstep in the snow. Madame Defarge. "I salute you, citizeness," from the Doctor. "I salute you, citizen." This in passing. Nothing more. Madame Defarge gone, like a shadow over the white road.

"Give me your arm, my love. Pass from here with an air of cheerfulness and courage, for his sake. That was well done;" they had left the spot; "it shall not be in vain. Charles is summoned for to-morrow."

"For to-morrow!"

"There is no time to lose. I am well prepared, but there are precautions to be taken, that could not be taken until he was actually summoned before the Tribunal. He has not received the notice yet, but I know that he will presently be summoned for to-morrow, and removed to the Conciergerie; I have timely information. You are not afraid?"

She could scarcely answer, "I trust in you."

"Do so, implicitly. Your suspense is nearly ended, my

darling; he shall be restored to you within a few hours; I have encompassed him with every protection. I must see Lorry."

He stopped. There was a heavy lumbering of wheels within hearing. They both knew too well what it meant. One. Two. Three. Three tumbrils faring away with their dread loads over the hushing snow.

"I must see Lorry," the Doctor repeated, turning her another way.

The staunch old gentleman was still in his trust; had never left it. He and his books were in frequent requisition as to property confiscated and made national. What he could save for the owners, he saved. No better man living to hold fast by what Tellson's had in keeping, and to hold his peace.

A murky red and yellow sky, and a rising mist from the Seine, denoted the approach of darkness. It was almost dark when they arrived at the Bank. The stately residence of Monseigneur was altogether blighted and deserted. Above a heap of dust and ashes in the court, ran the letters: National Property. Republic One and Indivisible. Liberty, Equality, Fraternity, or Death!

Who could that be with Mr. Lorry—the owner of the riding-coat upon the chair—who must not be seen? From whom newly arrived, did he come out, agitated and surprised, to take his favourite in his arms? To whom did he appear to repeat her faltering words, when, raising his voice and turning his head towards the door of the room from which he had issued, he said: "Removed to the Conciergerie, and summoned for to-morrow?"

CHAPTER VI.

TRIUMPH.

The dread Tribunal of five Judges, Public Prosecutor, and determined Jury, sat every day. Their lists went forth every evening, and were read out by the gaolers of the various prisons to their prisoners. The standard gaoler-joke was, "Come out and listen to the Evening Paper, you inside there!"

"Charles Evrémonde, called Darnay!"

So at last began the Evening Paper at La Force.

When a name was called, its owner stepped apart into a spot reserved for those who were announced as being thus fatally recorded. Charles Evrémonde, called Darnay, had reason to know the usage; he had seen hundreds pass away so.

His bloated gaoler, who wore spectacles to read with, glanced over them to assure himself that he had taken his place, and went through the list, making a similar short pause at each name. There were twenty-three names, but only twenty were responded to; for one of the prisoners so summoned had died in gaol and been forgotten, and two had already been guillotined and forgotten. The list was read, in the vaulted chamber where Darnay had seen the associated prisoners on the night of his arrival. Every one of those had perished in the massacre; every human creature he had since cared for and parted with, had died on the scaffold.

There were hurried words of farewell and kindness, but the parting was soon over. It was the incident of every day, and the society of La Force were engaged in the preparation of some games of forfeits and a little concert, for

that evening. They crowded to the gates and shed tears there; but, twenty places in the projected entertainments had to be refilled, and the time was, at best, short to the lock-up hour, when the common rooms and corridors would be delivered over to the great dogs who kept watch there through the night. The prisoners were far from insensible or unfeeling; their ways arose out of the condition of the time. Similarly, though with a subtle difference, a species of fervour or intoxication, known, without doubt, to have led some persons to brave the guillotine unnecessarily, and to die by it, was not mere boastfulness, but a wild infection of the wildly shaken public mind. In seasons of pestilence, some of us will have a secret attraction to the disease—a terrible passing inclination to die of it. And all of us have like wonders hidden in our breasts, only needing circumstances to evoke them.

The passage to the Conciergerie was short and dark; the night in its vermin-haunted cells was long and cold. Next day, fifteen prisoners were put to the bar before Charles Darnay's name was called. All the fifteen were condemned, and the trials of the whole occupied an hour and a half.

"Charles Evrémonde, called Darnay," was at length arraigned.

His judges sat upon the Bench in feathered hats; but the rough red cap and tricoloured cockade was the head-dress otherwise prevailing. Looking at the Jury and the turbulent audience, he might have thought that the usual order of things was reversed, and that the felons were trying the honest men. The lowest, cruellest, and worst populace of a city, never without its quantity of low, cruel, and bad, were the directing spirits of the scene: noisily commenting, applauding, disapproving, anticipating, and precipitating the result, without a check. Of the men, the greater part were armed in various ways; of the women, some wore knives, some daggers, some ate and drank as they looked on, many knitted. Among these last, was one, with a spare piece of knitting under her arm as she worked. She was in a front row, by the side of a man whom he had never seen since his arrival at the Barrier, but whom he directly remembered as Defarge. He noticed that she once or twice whispered in his ear, and that she seemed to be his wife; but, what he most noticed in the two figures was, that although they were posted as close to himself as they could be, they never looked towards him. They seemed to be waiting for something with a dogged determination, and they looked at the Jury, but at nothing else. Under the President sat Doctor Manette, in his usual quiet dress. As well as the prisoner could see, he and Mr. Lorry were the only men there, unconnected with the Tribunal, who wore their usual clothes, and had not assumed the coarse garb of the Carmagnole.

Charles Evrémonde, called Darnay, was accused by the public prosecutor as an emigrant, whose life was forfeit to the Republic, under the decree which banished all emigrants on pain of Death. It was nothing that the decree bore date since his return to France. There he was, and there was the decree; he had been taken in France, and his head was demanded.

"Take off his head!" cried the audience. "An enemy to the Republic!"

The President rang his bell to silence those cries, and asked the prisoner whether it was not true that he had lived many years in England?

Undoubtedly it was.

Was he not an emigrant then? What did he call himself?

Not an emigrant, he hoped, within the sense and spirit of the law.

Why not? the President desired to know.

Because he had voluntarily relinquished a title that was distasteful to him, and a station that was distasteful to him, and had left his country—he submitted before the word emigrant in the present acceptation by the Tribunal was in use—to live by his own industry in England, rather than on the industry of the overladen people of France.

What proof had he of this?

He handed in the names of two witnesses; Théophile Gabelle, and Alexandre Manette.

But he had married in England? the President reminded him.

True, but not an English woman.

A citizeness of France?

Yes. By birth.

Her name and family?

"Lucie Manette, only daughter of Doctor Manette, the good physician who sits there."

This answer had a happy effect upon the audience. Cries in exaltation of the well-known good physician rent the hall. So capriciously were the people moved, that tears immediately rolled down several ferocious countenances which had been glaring at the prisoner a moment before, as if with impatience to pluck him out into the streets and kill him.

On these few steps of his dangerous way, Charles Darnay had set his foot according to Doctor Manette's reiterated instructions. The same cautious counsel directed every step that lay before him, and had prepared every inch of his road.

The President asked, why had he returned to France when he did, and not sooner?

He had not returned sooner, he replied, simply because he had no means of living in France, save those he had resigned; whereas, in England, he lived by giving instruction in the French language and literature. He had returned when he did, on the pressing and written entreaty of a French citizen, who represented that his life was endangered by his absence. He had come back, to save a citizen's life, and to bear his testimony, at whatever personal hazard, to the truth. Was that criminal in the eyes of the Republic?

The populace cried enthusiastically, "No!" and the President rang his bell to quiet them. Which it did not, for they continued to cry "No!" until they left off, of their own will.

The President required the name of that citizen? The accused explained that the citizen was his first witness. He also referred with confidence to the citizen's letter, which had been taken from him at the Barrier, but which he did not doubt would be found among the papers then before the President.

The Doctor had taken care that it should be there—had assured him that it would be there—and at this stage of the proceedings it was produced and read. Citizen Gabelle was called to confirm it, and did so. Citizen Gabelle hinted, with infinite delicacy and politeness, that in the pressure of business imposed on the Tribunal by the multitude of enemies of the Republic with which it had to deal, he had been slightly overlooked in his prison of the Abbaye—in fact, had rather passed out of the Tribunal's patriotic remembrance—until three days ago; when he had been summoned before it, and had been set at liberty on the Jury's declaring themselves satisfied that the accusation against him was answered, as to himself, by the surrender of the citizen Evrémonde, called Darnay.

Doctor Manette was next questioned. His high personal popularity, and the clearness of his answers, made a great impression; but, as he proceeded, as he showed that the Accused was his first friend on his release from his long imprisonment; that, the accused had remained in England, always faithful and devoted to his daughter and himself in their exile; that, so far from being in favour with the Aristocrat government there, he had actually been tried for his life by it, as the foe of England and friend of the United States—as he brought these circumstances into view, with the greatest discretion and with the straightforward force of truth and earnestness, the Jury and the populace became one. At last, when he appealed by name to Monsieur Lorry, an English gentleman then and there present, who, like himself, had been a witness on that English trial and could corroborate his account of it, the Jury declared that they had heard enough, and that they were ready with their votes if the President were content to receive them.

At every vote (the Jurymen voted aloud and individually), the populace set up a shout of applause. All the voices were in the prisoner's favour, and the President declared him free.

Then, began one of those extraordinary scenes with which the populace sometimes gratified their fickleness, or their better impulses towards generosity and mercy, or which they regarded as some set-off against their swollen account of cruel rage. No man can decide now to which of these motives such extraordinary scenes were referable; it is probable, to a blending of all the three, with the second predominating. No sooner was the acquittal pronounced, than tears were shed as freely as blood at another time, and such fraternal embraces were bestowed upon the prisoner by as many of both sexes as could rush at him, that after his long and unwholesome confinement he was in danger of fainting from exhaustion; none the less because he knew very well, that the very same people, carried by another current, would have rushed at him with the very same intensity, to rend him to pieces and strew him over the streets.

His removal, to make way for other accused persons who were to be tried, rescued him from these caresses for the moment. Five were to be tried together, next, as enemies of the Republic, forasmuch as they had not assisted it by word or deed. So quick was the Tribunal to compensate itself and the nation for a chance lost, that these five came down to him before he left the place, condemned to die within twenty-four hours. The first of them told him so, with the customary prison sign of Death—a raised finger—and they all added in words, "Long live the Republic!"

The five had had, it is true, no audience to lengthen their proceedings, for when he and Doctor Manette emerged from the gate, there was a great crowd about it, in which there seemed to be every face he had seen in Court—except two, for which he looked in vain. On his coming out, the concourse made at him anew, weeping, embracing, and shouting, all by turns and all together, until the very tide of the river on the bank of which the mad scene was acted, seemed to run mad, like the people on the shore.

They put him into a great chair they had among them,

and which they had taken either out of the Court itself, or one of its rooms or passages. Over the chair they had thrown a red flag, and to the back of it they had bound a pike with a red cap on its top. In this car of triumph, not even the Doctor's entreaties could prevent his being carried to his home on men's shoulders, with a confused sea of red caps heaving about him, and casting up to sight from the stormy deep such wrecks of faces, that he more than once misdoubted his mind being in confusion, and that he was in the tumbril on his way to the Guillotine.

In wild dreamlike procession, embracing whom they met and pointing him out, they carried him on. Reddening the snowy streets with the prevailing Republican colour, in winding and tramping through them, as they had reddened them below the snow with a deeper dye, they carried him thus into the courtyard of the building where he lived. Her father had gone on before, to prepare her, and when her husband stood upon his feet, she dropped insensible in his arms.

As he held her to his heart and turned her beautiful head between his face and the brawling crowd, so that his tears and her lips might come together unseen, a few of the people fell to dancing. Instantly, all the rest fell to dancing, and the courtyard overflowed with the Carmagnole. Then, they elevated into the vacant chair a young woman from the crowd to be carried as the Goddess of Liberty, and then swelling and overflowing out into the adjacent streets, and along the river's bank, and over the bridge, the Carmagnole absorbed them every one and whirled them away.

After grasping the Doctor's hand, as he stood victorious and proud before him; after grasping the hand of Mr. Lorry, who came panting in breathless from his struggle against the waterspout of the Carmagnole; after kissing little Lucie, who was lifted up to clasp her arms round his neck; and after embracing the ever zealous and faithful Pross who lifted her; he took his wife in his arms, and carried her up to their rooms.

"Lucie! My own! I am safe."

"O dearest Charles, let me thank God for this on my knees as I have prayed to Him."

They all reverently bowed their heads and hearts. When she was again in his arms, he said to her:

"And now speak to your father, dearest. No other man in all this France could have done what he has done for me."

She laid her head upon her father's breast, as she had laid his poor head on her own breast, long, long ago. He was happy in the return he had made her, he was recompensed for his suffering, he was proud of his strength. "You must not be weak, my darling," he remonstrated; "don't tremble so. I have saved him."

CHAPTER VII

A KNOCK AT THE DOOR.

"I HAVE saved him." It was not another of the dreams in which he had often come back; he was really here. And yet his wife trembled, and a vague but heavy fear was upon her.

All the air round was so thick and dark, the people were so passionately revengeful and fitful, the innocent were so

constantly put to death on vague suspicion and black malice, it was so impossible to forget that many as blameless as her husband and as dear to others as he was to her, every day shared the fate from which he had been clutched, that her heart could not be as lightened of its load as she felt it ought to be. The shadows of the wintry afternoon were beginning to fall, and even now the dreadful carts were rolling through the streets. Her mind pursued them, looking for him among the Condemned; and then she clung closer to his real presence and trembled more.

Her father, cheering her, showed a compassionate superiority to this woman's weakness, which was wonderful to see. No garret, no shoemaking, no One Hundred and Five, North Tower, now! He had accomplished the task he had set himself, his promise was redeemed, he had saved Charles. Let them all lean upon him.

Their housekeeping was of a very frugal kind: not only because that was the safest way of life, involving the least offence to the people, but because they were not rich, and Charles, throughout his imprisonment, had had to pay heavily for his bad food, and for his guard, and towards the living of the poorer prisoners. Partly on this account and partly to avoid a domestic spy, they kept no servant; the citizen and citizeness who acted as porters at the courtyard gate, rendered them occasional service; and Jerry (almost wholly transferred to them by Mr. Lorry) had become their daily retainer, and had his bed there every night.

It was an ordinance of the Republic One and Indivisible of Liberty, Equality, Fraternity, or Death, that on the door or doorpost of every house, the name of every inmate must be legibly inscribed in letters of a certain size, at a certain convenient height from the ground. Mr. Jerry Cruncher's name, therefore, duly embellished the doorpost down below; and, as the afternoon shadows deepened, the owner of that name himself appeared, from overlooking a painter whom Doctor Manette had employed to add to the list the name of Charles Evrémonde, called Darnay.

In the universal fear and distrust that darkened the time, all the usual harmless ways of life were changed. In the Doctor's little household, as in very many others, the articles of daily consumption that were wanted were purchased every evening, in small quantities and at various small shops. To avoid attracting notice, and to give as little occasion as possible for talk and envy, was the general desire.

For some months past, Miss Pross and Mr. Cruncher had discharged the office of purveyors; the former carrying the money; the latter, the basket. Every afternoon at about the time when the public lamps were lighted, they fared forth on this duty, and made and brought home such purchases as were needful. Although Miss Pross, through her long association with a French family, might have known as much of their language as of her own, if she had had a mind, she had no mind in that direction; consequently she knew no more of that "nonsense" (as she was pleased to call it) than Mr. Cruncher did. So her manner of marketing was to plump a noun-substantive at the head of a shopkeeper without any introduction in the nature of an article, and, if it happened not to be the name of the thing she wanted, to look round for that thing, lay hold of it, and hold on by it until the bargain was concluded. She always made a bargain for it, by holding up, as a statement of its just price, one finger less than the merchant held up, whatever his number might be.

"Now, Mr. Cruncher," said Miss Pross, whose eyes were red with felicity; "if you are ready, I am."

Jerry hoarsely professed himself at Miss Pross's service. He had worn all his rust off long ago, but nothing would file his spiky head down.

"There's all manner of things wanted," said Miss Pross, "and we shall have a precious time of it. We want wine, among the rest. Nice toasts these Redheads will be drinking, wherever we buy it."

"It will be much the same to your knowledge, miss, I should think," retorted Jerry, "whether they drink your health or the Old Un's."

"Who's he?" said Miss Pross.

Mr. Cruncher, with some diffidence, explained himself as meaning "Old Nick's."

"Ha!" said Miss Pross, "it doesn't need an interpreter to explain the meaning of these creatures. They have but one, and it's Midnight Murder, and Mischief."

"Hush, dear! Pray, pray, be cautious!" cried Lucie.

"Yes, yes, yes, I'll be cautious," said Miss Pross; "but I may say among ourselves, that I do hope there will be no oniony and tobaccoey smotherings in the form of embracings all round, going on in the streets. Now, Ladybird, never you stir from that fire till I come back! Take care of the dear husband you have recovered, and don't move your pretty head from his shoulder as you have it now, till you see me again! May I ask a question, Doctor Manette, before I go?"

"I think you may take that liberty, the Doctor answered, smiling.

"For gracious sake, don't talk about Liberty; we have quite enough of that," said Miss Pross.

"Hush, dear! Again?" Lucie remonstrated.

"Well, my sweet," said Miss Pross, nodding her head emphatically, "the short and the long of it is, that I am a subject of His Most Gracious Majesty King George the Third;" Miss Pross curtseyed at the name; "and as such, my maxim is, Confound their politics, Frustrate their knavish tricks, On him our hopes we fix, God save the King!"

Mr. Cruncher, in an access of loyalty, growlingly repeated the words after Miss Pross, like somebody at church.

"I am glad you have so much of the Englishman in you, though I wish you had never taken that cold in your voice," said Miss Pross, approvingly. "But the question, Doctor Manette. Is there"—it was the good creature's way to affect to make light of anything that was a great anxiety with them all, and to come at it in this chance manner—"is there any prospect yet, of our getting out of this place?"

"I fear not yet. It would be dangerous for Charles yet."

"Heigh-ho-hum!" said Miss Pross, cheerfully repressing a sigh as she glanced at her darling's golden hair in the light of the fire, "then we must have patience and wait: that's all. We must hold up our heads and fight low, as my brother Solomon used to say. Now, Mr. Cruncher!— Don't you move, Ladybird!"

They went out, leaving Lucie, and her husband, her father, and the child, by a bright fire. Mr. Lorry was expected back presently from the Banking House. Miss Pross had lighted the lamp, but had put it aside in a corner, that they might enjoy the fire-light undisturbed. Little Lucie sat by her grandfather with her hands clasped through his arm: and he, in a tone not rising much above a whisper, began to tell her a story of a great and powerful Fairy who had opened a prison-wall and let out a captive who had once done the Fairy a service. All was subdued and quiet, and Lucie was more at ease than she had been.

"What is that?" she cried, all at once.

"My dear!" said her father, stopping in his story, and laying his hand on hers, "command yourself. What a disordered state you are in! The least thing—nothing—startles you! *You*, your father's daughter!"

"I thought, my father," said Lucie, excusing herself, with a pale face and in a faltering voice, "that I heard strange feet upon the stairs."

"My love, the staircase is as still as Death."

As he said the word a blow was struck upon the door.

"Oh father, father. What can this be! Hide Charles. Save him!"

"My child," said the Doctor, rising, and laying his hand upon her shoulder, "I *have* saved him. What weakness is this, my dear! Let me go to the door."

He took the lamp in his hand, crossed the two intervening outer rooms, and opened it. A rude clattering of feet over the floor, and four rough men in red caps, armed with sabres and pistols, entered the room.

"The Citizen Evrémonde, called Darnay," said the first.

"Who seeks him?" answered Darnay.

"I seek him. We seek him. I know you, Evrémonde; I saw you before the Tribunal to-day. You are again the prisoner of the Republic."

The four surrounded him, where he stood with his wife and child clinging to him.

"Tell me how and why am I again a prisoner?"

"It is enough that you return straight to the Conciergerie, and will know to-morrow. You are summoned for to-morrow."

Doctor Manette, whom this visitation had so turned into stone, that he stood with the lamp in his hand, as if he were a statue made to hold it, moved after these words were spoken, put the lamp down, and confronting the speaker, and taking him, not ungently, by the loose front of his red woollen shirt, said:

"You know him, you have said. Do you know me?"

"Yes, I know you, Citizen Doctor."

"We all know you, Citizen Doctor," said the other three.

He looked abstractedly from one to another, and said, in a lower voice, after a pause:

"Will you answer his question to me then? How does this happen?"

"Citizen Doctor," said the first, reluctantly, "he has been denounced to the Section of Saint Antoine. This citizen," pointing out the second who had entered, "is from Saint Antoine."

The citizen here indicated nodded his head, and added:

"He is accused by Saint Antoine."

"Of what?" asked the Doctor.

"Citizen Doctor," said the first, with his former reluctance, "ask no more. If the Republic demands sacrifices from you, without doubt you as a good patriot will be happy to make them. The Republic goes before all. The People is supreme. Evrémonde, we are pressed."

"One word," the Doctor entreated. "Will you tell me who denounced him?"

"It is against rule," answered the first; "but you can ask Him of Saint Antoine here."

The Doctor turned his eyes upon that man. Who moved uneasily on his feet, rubbed his beard a little, and at length said:

"Well! Truly it is against rule. But he is denounced —and gravely—by the Citizen and Citizeness Defarge. And by one other."

"What other?"

"Do *you* ask, Citizen Doctor?"

"Yes."

"Then," said he of Saint Antoine, with a strange look, "you will be answered to-morrow. Now, I am dumb!"

CHAPTER VIII.

A HAND AT CARDS.

HAPPILY unconscious of the new calamity at home, Miss Pross threaded her way along the narrow streets and crossed the river by the bridge of the Pont-Neuf, reckoning in her mind the number of indispensable purchases she had to make. Mr. Cruncher, with the basket, walked at her side. They both looked to the right and to the left into most of the shops they passed, had a wary eye for all gregarious assemblages of people, and turned out of their road to avoid any very excited group of talkers. It was a raw evening, and the misty river, blurred to the eye with blazing lights and to the ear with harsh noises, showed where the barges were stationed in which the smiths worked, making guns for the Army of the Republic. Woe to the man who played tricks with *that* Army, or got undeserved promotion in it! Better for him that his beard had never grown, for the National Razor shaved him close.

Having purchased a few small articles of grocery, and a measure of oil for the lamp, Miss Pross bethought herself of the wine they wanted. After peeping into several wine-shops, she stopped at the sign of the The Good Republican Brutus of Antiquity, not far from the National Palace, once (and twice) the Tuileries, where the aspect of things rather took her fancy. It had a quieter look than any other place of the same description they had passed, and, though red with patriotic caps, was not so red as the rest. Sounding Mr. Cruncher, and finding him of her opinion, Miss Pross resorted to The Good Republican Brutus of Antiquity, attended by her cavalier.

Slightly observant of the smoky lights; of the people, pipe in mouth, playing with limp cards and yellow dominoes; of the one bare-breasted, bare-armed, soot-begrimed workman reading a journal aloud, and of the others listening to him; of the weapons worn, or laid aside to be resumed; of the two or three customers fallen forward asleep, who in the popular high-shouldered shaggy black spencer looked, in that attitude, like slumbering bears or dogs; the two outlandish customers approached the counter, and showed what they wanted.

As their wine was measuring out, a man parted from another man, in a corner, and rose to depart. In going, he had to face Miss Pross. No sooner did he face her, than Miss Pross uttered a scream, and clapped her hands.

In a moment, the whole company were on their feet. That somebody was assassinated by somebody vindicating a difference of opinion was the likeliest occurrence. Everybody looked to see somebody fall, but only saw a man and a woman standing staring at each other; the man with all the outward aspect of a Frenchman and a thorough Republican; the woman, evidently English.

What was said in this disappointing anti-climax, by the disciples of the Good Republican Brutus of Antiquity, except that it was something very voluble and loud, would have been as so much Hebrew or Chaldean to Miss Pross and her protector, though they had been all ears. But, they had no ears for anything in their surprise. For, it must be recorded, that not only was Miss Pross lost in amazement and agitation, but, Mr. Cruncher—though it seemed on his own separate and individual account—was in a state of the greatest wonder.

"What is the matter?" said the man who had caused Miss Pross to scream; speaking in a vexed, abrupt voice (though in a low tone), and in English.

"Oh, Solomon, dear Solomon!" cried Miss Pross, clapping her hands again. "After not setting eyes upon you or hearing of you for so long a time, do I find you here!"

"Don't call me Solomon. Do you want to be the death of me?" asked the man, in a furtive, frightened way.

"Brother, brother!" cried Miss Pross, bursting into tears. "Have I ever been so hard with you that you ask me such a cruel question?"

"Then hold your meddlesome tongue," said Solomon, "and come out, if you want to speak to me. Pay for your wine, and come out. Who's this man?"

Miss Pross, shaking her loving and dejected head at her by no means affectionate brother, said through her tears, "Mr. Cruncher."

"Let him come out too," said Solomon. "Does he think me a ghost?"

Apparently, Mr. Cruncher did, to judge from his looks. He said not a word, however, and Miss Pross, exploring the depths of her reticule through her tears with great difficulty paid for her wine. As she did so, Solomon turned to the followers of the Good Republican Brutus of Antiquity, and offered a few words of explanation in the French language, which caused them all to relapse into their former places and pursuits.

"Now," said Solomon, stopping at the dark street corner, "what do you want?"

"How dreadfully unkind in a brother nothing has ever turned my love away from!" cried Miss Pross, "to give me such a greeting, and show me no affection."

"There. Con-found it! There," said Solomon, making a dab at Miss Pross's lips with his own. "Now are you content?"

Miss Pross only shook her head and wept in silence.

"If you expect me to be surprised," said her brother Solomon, "I am not surprised; I knew you were here; I know of most people who are here. If you really don't want to endanger my existence—which I half believe you do—go your ways as soon as possible, and let me go mine. I am busy. I am an official."

"My English brother Solomon," mourned Miss Pross, casting up her tear-fraught eyes, "that had the makings in him of one of the best and greatest of men in his native country, an official among foreigners, and such foreigners! I would almost sooner have seen the dear boy lying in his——"

"I said so!" cried her brother, interrupting. "I knew it. You want to be the death of me. I shall be rendered Suspected, by my own sister. Just as I am getting on!"

"The gracious and merciful Heavens forbid!" cried Miss Pross. "Far rather would I never see you again, dear Solomon, though I have ever loved you truly, and ever shall. Say but one affectionate word to me, and tell me there is nothing angry or estranged between us, and I will detain you no longer."

Good Miss Pross! As if the estangement between them had come of any culpability of hers. As if Mr. Lorry had not known it for a fact, years ago, in the quiet corner in Soho, that this precious brother had spent her money and left her!

He was saying the affectionate word, however, with a far more grudging condescension and patronage than he could have shown if their relative merits and positions had been reversed (which is invariably the case, all the world over), when Mr. Cruncher, touching him on the shoulder, hoarsely and unexpectedly interposed with the following singular question:

"I say! Might I ask the favour? As to whether your name is John Solomon, or Solomon John?"

The official turned towards him with sudden distrust. He had not previously uttered a word.

"Come!" said Mr. Cruncher. "Speak out, you know." (Which, by the way, was more than he could do himself.) "John Solomon, or Solomon John? She calls you Solomon, and she must know, being your sister. And I know you're John, you know. Which of the two goes first? And regarding that name of Pross, likewise. That warn't your name over the water."

"What do you mean?"

"Well, I don't know all I mean, for I can't call to mind what your name was, over the water."

"No?"

"No. But I'll swear it was a name of two syllables."

"Indeed?"

"Yes. T'other one's was one syllable. I know you. You was a spy-witness at the Bailey. What, in the name of the Father of Lies, own father to yourself, was you called at that time?"

"Barsad," said another voice, striking in.

"That's the name for a thousand pound!" cried Jerry.

The speaker who struck in, was Sydney Carton. He had his hands behind him under the skirts of his riding-coat, and he stood at Mr. Cruncher's elbow as negligently as he might have stood at the Old Bailey itself.

"Don't be alarmed, my dear Miss Pross. I arrived at Mr. Lorry's, to his surprise, yesterday evening; we agreed that I would not present myself elsewhere until all was well, or unless I could be useful; I present myself here, to beg a little talk with your brother. I wish you had a better employed brother than Mr. Barsad. I wish for your sake Mr. Barsad was not a Sheep of the Prisons."

Sheep was a cant word of the time for a spy, under the gaolers. The spy, who was pale, turned paler, and asked him how he dared——

"I'll tell you," said Sydney. "I lighted on you, Mr. Barsad, coming out of the prison of the Conciergerie while I was contemplating the walls, an hour or more ago. You have a face to be remembered, and I remember faces well. Made curious by seeing you in that connection, and having a reason, to which you are no stranger, for associating you with the misfortunes of a friend now very unfortunate, I walked in your direction. I walked into the wine-shop here, close after you, and sat near you. I had no difficulty in deducing from your unreserved conversation, and the rumour openly going about among your admirers, the nature of your calling. And gradually, what I had done at random, seemed to shape itself into a purpose, Mr. Barsad."

"What purpose?" the spy asked.

"It would be troublesome, and might be dangerous, to explain in the street. Could you favour me, in confidence, with some minutes of your company—at the office of Tellson's Bank, for instance?"

"Under a threat?"

"Oh! Did I say that?"

"Then, why should I go there?"

"Really, Mr. Barsad, I can't say, if you can't."

"Do you mean that you won't say, sir?" the spy irresolutely asked.

"You apprehend me very clearly, Mr. Barsad. I won't."

Carton's negligent recklessness of manner came powerfully in aid of his quickness and skill, in such a business as he had in his secret mind, and with such a man as he had to do with. His practised eye saw it, and made the most of it.

"Now, I told you so," said the spy, casting a reproachful look at his sister; "if any trouble comes of this, it's your doing."

"Come, come, Mr. Barsad!" exclaimed Sydney. "Don't be ungrateful. But for my great respect for your sister, I might not have led up so pleasantly to a little proposal that I wish to make for our mutual satisfaction. Do you go with me to the Bank?"

"I'll hear what you have got to say. Yes, I'll go with you."

"I propose that we first conduct your sister safely to the corner of her own street. Let me take your arm, Miss Pross. This is not a good city, at this time, for you to be out in, unprotected; and as your escort knows Mr. Barsad, I will invite him to Mr. Lorry's with us. Are we ready? Come then!"

Miss Pross recalled soon afterwards, and to the end of her life remembered, that as she pressed her hands on Sydney's arm and looked up in his face, imploring him to do no hurt to Solomon, there was a braced purpose in the arm and a kind of inspiration in the eyes, which not only contradicted his light manner, but changed and raised the man. She was too much occupied then with fears for the brother who so little deserved her affection, and with Sydney's friendly reassurances, adequately to heed what she observed.

They left her at her corner of the street, and Carton led the way to Mr. Lorry's, which was within a few minutes' walk. John Barsad, or Solomon Pross, walked at his side.

Mr. Lorry had just finished his dinner, and was sitting before a cheery little log or two of fire—perhaps looking into their blaze for the picture of that younger elderly gentleman from Tellson's, who had looked into the red coals at the Royal George at Dover, now a good many years ago. He turned his head as they entered, and showed the surprise with which he saw a stranger.

"Miss Pross's brother, sir," said Sydney. "Mr. Barsad."

"Barsad?" repeated the old gentleman, "Barsad? I have an association with the name—and with the face."

"I told you you had a remarkable face, Mr. Barsad," observed Carton, coolly. "Pray sit down."

As he took a chair himself, he supplied the link that Mr.

Lorry wanted, by saying to him with a frown, "Witness at that trial." Mr. Lorry immediately remembered, and regarded his new visitor with an undisguised look of abhorrence.

"Mr. Barsad has been recognised by Miss Pross as the affectionate brother you have heard of," said Sydney, "and has acknowledged the relationship. I pass to worse news. Darnay has been arrested again."

Struck with consternation, the old gentleman exclaimed, "What do you tell me! I left him safe and free within these two hours, and am about to return to him!"

"Arrested for all that. When was it done, Mr. Barsad?"

"Just now, if at all."

"Mr. Barsad is the best authority possible, sir," said Sydney, "and I have it from Mr. Barsad's communication to a friend and brother Sheep over a bottle of wine, that the arrest has taken place. He left the messengers at the gate, and saw them admitted by the porter. There is no earthly doubt that he is retaken."

Mr. Lorry's business eye read in the speaker's face that it was loss of time to dwell upon the point. Confused, but sensible that something might depend on his presence of mind, he commanded himself, and was silently attentive.

"Now, I trust," said Sydney to him, "that the name and influence of Doctor Manette may stand him in as good stead to-morrow—you said he would be before the Tribunal again to-morrow, Mr. Barsad?——"

"Yes; I believe so."

"—In as good stead to-morrow as to-day. But it may not be so. I own to you, I am shaken, Mr. Lorry, by Doctor Manette's not having had the power to prevent this arrest."

"He may not have known of it beforehand," said Mr. Lorry.

"But that very circumstance would be alarming, when we remember how identified he is with his son-in-law."

"That's true," Mr. Lorry acknowledged, with his troubled hand at his chin, and his troubled eyes on Carton.

"In short," said Sydney, "this is a desperate time, when desperate games are played for desperate stakes. Let the Doctor play the winning game; I will play the losing one. No man's life here is worth purchase. Any one carried home by the people to-day, may be condemned to-morrow. Now, the stake I have resolved to play for, in case of the worst, is a friend in the Conciergerie. And the friend I purpose to myself to win, is Mr. Barsad."

"You need have good cards, sir," said the spy.

"I'll run them over. I'll see what I hold,—Mr. Lorry, you know what a brute I am; I wish you'd give me a little brandy."

It was put before him, and he drank off a glassful—drank off another glassful—pushed the bottle thoughtfully away.

"Mr. Barsad," he went on, in the tone of one who really was looking over a hand at cards: "Sheep of the prisons, emissary of Republican committees, now turnkey, now prisoner, always spy and secret informer, so much the more valuable here for being English that an Englishman is less open to suspicion of subornation in those characters than a Frenchman, represents himself to his employers under a false name. That's a very good card. Mr. Bar-

sad, now in the employ of the republican French government, was formerly in the employ of the aristocratic English government, the enemy of France and freedom. That's an excellent card. Inference clear as day in this region of suspicion, that Mr. Barsad, still in the pay of the aristocratic English government, is the spy of Pitt, the treacherous foe of the Republic crouching in its bosom, the English traitor and agent of all mischief so much spoken of and so difficult to find. That's a card not to be beaten. Have you followed my hand, Mr. Barsad?"

"Not to understand your play," returned the spy, somewhat uneasily.

"I play my Ace, Denunciation of Mr. Barsad to the nearest Section Committee. Look over your hand, Mr. Barsad, and see what you have. Don't hurry."

He drew the bottle near, poured out another glassful of brandy, and drank it off. He saw that the spy was fearful of his drinking himself into a fit state for the immediate denunciation of him. Seeing it, he poured out and drank another glassful.

"Look over your hand carefully, Mr. Barsad. Take time."

It was a poorer hand than he suspected. Mr. Barsad saw losing cards in it that Sydney Carton knew nothing of. Thrown out of his honourable employment in England, through too much unsuccessful hard swearing there—not because he was not wanted there; our English reasons for vaunting our superiority to secrecy and spies are of very modern date—he knew that he had crossed the Channel, and accepted service in France: first, as a tempter and an eavesdropper among his own countrymen there: gradually, as a tempter and an eavesdropper among the natives. He knew that under the overthrown government he had been a spy upon Saint Antoine and Defarge's wine-shop; had received from the watchful police such heads of information concerning Doctor Manette's imprisonment, release, and history, as should serve him for an introduction to familiar conversation with the Defarges; and tried them on Madame Defarge, and had broken down with them signally. He always remembered with fear and trembling, that that terrible woman had knitted when he talked with her, and had looked ominously at him as her fingers moved. He had since seen her, in the Section of Saint Antoine, over and over again produce her knitted registers, and denounce people whose lives the guillotine then surely swallowed up. He knew, as every one employed as he was did, that he was never safe; that flight was impossible; that he was tied fast under the shadow of the axe; and that in spite of his utmost tergiversation and treachery in furtherance of the reigning terror, a word might bring it down upon him. Once denounced, and on such grave grounds as had just now been suggested to his mind, he foresaw that the dreadful woman of whose unrelenting character he had seen many proofs, would produce against him that fatal register, and would quash his last chance of life. Besides that all secret men are men soon terrified, here were surely cards enough of one black suit, to justify the holder in growing rather livid as he turned them over.

"You scarcely seem to like your hand," said Sydney, with the greatest composure. "Do you play?"

"I think, sir," said the spy, in the meanest manner, as he turned to Mr. Lorry, "I may appeal to a gentleman of your years and benevolence, to put it to this other gentleman, so much your junior, whether he can under any circumstances reconcile it to his station to play that Ace of which he has spoken. I admit that *I* am a spy, and that it is considered a discreditable station—though it must be filled by somebody; but this gentleman is no spy, and why should he so demean himself as to make himself one?"

"I play my Ace, Mr. Barsad," said Carton, taking the answer on himself, and looking at his watch, "without any scruple, in a very few minutes."

"I should have hoped, gentlemen both," said the spy, always striving to hook Mr. Lorry into the discussion, "that your respect for my sister——"

"I could not better testify my respect for your sister than by finally relieving her of her brother," said Sydney Carton.

"You think not, sir?"

"I have thoroughly made up my mind about it."

The smooth manner of the spy, curiously in dissonance with his ostentatiously rough dress, and probably with his usual demeanour, received such a check from the inscrutability of Carton,—who was a mystery to wiser and honester men than he,—that it faltered here and failed him. While he was at a loss, Carton said, resuming his former air of contemplating cards:

"And indeed, now I think again, I have a strong impression that I have another good card here, not yet enumerated. That friend and fellow-Sheep, who spoke of himself as pasturing in the country prisons; who was he?"

"French. You don't know him," said the spy, quickly.

"French, eh?" repeated Carton, musing, and not appearing to notice him at all, though he echoed his word. "Well; he may be."

"Is, I assure you," said the spy; "though it's not important."

"Though it's not important," repeated Carton, in the same mechanical way—"though it's not important——No, it's not important. No. Yet I know the face."

"I think not. I am sure not. It can't be," said the spy.

"It can't—be," muttered Sydney Carton, retrospectively, and filling his glass (which fortunately was a small one) again. "Can't—be. Spoke good French. Yet like a foreigner, I thought?"

"Provincial," said the spy.

"No. Foreign!" cried Carton, striking his open hand on the table, as a light broke clearly on his mind. "Cly! Disguised, but the same man. We had that man before us at the Old Bailey."

"Now, there you are hasty, sir," said Barsad, with a smile that gave his aquiline nose an extra inclination to one side; "there you really give me an advantage over you. Cly (who I will unreservedly admit, at this distance of time, was a partner of mine) has been dead several years. I attended him in his last illness. He was buried in London, at the church of Saint Pancras-in-the-Fields. His unpopularity with the blackguard multitude at the moment prevented my following his remains, but I helped to lay him in his coffin."

Here, Mr. Lorry became aware, from where he sat, of a most remarkable goblin shadow on the wall. Tracing it to its source, he discovered it to be caused by a sudden extraordinary rising and stiffening of all the risen and stiff hair on Mr. Cruncher's head.

"Let us be reasonable," said the spy, "and let us be fair. To show you how mistaken you are, and what an unfounded assumption yours is, I will lay before you a certificate of Cly's burial, which I happened to have carried in my pocket-book," with a hurried hand he produced and opened it, "ever since. There it is. Oh, look at it, look at it! You may take it in your hand; it's no forgery."

Here, Mr. Lorry perceived the reflection on the wall to elongate, and Mr. Cruncher rose and stepped forward. His hair could not have been more violently on end, if it had been that moment dressed by the Cow with the crumpled horn in the house that Jack built.

Unseen by the spy, Mr. Cruncher stood at his side, and touched him on the shoulder like a ghostly bailiff.

"That there Roger Cly, master," said Mr. Cruncher, with a taciturn and iron-bound visage. "So *you* put him in his coffin?"

"I did."

"Who took him out of it?"

Barsad leaned back in his chair, and stammered, "What do you mean?"

"I mean," said Mr. Cruncher, "that he warn't never in it. No! Not he! I'll have my head took off, if he was ever in it."

The spy looked round at the two gentlemen; they both looked in unspeakable astonishment at Jerry.

"I tell you," said Jerry, "that you buried paving-stones and earth in that there coffin. Don't go and tell *me* that you buried Cly. It was a take in. Me and two more knows it."

"How do you know it?"

"What's that to you? Ecod!" growled Mr. Cruncher, "it's you I have got a old grudge again, is it, with your shameful impositions upon tradesmen! I'd catch hold of your throat and choke you for half a guinea."

Sydney Carton, who, with Mr. Lorry, had been lost in amazement at this turn of the business, here requested Mr. Cruncher to moderate and explain himself.

"At another time, sir," he returned, evasively, "the present time is ill-convenient for explainin'. What I stand to, is, that he knows well wot that there Cly was never in that there coffin. Let him say he was, in so much as a word of one syllable, and I'll either catch hold of his throat and choke him for half a guinea;" Mr. Cruncher dwelt upon this as quite a liberal offer; "or I'll out and announce him."

"Humph! I see one thing," said Carton. "I hold another card, Mr. Barsad. Impossible, here in raging Paris, with Suspicion filling the air, for you to outlive denunciation, when you are in communication with another aristocratic spy of the same antecedents as yourself, who, moreover, has the mystery about him of having feigned death and come to life again! A plot in the prisons, of the foreigner against the Republic. A strong card—a certain Guillotine card! Do you play?"

"No!" returned the spy. "I throw up. I confess that we were so unpopular with the outrageous mob, that I only got away from England at the risk of being ducked to death, and that Cly was so ferreted up and down, that he never would have got away at all but for that sham. Though how this man knows it was a sham, is a wonder of wonders to me."

"Never you trouble your head about this man," retorted the contentious Mr. Cruncher; "you'll have trouble enough with giving your attention to that gentleman. And look here! Once more!"—Mr. Cruncher could not be restrained from making rather an ostentatious parade of his liberality —"I'd catch hold of your throat and choke you for half a guinea."

The Sheep of the prison turned from him to Sydney Carton, and said, with more decision, "It has come to a point. I go on duty soon, and can't overstay my time. You told me you had a proposal; what is it? Now, it is of no use asking too much of me. Ask me to do anything in my office, putting my head in great extra danger, and I had better trust my life to the chances of a refusal than the chances of consent. In short, I should make that choice. You talk of desperation. We are all desperate here. Remember! I may denounce you if I think proper, and I can swear my way through stone walls, and so can others. Now, what do you want with me?"

"Not very much. You are a turnkey at the Conciergerie?"

"I tell you once for all, there is no such thing as an escape possible," said the spy, firmly.

"Why need you tell me what I have not asked? You are a turnkey at the Conciergerie?"

"I am sometimes."

"You can be when you choose?"

"I can pass in and out when I choose."

Sydney Carton filled another glass with brandy, poured it slowly out upon the hearth, and watched it as it dropped. It being all spent, he said, rising:

"So far, we have spoken before these two, because it was as well that the merits of the cards should not rest solely between you and me. Come into the dark room here, and let us have one final word alone."

CHAPTER IX

THE GAME MADE.

WHILE Sydney Carton and the Sheep of the prisons were in the adjoining dark room, speaking so low that not a sound was heard, Mr. Lorry looked at Jerry in considerable doubt and mistrust. That honest tradesman's manner of receiving the look, did not inspire confidence; he changed the leg on which he rested, as often as if he had fifty of those limbs, and were trying them all; he examined his finger-nails with a very questionable closeness of attention; and whenever Mr. Lorry's eye caught his, he was taken with that peculiar kind of short cough requiring the hollow of a hand before it, which is seldom, if ever, known to be an infirmity attendant on perfect openness of character.

"Jerry," said Mr. Lorry. "Come here."

Mr. Cruncher came forward sideways, with one of his shoulders in advance of him.

"What have you been, besides a messenger?"

After some cogitation, accompanied with an intent look at his patron, Mr. Cruncher conceived the luminous idea of replying, "Agricultooral character."

"My mind misgives me much," said Mr. Lorry, angrily shaking a forefinger at him, "that you have used the respectable and great house of Tellson's as a blind, and that you have had an unlawful occupation of an infamous description. If you have, don't expect me to befriend you when you get back to England. If you have, don't expect me to keep your secret. Tellson's shall not be imposed upon."

"I hope, sir," pleaded the abashed Mr. Cruncher, "that

a gentleman like yourself wot I've had the honour of odd jobbing till I'm grey at it, would think twice about harming of me, even if it wos so—I don't say it is, but even if it wos. And which it is to be took into account that if it wos, it wouldn't, even then, be all o' one side. There'd be two sides to it. There might be medical doctors at the present hour, a picking up their guineas where a honest tradesman don't pick up his fardens—fardens! no, nor yet his half fardens—half fardens! no, nor yet his quarter—a banking away like smoke at Tellson's, and a cocking their medical eyes at that tradesman on the sly, a going in and going out to their own carriages—ah! equally like smoke, if not more so. Well, that 'ud be imposing, too, on Tellson's. For you cannot sarse the goose and not the gander. And here's Mrs. Cruncher, or leastways wos in the Old England times, and would be to-morrow, if cause given, a floppin' again the business to that degree as is ruinating —stark ruinating! Whereas them medical doctors' wives don't flop—catch 'em at it! Or, if they flop, their floppings goes in favour of more patients, and how can you rightly have one without the t'other? Then, wot with undertakers, and wot with parish clerks, and wot with sextons, and wot with private watchmen (all awaricious and all in it), a man wouldn't get much by it, even if it wos so. And wot little a man did get, would never prosper with him, Mr. Lorry. He'd never have no good of it; he'd want all along to be out of the line, if he could see his way out, being once in—even if it wos so."

"Ugh!" cried Mr. Lorry, rather relenting, nevertheless. "I am shocked at the sight of you."

"Now, what I would humbly offer to you, sir," pursued Mr. Cruncher, "even if it wos so, which I don't say it is—"

"Don't prevaricate," said Mr. Lorry.

"No, I will not, sir," returned Mr. Cruncher, as if nothing were further from his thoughts or practice—"which I don't say it is—wot I would humbly offer to you, sir, would be this. Upon that there stool, at that there Bar, sets that there boy of mine, brought up and growed up to be a man, wot will errand you, message you, general-light-job you, till your heels is where your head is, if such should be your wishes. If it wos so, which I still don't say it is (for I will not prevaricate to you, sir), let that there boy keep his father's place, and take care of his mother; don't blow upon that boy's father—do not do it, sir—and let that father go into the line of the reg'lar digging', and make amends for what he would have un-dug—if it wos so—by diggin' of 'em in with a will, and with convictions respectin' the futur' keepin' of 'em safe. That, Mr. Lorry," said Mr. Cruncher, wiping his forehead with his arm, as an announcement that he had arrived at the peroration of his discourse, "is wot I would respectfully offer to you, sir. A man don't see all this here a goin' on dreadful round him, in the way of Subjects without heads, dear me, plentiful enough fur to bring the price down to porterage and hardly that, without havin' his serious thoughts of things. And these here would be mine, if it wos so, entreatin' of you fur to bear in mind that wot I said just now, I up and said in the good cause when I might have kep' it back."

"That at least is true," said Mr. Lorry. "Say no more now. It may be that I shall yet stand your friend, if you deserve it, and repent in action—not in words. I want no more words."

Mr. Cruncher knuckled his forehead, as Sydney Carton

and the spy returned from the dark room. "Adieu, Mr. Barsad," said the former; "our arrangement thus made, you have nothing to fear from me."

He sat down in a chair on the hearth, over against Mr. Lorry. When they were alone, Mr. Lorry asked him what he had done?

"Not much. If it should go ill with the prisoner, I have ensured access to him, once."

Mr. Lorry's countenance fell.

"It is all I could do," said Carton. "To propose too much, would be to put this man's head under the axe, and, as he himself said, nothing worse could happen to him if he were denounced. It was obviously the weakness of the position. There is no help for it."

"But access to him," said Mr. Lorry, "if it should go ill before the Tribunal, will not save him."

"I never said it would."

Mr. Lorry's eyes gradually sought the fire; his sympathy with his darling, and the heavy disappointment of his second arrest, gradually weakened them; he was an old man now, overborne with anxiety of late, and his tears fell.

"You are a good man and a true friend," said Carton, in an altered voice. "Forgive me if I notice that you are affected. I could not see my father weep, and sit by, careless. And I could not respect your sorrow more, if you were my father. You are free from that misfortune, however."

Though he said the last words, with a slip into his usual manner, there was a true feeling and respect both in his tone and in his touch, that Mr. Lorry, who had never seen the better side of him, was wholly unprepared for. He gave him his hand, and Carton gently pressed it.

"To return to poor Darnay," said Carton. "Don't tell Her of this interview, or this arrangement. It would not enable Her to go to see him. She might think it was contrived, in case of the worst, to convey to him the means of anticipating the sentence."

Mr. Lorry had not thought of that, and he looked quickly at Carton to see if it were in his mind. It seemed to be; he returned the look, and evidently understood it.

"She might think a thousand things," Carton said, "and any of them would only add to her trouble. Don't speak of me to her. As I said to you when I first came, I had better not see her. I can put my hand out, to do any little helpful work for her that my hand can find to do, without that. You are going to her, I hope? She must be very desolate to-night."

"I am going now, directly."

"I am glad of that. She has such a strong attachment to you and reliance on you. How does she look?"

"Anxious and unhappy, but very beautiful."

"Ah!"

It was a long, grieving sound, like a sigh—almost like a sob. It attracted Mr. Lorry's eyes to Carton's face, which was turned to the fire. A light, or a shade (the old gentleman could not have said which), passed from it as swiftly as a change will sweep over a hill-side on a wild bright day, and he lifted his foot to put back one of the little flaming logs, which was tumbling forward. He wore the white riding-coat and top-boots, then in vogue, and the light of the fire touching their light surfaces made him look very pale, with his long brown hair, all untrimmed, hanging loose about him. His indifference to fire was sufficiently remarkable to elicit a word of remonstrance from

Mr. Lorry; his boot was still upon the hot embers of the flaming log, when it had broken under the weight of his foot.

"I forgot it," he said.

Mr. Lorry's eyes were again attracted to his face. Taking note of the wasted air which clouded the naturally handsome features, and having the expression of prisoners' faces fresh in his mind, he was strongly reminded of that expression.

"And your duties here have drawn to an end, sir?" said Carton, turning to him.

"Yes. As I was telling you last night when Lucie came in so unexpectedly, I have at length done all that I can do here. I hoped to have left them in perfect safety, and then to have quitted Paris. I have my Leave to Pass. I was ready to go."

They were both silent.

"Yours is a long life to look back upon, sir?" said Carton, wistfully.

"I am in my seventy-eighth year."

"You have been useful all your life; steadily and constantly occupied; trusted, respected, and looked up to?"

"I have been a man of business, ever since I have been a man. Indeed, I may say that I was a man of business when a boy."

"See what a place you fill at seventy-eight. How many people will miss you when you leave it empty!"

"A solitary old bachelor," answered Mr. Lorry, shaking his head. "There is nobody to weep for me."

"How can you say that? Wouldn't She weep for you? Wouldn't her child?"

"Yes, yes, thank God. I didn't quite mean what I said."

"It *is* a thing to thank God for; is it not?"

"Surely, surely."

"If you could say, with truth, to your own solitary heart, to-night, 'I have secured to myself the love and attachment, the gratitude or respect, of no human creature; I have won myself a tender place in no regard; I have done nothing good or serviceable to be remembered by!' your seventy-eight years would be seventy-eight heavy curses; would they not?"

"You say truly, Mr. Carton; I think they would be."

Sydney turned his eyes again upon the fire, and, after a silence of a few moments, said:

"I should like to ask you:—Does your childhood seem far off? Do the days when you sat at your mother's knee, seem days of very long ago?"

Responding to his softened manner, Mr. Lorry answered:

"Twenty years back, yes; at this time of my life, no. For, as I draw closer and closer to the end, I travel in the circle, nearer and nearer to the beginning. It seems to be one of the kind smoothings and preparings of the way. My heart is touched now, by many remembrances that had long fallen asleep, of my pretty young mother (and I so old!), and by many associations of the days when what we call the World was not so real with me, and my faults were not confirmed in me."

"I understand the feeling!" exclaimed Carton, with a bright flush. "And you are the better for it?"

"I hope so."

Carton terminated the conversation here, by rising to help him on with his outer coat; "but you," said Mr. Lorry, reverting to the theme, "you are young."

"Yes," said Carton. "I am not old, but my young way was never the way to age. Enough of me."

"And of me, I am sure," said Mr. Lorry. Are you going out?"

"I'll walk with you to her gate. You know my vagabond and restless habits. If I should prowl about the streets a long time, don't be uneasy; I shall reappear in the morning. You go to the Court to-morrow?"

"Yes, unhappily."

"I shall be there, but only as one of the crowd. My Spy will find a place for me. Take my arm, sir."

Mr. Lorry did so, and they went down-stairs and out in the streets. A few minutes brought them to Mr. Lorry's destination. Carton left him there; but lingered at a little distance, and turned back to the gate again when it was shut, and touched it. He had heard of her going to the prison every day. "She came out here, he said, looking about him, "turned this way, must have trod on these stones often. Let me follow in her steps."

It was ten o'clock at night when he stood before the prison of La Force, where she had stood hundreds of times. A little wood-sawyer, having closed his shop, was smoking his pipe at his shop-door.

"Good night, citizen," said Sydney Carton, pausing in going by; for, the man eyed him inquisitively.

"Good night, citizen."

"How goes the Republic?"

"You mean the Guillotine. Not ill. Sixty-three to-day. We shall mount to a hundred soon. Samson and his men complain sometimes, of being exhausted. Ha, ha, ha! He is so droll, that Samson. Such a Barber!"

"Do you often go to see him——"

"Shave? Always. Every day. What a barber! You have seen him at work?"

"Never."

"Go and see him when he has a good batch. Figure this to yourself, citizen; he shaved the sixty-three to-day, in less than two pipes! Less than two pipes! Word of honour!"

As the grinning little man held out the pipe he was smoking, to explain how he timed the executioner, Carton was so sensible of a rising desire to strike the life out of him, that he turned away.

"But you are not English," said the wood-sawyer, "though you wear English dress?"

"Yes," said Carton, pausing again, and answering over his shoulder.

"You speak like a Frenchman."

"I am an old student here."

"Aha, a perfect Frenchman! Good night, Englishman."

"Good night, citizen."

"But go and see that droll dog," the little man persisted, calling after him. "And take a pipe with you!"

Sydney had not gone far out of sight, when he stopped in the middle of the street under a glimmering lamp, and wrote with his pencil on a scrap of paper. Then, traversing with the decided step of one who remembered the way well, several dark and dirty streets—much dirtier than usual, for the best public thoroughfares remained uncleansed in those times of terror—he stopped at a chemist's shop, which the owner was closing with his own hands. A small, dim, crooked shop, kept in a tortuous, up-hill thoroughfare, by a small, dim, crooked man.

Giving this citizen, too, good night, as he confronted him at his counter, he laid the scrap of paper before him. "Whew!" the chemist whistled softly, as he read it. "Hi! hi! hi!"

Sydney Carton took no heed, and the chemist said:

"For you, citizen?"

"For me."

"You will be careful to keep them separate, citizen? You know the consequences of mixing them?"

"Perfectly."

Certain small packets were made and given to him. He put them, one by one, in the breast of his inner coat, counted out the money for them, and deliberately left the shop. "There is nothing more to do," said he, glancing upward at the moon, "until to-morrow. I can't sleep."

It was not a reckless manner, the manner in which he said these words aloud under the fast-sailing clouds, nor was it more expressive of negligence than defiance. It was the settled manner of a tired man, who had wandered and struggled and got lost, but who at length struck into his road and saw its end.

Long ago, when he had been famous among his earliest competitors as a youth of great promise, he had followed his father to the grave. His mother had died, years before. These solemn words, which had been read at his father's grave, arose in his mind as he went down the dark streets, among the heavy shadows, with the moon and the clouds sailing on high above him. "I am the resurrection and the life, saith the Lord: he that believeth in me, though he were dead, yet shall he live: and whosoever liveth and believeth in me, shall never die."

In a city dominated by the axe, alone at night, with natural sorrow rising in him for the sixty-three who had been that day put to death, and for to-morrow's victims then awaiting their doom in the prisons, and still of to-morrow's and to-morrow's, the chain of association that brought the words home, like a rusty old ship's anchor from the deep, might have been easily found. He did not seek it, but repeated them and went on.

With a solemn interest in the lighted windows where the people were going to rest, forgetful through a few calm hours of the horrors surrounding them; in the towers of the churches, where no prayers were said, for the popular revulsion had even travelled that length of self-destruction from years of priestly impostors, plunderers, and profligates; in the distant burial-places, reserved, as they wrote upon the gates, for Eternal Sleep; in the abounding gaols; and in the streets along which the sixties rolled to a death which had become so common and material, that no sorrowful story of a haunting Spirit ever arose among the people out of all the working of the Guillotine; with a solemn interest in the whole life and death of the city settling down to its short nightly pause in fury; Sydney Carton crossed the Seine again for the lighter streets.

Few coaches were abroad, for riders in coaches were liable to be suspected, and gentility hid its head in red nightcaps, and put on heavy shoes, and trudged. But, the theatres were all well filled, and the people poured cheerfully out as he passed, and went chatting home. At one of the theatre doors, there was a little girl with a mother, looking for a way across the street through the mud. He carried the child over, and before the timid arm was loosed from his neck asked her for a kiss.

"I am the resurrection and the life, saith the Lord: he that believeth in me, though he were dead, yet shall he live: and whosoever liveth and believeth in me, shall never die."

Now, that the streets were quiet, and the night wore on, the words were in the echoes of his feet, and were in the air. Perfectly calm and steady, he sometimes repeated them to himself as he walked; but, he heard them always.

The night wore out, and, as he stood upon the bridge listening to the water as it splashed the river-walls of the Island of Paris, where the picturesque confusion of houses and cathedral shone bright in the light of the moon, the day came coldly, looking like a dead face out of the sky. Then, the night, with the moon and the stars, turned pale and died, and for a little while it seemed as if Creation were delivered over to Death's dominion.

But, the glorious sun, rising, seemed to strike those words, that burden of the night, straight and warm to his heart in its long bright rays. And looking along them, with reverently shaded eyes, a bridge of light appeared to span the air between him and the sun, while the river sparkled under it.

The strong tide, so swift, so deep, and certain, was like a congenial friend, in the morning stillness. He walked by the stream, far from the houses, and in the light and warmth of the sun fell asleep on the bank. When he awoke and was afoot again, he lingered there yet a little longer, watching an eddy that turned and turned purposeless, until the stream absorbed it, and carried it on to the sea.—"Like me!"

A trading-boat, with a sail of the softened colour of a dead leaf, then glided into his view, floated by him, and died away. As its silent track in the water disappeared, the prayer that had broken up out of his heart for a merciful consideration of all his poor blindnesses and errors, ended in the words, "I am the resurrection and the life."

Mr. Lorry was already out when he got back, and it was easy to surmise where the good old man was gone. Sydney Carton drank nothing but a little coffee, ate some bread, and, having washed and changed to refresh himself, went out to the place of trial.

The court was all astir and a-buzz, when the black sheep —whom many fell away from in dread—pressed him into an obscure corner among the crowd. Mr. Lorry was there, and Doctor Manette was there. She was there, sitting beside her father.

When her husband was brought in, she turned a look upon him, so sustaining, so encouraging, so full of admiring love and pitying tenderness, yet so courageous for his sake, that it called the healthy blood into his face, brightened his glance, and animated his heart. If there had been any eyes to notice the influence of her look, on Sydney Carton, it would have been seen to be the same influence exactly.

Before that unjust Tribunal, there was little or no order of procedure, ensuring to any accused person any reasonable hearing. There could have been no such Revolution, if all laws, forms, and ceremonies, had not first been so monstrously abused, that the suicidal vengeance of the Revolution was to scatter them all to the winds.

Every eye was turned to the jury. The same determined patriots and good republicans as yesterday and the day before, and to-morrow and the day after. Eager and prominent among them, one man with a craving face, and his fingers perpetually hovering about his lips, whose appearance gave great satisfaction to the spectators. A life-thirsting, cannibal-looking, bloody-minded juryman, the Jacques Three of St. Antoine. The whole jury, as a jury of dogs empannelled to try the deer.

Every eye then turned to the five judges and the public prosecutor. No favourable leaning in that quarter to-day.

A fell, uncompromising, murderous business-meaning there. Every eye then sought some other eye in the crowd, and gleamed at it approvingly; and heads nodded at one another, before bending forward with a strained attention.

Charles Evrémonde, called Darnay. Released yesterday. Reaccused and retaken yesterday. Indictment delivered to him last night. Suspected and Denounced enemy of the Republic, Aristocrat, one of a family of tyrants, one of a race proscribed, for that they had used their abolished privileges to the infamous oppression of the people. Charles Evrémonde, called Darnay, in right of such proscription, absolutely Dead in Law.

To this effect, in as few or fewer words, the Public Prosecutor.

The President asked, was the Accused openly denounced or secretly?

"Openly, President."

"By whom?"

"Three voices. Ernest Defarge, wine-vender of St. Antoine."

"Good."

"Thérèse Defarge, his wife."

"Good."

"Alexandre Manette, physician."

A great uproar took place in the court, and in the midst of it, Doctor Manette was seen, pale and trembling, standing where he had been seated.

"President, I indignantly protest to you that this is a forgery and a fraud. You know the accused to be the husband of my daughter. My daughter, and those dear to her, are far dearer to me than my life. Who and where is the false conspirator who says that I denounce the husband of my child!"

"Citizen Manette, be tranquil. To fail in submission to the authority of the Tribunal would be to put yourself out of Law. As to what is dearer to you than life, nothing can be so dear to a good citizen as the Republic."

Loud acclamations hailed this rebuke. The President rang his bell, and with warmth resumed.

"If the Republic should demand of you the sacrifice of your child herself, you would have no duty but to sacrifice her. Listen to what is to follow. In the meanwhile, be silent!"

Frantic acclamations were again raised. Doctor Manette sat down, with his eyes looking around, and his lips trembling; his daughter drew closer to him. The craving man on the jury rubbed his hands together, and restored the usual hand to his mouth.

Defarge was produced, when the court was quiet enough to admit of his being heard, and rapidly expounded the story of the imprisonment, and of his having been a mere boy in the Doctor's service, and of the release, and of the state of the prisoner when released and delivered to him. This short examination followed, for the court was quick with its work.

"You did good service at the taking of the Bastille, citizen?"

"I believe so."

Here, an excited woman screeched from the crowd: "You were one of the best patriots there. Why not say so? You were a cannonier that day there, and you were among the first to enter the accursed fortress when it fell. Patriots, I speak the truth!"

It was The Vengeance who, amidst the warm commendations of the audience, thus assisted the proceedings. The

"THIS IS THAT WRITTEN PAPER."

President rang his bell; but, The Vengeance, warming with encouragement, shrieked, "I defy that bell!" wherein she was likewise much commended.

"Inform the Tribunal of what you did that day within the Bastille, citizen."

"I knew," said Defarge, looking down at his wife, who stood at the bottom of the steps on which he was raised, looking steadily up at him; "I knew that this prisoner, of whom I speak, had been confined in a cell known as One Hundred and Five, North Tower. I knew it from himself. He knew himself by no other name than One Hundred and Five, North Tower, when he made shoes under my care. As I serve my gun that day, I resolve, when the place shall fall, to examine that cell. It falls. I mount to the cell, with a fellow-citizen who is one of the Jury, directed by a gaoler. I examine it, very closely. In a hole in the chimney, where a stone has been worked out and replaced, I find a written paper. This is that written paper. I have made it my business to examine some specimens of the writing of Doctor Manette. This is the writing of Doctor Manette. I confide this paper, in the writing of Doctor Manette, to the hands of the President."

"Let it be read."

In a dead silence and stillness—the prisoner under trial looking lovingly at his wife, his wife only looking from him to look with solicitude at her father, Doctor Manette keeping his eyes fixed on the reader, Madame Defarge never taking hers from the prisoner, Defarge never taking his from his feasting wife, and all the other eyes there intent upon the Doctor, who saw none of them—the paper was read, as follows.

CHAPTER X.

THE SUBSTANCE OF THE SHADOW.

"I, ALEXANDRE MANETTE, unfortunate physician, native of Beauvais, and afterwards resident in Paris, write this melancholy paper in my doleful cell in the Bastille, during the last month of the year, 1767. I write it at stolen intervals, under every difficulty. I design to secrete it in the wall of the chimney, where I have slowly and laboriously made a place of concealment for it. Some pitying hand may find it there, when I and my sorrows are dust.

"These words are formed by the rusty iron point with which I write with difficulty in scrapings of soot and charcoal from the chimney, mixed with blood, in the last month of the tenth year of my captivity. Hope has quite departed from my breast. I know from terrible warnings I have noted in myself that my reason will not long remain unimpaired, but I solemnly declare that I am at this time in the possession of my right mind—that my memory is exact and circumstantial—and that I write the truth as I shall answer for these my last recorded words, whether they be ever read by men or not, at the Eternal Judgment-seat.

"One cloudy moonlight night, in the third week of December (I think the twenty-second of the month) in the year 1757, I was walking on a retired part of the quay by the Seine for the refreshment of the frosty air, at an hour's distance from my place of residence in the Street of the School of Medicine, when a carriage came along behind me, driven very fast. As I stood aside to let that carriage pass, apprehensive that it might otherwise run me down, a head was put out at the window, and a voice called to the driver to stop.

"The carriage stopped as soon as the driver could rein in his horses, and the same voice called to me by my name. I answered. The carriage was then so far in advance of me that two gentlemen had time to open the door and alight before I came up with it. I observed that they were both wrapped in cloaks, and appeared to conceal themselves. As they stood side by side near the carriage door, I also observed that they both looked of about my own age, or rather younger, and that they were greatly alike, in stature, manner, voice, and (as far as I could see) face too.

"'You are Doctor Manette?' said one.

"'I am.'

"'Doctor Manette, formerly of Beauvais,' said the other; 'the young physician, originally an expert surgeon, who within the last year or two has made a rising reputation in Paris?'

"'Gentlemen,' I returned, 'I am that Doctor Manette of whom you speak so graciously.'

"'We have been to your residence,' said the first, 'and not being so fortunate as to find you there, and being informed that you were probably walking in this direction, we followed, in the hope of overtaking you. Will you please to enter the carriage?'

"The manner of both was imperious, and they both moved, as these words were spoken, so as to place me between themselves and the carriage door. They were armed. I was not.

"'Gentlemen,' said I, 'pardon me; but I usually inquire who does me the honour to seek my assistance, and what is the nature of the case to which I am summoned.'

"The reply to this was made by him who had spoken second. 'Doctor, your clients are people of condition. As to the nature of the case, our confidence in your skill assures us that you will ascertain it for yourself better than we can describe it. Enough. Will you please to enter the carriage?'

"I could do nothing but comply, and I entered it in silence. They both entered after me—the last springing in, after putting up the steps. The carriage turned about, and drove on at its former speed.

"I repeat this conversation exactly as it occurred. I have no doubt that it is, word for word, the same. I describe everything exactly as it took place, constraining my mind not to wander from the task. Where I make the broken marks that follow here, I leave off for the time, and put my paper in its hiding-place. * * * *

"The carriage left the streets behind, passed the North Barrier, and emerged upon the country road. At two-thirds of a league from the Barrier—I did not estimate the distance at that time, but afterwards when I traversed it—it struck out of the main avenue, and presently stopped at a solitary house. We all three alighted, and walked, by a damp soft footpath in a garden where a neglected fountain had overflowed, to the door of the house. It was not opened immediately, in answer to the ringing of the bell, and one of my two conductors struck the man who opened it, with his heavy riding glove, across the face.

"There was nothing in this action to attract my particular attention, for I had seen common people struck more commonly than dogs. But, the other of the two, being angry likewise, struck the man in like manner with his arm; the look and bearing of the brothers were then so exactly alike, that I then first perceived them to be twin brothers.

"From the time of our alighting at the outer gate (which we found locked, and which one of the brothers had opened to admit us, and had relocked), I had heard cries proceeding from an upper chamber. I was conducted to this chamber straight, the cries growing louder as we ascended the stairs, and I found a patient in a high fever of the brain, lying on a bed.

"The patient was a woman of great beauty, and young; assuredly not much past twenty. Her hair was torn and ragged, and her arms were bound to her sides with sashes and handkerchiefs. I noticed that these bonds were all portions of a gentleman's dress. On one of them, which was a fringed scarf for a dress of ceremony, I saw the armorial bearings of a Noble, and the letter E.

"I saw this, within the first minute of my contemplation of the patient; for, in her restless strivings she had turned over on her face on the edge of the bed, had drawn the end of the scarf into her mouth, and was in danger of suffocation. My first act was to put out my hand to relieve her breathing; and in moving the scarf aside, the embroidery in the corner caught my sight.

"I turned her gently over, placed my hands upon her breast to calm her and keep her down, and looked into her face. Her eyes were dilated and wild, and she constantly uttered piercing shrieks, and repeated the words, 'My husband, my father, and my brother!' and then counted up to twelve, and said, 'Hush!' For an instant, and no more, she would pause to listen, and then the piercing shrieks would begin again, and she would repeat the cry 'My husband, my father, and my brother!' and would count up to twelve, and say, 'Hush!' There was no variation in the order, or the manner. There was no cessation, but the regular moment's pause, in the utterance of these sounds.

"'How long,' I asked, 'has this lasted?'

"To distinguish the brothers, I will call them the elder and the younger; by the elder, I mean him who exercised the most authority. It was the elder who replied, 'Since about this hour last night.'

"'She has a husband, a father, and a brother?'

"'A brother.'

"'I do not address her brother?'

"He answered with great contempt, 'No.'

"'She has some recent association with the number twelve?'

"The younger brother impatiently rejoined, 'With twelve o'clock?'

"'See, gentlemen,' said I, still keeping my hands upon her breast, 'how useless I am, as you have brought me! If I had known what I was coming to see, I could have come provided. As it is, time must be lost. There are no medicines to be obtained in this lonely place.'

"The elder brother looked to the younger, who said haughtily, 'There is a case of medicines here;' and brought it from a closet, and put it on the table. * * * *

"I opened some of the bottles, smelt them, and put the stoppers to my lips. If I had wanted to use anything save narcotic medicines that were poisons in themselves, I would not have administered any of those.

"'Do you doubt them?' asked the younger brother.

"'You see, monsieur, I am going to use them,' I replied, and said no more.

"I made the patient swallow, with great difficulty, and after many efforts, the dose that I desired to give. As I

intended to repeat it after a while, and as it was necessary to watch its influence, I then sat down by the side of the bed. There was a timid and suppressed woman in attendance (wife of the man down-stairs), who had retreated into a corner. The house was damp and decayed, indifferently furnished—evidently, recently occupied and temporarily used. Some thick old hangings had been nailed up before the windows, to deaden the sound of the shrieks. They continued to be uttered in their regular succession, with the cry, 'My husband, my father, and my brother!' the counting up to twelve, and 'Hush!' The frenzy was so violent, that I had not unfastened the bandages restraining the arms; but I had looked to them, to see that they were not painful. The only spark of encouragement in the case, was, that my hand upon the sufferer's breast had this much soothing influence, that for minutes at a time it tranquillised the figure. It had no effect upon the cries; no pendulum could be more regular.

"For the reason that my hand had this effect (I assume), I had sat by the side of the bed for half an hour, with the two brothers looking on, before the elder said:

"'There is another patient.'

"I was startled, and asked, 'Is it a pressing case?'

"'You had better see,' he carelessly answered; and took up a light. * * * *

"The other patient lay in a back room across a second staircase, which was a species of loft over a stable. There was a low plastered ceiling to a part of it; the rest was open, to the ridge of the tiled roof, and there were beams across. Hay and straw were stored in that portion of the place, fagots for firing, and a heap of apples in sand. I had to pass through that part, to get at the other. My memory is circumstantial and unshaken. I try it with these details, and I see them all, in this my cell in the Bastille, near the close of the tenth year of my captivity, as I saw them all that night.

"On some hay on the ground, with a cushion thrown under his head, lay a handsome peasant boy—a boy of not more than seventeen at the most. He lay on his back, with his teeth set, his right hand clenched on his breast, and his glaring eyes looking straight upward. I could not see where his wound was, as I kneeled on one knee over him; but, I could see that he was dying of a wound from a sharp point.

"'I am a doctor, my poor fellow,' said I. 'Let me examine it.'

"'I do not want it examined,' he answered; 'let it be.'

"It was under his hand, and I soothed him to let me move his hand away. The wound was a sword-thrust, received from twenty to twenty-four hours before, but no skill could have saved him if it had been looked to without delay. He was then dying fast. As I turned my eyes to the elder brother, I saw him looking down at this handsome boy whose life was ebbing out, as if he were a wounded bird, or hare, or rabbit; not at all as if he were a fellow-creature.

"'How has this been done, monsieur?' said I.

"'A crazed young common dog! A serf! Forced my brother to draw upon him, and has fallen by my brother's sword—like a gentleman.'

"There was no touch of pity, sorrow, or kindred humanity, in this answer. The speaker seemed to acknowledge that it was inconvenient to have that different order of creature dying there, and that it would have been better if he had died in the usual obscure routine of his vermin kind.

He was quite incapable of any compassionate feeling about the boy, or about his fate.

"The boy's eyes had slowly moved to him as he had spoken, and they now slowly moved to me.

"'Doctor, they are very proud, these Nobles; but we common dogs are proud too, sometimes. They plunder us, outrage us, beat us, kill us; but we have a little pride left, sometimes. She——have you seen her, Doctor?'

"The shrieks and the cries were audible there, though subdued by the distance. He referred to them, as if she were lying in our presence.

"I said, 'I have seen her.'

"'She is my sister, Doctor. They have had their shameful rights, these Nobles, in the modesty and virtue of our sisters, many years, but we have had good girls among us. I know it, and have heard my father say so. She was a good girl. She was betrothed to a good young man, too: a tenant of his. We were all tenants of his—that man's who stands there. The other is his brother, the worst of a bad race.'

"It was with the greatest difficulty that the boy gathered bodily force to speak; but, his spirit spoke with a dreadful emphasis.

"'We were so robbed by that man who stands there, as all we common dogs are by those superior Beings—taxed by him without mercy, obliged to work for him without pay, obliged to grind our corn at his mill, obliged to feed scores of his tame birds on our wretched crops, and forbidden for our lives to keep a single tame bird of our own, pillaged and plundered to that degree that when we chanced to have a bit of meat, we ate it in fear, with the door barred and the shutters closed, that his people should not see it and take it from us—I say, we were so robbed, and hunted, and were made so poor, that our father told us it was a dreadful thing to bring a child into the world, and that what we should most pray for, was, that our women might be barren and our miserable race die out!'

"I had never before seen the sense of being oppressed, bursting forth like a fire. I had supposed that it must be latent in the people somewhere; but, I had never seen it break out, until I saw it in the dying boy.

"'Nevertheless, Doctor, my sister married. He was ailing at that time, poor fellow, and she married her lover, that she might tend and comfort him in our cottage—our dog-hut, as that man would call it. She had not been married many weeks, when that man's brother saw her and admired her, and asked that man to lend her to him—for what are husbands among us! He was willing enough, but my sister was good and virtuous, and hated his brother with a hatred as strong as mine. What did the two then, to persuade her husband to use his influence with her, to make her willing?'

"The boy's eyes, which had been fixed on mine, slowly turned to the looker-on, and I saw in the two faces that all he said was true. The two opposing kinds of pride confronting one another, I can see, even in this Bastille; the gentleman's, all negligent indifference; the peasant's, all trodden-down sentiment, and passionate revenge.

"'You know, Doctor, that it is among the Rights of these Nobles to harness us common dogs to carts, and drive us. They so harnessed him and drove him. You know that it is among their Rights to keep us in their grounds all night, quieting the frogs, in order that their noble sleep may not be disturbed. They kept him out in the unwhole-some mists at night, and ordered him back into his harness in the day. But he was not persuaded. No! Taken out of harness one day at noon, to feed—if he could find food—he sobbed twelve times, once for every stroke of the bell, and died on her bosom.'

"Nothing human could have held life in the boy but his determination to tell all his wrong. He forced back the gathering shadows of death, as he forced his clenched right hand to remain clenched, and to cover his wound.

"'Then, with that man's permission and even with his aid, his brother took her away; in spite of what I know she must have told his brother—and what that is, will not be long unknown to you, Doctor, if it is now—his brother took her away—for his pleasure and diversion, for a little while. I saw her pass me on the road. When I took the tidings home, our father's heart burst; he never spoke one of the words that filled it. I took my young sister (for I have another) to a place beyond the reach of this man, and where, at least, she will never be *his* vassal. Then, I tracked the brother here, and last night climbed in—a common dog, but sword in hand.—Where is the loft window? It was somewhere here?'

"The room was darkening to his sight; the world was narrowing around him. I glanced about me, and saw that the hay and straw were trampled over the floor, as if there had been a struggle.

"'She heard me, and ran in. I told her not to come near us till he was dead. He came in and first tossed me some pieces of money; then struck at me with a whip. But I, though a common dog, so struck at him as to make him draw. Let him break into as many pieces as he will, the sword that he stained with my common blood; he drew to defend himself—thrust at me with all his skill for his life.'

"My glance had fallen, but a few moments before, on the fragments of a broken sword, lying among the hay. That weapon was a gentleman's. In another place, lay an old sword that seemed to have been a soldier's.

"'Now, lift me up, Doctor; lift me up. Where is he?'

"'He is not here,' I said, supporting the boy, and thinking that he referred to the brother.

"'He! Proud as these nobles are, he is afraid to see me. Where is the man who was here? Turn my face to him.'

"I did so, raising the boy's head against my knee. But, invested for the moment with extraordinay power, he raised himself completely: obliging me to rise too, or I could not have still supported him.

"'Marquis,' said the boy, turned to him with his eyes opened wide, and his right hand raised, 'in the days when all these things are to be answered for, I summon you and yours, to the last of your bad race, to answer for them. I mark this cross of blood upon you, as a sign that I do it. In the days when all these things are to be answered for, I summon your brother, the worst of the bad race, to answer for them separately. I mark this cross of blood upon him; as a sign that I do it.'

"Twice, he put his hand to the wound in his breast, and with his forefinger drew a cross in the air. He stood for an instant with the finger yet raised, and as it dropped, he dropped with it, and I laid him down dead. * * * *

"When I returned to the bedside of the young woman, I found her raving in precisely the same order of continuity. I knew that this might last for many hours, and that it would probably end in the silence of the grave.

"I repeated the medicines I had given her, and I sat at

the side of the bed until the night was far advanced. She never abated the piercing quality of her shrieks, never stumbled in the distinctness or the order of her words. They were always 'My husband, my father, and my brother! One, two, three, four, five, six, seven, eight, nine, ten, eleven, twelve. Hush!'

"This lasted twenty-six hours from the time when I first saw her. I had come and gone twice, and was again sitting by her, when she began to falter. I did what little could be done to assist that opportunity, and by-and-bye she sank into a lethargy, and lay like the dead.

"It was as if the wind and rain had lulled at last, after a long and fearful storm. I released her arms, and called the woman to assist me to compose her figure and the dress she had torn. It was then that I knew her condition to be that of one in whom the first expectations of being a mother have arisen; and it was then that I lost the little hope I had had of her.

"'Is she dead?' asked the Marquis, whom I will still describe as the elder brother, coming booted into the room from his horse.

"'Not dead,' said I; 'but like to die.'

"'What strength there is in these common bodies!' he said, looking down at her with some curiosity.

"'There is prodigious strength,' I answered him, 'in sorrow and despair.'

"He first laughed at my words, and then frowned at them. He moved a chair with his foot near to mine, ordered the woman away, and said in a subdued voice,

"'Doctor, finding my brother in this difficulty with these hinds, I recommended that your aid should be invited. Your reputation is high, and, as a young man with your fortune to make, you are probably mindful of your interest. The things that you see here, are things to be seen, and not spoken of.'

"I listened to the patient's breathing, and avoided answering.

"'Do you honour me with your attention, Doctor?'

"'Monsieur,' said I, 'in my profession, the communications of patients are always received in confidence.' I was guarded in my answer, for I was troubled in my mind with what I had heard and seen.

"Her breathing was so difficult to trace, that I carefully tried the pulse and the heart. There was life, and no more. Looking round as I resumed my seat, I found both the brothers intent upon me. * * * *

"I write with so much difficulty, the cold is so severe, I am so fearful of being detected and consigned to an underground cell and total darkness, that I must abridge this narrative. There is no confusion or failure in my memory; it can recall, and could detail, every word that was ever spoken between me and those brothers.

"She lingered for a week. Towards the last, I could understand some few syllables that she said to me, by placing my ear close to her lips. She asked me where she was, and I told her; who I was, and I told her. It was in vain that I asked her for her family name. She faintly shook her head upon the pillow, and kept her secret, as the boy had done.

"I had no opportunity of asking her any question, until I had told the brothers she was sinking fast, and could not live another day. Until then, though no one was ever presented to her consciousness save the woman and myself, one or other of them had always jealously sat behind the curtain at the head of the bed when I was there. But when it came to that, they seemed careless what communication I might hold with her; as if—the thought passed through my mind—I were dying too.

"I always observed that their pride bitterly resented the younger brother's (as I call him) having crossed swords with a peasant, and that peasant a boy. The only consideration that appeared to affect the mind of either of them was the consideration that this was highly degrading to the family, and was ridiculous. As often as I caught the younger brother's eyes, their expression reminded me that he disliked me deeply, for knowing what I knew from the boy. He was smoother and more polite to me than the elder; but I saw this. I also saw that I was an incumbrance in the mind of the elder, too.

"My patient died, two hours before midnight—at a time, by my watch, answering almost to the minute when I had first seen her. I was alone with her, when her forlorn young head drooped gently on one side, and all her earthly wrongs and sorrows ended.

"The brothers were waiting in a room down-stairs, impatient to ride away. I had heard them, alone at the bedside, striking their boots with their riding-whips, and loitering up and down.

"'At last she is dead?' said the elder, when I went in.

"'She is dead,' said I.

"'I congratulate you, my brother,' were his words as he turned round.

"He had before offered me money, which I had postponed taking. He now gave me a rouleau of gold. I took it from his hand, but laid it on the table. I had considered the question, and had resolved to accept nothing.

"'Pray excuse me,' said I. 'Under the circumstances, no.'

"They exchanged looks, but bent their heads to me as I bent mine to them, and we parted without another word on either side. * * * *

"I am weary, weary, weary—worn down by misery. I cannot read what I have written with this gaunt hand.

"Early in the morning, the rouleau of gold was left at my door in a little box, with my name on the outside. From the first, I had anxiously considered what I ought to do. I decided, that day, to write privately to the Minister, stating the nature of the two cases to which I had been summoned, and the place to which I had gone: in effect, stating all the circumstances. I knew what Court influence was, and what the immunities of the Nobles were, and I expected that the matter would never be heard of; but, I wished to relieve my own mind. I had kept the matter a profound secret, even from my wife; and this, too, I resolved to state in my letter. I had no apprehension whatever of my real danger; but I was conscious that there might be danger for others, if others were compromised by possessing the knowledge that I possessed.

"I was much engaged that day, and could not complete my letter that night. I rose long before my usual time next morning to finish it. It was the last day of the year. The letter was lying before me just completed, when I was told that a lady waited, who wished to see me. * * * *

"I am growing more and more unequal to the task I have set myself. It is so cold, so dark, my senses are so benumbed, and the gloom upon me is so dreadful.

"The lady was young, engaging, and handsome, but not

marked for long life. She was in great agitation. She presented herself to me as the wife of the Marquis St. Evrémonde. I connected the title by which the boy had addressed the elder brother, with the initial letter embroidered on the scarf, and had no difficulty in arriving at the conclusion that I had seen that nobleman very lately.

"My memory is still accurate, but I cannot write the words of our conversation. I suspect that I am watched more closely than I was, and I know not at what times I may be watched. She had in part suspected, and in part discovered, the main facts of the cruel story, of her husband's share in it, and my being resorted to. She did not know that the girl was dead. Her hope had been, she said in great distress, to show her, in secret, a woman's sympathy. Her hope had been to avert the wrath of Heaven from a House that had long been hateful to the suffering many.

"She had reasons for believing that there was a young sister living, and her greatest desire was, to help that sister. I could tell her nothing but that there was such a sister; beyond that, I knew nothing. Her inducement to come to me, relying on my confidence, had been the hope that I could tell her the name and place of abode. Whereas, to this wretched hour I am ignorant of both. * * * *

"These scraps of paper fail me. One was taken from me, with a warning, yesterday. I must finish my record to-day.

"She was a good, compassionate lady, and not happy in her marriage. How could she be! The brother distrusted and disliked her, and his influence was all opposed to her; she stood in dread of him, and in dread of her husband too. When I handed her down to the door, there was a child, a pretty boy from two to three years old, in her carriage.

"'For his sake, Doctor,' she said, pointing to him in tears, 'I would do all I can to make what poor amends I can. He will never prosper in his inheritance otherwise. I have a presentiment that if no other innocent atonement is made for this, it will one day be required of him. What I have left to call my own—it is little beyond the worth of a few jewels—I will make it the first charge of his life to bestow, with the compassion and lamenting of his dead mother, on this injured family, if the sister can be discovered.'

"She kissed the boy, and said, caressing him, 'It is for thine own dear sake. Thou wilt be faithful, little Charles?' The child answered her bravely, 'Yes!' I kissed her hand, and she took him in her arms, and went away caressing him. I never saw her more.

"As she had mentioned her husband's name in the faith that I knew it, I added no mention of it to my letter. I sealed my letter, and, not trusting it out of my own hands, delivered it myself that day.

"That night, the last night of the year, towards nine o'clock, a man in a black dress rang at my gate, demanded to see me, and softly followed my servant, Ernest Defarge, a youth, up-stairs. When my servant came into the room where I sat with my wife—O my wife, beloved of my heart! My fair young English wife!—we saw the man, who was supposed to be at the gate, standing silent behind him.

"An urgent case in the Rue St. Honoré, he said. It would not detain me, he had a coach in waiting.

"It brought me here, it brought me to my grave. When I was clear of the house, a black muffler was drawn tightly over my mouth from behind, and my arms were pinioned.

The two brothers crossed the road from a dark corner, and identified me with a single gesture. The Marquis took from his pocket the letter I had written, showed it me, burnt it in the light of a lantern that was held, and extinguished the ashes with his foot. Not a word was spoken. I was brought here, I was brought to my living grave.

"If it had pleased GOD to put it in the hard heart of either of the brothers, in all these frightful years, to grant me any tidings of my dearest wife—so much as to let me know by a word whether alive or dead—I might have thought that He had not quite abandoned them. But, now I believe that the mark of the red cross is fatal to them, and that they have no part in His mercies. And them and their descendants, to the last of their race, I, Alexandre Manette, unhappy prisoner, do this last night of the year 1767, in my unbearable agony, denounce to the times when all these things shall be answered for. I denounce them to Heaven and to earth."

A terrible sound arose when the reading of this document was done. A sound of craving and eagerness that had nothing articulate in it but blood. The narrative called up the most revengeful passions of the time, and there was not a head in the nation but must have dropped before it.

Little need, in presence of that tribunal and that auditory, to show how the Defarges had not made the paper public, with the other captured Bastille memorials borne in procession, and had kept it, biding their time. Little need to show that this detested family name had long been anathematised by Saint Antoine, and was wrought into the fatal register. The man never trod ground whose virtues and services would have sustained him in that place that day, against such denunciation.

And all the worse for the doomed man, that the denouncer was a well-known citizen, his own attached friend, the father of his wife. One of the frenzied aspirations of the populace was, for imitations of the questionable public virtues of antiquity, and for sacrifices and self-immolations on the people's altar. Therefore when the President said (else had his own head quivered on his shoulders), that the good physician of the Republic would deserve better still of the Republic by rooting out an obnoxious family of Aristocrats, and would doubtless feel a sacred glow and joy in making his daughter a widow and her child an orphan, there was wild excitement, patriotic fervour, not a touch of human sympathy.

"Much influence around him, has that Doctor?" murmured Madame Defarge, smiling to The Vengeance. "Save him now, my Doctor, save him!"

At every juryman's vote, there was a roar. Another and another. Roar and roar.

Unanimously voted. At heart and by descent an Aristocrat, an enemy of the Republic, a notorious oppressor of the People. Back to the Conciergerie, and Death within four-and-twenty hours!

CHAPTER XI.

DUSK.

THE wretched wife of the innocent man thus doomed to die, fell under the sentence, as if she had been mortally stricken. But, she uttered no sound; and so strong was the voice within her, representing that it was she of all the world who must uphold him in his misery and not augment it, that it quickly raised her, even from that shock.

The Judges having to take part in a public demonstration out of doors, the tribunal adjourned. The quick noise and movement of the court's emptying itself by many passages had not ceased, when Lucie stood stretching out her arms towards her husband, with nothing in her face but love and consolation.

"If I might touch him! If I might embrace him once! O, good citizens, if you would have so much compassion for us!"

There was but a gaoler left, along with two of the four men who had taken him last night, and Barsad. The people had all poured out to the show in the streets. Barsad proposed to the rest, "Let her embrace him then; it is but a moment." It was silently acquiesced in, and they passed her over the seats in the hall to a raised place, where he, by leaning over the dock, could fold her in his arms.

"Farewell, dear darling of my soul. My parting blessing on my love. We shall meet again, where the weary are at rest!"

They were her husband's words, as he held her to his bosom.

"I can bear it, dear Charles. I am supported from above: don't suffer for me. A parting blessing for our child."

"I send it to her by you. I kiss her by you. I say farewell to her by you."

"My husband. No! A moment!" He was tearing himself apart from her. "We shall not be separated long. I feel that this will break my heart by-and-bye; but I will do my duty while I can, and when I leave her, God will raise up friends for her, as He did for me."

Her father had followed her, and would have fallen on his knees to both of them, but that Darnay put out a hand and seized him, crying:

"No, no! What have you done, what have you done, that you should kneel to us! We know now, what a struggle you made of old. We know now, what you underwent when you suspected my descent, and when you knew it. We know now, the natural antipathy you strove against, and conquered, for her dear sake. We thank you with all our hearts, and all our love and duty. Heaven be with you!"

Her father's only answer was to draw his hands through his white hair, and wring them with a shriek of anguish.

"It could not be otherwise," said the prisoner. "All things have worked together as they have fallen out. It was the always-vain endeavour to discharge my poor mother's trust that first brought my fatal presence near you. Good could never come of such evil, a happier end was not in nature to so unhappy a beginning. Be comforted, and forgive me. Heaven bless you!"

As he was drawn away, his wife released him, and stood looking after him with her hands touching one another in the attitude of prayer, and with a radiant look upon her face, in which there was even a comforting smile. As he went out at the prisoners' door, she turned, laid her head lovingly on her father's breast, tried to speak to him, and fell at his feet.

Then, issuing from the obscure corner from which he had never moved, Sydney Carton came and took her up. Only her father and Mr. Lorry were with her. His arm trembled as it raised her, and supported her head. Yet, there was an air about him that was not all of pity—that had a flush of pride in it.

"Shall I take her to a coach? I shall never feel her weight."

He carried her lightly to the door, and laid her tenderly down in a coach. Her father and their old friend got into it, and he took his seat beside the driver.

When they arrived at the gateway where he had paused in the dark not many hours before, to picture to himself on which of the rough stones of the street her feet had trodden, he lifted her again, and carried her up the staircase to their rooms. There, he laid her down on a couch, where her child and Miss Pross wept over her.

"Don't recall her to herself," he said, softly, to the latter, "she is better so. Don't revive her to consciousness, while she only faints."

"Oh, Carton, Carton, dear Carton!" cried little Lucie, springing up and throwing her arms passionately round him, in a burst of grief. "Now that you have come, I think you will do something to help mamma, something to save papa! O, look at her, dear Carton! Can you, of all the people who love her, bear to see her so?"

He bent over the child, and laid her blooming cheek against his face. He put her gently from him, and looked at her unconscious mother.

"Before I go," he said, and paused—"I may kiss her?"

It was remembered afterwards that when he bent down and touched her face with his lips, he murmured some words. The child, who was nearest to him, told them afterwards, and told her grandchildren when she was a handsome old lady, that she heard him say, "A life you love."

When he had gone out into the next room, he turned suddenly on Mr. Lorry and her father, who were following, and said to the latter:

"You had great influence but yesterday, Doctor Manette; let it at least be tried. These judges, and all the men in power, are very friendly to you, and very recognisant of your services; are they not?"

"Nothing connected with Charles was concealed from me. I had the strongest assurances that I should save him; and I did." He returned the answer in great trouble, and very slowly.

"Try them again. The hours between this and to-morrow afternoon are few and short, but try."

"I intend to try. I will not rest a moment."

"That's well. I have known such energy as yours do great things before now—though never," he added, with a smile and a sigh together, "such great things as this. But try! Of little worth as life is when we misuse it, it is worth that effort. It would cost nothing to lay down if it were not."

"I will go," said Doctor Manette, "to the Prosecutor and the President straight, and I will go to others whom it is better not to name. I will write too, and——But stay! There is a celebration in the streets, and no one will be accessible until dark."

"That's true. Well! It is a forlorn hope at the best, and not much the forlorner for being delayed till dark. I should like to know how you speed; though, mind! I expect nothing! When are you likely to have seen these dread powers, Doctor Manette?"

"Immediately after dark, I should hope. Within an hour or two from this."

"It will be dark soon after four. Let us stretch the hour or two. If I go to Mr. Lorry's at nine, shall I hear what you have done, either from our friend or from yourself?"

"Yes."

"May you prosper!"

Mr. Lorry followed Sydney to the outer door, and, touching him on the shoulder as he was going away, caused him to turn.

"I have no hope," said Mr. Lorry, in a low and sorrowful whisper.

"Nor have I."

"If any one of these men, or all of these men, were disposed to spare him—which is a large supposition; for what is his life, or any man's to them!—I doubt if they durst spare him after the demonstration in the court."

"And so do I. I heard the fall of the axe in that sound."

Mr. Lorry leaned his arm upon the door-post, and bowed his face upon it.

"Don't despond," said Carton, very gently; "don't grieve. I encouraged Doctor Manette in this idea, because I felt that it might one day be consolatory to her. Otherwise, she might think 'his life was wantonly thrown away or wasted,' and that might trouble her."

"Yes, yes, yes," returned Mr. Lorry, drying his eyes, "you are right. But he will perish; there is no real hope."

"Yes. He will perish: there is no real hope," echoed Carton. And walked with a settled step, down-stairs.

CHAPTER XII.

DARKNESS.

SYDNEY CARTON paused in the street, not quite decided where to go. "At Tellson's banking-house at nine," he said, with a musing face. "Shall I do well, in the mean time, to show myself? I think so. It is best that these people should know there is such a man as I here; it is a sound precaution, and may be a necessary preparation. But care, care, care! Let me think it out!"

Checking his steps which had begun to tend towards an object, he took a turn or two in the already darkening street, and traced the thought in his mind to its possible consequences. His first impression was confirmed. "It is best," he said, finally resolved, "that these people should know there is such a man as I here." And he turned his face towards Saint Antoine.

Defarge had described himself, that day, as the keeper of a wine-shop in the Saint Antoine suburb. It was not difficult for one who knew the city well, to find his house without asking any question. Having ascertained its situation, Carton came out of those closer streets again, and dined at a place of refreshment and fell sound asleep after dinner. For the first time in many years, he had no strong drink. Since last night he had taken nothing but a little light thin wine, and last night he had dropped the brandy slowly down on Mr. Lorry's hearth like a man who had done with it.

It was as late as seven o'clock when he awoke refreshed, and went out into the streets again. As he passed along towards Saint Antoine, he stopped at a shop-window where there was a mirror, and slightly altered the disordered arrangement of his loose cravat, and his coat-collar, and his wild hair. This done, he went on direct to Defarge's, and went in.

There happened to be no customer in the shop but Jacques Three, of the restless fingers and the croaking voice. This man, whom he had seen upon the Jury, stood drinking at the little counter, in conversation with the Defarges, man and wife. The Vengeance assisted in the conversation, like a regular member of the establishment.

As Carton walked in, took his seat and asked (in very indifferent French) for a small measure of wine, Madame Defarge cast a careless glance at him, and then a keener, and then a keener, and then advanced to him herself, and asked him what it was he had ordered.

He repeated what he had already said.

"English?" asked Madame Defarge, inquisitively raising her dark eyebrows.

After looking at her, as if the sound of even a single French word were slow to express itself to him, he answered, in his former strong foreign accent. "Yes, madame, yes. I am English!"

Madame Defarge returned to her counter to get the wine, and, as he took up a Jacobin journal and feigned to pore over it puzzling out its meaning, he heard her say, "I swear to you, like Evrémonde!"

Defarge brought him the wine, and gave him Good Evening.

"How?"

"Good evening."

"Oh! Good evening, citizen," filling his glass. "Ah! and good wine. I drink to the Republic."

Defarge went back to the counter, and said, "Certainly, a little like." Madame sternly retorted, "I tell you a good deal like." Jacques Three pacifically remarked, "He is so much in your mind, see you, madame." The amiable Vengeance added, with a laugh "Yes, my faith! And you are looking forward with so much pleasure to seeing him once more to-morrow!"

Carton followed the lines and words of his paper, with a slow forefinger, and with a studious and absorbed face. They were all leaning their arms on the counter close together, speaking low. After a silence of a few moments, during which they all looked towards him without disturbing his outward attention from the Jacobin editor, they resumed their conversation.

"It is true what madame says," observed Jacques Three. "Why stop? There is great force in that. Why stop?"

"Well, well," reasoned Defarge, "but one must stop somewhere. After all, the question is still where?"

"At extermination," said madame.

"Magnificent!" croaked Jacques Three. The Vengeance, also, highly approved.

"Extermination is good doctrine, my wife," said Defarge, rather troubled; "in general, I say nothing against it. But this Doctor has suffered much; you have seen him to-day; you have observed his face when the paper was read."

"I have observed his face!" repeated madame, contemptuously and angrily. "Yes. I have observed his face. I have observed his face to be not the face of a true friend of the Republic. Let him take care of his face!"

"And you have observed, my wife," said Defarge, in a deprecatory manner, "the anguish of his daughter, which must be a dreadful anguish to him!"

"I have observed his daughter," repeated madame;

"yes, I have observed his daughter, more times than one. I have observed her to-day, and I have observed her other days. I have observed her in the court, and I have observed her in the street by the prison. Let me but lift my finger——!" She seemed to raise it (the listener's eyes were always on his paper), and to let it fall with a rattle on the ledge before her, as if the axe had dropped.

"The citizeness is superb!" croaked the Juryman.

"She is an Angel!" said The Vengeance, and embraced her.

"As to thee," pursued madame, implacably, addressing her husband, "if it depended on thee—which, happily, it does not—thou wouldst rescue this man even now."

"No!" protested Defarge. "Not if to lift this glass would do it! But I would leave the matter there. I say, stop there."

"See you then, Jacques," said Madame Defarge, wrathfully; "and see you, too, my little Vengeance; see you both! Listen! For other crimes as tyrants and oppressors, I have this race a long time on my register, doomed to destruction and extermination. Ask my husband, is that so?"

"It is so," assented Defarge, without being asked.

"In the beginning of the great days, when the Bastille falls, he finds this paper of to-day, and he brings it home, and in the middle of the night when this place is clear and shut, we read it, here on this spot, by the light of this lamp. Ask him, is that so."

"It is so," assented Defarge.

"That night, I tell him, when the paper is read through, and the lamp is burnt out, and the day is gleaming in above those shutters and between those iron bars, that I have now a secret to communicate. Ask him, is that so."

"It is so," assented Defarge again.

"I communicate to him that secret. I smite this bosom with these two hands as I smite it now, and I tell him, 'Defarge, I was brought up among the fishermen of the sea-shore, and that peasant family so injured by the two Evrémonde brothers, as that Bastille paper describes, is my family. Defarge, that sister of the mortally wounded boy upon the ground was my sister, that husband was my sister's husband, that unborn child was their child, that brother was my brother, that father was my father, those dead are my dead, and that summons to answer for those things descends to me!' Ask him, is that so."

"It is so," assented Defarge once more.

"Then tell Wind and Fire where to stop," returned madame; "but don't tell me."

Both her hearers derived a horrible enjoyment from the deadly nature of her wrath—the listener could feel how white she was, without seeing her—and both highly commended it. Defarge, a weak minority, interposed a few words for the memory of the compassionate wife of the Marquis; but only elicited from his own wife a repetition of her last reply. "Tell the Wind and the Fire where to stop; not me!"

Customers entered, and the group was broken up. The English customer paid for what he had had, perplexedly counted his change, and asked, as a stranger, to be directed towards the National Palace. Madame Defarge took him to the door, and put her arm on his, in pointing out the road. The English customer was not without his reflections then, that it might be a good deed to seize that arm, lift it, and strike under it sharp and deep.

But, he went his way, and was soon swallowed up in the shadow of the prison wall. At the appointed hour, he emerged from it to present himself in Mr. Lorry's room again, where he found the old gentleman walking to and fro in restless anxiety. He said he had been with Lucie until just now, and had only left her for a few minutes, to come and keep his appointment. Her father had not been seen, since he quitted the banking-house towards four o'clock. She had some faint hopes that his mediation might save Charles, but they were very slight. He had been more than five hours gone: where could he be?

Mr. Lorry waited until ten; but, Doctor Manette not returning, and he being unwilling to leave Lucie any longer, it was arranged that he should go back to her, and come to the banking-house again at midnight. In the meanwhile, Carton would wait alone by the fire for the Doctor.

He waited and waited, and the clock struck twelve; but Doctor Manette did not come back. Mr. Lorry returned, and found no tidings of him, and brought none. Where could he be?

They were discussing this question, and were almost building up some weak structure of hope on his prolonged absence, when they heard him on the stairs. The instant he entered the room, it was plain that all was lost.

Whether he had really been to any one, or whether he had been all that time traversing the streets, was never known. As he stood staring at them, they asked him no question, for his face told them everything.

"I cannot find it," said he, "and I must have it. Where is it?"

His head and throat were bare, and, as he spoke with a helpless look straying all around, he took his coat off, and let it drop on the floor.

"Where is my bench? I have been looking everywhere for my bench, and I can't find it. What have they done with my work? Time presses: I must finish those shoes."

They looked at one another, and their hearts died within them.

"Come, come!" said he, in a whimpering miserable way; "let me get to work. Give me my work."

Receiving no answer, he tore his hair, and beat his feet upon the ground, like a distracted child.

"Don't torture a poor forlorn wretch," he implored them, with a dreadful cry; "but give me my work! What is to become of us, if those shoes are not done to-night?"

Lost, utterly lost!

It was so clearly beyond hope to reason with him, or try to restore him,—that—as if by agreement—they each put a hand upon his shoulder, and soothed him to sit down before the fire, with a promise that he should have his work presently. He sank into the chair, and brooded over the embers, and shed tears. As if all that had happened since the garret time were a momentary fancy, or a dream, Mr. Lorry saw him shrink into the exact figure that Defarge had had in keeping.

Affected, and impressed with terror as they both were, by this spectacle of ruin, it was not a time to yield to such emotions. His lonely daughter, bereft of her final hope and reliance, appealed to them both too strongly. Again, as if by agreement, they looked at one another with one meaning in their faces. Carton was the first to speak:

"The last chance is gone: it was not much. Yes; he had better be taken to her. But, before you go, will you, for a moment, steadily attend to me? Don't ask me why

I make the stipulations I am going to make, and exact the promise I am going to exact; I have a reason—a good one."

"I do not doubt it," answered Mr. Lorry. "Say on."

The figure in the chair between them, was all the time monotonously rocking itself to and fro, and moaning. They spoke in such a tone as they would have used if they had been watching by a sick-bed in the night.

Carton stooped to pick up the coat, which lay almost entangling his feet. As he did so, a small case in which the Doctor was accustomed to carry the lists of his day's duties, fell lightly on the floor. Carton took it up, and there was a folded paper in it. "We should look at this! he said. Mr. Lorry nodded his consent. He opened it, and exclaimed, "Thank God!"

"What is it?" asked Mr. Lorry, eagerly.

"A moment! Let me speak of it in its place. First," he put his hand in his coat, and took another paper from it, "that is the certificate which enables me to pass out of this city. Look at it. You see—Sydney Carton, an Englishman?"

Mr. Lorry held it open in his hand, gazing in his earnest face.

"Keep it for me until to-morrow. I shall see him to-morrow, you remember, and I had better not take it into the prison."

"Why not?"

"I don't know; I prefer not to do so. Now, take this paper that Doctor Manette has carried about him. It is a similar certificate, enabling him and his daughter and her child, at any time, to pass the barrier and the frontier! You see?"

"Yes!"

"Perhaps he obtained it as his last and utmost precaution against evil yesterday. When is it dated? But no matter; don't stay to look; put it up carefully with mine and your own. Now, observe! I never doubted until within this hour or two, that he had, or could have such a paper. It is good, until recalled. But it may be soon recalled, and, I have reason to think, will be."

"They are not in danger?"

"They are in great danger. They are in danger of denunciation by Madame Defarge. I know it from her own lips. I have overheard words of that woman's, to-night, which have presented their danger to me in strong colours. I have lost no time, and since then, I have seen the spy. He confirms me. He knows that a wood-sawyer, living by the prison-wall, is under the control of the Defarges, and has been rehearsed by Madame Defarge as to his having seen Her"—he never mentioned Lucie's name—"making signs and signals to prisoners. It is easy to foresee that the pretence will be the common one, a prison plot, and that it will involve her life—and perhaps her child's —and perhaps her father's—for both have been seen with her at that place. Don't look so horrified. You will save them all."

"Heaven grant I may, Carton! But how?"

"I am going to tell you how. It will depend on you, and it could depend on no better man. This new denunciation will certainly not take place until after to-morrow; probably not until two or three days afterwards; more probably a week afterwards. You know it is a capital crime, to mourn for, or sympathise with, a victim of the Guillotine. She and her father would unquestionably be guilty of this crime, and this woman (the inveteracy of whose pursuit cannot be described) would wait to add that strength to her case, and make herself doubly sure. You follow me?"

"So attentively, and with so much confidence in what you say, that for the moment I lose sight," touching the back of the Doctor's chair, "even of this distress."

"You have money, and can buy the means of travelling to the sea-coast as quickly as the journey can be made. Your preparations have been completed for some days, to return to England. Early to-morrow have your horses ready, so that they may be in starting trim at two o'clock in the afternoon."

"It shall be done!"

His manner was so fervent and inspiring, that Mr. Lorry caught the flame, and was as quick as youth.

"You are a noble heart. Did I say we could depend upon no better man? Tell her, to-night, what you know of her danger as involving her child and her father. Dwell upon that, for she would lay her own fair head beside her husband's cheerfully." He faltered for an instant; then went on as before. "For the sake of her child and her father, press upon her the necessity of leaving Paris, with them and you, at that hour. Tell her that it was her husband's last arrangement. Tell her that more depends upon it than she dare believe, or hope. You think that her father, even in this sad state, will submit himself to her; do you not?"

"I am sure of it."

"I thought so. Quietly and steadily have all these arrangements made in the courtyard here, even to the taking of your own seat in the carriage. The moment I come to you, take me in, and drive away."

"I understand that I wait for you under all circumstances?"

"You have my certificate in your hand with the rest, you know, and will reserve my place. Wait for nothing but to have my place occupied, and then for England!"

"Why, then," said Mr. Lorry, grasping his eager but so firm and steady hand, "it does not all depend on one old man, but I shall have a young and ardent man at my side."

"By the help of Heaven you shall! Promise me solemnly that nothing will influence you to alter the course on which we now stand pledged to one another."

"Nothing, Carton."

"Remember these words to-morrow: change the course, or delay in it—for any reason—and no life can possibly be saved, and many lives must inevitably be sacrificed."

"I will remember them. I hope to do my part faithfully."

"And I hope to do mine. Now, good bye!"

Though he said it with a grave smile of earnestness, and though he even put the old man's hand to his lips, he did not part from him then. He helped him so far to arouse the rocking figure before the dying embers, as to get a cloak and hat put upon it, and to tempt it forth to find where the bench and work were hidden that it still moaningly besought to have. He walked on the other side of it and protected it to the courtyard of the house where the afflicted heart—so happy in the memorable time when he had revealed his own desolate heart to it—outwatched the awful night. He entered the courtyard and remained there for a few moments alone, looking up at the light in the window of her room. Before he went away, he breathed a blessing towards it, and a Farewell.

CHAPTER XIII.

FIFTY-TWO.

In the black prison of the Conciergerie, the doomed of the day awaited their fate. They were in number as the weeks of the year. Fifty-two were to roll that afternoon on the life-tide of the city to the boundless everlasting sea. Before their cells were quit of them, new occupants were appointed; before their blood ran into the blood spilled yesterday, the blood that was to mingle with theirs to-morrow was already set apart.

Two score and twelve were told off. From the farmer-general of seventy, whose riches could not buy his life, to the seamstress of twenty, whose poverty and obscurity could not save her. Physical diseases, engendered in the vices and neglects of men, will seize on victims of all degrees; and the frightful moral disorder, born of unspeakable suffering, intolerable oppression, and heartless indifference, smote equally without distinction.

Charles Darnay, alone in a cell, had sustained himself with no flattering delusion since he came to it from the Tribunal. In every line of the narrative he had heard, he had heard his condemnation. He had fully comprehended that no personal influence could possibly save him, that he was virtually sentenced by the millions, and that units could avail him nothing.

Nevertheless, it was not easy, with the face of his beloved wife fresh before him, to compose his mind to what it must bear. His hold on life was strong, and it was very, very hard, to loosen; by gradual efforts and degrees unclosed a little here, it clenched the tighter there; and when he brought his strength to bear on that hand and it yielded, this was closed again. There was a hurry, too, in all his thoughts, a turbulent and heated working of his heart, that contended against resignation. If, for a moment, he did feel resigned, then his wife and child who had to live after him, seemed to protest and to make it a selfish thing.

But, all this was at first. Before long, the consideration that there was no disgrace in the fate he must meet, and that numbers went the same road wrongfully, and trod it firmly every day, sprang up to stimulate him. Next followed the thought that much of the future peace of mind enjoyable by the dear ones, depended on his quiet fortitude. So, by degrees he calmed into the better state, when he could raise his thoughts much higher, and draw comfort down.

Before it had set in dark on the night of his condemnation, he had travelled thus far on his last way. Being allowed to purchase the means of writing, and a light, he sat down to write until such time as the prison lamps should be extinguished.

He wrote a long letter to Lucie, showing her that he had known nothing of her father's imprisonment, until he had heard of it from herself, and that he had been as ignorant as she of his father's and uncle's responsibility for that misery, until the paper had been read. He had already explained to her that his concealment from herself of the name he had relinquished, was the one condition—fully intelligible now—that her father had attached to their betrothal, and was the one promise he had still exacted on the morning of their marriage. He entreated her, for her father's sake, never to seek to know whether her father had become oblivious of the existence of the paper, or had had it recalled to him (for the moment, or for good), by the story of the Tower, on that old Sunday under the dear old plane-tree in the garden. If he had preserved any definite remembrance of it, there could be no doubt that he had supposed it destroyed with the Bastille, when he had found no mention of it among the relics of prisoners which the populace had discovered there, and which had been described to all the world. He besought her—though he added that he knew it was needless—to console her father, by impressing him through every tender means she could think of, with the truth that he had done nothing for which he could justly reproach himself, but had uniformly forgotten himself for their joint sakes. Next to her preservation of his own last grateful love and blessing, and her overcoming of her sorrow, to devote herself to their dear child, he adjured her, as they would meet in Heaven, to comfort her father.

To her father himself, he wrote in the same strain; but, he told her father that he expressly confided his wife and child to his care. And he told him this, very strongly, with the hope of rousing him from any despondency or dangerous retrospect towards which he foresaw he might be tending.

To Mr. Lorry, he commended them all, and explained his worldly affairs. That done, with many added sentences of grateful friendship and warm attachment, all was done. He never thought of Carton. His mind was so full of the others, that he never once thought of him.

He had time to finish these letters before the lights were put out. When he lay down on his straw bed, he thought he had done with this world.

But, it beckoned him back in his sleep, and showed itself in shining forms. Free and happy, back in the old house in Soho (though it had nothing in it like the real house), unaccountably released and light of heart, he was with Lucie again, and she told him it was all a dream, and he had never gone away. A pause of forgetfulness, and then he had even suffered, and had come back to her, dead and at peace, and yet there was no difference in him. Another pause of oblivion, and he awoke in the sombre morning, unconscious where he was or what had happened, until it flashed upon his mind, "this is the day of my death!"

Thus, had he come through the hours, to the day when the fifty-two heads were to fall. And now, while he was composed, and hoped that he could meet the end with quiet heroism, a new action began in his waking thoughts, which was very difficult to master.

He had never seen the instrument that was to terminate his life. How high it was from the ground, how many steps it had, where he would be stood, how he would be touched, whether the touching hands would be dyed red, which way his face would be turned, whether he would be the first, or might be the last: these and many similar questions, in nowise directed by his will, obtruded themselves over and over again, countless times. Neither were they connected with fear: he was conscious of no fear. Rather, they originated in a strange besetting desire to know what to do when the time came; a desire gigantically disproportionate to the few swift moments to which it referred; a wondering that was more like the wondering of some other spirit within his, than his own.

The hours went on as he walked to and fro, and the

clocks struck the numbers he would never hear again. Nine gone for ever, ten gone for ever, eleven gone for ever, twelve coming on to pass away. After a hard contest with that eccentric action of thought which had last perplexed him, he had got the better of it. He walked up and down, softly repeating their names to himself. The worst of the strife was over. He could walk up and down, free from distracting fancies, praying for himself and for them.

Twelve gone for ever.

He had been apprised that the final hour was Three, and he knew he would be summoned some time earlier, inasmuch as the tumbrils jolted heavily and slowly through the streets. Therefore, he resolved to keep Two before his mind, as the hour, and so to strengthen himself in the interval that he might be able, after that time, to strengthen others.

Walking regularly to and fro with his arms folded on his breast, a very different man from the prisoner, who had walked to and fro at La Force, he heard One struck away from him, without surprise. The hour had measured like most other hours. Devoutly thankful to Heaven for his recovered self-possession, he thought, "There is but another now," and turned to walk again.

Footsteps in the stone passage outside the door. He stopped.

The key was put in the lock, and turned. Before the door was opened, or as it opened, a man said in a low voice, in English: "He has never seen me here; I have kept out of his way. Go you in alone; I wait near. Lose no time!"

The door was quickly opened and closed, and there stood before him face to face, quiet, intent upon him, with the light of a smile on his features, and a cautionary finger on his lip, Sydney Carton.

There was something so bright and remarkable in his look, that, for the first moment, the prisoner misdoubted him to be an apparition of his own imagining. But, he spoke, and it was his voice; he took the prisoner's hand, and it was his real grasp.

"Of all the people upon earth, you least expected to see me?" he said.

"I could not believe it to be you. I can scarcely believe it now. You are not"—the apprehension came suddenly into his mind—"a prisoner?"

"No. I am accidentally possessed of a power over one of the keepers here, and in virtue of it I stand before you. I come from her—your wife, dear Darnay."

The prisoner wrung his hand.

"I bring you a request from her."

"What is it?"

"A most earnest, pressing, and emphatic entreaty, addressed to you in the most pathetic tones of the voice so dear to you, that you well remember."

The prisoner turned his face partly aside.

"You have no time to ask me why I bring it, or what it means; I have no time to tell you. You must comply with it—take off those boots you wear, and draw on these of mine."

There was a chair against the wall of the cell, behind the prisoner. Carton, pressing forward, had already, with the speed of lightning, got him down into it, and stood over him, barefoot.

"Draw on these boots of mine. Put your hands to them; put your will to them. Quick!"

"Carton, there is no escaping from this place; it never

can be done. You will only die with me. It is madness."

"It would be madness if I asked you to escape; but do I? When I ask you to pass out at that door, tell me it is madness and remain here. Change that cravat for this of mine, that coat for this of mine. While you do it, let me take this ribbon from your hair, and shake out your hair like this of mine!"

With wonderful quickness, and with a strength both of will and action, that appeared quite supernatural, he forced all these changes upon him. The prisoner was like a young child in his hands.

"Carton! Dear Carton! It is madness. It cannot be accomplished, it never can be done, it has been attempted, and has always failed. I implore you not to add your death to the bitterness of mine."

"Do I ask you, my dear Darnay, to pass the door? When I ask that, refuse. There are pen and ink and paper on this table. Is your hand steady enough to write?"

"It was when you came in."

"Steady it again, and write what I shall dictate. Quick, friend, quick!"

Pressing his hand to his bewildered head, Darnay sat down at the table. Carton, with his right hand in his breast, stood close beside him.

"Write exactly as I speak."

"To whom do I address it?"

"To no one." Carton still had his hand in his breast.

"Do I date it?"

"No."

The prisoner looked up, at each question. Carton, standing over him with his hand in his breast, looked down.

"'If you remember,'" said Carton, dictating, "'the words that passed between us, long ago, you will readily comprehend this when you see it. You do remember them, I know. It is not in your nature to forget them.'"

He was drawing his hand from his breast; the prisoner chancing to look up in his hurried wonder as he wrote, the hand stopped, closing upon something.

"Have you written 'forget them'?" Carton asked.

"I have. Is that a weapon in your hand?"

"No; I am not armed."

"What is it in your hand?"

"You shall know directly. Write on; there are but a few words more." He dictated again. "'I am thankful that the time has come, when I can prove them. That I do so is no subject for regret or grief.'" As he said these words with his eyes fixed on the writer, his hand slowly and softly moved down close to the writer's face.

The pen dropped from Darnay's fingers on the table, and he looked about him vacantly.

"What vapour is that?" he asked.

"Vapour?"

"Something that crossed me?"

"I am conscious of nothing; there can be nothing here. Take up the pen and finish. Hurry, hurry!"

As if his memory were impaired, or his faculties disordered, the prisoner made an effort to rally his attention. As he looked at Carton with clouded eyes and with an altered manner of breathing, Carton—his hand again in his breast—looked steadily at him.

"Hurry, hurry!"

The prisoner bent over the paper, once more.

"'If it had been otherwise;'" Carton's hand was again

watchfully and softly stealing down; "'I never should have used the longer opportunity. If it had been otherwise;'" the hand was at the prisoner's face; "'I should but have had so much the more to answer for. If it had been otherwise——'" Carton looked at the pen and saw it was trailing off into unintelligible signs.

Carton's hand moved back to his breast no more. The prisoner sprang up with a reproachful look, but Carton's hand was close and firm at his nostrils, and Carton's left arm caught him round the waist. For a few seconds he faintly struggled with the man who had come to lay down his life for him; but, within a minute or so, he was stretched insensible on the ground.

Quickly, but with hands as true to the purpose as his heart was, Carton dressed himself in the clothes the prisoner had laid aside, combed back his hair, and tied it with the ribbon the prisoner had worn. Then, he softly called, "Enter there! Come in!" and the Spy presented himself.

"You see?" said Carton, looking up, as he kneeled on one knee beside the insensible figure, putting the paper in the breast: "is your hazard very great?"

"Mr. Carton," the Spy answered, with a timid snap of his fingers, "my hazard is not *that*, in the thick of business here, if you are true to the whole of your bargain."

"Don't fear me. I will be true to the death."

"You must be, Mr. Carton, if the tale of fifty-two is to be right. Being made right by you in that dress, I shall have no fear."

"Have no fear! I shall soon be out of the way of harming you, and the rest will soon be far from here, please God! Now, get assistance and take me to the coach."

"You?" said the Spy nervously.

"Him, man, with whom I have exchanged. You go out at the gate by which you brought me in?"

"Of course."

"I was weak and faint when you brought me in, and I am fainter now you take me out. The parting interview has overpowered me. Such a thing has happened here, often, and too often. Your life is in your own hands. Quick! Call assistance!"

"You swear not to betray me?" said the trembling Spy, as he paused for a last moment.

"Man, man!" returned Carton, stamping his foot; "have I sworn by no solemn vow already, to go through with this, that you waste the precious moments now? Take him yourself to the courtyard you know of, place him yourself in the carriage, show him yourself to Mr. Lorry, tell him yourself to give him no restorative but air, and to remember my words of last night, and his promise of last night, and drive away!"

The Spy withdrew, and Carton seated himself at the table, resting his forehead on his hands. The Spy returned immediately, with two men.

"How, then?" said one of them, contemplating the fallen figure. "So afflicted to find that his friend has drawn a prize in the lottery of Sainte Guillotine?"

"A good patriot," said the other, "could hardly have been more afflicted if the Aristocrat had drawn a blank."

They raised the unconscious figure, placed it on a litter they had brought to the door, and bent to carry it away.

"The time is short, Evrémonde," said the Spy, in a warning voice.

"I know it well," answered Carton. "Be careful of my friend, I entreat you, and leave me."

"Come, then, my children," said Barsad. "Lift him, and come away!"

The door closed, and Carton was left alone. Straining his powers of listening to the utmost, he listened for any sound that might denote suspicion or alarm. There was none. Keys turned, doors clashed, footsteps passed along distant passages: no cry was raised, or hurry made, that seemed unusual. Breathing more freely in a little while, he sat down at the table, and listened again until the clock struck Two.

Sounds that he was not afraid of, for he divined their meaning, then began to be audible. Several doors were opened in succession, and finally his own. A gaoler, with a list in his hand, looked in, merely saying, "Follow me, Evrémonde!" and he followed into a large dark room, at a distance. It was a dark winter day, and what with the shadows within, and what with the shadows without, he could but dimly discern the others who were brought there to have their arms bound. Some were standing; some seated. Some were lamenting, and in restless motion; but, these were few. The great majority were silent and still, looking fixedly at the ground.

As he stood by the wall in a dim corner, while some of the fifty-two were brought in after him, one man stopped in passing, to embrace him, as having a knowledge of him. It thrilled him with a great dread of discovery; but the man went on. A very few moments after that, a young woman, with a slight girlish form, a sweet spare face in which there was no vestige of colour, and large widely opened patient eyes, rose from the seat where he had observed her sitting, and came to speak to him.

"Citizen Evrémonde," she said, touching him with her cold hand. "I am a poor little seamstress, who was with you in La Force."

He murmured for answer: "True. I forget what you were accused of?"

"Plots. Though the just Heaven knows that I am innocent of any. Is it likely? Who would think of plotting with a poor little weak creature like me?"

The forlorn smile with which she said it, so touched him, that tears started from his eyes.

"I am not afraid to die, Citizen Evrémonde, but I have done nothing. I am not unwilling to die, if the Republic which is to do so much good to us poor, will profit by my death; but I do not know how that can be, Citizen Evrémonde. Such a poor weak little creature!"

As the last thing on earth that his heart was to warm and soften to, it warmed and softened to this pitiable girl.

"I heard you were released, Citizen Evrémonde. I hoped it was true?"

"It was. But, I was again taken and condemned."

"If I may ride with you, Citizen Evrémonde, will you let me hold your hand? I am not afraid, but I am little and weak, and it will give me more courage."

As the patient eyes were lifted to his face, he saw a sudden doubt in them, and then astonishment. He pressed the work-worn, hunger-worn young fingers, and touched his lips.

"Are you dying for him?" she whispered.

"And his wife and child. Hush! Yes."

"O you will let me hold your brave hand, stranger?"

"Hush! Yes, my poor sister; to the last."

The same shadows that are falling on the prison, are

falling, in that same hour of the early afternoon, on the Barrier with the crowd about it, when a coach going out of Paris drives up to be examined.

"Who goes here? Whom have we within? Papers!" The papers are handed out, and read.

"Alexandre Manette. Physician. French. Which is he?"

This is he; this helpless, inarticulately murmuring, wandering old man pointed out.

"Apparently the Citizen-Doctor is not in his right mind? The Revolution-fever will have been too much for him?"

Greatly too much for him.

'Hah! Many suffer with it. Lucie. His daughter. French. Which is she?"

This is she.

"Apparently it must be. Lucie, the wife of Evrémonde; is it not?"

It is.

"Hah! Evrémonde has an assignation elsewhere. Lucie, her child. English. This is she?"

She and no other.

"Kiss me, child of Evrémonde. Now, thou hast kissed a good Republican; something new in thy family; remember it! Sydney Carton. Advocate. English. Which is he?"

He lies here, in this corner of the carriage. He, too, is pointed out.

"Apparently the English advocate is in a swoon?"

It is hoped he will recover in the fresher air. It is represented that he is not in strong health, and has separated sadly from a friend who is under the displeasure of the Republic.

"Is that all? It is not a great deal, that! Many are under the displeasure of the Republic, and must look out at the little window. Jarvis Lorry. Banker. English. Which is he?"

"I am he. Necessarily, being the last."

It is Jarvis Lorry who has replied to all the previous questions. It is Jarvis Lorry who has alighted and stands with his hand on the coach door, replying to a group of officials. They leisurely walk round the carriage and leisurely mount the box, to look at what little luggage it carries on the roof; the country-people hanging about, press nearer to the coach doors and greedily stare in; a little child, carried by its mother, has its short arm held out for it, that it may touch the wife of an aristocrat who has gone to the Guillotine.

"Behold your papers, Jarvis Lorry, countersigned."

"One can depart, citizen?"

"One can depart. Forward, my postilions! A good journey!"

"I salute you, citizens.—And the first danger passed!"

These are again the words of Jarvis Lorry, as he clasps his hands, and looks upward. There is terror in the carriage, there is weeping, there is the heavy breathing of the insensible traveller.

"Are we not going too slowly? Can they not be induced to go faster?" asks Lucie, clinging to the old man.

"It would seem like flight, my darling. I must not urge them too much; it would rouse suspicion."

"Look back, look back, and see if we are pursued!"

"The road is clear, my dearest. So far, we are not pursued."

Houses in twos and threes pass by us, solitary farms, ruinous buildings, dye-works, tanneries, and the like, open country, avenues of leafless trees. The hard uneven pavement is under us, the soft deep mud is on either side. Sometimes, we strike into the skirting mud, to avoid the stones that clatter us and shake us; sometimes, we stick in ruts and sloughs there. The agony of our impatience is then so great, that in our wild alarm and hurry we are for getting out and running—hiding—doing anything but stopping.

Out of the open country, in again among ruinous buildings, solitary farms, dye-works, tanneries, and the like, cottages in twos and threes, avenues of leafless trees. Have these men deceived us, and taken us back by another road? Is not this the same place twice over? Thank Heaven, no. A village. Look back, look back, and see if we are pursued! Hush! the posting-house.

Leisurely, our four horses are taken out; leisurely, the coach stands in the little street, bereft of horses, and with no likelihood upon it of ever moving again; leisurely, the new horses come into visible existence, one by one; leisurely, the new postilions follow, sucking and plaiting the lashes of their whips; leisurely, the old postilions count their money, make wrong additions, and arrive at dissatisfied results. All the time, our overfraught hearts are beating at a rate that would far outstrip the fastest gallop of the fastest horses ever foaled.

At length the new postilions are in their saddles, and the old are left behind. We are through the village, up the hill, and down the hill, and on the low watery grounds. Suddenly, the postilions exchange speech with animated gesticulation, and the horses are pulled up, almost on their haunches. We are pursued?

"Ho! Within the carriage there. Speak then!"

"What is it?" asks Mr. Lorry, looking out at window.

"How many did they say?"

"I do not understand you."

"——At the last post. How many to the Guillotine to-day?"

"Fifty-two."

"I said so! A brave number! My fellow-citizen here would have it forty-two; ten more heads are worth having. The Guillotine goes handsomely. I love it. Hi forward. Whoop!"

The night comes on dark. He moves more; he is beginning to revive, and to speak intelligibly; he thinks they are still together; he asks him, by his name, what he has in his hand. O pity us, kind Heaven, and help us! Look out, look out, and see if we are pursued.

The wind is rushing after us, and the clouds are flying after us, and the moon is plunging after us, and the whole wild night is in pursuit of us; but, so far, we are pursued by nothing else.

CHAPTER XIV.

THE KNITTING DONE.

IN that same juncture of time when the Fifty-Two awaited their fate Madame Defarge held darkly ominous council with The Vengeance and Jacques Three of the Revolutionary Jury. Not in the wine-shop did Madame Defarge confer with these ministers, but in the shed of the wood-sawyer, erst a mender of roads. The sawyer himself did not participate in the conference, but abided at a little distance, like an outer satellite who was not to speak until required, or to offer an opinion until invited.

"But our Defarge," said Jacques Three, "is undoubtedly a good Republican? Eh?"

"There is no better," the voluble Vengeance protested in her shrill notes, "in France."

"Peace, little Vengeance," said Madame Defarge, laying her hand with a slight frown on her 'lieutenant's lips, "hear me speak. My husband, fellow-citizen, is a good Republican and a bold man; he has deserved well of the Republic, and possesses its confidence. But my husband has his weaknesses, and he is so weak as to relent towards this Doctor."

"It is a great pity," croaked Jacques Three, dubiously shaking his head, with his cruel fingers at his hungry mouth; "it is not quite like a good citizen; it is a thing to regret."

"See you," said madame, "I care nothing for this Doctor, I. He may wear his head or lose it, for any interest I have in him; it is all one to me. But, the Evrémonde people are to be exterminated, and the wife and child must follow the husband and father."

"She has a fine head for it," croaked Jacques Three. "I have seen blue eyes and golden hair there, and they looked charming when Samson held them up." Ogre that he was, he spoke like an epicure.

Madame Defarge cast down her eyes, and reflected a little.

"The child also," observed Jacques Three, with a meditative enjoyment of his words, "has golden hair and blue eyes. And we seldom have a child there. It is a pretty sight!"

"In a word," said Madame Defarge, coming out of her short abstraction, "I cannot trust my husband in this matter. Not only do I feel, since last night, that I dare not confide to him the details of my projects; but also I feel that if I delay, there is danger of his giving warning, and then they might escape."

"That must never be," croaked Jacques Three; "no one must escape. We have not half enough as it is. We ought to have six score a day."

"In a word," Madame Defarge went on, "my husband has not my reason for pursuing this family to annihilation, and I have not his reason for regarding this Doctor with any sensibility. I must act for myself, therefore. Come hither, little citizen."

The wood-sawyer, who held her in the respect, and himself in the submission, of mortal fear, advanced with his hand to his red cap.

"Touching those signals, little citizen," said Madame Defarge, sternly, "that she made to the prisoners; you are ready to bear witness to them this very day?"

"Ay, ay, why not!" cried the sawyer. "Every day, in all weathers, from two to four, always signalling, sometimes with the little one, sometimes without. I know what I know. I have seen with my eyes."

He made all manner of gestures while he spoke, as if in incidental imitation of some few of the great diversity of signals that he had never seen.

"Clearly plots," said Jacques Three. "Transparently!"

"There is no doubt of the Jury?" inquired Madame Defarge, letting her eyes turn to him with a gloomy smile.

"Rely upon the patriotic Jury, dear citizeness. I answer for my fellow-Jurymen."

"Now, let me see," said Madame Defarge, pondering again. "Yet once more! Can I spare this Doctor to my husband? I have no feeling either way. Can I spare him?"

"He would count as one head," observed Jacques Three, in a low voice. "We really have not heads enough; it would be a pity, I think."

"He was signalling with her when I saw her," argued Madame Defarge; "I cannot speak of one without the other; and I must not be silent, and trust the case wholly to him, this little citizen here. For, I am not a bad witness."

The Vengeance and Jacques Three vied with each other in their fervent protestations that she was the most admirable and marvellous of witnesses. The little citizen, not to be outdone, declared her to be a celestial witness.

"He must take his chance," said Madame Defarge. "No, I cannot spare him! You are engaged at three o'clock; you are going to see the batch of to-day executed. —You?"

The question was addressed to the wood-sawyer, who hurriedly replied in the affirmative: seizing the occasion to add that he was the most ardent of Republicans, and that he would be in effect the most desolate of Republicans, if anything prevented him from enjoying the pleasure of smoking his afternoon pipe in the contemplation of the droll national barber. He was so very demonstrative herein, that he might have been suspected (perhaps was, by the dark eyes that looked contemptuously at him out of Madame Defarge's head) of having his small individual fears for his own personal safety, every hour in the day.

"I," said madame, "am equally engaged at the same place. After it is over—say at eight to-night—come you to me, in Saint Antoine, and we will give information against these people at my Section."

The wood-sawyer said he would be proud and flattered to attend the citizeness. The citizeness looking at him, he became embarrassed, evaded her glance as a small dog would have done, retreated among his wood, and hid his confusion over the handle of his saw.

Madame Defarge beckoned the Juryman and The Vengeance a little nearer to the door, and there expounded her further views to them thus:

"She will now be at home, awaiting the moment of his death. She will be mourning and grieving. She will be in a state of mind to impeach the justice of the Republic. She will be full of sympathy with its enemies. I will go to her."

"What an admirable woman; what an adorable woman!" exclaimed Jacques Three, rapturously. "Ah, my cherished!" cried The Vengeance; and embraced her.

"Take you my knitting," said Madame Defarge, placing it in her lieutenant's hands, "and have it ready for me in my usual seat. Keep me my usual chair. Go you there, straight, for there will probably be a greater concourse than usual, to-day."

"I willingly obey the orders of my Chief," said The Vengeance with alacrity, and kissing her cheek. "You will not be late?"

"I shall be there before the commencement."

"And before the tumbrils arrive. Be sure you are there, my soul," said The Vengeance, calling after her, for she had already turned into the street, "before the tumbrils arrive!"

Madame Defarge slightly waved her hand, to imply that she heard, and might be relied upon to arrive in good time, and so went through the mud, and round the corner of the prison wall. The Vengeance and the Juryman, looking after her as she walked away, were highly appreciative of her fine figure, and her superb moral endowments.

There were many women at that time, upon whom the time laid a dreadfully disfiguring hand; but, there was not one among them more to be dreaded than this ruthless woman, now taking her way along the streets. Of a strong and fearless character, of shrewd sense and readiness, of great determination, of that kind of beauty which not only seems to impart to its possessor firmness and animosity, but to strike into others an instinctive recognition of those qualities; the troubled time would have heaved her up, under any circumstances. But, imbued from her childhood with a brooding sense of wrong, and an inveterate hatred of a class, opportunity had developed her into a tigress. She was absolutely without pity. If she had ever had the virtue in her, it had quite gone out of her.

It was nothing to her, that an innocent man was to die for the sins of his forefathers; she saw, not him, but them. It was nothing to her, that his wife was to be made a widow and his daughter an orphan; that was insufficient punishment, because they were her natural enemies and her prey, and as such had no right to live. To appeal to her, was made hopeless by her having no sense of pity, even for herself. If she had been laid low in the streets, in any of the many encounters in which she had been engaged, she would not have pitied herself; nor, if she had been ordered to the axe to-morrow, would she have gone to it with any softer feeling than a fierce desire to change places with the man who sent her there.

Such a heart Madame Defarge carried under her rough robe. Carelessly worn, it was a becoming robe enough, in a certain weird way, and her dark hair looked rich under her coarse red cap. Lying hidden in her bosom, was a loaded pistol. Lying hidden at her waist, was a sharpened dagger. Thus accoutred, and walking with the confident tread of such a character, and with the supple freedom of a woman who had habitually walked in her girlhood, bare-foot and bare-legged, on the brown sea-sand, Madame Defarge took her way along the streets.

Now, when the journey of the travelling coach, at that very moment waiting for the completion of its load, had been planned out last night, the difficulty of taking Miss Pross in it had much engaged Mr. Lorry's attention. It was not merely desirable to avoid overloading the coach, but it was of the highest importance that the time occupied in examining it and its passengers, should be reduced to the utmost; since their escape might depend on the saving of only a few seconds here and there. Finally, he had proposed, after anxious consideration, that Miss Pross and Jerry, who were at liberty to leave the city, should leave it at three o'clock in the lightest-wheeled conveyance known to that period. Unencumbered with luggage, they would soon overtake the coach, and, passing it and preceding it on the road, would order its horses in advance, and greatly facilitate its progress during the precious hours of the night, when delay was the most to be dreaded.

Seeing in this arrangement the hope of rendering real service in that pressing emergency, Miss Pross hailed it with joy. She and Jerry had beheld the coach start, had known who it was that Solomon brought, had passed some ten minutes in tortures of suspense, and were now concluding their arrangements to follow the coach, even as Madame Defarge, taking her way through the streets, now drew nearer and nearer to the else-deserted lodging in which they held their consultation.

"Now what do you think, Mr. Cruncher," said Miss Pross, whose agitation was so great that she could hardly speak, or stand, or move, or live; "what do you think of our not starting from this courtyard? Another carriage having already gone from here to-day, it might awaken suspicion."

"My opinion, miss," returned Mr. Cruncher, "is as you're right. Likewise wot I'll stand by you, right or wrong."

"I am so distracted with fear and hope for our precious creatures," said Miss Pross, wildly crying, "that I am incapable of forming any plan. Are you capable of forming any plan, my dear good Mr. Cruncher?"

"Respectin' a future spear o' life, miss," returned Mr. Cruncher, "I hope so. Respectin' any present use o' this here blessed old head o' mine, I think not. Would you do me the favour, miss, to take notice o' two promises and wows wot it is my wishes fur to record in this here crisis?"

"Oh, for gracious sake!" cried Miss Pross, still wildly crying, "record them at once, and get them out of the way, like an excellent man."

"First," said Mr. Cruncher, who was all in a tremble, and who spoke with an ashy and solemn visage, "them poor things well out o' this, never no more will I do it, never no more!"

"I am quite sure, Mr. Cruncher," returned Miss Pross, "that you never will do it again, whatever it is, and I beg you not to think it necessary to mention more particularly what it is."

"No, miss," returned Jerry, "it shall not be named to you. Second: them poor things well out o' this, and never no more will I interfere with Mrs. Cruncher's flopping, never no more!"

"Whatever housekeeping arrangement that may be," said Miss Pross, striving to dry her eyes and compose herself, "I have no doubt it is best that Mrs. Cruncher should have it entirely under her own superintendence.—O my poor darlings!"

"I go so far as to say, miss, moreover," proceeded Mr. Cruncher, with a most alarming tendency to hold forth as from a pulpit—"and let my words be took down and took to Mrs. Cruncher through yourself—that wot my opinions respectin' flopping has undergone a change, and that wot I only hope with all my heart as Mrs. Cruncher may be a flopping at the present time."

"There, there, there! I hope she is, my dear man," cried the distracted Miss Pross, "and I hope she finds it answering her expectations."

"Forbid it," proceeded Mr. Cruncher, with additional solemnity, additional slowness, and additional tendency to hold forth and hold out, "as anything wot I have ever said or done should be wisited on my earnest wishes for them poor creeturs now! Forbid it as we shouldn't all flop (if it was anyways conwenient) to get 'em out o' this here dismal risk! Forbid it, miss! Wot I say, for—BID it!" This was Mr. Cruncher's conclusion after a protracted but vain endeavour to find a better one.

And still Madame Defarge, pursuing her way along the streets, came nearer and nearer.

"If we ever get back to our native land," said Miss Pross, "you may rely upon my telling Mrs. Cruncher as much as I may be able to remember and understand of what you have so impressively said; and at all events you may be sure that I shall bear witness to your being thoroughly in earnest at this dreadful time. Now, pray let us think! My esteemed Mr. Cruncher, let us think!"

Still, Madame Defarge, pursuing her way along the streets, came nearer and nearer.

"If you were to go before," said Miss Pross, "and stop the vehicle and horses from coming here, and were to wait somewhere for me; wouldn't that be best?"

Mr. Cruncher thought it might be best.

"Where could you wait for me?" asked Miss Pross.

Mr. Cruncher was so bewildered that he could think of no locality but Temple Bar. Alas! Temple Bar was hundreds of miles away, and Madame Defarge was drawing very near indeed.

"By the cathedral door," said Miss Pross. "Would it be much out of the way, to take me in, near the great cathedral door between the two towers?"

"No, miss," answered Mr. Cruncher.

"Then, like the best of men," said Miss Pross, "go to the posting-house straight, and make that change."

"I am doubtful," said Mr. Cruncher, hesitating and shaking his head, "about leaving of you, you see. We don't know what may happen."

"Heaven knows we don't," returned Miss Pross, "but have no fear for me. Take me at the cathedral, at Three o'Clock, or as near it as you can, and I am sure it will be better than our going from here. I feel certain of it. There! Bless you, Mr. Cruncher! Think—not of me, but of the lives that may depend on both of us!"

This exordium, and Miss Pross's two hands in quite agonised entreaty clasping his, decided Mr. Cruncher. With an encouraging nod or two, he immediately went out to alter the arrangements, and left her by herself to follow as she had proposed.

The having originated a precaution which was already in course of execution, was a great relief to Miss Pross. The necessity of composing her appearance so that it should attract no special notice in the streets, was another relief. She looked at her watch, and it was twenty minutes past two. She had no time to lose, but must get ready at once.

Afraid, in her extreme perturbation, of the loneliness of the deserted rooms, and of half-imagined faces peeping from behind every open door in them, Miss Pross got a basin of cold water and began laving her eyes, which were swollen and red. Haunted by her feverish apprehensions, she could not bear to have her sight obscured for a minute at a time by the dripping water, but constantly paused and looked round to see that there was no one watching her. In one of those pauses she recoiled and cried out, for she saw a figure standing in the room.

The basin fell to the ground broken, and the water flowed to the feet of Madame Defarge. By strange stern ways, and through much staining blood, those feet had come to meet that water.

Madame Defarge looked coldly at her, and said, "The wife of Evrémonde; where is she?"

It flashed upon Miss Pross's mind that the doors were all standing open, and would suggest the flight. Her first act was to shut them. There were four in the room, and she shut them all. She then placed herself before the door of the chamber which Lucie had occupied.

Madame Defarge's dark eyes followed her through this rapid movement, and rested on her when it was finished. Miss Pross had nothing beautiful about her; years had not tamed the wildness, or softened the grimness, of her appearance; but, she too was a determined woman in her different way, and she measured Madame Defarge with her eyes, every inch.

"You might, from your appearance, be the wife of Luci-fer," said Miss Pross, in her breathing. "Nevertheless, you shall not get the better of me. I am an Englishwoman."

Madame Defarge looked at her scornfully, but still with something of Miss Pross's own perception that they two were at bay. She saw a tight, hard, wiry woman before her, as Mr. Lorry had seen in the same figure a woman with a strong hand, in the years gone by. She knew full well that Miss Pross was the family's devoted friend; Miss Pross knew full well that Madame Defarge was the family's malevolent enemy.

"On my way yonder," said Madame Defarge, with a slight movement of her hand towards the fatal spot, "where they reserve my chair and my knitting for me, I am come to make my compliments to her in passing. I wish to see her."

"I know that your intentions are evil," said Miss Pross, "and you may depend upon it, I'll hold my own against them."

Each spoke in her own language; neither understood the other's words; both were very watchful, and intent to deduce from look and manner, what the unintelligible words meant.

"It will do her no good to keep herself concealed from me at this moment," said Madame Defarge. "Good patriots will know what that means. Let me see her. Go tell her that I wish to see her. Do you hear?"

"If those eyes of yours were bed-winches," returned Miss Pross, "and I was an English four-poster, they shouldn't loose a splinter of me. No, you wicked foreign woman; I am your match."

Madame Defarge was not likely to follow these idiomatic remarks in detail; but, she so far understood them as to perceive that she was set at naught.

"Woman imbecile and pig-like!" said Madame Defarge, frowning. "I take no answer from you. I demand to see her. Either tell her that I demand to see her, or stand out of the way of the door and let me go to her!" This, with an angry explanatory wave of her right arm.

"I little thought," said Miss Pross, "that I should ever want to understand your nonsensical language; but I would give all I have, except the clothes I wear, to know whether you suspect the truth, or any part of it."

Neither of them for a single moment released the other's eyes. Madame Defarge had not moved from the spot where she stood when Miss Pross first became aware of her; but, she now advanced one step.

"I am a Briton," said Miss Pross, "I am desperate. I don't care an English Twopence for myself. I know that the longer I keep you here, the greater hope there is for my Ladybird. I'll not leave a handful of that dark hair upon your head, if you lay a finger on me!"

Thus Miss Pross, with a shake of her head and a flash of her eyes between every rapid sentence, and every rapid sentence a whole breath. Thus Miss Pross, who had never struck a blow in her life.

But, her courage was of that emotional nature that it brought the irrepressible tears into her eyes. This was a courage that Madame Defarge so little comprehended as to mistake for weakness. "Ha, ha!" she laughed, "you poor wretch! What are you worth! I address myself to that Doctor." Then she raised her voice and called out, "Citizen Doctor! Wife of Evrémonde! Child of Evrémonde! Any person but this miserable fool, answer the Citizeness Defarge!"

Perhaps the following silence, perhaps some latent disclosure in the expression of Miss Pross's face, perhaps a sudden misgiving apart from either suggestion, whispered to Madame Defarge that they were gone. Three of the doors she opened swiftly, and looked in.

"Those rooms are all in disorder, there has been hurried packing, there are odds and ends upon the ground. There is no one in that room behind you! Let me look."

"Never!" said Miss Pross, who understood the request as perfectly as Madame Defarge understood the answer.

"If they are not in that room, they are gone, and can be pursued and brought back," said Madame Defarge to herself.

"As long as you don't know whether they are in that room or not, you are uncertain what to do," said Miss Pross to *herself*; "and you shall not know that, if I can prevent your knowing it; and know that, or not know that, you shall not leave here while I can hold you."

"I have been in the streets from the first, nothing has stopped me, I will tear you to pieces, but I will have you from that door," said Madame Defarge.

"We are alone at the top of a high house in a solitary courtyard, we are not likely to be heard, and I pray for bodily strength to keep you here, while every minute you are here is worth a hundred thousand guineas to my darling," said Miss Pross.

Madame Defarge made at the door. Miss Pross, on the instinct of the moment, seized her round the waist in both her arms, and held her tight. It was in vain for Madame Defarge to struggle and to strike; Miss Pross, with the vigorous tenacity of love, always so much stronger than hate, clasped her tight, and even lifted her from the floor in the struggle that they had. The two hands of Madame Defarge buffeted and tore her face; but Miss Pross, with her head down, held her round the waist, and clung to her with more than the hold of a drowning woman.

Soon, Madame Defarge's hands ceased to strike, and felt at her encircled waist. "It is under my arm," said Miss Pross, in smothered tones, "you shall not draw it. I am stronger than you, I bless Heaven for it. I hold you till one or other of us faints or dies!"

Madame Defarge's hands were at her bosom. Miss Pross looked up, saw what it was, struck at it, struck out a flash and a crash, and stood alone—blinded with smoke.

All this was in a second. As the smoke cleared, leaving an awful stillness, it passed out on the air, like the soul of the furious woman whose body lay lifeless on the ground.

In the first fright and horror of her situation, Miss Pross passed the body as far from it as she could, and ran down the stairs to call for fruitless help. Happily, she bethought herself of the consequences of what she did, in time to check herself and go back. It was dreadful to go in at the door again; but, she did go in, and even went near it, to get the bonnet and other things that she must wear. These she put on, out on the staircase, first shutting and locking the door and taking away the key. She then sat down on the stairs a few moments to breathe and to cry, and then got up and hurried away.

By good fortune she had a veil on her bonnet, or she could hardly have gone along the streets without being stopped. By good fortune, too, she was naturally so peculiar in appearance as not to show disfigurement like any other woman. She needed both advantages, for the marks of griping fingers were deep in her face, and her hair was torn, and her dress (hastily composed with unsteady hands) was clutched and dragged a hundred ways.

In crossing the bridge, she dropped the door key in the river. Arriving at the cathedral some few minutes before her escort, and waiting there, she thought, what if the key were already taken in a net, what if it were identified, what if the door were opened and the remains discovered, what if she were stopped at the gate, sent to prison, and charged with murder! In the midst of these fluttering thoughts, the escort appeared, took her in, and took her away.

"Is there any noise in the streets?" she asked him.

"The usual noises," Mr. Cruncher replied; and looked surprised by the question and by her aspect.

"I don't hear you," said Miss Pross. "What do you say?"

It was in vain for Mr. Cruncher to repeat what he said; Miss Pross could not hear him. "So I'll nod my head," thought Mr. Cruncher, amazed, "at all events she'll see that." And she did.

"Is there any noise in the streets now?" asked Miss Pross again, presently.

Again Mr. Cruncher nodded his head.

"I don't hear it."

"Gone deaf in an hour?" said Mr. Cruncher, ruminating, with his mind much disturbed; "wot's come to her?"

"I feel," said Miss Pross, "as if there had been a flash and a crash, and that crash was the last thing I should ever hear in this life."

"Blest if she ain't in a queer condition!" said Mr. Cruncher, more and more disturbed. "Wot can she have been a takin', to keep her courage up? Hark! There's the roll of them dreadful carts! You can hear that, miss?"

"I can hear," said Miss Pross, seeing that he spoke to her, "nothing. O, my good man, there was first a great crash, and then a great stillness, and that stillness seems to be fixed and unchangeable, never to be broken any more as long as my life lasts."

"If she don't hear the roll of those dreadful carts, now very nigh their journey's end," said Mr. Cruncher, glancing over his shoulder, "it's my opinion that indeed she never will hear anything else in this world."

And indeed she never did.

CHAPTER XV.

THE FOOTSTEPS DIE OUT FOREVER.

ALONG the Paris streets, the death-carts rumble, hollow and harsh. Six tumbrils carry the day's wine to La Guillotine. All the devouring and insatiate Monsters imagined since imagination could record itself, are fused in the one realisation, Guillotine. And yet there is not in France, with its rich variety of soil and climate, a blade, a leaf, a root, a sprig, a peppercorn, which will grow to maturity under conditions more certain than those that have produced this horror. Crush humanity out of shape once more, under similar hammers, and it will twist itself into the same tortured forms. Sow the same seed of rapacious license and oppression over again, and it will surely yield the same fruit according to its kind.

Six tumbrils roll along the streets. Change these back again to what they were, thou powerful enchanter, Time, and they shall be seen to be the carriages of absolute monarchs, the equipages of feudal nobles, the toilettes of flaring Jezebels, the churches that are not my father's house but dens of thieves, the huts of millions of starving peas-

"AND STOOD ALONE—BLINDED WITH SMOKE."

ants! No; the great magician who majestically works out the appointed order of the Creator, never reverses his transformations. "If thou be changed into this shape by the will of God," say the seers to the enchanted, in the wise Arabian stories, "then remain so! But, if thou wear this form through mere passing conjuration, then resume thy former aspect!" Changeless and hopeless, the tumbrils roll along.

As the sombre wheels of the six carts go round, they seem to plough up a long crooked furrow among the populace in the streets. Ridges of faces are thrown to this side and to that, and the ploughs go steadily onward. So used are the regular inhabitants of the houses to the spectacle, that in many windows there are no people, and in some the occupation of the hands is not so much as suspended, while the eyes survey the faces in the tumbrils. Here and there, the inmate has visitors to see the sight; then he points his finger, with something of the complacency of a curator or authorised exponent, to this cart and to this, and seems to tell who sat here yesterday, and who there the day before.

Of the riders in the tumbrils, some observe these things, and all things on their last roadside, with an impassive stare; others, with a lingering interest in the ways of life and men. Some, seated with drooping heads, are sunk in silent despair; again, there are some so heedful of their looks that they cast upon the multitude such glances as they have seen in theatres, and in pictures. Several close their eyes, and think, or try to get their straying thoughts together. Only one, and he a miserable creature, of a crazed aspect, is so shattered and made drunk by horror, that he sings, and tries to dance. Not one of the whole number appeals by look or gesture, to the pity of the people.

There is a guard of sundry horsemen riding abreast of the tumbrils, and faces are often turned up to some of them, and they are asked some question. It would seem to be always the same question, for, it is always followed by a press of people towards the third cart. The horsemen abreast of that cart, frequently point out one man in it with their swords. The leading curiosity is, to know which is he; he stands at the back of the tumbril with his head bent down, to converse with a mere girl who sits on the side of the cart, and holds his hand. He has no curiosity or care for the scene about him, and always speaks to the girl. Here and there in the long street of St. Honoré, cries are raised against him. If they move him at all, it is only to a quiet smile, as he shakes his hair a little more loosely about his face. He cannot easily touch his face, his arms being bound.

On the steps of a church, awaiting the coming-up of the tumbrils, stands the Spy and prison-sheep. He looks in to the first of them: not there. He looks into the second: not there. He already asks himself, "Has he sacrificed me?" when his face clears, as he looks into the third.

"Which is Evrémonde?" says a man behind him.

"That. At the back there."

"With his hand in the girl's?"

"Yes."

The man cries, "Down, Evrémonde! To the Guillotine all aristocrats! Down, Evrémonde!"

"Hush, hush!" the Spy entreats him, timidly.

"And why not, citizen?"

"He is going to pay the forfeit: it will be paid in five minutes more. Let him be at peace."

But the man continuing to exclaim, "Down Evrémonde!" the face of Evrémonde is for a moment turned towards him. Evrémonde then sees the Spy, and looks attentively at him, and goes his way.

The clocks are on the stroke of three, and the furrow ploughed among the populace is turning round, to come on into the place of execution, and end. The ridges thrown to this side and to that, now crumble in and close behind the last plough as it passes on, for all are following to the Guillotine. In front of it, seated in chairs, as in a garden of public diversion, are a number of women, busily knitting. On one of the foremost chairs, stands The Vengeance, looking about for her friend.

"Thérèse!" she cries, in her shrill tones. "Who has seen her? Thérèse Defarge!"

"She never missed before," says a knitting-woman of the sisterhood.

"No; nor will she miss now," cries The Vengeance, petulantly. "Thérèse."

"Louder," the woman recommends.

Ay! Louder, Vengeance, much louder, and still she will scarcely hear thee. Louder yet, Vengeance, with a little oath or so added, and yet it will hardly bring her. Send other women up and down to seek her, lingering somewhere; and yet, although the messengers have done dread deeds, it is questionable whether of their own wills they will go far enough to find her!

"Bad Fortune!" cries The Vengeance, stamping her foot in the chair, "and here are the tumbrils! And Evrémonde will be despatched in a wink, and she not here! See her knitting in my hand, and her empty chair ready for her. I cry with vexation and disappointment!"

As The Vengeance descends from her elevation to do it, the tumbrils begin to discharge their loads. The ministers of Sainte Guillotine are robed and ready. Crash!—A head is held up, and the knitting-women who scarcely lifted their eyes to look at it a moment ago when it could think and speak, count One.

The second tumbril empties and moves on; the third comes up. Crash!—And the knitting-women, never faltering or pausing in their work, count Two.

The supposed Evrémonde descends, and the seamstress is lifted out next after him. He has not relinquished her patient hand in getting out, but still holds it as he promised. He gently places her with her back to the crashing engine that constantly whirrs up and falls, and she looks into his face and thanks him.

"But for you, dear stranger, I should not be so composed, for I am naturally a poor little thing, faint of heart; nor should I have been able to raise my thoughts to Him who was put to death, that we might have hope and comfort here to-day. I think you were sent to me by Heaven."

"Or you to me," says Sydney Carton. "Keep your eyes upon me, dear child, and mind no other object."

"I mind nothing while I hold your hand. I shall mind nothing when I let it go, if they are rapid."

"They will be rapid. Fear not!"

The two stand in the fast-thinning throng of victims, but they speak as if they were alone. Eye to eye, voice to voice, hand to hand, heart to heart, these two children of the Universal Mother, else so wide apart and differing, have come together on the dark highway, to repair home together, and to rest in her bosom.

"Brave and generous friend, will you let me ask you one

last question? I am very ignorant, and it troubles me—just a little."

"Tell me what it is."

"I have a cousin, an only relative and an orphan, like myself, whom I love very dearly. She is five years younger than I, and she lives in a farmer's house in the south country. Poverty parted us, and she knows nothing of my fate—for I cannot write—and if I could, how should I tell her! It is better as it is."

"Yes, yes: better as it is."

"What I have been thinking as we came along, and what I am still thinking now, as I look into your kind strong face which gives me so much support, is this:—If the Republic really does good to the poor, and they come to be less hungry, and in all ways to suffer less, she may live a long time: she may even live to be old."

"What then, my gentle sister?"

"Do you think:" the uncomplaining eyes in which there is so much endurance, fill with tears, and the lips part a little more and tremble: "that it will seem long to me, while I wait for her in the better land where I trust both you and I will be mercifully sheltered?"

"It cannot be, my child; there is no Time there, and no trouble there."

"You comfort me so much! I am so ignorant. Am I to kiss you now? Is the moment come?"

"Yes."

She kisses his lips; he kisses hers; they solemnly bless each other. The spare hand does not tremble as he releases it; nothing worse than a sweet, bright constancy is in the patient face. She goes next before him—is gone; the knitting-women count Twenty-Two.

"I am the Resurrection and the Life, saith the Lord: he that believeth in me, though he were dead, yet shall he live: and whosoever liveth and believeth in me shall never die."

The murmuring of many voices, the upturning of many faces, the pressing on of many footsteps in the outskirts of the crowd, so that it swells forward in a mass, like one great heave of water, all flashes away. Twenty-Three.

They said of him, about the city that night, that it was the peacefullest man's face ever beheld there. Many added that he looked sublime and prophetic.

One of the most remarkable sufferers by the same axe—a woman—had asked at the foot of the same scaffold, not long before, to be allowed to write down the thoughts that were inspiring her. If he had given any utterance to his, and they were prophetic, they would have been these:

"I see Barsad, and Cly, Defarge, The Vengeance, the Juryman, the Judge, long ranks of the new oppressors who have risen on the destruction of the old, perishing by this retributive instrument, before it shall cease out of its present use. I see a beautiful city and a brilliant people rising from this abyss, and, in their struggles to be truly free, in their triumphs and defeats, through long long years to come, I see the evil of this time and of the previous time of which this is the natural birth, gradually making expiation for itself and wearing out.

"I see the lives for which I lay down my life, peaceful, useful, prosperous and happy, in that England which I shall see no more. I see Her with a child upon her bosom, who bears my name. I see her father, aged and bent, but otherwise restored, and faithful to all men in his healing office, and at peace. I see the good old man, so long their friend, in ten years' time enriching them with all he has, and passing tranquilly to his reward.

"I see that I hold a sanctuary in their hearts, and in the hearts of their descendants, generations hence. I see her, an old woman, weeping for me on the anniversary of this day. I see her and her husband, their course done, lying side by side in their last earthly bed, and I know that each was not more honoured and held sacred in the other's soul, than I was in the souls of both.

"I see that child who lay upon her bosom and who bore my name, a man winning his way up in that path of life which once was mine. I see him winning it so well, that my name is made illustrious there by the light of his. I see the blots I threw upon it, faded away. I see him, foremost of just judges and honoured men, bringing a boy of my name, with a forehead that I know and golden hair, to this place—then fair to look upon, with not a trace of this day's disfigurement—and I hear him tell the child my story, with a tender and a faltering voice.

"It is a far, far better thing that I do, than I have ever done; it is a far, far better rest that I go to than I have ever known."